LEO TOLSTOY

LIBRARY OF ESSENTIAL WRITERS

LEO TOLSTOY

THREE NOVELS

COMPLETE AND UNABRIDGED

The Cossacks • War and Peace • Anna Karenina

BARNES & NOBLE
NEW YORK

2007 Barnes & Noble, Inc.

ISBN-13: 978-0-7607-9278-0
ISBN-10: 0-7607-9278-X

Printed and bound in China

1 3 5 7 9 10 8 6 4 2

Contents

Introduction

Photographs of Leo Tolstoy from late in his life have stamped a lasting image of the man in the minds of readers. Old and gray, with a long white beard and bushy eyebrows, he looks to have all of Russian history etched into his visage. He appears as a man of his century, the seriousness of his expression capturing the grand accomplishments and intentions of his great works. Just as photographs of Walt Whitman reflect the vibrancy of his uniquely American life, Tolstoy's pictures are of a man who has lived through Russian winters. His life spanned more than eight decades and in that time he was witness to many sea changes in Russian life, and experienced personal transitions no less severe. Father, husband, aristocrat, prophet, and writer, he was regarded in his own time as an artist of profound achievement, and that estimation only grew in the twentieth century. He crafted two of the most influential novels in the history of literature and volumes of lesser work that would make almost any other writer jealous. His writing always reflected his life, and his struggle to understand and shape a life he felt worth living. For this, Tolstoy's major works, even the sweeping historical war epic *War and Peace,* are intensely personal, and reflect Tolstoy's own philosophical inquiries at the time of their writing. His early novel, *The Cossacks,* and his two later masterpieces, *War and Peace* and *Anna Karenina,* all show Tolstoy's high level of skill in channeling his ideas into vivid and engrossing narratives. His writing casts a staggeringly wide shadow over world literature.

Count Lev Nikolayevich Tolstoy (in English he is commonly called Leo) was born on August 28, 1828, at Yasnaya Polyana, his family's estate in Central Russia. In a country that was not merely class-conscious, but where one's class firmly established the pattern to be followed in life, Tolstoy's family was a part of the land-owning aristocracy. Tolstoy would never have to worry about a lack of money in his life, but later his economic fortune caused him to question the luck of birth and the need for material possessions. In Tolstoy's behavior in later life, one can sense possible feelings of guilt for having been born to advantage.

Despite his financial status, Tolstoy knew tragedy early. His mother died when he was only two. Tolstoy subsequently idealized his mother, and her presence is found in many of the angelic female characters of his novels. When Tolstoy was nine, his father was murdered while traveling away from the estate. Tolstoy was primarily raised by his aunt. It is not difficult to see the seeds of Tolstoy's future philosophical questionings in the deaths of his parents. The inexorable push of fate, and humanity's inability to be anything more than a pawn at fate's whim, emerges as a major theme in his novels. Tolstoy, who was rich because of nothing he had done, and an orphan because of nothing he had done, acutely felt the indifference of fate.

Tolstoy was a fairly unmotivated student. He studied law and Oriental languages at Kazan University but left in 1847 without having taken his degree. He lived a life of leisure in Moscow befitting his class, yet that life seemed hollow to him, and so he left for the Caucasus. He enlisted in the military in 1851 and served in the Crimean War. During his service he witnessed some exceptionally bloody conflict firsthand. His first novel, *Childhood,* was completed in 1852, and upon publication earned him a reputation as a writer of promise. His military service inspired his first significant published literary work, *Sevastopol Stories,* which appeared in 1855 and demonstrated his great skill at recording military life, battle, and death. The book was highly acclaimed, and even Tsar Alexander II is reported to have read and enjoyed it.

Upon leaving the military, Tolstoy traveled abroad. His trips to Europe further fueled his burgeoning beliefs that upper-class Western European societies, which the Russian aristocracy aspired to mimic, were spiritually empty. This idea took prominence in his short stories of the time. Tolstoy began to see more and more human value in the lives of the simple peasants. *The Cossacks,* his major work for this period, was published in 1863 and clearly expresses his beliefs.

The Cossacks was inspired by Tolstoy's own time in the Caucasus. It is not a novel that attempts to show a complete picture of a society or a period in time, the way that *War and Peace* and *Anna Karenina* do, yet it does captures a particular area and its people. It also is a clear indication of Tolstoy's turn away from his own class and toward those closer to the earth in Russia. The novel's main character is Olenin, a soldier who leaves Moscow to be stationed in the Caucasus. There, he befriends some Cossacks and begins to become enamored of their way of life. The theme of the purity and spiritual advantages of a simple way of life are obvious even on a superficial level. Tolstoy, through the magic of his prose goes deeper, though. The plot touts the value of the Cossack way of life as Olenin falls in love with a local girl, Marianka, betrothed to another. Olenin feels he must keep his love to himself and not disrupt the lives of his new friends. He becomes close to both Marianka and her fiancée, Luka, and contents himself with friendship and friendship alone. This relationship is disturbed, though, when Beletsky, another visitor from Moscow, arrives. Beletsky is not as open to the Cossacks; he holds on to the Western ways and attitudes. Beletsky keeps Olenin from making a clean break with his former self and ultimately corrupts him into professing his love for Marianka. The materialism of Moscow possesses Olenin, and the purity of the simple life is spoiled. In the end, Luka is killed but Marianka does not choose Olenin and he loses both friendship and love.

Tolstoy was a masterful chronicler of the actual world. He could render a setting, a place, a person, in such detail as to create it wholly in the reader's mind. He accomplished this by making the mundane and ordinary seem new. His remarkable eye for detail was not just a reporter's eye, documenting objects as though compiling a list; rather, he took what most readers were familiar with and forced them to see it in a different way. Compelled to see the everyday from a new angle, readers of his fiction see previously hidden details emerge suddenly as prominent features.

This skill is what caused his realistic writing to penetrate so deeply. It was both of the world and not of the world, all at once. Tolstoy conjures the natural world with such vivid imagery that its uniqueness shines through the mundane like a newly polished diamond. Tolstoy's descriptive prowess mirrors Olenin's transformation; the special character of the world in Tolstoy's prose gives us insight into how Olenin begins to understand and love his new home.

Ironically, the period of *The Cossacks* also marked the only time that Tolstoy actually actively mingled with the literary elite of Russia. He was welcomed by Turgenev and other renowned authors as a fellow artist. Turgenev heaped praise on *The Cossacks* in particular, yet the literary world held no tangible value for Tolstoy. To him, it was as unfulfilling as his trips abroad. He quarreled with Turgenev, challenging him to a duel, although he later apologized. Tolstoy was a man in search of a purpose beyond that of just being a writer. He sought a home, a place where he could feel both fulfilled and accepted. Surprisingly, he found that home in the next stage of his life as a father and a husband. This period of stability allowed him to produce his two unquestioned masterpieces.

In 1862, Tolstoy married Sofya Andreevna Behrs. He was thirty-four years old, and she was sixteen years younger than him. For almost the next two decades, Tolstoy contented himself with being the head of a household and with writing. They lived on a large estate and he even seemed to accept his position as landowner. He maintained his view of the purity of those less economically fortunate, and on his estate set up schools so the peasants could receive an education. Family life gave Tolstoy stability and routine and encouraged the expansion of his literary powers. Sofya was a great help to her husband: it is reported that she copied *War and Peace* seven times for him. They had thirteen children together, five of whom died in childhood. Family relationships and depictions of the family as a building block of society, seeped into Tolstoy's work at the time. In many ways, *War and Peace* is a family saga.

War and Peace is a literary accomplishment whose merits cannot be overstated. It is a work of brilliance, combining Tolstoy's unique powers of description with a long story that captures people in a particular period of time. In simple terms, it is on the very short list of greatest novels ever written. However, that has become easy to proclaim and its accepted status should not prevent readers from truly enjoying the simple pleasures the novel affords. Its story covers Napoleon's invasion of Russia. It was published in serial form between 1865 and 1869.

War and Peace achieves the broad sweep of history, examining the effect of the war on the lives of hundreds of characters. Focusing on a very dramatic period of time that gives his narrative tension and momentum, Tolstoy sought—and succeeded—in evoking a time and place in its totality. The novel is concerned primarily with several aristocratic families, their schemes, their betrayals, how they try to use the war to their advantage, and how some of them find true nobility through their actions. It offers portrayals of Napoleon, the Russian General Mikhail Kutuzov, and even Tsar Alexander I. Peasants take center stage in several sections, with Tolstoy once again showing the value of their simple lives, most notably in the character of Platon Karataev.

On one level, the novel is an indictment on the shallowness of the aristocracy. The character who comes closest to being the traditional protagonist is Pierre Bezukhov, a young man who inherits a great deal of money and finds himself suddenly thrust into the life of the very rich. Tolstoy masterfully uses this outsider to introduce this insular society, and as Pierre gets increasingly entangled in the manipulations of the rich, we, as well as Pierre, come to realize how corrupt their society is. Pierre can be seen as a surrogate of Tolstoy himself—a man who is part of the aristocracy due to his wealth, yet not a part of it owing to his innate character. Pierre, like Tolstoy, spent years living a life of leisure, but discards that when he comes to see the beauty of a simpler life. Surprisingly, he marries the vapid, yet beautiful, Helene; not surprisingly the union is a disaster. Helene's family, the Kuragins, embody all that is wrong with the aristocracy. They are cruel and continually strive to better themselves at the expense of others. Helene almost immediately has an affair with another man after marrying Pierre and this sends Pierre away from home. Pierre ultimately gets caught up in the events of history, becoming obsessed over the idea that he is the one to assassinate Napoleon. Eventually, the French capture him, but he is freed at the end and able to marry the angelic Natasha.

Throughout *War and Peace* Tolstoy uses a series of foils, contrasting one character against another and using the contrasts to highlight character faults. Natasha Rostov is a foil to Helene. She is innocent whereas Helene is sinister, and altruistic whereas Helene is increasingly selfish. The Rostov family itself is a larger foil to the Kuragins. The Rostovs embody the admirable qualities of the aristocracy, and possibly were for Tolstoy a way to defend his own station in life. The use of foils even extends to the major historical figures. The Russian General Kutuzov is a foil to Napoleon. The French Emperor's arrogance and cold logic lead him into a series of blunders, and despite initial success he abandons his men at the end, as the French try to escape from Russia.

Napoleon is a representative of Western corruption, a figure who prizes rational thought to the exclusion of all else. He is cold in his calculations and arrogant because of his faith in pure reason. He is what the Russian aristocracy can become in its desire to emulate Western society. Where Napoleon worships logic and materialism, Kutuzov is more in tune with the land and with his men. He is not distant from those who serve under him; he is neither rash nor headstrong. He sees the long view of the war and his patience, as opposed to Napoleon's impulsiveness, triumphs in the end.

Thematically, *War and Peace* expresses a fatalistic perspective on humanity's role in its own development. The characters in the novel, while possessing the ability to act of their own volition, are inevitably caught in the web of history, a process that they cannot control. Fate traps them, and while they cannot master fate, they can control how they react to it. For Tolstoy, mankind can not change history, but people can change how history affects them personally.

Tolstoy continued with his literature of totality in his second masterpiece, *Anna Karenina,* which was serialized between 1875 and 1877. The novel begins with one of the most famous lines in world literature: "Happy families are all alike; every unhappy family is unhappy in its own way." A look into the lives of some unhappy families ensues. Several families, torn apart by adultery and duplicity, are the foundations of the story. The title character's tragic end stems not from a religiously moral judgment of her actions, but from how they are viewed within her society. Adultery is a major element of the plot, not just for Anna, but for others as well, and it is presented as an affront to social decorum. Anna's husband's anger over his wife's actions is a result of his own embarrassment and the possibility that he will face public shame. Tolstoy's ire at the hypocrisy rampant in the aristocracy again is prominent in *Anna Karenina.*

In *Anna Karenina,* as in *War and Peace*, the momentum of history and the unavoidable turning of fate are the primary forces moving characters. Rather than a single historical event, though, Tolstoy places his characters in a period of change, a time when many in Russia were actively vocalizing a desire for more freedoms and a Westernized government. Tolstoy's characters face the complexities of these issues, striving for certain freedoms (such as a release from the restraints of marriage), yet they suffer from a myopia that compels them to value this kind of progress at the expense of historical memory. Anna wishes to be free from her marriage and to be with the man she loves. However, when she is able to be with Vronsky, she still cannot find happiness. She is too disconnected from the simple life to allow herself to feel contentment.

The character who does find contentment, Levin, is more directly tied to the earth and the lower classes. Levin's acceptance of the virtues of family life affirms the value of family, not in terms of societal mores but through the family's simply nobility and link to the land. Levin farms with peasants, and attempts to improve their productivity with Western techniques much to the peasants' chagrin. In this relationship he experiences a familial value that is not about appearances, but a shared commitment. Tolstoy himself had found familial stability and, at least at the time of writing, had achieved a balance between his station and his ideals. *Anna Karenina* reflects Tolstoy's feelings on how family, while never perfect, can be spiritually uplifting. Levin discovers at the end of the novel that the meaning of life is in what you make of it, having a family and serving them.

After *War and Peace* and *Anna Karenina,* Tolstoy continued to write, though he did not attempt capture the totality of life on such a broad scale again. He also went through a profound religious conversion, which he recorded in *A Confession* (1882). Subsequently, Tolstoy attracted disciples drawn to his new anti-materialistic and pacifist philosophy. In *The Kingdom of God is Within You* (1893), Tolstoy expressed more fully his religious beliefs and conversion to a form of radical Christianity mixed with strong Buddhist ideas. It was a form of Christianity that did not stress immortality or Christian traditions, but rather focused on the teachings of Jesus in the Gospels. This strict reading led Tolstoy to the conclusion that non-aggressive resistance was the best means of achieving change. It also enhanced his disdain for material goods. These new attitudes created friction with his wife and family. He remained married, but the marriage in the later years was a source of bitterness and suffering for Tolstoy because his wife did not embrace his beliefs.

Tolstoy's pacifist philosophy influenced prominent political leaders, including Gandhi. He was eventually excommunicated from the Russian Church, yet he never stopped writing. Even with his religious struggles, he continued to produce lucid, moving prose. *The Death of Ivan Ilyich* (1886) and *Hadji Murad* (published posthumously in 1912) are two major works crafted after Tolstoy's conversion. Late in life, his literary reputation already secured, he became a figure of controversy, scorned by the Russian church, yet embraced by followers seeking meaning in their lives. His life almost matched the works of art he created; a towering presence touching irrevocably all those who came into close contact. Tolstoy died on November 7, 1910.

TOMMY JENKINS

Tommy Jenkins is a published author and has taught creative writing for several years. He studied at the University of North Carolina as an undergraduate and holds a master's degree from Columbia University. He is currently studying and teaching creative writing at North Carolina State University.

THE COSSACKS

A TALE OF THE CAUCASUS IN 1852

Chapter I

MOSCOW HAS BECOME QUIET. ONLY VERY RARELY DOES ONE HEAR THE SOUND OF WHEELS in the wintry streets. There are no longer any lights in the windows, and the street lamps have been extinguished. From the church towers come the sound of bells which, borne over the sleepy city, remind one of morning. The streets are empty. Every now and then a sleigh ploughs its way through the mixture of snow and sand and, crossing over to another street corner, the driver stops to wait for another fare. An old woman passes by on her way to the church, where a few irregularly placed wax-candles are already burning with a red light which is reflected from the gilt mountings of the icons. Workmen are already getting up after their long winter night, and are going to their work. But for the gentlefolk it is still evening!

Through chinks beneath the shutters of Chevalier's Restaurant, lights—unlawful at this hour—are still visible. At the entrance stand, closely crowded, a carriage and a number of sleighs. Also a three-horsed post-sleigh is there. The yard-porter, muffled up and pinched with cold, seems to be hiding behind the corner of the house.

"And what's the good of all this jawing?" thinks the attendant who, with a haggard look on his face, is sitting in the hall. "This is what always happens when I am on duty!"

From the adjoining brightly illuminated little room are heard the voices of three young men. On the table in the room are the remnants of supper and wine. One, a plain clean thin little man sits looking with kindly, tired eyes at the friend about to depart. Another, a tall man, playing with his watch-key, is lying on a sofa near the table on which stand the empty bottles. The third, in a new sheepskin coat, is pacing up and down. Every now and then he stops to crack an almond between his fingers, which are strong and thick, with carefully cleaned nails. He is constantly smiling at something, and his eyes and face are all aglow. He speaks with warmth, and gesticulates; but evidently he cannot find the words he wants, and those that come to his lips seem inadequate to express all that fills his heart.

"Now I can speak out," says the traveler. "I am not defending myself, but I want you, at least, to understand me as I understand myself, and not to look at the matter superficially. You say, I've treated her badly?" he continues, addressing the man who was looking at him with kindly eyes.

"Yes, you are to blame," says the latter, and his look seems to express still more kindness and weariness.

"I know why you say that," continues the traveler. "You think that to be loved is as great a happiness as to love, and should suffice for a whole lifetime, once you have attained it."

"Yes, my dear fellow, it is quite sufficient, more than sufficient," insists the plain little man, opening and closing his eyes.

"But why should not a man also love?" says the traveler, thoughtfully, looking at his friend as if with pity, "Why shouldn't one love? Love doesn't come. . . . No, to be beloved is a misfortune! It is a misfortune when it makes you feel guilty because you do not, and cannot, give back what you receive. Ah, my God!" and he waves his arm. "If only these things happened logically! But it's all topsy-turvy, and doesn't depend on us—it comes as it will. Why, it's as if I had stolen that love! You think so too. Don't deny it, you must think so! But, will you believe it? Of all the stupid and horrid things I have found time to do in my life, this is one I do not and cannot repent of. Neither when it began, nor afterwards, did I consciously deceive myself or her. It seemed to me that I had at last fallen in love; but later on I discovered that I had been unconsciously deceiving myself—that it is impossible to love like that—and I could not go on, and then she went and . . . Is it my fault that I couldn't? What was I to do?"

"Well, anyhow, it's all over now!" says his friend, lighting a cigar to keep awake. "Only you have never yet loved and do not know what love is!"

The man in the sheepskin was going to speak again, and put his hands to his head, but could not express what he wanted to say.

"Never loved! . . . Yes, quite true, I never have! But after all, I have within me a desire to love, and nothing could be stronger than that desire! But then, again, does such love exist? There always remains something incomplete. Ah well! What's the use of talking? I've made an awful mess of life! But anyhow, it's all over now; you are quite right. And I feel that I am beginning a new life."

"Which you will again make a mess of," said the man who lay on the sofa playing with his watch-key. But the traveler did not listen to him.

"I am sad, and yet glad to go," he continued. "Why I am sad, I don't know."

And the traveler went on talking about himself, without noticing that this did not interest the others as much as it did him. A man is never such an egotist as at moments of spiritual ecstasy. At such times it seems to him that there is nothing on earth more splendid and interesting than himself.

"Dmitry Andreich! The coachman won't wait any longer!" said a young serf, entering the room in a sheepskin coat with a scarf tied round his head. "The horses have been standing since twelve, and it's now four o'clock!"

Dmitry Andreich looked at his serf, Vanyusha. The scarf round Vanyusha's head, his felt boots, and sleepy face, seemed to be calling his master to a new life of labor, hardship, and activity.

"True enough! Good-bye!" said he, feeling for the unfastened hook and eye on his coat.

In spite of advice to mollify the coachman by another tip, he put on his cap, and stood in the middle of the room. The friends kissed once, then again, and after a pause, a third time. The man in the sheepskin coat approached the table and emptied a champagne glass, then took the plain little man's hand and blushed.

"Ah well, I will speak out all the same. . . . I must, and will be frank with you, because I am fond of you. . . . Of course you love her—I always thought so—don't you?"

"Yes," answered his friend, smiling still more gently.

"And perhaps . . ."

"Please sir, I have orders to put out the candles," said the sleepy attendant, who has been listening to the last part of the conversation and wondering why gentlefolk always talk about one and the same thing. "To whom shall I make out the bill? To you, sir?" he added, knowing whom to address, and turning to the tall man.

"To me," replied the tall man. "How much?"

"Twenty-six rubles."

The tall man considered for a moment, but said nothing, and put the bill in his pocket.

The other two continued their talk.

"Good-bye, you are a capital fellow!" said the short plain man with the mild eyes.

Tears filled the eyes of both. They stepped into the porch.

"Oh, by the by," said the traveler, turning with a blush to the tall man, "will you settle Chevalier's bill, and write and let me know?"

"All right, all right!" said the tall man, pulling on his gloves. "How I envy you!" he added quite unexpectedly when they were out in the porch.

The traveler got into his sleigh, wrapped his sheepskin about him, and said: "Well then, come along!" He even moved a little to make room in the sleigh for the man who said he envied him; his voice trembled.

"Good-bye, Mitya! I hope that with God's help you . . ." said the tall one. But his wish was that the other would go away quickly, and so he could not finish the sentence.

They were silent a moment. Then someone again said. "Good-bye," and a voice cried, "Ready," and the coachman touched up the horses.

"Hy, Elisar!" one of the friends called out, and the other coachman and the sleigh-drivers begin moving, clicking their tongues and pulling at the reins. Then the stiffened carriage wheels rolled squeaking over the frozen snow.

"A fine fellow, that Olenin!" said one of the friends. "But what an idea, to go to the Caucasus—as a cadet, too! I wouldn't do it for a bob. . . . Are you dining at the club tomorrow?"

"Yes."

They separated.

The traveler felt warm, his sheepskin seemed too hot. He sat on the bottom of the sleigh and unfastened his coat, and the three shaggy post-horses dragged themselves out of one dark street into another, past houses he had never before seen. It seemed to Olenin that only travelers starting on a long journey went through those streets. All was dark and silent and dull around him, but his soul was full of memories, love, regrets, and a pleasant tearful feeling.

Chapter II

"I'M FOND OF THEM, VERY FOND! . . . FIRST-RATE FELLOWS! . . . FINE!" HE KEPT REPEATING, AND FELT ready to cry. But why he wanted to cry; who were the first-rate fellows; whom he was so fond of—was more than he quite knew. Now and then he looked round at some house and wondered why it was so curiously built; sometimes he began wondering why the postboy and Vanyusha, who were so different from him, sat so near, and together with him were being jerked about and swayed by the tugs the side-horses gave at the frozen traces: and again he repeated: "First rate . . . very fond!" and once more he even said: "And it seizes one . . . excellent!" and wondered what made him say it. "Dear me, am I drunk?" he asked himself. He had had a couple of bottles of wine, but it was not the wine alone that was having this effect on Olenin. He remembered all the words of friendship heartily, bashfully, spontaneously (as he believed) addressed to him on his departure. He remembered the clasp of hands, glances, the moments of silence, and the sound of a voice saying, "Good-bye, Mitya!" when he was already in the sleigh. He remembered his own deliberate frankness. And all this had a touching significance for him. Not only friends and relatives, not only people who had been indifferent to him, but even those who did not like him, seemed to have agreed to become fonder of him, or to forgive him, before his departure, as people do before confession or death.

"Perhaps I shall not return from the Caucasus," he thought. And he felt that he loved his friends and someone besides. He was sorry for himself. But it was not love for his friends that so stirred and uplifted his heart that he could not repress the meaningless words that seemed to rise of themselves to his lips; nor was it love for a woman (he had never yet been in love) that had brought on this mood. Love for himself, love full of hope—warm, young love for all that was good in his own soul (and at that moment it seemed to him that there was nothing but good in it)—compelled him to weep and to mutter incoherent words.

Olenin was a youth who had never completed his university course, never served anywhere (having only a nominal post in some government office or other), who had squandered half his fortune, and had reached the age of twenty-four without having done anything or even chosen a career. He was what in Moscow society is termed *un jeune homme*.

At the age of eighteen he was free—as only rich young Russians in the 'forties, who had lost their parents at an early age, could be. Neither physical nor moral fetters of any kind existed for him; he could do as he liked, lacking nothing and bound by nothing. Neither relatives, nor fatherland, nor religion, nor wants, existed for him. He believed in nothing and admitted nothing. But although he believed in nothing he was not a morose or blasé young man, nor argumentative, but on the contrary continually let himself be carried away. He had come to the conclusion that there is no such thing as love, yet his heart always overflowed in the presence of any young and attractive woman. He had long been aware that honours and position were nonsense, yet involuntarily he felt pleased when, at a ball, Prince Sergius came up and spoke to him affably. But he yielded to his impulses only in so far as they did not limit his freedom.

As soon as he had yielded to any influence and became conscious of its leading on to labour and struggle, he instinctively hastened to free himself from the feeling or activity into which he was being drawn, and to regain his freedom. In this way he experimented with society-life, the civil service, farming, music—to which at one time he intended to devote his life—and even with the love of women, in which he did not believe. He meditated on the use to which he should devote that power of youth which is granted to man only once in a lifetime: that force which gives a man the power of making himself, or even—as it seemed to him—of making the universe, into anything he wishes: should it be to art, to science, to love of woman, or to practical activities? It is true that some people are devoid of this impulse, and on entering life at once place their necks under the first yoke that offers itself, and honestly labor under it for the rest of their lives. But Olenin was too strongly conscious of the presence of that all-powerful God of Youth—of that capacity to be entirely transformed into an aspiration or idea—the capacity to wish and to do—to throw oneself headlong into a bottomless abyss without knowing why or wherefore. He bore this consciousness within himself, was proud of it, and, without knowing it, was happy in that consciousness. Up to that time he had loved only himself, and could not help loving himself, for he expected nothing but good of himself, and had not yet had time to be disillusioned. On leaving Moscow he was in that happy state of mind in which a young man, conscious of past mistakes, suddenly says to himself, "That was not the real thing." All that had gone before was accidental and unimportant. Till then he had not really tried to live, but now, with his departure from Moscow, a new life was beginning—a life in which there would be no mistakes, no remorse, and certainly nothing but happiness.

It is always the case on a long journey that, till the first two or three stages have been passed, imagination continues to dwell on the place left behind, but with the first morning on the road it leaps to the end of the journey, and there begins building castles in the air. So it happened to Olenin.

After leaving the town behind, he gazed at the snowy fields, and felt glad to be alone in their midst. Wrapping himself in his fur coat, he lay at the bottom of the sleigh, became tranquil, and fell into a doze. The parting with his friends had touched him deeply, and memories of that last winter spent in Moscow and images of the past, mingled with vague thoughts and regrets, rose unbidden in his imagination.

He remembered the friend who had seen him off, and his relations with the girl they had talked about. The girl was rich. "How could he love her, knowing that she loved me?" thought he, and evil suspicions crossed his mind. "There is much dishonesty in men, when one comes to reflect." Then he was confronted by the question: "But really, how is it I have never been in love? Everyone tells me that I never have. Can it be that I am a moral monstrosity?" And he began to recall all his infatuations. He recalled his entry into society, and a friend's sister with whom he spent several evenings at a table with a lamp on it which lit up her slender fingers busy with needlework, and the lower part of her pretty delicate face. He recalled their conversations, that dragged on like the game in which one passes on a stick which one keeps alight as long as possible, and the general awkwardness and restraint, and his continual feeling of rebellion at all that conventionality. Some voice had always whispered: "That's not it, that's not it," and so it had proved. Then he remembered a ball, and the mazurka he danced with the beautiful D——. "How much in love I was that night, and how happy! And how hurt and vexed I was next morning, when I woke and felt myself still free! Why does not love come and bind me hand and foot?" thought he. "No, there is no such thing as love! That neighbour who used to tell me, as she told Dubrovin and the Marshal, that she loved the stars, was not *it* either."

And now his farming and work in the country recurred to his mind, and in those recollections also there was nothing to dwell on with pleasure. "Will they long talk of my departure?" came into his head; but who "they" were, he did not quite know. Next came a thought that made him wince and mutter incoherently. It was the recollection of M. Cappel, the tailor, and the 678 rubles he still owed him, and he recalled the words in which he had begged him to wait another year, and the look of perplexity and resignation which had appeared on the tailor's face. "Oh, my God, my God!" he repeated, wincing and trying to drive away the intolerable thought. "All the same, and in spite of everything, she loved me," thought he of the girl they had talked about at the farewell supper. "Yes, had I married her I should not now be owing anything, and as it is I am in debt to Vasilyev." Then he remembered the last night he had played with Vasilyev at the club (just after leaving her), and he recalled his humiliating requests for another game, and the other's cold refusal. "A year's economizing, and they will all be paid, and the Devil take them!" . . . But despite this assurance he again began calculating his outstanding debts, their dates, and when he could hope to pay them off. "And I owe something to Morell as well as to Chevalier," thought he, recalling the night when he had run up so large a debt. It was at a drinking bout with the gipsies, arranged by some fellows from Petersburg: Sashka B——, an aide-de-camp to the Tsar, Prince D——, and that pompous old——. "How is it those gentlemen are so self-satisfied?" thought he, "and by what right do they form a clique, to which they think others must be highly flattered to be admitted? Can it be because they are aides-de-camp? Why, it's awful what fools and scoundrels they consider other people to be! But I showed them that I, on the contrary, at any rate, do not at all want their intimacy. All the same, I fancy Andrew, the steward, would be amazed to know that I am on familiar terms with a man like Sashka B——, a colonel and an aide-de-camp to the Tsar! Yes, and no one drank more than I did that evening, and I taught the gipsies a new song, and everyone listened to it. Though I have done many foolish things, all the same I am a very good fellow, thought he.

Morning found him at the third post-stage. He drank tea, and himself helped Vanyusha to move his bundles and trunks, and sat down among them, sensible, erect, and precise, knowing where all his belongings were, how much money he had and where it was, where he had put his passport and the post-horse requisition and toll-gate papers; and it all seemed to him so well arranged that he grew quite cheerful and the long journey before him seemed an extended pleasure-trip.

All that morning and noon he was deep in calculations of how many versts he had traveled, how many remained to the next stage, how many to the next town, to the place where he would dine, to the place where he would drink tea, and to Stavropol, and what fraction of the whole journey was already accomplished. He also calculated how much money he had with him, how much would be left over, how much would pay off all his debts, and what proportion of his income he would spend each month. Towards evening, after tea, he calculated that to Stavropol there still remained seven-elevenths of the whole journey; that his debts would require seven months' economy and one-eighth of his whole fortune; and then, tranquillized, he wrapped himself up, lay down in the sleigh, and again dozed off. His imagination was now turned to the future: to the Caucasus. All his dreams of the future were mingled with pictures of Amalat-Beks, Circassian women, mountains, precipices, terrible torrents, and dangers. All these things were vague and dim, but the love of fame and the danger of death furnished the interest of that future. Now, with unprecedented courage and a strength that amazed everyone, he slew and subdued an innumerable host of hillsmen; now he was himself a hillsman, and with them was maintaining their independence against the Russians. As soon as he pictured anything definite, familiar Moscow figures always appeared on the scene. Sashka B——fights with the Russians or the hillsmen against him. Even the tailor, Cappel, in some strange way, takes part in the conqueror's triumph. Amid all this he remembered his former humiliations, weaknesses, and mistakes, and the recollection was not disagreeable. It was clear that there among the mountains, waterfalls, fair Circassians, and dangers, such mistakes could not recur. Having once made full confession to himself, there was an end of it all. One other vision, the sweetest of them all, mingled with the young man's every thought of the future—the vision of a woman. And there, among the mountains, she appeared to his imagination as a Circassian slave, a fine figure with a long plait of hair and deep submissive eyes. He pictured a lonely hut in the mountains, and on the threshold *she* stands awaiting him, when, tired and covered with dust, blood, and fame, he returns to her. He is conscious of her kisses, her shoulders, her sweet voice, and her submissiveness. She is enchanting, but uneducated, wild, and rough. In the long winter evenings he begins her education. She is clever and gifted, and quickly acquires all the knowledge essential. Why not? She can quite easily learn foreign languages, read the French masterpieces and understand them: *Notre Dame de Paris,* for instance, is sure to please her. She can also speak French. In a drawing room she can show more innate dignity than a lady of the highest society. She can sing, simply, powerfully, and passionately. . . . "Oh, what nonsense!" said he to himself. But here they reached a post station, and he had to change into another sleigh and give some tips. But his fancy again began searching for the "nonsense" he had relinquished, and again fair Circassians, glory, and his return to Russia with an appointment as aide-de-camp and a lovely wife, rose before his imagination. "But there's no such thing as love," said he to himself. "Fame is all rubbish. But the 678 rubles? . . . And the conquered land, that will bring me more wealth than I need for a lifetime? It will not be right, though, to keep all that wealth for myself. I shall have to distribute it. But to whom? Well, 678 rubles to Cappel, and then we'll see." . . . Quite vague visions now cloud his mind, and only Vanyusha's voice and the interrupted motion of the sleigh break his healthy youthful slumber. Scarcely conscious, he changes into another sleigh at the next stage and continues his journey.

Next morning everything goes on just the same: the same kind of post stations and tea-drinking, the same moving horses' cruppers, the same short talks with Vanyusha, the same vague dreams and drowsiness, and the same tired, healthy, youthful sleep at night.

Chapter III

THE FARTHER OLENIN TRAVELED FROM CENTRAL RUSSIA, THE FARTHER HE LEFT HIS MEMORIES behind and the nearer he drew to the Caucasus, the lighter his heart became. "I'll stay away for good, and never return to show myself in society," was a thought that sometimes occurred to him. "These people whom I see here are *not* people. None of them know me, and none of them can ever enter the Moscow society I was in, or find out about my past. And no one in that society will ever know what I am doing, living among these people." And quite a new feeling of freedom from his whole past came over him among the rough beings he met on the road, whom he did not consider to be *people* in the sense that his Moscow acquaintances were.

The rougher the people and the fewer the signs of civilization, the freer he felt. Stavropol, through which he had to pass, irked him. The signboards, some of them even in French, ladies in carriages, cabs in the market-place, and a gentleman wearing a fur cloak and tall hat who was walking along the boulevard and staring at the passers-by, quite upset him. "Perhaps these people know some of my acquaintances," he thought; and the club, his tailor, cards, society . . . came back to his mind. But, after Stavropol, everything was satisfactory—wild and also beautiful and warlike, and Olenin felt happier and happier. All the Cossacks, post-boys and post station masters seemed to him simple folk, with whom he could jest and converse simply, without having to consider to what class they belonged. They all belonged to the human race, which, without his thinking about it, all appeared dear to Olenin; and they all treated him in a friendly way.

Already, in the province of the Don Cossacks, his sleigh had been exchanged for a cart; and beyond Stavropol it became so warm that Olenin traveled without wearing his sheepskin. It was already Spring—an unexpected joyous Spring for Olenin. At night he was no longer allowed to leave the Cossack villages, and they said it was dangerous to travel in the evening. Vanyusha began to be uneasy, and they carried a loaded gun in the cart. Olenin became still more joyful. At one of the post stations the postmaster told of a terrible murder that had been committed recently on the high road. They began to meet armed men. "So this is where it begins!" thought Olenin, and kept expecting to see the snowy mountains, of which mention was so often made. Once, towards evening, the Nogay driver pointed with his whip to the mountains shrouded in clouds. Olenin looked eagerly, but it was dull, and the mountains were almost hidden by the clouds. Olenin made out something gray and white and fleecy, but, try as he would, he could find nothing beautiful in the mountains of which he had so often read and heard. The mountains and the clouds appeared to him quite alike, and he thought the special beauty of the snow peaks, of which he had so often been told, was as much an invention as Bach's music and the love for women, which he did not believe in. So he gave up looking forward to see the mountains.

But early next morning, being awakened in his cart by the freshness of the air, he glanced carelessly to the right. The morning was perfectly clear. Suddenly he saw, about twenty paces away as it seemed to him at first glance, pure white gigantic masses with delicate contours, the distinct fantastic outlines of their summits showing sharply against the far-off sky. When he had realized the distance between himself and them and the sky, and the whole immensity of the mountains, and felt the infinitude of all that beauty, he became afraid that it was but a phantasm or a dream. He gave himself a shake to rouse himself, but the mountains were still the same.

"What's that? What is it?" he said to the driver.

"Why, the mountains," answered the Nogay driver with indifference.

"And I too have been looking at them for a long while," said Vanyusha. "Aren't they fine? They won't believe it at home."

The quick progress of the three-horsed cart along the smooth road caused the mountains to appear to be running along the horizon, while their rosy crests glittered in the light of the rising sun. At first Olenin was only astonished at the sight, then gladdened by it; but later on, gazing more and more intently at that snow-peaked chain, that seemed to rise not from behind other, black, mountains, but straight out of the plain, and to glide away into the distance, he began by slow degrees to be penetrated by their beauty, and at length to *feel* the mountains. From that moment all he saw, all he thought, and all he felt, acquired for him a new character, sternly majestic, like the mountains! All his Moscow reminiscences, shame and repentance, and his trivial dreams about the Caucasus, vanished and did not return. "Now it has begun," a solemn voice seemed to say to him. The road, and the Terek, just becoming visible in the distance, and the Cossack villages and the people, all no longer appeared to him as a joke. He looked at himself or Vanyusha, and again thought of the mountains. . . . Two Cossacks ride by, their guns in their cases swinging rhythmically behind their backs, the white and bay legs of their horses mingling confusedly . . . and the mountains! Beyond the Terek rises the smoke from a Tartar village . . . and the mountains! The sun has risen and glitters on the Terek now visible beyond the reeds . . . and the mountains! From the village comes a Tartar wagon, and women, beautiful young women, pass by . . . and the mountains! "*Abreks* canter about the plain, and here am I driving along and do not fear them! I have a gun, and strength, and youth . . . and the mountains!

Chapter IV

THAT WHOLE PART OF THE TEREK LINE (ABOUT FIFTY MILES) ALONG WHICH LIE THE VILLAGES OF the Grebensk Cossacks, is uniform in character, both as to the country and the inhabitants. The Terek, which separates the Cossacks from the hill-tribes, still flows turbid and rapid though already broad and smooth, always depositing grayish sand on its low reedy right bank, and washing away the steep, though not high, left bank, with its roots of century-old oaks, its rotting plane-trees and young brushwood. On the right bank lie the villages of pro-Russian, though still somewhat restless, Tartars. Along the left bank, back half a mile from the river and standing five or six miles apart from one another, are Cossack villages. In olden times most of these villages were situated on the banks of the river; but the Terek, shifting northward from the mountains year by year, washed away these banks, and now there remain only the ruins of the old villages, and of the gardens of pear and plum-trees and poplars, all overgrown with blackberry bushes and wild vines. No one lives there now, and one only sees the tracks of the deer, the wolves, the hares, and the pheasants, who have learned to love these places. From village to village runs a road cut through the forest as a cannon-shot might fly. Along the roads are cordons of Cossacks, and watch-towers with sentinels in them. Only a narrow strip of about seven hundred yards of fertile wooded soil belongs to the Cossacks. To the north of it begin the sand-drifts of the Nogay or Mozdok Steppes, which stretch far to the north and run, Heaven knows where, into the Trukhmen, Astrakhan and Kirghiz-Kaisatsk Steppes. To the south, beyond the Terek, are the great Chechnya river, the Kochkalov range, the Black Mountains, yet another range, and at last the snow mountains, which can just be seen but have never yet been scaled. In this fertile wooded strip, rich in vegetation, has delled, as far back as memory runs, the fine warlike and prosperous Russian tribe belonging to the sect of Old Believers, and called the Grebensk Cossacks.

Long long ago their Old Believer ancestors fled from Russia, and settled beyond the Terek among the Chechens on the Greben, the first range of wooded mountains of Chechnya. Living among the Chechens, the Cossacks intermarried with them, and adopted the manners and customs of the hill tribes, though they still retained the Russian language in all its purity, as well as their Old Faith. A tradition, still fresh among them, declares that Tsar John the Terrible came to the Terek, sent for their Elders, and gave them the land on this side of the river, exhorting them to remain friendly to Russia, and promising not to enforce his rule upon them nor oblige them to change their faith. Even now the Cossack families claim relationship with the Chechens, and the love of freedom, of leisure, of plunder and of war, still form their chief characteristics. Only the harmful side of Russian influence is apparent—by interference at elections, by confiscation of church bells, and by the troops who are quartered in the country, or march through it.

A Cossack is inclined to hate less the *dzhigit* hillsman, who maybe has killed his brother, than the soldier quartered on him to defend his village, but who has defiled his hut with tobacco-smoke. He respects his enemy the hillsman, and despises the soldier; who is in his eyes an alien and an oppressor. In reality, from a Cossack's point of view, a Russian peasant is a foreign, savage, despicable creature, of whom he sees a sample in the hawkers who come to the country, and in the Little-Russian immigrants whom the Cossack contemptuously calls "woolbeaters'. For him, to be smartly dressed, means to be dressed like a Circassian. The best weapons are obtained from the hillsmen, and the best horses are bought, or stolen, from them. A dashing young Cossack likes to show off his knowledge of Tartar, and when carousing talks Tartar even to his fellow Cossack.

In spite of all these things this small Christian clan, stranded in a tiny corner of the earth, surrounded by half-savage Mohammedan tribes and by soldiers, considers itself highly advanced, acknowledges none but Cossacks as human beings, and despises everybody else. The Cossack spends most of his time in the cordon, in action, or in hunting and fishing. He hardly ever works at home. When he stays in the village, it is an exception to the general rule, and then he is holiday-making. All Cossacks make their own wine, and drunkenness is not so much a general tendency as a rite, the non-fulfilment of which would be considered apostasy. The Cossack looks upon a woman as an instrument for his welfare; only the unmarried girls are allowed to amuse themselves. A married woman has to work for her husband from youth to very old age: his demands on her are the Oriental ones of submission and labour. In consequence of this outlook, women are strongly developed, both physically and mentally; and though they are—as everywhere in the East—nominally in subjection, they possess far greater influence and importance in family-life than Western women. The exclusion from public life and inurement to heavy male labour, give the women all the more power and importance in the household. A Cossack, who before strangers considers it improper to speak affectionately or needlessly to his wife, when alone with her is involuntarily conscious of her superiority. His house and all his property, in fact the entire homestead, has been acquired and is kept together solely by her labour and care. Though firmly convinced that labour is degrading to a Cossack, and is only proper for a Nogay labourer or a woman, he is vaguely aware of the fact that all he makes use of and calls his own is the result of that toil, and that it is in the power of the woman (his mother or his wife) whom he considers his slave, to deprive him of all he possesses. Besides, the continuous performance of man's heavy work and the responsibilities entrusted to her, have endowed the Grebensk women with a peculiarly independent, masculine character, and have remarkably developed their physical powers, common sense, resolution, and stability. The women are in most cases stronger, more intelligent, more developed, and handsomer, than the men. A striking feature of a Grebensk woman's beauty is the combination of the purest Circassian type of face with the broad and powerful build of Northern women. Cossack women wear the Circassian dress: a Tartar smock, *beshmet,* and soft slippers; but they tie their kerchiefs round their heads in the Russian fashion. Smartness, cleanliness and elegance in dress and in the arrangement of their huts, are with them a custom and a necessity. In their relations with men the women, and especially the unmarried girls, enjoy perfect freedom.

Novomlinsk village was considered the very heart of Grebensk Cossackdom. In it more than elsewhere the customs of the old Grebensk population have been preserved; and its women have from time immemorial been renowned all over the Caucasus for their beauty. A Cossack's livelihood is derived from vineyards, fruit-gardens, water melon and pumpkin plantations, from fishing, hunting, maize and millet growing, and from war plunder. Novomlinsk village lies about two and a half miles away from the Terek, from which it is separated by a dense forest. On one side of the road, which runs through the village, is the river; on the other, green vineyards and orchards, beyond which are seen the driftsands of the Nogay Steppe. The village is surrounded by earth-banks and prickly bramble hedges, and is entered by tall gates hung on posts, and covered with little reed-thatched roofs. Beside them stands, on a wooden gun-carriage, an unwieldy cannon, captured by the Cossacks at some time or other, and which has not been fired for a hundred years. A uniformed Cossack sentinel, with dagger and gun, sometimes stands, and sometimes does not stand, on guard beside the gate, and sometimes presents arms to a passing officer, and sometimes does not.

Below the roof of the gateway is written in black letters on a white board:

HOUSES 266: MALE INHABITANTS 897: FEMALE 1012.

The Cossacks' houses are all raised on pillars two-and-a-half feet from the ground. They are carefully thatched with reeds, and have large carved gables. If not new, they are at least all straight and clean, with high porches of different shapes; and they are not built close together but have ample space around them, and are all picturesquely placed along broad streets and lanes. In front of the large clear windows of many of the houses, beyond the kitchen gardens, dark green poplars and acacias with their delicate pale verdure and scented white blossoms overtop the houses, and beside them grow bold-faced yellow sunflowers, creepers, and grape vines. In the broad open square are three shops, where drapery, sunflower and pumpkin seeds, locust beans and gingerbreads are sold; and surrounded by a tall fence, loftier and larger than the other houses, stands, behind a row of tall poplars, the Regimental Commander's dwelling with its casement windows. Few people are to be seen in the streets of the village on weekdays, especially in summer. The young men are on duty in the cordons, or on military expeditions; the old ones are fishing or helping the women in the orchards and gardens. Only the very old, the sick, and the children, remain at home.

Chapter V

IT WAS ONE OF THOSE RARE EVENINGS THAT OCCUR ONLY IN THE CAUCASUS. THE SUN HAD SUNK behind the mountains, but it was yet light. The evening glow had spread over a third of the sky, and against its light the dull white immensity of the mountains was sharply defined. The air was rarefied, motionless, and full of sound. The shadow of the mountains reached for several miles over the steppe. The steppe, the opposite side of the river, and the roads, were all deserted. If, very occasionally, mounted men appeared, the Cossacks in the cordon and the Chechens in their *aouls* (villages) watched them with surprised curiosity, and tried to guess who those questionable men could be.

At nightfall people from fear of one another flock to their dwellings, and only birds and beasts fearless of man prowl in those deserted spaces. Talking merrily, the women, who have been tying up the vines, hurry away from the gardens before sunset. The vineyards, like all the surrounding district, are deserted, but the villages become very animated at that time of the evening. From all sides, walking, riding, or driving in their creaking carts, people move towards the village. Girls with their smocks tucked up and twigs in their hands, run chatting merrily to the village gates to meet the cattle that are crowding together in a cloud of dust and mosquitoes which they bring with them from the steppe. The well-fed cows and buffaloes disperse at a run all over the streets, and Cossack women in colored *beshmets* go to and fro among them. You can hear their merry laughter and shrieks mingling with the lowing of the cattle. There an armed and mounted Cossack, on leave from the cordon, rides up to a hut and, leaning towards the window, knocks. In answer to the knock the handsome head of a young woman appears at the window, and you can hear caressing, laughing voices. There a tattered Nogay laborer with prominent cheekbones, brings a load of reeds from the steppes, turns his creaking cart into the Cossack captain's broad and clean courtyard, and lifts the yoke off the oxen, that stand tossing their heads, while he and his master shout to one another in Tartar. Past a puddle that reaches nearly across the street, a barefooted Cossack woman, with a bundle of firewood on her back, makes her laborious way by clinging to the fences, holding her smock high and exposing her white legs. A Cossack returning from shooting calls out in jest: "Lift it higher, shameless thing!" and points his gun at her. The woman lets down her smock and drops the wood. An old Cossack, returning home from fishing with his trousers tucked up and his hairy gray chest uncovered, has a net across his shoulder containing silvery fish that are still struggling; and, to take a short cut, climbs over his neighbor's broken fence and gives a tug to his coat which has caught on the fence. There a woman is dragging a dry branch along, and from round the corner comes the sound of an ax. Cossack children, spinning their tops wherever there is a smooth place in the street, are shrieking; women are climbing over fences to avoid going round. From every chimney rises the scented *kisyak* smoke. From every homestead comes the sound of increased bustle, precursor to the stillness of night.

Granny Ulitka, the wife of the Cossack Cornet who is also Teacher in the regimental school, goes out to the gates of her yard, like the other women, and waits for the cattle which her daughter Maryanka is driving along the street. Before she has had time fully to open the wattle gate in the fence, an enormous buffalo cow, surrounded by mosquitoes, rushes up bellowing, and squeezes in. Several well-fed cows slowly follow her, their large eyes gazing with recognition at their mistress as they swish their sides with their tails.

The beautiful and shapely Maryanka enters at the gate and, throwing away her switch, quickly slams the gate to, and rushes with all the speed of her nimble feet to separate and drive the cattle into their sheds. "Take off your slippers, you devil's wench!" shouts her mother, "you'll wear them into holes!" Maryanka is not at all offended at being called a "devil's wench", but, accepting it as a term of endearment, cheerfully goes on with her task. Her face is covered with a kerchief tied round her head. She is wearing a pink smock and a green *beshmet*. She disappears inside the lean-to shed in the yard, following the big fat cattle; and from the shed comes her voice as she speaks gently and persuasively to the buffalo: "Won't she stand still? What a creature! Come now, come old dear!" Soon the girl and the old woman pass from the shed to the outhouse, carrying two large pots of milk, the day's yield. From the chimney of the outhouse rises a thin cloud of *kisyak* smoke: the milk is being used to make into clotted cream. The girl makes up the fire, while her mother goes to the gate. Twilight has fallen on the village. The air is full of the smell of vegetables, cattle, and scented *kisyak* smoke. From the gates and along the streets Cossack women come running, carrying burning rags. From the yards, one hears the snorting and quiet chewing of the cattle, eased of their milk; while in the street only the voices of women and children sound, as they call to one another. It is rare on a weekday to hear the drunken voice of a man.

One of the Cossack wives, a tall, masculine old woman, approaches Granny Ulitka from the homestead opposite, and asks her for a light. In her hand she holds a rag.

"Have you cleared up, Granny?"

"The girl is lighting the fire. Is it fire you want?" says Granny Ulitka, proud of being able to oblige her neighbour.

Both women enter the hut, and coarse hands, unused to dealing with small articles, tremblingly remove the lid of a match-box, which is rare in the Caucasus. The masculine-looking new-comer sits down on the door-step, with the evident intention of having a chat.

"And is your man at the school, Mother?" she asked.

"He's always teaching the youngsters, Mother. But he writes that he'll come home for the holidays," said the Teacher's wife.

"Yes, he's a clever man, one sees; it all comes useful."

"Of course it does."

And my Lukashka is at the cordon; they won't let him come home," said the visitor, though the Teacher's wife had known all this long ago. She wanted to talk about her Lukashka, whom she had lately fitted out for service in the Cossack regiment, and whom she wished to marry to the Teacher's daughter, Maryanka.

"So he's at the cordon?"

"He is, Mother. He's not been home since last holidays. The other day I sent him some shirts by Fomushkin. He says he's all right, and that his superiors are satisfied. He says they are looking out for *abreks* again. Lukashka is quite happy, he says."

"Ah well, thank God," said the Teacher's wife. "'Snatcher' is certainly the only word for him." Lukashka was surnamed "the Snatcher" because of his bravery in snatching a boy from a watery grave, and the Teacher's wife alluded to this, wishing in her turn to say something agreeable to Lukashka's mother.

"I thank God, Mother, that he's a good son! He's a fine fellow, everyone praises him," says Lukashka's mother. "All I wish is, to get him married; then I could die in peace."

"Well, aren't there plenty of young women in the village?" answered the Teacher's sly wife, as she carefully replaced the lid of the match-box with her horny hands.

"Plenty, Mother, plenty," remarked Lukashka's mother, shaking her head. "There's your girl now, your Maryanka—that's the sort of girl! You'd have to search through the whole place to find such another!"

The Teacher's wife knows what Lukashka's mother is after; but though she believes him to be a good Cossack, she hangs back: first because she is a Teacher's wife and rich, while Lukashka is the son of a simple Cossack and fatherless; secondly because she does not want to part with her daughter yet; but chiefly, because propriety demands it.

"Well, when Maryanka grows up she'll be marriageable too," she answers soberly and modestly.

"I'll send the matchmakers to you—I'll send them! Only let me get the vineyard done, and then we'll come and make our bows to you," says Lukashka's mother. "And we'll make our bows to Elias Vasilich too."

"Elias, indeed!" says the Teacher's wife, proudly. "It's to me you must speak! All in its own good time."

Lukashka's mother sees by the stern face of the Teacher's wife that it is not the time to say anything more just now, so she lights her rag with the match, and says, rising; "Don't refuse us, think of my words. I'll go; it is time to light the fire."

As she crosses the road, swinging the burning rag, she meets Maryanka, who bows.

"Ah, she's a regular queen, a splendid worker, that girl!" she thinks, looking at the beautiful maiden. "What need for her to grow anymore? It's time she were married, and into a good home; married to Lukashka!"

But Granny Ulitka had her own cares, and she remained sitting on the threshold, thinking hard about something, till the girl called her.

Chapter VI

THE MALE POPULATION OF THE VILLAGE SPEND THEIR TIME ON MILITARY EXPEDITIONS AND IN the cordon—or "at their posts", as the Cossacks say. Towards evening, that same Lukashka the Snatcher, about whom the old women had been talking, was standing on a watch-tower of the Nizhne-Prototsk post, situated on the very banks of the Terek. Leaning on the railing of the tower and screwing up his eyes, he looked, now far into the distance beyond the Terek, now down at his fellow-Cossacks, and occasionally he addressed the latter. The sun was already approaching the snowy range that gleamed white above the fleecy clouds. The clouds undulating at the base of the mountains grew darker and darker. The clearness of evening was noticeable in the air. A sense of freshness came from the woods, though round the post it was still hot. The voices of the talking Cossacks vibrated more sonorously than before. The moving mass of the Terek's rapid brown waters contrasted more vividly with its motionless banks. The waters were beginning to subside, and here and there the wet sands gleamed drab on the banks and in the shallows. The other side of the river, just opposite the cordon, was deserted; only an immense waste of low-growing reeds stretched far away to the very foot of the mountains. On the low bank, a little to one side, could be seen the flat-roofed clay houses and the funnel-shaped chimneys of a Chechen village. The sharp eyes of the Cossack who stood on the watch-tower followed, through the evening smoke of the pro-Russian village, the tiny moving figures of the Chechen women, visible in the distance in their red and blue garments.

Although the Cossacks expected *abreks* to cross over and attack them from the Tartar side at any moment, especially as it was May, when the woods by the Terek are so dense that it is difficult to pass through them on foot and the river is shallow enough in places for a horseman to ford it, and despite the fact that a couple of days before a Cossack had arrived with a circular from the Commander of the regiment, announcing that spies had reported the intention of a party of some eight men to cross the Terek, and ordering special vigilance—no special vigilance was being observed in the cordon. The Cossacks, unarmed and with their horses unsaddled, just as if they were at home, spent their time some in fishing, some in drinking, and some in hunting. Only the horse of the man on duty was saddled and, with its feet hobbled, was moving about by the brambles near the wood; and only the sentinel had his Circassian coat on and carried a gun and sword. The Corporal, a tall thin Cossack with an exceptionally long back and small hands and feet, was sitting on the earth-bank of a hut, with his *beshmet* unbuttoned. On his face was the lazy, bored expression of a superior, and, having shut his eyes, he dropped his head upon the palm, first of one hand and then of the other. An elderly Cossack, with a broad grayish-black beard, was lying in his shirt, girdled with a black strap, close to the river and gazing lazily at the waves of the Terek as they monotonously foamed and swirled. Others, also overcome by the heat and half naked, were rinsing clothes in the Terek, plaiting a fishing line, or humming tunes as they lay on the hot sand of the river bank. One Cossack, with a thin face burned black by the sun, lay near the hut, evidently dead-drunk, by a wall which, though it had been in shadow some two hours previously, was now exposed to the sun's fierce slanting rays.

Lukashka, who stood on the watch-tower, was a tall handsome lad about twenty years old, and very like his mother. His face and whole build, in spite of the angularity of youth, indicated great strength, both physical and moral. Though he had only lately joined the Cossacks at the front, it was evident from the expression of his face and the calm assurance of his attitude that he had already acquired the somewhat proud and warlike bearing peculiar to Cossacks and to men generally who continually carry arms; and that he felt he was a Cossack and fully knew his own value. His ample Circassian coat was torn in some places; his cap was on the back of his head, Chechen fashion, and his leggings had slipped below his knees. His clothing was not rich, but he wore it with that peculiar Cossack foppishness which consists in imitating the Chechen brave. Everything on a real brave is ample, ragged, and neglected; only his weapons are costly. But these ragged clothes and these weapons are belted and worn with a certain air and matched in a certain manner, neither of which can be acquired by everybody, and which at once strikes the eye of a Cossack or a hillsman. Lukashka had this resemblance to a brave. With his hands folded behind his cap, and his eyes nearly closed, he kept looking at the distant Tartar village. Taken separately, his features were not beautiful, but anyone who saw his stately carriage, and his dark-browed intelligent face, would involuntarily say "What a fine fellow!"

"Look at the women, what a lot of them are walking about in the village," said he in a sharp voice, languidly showing his brilliant white teeth, and not addressing anyone in particular. But Nazarka, who was lying below, immediately lifted his head, and remarked:

"They must be going for water."

"Supposing one scared them with a gun?" said Lukashka, laughing. "Wouldn't they be frightened?"

"It wouldn't reach."

"What! Mine would carry beyond. Just wait a bit, and when their feast comes round I'll go and visit Girey Khan and drink *buza* there," said Lukashka, angrily swishing away the mosquitoes which clung about him.

A rustling in the thicket drew the Cossack's attention. A pied mongrel half-setter, searching for a scent and violently wagging its scantily furred tail, came running to the cordon. Lukashka recognized the dog as one belonging to his neighbor, Uncle Eroshka, a hunter, and saw, following it through the thicket, the approaching figure of the hunter himself.

Uncle Eroshka was a gigantic Cossack with a broad, snow-white beard, and such broad shoulders and chest that in the wood where there was no one to compare him with, he did not look particularly tall, so well proportioned were his powerful limbs. He wore a tattered coat and, over the bands with which his legs were swathed, sandals made of undressed deer's hide, tied on with strings; while on his head he had a rough little white cap. He carried over one shoulder a screen to hide behind when shooting pheasants, and a bag containing a hen for luring hawks, and a small falcon; over the other shoulder, attached by a strap, was a wild cat he had killed; and stuck in his belt behind were some little bags containing bullets, gunpowder and bread; a horse's tail to swish away the mosquitoes, a large dagger in a torn scabbard smeared with old bloodstains, and two dead pheasants. Having glanced at the cordon, he halted.

"Hi, Lyam!" he called to the dog, in such a ringing bass that it awoke an echo far away in the wood; and throwing over his shoulder his big gun, of the kind the Cossacks call a "flint", he raised his cap.

"Had a good day, good people, eh?" he said, addressing the Cossacks in the same strong and cheerful voice, quite without effort but as loudly as if he were shouting to someone on the other bank of the river.

"Yes, yes, Uncle!" answered from all sides the voices of the young Cossacks.

"What have you seen? Tell us!" shouted Uncle Eroshka, wiping the sweat from his broad red face with the sleeve of his coat.

"Ah, there's a vulture living in the plane-tree here, Uncle. As soon as night comes he begins hovering round," said Nazarka, winking, and jerking his shoulder and leg.

"Come, come!" said the old man incredulously.

"Really, Uncle! You just watch," replied Nazarka, with a laugh.

The other Cossacks began laughing.

The wag had not seen any vulture at all, but it had long been the custom of the young Cossacks in the cordon to tease and mislead Uncle Eroshka every time he came to them.

"Eh, you fool, always lying!" exclaimed Lukashka from the tower to Nazarka.

Nazarka was immediately silenced.

"It must be watched. I'll watch," answered the old man, to the great delight of all the Cossacks. "But have you seen any boars?"

"Watching for boars, are you?" said the Corporal, bending forward and scratching his back with both hands, very pleased at the chance of some distraction. "It's *abreks* one has to hunt here, and not boars! You've not heard anything, Uncle, have you?" he added, needlessly screwing up his eyes, and showing his close-set white teeth.

"Abreks?" said the old man. "No, I've not. I say, have you any *chikhir.* Let me have a drink, there's a good man. I'm really quite done up. When the time comes, I'll bring you some fresh meat, I really will. Give me a drink!" he added.

"Well, and are you going to watch?" inquired the Corporal, as though he had not heard what the other said.

"I did mean to watch tonight," replied Uncle Eroshka. "Maybe, with God's help, I shall kill something for the holiday. Then you shall have a share, you shall indeed!"

"Uncle! Hallo, Uncle!" called out Lukashka sharply from above, attracting everybody's attention. All the Cossacks looked up at him. "Just go to the upper water course, there's a fine herd of boars there. I'm not inventing, really! The other day one of our Cossacks shot one there. I'm telling you the truth," added he, readjusting the musket at his back, and in a tone that showed he was not joking.

"Ah! Lukashka the Snatcher is here!" said the old man, looking up. "Where has he been shooting?"

"Haven't you seen? I suppose you're too young!" said Lukashka. "Close by the ditch," he went on seriously, with a shake of the head. "We were just going along the ditch when all at once we heard something crackling, but my gun was in its case. Elias fired suddenly. . . . But I'll show you the place, it's not far. You just wait a bit. I know everyone of their footpaths. . . . Daddy Mosev," said he, turning resolutely and almost commandingly to the Corporal, "its time to relieve guard!" and, holding aloft his gun, he began to descend from the watch-tower, without waiting for the order.

"Come down!" said the Corporal, after Lukashka had started, and glanced round. "Is it your turn, Gurka? Then go. . . . True enough, your Lukashka has become very skilful," he went on, addressing the old man. "He keeps going about just like you, he doesn't stay at home. The other day he killed a boar."

Chapter VII

THE SUN HAD ALREADY SET, AND THE SHADES OF NIGHT WERE RAPIDLY SPREADING FROM THE edge of the wood. The Cossacks finished their task round the cordon, and gathered in the hut for supper. Only the old man still stayed under the plane-tree, watching for the vulture and pulling the string tied to the falcon's leg, but though a vulture was really perching on the plane-tree it declined to swoop down on the lure. Lukashka, singing one song after another, was leisurely placing nets among the very thickest brambles to trap pheasants. In spite of his tall stature and big hands, every kind of work, both rough and delicate, prospered under Lukashka's fingers.

"Hallo, Luke!" came Nazarka's shrill, sharp voice calling him from the thicket close by. "The Cossacks have gone in to supper." And Nazarka, with a live pheasant under his arm, forced his way through the brambles, and emerged on the footpath.

"Oh!" said Lukashka, breaking off in his song, "where did you get that cock-pheasant? I suppose it was in my trap?"

Nazarka was of the same age as Lukashka, and had also only been at the front since the previous spring. He was plain, thin and puny, with a shrill voice that rang in one's ears. They were neighbours and comrades. Lukashka was sitting on the grass, cross-legged like a Tartar, adjusting his nets.

"I don't know whose it was—yours, I expect."

"Was it beyond the pit, by the plane-tree? Then it is mine! I set the nets last night."

Lukashka rose and examined the captured pheasant. After stroking the dark burnished head of the bird, which rolled its eyes and stretched out its neck in terror, Lukashka took the pheasant in his hands.

"We'll have it in a *pilav* tonight. You go and kill and pluck it."

"And shall we eat it ourselves, or give it to the Corporal?"

"He has plenty!"

"I don't like killing them," said Nazarka.

"Give it here!"

Lukashka drew a little knife from under his dagger and gave it a swift jerk. The bird fluttered, but before it could spread its wings the bleeding head bent and quivered. "That's how one should do it!" said Lukashka, throwing down the pheasant. "It will make a fat *pilav*."

Nazarka shuddered as he looked at the bird.

"I say, Lukashka, that fiend will be sending us to lie in ambush again tonight," he said, taking up the bird. (He was alluding to the Corporal.) "He has sent Fomushkin to get wine, and it ought to be his turn. He always puts it on us."

Luskashka went whistling along the cordon. "Take the string with you," he shouted; and Nazarka obeyed.

"I'll give him a bit of my mind, today, I really will," continued Nazarka. "Let's say we won't go; we're tired out, and there's an end of it! No, really, you tell them; they'll listen to you. It's too bad!"

"Get along with you! What a thing to make a fuss about!" said Lukashka, evidently thinking of something else. "What bosh! If he made us turn out of the village at night now, that would be annoying: there one can have some fun, but here, what is there? It's all one whether we're in the cordon or in ambush. What a chap you are!"

"And are you going to the village?"

"I'll go for the holidays."

"Gurka says your Dunayka is carrying on with Fomushkin," said Nazarka suddenly.

"Well, let her go to the devil," said Lukashka, showing his regular white teeth, though he did not laugh. "As if I couldn't find another!"

"Gurka says he went to her house. Her husband was out, and there was Fomushkin sitting and eating pie. Gurka stopped awhile and then went away, and passing by the window he heard her say, " He's gone, the fiend. . . . Why don't you eat your pie, my own? You needn't go home for the night," she says. And Gurka under the window, says to himself, "Fine, that!" '

"You're making it up."

"No, quite true, by Heaven!"

"Well, if she's found another, let her go to the devil," said Lukashka, after a pause. "There's no lack of girls, and I was sick of her anyway."

"Well, see what a devil you are!" said Nazarka. "You should make up to the Teacher's girl, Maryanka. Why doesn't she walk out with anyone?"

Lukashka frowned. "What of Maryanka? They're all alike," said he.

"Well, you just try . . ."

"What do you think? Are girls so scarce in the village?"

And Lukashka recommenced whistling, and went along the cordon, pulling leaves and branches from the bushes as he went. Suddenly, catching sight of a smooth sapling, he drew the knife from the handle of his dagger, and cut it down. "What a ramrod it will make," he said, swinging the sapling till it whistled through the air.

The Cossacks were sitting round a low Tartar table on the earthen floor of the clay-plastered outer room of the hut, when the question of whose turn it was to lie in ambush was raised.

"Who is to go tonight?" shouted one of the Cossacks, through the open door, to the Corporal in the next room.

"Who is to go?" the Corporal shouted back. "Uncle Burlak has been, and Fomushkin too," said he, not quite confidently. "You two had better go, you and Nazarka," he went on, addressing Lukashka. "And Ergushov must go too; surely he has slept it off?"

"You don't sleep it off yourself, so why should he?" said Nazarka in a subdued voice.

The Cossacks laughed.

Ergushov was the Cossack who had been lying drunk and asleep near the hut. He had only that moment staggered into the room, rubbing his eyes.

Lukashka had already risen, and was getting his gun ready.

"Be quick and go! Finish your supper and go!" said the Sergeant; and without waiting for an expression of consent he shut the door, evidently not expecting the Cossack to obey. "Of course," thought he, "if I hadn't been ordered to, I wouldn't send anyone; but an officer might turn up at any moment. As it is they say eight *abreks* have crossed over."

"Well, I suppose I must go," remarked Ergushov, "it's the regulation. Can't be helped! The times are such. I say, we must go."

Meanwhile Lukashka, holding a big piece of pheasant to his mouth with both hands, and glancing now at Nazarka, now at Ergushov, seemed quite indifferent to what passed, and only laughed at them both. Before the Cossacks were ready to go into ambush, Uncle Eroshka, who had been vainly waiting under the plane-tree till night fell, entered the dark outer room.

"Well, lads," his loud bass resounded through the low-roofed room, drowning all the other voices, "I'm going with you. You'll watch for Chechens, and I for boars!"

Chapter VIII

IT WAS QUITE DARK WHEN UNCLE EROSHKA AND THE THREE COSSACKS, IN THEIR CLOAKS AND shouldering their guns, left the cordon and went towards the place on the Terek where they were to lie in ambush.

Nazarka did not want to go at all, but Lukashka shouted at him, and they soon started. After they had gone a few steps in silence, the Cossacks turned aside from the ditch and went along a path almost hidden by reeds, till they reached the river. On its bank lay a thick black log cast up by the water. The reeds around it had been recently beaten down.

"Shall we lie here?" asked Nazarka.

"Why not?" answered Lukashka. "Sit down here, and I'll be back in a minute. I'll only show Daddy where to go."

"This is the best place; here we can see and not be seen," said Ergushov, "so it's here we'll lie. It's a first-rate place!"

Nazarka and Ergushov spread out their cloaks and settled down behind the log, while Lukashka went on with Uncle Eroshka.

"It's not far from here, Daddy," said Lukashka, stepping softly in front of the old man; "I'll show you where they've been—I'm the only one that knows, Daddy."

"Show me! You're a fine fellow, a regular Snatcher!" replied the old man, also whispering.

Having gone a few steps, Lukashka stopped, stooped down over a puddle, and whistled. "That's where they come to drink, d'you see?" He spoke in a scarcely audible voice, pointing to fresh hoof-prints.

"Christ bless you," answered the old man. "The boar will be in the hollow beyond the ditch," he added. "I'll watch, and you can go."

Lukashka pulled his cloak up higher and walked back alone, throwing swift glances, now to the left at the wall of reeds, now to the Terek rushing by below the bank. "I dare say he's watching or creeping along somewhere," thought he of a possible Chechen hillsman. Suddenly a loud rustling and a splash in the water made him start and seize his musket. From under the bank a boar leapt out—his dark outline showing for a moment against the glassy surface of the water and then disappearing among the reeds. Lukashka pulled out his gun and aimed; but, before he could fire, the boar had disappeared in the thicket. Lukashka spat with vexation, and went on. On approaching the ambuscade he halted again, and whistled softly. His whistle was answered and he stepped up to his comrades.

Nazarka, all curled up, was already asleep. Ergushov sat with his legs crossed, and moved slightly to make room for Lukashka.

"How jolly it is to sit here! It's really a good place," said he. "Did you take him there?"

"Showed him where," answered Lukashka, spreading out his cloak. "But what a big boar I roused just now, close to the water! I expect it was the very one! You must have heard the crash?"

"I did hear a beast crashing through. I knew at once it was a beast, I thought to myself:

'Lukashka has roused a beast,' " Ergushov said, wrapping himself up in his cloak. "Now I'll go to sleep," he added. "Wake me when the cocks crow. We must have discipline. I'll lie down and have a nap; and then you will have a nap and I'll watch—that's the way."

"Luckily, I don't want to sleep," answered Lukashka.

The night was dark, warm, and still. Only on one side of the sky the stars were shining; the other and greater part was overcast by one huge cloud, stretching from the mountain-tops. The black cloud, blending, in the absence of any wind, with the mountains, moved slowly onwards, its curved edges sharply defined against the deep starry sky. Only in front of him could the Cossack discern the Terek and the distance beyond. Behind, and on both sides, he was surrounded by a wall of reeds. Occasionally the reeds would sway and rustle against one another, apparently without cause. Seen from down below, against the clear part of the sky, their waving tufts looked like the feathery branches of trees. Close in front, at his very feet, was the bank, and at its base the rushing torrent. A little farther on was the moving mass of glassy brown water, which eddied rhythmically along the bank and round the shallows. Farther still, water, banks and cloud all merged together in impenetrable gloom. Along the surface of the water floated black shadows, in which the experienced eyes of the Cossack detected trees carried down by the current. Only very rarely sheet-lightning, mirrored in the water as in a black glass, disclosed the sloping bank opposite. The rhythmic sounds of night: the rustling of the reeds, the snoring of the Cossacks, the hum of mosquitoes, and the rushing water, were every now and then broken by a shot fired in the distance, or by the gurgling of water when a piece of bank slipped down, the splash of a big fish, or the crashing of an animal breaking through the thick undergrowth in the wood. Once an owl flew past along the Terek, flapping one wing against the other rhythmically at every second beat. Just above the Cossack's head it turned towards the wood, and then, striking its wings, no longer after every other flap but at every flap, it flew to an old plane-tree, where it rustled about for a long time before settling down among the branches. At everyone of these unexpected sounds the watching Cossack listened intently, straining his hearing, and his eyes screwed up while he deliberately felt for his musket.

The greater part of the night was past. The black cloud that had moved westward revealed, from under its torn edge, the clear starry sky, and the golden upturned crescent of the moon shone above the mountains with a reddish light. The cold began to be penetrating. Nazarka awoke, spoke a little, and fell asleep again. Lukashka, feeling bored, got up, drew the knife from his dagger-handle, and began to fashion his stick into a ramrod. His head was full of the Chechens who lived over there in the mountains, and of how their brave lads came across and were not afraid of the Cossacks, and might even now be crossing the river at some other spot. He thrust himself out of his hiding-place and looked along the river, but could see nothing. And as he continued looking out at intervals upon the river and at the opposite bank, now faintly distinguishable from the water in the faint moonlight, he no longer thought about the Chechens, but only of when it would be time to wake his comrades, and of going home to the village. In the village, he imagined Dunka, his "little soul," as the Cossacks call a man's mistress, and thought of her with vexation. Silvery mists, a sign of coming morning, glittered white above the water, and not far from him young eagles were whistling and flapping their wings. At last the crowing of a cock reached him from the distant village, followed by the long-sustained note of another, which was again answered by yet other voices.

"Time to wake them," thought Lukashka, who had finished his ramrod and felt his eyes growing heavy. Turning to his comrades he managed to make out which pair of legs belonged to whom, when it suddenly seemed to him that he heard something splash on the other side of the Terek. He turned again towards the horizon beyond the hills, where day was breaking under the upturned crescent, glanced at the outline of the opposite bank, at the Terek, and at the now distinctly visible driftwood upon it. For one instant it seemed to him that he was moving and that the Terek with the drifting wood remained stationary. Again he peered out. One large black log with a branch particularly attracted his attention. The tree was floating in a strange way right down the middle of the stream, neither rocking nor whirling. It even appeared not to be floating altogether with the current, but to be crossing it in the direction of the shallows. Lukashka, stretching out his neck, watched it intently. The tree floated to the shallows, stopped, and shifted in a peculiar manner. Lukashka thought he saw an arm stretched out from beneath the tree.

"Supposing I killed an *abrek* all by myself!" he thought, and seized his gun with a swift, unhurried movement, putting up his gun-rest, placing the gun upon it, and holding it noiselessly in position. Cocking the trigger, with bated breath he took aim, still peering out intently.

"I won't wake them," he thought. But his heart began beating so fast that he remained motionless, listening. Suddenly the trunk gave a plunge and began again to float across the stream towards our bank.

"Suppose I miss? . . ." thought he, and now by the faint light of the moon he caught a glimpse of a Tartar's head in front of the floating wood. He aimed straight at the head, which appeared to be quite near—just at the end of his musket's barrel. He glanced across. "Right enough, it is an *abrek!*" he thought joyfully, and suddenly, rising to his knees, he again took aim. Having found the mark, just visible in a line with the end of his gun, he said: "In the name of the Father and of the Son", in the Cossack way learned in his childhood, and pulled the trigger. A flash of lightning lit up for an instant the reeds and the water; and the sharp, abrupt report of the shot was carried across the river, changing into a prolonged roll somewhere in the far distance. The piece of driftwood now floated not across, but with, the current, rocking and whirling.

"Hold, I say!" exclaimed Ergushov, seizing his musket, and raising himself behind the log near which he was lying.

"Shut up, you devil!" whispered Lukashka, grinding his teeth. *"Abreks!"*

"Whom have you shot?" asked Nazarka. "Who was it, Lukashka?"

Lukashka did not answer. He was reloading his gun and watching the floating wood. A little way off, it stopped on a sandbank, and from behind it something large, that rocked in the water, came into view.

"What did you shoot? Why don't you speak?" insisted the Cossacks.

"*Abreks,* I tell you!" said Lukashka.

"Don't humbug! Did the gun go off? . . ."

"I've killed an *abrek,* that's what I fired at," muttered Lukashka in a voice choked by emotion, as he jumped to his feet. "A man was swimming . . ." he said, pointing to the sandbank. "I killed him. Just look there."

"Have done with your humbugging!" said Ergushov again, rubbing his eyes.

"Have done with what? Look there," said Lukashka, seizing him by the shoulders, and pulling him with such force that Ergushov groaned.

He looked in the direction in which Lukashka pointed, and discerning a body, immediately changed his tone.

"Oh my! But I say, more will come! I tell you the truth," said he softly, and began examining his musket. "That was a scout swimming across: either the others are here already, or are not far off on the other side—I tell you true!"

Lukashka was unfastening his belt and taking off his Circassian coat.

"What are you up to, you idiot?" exclaimed Ergushov. "Only show yourself, and you're lost, all for nothing, I tell you true! If you've killed him, he won't escape. Let me have a little powder for my musket-pan—you have some? Nazar, you go back to the cordon, and look alive; but don't go along the bank, or you'll be killed—I tell you true."

"Catch me going alone! Go yourself!" said Nazarka angrily.

Having taken off his coat, Lukashka went down to the bank.

"Don't go in, I tell you!" said Ergushov, putting some powder on the pan. "Look, he is not moving. I can see. It's nearly morning; wait till they come from the cordon. You go, Nazarka. You're afraid! Don't be afraid, I tell you."

"Luke, I say, Lukashka! Tell us how you did it!" said Nazarka.

Lukashka changed his mind about going into the water just then. "Go quick to the cordon, and I will watch. Tell the Cossacks to send out the patrol. If the *abreks* are on this side, they must be caught," said he.

"That's what I say. They'll get off," said Ergushov, rising. "True, they must be caught!"

Ergushov and Nazarka rose, and, crossing themselves, started off for the cordon—not along the river bank, but breaking their way through the brambles to reach a path in the wood.

"Now mind, Lukashka—they may cut you down here, so you'd best keep a sharp look-out, I tell you!"

"Go along; I know," muttered Lukashka; and having examined his gun again, he sat down behind the log.

Lukashka remained alone, and sat gazing at the shallows and listening for the Cossacks; but it was some distance to the cordon, and he was tormented by impatience. He kept thinking that the other *abreks* who were with the one he had killed would escape. He was vexed with the *abreks* who were going to escape, just as he had been with the boar that had escaped the evening before. He glanced round and at the opposite bank, expecting every moment to see a man; and having arranged his gun-rest, he was ready to fire. The idea that he might himself be killed never entered his head.

Chapter IX

IT WAS GROWING LIGHT. THE CHECHEN'S BODY, WHICH WAS GENTLY ROCKING IN THE SHALLOW water, was now clearly visible. Suddenly the reeds rustled not far from Luke, and he heard steps and saw the feathery tops of the reeds moving. He set his gun at full cock and muttered: "In the name of the Father and of the Son," but when the cock clicked, the sound of steps ceased.

"Hullo, Cossacks! Don't kill your Daddy!" calmly said a deep bass voice; and, moving the reeds apart, Daddy Eroshka came up close to Luke.

"I very nearly killed you, by God I did!" said Lukashka.

"What have you shot?" asked the old man. His sonorous voice resounded through the wood and downward along the river, suddenly dispelling the mysterious quiet of night around the Cossack. It was as if everything had suddenly become lighter and more distinct.

"There now, Uncle, you have not seen anything, but I've killed a beast," said Lukashka, uncocking is gun, and getting up with unnatural calmness.

The old man was staring intently at the white back, now clearly visible, against which rippled the Terek.

"He was swimming with a log on his back. I spied him out!. . . . Look there. There! He's got blue trousers, and a gun, I think. . . . Do you see?" inquired Luke.

"How can one help seeing?" said the old man angrily, and a serious and stern expression appeared on his face. "You've killed a brave," he said, apparently with regret.

"Well, I sat here, and suddenly saw something dark on the other side. I spied him when he was still over there. It was as if a man had come there and fallen in. Strange! And a piece of driftwood, a good-sized piece, comes floating, not with the stream, but across it; and what do I see but a head appearing from under it! Strange! I stretched out of the reeds, but could see nothing; then I rose, and he must have heard, the beast, and crept out into the shallow and looked about. " No, you don't!" I said, as soon as he landed and looked round, " you'll not get away!" Oh, there was something choking me! I got my gun ready, but did not stir, and looked out. He waited a little and then swam out again; and when he came into the moonlight I could see his whole back. " In the name of the Father and of the Son and of the Holy Ghost" . . . and through the smoke I see him struggling. He moaned, or so it seemed to me. " Ah," I thought, " the Lord be thanked, I've killed him!" And when he drifted on to the sandbank I could see him distinctly: he tried to get up, but couldn't. He struggled a bit, and then lay down. Everything could be seen. Look, he does not move—he must be dead! The Cossacks have gone back to the cordon in case there should be any more of them."

"And so you had him!" said the old man. "He is far away now, my lad! . . ." And again he shook his head sadly.

Just then the sound reached them of breaking bushes, and the loud voices of Cossacks approaching along the bank on horseback and on foot. "Are you bringing the skiff?" shouted Lukashka.

"You're a trump, Luke! Lug it to the bank!" shouted one of the Cossacks.

Without waiting for the skiff, Lukashka began to undress, keeping an eye all the while on his prey.

"Wait a bit, Nazarka is bringing the skiff," shouted the Corporal.

"You fool! Maybe he is alive and only pretending! Take your dagger with you!" shouted another Cossack.

"Get along," cried Luke, pulling off his trousers. He quickly undressed and, crossing himself, jumped, plunging with a splash into the river. Then with long strokes of his white arms, lifting his back high out of the water and breathing deeply, he swam across the current of the Terek towards the shallows. A crowd of Cossacks stood on the bank, talking loudly. Three horsemen rode off to patrol. The skiff appeared round a bend. Lukashka stood up on the sandbank, leaned over the body, and gave it a couple of shakes. "Quite dead!" he shouted, in a shrill voice.

The Chechen had been shot in the head. He had on a pair of blue trousers, a shirt, and a Circassian coat, and a gun and dagger were tied to his back. Above all these a large branch was tied, and that it was which at first had misled Lukashka.

"What a carp you've landed!" cried one of the Cossacks who had assembled in a circle, as the body, lifted out of the skiff, was laid on the bank, pressing down the grass.

"How yellow he is!" said another.

"Where have our fellows gone to search? I expect the rest of them are on the other bank. If this one had not been a scout he would not have swum that way. Why else should he swim alone?" said a third.

"Must have been a smart one, to offer himself before the others; a regular brave!" said Lukashka mockingly, as he stood shivering at the bottom of the bank, wringing out his wet clothes.

"His beard is dyed, and cropped."

"And he has tied a bag with a coat in it to his back."

"That would make it easier for him to swim," said someone.

"I say, Lukashka," said the Corporal, who was holding the dagger and gun taken from the dead man. "Keep the dagger for yourself and the coat too; but I'll give you three rubles for the gun. You see it has a hole in it," said he, blowing into the muzzle. "I want it just for a souvenir."

Lukashka did not answer. Evidently this sort of begging vexed him, but he knew it could not be avoided.

"See, what a devil!" said he, frowning and throwing down the Chechen's coat. "If at least it were a good coat, but it's a mere rag."

"It'll do to fetch firewood in," said one of the Cossacks.

"Mosev, I'll go home," said Lukashka, evidently forgetting his vexation and wishing to get some advantage out of having to give a present to his superior.

"All right, you may go!"

"Take the body beyond the cordon, lads," said the Corporal, still examining the gun, "and put a shelter over him from the sun. Perhaps they'll send from the mountains to ransom it."

"It isn't hot yet," said someone.

"And supposing a jackal tears him? Would that be well?" remarked another Cossack.

"We'll set a watch; for should they come to ransom him, it won't do for him to have been torn."

"Well, Lukashka, whatever you do, you must stand a pail of vodka for the lads," said the Corporal gaily.

"Of course! That's the custom," chimed in the Cossacks. "See what luck God has sent you! Without ever having seen anything of the kind before, you've killed a brave!"

"Buy the dagger and coat, and don't be stingy, and I'll let you have the trousers too," said Lukashka. "They're too tight for me; he was a thin devil."

One Cossack bought the coat for a ruble, and another gave the price of two-pails of vodka for the dagger.

"Drink, lads! I'll stand you a pail!" said Luke. "I'll bring it myself from the village."

"And cut up the trousers into kerchiefs for the girls!" said Nazarka.

The Cossacks burst out laughing.

"Have done laughing!" said the Corporal: "And take the body away. Why have you put the nasty thing by the hut?"

"What are you standing there for? Haul him along, lads!" shouted Lukashka in a commanding voice to the Cossacks, who reluctantly took hold of the body, obeying him as though he were their chief. After dragging the body along for a few steps, the Cossacks let fall the legs, which dropped with a lifeless jerk; and stepping apart they then stood silent for a few moments. Nazarka came up and straightened the head, which was turned to one side, so that the round wound above the temple and the whole of the dead man's face were visible.

"See what a mark he has made, right in the brain," he said. "He'll not get lost. His owners will always know him!"

No one answered, and again the Angel of Silence flew over the Cossacks.

The sun had risen high and its diverging beams were lighting up the dewy grass. Nearby, the Terek murmured in the awakened wood, and, greeting the morning, the pheasants called to one another. The Cossacks stood still and silent around the dead man, gazing at him. The brown body, with nothing on but the wet blue trousers held by a girdle over the sunken stomach, was well-shaped and handsome. The muscular arms lay stretched straight out by his sides; the blue, freshly shaven, round head with the clotted wound on one side of it, was thrown back. The smooth tanned forehead contrasted sharply with the shaven part of the head. The open glassy eyes with lowered pupils, stared upwards, seeming to gaze past everything. Under the red, trimmed moustache, the fine lips, drawn at the corners, seemed stiffened into a smile of good-natured subtle raillery. The fingers of the small hands, covered with red hairs, were bent inward, and the nails were dyed red.

Lukashka had not yet dressed. He was wet. His neck was redder and his eyes brighter than usual; his broad jaws twitched, and from his healthy body a hardly perceptible steam rose in the fresh morning air.

"He too was a man!" he muttered, evidently admiring the corpse.

"Yes, if you had fallen into his hands, you would have had short shrift," said one of the Cossacks.

The Angel of Silence had taken wing. The Cossacks began bustling about and talking. Two of them went to cut down bushes for a shelter, others strolled towards the cordon. Luke and Nazarka ran to get ready to go to the village.

Half an hour later Lukashka and Nazarka were on their way homewards, talking incessantly, and almost running through the dense woods which separated the Terek from the village.

"Mind, don't tell her I sent you, but just go and find out if her husband is at home," Luke was saying in his shrill voice.

"And I'll go round to Yamka too," said the devoted Nazarka. "We'll have a spree, shall we?"

"When should we have one, if not today?" replied Luke.

When they reached the village the two Cossacks drank, and lay down to sleep till evening.

Chapter X

ON THE THIRD DAY AFTER THE EVENTS ABOVE DESCRIBED, TWO COMPANIES OF A CAUCASIAN INfantry regiment arrived at the Cossack village of Novomlinsk. The horses had been unharnessed, and the companies' wagons were standing in the square. The cooks had dug a pit and with logs gathered from various yards (where they had not been sufficiently securely stored) were now cooking the food; the pay-sergeants were settling accounts with the soldiers. The Service Corps men were driving piles in the ground to which to tie the horses; and the quartermasters were going about the streets just as if they were at home, showing officers and men to their quarters. Here were green ammunition boxes in a line, artillery wagons, horses, and cauldrons in which buckwheat porridge was being cooked.

Here were the Captain and the Lieutenant and the Sergeant-Major, Onisim Mikhaylovich; and all this was in the Cossack village where it was reported that the companies were ordered to take up their quarters: therefore they were at home here.

But why they were stationed there; who the Cossacks were; and whether they wanted the troops to be there; and whether they were Old Believers or not—was all quite immaterial. Having received their pay and been dismissed tired out and covered with dust, the soldiers noisily and in disorder, like a swarm of bees about to settle, spread over the squares and streets.

Quite regardless of the Cossacks' ill-will, chattering merrily, and with their muskets clinking, by twos and threes they entered the huts and hung up their accoutrements, unpacked their bags, and joked with the women. At their favorite spot, round the porridge-cauldrons, a large group of soldiers assembled, and with little pipes between their teeth they gazed, now at the smoke which rose into the hot sky, becoming visible when it thickened into white clouds as it rose, and now at the camp fires which were quivering in the pure air, like molten glass; and bantered and made fun of the Cossack men and women, because they do not live at all like Russians. In all the yards one could see soldiers and hear their laughter, and the exasperated and shrill cries of Cossack women defending their houses and refusing to give the soldiers water or cooking utensils. Little boys and girls clinging to their mothers and to each other, followed all the movements of the troopers (never before seen by them) with frightened curiosity or ran after them at a respectful distance.

The old Cossacks came out silently and dismally and sat on the earthen embankments of their huts and watched the soldiers' activity with an air of leaving it all to the will of God, without understanding what would come of it.

Olenin, who had joined the Caucasian Army as a cadet three months before, was quartered in one of the best houses in the village, the house of the Teacher, Elias Vasilich—that is to say in Granny Ulitka's.

"Goodness knows what it will be like, Dmitry Andreich," said the panting Vanyusha to Olenin, who, dressed in a Circassian coat and mounted on a Kabarda horse which he had bought in Groznoe, was, after a five-hours' march, gaily entering the yard of the quarters assigned to him. "Why, what's the matter?" he asked, caressing his horse, and looking merrily at the perspiring, dishevelled, and worried Vanyusha, who had arrived with the baggage wagons and was unpacking.

Olenin looked quite a different man. In place of his clean-shaven lips and chin, he had a youthful mustache and a small beard. In place of his sallow complexion, the result of nights turned into day, his cheeks, his forehead, and the skin behind his ears were now red with healthy sunburn. In place of a clean new black suit, he wore a dirty white Circassian coat with a deeply pleated skirt, and he bore arms. Instead of a freshly starched collar, his neck was tightly clasped by the red band of his silk *beshmet.* He wore Circassian dress, but did not wear it well, and anyone would have known him for a Russian and not a Tartar-brave. It was the thing—but not the real thing. But for all that, his whole person breathed health, joy, and satisfaction.

"Yes, it seems funny to you," said Vanyusha; "but just try to talk to these people yourself: they set themselves against one and there's an end of it. You can't get as much as a word out of them." Vanyusha angrily threw down a pail on the threshold. "Somehow they don't seem like Russians."

"You should speak to the Chief of the Village!"

"But I don't know where he lives," said Vanyusha, in an offended tone.

"Who has upset you so much?" asked Olenin, looking round.

"The devil only knows. Faugh! There is no real master here. They say he has gone to some kind of *kriga,* and the old woman is a real devil. God preserve us!" answered Vanyusha putting his hands to his head. "How we shall live here, I don't know. They are worse than Tartars, I do declare—though they consider themselves Christians! A Tartar is bad enough, but all the same he is more noble. Gone to the *kriga* indeed! What this *kriga* they have invented is I don't know!" concluded Vanyusha, and turned aside.

"It's not as it is in the serfs' quarters at home, eh?" chaffed. Olenin without dismounting.

"Please sir, may I have your horse?" said Vanyusha, evidently perplexed by this new order of things, but resigning himself to his fate.

"So a Tartar is more noble, eh, Vanyusha?" repeated Olenin, dismounting and slapping the saddle.

"Yes, you're laughing! You think it funny," muttered Vanyusha angrily.

"Come, don't be angry, Vanyusha," replied Olenin, still smiling. "Wait a minute, I'll go and speak to the people of the house; you'll see I shall arrange everything. You don't know what a jolly life we shall have here. Only don't get upset."

Vanyusha did not answer. Screwing up his eyes, he looked contemptuously after his master, and shook his head. Vanyusha regarded Olenin as only his master, and Olenin regarded Vanyusha as only his servant; and they would both have been much surprised if anyone had told them that they were friends, as they really were without knowing it themselves. Vanyusha had been taken into his proprietor's house when he was only eleven, and when Olenin was the same age. When Olenin was fifteen he gave Vanyusha lessons for a time, and taught him to read French, of which the latter was inordinately proud; and when in specially good spirits he still let off French words, always laughing stupidly when he did so.

Olenin ran up the steps of the porch; and pushed open the door of the hut. Maryanka, wearing nothing but a pink smock, as all Cossack women do in the house, jumped, frightened, away from the door and pressing herself against the wall covered the lower part of her face with the broad sleeve of her Tartar smock. Having opened the door wider, Olenin, in the semi-darkness of the passage, saw the whole tall, shapely figure of the young Cossack girl. With the quick and eager curiosity of youth, he involuntarily noticed the firm maidenly form revealed by the fine print smock, and the beautiful black eyes fixed on him with childlike terror and wild curiosity.

"This is *she,*" thought Olenin. "But there will be many others like her," came at once into his head, and he opened the inner door.

Old Granny Ulitka, also dressed only in a smock, was stooping, with her back turned to him, sweeping the floor.

"Good day to you, Mother! I've come about my lodgings," he began.

The Cossack woman, without unbending, turned her severe but still handsome face towards him.

"What have you come here for? Want to mock at us, eh? I'll teach you to mock; may the black plague seize you!" she shouted, looking askance from under her frowning brow at the newcomer.

Olenin had at first imagined that the wayworn, gallant Caucasian Army (of which he was a member) would be everywhere received joyfully, and especially by the Cossacks, our comrades in the war; and he therefore felt perplexed by this reception. Without losing presence of mind, however, he tried to explain that he meant to pay for his lodgings, but the old woman would not give him a hearing.

"What have you come for? Who wants a pest like you, with your scraped face? You just wait a bit; when the master returns he'll show you your place. I don't want your dirty money! A likely thing—just as if we had never seen any! You'll stink the house out with your beastly tobacco, and want to put it right with money! Think we've never seen a pest! May you be shot in your bowels and your heart!" shrieked the old woman in a piercing voice, interrupting Olenin.

"It seems Vanyusha was right!" thought Olenin. " 'A Tartar would be nobler'," and, followed by Granny Ulitka's abuse, he went out of the hut. As he was leaving, Maryanka, still wearing only her pink smock, but with her face now hidden right up to her eyes in a white kerchief, suddenly slipped out from the passage past him. Pattering rapidly down the steps with her bare feet, she ran down from the porch, stopped, and, looking round hastily, with laughing eyes at the young man, vanished round the corner of the hut.

Her firm youthful step, the untamed look of the eyes glistening from under the white kerchief, and the firm stately build of the young beauty, struck Olenin even more powerfully than before.

"Yes, it must be *she,*" he thought, and troubling his head still less about the lodgings, he kept looking round at Maryanka as he approached Vanyusha.

"There you see, the girl too is quite savage, just like a wild filly!" said Vanyusha, who, though still busy with the luggage wagon, had now cheered up a bit. *"La fame!"* he added in a loud triumphant voice, and burst out laughing.

Chapter XI

TOWARDS EVENING THE MASTER OF THE HOUSE RETURNED FROM HIS FISHING, AND HAVING learned that the cadet would pay for the lodging, pacified the old woman and satisfied Vanyusha's demands.

Everything was settled in the new quarters. Their hosts moved into the winter hut, and let their summer hut to the cadet for three rubles a month. Olenin had something to eat and went to sleep. Towards evening he woke up, washed, and made himself tidy; dined and, having lit a cigarette, sat down by the window that looked on to the street. It was cooler. The slanting shadow of the hut with its ornamental gables fell across the dusty road, and even bent upwards at the base of the wall of the house opposite. The steep reed-thatched roof of that house shone in the rays of the setting sun. The air grew fresher. Everything was peaceful in the village. The soldiers had settled down and become quiet. The herds had not yet been driven home, and the people had not returned from their work.

Olenin's lodging was situated almost at the end of the village. At rare intervals, from somewhere far beyond the Terek in those parts whence Olenin had just come (the Chechen or the Kumytsk plain), came muffled sounds of firing. Olenin was feeling very well-contented after three months of bivouac life. His newly washed face was fresh and his powerful body clean (an unaccustomed sensation after the campaign) and in all his rested limbs he was conscious of a feeling of tranquility and strength. His mind, too, felt fresh and clear. He thought of the campaign and of past dangers. He remembered that he had faced them no worse than other men, and that he was accepted as a comrade among valiant Caucasians. His Moscow recollections were left behind, Heaven knows how far! The old life was wiped out, and a quite new life had begun in which there were, as yet, no mistakes. Here, as a new man among new men, he could gain a new and good reputation. He was conscious of a youthful and unreasoning joy of life. Looking now out of the window at the boys spinning their tops in the shadow of the house, now round his new little lodging, he thought how pleasantly he would settle down to this new Cossack village life. Now and then he glanced at the mountains and the blue sky, and an appreciation of the solemn grandeur of nature mingled with his reminiscences and dreams. His new life had begun, not as he imagined it would when he left Moscow, but unexpectedly well. "The mountains, the mountains, the mountains!" they permeated all his thoughts and feelings.

"He's drunk his bitch, and licked the jug! . . . Daddy Eroshka has drunk his bitch!" suddenly the little Cossacks, who had been spinning their tops under the window, shouted, looking towards the side street.

"He's drunk his bitch, and his dagger!" shouted the boys, crowding together and stepping backwards.

These shouts were addressed to Daddy Eroshka, who, with his gun on his shoulder and some pheasants hanging at his girdle, was returning from his shooting expedition.

"I have done wrong, lads, I have!" he said, vigorously swinging his arms and looking up at the windows on both sides of the street. "I have drunk the bitch; it was wrong," he repeated evidently vexed, but pretending not to care.

Olenin was surprised by the boys' behavior towards the old hunter, but was still more struck by the expressive, intelligent face and the powerful build of the man whom they called Daddy Eroshka.

"Here Daddy, here Cossack!" he called. "Come here!"

The old man looked into the window and stopped.

"Good evening, good man," he said, lifting his little cap off his cropped head.

"Good evening, good man," replied Olenin. "What is it the youngsters are shouting at you?"

Daddy Eroshka came up to the windows. "Why they're teasing the old man. No matter, I like it. Let them joke about their old daddy," he said with those firm musical intonations with which old and venerable people speak. "Are you an army commander?" he added.

"No, I am a cadet. But where did you kill those pheasants?" asked Olenin.

"I dispatched these three hens in the forest," answered the old man, turning his broad back towards the window, to show the hen-pheasants, which were hanging with their heads tucked into his belt and staining his coat with blood.

"Haven't you seen any?" he asked. "If you like, take a brace! Here you are," and he handed two of the pheasants in at the window. "Are you a sportsman yourself?" he asked.

"I am. During the campaign I killed four, myself."

"Four? What a lot!" said the old man sarcastically. "And are you a drinker? Do you drink *chikhir?*"

"Why not? I like a drink."

"Ah, I see you are a trump! We shall be *kunaks,* you and I," said Daddy Eroshka.

"Step in," said Olenin. "We'll have a drop of *chikhir.*"

"I might as well," said the old man, "but take the pheasants." The old man's face showed that he liked the cadet. He had seen at once that he could get free drinks from him, and that therefore it would be all right to give him a brace of pheasants.

Soon Daddy Eroshka's figure appeared in the doorway of the hut; and it was only then that

Olenin became fully conscious of the enormous size and sturdy build of this man, whose red-brown face, with its perfectly white broad beard, was all furrowed by deep lines produced by age and toil. For an old man, the muscles of his legs, arms, and shoulders were quite exceptionally large and prominent. There were deep scars on his head, under the short-cropped hair. His thick sinewy neck was covered with deep intersecting folds like a bull's. His horny hands were bruised and scratched. He stepped lightly and easily over the threshold, unslung his gun and placed it in a corner, and casting a rapid glance round the room noted the value of the goods and chattels deposited in the hut, and with out-turned toes stepped softly, in his sandals of raw hide, into the middle of the room. He brought with him a penetrating but not unpleasant smell of *chikhir* wine, vodka, gunpowder, and congealed blood.

Daddy Eroshka bowed down before the icons, smoothed his beard, and approaching Olenin, held out his thick brown hand. *"Koshkildy,"* said he: "That is Tartar for "Good day"—"Peace be unto you," it means in their tongue."

"*Koshkildy,* I know," answered Olenin, shaking hands.

"Eh, but you don't, you won't know the right order! Fool!" said Daddy Eroshka, shaking his head reproachfully. "If anyone says *"Koshkildy"* to you, you must say *"Allah rasi bo sun,"* that is, "God save you." That's the way, my dear fellow, and not *"Koshkildy."* But I'll teach you all about it. We had a fellow, Elias Mosevich here, one of your Russians, he and I were *kunaks.* He was a trump, a drunkard, a thief, a sportsman,—and what a sportsman! I taught him everything."

"And what will you teach me?" asked Olenin who was becoming more and more interested in the old man.

"I'll take you hunting, and teach you to fish. I'll show you Chechens, and find a girl for you, if you like—even that! That's the sort I am! I'm a wag!"—and the old man laughed. "I'll sit down. I'm tired. *Karga?"* he added, inquiringly.

"And what does *"Karga"* mean?" asked Olenin.

"Why, that means " all right" in Georgian. But I say it just so. It is a way I have, it's my favourite word. *Karga, Karga.* I say it just so; in fun I mean. Well, lad, won't you order the *chikhir?* You've got an orderly, haven't you?"

"Yes."

"Hey, Ivan!" shouted the old man. "All your soldiers are Ivans. Is yours Ivan?"

"True enough, his name is Ivan—Vanyusha. Here Vanyusha! Please get some *chikhir* from our landlady, and bring it here."

"Ivan or Vanyusha, that's all one. Why are all your soldiers Ivans? Ivan, old fellow," said the old man, "You tell them to give you some from the barrel that they have begun. They have the best *chikhir* in the village. But don't give more than thirty kopeks for the pint, mind, because that witch would be only too glad. . . . Our people are anathema people; stupid people," Daddy Eroshka continued in a confidential tone after Vanyusha had gone out. "They do not look upon you as on men; you are worse than a Tartar in their eyes. " Worldly Russians" they say. But as for me, though you are a soldier, you are still a man, and have a soul in you. Isn't that right? Elias Mosevich was a soldier, yet what a treasure of a man he was! Isn't that so, my dear fellow? That's why our people don't like me; but I don't care! I'm a merry fellow, and I like everybody. I'm Eroshka; yes, my dear fellow."

And the old Cossack patted the young man affectionately on the shoulder.

Chapter XII

VANYUSHA, WHO MEANWHILE HAD FINISHED HIS HOUSEKEEPING ARRANGEMENTS AND HAD EVEN got shaved by the company's barber and had pulled his trousers out of his high boots as a sign that the company was stationed in comfortable quarters, was in excellent spirits. He looked attentively, but not benevolently, at Eroshka, as at a wild beast he had never seen before, shook his head at the floor which the old man had dirtied, and, having taken two bottles from under a bench, went to the landlady.

"Good evening, kind people," he said, having made up his mind to be very gentle. "My master has sent me to get some *chikhir,* will you draw some for me, good folk?"

The old woman gave no answer. The girl, who was arranging the kerchief on her head before a little Tartar mirror, looked round at Vanyusha in silence.

"I'll pay money for it, honoured people," said Vanyusha, jingling the coppers in his pocket. "Be kind to us and we too will be kind to you," he added.

"How much?" asked the old woman abruptly.

"A pint."

"Go, my own, draw some for them," said Granny Ulitka to her daughter. "Take it from the cask that's begun, my precious."

The girl took the keys and a decanter, and went out of the hut with Vanyusha.

"Tell me, who is that young woman?" asked Olenin, pointing to Maryanka who was passing the window. The old man winked, and nudged the young man with his elbow.

"Wait a bit," said he, and reached out of the window. "Khm," he coughed, and bellowed, "Maryanka dear. Hallo, Maryanka, my girlie, won't you love me, darling? I'm a wag," he added in a whisper to Olenin. The girl, not turning her head and swinging her arms regularly and vigorously, passed the window with the peculiarly elegant and bold gait of a Cossack woman, and only turned her dark shaded eyes slowly towards the old man.

"Love me, and you'll be happy," shouted Eroshka, and, winking, he looked questioningly at the cadet.

"I'm a fine fellow, I'm a wag!" he added. "She's a regular queen, that girl. Eh?"

"She is lovely," said Olenin. "Call her here!"

"No, no," said the old man. "For that one, a match is being arranged with Lukashka, Luke, a fine Cossack, a brave, who killed an *abrek* the other day. I'll find you a better one. I'll find you one that will go about clothed in silk and silver. Once I've said it, I'll do it. I'll get you a regular beauty!"

"You, an old man—and say such things," replied Olenin. "Why, it's a sin!"

"A sin? Where's the sin?" said the old man emphatically. "A sin to look at a nice girl? A sin to have some fun with her? Or is it a sin to love her? Is that so in your parts? . . . No, my dear fellow, it's not a sin, it's salvation! God made you, and God made the girl too. He made it all; so it is no sin to look at a nice girl. That's what she was made for; to be loved and to give joy. That's how I judge it, my good fellow."

Having crossed the yard and entered a cool dark storeroom filled with barrels, Maryanka went up to one of them and repeating the usual prayer, plunged a dipper into it. Vanyusha, standing in the doorway, smiled as he looked at her. He thought it awfully funny that she had only a smock on, close-fitting behind and tucked up in front, and still funnier that she wore a necklace of silver coins. He thought this quite un-Russian, and that they would all laugh in the serfs' quarters at home, if they saw a girl like that. "*La fille comme c'est tres bien,* for a change," he thought. "I'll tell that to my master."

"What are you standing in the light for, you devil!" the girl suddenly shouted. "Why don't you hand me the decanter!"

Having filled the decanter with cool red wine, Maryanka handed it to Vanyusha.

"Give the money to Mammy," she said, pushing away the hand in which he held the money.

Vanyusha laughed. "Why are you so cross, little dear?" he said good-naturedly, irresolutely shuffling with his feet while the girl was covering the barrel.

She began to laugh.

"And you! Are you kind?"

"We, my master and I, are very kind," Vanyusha answered decidedly. "We are so kind, that wherever we have stayed our hosts were always very grateful. It's because he's a nobleman."

The girl stood listening.

"And is your master married?" she asked.

"No. The master is young and unmarried, because noble gentlemen can never marry young," said Vanyusha didactically.

"A likely thing! See what a fed-up buffalo he is, and too young to marry! Is he the chief of you all?" she asked.

"My master is a cadet; that means he's not yet an officer, but he's more important than a general—he's an important man! Because not only our colonel, but the Tsar himself, knows him," proudly explained Vanyusha. "We are not like those other beggars of the line regiment, and our papa himself was a Senator. He had more than a thousand serfs, all his own, and they send us a thousand rubles at a time. That's why everyone likes us. Another may be a captain, but have no money. What's the use of that?"

"Go, I'll lock up," said the girl, interrupting him.

Vanyusha brought Olenin the wine, and announced that *"La fille c'est tres joulie,"* and, laughing stupidly, at once went out.

Chapter XIII

MEANWHILE, THE TATTOO HAD SOUNDED IN THE VILLAGE SQUARE. THE PEOPLE HAD RETURNED from their work. The herd lowed, as in clouds of golden dust it crowded at the village gate. The girls and the women hurried through the streets and yards, turning in their cattle. The sun had quite hidden itself behind the distant snowy peaks. One pale bluish shadow spread over land and sky. Above the darkened gardens, stars just discernible were kindling, and the sounds were gradually hushed in the village. The cattle having been attended to and left for the night, the women came out and gathered at the corners of the streets and, cracking sunflower seeds with their teeth, settled down on the earthen embankments of the houses. Later on, Maryanka, having finished milking a buffalo and the two cows, also joined one of these groups. The group consisted of several women and girls and one old Cossack man. They were talking about the *abrek* who had been killed. The Cossack was narrating and the women questioning him.

"I expect he'll get a handsome reward," said one of the women.

"Of course. It's said that they'll send him a cross."

"Mosev did try to wrong him. Took the gun away from him; but the authorities at Kizlyar heard of it."

"A mean creature that Mosev is!"

"They say Lukashka has come home," remarked one of the girls.

"He and Nazarka are merry-making at Yamka's." (Yamka was an unmarried, disreputable Cossack woman who kept an illicit pot-house.) "I heard say they had drunk half a pailful."

"What luck that snatcher has," somebody remarked. "A real snatcher. But there's no denying he's a fine lad, smart enough for anything, a right-minded lad! His father was just such another, Daddy Kiryak was: he takes after his father. When he was killed the whole village howled. Look, there they are," added the speaker, pointing to the Cossacks who were coming down the street towards them. "And Ergushov has also managed to come along with them! The drunkard!"

Lukashka, Nazarka, and Ergushov, having emptied half a pail of vodka, were coming towards the girls. The faces of all three, but especially that of the old Cossack, were redder than usual. Ergushov was reeling, and kept laughing and nudging Nazarka in the ribs.

"Why are you not singing?" he shouted to the girls. "Sing to our merry-making, I tell you!"

They were welcomed with the words, "Had a good day? Had a good day?"

"Why sing? It's not a holiday," said one of the women. "You're tight, so you go and sing."

Ergushov roared with laughter, and nudged Nazarka. "You'd better sing. And I'll begin too. I'm clever, I tell you."

"Are you asleep, fair ones?" said Nazarka. "We've come from the cordon to drink your health. We've already drunk Lukashka's health."

Lukashka, when he reached the group, slowly raised his cap and stopped in front of the girls. His broad cheekbones and neck were red. He stood and spoke softly and sedately, but in his tranquillity and sedateness there was more of animation and strength than in all Nazarka's loquacity and bustle. He reminded one of a playful colt, that with a snort and a flourish of its tail suddenly stops short and stands as though nailed to the ground with all four feet. Lukashka stood quietly in front of the girls; his eyes laughed, and he spoke but little as he glanced now at his drunken companions and now at the girls.

When Maryanka joined the group he raised his cap with a firm deliberate movement, moved out of her way, and then stepped in front of her with one foot a little forward and with his thumbs in his belt, fingering his dagger. Maryanka answered his greeting with a leisurely bow of her head, settled down on the earth-bank, and took some seeds out of the bosom of her smock. Lukashka, keeping his eyes fixed on Maryanka, slowly cracked seeds and spat out the shells. All were quiet when Maryanka joined the group.

"Have you come for long?" asked a woman, breaking the silence.

"Till tomorrow morning," quietly replied Lukashka.

"Well, God willing, you've got a good chance," said the Cossack; "I'm glad of it, as I've just been saying."

"And I say so too," put in the tipsy Ergushov, laughing. "What a lot of visitors have come," he added, pointing to a soldier who was passing by. "The soldiers' vodka is good—I like it."

"They've sent three of the devils to us," said one of the women. "Grandad went to the village Elders, but they say nothing can be done."

"Ah, ha! Have you met with trouble?" said Ergushov.

"I expect they have smoked you out with their tobacco?" asked another woman. "Smoke as much as you like in the yard, I say, but we won't allow it inside the hut. Not if the Elder himself comes; I won't allow it. Besides, they may rob you. He's not quartered any of them on himself, no fear, that devil's son of an Elder."

"You don't like it?" Ergushov began again.

"And I've also heard say that the girls will have to make the soldiers' beds and offer them *chikhir* and honey," said Nazarka, putting one foot forward and tilting his cap like Lukashka.

Ergushov burst into a roar of laughter, and seizing the girl nearest to him, he embraced her. "I tell you true."

"Now then, you black pitch!" squealed the girl, "I'll tell your old woman."

"Tell her," shouted he, "That's quite right what Nazarka says; a circular has been sent round. He can read, you know. Quite true!" And he began embracing the next girl.

"Where are you getting to, you beast?" squealed the rosy, round-faced Ustenka, laughing and lifting her arm to hit him.

The Cossack stepped aside, and nearly fell. "There, they say girls have no strength, and you nearly killed me."

"Get away, you black pitch, what devil has brought you from the cordon?" said Ustenka, and turning away from him she again burst out laughing. "You were asleep and missed the *abrek*, didn't you? Suppose he had done for you; it would have been all the better."

"You'd have howled, I expect," said Nazarka, laughing.

"Howled! A likely thing."

"Just look, she doesn't care. She'd howl, Nazarka, eh? Would she?" said Ergushov.

Lukashka all this time had stood silently looking at Maryanka. His gaze evidently confused the girl. "Well, Maryanka! I hear they've quartered one of the chiefs on you?" he said, drawing nearer.

Maryanka, as was her wont, waited before she replied, and, slowly raising her eyes, looked at the Cossack. Lukashka's eyes were laughing, as if something special, apart from what was said, was taking place between himself and the girl.

"Yes, it's all right for them, as they have two huts," replied an old woman on Maryanka's behalf, "but at Fomushkin's now, they also have one of the chiefs quartered on them, and they say one whole corner is packed full with his things, and the family have nowhere to go. Was such a thing ever heard of, as that they should turn a whole horde loose in the village?" she said. "And what the plague are they going to do here?"

"I've heard say they'll build a bridge across the Terek," said one of the girls.

"And I've been told that they will dig a pit to put the girls in, because they don't love the lads," said Nazarka, approaching Ustenka; and he again made a whimsical gesture which set everybody laughing, and Ergushov, passing by Maryanka, who was next in turn, began to embrace an old woman.

"Why don't you hug Maryanka? You should do it to each in turn," said Nazarka.

"No, my old one is sweeter," shouted the Cossack, kissing the struggling old woman.

"You'll throttle me," she screamed, laughing.

The tramp of regular footsteps at the other end of the street interrupted their laughter. Three soldiers in their cloaks, with their muskets on their shoulders, were marching in step to relieve guard by the ammunition wagon.

The Corporal, an old cavalry man, looked angrily at the Cossacks and led his men straight along the road where Lukashka and Nazarka were standing, so that they should have to get out of the way. Nazarka moved, but Lukashka only screwed up his eyes and turned his broad back, without moving from his place. "People are standing here, so you go round," he muttered, only half turning his head and tossing it contemptuously in the direction of the soldiers. The soldiers passed by in silence, keeping step regularly along the dusty road. Maryanka began laughing, and all the other girls chimed in.

"What swells!" said Nazarka, "Just like long-skirted choristers," and he walked a few steps down the road, imitating the soldiers. Again everyone broke into peals of laughter.

Lukashka slowly came up to Maryanka. "And where have you put up the chief?" he asked.

Maryanka thought for a moment. "We've let him have the new hut," she said.

"And is he old or young," asked Lukashka, sitting down beside her.

"Do you think I've asked?" answered the girl. "I went to get him some *chikhir*, and saw him sitting by the window with Daddy Eroshka. Redheaded he seemed. They've brought a whole cartload of things"; and she dropped her eyes.

"Oh, how glad I am that I got leave from the cordon!" said Lukashka, moving closer to the girl, and looking straight in her eyes all the time.

"And have you come for long?" asked Maryanka, smiling slightly.

"Till the morning. Give me some seeds," he said, holding out his hand.

Maryanka now smiled outright, and unfastening the neckband of her smock, said, "Don't take them all."

"Really, I felt so dull all the time without you, I swear I did," he said in a restrained, calm whisper, helping himself to some seeds out of the bosom of the girl's smock; and stooping still closer over her, he continued with laughing eyes to talk to her in low tones.

"I won't come. I tell you," Maryanka suddenly said aloud, leaning away from him.

"No really . . . what I wanted to say to you," . . . whispered Lukashka. "By the Heavens! Do come!"

Maryanka shook her head, but did so with a smile.

"Nursey Maryanka! Hallo Nursey! Mammy is calling! Supper time!" shouted Maryanka's little brother, running towards the group.

"I'm coming," replied the girl, "Go, my dear, go alone—I'll come in a minute."

Lukashka rose and raised his cap.

"I expect I had better go home too, that will be best," he said, trying to appear unconcerned but hardly able to repress a smile, and he disappeared behind the corner of the house.

Meanwhile, night had entirely enveloped the village. Bright stars were scattered over the dark sky. The streets became dark and empty. Nazarka remained with the women on the earth-bank, and their laughter was still heard, but Lukashka, having slowly moved away from the girls, crouched down like a cat and then suddenly started running lightly, holding his dagger to steady it: not homeward, however, but towards the Teacher's house. Having passed two streets he turned into a lane, and lifting the skirt of his coat he sat down on the ground in the shadow of a fence. "A regular Teacher's daughter!" he thought about Maryanka. "Won't even have a lark—the devil! But just wait a bit."

The approaching footsteps of a woman attracted his attention. He began listening, and laughed all by himself.

Maryanka with bowed head, striking the pales of the fences with a switch, was walking with rapid regular strides straight towards him. Lukashka rose. Maryanka started and stopped.

"What an accursed devil! You frightened me! So you have not gone home?" she said, and laughed aloud.

Lukashka put one arm round her and with the other hand raised her face. "What I wanted to tell you, by Heaven!" his voice trembled and broke.

"What are you talking of, at night time!" answered Maryanka. "Mammy is waiting for me, and you'd better go to your sweetheart." And, freeing from his arms, she ran away a few steps. When she had reached the wattle fence of her home, she stopped and turned to the Cossack, who was running beside her and still trying to persuade her to stay a while with him.

"Well, what do you want to say, midnight-gadabout?" and she again began laughing.

"Don't laugh at me, Maryanka! By the Heaven! Well, what if I have a sweetheart? May the devil take her! Only say the word and now I'll love you—I'll do anything you wish. Here they are!" and he jingled the money in his pocket. "Now we can live splendidly. Others have pleasures, and I? I get no pleasure from you, Maryanka dear!"

The girl did not answer. She stood before him, breaking her switch into little bits with a rapid movement of her fingers.

Lukashka suddenly clenched his teeth and fists.

"And why keep waiting and waiting! Don't I love you, darling! You can do what you like with me," said he suddenly, frowning angrily and seizing both her hands.

The calm expression of Maryanka's face and voice did not change.

"Don't bluster, Lukashka, but listen to me," she answered, not pulling away her hands, but holding the Cossack at arm's length. "It's true I am a girl, but you listen to me! It does not depend on me, but if you love me I'll tell you this. Let go my hands, I'll tell you without.—I'll marry you, but you'll never get any nonsense from me," said Maryanka without turning her face.

"What, you'll marry me? Marriage does not depend on us. Love me yourself, Maryanka dear," said Lukashka, from sullen and furious becoming again gentle, submissive, and tender, and smiling as he looked closely into her eyes. Maryanka clung to him and kissed him firmly on the lips. "Brother dear!" she whispered, pressing him convulsively to her. Then, suddenly tearing herself away, she ran into the gate of her house without looking round.

In spite of the Cossack's entreaties to wait another minute to hear what he had to say, Maryanka did not stop.

"Go," she cried, "you'll be seen! I do believe that devil, our lodger, is walking about the yard."

"Teacher's daughter," thought Lukashka, "She will marry me. Marriage is all very well, but you just love me!"

He found Nazarka at Yamka's house, and after having a spree with him, went to Dunayka's house, where, in spite of her not being faithful to him, he spent the night.

Chapter XIV

IT WAS QUITE TRUE THAT OLENIN HAD BEEN WALKING ABOUT THE YARD WHEN MARYANKA ENTERED the gate, and had heard her say, "That devil, our lodger, is walking about." He had spent that evening with Daddy Eroshka in the porch of his new lodging. He had had a table, a samovar, wine and a lit candle, brought out, and over a cup of tea he listened to the tales the old man told seated on the threshold at his feet. Though the air was still, the candle dripped and flickered: now lighting up the post of the porch, now the table and crockery, now the cropped white head of the old man. Moths circled round the flame and, shedding the dust of their wings, fluttered on the table and in the glasses, flew into the candle flame, and disappeared in the black space beyond. Olenin and Eroshka had emptied five bottles of *chikhir.* Eroshka filled the glasses every time, offering one to Olenin, drinking his health, and talking untiringly. He told of Cossack life in the old days; of his father, "The Blood," who alone had carried on his back a boar's carcass weighing three hundredweight, and drank two pails of *chikhir* at one sitting. He told of his own days and his chum Girchik, with whom, during the plague, he used to smuggle felt cloaks across the Terek. He told how one morning he had killed two deer, and about his "little soul' who used to run to him at the cordon at night. He told all this so eloquently and picturesquely that Olenin did not notice how time passed. "Ah, yes, my dear fellow, you did not know me in my golden days; then I'd have shown you things. Today it's "Eroshka licks the jug," but then Eroshka was famous in the whole regiment. Whose was the finest horse? Who had a Gurda sword? To whom should one go to get a drink? With whom go on the spree? Who should be sent to the mountains to kill Ahmet Khan? Why, always Eroshka! Whom did the girls love? Always Eroshka had to answer for it. Because I was a real brave; a drinker; a thief (I used to seize herds of horses in the mountains); a singer; I was a master of every art! There are no Cossacks like that nowadays. It's disgusting to look at them. When they're that high (Eroshka held his hand three feet from the ground) they put on idiotic boots and keep looking at them—that's all the pleasure they know. Or they'll drink themselves foolish, not like men, but all wrong. And who was I? I was Eroshka, the thief; they knew me not only in this village, but up in the mountains. Tartar princes, my *kunaks,* used to come to see me! I used to be everybody's *kunak*. If he was a Tartar—with a Tartar; an Armenian—with an Armenian; a soldier—with a soldier; an officer—with an officer! I didn't care, as long as he was a drinker. He says you should cleanse yourself from intercourse with the world: not drink with soldiers, not eat with a Tartar."

"Who says all that?" asked Olenin.

"Why, our teacher! But listen to a Mullah or a Tartar Cadi. He says, " You unbelieving Giaours, why do you eat pig?" That shows that everyone has his own law. But I think it's all one. God has made everything for the joy of man. There is no sin in any of it."

"Take example from an animal. It lives in the Tartar's reeds, or in ours. Wherever it happens to go, there is its home! Whatever God gives it, that it eats! But our people say we have to lick red-hot plates in hell, for that. And I think it is all a fraud," he added after a pause.

"What is a fraud?" asked Olenin.

"Why, what the preachers say. We had an army captain in Chervlena who was my *kunak:* a fine fellow, just like me. He was killed in Chechnya. Well, he used to say that the preachers invent all that out of their own heads. " When you die the grass will grow on your grave, and that's all!" ' The old man laughed. "He was a desperate fellow."

"And how old are you?" asked Olenin.

"The Lord only knows! I must be about seventy. When a Tsaritsa reigned in Russia. I was no longer very little. So you can reckon it out. I must be seventy."

"Yes, you must, but you are still a fine fellow."

"Well, thank Heaven, I am healthy, quite healthy, except that a woman, a witch, has harmed me. . . ."

"How?"

"Oh, just harmed me."

"And so when you die, the grass will grow?" repeated Olenin.

Eroshka evidently did not wish to express his thought clearly. He was silent for a while. "And what did you think? Drink!" he shouted suddenly, smiling and handing Olenin some wine.

Chapter XV

WELL, WHAT WAS I SAYING?" HE CONTINUED, TRYING TO REMEMBER. "YES, THAT'S THE SORT OF man I am. I am a hunter. There is no hunter to equal me in the regiment. I will find and show you any animal, and any bird, and what, and where. I know it all! I have dogs, and two guns and nets, and a screen and a hawk. I have everything, thank the Lord! If you are not bragging but are a real sportsman, I'll show you everything. Do you know what a man I am! When I have found a track—I know the animal. I know where he will lie down, and where he'll drink or roll about. I make myself a perch and sit there all night, watching. What's the good of staying at home! One only gets into mischief, gets drunk. And here women come and chatter, and boys shout at me: enough to drive one mad.

"It's a different matter when you go out at nightfall, choose yourself a place, press down the reeds and sit there and sit, waiting, like a jolly fellow. One knows everything that goes on in the woods. One looks up at the sky: the stars move, you look at them and find out from them how the time goes. One looks round—the wood is rustling; one goes on waiting, now, there comes a crackling—a boar comes to rub himself; one listens to hear the young eaglets screech, and then the cocks give voice in the village, or the geese. When you hear the geese, you know it is not yet midnight. And I know all about it! Or when a gun is fired, somewhere far away, thoughts come to one. One thinks, who is that firing? Is it another Cossack like myself, who has been watching for some animal? And has he killed it? Or only wounded it, so that now the poor dear goes through the reeds smearing them with its blood all for nothing? I don't like that! Oh, how I dislike it! Why injure a beast? You fool, you fool! Or one thinks, "Maybe an *abrek* has killed some silly little Cossack." All this passes through one's mind. And once as I sat watching by the river, I saw a cradle floating down. It was sound, except for one corner which was broken off. Thoughts did come that time! I thought, some of your soldiers, the devils, must have got into a Tartar village and seized the Chechen women; and one of the devils has killed the little one: taken it by its legs, and hit its head against a wall. Don't they do such things? Sh! Men have no souls! And thoughts came to me that filled me with pity. I thought: they've thrown away the cradle and driven the wife out, and her brave has taken his gun and come across to our side to rob us. One watches and thinks. And when one hears a litter breaking through the thicket, something begins to knock inside one. Dear one, come this way! "They'll scent me," one thinks; and one sits and does not stir, while one's heart goes dun! dun! dun! and simply lifts you. Once this spring a fine litter came near me, I saw something black. "In the name of the Father and of the Son," and I was just about to fire when she grunts to her pigs: "Danger, children," she says, "there's a man here," and off they all ran, breaking through the bushes. I felt I should like to get my teeth into her."

"How could a sow tell her brood that a man was there?" asked Olenin.

"What do you think? You think, the beast's a fool? No, he is wiser than a man, though you do call him a pig! He knows everything.

"Take this, for instance. A man will pass along your track, and not notice it; but a pig as soon as it gets on to your track, turns and runs at once: that shows there is wisdom in him, since he scents your smell, and you don't. And there is this to be said too: you wish to kill it, and it wishes to go about the woods alive. You have one law, and it has another. It is a pig, but it is no worse than you— it too is God's creature. Ah, dear! Man is foolish, foolish, foolish!" The old man repeated this several times, and then letting his head drop, he sat thinking.

Olenin also became thoughtful, and descending from the porch, with his hands behind his back began pacing up and down the yard.

Eroshka, rousing himself, raised his head and began gazing intently at the moths circling round the flickering flame of the candle and burning themselves in it.

"Fool, fool!" he said. "Where are you flying to? Fool, fool!" He rose and with his thick fingers began to drive away the moths.

"You'll burn, little fool! Fly this way, there's plenty of room." He spoke tenderly, trying to catch them with his thick fingers delicately by their wings, and then letting them fly again. "You are killing yourself, and I am sorry for you!"

He sat a long time, chattering, and sipping out of the bottle. Olenin paced up and down the yard. Suddenly he was struck by the sound of whispering outside the gate. Involuntarily holding his breath, he heard a woman's laughter, a man's voice, and the sound of a kiss. Intentionally rustling the grass under his feet, he crossed to the opposite side of the yard; but after a while the wattle fence creaked. A Cossack in a dark Circassian coat and a white sheepskin cap passed along the other side of the fence (it was Luke), and a tall woman with a white kerchief on her head went past Olenin. "I and you have nothing to do with one another' was what Maryanka's firm step gave him to understand. He followed her with his eyes to the porch of the hut, and he even saw her, through the window, take off her kerchief and sit down. And suddenly a feeling of lonely depression, and some vague longings and hopes, and envy of someone or other, overcame the young man's soul.

The last lights had been put out in the huts. The last sounds had died away in the village. The wattle fences and the cattle gleaming white in the yards, the roofs of the houses and the stately poplars, all seemed to be sleeping the laborers' healthy peaceful sleep. Only the incessant ringing voices of frogs from the damp distance reached the young man. In the east the stars were growing fewer and seemed to be melting in the increasing light; but overhead they were denser and deeper than before. The old man was dozing with his head on his hand. A cock crowed in the yard opposite, but Olenin still paced the yard, thinking of something. The sound of a song sung by several voices reached him, and he stepped up to the fence and listened. The voices of several young Cossacks caroled a merry song, and one voice was distinguishable among them all by its firm strength.

"Do you know who is singing there?" said the old man, rousing himself. "It is the brave Lukashka. He has killed a Chechen, and now he rejoices. And what is there to rejoice at? . . . The fool, the fool!"

"And have you ever killed people?" asked Olenin.

"You devil!" shouted the old man. "What are you asking? One must not talk so. It is a serious thing to destroy a human being. . . . Ah, a very serious thing! Good-bye, my dear fellow. I've eaten my fill and am drunk," he said, rising. "Shall I come tomorrow, to go shooting?"

"Yes, come!"

"Mind, get up early; if you oversleep you will be fined!"

"Never fear, I'll be up before you," answered Olenin.

The old man left. The song ceased, but one could hear footsteps and merry talk. A little later the singing broke out again, but farther away, and Eroshka's loud voice chimed in with the other.

"What people, what a life!" thought Olenin with a sigh, as he returned alone to his hut.

Chapter XVI

DADDY EROSHKA WAS A SUPERANNUATED AND SOLITARY COSSACK: TWENTY YEARS AGO HIS WIFE went over to the Orthodox Church, and ran away from him and married a Russian sergeant-major, and he had no children. He was not bragging when he spoke of himself as having been the boldest dare-devil in the village when he was young. Everybody in the regiment knew of his old-time prowess. The death of more than one Russian, as well as Chechen, lay on his conscience. He used to go plundering in the mountains, and robbed the Russians too; and he had twice been in prison. The greater part of his life was spent in the forests, hunting. There he lived for days on a crust of bread and drank nothing but water. But, on the other hand, when he was in the village he made merry from morning to night. After leaving Olenin he slept for a couple of hours and awoke before it was light. He lay on his bed thinking of the man he had become acquainted with the evening before. Olenin's "simplicity" (simplicity in the sense of not grudging him a drink) pleased him very much, and so did Olenin himself. He wondered why the Russians were all "simple" and so rich, and why they knew nothing and yet were educated. He pondered on these questions, and also considered what he might get out of Olenin.

Daddy Eroshka's hut was of a good size and not old, but the absence of a woman was very noticeable in it. Contrary to the usual cleanliness of the Cossacks, the whole of this hut was filthy and exceedingly untidy. A bloodstained coat had been thrown on to the table; half a dough-cake lay beside a plucked and mangled crow with which to feed the hawk. Sandals of raw hide, a gun, a dagger, a little bag, wet clothes and sundry rags lay scattered on the benches. In a corner stood a tub with stinking water, in which another pair of sandals were being steeped; and nearby was a gun and a hunting-screen. On the floor a net had been thrown down and several dead pheasants lay there, while a hen tied by its leg was walking about near the table pecking among the dirt. In the unheated oven stood a broken pot with some kind of milky liquid. On the top of the oven a falcon was screeching and trying to break the cord by which it was tied, and a moulting hawk sat quietly on the edge of the oven, looking askance at the hen and occasionally bowing its head to right and left.

Daddy Eroshka, in his shirt, was lying prone on a short bed rigged up between the wall and the oven, with his strong legs raised and his feet on the oven. He was picking with his thick fingers at the scratches left on his hands by the hawk, which he was accustomed to carry without wearing gloves. The whole room, especially near the old man, was filled with that strong but not unpleasant mixture of smells that he always carried about with him.

"Uyde-ma, Daddy?" (Is Daddy in?) through the window came a sharp voice, which he at once recognized as Lukashka's. "Uyde, Uyde, Uyde."

"I am in!" shouted the old man. "Come in, neighbor Mark, Luke Mark. Come to see Daddy? On your way to the cordon?"

The hawk, at the sound of his master's shout, flapped his wings and pulled at his cord.

The old man was fond of Lukashka, who was the only man he excepted from his general contempt for the younger generation of Cossacks. Besides which, Lukashka and his mother, as near neighbors, often gave the old man wine, clotted cream, and other home produce which Eroshka did not possess. Daddy Eroshka, who all his life had allowed himself to get carried away, always explained his infatuations from a practical point of view. "Well, why not?" he used to say to himself. "I'll give them some fresh meat, or a bird, and they won't forget Daddy: they'll sometimes bring a cake or a piece of pie."

"Good morning, Mark! I am glad to see you," shouted the old man cheerfully, and, quickly putting down his bare feet, he jumped off his bed and walked a step or two along the creaking floor, looked down at his out-turned toes, and suddenly, amused by the appearance of his feet, he smiled, stamped with his bare heel on the ground, stamped again, and then performed a funny dance-step.

"That was clever, eh?" he asked, his small eyes glistening.

Lukashka smiled faintly.

"Going back to the cordon?" asked the old man.

"I have brought the *chikhir* I promised you when we were at the cordon."

"May Christ save you!" said the old man, who took up the extremely wide trousers that were lying on the floor and his *beshmet*, put them on, fastened a strap round his waist, poured some water over his hands from an earthenware pot, wiped them on the old trousers, smoothed his beard with a bit of comb, and stopped in front of Lukashka.

"Ready," he said.

Lukashka fetched a cup, wiped it, and filled it with wine, and then handed it to the old man.

"Your health! To the Father and the Son!" said the old man, accepting the wine with solemnity. "May you have what you desire, may you always be a hero, and receive the cross."

Lukashka also drank a little, after repeating a prayer, and then put the wine on the table.

The old man rose and brought out some dried fish which he laid on the threshold, where he beat it with a stick to make it tender; then, having put it with his horny hands on a blue plate (his only one), he placed it on the table.

"I have all I want. I have victuals, thank God!" he said proudly. "Well, and what of Mosev?" he added.

Lukashka, evidently wishing to know the old man's opinion, told him how the officer had taken the gun from him. "Never mind the gun," said the old man. "If you don't give away the gun, you will get no reward."

"But they say, Daddy, it's little reward a fellow gets when he is not yet a mounted Cossack; and the gun is a fine one, worth eighty rubles."

"Eh, let it go! I had a dispute like that with an officer: he wanted my horse. " Give it me and you'll be made a Teacher," says he. I wouldn't, and I got nothing!"

"Yes, Daddy, but you see I have to buy a horse; and they say you can't get one the other side of the river under fifty rubles, and mother has not yet sold our wine."

"Eh, we didn't bother," said the old man; "when Daddy Eroshka was your age, he already stole herds of horses from the Nogay folk, and drove them across the Terek. Sometimes we'd give a fine horse for a quart of vodka or a cloak."

"Why so cheap?" asked Lukashka.

"You're a fool, a fool, Mark," said the old man contemptuously. "Why, that's what one steals for, so as not to be stingy! As for you, I suppose you have not so much as seen how one drives off a herd of horses? Why don't you speak?"

"What's one to say, Daddy?" replied Lukashka. "It seems we are not the same sort of men as you were."

"You're a fool! Mark, a fool! not the same sort of men!" retorted the old man, mimicking the Cossack lad. "I was not that sort of Cossack at your age."

"How's that?" asked Lukashka.

The old man shook his head contemptuously. "Daddy Eroshka was *simple*; he did not grudge anything! That's why I was *kunak* with all Chechnya. A *kunak* would come to visit me, and I'd make him drunk with vodka and make him happy, and put him to sleep with me; and when I went to see him I'd take him a present—a dagger! That's the way it is done, and not as you do nowadays: the only amusement lads have now is to crack seeds and spit out the shells!" The old man finished contemptuously, imitating the present-day Cossacks cracking seeds and spitting out the shells.

"Yes, I know," said Lukashka; "that's so!"

"If you wish to be a fellow of the right sort, be a brave, and not a peasant! Because even a peasant can buy a horse—pay the money and take the horse."

They were silent for a while.

"Well, of course it is dull both in the village and the cordon, Daddy: but there's nowhere one can go for a bit of sport. All our fellows are so timid. Take Nazarka. The other day when we went to the Tartar village, Girey Khan asked us to come to Nogay to take some horses, but no one went; and how was I to go alone?"

"And what of Daddy? Do you think I am quite dried up? . . . No, I'm not dried up. Let me have a horse, and I'll be off to Nogay at once."

"What's the good of talking nonsense!" said Luke. "You'd better tell me what to do about Girey Khan. He says, " Only bring horses to the Terek, and then even if you bring a whole stud, I'll find a place for them." You see, he's also a shaven-headed Tartar,—how's one to believe him?"

"You may trust Girey Khan, all his kin were good people. His father too was a faithful *kunak*. But listen to Daddy and I won't teach you wrong: make him take an oath, then it will be all right. And if you go with him, have your pistol ready all the same; especially when it comes to dividing up the horses. I was nearly killed that way once by a Chechen. I wanted ten rubles from him for a horse. Trusting is all right, but don't go to sleep without a gun."

Lukashka listened attentively to the old man.

"I say, Daddy, have you any stone-break grass?" he asked after a pause.

"I have none, but I'll teach you how to get it. You're a good lad, and won't forget the old man. . . . Shall I tell you?"

"Tell me, Daddy."

"You know a tortoise? She's a devil, the tortoise is!"

"Of course I know!"

"Find her nest and fence it round, so that she can't get in. Well, she'll come, go round it, and will then go off to find the stone-break grass, and will bring some along and destroy the fence. Anyhow, next morning come in good time, and where the fence is broken, there you'll find the stone-break grass lying. Take it wherever you like. No lock and no bar will be able to stop you."

"Have you tried it yourself, Daddy?"

"As for trying, I have not tried it, but I was told of it by good people. I used only one charm: that was to repeat the " Hail Rhyme" when mounting my horse; and no one ever killed me!"

"What is the " Hail Rhyme," Daddy?"

"What, don't you know it? Oh, what people! You're right to ask Daddy. Well, listen, and repeat after me:

"Hail! Ye, living in Sion,
This is your King,
Our steeds we shall sit on,
Sophonia is weeping.
Zacharias is speaking,
Father Mandrych,
Mankind ever loving."

"Kind ever loving," the old man repeated. "Do you know it now? Try it."

Lukashka laughed.

"Come, Daddy, was it that that hindered their killing you? Maybe it just happened so!"

"You've grown too clever! You learn it all, and say it. It will do you no harm. Well, suppose you have sung "Mandrych," it's all right," and the old man himself began laughing.

"But just one thing! Luke, don't you go to Nogay!"

"Why?"

"Times have changed. You are not the same men. You've become rubbishy Cossacks! And see how many Russians have come down on us! You'd get to prison. Really, give it up! Just as if you could! Now Girchik and I, we used . . ." And the old man was about to begin one of his unending tales, but Lukashka glanced at the window and interrupted him.

"It is quite light, Daddy. It's time to be off. Look us up, someday."

"May Christ save you! I'll go to the army man; I promised to take him out shooting. He seems a good fellow."

Chapter XVII

FROM EROSHKA'S HUT LUKASHKA WENT HOME. AS HE RETURNED, THE DEWY MISTS WERE RISING from the ground and enveloped the village. Though the cattle were out of sight, you could hear them on all sides beginning to stir. The cocks called to one another with increasing frequency and insistence. The air was becoming more transparent, and the villagers were getting up. Not till he was close to it, could Lukashka discern the fence of his yard, all wet with dew, the porch of the hut and the open shed. From the misty yard he heard the sound of an ax chopping wood. Lukashka entered the hut. His mother was up, and stood at the oven, throwing wood into it. His little sister was still lying in bed asleep.

"Well, Lukashka, had enough holiday-making?" softly asked his mother. "Where did you spend the night?"

"I was in the village," reluctantly replied her son, reaching for his musket, which he drew from its cover and examined carefully.

His mother shook her head.

Lukashka poured a little gunpowder on to the pan, took out a little bag from which he drew some empty cartridge cases which he began filling, carefully plugging each one with a ball wrapped in a rag. Then, having tested the loaded cartridges with his teeth and examined them, he put down the bag.

"I say, Mother, I told you my socks wanted mending; have they been done?" he asked.

"Oh yes, our dumb girl was mending something last night. Why, is it time for you to be going back to the cordon? I haven't seen anything of you!"

"Yes, as soon as I have got ready I shall have to go," answered Lukashka, tying up the gunpowder. "And where is our dumb one? Outside?"

"Chopping wood, I expect. She kept fretting for you. " I shall not see him at all!" she said. She puts her hand to her face like this, and clicks her tongue, and presses her hands to her heart, as much as to say—"sorry." Shall I call her in? She understood all about the *abrek*."

"Call her," said Lukashka. "And I had some tallow there; bring it: I must grease my sword."

The old woman went out, and a few minutes later Lukashka's dumb sister came up the creaking steps and entered the hut. She was six years older than her brother, and would have been extremely like him, had it not been for the dull and coarsely changeable expression (common to all deaf and dumb people) of her face.

She wore a coarse smock all patched; her feet were bare and muddy, and on her head she had an old blue kerchief. Her neck, arms, and face were sinewy like a peasant's. Her clothing and her whole appearance indicated that she always did the hard work of a man.

She brought in a heap of logs, which she threw down by the oven. Then she went up to her brother, and with a joyful smile which made her whole face pucker up, touched him on the shoulder and began making rapid signs to him with her hands, her face, and whole body.

"That's right, that's right, Stepka is a trump!" answered the brother, nodding. "She's fetched everything, and mended everything, she's a trump! Here, take this for it!" He brought out two pieces of gingerbread from his pocket and gave them to her.

The dumb woman's face flushed with pleasure, and she began making a weird noise for joy. Having seized the gingerbread, she began to gesticulate still more rapidly, frequently pointing in one direction, and passing her thick finger over her eyebrows and her face. Lukashka understood her, and kept nodding, while he smiled slightly. She was telling him to give the girls dainties, and that the girls liked him, and that one girl, Maryanka—the best of them all—loved him. She indicated Maryanka by rapidly pointing in the direction of Maryanka's home and to her own eyebrows and face, and by smacking her lips and shaking her head. "Loves' she expressed by pressing her hands to her breast, kissing her hand, and pretending to embrace someone. Their mother returned to the hut, and seeing what her dumb daughter was saying, smiled and shook her head. Her daughter showed her the gingerbread, and again made the noise which expressed joy.

"I told Ulitka the other day that I'd send a matchmaker to them," said the mother. "She took my words well."

Lukashka looked silently at his mother. "But how about selling the wine, mother? I need a horse."

"I'll cart it when I have time. I must get the barrels ready," said the mother, evidently not wishing her son to meddle in domestic matters. "When you go out, you'll find a bag in the passage. I borrowed it from the neighbors, and got something for you to take back to the cordon; or shall I put it in your sack?"

"All right," answered Lukashka. "And if Girey Khan should come across the river, send him to me at the cordon, for I shall not get leave again for a long time now; I have some business with him."

He began to get ready to start.

"I will send him on," said the old woman. "It seems you have been spreeing at Yamka's all the time. I went out in the night to see to the cattle, and I think it was your voice I heard singing songs."

Lukashka did not reply, but went out into the passage, threw his bags over his shoulder, tucked up the skirts of his coat, took his musket, and then stopped for a moment on the threshold.

"Good-bye, mother!" he said as he closed the gate behind him. "Send me a small barrel with Nazarka. I promised it to the lads, and he'll call for it."

"May Christ keep you, Lukashka. God be with you! I'll send you some, some from the new barrel," said the old woman, going to the fence: "But listen," she added, leaning over the fence.

The Cossack stopped.

"You've been making merry here; well, that's all right. Why should not a young man amuse himself? God has sent you luck, and that's good. But now look out and mind, my son. Don't you go and get into mischief. Above all, honor your superiors: one has to! And I will sell the wine and find money for a horse, and will arrange a match with the girl for you."

"All right, all right!" answered her son, frowning.

His deaf sister shouted to attract his attention. She pointed to her head and the palm of her hand, to indicate the shaved head of a Chechen. Then she frowned and pretending to aim with a gun, she shrieked and began rapidly humming and shaking her head. This meant that Lukashka should kill another Chechen.

Lukashka understood. He smiled, and shifting the gun at his back under his cloak, stepped lightly and rapidly, and soon disappeared in the thick mist.

Silently the old woman, having stood a little while at the gate, returned to the hut and immediately began working.

Chapter XVIII

LUKASHKA RETURNED TO THE CORDON, AND AT THE SAME TIME DADDY EROSHKA WHISTLED TO his dogs and, climbing over his wattle fence, went to Olenin's lodging, passing by the back of the houses (he disliked meeting women before going out hunting or shooting).

He found Olenin still asleep, and even Vanyusha, though awake, was still in bed and was looking round the room, considering whether it was not time to get up, when Daddy Eroshka, gun on shoulder and in full hunter's trappings, opened the door. "A cudgel!" he shouted in his deep voice, "An alarm! The Chechens are upon us! Ivan! Get the samovar ready for your master; and get up yourself—quick!" cried the old man. "That's our way, my good man! Why, even the girls are already up! Look out of the window. See, she's going for water, and you're still sleeping!"

Olenin awoke and jumped up, feeling fresh and light-hearted at the sight of the old man and at the sound of his voice. "Quick, Vanyusha, quick!" he cried.

"Is that the way you go hunting?" said the old man. "Others are having their breakfast, and you are asleep! Lyam! Here!" he called to his dog.

"Is your gun ready?" he shouted, as loud as if a whole crowd were in the hut.

"Well, it's true I'm guilty, but it can't be helped! The powder, Vanyusha, and the wads!" said Olenin.

"A fine!" shouted the old man.

"Du tay voulay vou?" asked Vanyusha, grinning.

"You're not one of us, your gabble is not like our speech, you devil!" the old man shouted at Vanyusha, showing the stumps at his teeth.

"A first offense must be forgiven," said Olenin playfully, drawing on his high boots.

"The first offense shall be forgiven," answered Eroshka, "but if you oversleep another time you'll be fined a pail of *chikhir.* When it gets warmer you'll not find the deer."

"And even if we do find him, he is wiser than we are," said Olenin, repeating the words spoken by the old man the evening before, "and you can't deceive him!"

"Yes, laugh away! You kill one first, and then you may talk. Now then, hurry up! Look, there's the master himself coming to see you," added Eroshka, looking out of the window. "Just see how he's got himself up. He's put on a new coat so that you should see that he is an officer. Ah, these people, these people!" and, right enough, Vanyusha came in and announced that the master of the house wished to see Olenin.

"L'arjan!" he remarked profoundly, to forewarn his master of the meaning of this visitation.

Following him, the master of the house, in a new Circassian coat with an officer's stripes on the shoulders and with polished boots (quite exceptional among Cossacks) entered the room, swaying from side to side and congratulating his lodger on its being a holiday.

The Teacher, Elias Vasilich, was an *educated* Cossack. He had been to Russia proper, was a regimental school-teacher, and above all, he was noble. He wished to appear noble, but one could not help feeling that beneath his grotesque pretense of polish, his affectation, his self-confidence, and his absurd way of speaking, he was just the same as Daddy Eroshka. This could also clearly be seen by his sunburned face and his hands and his red nose. Olenin asked him to sit down.

"Good morning, Father Elias Vasilich," said Eroshka, rising with (or so it seemed to Olenin) an ironically low bow.

"Good morning, Daddy. So you're here already," said the Teacher, with a careless nod.

The Teacher was a man of about forty, with a gray pointed beard, skinny and lean, but handsome and very fresh-looking for his age. Having come to see Olenin, he was evidently afraid of being taken for an ordinary Cossack, and wanted to let Olenin feel his importance from the first.

"That's our Egyptian Nimrod," he remarked, addressing Olenin, and pointing to the old man with a self-satisfied smile. "A mighty hunter before the Lord! He's our foremost man on every hand. You've already been pleased to get acquainted with him."

Daddy Eroshka gazed at his feet, in their shoes of wet raw hide, and shook his head thoughtfully at the Teacher's ability and learning, and muttered to himself: "Gyptian Nimvrod! What things he invents!"

"Yes, you see, we mean to go hunting," answered Olenin.

"Yes, sir, exactly," said the Teacher, "but I have a small business with you."

"What do you want?"

"Seeing that you are a gentleman," began the Teacher, "and as I may understand myself to be in the rank of an officer too, and therefore we may always progressively negotiate, as gentlemen do . . ." (He stopped and looked with a smile at Olenin and at the old man.) "But if you have the desire with my consent, then, as my wife is a foolish woman of our class, she could not quite comprehend your words of yesterday's date. Therefore my quarters might be let for six rubles to the Regimental Adjutant, without the stables; but I can always avert it from myself free of charge. But, as you desire, therefore I, being myself of an officer's rank, can come to an agreement with you in everything, personally, as an inhabitant of this district, not according to our customs, but can maintain the conditions in every way. . . ."

"Speaks clearly!" muttered the old man.

The Teacher continued in the same strain for a long time. At last, not without difficulty, Olenin gathered that the Teacher wished to let his rooms to him, Olenin, for six rubles a month. The latter gladly agreed to this, and offered his visitor a glass of tea. The Teacher declined it.

"According to our silly custom we consider it a sort of sin to drink out of a "worldly" tumbler," he said. "Though, of course, with my education I may understand, but my wife from her human weakness . . ."

"Well then, will you have some tea?"

"If you will permit me, I will bring my own particular glass," answered the Teacher, and stepped out into the porch.

"Bring me my glass!" he cried.

In a few minutes the door opened, and a young sunburned arm in a print sleeve thrust itself in, holding a tumbler in the hand. The Teacher went up, took it, and whispered something to his daughter. Olenin poured tea for the Teacher into the latter's own "particular' glass, and for Eroshka into a "worldly' glass.

"However, I do not desire to detain you," said the Teacher, scalding his lips and emptying his tumbler. "I too have a great liking for fishing, and I am here, so to say, only on leave of absence for recreation from my duties. I too have the desire to tempt fortune and see whether some *Gifts of the Terek* may not fall to my share. I hope you too will come and see us and have a drink of our wine, according to the custom of our village," he added. The Teacher bowed, shook hands with Olenin, and went out. While Olenin was getting ready, he heard the Teacher giving orders to his family in an authoritative and sensible tone, and a few minutes later he saw him pass by the window in a tattered coat, with his trousers rolled up to his knees, and a fishing net over his shoulder.

"A rascal!" said Daddy Eroshka, emptying his "worldly' tumbler. "And will you really pay him six rubles? Was such a thing ever heard of? They would let you the best hut in the village for two rubles. What a beast! Why, I'd let you have mine for three!"

"No, I'll remain here," said Olenin.

"Six rubles! . . . Clearly it's a fool's money. Eh, eh, eh!" answered the old man. "Let's have some *chikhir,* Ivan!"

Having had a snack and a drink of vodka to prepare themselves for the road, Olenin and the old man went out together before eight o'clock. At the gate they came up against a wagon, to which a pair of oxen were harnessed. With a white kerchief tied round her head nearly to her eyes, a coat over her smock, and wearing high boots, Maryanka, with a long switch in her hand, was dragging the oxen by a cord tied to their horns.

"Mammy," said the old man, pretending that he was going to seize her.

Maryanka flourished her switch at him, and glanced merrily at them both with her beautiful eyes.

Olenin felt still more light-hearted.

"Now then, come on, come on," he said, throwing his gun on his shoulder and conscious of the girl's eyes upon him.

"Gee, gee!" sounded Maryanka's voice behind them, followed by the creak of the moving wagon.

As long as their road lay through the pastures at the back of the village, Eroshka went on talking. He could not forget the Teacher, and kept on abusing him.

"Why are you so angry with him?" asked Olenin.

"He's stingy. I don't like it," answered the old man. "He'll leave it all behind when he dies! Then who's he saving up for? He's built two houses, and he's got a second garden from his brother by a law-suit. And in the matter of papers what a dog he is! They come to him from other villages to fill up documents. As he writes it out, exactly so it happens. He gets it quite exact. But who is he saving for? He's only got one boy and the girl; when she is married who'll be left?"

"Well then, he's saving up for her dowry," said Olenin.

"What dowry? The girl is sought after, she's a fine girl. But he's such a devil that he must yet marry her to a rich fellow. He wants to get a big price for her. There's Luke, a Cossack, a neighbour and a nephew of mine, a fine lad. It's he who killed the Chechen—he has been wooing her for a long time, but he hasn't let him have her. He's given one excuse and another, and a third. "The girl's too young," he says. But I know what he is thinking. He wants to keep them bowing to him. What a lot of scandal there has been about her lately. Still they will get her for Lukashka, because he is the best Cossack in the village, a brave, who has killed an *abrek,* and will be rewarded with a cross."

"But how about this? When I was walking up and down the yard last night, I saw my landlord's daughter and some Cossack kissing," said Olenin.

"You're pretending!" cried the old man, stopping.

"On my word," said Olenin.

"Women are the devil," said Eroshka, pondering. "But what Cossack was it?"

"I couldn't see."

"Well, what sort of a cap had he, a white one?"

"Yes."

"And a red coat? About your height?"

"No, a bit taller."

"It's he!" and Eroshka burst out laughing. "It's himself, it's Mark. He is Luke, but I call him Mark for a joke. His very self! I love him. I was just such a one myself. What's the good of minding them? My sweetheart used to sleep with her mother and her sister-in-law, but I managed to get in. She used to sleep upstairs; that witch her mother was a regular demon; it's awful how she hated me. Well, I used to come with a chum, Girchik his name was. We'd come under her window, and I'd climb on his shoulders, push up the window and begin groping about. She used to sleep just there on a bench. Once I woke her up and she nearly called out. She had not recognized me. "Who is there?" she said, and I could not answer. Her mother was even beginning to stir, but I took off my cap and shoved it over her mouth; and she at once knew it, by a seam in it, and ran out to me. I used not to want anything then. She'd bring along clotted cream and grapes and everything," added Eroshka (who always explained things practically), "and she was not the only one. It was a life!"

"And what now?"

"Now we'll follow the dog, get a pheasant to settle on a tree, and then you may fire."

"Would you have made up to Maryanka?"

"Attend to the dogs. I'll tell you tonight," said the old man, pointing to his favourite dog, Lyamka.

After a pause they continued talking while they went about a hundred paces. Then the old man stopped again and pointed to a twig that lay across the path.

"What do you think of that?" he said. "You think it's nothing? It's bad that this stick is lying so."

"Why is it bad?"

He smiled.

"Ah, you don't know anything. Just listen to me. When a stick lies like that, don't you step across it, but go round it, or throw it off the path this way, and say "Father and Son and Holy Ghost," and then go on with God's blessing. Nothing will happen to you. That's what the old men used to teach me."

"Come, what rubbish!" said Olenin. "You'd better tell me more about Maryanka. Does she carry on with Lukashka?"

"Hush, . . . be quiet now!" the old man again interrupted in a whisper: "just listen, we'll go round by the wood."

And the old man, stepping quietly in his soft shoes, led the way by a narrow path into the dense, wild, overgrown forest. Now and again with a frown he turned to look at Olenin, who rustled and clattered with his heavy boots and, carrying his gun carelessly, several times caught the twigs of the trees that grew across the path.

"Don't make a noise. Step softly, soldier!" the old man whispered angrily.

There was a feeling in the air that the sun had risen. The mist was dissolving, but it still enveloped the tops of the trees. The forest looked terribly high. At every step the aspect changed: what had appeared like a tree proved to be a bush, and a reed looked like a tree.

Chapter XIX

IT WAS CALM. THE SOUNDS FROM THE VILLAGE, AUDIBLE AT FIRST, NOW NO LONGER REACHED THE sportsmen. Only the brambles cracked as the dogs ran under them, and now and then birds called to one another. Olenin knew that danger lurked in the forest, that *abreks* always hid in such places. But he knew too that in the forest, for a man on foot, a gun is a great protection. Not that he was afraid, but he felt that another in his place might be; and looking into the damp misty forest and listening to the rare and faint sounds with strained attention, he changed his hold on his gun and experienced a pleasant feeling that was new to him. Daddy Eroshka went in front, stopping and carefully scanning every puddle where an animal had left a double track, and pointing it out to Olenin. He hardly spoke at all, and only occasionally made remarks in a whisper. The track they were following had once been made by wagons, but the grass had long overgrown it. The elm and plane-tree forest, on both sides of them, was so dense and overgrown with creepers that it was impossible to see anything through it. Nearly every tree was enveloped from top to bottom with wild grape vines, and dark bramble bushes thickly covered the ground. Every little glade was overgrown with blackberry bushes and gray feathery reeds. In places large hoof-prints and small funnel-shaped pheasant trails led from the path into the thicket. The vigour of the growth of this forest untrampled by cattle, struck Olenin at every turn, for he had never seen anything like it. This forest, the danger, the old man and his mysterious whispering, Maryanka with her virile upright bearing, and the mountains—all this seemed to him like a dream.

"A pheasant has settled," whispered the old man, looking round and pulling his cap over his face—"Cover your mug! A pheasant!" he moved his arm angrily at Olenin, and pushed forward almost on all fours. "He don't like a man's mug."

Olenin was still behind him when the old man stopped and began examining a tree. A cock-pheasant on the tree clucked at the dog that was barking at it, and Olenin saw the pheasant; but at that moment a report, as of a cannon, came from Eroshka's enormous gun; the bird fluttered up and, losing some feathers, fell to the ground. Coming up to the old man, Olenin disturbed another, and raising his gun he aimed and fired. The pheasant flew swiftly up, and then, catching at the branches as he fell, dropped like a stone to the ground.

"Good man!" the old man (who could not hit a flying bird) shouted, laughing.

Having picked up the pheasants, they went on. Olenin, excited by the exercise and the praise, kept addressing remarks to the old man.

"Stop! Come this way," the old man interrupted. "I noticed the track of deer here, yesterday."

After they had turned into the thicket and gone some three hundred paces, they scrambled through into a glade overgrown with reeds and partly under water. Olenin failed to keep up with the old huntsman, and presently Daddy Eroshka, some twenty paces in front, stooped down, nodding and beckoning with his arm. On coming up with him, Olenin saw a man's footprint to which the old man was pointing.

"D'you see?"

"Yes, well?" said Olenin, trying to speak as calmly as he could. "A man's footstep!"

Involuntarily a thought of Cooper's *Pathfinder* and of *abreks* flashed through Olenin's mind, but noticing the mysterious manner with which the old man moved on, he hesitated to question him, and remained in doubt whether this mysteriousness was caused by fear of danger, or by the sport.

"No, it's my own footprint," the old man said quietly, and pointed to some grass, under which the track of an animal was just perceptible.

The old man went on, and Olenin kept up with him. Descending to lower ground some twenty paces farther on, they came upon a spreading pear-tree, under which, on the black earth, lay the fresh dung of some animal. The spot, all covered over with wild vines, was like a cosy arbor, dark and cool.

"He's been here this morning," said the old man with a sigh; "the lair is still damp; quite fresh."

Suddenly they heard a terrible crash in the forest some ten paces from where they stood. They both started and seized their guns, but they could see nothing and only heard the branches breaking. The rhythmical rapid thud of galloping was heard for a moment and then changed into a hollow rumble which resounded farther and farther off, re-echoing in wider and wider circles through the forest. Olenin felt as though something had snapped in his heart. He peered carefully, but vainly, into the green thicket, and then turned to the old man. Daddy Eroshka, with his gun pressed to his breast, stood motionless; his cap was thrust backwards, his eyes gleamed with an unwonted glow, and his mouth open, with its worn yellow teeth, seemed to have stiffened in that position.

"A horned stag!" he muttered, and throwing down his gun in despair he began pulling at his gray beard. "Here it stood. We should have come round by the path. . . . Fool! fool!" and he gave his beard an angry tug. "Fool! Pig!" he repeated, pulling painfully at his own beard.

Through the forest something seemed to fly away in the mist, and ever farther and farther off was heard the sound of the flight of the stag.

It was already dusk when, hungry, tired, but full of vigor, Olenin returned with the old man. Dinner was ready. He ate and drank with the old man till he felt warm and merry. Olenin then went out into the porch. Again westwards before his eyes rose the mountains. Again the old man told his endless stories of hunting, of *abreks,* of sweethearts, and of all that free and reckless life. Again the fair Maryanka went in and out and across the yard, and her smock outlined the powerful form of the beautiful maiden.

Chapter XX

THE NEXT DAY, OLENIN WENT ALONE TO THE SPOT WHERE HE AND THE OLD MAN HAD STARTLED the stag. Instead of passing round through the gate, he climbed over the prickly hedge, as everybody else did, and before he had had time to pull out the thorns that had caught in his coat, his dog, which had run on in front, started two pheasants. He had hardly stepped among the briers, when the pheasants began to rise at every step (the old man had not shown him that place the day before, as he meant to keep it for shooting from behind the screen). Olenin fired twelve times, and killed five pheasants, but clambering after them through the briers he got so fatigued that he was drenched with perspiration. He called off his dog, uncocked his gun, put in a bullet above the small shot, and, brushing away the mosquitoes with the wide sleeve of his Circassian coat, he went slowly to the spot where they had been the day before. It was, however, impossible to keep back the dog, who found trails on the very path, and Olenin killed two more pheasants, so that, after being detained by this, it was getting towards noon before he began to find the place he was looking for.

The day was perfectly clear, calm, and hot. The morning moisture had dried up even in the forest, and myriads of mosquitoes literally covered his face, his back, and his arms. His dog had turned from black to gray, its back being covered with mosquitoes, and so had Olenin's coat, through which the insects thrust their stings. Olenin was ready to run away from them, and it seemed to him that it was impossible to live in this country in the summer. He was about to go home, but remembering that other people managed to endure such pain, he resolved to bear it, and gave himself up to be devoured. And, strange to say, by noontime the feeling became actually pleasant. He even felt that without this mosquito-filled atmosphere around him, and that mosquito-paste mingled with perspiration which his hand smeared over his face, and that unceasing irritation all over his body, the forest would lose for him some of its character and charm. These myriads of insects were so well suited to that monstrously lavish wild vegetation, these multitudes of birds and beasts which filled the forest, this dark foliage, this hot scented air, these runlets filled with turbid water which everywhere soaked through from the Terek and gurgled here and there under the overhanging leaves, that the very thing which had at first seemed to him dreadful and intolerable, now seemed pleasant. After going round the place where yesterday they had found the animal, and not finding anything, he felt inclined to rest. The sun stood right above the forest and poured its perpendicular rays down on his back and head whenever he came out into a glade, or on to the road. The seven heavy pheasants dragged painfully at his waist. Having found the traces of yesterday's stag, he crept under a bush into the thicket just where the stag had lain, and lay down in its lair. He examined the dark foliage around him, the place marked by the stag's perspiration, and yesterday's dung, the imprint of the stag's knees, the bit of black earth it had kicked up, and his own footprints of the day before. He felt cool and comfortable and did not think of or wish for anything. And suddenly he was overcome by such a strange feeling of causeless joy, and of love for everything, that, from an old habit of his childhood, he began crossing himself and thanking someone. Suddenly, with extraordinary clearness, he thought: "Here am I, Dmitry Olenin, a being quite distinct from every other being, now lying all alone, Heaven only knows where—where a stag used to live—an old stag, a beautiful stag, who perhaps had never seen a man, and in a place where no human being has ever sat, or thought these thoughts. Here I sit, and around me stand old and young trees, one of them festooned with wild grape vines, and pheasants are fluttering, driving one another about and perhaps scenting their murdered brothers." He felt his pheasants, examined them, and wiped the warm blood off his hand on to his coat. "Perhaps the jackals scent them, and with dissatisfied faces go off in another direction: above me, flying in among the leaves, which to them seem enormous islands, mosquitoes hang in the air and buzz: one, two, three, four, a hundred, a thousand, a million mosquitoes, and all of them buzz something or other, and each one of them is separate from all else, and is just such a separate Dmitry Olenin as I am myself." He imagined vividly what the mosquitoes buzzed: "This way, this way, lads! Here's someone we can eat!" They buzzed, and stuck to him. And it was clear to him that he was not a Russian nobleman, a member of Moscow society, the friend and relation of so-and-so and so-and-so, but just such a mosquito, or pheasant, or deer, as those that were now living all round him. "Just as they, just as Daddy Eroshka, I shall live awhile and die, and as he says truly: grass will grow and nothing more."

"But what though the grass does grow?" he continued thinking, "Still I must live, and be happy, because happiness is all I desire. Never mind what I am—an animal like all the rest, above whom the grass will grow, and nothing more; or a frame in which a bit of the one God has been set—still I must live in the very best way. How then must I live to be happy, and why was I not happy before?" And he began to recall his former life, and he felt disgusted with himself. He appeared to himself to have been terribly exacting and selfish, though he now saw that all the while he really needed nothing for himself. And he looked round at the foliage with the light shining through it, at the setting sun and the clear sky, and he felt just as happy as before.

"Why am I happy, and what used I to live for?" thought he. "How much I exacted for myself; how I schemed and did not manage to gain anything but shame and sorrow! and, there now, I require nothing to be happy"; and suddenly a new light seemed to reveal itself to him. "Happiness is this!" he said to himself, "Happiness lies in living for others. That is evident. The desire for happiness is innate in every man; therefore it is legitimate. When trying to satisfy it selfishly—that is, by seeking for oneself riches, fame, comforts, or love—it may happen that circumstances arise which make it impossible to satisfy these desires. It follows that it is these desires that are illegitimate, but not the need for happiness. But what desires can always be satisfied, despite external circumstances? What are they? Love, self-sacrifice." He was so glad and excited when he had discovered this, as it seemed to him, new truth, that he jumped up and began impatiently seeking someone to sacrifice himself for, to do good to, and to love. "Since one wants nothing for oneself," he kept thinking, "why not live for others?"

He took up his gun with the intention of returning home quickly to think this out and to find an opportunity of doing good. He made his way out of the thicket.

When he had come out into the glade he looked around him; the sun was no longer visible above the treetops. It had grown cooler, and the place seemed to him quite strange, and not like the country round the village. Everything seemed changed—the weather and the character of the forest; the sky was wrapped in clouds, the wind was rustling in the treetops, and all around nothing was visible but reeds and dying broken-down trees. He called to his dog, who had run away to follow some animal, and his voice came back as in a desert. And suddenly he was seized with a terrible sense of weirdness. He grew frightened. He remembered the *abreks,* and the murders he had been told about, and he expected every moment that an *abrek* would spring from behind every bush, and he would have to defend his life and die, or be a coward. He thought of God and of the future life as for long he had not thought about them. And all around was that same gloomy stern wild nature. "And is it worthwhile living for oneself," thought he, "when at any moment you may die, and die without having done any good; and so that no one will know of it?" He went in the direction where he fancied the village lay. Of his shooting he had no further thought; but he felt tired to death, and peered round at every bush and tree with particular attention and almost with terror, every moment expecting to be called to account for his life. After having wandered about for a considerable time, he came upon a ditch down which was flowing cold sandy water from the Terek, and, not to go astray any longer, he decided to follow it. He went on, without knowing whither the ditch would lead him. Suddenly the reeds behind him crackled. He shuddered and seized his gun. He felt ashamed of himself: the over-excited dog, panting hard, had thrown itself into the cold water of the ditch, and was lapping it!

He too had a drink, and then followed the dog in the direction it wished to go, thinking it would lead him to the village. But despite the dog's company, everything around him seemed still more dreary. The forest grew darker, and the wind grew stronger and stronger in the tops of the broken old trees. Some large birds circled, screeching, round their nests in those trees. The vegetation grew poorer, and he came oftener and oftener upon rustling reeds and bare sandy spaces, covered with animal footprints. To the howling of the wind was added another kind of cheerless monotonous roar. Altogether his spirits became gloomy. Putting his hand behind him he felt his pheasants, and found one missing. It had broken off and was lost, and only the bleeding head and beak remained sticking in his belt. He felt more frightened than he had ever been before. He began to pray to God, and feared above all that he might die without having done anything good or kind; and he so wanted to live, and to live so as to perform a feat of self-sacrifice.

Chapter XXI

SUDDENLY IT WAS AS THOUGH THE SUN HAD SHONE INTO HIS SOUL. HE HEARD RUSSIAN BEING SPOken, and also heard the rapid smooth flow of the Terek, and a few steps farther in front of him saw the brown moving surface of the river with the dim-colored wet sand of its banks and shallows, the distant steppe, the cordon watch-tower outlined above the water, a saddled, hobbled horse among the brambles, and then the mountains opening out before him. The red sun appeared for an instant from under a cloud, and its last rays glittered brightly along the river over the reeds, on the watch-tower and on a group of Cossacks, among whom Lukashka's vigorous figure attracted Olenin's involuntary attention.

Olenin felt that he was again, without any apparent cause, perfectly happy. He had come upon the Nizhne-Prototsk post on the Terek, opposite a pro-Russian Tartar village on the other bank of the river. He accosted the Cossacks, but not finding as yet any excuse for doing anyone a kindness he entered the hut; nor in the hut did he find any such opportunity. The Cossacks received him coldly. On entering the mud hut he lit a cigarette. The Cossacks paid little attention to him, first because he was smoking a cigarette, and secondly because they had something else to divert them that evening. Some hostile Chechens, relatives of the *abrek* who had been killed, had come from the hills with a scout to ransom the body; and the Cossacks were waiting for their Commanding Officer's arrival from the village. The dead's man brother, tall and well-shaped, with a short cropped beard which was dyed red, despite his very tattered coat and cap was calm and majestic as a king. His face was very like that of the dead *abrek*. He did not deign to look at anyone and never once glanced at the dead body, but, sitting on his heels in the shade, he spat as he smoked his short pipe, and occasionally uttered some few guttural sounds of command, which were respectfully listened to by his companion. He was evidently a brave who had met Russians more than once before in quite other circumstances, and nothing about them could astonish or even interest him. Olenin was about to approach the dead body and had begun to look at it, when the brother, looking up at him from under his brows with calm contempt, said something sharply and angrily. The scout hastened to cover the dead's man face with his coat. Olenin was struck by the dignified and stern expression of the brave's face. He began to speak to him asking from what village he came, but the Chechen scarcely giving him a glance, spat contemptuously and turned away. Olenin was so surprised at the Chechen not being interested in him, that he could only put it down to the man's stupidity or ignorance of Russian; so he turned to the scout who also acted as interpreter. The scout was as ragged as the other, but instead of being red-haired he was black-haired, fidgety, with extremely white gleaming teeth and sparkling black eyes. The scout willingly entered into conversation, and asked for a cigarette.

"There were five brothers," began the scout in his broken Russian. "This is the third brother the Russians have killed, only two are left. He is a brave, a great brave!" he said, pointing to the Chechen. "When they killed Ahmet Khan (the dead brave) this one was sitting on the opposite bank among the reeds. He saw it all. Saw him laid in the skiff and brought to the bank. He sat there till the night and wished to kill the old man, but the others would not let him."

Lukashka went up to the speaker, and sat down.

"Of what village?" asked he.

"From there in the hills," replied the scout, pointing to the misty bluish gorge beyond the Terek. "Do you know Suzuk-su? It is about eight miles beyond that."

"Do you know Girey Khan in Suzuk-su?" asked Lukashka, evidently proud of the acquaintance. "He is my *kunak*."

"He is my neighbor," answered the scout.

"He's a trump!" and Lukashka, evidently much interested, began talking in Tartar to the scout.

Presently a Cossack captain and the head of the village arrived on horseback, with a suite of two Cossacks. The captain—one of the new type of Cossack officers—wished the Cossacks "Good health," but none shouted in reply, "Hail! Good health to your honor," as is customary in the Russian Army, and only a few replied with a bow. Some, and among them Lukashka, rose and stood erect. The corporal replied that all was well at the outposts. All this seemed ridiculous: it was as if these Cossacks were playing at being soldiers. But these formalities soon gave place to ordinary ways of behavior, and the captain, who was a smart Cossack, just like the others, began speaking fluently in Tartar to the interpreter. They filled in some document, gave it to the scout, and received from him some money. Then they approached the body.

"Which of you is Luke Gavrilov?" asked the captain.

Lukashka took off his cap and came forward.

"I have reported your exploit to the Commander. I don't know what will come of it. I have recommended you for a cross; you're too young to be made a sergeant. Can you read?"

"I can't."

"But what a fine fellow to look at!" said the captain, again playing the commander. "Put on your cap. Which of the Gavrilovs does he come of? . . . the Broad, eh?"

"His nephew," replied the corporal.

"I know, I know. Well, lend a hand, help them," he said, turning to the Cossacks.

Lukashka's face shone with joy and seemed handsomer than usual. He moved away from the corporal, and having put on his cap, sat down beside Olenin.

When the body had been carried to the skiff, the brother Chechen descended to the bank. The Cossacks involuntarily stepped aside to let him pass. He jumped into the boat, and pushed off from the bank with his powerful leg, and now, as Olenin noticed, for the first time threw a rapid glance at all the Cossacks, and then abruptly asked his companion a question. The latter answered something, and pointed to Lukashka. The Chechen looked at him and, turning slowly away, gazed at the opposite bank. That look expressed not hatred, but cold contempt. He again made some remark.

"What is he saying?" Olenin asked of the fidgety scout.

"Yours kill ours, ours slay yours. It's always the game," replied the scout, evidently inventing, and he smiled, showing his white teeth, as he jumped into the skiff.

The dead man's brother sat motionless, gazing at the opposite bank. He was so full of hatred and contempt that there was nothing on this side of the river that moved his curiosity. The scout, standing up at one end of the skiff and dipping his paddle now on one and then on the other, steered skillfully, while talking incessantly. The skiff became smaller and smaller as it moved obliquely across the stream; the voices became scarcely audible, and at last, still within sight, they landed on the opposite bank, where their horses stood waiting. There they lifted out the corpse, and (though the horse shied) laid it across one of the saddles, mounted, and rode at a footpace along the road past a Tartar village, from which a crowd came out to look at them.

The Cossacks on the Russian side of the river were highly satisfied and jolly. Laughter and jokes were heard on all sides. The captain and the head of the village entered the mud hut to regale themselves. Lukashka, vainly striving to impart a sedate expression to his merry face, sat down with his elbows on his knees beside Olenin, and whittled away at a stick.

"Why do you smoke?" he said with assumed curiosity. "Is it good?"

He evidently spoke because he noticed Olenin felt ill at ease and isolated among the Cossacks.

"It's just a habit," answered Olenin. "Why?"

"H'm, if one of us were to smoke there would be a row! Look there now, the mountains are not far off," continued Lukashka, "yet you can't get there! How will you get back alone? It's getting dark. I'll take you, if you like. You ask the corporal to give me leave."

"What a fine fellow!" thought Olenin, looking at the Cossack's bright face. He remembered Maryanka and the kiss he had heard by the gate, and he was sorry for Lukashka and his want of culture. "What confusion it is," he thought. "A man kills another, and is happy and satisfied with himself as if he had done something excellent. Can it be that nothing tells him that it is not a reason for any rejoicing, and that happiness lies not in killing, but in sacrificing oneself?"

"Well, you had better not meet him again now, mate!" said one of the Cossacks who had seen the skiff off, addressing Lukashka. "Did you hear him asking about you?"

Lukashka raised his head. "My godson?" said Lukashka, meaning by that word the dead Chechen.

"Your godson won't rise, but the red one is the godson's brother!"

"Let him thank God that he got off whole himself," replied Lukashka.

"What are you glad about?" asked Olenin. "Supposing your brother had been killed, would you be glad?"

The Cossack looked at Olenin with laughing eyes. He seemed to have understood all that Olenin wished to say to him, but to be above such considerations.

"Well, that happens too! Don't our fellows get killed, sometimes?"

Chapter XXII

THE CAPTAIN AND THE HEAD OF THE VILLAGE RODE AWAY; AND OLENIN, TO PLEASE LUKASHKA as well as to avoid going back alone through the dark forest, asked the corporal to give Lukashka leave, and the corporal did so. Olenin thought that Lukashka wanted to see Maryanka, and he was also glad of the companionship of such a pleasant-looking and sociable Cossack. Lukashka and Maryanka he involuntarily united in his mind, and he found pleasure in thinking about them. "He loves Maryanka," thought Olenin, "and I could love her," and a powerful novel emotion of tenderness overcame him as they walked homewards together through the dark forest. Lukashka too felt happy; something akin to love made itself felt between these two very different young men. Every time they glanced at one another they wanted to laugh.

"By which gates do you enter?" asked Olenin.

"By the middle ones. But I'll see you as far as the marsh. After that you have nothing to fear."

Olenin laughed.

"Do you think I am afraid? Go back, and thank you. I can get on alone."

"It's all right! What have I to do? And how can you help being afraid? Even we are afraid," said Lukashka to set Olenin's self-esteem at rest, and laughed too.

"Then come in with me. We'll have a talk and a drink, and in the morning you can go back."

"Couldn't I find a place to spend the night!" laughed Lukashka. "But the corporal asked me to go back."

"I heard you singing last night, and also saw you."

"Everyone . . ." and Luke moved his head.

"Is it true you are getting married?" asked Olenin.

"Mother wants me to marry. But I have not got a house yet."

"Aren't you in the regular service?"

"Oh dear no! I've only just joined, and have not got a horse yet, and don't know how to get one. That's why the marriage does not come off."

"And what would a horse cost?"

"We were bargaining for one beyond the river the other day, and they would not take sixty rubles for it, though it is a Nogay horse."

"Will you come and be my drabant?" (A drabant was a kind of orderly attached to an officer when campaigning.) "I'll get it arranged and will give you a horse," said Olenin suddenly. "Really now I have two and I don't want it."

"How—don't want it?" Lukashka said, laughing. "Why should you make us a present? We'll get on by ourselves, by God's help."

"No, really! Or don't you want to be a drabant?" said Olenin, glad that it had entered his head to give a horse to Lukashka, though, without his knowing why, he felt uncomfortable and confused and did not know what to say when he tried to speak.

Lukashka was the first to break the silence.

"Have you a house of your own in Russia?" he asked.

Olenin could not refrain from replying that he had not only one, but several houses.

"A good house? Bigger than ours?" asked Lukashka, good-naturedly.

"Much bigger; ten times as big, and three stories high," replied Olenin.

"And have you steeds such as ours?"

"I have a hundred horses, worth three or four hundred rubles each, but they are not like yours. They are trotters, you know! But still, I like the horses here best."

"Well, and did you come here of your own free will, or were you sent?" said Lukashka, laughing at him. "Look! that's where you lost your way," he added, "you should have turned to the right."

"I came by my own wish," replied Olenin. "I wanted to see your parts and to join some expeditions."

"I would go on an expedition any day," said Lukashka. "D'you hear the jackals howling?" he added, listening.

"I say, don't you feel any horror at having killed a man?" asked Olenin.

"What's there to be frightened about? But I should like to join an expedition," Lukashka repeated. "How I want to! How I want to!"

"Perhaps we may be going together. Our company is going before the holidays, and your hundred too."

"And what did you want to come here for? You've a house, and horses, and serfs. In your place I'd do nothing but make merry! And what is your rank?"

"I am a cadet, but have been presented for a commission."

"Well, if you're not bragging about your home, if I were you I'd never have left it! Yes, I'd never have gone away anywhere. Do you find it pleasant living among us?"

"Yes, very pleasant," answered Olenin.

It had grown quite dark before, talking in this way, they approached the village. They were still surrounded by the deep gloom of the forest. The wind howled through the treetops. The jackals suddenly seemed to be crying close beside them: howling, chuckling, and sobbing, but ahead of them in the village the sounds of women's voices and the barking of dogs could already be heard; the outlines of the huts were clearly to be seen; lights gleamed, and the air was filled with the peculiar smell of *kizyak* smoke. Olenin felt keenly, that night especially, that here in this village was his home, his family, all his happiness, and that he had never and would never live so happily anywhere as he did in this Cossack village. He was so fond of everybody and especially of Lukashka that night. On reaching home, to Lukashka's great surprise, Olenin led out of the shed with his own hands a horse he had bought in Groznoe—it was not the one he usually rode but another—not a bad horse though no longer young, and gave it to Lukashka.

"Why should you give me a present?" said Lukashka, "I have not yet done anything for you."

"Really it is nothing," answered Olenin. "Take it, and you will give me a present, and we'll go on an expedition against the enemy together."

Lukashka became confused.

"But what d'you mean by it? As if a horse were of small value," he said without looking at the horse.

"Take it, take it! If you don't, you will offend me. Vanyusha! Take the gray horse to his house."

Lukashka took hold of the halter.

"Well, then, thank you! This is something unexpected, undreamed of."

Olenin was as happy as a boy of twelve.

"Tie it up here. It's a good horse. I bought it in Groznoe; it gallops splendidly! Vanyusha, bring us some *chikhir.* Come into the hut."

The wine was brought. Lukashka sat down and took the wine-bowl.

"God willing, I'll find a way to repay you," he said, finishing his wine. "How are you called?"

"Dmitry Andreich."

"Well, 'Mitry Andreich, God bless you. We will be *kunaks.* Now you must come to see us. Though we are not rich people, still we can treat a *kunak,* and I will tell mother that if you need anything—clotted cream, or grapes—and if you come to the cordon I'm your servant to go hunting, or to go across the river, anywhere you like! There now, only the other day, what a boar I killed, and I divided it among the Cossacks; but if I had only known, I'd have given it to you."

"That's all right, thank you! But don't harness the horse, it has never been in harness."

"Why harness the horse? And there is something else I'll tell you, if you like," said Lukashka; bending his head. "I have a *kunak,* Girey Khan. He asked me to lie in ambush by the road where they come down from the mountains. Shall we go together? I'll not betray you. I'll be your *murid.*"

"Yes, we'll go; we'll go someday."

Lukashka seemed quite to have quieted down and to have understood Olenin's attitude towards him. His calmness, and the ease of his behaviour, surprised Olenin, and he even did not quite like it. They talked long, and it was late when Lukashka, not tipsy (he never was tipsy) but having drunk a good deal, left Olenin after shaking hands. Olenin looked out of the window to see what he would do. Lukashka went out hanging his head. Then, having led the horse out of the gate, he suddenly shook his head, sprang on to its back like a cat, gathered up the reins of the halter, gave a shout and galloped down the street.

Olenin expected that Lukashka would go to share his joy with Maryanka, but, though he did not do so, Olenin still felt his soul more at ease than ever before in his life. He was as delighted as a boy, and could not refrain from telling Vanyusha, not only that he had given Lukashka the horse, but also why he had done it, as well as his new theory of happiness.

Vanyusha did not approve of this theory, and announced that *"l'argent il n'y a pas!"* and that therefore it was all nonsense.

Lukashka rode home, jumped off the horse, and handed it over to his mother, telling her to let it out with the communal Cossack herd. He himself had to return to the cordon that same night. His deaf sister undertook to take the horse, and explained by signs that when she saw the man who had given the horse, she would bow down at his feet. The old woman only shook her head at her son's story, and decided in her own mind that he had stolen it. She therefore told the deaf girl to take it to the herd before daybreak.

Lukashka went back alone to the cordon pondering over Olenin's action. Though he did not consider the horse a good one, yet it was worth at least forty rubles and Lukashka was very glad to have the present. But why it had been given him he could not at all understand, and therefore he did not experience the least feeling of gratitude. On the contrary, vague suspicions that the cadet had some evil intentions filled his mind. What those intentions were he could not decide, but neither could he admit the idea that a stranger would give him a horse worth forty rubles, for nothing, just out of kindness; it seemed impossible. Had he been drunk, one might understand it! He might have wished to show off. But the cadet had been sober, and therefore must have wished to bribe him to do something wrong. "Eh, humbug!" thought Lukashka. "Haven't I got the horse, and we'll see later on. I'm not a fool myself, and we shall see who'll get the better of the other," he thought, feeling the necessity of being on his guard and therefore arousing in himself unfriendly feelings towards Olenin. He told no one how he had got the horse. To some he said he had bought it, to others he replied evasively. However, the truth soon got about in the village, and Lukashka's mother, and Maryanka, as well as Elias Vasilich and other Cossacks, when they heard of Olenin's unnecessary gift, were perplexed, and began to be on their guard against the Cadet. But despite their fears, his action aroused in them a great respect for his simplicity and wealth.

"Have you heard," said one, "that the cadet quartered on Elias Vasilich has thrown a forty-ruble horse at Lukashka?"

"He's rich! . . ."

"Yes, I heard of it," replied another profoundly, "he must have done him some great service. We shall see what will come of this cadet. Eh! what luck that snatcher has!"

"Those cadets are crafty, awfully crafty," said a third. "See if he don't go setting fire to a building, or doing something!"

Chapter XXIII

OLENIN'S LIFE WENT ON WITH MONOTONOUS REGULARITY. HE HAD LITTLE INTERCOURSE WITH the commanding officers or with his equals. The position of a rich cadet in the Caucasus was peculiarly advantageous in this respect. He was not sent out to work, or for training. As a reward for going on an expedition, he was recommended for a commission, and meanwhile he was left in peace. The officers regarded him as an aristocrat, and behaved towards him with dignity. Card-playing and the officers' carousals accompanied by the soldier-singers, of which he had had experience when he was with the detachment, did not seem to him attractive, and he also avoided the society and the life of the officers in the village. The life of officers stationed in a Cossack village has long had its own definite form. Just as every cadet or officer when in a fort regularly drinks porter, plays cards and discusses the rewards given for taking part in the expeditions, so in the Cossack villages he regularly drinks *chikhir* with his hosts, treats the girls to sweetmeats and honey, dangles after the Cossack women, and falls in love, and occasionally marries there. Olenin always took his own path and had an unconscious objection to the beaten tracks. And here, too, he did not follow the ruts of a Caucasian officer's life.

It came quite naturally to him to wake up at daybreak. After drinking tea and admiring from his porch the mountains, the morning, and Maryanka, he would put on a tattered ox-hide coat, sandals of soaked raw hide, buckle on a dagger, take a gun, with cigarettes and some lunch in a little bag, call his dog, and soon after five o'clock he would start for the forest beyond the village. Towards seven in the evening he returned tired and hungry, with five or six pheasants hanging from his belt (sometimes with some other animal) and with his bag of food and cigarettes untouched. If the thoughts in his head had lain like the lunch and cigarettes in the bag, one might have seen that during all those fourteen hours not a single thought had moved in it.

He returned morally fresh, strong, and perfectly happy, and he could not tell what he had been thinking about all the time. Were they ideas, memories, or dreams, that had been flitting through his mind? They were frequently all three. He would rouse himself and ask what he had been thinking about; and would see himself as a Cossack, working in a vineyard with his Cossack wife, or an *abrek* in the mountains, or a boar running away from himself. And all the time he kept peering and watching for a pheasant, a boar, or a deer.

In the evening, Daddy Eroshka would be sure to be sitting with him. Vanyusha would bring a jug of *chikhir,* and they would converse quietly, drink, and separate to go quite contentedly to bed. The next day he would again go shooting, again be healthily weary, again they would sit conversing and drink their fill, and again be happy. Sometimes, on a holiday or a day of rest, Olenin spent the whole day at home. Then his chief occupation was watching Maryanka, whose every movement, without realizing it himself, he followed greedily from his window or his porch. He regarded Maryanka and loved her (so he thought) just as he loved the beauty of the mountains and the sky, and he had no thought of entering into any relations with her. It seemed to him that between him and her such relations as there were between her and the Cossack Lukashka, could not exist, and still less, such as often existed between rich officers and other Cossack girls. It seemed to him that if he tried to do as his fellow-officers did, he would exchange his complete enjoyment of contemplation for an abyss of suffering, disillusionment and remorse. Besides, he had already achieved a triumph of self-sacrifice in connection with her, which had given him great pleasure; but above all he was in a way afraid of Maryanka, and would not for anything have ventured to utter a word of love to her lightly.

Once during the summer when Olenin had not gone out shooting but was sitting at home, quite unexpectedly a Moscow acquaintance, a very young man whom he had met in society, came in.

"Ah, *mon cher*, my dear fellow, how glad I was when I heard that you were here!" he began in his Moscow French, and he went on intermingling French words in his remarks. "They said, 'Olenin'. What Olenin? and I was so pleased. . . . Fancy fate bringing us together here! Well, and how are you? How? Why?" and Prince Beletsky told his whole story: how he had temporarily entered the regiment, how the Commander-in-Chief had offered to take him as an aide-de-camp, and how he would take up the post after this campaign, although personally he felt quite indifferent about it.

"Living here, in this hole, one must at least make a career—get a cross—or a rank—be transferred to the Guards. That is quite indispensable, not for myself, but for the sake of my relations and friends. The prince received me very well; he is a very decent fellow," said Beletsky, and went on unceasingly. "I have been recommended for the St. Ann's Cross, for the expedition. Now I shall stay here a bit until we start on the campaign. It's capital here. What women! Well, and how are you getting on? I was told by our captain, Startsev, you know, a kind-hearted, stupid creature . . . Well, he said you were living like an awful savage, seeing no one! I quite understand you don't want to be mixed up with the set of officers we have here. I am so glad now, you and I will be able to see something of one another. I have put up at the police officer's house. There is such a girl there, Ustenka! I tell you, she is just charming."

And more and more French and Russian words came pouring forth from that world which Olenin thought he had left forever.

The general opinion about Beletsky was that he was a nice good-natured fellow. Perhaps he really was; but in spite of his pretty, good-natured face, Olenin thought him extremely unpleasant. He seemed just to exhale that filthiness which Olenin had forsworn. What vexed him most, was that he could not—had not the strength—abruptly to repulse this man, who came from that world: as if that old world he used to belong to had an irresistible claim on him. Olenin felt angry with Beletsky and with himself, yet, against his wish, he introduced French phrases into his own conversation, was interested in the Commander-in-Chief and in their Moscow acquaintances, and because he and Beletsky in this Cossack village both spoke French, he spoke contemptuously of their fellow-officers, and of the Cossacks, and was friendly with Beletsky, promising to visit him and inviting him to drop in to see him. Olenin, however, did not himself go to see Beletsky.

Vanyusha for his part approved of Beletsky; remarking that he was a real gentleman.

Beletsky at once adopted the customary life of a rich officer in a Cossack village.

Before Olenin's eyes, in one month he came to be like an old resident of the village; he made the old men drunk, arranged evening parties, and himself went to parties arranged by the girls—bragged of his conquests, and even got so far that, for some unknown reason, the women and girls began calling him grandad, and the Cossacks, to whom a man who loved wine and women was clearly understandable, got used to him and even liked him better than they did Olenin, who was a puzzle to them.

Chapter XXIV

It was five in the morning. Vanyusha was in the porch heating the samovar, and using the leg of a long boot instead of bellows. Olenin had already ridden off to bathe in the Terek. (He had recently invented a new amusement: to swim his horse in the river.) His landlady was in her outhouse and the dense smoke of the kindling fire rose from the chimney. The girl was milking the buffalo-cow in the shed. "Can't keep quiet, the damned thing!" came her impatient voice, followed by the rhythmical sound of milking.

From the street in front of the house, horses' hoofs were heard clattering briskly, and Olenin, riding bareback on a handsome dark-gray horse which was still wet and shining, rode up to the gate. Maryanka's handsome head, tied round with a red kerchief, appeared from the shed, and again disappeared. Olenin was wearing a red silk shirt, a white Circassian coat girdled with a strap which carried a dagger, and a tall cap. He sat his wet, well-fed horse with a slightly conscious elegance and, holding his gun at his back, stooped to open the gate. His hair was still wet, and his face shone with youth and health. He thought himself handsome, agile, and like a brave; but he was mistaken. To any experienced Caucasian, he was still only a soldier.

When he noticed that the girl had put out her head, he stooped with particular smartness, threw open the gate and, tightening the reins, swished his whip and entered the yard. "Is tea ready, Vanyusha?" he cried gaily, not looking at the door of the shed. He felt with pleasure how his fine horse, pressing down its flanks, pulling at the bridle and with every muscle quivering, and with each foot ready to leap over the fence, pranced on the hard clay of the yard. *"C'est prêt,"* answered Vanyusha. Olenin felt as if Maryanka's beautiful head was still looking out of the shed, but he did not turn to look at her. As he jumped down from his horse he made an awkward movement, and caught his gun against the porch and turned a frightened look towards the shed, where there was no one to be seen and whence the sound of milking could still be heard.

Soon after he had entered the hut he came out again and sat down with his pipe and a book on the side of the porch which was not yet exposed to the rays of the sun. He meant not to go anywhere before dinner that day, and to write some long-postponed letters; but somehow he felt disinclined to leave his place in the porch, and he was as reluctant to go back into the hut as if it had been a prison. The housewife had heated her oven, and the girl, having driven the cattle, had come back and was collecting *kisyak* and heaping it up along the fence. Olenin went on reading but did not understand a word of what was written in the book that lay open before him. He kept lifting his eyes from it and looking at the powerful young woman who was moving about. Whether she stepped into the moist morning shadow thrown by the house, or went out into the middle of the yard lit up by the joyous young light so that the whole of her stately figure in its bright colored garment gleamed in the sunshine and cast a black shadow—always he feared to lose any one of her movements. It delighted him to see how freely and gracefully her figure bent: into what folds her only garment, a pink smock, draped itself on her bosom and down her shapely legs; how she drew herself up and her tight-drawn smock showed the outline of her breathing bosom; how the soles of her narrow feet in her worn red slippers stood on the ground without altering their shape; how her strong arms with the sleeves rolled up, exerting the muscles, used the spade almost as if in anger, and how her deep dark eyes sometimes glanced at him. Though the delicate brows frowned, yet her eyes expressed pleasure, and a knowledge of her own beauty.

"I say, Olenin, have you been up long?" said Beletsky, as he entered the yard, dressed in the coat of a Caucasian officer.

"Ah, Beletsky," replied Olenin, holding out his hand. "How is it you are out so early?"

"I had to. I was driven out; we are having a ball tonight. Maryanka,—of course you'll come to Ustenka's?" he added, turning to the girl. Olenin felt surprised that Beletsky could address this woman so easily. But Maryanka, as though she had not heard him, bent her head, and throwing the spade across her shoulder went with her firm masculine tread towards the outhouse.

"She's shy, the wench is shy," Beletsky called after her. "Shy of you," he added as, smiling gaily, he ran up the steps of the porch.

"How is it you are having a ball, and have been driven out?"

"It is at Ustenka's, at my landlady's, that the ball is, and you two are invited. A ball consists of a pie and a gathering of girls."

"What should we do there?"

Beletsky smiled knowingly and winked, jerking his head in the direction of the outhouse into which Maryanka had disappeared.

Olenin shrugged his shoulders and blushed.

"Well, really, you are a strange fellow!" said he.

"Come now, don't pretend!"

Olenin frowned, and Beletsky noticing this, smiled insinuatingly.

"Oh, come, what do you mean?" he said, "living in the same house—and such a fine girl, a splendid girl, a perfect beauty—"

"Wonderfully beautiful! I never saw such a woman before," replied Olenin.

"Well then?" said Beletsky, quite unable to understand the situation.

"It may be strange," replied Olenin, "but why should I not say what is true? Since I have lived here, women don't seem to exist for me. And it is so good, really! Now what can there be in common between us and women like these? Eroshka—that's a different matter! He and I have a passion in common—sport."

"There now! In common! And what have I in common with Amalia Ivanovna? It's the same thing! You may say they're not very clean; that's another matter . . . *A la guerre, comme à la guerre! . . .*"

"But I have never known any Amalia Ivanovnas, and have never known how to behave with women of that sort," replied Olenin. "One cannot respect them; but these I do respect."

"Well, go on respecting them! Who wants to prevent you?"

Olenin did not reply. He evidently wanted to complete what he had begun to say. It was very near to his heart.

"I know I am an exception . . ." He was visibly confused. "But my life has so shaped itself that I not only see no necessity to renounce my rules, but that I could not live here, let alone live as happily as I am doing, were I to live as you do. Therefore I look for something quite different from what you look for."

Beletsky raised his eyebrows incredulously. "Anyhow, come to me this evening; Maryanka will be there and I will make you acquainted. Do come, please! If you feel dull you can go away. Will you come?"

"I would come, but to speak frankly, I am afraid of being seriously carried away."

"Oh, oh, oh!" shouted Beletsky. "Only come, and I will comfort you. Will you? On your word?"

"I would come, but really I don't understand what we shall do; what part we shall play!"

"Please, I beg of you. You will come?"

"Yes, perhaps I'll come," said Olenin.

"Really now! Charming women such as one sees nowhere else, and to live like a monk! What an idea! Why spoil your life and not make use of what is at, hand? Have you heard that our company is ordered to Vozdvizhensk?"

"Hardly, I was told the 18th Company would be sent there," said Olenin.

"No. I have had a letter from the aide-de-camp. He writes that the Prince himself will take part in the campaign. I am very glad I shall see something of him. I'm beginning to get tired of this place."

"I hear we shall start on a raid soon."

"I have not heard of it; but I have heard that Krinovitsin has received the Order of St. Ann, for a raid. He expected a lieutenancy," said Beletsky, laughing. "He was let in! He has set off for headquarters."

It was growing dusk and Olenin began thinking about the party. The invitation he had received worried him. He felt inclined to go, but what might take place there seemed strange, absurd, and even rather alarming. He knew that neither Cossack men nor older women, nor anyone besides the girls, were to be there. What was going to happen? How was he to behave? What would they talk about? What connection was there between him and those wild Cossack girls? Beletsky had told him of such curious, cynical and yet rigid relations. It seemed strange to think that he would be there in the same hut with Maryana and perhaps might have to talk to her. It seemed to him impossible when he remembered her majestic bearing. But Beletsky spoke of it as if it were all perfectly simple. "Is it possible that Beletsky will treat Maryana in the same way? That is interesting," thought he. "No, better not go. It's all so horrid, so vulgar, and above all—it leads to nothing!" But again he was worried by the question of what would take place; and besides, he felt as if bound by a promise. He went out without having made up his mind one way or the other; but he walked as far as Beletsky's, and went in there.

The hut in which Beletsky lived was like Olenin's. It was raised nearly five feet from the ground on wooden piles, and had two rooms. In the first (which Olenin entered by the steep flight of steps) feather-beds, rugs, blankets and cushions were tastefully and handsomely arranged, Cossack fashion, along the main wall. On the side wall hung brass basins and weapons, while on the floor, under a bench, lay watermelons and pumpkins. In the second room there was a big brick oven, a table, and sectarian icons. It was here that Beletsky was quartered, with his camp-bed and his pack and trunks. His weapons hung on the wall with a little rug behind them, and on the table were his toilet appliances and some portraits. A silk dressing-gown had been thrown on to the bench. Beletsky himself, clean and good looking, lay on the bed in his underclothing, reading *Les Trois Mousquetaires*.

He jumped up.

"There, you see how I have arranged things. Fine! Well, that's right, that you have come. They are working furiously. Do you know what the pie is made of? Dough, with a stuffing of pork and grapes. But that's not the point. You just look at the commotion out there!"

And really, on looking out of the window they saw an unusual bustle going on in the hut. Girls ran in and out, now for one thing and now for another. "Will it soon be ready?" cried Beletsky.

"Very soon! Why? Is Grandad hungry?" and from the hut came the sounds of ringing laughter.

Ustenka, plump, small, rosy, and pretty, with her sleeves turned up, ran into Beletsky's hut to fetch some plates.

"Get away, or I shall smash the plates!" she squeaked, escaping from Beletsky. "You'd better come and help," she shouted, laughing, to Olenin. "And don't forget to get some refreshments for the girls." ("Refreshments" meaning spice-bread and sweets.)

"And has Maryana come?"

"Of course! She brought some dough."

"Do you know," said Beletsky, "if one were to dress Ustenka up and clean and polish her up a bit, she'd be better than all our beauties. Have you ever seen that Cossack woman who married a colonel; she was charming! Borsheva? What dignity! Where do they get it . . ."

"I have not seen Borsheva, but I think nothing could be better than the costume they wear here."

"Ah, I'm first rate at fitting into any kind of life," said Beletsky with a sigh of pleasure. "I'll go and see what they are up to." He threw his dressing-gown over his shoulders and ran out, shouting, "And you look after the " refreshments.""

Olenin sent Beletsky's orderly to buy spice-bread and honey; but it suddenly seemed to him so disgusting to give money (as if he were bribing someone) that he gave no definite reply to the orderly's question: "How much spice-bread with peppermint, and how much with honey?"

"Just as you please."

"Shall I spend all the money," asked the old soldier, impressively. "The peppermint is dearer. It's sixteen kopeks."

"Yes, yes, spend it all," answered Olenin, and sat down by the window, surprised that his heart was thumping as if he were preparing himself for something serious and wicked. He heard screaming and shrieking in the girls' hut when Beletsky went there, and a few moments later saw how, accompanied by shrieks, bustle, and laughter, he jumped out and ran down the steps. "Turned out," he said.

A little later Ustenka entered, and solemnly invited her visitors to come in: announcing that all was ready.

When they came into the room they saw that everything was really ready. Ustenka was rearranging the cushions along the wall. On the table, which was covered by a disproportionately small cloth, was a decanter of *chikhir* and some dried fish. The room smelled of dough and grapes. Some half dozen girls in smart tunics, with their heads not covered, as usual, with kerchiefs, were huddled together in a corner behind the oven, whispering, giggling, and spluttering with laughter.

"I humbly beg you to do honour to my patron saint," said Ustenka, inviting her guests to the table.

Olenin noticed Maryanka among the group of girls, who without exception were all handsome, and he felt vexed and hurt that he met her in such vulgar and awkward circumstances. He felt stupid and awkward, and made up his mind to do what Beletsky did. Beletsky stepped to the table somewhat solemnly, yet with confidence and ease, drank a glass of wine to Ustenka's health, and invited the others to do the same. Ustenka announced that girls don't drink.

"We might, with a little honey," exclaimed a voice from among the group of girls.

The orderly, who had just returned with the honey and spice-cakes, was called in. He looked askance (whether with envy or with contempt) at the gentlemen, who in his opinion were on the spree; and carefully and conscientiously handed over to them a piece of honeycomb and the cakes, wrapped up in a piece of grayish paper, and began explaining circumstantially all about the price and the change, but Beletsky sent him away. Having mixed honey with wine in the glasses, and having lavishly scattered the three pounds of spice-cakes on the table, Beletsky dragged the girls from their corners by force, made them sit down at the table, and began distributing the cakes among them. Olenin involuntarily noticed how Maryanka's sunburned but small hand closed on two round peppermint nuts and one brown one, and that she did not know what to do with them. The conversation was halting and ungenial, in spite of Ustenka's and Beletsky's free and easy manner and their wish to enliven the company, Olenin faltered and tried to think of something to say, feeling that he was exciting curiosity and perhaps provoking ridicule and infecting the others with his shyness. He blushed, and it seemed to him that Maryanka in particular was feeling uncomfortable. "Most likely they are expecting us to give them some money," thought he. "How are we to do it? And how can we manage quickest to give it and get away?"

Chapter XXV

"HOW IS IT YOU DON'T KNOW YOUR OWN LODGER?" SAID BELETSKY, ADDRESSING MARYANKA.

"How is one to know him if he never comes to see us?" answered Maryanka, with a look at Olenin.

Olenin felt frightened, he did not know of what. He flushed, and, hardly knowing what he was saying, remarked:

"I'm afraid of your mother. She gave me such a scolding the first time I went in."

Maryanka burst out laughing.

"And so you were frightened?" she said; and glanced at him and turned away.

It was the first time Olenin had seen the whole of her beautiful face. Till then he had seen her with her kerchief covering her to the eyes. It was not for nothing that she was reckoned the beauty of the village.

Ustenka was a pretty girl, small, plump, rosy, with merry brown eyes and red lips which were perpetually smiling and chattering. Maryanka, on the contrary, was certainly not pretty, but beautiful. Her features might have been considered too masculine and almost harsh, had it not been for her tall stately figure, her powerful chest and shoulders, and especially the severe yet tender expression of her long dark eyes, which were darkly shadowed beneath their black brows, and for the gentle expression of her mouth and smile. She rarely smiled, but her smile was always striking. She seemed to radiate virginal strength and health. All the girls were good-looking, but they themselves, and Beletsky, and the orderly when he brought in the spice-cakes, all involuntarily gazed at Maryanka, and anyone addressing the girls was sure to address her. She seemed a proud and happy queen among them.

Beletsky, trying to keep up the spirit of the party, chattered incessantly, made the girls hand round *chikhir*, fooled about with them, and kept making improper remarks in French about Maryanka's beauty to Olenin, calling her "yours" *(la vôtre)*, and advising him to behave as he did himself. Olenin felt more and more uncomfortable. He was devising an excuse to get out and run away, when Beletsky announced that Ustenka, whose saint's day it was, must offer *chikhir* to everybody with a kiss. She consented, on condition that they should put money on her plate, as is the custom at weddings.

"What fiend brought me to this disgusting feast!" thought Olenin, rising to go away.

"Where are you off to?"

"I'll fetch some tobacco," he said, meaning to escape; but Beletsky seized his hand, saying in French, "I have some money, one can't go away." "One has to pay here," thought Olenin bitterly, vexed at his own awkwardness. "Can't I really behave like Beletsky? I ought not to have come, but once I am here I must not spoil their fun. I must drink like a Cossack," and taking the wooden bowl (holding about eight tumblers) he almost filled it with *chikhir* and drank it up. The girls looked at him, surprised and almost frightened, while he drank. It seemed to them strange and not right. Ustenka brought them another glass each, and kissed them both.

"There girls, now we'll have some fun," she said, clinking on the plate the four rubles the men had put there. Olenin no longer felt awkward, but became talkative.

"Now, Maryanka, it's your turn to offer us wine and a kiss," said Beletsky, seizing her hand.

"Yes, I'll give you such a kiss!" she said, playfully, preparing to strike at him.

"One can kiss Grandad without payment," said another girl.

"There's a wise girl," said Beletsky, kissing the struggling girl. "No, you must offer it," he insisted, addressing Maryanka. "Offer a glass to your lodger."

And taking her by the hand he led her to the bench and sat her down beside Olenin.

"What a beauty," he said, turning her head to see it in profile.

Maryanka did not resist, but, proudly smiling, turned her long eyes towards Olenin.

"A beautiful girl," repeated Beletsky, and Maryanka's look seemed to affirm, "Yes, see what a beauty I am."

Without considering what he was doing, Olenin embraced Maryanka and was going to kiss her, but she suddenly extricated herself, upsetting Beletsky and pushing the top off the table, and sprang away towards the oven. There was much shouting and laughter. Then Beletsky whispered something to the girls, and suddenly they all ran out into the passage and locked the door behind them.

"Why did you kiss Beletsky and won't kiss me?" asked Olenin.

"Oh, just so. I don't want to; that's all!" she answered, pouting and frowning. "He's Grandad," she added with a smile. She went to the door and began to bang at it. "Why have you locked the door, you devils?"

"Well, let them be there, and us be here," said Olenin, drawing closer to her.

She frowned, and sternly pushed him away with her hand. And again she appeared so majestically handsome to Olenin, that he came to his senses and felt ashamed of what he was doing. He went to the door, and began pulling at it himself. "Beletsky! Open the door! What a stupid joke!"

Maryanka again gave a bright, happy laugh. "Ah, you're afraid of me?" she said.

"Yes, you know you're as cross as your mother."

"You spend more of your time with Eroshka; that will make the girls love you!" And she smiled, looking straight and close into his eyes. He did not know what to reply.

"And if I were to come to see you—" he let fall.

"That would be a different matter," she replied, tossing her head.

At that moment Beletsky pushed the door open, and Maryanka sprang away from Olenin, and in doing so her thigh struck his leg. "It's all nonsense what I have been thinking about, love and self-sacrifice and Lukashka. Happiness is the one thing. He who is happy is right," flashed through Olenin's mind, and with a strength unexpected to himself, he seized and kissed the beautiful Maryanka on her temple and her cheek. Maryanka was not angry, but only burst into a loud laugh and ran out to the other girls.

That was the end of the party. Ustenka's mother, returned from her work, gave all the girls a scolding, and turned them all out.

Chapter XXVI

"YES," THOUGHT OLENIN, AS HE WALKED HOME. "I NEED ONLY SLACKEN THE REINS A BIT AND I might fall desperately in love with this Cossack girl." He went to bed with these thoughts, but expected it all to blow over, and that he would continue to live as before. But the old life did not return. His relations to Maryanka were changed. The wall that had separated them was broken down. Olenin now greeted her every time they met.

The master of the house having returned to collect the rent, on hearing of Olenin's wealth and generosity, invited him to his hut. The old woman received him kindly and, from the day of the party onwards, Olenin often went in of an evening and sat with them till late at night. He seemed to be living in the village just as he used to, but within him everything had changed. He spent his days in the forest, and towards eight o'clock, when it began to grow dusk, he would go to see his hosts, alone or with Daddy Eroshka. They grew so used to him that they were surprised when he stayed away. He paid well for his wine, and was a quiet fellow. Vanyusha would bring him his tea, and he would sit down in a corner near the oven. The old woman did not mind him, but went on with her work, and they talked over their tea or their *chikhir* about Cossack affairs, about the neighbours, or about Russia: Olenin relating and the others inquiring. Sometimes he brought a book and read to himself. Maryanka crouched like a wild goat with her feet drawn up under her, sometimes on the top of the oven, sometimes in a dark corner. She did not take part in the conversations, but Olenin saw her eyes and face and heard her moving, or cracking sunflower seeds, and he felt that she listened with her whole being when he spoke, and was aware of his presence while he silently read to himself. Sometimes he thought her eyes were fixed on him and, meeting their radiance, he involuntarily became silent and gazed at her. Then she would instantly hide her face, and he would pretend to be deep in conversation with the old woman, while he listened all the time to her breathing and to her every movement, and waited for her to look at him again. In the presence of others she was generally bright and friendly with him, but when they were alone together she was shy and rough. Sometimes he came in before Maryanka had returned home. Suddenly he would hear her firm footsteps and catch a glimmer of her blue cotton smock at the open door. Then she would step into the middle of the hut; catch sight of him, and her eyes would give a scarcely perceptible kindly smile, and he would feel happy and frightened.

He neither sought for nor wished for anything from her, but every day her presence became more and more necessary to him.

Olenin had so fully entered into the life of the Cossack village that his past seemed quite foreign to him. As to the future, especially a future outside the world in which he was now living, it did not interest him at all. When he received letters from home, from relatives and friends, he was offended by the evident distress with which they regarded him as a lost man, while he, in his village, considered those as lost who did not live as he was living. He felt sure he would never repent of having broken away from his former surroundings and of having settled down in this village to such a solitary and original life. When out on expeditions and when quartered at one of the forts, he felt happy too; but it was here, from under Daddy Eroshka's wing, from the forest and from his hut at the end of the village, and especially when he thought of Maryanka and Lukashka, that he seemed to see the falseness of his former life. That falseness used to rouse his indignation even before, but now it seemed inexpressibly vile and ridiculous. Here he felt freer and freer every day, and more and more of a man. The Caucasus now appeared entirely different to what his imaginations had painted it. He had found nothing at all like his dreams, nor like the descriptions of the Caucasus he had heard and read. "There are none of all those chestnut-trees, precipices, Amalet Beks, heroes or villains," thought he. "The people live as nature lives: they die, are born, unite, and more are born—they fight, eat and drink, rejoice and die, without any restrictions but those that nature imposes on sun and grass, on animal and tree. They have no other laws." Therefore, these people, compared to himself, appeared to him beautiful, strong, and free, and the sight of them made him feel ashamed and sorry for himself. Often it seriously occurred to him to throw up everything, to get registered as a Cossack, to buy a hut and cattle, and marry a Cossack woman (only not Maryanka, whom he conceded to Lukashka), and to live with Daddy Eroshka, and go shooting and fishing with him, and go with the Cossacks on their expeditions. "Why ever don't I do it? What am I waiting for?" he asked himself, and he egged himself on, and shamed himself. "Am I afraid of doing what I hold to be reasonable and right? Is the wish to be a simple Cossack, to live close to nature, not to injure anyone, but even to do good to others, more stupid than my former dreams, such as those of becoming a minister of state, or a colonel?" but a voice seemed to say that he should wait and not take any decision. He was held back by a dim consciousness that he could not live altogether like Eroshka and Lukashka, because he had a different idea of happiness—he was held back by the thought that happiness lies in self-sacrifice. What he had done for Lukashka continued to give him joy. He kept looking for occasions to sacrifice himself for others, but did not meet with them. Sometimes he forgot this newly-discovered recipe for happiness, and considered himself capable of identifying his life with Daddy Eroshka's, but he then quickly bethought himself, and promptly clutched at the idea of conscious self-sacrifice, and from that basis looked calmly and proudly at all men and at their happiness.

Chapter XXVII

JUST BEFORE THE VINTAGE, LUKASHKA CAME ON HORSEBACK TO SEE OLENIN. HE LOOKED MORE dashing than ever.

"Well? Are you getting married?" asked Olenin, greeting him merrily.

Lukashka gave no direct reply. "There, I've exchanged your horse across the river. This *is* a horse! A Kabarda horse from the Lov stud. I know horses."

They examined the new horse and made him caracole about the yard. The horse really was an exceptionally fine one, a broad and long bay gelding, with glossy coat, thick silky tail and the soft fine mane and crest of a thoroughbred. He was so well fed that "you might go to sleep on his back' as Lukashka expressed it. His hoofs, eyes, teeth, were exquisitely shaped and sharply outlined, as one only finds them in very pure-bred horses. Olenin could not help admiring the horse; he had not yet met with such a beauty in the Caucasus.

"And how it goes!" said Lukashka, patting its neck. "What a step! And so clever—he simply runs after his master."

"Did you have to add much to make the exchange?" asked Olenin.

"I did not count it," answered Lukashka with a smile. "I got him from a *kunak*."

"A wonderfully beautiful horse! What would you take for it?" asked Olenin.

"I have been offered a hundred and fifty rubles for it, but I'll give it you for nothing," said Lukashka, merrily. "Only say the word, and it's yours. I'll unsaddle it, and you may take it. Only give me some sort of a horse for my duties."

"No, on no account."

"Well, then, here is a dagger I've brought you," said Lukashka, unfastening his girdle and taking out one of the two daggers which hung from it. "I got it from across the river."

"Oh, thank you!"

"And mother has promised to bring you some grapes herself."

"That's quite unnecessary. We'll balance up someday. You see I don't offer you any money for the dagger!"

"How could you, we are *kunaks*. It's just the same as when Girey Khan, across the river, took me into his home, and said, " Choose what you like!" So I took this sword. It's our custom."

They went into the hut and had a drink.

"Are you staying here awhile?" asked Olenin.

"No, I have come to say good-bye. They are sending me from the cordon to a company beyond the Terek. I am going tonight with my comrade, Nazarka."

"And when is the wedding to be?"

"I shall be coming back for the betrothal, and then I shall return to the company again," Lukashka replied, reluctantly.

"What, and see nothing of your betrothed?"

"Just so—what is the good of looking at her? When you go on campaign, ask in our company for Lukashka the Broad. But what a lot of boars there are in our parts! I've killed two. I'll take you. Well, good-bye! Christ save you." Lukashka mounted his horse, and without calling on Maryanka, rode caracoling down the street, where Nazarka was already awaiting him.

"I say, shan't we call round?" asked Nazarka, winking in the direction of Yamka's house.

"That's a good one!" said Lukashka. "Here, take my horse to her, and, if I don't come soon, give him some hay. I shall reach the company by the morning, any way."

"Hasn't the cadet given you anything more?"

"I am thankful to have paid him back with a dagger—he was going to ask for the horse," said Lukashka, dismounting and handing over the horse to Nazarka.

He darted into the yard, past Olenin's very window, and came up to the window of the teacher's hut. It was already quite dark. Maryanka, wearing only her smock, was combing her hair, preparing for bed. "It's I——" whispered the Cossack.

Maryanka's look was severely indifferent; but her face suddenly brightened up when she heard her name. She opened the window and leant out, frightened and joyous.

"What—what do you want?" she said.

"Open!" uttered Lukashka. "Let me in for a minute. I am so sick of waiting! It's awful!"

He took hold of her head through the window and kissed her.

"Really, do open!"

"Why do you talk nonsense? I've told you I won't? Have you come for long?"

He did not answer, but went on kissing her, and she did not ask again.

"There, through the window, one can't even hug you properly," said Lukashka.

"Maryanka dear!" came the voice of her mother, "who is that with you?"

Lukashka took off his cap, which might have been seen, and crouched down by the window.

"Go, be quick!" whispered Maryanka. "Lukashka has called round," she answered; "he is asking for Daddy."

"Well, then send him here!"

"He's gone; says he's in a hurry."

In fact, Lukashka, stooping as with big strides he passed under the windows, ran out through the yard and towards Yamka's house, unseen by anyone but Olenin. After drinking two bowls of *chikhir* he and Nazarka rode away to the outpost. The night was warm, dark, and calm. They rode in silence; only the footfall of their horses was heard. Lukashka started a song about the Cossack, Mingal, but stopped before he had finished the first verse, and, after a pause, turning to Nazarka; said:

"I say, she would'nt let me in!"

"Oh?" rejoined Nazarka. "I knew she wouldn't. D'you know what Yamka told me? The cadet has begun going to their house. Daddy Eroshka brags that he got a gun from the cadet for getting him Maryanka."

"He lies, the old devil!" said Lukashka, angrily. She's not such a girl. If he does not look out, I'll whallop the devil's sides," and he began his favorite song:

"From the village of Izmaylov,
From the master's favorite garden,
A bright-eyed falcon from his cage once flew there,
And soon after him a huntsman young came riding.
With his hand he beckoned to the bright-eyed falcon.
The bright-eyed falcon then made answer:
'In a golden cage you knew not how to keep me,
On your right hand you knew not how to hold me.
So now I'll fly to the blue sea, far far away,
And there I will kill a white swan for myself,
And I will get my fill of the sweet swan-flesh.' "

Chapter XXVIII

THE BETROTHAL WAS TAKING PLACE IN THE TEACHER'S HUT. LUKASHKA HAD RETURNED TO the village, but had not been to see Olenin; and Olenin had not gone to the betrothal though he had been invited. He was sad, as he had never been since he settled in this Cossack village. He had seen Lukashka earlier in the evening, and he was worried by the question why Lukashka was so cold towards him. Olenin shut himself up in his hut and began writing in his diary as follows:

"Many things have I pondered over lately, and much have I changed," wrote he, "and I have come back to the copy-book maxim: The one way to be happy is to love, to love self-denyingly, to love everybody and everything; to spread a web of love on all sides and to take all who come into it. In this way I caught Vanyusha, Daddy Eroshka, Lukashka, and Maryanka."

As Olenin was finishing this sentence, Daddy Eroshka entered the room.

Eroshka was in the happiest frame of mind. A few evenings before this, Olenin had gone to see him, and had found him with a proud and happy face deftly skinning the carcass of a boar with a small knife in the yard. The dogs (Lyamka his pet among them) were lying close by, watching what he was doing, and gently wagging their tails. The little boys were respectfully looking at him through the fence, and not even teasing him as was their wont. His women neighbours, who were as a rule not too gracious towards him, greeted him and brought him, one a jug of *chikhir*, another some clotted cream, and a third a little flour. The next day Eroshka sat in his storeroom, all covered with blood, and distributed pounds of boar-flesh, taking in payment, money from some and wine from others. His face clearly expressed, "God has sent me luck. I have killed a boar; so now I am wanted." Consequently he naturally began to drink, and had gone on for four days, never leaving the village. Beside which he had had something to drink at the betrothal.

He came to Olenin quite drunk: his face red his beard tangled, but wearing a new *beshmet* trimmed with gold braid; and he brought with him a *balalayka* which he had obtained beyond the river. He had long promised Olenin this treat, and felt in the mood for it, so that he was sorry to find Olenin writing.

"Write on, write on, my lad," he whispered, as if he thought that a spirit sat between him and the paper and must not be frightened away, and he softly and silently sat down on the floor. When Daddy Eroskha was drunk, his favourite position was on the floor. Olenin looked round, ordered some wine to be brought, and continued to write. Eroskha found it dull to drink by himself, and he wished to talk.

"I've been to the betrothal at the teacher's. But there! They're shwine!—Don't want them!—Have come to you."

"And where did you get your *balalayka?*" asked Olenin, still writing.

"I've been beyond the river and got it there, brother mine," he answered, also very quietly. "I'm a master at it. Tartar or Cossack, squire or peasant songs, any kind you please."

Olenin looked at him again, smiled, and went on writing.

That smile emboldened the old man.

"Come, leave off, my lad, leave off!" he said with sudden firmness.

"Well, perhaps I will."

"Come, people have injured you, but leave them alone, spit at them! Come, what's the use of writing and writing, what's the good?"

And he tried to mimic Olenin by tapping the floor with his thick fingers, and then twisted his big face to express contempt.

"What's the good of writing quibbles. Better have a spree and show you're a man!"

No other conception of writing found place in his head, except that of legal chicanery. Olenin burst out laughing and so did Eroshka. Then, jumping up from the floor, the latter began to show off his skill on the *balalayka*, and to sing Tartar songs.

"Why write, my good fellow! You'd better listen to what I'll sing to you. When you're dead you'll not hear any more songs. Make merry now!"

First he sang a song of his own composing, accompanied by a dance:

"Ah, dee, dee, dee, dee, dee, dim,
Say where did they last see him?
In a booth, at the fair,
He was selling pins, there."

Then he sang a song he had learned from his former sergeant-major:

> *"Deep I fell in love on Monday,*
> *Tuesday nothing did but sigh,*
> *Wednesday I popped the question,*
> *Thursday waited her reply.*
> *Friday, late, it came at last,*
> *Then all hope for me was past!*
> *Saturday my life to take*
> *I determined like a man,*
> *But for my salvation's sake*
> *Sunday morning changed my plan!"*

Then he sang again:

> *"Oh dee, dee, dee, dee, dee, dim,*
> *Say where did they last see him."*

And after that, winking, shrugging his shoulders and footing it to the tune he sang:

> *"I will kiss you and embrace,*
> *Ribbons red twine round you;*
> *And I'll call you little Grace.*
> *Oh! you little Grace now do*
> *Tell me, do you love me true?"*

And he became so excited that with a sudden daring movement he started dancing all alone around the room.

Songs like "Dee, dee, dee"—"gentlemen's songs"—he sang for Olenin's benefit, but after drinking three more tumblers of *chikhir* he remembered old times and began singing real Cossack and Tartar songs. In the midst of one of his favourite songs his voice suddenly trembled, and he ceased singing, and only continued strumming on the *balalayka.*

"Oh, my dear friend!" he said.

The peculiar sound of his voice made Olenin look round. The old man was weeping. Tears stood in his eyes, and one tear was running down his cheek. "You are gone, my young days, and will never come back!" he said, blubbering and halting. "Drink, why don't you drink!" he suddenly shouted with a deafening roar, without wiping away his tears.

There was one Tartar song that specially moved him. It had few words, but its charm lay in the sad refrain. "Ay day, dalalay!" Eroshka translated the words of the song: "A youth drove his sheep from the *aoul* to the mountains: the Russians came and burned the *aoul,* they killed all the men, and took all the women into bondage. The youth returned from the mountains. Where the *aoul* had stood was an empty space; his mother not there, nor his brothers, nor his house; one tree alone was left standing. The youth sat beneath the tree and wept. "Alone like thee, alone am I left," and Eroshka began singing: "Ay day, dalalay!" and the old man repeated several times this wailing, heart-rending refrain.

When he had finished the refrain, Eroshka suddenly seized a gun that hung on the wall, rushed hurriedly out into the yard, and fired off both barrels into the air. Then again he began, more dolefully, his "Ay day, dalalay—ah, ah," and ceased.

Olenin followed him into the porch and looked up into the starry sky in the direction where the shots had flashed. In the teacher's house there were lights, and the sound of voices. In the yard girls were crowding round the porch and the windows, and running backwards and forwards between the hut and the outhouse. Some Cossacks rushed out of the hut, and could not refrain from shouting, re-echoing the refrain of Daddy Eroshka's song and his shots.

"Why are you not at the betrothal?" asked Olenin.

"Never mind them! Never mind them!" muttered the old man, who had evidently been offended by something there. "Don't like them, I don't. Oh, those people! Come back into the hut! Let them make merry by themselves and we'll make merry by ourselves."

Olenin went in.

"And Lukashka, is he happy? Won't he come to see me?" he asked.

"What, Lukashka? They've lied to him and said I am getting his girl for you," whispered the old man. "But what's the girl? She will be ours if we want her. Give enough money—and she's ours. I'll fix it up for you. Really!"

"No, Daddy, money can do nothing if she does not love me. You'd better not talk like that!"

"We are not loved, you and I. We are forlorn," suddenly said Daddy Eroshka, and again he began to cry.

Listening to the old man's talk, Olenin had drunk more than usual. "So now my Lukashka is happy," thought he; yet he felt sad. The old man had drunk so much that evening that he fell down on the floor, and Vanyusha had to call soldiers in to help, and spat as they dragged the old man out. He was so angry with the old man for his bad behavior that he did not even say a single French word.

Chapter XXIX

IT WAS AUGUST. FOR DAYS THE SKY HAD BEEN CLOUDLESS; THE SUN SCORCHED UNBEARABLY, AND from early morning the warm wind raised a whirl of hot sand from the sand-drifts and from the road, and bore it in the air through the reeds, the trees, and the village.

The grass and the leaves on the trees were covered with dust; the roads and dried-up salt marshes were baked so hard that they rang when trodden on. The water had long since subsided in the Terek, and rapidly vanished and dried up in the ditches. The slimy banks of the pond near the village were trodden bare by the cattle, and all day long you could hear the splashing of water, and the shouting of bathing girls and boys. The sand-drifts and the reeds were already drying up in the steppes, and the cattle, lowing, ran into the fields in the day-time. The boars migrated into the distant reed-beds and to the hills beyond the Terek. Mosquitoes and gnats swarmed in thick clouds over the low lands and villages. The snow peaks were hidden in gray mist. The air was rarefied and smoky. It was said that *abreks* had crossed the now shallow river, and were prowling on this side of it. Every night the sun set in a glowing red blaze. It was the busiest time of the year. The villagers all swarmed in the plantations and the vineyards. The vineyards thickly overgrown with twining verdure lay in cool, deep shade. Everywhere between the broad translucent leaves, ripe, heavy, black clusters peeped out. Along the dusty road from the vineyards, slowly moved the creaking carts heaped up with black grapes. Clusters of them, crushed by the wheels, lay in the dirt. Boys and girls in smocks stained with grape-juice, with grapes in their hands and mouths, ran after their mothers. On the road you continually came across tattered laborers with baskets of grapes on their powerful shoulders; Cossack maidens, wrapped in kerchiefs to their eyes, drove bullocks harnessed to carts laden high with grapes. Soldiers who happened to meet these carts, asked for grapes, and these maidens, clambering up without stopping their carts, would take an armful of grapes and drop them into the skirts of the soldiers' coats. In some homesteads they had already begun pressing the grapes; and the smell of the emptied skins filled the air. One saw the blood-red troughs in the penthouses in the yards, and Nogay laborers with their trousers rolled up and their legs stained with the juice. Grunting pigs gorged themselves with the empty skins, and rolled about in them. The flat roofs of the outhouses were all spread over with black clusters that were drying in the sun. Daws and magpies crowded round the roofs, picking the seeds and fluttering from one place to another.

The fruits of the year's labor were being merrily gathered in; and this year the fruit was unusually fine and plentiful.

In the shady green vineyards, amid a sea of vines, on all sides laughter, songs, merriment, and the voices of women were to be heard and glimpses of their bright-colored garments could be seen.

Just at noon, Maryanka was sitting in their vineyard in the shade of a peach-tree, getting out the family dinner from under an unharnessed cart. Opposite her, on a spread-out horsecloth, sat the teacher (who had returned from the school) washing his hands by pouring water on them from a little jug. Her little brother, who had just come straight out of the pond, stood wiping his face with his wide sleeves, gazed anxiously at his sister and his mother and breathed deeply, awaiting his dinner. The old mother, with her sleeves rolled up over her strong sunburned arms, was arranging grapes, dried fish, and clotted cream on a little low circular Tartar table. The teacher wiped his hands, took off his cap, crossed himself, and moved nearer to the table. The boy seized the jug and eagerly began to drink. The mother and daughter crossed their legs under them and sat down by the table. Even in the shade it was intolerably hot. The air above the vineyard smelled unpleasant: the strong warm wind passing amid the branches brought no coolness, but only monotonously bent the tops of the pear, peach, and mulberry-trees with which the vineyard was sprinkled. The teacher, having crossed himself once more, took a little jug of *chikhir* that stood behind him covered with a vine-leaf, and having had a drink from the mouth of the jug passed it to the old woman. He had nothing on over his shirt, which was unfastened at the neck, and showing his shaggy muscular chest. His fine-featured cunning face looked cheerful; neither in his attitude nor in his words was his usual wiliness to be seen; he was cheerful and natural.

"Shall we finish the bit beyond the shed tonight?" he asked, wiping his wet beard.

"We'll manage it," replied his wife, "if only the weather does not hinder us. The Demkins have not half finished yet," she added. "Only Ustenka is at work there, wearing herself out."

"What can you expect of them?" said the old man proudly.

"Here, have a drink, Maryanka dear!" said the old woman, passing the jug to the girl. "God willing, we'll have enough to pay for the wedding feast," added the old woman.

"That's not yet awhile," said the teacher with a slight frown.

The girl hung her head.

"Why shouldn't we mention it?" said the old woman, "the affair is settled, and the time is drawing near too."

"Don't make plans beforehand," said the teacher. "Now we have the harvest to get in."

"Have you seen Lukashka's new horse?" asked the old woman. "That which Dmitry Andreich Olenin gave him is gone—he's exchanged it."

"No, I have not; but I spoke with the servant today," said the teacher, "and he said his master has again received a thousand rubles."

"Rolling in riches, in short," said the old woman.

The whole family felt cheerful and contented. The work was progressing successfully. The grapes were more abundant and finer than they had expected. After dinner Maryanka threw some grass to the oxen, folded her *beshmet* for a pillow, and lay down under the wagon on the juicy downtrodden grass. She had on only a red kerchief over her head, and a faded blue print smock; yet she felt unbearably hot. Her face was burning and she did not know where to put her feet; her eyes were moist with sleepiness and weariness; her lips parted involuntarily, and her chest heaved heavily and deeply.

The busy time of year had begun a fortnight ago, and the continuous heavy labour had filled the girl's life. At dawn she jumped up, washed her face with cold water, wrapped herself in a shawl, and ran out barefoot to see to the cattle. Then she hurriedly put on her shoes and her *beshmet* and, taking a small bundle of bread, she harnessed the bullocks and drove away to the vineyards for the whole day. There she cut the grapes and carried the baskets, with only one hour's interval for rest, and in the evening she returned to the village, bright and not tired, dragging the bullocks by a rope or driving them with a long stick. After attending to the cattle, she took some sunflower seeds in the wide sleeve of her smock and went to the corner of the street to crack them and have some fun with the other girls. But as soon as it was dusk, she returned home, and after having supper with her parents and her brother in the dark outhouse, she went into the hut, healthy, and free from care, and climbed on to the oven, where, half drowsing, she listened to their lodger's conversation. As soon as he went away, she would throw herself down on her bed and sleep soundly and quietly till morning. And so it went on day after day. She had not seen Lukashka since the day of their betrothal, but calmly awaited the wedding.

She had got used to their lodger and felt his intent looks with pleasure.

Chapter XXX

ALTHOUGH THERE WAS NO ESCAPE FROM THE HEAT, AND THE MOSQUITOES SWARMED IN THE COOL shadow of the wagons, and her little brother tossing about beside her kept pushing her, Maryanka, having drawn her kerchief over her head, was just falling asleep, when suddenly their neighbor Ustenka came running towards her, and, diving under the wagon, lay down beside her.

"Sleep, girls, sleep!" said Ustenka, making herself comfortable under the wagon. "Wait a bit," she exclaimed, "that won't do!" She jumped up, plucked some green branches, and stuck them through the wheels on both sides of the wagon, and hung her *beshmet* over them. "Let me in," she shouted to the little boy, as she again crept under the wagon. "Is this the place for a Cossack; with the girls? Go away!" When alone under the wagon with her friend, Ustenka suddenly put both her arms round her and clinging close to her, began kissing her cheeks and neck.

"Darling, brotherkin," she kept repeating, between bursts of shrill, clear laughter.

"Why, you've learned it from grandad," said Maryanka, struggling. "Stop it!"

And they both broke into such peals of laughter that Maryanka's mother shouted to them to be quiet."

"Are you envious?" asked Ustenka in a whisper.

"What humbug! Let us sleep. What have you come for?"

But Ustenka kept on, "I say! But I wanted to tell you such a thing."

Maryanka raised herself on her elbow and arranged the kerchief which had slipped off.

"Well, what is it?"

"I know something about your lodger!"

"There's nothing to know," said Maryanka.

"Oh, you rogue of a girl!" said Ustenka, nudging her with her elbow and laughing. "Won't tell anything. Does he come to you?"

"He does. What of that?" said Maryanka, with a sudden blush.

"Now I'm a simple lass. I tell everybody. Why should I pretend?" said Ustenka; and her bright rosy face suddenly became pensive. "Whom do I hurt? I love him, that's all about it."

"Grandad, do you mean?"

"Well, yes!"

"And the sin?"

"Ah, Maryanka! When is one to have a good time if not while one's still free? When I marry a Cossack, I shall bear children and shall have cares. There now, when you get married to Lukashka not even a thought of joy will enter your head: children will come, and work!"

"Well? Some who are married live happily. It makes no difference!" Maryanka replied quietly.

"Do tell me just this once, what has passed between you and Lukashka?"

"What has passed? A match was proposed. Father put it off for a year; but now it's been settled, and they'll marry us in autumn."

"But what did he say to you?"

Maryanka smiled.

"What should he say? He said he loved me. He kept asking me to come to the vineyards with him."

"Just see what pitch! But you did not go, did you? And what a dare-devil he has become: the first among the braves. He makes merry out there in the army too! The other day our Kirka came home; he says: What a horse Lukashka's got in exchange! But all the same I expect he frets after you. And what else did he say?"

"Must you know everything?" said Maryanka laughing. "One night he came to my window, tipsy, and asked me to let him in."

"And you didn't let him?"

"Let him, indeed! Once I have said a thing, I keep to it, firm as a rock," answered Maryanka seriously.

"A fine fellow! If he wanted her, no girl would refuse him."

"Well, let him go to the others," proudly replied Maryanka.

"You don't pity him?"

"I do pity him, but will have no nonsense. It is wrong."

Ustenka suddenly dropped her head on her friend's breast, seized hold of her and shook with smothered laughter. "You silly fool!" she exclaimed, quite out of breath. "You don't want to be happy," and she began tickling Maryanka.

"Ay, leave off!" said Maryanka, screaming and laughing. "You've crushed Lazutka."

"Hark at those young devils! Quite frisky! Not tired yet!" came the old woman's sleepy voice from the wagon.

"Don't want happiness," repeated Ustenka in a whisper, insistently. "But you are lucky, that you are! How they love you! You are so haughty, and yet they love you. Ah, were I in your place I'd soon turn the lodger's head! I noticed him when you were at our house. He was ready to eat you with his eyes. What things grandad has given me! And yours, they say, is the richest of the Russians. His orderly says they have serfs of their own."

Maryanka raised herself, and after thinking a moment, smiled.

"Do you know what he once told me: the lodger, I mean?" she said, biting a bit of grass. "He said, I'd like to be Lukashka the Cossack, or your brother Lazutka——. What do you think he meant?"

"Oh, just chattering what came into his head," answered Ustenka. "What does mine not say! Just as if he was possessed!"

Maryanka dropped her head on her folded *beshmet,* threw her arm over Ustenka's shoulder, and shut her eyes. "He wanted to come and work in the vineyard today: father asked him," she said, and after a short silence she fell asleep.

Chapter XXXI

THE SUN HAD COME OUT FROM BEHIND THE PEAR-TREE THAT HAD SHADED THE WAGON, AND, even through the branches that Ustenka had fixed up, it scorched the faces of the sleeping girls. Maryanka woke up and began arranging the kerchief on her head. Looking about her, beyond the pear-tree, she noticed their lodger, who, with his gun on his shoulder, stood talking to her father. She nudged Ustenka and smilingly pointed him out to her.

"I went yesterday, and didn't find a single one," Olenin was saying as he looked about uneasily, not seeing Maryanka through the branches.

"Ah, you should go out there, to that direction, go right round as by compasses, there, in a disused vineyard, denominated as the Waste, hares are always to be found," said the teacher, having at once changed his manner of speech.

"A fine thing to go looking for hares in these busy times! You had better come and help us, and do some work with the girls," the old woman said merrily. "Now then, girls, up with you!" she cried.

Maryanka and Ustenka under the cart were whispering, and could hardly restrain their laughter.

Since it had become known that Olenin had given a horse worth fifty rubles to Lukashka, his hosts had become more amiable, and the teacher in particular saw with pleasure his daughter's growing intimacy with Olenin.

"But I don't know how to do the work," replied Olenin, trying not to look through the green branches under the wagon, where he had now noticed Maryanka's blue smock and red kerchief.

"Come, I'll give you some peaches," said the old woman.

"It's only according to the ancient Cossack hospitality. It's her old woman's silliness," said the teacher, explaining, and apparently correcting, his wife's words. "In Russia, I expect, it's not so much peaches as pine-apple jam and preserves you have been accustomed to eat at your pleasure."

"So you say hares are to be found in the disused vineyard?" asked Olenin. "I will go there," and throwing a hasty glance through the green branches, he raised his cap and disappeared between the regular rows of green vines.

The sun had already sunk behind the fence of the vineyards, and its broken rays glittered through the translucent leaves, when Olenin returned to his host's vineyard. The wind was falling, and a cool freshness was beginning to spread around. By some instinct Olenin recognized from afar Maryanka's blue smock among the rows of vine, and, picking grapes on his way, he approached her. His highly excited dog also now and then seized a low-hanging cluster of grapes in his slobbering mouth.

Maryanka, her face flushed, her sleeves rolled up, and her kerchief down below her chin, was rapidly cutting the heavy clusters and laying them in a basket. Without letting go of the vine she had hold of, she stopped to smile pleasantly at him, and resumed her work. Olenin drew near, and threw his gun behind his back to have his hands free. "Where are your people? May God aid you! Are you alone?" he meant to say, but did not say, and only raised his cap in silence.

"You'll be shooting the women with your gun like that," said Maryanka.

"No, I shan't shoot them." They were both silent, and then, after a pause, she said: "You should help me." He took out his knife and began silently to cut off the clusters. He reached from under the leaves, low down, a thick bunch, weighing about three pounds, the grapes of which grew so close that they flattened each other for want of space. He showed it to Maryanka.

"Must they all be cut? Isn't this one too green?"

"Give it here."

Their hands touched. Olenin took her hand, and she looked at him smiling.

"Are you going to be married soon?" he asked.

She did not answer, but turned away with a stern look.

"Do you love Lukashka?"

"What's that to you?"

"I envy him!"

"Very likely!"

"No, really. You are so beautiful!"

And he suddenly felt terribly ashamed of having said it, so commonplace did the words seem to him. He flushed, lost control of himself, and seized both her hands. "Whatever I am, I'm not for you. Why do you make fun of me?" replied Maryanka, but her look showed how certainly she knew he was not making fun.

"Making fun? If you only knew how I—"

The words sounded still more commonplace, they accorded still less with what he felt; but yet he continued, "I don't know what I would not do for you—"

"Leave me alone, you pitch!"

But her face, her shining eyes, her swelling bosom, her shapely legs, said something quite different. It seemed to him that she understood how petty were all the things he had said, but that she was superior to such considerations. It seemed to him she had long known all he wished, and was not able, to tell her, but wanted to hear how he would say it.

"And how can she help knowing," he thought, "since I only want to tell her all that she herself is? But she does not wish to understand, does not wish to reply."

"Hullo!" suddenly came from behind the vine at no great distance Ustenka's high voice, followed by her shrill laugh. "Come and help me, Dmitry Andreich. I am all alone," she cried, thrusting her round, naïve little face through the vines.

Olenin did not answer, nor move from his place.

Maryanka went on cutting and continually looked up at Olenin. He was about to say something, but stopped, shrugged his shoulders and, having jerked up his gun, with rapid strides walked out of the vineyard.

Chapter XXXII

He stopped once or twice, listening to the ringing laughter of Maryanka and Ustenka who, having come together, were shouting something. Olenin spent the whole evening hunting in the forest. Without having killed anything, he returned home at dusk. When crossing the road, he noticed her open the door of the outhouse, and her blue smock showed through it. He called to Vanyusha very loud, so as to let her know that he was back, and then sat down in the porch in his usual place. His hosts now returned from the vineyard; they came out of the outhouse and into their hut, but did not ask him in. Maryanka went twice out of the gate. Once in the twilight it seemed to him that she was looking at him. He eagerly followed her every movement, but could not make up his mind to approach her. When she disappeared into the hut he left the porch and began pacing up and down the yard; but Maryanka did not again come out. Olenin spent the whole sleepless night out in the yard, listening to every sound in his hosts' hut. He heard them talking early in the evening, heard them having their supper, and pulling out their cushions, and going to bed; he heard Maryanka laughing at something, and then heard everything growing gradually quiet.

The teacher and his wife talked a while in whispers, and someone was breathing. Olenin re-entered his hut. Vanyusha lay asleep in his clothes. Olenin envied him, and again went out to pace the yard, always expecting something, but no one came, no one moved, and he only heard the regular breathing of three people. He knew Maryanka's breathing and listened to it and to the beating of his own heart. In the village everything was quiet. The waning moon rose late and the deep-breathing cattle in the yard became more visible as they lay down and slowly rose. Olenin angrily asked himself, "What is it I want?" but could not tear himself away from the enchantment of the night. Suddenly he thought he distinctly heard the floor creak and the sound of footsteps in his hosts' hut. He rushed to the door, but all was silent again, except for the sound of regular breathing, and in the yard the buffalo-cow, after a deep sigh, again moved, rose on her front knees and then on her feet, swished her tail, and something splashed steadily on the dry clay ground, and then she lay down again in the dim moonlight. He asked himself: "What am I to do?" and definitely decided to go to bed, but again he heard a sound, and in his imagination there rose the image of Maryanka coming out into this moonlit misty night, and again he rushed to her window, and again heard the sound of footsteps. Not till just before dawn did he go up to her window and push at the shutter and then run to the door, and this time he really heard Maryanka's deep breathing and her footsteps. He took hold of the latch and knocked. The floor hardly creaked under the bare cautious footsteps which approached the door. The latch clicked, the door creaked, and he noticed a faint smell of marjoram and pumpkin, and Maryanka's whole figure appeared in the doorway. He saw her only for an instant in the moonlight. She slammed the door and, muttering something, ran lightly back again. Olenin began rapping softly, but nothing responded. He ran to the window and listened. Suddenly he was startled by a shrill squeaky man's voice.

"Fine!" exclaimed a rather small young Cossack, in a white cap, coming across the yard close to Olenin. "I saw . . . fine!"

Olenin recognized Nazarka, and was silent, not knowing what to do or say.

"Fine! I'll go and tell them at the office, and I'll tell her father! That's a fine teacher's daughter! One's not enough for her."

"What do you want of me, what are you after?" uttered Olenin.

"Nothing; only I'll tell them at the office."

Nazarka spoke very loud, and evidently did so intentionally, adding: "Just see what a clever cadet!"

Olenin trembled and grew pale. "Come here, here!"

He seized the Cossack firmly by the arm, and drew him towards his hut: "Nothing happened, she did not let me in and I, too, mean no harm. She is an honest girl—"

"Eh, discuss—"

"Yes; but all the same I'll give you something now. Wait a bit!"

Nazarka said nothing. Olenin ran into his hut and brought out ten rubles, which he gave to the Cossack.

"Nothing happened, but still I was to blame, so I give this!—Only for God's sake don't let anyone know, for nothing happened—"

"I wish you joy," said Nazarka, laughing, and went away.

Nazarka had come to the village that night, at Lukashka's bidding, to find a place to hide a stolen horse, and now, passing by on his way home, had heard the sound of footsteps. When he returned next morning to his company, he bragged to his chum, and told him how cleverly he had got ten rubles.

Next morning Olenin met his hosts, and they knew nothing about the events of the night. He did not speak to Maryanka, and she only laughed a little when she looked at him. Next night he also passed without sleep, vainly wandering about the yard. The day after, he purposely spent shooting, and in the evening he went to see Beletsky, to escape from his own thoughts. He was afraid of himself, and promised himself not to go to his hosts' hut anymore.

That night he was roused by the sergeant-major. His company was ordered to start at once on a raid.

Olenin was glad this had happened, and thought he would not again return to the village.

The raid lasted four days. The commander, who was a relative of Olenin's, wished to see him, and offered to let him remain with the staff, but this Olenin declined. He found that he could not live away from the village, and asked to be allowed to return to it. For having taken part in the raid, he received a soldier's cross, which he had formerly so much desired. Now he was quite indifferent about it, and even more indifferent about his promotion, the order for which had still not arrived.

Accompanied by Vanyusha, he rode back to the cordon without any accident, several hours in advance of the rest of the company. He spent the whole evening in his porch, watching Maryanka, and he again walked about the yard, without aim or thought, all night.

Chapter XXXIII

IT WAS LATE WHEN HE AWOKE THE NEXT DAY. HIS HOSTS WERE NO LONGER IN. HE DID NOT GO shooting, but now took up a book, and now went out into the porch, and now again re-entered the hut and lay down on the bed. Vanusha thought he was ill.

Towards evening Olenin got up, resolutely began writing, and wrote on till late at night. He wrote a letter, but did not post it, because he felt that no one would have understood what he wanted to say; and, besides, it was not necessary that anyone but himself should understand it.

This is what he wrote:

"I receive letters of condolence from Russia. They are afraid that I shall perish, buried in these wilds. They say about me: " He will become coarse; he will be behind the times in every thing; he will take to drink, and who knows but that he may marry a Cossack girl." It was not for nothing, they say, that Ermolov declared: " Anyone serving in the Caucasus for ten years, either becomes a confirmed drunkard, or marries a loose woman." How terrible! Indeed, it won't do for me to ruin myself when I might have the great happiness of even becoming the Countess B——'s husband or a Court chamberlain, or a *Maréchal de noblesse* of my district. Oh, how repulsive and pitiable you all seem to me! You do not know what happiness is, and what life is! One must once taste life in all its natural beauty! Must see and understand what I see every day before me; those eternally unapproachable snowy peaks, and a majestic woman in that primitive beauty in which the first woman must have come from her Creator's hands—and then it becomes clear who is ruining himself, and who is living truly or falsely: you or I. If you only knew how despicable and pitiable you, in your delusions, seem to me! When I picture to myself, in place of my hut, my forests, and my love, those drawing rooms, those women with their pomatum-greased hair eked out with false curls, these unnaturally grimacing lips, these hidden, feeble, distorted limbs, and that chatter of obligatory drawing room conversation, which has no right to the name—I feel unendurably revolted. I then see before me those obtuse faces, those rich eligible girls, whose looks seem to say: " It's all right, you may come near, though I am rich and eligible,"—and that arranging and rearranging of seats, that shameless matchmaking, and that eternal tittle-tattle and pretense; those rules—with whom to shake hands, to whom only to nod, with whom to converse (and all this done deliberately with a conviction of its inevitability), that continual ennui in the blood passing on from generation to generation. Try to understand or believe just this one thing: you need only see and comprehend what truth and beauty are, and all that you now say and think, and all your wishes for me and for yourselves will fly to atoms!

"Happiness is being with nature, seeing her, and conversing with her. " He may even (God forbid) marry a common Cossack girl, and be quite lost socially," I can imagine them saying of me with sincere pity! Yet the one thing I desire is to be quite " lost," in your sense of the word. I wish to marry a common Cossack girl, and dare not, because it would be a height of happiness of which I am unworthy.

"Three months have passed since I first saw the Cossack girl, Maryanka. The views and prejudices of the world I had left were still fresh in me. I did not then believe that I could love that woman. I delighted in her beauty just as I delighted in the beauty of the mountains and the sky, nor could I help delighting in her, for she is as beautiful as they. I found that the sight of her beauty had become a necessity of my life, and I began asking myself whether I did not love her. But I could find nothing within myself at all like love, as I had imagined it to be. Mine was not the restlessness of loneliness and desire for marriage, nor was it platonic, still less a carnal love, such as I have experienced. I needed only to see her, to hear her, to know that she was near; and if I was not happy, I was at peace.

"After an evening gathering at which I met her and touched her, I felt that between that woman and myself there existed an indissoluble though unacknowledged bond against which I could not struggle, yet I did struggle. I asked myself: " Is it possible to love a woman who will never understand the profoundest interests of my life? Is it possible to love a woman simply for her beauty, to love the statue of a woman?" But I was already in love with her; though I did not yet trust to my feelings.

"After that evening, when I first spoke to her, our relations changed. Before that, she had been to me an extraneous but majestic object of external nature: but since that, she has become a human being. I began to meet her, to talk to her, and sometimes to go to work for her father and to spend whole evenings with them, and in this intimate intercourse she remained still in my eyes just as pure, inaccessible, and majestic. She always responded with equal calm, pride, and cheerful equanimity. Sometimes she was friendly, but generally her every look, every word, and her every movement expressed equanimity—not contemptuous, but crushing and bewitching. Every day, with a feigned smile on my lips, I tried to play a part, and with torments of passion and desire in my heart I spoke banteringly to her. She saw that I was dissembling, but looked straight at me, cheerfully and simply. This position became unbearable. I wished not to deceive her, but to tell her all I felt and thought. I was extremely agitated. We were in the vineyard when I began to tell her of my love, in words I am now ashamed to remember. I am ashamed because I ought not to have dared to speak so to her, because she stood far above such words, and above the feeling they were meant to express. I said no more, but from that day my position has been intolerable. I did not wish to demean myself by continuing our former flippant relations, and at the same time I felt that I had not yet reached the level of straight and simple relations with her. I asked myself despairingly, " What am I to do?" In foolish dreams I imagined her, now as my mistress and now as my wife, but rejected both ideas with disgust. To make her a wanton woman would be dreadful. It would be murder. To turn her into a fine lady, the wife of Dmitry Andreich Olenin, like a Cossack woman here who is married to one of our officers, would be still worse. Now could I turn Cossack, like Lukashka, and steal horses, get drunk on *chikhir,* sing rollicking songs, kill people, and when drunk climb up at her window for the night without a thought of who and what I am, it would be different: then we might understand one another, and I might be happy.

"I tried to throw myself into that kind of life, but was still more conscious of my own weakness and artificiality. I cannot forget myself and my complex, distorted past; and my future appears to me still more hopeless. Every day I have before me the distant snowy mountains, and this majestic, happy woman. But not for me is the only happiness possible in the world; I cannot have this woman! What is most terrible and yet sweetest in my condition is that I feel that I understand her, but that she will never understand me; not because she is inferior: on the contrary she ought not to understand me. She is happy, she is like nature: consistent, calm, and self-contained; and I, a weak distorted being, want her to understand my deformity and my torments! I have not slept at night, but have aimlessly passed under her windows, not rendering account to myself of what was happening to me.

"On the 8th our company started on a raid, and I spent three days away from the village. I was sad and apathetic, the usual songs, cards, drinking-bouts, and talk of rewards in the regiment, were more repulsive than usual to me. Yesterday I returned home, and saw her, my hut, Daddy Eroshka, and the snowy, mountains from my porch, and was seized by such a strong, new feeling of joy that I understood it all. I love this woman; I feel real love for the first and only time in my life. I know what has befallen me. I do not fear to be degraded by this feeling; I am not ashamed of my love, I am proud of it. It is not my fault that I love. It has come about against my will. I tried to escape from my love by self-renunciation, and tried to devise a joy in the Cossack Lukashka's and Maryanka's love, but thereby only stirred up my own love and jealousy.

"This is not the ideal, the so-called exalted love, which I have known before; not that sort of attachment in which you admire your own love, and feel that the source of your emotion is within yourself, and do everything yourself. I have felt that too. It is still less a desire for enjoyment: it is something different. Perhaps in her I love nature: the personification of all that is beautiful in nature; but yet I am not acting by my own will, but some elemental force loves through me; the whole of God's world, all nature, presses this love into my soul, and says, " Love her." I love her not with my mind, or my imagination, but with my whole being. Loving her, I feel myself to be an integral part of all God's joyous world.

"I wrote before about the new convictions to which my solitary life had brought me; but no one knows with what labour they shaped themselves within me, and with what joy I realized them, and saw a new way of life opening out before me; nothing was dearer to me than those convictions. . . . Well! . . . love has come, and neither they, nor any regrets for them, remain!

"It is even difficult for me to believe that I could prize such a one-sided, cold, and abstract state of mind. Beauty came and scattered to the winds all that laborious inward toil; and no regret remains for what has vanished! Self-renunciation is all nonsense and absurdity! That is pride, a refuge from well-merited unhappiness, and salvation from the envy of other's happiness: " Live for others, and do good!"—Why? when in my soul there is only love for myself, and the desire to love her, and to live her life with her. Not for others, not for Lukashka, I now desire happiness. I do not now love those others. Formerly I should have told myself that this is wrong. I should have tormented myself with the questions: What will become of her, of me, and of Lukashka? Now I don't care. I do not live my own life, there is something stronger than me which directs me. I suffer; but formerly I was dead, and only now do I live. Today I will go to their house, and will tell her everything."

Chapter XXXIV

LATE THAT EVENING, AFTER WRITING THIS LETTER, OLENIN WENT TO HIS HOSTS' HUT. THE OLD woman was sitting on a bench behind the oven, unwinding cocoons. Maryana, with her head uncovered, sat sewing by the light of a candle. On seeing Olenin she jumped up, took her kerchief and stepped to the oven.

"Maryana, dear," said her mother, "won't you sit here with me a bit?"

"No, I'm bareheaded," she replied, and sprang up on the oven.

Olenin could only see a knee and one of her shapely legs hanging down from the oven. He treated the old woman to tea. She treated her guest to clotted cream, which she sent Maryana to fetch. But, having put a plateful on the table, Maryana again sprang on the oven, from whence Olenin felt her eyes upon him. They talked about household matters. Granny Ulita became animated, and went into raptures of hospitality. She brought Olenin preserved grapes and a grape tart, and some of her best wine, and pressed him to eat and drink with the rough yet proud hospitality of country folk, only found among those who produce their bread by the labor of their own hands.

The old woman, who had at first struck Olenin so much by her rudeness, now often touched him by her simple tenderness towards her daughter.

"Yes, we need not offend the Lord by grumbling! We have enough of everything, thank God. We have pressed sufficient *chikhir,* and have preserved, and shall sell, three or four barrels of grapes, and have enough left to drink. Don't be in a hurry to leave us. We will make merry together at the wedding."

"And when is the wedding to be?" asked Olenin, feeling his blood suddenly rush to his face, while his heart beat irregularly and painfully. He heard a movement on the oven, and the sound of seeds being cracked.

"Well, you know, it ought to be next week. We are quite ready," replied the old woman, as simply and quietly as though Olenin did not exist. "I have prepared, and have procured everything for Maryana. We will give her away properly. Only there's one thing not quite right. Our Lukashka has been running rather wild. He has been too much on the spree! He's up to tricks! The other day a Cossack came here from his company and said he had been to Nogay."

"He must mind he does not get caught," said Olenin.

"Yes, that's what I tell him. "Mind Lukashka, don't you get into mischief. Well, of course a young fellow naturally wants to cut a dash. But there's a time for everything. Well, you've captured or stolen something, and killed an *abrek!* Well, you're a fine fellow! But now you should live quietly for a bit, or else there'll be trouble." '

"Yes, I saw him a time or two in the division; he was always merry-making. He has sold another horse," said Olenin, and glanced towards the oven.

A pair of large, dark, and hostile eyes glittered as they gazed severely at him.

He became ashamed of what he had said "What of it? He does no one any harm," suddenly remarked Maryana. "He makes merry with his own money," and lowering her legs she jumped down from the oven and went out, banging the door. Olenin followed her with his eyes as long as she was in the hut; and then looked at the door and waited, understanding nothing of what Granny Ulita was telling him.

A few minutes later some visitors arrived: an old man, Granny Ulitka's brother, with Daddy Eroshka, and following them came Maryana and Ustenka.

"Good evening," squeaked Ustenka. "Still on holiday?" she added, turning to Olenin. "Yes, still on holiday," he replied, and felt, he did not know why, ashamed and ill at ease.

He wished to go away, but could not. It also seemed to him impossible to keep silent. The old man helped him by asking for a drink, and they had a drink. Olenin drank with Eroshka, with the other Cossack, and again with Eroshka, and the more he drank the heavier was his heart. But the two old men grew merry. The girls climbed to the oven, where they sat whispering and looking at the men, who drank till it was late. Olenin did not talk, but drank more than the others. The Cossacks were shouting. The old woman would not let them have any more *chikhir,* and at last turned them out. The girls laughed at Daddy Eroshka, and it was past ten when they all went out into the porch. The old men invited themselves to finish their merry-making at Olenin's. Ustenka ran off home, and Eroshka led the old Cossack to Vanyusha. The old woman went out to tidy up the shed. Maryana remained alone in the hut. Olenin felt fresh and joyous, as if he had only just woke up. He noticed everything, and having let the old men pass ahead, he turned back to the hut where Maryana was preparing for bed. He went up to her and wished to say something, but his voice broke. She moved away from him, sat down cross-legged on her bed in the corner, and silently looked at him with wild and frightened eyes. She was evidently afraid of him. Olenin felt this. He felt sorry and ashamed of himself, and at the same time felt proud and pleased that he aroused even that feeling in her.

"Maryana!" he said, "Will you never take pity on me? I can't tell you how I love you."

She moved still farther away and said: "Just hear how the wine is speaking! . . . You'll get nothing from me!"

"No, it is not the wine. Do not marry Lukashka. I will marry you. What am I saying," he thought as he uttered these words. "Shall I be able to say the same tomorrow?" "Yes, I shall, I am sure I shall, and I will repeat them now," replied an inner voice.

"Will you marry me?"

She looked at him seriously, and her fear seemed to have passed.

"Maryanka, I shall go out of my mind! I am not myself. I will do whatever you command," and madly tender words came from his lips of their own accord.

"Now then, what are you drivelling about?" she interrupted, suddenly seizing the arm he was stretching towards her. She did not push his arm away, but pressed it firmly with her strong hard fingers.

"Do gentlemen marry Cossack girls? Go away!"

"But will you? Everything . . ."

"And what shall we do with Lukashka?" said she, laughing.

He snatched away the arm she was holding, and firmly embraced her young body, but she sprang away like a fawn and ran barefooted into the porch: Olenin came to his senses and was terrified at himself. He again felt himself inexpressibly vile compared to her, yet not repenting for an instant of what he had said, he went home and, without even glancing at the old men who were drinking in his room, he lay down and fell asleep more soundly than he had done for a long time.

Chapter XXXV

THE NEXT DAY WAS A HOLIDAY. IN THE EVENING ALL THE VILLAGERS, THEIR HOLIDAY CLOTHES shining in the sunset, were out in the street. That season more wine than usual had been produced, and the people were now free from their labors. In a month the Cossacks were to start on a campaign, and in many families preparations were being made for weddings.

Most of the people were standing in the square, in front of the Cossack Government Office and near the two shops, in one of which cakes and pumpkin seeds were sold, in the other kerchiefs and cotton prints. On the earth-embankment of the office-building sat or stood the old men in sober gray or black coats, without gold trimmings or any kind of ornament. They conversed among themselves quietly, in measured tones, about the harvest, about the young folk, about village affairs, and about old times, looking with dignified equanimity at the younger generation. Passing by them, the women and girls stopped and bent their heads. The young Cossacks respectfully slackened their pace and raised their caps, holding them for a while over their heads. The old men then stopped speaking. Some of them watched the passers-by severely, others kindly, and in their turn slowly took off their caps and put them on again.

The Cossack girls had not yet started dancing their *horovods,* but having gathered in groups, they in their bright colored *beshmets,* with white kerchiefs on their heads pulled down to their eyes, sat, either on the ground or on the earth-banks about the huts, sheltered from the oblique rays of the sun, and laughed and chattered in their ringing voices. Little boys and girls, playing in the square, sent their balls high up into the clear sky, and ran about squealing and shouting. The rather older girls had started dancing their *horovods*; and were timidly singing in their thin shrill voices. Clerks, lads not in the service, or home for the holiday, bright-faced, and wearing smart white or new red Circassian gold-trimmed coats, went about arm in arm, in twos or threes, from one group of women or girls to another, and stopped, joking and chatting with the Cossack girls. The Armenian shopkeeper, in a gold-trimmed coat of fine blue cloth, stood at the open door, through which piles of folded bright-colored kerchiefs were visible, and conscious of his own importance and with the pride of an Oriental tradesman, waited for customers. Two red-bearded, barefooted Chechens, who had come from beyond the Terek to see the fête, sat on their heels outside the house of a friend, negligently smoking their little pipes and occasionally spitting, watching the villagers and exchanging remarks with one another in their rapid guttural speech. Occasionally a workaday-looking soldier in an old overcoat passed among the bright-clad girls. Here and there the songs of tipsy Cossacks who were merry-making, could already be heard. All the huts were locked up; the porches had been scrubbed clean the day before. Even the old women were out in the street, which was everywhere sprinkled with pumpkin and melon seed-shells. The air was warm and still, the sky deep and clear. Beyond the roofs the dead-white mountain range, which seemed very near, was turning rosy in the glow of the evening sun. Now and then, from the other side of the river, came the distant roar of a cannon, but above the village, mingling with one another, floated all sorts of merry holiday sounds.

Olenin had been pacing the yard all that morning, hoping to see Maryana. But she went to Mass at the chapel, and afterwards sat with the other girls on an earth-embankment, cracking seeds; sometimes, again, together with her companions, she ran home, and each time gave the lodger a bright and kindly look. Olenin felt afraid to address her playfully, or in the presence of others. He wished to finish telling her what he had begun to say the night before, and to get her to give him a definite answer. He waited for another moment like that of yesterday evening; but the moment did not come, and he felt that he could not remain any longer in this uncertainty. She went out into the street again, and after waiting a while he too went out, and without knowing where he was going he followed her. He passed by the corner where she was sitting in her shining blue satin *beshmet*, and with an aching heart he heard behind him the girls laughing.

Beletsky's hut looked out on to the square. As Olenin was passing it he heard Beletsky's voice calling to him, "Come in," and in he went.

After a short talk they both sat down by the window, and were soon joined by Eroshka, who entered, dressed in a new *beshmet*, and sat down on the floor beside them.

"There, that's the aristocratic party," said Beletsky, pointing with his cigarette to a brightly-coloured group at the corner. "Mine is there too. Do you see her? in red. That's a new *beshmet*." "Why don't you start the *horovod?*" he shouted, leaning out of the window. "Wait a bit, and then, when it grows dark, let us go too. Then we will invite them to Ustenka's. We must arrange a ball for them!"

"And I will come to Ustenka's," said Olenin in a decided tone. "Will Maryana be there?"

"Yes, she'll be there. Do come!" said Beletsky, without the least surprise. "But isn't it a pretty picture?" he added, pointing to the motley crowds.

"Yes, very!" Olenin assented, trying to appear indifferent. "Holidays of this kind," he added, "always make me wonder why all these people should suddenly be contented and jolly. Today, for instance, just because it happens to be the fifteenth of the month, everything is festive. Eyes and faces, and voices and movements and garments, and the air and the sun, are all in a holiday mood. And we have no longer any holidays!"

"Yes," said Beletsky, who did not like such reflections. "And why are you not drinking, old fellow?" he said, turning to Eroshka.

Eroshka winked at Olenin, pointing to Beletsky. "Eh, he's a proud one, that *kunak* of yours," he said.

Beletsky raised his glass.

"Allah birdy!" he said, emptying his glass. (*Allah birdy,* "God gave," is the usual greeting of Caucasians, when drinking together.)

"Sau bul" ("Your health'), answered Eroshka smiling, and emptied his glass.

"Talking about holidays!" he said, turning to Olenin as he rose and looked out of the window. "What sort of holiday is that? You should have seen them make merry in the old days! The women used to come out in their gold-trimmed *sarafans.* Two rows of gold coins hanging round their necks, and gold-cloth diadems on their heads, and when they passed they made a noise, " flu, flu," with their dresses.

"Every woman looked like a princess. Sometimes they'd come out, a whole herd of them, and begin singing songs so that the air seemed to rumble, and they went on making merry all night. And the Cossacks would roll out a barrel into the yards, and sit down and drink till break of day, or they would go hand-in-hand sweeping the village. Whoever they met they seized and took along with them, and went from house to house. Sometimes they used to make merry for three days on end. Father used to come home—I still remember it—quite red and swollen, without a cap, having lost everything: he'd come and lie down. Mother knew what to do: she would bring him some fresh caviar, and a little *chikhir* to sober him up, and would herself run about in the village looking for his cap. Then he'd sleep for two days! That's the fellows they were then! But now what are they?"

"Well, and the girls in the *sarafans,* did they make merry all by themselves?" asked Beletsky.

"Yes, they did! Sometimes Cossacks would come on foot or on horse, and say, " Let's break up the *horovods*" and they'd go, but the girls would take up cudgels. Carnival week, some young fellow would come galloping up, and they'd cudgel his horse and cudgel him too. But he'd break through, seize the one he loved, and carry her off. "Mammy, darling! . . ." Oh! how he would love her! Yes, the girls in those days, they were regular queens!"

Chapter XXXVI

JUST THEN TWO MEN RODE OUT OF THE SIDE STREET INTO THE square. ONE OF THEM WAS NAZARKA. The other, Lukashka, sat slightly sideways on his well-fed bay Kabarda horse, which stepped lightly over the hard road, jerking its beautiful head with the fine glossy crest. The well-adjusted gun in its cover, the pistol at his back, and the cloak rolled up behind the saddle, showed that Lukashka had not come from a peaceful place, or from one nearby. The smart way in which he sat a little sideways on his horse, the careless motion with which he touched the horse under its belly with his whip, and especially his half-closed black eyes, glistening as he looked proudly around him, all expressed the conscious strength and self-confidence of youth. "Ever seen as fine a lad?" his eyes, looking from side to side, seemed to say. The elegant horse with its silver ornaments and trappings, the weapons, and the handsome Cossack himself, attracted the attention of everyone in the square. Nazarka, lean and short, was much less well dressed. As he rode past the old men, Lukashka paused and raised his curly, white, sheepskin cap above his closely cropped black head.

"Well, have you carried off many Nogay horses?" asked a lean old man, with a frowning, lowering look.

"Have you counted them, Grandad, that you ask?" replied Lukashka, turning away.

"That's all very well, but you need not take my lad along with you," the old man muttered, with a still darker frown.

"Just see the old devil, he knows everything," muttered Lukashka to himself, and a worried expression came over his face; but then, noticing a corner where a number of Cossack girls were standing, he turned his horse towards them.

"Good evening, girls!" he shouted in his powerful, resonant voice, suddenly checking his horse. "You've grown old, without me, you witches!" and he laughed.

"Good evening, Lukashka! Good evening, laddie!" the merry voices answered.

"Have you brought much money? Buy some sweets for the girls! . . . Have you come for long? True enough, it's long since we saw you. . . ."

"Nazarka and I have just flown across to make a night of it," replied Lukashka, raising his whip and riding straight at the girls.

"Why, Maryanka has quite forgotten you," said Ustenka, nudging Maryanka with her elbow and breaking into a shrill laugh.

Maryana moved away from the horse and, throwing back her head, calmly looked at the Cossack with her large sparkling eyes.

"True enough, you have not been, for a long time! Why are you trampling us under your horse?" she remarked dryly, and turned away.

Lukashka had appeared particularly merry. His face shone with audacity and joy. Obviously staggered by Maryana's cold reply, he suddenly knitted his brow.

"Step up on my stirrup and I'll carry you away to the mountains, Mammy!" he suddenly exclaimed, and, as if to disperse his dark thoughts, he caracoled among the girls. Stooping down towards Maryana, he said, "I'll kiss, oh, how I'll kiss you! . . ."

Maryana's eyes met his, and she suddenly blushed and stepped back.

"Oh, bother you! you'll crush my feet," she said, and bending her head looked at her well-shaped feet in their tightly-fitting light blue stockings with clocks, and her new red slippers trimmed with narrow silver braid.

Lukashka turned towards Ustenka, and Maryana sat down next to a woman with a baby in her arms. The baby stretched his plump little arms towards the girl, and seized the string of coins that hung down on to her blue *beshmet.* Maryana bent towards the child and glanced at Lukashka from the corner of her eyes. Lukashka just then was getting out from under his coat, out of the pocket of his black *beshmet,* a bundle of sweetmeats and seeds.

"There, I give them to all of you," he said, handing the bundle to Ustenka and smiling at Maryana.

A confused expression again appeared on the girl's face. It was as though a mist gathered over her beautiful eyes. She drew her kerchief down from her lips, and leaning her head over the fair-skinned face of the baby that still held her by her coin necklace, she suddenly began to kiss it greedily. The baby pressed his little hands against the girl's high breasts, and opening his toothless mouth, screamed loudly.

"You're smothering the boy!" said the little one's mother, taking him away; and she unfastened her *beshmet* to give him the breast. "You'd better go and welcome the lad."

"I'll only go and put up my horse, and then Nazarka and I will come back; we'll make merry all night," said Lukashka, touching his horse with his whip and riding away from the girls. Turning into a side street, he and Nazarka rode up to two huts that stood side by side.

"Here we are, all right, old fellow! Be quick and come soon!" called Lukashka to his comrade, dismounting in front of one of the huts; then he carefully led his horse in at the gate of the wattle fence of his own home.

"How d'you do, Stepka?" he said to his dumb sister, who, smartly dressed like the others, came in from the street to take his horse; and he made signs to her to take the horse to the hay, but not to unsaddle it.

The dumb girl made her usual humming noise, smacked her lips as she pointed to the horse, and kissed it on the nose, as much as to say that she loved it and that it was a fine horse.

"How d'you do, mother? How is it that you have not gone out yet?" shouted Lukashka, holding his gun in place, as he mounted the steps of the porch.

His old mother opened the door. "Dear me! I never expected, never thought, you'd come," said the old woman. "Why, Kirka said you'd not be here."

"Go and bring some *chikhir,* mother. Nazarka is coming here and we will celebrate the feast day."

"Directly, Lukashka, directly!" answered the old woman. "Our women are making merry. I expect our dumb one has gone too."

She took her keys, and hurriedly went to the outhouse.

Nazarka, after putting up his horse and taking the gun off his shoulder, returned to Lukashka's house and went in.

Chapter XXXVII

"YOUR HEALTH!" SAID LUKASHKA, TAKING FROM HIS MOTHER'S HANDS A CUP FILLED TO THE, BRIM with *chikhir,* and carefully raising it to his bowed head.

"A bad business!" said Nazarka. "You heard how Daddy Burlak said, " Have you stolen many horses?" He seems to know!"

"A regular wizard!" Lukashka replied shortly. "But what of that!" he added, tossing his head. "They are across the river by now. Go and find them."

"Still, it's a bad lookout."

"What's a bad lookout? Go and take some *chikhir* to him tomorrow, and nothing will come of it. Now let's make merry. Drink!" shouted Lukashka, just in the tone in which old Eroshka uttered the word. "We'll go out into the street and make merry with the girls. You go and get some honey; or no, I'll send our dumb wench. We'll make merry till morning."

Nazarka smiled. "Are we stopping here long?" he asked.

"Till we've had a bit of fun. Run and get some vodka. Here's the money."

Nazarka ran off obediently to get the vodka from Yamka's.

Daddy Eroshka and Ergushov, like birds of prey, scenting where the merry-making was going on, tumbled into the hut one after the other, both tipsy.

"Bring us another half-pail," shouted Lukashka to his mother, by way of reply to their greeting.

"Now then, tell us, where did you steal them, you devil?" shouted Eroshka. "Fine fellow, I'm fond of you!"

"Fond indeed . . ." answered Lukashka, laughing, "carrying sweets from cadets to lasses! Eh, you old . . ."

"That's not true, not true! . . . Oh, Mark," and the old man burst out laughing. "And how that devil begged me. " Go," he said, " and arrange it." He offered me a gun! But, no. I'd have managed it, but I feel for you. Now tell us, where have you been?" And the old man began speaking in Tartar.

Lukashka answered him promptly.

Ergushov, who did not know much Tartar, only occasionally put in a word in Russian:

"What I say is, he's driven away the horses. I know it for a fact," he chimed in.

"Girey and I went together." (His speaking of Girey Khan as "Girey' was, to the Cossack mind, evidence of his boldness.) "Just beyond the river he kept bragging that he knew the whole of the steppe, and would lead the way straight, but we rode on and the night was dark, and my Girey lost his way, and began wandering in a circle without getting anywhere: couldn't find the village, and there we were. We must have gone too much to the right. I believe we wandered about well-nigh till midnight. Then, thank goodness, we heard dogs howling."

"Fools!" said Daddy Eroshka. "There now, we too used to lose our way in the steppe. (Who the devil can follow it?) But I used to ride up a hillock and start howling like the wolves, like this!" He placed his hands before his mouth, and howled like a pack of wolves, all on one note. "The dogs would answer at once. . . . Well, go on—so you found them?"

"We soon led them away! Nazarka was nearly caught by some Nogay women, he was!"

"Caught, indeed," Nazarka, who had just come back, said in an injured tone.

"We rode off again, and again Girey lost his way, and almost landed us among the sand-drifts. We thought we were just getting to the Terek, but we were riding away from it all the time!"

"You should have steered by the stars," said Daddy Eroshka.

"That's what I say," interjected Ergushov.

"Yes, steer when all is black; I tried and tried all about . . . and at last I put the bridle on one of the mares, and let my own horse go free—thinking he'll lead us out; and what do you think! he just gave a snort or two with his nose to the ground, galloped ahead, and led us straight to our village. Thank goodness!"

"It was getting quite light. We barely had time to hide them in the forest. Nagim came across the river, and took them away."

Ergushov shook his head. "It's just what I said. Smart. Did you get much for them?"

"It's all here," said Lukashka, slapping his pocket.

Just then his mother came into the room, and Lukashka did not finish what he was saying.

"Drink!" he shouted.

"We too, Girich and I, rode out late one night . . ." began Eroshka.

"Oh, bother, we'll never hear the end of you!" said Lukashka. "I am going." And having emptied his cup and tightened the strap of his belt, he went out.

Chapter XXXVIII

IT WAS ALREADY DARK WHEN LUKASHKA WENT OUT INTO THE STREET. THE AUTUMN NIGHT WAS fresh and calm. The full golden moon floated up behind the tall dark poplars that grew on one side of the square. From the chimneys of the outhouses smoke rose and spread above the village, mingling with the mist. Here and there lights shone through the windows, and the air was laden with the smell of *kisyak*, grape-pulp, and mist. The sounds of voices, laughter, songs, and the cracking of seeds, mingled just as they had done in the daytime, but were now more distinct. Clusters of white kerchiefs and caps gleamed through the darkness near the houses and by the fences.

In the square, before the shop door, which was lit up and open, the black and white figures of Cossack men and maids showed through the darkness, and one heard from afar their loud songs and laughter and talk. The girls, hand in hand, went round and round in a circle, stepping lightly in the dusty square. A skinny girl, the plainest of them all, set the tune:

"From beyond the wood, from the forest dark,
From the garden green, and the shady park,
There came out, there came two young fellows gay.

They were brave and smart, bach'lors both were they!
And they walked and walked, then stood still, each man,
So they stood and soon to dispute began!
Then a maid came out; as she came along,
Said, 'To one of you, I shall soon belong!'
'Twas the fair-faced lad got the maiden fair,
Yes, the fair-faced lad with the golden hair!
Her right hand so white, in his own took he,
And he led her round, for his mates to see!
And he said, 'Have you, mates, in all your life,
Met a lass as fair as my little wife?' "

The old women stood round, listening to the songs. The little boys and girls ran about chasing one another in the dark. The men stood by, catching at the girls as the latter moved round, and sometimes breaking the ring and entering it. On the dark side of the doorway stood Beletsky and Olenin, in their Circassian coats and sheepskin caps, and in a style of speech unlike that of the Cossacks talked together in low but distinct tones, conscious that they were attracting attention.

Next to one another, in the *horovod* circle, moved plump little Ustenka in her red *beshmet* and the stately Maryanka in her new smock and *beshmet.* Olenin and Beletsky were discussing how to snatch Ustenka and Maryanka out of the ring. Beletsky thought that Olenin wished only to amuse himself, while Olenin was expecting his fate to be decided. He wanted, at any cost, to see Maryanka alone that very day, and to tell her everything, and ask her whether she could and would be his wife. Although that question had long been answered in the negative in his own mind, he hoped he would be able to tell her all he felt, and that she would understand him.

"Why did you not tell me sooner?" said Beletsky. "I would have got Ustenka to arrange it for you. You are such a queer fellow! . . ."

"What's to be done! . . . Some day, very soon, I'll tell you all about it. Only now, for Heaven's sake arrange so that she should come to Ustenka's."

"All right, that's easily done! Well, Maryanka, will you belong to the 'fair-faced lad,' and not to Lukashka?" said Beletsky, speaking to Maryanka first for propriety's sake, but, having received no reply, he went up to Ustenka and begged her to bring Maryanka home with her. He had hardly time to finish what he was saying before the leader began another song, and the girls started pulling each other round in the ring by the hand. They sang:

"Past the garden, the garden,
A young lad came strolling down,
Up the street and through the town;
And the first time, as he passed,
He did wave his strong right hand.
As the second time he passed
Waved his hat with silken band.
And the third time as he passed
He stood still: did not depart.
He this time did not depart, but he made himself look smart.

'I have wished to come to thee
Just to have a bit of talk.
Why is it that thou, my dear,
In the park don't come to walk?

'Come now, answer me, my dear,
Dost thou hold me in contempt?
Later on, thou knowest, dear,
Thou'lt get sober and repent.
Soon to woo thee, I will come,
And when we shall married be,
Thou shalt weep because of me!'

Though I knew what to reply,
Yet I dared not him deny,
No I dared not him deny!
In the park to walk went I,
In the park my lad to meet,
There my dear one I did greet.
As I bowed, so it befell,
To the ground my kerchief fell.

Up he picked it, where it lay,
'In thy white hand take it, pray.
Please accept it, dear, from me,
Say I am beloved by thee,
I don't know at all, I fear,
What I am to give thee, dear!
To my dear I think I will
Of a shawl a present make—
Kisses five for it I'll take.' "

Lukashka and Nazarka broke into the ring and started walking about among the girls. Lukashka joined in the singing, taking seconds in his clear voice as he walked in the middle of the ring swinging his arms.

"Well, come in, one of you!" he said. The other girls pushed Maryanka, but she would not enter the ring. The sound of shrill laughter, slaps, kisses, and whispers, mingled with the singing. As he went past Olenin, Lukashka gave a friendly nod.

"Dmitry Andreich! Have you, too, come to have a look?" he said.

"Yes," answered Olenin, dryly.

Beletsky stooped and whispered something into Ustenka's ear. She had not time to reply till she came round again, when she said, "All right, we'll come."

"And Maryanka too?"

Olenin stooped towards Maryanka. "You'll come? Please do, if only for a minute. I must speak to you."

"If the other girls come, I will."

"Will you answer my question?" said he, bending towards her. "You are in good spirits today."

She had already moved past him. He went after her. "Will you?"

"What question?"

"The one I asked you the other day," said Olenin, stooping to her ear. "Will you marry me?"

Maryanka thought for a moment. "I'll tell you," said she, "I'll tell you tonight," and through the darkness her eyes gleamed brightly and kindly at the young man.

He still followed her. He enjoyed stooping closer to her.

But Lukashka, without ceasing to sing, suddenly seized her firmly by the hand and pulled her from her place in the ring of girls, into the middle. Olenin had only time to say, "Come to Ustenka's," and stepped back to his companion. The song came to an end. Lukashka wiped his lips, Maryanka did the same, and they kissed.

"No, no, kisses five!" said Lukashka. Chatter, laughter, and running about, succeeded to the rythmic movements and sound. Lukashka, who seemed to have drunk a great deal, began to distribute sweetmeats to the girls. "I offer them to everyone!" he said, with proud, comically pathetic self-admiration. "But anyone who goes after soldiers, get out of the ring!" he suddenly added with an angry glance at Olenin.

The girls grabbed his sweetmeats from him, and laughing, struggled for them among themselves. Beletsky and Olenin stepped aside.

Lukashka, as if ashamed of his generosity, took off his cap and wiping his forehead with his sleeve, came up to Maryanka and Ustenka. "Answer me, my dear, dost thou hold me in contempt?" he said, in the words of the song they had just been singing, and turning to Maryanka, he angrily repeated the words: "Dost thou hold me in contempt? When we shall married be, thou shalt weep because of me!" he added, embracing Ustenka and Maryanka both together. Ustenka tore herself away, and swinging her arm gave him such a blow on the back that she hurt her hand.

"Well, are you going to have another turn?" he asked.

"The other girls may if they like," answered Ustenka, "but I am going home, and Maryanka was coming to our house too."

With his arm still round her, Lukashka led Maryanka away from the crowd to the darker corner of a house.

"Don't go, Maryanka," he said, "let's have some fun for the last time. Go home and I will come to you!"

"What am I to do at home? Holidays are meant for merry-making. I am going to Ustenka's," replied Maryanka.

"I'll marry you, all the same, you know!"

"All right," said Maryanka, "we shall see when the time comes."

"So you are going," said Lukashka sternly, and, pressing her close, he kissed her on the cheek.

"There, leave off! Don't bother," and Maryanka, wrenching herself from his arms, moved away.

"Ah, my girl, it will turn out badly," said Lukashka reproachfully, and stood still shaking his head. "Thou shalt weep because of me . . ." and turning away from her, he shouted to the other girls.

"Now then! Play away!"

What he had said seemed to have frightened and vexed Maryanka. She stopped, "What will turn out badly?"

"Why, that!"

"That what?"

"Why, that you keep company with a soldier-lodger and no longer care for me!"

"I'll care just as long as I choose. You're not my father, nor my mother. What do you want. I'll care for whom I like!"

"Well, all right . . ." said Lukashka, "but remember!" He moved towards the shop. "Girls!" he shouted, "why have you stopped? Go on dancing. Nazarka, fetch some more *chikhir*."

"Well, will they come?" asked Olenin, addressing Beletsky.

"They'll come directly," replied Beletsky. "Come along, we must prepare the ball."

Chapter XXXIX

It was already late in the night when Olenin came out of Beletsky's hut, following Maryanka and Ustenka. He saw in the dark street before him the gleam of the girl's white kerchief. The golden moon was descending towards the steppe. A silvery mist hung over the village. All was still; there were no lights anywhere, and one heard only the retreating footsteps of the young women. Olenin's heart beat fast. The fresh moist atmosphere cooled his burning face. He glanced at the sky and turned to look at the hut he had just come out of: the candle was already out. Then he again peered through the darkness at the girls' retreating shadows. The white kerchief disappeared in the mist. He was afraid to remain alone, he was so happy. He jumped down from the porch and ran after the girls.

"Bother you, someone may see . . ." said Ustenka.

"Never mind!"

Olenin ran up to Maryanka, and embraced her. Maryanka did not resist.

"Haven't you kissed enough yet?" said Ustenka. "Marry and then kiss, but now you'd better wait."

"Good night, Maryanka, tomorrow I will come to see your father, and tell him. Don't you say anything."

"Why should I!" answered Maryanka.

Both the girls started running. Olenin went on by himself, thinking over all that had happened. He had spent the whole evening alone with her in a corner by the oven. Ustenka had not left the hut for a single moment, but had romped about with the other girls and with Beletsky all the time. Olenin had talked in whispers to Maryanka.

"Will you marry me?" he had asked.

"You'll deceive me and not have me," she replied cheerfully and calmly.

"But do you love me? Tell me for God's sake!"

"Why shouldn't I love you? You don't squint," answered Maryanka, laughing, and with her hard hands squeezing his . . .

"What whi-ite, whi-i-ite, soft hands you've got—so like clotted cream," she said.

"I am in earnest. Tell me, will you marry me?"

"Why not, if father gives me to you?"

"Well then, remember, I shall go mad if you deceive me. Tomorrow I will tell your mother and father. I shall come and propose."

Maryanka suddenly burst out laughing.

"What's the matter?"

"It seems so funny!"

"It's true! I will buy a vineyard and a house, and will enroll myself as a Cossack."

"Mind you don't go after other women, then. I am severe about that."

Olenin joyfully repeated all these words to himself. The memory of them now gave him pain, and now such joy that it took away his breath. The pain was because she had remained as calm as usual while talking to him. She did not seem at all agitated by these new conditions. It was as if she did not trust him, and did not think of the future. It seemed to him that she only loved him for the present moment, and that in her mind there was no future with him. He was happy, because her words sounded to him true, and she had consented to be his.

"Yes," thought he to himself, "we shall only understand one another when she is quite mine. For such love, there are no words. It needs life—the whole of life. Tomorrow everything will be cleared up. I cannot live like this any longer; tomorrow I will tell everything to her father, to Beletsky, and to the whole village."

Lukashka, after two sleepless nights, had drunk so much at the fête, that for the first time in his life, his feet would not carry him, and he slept in Yamka's house.

Chapter XL

THE NEXT DAY OLENIN AWOKE EARLIER THAN USUAL AND IMMEDIATELY REMEMBERED WHAT LAY before him, and he joyfully recalled her kisses, the pressure of her hard hands, and her words, "What white hands you have!"

He jumped up and wished to go at once to his hosts' hut to ask for their consent to his marriage with Maryanka. The sun had not yet risen, but it seemed that there was an unusual bustle in the street and side street: people were moving about on foot and on horseback, and talking. He threw on his Circassian coat and hastened out into the porch. His hosts were not yet up. Five Cossacks were riding past and talking loudly together. In front rode Lukashka, on his broad-backed Kabarda horse. The Cossacks were all speaking and shouting so that it was impossible to make out exactly what they were saying.

"Ride to the Upper Post," shouted one.

"Saddle, and catch us up, be quick," said another.

"It's nearer through the other gate!"

"What are you talking about!" cried Lukashka, "We must go through the middle gates, of course."

"So we must, it's nearer that way," said one of the Cossacks, who was covered with dust and rode a perspiring horse.

Lukashka's face was red and swollen after the drinking of the previous night, and his cap was pushed to the back of his head. He was calling out with authority, as though he were an officer.

"What is the matter? Where are you going?" asked Olenin, with difficulty attracting the Cossacks' attention.

"We are off to catch *abreks*. They're hiding among the sand-drifts. We are just off, but there are not enough of us yet." And the Cossacks continued to shout, more and more of them joining as they rode down the street. It occurred to Olenin that it would not look well for him to stay behind; besides he thought he could soon come back. He dressed, loaded his gun with bullets, jumped on to his horse, which Vanyusha had saddled more or less well, and overtook the Cossacks at the village gates. The Cossacks had dismounted, and filling a wooden bowl with *chikhir* from a little cask which they had brought with them, they passed the bowl round to one another, and drank to the success of their expedition. Among them was a smartly-dressed young Teacher, who happened to be in the village and who took command of the group of nine Cossacks who had joined for the expedition. All these Cossacks were privates, and although the Teacher assumed the airs of a commanding officer, they only obeyed Lukashka.

Of Olenin they took no notice at all, and when they had all mounted and started, and Olenin rode up to the Teacher and began asking him what was taking place, the Teacher, who was usually quite friendly, treated him with marked condescension. It was with great difficulty that Olenin managed to find out from him what was happening. Scouts, who had been sent out to search for *abreks*, had come upon several hillsmen some six miles from the village. These *abreks* had taken shelter in pits and had fired at the scouts, declaring they would not surrender. A corporal, who had been scouting with two Cossacks, had remained to watch the *abreks* and had sent one Cossack back to get help.

The sun was just rising. Three miles beyond the village the steppe spread out and nothing was visible except the dry, monotonous, sandy, dismal plain covered with the footmarks of cattle, and here and there with tufts of withered grass, with low reeds in the flats, and rare, little-trodden footpaths, and the camps of the nomad Nogay tribe just visible far away. The absence of shade and the austere aspect of the place were striking. The sun always rises and sets red in the steppe. When it is windy whole hills of sand are carried by the wind from place to place. When it is calm, as it was that morning, the silence, uninterrupted by any movement or sound, is peculiarly striking. That morning in the steppe it was quiet and dull, though the sun had already risen. It all seemed specially soft and desolate. The air was hushed; the footfalls and the snorting of the horses were the only sounds to be heard, and even they quickly died away. The men rode almost silently. A Cossack always carries his weapons so that they neither jingle nor rattle. Jingling weapons are a terrible disgrace to a Cossack. Two other Cossacks from the village caught the party up and exchanged a few words. Lukashka's horse either stumbled or caught its foot in some grass, and became restive—which is a sign of bad luck among the Cossacks, and at such a time was of special importance. The others exchanged glances, and turned away, trying not to notice what had happened. Lukashka pulled at the reins, frowned sternly, set his teeth, and flourished his whip above his head. His good Kabarda horse, prancing from one foot to another, not knowing with which to start, seemed to wish to fly upwards on wings. But Lukashka hit its well-fed sides with his whip once, then again, and a third time, and the horse, showing its teeth and spreading out its tail, snorted and reared and stepped on its hind legs a few paces away from the others. "Ah, a good steed that!" said the Teacher. That he said *steed* instead of *horse,* indicated special praise.

"A lion of a horse," assented one of the others, an old Cossack.

The Cossacks rode silently forward, now at a footpace, then at a trot, and these changes were the only incidents that for a moment interrupted the stillness and solemnity of their movements.

Riding through the steppe for about six miles, they passed nothing but one Nogay tent, placed on a cart and moving slowly along at a distance of about a mile from them. A Nogay family was moving from one part of the steppe to another. Afterwards they met two tattered Nogay women with high cheekbones, who with baskets on their backs were gathering dung left by the cattle that wandered over the steppe. The Teacher, who did not know their language well, tried to question them, but they did not understand him, and obviously frightened, looked at one another.

Lukashka rode up to them both, stopped his horse and promptly uttered the usual greeting. The Nogay women were evidently relieved, and began speaking to him quite freely as to a brother.

"Ay-ay, kop abrek!" they said plaintively, pointing in the direction in which the Cossacks were going. Olenin understood that they were saying, "Many *abreks.*"

Never having seen an engagement of that kind, and having formed an idea of them only from Daddy Eroshka's tales, Olenin wished not to be left behind by the Cossacks, but wanted to see it all. He admired the Cossacks, and was on the watch, looking and listening and making his own observations. Though he had brought his sword and a loaded gun with him, when he noticed that the Cossacks avoided him he decided to take no part in the action, as in his opinion his courage had already been sufficiently proved when he was with his detachment, and also because he was very happy. Suddenly a shot was heard in the distance. The Teacher became excited, and began giving orders to the Cossacks as to how they should divide and from which side they should approach. But the Cossacks did not appear to pay any attention to these orders, listening only to what Lukashka said, and looking to him alone. Lukashka's face and figure were expressive of calm solemnity. He put his horse to a trot with which the others were unable to keep pace, and screwing up his eyes, he kept looking ahead.

"There's a man on horseback," he said, reining in his horse and keeping in line with the others.

Olenin looked intently, but could not see anything.

The Cossacks soon distinguished two riders, and quietly rode straight towards them.

"Are those the *abreks?*" asked Olenin.

The Cossacks did not answer his question, which appeared quite meaningless to them. The *abreks* would have been fools to venture across the river on horseback.

"That's friend Rodka waving to us, I do believe," said Lukashka, pointing to the two mounted men, who were now clearly visible. "Look, he's coming to us."

A few minutes later it became plain that the two horsemen were the Cossack scouts. The corporal rode up to Lukashka.

Chapter XLI

"ARE THEY FAR?" WAS ALL LUKASHKA SAID.

Just then they heard a sharp shot, some thirty paces off. The corporal smiled slightly. "Our Gurka is having shots at them," he said, nodding in the direction of the shot.

Having gone a few paces farther, they saw Gurka sitting behind a sand-hillock and loading his gun. To while away the time, he was exchanging shots with the *abreks,* who were behind another sand-heap. A bullet came whistling from their side. The Teacher was pale and grew confused. Lukashka dismounted from his horse, threw the reins to one of the other Cossacks, and went up to Gurka. Olenin also dismounted, and bending down, followed Lukashka. They had hardly reached Gurka when two bullets whistled above them. Lukashka looked around laughing at Olenin, and stooped a little. "Look out, or they will kill you, Dmitry Andreich," he said. "You'd better go away—you have no business here."

But Olenin wanted absolutely to see the *abreks.* From behind the mound he saw caps and muskets some two hundred paces off. Suddenly a little cloud of smoke appeared from thence, and again a bullet whistled past. The *abreks* were hiding in a marsh at the foot of the hill. Olenin was much impressed by the place in which they sat. In reality it was very much like the rest of the steppe, but because the *abreks* sat there, it seemed to detach itself from all the rest and to have become distinguished. Indeed it appeared to Olenin that it was the very spot for *abreks* to occupy. Lukashka went back to his horse, and Olenin followed him.

"We must get a hay-cart," said Lukashka, "or they will be killing some of us. There, behind that mound, is a Nogay cart with a load of hay." The Teacher listened to him, and the Corporal agreed. The cart of hay was fetched, and the Cossacks, hiding behind it, pushed it forward. Olenin rode up a hillock from whence he could see everything. The hay-cart moved on, and the Cossacks crowded together behind it. The Cossacks advanced, but the Chechens, of whom there were nine, sat with their knees in a row and did not fire.

All was quiet. Suddenly from the Chechens arose the sound of a mournful song, something like Daddy Eroshka's "Ay day, dalalay." The Chechens knew that they could not escape, and to prevent themselves from being tempted to take to flight they had strapped themselves together knee to knee, had got their guns ready, and were singing their death-song.

The Cossacks with their hay-cart drew closer and closer, and Olenin expected the firing to begin any moment, but the silence was only broken by the *abreks'* mournful song. Suddenly the song ceased; there was a sharp report, a bullet struck the front of the cart, and Chechen curses and yells broke the silence, and shot followed on shot, and one bullet after another struck the cart. The Cossacks did not fire, and were now only five paces distant.

Another moment passed, and the Cossacks with a whoop rushed out on both sides, from behind the cart—Lukashka in front of them. Olenin heard only a few shots, then shouting and moans. He thought he saw smoke and blood, and abandoning his horse and quite beside himself, he ran towards the Cossacks. Horror seemed to blind him. He could not make out anything, but understood that all was over. Lukashka, pale as death, was holding a wounded Chechen by the arms, and shouting, "Don't kill him. I'll take him alive!" The Chechen was the red-haired man who had fetched his brother's body away after Lukashka had killed him. Lukashka was twisting his arms. Suddenly the Chechen wrenched himself free and fired his revolver. Lukashka fell and blood began to flow from his stomach. He jumped up, but fell again, swearing in Russian and in Tartar. More and more blood appeared on his clothes and under him. Some Cossack approached him and began loosening his girdle. One of them, Nazarka, before beginning to help, fumbled for some time, unable to put his sword in its sheath: it would not go the right way. The blade of the sword was blood-stained.

The Chechens, with their red hair and clipped mustaches, lay dead and hacked about. Only the one we know of, who had fired at Lukashka, though wounded in many places was still alive. Like a wounded hawk, all covered with blood (blood was flowing from a wound under his right eye), pale and gloomy, he looked about him with wide-open excited eyes and clenched teeth, as he crouched, dagger in hand, still prepared to defend himself. The Teacher went up to him as if intending to pass by, and with a quick movement shot him in the ear. The Chechen started up, but it was too late, and he fell.

The Cossacks, quite out of breath, dragged the bodies aside and took the weapons from them. Each of the red-haired Chechens had been a man, and each one had his own individual expression. Lukashka was carried to the cart. He continued to swear in Russian and in Tartar.

"No fear, I'll strangle him with my hands. *Anna seni!*" he cried, struggling. But he soon became quiet from weakness.

Olenin rode home. In the evening he was told that Lukashka was at death's door, but that a Tartar from beyond the river had undertaken to cure him with herbs.

The bodies were brought to the village office. The women and the little boys hastened to look at them.

It was growing dark when Olenin returned, and he could not collect himself after what he had seen. But towards night memories of the evening before came rushing to his mind. He looked out of the window, Maryanka was passing to and fro, from the house to the cowshed, putting things straight. Her mother had gone to the vineyard and her father to the office. Olenin could not wait till she had quite finished her work, but went out to meet her. She was in the hut, standing with her back towards him. Olenin thought she felt shy.

"Maryanka," said he, "I say, Maryanka! May I come in?"

She suddenly turned. There was a scarcely perceptible trace of tears in her eyes, and her face was beautiful in its sadness. She looked at him in silent dignity.

Olenin again said: "Maryanka, I have come—"

"Leave me alone!" she said. Her face did not change, but the tears ran down her cheeks.

"What are you crying for? What is it?"

"What?" she repeated in a rough voice. Cossacks have been killed, that's all."

"Lukashka?" said Olenin.

"Go away! What do you want?"

"Maryanka!" said Olenin, approaching her.

"You will never get anything from me!"

"Maryanka, don't speak like that," Olenin entreated.

"Get away. I'm sick of you!" shouted the girl, stamping her foot, and moved threateningly towards him. And her face expressed such abhorrence, such contempt, and such anger, that Olenin suddenly understood that there was no hope for him, and that his first impression of this woman's inaccessibility had been perfectly correct.

Olenin said nothing more, but ran out of the hut.

Chapter XLII

FOR TWO HOURS AFTER RETURNING HOME HE LAY ON HIS BED MOTIONLESS. THEN HE WENT TO his company commander and obtained leave to join the staff. Without taking leave of anyone, and sending Vanyusha to settle his accounts with his landlord, he prepared to leave for the fort where his regiment was stationed. Daddy Eroshka was the only one to see him off. They had a drink, and then a second, and then yet another. Again, as on the night of his departure from Moscow, a three-horsed post-chaise stood waiting at the door. But Olenin did not confer with himself as he had done then, and did not say to himself that all he had thought and done here was "not it." He did not promise himself a new life. He loved Maryanka more than ever, and knew that he could never be loved by her.

"Well, good-bye, my lad!" said Daddy Eroshka. "When you go on an expedition, be wise, and listen to my words—the words of an old man. When you are out on a raid, or the like (you know I'm an old wolf and have seen things), and when they begin firing, don't get into a crowd, where there are many men. When you fellows get frightened, you always try to get close together with a lot of others. You think it is merrier to be with others, but that's where it is worst of all! They always aim at a crowd. Now I used to keep farther away from the others, and went alone, and I've never been wounded. Yet what things haven't I seen in my day?"

"But you've got a bullet in your back," remarked Vanyusha, who was clearing up the room.

"That was the Cossacks fooling about," answered Eroshka.

"Cossacks? How was that?" asked Olenin.

"Oh, just so. We were drinking. Vanka Sitkin, one of the Cossacks, got merry, and puff! he gave me one from his pistol, just here."

"Yes, and did it hurt?" asked Olenin. "Vanyusha, will you soon be ready?" he added.

"Ah, where's the hurry! Let me tell you. When he banged into me, the bullet did not break the bone, but remained here. And I say: 'You've killed me, brother. Eh? What have you done to me? I won't let you off! You'll have to stand me a pailful!' "

"Well, but did it hurt?" Olenin asked again, scarcely listening to the tale.

"Let me finish. He stood a pailful; and we drank it, but the blood went on flowing. The whole room was drenched and covered with blood. Grandad Burlak, he says, " The lad will give up the ghost. Stand a bottle of the sweet sort, or we shall have you taken up!" They brought more drink, and boozed and boozed—"

"Yes, but did it hurt you much?" Olenin asked once more.

"Hurt, indeed! Don't interrupt: I don't like it. Let me finish. We boozed and boozed till morning, and I fell asleep on the top of the oven, drunk. When I woke in the morning I could not unbend myself anyhow—"

"Was it very painful?" repeated Olenin, thinking that now he would at last get an answer to his question.

"Did I tell you it was painful? I did not say it was painful, but I could not bend and could not walk."

"And then it healed up?" said Olenin, not even laughing, so heavy was his heart.

"It healed up, but the bullet is still there. Just feel it!" And lifting his shirt he showed his powerful back, where just near the bone a bullet could be felt and rolled about.

"Feel how it rolls," he said, evidently amusing himself with the bullet as with a toy. "There now, it has rolled to the back."

"And Lukashka, will he recover?" asked Olenin.

"Heaven only knows! There's no doctor. They've gone for one."

"Where will they get one? From Groznoe?" asked Olenin.

"No, my lad. Were I the Tzar, I'd have hung all your Russian doctors long ago. Cutting is all they know! There's our Cossack Baklashka, no longer a real man now that they've cut off his leg! That shows they're fools! What's Baklashka good for now? No, my lad, in the mountains there are real doctors. There was my chum, Vorchik, he was on an expedition and was wounded just here in the chest. Well, your doctors gave him up, but one of theirs came from the mountains and cured him! They understand herbs, my lad!"

"Come, stop talking rubbish," said Olenin. "I'd better send a doctor from head-quarters."

"Rubbish!" the old man said, mockingly. "Fool, fool! Rubbish. You'll send a doctor!—If yours cured people, Cossacks and Chechens would go to you for treatment, but, as it is, your officers and colonels send to the mountains for doctors. Yours are all humbugs, all humbugs."

Olenin did not answer. He agreed, only too fully, that all was humbug in the world in which he had lived and to which he was now returning.

"How is Lukashka? You've been to see him?" he asked.

"He just lies as if he were dead. He does not eat nor drink. Vodka is the only thing his soul accepts. But as long as he drinks vodka, it's well. I'd be sorry to lose the lad. A fine lad—a brave, like me. I too lay dying like that once. The old women were already wailing. My head was burning. They had already laid me out under the holy icons. So I lay there and above me, on the oven—little drummers, no bigger than this, beat the tattoo. I shout at them and they drum all the harder." (The old man laughed.) "The women brought our church elder. They were getting ready to bury me. They said, "he defiled himself with worldly unbelievers; he made merry with women; he ruined people; he did not fast, and he played the *balalayka*." "Confess," they said. So I began to confess. "I've sinned!" I said. Whatever the priest said, I always answered " I've sinned." He began to ask me about the *balalayka*. "Where is the accursed thing," he says. "Show it me and smash it." But I say, "I've not got it." I'd hidden it myself in a net in the outhouse. I knew they could not find it. So they left me. Yet after all I recovered. When I went for my *balalayka*——What was I saying?" he continued. "Listen to me, and keep farther away from the other men, or you'll get killed foolishly. I feel for you, truly: you are a drinker—I love you! And fellows like you like riding up the mounds. There was one who lived here, who had come from Russia, he always would ride up the mounds (he called the mounds so funnily, "hillocks"). Whenever he saw a mound, off he'd gallop. Once he galloped off that way and rode to the top, quite pleased, but a Chechen fired at him, and killed him! Ah, how well they shoot from their gun-rests, those Chechens! Some of them shoot even better than I do. I don't like it when a fellow gets killed so foolishly! Sometimes I used to look at your soldiers and wonder at them. There's foolishness for you! They go, the poor fellows, all in a clump, and even sew red collars to their coats! How can they help being hit! One gets killed, they drag him away, and another takes his place! What foolishness!" the old man repeated, shaking his head. "Why not scatter and go one by one? So you just go like that, and they'll not notice you. That's what you must do."

"Well, thank you! Good-bye, Daddy. God willing, we may meet again," said Olenin, getting up and moving towards the passage. The old man, who was sitting on the floor, did not rise.

"Is that the way one says "Good-bye"? Fool, fool!" he began. "Oh dear, what has come to people! We've kept company, kept company for wellnigh a year, and now "Good-bye!" and off he goes! Why, I love you, and how I pity you! You are so forlorn, always alone, always alone. You're somehow so unsociable. At times I can't sleep for thinking about you. I am so sorry for you. As the song has it:

It is very hard, dear brother,
In a foreign land to live.

So it is with you."

"Well, good-bye," said Olenin again.

The old man rose and held out his hand. Olenin pressed it and turned to go.

"Give us your mug, your mug!" And the old man took Olenin by the head with both hands and kissed him three times with wet mustaches and lips, and began to cry.

"I love you, good-bye!"

Olenin got into the post-chaise.

"Well, is that how you're going? You might give me something for a remembrance. Give me a gun! What do you want two for?" said the old man, sobbing quite sincerely.

Olenin got out a musket and gave it to him.

"What a lot you've given the old fellow," murmured Vanyusha, "he'll never have enough! A regular old beggar. They are all such irregular people," he remarked, as he wrapped himself in his overcoat and took his seat on the box.

"Hold your tongue, swine!" exclaimed the old man, laughing. "What a stingy fellow!"

Maryanka came out of the cowshed, glanced indifferently at the post-chaise, bowed and went towards the hut.

"La fille!" said Vanyusha, with a wink, and burst out into a silly laugh.

"Go on!" shouted Olenin, angrily.

"Good-bye, my lad! Good-bye. I won't forget you!" shouted Eroshka.

Olenin turned round. Daddy Eroshka was talking to Maryanka, evidently about his own affairs, and neither the old man nor the girl looked at Olenin.

WAR AND PEACE

Contents

Part One

Chapter I

"WELL, PRINCE, SO GENOA AND LUCCA ARE NOW JUST FAMILY ESTATES OF THE BUONAPARTES. But I warn you, if you don't tell me that this means war, if you still try to defend the infamies and horrors perpetrated by that Antichrist—I really believe he is Antichrist—I will have nothing more to do with you and you are no longer my friend, no longer my 'faithful slave,' as you call yourself! But how do you do? I see I have frightened you—sit down and tell me all the news."

It was in July 1805, and the speaker was the well-known Anna Pávlovna Scherer, maid of honor and favorite of the Empress Márya Fëdorovna. With these words she greeted Prince Vasíli, a man of high rank and importance, who was the first to arrive at her reception. Anna Pávlovna had had a cough for some days. She was, as she said, suffering from *la grippe*; *grippe* being then a new word in St. Petersburg, used only by the *élite*.

All her invitations without exception, written in French, and delivered by a scarlet-liveried footman that morning, ran as follows:

"If you have nothing better to do, Count (or Prince), and if the prospect of spending an evening with a poor invalid is not too terrible, I shall be very charmed to see you tonight between 7 and 10—Annette Scherer."

"Heavens! what a virulent attack!" replied the prince, not in the least disconcerted by this reception. He had just entered, wearing an embroidered court uniform, knee-breeches, and shoes, and had stars on his breast and a serene expression on his flat face. He spoke in that refined French in which our grandfathers not only spoke but thought, and with the gentle, patronizing intonation natural to a man of importance who had grown old in society and at court. He went up to Anna Pávlovna, kissed her hand, presenting to her his bald, scented and shining head, and complacently seated himself on the sofa.

"First of all, dear friend, tell me how you are. Set your friend's mind at rest," said he without altering his tone, beneath the politeness and affected sympathy of which indifference and even irony could be discerned.

"Can one be well while suffering morally? Can one be calm in times like these if one has any feeling?" said Anna Pávlovna. "You are staying the whole evening, I hope?"

"And the fête at the English Ambassador's? Today is Wednesday. I must put in an appearance there," said the prince. "My daughter is coming for me to take me there."

"I thought today's fête had been canceled. I confess all these festivities and fireworks are becoming wearisome."

"If they had known that you wished it, the entertainment would have been put off," said the prince, who, like a wound-up clock, by force of habit said things he did not even wish to be believed.

"Don't tease! Well, and what has been decided about Novosíltsev's dispatch? You know everything."

"What can one say about it?" replied the prince in a cold, listless tone. "What has been decided? They have decided that Buonaparte has burned his boats, and I believe that we are ready to burn ours."

Prince Vasíli always spoke languidly, like an actor repeating a stale part. Anna Pávlovna Scherer on the contrary, despite her forty years, overflowed with animation and impulsiveness. To be an enthusiast had become her social vocation and, sometimes even when she did not feel like it, she became enthusiastic in order not to disappoint the expectations of those who knew her. The subdued smile which, though it did not suit her faded features, always played round her lips expressed, as in a spoiled child, a continual consciousness of her charming defect, which she neither wished, nor could, nor considered it necessary, to correct.

In the midst of a conversation on political matters Anna Pávlovna burst out:

"Oh, don't speak to me of Austria. Perhaps I don't understand things, but Austria never has wished, and does not wish, for war. She is betraying us! Russia alone must save Europe. Our gracious sovereign recognizes his high vocation and will be true to it. That is the one thing I have faith in! Our good and wonderful sovereign has to perform the noblest rôle on earth, and he is so virtuous and noble that God will not forsake him. He will fulfill his vocation and crush the hydra of revolution, which has become more terrible than ever in the person of this murderer and villain! We alone must avenge the blood of the just one. . . . Whom, I ask you, can we rely on? . . . England with her commercial spirit will not and cannot understand the Emperor Alexander's loftiness of soul. She has refused to evacuate Malta. She wanted to find, and still seeks, some secret motive in our actions. What answer did Novosíltsev get? None. The English have not understood and cannot understand the self-abnegation of our Emperor who wants nothing for himself, but only desires the good of mankind. And what have they promised? Nothing! And what little they have promised they will not perform! Prussia has always declared that Buonaparte is invincible, and that all Europe is powerless before him. . . . And I don't believe a word that Hardenburg says, or Haugwitz either. This famous Prussian neutrality is just a trap. I have faith only in God and the lofty destiny of our adored monarch. He will save Europe!"

She suddenly paused, smiling at her own impetuosity.

"I think," said the prince with a smile, "that if you had been sent instead of our dear Wintzingerode you would have captured the King of Prussia's consent by assault. You are so eloquent. Will you give me a cup of tea?"

"In a moment. *A propos,*" she added, becoming calm again, "I am expecting two very interesting men tonight, le Vicomte de Mortemart, who is connected with the Montmorencys through the Rohans, one of the best French families. He is one of the genuine *émigrés,* the good ones. And also the Abbé Morio. Do you know that profound thinker? He has been received by the Emperor. Had you heard?"

"I shall be delighted to meet them," said the prince. "But tell me," he added with studied carelessness as if it had only just occurred to him, though the question he was about to ask was the chief motive of his visit, "is it true that the Dowager Empress wants Baron Funke to be appointed first secretary at Vienna? The baron by all accounts is a poor creature."

Prince Vasíli wished to obtain this post for his son, but others were trying through the Dowager Empress Márya Fëdorovna to secure it for the baron.

Anna Pávlovna almost closed her eyes to indicate that neither she nor anyone else had a right to criticize what the Empress desired or was pleased with.

"Baron Funke has been recommended to the Dowager Empress by her sister," was all she said, in a dry and mournful tone.

As she named the Empress, Anna Pávlovna's face suddenly assumed an expression of profound and sincere devotion and respect mingled with sadness, and this occurred every time she mentioned her illustrious patroness. She added that her Majesty had deigned to show Baron Funke *beaucoup d'estime,* and again her face clouded over with sadness.

The prince was silent and looked indifferent. But, with the womanly and courtierlike quickness and tact habitual to her, Anna Pávlovna wished both to rebuke him (for daring to speak he had done of a man recommended to the Empress) and at the same time to console him, so she said—

"Now about your family. Do you know that since your daughter came out everyone has been enraptured by her? They say she is amazingly beautiful."

The prince bowed to signify his respect and gratitude.

"I often think," she continued after a short pause, drawing nearer to the prince and smiling amiably at him as if to show that political and social topics were ended and the time had come for intimate conversation—"I often think how unfairly sometimes the joys of life are distributed. Why has fate given you two such splendid children? I don't speak of Anatole, your youngest. I don't like him," she added in a tone admitting of no rejoinder and raising her eyebrows. "Two such charming children. And really you appreciate them less than anyone, and so you don't deserve to have them."

And she smiled her ecstatic smile.

"I can't help it," said the prince. "Lavater would have said I lack the bump of paternity."

"Don't joke; I mean to have a serious talk with you. Do you know I am dissatisfied with your younger son? Between ourselves," (and her face assumed its melancholy expression) "he was mentioned at her Majesty's and you were pitied. . . ."

The prince answered nothing, but she looked at him significantly, awaiting a reply. He frowned.

"What would you have me do?" he said at last. "You know I did all a father could for their education, and they have both turned out fools. Hippolyte is at least a quiet fool, but Anatole is an active one. That is the only difference between them." He said this smiling in a way more natural and animated than usual, so that the wrinkles round his mouth very clearly revealed something unexpectedly coarse and unpleasant.

"And why are children born to such men as you? If you were not a father there would be nothing I could reproach you with," said Anna Pávlovna, looking up pensively.

"I am your faithful slave and to you alone I can confess that my children are the bane of my life. It is the cross I have to bear. That is how I explain it to myself. It can't be helped!"

He said no more, but expressed his resignation to cruel fate by a gesture. Anna Pávlovna meditated.

"Have you never thought of marrying your prodigal son Anatole?" she asked. "They say old maids have a mania for match-making, and though I don't feel that weakness in myself as yet, I know a little person who is very unhappy with her father. She is a relation of yours, Princess Mary Bolkónskaya."

Prince Vasíli did not reply, though, with the quickness of memory and perception befitting a man of the world, he indicated by a movement of the head that he was considering this information.

"Do you know," he said at last, evidently unable to check the sad current of his thoughts, "that Anatole is costing me forty thousand rubles a year? And," he went on after a pause, "what will it be in five years, if he goes on like this?" Presently he added: "That's what we fathers have to put up with. . . . Is this princess of yours rich?"

"Her father is very rich and stingy. He lives in the country. He is the well-known Prince Bolkónski who had to retire from the army under the late Emperor, and was nicknamed 'the King of Prussia.' He is very clever but eccentric, and a bore. The poor girl is very unhappy. She has a brother; I think you know him, he married Lise Meinen lately. He is an aide-de-camp of Kutúzov's and will be here tonight."

"Listen, dear Annette," said the prince, suddenly taking Anna Pávlovna's hand and for some reason drawing it downward. "Arrange that affair for me and I shall always be your most devoted slave—*slafe* with an f, as a village elder of mine writes in his reports. She is rich and of good family and that's all I want."

And with the familiarity and easy grace peculiar to him, he raised the maid of honor's hand to his lips, kissed it, and swung it to and fro as he lay back in his arm-chair, looking in another direction.

"*Attendez*," said Anna Pávlovna, reflecting, "I'll speak to Lise, young Bolkónski's wife, this very evening, and perhaps the thing can be arranged. It shall be on your family's behalf that I'll start my apprenticeship as old maid."

Chapter II

ANNA PÁVLOVNA'S DRAWING ROOM WAS GRADUALLY FILLING. THE HIGHEST PETERSBURG SOCIety was assembled there: people differing widely in age and character but alike in the social circle to which they belonged. Prince Vasíli's daughter, the beautiful Hélène, came to take her father to the ambassador's entertainment; she wore a ball dress and her badge as maid of honor. The youthful little Princess Bolkónskaya, known as *la femme la plus séduisante de Pétersbourg,* was also there. She had been married during the previous winter, and being pregnant did not go to any large gatherings, but only to small receptions. Prince Vasíli's son, Hippolyte, had come with Mortemart, whom he introduced. The Abbé Morio and many others had also come.

To each new arrival Anna Pávlovna said, "You have not yet seen my aunt," or "You do not know my aunt?" and very gravely conducted him or her to a little old lady, wearing large bows of ribbon in her cap, who had come sailing in from another room as soon as the guests began to arrive; and slowly turning her eyes from the visitor to her aunt, Anna Pávlovna mentioned each one's name and then left them.

Each visitor performed the ceremony of greeting this old aunt whom not one of them knew, not one of them wanted to know, and not one of them cared about; Anna Pávlovna observed these greetings with mournful and solemn interest and silent approval. The aunt spoke to each of them in the same words, about their health and her own, and the health of her Majesty, "who, thank God, was better today." And each visitor, though politeness prevented his showing impatience, left the old woman with a sense of relief at having performed a vexatious duty and did not return to her the whole evening.

The young Princess Bolkónskaya had brought some work in a gold-embroidered velvet bag. Her pretty little upper lip, on which a delicate dark brown was just perceptible, was too short for her teeth, but it lifted all the more sweetly, and was especially charming when she occasionally drew it down to meet the lower lip. As is always the case with a thoroughly attractive woman, her defect—the shortness of her upper lip and her half-open mouth—seemed to be her own special and peculiar form of beauty. Everyone brightened at the sight of this pretty young woman, so soon to become a mother, so full of life and health, and carrying her burden so lightly. Old men and dull dispirited young ones who looked at her, after being in her company and talking to her a little while, felt as if they too were becoming, like her, full of life and health. All who talked to her, and at each word saw her bright smile and the constant gleam of her white teeth, thought that they were in a specially amiable mood that day.

The little princess went round the table with quick short swaying steps, her workbag on her arm, and gaily spreading out her dress sat down on a sofa near the silver samovar, as if all she was doing was a pleasure to herself and to all around her. "I have brought my work," said she in French, displaying her bag and addressing all present. "Mind, Annette, I hope you have not played a wicked trick on me," she added, turning to her hostess. "You wrote that it was to be quite a small reception, and just see how badly I am dressed." And she spread out her arms to show her short-waisted, lace-trimmed, dainty gray dress, girdled with a broad ribbon just below the breast.

"*Soyez tranquille, Lise,* you will always be prettier than anyone else," replied Anna Pávlovna.

"You know," said the princess in the same tone of voice and still in French, turning to a general, "my husband is deserting me? He is going to get himself killed. Tell me what this wretched war is for?" she added, addressing Prince Vasíli, and without waiting for an answer she turned to speak to his daughter, the beautiful Hélène.

"What a delightful woman this little princess is!" said Prince Vasíli to Anna Pávlovna.

One of the next arrivals was a stout, heavily built young man with close cropped hair, spectacles, the light-colored breeches fashionable at that time, a very high ruffle, and a brown dress-coat. This stout young man was an illegitimate son of Count Bezúkhov, a well-known grandee of Catherine's time who now lay dying in Moscow. The young man had not yet entered either the military or civil service, as he had only just returned from abroad where he had been educated, and this was his first appearance in society. Anna Pávlovna greeted him with the nod she accorded to the lowest hierarchy in her drawing room. But in spite of this lowest grade greeting, a look of anxiety and fear, as at the sight of something too large and unsuited to the place, came over her face when she saw Pierre enter. Though he was certainly rather bigger than the other men in the room, her anxiety could only have reference to the clever though shy, but observant and natural, expression which distinguished him from everyone else in that drawing room.

"It is very good of you, Monsieur Pierre, to come and visit a poor invalid," said Anna Pávlovna, exchanging an alarmed glance with her aunt as she conducted him to her.

Pierre murmured something unintelligible, and continued to look round as if in search of something. On his way to the aunt he bowed to the little princess with a pleased smile, as to an intimate acquaintance.

Anna Pávlovna's alarm was justified, for Pierre turned away from the aunt without waiting to hear her speech about her Majesty's health. Anna Pávlovna in dismay detained him with the words:

"Do you know the Abbé Morio? He is a most interesting man."

"Yes, I have heard of his scheme for perpetual peace, and it is very interesting but hardly feasible."

"You think so?" rejoined Anna Pávlovna in order to say something and get away to attend to her duties as hostess. But Pierre now committed a reverse act of impoliteness. First he had left a lady before she had finished speaking to him, and now he continued to speak to another who wished to get away. With his head bent, and his big feet spread apart, he began explaining his reasons for thinking the abbé's plan chimerical.

"We will talk of it later," said Anna Pávlovna with a smile.

And having got rid of this young man who did not know how to behave, she resumed her duties as hostess and continued to listen and watch, ready to help at any point where the conversation might happen to flag. As the foreman of a spinning mill when he has set the hands to work, goes round and notices here a spindle that has stopped or there one that creaks or makes more noise than it should, and hastens to check the machine or set it in proper motion, so Anna Pávlovna moved about her drawing room, approaching now a silent, now a too noisy group, and by a word or slight rearrangement kept the conversational machine in steady, proper, and regular motion. But amid these cares her anxiety about Pierre was evident. She kept an anxious watch on him when he approached the group round Mortemart to listen to what was being said there, and again when he passed to another group whose center was the abbé.

Pierre had been educated abroad, and this reception at Anna Pávlovna's was the first he had attended in Russia. He knew that all the intellectual lights of Petersburg were gathered there, and like a child in a toy shop, did not know which way to look, afraid of missing any clever conversation that was to be heard. Seeing the self-confident and refined expression on the faces of those present he was always expecting to hear something very profound. At last he came up to Morio. Here the conversation seemed interesting and he stood waiting for an opportunity to express his own views, as young people are fond of doing.

Chapter III

ANNA PÁVLOVNA'S RECEPTION WAS IN FULL SWING. THE SPINDLES HUMMED STEADILY AND CEASElessly on all sides. With the exception of the aunt, beside whom sat only one elderly lady, who with her thin careworn face was rather out of place in this brilliant society, the whole company had settled into three groups. One, chiefly masculine, had formed round the abbé. Another, of young people, was grouped round the beautiful Princess Hélène, Prince Vasíli's daughter, and the little Princess Bolkónskaya, very pretty and rosy, though rather too plump for her age. The third group was gathered round Mortemart and Anna Pávlovna.

The vicomte was a nice-looking young man with soft features and polished manners, who evidently considered himself a celebrity but out of politeness modestly placed himself at the disposal of the circle in which he found himself. Anna Pávlovna was obviously serving him up as a treat to her guests. As a clever *maître d'hôtel* serves up as a specially choice delicacy a piece of meat that no one who had seen it in the kitchen would have cared to eat, so Anna Pávlovna served up to her guests, first the vicomte and then the abbé, as peculiarly choice morsels. The group about Mortemart immediately began discussing the murder of the Duc d'Enghien. The vicomte said that the Duc d'Enghien had perished by his own magnanimity, and that there were particular reasons for Buonaparte's hatred of him.

"Ah, yes! Do tell us all about it, vicomte," said Anna Pávlovna, with a pleasant feeling that there was something *à la Louis XV* in the sound of that sentence: *"Contez nous cela, vicomte."*

The vicomte bowed and smiled courteously in token of his willingness to comply. Anna Pávlovna arranged a group round him, inviting everyone to listen to his tale.

"The vicomte knew the duc personally," whispered Anna Pávlovna to of the guests. "The vicomte is a wonderful *raconteur,*" said she to another. "How evidently he belongs to the best society," said she to a third; and the vicomte was served up to the company in the choicest and most advantageous style, like a well-garnished joint of roast beef on a hot dish.

The vicomte wished to begin his story and gave a subtle smile.

"Come over here, Hélène, dear," said Anna Pávlovna to the beautiful young princess who was sitting some way off, the center of another group.

The princess smiled. She rose with the same unchanging smile with which she had first entered the room—the smile of a perfectly beautiful woman. With a slight rustle of her white dress trimmed with moss and ivy, with a gleam of white shoulders, glossy hair and sparkling diamonds, she passed between the men who made way for her, not looking at any of them but smiling on all, as if graciously allowing each the privilege of admiring her beautiful figure and shapely shoulders, back, and bosom—which in the fashion of those days were very much exposed—and she seemed to bring the glamour of a ballroom with her as she moved toward Anna Pávlovna. Hélène was so lovely that not only did she not show any trace of coquetry, but on the contrary she even appeared shy of her unquestionable and all too victorious beauty. She seemed to wish, but to be unable, to diminish its effect.

"How lovely!" said everyone who saw her; and the vicomte lifted his shoulders and dropped his eyes as if startled by something extraordinary when she took her seat opposite and beamed upon him also with her unchanging smile.

"Madame, I doubt my ability before such an audience," said he, smilingly inclining his head.

The princess rested her bare round arm on a little table and considered a reply unnecessary. She smilingly waited. All the time the story was being told she sat upright, glancing now at her beautiful round arm, altered in shape by its pressure on the table, now at her still more beautiful bosom, on which she readjusted a diamond necklace. From time to time she smoothed the folds of her dress, and whenever the story produced an effect she glanced at Anna Pávlovna, at once adopted just the expression she saw on the maid of honor's face, and again relapsed into her radiant smile.

The little princess had also left the tea-table and followed Hélène.

"Wait a moment, I'll get my work. . . . Now then, what are you thinking of?" she went on, turning to Prince Hippolyte. "Fetch me my workbag."

There was a general movement as the princess, smiling and talking merrily to everyone at once, sat down and gaily arranged herself in her seat.

"Now I am all right," she said, and asking the vicomte to begin, she took up her work.

Prince Hippolyte, having brought the workbag, joined the circle and moving a chair close to hers seated himself beside her.

Le charmant Hippolyte was surprising by his extraordinary resemblance to his beautiful sister, but yet more by the fact that in spite of this resemblance he was exceedingly ugly. His features were like his sister's, but while in her case everything was lit up by a joyous, self-satisfied, youthful, and constant smile of animation, and by the wonderful classic beauty of her figure, his face on the contrary was dulled by imbecility and a constant expression of sullen self-confidence, while his body was thin and weak. His eyes, nose, and mouth all seemed puckered into a vacant, wearied grimace, and his arms and legs always fell into unnatural positions.

"It's not going to be a ghost story?" said he, sitting down beside the princess and hastily adjusting his lorgnette, as if without this instrument he could not begin to speak.

"Why no, my dear fellow," said the astonished narrator, shrugging his shoulders.

"Because I hate ghost stories," said Prince Hippolyte in a tone which showed that he only understood the meaning of his words after he had uttered them.

He spoke with such self-confidence that his hearers could not be sure whether what he said was very witty or very stupid. He was dressed in a dark-green dress-coat, knee-breeches of the color of *cuisse de nymphe effrayée,* as he called it, shoes, and silk stockings.

The vicomte told his tale very neatly. It was an anecdote, then current, to the effect that the Duc d'Enghien had gone secretly to Paris to visit Mademoiselle George; that at her house he came upon Bonaparte, who also enjoyed the famous actress' favors, and that in his presence Napoleon happened to fall into one of the fainting fits to which he was subject, and was thus at the duc's mercy. The latter spared him, and this magnanimity Bonaparte subsequently repaid by death.

The story was very pretty and interesting, especially at the point where the rivals suddenly recognized one another; and the ladies looked agitated.

"Charming!" said Anna Pávlovna with an inquiring glance at the little princess.

"Charming!" whispered the little princess, sticking the needle into her work as if to testify that the interest and fascination of the story prevented her from going on with it.

The vicomte appreciated this silent praise and smiling gratefully prepared to continue, but just then Anna Pávlovna, who had kept a watchful eye on the young man who so alarmed her, noticed that he was talking too loudly and vehemently with the abbé, so she hurried to the rescue. Pierre had managed to start a conversation with the abbé about the balance of power, and the latter, evidently interested by the young man's simple-minded eagerness, was explaining his pet theory. Both were talking and listening too eagerly and too naturally, which was why Anna Pávlovna disapproved.

"The means are . . . the balance of power in Europe and the rights of the people," the abbé was saying. "It is only necessary for one powerful nation like Russia—barbaric as she is said to be—to place herself disinterestedly at the head of an alliance having for its object the maintenance of the balance of power of Europe, and it would save the world!"

"But how are you to get that balance?" Pierre was beginning.

At that moment Anna Pávlovna came up and, looking severely at Pierre, asked the Italian how he stood Russian climate. The Italian's face instantly changed and assumed an offensively affected, sugary expression, evidently habitual to him when conversing with women.

"I am so enchanted by the brilliancy of the wit and culture of the society, more especially of the feminine society, in which I have had the honor of being received, that I have not yet had time to think of the climate," said he.

Not letting the abbé and Pierre escape, Anna Pávlovna, the more conveniently to keep them under observation, brought them into the larger circle.

Chapter IV

JUST THEN ANOTHER VISITOR ENTERED THE DRAWING ROOM: PRINCE ANDREW BOLKÓNSKI, THE LITtle princess's husband. He was a very handsome young man, of medium height, with firm, clear-cut features. Everything about him, from his weary, bored expression to his quiet, measured step, offered a most striking contrast to his lively little wife. It was evident that he not only knew everyone in the drawing room, but had found them to be so tiresome that it wearied him to look at or listen to them. And among all these faces that he found so tedious, none seemed to bore him so much as that of his pretty wife. He turned away from her with a grimace that distorted his handsome face, kissed Anna Pávlovna's hand, and screwing up his eyes scanned the whole company.

"You are off to the war, prince?" said Anna Pávlovna.

"General Kutúzov," said Bolkónski, speaking French and stressing the last syllable of the general's name like a Frenchman, "has been pleased to take me as an aide-de-camp. . . ."

"And Lise, your wife?"

"She will go to the country."

"Are you not ashamed to deprive us of your charming wife?"

"André," said his wife, addressing her husband in the same coquettish manner in which she spoke to other men, "the vicomte has been telling us such a tale about Mademoiselle George and Buonaparte!"

Prince Andrew screwed up his eyes and turned away. Pierre, who from the moment Prince Andrew entered the room had watched him with glad, affectionate eyes, now came up and took his arm. Before he looked round Prince Andrew frowned again, expressing his annoyance with whoever was touching his arm, but when he saw Pierre's beaming face he gave him an unexpectedly kind and pleasant smile.

"There now! . . . So you, too, are in the great world?" said he to Pierre.

"I knew you would be here," replied Pierre. "I will come to supper with you. May I?" he added in a low voice so as not to disturb the vicomte who was continuing his story.

"No, impossible!" said Prince Andrew, laughing and pressing Pierre's hand to show that there was no need to ask the question. He wished to say something more, but at that moment Prince Vasíli and his daughter got up to go and the two young men rose to let them pass.

"You must excuse me, dear Vicomte," said Prince Vasíli to the Frenchman, holding him down by the sleeve in a friendly way to prevent his rising. "This unfortunate fête at the ambassador's deprives me of a pleasure, and obliges me to interrupt you. I am very sorry to leave your enchanting party," said he, turning to Anna Pávlovna.

His daughter, Princess Hélène, passed between the chairs, lightly holding up the folds of her dress, and the smile shone still more radiantly on her beautiful face. Pierre gazed at her with rapturous, almost frightened, eyes as she passed him.

"Very lovely," said Prince Andrew.

"Very," said Pierre.

In passing, Prince Vasíli seized Pierre's hand and said to Anna Pávlovna:

"Educate this bear for me! He has been staying with me a whole month and this is the first time I have seen him in society. Nothing is so necessary for a young man as the society of clever women."

Chapter V

Anna Pávlovna smiled and promised to take Pierre in hand. She knew his father to be a connection of Prince Vasíli's. The elderly lady who had been sitting with the old aunt rose hurriedly and overtook Prince Vasíli in the anteroom. All the affectation of interest she had assumed had left her kindly and tear-worn face and it now expressed only anxiety and fear.

"How about my son Borís, prince?" said she, hurrying after him into the anteroom. "I can't remain any longer in Petersburg. Tell me what news I may take back to my poor boy."

Although Prince Vasíli listened reluctantly and not very politely to the elderly lady, even betraying some impatience, she gave him an ingratiating and appealing smile, and took his hand that he might not go away.

"What would it cost you to say a word to the Emperor, and then he would be transferred to the Guards at once?" said she.

"Believe me, princess I am ready to do all I can," answered Prince Vasíli, "but it is difficult for me to ask the Emperor. I should advise you to appeal to Rumyántsev through Prince Golítsyn. That would be the best way."

The elderly lady was a Princess Drubetskáya, belonging to one of the best families in Russia, but she was poor, and having long been out of society had lost her former influential connections. She had now come to Petersburg to procure an appointment in the Guards for her only son. It was, in fact, solely to meet Prince Vasíli that she had obtained an invitation to Anna Pávlovna's reception, and had sat listening to the vicomte's story. Prince Vasíli's words frightened her, an embittered look clouded her once handsome face, but only for a moment; then she smiled again and clutched Prince Vasíli's arm more tightly.

"Listen to me, prince," said she. "I have never yet asked you for anything and I never will again, nor have I ever reminded you of my father's friendship for you; but now I entreat you for God's sake to do this for my son—and I shall always regard you as a benefactor," she added hurriedly. "No, don't be angry, but promise! I have asked Golítsyn and he has refused. Be the kind-hearted man you always were," she said, trying to smile though tears were in her eyes.

"Papa, we shall be late," said Princess Hélène, turning her beautiful head and looking over her classically molded shoulder as she stood waiting by the door.

Influence in society, however, is capital which has to be economized if it is to last. Prince Vasíli knew this, and having once realized that if he asked on behalf of all who begged of him, he would soon be unable to ask for himself, he became chary of using his influence. But in Princess Drubetskáya's case he felt, after her second appeal, something like qualms of conscience. She had reminded him of what was quite true; he had been indebted to her father for the first steps in his career. Moreover, he could see by her manners that she was one of those women—mostly mothers—who, having once made up their minds, will not rest until they have gained their end, and are prepared if necessary to go on insisting day after day and hour after hour, and even to make scenes. This last consideration moved him.

"My dear Anna Mikháylovna," said he with his usual familiarity and weariness of tone, "it is almost impossible for me to do what you ask; but to prove my devotion to you and how I respect your father's memory, I will do the impossible—your son shall be transferred to the Guards. Here is my hand on it. Are you satisfied?"

"My dear benefactor! This is what I expected from you—I knew your kindness!" He turned to go.

"Wait—just a word! When he has been transferred to the Guards . . ." she faltered. "You are on good terms with Michael Ilariónovich Kutúzov . . . recommend Borís to him as adjutant! Then I shall be at rest, and then . . ."

Prince Vasíli smiled.

"No, I won't promise that. You don't know how Kutúzov is pestered since his appointment as Commander-in-Chief. He told me himself that all the Moscow ladies have conspired to give him all their sons as adjutants."

"No, but do promise! I won't let you go! My dear benefactor . . ."

"Papa," said his beautiful daughter in the same tone as before, "we shall be late."

"Well, *au revoir!* Good-bye! You hear her?"

"Then tomorrow you will speak to the Emperor?"

"Certainly; but about Kutúzov, I don't promise."

"Do promise, do promise, Vasíli!" cried Anna Mikháylovna as he went, with the smile of a coquettish girl, which at one time probably came naturally to her, but was now very ill-suited to her care-worn face.

Apparently she had forgotten her age and by force of habit employed all the old feminine arts. But as soon as the prince had gone her face resumed its former cold, artificial expression. She returned to the group where the vicomte was still talking, and again pretended to listen, while waiting till it would be time to leave. Her task was accomplished.

"And what do you think of this latest comedy, the coronation at Milan?" asked Anna Pávlovna, "and of the comedy of the people of Genoa and Lucca laying their petitions before Monsieur Buonaparte, and Monsieur Buonaparte sitting on a throne and granting the petitions of the nations? Adorable! It is enough to make one's head whirl! It is as if the whole world had gone crazy."

Prince Andrew looked Anna Pávlovna straight in the face with a sarcastic smile.

"*'Dieu me la donne, gare à qui la touche!'* (Bonaparte's words at his coronation). They say he was very fine when he said that," he remarked, repeating the words in Italian: "*'Dio mi l'ha dato. Guai a chi la tocchi!'*"

"I hope this will prove the last drop that will make the glass run over," Anna Pávlovna continued. "The sovereigns will not be able to endure this man who is a menace to everything."

"The sovereigns? I do not speak of Russia," said the vicomte, polite but hopeless: "The sovereigns, madame . . . What have they done for Louis XVII, for the Queen, or for Madame Elizabeth? Nothing!" and he became more animated. "And believe me, they are reaping the reward of their betrayal of the Bourbon cause. The sovereigns! Why, they are sending ambassadors to compliment the usurper."

And sighing disdainfully, he again changed his position.

Prince Hippolyte, who had been gazing at the vicomte for some time through his lorgnette, suddenly turned completely round toward the little princess, and having asked for a needle began tracing the Condé coat-of-arms on the table. He explained this to her with as much gravity as if she had asked him to do it.

"*Bâton de gueules, engrêlé de gueules d'azur—maison Condé,*" said he.

The princess listened, smiling.

"If Buonaparte remains on the throne of France a year longer," the vicomte continued, with the air of a man who, in a matter with which he is better acquainted than anyone else, does not listen to others but follows the current of his own thoughts, "things will have gone too far. By intrigues, violence, exile, and executions, French society—I mean good French society—will have been forever destroyed, and then . . ."

He shrugged his shoulders and spread out his hands. Pierre wished to make a remark for the conversation interested him, but Anna Pávlovna, who had him under observation, interrupted:

"The Emperor Alexander," said she, with the melancholy which always accompanied any reference of hers to the Imperial family, "has declared that he will leave it to the French people themselves to choose their own form of government; and I believe that once free from the usurper, the whole nation will certainly throw itself into the arms of its rightful king," she concluded, trying to be amiable to the royalist emigrant.

"That is doubtful," said Prince Andrew. "Monsieur le Vicomte quite rightly supposes that matters have already gone too far. I think it will be difficult to return to the old regime."

"From what I have heard," said Pierre, blushing and breaking into the conversation, "almost all the aristocracy has already gone over to Bonaparte's side."

"It is the Buonapartists who say that," replied the vicomte without looking at Pierre. "At the present time it is difficult to know the real state of French public opinion."

"Bonaparte has said so," remarked Prince Andrew with a sarcastic smile.

It was evident that he did not like the vicomte and was aiming his remarks at him, though without looking at him.

" 'I showed them the path to glory, but they did not follow it,' " Prince Andrew continued after a short silence, again quoting Napoleon's words. " 'I opened my antechambers and they crowded in.' I do not know how far he was justified in saying so."

"Not in the least," replied the vicomte. "After the murder of the duc even the most partial ceased to regard him as a hero. If to some people," he went on, turning to Anna Pávlovna, "he ever was a hero, after the murder of the duc there was one martyr more in heaven and one hero less on earth."

Before Anna Pávlovna and the others had time to smile their appreciation of the vicomte's epigram, Pierre again broke into the conversation, and though Anna Pávlovna felt sure he would say something inappropriate, she was unable to stop him.

"The execution of the Duc d'Enghien," declared Monsieur Pierre, "was a political necessity, and it seems to me that Napoleon showed greatness of soul by not fearing to take on himself the whole responsibility of that deed."

"Dieu! Mon Dieu!" muttered Anna Pávlovna in a terrified whisper.

"What, Monsieur Pierre . . . Do you consider that assassination shows greatness of soul?" said the little princess, smiling and drawing her work nearer to her.

"Oh! Oh!" exclaimed several voices.

"Capital!" said Prince Hippolyte in English, and began slapping his knee with the palm of his hand.

The vicomte merely shrugged his shoulders. Pierre looked solemnly at his audience over his spectacles and continued.

"I say so," he continued desperately, "because the Bourbons fled from the Revolution leaving the people to anarchy, and Napoleon alone understood the Revolution and quelled it, and so for the general good, he could not stop short for the sake of one man's life."

"Won't you come over to the other table?" suggested Anna Pávlovna.

But Pierre continued his speech without heeding her.

"No," cried he, becoming more and more eager, "Napoleon is great because he rose superior to the Revolution, suppressed its abuses, preserved all that was good in it—equality of citizenship and freedom of speech and of the press—and only for that reason did he obtain power."

"Yes, if having obtained power, without availing himself of it to commit murder he had restored it to the rightful king, I should have called him a great man," remarked the vicomte.

"He could not do that. The people only gave him power that he might rid them of the Bourbons and because they saw that he was a great man. The Revolution was a grand thing!" continued Monsieur Pierre, betraying by this desperate and provocative proposition his extreme youth and his wish to express all that was in his mind.

"What? Revolution and regicide a grand thing? . . . Well, after that . . . But won't you come to this other table?" repeated Anna Pávlovna.

"Rousseau's *Contrat Social*," said the vicomte with a tolerant smile.

"I am not speaking of regicide, I am speaking about ideas."

"Yes: ideas of robbery, murder, and regicide," again interjected an ironical voice.

"Those were extremes, no doubt, but they are not what is most important. What is important are the rights of man, emancipation from prejudices, and equality of citizenship, and all these ideas Napoleon has retained in full force."

"Liberty and equality," said the vicomte contemptuously, as if at last deciding seriously to prove to this youth how foolish his words were, "high-sounding words which have long been discredited. Who does not love Liberty and Equality? Even our Saviour preached liberty and equality. Have people since the Revolution become happier? On the contrary. We wanted liberty, but Buonaparte has destroyed it."

Prince Andrew kept looking with an amused smile from Pierre to the vicomte and from the vicomte to their hostess. In the first moment of Pierre's outburst Anna Pávlovna, despite her social experience, was horror-struck. But when she saw that Pierre's sacrilegious words had not exasperated the vicomte, and had convinced herself that it was impossible to stop him, she rallied her forces and joined the vicomte in a vigorous attack on the orator.

"But, my dear Monsieur Pierre," said she, "how do you explain the fact of a great man executing a duc—or even an ordinary man who—is innocent and untried?"

"I should like," said the vicomte, "to ask how monsieur explains the 18th Brumaire; was not that an imposture? It was a swindle, and not at all like the conduct of a great man!"

"And the prisoners he killed in Africa? That was horrible!" said the little princess, shrugging her shoulders.

"He's a low fellow, say what you will," remarked Prince Hippolyte.

Pierre, not knowing whom to answer, looked at them all and smiled. His smile was unlike the half-smile of other people. When he smiled his grave, even rather gloomy, look was instantaneously replaced by another—a childlike, kindly, even rather silly look, which seemed to ask forgiveness.

The vicomte who was meeting him for the first time saw clearly that this young Jacobin was not so terrible as his words suggested. All were silent.

"How do you expect him to answer you all at once?" said Prince Andrew. "Besides, in the actions of a statesman one has to distinguish between his acts as a private person, as a general, and as an emperor. So it seems to me."

"Yes, yes, of course!" Pierre chimed in, pleased at the arrival of this reinforcement.

"One must admit," continued Prince Andrew, "that Napoleon as a man was great on the bridge of Arcola, and in the hospital at Jaffa where he gave his hand to the plague-stricken; but . . . but there are other acts which it is difficult to justify."

Prince Andrew, who had evidently wished to tone down the awkwardness of Pierre's remarks, rose and made a sign to his wife that it was time to go.

Suddenly Prince Hippolyte started up making signs to everyone to attend, and asking them all to be seated began:

"I was told a charming Moscow story today and must treat you to it. Excuse me, vicomte—I must tell it in Russian or the point will be lost. . . ." And Prince Hippolyte began to tell his story in such Russian as a Frenchman would speak after spending about a year in Russia. Everyone waited, so emphatically and eagerly did he demand their attention to his story.

"There is in Moscow a lady, *une dame,* and she is very stingy. She must have two footmen behind her carriage, and very big ones. That was her taste. And she had a lady's maid, also big. She said . . ."

Here Prince Hippolyte paused, evidently collecting his ideas with difficulty.

"She said . . . Oh yes! She said, 'Girl,' to the maid, 'put on a livery, get up behind the carriage, and come with me while I make some calls.' "

Here Prince Hippolyte spluttered and burst out laughing long before his audience, which produced an effect unfavorable to the narrator. Several persons, among them the elderly lady and Anna Pávlovna, did however smile.

"She went. Suddenly there was a great wind. The girl lost her hat and her long hair came down. . . ." Here he could contain himself no longer and went on, between gasps of laughter: "And the whole world knew. . . ."

And so the anecdote ended. Though it was unintelligible why he had told it, or why it had to be told in Russian, still Anna Pávlovna and the others appreciated Prince Hippolyte's social tact in so agreeably ending Pierre's unpleasant and unamiable outburst. After the anecdote the conversation broke up into insignificant small talk about the last and next balls, about theatricals, and who would meet whom, and when and where.

Chapter VI

HAVING THANKED ANNA PÁVLOVNA FOR HER CHARMING SOIREÉ, THE GUESTS BEGAN TO TAKE their leave.

Pierre was ungainly. Stout, about the average height, broad, with huge red hands; he did not know, as the saying is, how to enter a drawing room and still less how to leave one; that is, how to say something particularly agreeable before going away. Besides this he was absent-minded. When he rose to go, he took up instead of his own, the general's three-cornered hat, and held it, pulling at the plume, till the general asked him to restore it. All his absent-mindedness and inability to enter a room and converse in it was however redeemed by his kindly, simple, and modest expression. Anna Pávlovna turned toward him and, with a Christian mildness that expressed forgiveness of his indiscretion, nodded and said: "I hope to see you again, but I also hope you will change your opinions, my dear Monsieur Pierre."

When she said this, he did not reply and only bowed, but again everybody saw his smile, which said nothing, unless perhaps, "Opinions are opinions, but you see what a capital, good-natured fellow I am." And everyone, including Anna Pávlovna, felt this.

Prince Andrew had gone out into the hall, and, turning his shoulders to the footman who was helping him on with his cloak, listened indifferently to his wife's chatter with Prince Hippolyte who had also come into the hall. Prince Hippolyte stood close to the pretty, pregnant princess, and stared fixedly at her through his eyeglass.

"Go in, Annette, or you will catch cold," said the little princess, taking leave of Anna Pávlovna. "It is settled," she added in a low voice.

Anna Pávlovna had already managed to speak to Lise about the match she contemplated between Anatole and the little princess's sister-in-law.

"I rely on you, my dear," said Anna Pávlovna, also in a low tone. "Write to her and let me know how her father looks at the matter. *Au revoir!*"—and she left the hall.

Prince Hippolyte approached the little princess and, bending his face close to her, began to whisper something.

Two footmen, the princess's and his own, stood holding a shawl and a cloak, waiting for the conversation to finish. They listened to the French sentences which to them were meaningless, with an air of understanding but not wishing to appear to do so. The princess as usual spoke smilingly and listened with a laugh.

"I am very glad I did not go to the ambassador's," said Prince Hippolyte—"so dull—. It has been a delightful evening, has it not? Delightful!"

"They say the ball will be very good," replied the princess, drawing up her downy little lip. "All the pretty women in society will be there."

"Not all, for you will not be there; not all," said Prince Hippolyte smiling joyfully; and snatching the shawl from the footman, whom he even pushed aside, he began wrapping it round the princess. Either from awkwardness or intentionally (no one could have said which) after the shawl had been adjusted he kept his arm around her for a long time, as though embracing her.

Still smiling, she gracefully moved away, turning and glancing at her husband. Prince Andrew's eyes were closed, so weary and sleepy did he seem.

"Are you ready?" he asked his wife, looking past her.

Prince Hippolyte hurriedly put on his cloak, which in the latest fashion reached to his very heels, and stumbling in it, ran out into the porch following the princess, whom a footman was helping into the carriage.

"Princesse, au revoir," cried he, stumbling with his tongue as well as with his feet.

The princess, picking up her dress was taking her seat in the dark carriage, her husband was adjusting his saber; Prince Hippolyte, under pretense of helping, was in everyone's way.

"Allow me, sir," said Prince Andrew in Russian in a cold, disagreeable tone to Prince Hippolyte who was blocking his path.

"I am expecting you, Pierre," said the same voice, but gently and affectionately.

The postilion started, the carriage wheels rattled. Prince Hippolyte laughed spasmodically as he stood in the porch waiting for the vicomte whom he had promised to take home.

"Well, *mon cher,*" said the vicomte, having seated himself beside Hippolyte in the carriage, "your little princess is very nice, very nice indeed, quite French," and he kissed the tips of his fingers. Hippolyte burst out laughing.

"Do you know, you are a terrible chap for all your innocent airs," continued the vicomte. "I pity the poor husband, that little officer who gives himself the airs of a monarch."

Hippolyte spluttered again, and amid his laughter said, "And you were saying that the Russian ladies are not equal to the French? One has to know how to deal with them."

Pierre reaching the house first went into Prince Andrew's study like one quite at home, and from habit immediately lay down on the sofa, took from the shelf the first book that came to his hands (it was Caesar's *Commentaries*) and resting on his elbow, began reading it in the middle.

"What have you done to Mlle. Scherer? She will be quite ill now," said Prince Andrew, as he entered the study, rubbing his small white hands.

Pierre turned his whole body, making the sofa creak. He lifted his eager face to Prince Andrew, smiled, and waved his hand.

"That abbé is very interesting but he does not see the thing in the right light. . . . In my opinion perpetual peace is possible but—I do not know how to express it . . . not by a balance of political power. . . ."

It was evident that Prince Andrew was not interested in such abstract conversation.

"One can't everywhere say all one thinks, *mon cher.* Well, have you at last decided on anything? Are you going to be a guardsman or a diplomatist?" asked Prince Andrew after a momentary silence.

Pierre sat up on the sofa, with his legs tucked under him.

"Really, I don't yet know. I don't like either the one or the other."

"But you must decide on something! Your father expects it."

Pierre at the age of ten had been sent abroad with an abbé as tutor, and had remained away till he was twenty. When he returned to Moscow his father dismissed the abbé and said to the young man, "Now go to Petersburg, look round, and choose your profession. I will agree to anything. Here is a letter to Prince Vasíli, and here is money. Write to me all about it, and I will help you in everything." Pierre had already been choosing a career for three months, and had not decided on anything. It was about this choice that Prince Andrew was speaking. Pierre rubbed his forehead.

"But he must be a freemason," said he, referring to the abbé whom he had met that evening.

"That is all nonsense." Prince Andrew again interrupted him, "let us talk business. Have you been to the Horse-Guards?"

"No, I have not; but this is what I have been thinking and wanted to tell you. There is a war now against Napoleon. If it were a war for freedom I could understand it and should be the first to enter the army; but to help England and Austria against the greatest man in the world is not right."

Prince Andrew only shrugged his shoulders at Pierre's childish words. He put on the air of one who finds it impossible to reply to such nonsense, but it would in fact have been difficult to give any other answer than the one Prince Andrew gave to this naïve question.

"If no one fought except on his own conviction, there would be no wars," he said.

"And that would be splendid," said Pierre.

Prince Andrew smiled ironically.

"Very likely it would be splendid, but it will never come about. . . ."

"Well, why are *you* going to the war?" asked Pierre.

"What for? I don't know. I must. Besides that I am going . . ." He paused. "I am going because the life I am leading here does not suit me!"

Chapter VII

THE RUSTLE OF A WOMAN'S DRESS WAS HEARD IN THE NEXT ROOM. PRINCE ANDREW SHOOK HIMself as if waking up, and his face assumed the look it had had in Anna Pávlovna's drawing room. Pierre removed his feet from the sofa. The princess came in. She had changed her gown for a house dress as fresh and elegant as the other. Prince Andrew rose and politely placed a chair for her.

"How is it," she began, as usual in French, settling down briskly and fussily in the easy chair, "how is it Annette never got married? How stupid you men all are not to have married her! Excuse me for saying so, but you have no sense about women. What an argumentative fellow you are, Monsieur Pierre!"

"And I am still arguing with your husband. I can't understand why he wants to go to the war," replied Pierre, addressing the princess with none of the embarrassment so commonly shown by young men in their intercourse with young women.

The princess started. Evidently Pierre's words touched her to the quick.

"Ah, that is just what I tell him!" said she. "I don't understand it; I don't in the least understand why men can't live without wars. How is it that we women don't want anything of the kind, don't need it? Now you shall judge between us. I always tell him: here he is uncle's aide-de-camp, a most brilliant position. He is so well known, so much appreciated by everyone. The other day at the Apráksins' I heard a lady asking, 'Is that the famous Prince Andrew?' I did indeed." She laughed. "He is so well received everywhere. He might easily become aide-de-camp to the Emperor. You know the Emperor spoke to him most graciously. Annette and I were speaking of how to arrange it. What do you think?"

Pierre looked at his friend, and noticing that he did not like the conversation, gave no reply.

"When are you starting?" he asked.

"Oh, don't speak of his going, don't! I won't hear it spoken of," said the princess in the same petulantly playful tone in which she had spoken to Hippolyte in the drawing room and which was so plainly ill-suited to the family circle of which Pierre was almost a member. "Today when I remembered that all these delightful associations must be broken off . . . and then you know, André . . . (she looked significantly at her husband) I'm afraid, I'm afraid!" she whispered, and a shudder ran down her back.

Her husband looked at her as if surprised to notice that someone besides Pierre and himself was in the room, and addressed her in a tone of frigid politeness.

"What is it you are afraid of, Lise? I don't understand," said he.

"There, what egotists men all are: all, all egotists! Just for a whim of his own, goodness only knows why, he leaves me and locks me up alone in the country."

"With my father and sister, remember," said Prince Andrew gently.

"Alone all the same, without *my* friends. . . . And he expects me not to be afraid."

Her tone was now querulous and her lip drawn up, giving her not a joyful, but an animal, squirrel-like expression. She paused as if she felt it indecorous to speak of her pregnancy before Pierre, though the gist of the matter lay in that.

"I still can't understand what you are afraid of," said Prince Andrew slowly, not taking his eyes off his wife.

The princess blushed, and raised her arms with a gesture of despair.

"No, Andrew, I must say you have changed. Oh, how you have . . ."

"Your doctor tells you to go to bed earlier," said Prince Andrew. "You had better go."

The princess said nothing, but suddenly her short downy lip quivered. Prince Andrew rose, shrugged his shoulders, and walked about the room.

Pierre looked over his spectacles with naïve surprise, now at him and now at her, moved as if about to rise too, but changed his mind.

"Why should I mind Monsieur Pierre being here?" exclaimed the little princess suddenly, her pretty face all at once distorted by a tearful grimace. "I have long wanted to ask you, Andrew, why you have changed so to me? What have I done to you? You are going to the war and have no pity for me. Why is it?"

"Lise!" was all Prince Andrew said. But that one word expressed an entreaty, a threat, and above all conviction that she would herself regret her words. But she went on hurriedly:

"You treat me like an invalid or a child. I see it all! Did you behave like that six months ago?"

"Lise, I beg you to desist," said Prince Andrew still more emphatically.

Pierre, who had been growing more and more agitated as he listened to all this, rose and approached the princess. He seemed unable to bear the sight of tears, and was ready to cry himself.

"Calm yourself, princess! It seems so to you because . . . I assure you I myself have experienced . . . and so . . . because . . . No, excuse me! An outsider is out of place here . . . No, don't distress yourself . . . Good-bye!"

Prince Andrew caught him by the hand.

"No, wait, Pierre! The Princess is too kind to wish to deprive me of the pleasure of spending the evening with you."

"No, he thinks only of himself," muttered the princess without restraining her angry tears.

"Lise!" said Prince Andrew dryly, raising his voice to the pitch which indicates that patience is exhausted.

Suddenly the angry, squirrel-like expression of the princess's pretty face changed into a winning and piteous look of fear. Her beautiful eyes glanced askance at her husband's face, and her own assumed the timid, deprecating expression of a dog when it rapidly but feebly wags its drooping tail.

"Mon Dieu, mon Dieu!" she muttered, and lifting her dress with one hand she went up to her husband and kissed him on the forehead.

"Good night, Lise," said he, rising and courteously kissing her hand as he would have done to a stranger.

Chapter VIII

THE FRIENDS WERE SILENT. NEITHER CARED TO BEGIN TALKING. PIERRE CONTINUALLY GLANCED at Prince Andrew; Prince Andrew rubbed his forehead with his small hand.

"Let us go and have supper," he said with a sigh, going to the door.

They entered the elegant, newly decorated, and luxurious dining room. Everything from the table napkins to the silver, china, and glass, bore that imprint of newness found in the households of the newly married. Halfway through supper Prince Andrew leaned his elbows on the table, and with a look of nervous agitation such as Pierre had never before seen on his face, began to talk—as one who has long had something on his mind and suddenly determines to speak out.

"Never, never marry, my dear fellow! That's my advice: never marry till you can say to yourself that you have done all you are capable of, and until you have ceased to love the woman of your choice and have seen her plainly as she is, or else you will make a cruel and irrevocable mistake. Marry when you are old and good for nothing—or all that is good and noble in you will be lost. It will all be wasted on trifles. Yes! Yes! Yes! Don't look at me with such surprise. If you marry expecting anything from yourself in the future you will feel at every step that for you all is ended, all is closed except the drawing room, where you will be ranged side by side with a court lackey and an idiot! . . . But what's the good? . . ." and he waved his arm.

Pierre took off his spectacles, which made his face seem different and the good-natured expression still more apparent, and gazed at his friend in amazement.

"My wife," continued Prince Andrew, "is an excellent woman, one of those rare women with whom a man's honor is safe; but O God, what would I not give now to be unmarried! You are the first and only one to whom I mention this, because I like you."

As he said this Prince Andrew was less than ever like that Bolkónski who had lolled in Anna Pávlovna's easy chairs and with half-closed eyes had uttered French phrases between his teeth. Every muscle of his thin face was now quivering with nervous excitement; his eyes, in which the fire of life had seemed extinguished, now flashed with brilliant light. It was evident that the more lifeless he seemed at ordinary times, the more impassioned he became in these moments of almost morbid irritation.

"You don't understand why I say this," he continued, "but it is the whole story of life. You talk of Bonaparte and his career," said he (though Pierre had not mentioned Bonaparte), "but Bonaparte when he worked went step by step toward his goal. He was free, he had nothing but his aim to consider, and he reached it. But tie yourself up with a woman, and like a chained convict you lose all freedom! And all you have of hope and strength merely weighs you down and torments you with regret. Drawing rooms, gossip, balls, vanity, and triviality—these are the enchanted circle I cannot escape from. I am now going to the war, the greatest war there ever was, and I know nothing and am fit for nothing. I am very amiable and have a caustic wit," continued Prince Andrew, "and at Anna Pávlovna's they listen to me. And that stupid set without whom my wife cannot exist, and those women . . . If you only knew what those society women are, and women in general! My father is right. Selfish, vain, stupid, trivial in everything—that's what women are when you see them in their true colors! When you meet them in society it seems as if there were something in them, but there's nothing, nothing, nothing! No, don't marry, my dear fellow; don't marry!" concluded Prince Andrew.

"It seems funny to me," said Pierre, "that *you, you* should consider yourself incapable and your life a spoiled life. You have everything before you, everything. And you . . ."

He did not finish his sentence, but his tone showed how highly he thought of his friend and how much he expected of him in the future.

"How can he talk like that?" thought Pierre. He considered his friend a model of perfection because Prince Andrew possessed in the highest degree just the very qualities Pierre lacked, and which might be best described as strength of will. Pierre was always astonished at Prince Andrew's calm manner of treating everybody, his extraordinary memory, his extensive reading (he had read everything, knew everything, and had an opinion about everything), but above all at his capacity for work and study. And if Pierre was often struck by Andrew's lack of capacity for philosophical meditation (to which he himself was particularly addicted), he regarded even this not as a defect but as a sign of strength.

Even in the best, most friendly and simplest relations of life, praise and commendation are essential, just as grease is necessary to wheels that they may run smoothly.

"My part is played out," said Prince Andrew. "What's the use of talking about me? Let us talk about you," he added after a silence, smiling at his reassuring thoughts.

That smile was immediately reflected on Pierre's face.

"But what is there to say about me?" said Pierre, his face relaxing into a careless, merry smile. "What am I? An illegitimate son!" He suddenly blushed crimson, and it was plain that he had made a great effort to say this. "Without a name and without means . . . And it really . . ." But he did not say what "it really" was. "For the present I am free and am all right. Only I haven't the least idea what I am to do; I wanted to consult you seriously."

Prince Andrew looked kindly at him, yet his glance—friendly and affectionate as it was—expressed a sense of his own superiority.

"I am fond of you, especially as you are the one live man among our whole set. Yes, you're all right! Choose what you will; it's all the same. You'll be all right anywhere. But look here: give up visiting those Kurágins and leading that sort of life. It suits you so badly—all this debauchery, dissipation, and the rest of it!"

"What would you have, my dear fellow?" answered Pierre, shrugging his shoulders. "Women, my dear fellow; women!"

"I don't understand it," replied Prince Andrew. "Women who are *comme il faut,* that's a different matter; but the Kurágins' set of women, 'women and wine,' I don't understand!"

Pierre was staying at Prince Vasíli Kurágin's and sharing the dissipated life of his son Anatole, the son whom they were planning to reform by marrying him to Prince Andrew's sister.

"Do you know?" said Pierre, as if suddenly struck by a happy thought, "seriously, I have long been thinking of it. . . . Leading such a life I can't decide or think properly about anything. One's head aches, and one spends all one's money. He asked me for tonight, but I won't go."

"You give me your word of honor not to go?"

"On my honor!"

Chapter IX

It was past one o'clock when Pierre left his friend. It was a cloudless, northern, summer night. Pierre took an open cab intending to drive straight home. But the nearer he drew to the house the more he felt the impossibility of going to sleep on such a night. It was light enough to see a long way in the deserted street and it seemed more like morning or evening than night. On the way Pierre remembered that Anatole Kurágin was expecting the usual set for cards that evening, after which there was generally a drinking bout, finishing with visits of a kind Pierre was very fond of.

"I should like to go to Kurágin's," thought he.

But he immediately recalled his promise to Prince Andrew not to go there. Then, as happens to people of weak character, he desired so passionately once more to enjoy that dissipation he was so accustomed to, that he decided to go. The thought immediately occurred to him that his promise to Prince Andrew was of no account, because before he gave it he had already promised Prince Anatole to come to his gathering; "besides," thought he, "all such 'words of honor' are conventional things with no definite meaning, especially if one considers that by tomorrow one may be dead, or something so extraordinary may happen to one that honor and dishonor will be all the same!" Pierre often indulged in reflections of this sort, nullifying all his decisions and intentions. He went to Kurágin's.

Reaching the large house near the Horse-Guards' barracks, in which Anatole lived, Pierre entered the lit porch, ascended the stairs, and went in at the open door. There was no one in the anteroom; empty bottles, cloaks, and overshoes were lying about; there was a smell of alcohol, and sounds of voices and shouting in the distance.

Cards and supper were over, but the visitors had not yet dispersed. Pierre threw off his cloak and entered the first room, in which were the remains of supper. A footman, thinking no one saw him, was drinking on the sly what was left in the glasses. From the third room came sounds of laughter, the shouting of familiar voices, the growling of a bear, and general commotion. Some eight or nine young men were crowding anxiously round an open window. Three others were romping with a young bear, one pulling him by the chain and trying to set him at the others.

"I bet a hundred on Stevens!" shouted one.

"Mind, no holding on!" cried another.

"I bet on Dólokhov!" cried a third. "Kurágin, you part our hands."

"There, leave Bruin alone; here's a bet on."

"At one draught, or he loses!" shouted a fourth.

"Jacob, bring a bottle!" shouted the host, a tall, handsome fellow who stood in the midst of the group, without a coat, and with his fine linen shirt unfastened in front. "Wait a bit, you fellows. . . . Here is Pétya! Good man!" cried he, addressing Pierre.

Another voice, from a man of medium height with clear blue eyes, particularly striking among all these drunken voices by its sober ring, cried from the window: "Come here; part the bets!" This was Dólokhov, an officer of the Semënov regiment, a notorious gambler and duelist, who was living with Anatole. Pierre smiled, looking about him merrily.

"I don't understand. What's it all about?"

"Wait a bit, he is not drunk yet! A bottle here," said Anatole, taking a glass from the table he went up to Pierre.

"First of all you must drink!"

Pierre drank one glass after another, looking from under his brows at the tipsy guests who were again crowding round the window, and listening to their chatter. Anatole kept on refilling

Pierre's glass while explaining that Dólokhov was betting with Stevens, an English naval officer, that he would drink a bottle of rum sitting on the outer ledge of the third-floor window with his legs hanging out.

"Go on, you must drink it all," said Anatole, giving Pierre the last glass, "or I won't let you go!"

"No, I won't," said Pierre, pushing Anatole aside, and he went up to the window.

Dólokhov was holding the Englishman's hand and clearly and distinctly repeating the terms of the bet, addressing himself particularly to Anatole and Pierre.

Dólokhov was of medium height, with curly hair and light blue eyes. He was about five-and-twenty. Like all infantry officers he wore no mustache, so that his mouth, the most striking feature of his face, was clearly seen. The lines of that mouth were remarkably finely curved. The middle of the upper lip formed a sharp wedge and closed firmly on the firm lower one, and something like two distinct smiles played continually round the two corners of the mouth; this, together with the resolute, insolent intelligence of his eyes, produced an effect which made it impossible not to notice his face. Dólokhov was a man of small means and no connections. Yet though Anatole spent tens of thousands of rubles, Dólokhov lived with him and had placed himself on such a footing that all who knew them, including Anatole himself, respected him more than they did Anatole. Dólokhov could play all games and nearly always won. However much he drank he never lost his clear-headedness. Both Kurágin and Dólokhov were at that time notorious among the rakes and scape-graces of Petersburg.

The bottle of rum was brought. The window frame which prevented anyone from sitting on the outer sill, was being forced out by two footmen, who were evidently flurried and intimidated by the directions and shouts of the gentlemen around.

Anatole with his swaggering air strode up to the window. He wanted to smash something. Pushing away the footmen he tugged at the frame, but could not move it. He smashed a pane.

"You have a try, Hercules," said he, turning to Pierre.

Pierre seized the crossbeam, tugged, and wrenched the oak frame out with a crash.

"Take it right out, or they'll think I'm holding on," said Dólokhov.

"Is the Englishman bragging? . . . Eh? Is it all right?" said Anatole.

"First rate," said Pierre, looking at Dólokhov, who with a bottle of rum in his hand was approaching the window, from which the light of the sky, the dawn merging with the afterglow of sunset, was visible.

Dólokhov, the bottle of rum still in his hand, jumped onto the window sill. "Listen!" cried he, standing there and addressing those in the room. All were silent.

"I bet fifty imperials"—he spoke French that the Englishman might understand him, but he did not speak it very well—"I bet fifty imperials . . . or do you wish to make it a hundred?" added he, addressing the Englishman.

"No, fifty," replied the latter.

"All right. Fifty imperials . . . that I will drink a whole bottle of rum without taking it from my mouth, sitting outside the window on this spot" (he stooped and pointed to the sloping ledge outside the window) "and without holding on to anything. Is that right?"

"Quite right," said the Englishman.

Anatole turned to the Englishman and taking him by one of the buttons of his coat and looking down at him—the Englishman was short—began repeating the terms of the wager to him in English.

"Wait!" cried Dólokhov, hammering with the bottle on the window sill to attract attention. "Wait a bit, Kurágin. Listen! If anyone else does the same, I will pay him a hundred imperials. Do you understand?"

The Englishman nodded, but gave no indication whether he intended to accept this challenge or not. Anatole did not release him, and though he kept nodding to show that he understood, Anatole went on translating Dólokhov's words into English. A thin young lad, a hussar of the Life Guards, who had been losing that evening, climbed on the window sill, leaned over, and looked down.

"Oh! Oh! Oh!" he muttered, looking down from the window at the stones of the pavement.

"Shut up!" cried Dólokhov, pushing him away from the window. The lad jumped awkwardly back into the room, tripping over his spurs.

Placing the bottle on the window sill where he could reach it easily, Dólokhov climbed carefully and slowly through the window and lowered his legs. Pressing against both sides of the window, he adjusted himself on his seat, lowered his hands, moved a little to the right and then to the left and took up the bottle. Anatole brought two candles and placed them on the window sill, though it was already quite light. Dólokhov's back in his white shirt, and his curly head, were lit up from both sides. Everyone crowded to the window, the Englishman in front. Pierre stood smiling but silent. One man, older than the others present, suddenly pushed forward with a scared and angry look and wanted to seize hold of Dólokhov's shirt.

"I say, this is folly! He'll be killed," said this more sensible man.

Anatole stopped him.

"Don't touch him! You'll startle him and then he'll be killed. Eh? . . . What then? . . . Eh?"

Dólokhov turned round, and again holding on with both hands, arranged himself on his seat.

"If anyone comes meddling again," said he, emitting the words separately through his thin compressed lips, "I will throw him down there. Now then!"

Saying this he again turned round, dropped his hands, took the bottle and lifted it to his lips, threw back his head, and raised his free hand to balance himself. One of the footmen who had stooped to pick up some broken glass, remained in that position without taking his eyes from the window and from Dólokhov's back. Anatole stood erect with staring eyes. The Englishman looked on sideways, pursing up his lips. The man who had wished to stop the affair ran to a corner of the room and threw himself on a sofa with his face to the wall. Pierre hid his face, from which a faint smile forgot to fade though his features now expressed horror and fear. All were still. Pierre took his hands from his eyes. Dólokhov still sat in the same position, only his head was thrown further back till his curly hair touched his shirt collar, and the hand holding the bottle was lifted higher and higher and trembled with the effort. The bottle was emptying perceptibly and rising still higher and his head tilting yet further back. "Why is it so long?" thought Pierre. It seemed to him that more than half an hour had elapsed. Suddenly Dólokhov made a backward movement with his spine, and his arm trembled nervously; this was sufficient to cause his whole body to slip as he sat on the sloping ledge. As he began slipping down, his head and arm wavered still more with the strain. One hand moved as if to clutch the window sill, but refrained from touching it. Pierre again covered his eyes and thought he would never open them again. Suddenly he was aware of a stir all around. He looked up: Dólokhov was standing on the window sill, with a pale but radiant face.

"It's empty!"

He threw the bottle to the Englishman, who caught it neatly. Dólokhov jumped down. He smelled strongly of rum.

"Well done! . . . Fine fellow! . . . There's a bet for you! . . . Devil take you!" came from different sides.

The Englishman took out his purse and began counting out the money. Dólokhov stood frowning and did not speak. Pierre jumped upon the window sill.

"Gentlemen, who wishes to bet with me? I'll do the same thing!" he suddenly cried. "Even without a bet, there! Tell them to bring me a bottle. I'll do it. . . . Bring a bottle!"

"Let him do it, let him do it," said Dólokhov, smiling.

"What next? Have you gone mad? . . . No one would let you! . . . Why, you go giddy even on a staircase," exclaimed several voices.

"I'll drink it! Let's have a bottle of rum!" shouted Pierre, banging the table with a determined and drunken gesture and preparing to climb out of the window.

They seized him by his arms; but he was so strong that everyone who touched him was sent flying.

"No, you'll never manage him that way," said Anatole. "Wait a bit and I'll get round him. . . . Listen! I'll take your bet tomorrow, but now we are all going to ——'s."

"Come on then," cried Pierre. "Come on! . . . And we'll take Bruin with us."

And he caught the bear, took it in his arms, lifted it from the ground, and began dancing round the room with it.

Chapter X

PRINCE VASÍLI KEPT THE PROMISE HE HAD GIVEN TO PRINCESS DRUBETSKÁYA WHO HAD SPOKEN to him on behalf of her only son Borís on the evening of Anna Pávlovna's soireé. The matter was mentioned to the Emperor, an exception made, and Borís transferred into the regiment of Semënov Guards with the rank of cornet. He received, however, no appointment to Kutúzov's staff despite all Anna Mikháylovna's endeavors and entreaties. Soon after Anna Pávlovna's reception Anna Mikháylovna returned to Moscow, and went straight to her rich relations the Rostóvs, with whom she stayed when in the town and where her darling Bóry, who had only just entered a regiment of the line and was being at once transferred to the Guards as a cornet, had been educated from childhood and lived for years at a time. The Guards had already left Petersburg on the 10th of August, and her son, who had remained in Moscow for his equipment, was to join them on the march to Radzivílov.

It was St. Natalia's day and the name-day of two of the Rostóvs—the mother and the youngest daughter—both named Nataly. Ever since the morning, carriages with six horses had been coming and going continually, bringing visitors to the Countess Rostóva's big house on the Povarskáya, so well known to all Moscow. The countess herself and her handsome eldest daughter were in the drawing room with the visitors who came to congratulate, and who constantly succeeded one another in relays.

The countess was a woman of about forty-five, with a thin Oriental type of face, evidently worn out with child-bearing—she had had twelve. A languor of motion and speech, resulting from weakness, gave her a distinguished air which inspired respect. Princess Anna Mikháylovna Drubetskáya, who as a member of the household was also seated in the drawing room, helped to receive and entertain the visitors. The young people were in one of the inner rooms, not considering it necessary to take part in receiving the visitors. The count met the guests and saw them off, inviting them all to dinner.

"I am very, very grateful to you, *mon cher,*" or *"ma chère"*—he called everyone without exception and without the slightest variation in his tone, "my dear," whether they were above or below him in rank—"I thank you for myself and for our two dear ones whose name-day we are keeping. But mind you come to dinner or I shall be offended, *ma chère!* On behalf of the whole family I beg you to come, *mon cher!*" These words he repeated to everyone without exception or variation, and with the same expression on his full, cheerful, clean-shaven face, the same firm pressure of the hand and the same quick, repeated bows. As soon as he had seen a visitor off he returned to one of those who were still in the drawing room, drew a chair toward him or her, and jauntily spreading out his legs and putting his hands on his knees with the air of a man who enjoys life and knows how to live, he swayed to and fro with dignity, offered surmises about the weather, or touched on questions of health, sometimes in Russian and sometimes in very bad but self-confident French; then again, like a man weary but unflinching in the fulfillment of duty, he rose to see some visitors off, and stroking his scanty gray hairs over his bald patch, also asked them to dinner. Sometimes on his way back from the anteroom he would pass through the conservatory and pantry into the large marble dining hall, where tables were being set out for eighty people; and looking at the footmen, who were bringing in silver and china, moving tables, and unfolding damask table-linen, he would call Dmítri Vasílevich, a man of good family and the manager of all his affairs, and while looking with pleasure at the enormous table would say: "Well, Dmítri, you'll see that things are all as they should be? That's right! The great thing is the serving, that's it." And with a complacent sigh he would return to the drawing room.

"Márya Lvóvna Karágina and her daughter!" announced the countess's gigantic footman in his bass voice, entering the drawing room. The countess reflected a moment and took a pinch from a gold snuffbox with her husband's portrait on it.

"I'm quite worn out by these callers. However, I'll see her and no more. She is so affected. Ask her in," she said to the footman in a sad voice, as if saying: "Very well, finish me off."

A tall, stout, and proud-looking woman, with a round-faced smiling daughter, entered the drawing room, their dresses rustling.

"Dear countess, what an age . . . She has been laid up, poor child . . . at the Razumóvski's ball . . . and Countess Apráksina . . . I was so delighted . . ." came the sounds of animated feminine voices, interrupting one another and mingling with the rustling of dresses and the scraping of chairs. Then one of those conversations began which last out until, at the first pause, the guests rise with a rustle of dresses and say, "I am so delighted . . . Mamma's health . . . and Countess Apráksina . . ." and then, again rustling, pass into the anteroom, put on cloaks or mantles, and drive away. The conversation was on the chief topic of the day: the illness of the wealthy and celebrated beau of Catherine's day, Count Bezúkhov, and about his illegitimate son Pierre, the one who had behaved so improperly at Anna Pávlovna's reception.

"I am so sorry for the poor count," said the visitor. "He is in such bad health, and now this vexation about his son is enough to kill him!"

"What is that?" asked the countess as if she did not know what the visitor alluded to, though she had already heard about the cause of Count Bezúkhov's distress some fifteen times.

"That's what comes of a modern education," exclaimed the visitor. "It seems that while he was abroad this young man was allowed to do as he liked, now in Petersburg I hear he has been doing such terrible things that he has been expelled by the police."

"You don't say so!" replied the countess.

"He chose his friends badly," interposed Anna Mikháylovna. "Prince Vasíli's son, he, and a certain Dólokhov have, it is said, been up to heaven only knows what! And they have had to suffer for it. Dólokhov has been degraded to the ranks and Bezúkhov's son sent back to Moscow. Anatole Kurágin's father managed somehow to get his son's affair hushed up, but even he was ordered out of Petersburg."

"But what have they been up to?" asked the countess.

"They are regular brigands, especially Dólokhov," replied the visitor. "He is a son of Márya Ivánovna Dólokhova, such a worthy woman, but there, just fancy! Those three got hold of a bear somewhere, put it in a carriage, and set off with it to visit some actresses! The police tried to interfere, and what did the young men do? They tied a policeman and the bear back to back and put the bear into the Moyka Canal. And there was the bear swimming about with the policeman on his back!"

"What a nice figure the policeman must have cut, my dear!" shouted the count, dying with laughter.

"Oh, how dreadful! How can you laugh at it, count?"

Yet the ladies themselves could not help laughing.

"It was all they could do to rescue the poor man," continued the visitor. "And to think it is Cyril Vladímirovich Bezúkhov's son who amuses himself in this sensible manner! And he was said to be so well educated and clever. This is all that his foreign education has done for him! I hope that here in Moscow no one will receive him, in spite of his money. They wanted to introduce him to me, but I quite declined: I have my daughters to consider."

"Why do you say this young man is so rich?" asked the countess, turning away from the girls, who at once assumed an air of inattention. "His children are all illegitimate. I think Pierre also is illegitimate."

The visitor made a gesture with her hand.

"I should think he has a score of them."

Princess Anna Mikháylovna intervened in the conversation, evidently wishing to show her connections and knowledge of what went on in society.

"The fact of the matter is," said she significantly, and also in a half whisper, "everyone knows Count Cyril's reputation. . . . He has lost count of his children, but this Pierre was his favorite."

"How handsome the old man still was only a year ago!" remarked the countess. "I have never seen a handsomer man."

"He is very much altered now," said Anna Mikháylovna. "Well, as I was saying, Prince Vasíli is the next heir through his wife, but the count is very fond of Pierre, looked after his education, and wrote to the Emperor about him; so that in the case of his death—and he is so ill that he may die at any moment, and Dr. Lorrain has come from Petersburg—no one knows who will inherit his immense fortune, Pierre or Prince Vasíli. Forty thousand serfs and millions of rubles! I know it all very well for Prince Vasíli told me himself. Besides, Cyril Vladímirovich is my mother's second cousin. He's also my Bóry's godfather," she added, as if she attached no importance at all to the fact.

"Prince Vasíli arrived in Moscow yesterday. I hear he has come on some inspection business," remarked the visitor.

"Yes, but between ourselves," said the princess, "that is a pretext. The fact is he has come to see Count Cyril Vladímirovich, hearing how ill he is."

"But do you know, my dear, that was a capital joke," said the count; and seeing that the elder visitor was not listening, he turned to the young ladies. "I can just imagine what a funny figure that policeman cut!"

And as he waved his arms to impersonate the policeman, his portly form again shook with a deep ringing laugh, the laugh of one who always eats well and, in particular, drinks well. "So do come and dine with us!" he said.

Chapter XI

A SILENCE ENSUED. THE COUNTESS LOOKED AT HER CALLERS, SMILING AFFABLY, BUT NOT CONcealing the fact that she would not be distressed if they now rose and took their leave. The visitor's daughter was already smoothing down her dress with an inquiring look at her mother, when suddenly from the next room were heard the footsteps of boys and girls running to the door and the noise of a chair falling over, and a girl of thirteen, hiding something in the folds of her short muslin frock, darted in and stopped short in the middle of the room. It was evident that she had not intended her flight to bring her so far. Behind her in the doorway appeared a student with a crimson coatcollar, an officer of the Guards, a girl of fifteen, and a plump rosy-faced boy in a short jacket.

The count jumped up and, swaying from side to side, spread his arms wide and threw them round the little girl who had run in.

"Ah, here she is!" he exclaimed laughing. "My pet, whose name-day it is. My dear pet!"

"*Ma chère,* there is a time for everything," said the countess with feigned severity. "You spoil her, Ilyá," she added, turning to her husband.

"How do you do, my dear? I wish you many happy returns of your name-day," said the visitor. "What a charming child," she added, addressing the mother.

This black-eyed, wide-mouthed girl, not pretty but full of life, with childish bare shoulders which after her run heaved and shook her bodice, with black curls tossed backward, thin bare arms, little legs in lace-frilled drawers, and feet in low slippers—was just at that charming age when a girl is no longer a child, though the child is not yet a young woman. Escaping from her father she ran to hide her flushed face in the lace of her mother's mantilla—not paying the least attention to her severe remark—and began to laugh. She laughed, and in fragmentary sentences tried to explain about a doll which she produced from the folds of her frock.

"Do you see? . . . My doll . . . Mimi . . . You see . . ." was all Natásha managed to utter (to her everything seemed funny). She leaned against her mother and burst into such a loud, ringing fit of laughter that even the prim visitor could not help joining in.

"Now then, go away and take your monstrosity with you," said the mother, pushing away her daughter with pretended sternness, and turning to the visitor she added: "She is my youngest girl."

Natásha, raising her face for a moment from her mother's mantilla, glanced up at her through tears of laughter, and again hid her face.

The visitor, compelled to look on at this family scene, thought it necessary to take some part in it.

"Tell me, my dear," said she to Natásha, "is Mimi a relation of yours? A daughter, I suppose?"

Natásha did not like the visitor's tone of condescension to childish things. She did not reply, but looked at her seriously.

Meanwhile the younger generation: Borís, the officer, Anna Mikháylovna's son; Nicholas, the undergraduate, the count's eldest son; Sónya, the count's fifteen-year-old niece, and little Pétya, his youngest boy, had all settled down in the drawing room and were obviously trying to restrain within the bounds of decorum the excitement and mirth that shone in all their faces. Evidently in the back rooms, from which they had dashed out so impetuously, the conversation had been more amusing than the drawing room talk of society scandals, the weather, and Countess Apráksina. Now and then they glanced at one another, hardly able to suppress their laughter.

The two young men, the student and the officer, friends from childhood, were of the same age and both handsome fellows, though not alike. Borís was tall and fair, and his calm and handsome face had regular, delicate features. Nicholas was short with curly hair and an open expression. Dark hairs were already showing on his upper lip, and his whole face expressed impetuosity and enthusiasm. Nicholas blushed when he entered the drawing room. He evidently tried to find something to say, but failed. Borís on the contrary at once found his footing, and related quietly and humorously how he had know that doll Mimi when she was still quite a young lady, before her nose was broken; how she had aged during the five years he had known her, and how her head had cracked right across the skull. Having said this he glanced at Natásha. She turned away from him and glanced at her younger brother, who was screwing up his eyes and shaking with suppressed laughter, and unable to control herself any longer, she jumped up and rushed from the room as fast as her nimble little feet would carry her. Borís did not laugh.

"You were meaning to go out, weren't you, Mamma? Do you want the carriage?" he asked his mother with a smile.

"Yes, yes, go and tell them to get it ready," she answered, returning his smile.

Borís quietly left the room and went in search of Natásha. The plump boy ran after them angrily, as if vexed that their program had been disturbed.

Chapter XII

THE ONLY YOUNG PEOPLE REMAINING IN THE DRAWING ROOM, NOT COUNTING THE YOUNG LADY visitor and the countess's eldest daughter (who was four years older than her sister and behaved already like a grown-up person), were Nicholas and Sónya, the niece. Sónya was a slender little brunette with a tender look in her eyes which were veiled by long lashes, thick black plaits coiling twice round her head, and a tawny tint in her complexion and especially in the color of her slender but graceful and muscular arms and neck. By the grace of her movements, by the softness and flexibility of her small limbs, and by a certain coyness and reserve of manner, she reminded one of a pretty, half-grown kitten which promises to become a beautiful little cat. She evidently considered it proper to show an interest in the general conversation by smiling, but in spite of herself her eyes under their thick long lashes watched her cousin who was going to join the army, with such passionate girlish adoration that her smile could not for a single instant impose upon anyone, and it was clear that the kitten had settled down only to spring up with more energy and again play with her cousin as soon as they too could, like Natásha and Borís, escape from the drawing room.

"Ah yes, my dear," said the count, addressing the visitor and pointing to Nicholas, "his friend Borís has become an officer, and so for friendship's sake he is leaving the university and me, his old father, and entering the military service, my dear. And there was a place and everything waiting for him in the Archives Department! Isn't that friendship?" remarked the count in an inquiring tone.

"But they say that war has been declared," replied the visitor.

"They've been saying so a long while," said the count, "and they'll say so again and again, and that will be the end of it. My dear, there's friendship for you," he repeated. "He's joining the hussars."

The visitor, not knowing what to say, shook her head.

"It's not at all from friendship," declared Nicholas, flaring up and turning away as if from a shameful aspersion. "It is not from friendship at all; I simply feel that the army is my vocation."

He glanced at his cousin and the young lady visitor; and they were both regarding him with a smile of approbation.

"Schubert, the colonel of the Pávlograd Hussars, is dining with us today. He has been here on leave and is taking Nicholas back with him. It can't be helped!" said the count, shrugging his shoulders and speaking playfully of a matter that evidently distressed him.

"I have already told you, Papa," said his son, "that if you don't wish to let me go, I'll stay. But I know I am no use anywhere except in the army; I am not a diplomat nor a government clerk.—I don't know how to hide what I feel." As he spoke he kept glancing with the flirtatiousness of a handsome youth at Sónya and the young lady visitor.

The little kitten, feasting her eyes on him, seemed ready at any moment to start her gambols again and display her kittenish nature.

"All right, all right!" said the old count. "He always flares up! This Buonaparte has turned all their heads; they all think of how he rose from an ensign and became Emperor. Well, well, God grant it," he added, not noticing his visitor's sarcastic smile.

The elders began talking about Bonaparte. Julie Karágina turned to young Rostóv.

"What a pity you weren't at the Arkharovs' on Thursday. It was so dull without you," said she, giving him a tender smile.

The young man, flattered, sat down nearer to her with a coquettish smile, and engaged the smiling Julie in a confidential conversation without at all noticing that his involuntary smile had stabbed the heart of Sónya, who blushed and smiled unnaturally. In the midst of his talk he glanced round at her. She gave him a passionately angry glance, and hardly able to restrain her tears and maintain the artificial smile on her lips, she got up and left the room. All Nicholas's animation vanished. He waited for the first pause in the conversation, and then with a distressed face left the room to find Sónya.

"How plainly all these young people wear their hearts on their sleeves!" said Anna Mikháylovna, pointing to Nicholas as he went out. *"Cousinage—dangereux voisinage,"* she added.

"Yes," said the countess when the brightness these young people had brought into the room had vanished; and as if answering a question no one had put but which was always in her mind, "and how much suffering, how much anxiety one has had to go through that we might rejoice in them now! And yet really the anxiety is greater now than the joy. One is always, always anxious! Especially just at this age, so dangerous both for girls and boys."

"It all depends on the bringing up," remarked the visitor.

"Yes, you're quite right," continued the countess. "Till now I have always, thank God, been my children's friend and had their full confidence," said she, repeating the mistake of so many parents who imagine that their children have no secrets from them. "I know I shall always be my daughters' first confidante, and that if Nicholas, with his impulsive nature, does get into mischief (a boy can't help it) he will all the same never be like those Petersburg young men."

"Yes, they are splendid, splendid youngsters," chimed in the count, who always solved questions that seemed to him perplexing by deciding that everything was splendid. "Just fancy: wants to be a hussar. What's one to do, my dear?"

"What a charming creature your younger girl is," said the visitor; "a little volcano!"

"Yes, a regular volcano," said the count. "Takes after me! And what a voice she has; though she's my daughter, I tell the truth when I say she'll be a singer, a second Salomoni! We have engaged an Italian to give her lessons."

"Isn't she too young? I have heard that it harms the voice to train it at that age."

"Oh no, not at all too young!" replied the count. "Why, our mothers used to be married at twelve or thirteen."

"And she's in love with Borís already. Just fancy!" said the countess with a gentle smile, looking at Borís's mother, and went on, evidently concerned with a thought that always occupied her: "Now you see if I were to be severe with her and to forbid it . . . goodness knows what they might be up to on the sly" (she meant that they would be kissing), "but as it is, I know every word she utters. She will come running to me of her own accord in the evening and tell me everything. Perhaps I spoil her, but really that seems the best plan. With her elder sisters I was stricter."

"Yes, I was brought up quite differently," remarked the handsome elder daughter, Countess Véra, with a smile.

But the smile did not enhance Véra's beauty as smiles generally do; on the contrary it gave her an unnatural, and therefore unpleasant, expression. Véra was good-looking, not at all stupid, quick at learning, was well brought up, and had a pleasant voice; what she said was true and appropriate, yet, strange to say, everyone—the visitors and countess alike—turned to look at her as if wondering why she had said it, and they all felt awkward.

"People are always too clever with their eldest children and try to make something exceptional of them," said the visitor.

"What's the good of denying it, my dear? Our dear countess was too clever with Véra," said the count. "Well, what of that? She's turned out splendidly all the same," he added, winking at Véra.

The guests got up and took their leave, promising to return to dinner.

"What manners! I thought they would never go," said the countess, when she had seen her guests out.

Chapter XIII

When Natásha ran out of the drawing room she only went as far as the conservatory. There she paused and stood listening to the conversation in the drawing room, waiting for Borís to come out. She was already growing impatient, and stamped her foot, ready to cry at his not coming at once, when she heard the young man's discreet steps approaching neither quickly nor slowly. At this Natásha dashed swiftly among the flower-tubs and hid there.

Borís paused in the middle of the room, looked around, brushed a little dust from the sleeve of his uniform, and going up to a mirror examined his handsome face. Natásha, very still, peered out from her ambush, waiting to see what he would do. He stood a little while before the glass, smiled, and walked toward the other door. Natásha was about to call him but changed her mind. "Let him look for me," thought she. Hardly had Borís gone than Sónya, flushed, in tears, and muttering angrily, came in at the other door. Natásha checked her first impulse to run out to her, and remained in her hiding place, watching—as under an invisible cap—to see what went on in the world. She was experiencing a new and peculiar pleasure. Sónya, muttering to herself, kept looking round toward the drawing room door. It opened and Nicholas came in.

"Sónya, what is the matter with you? How can you?" said he, running up to her.

"It's nothing, nothing; leave me alone!" sobbed Sónya.

"Ah, I know what it is."

"Well, if you do, so much the better, and you can go back to her!"

"So-o-onya! Look here! How can you torture me and yourself like that, for a mere fancy?" said Nicholas taking her hand.

Sónya did not pull it away, and left off crying. Natásha, not stirring and scarcely breathing, watched from her ambush with sparkling eyes. "What will happen now?" thought she.

"Sónya! What is anyone in the world to me? You alone are everything!" said Nicholas. "And I will prove it to you."

"I don't like you to talk like that."

"Well, then, I won't; only forgive me, Sónya!" He drew her to him and kissed her.

"Oh, how nice," thought Natásha; and when Sónya and Nicholas had gone out of the conservatory she followed and called Borís to her.

"Borís, come here," said she with a sly and significant look. "I have something to tell you. Here, here!" and she led him into the conservatory to the place among the tubs where she had been hiding.

Borís followed her, smiling.

"What is the *something?*" asked he.

She grew confused, glanced round, and, seeing the doll she had thrown down on one of the tubs, picked it up.

"Kiss the doll," said she.

Borís looked attentively and kindly at her eager face, but did not reply.

"Don't you want to? Well then, come here," said she, and went further in among the plants and threw down the doll. "Closer, closer!" she whispered.

She caught the young officer by his cuffs, and a look of solemnity and fear appeared on her flushed face.

"And me? Would you like to kiss me?" she whispered almost inaudibly, glancing up at him from under her brows, smiling, and almost crying from excitement.

Borís blushed.

"How funny you are!" he said, bending down to her and blushing still more, but he waited and did nothing.

Suddenly she jumped up onto a tub to be higher than he, embraced him so that both her slender bare arms clasped him above his neck, and, tossing back her hair, kissed him full on the lips.

Then she slipped down among the flower pots on the other side of the tubs and stood, hanging her head.

"Natásha," he said, "you know that I love you, but . . ."

"You are in love with me?" Natásha broke in.

"Yes, I am, but please don't let us do like that. . . . In another four years . . . then I will ask for your hand."

Natásha considered.

"Thirteen, fourteen, fifteen, sixteen," she counted on her slender little fingers. "All right! Then it's settled?"

A smile of joy and satisfaction lit up her eager face.

"Settled!" replied Borís.

"Forever?" said the little girl. "Till death itself?"

She took his arm and with a happy face went with him into the adjoining sitting room.

Chapter XIV

After receiving her visitors the countess was so tired that she gave orders to admit no more, but the porter was told to be sure to invite to dinner all who came "to congratulate." The countess wished to have a tête-à-tête talk with the friend of her childhood, Princess Anna Mikháylovna, whom she had not seen properly since she returned from Petersburg. Anna Mikháylovna, with her tear-worn but pleasant face, drew her chair nearer to that of the countess.

"With you I will be quite frank," said Anna Mikháylovna. "There are not many left of us old friends! That's why I so value your friendship."

Anna Mikháylovna looked at Véra and paused. The countess pressed her friend's hand.

"Véra," she said to her eldest daughter who was evidently not a favorite, "how is it you have so little tact? Don't you see you are not wanted here? Go to the other girls, or . . ."

The handsome Véra smiled contemptuously but did not seem at all hurt.

"If you had told me sooner, Mamma, I would have gone," she replied as she rose to go to her own room.

But as she passed the sitting room she noticed two couples sitting, one pair at each window. She stopped and smiled scornfully. Sónya was sitting close to Nicholas who was copying out some verses for her, the first he had ever written. Borís and Natásha were at the other window and ceased talking when Véra entered. Sónya and Natásha looked at Véra with guilty, happy faces.

It was pleasant and touching to see these little girls in love; but apparently the sight of them roused no pleasant feeling in Véra.

"How often have I asked you not to take my things?" she said. "You have a room of your own," and she took the inkstand from Nicholas.

"In a minute, in a minute," he said, dipping his pen.

"You always manage to do things at the wrong time," continued Véra. "You came rushing into the drawing room so that everyone felt ashamed of you."

Though what she said was quite just, perhaps for that very reason no one replied, and the four simply looked at one another. She lingered in the room with the inkstand in her hand.

"And at your age what secrets can there be between Natásha and Borís, or between you two? It's all nonsense!"

"Now, Véra, what does it matter to you?" said Natásha in defense, speaking very gently.

She seemed that day to be more than ever kind and affectionate to everyone.

"Very silly," said Véra. "I am ashamed of you. Secrets indeed!"

"All have secrets of their own," answered Natásha, getting warmer. "We don't interfere with you and Berg."

"I should think not," said Véra, "because there can never be anything wrong in my behavior. But I'll tell Mamma how you are behaving with Borís."

"Natálya Ilyínichna behaves very well to me," remarked Borís. "I have nothing to complain of."

"Don't, Borís! You are such a diplomat that it is really tiresome," said Natásha in a mortified voice that trembled slightly. (She used the word "diplomat," which was just then much in vogue among the children, in the special sense they attached to it.) "Why does she bother me?" And she added, turning to Véra, "You'll never understand it, because you've never loved anyone. You have no heart! You are a Madame de Genlis and nothing more" (this nickname, bestowed on Véra by Nicholas, was considered very stinging) "and your greatest pleasure is to be unpleasant to people! Go and flirt with Berg as much as you please," she finished quickly.

"I shall at any rate not run after a young man before visitors . . ."

"Well, now you've done what you wanted," put in Nicholas—"said unpleasant things to everyone and upset them. Let's go to the nursery."

All four, like a flock of scared birds, got up and left the room.

"The unpleasant things were said to me," remarked Véra, "I said none to anyone."

"Madame de Genlis! Madame de Genlis!" shouted laughing voices through the door.

The handsome Véra, who produced such an irritating and unpleasant effect on everyone, smiled, and evidently unmoved by what had been said to her, went to the looking-glass and arranged her hair and scarf. Looking at her own handsome face she seemed to become still colder and calmer.

In the drawing room the conversation was still going on.

"Ah, my dear," said the countess, "my life is not all roses either. Don't I know that at the rate we are living our means won't last long? It's all the Club and his easy-going nature. Even in the country do we get any rest? Theatricals, hunting, and heaven knows what besides! But don't let's talk about me; tell me how you managed everything. I often wonder at you, Annette—how at your age you can rush off alone in a carriage to Moscow, to Petersburg, to those ministers and great people, and know how to deal with them all! It's quite astonishing. How did you get things settled? I couldn't possibly do it."

"Ah, my love," answered Anna Mikháylovna, "God grant you never know what it is to be left a widow without means and with a son you love to distraction! One learns many things then," she added with a certain pride. "That lawsuit taught me much. When I want to see one of those big people I write a note: 'Princess So-and-So desires an interview with So and-So,' and then I take a cab and go myself two, three, or four times—till I get what I want. I don't mind what they think of me."

"Well, and to whom did you apply about Bóry?" asked the countess. "You see yours is already an officer in the Guards, while my Nicholas is going as a cadet. There's no one to interest himself for him. To whom did you apply?"

"To Prince Vasíli. He was so kind. He at once agreed to everything, and put the matter before the Emperor," said Princess Anna Mikháylovna enthusiastically, quite forgetting all the humiliation she had endured to gain her end.

"Has Prince Vasíli aged much?" asked the countess. "I have not seen him since we acted together at the Rumyántsovs' theatricals. I expect he has forgotten me. He paid me attentions in those days," said the countess, with a smile.

"He is just the same as ever," replied Anna Mikháylovna, "overflowing with amiability. His position has not turned his head at all. He said to me, 'I am sorry I can do so little for you, dear princess. I am at your command.' Yes, he is a fine fellow and a very kind relation. But, Nataly, you know my love for my son: I would do anything for his happiness! And my affairs are in such a bad way that my position is now a terrible one," continued Anna Mikháylovna, sadly, dropping her voice. "My wretched lawsuit takes all I have and makes no progress. Would you believe it, I have literally not a penny and don't know how to equip Borís." She took out her handkerchief and began to cry. "I need five hundred rubles, and have only one twenty-five-ruble note. I am in such a state. . . . My only hope now is in Count Cyril Vladímirovich Bezúkhov. If he will not assist his godson—you know he is Bóry's godfather—and allow him something for his maintenance, all my trouble will have been thrown away. . . . I shall not be able to equip him."

The countess's eyes filled with tears and she pondered in silence.

"I often think, though perhaps it's a sin," said the princess, "that here lives Count Cyril Vladímirovich Bezúkhov so rich, all alone . . . that tremendous fortune . . . and what is his life worth? It's a burden to him, and Bóry's life is only just beginning. . . ."

"Surely he will leave something to Borís," said the countess.

"Heaven only knows, my dear! These rich grandees are so selfish. Still, I will take Borís and go to see him at once, and I shall speak to him straight out. Let people think what they will of me, it's really all the same to me when my son's fate is at stake." The princess rose. "It's now two o'clock and you dine at four. There will just be time."

And like a practical Petersburg lady who knows how to make the most of time, Anna Mikháylovna sent someone to call her son, and went into the anteroom with him.

"Good-bye, my dear," said she to the countess who saw her to the door, and added in a whisper so that her son should not hear, "Wish me good luck."

"Are you going to Count Cyril Vladímirovich, my dear?" said the count coming out from the dining hall into the anteroom, and he added: "If he is better, ask Pierre to dine with us. He has been to the house, you know, and danced with the children. Be sure to invite him, my dear. We will see how Tarás distinguishes himself today. He says Count Orlóv never gave such a dinner as ours will be!"

Chapter XV

"MY DEAR BORÍS," SAID PRINCESS ANNA MIKHÁYLOVNA TO HER SON AS COUNTESS ROSTÓVA'S CARriage in which they were seated drove over the straw-covered street and turned into the wide courtyard of Count Cyril Vladímirovich Bezúkhov's house. "My dear Borís," said the mother, drawing her hand from beneath her old mantle and laying it timidly and tenderly on her son's arm, "be affectionate and attentive to him. Count Cyril Vladímirovich is your godfather after all, and your future depends on him. Remember that, my dear, and be nice to him, as you so well know how to be."

"If only I knew that anything besides humiliation would come of it . . ." answered her son coldly. "But I have promised and will do it for your sake."

Although the hall-porter saw someone's carriage standing at the entrance, after scrutinizing the mother and son (who without asking to be announced had passed straight through the glass porch between the rows of statues in niches) and looking significantly at the lady's old cloak, he asked whether they wanted the count or the princesses, and, hearing that they wished to see the count, said his excellency was worse today, and that his excellency was not receiving anyone.

"We may as well go back," said the son in French.

"My dear!" exclaimed his mother imploringly, again laying her hand on his arm as if that touch might soothe or rouse him.

Borís said no more, but looked inquiringly at his mother without taking off his cloak.

"My friend," said Anna Mikháylovna in gentle tones, addressing the hall-porter, "I know Count Cyril Vladímirovich is very ill . . . that's why I have come . . . I am a relation. I shall not disturb him, my friend . . . I only need see Prince Vasíli Sergéevich: he is staying here, is he not? Please announce me."

The hall-porter sullenly pulled a bell that rang upstairs, and turned away.

"Princess Drubetskáya to see Prince Vasíli Sergéevich," he called to a footman dressed in knee-breeches, shoes, and a swallow-tail coat, who ran downstairs and looked over from the halfway landing.

The mother smoothed the folds of her dyed silk dress before a large Venetian mirror in the wall, and in her trodden-down shoes briskly ascended the carpeted stairs.

"My dear," she said to her son, once more stimulating him by a touch, "you promised me!"

The son, lowering his eyes, followed her quietly.

They entered the large hall, from which one of the doors led to the apartments assigned to Prince Vasíli.

Just as the mother and son, having reached the middle of the hall, were about to ask their way of an elderly footman who had sprung up as they entered, the bronze handle of one of the doors turned and Prince Vasíli came out—wearing a velvet coat with a single star on his breast, as was his custom when at home—taking leave of a good-looking, dark-haired man. This was the celebrated Petersburg doctor, Lorrain.

"Then it is certain?" said the prince.

"Prince, *humanum est errare,* but . . ." replied the doctor, swallowing his *r's,* and pronouncing the Latin words with a French accent.

"Very well, very well . . ."

Seeing Anna Mikháylovna and her son, Prince Vasíli dismissed the doctor with a bow and approached them silently and with a look of inquiry. The son noticed that an expression of profound sorrow suddenly clouded his mother's face, and he smiled slightly.

"Ah, prince! In what sad circumstances we meet again! And how is our dear invalid?" said she, as though unaware of the cold offensive look fixed on her.

Prince Vasíli stared at her and at Borís questioningly and perplexed. Borís bowed politely. Prince Vasíli without acknowledging the bow turned to Anna Mikháylovna, answering her query by a movement of the head and lips indicating very little hope for the patient.

"Is it possible?" exclaimed Anna Mikháylovna. "Oh, how awful! It is terrible to think. . . . This is my son," she added, indicating Borís. "He wanted to thank you himself."

Borís bowed again politely.

"Believe me, prince, a mother's heart will never forget what you have done for us."

"I am glad I was able to do you a service, my dear Anna Mikháylovna," said Prince Vasíli, arranging his lace frill, and in tone and manner, here in Moscow to Anna Mikháylovna whom he had placed under an obligation, assuming an air of much greater importance than he had done in Petersburg at Anna Scherer's reception.

"Try to serve well and show yourself worthy," added he, addressing Borís with severity. "I am glad. . . . Are you here on leave?" he went on in his usual tone of indifference.

"I am awaiting orders to join my new regiment, your excellency," replied Borís, betraying neither annoyance at the prince's brusque manner nor a desire to enter into conversation, but speaking so quietly and respectfully that the prince gave him a searching glance.

"Are you living with your mother?"

"I am living at Countess Rostóva's," replied Borís, again adding, "your excellency."

"That is, with Ilyá Rostóv who married Nataly Shinshiná," said Anna Mikháylovna.

"I know, I know," answered Prince Vasíli in his monotonous voice. "I never could understand how Nataly made up her mind to marry that unlicked bear! A perfectly absurd and stupid fellow, and a gambler too, I am told."

"But a very kind man, prince," said Anna Mikháylovna with a pathetic smile, as though she too knew that Count Rostóv deserved this censure, but asked him not to be too hard on the poor old man. "What do the doctors say?" asked the princess after a pause, her worn face again expressing deep sorrow.

"They give little hope," replied the prince.

"And I should so like to thank *Uncle* once for all his kindness to me and Borís. He is his godson," she added, her tone suggesting that this fact ought to give Prince Vasíli much satisfaction.

Prince Vasíli became thoughtful and frowned. Anna Mikháylovna saw that he was afraid of finding in her a rival for Count Bezúkhov's fortune, and hastened to reassure him.

"If it were not for my sincere affection and devotion to *Uncle*," said she, uttering the word with peculiar assurance and unconcern, "I know his character: noble, upright . . . but you see he has no one with him except the young princesses. . . . They are still young. . . ." She bent her head and continued in a whisper: "Has he performed his final duty, prince? How priceless are those last moments! It can make things no worse, and it is absolutely necessary to prepare him if he is so ill. We women, prince," and she smiled tenderly, "always know how to say these things. I absolutely must see him, however painful it may be for me. I am used to suffering."

Evidently the prince understood her, and also understood, as he had done at Anna Pávlovna's, that it would be difficult to get rid of Anna Mikháylovna.

"Would not such a meeting be too trying for him, dear Anna Mikháylovna?" said he. "Let us wait until evening. The doctors are expecting a crisis."

"But one cannot delay, prince, at such a moment! Consider that the welfare of his soul is at stake. Ah, it is awful: the duties of a Christian . . ."

A door of one of the inner rooms opened and one of the princesses, the count's niece, entered with a cold stern face. The length of her body was strikingly out of proportion to her short legs. Prince Vasíli turned to her.

"Well, how is he?"

"Still the same; but what can you expect, this noise . . ." said the princess, looking at Anna Mikháylovna as at a stranger.

"Ah, my dear, I hardly knew you," said Anna Mikháylovna with a happy smile, ambling lightly up to the count's niece. "I have come, and am at your service to help you nurse *my uncle*. I imagine what you have gone through," and she sympathetically turned up her eyes.

The princess gave no reply and did not even smile, but left the room at once. Anna Mikháylovna took off her gloves, and occupying the position she had conquered, settled down in an arm-chair, inviting Prince Vasíli to take a seat beside her.

"Borís," she said to her son with a smile, "I shall go in to see the count, my uncle; but you, my dear, had better go to Pierre meanwhile and don't forget to give him the Rostóvs' invitation. They ask him to dinner. I suppose he won't go?" she continued, turning to the prince.

"On the contrary," replied the prince, who had plainly become depressed, "I shall be only too glad if you relieve me of that young man. . . . Here he is, and the count has not once asked for him."

He shrugged his shoulders. A footman conducted Borís down one flight of stairs and up another, to Pierre's rooms.

Chapter XVI

PIERRE, AFTER ALL, HAD NOT MANAGED TO CHOOSE A CAREER FOR HIMSELF IN PETERSBURG, AND had been expelled from there for riotous conduct and sent to Moscow. The story told about him at Count Rostóv's was true. Pierre had taken part in tying a policeman to a bear. He had now been for some days in Moscow and was staying as usual at his father's house. Though he expected that the story of his escapade would be already known in Moscow and that the ladies about his father—who were never favorably disposed toward him—would have used it to turn the count against him, he nevertheless on the day of his arrival went to his father's part of the house. Entering the drawing room, where the princesses spent most of their time, he greeted the ladies, two of whom were sitting at embroidery frames while a third read aloud. It was the eldest who was reading—the one who had met Anna Mikháylovna. The two younger ones were embroidering: both were rosy and pretty and they differed only in that one had a little mole on her lip which made her much prettier. Pierre was received as if he were a corpse or a leper. The eldest princess paused in her reading and silently stared at him with frightened eyes: the second assumed precisely the same expression: while the youngest, the one with the mole, who was of a cheerful and lively disposition, bent over her frame to hide a smile probably evoked by the amusing scene she foresaw. She drew her wool down through the canvas and, scarcely able to refrain from laughing, stooped as if trying to make out the pattern.

"How do you do, cousin?" said Pierre. "You don't recognize me?"

"I recognize you only too well, too well."

"How is the count? Can I see him?" asked Pierre, awkwardly as usual, but unabashed.

"The count is suffering physically and mentally, and apparently you have done your best to increase his mental sufferings."

"Can I see the count?" Pierre again asked.

"H'm. . . . If you wish to kill him, to kill him outright, you can see him . . . Olga, go and see whether uncle's beef tea is ready—it is almost time," she added, giving Pierre to understand that they were busy, and busy making his father comfortable, while evidently he, Pierre, was only busy causing him annoyance.

Olga went out. Pierre stood looking at the sisters; then he bowed and said:

"Then I will go to my rooms. You will let me know when I can see him."

And he left the room, followed by the low but ringing laughter of the sister with the mole.

Next day Prince Vasíli had arrived and settled in the count's house. He sent for Pierre and said to him:

"My dear fellow, if you are going to behave here as you did in Petersburg, you will end very badly; that is all I have to say to you. The count is very, very ill, and you must not see him at all."

Since then Pierre had not been disturbed and had spent the whole time in his rooms upstairs.

When Borís appeared at his door Pierre was pacing up and down his room, stopping occasionally at a corner to make menacing gestures at the wall, as if running a sword through an invisible foe, and glaring savagely over his spectacles, and then again resuming his walk, muttering indistinct words, shrugging his shoulders and gesticulating.

"England is done for," said he, scowling and pointing his finger at someone unseen. "Mr. Pitt, as a traitor to the nation and to the rights of man, is sentenced to . . ." But before Pierre—who at that moment imagined himself to be Napoleon in person and to have just effected the dangerous crossing of the Straits of Dover and captured London—could pronounce Pitt's sentence, he saw a well-built and handsome young officer entering his room. Pierre paused. He had left Moscow when Borís was a boy of fourteen, and had quite forgotten him, but in his usual impulsive and hearty way he took Borís by the hand with a friendly smile.

"Do you remember me?" asked Borís quietly with a pleasant smile. "I have come with my mother to see the count, but it seems he is not well."

"Yes, it seems he is ill. People are always disturbing him," answered Pierre, trying to remember who this young man was.

Borís felt that Pierre did not recognize him but did not consider it necessary to introduce himself, and without experiencing the least embarrassment looked Pierre straight in the face.

"Count Rostóv asks you to come to dinner today," said he, after a considerable pause which made Pierre feel uncomfortable.

"Ah, Count Rostóv!" exclaimed Pierre joyfully. "Then you are his son, Ilyá? Only fancy, I didn't know you at first. Do you remember how we went to the Sparrow Hills with Madame Jacquot? . . . It's such an age . . ."

"You are mistaken," said Borís deliberately, with a bold and slightly sarcastic smile. "I am Borís, son of Princess Anna Mikháylovna Drubetskáya. Rostóv, the father, is Ilyá, and his son is Nicholas. I never knew any Madame Jacquot."

Pierre shook his head and arms as if attacked by mosquitoes or bees.

"Oh dear, what am I thinking about? I've mixed everything up. One has so many relatives in Moscow! So you are Borís? Of course. Well, now we know where we are. And what do you think of the Boulogne expedition? The English will come off badly, you know, if Napoleon gets across the Channel. I think the expedition is quite feasible. If only Villeneuve doesn't make a mess of things!"

Borís knew nothing about the Boulogne expedition; he did not read the papers and it was the first time he had heard Villeneuve's name.

"We here in Moscow are more occupied with dinner parties and scandal than with politics," said he in his quiet ironical tone. "I know nothing about it and have not thought about it. Moscow is chiefly busy with gossip," he continued. "Just now they are talking about you and your father."

Pierre smiled in his good-natured way as if afraid for his companion's sake that the latter might say something he would afterward regret. But Borís spoke distinctly, clearly and dryly, looking straight into Pierre's eyes.

"Moscow has nothing else to do but gossip," Borís went on. "Everybody is wondering to whom the count will leave his fortune though he may perhaps outlive us all, as I sincerely hope he will . . ."

"Yes, it is all very horrid," interrupted Pierre, "very horrid."

Pierre was still afraid that this officer might inadvertently say something disconcerting to himself.

"And it must seem to you," said Borís flushing slightly, but not changing his tone or attitude, "it must seem to you that everyone is trying to get something out of the rich man?"

"So it does," thought Pierre.

"But I just wish to say, to avoid misunderstandings, that you are quite mistaken if you reckon me or my mother among such people. We are very poor, but for my own part at any rate, for the very reason that your father is rich I don't regard myself as a relation of his, and neither I nor my mother would ever ask or take anything from him."

For a long time Pierre could not understand, but when he did, he jumped up from the sofa, seized Borís under the elbow in his quick, clumsy way, and, blushing far more than Borís, began to speak with a feeling of mingled shame and vexation.

"Well, this is strange! Do you suppose I . . . who could think? . . . I know very well . . ."

But Borís again interrupted him.

"I am glad I have spoken out fully. Perhaps you did not like it? You must excuse me," said he, putting Pierre at ease instead of being put at ease by him, "but I hope I have not offended you. I always make it a rule to speak out . . . Well, what answer am I to take? Will you come to dinner at the Rostóvs'?"

And Borís, having apparently relieved himself of an onerous duty and extricated himself from an awkward situation and placed another in it, became quite pleasant again.

"No, but I say," said Pierre, calming down, "you are a wonderful fellow! What you have just said is good, very good. Of course you don't know me. We have not met for such a long time . . . not since we were children. You might think that I . . . I understand, quite understand. I could not have done it myself, I should not have had the courage, but it's splendid. I am very glad to have made your acquaintance. It's queer," he added after a pause, "that you should have suspected me!" He began to laugh. "Well, what of it! I hope we'll get better acquainted," and he pressed Borís's hand. "Do you know, I have not once been in to see the count. He has not sent for me. . . . I am sorry for him as a man, but what can one do?"

"And so you think Napoleon will manage to get an army across?" asked Borís with a smile.

Pierre saw that Borís wished to change the subject, and being of the same mind he began explaining the advantages and disadvantages of the Boulogne expedition.

A footman came in to summon Borís—the princess was going. Pierre, in order to make Borís's better acquaintance, promised to come to dinner, and warmly pressing his hand looked affectionately over his spectacles into Borís's eyes. After he had gone Pierre continued pacing up and down the room for a long time, no longer piercing an imaginary foe with his imaginary sword, but smiling at the remembrance of that pleasant, intelligent and resolute young man.

As often happens in early youth, especially to one who leads a lonely life, he felt an unaccountable tenderness for this young man and made up his mind that they would be friends.

Prince Vasíli saw the princess off. She held a handkerchief to her eyes and her face was tearful.

"It is dreadful, dreadful!" she was saying, "but cost me what it may I shall do my duty. I will come and spend the night. He must not be left like this. Every moment is precious. I can't think why his nieces put it off. Perhaps God will help me to find a way to prepare him! . . . Adieu, prince! May God support you . . ."

"Adieu, ma bonne," answered Prince Vasíli turning away from her.

"Oh, he is in a dreadful state," said the mother to her son when they were in the carriage. "He hardly recognizes anybody."

"I don't understand, Mamma—what is his attitude to Pierre?" asked the son.

"The will will show that, my dear; our fate also depends on it."

"But why do you expect that he will leave us anything?"

"Ah, my dear! He is so rich, and we are so poor!"

"Well, that is hardly a sufficient reason, Mamma . . ."

"Oh Heaven! How ill he is," exclaimed the mother.

Chapter XVII

After Anna Mikháylovna had driven off with her son to visit Count Cyril Vladímirovich Bezúkhov, Countess Rostóva sat for a long time all alone applying her handkerchief to her eyes. At last she rang.

"What is the matter with you, my dear?" she said crossly to the maid who kept her waiting some minutes. "Don't you wish to serve me? Then I'll find you another place."

The countess was upset by her friend's sorrow and humiliating poverty, and was therefore out of sorts, a state of mind which with her always found expression in calling her maid "my dear" and speaking to her with exaggerated politeness.

"I am very sorry, ma'am," answered the maid.

"Ask the count to come to me."

The count came waddling in to see his wife with a rather guilty look as usual.

"Well, little countess? What a *sauté* of game *au madère* we are to have, my dear! I tasted it. The thousand rubles I paid for Tarás were not ill-spent. He is worth it!"

He sat down by his wife, his elbows on his knees and his hands ruffling his gray hair.

"What are your commands, little countess?"

"You see, my dear . . . What's that mess?" she said, pointing to his waistcoat. "It's the *sauté*, most likely," she added with a smile. "Well, you see, count, I want some money."

Her face became sad.

"Oh, little countess!" . . . and the count began bustling to get out his pocketbook.

"I want a great deal, count! I want five hundred rubles," and taking out her cambric handkerchief she began wiping her husband's waistcoat.

"Yes, immediately, immediately! Hey, who's there?" he called out in a tone only used by persons who are certain that those they call will rush to obey the summons. "Send Dmítri to me!"

Dmítri, a man of good family who had been brought up in the count's house and now managed all his affairs, stepped softly into the room.

"This is what I want, my dear fellow," said the count to the deferential young man who had entered. "Bring me . . ." he reflected a moment, "Yes, bring me seven hundred rubles, yes! But mind, don't bring me such tattered and dirty notes as last time, but nice clean ones for the countess."

"Yes, Dmítri, clean ones, please," said the countess, sighing deeply.

"When would you like them, your excellency?" asked Dmítri. "Allow me to inform you . . . But, don't be uneasy," he added, noticing that the count was beginning to breathe heavily and quickly which was always a sign of approaching anger. "I was forgetting . . . Do you wish it brought at once?"

"Yes, yes; just so! Bring it. Give it to the countess."

"What a treasure that Dmítri is," added the count with a smile when the young man had departed. "There is never any 'impossible' with him. That's a thing I hate! Everything is possible."

"Ah, money, count, money! How much sorrow it causes in the world," said the countess. "But I am in great need of this sum."

"You, my little countess, are a notorious spendthrift," said the count, and having kissed his wife's hand he went back to his study.

When Anna Mikháylovna returned from Count Bezúkhov's the money, all in clean notes, was lying ready under a handkerchief on the countess's little table, and Anna Mikháylovna noticed that something was agitating her.

"Well, my dear?" asked the countess.

"Oh, what a terrible state he is in! One would not know him, he is so ill! I was only there a few moments and hardly said a word . . ."

"Annette, for heaven's sake don't refuse me," the countess began, with a blush that looked very strange on her thin, dignified, elderly face, and she took the money from under the handkerchief.

Anna Mikháylovna instantly guessed her intention and stooped to be ready to embrace the countess at the appropriate moment.

"This is for Borís from me, for his outfit."

Anna Mikháylovna was already embracing her and weeping. The countess wept too. They wept because they were friends, and because they were kind-hearted, and because they—friends from childhood—had to think about such a base thing as money, and because their youth was over. . . . But those tears were pleasant to them both.

Chapter XVIII

COUNTESS ROSTÓVA, WITH HER DAUGHTERS AND A LARGE NUMBER OF GUESTS, WAS ALREADY seated in the drawing room. The count took the gentlemen into his study and showed them his choice collection of Turkish pipes. From time to time he went out to ask: "Hasn't she come yet?" They were expecting Márya Dmítrievna Akhrosímova, known in society as *le terrible dragon*, a lady distinguished not for wealth or rank, but for common sense and frank plainness of speech. Márya Dmítrievna was known to the Imperial family as well as to all Moscow and Petersburg, and both cities wondered at her, laughed privately at her rudenesses, and told good stories about her, while none the less all without exception respected and feared her.

In the count's room, which was full of tobacco-smoke, they talked of war that had been announced in a manifesto, and about the recruiting. None of them had yet seen the manifesto, but they all knew it had appeared. The count sat on the sofa between two guests who were smoking and talking. He neither smoked nor talked, but bending his head first to one side and then to the other watched the smokers with evident pleasure and listened to the conversation of his two neighbors, whom he egged on against each other.

One of them was a sallow, clean-shaven civilian with a thin and wrinkled face, already growing old, though he was dressed like a most fashionable young man. He sat with his legs up on the sofa as if quite at home, and having stuck an amber mouthpiece far into his mouth, was inhaling the smoke spasmodically and screwing up his eyes. This was an old bachelor, Shinshín, a cousin of the countess', a man with "a sharp tongue" as they said in Moscow society. He seemed to be condescending to his companion. The latter, a fresh, rosy officer of the Guards, irreproachably washed, brushed and buttoned, held his pipe in the middle of his mouth and with red lips gently inhaled the smoke, letting it escape from his handsome mouth in rings. This was Lieutenant Berg, an officer in the Semënov regiment with whom Borís was to travel to join the army, and about whom Natásha had, teased her elder sister Véra, speaking of Berg as her "intended." The count sat between them and listened attentively. His favorite occupation when not playing boston, a card game he was very fond of, was that of listener, especially when he succeeded in setting two loquacious talkers at one another.

"Well, then, old chap, *mon très honorable* Alphonse Kárlovich," said Shinshín, laughing ironically and mixing the most ordinary Russian expressions with the choicest French phrases—which was a peculiarity of his speech. "*Vous comptez vous faire des rentes sur l'État*; you want to make something out of your company?"

"No, Peter Nikoláevich; I only want to show that in the cavalry the advantages are far less than in the infantry. Just consider my own position now, Peter Nikoláevich . . ."

Berg always spoke quietly, politely, and with great precision. His conversation always related entirely to himself; he would remain calm and silent when the talk related to any topic that had no direct bearing on himself. He could remain silent for hours without being at all put out of countenance himself or making others uncomfortable, but as soon as the conversation concerned himself he would begin to talk circumstantially and with evident satisfaction.

"Consider my position, Peter Nikoláevich. Were I in the cavalry I should get not more than two hundred rubles every four months, even with the rank of lieutenant; but as it is I receive two hundred and thirty," said he, looking at Shinshín and the count with a joyful, pleasant smile, as if it were obvious to him that his success must always be the chief desire of everyone else.

"Besides that, Peter Nikoláevich, by exchanging into the Guards I shall be in a more prominent position," continued Berg, "and vacancies occur much more frequently in the Foot Guards. Then just think what can be done with two hundred and thirty rubles! I even manage to put a little aside and to send something to my father," he went on, emitting a smoke ring.

"*La balance y est.* . . . A German knows how to skin a flint, as the proverb says," remarked Shinshín, moving his pipe to the other side of his mouth and winking at the count.

The count burst out laughing. The other guests seeing that Shinshín was talking came up to listen. Berg, oblivious of irony or indifference, continued to explain how by exchanging into the Guards he had already gained a step on his old comrades of the Cadet Corps; how in wartime the company commander might get killed and he, as senior in the company, might easily succeed to the post; how popular he was with everyone in the regiment, and how satisfied his father was with him. Berg evidently enjoyed narrating all this, and did not seem to suspect that others, too, might have their own interests. But all he said was so prettily sedate, and the *naïveté* of his youthful egotism was so obvious, that he disarmed his hearers.

"Well, my boy, you'll get along wherever you go—foot or horse—that I'll warrant," said Shinshín, patting him on the shoulder and taking his feet off the sofa.

Berg smiled joyously. The count, followed by his guests, went into the drawing room.

It was just the moment before a big dinner when the assembled guests, expecting the summons to *zakúska,* avoid engaging in any long conversation but think it necessary to move about and talk, in order to show that they are not at all impatient for their food. The host and hostess look toward the door, and now and then glance at one another, and the visitors try to guess from these glances who, or what, they are waiting for—some important relation who has not yet arrived, or a dish that is not yet ready.

Pierre had come just at dinnertime, and was sitting awkwardly in the middle of the drawing room on the first chair he had come across, blocking the way for everyone. The countess tried to make him talk, but he went on naïvely looking around through his spectacles as if in search of somebody and answered all her questions in monosyllables. He was in the way and was the only one who did not notice the fact. Most of the guests, knowing of the affair with the bear, looked with curiosity at this big, stout, quiet man, wondering how such a clumsy, modest fellow could have played such a prank on a policeman.

"You have only lately arrived?" the countess asked him.

"*Oui, madame,*" replied he, looking around him.

"You have not yet seen my husband?"

"*Non, madame.*" He smiled quite inappropriately.

"You have been in Paris recently I believe? I suppose it's very interesting."

"Very interesting."

The countess exchanged glances with Anna Mikháylovna. The latter understood that she was being asked to entertain this young man, and sitting down beside him she began to speak about his father; but he answered her, as he had the countess, only in monosyllables. The other guests were all conversing with one another. "The Razumóvskis . . . It was charming . . . You are very kind . . . Countess Apráksina . . ." was heard on all sides. The countess rose and went into the ballroom.

"Márya Dmítrievna?" came her voice from there.

"Herself," came the answer in a rough voice, and Márya Dmítrievna entered the room.

All the unmarried ladies and even the married ones except the very oldest rose. Márya Dmítrievna paused at the door. Tall and stout, holding high her fifty-year-old head with its gray curls, she stood surveying the guests, and leisurely arranged her wide sleeves as if rolling them up. Márya Dmítrievna always spoke in Russian.

"Health and happiness to her whose name-day we are keeping and to her children," she said, in her loud, full-toned voice which drowned all others. "Well, you old sinner," she went on, turning to the count who was kissing her hand, "you're feeling dull in Moscow, I dare say? Nowhere to hunt with your dogs? But what is to be done, old man? Just see how these nestlings are growing up," and she pointed to the girls. "You must look for husbands for them whether you like it or not."

"Well," said she, "how's my Cossack?" (Márya Dmítrievna always called Natásha a Cossack) and she stroked the child's arm as she came up fearless and gay to kiss her hand. "I know she's a scamp of a girl, but I like her."

She took a pair of pear-shaped ruby earrings from her huge reticule, and having given them to the rosy Natásha, who beamed with the pleasure of her saint's-day fête, turned away at once and addressed herself to Pierre.

"Eh, eh, friend! Come here a bit," said she, assuming a soft high tone of voice. "Come here, my friend . . ." and she ominously tucked up her sleeves still higher. Pierre approached, looking at her in a childlike way through his spectacles.

"Come nearer, come nearer, friend! I used to be the only one to tell your father the truth when he was in favor, and in your case it's my evident duty."

She paused. All were silent, expectant of what was to follow, for this was clearly only a prelude.

"A fine lad! My word! A fine lad! . . . His father lies on his deathbed and he amuses himself setting a policeman astride a bear! For shame, sir, for shame! It would be better if you went to the war."

She turned away and gave her hand to the count, who could hardly keep from laughing.

"Well, I suppose it is time we were at table?" said Márya Dmítrievna.

The count went in first with Márya Dmítrievna, the countess followed on the arm of a colonel of hussars, a man of importance to them because Nicholas was to go with him to the regiment; then came Anna Mikháylovna with Shinshín. Berg gave his arm to Véra. The smiling Julie Karágina went in with Nicholas. After them other couples followed, filling the whole dining hall, and last of all the children, tutors and governesses followed singly. The footmen began moving about, chairs scraped, the band struck up in the gallery, and the guests settled down in their places. Then the strains of the count's household band were replaced by the clatter of knives and forks, the voices of visitors, and the soft steps of the footmen. At one end of the table sat the countess with Márya Dmítrievna on her right and Anna Mikháylovna on her left, the other lady visitors were farther down. At the other end sat the count, with the hussar colonel on his left and Shinshín and the other male visitors on his right. Midway down the long table on one side sat the grown-up young people: Véra beside Berg, and Pierre beside Borís; and on the other side, the children, tutors and governesses. From behind the crystal decanters and fruit-vases the count kept glancing at his wife and her tall cap with its light-blue ribbons, and busily filled his neighbors' glasses, not neglecting his own. The countess in turn, without omitting her duties as hostess, threw significant glances from behind the pineapples at her husband whose face and bald head seemed by their redness to contrast more than usual with his gray hair. At the ladies' end an even chatter of voices was heard all the time, at the men's end the voices sounded louder and louder, especially that of the colonel of hussars, who growing more and more flushed, ate and drank so much that the count held him up as a pattern to the other guests. Berg with tender smiles was saying to Véra that love is not an earthly but a heavenly feeling. Borís was telling his new friend Pierre who the guests were and exchanging glances with Natásha, who was sitting opposite. Pierre spoke little but examined the new faces, and ate a great deal. Of the two soups he chose turtle with savory patties and went on to the game without omitting a single dish or one of the wines. These latter the butler thrust mysteriously forward, wrapped in a napkin, from behind the next man's shoulders and whispered: "Dry madeira" . . . "Hungarian" . . . or "Rhine-wine" as the case might be. Of the four crystal glasses engraved with the count's monogram that stood before his plate, Pierre held out one at random and drank with enjoyment, gazing with ever-increasing amiability at the other guests. Natásha, who sat opposite, was looking at Borís as girls of thirteen look at the boy they are in love with and have just kissed for the first time. Sometimes that same look fell on Pierre, and that funny lively little girl's look made him inclined to laugh without knowing why.

Nicholas sat at some distance from Sónya, beside Julie Karágina, to whom he was again talking with the same involuntary smile. Sónya wore a company smile but was evidently tormented by jealousy; now she turned pale, now blushed and strained every nerve to overhear what Nicholas and

Julie were saying to one another. The governess kept looking round uneasily as if preparing to resent any slight that might be put upon the children. The German tutor was trying to remember all the dishes, wines and kinds of dessert, in order to send a full description of the dinner to his people in Germany; and he felt greatly offended when the butler with a bottle wrapped in a napkin passed him by. He frowned, trying to appear as if he did not want any of that wine, but was mortified because no one would understand that it was not to quench his thirst or from greediness that he wanted it, but simply from a conscientious desire for knowledge.

Chapter XIX

At the men's end of the table the talk grew more and more animated. The colonel told them that the declaration of war had already appeared in Petersburg and that a copy, which he had himself seen, had that day been forwarded by courier to the commander-in-chief.

"And why the deuce are we going to fight Bonaparte?" remarked Shinshín. "He has stopped Austria's cackle and I fear it will be our turn next."

The colonel was a stout, tall, plethoric German, evidently devoted to the service and patriotically Russian. He resented Shinshín's remark.

"It is for the reason, my goot sir," said he, speaking with a German accent, "for the reasson zat ze Emperor knows zat. He declares in ze manifessto zat he cannot fiew wiz indifference ze danger vreatening Russia and zat ze safety and dignity of ze Empire as vell as ze sanctity of its *alliances* . . ." he spoke this last word with particular emphasis as if in it lay the gist of the matter.

Then with the unerring official memory that characterized him he repeated from the opening words of the manifesto:

". . . and the wish, which constitutes the Emperor's sole and absolute aim—to establish peace in Europe on firm foundations—has now decided him to dispatch part of the army abroad and to create a new condition for the attainment of that purpose."

"Zat, my dear sir, is vy . . ." he concluded, drinking a tumbler of wine with dignity and looking to the count for approval.

"*Connaissez-vous le proverbe*: 'Jerome, Jerome, do not roam, but turn spindles at home!'?" said Shinshín, puckering his brows and smiling. "*Cela nous convient à merveille*. Suvórov now—he knew what he was about; yet they beat him *à plate couture*, and where are we to find Suvórovs now? *Je vous demande un peu,*" said he, continually changing from French to Russian.

"Ve must vight to the last tr-r-op of our plood!" said the colonel, thumping the table; "and ve must tie for our Emperor, and zen all vill pe vell. And ve must discuss it as little as po-o-ossible" . . . he dwelled particularly on the word *possible* . . . "as po-o-ossible," he ended, again turning to the count. "Zat is how ve old hussars look at it, and zere's an end of it! And how do you, a young man and a young hussar, how do you judge of it?" he added, addressing Nicholas, who when he heard that the war was being discussed had turned from his partner with eyes and ears intent on the colonel.

"I am quite of your opinion," replied Nicholas, flaming up, turning his plate round and moving his wine glasses about with as much decision and desperation as though he were at that moment facing some great danger. "I am convinced that we Russians must die or conquer," he concluded, conscious—as were others—after the words were uttered that his remarks were too enthusiastic and emphatic for the occasion and were therefore awkward.

"What you said just now was splendid!" said his partner Julie.

Sónya trembled all over and blushed to her ears and behind them and down to her neck and shoulders while Nicholas was speaking.

Pierre listened to the colonel's speech and nodded approvingly.

"That's fine," said he.

"The young man's a real hussar!" shouted the colonel, again thumping the table.

"What are you making such a noise about over there?" Márya Dmítrievna's deep voice suddenly inquired from the other end of the table. "What are you thumping the table for?" she demanded of the hussar, "and why are you exciting yourself? Do you think the French are here?"

"I am speaking ze truce," replied the hussar with a smile.

"It's all about the war," the count shouted down the table. "You know my son's going, Márya Dmítrievna? My son is going."

"I have four sons in the army but still I don't fret. It is all in God's hands. You may die in your bed or God may spare you in a battle," replied Márya Dmítrievna's deep voice, which easily carried the whole length of the table.

"That's true!"

Once more the conversations concentrated, the ladies' at the one end and the men's at the other.

"You won't ask," Natásha's little brother was saying; "I know you won't ask!"

"I will," replied Natásha.

Her face suddenly flushed with reckless and joyous resolution. She half rose, by a glance inviting Pierre, who sat opposite, to listen to what was coming, and turning to her mother:

"Mamma!" rang out the clear contralto notes of her childish voice, audible the whole length of the table.

"What is it?" asked the countess, startled; but seeing by her daughter's face that it was only mischief, she shook a finger at her sternly with a threatening and forbidding movement of her head.

The conversation was hushed.

"Mamma! What sweets are we going to have?" and Natásha's voice sounded still more firm and resolute.

The countess tried to frown, but could not. Márya Dmítrievna shook her fat finger.

"Cossack!" she said threateningly.

Most of the guests, uncertain how to regard this sally, looked at the elders.

"You had better take care!" said the countess.

"Mamma! What sweets are we going to have?" Natásha again cried boldly, with saucy gaiety, confident that her prank would be taken in good part.

Sónya and fat little Pétya doubled up with laughter.

"You see! I *have* asked," whispered Natásha to her little brother and to Pierre, glancing at him again.

"Ice pudding, but you won't get any," said Márya Dmítrievna.

Natásha saw there was nothing to be afraid of and so she braved even Márya Dmítrievna.

"Márya Dmítrievna! What kind of ice pudding? I don't like ice cream."

"Carrot-ices."

"No! What kind, Márya Dmítrievna? What kind?" she almost screamed; "I want to know!"

Márya Dmítrievna and the countess burst out laughing, and all the guests joined in. Everyone laughed, not at Márya Dmítrievna's answer but at the incredible boldness and smartness of this little girl who had dared to treat Márya Dmítrievna in this fashion.

Natásha only desisted when she had been told that there would be pineapple ice. Before the ices, champagne was served round. The band again struck up, the count and countess kissed, and the guests, leaving their seats, went up to "congratulate" the countess, and reached across the table to clink glasses with the count, with the children, and with one another. Again the footmen rushed about, chairs scraped, and in the same order in which they had entered but with redder faces, the guests returned to the drawing room and to the count's study.

Chapter XX

THE CARD-TABLES WERE DRAWN OUT, SETS MADE UP FOR BOSTON, AND THE COUNT'S VISITORS settled themselves, some in the two drawing rooms, some in the sitting room, some in the library.

The count, holding his cards fanwise, kept himself with difficulty from dropping into his usual after-dinner nap, and laughed at everything. The young people, at the countess's instigation, gathered round the clavichord and harp. Julie by general request played first. After she had played a little air with variations on the harp, she joined the other young ladies in begging Natásha and Nicholas, who were noted for their musical talent, to sing something. Natásha, who was treated as though she were grown up, was evidently very proud of this but at the same time felt shy.

"What shall we sing?" she said.

" 'The Brook,' " suggested Nicholas.

"Well, then, let's be quick. Borís, come here," said Natásha. "But where is Sónya?"

She looked round and seeing that her friend was not in the room ran to look for her.

Running into Sónya's room and not finding her there, Natásha ran to the nursery, but Sónya was not there either. Natásha concluded that she must be on the chest in the passage. The chest in the passage was the place of mourning for the younger female generation in the Rostóv household. And there in fact was Sónya lying face downward on Nurse's dirty feather-bed on the top of the chest, crumpling her gauzy pink dress under her, hiding her face with her slender fingers, and sobbing so convulsively that her bare little shoulders shook. Natásha's face which had been so radiantly happy all that saint's-day, suddenly changed: her eyes became fixed, and then a shiver passed down her broad neck and the corners of her mouth drooped.

"Sónya! What is it? What is the matter? . . . Oo . . . Oo . . . Oo . . . !" And Natásha's large mouth widened, making her look quite ugly, and she began to wail like a baby without knowing why, except that Sónya was crying. Sónya tried to lift her head to answer but could not, and hid her face still deeper in the bed. Natásha wept, sitting on the blue-striped feather-bed and hugging her friend. With an effort Sónya sat up and began wiping her eyes and explaining.

"Nicholas is going away in a week's time, his . . . papers . . . have come . . . he told me himself . . . but still I should not cry," and she showed a paper she held in her hand—with the verses Nicholas had written, "still, I should not cry, but you can't . . . no one can understand . . . what a soul he has!"

And she began to cry again because he had such a noble soul.

"It's all very well for you . . . I am not envious . . . I love you and Borís also," she went on, gaining a little strength; "he is nice . . . there are no difficulties in your way. . . . But Nicholas is my cousin . . . one would have to . . . the Metropolitan himself . . . and even then it can't be done. And besides, if she tells Mamma" (Sónya looked upon the countess as her mother and called her so) "that I am spoiling Nicholas's career and am heartless and ungrateful, while truly . . . God is my witness," and she made the sign of the cross, "I love her so much, and all of you, only Véra . . . And what for? What have I done to her? I am so grateful to you that I would willingly sacrifice everything, only I have nothing. . . ."

Sónya could not continue, and again hid her face in her hands and in the feather-bed. Natásha began consoling her, but her face showed that she understood all the gravity of her friend's trouble.

"Sónya," she suddenly exclaimed, as if she had guessed the true reason of her friend's sorrow, "I'm sure Véra has said something to you since dinner? Hasn't she?"

"Yes, these verses Nicholas wrote himself and I copied some others, and she found them on my table and said she'd show them to Mamma, and that I was ungrateful, and that Mamma would never allow him to marry me, but that he'll marry Julie. You see how he's been with her all day . . . Natásha, what have I done to deserve it? . . ."

And again she began to sob, more bitterly than before. Natásha lifted her up, hugged her, and smiling through her tears, began comforting her.

"Sónya, don't believe her, darling! Don't believe her! Do you remember how we and Nicholas, all three of us, talked in the sitting room after supper? Why, we settled how everything was to be. I don't quite remember how, but don't you remember that it could all be arranged and how nice it all was? There's Uncle Shinshín's brother has married his first cousin? And we are only second cousins, you know. And Borís says it is quite possible. You know I have told him all about it. And he is so clever and so good!" said Natásha. "Don't you cry, Sónya, dear love, darling Sónya!" and she kissed her and laughed. "Véra's spiteful; never mind her! And all will come right and she won't say anything to Mamma. Nicholas will tell her himself, and he doesn't care at all for Julie."

Natásha kissed her on the hair.

Sónya sat up. The little kitten brightened, its eyes shone, and it seemed ready to lift its tail, jump down on its soft paws, and begin playing with the ball of worsted as a kitten should.

"Do you think so? . . . Really? Truly?" she said, quickly smoothing her frock and hair.

"Really, truly!" answered Natásha, pushing in a crisp lock that had strayed from under her friend's plaits.

Both laughed.

"Well, let's go and sing 'The Brook.' "

"Come along!"

"Do you know, that fat Pierre who sat opposite me is so funny!" said Natásha, stopping suddenly. "I feel so happy!"

And she set off at a run along the passage.

Sónya, shaking off some down which clung to her and tucking away the verses in the bosom of her dress close to her bony little chest, ran after Natásha down the passage into the sitting room with flushed face and light, joyous steps. At the visitors' request the young people sang the quartette, "The Brook," with which everyone was delighted. Then Nicholas sang a song he had just learned:

"At night time in the moon's fair glow
How sweet, as fancies wander free,
To feel that in this world there's one
Who still is thinking but of thee!

That while her fingers touch the harp
Wafting sweet music o'er the lea,
It is for thee thus swells her heart,
Sighing its message out to thee. . . .

A day, or two, then bliss unspoilt,
But oh! till then I cannot live! . . ."

He had not finished the last verse before the young people began to get ready to dance in the large hall, and the sound of the feet and the coughing of the musicians were heard from the gallery.

Pierre was sitting in the drawing room where Shinshín had engaged him, as a man recently returned from abroad, in a political conversation in which several others joined but which bored Pierre. When the music began Natásha came in and walking straight up to Pierre said, laughing and blushing:

"Mamma told me to ask you to join the dancers."

"I am afraid of mixing the figures," Pierre replied; "but if you will be my teacher . . ." And lowering his big arm he offered it to the slender little girl.

While the couples were arranging themselves and the musicians tuning up, Pierre sat down with his little partner. Natásha was perfectly happy; she was dancing with a *grown-up* man, who had been *abroad*. She was sitting in a conspicuous place and talking to him like a grown-up lady. She had a fan in her hand that one of the ladies had given her to hold. Assuming quite the pose of a society woman (heaven knows when and where she had learned it) she talked with her partner, fanning herself and smiling over the fan.

"Dear, dear! Just look at her!" exclaimed the countess as she crossed the ballroom, pointing to Natásha.

Natásha blushed and laughed.

"Well, really, Mamma! Why should you? What is there to be surprised at?"

In the midst of the third *écossaise* there was a clatter of chairs being pushed back in the sitting room where the count and Márya Dmítrievna had been playing cards with the majority of the more distinguished and older visitors. They now, stretching themselves after sitting so long, and replacing their purses and pocketbooks, entered the ballroom. First came Márya Dmítrievna and the count, both with merry countenances. The count, with playful ceremony somewhat in *ballet* style, offered his bent arm to Márya Dmítrievna. He drew himself up, a smile of debonair gallantry lit up his face, and as soon as the last figure of the *écossaise* was ended, he clapped his hands to the musicians and shouted up to their gallery, addressing the first violin:

"Simën! Do you know the *Daniel Cooper?*"

This was the count's favorite dance, which he had danced in his youth. (Strictly speaking, *Daniel Cooper* was one figure of the *anglaise.*)

"Look at Papa!" shouted Natásha to the whole company, and quite forgetting that she was dancing with a grown-up partner she bent her curly head to her knees and made the whole room ring with her laughter.

And indeed everybody in the room looked with a smile of pleasure at the jovial old gentleman, who standing beside his tall and stout partner, Márya Dmítrievna, curved his arms, beat time, straightened his shoulders, turned out his toes, tapped gently with his foot, and by a smile that broadened his round face more and more, prepared the onlookers for what was to follow. As soon as the provocatively gay strains of *Daniel Cooper* (somewhat resembling those of a merry peasant dance) began to sound, all the doorways of the ballroom were suddenly filled by the domestic serfs—the men on one side and the women on the other—who with beaming faces had come to see their master making merry.

"Just look at the master! A regular eagle he is!" loudly remarked the nurse, as she stood in one of the doorways.

The count danced well and knew it. But his partner could not and did not want to dance well. Her enormous figure stood erect, her powerful arms hanging down (she had handed her reticule to the countess), and only her stern but handsome face really joined in the dance. What was expressed by the whole of the count's plump figure, in Márya Dmítrievna found expression only in her more and more beaming face and quivering nose. But if the count, getting more and more into the swing of it, charmed the spectators by the unexpectedness of his adroit maneuvers and the agility with which he capered about on his light feet, Márya Dmítrievna produced no less impression by slight exertions—the least effort to move her shoulders or bend her arms when turning, or stamp her foot—which everyone appreciated in view of her size and habitual severity. The dance grew livelier and livelier. The other couples could not attract a moment's attention to their own evolutions and did not even try to do so. All were watching the count and Márya Dmítrievna. Natásha kept pulling everyone by sleeve or dress, urging them to "look at Papa!" though as it was they never took their eyes off the couple. In the intervals of the dance the count, breathing deeply, waved and shouted to the musicians to play faster. Faster, faster and faster; lightly, more lightly and yet more lightly whirled the count, flying round Márya Dmítrievna, now on his toes, now on his heels; until, turning his partner round to her seat, he executed the final *pas,* raising his soft foot backward, bowing his perspiring head, smiling and making a wide sweep with his arm, amid a thunder of applause and laughter led by Natásha. Both partners stood still, breathing heavily and wiping their faces with their cambric handkerchiefs.

"That's how we used to dance in our time, *ma chère,*" said the count.

"That *was* a *Daniel Cooper!*" exclaimed Márya Dmítrievna, tucking up her sleeves and puffing heavily.

Chapter XXI

WHILE IN THE ROSTÓVS' BALLROOM THE SIXTH ANGLAISE WAS BEING DANCED, TO A TUNE IN which the weary musicians blundered, and while tired footmen and cooks were getting the supper, Count Bezúkhov had a sixth stroke. The doctors pronounced recovery impossible. After a mute confession, Communion was administered to the dying man, preparations made for the sacrament of Unction, and in his house there was the bustle and thrill of suspense usual at such moments. Outside the house, beyond the gates, a group of undertakers, who hid whenever a carriage drove up, waited in expectation of an important order for an expensive funeral. The Military Governor of Moscow, who had been assiduous in sending aides-de-camp to inquire after the count's health, came himself that evening to bid a last farewell to the celebrated grandee of Catherine's court, Count Bezúkhov.

The magnificent reception room was crowded. Everyone stood up respectfully when the Military Governor, having stayed about half an hour alone with the dying man, passed out, slightly acknowledging their bows and trying to escape as quickly as from the glances fixed on him by the doctors, clergy and relatives of the family. Prince Vasíli, who had grown thinner and paler during the last few days, escorted him to the door, repeating something to him several times in low tones.

When the Military Governor had gone, Prince Vasíli sat down all alone on a chair in the ballroom, crossing one leg high over the other, leaning his elbow on his knee and covering his face with his hand. After sitting so for a while he rose, and, looking about him with frightened eyes, went with unusually hurried steps down the long corridor leading to the back of the house, to the room of the eldest princess.

Those who were in the dimly-lit reception room spoke in nervous whispers, and whenever anyone went into or came from the dying man's room, grew silent and gazed with eyes full of curiosity or expectancy at his door, which creaked slightly when opened.

"The limits of human life . . . are fixed and may not be o'er-passed," said an old priest to a lady who had taken a seat beside him and was listening naïvely to his words.

"I wonder, is it not too late to administer Unction?" asked the lady, adding the priest's clerical title, as if she had no opinion of her own on the subject.

"Ah, madam, it is a great sacrament," replied the priest, passing his hand over the thin grizzled strands of hair combed back across his bald head.

"Who was that? The Military Governor himself?" was being asked at the other side of the room. "How young-looking he is!"

"Yes, and he is over sixty. I hear the count no longer recognizes anyone? They wished to administer the sacrament of Unction."

"I knew someone who received that sacrament seven times."

The second princess had just come from the sick room with her eyes red from weeping and sat down beside Doctor Lorrain, who was sitting in a graceful pose under a portrait of Catherine, leaning his elbow on a table.

"Beautiful," said the doctor in answer to a remark about the weather. "The weather is beautiful, princess; and besides, in Moscow one feels as if one were in the country."

"Yes, indeed," replied the princess with a sigh. "So he may have something to drink?"

Lorrain considered.

"Has he taken his medicine?"

"Yes."

The doctor glanced at his watch.

"Take a glass of boiled water and put in a pinch of cream of tartar," and he indicated with his delicate fingers what he meant by a pinch.

"Dere has neffer been a gase," a German doctor was saying to an aide-de-camp, "dat one liffs after de sird sdroke."

"And what a well-preserved man he was!" remarked the aide-de-camp. "And who will inherit his wealth?" he added in a whisper.

"It von't go begging," replied the German with a smile.

Everyone again looked toward the door, which creaked as the second princess went in with the drink she had prepared according to Lorrain's instructions. The German doctor went up to Lorrain.

"Do you think he can last till morning?" asked the German, addressing Lorrain in French which he pronounced badly.

Lorrain, pursing up his lips, waved a severely negative finger before his nose.

"Tonight, not later," said he in a low voice, and he moved away with a decorous smile of self-satisfaction at being able clearly to understand and state the patient's condition.

Meanwhile Prince Vasíli had opened the door into the princess's room.

In this room it was almost dark; only two tiny lamps were burning before the icons and there was a pleasant scent of flowers and burned pastilles. The room was crowded with small pieces of furniture, whatnots, cupboards and little tables. The quilt of a high, white feather-bed was just visible behind a screen. A small dog began to bark.

"Ah, is it you, cousin?"

She rose and smoothed her hair, which was as usual so extremely smooth that it seemed to be made of one piece with her head and covered with varnish.

"Has anything happened?" she asked. "I am so terrified."

"No, there is no change. I only came to have a talk about business, Catiche," muttered the prince, seating himself wearily on the chair she had just vacated. "You have made the place warm, I must say," he remarked. "Well, sit down: let's have a talk."

"I thought perhaps something had happened," she said with her unchanging stonily severe expression; and, sitting down opposite the prince, she prepared to listen.

"I wished to get a nap, *mon cousin,* but I can't."

"Well, my dear?" said Prince Vasíli, taking her hand and bending it downward as was his habit.

It was plain that this "well?" referred to much that they both understood without naming.

The princess, who had a straight, rigid body, abnormally long for her legs, looked directly at Prince Vasíli with no sign of emotion in her prominent gray eyes. Then she shook her head and glanced up at the icons with a sigh. This might have been taken as an expression of sorrow and devotion, or of weariness and hope of resting before long. Prince Vasíli understood it as an expression of weariness.

"And I?" he said; "do you think it is easier for me? I am as worn out as a post-horse, but still I must have a talk with you, Catiche, a very serious talk."

Prince Vasíli said no more and his cheeks began to twitch nervously, now on one side, now on the other, giving his face an unpleasant expression which was never to be seen on it in a drawing room. His eyes too seemed strange; at one moment they looked impudently sly and at the next glanced round in alarm.

The princess, holding her little dog on her lap with her thin bony hands, looked attentively into Prince Vasíli's eyes evidently resolved not to be the first to break silence, if she had to wait till morning.

"Well, you see, my dear princess and cousin, Catherine Semënovna," continued Prince Vasíli, returning to his theme, apparently not without an inner struggle; "at such a moment as this one must think of everything. One must think of the future, of all of you . . . I love you all, like children of my own, as you know."

The princess continued to look at him without moving, and with the same dull expression.

"And then of course my family has also to be considered," Prince Vasíli went on, testily pushing away a little table without looking at her. "You know, Catiche, that we—you three sisters, Mámontov, and my wife—are the count's only direct heirs. I know, I know how hard it is for you to talk or think of such matters. It is no easier for me; but, my dear, I am getting on for sixty and must be prepared for anything. Do you know I have sent for Pierre? The count," pointing to his portrait, "definitely demanded that he should be called."

Prince Vasíli looked questioningly at the princess, but could not make out whether she was considering what he had just said or whether she was simply looking at him.

"There is one thing I constantly pray God to grant, *mon cousin*," she replied, "and it is that He would be merciful to him and would allow his noble soul peacefully to leave this . . ."

"Yes, yes, of course," interrupted Prince Vasíli impatiently, rubbing his bald head and angrily pulling back toward him the little table that he had pushed away. "But . . . in short, the fact is . . . you know yourself that last winter the count made a will by which he left all his property, not to us his direct heirs, but to Pierre."

"He has made wills enough!" quietly remarked the princess. "But he cannot leave the estate to Pierre. Pierre is illegitimate."

"But, my dear," said Prince Vasíli suddenly, clutching the little table and becoming more animated and talking more rapidly: "what if a letter has been written to the Emperor in which the count asks for Pierre's legitimation? Do you understand that in consideration of the count's services, his request would be granted? . . ."

The princess smiled as people do who think they know more about the subject under discussion than those they are talking with.

"I can tell you more," continued Prince Vasíli, seizing her hand, "that letter was written, though it was not sent, and the Emperor knew of it. The only question is, has it been destroyed or not? If not, then as soon as *all is over*," and Prince Vasíli sighed to intimate what he meant by the words *all is over*, "and the count's papers are opened, the will and letter will be delivered to the Emperor, and the petition will certainly be granted. Pierre will get everything as the legitimate son."

"And our share?" asked the princess smiling ironically, as if anything might happen, only not that.

"But, my poor Catiche, it is as clear as daylight! He will then be the legal heir to everything and you won't get anything. You must know, my dear, whether the will and letter were written, and whether they have been destroyed or not. And if they have somehow been overlooked, you ought to know where they are, and must find them, because . . ."

"What next?" the princess interrupted, smiling sardonically and not changing the expression of her eyes. "I'm a woman, and you think we are all stupid; but I know this: an illegitimate son cannot inherit . . . *un bâtard!*" she added, as if supposing that this translation of the word would effectively prove to Prince Vasíli the invalidity of his contention.

"Well, really, Catiche! Can't you understand! You are so intelligent, how is it you don't see that if the count has written a letter to the Emperor begging him to recognize Pierre as legitimate, it follows that Pierre will not be Pierre but will become Count Bezúkhov, and will then inherit everything under the will? And if the will and letter are not destroyed, then you will have nothing but the consolation of having been dutiful *et tout ce qui s'ensuit!* That's certain."

"I know the will was made, but I also know that it is invalid; and you, *mon cousin,* seem to consider me a perfect fool," said the princess with the expression women assume when they suppose they are saying something witty and stinging.

"My dear Princess Catherine Semënovna," began Prince Vasíli impatiently, "I came here not to wrangle with you, but to talk about your interests as with a kinswoman, a good, kind, true relation. And I tell you for the tenth time, that if the letter to the Emperor and the will in Pierre's favor are among the count's papers, then, my dear girl, you and your sisters are not heiresses! If you don't believe me, then believe an expert. I have just been talking to Dmítri Onúfrich" (the family solicitor) "and he says the same."

At this a sudden change evidently took place in the princess's ideas; her thin lips grew white, though her eyes did not change, and her voice when she began to speak passed through such transitions as she herself evidently did not expect.

"That would be a fine thing!" said she. "I never wanted anything and I don't now."

She pushed the little dog off her lap and smoothed her dress.

"And this is gratitude—this is recognition for those who have sacrificed everything for his sake!" she cried. "It's splendid! Fine! I don't want anything, prince."

"Yes, but you are not the only one. There are your sisters . . ." replied Prince Vasíli.

But the princess did not listen to him.

"Yes, I knew it long ago but had forgotten. I knew that I could expect nothing but meanness, deceit, envy, intrigue, and ingratitude—the blackest ingratitude—in this house . . ."

"Do you or do you not know where that will is?" insisted Prince Vasíli, his cheeks twitching more than ever.

"Yes, I was a fool! I still believed in people, loved them, and sacrificed myself. But only the base, the vile succeed! I know who has been intriguing!"

The princess wished to rise, but the prince held her by the hand. She had the air of one who has suddenly lost faith in the whole human race. She gave her companion an angry glance.

"There is still time, my dear. You must remember, Catiche, that it was all done casually in a moment of anger, of illness, and was afterward forgotten. Our duty, my dear, is to rectify his mistake, to ease his last moments by not letting him commit this injustice, and not to let him die feeling that he is rendering unhappy those who . . ."

"Who sacrificed everything for him," chimed in the princess, who would again have risen had not the prince still held her fast, "though he never could appreciate it. No, *mon cousin,*" she added with a sigh, "I shall always remember that in this world one must expect no reward, that in this world there is neither honor nor justice. In this world one has to be cunning and cruel."

"Now come, come! Be reasonable. I know your excellent heart."

"No, I have a wicked heart."

"I know your heart," repeated the prince. "I value your friendship and wish you to have as good an opinion of me. Don't upset yourself, and let us talk sensibly while there is still time, be it a day or be it but an hour. . . . Tell me all you know about the will, and above all where it is. You must know. We will take it at once and show it to the count. He has, no doubt forgotten it and will wish to destroy it. You understand that my sole desire is conscientiously to carry out his wishes; that is my only reason for being here. I came simply to help him and you."

"Now I see it all! I know who has been intriguing—I know!" cried the princess.

"That's not the point, my dear."

"It's that protégé of yours, that sweet Princess Drubetskáya, that Anna Mikháylovna whom I would not take for a housemaid . . . the infamous, vile woman!"

"Do not let us lose any time . . ."

"Ah, don't talk to me! Last winter she wheedled herself in here and told the count such vile, disgraceful things about us, especially about Sophie—I can't repeat them—that it made the count quite ill and he would not see us for a whole fortnight. I know it was then he wrote this vile, infamous paper, but I thought the thing was invalid."

"We've got to it at last—why did you not tell me about it sooner?"

"It's in the inlaid portfolio that he keeps under his pillow," said the princess, ignoring his question. "Now I know! Yes; if I have a sin, a great sin, it is hatred of that vile woman!" almost shrieked the princess, now quite changed. "And what does she come worming herself in here for? But I will give her a piece of my mind. The time will come!"

Chapter XXII

While these conversations were going on in the reception room and the princess's room, a carriage containing Pierre (who had been sent for) and Anna Mikháylovna (who found it necessary to accompany him) was driving into the court of Count Bezúkhov's house. As the wheels rolled softly over the straw beneath the windows, Anna Mikháylovna, having turned with words of comfort to her companion realized that he was asleep in his corner and woke him up. Rousing himself, Pierre followed Anna Mikháylovna out of the carriage, and only then began to think of the interview with his dying father which awaited him. He noticed that they had not come to the front entrance but to the back door. While he was getting down from the carriage steps two men, who looked like tradespeople, ran hurriedly from the entrance and hid in the shadow of the wall. Pausing for a moment, Pierre noticed several other men of the same kind hiding in the shadow of the house on both sides. But neither Anna Mikháylovna nor the footman nor the coachman, who could not help seeing these people, took any notice of them. "It seems to be all right," Pierre concluded, and followed Anna Mikháylovna. She hurriedly ascended the narrow dimly-lit stone staircase, calling to Pierre, who was lagging behind, to follow. Though he did not see why it was necessary for him to go to the count at all, still less why he had to go by the back stairs, yet judging by Anna Mikháylovna's air of assurance and haste, Pierre concluded that it was all absolutely necessary. Halfway up the stairs they were almost knocked over by some men who, carrying pails, came running downstairs, their boots clattering. These men pressed close to the wall to let Pierre and Anna Mikháylovna pass and did not evince the least surprise at seeing them there.

"Is this the way to the princesses' apartments?" asked Anna Mikháylovna of one of them.

"Yes," replied a footman in a bold loud voice, as if anything were now permissible; "the door to the left, ma'am."

"Perhaps the count did not ask for me," said Pierre when he reached the landing. "I'd better go to my own room."

Anna Mikháylovna paused and waited for him to come up.

"Ah, my friend!" she said, touching his arm as she had done her son's when speaking to him that afternoon, "believe me I suffer no less than you do, but be a man!"

"But really, hadn't I better go away?" he asked, looking kindly at her over his spectacles.

"Ah, my dear friend! Forget the wrongs that may have been done you. Think that he is your father . . . perhaps in the agony of death." She sighed. "I have loved you like a son from the first. Trust yourself to me, Pierre. I shall not forget your interests."

Pierre did not understand a word, but the conviction that all this had to be grew stronger, and he meekly followed Anna Mikháylovna who was already opening a door.

This door led into a back anteroom. An old man, a servant of the princesses, sat in a corner knitting a stocking. Pierre had never been in this part of the house and did not even know of the existence of these rooms. Anna Mikháylovna, addressing a maid who was hurrying past with a decanter on a tray as "my dear" and "my sweet," asked about the princesses' health and then led Pierre along a stone passage. The first door on the left led into the princesses' apartments. The maid with the decanter in her haste had not closed the door (everything in the house was done in haste at that time) and Pierre and Anna Mikháylovna in passing instinctively glanced into the room, where Prince Vasíli and the eldest princess were sitting close together talking. Seeing them pass, Prince Vasíli drew back with obvious impatience, while the princess jumped up and with a gesture of desperation slammed the door with all her might.

This action was so unlike her usual composure and the fear depicted on Prince Vasíli's face so out of keeping with his dignity that Pierre stopped and glanced inquiringly over his spectacles at his guide. Anna Mikháylovna evinced no surprise, she only smiled faintly and sighed, as if to say that this was no more than she had expected.

"Be a man, my friend. I will look after your interests," said she in reply to his look, and went still faster along the passage.

Pierre could not make out what it was all about, and still less what "watching over his interests" meant, but he decided that all these things had to be. From the passage they went into a large dimly-lit room adjoining the count's reception room. It was one of those sumptuous but cold apartments known to Pierre only from the front approach, but even in this room there now stood an empty bath, and water had been spilled on the carpet. They were met by a deacon with a censer and by a servant who passed out on tiptoe without heeding them. They went into the reception room familiar to Pierre, with two Italian windows opening into the conservatory, with its large bust and full-length portrait of Catherine the Great. The same people were still sitting here in almost the same positions as before, whispering to one another. All became silent and turned to look at the pale tear-worn Anna Mikháylovna as she entered, and at the big stout figure of Pierre who, hanging his head, meekly followed her.

Anna Mikháylovna's face expressed a consciousness that the decisive moment had arrived. With the air of a practical Petersburg lady she now, keeping Pierre close beside her, entered the room even more boldly than that afternoon. She felt that as she brought with her the person the dying man wished to see, her own admission was assured. Casting a rapid glance at all those in the room and noticing the count's confessor there, she glided up to him with a sort of amble, not exactly bowing, yet seeming to grow suddenly smaller, and respectfully received the blessing first of one and then of another priest.

"God be thanked that you are in time," said she to one of the priests; "all we relatives have been in such anxiety. This young man is the count's son," she added more softly. "What a terrible moment!"

Having said this she went up to the doctor.

"Dear doctor," said she, "this young man is the count's son. Is there any hope?"

The doctor cast a rapid glance upward and silently shrugged his shoulders. Anna Mikháylovna with just the same movement raised her shoulders and eyes, almost closing the latter, sighed and moved away from the doctor to Pierre. To him, in a particularly respectful and tenderly sad voice, she said:

"Trust in His mercy!" and pointing out a small sofa for him to sit and wait for her, she went silently toward the door that everyone was watching and it creaked very slightly as she disappeared behind it.

Pierre having made up his mind to obey his monitress implicitly, moved toward the sofa she had indicated. As soon as Anna Mikháylovna had disappeared he noticed that the eyes of all in the room turned to him with something more than curiosity and sympathy. He noticed that they whispered to one another, casting significant looks at him with a kind of awe and even servility. A deference such as he had never before received was shown him. A strange lady, the one who had been talking to the priests, rose and offered him her seat; an aide-de-camp picked up and returned a glove Pierre had dropped; the doctors became respectfully silent as he passed by, and moved to make way for him. At first Pierre wished to take another seat so as not to trouble the lady, and also to pick up the glove himself and to pass round the doctors who were not even in his way; but all at once he felt that this would not do, and that tonight he was a person obliged to perform some sort of awful rite which everyone expected of him, and that he was therefore bound to accept their services. He took the glove in silence from the aide-de-camp, and sat down in the lady's chair, placing his huge hands symmetrically on his knees in the naïve attitude of an Egyptian statue, and decided in his own mind that all was as it should be, and that in order not to lose his head and do foolish things he must not act on his own ideas tonight, but must yield himself up entirely to the will of those who were guiding him.

Not two minutes had passed before Prince Vasíli with head erect majestically entered the room. He was wearing his long coat with three stars on his breast. He seemed to have grown thinner since the morning; his eyes seemed larger than usual when he glanced round and noticed Pierre. He went up to him, took his hand (a thing he never used to do) and drew it downward as if wishing to ascertain whether it was firmly fixed on.

"Courage, courage, my friend! He has asked to see you. That is well!" and he turned to go.

But Pierre thought it necessary to ask: "How is . . ." and hesitated, not knowing whether it would be proper to call the dying man "the count," yet ashamed to call him "father."

"He had another stroke about half an hour ago. Courage, my friend . . ."

Pierre's mind was in such a confused state that the word "stroke" suggested to him a blow from something. He looked at Prince Vasíli in perplexity, and only later grasped that a stroke was an attack of illness. Prince Vasíli said something to Lorrain in passing and went through the door on tiptoe. He could not walk well on tiptoe and his whole body jerked at each step. The eldest princess followed him, and the priests and deacons and some servants also went in at the door. Through that door was heard a noise of things being moved about, and at last Anna Mikháylovna, still with the same expression, pale but resolute in the discharge of duty, ran out and touching Pierre lightly on the arm said:

"The divine mercy is inexhaustible! Unction is about to be administered. Come."

Pierre went in at the door, stepping on the soft carpet, and noticed that the strange lady, the aide-de-camp, and some of the servants, all followed him in, as if there were now no further need for permission to enter that room.

Chapter XXIII

PIERRE WELL KNEW THIS LARGE ROOM DIVIDED BY COLUMNS AND AN ARCH, ITS WALLS HUNG round with Persian carpets. The part of the room behind the columns, with a high silk-curtained mahogany bedstead on one side and on the other an immense case containing icons, was brightly illuminated with red light like a Russian church during evening service. Under the gleaming icons stood a long invalid chair, and in that chair on snowy white smooth pillows, evidently freshly changed, Pierre saw—covered to the waist by a bright green quilt—the familiar, majestic figure of his father, Count Bezúkhov, with that gray mane of hair above his broad forehead which reminded one of a lion, and the deep characteristically noble wrinkles of his handsome, ruddy face. He lay just under the icons; his large thick hands outside the quilt. Into the right hand, which was lying palm downward, a wax taper had been thrust between forefinger and thumb, and an old servant, bending over from behind the chair, held it in position. By the chair stood the priests, their long hair falling over their magnificent glittering vestments, with lit tapers in their hands, slowly and solemnly conducting the service. A little behind them stood the two younger princesses holding handkerchiefs to their eyes, and just in front of them their eldest sister, Catiche, with a vicious and determined look steadily fixed on the icons, as though declaring to all that she could not answer for herself should she glance round. Anna Mikháylovna, with a meek, sorrowful and all-forgiving expression on her face, stood by the door near the strange lady. Prince Vasíli in front of the door, near the invalid chair, a wax taper in his left hand, was leaning his left arm on the carved back of a velvet chair he had turned round for the purpose, and was crossing himself with his right hand, turning his eyes upward each time he touched his forehead. His face wore a calm look of piety and resignation to the will of God. "If you do not understand these sentiments," he seemed to be saying, "so much the worse for you!"

Behind him stood the aide-de-camp, the doctors, and the menservants; the men and women had separated as in church. All were silently crossing themselves, and the reading of the church service, the subdued chanting of deep bass voices, and in the intervals sighs and the shuffling of feet, were the only sounds that could be heard. Anna Mikháylovna, with an air of importance that showed that she felt she quite knew what she was about, went across the room to where Pierre was standing and gave him a taper. He lit it and, distracted by observing those around him, began crossing himself with the hand that held the taper.

Sophie, the rosy, laughter-loving, youngest princess with the mole, watched him. She smiled, hid her face in her handkerchief, and remained with it hidden for awhile; then looking up and seeing Pierre she again began to laugh. She evidently felt unable to look at him without laughing, but could not resist looking at him: so to be out of temptation she slipped quietly behind one of the columns. In the midst of the service the voices of the priests suddenly ceased, they whispered to one another, and the old servant who was holding the count's hand got up and said something to the ladies. Anna Mikháylovna stepped forward and, stooping over the dying man, beckoned to Lorrain from behind her back. The French doctor held no taper; he was leaning against one of the columns in a respectful attitude implying that he, a foreigner, in spite of all differences of faith, understood the full importance of the rite now being performed and even approved of it. He now approached the sick man with the noiseless step of one in full vigor of life, with his delicate white fingers raised from the green quilt the hand that was free, and turning sideways felt the pulse and reflected a moment. The sick man was given something to drink, there was a stir around him, then the people resumed their places and the service continued. During this interval Pierre noticed that Prince Vasíli left the chair on which he had been leaning, and—with air which intimated that he knew what he was about and if others did not understand him it was so much the worse for them—did not go up to the dying man, but passed by him, joined the eldest princess, and moved with her to the side of the room where stood the high bedstead with its silken hangings. On leaving the bed both Prince Vasíli and the princess passed out by a back door, but returned to their places one after the other before the service was concluded. Pierre paid no more attention to this occurrence than to the rest of what went on, having made up his mind once for all that what he saw happening around him that evening was in some way essential.

The chanting of the service ceased, and the voice of the priest was heard respectfully congratulating the dying man on having received the sacrament. The dying man lay as lifeless and immovable as before. Around him everyone began to stir: steps were audible and whispers, among which Anna Mikháylovna's was the most distinct.

Pierre heard her say:

"Certainly he must be moved onto the bed; here it will be impossible . . ."

The sick man was so surrounded by doctors, princesses, and servants, that Pierre could no longer see the reddish-yellow face with its gray mane—which, though he saw other faces as well, he had not lost sight of for a single moment during the whole service. He judged by the cautious movements of those who crowded round the invalid chair that they had lifted the dying man and were moving him.

"Catch hold of my arm or you'll drop him!" he heard one of the servants say in a frightened whisper. "Catch hold from underneath. Here!" exclaimed different voices; and the heavy breathing of the bearers and the shuffling of their feet grew more hurried, as if the weight they were carrying were too much for them.

As the bearers, among whom was Anna Mikháylovna, passed the young man he caught a momentary glimpse between their heads and backs of the dying man's high, stout, uncovered chest and powerful shoulders, raised by those who were holding him under the armpits, and of his gray, curly, leonine head. This head, with its remarkably broad brow and cheekbones, its handsome, sensual mouth, and its cold, majestic expression, was not disfigured by the approach of death. It was the same as Pierre remembered it three months before, when the count had sent him to Petersburg. But now this head was swaying helplessly with the uneven movements of the bearers, and the cold listless gaze fixed itself upon nothing.

After a few minutes' bustle beside the high bedstead, those who had carried the sick man dispersed. Anna Mikháylovna touched Pierre's hand and said "Come." Pierre went with her to the bed on which the sick man had been laid in a stately pose in keeping with the ceremony just completed. He lay with his head propped high on the pillows. His hands were symmetrically placed on the green silk quilt, the palms downward. When Pierre came up the count was gazing straight at him, but with a look the significance of which could not be understood by mortal man. Either this look meant nothing but that as long as one has eyes they must look somewhere, or it meant too much. Pierre hesitated, not knowing what to do, and glanced inquiringly at his guide. Anna Mikháylovna made a hurried sign with her eyes, glancing at the sick man's hand and moving her lips as if to send it a kiss. Pierre carefully stretching his neck so as not to touch the quilt, followed her suggestion and pressed his lips to the large-boned, fleshy hand. Neither the hand nor a single muscle of the count's face stirred. Once more Pierre looked questioningly at Anna Mikháylovna to see what he was to do next. Anna Mikháylovna with her eyes indicated a chair that stood beside the bed. Pierre obediently sat down, his eyes asking if he were doing right. Anna Mikháylovna nodded approvingly. Again Pierre fell into the naïvely symmetrical pose of an Egyptian statue, evidently distressed that his stout and clumsy body took up so much room and doing his utmost to look as small as possible. He looked at the count, who still gazed at the spot where Pierre's face had been before he sat down. Anna Mikháylovna indicated by her attitude her consciousness of the pathetic importance of these last moments of meeting between the father and son. This lasted about two minutes, which to Pierre seemed an hour. Suddenly the broad muscles and lines of the count's face began to twitch. The twitching increased, the handsome mouth was drawn to one side (only now did Pierre realize how near death his father was), and from that distorted mouth issued an indistinct, hoarse sound. Anna Mikháylovna looked attentively at the sick man's eyes, trying to guess what he wanted; she pointed first to Pierre, then to some drink, then named Prince Vasíli in an inquiring whisper, then pointed to the quilt. The eyes and face of the sick man showed impatience. He made an effort to look at the servant who stood constantly at the head of the bed.

"Wants to turn on the other side," whispered the servant, and got up to turn the count's heavy body toward the wall.

Pierre rose to help him.

While the count was being turned over, one of his arms fell back helplessly and he made a fruitless effort to pull it forward. Whether he noticed the look of terror with which Pierre regarded that lifeless arm, or whether some other thought flitted across his dying brain, at any rate he glanced at the refractory arm, at Pierre's terror-stricken face, and again at the arm, and on his face a feeble, piteous smile appeared, quite out of keeping with his features, that seemed to deride his own helplessness. At sight of this smile Pierre felt an unexpected quivering in his breast and a tickling in his nose, and tears dimmed his eyes. The sick man was turned onto his side with his face to the wall. He sighed.

"He is dozing," said Anna Mikháylovna, observing that one of the princesses was coming to take her turn at watching. "Let us go."

Pierre went out.

Chapter XXIV

THERE WAS NOW NO ONE IN THE RECEPTION ROOM EXCEPT PRINCE VASÍLI AND THE ELDEST princess, who were sitting under the portrait of Catherine the Great and talking eagerly. As soon as they saw Pierre and his companion they became silent, and Pierre thought he saw the princess hide something as she whispered:

"I can't bear the sight of that woman."

"Catiche has had tea served in the small drawing room," said Prince Vasíli to Anna Mikháylovna. "Go and take something, my poor Anna Mikháylovna, or you will not hold out."

To Pierre he said nothing, merely giving his arm a sympathetic squeeze below the shoulder. Pierre went with Anna Mikháylovna into the small drawing room.

"There is nothing so refreshing after a sleepless night as a cup of this delicious Russian tea," Lorrain was saying with an air of restrained animation as he stood sipping tea from a delicate Chinese handleless cup before a table on which tea and a cold supper were laid in the small circular room. Around the table all who were at Count Bezúkhov's house that night had gathered to fortify themselves. Pierre well remembered this small circular drawing room with its mirrors and little tables. During balls given at the house Pierre, who did not know how to dance, had liked sitting in this room to watch the ladies who, as they passed through in their ball dresses with diamonds and pearls on their bare shoulders, looked at themselves in the brilliantly lit mirrors which repeated their reflections several times. Now this same room was dimly lit by two candles. On one small table tea things and supper-dishes stood in disorder, and in the middle of the night a motley throng of people sat there, not merrymaking, but somberly whispering, and betraying by every word and movement that they none of them forgot what was happening and what was about to happen in the bedroom. Pierre did not eat anything though he would very much have liked to. He looked inquiringly at his monitress, and saw that she was again going on tiptoe to the reception room where they had left Prince Vasíli and the eldest princess. Pierre concluded that this also was essential, and after a short interval followed her. Anna Mikháylovna was standing beside the princess, and they were both speaking in excited whispers.

"Permit me, princess, to know what is necessary and what is not necessary," said the younger of the two speakers, evidently in the same state of excitement as when she had slammed the door of her room.

"But, my dear princess," answered Anna Mikháylovna blandly but impressively, blocking the way to the bedroom and preventing the other from passing, "won't this be too much for poor uncle at a moment when he needs repose? Worldly conversation at a moment when his soul is already prepared . . ."

Prince Vasíli was seated in an easy chair in his familiar attitude, with one leg crossed high above the other. His cheeks, which were so flabby that they looked heavier below, were twitching violently; but he wore the air of a man little concerned in what the two ladies were saying.

"Come, my dear Anna Mikháylovna, let Catiche do as she pleases. You know how fond the count is of her."

"I don't even know what is in this paper," said the younger of the two ladies, addressing Prince Vasíli and pointing to an inlaid portfolio she held in her hand. "All I know is that his real will is in his writing-table, and this is a paper he has forgotten. . . ."

She tried to pass Anna Mikháylovna, but the latter sprang so as to bar her path.

"I know, my dear, kind princess," said Anna Mikháylovna, seizing the portfolio so firmly that it was plain she would not let go easily. "Dear princess, I beg and implore you, have some pity on him! *Je vous en conjure . . .*"

The princess did not reply. Their efforts in the struggle for the portfolio were the only sounds audible, but it was evident that if the princess did speak, her words would not be flattering to Anna Mikháylovna. Though the latter held on tenaciously, her voice lost none of its honeyed firmness and softness.

"Pierre, my dear, come here. I think he will not be out of place in a family consultation; is it not so, prince?"

"Why don't you speak, cousin?" suddenly shrieked the princess so loud that those in the drawing room heard her and were startled. "Why do you remain silent when heaven knows who permits herself to interfere, making a scene on the very threshold of a dying man's room? Intriguer!" she hissed viciously, and tugged with all her might at the portfolio.

But Anna Mikháylovna went forward a step or two to keep her hold on the portfolio, and changed her grip.

Prince Vasíli rose. "Oh!" said he with reproach and surprise, "this is absurd! Come, let go I tell you."

The princess let go.

"And you too!"

But Anna Mikháylovna did not obey him.

"Let go, I tell you! I will take the responsibility. I myself will go and ask him, I! . . . does that satisfy you?"

"But, prince," said Anna Mikháylovna, "after such a solemn sacrament, allow him a moment's peace! Here, Pierre, tell them your opinion," said she, turning to the young man who, having come quite close, was gazing with astonishment at the angry face of the princess which had lost all dignity, and at the twitching cheeks of Prince Vasíli.

"Remember that you will answer for the consequences," said Prince Vasíli severely. "You don't know what you are doing."

"Vile woman!" shouted the princess, darting unexpectedly at Anna Mikháylovna and snatching the portfolio from her.

Prince Vasíli bent his head and spread out his hands.

At this moment that terrible door, which Pierre had watched so long and which had always opened so quietly, burst noisily open and banged against the wall, and the second of the three sisters rushed out wringing her hands.

"What are you doing!" she cried vehemently. "He is dying and you leave me alone with him!"

Her sister dropped the portfolio. Anna Mikháylovna, stooping, quickly caught up the object of contention and ran into the bedroom. The eldest princess and Prince Vasíli, recovering themselves, followed her. A few minutes later the eldest sister came out with a pale hard face, again biting her underlip. At sight of Pierre her expression showed an irrepressible hatred.

"Yes, now you may be glad!" said she; "this is what you have been waiting for." And bursting into tears she hid her face in her handkerchief and rushed from the room.

Prince Vasíli came next. He staggered to the sofa on which Pierre was sitting and dropped onto it, covering his face with his hand. Pierre noticed that he was pale and that his jaw quivered and shook as if in an ague.

"Ah, my friend!" said he, taking Pierre by the elbow; and there was in his voice a sincerity and weakness Pierre had never observed in it before. "How often we sin, how much we deceive, and all for what? I am near sixty, dear friend . . . I too . . . All will end in death, all! Death is awful . . ." and he burst into tears.

Anna Mikháylovna came out last. She approached Pierre with slow, quiet steps.

"Pierre!" she said.

Pierre gave her an inquiring look. She kissed the young man on his forehead, wetting him with her tears. Then after a pause she said:

"He is no more. . . ."

Pierre looked at her over his spectacles.

"Come, I will go with you. Try to weep, nothing gives such relief as tears."

She led him into the dark drawing room and Pierre was glad no one could see his face. Anna Mikháylovna left him, and when she returned he was fast asleep with his head on his arm.

In the morning Anna Mikháylovna said to Pierre:

"Yes, my dear, this is a great loss for us all, not to speak of you. But God will support you: you are young, and are now I hope in command of an immense fortune. The will has not yet been opened. I know you well enough to be sure that this will not turn your head, but it imposes duties on you, and you must be a man."

Pierre was silent.

"Perhaps later on I may tell you, my dear boy, that if I had not been there, God only knows what would have happened! You know, uncle promised me only the day before yesterday not to forget Borís. But he had no time. I hope, my dear friend, you will carry out your father's wish?"

Pierre understood nothing of all this and coloring shyly looked in silence at Princess Anna Mikháylovna. After her talk with Pierre, Anna Mikháylovna returned to the Rostóvs' and went to bed. On waking in the morning she told the Rostóvs and all her acquaintances the details of Count Bezúkhov's death. She said the count had died as she would herself wish to die, that his end was not only touching but edifying. As to the last meeting between father and son, it was so touching that she could not think of it without tears, and did not know which had behaved better during those awful moments—the father who so remembered everything and everybody at last and had spoken such pathetic words to the son, or Pierre, whom it had been pitiful to see, so stricken was he with grief, though he tried hard to hide it in order not to sadden his dying father. "It is painful, but it does one good. It uplifts the soul to see such men as the old count and his worthy son," said she. Of the behavior of the eldest princess and Prince Vasíli she spoke disapprovingly, but in whispers and as a great secret.

Chapter XXV

At Bald Hills, Prince Nicholas Andréevich Bolkónski's estate, the arrival of young Prince Andrew and his wife was daily expected, but this expectation did not upset the regular routine of life in the old prince's household. General-in-Chief Prince Nicholas Andréevich (nicknamed in society, "the King of Prussia") ever since the Emperor Paul had exiled him to his country estate had lived there continuously with his daughter, Princess Mary, and her companion Mademoiselle Bourienne. Though in the new reign he was free to return to the capitals he still continued to live in the country, remarking that anyone who wanted to see him could come the hundred miles from Moscow to Bald Hills, while he himself needed no one and nothing. He used to say that there are only two sources of human vice—idleness and superstition, and only two virtues—activity and intelligence. He himself undertook his daughter's education, and to develop these two cardinal virtues in her gave her lessons in algebra and geometry till she was twenty, and arranged her life so that her whole time was occupied. He was himself always occupied: writing his memoirs, solving problems in higher mathematics, turning snuffboxes on a lathe, working in the garden, or superintending the building that was always going on at his estate. As regularity is a prime condition facilitating activity, regularity in his household was carried to the highest point of exactitude. He always came to table under precisely the same conditions, and not only at the same hour but at the same minute. With those about him, from his daughter to his serfs, the prince was sharp and invariably exacting, so that without being a hard-hearted man he inspired such fear and respect as few hard-hearted men would have aroused. Although he was in retirement and had now no influence in political affairs, every high official appointed to the province in which the prince's estate lay considered it his duty to visit him and waited in the lofty antechamber just as the architect, gardener, or Princess Mary did, till the prince appeared punctually to the appointed hour. Everyone sitting in this antechamber experienced the same feeling of respect and even fear when the enormously high study door opened and showed the figure of a rather small old man, with powdered wig, small withered hands, and bushy gray eyebrows which, when he frowned, sometimes hid the gleam of his shrewd, youthfully glittering eyes.

On the morning of the day that the young couple were to arrive, Princess Mary entered the antechamber as usual at the time appointed for the morning greeting, crossing herself with trepidation and repeating a silent prayer. Every morning she came in like that, and every morning prayed that the daily interview might pass off well.

An old powdered manservant who was sitting in the antechamber rose quietly and said in a whisper: "Please walk in."

Through the door came the regular hum of a lathe. The princess timidly opened the door which moved noiselessly and easily. She paused at the entrance. The prince was working at the lathe and after glancing round continued his work.

The enormous study was full of things evidently in constant use. The large table covered with books and plans, the tall glass-fronted bookcases with keys in the locks, the high desk for writing while standing up, on which lay an open exercise-book, and the lathe with tools laid ready to hand and shavings scattered around—all indicated continuous, varied, and orderly activity. The motion of the small foot shod in a Tartar boot embroidered with silver, and the firm pressure of the lean sinewy hand, showed that the prince still possessed the tenacious endurance and vigor of hardy old age. After a few more turns of the lathe he removed his foot from the pedal, wiped his chisel, dropped it into a leather pouch attached to the lathe, and approaching the table, summoned his daughter. He never gave his children a blessing, so he simply held out his bristly cheek (as yet unshaven) and regarding her tenderly and attentively, said severely:

"Quite well? All right then, sit down." He took the exercise-book containing lessons in geometry written by himself, and drew up a chair with his foot.

"For tomorrow!" said he, quickly finding the page and making a scratch from one paragraph to another with his hard nail.

The princess bent over the exercise-book on the table.

"Wait a bit, here's a letter for you," said the old man suddenly, taking a letter addressed in a woman's hand from a bag hanging above the table, onto which he threw it.

At the sight of the letter red patches showed themselves on the princess's face. She took it quickly and bent her head over it.

"From Héloïse?" asked the prince with a cold smile that showed his still sound, yellowish teeth.

"Yes, it's from Julie," replied the princess with a timid glance and a timid smile.

"I'll let two more letters pass, but the third I'll read," said the prince sternly; "I'm afraid you write much nonsense. I'll read the third!"

"Read this if you like, father," said the princess, blushing still more and holding out the letter.

"The third, I said the third!" cried the prince abruptly, pushing the letter away, and leaning his elbows on the table he drew toward him the exercise-book containing geometrical figures.

"Well, madam," he began, stooping over the book close to his daughter and placing an arm on the back of the chair on which she sat, so that she felt herself surrounded on all sides by the acrid scent of old age and tobacco, which she had known so long. "Now, madam, these triangles are equal; please note that the angle *ABC* . . ."

The princess looked in a scared way at her father's eyes glittering close to her; the red patches on her face came and went, and it was plain that she understood nothing and was so frightened that her fear would prevent her understanding any of her father's further explanations, however clear they might be. Whether it was the teacher's fault or the pupil's, this same thing happened every day: the princess's eyes grew dim, she could not see and could not hear anything, but was only conscious of her stern father's withered face close to her, of his breath and the smell of him, and could think only of how to get away quickly to her own room to make out the problem in peace. The old man was beside himself: moved the chair on which he was sitting noisily backward and forward, made efforts to control himself and not become vehement, but almost always did become vehement, scolded, and sometimes flung the exercise-book away.

The princess gave a wrong answer.

"Well now, isn't she a fool!" shouted the prince, pushing the book aside and turning sharply away; but rising immediately, he paced up and down, lightly touched his daughter's hair and sat down again.

He drew up his chair, and continued to explain.

"This won't do, princess; it won't do," said he, when Princess Mary, having taken and closed the exercise-book with the next day's lesson, was about to leave: "Mathematics are most important, madam! I don't want to have you like our silly ladies. Get used to it and you'll like it," and he patted her cheek. "It will drive all the nonsense out of your head."

She turned to go, but he stopped her with a gesture and took an uncut book from the high desk.

"Here is some sort of *Key to the Mysteries* that your Héloïse has sent you. Religious! I don't interfere with anyone's belief . . . I have looked at it. Take it. Well, now go. Go."

He patted her on the shoulder and himself closed the door after her.

Princess Mary went back to her room with the sad, scared expression that rarely left her and which made her plain, sickly face yet plainer. She sat down at her writing-table, on which stood miniature portraits and which was littered with books and papers. The princess was as untidy as her father was tidy. She put down the geometry-book and eagerly broke the seal of her letter. It was from her most intimate friend from childhood; that same Julie Karágina who had been at the Rostóvs' name-day party.

Julie wrote in French:

DEAR AND PRECIOUS FRIEND—How terrible and frightful a thing is separation! Though I tell myself that half my life and half my happiness are wrapped up in you, and that in spite of the distance separating us our hearts are united by indissoluble bonds, my heart rebels against fate and in spite of the pleasures and distractions around me I cannot overcome a certain secret sorrow that has been in my heart ever since we parted. Why are we not together as we were last summer, in your big study, on the blue sofa, the confidential sofa? Why cannot I now, as three months ago, draw fresh moral strength from your look, so gentle, calm, and penetrating, a look I loved so well and seem to see before me as I write?

Having read thus far, Princess Mary sighed and glanced into the mirror which stood on her right. It reflected a weak, ungraceful figure and thin face. Her eyes, always sad, now looked with particular hopelessness at her reflection in the glass. "She flatters me," thought the princess, turning away and continuing to read. But Julie did not flatter her friend; the princess's eyes—large, deep and luminous (it seemed as if at times there radiated from them shafts of warm light)—were so beautiful that very often in spite of the plainness of her face they gave her an attraction more powerful than that of beauty. But the princess never saw the beautiful expression of her own eyes—the look they had when she was not thinking of herself. As with everyone, her face assumed a forced unnatural expression as soon as she looked in a glass. She went on reading:

All Moscow talks of nothing but war. One of my two brothers is already abroad, the other is with the Guards, who are starting on their march to the frontier. Our dear Emperor has left Petersburg and it is thought intends to expose his precious person to the chances of war. God grant that the Corsican monster who is destroying the peace of Europe may be overthrown by the angel whom it has pleased the Almighty, in His goodness, to give us as sovereign! To say nothing of my brothers, this war has deprived me of one of the associations nearest my heart. I mean young Nicholas Rostóv, who with his enthusiasm could not bear to remain inactive and has left the university to join the army. I will confess to you, dear Mary, that in spite of his extreme youth his departure for the army was a great grief to me. This young man, of whom I spoke to you last summer, is so noble-minded and full of that real youthfulness which one seldom finds nowadays among our old men of twenty and, particularly, he is so frank and has so much heart. He is so pure and poetic that my relations with him, transient as they were, have been one of the sweetest comforts to my poor heart, which has already suffered so much. Someday I will tell you about our parting and all that was said then. That is still too fresh. Ah, dear friend, you are happy not to know these poignant joys and sorrows. You are fortunate, for the latter are generally the stronger! I know very well that Count Nicholas is too young ever to be more to me than a friend, but this sweet friendship, this poetic and pure intimacy, were what my heart needed. But enough of this! The chief news, about which all Moscow gossips, is the death of old Count Bezúkhov, and his inheritance. Fancy! The three princesses have received very little, Prince Vasíli nothing, and it is Monsieur Pierre who has inherited all the property and has besides been recognized as legitimate; so that he is now Count Bezúkhov and possessor of the finest fortune in Russia. It is rumored that Prince Vasíli played a very despicable part in this affair and that he returned to Petersburg quite crestfallen.

I confess I understand very little about all these matters of wills and inheritance; but I do know that since this young man, whom we all used to know as plain Monsieur Pierre, has become Count Bezúkhov and the owner of one of the largest fortunes in Russia, I am much amused to watch the change in the tone and manners of the Mammas burdened by marriageable daughters, and of the young ladies themselves, toward him, though, between you and me, he always seemed to me a poor sort of fellow. As for the past two years people have amused themselves by finding husbands for me (most of whom I don't even know), the matchmaking chronicles of Moscow now speak of me as the future Countess Bezúkhova. But you will understand that I have no desire for the post. *A propos* of marriages: do you know that a while ago that *universal auntie* Anna Mikháylovna told me, under the seal of strict secrecy, of a plan of marriage for you. It is neither more nor less than with Prince Vasíli's son Anatole, whom they wish to reform by marrying him to someone rich and *distingueé*, and it is on you that his relations' choice has fallen. I don't know what you will think of it, but I consider it my duty to let you know of it. He is said to be very handsome and a terrible scapegrace. That is all I have been able to find out about him.

But enough of gossip. I am at the end of my second sheet of paper, and Mamma has sent for me to go and dine at the Apráksins'. Read the mystical book I am sending you; it has an enormous success here. Though there are things in it difficult for the feeble human mind to grasp, it is an admirable book which calms and elevates the soul. Adieu! Give my respects to monsieur your father and my compliments to Mademoiselle Bourienne. I embrace you as I love you.

JULIE

P.S. Let me have news of your brother and his charming little wife.

The princess pondered awhile with a thoughtful smile and her luminous eyes lit up so that her face was entirely transformed. Then she suddenly rose and with her heavy tread went up to the table. She took a sheet of paper and her hand moved rapidly over it. This is the reply she wrote, also in French:

DEAR AND PRECIOUS FRIEND—Your letter of the 13th has given me great delight. So you still love me, my romantic Julie? Separation, of which you say so much that is bad, does not seem to have had its usual effect on you. You complain of our separation. What then should I say, if I *dared* complain, I who am deprived of all who are dear to me? Ah, if we had not religion to console us life would be very sad. Why do you suppose that I should look severely on your affection for that young man? On such matters I am only severe with myself. I understand such feelings in others, and if never having felt them I cannot approve of them, neither do I condemn them. Only it seems to me that Christian love, love of one's neighbor, love of one's enemy, is worthier, sweeter and better than the feelings which the beautiful eyes of a young man can inspire in a romantic and loving young girl like yourself.

The news of Count Bezúkhov's death reached us before your letter and my father was much affected by it. He says the count was the last representative but one of the great century, and that it is his own turn now, but that he will do all he can to let his turn come as late as possible. God preserve us from that terrible misfortune!

I cannot agree with you about Pierre, whom I knew as a child. He always seemed to me to have an excellent heart, and that is the quality I value most in people. As to his inheritance and the part played by Prince Vasíli, it is very sad for both. Ah, my dear friend, our divine Saviour's words, that it is easier for a camel to go through the eye of a needle than for a rich man to enter the Kingdom of God, are terribly true. I pity Prince Vasíli but am still more sorry for Pierre. So young, and burdened with such riches—to what temptations he will be exposed! If I were asked what I desire most on earth, it would be to be poorer than the poorest beggar. A thousand thanks, dear friend, for the volume you have sent me and which has such success in Moscow. Yet since you tell me that among some good things it contains others which our weak human understanding cannot grasp, it seems to me rather useless to spend time in reading what is unintelligible and can therefore bear no fruit. I never could understand the fondness some people have for confusing their minds by dwelling on mystical books that merely awaken their doubts and excite their imagination, giving them a bent for exaggeration quite contrary to Christian simplicity. Let us rather read the Epistles and Gospels. Let us not seek to penetrate what mysteries they contain; for how can we, miserable sinners that we are, know the terrible and holy secrets of Providence while we remain in this flesh which forms an impenetrable veil between us and the Eternal? Let us rather confine ourselves to studying those sublime rules which our divine Saviour has left for our guidance here below. Let us try to conform to them and follow them, and let us be persuaded that the less we let our feeble human minds roam, the better we shall please God, who rejects all knowledge that does not come from Him; and the less we seek to fathom what He has been pleased to conceal from us, the sooner will He vouchsafe its revelation to us through His divine Spirit.

My father has not spoken to me of a suitor, but has only told me that he has received a letter and is expecting a visit from Prince Vasíli. In regard to this project of marriage for me, I will tell you, dear sweet friend, that I look on marriage as a divine institution to which we must conform. However painful it may be to me, should the Almighty lay the duties of wife and mother upon me

I shall try to perform them as faithfully as I can, without disquieting myself by examining my feelings toward him whom He may give me for husband.

I have had a letter from my brother, who announces his speedy arrival at Bald Hills with his wife. This pleasure will be but a brief one, however, for he will leave us again to take part in this unhappy war into which we have been drawn, God knows how or why. Not only where you are—at the heart of affairs and of the world—is the talk all of war, even here amid field-work and the calm of nature—which townsfolk consider characteristic of the country—rumors of war are heard and painfully felt. My father talks of nothing but marches and counter-marches, things of which I understand nothing; and the day before yesterday during my daily walk through the village I witnessed a heartrending scene. . . . It was a convoy of conscripts enrolled from our people and starting to join the army. You should have seen the state of the mothers, wives, and children of the men who were going and should have heard the sobs. It seems as though mankind has forgotten the laws of its divine Saviour, Who preached love and forgiveness of injuries—and that men attribute the greatest merit to skill in killing one another.

Adieu, dear and kind friend; may our divine Saviour and His most Holy Mother keep you in their holy and all-powerful care!

MARY

"Ah, you are sending off a letter, princess? I have already dispatched mine. I have written to my poor mother," said the smiling Mademoiselle Bourienne rapidly, in her pleasant mellow tones and with guttural *r*'s. She brought into Princess Mary's strenuous, mournful and gloomy world a quite different atmosphere, careless, light-hearted and self-satisfied.

"Princess, I must warn you," she added, lowering her voice and evidently listening to herself with pleasure, and speaking with exaggerated *grasseyement*, "the prince has been scolding Michael Ivánovich. He is in a very bad humor, very morose. Be prepared."

"Ah, dear friend," replied Princess Mary, "I have asked you never to warn me of the humor my father is in. I do not allow myself to judge him and would not have others do so."

The princess glanced at her watch and seeing that she was five minutes late in starting her practice on the clavichord, went into the sitting room with a look of alarm. Between twelve and two o'clock, as the day was mapped out, the prince rested and the princess played the clavichord.

Chapter XXVI

THE GRAY-HAIRED VALET WAS SITTING DROWSILY LISTENING TO THE SNORING OF THE PRINCE, who was in his large study. From the far side of the house through the closed doors came the sound of difficult passages—twenty times repeated—of a sonata by Dussek.

Just then a closed carriage and another with a hood drove up to the porch. Prince Andrew got out of the carriage, helped his little wife to alight, and let her pass into the house before him. Old Tíkhon, wearing a wig, put his head out of the door of the antechamber, reported in a whisper that the prince was sleeping, and hastily closed the door. Tíkhon knew that neither the son's arrival nor any other unusual event must be allowed to disturb the appointed order of the day. Prince Andrew apparently knew this as well as Tíkhon; he looked at his watch as if to ascertain whether his father's habits had changed since he was at home last, and, having assured himself that they had not, he turned to his wife.

"He will get up in twenty minutes. Let us go across to Mary's room," he said.

The little princess had grown stouter during this time, but her eyes and her short, downy, smiling lip lifted when she began to speak just as merrily and prettily as ever.

"Why, this is a palace!" she said to her husband, looking around with the expression with which people compliment their host at a ball. "Let's come, quick, quick!" And with a glance round, she smiled at Tíkhon, at her husband, and at the footman who accompanied them.

"Is that Mary practicing? Let's go quietly and take her by surprise."

Prince Andrew followed her with a courteous but sad expression.

"You've grown older, Tíkhon," he said in passing to the old man, who kissed his hand.

Before they reached the room from which the sounds of the clavichord came, the pretty, fair-haired Frenchwoman, Mademoiselle Bourienne, rushed out apparently beside herself with delight.

"Ah! what joy for the princess!" exclaimed she: "At last! I must let her know."

"No, no, please not . . . You are Mademoiselle Bourienne," said the little princess, kissing her. "I know you already through my sister-in-law's friendship for you. She was not expecting us?"

They went up to the door of the sitting room from which came the sound of the oft-repeated passage of the sonata. Prince Andrew stopped and made a grimace, as if expecting something unpleasant.

The little princess entered the room. The passage broke off in the middle, a cry was heard, then Princess Mary's heavy tread and the sound of kissing. When Prince Andrew went in the two princesses, who had only met once before for a short time at his wedding, were in each other's arms warmly pressing their lips to whatever place they happened to touch. Mademoiselle Bourienne stood near them pressing her hand to her heart, with a beatific smile and obviously equally ready to cry or to laugh. Prince Andrew shrugged his shoulders and frowned, as lovers of music do when they hear a false note. The two women let go of one another, and then as if afraid of being too late, seized each other's hands, kissing them and pulling them away, and again began kissing each other on the face, and then to Prince Andrew's surprise both began to cry and kissed again. Mademoiselle Bourienne also began to cry. Prince Andrew evidently felt ill at ease, but to the two women it seemed quite natural that they should cry, and apparently it never entered their heads that it could have been otherwise at this meeting.

"Ah! my dear! . . . Ah! Mary . . ." they suddenly exclaimed, and then laughed. "I dreamed last night . . ."—"You were not expecting us? . . ."—"Ah! Mary, you have got thinner! . . ." "And you have grown stouter! . . ."

"I knew the princess at once," put in Mademoiselle Bourienne.

"And I had no idea! . . ." exclaimed Princess Mary. "Ah, Andrew, I did not see you."

Prince Andrew and his sister, hand in hand, kissed one another, and he told her she was still the same cry-baby as ever. Princess Mary had turned toward her brother, and through her tears the loving warm gentle look of her large luminous eyes, very beautiful at that moment, rested on Prince Andrew's face.

The little princess talked incessantly, her short downy upper lip continually and rapidly touching her rosy nether lip when necessary and drawing up again next moment when her face broke into a smile of glittering teeth and sparkling eyes. She told of an accident they had had on the Spásski Hill which might have been serious for her in her condition, and immediately after that informed them that she had left all her clothes in Petersburg and that heaven knew what she would have to dress in here; and that Andrew had quite changed, and that Kitty Odýntsova had married an old man, and that there was a suitor for Mary, a real one, but that they would talk of that later. Princess Mary was still looking silently at her brother and her beautiful eyes were full of love and sadness. It was plain that she was following a train of thought independent of her sister-in-law's words. In the midst of a description of the last Petersburg fête she addressed her brother:

"So you are really going to the war, Andrew?" she said sighing.

Lise sighed too.

"Yes, and even tomorrow," replied her brother.

"He is leaving me here, God knows why, when he might have had promotion . . ."

Princess Mary did not listen to the end, but continuing her train of thought turned to her sister-in-law with a tender glance at her figure.

"Is it certain?" she said.

The face of the little princess changed. She sighed and said:

"Yes, quite certain. Ah! it is very dreadful . . ."

Her lip descended. She brought her face close to her sister-in-law's, and unexpectedly again began to cry.

"She needs rest," said Prince Andrew with a frown. "Don't you, Lise? Take her to your room and I'll go to father. How is he? Just the same?"

"Yes, just the same. Though I don't know what your opinion will be," answered the princess joyfully.

"And are the hours the same? And the walks in the avenues? And the lathe?" asked Prince Andrew with a scarcely perceptible smile which showed that, in spite of all his love and respect for his father, he was aware of his weaknesses.

"The hours are the same, and the lathe, and also the mathematics and my geometry lessons," said Princess Mary gleefully, as if her lessons in geometry were among the greatest delights of her life.

When the twenty minutes had elapsed and the time had come for the old prince to get up, Tíkhon came to call the young prince to his father. The old man made a departure from his usual routine in honor of his son's arrival: he gave orders to admit him to his apartments while he dressed for dinner. The old prince always dressed in old-fashioned style, wearing an antique coat and powdered hair; and when Prince Andrew entered his father's dressing room (not with the contemptuous look and manner he wore in drawing rooms, but with the animated face with which he talked to Pierre) the old man was sitting on a large leather-covered chair, wrapped in a powdering mantle, entrusting his head to Tíkhon.

"Ah! here's the warrior! Wants to vanquish Buonaparte?" said the old man, shaking his powdered head as much as the tail, which Tíkhon was holding fast to plait, would allow.

"You at least must tackle him properly, or else if he goes on like this he'll soon have us, too, for his subjects! How are you?" And he held out his cheek.

The old man was in a good temper after his nap before dinner. (He used to say that a nap "after dinner was silver—before dinner, golden.") He cast happy, sidelong glances at his son from under his thick, bushy eyebrows. Prince Andrew went up and kissed his father on the spot indicated to him. He made no reply on his father's favorite topic—making fun of the military men of the day, and more particularly of Bonaparte.

"Yes, father, I have come come to you and brought my wife who is pregnant," said Prince Andrew, following every movement of his father's face with an eager and respectful look. "How is your health?"

"Only fools and rakes fall ill, my boy. You know me: I am busy from morning till night and abstemious, so of course I am well."

"Thank God," said his son smiling.

"God has nothing to do with it! Well, go on," he continued, returning to his hobby; "tell me how the Germans have taught you to fight Bonaparte by this new science you call 'strategy.' "

Prince Andrew smiled.

"Give me time to collect my wits, father," said he, with a smile that showed that his father's foibles did not prevent his son from loving and honoring him. "Why, I have not yet had time to settle down!"

"Nonsense, nonsense!" cried the old man, shaking his pigtail to see whether it was firmly plaited, and grasping his by the hand. "The house for your wife is ready. Princess Mary will take her there and show her over, and they'll talk nineteen to the dozen. That's their woman's way! I am glad to have her. Sit down and talk. About Mikhelson's army I understand—Tolstóy's too . . . a simultaneous expedition. . . . But what's the southern army to do? Prussia is neutral . . . I know that. What about Austria?" said he, rising from his chair and pacing up and down the room followed by Tíkhon, who ran after him, handing him different articles of clothing. "What of Sweden? How will they cross Pomerania?"

Prince Andrew, seeing that his father insisted, began—at first reluctantly, but gradually with more and more animation, and from habit changing unconsciously from Russian to French as he went on—to explain the plan of operation for the coming campaign. He explained how an army, ninety thousand strong, was to threaten Prussia so as to bring her out of her neutrality and draw her into the war; how part of that army was to join some Swedish forces at Stralsund; how two hundred and twenty thousand Austrians, with a hundred thousand Russians, were to operate in Italy and on the Rhine; how fifty thousand Russians and as many English were to land at Naples, and how a total force of five hundred thousand men was to attack the French from different sides. The old prince did not evince the least interest during this explanation, but as if he were not listening to it continued to dress while walking about, and three times unexpectedly interrupted. Once he stopped it by shouting: "The white one, the white one!"

This meant that Tíkhon was not handing him the waistcoat he wanted. Another time he interrupted, saying:

"And will she soon be confined?" and shaking his head reproachfully said: "That's bad! Go on, go on."

The third interruption came when Prince Andrew was finishing his description. The old man began to sing, in the cracked voice of old age: *"Malbrook s'en va-t-en-guerre. Dieu sait quand reviendra."*

His son only smiled.

"I don't say it's a plan I approve of," said the son: "I am only telling you what it is. Napoleon has also formed his plan by now, not worse than this one."

"Well you've told me nothing new," and the old man repeated, meditatively and rapidly:

"*Dieu sait quand reviendra*. Go to the dining room."

Chapter XXVII

AT THE APPOINTED HOUR THE PRINCE, POWDERED AND SHAVEN, ENTERED THE DINING ROOM where his daughter-in-law, Princess Mary and Mademoiselle Bourienne, were already awaiting him together with his architect, who by a strange caprice of his employer's was admitted to table though the position of that insignificant individual was such as could certainly not have caused him to expect that honor. The prince, who generally kept very strictly to social distinctions and rarely admitted even important government officials to his table, had unexpectedly selected Michael Ivánovich (who always went into a corner to blow his nose on his checked handkerchief) to illustrate the theory that all men are equals, and had more than once impressed on his daughter that Michael Ivánovich was "not a whit worse than you or I." At dinner the prince usually spoke to the taciturn Michael Ivánovich more often than to anyone else.

In the dining room, which like all the rooms in the house was exceedingly lofty, the members of the household and the footmen—one behind each chair—stood waiting for the prince to enter. The head butler, napkin on arm, was scanning the setting of the table, making signs to the footmen, and anxiously glancing from the clock to the door by which the prince was to enter. Prince Andrew was looking at a large gilt frame, new to him, containing the genealogical tree of the Princes

Bolkónski, opposite which hung another such frame with a badly-painted portrait (evidently by the hand of the artist belonging to the estate) of a ruling prince, in a crown—an alleged descendant of Rúrik and ancestor of the Bolkónskis. Prince Andrew, looking again at that genealogical tree, shook his head, laughing as a man laughs who looks at a portrait so characteristic of the original as to be amusing.

"How thoroughly like him that is!" he said to Princess Mary, who had come up to him.

Princess Mary looked at her brother in surprise. She did not understand what he was laughing at. Everything her father did inspired her with reverence and was beyond question.

"Everyone has his Achilles' heel," continued Prince Andrew. "Fancy, with *his* powerful mind, indulging in such nonsense!"

Princess Mary could not understand the boldness of her brother's criticism and was about to reply, when the expected footsteps were heard coming from the study. The prince walked in quickly and jauntily as was his wont, as if intentionally contrasting the briskness of his manners with the strict formality of his house. At that moment the great clock struck two, and another with a shrill tone joined in from the drawing room. The prince stood still; his lively glittering eyes from under their thick, bushy eyebrows sternly scanned all present and rested on the little princess. She felt, as courtiers do when the Tsar enters, the sensation of fear and respect which the old man inspired in all around him. He stroked her hair, and then patted her awkwardly on the back of her neck.

"I'm glad, glad, to see you," he said, looking attentively into her eyes, and then quickly went to his place and sat down. "Sit down, sit down! Sit down, Michael Ianovich!"

He indicated a place beside him to his daughter-in-law. A footman moved the chair for her.

"Ho, ho!" said the old man, casting his eyes on her rounded figure. "You've been in a hurry. That's bad!"

He laughed in his usual dry, cold, unpleasant way, with his lips only and not with his eyes.

"You must walk, walk as much as possible, as much as possible," he said.

The little princess did not, or did not wish to, hear his words. She was silent and seemed confused. The prince asked her about her father, and she began to smile and talk. He asked about mutual acquaintances, and she became still more animated and chattered away giving him greetings from various people and retailing the town gossip.

"Countess Apráksina, poor thing, has lost her husband and she has cried her eyes out," she said, growing more and more lively.

As she became animated the prince looked at her more and more sternly, and suddenly, as if he had studied her sufficiently and had formed a definite idea of her, he turned away and addressed Michael Ivánovich.

"Well, Michael Ivánovich, our Bonaparte will be having a bad time of it. Prince Andrew" (he always spoke thus of his son) "has been telling me what forces are being collected against him! While you and I never thought much of him."

Michael Ivánovich did not at all know when "you and I" had said such things about Bonaparte, but understanding that he was wanted as a peg on which to hang the prince's favorite topic, he looked inquiringly at the young prince, wondering what would follow.

"He is a great tactician!" said the prince to his son, pointing to the architect.

And the conversation again turned on the war, on Bonaparte, and the generals and statesmen of the day. The old prince seemed convinced not only that all the men of the day were mere babies who did not know the A B C of war or of politics, and that Bonaparte was an insignificant little Frenchy, successful only because there were no longer any Potëmkins or Suvórovs left to oppose him; but he was also convinced that there were no political difficulties in Europe and no real war, but only a sort of puppet-show at which the men of the day were playing, pretending to do something real. Prince Andrew gaily bore with his father's ridicule of the new men, and drew him on and listened to him with evident pleasure.

"The past always seems good," said he, "but did not Suvórov himself fall into a trap Moreau set him, and from which he did not know how to escape?"

"Who told you that? Who?" cried the prince. "Suvórov!" And he jerked away his plate, which Tíkhon briskly caught. "Suvórov! . . . Consider, Prince Andrew! Two . . . Frederick and Suvórov; Moreau! . . . Moreau would have been a prisoner if Suvórov had had a free hand; but he had the Hofs-kriegs-wurst-schnapps-Rath on his hands. It would have puzzled the devil himself! When you get there you'll find out what those Hofs-kriegs-wurst-Raths are! Suvórov couldn't manage them so what chance has Michael Kutúzov? No, my dear boy," he continued, "you and your generals won't get on against Buonaparte; you'll have to call in the French, so that birds of a feather may fight together. The German, Pahlen, has been sent to New York in America, to fetch the Frenchman, Moreau," he said, alluding to the invitation made that year to Moreau to enter the Russian service. . . . "Wonderful! . . . Were the Potëmkins, Suvórovs and Orlóvs Germans? No, lad, either you fellows have all lost your wits, or I have outlived mine. May God help you, but we'll see what will happen. Buonaparte has become a great commander among them! Hm! . . ."

"I don't at all say that all the plans are good," said Prince Andrew, "I am only surprised at your opinion of Bonaparte. You may laugh as much as you like, but all the same Bonaparte is a great general!"

"Michael Ivánovich!" cried the old prince to the architect who, busy with his roast meat, hoped he had been forgotten: "Didn't I tell you Buonaparte was a great tactician? Here, he says the same thing."

"To be sure, your excellency." replied the architect.

The prince again laughed his frigid laugh.

"Buonaparte was born with a silver spoon in his mouth. He has got splendid soldiers. Besides he began by attacking Germans. And only idlers have failed to beat the Germans. Since the world began everybody has beaten the Germans. They beat no one—except one another. He made his reputation fighting them."

And the prince began explaining all the blunders which, according to him, Bonaparte had made in his campaigns and even in politics. His son made no rejoinder, but it was evident that whatever arguments were presented he was as little able as his father to change his opinion. He listened, refraining from a reply, and involuntarily wondered how this old man, living alone in the country for so many years, could know and discuss so minutely and acutely all the recent European military and political events.

"You think I'm an old man and don't understand the present state of affairs?" concluded his father. "But it troubles me. I don't sleep at night. Come now, where has this great commander of yours shown his skill?" he concluded.

"That would take too long to tell," answered the son.

"Well, then go to your Buonaparte! Mademoiselle Bourienne, here's another admirer of that powder-monkey emperor of yours," he exclaimed in excellent French.

"You know, prince, I am not a Bonapartist!"

"Dieu sait quand reviendra" . . . hummed the prince out of tune and, with a laugh still more so, he quitted the table.

The little princess during the whole discussion and the rest of the dinner sat silent, glancing with a frightened look now at her father-in-law and now at Princess Mary. When they left the table she took her sister-in-law's arm and drew her into another room.

"What a clever man your father is," said she; "perhaps that is why I am afraid of him."

"Oh, he is so kind!" answered Princess Mary.

Chapter XXVIII

PRINCE ANDREW WAS TO LEAVE NEXT EVENING. THE OLD PRINCE, NOT ALTERING HIS ROUTINE, retired as usual after dinner. The little princess was in her sister-in-law's room. Prince Andrew in a traveling coat without epaulets had been packing with his valet in the rooms assigned to him. After inspecting the carriage himself and seeing the trunks put in, he ordered the horses to be harnessed. Only those things he always kept with him remained in his room; a small box, a large canteen fitted with silver plate, two Turkish pistols and a saber—a present from his father who had brought it from the siege of Ochákov. All these traveling effects of Prince Andrew's were in very good order: new, clean, and in cloth covers carefully tied with tapes.

When starting on a journey or changing their mode of life, men capable of reflection are generally in a serious frame of mind. At such moments one reviews the past and plans for the future. Prince Andrew's face looked very thoughtful and tender. With his hands behind him he paced briskly from corner to corner of the room looking straight before him and thoughtfully shaking his head. Did he fear going to the war, or was he sad at leaving his wife?—perhaps both, but evidently he did not wish to be seen in that mood, for hearing footsteps in the passage he hurriedly unclasped his hands, stopped at a table as if tying the cover of the small box, and assumed his usual tranquil and impenetrable expression. It was the heavy tread of Princess Mary that he heard.

"I hear you have given orders to harness," she cried, panting (she had apparently been running), "and I did so wish to have another talk with you alone! God knows how long we may again be parted. You are not angry with me for coming? You have changed so, Andrúsha," she added, as if to explain such a question.

She smiled as she uttered his pet name, "Andrúsha." It was obviously strange to her to think that this stern handsome man should be Andrúsha—the slender mischievous boy who had been her playfellow in childhood.

"And where is Lise?" he asked, answering her question only by a smile.

"She was so tired that she has fallen asleep on the sofa in my room. Oh, Andrew! What a treasure of a wife you have," said she, sitting down on the sofa, facing her brother. "She is quite a child: such a dear, merry child. I have grown so fond of her."

Prince Andrew was silent, but the princess noticed the ironical and contemptuous look that showed itself on his face.

"One must be indulgent to little weaknesses; who is free from them, Andrew? Don't forget that she has grown up and been educated in society, and so her position now is not a rosy one. We should enter into everyone's situation. *Tout comprendre, c'est tout pardonner.* Think it must be for her, poor thing, after what she has been used to, to be parted from her husband and be left alone in the country, in her condition! It's very hard."

Prince Andrew smiled as he looked at his sister, as we smile at those we think we thoroughly understand.

"You live in the country and don't think the life terrible," he replied.

"I . . . that's different. Why speak of me? I don't want any other life, and can't, for I know no other. But think, Andrew: for a young society woman to be buried in the country during the best years of her life, all alone—for Papa is always busy, and I . . . well, you know what poor resources I have for entertaining a woman used to the best society. There is only Mademoiselle Bourienne. . . ."

"I don't like your Mademoiselle Bourienne at all," said Prince Andrew.

"No? She is very nice and kind, and above all, she's much to be pitied. She has no one, no one. To tell the truth, I don't need her, and she's even in my way. You know I always was a savage, and now am even more so. I like being alone. . . . Father likes her very much. She and Michael Ivánovich are the two people to whom he is always gentle and kind, because he has been a benefactor to them both. As Sterne says: 'We don't love people so much for the good they have done us, as for the good we have done them.' Father took her when she was homeless after losing her own father. She is very good-natured, and my father likes her way of reading. She reads to him in the evenings and reads splendidly."

"To be quite frank, Mary, I expect father's character sometimes makes things trying for you, doesn't it?" Prince Andrew asked suddenly.

Princess Mary was first surprised and then aghast at this question.

"For me? For me? . . . Trying for me! . . ." said she.

"He always was rather harsh; and now I should think he's getting very trying," said Prince Andrew, apparently speaking lightly of their father in order to puzzle or test his sister.

"You are good in every way, Andrew, but you have a kind of intellectual pride," said the princess, following the train of her own thoughts rather than the trend of the conversation—"and that's a great sin. How can one judge father? But even if one might, what feeling except veneration could such a man as my father evoke? And I am so contented and happy with him. I only wish you were all as happy as I am."

Her brother shook his head incredulously.

"The only thing that is hard for me . . . I will tell you the truth, Andrew—is father's way of treating religious subjects. I don't understand how a man of his immense intellect can fail to see what is as clear as day, and can go so far astray. That is the only thing that makes me unhappy. But even in this I can see lately a shade of improvement. His satire has been less bitter of late, and there was a monk he received and had a long talk with."

"Ah! my dear, I am afraid you and your monk are wasting your powder," said Prince Andrew banteringly yet tenderly.

"Ah! *mon ami*, I only pray, and hope that God will hear me. Andrew . . ." she said timidly after a moment's silence, "I have a great favor to ask of you."

"What is it, dear?"

"No—promise that you will not refuse! It will give you no trouble and is nothing unworthy of you, but it will comfort me. Promise, Andrúsha! . . ." said she, putting her hand in her reticule but not yet taking out what she was holding inside it, as if what she held were the subject of her request and must not be shown before the request was granted.

She looked timidly at her brother.

"Even if it were a great deal of trouble . . ." answered Prince Andrew, as if guessing what it was about.

"Think what you please! I know you are just like father. Think as you please, but do this for my sake! Please do! Father's father, our grandfather, wore it in all his wars." (She still did not take out what she was holding in her reticule.) "So you promise?"

"Of course. What is it?"

"Andrew, I bless you with this icon and you must promise me you will never take it off. Do you promise?"

"If it does not weigh a hundredweight and won't break my neck . . . To please you . . ." said Prince Andrew. But immediately, noticing the pained expression his joke had brought to his sister's face, he repented and added: "I am glad; really dear, I am very glad."

"Against your will He will save and have mercy on you and bring you to Himself, for in Him alone is truth and peace," said she in a voice trembling with emotion, solemnly holding up in both hands before her brother a small, oval, antique, dark-faced icon of the Saviour in a gold setting, on a finely wrought silver chain.

She crossed herself, kissed the icon, and handed it to Andrew.

"Please, Andrew, for my sake! . . ."

Rays of gentle light shone from her large timid eyes. Those eyes lit up the whole of her thin sickly face and made it beautiful. Her brother would have taken the icon, but she stopped him. Andrew understood, crossed himself and kissed the icon. There was a look of tenderness, for he was touched, but also a gleam of irony on his face.

"Thank you, my dear." She kissed him on the forehead and sat down again on the sofa. They were silent for a while.

"As I was saying to you, Andrew, be kind and generous as you always used to be. Don't judge Lise harshly," she began. "She is so sweet, so good-natured and her position now is a very hard one."

"I do not think I have complained of my wife to you, Másha, or blamed her. Why do you say all this to me?"

Red patches appeared on Princess Mary's face and she was silent as if she felt guilty.

"I have said nothing to you, but you have already been talked to. And I am sorry for that," he went on.

The patches grew deeper on her forehead, neck and cheeks. She tried to say something but could not. Her brother had guessed right: the little princess had been crying after dinner and had spoken of her forebodings about her confinement, and how she dreaded it, and had complained of her fate, her father-in-law and her husband. After crying she had fallen asleep. Prince Andrew felt sorry for his sister.

"Know this, Másha: I can't reproach, have not reproached, and never shall reproach *my wife* with anything, and I cannot reproach myself with anything in regard to her; and that always will be so in whatever circumstances I may be placed. But if you want to know the truth . . . if you want to know whether I am happy? No! Is she happy? No! But why this is so I don't know . . ."

As he said this he rose, went to his sister and, stooping, kissed her forehead. His fine eyes lit up with a thoughtful, kindly and unaccustomed brightness, but he was looking not at his sister but over her head toward the darkness of the open doorway.

"Let us go to her, I must say good-bye. Or—go and wake and I'll come in a moment. Petrúshka!" he called to his valet: "Come here, take these away. Put this on the seat and this to the right."

Princess Mary rose and moved to the door, then stopped and said:

"Andrew, if you had faith you would have turned to God and asked Him to give you the love you do not feel, and your prayer would have been answered."

"Well, may be!" said Prince Andrew. "Go, Másha; I'll come immediately."

On the way to his sister's room, in the passage which connected one wing with the other, Prince Andrew met Mademoiselle Bourienne smiling sweetly. It was the third time that day that, with an ecstatic and artless smile, she had met him in secluded passages.

"Oh! I thought you were in your room," she said, for some reason blushing and dropping her eyes.

Prince Andrew looked sternly at her and an expression of anger suddenly came over his face. He said nothing to her but looked at her forehead and hair without looking at her eyes, with such contempt that the Frenchwoman blushed and went away without a word. When he reached his sister's room his wife was already awake and her merry voice, hurrying one word after another, came through the open door. She was speaking as usual in French, and as if after long self-restraint she wished to make up for lost time.

"No, but imagine the old Countess Zúbova, with false curls and her mouth full of false teeth, as if she were trying to cheat old age. . . . Ha, ha, ha! Mary!"

This very sentence about Countess Zúbova and this same laugh Prince Andrew had already heard from his wife in the presence of others some five times. He entered the room softly. The little princess, plump and rosy, was sitting in an easy chair with her work in her hands, talking incessantly, repeating Petersburg reminiscences and even phrases. Prince Andrew came up, stroked her hair, and asked if she felt rested after their journey. She answered him, and continued her chatter.

The coach with six horses was waiting at the porch. It was an autumn night, so dark that the coachman could not see the carriage-pole. Servants with lanterns were bustling about in the porch. The immense house was brilliant with lights shining through its lofty windows. The domestic serfs were crowding in the hall, waiting to bid good-bye to the young prince. The members of the household were all gathered in the reception hall: Michael Ivánovich, Mademoiselle Bourienne, Princess Mary and the little princess. Prince Andrew had been called to his father's study as the latter wished to say good-bye to him alone. All were waiting for them to come out.

When Prince Andrew entered the study the old man in his old-age spectacles and white dressing-gown, in which he received no one but his son, sat at the table writing. He glanced round.

"Going?" And he went on writing.

"I've come to say good-bye."

"Kiss me here," and he touched his cheek: "Thanks, thanks!"

"What do you thank me for?"

"For not dilly-dallying and not hanging to a woman's apron-strings. The Service before everything. Thanks, thanks!" And he went on writing, so that his quill spluttered and squeaked. "If you have anything to say, say it. These two things can be done together," he added.

"About my wife . . . I am ashamed as it is to leave her on your hands . . ."

"Why talk nonsense? Say what you want."

"When her confinement is due, send to Moscow for an *accoucheur*. . . . Let him be here. . . ."

The old prince stopped writing and, as if not understanding, fixed his stern eyes on his son.

"I know that no one can help if nature does not do her work," said Prince Andrew, evidently confused. "I know that out of a million cases only one goes wrong, but it is her fancy and mine. They have been telling her things. She has had a dream and is frightened."

"Hm . . . Hm . . ." muttered the old prince to himself, finishing what he was writing. "I'll do it."

He signed with a flourish and suddenly turning to his son began to laugh.

"It's a bad business, eh?"

"What is bad, father?"

"The wife!" said the old prince, briefly and significantly.

"I don't understand!" said Prince Andrew.

"No, it can't be helped, lad," said the prince. "They're all like that; one can't unmarry. Don't be afraid; I won't tell anyone, but you know it yourself."

He seized his son by the hand with small bony fingers, shook it, looked straight into his son's face with keen eyes which seemed to see through him, and again laughed his frigid laugh.

The son sighed, thus admitting that his father had understood him. The old man continued to fold and seal his letter, snatching up and throwing down the wax, the seal, and the paper, with his accustomed rapidity.

"What's to be done? She's pretty! I will do everything. Make your mind easy," said he in abrupt sentences while sealing his letter.

Andrew did not speak; he was both pleased and displeased that his father understood him. The old man got up and gave the letter to his son.

"Listen!" said he; "don't worry about your wife: what can be done shall be. Now listen! Give this letter to Michael Ilariónovich. I have written that he should make use of you in proper places and not keep you long as an adjutant: a bad position! Tell him I remember and like him. Write and tell me how he receives you. If he is all right—serve him. Nicholas Bolkónski's son need not serve under anyone if he is in disfavor. Now come here."

He spoke so rapidly that he did not finish half his words, but his son was accustomed to understand him. He led him to the desk, raised the lid, drew out a drawer, and took out an exercise-book filled with his bold, tall, close handwriting.

"I shall probably die before you. So remember, these are my memoirs; hand them to the Emperor after my death. Now here is a Lombard-bond and a letter; it is a premium for the man who writes a history of Suvórov's wars. Send it to the Academy. Here are some jottings for you to read when I am gone. You will find them useful."

Andrew did not tell his father that he would no doubt live a long time yet. He felt that he must not say it.

"I will do it all, father," he said.

"Well, now, good-bye!" He gave his son his hand to kiss, and embraced him. "Remember this, Prince Andrew, if they kill you it will hurt me, your old father . . ." he paused unexpectedly, and then in a querulous voice suddenly shrieked: "but if I hear that you have not behaved like a son of Nicholas Bolkónski, I shall be ashamed!"

"You need not have said that to me, father," said the son with a smile.

The old man was silent.

"I also wanted to ask you," continued Prince Andrew, "if I'm killed and if I have a son, do not let him be taken away from you—as I said yesterday . . . let him grow up with you . . . Please."

"Not let the wife have him?" said the old man, and laughed.

They stood silent, facing one another. The old man's sharp eyes were fixed straight on his son's. Something twitched in the lower part of the old prince's face.

"We've said good-bye. Go!" he suddenly shouted in a loud, angry voice, opening his door.

"What is it? What?" asked both princesses when they saw for a moment at the door Prince Andrew and the figure of the old man in a white dressing-gown, spectacled and wigless, shouting in an angry voice.

Prince Andrew sighed and made no reply.

"Well!" he said, turning to his wife.

And this "Well!" sounded coldly ironic, as if he were saying,: "Now go through your performance."

"Andrew, already!" said the little princess, turning pale and looking with dismay at her husband.

He embraced her. She screamed and fell unconscious on his shoulder.

He cautiously released the shoulder she leaned on, looked into her face, and carefully placed her in an easy chair.

"Adieu, Mary," said he gently to his sister, taking her by the hand and kissing her, and then he left the room with rapid steps.

The little princess lay in the arm-chair, Mademoiselle Bourienne chafing her temples. Princess Mary, supporting her sister-in-law, still looked with her beautiful eyes full of tears at the door through which Prince Andrew had gone and made the sign of the cross in his direction. From the study, like pistol shots, came the frequent sound of the old man angrily blowing his nose. Hardly had Prince Andrew gone when the study door opened quickly, and the stern figure of the old man in the white dressing-gown looked out.

"Gone? That's all right!" said he; and looking angrily at the unconscious little princess, he shook his head reprovingly and slammed the door.

Part Two

Chapter I

In October 1805 a Russian army was occupying the villages and towns of the Archduchy of Austria, and yet other regiments freshly arriving from Russia were settling near the fortress of Braunau and burdening the inhabitants on whom they were quartered. Braunau was the headquarters of the commander-in-chief, Kutúzov.

On October 11th, 1805, one of the infantry regiments that had just reached Braunau had halted half a mile from the town, waiting to be inspected by the commander-in-chief. Despite the un-Russian appearance of the locality and surroundings—fruit gardens, stone fences, tiled roofs, and hills in the distance—and despite the fact that the inhabitants (who gazed with curiosity at the soldiers) were not Russians, the regiment had just the appearance of any Russian regiment preparing for an inspection anywhere in the heart of Russia.

On the evening of the last day's march an order had been received that the commander-in-chief would inspect the regiment on the march. Though the words of the order were not clear to the regimental commander, and the question arose whether the troops were to be in marching order or not, it was decided at a consultation between the battalion commanders, to present the regiment in parade order, on the principle that it is always better to "bow too low than not bow low enough." So the soldiers, after a twenty-mile march, were kept mending and cleaning all night long without closing their eyes, while the adjutants and company-commanders calculated and reckoned, and by morning the regiment—instead of the straggling, disorderly crowd it had been on its last march the day before—presented a well-ordered array of two thousand men each of whom knew his place and his duty, had every button and every strap in place, and shone with cleanliness. And not only externally was all in order, but had it pleased the commander-in-chief to look under the uniforms he would have found on every man a clean shirt, and in every knapsack the appointed number of articles, "awl, soap, and all," as the soldiers say. There was only one circumstance concerning which no one could be at ease. It was the state of the soldiers' boots. More than half the men's boots were in holes. But this defect was not due to any fault of the regimental commander, for in spite of repeated demands boots had not been issued by the Austrian commissariat, and the regiment had marched some seven hundred miles.

The commander of the regiment was an elderly, choleric, stout and thick-set general with grizzled eyebrows and whiskers, and wider from chest to back than across the shoulders. He had on a brand new uniform showing the creases where it had been folded, and thick gold epaulets which seemed to stand rather than lie down on his massive shoulders. He had the air of a man happily performing one of the most solemn duties of his life. He walked about in front of the line and at every step pulled himself up, slightly arching his back. It was plain that the commander admired his regiment, rejoiced in it, and that his whole mind was engrossed by it, yet his strut seemed to indicate that, besides military matters, social interests and the fair sex occupied no small part of his thoughts.

"Well, Michael Mítrich, sir?" he said, addressing one of the battalion commanders who smilingly pressed forward (it was plain that they both felt happy). "We had our hands full last night. However, I think the regiment is not a bad one, eh?"

The battalion commander perceived the jovial irony and laughed.

"It would not be turned off the field even on the Tsarítsin Meadow."

"What?" asked the commander.

At that moment, on the road from the town on which signalers had been posted, two men appeared on horseback. They were an aide-de-camp followed by a Cossack.

The aide-de-camp was sent to confirm the order which had not been clearly worded the day before, namely, that the commander-in-chief wished to see the regiment just in the state in which it had been on the march: in their greatcoats, and packs, and without any preparation whatever.

A member of the Hofkriegsrath from Vienna had come to Kutúzov the day before with proposals and demands for him to join up with the army of the Archduke Ferdinand and Mack, and Kutúzov, not considering this junction advisable, meant among other arguments in support of his view, to show the Austrian general the wretched state in which the troops arrived from Russia. With this object he intended to meet the regiment; so the worse the condition it was in, the better pleased the commander-in-chief would be. Though the aide-de-camp did not know these circumstances, he nevertheless delivered the definite order that the men should be in their greatcoats and in marching-order, and that the commander-in-chief would otherwise be dissatisfied. On hearing this the regimental commander hung his head, silently shrugged his shoulders, and spread out his arms with a choleric gesture.

"A fine mess we've made of it!" he remarked.

"There now! Didn't I tell you, Michael Mítrich, that if it was said 'on the march' it meant in greatcoats?" said he reproachfully to the battalion commander. "Oh, my God!" he added stepping resolutely forward. "Company commanders!" he shouted in a voice accustomed to command. "Sergeant-majors! . . . How soon will he be here?" he asked the aide-de-camp with a respectful politeness evidently relating to the personage he was referring to.

"In an hour's time, I should say."

"Shall we have time to change clothes?"

"I don't know, general. . . ."

The regimental commander, going up to the line himself, ordered the soldiers to change into their greatcoats. The company commanders ran off to their companies, the sergeant-majors began bustling (the greatcoats were not in very good condition), and instantly the squares that had up to then been in regular order and silent, began to sway and stretch and hum with voices. On all sides soldiers were running to and fro, throwing up their knapsacks with a jerk of their shoulders and pulling the straps over their heads, unstrapping their overcoats and drawing the sleeves on with upraised arms.

In half an hour all was again in order, only the squares had become gray instead of black. The regimental commander walked with his jerky steps to the front of the regiment and examined it from a distance.

"Whatever is this? This!" he shouted and stood still. "Commander of the third company!"

"Commander of the third company wanted by the general! . . . commander to the general . . . third company to the commander." The words passed along the lines and an adjutant ran to look for the missing officer.

When the eager but misrepeated words had reached their destination in a cry of: "The general to the third company," the missing officer appeared from behind his company and, though he was a middle-aged man and not in the habit of running, trotted awkwardly stumbling on his toes toward the general. The captain's face showed the uneasiness of a schoolboy who is told to repeat a lesson he has not learned. Spots appeared on his nose, the redness of which was evidently due to intemperance, and his mouth twitched nervously. The general looked the captain up and down as he came up panting, slackening his pace as he approached.

"You will soon be dressing your men in petticoats! What is this?" shouted the regimental commander, thrusting forward his jaw and pointing at a soldier in the ranks of the third company in a greatcoat of bluish cloth, which contrasted with the others. "What have you been after? The commander-in-chief is expected and you leave your place? Eh? I'll teach you to dress the men in fancy coats for a parade. . . . Eh . . . ?"

The commander of the company, with his eyes fixed on his superior pressed two fingers more and more rigidly to his cap, as if in this pressure lay his only hope of salvation.

"Well, why don't you speak? Whom have you got there dressed up as a Hungarian?" said the commander with an austere gibe.

"Your excellency . . ."

"Well, your excellency what? Your excellency! But what about your excellency? . . . nobody knows."

"Your excellency, it's the officer Dólokhov, who has been reduced to the ranks," said the captain softly.

"Well? Has he been degraded into a field marshal, or into a soldier? If a soldier, he should be dressed in regulation uniform like the others."

"Your excellency, you gave him leave yourself, on the march."

"Gave him leave? Leave? That's just like you young men," said the regimental commander cooling down a little. "Leave indeed. . . . One says a word to you and you . . . What?" he added with renewed irritation, "I beg you to dress your men decently."

And the commander, turning to look at the adjutant, directed his jerky steps down the line. He was evidently pleased at his own display of anger and walking up to the regiment wished to find a further excuse for wrath. Having snapped at an officer for an unpolished badge, at another because his line was not straight, he reached the third company.

"H-o-o-w are you standing? Where's your leg? Your leg?" shouted the commander with a tone of suffering in his voice, while there were still five men between him and Dólokhov with his bluish-gray uniform.

Dólokhov slowly straightened his bent knee, looking straight with his clear, insolent eyes in the general's face.

"Why a blue coat? Off with it . . . Sergeant-major! Change his coat . . . the ras . . ." he did not finish.

"General, I must obey orders, but I am not bound to endure . . ." Dólokhov hurriedly interrupted.

"No talking in the ranks! . . . No talking, no talking!"

"Not bound to endure insults," Dólokhov concluded in loud, ringing tones.

The eyes of the general and the soldier met. The general became silent, angrily pulling down his tight scarf.

"I request you to have the goodness to change your coat," he said as he turned away.

Chapter II

HE'S COMING!" SHOUTED THE SIGNALER AT THAT MOMENT.

The regimental commander, flushing, ran to his horse, seized the stirrup with trembling hands, threw his body across the saddle, righted himself, drew his saber, and with a happy and resolute countenance, opening his mouth awry, prepared to shout. The regiment fluttered like a bird preening its plumage, and became motionless.

"Att-ention!" shouted the regimental commander in a soul-shaking voice which expressed joy for himself, severity for the regiment, and welcome for the approaching chief.

Along the broad country road, edged on both sides by trees, came a high, light-blue Viennese calèche, slightly creaking on its springs and drawn by six horses at a smart trot. Behind the calèche galloped the suite and a convoy of Croats. Beside Kutúzov sat an Austrian general, in a white uniform that looked strange among the Russian black ones. The calèche stopped in front of the regiment. Kutúzov and the Austrian general were talking in low voices and Kutúzov smiled slightly as treading heavily he stepped down from the carriage just as if those two thousand men breathlessly gazing at him and the regimental commander did not exist.

The word of command rang out, and again the regiment quivered, as with a jingling sound it presented arms. Then amidst a dead silence the feeble voice of the commander-in-chief was heard. The regiment roared, "Health to your Ex . . . len . . . len . . . lency!" and again all became silent. At first Kutúzov stood still while the regiment moved; then he and the general in white, accompanied by the suite, walked between the ranks.

From the way the regimental commander saluted the commander-in-chief and devoured him with his eyes, drawing himself up obsequiously, and from the way he walked through the ranks behind the generals, bending forward and hardly able to restrain his jerky movements, and from the way he darted forward at every word or gesture of the commander-in-chief, it was evident that he performed his duty as a subordinate with even greater zeal than his duty as a commander. Thanks to the strictness and assiduity of its commander the regiment, in comparison with others that had reached Braunau at the same time, was in splendid condition. There were only 217 sick and stragglers. Everything was in good order except the boots.

Kutúzov walked through the ranks, sometimes stopping to say a few friendly words to officers he had known in the Turkish war, sometimes also to the soldiers. Looking at their boots he several times shook his head sadly, pointing them out to the Austrian general with an expression which seemed to say that he was not blaming anyone, but could not help noticing what a bad state of things it was. The regimental commander ran forward on each such occasion fearing to miss a single word of the commander-in-chief's regarding the regiment. Behind Kutúzov, at a distance that allowed every softly spoken word to be heard, followed some twenty men of his suite. These gentlemen talked among themselves and sometimes laughed. Nearest of all to the commander-in-chief walked a handsome adjutant. This was Prince Bolkónski. Beside him was his comrade Nesvítski, a tall staff-officer, extremely stout, with a kindly, smiling, handsome face and moist eyes. Nesvítski could hardly keep from laughter provoked by a swarthy hussar officer who walked beside him. This hussar, with a grave face and without a smile or a change in the expression of his fixed eyes, watched the regimental commander's back and mimicked his every movement. Each time the commander started and bent forward, the hussar started and bent forward in exactly the same manner. Nesvítski laughed and nudged the others to make them look at the wag.

Kutúzov walked slowly and languidly past thousands of eyes which were starting from their sockets to watch their chief. On reaching the third company he suddenly stopped. His suite, not having expected this, involuntarily came closer to him.

"Ah, Timókhin!" said he, recognizing the red-nosed captain who had been reprimanded on account of the blue greatcoat.

One would have thought it impossible for a man to stretch himself more than Timókhin had done when he was reprimanded by the regimental commander, but now that the commander-in-chief addressed him he drew himself up to such an extent that it seemed he could not have sustained it had the commander-in-chief continued to look at him, and so Kutúzov, who evidently understood his case and wished him nothing but good, quickly turned away, a scarcely perceptible smile flitting over his scarred and puffy face.

"Another Ismail comrade," said he. "A brave officer! Are you satisfied with him?" he asked the regimental commander.

And the latter—unconscious that he was being reflected in the hussar officer as in a looking-glass—started, moved forward, and answered: "Highly satisfied, your excellency!"

"We all have our weaknesses," said Kutúzov smiling and walking away from him. "He used to have a predilection for Bacchus."

The regimental commander was afraid he might be blamed for this, and did not answer. The hussar at that moment noticed the face of the red-nosed captain and his drawn-in stomach, and mimicked his expression and pose with such exactitude that Nesvítski could not help laughing. Kutúzov turned round. The officer evidently had complete control of his face, and while Kutúzov was turning managed to make a grimace and then assume a most serious, deferential, and innocent expression.

The third company was the last, and Kutúzov pondered, apparently trying to recollect something. Prince Andrew stepped forward from among the suite and said in French:

"You told me to remind you of the officer Dólokhov, reduced to the ranks in this regiment."

"Where is Dólokhov?" asked Kutúzov.

Dólokhov, who had already changed into a soldier's gray greatcoat, did not wait to be called. The shapely figure of the fair-haired soldier, with his clear blue eyes, stepped forward from the ranks, went up to the commander-in-chief, and presented arms.

"Have you a complaint to make?" Kutúzov asked with a slight frown.

"This is Dólokhov," said Prince Andrew.

"Ah!" said Kutúzov. "I hope this will be a lesson to you. Do your duty. The Emperor is gracious, and I shan't forget you if you deserve well."

The clear blue eyes looked at the commander-in-chief just as boldly as they had looked at the regimental commander, seeming by their expression to tear open the veil of convention that separates a commander-in-chief so widely from a private.

"One thing I ask of your excellency," Dólokhov said in his firm, ringing, deliberate voice. "I ask an opportunity to atone for my fault and prove my devotion to his Majesty the Emperor and to Russia!"

Kutúzov turned away. The same smile of the eyes with which he had turned from Captain Timókhin again flitted over his face. He turned away with a grimace as if to say that everything Dólokhov had said to him and everything he could say had long been known to him, that he was weary of it and it was not at all what he wanted. He turned away and went to the carriage.

The regiment broke up into companies, which went to their appointed quarters near Braunau, where they hoped to receive boots and clothes and to rest after their hard marches.

"You won't bear me a grudge, Prokhór Ignátych?" said the regimental commander, overtaking the third company on its way to its quarters and riding up to Captain Timókhin who was walking in front. (The regimental commander's face now that the inspection was happily over beamed with irrepressible delight.) "It's in the Emperor's service . . . it can't be helped . . . one is sometimes a bit hasty on parade . . . I am the first to apologize, you know me! . . . He was very pleased!" And he held out his hand to the captain.

"Don't mention it, general, as if I'd be so bold!" replied the captain, his nose growing redder as he gave a smile which showed where two front teeth were missing that had been knocked out by the butt end of a gun at Ismail.

"And tell Mr. Dólokhov that I won't forget him—he may be quite easy. And tell me, please—I've been meaning to ask—how is he behaving himself, and in general . . ."

"As far as the service goes he is quite punctilious, your excellency; but his character . . ." said Timókhin.

"And what about his character?" asked the regimental commander.

"It's different on different days," answered the captain. "One day he is sensible, well educated and good-natured, and the next he's a wild beast. . . . In Poland, if you please, he nearly killed a Jew."

"Oh, well, well!" remarked the regimental commander. "Still, one must have pity on a young man in misfortune. You know he has important connections . . . Well, then, you just . . ."

"I will, your excellency," said Timókhin, showing by his smile that he understood his commander's wish.

"Well, of course, of course!"

The regimental commander sought out Dólokhov in the ranks, and reining in his horse, said to him:

"After the next affair . . . epaulets."

Dólokhov looked round but did not say anything, nor did the mocking smile on his lips change.

"Well, that's all right," continued the regimental commander. "A cup of vodka for the men from me," he added so that the soldiers could hear. "I thank you all! God be praised!" and he rode past that company and overtook the next one.

"Well, he's really a good fellow, one can serve under him," said Timókhin to the subaltern beside him.

"In a word, a hearty one . . ." said the subaltern, laughing (the regimental commander was nicknamed *King of Hearts*).

The cheerful mood of their officers after the inspection infected the soldiers. The company marched on gaily. The soldiers' voices could be heard on every side.

"And they said Kutúzov was blind of one eye?"

"And so he is! Quite blind!"

"No, friend, he is sharper eyed than you are. Boots and legbands . . . he noticed everything . . ."

"When he looked at my feet, friend . . . well, thinks I . . ."

"And that other one with him, the Austrian, looked as if he were smeared with chalk—as white as flour! I suppose they polish him up as they do the guns."

"I say, Fédeshon! . . . Did he say when the battles are to begin? You were near him. Everybody said that Buonaparte himself was at Braunau."

"Buonaparte himself! . . . Just listen to the fool, what he doesn't know! The Prussians are up in arms now. The Austrians, you see, are putting them down. When they've been put down, the war with Buonaparte will begin. And he says Buonaparte is in Braunau! Shows you're a fool. You'd better listen more carefully!"

"What devils these quartermasters are! See, the fifth company is turning into the village already . . . they will have their buckwheat cooked before we reach our quarters."

"Give me a biscuit, you devil!"

"And did you give me tobacco yesterday? That's just it, friend! Ah, well, never mind, here you are."

"They might call a halt here or we'll have to do another four miles without eating."

"Wasn't it fine when those Germans gave us lifts! You just sit still and are drawn along."

"And here, friend, the people are quite beggarly. There they all seemed to be Poles—all under the Russian crown—but here they're all regular Germans."

"Singers to the front " came the captain's order.

And from the different ranks some twenty men ran to the front. A drummer, their leader, turned round facing the singers, and flourishing his arm began a long-drawn-out soldiers' song, commencing with the words: *"Morning dawned, the sun was rising,"* and concluding: *"On then, brothers, on to glory, led by Father Kámenski."* This song had been composed in the Turkish campaign and now being sung in Austria, the only change being that the words "Father Kámenski" were replaced by "Father Kutúzov."

Having jerked out these last words as soldiers do and waved his arms as if flinging something to the ground, the drummer—a lean, handsome soldier of forty—looked sternly at the singers and screwed up his eyes. Then having satisfied himself that all eyes were fixed on him, he raised both arms as if carefully lifting some invisible but precious object above his head and, holding it there for some seconds, suddenly flung it down and began:

"Oh, my bower, oh, my bower . . . !"

"Oh, my bower new . . . !" chimed in twenty voices, and the castanet-player in spite of the burden of his equipment rushed out to the front and walking backward before the company, jerked his shoulders and flourished his castanets as if threatening someone. The soldiers, swinging their arms and keeping time spontaneously, marched with long steps. Behind the company the sound of wheels, the creaking of springs, and the tramp of horses' hoofs were heard. Kutúzov and his suite were returning to the town. The commander-in-chief made a sign that the men should continue to march at ease, and he and all his suite showed pleasure at the sound of the singing and the sight of the dancing soldier and the gay and smartly marching men. In the second file from the right flank, beside which the carriage passed the company, a blue-eyed soldier involuntarily attracted notice. It was Dólokhov marching with particular grace and boldness in time to the song and looking at those driving past as if he pitied all who were not at that moment marching with the company. The hussar cornet of Kutúzov's suite who had mimicked the regimental commander, fell back from the carriage and rode up to Dólokhov.

Hussar cornet Zherkóv had at one time, in Petersburg, belonged to the wild set led by Dólokhov. Zherkóv had met Dólokhov abroad as a private and had not seen fit to recognize him. But now that Kutúzov had spoken to the gentleman-ranker, he addressed him with the cordiality of an old friend.

"My dear fellow, how are you?" said he through the singing, making his horse keep pace with the company.

"How am I?" Dólokhov answered coldly. "I am as you see."

The lively song gave a special flavor to the tone of free and easy gaiety with which Zherkóv spoke, and to the intentional coldness of Dólokhov's reply.

"And how do you get on with the officers?" inquired Zherkóv.

"All right. They are good fellows. And how have you wriggled onto the staff?"

"I was attached; I am on duty."

Both were silent.

"She let the hawk fly upward from her wide right sleeve," went the song, arousing an involuntary sensation of courage and cheerfulness. Their conversation would probably have been different but for the effect of that song.

"Is it true that Austrians have been beaten?" asked Dólokhov.

"The devil only knows! They say so."

"I'm glad," answered Dólokhov briefly and clearly, as the song demanded.

"I say, come round some evening and we'll have a game of faro!" said Zherkóv.

"Why, have you too much money?"

"Do come."

"I can't. I've sworn not to. I won't drink and won't play till I get reinstated."

"Well that's only till the first engagement."

"We shall see."

They were again silent.

"Come if you need anything. One can at least be of use on the staff . . ."

Dólokhov smiled. "Don't trouble. If I want anything, I won't beg—I'll take it!"

"Well, never mind; I only . . ."

"And I only . . ."

"Good-bye."

"Good health . . ."

It's a long, long way
To my native land . . .

Zherkóv touched his horse with the spurs; it pranced excitedly from foot to foot uncertain with which to start, then settled down, galloped past the company, and overtook the carriage, still keeping time to the song.

Chapter III

On returning from the review Kutúzov took the Austrian general into his private room, and calling his adjutant, asked for some papers relating to the condition of the troops on their arrival, and the letters that had come from the Archduke Ferdinand, who was in command of the advanced army. Prince Andrew Bolkónski came into the room with the required papers. Kutúzov and the Austrian member of the Hofkriegsrath were sitting at the table on which a plan was spread out.

"Ah! . . ." said Kutúzov glancing at Bolkónski as if by this exclamation he was asking the adjutant to wait, and he went on with the conversation in French.

"All I can say, general," said he with a pleasant elegance of expression and intonation that obliged one to listen to each deliberately spoken word. It was evident that Kutúzov himself listened with pleasure to his own voice. "All I can say, general, is that if the matter depended on my personal wishes, the will of his Majesty the Emperor Francis would have been fulfilled long ago. I should long ago have joined the archduke. And believe me on my honor that to me personally it would be a pleasure to hand over the supreme command of the army into the hands of a better informed and more skillful general—of whom Austria has so many—and to lay down all this heavy responsibility. But circumstances are sometimes too strong for us, general."

And Kutúzov smiled in a way that seemed to say, "You are quite at liberty not to believe me and I don't even care whether you do or not, but you have no grounds for telling me so. And that is the whole point."

The Austrian general looked dissatisfied, but had no option but to reply in the same tone.

"On the contrary," he said, in a querulous and angry tone that contrasted with his flattering words, "on the contrary, your excellency's participation in the common action is highly valued by his Majesty; but we think the present delay is depriving the splendid Russian troops and their commander of the laurels they have been accustomed to win in their battles," he concluded his evidently prearranged sentence.

Kutúzov bowed with the same smile.

"But that is my conviction, and judging by the last letter with which his Highness the Archduke Ferdinand has honored me, I imagine that the Austrian troops, under the direction of so skillful a leader as General Mack have by now already gained a decisive victory and no longer need our aid," said Kutúzov.

The general frowned. Though there was no definite news of an Austrian defeat, there were many circumstances confirming the unfavorable rumors that were afloat, and so Kutúzov's suggestion of an Austrian victory sounded much like irony. But Kutúzov went on blandly smiling with the same expression, which seemed to say that he had a right to suppose so. And in fact the last letter he had received from Mack's army informed him of a victory and stated that strategically the position of the army was very favorable.

"Give me that letter," said Kutúzov turning to Prince Andrew. "Please have a look at it"—and Kutúzov with an ironical smile about the corners of his mouth read to the Austrian general the following passage, in German, from the Archduke Ferdinand's letter.

"We have fully concentrated forces of nearly seventy thousand men with which to attack and defeat the enemy should he cross the Lech. Also, as we are masters of Ulm, we cannot be deprived of the advantage of commanding both sides of the Danube, so that should the enemy not cross the Lech, we can cross the Danube, throw ourselves on his line of communications, recross the river lower down, and frustrate his intention should he try to direct his whole force against our faithful ally. We shall therefore confidently await

the moment when the Imperial Russian army will be fully equipped, and shall then, in conjunction with it, easily find a way to prepare for the enemy the fate he deserves."

Kutúzov sighed deeply on finishing this paragraph and looked at the member of the Hofkriegsrath mildly and attentively.

"But you know the wise maxim, your excellency, advising one to expect the worst," said the Austrian general, evidently wishing to have done with jests and to come to business. He involuntarily looked round at the aide-de-camp.

"Excuse me, general," interrupted Kutúzov, also turning to Prince Andrew. "Look here, my dear fellow, get from Kozlóvski all the reports from our scouts. Here are two letters from Count Nostitz and here is one from his Highness the Archduke Ferdinand and here are these," he said, handing him several papers, "make a neat memorandum in French out of all this, showing all the news we have had of the movements of the Austrian army, and then give it to his excellency."

Prince Andrew bowed his head in token of having understood from the first not only what had been said but also what Kutúzov would have liked to tell him. He gathered up the papers and, with a bow to both, stepped softly over the carpet and went out into the waiting room.

Though not much time had passed since Prince Andrew had left Russia, he had changed greatly during that period. In the expression of his face, in his movements, in his walk, scarcely a trace was left of his former affected languor and indolence. He now looked like a man who has time to think of the impression he makes on others, but is occupied with agreeable and interesting work. His face expressed more satisfaction with himself and those around him, his smile and glance were brighter and more attractive.

Kutúzov whom he had overtaken in Poland, had received him very kindly, promised not to forget him, distinguished him above the other adjutants, and had taken him to Vienna and given him the more serious commissions. From Vienna Kutúzov wrote to his old comrade, Prince Andrew's father:

Your son bids fair to become an officer distinguished by his industry, firmness, and expedition. I consider myself fortunate to have such a subordinate by me.

On Kutúzov's staff, among his fellow-officers and in the army generally, Prince Andrew had, as he had had in Petersburg society, two quite opposite reputations. Some, a minority, acknowledged him to be different from themselves and from everyone else, expected great things of him, listened to him, admired, and imitated him, and with them Prince Andrew was natural and pleasant. Others, the majority, disliked him and considered him conceited, cold, and disagreeable. But among these people Prince Andrew knew how to take his stand so that they respected and even feared him.

Coming out of Kutúzov's room into the waiting room with the papers in his hand Prince Andrew came up to his comrade, the aide-de-camp on duty, Kozlóvski, who was sitting at the window with a book.

"Well, prince?" asked Kozlóvski.

"I am ordered to write a memorandum explaining why we are not advancing."

"And why is it?"

Prince Andrew shrugged his shoulders.

"Any news from Mack?"

"No."

"If it were true that he has been beaten, news would have come."

"Probably," said Prince Andrew moving toward the outer door.

But at that instant a tall Austrian general in a greatcoat, with the order of Maria Theresa on his neck and a black bandage round his head, who had evidently just arrived, entered quickly, slamming the door. Prince Andrew stopped short.

"Commander-in-Chief Kutúzov?" said the newly-arrived general speaking quickly with a harsh German accent, looking to both sides and advancing straight toward the inner door.

"The commander-in-chief is engaged," said Kozlóvski, going hurriedly up to the unknown general and blocking his way to the door. "Whom shall I announce?"

The unknown general looked disdainfully down at Kozlóvski, who was rather short, as if surprised that anyone should not know him.

"The commander-in-chief is engaged," repeated Kozlóvski calmly.

The general's face clouded, his lips quivered and trembled. He took out a notebook, hurriedly scribbled something in pencil, tore out the leaf, gave it to Kozlóvski, stepped quickly to the window and threw himself into a chair, gazing at those in the room as if asking, "Why do they look at me?" Then he lifted his head, stretched his neck as if he intended to say something, but immediately, with affected indifference, began to hum to himself, producing a queer sound which immediately broke off. The door of the private room opened and Kutúzov appeared in the doorway. The general with the bandaged head bent forward as though running away from some danger, and making long quick strides with his thin legs, went up to Kutúzov.

"Vous voyez le malheureux Mack," he uttered in a broken voice.

Kutúzov's face as he stood in the open doorway remained perfectly immobile for a few moments. Then wrinkles ran over his face like a wave and his forehead became smooth again, he bowed his head respectfully, closed his eyes, silently let Mack enter his room before him, and closed the door himself behind him.

The report which had been circulated that the Austrians had been beaten and that the whole army had surrendered at Ulm proved to be correct. Within half an hour adjutants had been sent in various directions with orders which showed that the Russian troops, who had hitherto been inactive, would also soon have to meet the enemy.

Prince Andrew was one of those rare staff-officers whose chief interest lay in the general progress of the war. When he saw Mack and heard the details of his disaster he understood that half the campaign was lost, understood all the difficulties of the Russian army's position, and vividly imagined what awaited it and the part he would have to play. Involuntarily he felt a joyful agitation at the thought of the humiliation of arrogant Austria and that in a week's time he might, perhaps, see and take part in the first Russian encounter with the French since Suvórov met them. He feared that Bonaparte's genius might outweigh all the courage of the Russian troops, and at the same time could not admit the idea of his hero being disgraced.

Excited and irritated by these thoughts Prince Andrew went toward his room to write to his father, to whom he wrote every day. In the corridor he met Nesvítski with whom he shared a room, and the wag Zherkóv; they were as usual laughing.

"Why are you so glum?" asked Nesvítski noticing Prince Andrew's pale face and glittering eyes.

"There's nothing to be gay about," answered Bolkónski.

Just as Prince Andrew met Nesvítski and Zherkóv, there came toward them from the other end of the corridor, Strauch, an Austrian general who was on Kutúzov's staff in charge of the provisioning of the Russian army, and the member of the Hofkriegsrath who had arrived the previous evening. There was room enough in the wide corridor for the generals to pass the three officers quite easily, but Zherkóv, pushing Nesvítski aside with his arm, said in a breathless voice,

"They're coming! . . . they're coming! . . . Stand aside, make way, please make way!"

The generals were passing by, looking as if they wished to avoid embarrassing attentions. On the face of the wag Zherkóv there suddenly appeared a stupid smile of glee which he seemed unable to suppress.

"Your excellency," said he in German, stepping forward and addressing the Austrian general, "I have the honor to congratulate you."

He bowed his head and scraped first with one boot and then with the other, awkwardly, like a child at a dancing lesson.

The member of the Hofkriegsrath looked at him severely, but seeing the seriousness of his stupid smile, could not but give him a moment's attention. He screwed up his eyes showing that he was listening.

"I have the honor to congratulate you. General Mack has arrived, quite well, only a little bruised just here," he added, pointing with a beaming smile to his head.

The general frowned, turned away, and went on.

"Gott, wie naiv!" said he angrily, after he had gone a few steps.

Nesvítski with a laugh threw his arms round Prince Andrew, but Bolkónski turning still paler, pushed him away with an angry look and turned to Zherkóv. The nervous irritation aroused by the appearance of Mack, the news of his defeat, and the thought of what lay before the Russian army, found vent in anger at Zherkóv's untimely jest.

"If you, sir, choose to make a *buffoon* of yourself," he said sharply, with a slight trembling of the lower jaw, "I can't prevent your doing so; but I warn you that if you dare to play the fool in my presence, I will teach you to behave yourself."

Nesvítski and Zherkóv were so surprised by this outburst that they gazed at Bolkónski silently with wide-open eyes.

"What's the matter? I only congratulated them," said Zherkóv.

"I am not jesting with you; please be silent!" cried Bolkónski, and taking Nesvítski's arm he left Zherkóv, who did not know what to say.

"Come, what's the matter, old fellow?" said Nesvítski trying to soothe him.

"What's the matter?" exclaimed Prince Andrew standing still in his excitement. "Don't you understand that either we are officers serving our Tsar and our country, rejoicing in the successes and grieving at the misfortunes of our common cause, or we are merely lackeys who care nothing for their master's business. *Quarante mille hommes massacrés et l'armée de nos alliés détruite, et vous trouvez là le mot pour rire,*" he said, as if strengthening his views by this French sentence. "*C'est bien pour un garçon de rien comme cet individu dont vous avez fait un ami, mais pas pour vous, pas pour vous.* Only a *hobbledehoy* could amuse himself in this way," he added in Russian—but pronouncing the word with a French accent—having noticed that Zherkóv could still hear him.

He waited a moment to see whether the cornet would answer, but he turned and went out of the corridor.

Chapter IV

THE PÁVLOGRAD HUSSARS WERE STATIONED TWO MILES FROM BRAUNAU. THE SQUADRON IN which Nicholas Rostóv served as a cadet was quartered in the German village of Salzeneck. The best quarters in the village were assigned to cavalry-captain Denísov, the squadron commander, known throughout the whole cavalry division as Váska Denísov. Cadet Rostóv ever since he had overtaken the regiment in Poland had lived with the squadron commander.

On October 11th, the day when all was astir at headquarters over the news of Mack's defeat, the camp life of the officers of this squadron was proceeding as usual. Denísov, who had been losing at cards all night, had not yet come home when Rostóv rode back early in the morning from a foraging expedition. Rostóv in his cadet uniform, with a jerk to his horse rode up to the porch, swung his leg over the saddle with a supple youthful movement, stood for a moment in the stirrup as if loathe to part from his horse, and at last sprang down and called to his orderly.

"Ah, Bondarénko, dear friend!" said he to the hussar who rushed up headlong to the horse. "Walk him up and down, my dear fellow," he continued, with that gay brotherly cordiality which good-hearted young people show to everyone when they are happy.

"Yes, your excellency," answered the Ukrainian gaily, tossing his head.

"Mind, walk him up and down well!"

Another hussar also rushed toward the horse, but Bondarénko had already thrown the reins of the snaffle-bridle over the horse's head. It was evident that the cadet was liberal with his tips and that it paid to serve him. Rostóv patted the horse's neck and then his flank, and lingered for a moment.

"Splendid! What a horse he will be!" he thought with a smile, and holding up his saber, his spurs jingling, he ran up the steps of the porch. His landlord, who in a waistcoat and a pointed cap, pitchfork in hand, was clearing manure from the cow house, looked out, and his face immediately brightened on seeing Rostóv. *"Schön gut Morgen! Schön gut Morgen!"* he said winking with a merry smile, evidently pleased to greet the young man.

"Schön fleissig?" said Rostóv with the same gay brotherly smile which did not leave his eager face. *"Hoch Oestreicher! Hoch Russen! Kaiser Alexander hoch!"* said he, quoting words often repeated by the German landlord.

The German laughed, came out of the cowshed, pulled off his cap, and waving it above his head cried:

"Und die ganze Welt hoch!"

Rostóv waved his cap above his head like the German and cried laughing, *"Und vivat die ganze Welt!"* Though neither the German cleaning his cowshed, nor Rostóv back with his platoon from foraging for hay, had any reason for rejoicing, they looked at each other with joyful delight and brotherly love, wagged their heads in token of their mutual affection, and parted smiling, the German returning to his cowshed and Rostóv going to the cottage he occupied with Denísov.

"What about your master?" he asked Lavrúshka, Denísov's orderly, whom all the regiment knew for a rogue.

"Hasn't been in since the evening. Must have been losing," answered Lavrúshka. "I know by now, if he wins he comes back early to brag about it, but if he stays out till morning it means he's lost and will come back in a rage. Will you have coffee?"

"Yes, bring some."

Ten minutes later Lavrúshka brought the coffee. "He's coming!" said he. "Now for trouble!" Rostóv looked out of the window and saw Denísov coming home. Denísov was a small man with a red face, sparkling black eyes, and black tousled mustache and hair. He wore an unfastened cloak, wide breeches hanging down in creases, and a crumpled shako on the back of his head. He came up to the porch gloomily, hanging his head.

"Lavwúska!" he shouted loudly and angrily, "take it off, block-head!"

"Well, I am taking it off," replied Lavrúshka's voice.

"Ah, you're up already," said Denísov, entering the room.

"Long ago," answered Rostóv, "I have already been for the hay, and have seen Fräulein Mathilde."

"Weally! And I've been losing, bwother. I lost yesterday like a damned fool!" cried Denísov, not pronouncing his *r*'s. "Such ill luck! Such ill luck. As soon as you left, it began and went on. Hullo there! Tea!"

Puckering up his face though smiling, and showing his short strong teeth, he began with stubby fingers of both hands to ruffle up his thick tangled black hair.

"And what devil made me go to that wat?" (an officer nicknamed "the rat") he said, rubbing his forehead and whole face with both hands. "Just fancy, he didn't let me win a single cahd, not one cahd."

He took the lit pipe that was offered to him, gripped it in his fist, and tapped it on the floor, making the sparks fly, while he continued to shout.

"He lets one win the singles and collahs it as soon as one doubles it; gives the singles and snatches the doubles!"

He scattered the burning tobacco, smashed the pipe, and threw it away. Then he remained silent for a while, and all at once looked cheerfully with his glittering, black eyes at Rostóv.

"If at least we had some women here; but there's nothing foh one to do but dwink. If we could only get to fighting soon. Hullo, who's there?" he said, turning to the door as he heard a tread of heavy boots and the clinking of spurs that came to a stop, and a respectful cough.

"The squadron quartermaster!" said Lavrúshka.

Denísov's face puckered still more.

"Wetched!" he muttered, throwing down a purse with some gold in it. "Wostóv, deah fellow, just see how much there is left and shove the purse undah the pillow," he said, and went out to the quartermaster.

Rostóv took the money and, mechanically arranging the old and new coins in separate piles, began counting them.

"Ah! Telyánin! How d'ye do? They plucked me last night," came Denísov's voice from the next room.

"Where? At Bykov's, at the rat's . . . I knew it," replied a piping voice, and Lieutenant Telyánin, a small officer of the same squadron, entered the room.

Rostóv thrust the purse under the pillow and shook the damp little hand which was offered him. Telyánin for some reason had been transferred from the Guards just before this campaign. He behaved very well in the regiment but was not liked: Rostóv especially detested him and was unable to overcome or conceal his groundless antipathy to the man.

"Well, young cavalryman, how is my Rook behaving?" he asked. (Rook was a young horse Telyánin had sold to Rostóv.)

The lieutenant never looked the man he was speaking to straight in the face; his eyes continually wandered from one object to another.

"I saw you riding this morning . . ." he added.

"Oh, he's all right, a good horse," answered Rostóv, though the horse for which he had paid seven hundred rubbles was not worth half that sum. "He's begun to go a little lame on the left foreleg," he added.

"The hoof's cracked! That's nothing. I'll teach you what to do and show you what kind of rivet to use."

"Yes, please do," said Rostóv.

"I'll show you, I'll show you! It's not a secret. And it's a horse you'll thank me for."

"Then I'll have it brought round," said Rostóv wishing to avoid Telyánin, and he went out to give the order.

In the passage Denísov, with a pipe, was squatting on the threshold facing the quartermaster who was reporting to him. On seeing Rostóv, Denísov screwed up his face and pointing over his shoulder with his thumb to the room where Telyánin was sitting, he frowned and gave a shudder of disgust.

"Ugh! I don't like that fellow," he said, regardless of the quartermaster's presence.

Rostóv shrugged his shoulders as much as to say: "Nor do I, but what's one to do?" and, having given his order, he returned to Telyánin.

Telyánin was sitting in the same indolent pose in which Rostóv had left him, rubbing his small white hands.

"Well there certainly are disgusting people," thought Rostóv as he entered.

"Have you told them to bring the horse?" asked Telyánin, getting up and looking carelessly about him.

"I have."

"Let us go ourselves. I only came round to ask Denísov about yesterday's order. Have you got it, Denísov?"

"Not yet. But where are you off to?"

"I want to teach this young man how to shoe a horse," said Telyánin.

They went through the porch and into the stable. The lieutenant explained how to rivet the hoof and went away to his own quarters.

When Rostóv went back there was a bottle of vodka and a sausage on the table. Denísov was sitting there scratching with his pen on a sheet of paper. He looked gloomily in Rostóv's face and said:

"I am witing to her."

He leaned his elbows on the table with his pen in his hand, and evidently glad of a chance to say quicker in words what he wanted to write, told Rostóv the contents of his letter.

"You see, my fwiend," he said, "we sleep when we don't love. We are childwen of the dust . . . but one falls in love and one is a God, one is pua' as on the first day of cweation . . . Who's that now? Send him to the devil, I'm busy!" he shouted to Lavrúshka, who went up to him not in the least abashed.

"Who should it be? You yourself told him to come. It's the quartermaster for the money."

Denísov frowned and was about to shout some reply but stopped.

"Wetched business," he muttered to himself. "How much is left in the puhse?" he asked, turning to Rostóv.

"Seven new and three old imperials."

"Oh, it's wetched! Well, what are you standing there for, you sca'cwow? Call the quahtehmasteh," he shouted to Lavrúshka.

"Please, Denísov, let me lend you some: I have some, you know," said Rostóv blushing.

"Don't like bowowing from my own fellows, I don't," growled Denísov.

"But if you won't accept money from me like a comrade, you will offend me. Really I have some," Rostóv repeated.

"No, I tell you."

And Denísov went to the bed to get the purse from under the pillow.

"Where have you put it, Wostóv?"

"Under the lower pillow."

"It's not there."

Denísov threw both pillows on the floor. The purse was not there.

"That's a miwacle."

"Wait, haven't you dropped it?" said Rostóv, picking up the pillows one at a time and shaking them.

He pulled off the quilt and shook it. The purse was not there.

"Dear me, can I have forgotten? No, I remember thinking that you kept it under your head like a treasure," said Rostóv. "I put it just here. Where is it?" he asked, turning to Lavrúshka.

"I haven't been in the room. It must be where you put it."

"But it isn't? . . ."

"You're always like that; you thwow a thing down anywhere and forget it. Feel in your pockets."

"No, if I hadn't thought of it being a treasure," said Rostóv, "but I remember putting it there."

Lavrúshka turned all the bedding over, looked under the bed and under the table, searched everywhere, and stood still in the middle of the room. Denísov silently watched Lavrúshka's movements, and when the latter threw up his arms in surprise saying it was nowhere to be found Denísov glanced at Rostóv.

"Wostóv, you've not been playing schoolboy twicks . . ."

Rostóv felt Denísov's gaze fixed on him, raised his eyes, and instantly dropped them again. All the blood which had seemed congested somewhere below his throat rushed to his face and eyes. He could not draw breath.

"And there hasn't been anyone in the room except the lieutenant and yourselves. It must be there somewhere," said Lavrúshka.

"Now then, you devil's puppet, look alive and hunt for it!" shouted Denísov suddenly, turning purple and rushing at the man with a threatening gesture. "If the purse isn't found I'll flog you. I'll flog you all."

Rostóv, his eyes avoiding Denísov, began buttoning his coat, buckled on his saber, and put on his cap.

"I must have that purse, I tell you," shouted Denísov, shaking his orderly by the shoulders and knocking him against the wall.

"Denísov, let him alone, I know who has taken it," said Rostóv, going toward the door without raising his eyes.

Denísov paused, thought a moment, and, evidently understanding what Rostóv hinted at, seized his arm.

"Nonsense!" he cried, and the veins on his forehead and neck stood out like cords. "You are mad, I tell you. I won't allow it. The purse is here! I'll flay this scoundwel alive, and it will be found."

"I know who has taken it," repeated Rostóv in an unsteady voice, and went to the door.

"And I tell you, don't you dahe to do it!" shouted Denísov, rushing at the cadet to restrain him.

But Rostóv pulled away his arm and with as much anger as though Denísov were his worst enemy firmly fixed his eyes directly on his face.

"Do you understand what you're saying?" he said in a trembling voice. "There was no one else in the room except myself. So that if it is not so, then . . ."

He could not finish, and ran out of the room.

"Ah, may the devil take you and evewybody," were the last words Rostóv heard.

Rostóv went to Telyánin's quarters.

"The master is not in, he's gone to headquarters," said Telyánin's orderly. "Has something happened?" he added, surprised at the cadet's troubled face.

"No, nothing."

"You've only just missed him," said the orderly.

The headquarters were situated two miles away from Salzeneck, and Rostóv, without returning home, took a horse and rode there. There was an inn in the village which the officers frequented. Rostóv rode up to it and saw Telyánin's horse at the porch.

In the second room of the inn the lieutenant was sitting over a dish of sausages and a bottle of wine.

"Ah, you've come here too, young man!" he said, smiling and raising his eyebrows.

"Yes," said Rostóv as if it cost him a great deal to utter the word; and he sat down at the nearest table.

Both were silent. There were two Germans and a Russian officer in the room. No one spoke and the only sounds heard were the clatter of knives and the munching of the lieutenant.

When Telyánin had finished his lunch he took out of his pocket a double purse, and drawing its rings aside with his small, white, turned-up fingers, drew out a gold imperial, and lifting his eyebrows gave it to the waiter.

"Please be quick," he said.

The coin was a new one. Rostóv rose and went up to Telyánin.

"Allow me to look at your purse," he said in a low, almost inaudible, voice.

With shifting eyes but eyebrows still raised, Telyánin handed him the purse.

"Yes, it's a nice purse. Yes, yes," he said growing suddenly pale, and added, "Look at it, young man."

Rostóv took the purse in his hand, examined it and the money in it, and looked at Telyánin. The lieutenant was looking about in his usual way and suddenly seemed to grow very merry.

"If we get to Vienna I'll get rid of it there but in these wretched little towns there's nowhere to spend it," said he. "Well, let me have it, young man, I'm going."

Rostóv did not speak.

"And you? Are you going to have lunch too? They feed you quite decently here," continued Telyánin. "Now then, let me have it."

He stretched out his hand to take hold of the purse. Rostóv let go of it. Telyánin took the purse and began carelessly slipping it into the pocket of his riding-breeches, with his eyebrows lifted and his mouth slightly open, as if to say, "Yes, yes, I am putting my purse in my pocket and that's quite simple and is no else's business."

"Well, young man?" he said with a sigh, and from under his lifted brows he glanced into Rostóv's eyes.

Some flash as of an electric spark shot from Telyánin's eyes to Rostóv's and back, and back again and again in an instant.

"Come here," said Rostóv, catching hold of Telyánin's arm and almost dragging him to the window. "That money is Denísov's; you took it . . ." he whispered just above Telyánin's ear.

"What? What? How dare you? What?" said Telyánin.

But these words came like a piteous, despairing cry and an entreaty for pardon. As soon as Rostóv heard them, an enormous load of doubt fell from him. He was glad, and at the same instant began to pity the miserable man who stood before him, but the task he had begun had to be completed.

"Heaven only knows what the people here may imagine," muttered Telyánin, taking up his cap and moving toward a small empty room. "We must have an explanation . . ."

"I know it and shall prove it," said Rostóv.

"I . . ."

Every muscle of Telyánin's pale terrified face began to quiver, his eyes still shifted from side to side but with a downward look not rising to Rostóv's face, and his sobs were audible.

"Count! . . . Don't ruin a young fellow . . . here is this wretched money, take it . . ." He threw it on the table. "I have an old father and mother! . . ."

Rostóv took the money, avoiding Telyánin's eyes, and went out of the room without a word. But at the door he stopped and then retraced his steps. "O God," he said with tears in his eyes, "how could you do it?"

"Count . . ." said Telyánin drawing nearer to him.

"Don't touch me," said Rostóv, drawing back. "If you need it, take the money," and he threw the purse to him and ran out of the inn.

Chapter V

THAT SAME EVENING THERE WAS AN ANIMATED DISCUSSION AMONG THE SQUADRON'S OFFICERS in Denísov's quarters.

"And I tell you, Rostóv, that you must apologize to the colonel!" said a tall, grizzly-haired staff-captain with enormous mustaches and many wrinkles on his large features, to Rostóv who was crimson with excitement.

The staff-captain, Kirsten, had twice been reduced to the ranks for affairs of honor and had twice regained his commission.

"I will allow no one to call me a liar!" cried Rostóv. "He told me I lied, and I told him he lied. And there it rests. He may keep me on duty every day, or may place me under arrest, but no one can make me apologize, because if he, as commander of this regiment, thinks it beneath his dignity to give me satisfaction, then . . ."

"You just wait a moment, my dear fellow, and listen," interrupted the staff-captain in his deep bass, calmly stroking his long mustache. "You tell the colonel in the presence of other officers that an officer has stolen . . ."

"I'm not to blame that the conversation began in the presence of other officers. Perhaps I ought not to have spoken before them, but I am not a diplomatist. That's why I joined the hussars, thinking that here one would not need finesse; and he tells me that I am lying—so let him give me satisfaction . . ."

"That's all right. No one thinks you a coward, but that's not the point. Ask Denísov whether it is not out of the question for a cadet to demand satisfaction of his regimental commander?"

Denísov sat gloomily biting his mustache and listening to the conversation, evidently with no wish to take part in it. He answered the staff-captain's question by a disapproving shake of his head.

"You speak to the colonel about this nasty business before other officers," continued the staff-captain, "and Bogdánich" (the colonel was called Bogdánich) "shuts you up."

"He did not shut me up, he said I was telling an untruth."

"Well, have it so, and you talked a lot of nonsense to him and must apologize."

"Not on any account!" exclaimed Rostóv.

"I did not expect this of you," said the staff-captain seriously and severely. "You don't wish to apologize, but, man, it's not only to him but to the whole regiment—all of us—you're to blame all round. The case is this: you ought to have thought the matter over and taken advice; but no, you go and blurt it all straight out before the officers. Now what was the colonel to do? Have the officer tried and disgrace the whole regiment? Disgrace the whole regiment because of one scoundrel? Is that how you look at it? We don't see it like that. And Bogdánich was a brick: he told you you were saying what was not true. It's not pleasant, but what's to be done, my dear fellow? You landed yourself in it. And now, when one wants to smooth the thing over, some conceit prevents your apologizing, and you wish to make the whole affair public. You are offended at being put on duty a bit, but why not apologize to an old and honorable officer? Whatever Bogdánich may be, anyway he is an honorable and brave old colonel! You're quick at taking offense, but you don't mind disgracing the whole regiment!" The staff-captain's voice began to tremble. "You have been in the regiment next to no time, my lad, you're here today and tomorrow you'll be appointed adjutant somewhere and can snap your fingers when it is said, 'There are thieves among the Pávlograd officers!' But it's not all the same to us! Am I not right, Denísov? It's not the same!"

Denísov remained silent and did not move, but occasionally looked with his glittering black eyes at Rostóv.

"You value your own pride and don't wish to apologize," continued the staff-captain, "but we old fellows, who have grown up in and, God willing, are going to die in the regiment, we prize the honor of the regiment, and Bogdánich knows it. Oh, we do prize it, old fellow! And all this is not right, it's not right! You may take offense or not but I always stick to mother truth. It's not right!"

And the staff-captain rose and turned away from Rostóv.

"That's twue, devil take it!" shouted Denísov, jumping up. "Now then, Wostóv, now then!"

Rostóv, growing red and pale alternately, looked first at one officer and then at the other.

"No, gentlemen, no . . . you mustn't think . . . I quite understand. You're wrong to think that of me . . . I . . . for me . . . for the honor of the regiment I'd . . . Ah well, I'll show that in action, and for me the honor of the flag . . . Well, never mind, it's true I'm to blame, to blame all round. Well, what else do you want? . . ."

"Come, that's right, count!" cried the staff-captain, turning round and clapping Rostóv on the shoulder with his big hand.

"I tell you," shouted Denísov, "he's a fine fellow."

"That's better, count," said the staff-captain, beginning to address Rostóv by his title, as if in recognition of his confession. "Go and apologize, your excellency. Yes, go!"

"Gentlemen, I'll do anything. No one shall hear a word from me," said Rostóv in an imploring voice, "but I can't apologize, by God I can't, do what you will! How can I go and apologize like a little boy asking forgiveness?"

Denísov began to laugh.

"It'll be worse for you. Bogdánich is vindictive and you'll pay for your obstinacy," said Kírsten.

"No, on my word it's not obstinacy! I can't describe the feeling. I can't . . ."

"Well, it's as you like," said the staff-captain. "And what has become of that scoundrel?" he asked Denísov.

"He has weported himself sick, he's to be stwuck off the list tomowwow," muttered Denísov.

"It is an illness, there's no other way of explaining it," said the staff-captain.

"Illness or not, he'd better not cwoss my path. I'd kill him!" shouted Denísov in a bloodthirsty tone.

Just then Zherkóv entered the room.

"What brings you here?" cried the officers turning to the newcomer.

"We're to go into action, gentlemen! Mack has surrendered with his whole army."

"It's not true!"

"I've seen him myself!"

"What? Saw the real Mack? With hands and feet?"

"Into action! Into action! Bring him a bottle for such news! But how did you come here?"

"I've been sent back to the regiment all on account of that devil, Mack. An Austrian general complained of me. I congratulated him on Mack's arrival . . . What's the matter, Rostóv? You look as if you'd just come out of a hot bath."

"Oh, my dear fellow, we're in such a stew here these last two days."

The regimental adjutant came in and confirmed the news brought by Zherkóv. They were under orders to advance next day.

"We're going into action, gentlemen!"

"Well, thank God! We've been sitting here too long!"

Chapter VI

KUTÚZOV FELL BACK TOWARD VIENNA, DESTROYING BEHIND HIM THE BRIDGES OVER THE RIVERS Inn (at Braunau) and Traun (near Linz). On October 23rd, the Russian troops were crossing the river Enns. At midday the Russian baggage-train, the artillery, and columns of troops were defiling through the town of Enns on both sides of the bridge.

It was a warm, rainy, autumnal day. The wide expanse that opened out before the heights on which the Russian batteries stood guarding the bridge, was at times veiled by a diaphanous curtain of slanting rain, and then, suddenly spread out in the sunlight, far-distant objects could be clearly seen glittering as though freshly varnished. Down below, the little town could be seen with its white, red-roofed houses, its cathedral, and its bridge, on both sides of which streamed jostling masses of Russian troops. At the bend of the Danube, vessels, an island, and a castle with a park surrounded by the waters of the confluence of the Enns and the Danube, became visible, and the rocky left bank of the Danube covered with pine forests, with a mystic background of green tree-tops and bluish gorges. The turrets of a convent stood out beyond a wild virgin pine-forest, and far away on the other side of the Enns the enemy's horse patrols could be discerned.

Among the field-guns on the brow of the hill the general in command of the rearguard stood with a staff-officer, scanning the country through his field-glass. A little behind them Nesvítski, who had been sent to the rearguard by the commander-in-chief, was sitting on the trail of a gun carriage. A Cossack who accompanied him had handed him a knapsack and a flask, and Nesvítski was treating some officers to pies and real *doppel-kümmel*. The officers gladly gathered round him, some on their knees, some squatting Turkish fashion on the wet grass.

"Yes, the Austrian prince who built that castle was no fool. It's a fine place! Why are you not eating anything, gentlemen?" Nesvítski was saying.

"Thank you very much, prince," answered one of the officers, pleased to be talking to a staff-officer of such importance. "It's a lovely place! We passed close to the park and saw two deer . . . and what a splendid house!"

"Look, prince," said another, who would have dearly liked to take another pie but felt shy, and therefore pretended to be examining the countryside—"See, our infantrymen have already got there. Look there in the meadow behind the village, three of them are dragging something. They'll ransack that castle," he remarked with evident approval.

"So they will," said Nesvítski. "No, but what I should like," added he, munching a pie in his moist-lipped handsome mouth, "would be to slip in over there."

He pointed with a smile to a turreted nunnery, and his eyes narrowed and gleamed.

"That would be fine, gentlemen!"

The officers laughed.

"Just to flutter the nuns a bit. They say there are Italian girls among them. On my word I'd give five years of my life for it!"

"They must be feeling dull, too," said one of the bolder officers, laughing.

Meanwhile the staff-officer standing in front pointed out something to the general, who looked through his field-glass.

"Yes, so it is, so it is," said the general angrily, lowering the field-glass and shrugging his shoulders, "so it is! They'll be fired on at the crossing. And why are they dawdling there?"

On the opposite side the enemy could be seen by the naked eye, and from their battery a milk-white cloud arose. Then came the distant report of a shot, and our troops could be seen hurrying to the crossing.

Nesvítski rose puffing, and went up to the general smiling.

"Would not your excellency like a little refreshment?" he said.

"It's a bad business," said the general without answering him, "our men have been wasting time."

"Hadn't I better ride over, your excellency?" asked Nesvítski.

"Yes, please do," answered the general, and he repeated the order that had already once been given in detail: "and tell the hussars that they are to cross fast and to fire the bridge as I ordered; and the inflammable material on the bridge must be reinspected."

"Very good," answered Nesvítski.

He called the Cossack with his horse, told him to put away the knapsack and flask, and swung his heavy person easily into the saddle.

"I'll really call in on the nuns," he said to the officers who watched him smilingly, and he rode off by the winding path down the hill.

"Now then, let's see how far it will carry, captain. Just try!" said the general, turning to an artillery officer. "Have a little fun to pass the time."

"Crew, to your guns!" commanded the officer.

In a moment the men came running gaily from their campfires and began loading.

"One!" came the command.

Number one jumped briskly aside. The gun rang out with a deafening metallic roar, and a whistling grenade flew above the heads of our troops below the hill and fell far short of the enemy, a little smoke showing the spot where it burst.

The faces of officers and men brightened up at the sound. Everyone got up and began watching the movements of our troops below, as plainly visible as if but a stone's throw away, and the movements of the approaching enemy farther off. At the same instant the sun came fully out from behind the clouds, and the clear sound of the solitary shot and the brilliance of the bright sunshine merged in a single joyous and spirited impression.

Chapter VII

Two of the enemy's shots had already flown across the bridge, where there was a crush. Halfway across stood Prince Nesvítski, who had alighted from his horse and whose big body was jammed against the railings. He looked back laughing to the Cossack who stood a few steps behind him holding two horses by their bridles. Each time Prince Nesvítski tried to move on, soldiers and carts pushed him back again and pressed him against the railings, and all he could do was to smile.

"What a fellow you are, friend!" said the Cossack to a convoy-soldier with a wagon, who was pressing onto the infantrymen who were crowded together close to his wheels and his horses. "What a fellow! You can't wait a moment! Don't you see the general wants to pass?"

But the convoyman took no notice of the word "General" and shouted at the soldiers who were blocking his way. "Hi there, boys! Keep to the left! Wait a bit." But the soldiers, crowded together shoulder to shoulder, their bayonets interlocking, moved over the bridge in a dense mass. Looking down over the rails Prince Nesvítski saw the rapid, noisy little waves of the Enns, which rippling and eddying round the piles of the bridge chased each other along. Looking on the bridge he saw equally uniform living waves of soldiers, shoulder-straps, covered shakos, knapsacks, bayonets, long muskets, and, under the shakos, faces with broad cheekbones, sunken cheeks, and listless tired expressions, and feet that moved through the sticky mud that covered the planks of the bridge. Sometimes through the monotonous waves of men, like a fleck of white foam on the waves of the Enns, an officer in a cloak and with a type of face different from that of the men, squeezed his way along; sometimes like a chip of wood whirling in the river, a hussar on foot, an orderly, or a townsman, was carried through the waves of infantry; and sometimes like a log floating down the river, an officers' or company's baggage-wagon, piled high, leather-covered, and hemmed in on all sides, moved across the bridge.

"It's as if a dam had burst," said the Cossack hopelessly. "Are there many more of you to come?"

"A million all but one!" replied a waggish soldier in a torn coat, with a wink, and passed on followed by another, an old man.

"If *he*" (*he* meant the enemy) "begins popping at the bridge now," said the old soldier dismally to a comrade, "you'll forget to scratch yourself."

That soldier passed on, and after him came another sitting on a cart.

"Where the devil have the legbands been shoved to?" said an orderly, running behind the cart and fumbling in the back of it.

And he also passed on with the wagon. Then came some merry soldiers who had evidently been drinking.

"And then, old fellow, he gives him one in the teeth with the butt end of his gun . . ." a soldier whose greatcoat was well tucked up said gaily, with a wide swing of his arm.

"Yes, the ham was just delicious . . ." answered another with a loud laugh. And they, too, passed on, so that Nesvítski did not learn who had been struck on the teeth, or what the ham had to do with it.

"Bah! How they scurry. He just sends a ball and they think they'll all be killed," a sergeant was saying angrily and reproachfully.

"As it flies past me, Daddy, the ball I mean," said a young soldier with an enormous mouth, hardly refraining from laughing, "I felt like dying of fright. I did, 'pon my word, I got that frightened!" said he, as if bragging of having been frightened.

That one also passed. Then followed a cart unlike any that had gone before. It was a German cart with a pair of horses led by a German, and seemed loaded with a whole houseful of effects. A fine brindled cow with a large udder was attached to the cart behind. A woman with an unweaned baby, an old woman, and a healthy German girl with bright red cheeks, were sitting on some feather-beds. Evidently these fugitives were allowed to pass by special permission. The eyes of all the soldiers turned toward the women, and while the vehicle was passing at footpace all the soldiers' remarks related to the two young ones. Every face bore almost the same smile, expressing unseemly thoughts about the women.

"Just see, the German sausage is making tracks, too!"

"Sell me the missis," said another soldier, addressing the German, who, angry and frightened, strode energetically along with downcast eyes.

"See how smart she's made herself! Oh, the devils!"

"There, Fedótov, you should be quartered on them!"

"I have seen as much before now, mate!"

"Where are you going?" asked an infantry officer who was eating an apple, also half smiling as he looked at the handsome girl.

The German closed his eyes, signifying that he did not understand.

"Take it if you like," said the officer, giving the girl an apple.

The girl smiled and took it. Nesvítski like the rest of the men on the bridge did not take his eyes off the women till they had passed. When they had gone by, the same stream of soldiers followed, with the same kind of talk, and at last all stopped. As often happens, the horses of a convoy-wagon became restive at the end of the bridge, and the whole crowd had to wait.

"And why are they stopping? There's no proper order!" said the soldiers. "Where are you shoving to? Devil take you! Can't you wait? It'll be worse if he fires the bridge. See, here's an officer jammed in too"—different voices were saying in the crowd, as the men looked at one another, and all pressed toward the exit from the bridge.

Looking down at the waters of the Enns under the bridge, Nesvítski suddenly heard a sound new to him, of something swiftly approaching . . . something big, that splashed into the water.

"Just see where it carries to!" a soldier nearby said sternly, looking round at the sound.

"Encouraging us to get along quicker," said another uneasily.

The crowd moved on again. Nesvítski realized that it was a cannon-ball.

"Hey, Cossack, my horse!" he said. "Now, then, you there! get out of the way! Make way!"

With great difficulty he managed to get to his horse, and shouting continually he moved on. The soldiers squeezed themselves to make way for him, but again pressed on him so that they jammed his leg, and those nearest him were not to blame for they were themselves pressed still harder from behind.

"Nesvítski, Nesvítski! you numskull!" came a hoarse voice from behind him.

Nesvítski looked round and saw, some fifteen paces away but separated by the living mass of moving infantry, Váska Denísov, red and shaggy, with his cap on the back of his black head and a cloak hanging jauntily over his shoulder.

"Tell these devils, these fiends, to let me pass!" shouted Denísov evidently in a fit of rage, his coal-black eyes with their bloodshot whites glittering and rolling as he waved his sheathed saber in a small bare hand as red as his face.

"Ah, Váska!" joyfully replied Nesvítski. "What's up with you?"

"The squadwon can't pass," shouted Váska Denísov, showing his white teeth fiercely and spurring his black thoroughbred Arab, which twitched its ears as the bayonets touched it, and snorted, spurting white foam from his bit, tramping the planks of the bridge with his hoofs, and apparently ready to jump over the railings had his rider let him. "What is this? They're like sheep! Just like sheep! Out of the way! . . . Let us pass! . . . Stop there, you devil with the cart! I'll hack you with my saber!" he shouted, actually drawing his saber from its scabbard and flourishing it.

The soldiers crowded against one another with terrified faces, and Denísov joined Nesvítski.

"How's it you're not drunk today?" said Nesvítski when the other had ridden up to him.

"They don't even give one time to dwink!" answered Váska Denísov. "They keep dwagging the wegiment to and fwo all day. If they mean to fight, let's fight. But the devil knows what this is."

"What a dandy you are today!" said Nesvítski, looking at Denísov's new cloak and saddle-cloth.

Denísov smiled, took out of his sabertache a handkerchief that diffused a smell of perfume, and put it to Nesvítski's nose.

"Of course. I'm going into action! I've shaved, bwushed my teeth, and scented myself."

The imposing figure of Nesvítski followed by his Cossack, and the determination of Denísov who flourished his sword and shouted frantically, had such an effect that they managed to squeeze through to the farther side of the bridge and stopped the infantry. Beside the bridge Nesvítski found the colonel to whom he had to deliver the order, and having done this he rode back.

Having cleared the way Denísov stopped at the end of the bridge. Carelessly holding in his stallion that was neighing and pawing the ground eager to rejoin its fellows, he watched his squadron draw nearer. Then the clang of hoofs, as of several horses galloping, resounded on the planks of the bridge, and the squadron, officers in front and men four abreast, spread across the bridge and began to emerge on his side of it.

The infantry who had been stopped crowded near the bridge in the trampled mud, and gazed with that particular feeling of ill-will, estrangement, and ridicule with which troops of different arms usually encounter one another, at the clean smart hussars who moved past them in regular order.

"Smart lads! Only fit for a fair!" said one.

"What good are they? They're led about just for show!" remarked another.

"Don't kick up the dust, you infantry!" jested a hussar whose prancing horse had splashed mud over some foot-soldiers.

"I'd like to put you on a two-days' march with a knapsack! Your fine cords would soon get a bit rubbed," said an infantryman, wiping the mud off his face with his sleeve. "Perched up there, you're more like a bird than a man."

"There now, Zíkin, they ought to put you on a horse. You'd look fine," said a corporal, chaffing a thin little soldier who bent under the weight of his knapsack.

"Take a stick between your legs, that'll suit you for a horse!" the hussar shouted back.

Chapter VIII

The last of the infantry hurriedly crossed the bridge, squeezing together as they approached it as if passing through a funnel. At last the baggage-wagons had all crossed, the crush was less, and the last battalion came onto the bridge. Only Denísov's squadron of hussars remained on the farther side of the bridge facing the enemy, who could be seen from the hill on the opposite bank but was not yet visible from the bridge, for the horizon as seen from the valley through which the river flowed was formed by the rising ground only half a mile away. At the foot of the hill lay waste land over which a few groups of our Cossack scouts were moving. Suddenly on the road at the top of the high ground, artillery and troops in blue uniform were seen. These were the French. A group of Cossack scouts retired down the hill at a trot. All the officers and men of Denísov's squadron, though they tried to talk of other things and to look in other directions, thought only of what was there on the hilltop, and kept constantly looking at the patches appearing on the sky-line, which they knew to be the enemy's troops. The weather had cleared again since noon and the sun was descending brightly upon the Danube and the dark hills around it. It was calm, and at intervals the bugle-calls and the shouts of the enemy could be heard from the hill. There was no one now between the squadron and the enemy except a few scattered skirmishers. An empty space of some seven hundred yards was all that separated them. The enemy ceased firing, and that stern, threatening, inaccessible and intangible line which separates two hostile armies was all the more clearly felt.

"One step beyond that boundary line which resembles the line dividing the living from the dead, lies uncertainty, suffering, and death. And what is there? Who is there?—there beyond that field, that tree, that roof lit up by the sun? No one knows, but one wants to know. You fear and yet long to cross that line, and know that sooner or later it must be crossed and you will have to find out what is there, just as you will inevitably have to learn what lies the other side of death. But you are strong, healthy, cheerful, and excited, and are surrounded by other such excitedly-animated and healthy men." So thinks, or at any rate feels, anyone who comes in sight of the enemy, and that feeling gives a particular glamour and glad keenness of impression to everything that takes place at such moments.

On the high ground where the enemy was, the smoke of a cannon rose, and a ball flew whistling over the heads of the hussar squadron. The officers who had been standing together rode off to their places. The hussars began carefully aligning their horses. Silence fell on the whole squadron. All were looking at the enemy in front and at the squadron commander, awaiting the word of command. A second and a third cannon-ball flew past. Evidently they were firing at the hussars, but the balls with rapid rhythmic whistle flew over the heads of the horsemen and fell somewhere beyond them. The hussars did not look round, but at the sound of each shot, as at the word of command, the whole squadron with its rows of faces so alike yet so different, holding its breath while the ball flew past, rose in the stirrups and sank back again. The soldiers without turning their heads glanced at one another, curious to see their comrades' impression. Every face, from Denísov's to that of the bugler, showed one common expression of conflict, irritation, and excitement, around chin and mouth. The quartermaster frowned, looking at the soldiers as if threatening to punish them. Cadet Mirónov ducked every time a ball flew past. Rostóv on the left flank, mounted on his Rook—a handsome horse despite its game leg—had the happy air of a schoolboy called up before a large audience for an examination in which he feels sure he will distinguish himself. He was glancing at everyone with a clear bright expression, as if asking them to notice how calmly he sat under fire. But despite himself, on his face too that same indication of something new and stern showed round the mouth.

"Who's that curtseying there? Cadet Miwónov! That's not wight! Look at me," cried Denísov, who unable to keep still on one spot, kept turning his horse in front of the squadron.

The black, hairy, snub-nosed face of Váska Denísov, and his whole short sturdy figure with the sinewy hairy hand and stumpy fingers in which he held the hilt of his naked saber, looked just as it usually did, especially toward evening when he had emptied his second bottle; he was only redder than usual. With his shaggy head thrown back like birds when they drink, pressing his spurs mercilessly into the sides of his good horse, Bedouin, and sitting as though falling backward in the saddle, he galloped to the other flank of the squadron and shouted in a hoarse voice to the men to look to their pistols. He rode up to Kirsten. The staff-captain on his broad-backed steady mare came at a walk to meet him. His face with its long mustache was serious as always, only his eyes were brighter than usual.

"Well, what about it?" said he to Denísov. "It won't come to a fight. You'll see—we shall retire."

"The devil only knows what they're about!" muttered Denísov. "Ah, Wostóv," he cried noticing the cadet's bright face, "you've got it at last."

And he smiled approvingly, evidently pleased with the cadet. Rostóv felt perfectly happy. Just then the commander appeared on the bridge. Denísov galloped up to him.

"Your excellency! Let us attack them! I'll dwive them off."

"Attack indeed!" said the colonel in a bored voice, puckering up his face as if driving off a troublesome fly. "And why are you stopping here? Don't you see the skirmishers are retreating? Lead the squadron back."

The squadron crossed the bridge and drew out of range of fire without having lost a single man. The second squadron that had been in the front line followed them across and the last Cossacks quitted the farther side of the river.

The two Pávlograd squadrons, having crossed the bridge, retired up the hill one after the other. Their colonel, Karl Bogdánich Schubert, came up to Denísov's squadron and rode at a footpace not far from Rostóv, without taking any notice of him although they were now meeting for the first time since their encounter concerning Telyánin. Rostóv feeling that he was at the front and in the power of a man toward whom he now admitted that he had been to blame, did not lift his eyes from the colonel's athletic back, his nape covered with light hair, and his red neck. It seemed to Rostóv that Bogdánich was only pretending not to notice him, and that his whole aim now was to test the cadet's courage, so he drew himself up and looked around him merrily; then it seemed to him that Bogdánich rode so near in order to show him his courage. Next he thought that his enemy would send the squadron on a desperate attack just to punish him—Rostóv. Then he imagined how, after the attack, Bogdánich would come up to him as he lay wounded and would magnanimously extend the hand of reconciliation.

The high-shouldered figure of Zherkóv, familiar to the Pávlograds as he had but recently left their regiment, rode up to the colonel. After his dismissal from headquarters Zherkóv had not remained in the regiment, saying he was not such a fool as to slave at the front when he could get more rewards by doing nothing on the staff, and had succeeded in attaching himself as an orderly officer to Prince Bagratión. He now came to his former chief with an order from the commander of the rearguard.

"Colonel," he said, addressing Rostóv's enemy with an air of gloomy gravity and glancing round at his comrades, "there is an order to stop and fire the bridge."

"An order to who?" asked the colonel morosely.

"I don't myself know 'to who,' " replied the cornet in a serious tone, "but the prince told me to 'go and tell the colonel that the hussars must return quickly and fire the bridge.' "

Zherkóv was followed by an officer of the suite who rode up to the colonel of hussars with the same order. After him the stout Nesvítski came galloping up on a Cossack horse that could scarcely carry his weight.

"How's this, colonel?" he shouted as he approached. "I told you to fire the bridge, and now someone has gone and blundered; they are all beside themselves over there and one can't make anything out."

The colonel deliberately stopped the regiment and turned to Nesvítski.

"You spoke to me of inflammable material," said he, "but you said nothing about firing it."

"But, my dear sir," said Nesvítski as he drew up, taking off his cap and smoothing his hair wet with perspiration with his plump hand, "wasn't I telling you to fire the bridge, when inflammable material had been put in position?"

"I am not your 'dear sir,' Mr. Staff-officer, and you did not tell me to burn the bridge! I know the service, and it is my habit orders strictly to obey. You said the bridge would be burned, but who would it burn, I could not know by the holy spirit!"

"Ah, that's always the way!" said Nesvítski with a wave of the hand. "How did you get here?" said he, turning to Zherkóv.

"On the same business. But you *are* damp! Let me wring you out!"

"You were saying, Mr. Staff-officer . . ." continued the colonel in an offended tone.

"Colonel," interrupted the officer of the suite, "you must be quick or the enemy will bring up his guns to use grapeshot."

The colonel looked silently at the officer of the suite, at the stout staff-officer, and at Zherkóv, and he frowned.

"I will the bridge fire," he said in a solemn tone as if to announce that in spite of all the unpleasantness he had to endure he would still do the right thing.

Striking his horse with his long muscular legs as if it were to blame for everything, the colonel moved forward and ordered the second squadron, that in which Rostóv was serving under Denísov, to return to the bridge.

"There, it's just as I thought," said Rostóv to himself. "He wishes to test me!" His heart contracted and the blood rushed to his face. "Let him see whether I am a coward!" he thought.

Again on all the bright faces of the squadron the serious expression appeared that they had worn when under fire. Rostóv watched his enemy, the colonel, closely—to find in his face confirmation of his own conjecture, but the colonel did not once glance at Rostóv, and looked as he always did when at the front, solemn and stern. Then came the word of command.

"Look sharp! Look sharp!" several voices repeated around him.

Their sabers catching in the bridles and their spurs jingling, the hussars hastily dismounted, not knowing what they were to do. The men were crossing themselves. Rostóv no longer looked at the colonel, he had no time. He was afraid of falling behind the hussars, so much afraid that his heart stood still. His hand trembled as he gave his horse into an orderly's charge, and he felt the blood rush to his heart with a thud. Denísov rode past him, leaning back and shouting something.

Rostóv saw nothing but the hussars running all around him, their spurs catching and their sabers clattering.

"Stretchers!" shouted someone behind him.

Rostóv did not think what this call for stretchers meant; he ran on, trying only to be ahead of the others; but just at the bridge, not looking at the ground, he came on some sticky, trodden mud, stumbled, and fell on his hands. The others outstripped him.

"At boss zides, captain," he heard the voice of the colonel, who, having ridden ahead, had pulled up his horse near the bridge, with a triumphant, cheerful face.

Rostóv wiping his muddy hands on his breeches looked at his enemy, and was about to run on, thinking that the farther he went to the front the better. But Bogdánich, without looking at or recognizing Rostóv, shouted to him:

"Who's that running on the middle of the bridge? To the right! Come back, cadet!" he cried angrily; and turning to Denísov, who, showing off his courage, had ridden on to the planks of the bridge:

"Why run risks, captain? You should dismount," he said.

"Oh, every bullet has its billet," answered Váska Denísov, turning in his saddle.

Meanwhile Nesvítski, Zherkóv, and the officer of the suite were standing together out of range of the shots, watching, now the small group of men with yellow shakos, dark-green jackets braided with cord, and blue riding-breeches, who were swarming near the bridge, and then at what was approaching in the distance from the opposite side—the blue uniforms and groups with horses, easily recognizable as artillery.

"Will they burn the bridge or not? Who'll get there first? Will they get there and fire the bridge or will the French get within grapeshot range and wipe them out?" These were the questions each man of the troops on the high ground above the bridge involuntarily asked himself with a sinking heart—watching the bridge and the hussars in the bright evening light and the blue tunics advancing from the other side with their bayonets and guns.

"Ugh. The hussars will get it hot!" said Nesvítski; "they are within grapeshot range now."

"He shouldn't have taken so many men," said the officer of the suite.

"True enough," answered Nesvítski; "two smart fellows could have done the job just as well."

"Ah, your excellency," put in Zherkóv, his eyes fixed on the hussars, but still with that naïve air that made it impossible to know whether he was speaking in jest or in earnest. "Ah, your excellency! How you look at things! Send two men? And who then would give us the Vladímir medal and ribbon? But now, even if they do get peppered, the squadron may be recommended for honors and he may get a ribbon. Our Bogdánich knows how things are done."

"There now!" said the officer of the suite, "that's grapeshot."

He pointed to the French guns, the limbers of which were being detached and hurriedly removed.

On the French side, amid the groups with cannon, a cloud of smoke appeared, then a second and a third almost simultaneously, and at the moment when the first report was heard a fourth was seen. Then two reports one after another, and a third.

"Oh! Oh!" groaned Nesvítski as if in fierce pain, seizing the officer of the suite by the arm. "Look! A man has fallen! Fallen, fallen!"

"Two, I think."

"If I were Tsar I would never go to war," said Nesvítski, turning away.

The French guns were hastily reloaded. The infantry in their blue uniforms advanced toward the bridge at a run. Smoke appeared again but at irregular intervals, and grapeshot cracked and rattled onto the bridge. But this time Nesvítski could not see what was happening there, as a dense cloud of smoke arose from it. The hussars had succeeded in setting it on fire and the French batteries were now firing at them, no longer to hinder them but because the guns were trained and there was someone to fire at.

The French had time to fire three rounds of grapeshot before the hussars got back to their horses. Two were misdirected and the shot went too high, but the last round fell in the midst of a group of hussars and knocked three of them over.

Rostóv absorbed by his relations with Bogdánich had paused on the bridge not knowing what to do. There was no one to hew down (as he had always imagined battles to himself), nor could he help to fire the bridge because he had not brought any burning straw with him like the other soldiers. He stood looking about him, when suddenly he heard a rattle on the bridge as if nuts were being split, and the hussar nearest to him fell against the rails with a groan. Rostóv ran up to him with the others. Again someone shouted, "Stretchers!" Four men seized the hussar and began lifting him.

"Oooh! For Christ's sake let me alone!" cried the wounded man, but still he was lifted and laid on the stretcher.

Nicholas Rostóv turned away and, as if searching for something, gazed into the distance, at the waters of the Danube, at the sky, and at the sun. How beautiful the sky looked; how blue, how calm, and how deep! How bright and glorious was the setting sun! With what soft glitter the waters of the distant Danube shone. And fairer still were the far away blue mountains beyond the river, the nunnery, the mysterious gorges, and the pine forests veiled in the mist of their summits . . . There was peace and happiness . . . "I should wish for nothing else, nothing, if only I were there," thought Rostóv. "In myself alone and in that sunshine there is so much happiness; but here . . . groans, suffering, fear, and this uncertainty and hurry . . . There—they are shouting again, and again are all running back somewhere, and I shall run with them, and it, death, is here above me and around . . . Another instant and I shall never again see the sun, this water, that gorge! . . ."

At that instant the sun began to hide behind the clouds, and other stretchers came into view before Rostóv. And the fear of death and of the stretchers, and love of the sun and of life, all merged into one feeling of sickening agitation.

"O Lord God! Thou who art in that heaven, save, forgive, and protect me!" Rostóv whispered.

The hussars ran back to the men who held their horses; their voices sounded louder and calmer, the stretchers disappeared from sight.

"Well, fwiend? So you've smelt powdah!" shouted Váska Denísov just above his ear.

"It's all over; but I am a coward—yes, a coward!" thought Rostóv, and sighing deeply he took Rook, his horse, which stood resting one foot, from the orderly, and began to mount.

"Was that grapeshot?" he asked Denísov.

"Yes and no mistake!" cried Denísov. "You worked like wegular bwicks and it's nasty work! An attack's pleasant work! Hacking away at the dogs! But this sort of thing is the very devil, with them shooting at you like a target."

And Denísov rode up to a group that had stopped near Rostóv, composed of the colonel, Nesvítski, Zherkóv, and the officer from the suite.

"Well it seems that no one has noticed," thought Rostóv. And this was true. No one had taken any notice, for everyone knew the sensation which the cadet under fire for the first time had experienced.

"Here's something for you to report," said Zherkóv. "See if I don't get promoted to a sublieutenancy."

"Inform the prince that I the bridge fired!" said the colonel triumphantly and gaily.

"And if he asks about the losses?"

"A trifle," said the colonel in his bass voice: "two hussars wounded, and one knocked out," he added, unable to restrain a happy smile, and pronouncing the phrase "knocked out" with ringing distinctness.

Chapter IX

PURSUED BY THE FRENCH ARMY OF A HUNDRED THOUSAND MEN UNDER THE COMMAND OF BONAparte, encountering a population that was unfriendly to it, losing confidence in its allies, suffering from shortness of supplies, and compelled to act under conditions of war unlike anything that had been foreseen, the Russian army of thirty-five thousand men commanded by Kutúzov was hurriedly retreating along the Danube, stopping where overtaken by the enemy and fighting rearguard actions only as far as necessary to enable it to retreat without losing its heavy equipment. There had been actions at Lambach, Amstetten, and Melk; but despite the courage and endurance—acknowledged even by the enemy—with which the Russians fought, the only consequence of these actions was a yet more rapid retreat. Austrian troops that had escaped capture at Ulm and had joined Kutúzov at Braunau, now separated from the Russian army, and Kutúzov was left with only his own weak and exhausted forces. The defense of Vienna was no longer to be thought of. Instead of an offensive, the plan of which, carefully prepared in accord with the modern science of strategics, had been handed to Kutúzov when he was in Vienna by the Austrian Hofkriegsrath, the sole and almost unattainable aim remaining for him was to effect a junction with the forces that were advancing from Russia, without losing his army as Mack had done at Ulm.

On the 28th of October Kutúzov with his army crossed to the left bank of the Danube and took up a position for the first time with the river between himself and the main body of the French. On the 30th he attacked Mortier's division which was on the left bank, and broke it up. In this action for the first time trophies were taken; banners, cannon, and two enemy generals. For the first time, after a fortnight's retreat, the Russian troops had halted and after a fight had not only held the field but had repulsed the French. Though the troops were ill-clad, exhausted, and had lost a third of their number in killed, wounded, sick, and stragglers; though a number of sick and wounded had been abandoned on the other side of the Danube with a letter in which Kutúzov entrusted them to the humanity of the enemy; and though the big hospitals and the houses in Krems converted into military hospitals could no longer accommodate all the sick and wounded, yet the stand made at Krems and the victory over Mortier raised the spirits of the army considerably. Throughout the whole army and at headquarters most joyful though erroneous rumors were rife of the imaginary approach of columns from Russia, of some victory gained by the Austrians, and of the retreat of the frightened Bonaparte.

Prince Andrew during the battle had been in attendance on the Austrian General Schmidt, who was killed in the action. His horse had been wounded under him and his own arm slightly grazed by a bullet. As a mark of the commander-in-chief's special favor he was sent with the news of this victory to the Austrian court, now no longer at Vienna (which was threatened by the French) but at Brünn. Despite his apparently delicate build Prince Andrew could endure physical fatigue far better than many very muscular men, and on the night of the battle, having arrived at Krems excited but not weary, with dispatches from Dokhtúrov to Kutúzov, he was sent immediately with a special dispatch to Brünn. To be so sent meant not only a reward but an important step toward promotion.

The night was dark but starry, the road showed black in the snow that had fallen the previous day—the day of the battle. Reviewing his impressions of the recent battle, picturing pleasantly to himself the impression his news of a victory would create, or recalling the send-off given him by the commander-in-chief and his fellow-officers, Prince Andrew was galloping along in a postchaise enjoying the feelings of a man who has at length begun to attain a long-desired happiness. As soon as he closed his eyes his ears seemed filled with the rattle of the wheels and the sensation of victory. Then he began to imagine that the Russians were running away and that he himself was killed, but he quickly roused himself with a feeling of joy, as if learning afresh that this was not so but that on the contrary the French had run away. He again recalled all the details of the victory and his own calm courage during the battle, and feeling reassured he dozed off. . . . The dark starry night was followed by a bright cheerful morning. The snow was thawing in the sunshine, the horses galloped quickly, and on both sides of the road were forests of different kinds, fields, and villages.

At one of the post stations he overtook a convoy of Russian wounded. The Russian officer in charge of the transport lolled back in the front cart, shouting and scolding a soldier with coarse abuse. In each of the long German carts six or more pale, dirty, bandaged men were being jolted over the stony road. Some of them were talking (he heard Russian words), others were eating bread; the more severely wounded looked silently, with the languid interest of sick children, at the envoy hurrying past them.

Prince Andrew told his driver to stop, and asked a soldier in what action they had been wounded. "Day before yesterday, on the Danube," answered the soldier. Prince Andrew took out his purse and gave the soldier three gold pieces.

"That's for them all," he said to the officer who came up.

"Get well soon, lads!" he continued, turning to the soldiers. "There's plenty to do still."

"What news, sir?" asked the officer, evidently anxious to start a conversation.

"Good news! . . . Go on!" he shouted to the driver, and they galloped on.

It was already quite dark when Prince Andrew rattled over the paved streets of Brnn and found himself surrounded by high buildings, the lights of shops, houses, and street lamps, fine carriages, and all that atmosphere of a large and active town which is always so attractive to a soldier after camp life. Despite his rapid journey and sleepless night, Prince Andrew when he drove up to the palace felt even more vigorous and alert than he had done the day before. Only his eyes gleamed feverishly and his thoughts followed one another with extraordinary clearness and rapidity. He again vividly recalled the details of the battle, no longer dim, but definite and in the concise form in which he imagined himself stating them to the Emperor Francis. He vividly imagined the casual questions that might be put to him and the answers he would give. He expected to be at once presented to the Emperor. At the chief entrance to the palace, however, an official came running out to meet him, and learning that he was a special messenger led him to another entrance.

"To the right from the corridor, *Euer Hochgeboren!* There you will find the adjutant on duty," said the official. "He will conduct you to the Minister of War."

The adjutant on duty, meeting Prince Andrew, asked him to wait, and went in to the Minister of War. Five minutes later he returned and bowing with particular courtesy ushered Prince Andrew before him along a corridor to the cabinet where the Minister of War was at work. The adjutant by his elaborate courtesy appeared to wish to ward off any attempt at familiarity on the part of the Russian messenger.

Prince Andrew's joyous feeling was considerably weakened as he approached the door of the minister's room. He felt offended, and without his noticing it the feeling of offense immediately turned into one of disdain which was quite uncalled for. His fertile mind instantly suggested to him a point of view which gave him a right to despise the adjutant and the minister. "Away from the smell of powder, they probably think it easy to gain victories!" he thought. His eyes narrowed disdainfully, he entered the room of the Minister of War with peculiarly deliberate steps. This feeling of disdain was heightened when he saw the minister seated at a large table reading some papers and making pencil notes on them, and for the first two or three minutes taking no notice of his arrival. A wax candle stood at each side of the minister's bent bald head with its gray temples. He went on reading to the end, without raising his eyes at the opening of the door and the sound of footsteps.

"Take this and deliver it," said he to his adjutant, handing him the papers and still taking no notice of the special messenger.

Prince Andrew felt that either the actions of Kutúzov's army interested the Minister of War less than any of the other matters he was concerned with, or he wanted to give the Russian special messenger that impression. "But that is a matter of perfect indifference to me," he thought. The minister drew the remaining papers together, arranged them evenly, and then raised his head. He had an intellectual and distinctive head, but the instant he turned to Prince Andrew the firm, intelligent expression on his face changed in a way evidently deliberate and habitual to him. His face took on the stupid artificial smile (which does not even attempt to hide its artificiality) of a man who is continually receiving many petitioners one after another.

"From General Field Marshal Kutúzov?" he asked. "I hope it is good news? There has been an encounter with Mortier? A victory? It was high time!"

He took the dispatch which was addressed to him and began to read it with a mournful expression.

"Oh, my God! My God! Schmidt!" he exclaimed in German. "What a calamity! What a calamity!"

Having glanced through the dispatch he laid it on the table and looked at Prince Andrew, evidently considering something.

"Ah, what a calamity! You say the affair was decisive? But Mortier is not captured." Again he pondered. "I am very glad you have brought good news, though Schmidt's death is a heavy price to pay for the victory. His Majesty will no doubt wish to see you, but not today. I thank you! You must have a rest. Be at the levee tomorrow after the parade. However I will let you know."

The stupid smile, which had left his face while he was speaking, reappeared.

"*Au revoir!* Thank you very much. his Majesty will probably desire to see you," he added, bowing his head.

When Prince Andrew left the palace he felt that all the interest and happiness the victory had afforded him had been now left in the indifferent hands of the Minister of War and the polite adjutant. The whole tenor of his thoughts instantaneously changed; the battle seemed the memory of a remote event long past.

Chapter X

PRINCE ANDREW STAYED AT BRÜNN WITH BILÍBIN, A RUSSIAN ACQUAINTANCE OF HIS IN THE DIPLOmatic service.

"Ah, my dear prince! I could not have a more welcome visitor," said Bilíbin as he came out to meet Prince Andrew. "Franz, put the prince's things in my bedroom," said he to the servant who was ushering Bolkónski in. "So you're a messenger of victory, eh? Splendid! And I am sitting here ill, as you see."

After washing and dressing, Prince Andrew came into the diplomat's luxurious study and sat down to the dinner prepared for him. Bilíbin settled down comfortably beside the fire.

After his journey and the campaign during which he had been deprived of all the comforts of cleanliness and all the refinements of life, Prince Andrew felt a pleasant sense of repose among luxurious surroundings such as he had been accustomed to from childhood. Besides it was pleasant, after his reception by the Austrians, to speak if not in Russian (for they were speaking French) at least with a Russian who would, he supposed, share the general Russian antipathy to the Austrians which was then particularly strong.

Bilíbin was a man of thirty-five, a bachelor and of the same circle as Prince Andrew. They had known each other previously in Petersburg, but had become more intimate when Prince Andrew was in Vienna with Kutúzov. Just as Prince Andrew was a young man who gave promise of rising high in the military profession, so to an even greater extent Bilíbin gave promise of rising in his diplomatic career. He still a young man but no longer a young diplomat, as he had entered the service at the age of sixteen, had been in Paris and Copenhagen, and now held a rather important post in Vienna. Both the foreign minister and our ambassador in Vienna knew him and valued him. He was not one of those many diplomats who are esteemed because they have certain negative qualities, avoid doing certain things, and speak French. He was one of those, who, liking work, knew how to do it, and despite his indolence would sometimes spend a whole night at his writing-table. He worked equally well whatever the import of his work. It was not the question "What for?" but the question "How?" that interested him. What the diplomatic matter might be he did not care, but it gave him great pleasure to prepare a circular, memorandum, or report, skillfully, pointedly and elegantly. Bilíbin's services were valued not only for what he wrote, but also for his skill in dealing and conversing with those in the highest spheres.

Bilíbin liked conversation as he liked work, only when it could be made elegantly witty. In society he always awaited an opportunity to say something striking, and took part in a conversation only when that was possible. His conversation was always sprinkled with wittily original, finished phrases of general interest. These sayings were prepared in the inner laboratory of his mind in a portable form as if intentionally, so that insignificant society people might carry them from drawing room to drawing room. And in fact Bilíbin's witticisms were hawked about in the Viennese drawing rooms and often had an influence on matters considered important.

His thin, worn, sallow face was covered with deep wrinkles, which always looked as clean and well washed as the tips of one's fingers after a Russian bath. The movement of these wrinkles formed the principal play of expression on his face. Now his forehead would pucker into deep folds and his eyebrows were lifted, then his eyebrows would descend and deep wrinkles would crease his cheeks. His small, deep-set eyes always twinkled and looked out straight.

"Well, now tell me about your exploits," said he.

Bolkónski, very modestly without once mentioning himself, described the engagement and his reception by the Minister of War.

"They received me and my news as one receives a dog in a game of skittles," said he in conclusion.

Bilíbin smiled and the wrinkles on his face disappeared.

"Cependant, mon cher," he remarked, examining his nails from a distance and puckering the skin above his left eye, *"malgré la haute estime que je professe pour* the Orthodox Russian army, *j'avoue que votre victoire n'est pas des plus victorieuses."*

He went on talking in this way in French, uttering only those words in Russian on which he wished to put a contemptuous emphasis.

"Come now! You with all your forces fall on the unfortunate Mortier and his one division, and even then Mortier slips through your fingers! Where's the victory?"

"But seriously," said Prince Andrew, "we can at any rate say without boasting that it was a little better than at Ulm . . ."

"Why didn't you capture one, just one, marshal for us?"

"Because not everything happens as one expects or with the smoothness of a parade. We had expected, as I told you, to get at their rear by seven in the morning but had not reached it by five in the afternoon."

"And why didn't you do it at seven in the morning? You ought to have been there at seven in the morning," returned Bilíbin with a smile. "You ought to have been there at seven in the morning."

"Why did you not succeed in impressing on Bonaparte by diplomatic methods that he had better leave Genoa alone?" retorted Prince Andrew in the same tone.

"I know," interrupted Bilíbin, "you're thinking it's very easy to take marshals, sitting on a sofa by the fire! That is true, but still why didn't you capture him? So don't be surprised if not only the

Minister of War but also his Most August Majesty the Emperor and King Francis is not much delighted by your victory. Even I, a poor secretary of the Russian Embassy, do not feel any need in token of my joy to give my Franz a *thaler*, or let him go with his *Liebchen* to the Prater . . . True, we have no Prater here . . ."

He looked straight at Prince Andrew and suddenly unwrinkled his forehead.

"It is now my turn to ask you 'why?' *mon cher*," said Bolkónski. "I confess I do not understand: perhaps there are diplomatic subtleties here beyond my feeble intelligence, but I can't make it out. Mack loses a whole army, the Archduke Ferdinand and the Archduke Karl give no signs of life and make blunder after blunder. Kutúzov alone at last gains a real victory, destroying the spell of the invincibility of the French, and the Minister of War does not even care to hear the details."

"That's just it, my dear fellow. You see it's *hurrah* for the Tsar, for Russia, for the Orthodox Greek faith! All that is beautiful, but what do we, I mean the Austrian Court, care for your victories? Bring us nice news of a victory by the Archduke Karl or Ferdinand (one archduke's as good as another, as you know) and even if it is only over a fire-brigade of Bonaparte's, that will be another story and we'll fire off some cannon! But this sort of thing seems done on purpose to vex us. The Archduke Karl does nothing, the Archduke Ferdinand disgraces himself. You abandon Vienna, give up its defense—as much as to say: 'Heaven is with us, but heaven help you and your capital!' The one general whom we all loved, Schmidt, you expose to a bullet, and then you congratulate us on the victory! Admit that more irritating news than yours could not have been conceived. It's as if it had been done on purpose, on purpose. Besides, suppose you did gain a brilliant victory, if even the Archduke Karl gained a victory, what effect would that have on the general course of events? It's too late now when Vienna is occupied by the French army!"

"What? Occupied? Vienna occupied?"

"Not only occupied, but Bonaparte is at Schönbrunn, and the count, our dear Count Vrbna, goes to him for orders."

After the fatigues and impressions of the journey, his reception, and especially after having dined, Bolkónski felt that he could not take in the full significance of the words he heard.

"Count Lichtenfels was here this morning," Bilíbin continued, "and showed me a letter in which the parade of the French in Vienna was fully described: Prince Murat *et tout le tremblement* . . . You see that your victory is not a matter for great rejoicing and that you can't be received as a savior."

"Really I don't care about that, I don't care at all," said Prince Andrew, beginning to understand that his news of the battle before Krems was really of small importance in view of such events as the fall of Austria's capital. "How is it Vienna was taken? What of the bridge and its celebrated bridge-head and Prince Auersperg? We heard reports that Prince Auersperg was defending Vienna?" he said.

"Prince Auersperg is on this, on our side of the river, and is defending us—doing it very badly, I think, but still he is defending us. But Vienna is on the other side. No, the bridge has not yet been taken and I hope it will not be, for it is mined and orders have been given to blow it up. Otherwise we should long ago have been in the mountains of Bohemia, and you and your army would have spent a bad quarter of an hour between two fires."

"But still this does not mean that the campaign is over," said Prince Andrew.

"Well, I think it is. The bigwigs here think so too, but they daren't say so. It will be as I said at the beginning of the campaign, it won't be your skirmishing at Drrenstein, or gunpowder at all that will decide the matter, but those who devised it," said Bilíbin quoting one of his own *mots*, releasing the wrinkles on his forehead, and pausing. "The only question is what will come of the meeting between the Emperor Alexander and the King of Prussia in Berlin? If Prussia joins the allies, Austria's hand will be forced and there will be war. If not it is merely a question of settling where the preliminaries of the new Campo Formio are to be drawn up."

"What an extraordinary genius!" Prince Andrew suddenly exclaimed, clenching his small hand and striking the table with it, "and what luck the man has!"

"Buonaparte?" said Bilíbin inquiringly, puckering up his forehead to indicate that he was about to say something witty. "Buonaparte?" he repeated, accentuating the *u:* "I think, however, now that he lays down laws for Austria at Schönbrunn, *il faut lui faire grâce de l'u!* I shall certainly adopt an innovation and call him simply Bonaparte!"

"But joking apart," said Andrew, "do you really think the campaign is over?"

"This is what I think. Austria has been made a fool of, and she is not used to it. She will retaliate. And she has been fooled in the first place because her provinces have been pillaged—they say the Holy Russian army loots terribly—her army is destroyed, her capital taken, and all this for the *beaux yeux* of His Sardinian Majesty. And therefore—this is between ourselves—I instinctively feel that we are being deceived, my instinct tells me of negotiations with France and projects for peace, a secret peace concluded separately."

"Impossible!" cried Prince Andrew. "That would be too base."

"If we live we shall see," replied Bilíbin, his face again becoming smooth as a sign that the conversation was at an end.

When Prince Andrew reached the room prepared for him and lay down in a clean shirt on the feather-bed with its warmed and fragrant pillows, he felt that the battle of which he had brought tidings was far far away from him. The alliance with Prussia, Austria's treachery, Bonaparte's new triumph, tomorrow's levee and parade, and the audience with the Emperor Francis, occupied his thoughts.

He closed his eyes, and immediately a sound of cannonading, of musketry and the rattling of carriage wheels seemed to fill his ears, and now again drawn out in a thin line the musketeers were descending the hill, the French were firing, and he felt his heart palpitating as he rode forward beside Schmidt with the bullets merrily whistling all around, and he experienced tenfold the joy of living, as he had not done since childhood.

He woke up . . .

"Yes, that all happened!" he said, and, smiling happily to himself like a child, he fell into a deep youthful slumber.

Chapter XI

NEXT DAY HE WOKE LATE. RECALLING HIS RECENT IMPRESSIONS THE FIRST THOUGHT THAT CAME into his mind was that today he had to be presented to the Emperor Francis; he remembered the Minister of War, the polite Austrian adjutant, Bilíbin, and last night's conversation. Having dressed for his attendance at court in full parade uniform, which he had not worn for a long time, he went into Bilíbin's study fresh, animated and handsome, with his hand bandaged. In the study were four gentlemen of the diplomatic corps. With Prince Hippolyte Kurágin, who was a secretary to the embassy, Bolkónski was already acquainted. Bilíbin introduced him to the others.

The gentlemen assembled at Bilíbin's were young, wealthy, gay society men, who here, as in Vienna, formed a special set which Bilíbin, their leader, called *les nôtres.* This set, consisting almost exclusively of diplomats, evidently had its own interests which had nothing to do with war or politics but related to high society, to certain women, and to the official side of the service. These gentlemen received Prince Andrew as one of themselves, an honor they did not extend to many. From politeness and to start conversation, they asked him a few questions about the army and the battle, and then the talk went off into merry jests and gossip.

"But the best of it was," said one, telling of the misfortune of a fellow-diplomat, "that the Chancellor told him flatly that his appointment to London was a promotion and that he was so to regard it. Can you fancy the figure he cut? . . ."

"But the worst of it, gentlemen—I am giving Kurágin away to you—is that that man suffers, and this Don Juan, wicked fellow, is taking advantage of it!"

Prince Hippolyte was lolling in a lounge chair with his legs over its arm. He began to laugh.

"Tell me about that!" he said.

"Oh, you Don Juan! You serpent!" cried several voices.

"You, Bolkónski, don't know," said Bilíbin turning to Prince Andrew, "that all the atrocities of the French army (I nearly said of the Russian army) are nothing compared to what this man has been doing among the women!"

"La femme est la compagne de l'homme," announced Prince Hippolyte, and began looking through a lorgnette at his elevated legs.

Bilíbin and the rest of "ours" burst out laughing in Hippolyte's face, and Prince Andrew saw that Hippolyte, of whom—he had to admit—he had almost been jealous on his wife's account, was the butt of this set.

"Oh, I must give you a treat," Bilíbin whispered to Bolkónski. "Kurágin is exquisite when he discusses politics—you should see his gravity!"

He sat down beside Hippolyte and wrinkling his forehead began talking to him about politics. Prince Andrew and the others gathered round these two.

"The Berlin cabinet cannot express a feeling of alliance," began Hippolyte gazing round with importance at the others, "without expressing . . . as in its last note . . . you understand . . . Besides, unless his Majesty the Emperor derogates from the principle of our alliance . . ."

"Wait, I have not finished . . ." he said to Prince Andrew, seizing him by the arm, "I believe that intervention will be stronger than non-intervention. And . . ." he paused. "Finally one cannot impute the non-receipt of our dispatch of November 18. That is how it will end." And he released Bolkónski's arm to indicate that he had now quite finished.

"Demosthenes, I know thee by the pebble thou secretest in thy golden mouth!" said Bilíbin, and the mop of hair on his head moved with satisfaction.

Everybody laughed, and Hippolyte louder than anyone. He was evidently distressed, and breathed painfully, but could not restrain the wild laughter that convulsed his usually impassive features.

"Well now, gentlemen," said Bilíbin, "Bolkónski is my guest in this house and in Brnn itself. I want to entertain him as far as I can, with all the pleasures of life here. If we were in Vienna it would be easy, but here, in this wretched Moravian hole, it is more difficult, and I beg you all to help me. Brnn's attractions must be shown him. You can undertake the theater, I society, and you, Hippolyte, of course the women."

"We must let him see Amelie, she's exquisite!" said one of "ours," kissing his finger-tips.

"In general we must turn this bloodthirsty soldier to more humane interests," said Bilíbin.

"I shall scarcely be able to avail myself of your hospitality, gentlemen, it is already time for me to go," replied Prince Andrew looking at his watch.

"Where to?"

"To the Emperor."

"Oh! Oh! Oh!"

"Well, *au revoir,* Bolkónski! *Au revoir,* prince! Come back early to dinner," cried several voices. "We'll take you in hand."

"When speaking to the Emperor, try as far as you can to praise the way that provisions are supplied and the routes indicated," said Bilíbin, accompanying him to the hall.

"I should like to speak well of them, but as far as I the facts, I can't," replied Bolkónski, smiling.

"Well, talk as much as you can, anyway. He has a passion for giving audiences, but he does not like talking himself and can't do it, as you will see."

Chapter XII

At the levee Prince Andrew stood among the Austrian officers as he had been told to, and the Emperor Francis merely looked fixedly into his face and just nodded to him with to him with his long head. But after it was over the adjutant he had seen the previous day ceremoniously informed Bolkónski that the Emperor desired to give him an audience. The Emperor Francis received him standing in the middle of the room. Before the conversation began Prince Andrew was struck by the fact that the Emperor seemed confused and blushed as if not knowing what to say.

"Tell me, when did the battle begin?" he asked hurriedly.

Prince Andrew replied. Then followed other questions just as simple: "Was Kutúzov well? When had he left Krems?" and so on. The Emperor spoke as if his sole aim were to put a given number of questions—the answers to these questions, as was only too evident, did not interest him.

"At what o'clock did the battle begin?" asked the Emperor.

"I cannot inform your Majesty at what o'clock the battle began at the front, but at Drrenstein, where I was, our attack began after five in the afternoon," replied Bolkónski growing more animated and expecting that he would have a chance to give a reliable account, which he had ready in his mind, of all he knew and had seen. But the Emperor smiled and interrupted him.

"How many miles?"

"From where to where, your Majesty?"

"From Drrenstein to Krems."

"Three and a half miles, your Majesty."

"The French have abandoned the left bank?"

"According to the scouts the last of them crossed on rafts during the night."

"Is there sufficient forage in Krems?"

"Forage has not been supplied to the extent . . ."

The Emperor interrupted him.

"At what o'clock was General Schmidt killed?"

"At seven o'clock, I believe."

"At seven o'clock? It's very sad, very sad!"

The Emperor thanked Prince Andrew and bowed. Prince Andrew withdrew and was immediately surrounded by courtiers on all sides. Everywhere he saw friendly looks and heard friendly words. Yesterday's adjutant reproached him for not having stayed at the palace, and offered him his own house. The Minister of War came up and congratulated him on the Maria Theresa Order of the third grade, which the Emperor was conferring on him. The Empress's chamberlain invited him to see her Majesty. The archduchess also wished to see him. He did not know whom to answer, and for a few seconds collected his thoughts. Then the Russian ambassador took him by the shoulder, led him to the window, and began to talk to him.

Contrary to Bilíbin's forecast the news he had brought was joyfully received. A thanksgiving service was arranged, Kutúzov was awarded the Grand Cross of Maria Theresa, and the whole army received rewards. Bolkónski was invited everywhere, and had to spend the whole morning calling on the principal Austrian dignitaries. Between four and five in the afternoon, having made all his calls, he was returning to Bilíbin's house thinking out a letter to his father about the battle and his visit to Brnn. At the door he found a vehicle half full of luggage. Franz, Bilíbin's man, was dragging a portmanteau with some difficulty out of the front door.

Before returning to Bilíbin's Prince Andrew had gone to bookshop to provide himself with some books for the campaign, and had spent some time in the shop.

"What is it?" he asked.

"Oh, your excellency!" said Franz, with difficulty rolling the portmanteau into the vehicle, "we are to move on still farther. The scoundrel is again at our heels!"

"Eh? What?" asked Prince Andrew.

Bilíbin came out to meet him. His usually calm face showed excitement.

"There now! Confess that this is delightful," said he. "This affair of the Thabor Bridge, at Vienna. . . . They have crossed without striking a blow!"

Prince Andrew could not understand.

"But where do you come from not to know what every coachman in the town knows?"

"I come from the archduchess's. I heard nothing there."

"And you didn't see that everybody is packing up?"

"I did not . . . What is it all about?" inquired Prince Andrew impatiently.

"What's it all about? Why, the French have crossed the bridge that Auersperg was defending, and the bridge was not blown up: so Murat is now rushing along the road to Brnn and will be here in a day or two."

"What? Here? But why did they not blow up the bridge, if it was mined?"

"That is what I ask you. No one, not even Bonaparte, knows why."

Bolkónski shrugged his shoulders.

"But if the bridge is crossed it means that the army too is lost? It will be cut off," said he.

"That's just it," answered Bilíbin. "Listen! The French entered Vienna as I told you. Very well. Next day, which was yesterday, those gentlemen, *messieurs les maréchaux,* Murat, Lannes, and Belliard, mount and ride to bridge. (Observe that all three are Gascons.) 'Gentlemen,' says one of them, 'you know the Thabor Bridge is mined and doubly mined and that there are menacing fortifications at its head and an army of fifteen thousand men has been ordered to blow up the bridge and not let us cross? But it will please our sovereign the Emperor Napoleon if we take this bridge, so let us three go and take it!' 'Yes, let's!' say the others. And off they go and take the bridge, cross it, and now with their whole army are on this side of the Danube, marching on us, you, and your lines of communication."

"Stop jesting," said Prince Andrew sadly and seriously. This news grieved him and yet he was pleased.

As soon as he learned that the Russian army was in such a hopeless situation it occurred to him that it was he who was destined to lead it out of this position; that here was the Toulon that would lift him from the ranks of obscure officers and offer him the first step to fame! Listening to Bilíbin he was already imagining how on reaching the army he would give an opinion at the war council which would be the only one that could save the army, and how he alone would be entrusted with the executing of the plan.

"Stop this jesting," he said

"I am not jesting," Bilíbin went on. "Nothing is truer or sadder. These gentlemen ride onto the bridge alone and wave white handkerchiefs; they assure the officer on duty that they, the marshals, are on their way to negotiate with Prince Auersperg. He lets them enter the *tête-de-pont*. They spin him a thousand gasconades, saying that the war is over, that the Emperor Francis is arranging a meeting with Bonaparte, that they desire to see Prince Auersperg, and so on. The officer sends for Auersperg; these gentlemen embrace the officers, crack jokes, sit on the cannon, and meanwhile a

French battalion gets to the bridge unobserved, flings the bags of incendiary material into the water, and approaches the *tête-de-pont*. At length appears the lieutenant-general, our dear Prince Auersperg von Mautern himself. 'Dearest foe! Flower of the Austrian army, hero of the Turkish wars! Hostilities are ended, we can shake one another's hand. . . . The Emperor Napoleon burns with impatience to make Prince Auersperg's acquaintance.' In a word those gentlemen, Gascons indeed, so bewildered him with fine words, and he is so flattered by his rapidly established intimacy with the French marshals, and so dazzled by the sight of Murat's mantle and ostrich plumes, *qu'il n'y voit que du feu, et oublie celui qu'il devait faire faire sur l'ennemi!*" In spite of the animation of his speech Bilíbin did not forget to pause after this *mot* to give time for its due appreciation. "The French battalion rushes to the bridgehead, spikes the guns, and the bridge is taken! But what is best of all," he went on, his excitement subsiding under the delightful interest of his own story, "is that the sergeant in charge of the cannon which was to give the signal to fire the mines and blow up the bridge, this sergeant seeing that the French troops were running onto the bridge, was about to fire, but Lannes stayed his hand. The sergeant, who was evidently wiser than his general, goes up to Auersperg and says: 'Prince, you are being deceived, here are the French!' Murat, seeing that all is lost if the sergeant is allowed to speak, turns to Auersperg with feigned astonishment (he is a true Gascon) and says: 'I don't recognize the world-famous Austrian discipline, if you allow a subordinate to address you like that!' It was a stroke of genius. Prince Auersperg feels his dignity at stake and orders the sergeant to be arrested. Come, you must own that this affair of the Thabor Bridge is delightful! It is not exactly stupidity, nor rascality. . . ."

"It may be treachery," said Prince Andrew, vividly imagining the gray overcoats, wounds, the smoke of gunpowder, the sounds of firing and the glory that awaited him.

"Not that either. That puts the court in too bad a light," replied Bilíbin. "It's not treachery nor rascality nor stupidity: it is just as at Ulm . . . it is . . ."—he seemed to be trying to find the right expression. *"C'est . . . c'est du Mack. Nous sommes mackés,"* he concluded, feeling that he had produced a good epigram, a fresh one that would be repeated. His hitherto puckered brow became smooth as a sign of pleasure, and with a slight smile he began to examine his nails.

"Where are you off to?" he said suddenly to Prince Andrew who had risen and was going toward his room.

"I am going away."

"Where to?"

"To the army."

"But you meant to stay another two days?"

"But now I am off at once."

And Prince Andrew after giving directions about his departure went to his room.

"Do you know, *mon cher,*" said Bilíbin following him, "I have been thinking about you. Why are you going?"

And in proof of the conclusiveness of his opinion all the wrinkles vanished from his face.

Prince Andrew looked inquiringly at him and gave no reply.

"Why are you going? I know you think it your duty to gallop back to the army now that it is in danger. I understand that. *Mon cher,* it is heroism!"

"Not at all," said Prince Andrew.

"But as you are a philosopher, be a consistent one, look at the other side of the question and you will see that your duty, on the contrary, is to take care of yourself. Leave it to those who are no longer fit for anything else. . . . You have not been ordered to return and have not been dismissed from here; therefore you can stay and go with us wherever our ill-luck takes us. They say we are going to Olmütz, and Olmütz is a very decent town. You and I will travel comfortably in my calèche."

"Do stop joking, Bilíbin," cried Bolkónski.

"I am speaking sincerely as a friend! Consider! Where and why are you going, when you might remain here? You are faced by one of two things," and the skin over his left temple puckered, "either you will not reach your regiment before peace is concluded, or you will share defeat and disgrace with Kutúzov's whole army."

And Bilíbin unwrinkled his temple, feeling that the dilemma was insoluble.

"I cannot argue about it," replied Prince Andrew coldly, but he thought: "I am going to save the army."

"My dear fellow, you are a hero!" said Bilíbin.

Chapter XIII

THAT SAME NIGHT, HAVING TAKEN LEAVE OF THE MINISTER OF WAR, BOLKÓNSKI SET OFF TO REjoin the army, not knowing where he would find it and fearing to be captured by the French on the way to Krems.

In Brünn everybody attached to the court was packing up, and the heavy baggage was already being dispatched to Olmütz. Near Hetzelsdorf Prince Andrew struck the highroad along which the Russian army was moving with great haste and in the greatest disorder. The road was so obstructed with carts that it was impossible to get by in a carriage. Prince Andrew took a horse and a Cossack from a Cossack commander, and hungry and weary, making his way past the baggage-wagons, rode in search of the commander-in-chief and of his own luggage. Very sinister reports of the position of the army reached him as he went along, and the appearance of the troops in their disorderly flight confirmed these rumors.

"Cette armée russe que l'or de l'Angleterre a transportée des extrémités de l'univers, nous allons lui faire éprouver le même sort—(le sort de l'armée d'Ulm)." He remembered these words in Bonaparte's address to his army at the beginning of the campaign, and they awoke in him astonishment at the genius of his hero, a feeling of wounded pride, and a hope of glory. "And should there be nothing left but to die?" he thought. "Well, if need be, I shall do it no worse than others."

He looked with disdain at the endless confused mass of detachments, carts, guns, artillery and again baggage-wagons and vehicles of all kinds overtaking one another and blocking the muddy road, three and sometimes four abreast. From all sides, behind and before, as far as ear could reach, there was the rattle of wheels, the creaking of carts and gun-carriages, the tramp of horses, the crack of whips, shouts, the urging of horses, and the swearing of soldiers, orderlies and officers. All along the sides of the road fallen horses were to be seen, some flayed, some not, and broken-down carts beside which solitary soldiers sat waiting for something, and again soldiers straggling from their companies, crowds of whom set off to the neighboring villages, or returned from them dragging sheep, fowls, hay and bulging sacks. At each ascent or descent of the road the crowds were yet denser and the din of shouting more incessant. Soldiers floundering knee-deep in mud pushed the guns and wagons themselves. Whips cracked, hoofs slipped, traces broke and lungs were strained with shouting. The officers directing the march rode backward and forward between the carts. Their voices were but feebly heard amid the uproar and one saw by their faces that they despaired of the possibility of checking this disorder.

"Here is our dear Orthodox Russian army," thought Bolkónski, recalling Bilíbin's words.

Wishing to find out where the commander-in-chief was, he rode up to a convoy. Directly opposite to him came a strange one-horse vehicle, evidently rigged up by soldiers out of any available materials and looking like something between a cart, a cabriolet and a calèche. A soldier was driving, and a woman enveloped in shawls sat behind the apron under the leather hood of the vehicle.

Prince Andrew rode up and was just putting his question to a soldier when his attention was diverted by the desperate shrieks of the woman in the vehicle. An officer in charge of transport was beating the soldier who was driving the woman's vehicle for trying to get ahead of others, and the strokes of his whip fell on the apron of the equipage. The woman screamed piercingly. Seeing Prince Andrew she leaned out from behind the apron, and waving her thin arms from under the woolen shawl, cried:

"Mr. Aide-de-camp! Mr. Aide-de-camp! . . . For heaven's sake . . . Protect me! What will become of us? I am the wife of the doctor of the Seventh Chasseurs. . . . They won't let us pass, we are left behind and have lost our people . . ."

"I'll flatten you into a pancake!" shouted the angry officer to the soldier. "Turn back with your slut!"

"Mr. Aide-de-camp! Help me! . . . What does it all mean?" screamed the doctor's wife.

"Kindly let this cart pass. Don't you see it's a woman?" said Prince Andrew riding up to the officer.

The officer glanced at him, and without replying turned again to the soldier. "I'll teach you to push on! . . . Back!"

"Let them pass, I tell you!" repeated Prince Andrew, compressing his lips.

"And who are you?" cried the officer, turning on him with tipsy rage, "who are *you?* Are you in command here? Eh? I am commander here, not you! Go back or I'll flatten you into a pancake," repeated he. This expression evidently pleased him.

"That was a nice snub for the little aide-de-camp," came a voice from behind.

Prince Andrew saw that the officer was in that state of senseless tipsy rage when a man does not know what he is saying. He saw that his championship of the doctor's wife in her queer trap might expose him to what he dreaded more than anything in the world—to ridicule; but his instinct urged him on. Before the officer finished his sentence Prince Andrew, his face distorted with fury, rode up to him and raised his riding-whip.

"Kind . . . ly let—them—pass!"

The officer flourished his arm and hastily rode away.

"It's all the fault of these fellows on the staff that there's this disorder," he muttered. "Do as you like."

Prince Andrew without lifting his eyes rode hastily away from the doctor's wife, who was calling him her deliverer, and recalling with a sense of disgust the minutest details of this humiliating scene he galloped on to the village where he was told that the commander-in-chief was.

On reaching the village he dismounted and went to the nearest house, intending to rest if but for a moment, eat something, and try to sort out the stinging and tormenting thoughts that confused his mind. "This is a mob of scoundrels and not an army," he was thinking as he went up to the window of the first house, when a familiar voice called him by name.

He turned round. Nesvítski's handsome face looked out of the little window. Nesvítski, moving his moist lips as he chewed something, and flourishing his arm, called him to enter.

"Bolkónski! Bolkónski! . . . Don't you hear? Eh? Come quick . . ." he shouted.

Entering the house, Prince Andrew saw Nesvítski and another adjutant having something to eat. They hastily turned round to him asking if he had any news. On their familiar faces he read agitation and alarm. This was particularly noticeable on Nesvítski's usually laughing countenance.

"Where is the commander-in-chief?" asked Bolkónski.

"Here, in that house," answered the adjutant.

"Well, is it true that it's peace and capitulation?" asked Nesvítski.

"I was going to ask you. I know nothing except that it was all I could do to get here."

"And we, my dear boy! It's terrible! I was wrong to laugh at Mack, we're getting it still worse," said Nesvítski. "But sit down and have something to eat."

"You won't be able to find either your baggage or anything else now, prince. And God only knows where your man Peter is," said the other adjutant.

"Where are headquarters?"

"We are to spend the night in Znaim."

"Well, I have got all I need into packs for two horses," said Nesvítski. "They've made up splendid packs for me—fit to cross the Bohemian mountains with. It's a bad look-out, old fellow! But what's the matter with you? You must be ill to shiver like that," he added, noticing that Prince Andrew winced as at an electric shock.

"It's nothing," replied Prince Andrew.

He had just remembered his recent encounter with the doctor's wife and the convoy officer.

"What is the commander-in-chief doing here?" he asked.

"I can't make out at all," said Nesvítski.

"Well, all I can make out is that everything is abominable, abominable, quite abominable!" said Prince Andrew, and he went off to the house where the commander-in-chief was.

Passing by Kutúzov's carriage and the exhausted saddle-horses of his suite, with their Cossacks who were talking loudly together, Prince Andrew entered the passage. Kutúzov himself, he was told, was in the house with Prince Bagratión and Weyrother. Weyrother was the Austrian general who had succeeded Schmidt. In the passage little Kozlóvski was squatting on his heels in front of a clerk. The clerk, with cuffs turned up, was hastily writing at a tub turned bottom upward. Kozlóvski's face looked worn—he too had evidently not slept all night. He glanced at Prince Andrew and did not even nod to him.

"Second line . . . have you written it?" he continued dictating to the clerk. "The Kiev Grenadiers, Podolian . . ."

"One can't write so fast, your honor," said the clerk, glancing angrily and disrespectfully at Kozlóvski.

Through the door came the sounds of Kutúzov's voice, excited and dissatisfied, interrupted by another, an unfamiliar voice. From the sound of these voices, the inattentive way Kozlóvski looked at him, the disrespectful manner of the exhausted clerk, the fact that the clerk and Kozlóvski were squatting on the floor by a tub so near to the commander-in-chief, and from the noisy laughter of the Cossacks holding the horses near the window, Prince Andrew felt that something important and disastrous was about to happen.

He turned to Kozlóvski with urgent questions.

"Immediately, prince," said Kozlóvski. "Dispositions for Bagratión."

"What about capitulation?"

"Nothing of the sort. Orders are issued for a battle."

Prince Andrew moved toward the door from whence voices were heard. Just as he was going to open it the sounds ceased, the door opened, and Kutúzov with his eagle nose and puffy face appeared in the doorway. Prince Andrew stood right in front of Kutúzov but the expression of the commander-in-chief's one sound eye showed him to be so preoccupied with thoughts and anxieties as to be oblivious of his presence. He looked straight at his adjutant's face without recognizing him.

"Well, have you finished?" said he to Kozlóvski.

"One moment, your excellency."

Bagratión, a gaunt middle-aged man of medium height with a firm, impassive face of Oriental type, came out after the commander-in-chief.

"I have the honor to present myself," repeated Prince Andrew rather loudly, handing Kutúzov an envelope.

"Ah, from Vienna? Very good. Later, later!"

Kutúzov went out into the porch with Bagratión.

"Well, good-bye, prince," said he to Bagratión. "My blessing, and may Christ be with you in your great endeavor!"

His face suddenly softened and tears came into his eyes. With his left hand he drew Bagratión toward him, and with his right, on which he wore a ring, he made the sign of the cross over him with a gesture evidently habitual, offering his puffy cheek, but Bagratión kissed him on the neck instead.

"Christ be with you!" Kutúzov repeated and went toward his carriage. "Get in with me," said he to Bolkónski.

"Your excellency, I should like to be of use here. Allow me to remain with Prince Bagratión's detachment."

"Get in," said Kutúzov, and noticing that Bolkónski still delayed, he added: "I need good officers myself, need them myself!"

They got into the carriage and drove for a few minutes in silence.

"There is still much, much before us," he said, as if with an old man's penetration he understood all that was passing in Bolkónski's mind. "If a tenth part of his detachment returns I shall thank God," he added as if speaking to himself.

Prince Andrew glanced at Kutúzov's face only a foot distant from him and involuntarily noticed the carefully washed seams of the scar near his temple, where an Ismail bullet had pierced his skull, and the empty eye-socket. "Yes, he has a right to speak so calmly of those men's death," thought Bolkónski.

"That is why I beg to be sent to that detachment," he said.

Kutúzov did not reply. He seemed to have forgotten what he had been saying, and sat plunged in thought. Five minutes later, gently swaying on the soft springs of the carriage, he turned to Prince Andrew. There was not a trace of agitation on his face. With delicate irony he questioned Prince Andrew about the details of his interview with the Emperor, about the remarks he had heard at court concerning the Krems affair, and about some ladies they both knew.

Chapter XIV

On November 1st Kutúzov had received, through a spy, news that the army he commanded was in an almost hopeless position. The spy reported that the French, after crossing the bridge at Vienna, were advancing in immense force upon Kutúzov's line of communication with the troops that were arriving from Russia. If Kutúzov decided to remain at Krems, Napoleon's army of one hundred and fifty thousand men would cut him off completely and surround his exhausted army of forty thousand, and he would find himself in the position of Mack at Ulm. If Kutúzov decided to abandon the road connecting him with the troops arriving from Russia, he would have to march with no road into unknown parts of the Bohemian mountains defending himself against superior forces of the enemy and abandoning all hope of a junction with Buxhöwden. If Kutúzov decided to retreat along the road from Krems to Olmütz, to unite with the troops arriving from Russia, he risked being forestalled on that road by the French who had crossed the Vienna bridge, and encumbered by his baggage and transport, having to accept battle on the march against an enemy three times as strong, who would hem him in from two sides.

Kutúzov chose this latter course.

The French, the spy reported, having crossed the Vienna bridge were advancing by forced marches toward Znaim, which lay a hundred versts off on the line of Kutúzov's retreat. If he reached Znaim before the French, there would be great hope of saving the army; to let the French forestall him at Znaim meant the exposure of his whole army to a disgrace such as that of Ulm, or to utter destruction. But to forestall the French with his whole army was impossible. The road for the French from Vienna to Znaim was shorter and better than the road for the Russians from Krems to Znaim.

The night he received the news, Kutúzov sent Bagratión's vanguard, four thousand strong, to the right across the hills from the Krems-Znaim to the Vienna-Znaim road. Bagratión was to make this march without resting, and to halt facing Vienna with Znaim to his rear, and if he succeeded in forestalling the French he was to delay them as long as possible. Kutúzov himself with all his transport took the road to Znaim.

Marching thirty miles that stormy night across roadless hills, with his hungry, ill-shod soldiers, and losing a third of his men as stragglers by the way, Bagratión came out on the Vienna-Znaim road at Hollabrnn a few hours ahead of the French who were approaching Hollabrnn from Vienna. Kutúzov with his transport had still to march for some days before he could reach Znaim. Hence Bagratión with his four thousand hungry, exhausted men, would have to detain for days the whole enemy army that came upon him at Hollabrnn, which was clearly impossible. But a freak of fate made the impossible possible. The success of the trick that had placed the Vienna bridge in the hands of the French without a fight, led Murat to try to deceive Kutúzov in a similar way. Meeting Bagratión's weak detachment on the Znaim road he supposed it to be Kutúzov's whole army. To be able to crush it absolutely he awaited the arrival of the rest of the troops who were on their way from Vienna, and with this object offered a three days' truce on condition that both armies should remain in position without moving. Murat declared that negotiations for peace were already proceeding, and that he therefore offered this truce to avoid unnecessary bloodshed. Count Nostitz, the Austrian general occupying the advanced posts, believed Murat's emissary and retired, leaving Bagratión's division exposed. Another emissary rode to the Russian line to announce the peace negotiations and to offer the Russian army the three days' truce. Bagratión replied that he was not authorized either to accept or refuse a truce, and sent his adjutant to Kutúzov to report the offer he had received.

A truce was Kutúzov's sole chance of gaining time, giving Bagratión's exhausted troops some rest, and letting the transport and heavy convoys (whose movements were concealed from the French) advance if but one stage nearer Znaim. The offer of a truce gave the only, and a quite unexpected, chance of saving the army. On receiving the news he immediately dispatched Adjutant-General Wintzingerode, who was in attendance on him, to the enemy camp. Wintzingerode was not merely to agree to the truce but also to offer terms of capitulation, and meanwhile Kutúzov sent his adjutants back to hasten to the utmost the movements of the baggage-trains of the entire army along the Krems-Znaim road. Bagratión's exhausted and hungry detachment which alone covered this movement of the transport and of the whole army, had to remain stationary in face of an enemy eight times as strong as itself.

Kutúzov's expectations that the proposals of capitulation (which were in no way binding) might give time for part of the transport to pass, and also that Murat's mistake would very soon be discovered, proved correct. As soon as Bonaparte (who was at Schönbrunn, sixteen miles from Hollabrnn) received Murat's dispatch with the proposal of a truce and a capitulation, he detected a ruse and wrote the following letter to Murat:

Schönbrunn, 25th Brumaire, 1805,
at eight o'clock in the morning.

TO PRINCE MURAT—I cannot find words to express to you my displeasure. You command only my advance guard, and have no right to arrange an armistice without my order. You are causing me to lose the fruits of a campaign. Break the armistice immediately and march on the enemy. Inform him that the general who signed that capitulation had no right to do so, and that no one but the Emperor of Russia has that right.

If, however, the Emperor of Russia ratifies that convention, I will ratify it; but it is only a trick. March on, destroy the Russian army. . . . You are in a position to seize its baggage and artillery.

The Russian Emperor's aide-de-camp is an impostor. Officers are nothing when they have no powers; this one had none. . . . The Austrians let themselves be tricked at the crossing of the Vienna bridge, you are letting yourself be tricked by an aide-de-camp of the Emperor.

NAPOLEON

Bonaparte's adjutant rode full gallop with this menacing letter to Murat. Bonaparte himself, not trusting to his generals, moved with all the Guards to the field of battle, afraid of letting a ready victim escape, and Bagratión's four thousand men merrily lit campfires, dried and warmed themselves, cooked their porridge for the first time for three days, and not one of them knew or imagined what was in store for him.

Chapter XV

BETWEEN THREE AND FOUR O'CLOCK IN THE AFTERNOON PRINCE ANDREW, WHO HAD PERSISTED in his request to Kutúzov, arrived at Grunth and reported himself to Bagratión. Bonaparte's adjutant had not yet reached Murat's detachment and the battle had not yet begun. In Bagratión's detachment no one knew anything of the general position of affairs. They talked of peace but did not believe in its possibility; others talked of a battle but also disbelieved in the nearness of an engagement. Bagratión, knowing Bolkónski to be a favorite and trusted adjutant, received him with distinction and special marks of favor, explaining to him that there would probably be an engagement that day or the next, and giving him full liberty to remain with him during the battle or to join the rearguard and have an eye on the order of retreat, "which is also very important."

"However there will hardly be an engagement today," said Bagratión as if to reassure Prince Andrew.

"If he is one of the ordinary little staff-dandies sent to earn a medal he can get his reward just as well in the rearguard, but if he wishes to stay with me, let him . . . he'll be of use here if he's a brave officer," thought Bagratión. Prince Andrew, without replying, asked the prince's permission to ride round the position to see the disposition of the forces, so as to know his bearings should he be sent to execute an order. The officer on duty, a handsome, elegantly dressed man with a diamond ring on his forefinger, who was fond of speaking French though he spoke it badly, offered to conduct Prince Andrew.

On all sides they saw rain-soaked officers with dejected faces who seemed to be seeking something, and soldiers dragging doors, benches and fencing from the village.

"There now, prince! We can't stop those fellows," said the staff-officer pointing to the soldiers. "The officers don't keep them in hand. And there," he pointed to a sutler's tent, "they crowd in and sit. This morning I turned them all out and now look, it's full again. I must go there, prince, and scare them a bit. It won't take a moment."

"Yes, let's go in and I will get myself a roll and some cheese," said Prince Andrew who had not yet had time to eat anything.

"Why didn't you mention it, prince? I would have offered you something."

They dismounted and entered the tent. Several officers, with flushed and weary faces, were sitting at the table eating and drinking.

"Now what does this mean, gentlemen?" said the staff-officer, in the reproachful tone of a man who has repeated the same thing more than once. "You know it won't do to leave your posts like this. The prince gave orders that no one should leave his post. Now you, captain," and he turned to a thin, dirty little artillery officer who without his boots (he had given them to the canteen-keeper to dry), in only his stockings, rose when they entered, smiling not altogether comfortably.

"Well, aren't you ashamed of yourself, Captain Túshin?" he continued. "One would think that as an artillery officer you would set a good example, yet here you are without your boots! The alarm will be sounded and you'll be in a pretty position without your boots!" (The staff-officer smiled.) "Kindly return to your posts, gentlemen, all of you, all!" he added in a tone of command.

Prince Andrew smiled involuntarily as he looked at the artillery officer Túshin, who silent and smiling, shifting from one stockinged foot to the other, glanced inquiringly with his large, intelligent, kindly eyes from Prince Andrew to the staff-officer.

"The soldiers say it feels easier without boots," said Captain Túshin smiling shyly in his uncomfortable position, evidently wishing to adopt a jocular tone. But before he had finished he felt that his jest was unacceptable and had not come off. He grew confused.

"Kindly return to your posts," said the staff-officer trying to preserve his gravity.

Prince Andrew glanced again at the artillery officer's small figure. There was something peculiar about it, quite unsoldierly, rather comic, but extremely attractive.

The staff-officer and Prince Andrew mounted their horses and rode on.

Having ridden beyond the village, continually meeting and overtaking soldiers and officers of various regiments, they saw on their left some entrenchments being thrown up, the freshly-dug clay of which showed up red. Several battalions of soldiers, in their shirt-sleeves despite the cold wind, swarmed in these earth-works like a host of white ants; spadefuls of red clay were continually being thrown up from behind the bank by unseen hands. Prince Andrew and the officer rode up, looked at the entrenchment, and went on again. Just behind it they came upon some dozens of soldiers, continually replaced by others, who ran from the entrenchment. They had to hold their noses and put their horses to a trot to escape from the poisoned atmosphere of these latrines.

"Voilà l'agrément des camps, monsieur le prince," said the staff-officer.

They rode up the opposite hill. From there the French could already be seen. Prince Andrew stopped and began examining the position.

"That's our battery," said the staff-officer indicating the highest point. "It's in charge of the queer fellow we saw without his boots. You can see everything from there; let's go there, prince."

"Thank you very much, I will go on alone," said Prince Andrew, wishing to rid himself of this staff-officer's company, "please don't trouble yourself further."

The staff-officer remained behind and Prince Andrew rode on alone.

The farther forward and nearer the enemy he went, the more orderly and cheerful were the troops. The greatest disorder and depression had been in the baggage-train he had passed that morning on the Znaim road seven miles away from the French. At Grunth also some apprehension and alarm could be felt, but the nearer Prince Andrew came to the French lines the more confident was the appearance of our troops. The soldiers in their greatcoats were ranged in lines, the sergeant-majors and company officers were counting the men, poking the last man in each section in the ribs and telling him to hold his hand up. Soldiers scattered over the whole place were dragging logs and brushwood and were building shelters with merry chatter and laughter; around the fires sat others, dressed and undressed, drying their shirts and legbands or mending boots or overcoats and crowding round the boilers and porridge-cookers. In one company dinner was ready, and the soldiers were gazing eagerly at the steaming boiler, waiting till the sample, which a quartermaster-sergeant was carrying in a wooden bowl to an officer who sat on a log before his shelter, had been tasted.

Another company, a lucky one for not all the companies had vodka, crowded round a pockmarked, broad-shouldered sergeant-major who, tilting a keg, filled one after another the canteen-lids held out to him. The soldiers lifted the canteen-lids to their lips with reverential faces, emptied them, rolling the vodka in their mouths, and walked away from the sergeant-major with brightened expressions, licking their lips and wiping them on the sleeves of their greatcoats. All their faces were as serene as if all this were happening at home awaiting peaceful encampment, and not within sight of the enemy before an action in which at least half of them would be left on the field. After passing a chasseur regiment and in the lines of the Kiev grenadiers—fine fellows busy with similar peaceful affairs—near the shelter of the regimental commander, higher than and different from the others, Prince Andrew came out in front of a platoon of grenadiers before whom lay a naked man. Two soldiers held him while two others were flourishing their switches and striking him regularly on his bare back. The man shrieked unnaturally. A stout major was pacing up and down the line, and regardless of the screams kept repeating:

"It's a shame for a soldier to steal; a soldier must be honest, honorable and brave, but if he robs his fellows there is no honor in him, he's a scoundrel. Go on! Go on!"

So the swishing sound of the strokes, and the desperate but unnatural screams, continued.

"Go on, go on!" said the major.

A young officer with a bewildered and pained expression on his face stepped away from the man and looked round inquiringly at the adjutant as he rode by.

Prince Andrew, having reached the front line, rode along it. Our front line and that of the enemy were far apart on the right and left flanks, but in the center where the men with a flag of truce had passed that morning, the lines were so near together that the men could see one another's faces and speak to one another. Besides the soldiers who formed the picket line on either side, there were many curious onlookers who, jesting and laughing, stared at their strange foreign enemies.

Since early morning—despite an injunction not to approach the picket line—the officers had been unable to keep sightseers away. The soldiers forming the picket line, like showmen exhibiting a curiosity, no longer looked at the French but paid attention to the sightseers and grew weary waiting to be relieved. Prince Andrew halted to have a look at the French.

"Look! Look there!" one soldier was saying to another, pointing to a Russian musketeer who had gone up to the picket line with an officer and was rapidly and excitedly talking to a French grenadier. "Hark to him jabbering! Fine, isn't it? It's all the Frenchy can do to keep up with him. There now, Sídorov!"

"Wait a bit and listen. It's fine!" answered Sídorov, who was considered an adept at French.

The soldier to whom the laughers referred was Dólokhov. Prince Andrew recognized him and stopped to listen to what he was saying. Dólokhov had come from the left flank where their regiment was stationed, with his captain.

"Now then, go on, go on!" incited the officer, bending forward and trying not to lose a word of the speech which was incomprehensible to him. "More, please: more! What's he saying?"

Dólokhov did not answer the captain; he had been drawn into a hot dispute with the French grenadier. They were naturally talking about the campaign. The Frenchman, confusing the Austrians with the Russians, was trying to prove that the Russians had surrendered and had fled all the way from Ulm, while Dólokhov maintained that the Russians had not surrendered but had beaten the French.

"We have orders to drive you off here, and we shall drive you off," said Dólokhov.

"Only take care you and your Cossacks are not all captured!" said the French grenadier.

The French onlookers and listeners laughed.

"We'll make you dance as we did under Suvórov . . . (*on vous fera danser*)," said Dólokhov.

"*Qu'est-ce qu'il chante?* (What's he singing about?)" asked a Frenchman.

"It's ancient history," said another, guessing that it referred to a former war. "The Emperor will teach your Suvara as he has taught the others . . ."

"Bonaparte . . ." began Dólokhov, but the Frenchman interrupted him.

"Not Bonaparte. He is the Emperor! *Sacré nom* . . . !" cried he angrily.

"The devil skin your Emperor."

And Dólokhov swore at him in coarse soldier's Russian and shouldering his musket walked away.

"Let us go, Iván Lukích," he said to the captain.

"Ah, that's the way to talk French," said the picket soldiers. "Now, Sídorov, you have a try!"

Sídorov, turning to the French, winked, and began to jabber meaningless sounds very fast: *"Kari, mala, tafa, safi, muter, Kaská,"* he said, trying to give an expressive intonation to his voice.

"Ho! ho! ho! Ha! ha! ha! ha! Ouh! ouh!" came peals of such healthy and good-humored laughter from the soldiers that it infected the French involuntarily, so much so that the only thing left to do seemed to be to unload the muskets, explode the ammunition, and all return home as quickly as possible.

But the guns remained loaded, the loop-holes in block houses and entrenchments looked out just as menacingly, and the unlimbered cannon confronted one another as before.

Chapter XVI

HAVING RIDDEN ROUND THE WHOLE LINE FROM RIGHT FLANK TO LEFT, PRINCE ANDREW MADE his way up to the battery from which the staff-officer had told him the whole field could be seen. Here he dismounted, and stopped beside the farthest of the four unlimbered cannon. Before the guns an artillery sentry was pacing up and down; he stood at attention when the officer arrived, but at a sign resumed his measured, monotonous pacing. Behind the guns were their limbers, and still farther back picket-ropes and artillerymen's bonfires. To the left, not far from the farthest cannon, was a small, newly-constructed wattle-shed from which came the sound of officers' voices in eager conversation.

It was true that a view over nearly the whole Russian position and the greater part of the enemy's opened out from this battery. Just facing it, on the crest of the opposite hill, the village of Schön Grabern could be seen, and in three places to left and right the French troops amid the smoke of their campfires, the greater part of whom were evidently in the village itself and behind the hill. To the left from that village, amid the smoke, was something resembling a battery, but it was impossible to see it clearly with the naked eye. Our right flank was posted on a rather steep incline which dominated the French position. Our infantry were stationed there, and at the farthest point the dragoons. In the center, where Túshin's battery stood and from which Prince Andrew was surveying the position, was the easiest and most direct descent and ascent to the brook separating us from Schön Grabern. On the left our troops were close to a copse, in which smoked the bonfires of our infantry who were felling wood. The French line was wider than ours, and it was plain that they could easily outflank us on both sides. Behind our position was a steep and deep dip, making it difficult for artillery and cavalry to retire. Prince Andrew took out his notebook, and leaning on the cannon, sketched a plan of the position. He made some notes on two points, intending to mention them to Bagratión. His idea was, first to concentrate all the artillery in the center, and secondly, to withdraw the cavalry to the other side of the dip. Prince Andrew, being always near the commander-in-chief, closely following the mass movements and general orders, and constantly studying historical accounts of battles, involuntarily pictured to himself the course of events in the forthcoming action in broad outline. He imagined only important possibilities: "If the enemy attacks the right flank," he said to himself, "the Kiev grenadiers and the Podólsk chasseurs must hold their position till reserves from the center come up. In that case the dragoons could successfully make a flank counterattack. If they attack our center we, having the center battery on this high ground, shall withdraw the left flank under its cover, and retreat to the dip by echelons." So he reasoned. . . . All the time he had been beside the gun he had heard the voices of the officers distinctly, but as often happens had not understood a word of what they were saying. Suddenly however he was struck by a voice coming from the shed, and its tone was so sincere that he could not but listen.

"No, friend," said a pleasant and as it seemed to Prince Andrew a familiar voice, "what I say is that if it were possible to know what is beyond death, none of us would be afraid of it. That's so, friend."

Another, a younger voice, interrupted him:

"Afraid or not, you can't escape it anyhow."

"All the same, one is afraid! Oh, you clever people," said a third manly voice interrupting them both. "Of course you artillery men are very wise, because you can take everything along with you—vodka and snacks."

And the owner of the manly voice, evidently an infantry officer, laughed.

"Yes, one is afraid," continued the first speaker, he of the familiar voice. "One is afraid of the unknown, that's what it is. Whatever we may say about the soul going to the sky . . . we know there is no sky but only an atmosphere."

The manly voice again interrupted the artillery officer.

"Well, stand us some of your herb vodka, Túshin," it said.

"Why," thought Prince Andrew, "that's the captain who stood up in the sutler's hut without his boots." He recognized the agreeable philosophizing voice with pleasure.

"Some herb vodka? Certainly!" said Túshin—"but still, to conceive a future life . . ."

He did not finish. Just then there was a whistle in the air; nearer and nearer, faster and louder, louder and faster, a cannon-ball, as if it had not finished saying what was necessary, thudded into the ground near the shed with super-human force, throwing up a mass of earth. The ground seemed to groan at the terrible impact.

And immediately Túshin, with a short pipe in the corner of his mouth and his kind intelligent face rather pale, rushed out of the shed followed by the owner of the manly voice, a dashing infantry officer who hurried off to his company, buttoning up his coat as he ran.

Chapter XVII

MOUNTING HIS HORSE AGAIN PRINCE ANDREW LINGERED WITH THE BATTERY, LOOKING AT THE puff from the gun that had sent the ball. His eyes ran rapidly over the wide space, but he only saw that the hitherto motionless masses of the French now swayed and that there really was a battery to their left. The smoke above it had not yet dispersed. Two mounted Frenchmen, probably adjutants, were galloping up the hill. A small but distinctly visible enemy column was moving down the hill, probably to strengthen the front line. The smoke of the first shot had not yet dispersed before another puff appeared, followed by a report. The battle had begun! Prince Andrew turned his horse and galloped back to Grunth to find Prince Bagratión. He heard the cannonade behind him growing louder and more frequent. Evidently our guns had begun to reply. From the bottom of the slope, where the parleys had taken place, came the report of musketry.

Lemarrois had just arrived at a gallop with Bonaparte's stern letter, and Murat, humiliated and anxious to expiate his fault, had at once moved his forces to attack the center and outflank both the

Russian wings, hoping before evening and before the arrival of the Emperor to crush the contemptible detachment that stood before him.

"It has begun. Here it is!" thought Prince Andrew, feeling the blood rush to his heart. "But where and how will my Toulon present itself?"

Passing between the companies that had been eating porridge and drinking vodka a quarter of an hour before, he saw everywhere the same rapid movement of soldiers forming ranks and getting their muskets ready, and on all their faces he recognized the same eagerness that filled his heart. "It has begun! Here it is, dreadful but enjoyable!" was what the face of each soldier and each officer seemed to say.

Before he had reached the embankments that were being thrown up, he saw, in the light of the dull autumn evening, mounted men coming toward him. The foremost, wearing a Cossack cloak and lambskin cap and riding a white horse, was Prince Bagratión. Prince Andrew stopped, waiting for him to come up; Prince Bagratión reined in his horse and recognizing Prince Andrew nodded to him. He still looked ahead while Prince Andrew told him what he had seen.

The feeling, "It has begun! Here it is!" was seen even on Prince Bagratión's hard brown face with its half-closed dull sleepy eyes. Prince Andrew gazed with anxious curiosity at that impassive face and wished he could tell what, if anything, this man was thinking and feeling at that moment. "Is there anything at all behind that impassive face?" Prince Andrew asked himself as he looked. Prince Bagratión bent his head in sign of agreement with what Prince Andrew told him, and said, "Very good!" in a tone that seemed to imply that everything that took place and was reported to him was exactly what he had foreseen. Prince Andrew, out of breath with his rapid ride, spoke quickly. Prince Bagratión, uttering his words with an Oriental accent, spoke particularly slowly, as if to impress the fact that there was no need to hurry. However he put his horse to a trot in the direction of Túshin's battery. Prince Andrew followed with the suite. Behind Prince Bagratión rode an officer of the suite, the prince's personal adjutant, Zherkóv, an orderly officer, the staff-officer on duty, riding a fine bob-tailed horse, and a civilian—an accountant who had asked permission to be present at the battle out of curiosity. The accountant, a stout full-faced man, looked around him with a naïve smile of satisfaction and presented a strange appearance among the hussars, Cossacks and adjutants, in his camlet coat as he jolted on his horse with a convoy-officer's saddle.

"He wants to see a battle," said Zherkóv to Bolkónski, pointing to the accountant, "but he feels a pain in the pit of his stomach already."

"Oh, leave off!" said the accountant with a beaming but rather cunning smile, as if flattered at being made the subject of Zherkóv's joke, and purposely trying to appear stupider than he really was.

"It is very strange, *mon Monsieur Prince,*" said the staff-officer. (He remembered that in French there is some peculiar way of addressing a prince, but could not get it quite right.)

By this time they were all approaching Túshin's battery, and a ball struck the ground in front of them.

"What's that that has fallen?" asked the accountant with a naïve smile.

"A French pancake," answered Zherkóv.

"So that's what they hit with?" asked the accountant. "How awful!"

He seemed to swell with satisfaction. He had hardly finished speaking when they again heard an unexpectedly violent whistling which suddenly ended with a thud into something soft . . . *f-f-flop!* and a Cossack, riding a little to their right and behind the accountant, crashed to earth with his horse. Zherkóv and the staff-officer bent over their saddles and turned their horses away. The accountant stopped facing the Cossack and examined him with attentive curiosity. The Cossack was dead, but the horse still struggled.

Prince Bagratión screwed up his eyes, looked round, and, seeing the cause of the confusion, turned away with indifference, as if to say, "Is it worthwhile noticing trifles?" He reined in his horse with the case of a skillful rider, and slightly bending over, disengaged his saber which had caught in his cloak. It was an old-fashioned saber of a kind no longer in general use. Prince Andrew remembered the story of Suvórov giving his saber to Bagratión in Italy, and the recollection was particularly pleasant at that moment. They had reached the battery at which Prince Andrew had been when he examined the battlefield.

"Whose company?" asked Prince Bagratión of an artilleryman standing by the ammunition-wagon.

He asked, "Whose company?" but he really meant, "Are you frightened here?" and the artilleryman understood him.

"Captain Túshin's, your excellency!" shouted the red-haired, freckled gunner in a merry voice, standing to attention.

"Yes, yes," muttered Bagratión as if considering something, and he rode past the limbers to the farthest cannon.

As he approached, a ringing shot issued from it deafening him and his suite, and in the smoke that suddenly surrounded the gun they could see the gunners who had seized it straining to roll it quickly back to its former position. A huge, broad-shouldered gunner, Number One, holding a mop, his legs far apart, sprang to the wheel; while Number Two with a trembling hand placed a charge in the cannon's mouth. The short round-shouldered Captain Túshin, stumbling over the tail of the gun-carriage, moved forward, and not noticing the general, looked out shading his eyes with his small hand.

"Lift it two lines more and it will be just right," cried he in a feeble voice to which he tried to impart a dashing note, ill suited to his weak figure. "Number Two!" he squeaked. "Fire Medvédev!"

Bagratión called to him, and Túshin, raising three fingers to his cap with a bashful and awkward gesture not at all like a military salute but like a priest's benediction, approached the general. Though Túshin's guns had been intended to cannonade the valley, he was firing incendiary balls at the village of Schön Grabern visible just opposite, in front of which large masses of French were advancing.

No one had given Túshin orders where and at what to fire, but after consulting his sergeant-major, Zakharchénko, for whom he had great respect, he had decided that it would be a good thing to set fire to the village. "Very good!" said Bagratión in reply to the officer's report, and began deliberately to examine the whole battlefield extended before him. The French had advanced nearest on our right. Below the height on which the Kiev regiment was stationed, in the hollow where the rivulet flowed, the soul-stirring rolling and crackling of musketry was heard, and much farther to the right beyond the dragoons, the officer of the suite pointed out to Bagratión a French column that was outflanking us. To the left the horizon bounded by the adjacent wood. Prince Bagratión ordered two battalions from the center to be sent to reinforce the right flank. The officer of the suite ventured to remark to the prince that if these battalions went away, the guns would remain without support. Prince Bagratión turned to the officer and with his dull eyes looked at him in silence. It seemed to Prince Andrew that the officer's remark was just and that really no answer could be made to it. But at that moment an adjutant galloped up with a message from the commander of the regiment in the hollow and news that immense masses of the French were coming down upon them, and that his regiment was in disorder and was retreating upon the Kiev grenadiers. Prince Bagratión bowed his head in sign of assent and approval. He rode off at a walk to the right and sent an adjutant to the dragoons with orders to attack the French. But this adjutant returned half an hour later with the news that the commander of the dragoons had already retreated beyond the dip in the ground, as a heavy fire had been opened on him and he was losing men uselessly, and so had hastened to throw some sharpshooters into the wood.

"Very good!" said Bagratión.

As he was leaving the battery, firing was heard on the left also, and as it was too far to the left flank for him to have time to go there himself, Prince Bagratión sent Zherkóv to tell the general in command (the one who had paraded his regiment before Kutúzov at Braunau) that he must retreat as quickly as possible behind the hollow in the rear, as the right flank would probably not be able to withstand the enemy's attack very long. About Túshin and the battalion that had been in support of his battery all was forgotten. Prince Andrew listened attentively to Bagratión's colloquies with the commanding officers and the orders he gave them, and to his surprise found that no orders were really given, but that Prince Bagratión tried to make it appear that everything done by necessity, by accident, or by the will of subordinate commanders, was done, if not by his direct command at least in accord with his intentions. Prince Andrew noticed however that though what happened was due to chance and was independent of the commander's will, owing to the tact Bagratión showed his presence was very valuable. Officers who approached him with disturbed countenances became calm; soldiers and officers greeted him gaily, grew more cheerful in his presence, and were evidently anxious to display their courage before him.

Chapter XVIII

PRINCE BAGRATIÓN HAVING REACHED THE HIGHEST POINT OF OUR RIGHT FLANK, BEGAN RIDING downhill to where the roll of musketry was heard but where on account of the smoke nothing could be seen. The nearer they got to the hollow the less they could see but the more they felt the nearness of the actual battlefield. They began to meet wounded men. One with a bleeding head and no cap was being dragged along by two soldiers who supported him under the arms. There was a gurgle in his throat and he was spitting blood. A bullet had evidently hit him in the throat or mouth. Another was walking sturdily by himself but without his musket, groaning aloud and swinging his arm which had just been hurt, while blood from it was streaming over his greatcoat as from a bottle. He had that moment been wounded and his face showed fear rather than suffering. Crossing a road they descended a steep incline and saw several men lying on the ground, they also met a crowd of soldiers some of whom were unwounded. The soldiers were ascending the hill breathing heavily, and despite the general's presence were talking loudly and gesticulating. In front of them rows of gray cloaks were already visible through the smoke, and an officer catching sight of Bagratión rushed shouting after the crowd of retreating soldiers, ordering them back. Bagratión rode up to the ranks along which shots crackled now here and now there, drowning the sound of voices and the shouts of command. The whole air reeked with smoke. The excited faces of the soldiers were blackened with it. Some were using their ramrods, others putting powder on the touch-pans or taking charges from their pouches, while others were firing, though who they were firing at could not be seen for the smoke which there was no wind to carry away. A pleasant humming and whistling of bullets were often heard. "What is this?" thought Prince Andrew approaching the crowd of soldiers. "It can't be an attack, for they are not moving; it can't be a square—for they are not drawn up for that."

The commander of the regiment, a thin, feeble-looking old man with a pleasant smile—his eyelids drooping more than half over his old eyes giving him a mild expression, rode up to Bagratión and welcomed him as a host welcomes an honored guest. He reported that his regiment had been attacked by French cavalry and that, though the attack had been repulsed, he had lost more than half his men. He said the attack had been repulsed, employing this military term to describe what had occurred to his regiment, but in reality he did not himself know what had happened during that half-hour to the troops entrusted to him, and could not say with certainty whether the attack had been repulsed or his regiment had been broken up. All he knew was that at the commencement of the action balls and shells began flying all over his regiment and hitting men, and that afterward someone had shouted "Cavalry!" and our men had begun firing. They were still firing, not at the cavalry which had disappeared, but at French infantry who had come into the hollow and were firing at our men. Prince Bagratión bowed his head as a sign that this was exactly what he had desired and expected. Turning to his adjutant he ordered him to bring down the two battalions of the Sixth Chasseurs whom they had just passed. Prince Andrew was struck by the changed expression on Prince Bagratión's face at this moment. It expressed the concentrated and happy resolution you see on the face of a man who on a hot day takes a final run before plunging into the water. The dull sleepy expression was no longer there, nor the affectation of profound thought. The round, steady, hawk's eyes looked before him eagerly and rather disdainfully, not resting on anything although his movements were still slow and measured.

The commander of the regiment turned to Prince Bagratión, entreating him to go back as it was too dangerous to remain where they were. "Please, your excellency, for God's sake!" he kept saying, glancing for support at an officer of the suite who turned away from him. "There, you see!" and he drew attention to the bullets whistling, singing and hissing continually around them. He spoke in the tone of entreaty and reproach that a carpenter uses to a gentleman who has picked up an axe: "We are used to it, but you sir, will blister your hands." He spoke as if those bullets could not kill him, and his half-closed eyes gave still more persuasiveness to his words. The staff-officer joined in the colonel's appeals, but Bagratión did not reply; he only gave an order to cease firing and re-form, so as to give room for the two approaching battalions. While he was speaking the curtain of smoke that had concealed the hollow, driven by a rising wind, began to move from right to left as if drawn by an invisible hand, and the hill opposite, with the French moving about on it, opened out before them. All eyes fastened involuntarily on this French column advancing against them and winding down over the uneven ground. One could already see the soldiers' shaggy caps, distinguish the officers from the men, and see the standard flapping against its staff.

"They march splendidly," remarked someone in Bagratión's suite.

The head of the column had already descended into the hollow. The clash would take place on this side of it . . .

The remains of our regiment which had been in action rapidly formed up and moved to the right; from behind it, dispersing the laggards, came two battalions of the Sixth Chasseurs in fine order. Before they had reached Bagratión, the weighty tread of the mass of men marching in step could be heard. On their left flank, nearest to Bagratión, marched a company commander, a fine round-faced man, with a stupid and happy expression—the same man who had rushed out of the wattle-shed. At that moment he was clearly thinking of nothing but how dashing a fellow he would appear as he passed the commander.

With the self-satisfaction of a man on parade, he stepped lightly with his muscular legs as if sailing along, stretching himself to his full height without the smallest effort, his ease contrasting with the heavy tread of the soldiers who were keeping step with him. He carried close to his leg a narrow unsheathed sword (small, curved, and not like a real weapon) and looked now at the superior officers and now back at the men without losing step, his whole powerful body turning flexibly. It was as if all the powers of his soul were concentrated on passing the commander in the best possible manner, and feeling that he was doing it well he was happy. "Left . . . left . . . left . . ." he seemed to repeat to himself at each alternate step; and in time to this, with stern but varied faces, the wall of soldiers burdened with knapsacks and muskets marched in step, and each one of these hundreds of soldiers seemed to be repeating to himself at each alternate step, "Left . . . left . . . left . . ." A fat major skirted a bush, puffing and falling out of step; a soldier who had fallen behind, his face showing alarm at his defection, ran at a trot, panting to catch up with his company. A cannon-ball cleaving the air, flew over the heads of Bagratión and his suite and fell into the column to the measure of *"Left . . . left!"* "Close up!" came the company commander's voice in jaunty tones. The soldiers passed in a semicircle round something where the ball had fallen, and an old trooper on the flank, a non-commissioned officer who had stopped beside the dead men, ran to catch up his line and falling into step with a hop, looked back angrily, and through the ominous silence and the regular tramp of feet beating the ground in unison, one seemed to hear *left* . . . *left* . . . *left*.

"Well done, lads!" said Prince Bagratión.

"Glad to do our best, your ex'len-lency!" came a confused shout from the ranks. A morose soldier marching on the left turned his eyes on Bagratión as he shouted, with an expression that seemed to say: "We know that ourselves!" Another, without looking round, as though fearing to relax, shouted with his mouth wide-open and passed on.

The order was given to halt and down knapsacks.

Bagratión rode round the ranks that had marched past him and dismounted. He gave the reins to a Cossack, took off and handed over his felt coat, stretched his legs, and set his cap straight. The head of the French column, with its officers leading, appeared from below the hill.

"Forward, with God!" said Bagratión, in a resolute sonorous voice, turning for a moment to the front line, and slightly swinging his arms, he went forward uneasily over the rough field with the awkward gait of a cavalryman. Prince Andrew felt that an invisible power was leading him forward, and experienced great happiness.

The French were already near. Prince Andrew, walking beside Bagratión, could clearly distinguish their bandoliers, red epaulets, and even their faces. (He distinctly saw an old French officer who, with gaitered legs and turned-out toes climbed the hill with difficulty.) Prince Bagratión gave no further orders and silently continued to walk on in front of the ranks. Suddenly one shot after another rang out from the French, smoke appeared all along their uneven ranks, and musket shots sounded. Several of our men fell, among them the round-faced officer who had marched so gaily and complacently. But at the moment the first report was heard, Bagratión looked round and shouted, "Hurrah!"

"Hurrah—ah!—ah!" rang a long-drawn shout from our ranks, and passing Bagratión and racing one another they rushed in an irregular but joyous and eager crowd down the hill at their disordered foe.

Chapter XIX

THE ATTACK OF THE SIXTH CHASSEURS SECURED THE RETREAT OF OUR RIGHT FLANK. IN THE CENter Túshin's forgotten battery, which had managed to set fire to the Schön Grabern village, delayed the French advance. The French were putting out the fire which the wind was spreading, and thus gave us time to retreat. The retirement of the center to the other side of the dip in the ground at the rear was hurried and noisy, but the different companies did not get mixed. But our left—which consisted of the Azóv and Podólsk infantry and the Pávlograd hussars—was simultaneously attacked and outflanked by superior French forces under Lannes, and was thrown into confusion. Bagratión had sent Zherkóv to the general commanding that left flank with orders to retreat immediately.

Zherkóv, not removing his hand from his cap, turned his horse about and galloped off. But no sooner had he left Bagratión than his courage failed him. He was seized by panic and could not go where it was dangerous.

Having reached the left flank, instead of going to the front where the firing was, he began to look for the general and his staff where they could not possibly be, and so did not deliver the order.

The command of the left flank belonged by seniority to the commander of the regiment Kutúzov had reviewed at Braunau and in which Dólokhov was serving as a private. But the command of the extreme left flank had been assigned to the commander of the Pávlograd regiment in which Rostóv was serving, and a misunderstanding arose. The two commanders were much exasperated with one another and long after the action had begun on the right flank and the French were already advancing, were engaged in discussion with the sole object of offending one another. But the regiments, both cavalry and infantry, were by no means ready for the impending action. From privates to general they were not expecting a battle and were engaged in peaceful occupations, the cavalry feeding the horses and the infantry collecting wood.

"He higher iss dan I in rank," said the German colonel of the hussars, flushing and addressing an adjutant who had ridden up, "so let him do vhat he vill, but I cannot sacrifice my hussars . . . Bugler, sount ze retreat!"

But haste was becoming imperative. Cannon and musketry mingling together, thundered on the right and in the center, while the capotes of Lannes' sharpshooters were already seen crossing the mill-dam and forming up within twice the range of a musket shot. The general in command of the infantry went toward his horse with jerky steps, and having mounted drew himself up very straight and tall and rode to the Pávlograd commander. The commanders met with polite bows but with secret malevolence in their hearts.

"Once again, colonel," said the general, "I can't leave half my men in the wood. I *beg* of you, I *beg* of you," he repeated, "to occupy the *position* and prepare for an attack."

"I peg of you yourself not to mix in vot is not your pusiness!" suddenly replied the irate colonel. "If you vere in the cavalry . . ."

"I am not in the cavalry, colonel, but I am a Russian general and if you are not aware of the fact . . ."

"Quite avare, your excellency," suddenly shouted the colonel, touching his horse and turning purple in the face. "Vil you be so goot to come to ze front and see dat zis position iss no goot? I don't vish to destroy my men for your pleasure!"

"You forget yourself, colonel. I am not considering my own pleasure and I won't allow it to be said!"

Taking the colonel's outburst as a challenge to his courage, the general expanded his chest and rode, frowning, beside him to the front line, as if their differences would be settled there amongst the bullets. They reached the front, several bullets sped over them, and they halted in silence. There was nothing fresh to be seen from the line, for from where they had been before it had been evident that it was impossible for cavalry to act among the bushes and broken ground, as well as that the French were out-flanking our left. The general and colonel looked sternly and significantly at one another like two fighting-cocks preparing for battle, each vainly trying to detect signs of cowardice in the other. Both passed the examination successfully. As there was nothing to be said, and neither wished to give occasion for it to be alleged that he had been the first to leave the range of fire, they would have remained there for a long time testing each other's courage, had it not been that just then they heard the rattle of musketry and a muffled shout almost behind them in the wood. The French had attacked the men collecting wood in the copse. It was no longer possible for the hussars to retreat with the infantry. They were cut off from the line of retreat on the left by the French. However inconvenient the position, it was now necessary to attack in order to cut a way through for themselves.

The squadron in which Rostóv was serving had scarcely time to mount before it was halted facing the enemy. Again, as at the Enns bridge, there was nothing between the squadron and the enemy, and again that terrible dividing line of uncertainty and fear—resembling the line separating the living from the dead—lay between them. All were conscious of this unseen line, and the question whether they would cross it or not, and how they would cross it, agitated them all.

The colonel rode to the front, angrily gave some reply to questions put to him by the officers, and, like a man desperately insisting on having his own way, gave an order. No one said anything definite, but the rumor of an attack spread through the squadron. The command to form up rang out and the sabers whizzed as they were drawn from their scabbards. Still no one moved. The troops of the left flank, infantry and hussars alike, felt that the commander did not himself know what to do, and this irresolution communicated itself to the men.

"If only they would be quick!" thought Rostóv, feeling that at last the time had come to experience the joy of an attack of which he had so often heard from his fellow hussars.

"Fo'ward, with God, lads!" rang out Denísov's voice. "At a twot fo'ward!"

The horses' croups began to sway in the front line. Rook pulled at the reins and started of his own accord.

Before him, on the right, Rostóv saw the front lines of his hussars, and still farther ahead a dark line which he could not see distinctly but took to be the enemy. Shots could be heard, but some way off.

"Faster!" came the word of command, and Rostóv felt Rook's flanks drooping as he broke into a gallop.

Rostóv anticipated his horse's movements and became more and more elated. He had noticed a solitary tree ahead of him. This tree had been in the middle of the line that had seemed so terrible—and now he had crossed that line and not only was there nothing terrible, but everything was becoming more and more happy and animated. "Oh, how I will slash at him!" thought Rostóv, gripping the hilt of his saber.

"Hur-a-a-a-ah!" came a roar of voices. "Let anyone come my way now," thought Rostóv driving his spurs into Rook and letting him go at a full gallop so that he outstripped the others. Ahead, the enemy was already visible. Suddenly something like a birch-broom seemed to sweep over the squadron. Rostóv raised his saber, ready to strike, but at that instant the trooper Nikítenko, who was galloping ahead, shot away from him, and Rostóv felt as in a dream that he continued to be carried forward with unnatural speed but yet stayed on the same spot. From behind him Bondarchúk, a hussar he knew, jolted against him and looked angrily at him. Bondarchúk's horse swerved and galloped past.

"How is it I am not moving? I have fallen, I am killed!" Rostóv asked and answered at the same instant. He was alone in the middle of a field. Instead of the moving horses and hussars' backs, he saw nothing before him but the motionless earth and the stubble around him. There was warm blood under his arm. "No, I am wounded and the horse is killed." Rook tried to rise on his forelegs but fell back, pinning his rider's leg. Blood was flowing from his head, he struggled but could not rise. Rostóv also tried to rise but fell back, his sabertache having become entangled in the saddle. Where our men were, and where the French, he did not know. There was no one near.

Having disentangled his leg, he rose. "Where, on which side, was now the line that had so sharply divided the two armies?" he asked himself and could not answer. "Can something bad have happened to me?" he wondered as he got up: and at that moment he felt that something superfluous was hanging on his benumbed left arm. The wrist felt as if it were not his. He examined his hand carefully, vainly trying to find blood on it. "Ah, here are people coming," he thought joyfully, seeing some men running toward him. "They will help me!" In front came a man wearing a strange shako and a blue cloak, swarthy, sunburned, and with a hooked nose. Then came two more, and many more running behind. One of them said something strange, not in Russian. In among the hindmost of these men wearing similar shakos, was a Russian hussar. He was being held by the arms and his horse was being led behind him.

"It must be one of ours, a prisoner. Yes. Can it be that they will take me too? Who are these men?" thought Rostóv, scarcely believing his eyes. "Can they be French?" He looked at the approaching Frenchmen, and though but a moment before he had been galloping to get at them and hack them to pieces, their proximity now seemed so awful that he could not believe his eyes. "Who are they? Why are they running? Can they be coming at me? And why? To kill me? *Me* whom everyone is so fond of?" He remembered his mother's love for him, and his family's, and his friends', and the enemy's intention to kill him seemed impossible. "But perhaps they may do it!" For more than ten seconds he stood not moving from the spot or realizing the situation. The foremost Frenchman, the one with the hooked nose, was already so close that the expression of his face could be seen. And the excited, alien face of that man, his bayonet hanging down, holding his breath, and running so lightly, frightened Rostóv. He seized his pistol, and instead of firing it, flung it at the Frenchman and ran with all his might toward the bushes. He did not now run with the feeling of doubt and conflict with which he had trodden the Enns bridge, but with the feeling of a hare fleeing from the hounds. One single sentiment, that of fear for his young and happy life, possessed his whole being. Rapidly leaping the furrows, he fled across the field with the impetuosity he used to show at catchplay, now and then turning his good-natured, pale, young face to look back. A shudder of terror went through him. "No, better not look," he thought, but having reached the bushes he glanced round once more. The French had fallen behind, and just as he looked round the first man changed his run to a walk, and turning, shouted something loudly to a comrade farther back. Rostóv paused. "No, there's some mistake," thought he. "They can't have wanted to kill me." But at the same time, his left arm felt as heavy as if a five-stone weight were tied to it. He could run no more. The Frenchman also stopped and took aim. Rostóv closed his eyes and stooped down. One bullet and then another whistled past him. He mustered his last remaining strength, took hold of his left hand with his right and reached the bushes. Behind these were some Russian sharpshooters.

Chapter XX

THE INFANTRY REGIMENTS THAT HAD BEEN CAUGHT UNAWARES IN THE OUTSKIRTS OF THE WOOD ran out of it, the different companies getting mixed, and retreated as a disorderly crowd. One soldier, in his fear, uttered the senseless cry, "Cut off!" that is so terrible in battle, and that word infected the whole crowd with a feeling of panic.

"Surrounded! Cut off! We're lost!" shouted the fugitives.

The moment he heard the firing and the cry from behind, the general realized that something dreadful had happened to his regiment, and the thought that he, an exemplary officer of many years' service who had never been to blame, might be held responsible at headquarters for negligence or inefficiency, so staggered him that forgetting the recalcitrant cavalry colonel, his own dignity as a general, and above all quite forgetting the danger and all regard for self-preservation, he clutched the crupper of his saddle, and spurring his horse galloped to the regiment under a hail of bullets which fell around, but fortunately missed him. His one desire was to know what was happening and at any cost correct, or remedy, the mistake if he had made one, so that he, an exemplary officer of twenty-two years' service, who had never been censured, should not be held to blame.

Having galloped safely through the French, he reached a field behind the copse across which our men, regardless of orders, were running and descending the valley. That moment of moral hesitation which decides the fate of battles had arrived. Would this disorderly crowd of soldiers attend to the voice of their commander, or would they, disregarding him, continue their flight? Despite his desperate shouts that used to seem so terrible to the soldiers, despite his furious purple countenance distorted out of all likeness to his former self, and the flourishing of his saber, the soldiers all continued to run, talking, firing into the air and disobeying orders. The moral hesitation which decided the fate of battles was evidently culminating in a panic.

The general had a fit of coughing as a result of shouting and of the powder-smoke, and stopped in despair. Everything seemed lost. But at that moment the French who were attacking, suddenly and without any apparent reason, ran back and disappeared from the outskirts, and Russian sharpshooters showed themselves in the copse. It was Timókhin's company, which alone had maintained its order in the wood, and having lain in ambush in a ditch now attacked the French unexpectedly. Timókhin armed only with a sword, had rushed at the enemy with such a desperate cry and such mad drunken determination, that taken by surprise, the French had thrown down their muskets and run. Dólokhov, running beside Timókhin, killed a Frenchman at close quarters and was the first to seize the surrendering French officer by his collar. Our fugitives returned, the battalions re-formed, and the French who had nearly cut our left flank in half, were for the moment repulsed. Our reserve units were able to join up, and the fight was at an end. The regimental commander and Major Ekonómov had stopped beside a bridge, letting the retreating companies pass by them, when a soldier came up and took hold of the commander's stirrup, almost leaning against him. The man was wearing a bluish coat of broadcloth, he had no knapsack or cap, his head was bandaged, and over his shoulder, a French munition pouch was slung. He had an officer's sword in his hand. The soldier was pale, his blue eyes looked impudently into the commander's face and his lips were smiling. Though the commander was occupied in giving instructions to Major Ekonómov, he could not help taking notice of the soldier.

"Your excellency, here are two trophies," said Dólokhov, pointing to the French sword and pouch. "I have taken an officer prisoner. I stopped the company." Dólokhov breathed heavily from weariness and spoke in abrupt sentences. "The whole company can bear witness. I beg you will remember this, your excellency!"

"All right, all right," replied the commander, and turned to Major Ekonómov.

But Dólokhov did not go away; he untied the handkerchief around his head, pulled it off, and showed the blood congealed on his hair.

"A bayonet wound. I remained at the front. Remember, your excellency!"

Túshin's battery had been forgotten and only at the very end of the action did Prince Bagratión, still hearing the cannonade in the center, send his orderly staff-officer and later Prince Andrew also, to order the battery to retire as quickly as possible. When the supports attached to Túshin's battery had been moved away in the middle of the action by someone's order, the battery had continued firing and was only not captured by the French because the enemy could not surmise that anyone could have the effrontery to continue firing from four quite undefended guns. On the contrary the energetic action of that battery led the French to suppose that here—in the center—the main Russian forces were concentrated. Twice they had attempted to attack this point, but on each occasion had been driven back by grapeshot from the four isolated guns on the hillock.

Soon after Prince Bagratión had left him, Túshin had succeeded in setting fire to Schön Grabern.

"Look at them scurrying! It's burning! Just see the smoke! Fine! Grand! Look at the smoke, the smoke!" exclaimed the artillerymen brightening up.

All the guns, without waiting for orders, were being fired in the direction of the conflagration. As if urging each other on, the soldiers cried at each shot: "Fine! That's good! Look at it . . . Grand!" The fire, fanned by the breeze, was rapidly spreading. The French columns that had advanced beyond the village went back; but as though in revenge for this failure, the enemy placed ten guns to the right of the village and began firing them at Túshin's battery.

In their childlike glee, aroused by the fire and their luck in successfully cannonading the French, our artillerymen only noticed this battery when two balls, and then four more, fell among our guns, one knocking over two horses and another tearing off a munition-wagon driver's leg. Their spirits once roused were, however, not diminished, but only changed character. The horses were replaced by others from a reserve gun-carriage, the wounded were carried away, and the four guns were turned against the ten-gun battery. Túshin's companion officer had been killed at the beginning of the engagement and within an hour seventeen of the forty men of the guns' crews had been disabled, but the artillerymen were still as merry and lively as ever. Twice they noticed the French appearing below them, and then they fired grapeshot at them.

Little Túshin, moving feebly and awkwardly, kept telling his orderly to "refill my pipe for that one!" and then scattering sparks from it, ran forward shading his eyes with his small hand to look at the French.

"Smack at 'em, lads!" he kept saying, seizing the guns by the wheels and working the screws himself.

Amid the smoke, deafened by the incessant reports which always made him jump, Túshin not taking his pipe from his mouth ran from gun to gun, now aiming, now counting the charges, now giving orders about replacing dead or wounded horses and harnessing fresh ones, and shouting in his feeble voice, so high-pitched and irresolute. His face grew more and more animated. Only when a man was killed or wounded did he frown and turn away from the sight, shouting angrily at the men who, as is always the case, hesitated about lifting the injured or dead. The soldiers, for the most part handsome fellows and, as is always the case in an artillery company, a head and shoulders taller and twice as broad as their officer—all looked at their commander like children in an embarrassing situation, and the expression on his face was invariably reflected on theirs.

Owing to the terrible uproar and the necessity for concentration and activity, Túshin did not experience the slightest unpleasant sense of fear, and the thought that he might be killed or badly wounded never occurred to him. On the contrary, he became more and more elated. It seemed to him that it was a very long time ago, almost a day, since he had first seen the enemy and fired the first shot, and that the corner of the field he stood on was well known and familiar ground. Though he thought of everything, considered everything, and did everything the best of officers could do in his position, he was in a state akin to feverish delirium or drunkenness.

From the deafening sounds of his own guns around him, the whistle and thud of the enemy's cannon-balls, from the flushed and perspiring faces of the crew bustling round the guns, from the sight of the blood of men and horses, from the little puffs of smoke on the enemy's side (always followed by a ball flying past and striking the earth, a man, a gun, a horse), from the sight of all these things a fantastic world of his own had taken possession of his brain and at that moment afforded him pleasure. The enemy's guns were in his fancy not guns but pipes from which occasional puffs were blown by an invisible smoker.

"There . . . he's puffing again," muttered Túshin to himself, as a small cloud rose from the hill and was borne in a streak to the left by the wind. "Now look out for the ball . . . we'll throw it back."

"What do you want, your honor?" asked an artilleryman, standing close by, who heard him muttering.

"Nothing . . . only a shell . . ." he answered.

"Come along, our Matvévna!" he said to himself. "Matvévna" (daughter of Matthew) was the name his fancy gave to the farthest gun of the battery, which was large and of an old pattern. The French swarming round their guns seemed to him like ants. In that world, the handsome drunkard Number One of the second gun's crew was "uncle"; Túshin looked at him more often than at anyone else and took delight in his every movement. The sound of musketry at the foot of the hill, now diminishing now increasing, seemed like someone's breathing. He listened intently to the ebb and flow of these sounds.

"Ah! Breathing again, breathing!" he muttered to himself.

He imagined himself as an enormously tall, powerful man who was throwing cannon-balls at the French with both hands.

"Now then, Matvévna, dear old lady, don't let me down!" he was saying as he moved from the gun, when a strange, unfamiliar voice called above his head: "Captain Túshin! Captain!"

Túshin turned round in dismay. It was the staff-officer who had turned him out of the booth at Grunth. He was shouting in a gasping voice:

"Are you mad? You have twice been ordered to retreat, and you . . ."

"Why are they down on me?" thought Túshin, looking in alarm at his superior.

"I . . . don't . . ." he muttered, holding up two fingers to his cap. "I . . ."

But the staff-officer did not finish what he wanted to say. A cannon-ball flying close to him, caused him to duck and bend over his horse. He paused, and just as he was about to say something more, another ball stopped him. He turned his horse and galloped off.

"Retire! All to retire!" he shouted from a distance.

The soldiers laughed. A moment later, an adjutant arrived with the same order.

It was Prince Andrew. The first thing he saw on riding up to the space where Túshin's guns were stationed was an unharnessed horse with a broken leg, that lay screaming piteously beside the harnessed horses. Blood was gushing from its leg as from a spring. Among the limbers lay several dead men. One ball after another passed over as he approached and he felt a nervous shudder run down his spine. But the mere thought of being afraid roused him again. "I cannot be afraid," thought he, and dismounted slowly among the guns. He delivered the order and did not leave the battery. He decided to have the guns removed from their positions and withdrawn in his presence. Together with Túshin, stepping across the bodies and under a terrible fire from the French, he attended to the removal of the guns.

"A staff-officer was here a minute ago, but skipped off," said an artilleryman to Prince Andrew. "Not like your honor!"

Prince Andrew said nothing to Túshin. They were both so busy as to seem not to notice one another. When having limbered up the only two cannon that remained uninjured out of the four, they began moving down the hill (one shattered gun and one unicorn were left behind), Prince Andrew rode up to Túshin.

"Well, till we meet again . . ." he said, holding out his hand to Túshin.

"Good-bye, my dear fellow," said Túshin. "Dear soul! Good-bye, my dear fellow!" and for some unknown reason tears suddenly filled his eyes.

Chapter XXI

THE WIND HAD FALLEN AND BLACK CLOUDS, MERGING WITH THE POWDER SMOKE, HUNG LOW over the field of battle on the horizon. It was growing dark and the glow of two conflagrations was the more conspicuous. The cannonade was dying down, but the rattle of musketry behind and on the right sounded oftener and nearer. As soon as Túshin with his guns, continually driving round or coming upon wounded men, was out of range of fire and had descended into the dip, he was met by some of the staff, among them the staff-officer and Zherkóv, who had been twice sent to Túshin's battery but had never reached it. Interrupting one another, they all gave, and transmitted, orders as to how to proceed, reprimanding and reproaching him. Túshin gave no orders, and silently—fearing to speak because at every word he felt ready to weep without knowing why—rode behind on his artillery nag. Though the orders were to abandon the wounded, many of them dragged themselves after troops and begged for seats on the gun-carriages. The jaunty infantry officer who just before the battle had rushed out of Túshin's wattle-shed was laid, with a bullet in his stomach, on Matvévna's carriage. At the foot of the hill, a pale hussar cadet, supporting one hand with the other, came up to Túshin and asked for a seat.

"Captain, for God's sake! I've hurt my arm," he said timidly. "For God's sake . . . I can't walk. For God's sake!"

It was plain that this cadet had already repeatedly asked for a lift and been refused. He asked in a hesitating, piteous voice.

"Tell them to give me a seat, for God's sake!"

"Give him a seat," said Túshin. "Lay a cloak for him to sit on, lad," he said, addressing his favorite soldier. "And where is the wounded officer?"

"He has been set down. He died," replied someone.

"Help him up. Sit down, dear fellow, sit down! Spread out the cloak, Antónov."

The cadet was Rostóv. With one hand he supported the other; he was pale and his jaw trembled, shivering feverishly. He was placed on "Matvévna," the gun from which they had removed the dead officer. The cloak they spread under him was wet with blood which stained his breeches and arm.

"What, are you wounded, my lad?" said Túshin, approaching the gun on which Rostóv sat.

"No, it's a sprain."

"Then what is this blood on the gun-carriage?" inquired Túshin.

"It was the officer, your honor, stained it," answered the artilleryman, wiping away the blood with his coat-sleeve, as if apologizing for the state of his gun.

It was all that they could do to get the guns up the rise aided by the infantry, and having reached the village of Gruntersdorf they halted. It had grown so dark that one could not distinguish the uniforms ten paces off, and the firing had begun to subside. Suddenly, nearby on the right, shouting and firing were again heard. Flashes of shot gleamed in the darkness. This was the last French attack, and was met by soldiers who had sheltered in the village houses. They all rushed out of the village again, but Túshin's guns could not move, and the artillerymen, Túshin, and the cadet, exchanged silent glances as they awaited their fate. The firing died down and soldiers talking eagerly, streamed out of a side-street.

"Not hurt, Petróv?" asked one.

"We've given it 'em hot, mate! They won't make another push now," said another.

"You couldn't see a thing. How they shot at their own fellows! Nothing could be seen. Pitch-dark, brother! Isn't there something to drink?"

The French had been repulsed for the last time. And again and again in the complete darkness Túshin's guns moved forward, surrounded by the humming infantry as by a frame.

In the darkness, it seemed as though a gloomy unseen river was flowing always in one direction, humming with whispers and talk and the sound of hoofs and wheels. Amid the general rumble, the groans and voices of the wounded were more distinctly heard than any other sound in the darkness of the night. The gloom that enveloped the army was filled with their groans, which seemed to melt into one with the darkness of the night. After a while the moving mass became agitated, someone rode past on a white horse followed by his suite, and said something in passing: "What did he say? Where to, now? Halt, is it? Did he thank us?" came eager questions from all sides. The whole moving mass began pressing closer together and a report spread that they were ordered to halt: evidently those in front had halted. All remained where they were in the middle of the muddy road.

Fires were lit and the talk became more audible. Captain Túshin, having given orders to his company, sent a soldier to find a dressing-station or a doctor for the cadet, and sat down by a bonfire the soldiers had kindled on the road. Rostóv, too, dragged himself to the fire. From pain, cold and damp, a feverish shivering shook his whole body. Drowsiness was irresistibly mastering him, but he was kept awake by an excruciating pain in his arm, for which he could find no satisfactory position. He kept closing his eyes and then again looking at the fire, which seemed to him dazzlingly red, and at the feeble, round-shouldered figure of Túshin who was sitting cross-legged like a Turk beside him. Túshin's large, kind, intelligent eyes were fixed with sympathy and commiseration on Rostóv, who saw that Túshin with his whole heart wished to help him but could not.

From all sides were heard the footsteps and talk of the infantry, who were walking, driving past, and settling down all around. The sound of voices, the tramping feet, the horses' hoofs moving in mud, the crackling of wood fires near and afar, merged into one tremulous rumble.

It was no longer, as before, a dark, unseen river flowing through the gloom, but a dark sea swelling and gradually subsiding after a storm. Rostóv looked at and listened listlessly to what passed before and around him. An infantryman came to the fire, squatted on his heels, held his hands to the blaze, and turned away his face.

"You don't mind, your honor?" he asked Túshin. "I've lost my company, your honor. I don't know where . . . such bad luck!"

With the soldier, an infantry officer with a bandaged cheek came up to the bonfire, and addressing Túshin asked him to have the guns moved a trifle to let a wagon go past. After he had gone, two soldiers rushed to the campfire. They were quarreling and fighting desperately, each trying to snatch from the other a boot they were both holding on to.

"You picked it up? . . . I dare say! You're very smart!" one of them shouted hoarsely.

Then a thin, pale soldier, his neck bandaged with a bloodstained legband, came up and in angry tones asked the artillerymen for water.

"Must one die like a dog?" said he.

Túshin told them to give the man some water. Then a cheerful soldier ran up, begging a little fire for the infantry.

"A nice little hot torch for the infantry! Good luck to you, fellow-countrymen. Thanks for the fire—we'll return it with interest," said he, carrying away into the darkness a glowing stick.

Next came four soldiers carrying something heavy on a cloak, and passed by the fire. One of them stumbled.

"Who the devil has put the logs on the road?" snarled he.

"He's dead—why carry him?" said another.

"Shut up!"

And they disappeared into the darkness with with their load.

"Still aching?" Túshin asked Rostóv in a whisper.

"Yes."

"Your honor, you're wanted by the general. He is in the hut here," said a gunner, coming up to Túshin.

"Coming, friend."

Túshin rose and buttoning his greatcoat and pulling it straight, walked away from the fire.

Not far from the artillery campfire, in a hut that had been prepared for him, Prince Bagratión sat at dinner, talking with some commanding officers who had gathered at his quarters. The little old man with the half-closed eyes was there greedily gnawing a mutton bone, and the general who had served blamelessly for twenty-two years, flushed by a glass of vodka and the dinner; and the staff-officer with the signet-ring, and Zherkóv, uneasily glancing at them all, and Prince Andrew, pale, with compressed lips and feverishly glittering eyes.

In a corner of the hut stood a standard captured from the French, and the accountant with the naïve face, was feeling its texture, shaking his head in perplexity—perhaps because the banner really interested him, perhaps because it was hard for him, hungry as he was, to look on at a dinner where there was no place for him. In the next hut there was a French colonel who had been taken prisoner by our dragoons. Our officers were flocking in to look at him. Prince Bagratión was thanking the individual commanders and inquiring into details of the action and our losses. The general whose regiment had been inspected at Braunau was informing the prince that as soon as the action began he had withdrawn from the wood, mustered the men who were wood-cutting, and, allowing the French to pass him, had made a bayonet charge with two battalions and had broken up the French troops.

"When I saw, your excellency, that their first battalion was disorganized, I stopped in the road and thought: 'I'll let them come on and will meet them with the fire of the whole battalion'—and that's what I did."

The general had so wished to do this and was so sorry he had not managed to do it, that it seemed to him as if it had really happened. Perhaps it might really have been so? Could one possibly make out amid all that confusion what did or did not happen?

"By the way, your excellency, I should inform you," he continued—remembering Dólokhov's conversation with Kutúzov and his last interview with the gentleman-ranker—"that Private Dólokhov, who was reduced to the ranks, took a French officer prisoner in my presence and particularly distinguished himself."

"I saw the Pávlograd hussars attack there, your excellency," chimed in Zherkóv, looking uneasily around. He had not seen the hussars all that day, but had heard about them from an infantry officer. "They broke up two squares, your excellency."

Several of those present smiled at Zherkóv's words expecting one of his usual jokes, but noticing that what he was saying redounded to the glory of our arms and of the day's work, they assumed a serious expression, though many of them knew that what he was saying was a lie devoid of any foundation. Prince Bagratión turned to the old colonel:

"Gentlemen, I thank you all; all arms have behaved heroically: infantry, cavalry, and artillery. How was it that two guns were abandoned in the center?" he inquired, searching with his eyes for someone. (Prince Bagratión did not ask about the guns on the left flank; he knew that all the guns there had been abandoned at the very beginning of the action.) "I think I sent you?" he added, turning to the staff-officer on duty.

"One was damaged," answered the staff-officer, "and the other I can't understand. I was there all the time giving orders and had only just left. . . . It is true that it was hot there," he added, modestly.

Someone mentioned that Captain Túshin was bivouacking close to the village and had already been sent for.

"Oh, but you were there?" said Prince Bagratión, addressing Prince Andrew.

"Of course, we only just missed one another," said the staff-officer, with a smile to Bolkónski.

"I had not the pleasure of seeing you," said Prince Andrew, coldly and abruptly.

All were silent. Túshin appeared at the threshold and made his way timidly from behind the backs of the generals. As he stepped past the generals, in the crowded hut, feeling embarrassed as he always was by the sight of his superiors he did not notice the staff of the banner and stumbled over it. Several of those present laughed.

"How was it a gun was abandoned?" asked Bagratión, frowning, not so much at the captain as at those who were laughing, among whom Zherkóv laughed loudest.

Only now, when he was confronted by the stern authorities, did his guilt and the disgrace of having lost two guns and yet remaining alive, present themselves to Túshin in all their horror. He had been so excited that he had not thought about it until that moment. The officers' laughter confused him still more. He stood before Bagratión with his lower jaw trembling, and was hardly able to mutter:

"I don't know . . . your excellency . . . I had no men . . . your excellency."

"You might have taken some from the covering troops."

Túshin did not say that there were no covering troops though that was perfectly true. He was afraid of getting some other officer into trouble, and silently fixed his eyes on Bagratión as a schoolboy who has blundered looks at an examiner.

The silence lasted some time. Prince Bagratión, apparently not wishing to be severe, found nothing to say, the others did not venture to intervene. Prince Andrew looked at Túshin from under his brows and his fingers twitched nervously.

"Your excellency!" Prince Andrew broke the silence with his abrupt voice, "you were pleased to send me to Captain Túshin's battery. I went there and found two-thirds of the men and horses knocked out, two guns smashed, and no supports at all."

Prince Bagratión and Túshin looked with equal intentness at Bolkónski, who spoke with suppressed agitation.

"And, if your excellency will allow me to express my opinion," he continued, "we owe today's success chiefly to the action of that battery and the heroic endurance of Captain Túshin and his company," and without awaiting a reply, Prince Andrew rose and left the table.

Prince Bagratión looked at Túshin, evidently reluctant to show distrust in Bolkónski's emphatic opinion yet not feeling able fully to credit it, bent his head, and told Túshin that he could go. Prince Andrew went out with him.

"Thank you; you saved me, my dear fellow!" said Túshin.

Prince Andrew gave him a look, but said nothing and went away. He felt sad and depressed. It was all so strange, so unlike what he had hoped.

"Who are they? Why are they here? What do they want? And when will all this end?" thought Rostóv, looking at the changing shadows before him. The pain in his arm became more and more intense. Irresistible drowsiness overpowered him, red rings danced before his eyes, and the impression of those voices and faces and a sense of loneliness merged with the physical pain. It was they, these soldiers—wounded and unwounded—it was they who were crushing, weighing down and twisting the sinews and scorching the flesh of his sprained arm and shoulder. To rid himself of them, he closed his eyes.

For a moment he dozed, but in that short interval innumerable things appeared to him in a dream: his mother and her large white hands, Sónya's thin little shoulders, Natásha's eyes and laughter, Denísov with his voice and mustache, and Telyánin and all that affair with Telyánin and Bogdánich. That affair was the same thing as this soldier with the harsh voice, and it was that affair and this soldier that were so agonizingly, incessantly, pulling and pressing his arm and always dragging it in one direction. He tried to get away from them, but they would not for an instant let his shoulder move a hair's breadth. It would not ache—it would be well—if only they did not pull it, but it was impossible to get rid of them.

He opened his eyes and looked up. The black canopy of night hung less than a yard above the glow of the charcoal. Flakes of falling snow were fluttering in that light. Túshin had not returned, the doctor had not come. He was alone now, except for a soldier who was sitting naked at the other side of the fire, warming his thin yellow body.

"Nobody wants me!" thought Rostóv. "There is no one to help me or pity me. Yet I was once at home, strong, happy, and loved." He sighed, and, doing so, groaned involuntarily.

"Eh, is anything hurting you?" asked the soldier, shaking his shirt out over the fire, and not waiting for an answer he gave a grunt and added: "What a lot of men have been crippled today—frightful!"

Rostóv did not listen to the soldier. He looked at the snowflakes fluttering above the fire and remembered a Russian winter at his warm, bright home, his fluffy fur coat, his quickly-gliding sleigh, his healthy body and all the affection and care of his family. "And why did I come here?" he wondered.

Next day the French army did not renew their attack, and the remnant of Bagratión's detachment was reunited to Kutúzov's army.

Part Three

Chapter I

PRINCE VASÍLI WAS NOT A MAN WHO DELIBERATELY THOUGHT OUT HIS PLANS. STILL LESS DID he think of injuring anyone for his own advantage. He was merely a man of the world who had got on and to whom getting on had become a habit. Schemes and devices for which he never rightly accounted to himself, but which formed the whole interest of his life, were constantly shaping themselves in his mind, arising from the circumstances and persons he met. Of these plans he had not merely one or two in his head but dozens, some only beginning to form themselves, some approaching achievement, and some in course of disintegration. He did not, for instance, say to himself: "This man now has influence, I must gain his confidence and friendship and through him obtain a special grant." Nor did he say to himself: "Pierre is a rich man, I must entice him to marry my daughter and lend me the forty thousand rubles I need." But when he came across a man of position his instinct immediately told him that this man could be useful, and without any premeditation Prince Vasíli took the first opportunity to gain his confidence, flatter him, become intimate with him, and finally make his request.

He had Pierre at hand in Moscow and procured for him an appointment as Gentleman of the Bed-chamber, which at that time conferred the status of Councilor of State, and insisted on the young man accompanying him to Petersburg and staying at his house. With apparent absent-mindedness, yet with unhesitating assurance that he was doing the right thing, Prince Vasíli did everything to get Pierre to marry his daughter. Had he thought out his plans beforehand he could not have been so natural and shown such unaffected familiarity in intercourse with everybody both above and below him in social standing. Something always drew him toward those richer and more powerful than himself and he had rare skill in seizing the most opportune moment for making use of people.

Pierre on unexpectedly becoming Count Bezúkhov and a rich man, felt himself after his recent loneliness and freedom from cares, so beset and preoccupied that only in bed was he able to be by himself. He had to sign papers, to present himself at government offices the purpose of which was not clear to him, to question his chief steward, to visit his estate near Moscow, and to receive many people who formerly did not even wish to know of his existence but would now have been offended and grieved had he chosen not to see them. These different people—business men, relations, and acquaintances alike—were all disposed to treat the young heir in the most friendly and flattering manner: they were all evidently firmly convinced of Pierre's noble qualities. He was always hearing such words as: "With your remarkable kindness," or, "With your excellent heart," "You are yourself so honorable, count," or, "Were he as clever as you," and so on, till he began sincerely to believe in his own exceptional kindness and extraordinary intelligence, the more so as in the depth of his heart it had always seemed to him that he really was very kind and intelligent. Even people who had formerly been spiteful toward him and evidently unfriendly now became gentle and affectionate. The angry eldest princess, with the long waist and hair plastered down like a doll's, had come into Pierre's room after the funeral. With drooping eyes and frequent blushes she told him she was very sorry about their past misunderstandings and did not now feel she had a right to ask him for anything, except only for permission, after the blow she had received, to remain for a few weeks longer in the house she so loved and where she had sacrificed so much. She could not refrain from weeping at these words. Touched that this statuesque princess could so change, Pierre took her hand and begged her forgiveness, without knowing what for. From that day the eldest princess quite changed toward Pierre and began knitting a striped scarf for him.

"Do this for my sake, *mon cher*; after all, she had to put up with a great deal from the deceased," said Prince Vasíli to him, handing him a deed to sign for the princess's benefit.

Prince Vasíli had come to the conclusion that it was necessary to throw this bone—a bill for thirty thousand rubles—to the poor princess, that it might not occur to her to speak of his share in the affair of the inlaid portfolio. Pierre signed the deed and after that the princess grew still kinder. The younger sisters also became affectionate to him, especially the youngest, the pretty one with the mole, who often made him feel confused by her smiles and her own confusion when meeting him.

It seemed so natural to Pierre that everyone should like him, and it would have seemed so unnatural had anyone disliked him, that he could not but believe in the sincerity of those around him. Besides, he had no time to ask himself whether these people were sincere or not. He was always busy and always felt in a state of mild and cheerful intoxication. He felt as though he were the center of some important and general movement; that something was constantly expected of him, that if he did not do it he would grieve and disappoint many people, but if he did this and that, all would be well; and he did what was demanded of him, but still that happy result always remained in the future.

More than anyone else, Prince Vasíli took possession of Pierre's affairs and of Pierre himself in those early days. From the death of Count Bezúkhov he did not let go his hold of the lad. He had the air of a man oppressed by business, weary and suffering, who yet would not, for pity's sake, leave this helpless youth who, after all, was the son of his old friend and the possessor of such enormous wealth, to the caprice of fate and the designs of rogues. During the few days he spent in Moscow after the death of Count Bezúkhov, he would call Pierre, or go to him himself, and tell him what ought to be done in a tone of weariness and assurance, as if he were adding every time: "You know I am overwhelmed with business and it is purely out of charity that I trouble myself about you, and you also know quite well that what I propose is the only thing possible."

"Well, my dear fellow, tomorrow we are off at last," said Prince Vasíli one day, closing his eyes and fingering Pierre's elbow, speaking as if he were saying something which had long since been agreed upon and could not now be altered. "We start tomorrow and I'm giving you a place in my carriage. I am very glad. All our important business here is now settled, and I ought to have been off long ago. Here is something I have received from the chancellor. I asked him for you, and you have been entered in the diplomatic corps and made a Gentleman of the Bed-chamber. The diplomatic career now lies open before you."

Notwithstanding the tone of wearied assurance with which these words were pronounced, Pierre, who had so long been considering his career, wished to make some suggestion. But Prince Vasíli interrupted him in the special deep cooing tone, precluding the possibility of interrupting his speech, which he used in extreme cases when special persuasion was needed.

"*Mais, mon cher,* I did this for my own sake, to satisfy my conscience, and there is nothing to thank me for. No one has ever complained yet of being too much loved; and besides, you are free, you could throw it up tomorrow. But you will see everything for yourself when you get to Petersburg. It is high time for you to get away from these terrible recollections." Prince Vasíli sighed. "Yes, yes, my boy. And my valet can go in your carriage. Ah! I was nearly forgetting," he added. "You know, *mon cher,* your father and I had some accounts to settle, so I have received what was due from the Ryazán estate and will keep it; you won't require it. We'll go into the accounts later."

By "what was due from the Ryazán estate" Prince Vasíli meant several thousand rubles quitrent received from Pierre's peasants, which the prince had retained for himself.

In Petersburg, as in Moscow, Pierre found the same atmosphere of gentleness and affection. He could not refuse the post, or rather the rank (for he did nothing), that Prince Vasíli had procured for him, and acquaintances, invitations, and social occupations were so numerous that, even more than in Moscow, he felt a sense of bewilderment, bustle, and continual expectation of some good, always in front of him but never attained.

Of his former bachelor acquaintances many were no longer in Petersburg. The Guards had gone to the front; Dólokhov had been reduced to the ranks; Anatole was in the army somewhere in the provinces; Prince Andrew was abroad; so Pierre had not the opportunity to spend his nights as he used to like to spend them, or to open his mind by intimate talks with a friend older than himself and whom he respected. His whole time was taken up with dinners and balls, and was spent chiefly at Prince Vasíli's house in the company of the stout princess, his wife, and his beautiful daughter Hélène.

Like the others, Anna Pávlovna Schérer showed Pierre the change of attitude toward him that had taken place in society.

Formerly in Anna Pávlovna's presence, Pierre had always felt that what he was saying was out of place, tactless and unsuitable, that remarks which seemed to him clever while they formed in his mind became foolish as soon as he uttered them, while on the contrary Hippolyte's stupidest remarks came out clever and apt. Now everything Pierre said was *charmant*. Even if Anna Pávlovna did not say so, he could see that she wished to, and only refrained out of regard for his modesty.

In the beginning of the winter of 1805-6 Pierre received one of Anna Pávlovna's usual pink notes with an invitation to which was added: "You will find the beautiful Hélène here, whom it is always delightful to see."

When he read that sentence, Pierre felt for the first time that some link which other people recognized, had grown up between himself and Hélène, and that thought both alarmed him, as if some obligation were being imposed on him which he could not fulfill, and pleased him as an entertaining supposition.

Anna Pávlovna's "At Home" was like the former one, only the novelty she offered her guests this time was not Mortemart, but a diplomatist fresh from Berlin with the very latest details of the Emperor Alexander's visit to Potsdam, and of how the two august friends had pledged themselves in an indissoluble alliance to uphold the cause of justice against the enemy of the human race. Anna Pávlovna received Pierre with a shade of melancholy, evidently relating to the young man's recent loss by the death of Count Bezúkhov (everyone constantly considered it a duty to assure Pierre that he was greatly afflicted by the death of the father he had hardly known), and her melancholy was just like the august melancholy she showed at the mention of her most august Majesty the Empress Márya Fëdorovna. Pierre felt flattered by this. Anna Pávlovna arranged the different groups in her drawing room with her habitual skill. The large group, in which were Prince Vasíli and the generals, had the benefit of the diplomat. Another group was at the tea-table. Pierre wished to join the former, but Anna Pávlovna—who was in the excited condition of a commander on a battlefield to whom thousands of new and brilliant ideas occur which there is hardly time to put in action—seeing Pierre, touched his sleeve with her finger, saying:

"Wait a bit, I have something in view for you this evening." (She glanced at Hélène and smiled at her.) "My dear Hélène, be charitable to my poor aunt who adores you. Go and keep her company for ten minutes. And that it will not be too dull, here is the dear count who will not refuse to accompany you."

The beauty went to the aunt, but Anna Pávlovna detained Pierre, looking as if she had to give some final necessary instructions.

"Isn't she exquisite?" she said to Pierre, pointing to the stately beauty as she glided away. "And how she carries herself! For so young a girl, such tact, such masterly perfection of manner! It comes from her heart. Happy the man who wins her! With her the least worldly of men would occupy a most brilliant position in society. Don't you think so? I only wanted to know your opinion," and Anna Pávlovna let Pierre go.

Pierre, in reply, sincerely agreed with her as to Hélène's perfection of manner. If he ever thought of Hélène, it was just of her beauty and her remarkable skill in appearing silently dignified in society.

The old aunt received the two young people in her corner, but seemed desirous of hiding her adoration for Hélène and inclined rather to show her fear of Anna Pávlovna. She looked at her niece, as if inquiring what she was to do with these people. On leaving them, Anna Pávlovna again touched Pierre's sleeve, saying: "I hope you won't say that it is dull in my house again," and she glanced at Hélène.

Hélène smiled, with a look implying that she did not admit the possibility of anyone seeing her without being enchanted. The aunt coughed, swallowed, and said in French that she was very pleased to see Hélène, then she turned to Pierre with the same words of welcome and the same look. In the middle of a dull and halting conversation, Hélène turned to Pierre with the beautiful bright smile that she gave to everyone. Pierre was so used to that smile, and it had so little meaning for him, that he paid no attention to it. The aunt was just speaking of a collection of snuffboxes that had belonged to Pierre's father, Count Bezúkhov, and showed them her own box. Princess Hélène asked to see the portrait of the aunt's husband on the box-lid.

"That is probably the work of Vinesse," said Pierre, mentioning a celebrated miniaturist, and he leaned over the table to take the snuffbox while trying to hear what was being said at the other table.

He half rose, meaning to go round, but the aunt handed him the snuffbox, passing it across Hélène's back. Hélène stooped forward to make room, and looked round with a smile. She was, as always at evening parties, wearing a dress such as was then fashionable, cut very low at front and back. Her bust, which had always seemed like marble to Pierre, was so close to him that his short-sighted eyes could not but perceive the living charm of her neck and shoulders, so near to his lips that he need only have bent his head a little to have touched them. He was conscious of the warmth of her body, the scent of perfume, and the creaking of her corset as she moved. He did not see her marble beauty forming a complete whole with her dress, but all the charm of her body only covered by her garments. And having once seen this he could not help being aware it, just as we cannot renew an illusion we have once seen through.

"So you have never noticed before how beautiful I am?" Hélène seemed to say. "You had not noticed that I am a woman? Yes, I am a woman who may belong to anyone—to you too," said her glance. And at that moment Pierre felt that Hélène not only could, but must, be his wife, and that it could not be otherwise.

He knew this at that moment as surely as if he had been standing at the altar with her. How and when this would be he did not know, he did not even know if it would be a good thing (he even felt, he knew not why, that it would be a bad thing), but he knew it would happen.

Pierre dropped his eyes, lifted them again, and wished once more to see her as a distant beauty far removed from him, as he had seen her every day until then, but he could no longer do it. He could not, any more than a man who has been looking at a tuft of steppe grass through the mist and taking it for a tree, can again take it for a tree after he has once recognized it to be a tuft of grass. She was terribly close to him. She already had power over him, and between them there was no longer any barrier except the barrier of his own will.

"Well, I will leave you in your little corner," came Anna Pávlovna's voice, "I see you are all right there."

And Pierre, anxiously trying to remember whether he had done anything reprehensible, looked round with a blush. It seemed to him that everyone knew what had happened to him as he knew it himself.

A little later when he went up to the large circle, Anna Pávlovna said to him: "I hear you are refitting your Petersburg house?"

This was true. The architect had told him that it was necessary, and Pierre, without knowing why, was having his enormous Petersburg house done up.

"That's a good thing, but don't move from Prince Vasíli's. It is good to have a friend like the prince," she said, smiling at Prince Vasíli. "I know something about that. Don't I? And you are still so young. You need advice. Don't be angry with me for exercising an old woman's privilege."

She paused, as women always do, expecting something after they have mentioned their age. "If you marry it will be a different thing," she continued, uniting them both in one glance. Pierre did not look at Hélène nor she at him. But she was just as terribly close to him. He muttered something, and colored.

When he got home he could not sleep for a long time for thinking of what had happened. What had happened? Nothing. He had merely understood that the woman he had known as a child, of whom when her beauty was mentioned he had said absent-mindedly: "Yes, she's good looking," he had understood that this woman might belong to him.

"But she's stupid. I have myself said she is stupid," he thought. "There is something nasty, something wrong, in the feeling she excites in me. I have been told that her brother Anatole was in love with her and she with him, that there was quite a scandal and that that's why he was sent away. Hippolyte is her brother . . . Prince Vasíli is her father . . . It's bad. . . ." he reflected, but while he was thinking this (the reflection was still incomplete), he caught himself smiling and was conscious that another line of thought had sprung up, and while thinking of her worthlessness he was also dreaming of how she would be his wife, how she would love him and become quite different, and how all he had thought and heard of her might be false. And he again saw her not as the daughter of Prince Vasíli, but visualized her whole body only veiled by its gray dress. "But no! Why did this thought never occur to me before?" and again he told himself that it was impossible, that there would be something unnatural, and as it seemed to him dishonorable, in this marriage. He recalled her former words and looks and the words and looks of those who had seen them together. He recalled Anna Pávlovna's words and looks when she spoke to him about his house, recalled thousands of such hints from Prince Vasíli and others, and was seized by terror lest he had already, in some way, bound himself to do something that was evidently wrong, and that he ought not to do. But at the very time he was expressing this conviction to himself, in another part of his mind her image rose in all its womanly beauty.

Chapter II

In November 1805, Prince Vasíli had to go on a tour of inspection in four different provinces. He had arranged this for himself so as to visit his neglected estates at the same time and pick up his son Anatole where his regiment was stationed, and take him to visit Nicholas Bolkónski in order to arrange a match for him with the daughter of that rich old man. But before leaving home and undertaking these new affairs, Prince Vasíli had to settle matters with Pierre, who, it is true, had latterly spent whole days at home, that is in Prince Vasíli's house where he was staying, and had been absurd, excited, and foolish in Hélène's presence (as a lover should be), but had not yet proposed to her.

"This is all very fine, but things must be settled," said Prince Vasíli to himself, with a sorrowful sigh, one morning, feeling that Pierre who was under such obligations to him ("But never mind that") was not behaving very well in this matter. "Youth, frivolity . . . well, God be with him," thought he, relishing his own goodness of heart, "but it must be brought to a head. The day after tomorrow will be Lëlya's name-day. I will invite two or three people, and if he does not understand what he ought to do then it will be my affair—yes, my affair. I am her father."

Six weeks after Anna Pávlovna's "At Home" and after the sleepless night when he had decided that to marry Hélène would be a calamity and that he ought to avoid her and go away, Pierre, despite that decision, had not left Prince Vasíli's and felt with terror that in people's eyes he was every day more and more connected with her, that it was impossible for him to return to his former conception of her, that he could not break away from her, and that though it would be a terrible thing he would have to unite his fate with hers. He might perhaps have been able to free himself but that Prince Vasíli (who had rarely before given receptions) now hardly let a day go by without having an evening party at which Pierre had to be present unless he wished to spoil the general pleasure and disappoint everyone's expectation. Prince Vasíli in the rare moments when he was at home, would take Pierre's hand in passing and draw it downward, or absent-mindedly hold out his wrinkled clean-shaven cheek for Pierre to kiss and would say: "Till tomorrow," or, "Be in to dinner or I shall not see you," or, "I am staying in for your sake," and so on. And though Prince Vasíli, when he stayed in (as he said) for Pierre's sake, hardly exchanged a couple of words with him, Pierre felt unable to disappoint him. Every day he said to himself one and the same thing: "It is time I understood her and made up my mind what she really is. Was I mistaken before, or am I mistaken now? No, she is not stupid, she is an excellent girl," he sometimes said to himself, "she never makes a mistake, never says anything stupid. She says little, but what she does say is always clear and simple, so she is not stupid. She never was abashed and is not abashed now, so she cannot be a bad woman!" He had often begun to make reflections or think aloud in her company, and she had always answered him either by a brief but appropriate remark—showing that it did not interest her—or by a silent look and smile which more palpably than anything else showed Pierre her superiority. She was right in regarding all arguments as nonsense in comparison with that smile.

She always addressed him with a radiantly confiding smile meant for him alone, in which there was something more significant than in the general smile that usually brightened her face. Pierre knew that everyone was waiting for him to say a word and cross a certain line, and he knew that sooner or later he would step across it, but an incomprehensible terror seized him at the thought of that dreadful step. A thousand times during that month and a half while he felt himself drawn nearer and nearer to that dreadful abyss, Pierre said to himself: "What am I doing? I need resolution. Can it be that I have none?"

He wished to take a decision, but felt with dismay that in this matter he lacked that strength of will which he had known in himself and really possessed. Pierre was one of those who are only strong when they feel themselves quite innocent, and since that day when he was overpowered by a feeling of desire while stooping over the snuffbox at Anna Pávlovna's, an unacknowledged sense of the guilt of that desire paralyzed his will.

On Hélène's name-day, a small party of just their own people—as his wife said—met for supper at Prince Vasíli's. All these friends and relations had been given to understand that the fate of the young girl would be decided that evening. The visitors were seated at supper. Princess Kurágina, a portly imposing woman who had once been handsome, was sitting at the head of the table. On either side of her sat the more important guests—an old general and his wife, and Anna Pávlovna Schérer. At the other end sat the younger and less important guests, and there too sat the members of the family, and Pierre and Hélène, side by side. Prince Vasíli was not having any supper: he went round the table in a merry mood, sitting down now by one, now by another, of the guests. To each of them he made some careless and agreeable remark except to Pierre and Hélène, whose presence he seemed not to notice. He enlivened the whole party. The wax candles burned brightly, the silver and crystal gleamed, so did the ladies' toilets and the gold and silver of the men's epaulets; servants in scarlet liveries moved round the table, the clatter of plates, knives, and glasses mingled with the animated hum of several conversations. At one end of the table, the old chamberlain was heard assuring an old baroness that he loved her passionately, at which she laughed; at the other could be heard the story of the misfortunes of some Mary Víktorovna or other. At the center of the table, Prince Vasíli attracted everybody's attention. With a facetious smile on his face, he was telling the ladies about last Wednesday's meeting of the Imperial Council, at which Sergéy Kuzmích Vyazmítinov, the new military governor-general of Petersburg, had received and read the then famous rescript of the Emperor Alexander from the army to Sergéy Kuzmích, in which the

Emperor said that he was receiving from all sides declarations of the people's loyalty, that the declaration from Petersburg gave him particular pleasure, and that he was proud to be at the head of such a nation and would endeavor to be worthy of it. This rescript began with the words: "Sergéy Kuzmích, From all sides reports reach me," etc.

"Well, and so he never got farther than: 'Sergéy Kuzmích'?" asked one of the ladies.

"Exactly, not a hair's breadth farther," answered Prince Vasíli, laughing, " 'Sergéy Kuzmích . . . From all sides . . . From all sides . . . Sergéy Kuzmích . . . ' Poor Vyazmítinov could not get any farther. He began the rescript again and again, but as soon as he uttered *'Sergéy'* he sobbed, *'Kuz-mí-ch,'* tears, and *'From all sides'* was smothered in sobs and he could get no farther. And again his handkerchief, and again: *'Sergéy Kuzmích, From all sides,'* . . . and tears, till at last somebody else was asked to read it."

"Kuzmích . . . From all sides . . . and then tears," someone repeated laughing.

"Don't be unkind," cried Anna Pávlovna from her end of the table holding up a threatening finger. "He is such a worthy and excellent man, our dear Vyazmítinov. . . ."

Everybody laughed a great deal. At the head of the table, where the honored guests sat, everyone seemed to be in high spirits and under the influence of a variety of exciting sensations. Only Pierre and Hélène sat silently side by side almost at the bottom of the table, a suppressed smile brightening both their faces, a smile that had nothing to do with Sergéy Kuzmích—a smile of bashfulness at their own feelings. But much as all the rest laughed, talked, and joked, much as they enjoyed their Rhine wine, *sauté,* and ices, and however they avoided looking at the young couple, and heedless and unobservant as they seemed of them, one could feel by the occasional glances they gave that the story about Sergéy Kuzmích, the laughter, and the food, were all a pretense, and that the whole attention of that company was directed to—Pierre and Hélène. Prince Vasíli mimicked the sobbing of Sergéy Kuzmích and at the same time his eyes glanced toward his daughter, and while he laughed the expression on his face clearly said: "Yes . . . it's getting on, it will all be settled today." Anna Pávlovna threatened him on behalf of "our dear Vyazmítinov," and in her eyes, which, for an instant, glanced at Pierre, Prince Vasíli read a congratulation on his future son-in-law and on his daughter's happiness. The old princess sighed sadly as she offered some wine to the old lady next to her and glanced angrily at her daughter, and her sigh seemed to say: "Yes, there's nothing left for you and me but to sip sweet wine, my dear, now that the time has come for these young ones to be thus boldly, provocatively happy." "And what nonsense all this is that I am saying!" thought a diplomatist, glancing at the happy faces of the lovers. "That's happiness!"

Into the insignificant, trifling, and artificial interests uniting that society, had entered the simple feeling of the attraction of a healthy and handsome young man and woman for one another. And this human feeling dominated everything else and soared above all their affected chatter. Jests fell flat, news was not interesting, and the animation was evidently forced. Not only the guests but even the footmen waiting at table seemed to feel this, and they forgot their duties as they looked at the beautiful Hélène with her radiant face and at the red, broad, and happy though uneasy face of Pierre. It seemed as if the very light of the candles was focused on those two happy faces alone.

Pierre felt that he was the center of it all, and this both pleased and embarrassed him. He was like a man entirely absorbed in some occupation. He did not see, hear, or understand anything clearly. Only now and then detached ideas and impressions from the world of reality shot unexpectedly through his mind.

"So it is all finished!" he thought. "And how has it all happened? How quickly! Now I know that not because of her alone, nor of myself alone, but because of everyone, *it* must inevitably come about. They are all expecting *it,* they are so sure that it will happen that I cannot, I cannot, disappoint them. But how will it be? I do not know, but it will certainly happen!" thought Pierre, glancing at those dazzling shoulders close to his eyes.

Or he would suddenly feel ashamed of he knew not what. He felt it awkward to attract everyone's attention and to be considered a lucky man and, with his plain face, to be looked on as a sort of Paris possessed of a Helen. "But no doubt it always is and must be so!" he consoled himself. "And besides, what have I done to bring it about? How did it begin? I traveled from Moscow with Prince Vasíli. Then there was nothing. So why should I not stay at his house? Then I played cards with her and picked up her reticule and drove out with her. How did it begin, when did it all come about?" And here he was sitting by her side as her betrothed, seeing, hearing, feeling her nearness, her breathing, her movements, her beauty. Then it would suddenly seem to him that it was not she but he was so unusually beautiful, and that that was why they all looked so at him, and flattered by this general admiration he would expand his chest, raise his head, and rejoice at his good fortune. Suddenly he heard a familiar voice repeating something to him a second time. But Pierre was so absorbed that he did not understand what was said.

"I am asking you when you last heard from Bolkónski," repeated Prince Vasíli a third time. "How absent-minded you are, my dear fellow."

Prince Vasíli smiled, and Pierre noticed that everyone was smiling at him and Hélène. "Well, what of it, if you all know it?" thought Pierre. "What of it? It's the truth!" and he himself smiled his gentle childlike smile, and Hélène smiled too.

"When did you get the letter? Was it from Olmütz?" repeated Prince Vasíli, who pretended to want to know this in order to settle a dispute.

"How can one talk or think of such trifles?" thought Pierre.

"Yes, from Olmütz," he answered, with a sigh.

After supper Pierre with his partner followed the others into the drawing room. The guests began to disperse, some without taking leave of Hélène. Some, as if unwilling to distract her from an important occupation, came up to her for a moment and made haste to go away, refusing to let her see them off. The diplomatist preserved a mournful silence as he left the drawing room. He pictured the vanity of his diplomatic career in comparison with Pierre's happiness. The old general grumbled at his wife when she asked how his leg was. "Oh, the old fool," he thought. "That Princess Hélène will be beautiful still when she's fifty."

"I think I may congratulate you," whispered Anna Pávlovna to the old princess, kissing her soundly. "If I hadn't this headache I'd have stayed longer."

The old princess did not reply, she was tormented by jealousy of her daughter's happiness.

While the guests were taking their leave, Pierre remained for a long time alone with Hélène in the little drawing room where they were sitting. He had often before, during the last six weeks, remained alone with her, but had never spoken to her of love. Now he felt that it was inevitable, but he could not make up his mind to take the final step. He felt ashamed; he felt that he was occupying someone else's place here beside Hélène. "This happiness is not for you," some inner voice whispered to him. "This happiness is for those who have not in them what there is in you."

But, as he had to say something, he began by asking her whether she was satisfied with the party. She replied in her usual simple manner that this name-day of hers had been one of the pleasantest she had ever had.

Some of the nearest relatives had not yet left. They were sitting in the large drawing room. Prince Vasíli came up to Pierre with languid footsteps. Pierre rose, and said it was getting late. Prince Vasíli gave him a look of stern inquiry, as though what Pierre had just said was so strange that one could not take it in. But then the expression of severity changed, and he drew Pierre's hand downward, made him sit down, and smiled affectionately.

"Well, Lëlya?" he asked, turning instantly to his daughter and addressing her with the careless tone of habitual tenderness natural to parents who have petted their children from babyhood, but which Prince Vasíli had only acquired by imitating other parents.

And he again turned to Pierre.

"Sergéy Kuzmích—from all sides—" he said unbuttoning the top button of his waistcoat.

Pierre smiled, but his smile showed that he knew it was not the story about Sergéy Kuzmích that interested Prince Vasíli just then, and Prince Vasíli saw that Pierre knew this. He suddenly muttered something and went away. It seemed to Pierre that even the prince was disconcerted. The sight of the discomposure of that old man of the world touched Pierre: he looked at Hélène and she too seemed disconcerted, and her look seemed to say: "Well, it is your own fault."

"The step must be taken but I cannot, I cannot!" thought Pierre, and he again began speaking about indifferent matters, about Sergéy Kuzmích, asking what the point of the story was as he had not heard it properly. Hélène answered with a smile that she too had missed it.

When Prince Vasíli returned to the drawing room, the princess, his wife, was talking in low tones to the elderly lady about Pierre.

"Of course, it is a very brilliant match, but happiness, my dear . . ."

"Marriages are made in heaven," replied the elderly lady.

Prince Vasíli passed by, seeming not to hear the ladies, and sat down on a sofa in a far corner of the room. He closed his eyes and seemed to be dozing. His head sank forward and then he roused himself.

"Aline," he said to his wife, "go and see what they are about."

The princess went up to the door, passed by it with a dignified and indifferent air and glanced into the little drawing room. Pierre and Hélène still sat talking just as before.

"Still the same," she said to her husband.

Prince Vasíli frowned, twisting his mouth, his cheeks quivered and his face assumed the coarse unpleasant expression peculiar to him. Shaking himself, he rose, threw back his head and with resolute steps went past the ladies into the little drawing room. With quick steps he went joyfully up to Pierre. His face was so unusually triumphant that Pierre rose in alarm on seeing it.

"Thank God!" said Prince Vasíli. "My wife has told me everything!"—(He put one arm around Pierre and the other around his daughter.)—"My dear boy . . . Lëlya . . . I am very pleased." (His voice trembled.) "I loved your father . . . and she will make you a good wife . . . God bless you! . . ."

He embraced his daughter, and then again Pierre, and kissed him with his malodorous mouth. Tears actually moistened his cheeks.

"Princess, come here!" he shouted.

The old princess came in, and also wept. The elderly lady was using her handkerchief too. Pierre was kissed, and he kissed the beautiful Hélène's hand several times. After a while they were left alone again.

"All this had to be and could not be otherwise," thought Pierre, "so it is useless to ask whether it is good or bad. It is good because it's definite and one is rid of the old tormenting doubt." Pierre held the hand of his betrothed in silence, looking at her beautiful bosom as it rose and fell.

"Hélène!" he said aloud and paused.

"Something special is always said in such cases," he thought, but could not remember what it was that people say. He looked at her face. She drew nearer to him. Her face flushed.

"Oh, take those off . . . those . . ." she said, pointing to his spectacles.

Pierre took them off, and his eyes besides the strange look eyes have from which spectacles have just been removed, had also a frightened and inquiring look. He was about to stoop over her hand and kiss it, but with a rapid, almost brutal movement of her head, she intercepted his lips and met them with her own. Her face struck Pierre, by its altered, unpleasantly excited expression.

"It is too late now, it's done; besides I love her," thought Pierre.

"Je vous aime!" he said, remembering what has to be said at such moments: but his words sounded so weak that he felt ashamed of himself.

Six weeks later he was married, and settled in Count Bezúkhov's large newly-furnished Petersburg house, the happy possessor, as people said, of a wife who was a celebrated beauty, and of millions of money.

Chapter III

OLD PRINCE NICHOLAS BOLKÓNSKI RECEIVED A LETTER FROM PRINCE VASÍLI IN NOVEMBER, 1805, announcing that he and his son would be paying him a visit. "I am starting on a journey of inspection, and of course I shall think nothing of an extra seventy miles to come and see you at the same time, my honored benefactor," wrote Prince Vasíli. "My son Anatole is accompanying me on his way to the army, so I hope you will allow him personally to express the deep respect that, emulating his father, he feels for you."

"It seems that there will be no need to bring Mary out, suitors are coming to us of their own accord," incautiously remarked the little princess on hearing the news.

Prince Nicholas frowned, but said nothing.

A fortnight after the letter Prince Vasíli's servants came one evening in advance of him, and he and his son arrived next day.

Old Bolkónski had always had a poor opinion of Prince Vasíli's character, but more so recently, since in the new reigns of Paul and Alexander Prince Vasíli had risen to high position and honors. And now, from the hints contained in his letter and given by the little princess, he saw which way the wind was blowing, and his low opinion changed into a feeling of contemptuous ill will. He snorted whenever he mentioned him. On the day of Prince Vasíli's arrival, Prince Bolkónski was particularly discontented and out of temper. Whether he was in a bad temper because Prince Vasíli was coming, or whether his being in a bad temper made him specially annoyed at Prince Vasíli's visit, he was in a bad temper, and in the morning Tíkhon had already advised the architect not to go to the prince with his report.

"Do you hear how he's walking?" said Tíkhon, drawing the architect's attention to the sound of the prince's footsteps. "Stepping flat on his heels—we know what that means. . . ."

However at nine o'clock the prince, in his velvet coat with a sable collar and cap, went out for his usual walk. It had snowed the day before and the path to the hothouse, along which the prince was in the habit of walking, had been swept: the marks of the broom were still visible in the snow and a shovel had been left sticking in one of the soft snowbanks that bordered both sides of the path. The prince went through the conservatories, the serfs' quarters and the outbuildings, frowning and silent.

"Can a sleigh pass?" he asked his overseer, a venerable man, resembling his master in manners and looks, who was accompanying him back to the house.

"The snow is deep. I am having the avenue swept, your honor."

The prince bowed his head and went up to the porch. "God be thanked," thought the overseer, "the storm has blown over!"

"It would have been hard to drive up, your honor," he added. "I heard, your honor, that a minister is coming to visit your honor."

The prince turned round to the overseer and fixed his eyes on him, frowning.

"What? A minister? What minister? Who gave orders?" he said in his shrill harsh voice. "The road is not swept for the princess my daughter, but for a minister! For me, there are no ministers!"

"Your honor, I thought . . ."

"You thought!" shouted the prince, his words coming more and more rapidly and indistinctly. "You thought! . . . Rascals! Blackgaurds! . . . I'll teach you to think!" and lifting his stick he swung it and would have hit Alpátych, the overseer, had not the latter instinctively avoided the blow. "Thought . . . Blackguards . . ." shouted the prince rapidly.

But although Alpátych, frightened at his own temerity in avoiding the stroke, came up to the prince, bowing his bald head resignedly before him, or perhaps for that very reason, the prince, though he continued to shout: "Blackgaurds! . . . Throw the snow back on the road!" did not lift his stick again but hurried into the house.

Before dinner, Princess Mary and Mademoiselle Bourienne, who knew that the prince was in a bad humor, stood awaiting him; Mademoiselle Bourienne with a radiant face that said: "I know nothing, I am the same as usual," and Princess Mary pale, frightened and with downcast eyes. What she found hardest to bear was to know that on such occasions she ought to behave like Mademoiselle Bourienne, but could not. She thought: "If I seem not to notice he will think that I do not sympathize with him; if I seem sad and out of spirits myself, he will say (as he has done before) that I'm in the dumps."

The prince looked at his daughter's frightened face and snorted.

"Fool . . . or dummy!" he muttered.

"And the other one is not here. They've been telling tales," he thought—referring to the little princess who was not in the dining room.

"Where is the princess?" he asked. "Hiding?"

"She is not very well," answered Mademoiselle Bourienne with a bright smile, "so she won't come down. It is natural in her state."

"Hm! Hm!" muttered the prince, sitting down.

His plate seemed to him not quite clean, and pointing to a spot he flung it away. Tíkhon caught it and handed it to a footman. The little princess was not unwell, but had such an overpowering fear of the prince that, hearing he was in a bad humor, she had decided not to appear.

"I am afraid for the baby," she said to Mademoiselle Bourienne: "Heaven knows what a fright might do."

In general at Bald Hills the little princess lived in constant fear, and with a sense of antipathy to the old prince which she did not realize because the fear was so much the stronger feeling. The prince reciprocated this antipathy, but it was overpowered by his contempt for her. When the little princess had grown accustomed to life at Bald Hills, she took a special fancy to Mademoiselle Bourienne, spent whole days with her, asked her to sleep in her room, and often talked with her about the old prince and criticized him.

"So we are to have visitors, *mon prince?*" remarked Mademoiselle Bourienne, unfolding her white napkin with her rosy fingers. "His Excellency Prince Vasíli Kurágin and his son, I understand?" she said inquiringly.

"Hm!—his excellency is a puppy. . . . I got him his appointment in the service," said the prince disdainfully. "Why his son is coming I don't understand. Perhaps Princess Elizabeth and Princess Mary know. I don't want him." (He looked at his blushing daughter.) "Are you unwell today? Eh? Afraid of the 'minister' as that idiot Alpátych called him this morning?"

"No, *mon père.*"

Though Mademoiselle Bourienne had been so unsuccessful in her choice of a subject, she did not stop talking, but chattered about the conservatories and the beauty of a flower that had just opened, and after the soup the prince became more genial.

After dinner, he went to see his daughter-in-law. The little princess was sitting at a small table, chattering with Másha, her maid. She grew pale on seeing her father-in-law.

She was much altered. She was now plain rather than pretty. Her cheeks had sunk, her lip was drawn up, and her eyes drawn down.

"Yes, I feel a kind of oppression," she said in reply to the prince's question as to how she felt.

"Do you want anything?"

"No, *merci, mon père.*"

"Well, all right, all right."

He left the room and went to the waiting room where Alpátych stood with bowed head.

"Has the snow been shoveled back?"

"Yes, your excellency. Forgive me for heaven's sake . . . It was only my stupidity."

"All right, all right," interrupted the prince, and laughing in his unnatural way, he stretched out his hand for Alpátych to kiss, and then proceeded to his study.

Prince Vasíli arrived that evening. He was met in the avenue by coachmen and footmen, who, with loud shouts, dragged his sleighs up to one of the lodges over the road purposely laden with snow.

Prince Vasíli and Anatole had separate rooms assigned to them.

Anatole, having taken off his overcoat, sat with arms akimbo before a table on a corner of which he smilingly and absent-mindedly fixed his large and handsome eyes. He regarded his whole life as a continual round of amusement which someone for some reason had to provide for him. And he looked on this visit to a churlish old man and a rich and ugly heiress in the same way. All this might, he thought, turn out very well and amusingly. "And why not marry her if she really has so much money? That never does any harm," thought Anatole.

He shaved and scented himself with the care and elegance which had become habitual to him and, his handsome head held high, entered his father's room with the good-humored and victorious air natural to him. Prince Vasíli's two valets were busy dressing him, and he looked round with much animation and cheerfully nodded to his son as the latter entered, as if to say: "Yes, that's how I want you to look."

"I say, father, joking apart, is she very hideous?" Anatole asked, as if continuing a conversation the subject of which had often been mentioned during the journey.

"Enough! What nonsense! Above all, try to be respectful and cautious with the old prince."

"If he starts a row I'll go away," said Prince Anatole. "I can't bear those old men! Eh?"

"Remember, for you everything depends on this."

In the meantime, not only was it known in the maidservants' rooms that the minister and his son had arrived, but the appearance of both had been minutely described. Princess Mary was sitting alone in her room, vainly trying to master her agitation.

"Why did they write, why did Lise tell me about it? It can never happen!" she said, looking at herself in the glass. "How shall I enter the drawing room? Even if I like him I can't now be myself with him." The mere thought of her father's look filled her with terror. The little princess and Mademoiselle Bourienne had already received from Másha, the lady's maid, the necessary report of how handsome the minister's son was, with his rosy cheeks and dark eyebrows, and with what difficulty the father had dragged his legs upstairs while the son had followed him like an eagle, three steps at a time. Having received this information, the little princess and Mademoiselle Bourienne, whose chattering voices had reached her from the corridor, went into Princess Mary's room.

"You know they've come, Marie?" said the little princess, waddling in, and sinking heavily into an arm-chair.

She was no longer in the loose gown she generally wore in the morning, but had on one of her best dresses. Her hair was carefully done and her face was animated, which, however, did not conceal its sunken and faded outlines. Dressed as she used to be in Petersburg society, it was still more noticeable how much plainer she had become. Some unobtrusive touch had been added to Mademoiselle Bourienne's toilet which rendered her fresh and pretty face yet more attractive.

"What! Are you going to remain as you are, dear princess?" she began. "They'll be announcing that the gentlemen are in the drawing room and we shall have to go down, and you have not smartened yourself up at all!"

The little princess got up, rang for the maid, and hurriedly and merrily began to devise and carry out a plan of how Princess Mary should be dressed. Princess Mary's self-esteem was wounded by the fact that the arrival of a suitor agitated her, and still more so by both her companions not having the least conception that it could be otherwise. To tell them that she felt ashamed for herself and for them would be to betray her agitation, while to decline their offers to dress her would prolong their banter and insistence. She flushed, her beautiful eyes grew dim, red blotches came on her face and it took on the unattractive martyrlike expression it so often wore, as she submitted herself to Mademoiselle Bourienne and Lise. Both these women *quite sincerely* tried to make her look pretty. She was so plain that neither of them could think of her as a rival, so they began dressing her with perfect sincerity, and with the naïve and firm conviction women have that dress can make a face pretty.

"No really, my dear, this dress is not pretty," said Lise, looking sideways at Princess Mary from a little distance. "You have a maroon dress, have it fetched. Really! You know the fate of your whole life may be at stake. But this one is too light, it's not becoming!"

It was not the dress, but the face and whole figure of Princess Mary that was not pretty, but neither Mademoiselle Bourienne nor the little princess felt this, they still thought that if a blue ribbon were placed in the hair, the hair combed up, and the blue scarf arranged lower on the best maroon dress, and so on, all would be well. They forgot that the frightened face and the figure could not be altered, and that however they might change the setting and adornment of that face, it would still remain piteous and plain. After two or three changes to which Princess Mary meekly submitted, just as her hair had been arranged on the top of her head (a style that quite altered and spoiled her looks) and she had put on a maroon dress with a pale-blue scarf, the little princess walked twice round her, now adjusting a fold of the dress with her little hand, now arranging the scarf and looking at her with her head bent first on one side and then on the other.

"No, it will not do," she said decidedly, clasping her hands. "No, Mary, really this dress does not suit you. I prefer you in your little gray everyday dress. Now please, do it for my sake. Katie," she said to the maid, "bring the princess her gray dress, and you'll see, Mademoiselle Bourienne, how I shall arrange it," she added, smiling with a foretaste of artistic pleasure.

But when Katie brought the required dress, Princess Mary remained sitting motionless before the glass, looking at her face, and saw in the mirror her eyes full of tears and her mouth quivering, ready to burst into sobs.

"Come, dear princess," said Mademoiselle Bourienne, "just one more little effort."

The little princess, taking the dress from the maid, came up to Princess Mary.

"Well, now we'll arrange something quite simple and becoming," she said.

The three voices, hers, Mademoiselle Bourienne's, and Katie's, who was laughing at something, mingled in a merry sound, like the chirping of birds.

"No, leave me alone," said Princess Mary.

Her voice sounded so serious and so sad that the chirping of the birds was silenced at once. They looked at the beautiful, large, thoughtful eyes full of tears and of thoughts, gazing shiningly and imploringly at them, and understood that it was useless and even cruel to insist.

"At least, change your coiffure," said the little princess. "Didn't I tell you," she went on, turning reproachfully to Mademoiselle Bourienne, "Mary's is a face which such a coiffure does not suit in the least. Not in the least! Please change it."

"Leave me alone, please leave me alone! It is all quite the same to me," answered a voice struggling with tears.

Mademoiselle Bourienne and the little princess had to own to themselves that Princess Mary in this guise looked very plain, worse than usual, but it was too late. She was looking at them with an expression they both knew, an expression thoughtful and sad. This expression in Princess Mary did not frighten them (she never inspired fear in anyone), but they knew that when it appeared on her face, she became mute and was not to be shaken in her determination.

"You will change it, won't you?" said Lise. And as Princess Mary gave no answer, she left the room.

Princess Mary was left alone. She did not comply with Lise's request, she not only left her hair as it was, but did not even look in her glass. Letting her arms fall helplessly, she sat with downcast eyes and pondered. A husband, a man, a strong dominant and strangely attractive being rose in her imagination, and carried her into a totally different happy world of his own. She fancied a child, *her own*—such as she had seen the day before in the arms of her nurse's daughter—at her own breast, the husband standing by and gazing tenderly at her and the child. "But no, it is impossible, I am too ugly," she thought.

"Please come to tea. The prince will be out in a moment," came the maid's voice at the door.

She roused herself, and felt appalled at what she had been thinking, and before going down she went into the room where the icons hung and, her eyes fixed on the dark face of a large icon of the Saviour lit by a lamp, she stood before it with folded hands for a few moments. A painful doubt filled her soul. Could the joy of love, of earthly love for a man, be for her? In her thoughts of marriage Princess Mary dreamed of happiness and of children, but her strongest, most deeply-hidden longing was for earthly love. The more she tried to hide this feeling from others and even from herself, the stronger it grew. "O God," she said, "how am I to stifle in my heart these temptations of the devil? How am I to renounce forever these vile fancies, so as peacefully to fulfill Thy will?" And scarcely had she put that question than God gave her the answer in her own heart. "Desire nothing for thyself, seek nothing, be not anxious or envious. Man's future and thy own fate must remain hidden from thee, but live so that thou mayest be ready for anything. If it be God's will to prove thee in the duties of marriage, be ready to fulfill His will." With this consoling thought (but yet with a hope for the fulfillment of her forbidden earthly longing) Princess Mary sighed, and having crossed herself went down, thinking neither of her gown and coiffure, nor of how she would go in nor of what she would say. What could all that matter in comparison with the will of God, without Whose care not a hair of man's head can fall?

Chapter IV

When princess Mary came down, prince Vasíli and his son were already in the drawing room, talking to the little princess and Mademoiselle Bourienne. When she entered with her heavy step, treading on her heels, the gentlemen and Mademoiselle Bourienne rose and the little princess, indicating her to the gentlemen, said: *"Voilà Marie!"* Princess Mary saw them all and saw them in detail. She saw Prince Vasíli's face, serious for an instant at the sight of her, but immediately smiling again, and the little princess curiously noting the impression "Marie" produced on the visitors. And she saw Mademoiselle Bourienne, with her ribbon and pretty face, and her unusually animated look which was fixed on *him*, but *him* she could not see, she only saw something large, brilliant, and handsome moving toward her as she entered the room. Prince Vasíli approached first, and she kissed the bald forehead that bent over her hand and answered his question by saying that, on the contrary, she remembered him quite well. Then Anatole came up to her. She still could not see him. She only felt a soft hand taking hers firmly, and she touched with her lips a white forehead, over which was beautiful light-brown hair smelling of pomade. When she looked up at him she was struck by his beauty. Anatole stood with his right thumb under a button of his uniform, his chest expanded and his back drawn in, slightly swinging one foot and, with his head a little bent, looked with beaming face at the princess without speaking and evidently not thinking about her at all. Anatole was not quick-witted, nor ready or eloquent in conversation, but he had the faculty, so invaluable in society, of composure and imperturbable self-possession. If a man lacking in self-confidence remains dumb on a first introduction and betrays a consciousness of the impropriety of such silence and an anxiety to find something to say, the effect is bad. But Anatole was dumb, swung his foot, and smilingly examined the princess's hair. It was evident that he could be silent in this way for a very long time. "If anyone finds this silence inconvenient, let him talk, but I don't want to," he seemed to say. Besides this, in his behavior to women Anatole had a manner which particularly inspired in them curiosity, awe, and even love—a supercilious consciousness of his own superiority. It was was as if he said to them: "I know you, I know you, but why should I bother about you? You'd be only too glad, of course." Perhaps he did not really think this when he met women—even probably he did not, for in general he thought very little—but his looks and manner gave that impression. The princess felt this, and as if wishing to show him that she did not even dare expect to interest him, she turned to his father. The conversation was general and animated, thanks to Princess Lise's voice and little downy lip that lifted over her white teeth. She met Prince Vasíli with that playful manner often employed by lively chatty people, and consisting in the assumption that between the person they so address and themselves there are some semi-private long-established jokes and amusing reminiscences, though no such reminiscences really exist—just as none existed in this case. Prince Vasíli readily adopted her tone and the little princess also drew Anatole, whom she hardly knew, into these amusing recollections of things that had never occurred. Mademoiselle Bourienne also shared them and even Princess Mary felt herself pleasantly made to share in these merry reminiscences.

"Here at least we shall have the benefit of your company all to ourselves, dear prince," said the little princess (of course, in French) to Prince Vasíli. "It's not as at Annette's receptions where you always ran away; you remember *cette chère Annette!*"

"Ah, but you won't talk politics to me like Annette!"

"And our little tea-table?"

"Oh, yes!"

"Why is it you were never at Annette's?" the little princess asked Anatole. "Ah, I know, I know," she said with a sly glance, "your brother Hippolyte told me about your goings on. Oh!" and she shook her finger at him, "I have even heard of your doings in Paris!"

"And didn't Hippolyte tell you?" asked Prince Vasíli, turning to his son and seizing the little princess's arm as if she would have run away and he had just managed to catch her, "didn't he tell you how he himself was pining for the dear princess, and how she showed him the door? Oh, she is a pearl among women, princess," he added, turning to Princess Mary.

When Paris was mentioned, Mademoiselle Bourienne for her part seized the opportunity of joining in the general current of recollections.

She took the liberty of inquiring whether it was long since Anatole had left Paris and how he had liked that city. Anatole answered the Frenchwoman very readily and, looking at her with a smile, talked to her about her native land. When he saw the pretty little Bourienne, Anatole came to the conclusion that he would not find Bald Hills dull either. "Not at all bad!" he thought, examining her, "not at all bad, that little companion! I hope she will bring her along with her when we're married, *la petite est gentille.*"

The old prince dressed leisurely in his study, frowning and considering what he was to do. The coming of these visitors annoyed him. "What are Prince Vasíli and that son of his to me? Prince Vasíli is a shallow braggart and his son, no doubt, is a fine specimen," he grumbled to himself. What angered him was that the coming of these visitors revived in his mind an unsettled question he always tried to stifle, one about which he always deceived himself. The question was whether he could ever bring himself to part from his daughter and give her to a husband. The prince never directly asked himself that question, knowing beforehand that he would have to answer it justly, and justice clashed not only with his feelings but with the very possibility of life. Life without Princess Mary, little as he seemed to value her, was unthinkable to him. "And why should she marry?" he thought. "To be unhappy for certain. There's Lise, married to Andrew—a better husband one would think could hardly be found nowadays—but is she contented with her lot? And who would marry Marie for love? Plain and awkward! They'll take her for her connections and wealth. Are there no women living unmarried, and even the happier for it?" So thought Prince Bolkónski while dressing, and yet the question he was always putting off demanded an immediate answer. Prince Vasíli had brought his son with the evident intention of proposing, and today or tomorrow he would probably ask for an answer. His birth and position in society were not bad. "Well, I've nothing against it," the prince said to himself, "but he must be worthy of her. And that is what we shall see."

"That is what we shall see! That is what we shall see!" he added aloud.

He entered the drawing room with his usual alert step, glancing rapidly round the company. He noticed the change in the little princess's dress, Mademoiselle Bourienne's ribbon, Princess Mary's unbecoming coiffure, Mademoiselle Bourienne's and Anatole's smiles, and the loneliness of his daughter amid the general conversation. "Got herself up like a fool!" he thought, looking irritably at her. "She is shameless, and he ignores her!"

He went straight up to Prince Vasíli.

"Well! How d'ye do? How d'ye do? Glad to see you!"

"Friendship laughs at distance," began Prince Vasíli in his usual rapid, self-confident, familiar tone. "Here is my second son; please love and befriend him."

Prince Bolkónski surveyed Anatole.

"Fine young fellow! Fine young fellow!" he said. "Well, come and kiss me," and he offered his cheek.

Anatole kissed the old man, and looked at him with curiosity and perfect composure, waiting for a display of the eccentricities his father had told him to expect.

Prince Bolkónski sat down in his usual place in the corner of the sofa, and drawing up an armchair for Prince Vasíli, pointed to it and began questioning him about political affairs and news. He seemed to listen attentively to what Prince Vasíli said, but kept glancing at Princess Mary.

"And so they are writing from Potsdam already?" he said, repeating Prince Vasíli's last words. Then rising, he suddenly went up to his daughter.

"Is it for visitors you've got yourself up like that, eh?" said he. "Fine, very fine! You have done up your hair in this new way for the visitors, and before the visitors I tell you that in future you are never to dare to change your way of dress without my consent."

"It was my fault, *mon père,*" interceded the little princess, with a blush.

"*You* must do as you please," said Prince Bolkónski, bowing to his daughter-in-law, "but she need not make a fool of herself, she's plain enough as it is."

And he sat down again, paying no more attention to his daughter, who was reduced to tears.

"On the contrary, that coiffure suits the princess very well," said Prince Vasíli.

"Now you, young prince, what's your name?" said Prince Bolkónski, turning to Anatole, "come here, let us talk and get acquainted."

"Now the fun begins," thought Anatole, sitting down with a smile beside the old prince.

"Well, my dear boy, I hear you've been educated abroad, not taught to read and write by the deacon, like your father and me. Now tell me, my dear boy, are you serving in the Horse-Guards?" asked the old man, scrutinizing Anatole closely and intently.

"No, I have been transferred to the line," said Anatole, hardly able to restrain his laughter.

"Ah! That's a good thing. So, my dear boy, you wish to serve the Tsar and the country? It is war time. Such a fine fellow must serve. Well, are you off to the front?"

"No, prince, our regiment has gone to the front, but I am attached . . . what is it I am attached to, Papa?" said Anatole, turning to his father with a laugh.

"A splendid soldier, splendid! 'What am I attached to!' Ha, ha, ha!" laughed Prince Bolkónski, and Anatole laughed still louder. Suddenly Prince Bolkónski frowned.

"You may go," he said to Anatole.

Anatole returned smiling to the ladies.

"And so you've had him educated abroad, Prince Vasíli, haven't you?" said the old prince to Prince Vasíli.

"I have done my best for him, and I can assure you the education there is much better than ours."

"Yes, everything is different nowadays, everything is changed. The lad's a fine fellow, a fine fellow! Well, come with me now." He took Prince Vasíli's arm and led him to his study. As soon as they were alone together, Prince Vasíli announced his hopes and wishes to the old prince.

"Well, do you think I shall prevent her, that I can't part from her?" said the old prince angrily. "What an idea! I'm ready for it tomorrow! Only let me tell you, I want to know my son-in-law better. You know my principles—everything above-board? I will ask her tomorrow in your presence; if she is willing, then he can stay on. He can stay and I'll see." The old prince snorted. "Let her marry, it's all the same to me!" he screamed in the same piercing tone as when parting from his son.

"I will tell you frankly," said Prince Vasíli in the tone of a crafty man convinced of the futility of being cunning with so keen-sighted a companion. "You know, you see right through people. Anatole is no genius, but he is an honest, good-hearted lad; an excellent son or kinsman."

"All right, all right, we'll see!"

As always happens when women lead lonely lives for any length of time without male society, on Anatole's appearance all the three women of Prince Bolkónski's household felt that their life had not been real till then. Their powers of reasoning, feeling, and observing, immediately increased tenfold, and their life, which seemed to have been passed in darkness, was suddenly lit up by a new brightness, full of significance.

Princess Mary grew quite unconscious of her face and coiffure. The handsome open face of the man who might perhaps be her husband absorbed all her attention. He seemed to her kind, brave, determined, manly, and magnanimous. She felt convinced of that. Thousands of dreams of a future family life continually rose in her imagination. She drove them away and tried to conceal them.

"But am I not too cold with him?" thought the princess. "I try to be reserved because in the depth of my soul I feel too near to him already, but then he cannot know what I think of him and may imagine that I do not like him."

And Princess Mary tried, but could not manage, to be cordial to her new guest. "Poor girl, she's devilish ugly!" thought Anatole.

Mademoiselle Bourienne, also roused to great excitement by Anatole's arrival, thought in another way. Of course, she, a handsome young woman without any definite position, without relations or even a country, did not intend to devote her life to serving Prince Bolkónski, to reading aloud to him and being friends with Princess Mary. Mademoiselle Bourienne had long been waiting for a Russian prince who, able to appreciate at a glance her superiority to the plain, badly dressed, ungainly Russian princesses, would fall in love with her and carry her off; and here at last was a Russian prince. Mademoiselle Bourienne knew a story, heard from her aunt but finished in her own way, which she liked to repeat to herself. It was the story of a girl who had been seduced, and to whom her poor mother (*sa pauvre mère*) appeared, and reproached her for yielding to a man without being married. Mademoiselle Bourienne was often touched to tears as in imagination she told this story to *him*, her seducer. And now *he*, a real Russian prince, had appeared. He would carry her away and then *sa pauvre mère* would appear and he would marry her. So her future shaped itself in Mademoiselle Bourienne's head at the very time she was talking to Anatole about Paris. It was not calculation that guided her (she did not even for a moment consider what she should do) but all this had long been familiar to her, and now that Anatole had appeared it just grouped itself around him and she wished and tried to please him as much as possible.

The little princess, like an old war-horse that hears the trumpet, unconsciously and quite forgetting her condition, prepared for the familiar gallop of coquetry, without any ulterior motive or any struggle, but with naïve and light-hearted gaiety.

Although in female society Anatole usually assumed the rôle of a man tired of being run after by women, his vanity was flattered by the spectacle of his power over these three women. Besides that, he was beginning to feel for the pretty and provocative Mademoiselle Bourienne that passionate animal feeling which was apt to master him with great suddenness and prompt him to the coarsest and most reckless actions.

After tea, the company went into the sitting room and Princess Mary was asked to play on the clavichord. Anatole, laughing and in high spirits, came and leaned on his elbows, facing her and beside Mademoiselle Bourienne. Princess Mary felt his look with a painfully joyous emotion. Her favorite sonata bore her into a most intimately poetic world and the look she felt upon her made that world still more poetic. But Anatole's expression, though his eyes were fixed on her, referred not to her but to the movements of Mademoiselle Bourienne's little foot, which he was then touching with his own under the clavichord. Mademoiselle Bourienne was also looking at Princess Mary, and in her lovely eyes there was a look of fearful joy and hope that was also new to the princess.

"How she loves me!" thought Princess Mary. "How happy I am now, and how happy I may be with such a friend and such a husband! Husband? Can it be possible?" she thought, not daring to look at his face, but still feeling his eyes gazing at her.

In the evening, after supper, when all were about to retire, Anatole kissed Princess Mary's hand. She did not know how she found the courage, but she looked straight into his handsome face as it came near to her short-sighted eyes. Turning from Princess Mary he went up and kissed Mademoiselle Bourienne's hand. (This was not etiquette, but then he did everything so simply and with such assurance!) Mademoiselle Bourienne flushed, and gave the princess a frightened look.

"What delicacy!" thought the princess. "Is it possible that Amélie" (Mademoiselle Bourienne) "thinks I could be jealous of her, and not value her pure affection and devotion to me?" She went up to her and kissed her warmly. Anatole went up to kiss the little princess's hand.

"No! No! No! When your father writes to tell me that you are behaving well I will give you my hand to kiss. Not till then!" she said. And smilingly raising a finger at him, she left the room.

Chapter V

THEY ALL SEPARATED, BUT, EXCEPT ANATOLE WHO FELL ASLEEP AS SOON AS HE GOT INTO BED, all kept awake a long time that night.

"Is he really to be my husband, this stranger who is so kind—yes, kind, that is the chief thing," thought Princess Mary; and fear, which she had seldom experienced, came upon her. She feared to look round, it seemed to her that someone was there standing behind the screen in the dark corner. And this same one was *he*—the devil—and *he* was also this man with the white forehead, black eyebrows, and red lips.

She rang for her maid and asked her to sleep in her room.

Mademoiselle Bourienne walked up and down the conservatory for a long time that evening, vainly expecting someone, now smiling at someone, now working herself up to tears with the imaginary words of her *pauvre mère* rebuking her for her fall.

The little princess grumbled to her maid that her bed was badly made. She could not lie either on her face or on her side. Every position was awkward and uncomfortable, and her burden oppressed her now more than ever because Anatole's presence had vividly recalled to her the time when she was not like that, and when everything was light and gay. She sat in an arm-chair in her dressing-jacket and nightcap and Katie, sleepy and disheveled, beat and turned the heavy featherbed for the third time, muttering to herself.

"I told you it was all lumps and holes!" the little princess repeated. "I should be glad enough to fall asleep, so it's not my fault!" and her voice quivered like that of a child about to cry.

The old prince did not sleep either. Tíkhon, half asleep, heard him pacing angrily about and snorting. The old prince felt as though he had been insulted through his daughter. The insult was the more pointed because it concerned not himself but another, his daughter, whom he loved more than himself. He kept telling himself that he would consider the whole matter and decide what was right and how he should act, but instead of that he only excited himself more and more.

"The first man that turns up—she forgets her father and everything else, runs upstairs and does up her hair and wags her tail and is unlike herself! Glad to throw her father over! And she knew I should notice it. Fr . . . fr . . . fr . . . ! And don't I see that that idiot had eyes only for Bourienne—I shall have to get rid of her. And how is it she has not pride enough to see it? If she has no pride for herself she might at least have some for my sake! She must be shown that the blockhead thinks nothing of her and looks only at Bourienne. No, she has no pride . . . but I'll let her see. . . ."

The old prince knew that if he told his daughter she was making a mistake and that Anatole meant to flirt with Mademoiselle Bourienne, Princess Mary's self-esteem would be wounded and his point (not to be parted from her) would be gained, so pacifying himself with this thought, he called Tíkhon and began to undress.

"What devil brought them here?" thought he, while Tíkhon was putting the nightshirt over his dried-up old body and gray-haired chest. "I never invited them. They came to disturb my life—and there is not much of it left."

"Devil take 'em!" he muttered, while his head was still covered by the shirt.

Tíkhon knew his master's habit of sometimes thinking aloud, and therefore met with unaltered looks the angrily inquisitive expression of the face that emerged from the shirt.

"Gone to bed?" asked the prince.

Tíkhon, like all good valets, instinctively knew the direction of his master's thoughts. He guessed that the question referred to Prince Vasíli and his son.

"They have gone to bed and put out their lights, your excellency."

"No good . . . no good . . ." said the prince rapidly, and thrusting his feet into his slippers and his arms into the sleeves of his dressing-gown, he went to the couch on which he slept.

Though no words had passed between Anatole and Mademoiselle Bourienne, they quite understood one another as to the first part of their romance, up to the appearance of the *pauvre mère*; they understood that they had much to say to one another in private and so they had been seeking an opportunity since morning to meet one another alone. When Princess Mary went to her father's room at the usual hour, Mademoiselle Bourienne and Anatole met in the conservatory.

Princess Mary went to the door of the study with special trepidation. It seemed to her that not only did everybody know that her fate would be decided that day, but that they also knew what she thought about it. She read this in Tíkhon's face and in that of Prince Vasíli's valet, who made her a low bow when she met him in the corridor carrying hot water.

The old prince was very affectionate and careful in his treatment of his daughter that morning. Princess Mary well knew this painstaking expression of her father's. His face wore that expression when his dry hands clenched with vexation at her not understanding a sum in arithmetic, when rising from his chair he would walk away from her, repeating in a low voice the same words several times over.

He came to the point at once, treating her ceremoniously.

"I have had a proposition made me concerning you," he said with an unnatural smile. "I expect you have guessed that Prince Vasíli has not come and brought his pupil with him" (for some reason Prince Bolkónski referred to Anatole as a "pupil") "for the sake of my beautiful eyes. Last night a proposition was made me on your account and, as you know my principles, I refer it to you."

"How am I to understand you, *mon père?*" said the princess, growing pale and then blushing.

"How understand me!" cried her father angrily. "Prince Vasíli finds you to his taste as a daughter-in-law and makes a proposal to you on his pupil's behalf. That's how it's to be understood! 'How understand it'! . . . And I ask you!"

"I do not know what you think, father," whispered the princess.

"I? I? What of me? Leave me out of the question. I'm not going to get married. What about *you?* That's what I want to know."

The princess saw that her father regarded the matter with disapproval, but at that moment the thought occurred to her that her fate would be decided now or never. She lowered her eyes so as not to see the gaze under which she felt that she could not think, but would only be able to submit from habit, and she said:

"I wish only to do your will, but if I had to express my own desire . . ." She had no time to finish. The old prince interrupted her.

"That's admirable!" he shouted. "He will take you with your dowry and take Mademoiselle Bourienne into the bargain. She'll be the wife, while you . . ."

The prince stopped. He saw the effect these words had produced on his daughter. She lowered her head and was ready to burst into tears.

"Now then, now then, I'm only joking!" he said. "Remember this, princess, I hold to the principle that a maiden has a full right to choose. I give you freedom. Only remember that your life's happiness depends on your decision. Never mind me!"

"But I do not know, father!"

"There's no need to talk! He receives his orders and will marry you or anybody; but you are free to choose. . . . Go to your room, think it over, and come back in an hour and tell me in his presence: yes or no. I know you will pray over it. Well, pray if you like, but you had better think it over. Go! Yes or no, yes or no, yes or no!" he still shouted when the princess, as if lost in a fog, had already staggered out of the study.

Her fate was decided and happily decided. But what her father had said about Mademoiselle Bourienne was dreadful. It was untrue to be sure, but still it was terrible, and she could not help thinking of it. She was going straight on through the conservatory, neither seeing nor hearing anything, when suddenly the well-known whispering of Mademoiselle Bourienne aroused her. She raised her eyes, and two steps away saw Anatole embracing the Frenchwoman and whispering something to her. With a horrified expression on his handsome face, Anatole looked at Princess Mary, but did not at once take his arm from the waist of Mademoiselle Bourienne who had not yet seen her.

"Who's that? Why? Wait a moment!" Anatole's face seemed to say. Princess Mary looked at them in silence. She could not understand it. At last Mademoiselle Bourienne gave a scream and ran away. Anatole bowed to Princess Mary with a gay smile, as if inviting her to join in a laugh at this strange incident, and then shrugging his shoulders went to the door that led to his own apartments.

An hour later, Tíkhon came to call Princess Mary to the old prince; he added that Prince Vasíli was also there. When Tíkhon came to her Princess Mary was sitting on the sofa in her room, holding the weeping Mademoiselle Bourienne in her arms and gently stroking her hair. The princess's beautiful eyes with all their former calm radiance were looking with tender affection and pity at Mademoiselle Bourienne's pretty face.

"No, princess, I have lost your affection forever!" said Mademoiselle Bourienne.

"Why? I love you more than ever," said Princess Mary, "and I will try to do all I can for your happiness."

"But you despise me. You who are so pure can never understand being so carried away by passion. Oh, only my poor mother . . ."

"I quite understand," answered Princess Mary, with a sad smile. "Calm yourself, my dear. I will go to my father," she said, and went out.

Prince Vasíli, with one leg thrown high over the other and a snuffbox in his hand, was sitting there with a smile of deep emotion on his face, as if stirred to his heart's core and himself regretting and laughing at his own sensibility, when Princess Mary entered. He hurriedly took a pinch of snuff.

"Ah, my dear, my dear!" he began, rising and taking her by both hands. Then, sighing, he added: "My son's fate is in your hands. Decide, my dear, good, gentle Marie, whom I have always loved as a daughter!"

He drew back and a real tear appeared in his eye.

"Fr . . . fr . . ." snorted Prince Bolkónski. "The prince is making a proposition to you in his pupil's—I mean, his son's—name. Do you wish or not to be Prince Anatole Kurágin's wife? Reply: yes or no," he shouted, "and then I shall reserve the right to state my opinion also. Yes, my opinion, and only my opinion," added Prince Bolkónski, turning to Prince Vasíli and answering his imploring look. "Yes, or no?"

"My desire is never to leave you, father, never to separate my life from yours. I don't wish to marry," she answered positively, glancing at Prince Vasíli and at her father with her beautiful eyes.

"Humbug! Nonsense! Humbug, humbug, humbug!" cried Prince Bolkónski, frowning and taking his daughter's hand, he did not kiss her, but only bending his forehead to hers just touched it, and pressed her hand so that she winced and uttered a cry.

Prince Vasíli rose.

"My dear, I must tell you that this is a moment I shall never, never forget. But, my dear, will you not give us a little hope of touching this heart, so kind and generous? Say 'perhaps' . . . The future is so long. Say 'perhaps.' "

"Prince, what I have said is all there is in my heart. I thank you for the honor, but I shall never be your son's wife."

"Well, so that's finished, my dear fellow! I am very glad to have seen you. Very glad! Go back to your rooms, princess. Go!" said the old prince. "Very, very glad to have seen you," repeated he, embracing Prince Vasíli.

"My vocation is a different one," thought Princess Mary. "My vocation is to be happy with another kind of happiness, the happiness of love and self-sacrifice. And cost what it may, I will arrange poor Amélie's happiness, she loves him so passionately, and so passionately repents. I will do all I can to arrange the match between them. If he is not rich I will give her the means; I will ask my father and Andrew. I shall be so happy when she is his wife. She is so unfortunate, a stranger, alone, helpless! And, oh God, how passionately she must love him if she could so far forget herself! Perhaps I might have done the same! . . ." thought Princess Mary.

Chapter VI

IT WAS LONG SINCE THE ROSTÓVS HAD NEWS OF NICHOLAS. NOT TILL MID-WINTER WAS THE COUNT at last handed a letter addressed in his son's handwriting. On receiving it, he ran on tiptoe to his study in alarm and haste, trying to escape notice, closed the door, and began to read the letter.

Anna Mikháylovna, who always knew everything that passed in the house, on hearing of the arrival of the letter went softly into the room and found the count with it in his hand, sobbing and laughing at the same time.

Anna Mikháylovna, though her circumstances had improved, was still living with the Rostóvs.

"My dear friend?" said she, in a tone of pathetic inquiry, prepared to sympathize in any way.

The count sobbed yet more.

"Nikólenka . . . a letter . . . wa . . . a . . . s . . . wounded . . . my darling boy . . . the countess . . . promoted to be an officer . . . thank God . . . How tell the little countess!"

Anna Mikháylovna sat down beside him, with her own handkerchief wiped the tears from his eyes and from the letter, then having dried her own eyes she comforted the count, and decided that at dinner and till teatime she would prepare the countess, and after tea, with God's help, would inform her.

At dinner Anna Mikháylovna talked the whole time about the war news and about Nikólenka, twice asked when the last letter had been received from him, though she knew that already, and remarked that they might very likely be getting a letter from him that day. Each time that these hints began to make the countess anxious and she glanced uneasily at the count and at Anna Mikháylovna, the latter very adroitly turned the conversation to insignificant matters. Natásha, who, of the whole family, was the most gifted with a capacity to feel any shades of intonation, look, and expression, pricked up her ears from the beginning of the meal, and was certain that there was some secret between her father and Anna Mikháylovna, that it had something to do with her brother and that Anna Mikháylovna was preparing them for it. Bold as she was, Natásha, who knew how sensitive her mother was to anything relating to Nikólenka, did not venture to ask any questions at dinner, but she was too excited to eat anything and kept wriggling about on her chair regardless of her governess's remarks. After dinner, she rushed headlong after Anna Mikháylovna, and dashing at her, flung herself on her neck as soon as she overtook her in the sitting room.

"Auntie, darling, do tell me what it is!"

"Nothing, my dear."

"No, dearest, sweet one, honey, I won't give up—I know you know something."

Anna Mikháylovna shook her head.

"You are a little sly-boots," she said.

"A letter from Nikólenka! I'm sure of it!" exclaimed Natásha, reading confirmation in Anna Mikháylovna's face.

"But for God's sake, be careful, you know how it may affect your Mamma."

"I will, I will, only tell me! You won't? Then I will go and tell at once."

Anna Mikháylovna, in a few words, told her the contents of the letter, on condition that she should tell no one.

"No, on my true word of honor," said Natásha, crossing herself, "I won't tell anyone!" and she ran off at once to Sónya.

"Nikólenka . . . wounded . . . a letter," she announced in gleeful triumph.

"Nicholas!" was all Sónya said, instantly turning white.

Natásha, seeing the impression the of her brother's wound produced on Sónya, felt for the first time the sorrowful side of the news.

She rushed to Sónya, hugged her, and began to cry.

"A little wound, but he has been made an officer; he is well now, he wrote himself," said she through her tears.

"There now! It's true that all you women are cry-babies," remarked Pétya, pacing the room with large, resolute strides. "Now I'm very glad, very glad indeed, that my brother has distinguished himself so. You are all blubberers and understand nothing."

Natásha smiled through her tears.

"You haven't read the letter?" asked Sónya.

"No, but she said that it was all over and that he's now an officer."

"Thank God!" said Sónya, crossing herself. "But perhaps she deceived you. Let us go to Mamma."

Pétya paced the room in silence for a time.

"If I'd been in Nikólenka's place I would have killed even more of these Frenchmen," he said. "What nasty brutes they are! I'd have killed so many that there'd have been a heap of them."

"Hold your tongue, Pétya, what a goose you are!"

"I'm not a goose, but they are who cry about trifles," said Pétya.

"Do you remember him?" Natásha suddenly asked, after a moment's silence.

Sónya smiled.

"Do I remember *Nicholas?*"

"No, Sónya, but do you remember so that you remember him perfectly, remember everything?" said Natásha, with an expressive gesture, evidently wishing to give her words a very definite meaning. "I remember Nikólenka too, I remember him well," she said. "But I don't remember Borís. I don't remember him a bit."

"What! You don't remember Borís?" asked Sónya in surprise.

"It's not that I don't remember—I know what he is like, but not as I remember Nikólenka. Him—I just shut my eyes and remember, but Borís . . . No!" (She shut her eyes.) "No! there's nothing at all."

"Oh, Natásha!" said Sónya, looking ecstatically and earnestly at her friend as if she did not consider her worthy to hear what she meant to say and as if she were saying it to someone else, with whom joking was out of the question, "I am in love with your brother once for all and, whatever may happen to him or to me, shall never cease to love him as long as I live."

Natásha looked at Sónya with wondering and inquisitive eyes, and said nothing. She felt that Sónya was speaking the truth, that there was such love as Sónya was speaking of. But Natásha had not yet felt anything like it. She believed it could be, but did not understand it.

"Shall you write to him?" she asked.

Sónya became thoughtful. The question of how to write to *Nicholas,* and whether she ought to write, tormented her. Now that he was already an officer and a wounded hero, would it be right to remind him of herself and, as it might seem, of the obligations to her he had taken on himself?

"I don't know. I think if he writes, I will write too," she said, blushing.

"And you won't feel ashamed to write to him?"

Sónya smiled.

"No."

"And I should be ashamed to write to Borís. I'm not going to."

"Why should you be ashamed?"

"Well, I don't know. It's awkward, and would make me ashamed."

"And I know why she'd be ashamed," said Pétya, offended by Natásha's previous remark. "It's because she was in love with that fat one in spectacles" (that was how Pétya described his namesake, the new Count Bezúkhov) "and now she's in love with that singer" (he meant Natásha's Italian singing master), "that's why she's ashamed!"

"Pétya, you're a stupid!" said Natásha.

"Not more stupid than you, madam," said the nine-year-old Pétya, with the air of an old brigadier.

The countess had been prepared by Anna Mikháylovna's hints at dinner. On retiring to her own room, she sat in an arm-chair, her eyes fixed on a miniature portrait of her son on the lid of a snuffbox, while the tears kept coming into her eyes. Anna Mikháylovna, with the letter, came on tiptoe to the countess's door and paused.

"Don't come in," she said to the old count who was following her. "Come later." And she went in, closing the door behind her.

The count put his ear to the keyhole and listened.

At first he heard the sound of indifferent voices, then Anna Mikháylovna's voice alone in a long speech, then a cry, then silence, then both voices together with glad intonations, and then footsteps. Anna Mikháylovna opened the door. Her face wore the proud expression of a surgeon who has just performed a difficult operation and admits the public to appreciate his skill.

"It is done!" she said to the count, pointing triumphantly to the countess, who sat holding in one hand the snuffbox with its portrait and in the other the letter, and pressing them alternately to her lips.

When she saw the count, she stretched out her arms to him, embraced his bald head, over which she again looked at the letter and the portrait, and in order to press them again to her lips, she slightly pushed away the bald head. Véra, Natásha, Sónya, and Pétya now entered the room, and the reading of the letter began. After a brief description of the campaign and the two battles in which he had taken part, and his promotion, Nicholas said that he kissed his father's and mother's hand asking for their blessing, and that he kissed Véra, Natásha, and Pétya. Besides that, he sent greetings to Monsieur Schelling, Madame Schoss and his old nurse, and asked them to kiss for him "dear Sónya, whom he loved and thought of just the same as ever." When she heard this Sónya blushed so that tears came into her eyes, and unable to bear the looks turned upon her, ran away into the dancing hall, whirled round it at full speed with her dress puffed out like a balloon, and flushed and smiling, plumped down on the floor. The countess was crying.

"Why are you crying, Mamma?" asked Véra. "From all he says one should be glad and not cry."

This was quite true, but the count, the countess, and Natásha, looked at her reproachfully. "And who is it she takes after?" thought the countess.

Nicholas's letter was read over hundreds of times, and those who were considered worthy to hear it had to come to the countess, for she did not let it out of her hands. The tutors came, and the nurses, and Dmítri, and several acquaintances, and the countess reread the letter each time with fresh pleasure and each time discovered in it fresh proofs of Nikólenka's virtues. How strange, how extraordinary, how joyful it seemed, that her son, the scarcely perceptible motion of whose tiny limbs she had felt twenty years ago within her, that son about whom she used to have quarrels with the too indulgent count, that son who had first learned to say "pear" and then "granny," that this son should now be away in a foreign land amid strange surroundings, a manly warrior doing some kind of man's work of his own, without help or guidance. The universal experience of ages, showing that children do grow imperceptibly from the cradle to manhood, did not exist for the countess. Her son's growth toward manhood, at each of its stages, had seemed as extraordinary to her as if there had never existed the millions of human beings who grew up in the same way. As twenty years before, it seemed impossible that the little creature who lived somewhere under her heart would ever cry, suck her breast, and begin to speak, so now she could not believe that that little creature could be this strong, brave man, this model son and officer that, judging by this letter, he now was.

"What a *style!* How charmingly he describes!" said she, reading the descriptive part of the letter. "And what a soul! Not a word about himself. . . . Not a word! About some Denísov or other, though he himself, I dare say, is braver than any of them. He says nothing about his sufferings. What a heart! How like him it is! And how he has remembered everybody! Not forgetting anyone. I always said when he was only so high—I always said. . . ."

For more than a week preparations were being made, rough drafts of letters to Nicholas from all the household were written and copied out, while under the supervision of the countess and the solicitude of the count, money and all things necessary for the uniform and equipment of the newly commissioned officer were collected. Anna Mikháylovna, practical woman that she was, had even managed by favor with army authorities to secure advantageous means of communication for herself and her son. She had opportunities of sending her letters to the Grand Duke Constantine Pávlovich, who commanded the Guards. The Rostóvs supposed that *The Russian Guards, Abroad,* was quite a definite address, and that if a letter reached the Grand Duke in command of the Guards there was no reason why it should not reach the Pávlograd regiment, which was presumably somewhere in the same neighborhood. And so it was decided to send the letters and money by the Grand Duke's courier to Borís and Borís was to forward them to Nicholas. The letters were from the old count, the countess, Pétya, Véra, Natásha and Sónya, and finally there were six thousand rubles for his outfit and various other things the old count sent to his son.

Chapter VII

On the 12th of November, Kutúzov's active army, in camp before Olmütz, was preparing to be reviewed next day by the two Emperors—the Russian and the Austrian. The Guards, just arrived from Russia, spent the night ten miles from Olmütz, and next morning were to come straight to the review, reaching the field at Olmütz by ten o'clock.

That day Nicholas Rostóv received a letter from Borís, telling him that the Ismáylov regiment was quartered for the night ten miles from Olmütz and that he wanted to see him as he had a letter and money for him. Rostóv was particularly in need of money now that the troops, after their active service, were stationed near Olmütz and the camp swarmed with well-provisioned sutlers and Austrian Jews offering all sorts of tempting wares. The Pávlograds held feast after feast, celebrating awards they had received for the campaign, and made expeditions to Olmütz to visit a certain Caroline the Hungarian, who had recently opened a restaurant there with girls as waitresses. Rostóv, who had just celebrated his promotion to a cornetcy and bought Denísov's horse, Bedouin, was in debt all round, to his comrades and the sutlers. On receiving Borís's letter he rode with a fellow-officer to Olmütz, dined there, drank a bottle of wine, and then set off alone to the Guards' camp to find his old playmate. Rostóv had not yet had time to get his uniform. He had on a shabby cadet jacket, decorated with a soldier's cross, equally shabby cadet's riding-breeches lined with worn leather, and an officer's saber with a sword-knot. The Don horse he was riding was one he had bought from a Cossack during the campaign, and he wore a crumpled hussar cap stuck jauntily back on one side of his head. As he rode up to the camp he thought how he would impress Borís and all his comrades of the Guards by his appearance—that of a fighting hussar who had been under fire.

The Guards had made their whole march as if on a pleasure trip, parading their cleanliness and discipline. They had come by easy stages, their knapsacks conveyed on carts, and the Austrian authorities had provided excellent dinners for the officers at every halting place. The regiments had entered and left the town with their bands playing, and by the Grand Duke's orders the men had marched all the way in step (a practice on which the Guards prided themselves), the officers on foot and at their proper posts. Borís had been quartered, and had marched all the way, with Berg who was already in command of a company. Berg, who had obtained his captaincy during the campaign, had gained the confidence of his superiors by his promptitude and accuracy and had arranged his money matters very satisfactorily. Borís, during the campaign, had made the acquaintance of many persons who might prove useful to him, and by a letter of recommendation he had brought from Pierre had become acquainted with Prince Andrew Bolkónski, through whom he hoped to obtain a post on the commander-in-chief's staff. Berg and Borís having rested after yesterday's march, were sitting, clean and neatly dressed, at a round table in the clean quarters allotted to them, playing chess. Berg held a smoking pipe between his knees. Borís, in the accurate way characteristic of him, was building a little pyramid of chessmen with his delicate white fingers while awaiting Berg's move, and watched his opponent's face, evidently thinking about the game as he always thought only of whatever he was engaged on.

"Well, how are you going to get out of that?" he remarked.

"We'll try to," replied Berg, touching a pawn and then removing his hand.

At that moment the door opened.

"Here he is at last!" shouted Rostóv. "And Berg too! Oh, you *petisenfans, allay cushay dormir!*" he exclaimed, imitating his Russian nurse's French, at which he and Borís used to laugh long ago.

"Dear me, how you have changed!"

Borís rose to meet Rostóv, but in doing so did not omit to steady and replace some chessmen that were falling. He was about to embrace his friend, but Nicholas avoided him. With that peculiar feeling of youth, that dread of beaten tracks, and wish to express itself in a manner different from that of its elders which is often insincere, Nicholas wished to do something special on meeting his friend. He wanted to pinch him, push him, do anything but kiss him—a thing everybody did. But notwithstanding this, Borís embraced him in a quiet friendly way and kissed him three times.

They had not met for nearly half a year and, being at the age when young men take their first steps on life's road, each saw immense changes in the other, quite a new reflection of the society in which they had taken those first steps. Both had changed greatly since they last met and both were in a hurry to show the changes that had taken place in them.

"Oh, you damned dandies! Clean and fresh as if you'd been to a fête, not like us sinners of the line," cried Rostóv, with martial swagger and with baritone notes in his voice, new to Borís, pointing to his own mud-bespattered breeches. The German landlady, hearing Rostóv's loud voice, popped her head in at the door.

"Eh, is she pretty?" he asked with a wink.

"Why do you shout so? You'll frighten them!" said Borís. "I did not expect you today," he added. "I only sent you the note yesterday by Bolkónski—an adjutant of Kutúzov's, who's a friend of mine. I did not think he would get it to you so quickly. . . . Well, how are you? Been under fire already?" asked Borís.

Without answering, Rostóv shook the soldier's Cross of St. George fastened to the cording of his uniform and, indicating a bandaged arm, glanced at Berg with a smile.

"As you see," he said.

"Indeed? Yes, yes!" said Borís, with a smile. "And we too have had a splendid march. You know, of course, that his Imperial Highness rode with our regiment all the time, so that we had every comfort and every advantage. What receptions we had in Poland! What dinners and balls! I can't tell you. And the Tsarévich was very gracious to all our officers."

And the two friends told each other of their doings, the one of his hussar revels, and life in the fighting line, the other of the pleasures and advantages of service under members of the Imperial family.

"Oh, you Guards!" said Rostóv. "I say, send for some wine."

Borís made a grimace.

"If you really want it," said he.

He went to his bed, drew a purse from under the clean pillow, and sent for wine.

"Yes, and I have some money and a letter to give you," he added.

Rostóv took the letter, and throwing the money on the sofa, put both arms on the table and began to read. After reading a few lines, he glanced angrily at Berg, then, meeting his eyes, hid his face behind the letter.

"Well, they've sent you a tidy sum," said Berg, eying the heavy purse that sank into the sofa. "As for us, count, we get along on our pay. I can tell you for myself . . ."

"I say, Berg, my dear fellow," said Rostóv, "when you get a letter from home and meet one of your own people whom you want to talk everything over with, and I happen to be there, I'll go at once, to be out of your way! Do go somewhere, anywhere . . . to the devil!" he exclaimed, and immediately seizing him by the shoulder and looking amiably into his face, evidently wishing to soften the rudeness of his words, he added, "Don't be hurt, my dear fellow; you know I speak from my heart as to an old acquaintance."

"Oh, don't mention it, count! I quite understand," said Berg, getting up and speaking in a muffled and guttural voice.

"Go across to our hosts': they invited you," added Borís.

Berg put on the cleanest of coats, without a spot or speck of dust, stood before a looking-glass and brushed the hair on his temples upward, in the way affected by the Emperor Alexander, and, having assured himself from the way Rostóv looked at it that his coat had been noticed, left the room with a pleasant smile.

"Oh dear, what a beast I am!" muttered Rostóv, as he read the letter.

"Why?"

"Oh, what a pig I am, not to have written and to have given them such a fright! Oh, what a pig I am!" he repeated, flushing suddenly. "Well, have you sent Gabriel for some wine? All right let's have some!"

In the letter from his parents was enclosed a letter of recommendation to Bagratión which the old countess at Anna Mikháylovna's advice had obtained through an acquaintance and sent to her son, asking him to take it to its destination and make use of it.

"What nonsense! Much I need it!" said Rostóv, throwing the letter under the table.

"Why have you thrown that away?" asked Borís.

"It is some letter of recommendation . . . what the devil do I want it for!"

"Why 'What the devil'?" said Borís, picking it up and reading the address. "This letter would be of great use to you."

"I want nothing, and I won't be anyone's adjutant."

"Why not?" inquired Borís.

"It's a lackey's job!"

"You are still the same dreamer, I see," remarked Borís, shaking his head.

"And you're still the same diplomatist! But that's not the point. . . . Come, how are you?" asked Rostóv.

"Well, as you see. So far everything's all right, but I confess I should much like to be an adjutant and not remain at the front."

"Why?"

"Because when once a man starts on military service, he should try to make as successful a career of it as possible."

"Oh, that's it!" said Rostóv, evidently thinking of something else.

He looked intently and inquiringly into his friend's eyes, evidently trying in vain to find the answer to some question.

Old Gabriel brought in the wine.

"Shouldn't we now send for Berg?" asked Borís. "He would drink with you. I can't."

"Well, send for him . . . and how do you get on with that German?" asked Rostóv, with a contemptuous smile.

"He is a very, very nice, honest, and pleasant fellow," answered Borís.

Again Rostóv looked intently into Borís's eyes and sighed. Berg returned, and over the bottle of wine conversation between the three officers became animated. The Guardsmen told Rostóv of their march and how they had been made much of in Russia, Poland, and abroad. They spoke of the sayings and doings of their commander, the Grand Duke, and told stories of his kindness and irascibility. Berg, as usual, kept silent when the subject did not relate to himself, but in connection with the stories of the Grand Duke's quick temper he related with gusto how in Galicia he had managed to deal with the Grand Duke when the latter made a tour of the regiments and was annoyed at the irregularity of a movement. With a pleasant smile Berg related how the Grand Duke had ridden up to him in a violent passion, shouting: "Arnauts!" (Arnauts was the Tsarévich's favorite expression when he was in a rage) and called for the company commander.

"Would you believe it, count, I was not at all alarmed, because I knew I was right. Without boasting, you know, I may say that I know the Army Orders by heart and know the Regulations as well as I do the Lord's Prayer. So, count, there never is any negligence in my company, and so my conscience was at ease. I came forward. . . ." (Berg stood up and showed how he presented himself, with his hand to his cap, and really it would have been difficult for a face to express greater respect and self-complacency than his did.) "Well, he stormed at me, as the saying is, stormed and stormed and stormed! It was not a matter of life but rather of death, as the saying is. 'Albanians!' and 'devils!' and 'To Siberia!' " said Berg with a sagacious smile. "I knew I was in the right so I kept silent; was not that best, count? . . . 'Hey, are you dumb?' he shouted. Still I remained silent. And what do you think, count? The next day it was not even mentioned in the Orders of the Day. That's what keeping one's head means. That's the way, count," said Berg, lighting his pipe and emitting rings of smoke.

"Yes, that was fine," said Rostóv, smiling.

But Borís noticed that he was preparing to make fun of Berg, and skillfully changed the subject. He asked him to tell them how and where he got his wound. This pleased Rostóv and he began talking about it, and as he went on became more and more animated. He told them of his Schön Grabern affair, just as those who have taken part in a battle generally do describe it, that is, as they would like it to have been, as they have heard it described by others, and as sounds well, but not at all as it really was. Rostóv was a truthful young man and would on no account have told a deliberate lie. He began his story meaning to tell everything just as it happened, but imperceptibly, involuntarily, and inevitably he lapsed into falsehood. If he had told the truth to his hearers—who like himself had often heard stories of attacks and had formed a definite idea of what an attack was and were expecting to hear just such a story—they would either not have believed him or, still worse, would have thought that Rostóv was himself to blame since what generally happens to the narrators of cavalry attacks had not happened to him. He could not tell them simply that everyone went at a trot and that he fell off his horse and sprained his arm and then ran as hard as he could from a Frenchman into the wood. Besides, to tell everything as it really happened, it would have been necessary to make an effort of will to tell only what happened. It is very difficult to tell the truth, and young people are rarely capable of it. His hearers expected a story of how beside himself and all aflame with excitement, he had flown like a storm at the square, cut his way in, slashed right and left, how his saber had tasted flesh and he had fallen exhausted, and so on. And so he told them all that.

In the middle of his story, just as he was saying: "You cannot imagine what a strange frenzy one experiences during an attack," Prince Andrew, whom Borís was expecting, entered the room. Prince Andrew, who liked to help young men, was flattered by being asked for his assistance and being well-disposed toward Borís, who had managed to please him the day before, he wished to do what the young man wanted. Having been sent with papers from Kutúzov to the Tsarévich, he looked in on Borís, hoping to find him alone. When he came in and saw a hussar of the line recounting his military exploits (Prince Andrew could not endure that sort of man), he gave Borís a pleasant smile, frowned as with half-closed eyes he looked at Rostóv, bowed slightly and wearily and sat down languidly on the sofa: he felt it unpleasant to have dropped in on bad company. Rostóv flushed up on noticing this, but he did not care, this was a mere stranger. Glancing, however, at Borís, he saw that he too seemed ashamed of the hussar of the line.

In spite of Prince Andrew's disagreeable, ironical tone, in spite of the contempt with which Rostóv, from his *fighting* army point of view, regarded all these little adjutants on the staff, of whom the newcomer was evidently one, Rostóv felt confused, blushed, and became silent. Borís inquired what news there might be on the staff, and what, without indiscretion, one might ask about our plans.

"We shall probably advance," replied Bolkónski, evidently reluctant to say more in the presence of a stranger.

Berg took the opportunity to ask, with great politeness, whether, as was rumored, the allowance of forage-money to captains of companies would be doubled. To this Prince Andrew answered with a smile that he could give no opinion on such an important government order, and Berg laughed gaily.

"As to your business," Prince Andrew continued, addressing Borís, "we will talk of it later" (and he looked round at Rostóv). "Come to me after the review and we will do what is possible."

And, having glanced round the room, Prince Andrew turned to Rostóv, whose state of unconquerable childish embarrassment now changing to anger he did not condescend to notice, and said:

"I think you were talking of the Schön Grabern affair? Were you there?"

"I was there," said Rostóv angrily, as if intending to insult the aide-de-camp.

Bolkónski noticed the hussar's state of mind, and it amused him. With a slightly contemptuous smile, he said:

"Yes, there are many stories now told about that affair!"

"Yes, stories!" repeated Rostóv loudly, looking with eyes suddenly grown furious, now at Borís, now at Bolkónski. "Yes, many stories! But our stories are the stories of men who have been under the enemy's fire! *Our* stories have some weight, not like the stories of those fellows on the staff who get rewards without doing anything!"

"Of whom you imagine me to be one?" said Prince Andrew, with a quiet and particularly amiable smile.

A strange feeling of exasperation and yet of respect for this man's self-possession mingled at that moment in Rostóv's soul.

"I am not talking about you," he said, "I don't know you and, frankly, I don't want to. I am speaking of the staff in general."

"And I will tell you this," Prince Andrew interrupted in a tone of quiet authority, "you wish to insult me, and I am ready to agree with you that it would be very easy to do so if you haven't sufficient self-respect, but admit that the time and place are very badly chosen. In a day or two we shall all have to take part in a greater and more serious duel, and besides, Drubetskóy, who says he is an old friend of yours, is not at all to blame that my face has the misfortune to displease you. However," he added rising, "you know my name and where to find me, but don't forget that I do not regard either myself or you as having been at all insulted, and as a man older than you, my advice is to let the matter drop. Well then, on Friday after the review I shall expect you, Drubetskóy. *Au revoir!*" exclaimed Prince Andrew, and with a bow to them both he went out.

Only when Prince Andrew was gone did Rostóv think of what he ought to have said. And he was still more angry at having omitted to say it. He ordered his horse at once, and coldly taking leave of Borís, rode home. Should he go to headquarters next day and challenge that affected adjutant, or really let the matter drop, was the question that worried him all the way. He thought angrily of the pleasure he would have at seeing the fright of that small and frail but proud man when covered by his pistol, and then he felt with surprise that of all the men he knew there was none he would so much like to have for a friend as that very adjutant whom he so hated.

Chapter VIII

THE DAY AFTER ROSTÓV HAD BEEN TO SEE BORÍS, A REVIEW WAS HELD OF THE AUSTRIAN AND Russian troops, both those freshly arrived from Russia and those who had been campaigning under Kutúzov. The two Emperors, the Russian with his heir the Tsarévich, and the Austrian with the Archduke, inspected the Allied army of eighty thousand men.

From early morning the smart clean troops were on the move, forming up on the field before the fortress. Now thousands of feet and bayonets moved and halted at the officers' command, turned with banners flying, formed up at intervals, and wheeled round other similar masses of infantry in different uniforms; now was heard the rhythmic beat of hoofs and the jingling of showy cavalry in blue, red and green braided uniforms, with smartly dressed bandsmen in front mounted on black, roan, or gray horses; then again, spreading out with the brazen clatter of the polished shining cannon that quivered on the gun-carriages and with the smell of linstocks, came the artillery which crawled between the infantry and cavalry and took up its appointed position. Not only the generals in full parade uniforms, with their thin or thick waists drawn in to the utmost, their red necks squeezed into their stiff collars, and wearing scarves and all their decorations, not only the elegant, pomaded officers, but every soldier with his freshly washed and shaven face and his weapons clean and polished to the utmost, and every horse groomed till its coat shone like satin and every hair of its wetted mane lay smooth—felt that no small matter was happening, but an important and solemn affair. Every general and every soldier was conscious of his own insignificance, aware of being but a drop in that ocean of men, and yet at the same time was conscious of his strength as a part of that enormous whole.

From early morning strenuous activities and efforts had begun and by ten o'clock all had been brought into due order. The ranks were drown up on the vast field. The whole army was extended in three lines: the cavalry in front, behind it the artillery, and behind that again the infantry.

A space like a street was left between each two lines of troops. The three parts of that army were sharply distinguished: Kutúzov's fighting army (with the Pávlograds on the right flank of the front); those recently arrived from Russia, both Guards and regiments of the line; and the Austrian troops. But they all stood in the same lines, under one command, and in a like order.

Like wind over leaves ran an excited whisper: "They're coming! They're coming!" Alarmed voices were heard, and a stir of final preparation swept over all the troops.

From the direction of Olmütz in front of them, a group was seen approaching. And at that moment, though the day was still, a light gust of wind blowing over the army slightly stirred the streamers on the lances and the unfolded standards fluttered against their staffs. It looked as if by that slight motion the army itself was expressing its joy at the approach of the Emperors. One voice was heard shouting: "Eyes front!" Then, like the crowing of cocks at sunrise, this was repeated by others from various sides and all became silent.

In the deathlike stillness only the tramp of horses was heard. This was the Emperors' suites. The Emperors rode up to the flank, and the trumpets of the first cavalry regiment played the general march. It seemed as though not the trumpeters were playing, but as if the army itself, rejoicing at the Emperors' approach, had naturally burst into music. Amid these sounds, only the youthful kindly voice of the Emperor Alexander was clearly heard. He gave the words of greeting, and the first regiment roared "hurrah!" so deafeningly, continuously and joyfully that the men themselves were awed by their multitude and the immensity of the power they constituted.

Rostóv standing in the front lines of Kutúzov's army which the Tsar approached first, experienced the same feeling as every other man in that army: a feeling of self-forgetfulness, a proud consciousness of might, and a passionate attraction to him who was the cause of this triumph.

He felt that at a single word from that man all this vast mass (and he himself an insignificant atom in it) would go through fire and water, commit crime, die, or perform deeds of highest heroism, and so he could not but tremble and his heart stand still at the imminence of that word.

"Hurrah! Hurrah! Hurrah!" thundered from all sides, one regiment after another greeting the Tsar with the strains of the march, and then "hurrah!" . . . Then the general march, and again "hurrah! hurrah!" growing ever stronger and fuller, and merging into a deafening roar.

Till the Tsar reached it, each regiment in its silence and immobility seemed like a lifeless body, but as soon as he came up it became alive, its thunder joining the roar of the whole line along which he had already passed. Through the terrible and deafening roar of those voices, amid the square masses of troops standing motionless as if turned to stone, hundreds of riders composing the suites moved carelessly but symmetrically and above all freely, and in front of them two men—the Emperors. Upon them the undivided, tensely passionate attention of that whole mass of men was concentrated.

The handsome young Emperor Alexander, in the uniform of the Horse-Guards, wearing a cocked hat with its peaks front and back, with his pleasant face and resonant though not loud voice, attracted everyone's attention.

Rostóv was not far from the trumpeters, and with his keen sight had recognized the Tsar and watched his approach. When he was within twenty paces, and Nicholas could clearly distinguish every detail of his handsome, happy young face, he experienced a feeling tenderness and ecstasy such as he had never before known. Every trait and every movement of the Tsar's seemed to him enchanting.

Stopping in front of the Pávlograds, the Tsar said something in French to the Austrian Emperor and smiled.

Seeing that smile, Rostóv involuntarily smiled himself and felt a still stronger flow of love for his sovereign. He longed to show that love in some way, and knowing that this was impossible was ready to cry. The Tsar called the colonel of the regiment and said a few words to him.

"Oh God, what would happen to me if the Emperor spoke to me?" thought Rostóv. "I should die of happiness!"

The Tsar addressed the officers also: "I thank you all, gentlemen, I thank you with my whole heart." To Rostóv every word sounded like a voice from heaven. How gladly would he have died at once for his Tsar!

"You have earned the St. George's standards and will be worthy of them."

"Oh, to die, to die for him," thought Rostóv.

The Tsar said something more which Rostóv did not hear, and the soldiers, straining their lungs, shouted "hurrah!"

Rostóv too, bending over his saddle, shouted "hurrah!" with all his might, feeling that he would like to injure himself by that shout, if only to express his rapture fully.

The Tsar stopped a few minutes in front of the hussars as if undecided.

"How can the Emperor be undecided?" thought Rostóv, but then even this indecision appeared to him majestic and enchanting, like everything else the Tsar did.

That hesitation lasted only an instant. The Tsar's foot, in the narrow pointed boot then fashionable, touched the groin of the bob-tailed bay mare he rode, his hand in a white glove gathered up the reins, and he moved off accompanied by an irregularly swaying sea of aides-de-camp. Farther and farther he rode away, stopping at other regiments, till at last only his white plumes were visible to Rostóv from amid the suites that surrounded the Emperors.

Among the gentlemen of the suite, Rostóv noticed Bolkónski, sitting his horse indolently and carelessly. Rostóv recalled their quarrel of yesterday and the question presented itself whether he ought or ought not to challenge Bolkónski. "Of course not!" he now thought. "Is it worth thinking or speaking of it at such a moment? At a time of such love, such rapture, and such self-sacrifice, what do any of our quarrels and affronts matter? I love and forgive everybody now."

When the Emperor had passed nearly all the regiments, the troops began a ceremonial march past him, and Rostóv on Bedouin, recently purchased from Denísov, rode past too, at the rear of his squadron—that is, alone and in full view of the Emperor.

Before he reached him, Rostóv, who was a splendid horseman, spurred Bedouin twice and successfully put him to the showy trot in which the animal went when excited. Bending his foaming muzzle to his chest, his tail extended, Bedouin, as if also conscious of the Emperor's eye upon him, passed splendidly, lifting his feet with a high and graceful action, as if flying through the air without touching the ground.

Rostóv himself, his legs well back and his stomach drawn in and feeling himself one with his horse, rode past the Emperor with a frowning but blissful face "like a vewy devil," as Denísov expressed it.

"Fine fellows, the Pávlograds!" remarked the Emperor.

"My God, how happy I should be if he ordered me to leap into the fire this instant!" thought Rostóv.

When the review was over, the newly arrived officers, and also Kutzov's, collected in groups and began to talk about the awards, about the Austrians and their uniforms, about their lines, about Bonaparte, and how badly the latter would fare now, especially if the Essen corps arrived and Prussia took our side.

But the talk in every group was chiefly about the Emperor Alexander. His every word and movement was described with ecstasy.

They all had but one wish: to advance as soon as possible against the enemy under the Emperor's command. Commanded by the Emperor himself they could not fail to vanquish anyone, be it whom it might: so thought Rostóv and most of the officers after the review.

All were then more confident of victory than the winning of two battles would have made them.

Chapter IX

THE DAY AFTER THE REVIEW, BORÍS IN HIS BEST UNIFORM AND WITH HIS COMRADE BERG'S BEST wishes for success, rode to Olmütz to see Bolkónski, wishing to profit by his friendliness and obtain for himself the best post he could—preferably that of adjutant to some important personage, a position in the army which seemed to him most attractive. "It is all very well for Rostóv, whose father sends him ten thousand rubles at a time, to talk about not wishing to cringe to anybody and not be anyone's lackey, but I who have nothing but my brains, have to make a career, and must not miss opportunities, but must avail myself of them!" he reflected.

He did not find Prince Andrew in Olmütz that day, but the appearance of the town where the headquarters and the diplomatic corps were stationed, and the two Emperors were living with their suites, households, and courts, only strengthened his desire to belong to that higher world.

He knew no one, and despite his smart Guardsman's uniform, all these exalted personages passing in the streets in their elegant carriages with their plumes, ribbons, and medals, both courtiers and military men, seemed so immeasurably above him, an insignificant officer of the Guards, that they not only did not wish to, but simply could not, be aware of his existence. At the quarters of the commander-in-chief, Kutúzov, where he inquired for Bolkónski, all the adjutants and even the orderlies looked at him as if they wished to impress on him that a great many officers like him were always coming there and that everybody was heartily sick of them. In spite of this, or rather because of it, next day, November the 15th, after dinner he again went to Olmütz, and entering the house occupied by Kutúzov, asked for Bolkónski. Prince Andrew was in and Borís was shown into a large hall probably formerly used for dancing, but in which five beds now stood, and furniture of various kinds: a table, chairs, and a clavichord. One adjutant, nearest the door, was sitting at the table in a Persian dressing-gown, writing. Another, the red, stout Nesvítski, lay on a bed with his arms under his head, laughing with an officer who had sat down beside him. A third was playing a Viennese valse on the clavichord, while a fourth, lying on the clavichord, sang the tune. Bolkónski was not there. None of these gentlemen changed his position on seeing Borís. The one who was writing and whom Borís addressed, turned round crossly and told him Bolkónski was on duty and that he should go through the door on the left into the reception room if he wished to see him. Borís thanked him and went to the reception room, where he found some ten officers and generals.

When he entered, Prince Andrew, his eyes drooping contemptuously (with that peculiar expression of polite weariness which plainly says, "If it were not my duty I would not talk to you for a moment"), was listening to an old Russian general with decorations, who stood very erect, almost on tiptoe, with a soldier's obsequious expression on his purple face, reporting something.

"Very well, then, be so good as to wait," said Prince Andrew to the general, in Russian, speaking with the French intonation he affected when he wished to speak contemptuously, and noticing Borís, Prince Andrew, paying no more heed to the general who ran after him imploring him to hear something more, nodded and turned to him with a cheerful smile.

At that moment Borís clearly realized what he had before surmized, that in the army, besides the subordination and discipline prescribed in the military code, which he and the others knew in the regiment, there was another, more important, subordination, which made this tight-laced, purple-faced general wait respectfully while Captain Prince Andrew, for his own pleasure, chose to chat with Lieutenant Drubetskóy. More than ever was Borís resolved to serve in future not according to the written code, but under this unwritten law. He felt now that merely by having been recommended to Prince Andrew he had already risen above the general who at the front had the power to annihilate him, a lieutenant of the Guards. Prince Andrew came up to him and took his hand.

"I am very sorry you did not find me in yesterday. I was fussing about with Germans all day. We went with Weyrother to survey the dispositions. When Germans start being accurate, there's no end to it!"

Borís smiled, as if he understood what Prince Andrew was alluding to as something generally known. But it the first time he had heard Weyrother's name, or even the term "dispositions."

"Well, my dear fellow, so you still want to be an adjutant? I have been thinking about you."

"Yes, I was thinking"—for some reason Borís could not help blushing—"of asking the commander-in-chief. He has had a letter from Prince Kurágin about me. I only wanted to ask because I fear the Guards won't be in action," he added as if in apology.

"All right, all right. We'll talk it over," replied Prince Andrew. "Only let me report this gentleman's business, and I shall be at your disposal."

While Prince Andrew went to report about the purple-faced general, that gentleman—evidently not sharing Borís's conception of the advantages of the unwritten code of subordination—looked so fixedly at the presumptuous lieutenant who had prevented his finishing what he had to say to the adjutant, that Borís felt uncomfortable. He turned away and waited impatiently for Prince Andrew's return from the commander-in-chief's room.

"You see, my dear fellow, I have been thinking about you," said Prince Andrew when they had gone into the large room where the clavichord was. "It's no use your going to the commander-in-chief. He would say a lot of pleasant things, ask you to dinner" ("that would not be bad as regards the unwritten code," thought Borís), "but nothing more would come of it. There will soon be a battalion of us aides-de-camp and adjutants! But this is what we'll do: I have a good friend, an adjutant-general and an excellent fellow, Prince Dolgorúkov; and though you may not know it, the fact is that now Kutúzov with his staff and all of us count for nothing. Everything is now centered round the Emperor. So we will go to Dolgorúkov; I have to go there anyhow, and I have already spoken to him about you. We shall see whether he cannot attach you to himself or find a place for you somewhere nearer the sun."

Prince Andrew always became specially keen when he had to guide a young man and help him to worldly success. Under cover of obtaining help of this kind for another, which from pride he would never accept for himself, he kept in touch with the circle which confers success and which attracted him. He very readily took up Borís's cause and went with him to Dolgorúkov.

It was late in the evening when they entered the palace at Olmütz occupied by the Emperors and their retinues.

That same-day a council of war had been held in which all the members of the Hofkriegsrath and both Emperors took part. At that council, contrary to the views of the old generals Kutúzov and Prince Schwartzenberg, it had been decided to advance immediately and give battle to Bonaparte. The council of war was just over when Prince Andrew accompanied by Borís arrived at the palace to find Dolgorúkov. Everyone at headquarters was still under the spell of the day's council, at which the party of the young had triumphed. The voices of those who counseled delay and advised waiting for something else before advancing had been so completely silenced and their arguments confuted by such conclusive evidence of the advantages of attacking that what had been discussed at the council—the coming battle and the victory that would certainly result from it—no longer seemed to be in the future but in the past. All the advantages were on our side. Our enormous forces, undoubtedly superior to Napoleon's, were concentrated in one place, the troops inspired by the Emperors' presence were eager for action. The strategic position where the operations would take place was familiar in all its details to the Austrian General Weyrother: a lucky accident had ordained that the Austrian army should maneuver the previous year on the very fields where the French had now to be fought; the adjacent locality was known and shown in every detail on the maps, and Bonaparte, evidently weakened, was undertaking nothing.

Dolgorúkov, one of the warmest advocates of an attack, had just returned from the council, tired and exhausted but eager and proud of the victory that had been gained. Prince Andrew introduced his protégé, but Prince Dolgorúkov politely and firmly pressing his hand said nothing to Borís, and evidently unable to suppress the thoughts which were uppermost in his mind at that moment, addressed Prince Andrew in French.

"Ah, my dear fellow, what a battle we have gained! God grant that the one that will result from it will be as victorious! However, dear fellow," he said abruptly and eagerly, "I must confess to having been unjust to the Austrians and especially to Weyrother. What exactitude, what minuteness, what knowledge of the locality, what foresight for every eventuality, every possibility even to the smallest detail! No, my dear fellow, no conditions better than our present ones could have been devised. This combination of Austrian precision with Russian valor—what more could be wished for?"

"So the attack is definitely resolved on?" asked Bolkónski.

"And do you know, my dear fellow, it seems to me that Bonaparte has decidedly lost his bearings, you know that a letter was received from him today for the Emperor." Dolgorúkov smiled significantly.

"Is that so? And what did he say?" inquired Bolkónski.

"What can he say? Tra-di-ri-di-ra and so on . . . merely to gain time. I tell you he is in our hands, that's certain! But what was most amusing," he continued, with a sudden, good-natured laugh, "was that we could not think how to address the reply! If not as 'Consul' and of course not as 'Emperor,' it seemed to me it should be to 'General Bonaparte.' "

"But between not recognizing him as Emperor and calling him General Bonaparte, there is a difference," remarked Bolkónski.

"That's just it," interrupted Dolgorúkov quickly, laughing. "You know Bilíbin—he's a very clever fellow. He suggested addressing him as 'Usurper and Enemy of Mankind.' "

Dolgorúkov laughed merrily.

"Only that?" said Bolkónski.

"All the same, it was Bilíbin who found a suitable form for the address. He is a wise and clever fellow."

"What was it?"

"To the Head of the French Government . . . *Au chef du gouvernement français,*" said Dolgorúkov, with grave satisfaction. "Good, wasn't it?"

"Yes, but he will dislike it extremely," said Bolkónski.

"Oh yes, very much! My brother knows him, he's dined with him—the present Emperor—more than once in Paris, and tells me he never met a more cunning or subtle diplomatist—you know, a combination of French adroitness and Italian play-acting! Do you know the tale about him and Count Markóv? Count Markóv was the only man who knew how to handle him. You know the story of the handkerchief? It is delightful!"

And the talkative Dolgorúkov, turning now to Borís, now to Prince Andrew, told how Bonaparte wishing to test Markóv, our ambassador, purposely dropped a handkerchief in front of him and stood looking at Markóv, probably expecting Markóv to pick it up for him, and how Markóv immediately dropped his own beside it and picked it up without touching Bonaparte's.

"Delightful!" said Bolkónski. "But I have come to you, prince, as a petitioner on behalf of this young man. You see . . ." but before Prince Andrew could finish, an aide-de-camp came in to summon Dolgorúkov to the Emperor.

"Oh, what a nuisance," said Dolgorúkov, getting up hurriedly and pressing the hands of Prince Andrew and Borís. "You know I should be very glad to do all in my power both for you and for this dear young man." Again he pressed the hand of the latter with an expression of good-natured, sincere, and animated levity. "But you see . . . another time!"

Borís was excited by the thought of being so close to the higher powers as he felt himself to be at that moment. He was conscious that here he was in contact with the springs that set in motion the enormous movements of the mass of which in his regiment he felt himself a tiny, obedient, and insignificant atom. They followed Prince Dolgorúkov out into the corridor, and met—coming out of the door of the Emperor's room by which Dolgorúkov had entered—a short man in civilian clothes with a clever face and sharply projecting jaw which, without spoiling his face, gave him a peculiar vivacity and shiftiness of expression. This short man nodded to Dolgorúkov as to an intimate friend, and stared at Prince Andrew with cool intensity, walking straight toward him and evidently expecting him to bow or to step out of his way. Prince Andrew did neither: a look of animosity appeared on his face and the other turned away and went down the side of the corridor.

"Who was that?" asked Borís.

"He is one of the most remarkable, but to me most unpleasant of men—the Minister of Foreign Affairs, Prince Adam Czartoryski. . . . It is such men as he who decide the fate of nations," added Bolkónski with a sigh he could not suppress, as they passed out of the palace.

Next day, the army began its campaign, and up to the very battle of Austerlitz, Borís was unable to see either Prince Andrew or Dolgorúkov again, and remained for a while with the Ismáylov regiment.

Chapter X

At dawn on the 16th of November, Denísov's squadron, in which Nicholas Rostóv served and which was in Prince Bagratión's detachment, moved from the place where it had spent the night, advancing into action as arranged, and after going behind other columns for about a verst, was stopped on the highroad. Rostóv saw the Cossacks and then the first and second squadrons of hussars, and infantry battalions and artillery pass by and go forward, and then Generals Bagratión and Dolgorúkov ride past with their adjutants. All the fear before action which he had experienced as previously, all the inner struggle to conquer that fear, all his dreams of distinguishing himself as a true hussar in this battle, had been wasted. Their squadron remained in reserve and Nicholas Rostóv spent that day in a dull and wretched mood. At nine in the morning, he heard firing in front and shouts of *hurrah,* and saw wounded being brought back (there were not many of them), and at last he saw how a whole detachment of French cavalry was brought in, convoyed by a sótnya of Cossacks. Evidently the affair was over, and though not big, had been a successful engagement. The men and officers returning spoke of a brilliant victory, of the occupation of the town of Wischau and the capture of a whole French squadron. The day was bright and sunny after a sharp night frost, and the cheerful glitter of that autumn day was in keeping with the news of victory which was conveyed, not only by the tales of those who had taken part in it, but also by the joyful expression on the faces of soldiers, officers, generals, and adjutants, as they passed Rostóv going or coming. And Nicholas, who had vainly suffered all the dread that precedes a battle and had spent that happy day in inactivity, was all the more depressed.

"Come here, Wostóv. Let's dwink to dwown our gwief!" shouted Denísov, who had settled down by the roadside with a flask and some food.

The officers gathered round Denísov's canteen, eating and talking.

"There! They are bringing another!" cried one of the officers, indicating a captive French dragoon who was being brought in on foot by two Cossacks.

One of them was leading by the bridle a fine large French horse he had taken from the prisoner.

"Sell us that horse!" Denísov called out to the Cossacks.

"If you like, your honor!"

The officers got up and stood round the Cossacks and their prisoner. The French dragoon was a young Alsatian who spoke French with a German accent. He was breathless with agitation, his face was red, and when he heard some French spoken he at once began speaking to the officers, addressing first one, then another. He said he would not have been taken, it was not his fault but the corporal's who had sent him to seize some horsecloths, though he had told him the Russians were there. And at every word he added: "But don't hurt my little horse!" and stroked the animal. It was plain that he did not quite grasp where he was. Now he excused himself for having been taken prisoner, and now imagining himself before his own officers, insisted on his soldierly discipline and zeal in the service. He brought with him into our rearguard all the freshness of atmosphere of the French army, which was so alien to us.

The Cossacks sold the horse for two gold pieces, and Rostóv, being the richest of the officers now that he had received his money, bought it.

"But don't hurt my little horse!" said the Alsatian good-naturedly to Rostóv when the animal was handed over to the hussar.

Rostóv smilingly reassured the dragoon and gave him money.

"Alley! Alley!" said the Cossack, touching the prisoner's arm to make him go on.

"The Emperor! The Emperor!" was suddenly heard among the hussars.

All began to run and bustle, and Rostóv saw coming up the road behind him several riders with white plumes in their hats. In a moment everyone was in his place, waiting.

Rostóv did not know or remember how he ran to his place and mounted. Instantly his regret at not having been in action and his dejected mood amid people of whom he was weary, had gone, instantly every thought of himself had vanished. He was filled with happiness at his nearness to the Emperor. He felt that this nearness by itself made up to him for the day he had lost. He was happy as a lover when the longed-for moment of meeting arrives. Not daring to look round and without looking round, he was ecstatically conscious of *his* approach. He felt it not only from the sound of the hoofs of the approaching cavalcade, but because as *he* drew near everything grew brighter, more joyful, more significant, and more festive around him. Nearer and nearer to Rostóv came that sun shedding beams of mild and majestic light around, and already he felt himself enveloped in those beams, he heard *his* voice, that kindly, calm, and majestic voice, that was yet so simple! And as if in accord with Rostóv's feeling, there was a deathly stillness amid which was heard the Emperor's voice.

"The Pávlograd hussars?" he inquired.

"The reserves, sire!" replied a voice, a very human one compared to that which had said: "The Pávlograd hussars?"

The Emperor drew level with Rostóv and halted. Alexander's face was even more beautiful than it had been three days before at the review. It shone with such gaiety and youth, such innocent youth, that it suggested the liveliness of a fourteen-year-old boy, and yet it was the face of the majestic Emperor. Casually, while surveying the squadron, the Emperor's eyes met Rostóv's and rested on them for not more than two seconds. Whether or no the Emperor understood what was going on in Rostóv's soul (it seemed to Rostóv that he understood everything), at any rate his light-blue eyes gazed for about two seconds into Rostóv's face. A gentle, mild light poured from them. Then all at once he raised his eyebrows, abruptly touched his horse with his left foot, and galloped on.

The younger Emperor could not restrain his wish to be present at the battle and, in spite of the remonstrances of his courtiers, at twelve o'clock left the third column with which he had been and galloped toward the vanguard. Before he came up with the hussars, several adjutants met him with news of the successful result of the action.

This battle, which consisted in the capture of a French squadron, was represented as a brilliant victory over the French, and so the Emperor and the whole army, especially while the smoke hung over the battlefield, believed that the French had been defeated and were retreating against their will. A few minutes after the Emperor had passed, the Pávlograd division was ordered to advance. In Wischau itself, a petty German town, Rostóv saw the Emperor again. In the market-place, where there had been some rather heavy firing before the Emperor's arrival, lay several killed and wounded soldiers whom there had not been time to move. The Emperor, surrounded by his suite of officers and courtiers, was riding a bob-tailed chestnut mare, a different one from that which he had ridden at the review, and bending to one side he gracefully held a gold lorgnette to his eyes and looked at a soldier who lay prone, with blood on his uncovered head. The wounded soldier was so dirty, coarse, and revolting, that his proximity to the Emperor shocked Rostóv. Rostóv saw how the Emperor's rather round shoulders shuddered as if a cold shiver had run down them, how his left foot began convulsively tapping the horse's side with the spur, and how the well-trained horse looked round unconcerned and did not stir. An adjutant, dismounting, lifted the soldier under the arms to place him on a stretcher that had been brought. The soldier groaned.

"Gently, gently! Can't you do it more gently?" said the Emperor apparently suffering more than the dying soldier, and he rode away.

Rostóv saw tears filling the Emperor's eyes and heard him, as he was riding away, say to Czartoryski:

"What a terrible thing war is: what a terrible thing! *Quelle terrible chose que la guerre!*"

The troops of the vanguard were stationed before Wischau, within sight of the enemy's lines, which all day long had yielded ground to us at the least firing. The Emperor's gratitude was announced to the vanguard, rewards were promised and the men received a double ration of vodka. The campfires crackled and the soldiers' songs resounded even more merrily than on the previous night. Denísov celebrated his promotion to the rank of major, and Rostóv, who had already drunk enough, at the end of the feast proposed the Emperor's health. "Not 'our Sovereign, the Emperor,' as they say at official dinners," said he, "but the health of our Sovereign, that good, enchanting, and great man! Let us drink to his health and to the certain defeat of the French!"

"If we fought before," he said, "not letting the French pass, as at Schön Grabern, what shall we not do now when *he* is at the front? We will all die for him gladly! Is it not so, gentlemen? Perhaps I am not saying it right, I have drunk a good deal—but that is how I feel, and so do you too! To the health of Alexander the First! Hurrah!"

"Hurrah!" rang the enthusiastic voices of the officers.

And the old cavalry captain, Kirsten, shouted enthusiastically and no less sincerely than the twenty-year-old Rostóv.

When the officers had emptied and smashed their glasses, Kirsten filled others, and in shirt-sleeves and breeches, went glass in hand to the soldiers' bonfires and with his long gray mustache, his white chest showing under his open shirt, he stood in a majestic pose in the light of the campfire, waving his uplifted arm.

"Lads! here's to our Sovereign, the Emperor, and victory over our enemies! Hurrah!" he exclaimed in his dashing, old, hussar's baritone.

The hussars crowded round and responded heartily with loud shouts.

Late that night, when all had separated, Denísov with his short hand patted his favorite, Rostóv, on the shoulder.

"As there's no one to fall in love with on campaign, he's fallen in love with the Tsar," he said.

"Denísov, don't make fun of it!" cried Rostóv. "It is such a lofty, beautiful feeling, such a . . ."

"I believe it, I believe it, fwiend, and I share and appwove . . ."

"No, you don't understand!"

And Rostóv got up and went wandering among the campfires, dreaming of what happiness it would be to die—not in saving the Emperor's life (he did not even dare to dream of that), but simply to die before his eyes. He really was in love with the Tsar and the glory of the Russian arms and the hope of future triumph. And he was not the only man to experience that feeling during those memorable days preceding the battle of Austerlitz: nine-tenths of the men in the Russian army were then in love, though less ecstatically, with their Tsar and the glory of the Russian arms.

Chapter XI

THE NEXT DAY THE EMPEROR STOPPED AT WISCHAU, AND VILLIER, HIS PHYSICIAN, WAS REPEATedly summoned to see him. At headquarters and among the troops nearby the news spread that the Emperor was unwell. He ate nothing and had slept badly that night, those around him reported. The cause of this indisposition was the strong impression made on his sensitive mind by the sight of the killed and wounded.

At daybreak on the 17th, a French officer who had come with a flag of truce, demanding an audience with the Russian Emperor, was brought into Wischau from our outposts. This officer was Savary. The Emperor had only just fallen asleep and so Savary had to wait. At midday he was admitted to the Emperor, and an hour later he rode off with Prince Dolgorúkov to the advanced post of the French army.

It was rumored that Savary had been sent to propose to Alexander a meeting with Napoleon. To the joy and pride of the whole army, a personal interview was refused, and instead of the Sovereign, Prince Dolgorúkov, the victor at Wischau, was sent with Savary to negotiate with Napoleon if, contrary to expectations, these negotiations were actuated by a real desire for peace.

Toward evening Dolgorúkov came back, went straight to the Tsar, and remained alone with him for a long time.

On the 18th and 19th of November, the army advanced two days' march and the enemy's outposts after a brief interchange of shots retreated. In the highest army circles from midday on the 19th, a great, excitedly bustling activity began which lasted till the morning of the 20th, when the memorable battle of Austerlitz was fought.

Till midday on the 19th, the activity, the eager talk, running to and fro, and dispatching of adjutants, was confined to the Emperor's headquarters. But on the afternoon of that day, this activity reached Kutúzov's headquarters and the staffs of the commanders of columns. By evening, the adjutants had spread it to all ends and parts of the army, and in the night from the 19th to the 20th, the whole eighty thousand allied troops rose from their bivouacs to the hum of voices, and the army swayed and started in one enormous mass six miles long.

The concentrated activity which had begun at the Emperor's headquarters in the morning and had started the whole movement that followed, was like the first movement of the main wheel of a large tower-clock. One wheel slowly moved, another was set in motion, and a third, and wheels began to revolve faster and faster, levers and cogwheels to work, chimes to play, figures to pop out, and the hands to advance with regular motion as a result of all that activity.

Just as in the mechanism of a clock, so in the mechanism of the military machine, an impulse once given leads to the final result; and just as indifferently quiescent till the moment when motion is transmitted to them are the parts of the mechanism which the impulse has not yet reached. Wheels creak on their axles as the cogs engage one another and the revolving pulleys whirr with the rapidity of their movement, but a neighboring wheel is as quiet and motionless as though it were prepared to remain so for a hundred years; but the moment comes when the lever catches it and obeying the impulse that wheel begins to creak and joins in the common motion the result and aim of which are beyond its ken.

Just as in a clock, the result of the complicated motion of innumerable wheels and pulleys is merely a slow and regular movement of the hands which show the time, so the result of all the complicated human activities of 160,000 Russians and French—all their passions, desires, remorse, humiliations, sufferings, outbursts of pride, fear, and enthusiasm—was only the loss of the battle of Austerlitz, the so-called battle of the three Emperors—that is to say, a slow movement of the hand on the dial of human history.

Prince Andrew was on duty that day and in constant attendance on the commander-in-chief.

At six in the evening, Kutúzov went to the Emperor's headquarters and after staying but a short time with the Tsar went to see the grand marshal of the court, Count Tolstóy.

Bolkónski took the opportunity to go in to get some details of the coming action from Dolgorúkov. He felt that Kutúzov was upset and dissatisfied about something and that at headquarters they were dissatisfied with him, and also that at the Emperor's headquarters, everyone adopted toward him the tone of men who know something others do not know: he therefore wished to speak to Dolgorúkov.

"Well, how d'you do, my dear fellow?" said Dolgorúkov, who was sitting at tea with Bilíbin. "The fête is for tomorrow. How is your old fellow? Out of sorts?"

"I won't say he is out of sorts, but I fancy he would like to be heard."

"But they heard him at the council of war and will hear him when he talks sense, but to temporize and wait for something now when Bonaparte fears nothing so much as a general battle is impossible."

"Yes, you have seen him?" said Prince Andrew. "Well, what is Bonaparte like? How did he impress you?"

"Yes, I saw him, and am convinced that he fears nothing so much as a general engagement," repeated Dolgorúkov, evidently prizing this general conclusion which he had arrived at from his interview with Napoleon. "If he weren't afraid of a battle why did he ask for that interview? Why negotiate, and above all why retreat, when to retreat is so contrary to his method of conducting war? Believe me he is afraid, afraid of a general battle. His hour has come! Mark my words!"

"But tell me, what is he like, eh?" said Prince Andrew again.

"He is a man in a gray overcoat, very anxious that I should call him 'Your Majesty,' but who, to his chagrin, got no title from me! That's the sort of man he is, and nothing more," replied Dolgorúkov, looking round at Bilíbin with a smile.

"Despite my great respect for old Kutúzov," he continued, "we should be a nice set of fellows if we were to wait about and so give him a chance to escape, or to trick us, now that we certainly have him in our hands! No, we mustn't forget Suvórov and his rule—not to put yourself in a position to be attacked, but yourself to attack. Believe me in war the energy of young men often shows the way better than all the experience of old Cunctators."

"But in what position are we going to attack him? I have been at the outposts today and it is impossible to say where his chief forces are situated," said Prince Andrew.

He wished to explain to Dolgorúkov a plan of attack he had himself formed.

"Oh, that is all the same," Dolgorúkov said quickly, and getting up he spread a map on the table. "All eventualities have been foreseen. If he is standing before Brünn . . ."

And Prince Dolgorúkov rapidly but indistinctly explained Weyrother's plan of a flanking movement.

Prince Andrew began to reply and to state his own plan, which might have been as good as Weyrother's, but for the disadvantage that Weyrother's had already been approved. As soon as Prince Andrew began to demonstrate the defects of the latter and the merits of his own plan, Prince Dolgorúkov ceased to listen to him and gazed absent-mindedly not at the map, but at Prince Andrew's face.

"There will be a counseil of war at Kutúzov's tonight, though; you can say all this there," remarked Dolgorúkov.

"I will do so," said Prince Andrew, moving away from the map.

"Whatever are you bothering about, gentlemen?" said Bilíbin, who, till then, had listened with an amused smile to their conversation and now was evidently ready with a joke. "Whether tomorrow brings victory or defeat, the glory of our Russian arms is secure. Except your Kutúzov, there is not a single Russian in command of a column! The commanders are: Herr General Wimpfen, le Comte de Langeron, le Prince de Lichtenstein, le Prince de Hohenlohe, and finally Prishprish, and so on like all those Polish names."

"Be quiet, backbiter!" said Dolgorúkov. "It is not true; there are now two Russians, Milorádovich, and Dokhtúrov, and there would be a third, Count Arakchéev, if his nerves were not too weak."

"However, I think General Kutúzov has come out," said Prince Andrew. "I wish you good luck and success, gentlemen!" he added and went out after shaking hands with Dolgorúkov and Bilíbin.

On the way home, Prince Andrew could not refrain from asking Kutúzov, who was sitting silently beside him, what he thought of tomorrow's battle.

Kutúzov looked sternly at his adjutant and, after a pause, replied: "I think the battle will be lost, and so I told Count Tolstóy and asked him to tell the Emperor. What do you think he replied? 'But, my dear general, I am engaged with rice and cutlets, look after military matters yourself!' Yes . . . That was the answer I got!"

Chapter XII

SHORTLY AFTER NINE O'CLOCK THAT EVENING, WEYROTHER DROVE WITH HIS PLANS TO KUTÚZOV's quarters where the council of war was to be held. All the commanders of columns were summoned to the commander-in-chief's and with the exception of Prince Bagratión, who declined to come, were all there at the appointed time.

Weyrother, who was in full control of the proposed battle, by his eagerness and briskness presented a marked contrast to the dissatisfied and drowsy Kutúzov, who reluctantly played the part of chairman and president of the council of war. Weyrother evidently felt himself to be at the head of a movement that had already become unrestrainable. He was like a horse running downhill harnessed to a heavy cart. Whether he was pulling it or being pushed by it he did not know, but rushed along at headlong speed with no time to consider what this movement might lead to. Weyrother had been twice that evening to the enemy's picket line to reconnoiter personally, and twice to the Emperors, Russian and Austrian, to report and explain, and to his headquarters where he had dictated the dispositions in German, and now, much exhausted he arrived at Kutúzov's.

He was evidently so busy that he even forgot to be polite to the commander-in-chief. He interrupted him, talked rapidly and indistinctly, without looking at the man he was addressing, and did not reply to questions put to him. He was bespattered with mud and had a pitiful, weary, and distracted air, though at the same time he was haughty and self-confident.

Kutúzov was occupying a nobleman's castle of modest dimensions near Austerlitz. In the large drawing room which had become the commander-in-chief's office, were gathered Kutúzov himself, Weyrother, and the members of the council of war. They were drinking tea, and only awaited Prince Bagratión to begin the council. At last Bagratión's orderly came with the news that the prince could not attend. Prince Andrew came in to inform the commander-in-chief of this, and availing himself of permission previously given him by Kutúzov to be present at the council, he remained in the room.

"Since Prince Bagratión is not coming, we may begin," said Weyrother, hurriedly rising from his seat and going up to the table on which an enormous map of the environs of Brnn was spread out.

Kutúzov, with his uniform unbuttoned so that his fat neck bulged over his collar as if escaping, was sitting almost asleep in a low chair, with his podgy old hands resting symmetrically on its arms. At the sound of Weyrother's voice, he opened his one eye with an effort.

"Yes, yes, if you please! It is already late," said he, and nodding his head he let it droop and again closed his eye.

If at first the members of the council thought that Kutúzov was pretending to sleep, the sounds his nose emitted during the reading that followed, proved that the commander-in-chief at that moment was absorbed by a far more serious matter than a desire to show his contempt for the dispositions or anything else—he was engaged in satisfying the irresistible human need for sleep. He really was asleep. Weyrother, with the gesture of a man too busy to lose a moment, glanced at Kutúzov and having convinced himself that he was asleep, took up a paper and in a loud monotonous voice began to read out the dispositions for the impending battle, under a heading which he also read out:

"Dispositions for an attack on the enemy position behind Kobenitz and Sokolnitz, November 30th, 1805."

The dispositions were very complicated and difficult. They began as follows:

"As the enemy's left wing rests on wooded hills and his right extends along Kobenitz and Sokolnitz behind the ponds that are there, while we, on the other hand, with our left wing by far outflank his right, it is advantageous to attack the enemy's latter wing especially if we occupy the villages of Sokolnitz and Kobenitz, whereby we can both fall on his flank and pursue him over the plain between Schlappanitz and the Thuerassa forest, avoiding the defiles of Schlappanitz and Bellowitz which cover the enemy's front. For this object it is necessary that . . . The first column marches . . . The second column marches . . . The third column marches . . ." and so on, read Weyrother.

The generals seemed to listen reluctantly to the difficult dispositions. The tall fair-haired General Buxhöwden stood, leaning his back against the wall, his eyes fixed on a burning candle, and seemed not to listen or even to wish to be thought to listen. Exactly opposite Weyrother, with his glistening wide-open eyes fixed upon him and his mustache twisted upward, sat the ruddy Milorádovich in a military pose, his elbows turned outward, his hands on his knees, and his shoulders raised. He remained stubbornly silent, gazing at Weyrother's face, and only turned away his eyes when the Austrian chief-of-staff finished reading. Then Milorádovich looked round significantly at the other generals. But one could not tell from that significant look whether he agreed or disagreed and was satisfied or not with the arrangements. Next to Weyrother sat Count Langeron who, with a subtle smile that never left his typically southern French face during the whole time of the reading, gazed at his delicate fingers which rapidly twirled by its corners a gold snuffbox on which was a portrait. In the middle of one of the longest sentences, he stopped the rotary motion of the snuffbox, raised his head, and with inimical politeness lurking in the corners of his thin lips, interrupted Weyrother, wishing to say something. But the Austrian general continuing to read, frowned angrily and jerked his elbows, as if to say: "You can tell me your views later, but now be so good as to look at the map and listen." Langeron lifted his eyes with an expression of perplexity, turned round to Milorádovich as if seeking an explanation, but meeting the latter's impressive but meaningless gaze, drooped his eyes sadly and again took to twirling his snuffbox.

"A geography lesson!" he muttered as if to himself, but loud enough to be heard.

Przebyszéwski, with respectful but dignified politeness, held his hand to his ear toward Weyrother, with the air of a man absorbed in attention. Dohktúrov, a little man, sat opposite Weyrother, with an assiduous and modest mien, and stooping over the outspread map conscientiously studied the dispositions and the unfamiliar locality. He asked Weyrother several times to repeat words he had not clearly heard and the difficult names of villages. Weyrother complied and Dohktúrov noted them down.

When the reading which lasted more than an hour was over, Langeron again brought his snuffbox to rest and, without looking at Weyrother or at anyone in particular, began to say how difficult it was to carry out such a plan in which the enemy's position was assumed to be known, whereas it was perhaps not known, since the enemy was in movement. Langeron's objections were valid but it was obvious that their chief aim was to show General Weyrother—who had read his dispositions with as much self-confidence as if he were addressing school-children—that he had to do, not with fools, but with men who could teach him something in military matters.

When the monotonous sound of Weyrother's voice ceased, Kutúzov opened his eye as a miller wakes up when the soporific drone of the mill-wheel is interrupted. He listened to what Langeron said, as if remarking, "So you are still at that silly business!" quickly closed his eye again and let his head sink still lower.

Langeron, trying as virulently as possible to sting Weyrother's vanity as author of the military plan, argued that Bonaparte might easily attack instead of being attacked, and so render the whole of this plan perfectly worthless. Weyrother met all objections with a firm and contemptuous smile, evidently prepared beforehand to meet all objections be they what they might.

"If he could attack us, he would have done so today," said he.

"So you think he is powerless?" said Langeron.

"He has forty thousand men at most," replied Weyrother, with the smile of a doctor to whom an old wife wishes to explain the treatment of a case.

"In that case he is inviting his doom by awaiting our attack," said Langeron, with a subtly ironical smile, again glancing round for support to Milorádovich who was near him.

But Milorádovich was at that moment evidently thinking of anything rather than of what the generals were disputing about.

"Ma foi!" said he, "tomorrow we shall see all that on the battlefield."

Weyrother again gave that smile which seemed to say that to him it was strange and ridiculous to meet objections from Russian generals, and to have to prove to them what he had not merely convinced himself of, but had also convinced the sovereign Emperors of.

"The enemy has quenched his fires and a continual noise is heard from his camp," said he. "What does that mean? Either he is retreating, which is the only thing we need fear, or he is changing his position." (He smiled ironically.) "But even if he also took up a position in the Thuerassa, he merely saves us a great deal of trouble and all our arrangements to the minutest detail remain the same."

"How is that? . . ." began Prince Andrew, who had for long been waiting an opportunity to express his doubts.

Kutúzov here woke up, coughed heavily, and looked round at the generals.

"Gentlemen, the dispositions for tomorrow—or rather for today, for it is past midnight—cannot now be altered," said he. "You have heard them, and we shall all do our duty. But before a battle, there is nothing more important . . ." he paused, "than to have a good sleep."

He moved as if to rise. The generals bowed and retired. It was past midnight. Prince Andrew went out.

The council of war, at which Prince Andrew had not been able to express his opinion as he had hoped to, left on him a vague and uneasy impression. Whether Dolgorúkov and Weyrother, or Kutúzov, Langeron, and the others who did not approve of the plan of attack, were right—he did not know. "But was it really not possible for Kutúzov to state his views plainly to the Emperor? Is it possible that on account of court and personal considerations tens of thousands of lives, and my life, *my* life," he thought, "must be risked?"

"Yes, it is very likely that I shall be killed tomorrow," he thought. And suddenly, at this thought of death, a whole series of most distant, most intimate, memories rose in his imagination: he remembered his last parting from his father and his wife; he remembered the days when he first loved her. He thought of her pregnancy and felt sorry for her and for himself, and in a nervously emotional and softened mood he went out of the hut in which he was billeted with Nesvítski and began to walk up and down before it.

The night was foggy and through the fog the moonlight gleamed mysteriously. "Yes, tomorrow, tomorrow!" he thought. "Tomorrow everything may be over for me! All these memories will be no more, none of them will have any meaning for me. Tomorrow perhaps, even certainly, I have a presentiment that for the first time I shall have to show all I can do." And his fancy pictured the battle, its loss, the concentration of fighting at one point, and the hesitation of all the commanders. And then that happy moment, that Toulon for which he had so long waited, presents itself to him at last. He firmly and clearly expresses his opinion to Kutúzov, to Weyrother, and to the Emperors. All are struck by the justness of his views, but no one undertakes to carry them out, so he takes a regiment, a division—stipulates that no one is to interfere with his arrangements—leads his division to the decisive point, and gains the victory alone. "But death and suffering?" suggested another voice. Prince Andrew, however, did not answer that voice and went on dreaming of his triumphs. The dispositions for the next battle are planned by him alone. Nominally he is only an adjutant on Kutúzov's staff, but he does everything alone. The next battle is won by him alone. Kutúzov is removed and he is appointed . . . "Well and then?" asked the other voice. "If before that you are not ten times wounded, killed, or betrayed, well . . . what then? . . ." "Well then," Prince Andrew answered himself, "I don't know what will happen and don't want to know, and can't, but if I want this—want glory, want to be known to men, want to be loved by them, it is not my fault that I want it and want nothing but that and live only for that. Yes, for that alone! I shall never tell anyone, but, oh God! what am I to do if I love nothing but fame and men's esteem? Death, wounds, the loss of family—I fear nothing. And precious and dear as many persons are to me—father, sister, wife—those dearest to me—yet dreadful and unnatural as it seems, I would give them all at once for a moment of glory, of triumph over men, of love from men I don't know and never shall know, for the love of these men here," he thought, as he listened to voices in Kutúzov's courtyard. The voices were those of the orderlies who were packing up; one voice, probably a coachman's, was teasing Kutúzov's old cook whom Prince Andrew knew, and who was called Tit. He was saying, "Tit, I say, Tit!"

"Well?" returned the old man.

"Go, Tit, thresh a bit!" said the wag.

"Oh, go to the devil!" called out a voice, drowned by the laughter of the orderlies and servants.

"All the same, I love and value nothing but triumph over them all, I value this mystic power and glory that is floating here above me in this mist!"

Chapter XIII

THAT SAME NIGHT, ROSTÓV WAS WITH A PLATOON ON SKIRMISHING DUTY IN FRONT OF Bagratión's detachment. His hussars were placed along the line in couples and he himself rode along the line trying to master the sleepiness that kept coming over him. An enormous space, with our army's campfires dimly glowing in the fog, could be seen behind him, in front of him was misty darkness. Rostóv could see nothing, peer as he would into that foggy distance: now something gleamed gray, now there was something black, now little lights seemed to glimmer where the enemy ought to be, now he fancied it was only something in his own eyes. His eyes kept closing, and in his fancy appeared—now the Emperor, now Denísov, and now Moscow memories—and he again hurriedly opened his eyes and saw close before him the head and ears of the horse he was riding, and sometimes when he came within six paces of them, the black figures of hussars, but in the distance was still the same misty darkness. "Why not? . . . It might easily happen," thought Rostóv, "that the Emperor will meet me and give me an order as he would to any other officer; he'll say: 'Go and find out what's there.' There are many stories of his getting to know an officer in just such a chance way and attaching him to himself! What if he gave me a place near him? Oh, how I would guard him, how I would tell him the truth, how I would unmask his deceivers!" And in order to realize vividly his love devotion to the sovereign, Rostóv pictured to himself an enemy or a deceitful German, whom he would not only kill with pleasure but whom he would slap in the face before the Emperor. Suddenly a distant shout aroused him. He started and opened his eyes.

"Where am I? Oh yes, in the skirmishing line . . . pass and watchword—*shaft, Olmütz*. What a nuisance that our squadron will be in reserve tomorrow," he thought. "I'll ask leave to go to the front, this may be my only chance of seeing the Emperor. It won't be long now before I am off duty. I'll take another turn and when I get back I'll go to the general and ask him." He readjusted himself in the saddle and touched up his horse to ride once more round his hussars. It seemed to him that it was getting lighter. To the left he saw a sloping descent lit up, and facing it a black knoll that seemed as steep as a wall. On this knoll there was a white patch that Rostóv could not at all make out: was it a glade in the wood lit up by the moon, or some unmelted snow, or some white houses?

He even thought something moved on that white spot. "I expect it's snow . . . that spot . . . a spot—*une tache,*" he thought. "There now . . . it's not a *tache* . . . Natásha . . . sister, black eyes . . . Na . . . tásha . . . (won't she be surprised when I tell her how I've seen the Emperor?) Natásha . . . take my *sabertache* . . ."—"Keep to the right, your honor, there are bushes here," came the voice of a hussar, past whom Rostóv was riding in the act of falling asleep. Rostóv lifted his head that had sunk almost to his horse's mane and pulled up beside the hussar. He was succumbing to irresistible, youthful, childish drowsiness. "But what was I thinking? I mustn't forget. How shall I speak to the Emperor? No, that's not it—that's tomorrow. Oh yes! Natásha . . . *sabertache* . . . saber them . . . Whom? The hussars . . . Ah, the hussars with mustaches. Along the Tverskáya Street rode the hussar with mustaches . . . I thought about him too, just opposite Gúryev's house . . . Old Gúryev. . . . Oh, but Denísov's a fine fellow. But that's all nonsense. The chief thing is that the Emperor is here. How he looked at me and wished to say something, but dared not. . . . No, it was I who dared not. But that's nonsense, the chief thing is not to forget the important thing I was thinking of. Yes, Natásha, *sabertache,* oh, yes, yes! That's right!" And his head once more sank to his horse's neck. All at once it seemed to him that he was being fired at. "What? What? What? . . . Cut them down! What? . . ." said Rostóv, waking up. At the moment he opened his eyes he heard in front of him, where the enemy was, the long-drawn shouts of thousands of voices. His horse and the horse of the hussar near him pricked their ears at these shouts. Over there, where the shouting came from, a fire flared up and went out again, then another, and all along the French line on the hill fires flared up and the shouting grew louder and louder. Rostóv could hear the sound of French words but could not distinguish them. The din of many voices was too great; all he could hear was: "ahahah!" and "rrrr!"

"What's that? What do you make of it?" said Rostóv to the hussar beside him. "That must be the enemy's camp!"

The hussar did not reply.

"Why, don't you hear it?" Rostóv asked again, after waiting for a reply.

"Who can tell, your honor?" replied the hussar reluctantly.

"From the direction, it must be the enemy," repeated Rostóv.

"It may be *he* or it may be nothing," muttered the hussar. "It's dark . . . Steady!" he cried to his fidgeting horse.

Rostóv's horse was also getting restive: it pawed the frozen ground, pricking its ears at the noise and looking at the lights. The shouting grew still louder and merged into a general roar that only an army of several thousand men could produce. The lights spread farther and farther, probably along the line of the French camp. Rostóv no longer wanted to sleep. The gay triumphant shouting of the enemy army had a stimulating effect on him. *"Vive l'Empereur! l'Empereur!"* he now heard distinctly.

"They can't be far off, probably just beyond the stream," he said to the hussar beside him.

The hussar only sighed without replying and coughed angrily. The sound of horse's hoofs approaching at a trot along the line of hussars was heard, and out of the foggy darkness the figure of a sergeant of hussars suddenly appeared, looming huge as an elephant.

"Your honor, the generals!" said the sergeant, riding up to Rostóv.

Rostóv, still looking round toward the fires and the shouts, rode with the sergeant to meet some mounted men who were riding along the line. One was on a white horse. Prince Bagratión and Prince Dolgorúkov with their adjutants had come to witness the curious phenomenon of the lights and shouts in the enemy's camp. Rostóv rode up to Bagratión, reported to him, and then joined the adjutants listening to what the generals were saying.

"Believe me," said Prince Dolgorúkov, addressing Bagratión, "it is nothing but a trick! He has retreated and ordered the rearguard to kindle fires and make a noise to deceive us."

"Hardly," said Bagratión. "I saw them this evening on that knoll; if they had retreated they would have withdrawn from that too. . . . Officer!" said Bagratión to Rostóv, "are the enemy's skirmishers still there?"

"They were there this evening, but now I don't know, your excellency. Shall I go with some of my hussars to see?" replied Rostóv.

Bagratión stopped and, before replying, tried to see Rostóv's face in the mist.

"Well, go and see," he said, after a pause.

"Yes, sir."

Rostóv spurred his horse, called to Sergeant Fédchenko and two other hussars, told them to follow him, and trotted downhill in the direction from which the shouting came. He felt both frightened and pleased to be riding alone with three hussars into that mysterious and dangerous misty distance where no one had been before him. Bagratión called to him from the hill not to go beyond the stream, but Rostóv pretended not to hear him and did not stop but rode on and on, continually mistaking bushes for trees and gullies for men, and continually discovering his mistakes. Having descended the hill at a trot, he no longer saw either our own or the enemy's fires, but heard the shouting of the French more loudly and distinctly. In the valley he saw before him something like a river, but when he reached it he found it was a road. Having come out onto the road he reined in his horse, hesitating whether to ride along it or cross it and ride over the black field up the hillside. To keep to the road which gleamed white in the mist would have been safer because it would be easier to see people coming along it. "Follow me!" said he, crossed the road, and began riding up the hill at a gallop toward the point where the French pickets had been standing that evening.

"Your honor, there he is!" cried one of the hussars behind him. And before Rostóv had time to make out what the black thing was that had suddenly appeared in the fog, there was a flash, followed by a report, and a bullet whizzing high up in the mist with a plaintive sound passed out of hearing. Another musket missed fire but flashed in the pan. Rostóv turned his horse and galloped back. Four more reports followed at intervals, and the bullets passed somewhere in the fog singing in different tones. Rostóv reined in his horse, whose spirits had risen, like his own, at the firing, and went back at a footpace. "Well, some more! Some more!" a merry voice was saying in his soul. But no more shots came.

Only when approaching Bagratión did Rostóv let his horse gallop again, and with his hand at the salute rode up to the general.

Dolgorúkov was still insisting that the French had retreated and had only lit fires to deceive us.

"What does that prove?" he was saying as Rostóv rode up. "They might retreat and leave the pickets."

"It's plain that they have not all gone yet, prince," said Bagratión. "Wait till tomorrow morning, we'll find out everything tomorrow."

"The picket is still on the hill, your excellency, just where it was in the evening," reported Rostóv, stooping forward with his hand at the salute and unable to repress the smile of delight induced by his ride and especially by the sound of the bullets.

"Very good, very good," said Bagratión. "Thank you, officer."

"Your excellency," said Rostóv, "may I ask a favor?"

"What is it?"

"Tomorrow our squadron is to be in reserve. May I ask to be attached to the first squadron?"

"What's your name?"

"Count Rostóv."

"Oh, very well, you may stay in attendance on me."

"Count Ilyá Rostóv's son?" asked Dolgorúkov.

But Rostóv did not reply.

"Then I may reckon on it, your excellency?"

"I will give the order."

"Tomorrow very likely I may be sent with some message to the Emperor," thought Rostóv. "Thank God!"

The fires and shouting in the enemy's army were occasioned by the fact that while Napoleon's proclamation was being read to the troops the Emperor himself rode round his bivouacs. The soldiers, on seeing him, lit wisps of straw and ran after him, shouting, *"Vive l'Empereur!"* Napoleon's proclamation was as follows:

> Soldiers! The Russian army is advancing against you to avenge the Austrian army of Ulm. They are the same battalions you broke at Hollabrnn and have pursued ever since to this place. The position we occupy is a strong one, and while they are marching to go round me on the right they will expose a flank to me. Soldiers! I will myself direct your battalions. I will keep out of fire if you with your habitual valor carry disorder and confusion into the enemy's ranks, but should victory be in doubt, even for a moment, you will see your Emperor exposing himself to the first blows of the enemy, for there must be no doubt of victory, especially on this day when what is at stake is the honor of the French infantry, so necessary to the honor of our nation.
>
> Do not break your ranks on the plea of removing the wounded! Let every man be fully imbued with the thought that we must defeat these hirelings of England, inspired by such hatred of our nation! This victory will conclude our campaign and we can return to winter quarters, where fresh French troops who are being raised in France will join us, and the peace I shall conclude will be worthy of my people, of you, and of myself.
>
> NAPOLEON

Chapter XIV

AT FIVE IN THE MORNING IT WAS STILL QUITE DARK. THE TROOPS OF THE CENTER, THE RESERVES, and Bagratión's right flank, had not yet moved, but on the left flank the columns of infantry, cavalry and artillery which were to be the first to descend the heights to attack the French right flank and drive it into the Bohemian mountains according to plan, were already up and astir. The smoke of the campfires, into which they were throwing everything superfluous, made the eyes smart. It was cold and dark. The officers were hurriedly drinking tea and breakfasting, the soldiers, munching biscuit and beating a tattoo with their feet to warm themselves, gathering round the fires throwing into the flames the remains of sheds, chairs, tables, wheels, tubs and everything that they did not want or could not carry away with them. Austrian column-guides were moving in and out among the Russian troops and served as heralds of the advance. As soon as an Austrian officer showed himself near a commanding officer's quarters, the regiment began to move: the soldiers ran from the fires, thrust their pipes into their boots, their bags into the carts, got their muskets ready, and formed rank. The officers buttoned up their coats, buckled on their swords and pouches, and moved along the ranks shouting. The train-drivers and orderlies harnessed and packed the wagons and tied on the loads. The adjutants and battalion and regimental commanders mounted, crossed themselves, gave final instructions, orders and commissions to the baggage men who remained behind, and the monotonous tramp of thousands of feet resounded. The column moved forward without knowing where, and unable from the masses around them, the smoke and the increasing fog, to see either the place they were leaving or that to which they were going.

A soldier on the march is hemmed in and borne along by his regiment as much as a sailor is by his ship. However far he has walked, whatever strange, unknown and dangerous places he reaches, just as a sailor is always surrounded by the same decks, masts and rigging of his ship, so the soldier always has around him the same comrades, the same ranks, the same sergeant-major Iván Mítrich, the same company dog Jack, and the same commanders. The sailor rarely cares to know the latitude in which his ship is sailing, but on the day of battle—heaven knows how and whence—a stern note of which all are conscious sounds in the moral atmosphere of an army, announcing the approach of something decisive and solemn, and awakening in the men an unusual curiosity. On the day of battle the soldiers excitedly try to get beyond the interests of their regiment, they listen intently, look about and eagerly ask concerning what is going on around them.

The fog had grown so dense that though it was growing light they could not see ten paces ahead. Bushes looked like gigantic trees and level ground like cliffs and slopes. Anywhere, on any side, one might encounter an enemy invisible ten paces off. But the columns advanced for a long time, always in the same fog, descending and ascending hills, avoiding gardens and enclosures, going over new and unknown ground, and nowhere encountering the enemy. On the contrary, the soldiers became aware that in front, behind and on all sides, other Russian columns were moving in the same direction. Every soldier felt glad to know that to the unknown place where he was going, many more of our men were going too.

"There now, the Kúrskies have also gone past," was being said in the ranks.

"It's wonderful what a lot of our troops have gathered, lads! Last night I looked at the campfires and there was no end of them. A regular Moscow!"

Though none of the column commanders rode up to the ranks or talked to the men (the commanders, as we saw at the council of war, were out of humor and dissatisfied with the affair, and so did not exert themselves to cheer the men but merely carried out the orders), yet the troops marched gaily, as they always do when going into action, especially to an attack. But when they had marched for about an hour in the dense fog, the greater part of the men had to halt, and an unpleasant consciousness of some dislocation and blunder spread through the ranks. How such a consciousness is communicated is very difficult to define, but it certainly is communicated very surely, and flows rapidly, imperceptibly, and irrepressibly, as water does in a creek. Had the Russian army been alone without any allies, it might perhaps have been a long time before this consciousness of mismanagement became a general conviction, but as it was, the disorder was readily and naturally attributed to the stupid Germans, and everyone was convinced that a dangerous muddle had been occasioned by the sausage-eaters.

"Why have we stopped? Is the way blocked? Or have we already come up against the French?"

"No, one can't hear them. They'd be firing if we had."

"They were in a hurry enough to start us, and now here we stand in the middle of a field without rhyme or reason. It's all those damned Germans' muddling! What stupid devils!"

"Yes, I'd send them on in front, but no fear, they're crowding up behind. And now here we stand hungry."

"I say, shall we soon be clear? They say the cavalry are blocking the way," said an officer.

"Ah, those damned Germans! They don't know their own country!" said another.

"What division are you?" shouted an adjutant, riding up.

"The Eighteenth."

"Then why are you here? You should have gone on long ago, now you won't get there till evening."

"What stupid orders! They don't themselves know what they are doing!" said the officer and rode off.

Then a general rode past shouting something angrily, not in Russian.

"Tafa-lafa! But what he's jabbering no one can make out," said a soldier, mimicking the general who had ridden away. "I'd shoot them, the scoundrels!"

"We were ordered to be at the place before nine, but we haven't got halfway. Fine orders!" was being repeated on different sides.

And the feeling of energy with which the troops had started began to turn into vexation and anger at the stupid arrangements and at the Germans.

The cause of the confusion was that while the Austrian cavalry was moving toward our left flank, the higher command found that our center was too far separated from our right flank and the cavalry were all ordered to turn back to the right. Several thousand cavalry crossed in front of the infantry, who had to wait.

At the front an altercation occurred between an Austrian guide and a Russian general. The general shouted a demand that the cavalry should be halted, the Austrian argued that not he, but the higher command, was to blame. The troops meanwhile stood growing listless and dispirited. After an hour's delay they at last moved on, descending the hill. The fog that was dispersing on the hill lay still more densely below, where they were descending. In front in the fog a shot was heard and then another, at first irregularly at varying intervals—trata . . . tat—and then more and more regularly and rapidly, and the action at the Goldbach stream began.

Not expecting to come on the enemy down by the stream, and having stumbled on him in the fog, hearing no encouraging word from their commanders, and with a consciousness of being too late spreading through the ranks, and above all being unable to see anything in front or around them in the thick fog, the Russians exchanged shots with the enemy lazily, and advanced and again halted, receiving no timely orders from the officers or adjutants who wandered about in the fog in those unknown surroundings unable to find their own regiments. In this way the action began for the first, second and third columns, which had gone down into the valley. The fourth column, with which Kutúzov was, stood on the Pratzen heights.

Below, where the fight was beginning, there was still thick fog; on the higher ground it was clearing, but nothing could be seen of what was going on in front. Whether all the enemy forces were, as we supposed, six miles away, or whether they were nearby in that sea of mist, no one knew till after eight o'clock.

It was nine o'clock in the morning. The fog lay unbroken like a sea down below, but higher up at the village of Schlappanitz where Napoleon stood with his marshals around him, it was quite light. Above him was a clear blue sky, and the sun's vast orb quivered like a huge hollow, crimson float on the surface of that milky sea of mist. The whole French army, and even Napoleon himself with his staff, were not on the far side of the streams and hollows of Sokolnitz and Schlappanitz beyond which we intended to take up our position and begin the action, but were on this side, so close to our own forces that Napoleon with the naked eye could distinguish a mounted man from one on foot. Napoleon, in the blue cloak which he had worn on his Italian campaign, sat on his small gray Arab horse a little in front of his marshals. He gazed silently at the hills which seemed to rise out of the sea of mist and on which the Russian troops were moving in the distance, and he listened to the sounds of firing in the valley. Not a single muscle of his face—which in those days was still thin—moved. His gleaming eyes were fixed intently on one spot. His predictions were being justified. Part of the Russian force had already descended into the valley toward the ponds and lakes, and part were leaving these Pratzen Heights which he intended to attack and regarded as the key to the position. He saw over the mist that in a hollow between two hills near the village of Pratzen, the Russian columns, their bayonets glittering, were moving continuously in one direction toward the valley and disappearing one after another into the mist. From information he had received the evening before, from the sound of wheels and footsteps heard by the outposts during the night, by the disorderly movement of the Russian columns, and from all indications, he saw clearly that the allies believed him to be far away in front of them, and that the columns moving near Pratzen constituted the center of the Russian army, and that that center was already sufficiently weakened to be successfully attacked. But still he did not begin the engagement.

Today was a great day for him—the anniversary of his coronation. Before dawn he had slept for a few hours, and refreshed, vigorous and in good spirits, he mounted his horse and rode out into the field in that happy mood in which everything seems possible and everything succeeds. He sat motionless, looking at the heights visible above the mist, and his cold face wore that special look of confident, self-complacent happiness that one sees on the face of a boy happily in love. The marshals stood behind him not venturing to distract his attention. He looked now at the Pratzen Heights, now at the sun floating up out of the mist.

When the sun had entirely emerged from the fog, and fields and mist were aglow with dazzling light—as if he had only awaited this to begin the action—he drew the glove from his shapely white hand, made a sign with it to the marshals, and ordered the action to begin. The marshals, accompanied by adjutants, galloped off in different directions, and a few minutes later the chief forces of the French army moved rapidly toward those Pratzen Heights which were being more and more denuded by Russian troops moving down the valley to their left.

Chapter XV

At eight o'clock Kutúzov rode to Pratzen at the head of the fourth column, Milorádovich's, the one that was to take the place of Przebyszéwski's and Langeron's columns which had already gone down into the valley. He greeted the men of the foremost regiment and gave them the order to march, thereby indicating that he intended to lead that column himself. When he had reached the village of Pratzen he halted. Prince Andrew was behind, among the immense number forming the commander-in-chief's suite. He was in a state of suppressed excitement and irritation, though controlledly calm as a man is at the approach of a long-awaited moment. He was firmly convinced that this was the day of his Toulon, or his bridge of Arcola. How it would come about he did not know, but he felt sure it would do so. The locality and the position of our troops were known to him as far as they could be known to anyone in our army. His own strategic plan, which obviously could not now be carried out, was forgotten. Now, entering into Weyrother's plan, Prince Andrew considered possible contingencies and formed new projects such as might call for his rapidity of perception and decision.

To the left down below in the mist, the musketry fire of unseen forces could be heard. It was there Prince Andrew thought the fight would concentrate. "There we shall encounter difficulties, and there," thought he, "I shall be sent with a brigade or division, and there, standard in hand, I shall go forward and break whatever is in front of me."

He could not look calmly at the standards of the passing battalions. Seeing them he kept thinking, "That may be the very standard with which I shall lead the army."

In the morning all that was left of the night-mist on the heights was a hoarfrost now turning to dew, but in the valleys it still lay like a milk-white sea. Nothing was visible in the valleys to the left into which our troops had descended and from whence came the sounds of firing. Above the heights was the dark clear sky, and to the right the vast orb of the sun. In front, far off on the farther shore of that sea of mist some wooded hills were discernible, and it was there the enemy probably was, for something could be descried. On the right the Guards were entering the misty region with a sound of hoofs and wheels and now and then a gleam of bayonets; to the left beyond the village similar masses of cavalry came up and disappeared in the sea of mist. In front and behind moved infantry. The commander-in-chief was standing at the end of the village letting the troops pass by him. That morning Kutúzov seemed worn and irritable. The infantry passing before him came to a halt without any command being given, apparently obstructed by something in front.

"Do order them to form into battalion columns and go round the village!" he said angrily to a general who had ridden up. "Don't you understand, your excellency, my dear sir, that you must not defile through narrow village streets when we are marching against the enemy?"

"I intended to re-form them beyond the village, your excellency," answered the general.

Kutúzov laughed bitterly.

"You'll make a fine thing of it, deploying in sight of the enemy! Very fine!"

"The enemy is still far away, your excellency. According to the dispositions . . ."

"The dispositions!" exclaimed Kutúzov bitterly. "Who told you that? . . . Kindly do as you are ordered."

"Yes, sir."

"My dear fellow," Nesvítski whispered to Prince Andrew, "the old man is as surly as a dog."

An Austrian officer in a white uniform with green plumes in his hat galloped up to Kutúzov and asked in the Emperor's name, had the fourth column advanced into action?

Kutúzov turned round without answering and his eye happened to fall upon Prince Andrew, who was beside him. Seeing him, Kutúzov's malevolent and caustic expression softened, as if admitting that what was being done was not his adjutant's fault, and still not answering the Austrian adjutant, he addressed Bolkónski.

"Go, my dear fellow, and see whether the third division has passed the village. Tell it to stop and await my orders."

Hardly had Prince Andrew started than he stopped him.

"And ask whether sharpshooters have been posted," he added. "What are they doing? What are they doing?" he murmured to himself, still not replying to the Austrian.

Prince Andrew galloped off to execute the order.

Overtaking the battalions that continued to advance, he stopped the third division and convinced himself that there really were no sharpshooters in front of our columns. The colonel at the head of the regiment was much surprised at the commander-in-chief's order to throw out skirmishers. He had felt perfectly sure that there were other troops in front of him and that the enemy must be at least six miles away. There was really nothing to be seen in front except a barren descent hidden by dense mist. Having given orders in the commander-in-chief's name to rectify this omission, Prince Andrew galloped back. Kutúzov still in the same place, his stout body resting heavily in the saddle with the lassitude of age, sat yawning wearily with closed eyes. The troops were no longer moving, but stood with the butts of their muskets on the ground.

"All right, all right!" he said to Prince Andrew, and turned to a general who, watch in hand, was saying it was time they started as all the left flank columns had already descended.

"Plenty of time, your excellency," muttered Kutúzov in the midst of a yawn. "Plenty of time," he repeated.

Just then at a distance behind Kutúzov was heard the sound of regiments saluting, and this sound rapidly came nearer along the whole extended line of the advancing Russian columns. Evidently the person they were greeting was riding quickly. When the soldiers of the regiment in front of which Kutúzov was standing began to shout, he rode a little to one side and looked round with a frown. Along the road from Pratzen galloped what looked like a squadron of horsemen in various uniforms. Two of them rode side by side in front, at full gallop. One in a black uniform with white plumes in his hat rode a bob-tailed chestnut horse, the other who was in a white uniform, rode a black one. These were the two Emperors followed by their suites. Kutúzov, affecting the manners of an old soldier at the front, gave the command "Attention!" and rode up to the Emperors with a salute. His whole appearance and manner were suddenly transformed. He put on the air of a subordinate who obeys without reasoning. With an affectation of respect which evidently struck Alexander unpleasantly, he rode up and saluted.

This unpleasant impression merely flitted over the young and happy face of the Emperor like a cloud of haze across a clear sky, and vanished. After his illness he looked rather thinner that day than on the field of Olmütz where Bolkónski had seen him for the first time abroad, but there was still the same bewitching combination of majesty and mildness in his fine gray eyes, and on his delicate lips the same capacity for varying expression and the same prevalent appearance of good-hearted innocent youth.

At the Olmütz review he had seemed more majestic, here he seemed brighter and more energetic. He was slightly flushed after galloping two miles, and reining in his horse he sighed restfully and looked round at the faces of his suite, young and animated as his own. Czartoryski, Novosíltsev, Prince Volkónsky, Strógonov and the others, all richly dressed gay young men on splendid, well-groomed, fresh, only slightly heated horses, exchanging remarks and smiling, had stopped behind the Emperor. The Emperor Francis, a rosy long-faced young man, sat very erect on his handsome black horse looking about him in a leisurely and preoccupied manner. He beckoned to one of his white adjutants and asked some question—"Most likely he is asking at what o'clock they started," thought Prince Andrew, watching his old acquaintance with a smile he could not repress as he recalled his reception at Brnn. In the Emperors' suite were the picked young orderly officers of the Guard and line regiments, Russian and Austrian. Among them were grooms leading the Tsar's beautiful relay horses covered with embroidered cloths.

As when a window is opened a whiff of fresh air from the fields enters a stuffy room, so a whiff of youthfulness, energy and confidence of success reached Kutúzov's cheerless staff with the galloping advent of all these brilliant young men.

"Why aren't you beginning, Michael Ilariónovich?" said the Emperor Alexander hurriedly to Kutúzov, glancing courteously at the same time at the Emperor Francis.

"I am waiting, your Majesty," answered Kutúzov, bending forward respectfully.

The Emperor, frowning slightly, bent his ear forward as if he had not quite heard.

"Waiting, your Majesty," repeated Kutúzov. (Prince Andrew noted that Kutúzov's upper lip twitched unnaturally as he said the word "waiting.") "Not all the columns have formed up yet, your Majesty."

The Tsar heard but obviously did not like the reply; he shrugged his rather round shoulders and glanced at Novosíltsev who was near him, as if complaining of Kutúzov.

"You know, Michael Ilariónovich, we are not on the Empress's Field where a parade does not begin till all the troops are assembled," said the Tsar with another glance at the Emperor Francis, as if inviting him if not to join in at least to listen to what he was saying. But the Emperor Francis continued to look about him and did not listen.

"That is just why I do not begin, sire," said Kutúzov in a resounding voice, apparently to preclude the possibility of not being heard, and again something in his face twitched—"That is just why I do not begin, sire, because we are not on parade and not on the Empress's Field," said he clearly and distinctly.

In the Emperor's suite all exchanged rapid looks that expressed dissatisfaction and reproach. "Old though he may be, he should not, he certainly should not, speak like that," their glances seemed to say.

The Tsar looked intently and observantly into Kutúzov's eye waiting to hear whether he would say anything more. But Kutúzov, with respectfully bowed head, seemed also to be waiting. The silence lasted for about a minute.

"However, if you command it, your Majesty," said Kutúzov, lifting his head and again assuming his former tone of a dull, unreasoning, but submissive general.

He touched his horse and having called Milorádovich, the commander of the column, gave him the order to advance.

The troops again began to move, and two battalions of the Nóvgorod and one of the œpsheron regiment went forward past the Emperor.

As this Ápsheron battalion marched by, the red-faced Milorádovich, without his greatcoat, with his Orders on his breast and an enormous tuft of plumes in his cocked hat worn on one side with its corners front and back, galloped strenuously forward, and with a dashing salute reined in his horse before the Emperor.

"God be with you, general!" said the Emperor.

"Ma foi, sire, nous ferons ce qui sera dans notre possibilité, sire," he answered gaily, raising nevertheless ironic smiles among the gentlemen of the Tsar's suite by his poor French.

Milorádovich wheeled his horse sharply and stationed himself a little behind the Emperor. The œpsheron men, excited by the Tsar's presence, passed in step before the Emperors and their suites at a bold brisk pace.

"Lads!" shouted Milorádovich in a loud self-confident and cheery voice, obviously so elated by the sound of firing, by the prospect of battle, and by the sight of the gallant Ápsherons, his comrades in Suvórov's time, now passing so gallantly before the Emperors, that he forgot the sovereigns' presence. "Lads, it's not the first village you've had to take," cried he.

"Glad to do our best!" shouted the soldiers.

The Emperor's horse started at the sudden cry. This horse that had carried the sovereign at reviews in Russia bore him also here on the field of Austerlitz, enduring the heedless blows of his left foot and pricking its ears at the sound of shots just as it had done on the Empress's Field, not understanding the significance of the firing, nor of the nearness of the Emperor Francis's black cob, nor of all that was being said, thought, and felt that day by its rider.

The Emperor turned with a smile to one of his followers and made a remark to him, pointing to the gallant Ápsherons.

Chapter XVI

KUTÚZOV ACCOMPANIED BY HIS ADJUTANTS RODE AT A WALKING PACE BEHIND THE CARABINEERS.

When he had gone less than half a mile in the rear of the column he stopped at a solitary, deserted house that had probably once been an inn, where two roads parted. Both of them led downhill and troops were marching along both.

The fog had begun to clear and enemy troops were already dimly visible about a mile and a half off on the opposite heights. Down below, on the left, the firing became more distinct. Kutúzov had stopped and was speaking to an Austrian general. Prince Andrew, who was a little behind and looking at them, turned to an adjutant to ask him for a field-glass.

"Look, look!" said this adjutant, looking not at the troops in the distance, but down the hill before him. "It's the French!"

The two generals and the adjutant took hold of the field-glass, trying to snatch it from one another. The expression on all their faces suddenly changed to one of horror. The French were supposed to be a mile and a half away, but had suddenly and unexpectedly appeared just in front of us.

"It's the enemy? . . . No! . . . Yes, see it is! . . . for certain. . . . But how is that?" said different voices.

With the naked eye Prince Andrew saw below them to the right, not more than five hundred paces from where Kutúzov was standing, a dense French column coming up to meet the Ápsherons.

"Here it is! The decisive moment has arrived. My turn has come," thought Prince Andrew, and striking his horse he rode up to Kutúúzov.

"The Ápsherons must be stopped, your excellency," cried he. But at that very instant a cloud of smoke spread all round, firing was heard quite close at hand and a voice of naïve terror barely two steps from Prince Andrew, shouted, "Brothers! All's lost!" And at this voice, as if at a command, everyone began to run.

Confused and ever-increasing crowds were running back to where five minutes before the troops had passed the Emperors. Not only would it have been difficult to stop that crowd, it was even impossible not to be carried back with it oneself. Bolkónski only tried not to lose touch with it, and looked around bewildered and unable to grasp what was happening in front of him. Nesvítski with an angry face, red and unlike himself, was shouting to Kutúzov that if he did not ride away at once he would certainly be taken prisoner. Kutúzov remained in the same place, and without answering drew out a handkerchief. Blood was flowing from his cheek. Prince Andrew forced his way to him.

"You are wounded?" he asked, hardly able to master the trembling of his lower jaw.

"The wound is not here, it is there!" said Kutúzov, pressing the handkerchief to his wounded cheek and pointing to the fleeing soldiers. "Stop them!" he shouted, and at the same moment, probably realizing that it was impossible to stop them, spurred his horse and rode to the right.

A fresh wave of the flying mob caught him and bore him back with it.

The troops were running in such a dense mass that once surrounded by them it was difficult to get out again. One was shouting, "Get on! Why are you hindering us?" Another in the same place turned round and fired in the air; a third was striking the horse Kutúzov himself rode. Having by a great effort got away to the left from that flood of men, Kutúzov, with his suite diminished by more than half, rode toward a sound of artillery fire nearby. Having forced his way out of the crowd of fugitives, Prince Andrew, trying to keep near Kutúzov, saw on the slope of the hill amid the smoke a Russian battery that was still firing and Frenchmen running toward it. Higher up stood some Russian infantry, neither moving forward to protect the battery nor backward with the fleeing crowd. A mounted general separated himself from the infantry and approached Kutúzov. Of Kutúzov's suite only four remained. They were all pale and exchanged looks in silence.

"Stop those wretches!" gasped Kutúzov to the regimental commander, pointing to the flying soldiers; but at that instant, as if to punish him for those words, bullets flew hissing across the regiment and across Kutúzov's suite like a flock of little birds.

The French had attacked the battery, and seeing Kutúzov, were firing at him. After this volley the regimental commander clutched at his leg; several soldiers fell, and a second lieutenant who was holding the flag let it fall from his hands. It swayed and fell, but caught on the muskets of the nearest soldiers. The soldiers started firing without orders.

"Oh! Oh! Oh!" groaned Kutúzov despairingly and looked around. . . . "Bolkónski!" he whispered, his voice trembling from a consciousness of the feebleness of age, "Bolkónski!" he whispered pointing to the disordered battalion and at the enemy, "What's that?"

But before he had finished speaking, Prince Andrew, feeling tears of shame and anger choking him, had already leapt from his horse and run to the standard.

"Forward, lads!" he shouted in a voice piercing as a child's.

"Here it is!" thought he, seizing the staff of the standard and hearing with pleasure the whistle of bullets evidently aimed at him. Several soldiers fell.

"Hurrah!" shouted Prince Andrew, and, scarcely able to hold up the heavy standard, he ran forward with full confidence that the whole battalion would follow him.

And really he only ran a few steps alone. One soldier moved and then another and soon the whole battalion ran forward shouting "hurrah!" and overtook him. A sergeant of the battalion ran up and took the flag that was swaying from its weight in Prince Andrew's hands, but he was immediately killed. Prince Andrew again seized the standard, and dragging it by the staff ran on with the battalion. In front he saw our artillerymen, some of whom were fighting, while others having abandoned their guns were running toward him. He also saw French infantry soldiers who were seizing the artillery horses and turning the guns round. Prince Andrew and the battalion were already within twenty paces of the cannon. He heard the whistle of bullets above him unceasingly and to right and left of him soldiers continually groaned and dropped. But he did not look at them: he looked only at what was going on in front of him—at the battery. He now saw clearly the figure of a red-haired gunner with his shako knocked awry, pulling one end of a mop while a French soldier tugged at the other. He could distinctly see the distraught yet angry expression on the faces of these two men, who evidently did not realize what they were doing.

"What are they about?" thought Prince Andrew as he gazed at them. "Why doesn't the red-haired gunner run away as he is unarmed? Why doesn't the Frenchman stab him? He will not get away before the Frenchman remembers his bayonet and stabs him. . . ."

And really another French soldier, trailing his musket, ran up to the struggling men and the fate of the red-haired gunner who had triumphantly secured the mop and still did not realize what awaited him, was about to be decided. But Prince Andrew did not see how it ended. It seemed to him as though one of the soldiers near him hit him on the head with the full swing of a bludgeon. It hurt a little, but the worst of it was that the pain distracted him and prevented his seeing what he had been looking at.

"What's this? Am I falling? My legs are giving way," thought he, and fell on his back. He opened his eyes, hoping to see how the struggle of the Frenchmen with the gunners ended, whether the red-haired gunner had been killed or not and whether the cannon had been captured or saved. But he saw nothing. Above him there was now nothing but the sky—the lofty sky, not clear yet still immeasurably lofty, with gray clouds gliding slowly across it. "How quiet, peaceful and solemn; not at all as I ran," thought Prince Andrew—"not as we ran, shouting and fighting, not at all as the gunner and the Frenchman with frightened and angry faces struggled for the mop: how differently do those clouds glide across that lofty infinite sky! How was it I did not see that lofty sky before? And how happy I am to have found it at last! Yes! All is vanity, all falsehood, except that infinite sky. There is nothing, nothing, but that. But even it does not exist, there is nothing but quiet and peace. Thank God! . . ."

Chapter XVII

On our right flank commanded by Bagratión, at nine o'clock the battle had not yet begun. Not wishing to agree to Dolgorúkov's demand to commence the action, and wishing to avert responsibility from himself, Prince Bagratión proposed to Dolgorúkov to send to inquire of the commander-in-chief. Bagratión knew that as the distance between the two flanks was more than six miles, even if the messenger were not killed (which he very likely would be), and found the commander-in-chief (which would be very difficult), he would not be able to get back before evening.

Bagratión cast his large, expressionless, sleepy eyes round his suite, and the boyish face of Rostóv, breathless with excitement and hope, was the first to catch his eye. He sent him.

"And if I should meet his Majesty before I meet the commander-in-chief, your excellency?" said Rostóv, with his hand to his cap.

"You can give the message to his Majesty," said Dolgorúkov, hurriedly interrupting Bagratión.

On being relieved from picket duty Rostóv had managed to get a few hours' sleep before morning, and felt cheerful, bold and resolute, with elasticity of movement, faith in his good fortune and generally in that state of mind which makes everything seem possible, pleasant and easy.

All his wishes were being fulfilled that morning: there was to be a general engagement in which he was taking part, more than that, he was orderly to the bravest general, and still more, he was going with a message to Kutúzov, perhaps even to the sovereign himself. The morning was bright, he had a good horse under him, and his heart was full of joy and happiness. On receiving the order he gave his horse the rein and galloped along the line. At first he rode along the line of Bagratión's troops, which had not yet advanced into action but were standing motionless; then he came to the region occupied by Uvárov's cavalry and here he noticed a stir and signs of preparation for battle; having passed Uvárov's cavalry he clearly heard the sound of cannon and musketry ahead of him. The firing grew louder and louder.

In the fresh morning air were now heard, not two or three musket shots at irregular intervals as before, followed by one or two cannon shots, but a roll of volleys of musketry from the slopes of the hill before Pratzen, interrupted by such frequent reports of cannon that sometimes several of them were not separated from one another but merged into a general roar.

He could see puffs of musketry smoke that seemed to chase one another down the hillsides, and clouds of cannon smoke rolling, spreading and mingling with one another. He could also, by the gleam of bayonets visible through the smoke, make out moving masses of infantry and narrow lines of artillery with green caissons.

Rostóv stopped his horse for a moment on a hillock to see what was going on, but strain his attention as he would he could not understand or make out anything of what was happening: there in the smoke men of some sort were moving about, in front and behind moved lines of troops; but why, whither and who they were, it was impossible to make out. These sights and sounds had no depressing or intimidating effect on him, on the contrary they stimulated his energy and determination.

"Go on! Go on! Give it them!" he mentally exclaimed at these sounds, and again proceeded to gallop along the line, penetrating farther and farther into the region where the army was already in action.

"How it will be there I don't know, but all will be well!" thought Rostóv.

After passing some Austrian troops he noticed that the next part of the line (the Guards) was already in action.

"So much the better! I shall see it close," he thought.

He was riding almost along the front line. A handful of men came galloping toward him. They were our Uhlans who with disordered ranks were returning from the attack. Rostóv got out of their way, involuntarily noticed that one of them was bleeding, and galloped on.

"That is no business of mine," he thought. He had not ridden many hundred yards after that before he saw to his left, across the whole width of the field, an enormous mass of cavalry in brilliant white uniforms, mounted on black horses, trotting straight toward him and across his path. Rostóv put his horse to full gallop to get out of the way of these men, and he would have got clear had they continued at the same speed, but they kept increasing their pace, so that some of the horses were already galloping. Rostóv heard the thud of their hoofs and the jingle of their weapons and saw their horses, their figures and even their faces, more and more distinctly. They were our Horse-Guards, advancing to attack the French cavalry that was coming to meet them.

The Horse-Guards were galloping, but still holding in their horses. Rostóv could already see their faces and heard the command: "Charge!" shouted by an officer who was urging his thoroughbred to full speed. Rostóv fearing to be crushed or swept into the attack on the French, galloped along the front as hard as his horse could go, but still was not in time to avoid them.

The last of the Horse-Guards, a huge pockmarked fellow, frowned angrily on seeing Rostóv before him, with whom he would inevitably collide. This Guardsman would certainly have bowled Rostóv and his Bedouin over (Rostóv felt himself quite tiny and weak compared to these gigantic men and horses) had it not occurred to Rostóv to flourish his whip before the eyes of the Guardsman's horse. The heavy black horse, sixteen hands high, shied, throwing back its ears; but the pockmarked Guardsman drove his huge spurs in violently, and the horse flourishing its tail and extending its neck, galloped on yet faster. Hardly had the Horse-Guards passed Rostóv before he heard them shout, "Hurrah!" and looking back saw that their foremost ranks were mixed up with some foreign cavalry with red epaulets, probably French. He could see nothing more, for immediately afterward cannon began firing from somewhere and smoke enveloped everything.

At that moment, as the Horse-Guards having passed him disappeared in the smoke, Rostóv hesitated whether to gallop after them or to go where he was sent. This was the brilliant charge of the Horse-Guards that amazed the French themselves. Rostóv was horrified to hear later that of all that mass of huge and handsome men, of all those brilliant, rich youths, officers and cadets, who had galloped past him on their thousand-ruble horses, only eighteen were left after the charge.

"Why should I envy them? My chance is not lost, and maybe I shall see the Emperor immediately!" thought Rostóv and galloped on.

When he came level with the Foot Guards he noticed that about them and around them cannon-balls were flying, of which he was aware not so much because he heard their sound as because he saw uneasiness on the soldiers' faces, and unnatural warlike solemnity on those of the officers.

Passing behind one of the lines of a regiment of Foot Guards he heard a voice calling him by name.

"Rostóv!"

"What?" he answered, not recognizing Borís.

"I say, we've been in the front line! Our regiment attacked!" said Borís with the happy smile seen on the faces of young men who have been under fire for the first time.

Rostóv stopped.

"Have you?" he said. "Well, how did it go?"

"We drove them back!" said Borís with animation, growing talkative. "Can you imagine it?" and he began describing how the Guards having taken up their position and seeing troops before them, thought they were Austrians, and all at once discovered from the cannon-balls discharged by those troops, that they were themselves in the front line and had unexpectedly to go into action. Rostóv without hearing Borís to the end spurred his horse.

"Where are you off to?" asked Borís.

"With a message to his Majesty."

"There he is!" said Borís, thinking Rostóv had said "His Highness," and pointing to the Grand Duke who with his high shoulders and frowning brows stood a hundred paces away from them in his helmet and horse-guards' jacket, shouting something to a pale, white uniformed Austrian officer.

"But that's the Grand Duke, and I want the commander-in-chief or the Emperor," said Rostóv, and was about to spur his horse.

"Count! Count!" shouted Berg who ran up from the other side as eager as Borís. "Count! I am wounded in my right hand" (and he showed his bleeding hand with a handkerchief tied round it) "and I remained at the front. I held my sword in my left hand, count. All our family—the von Bergs—have been knights!"

He said something more, but Rostóv did not wait to hear it and rode away.

Having passed the Guards and traversed an empty space, Rostóv to avoid again getting in front of the first line as he had done when the Horse-Guards charged, followed the line of reserves, going far round the place where the hottest musket-fire and cannonade was heard. Suddenly he heard musket-fire quite close in front of him and behind our troops, where he could never have expected the enemy to be.

"What can it be?" he thought. "The enemy in the rear of our army? Impossible!" And suddenly he was seized by a panic of fear for himself and for the issue of the whole battle. "But be that what it may," he reflected, "there is no riding round it now. I must look for the commander-in-chief here, and if all is lost it is for me to perish with the rest."

The foreboding of evil that had suddenly come over Rostóv was more and more confirmed the farther he rode into the region behind the village of Pratzen, which was full of troops of all kinds.

"What does it mean? What is it? Whom are they firing at? Who is firing?" Rostóv kept asking as he came up to Russian and Austrian soldiers running in confused crowds across his path.

"The devil knows! They've killed everybody! It's all up now!" he was told in Russian, German and Czech, by the crowd of fugitives who understood what was happening as little as he did.

"Kill the Germans!" shouted one.

"May the devil take them—the traitors!"

"Zum Henker diese Russen!" muttered a German.

Several wounded men passed along the road, and words of abuse, screams and groans mingled in a general hubbub, then the firing died down. Rostóv learned later that Russian and Austrian soldiers had been firing at one another.

"My God! What does it all mean?" thought he. "And here, where at any moment the Emperor may see them. . . . But no, these must be only a handful of scoundrels. It will soon be over, it can't be *that*, it can't be! Only to get past them quicker, quicker!"

The idea of defeat and flight could not enter Rostóv's head. Though he saw French cannon and French troops on the Pratzen Heights just where he had been ordered to look for the commander-in-chief, he could not, did not wish to, believe *that*.

Chapter XVIII

ROSTÓV HAD BEEN ORDERED TO LOOK FOR KUTÚZOV AND THE EMPEROR NEAR THE VILLAGE OF Pratzen. But neither they nor a single commanding officer were there, only disorganized crowds of troops of various kinds. He urged on his already weary horse to get quickly past these crowds, but the farther he went the more disorganized they were. The highroad on which he had come out was thronged with calèches, carriages of all sorts, and Russian and Austrian soldiers of all arms, some wounded and some not. This whole mass droned and jostled in confusion under the dismal influence of cannon-balls flying from the French batteries stationed on the Pratzen heights.

"Where is the Emperor? Where is Kutúzov?" Rostóv kept asking everyone he could stop, but got no answer from anyone.

At last seizing a soldier by his collar he forced him to answer.

"Eh, brother! They've all bolted long ago!" said the soldier, laughing for some reason and shaking himself free.

Having left that soldier who was evidently drunk, Rostóv stopped the horse of a batman or groom of some important personage and began to question him. The man announced that the Tsar had been driven in a carriage at full speed about an hour before along that very road and that he was dangerously wounded.

"It can't be!" said Rostóv. "It must have been someone else."

"I saw him myself," replied the man with a self-confident smile of derision. "I ought to know the Emperor by now, after the times I've seen him in Petersburg. I saw him just as I see you. . . . There he sat in the carriage as pale as anything. How they made the four black horses fly! Gracious me, they did rattle past! It's time I knew the imperial horses and Ilyá Iványch. I don't think Ilyá drives anyone except the Tsar!"

Rostóv let go of the horse and was about to ride on, when a wounded officer passing by addressed him:

"Who is it you want?" he asked. "The commander-in-chief? He was killed by a cannon-ball—struck in the breast before our regiment."

"Not killed—wounded!" another officer corrected him.

"Who? Kutúzov?" asked Rostóv.

"Not Kutúzov, but what's his name—well, never mind . . . there are not many left alive. Go that way, to that village, all the commanders are there," said the officer, pointing to the village of Hosjeradek, and he walked on.

Rostóv rode on at a footpace not knowing why or to whom he was now going. The Emperor was wounded, the battle lost. It was impossible to doubt it now. Rostóv rode in the direction pointed out to him, in which he saw turrets and a church. What need to hurry? What was he now to say to the Tsar or to Kutúzov, even if they were alive and unwounded?

"Take this road, your honor, that way you will be killed at once!" a soldier shouted to him. "They'd kill you there!"

"Oh, what are you talking about?" said another. "Where is he to go? That way is nearer."

Rostóv considered, and then went in the direction where they said he would be killed.

"It's all the same now. If the Emperor is wounded, am I to try to save myself?" he thought. He rode on to the region where the greatest number of men had perished in fleeing from Pratzen. The French had not yet occupied that region, and the Russians—the uninjured and slightly wounded—had left it long ago. All about the field, like heaps of manure on well-kept plowland, lay from ten to fifteen dead and wounded to each couple of acres. The wounded crept together in twos and threes and one could hear their distressing screams and groans, sometimes feigned—or so it seemed to Rostóv. He put his horse to a trot to avoid seeing all these suffering men, and he felt afraid—afraid not for his life, but for the courage he needed and which he knew would not stand the sight of these unfortunates.

The French, who had ceased firing at this field strewn with dead and wounded where there was no one left to fire at, on seeing an adjutant riding over it trained a gun on him and fired several shots. The sensation of those terrible whistling sounds and of the corpses around him merged in Rostóv's mind into a single feeling of terror and pity for himself. He remembered his mother's last letter. "What would she feel," thought he, "if she saw me here now on this field with the cannon aimed at me?"

In the village of Hosjeradek there were Russian troops retiring from the field of battle, who though still in some confusion were less disordered. The French cannon did not reach there and the musketry fire sounded far away. Here everyone clearly saw and said that the battle was lost. No one whom Rostóv asked could tell him where the Emperor or Kutúzov was. Some said the report that the Emperor was wounded was correct, others that it was not, and explained the false rumor that had spread by the fact that the Emperor's carriage had really galloped from the field of battle with the pale and terrified Ober-Hofmarschal Count Tolstóy, who had ridden out to the battlefield with others in the Emperor's suite. One officer told Rostóv that he had seen someone from headquarters behind the village to the left, and thither Rostóv rode, not hoping to find anyone but merely to ease his conscience. When he had ridden about two miles and had passed the last of the Russian troops, he saw, near a kitchen-garden with a ditch round it, two men on horseback facing the ditch. One with a white plume in his hat seemed familiar to Rostóv; the other on a beautiful chestnut horse (which Rostóv fancied he had seen before) rode up to the ditch, struck his horse with his spurs, and giving it the rein leaped lightly over. Only a little earth crumbled from the bank under the horse's hind hoofs. Turning the horse sharply, he again jumped the ditch, and deferentially addressed the horseman with the white plumes, evidently suggesting that he should do the same. The rider, whose figure seemed familiar to Rostóv and involuntarily riveted his attention, made a gesture of refusal with his head and hand and by that gesture Rostóv instantly recognized his lamented and adored monarch.

"But it can't be he, alone in the midst of this empty field!" thought Rostóv. At that moment Alexander turned his head and Rostóv saw the beloved features that were so deeply engraved on his memory. The Emperor was pale, his cheeks sunken and his eyes hollow, but the charm, the mildness of his features, was all the greater. Rostóv was happy in the assurance that the rumors about the Emperor being wounded were false. He was happy to be seeing him. He knew that he might, and even ought, to go straight to him and give the message Dolgorúkov had ordered him to deliver.

But as a youth in love trembles, is unnerved, and dares not utter the thoughts he has dreamed of for nights, but looks around for help or a chance of delay and flight when the longed-for moment comes and he is alone with *her*, so Rostóv, now that he had attained what he had longed for more than anything else in the world, did not know how to approach the Emperor, and a thousand reasons occurred to him why it would be inconvenient, unseemly and impossible to do so.

"What! It is as if I were glad of a chance to take advantage of his being alone and despondent! A strange face may seem unpleasant or painful to him at this moment of sorrow; besides, what can I say to him now, when my heart fails me and my mouth feels dry at the mere sight of him?" Not one of the innumerable speeches addressed to the Emperor that he had composed in his imagination could he now recall. Those speeches were intended for quite other conditions, they were for the most part to be spoken at a moment of victory and triumph, generally when he was dying of wounds and the sovereign had thanked him for heroic deeds, and while dying he expressed the love his actions had proved.

"Besides how can I ask the Emperor for his instructions for the right flank now that it is nearly four o'clock and the battle is lost? No, certainly I must not approach him, I must not intrude on his reflections. Better die a thousand times than risk receiving an unkind look or bad opinion from him," Rostóv decided; and sorrowfully and with a heart full despair he rode away, continually looking back at the Tsar, who still remained in the same attitude of indecision.

While Rostóv was thus arguing with himself and riding sadly away, Captain von Toll chanced to ride to the same spot, and seeing the Emperor at once rode up to him, offered his services, and assisted him to cross the ditch on foot. The Emperor, wishing to rest and feeling unwell, sat down under an apple tree and von Toll remained beside him. Rostóv from a distance saw with envy and remorse how von Toll spoke long and warmly to the Emperor and how the Emperor, evidently weeping, covered his eyes with his hand and pressed von Toll's hand.

"And I might have been in his place!" thought Rostóv, and hardly restraining his tears of pity for the Emperor, he rode on in utter despair, not knowing where to or why he was now riding.

His despair was all the greater from feeling that his own weakness was the cause his grief.

He might . . . not only might but should, have gone up to the sovereign. It was a unique chance to show his devotion to the Emperor and he had not made use of it. . . . "What have I done?" thought he. And he turned round and galloped back to the place where he had seen the Emperor, but there was no one beyond the ditch now. Only some carts and carriages were passing by. From one of the drivers he learned that Kutúzov's staff were not far off, in the village the vehicles were going to. Rostóv followed them. In front of him walked Kutúzov's groom leading horses in horsecloths. Then came a cart, and behind that walked an old, bandy-legged domestic serf in a peaked cap and sheepskin coat.

"Tit! I say, Tit!" said the groom.

"What?" answered the old man absent-mindedly.

"Go, Tit! Thresh a bit!"

"Oh, you fool!" said the old man, spitting angrily. Some time passed in silence, and then the same joke was repeated.

Before five in the evening the battle had been lost at all points. More than a hundred cannon were already in the hands of the French.

Przebyszéwski and his corps had laid down their arms. Other columns after losing half their men were retreating in disorderly confused masses.

The remains of Langeron's and Dokhtúrov's mingled forces were crowding around the dams and banks of the ponds near the village of Augesd.

After five o'clock it was only at the Augesd Dam that a hot cannonade (delivered by the French alone) was still to be heard from numerous batteries ranged on the slopes of the Pratzen Heights, directed at our retreating forces.

In the rearguard Dokhtúrov and others rallying some battalions kept up a musketry fire at the French cavalry that was pursuing our troops. It was growing dusk. On the narrow Augesd Dam where for so many years the old miller had been accustomed to sit in his tasseled cap peacefully angling, while his grandson, with shirt-sleeves rolled up, handled the floundering silvery fish in the watering-can, on that dam over which for so many years Moravians in shaggy caps and blue jackets had peacefully driven their two-horse carts loaded with wheat and had returned dusty with flour whitening their carts—on that narrow dam amid the wagons and the cannon, under the horses' hoofs and between the wagon wheels, men disfigured by fear of death now crowded together, crushing one another, dying, stepping over the dying and killing one another, only to move on a few steps and be killed themselves in the same way.

Every ten seconds a cannon-ball flew compressing the air around, or a shell burst in the midst of that dense throng, killing some and splashing with blood those near them.

Dólokhov—now an officer—wounded in the arm, and on foot, with the regimental commander on horseback and some ten men of his company, represented all that was left of that whole regiment. Impelled by the crowd, they had got wedged in at the approach to the dam and, jammed in on all sides, had stopped because a horse in front had fallen under a cannon and the crowd were dragging it out. A cannon-ball killed someone behind them, another fell in front and splashed Dólokhov with blood. The crowd, pushing forward desperately, squeezed together, moved a few steps, and again stopped.

"Move on a hundred yards and we are certainly saved, remain here another two minutes and it is certain death," thought each one.

Dólokhov who was in the midst of the crowd forced his way to the edge of the dam, throwing two soldiers off their feet, and ran onto the slippery ice that covered the mill-pool.

"Turn this way!" he shouted, jumping over the ice which creaked under him; "turn this way!" he shouted to those with the gun. "It bears! . . ."

The ice bore him but it swayed and creaked, and it was plain that it would give way not only under a cannon or a crowd, but very soon even under his weight alone. The men looked at him and pressed to the bank, hesitating to step onto the ice. The general on horseback at the entrance to the dam, raised his hand and opened his mouth to address Dólokhov. Suddenly a cannon-ball hissed so low above the crowd that everyone ducked. It flopped into something moist, and the general fell from his horse in a pool of blood. Nobody gave him a look or thought of raising him.

"Get onto the ice, over the ice! Go on! Turn! Don't you hear? Go on!" innumerable voices suddenly shouted after the ball had struck the general, the men themselves not knowing what, or why, they were shouting.

One of the hindmost guns that was going onto the dam turned off onto the ice. Crowds of soldiers from the dam began running onto the frozen pond. The ice gave way under one of the foremost soldiers, and one leg slipped into the water. He tried to right himself but fell in up to his waist. The nearest soldiers shrank back, the gun-driver stopped his horse, but from behind still came the shouts: "Onto the ice, why do you stop? Go on! Go on!" And cries of horror were heard in the crowd. The soldiers near the gun waved their arms and beat the horses to make them turn and move on. The horses moved off the bank. The ice, that had held under those on foot, collapsed in a great mass, and some forty men who were on it dashed, some forward and some back, drowning one another.

Still the cannon-balls continued regularly to whistle and flop onto the ice and into the water, and oftenest of all among the crowd that covered the dam, the pond, and the bank.

Chapter XIX

ON THE PRATZEN HEIGHTS, WHERE HE HAD FALLEN WITH THE FLAGSTAFF IN HIS HAND, LAY Prince Andrew Bolkónski bleeding profusely and unconsciously uttering a gentle, piteous, and childlike moan.

Toward evening he ceased moaning and became quite still. He did not know how long his unconsciousness lasted. Suddenly he again felt that he was alive and suffering from a burning, lacerating pain in his head.

"Where is it, that lofty sky that I did not know till now, but saw today?" was his first thought. "And I did not know this suffering either," he thought. "Yes, I did not know anything, anything at all till now. But where am I?"

He listened, and heard the sound of approaching horses, and voices speaking French. He opened his eyes. Above him again was the same lofty sky with clouds that had risen and were floating still higher, and between them gleamed blue infinity. He did not turn his head and did not see those who, judging by the sound of hoofs and voices, had ridden up and stopped near him.

It was Napoleon accompanied by two aides-de-camp. Bonaparte riding over the battlefield had given final orders to strengthen the batteries firing at the Augesd Dam and was looking at the killed and wounded left on the field.

"Fine men!" remarked Napoleon, looking at a dead Russian grenadier, who with his face buried in the ground and a blackened nape, lay on his stomach with an already stiffened arm flung wide.

"The ammunition for the guns in position is exhausted, your Majesty," said an adjutant who had come from the batteries that were firing at Augesd.

"Have some brought from the reserve," said Napoleon, and having gone on a few steps he stopped before Prince Andrew, who lay on his back with the flagstaff that had been dropped beside him. (The flag had already been taken by the French as a trophy.)

"That's a fine death!" said Napoleon as he gazed at Bolkónski.

Prince Andrew understood that this was said of him, and that it was Napoleon who said it. He heard the speaker addressed as *Sire*. But he heard the words as he might have heard the buzzing of a fly. Not only did they not interest him, but he took no notice of them and at once forgot them. His head was burning, he felt himself bleeding to death, and he saw above him the remote, lofty and everlasting sky. He knew it was Napoleon—his hero—but at that moment Napoleon seemed to him such a small insignificant creature compared with what was passing now between himself and that lofty infinite sky with the clouds flying over it. At that moment it meant nothing to him who might be standing over him, or what was said of him; he was only glad that people were standing near him, and only wished that they would help him and bring him back to life, which seemed to him so beautiful now that he had today learned to understand it so differently. He collected all his strength, to stir and utter a sound. He feebly moved his leg, and uttered a weak sickly groan which aroused his own pity.

"Ah! He is alive," said Napoleon. "Lift this young man up and carry him to the dressing-station."

Having said this, Napoleon rode on to meet Marshal Lannes, who, hat in hand, rode up smiling to the Emperor to congratulate him on the victory.

Prince Andrew remembered nothing more: he lost consciousness from the terrible pain of being lifted onto the stretcher, the jolting while being moved, and the probing of his wound at the dressing-station. He did not regain consciousness till late in the day, when with other wounded and captured Russian officers he was carried to the hospital. During this transfer he felt a little stronger and was able to look about him and even speak.

The first words he heard on coming to his senses were those of a French convoy officer, who said rapidly:

"We must halt here: the Emperor will pass here immediately; it will please him to see these gentlemen prisoners."

"There are so many prisoners today, nearly the whole Russian army, that he is probably tired of them," said another officer.

"All the same! They say this one is the commander of all the Emperor Alexander's Guards," said the first one, indicating a Russian officer in the white uniform of the Horse-Guards.

Bolkónski recognized Prince Repnín whom he had met in Petersburg society. Beside him stood a lad of nineteen, also a wounded officer of the Horse-Guards.

Bonaparte, having come up at a gallop, stopped his horse.

"Which is the senior?" he asked, on seeing the prisoners.

They named the colonel, Prince Repnín.

"You are the commander of the Emperor Alexander's regiment of Horse-Guards?" asked Napoleon.

"I commanded a squadron," replied Repnín.

"Your regiment fulfilled its duty honorably," said Napoleon.

"The praise of a great commander is a soldier's highest reward," said Repnín.

"I bestow it with pleasure," said Napoleon. "And who is that young man beside you?"

Prince Repnín named Lieutenant Sukhtélen.

After looking at him Napoleon smiled.

"He's very young to come to meddle with us."

"Youth is no hindrance to courage," muttered Sukhtélen in a failing voice.

"A splendid reply!" said Napoleon. "Young man, you will go far!"

Prince Andrew, who had also been brought forward before the Emperor's eyes to complete the show of prisoners, could not fail to attract his attention. Napoleon apparently remembered seeing him on the battlefield, and addressing him, again used the epithet "young man" that was connected in his memory with Prince Andrew.

"Well, and you, young man," said he. "How do you feel, *mon brave?*"

Though five minutes before, Prince Andrew had been able to say a few words to the soldiers who were carrying him, now with his eyes fixed straight on Napoleon, he was silent. . . . So insignificant at that moment seemed to him all the interests that engrossed Napoleon, so mean did his hero himself with his paltry vanity and joy in victory appear, compared to the lofty, equitable and kindly sky which he had seen and understood—that he could not answer him.

Everything seemed so futile and insignificant in comparison with the stern and solemn train of thought that weakness from loss of blood, suffering and the nearness of death, aroused in him. Looking into Napoleon's eyes Prince Andrew thought of the insignificance of greatness, the unimportance of life which no one could understand, and the still greater unimportance of death, the meaning of which no one alive could understand or explain.

The Emperor without waiting for an answer turned away, and said to one of the officers as he went:

"Have these gentlemen attended to and taken to my bivouac; let my doctor, Larrey examine their wounds. *Au revoir,* Prince Repnín!" and he spurred his horse and galloped away.

His face shone with self-satisfaction and pleasure.

The soldiers who had carried Prince Andrew had noticed and taken the little gold icon Princess Mary had hung round her brother's neck, but seeing the favor the Emperor showed the prisoners, they now hastened to return the holy image. Prince Andrew did not see how and by whom it was replaced, but the little icon with its thin gold chain suddenly appeared upon his chest outside his uniform.

"It would be good," thought Prince Andrew, glancing at the icon his sister had hung round his neck with such emotion and reverence, "it would be good if everything were as clear and simple as it seems to Mary. How good it would be to know where to seek for help in this life, and what to expect after it beyond the grave! How happy and calm I should be if I could now say: 'Lord, have mercy on me!' . . . But to whom should I say that? Either to a Power indefinable, incomprehensible, which I not only cannot address but which I cannot even express in words—the Great All or Nothing—" said he to himself, "or to that God who has been sewn into this amulet by Mary! There is nothing certain, nothing at all except the unimportance of everything I understand, and the greatness of something incomprehensible but all-important."

The stretchers moved on. At every jolt he again felt unendurable pain; his feverishness increased and he grew delirious. Visions of his father, wife, sister and future son, and the tenderness he had felt the night before the battle, the figure of the insignificant little Napoleon, and above all this the lofty sky, formed the chief subjects of his delirious fancies.

The quiet home life and peaceful happiness of Bald Hills presented itself to him. He was already enjoying that happiness when that little Napoleon had suddenly appeared with his unsympathizing look of short-sighted delight at the misery of others, and doubts and torments had followed, and only the heavens promised peace. Toward morning all these dreams melted and merged into the chaos and darkness of unconciousness and oblivion, which in the opinion of Napoleon's doctor, Larrey, was much more likely to end in death than in convalescence.

"He is a nervous, bilious subject," said Larrey, "and will not recover."

And Prince Andrew, with others fatally wounded, was left to the care of the inhabitants of the district.

Part Four

Chapter I

EARLY IN THE YEAR 1806 NICHOLAS ROSTÓV RETURNED HOME ON LEAVE. DENÍSOV WAS GOING home to Vorónezh and Rostóv persuaded him to travel with him as far as Moscow and to stay with him there. Meeting a comrade at the last post station but one before Moscow, Denísov had drunk three bottles of wine with him, and despite the jolting ruts across the snow-covered road, did not once wake up on the way to Moscow, but lay at the bottom of the sleigh beside Rostóv, who grew more and more impatient the nearer they got to Moscow.

"How much longer? How much longer? Oh, these insufferable streets, shops, bakers' signboards, street lamps and sleighs!" thought Rostóv, when their leave-permits had been passed at the town gate and they had entered Moscow.

"Denísov! We're here? He's asleep," he added, leaning forward with his whole body as if in that position he hoped to hasten the speed of the sleigh.

Denísov gave no answer.

"There's the corner at the crossroads, where the cabman, Zakhár, has his stand, and there's Zakhár himself and still the same horse! And here's the little shop where we used to buy gingerbread! Can't you hurry up? Now then!"

"Which house is it?" asked the driver.

"Why, that one, right at the end, the big one. Don't you see? That's our house," said Rostóv. "Of course, it's our house! Denísov, Denísov! We're almost there!"

Denísov raised his head, coughed, and made no answer.

"Dmítri," said Rostóv to his valet on the box, "those lights are in our house, aren't they?"

"Yes, sir, and there's a light in your father's study."

"Then they've not gone to bed yet? What do you think? Mind now, don't forget to put out my new coat," added Rostóv, fingering his new mustache. "Now then, get on," he shouted to the driver. "Do wake up, Váska!" he went on, turning to Denísov, whose head was again nodding. "Come, get on! You shall have three rubles for vodka—get on!" Rostóv shouted, when the sleigh was only three houses from his door. It seemed to him the horses were not moving at all. At last the sleigh bore to the right, drew up at an entrance, and Rostóv saw overhead the old familiar cornice with a bit of plaster broken off, the porch, and the post by the side of the pavement. He sprang out before the sleigh stopped, and ran into the hall. The house stood cold and silent, as if quite regardless of who had come to it. There was no one in the hall. "Oh God! Is everyone all right?" he thought, stopping for a moment with a sinking heart, and then immediately starting to run along the hall and up the warped steps of the familiar staircase. The well-known old door handle, which always angered the countess when it was not properly cleansed, turned as loosely as ever. A solitary tallow candle burned in the anteroom.

Old Michael was asleep on the chest. Prokófy, the footman, who was so strong that he could lift the back of the carriage from behind, sat plaiting slippers out of cloth selvedges. He looked up at the opening door and his expression of sleepy indifference suddenly changed to one of delighted amazement.

"Gracious heavens! The young count!" he cried, recognizing his young master. "Can it be? My treasure!" and Prokófy, trembling with excitement, rushed toward the drawing room door, probably in order to announce him, but, changing his mind, came back and stooped to kiss the young man's shoulder.

"All well?" asked Rostóv, drawing away his arm.

"Yes, God be thanked! Yes! They've just finished supper. Let me have a look at you, your excellency."

"Is everything quite all right?"

"The Lord be thanked, yes!"

Rostóv, who had completely forgotten Denísov, not wishing anyone to forestall him, threw off his fur coat and ran on tiptoe through the large dark ballroom. All was the same: there were the same old card-tables and the same chandelier with a cover over it; but someone had already seen the young master, and before he had reached the drawing room, something flew out from a side door like a tornado and began hugging and kissing him. Another and yet another creature of the same kind sprang from a second door and a third; more hugging, more kissing, more outcries, and tears of joy. He could not distinguish which was Papa, which Natásha, and which Pétya. Everyone shouted, talked, and kissed him at the same time. Only his mother was not there, he noticed that.

"And I did not know . . . Nicholas . . . My darling! . . ."

"Here he is . . . our own . . . Kólya, dear fellow . . . How he has changed! . . . Where are the candles? . . . Tea! . . ."

"And me, kiss me!"

"Dearest . . . and me!"

Sónya, Natásha, Pétya, Anna Mikháylovna, Véra, and the old count were all hugging him, and the serfs, men and maids, flocked into the room, exclaiming and oh-ing and ah-ing.

Pétya, clinging to his legs, kept shouting, "And me too!"

Natásha, after she had pulled him down toward her and covered his face with kisses, holding him tight by the skirt of his coat, sprang away and pranced up and down in one place like a goat, and shrieked piercingly.

All around were loving eyes glistening with tears of joy, and all around were lips seeking a kiss.

Sónya too, all rosy red, clung to his arm and, radiant with bliss, looked eagerly toward his eyes, waiting for the look for which she longed. Sónya now was sixteen and she was very pretty, especially at this moment of happy rapturous excitement. She gazed at him, not taking her eyes off him, and smiling and holding her breath. He gave her a grateful look, but was still expectant and looking for someone. The old countess had not yet come. But now steps were heard at the door, steps so rapid that they could hardly be his mother's.

Yet it was she, dressed in a new gown which he did not know, made since he had left. All the others let him go, and he ran to her. When they met, she fell on his breast, sobbing. She could not lift her face, but only pressed it to the cold braiding of his hussar's jacket. Denísov, who had come into the room unnoticed by anyone, stood there and wiped his eyes at the sight.

"Vasíli Denísov, your son's friend," he said, introducing himself to the count, who was looking inquiringly at him.

"You are most welcome! I know, I know," said the count, kissing and embracing Denísov. "Nicholas wrote us . . . Natásha, Véra, look! Here is Denísov!"

The same happy rapturous faces turned to the shaggy figure of Denísov.

"Darling Denísov!" screamed Natásha, beside herself with rapture, springing to him, putting her arms round him, and kissing him. This escapade made everybody feel confused. Denísov blushed too, but smiled, and taking Natásha's hand, kissed it.

Denísov was shown to the room prepared for him, and the Rostóvs all gathered round Nicholas in the sitting room.

The old countess, not letting go of his hand and kissing it every moment, sat beside him: the rest, crowding round him, watched every movement, word, or look of his, never taking their blissfully adoring eyes off him. His brother and sisters struggled for the places nearest to him, and disputed with one another who should bring him his tea, handkerchief, and pipe.

Rostóv was very happy in the love they showed him; but the first moment of meeting had been so beatific that his present joy seemed insufficient, and he kept expecting something more, more and yet more.

Next morning, after the fatigues of their journey, the travelers slept till ten o'clock.

In the room next their bedroom there was a confusion of sabers, satchels, sabertaches, open portmanteaus, and dirty boots. Two freshly cleaned pairs with spurs had just been placed by the wall. The servants were bringing in jugs and basins, hot water for shaving, and their well-brushed clothes. There was a masculine odor and a smell of tobacco.

"Hallo, Gwíska—my pipe!" came Vasíli Denísov's husky voice. "Wostóv, get up!"

Rostóv, rubbing his eyes that seemed glued together, raised his disheveled head from the hot pillow.

"Why, is it late?"

"Late! It's nearly ten o'clock," answered Natásha's voice. A rustle of starched petticoats and the whispering and laughter of girls' voices came from the adjoining room. The door was opened a crack and there was a glimpse of something blue, of ribbons, black hair and merry faces. It was Natásha, Sónya, and Pétya, who had come to see whether they were getting up.

"Nicholas! Get up!" Natásha's voice was again heard at the door.

"Directly!"

Meanwhile, Pétya, having found and seized the sabers in the outer room, with the delight boys feel at the sight of a military elder brother, and forgetting that it was unbecoming for the girls to see men undressed, opened the bedroom door.

"Is this your saber?" he shouted.

The girls sprang aside. Denísov hid his hairy legs under the blanket, looking with a scared face at his comrade for help. The door, having let Pétya in, closed again. A sound of laughter came from behind it.

"Nicholas! Come out in your dressing-gown!" said Natásha's voice.

"Is this your saber?" asked Pétya. "Or is it yours?" he said, addressing the black-mustached Denísov with servile deference.

Rostóv hurriedly put something on his feet, drew on his dressing-gown, and went out. Natásha had put on one spurred boot and was just getting her foot into the other. Sónya, when he came in was twirling round and was about to expand her dresses into a balloon and sit down. They were dressed alike, in new pale-blue frocks, and were both fresh, rosy, and bright. Sónya ran away, but Natásha, taking her brother's arm, led him into the sitting room, where they began talking. They hardly gave one another time to ask questions and give replies concerning a thousand little matters which could not interest anyone but themselves. Natásha laughed at every word he said or that she said herself, not because what they were saying was amusing, but because she felt happy and was unable to control her joy which expressed itself by laughter.

"Oh, how nice, how splendid!" she said to everything.

Rostóv felt that under the influence of the warm rays of love, that childlike smile which had not once appeared on his face since he left home, now for the first time after eighteen months again brightened his soul and his face.

"No, but listen," she said, "now you are quite a man, aren't you? I'm awfully glad you're my brother." She touched his mustache. "I want to know what you men are like. Are you the same as we? No?"

"Why did Sónya run away?" asked Rostóv.

"Ah, yes! That's a whole long story! How are you going to speak to her—*Thou* or *you?*"

"As may happen," said Rostóv.

"No, call her *you,* please! I'll tell you all about it some other time. No, I'll tell you now. You know Sónya's my dearest friend. Such a friend that I burned my arm for her sake. Look here!"

She pulled up her muslin sleeve and showed him a red scar on her long, slender, delicate arm, high above the elbow on that part that is covered even by a ball dress.

"I burned this to prove my love for her. I just heated a ruler in the fire and pressed it there!"

Sitting on the sofa with the little cushions on its arms, in what used to be his old schoolroom, and looking into Natásha's wildly bright eyes, Rostóv re-entered that world of home and childhood which had no meaning for anyone else, but gave him some of the best joys of his life; and the burning of an arm with a ruler as a proof of love did not seem to him senseless, he understood and was not surprised at it.

"Well, and is that all?" he asked.

"We are such friends, such friends! All that ruler business was just nonsense, but we are friends forever. She, if she loves anyone, does it for life, but I don't understand that, I forget quickly."

"Well, what then?"

"Well, she loves me and you like that."

Natásha suddenly flushed.

"Why, you remember before you went away? . . . Well, she says you are to forget all that. . . . She says: 'I shall love him always, but let him be free.' Isn't that lovely and noble! Yes, very noble? Isn't it?" asked Natásha, so seriously and excitedly that it was evident that what she was now saying she had talked of before, with tears.

Rostóv became thoughtful.

"I never go back on my word," he said. "Besides, Sónya is so charming that only a fool would renounce such happiness."

"No, no!" cried Natásha, "she and I have already talked it over. We knew you'd say so. But it won't do, because you see, if you say that—if you consider yourself bound by your promise—it will seem as if she had not meant it seriously. It makes it as if you were marrying her because you must, and that wouldn't do at all."

Rostóv saw that it had been well considered by them. Sónya had already struck him by her beauty on the preceding day. Today, when he had caught a glimpse of her, she seemed still more lovely. She was a charming girl of sixteen, evidently passionately in love with him (he did not doubt that for an instant). Why should he not love her now, and even marry her, Rostóv thought, but just now there were so many other pleasures and interests before him! "Yes, they have taken a wise decision," he thought, "I must remain free."

"Well then, that's excellent," said he. "We'll talk it over later on. Oh, how glad I am to have you!"

"Well, and are you still true to Borís?" he continued.

"Oh, what nonsense!" cried Natásha, laughing. "I don't think about him or anyone else, and I don't want anything of the kind."

"Dear me! Then what are you up now?"

"Now?" repeated Natásha, and a happy smile lit up her face. "Have you seen Duport?"

"No."

"Not seen Duport—the famous dancer? Well then, you won't understand. That's what I'm up to."

Curving her arms, Natásha held out her skirts as dancers do, ran back a few steps, turned, cut a caper, brought her little feet sharply together, and made some steps on the very tips of her toes.

"See, I'm standing! See!" she said, but could not maintain herself on her toes any longer. "So that's what I'm up to! I'll never marry anyone, but will be a dancer. Only don't tell anyone."

Rostóv laughed so loud and merrily that Denísov, in his bedroom, felt envious and Natásha could not help joining in.

"No, but don't you think it's nice?" she kept repeating.

"Nice! And so you no longer wish to marry Borís?"

Natásha flared up. "I don't want to marry anyone. And I'll tell him so when I see him!"

"Dear me!" said Rostóv.

"But that's all rubbish," Natásha chattered on. "And is Denísov nice?" she asked.

"Yes, indeed!"

"Oh, well then, good-bye: go and dress. Is he very terrible, Denísov?"

"Why terrible?" asked Nicholas. "No, Váska is a splendid fellow."

"You call him Váska? That's funny! And is he very nice?"

"Very."

"Well then, be quick. We'll all have breakfast together."

And Natásha rose and went out of the room on tiptoe, like a ballet dancer, but smiling as only happy girls of fifteen can smile. When Rostóv met Sónya in the drawing room, he reddened. He did not know how to behave with her. The evening before, in the first happy moment of meeting, they had kissed each other, but today they felt it could not be done; he felt that everybody, including his mother and sisters, was looking inquiringly at him and watching to see how he would behave with her. He kissed her hand and addressed her not as *thou* but as *you—Sónya*. But their eyes met and said *thou,* and exchanged tender kisses. Her looks asked him to forgive her for having dared, by Natásha's intermediacy, to remind him of his promise, and then thanked him for his love. His looks thanked her for offering him his freedom, and told her that one way or another he would never cease to love her, for that would be impossible.

"How strange it is," said Véra, selecting a moment when all were silent, "that Sónya and Nicholas now say *you* to one another and meet like strangers."

Véra's remark was correct, as her remarks always were, but, like most of her observations, it made everyone feel uncomfortable, not only Sónya, Nicholas, and Natásha, but even the old countess, who—dreading this love affair which might hinder Nicholas from making a brilliant match—blushed like a girl.

Denísov, to Rostóv's surprise, appeared in the drawing room with pomaded hair, perfumed, and in a new uniform, looking just as smart as he made himself when going into battle, and he was more amiable to the ladies and gentlemen than Rostóv had ever expected to see him.

Chapter II

On his return to Moscow from the army, Nicholas Rostóv was welcomed by his home circle as the best of sons, a hero, and their darling Nikólenka; by his relations as a charming, attractive, and polite young man; by his acquaintances as a handsome lieutenant of hussars, a good dancer, and one of the best matches in the city.

The Rostóvs knew everybody in Moscow. The old count had money enough that year, as all his estates had been remortgaged, and so Nicholas, acquiring a trotter of his own, very stylish riding-breeches of the latest cut, such as no one else yet had in Moscow, and boots of the latest fashion, with extremely pointed toes and small silver spurs, passed his time very gaily. After a short period of adapting himself to the old conditions of life, Nicholas found it very pleasant to be at home again. He felt that he had grown up and matured very much. His despair at failing in a Scripture examination, his borrowing money from Gavríl to pay a sleigh-driver, his kissing Sónya on the sly—he now recalled all this as childishness he had left immeasurably behind. Now he was a lieutenant of hussars, in a jacket laced with silver, and wearing the Cross of St. George, awarded to soldiers for bravery in action, and in the company of well-known, elderly and respected racing-men was training a trotter of his own for a race. He knew a lady on one of the boulevards whom he visited of an evening. He led the mazurka at the Arkhárovs' ball, talked about the war with Field Marshal Kámenski, visited the English Club, and was on intimate terms with a colonel of forty to whom Denísov had introduced him.

His passion for the Emperor had cooled somewhat in Moscow. But still, as he did not see him and had no opportunity of seeing him, he often spoke about him and about his love for him, letting it be understood that he had not told all and that there was something in his feelings for the Emperor not everyone could understand, and with his whole soul he shared the adoration then common in Moscow for the Emperor, who was spoken of as the "angel incarnate."

During Rostóv's short stay in Moscow, before rejoining the army, he did not draw closer to Sónya, but rather drifted away from her. She was very pretty and sweet, and evidently deeply in love with him, but he was at the period of youth when there seems so much to do that there is *no time* for that sort of thing and a young man fears to bind himself, and prizes his freedom which he needs for so many other things. When he thought of Sónya, during this stay in Moscow, he said to himself, "Ah, there will be, and there are, many more such girls somewhere whom I do not yet know. There will be time enough to think about love when I want to, but now I have no time." Besides, it seemed to him that the society of women was rather derogatory to his manhood. He went to balls and into ladies' society with an affectation of doing so against his will. The races, the English Club, sprees with Denísov and visits to a certain house—that was another matter and quite the thing for a dashing young hussar!

At the beginning of March, old Count Ilyá Rostóv was very busy arranging a dinner in honor of Prince Bagratión at the English Club.

The count walked up and down the hall in his dressing-gown, giving orders to the club steward and to the famous Feoktíst, the Club's head cook, about asparagus, fresh cucumbers, strawberries, veal, and fish for this dinner. The count had been a member and on the committee of the Club from the day it was founded. To him the Club entrusted the arrangement of the festival in honor of Bagratión, for few men knew so well how to arrange a feast on an open-handed, hospitable scale, and still fewer men would be so well able and willing to make up out of their own resources what might be needed for the success of the fête. The club cook and the steward listened to the count's orders with pleased faces, for they knew that under no other management could they so easily extract a good profit for themselves from a dinner costing several thousand rubles.

"Well then, mind and have cocks' comb in the turtle soup, you know!"

"Shall we have three cold dishes then?" asked the cook.

The count considered.

"We can't have less—yes three . . . the mayonnaise, that's one," said he, bending down a finger.

"Then am I to order those large sterlets?" asked the steward.

"Yes, it can't be helped if they won't take less. Ah, dear me! I was forgetting. We must have another entrée. Ah, goodness gracious!" he clutched at his head. "Who is going to get me the flowers? Dmítri! Eh, Dmítri! Gallop off to our Moscow estate," he said to the factotum who appeared at his call. "Hurry off and tell Maksím, the gardener, to set the serfs to work. Say that everything out of the hothouses must be brought here well wrapped up in felt. I must have two hundred pots here on Friday."

Having given several more orders, he was about to go to his "little countess" to have a rest, but remembering something else of importance, he returned again, called back the cook and the club steward, and again began giving orders. A light footstep and the clinking of spurs were heard at the door, and the young count, handsome, rosy, with a dark little mustache, evidently rested and made sleeker by his easy life in Moscow, entered the room.

"Ah, my boy, my head's in a whirl!" said the old man with a smile, as if he felt a little confused before his son. "Now, if you would only help a bit! I must have singers too. I shall have my own orchestra, but shouldn't we get the gypsy singers as well? You military men like that sort of thing."

"Really, Papa, I believe Prince Bagratión worried himself less before the battle of Schön Grabern than you do now," said his son with a smile.

The old count pretended to be angry.

"Yes, you talk, but try it yourself!"

And the count turned to the cook, who, with a shrewd and respectful expression, looked observantly and sympathetically at the father and son.

"What have the young people come to nowadays, eh, Feoktíst?" said he—"laughing at us old fellows!"

"That's so, your excellency, all they have to do is to eat a good dinner, but providing it and serving it all up, that's not their business!"

"That's it, that's it!" exclaimed the count, and gaily seizing his son by both hands, he cried, "Now I've got you, so take the sleigh and pair at once, and go to Bezúkhov's, and tell him 'Count Ilyá has sent you to ask for strawberries and fresh pineapples.' We can't get them from anyone else. He's not there himself, so you'll have to go in and ask the princesses; and from there go on to the Rasgulyáy—the coachman Ipátka knows—and look up the gypsy Ilyúshka, the one who danced at Count Orlóv's, you remember, in a white Cossack coat, and bring him along to me."

"And am I to bring the gypsy girls along with him?" asked Nicholas, laughing. "Dear, dear! . . ."

At that moment, with noiseless footsteps and with the businesslike, preoccupied, yet meekly Christian look which never left her face, Anna Mikháylovna entered the hall. Though she came upon the count in his dressing-gown every day, he invariably became confused and begged her to excuse his costume.

"No matter at all, my dear count," she said, meekly closing her eyes. "But I'll go to Bezúkhov's myself. Pierre has arrived, and now we shall get anything we want from his hothouses. I have to see him in any case. He has forwarded me a letter from Borís. Thank God, Borís is now on the staff."

The count was delighted at Anna Mikháylovna's taking upon herself one of his commissions, and ordered the small closed carriage for her.

"Tell Bezúkhov to come. I'll put his name down. Is his wife with him?" he asked.

Anna Mikháylovna turned up her eyes, and profound sadness was depicted on her face.

"Ah, my dear friend, he is very unfortunate," she said. "If what we hear is true, it is dreadful. How little we dreamed of such a thing when we were rejoicing at his happiness! And such a lofty angelic soul as young Bezúkhov! Yes, I pity him from my heart, and shall try to give him what consolation I can."

"Wh-what is the matter?" asked both the young and old Rostóv.

Anna Mikháylovna sighed deeply.

"Dólokhov, Mary Ivánovna's son," she said in a mysterious whisper, "has compromised her completely, they say. Pierre took him up, invited him to his house in Petersburg, and now . . . she has come here and that dare-devil after her!" said Anna Mikháylovna, wishing to show her sympathy for Pierre, but by involuntary intonations and a half-smile betraying her sympathy for the "dare-devil," as she called Dólokhov. "They say Pierre is quite broken by his misfortune."

"Dear, dear! But still tell him to come to the Club—it will all blow over. It will be a tremendous banquet."

Next day, the 3rd of March, soon after one o'clock, two hundred and fifty members of the English Club and fifty guests were awaiting the guest of honor and hero of the Austrian campaign, Prince Bagratión, to dinner.

On the first arrival of the news of the battle of Austerlitz, Moscow had been bewildered. At that time, the Russians were so used to victories that on receiving news of the defeat some would simply not believe it, while others sought some extraordinary explanation of so strange an event. In the English Club, where all who were distinguished, important, and well-informed foregathered when the news began to arrive in December, nothing was said about the war and the last battle, as though all were in a conspiracy of silence. The men who set the tone in conversation—Count Rostopchín, Prince Yúri Dolgorúkov, Valúev, Count Markóv and Prince Vyázemski—did not show themselves at the Club, but met in private houses in intimate circles, and the Muscovites who took their opinions from others—Ilyá Rostóv among them—remained for a while without any definite opinion on the subject of the war, and without leaders. The Muscovites felt that something was wrong, and that to discuss the bad news was difficult, and so it was best to be silent. But after a while, just as a jury comes out of its room, the bigwigs who guided the Club's opinion reappeared, and everybody began speaking clearly and definitely. Reasons were found for the incredible, unheard-of, and impossible event of a Russian defeat, everything became clear, and in all corners of Moscow the same things began to be said. These reasons were the treachery of the Austrians, a defective commissariat, the treachery of the Pole Przebyszéwski and of the Frenchman Langeron, Kutúzov's incapacity, and (it was whispered) the youth and inexperience of the sovereign, who had trusted worthless and insignificant people. But the army, the Russian army, everyone declared was extraordinary, and had achieved miracles of valor. The soldiers, officers, and generals were heroes. But the hero of heroes was Prince Bagratión, distinguished by his Schön Grabern affair and by the retreat from Austerlitz, where he alone had withdrawn his column unbroken and had all day beaten back an enemy force twice as numerous as his own. What also conduced to Bagratión's being selected as Moscow's hero was the fact that he had no connections in the city and was a stranger there. In his person, honor was shown to a simple fighting Russian soldier without connections and intrigues, and to one who was associated by memories of the Italian campaign with the name of Suvórov. Moreover, paying such honor to Bagratión was the best way of expressing disapproval and dislike of Kutúzov.

"Had there been no Bagratión, it would have been necessary to invent him," said the wit Shinshín, parodying the words of Voltaire. Kutúzov no one spoke of, except some who abused him in whispers, calling him a court-weathercock and an old satyr.

All Moscow repeated Prince Dolgorúkov's saying: "If you go on modeling and modeling you must get smeared with clay," suggesting consolation for our defeat by the memory of former victories; and the words of Rostopchín, that French soldiers have to be incited to battle by high-falutin' words, and Germans by logical arguments to show them that it is more dangerous to run away than to advance, but that Russian soldiers only need to be restrained and held back! On all sides, new and fresh anecdotes were heard of individual examples of heroism shown by our officers and men at Austerlitz. One had saved a standard, another had killed five Frenchmen, a third had loaded five cannon single-handed. Berg was mentioned by those who did not know him, as having when wounded in the right hand, taken his sword in the left, and gone forward. Of Bolkónski, nothing was said, and only those who knew him intimately regretted that he had died so young, leaving a pregnant wife with his eccentric father.

Chapter III

On that 3rd of March, all the rooms in the English Club were filled with a hum of conversation, like the hum of bees swarming in springtime. The members and guests of the club wandered hither and thither, sat, stood, met, and separated, some in uniform and some in evening dress, and a few here and there with powdered hair and in Russian *kaftáns*. Powdered footmen, in livery with buckled shoes and smart stockings, stood at every door anxiously noting visitors' every movement in order to offer their services. Most of those present were elderly, respected men with broad, self-confident faces, fat fingers, and resolute gestures and voices. This class of guests and members sat in certain habitual places and met in certain habitual groups. A minority of those present were casual guests—chiefly young men, among whom were Denísov, Rostóv and Dólokhov—who was now again an officer in the Semënov regiment. The faces of these young people, especially those who were military men, bore that expression of condescending respect for their elders which seems to say to the older generation, "We are prepared to respect and honor you, but all the same remember that the future belongs to us."

Nesvítski was there as an old member of the club. Pierre, who at his wife's command had let his hair grow and abandoned his spectacles, went about the rooms fashionably dressed but looking sad and dull. Here, as elsewhere, he was surrounded by an atmosphere of subservience to his wealth, and being in the habit of lording it over these people, he treated them with absent-minded contempt.

By his age he should have belonged to the younger men, but by his wealth and connections he belonged to the groups old and honored guests, and so he went from one group to another. Some of the most important old men were the center of groups which even strangers approached respectfully to hear the voices of well-known men. The largest circles formed round Count Rostopchín, Valúev, and Narýshkin. Rostopchín was describing how the Russians had been overwhelmed by flying Austrians and had had to force their way through them with bayonets.

Valúev was confidentially telling that Uvárov had been sent from Petersburg to ascertain what Moscow was thinking about Austerlitz.

In the third circle, Naryshkin was speaking of the meeting of the Austrian Council of War at which Suvórov crowed like a cock in reply to the nonsense talked by the Austrian generals. Shinshín, standing close by, tried to make a joke, saying that Kutúzov had evidently failed to learn from Suvórov even so simple a thing as the art of crowing like a cock, but the elder members glanced severely at the wit, making him feel that in that place and on that day, it was improper to speak so of Kutúzov.

Count Ilyá Rostóv, hurried and preoccupied, went about in his soft boots between the dining and drawing rooms, hastily greeting the important and unimportant, all of whom he knew, as if they were all equals, while his eyes occasionally sought out his fine well-set-up young son, resting on him and winking joyfully at him. Young Rostóv stood at a window with Dólokhov, whose acquaintance he had lately made and highly valued. The old count came up to them and pressed Dólokhov's hand.

"Please come and visit us . . . you know my brave boy . . . been together out there . . . both playing the hero . . . Ah, Vasíli Ignátovich . . . How d'ye do, old fellow?" he said, turning to an old man who was passing, but before he had finished his greeting there was a general stir, and a footman who had run in, announced, with a frightened face: "He's arrived!"

Bells rang, the stewards rushed forward, and—like rye shaken together in a shovel—the guests who had been scattered about in different rooms came together and crowded in the large drawing room by the door of the ballroom.

Bagratión appeared in the doorway of the anteroom without hat or sword, which, in accord with the Club custom, he had given up to the hall-porter. He had no lambskin cap on his head, nor had he a loaded whip over his shoulder, as when Rostóv had seen him on the eve of the battle of Austerlitz, but wore a tight new uniform with Russian and foreign Orders, and the Star of St. George on his left breast. Evidently just before coming to the dinner he had had his hair and whiskers trimmed, which changed his appearance for the worse. There was something naïvely festive in his air, which, in conjunction with his firm and virile features, gave him a rather comical expression. Bekleshëv and Theodore Uvárov, who had arrived with him, paused at the doorway to allow him, as the guest of honor, to enter first. Bagratión was embarrassed, not wishing to avail himself of their courtesy, and this caused some delay at the doors, but after all he did at last enter first. He walked shyly and awkwardly over the parquet floor of the reception room, not knowing what to do with his hands; he was more accustomed to walk over a plowed field under fire, as he had done at the head of the Kursk regiment at Schön Grabern—and he would have found that easier. The committee-men met him at the first door and, expressing their delight at seeing such a highly honored guest, took possession of him as it were, without waiting for his reply, surrounded him, and led him to the drawing room. It was at first impossible to enter the drawing room door for the crowd of members and guests jostling one another and trying to get a good look at Bagratión over each other's shoulders, as if he were some rare animal. Count Ilyá Rostóv, laughing and repeating the words, "Make way, dear boy! Make way, make way!" pushed through the crowd more energetically than anyone, led the guests into the drawing room, and seated them on the center sofa. The bigwigs, the most respected members of the Club, beset the new arrivals. Count Ilyá again thrusting his way through the crowd, went out of the drawing room, and reappeared a minute later with another committee-man, carrying a large silver salver which he presented to Prince Bagratión. On the salver lay some verses composed and printed in the hero's honor. Bagratión, on seeing the salver, glanced around in dismay, as though seeking help. But all eyes demanded that he should submit. Feeling himself in their power, he resolutely took the salver with both hands and looked sternly and reproachfully at the count who had presented it to him. Someone obligingly took the dish from Bagratión (or he would, it seemed, have held it till evening and have gone in to dinner with it) and drew his attention to the verses.

"Well, I will read them, then!" Bagratión seemed to say, and, fixing his weary eyes on the paper, began to read them with a fixed and serious expression. But the author himself took the verses and began reading them aloud. Bagratión bowed his bead and listened:

"Bring glory then to Alexander's reign
And on the throne our Titus shield.
A dreaded foe be thou, kind-hearted as a man,
A Rhipheus at home, a Caesar in the field!
E'en fortunate Napoleon
Knows by experience, now, Bagratión,
And dare not Herculean Russians trouble . . ."

But before he had finished reading, a stentorian major-domo announced that dinner was ready! The door opened, and from the dining room came the resounding strains of the Polonaise:

"Conquest's joyful thunder waken,
Triumph, valiant Russians, now! . . ."

and Count Rostóv, glancing angrily at the author who went on reading his verses, bowed to Bagratión. Everyone rose, feeling that dinner was more important than verses, and Bagratión, again preceding all the rest, went in to dinner. He was seated in the place of honor between two Alexanders—Bekleshëv and Naryshkin—which was a significant allusion to the name of the sovereign. Three hundred persons took their seats in the dining room, according to their rank and importance: the more important nearer to the honored guest, as naturally as water flows deepest where the land lies lowest.

Just before dinner, Count Ilyá Rostóv presented his son to Bagratión, who recognized him and said a few words to him, disjointed and awkward, as were all the words he spoke that day, and Count Ilyá looked joyfully and proudly around while Bagratión spoke to his son.

Nicholas Rostóv, with Denísov and his new acquaintance, Dólokhov, sat almost at the middle of the table. Facing them sat Pierre, beside Prince Nesvítski. Count Ilyá Rostóv with the other members of the committee sat facing Bagratión, and as the very personification of Moscow hospitality, did the honors to the prince.

His efforts had not been in vain. The dinner, both the lenten and the other fare, was splendid, yet he could not feel quite at ease till the end of the meal. He winked at the butler, whispered directions to the footmen, and awaited each expected dish with some anxiety. Everything was excellent. With the second course, a gigantic sterlet (at sight of which Ilyá Rostóv blushed with self-conscious pleasure), the footmen began popping corks and filling the champagne glasses. After the fish, which made a certain sensation, the count exchanged glances with the other committeemen. "There will be many toasts, it's time to begin," he whispered, and taking up his glass, he rose. All were silent, waiting for what he would say.

"To the health of our Sovereign, the Emperor!" he cried, and at the same moment his kindly eyes grew moist with tears of joy and enthusiasm. The band immediately struck up "Conquest's joyful thunder waken . . ." All rose and cried "hurrah!" Bagratión also rose, and shouted "hurrah!" in exactly the same voice in which he had shouted it on the field at Schön Grabern. Young Rostóv's ecstatic voice could be heard above the three hundred others. He nearly wept. "To the health of our Sovereign, the Emperor!" he roared, "hurrah!" and emptying his glass at one gulp he dashed it to the floor. Many followed his example, and the loud shouting continued for a long time. When the voices subsided, the footmen cleared away the broken glass and everybody sat down again, smiling at the noise they had made and exchanging remarks. The old count rose once more, glanced at a note lying beside his plate, and proposed a toast, "To the health of the hero of our last campaign, Prince Peter Ivánovich Bagratión!" and again his blue eyes grew moist. "Hurrah!" cried the three hundred voices again, but instead of the band a choir began singing a cantata composed by Paul Ivánovich Kutúzov:

Russians! O'er all barriers on!
Courage conquest guarantees;
Have we not Bagratión?
He brings foemen to their knees, . . . etc.

As soon as the singing was over, another and another toast was proposed and Count Ilyá Rostóv became more and more moved, more glass was smashed and the shouting grew louder. They drank to Bekleshëv, Naryshkin, Uvárov, Dolgorúkov, Apráksin, Valúev, to the committee, to all the Club members and to all the Club guests, and finally to Count Ilyá Rostóv separately, as the organizer of the banquet. At that toast, the count took out his handkerchief and, covering his face, wept outright.

Chapter IV

PIERRE SAT OPPOSITE DÓLOKHOV AND NICHOLAS ROSTÓV. AS USUAL, HE ATE AND DRANK MUCH, and eagerly. But those who knew him intimately noticed that some great change had come over him that day. He was silent all through dinner and looked about, blinking and scowling, or with fixed eyes and a look of complete absent-mindedness, kept rubbing the bridge of his nose. His face was depressed and gloomy. He seemed to see and hear nothing of what was going on around him, and to be absorbed by some depressing and unsolved problem.

The unsolved problem that tormented him was caused by hints given by the princess, his cousin, at Moscow, concerning Dólokhov's intimacy with his wife, and by an anonymous letter he had received that morning, which in the mean jocular way common to anonymous letters said that he saw badly through his spectacles, but that his wife's connection with Dólokhov was a secret to no one but himself. Pierre absolutely disbelieved both the princess's hints and the letter, but he feared now to look at Dólokhov, who was sitting opposite him. Every time he chanced to meet Dólokhov's handsome insolent eyes, Pierre felt something terrible and monstrous rising in his soul and turned quickly away. Involuntarily recalling his wife's past and her relations with Dólokhov, Pierre saw clearly that what was said in the letter might be true, or might at least seem to be true had it not referred to *his wife*. He involuntarily remembered how Dólokhov who had fully recovered his former position after the campaign, had returned to Petersburg and come to him. Availing himself of his friendly relations with Pierre as a boon companion, Dólokhov had come straight to his house, and Pierre had put him up and lent him money. Pierre recalled how Hélène had smilingly expressed disapproval of Dólokhov's living at their house, and how cynically Dólokhov had praised his wife's beauty to him and from that time till they came to Moscow had not left them for a day.

"Yes, he is very handsome," thought Pierre, "and I know him. It would be particularly pleasant to him to dishonor my name and ridicule me, just because I have exerted myself on his behalf, befriended him and helped him. I know and understand what a spice that would add to the pleasure of deceiving me, if it really were true. Yes, if it were true, but I do not believe it. I have no right to, and can't, believe it." He remembered the expression Dólokhov's face assumed in his moments of cruelty, as when tying the policeman to the bear and dropping them into the water, or when he challenged a man to a duel without any reason, or shot a post-boy's horse with a pistol. That expression was often on Dólokhov's face when looking at him. "Yes, he is a bully," thought Pierre, "to kill a man means nothing to him. It must seem to him that everyone is afraid of him, and that must please him. He must think that I, too, am afraid of him—and in fact I am afraid of him," he thought, and again he felt something terrible and monstrous rising in his soul. Dólokhov, Denísov and Rostóv were now sitting opposite Pierre and seemed very gay. Rostóv was talking merrily to his two friends, one of whom was a dashing hussar and the other a notorious duelist and rake, and every now and then he glanced ironically at Pierre, whose preoccupied, absent-minded, and massive figure was a very noticeable one at the dinner. Rostóv looked inimically at Pierre, first because Pierre appeared to his hussar eyes as a rich civilian, the husband of a beauty, and in a word—an old woman, and secondly because Pierre in his preoccupation and absent-mindedness had not recognized Rostóv and had not responded to his greeting. When the Emperor's health was drunk, Pierre, lost in thought, did not rise or lift his glass.

"What are you about?" shouted Rostóv, looking at him in an ecstasy of exasperation. "Don't you hear it's his Majesty the Emperor's health?"

Pierre sighed, rose submissively, emptied his glass, and waiting till all were seated again, turned with his kindly smile to Rostóv.

"Why, I didn't recognize you!" he said. But Rostóv was otherwise engaged; he was shouting "hurrah!"

"Why don't you renew the acquaintance?" said Dólokhov to Rostóv.

"Confound him, he's a fool!" said Rostóv.

"One should make up to the husbands of pretty women," said Denísov.

Pierre did not catch what they were saying, but knew they were talking about him. He reddened and turned away.

"Well, now to the health of handsome women!" said Dólokhov, and with a serious expression, but with a smile lurking at the corners of his mouth, he turned with his glass to Pierre.

"Here's to the health of lovely women, Peterkin—and their lovers!" he added.

Pierre, with downcast eyes, drank out of his glass without looking at Dólokhov or answering him. The footman, who was distributing leaflets with Kutúzov's cantata, laid one before Pierre as one of the principal guests. He was just going to take it when Dólokhov, leaning across, snatched it from his hand and began reading it. Pierre looked at Dólokhov and his eyes dropped, the something terrible and monstrous that had tormented him all dinnertime rose and took possession of him. He leaned his whole massive body across the table.

"How dare you take it?" he shouted.

Hearing that cry and seeing to whom it was addressed, Nesvítski and the neighbor on his right quickly turned in alarm to Bezúkhov.

"Don't! Don't! What are you about?" whispered their frightened voices.

Dólokhov looked at Pierre with clear mirthful cruel eyes, and that smile of his which seemed to say, "Ah! This is what I like!"

"You shan't have it!" he said distinctly.

Pale, with quivering lips, Pierre snatched the copy.

"You . . . ! you . . . scoundrel! I challenge you!" he ejaculated, and, pushing back his chair, he rose from the table.

At the very instant he did this and uttered those words, Pierre felt that the question of his wife's guilt which had been tormenting him the whole day, was finally and indubitably answered in the affirmative. He hated her and was forever sundered from her. Despite Denísov's request that he would take no part in the matter, Rostóv agreed to be Dólokhov's second, and after dinner he discussed the arrangements for the duel with Nesvítski, Bezúkhov's second. Pierre went home, but Rostóv with Dólokhov and Denísov stayed on at the Club till late, listening to the gypsies and other singers.

"Well then, till tomorrow at Sokólniki," said Dólokhov, as he took leave of Rostóv in the Club porch.

"And do you feel quite calm?" Rostóv asked.

Dólokhov paused.

"Well, you see, I'll tell you the whole secret of dueling in two words. If you are going to fight a duel, and you make a will and write affectionate letters to your parents, and if you think you may be killed, you are a fool and are lost for certain. But go with the firm intention of killing your man as quickly and surely as possible, and then all will be right, as our bear huntsman at Kostromá used to tell me. 'Everyone fears a bear,' he says, 'but when you see one your fear's all gone, and your only thought is not to let him get away!' And that's how it is with me. A *demain, mon cher.*"

Next day, at eight in the morning, Pierre and Nesvítski drove to the Sokólniki forest and found Dólokhov, Denísov and Rostóv already there. Pierre had the air of a man preoccupied with considerations which had no connection with the matter in hand. His haggard face was yellow. He had evidently not slept that night. He looked about distractedly and screwed up his eyes as if dazzled by the sun. He was entirely absorbed by two considerations: his wife's guilt, of which after his sleepless night he had not the slightest doubt, and the guiltlessness of Dólokhov, who had no reason to preserve the honor of a man who was nothing to him. . . . "I should perhaps have done the same thing in his place," thought Pierre. "It's even certain that I should have done the same, then why this duel, this murder? Either I shall kill him, or he will hit me in the head, or elbow, or knee. Can't I go away from here, run away, bury myself somewhere?" passed through his mind. But just at moments when such thoughts occurred to him, he would ask in a particularly calm and absent-minded way, which inspired the respect of the onlookers, "Will it be long? Are things ready?"

When all was ready, the sabers stuck in the snow to mark the barriers, and the pistols loaded, Nesvítski went up to Pierre.

"I should not be doing my duty, count," he said in timid tones, "and should not justify your confidence and the honor you have done me in choosing me for your second, if at this grave, this very grave, moment I did not tell you the whole truth. I think there is no sufficient ground for this affair, or for blood to be shed over it. . . . You were not right, not quite in the right, you were impetuous . . ."

"Oh yes, it is horribly stupid," said Pierre.

"Then allow me to express your regrets, and I am sure your opponent will accept them," said Nesvítski (who like the others concerned in the affair, and like everyone in similar cases, did not yet believe that the affair had come to an actual duel). "You know, count, it is much more honorable to admit one's mistake than to let matters become irreparable. There was no insult on either side. Allow me to convey. . . ."

"No! What is there to talk about?" said Pierre. "It's all the same. . . . Is everything ready?" he added. "Only tell me where to go and where to shoot," he said with an unnaturally gentle smile.

He took the pistol in his hand and began asking about the working of the trigger, as he had not before held a pistol in his hand—a fact that he did not to confess.

"Oh yes, like that, I know, I only forgot," said he.

"No apologies, none whatever," said Dólokhov to Denísov (who on his side had been attempting a reconciliation), and he also went up to the appointed place.

The spot chosen for the duel was some eighty paces from the road, where the sleighs had been left, in a small clearing in the pine forest covered with melting snow, the frost having begun to break up during the last few days. The antagonists stood forty paces apart at the farther edge of the clearing. The seconds, measuring the paces, left tracks in the deep wet snow between the place where they had been standing and Nesvítski's and Dólokhov's sabers, which were stuck into the ground ten paces apart to mark the barrier. It was thawing and misty; at forty paces' distance nothing could be seen. For three minutes all had been ready, but they still delayed and all were silent.

Chapter V

"WELL BEGIN!" SAID DÓLOKHOV.

"All right," said Pierre, still smiling in the same way. A feeling of dread was in the air. It was evident that the affair so lightly begun could no longer be averted but was taking its course independently of men's will. Denísov first went to the barrier and announced:

"As the adve'sawies have wefused a weconciliation, please pwoceed. Take your pistols, and at the word *thwee* begin to advance."

"O-ne! T-wo! Thwee!" he shouted angrily and stepped aside.

The combatants advanced along the trodden tracks, nearer and nearer to one another, beginning to see one another through the mist. They had the right to fire when they liked as they approached the barrier. Dólokhov walked slowly without raising his pistol, looking intently with his bright sparkling blue eyes into his antagonist's face. His mouth wore its usual semblance of a smile.

"So I can fire when I like!" said Pierre, and at the word "three," he went quickly forward, missing the trodden path and stepping into the deep snow. He held the pistol in his right hand at arm's length, apparently afraid of shooting himself with it. His left hand he held carefully back, because he wished to support his right hand with it and knew he must not do so. Having advanced six paces and strayed off the track into the snow, Pierre looked down at his feet, then quickly glanced at Dólokhov and, bending his finger as he had been shown, fired. Not at all expecting so loud a report, Pierre shuddered at the sound, and then smiling at his own sensations, stood still. The smoke, rendered denser by the mist, prevented him from seeing anything for an instant, but there was no second report as he had expected. He only heard Dólokhov's hurried steps, and his figure came in view through the smoke. He was pressing one hand to his left side, while the other clutched his drooping pistol. His face was pale. Rostóv ran toward him and said something.

"No-o-o!" muttered Dólokhov through his teeth, "no, it's not over." And after stumbling a few staggering steps right up to the saber, he sank on the snow beside it. His left hand was bloody; he wiped it on his coat and supported himself with it. His frowning face was pallid and quivered.

"Plea . . ." began Dólokhov, but could not at first pronounce the word.

"Please," he uttered with an effort.

Pierre, hardly restraining his sobs, began running toward Dólokhov and was about to cross the space between the barriers, when Dólokhov cried:

"To your barrier!" and Pierre, grasping what was meant, stopped by his saber. Only ten paces divided them. Dólokhov lowered his head to the snow, greedily bit at it, again raised his head, adjusted himself, drew in his legs and sat up, seeking a firm center of gravity. He sucked and swallowed the cold snow, his lips quivered, but his eyes, still smiling, glittered with effort and exasperation as he mustered his remaining strength. He raised his pistol and aimed.

"Sideways! Cover yourself with your pistol!" ejaculated Nesvítski.

"Cover yourself!" even Denísov cried to his adversary.

Pierre, with a gentle smile of pity and remorse, his arms and legs helplessly spread out, stood with his broad chest directly facing Dólokhov looked sorrowfully at him. Denísov, Rostóv and Nesvítski closed their eyes. At the same instant they heard a report and Dólokhov's angry cry.

"Missed!" shouted Dólokhov, and he lay helplessly, face downward on the snow.

Pierre clutched his temples, and turning round went into the forest, trampling through the deep snow, and muttering incoherent words:

"Folly . . . folly! Death . . . lies . . ." he repeated, puckering his face.

Nesvítski stopped him and took him home.

Rostóv and Denísov drove away with the wounded Dólokhov.

The latter lay silent in the sleigh with closed eyes, and did not answer a word to the questions addressed to him. But on entering Moscow he suddenly came to, and lifting his head with an effort, took Rostóv, who was sitting beside him, by the hand. Rostóv was struck by the totally altered and unexpectedly rapturous and tender expression on Dólokhov's face.

"Well? How do you feel?" he asked.

"Bad! But it's not that, my friend—" said Dólokhov with a gasping voice. "Where are we? In Moscow, I know. I don't matter, but I have killed her, killed . . . She won't get over it! She won't survive. . . ."

"Who?" asked Rostóv.

"My mother! My mother, my angel, my adored angel mother," and Dólokhov pressed Rostóv's hand and burst into tears.

When he had become a little quieter, he explained to Rostóv that he was living with his mother, who, if she saw him dying, would not survive it. He implored Rostóv to go on and prepare her.

Rostóv went on ahead to do what was asked, and to his great surprise learned that Dólokhov the brawler, Dólokhov the bully, lived in Moscow with an old mother and a hunchback sister, and was the most affectionate of sons and brothers.

Chapter VI

Pierre had of late rarely seen his wife alone. Both in Petersburg and in Moscow their house was always full of visitors. The night after the duel he did not go to his bedroom, but as he often did, remained in his father's room, that huge room in which Count Bezúkhov had died.

He lay down on the sofa meaning to fall asleep and forget all that had happened to him, but could not do so. Such a storm of feelings, thoughts, and memories suddenly arose within him, that he could not fall asleep, nor even remain in one place, but had to jump up and pace the room with rapid steps. Now he seemed to see her in the early days of their marriage, with bare shoulders and a languid, passionate look on her face, and then immediately he saw beside her Dólokhov's handsome, insolent, hard and mocking face as he had seen it at the banquet, and then that same face pale, quivering, and suffering, as it had been when he reeled and sank on the snow.

"What has happened?" he asked himself. "I have killed her *lover,* yes, killed my wife's lover. Yes, that was it! And why? How did I come to do it?"—"Because you married her," answered an inner voice.

"But in what was I to blame?" he asked. "In marrying her without loving her; in deceiving yourself and her." And he vividly recalled that moment after supper at Prince Vasíli's, when he spoke those words he had found so difficult to utter: "I love you." "It all comes from that! Even then I felt it," he thought. "I felt then that it was not so, that I had no right to do it. And so it turns out."

He remembered his honeymoon, and blushed at the recollection. Particularly vivid, humiliating and shameful was the recollection of how one day soon after his marriage he came out of the bedroom into his study a little before noon in his silk dressing-gown, and found his head-steward there, who, bowing respectfully, looked into his face and at his dressing-gown, and smiled slightly, as if expressing respectful understanding of his employer's happiness.

"But how often I have felt proud of her, proud of her majestic beauty and social tact," thought he; "been proud of my house, in which she received all Petersburg, proud of her unapproachability and beauty. So this is what I was proud of! I then thought that I did not understand her. How often when considering her character I have told myself that I was to blame for not understanding her, for not understanding that constant composure and complacency and lack of all interests or desires, and the whole secret lies in the terrible truth that she is a depraved woman. Now I have spoken that terrible word to myself all has become clear.

"Anatole used to come to borrow money from her and used to kiss her naked shoulders. She did not give him the money, but let herself be kissed. Her father in jest tried to rouse her jealousy, and she replied with a calm smile that she was not so stupid as to be jealous: 'Let him do what he pleases,' she used to say of me. One day I asked her if she felt any symptoms of pregnancy. She laughed contemptuously and said she was not a fool to want to have children, and that she was not going to have any children by *me.*"

Then he recalled the coarseness and bluntness of her thoughts and the vulgarity of the expressions that were natural to her, though she had been brought up in the most aristocratic circles.

"I'm not such a fool. . . . Just you try it on. . . . *Allez-vous promener,*" she used to say. Often seeing the success she had with young and old men and women Pierre could not understand why he did not love her.

"Yes, I never loved her," said he to himself; "I knew she was a depraved woman," he repeated, "but dared not admit it to myself. And now there's Dólokhov sitting in the snow with a forced smile and perhaps dying, while meeting my remorse with some forced bravado!"

Pierre was one of those people who, in spite of an appearance of what is called weak character, do not seek a confidant in their troubles. He digested his sufferings alone.

"It is all, all her fault," he said to himself; "but what of that? Why did I bind myself to her? Why did I say '*Je vous aime*' to her, which was a lie, and worse than a lie? I am guilty and must endure . . . what? A slur on my name? A misfortune for life? Oh, that's nonsense," he thought. "The slur on my name and honor—that's all apart from myself."

"Louis XVI was executed because they said he was dishonorable and a criminal," came into Pierre's head, "and from their point of view they were right, as were those too who canonized him and died a martyr's death for his sake. Then Robespierre was beheaded for being a despot. Who is right and who is wrong? No one! But if you are alive—live: tomorrow you'll die as I might have died an hour ago. And is it worth tormenting oneself, when one has only a moment of life in comparison with eternity?"

But at the moment when he imagined himself calmed by such reflections, *she* suddenly came into his mind as she was at the moments when he had most strongly expressed his insincere love for her, and he felt the blood rush to his heart and had again to get up and move about and break and tear whatever came to his hand. "Why did I tell her that *'Je vous aime'*?" he kept repeating to himself. And when he had said it for the tenth time, Molibre's words: *"Mais que diable allait-il faire dans cette galère?"* occurred to him, and he began to laugh at himself.

In the night he called his valet and told him to pack up to go to Petersburg. He could not imagine how he could speak to her now. He resolved to go away next day and leave a letter informing her of his intention to part from her forever.

Next morning when the valet came into the room with his coffee, Pierre was lying asleep on the ottoman with an open book in his hand.

He woke up and looked round for a while with a startled expression, unable to realize where he was.

"The countess told me to inquire whether your excellency was at home," said the valet.

But before Pierre could decide what answer he would send, the countess herself in a white satin dressing-gown embroidered with silver and with simply dressed hair (two immense plaits twice round her lovely head like a coronet) entered the room, calm and majestic, except that there was a wrathful wrinkle on her rather prominent marble brow. With her imperturbable calm she did not begin to speak in front of the valet. She knew of the duel and had come to speak about it. She waited till the valet had set down the coffee things and left the room. Pierre looked at her timidly over his spectacles, and like a hare surrounded by hounds who lays back her ears and continues to crouch motionless before her enemies, he tried to continue reading. But feeling this to be senseless and impossible, he again glanced timidly at her. She did not sit down but looked at him with a contemptuous smile, waiting for the valet to go.

"Well, what's this now? What have you been up to now, I should like to know?" she asked sternly.

"I? What have I . . . ?" stammered Pierre.

"So it seems you're a hero, eh? Come now, what was this duel about? What is it meant to prove? What? I ask you."

Pierre turned over heavily on the ottoman and opened his mouth, but could not reply.

"If you won't answer, I'll tell you . . ." Hélène went on. "You believe everything you're told. You were told . . ." Hélène laughed, "that Dólokhov was my lover," she said in French with her coarse plainness of speech, uttering the word *amant* as casually as any other word, "and you believed it! Well, what have you proved? What does this duel prove? That you're a fool, *que vous êtes un sot,* but everybody knew that. What will be the result? That I shall be the laughing-stock of all Moscow, that everyone will say that you, drunk and not knowing what you were about, challenged a man you are jealous of without cause." Hélène raised her voice and became more and more excited, "A man who's a better man than you in every way . . ."

"Hm . . . Hm . . . !" growled Pierre, frowning without looking at her, and not moving a muscle.

"And how could you believe he was my lover? Why? Because I like his company? If you were cleverer and more agreeable, I should prefer yours."

"Don't speak to me . . . I beg you," muttered Pierre hoarsely.

"Why shouldn't I speak? I can speak as I like, and I tell you plainly that there are not many wives with husbands such as you who would not have taken lovers (*des amants*), but I have not done so," said she.

Pierre wished to say something, looked at her with eyes whose strange expression she did not understand, and lay down again. He was suffering physically at that moment, there was a weight on his chest and he could not breathe. He knew that he must do something to put an end to this suffering, but what he wanted to do was too terrible.

"We had better separate," he muttered in a broken voice.

"Separate? Very well, but only if you give me a fortune," said Hélène. "Separate! That's a thing to frighten me with!"

Pierre leaped up from the sofa and rushed staggering toward her.

"I'll kill you!" he shouted, and seizing the marble top of a table with a strength he had never before felt, he made a step toward her brandishing the slab.

Hélène's face became terrible, she shrieked and sprang aside. His father's nature showed itself in Pierre. He felt the fascination and delight of frenzy. He flung down the slab, broke it, and swooping down on her with outstretched hands shouted, "Get out!" in such a terrible voice that the whole house heard it with horror. God knows what he would have done at that moment had Hélène not fled from the room.

A week later Pierre gave his wife full power to control all his estates in Great Russia, which formed the larger part of his property, and left for Petersburg alone.

Chapter VII

TWO MONTHS HAD ELAPSED SINCE THE NEWS OF THE BATTLE OF AUSTERLITZ AND THE LOSS OF Prince Andrew had reached Bald Hills, and in spite of the letters sent through the embassy and all the searches made, his body had not been found nor was he on the list of prisoners. What was worst of all for his relations was the fact that there was still a possibility of his having been picked up on the battlefield by the people of the place and that he might now be lying, recovering or dying, alone among strangers and unable to send news of himself. The gazettes from which the old prince first heard of the defeat at Austerlitz stated, as usual very briefly and vaguely, that after brilliant engagements the Russians had had to retreat and had made their withdrawal in perfect order. The old prince understood from this official report that our army had been defeated. A week after the gazette report of the battle of Austerlitz came a letter from Kutúzov informing the prince of the fate that had befallen his son.

"Your son," wrote Kutúzov, "fell before my eyes, a standard in his hand and at the head of a regiment—he fell as a hero, worthy of his father and his fatherland. To the great regret of myself and of the whole army it is still uncertain whether he is alive or not. I comfort myself and you with the hope that your son is alive, for otherwise he would have been mentioned among the officers found on the field of battle, a list of whom has been sent me under flag of truce."

After receiving this news late in the evening, when he was alone in his study, the old prince went for his walk as usual next morning, but he was silent with his steward, the gardener, and the architect, and though he looked very grim he said nothing to anyone.

When Princess Mary went to him at the usual hour he was working at his lathe and, as usual, did not look round at her.

"Ah, Princess Mary!" he said suddenly in an unnatural voice, throwing down his chisel. (The wheel continued to revolve by its own impetus, and Princess Mary long remembered the dying creak of that wheel, which merged in her memory with what followed.)

She approached him, saw his face, and something gave way within her. Her eyes grew dim. By the expression of her father's face, not sad, not crushed, but angry and working unnaturally, she saw that hanging over her and about to crush her was some terrible misfortune, the worst in life, one she had not yet experienced, irreparable and incomprehensible—the death of one she loved.

"Father! Andrew!"—said the ungraceful, awkward princess with such an indescribable charm of sorrow and self-forgetfulness that her father could not bear her look but turned away with a sob.

"Bad news! He's not among the prisoners nor among the killed! Kutúzov writes . . ." and he screamed as piercingly as if he wished to drive the princess away by that scream . . . "Killed!"

The princess did not fall down or faint. She was already pale, but on hearing these words her face changed and something brightened in her beautiful radiant eyes. It was as if joy—a supreme joy apart from the joys and sorrows of this world—overflowed the great grief within her. She forgot all fear of her father, went up to him, took his hand, and drawing him down put her arm round his thin, scraggy neck.

"Father," she said, "do not turn away from me, let us weep together."

"Scoundrels! Blackguards!" shrieked the old man, turning his face away from her. "Destroying the army, destroying the men! And why? Go, go and tell Lise."

The princess sank helplessly into an arm-chair beside her father and wept. She saw her brother now as he had been at the moment when he took leave of her and of Lise, his look tender yet proud. She saw him tender and amused as he was when he put on the little icon. "Did he believe? Had he repented of his unbelief? Was he now there? There in the realms of eternal peace and blessedness?" she thought.

"Father, tell me how it happened," she asked through her tears.

"Go! Go! Killed in battle, where the best of Russian men and Russia's glory were led to destruction. Go, Princess Mary. Go and tell Lise. I will follow."

When Princess Mary returned from her father, the little princess sat working, and looked up with that curious expression of inner, happy calm peculiar to pregnant women. It was evident that her eyes did not see Princess Mary but were looking within . . . into herself . . . at something joyful and mysterious taking place within her.

"Mary," she said, moving away from the embroidery-frame and lying back, "give me your hand." She took her sister-in-law's hand and held it below her waist.

Her eyes were smiling expectantly, her downy lip rose, and remained lifted in childlike happiness.

Princess Mary knelt down before her and hid her face in the folds of her sister-in-law's dress.

"There, there! Do you feel it? I feel so strange. And do you know, Mary, I am going to love him very much," said Lise, looking with bright and happy eyes at her sister-in-law.

Princess Mary could not lift her head, she was weeping.

"What is the matter, Mary?"

"Nothing . . . only I feel sad . . . sad about Andrew," she said, wiping away her tears on her sister-in-law's knee.

Several times in the course of the morning Princess Mary began trying to prepare her sister-in-law, and every time began to cry. Unobservant as was the little princess, these tears, the cause of which she did not understand, agitated her. She said nothing but looked about uneasily as if in search of something. Before dinner the old prince, of whom she was always afraid, came into her room with a peculiarly restless and malign expression, and went out again without saying a word. She looked at Princess Mary, then sat thinking for a while with that expression of attention to something within her that is only seen in pregnant women, and suddenly began to cry.

"Has anything come from Andrew?" she asked.

"No, you know it's too soon for news. But my father is anxious and I feel afraid."

"So there's nothing?"

"Nothing," answered Princess Mary, looking firmly with her radiant eyes at her sister-in-law. She had determined not to tell her, and persuaded her father to hide the terrible news from her till after her confinement, which was expected within a few days. Princess Mary and the old prince each bore and hid their grief in their own way. The old prince would not cherish any hope: he made up his mind that Prince Andrew had been killed, and though he sent an official to Austria to seek for traces of his son, he ordered a monument from Moscow which he intended to erect in his own garden to his memory, and he told everybody that his son had been killed. He tried not to change his former way of life, but his strength failed him. He walked less, ate less, slept less, and became weaker every day. Princess Mary hoped. She prayed for her brother as living, and was always awaiting news of his return.

Chapter VIII

"DEAREST," SAID THE LITTLE PRINCESS AFTER BREAKFAST ON THE MORNING OF THE 19TH OF March, and her downy little lip rose from old habit, but as sorrow was manifest in every smile, the sound of every word, and even every footstep in that house since the terrible news had come, so now the smile of the little princess—influenced by the general mood though without knowing its cause—was such as to remind one still more of the general sorrow.

"Dearest, I'm afraid this morning's fruschtique—as Fóka the cook calls it—has disagreed with me."

"What is the matter with you, my darling? You look pale. Oh, you are very pale!" said Princess Mary in alarm, running with her soft, ponderous steps up to her sister-in-law.

"Your excellency, should not Mary Bogdánovna be sent for?" said one of the maids who was present. (Mary Bogdánovna was a midwife from the neighboring town, who had been at Bald Hills for the last fortnight.)

"Oh yes," assented Princess Mary, "perhaps that's it. I'll go. Courage, my angel." She kissed Lise and was about to leave the room.

"Oh, no, no!" And besides the pallor and the physical suffering on the little princess's face, an expression of childish fear of inevitable pain showed itself.

"No, it's only indigestion! . . . Say it's only indigestion, say so, Mary! Say . . ." And the little princess began to cry capriciously like a suffering child, and to wring her little hands even with some affectation. Princess Mary ran out of the room to fetch Mary Bogdánovna.

"*Mon Dieu! Mon Dieu!* Oh!" she heard as she left the room.

The midwife was already on her way to meet her, rubbing her small plump white hands with an air of calm importance.

"Mary Bogdánovna, I think it's beginning!" said Princess Mary looking at the midwife with wide-open eyes of alarm.

"Well, the Lord be thanked, princess," said Mary Bogdánovna, not hastening her steps. "You young ladies should not know anything about it."

"But how is it the doctor from Moscow is not here yet?" said the princess. (In accordance with Lise's and Prince Andrew's wishes they had sent in good time to Moscow for a doctor and were expecting him at any moment.)

"No matter, princess, don't be alarmed," said Mary Bogdánovna. "We'll manage very well without a doctor."

Five minutes later Princess Mary from her room heard something heavy being carried by. She looked out. The menservants were carrying the large leather sofa from Prince Andrew's study into the bedroom. On their faces was a quiet and solemn look.

Princess Mary sat alone in her room listening to the sounds in the house, now and then opening her door when someone passed and watching what was going on in the passage. Some women passing with quiet steps in and out of the bedroom glanced at the princess and turned away. She did not venture to ask any questions, and shut the door again, now sitting down in her easy chair, now taking her prayer book, now kneeling before the icon-stand. To her surprise and distress she found that her prayers did not calm her excitement. Suddenly her door opened softly and her old nurse, Praskóvya Sávishna, who hardly ever came to that room as the old prince had forbidden it, appeared on the threshold with a shawl round her head.

"I've come to sit with you a bit, Másha," said the nurse, "and here I've brought the prince's wedding candles to light before his saint, my angel," she said with a sigh.

"Oh, nurse, I'm so glad!"

"God is merciful, birdie."

The nurse lit the gilt candles before the icons and sat down by the door with her knitting. Princess Mary took a book and began reading. Only when footsteps or voices were heard did they look at one another, the princess anxious and inquiring, the nurse encouraging. Everyone in the house was dominated by the same feeling that Princess Mary experienced as she sat in her room. But owing to the superstition that the fewer the people who know of it the less a woman in travail suffers, everyone tried to pretend not to know; no one spoke of it, but apart from the ordinary staid and respectful good manners habitual in the prince's household, a common anxiety, a softening of the heart, and a consciousness that something great and mysterious was being accomplished at that moment, made itself felt.

There was no laughter in the maids' large hall. In the menservants' hall all sat waiting, silently and alert. In the outlying serfs' quarters torches and candles were burning and no one slept. The old prince, stepping on his heels, paced up and down his study and sent Tíkhon to ask Mary Bogdánovna what news—"Say only that 'the prince told me to ask,' and come and tell me her answer."

"Inform the prince that labor has begun," said Mary Bogdánovna, giving the messenger a significant look.

Tíkhon went and told the prince.

"Very good!" said the prince closing the door behind him, and Tíkhon did not hear the slightest sound from the study after that.

After a while he re-entered it as if to snuff the candles, and seeing the prince was lying on the sofa, looked at him, noticed his perturbed face, shook his head, and going up to him silently kissed him on the shoulder and left the room without snuffing the candles or saying why he had entered. The most solemn mystery in the world continued its course. Evening passed, night came, and the feeling of suspense and softening of heart in the presence of the unfathomable did not lessen but increased. No one slept.

It was one of those March nights when winter seems to wish to resume its sway and scatters its last snows and storms with desperate fury. A relay of horses had been sent up the highroad to meet the German doctor from Moscow who was expected every moment, and men on horseback with lanterns were sent to the crossroads to guide him over the country road with its hollows and snow-covered pools of water.

Princess Mary had long since put aside her book: she sat silent, her luminous eyes fixed on her nurse's wrinkled face (every line of which she knew so well), on the lock of gray hair that escaped from under the kerchief, and the loose skin that hung under her chin.

Nurse Sávishna, knitting in hand, was telling in low tones, scarcely hearing or understanding her own words, what she had told hundreds of times before: how the late princess had given birth to Princess Mary in Kishenëv with only a Moldavian peasant woman to help instead of a midwife.

"God is merciful, doctors are never needed," she said.

Suddenly a gust of wind beat violently against the casement of the window, from which the double frame had been removed (by order of the prince, one window frame was removed in each room as soon as the larks returned), and, forcing open a loosely closed latch, set the damask curtain flapping and blew out the candle with its chill, snowy draft. Princess Mary shuddered; her nurse putting down the stocking she was knitting, went to the window and leaning out tried to catch the open casement. The cold wind flapped the ends of her kerchief and her loose locks of gray hair.

"Princess, my dear, there's someone driving up the avenue!" she said, holding the casement and not closing it. "With lanterns. Most likely the doctor."

"Oh, my God! thank God!" said Princess Mary. "I must go and meet him, he does not know Russian."

Princess Mary threw a shawl over her head and ran to meet the newcomer. As she was crossing the anteroom she saw through the window a carriage with lanterns, standing at the entrance. She went out on the stairs. On a banister-post stood a tallow candle which guttered in the draft. On the landing below, Philip, the footman, stood looking scared and holding another candle. Still lower, beyond the turn of the staircase, one could hear the footstep of someone in thick felt boots, and a voice that seemed familiar to Princess Mary was saying something.

"Thank God!" said the voice. "And father?"

"Gone to bed," replied the voice of Demyán the house-steward, who was downstairs.

Then the voice said something more, Demyán replied, and the steps in the felt boots approached the unseen bend of the staircase more rapidly.

"It's Andrew!" thought Princess Mary. "No it can't be, that would be too extraordinary," and at the very moment she thought this, the face and figure of Prince Andrew, in a fur cloak the deep collar of which covered with snow, appeared on the landing where the footman stood with the candle. Yes, it was he, pale, thin, with a changed and strangely softened but agitated expression on his face. He came up the stairs and embraced his sister.

"You did not get my letter?" he asked, and not waiting for a reply—which he would not have received, for the princess was unable to speak—he turned back, rapidly mounted the stairs again with the doctor who had entered the hall after him (they had met at the last post station) and again embraced his sister.

"What a strange fate, Másha darling!" And having taken off his cloak and felt boots, he went to the little princess's apartment.

Chapter IX

THE LITTLE PRINCESS LAY SUPPORTED BY PILLOWS, WITH A WHITE CAP ON HER HEAD (THE PAINS had just left her). Strands of her black hair lay round her inflamed and perspiring cheeks, her charming rosy mouth with its downy lip was open and she was smiling joyfully. Prince Andrew entered and paused facing her at the foot of the sofa on which she was lying. Her glittering eyes, filled with childlike fear and excitement, rested on him without changing their expression. "I love you all and have done no harm to anyone; why must I suffer so? Help me!" her look seemed to say. She saw her husband, but did not realize the significance of his appearance before her now. Prince Andrew went round the sofa and kissed her forehead.

"My darling!" he said—a word he had never used to her before. "God is merciful. . . ."

She looked at him inquiringly and with childlike reproach.

"I expected help from you and I get none, none from you either!" said her eyes. She was not surprised at his having come; she did not realize that he had come. His coming had nothing to do with her sufferings or with their relief. The pangs began again and Mary Bogdánovna advised Prince Andrew to leave the room.

The doctor entered. Prince Andrew went out, and meeting Princess Mary again joined her. They began talking in whispers, but their talk broke off at every moment. They waited and listened.

"Go, dear," said Princess Mary.

Prince Andrew went again to his wife and sat waiting in the room next to hers. A woman came from the bedroom with a frightened face and became confused when she saw Prince Andrew. He covered his face with his hands and remained so for some minutes. Piteous, helpless, animal moans came through the door. Prince Andrew got up, went to the door, and tried to open it. Someone was holding it shut.

"You can't come in! You can't!" said a terrified voice from within.

He began pacing the room. The screaming ceased, and a few more seconds went by. Then suddenly a terrible shriek—it could not be hers, she could not scream like that—came from the bedroom. Prince Andrew ran to the door; the scream ceased and he heard the wail of an infant.

"What have they taken a baby in there for?" thought Prince Andrew in the first second. "A baby? What baby . . . ? Why is there a baby there? Or is the baby born?"

Then suddenly he realized the joyful significance of that wail; tears choked him, and leaning his elbows on the window sill be began to cry, sobbing like a child. The door opened. The doctor with his shirt-sleeves tucked up, without a coat, pale and with a trembling jaw came out of the room. Prince Andrew turned to him, but the doctor gave him a bewildered look and passed by without a word. A woman rushed out and seeing Prince Andrew stopped, hesitating on the threshold. He went into his wife's room. She was lying dead, in the same position he had seen her in five minutes before and, despite the fixed eyes and the pallor of the cheeks, the same expression was on her charming childlike face with its upper lip covered with tiny black hair.

"I love you all, and have done no harm to anyone; and what have you done to me?"— said her charming, pathetic, dead face.

In a corner of the room something red and tiny gave a grunt and squealed in Mary Bogdánovna's trembling white hands.

Two hours later Prince Andrew, stepping softly, went into his father's room. The old man already knew everything. He was standing close to the door and as soon as it opened his rough old arms closed like a vise round his son's neck, and without a word he began to sob like a child.

Three days later the little princess was buried, and Prince Andrew went up the steps to where the coffin stood, to give her the farewell kiss. And there in the coffin was the same face, though with closed eyes. "Ah, what have you done to me?" it still seemed to say, and Prince Andrew felt that something gave way in his soul and that he was guilty of a sin he could neither remedy nor forget. He could not weep. The old man too came up and kissed the waxen little hands that lay quietly crossed one on the other on her breast, and to him, too, her face seemed to say: "Ah, what have you done to me, and why?" And at the sight the old man turned angrily away.

Another five days passed, and then the young Prince Nicholas Andréevich was baptized. The wet-nurse supported the coverlet with her chin, while the priest with a goose feather anointed the boy's little red and wrinkled soles and palms.

His grandfather, who was his godfather, trembling and afraid of dropping him, carried the infant round the battered tin font and handed him over to the godmother, Princess Mary. Prince Andrew sat in another room, faint with fear lest the baby should be drowned in the font, and awaited the termination of the ceremony. He looked up joyfully at the baby when the nurse brought it to him, and nodded approval when she told him that the wax with the baby's hair had not sunk in the font but had floated.

Chapter X

ROSTÓV'S SHARE IN DÓLOKHOV'S DUEL WITH BEZÚKHOV WAS HUSHED UP BY THE EFFORTS OF THE old count, and instead of being degraded to the ranks as he expected he was appointed an adjutant to the governor-general of Moscow. As a result he could not go to the country with the rest of the family, but was kept all summer in Moscow by his new duties. Dólokhov recovered, and Rostóv became very friendly with him during his convalescence. Dólokhov lay ill at his mother's who loved him passionately and tenderly, and old Mary Ivánovna, who had grown fond of Rostóv for his friendship to her Fédya, often talked to him about her son.

"Yes, count," she would say, "he is too noble and pure-souled for our present, depraved world. No one now loves virtue, it seems like a reproach to everyone. Now tell me, count, was it right, was it honorable, of Bezúkhov? And Fédya, with his noble spirit, loved him and even now never says a word against him. Those pranks in Petersburg when they played some tricks on a policeman, didn't they do it together? And there! Bezúkhov got off scot free, while Fédya had to bear the whole burden on his shoulders. Fancy what he had to go through! It's true he has been reinstated, but how could they fail to do that? I think there were not many such gallant sons of the fatherland out there as he. And now—this duel! Have these people no feeling, no honor? Knowing him to be an only son, to challenge him and shoot so straight! It's well God had mercy on us. And what was it for? Who doesn't have intrigues nowadays? Why, if he was so jealous, as I see things he should have shown it sooner, but he lets it go on for months. And then to call him out, reckoning on Fédya not fighting because he owed him money! What baseness! What meanness! I know you understand Fédya, my dear count; that, believe me, is why I am so fond of you. Few people do understand him. He is such a lofty, heavenly soul!"

Dólokhov himself during his convalescence spoke to Rostóv in a way no one would have expected of him.

"I know people consider me a bad man!" he said. "Let them! I don't care a straw about anyone but those I love; but those I love, I love so that I would give my life for them, and the others I'd throttle if they stood in my way. I have an adored, a priceless mother, and two or three friends—you among them, and as for the rest I only care about them in so far as they are harmful or useful. And most of them are harmful, especially the women. Yes, dear boy," he continued, "I have met loving, noble-minded men, but I have not yet met any women—countesses or cooks—who were not venal. I have not yet met that divine purity and devotion I look for in woman. If I found such a one I'd give my life for her! But those! . . ." and he made a gesture of contempt. "And believe me, if I still value my life it is only because I still hope to meet such a divine creature, who will regenerate, purify and elevate me. But you don't understand it."

"Oh, yes, I quite understand," answered Rostóv, who was under his new friend's influence.

In the autumn the Rostóvs returned to Moscow. Early in the winter Denísov also came back and stayed with them. The first half of the winter of 1806 which Nicholas Rostóv spent in Moscow, was one of the happiest, merriest times for him and the whole family. Nicholas brought many young men to his parents' house. Véra was a handsome girl of twenty; Sónya a girl of sixteen with all the charm of an opening flower; Natásha, half grown-up and half child, was now childishly amusing, now girlishly enchanting.

At that time in the Rostóvs' house there prevailed an amorous atmosphere characteristic of homes where there are very young and very charming girls. Every young man who came to the house, seeing those impressionable, smiling young faces (smiling probably at their own happiness), feeling the eager bustle around him, and hearing the fitful bursts of song and music and the inconsequent but friendly prattle of young girls ready for anything and full of hope—experienced the same feeling; sharing with the young folk of the Rostóvs' household a readiness to fall in love and an expectation of happiness.

Among the young men introduced by Rostóv one of the first was Dólokhov, whom everyone in the house liked except Natásha. She almost quarreled with her brother about him. She insisted that he was a bad man, and that in the duel with Bezúkhov, Pierre was right and Dólokhov wrong, and further that he was disagreeable and unnatural.

"There's nothing for me to understand," cried out with resolute self-will, "he is wicked and heartless. There now, I like your Denísov though he is a rake and all that, but I like him; so you see I do understand. I don't know how to put it . . . with this one everything is calculated, and I don't like that. But Denísov . . ."

"Oh, Denísov is quite different," replied Nicholas—implying that even Denísov was nothing compared to Dólokhov—"you must understand what a soul there is in Dólokhov, you should see him with his mother. What a heart!"

"Well, I don't know about that, but I am uncomfortable with him. And do you know he has fallen in love with Sónya?"

"What nonsense . . ."

"I'm certain of it, you'll see."

Natásha's prediction proved true. Dólokhov, who did not usually care for the society of ladies, began to come often to the house, and the question for whose sake he came (though no one spoke of it) was soon settled. He came because of Sónya. And Sónya, though she would never have dared to say so, knew it and blushed scarlet every time Dólokhov appeared.

Dólokhov often dined at the Rostóvs', never missed a performance at which they were present, and went to Iogel's balls for young people which the Rostóvs always attended. He was pointedly attentive to Sónya, and looked at her in such a way that not only could she not bear his glances without coloring, but even the old countess and Natásha blushed when they saw his looks.

It was evident that this strange, strong man was under the irresistible influence of the dark graceful girl who loved another.

Rostóv noticed something new in Dólokhov's relations with Sónya, but he did not explain to himself what these new relations were. "They're always in love with someone," he thought of Sónya and Natásha. But he was not as much at ease with Sónya and Dólokhov as before, and was less frequently at home.

In the autumn of 1806 everybody had again begun talking of the war with Napoleon with even greater warmth than the year before. Orders were given to raise recruits, ten men in every thousand for the regular army, and besides this, nine men in every thousand for the militia. Everywhere Bonaparte was anathematized and in Moscow nothing but the coming war was talked of. For the Rostóv family the whole interest of these preparations for war lay in the fact that Nicholas would not hear of remaining in Moscow, and only awaited the termination of Denísov's furlough after Christmas, to return with him to their regiment. His approaching departure did not prevent his amusing himself, but rather gave zest to his pleasures. He spent the greater part of his time away from home, at dinners, parties and balls.

Chapter XI

On the third day after Christmas Nicholas dined at home, a thing he had rarely done of late. It was a grand farewell dinner, as he and Denísov were leaving to join their regiment after Epiphany. About twenty people were present, including Dólokhov and Denísov.

Never had love been so much in the air, and never had the amorous atmosphere made itself so strongly felt in the Rostóvs' house as at this holiday time. "Seize the moments of happiness, love and be loved! That is the only reality in the world, all else is folly. It is the one thing we are interested in here," said the spirit of the place.

Nicholas, having as usual exhausted two pairs of horses, without visiting all the places he meant to go to and where he had been invited, returned home just before dinner. As soon as he entered he noticed and felt the tension of the amorous air in the house, and also noticed a curious embarrassment among some of those present. Sónya, Dólokhov and the old countess were especially disturbed, and to a lesser degree Natásha. Nicholas understood that something must have happened between Sónya and Dólokhov before dinner, and with the kindly sensitiveness natural to him was very gentle and wary with them both at dinner. On that same evening there was to be one of the balls that Iogel (the dancing master) gave for his pupils durings the holidays.

"Nicholas, will you come to Iogel's? Please do!" said Natásha. "He asked you, and Vasíli Dmítrich (Denísov) is also going."

"Where would I not go at the countess's command!" said Denísov, who at the Rostóvs' had jocularly assumed the rôle of Natásha's knight. "I'm even weady to dance the *pas de châle.*"

"If I have time," answered Nicholas. "But I promised the Arkhárovs; they have a party."

"And you?" he asked Dólokhov, but as soon as he had asked the question he noticed that it should not have been put.

"Perhaps," coldly and angrily replied Dólokhov, glancing at Sónya, and, scowling, he gave Nicholas just such a look as he had given Pierre at the Club dinner.

"There is something up," thought Nicholas, and he was further confirmed in this conclusion by the fact that Dólokhov left immediately after dinner. He called Natásha and asked her what was the matter.

"And I was looking for you," said Natásha running out to him. "I told you, but you would not believe it," she said triumphantly. "He has proposed to Sónya!"

Little as Nicholas had occupied himself with Sónya of late, something seemed to give way within him at this news. Dólokhov was a suitable and in some respects a brilliant match for the dowerless, orphan girl. From the point of view of the old countess and of society it was out of the question for her to refuse him. And therefore Nicholas's first feeling on hearing the news was one of anger with Sónya. . . . He tried to say, "That's capital; of course she'll forget her childish promises and accept the offer," but before he had time to say it Natásha began again.

"And fancy! she refused him quite definitely!" adding, after a pause, "she told him she loved another."

"Yes, my Sónya could not have done otherwise!" thought Nicholas.

"Much as Mamma pressed her, she refused, and I know she won't change once she has said . . ."

"And Mamma pressed her!" said Nicholas reproachfully.

"Yes," said Natásha. "Do you know, Nicholas—don't be angry—but I know you will not marry her. I know, Heaven knows how, but I know for certain that you won't marry her."

"Now you don't know that at all!" said Nicholas. "But I must talk to her. What a darling Sónya is!" he added with a smile.

"Ah, she is indeed a darling! I'll send her to you."

And Natásha kissed her brother and ran away.

A minute later Sónya came in with a frightened, guilty and scared look. Nicholas went up to her and kissed her hand. This was the first time since his return that they had talked alone and about their love.

"Sophie," he began, timidly at first and then more and more boldly, "if you wish to refuse one who is not only a brilliant and advantageous match but a splendid, noble fellow . . . he is my friend . . ."

Sónya interrupted him.

"I have already refused," she said hurriedly.

"If you are refusing for my sake, I am afraid that I . . ."

Sónya again interrupted. She gave him an imploring, frightened look.

"Nicholas, don't tell me that!" she said.

"No, but I must. It may be arrogant of me, but still it is best to say it. If you refuse him on my account, I must tell you the whole truth. I love you, and I think I love you more than anyone else. . . ."

"That is enough for me," said Sónya, blushing.

"No, but I have been in love a thousand times and shall fall in love again, though for no one have I such a feeling of friendship, confidence and love as I have for you. Then I am young. Mamma does not wish it. In a word, I make no promise. And I beg you to consider Dólokhov's offer," he said, articulating his friend's name with difficulty.

"Don't say that to me! I want nothing. I love you as a brother and always shall, and I want nothing more."

"You are an angel: I am not worthy of you, but I am afraid of misleading you."

And Nicholas again kissed her hand.

Chapter XII

IOGEL'S WERE THE MOST ENJOYABLE BALLS IN MOSCOW. SO SAID THE MOTHERS AS THEY WATCHED their young people executing their newly-learned steps, and so said the youths and maidens themselves as they danced till they were ready to drop, and so said the grown-up young men and women who came to these balls with an air of condescension, and found them most enjoyable. That year two marriages had come of these balls. The two pretty young Princesses Gorchakóv met suitors there and were married, and so further increased the fame of these dances. What distinguished them from others was the absence of host or hostess and the presence of the good-natured Iogel, flying about like a feather and bowing according to the rules of his art, as he collected the tickets from all his visitors. There was the fact that only those came who wished to dance and amuse themselves as girls of thirteen and fourteen do who are wearing long dresses for the first time. With scarcely any exceptions they all were, or seemed to be, pretty—so rapturous were their smiles and so sparkling their eyes. Sometimes the best of the pupils, of whom Natásha, who was exceptionally graceful, was first, even danced the *pas de châle,* but at this last ball only the écossaise, the anglaise, and the mazurka which was just coming into fashion, were danced. Iogel had taken a ballroom in Bezúkhov's house, and the ball, as everyone said, was a great success. There were many pretty girls and the Rostóv girls were among the prettiest. They were both particularly happy and gay. That evening, proud of Dólokhov's proposal, her refusal, and her explanation with Nicholas, Sónya twirled about before she left home so that the maid could hardly get her hair plaited, and she was transparently radiant with impulsive joy.

Natásha no less proud of her first long dress and of being at a real ball was even happier. They were both dressed in white muslin with pink ribbons.

Natásha fell in love the very moment she entered the ballroom. She was not in love with anyone in particular, but with everyone. Whatever person she happened to look at she was in love with for that moment.

"Oh, how delightful it is!" she kept saying, running up to Sónya.

Nicholas and Denísov were walking up and down, looking with kindly patronage at the dancers.

"How sweet she is—she will be a weal beauty!" said Denísov.

"Who?"

"Countess Natásha," answered Denísov.

"And how she dances! What gwace!" he said again after a pause.

"Who are you talking about?"

"About your sister," ejaculated Denísov testily.

Rostóv smiled.

"My dear count, you were one of my best pupils—you must dance," said little Iogel coming up to Nicholas. "Look how many charming young ladies—" He turned with the same request to Denísov who was also a former pupil of his.

"No, my dear fellow, I'll be a wallflower," said Denísov. "Don't you wecollect what bad use I made of your lessons?"

"Oh no!" said Iogel, hastening to reassure him. "You were only inattentive, but you had talent—oh yes, you had talent!"

The band struck up the newly introduced mazurka. Nicholas could not refuse Iogel, and asked Sónya to dance. Denísov sat down by the old ladies and, leaning on his saber and beating time with his foot, told them something funny and kept them amused, while he watched the young people dancing. Iogel with Natásha, his pride and his best pupil, were the first couple. Noiselessly, skillfully stepping with his little feet in low shoes, Iogel flew first across the hall with Natásha, who though shy, went on carefully executing her steps. Denísov did not take his eyes off her and beat time with his saber in a way that clearly indicated that if he was not dancing it was because he would not and not because he could not. In the middle of a figure he beckoned to Rostóv who was passing:

"This is not at all the thing," he said. "What sort of Polish mazuwka is this? But she does dance splendidly."

Knowing that Denísov had a reputation even in Poland for the masterly way in which he danced the mazurka, Nicholas ran up to Natásha:

"Go and choose Denísov. He is a real dancer, a wonder!" he said.

When it came to Natásha's turn to choose a partner, she rose and, tripping rapidly across in her little shoes trimmed with bows, ran timidly to the corner where Denísov sat. She saw that everybody was looking at her and waiting. Nicholas saw that Denísov was refusing though he smiled delightedly. He ran up to them.

"Please, Vasíli Dmítrich," Natásha was saying, "do come!"

"Oh no, let me off, countess," Denísov replied.

"Now then, Váska," said Nicholas.

"They coax me as if I were Váska the cat!" said Denísov jokingly.

"I'll sing for you a whole evening," said Natásha.

"Oh, the faiwy! She can do anything with me!" said Denísov, and he unhooked his saber. He came out from behind the chairs, clasped his partner's hand firmly, threw back his head, and advanced his foot, waiting for the beat. Only on horseback and in the mazurka was Denísov's short stature not noticeable and he looked the fine fellow he felt himself to be. At the right beat of the music he looked sideways at his partner with a merry and triumphant air, suddenly stamped with one foot, bounded from the floor like a ball, and flew round the room taking his partner with him. He glided silently on one foot half across the room, and seeming not to notice the chairs was dashing straight at them, when suddenly, clinking his spurs and spreading out his legs, he stopped short on his heels, stood so a second, stamped on the spot clanking his spurs, whirled rapidly round, and, striking his left heel against his right, flew round again in a circle. Natásha guessed what he meant to do, and abandoning herself to him followed his lead hardly knowing how. First he spun her round, holding her now with his left now with his right hand, then falling on one knee he twirled her round him, and again jumping up, dashed so impetuously forward that it seemed as if he would rush through the whole suite of rooms without drawing breath, and then he suddenly stopped and performed some new and unexpected steps. When at last, smartly whirling his partner round in front of her chair, he drew up with a click of his spurs and bowed to her, Natásha did not even make him a curtsey. She fixed her eyes on him in amazement, smiling as if she did not recognize him.

"What does this mean?" she brought out.

Although Iogel did not acknowledge this to be the real mazurka, everyone was delighted with Denísov's skill, he was asked again and again as a partner, and the old men began smilingly to talk about Poland and the good old days. Denísov, flushed after the mazurka and mopping himself with his handkerchief, sat down by Natásha and did not leave her for the rest of the evening.

Chapter XIII

For two days after that Rostóv did not see Dólokhov at his own or at Dólokhov's home: on the third day he received a note from him:

As I do not intend to be at your house again for reasons you know of, and am going to rejoin my regiment, I am giving a farewell supper tonight to my friends—come to the English Hotel.

About ten o'clock Rostóv went to the English Hotel straight from the theater, where he had been with his family and Denísov. He was at once shown to the best room, which Dólokhov had taken for that evening. Some twenty men were gathered round a table at which Dólokhov sat between two candles. On the table was a pile of gold and paper money, and he was keeping the bank. Rostóv had not seen him since his proposal and Sónya's refusal, and felt uncomfortable at the thought of how they would meet.

Dólokhov's clear cold glance met Rostóv as soon as he entered the door, as though he had long expected him.

"It's a long time since we met," he said. "Thanks for coming. I'll just finish dealing, and then Ilyúshka will come with his chorus."

"I called once or twice at your house," said Rostóv, reddening.

Dólokhov made no reply.

"You may punt," he said.

Rostóv recalled at that moment a strange conversation he had once had with Dólokhov. "None but fools trust to luck in play," Dólokhov had then said.

"Or are you afraid to play with me?" Dólokhov now asked as if guessing Rostóv's thought.

Beneath his smile Rostóv saw in him the mood he had shown at the Club dinner and at other times, when as if tired of everyday life he had felt a need to escape from it by some strange, and usually cruel, action.

Rostóv felt ill at ease. He tried, but failed, to find some joke with which to reply to Dólokhov's words. But before he had thought of anything, Dólokhov, looking straight in his face, said slowly and deliberately so that everyone could hear:

"Do you remember we had a talk about cards . . . 'He's a fool who trusts to luck, one should make certain,' and I want to try."

"To try his luck or the certainty?" Rostóv asked himself.

"Well, you'd better not play," Dólokhov added, and springing a new pack of cards said: "Bank, gentlemen!"

Moving the money forward he prepared to deal. Rostóv sat down by his side and at first did not play. Dólokhov kept glancing at him.

"Why don't you play?" he asked.

And strange to say Nicholas felt that he could not help taking up a card, putting a small stake on it, and beginning to play.

"I have no money with me," he said.

"I'll trust you."

Rostóv staked five rubles on a card and lost, staked again, and again lost. Dólokhov "killed," that is, beat, ten cards of Rostóv's running.

"Gentlemen," said Dólokhov after he had dealt for some time. "Please place your money on the cards or I may get muddled in the reckoning."

One of the players said he hoped he might be trusted.

"Yes, you might, but I am afraid of getting the accounts mixed. So I ask you to put the money on your cards," replied Dólokhov. "Don't stint yourself, we'll settle afterward," he added, turning to Rostóv.

The game continued; a waiter kept handing round champagne.

All Rostóv's cards were beaten and he had eight hundred rubles scored up against him. He wrote "800 rubles" on a card, but while the waiter filled his glass he changed his mind and altered it to his usual stake of twenty rubles.

"Leave it," said Dólokhov, though he did not seem to be even looking at Rostóv, "you'll win it back all the sooner. I lose to the others but win from you. Or are you afraid of me?" he asked again.

Rostóv submitted. He let the eight hundred remain and laid down a seven of hearts with a torn corner, which he had picked up from the floor. He well remembered that seven afterward. He laid down the seven of hearts, on which with a broken bit of chalk he had written "800 rubles" in clear upright figures; he emptied the glass of warm champagne that was handed him, smiled at Dólokhov's words, and with a sinking heart, waiting for a seven to turn up, gazed at Dólokhov's hands which held the pack. Much depended on Rostóv's winning or losing on that seven of hearts. On the previous Sunday the old count had given his son two thousand rubles, and though he always disliked speaking of money difficulties had told Nicholas that this was all he could let him have till May, and asked him to be more economical this time. Nicholas had replied that it would be more than enough for him, and that he gave his word of honor not to take anything more till the spring. Now only twelve hundred rubles was left of that money, so that this seven of hearts meant for him not only the loss of sixteen hundred rubles, but the necessity of going back on his word. With a sinking heart he watched Dólokhov's hands and thought, "Now then, make haste and let me have this card and I'll take my cap and drive home to supper with Denísov, Natásha and Sónya, and will certainly never touch a card again." At that moment his home life, jokes with Pétya, talks with Sónya, duets with Natásha, picquet with his father, and even his comfortable bed in the house on the Povarskáya rose before him with such vividness, clearness and charm that it seemed as if it were all a lost and unappreciated bliss, long past. He could not conceive that a stupid chance, letting the seven be dealt to the right rather than to the left, might deprive him of all this happiness, newly appreciated and newly illumined, and plunge him into the depths of unknown and undefined misery.

That could not be, yet he awaited with a sinking heart the movement of Dólokhov's hands. Those broad, reddish hands, with hairy wrists visible from under the shirt-cuffs, laid down the pack and took up a glass and a pipe that were handed him.

"So you are not afraid to play with me?" repeated Dólokhov, and as if about to tell a good story he put down the cards, leaned back in his chair, and began deliberately with a smile:

"Yes, gentlemen, I've been told there's a rumor going about Moscow that I'm a sharper, so I advise you to be careful."

"Come now, deal!" exclaimed Rostóv.

"Oh, those Moscow gossips!" said Dólokhov, and he took up the cards with a smile.

"Aah!" Rostóv almost screamed lifting both hands to his head. The seven he needed was lying uppermost, the first card in the pack. He had lost more than he could pay.

"Still, don't ruin yourself!" said Dólokhov with a side glance at Rostóv as he continued to deal.

Chapter XIV

An hour and a half later most of the players were but little interested in their own play.

The whole interest was concentrated on Rostóv. Instead of sixteen hundred rubles he had a long column of figures scored against him, which he had reckoned up to ten thousand, but that now, as he vaguely supposed, must have risen to fifteen thousand. In reality it already exceeded twenty thousand rubles. Dólokhov was no longer listening to stories or telling them, but followed every movement of Rostóv's hands and occasionally ran his eyes over the score against him. He had decided to play until that score reached forty-three thousand. He had fixed on that number because forty-three was the sum of his and Sónya's joint ages. Rostóv, leaning his head on both hands, sat at the table which was scrawled over with figures, wet with spilled wine, and littered with cards. One tormenting impression did not leave him: that those broad-boned reddish hands with hairy wrists visible from under the shirt-sleeves, those hands which he loved and hated, held him in their power.

"Six hundred rubles, ace, a corner, a nine . . . winning it back's impossible . . . Oh, how pleasant it was at home! . . . The knave, double or quits . . . it can't be! . . . And why is he doing this to me?" Rostóv pondered. Sometimes he staked a large sum, but Dólokhov refused to accept it and fixed the stake himself. Nicholas submitted to him, and at one moment prayed to God as he had done on the battlefield at the bridge over the Enns, and then guessed that the card that came first to hand from the crumpled heap under the table would save him, now counted the cords on his coat and took a card with that number and tried staking the total of his losses on it, then he looked round for aid from the other players, or peered at the now cold face of Dólokhov and tried to read what was passing in his mind.

"He knows of course what this loss means to me. He can't want my ruin. Wasn't he my friend? Wasn't I fond of him? But it's not his fault. What's he to do if he has such luck? . . . And it's not my fault either," he thought to himself, "I have done nothing wrong. Have I killed anyone, or insulted or wished harm to anyone? Why such a terrible misfortune? And when did it begin? Such a little while ago I came to this table with the thought of winning a hundred rubles to buy that casket for Mamma's name-day and then going home. I was so happy, so free, so light-hearted! And I did not realize how happy I was! When did that end and when did this new, terrible state of things begin? What marked the change? I sat all the time in this same place at this table, chose and placed cards, and watched those broad-boned agile hands in the same way. When did it happen and what has happened? I am well and strong, and still the same and in the same place. No, it can't be! Surely it will all end in nothing!"

He was flushed and bathed in perspiration, though the room was not hot. His face was terrible and piteous to see, especially from its helpless efforts to seem calm.

The score against him reached the fateful sum of forty-three thousand. Rostóv had just prepared a card, by bending the corner of which he meant to double the three thousand just put down to his score, when Dólokhov, slamming down the pack of cards, put it aside and began rapidly adding up the total of Rostóv's debt, breaking the chalk as he marked the figures in his clear, bold hand.

"Supper, it's time for supper! And here are the gypsies!"

Some swarthy men and women were really entering from the cold outside, and saying something in their gypsy accents. Nicholas understood that it was all over; but he said in an indifferent tone:

"Well, won't you go on? I had a splendid card all ready," as if it were the fun of the game which interested him most.

"It's all up! I'm lost!" thought he. "Now a bullet through my brain—that's all that's left me!" And at the same time he said in a cheerful voice:

"Come now, just this one more little card!"

"All right!" said Dólokhov, having finished the addition. "All right! Twenty-one rubles," he said, pointing to the figure twenty-one by which the total exceeded the round sum of forty-three thousand; and taking up a pack he prepared to deal. Rostóv submissively unbent the corner of his card and, instead of the six thousand he had intended, carefully wrote twenty-one.

"It's all the same to me," he said. "I only want to see whether you will let me win this ten, or beat it."

Dólokhov began to deal seriously. Oh, how Rostóv detested at that moment those hands with their short reddish fingers and hairy wrists, which held him in their power. . . . The ten fell to him.

"You owe forty-three thousand, count," said Dólokhov, and stretching himself he rose from the table. "One does get tired sitting so long," he added.

"Yes, I'm tired too," said Rostóv.

Dólokhov cut him short, as if to remind him that it was not for him to jest.

"When am I to receive the money, count?"

Rostóv flushing, drew Dólokhov into the next room.

"I cannot pay it all immediately. Will you take an I.O.U.?" he said.

"I say, Rostóv," said Dólokhov clearly, smiling and looking Nicholas straight in the eyes, "you know the saying, 'Lucky in love unlucky at cards.' Your cousin is in love with you, I know."

"Oh, it's terrible to feel oneself so in this man's power," thought Rostóv. He knew what a shock he would inflict on his father and mother by the news of this loss, he knew what a relief it would be to escape it all, and felt that Dólokhov knew that he could save him from all this shame and sorrow, but wanted now to play with him as a cat does with a mouse.

"Your cousin . . ." Dólokhov started to say, but Nicholas interrupted him.

"My cousin has nothing to do with this and it's not necessary to mention her!" he exclaimed fiercely.

"Then when am I to have it?"

"Tomorrow," replied Rostóv and left the room.

Chapter XV

To say "tomorrow" and keep up a dignified tone was not difficult, but to go home alone, see his sisters, brother, mother, and father, confess and ask for money he had no right to after giving his word of honor, was terrible.

At home, they had not yet gone to bed. The young people, after returning from the theater, had had supper, and were grouped round the clavichord. As soon as Nicholas entered, he was enfolded in that poetic atmosphere of love which pervaded the Rostóv household that winter and, now after Dólokhov's proposal and Iogel's ball, seemed to have grown thicker round Sónya and Natásha as the air does before a thunderstorm. Sónya and Natásha, in the light blue dresses they had worn at the theater, looking pretty and conscious of it, were standing by the clavichord, happy and smiling. Véra was playing chess with Shinshín in the drawing room. The old countess, waiting for the return of her husband and son, sat playing patience with the old gentlewoman who lived in their house. Denísov, with sparkling eyes and ruffled hair, sat at the clavichord striking chords with his short fingers, his legs thrown back and his eyes rolling as he sang, with his small, husky, but true voice, some verses called "Enchantress," which he had composed, and to which he was trying to fit music.

Enchantress say, to my forsaken lyre
What magic power is this recalls me still?
What spark has set my inmost soul on fire,
What is this bliss that makes my fingers thrill?

—He was singing in passionate tones, gazing with his sparkling black agate eyes at the frightened and happy Natásha.

"Splendid! Excellent!" exclaimed Natásha. "Another verse," she said, without noticing Nicholas.

"Everything's still the same with them," thought Nicholas, glancing into the drawing room, where he saw Véra and his mother with the old lady.

"Ah, and here's Nicholas!" cried Natásha, running up to him.

"Is Papa at home?" he asked.

"I am so glad you've come!" said Natásha, without answering him. "We *are* enjoying ourselves! Vasíli Dmítrich is staying a day longer for my sake! Did you know?"

"No, Papa is not back yet," said Sónya.

"Nicholas, have you come? Come here, dear!" called the old countess from the drawing room.

Nicholas went to her, kissed her hand, and sitting down silently at her table, began to watch her hands arranging the cards. From the dancing room, they still heard the laughter and merry voices trying to persuade Natásha to sing.

"All wight! All wight!" shouted Denísov. "It's no good making excuses now! It's your turn to sing the ba'cawolla—I entweat you!"

The countess glanced at her silent son.

"What is the matter?" she asked.

"Oh, nothing," said he, as if weary of being continually asked the same question. "Will Papa be back soon?"

"I expect so."

"Everything's the same with them. They know nothing about it! Where am I to go?" thought Nicholas, and went again into the dancing room where the clavichord stood.

Sónya was sitting at the clavichord, playing the prelude to Denísov's favorite barcarolle. Natásha was preparing to sing. Denísov was looking at her with enraptured eyes.

Nicholas began pacing up and down the room.

"Why do they want to make her sing? How can she sing? There's nothing to be happy about!" thought he.

Sónya struck the first chord of the prelude.

"My God, I'm a ruined and dishonored man! A bullet through my brain is the only thing left me—not singing!" his thoughts ran on. "Go away? But where to? It's all one—let them sing!"

He continued to pace the room, looking gloomily at Denísov and the girls and avoiding their eyes.

"Nikólenka, what is the matter?" Sónya's eyes fixed on him seemed to ask. She noticed at once that something had happened to him.

Nicholas turned away from her. Natásha too, with her quick instinct, had instantly noticed her brother's condition. But, though she noticed it, she was herself in such high spirits at that moment, so far from sorrow, sadness or self-reproach, that she purposely deceived herself as young people often do. "No, I am too happy now to spoil my enjoyment by sympathy with anyone's sorrow," she felt, and she said to herself: "No, I must be mistaken, he must be feeling happy, just as I am."

"Now Sónya!" she said, going to the very middle of the room, where she considered the resonance was best.

Having lifted her head and let her arms droop lifelessly, as ballet dancers do, Natásha, rising energetically from her heels to her toes, stepped to the middle of the room and stood still.

"Yes, that's me!" she seemed to say, answering the rapt gaze with which Denísov followed her.

"And what is she so pleased about?" thought Nicholas, looking at his sister. "Why isn't she dull and ashamed?"

Natásha took the first note, her throat swelled, her chest rose, her eyes became serious. At that moment she was oblivious of her surroundings, and from her smiling lips flowed sounds which anyone may produce at the same intervals hold for the same time, but which leave you cold a thousand times and the thousand and first time thrill you and make you weep.

Natásha, that winter, had for the first time begun to sing seriously, mainly because Denísov so delighted in her singing. She no longer sang as a child, there was no longer in her singing that comical, childish, painstaking effect that had been in it before; but she did not yet sing well, as all the connoisseurs who heard her said: "It is not trained, but it is a beautiful voice that must be trained." Only they generally said this some time after she had finished singing. While that untrained voice, with its incorrect breathing and labored transitions, was sounding, even the connoisseurs said nothing, but only delighted in it and wished to hear it again. In her voice there was a virginal freshness, an unconsciousness of her own powers, and an as yet untrained velvety softness, which so mingled with her lack of art in singing that it seemed as if nothing in that voice could be altered without spoiling it.

"What is this?" thought Nicholas, listening to her with widely opened eyes. "What has happened to her? How she is singing today!" And suddenly the whole world centered for him on anticipation of the next note, the next phrase, and everything in the world was divided into three beats: *Oh mio crudele affetto* . . . One, two, three . . . one, two, three . . . One . . . *Oh mio crudele affetto* . . . One, two, three . . . One. "Oh, this senseless life of ours!" thought Nicholas. "All this misery, and money, and Dólokhov, and anger, and honor—it's all nonsense . . . but this is real. . . . Now then, Natásha, now then, dearest! Now then, darling! How will she take that *si?* She's taken it! Thank God!" And without noticing that he was singing, to strengthen the *si* he sung a second, a third below the high note. "Ah, God! How fine! Did I really take it? How fortunate!" he thought.

Oh, how that chord vibrated, and how moved was something that was finest in Rostóv's soul! And this something was apart from everything else in the world and above everything in the world. "What were losses, and Dólokhov, and words of honor? . . . All nonsense! One might kill and rob and yet be happy . . ."

Chapter XVI

IT WAS LONG SINCE ROSTÓV HAD FELT SUCH ENJOYMENT FROM MUSIC AS HE DID THAT DAY. BUT NO sooner had Natásha finished her barcarolle than reality again presented itself. He got up without saying a word and went downstairs to his own room. A quarter of an hour later the old count came in from his Club, cheerful and contented. Nicholas, hearing him drive up, went to meet him.

"Well—had a good time?" said the old count, smiling gaily and proudly at his son.

Nicholas tried to say "Yes," but could not: and he nearly burst into sobs. The count was lighting his pipe and did not notice his son's condition.

"Ah, it can't be avoided!" thought Nicholas, for the first and last time. And suddenly, in the most casual tone, which made him feel ashamed of himself, he said, as if merely asking his father to let him have the carriage to drive to town:

"Papa, I have come on a matter of business. I was nearly forgetting. I need some money."

"Dear me!" said his father, who was in a specially good humor. "I told you it would not be enough. How much?"

"Very much," said Nicholas flushing, and with a stupid careless smile, for which he was long unable to forgive himself, "I have lost a little, I mean a good deal, a great deal—forty-three thousand."

"What! To whom? . . . Nonsense!" cried the count, suddenly reddening with an apoplectic flush over neck and nape as old people do.

"I promised to pay tomorrow," said Nicholas.

"Well! . . ." said the old count, spreading out his arms and sinking helplessly on the sofa.

"It can't be helped It happens to everyone!" said the son, with a bold, free and easy tone, while in his soul he regarded himself as a worthless scoundrel whose whole life could not atone for his crime. He longed to kiss his father's hands and kneel to beg his forgiveness, but said, in a careless and even rude voice, that it happens to everyone!

The old count cast down his eyes on hearing his son's words and began bustlingly searching for something.

"Yes, yes," he muttered, "it will be difficult, I fear, difficult to raise . . . happens to everybody! Yes, who has not done it?"

And with a furtive glance at his son's face, the count went out of the room. . . . Nicholas had been prepared for resistance, but had not at all expected this.

"Papa! Pa-pa!" he called after him, sobbing, "forgive me!" And seizing his father's hand, he pressed it to his lips and burst into tears.

While father and son were having their explanation, the mother and daughter were having one not less important. Natásha came running to her mother, quite excited.

"Mamma! . . . Mamma! . . . He has made me . . ."

"Made what?"

"Made, made me an offer, Mamma! Mamma!" she exclaimed.

The countess did not believe her ears. Denísov had proposed. To whom? To this chit of a girl, Natásha, who not so long ago was playing with dolls and who was still having lessons.

"Don't, Natásha! What nonsense!" she said, hoping it was a joke.

"Nonsense, indeed! I am telling you the fact," said Natásha indignantly. "I come to ask you what to do, and you call it 'nonsense!' "

The countess shrugged her shoulders.

"If it true that Monsieur Denísov has made you a proposal, tell him he is a fool, that's all!"

"No, he's not a fool!" replied Natásha indignantly and seriously.

"Well then, what do you want? You're all in love nowadays. Well, if you are in love, marry him!" said the countess, with a laugh of annoyance. "Good luck to you!"

"No, Mamma, I'm not in love with him, I suppose I'm not in love with him."

"Well then, tell him so."

"Mamma, are you cross? Don't be cross, dear! Is it my fault?"

"No, but what is it, my dear? Do you want me to go and tell him?" said the countess smiling.

"No, I will do it myself, only tell me what to say. It's all very well for you," said Natásha, with a responsive smile. "You should have seen how he said it! I know he did not mean to say it, but it came out accidently."

"Well, all the same, you must refuse him."

"No, I mustn't. I am so sorry for him! He's so nice."

"Well then, accept his offer. It's high time for you to be married," answered the countess sharply and sarcastically.

"No, Mamma, but I'm so sorry for him. I don't know how I'm to say it."

"And there's nothing for you to say. I shall speak to him myself," said the countess, indignant that they should have dared to treat this little Natásha as grown-up.

"No, not on any account! I will tell him myself, and you'll listen at the door," and Natásha ran across the drawing room to the dancing hall, where Denísov was sitting on the same chair by the clavichord with his face in his hands.

He jumped up at the sound of her light step.

"Natalie," he said, moving with rapid steps toward her, "decide my fate. It is in your hands."

"Vasíli Dmítrich, I'm so sorry for you! . . . No, but you are so nice . . . but it won't do . . . not that . . . but as a friend, I shall always love you."

Denísov bent over her hand and she heard strange sounds she did not understand. She kissed his rough curly black head. At this instant, they heard the quick rustle of the countess's dress. She came up to them.

"Vasíli Dmítrich, I thank you for the honor," she said, with an embarrassed voice, though it sounded severe to Denísov—"but my daughter is so young, and I thought that, as my son's friend, you would have addressed yourself first to me. In that case you would not have obliged me to give this refusal."

"Countess . . ." said Denísov, with downcast eyes and a guilty face. He tried to say more, but faltered.

Natásha could not remain calm, seeing him in such a plight. She began to sob aloud.

"Countess, I have done w'ong," Denísov went on in an unsteady voice, "but believe me, I so adore your daughter and all your family that I would give my life twice over . . ." He looked at the countess, and seeing her severe face said: "Well, good-bye, countess," and kissing her hand, he left the room with quick resolute strides, without looking at Natásha.

Next day Rostóv saw Denísov off. He not wish to stay another day in Moscow. All Denísov's Moscow friends gave him a farewell entertainment at the gypsies', with the result that he had no recollection of how he was put in the sleigh or of the first three stages of his journey.

After Denísov's departure, Rostóv spent another fortnight in Moscow, without going out of the house, waiting for the money his father could not at once raise, and he spent most of his time in the girls' room.

Sónya was more tender and devoted to him than ever. It was as if she wanted to show him that his losses were an achievement that made her love him all the more, but Nicholas now considered himself unworthy of her.

He filled the girls' albums with verses and music, and having at last sent Dólokhov the whole forty-three thousand rubles and received his receipt, he left at the end of November without taking leave of any of his acquaintances, to overtake his regiment which was already in Poland.

Part Five

Chapter I

After his interview with his wife Pierre left for Petersburg. At the Torzhók post station, either there were no horses or the postmaster would not supply them. Pierre was obliged to wait. Without undressing, he lay down on the leather sofa in front of a round table, put his big feet in their over-boots on the table and began to reflect.

"Will you have the portmanteaux brought in? And a bed got ready, and tea?" asked his valet.

Pierre gave no answer, for he neither heard nor saw anything. He had begun to think of the last station and was still pondering on the same question—one so important that he took no notice of what went on around him. Not only was he indifferent as to whether he got to Petersburg earlier or later, or whether he secured accommodation at this station, but compared to the thoughts that now occupied him it was a matter of indifference whether he remained there for a few hours or for the rest of his life.

The postmaster, his wife, the valet, and a peasant woman selling Torzhók embroidery, came into the room offering their services. Without changing his careless attitude, Pierre looked at them over his spectacles unable to understand what they wanted or how they could go on living without having solved the problems that so absorbed him. He had been engrossed by the same thoughts ever since the day he returned from Sokólniki after the duel and had spent that first agonizing, sleepless night. But now, in the solitude of the journey, they seized him with special force. No matter what he thought about, he always returned to these same questions which he could not solve and yet could not cease to ask himself. It was as if the thread of the chief screw which held his life together were stripped, so that the screw could not get in or out, but went on turning uselessly in the same place.

The postmaster came in and began obsequiously to beg his excellency to wait only two hours, when, come what might, he would let his excellency have the courier-horses. It was plain that he was lying and only wanted to get more money from the traveler.

"Is this good or bad?" Pierre asked himself. "It is good for me, bad for another traveler and for himself it's unavoidable, because he needs money for food; the man said an officer had once given him a thrashing for letting a private traveler have the courier-horses. But the officer thrashed him because he had to get on as quickly as possible. And I," continued Pierre, "shot Dólokhov because I considered myself injured, and Louis XVI was executed because they considered him a criminal, and a year later they executed those who executed him—also for some reason. What is bad? What is good? What should one love and what hate? What does one live for? And what am I? What is life, and what is death? What Power governs all?"

There was no answer to any of these questions, except one, and that not a logical answer and not at all a reply to them. The answer was: "You'll die and all will end. You'll die and know all, or cease asking." But dying was also dreadful.

The Torzhók peddler woman, in a whining voice, went on offering her wares, especially a pair of goatskin slippers. "I have hundreds of rubles I don't know what to do with, and she stands in her tattered cloak looking timidly at me," he thought. "And what does she want the money for? As if that money could add a hair's breadth to her happiness or peace of mind. Can anything in the world make her or me less a prey to evil and death?—death which ends all and must come today or tomorrow—at any rate, in an instant as compared with eternity." And again he twisted the screw with the stripped thread, and again it turned uselessly in the same place.

His servant handed him a half-cut novel, in the form of letters, by Madame de Souza. He began reading about the sufferings and virtuous struggles of a certain Emilie de Mansfeld. "And why did she resist her seducer when she loved him?" he thought. "God could not have put into her heart an impulse that was against His will. My wife—as she once was—did not struggle, and perhaps she was right. Nothing has been found out, nothing discovered," Pierre again said to himself. "All we can know is that we know nothing. And that's the height of human wisdom."

Everything within and around him seemed confused, senseless, and repellent. Yet in this very repugnance to all his circumstances Pierre found a kind of tantalizing satisfaction.

"I make bold to ask your excellency to move a little for this gentleman," said the postmaster, entering the room followed by another traveler, also detained for lack of horses.

The newcomer was a short, large-boned, yellow-faced wrinkled old man, with gray bushy eyebrows overhanging bright eyes of an indefinite grayish color.

Pierre took his feet off the table, stood up, and lay down on a bed that had been got ready for him, glancing now and then at the newcomer, who, with a gloomy and tired face, was wearily taking off his wraps with the aid of his servant, and not looking at Pierre. With a pair of felt boots on his thin bony legs, and keeping on a worn, nankeen-covered, sheepskin coat, the traveler sat down on the sofa, leaned back his big head with its broad temples and close-cropped hair and looked at Bezúkhov. The stern, shrewd, and penetrating expression of that look struck Pierre. He felt a wish to speak to the stranger, but by the time he had made up his mind to ask him a question about the roads, the traveler had closed his eyes. His shriveled old hands were folded and on the finger of one of them Pierre noticed a large cast-iron ring with a seal representing a death's head. The stranger sat without stirring, either resting or, as it seemed to Pierre, sunk in profound and calm meditation. His servant was also a yellow, wrinkled old man, without beard or mustache, evidently not because he was shaven but because they had never grown. This active old servant was unpacking the traveler's canteen and preparing tea. He brought in a boiling samovar. When everything was ready, the stranger opened his eyes, moved to the table, filled a tumbler with tea for himself and one for the beardless old man to whom he passed it. Pierre began to feel a sense of uneasiness, and the need, even the inevitability, of entering into conversation with this stranger.

The servant brought back his tumbler turned upside down, with an unfinished bit of nibbled sugar, and asked if anything more would be wanted.

"No. Give me the book," said the stranger.

The servant handed him a book which Pierre took to be a devotional work, and the traveler became absorbed in it. Pierre looked at him. All at once the stranger closed the book, putting in a marker, and again, leaning with his arms on the back of the sofa, sat in his former position with his eyes shut. Pierre looked at him and had not time to turn away when the old man, opening his eyes, fixed his steady and severe gaze straight on Pierre's face.

Pierre felt confused and wished to avoid that look, but the bright old eyes attracted him irresistibly.

Chapter II

"I HAVE THE PLEASURE OF ADDRESSING COUNT BEZÚKHOV, IF I AM NOT MISTAKEN," SAID THE stranger in a deliberate and loud voice.

Pierre looked silently and inquiringly at him over his spectacles.

"I have heard of you, my dear sir," continued the stranger, "and of your misfortune." He seemed to emphasize the last word, as if to say—"Yes, misfortune! Call it what you please, I know that what happened to you in Moscow was a misfortune."—"I regret it very much, my dear sir."

Pierre flushed, and hurriedly putting his legs down from the bed, bent forward toward the old man with a forced and timid smile.

"I have not referred to this out of curiosity, my dear sir, but for greater reasons."

He paused, his gaze still on Pierre, and moved aside on the sofa by way of inviting the other to take a seat beside him. Pierre felt reluctant to enter into conversation with this old man, but, submitting to him involuntarily, came up and sat down beside him.

"You are unhappy, my dear sir," the stranger continued. "You are young and I am old. I should like to help you as far as lies in my power."

"Oh, yes!" said Pierre, with a forced smile. "I am very grateful to you. Where are you traveling from?"

The stranger's face was not genial, it was even cold and severe, but in spite of this, both the face and words of his new acquaintance were irresistibly attractive to Pierre.

"But if for reason you don't feel inclined to talk to me," said the old man, "say so, my dear sir." And he suddenly smiled, in an unexpected and tenderly paternal way.

"Oh no, not at all! On the contrary, I am very glad to make your acquaintance," said Pierre. And again, glancing at the stranger's hands, he looked more closely at the ring, with its skull—a masonic sign.

"Allow me to ask," he said, "are you a mason?"

"Yes, I belong to the Brotherhood of the Freemasons," said the stranger, looking deeper and deeper into Pierre's eyes. "And in their name and my own I hold out a brotherly hand to you."

"I am afraid," said Pierre, smiling, and wavering between the confidence the personality of the freemason inspired in him and his own habit of ridiculing the masonic beliefs—"I am afraid I am very far from understanding—how am I to put it?—I am afraid my way of looking at the world is so opposed to yours that we shall not understand one another."

"I know your outlook," said the mason, "and the view of life you mention, and which you think is the result of your own mental efforts, is the one held by the majority of people, and is the invariable fruit of pride, indolence, and ignorance. Forgive me, my dear sir, but if I had not known it I should not have addressed you. Your view of life is a regrettable delusion."

"Just as I may suppose you to be deluded," said Pierre, with a faint smile.

"I should never dare to say that I know the truth," said the mason, whose words struck Pierre more and more by their precision and firmness. "No one can attain to truth by himself. Only by laying stone on stone with the cooperation of all, by the millions of generations from our forefather Adam to our own times is that temple reared which is to be a worthy dwelling-place of the Great God," he added, and closed his eyes.

"I ought to tell you that I do not believe . . . do not believe in God," said Pierre, regretfully and with an effort, feeling it essential to speak the whole truth.

The mason looked intently at Pierre and smiled as a rich man with millions in hand might smile at a poor fellow who told him that he, poor man, had not the five rubles that would make him happy.

"Yes, you do not know Him, my dear sir," said the mason. "You cannot know Him. You do not know Him and that is why you are unhappy."

"Yes, yes, I am unhappy," assented Pierre. "But what am I to do?"

"You know Him not, my dear sir, and so you are very unhappy. You do not know Him, but He is here, He is in me, He is in my words, He is in thee, and even in those blasphemous words thou hast just uttered!" pronounced the mason in a stern and tremulous voice.

He paused and sighed, evidently trying to calm himself.

"If He were not," he said quietly, "you and I would not be speaking of Him, my dear sir. Of what, of whom, are we speaking? Whom hast thou denied?" he suddenly asked with exulting austerity and authority in his voice. "Who invented Him, if He did not exist? Whence came thy conception of the existence of such an incomprehensible Being? Why didst thou, and why did the whole world, conceive the idea of the existence of such an incomprehensible Being, a Being all-powerful, eternal, and infinite in all His attributes? . . ."

He stopped and remained silent for a long time.

Pierre could not and did not wish to break this silence.

"He exists, but to understand Him is hard," the mason began again, looking not at Pierre but straight before him, and turning the leaves of his book with his old hands which from excitement he could not keep still. "If it were a man whose existence thou didst doubt I could bring him to thee, could take him by the hand and show him to thee. But how can I, an insignificant mortal, show His omnipotence, His infinity, and all His mercy to one who is blind, or who shuts his eyes that he may not see or understand Him and may not see or understand his own vileness and sinfulness?" He paused again. "Who art thou? Thou dreamest that thou art wise because thou couldst utter those blasphemous words," he went on, with a somber and scornful smile. "And thou art more foolish and unreasonable than a little child, who playing with the parts of a skillfully made watch, dares to say that, as he does not understand its use, he does not believe in the master who made it. To know Him is hard. . . . For ages, from our forefather Adam to our own day, we labor to attain that knowledge and are still infinitely far from our aim; but in our lack of understanding we see only our weakness and His greatness. . . ."

Pierre listened with swelling heart, gazing into the mason's face with shining eyes, not interrupting or questioning him, but believing with his whole soul what the stranger said. Whether he accepted the wise reasoning contained in the mason's words, or believed as a child believes, in the speaker's tone of conviction and earnestness or the tremor of the speaker's voice—which sometimes almost broke—or those brilliant aged eyes grown old in this conviction, or the calm firmness and certainty of his vocation, which radiated from his whole being (and which struck Pierre especially by contrast with his own dejection and hopelessness)—at any rate, Pierre longed with his whole soul to believe and he did believe, and felt a joyful sense of comfort, regeneration, and return to life.

"He is not to be apprehended by reason, but by life," said the mason.

"I do not understand," said Pierre, feeling with dismay doubts reawakening. He was afraid of any want of clearness, any weakness, in the mason's arguments, he dreaded not to be able to believe in him. "I don't understand," he said, "how it is that the mind of man cannot attain the knowledge of which you speak?"

The mason smiled with his gentle fatherly smile.

"The highest wisdom and truth are like the purest liquid we may wish to imbibe," he said. "Can I receive that pure liquid into an impure vessel and judge of its purity? Only by the inner purification of myself can I retain in some degree of purity the liquid I receive."

"Yes, yes, that is so," said Pierre joyfully.

"The highest wisdom is not founded on reason alone, not on those worldly sciences of physics, history, chemistry, and the like, into which intellectual knowledge is divided. The highest wisdom is one. The highest wisdom has but one science—the science of the whole—the science explaining the whole creation and man's place in it. To receive that science it is necessary to purify and renew one's inner self, and so before one can know, it is necessary to believe and to perfect one's self. And to attain this end, we have the light called conscience, that God has implanted in our souls."

"Yes, yes," assented Pierre.

"Look then at thy inner self with the eyes of the spirit, and ask thyself whether thou art content with thyself. What hast thou attained relying on reason only? What art thou? You are young, you are rich, you are clever, you are well educated. And what have you done with all these good gifts? Are you content with yourself and with your life?"

"No, I hate my life," Pierre muttered, wincing.

"Thou hatest it. Then change it, purify thyself; and as thou art purified, thou wilt gain wisdom. Look at your life, my dear sir. How have you spent it? In riotous orgies and debauchery, receiving everything from society and giving nothing in return. You have become the possessor of wealth. How have you used it? What have you done for your neighbor? Have you ever thought of your tens of thousands of slaves? Have you helped them physically and morally? No! You have profited by their toil to lead a profligate life. That is what you have done. Have you chosen a post in which you might be of service to your neighbor? No! You have spent your life in idleness. Then you married, my dear sir—took on yourself responsibility for the guidance of a young woman; and what have you done? You have not helped her to find the way of truth, my dear sir, but have thrust her into an abyss of deceit and misery. A man offended you and you shot him, and you say you do not know God and hate your life. There is nothing strange in that, my dear sir!"

After these words, the mason, as if tired by his long discourse, again leaned his arms on the back of the sofa and closed his eyes. Pierre looked at that aged, stern, motionless, almost lifeless face and moved his lips without uttering a sound. He wished to say, "Yes, a vile, idle, vicious life!" but dared not break the silence.

The mason cleared his throat huskily, as old men do, and called his servant.

"How about the horses?" he asked, without looking at Pierre.

"The exchange horses have just come," answered the servant. "Will you not rest here?"

"No, tell them to harness."

"Can he really be going away leaving me alone without having told me all, and without promising to help me?" thought Pierre, rising with downcast head; and he began to pace the room, glancing occasionally at the mason. "Yes, I never thought of it, but I have led a contemptible and profligate life, though I did not like it and did not want to," thought Pierre. "But this man knows the truth, and if he wished to, could disclose it to me."

Pierre wished to say this to the mason, but did not dare to. The traveler, having packed his things with his practiced hands, began fastening his coat. When he had finished, he turned to Bezúkhov, and said in a tone of indifferent politeness:

"Where are you going to now, my dear sir?"

"I? . . . I'm going to Petersburg," answered Pierre, in a childlike, hesitating voice. "I thank you. I agree with all you have said. But do not suppose me to be so bad. With my whole soul I wish to be what you would have me be, but I have never had help from anyone. . . . But it is I, above all, who am to blame for everything. Help me, teach me, and perhaps I may . . ."

Pierre could not go on. He gulped and turned away.

The mason remained silent for a long time, evidently considering.

"Help comes from God alone," he said, "but such measure of help as our Order can bestow it will render you, my dear sir. You are going to Petersburg. Hand this to Count Willarski" (he took out his notebook and wrote a few words on a large sheet of paper folded in four). "Allow me to give you a piece of advice. When you reach the capital, first of all devote some time to solitude and self-examination and do not resume your former way of life. And now I wish you a good journey, my dear sir," he added, seeing that his servant had entered . . . "and success."

The traveler was Joseph Alexéevich Bazdéev, as Pierre saw from the postmaster's book. Bazdéev had been one of the best-known freemasons and Martinists, even in Novíkov's time. For a long while after he had gone, Pierre did not go to bed or order horses but paced up and down the room, pondering over his vicious past, and with a rapturous sense of beginning anew, pictured to himself the blissful irreproachable virtuous future that seemed to him so easy. It seemed to him that he had been vicious only because he had somehow forgotten how good it is to be virtuous. Not a trace of his former doubts remained in his soul. He firmly believed in the possibility of the brotherhood of men united in the aim of supporting one another in the path of virtue, and that is how freemasonry presented itself to him.

Chapter III

On reaching Petersburg Pierre did not let anyone know of his arrival, he went nowhere and spent whole days in reading Thomas à Kempis, whose book had been sent him by someone unknown. One thing he continually realized as he read that book: the joy, hitherto unknown to him, of believing in the possibility of attaining perfection, and in the possibility of active brotherly love among men, which Joseph Alexéevich had revealed to him. A week after his arrival, the young Polish count, Willarski, whom Pierre had known slightly in Petersburg society, came into his room one evening in the official and ceremonious manner in which Dólokhov's second had called on him, and having closed the door behind him and satisfied himself that there was nobody else in the room, addressed Pierre.

"I have come to you with a message and an offer, count," he said without sitting down. "A person of very high standing in our Brotherhood has made application for you to be received into our Order before the usual term, and has proposed to me to be your sponsor. I consider it a sacred duty to fulfill that person's wishes. Do you wish to enter the Brotherhood of Freemasons under my sponsorship?"

The cold austere tone of this man, whom he had almost always before met at balls, amiably smiling in the society of the most brilliant women, surprised Pierre.

"Yes, I do wish it," said he.

Willarski bowed his head.

"One more question, count," he said, "which beg you to answer in all sincerity—not as a future mason but as an honest man: have you renounced your former convictions—do you believe in God?"

Pierre considered.

"Yes . . . yes, I believe in God," he said.

"In that case . . ." began Willarski, but Pierre interrupted him.

"Yes, I do believe in God," he repeated.

"In that case we can go," said Willarski. "My carriage is at your service."

Willarski was silent throughout the drive. To Pierre's inquiries as to what he must do and how he should answer, Willarski only replied that brothers more worthy than he would test him, and that Pierre had only to tell the truth.

Having entered the courtyard of a large house where the Lodge had its headquarters, and having ascended a dark staircase, they entered a small well-lit anteroom where they took off their cloaks without the aid of a servant. From there they passed into another room. A man in strange attire appeared at the door. Willarski, stepping toward him, said something to him in French in an undertone and then went up to a small wardrobe in which Pierre noticed garments such as he had never seen before. Having taken a kerchief from the cupboard, Willarski bound Pierre's eyes with it and tied it in a knot behind, catching some hairs painfully in the knot. Then he drew his face down, kissed him, and taking him by the hand led him forward. The hairs tied in the knot hurt Pierre and there were lines of pain on his face and a shamefaced smile. His huge figure, with arms hanging down and with a puckered, though smiling face, moved after Willarski with uncertain timid steps.

Having led him about ten paces, Willarski stopped.

"Whatever happens to you," he said, "you must bear it all manfully if you have firmly resolved to join our Brotherhood." (Pierre nodded affirmatively.) "When you hear a knock at the door, you will uncover your eyes," added Willarski. "I wish you courage and success," and pressing Pierre's hand, he went out.

Left alone, Pierre went on smiling in the same way. Once or twice he shrugged his and raised his hand to the kerchief, as if wishing to take it off, but let it drop again. The five minutes spent with his eyes bandaged seemed to him an hour. His arms felt numb, his legs almost gave way, it seemed to him that he was tired out. He experienced a variety of most complex sensations. He felt afraid of what would happen to him, and still more afraid of showing his fear. He felt curious to know what was going to happen and what would be revealed to him; but most of all, he felt joyful that the moment had come when he would at last start on that path of regeneration and on the actively virtuous life of which he had been dreaming since he met Joseph Alexéevich. Loud knocks were heard at the door. Pierre took the bandage off his eyes and glanced around him. The room was in black darkness, only a small lamp was burning inside something white. Pierre went nearer and saw that the lamp stood on a black table on which lay an open book. The book was the Gospel, and the white thing with the lamp inside was a human skull with its cavities and teeth. After reading the first words of the Gospel: "In the beginning was the Word and the Word was with God," Pierre went round the table and saw a large open box filled with something. It was a coffin with bones inside. He was not at all surprised by what he saw. Hoping to enter on an entirely new life quite unlike the old one, he expected everything to be unusual, even more unusual than what he was seeing. A skull, a coffin, the Gospel—it seemed to him that he had expected all this and even more. Trying to stimulate his emotions he looked around. "God, death, love, the brotherhood of man," he kept saying to himself, associating these words with vague yet joyful ideas. The door opened and someone came in.

By the dim light, to which Pierre had already become accustomed, he saw rather short man. Having evidently come from the light into the darkness, the man paused, then moved with cautious steps toward the table and placed on it his small leather-gloved hands.

This short man had on a white leather apron which covered his chest and part of his legs, he had on a kind of necklace above which rose a high white ruffle, outlining his rather long face which was lit up from below.

"For what have you come hither?" asked the newcomer, turning in Pierre's direction at a slight rustle made by the latter. "Why have you, who do not believe in the truth of the light and who have not seen the light, come here? What do you seek from us? Wisdom, virtue, enlightenment?"

At the moment the door opened and the stranger came in, Pierre felt a sense of awe and veneration such as he had experienced in his boyhood at confession; he felt himself in the presence of one socially a complete stranger, yet nearer to him through the brotherhood of man. With bated breath and beating heart he moved toward the Rhetor (by which name the brother who prepared a seeker for entrance into the Brotherhood was known). Drawing nearer, he recognized in the Rhetor a man he knew, Smolyanínov, and it mortified him to think that the newcomer was an acquaintance—he wished him simply a brother and a virtuous instructor. For a long time he could not utter a word, so that the Rhetor had to repeat his question.

"Yes . . . I . . . I . . . desire regeneration," Pierre uttered with difficulty.

"Very well," said Smolyanínov, and went on at once: "Have you any idea of the means by which our holy Order will help you to reach your aim?" said he quietly and quickly.

"I . . . hope . . . for guidance . . . help . . . in regeneration," said Pierre, with a trembling voice and some difficulty in utterance due to his excitement, and to being unaccustomed to speak of abstract matters in Russian.

"What is your conception of freemasonry?"

"I imagine that freemasonry is the fraternity and equality of men who have virtuous aims," said Pierre, feeling ashamed of the inadequacy of his words for the solemnity of the moment, as he spoke. "I imagine . . ."

"Good!" said the Rhetor quickly, apparently satisfied with this answer. "Have you sought for means of attaining your aim in religion?"

"No, I considered it erroneous and did not follow it," said Pierre, so softly that the Rhetor did not hear him and asked him what he was saying. "I have been an atheist," answered Pierre.

"You are seeking for truth in order to follow its laws in your life, therefore you seek wisdom and virtue. Is that not so?" said the Rhetor, after a moment's pause.

"Yes, yes," assented Pierre.

The Rhetor cleared his throat, crossed his gloved hands on his breast and began to speak.

"Now I must disclose to you the chief aim of our Order," he said, "and if this aim coincides with yours, you may enter our Brotherhood with profit. The first and chief object of our Order, the foundation on which it rests and which no human power can destroy, is the preservation and handing on to posterity of a certain important mystery . . . which has come down to us from the remotest ages, even from the first man—a mystery on which perhaps the fate of mankind depends. But since this mystery is of such a nature that nobody can know or use it unless he be prepared by long and diligent self-purification, not everyone can hope to attain it quickly. Hence we have a secondary aim, that of preparing our members as much as possible to reform their hearts, to purify and enlighten their minds, by means handed on to us by tradition from those who have striven to attain this mystery, and thereby to render them capable of receiving it.

"By purifying and regenerating our members we try, thirdly, to improve the whole human race, offering it in our members an example of piety and virtue, and thereby try with all our might to combat the evil which sways the world. Think this over and I will come to you again."

"To combat the evil which sways the world . . ." Pierre repeated, and a mental image of his future activity in this direction rose in his mind. He imagined men such as he had himself been a fortnight ago, and he addressed an edifying exhortation to them. He imagined to himself vicious and unfortunate people whom he would assist by word and deed, imagined oppressors whose victims he would rescue. Of the three objects mentioned by the Rhetor, this last, that of improving mankind, especially appealed to Pierre. The important mystery mentioned by the Rhetor, though it aroused his curiosity, did not seem to him essential, and the second aim, that of purifying and regenerating himself, did not much interest him because at that moment he felt with delight that he was already perfectly cured of his former faults and was ready for all that was good.

Half an hour later, the Rhetor returned to inform the seeker of the seven virtues, corresponding to the seven steps of Solomon's temple, which every freemason should cultivate in himself. These virtues were: 1. *Discretion,* the keeping of the secrets of the Order. 2. *Obedience* to those of higher ranks in the Order. 3. *Morality.* 4. *Love of mankind.* 5. *Courage.* 6. *Generosity.* 7. *The love of death.*

"In the *seventh* place, try, by the frequent thought of death," the Rhetor said, "to bring yourself to regard it not as a dreaded foe, but as a friend that frees the soul grown weary in the labors of virtue from this distressful life, and leads it to its place of recompense and peace."

"Yes, that must be so," thought Pierre, when after these words the Rhetor went away, leaving him to solitary meditation. "It must be so, but I am still so weak that I love my life, the meaning of which is only now gradually opening before me." But five of the other virtues which Pierre recalled, counting them on his fingers, he felt already in his soul: *Courage, generosity, morality, love of mankind,* and especially *obedience*—which did not even seem to him a virtue, but a joy. (He now felt so glad to be free from his own lawlessness and to submit his will to those who knew the indubitable truth.) He forgot what the seventh virtue was, and could not recall it.

The third time the Rhetor came back more quickly, and asked Pierre whether he was still firm in his intention and determined to submit to all that would be required of him.

"I am ready for everything," said Pierre.

"I must also inform you," said the Rhetor, "that our Order delivers its teaching not in words only but also by other means, which may perhaps have a stronger effect on the sincere seeker after wisdom and virtue than mere words. This chamber with what you see therein, should already have suggested to your heart, if it is sincere, more than words could do. You will perhaps also see in your further initiation a like method of enlightenment. Our Order imitates the ancient societies that explained their teaching by hieroglyphics. A hieroglyph," said the Rhetor, "is an emblem of something not cognizable by the senses but which possesses qualities resembling those of the symbol."

Pierre knew very well what a hieroglyph was, but dared not speak. He listened to the Rhetor in silence, feeling from all he said that his ordeal was about to begin.

"If you are resolved, I must begin your initiation," said the Rhetor coming closer to Pierre. "In token of generosity I ask you to give me all your valuables."

"But I have nothing here," replied Pierre, supposing that he was asked to give up all he possessed.

"What you have with you: watch, money, rings. . . ."

Pierre quickly took out his purse and watch, but could not manage for some time to get the wedding ring off his fat finger. When that had been done, the Rhetor said:

"In token of obedience, I ask you to undress."

Pierre took off his coat, waistcoat, and left boot according to the Rhetor's instructions. The mason drew the shirt back from Pierre's left breast, and stooping down pulled up the left leg of his trousers to above the knee. Pierre hurriedly began taking off his right boot also and was going to tuck up the other trouser-leg to save this stranger the trouble, but the mason told him that was not necessary and gave him a slipper for his left foot. With a childlike smile of embarrassment, doubt, and self-derision, which appeared on his face against his will, Pierre stood with his arms hanging down and legs apart, before his brother Rhetor, and awaited his further commands.

"And now, in token of candor, I ask you to reveal to me your chief passion," said the latter.

"My passion! I have had so many," replied Pierre.

"That passion which more than all others caused you to waver on the path of virtue," said the mason.

Pierre paused, seeking a reply.

"Wine? Gluttony? Idleness? Laziness? Irritability? Anger? Women?" He went over his vices in his mind, not knowing to which of them to give the pre-eminence.

"Women," he said in a low, scarcely audible voice.

The mason did not move and for a long time said nothing after this answer. At last he moved up to Pierre and, taking the kerchief that lay on the table, again bound his eyes.

"For the last time I say to you—turn all your attention upon yourself, put a bridle on your senses, and seek blessedness, not in passion but in your own heart. The source of blessedness is not without us but within. . . ."

Pierre had already long been feeling in himself that refreshing source of blessedness which now flooded his heart with glad emotion.

Chapter IV

SOON AFTER THIS THERE CAME INTO THE DARK CHAMBER TO FETCH PIERRE, NOT THE RHETOR BUT Pierre's sponsor, Willarski, whom he recognized by his voice. To fresh questions as to the firmness of his resolution Pierre replied: "Yes, yes, I agree," and with a beaming, childlike smile, his fat chest uncovered, stepping unevenly and timidly in one slippered and one booted foot, he advanced, while Willarski held a sword to his bare chest. He was conducted from that room along passages that turned backward and forward, and was at last brought to the doors of the Lodge. Willarski coughed, he was answered by the masonic knock with mallets, the doors opened before them. A bass voice (Pierre was still blindfolded) questioned him as to who he was, when and where he was born, and so on. Then he was again led somewhere still blindfolded, and as they went along he was told allegories of the toils of his pilgrimage, of holy friendship, of the Eternal Architect of the universe, and of the courage with which he should endure toils and dangers. During these wanderings, Pierre noticed that he was spoken of now as the "Seeker," now as the "Sufferer," and now as the "Postulant," to the accompaniment of various knockings with mallets and swords. As he was being led up to some object he noticed a hesitation and uncertainty among his conductors. He heard those around him disputing in whispers and one of them insisting that he should be led along a certain carpet. After that they took his right hand, placed it on something, and told him to hold a pair of compasses to his left breast with the other hand and to repeat after someone who read aloud, an oath of fidelity to the laws of the Order. The candles were then extinguished and some spirit lit, as Pierre knew by the smell, and he was told that he would now see the lesser light. The bandage was taken off his eyes and, by the faint light of the burning spirit, Pierre, as in a dream, saw several men standing before him, wearing aprons like the Rhetor's and holding swords in their hands pointed at his breast. Among them stood a man whose white shirt was stained with blood. On seeing this, Pierre moved forward with his breast toward the swords, meaning them to pierce it. But the swords were drawn back from him and he was at once blindfolded again.

"Now thou hast seen the lesser light," uttered a voice. Then the candles were relit and he was told that he would see the full light; the bandage was again removed and more than ten voices said together: *"Sic transit gloria mundi."*

Pierre gradually began to recover himself, and looked about at the room and at the people in it. Round a long table covered with black sat some twelve men in garments like those he had already seen. Some of them Pierre had met in Petersburg society. In the President's chair sat a young man he did not know, with a peculiar cross hanging from his neck. On his right sat the Italian abbé whom Pierre had met at Anna Pávlovna's two years before. There were also present a very distinguished dignitary and a Swiss who had formerly been tutor at the Kurágins. All maintained a solemn silence, listening to the words of the President, who held a mallet in his hand. Let into the wall was a star-shaped light. At one side of the table was a small carpet with various figures worked upon it, at the other was something resembling an altar on which lay a Testament and a skull. Round it stood seven large candlesticks like those used in churches. Two of the brothers led Pierre up to the altar, placed his feet at right angles and bade him lie down, saying that he must prostrate himself at the Gates of the Temple.

"He must first receive the trowel," whispered one of the brothers.

"Oh, hush, please!" said another.

Pierre, perplexed, looked round with his short-sighted eyes without obeying, and suddenly doubts arose in his mind. "Where am I? What am I doing? Aren't they laughing at me? Shan't I be ashamed to remember this?" But these doubts only lasted a moment. Pierre glanced at the serious faces of those around, remembered all he had already gone through, and realized that he could not stop halfway. He was aghast at his hesitation, and trying to arouse his former devotional feeling, prostrated himself before the Gates of the Temple. And really, the feeling of devotion returned to him even more strongly than before. When he had lain there some time, he was told to get up, and a white leather apron, such as the others wore, was put on him: he was given a trowel and three pairs of gloves, and then the Grand Master addressed him. He told him that he should try to do nothing to stain the whiteness of that apron, which symbolized strength and purity; then of the unexplained trowel, he told him to toil with it to cleanse his own heart from vice, and indulgently to smooth with it the heart of his neighbor. As to the first pair of gloves, a man's, he said that Pierre could not know their meaning but must keep them. The second pair of man's gloves he was to wear at the meetings, and finally of the third, a pair of women's gloves, he said: "Dear brother, these women's gloves are intended for you too. Give them to the woman whom you shall honor most of all. This gift will be a pledge of your purity of heart to her whom you select to be your worthy helpmeet in masonry." And after a pause, he added: "But beware, dear brother, that these gloves do not deck hands that are unclean." While the Grand Master said these last words it seemed to Pierre that he grew embarrassed. Pierre himself grew still more confused, blushed like a child till tears came to his eyes, began looking about him uneasily, and an awkward pause followed.

This silence was broken by one of the Brethren, who led Pierre up to the rug and began reading to him from a manuscript book an explanation of all the figures on it: the sun, the moon, a hammer, a plumb-line, a trowel, a rough stone and a squared stone, a pillar, three windows, and so on. Then a place was assigned to Pierre, he was shown the signs of the Lodge, told the password, and at last was permitted to sit down. The Grand Master began reading the statutes. They were very long, and Pierre, from joy, agitation, and embarrassment, was not in a state to understand what was being read. He managed to follow only the last words of the statutes and these remained in his mind.

"In our temples we recognize no other distinctions," read the Grand Master, "but those between virtue and vice. Beware of making any distinctions which may infringe equality. Fly to a brother's aid whoever he may be, exhort him who goeth astray, raise him that falleth, never bear malice or enmity toward thy brother. Be kindly and courteous. Kindle in all hearts the flame of virtue. Share thy happiness with thy neighbor, and may envy never dim the purity of that bliss. Forgive thy enemy, do not avenge thyself except by doing him good. Thus fulfilling the highest law thou shalt regain traces of the ancient dignity which thou hast lost."

He finished, and getting up, embraced and kissed Pierre, who, with tears of joy in his eyes, looked round him, not knowing how to answer the congratulations and greetings from acquaintances that met him on all sides. He acknowledged no acquaintances but saw in all these men only brothers, and burned with impatience to set to work with them.

The Grand Master rapped with his mallet. All the masons sat down in their places, and one of them read an exhortation on the necessity of humility.

The Grand Master proposed that the last duty should be performed, and the distinguished dignitary who bore the title of "Collector of Alms," went round to all the brothers. Pierre would have liked to subscribe all he had, but fearing that it might look like pride, subscribed the same amount as the others.

The meeting was at an end, and on reaching home Pierre felt as if he had returned from a long journey on which he had spent dozens of years, had become completely changed and had quite left behind him his former habits and way of life.

Chapter V

THE DAY AFTER HE HAD BEEN RECEIVED INTO THE LODGE, PIERRE WAS SITTING AT HOME READING a book and trying to fathom the significance of the Square, one side of which symbolized God, another moral things, a third physical things, and the fourth a combination of these. Now and then his attention wandered from the book and the Square and he formed in imagination a new plan of life. On the previous evening at the Lodge, he had heard that a rumor of his duel had reached the Emperor, and that it would be wiser for him to leave Petersburg. Pierre proposed going to his estates in the south and there attending to the welfare of his serfs. He was joyfully planning this new life, when Prince Vasíli suddenly entered the room.

"My dear fellow, what have you been up to in Moscow? Why have you quarreled with Hélène, *mon cher?* You are under a delusion," said Prince Vasíli, as he entered. "I know all about it, and I can tell you positively that Hélène is as innocent before you as Christ was before the Jews."

Pierre was about to reply, but Prince Vasíli interrupted him.

"And why didn't you simply come straight to me as to a friend? I know all about it and understand it all," he said. "You behaved as becomes a man values his honor, perhaps too hastily, but we won't go into that. But consider the position in which you are placing her and me in the eyes of society, and even of the Court," he added, lowering his voice. "She is living in Moscow and you are here. Remember, dear boy," and he drew Pierre's arm downward, "it is simply a misunderstanding. I expect you feel it so yourself. Let us write her a letter at once, and she'll come here and all will be explained, or else, my dear boy, let me tell you it's quite likely you'll have to suffer for it."

Prince Vasíli gave Pierre a significant look.

"I know from reliable sources that the Dowager Empress is taking a keen interest in the whole affair. You know she is very gracious to Hélène."

Pierre tried several times to speak, but, on one hand, Prince Vasíli did not let him and, on the other, Pierre himself feared to begin to speak in the tone of decided refusal and disagreement in which he had firmly resolved to answer his father-in-law. Moreover, the words of the masonic statutes, "be kindly and courteous," recurred to him. He blinked, went red, got up and sat down again, struggling with himself to do what was for him the most difficult thing in life—to say an unpleasant thing to a man's face, to say what the other, whoever he might be, did not expect. He was so used to submitting to Prince Vasíli's tone of careless self-assurance that he felt he would be unable to withstand it now, but he also felt that on what he said now his future depended—whether he would follow the same old road, or that new path so attractively shown him by the masons, on which he firmly believed he would be reborn to a new life.

"Now, dear boy," said Prince Vasíli playfully, "say 'yes,' and I'll write to her myself, and we will kill the fatted calf."

But before Prince Vasíli had finished his playful speech, Pierre, without looking at him, and with a kind of fury that made him like his father, muttered in a whisper:

"Prince, I did not ask you here. Go, please go!" And he jumped up and opened the door for him.

"Go!" he repeated, amazed at himself and glad to see the look of confusion and fear that showed itself on Prince Vasíli's face.

"What's the matter with you? Are you ill?"

"Go!" the quivering voice repeated. And Prince Vasíli had to go without receiving any explanation.

A week later, Pierre, having taken leave of his new friends, the masons, and leaving large sums of money with them for alms, went away to his estates. His new brethren gave him letters to the Kiev and Odessa masons and promised to write to him and guide him in his new activity.

Chapter VI

THE DUEL BETWEEN PIERRE AND DÓLOKHOV WAS HUSHED UP AND, IN SPITE OF THE EMPEROR'S severity regarding duels at that time, neither the principals nor their seconds suffered for it. But the story of the duel, confirmed by Pierre's rupture with his wife, was the talk of society. Pierre who had been regarded with patronizing condescension when he was an illegitimate son, and petted and extolled when he was the best match in Russia, had sunk greatly in the esteem of society after his marriage—when the marriageable daughters and their mothers had nothing to hope from him—especially as he did not know how, and did not wish, to court society's favor. Now he alone was blamed for what had happened, he was said to be insanely jealous, and subject like his father to fits of bloodthirsty rage. And when after Pierre's departure Hélène returned to Petersburg, she was received by all her acquaintances not only cordially, but even with a shade of deference due to her misfortune. When conversation turned on her husband Hélène assumed a dignified expression, which with characteristic tact she had acquired though she did not understand its significance. This expression suggested that she had resolved to endure her troubles uncomplainingly, and that her husband was a cross laid upon her by God. Prince Vasíli expressed his opinion more openly. He shrugged his shoulders when Pierre was mentioned and, pointing to his forehead, remarked:

"A bit touched—I always said so."

"I said from the first," declared Anna Pávlovna referring to Pierre, "I said at the time and before anyone else" (she insisted on her priority) "that that senseless young man was spoiled by the depraved ideas of these days. I said so even at the time when everybody was in raptures about him, when he had just returned from abroad and when, if you remember, he posed as a sort of Marat at one of my soirées. And how has it ended? I was against this marriage even then, and foretold all that has happened."

Anna Pávlovna continued to give on free evenings the same kind of soirées as before—such as she alone had the gift of arranging—at which was to be found "the cream of really good society, the bloom of the intellectual essence of Petersburg," as she herself put it. Besides this refined selection of society Anna Pávlovna's receptions were also distinguished by the fact that she always presented some new and interesting person to the visitors, and that nowhere else was the state of the political thermometer of legitimate Petersburg Court society so clearly and distinctly indicated.

Toward the end of 1806, when all the sad details of Napoleon's destruction of the Prussian Army at Jena and Auerstadt and the surrender of most of the Prussian fortresses had been received, when our troops had already entered Prussia and our second war with Napoleon was beginning, Anna Pávlovna gave one of her soireés. The "cream of really good society" consisted of the fascinating Hélène, forsaken by her husband, Mortemart, the delightful Prince Hippolyte who had just returned from Vienna, two diplomatists, the old aunt, a young man referred to in that drawing room as "a man of great merit" (*un homme de beaucoup de mérite*), a newly-appointed maid of honor and her mother, and several other less noteworthy persons.

The novelty Anna Pávlovna was setting before her guests that evening was Borís Drubetskóy, who had just arrived as a special messenger from the Prussian army and was aide-de-camp to a very important personage.

The temperature shown by the political thermometer to the company that evening was this:

"Whatever the European sovereigns and commanders may do to countenance Bonaparte, and to cause *me*, and *us* in general, annoyance and mortification, our opinion of Bonaparte cannot alter. We shall not cease to express our sincere views on that subject, and can only say to the King of Prussia and others: 'So much the worse for you. *Tu l'as voulu, George Dandin,*' that's all we have to say about it!"

When Borís, who was to be served up to the guests, entered the drawing room, almost all the company had assembled, and the conversation, guided by Anna Pávlovna, was about our diplomatic relations with Austria and the hope of an alliance with her.

Borís, grown more manly and looking fresh, rosy and self-possessed, entered the drawing room elegantly dressed in the uniform of an aide-de-camp, and was duly conducted to pay his respects to the aunt and then brought back to the general circle.

Anna Pávlovna gave him her shriveled hand to kiss, and introduced him to several persons whom he did not know, giving him a whispered description of each.

"Prince Hippolyte Kurágin—charming young fellow; M. Kronq—the *chargé d'affaires* from Copenhagen—a profound intellect," and simply, "Mr. Shítov—a man of great merit"—this of the man usually so described.

Thanks to Anna Mikháylovna's efforts, his own tastes, and the peculiarities of his reserved nature, Borís had managed during his service to place himself very advantageously. He was aide-de-camp to a very important personage, had been sent on a very important mission to Prussia, and had just returned from there as a special messenger. He had become thoroughly conversant with that unwritten code with which he had been so pleased at Olmütz and according to which an ensign might rank incomparably higher than a general, and according to which what was needed for success in the service was not effort or work, or courage, or perseverance, but only the knowledge of how to get on with those who can grant rewards, and he was himself often surprised at the rapidity of his success, and at the inability of others to understand these things. In consequence of this discovery his whole manner of life, all his relations with old friends, all his plans for his future, were completely altered. He was not rich, but would spend his last groat to be better dressed than others, and would rather deprive himself of many pleasures than allow himself to be seen in a shabby equipage or appear in the streets of Petersburg in an old uniform. He made friends with and sought the acquaintance of only those above him in position and who could therefore be of use to him. He liked Petersburg and despised Moscow. The remembrance of the Rostóvs' house and of his childish love for Natásha was unpleasant to him and he had not once been to see the Rostóvs since the day of his departure for the army. To be in Anna Pávlovna's drawing room he considered an important step up in the service, and he at once understood his rôle, letting his hostess make use of whatever interest he had to offer. He himself carefully scanned each face, appraising the possibilities of establishing intimacy with each of those present, and the advantages that might accrue. He took the seat indicated to him beside the fair Hélène, and listened to the general conversation.

"Vienna considers the bases of the proposed treaty so unattainable that not even a continuity of most brilliant successes would secure them, and she doubts the means we have of gaining them. That is the actual phrase used by the Vienna cabinet," said the Danish *chargé d'affaires.*

"The doubt is flattering," said "the man of profound intellect," with a subtle smile.

"We must distinguish between the Vienna cabinet and the Emperor of Austria," said Mortemart. "The Emperor of Austria can never have thought of such a thing, it is only the cabinet that says it."

"Ah, my dear Vicomte," put in Anna Pávlovna, *"L'Urope"* (for some reason she called it *Urope* as if that were a specially refined French pronunciation which she could allow herself when conversing with a Frenchman), *"L'Urope ne sera jamais notre alliée sincere."*

After that Anna Pávlovna led up to the courage and firmness of the King of Prussia, in order to draw Borís into the conversation.

Borís listened attentively to each of the speakers, awaiting his turn, but managed meanwhile to look round repeatedly at his neighbor, the beautiful Hélène, whose eyes several times met those of the handsome young aide-de-camp with a smile.

Speaking of the position of Prussia, Anna Pávlovna very naturally asked Borís to tell them about his journey to Glogau and in what state he found the Prussian army. Borís, speaking with deliberation, told them in pure correct French many interesting details about the armies and the Court, carefully abstaining from expressing an opinion of his own about the facts he was recounting. For some time he engrossed the general attention, and Anna Pávlovna felt that the novelty she had served up was received with pleasure by all her visitors. The greatest attention of all to Borís's narrative was shown by Hélène. She asked him several questions about his journey and seemed greatly interested in the state of the Prussian army. As soon as he had finished she turned to him with her usual smile.

"You absolutely must come and see me," she said in a tone that implied that, for certain considerations he could not know of, this was absolutely necessary.

"On Tuesday between eight and nine. It will give me great pleasure."

Borís promised to fulfill her wish and was about to begin a conversation with her, when Anna Pávlovna called him away on the pretext that her aunt wished to hear him.

"You know her husband, of course?" said Anna Pávlovna, closing her eyes and indicating Hélène with a sorrowful gesture. "Ah, she is such an unfortunate and charming woman! Don't mention him before her—please don't! It is too painful for her!"

Chapter VII

WHEN BORÍS AND ANNA PÁVLOVNA RETURNED TO THE OTHERS PRINCE HIPPOLYTE HAD THE EAR of the company.

Bending forward in his arm-chair he said: *"Le Roi de Prusse!"* and having said this laughed. Everyone turned toward him.

"Le Roi de Prusse?" Hippolyte said interrogatively, again laughing, and then calmly and seriously sat back in his chair. Anna Pávlovna waited for him to go on, but as he seemed quite decided to say no more she began to tell of how at Potsdam the impious Bonaparte had stolen the sword of Frederick the Great.

"It is the sword of Frederick the Great which I . . ." she began, but Hippolyte interrupted her with the words: *"Le Roi de Prusse . . ."* and again, as soon as all turned toward him, excused himself and said no more.

Anna Pávlovna frowned. Mortemart, Hippolyte's friend, addressed him firmly.

"Come now, what about your *Roi de Prusse?"*

Hippolyte laughed as if ashamed of laughing.

"Oh, it's nothing. I only wished to say . . ." (he wanted to repeat a joke he had heard in Vienna and which he had been trying all that evening to get in) "I only wished to say that we are wrong to fight *pour le Roi de Prusse!"*

Borís smiled circumspectly, so that it might be taken as ironical or appreciative according to the way the joke was received. Everybody laughed.

"Your joke is too bad, it's witty but unjust," said Anna Pávlovna, shaking her little shriveled finger at him.

"We are not fighting *pour le Roi de Prusse,* but for right principles. Oh, that wicked Prince Hippolyte!" she said.

The conversation did not flag all evening and turned chiefly on the political news. It became particularly animated toward the end of the evening when the rewards bestowed by the Emperor were mentioned.

"You know N——N——received a snuffbox with the portrait last year?" said "the man of profound intellect." "Why shouldn't S——S——get the same distinction?"

"Pardon me! A snuffbox with the Emperor's portrait is a reward but not a distinction," said the diplomatist—"A gift, rather."

"There are precedents, I may mention Schwarzenberg."

"It's impossible," replied another.

"Will you bet? The ribbon of the order is a different matter. . . ."

When everybody rose to go, Hélène who had spoken very little all the evening again turned to Borís, asking him in a tone of caressing significant command, to come to her on Tuesday.

"It is of great importance to me," she said, turning with a smile toward Anna Pávlovna, and Anna Pávlovna with the same sad smile with which she spoke of her exalted patroness, supported Hélène's wish.

It seemed as if from some words Borís had spoken that evening about the Prussian army, Hélène had suddenly found it necessary to see him. She seemed to promise to explain that necessity to him when he came on Tuesday.

But on Tuesday evening, having come to Hélène's splendid salon, Borís received no clear explanation of why it had been necessary for him to come. There were other guests and the countess talked little to him, and only as he kissed her hand on taking leave, said unexpectedly and in a whisper, with a strangely unsmiling face: "Come to dinner tomorrow . . . in the evening. You must come. . . . Come!"

During that stay in Petersburg, Borís became an intimate in the countess's house.

Chapter VIII

THE WAR WAS FLAMING UP AND NEARING THE RUSSIAN FRONTIER. EVERYWHERE ONE HEARD curses on Bonaparte, "the enemy of mankind." Militiamen and recruits were being enrolled in the villages, and from the seat of war came contradictory news, false as usual and therefore variously interpreted.

The life of old Prince Bolkónski, Prince Andrew and Princess Mary, had greatly changed since 1805.

In 1806 the old prince was made one of the eight commanders in chief then appointed to supervise the enrollment decreed throughout Russia. Despite the weakness of age, which had become particularly noticeable since the time when he thought his son had been killed, he did not think it right to refuse a duty to which he had been appointed by the Emperor himself, and this fresh opportunity for action gave him new energy and strength. He was continually traveling through the three provinces entrusted to him, was pedantic in the fulfillment of his duties, severe to cruelty with his subordinates, and went into everything down to the minutest details himself. Princess Mary had ceased taking lessons in mathematics from her father, and when the old prince was at home went to his study with the wet-nurse and little Prince Nicholas (as his grandfather called him). The baby Prince Nicholas lived with his wet-nurse and nurse Sávishna in the late princess's rooms and Princess Mary spent most of the day in the nursery, taking a mother's place to her little nephew as best she could. Mademoiselle Bourienne, too, seemed passionately fond of the boy, and Princess Mary often deprived herself to give her friend the pleasure of dandling the little *angel*—as she called her nephew—and playing with him.

Near the altar of the church at Bald Hills there was a chapel over the tomb of the little princess, and in this chapel was a marble monument brought from Italy, representing an angel with outspread wings ready to fly upward. The angel's upper lip was slightly raised as though about to smile, and once on coming out of the chapel Prince Andrew and Princess Mary admitted to one another that the angel's face reminded them strangely of the little princess. But what was still stranger, though of this Prince Andrew said nothing to his sister, was that in the expression the sculptor had happened to give the angel's face, Prince Andrew read the same mild reproach he had read on the face of his dead wife: "Ah, why have you done this to me?"

Soon after Prince Andrew's return the old prince made over to him a large estate, Boguchárovo, about twenty-five miles from Bald Hills. Partly because of the depressing memories associated with Bald Hills, partly because Prince Andrew did not always feel equal to bearing with his father's peculiarities, and partly because he needed solitude, Prince Andrew made use of Boguchárovo, began building and spent most of his time there.

After the Austerlitz campaign Prince Andrew had firmly resolved not to continue his military service, and when the war recommenced and everybody had to serve, he took a post under his father in the recruitment so as to avoid active service. The old prince and his son seemed to have changed rôles since the campaign of 1805. The old man, roused by activity, expected the best results from the new campaign, while Prince Andrew on the contrary, taking no part in the war and secretly regretting this, saw only the dark side.

On 26th February 1807 the old prince set off on one of his circuits. Prince Andrew remained at Bald Hills as usual during his father's absence. Little Nicholas had been unwell for four days. The coachman who had driven the old prince to town returned bringing papers and letters for Prince Andrew.

Not finding the young prince in his study the valet went with the letters to Princess Mary's apartments, but did not find him there. He was told that the prince had gone to the nursery.

"If you please, your excellency, Petrúsha has brought some papers," said one of the nursemaids to Prince Andrew who was sitting on a child's little chair while, frowning and with trembling hands, he poured drops from a medicine bottle into a wine glass half full of water.

"What is it?" he said crossly, and his hand shaking unintentionally, he poured too many drops into the glass. He threw the mixture onto the floor and asked for some more water. The maid brought it.

There were in the room a child's cot, two boxes, two arm-chairs, a table, a child's table and the little chair on which Prince Andrew was sitting. The curtains were drawn, and a single candle was burning on the table, screened by a bound music-book so that the light did not fall on the cot.

"My dear," said Princess Mary, addressing her brother from beside the cot where she was standing, "better wait a bit . . . later . . ."

"Oh, leave off, you always talk nonsense and keep putting things off—and this is what comes of it!" said Prince Andrew in an exasperated whisper, evidently meaning to wound his sister.

"My dear, really . . . it's better not to wake him . . . he's asleep," said the princess in a tone of entreaty.

Prince Andrew got up, and went on tiptoe up to the little bed, wine glass in hand.

"Perhaps we'd really better not wake him," he said hesitating.

"As you please . . . really . . . I think so . . . but as you please," said Princess Mary, evidently intimidated and confused that her opinion had prevailed. She drew her brother's attention to the maid who was calling him in a whisper.

It was the second night that neither of them had slept, watching the boy who was in a high fever. These last days, mistrusting their household doctor and expecting another for whom they had sent to town, they had been trying first one remedy and then another. Worn out by sleeplessness and anxiety they threw their burden of sorrow on one another and reproached and disputed with each other.

"Petrúsha has come with papers from your father," whispered the maid.

Prince Andrew went out.

"Devil take them!" he muttered, and after listening to the verbal instructions his father had sent and taking the correspondence and his father's letter, he returned to the nursery.

"Well?" he asked.

"Still the same. Wait, for heaven's sake. Karl Ivaních always says that sleep is more important than anything," whispered Princess Mary with a sigh.

Prince Andrew went up to the child and felt him. He was burning hot.

"Confound you and your Karl Ivaních!" He took the glass with the drops and again went up to the cot.

"Andrew, don't!" said Princess Mary.

But he scowled at her angrily though also with suffering in his eyes, and stooped glass in hand over the infant.

"But I wish it," he said. "I beg you—give it him!"

Princess Mary shrugged her shoulders but took the glass submissively, and calling the nurse began giving the medicine. The child screamed hoarsely. Prince Andrew winced, and clutching his head, went out and sat down on a sofa in the next room.

He still had all the letters in his hand. Opening them mechanically he began reading. The old prince, now and then using abbreviations, wrote in his large elongated hand on blue paper as follows:

Have just this moment received by special messenger very joyful news—if it's not false. Bennigsen seems to have obtained a complete victory over Buonaparte at Eylau. In Petersburg everyone is rejoicing, and the rewards sent to the army are innumerable. Though he is a German—I congratulate him! I can't make out what the commander at Kórchevo—a certain Khandrikóv—is up to; till now the additional men and provisions have not arrived. Gallop off to him at once and say I'll have his head off if everything is not here in a week. Have received another letter about the Preussisch-Eylau battle from Pétenka—he took part in it—and it's all true. When mischief-makers don't meddle even a German beats Buonaparte. He is said to be fleeing in great disorder. Mind you gallop off to Kórchevo without delay and carry out instructions!

Prince Andrew sighed and broke the seal of another envelope. It was a closely written letter of two sheets from Bilíbin. He folded it up without reading it and reread his father's letter, ending with the words: "Gallop off to Kórchevo and carry out instructions!"

"No, pardon me, I won't go now till the child is better," thought he, going to the door and looking into the nursery.

Princess Mary was still standing by the cot, gently rocking the baby.

"Ah yes, and what else did he say that's unpleasant?" thought Prince Andrew, recalling his father's letter. "Yes, we have gained a victory over Bonaparte, just when I'm not serving. Yes, yes, he's always poking fun at me. . . . Ah, well! Let him!" and he began reading Bilíbin's letter which was written in French. He read without understanding half of it, read only to forget, if but for a moment, what he had too long been thinking of so painfully to the exclusion of all else.

Chapter IX

BILÍBIN WAS NOW AT ARMY HEADQUARTERS IN A DIPLOMATIC CAPACITY, AND THOUGH HE WROTE in French and used French jests and French idioms, he described the whole campaign with a fearless self-censure and self-derision genuinely Russian. Bilíbin wrote that the obligation of diplomatic discretion tormented him, and he was happy to have in Prince Andrew a reliable correspondent to whom he could pour out the bile he had accumulated at the sight of all that was being done in the army. The letter was old, having been written before the battle at Preussisch-Eylau.

"Since the day of our brilliant success at Austerlitz," wrote Bilíbin, "as you know, my dear prince, I never leave headquarters. I have certainly acquired a taste for war, and it is just as well for me; what I have seen during these last three months is incredible.

"I begin *ab ovo.* 'The enemy of the human race,' as you know, attacks the Prussians. The Prussians are our faithful allies who have only betrayed us three times in three years. We take up their cause, but it turns out that 'the enemy of the human race' pays no heed to our fine speeches and in his rude and savage way throws himself on the Prussians without giving them time to finish the parade they had begun, and in two twists of the hand he breaks them to smithereens and installs himself in the palace at Potsdam.

" 'I most ardently desire,' writes the King of Prussia to Bonaparte, 'that your Majesty should be received and treated in my palace in a manner agreeable to yourself, and in so far as circumstances allowed, I have hastened to take all steps to that end. May I have succeeded!' The Prussian generals pride themselves on being polite to the French and lay down their arms at the first demand.

"The head of the garrison at Glogau, with ten thousand men, asks the King of Prussia what he is to do if he is summoned to surrender. . . . All this is absolutely true.

"In short, hoping to settle matters by taking up a warlike attitude, it turns out that we have landed ourselves in war, and what is more, in war on our own frontiers, *with* and *for* the King of Prussia. We have everything in perfect order, only one little thing is lacking, namely, a commander-in-chief. As it was considered that the Austerlitz success might have been more decisive had the commander-in-chief not been so young, all our octogenarians were reviewed, and of Prozoróvski and Kámenski the latter was preferred. The general comes to us, Suvórov-like, in a *kibítka,* and is received with acclamations of joy and triumph.

"On the 4th, the first courier arrives from Petersburg. The mails are taken to the field marshal's room, for he likes to do everything himself. I am called in to help sort the letters and take those meant for us. The field marshal looks on and waits for letters addressed to him. We search, but none are to be found. The field marshal grows impatient and sets to work himself, and finds letters from the Emperor to Count T., Prince V., and others. Then he bursts into one of his wild furies and rages at everyone and everything, seizes the letters, opens them and reads those from the Emperor addressed to others. 'Ah! So that's the way they treat me! No confidence in me! Ah, ordered to keep an eye on me! Very well then! Get along with you!' So he writes the famous order of the day to General Bennigsen:

" 'I am wounded and cannot ride, consequently cannot command the army. You have brought your army corps to Pultúsk, routed: here it is exposed, and without fuel or forage, so something must be done, and, as you yourself reported to Count Buxhöwden yesterday, you must think of retreating to our frontier—which do today.'

" 'From all my riding,' he writes to the Emperor, 'I have got a saddle-sore which, coming after all my previous journeys, quite prevents my riding and commanding so vast an army, so I have passed on the command to the general next in seniority, Count Buxhöwden, having sent him my whole staff and all that belongs to it, advising him if there is a lack of bread, to move farther into the interior of Prussia, for only one day's ration of bread remains, and in some regiments none at all, as reported by the division commanders, Ostermann and Sedmorétzki, and all that the peasants had has been eaten up. I myself will remain in hospital at Ostrolenka till I recover. In regard to which I humbly submit my report, with the information that if the army remains in its present bivouac another fortnight there will not be a healthy man left in it by spring.

" 'Grant leave to retire to his country seat to an old man who is already in any case dishonored by being unable to fulfill the great and glorious task for which he was chosen. I shall await your most gracious permission here in hospital, that I may not have to play the part of a *secretary* rather than *commander* in the army. My removal from the army does not produce the slightest stir—a blind man has left it. There are thousands such as I in Russia.'

"The field marshal is angry with the Emperor and he punishes us all, isn't it logical?

"This is the first act. Those that follow are naturally increasingly interesting and entertaining. After the field marshal's departure it appears that we are within sight of the enemy and must give battle. Buxhöwden is commander-in-chief by seniority, but General Bennigsen does not quite see it; more particularly as it is he and his corps who are within sight of the enemy and he wishes to profit by the opportunity to fight a battle 'on his own hand' as the Germans say. He does so. This is the battle of Pultúsk, which is considered a great victory but in my opinion was nothing of the kind. We civilians, as you know, have a very bad way of deciding whether a battle was won or lost. Those who retreat after a battle have lost it is what we say; and according to that it is we who lost the battle of Pultúsk. In short, we retreat after the battle but send a courier to Petersburg with news of a victory, and General Bennigsen hoping to receive from Petersburg the post of commander-in-chief as a reward for his victory, does not give up the command of the army to General Buxhöwden. During this interregnum we begin a very original and interesting series of maneuvers. Our aim is no longer, as it should be, to avoid or attack the enemy, but solely to avoid General Buxhöwden who by right of seniority should be our chief. So energetically do we pursue this aim that after crossing an unfordable river we burn the bridges to separate ourselves from our enemy, who at the moment is not Bonaparte but Buxhöwden. General Buxhöwden was all but attacked and captured by a superior enemy force as a result of one of these maneuvers that enabled us to escape him. Buxhöwden pursues us—we scuttle. He hardly crosses the river to our side before we recross to the other. At last our enemy, Buxhöwden, catches us and attacks. Both generals are angry, and the result is a challenge on Buxhöwden's part and an epileptic fit on Bennigsen's. But at the critical moment the courier who carried the news of our victory at Pultúsk to Petersburg, returns bringing our appointment as commander-in-chief, and our first foe, Buxhöwden, is vanquished; we can now turn our thoughts to the second, Bonaparte. But as it turns out, just at that moment a third enemy rises before us—namely the *Orthodox Russian soldiers,* loudly demanding bread, meat, biscuits, fodder and what not! The stores are empty, the roads impassable. The Orthodox begin looting, and in a way of which our last campaign can give you no idea. Half the regiments form bands and scour the countryside and put everything to fire and sword. The inhabitants are totally ruined, the hospitals overflow with sick, and famine is everywhere. Twice the marauders even attack our headquarters, and the commander-in-chief has to ask for a battalion to disperse them. During one of these attacks they carried off my empty portmanteau and my dressing-gown. The Emperor proposes to give all commanders of divisions the right to shoot marauders, but I much fear this will oblige one-half the army to shoot the other."

At first Prince Andrew read with his eyes only, but after a while, in spite of himself (although he knew how far it was safe to trust Bilíbin) what he had read began to interest him more and more. When he had read thus far, he crumpled the letter up and threw it away. It was not what he had read that vexed him, but the fact that the life out there in which he had now no part could perturb him. He shut his eyes, rubbed his forehead as if to rid himself of all interest in what he had read, and listened to what was passing in the nursery. Suddenly he thought he heard a strange noise through the door. He was seized with alarm lest something should have happened to the child while he was reading the letter. He went on tiptoe to the nursery door and opened it.

Just as he went in he saw that the nurse was hiding something from him with a scared look, and that Princess Mary was no longer by the cot.

"My dear," he heard what seemed to him her despairing whisper behind him.

As often happens after long sleeplessness and long anxiety, he was seized by an unreasoning panic—it occurred to him that the child was dead. All that he saw and heard seemed to confirm this terror.

"All is over," he thought, and a cold sweat broke out on his forehead. He went to the cot in confusion, sure that he would find it empty and that the nurse had been hiding the dead baby. He drew the curtain aside and for some time his frightened, restless eyes could not find the baby. At last he saw him: the rosy boy had tossed about till he lay across the bed with his head lower than the pillow, and was smacking his lips in his sleep and breathing evenly.

Prince Andrew was as glad to find the boy like that, as if he had already lost him. He bent over him and, as his sister had taught him, tried with his lips whether the child was still feverish. The soft forehead was moist. Prince Andrew touched the head with his hand; even the hair was wet, so profusely had the child perspired. He was not dead, but evidently the crisis was over and he was convalescent. Prince Andrew longed to snatch up, to squeeze, to hold to his heart, this helpless little creature, but dared not do so. He stood over him, gazing at his head and at the little arms and legs which showed under the blanket. He heard a rustle behind him and a shadow appeared under the curtain of the cot. He did not look round, but still gazing at the infant's face listened to his regular breathing. The dark shadow was Princess Mary, who had come up to the cot with noiseless steps, lifted the curtain, and dropped it again behind her. Prince Andrew recognized her without looking and held out his hand to her. She pressed it.

"He has perspired," said Prince Andrew.

"I was coming to tell you so."

The child moved slightly in his sleep, smiled and rubbed his forehead against the pillow.

Prince Andrew looked at his sister. In the dim shadow of the curtain her luminous eyes shone more brightly than usual from the tears of joy that were in them. She leaned over to her brother and kissed him, slightly catching the curtain of the cot. Each made the other a warning gesture, and stood still in the dim light beneath the curtain as if not wishing to leave that seclusion where they three were shut off from all the world. Prince Andrew was the first to move away, ruffling his hair against the muslin of the curtain.

"Yes, this is the one thing left me now," he said with a sigh.

Chapter X

SOON AFTER HIS ADMISSION TO THE MASONIC BROTHERHOOD PIERRE WENT TO THE KIEV PROVINCE, where he had the greatest number of serfs, taking with him full directions which he had written down for his own guidance as to what he should do on his estates.

When he reached Kiev he sent for all his stewards to the head office and explained to them his intentions and wishes. He told them that steps would be taken immediately to free his serfs—and that till then they were not to be overburdened with labor, women while nursing their babies were not to be sent to work, assistance was to be given to the serfs, punishments were to be admonitory and not corporal, and hospitals, asylums and schools were to be established on all the estates. Some of the stewards (there were semi-literate foremen among them) listened with alarm, supposing these words to mean that the young count was displeased with their management and embezzlement of money, some after their first fright were amused by Pierre's lisp and the new words they had not heard before, others simply enjoyed hearing how the master talked, while the cleverest among them, including the chief steward, understood from this speech how they could best handle the master for their own ends.

The chief steward expressed great sympathy with Pierre's intentions, but remarked that besides these changes it would be necessary to go into the general state of affairs which was far from satisfactory.

Despite Count Bezúkhov's enormous wealth, since he had come into an income which was said to amount to five hundred thousand rubles a year, Pierre felt himself far poorer than when his father had made him an allowance of ten thousand rubles. He had a dim perception of the following budget:

About 80,000 went in payment on all the estates to the Land Bank, about 30,000 went for the upkeep of the estate near Moscow, the town and the allowance to the three princesses; about 15,000 was given in pensions and the same amount for asylums; 150,000 alimony was sent to the countess; about 70,00 went for interest on debts. The building of a new church previously begun, had cost about 10,000 in each of the last two years, and he did not know how the rest, about 100,000 rubles, was spent, and almost every year he was obliged to borrow. Besides this the chief steward wrote every year telling him of fires and bad harvests, or of the necessity of rebuilding factories and workshops. So the first task Pierre had to face was one for which he had very little aptitude or inclination—practical business.

He discussed estate affairs every day with his chief steward. But he felt that this did not forward matters at all. He felt that these consultations were detached from real affairs and did not link up with them or make them move. On the one hand the chief steward put the state of things to him in the very worst light, pointing out the necessity of paying off the debts and undertaking new activities with serf-labor, to which Pierre did not agree. On the other hand Pierre demanded that steps should be taken to liberate the serfs, which the steward met by showing the necessity of first paying off the loans from the Land Bank, and the consequent impossibility of a speedy emancipation.

The steward did not say it was quite impossible, but suggested selling the forests in the province of Kostromá, the land lower down the river, and the Crimean estate, in order to make it possible: all of which operations according to him were connected with such complicated measures—the removal of injunctions, petitions, permits and so on—that Pierre became quite bewildered and only replied:

"Yes, yes, do so."

Pierre had none of the practical persistence that would have enabled him to attend to the business himself, and so he disliked it and only tried to pretend to the steward that he was attending to it. The steward for his part tried to pretend to the count that he considered these consultations very valuable for the proprietor and troublesome to himself.

In Kiev Pierre found some people he knew, and strangers hastened to make his acquaintance and joyfully welcomed the rich newcomer, the largest landowner of the province. Temptations to Pierre's greatest weakness—the one to which he had confessed when admitted to the Lodge—were so strong that he could not resist them. Again whole days, weeks and months of his life passed in as great a rush, and were as much occupied with evening parties, dinners, lunches and balls, giving him no time for reflection, as in Petersburg. Instead of the new life he had hoped to lead he still lived the old life, only in new surroundings.

Of the three precepts of freemasonry Pierre realized that he did not fulfill the one which enjoined every mason to set an example of moral life, and that of the seven virtues he lacked two—morality and the love of death. He consoled himself with the thought that he fulfilled another of the precepts—that of reforming the human race—and had other virtues—love of his neighbor, and especially generosity.

In the spring of 1807 he decided to return to Petersburg. On the way he intended to visit all his estates and see for himself how far his orders had been carried out and in what state were the serfs whom God had entrusted to his care and whom he intended to benefit.

The chief steward, who considered the young count's attempts almost insane—unprofitable to himself, to the count, and to the serfs—made some concessions. Continuing to represent the liberation of the serfs as impracticable, he arranged for the erection of large buildings—schools, hospitals and asylums—on all the estates before the master arrived. Everywhere preparations were made not for ceremonious welcomes (which he knew Pierre would not like), but for just such gratefully religious ones, with offerings of icons and the bread and salt of hospitality, as, according to his understanding of his master, would touch and delude him.

The southern spring, the comfortable rapid traveling in a Vienna carriage, and the solitude of the road, all had a gladdening effect on Pierre. The estates he had not before visited were each more picturesque than the other; the serfs everywhere seemed thriving and touchingly grateful for the benefits conferred on them. Everywhere were receptions, which though they embarrassed Pierre awakened a joyful feeling in the depth of his heart. In one place the peasants presented him with bread and salt and an icon of St. Peter and St. Paul, asking permission, as a mark of their gratitude for the benefits he had conferred on them, to build a new chantry to the church at their own expense in honor of Peter and Paul, his patron saints. In another place the women with infants in arms met him to thank him for releasing them from hard work. On a third estate the priest, bearing a cross, came to meet him surrounded by children whom, by the count's generosity, he was instructing in reading, writing and religion. On all his estates Pierre saw with his own eyes brick buildings erected or in course of erection, all on one plan, for hospitals, schools, and almshouses, which were soon to be opened. Everywhere he saw the stewards' accounts, according to which the serfs' manorial labor had been diminished, and heard the touching thanks of deputations of serfs in their full-skirted blue coats.

What Pierre did not know was, that the place where they presented him with bread and salt and wished to build a chantry in honor of Peter and Paul was a market-village where a fair was held on St. Peter's day, and that the richest peasants (who formed the deputation) had begun the chantry long before, but that nine-tenths of the peasants in that villages were in a state of the greatest poverty. He did not know that since the nursing mothers were no longer sent to work on his land, they did still harder work on their own land. He did not know that the priest who met him with the cross oppressed the peasants by his exactions, and that the pupils' parents wept at having to let him take their children and secured their release by heavy payments. He did not know that the brick buildings, built to plan, were being built by serfs whose manorial labor was thus increased, though lessened on paper. He did not know that where the steward had shown him in the accounts that the serfs' payments had been diminished by a third, their obligatory manorial work had been increased by a half. And so Pierre was delighted with his visit to his estates and quite recovered the philanthropic mood in which he had left Petersburg, and wrote enthusiastic letters to his "brother-instructor" as he called the Grand Master.

"How easy it is, how little effort it needs, to do so much good," thought Pierre, "and how little attention we pay to it!"

He was pleased at the gratitude he received, but felt abashed at receiving it. This gratitude reminded him of how much more he might do for these simple kindly people.

The chief steward, a very stupid but cunning man who saw perfectly through the naïve and intelligent count and played with him as with a toy, seeing the effect these prearranged receptions had on Pierre, pressed him still harder with proofs of the impossibility and above all the uselessness of freeing the serfs, who were quite happy as it was.

Pierre in his secret soul agreed with the steward that it would be difficult to imagine happier people, and that God only knew what would happen to them when they were free, but he insisted, though reluctantly, on what he thought right. The steward promised to do all in his power to carry out the count's wishes, seeing clearly that not only would the count never be able to find out whether all measures had been taken for the sale of the land and forests and to release them from the Land Bank, but would probably never even inquire, and would never know that the newly-erected buildings were standing empty, and that the serfs continued to give in money and work all that other people's serfs gave—that is to say, all that could be got out of them.

Chapter XI

RETURNING FROM HIS JOURNEY THROUGH SOUTH RUSSIA IN THE HAPPIEST STATE OF MIND, PIERRE carried out an intention he had long had of visiting his friend Bolkónski, whom he had not seen for two years.

Boguchárovo lay in a flat uninteresting part of the country among fields and forests of fir and birch, which were partly cut down. The house lay behind a newly-dug pond filled with water to the brink and with banks still bare of grass. It was at the end of a village that stretched along the highroad in the midst of a young copse in which were a few fir trees.

The homestead consisted of a threshing floor, outhouses, stables, a bathhouse, a lodge and a large brick house with semicircular façade still in course of construction. Round the house was a garden newly laid out. The fences and gates were new and solid; two fire pumps and a water-cart, painted green, stood in a shed; the paths were straight, the bridges were strong and had hand-rails. Everything bore an impress of tidiness and good management. Some domestic serfs Pierre met, in reply to inquiries as to where the prince lived, pointed out a small newly-built lodge close to the pond. Antón, a man who had looked after Prince Andrew in his boyhood, helped Pierre out of his carriage, said that the prince was at home, and showed him into a clean little anteroom.

Pierre was struck by the modesty of the small though clean house after the brilliant surroundings in which he had last met his friend in Petersburg.

He quickly entered the small reception room with its still unplastered wooden walls redolent of pine, and would have gone farther, but Antón ran ahead on tiptoe and knocked at a door.

"Well, what is it?" came a sharp, unpleasant voice.

"A visitor," answered Antón.

"Ask him to wait," and the sound was heard of a chair being pushed back.

Pierre went with rapid steps to the door and suddenly came face to face with Prince Andrew, who came out frowning and looking old. Pierre embraced him, and lifting his spectacles kissed his friend on the cheek and looked at him closely.

"Well, I did not expect you, I am very glad," said Prince Andrew.

Pierre said nothing; he looked fixedly at his friend with surprise. He was struck by the change in him. His words were kindly and there was a smile on his lips and face, but his eyes were dull and lifeless and in spite of his evident wish to do so he could not give them a joyous and glad sparkle. Prince Andrew had grown thinner, paler, and more manly looking, but what amazed and estranged Pierre till he got used to it were his inertia and a wrinkle on his brow indicating prolonged concentration on some one thought.

As is usually the case with people meeting after a prolonged separation, it was long before their conversation could settle on anything. They put questions and gave brief replies about things they knew ought to be talked over at length. At last the conversation gradually settled on some of the topics at first lightly touched on: their past life, plans for the future, Pierre's journeys and occupations, the war, and so on. The preoccupation and despondency which Pierre had noticed in his friend's look was now still more clearly expressed in the smile with which he listened to Pierre, especially when he spoke with joyful animation of the past or the future. It was as if Prince Andrew would have liked to sympathize with what Pierre was saying, but could not. The latter began to feel that it was in bad taste to speak of his enthusiasms, dreams and hopes of happiness or goodness, in Prince Andrew's presence. He was ashamed to express his new masonic views, which had been particularly revived and strengthened by his late tour. He checked himself, fearing to seem naïve, yet he felt an irresistible desire to show his friend as soon as possible that he was now a quite different, and better, Pierre than he had been in Petersburg.

"I can't tell you how much I have lived through since then. I hardly know myself again."

"Yes, we have altered much, very much, since then," said Prince Andrew.

"Well, and you? What are your plans?"

"Plans!" repeated Prince Andrew ironically. "My plans?" he said, as if astonished at the word. "Well, you see, I'm building. I mean to settle here altogether next year. . . ."

Pierre looked silently and searchingly into Prince Andrew's face, which had grown much older.

"No, I meant to ask . . ." Pierre began, but Prince Andrew interrupted him.

"But why talk of me? . . . Talk *to* me, yes, tell me about your travels and all you have been doing on your estates."

Pierre began describing what he had done on his estates, trying as far as possible to conceal his own part in the improvements that had been made. Prince Andrew several times prompted Pierre's story of what he had been doing, as though it were all an old-time story, and he listened not only without interest but even as if ashamed of what Pierre was telling him.

Pierre felt uncomfortable and even depressed in his friend's company and at last became silent.

"I'll tell you what, my dear fellow," said Prince Andrew, who evidently also felt depressed and constrained with his visitor, "I am only bivouacking here, and have just come to look round. I am going back to my sister today. I will introduce you to her. But of course you know her already," he said, evidently trying to entertain a visitor with whom he now found nothing in common. "We will go after dinner. And would you now like to look round my place?"

They went out and walked about till dinnertime, talking of the political news and common acquaintances like people who do not know each other intimately. Prince Andrew spoke with some animation and interest only of the new homestead he was constructing and its buildings, but even here, while on the scaffolding, in the midst of a talk explaining the future arrangements of the house, he interrupted himself:

"However, this is not at all interesting. Let us have dinner, and then we'll set off."

At dinner, conversation turned on Pierre's marriage.

"I was very much surprised when I heard of it," said Prince Andrew.

Pierre blushed, as he always did when it was mentioned, and said hurriedly:

"I will tell you some time how it all happened. But you know it is all over, and forever."

"Forever?" said Prince Andrew. "Nothing's forever."

"But you know how it all ended, don't you? You heard of the duel?"

"And so you had to go through that too!"

"One thing I thank God for, is that I did not kill that man," said Pierre.

"Why so?" asked Prince Andrew. "To kill a vicious dog is a very good thing really."

"No, to kill a man is bad—wrong."

"Why is it wrong?" urged Prince Andrew. "It is not given to man to know what is right and what is wrong. Men always did and always will err, and in nothing more than in what they consider right and wrong."

"What does harm to another is wrong," said Pierre, feeling with pleasure that for the first time since his arrival Prince Andrew was roused, had begun to talk, and wanted to express what had brought him to his present state.

"And who has told you what is bad for another man?" he asked.

"Bad! Bad!" exclaimed Pierre. "We all know what is bad for ourselves."

"Yes, we know that, but the harm I am conscious of in myself is something I cannot inflict on others," said Prince Andrew, growing more and more animated and evidently wishing to express his new outlook to Pierre. He spoke in French. "I only know two very real evils in life: remorse and illness. The only good is the absence of those evils. To live for myself avoiding those two evils is my whole philosophy now."

"And love of one's neighbor, and self-sacrifice?" began Pierre. "No, I can't agree with you! To live only so as not to do evil and not to have to repent, is not enough. I lived like that, I lived for myself and ruined my life. And only now when I am living, or at least trying" (Pierre's modesty made him correct himself) "to live for others, only now have I understood all the happiness of life. No, I shall not agree with you, and you do not really believe what you are saying."

Prince Andrew looked silently at Pierre with an ironic smile.

"When you see my sister, Princess Mary, you'll get on with her," he said. "Perhaps you are right for yourself," he added after a short pause, "but everyone lives in his own way. You lived for yourself and say you nearly ruined your life and only found happiness when you began living for others. I experienced just the reverse. I lived for glory.—And after all what is glory? The same love of others, a desire to do something for them, a desire for their approval.—So I lived for others, and not almost, but quite, ruined my life. And I have become calmer since I began to live only for myself."

"But what do you mean by living only for yourself?" asked Pierre growing excited. "What about your son, your sister and your father?"

"But that's just the same as myself—they are not *others,*" explained Prince Andrew. "The others, one's neighbors, *le prochain,* as you and Princess Mary call it, are the chief source of all error and evil. *Le prochain*—your Kiev peasants to whom you want to do good."

And he looked at Pierre with a mocking, challenging expression. He evidently wished to draw him on.

"You are joking," replied Pierre, growing more and more excited. "What error or evil can there be in my wishing to do good, and even doing a little—though I did very little and did it very badly?—What evil can there be in it if unfortunate people, our serfs, people like ourselves, were growing up and dying with no idea of God and truth beyond ceremonies and meaningless prayers and are now instructed in a comforting belief in future life, retribution, recompense and consolation? What evil and error are there in it, if people were dying of disease without help while material assistance could so easily be rendered, and I supplied them with a doctor, a hospital and an asylum for the aged? And is it not a palpable, unquestionable good if a peasant, or a woman with a baby, has no rest day or night and I give them rest and leisure?" said Pierre, hurrying and lisping. "And I have done that though badly and to a small extent; but I have done something toward it and you cannot persuade me that it was not a good action, and more than that, you can't make me believe that you do not think so yourself. And the main thing is," he continued, "that I know, and know for certain, that the enjoyment of doing this good is the only sure happiness in life."

"Yes, if you put it like that it's quite a different matter," said Prince Andrew. "I build a house and lay out a garden, and you build hospitals. The one and the other may serve as a pastime. But what's right and what's good must be judged by one who knows all, but not by us. Well, you want an argument," he added, "come on then."

They rose from the table and sat down in the entrance porch which served as a veranda.

"Come, let's argue then," said Prince Andrew, "You talk of schools," he went on, crooking a finger, "education and so forth; that is, you want to raise him" (pointing to a peasant who passed by them taking off his cap) "from his animal condition and awaken in him spiritual needs, while it seems to me that animal happiness is the only happiness possible, and that is just what you want to deprive him of. I envy him, but you want to make him what I am, without giving him my means. Then you say, 'lighten his toil.' But as I see it, physical labor is as essential to him, as much a condition of his existence, as mental activity is to you or me. You can't help thinking. I go to bed after two in the morning, thoughts come and I can't sleep but toss about till dawn, because I think and can't help thinking, just as he can't help plowing and mowing; if he didn't, he would go to the drink shop or fall ill. Just as I could not stand his terrible physical labor but should die of it in a week, so he could not stand my physical idleness, but would grow fat and die. The third thing—what else was it you talked about?" and Prince Andrew crooked a third finger. "Ah, yes, hospitals, medicine. He has a fit, he is dying, and you come and bleed him and patch him up. He will drag about as a cripple, a burden to everybody, for another ten years. It would be far easier and simpler for him to die. Others are being born and there are plenty of them as it is. It would be different if you grudged losing a laborer—that's how I regard him—but you want to cure him from love of him. And he does not want that. And besides, what a notion that medicine ever cured anyone! Killed them, yes!" said he, frowning angrily and turning away from Pierre.

Prince Andrew expressed his ideas so clearly and distinctly that it was evident he had reflected on this subject more than once, and he spoke readily and rapidly like a man who has not talked for a long time. His glance became more animated as his conclusions became more hopeless.

"Oh, that is dreadful, dreadful!" said Pierre. "I don't understand how one can live with such ideas. I had such moments myself not long ago, in Moscow and when traveling, but at such times I collapsed so that I don't live at all—everything seems hateful to me . . . myself most of all. Then I don't eat, don't wash . . . and how is it with you? . . ."

"Why not wash? That is not cleanly," said Prince Andrew; "on the contrary one must try to make one's life as pleasant as possible. I'm alive, that is not my fault, so I must live out my life as best I can without hurting others."

"But with such ideas what motive have you for living? One would sit without moving, undertaking nothing. . . ."

"Life as it is leaves one no peace. I should be thankful to do nothing, but here on the one hand the local nobility have done me the honor to choose me to be their marshal; it was all I could do to get out of it. They could not understand that I have not the necessary qualifications for it—the kind of good-natured, fussy shallowness necessary for the position. Then there's this house, which must be built in order to have a nook of one's own in which to be quiet. And now there's this recruiting."

"Why aren't you serving in the army?"

"After Austerlitz!" said Prince Andrew gloomily. "No, thank you very much! I have promised myself not to serve again in the active Russian army. And I won't—not even if Bonaparte were here at Smolénsk threatening Bald Hills—even then I wouldn't serve in the Russian army! Well, as I was saying," he continued, recovering his composure, "now there's this recruiting. My father is chief in command of the 3rd District, and my only way of avoiding active service is to serve under him."

"Then you are serving?"

"I am."

He paused a little while.

"And why do you serve?"

"Why, for this reason! My father is one of the most remarkable men of his time. But he is growing old, and though not exactly cruel he has too energetic a character. He is so accustomed to unlimited power that he is terrible, and now he has this authority of a commander-in-chief of the recruiting, granted by the Emperor. If I had been two hours late a fortnight ago he would have had a paymaster's clerk at Yúkhnovna hanged," said Prince Andrew with a smile. "So I am serving because I alone have any influence with my father, and now and then can save him from actions which would torment him afterwards."

"Well, there you see!"

"Yes, but it is not as you imagine," Prince Andrew continued. "I did not, and do not, in the least care about that scoundrel of a clerk who had stolen some boots from the recruits; I should even have been very glad to see him hanged, but I was sorry for my father—that again is for myself."

Prince Andrew grew more and more animated. His eyes glittered feverishly while he tried to prove to Pierre that in his actions there was no desire to do good to his neighbor.

"There now, you wish to liberate your serfs," he continued; "that is very good, but not for you—I don't suppose you ever had anyone flogged or sent to Siberia—and still less for your serfs. If they are beaten, flogged or sent to Siberia, I don't suppose they are any the worse off. In Siberia they lead the same animal life, and the stripes on their bodies heal, and they are happy as before. But it is a good thing for proprietors who perish morally, bring remorse upon themselves, stifle this remorse and grow callous, as a result of being able to inflict punishments justly and unjustly. It is those people I pity, and for their sake I should like to liberate the serfs. You may not have seen, but I have seen, how good men brought up in those traditions of unlimited power, in time when they grow more irritable, become cruel and harsh, are conscious of it, but cannot restrain themselves and grow more and more miserable."

Prince Andrew spoke so earnestly that Pierre could not help thinking that these thoughts had been suggested to Prince Andrew by his father's case.

He did not reply.

"So that's what I'm sorry for—human dignity, peace of mind, purity, and not the serfs' backs and foreheads, which, beat and shave as you may, always remain the same backs and foreheads."

"No, no! A thousand times no! I shall never agree with you," said Pierre.

Chapter XII

IN THE EVENING ANDREW AND PIERRE GOT INTO THE OPEN CARRIAGE AND DROVE TO BALD HILLS. Prince Andrew, glancing at Pierre, broke the silence now and then with remarks which showed that he was in a good temper.

Pointing to the fields, he spoke of the improvements he was making in his husbandry.

Pierre remained gloomily silent, answering in monosyllables and apparently immersed in his own thoughts.

He was thinking that Prince Andrew was unhappy, had gone astray, did not see the true light, and that he, Pierre, ought to aid, enlighten, and raise him. But as soon as he thought of what he should say, he felt that Prince Andrew with one word, one argument, would upset all his teaching, and he shrank from beginning, afraid of exposing to possible ridicule what to him was precious and sacred.

"No, but why do you think so?" Pierre suddenly began lowering his head and looking like a bull about to charge, "why do you think so? You should not think so."

"Think? What about?" asked Prince Andrew with surprise.

"About life, about man's destiny. It can't be so. I myself thought like that, and do you know what saved me? Freemasonry! No, don't smile. Freemasonry is not a religious ceremonial sect, as I thought it was: Freemasonry is the best expression of the best, the eternal, aspects of humanity."

And he began to explain freemasonry as he understood it to Prince Andrew. He said that freemasonry is the teaching of Christianity freed from the bonds of State and Church, a teaching of equality, brotherhood, and love.

"Only our holy brotherhood has the real meaning of life, all the rest is a dream," said Pierre. "Understand, my dear fellow, that outside this union all is filled with deceit and falsehood and I agree with you that nothing is left for an intelligent and good man but to live out his life, like you, merely trying not to harm others. But make our fundamental convictions your own, join our brotherhood, give yourself up to us, let yourself be guided, and you will at once feel yourself, as I have felt myself, a part of that vast invisible chain the beginning of which is hidden in Heaven," said Pierre.

Prince Andrew, looking straight in front of him, listened in silence to Pierre's words. More than once, when the noise of the wheels prevented his catching what Pierre said, he asked him to repeat it, and by the peculiar glow that came into Prince Andrew's eyes and by his silence, Pierre saw that his words were not in vain and that Prince Andrew would not interrupt him or laugh at what he said.

They reached a river that had overflowed its banks and which they had to cross by ferry. While the carriage and horses were being placed on it, they also stepped on the raft.

Prince Andrew, leaning his arms on the raft railing, gazed silently at the flooding waters glittering in the setting sun.

"Well, what do you think about it?" Pierre asked. "Why are you silent?"

"What do I think about it? I am listening to you. It's all very well. . . . You say: join our Brotherhood and we will show you the aim of life, the destiny of man, and the laws which govern the world. But who are *we?* Men. How is it you know everything? Why do I alone not see what you see? You see a reign of goodness and truth on earth, but I don't see it."

Pierre interrupted him.

"Do you believe in a future life?" he asked.

"A future life?" Prince Andrew repeated, but Pierre, giving him no time to reply, took the repetition for a denial, the more readily as he knew Prince Andrew's former atheistic convictions.

"You say you can't see a reign of goodness and truth on earth. Nor could I, and it cannot be seen if one looks on our life here as the end of everything. On *earth,* here on this earth" (Pierre pointed to the fields), "there is no truth, all is false and evil; but in the universe, in the whole universe there is a kingdom of truth, and we who are now the children of earth are—eternally—children of the whole universe. Don't I feel in my soul that I am part of this vast harmonious whole? Don't I feel that I form one link, one step, between the lower and higher beings, in this vast harmonious multitude of beings in whom the Deity—the Supreme Power if you prefer the term—is manifest? If I see, clearly see, that ladder leading from plant to man, why should I suppose it breaks off at me and does not go farther and farther? I feel that I cannot vanish, since nothing vanishes in this world, but that I shall always exist and always have existed. I feel that beyond me and above me there are spirits, and that in this world there is truth."

"Yes, that is Herder's theory," said Prince Andrew, "but it is not that which can convince me, dear friend—life and death are what convince. What convinces is when one sees a being dear to one, bound up with one's own life, before whom one was to blame and had hoped to make it right" (Prince Andrew's voice trembled and he turned away), "and suddenly that being is seized with pain, suffers, and ceases to exist. . . . Why? It cannot be that there is no answer. And I believe there is. . . . That's what convinces, that is what has convinced me," said Prince Andrew.

"Yes, yes, of course," said Pierre, "isn't that what I'm saying?"

"No. All I say is that it is not argument that convinces me of the necessity of a future life, but this: when you go hand in hand with someone and all at once that person vanishes *there, into nowhere,* and you yourself are left facing that abyss, and look in. And I have looked in. . . ."

"Well, that's it then! You know that there is a *there* and there is a *Someone? There* is the future life. The *Someone* is—God."

Prince Andrew did not reply. The carriage and horses had long since been taken off, onto the farther bank, and reharnessed. The sun had sunk half below the horizon and an evening frost was starring the puddles near the ferry, but Pierre and Andrew to the astonishment of the footmen, coachmen, and ferrymen, still stood on the raft and talked.

"If there is a God and future life, there is truth and good, and man's highest happiness consists in striving to attain them. We must live, we must love, and we must believe that we live not only today on this scrap of earth, but have lived and shall live forever, there, in the Whole," said Pierre, and he pointed to the sky.

Prince Andrew stood leaning on the railing of the raft listening to Pierre, and he gazed with his eyes fixed on the red reflection of the sun gleaming on the blue waters. There was perfect stillness. Pierre became silent. The raft had long since stopped and only the waves of the current beat softly against it below. Prince Andrew felt as if the sound of the waves kept up a refrain to Pierre's words, whispering:

"It is true, believe it."

He sighed, and glanced with a radiant, childlike, tender look at Pierre's face, flushed and rapturous, but yet shy before his superior friend.

"Yes, if it only were so!" said Prince Andrew. "However, it is time to get on," he added, and stepping off the raft, he looked up at the sky to which Pierre had pointed, and for the first time since Austerlitz saw that high, everlasting sky he had seen while lying on that battlefield; and something that had long been slumbering, something that was best within him, suddenly awoke, joyful and youthful, in his soul. It vanished as soon as he returned to the customary conditions of his life, but he knew that this feeling which he did not know how to develop, existed within him. His meeting with Pierre formed an epoch in Prince Andrew's life. Though outwardly he continued to live in the same old way, inwardly he began a new life.

Chapter XIII

IT WAS GETTING DUSK WHEN PRINCE ANDREW AND PIERRE DROVE UP TO THE FRONT ENTRANCE OF the house at Bald Hills. As they approached the house, Prince Andrew with a smile drew Pierre's attention to a commotion going on at the back porch. A woman, bent with age with a wallet on her back, and a short, long-haired, young man in a black garment, had rushed back to the gate on seeing the carriage driving up. Two women ran out after them, and all four, looking round at the carriage, ran in dismay up the steps of the back porch.

"Those are Mary's 'God's folk,' " said Prince Andrew. "They have mistaken us for my father. This is the one matter in which she disobeys him. He orders these pilgrims to be driven away, but she receives them."

"But what are 'God's folk'?" asked Pierre.

Prince Andrew had no time to answer. The servants came out to meet them, and he asked where the old prince was and whether he was expected back soon.

The old prince had gone to the town and was expected back any minute.

Prince Andrew led Pierre to his own apartments, which were always kept in perfect order and readiness for him in his father's house; he himself went to the nursery.

"Let us go and see my sister," he said to Pierre when he returned. "I have not found her yet, she is hiding now, sitting with her 'God's folk.' It will serve her right, she will be confused, but you will see her 'God's folk.' It's really very curious."

"What are 'God's folk'?" asked Pierre.

"Come, and you'll see for yourself."

Princess Mary really was disconcerted and red patches came on her face when they went in. In her snug room, with lamps burning before the icon-stand, a young lad with a long nose and long hair, wearing a monk's cassock, sat on the sofa beside her, behind a samovar. Near them, in an armchair, sat a thin, shriveled, old woman, with a meek expression on her childlike face.

"Andrew, why didn't you warn me?" said the princess, with mild reproach, as she stood before her pilgrims like a hen before her chickens.

"Charmée de vous voir. Je suis très contente de vous voir," she said to Pierre as he kissed her hand. She had known him as a child, and now his friendship with Andrew, his misfortune with his wife, and above all his kindly, simple face, disposed her favorably toward him. She looked at him with her beautiful radiant eyes and seemed to say, "I like you very much, but please don't laugh at my people." After exchanging the first greetings, they sat down.

"Ah, and Ivánushka is here too!" said Prince Andrew, glancing with a smile at the young pilgrim.

"Andrew!" said Princess Mary, imploringly.

"Il faut que vous sachiez que c'est une femme," said Prince Andrew to Pierre.

"Andrew, *au nom de Dieu!*" Princess Mary repeated.

It was evident that Prince Andrew's ironical tone toward the pilgrims and Princess Mary's helpless attempts to protect them, were their customary long-established relations on the matter.

"Mais, ma bonne amie," said Prince Andrew, *"vous devriez au contraire m'être reconnaissante de ce que j'explique à Pierre votre intimité avec ce jeune homme."*

"Really?" said Pierre, gazing over his spectacles with curiosity and seriousness (for which Princess Mary was specially grateful to him) into Ivánushka's face, who, seeing that she was being spoken about, looked round at them all with crafty eyes.

Princess Mary's embarrassment on *her people's* account was quite unnecessary. They were not in the least abashed. The old woman, lowering her eyes but casting side-glances at the newcomers, had turned her cup upside down and placed a nibbled bit of sugar beside it, and sat quietly in her arm-chair, though hoping to be offered another cup of tea. Ivánushka, sipping out of her saucer, looked with sly womanish eyes from under her brows at the young men.

"Where have you been? To Kiev?" Prince Andrew asked the old woman.

"I have, good sir," she answered garrulously. "Just at Christmas time I was deemed worthy to partake of the holy and heavenly sacrament at the shrine of the saint. And now I'm from Kolyázin, master, where a great and wonderful blessing has been revealed."

"And was Ivánushka with you?"

"I go by myself, benefactor," said Ivánushka, trying to speak in a bass voice. "I only came across Pelagéya in Yúkhnovo . . ."

Pelagéya interrupted her companion; she evidently wished to tell what she had seen.

"In Kolyázin, master, a wonderful blessing has been revealed."

"What is it? Some new relics?" asked Prince Andrew.

"Andrew, do leave off," said Princess Mary. "Don't tell him, Pelagéya."

"No . . . why not, my dear, why shouldn't I? I like him. He is kind, he is one of God's chosen, he's a benefactor, he once gave me ten rubles, I remember. When I was in Kiev, Crazy Cyril says to me (he's one of God's own and goes barefoot summer and winter), he says, 'Why are you not going to the right place? Go to Kolyázin where a wonder-working icon of the Holy Mother of God has been revealed.' On hearing those words I said good-bye to the holy folk and went."

All were silent, only the pilgrim woman went on in measured tones, drawing in her breath.

"So I come, master, and the people say to me: 'A great blessing has been revealed, holy oil trickles from the cheeks of our blessed Mother, the Holy Virgin Mother of God.' . . ."

"All right, all right, you can tell us afterward," said Princess Mary, blushing.

"Let me ask her," said Pierre. "Did you see it yourselves?" he inquired.

"Oh, yes, master, I was found worthy. Such a brightness on the face like the light of heaven, and from the blessed Mother's cheek it drops and drops. . . ."

"But, dear me, that must be a fraud!" said Pierre, naïvely, who had listened attentively to the pilgrim.

"Oh, master, what are you saying?" exclaimed the horrified Pelagéya, turning to Princess Mary for support.

"They impose on the people," he repeated.

"Lord Jesus Christ!" exclaimed the pilgrim woman, crossing herself. "Oh, don't speak so, master! There was a general who did not believe, and said, 'The monks cheat,' and as soon as he'd said it he went blind. And he dreamed that the Holy Virgin Mother of the Kiev catacombs came to him and said, 'Believe in me and I will make you whole.' So he begged: 'Take me to her, take me to her.' It's the real truth I'm telling you, I saw it myself. So he was brought, quite blind, straight to her, and he goes up to her and falls down and says, 'Make me whole,' says he, 'and I'll give thee what the Tsar bestowed on me.' I saw it myself, master, the star is fixed into the icon. Well, and what do you think? He received his sight! It's a sin to speak so. God will punish you," she said admonishingly, turning to Pierre.

"How did the star get into the icon?" Pierre asked.

"And was the Holy Mother promoted to the rank of general?" said Prince Andrew, with a smile.

Pelagéya suddenly grew quite pale and clasped her hands.

"Oh, master, master, what a sin! And you who have a son!" she began, her pallor suddenly turning to a vivid red. "Master, what have you said? God forgive you!" And she crossed herself. "Lord forgive him! My dear, what does it mean? . . ." she asked, turning to Princess Mary. She got up and, almost crying, began to arrange her wallet. She evidently felt frightened and ashamed to have accepted charity in a house where such things could be said, and was at the same time sorry to have now to forgo the charity of this house.

"Now, why need you do it?" said Princess Mary. "Why did you come to me? . . ."

"Come, Pelagéya, I was joking," said Pierre. "*Princesse, ma parole, je n'ai pas voulu l'offenser.* I did not mean anything, I was only joking," he said, smiling shyly and trying to efface his offense. "It was all my fault, and Andrew was only joking."

Pelagéya stopped doubtfully, but in Pierre's face there was such a look of sincere penitence, and Prince Andrew glanced so meekly now at her and now at Pierre, that she was gradually reassured.

Chapter XIV

THE PILGRIM WOMAN WAS APPEASED, AND BEING ENCOURAGED TO TALK, GAVE A LONG ACCOUNT of Father Amphilochus, who led so holy a life that his hands smelled of incense, and how on her last visit to Kiev some monks she knew let her have the keys of the catacombs, and how she, taking some dried bread with her, had spent two days in the catacombs with the saints. "I'd pray awhile to one, ponder awhile, then go on to another. I'd sleep a bit and then again go and kiss the relics, and there was such peace all around, such blessedness, that one don't want to come out, even into the light of heaven again."

Pierre listened to her attentively and seriously. Prince Andrew went out of the room, and then, leaving "God's folk" to finish their tea, Princess Mary took Pierre into the drawing room.

"You are very kind," she said to him.

"Oh, I really did not mean to hurt her feelings. I understand them so well and have the greatest respect for them."

Princess Mary looked at him silently and smiled affectionately.

"I have known you a long time, you see, and am as fond of you as of a brother," she said. "How do you find Andrew?" she added hurriedly, not giving him time to reply to her affectionate words. "I am very anxious about him. His health was better in the winter, but last spring his wound reopened and the doctor said he ought to go away for a cure. And I am also very much afraid for him spiritually. He has not a character like us women who, when we suffer, can weep away our sorrows. He keeps it all within him. Today he is cheerful and in good spirits, but that is the effect of your visit—he is not often like that. If you could persuade him to go abroad. He needs activity, and this quiet regular life is very bad for him. Others don't notice it, but I see it."

Toward ten o'clock the menservants rushed to the front door, hearing the bells of the old prince's carriage approaching. Prince Andrew and Pierre also went out into the porch.

"Who's that?" asked the old prince, noticing Pierre as he got out of, the carriage.

"Ah! Very glad! Kiss me," he said, having learned who the young stranger was.

The old prince was in a good temper and very gracious to Pierre.

Before supper, Prince Andrew, coming back to his father's study, found him disputing hotly with his visitor. Pierre was maintaining that a time would come when there would be no more wars. The old prince disputed it chaffingly, but without getting angry.

"Drain the blood from men's veins and put in water instead, then there will be no more war! Old women's nonsense—old women's nonsense!" he repeated, but still he patted Pierre affectionately on the shoulder, and then went up to the table where Prince Andrew, evidently not wishing to join in the conversation, was looking over the papers his father had brought from town. The old prince went up to him and began to talk business.

"The marshal, a Count Rostóv, hasn't sent half his contingent. He came to town and wanted to invite me to dinner—I gave him a pretty dinner! . . . And there, look at this. . . . Well, my boy," the old prince went on, addressing his son and patting Pierre on the shoulder. "A fine fellow—your friend—I like him! He stirs me up. Another says clever things and one doesn't care to listen, but this one talks rubbish yet stirs an old fellow up. Well, go! Get along! Perhaps I'll come and sit with you at supper. We'll have another dispute. Make friends with my little fool, Princess Mary," he shouted after Pierre, through the door.

Only now, on his visit to Bald Hills, did Pierre fully realize the strength and charm of his friendship with Prince Andrew. That charm was not expressed so much in his relations with him, as with all his family and with the household. With the stern old prince and the gentle, timid Princess Mary, though he had scarcely known them, Pierre at once felt like an old friend. They were all fond of him already. Not only Princess Mary, who had been won by his gentleness with the pilgrims, gave him her most radiant looks, but even the one-year-old "Prince Nicholas" (as his grandfather called him) smiled at Pierre and let himself be taken in his arms, and Michael Ivánovich and Mademoiselle Bourienne looked at him with pleasant smiles when he talked to the old prince.

The old prince came in to supper; this was evidently on Pierre's account. And during the two days of the young man's visit he was extremely kind to him, and told him to visit them again.

When Pierre had gone and the members of the household met together, they began to express their opinions of him as people always do after a new acquaintance has left, but as seldom happens, no one said anything but what was good of him.

Chapter XV

When returning from his leave, Rostóv felt, for the first time, how close was the bond that united him to Denísov and and the whole regiment.

On approaching it, Rostóv felt as he had done when approaching his home in Moscow. When he saw the first hussar with the unbuttoned uniform of his regiment, when he recognized red-haired Deméntyev and saw the picket ropes of the roan horses, when Lavrúshka gleefully shouted to his master, "The count has come!" and Denísov, who had been asleep on his bed, ran all disheveled out of the mud hut to embrace him, and the officers collected round to greet the new arrival, Rostóv experienced the same feeling as when his mother, his father, and his sister had embraced him, and tears of joy choked him so that he could not speak. The regiment was also a home, and as unalterably dear and precious as his parents' house.

When he had reported himself to the commander of the regiment and had been reassigned to his former squadron, had been on duty and had gone out foraging, when he had again entered into all the little interests of the regiment and felt himself deprived of liberty and bound in one narrow, unchanging frame, he experienced the same sense of peace, of moral support, and the same sense of being at home here in his own place, as he had felt under the parental roof. But here was none of all that turmoil of the world at large, where he did not know his right place and took mistaken decisions; here was no Sónya with whom he ought, or ought not, to have an explanation; here was no possibility of going there or not going there; here there were not twenty-four hours in the day which could be spent in such a variety of ways; there was not that innumerable crowd of people of whom not one was nearer to him or farther from him than another; there were none of those uncertain and undefined money relations with his father, and nothing to recall that terrible loss to Dólokhov. Here, in the regiment, all was clear and simple. The whole world was divided into two unequal parts: one, our Pávlograd regiment; the other, all the rest. And the rest was no concern of his. In the regiment, everything was definite: who was lieutenant, who captain, who was a good fellow, who a bad one, and most of all, who was a comrade. The canteen-keeper gave one credit, one's pay came every four months, there was nothing to think out or decide, you had only to do nothing that was considered bad in the Pávlograd regiment and, when given an order, to do what was clearly, distinctly, and definitely ordered—and all would be well.

Having once more entered into the definite conditions of this regimental life, Rostóv felt the joy and relief a tired man feels on lying down to rest. Life in the regiment, during this campaign, was all the pleasanter for him, because, after his loss to Dólokhov (for which, in spite of all his family's efforts to console him, he could not forgive himself), he had made up his mind to atone for his fault by serving, not as he had done before, but really well, and by being a perfectly first rate comrade and officer—in a word, a splendid man altogether, a thing which seemed so difficult out *in the world,* but so possible in the regiment.

After his losses, he had determined to pay back his debt to his parents in five years. He received ten thousand rubles a year, but now resolved to take only two thousand and leave the rest to repay the debt to his parents.

Our army, after repeated retreats and advances and battles at Pultúsk and Preussisch-Eylau, was concentrated near Bartenstein. It was awaiting the Emperor's arrival and the beginning of a new campaign.

The Pávlograd regiment, belonging to that part of the army which had served in the 1805 campaign, had been recruiting up to strength in Russia, and arrived too late to take part in the first actions of the campaign. It had been neither at Pultúsk nor at Preussisch-Eylau and, when it joined the army in the field in the second half of the campaign, was attached to Plátov's division.

Plátov's division was acting independently of the main army. Several times parts of the Pávlograd regiment had exchanged shots with the enemy, had taken prisoners, and once had even captured Marshal Oudinot's carriages. In April the Pávlograds were stationed immovably for some weeks near a totally ruined and deserted German village.

A thaw had set in, it was muddy and cold, the ice on the river broke and the roads became impassable. For days neither provisions for the men nor fodder for the horses had been issued. As no transports could arrive, the men dispersed about the abandoned and deserted villages, searching for potatoes, but found few even of these.

Everything had been eaten up and the inhabitants had all fled—if any remained, they were worse than beggars and nothing more could be taken from them; even the soldiers, usually pitiless enough, instead of taking anything from them, often gave them the last of their rations.

The Pávlograd regiment had had only two men wounded in action, but had lost nearly half its men from hunger and sickness. In the hospitals, death was so certain that soldiers suffering from fever, or the swelling that came from bad food, preferred to remain on duty, and hardly able to drag their legs went to the front rather than to the hospitals. When spring came on, the soldiers found a plant just showing out of the ground that looked like asparagus, which for some reason, they called "Máshka's sweet root." It was very bitter, but they wandered about the fields seeking it and dug it out with their sabers and ate it, though they were ordered not to do so, as it was a noxious plant. That spring a new disease broke out among the soldiers, a swelling of the arms, legs, and face, which the doctors attributed to eating this root. But in spite of all this, the soldiers of Denísov's squadron fed chiefly on "Máshka's sweet root," because it was the second week that the last of the biscuits were being doled out at the rate of half a pound a man and the last potatoes received had sprouted and frozen.

The horses also had been fed for a fortnight on straw from the thatched roofs, and had become terribly thin, though still covered with tufts of felty winter hair.

Despite this destitution, the soldiers and officers went on living just as usual. Despite their pale swollen faces and tattered uniforms, the hussars formed line for roll-call, kept things in order, groomed their horses, polished their arms, brought in straw from the thatched roofs in place of fodder, and sat down to dine round the caldrons from which they rose up hungry, joking about their nasty food and their hunger. As usual, in their spare time, they lit bonfires, steamed themselves before them naked; smoked, picked out and baked sprouting rotten potatoes, told and listened to stories of Potëmkin's and Suvórov's campaigns, or to legends of Alësha the Sly, or the priest's laborer Mikólka.

The officers, as usual, lived in twos and threes in the roofless, half-ruined houses. The seniors tried to collect straw and potatoes and, in general, food for the men. The younger ones occupied themselves as before, some playing cards (there was plenty of money, though there was no food), some with more innocent games, such as quoits and skittles. The general trend of the campaign was rarely spoken of, partly because nothing certain was known about it, partly because there was a vague feeling that in the main it was going badly.

Rostóv lived, as before, with Denísov, and since their furlough they had become more friendly than ever. Denísov never spoke of Rostóv's family, but by the tender friendship his commander showed him, Rostóv felt that the elder hussar's luckless love for Natásha played a part in strengthening their friendship. Denísov evidently tried to expose Rostóv to danger as seldom as possible, and after an action greeted his safe return with evident joy. On one of his foraging expeditions, in a deserted and ruined village to which he had come in search of provisions, Rostóv found a family consisting of an old Pole and his daughter with an infant in arms. They were half-clad, hungry, too weak to get away on foot and had no means of obtaining a conveyance. Rostóv brought them to his quarters, placed them in his own lodging, and kept them for some weeks while the old man was recovering. One of his comrades, talking of women, began chaffing Rostóv, saying that he was more wily than any of them and that it would not be a bad thing if he introduced to them the pretty Polish girl he had saved. Rostóv took the joke as an insult, flared up, and said such unpleasant things to the officer that it was all Denísov could do to prevent a duel. When the officer had gone away, Denísov, who did not himself know what Rostóv's relations with the Polish girl might be, began to upbraid him for his quickness of temper, and Rostóv replied:

"Say what you like. . . . She is like a sister to me, and I can't tell you how it offended me . . . because . . . well, for that reason. . . ."

Denísov patted him on the shoulder, and began rapidly pacing the room without looking at Rostóv, as was his way at moments of deep feeling.

"Ah, what a mad bweed you Wostóvs are!" he muttered, and Rostóv noticed tears in his eyes.

Chapter XVI

In April the troops were enlivened by news of the emperor's arrival, but Rostóv had no chance of being present at the review he held at Bartenstein, as the Pávlograds were at the outposts far beyond that place.

They were bivouacking. Denísov and Rostóv were living in an earth hut, dug out for them by the soldiers and roofed with branches and turf. The hut was made in the following manner, which had then come into vogue. A trench was dug three and a half feet wide, four feet eight inches deep, and eight feet long. At one end of the trench, steps were cut out and these formed the entrance and vestibule. The trench itself was the room, in which the lucky ones, such as the squadron commander, had a board, lying on piles at the end opposite the entrance, to serve as a table. On each side of the trench, the earth was cut out to a breadth of about two and a half feet, and this did duty for bedsteads and couches. The roof was so constructed that one could stand up in the middle of the trench and could even sit up on the beds if one drew close to the table. Denísov, who was living luxuriously because the soldiers of his squadron liked him, had also a board in the roof at the farther end, with a piece of (broken but mended) glass in it for a window. When it was very cold, embers from the soldiers' campfire were placed on a bent sheet of iron on the steps in the "reception room"— as Denísov called that part of the hut—and it was then so warm that the officers, of whom there were always some with Denísov and Rostóv, sat in their shirt-sleeves.

In April, Rostóv was on orderly duty. One morning, between seven and eight, returning after a sleepless night, he sent for embers, changed his rain-soaked underclothes, said his prayers, drank tea, got warm, then tidied up the things on the table and in his own corner and, his face glowing from exposure to the wind and with nothing on but his shirt, lay down on his back, putting his arms under his head. He was pleasantly considering the probability of being promoted in a few days for his last reconnoitering expedition, and was awaiting Denísov, who had gone out somewhere and with whom he wanted a talk.

Suddenly he heard Denísov shouting in a vibrating voice behind the hut, evidently much excited. Rostóv moved to the window to see whom he was speaking to, and saw the quartermaster, Topchéenko.

"I ordered you not to let them eat that Máshka woot stuff!" Denísov was shouting. "And I saw with my own eyes how Lazarchúk bwought some fwom the fields."

"I have given the order again and again, your honor, but they don't obey," answered the quartermaster.

Rostóv lay down again on his bed, and thought complacently: "Let him fuss and bustle now, my job's done and I'm lying down—capitally!" He could hear that Lavrúshka—that sly, bold orderly of Denísov's—was talking, as well as the quartermaster. Lavrúshka was saying something about loaded wagons, biscuits and oxen he had seen when he had gone out for provisions.

Then Denísov's voice was heard shouting farther and farther away. "Saddle! Second platoon!"

"Where are they off to now?" thought Rostóv.

Five minutes later, Denísov came into the hut, climbed with muddy boots on the bed, lit his pipe, furiously scattered his things about, took his leaded whip, buckled on his saber, and went out again. In answer to Rostóv's inquiry where he was going, he answered vaguely and crossly that he had some business.

"Let God and our gweat monarch judge me afterward!" said Denísov going out, and Rostóv heard the hoofs of several horses splashing through the mud. He did not even trouble to find out where Denísov had gone. Having got warm in his corner, he fell asleep and did not leave the hut till toward evening. Denísov had not yet returned. The weather had cleared up, and near the next hut two officers and a cadet were playing sváyka, laughing as they threw their missiles which buried themselves in the soft mud. Rostóv joined them. In the middle of the game, the officers saw some wagons approaching with fifteen hussars on their skinny horses behind them. The wagons escorted by the hussars drew up to the picket ropes and a crowd of hussars surrounded them.

"There now, Denísov has been worrying," said Rostóv, "and here are the provisions."

"So they are!" said the officers. "Won't the soldiers be glad!"

A little behind the hussars came Denísov, accompanied by two infantry officers with whom he was talking.

Rostóv went to meet them.

"I warn you, captain," one of the officers, a short thin man, evidently very angry, was saying.

"Haven't I told you I won't give them up?" replied Denísov.

"You will answer for it, captain. It is mutiny—seizing the transport of one's own army. Our men have had nothing to eat for two days."

"And mine have had nothing for two weeks," said Denísov.

"It is robbery! You'll answer for it, sir!" said the infantry officer, raising his voice.

"Now, what are you pestewing me for?" cried Denísov, suddenly losing his temper. "I shall answer for it and not you, and you'd better not buzz about here till you get hurt. Be off! Go!" he shouted at the officers.

"Very well, then!" shouted the little officer, undaunted and not riding away. "If you are determined to rob, I'll . . ."

"Go to the devil! Quick ma'ch, while you're safe and sound!" and Denísov turned his horse on the officer.

"Very well, very well!" muttered the officer threateningly, and turning his horse he trotted away, jolting in his saddle.

"A dog astwide a fence! A weal dog astwide a fence!" shouted Denísov after him (the most insulting expression a cavalryman can address to a mounted infantryman) and riding up to Rostóv, he burst out laughing.

"I've taken twansports from the infantwy by force!" he said. "After all, can't let our men starve."

The wagons that had reached the hussars had been consigned to an infantry regiment, but learning from Lavrúshka that the transport was unescorted, Denísov with his hussars had seized it by force. The soldiers had biscuits dealt out to them freely, and they even shared them with the other squadrons.

The next day the regimental commander sent for Denísov, and holding his fingers spread out before his eyes said:

"This is how I look at this affair: I know nothing about it and won't begin proceedings, but I advise you to ride over to the staff, and settle the business there in the commissariat department and if possible sign a receipt for such and such stores received. If not, as the demand was booked against an infantry regiment, there will be a row and the affair may end badly."

From the regimental commander's, Denísov rode straight to the staff with a sincere desire to act on this advice. In the evening he came back to his dug-out in a state such as Rostóv had never yet seen him in. Denísov could not speak, and gasped for breath. When Rostóv asked what was the matter, he only uttered some incoherent oaths and threats in a hoarse feeble voice.

Alarmed at Denísov's condition, Rostóv suggested that he should undress, drink some water and send for the doctor.

"Twy me for wobbewy . . . oh! Some more water . . . Let them twy me, but I'll always thwash scoundwels . . . and I'll tell the Empewo' . . . Ice . . ." he muttered.

The regimental doctor, when he came, said it was absolutely necessary to bleed Denísov. A deep saucer of black blood was taken from his hairy arm, and only then was he able to relate what had happened to him.

"I get there," began Denísov. " 'Now then, where's your chief's quarters?' They were pointed out. 'Please to wait.' 'I've widden twenty miles and have duties to attend to and no time to wait. Announce me.' Vewy well, so out comes their head thief—also took it into his head to lecture me: 'It's wobbewy!'—'Wobbewy,' I say, 'is not done by man who seizes pwovisions to feed his soldiers, but by him who takes them to fill his own pockets!' 'Will you please be silent?' 'Vewy good!' Then he says: 'Go and give a weceipt to the commissioner, but your affair will be passed on to headquarters.' I go to the commissioner. I enter, and at the table . . . who do you think? No, but wait a bit! . . . Who is it that's starving us?" shouted Denísov, hitting the table with the fist of his newly-bled arm so violently that the table nearly broke down and the tumblers on it jumped about. "Telyánin! 'What? So it's you who's starving us to death! Is it? Take this and this!' and I hit him so pat, stwaight on his snout . . . 'Ah, what a . . . what a . . . !' and I sta'ted fwashing him . . . Well, I've had a bit of fun I can tell you!" cried Denísov, gleeful and yet angry, his white teeth showing under his black mustache. "I'd have killed him if they hadn't taken him away!"

"But what are you shouting for? Calm yourself," said Rostóv. "You've set your arm bleeding afresh. Wait, we must tie it up again."

Denísov was bandaged up again and put to bed. Next day he woke calm and cheerful.

But at noon the adjutant of the regiment came into Rostóv's and Denísov's dug-out with a grave and serious face, and regretfully showed them a paper addressed to Major Denísov from the regimental commander in which inquiries were made about yesterday's occurrence. The adjutant told them that the affair was likely to take a very bad turn: that a court-martial had been appointed, and that in view of the severity with which marauding and insubordination were now regarded, degradation to the ranks would be the best that could be hoped for.

The case, as represented by the offended parties, was that, after seizing the transport, Major Denísov, being drunk, went to the chief quartermaster and without any provocation called him a thief, threatened to strike him, and on being led out had rushed into the office and given two officials a thrashing, and dislocated the arm of one of them.

In answer to Rostóv's renewed questions, Denísov said, laughing, that he thought he remembered that some other fellow had got mixed up in it, but that it was all nonsense and rubbish, and he did not in the least fear any kind of trial, and that if those scoundrels dared attack him he would give them an answer that they would not easily forget.

Denísov spoke contemptuously of the whole matter, but Rostóv knew him too well not to detect that (while hiding it from others) at heart he feared a court-martial and was worried over the affair, which was evidently taking a bad turn. Every day, letters of inquiry and notices from the Court arrived, and on the first of May, Denísov was ordered to hand the squadron over to the next in seniority and appear before the staff of his division to explain his violence at the commissariat office. On the previous day Plátov reconnoitered with two Cossack regiments and two squadrons of hussars. Denísov, as was his wont, rode out in front of the outposts parading his courage. A bullet fired by a French sharpshooter hit him in the fleshy part of his leg. Perhaps at another time Denísov would not have left the regiment for so slight a wound, but now he took advantage of it to excuse himself from appearing at the staff, and went into hospital.

Chapter XVII

In June the battle of Friedland was fought, in which the Pávlograds did not take part, and after that an armistice was proclaimed. Rostóv, who felt his friend's absence very much, having no news of him since he left and feeling very anxious about his wound and the progress of his affairs, took advantage of the armistice to get leave to visit Denísov in hospital.

The hospital was in a small Prussian town that had been twice devastated by Russian and French troops. Because it was summer, when it is so beautiful out in the fields, the little town presented a particularly dismal appearance with its broken roofs and fences, its foul streets, tattered inhabitants, and the sick and drunken soldiers wandering about.

The hospital was in a brick building with some of the window frames and panes broken, and a courtyard surrounded by the remains of a wooden fence that had been pulled to pieces. Several bandaged soldiers, with pale swollen faces, were sitting or walking about in the sunshine in the yard.

Directly Rostóv entered the door he was enveloped by a smell of putrefaction and hospital air. On the stairs he met a Russian army doctor smoking a cigar. The doctor was followed by a Russian assistant.

"I can't tear myself to pieces," the doctor was saying. "Come to Makár Alexéevich in the evening. I shall be there."

The assistant asked some further questions.

"Oh, do the best you can! Isn't it all the same?" The doctor noticed Rostóv coming upstairs.

"Who do you want, sir?" said the doctor. "What do you want? The bullets having spared you, do you want to try typhus? This is a pest house, sir."

"How so?" asked Rostóv.

"Typhus, sir. It's death to go in. Only we two, Makéev and I" (he pointed to the assistant), "keep on here. Some five of us doctors have died in this place. . . . When a new one comes he is done for in a week," said the doctor with evident satisfaction. "Prussian doctors have been invited here, but our allies don't like it at all."

Rostóv explained that he wanted to see Major Denísov of the hussars, who was wounded.

"I don't know. I can't tell you, sir. Only think! I am alone in charge of three hospitals with more than four hundred patients! It's well that the charitable Prussian ladies send us two pounds of coffee and some lint each month or we should be lost!" he laughed. "Four hundred, sir, and they're always sending me fresh ones. There *are* four hundred? Eh?" he asked, turning to the assistant.

The assistant looked fagged out. He was evidently vexed, and impatient for the talkative doctor to go.

"Major Denísov," Rostóv said again. "He was wounded at Molliten."

"Dead, I fancy. Eh, Makéev?" queried the doctor, in a tone of indifference.

The assistant, however, did not confirm the doctor's words.

"Is he tall and with reddish hair?" asked the doctor.

Rostóv described Denísov's appearance.

"There was one like that," said the doctor, as if pleased. "That one is dead, I fancy. However, I'll look up our list. We had a list. Have you got it, Makéev?"

"Makár Alexéevich has the list," answered the assistant. "But if you'll step into the officers' wards you'll see for yourself," he added, turning to Rostóv.

"Ah, you'd better not go, sir," said the doctor, "or you may have to stay here yourself."

But Rostóv bowed himself away from the doctor and asked the assistant to show him the way.

"Only don't blame me!" the doctor shouted up after him.

Rostóv and the assistant went into the dark corridor. The smell was so strong there that Rostóv held his nose, and had to pause and collect his strength before he could go on. A door opened to the right, and an emaciated sallow man on crutches, barefoot and in underclothing, limped out, and leaning against the doorpost, looked with glittering envious eyes at those who were passing. Glancing in at the door, Rostóv saw that the sick and wounded were lying on the floor on straw and overcoats.

"May I go in and look?"

"What is there to see?" said the assistant.

But, just because the assistant evidently did not want him to go in, Rostóv entered the soldiers' ward. The foul air to which he had already begun to get used in the corridor, was still stronger here. It was a little different, more pungent, and one felt that this was where it originated.

In the long room, brightly lit up by the sun through the large windows, the sick and wounded lay in two rows with their heads to the walls, and leaving a passage in the middle. Most of them were unconscious and paid no attention to the newcomers. Those who were conscious raised themselves or lifted their thin yellow faces, and all looked intently at Rostóv with the same expression of hope, of relief, reproach, and envy of another's health. Rostóv went to the middle of the room, and looking through the open doors into the two adjoining rooms saw the same thing there. He stood still, looking silently around. He had not at all expected such a sight. Just before him, almost across the middle of the passage on the bare floor, lay a sick man, probably a Cossack to judge by the cut of his hair. The man lay on his back, his huge arms and legs outstretched. His face was purple, his eyes were rolled back so that only the whites were seen, and on his bare legs and arms which were still red, the veins stood out like cords. He was knocking the back of his head against the floor, hoarsely uttering some word which he kept repeating. Rostóv listened and made out the word. It was "drink, drink, a drink!" Rostóv glanced round, looking for someone who would put this man back in his place and bring him water.

"Who looks after the sick here?" he asked the assistant.

Just then a commissariat soldier, a hospital orderly, came in from the next room, marching stiffly, and drew up in front of Rostóv.

"Good day, your honor!" he shouted, rolling his eyes at Rostóv and evidently mistaking him for one of the hospital authorities.

"Get him to his place and give him some water," said Rostóv, pointing to the Cossack.

"Yes, your honor," the soldier replied complacently, and rolling his eyes more than ever he drew himself up still straighter, but did not move.

"No, it's impossible to do anything here," thought Rostóv, lowering his eyes, and he was going out, but became aware of an intense look fixed on him on his right, and he turned. Close to the corner, on an overcoat, sat an old, unshaven, gray-bearded soldier as thin as a skeleton, with a stern sallow face and eyes intently fixed on Rostóv. The man's neighbor on one side whispered something to him, pointing at Rostóv, who noticed that the old man wanted to speak to him. He drew nearer and saw that the old man had only one leg bent under him, the other had been amputated above the knee. His neighbor on the other side, who lay motionless some distance from him with his head thrown back, was a young soldier with a snub nose. His pale waxen face was still freckled and his eyes were rolled back. Rostóv looked at the young soldier and a cold chill ran down his back.

"Why, this one seems . . ." he began, turning to the assistant.

"And how we've been begging, your honor," said the old soldier, his jaw quivering. "He's been dead since morning. After all we're men, not dogs."

"I'll send someone at once. He shall be taken away—taken away at once," said the assistant hurriedly. "Let us go, your honor."

"Yes, yes, let us go," said Rostóv hastily, and lowering his eyes and shrinking, he tried to pass unnoticed between the rows of reproachful envious eyes that were fixed upon him, and went out of the room.

Chapter XVIII

GOING ALONG THE CORRIDOR, THE ASSISTANT LED ROSTÓV TO THE OFFICERS' WARDS, CONSISTing of three rooms, the doors of which stood open. There were beds in these rooms and the sick and wounded officers were lying or sitting on them. Some were walking about the rooms in hospital dressing-gowns. The first person Rostóv met in the officers' ward was a thin little man with one arm, who was walking about the first room in a nightcap and hospital dressing-gown, with a pipe between his teeth. Rostóv looked at him, trying to remember where he had seen him before.

"See where we've met again!" said the little man. "Túshin, Túshin, don't you remember, who gave you a lift at Schön Grabern? And I've had a bit cut off, you see . . ." he went on with a smile, pointing to the empty sleeve of his dressing-gown. "Looking for Vasíli Dmítrich Denísov? My neighbor," he added, when he heard who Rostóv wanted. "Here, here," and Túshin led him into the next room, from whence came sounds of several laughing voices.

"How can they laugh, or even live at all here?" thought Rostóv, still aware of that smell of decomposing flesh that had been so strong in the soldiers' ward, and still seeming to see fixed on him those envious looks which had followed him out from both sides, and the face of that young soldier with eyes rolled back.

Denísov lay asleep on his bed with his head under the blanket, though it was nearly noon.

"Ah, Wostóv? How are you, how are you?" he called out, still in the same voice as in the regiment, but Rostóv noticed sadly that under this habitual ease and animation some new, sinister, hidden feeling showed itself in the expression of Denísov's face and the intonations of his voice.

His wound, though a slight one, had not yet healed even now, six weeks after he had been hit. His face had the same swollen pallor as the faces of the other hospital patients, but it was not this that struck Rostóv. What struck him was that Denísov did not seem glad to see him, and smiled at him unnaturally. He did not ask about the regiment, nor about the general state of affairs, and when Rostóv spoke of these matters did not listen.

Rostóv even noticed that Denísov did not like to be reminded of the regiment, or in general of that other free life which was going on outside the hospital. He seemed to try to forget that old life and was only interested in the affair with the commissariat officers. On Rostóv's inquiry as to how the matter stood, he at once produced from under his pillow a paper he had received from the commission and the rough draft of his answer to it. He became animated when he began reading his paper, and specially drew Rostóv's attention to the stinging rejoinders he made to his enemies. His hospital companions, who had gathered round Rostóv—a fresh arrival from the world outside—gradually began to disperse as soon as Denísov began reading his answer. Rostóv noticed by their faces that all those gentlemen had already heard that story more than once and were tired of it. Only the man who had the next bed, a stout Uhlan, continued to sit on his bed, gloomily frowning and smoking a pipe, and little one-armed Túshin still listened, shaking his head disapprovingly. In the middle of the reading, the Uhlan interrupted Denísov.

"But what I say is," he said, turning to Rostóv, "it would be best simply to petition the Emperor for pardon. They say great rewards will now be distributed, and surely a pardon would be granted. . . ."

"Me petition the Empewo'!" exclaimed Denísov, in a voice to which he tried hard to give the old energy and fire, but which sounded like an expression of irritable impotence. "What for? If I were a wobber I would ask mercy, but I'm being court-martialed for bwinging wobbers to book. Let them twy me, I'm not afwaid of anyone. I've served the Tsar and my countwy honowably and have not stolen! And am I to be degwaded? . . . Listen, I'm w'iting to them stwaight. This is what I say: 'If I had wobbed the Tweasuwy . . . ' "

"It's certainly well written," said Túshin, "but that's not the point, Vasíli Dmítrich," and he also turned to Rostóv. "One has to submit, and Vasíli Dmítrich doesn't want to. You know the auditor told you it was a bad business."

"Well, let it be bad," said Denísov.

"The auditor wrote out a petition for you," continued Túshin, "and you ought to sign it and ask this gentleman to take it. No doubt he" (indicating Rostóv) "has connections on the staff. You won't find a better opportunity."

"Haven't I said I'm not going to gwovel?" Denísov interrupted him, and went on reading his paper.

Rostóv had not the courage to persuade Denísov, though he instinctively felt that the way advised by Túshin and the other officers was the safest, and though he would have been glad to be of service to Denísov. He knew his stubborn will and straightforward hasty temper.

When the reading of Denísov's virulent reply, which took more than an hour, was over, Rostóv said nothing, and he spent the rest of the day in a most dejected state of mind amid Denísov's hospital comrades, who had gathered round him, telling them what he knew and listening to their stories. Denísov was moodily silent all the evening.

Late in the evening, when Rostóv was about to leave, he asked Denísov whether he had no commission for him.

"Yes, wait a bit," said Denísov, glancing round at the officers, and taking his papers from under his pillow he went to the window, where he had an inkpot, and sat down to write.

"It seems it's no use knocking one's head against a wall!" he said, coming from the window and giving Rostóv a large envelope. In it was the petition to the Emperor drawn up by the auditor, in which Denísov, without alluding to the offenses of the commissariat officials, simply asked for pardon.

"Hand it in. It seems . . ."

He did not finish, but gave a painfully unnatural smile.

Chapter XIX

Having returned to the regiment and told the commander the state of Denísov's affairs, Rostóv rode to Tilsit with the letter to the Emperor.

On the 13th of June the French and Russian Emperors arrived in Tilsit. Borís Drubetskóy had asked the important personage on whom he was in attendance, to include him in the suite appointed for the stay at Tilsit.

"I should like to see the great man," he said alluding to Napoleon, whom hitherto he, like everyone else, had always called Buonaparte.

"You are speaking of Buonaparte?" asked the general, smiling.

Borís looked at his general inquiringly and immediately saw that he was being tested.

"I am speaking, prince, of the Emperor Napoleon," he replied. The general patted him on the shoulder, with a smile.

"You will go far," he said, and took him to Tilsit with him.

Borís was among the few present at the Niemen on the day the two Emperors met. He saw the raft, decorated with monograms, saw Napoleon pass before the French Guards on the farther bank of the river, saw the pensive face of the Emperor Alexander as he sat in silence in a tavern on the bank of the Niemen awaiting Napoleon's arrival, saw both Emperors get into boats, and saw how Napoleon—reaching the raft first—stepped quickly forward to meet Alexander and held out his hand to him, and how they both retired into the pavilion. Since he had begun to move in the highest circles Borís had made it his habit to watch attentively all that went on around him and to note it down. At the time of the meeting at Tilsit he asked the names of those who had come with Napoleon and about the uniforms they wore, and listened attentively to words spoken by important personages. At the moment the Emperors went into the pavilion he looked at his watch, and did not forget to look at it again when Alexander came out. The interview had lasted an hour and fifty-three minutes. He noted this down that same evening, among other facts he felt to be of historic importance. As the Emperor's suite was a very small one, it was a matter of great importance, for a man who valued his success in the service, to be at Tilsit on the occasion of this interview between the two Emperors, and having succeeded in this, Borís felt that henceforth his position was fully assured. He had not only become known, but people had grown accustomed to him and accepted him. Twice he had executed commissions to the Emperor himself, so that the latter knew his face, and all those at Court, far from cold-shouldering him as at first when they considered him a newcomer, would now have been surprised had he been absent.

Borís lodged with another adjutant, the Polish Count Zhilínski. Zhilínski, a Pole brought up in Paris, was rich, and passionately fond of the French, and almost every day of the stay at Tilsit, French officers of the Guard and from French headquarters were dining and lunching with him and Borís.

On the evening of the 24th of June, Count Zhilínski arranged a supper for his French friends. The guest of honor was an aide-de-camp of Napoleon's, there were also several French officers of the Guard, and a page of Napoleon's, a young lad of an old aristocratic French family. That same-day, Rostóv, profiting by the darkness to avoid being recognized in civilian dress, came to Tilsit and went to the lodging occupied by Borís and Zhilínski.

Rostóv, in common with the whole army from which he came, was far from having experienced the change of feeling toward Napoleon and the French—who from being foes had suddenly become friends—that had taken place at headquarters and in Borís. In the army, Bonaparte and the French were still regarded with mingled feelings of anger, contempt, and fear. Only recently, talking with one of Plátov's Cossack officers, Rostóv had argued that if Napoleon were taken prisoner he would be treated not as a sovereign, but as a criminal. Quite lately, happening to meet a wounded French colonel on the road, Rostóv had maintained with heat that peace was impossible between a legitimate sovereign and the criminal Bonaparte. Rostóv was therefore unpleasantly struck by the presence of French officers in Borís's lodging, dressed in uniforms he had been accustomed to see from quite a different point of view from the outposts of the flank. As soon as he noticed a French officer, who thrust his head out of the door, that warlike feeling of hostility which he always experienced at the sight of the enemy, suddenly seized him. He stopped at the threshold and asked in Russian whether Drubetskóy lived there. Borís, hearing a strange voice in the anteroom, came out to meet him. An expression of annoyance showed itself for a moment on his face on first recognizing Rostóv.

"Ah, it's you? Very glad, very glad to see you," he said however, coming toward him with a smile. But Rostóv had noticed his first impulse.

"I've come at a bad time I think. I should not have come, but I have business," he said coldly.

"No, I only wonder how you managed to get away from your regiment. *Dans un moment je suis à vous,*" he said, answering someone who called him.

"I see I'm intruding," Rostóv repeated.

The look of annoyance had already disappeared from Borís's face: having evidently reflected and decided how to act, he very quietly took both Rostóv's hands and led him into the next room. His eyes, looking serenely and steadily at Rostóv, seemed to be veiled by something, as if screened by blue spectacles of conventionality. So it seemed to Rostóv.

"Oh, come now! As if you could come at a wrong time!" said Borís, and he led him into the room where the supper table was laid and introduced him to his guests, explaining that he was not a civilian, but a hussar officer, and an old friend of his.

"Count Zhilínski—*le Comte N. N.—le Capitaine S. S.,*" said he, naming his guests. Rostóv looked frowningly at the Frenchmen, bowed reluctantly, and remained silent.

Zhilínski evidently did not receive this new Russian person very willingly into his circle, and did not speak to Rostóv. Borís did not appear to notice the constraint the newcomer produced, and with the same pleasant composure and the same veiled look in his eyes with which he had met Rostóv, tried to enliven the conversation. One of the Frenchmen, with the politeness characteristic of his countrymen, addressed the obstinately taciturn Rostóv, saying that the latter had probably come to Tilsit to see the Emperor.

"No, I came on business," replied Rostóv, briefly.

Rostóv had been out of humor from the moment he noticed the look of dissatisfaction on

Borís's face, and as always happens to those in a bad humor, it seemed to him that everyone regarded him with aversion and that he was in everybody's way. He really was in their way, for he alone took no part in the conversation which again became general. The looks the visitors cast on him seemed to say: "And what is he sitting here for?" He rose and went up to Borís.

"Anyhow, I'm in your way," he said in a low tone. "Come and talk over my business and I'll go away."

"Oh, no, not at all," said Borís. "But if you are tired, come and lie down in my room and have a rest."

"Yes, really . . ."

They went into the little room where Borís slept. Rostóv, without sitting down, began at once, irritably (as if Borís were to blame in some way) telling him about Denísov's affair, asking him whether, through his general, he could and would intercede with the Emperor on Denísov's behalf and get Denísov's petition handed in. When he and Borís were alone, Rostóv felt for the first time that he could not look Borís in the face without a sense of awkwardness. Borís, with one leg crossed over the other and stroking his left hand with the slender fingers of his right, listened to Rostóv as a general listens to the report of a subordinate, now looking aside and now gazing straight into Rostóv's eyes with the same veiled look. Each time this happened Rostóv felt uncomfortable and cast down his eyes.

"I have heard of such cases and know that his Majesty is very severe in such affairs. I think it would be best not to bring it before the Emperor, but to apply to the commander of the corps. . . . But in general, I think . . ."

"So you don't want to do anything? Well then, say so!" Rostóv almost shouted, not looking Borís in the face.

Borís smiled.

"On the contrary, I will do what I can. Only I thought . . ."

At that moment Zhilínski's voice was heard calling Borís.

"Well then, go, go, go . . ." said Rostóv, and refusing supper and remaining alone in the little room, he walked up and down for a long time, hearing the light-hearted French conversation from the next room.

Chapter XX

Rostóv had come to Tilsit the day least suitable for a petition on Denísov's behalf. He could not himself go to the general in attendance as he was in mufti and had come to Tilsit without permission to do so, and Borís, even had he wished to, could not have done so on the following day. On that day, June 27th, the preliminaries of peace were signed. The Emperors exchanged decorations: Alexander received the Cross of the Legion of Honor, and Napoleon the Order of St. Andrew of the First Degree, and a dinner had been arranged for the evening, given by a battalion of the French Guards to the Preobrazhénsk battalion. The Emperors were to be present at that banquet.

Rostóv felt so ill at ease and uncomfortable with Borís, that, when the latter looked in after supper, he pretended to be asleep, and early next morning went away, avoiding Borís. In his civilian clothes and a round hat, he wandered about the town, staring at the French and their uniforms and at the streets and houses where the Russian and French Emperors were staying. In a square he saw tables being set up and preparations made for the dinner; he saw the Russian and French colors draped from side to side of the streets, with huge monograms A. and N. In the windows of the houses also flags and bunting were displayed.

"Borís doesn't want to help me and I don't want to ask him. That's settled," thought Nicholas. "All is over between us, but I won't leave here without having done all I can for Denísov and certainly not without getting his letter to the Emperor. The Emperor! . . . He is here!" thought Rostóv, who had unconsciously returned to the house where Alexander lodged.

Saddled horses were standing before the house and the suite were assembling, evidently preparing for the Emperor to come out.

"I may see him at any moment," thought Rostóv. "If only I were to hand the letter direct to him and tell him all . . . could they really arrest me for my civilian clothes? Surely not! He would understand on whose side justice lies. He understands everything, knows everything. Who can be more just, more magnanimous than he? And even if they did arrest me for being here, what would it matter?" thought he, looking at an officer who was entering the house the Emperor occupied. "After all, people do go in. . . . It's all nonsense! I'll go in and hand the letter to the Emperor myself, so much the worse for Drubetskóy who drives me to it!" And suddenly with a determination he himself did not expect, Rostóv felt for the letter in his pocket and went straight to the house.

"No, I won't miss my opportunity now, as I did after Austerlitz," he thought, expecting every moment to meet the monarch, and conscious of the blood that rushed to his heart at the thought. "I will fall at his feet and beseech him. He will lift me up, will listen, and will even thank me. 'I am happy when I can do good, but to remedy injustice is the greatest happiness,' " Rostóv fancied the sovereign saying. And passing people who looked after him with curiosity, he entered the porch of the Emperor's house.

A broad staircase led straight up from the entry, and to the right he saw a closed door. Below, under the staircase, was a door leading to the lower floor.

"Whom do you want?" someone inquired.

"To hand in a letter, a petition, to his Majesty," said Nicholas, with a tremor in his voice.

"A petition? This way, to the officer on duty" (he was shown the door leading downstairs), "only it won't be accepted."

On hearing this indifferent voice, Rostóv grew frightened at what he was doing; the thought of meeting the Emperor at any moment was so fascinating and consequently so alarming that he was ready to run away, but the official who had questioned him opened the door, and Rostóv entered.

A short stout man of about thirty, in white breeches and high boots and a batiste shirt that he had evidently only just put on, was standing in that room, and his valet was buttoning on to the back of his breeches a new pair of handsome silk-embroidered braces that, for some reason, attracted Rostóv's attention. This man was was speaking to someone in the adjoining room.

"A good figure and in her first bloom," he was saying, but on seeing Rostóv, he stopped short and frowned.

"What is it? A petition?"

"What is it?" asked the person in the other room.

"Another petitioner," answered the man with the braces.

"Tell him to come later. He'll be coming out directly, we must go."

"Later . . . later! Tomorrow. It's too late . . ."

Rostóv turned and was about to go, but the man in the braces stopped him.

"Whom have you come from? Who are you?"

"I come from Major Denísov," answered Rostóv.

"Are you an officer?"

"Lieutenant Count Rostóv."

"What audacity! Hand it in through your commander. And go along with you . . . go," and he continued to put on the uniform the valet handed him.

Rostóv went back into the hall and noticed that in the porch there were many officers and generals in full parade uniform, whom he had to pass.

Cursing his temerity, his heart sinking at the thought of finding himself at any moment face to face with the Emperor and being put to shame and arrested in his presence, fully alive now to the impropriety of his conduct and repenting of it, Rostóv, with downcast eyes, was making his way out of the house through the brilliant suite when a familiar voice called him and a hand detained him.

"What are you doing here, sir, in civilian dress?" asked a deep voice.

It was a cavalry general who had obtained the Emperor's special favor during this campaign, and who had formerly commanded the division in which Rostóv was serving.

Rostóv, in dismay, began justifying himself, but seeing the kindly, jocular face of the general, he took him aside and in an excited voice told him the whole affair, asking him to intercede for Denísov, whom the general knew. Having heard Rostóv to the end, the general shook his head gravely.

"I'm sorry, sorry for that fine fellow. Give me the letter."

Hardly had Rostóv handed him the letter and finished explaining Denísov's case, when hasty steps and the jingling of spurs were heard on the stairs, and the general, leaving him, went to the porch. The gentlemen of the Emperor's suite ran down the stairs, and went to their horses. Hayne, the same groom who had been at Austerlitz, led up the Emperor's horse, and the faint creak of a footstep Rostóv knew at once, was heard on the stairs. Forgetting the danger of being recognized, Rostóv went close to the porch, together with some inquisitive civilians, and again, after two years, saw those features he adored: that same face and same look and step, and the same union of majesty and mildness. . . . And the feeling of enthusiasm and love for his sovereign rose again in Rostóv's soul in all its old force. In the uniform of the Preobrazhénsk regiment—white chamois-leather breeches and high boots—and wearing a star Rostóv did not know (it was that of the *Légion d'honneur*), the monarch came out into the porch, putting on his gloves and carrying his hat under his arm. He stopped and looked about him, brightening everything around by his glance. He spoke a few words to some of the generals, and recognizing the former commander of Rostóv's division, smiled and beckoned to him.

All the suite drew back and Rostóv saw the general talking for some time to the Emperor.

The Emperor said a few words to him and took a step toward his horse. Again the crowd of members of the suite and street-gazers (among whom was Rostóv) moved nearer to the Emperor. Stopping beside his horse, with his hand on the saddle, the Emperor turned to the cavalry general and said in a loud voice, evidently wishing to be heard by all:

"I cannot do it, general. I cannot, because the law is stronger than I," and he raised his foot to the stirrup.

The general bowed his head respectfully, and the monarch mounted and rode down the street at a gallop. Beside himself with enthusiasm, Rostóv ran after him with the crowd.

Chapter XXI

THE EMPEROR RODE TO THE SQUARE WHERE, FACING ONE ANOTHER, A BATTALION OF THE PREobrazhénsk regiment stood on the right and a battalion of the French Guards in their bearskin caps on the left.

As the Tsar rode up to one flank of the battalions, which presented arms, another group of horsemen galloped up to the opposite flank, and at the head of them Rostóv recognized Napoleon.

It could be no one else. He came at a gallop, wearing a small hat, a blue uniform open over a white vest, and the St. Andrew ribbon over his shoulder. He was riding a very fine thoroughbred gray Arab horse with a crimson gold-embroidered saddle-cloth. On approaching Alexander he raised his hat, and as he did so, Rostóv, with his cavalryman's eye, could not help noticing that Napoleon did not sit well or firmly in the saddle. The battalions shouted "Hurrah!" and *"Vive l'Empereur!"* Napoleon said something to Alexander, and both Emperors dismounted and took each other's hands. Napoleon's face wore an unpleasant and artificial smile. Alexander was saying something affable to him.

In spite of the trampling of the French gendarmes' horses, which were pushing back the crowd, Rostóv kept his eyes on every movement of Alexander and Bonaparte. It struck him as a surprise that Alexander treated Bonaparte as an equal and that the latter was quite at ease with the Tsar, as if such relations with an Emperor were an everyday matter to him.

Alexander and Napoleon, with the long train of their suites, approached the right flank of the Preobrazhénsk battalion and came straight up to the crowd standing there. The crowd unexpectedly found itself so close to the Emperors that Rostóv, standing in the front row, was afraid he might be recognized.

"Sire, I ask your permission to present the Legion of Honor to the bravest of your soldiers," said a sharp, precise voice, articulating every letter.

This was said by the undersized Napoleon, looking up straight into Alexander's eyes. Alexander listened attentively to what was said to him, and bending his head, smiled pleasantly.

"To him who has borne himself most bravely in this last war," added Napoleon, accentuating each syllable, as with a composure and assurance exasperating to Rostóv, he ran his eyes over the Russian ranks drawn up before him, who all presented arms with their eyes fixed on their Emperor.

"Will your Majesty allow me to consult the colonel?" said Alexander and took a few hasty steps toward Prince Kozlóvski, the commander of the battalion.

Bonaparte meanwhile began taking the glove off his small white hand, tore it in doing so, and threw it away. An aide-de-camp behind him rushed forward and picked it up.

"To whom shall it be given?" the Emperor Alexander asked Kozlóvski, in Russian in a low voice.

"To whomever your Majesty commands."

The Emperor knit his brows with dissatisfaction, and glancing back, remarked:

"But we must give him an answer."

Kozlóvski scanned the ranks resolutely, and included Rostóv in his scrutiny.

"Can it be me?" thought Rostóv.

"Lázarev!" the colonel called, with a frown, and Lázarev, the first soldier in the rank, stepped briskly forward.

"Where are you off to? Stop here!" voices whispered to Lázarev who did not know where to go. Lázarev stopped, casting a side-long look at his colonel in alarm. His face twitched, as often happens to soldiers called before the ranks.

Napoleon slightly turned his head, and put his plump little hand out behind him as if to take something. The members of his suite, guessing at once what he wanted, moved about and whispered as they passed something from one to another, and a page—the same one Rostóv had seen the previous evening at Borís's—ran forward, and bowing respectfully over the outstretched hand and not keeping it waiting a moment, laid in it an Order on a red ribbon. Napoleon, without looking, pressed two fingers together and the badge was between them. Then he approached Lázarev (who rolled his eyes and persistently gazed at his own monarch), looked round at the Emperor Alexander to imply that what he was now doing was done for the sake of his ally, and the small white hand holding the Order touched one of Lázarev's buttons. It was as if Napoleon knew that it was only necessary for his hand to deign to touch that soldier's breast for the soldier to be forever happy, rewarded, and distinguished from everyone else in the world. Napoleon merely laid the cross on Lázarev's breast and, dropping his hand, turned toward Alexander as though sure that the cross would adhere there. And it really did.

Officious hands, Russian and French, immediately seized the cross and fastened it to the uniform. Lázarev glanced morosely at the little man with white hands who was doing something to him, and still standing motionless presenting arms, looked again straight into Alexander's eyes, as if asking whether he should stand there, or go away, or do something else. But receiving no orders, he remained for some time in that rigid position.

The Emperors remounted and rode away. The Preobrazhénsk battalion, breaking rank, mingled with the French Guards and sat down at the tables prepared for them.

Lázarev sat in the place of honor. Russian and French officers embraced him, congratulated him, and pressed his hands. Crowds of officers and civilians drew near merely to see him. A rumble of Russian and French voices and laughter filled the air round the tables in the square. Two officers with flushed faces, looking cheerful and happy, passed by Rostóv.

"What d'you think of the treat? All on silver plate," one of them was saying. "Have you seen Lázarev?"

"I have."

"Tomorrow, I hear, the Preobrazhénskis will give them a dinner."

"Yes, but what luck for Lázarev! Twelve hundred francs pension for life."

"Here's a cap, lads!" shouted a Preobrazhénsk soldier, donning a shaggy French cap.

"It's a fine thing! First rate!"

"Have you heard the password?" asked one Guards' officer of another. "The day before yesterday it was '*Napoleon, France, bravoure*'; yesterday, '*Alexandre, Russie, grandeur.*' One day our Emperor gives it and next day Napoleon. Tomorrow our Emperor will send a St. George's Cross to the bravest of the French Guards. It has to be done. He must respond in kind."

Borís, too, with his friend Zhilínski, came to see the Preobrazhénsk banquet. On his way back, he noticed Rostóv standing by the corner of a house.

"Rostóv! How d'you do? We missed one another," he said, and could not refrain from asking what was the matter, so strangely dismal and troubled was Rostóv's face.

"Nothing, nothing," replied Rostóv.

"You'll call round?"

"Yes, I will."

Rostóv stood at that corner for a long time, watching the feast from a distance. In his mind, a painful process was going on which he could not bring to a conclusion. Terrible doubts rose in his soul. Now he remembered Denísov with his changed expression, his submission, and the whole hospital, with arms and legs torn off and its dirt and disease. So vividly did he recall that hospital stench of dead flesh that he looked round to see where the smell came from. Next he thought of that self-satisfied Bonaparte, with his small white hand, who was now an Emperor, liked and respected by Alexander. Then why those severed arms and legs and those dead men? . . . Then again he thought of Lázarev rewarded and Denísov punished and unpardoned. He caught himself harboring such strange thoughts that he was frightened.

The smell of the food the Preobrazhénskis were eating and a sense of hunger, recalled him from these reflections; he had to get something to eat before going away. He went to a hotel he had noticed that morning. There he found so many people, among them officers who, like himself, had come in civilian clothes, that he had difficulty in getting a dinner. Two officers of his own division joined him. The conversation naturally turned on the peace. The officers, his comrades, like most of the army, were dissatisfied with the peace concluded after the battle of Friedland. They said that had we held out a little longer Napoleon would have been done for, as his troops had neither provisions nor ammunition. Nicholas ate and drank (chiefly the latter) in silence. He finished a couple of bottles of wine by himself. The process in his mind went on tormenting him without reaching a conclusion. He feared to give way to his thoughts, yet could not get rid of them. Suddenly, on one of the officers saying that it was humiliating to look at the French, Rostóv began shouting with uncalled-for wrath, and therefore much to the surprise of the officers:

"How can you judge what's best?" he cried, the blood suddenly rushing to his face. "How can you judge the Emperor's actions? What right have we to argue? We cannot comprehend either the Emperor's aims or his actions!"

"But I never said a word about the Emperor!" said the officer, justifying himself, and unable to understand Rostóv's outburst, except on the supposition that he was drunk.

But Rostóv did not listen to him.

"We are not diplomatic officials, we are soldiers and nothing more," he went on. "If we are ordered to die, we must die. If we're punished, it means that we have deserved it, it's not for us to judge. If the Emperor pleases to recognize Bonaparte as Emperor and to conclude an alliance with him, it means that that is the right thing to do. If once we begin judging and arguing about everything, nothing sacred will be left! That way we shall be saying there is no God—nothing!" shouted Nicholas, banging the table—very little to the point as it seemed to his listeners, but quite relevantly to the course of his own thoughts.

"Our business is to do our duty, to fight and not to think! That's all. . . ." said he.

"And to drink," said one of the officers, not wishing to quarrel.

"Yes, and to drink," assented Nicholas. "Hullo there! Another bottle!" he shouted.

Part Six

Chapter I

IN 1808 THE EMPEROR ALEXANDER WENT TO ERFURT FOR A FRESH INTERVIEW WITH THE EMPEROR Napoleon, and in the upper circles of Petersburg there was much talk of the grandeur of this important meeting.

In 1809 the intimacy between "the world's two arbiters," as Napoleon and Alexander were called, was such that when Napoleon declared war on Austria a Russian corps crossed the frontier to cooperate with our old enemy Bonaparte against our old ally the Emperor of Austria, and in court circles the possibility of marriage between Napoleon and one of Alexander's sisters was spoken of. But besides considerations of foreign policy, the attention of Russian society was at that time keenly directed on the internal changes that were being undertaken in all the departments of government.

Life meanwhile—real life, with its essential interests of health and sickness, toil and rest, and its intellectual interests in thought, science, poetry, music, love, friendship, hatred and passions—went on as usual, independently of and apart from political friendship or enmity with Napoleon Bonaparte and from all the schemes of reconstruction.

Prince Andrew had spent two years continuously in the country.

All the plans Pierre had attempted on his estates—and constantly changing from one thing to another had never accomplished—were carried out by Prince Andrew without display and without perceptible difficulty.

He had in the highest degree a practical tenacity which Pierre lacked, and without fuss or strain on his part this set things going.

On one of his estates the three hundred serfs were liberated and became free agricultural laborers—this being one of the first examples of the kind in Russia. On other estates the serfs' compulsory labor was commuted for a quitrent. A trained midwife was engaged for Bogucharovo at his expense, and a priest was paid to teach reading and writing to the children of the peasants and household serfs.

Prince Andrew spent half his time at Bald Hills with his father and his son, who was still in the care of nurses. The other half he spent in "Bogucharovo Cloister," as his father called Prince Andrew's estate. Despite the indifference to the affairs of the world he had expressed to Pierre, he diligently followed all that went on, received many books, and to his surprise noticed that when he or his father had visitors from Petersburg, the very vortex of life, these people lagged behind himself—who never left the country—in knowledge of what was happening in home and foreign affairs.

Besides being occupied with his estates and reading a great variety of books, Prince Andrew was at this time busy with a critical of survey our last two unfortunate campaigns, and with drawing up a proposal for a reform of the army rules and regulations.

In the spring of 1809 he went to visit the Ryazán estates which had been inherited by his son, whose guardian he was.

Warmed by the spring sunshine he sat in the calèche looking at the new grass, the first leaves on the birches, and the first puffs of white spring clouds floating across the clear blue sky. He was not thinking of anything, but looked absent-mindedly and cheerfully from side to side.

They crossed the ferry where he had talked with Pierre the year before. They went through the muddy village, past threshing floors and green fields of winter rye, downhill where snow still lodged near the bridge, uphill where the clay had been liquefied by the rain, past strips of stubble land and bushes touched with green here and there, and into a birch forest growing on both sides of the road. In the forest it was almost hot, no wind could be felt. The birches with their sticky green leaves were motionless, and lilac-colored flowers and the first blades of green grass were pushing up and lifting last year's leaves. The coarse evergreen color of the small fir trees scattered here and there among the birches was an unpleasant reminder of winter. On entering the forest the horses began to snort, and sweated visibly.

Peter the footman made some remark to the coachman; the latter assented. But apparently the coachman's sympathy was not enough for Peter, and he turned on the box toward his master.

"How pleasant it is, your excellency!" he said with a respectful smile.

"What?"

"It's pleasant, your excellency!"

"What is he talking about?" thought Prince Andrew. "Oh, the spring, I suppose," he thought as he turned round. "Yes, really everything is green already. . . . How early! The birches and cherry and alders too are coming out. . . . But the oaks show no sign yet. Ah, here is one oak!"

At the edge of the road stood an oak. Probably ten times the age of the birches that formed the forest, it was ten times as thick and twice as tall as they. It was an enormous tree, its girth twice as great as a man could embrace, and evidently long ago some of its branches had been broken off and its bark scarred. With its huge ungainly limbs sprawling unsymmetrically, and its gnarled hands and fingers, it stood an aged, stern, and scornful monster among the smiling birch trees. Only the dead-looking evergreen firs dotted about in the forest, and this oak, refused to yield to the charm of spring or notice either the spring or the sunshine.

"Spring, love, happiness!" this oak seemed to say. "Are you not weary of that stupid, meaningless, constantly repeated fraud? Always the same and always a fraud! There is no spring, no sun, no happiness! Look at those cramped dead firs, ever the same, and at me too, sticking out my broken and barked fingers just where they have grown, whether from my back or my sides: as they have grown so I stand, and I do not believe in your hopes and your lies."

As he passed through the forest Prince Andrew turned several times to look at that oak, as if expecting something from it. Under the oak, too, were flowers and grass, but it stood among them scowling, rigid, misshapen and grim as ever.

"Yes, the oak is right, a thousand times right," thought Prince Andrew. "Let others—the young—yield afresh to that fraud, but we know life, our life is finished!"

A whole sequence of new thoughts, hopeless but mournfully pleasant, rose in his soul in connection with that tree. During this journey he, as it were, considered his life afresh and arrived at his old conclusion, restful in its hopelessness: that it was not for him to begin anything anew—but that he must live out his life, content to do no harm, and not disturbing himself or desiring anything.

Chapter II

PRINCE ANDREW HAD TO SEE THE MARSHAL OF THE NOBILITY FOR THE DISTRICT IN CONNECTION with the affairs of the Ryazán estate of which he was trustee. This Marshal was Count Ilyá Rostóv, and in the middle of May Prince Andrew went to visit him.

It was now hot spring weather. The whole forest was already clothed in green. It was dusty, and so hot that on passing near water one longed to bathe.

Prince Andrew, depressed and preoccupied with the business about which he had to speak to the Marshal, was driving up the avenue in the grounds of the Rostóvs' house at Otrádnoe. He heard merry girlish cries behind some trees on the right, and saw a group of girls running to cross the path of his calèche. Ahead of the rest and nearer to him ran a dark-haired, remarkably slim, pretty girl in a yellow chintz dress, with a white handkerchief on her head from under which loose locks of hair escaped. The girl was shouting something, but seeing that he was a stranger, ran back laughing without looking at him.

Suddenly, he did not know why, he felt a pang. The day was so beautiful, the sun so bright, everything around so gay, but that slim pretty girl did not know, or wish to know, of his existence and was contented and cheerful in her own separate—probably foolish—but bright and happy life. "What is she so glad about? What is she thinking of? Not of the military regulations or of the arrangement of the Ryazán serfs' quitrents. Of what is she thinking? Why is she so happy?" Prince Andrew asked himself with instinctive curiosity.

In 1809 Count Ilyá Rostóv was living at Otrádnoe just as he had done in former years, that is, entertaining almost the whole province with hunts, theatricals, dinners and music. He was glad to see Prince Andrew, as he was to see any new visitor, and insisted on his staying the night.

During the dull day, in the course of which he was entertained by his elderly hosts and by the more important of the visitors (the old count's house was crowded on account of an approaching name-day), Prince Andrew repeatedly glanced at Natásha, gay and laughing among the younger members of the company, and asked himself each time, "What is she thinking about? Why is she so glad?"

That night, alone in new surroundings, he was long unable to sleep. He read awhile and then put out his candle, but relit it. It was hot in the room, the inside shutters of which were closed. He was cross with the stupid old man (as he called Rostóv), who had made him stay by assuring him that some necessary documents had not yet arrived from town, and he was vexed with himself for having stayed.

He got up and went to the window to open it. As soon as he opened the shutters the moonlight, as if it had long been watching for this, burst into the room. He opened the casement. The night was fresh, bright and very still. Just before the window was a row of pollard trees, looking black on one side and with a silvery light on the other. Beneath the trees grew some kind of lush, wet, bushy vegetation with silver-lit leaves and stems here and there. Farther back beyond the dark trees a roof glittered with dew, to the right was a leafy tree with brilliantly white trunk and branches, and above it shone the moon, nearly at its full, in a pale, almost starless, spring sky. Prince Andrew leaned his elbows on the window-ledge and his eyes rested on that sky.

His room was on the first floor. Those in the rooms above were also awake. He heard female voices overhead.

"Just once more," said a girlish voice above him which Prince Andrew recognized at once.

"But when are you coming to bed?" replied another voice.

"I won't, I can't sleep, what's the use? Come now for the last time."

Two girlish voices sang a musical passage—the end of some song.

"Oh, how lovely! Now go to sleep, and there's an end of it."

"You go to sleep, but I can't," said the first voice, coming nearer to the window. She was evidently leaning right out, for the rustle of her dress and even her breathing could be heard. Everything was stone-still, like the moon and its light and the shadows. Prince Andrew, too, dared not stir, for fear of betraying his unintentional presence.

"Sónya! Sónya!" he again heard the first speaker. "Oh, how can you sleep? Only look how glorious it is! Ah, how glorious! Do wake up, Sónya!" she said almost with tears in her voice. "There never, never was such a lovely night before!"

Sónya made some reluctant reply.

"Do just come and see what a moon! . . . Oh, how lovely! Come here. . . . Darling, sweetheart, come here! There, you see? I feel like sitting down on my heels, putting my arms round my knees like this, straining tight, as tight as possible, and flying away! Like this. . . ."

"Take care, you'll fall out."

He heard the sound of a scuffle and Sónya's disapproving voice: "It's past one o'clock."

"Oh, you only spoil things for me. All right, go, go!"

Again all was silent, but Prince Andrew knew she was still sitting there. From time to time he heard a soft rustle, and at times a sigh.

"O God, O God! What does it mean?" she suddenly exclaimed. "To bed then, if it must be!" and she slammed the casement.

"For her I might as well not exist!" thought Prince Andrew while he listened to her voice, for some reason expecting yet fearing that she might say something about him. "There she is again! As if it were on purpose," thought he.

In his soul there suddenly arose such an unexpected turmoil of youthful thoughts and hopes, contrary to the whole tenor of his life, that unable to explain his condition to himself he lay down and fell asleep at once.

Chapter III

NEXT MORNING, HAVING TAKEN LEAVE OF NO ONE BUT THE COUNT, AND NOT WAITING FOR THE ladies to appear, Prince Andrew set off for home.

It was already the beginning of June when on his return journey he drove into the birch forest where the gnarled old oak had made so strange and memorable an impression on him. In the forest the harness-bells sounded yet more muffled than they had done six weeks before, for now all was thick, shady, and dense, and the young firs dotted about in the forest did not jar on the general beauty but, lending themselves to the mood around, were delicately green with fluffy young shoots.

The whole day had been hot. Somewhere a storm was gathering, but only a small cloud had scattered some raindrops lightly, sprinkling the road and the sappy leaves. The left side of the forest was dark in the shade, the right side glittered in the sunlight, wet and shiny and scarcely swayed by the breeze. Everything was in blossom, the nightingales trilled, and their voices reverberated now near now far away.

"Yes, here in this forest was that oak with which I agreed," thought Prince Andrew. "But where is it?" he again wondered, gazing at the left side of the road, and without recognizing it he looked with admiration at the very oak he sought. The old oak, quite transfigured, spreading out a canopy of sappy dark-green foliage, stood rapt and slightly trembling in the rays of the evening sun. Neither gnarled fingers nor old scars nor old doubts and sorrows were any of them in evidence now. Through the hard century-old bark, even where there were no twigs, leaves had sprouted such as one could hardly believe the old veteran could have produced.

"Yes, it is the same oak," thought Prince Andrew, and all at once he was seized by an unreasoning springtime feeling of joy and renewal. All the best moments of his life suddenly rose to his memory. Austerlitz with the lofty heavens, his wife's dead reproachful face, Pierre at the ferry, that girl thrilled by the beauty of the night, and that night itself and the moon, and. . . . all this rushed suddenly to his mind.

"No, life is not over at thirty-one!" Prince Andrew suddenly decided finally and decisively. "It is not enough for me to know what I have in me—everyone must know it: Pierre, and that young girl who wanted to fly away into the sky, everyone must know me, so that my life may not be lived for myself alone while others live so apart from it, but so that it may be reflected in them all, and they and I may live in harmony!"

On reaching home Prince Andrew decided to go to Petersburg that autumn and found all sorts of reasons for this decision. A whole series of sensible and logical considerations showing it to be essential for him to go to Petersburg, and even to re-enter the service, kept springing up in his mind. He could not now understand how he could ever even have doubted the necessity of taking an active share in life, just as a month before he had not understood how the idea of leaving the quiet country could ever enter his head. It now seemed clear to him that all his experience of life must be senselessly wasted unless he applied it to some kind of work and again played an active part in life. He did not even remember how formerly, on the strength of similar wretched logical arguments, it had seemed obvious that he would be degrading himself if he now, after the lessons he had had in life, allowed himself to believe in the possibility of being useful and in the possibility of happiness or love. Now reason suggested quite the opposite. After that journey to Ryazán he found the country dull; his former pursuits no longer interested him, and often when sitting alone in his study he got up, went to the mirror and gazed a long time at his own face. Then he would turn away to the portrait of his dead Lise, who with hair curled *à la grecque* looked tenderly and gaily at him out of the gilt frame. She did not now say those former terrible words to him, but looked simply, merrily, and inquisitively at him. And Prince Andrew, crossing his arms behind him, long paced the room, now frowning now smiling, as he reflected on those irrational, inexpressible thoughts, secret as a crime, which altered his whole life and were connected with Pierre, with fame, with the girl at the window, the oak, and woman's beauty and love. And if anyone came into his room at such moments he was particularly cold, stern, and above all unpleasantly logical.

"My dear," Princess Mary entering at such a moment would say, "little Nicholas can't go out today, it's very cold."

"If it were hot," Prince Andrew would reply at such times very dryly to his sister, "he could go out in his smock, but as it is cold he must wear warm clothes, which were designed for that purpose. That is what follows from the fact that it is cold; and not that a child who needs fresh air should remain at home," he would add with extreme logic, as if punishing someone for those secret illogical emotions that stirred within him.

At such moments Princess Mary would think how intellectual work dries men up.

Chapter IV

PRINCE ANDREW ARRIVED IN PETERSBURG IN AUGUST 1809. IT WAS THE TIME WHEN THE YOUTHFUL Speránski was at the zenith of his fame and his reforms were being pushed forward with the greatest energy. That same August the Emperor was thrown from his calèche, injured his leg, and remained three weeks at Peterhof, receiving Speránski every day and no one else. At that time the two famous decrees were being prepared that so agitated society—abolishing court ranks and introducing examinations to qualify for the grades of Collegiate Assessor and State Councilor—and not merely these but a whole State constitution, intended to change the existing order of government in Russia: legal, administrative and financial, from the Council of State down to the district tribunals. Now those vague liberal dreams with which the Emperor Alexander had ascended the throne, and which he had tried to put into effect with the aid of his associates, Czartorýski, Novosíltsev, Kochubéy and Stróganov—whom he himself in jest had called his *Comité de salut public*—were taking shape and being realized.

Now all these men were replaced by Speránski on the civil side, and Arakchéev on the military. Soon after his arrival Prince Andrew, as a gentleman of the chamber, presented himself at court and at a levée. The Emperor, though he met him twice, did not favor him with a single word. It had always seemed to Prince Andrew before that he was antipathetic to the Emperor and that the latter disliked his face and personality generally, and in the cold, repellent glance the Emperor gave him, he now found further confirmation of this surmise. The courtiers explained the Emperor's neglect of him by his Majesty's displeasure at Bolkónski's not having served since 1805.

"I know myself that one cannot help one's sympathies and antipathies," thought Prince Andrew, "so it will not do to present my proposal for the reform of the army regulations to the Emperor personally, but the project will speak for itself."

He mentioned what he had written to an old field marshal, a friend of his father's. The field marshal made an appointment to see him, received him graciously, and promised to inform the Emperor. A few days later Prince Andrew received notice that he was to go to see the Minister of War, Count Arakchéev.

On the appointed day Prince Andrew entered Count Arakchéev's waiting room at nine in the morning.

He did not know Arakchéev personally, had never seen him, and all he had heard of him inspired him with but little respect for the man.

"He is Minister of War, a man trusted by the Emperor, and I need not concern myself about his personal qualities: he has been commissioned to consider my project, so he alone can get it adopted," thought Prince Andrew as he waited among a number of important and unimportant people in Count Arakchéev's waiting room.

During his service, chiefly as an adjutant, Prince Andrew had seen the anterooms of many important men, and the different types of such rooms were well known to him. Count Arakchéev's anteroom had quite a special character. The faces of the unimportant people awaiting their turn for an audience showed embarrassment and servility; the faces of those of higher rank expressed a common feeling of awkwardness, covered by a mask of unconcern and ridicule of themselves, their situation, and the person for whom they were waiting. Some walked thoughtfully up and down, others whispered and laughed. Prince Andrew heard the nickname "Síla Andréevich" and the words, "*Uncle* will give it us hot," in reference to Count Arakchéev. One general (an important personage) evidently feeling offended at having to wait so long, sat crossing and uncrossing his legs and smiling contemptuously to himself.

But the moment the door opened one feeling alone appeared on all faces—that of fear. Prince Andrew for the second time asked the adjutant on duty to take in his name, but received an ironical look and was told that his turn would come in due course. After some others had been shown in and out of the minister's room by the adjutant on duty, an officer who struck Prince Andrew by his humiliated and frightened air was admitted at that terrible door. This officer's audience lasted a long time. Then suddenly the grating sound of a harsh voice was heard from the other side of the door, and the officer—with pale face and trembling lips—came out and passed through the waiting room clutching his head.

After this Prince Andrew was conducted to the door and the officer on duty said in a whisper, "To the right, at the window."

Prince Andrew entered a plain tidy room and saw at the table a man of forty with a long waist, a long closely cropped head, deep wrinkles, scowling brows above dull greenish-hazel eyes and an overhanging red nose. Arakchéev turned his head toward him without looking at him.

"What is your petition?" asked Arakchéev.

"I am not petitioning, your excellency," returned Prince Andrew quietly.

Arakchéev's eyes turned toward him.

"Sit down," said he. "Prince Bolkónski?"

"I am not petitioning about anything. His Majesty the Emperor has deigned to send your excellency a project submitted by me . . ."

"You see, my dear sir, I have read your project," interrupted Arakchéev, uttering only the first words amiably and then—again without looking at Prince Andrew—relapsing gradually into a tone of grumbling contempt. "You are proposing new military laws? There are many laws but no one to carry out the old ones. Nowadays everybody designs laws, it is easier writing than doing."

"I came at his Majesty the Emperor's wish to learn from your excellency how you propose to deal with the memorandum I have presented," said Prince Andrew politely.

"I have endorsed a resolution on your memorandum and sent it to the committee. I do *not* approve of it," said Arakchéev rising and taking a paper from his writing-table. "Here!" and he handed it to Prince Andrew.

Across the paper was scrawled in pencil, without capital letters, misspelled, and without punctuation: "Unsoundly constructed because resembles an imitation of the French military code and from the Articles of War needlessly deviating."

"To what committee has the memorandum been referred?" inquired Prince Andrew.

"To the Committee on Army Regulations, and I have recommended that your honor should be appointed a member, but without a salary."

Prince Andrew smiled.

"I don't want one."

"A member without salary," repeated Arakchéev. "I have the honor . . . Eh! Call the next one! Who else is there?" he shouted, bowing to Prince Andrew.

Chapter V

WHILE WAITING FOR THE ANNOUNCEMENT OF HIS APPOINTMENT TO THE COMMITTEE PRINCE Andrew looked up his former acquaintances, particularly those he knew to be in power and whose aid he might need. In Petersburg he now experienced the same feeling he had had on the eve of a battle, when troubled by anxious curiosity and irresistibly attracted to the ruling circles where the future, on which the fate of millions depended, was being shaped. From the irritation of the older men, the curiosity of the uninitiated, the reserve of the initiated, the hurry and preoccupation of everyone and the innumerable committees and commissions of whose existence he learned every day, he felt that now, in 1809, here in Petersburg a vast civil conflict was in preparation, the commander-in-chief of which was a mysterious person he did not know, but who was supposed to be a man of genius—Speránski. And this movement of reconstruction of which Prince Andrew had a vague idea, and Speránski its chief promoter, began to interest him so keenly that the question of the army regulations quickly receded to a secondary place in his consciousness.

Prince Andrew was most favorably placed to secure good reception in the highest and most diverse Petersburg circles of the day. The reforming party cordially welcomed and courted him, the first place because he was reputed to be clever and very well-read, and secondly because by liberating his serfs he had obtained the reputation of being a liberal. The party of the old and dissatisfied who censured the innovations, turned to him expecting his sympathy in their disapproval of the reforms, simply because he was the son of his father. The feminine society world welcomed him gladly, because he was rich, distinguished, a good match, and almost a newcomer, with a halo of romance on account of his supposed death and the tragic loss of his wife. Besides this the general opinion of all who had known him previously was that he had greatly improved during these last five years, having softened and grown more manly, lost his former affectation, pride and contemptuous irony, and acquired the serenity that comes with years. People talked about him, were interested in him and wanted to meet him.

The day after his interview with Count Arakchéev, Prince Andrew spent the evening at Count Kochubéy's. He told the count of his interview with Síla Andréevich (Kochubéy spoke of Arakchéev by that nickname with the same vague irony Prince Andrew had noticed in the Minister of War's anteroom).

"*Mon cher,* even in this case you can't do without Michael Mikháylovich Speránski. He manages everything. I'll speak to him. He has promised to come this evening."

"What has Speránski to do with the army regulations?" asked Prince Andrew.

Kochubéy shook his head smilingly, as if surprised at Bolkónski's simplicity.

"We were talking to him about you a few days ago," Kochubéy continued, "and about your freed plowmen."

"Oh, is it you, prince, who have freed your serfs?" said an old man of Catherine's day, turning contemptuously toward Bolkónski.

"It was a small estate that brought in no profit," replied Prince Andrew, trying to extenuate his action so as not to irritate the old man uselessly.

"Afraid of being late . . ." said the old man, looking at Kochubéy.

"There's one thing I don't understand," he continued. "Who will plow the land if they are set free? It is easy to write laws, but difficult to rule. . . . Just the same as now—I ask you, count—who will be heads of the departments when everybody has to pass examinations?"

"Those who pass the examinations, I suppose," replied Kochubéy crossing his legs and glancing round.

"Well, I have Pryánichnikov serving under me, a splendid man, a priceless man, but he's sixty. Is he to go up for examination?"

"Yes, that's a difficulty, as education is not at all general, but . . ."

Count Kochubéy did not finish. He rose, took Prince Andrew by the arm, and went to meet a tall, bald man of about forty with a large open forehead and a long face of unusual and peculiar whiteness, who was just entering. The newcomer wore a blue swallow-tail coat with a cross suspended from his neck and a star on his left breast. It was Speránski. Prince Andrew recognized him at once, and felt a throb within him, as happens at critical moments of life. Whether it was from respect, envy, or anticipation, he did not know. Speránski's whole figure was of a peculiar type that made him easily recognizable. In the society in which Prince Andrew lived he had never seen anyone who together with awkward and clumsy gestures possessed such calmness and self-assurance; he had never seen so resolute yet gentle an expression as that in those half-closed, rather humid eyes, or so firm a smile that expressed nothing; nor had he heard such a refined, smooth, soft voice; above all he had never seen such delicate whiteness of face or hands—hands which were broad, but very plump, soft and white. Such whiteness and softness Prince Andrew had only seen on the faces of soldiers who had been long in hospital. This was Speránski, Secretary of State, reporter to the Emperor and his companion at Erfurt, where he had more than once met and talked with Napoleon.

Speránski did not shift his eyes from one face to another as people involuntarily do on entering a large company, and was in no hurry to speak. He spoke slowly, with assurance that he would be listened to, and he looked only at the person with whom he was conversing.

Prince Andrew followed Speránski's every word and movement with particular attention. As happens to some people, especially to men who judge those near to them severely, he was always on meeting anyone new—especially anyone whom, like Speránski, he knew by reputation—expected to discover in him the perfection of human qualities.

Speránski told Kochubéy he was sorry he had been unable to come sooner as he had been detained at the palace. He did not say that the Emperor had kept him, and Prince Andrew noticed this affectation of modesty. When Kochubéy introduced Prince Andrew, Speránski slowly turned his eyes to Bolkónski with his customary smile and looked at him in silence.

"I am very glad to make your acquaintance. I had heard of you, as everyone has," he said after a pause.

Kochubéy said a few words about the reception Arakchéev had given Bolkónski. Speránski smiled more markedly.

"The chairman of the Committee on Army Regulations is my good friend Monsieur Magnítski," he said, fully articulating every word and syllable, "and if you like I can put you in touch with him." He paused at the full stop. "I hope you will find him sympathetic and ready to cooperate in promoting all that is reasonable."

A circle soon formed round Speránski, and the old man who had talked about his subordinate Pryánichnikov addressed a question to him.

Prince Andrew without joining in the conversation watched every movement of Speránski's: this man, not long since an insignificant divinity student, who now, Bolkónski thought, held in his hands—those plump white hands—the fate of Russia. Prince Andrew was struck by the extraordinarily disdainful composure with which Speránski answered the old man. He appeared to address condescending words to him from an immeasurable height. When the old man began to speak too loud, Speránski smiled and said he could not judge of the advantage or disadvantage of what pleased the sovereign.

Having talked for a little while in the general circle, Speránski rose and coming up to Prince Andrew took him along to the other end of the room. It was clear that he thought it necessary to interest himself in Bolkónski.

"I had no chance to talk with you, prince, during the animated conversation in which that venerable gentleman involved me," he said with a mildly contemptuous smile, as if intimating by that smile that he and Prince Andrew understood the insignificance of the people with whom he had just been talking. This flattered Prince Andrew. "I have known of you for a long time: first from your action with regard to your serfs, a first example, of which it is very desirable that there should be more imitators; and secondly because you are one of those gentlemen of the chamber who have not considered themselves offended by the new decree concerning the ranks allotted to courtiers, which is causing so much gossip and tittle-tattle."

"No," said Prince Andrew, "my father did not wish me to take advantage of the privilege. I began the service from the lower grade."

"Your father, a man of the last century, evidently stands above our contemporaries who so condemn this measure which merely re-establishes natural justice."

"I think, however, that these condemnations have some ground," returned Prince Andrew, trying to resist Speránski's influence, of which he began to be conscious. He did not like to agree with him in everything and felt a wish to contradict. Though he usually spoke easily and well, he felt a difficulty in expressing himself now while talking with Speránski. He was too much absorbed in observing the famous man's personality.

"Grounds of personal ambition maybe," Speránski put in quietly.

"And of State interest to some extent," said Prince Andrew.

"What do you mean?" asked Speránski quietly, lowering his eyes.

"I am an admirer of Montesquieu," replied Prince Andrew, "and his idea that *le principe des monarchies est l'honneur, me paraît incontestable. Certains droits et privilèges de la noblesse me paraissent être des moyens de soutenir ce sentiment.*"

The smile vanished from Speránski's white face, which was much improved by the change. Probably Prince Andrew's thought interested him.

"Si vous envisagez la question sous ce point de vue," he began, pronouncing French with evident difficulty, and speaking even slower than in Russian but quite calmly.

Speránski went on to say that honor, *l'honneur,* cannot be upheld by privileges harmful to the service; that honor, *l'honneur,* is either a negative concept of not doing what is blameworthy or it is a source of emulation in pursuit of commendation and rewards, which recognize it. His arguments were concise, simple and clear.

"An institution upholding honor, the source of emulation, is one similar to the *Légion d'honneur* of the great Emperor Napoleon, not harmful but helpful to the success of the service, but not a class or court privilege."

"I do not dispute that, but it cannot be denied that court privileges have attained the same end," returned Prince Andrew. "Every courtier considers himself bound to maintain his position worthily."

"Yet you do not care to avail yourself of the privilege, prince," said Speránski, indicating by a smile that he wished to finish amiably an argument which was embarrassing for his companion. "If you will do me the honor of calling on me on Wednesday," he added, "I will, after talking with Magnítski, let you know what may interest you, and shall also have the pleasure of a more detailed chat with you."

Closing his eyes, he bowed *à la française,* without taking leave, and trying to attract as little attention as possible, he left the room.

Chapter VI

DURING THE FIRST WEEKS OF HIS STAY IN PETERSBURG PRINCE ANDREW FELT THE WHOLE TREND of thought he had formed during his life of seclusion quite overshadowed by the trifling cares that engrossed him in that city.

On returning home in the evening he would jot down in his notebook four or five necessary calls or appointments for certain hours. The mechanism of life, the arrangement of the day so as to be in time everywhere, absorbed the greater part of his vital energy. He did nothing, did not even think or find time to think, but only talked, and talked successfully, of what he had thought while in the country.

He sometimes noticed with dissatisfaction that he repeated the same remark on the same-day in different circles. But he was so busy for whole days together that he had no time to notice that he was thinking of nothing.

As he had done on their first meeting at Kochubéy's, Speránski produced a strong impression on Prince Andrew on the Wednesday, when he received him *tête-à-tête* at his own house and talked to him long and confidentially.

To Bolkónski so many people appeared contemptible and insignificant creatures, and he so longed to find in someone the living ideal of that perfection toward which he strove, that he readily believed that in Speránski he had found this ideal of a perfectly rational and virtuous man. Had Speránski sprung from the same class as himself and possessed the same breeding and traditions, Bolkónski would soon have discovered his weak, human, unheroic sides; but as it was, Speránski's strange and logical turn of mind inspired him with respect all the more because he did not quite understand him. Moreover, Speránski, either because he appreciated the other's capacity or because he considered it necessary to win him to his side, showed off his dispassionate calm reasonableness before Prince Andrew and flattered him with that subtle flattery which goes hand in hand with self-assurance, and consists in a tacit assumption that one's companion is the only man besides oneself capable of understanding the folly of the rest of mankind and the reasonableness and profundity of one's own ideas.

During their long conversation on Wednesday evening, Speránski more than once remarked: "*We* regard everything that is above the common level of rooted custom . . ." or, with a smile: "But *we* want the wolves to be fed and the sheep to be safe . . ." or: "*They* cannot understand this . . ." and all in a way that seemed to say: "*We*, you and I, understand what *they* are and who *we* are."

This first long conversation with Speránski only strengthened in Prince Andrew the feeling he had experienced toward him at their first meeting. He saw in him a remarkable, clear-thinking man of vast intellect who by his energy and persistence had attained power, which he was using solely for the welfare of Russia. In Prince Andrew's eyes Speránski was the man he would himself have wished to be—one who explained all the facts of life reasonably, considered important only what was rational, and was capable of applying the standard of reason to everything. Everything seemed so simple and clear in Speránski's exposition that Prince Andrew involuntarily agreed with him about everything. If he replied and argued, it was only because he wished to maintain his independence and not submit to Speránski's opinions entirely. Everything was right and everything was as it should be: only one thing disconcerted Prince Andrew. This was Speránski's cold, mirrorlike look, which did not allow one to penetrate to his soul, and his delicate white hands, which Prince Andrew involuntarily watched as one does watch the hands of those who possess power. This mirrorlike gaze and those delicate hands irritated Prince Andrew, he knew not why. He was unpleasantly struck, too, by the excessive contempt for others that he observed in Speránski, and by the diversity of lines of argument he used to support his opinions. He made use of every kind of mental device, except analogy, and passed too boldly, it seemed to Prince Andrew, from one to another. Now he would take up the position of a practical man and condemn dreamers; now that of a satirist, and laugh ironically at his opponents; now grow severely logical, or suddenly rise to the realm of metaphysics. (This last resource was one he very frequently employed.) He would transfer a question to metaphysical heights, pass on to definitions of space, time and thought, and having deduced the refutation he needed, would again descend to the level of the original discussion.

In general the trait of Speránski's mentality which struck Prince Andrew most was his absolute and unshakable belief in the power and authority of reason. It was evident that the thought could never occur to him which to Prince Andrew seemed so natural, namely, that it is after all impossible to express all one thinks; and that he had never felt the doubt, "Is not all I think and believe nonsense?" And it was just this peculiarity of Speránski's mind that particularly attracted Prince Andrew.

During the first period of their acquaintance Bolkónski felt a passionate admiration for him similar to that which he had once felt for Bonaparte. The fact that Speránski was the son of a village priest, and that stupid people might meanly despise him on account of his humble origin (as in fact many did), caused Prince Andrew to cherish his sentiment for him the more, and unconsciously to strengthen it.

On that first evening Bolkónski spent with him, having mentioned the Commission for the Revision of the Code of Laws, Speránski told him sarcastically that the Commission had existed for a hundred and fifty years, had cost millions, and had done nothing except that Rosenkampf had stuck labels on the corresponding paragraphs of the different codes.

"And that is all the State has for the millions it has spent," said he. "We want to give the Senate new juridical powers, but we have no laws. That is why it is a sin for men like you, prince, not to serve in these times!"

Prince Andrew said that for that work an education in jurisprudence was needed which he did not possess.

"But nobody possesses it, so what would you have? It is a vicious circle from which we must break a way out."

A week later Prince Andrew was a member of the Committee on Army Regulations, and—what he had not at all expected—was chairman of a section of the committee for the revision of the laws. At Speránski's request he took the first part of the Civil Code that was being drawn up, and with the aid of the *Code Napoléon* and the Institutes of Justinian he worked at formulating the section on Personal Rights.

Chapter VII

NEARLY TWO YEARS BEFORE THIS, IN 1808, PIERRE ON RETURNING TO PETERSBURG AFTER VISITing his estates had involuntarily found himself in a leading position among the Petersburg freemasons. He arranged dining and funeral Lodge meetings, enrolled new members, and busied himself uniting various Lodges and acquiring authentic charters. He gave money for the erection of temples, and supplemented as far as he could the collection of alms, in regard to which the majority of members were stingy and irregular. He supported almost single-handed a poorhouse the Order had founded in Petersburg.

His life meanwhile continued as before, with the same infatuations and dissipations. He liked to dine and drink well, and though he considered it immoral and humiliating could not resist the temptations of the bachelor circles in which he moved.

Amid the turmoil of his activities and distractions however, Pierre at the end of a year began to feel that the more firmly he tried to rest upon it, the more the masonic ground on which he stood gave way under him. At the same time he felt that the deeper the ground sank under him the closer bound he involuntarily became to the Order. When he had joined the freemasons he had experienced the feeling of one who confidently steps onto the smooth surface of a bog. When he put his foot down it sank in. To make quite sure of the firmness the ground, he put his other foot down and sank deeper still, became stuck in it, and involuntarily waded knee-deep in the bog.

Joseph Alexéevich was not in Petersburg—he had of late stood aside from the affairs of the Petersburg Lodges and lived almost entirely in Moscow. All the members of the lodges were men Pierre knew in ordinary life, and it was difficult for him to regard them merely as Brothers in Freemasonry and not as Prince B. or Iván Vasílevich D., whom he knew in society mostly as weak and insignificant men. Under the masonic aprons and insignia he saw the uniforms and decorations at which they aimed in ordinary life. Often after collecting alms, and reckoning up twenty to thirty rubles received for the most part in promises from a dozen members, of whom half were as well able to pay as himself, Pierre remembered the masonic vow in which each Brother promised to devote all his belongings to his neighbor, and doubts on which he tried not to dwell arose in his soul.

He divided the Brothers he knew into four categories. In the first he put those who did not take an active part in the affairs of the Lodges or in human affairs, but were exclusively occupied with the mystical science of the Order: with questions of the threefold designation of God, the three primordial elements—sulfur, mercury and salt—or the meaning of the square and all the various figures of the temple of Solomon. Pierre respected this class of Brothers to which the elder ones chiefly belonged, including, Pierre thought, Joseph Alexéevich himself, but he did not share their interests. His heart was not in the mystical aspect of freemasonry.

In the second category Pierre reckoned himself and others like him, seeking and vacillating, who had not yet found in freemasonry a straight and comprehensible path, but hoped to do so.

In the third category he included those Brothers (the majority) who saw nothing in freemasonry but the external forms and ceremonies, and prized the strict performance of these forms without troubling about their purport or significance. Such were Willarski and even the Grand Master of the principal Lodge.

Finally, to the fourth category also a great many Brothers belonged, particularly those who had lately joined. These according to Pierre's observations were men who had no belief in anything, nor desire for anything, but joined the freemasons merely to associate with the wealthy young Brothers who were influential through their connections or rank, and of whom there were very many in the Lodge.

Pierre began to feel dissatisfied with what he was doing. Freemasonry, at any rate as he saw it here, sometimes seemed to him based merely on externals. He did not think of doubting freemasonry itself, but suspected that Russian Masonry had taken a wrong path and deviated from its original principles. And so toward the end of the year he went abroad to be initiated into the higher secrets of the Order.

In the summer of 1809 Pierre returned to Petersburg. Our freemasons knew from correspondence with those abroad that Bezúkhov had obtained the confidence of many highly placed persons, had been initiated into many mysteries, had been raised to a higher grade, and was bringing back with him much that might conduce to the advantage of the masonic cause in Russia. The Petersburg freemasons all came to see him, tried to ingratiate themselves with him, and it seemed to them all that he was preparing something for them and concealing it.

A solemn meeting of the Lodge of the second degree was convened, at which Pierre promised to communicate to the Petersburg Brothers what he had to deliver to them from the highest leaders of their Order. The meeting was a full one. After the usual ceremonies Pierre rose and began his address.

"Dear Brothers," he began, blushing and stammering, with a written speech in his hand, "it is not sufficient to observe our mysteries in the seclusion of our Lodge—we must act—act! We are drowsing, but we must act." Pierre raised his notebook and began to read.

"For the dissemination of pure truth and to secure the triumph of virtue," he read, "we must cleanse men from prejudice, diffuse principles in harmony with the spirit of the times, undertake the education of the young, unite ourselves in indissoluble bonds with the wisest men, boldly yet prudently overcome superstitions, infidelity and folly, and form of those devoted to us a body linked together by unity of purpose and possessed of authority and power.

"To attain this end we must secure a preponderance of virtue over vice, and must endeavor to secure that the honest man may, even in this world, receive a lasting reward for his virtue. But in these great endeavors we are gravely hampered by the political institutions of today. What is to be done in these circumstances? To favor revolutions, overthrow everything, repel force by force? . . . No! We are very far from that. Every violent reform deserves censure, for it quite fails to remedy evil while men remain what they are, and also because wisdom needs no violence.

"The whole plan of our Order should be based on the idea of preparing men of firmness and virtue bound together by unity of conviction—aiming at the punishment of vice and folly, and patronizing talent and virtue: raising worthy men from the dust and attaching them to our Brotherhood. Only then will our order have the power unobtrusively to bind the hands of the protectors of disorder and to control them without their being aware of it. In a word, we must found a form of government holding universal sway, which should be diffused over the whole world without destroying the bonds of citizenship, and besides which all other governments can continue in their customary course and do everything except what impedes the great aim of our Order, which is to obtain for virtue the victory over vice. This aim was that of Christianity itself. It taught men to be wise and good, and for their own benefit to follow the example and instruction of the best and wisest men.

"At that time, when everything was plunged in darkness, preaching alone was of course sufficient. The novelty of Truth endowed her with special strength, but now we need much more powerful methods. It is now necessary that man, governed by his senses, should find in virtue a charm palpable to those senses. It is impossible to eradicate the passions; but we must strive to direct them to a noble aim, and it is therefore necessary that everyone should be able to satisfy his passions within the limits of virtue. Our Order should provide means to that end.

"As soon as we have a certain number of worthy men in every State, each of them again training two others and all being closely united, everything will be possible for our Order, which has already in secret accomplished much for the welfare of mankind."

This speech not only made a strong impression, but created excitement in the Lodge. The majority of the Brothers, seeing in it dangerous designs of Illuminism, met it with a coldness that surprised Pierre. The Grand Master began answering him, and Pierre began developing his views with more and more warmth. It was long since there had been so stormy a meeting. Parties were formed, some accusing Pierre of Illuminism, others supporting him. At that meeting he was struck for the first time by the endless variety of men's minds, which prevents a truth from ever presenting itself identically to two persons. Even those members who seemed to be on his side understood him in their own way with limitations and alterations he could not agree to, as what he always wanted most was to convey his thought to others just as he himself understood it.

At the end of the meeting the Grand Master with irony and ill-will reproved Bezúkhov for his vehemence, and said it was not love of virtue alone, but also a love of strife that had moved him in the dispute. Pierre did not answer him and asked briefly whether his proposal would be accepted. He was told that it would not, and without waiting for the usual formalities he left the Lodge and went home.

Chapter VIII

AGAIN PIERRE WAS OVERTAKEN BY THE DEPRESSION HE SO DREADED. FOR THREE DAYS AFTER THE delivery of his speech at the Lodge he lay on a sofa at home receiving no one and going nowhere.

It was just then that he received a letter from his wife, who implored him to see her, telling him how grieved she was about him and how she wished to devote her whole life to him.

At the end of the letter she informed him that in a few days she would return to Petersburg from abroad.

Following this letter one of the Masonic Brothers whom Pierre respected less than the others forced his way in to see him and, turning the conversation upon Pierre's matrimonial affairs, by way of fraternal advice expressed the opinion that his severity to his wife was wrong, and that he was neglecting one of the first rules of freemasonry by not forgiving the penitent.

At the same time his mother-in-law, Prince Vasíli's wife, sent to him imploring him to come if only for a few minutes to discuss a most important matter. Pierre saw that there was a conspiracy against him and that they wanted to reunite him with his wife, and in the mood he then was, this was not even unpleasant to him. Nothing mattered to him. Nothing in life seemed to him of much importance, and under the influence of the depression that possessed him he valued neither his liberty nor his resolution to punish his wife.

"No one is right and no one is to blame; so she too is not to blame," he thought.

If he did not at once give his consent to a reunion with his wife, it was only because in his state of depression he did not feel able to take any step. Had his wife come to him, he would not have turned her away. Compared to what preoccupied him, was it not a matter of indifference whether he lived with his wife or not?

Without replying either to his wife or his mother-in-law, Pierre late one night prepared for a journey and started for Moscow to see Joseph Alexéevich. This is what he noted in his diary:

Moscow, November 17th

I have just returned from my benefactor, and hasten to write down what I have experienced. Joseph Alexéevich is living poorly and has for three years been suffering from a painful disease of the bladder. No one has ever heard him utter a groan or a word of complaint. From morning till late at night, except when he eats his very plain food, he is working at science. He received me graciously and made me sit down on the bed on which he lay. I made the sign of the Knights of the East and of Jerusalem, and he responded in the same manner, asking me with a mild smile what I had learned and gained in the Prussian and Scottish Lodges. I told him everything as best I could, and told him what I had proposed to our Petersburg Lodge, of the bad reception I had encountered, and of my rupture with the Brothers. Joseph Alexéevich, having remained silent and thoughtful for a good while, told me his view of the matter, which at once lit up for me my whole past, and the future path I should follow. He surprised me by asking whether I remembered the threefold aim of the Order: (1) The preservation and study of the mystery. (2) The purification and reformation of oneself for its reception, and (3) The improvement of the human race by striving for such purification. Which is the principal *aim* of these three? Certainly self-reformation and self-purification. Only to this aim can we always strive independently of circumstances. But at the same time just this aim demands the greatest efforts of us; and so, led astray by pride, losing sight of this aim, we occupy ourselves either with the mystery which in our impurity we are unworthy to receive, or seek the reformation of the human race while ourselves setting an example of baseness and profligacy. Illuminism is not a pure doctrine, just because it is attracted by social activity and puffed up by pride. On this ground Joseph Alexéevich condemned my speech and my whole activity, and in the depth of my soul I agreed with him. Talking of my family affairs he said to me, "the chief duty of a true mason, as I have told you, lies in perfecting himself. We often think that by removing all the difficulties of our life we shall more quickly reach our aim, but on the contrary, my dear sir, it is only in the midst of worldly cares that we can attain our three chief aims: (1) Self-knowledge—for man can only know himself by comparison, (2) Self-perfecting, which can only be attained by conflict, and (3) The attainment of the chief virtue—love of death. Only the vicissitudes of life can show us its vanity and develop our innate love of death or of rebirth to a new life." These words are all the more remarkable because, in spite of his great physical sufferings, Joseph Alexéevich is never weary of life though he loves death, for which—in spite of the purity and loftiness of his inner man—he does not yet feel himself sufficiently prepared. My benefactor then explained to me fully the meaning of the Great Square of creation, and pointed out to me that the numbers three and seven are the basis of everything. He advised me not to avoid intercourse with the Petersburg Brothers, but to take up only second-grade posts in the Lodge, to try, while diverting the Brothers from pride, to turn them toward the true paths of self-knowledge and self-perfecting. Besides this he advised me for myself personally above all to keep a watch over myself, and to that end he gave me a notebook, the one I am now writing in, and in which I will in future note down all my actions.

Petersburg, November 23rd

I am again living with my wife. My mother-in-law came to me in tears and said that Hélène was here and that she implored me to hear her; that she was innocent and unhappy at my desertion, and much more. I knew that if I once let myself see her I should not have strength to go on refusing what she wanted. In my perplexity I did not know whose aid and advice to seek. Had my benefactor been here he would have told me what to do. I went to my room and reread Joseph Alexéevich's letter and recalled my conversations with him, and deduced from it all that I ought not to refuse a suppliant, and ought to reach a helping hand to everyone—especially to one so closely bound to me—and that I must bear my cross. But if I forgive her for the sake of doing right, then let union with her have only a spiritual aim. That is what I decided, and what I wrote to Joseph Alexéevich. I told my wife that I begged her to forget the past, to forgive me whatever wrong I may have done her, and that I have nothing to forgive. It gave me joy to tell her this. She need not know how hard it was for me to see her again. I have settled on the upper floor of this big house, and am experiencing a happy feeling of regeneration.

Chapter IX

AT THAT TIME, AS ALWAYS HAPPENS, THE HIGHEST SOCIETY THAT MET AT COURT AND AT THE grand balls was divided into several circles, each with its own particular tone. The largest of these was the French circle of the Napoleonic alliance, the circle of Count Rumyántsev and Caulaincourt. In this group Hélène, as soon as she had settled in Petersburg with her husband, took a very prominent place. She was visited by the members of the French embassy and by many belonging to that circle and noted for their intellect and polished manners.

Hélène had been at Erfurt during the famous meeting of the Emperors, and had brought from there these connections with the Napoleonic notabilities. At Erfurt her success had been brilliant. Napoleon himself had noticed her in the theater, and said of her: *"C'est un superbe animal."* Her success as a beautiful and elegant woman did not surprise Pierre, for she had become even handsomer than before. What did surprise him was that during these last two years his wife had succeeded in gaining the reputation *"d'une femme charmante, aussi spirituelle que belle."* The distinguished Prince de Ligne wrote her eight-page letters. Bilíbin saved up his epigrams to produce them in Countess Bezúkhov's presence. To be received in the Countess Bezúkhov's salon was regarded as a diploma of intellect. Young men read books before attending Hélène's evenings, to have something to say in her salon, and secretaries of the embassy, and even ambassadors, confided diplomatic secrets to her, so that in a way Hélène was a power. Pierre, who knew she was very stupid, sometimes attended, with a strange feeling of perplexity and fear, her evenings and dinner parties, where politics, poetry and philosophy were discussed. At these parties his feelings were like those of a conjuror who always expects his trick to be found out at any moment. But whether because stupidity was just what was needed to run such a salon, or because those who were deceived found pleasure in the deception, at any rate it remained unexposed and Hélène Bezúkhova's reputation as a lovely and clever woman became so firmly established that she could say the emptiest and stupidest things and yet everybody would go into raptures over every word of hers, and look for a profound meaning in it of which she herself had no conception.

Pierre was just the husband needed for a brilliant society woman. He was that absent-minded crank, a *grand seigneur* husband who was in no one's way, and far from spoiling the high tone and general impression of the drawing room, he served, by the contrast he presented to her, as an advantageous background to his elegant and tactful wife. Pierre during the last two years, as a result of his continual absorption in abstract interests and his sincere contempt for all else, had acquired in his wife's circle, which did not interest him, that air of unconcern, indifference, and benevolence toward all, which cannot be acquired artificially and therefore inspires involuntary respect. He entered his wife's drawing room as one enters a theater, was acquainted with everybody, equally pleased to see everyone and equally indifferent to them all. Sometimes he joined in a conversation which interested him and, regardless of whether any "gentlemen of the embassy" were present or not, lispingly expressed his views, which were sometimes not at all in accord with the accepted tone of the moment. But the general opinion concerning the queer husband of "the most distinguished woman in Petersburg" was so well established that no one took his freaks seriously.

Among the many young men who frequented her house every day, Borís Drubetskóy, who had already achieved great success in the service, was the most intimate friend of the Bezúkhov household since Hélène's return from Erfurt. Hélène spoke of him as *"mon page"* and treated him like a child. Her smile for him was the same as for everybody, but sometimes that smile made Pierre uncomfortable. Toward him Borís behaved with a particularly dignified and sad deference. This shade of deference also disturbed Pierre. He had suffered so painfully three years before from the mortification to which his wife had subjected him, that he now protected himself from the danger of its repetition, first by not being a husband to his wife, and secondly by not allowing himself to suspect.

"No, now that she has become a blue-stocking she has finally renounced her former infatuations," he told himself. "There has never been an instance of a blue-stocking being carried away by affairs of the heart"—a statement which, though gathered from an unknown source, he believed implicitly. Yet strange to say Borís's presence in his wife's drawing room (and he was almost always there) had a physical effect upon Pierre; it constricted his limbs and destroyed the unconsciousness and freedom of his movements.

"What a strange antipathy," thought Pierre, "yet I used to like him very much."

In the eyes of the world Pierre was a great gentleman, the rather blind and absurd husband of a distinguished wife, a clever crank who did nothing but harmed nobody, and was a first rate, good-natured fellow. But a complex and difficult process of internal development was taking place all this time in Pierre's soul, revealing much to him and causing him many spiritual doubts and joys.

Chapter X

PIERRE WENT ON WITH HIS DIARY, AND THIS IS WHAT HE WROTE IN IT DURING THAT TIME:

November 24th.

Got up at eight, read the Scriptures, then went to my duties. (By Joseph Alexéevich's advice Pierre had entered the service of the state and served on one of the committees.) Returned home for dinner and dined alone—the countess had many visitors I do not like. I ate and drank moderately, and after dinner copied out some passages for the Brothers. In the evening I went down to the countess and told a funny story about B., and only remembered that I ought not to have done so when everybody laughed loudly at it.

I am going to bed with a happy and tranquil mind. Great God, help me to walk in Thy paths, (1) to conquer anger by calmness and deliberation, (2) to vanquish lust by self-restraint and repulsion, (3) to withdraw from worldliness, but not avoid (*a*) the service of the State, (*b*) family duties, (*c*) relations with my friends, and (*d*) the management of my affairs.

November 27th.

I got up late. On waking I lay long in bed yielding to sloth. O God, help and strengthen me that I may walk in Thy ways! Read the Scriptures, but without proper feeling. Brother Urúsov came and we talked about worldly vanities. He told me of the Emperor's new projects. I began to criticize them, but remembered my rules and my benefactor's words—that a true freemason should be a zealous worker for the State when his aid is required and a quiet onlooker when not called on to assist. My tongue is my enemy. Brothers G. V. and O. visited me and we had a preliminary talk about the reception of a new Brother. They laid on me the duty of Rhetor. I feel myself weak and unworthy. Then our talk turned to the interpretation of the seven pillars and steps of the Temple, the seven sciences, the seven virtues, the seven vices and the seven gifts of the Holy Spirit. Brother O. was very eloquent. In the evening the admission took place. The new decoration of the premises contributed much to the magnificence of the spectacle. It was Borís Drubetskóy who was admitted. I nominated him and was the Rhetor. A strange feeling agitated me all the time I was alone with him in the dark chamber. I caught myself harboring a feeling of hatred toward him which I vainly tried to overcome. That is why I should really like to save him from evil and lead him into the path of truth, but evil thoughts of him did not leave me. It seemed to me that his object in entering the Brotherhood was merely to be intimate and in favor with members of our Lodge. Apart from the fact that he had asked me several times whether N. and S. were members of our Lodge (a question to which I could not reply) and that according to my observation he is incapable of feeling respect for our holy Order and is too preoccupied and satisfied with the outer man to desire spiritual improvement, I had no cause to doubt him, but he seemed to me insincere, and all the time I stood alone with him in the dark temple it seemed to me that he was smiling contemptuously at my words, and I wished really to stab his bare breast with the sword I held to it. I could not be eloquent, nor could I frankly mention my doubts to the Brothers and to the Grand Master. Great Architect of Nature, help me to find the true path out of the labyrinth of lies!

After this, three pages were left blank in the diary, and then the following was written:

I have had a long and instructive talk alone with Brother V., who advised me to hold fast by Brother A. Though I am unworthy, much was revealed to me. Adonai is the name of the creator of the world. Elohim is the name of the ruler of all. The third name is the name unutterable which means the *All.* Talks with Brother V. strengthen, refresh and support me in the path of virtue. In his presence doubt has no place. The distinction between the poor teachings of mundane science and our sacred all-embracing teaching is clear to me. Human sciences dissect everything to comprehend it, and kill everything to examine it. In the holy science of our order all is one, all is known in its entirety and life. The Trinity—the three elements of matter—are sulfur, mercury and salt. Sulfur is of an oily and fiery nature; in combination with salt by its fiery nature it arouses a desire in the latter by means of which it attracts mercury, seizes it, holds it, and in combination produces other bodies. Mercury is a fluid, volatile, spiritual essence. Christ, the Holy Spirit, Him! . . .

3rd December.

Awoke late, read the Scriptures but was apathetic. Afterward went and paced up and down the large hall. I wished to meditate, but instead my imagination pictured an occurrence of four years ago, when Dólokhov, meeting me in Moscow after our duel, said he hoped I was enjoying perfect peace of mind in spite of my wife's absence. At the time I gave him no answer. Now I recalled every detail of that meeting and in my mind gave him the most malevolent and bitter replies. I recollected myself and drove away that thought only when I found myself glowing with anger, but I did not sufficiently repent. Afterward Borís Drubetskóy came and began relating various adventures. His coming vexed me from the first, and I said something disagreeable to him. He replied. I flared up and said much that was unpleasant and even rude to him. He became silent, and I recollected myself only when it was too late. My God, I cannot get on with him at all. The cause of this is my egotism. I set myself above him and so become much worse than he, for he is lenient to my rudeness while I on the contrary nourish contempt for him. O God, grant that in his presence I may rather see my own vileness, and behave so that he too may benefit. After dinner I fell asleep and as I was drowsing off I clearly heard a voice saying in my left ear, "Thy day!"

I dreamed that I was walking in the dark and was suddenly surrounded by dogs, but I went on undismayed. Suddenly a smallish dog seized my left thigh with its teeth and would not let go. I began to throttle it with my hands. Scarcely had I torn it off before another, a bigger one, began biting me. I lifted it up but the higher I lifted it the bigger and heavier it grew. And suddenly Brother A. came and, taking my arm, led me to a building to enter which we had to pass along a narrow plank. I stepped on it, but it bent and gave way and I began to clamber up a fence which I could scarcely reach with my hands. After much effort I dragged myself up, so that my legs hung down on one side and my body on the other. I looked round and saw Brother A. standing on the fence and pointing me to a broad avenue and garden, and in the garden was a large and beautiful building. I woke up. O Lord, great Architect of Nature, help me to tear from myself these dogs—my passions—especially the last, which unites in itself the strength of all the former ones, and aid me to enter that temple of virtue to a vision of which I attained in my dream.

7th December.

I dreamed that Joseph Alexéevich was sitting in my house, and that I was very glad and wished to entertain him. It seemed as if I chattered incessantly with other people and suddenly remembered that this could not please him, and I wished to come close to him and embrace him. But as soon as I drew near I saw that his face had changed and grown young, and he was quietly telling me something about the teaching of our Order, but so softly that I could not hear it. Then it seemed that we all left the room and something strange happened. We were sitting or lying on the floor. He was telling me something, and I wished to show him my sensibility, and not listening to what he was saying I began picturing to myself the condition of my inner man and the grace of God sanctifying me. And tears came into my eyes, and I was glad he noticed this. But he looked at me with vexation and jumped up, breaking off his remarks. I felt abashed and asked whether what he had been saying did not concern me; but he did not reply, gave me a kind look, and then we suddenly found ourselves in my bedroom where there is a double bed. He lay down on the edge of it and I burned with longing to caress him and lie down too. And he said, "Tell me frankly what is your chief temptation? Do you know it? I think you know it already." Abashed by this question, I replied that sloth was my chief temptation. He shook his head incredulously; and even more abashed, I said that though I was living with my wife as he advised, I was not living with her as her husband. To this he replied that one should not deprive a wife of one's embraces, and gave me to understand that that was my duty. But I replied that I should be ashamed to do it, and suddenly everything vanished. And I awoke and found in my mind the text from the Gospel: "The life was the light of men. And the light shineth in darkness; and the darkness comprehended it not." Joseph Alexéevich's face had looked young and bright. That day I received a letter from my benefactor in which he wrote about "conjugal duties."

9th December.

I had a dream from which I awoke with a throbbing heart. I saw that I was in Moscow in my house, in the big sitting room, and Joseph Alexéevich came in from the drawing room. I seemed to know at once that the process of regeneration had already taken place in him, and I rushed to meet him. I embraced him and kissed his hands, and he said, "Hast thou noticed that my face is different?" I looked at him, still holding him in my arms, and saw that his face was young, but that he had no hair on his head and his features were quite changed. And I said, "I should have known you had I met you by chance," and I thought to myself, "Am I telling the truth?" And suddenly I saw him lying like a dead body; then he gradually recovered and went with me into my study carrying a large book of sheets of drawing paper; I said, "I drew that," and he answered by bowing his head. I opened the book, and on all the pages there were excellent drawings. And in my dream I knew that these drawings represented the love adventures of the soul with its beloved. And on its pages I saw a beautiful representation of a maiden in transparent garments and with a transparent body, flying up to the clouds. And I seemed to know that this maiden was nothing else than a representation of the Song of Songs. And looking at those drawings I dreamed I felt that I was doing wrong, but could not tear myself away from them. Lord, help me! My God, if Thy forsaking me is Thy doing, Thy will be done; but if I am myself the cause, teach me what I should do! I shall perish of my debauchery if Thou utterly desertest me!

Chapter XI

THE ROSTÓVS' MONETARY AFFAIRS HAD NOT IMPROVED DURING THE TWO YEARS THEY HAD SPENT in the country.

Though Nicholas Rostóv had kept firmly to his resolution and was still serving modestly in an obscure regiment, spending comparatively little, the way of life at Otrádnoe—Mítinka's management of affairs, in particular—was such that the debts inevitably increased every year. The only resource obviously presenting itself to the old count was to apply for an official post, so he had come to Petersburg to look for one and also, as he said, to let the lassies enjoy themselves for the last time.

Soon after their arrival in Petersburg Berg proposed to Véra and was accepted.

Though in Moscow the Rostóvs belonged to the best society without themselves giving it a thought, yet in Petersburg their circle of acquaintances was a mixed and indefinite one. In Petersburg they were provincials, and the very people they had entertained in Moscow without inquiring to what set they belonged, here looked down on them.

The Rostóvs lived in the same hospitable way in Petersburg as in Moscow, and the most diverse people met at their suppers. Country neighbors from Otrádnoe, impoverished old squires and their daughters, Perónskaya a maid of honor, Pierre Bezúkhov, and the son of their district postmaster who had obtained a post in Petersburg. Among the men who very soon became frequent visitors at the Rostóvs' house in Petersburg were Borís, Pierre whom the count had met in the street and dragged home with him, and Berg who spent whole days at the Rostóvs' and paid the eldest daughter, Countess Véra, the attentions a young man pays when he intends to propose.

Not in vain had Berg shown everybody his right hand wounded at Austerlitz and held a perfectly unnecessary sword in his left. He narrated that episode so persistently and with so important an air that everyone believed in the merit and usefulness of his deed, and he had obtained two decorations for Austerlitz.

In the Finnish war he also managed to distinguish himself. He had picked up the scrap of a grenade that had killed an aide-de-camp standing near the commander-in-chief, and had taken it to his commander. Just as he had done after Austerlitz, he related this occurrence at such length and so insistently that everyone again believed it had been necessary to do this, and he received two decorations for the Finnish war also. In 1809 he was a captain in the Guards, wore medals, and held some special lucrative posts in Petersburg.

Though some skeptics smiled when told of Berg's merits, it could not be denied that he was a painstaking and brave officer, on excellent terms with his superiors, and a moral young man with a brilliant career before him and an assured position in society.

Four years before, meeting a German comrade in the stalls of a Moscow theater, Berg had pointed out Véra Rostóva to him and had said in German, *"das soll mein Weib werden,"* and from that moment had made up his mind to marry her. Now in Petersburg, having considered the Rostóvs' position and his own, he decided that the time had come to propose.

Berg's proposal was at first received with a perplexity that was not flattering to him. At first it seemed strange that the son of an obscure Livonian gentleman should propose marriage to a Countess Rostóva; but Berg's chief characteristic was such a naïve and good-natured egotism that the Rostóvs involuntarily came to think it would be a good thing, since he himself was so firmly convinced that it was good, indeed excellent. Moreover, the Rostóvs' affairs were seriously embarrassed, as the suitor could not but know; and above all, Véra was twenty-four, had been taken out everywhere, and though she was certainly good-looking and sensible, no one up to now had proposed to her. So they gave their consent.

"You see," said Berg to his comrade, whom he called "friend" only because he knew that everyone has friends, "you see, I have considered it all, and should not marry if I had not thought it all out or if it were in any way unsuitable. But on the contrary, my Papa and Mamma are now provided for—I have arranged that rent for them in the Baltic Provinces—and I can live in Petersburg on my pay, and with her fortune and my good management we can get along nicely. I am not marrying for money—I consider that dishonorable—but a wife should bring her share and a husband his. I have my position in the service, she has connections and some means. In our times that is worth something, isn't it? But above all, she is a handsome, estimable girl, and she loves me . . ."

Berg blushed and smiled.

"And I love her, because her character is sensible and very good. Now the other sister, though they are the same family, is quite different—an unpleasant character and has not the same intelligence. She is so . . . you know? . . . Unpleasant . . . But my fiancée! . . . Well, you will be coming" he was going to say "to dine," but changed his mind and said "to take tea with us," and quickly doubling up his tongue he blew a small round ring of tobacco smoke, perfectly embodying his dream of happiness.

After the first feeling of perplexity aroused in the parents by Berg's proposal, the holiday tone of joyousness usual at such times took possession of the family, but the rejoicing was external and insincere. In the family's feeling toward this wedding a certain awkwardness and constraint was evident, as if they were ashamed of not having loved Véra sufficiently and of being so ready to get her off their hands. The old count felt this most. He would probably have been unable to state the cause of his embarrassment, but it resulted from the state of his affairs. He did not know at all how much he had, what his debts amounted to, or what dowry he could give Véra. When his daughters were born he had assigned to each of them, for her dowry, an estate with three hundred serfs; but one of these estates had already been sold, and the other was mortgaged, and the interest so much in arrears that it would have to be sold, so that it was impossible to give it to Véra. Nor had he any money.

Berg had already been engaged a month, and only a week remained before the wedding, but the count had not yet decided in his own mind the question of the dowry, nor spoken to his wife about it. At one time the count thought of giving her the Ryazán estate or of selling a forest, at another time of borrowing money on a note of hand. A few days before the wedding Berg entered the count's study early one morning, and with a pleasant smile respectfully asked his future father-in-law to let him know what Véra's dowry would be. The count was so disconcerted by this long-foreseen inquiry that without consideration he gave the first reply that came into his head. "I like your being businesslike about it. . . . I like it. You shall be satisfied. . . ."

And patting Berg on the shoulder he got up, wishing to end the conversation. But Berg, smiling pleasantly, explained that if he did not know for certain how much Véra would have and did not receive at least part of the dowry in advance, he would have to break matters off.

"Because, consider, count—if I allowed myself to marry now without having definite means to maintain my wife, I should be acting badly. . . ."

The conversation ended by the count, who wished to be generous and to avoid further importunity, saying that he would give a note of hand for eighty thousand rubles. Berg smiled meekly, kissed the count on the shoulder, and said that he was very grateful, but that it was impossible for him to arrange his new life without receiving thirty thousand in ready money. "Or at least twenty thousand, count," he added, "and then a note of hand for only sixty thousand."

"Yes, yes, all right!" said the count hurriedly. "Only excuse me, my dear fellow, I'll give you twenty thousand and a note of hand for eighty thousand as well. Yes, yes! Kiss me."

Chapter XII

NATÁSHA WAS SIXTEEN AND IT WAS THE YEAR 1809, THE VERY YEAR TO WHICH SHE HAD COUNTED on her fingers with Borís after they had kissed four years ago. Since then she had not seen him. Before Sónya and her mother, if Borís happened to be mentioned, she spoke quite freely of that episode as of some childish, long-forgotten matter that was not worth mentioning. But in the secret depths of her soul the question whether her engagement to Borís was a jest or an important, binding promise tormented her.

Since Borís left Moscow in 1805 to join the army he had had not seen the Rostóvs. He had been in Moscow several times, and had passed near Otrádnoe, but had never been to see them.

Sometimes it occurred to Natásha that he not wish to see her, and this conjecture was confirmed by the sad tone in which her elders spoke of him.

"Nowadays old friends are not remembered," the countess would say when Borís was mentioned.

Anna Mikháylovna also had of late visited them less frequently, seemed to hold herself with particular dignity, and always spoke rapturously and gratefully of the merits of her son and the brilliant career on which he had entered. When the Rostóvs came to Petersburg Borís called on them.

He drove to their house in some agitation. The memory of Natásha was his most poetic recollection. But he went with the firm intention of letting her and her parents feel that the childish relations between himself and Natásha could not be binding either on her or on him. He had a brilliant position in society thanks to his intimacy with Countess Bezúkhova, a brilliant position in the service thanks to the patronage of an important personage whose complete confidence he enjoyed, and he was beginning to make plans for marrying one of the richest heiresses in Petersburg, plans which might very easily be realized. When he entered the Rostóvs' drawing room Natásha was in her own room. When she heard of his arrival she almost ran into the drawing room, flushed and beaming with a more than cordial smile.

Borís remembered Natásha in a short dress, with dark eyes shining from under her curls and boisterous, childish laughter, as he had known her four years before; and so he was taken aback when quite a different Natásha entered, and his face expressed rapturous astonishment. This expression on his face pleased Natásha.

"Well, do you recognize your little madcap playmate?" asked the countess.

Borís kissed Natásha's hand and said that he was astonished at the change in her.

"How handsome you have grown!"

"I should think so!" replied Natásha's laughing eyes.

"And is Papa older?" she asked.

Natásha sat down and, without joining in Borís's conversation with the countess, silently and minutely studied her childhood's suitor. He felt the weight of that resolute and affectionate scrutiny and glanced at her occasionally.

Borís's uniform, spurs, tie, and the way his hair was brushed, were all *comme il faut* and in the latest fashion. This Natásha noticed at once. He sat rather sideways in the arm-chair next to the countess, arranging with his right hand the cleanest of gloves that fitted his left hand like a skin, and he spoke with a particularly refined compression of his lips about the amusement of the highest Petersburg society, recalling with mild irony old times in Moscow and Moscow acquaintances. It was not accidentally, Natásha felt, that he alluded, when speaking of the highest aristocracy, to an ambassador's ball he had attended, and to invitations he had received from N. N. and S. S.

All this time Natásha sat silent, glancing up at him from under her brows. This gaze disturbed and confused Borís more and more. He looked round more frequently toward her, and broke off in what he was saying. He did not stay more than ten minutes, then rose and took his leave. The same inquisitive, challenging and rather mocking eyes still looked at him. After his first visit Borís said to himself that Natásha attracted him just as much as ever, but that he must not yield to that feeling, because to marry her, a girl almost without fortune, would mean ruin to his career, while to renew their former relations without intending to marry her would be dishonorable. Borís made up his mind to avoid meeting Natásha, but despite that resolution he called again a few days later, and began calling often and spending whole days at the Rostóvs'. It seemed to him that he ought to have an explanation with Natásha and tell her that the old times must be forgotten, that in spite of everything . . . she could not be his wife, that he had no means, and they would never let her marry him. But he failed to do so and felt awkward about entering on such an explanation. From day to day he became more and more entangled. It seemed to her mother and Sónya that Natásha was in love with Borís as of old. She sang him his favorite songs, showed him her album, making him write in it, did not allow him to allude to the past, letting it be understood how delightful was the present; and every day he went away in a fog, without having said what he meant to, and not knowing what he was doing or why he came, or how it would all end. He left off visiting Hélène and received reproachful notes from her every day, and yet he continued to spend whole days with the Rostóvs.

Chapter XIII

One night when the old countess, in nightcap and dressing-jacket, without her false curls, and with her poor little knob of hair showing under her white cotton cap, knelt sighing and groaning on a rug and bowing to the ground in prayer, her door creaked and Natásha, also in a dressing-jacket with slippers on her bare feet and her hair in curl-papers, ran in. The countess—her prayerful mood dispelled—looked round and frowned. She was finishing her last prayer: "Can it be that this couch will be my grave?" Natásha, flushed and eager, seeing her mother in prayer, suddenly checked her rush, half sat down, and unconsciously put out her tongue as if chiding herself. Seeing that her mother was still praying she ran on tiptoe to the bed and, rapidly slipping one little foot against the other, pushed off her slippers and jumped onto the bed the countess had feared might become her grave. This couch was high, with a feather-bed and five pillows each smaller than the one below. Natásha jumped on it, sank into the feather-bed, rolled over to the wall and began snuggling up the bedclothes as she settled down, raising her knees to her chin, kicking out and laughing almost inaudibly, now covering herself up head and all, and now peeping at her mother.

The countess finished her prayers and came to the bed with a stern face, but seeing that Natásha's head was covered, she smiled in her kind, weak way.

"Now then, now then!" said she.

"Mamma, can we have a talk? Yes?" said Natásha. "Now just one on your throat and another . . . that'll do!" And seizing her mother round the neck, she kissed her on the throat. In her behavior to her mother Natásha seemed rough, but she was so sensitive and tactful that however she clasped her mother she always managed to do it without hurting her or making her feel uncomfortable or displeased.

"Well, what is it tonight?" said the mother, having arranged her pillows and waited until Natásha, after turning over a couple of times, had settled down beside her under the quilt, spread out her arms, and assumed a serious expression.

These visits of Natásha's at night before the count returned from his club, were one of the greatest pleasures of both mother and daughter.

"What is it tonight?—But I have to tell you . . ."

Natásha put her hand on her mother's mouth.

"About Borís . . . I know," she said seriously; "that's what I have come about. Don't say it—I know. No, do tell me!" and she removed her hand. "Tell me, Mamma! He's nice?"

"Natásha, you are sixteen. At your age I was married. You say Borís is nice. He is very nice, and I love him like a son. But what then? . . . What are you thinking about? You have quite turned his head, I can see that. . . ."

As she said this the countess looked round at her daughter. Natásha was lying looking steadily straight before her at one of the mahogany sphinxes carved on the corners of the bedstead, so that the countess only saw her daughter's face in profile. That face struck her by its peculiarly serious and concentrated expression.

Natásha was listening and considering.

"Well, what then?" said she.

"You have quite turned his head, and why? What do you want of him? You know you can't marry him."

"Why not?" said Natásha, without changing her position.

"Because he is young, because he is poor, because he is a relation . . . and because you yourself don't love him."

"How do you know?"

"I know. It is not right, darling!"

"But if I want to . . ." said Natásha.

"Leave off talking nonsense," said the countess.

"But if I want to . . ."

"Natásha, I am in earnest . . ."

Natásha did not let her finish. She drew the countess's large hand to her, kissed it on the back and then on the palm, then again turned it over and began kissing first one knuckle, then the space between the knuckles, then the next knuckle, whispering, "January, February, March, April, May. Speak, Mamma, why don't you say anything? Speak!" said she, turning to her mother, who was tenderly gazing at her daughter and in that contemplation seemed to have forgotten all she had wished to say.

"It won't do, my love! Not everyone will understand this friendship dating from your childish days, and to see him so intimate with you may injure you in the eyes of other young men who visit us, and above all it torments him for nothing. He may already have found a suitable and wealthy match, and now he's half crazy."

"Crazy?" repeated Natásha.

"I'll tell you some things about myself. I had a cousin . . ."

"I know! Cyril Matvéich . . . but he is old."

"He was not always old. But this is what I'll do, Natásha, I'll have a talk with Borís. He need not come so often. . . ."

"Why not, if he likes to?"

"Because I know it will end in nothing. . . ."

"How can you know? No, Mamma, don't speak to him! What nonsense!" said Natásha in the tone of one being deprived of her property. "Well, I won't marry, but let him come if he enjoys it and I enjoy it." Natásha smiled and looked at her mother. "Not to marry, but just *so,*" she added.

"How *so,* my pet?"

"Just *so.* There's no need for me to marry him. But . . . just *so.*"

"Just so, just so," repeated the countess, and shaking all over, she went off into a good-humored, unexpected, elderly laugh.

"Don't laugh, stop!" cried Natásha. "You're shaking the whole bed! You're awfully like me, just such another giggler. . . . Wait . . ." and she seized the countess's hands and kissed a knuckle of the little finger, saying, "June," and continued, kissing, "July, August," on the other hand. "But, Mamma, is he very much in love? What do you think? Was anybody ever so much in love with you? And he's very nice, very, very nice. Only not quite my taste—he is so narrow, like the dining room clock. . . . Don't you understand? Narrow, you know—gray, light gray . . ."

"What rubbish you're talking!" said the countess.

Natásha continued:

"Don't you really understand? Nicholas would understand. . . . Bezúkhov, now, is blue, dark-blue and red, and he is square."

"You flirt with him too," said the countess, laughing.

"No, he is a freemason, I have found out. He is fine, dark-blue and red. . . . How can I explain it to you?"

"Little countess!" the count's voice called from behind the door. "You're not asleep?" Natásha jumped up, snatched up her slippers, and ran barefoot to her own room.

It was a long time before she could sleep. She kept thinking that no one could understand all that she understood and all there was in her.

"Sónya?" she thought, glancing at that curled-up, sleeping little kitten with her enormous plait of hair. "No, how could she? She's virtuous. She fell in love with Nicholas and does not wish to know anything more. Even Mamma does not understand. It is wonderful how clever I am and how . . . charming she is," she went on, speaking of herself in the third person, and imagining it was some very wise man—the wisest and best of men—who was saying it of her. "There is everything, everything in her," continued this man. "She is unusually intelligent, charming . . . and then she is pretty, uncommonly pretty, and agile—she swims and rides splendidly . . . and her voice! One can really say it's a wonderful voice!"

She hummed a scrap from her favorite opera by Cherubini, threw herself on her bed, laughed at the pleasant thought that she would immediately fall asleep, called Dunyásha the maid to put out the candle, and before Dunyásha had left the room had already passed into yet another happier world of dreams, where everything was as light and beautiful as in reality, and even more so because it was different.

Next day the countess called Borís aside and had a talk with him, after which he ceased coming to the Rostóvs'.

Chapter XIV

ON THE 31ST OF DECEMBER, NEW YEAR'S EVE 1810, AN OLD GRANDEE OF CATHERINE'S DAY WAS giving a ball and midnight supper. The diplomatic corps and the Emperor himself were to be present.

The grandee's well-known mansion on the English Quay glittered with innumerable lights. Police were stationed at the brightly lit entrance which was carpeted with red baize, and not only gendarmes but dozens of police officers and even the policemaster himself stood at the porch. Carriages kept driving away and fresh ones arriving, with red-liveried footmen and footmen in plumed hats. From the carriages emerged men wearing uniforms, stars and ribbons, while ladies in satin and ermine cautiously descended the carriage steps which were let down for them with a clatter, and then walked hurriedly and noiselessly over the baize at the entrance.

Almost every time a new carriage drove up a whisper ran through the crowd and caps were doffed.

"The Emperor? . . . No, a minister . . . prince . . . ambassador. Don't you see the plumes? . . ." was whispered among the crowd.

One person, better dressed than the rest, seemed to know everyone and mentioned by name the greatest dignitaries of the day.

A third of the visitors had already arrived, but the Rostóvs, who were to be present, were still hurrying to get dressed.

There had been many discussions and preparations for this ball in the Rostóv family, many fears that the invitation would not arrive, that the dresses would not be ready, or that something would not be arranged as it should be.

Márya Ignátevna Perónskaya, a thin and sallow maid of honor at the court of the Dowager Empress, who was a friend and relation of the countess and piloted the provincial Rostóvs in Petersburg high society, was to accompany them to the ball.

They were to call for her at her house in the Taurida Gardens at ten o'clock, but it was already five minutes to ten and the girls were not yet dressed.

Natásha was going to her first grand ball. She had got up at eight that morning and had been in a fever of excitement and activity all day. All her powers since morning had been concentrated on ensuring that they all—she herself, Mamma and Sónya—should be as well dressed as possible. Sónya and her mother put themselves entirely in her hands. The countess was to wear a claret-colored velvet dress, and the two girls white gauze over pink silk slips, with roses on their bodices and their hair dressed *à la grecque*.

Everything essential had already been done; feet, hands, necks and ears washed, perfumed and powdered, as befits a ball; the open-work silk stockings and white satin shoes with ribbons were already on; the hairdressing was almost done. Sónya was finishing dressing and so was the countess, but Natásha, who had bustled about helping them all, was behindhand. She was still sitting before a looking-glass with a dressing-jacket thrown over her slender shoulders. Sónya stood ready dressed in the middle of the room, and pressing the head of a pin till it hurt her dainty fingers, was fixing on a last ribbon that squeaked as the pin went through it.

"That's not the way, that's not the way, Sónya!" cried Natásha turning her head and clutching with both hands at her hair which the maid who was dressing it had not time to release. "That bow is not right. Come here!"

Sónya sat down and Natásha pinned the ribbon on differently.

"Allow me, Miss! I can't do it like that," said the maid who was holding Natásha's hair.

"Oh, dear! Well then, wait. That's right, Sónya."

"Aren't you ready? It is nearly ten," came the countess's voice.

"Directly! Directly! And you, Mamma?"

"I have only my cap to pin on."

"Don't do it without me!" called Natásha. "You won't do it right."

"But it's already ten."

They had decided to be at the ball by half-past ten, and Natásha had still to get dressed and they had to call at the Taurida Gardens.

When her hair was done, Natásha, in her short petticoat from under which her dancing shoes showed, and in her mother's dressing-jacket, ran up to Sónya, scrutinized her, and then ran to her mother. Turning her mother's head this way and that, she fastened on the cap and hurriedly kissing her gray hair, ran back to the maids who were turning up the hem of her skirt.

The cause of the delay was Natásha's skirt, which was too long. Two maids were turning up the hem and hurriedly biting off the ends of thread. A third with pins in her mouth was running about between the countess and Sónya, and a fourth held the whole of the gossamer garment up high on one uplifted hand.

"Mávra, quicker, darling!"

"Give me my thimble, Miss, from there . . ."

"Whenever will you be ready?" asked the count coming to the door. "Here is some scent. Perónskaya must be tired of waiting."

"It's ready, Miss," said the maid, holding up the shortened gauze dress with two fingers, and blowing and shaking something off it, as if by this to express a consciousness of the airiness and purity of what she held.

Natásha began putting on the dress.

"In a minute! In a minute! Don't come in, Papa!" she cried to her father as he opened the door—speaking from under the filmy skirt which still covered her whole face.

Sónya slammed the door to. A minute later they let the count in. He was wearing a blue swallow-tail coat, shoes and stockings, and was perfumed and his hair pomaded.

"Oh, Papa! how nice you look! Charming!" cried Natásha, as she stood in the middle of the room smoothing out the folds of the gauze.

"If you please, Miss! allow me," said the maid, who on her knees was pulling the skirt straight and shifting the pins from one side of her mouth to the other with her tongue.

"Say what you like," exclaimed Sónya, in a despairing voice as she looked at Natásha, "say what you like, it's still too long."

Natásha stepped back to look at herself in the pier-glass. The dress *was* too long.

"Really, madam, it is not at all too long," said Mávra, crawling on her knees after her young lady.

"Well, if it's too long we'll take it up . . . we'll tack it up in one minute," said the resolute Dunyásha taking a needle that was stuck on the front of her little shawl and, still kneeling on the floor, set to work once more.

At that moment, with soft steps, the countess came in shyly, in her cap and velvet gown.

"Oo-oo, my beauty!" exclaimed the count, "she looks better than any of you!"

He would have embraced her but, blushing, she stepped aside fearing to be rumpled.

"Mamma, your cap, more to this side," said Natásha. "I'll arrange it," and she rushed forward so that the maids who were tacking up her skirt could not move fast enough and a piece of gauze was torn off.

"Oh goodness! What has happened? Really it was not my fault!"

"Never mind, I'll run it up, it won't show," said Dunyásha.

"What a beauty—a very queen!" said the nurse as she came to the door. "And Sónya! They are lovely!"

At a quarter past ten they at last got into their carriages and started. But they had still to call at the Taurida Gardens.

Perónskaya was quite ready. In spite of her age and plainness she had gone through the same process as the Rostóvs, but with less flurry—for to her it was a matter of routine. Her ugly old body was washed, perfumed and powdered in just the same way. She had washed behind her ears just as carefully, and when she entered her drawing room in her yellow dress, wearing her badge as maid of honor, her old lady's maid was as full of rapturous admiration as the Rostóvs' servants had been.

She praised the Rostóvs' toilets. They praised her taste and toilet, and at eleven o'clock, careful of their *coiffures* and dresses, they settled themselves in their carriages and drove off.

Chapter XV

NATÁSHA HAD NOT HAD A MOMENT FREE SINCE EARLY MORNING AND HAD NOT ONCE HAD TIME to think of what lay before her.

In the damp chill air and crowded closeness of the swaying carriage, she for the first time vividly imagined what was in store for her there at the ball, in those brightly lit rooms—with music, flowers, dances, the Emperor and all the brilliant young people of Petersburg. The prospect was so splendid that she hardly believed it would come true, so out of keeping was it with the chill darkness and closeness of the carriage. She understood all that awaited her only when, after stepping over the red baize at the entrance, she entered the hall, took off her fur cloak and, beside Sónya and in front of her mother, mounted the brightly illuminated stairs between the flowers. Only then did she remember how she must behave at a ball, and tried to assume the majestic air she considered indispensable for a girl on such an occasion. But, fortunately for her, she felt her eyes growing misty, she saw nothing clearly, her pulse beat a hundred to the minute and the blood throbbed at her heart. She could not assume that pose, which would have made her ridiculous, and she moved on almost fainting from excitement and trying with all her might to conceal it. And this was the very attitude that became her best. Before and behind them other visitors were entering, also talking in low tones and wearing ball dresses. The mirrors on the landing reflected ladies in white, pale blue, and pink dresses, with diamonds and pearls on their bare necks and arms.

Natásha looked in the mirrors and could not distinguish her reflection from the others. All was blended into one brilliant procession. On entering the ballroom the regular hum of voices, footsteps and greetings deafened Natásha, and the light and glitter dazzled her still more. The host and hostess, who had already been standing at the door for half an hour repeating the same words to the various arrivals, *"Charmé de vous voir,"* greeted the Rostóvs and Perónskaya in the same manner.

The two girls in their white dresses, each with a rose in her black hair, both curtsied in the same way, but the hostess's eye involuntarily rested longer on the slim Natásha. She looked at her and gave her alone a special smile in addition to her usual smile as hostess. Looking at her she may have recalled the golden, irrecoverable days of her own girlhood and her own first ball. The host also followed Natásha with his eyes and asked the count which was his daughter.

"Charming!" said he, kissing the tips of his fingers.

In the ballroom guests stood crowding at the entrance doors awaiting the Emperor. The countess took up a position in one of the front rows of that crowd. Natásha heard and felt that several people were asking about her and looking at her. She realized that those noticing her liked her, and this observation helped to calm her.

"There are some like ourselves and some worse," she thought.

Perónskaya was pointing out to the countess the most important people at the ball.

"That is the Dutch ambassador, do you see? That gray-haired man," she said, indicating an old man with a profusion of silver-gray curly hair, who was surrounded by ladies laughing at something he said.

"Ah, here she is, the Queen of Petersburg, Countess Bezúkhova," said Perónskaya, indicating Hélène who had just entered. "How lovely! She is quite equal to Márya Antónovna. See how the men, young and old, pay court to her. Beautiful and clever . . . they say Prince——is quite mad about her. But see, those two, though not good-looking, are even more run after."

She pointed to a lady who was crossing the room followed by a very plain daughter.

"She is a splendid match, a millionairess," said Perónskaya. "And look, here come her suitors."

"That is Bezúkhova's brother, Anatole Kurágin," she said, indicating a handsome officer of the Horse-Guards who passed by them with head erect, looking at something over the heads of the ladies. "He's handsome, isn't he? I hear they will marry him to that rich girl. But your cousin, Drubetskóy, is also very attentive to her. They say she has millions. Oh yes, that's the French ambassador himself!" she replied to the countess's inquiry about Caulaincourt. "Looks as if he were a king! All the same, the French are charming, very charming. No one more charming in society. Ah, here she is! Yes, she is still the most beautiful of them all, our Márya Antónovna! And how simply she is dressed! Lovely! And that stout one in spectacles is the universal freemason," she went on, indicating Pierre. "Put him beside his wife and he looks a regular buffoon!"

Pierre, swaying his stout body, advanced making way through the crowd and nodding to right and left as casually and good-naturedly as if he were passing through a crowd at a fair. He pushed through, evidently looking for someone.

Natásha looked joyfully at the familiar face of Pierre, "the buffoon," as Perónskaya had called him, and knew he was looking for them, and for her in particular. He had promised to be at the ball and introduce partners to her.

But before he reached them Pierre stopped beside a very handsome, dark man of middle height, and in a white uniform, who stood by a window talking to a tall man wearing stars and a ribbon. Natásha at once recognized the shorter and younger man in the white uniform: it was Bolkónski, who seemed to her to have grown much younger, happier and better-looking.

"There's someone else we know—Bolkónski, do you see, Mamma?" said Natásha, pointing out Prince Andrew. "You remember, he stayed a night with us at Otrádnoe."

"Oh, you know him?" said Perónskaya. "I can't bear him. *Il fait à présent la pluie et le beau temps.* He's too proud for anything. Takes after his father. And he's hand in glove with Speránski, writing some project or other. Just look how he treats the ladies! There's one talking to him and he has turned away," she said, pointing at him. "I'd give it to him if he treated me as he does those ladies."

Chapter XVI

SUDDENLY EVERYBODY STIRRED, BEGAN TALKING, AND PRESSED FORWARD AND THEN BACK, AND between the two rows, which separated, the Emperor entered to the sounds of music that had immediately struck up. Behind him walked his host and hostess. He walked in rapidly, bowing to right and left as if anxious to get the first moments of the reception over. The band played the polonaise in vogue at that time on account of the words that had been set to it, beginning: "Alexander, Elisaveta, all our hearts you ravish quite . . ." The Emperor passed on to the drawing room, the crowd made a rush for the doors, and several persons with excited faces hurried there and back again. Then the crowd hastily retired from the drawing room door, at which the Emperor reappeared talking to the hostess. A young man, looking distraught, pounced down on the ladies, asking them to move aside. Some ladies, with faces betraying complete forgetfulness of all the rules of decorum, pushed forward to the detriment of their toilets. The men began to choose partners and take their places for the polonaise.

Everyone moved back, and the Emperor came smiling out of the drawing room leading his hostess by the hand but not keeping time to the music. The host followed with Márya Antónovna Narýshkina; then came ambassadors, ministers and various generals, whom Perónskaya diligently named. More than half the ladies already had partners and were taking up, or preparing to take up, their positions for the polonaise. Natásha felt that she would be left with her mother and Sónya among a minority of women who crowded near the wall, not having been invited to dance. She stood with her slender arms hanging down, her scarcely defined bosom rising and falling regularly, and with bated breath and glittering, frightened eyes gazed straight before her, evidently prepared for the height of joy or misery. She was not concerned about the Emperor or any of those great people whom Perónskaya was pointing out—she had but one thought: "Is it possible no one will ask me, that I shall not be among the first to dance? Is it possible that not one of all these men will notice me? They do not even seem to see me, or if they do they look as if they were saying, 'Ah, she's not the one I'm after, so it's not worth looking at her!' No, it's impossible," she thought. "They must know how I long to dance, how splendidly I dance, and how they would enjoy dancing with me."

The strains of the polonaise, which had continued for a considerable time, had begun to sound like a sad reminiscence in Natásha's ears. She wanted to cry. Perónskaya had left them. The count was at the other end of the room. She and the countess and Sónya were standing by themselves as in the depths of a forest amid that crowd of strangers, with no one interested in them and not wanted by anyone. Prince Andrew with a lady passed by, evidently not recognizing them. The handsome Anatole was smilingly talking to a partner on his arm, and looked at Natásha as one looks at a wall. Borís passed them twice and each time turned away. Berg and his wife, who were not dancing, came up to them.

This family gathering seemed humiliating to Natásha—as if there were nowhere else for the family to talk but here at the ball. She did not listen to or look at Véra, who was telling her something about her own green dress.

At last the Emperor stopped beside his last partner (he had danced with three) and the music ceased. A worried aide-de-camp ran up to the Rostóvs requesting them to stand farther back, though as it was they were already close to the wall, and from the gallery resounded the distinct, precise, enticingly rhythmical strains of a valse. The Emperor looked smilingly down the room. A minute passed but no one had yet begun dancing. An aide-de-camp, the Master of Ceremonies, went up to Countess Bezúkhova and asked her to dance. She smilingly raised her hand and laid it on his shoulder without looking at him. The aide-de-camp, an adept in his art, grasping his partner firmly round her waist, with confident deliberation started smoothly, gliding first round the edge of the circle, then at the corner of the room he caught Hélène's left hand and turned her, the only sound audible, apart from the ever-quickening music, being the rhythmic click of the spurs on his rapid, agile feet, while at every third beat his partner's velvet dress spread out and seemed to flash as she whirled round. Natásha gazed at them and was ready to cry because it was not she who was dancing that first turn of the valse.

Prince Andrew, in the white uniform of a cavalry colonel, wearing stockings and dancing shoes, stood looking animated and bright in the front row of the circle not far from the Rostóvs. Baron Firhoff was talking to him about the first sitting of the Council of State to be held next day. Prince Andrew, as one closely connected with Speránski and participating in the work of the legislative commission, could give reliable information about that sitting, concerning which various rumors were current. But not listening to what Firhoff was saying, he was gazing now at the sovereign, and now at the men intending to dance who had not yet gathered courage to enter the circle.

Prince Andrew was watching these men abashed by the Emperor's presence, and the women who were breathlessly longing to be asked to dance.

Pierre came up to him and caught him by the arm.

"You always dance. I have a protégée, the young Rostóva, here. Ask her," he said.

"Where is she?" asked Bolkónski. "Excuse me!" he added, turning to the baron, "we will finish this conversation elsewhere—at a ball one must dance." He stepped forward in the direction Pierre indicated. The despairing, dejected expression of Natásha's face caught his eye. He recognized her, guessed her feelings, saw that it was her debut, remembered her conversation at the window, and with an expression of pleasure on his face approached Countess Rostóva.

"Allow me to introduce you to my daughter," said the countess, with heightened color.

"I have the pleasure of being already acquainted, if the countess remembers me," said Prince Andrew with a low and courteous bow quite belying Perónskaya's remarks about his rudeness, and approaching Natásha he held out his arm to grasp her waist before he had completed his invitation. He asked her to waltz. That tremulous expression on Natásha's face, prepared either for despair or rapture, suddenly brightened into a happy, grateful, childlike smile.

"I have long been waiting for you," that frightened happy little girl seemed to say by the smile that replaced the threatened tears, as she raised her hand to Prince Andrew's shoulder. They were the second couple to enter the circle. Prince Andrew was one of the best dancers of his day and Natásha danced exquisitely. Her little feet in their white satin dancing-shoes did their work swiftly, lightly and independently of herself, while her face beamed with ecstatic happiness. Her slender bare arms and neck were not beautiful—compared to Hélène's her shoulders looked thin and her bosom undeveloped. But Hélène seemed, as it were, hardened by a varnish left by the thousands of looks that had scanned her person, while Natásha was like a girl exposed for the first time, who would have felt very much ashamed had she not been assured that this was absolutely necessary.

Prince Andrew liked dancing, and wishing to escape as quickly as possible from the political and clever talk which everyone addressed to him, wishing also to break up the circle of restraint he disliked, caused by the Emperor's presence, he danced, and had chosen Natásha because Pierre pointed her out to him and because she was the first pretty girl who caught his eye; but scarcely had he embraced that slender supple figure and felt her stirring so close to him and smiling so near him, than the wine of her charm rose to his head, and he felt himself revived and rejuvenated when after leaving her he stood breathing deeply and watching the other dancers.

Chapter XVII

After Prince Andrew, Borís came up to ask Natásha for a dance, and then the aide-de-camp who had opened the ball, and several other young men, so that, flushed and happy, and passing on her superfluous partners to Sónya, she did not cease dancing all the evening. She noticed and saw nothing of what occupied everyone else. Not only did she fail to notice that the Emperor talked a long time with the French ambassador, and how particularly gracious he was to a certain lady, or that Prince So-and-so and So-and-so did and said this and that, and that Hélène had great success and was honored was by the special attention of So-and-so, but she did not even see the Emperor, and only noticed that he had gone because the ball became livelier after his departure. For one of the merry cotillions before supper Prince Andrew was again her partner. He reminded her of their first encounter in the Otrádnoe avenue, and how she had been unable to sleep that moonlight night, and told her how he had involuntarily overheard her. Natásha blushed at that recollection and tried to excuse herself, as if there had been something to be ashamed of in what Prince Andrew had overheard.

Like all men who have grown up in society, Prince Andrew liked meeting someone there not of the conventional society stamp. And such was Natásha, with her surprise, her delight, her shyness and even her mistakes in speaking French. With her he behaved with special care and tenderness, sitting beside her and talking of the simplest and most unimportant matters; he admired her shy grace. In the middle of the cotillion, having completed one of the figures, Natásha, still out of breath, was returning to her seat when another dancer chose her. She was tired and panting and evidently thought of declining, but immediately put her hand gaily on the man's shoulder, smiling at Prince Andrew.

"I'd be glad to sit beside you and rest: I'm tired; but you see how they keep asking me, and I'm glad of it, I'm happy and I love everybody, and you and I understand it all," and much, much more was said in her smile. When her partner left her Natásha ran across the room to choose two ladies for the figure.

"If she goes to her cousin first and then to another lady, she will be my wife," said Prince Andrew to himself quite to his own surprise, as he watched her. She did go first to her cousin.

"What rubbish sometimes enters one's head!" thought Prince Andrew, "but what is certain is that that girl is so charming, so original, that she won't be dancing here a month before she will be married. . . . Such as she are rare here," he thought, as Natásha, readjusting a rose that was slipping on her bodice, settled herself beside him.

When the cotillion was over the old count in his blue coat came up to the dancers. He invited Prince Andrew to come and see them, and asked his daughter whether she was enjoying herself. Natásha did not answer at once but only looked up with a smile that said reproachfully: "How can you ask such a question?"

"I have never enjoyed myself so much before!" she said, and Prince Andrew noticed how her thin arms rose quickly as if to embrace her father, and instantly dropped again. Natásha was happier than she had ever been in her life. She was at that height of bliss when one becomes completely kind and good and does not believe in the possibility of evil, unhappiness, or sorrow.

At that ball Pierre for the first time felt humiliated by the position his wife occupied in court circles. He was gloomy and absent-minded. A deep furrow ran across his forehead, and standing by a window he stared over his spectacles seeing no one.

On her way to supper Natásha passed him.

Pierre's gloomy, unhappy look struck her. She stopped in front of him. She wished to help him, to bestow on him the superabundance of her own happiness.

"How delightful it is, count!" said she. "Isn't it?"

Pierre smiled absent-mindedly, evidently not grasping what she said.

"Yes, I am very glad," he said.

"How can people be dissatisfied with anything?" thought Natásha. "Especially such a capital fellow as Bezúkhov!" In Natásha's eyes all the people at the ball alike were good, kind and splendid people, loving one another; none of them capable of injuring another—and so they ought all to be happy.

Chapter XVIII

NEXT DAY PRINCE ANDREW THOUGHT OF THE BALL, BUT HIS MIND DID NOT DWELL ON IT LONG. "Yes, it was a very brilliant ball," and then . . . "Yes, that little Rostóva is very charming. There's something fresh, original, un-Petersburg-like about her that distinguishes her." That was all he thought about yesterday's ball, and after his morning tea he set to work.

But either from fatigue or want of sleep he was ill-disposed for work and could get nothing done. He kept criticizing his own work as he often did, and was glad when he heard someone coming.

The visitor was Bítski, who served on various committees, frequented all the societies in Petersburg, and a passionate devotee of the new ideas and of Speránski, and a diligent Petersburg newsmonger—one of those men who choose their opinions like their clothes according to the fashion, but who for that very reason appear to be the warmest partisans. Hardly had he got rid of his hat before he ran into Prince Andrew's room with a preoccupied air and at once began talking. He had just heard particulars of that morning's sitting of the Council of State opened by the Emperor, and he spoke of it enthusiastically. The Emperor's speech had been extraordinary. It had been a speech such as only constitutional monarchs deliver. "The Sovereign plainly said that the Council and Senate are *estates* of the realm, he said that the government must rest not on authority but on secure bases. The Emperor said that the fiscal system must be reorganized and the accounts published," recounted Bítski, emphasizing certain words and opening his eyes significantly.

"Ah, yes! today's events mark an epoch, the greatest epoch in our history," he concluded.

Prince Andrew listened to the account of the opening of the Council of State, which he had so impatiently awaited and to which he had attached such importance, and was surprised that this event, now that it had taken place, did not affect him, and even seemed quite insignificant. He listened with quiet irony to Bítski's enthusiastic account of it. A very simple thought occurred to him: "What does it matter to me or to Bítski what the Emperor was pleased to say at the Council? Can all that make me any happier or better?"

And this simple reflection suddenly destroyed all the interest Prince Andrew had felt in the impending reforms. He was going to dine that evening at Speránski's, "with only a few friends," as the host had said when inviting him. The prospect of that dinner in the intimate home circle of the man he so admired, had greatly interested Prince Andrew, especially as he had not yet seen Speránski in his domestic surroundings, but now he felt disinclined to go to it.

At the appointed hour however he entered the modest house Speránski owned in the Taurida Gardens. In the parqueted dining room of this small house, remarkable for its extreme cleanliness (suggesting that of a monastery), Prince Andrew, who was rather late, found the friendly gathering of Speránski's intimate acquaintances already assembled at five o'clock. There were no ladies present except Speránski's little daughter (long-faced like her father) and her governess. The other guests were Gervais, Magnítski and Stolypin. While still in the anteroom Prince Andrew heard loud voices and a ringing staccato laugh—a laugh such as one hears on the stage. Someone—it sounded like Speránski—was distinctly ejaculating *ha-ha-ha*. Prince Andrew had never before heard Speránski's famous laugh, and this ringing, high-pitched laughter from a statesman made a strange impression on him.

He entered the dining room. The whole company were standing between two windows at a small table laid with hors-d'oeuvres. Speránski, wearing a gray swallow-tail coat with a star on the breast, and evidently still the same waistcoat and high white stock he had worn at the meeting of the Council of State, stood at the table with a beaming countenance. His guests surrounded him. Magnítski, addressing himself to Speránski, was relating an anecdote, and Speránski was laughing in advance at what Magnítski was going to say. When Prince Andrew entered the room Magnítski's words were again crowned by laughter. Stolypin gave a deep bass guffaw as he munched a piece of bread and cheese. Gervais laughed softly with a hissing chuckle, and Speránski in a high-pitched staccato manner.

Still laughing, Speránski held out his soft white hand to Prince Andrew.

"Very pleased to see you, prince," he said. "One moment . . ." he went on, turning to Magnítski and interrupting his story. "We have agreed that this is a dinner for recreation, with not a word about business!" and turning again to the narrator he began to laugh afresh.

Prince Andrew looked at the laughing Speránski with astonishment, regret, and disillusionment. It seemed to him that this was not Speránski but someone else. Everything that had formerly appeared mysterious and fascinating in Speránski suddenly became plain and unattractive.

At dinner the conversation did not cease for a moment and seemed to consist of the contents of a book of funny anecdotes. Before Magnítski had finished his story someone else was anxious to relate something still funnier. Most of the anecdotes, if not relating to the State service, related to people in the service. It seemed that in this company the insignificance of those people was so definitely accepted that the only possible attitude toward them was one of good-humored ridicule. Speránski related how at the Council that morning a deaf dignitary, when asked his opinion, replied that he thought so too. Gervais gave a long account of an official revision, remarkable for the stupidity of everybody concerned. Stolypin, stuttering, broke into the conversation and began excitedly talking of the abuses that existed under the former order of things—threatening to give a serious turn to the conversation. Magnítski starting quizzing Stolypin about his vehemence. Gervais intervened with a joke, and the talk reverted to its former lively tone.

Evidently Speránski liked to rest after his labors and find amusement in a circle of friends, and his guests, understanding his wish, tried to enliven him and amuse themselves. But their gaiety seemed to Prince Andrew mirthless and tiresome. Speránski's high-pitched voice struck him unpleasantly, and the incessant laughter grated on him like a false note. Prince Andrew did not laugh and feared that he would be a damper on the spirits of the company, but no one took any notice of his being out of harmony with the general mood. They all seemed very gay.

He tried several times to join in the conversation, but his remarks were tossed aside each time like a cork thrown out of the water, and he could not jest with them.

There was nothing wrong or unseemly in what they said, it was witty and might have been funny, but it lacked just that something which is the salt of mirth, and they were not even aware that such a thing existed.

After dinner Speránski's daughter and her governess rose. He patted the little girl with his white hand and kissed her. And that gesture, too, seemed unnatural to Prince Andrew.

The men remained at table over their port—English fashion. In the midst of a conversation that was started about Napoleon's Spanish affairs, which they all agreed in approving, Prince Andrew began to express a contrary opinion. Speránski smiled and, with an evident wish to prevent the conversation from taking an unpleasant course, told a story that had no connection with the previous conversation. For a few moments all were silent.

Having sat some time at table, Speránski corked a bottle of wine, and remarking, "Nowadays good wine rides in a carriage and pair," passed it to the servant and got up. All rose and continuing to talk loudly went into the drawing room. Two letters brought by a courier were handed to Speránski and he took them to his study. As soon as he had left the room the general merriment stopped and the guests began to converse sensibly and quietly with one another.

"Now for the recitation!" said Speránski on returning from his study. "A wonderful talent!" he said to Prince Andrew, and Magnítski immediately assumed a pose and began reciting some humorous verses in French which he had composed about various well-known Petersburg people. He was interrupted several times by applause. When the verses were finished Prince Andrew went up to Speránski and took his leave.

"Where are you off to so early?" asked Speránski.

"I promised to go to a reception."

They said no more. Prince Andrew looked closely into those mirrorlike, impenetrable eyes, and felt that it had been ridiculous of him to have expected anything from Speránski and from any of his own activities connected with him, or ever to have attributed importance to what Speránski was doing. That precise, mirthless laughter rang in Prince Andrew's ears long after he had left the house.

When he reached home Prince Andrew began thinking of his life in Petersburg during those last four months as if it were something new. He recalled his exertions and solicitations, and the history of his project of army reform, which had been accepted for consideration and which they were trying to pass over in silence simply because another, a very poor one, had already been prepared and submitted to the Emperor. He thought of the meetings of a committee of which Berg was a member. He remembered how carefully and at what length everything relating to form and procedure was discussed at those meetings, and how sedulously and promptly all that related to the gist of the business was evaded. He recalled his labors on the Legal Code, and how painstakingly he had translated the articles of the Roman and French codes into Russian, and he felt ashamed of himself. Then he vividly pictured to himself Boguchárovo, his occupations in the country, his journey to Ryazán; he remembered the peasants and Dron the village elder, and mentally applying to them the Personal Rights he had divided into paragraphs, he felt astonished that he could have spent so much time on such useless work.

Chapter XIX

NEXT DAY PRINCE ANDREW CALLED AT A FEW HOUSES HE HAD NOT VISITED BEFORE, AND AMONG them at the Rostóvs' with whom he had renewed acquaintance at the ball. Apart from considerations of politeness which demanded the call, he wanted to see that original, eager girl who had left such a pleasant impression on his mind, in her own home.

Natásha was one of the first to meet him. She was wearing a dark blue house dress in which Prince Andrew thought her even prettier than in her ball dress. She and all the Rostóv family welcomed him as an old friend, simply and cordially. The whole family, whom he had formerly judged severely, now seemed to him to consist of excellent, simple and kindly people. The old count's hospitality and good nature which struck one especially in Petersburg as a pleasant surprise, were such that Prince Andrew could not refuse to stay to dinner. "Yes," he thought, "they are capital people, who of course have not the slightest idea what a treasure they possess in Natásha; but they are kindly folk and form the best possible setting for this strikingly poetic, charming girl, overflowing with life!"

In Natásha Prince Andrew was conscious of a strange world completely alien to him and brimful of joys unknown to him, a different world, that in the Otrádnoe avenue and at the window that moonlight night had already begun to disconcert him. Now this world disconcerted him no longer and was no longer alien to him, but he himself having entered it found in it a new enjoyment.

After dinner Natásha, at Prince Andrew's request, went to the clavichord and began singing. Prince Andrew stood by a window talking to the ladies and listened to her. In the midst of a phrase he ceased speaking and suddenly felt tears choking him, a thing he had thought impossible for him. He looked at Natásha as she sang, and something new and joyful stirred in his soul. He felt happy and at the same time sad. He had absolutely nothing to weep about yet he was ready to weep. What about? His former love? The little princess? His disillusionments? . . . His hopes for the future? . . . Yes and no. The chief reason was a sudden, vivid sense of the terrible contrast between something infinitely great and illimitable within him, and that limited and material something that he, and even she, was. This contrast weighed on and yet cheered him while she sang.

As soon as Natásha had finished she went up to him and asked how he liked her voice. She asked this and then became confused, feeling that she ought not to have asked it. He smiled, looking at her, and said he liked her singing as he liked everything she did.

Prince Andrew left the Rostóvs' late in the evening. He went to bed from habit, but soon realized that he could not sleep. Having lit his candle he sat up in bed, then got up, then lay down again not at all troubled by his sleeplessness: his soul was as fresh and joyful as if he had stepped out of a stuffy room into God's own fresh air. It did not enter his head that he was in love with Natásha; he was not thinking about her, but only picturing her to himself, and in consequence all life appeared in a new light. "Why do I strive, why do I toil in this narrow, confined frame, when life, all life with all its joys, is open to me?" said he to himself. And for the first time for a very long while he began making happy plans for the future. He decided that he must attend to his son's education by finding a tutor and putting the boy in his charge, then he ought to retire from the service and go abroad, and see England, Switzerland and Italy. "I must use my freedom while I feel so much strength and youth in me," he said to himself. "Pierre was right when he said one must believe in the possibility of happiness in order to be happy, and now I do believe in it. Let the dead bury their dead, but while one has life one must live and be happy!" thought he.

Chapter XX

One morning Colonel Adolf Berg, whom Pierre knew as he knew everybody in Moscow and Petersburg, came to see him. Berg arrived in an immaculate brand-new uniform, with his hair pomaded and brushed forward over his temples as the Emperor Alexander wore his hair.

"I have just been to see the countess, your wife. Unfortunately she could not grant my request, but I hope, count, I shall be more fortunate with you," he said with a smile.

"What is it you wish, colonel? I am at your service."

"I have now quite settled in my new rooms, count" (Berg said this with perfect conviction that this information could not but be agreeable), "and so I wish to arrange just a small party for my own and my wife's friends." (He smiled still more pleasantly.) "I wished to ask the countess and you to do me the honor of coming to tea and to supper."

Only Countess Hélène, considering the society of such people as the Bergs beneath her, could be cruel enough to refuse such an invitation. Berg explained so clearly why he wanted to collect at his house a small but select company, and why this would give him pleasure, and why though he grudged spending money on cards or anything harmful, he was prepared to run into some expense for the sake of good society—that Pierre could not refuse, and promised to come.

"But don't be late, count, if I may venture to ask; about ten minutes to eight, please. We shall make up a rubber. Our general is coming. He is very good to me. We shall have supper, count. So you will do me the favor."

Contrary to his habit of being late, Pierre on that day arrived at the Bergs' house, not at ten but at fifteen minutes to eight.

Having prepared everything necessary for the party, the Bergs were ready for their guests' arrival.

In their new, clean and light study with its small busts and pictures and new furniture, sat Berg and his wife. Berg, closely buttoned up in his new uniform, sat beside his wife explaining to her that one always could and should be acquainted with people above one, because only then does one get satisfaction from acquaintances.

"You can get to know something, you can ask for something. See how I managed from my first promotion." (Berg measured his life not by years but by promotions.) "My comrades are still nobodies, while I am only waiting for a vacancy to command a regiment, and have the happiness to be your husband." (He rose and kissed Véra's hand, and on the way to her straightened out a turned-up corner of the carpet.) "And how have I obtained all this? Chiefly by knowing how to choose my aquaintances. It goes without saying that one must be conscientious and methodical."

Berg smiled with a sense of his superiority over a weak woman, and paused, reflecting that this dear wife of his was after all but a weak woman who could not understand all that constitutes a man's dignity, what it was *ein Mann zu sein*. Véra at the same time smiling with a sense of superiority over her good, conscientious husband, who all the same understood life wrongly, as according to Véra all men did. Berg, judging by his wife, thought all women weak and foolish. Véra, judging only by her husband and generalizing from that observation, supposed that all men, though they understand nothing and are conceited and selfish, ascribe common sense to themselves alone.

Berg rose and embraced his wife carefully, so as not to crush her lace fichu for which he had paid a good price, kissing her straight on the lips.

"The only thing is, we mustn't have children too soon," he continued, following an unconscious sequence of ideas.

"Yes," answered Véra, "I don't at all want that. We must live for society."

"Princess Yusupova wore one exactly like this," said Berg, pointing to the fichu with a happy and kindly smile.

Just then Count Bezúkhov was announced. Husband and wife glanced at one another, both smiling with self-satisfaction, and each mentally claiming the honor of this visit.

"This is what comes of knowing how to make acquaintances," thought Berg. "This is what comes of knowing how to conduct oneself."

"But please don't interrupt me when I am entertaining the guests," said Véra, "because I know what interests each of them and what to say to different people."

Berg smiled again.

"It can't be helped: men must sometimes have masculine conversation," said he.

They received Pierre in their small, new drawing room, where it was impossible to sit down anywhere without disturbing its symmetry, neatness and order; so it was quite comprehensible and not strange that Berg, having generously offered to disturb the symmetry of an arm-chair or of the sofa for his dear guest, but being apparently painfully undecided on the matter himself, eventually left the visitor to settle the question of selection. Pierre disturbed the symmetry by moving a chair for himself, and Berg and Véra immediately began their evening party, interrupting each other in their efforts to entertain their guest.

Véra, having decided in her own mind that Pierre ought to be entertained with conversation about the French embassy, at once began accordingly. Berg, having decided that masculine conversation was required, interrupted his wife's remarks and touched on the question of the war with Austria, and unconsciously jumped from the general subject to personal considerations as to the proposals made him to take part in the Austrian campaign and the reasons why he had declined them. Though the conversation was very incoherent and Véra was angry at the intrusion of the masculine element, both husband and wife felt with satisfaction that, even if only one guest was present, their evening had begun very well and was as like as two peas to every other evening party with its talk, tea, and lit candles.

Before long Borís, Berg's old comrade, arrived. There was a shade of condescension and patronage in his treatment of Berg and Véra. After Borís came a lady with the colonel, then the general himself, then the Rostóvs, and the party became unquestionably exactly like all other evening parties. Berg and Véra could not repress their smiles of satisfaction at the sight of all this movement in their drawing room, at the sound of the disconnected talk, the rustling of dresses, and the bowing and scraping. Everything was just as everybody always has it, especially so the general, who admired the apartment, patted Berg on the shoulder, and with parental authority superintended the setting out of the table for boston. The general sat down by Count Ilyá Rostóv, who was next to himself the most important guest. The old people sat with the old, the young with the young, and the hostess at the tea-table, on which stood exactly the same kind of cakes in a silver cake-basket as the Pánins had at their party. Everything was just as it was everywhere else.

Chapter XXI

PIERRE, AS ONE OF THE PRINCIPAL GUESTS, HAD TO SIT DOWN TO BOSTON WITH COUNT ROSTÓV, the general and the colonel. At the card-table he happened to be directly facing Natásha, and was struck by a curious change that had come over her since the ball. She was silent, and not only less pretty than at the ball, but only redeemed from plainness by her look of gentle indifference to everything around.

"What's the matter with her?" thought Pierre, glancing at her. She was sitting by her sister at the tea-table, and reluctantly, without looking at him, made some reply to Borís who sat down beside her. After playing out a whole suit and to his partner's delight taking five tricks, Pierre, hearing greetings and the steps of someone who had entered the room while he was picking up his tricks, glanced again at Natásha.

"What has happened to her?" he asked himself with still greater surprise.

Prince Andrew was standing before her, saying something to her with a look of tender solicitude. She having raised her head was looking up at him, flushed and evidently trying to master her rapid breathing. And the bright glow of some inner fire that had been suppressed was again alight in her. She was completely transformed, and from a plain girl had again become what she had been at the ball.

Prince Andrew went up to Pierre, and the latter noticed a new and youthful expression in his friend's face.

Pierre changed places several times during the game, sitting now with his back to Natásha and now facing her, but during the whole of the six rubbers he watched her and his friend.

"Something very important is happening between them," thought Pierre, and a feeling that was both joyful and painful agitated him and made him neglect the game.

After six rubbers the general got up, saying that it was no use playing like that, and Pierre was released. Natásha on one side was talking with Sónya and Borís, and Véra with a subtle smile was saying something to Prince Andrew. Pierre went up to his friend, and asking whether they were talking secrets, sat down beside them. Véra, having noticed Prince Andrew's attentions to Natásha, decided that at a party, a real evening party, subtle allusions to the tender passion were absolutely necessary, and seizing a moment when Prince Andrew was alone, began a conversation with him about feelings in general and about her sister. With so intellectual a guest as she considered Prince Andrew to be, she felt that she had to employ her diplomatic tact.

When Pierre went up to them he noticed that Véra was being carried away by her self-satisfied talk, but that Prince Andrew seemed embarrassed, a thing that rarely happened with him.

"What do you think?" Véra was saying with an arch smile. "You are so discerning, prince, and understand people's characters so well at a glance. What do you think of Natalie? Could she be constant in her attachments? Could she, like other women" (Véra meant herself), "love a man once for all and remain true to him forever? That is what I consider true love. What do you think, prince?"

"I know your sister too little," replied Prince Andrew, with a sarcastic smile under which he wished to hide his embarrassment, "to be able to solve so delicate a question, and then I have noticed that the less attractive a woman is the more constant she is likely to be," he added, and looked up Pierre who was just approaching them.

"Yes, that is true, prince. In our days," continued Véra—mentioning "our days" as people of limited intelligence are fond of doing, imagining that they have discovered and appraised the peculiarities of "our days" and that human characteristics change with the times—"in our days a girl has so much freedom that the pleasure of being courted often stifles real feeling in her. And it must be confessed that Natalie is very susceptible." This return to the subject of Natalie caused Prince Andrew to knit his brows with discomfort: he was about to rise, but Véra continued with a still more subtle smile:

"I think no one has been more courted than she," she went on, "but till quite lately she never cared seriously for anyone. Now you know, count," she said to Pierre, "even our dear cousin Borís, who, between ourselves, was very far gone in the land of tenderness . . ." (alluding to a map of love much in vogue at that time).

Prince Andrew frowned and remained silent.

"You are friendly with Borís, aren't you?" asked Véra.

"Yes, I know him . . ."

"I expect he has told you of his childish love for Natásha?"

"Oh, there was childish love?" suddenly asked Prince Andrew, blushing unexpectedly.

"Yes, you know between cousins intimacy often leads to love. *Le cousinage est un dangereux voisinage.* Don't you think so?"

"Oh, undoubtedly!" said Prince Andrew, and with sudden and unnatural liveliness he began chaffing Pierre about the need to be very careful with his fifty-year-old Moscow cousins, and in the midst of these jesting remarks he rose, taking Pierre by the arm, and drew him aside.

"Well?" asked Pierre, seeing his friend's strange animation with surprise, and noticing the glance he turned on Natásha as he rose.

"I must . . . I must have a talk with you," said Prince Andrew. "You know that pair of women's gloves?" (He referred to the masonic gloves given to a newly initiated Brother to present to the woman he loved.) "I . . . but no, I will talk to you later on," and with a strange light in his eyes and restlessness in his movements, Prince Andrew approached Natásha and sat down beside her. Pierre saw how Prince Andrew asked her something and how she flushed as she replied.

But at that moment Berg came to Pierre and began insisting that he should take part in an argument between the general and the colonel on the affairs in Spain.

Berg was satisfied and happy. The smile of pleasure never left his face. The party was very successful and quite like other parties he had seen. Everything was similar: the ladies' subtle talk, the cards, the general raising his voice at the card table, and the samovar and the tea-cakes; only one thing was lacking that he had always seen at the evening parties he wished to imitate. They had not yet had a loud conversation among the men and a dispute about something important and clever. Now the general had begun such a discussion and so Berg drew Pierre to it.

Chapter XXII

NEXT DAY, HAVING BEEN INVITED BY THE COUNT, PRINCE ANDREW DINED WITH THE ROSTÓVS and spent the rest of the day there.

Everyone in the house realized for whose sake Prince Andrew came, and without concealing it he tried to be with Natásha all day. Not only in the soul of the frightened yet happy and enraptured Natásha, but in the whole house, there was a feeling of awe at something important that was bound to happen. The countess looked with sad and sternly serious eyes at Prince Andrew when he talked to Natásha, and timidly started some artificial conversation about trifles as soon as he looked her way. Sónya was afraid to leave Natásha and afraid of being in the way when she was with them. Natásha grew pale, in a panic of expectation, when she remained alone with him for a moment. Prince Andrew surprised her by his timidity. She felt that he wanted to say something to her but could not bring himself to do so.

In the evening, when Prince Andrew had left, the countess went up to Natásha and whispered: "Well, what?"

"Mamma! For heaven's sake don't ask me anything now! One can't talk about that," said Natásha.

But all the same that night Natásha, now agitated and now frightened, lay a long time in her mother's bed gazing straight before her. She told her how he had complimented her, how he told her he was going abroad, asked her where they were going to spend the summer, and then how he had asked her about Borís.

"But such a . . . such a . . . never happened to me before!" she said. "Only I feel afraid in his presence. I am always afraid when I'm with him. What does that mean? Does it mean that it's the real thing? Yes? Mamma, are you asleep?"

"No, my love; I am frightened myself," answered her mother. "Now go!"

"All the same I shan't sleep. What silliness, to sleep! Mummy! Mummy! such a thing never happened to me before," she said, surprised and alarmed at the feeling she was aware of in herself. "And could we ever have thought! . . ."

It seemed to Natásha that even at the time she first saw Prince Andrew at Otrádnoe she had fallen in love with him. It was as if she feared this strange, unexpected happiness of meeting again the very man she had then chosen (she was firmly convinced she had done so) and of finding him, as it seemed, not indifferent to her.

"And it had to happen that he should come specially to Petersburg while we are here. And it had to happen that we should meet at that ball. It is fate. Clearly it is fate that everything led up to this! Already *then*, directly I saw him I felt something peculiar."

"What else did he say to you? What are those verses? Read them . . ." said her mother, thoughtfully, referring to some verses Prince Andrew had written in Natásha's album.

"Mamma, one need not be ashamed of his being a widower?"

"Don't, Natásha! Pray to God. 'Marriages are made in heaven,' " said her mother.

"Darling Mummy, how I love you! How happy I am!" cried Natásha, shedding tears of joy and excitement and embracing her mother.

At that very time Prince Andrew was sitting with Pierre and telling him of his love for Natásha and his firm resolve to make her his wife.

That day Countess Hélène had a reception at her house. The French ambassador was there, and a foreign Prince of the Blood who had of late become a frequent visitor of hers, and many brilliant ladies and gentlemen. Pierre, who had come downstairs, walked through the rooms and struck everyone by his preoccupied, absent-minded and morose air.

Since the ball he had felt the approach of a fit of nervous depression and had made desperate efforts to combat it. Since the intimacy of his wife with the royal Prince, Pierre had unexpectedly been made a gentleman of the bedchamber, and from that time he had begun to feel oppressed and ashamed in court society, and dark thoughts of the vanity of all things human came to him oftener than before. At the same time the feeling he had noticed between his protégée Natásha and Prince Andrew accentuated his gloom by the contrast between his own position and his friend's. He tried equally to avoid thinking about his wife, and about Natásha and Prince Andrew; and again everything seemed to him insignificant in comparison with eternity; again the question: For what? presented itself; and he forced himself to work day and night at masonic labors, hoping to drive away the evil spirit that threatened him. Toward midnight, after he had left the countess's apartments, he was sitting upstairs in a shabby dressing-gown, copying out the original transaction of the Scottish Lodge of Freemasons at a table in his low room cloudy with tobacco smoke, when someone came in. It was Prince Andrew.

"Ah, it's you!" said Pierre with a preoccupied, dissatisfied air. "And I, you see, am hard at it." He pointed to his manuscript-book with that air of escaping from the ills of life with which unhappy people look at their work.

Prince Andrew, with a beaming, ecstatic expression of renewed life on his face, paused in front of Pierre and, not noticing his sad look, smiled at him with the egotism of joy.

"Well, dear heart," said he, "I wanted to tell you about it yesterday and I have come to do so today. I never experienced anything like it before. I am in love, my friend!"

Suddenly Pierre heaved a deep sigh and dumped his heavy person down on the sofa beside Prince Andrew.

"With Natásha Rostóva, yes?" said he.

"Yes, yes! Who else should it be? I should never have believed it, but the feeling is stronger than I. Yesterday I tormented myself and suffered, but I would not exchange even that torment for anything in the world, I have not lived till now. At last I live, but I can't live without her! But can she love me? . . . I am too old for her. . . . Why don't you speak?"

"I? I? What did I tell you?" said Pierre suddenly, rising and beginning to pace up and down the room. "I always thought it. . . . That girl is such a treasure . . . she is a rare girl. . . . My dear friend, I entreat you, don't philosophize, don't doubt, marry, marry, marry. . . . And I am sure there will not be a happier man than you."

"But what of her?"

"She loves you."

"Don't talk rubbish . . ." said Prince Andrew, smiling and looking into Pierre's eyes.

"She does, I know," Pierre cried fiercely.

"But do listen," returned Prince Andrew, holding him by the arm. "Do you know the condition I am in? I must talk about it to someone."

"Well, go on, go on. I am very glad," said Pierre, and his face really changed, his brow became smooth and he listened gladly to Prince Andrew. Prince Andrew seemed, and really was, quite a different, quite a new man. Where was his spleen, his contempt for life, his disillusionment? Pierre was the only person to whom he made up his mind to speak openly; and to him he told all that was in his soul. Now he boldly and lightly made plans for an extended future, said he could not sacrifice his own happiness to his father's caprice, and spoke of how he would either make his father consent to this marriage and love her, or would do without his consent; then he marveled at the feeling that had mastered him as at something strange, apart from and independent of himself.

"I should not have believed anyone who told me that I was capable of such love," said Prince Andrew. "It is not at all the same feeling that I knew in the past. The whole world is now for me divided into two halves: one half is she, and there all is joy, hope, light: the other half is everything where she is not, and there all is gloom and darkness. . . ."

"Darkness and gloom," reiterated Pierre: "yes, yes, I understand that."

"I cannot help loving the light, it is not my fault. And I am very happy! You understand me? I know you are glad for my sake."

"Yes, yes," Pierre assented, looking at his friend with a touched and sad expression in his eyes. The brighter Prince Andrew's lot appeared to him, the gloomier seemed his own.

Chapter XXIII

PRINCE ANDREW NEEDED HIS FATHER'S CONSENT TO HIS MARRIAGE, AND TO OBTAIN THIS HE started for the country next day.

His father received his son's communication with external composure, but inward wrath. He could not comprehend how anyone could wish to alter his life or introduce anything new into it, when his own life was already ending. "If only they would let me end my days as I want to," thought the old man, "then they might do as they please." With his son however he employed the diplomacy he reserved for important occasions and, adopting a quiet tone, discussed the whole matter.

In the first place the marriage was not a brilliant one as regards birth, wealth or rank. Secondly, Prince Andrew was no longer as young as he had been and his health was poor (the old man laid special stress on this), while she was very young. Thirdly, he had a son whom it would be a pity to entrust to a chit of a girl. "Fourthly and finally," the father said, looking ironically at his son, "I beg you to put it off for a year: go abroad, take a cure, look out as you wanted to for a German tutor for Prince Nicholas. Then if your love or passion or obstinacy—as you please—is still as great, marry! And that's my last word on it. Mind, the last! . . ." concluded the prince, in a tone which showed that nothing would make him alter his decision.

Prince Andrew saw clearly that the old man hoped that his feelings, or his fiancée's, would not stand a year's test, or that he (the old prince himself) would die before then, and he decided to conform to his father's wish—to propose, and postpone the wedding for a year.

Three weeks after the last evening he had spent with the Rostóvs, Prince Andrew returned to Petersburg.

Next day after her talk with her mother Natásha expected Bolkónski all day, but he did not come. On the second and third day it was the same. Pierre did not come either and Natásha, not knowing that Prince Andrew had gone to see his father, could not explain his absence to herself.

Three weeks passed in this way. Natásha had no desire to go out anywhere and wandered from room to room like a shadow, idle and listless; she wept secretly at night and did not go to her mother in the evenings. She blushed continually and was irritable. It seemed to her that everybody knew about her disappointment and was laughing at her and pitying her. Strong as was her inward grief, this wound to her vanity intensified her misery.

Once she came to her mother, tried to say something, and suddenly began to cry. Her tears were those of an offended child who does not know why it is being punished.

The countess began to soothe Natásha, who after first listening to her mother's words, suddenly interrupted her:

"Leave off, Mamma! I don't think, and don't want to think about it! He just came and then left off, left off . . ."

Her voice trembled, and she again nearly cried, but recovered and went on quietly:

"And I don't at all want to get married. And I am afraid of him; I have now become quite calm, quite calm."

The day after this conversation Natásha put on the old dress which she knew had the peculiar property of conducing to cheerfulness in the mornings, and that day she returned to the old way of life which she had abandoned since the ball. Having finished her morning tea she went to the ballroom, which she particularly liked for its loud resonance, and began singing her solfeggio. When she had finished her first exercise she stood still in the middle of the room and sang a musical phrase that particularly pleased her. She listened joyfully (as though she had not expected it) to the charm of the notes reverberating, filling the whole empty ballroom, and slowly dying away; and all at once she felt cheerful. "What's the good of making so much of it? Things are nice as it is," she said to herself, and she began walking up and down the room, not stepping simply on the resounding parquet but treading with each step from the heel to the toe (she had on a new and favorite pair of shoes) and listening to the regular tap of the heel and creak of the toe as gladly as she had to the sounds of her own voice. Passing a mirror she glanced into it. "There, that's me!" the expression of her face seemed to say as she caught sight of herself. "Well, and very nice too! I need nobody."

A footman wanted to come in to clear away something in the room but she would not let him, and having closed the door behind him continued her walk. That morning she had returned to her favorite mood—love of, and delight in, herself. "How charming that Natásha is!" she said again, speaking as some third, collective, male person. "Pretty, a good voice, young, and in nobody's way if only they leave her in peace." But however much they left her in peace she could not now be at peace, and immediately felt this.

In the hall the porch door opened, and someone asked, "At home?" and then footsteps were heard. Natásha was looking at the mirror, but did not see herself. She listened to the sounds in the hall. When she saw herself, her face was pale. It was *he*. She knew this for certain, though she hardly heard his voice through the closed doors.

Pale and agitated, Natásha ran into the drawing room.

"Mamma! Bolkónski has come!" she said. "Mamma, it is awful, it is unbearable! I don't want . . . to be tormented? What am I to do? . . ."

Before the countess could answer, Prince Andrew entered the room with an agitated and serious face. As soon as he saw Natásha his face brightened. He kissed the countess's hand and Natásha's, and sat down beside the sofa.

"It is long since we had the pleasure . . ." began the countess, but Prince Andrew interrupted her by answering her intended question, obviously in haste to say what he had to.

"I have not been to see all this time because I have been at my father's. I had to talk over a very important matter with him. I only got back last night," he said glancing at Natásha; "I want to have a talk with you, countess," he added after a moment's pause.

The countess lowered her eyes, sighing deeply.

"I am at your disposal," she murmured.

Natásha knew that she ought to go away, but was unable to do so: something gripped her throat, and regardless of manners she stared straight at Prince Andrew with wide-open eyes.

"At once? This instant! . . . No, it can't be!" she thought.

Again he glanced at her, and that glance convinced her that she was not mistaken. Yes, at once, that very instant, her fate would be decided.

"Go, Natásha! I will call you," said the countess in a whisper.

Natásha glanced with frightened imploring eyes at Prince Andrew and at her mother and went out.

"I have come, countess, to ask for your daughter's hand," said Prince Andrew.

The countess's face flushed hotly, but she said nothing.

"Your offer . . ." she began at last sedately. He remained silent, looking into her eyes. "Your offer . . ." (she grew confused) "is agreeable to us, and . . . I accept your offer. I am glad. And my husband . . . I hope . . . but it will depend on her . . ."

"I will speak to her when I have your consent. . . . Do you give it to me?" said Prince Andrew.

"Yes," replied the countess. She held out her hand to him, and with a mixed feeling of estrangement and tenderness pressed her lips to his forehead as he stooped to kiss her hand. She wished to love him as a son, but felt that to her he was a stranger and a terrifying man. "I am sure my husband will consent," said the countess, "but your father . . ."

"My father, to whom I have told my plans, has made it an express condition of his consent that the wedding is not to take place for a year. And I wished to tell you of that," said Prince Andrew.

"It is true that Natásha is still young, but—so long as that? . . ."

"It is unavoidable," said Prince Andrew with a sigh.

"I will send her to you," said the countess, and left the room.

"Lord have mercy upon us!" she repeated while seeking her daughter.

Sónya said that Natásha was in her bedroom. Natásha was sitting on the bed, pale and dry-eyed, and was gazing at the icons and whispering something as she rapidly crossed herself. Seeing her mother she jumped up and flew to her.

"Well, Mamma? . . . Well? . . ."

"Go, go to him. He is asking for your hand," said the countess, coldly it seemed to Natásha. "Go . . . go," said the mother, sadly and reproachfully, with a deep sigh, as her daughter ran away.

Natásha never remembered how she entered the drawing room. When she came in and saw him she paused. "Is it possible that this stranger has now become *everything* to me?" she asked herself, and immediately answered "Yes, everything! He alone is now dearer to me than everything in the world." Prince Andrew came up to her with downcast eyes.

"I have loved you from the very first moment I saw you. May I hope?"

He looked at her and was struck by the serious impassioned expression of her face. Her face said: "Why ask? Why doubt what you cannot but know? Why speak, when words cannot express what one feels?"

She drew near to him and stopped. He took her hand and kissed it.

"Do you love me?"

"Yes, yes!" Natásha murmured as if in vexation. Then she sighed loudly and, catching her breath more and more quickly, began to sob.

"What is it? What's the matter?"

"Oh, I am so happy!" she replied, smiled through her tears, bent over closer to him, paused for an instant as if asking herself whether she might, and then kissed him.

Prince Andrew held her hands, looked into her eyes, and did not find in his heart his former love for her. Something in him had suddenly changed; there was no longer the former poetic and mystic charm of desire, but there was pity for her feminine and childish weakness, fear at her devotion and trustfulness, and an oppressive yet joyful sense of the duty that now bound him to her forever. The present feeling, though not so bright and poetic as the former, was stronger and more serious.

"Did your mother tell you that it cannot be for a year?" asked Prince Andrew, still looking into her eyes.

"Is it possible that I—the 'chit of a girl,' as everybody called me," thought Natásha—"is it possible that I am now to be the *wife* and the equal of this strange, dear, clever man whom even my father looks up to? Can it be true? Can it be true that there can be no more playing with life, that now I am grown-up, that on me now lies a responsibility for my every word and deed? Yes, but what did he ask me?"

"No," she replied, but she had not understood his question.

"Forgive me!" he said. "But you are so young, and I have already been through so much in life. I am afraid for you, you do not yet know yourself."

Natásha listened with concentrated attention, trying but failing to take in the meaning of his words.

"Hard as this year which delays my happiness will be," continued Prince Andrew, "it will give you time to be sure of yourself. I ask you to make me happy in a year, but you are free: our engagement shall remain a secret, and should you find that you do not love me, or should you come to love . . ." said Prince Andrew with an unnatural smile.

"Why do you say that?" Natásha interrupted him. "You know that from the very day you first came to Otrádnoe I have loved you," she cried, quite convinced that she spoke the truth.

"In a year you will learn to know yourself. . . ."

"A whole year!" Natásha repeated suddenly, only now realizing that the marriage was to be postponed for a year. "But why a year? Why a year? . . ."

Prince Andrew began to explain to her the reasons for this delay. Natásha did not hear him.

"And can't it be helped?" she asked. Prince Andrew did not reply, but his face expressed the impossibility of altering that decision.

"It's awful! Oh, it's awful! awful!" Natásha suddenly cried, and again burst into sobs. "I shall die, waiting a year: it's impossible, it's awful!" She looked into her lover's face and saw in it a look of commiseration and perplexity.

"No, no! I'll do anything!" she said, suddenly checking her tears. "I am so happy."

The father and mother came into the room and gave the betrothed couple their blessing.

From that day Prince Andrew began to frequent the Rostóvs' as Natásha's affianced lover.

Chapter XXIV

No betrothal ceremony took place and Natásha's engagement to Bolkónski was not announced; Prince Andrew insisted on that. He said that as he was responsible for the delay he ought to bear the whole burden of it; that he had given his word and bound himself forever, but that he did not wish to bind Natásha and gave her perfect freedom. If after six months she felt that she did not love him she would have full right to reject him. Naturally neither Natásha nor her parents wished to hear of this, but Prince Andrew was firm. He came every day to the Rostóvs', but did not behave to Natásha as an affianced lover: he did not use the familiar *thou*, but said *you* to her, and kissed only her hand. After their engagement, quite different, intimate and natural relations sprang up between them. It was as if they had not known each other till now. Both liked to recall how they had regarded each other when as yet they were *nothing* to one another; they felt themselves now quite different beings: then they were artificial, now natural and sincere. At first the family felt some constraint in intercourse with Prince Andrew; he seemed a man from another world, and for a long time Natásha trained the family to get used to him, proudly assuring them all that he only appeared to be different, but was really just like all of them, and that she was not afraid of him and no one else ought to be. After a few days they grew accustomed to him, and without restraint in his presence pursued their usual way of life, in which he took his part. He could talk about rural economy with the count, fashions with the countess and Natásha, and about albums and fancy-work with Sónya. Sometimes the household both among themselves and in his presence expressed their wonder at how it had all happened, and at the evident omens there had been of it: Prince Andrew's coming to Otrádnoe and their coming to Petersburg, and the likeness between Natásha and Prince Andrew which her nurse had noticed on his first visit, and Andrew's encounter with Nicholas in 1805, and many other incidents betokening that it had to be.

In the house that poetic dullness and quiet reigned which always accompanies the presence of a betrothed couple. Often when all sitting together everyone kept silent. Sometimes the others would get up and go away and the couple, left alone, still remained silent. They rarely spoke of their future life. Prince Andrew was afraid and ashamed to speak of it. Natásha shared this as she did all his feelings, which she constantly divined. Once she began questioning him about his son. Prince Andrew blushed, as he often did now—Natásha particularly liked it in him—and said that his son would not live with them.

"Why not?" asked Natásha in a frightened tone.

"I cannot take him away from his grandfather, and besides . . ."

"How I should have loved him!" said Natásha, immediately guessing his thought; "but I know you wish to avoid any pretext for finding fault with us."

Sometimes the old count would come up, kiss Prince Andrew, and ask his advice about Pétya's education or Nicholas's service. The old countess sighed as she looked at them; Sónya was always getting frightened lest she should be in the way and tried to find excuses for leaving them alone, even when they did not wish it. When Prince Andrew spoke (he could tell a story very well), Natásha listened to him with pride; when she spoke she noticed with fear and joy that he gazed attentively and scrutinizingly at her. She asked herself in perplexity: "What does he look for in me? He is trying to discover something by looking at me! What if what he seeks in me is not there?" Sometimes she fell into one of the mad, merry moods characteristic of her, and then she particularly loved to hear and see how Prince Andrew laughed. He seldom laughed, but when he did he abandoned himself entirely to his laughter, and after such a laugh she always felt nearer to him. Natásha would have been completely happy if the thought of the separation awaiting her and drawing near had not terrified her, just as the mere thought of it made him turn pale and cold.

On the eve of his departure from Petersburg Prince Andrew brought with him Pierre, who had not been to the Rostóvs' once since the ball. Pierre seemed disconcerted and embarrassed. He was talking to the countess, and Natásha sat down beside a little chess-table with Sónya, thereby inviting Prince Andrew to come too. He did so.

"You have known Bezúkhov a long time?" he asked. "Do you like him?"

"Yes, he's a dear, but very absurd."

And as usual when speaking of Pierre, she began to tell anecdotes of his absent-mindedness, some of which had even been invented about him.

"Do you know I have entrusted him with our secret? I have known him from childhood. He has a heart of gold. I beg you, Natalie," Prince Andrew said with sudden seriousness—"I am going away and heaven knows what may happen. You may cease to . . . all right, I know I am not to say that. Only this, then: whatever may happen to you when I am not here . . ."

"What can happen?"

"Whatever trouble may come," Prince Andrew continued, "I beg you, Mademoiselle Sophie, whatever may happen, to turn to him alone for advice and help! He is a most absent-minded and absurd fellow, but he has a heart of gold."

Neither her father, nor her mother, nor Sónya, nor Prince Andrew himself, could have foreseen how the separation from her lover would act on Natásha. Flushed and agitated she went about the house all that day, dry-eyed, occupied with most trivial matters as if not understanding what awaited her. She did not even cry when, on taking leave, he kissed her hand for the last time. "Don't go!" she said in a tone that made him wonder whether he really ought not to stay and which he remembered long afterward. Nor did she cry when he was gone; but for several days she sat in her room dry-eyed, taking no interest in anything and only saying now and then, "Oh, why did he go away?"

But a fortnight after his departure, to the surprise of those around her, she recovered from her mental sickness just as suddenly and became her old self again, but with a change in her moral physiognomy, as a child gets up after a long illness with a changed expression of face.

Chapter XXV

During that year after his son's departure, Prince Nicholas Bolkónski's health and temper became much worse. He grew still more irritable, and it was Princess Mary who generally bore the brunt of his frequent fits of unprovoked anger. He seemed carefully to seek out her tender spots so as to torture her mentally as harshly as possible. Princess Mary had two passions and consequently two joys—her nephew, little Nicholas, and religion—and these were the favorite subjects of the prince's attacks and ridicule. Whatever was spoken of he would bring round to the superstitiousness of old maids, or the petting and spoiling of children. "You want to make him"—little Nicholas—"into an old maid like yourself! A pity! Prince Andrew wants a son and not an old maid," he would say. Or, turning to Mademoiselle Bourienne, he would ask her in Princess Mary's presence how she liked our village priests and icons and would joke about them.

He continually hurt Princess Mary's feelings and tormented her, but it cost her no effort to forgive him. Could he be to blame toward her, or could her father, whom she knew loved her in spite of it all, be unjust? And what is justice? The princess never thought of that proud word "justice." All the complex laws of man centered for her in one clear and simple law—the law of love and self-sacrifice taught us by Him who lovingly suffered for mankind though He Himself was God. What had she to do with the justice or injustice of other people? She had to endure and love, and that she did.

During the winter Prince Andrew had come to Bald Hills and had been gay, gentle, and more affectionate than Princess Mary had known him for a long time past. She felt that something had happened to him, but he said nothing to her about his love. Before he left he had a long talk with his father about something, and Princess Mary noticed that before his departure they were dissatisfied with one another.

Soon after Prince Andrew had gone, Princess Mary wrote to her friend Julie Karágina in Petersburg, whom she had dreamed (as all girls dream) of marrying to her brother, and who was at that time in mourning for her own brother, killed in Turkey.

Sorrow, it seems, is our common lot, my dear, tender friend Julie.

Your loss is so terrible that I can only explain it to myself as a special providence of God who, loving you, wishes to try you and your excellent mother. Oh, my friend! Religion, and religion alone, can—I will not say comfort us—but save us from despair. Religion alone can explain to us what without its help man cannot comprehend: why, for what cause, kind and noble beings able to find happiness in life—not merely harming no one but necessary to the happiness of others—are called away to God, while cruel, useless, harmful persons, or such as are a burden to themselves and to others, are left living. The first death I saw, and one I shall never forget—that of my dear sister-in-law—left that impression on me. Just as you ask destiny why your splendid brother had to die, so I asked why that angel Lise, who not only never wronged anyone, but in whose soul there were never any unkind thoughts, had to die. And what do you think, dear friend? Five years have passed since then, and already I, with my petty understanding, begin to see clearly why she had to die, and in what way that death was but an expression of the infinite goodness of the Creator, whose every action, though generally incomprehensible to us, is but a manifestation of His infinite love for His creatures. Perhaps, I often think, she was too angelically innocent to have the strength to perform all a mother's duties. As a young wife she was irreproachable; perhaps she could not have been so as a mother. As it is, not only has she left us, and particularly Prince Andrew, with the purest regrets and memories, but probably she will there receive a place I dare not hope for myself. But not to speak of her alone, that early and terrible death has had the most beneficent influence on me and on my brother in spite of all our grief. Then, at the moment of our loss, these thoughts could not occur to me; I should then have dismissed them with horror, but now they are very clear and certain. I write all this to you, dear friend, only to convince you of the Gospel truth which has become for me a principle of life: not a single hair of our heads will fall without His will. And His will is governed only by infinite love for us, and so whatever befalls us is for our good.

You ask whether we shall spend next winter in Moscow. In spite of my wish to see you, I do not think so and do not want to do so. You will be surprised to hear that the reason for this is Buonaparte! The case is this: my father's health is growing noticeably worse, he cannot stand any contradiction and is becoming irritable. This irritability is, as you know, chiefly directed to political questions. He cannot endure the notion that Buonaparte is negotiating on equal terms with all the sovereigns of Europe and particularly with our own, the grandson of the Great Catherine! As you know, I am quite indifferent to politics, but from my father's remarks and his talks with Michael Ivánovich I know all that goes on in the world and especially about the honors conferred on Buonaparte, who only at Bald Hills in the whole world, it seems, is not accepted as a great man, still less as Emperor of France. And my father cannot stand this. It seems to me that it is chiefly because of his political views that my father is reluctant to speak of going to Moscow; for he foresees the encounters that would result from his way of expressing his views regardless of anybody. All the benefit he might derive from a course of treatment he would lose as a result of the disputes about Buonaparte which would be inevitable. In any case it will be decided very shortly.

Our family life goes on in the old way except for my brother Andrew's absence. He, as I wrote you before, has changed very much of late. After his sorrow he only this year quite recovered his spirits. He has again become as I used to know him when a child: kind, affectionate, with that heart of gold to which I know no equal. He has realized, it seems to me, that life is not over for him. But together with this mental change he has grown physically much weaker. He has become thinner and more nervous. I am anxious about him and glad he is taking this trip abroad which the doctors recommended long ago. I hope it will cure him. You write that in Petersburg he is spoken of as one of the most active, cultivated and capable of the young men. Forgive my vanity as a relation, but I never doubted it. The good he has done to everybody here, from his peasants up to the gentry, is incalculable. On his arrival in Petersburg he received only his due. I always wonder at the way rumors fly from Petersburg to Moscow, especially such false ones as that you write about—I mean the report of my brother's betrothal to the little Rostóva. I do not think my brother will ever marry again, and certainly not her; and this is why: first, I know that though he rarely speaks about the wife he has lost, the grief of that loss has gone too deep in his heart for him ever to decide to give her a successor and our little angel a stepmother. Secondly because, as far as I know, that girl is not the kind of girl who could please Prince Andrew. I do not think he would choose her for a wife, and frankly I do not wish it. But I am running on too long and am at the end of my second sheet. Good-bye, my dear friend. May God keep you in His holy and mighty care. My dear friend, Mademoiselle Bourienne, sends you kisses.

MARY

Chapter XXVI

IN THE MIDDLE OF THE SUMMER PRINCESS MARY RECEIVED AN UNEXPECTED LETTER FROM PRINCE Andrew in Switzerland in which he gave her strange and surprising news. He informed her of his engagement to Natásha Rostóva. The whole letter breathed loving rapture for his betrothed, and tender and confiding affection for his sister. He wrote that he had never loved as he did now, and that only now did he understand and know what life was. He asked his sister to forgive him for not having told her of his resolve when he had last visited Bald Hills, though he had spoken of it to his father. He had not done so for fear Princess Mary should ask her father to give his consent, irritating him and having to bear the brunt of his displeasure without attaining her object. "Besides," he wrote, "the matter was not then so definitely settled as it is now. My father then insisted on a delay of a year and now already *six months,* half of that period, has passed, and my resolution is firmer than ever. If the doctors did not keep me here at the spas I should be back in Russia, but as it is I have to postpone my return for three months. You know me and my relations with Father. I want nothing from him. I have been and always shall be independent; but to go against his will and arouse his anger, now that he may perhaps remain with us such a short time, would destroy half my happiness. I am now writing to him about the same question, and beg you to choose a good moment to hand him the letter, and to let me know how he looks at the whole matter and whether there is hope that he may consent to reduce the term by four months."

After long hesitations, doubts and prayers, Princess Mary gave the letter to her father. The next day the old prince said to her quietly:

"Write and tell your brother to wait till I am dead. . . . It won't be long—I shall soon set him free."

The princess was about to reply, but her father would not let her speak and raising his voice more and more cried:

"Marry, marry, my boy! . . . A good family! . . . Clever people, eh? Rich, eh? Yes, a nice stepmother little Nicholas will have! Write and tell him that he may marry tomorrow if he likes. She will be little Nicholas's stepmother and I'll marry Bourienne! . . . Ha, ha, ha! He mustn't be without a stepmother either! Only one thing, no more women are wanted in my house—let him marry and live by himself. Perhaps you will go and live with him too?" he added, turning to Princess Mary. "Go in heavens name! Go out into the frost . . . the frost . . . the frost!"

After this outburst the prince did not speak anymore about the matter. But repressed vexation at his son's poor-spirited behavior found expression in his treatment of his daughter. To his former pretexts for irony a fresh one was now added—allusions to stepmothers, and amiabilities to Mademoiselle Bourienne.

"Why shouldn't I marry her?" he asked his daughter. "She'll make a splendid princess!"

And latterly, to her surprise and bewilderment, Princess Mary noticed that her father was really associating more and more with the Frenchwoman. She wrote to Prince Andrew about the reception of his letter, but comforted him with hopes of reconciling their father to the idea.

Little Nicholas and his education, her brother Andrew, and religion, were Princess Mary's joys and consolations; but besides that, since everyone must have personal hopes, Princess Mary in the profoundest depths of her heart had a hidden dream and hope that supplied the chief consolation of her life. This comforting dream and hope were given her by *God's folk*—the half-witted and other pilgrims who visited her without the prince's knowledge. The longer she lived, the more experience and observation she had of life, the greater was her wonder at the short-sightedness of men who seek enjoyment and happiness here on earth: toiling, suffering, struggling and harming one another, to obtain that impossible, visionary, sinful happiness. Prince Andrew had loved his wife, she died, but that was not enough: he wanted to bind his happiness to another woman. Her father objected to this because he wanted a more distinguished and wealthier match for Andrew. And they all struggled and suffered and tormented one another and injured their souls, their eternal souls, for the attainment of benefits which endure but for an instant. Not only do we know this ourselves, but Christ, the Son of God, came down to earth and told us that this life is but for a moment and is a probation; yet we cling to it and think to find happiness in it. "How is it that no one realizes this?" thought Princess Mary. "No one except these despised *God's folk* who, wallet on back, come to me by the back door, afraid of being seen by the prince, not for fear of ill-usage by him but for fear of causing him to sin. To leave family, home and all the cares of worldly welfare, in order without clinging to anything to wander in hempen rags from place to place under an assumed name, doing no one any harm but praying for all—for those who drive one away as well as for those who protect one: higher than that life and truth there is no life or truth!"

There was one pilgrim, a quiet pockmarked little woman of fifty called Theodosia, who for over thirty years had gone about barefoot and worn heavy chains. Princess Mary was particularly fond of her. Once, when in a room with a lamp dimly lit before the icon Theodosia was talking of her life, the thought that Theodosia alone had found the true path of life suddenly came to Princess Mary with such force that she resolved to become a pilgrim herself. When Theodosia had gone to sleep Princess Mary thought about this for a long time, and at last made up her mind that, strange as it might seem, she must go on pilgrimage. She disclosed this thought to no one but to her confessor, Father Akínfi, the monk, and he approved of her intention. Under guise of a present for the pilgrims, Princess Mary prepared a pilgrim's complete costume for herself: a coarse smock, bast shoes, a rough coat and a black kerchief. Often, approaching the chest of drawers containing this secret treasure, Princess Mary paused, uncertain whether the time had not already come to put her project into execution.

Often, listening to the pilgrims' tales she was so stimulated by their simple speech, mechanical to them but to her so full of deep meaning, that several times she was on the point of abandoning everything and running away from home. In imagination she already pictured herself by Theodosia's side, dressed in coarse rags, walking with a staff, a wallet on her back, along the dusty road, directing her wanderings from one saint's shrine to another, free from envy, earthly love or desire, and reaching at last the place where there is no more sorrow or sighing, but eternal joy and bliss.

"I shall come to a place and pray there, and before having time to get used to it or getting to love it, I shall go farther. I will go on till my legs fail, and I'll lie down and die somewhere, and shall at last reach that eternal, quiet haven, where there is neither sorrow nor sighing . . ." thought Princess Mary.

But afterward, when she saw her father and especially little Koko (Nicholas), her resolve weakened. She wept quietly, and felt that she was a sinner who loved her father and little nephew more than God.

PART SEVEN

Chapter I

THE BIBLE LEGEND TELLS US THAT THE ABSENCE OF LABOR—IDLENESS—WAS A CONDITION of the first man's blessedness before the Fall. Fallen man has retained a love of idleness, but the curse weighs on the race not only because we have to seek our bread in the sweat of our brows, but because our moral nature is such that we cannot be both idle and at ease. An inner voice tells us we are in the wrong if we are idle. If man could find a state in which he felt that though idle he was fulfilling his duty, he would have found one of the conditions of man's primitive blessedness. And such a state of obligatory and irreproachable idleness is the lot of a whole class—the military. The chief attraction of military service has consisted and will consist in this compulsory and irreproachable idleness.

Nicholas Rostóv experienced this blissful condition to the full when, after 1807, he continued to serve in the Pávlograd regiment, in which he already commanded the squadron he had taken over from Denísov.

Rostóv had become a bluff, good-natured fellow, whom his Moscow acquaintances would have considered rather bad form, but who was liked and respected by his comrades, subordinates, and superiors, and was well contented with his life. Of late, in 1809, he found in letters from home more frequent complaints from his mother that their affairs were falling into greater and greater disorder, and that it was time for him to come back to gladden and comfort his old parents.

Reading these letters, Nicholas felt a dread of their wanting to take him away from surroundings in which, protected from all the entanglements of life, he was living so calmly and quietly. He felt that sooner or later he would have to re-enter that whirlpool of life, with its embarrassments and affairs to be straightened out, its accounts with stewards, quarrels, and intrigues, its ties, society, and with Sónya's love and his promise to her. It was all dreadfully difficult and complicated; and he replied to his mother in cold, formal letters in French, beginning: "My dear Mamma," and ending: "Your obedient son," which said nothing of when he would return. In 1810 he received letters from his parents, in which they told him of Natásha's engagement to Bolkónski, and that the wedding would be in a year's time because the old prince made difficulties. This letter grieved and mortified Nicholas. In the first place he was sorry that Natásha, for whom he cared more than for anyone else in the family, should be lost to the home; and secondly, from his hussar point of view, he regretted not to have been there to show that fellow Bolkónski that connection with him was no such great honor after all, and that if he loved Natásha he might dispense with permission from his dotard father. For a moment he hesitated whether he should not apply for leave in order to see Natásha before she was married, but then came the maneuvers, and considerations about Sónya and about the confusion of their affairs, and Nicholas again put it off. But in the spring of that year, he received a letter from his mother, written without his father's knowledge, and that letter persuaded him to return. She wrote that if he did not come and take matters in hand, their whole property would be sold by auction and they would all have to go begging. The count was so weak, and trusted Mítenka so much, and was so good-natured, that everybody took advantage of him and things were going from bad to worse. "For God's sake, I implore you, come at once if you do not wish to make me and the whole family wretched," wrote the countess.

This letter touched Nicholas. He had that common sense of a matter-of-fact man which showed him what he ought to do.

The right thing now was, if not to retire from the service, at any rate to go home on leave. Why he had to go he did not know; but after his after-dinner nap he gave orders to saddle Mars, an extremely vicious gray stallion that had not been ridden for a long time, and when he returned with the horse all in a lather, he informed Lavrúshka (Denísov's servant who had remained with him) and his comrades who turned up in the evening that he was applying for leave and was going home. Difficult and strange as it was for him to reflect that he would go away without having heard from the staff—and this interested him extremely—whether he was promoted to a captaincy or would receive the Order of St. Anne for the last maneuvers; strange as it was to think that he would go away without having sold his three roans to the Polish Count Golukhovski, who was bargaining for the horses Rostóv had betted he would sell for two thousand rubles; incomprehensible as it seemed that the ball the hussars were giving in honor of the Polish Mademoiselle Przazdziecka (out of rivalry to the Uhlans who had given one in honor of their Polish Mademoiselle Borzozowska) would take place without him—he knew he must go away from this good, bright world, to somewhere where everything was stupid and confused. A week later he obtained his leave. His hussar comrades—not only those of his own regiment, but the whole brigade—gave Rostóv a dinner to which the subscription was fifteen rubles a head, and at which there were two bands and two choirs of singers. Rostóv danced the Trepák with Major Básov; the tipsy officers tossed, embraced, and dropped Rostóv; the soldiers of the third squadron tossed him too, and shouted "hurrah!" and then they put him in his sleigh and escorted him as far as the first post station.

During the first half of the journey—from Kremenchug to Kiev—all Rostóv's thoughts, as is usual in such cases, were behind him, with the squadron; but when he had gone more than halfway he began to forget his three roans and Dozhoyvéyko, his quartermaster, and to wonder anxiously how things would be at Otrádnoe and what he would find there. Thoughts of home grew stronger the nearer he approached it—far stronger, as though this feeling of his was subject to the law by which the force of attraction is in inverse proportion to the square of the distance. At the last post station before Otrádnoe he gave the driver a three-ruble tip, and on arriving he ran breathlessly, like a boy, up the steps of his home.

After the rapture of meeting, and after that odd feeling of unsatisfied expectation—the feeling that "everything is just the same, so why did I hurry?"—Nicholas began to settle down in his old home world. His father and mother were much the same, only a little older. What was new in them was a certain uneasiness and occasional discord, which there used not to be, and which, as Nicholas soon found out, was due to the bad state of their affairs. Sónya was nearly twenty; she had stopped growing prettier and promised nothing more than she was already, but that was enough. She exhaled happiness and love from the time Nicholas returned, and the faithful, unalterable love of this girl had a gladdening effect on him. Pétya and Natásha surprised Nicholas most. Pétya was a big handsome boy of thirteen, merry, witty, and mischievous, with a voice that was already breaking. As for Natásha, for a long while Nicholas wondered and laughed whenever he looked at her.

"You're not the same at all," he said.

"How? Am I uglier?"

"On the contrary, but what dignity! A princess!" he whispered to her.

"Yes, yes, yes!" cried Natásha, joyfully.

She told him about her romance with Prince Andrew and of his visit to Otrádnoe and showed him his last letter.

"Well, are you glad?" Natásha asked. "I am so tranquil and happy now."

"Very glad," answered Nicholas. "He is an excellent fellow. . . . And are you very much in love?"

"How shall I put it?" replied Natásha. "I was in love with Borís, with my teacher, and with Denísov, but this is quite different. I feel at peace and settled. I know that no better man than he exists, and I am calm and contented now. Not at all as before."

Nicholas expressed his disapproval of the postponement of the marriage for a year; but Natásha attacked her brother with exasperation, proving to him that it could not be otherwise, and that it would be a bad thing to enter a family against the father's will, and that she herself wished it so.

"You don't at all understand," she said.

Nicholas was silent and agreed with her.

Her brother often wondered as he looked at her. She did not seem at all like a girl in love and parted from her affianced husband. She was even-tempered and calm, and quite as cheerful as of old. This amazed Nicholas and even made him regard Bolkónski's courtship skeptically. He could not believe that her fate was sealed, especially as he had not seen her with Prince Andrew. It always seemed to him that there was something not quite right about this intended marriage.

"Why this delay? Why no betrothal?" he thought. Once, when he had touched on this topic with his mother, he discovered, to his surprise and somewhat to his satisfaction, that in the depth of her soul she too had doubts about this marriage.

"You see he writes," said she, showing her son a letter of Prince Andrew's, with that latent grudge a mother always has in regard to a daughter's future married happiness, "he writes that he won't come before December. What can be keeping him? Illness, probably! His health is very delicate. Don't tell Natásha. And don't attach importance to her being so bright: that's because she's living through the last days of her girlhood, but I know what she is like every time we receive a letter from him! However, God grant that everything turns out well!" (she always ended with these words.) "He is an excellent man!"

Chapter II

After reaching home Nicholas was at first serious and even dull. He was worried by the impending necessity of interfering in the stupid business matters for which his mother had called him home. To throw off this burden as quickly as possible, on the third day after his arrival he went, angry and scowling and without answering questions as to where he was going, to Mítenka's lodge and demanded an *account of everything*. But what an *account of everything* might be Nicholas knew even less than the frightened and bewildered Mítenka. The conversation and the examination of the accounts with Mítenka did not last long. The village elder, a peasant delegate, and the village clerk, who were waiting in the passage, heard with fear and delight first the young count's voice roaring and snapping and rising louder and louder, and then words of abuse, dreadful words, ejaculated one after the other.

"Robber! . . . Ungrateful wretch! . . . I'll hack the dog to pieces! I'm not my father! . . . Robbing us! . . ." and so on.

Then with no less fear and delight they saw how the young count, red in the face and with bloodshot eyes, dragged Mítenka out by the scruff of the neck and applied his foot and knee to his behind with great agility at convenient moments between the words, shouting, "Be off! Never let me see your face here again, you villain!"

Mítenka flew headlong down the six steps and ran away into the shrubbery. (This shrubbery was a well-known haven of refuge for culprits at Otrádnoe. Mítenka himself, returning tipsy from the town, used to hide there, and many of the residents at Otrádnoe, hiding from Mítenka, knew of its protective qualities.)

Mítenka's wife and sisters-in-law thrust their heads and frightened faces out of the door of a room where a bright samovar was boiling and where the steward's high bedstead stood with its patchwork quilt.

The young count paid no heed to them, but breathing hard, passed by with resolute strides and went into the house.

The countess, who heard at once from the maids what had happened at the lodge, was calmed by the thought that now their affairs would certainly improve, but on the other hand felt anxious as to the effect this excitement might have on her son. She went several times to his door on tiptoe and listened, as he lit one pipe after another.

Next day the old count called his son aside and, with an embarrassed smile, said to him:

"But you know, my dear boy, it's a pity you got excited! Mítenka has told me all about it."

"I knew," thought Nicholas, "that I should never understand anything in this crazy world."

"You were angry that he had not entered those 700 rubles. But they were carried forward—and you did not look at the other page."

"Papa, he is a blackguard and a thief! I know he is! And what I have done, I have done; but, if you like, I won't speak to him again."

"No, my dear boy" (the count, too, felt embarrassed. He knew he had mismanaged his wife's property and was to blame toward his children, but he did not know how to remedy it). "No, I beg you to attend to the business. I am old. I . . ."

"No, Papa. Forgive me if I have caused you unpleasantness. I understand it all less than you do."

"Devil take all these peasants, and money matters, and carryings forward from page to page," he thought. "I used to understand what a 'corner' and the stakes at cards meant, but carrying forward to another page I don't understand at all," said he to himself, and after that he did not meddle in business affairs. But once the countess called her son and informed him that she had a promissory note from Anna Mikháylovna for two thousand rubles, and asked him what he thought of doing with it.

"This," answered Nicholas. "You say it rests with me. Well, I don't like Anna Mikháylovna and I don't like Borís, but they were our friends and poor. Well then, this!" and he tore up the note, and by so doing caused the old countess to weep tears of joy. After that, young Rostóv took no further part in any business affairs, but devoted himself with passionate enthusiasm to what was to him a new pursuit—the chase—for which his father kept a large establishment.

Chapter III

THE WEATHER WAS ALREADY GROWING WINTRY AND MORNING FROSTS CONGEALED AN EARTH saturated by autumn rains. The verdure had thickened and its bright green stood out sharply against the brownish strips of winter rye trodden down by the cattle, and against the pale yellow stubble of the spring sowing and the reddish strips of buckwheat. The wooded ravines and the copses, which at the end of August had still been green islands amid black fields and stubble, had become golden and bright-red islands amid the green winter rye. The hares had already half changed their summer coats, the fox cubs were beginning to scatter, and the young wolves were bigger than dogs. It was the best time of the year for the chase. The hounds of that ardent young sportsman Rostóv had not merely reached hard winter condition, but were so jaded that at a meeting of the huntsmen it was decided to give them a three days' rest and then, on the 16th of September, to go on a distant expedition, starting from the oak grove where there was an undisturbed litter of wolf cubs.

All that day the hounds remained at home. It was frosty and the air was sharp, but toward evening the sky became overcast and it began to thaw. On the 15th, when young Rostóv, in his dressing-gown, looked out of the window, he saw it was an unsurpassable morning for hunting: it was as if the sky were melting and sinking to the earth without any wind. The only motion in the air was that of the dripping, microscopic particles of drizzling mist. The bare twigs in the garden were hung with transparent drops which fell on the freshly fallen leaves. The earth in the kitchen-garden looked wet and black and glistened like poppy-seed and at a short distance merged into the dull, moist veil of mist. Nicholas went out into the wet and muddy porch. There was a smell of decaying leaves and of dog. Mílka, a black-spotted, broad-haunched bitch with prominent black eyes, got up on seeing her master, stretched her hind legs, lay down like a hare and then suddenly jumped up and licked him right on his nose and mustache. Another borzoi, a dog, catching sight of his master from the garden path, arched his back and rushing headlong toward the porch with lifted tail, began rubbing himself against his legs.

"O-hoy!" came at that moment that inimitable huntsman's call which unites the deepest bass with the shrillest tenor, and round the corner came Daniel the head huntsman and head kennelman, a gray, wrinkled old man with hair cut straight over his forehead, Ukrainian fashion, a long bent whip in his hand, and that look of independence and scorn of everything that is only seen in huntsmen. He doffed his Circassian cap to his master and looked at him scornfully. This scorn was not offensive to his master. Nicholas knew that this Daniel, disdainful of everybody and who considered himself above them, was all the same his serf and huntsman.

"Daniel!" Nicholas said timidly, conscious at the sight of the weather, the hounds, and the huntsman, that he was being carried away by that irresistible passion for sport which makes a man forget all his previous resolutions, as a lover forgets in the presence of his mistress.

"What orders, your excellency?" said the huntsman in his deep bass, deep as a proto-deacon's and hoarse with hallooing—and two flashing black eyes gazed from under his brows at his master, who was silent. "Can you resist it?" those eyes seemed to be asking.

"It's a good day, eh? For a hunt and a gallop, eh?" asked Nicholas, scratching Mílka behind the ears.

Daniel did not answer, but winked instead.

"I sent Uvárka at dawn to listen," his bass boomed out after a minute's pause. "He says *she's moved them* into the Otrádnoe enclosure. They were howling there." (This meant that the she-wolf, about whom they both knew, had moved with her cubs to the Otrádnoe copse, a small place two versts from the house.)

"We ought to go, don't you think so?" said Nicholas. "Come to me with Uvárka."

"As you please."

"Then put off feeding them."

"Yes, sir."

Five minutes later Daniel and Uvárka were standing in Nicholas's big study. Though Daniel was not a big man, to see him in a room was like seeing a horse or a bear on the floor among the furniture and surroundings of human life. Daniel himself felt this, and as usual stood just inside the door, trying to speak softly and not move, for fear of breaking something in the master's apartment, and he hastened to say all that was necessary so as to get from under that ceiling, out into the open under the sky once more.

Having finished his inquiries and extorted from Daniel an opinion that the hounds were fit (Daniel himself wished to go hunting), Nicholas ordered the horses to be saddled. But just as Daniel was about to go Natásha came in with rapid steps, not having done up her hair or finished dressing and with her old nurse's big shawl wrapped round her. Pétya ran in at the same time.

"You are going?" asked Natásha. "I knew you would! Sónya said you wouldn't go, but I knew that today is the sort of day when you couldn't help going."

"Yes, we are going," replied Nicholas reluctantly, for today, as he intended to hunt seriously, he did not want to take Natásha and Pétya. "We are going, but only wolf-hunting: it would be dull for you."

"You know it is my greatest pleasure," said Natásha. "It's not fair; you are going by yourself, are having the horses saddled and said nothing to us about it."

" 'No barrier bars a Russian's path'—we'll go!" shouted Pétya.

"But you can't. Mamma said you mustn't," said Nicholas to Natásha.

"Yes, I'll go. I shall certainly go," said Natásha decisively. "Daniel, tell them to saddle for us, and Michael must come with my dogs," she added to the huntsman.

It seemed to Daniel irksome and improper to be in a room at all, but to have anything to do with a young lady seemed to him impossible. He cast down his eyes and hurried out as if it were none of his business, careful as he went not to inflict any accidental injury on the young lady.

Chapter IV

THE OLD COUNT, WHO HAD ALWAYS KEPT UP AN ENORMOUS HUNTING ESTABLISHMENT BUT HAD now handed it all completely over to his son's care, being in very good spirits on this 15th of September, prepared to go out with the others.

In an hour's time the whole hunting party was at the porch. Nicholas, with a stern and serious air which showed that now was no time for attending to trifles, went past Natásha and Pétya who were trying to tell him something. He had a look at all the details of the hunt, sent a pack of hounds and huntsmen on ahead to find the quarry, mounted his chestnut Donéts, and whistling to his own leash of borzois, set off across the threshing-ground to a field leading to the Otrádnoe wood. The old count's horse, a sorrel gelding called Viflyánka, was led by the groom in attendance on him, while the count himself was to drive in a small trap straight to a spot reserved for him.

They were taking fifty-four hounds, with six hunt-attendants and whippers-in. Besides the family, there were eight borzoi kennel-men and more than forty borzois, so that, with the borzois on the leash belonging to members of the family, there were about a hundred and thirty dogs and twenty horsemen.

Each dog knew its master and its call. Each man in the hunt knew his business, his place, what he had to do. As soon as they had passed the fence they all spread out evenly and quietly, without noise or talk, along the road and field leading to the Otrádnoe covert.

The horses stepped over the field as over a thick carpet, now and then splashing into puddles as they crossed a road. The misty sky still seemed to descend evenly and imperceptibly toward the earth, the air was still, warm, and silent. Occasionally the whistle of a huntsman, the snort of a horse, the crack of a whip, or the whine of a straggling hound, could be heard.

When they had gone about a verst, five more riders with dogs appeared out of the mist, approaching the Rostóvs. In front rode a fresh-looking, handsome old man with a large gray mustache.

"Good morning, Uncle!" said Nicholas, when the old man drew near.

"That's it. Come on! . . . I was sure of it," began "Uncle." (He was a distant relative of the Rostóvs', a man of small means, and their neighbor.) "I knew you wouldn't be able to resist it and it's a good thing you're going. That's it! Come on!" (This was "Uncle's" favorite expression.) "Take the covert at once, for my Gírchik says the Ilágins are at Korniki with their hounds. That's it. Come on! . . . They'll take the cubs from under your very nose."

"That's where I'm going. Shall we join up our packs?" asked Nicholas.

The hounds were joined into one pack, and "Uncle" and Nicholas rode on side by side. Natásha, muffled up in shawls which did not hide her eager face and shining eyes, galloped up to them. She was followed by Pétya who always kept close to her, by Michael, a huntsman, and by a groom appointed to look after her. Pétya, who was laughing, whipped and pulled at his horse. Natásha sat easily and confidently on her black Arábchik and reined him in without effort with a firm hand.

"Uncle" looked round disapprovingly at Pétya and Natásha. He did not like to combine frivolity with the serious business of hunting.

"Good morning, Uncle! We are going too!" shouted Pétya.

"Good morning, good morning! But don't go over-riding the hounds," said "Uncle" sternly.

"Nicholas, what a fine dog Truníla is! He knew me," said Natásha, referring to her favorite hound.

"In the first place, Truníla is not a 'dog,' but a harrier," thought Nicholas, and looked sternly at his sister, trying to make her feel the distance that ought to separate them at that moment. Natásha understood it.

"You mustn't think we'll be in anyone's way, Uncle," she said. "We'll go to our places and won't budge."

"A good thing too, little countess," said "Uncle," "only mind you don't fall off your horse," he added, "because—that's it, come on!—you've nothing to hold on to."

The oasis of the Otrádnoe covert came in sight a few hundred yards off, the huntsmen were already nearing it. Rostóv, having finally settled with "Uncle" where they should set on the hounds, and having shown Natásha where she was to stand—a spot where nothing could possibly run out—went round above the ravine.

"Well, nephew, you're going for a big wolf," said "Uncle." "Mind and don't let her slip!"

"That's as may happen," answered Rostóv. "Karáy, here!" he shouted, answering "Uncle's" remark by this call to his borzoi. Karáy was a shaggy old dog with a hanging jowl, famous for having tackled a big wolf unaided. They all took up their places.

The old count, knowing his son's ardor in the hunt, hurried so as not to be late, and the huntsmen had not yet reached their places when Count Ilyá Rostóv, cheerful, flushed, and with quivering cheeks, drove up with his black horses over the winter rye to the place reserved for him, where a wolf might come out. Having straightened his coat and fastened on his hunting-knives and horn, he mounted his good, sleek, well-fed and comfortable horse, Viflyánka, which was turning gray like himself. His horses and trap were sent home. Count Ilyá Rostóv, though not at heart a keen sportsman, knew the rules of the hunt well, and rode to the bushy edge of the road where he was to stand, arranged his reins, settled himself in the saddle, and, feeling that he was ready, looked about with a smile.

Beside him was Simon Chekmár, his personal attendant, an old horseman now somewhat stiff in the saddle. Chekmár held in leash three formidable wolf-hounds, who had, however, grown fat like their master and his horse. Two wise old dogs lay down unleashed. Some hundred paces farther along the edge of the wood stood Mítka, the count's other groom, a daring horseman and keen rider to hounds. Before the hunt, by old custom, the count had drunk a silver cupful of mulled brandy, taken a snack, and washed it down with half a bottle of his favorite Bordeaux.

He was somewhat flushed with the wine and the drive. His eyes were rather moist and glittered more than usual, and as he sat in his saddle, wrapped up in his fur coat, he looked like a child taken out for an outing.

The thin, hollow-cheeked Chekmár, having got everything ready, kept glancing at his master with whom he had lived on the best of terms for thirty years, and understanding the mood he was in expected a pleasant chat. A third person rode up circumspectly through the wood (it was plain that he had had a lesson) and stopped behind the count. This person was a gray-bearded old man in a woman's cloak, with a tall peaked cap on his head. He was the buffoon, who went by a woman's name, Nastásya Ivánovna.

"Well, Nastásya Ivánovna!" whispered the count, winking at him. "If you scare away the beast, Daniel'll give it you!"

"I know a thing or two myself!" said Nastásya Ivánovna.

"Hush!" whispered the count and turned to Simon. "Have you seen the young countess?" he asked. "Where is she?"

"With young Count Peter, by the Zhárov rank grass," answered Simon, smiling. "Though she's a lady, she's very fond of hunting."

"And you're surprised at the way she rides, Simon, eh?" said the count. "She's as good as many a man!"

"Of course! It's marvelous. So bold, so easy!"

"And Nicholas? Where is he? By the Lyádov upland, isn't he?"

"Yes, sir. He knows where to stand. He understands the matter so well that Daniel and I are often quite astounded," said Simon, well knowing what would please his master.

"Rides well, eh? And how well he looks on his horse, eh?"

"A perfect picture! How he chased a fox out of the rank grass by the Zavárzinsk thicket the other day! Leaped a fearful place; what a sight when they rushed from the covert . . . the horse worth a thousand rubles and the rider beyond all price! Yes, one would have to search far to find another as smart."

"To search far . . ." repeated the count, evidently sorry Simon had not said more. "To search far," he said, turning back the skirt of his coat to get at his snuffbox.

"The other day when he came out from Mass in full uniform, Michael Sidórych . . ." Simon did not finish, for on the still air he had distinctly caught the music of the hunt with only two or three hounds giving tongue. He bent down his head and listened, shaking a warning finger at his master. "They are on the scent of the cubs . . ." he whispered, "straight to the Lyádov uplands."

The count, forgetting to smooth out the smile on his face, looked into the distance straight before him, down the narrow open space, holding the snuffbox in his hand but not taking any. After the cry of the hounds came the deep tones of the wolf-call from Daniel's hunting-horn; the pack joined the first three hounds and they could be heard in full cry, with that peculiar lift in the note that indicates that they are after a wolf. The whippers-in no longer set on the hounds, but changed to the cry of *ulyulyu,* and above the others rose Daniel's voice, now a deep bass, now piercingly shrill. His voice seemed to fill the whole wood and carried far beyond out into the open field.

After listening a few moments in silence, the count and his attendant convinced themselves that the hounds had separated into two packs: the sound of the larger pack, eagerly giving tongue, began to die away in the distance, the other pack rushed by the wood past the count, and it was with this that Daniel's voice was heard calling *ulyulyu.* The sounds of both packs mingled and broke apart again, but both were becoming more distant.

Simon sighed and stooped to straighten the leash a young borzoi had entangled, the count too sighed, and noticing the snuffbox in his hand, opened it and took a pinch. "Back!" cried Simon to a borzoi that was pushing forward out of the wood. The count started and dropped the snuffbox. Nastásya Ivánovna dismounted to pick it up. The count and Simon were looking at him.

Then, unexpectedly, as often happens, the sound of the hunt suddenly approached, as if the hounds in full cry and Daniel *ulyulyuing* were just in front of them.

The count turned and saw on his right Mítka staring at him with eyes starting out of his head, raising his cap and pointing before him to the other side.

"Look out!" he shouted, in a voice plainly showing that he had long fretted to utter that word, and letting the borzois slip he galloped toward the count.

The count and Simon galloped out of the wood, and saw on their left a wolf which, softly swaying from side to side, was coming at a quiet lope farther to the left to the very place where they were standing. The angry borzois whined, and getting free of the leash rushed past the horses' feet at the wolf.

The wolf paused, turned its heavy forehead toward the dogs awkwardly, like a man suffering from the quinsy, and still slightly swaying from side to side, gave a couple of leaps and with a swish of its tail disappeared into the skirt of the wood. At the same instant, with a cry like a wail, first one hound, then another, and then another, sprang helter-skelter from the wood opposite and the whole pack rushed across the field toward the very spot where the wolf had disappeared. The hazel bushes parted behind the hounds and Daniel's chestnut horse appeared, dark with sweat. On its long back sat Daniel, hunched forward, capless, his disheveled gray hair hanging over his flushed, perspiring face.

"Ulyulyulyu! ulyulyu! . . ." he cried. When he caught sight of the count his eyes flashed lightning.

"Blast you!" he shouted, holding up his whip threateningly at the count.

"You've let the wolf go! . . . What sportsmen!" and as if scorning to say more to the frightened and shamefaced count, he lashed the heaving flanks of his sweating chestnut gelding with all the anger the count had aroused, and flew off after the hounds. The count, like a punished schoolboy, looked round, trying by a smile to win Simon's sympathy for his plight. But Simon was no longer there. He was galloping round by the bushes while the field was coming up on both sides, all trying to head the wolf, but it vanished into the wood before they could do so.

Chapter V

NICHOLAS ROSTÓV MEANWHILE REMAINED AT HIS POST, WAITING FOR THE WOLF. BY THE WAY the hunt approached and receded, by the cries of the dogs whose notes were familiar to him, by the way the voices of the huntsmen approached, receded, and rose, he realized what was happening at the copse. He knew that young and old wolves were there, that the hounds had separated into two packs, that somewhere a wolf was being chased, and that something had gone wrong. He expected the wolf to come his way any moment. He made thousands of different conjectures as to where and from what side the beast would come and how he would set upon it. Hope alternated with despair. Several times he addressed a prayer to God that the wolf should come his way. He prayed with that passionate and shamefaced feeling with which men pray at moments of great excitement arising from trivial causes. "What would it be to Thee to do this for me?" he said to God. "I know Thou art great, and that it is a sin to ask this of Thee, but for God's sake do let the old wolf come my way and let Karáy spring at it—in sight of 'Uncle' who is watching from over there—and seize it by the throat in a death-grip!" A thousand times during that half-hour Rostóv cast eager and restless glances over the edge of the wood, with the two scraggy oaks rising above the aspen undergrowth and the gully with its water-worn side and "Uncle's" cap just visible above the bush on his right.

"No, I shan't have such luck," thought Rostóv, "yet what wouldn't it be worth! It is not to be! Everywhere, at cards and in war, I am always unlucky." Memories of Austerlitz and of Dólokhov flashed rapidly and clearly through his mind. "Only once in my life to get an old wolf, I want only that!" thought he, straining eyes and ears and looking to the left and then to the right and listening to the slightest variation of note in the cries of the dogs.

Again he looked to the right and saw something running toward him across the deserted field. "No, it can't be!" thought Rostóv, taking a deep breath, as a man does at the coming of something long hoped for. The height of happiness was reached—and so simply, without warning, or noise, or display, that Rostóv could not believe his eyes and remained in doubt for over a second. The wolf ran forward and jumped heavily over a gully that lay in her path. She was an old animal with a gray back and big reddish belly. She ran without hurry, evidently feeling sure that no one saw her. Rostóv, holding his breath, looked round at the borzois. They stood or lay not seeing the wolf or understanding the situation. Old Karáy had turned his head and was angrily searching for fleas, baring his yellow teeth and snapping at his hind legs.

"Ulyulyulyu!" whispered Rostóv, pouting his lips. The borzois jumped up, jerking the rings of

the leashes and pricking their ears. Karáy finished scratching his hindquarters, and cocking his ears, got up with quivering tail from which tufts of matted hair hung down.

"Shall I loose them or not?" Nicholas asked himself as the wolf approached him coming from the copse. Suddenly the wolf's whole physiognomy changed: she shuddered, seeing what she had probably never seen before—human eyes fixed upon her, and turning her head a little toward Rostóv, she paused.

"Back or forward? Eh, no matter, forward . . ." the wolf seemed to say to herself, and she moved forward without again looking round and with a quiet, long, easy yet resolute lope.

"Ulyulyu!" cried Nicholas, in a voice not his own, and of its own accord his good horse darted headlong downhill, leaping over gullies to head off the wolf, and the borzois passed it, running faster still. Nicholas did not hear his own cry nor feel that he was galloping, nor see the borzois, nor the ground over which he went: he saw only the wolf, who, increasing her speed, bounded on in the same direction along the hollow. The first to come into view was Mílka, with her black markings and powerful quarters, gaining upon the wolf. Nearer and nearer . . . now she was ahead of it; but the wolf turned its head to face her, and instead of putting on speed as she usually did Mílka suddenly raised her tail and stiffened her forelegs.

"Ulyulyulyulyu!" shouted Nicholas.

The reddish Lyubím rushed forward from behind Mílka, sprang impetuously at the wolf and seized it by its hindquarters, but immediately jumped aside in terror. The wolf crouched, gnashed her teeth, and again rose and bounded forward, followed at the distance of a couple of feet by all the borzois, who did not get any closer to her.

"She'll get away! No, it's impossible!" thought Nicholas, still shouting with a hoarse voice.

"Karáy, *ulyulyu!* . . ." he shouted, looking round for the old borzoi who was now his only hope. Karáy, with all the strength age had left him, stretched himself to the utmost, and watching the wolf, galloped heavily aside to intercept it. But the quickness of the wolf's lope and the borzoi's slower pace made it plain that Karáy had miscalculated. Nicholas could already see not far in front of him the wood where the wolf would certainly escape should she reach it. But, coming toward him, he saw hounds and a huntsman galloping almost straight at the wolf. There was still hope. A long, yellowish young borzoi, one Nicholas did not know, from another leash, rushed impetuously at the wolf from in front and almost knocked her over. But the wolf jumped up more quickly than anyone could have expected and, gnashing her teeth, flew at the yellowish borzoi, which, with a piercing yelp, fell with its head on the ground, bleeding from a gash in its side.

"Karáy? Old fellow! . . ." wailed Nicholas.

Thanks to the delay caused by this crossing of the wolf's path, the old dog with its felted hair hanging from its thigh was within five paces of it. As if aware of her danger, the wolf turned her eyes on Karáy, tucked her tail yet further between her legs, and increased her speed. But here Nicholas only saw that something happened to Karáy—the borzoi was suddenly on the wolf, and they rolled together down into a gully just in front of them.

That instant, when Nicholas saw the wolf struggling in the gully with the dogs, while from under them could be seen her gray hair and outstretched hind leg and her frightened choking head, with her ears laid back (Karáy was pinning her by the throat), was the happiest moment of his life. With his hand on his saddle-bow, he was ready to dismount and stab the wolf, when she suddenly thrust her head up from among that mass of dogs, and then her forepaws were on the edge of the gully. She clicked her teeth (Karáy no longer had her by the throat), leaped with a movement of her hind legs out of the gully, and having disengaged herself from the dogs, with tail tucked in again, went forward. Karáy, his hair bristling, and probably bruised or wounded, climbed with difficulty out of the gully.

"Oh my God! Why?" Nicholas cried in despair.

"Uncle's" huntsman was galloping from the other side across the wolf's path and his borzois once more stopped the animal's advance. She was again hemmed in.

Nicholas and his attendant, with "Uncle" and his huntsman, were all riding round the wolf, crying *"ulyulyu!"* shouting and preparing to dismount each moment that the wolf crouched back, and starting forward again every time she shook herself and moved toward the wood where she would be safe.

Already, at the beginning of this chase, Daniel, hearing the *ulyulyuing,* had rushed out from the wood. He saw Karáy seize the wolf, and checked his horse supposing the affair to be over. But when he saw that the horsemen did not dismount and that the wolf shook herself and ran for safety, Daniel set his chestnut galloping, not at the wolf but straight toward the wood, just as Karáy had run to cut the animal off. As a result of this, he galloped up to the wolf just when she had been stopped a second time by "Uncle's" borzois.

Daniel galloped up silently, holding a naked dagger in his left hand and thrashing the laboring sides of his chestnut horse with his whip as if it were a flail.

Nicholas neither saw nor heard Daniel until the chestnut, breathing heavily, panted past him, and he heard the fall of a body and saw Daniel lying on the wolf's back among the dogs, trying to seize her by the ears. It was evident to the dogs, the hunters, and to the wolf herself, that all was now over. The terrified wolf pressed back her ears and tried to rise, but the borzois stuck to her. Daniel rose a little, took a step, and with his whole weight, as if lying down to rest, fell on the wolf, seizing her by the ears. Nicholas was about to stab her, but Daniel whispered, "Don't, we'll gag her!" and changing his position, set his foot on the wolf's neck. A stick was thrust between her jaws and she was fastened with a leash, as if bridled, her legs were bound together, and Daniel rolled her over once or twice from side to side.

With happy, exhausted faces, they laid the old wolf, alive, on a shying and snorting horse, and accompanied by the dogs yelping at her, took her to the place where they were all to meet. The hounds had killed two of the cubs and the borzois three. The huntsmen assembled with their booty and their stories, and all came to look at the wolf, which, with her broad-browed head hanging down and the bitten stick between her jaws, gazed with great glassy eyes at this crowd of dogs and men surrounding her. When she was touched, she jerked her bound legs and looked wildly yet simply at everybody. Old Count Rostóv also rode up and touched the wolf.

"Oh, what a formidable one!" said he. "A formidable one, eh?" he asked Daniel, who was standing near.

"Yes, your excellency," answered Daniel, quickly doffing his cap.

The count remembered the wolf he had let slip and his encounter with Daniel.

"Ah, but you are a crusty fellow, friend!" said the count.

For sole reply Daniel gave him a shy, childlike, meek and amiable smile.

Chapter VI

THE OLD COUNT WENT HOME AND NATÁSHA AND PÉTYA PROMISED TO RETURN VERY SOON, BUT as it was still early the hunt went farther. At midday they put the hounds into a ravine thickly overgrown with young trees. Nicholas standing in a fallow field could see all his whips.

Facing him lay a field of winter rye, there his own huntsman stood alone in a hollow behind a hazel bush. The hounds had scarcely been loosed before Nicholas heard one he knew, Voltórn, giving tongue at intervals; other hounds joined in, now pausing and now again giving tongue. A moment later he heard a cry from the wooded ravine that a fox had been found, and the whole pack, joining together, rushed along the ravine toward the ryefield and away from Nicholas.

He saw the whips in their red caps galloping along the edge of the ravine, he even saw the hounds, and was expecting a fox to show itself at any moment on the ryefield opposite.

The huntsman standing in the hollow moved and loosed his borzois, and Nicholas saw a queer, short-legged red fox with a fine brush, going hard across the field. The borzois bore down on it. . . . Now they drew close to the fox which began to dodge between the field in sharper and sharper curves, trailing its brush, when suddenly a strange white borzoi dashed in followed by a black one, and everything was in confusion; the borzois formed a star-shaped figure, scarcely swaying their bodies and with tails turned away from the center of the group. Two huntsmen galloped up to the dogs; one in a red cap, the other, a stranger, in a green coat.

"What's this?" thought Nicholas. "Where's that huntsman from? He is not 'Uncle's' man."

The huntsmen got the fox, but stayed there a long time without strapping it to the saddle. Their horses, bridled and with high saddles, stood near them and there too the dogs were lying. The huntsmen waved their arms and did something to the fox. Then from that spot came the sound of a horn, with the signal agreed on in case of a fight.

"That's Ilágin's huntsman having a row with our Iván," said Nicholas's groom.

Nicholas sent the man to call Natásha and Pétya to him, and rode at a footpace to the place where the whips were getting the hounds together. Several of the field galloped to the spot where the fight was going on.

Nicholas dismounted, and with Natásha and Pétya, who had ridden up, stopped near the hounds, waiting to see how the matter would end. Out of the bushes came the huntsman who had been fighting, and rode toward his young master, with the fox tied to his crupper. While still at a distance he took off his cap and tried to speak respectfully, but he was pale and breathless and his face was angry. One of his eyes was black, but he probably was not even aware of it.

"What has happened?" asked Nicholas.

"A likely thing, killing a fox our dogs had hunted! And it was my gray bitch that caught it! Go to law, indeed! . . . He snatches at the fox! I gave him one with the fox. Here it is on my saddle! Do you want a taste of this? . . ." said the huntsman, pointing to his dagger and probably imagining himself still speaking to his foe.

Nicholas, not stopping to talk to the man, asked his sister and Pétya to wait for him and rode to the spot where the enemy's, Ilágin's, hunting-party was.

The victorious huntsman rode off to join the field, and there, surrounded by inquiring sympathizers, recounted his exploits.

The facts were that Ilágin, with whom the Rostóvs had a quarrel and were at law, hunted over places that belonged by custom to the Rostóvs, and had now, as if purposely, sent his men to the very woods the Rostóvs were hunting, and let his man snatch a fox their dogs had chased.

Nicholas, though he had never seen Ilágin, with his usual absence of moderation in judgment, hated him cordially from reports of his arbitrariness and violence, and regarded him as his bitterest foe. He rode in angry agitation toward him, firmly grasping his whip and fully prepared to take the most resolute and desperate steps to punish his enemy.

Hardly had he passed an angle of the wood before a stout gentleman in a beaver cap came riding toward him on a handsome raven-black horse, accompanied by two hunt-servants.

Instead of an enemy, Nicholas found in Ilágin a stately and courteous gentleman who was particularly anxious to make the young count's acquaintance. Having ridden up to Nicholas, Ilágin raised his beaver cap and said he much regretted what had occurred and would have the man punished who had allowed himself to seize a fox hunted by someone else's borzois. He hoped to become better acquainted with the count and invited him to draw his covert.

Natásha, afraid that her brother would do something dreadful, had followed him in some excitement. Seeing the enemies exchanging friendly greetings, she rode up to them. Ilágin lifted his beaver cap still higher to Natásha and said, with a pleasant smile, that the young countess resembled Diana in her passion for the chase as well as in her beauty, of which he had heard much.

To expiate his huntsman's offense, Ilágin pressed the Rostóvs to come to an upland of his about a verst away which he usually kept for himself and which, he said, swarmed with hares. Nicholas agreed, and the hunt, now doubled, moved on.

The way to Iligin's upland was across the fields. The hunt-servants fell into line. The masters rode together. "Uncle," Rostóv, and Ilágin kept stealthily glancing at one another's dogs, trying not to be observed by their companions and searching uneasily for rivals to their own borzois.

Rostóv was particularly struck by the beauty of a small, pure-bred, red-spotted bitch on Ilágin's leash, slender but with muscles like steel, a delicate muzzle and prominent black eyes. He had heard of the swiftness of Ilágin's borzois, and in that beautiful bitch saw a rival to his own Mílka.

In the middle of a sober conversation begun by Ilágin about the year's harvest, Nicholas pointed to the red-spotted bitch.

"A fine little bitch, that!" said he in a careless tone. "Is she swift?"

"That one? Yes, she's a good dog, gets what she's after," answered Ilágin indifferently, of the red-spotted bitch Erzá, for which, a year before, he had given a neighbor three families of house serfs. "So in your parts, too, the harvest is nothing to boast of, count?" he went on, continuing the conversation they had begun. And considering it polite to return the young count's compliment, Ilágin looked at his borzois and picked out Mílka who attracted his attention by her breadth. "That black-spotted one of yours is fine—well-shaped!" said he.

"Yes, she's fast enough," replied Nicholas, and thought: "If only a full-grown hare would cross the field now I'd show you what sort of borzoi she is," and turning to his groom, he said he would give a ruble to anyone who found a hare.

"I don't understand," continued Ilágin, "how some sportsmen can be so jealous about game and dogs. For myself, I can tell you, count, I enjoy riding in company such as this . . . what could be better?" (he again raised his cap to Natásha) "but as for counting skins and what one takes, I don't care about that."

"Of course not!"

"Or being upset because someone else's borzoi and not mine catches something. All I care about is to enjoy seeing the chase, is it not so, count? For I consider that . . ."

"A-tu!" came the long-drawn cry of one of the borzoi-whippers-in, who had halted. He stood on a knoll in the stubble, holding his whip aloft, and again repeated his long-drawn cry, *"A-tu!"* (This call and the uplifted whip meant that he saw a sitting hare.)

"Ah, he has found one, I think," said Ilágin carelessly. "Well, let us course it, count."

"Yes, we must ride up. . . . Shall we both course it?" answered Nicholas, seeing in Erza and "Uncle's" red Rugáy two rivals he had never yet had a chance of pitting against his own borzois. "And suppose they outdo my Mílka at once!" he thought as he rode with "Uncle" and Ilágin toward the hare.

"A full-grown one?" asked Ilágin as he approached the whip who had sighted the hare—and not without agitation he looked round and whistled to Erza.

"And you, Michael Nikanórovich?" he said, addressing "Uncle."

The latter was riding with a sullen expression on his face.

"How can I join in? Why, you've given a village for each of your borzois! That's it, come on! Yours are worth thousands. Try yours against one another, you two, and I'll look on!"

"Rugáy, hey, hey!" he shouted. "Rugayushka!" he added, involuntarily by this diminutive expressing his affection and the hopes he placed on this red borzoi. Natásha saw and felt the agitation the two elderly men and her brother were trying to conceal, and was herself excited by it.

The huntsman stood halfway up the knoll holding up his whip and the gentlefolk rode up to him at a footpace; the hounds that were far off on the horizon turned away from the hare, and the whips, but not the gentlefolk, also moved away. All were moving slowly and sedately.

"How is it pointing?" asked Nicholas, riding a hundred paces toward the whip who had sighted the hare.

But before the whip could reply, the hare, scenting the frost coming next morning, was unable to rest and leaped up. The pack on leash rushed downhill in full cry after the hare, and from all sides the borzois that were not on leash darted after the hounds and the hare. All the hunt, who had been moving slowly, shouted "Stop!" calling in the hounds, while the borzoi-whips, with a cry of *"A-tu!"* galloped across the field setting the borzois on the hare. The tranquil Ilágin, Nicholas, Natásha, and "Uncle," flew, reckless of where and how they went, seeing only the borzois and the hare and fearing only to lose sight even for an instant of the chase. The hare they had started was a strong and swift one. When he jumped up he did not run at once, but pricked his ears listening to the shouting and trampling that resounded from all sides at once. He took a dozen bounds, not very quickly, letting the borzois gain on him, and finally having chosen his direction and realized his danger, laid back his ears and rushed off headlong. He had been lying in the stubble, but in front of him was the autumn-sowing where the ground was soft. The two borzois of the huntsman who had sighted him, having been the nearest, were the first to see and pursue him, but they had not gone far before Ilágin's red-spotted Erza passed them, got within a length, flew at the hare with terrible swiftness aiming at his scut and, thinking she had seized him, rolled over like a ball. The hare arched his back and bounded off yet more swiftly. From behind Erza rushed the broad-haunched, black-spotted Mílka and began rapidly gaining on the hare.

"Miláshka, dear!" rose Nicholas's triumphant cry. It looked as if Mílka would immediately pounce on the hare, but she overtook him and flew past. The hare had squatted. Again the beautiful Erza reached him, but when close to the hare's scut paused as if measuring the distance, so as not to make a mistake this time but seize his hind leg.

"Erza, darling!" Ilágin wailed in a voice unlike his own. Erza did not hearken to his appeal. At the very moment when she would have seized her prey, the hare moved and darted along the balk between the winter rye and the stubble. Again Erza and Mílka were abreast, running like a pair of carriage horses, and began to overtake the hare, but it was easier for the hare to run on the balk and the borzois did not overtake him so quickly.

"Rugáy, Rugayushka! That's it, come on!" came a third voice just then, and "Uncle's" red borzoi, straining and curving its back, caught up with the two foremost borzois, pushed ahead of them regardless of the terrible strain, put on speed close to the hare, knocked it off the balk onto the ryefield, again put on speed still more viciously, sinking to his knees in the muddy field, and all one could see was how, muddying his back, he rolled over with the hare. A ring of borzois surrounded him. A moment later everyone had drawn up round the crowd of dogs. Only the delighted "Uncle" dismounted, and cut off a pad, shaking the hare for the blood to drip off, and anxiously glancing round with restless eyes while his arms and legs twitched. He spoke without himself knowing whom to or what about. "That's it, come on! That's a dog! . . . There, it has beaten them all, the thousand-ruble as well as the one-ruble borzois. That's it, come on!" said he, panting and looking wrathfully around as if he were abusing someone, as if they were all his enemies and had insulted him, and only now had he at last succeeded in justifying himself. "There are your thousand-ruble ones. . . . That's it, come on! . . ."

"Rugáy, here's a pad for you!" he said, throwing down the hare's muddy pad. "You've deserved it, that's it, come on!"

"She'd tired herself out, she'd run it down three times by herself," said Nicholas, also not listening to anyone and regardless of whether he were heard or not.

"But what is there in running across it like that?" said Ilágin's groom.

"Once she had missed it and turned it away, any mongrel could take it," Ilágin was saying at the same time, breathless from his gallop and his excitement. At the same moment Natásha, without drawing breath, screamed joyously, ecstatically, and so piercingly that it set everyone's ear tingling. By that shriek she expressed what the others expressed by all talking at once, and it was so strange that she must herself have been ashamed of so wild a cry and everyone else would have been amazed at it at any other time. "Uncle" himself twisted up the hare, threw it neatly and smartly across his horse's back as if by that gesture he meant to rebuke everybody and, with an air of not wishing to speak to anyone, mounted his bay and rode off. The others all followed, dispirited and shamefaced, and only much later were they able to regain their former affectation of indifference. For a long time they continued to look at red Rugáy who, his arched back spattered with mud and clanking the ring of his leash, walked along just behind "Uncle's" horse with the serene air of a conqueror.

"Well, I am like any other dog as long as it's not a question of coursing. But when it is, then look out!" his appearance seemed to Nicholas to be saying.

When, much later, "Uncle" rode up to Nicholas and began talking to him, he felt flattered that, after what had happened, "Uncle" deigned to speak to him.

Chapter VII

Toward evening Ilágin took leave of Nicholas, who found that they were so far from home that he accepted "Uncle's" offer that the hunting-party should spend the night in his little village of Mikháylovna.

"And if you put up at my house that will be better still. That's it, come on!" said "Uncle." "You see it's damp weather, and you could rest, and the little countess could be driven home in a trap."

"Uncle's" offer was accepted. A huntsman was sent to Otrádnoe for a trap, while Nicholas rode with Natásha and Pétya to "Uncle's" house.

Some five male domestic serfs, big and little, rushed out to the front porch to meet their master. A score of women serfs, old and young, as well as children, popped out from the back entrance to have a look at the hunters who were arriving. The presence of Natásha—a woman, a lady, and on horseback—raised the curiosity of the serfs to such a degree that many of them came up to her, stared her in the face, and unabashed by her presence made remarks about her as though she were some prodigy on show, and not a human being able to hear or understand what was said about her.

"Arínka! Look, she sits sideways! There she sits and her skirt dangles. . . . See, she's got a little hunting-horn!"

"Goodness gracious! See her knife? . . ."

"Isn't she a Tartar!"

"How is it you didn't go head over heels?" asked the boldest of all, addressing Natásha directly.

"Uncle" dismounted at the porch of his little wooden house which stood in the midst of an overgrown garden and, after a glance at his retainers, shouted authoritatively that the superfluous ones should take themselves off and that all necessary preparations should be made to receive the guests and the visitors.

The serfs all dispersed. "Uncle" lifted Natásha off her horse, and taking her hand led her up the rickety wooden steps of the porch. The house, with its bare unplastered log-walls, was not overclean—it did not seem that those living in it aimed at keeping it spotless—but neither was it noticeably neglected. In the entry there was a smell of fresh apples, and wolf and fox skins hung about.

"Uncle" led the visitors through the anteroom into a small hall with a folding table and red chairs, then into the drawing room with a round birch-wood table and a sofa, and finally into his private room where there was a tattered sofa, a worn carpet, and portraits of Suvórov, of the host's father and mother, and of himself in military uniform. The study smelled strongly of tobacco and dogs. "Uncle" asked his visitors to sit down and make themselves at home, and then went out of the room. Rugáy, his back still muddy, came into the room and lay down on the sofa, cleaning himself with his tongue and teeth. Leading from the study was a passage in which a partition with ragged curtains could be seen. From behind this came women's laughter and whispers. Natásha, Nicholas, and Pétya, took off their wraps and sat down on the sofa. Pétya, leaning on his elbow, fell asleep at once. Natásha and Nicholas were silent. Their faces glowed, they were hungry and very cheerful. They looked at one another (now that the hunt was over and they were in the house, Nicholas no longer considered it necessary to show his manly superiority over his sister), Natásha gave him a wink, and neither refrained long from bursting into a peal of ringing laughter even before they had a pretext ready to account for it.

After a while "Uncle" came in, in a Cossack coat, blue trousers and small top-boots. And Natásha felt that this costume, the very one she had regarded with surprise and amusement at Otrádnoe, was just the right thing and not at all worse than a swallow-tail or frock-coat. "Uncle" too was in high spirits and far from being offended by the brother's and sister's laughter (it could never enter his head that they might be laughing at his way of life) he himself joined in the merriment.

"That's right, young countess, that's it, come on! I never saw anyone like her!" said he, offering Nicholas a pipe with a long stem and, with a practiced motion of three fingers, taking down another that had been cut short. "She's ridden all day like a man, and is as fresh as ever!"

Soon after "Uncle's" reappearance the door was opened, evidently from the sound by a barefooted girl, and a stout, rosy, good-looking woman of about forty, with a double chin and full red lips, entered carrying a large loaded tray. With hospitable dignity and cordiality in her glance and in every motion, she looked at the visitors and, with a pleasant smile, bowed respectfully. In spite of her exceptional stoutness, which caused her to protrude her chest and stomach and throw back her head, this woman (who was "Uncle's" housekeeper) trod very lightly. She went to the table, set down the tray, and with her plump white hands deftly took from it the bottles and various hors d'oeuvres and dishes, and arranged them on the table. When she had finished, she stepped aside and stopped at the door with a smile on her face. "Here I am. I am she! Now do you understand 'Uncle'?" her expression said to Rostóv. How could one help understanding? Not only Nicholas, but even Natásha understood the meaning of his puckered brow and the happy complacent smile that slightly puckered his lips when Anísya Fëdorovna entered. On the tray was a bottle of herb wine, different kinds of vodka, pickled mushrooms, rye-cakes made with buttermilk, honey in the comb, still mead and sparkling mead, apples, nuts (raw and roasted), and nut-and-honey sweets. Afterward she brought a freshly roasted chicken, ham, preserves made with honey, and preserves made with sugar.

All this was the fruit of Anísya Fëdorovna's housekeeping, gathered and prepared by her. The smell and taste of it all had a smack of Anísya Fëdorovna herself: a savor of juiciness, cleanliness, whiteness, and pleasant smiles.

"Take this, little Lady-Countess!" she kept saying, as she offered Natásha first one thing and then another.

Natásha ate of everything and thought she had never seen or eaten such buttermilk-cakes, such aromatic jam, such honey-and-nut sweets, or such a chicken anywhere. Anísya Fëdorovna left the room.

After supper, over their cherry brandy, Rostóv and "Uncle" talked of past and future hunts, of Rugáy and Ilágin's dogs, while Natásha sat upright on the sofa and listened with sparkling eyes. She tried several times to wake Pétya that he might eat something, but he only muttered incoherent words without waking up. Natásha felt so light-hearted and happy in these novel surroundings that she only feared the trap would come for her too soon. After a casual pause, such as often occurs when receiving friends for the first time in one's own house, "Uncle," answering a thought that was in his visitors' mind, said:

"This, you see, is how I am finishing my days . . . Death will come. That's it, come on! Nothing will remain. Then why harm anyone?"

"Uncle's" face was very significant and even handsome as he said this. Involuntarily Rostóv recalled all the good he had heard about him from his father and the neighbors. Throughout the whole province "Uncle" had the reputation of being the most honorable and disinterested of cranks. They called him in to decide family disputes, chose him as executor, confided secrets to him, elected him to be a justice and to other posts; but he always persistently refused public appointments, passing the autumn and spring in the fields on his bay gelding, sitting at home in winter, and lying in his overgrown garden in summer.

"Why don't you enter the service, Uncle?"

"I did once, but gave it up. I am not fit for it. That's it, come on! I can't make head or tail of it. That's for you—I haven't brains enough. Now, hunting is another matter—that's it, come on! Open the door, there!" he shouted. "Why have you shut it?"

The door at the end of the passage led to the huntsmen's room, as they called the room for the hunt servants.

There was a rapid patter of bare feet, and an unseen hand opened the door into the huntsmen's room, from which came the clear sounds of a balaláyka on which someone, who was evidently a master of the art, was playing. Natásha had been listening to those strains for some time and now went out into the passage to hear better.

"That's Mítka, my coachman. . . . I have got him a good balaláyka. I'm fond of it," said "Uncle."

It was the custom for Mítka to play the balaláyka in the huntsmen's room when "Uncle" returned from the chase. "Uncle" was fond of such music.

"How good! Really very good!" said Nicholas with some unintentional superciliousness, as if ashamed to confess that the sounds pleased him very much.

"Very good?" said Natásha reproachfully, noticing her brother's tone. "Not 'very good'—it's simply delicious!"

Just as "Uncle's" pickled mushrooms, honey, and cherry brandy had seemed to her the best in the world, so also that song, at that moment, seemed to her the acme of musical delight.

"More, please, more!" cried Natásha at the door as soon as the balaláyka ceased. Mítka tuned up afresh, and recommenced thrumming the balaláyka to the air of *My Lady,* with trills and variations. "Uncle" sat listening, slightly smiling, with his head on one side. The air was repeated a hundred times. The balaláyka was retuned several times and the same notes were thrummed again, but the listeners did not grow weary of it and wished to hear it again and again. Anísya Fëdorovna came in and leaned her portly person against the doorpost.

"You like listening?" she said to Natásha, with a smile extremely like "Uncle's." "That's a good player of ours," she added.

"He doesn't play that part right!" said "Uncle" suddenly, with an energetic gesture. "Here he ought to burst out—that's it, come on!—ought to burst out."

"Do you play then?" asked Natásha.

"Uncle" did not answer, but smiled.

"Anísya, go and see if the strings of my guitar are all right. I haven't touched it for a long time. That's it—come on! I've given it up."

Anísya Fëdorovna, with her light step, willingly went to fulfill her errand, and brought back the guitar.

Without looking at anyone, "Uncle" blew the dust off it and, tapping the case with his bony fingers, tuned the guitar and settled himself in his arm-chair. He took the guitar a little above the finger-board, arching his left elbow with a somewhat theatrical gesture and, with a wink at Anísya Fëdorovna, struck a single chord, pure and sonorous, and then quietly, smoothly, and confidently, began playing in very slow time, not *My Lady,* but the well-known song: *Came a maiden down the street.* The tune, played with precision and in exact time, began to thrill in the hearts of Nicholas and Natásha, arousing in them the same kind of sober mirth as radiated from Anísya Fëdorovna's whole being. Anísya Fëdorovna flushed, and drawing her kerchief over her face went laughing out of the room. "Uncle" continued to play correctly, carefully, with energetic firmness, looking with a changed and inspired expression at the spot where Anísya Fëdorovna had just stood. Something seemed to be laughing a little on one side of his face under his gray mustaches, especially as the song grew brisker and the time quicker and when, here and there, as he ran his fingers over the strings, something seemed to snap.

"Lovely, lovely! Go on, Uncle, go on!" shouted Natásha as soon as he had finished. She jumped up and hugged and kissed him. "Nicholas, Nicholas!" she said, turning to her brother, as if asking him: "What is it moves me so?"

Nicholas too was greatly pleased by "Uncle's" playing, and "Uncle" played the piece over again. Anísya Fëdorovna's smiling face reappeared in the doorway and behind hers other faces. . . .

Fetching water clear and sweet,
Stop, dear maiden, I entreat—

played "Uncle" once more, running his fingers skillfully over the strings, and then he stopped short and jerked his shoulders.

"Go on, Uncle dear," Natásha wailed in an imploring tone as if her life depended on it.

"Uncle" rose, and it was as if there were two men in him: one of them smiled seriously at the merry fellow, while the merry fellow struck a naïve and precise attitude preparatory to a folk-dance.

"Now, then, niece!" he exclaimed, waving to Natásha the hand that had just struck a chord.

Natásha threw off the shawl from her shoulders, ran forward to face "Uncle," and setting her arms akimbo, also made a motion with her shoulders and struck an attitude.

Where, how, and when, had this young countess, educated by an *émigrée* French governess, imbibed from the Russian air she breathed that spirit, and obtained that manner which the *pas de châle* would, one would have supposed, long ago have effaced? But the spirit and the movements were those inimitable and unteachable Russian ones that "Uncle" had expected of her. As soon as she had struck her pose, and smiled triumphantly, proudly, and with sly merriment, the fear that had at first seized Nicholas and the others that she might not do the right thing was at an end, and they were already admiring her.

She did the right thing with such precision, such complete precision, that Anísya Fëdorovna, who had at once handed her the handkerchief she needed for the dance, had tears in her eyes, though she laughed as she watched this slim, graceful countess, reared in silks and velvets and so different from herself, who yet was able to understand all that was in Anísya and in Anísya's father and mother and aunt, and in every Russian man and woman.

"Well, little countess; that's it—come on!" cried "Uncle," with a joyous laugh, having finished the dance. "Well done, niece! Now a fine young fellow must be found as husband for you. That's it—come on!"

"He's chosen already," said Nicholas smiling.

"Oh?" said "Uncle" in surprise, looking inquiringly at Natásha, who nodded her head with a happy smile.

"And such a one!" she said. But as soon as she had said it a new train of thoughts and feelings arose in her. "What did Nicholas's smile mean when he said 'Chosen already'? Is he glad of it or not? It is as if he thought my Bolkónski would not approve of or understand our gaiety. But he would understand it all. Where is he now?" she thought, and her face suddenly became serious. But this lasted only a second. "Don't dare to think about it," she said to herself, and sat down again smilingly beside "Uncle," begging him to play something more.

"Uncle" played another song and a valse; then after a pause he cleared his throat, and sang his favorite hunting song:

As 'twas growing dark last night
Fell the snow so soft and light . . .

"Uncle" sang as peasants sing, with full and naïve conviction that the whole meaning of a song lies in the words and that the tune comes of itself, and that apart from the words there is no tune, which exists only to give measure to the words. As a result of this the unconsidered tune, like the song of a bird, was extraordinarily good. Natásha was in ecstasies over "Uncle's" singing. She resolved to give up learning the harp and to play only the guitar. She asked "Uncle" for his guitar and at once found the chords of the song.

After nine o'clock two traps and three mounted men, who had been sent to look for them, arrived to fetch Natásha and Pétya. The count and countess did not know where they were and were very anxious, said one of the men.

Pétya was carried out like a log and laid in the larger of the two traps. Natásha and Nicholas got into the other. "Uncle" wrapped Natásha up warmly, and took leave of her with quite a new tenderness. He accompanied them on foot as far as the bridge that could not be crossed, so that they had to go round by the ford, and he sent huntsmen to ride in front with lanterns.

"Good-bye, dear niece," his voice called out of the darkness—not the voice Natásha had known previously, but the one that had sung *As 'twas growing dark last night*.

In the village through which they passed there were red lights and a cheerful smell of smoke.

"What a darling "Uncle" is!" said Natásha, when they had come out onto the highroad.

"Yes," returned Nicholas. "You're not cold?"

"No. I'm quite, quite all right. I feel so comfortable!" answered Natásha, almost perplexed by her feelings. They remained silent a long while. The night was dark and damp. They could not see the horses, but only heard them splashing through the unseen mud.

What was passing in that receptive childlike soul that so eagerly caught and assimilated all the diverse impressions of life? How did they all find place in her? But she was very happy. As they were nearing home she suddenly struck up the air of *As 'twas growing dark last night*—the tune of which she had all the way been trying to get, and had at last caught.

"Got it?" said Nicholas.

"What were you thinking about just now, Nicholas?" inquired Natásha.

They were fond of asking one another that question.

"I?" said Nicholas, trying to remember. "Well, you see, first I thought that Rugáy, the red hound, was like "Uncle," and that if he were a man he would always keep "Uncle" near him, if not for his riding, then for his manner. What a good fellow "Uncle" is! Don't you think so? . . . Well, and you?"

"I? Wait a bit, wait. . . . Yes, first I thought that we are driving along and imagining that we are going home, but that heaven knows where we are really going in the darkness, and that we shall arrive and suddenly find that we are not in Otrádnoe, but in Fairyland. And then I thought . . . No, nothing else."

"I know, I expect you thought of him," said Nicholas, smiling as Natásha knew by the sound of his voice.

"No," said Natásha, though she had in reality been thinking about Prince Andrew at the same time as of the rest, and of how he would have liked "Uncle." "And then I was saying to myself all the way, 'How well Anísya carried herself, how well!' " And Nicholas heard her spontaneous, happy, ringing laughter. "And do you know," she suddenly said, "I know that I shall never again be as happy and tranquil as I am now."

"Rubbish, nonsense, humbug!" exclaimed Nicholas, and he thought: "How charming this Natásha of mine is! I have no other friend like her, and never shall have. Why should she marry? We might always drive about together!"

"What a darling this Nicholas of mine is!" thought Natásha.

"Ah, there are still lights in the drawing room!" she said, pointing to the windows of the house that gleamed invitingly in the moist velvety darkness of the night.

Chapter VIII

COUNT ILYÁ ROSTÓV HAD RESIGNED THE POSITION OF MARSHAL OF THE NOBILITY BECAUSE IT INvolved him in too much expense, but still his affairs did not improve. Natásha and Nicholas often noticed their parents conferring together anxiously and privately, and heard suggestions of selling the fine ancestral Rostóv house and estate near Moscow. It was not necessary to entertain so freely as when the count had been Marshal, and life at Otrádnoe was quieter than in former years, but still the enormous house and its lodges were full of people and more than twenty sat down to table every day. These were all their own people who had settled down in the house almost as members of the family, or persons who were, it seemed, obliged to live in the count's house. Such were Dimmler the musician and his wife, Vogel the dancing master and his family, Belóva, an old maiden lady, an inmate of the house, and many others such as Pétya's tutors, the girls' former governess, and other people who simply found it preferable and more advantageous to live in the count's house than at home. They had not as many visitors as before, but the old habits of life without which the count and countess could not conceive of existence, remained unchanged. There was still the hunting establishment which Nicholas had even enlarged, the same fifty horses and fifteen grooms in the stables, the same expensive presents and dinner-parties to the whole district on name-days; there were still the count's games of whist and boston, at which—spreading out his cards so that everybody could see them—he let himself be plundered of hundreds of rubles every day by his neighbors, who looked upon an opportunity to play a rubber with Count Rostóv as a most profitable source of income.

The count moved in his affairs as in a huge net, trying not to believe that he was entangled but becoming more and more so at every step, and feeling too feeble to break the meshes or to set to work carefully and patiently to disentangle them. The countess, with her loving heart, felt that her children were being ruined, that it was not the count's fault for he could not help being what he was—that (though he tried to hide it) he himself suffered from the consciousness of his own and his children's ruin, and she tried to find means of remedying the position. From her feminine point of view she could see only one solution, namely, for Nicholas to marry a rich heiress. She felt this to be their last hope and that if Nicholas refused the match she had found for him, she would have to abandon the hope of ever getting matters right. This match was with Julie Karágina, the daughter of excellent and virtuous parents, a girl the Rostóvs had known from childhood, and who had now become a wealthy heiress through the death of the last of her brothers.

The countess had written direct to Julie's mother in Moscow suggesting a marriage between their children, and had received a favorable answer from her. Karágina had replied that for her part she was agreeable, and everything would depend on her daughter's inclination. She invited Nicholas to come to Moscow.

Several times the countess, with tears in her eyes, told her son that now both her daughters were settled, her only wish was to see him married. She said she could lie down in her grave peacefully if that were accomplished. Then she told him that she knew of a splendid girl, and tried to discover what he thought about marriage.

At other times she praised Julie to him, and advised him to go to Moscow during the holidays to amuse himself. Nicholas guessed what his mother's remarks were leading to, and during one of these conversations induced her to speak quite frankly. She told him that her only hope of getting their affairs disentangled, now lay in his marrying Julie Karágina.

"But, Mamma, suppose I loved a girl who has no fortune, would you expect me to sacrifice my feelings and my honor for the sake of money?" he asked his mother, not realizing the cruelty of his question and only wishing to show his noble-mindedness.

"No, you have not understood me," said his mother, not knowing how to justify herself. "You have not understood me, Nikólenka. It is your happiness I wish for," she added, feeling that she was telling an untruth and was becoming entangled. She began to cry.

"Mamma, don't cry! Only tell me that you wish it, and you know I will give my life, anything, to put you at ease," said Nicholas. "I would sacrifice anything for you—even my feelings."

But the countess did not want the question put like that: she did not want a sacrifice from her son, she herself wished to make a sacrifice for him.

"No, you have not understood me, don't let us talk about it," she replied, wiping away her tears.

"Maybe I do love a poor girl," said Nicholas to himself. "Am I to sacrifice my feelings and my honor for money? I wonder how Mamma could speak so to me. Because Sónya is poor I must not love her," he thought, "must not respond to her faithful, devoted love? Yet I should certainly be happier with her than with some doll-like Julie. I can always sacrifice my feelings for my family's welfare," he said to himself, "but I can't coerce my feelings. If I love Sónya, that feeling is for me stronger and higher than all else."

Nicholas did not go to Moscow, and the countess did not renew the conversation with him about marriage. She saw with sorrow, and sometimes with exasperation, symptoms of a growing attachment between her son and the portionless Sónya. Though she blamed herself for it, she could not refrain from grumbling at and worrying Sónya, often pulling her up without reason, addressing her stiffly as "my dear," and using the formal "you" instead of the intimate "thou" in speaking to her. The kind-hearted countess was the more vexed with Sónya because that poor, dark-eyed niece of hers was so meek, so kind, so devotedly grateful to her benefactors, and so faithfully, unchangingly and unselfishly in love with Nicholas, that there were no grounds for finding fault with her.

Nicholas was spending the last of his leave at home. A fourth letter had come from Prince Andrew, from Rome, in which he wrote that he would have been on his way back to Russia long ago had not his wound unexpectedly reopened in the warm climate, which obliged him to defer his return till the beginning of the new year. Natásha was still as much in love with her betrothed, found the same comfort in that love, and was still as ready to throw herself into all the pleasures of life as before; but at the end of the fourth month of their separation she began to have fits of depression which she could not master. She felt sorry for herself: sorry that she was being wasted all this time and of no use to anyone—while she felt herself so capable of loving and being loved.

Things were not cheerful in the Rostóvs' home.

Chapter IX

CHRISTMAS CAME AND EXCEPT FOR THE CEREMONIAL MASS, THE SOLEMN AND WEARISOME Christmas congratulations from neighbors and servants, and the new dresses everyone put on, there were no special festivities, though the calm frost of twenty degrees Réaumur, the dazzling sunshine by day and the starlight of the winter nights, seemed to call for some special celebration of the season.

On the third day of Christmas week, after the midday dinner, all the inmates of the house dispersed to various rooms. It was the dullest time of the day. Nicholas, who had been visiting some neighbors that morning, was asleep on the sitting room sofa. The old count was resting in his study. Sónya sat in the drawing room at the round table, copying a design for embroidery. The countess was playing patience. Nastásya Ivánovna the buffoon sat with a sad face at the window with two old ladies. Natásha came into the room, went up to Sónya, glanced at what she was doing, and then went up to her mother and stood without speaking.

"Why are you wandering about like an outcast?" asked her mother. "What do you want?"

"*Him* . . . I want him . . . now, this minute! I want *him!*" said Natásha, with glittering eyes and no sign of a smile.

The countess lifted her head and looked attentively at her daughter.

"Don't look at me, Mamma! Don't look; I shall cry directly."

"Sit down with me a little," said the countess.

"Mamma, I want *him*. Why should I be wasted like this, Mamma?"

Her voice broke, tears gushed from her eyes, and she turned quickly to hide them and left the room.

She passed into the sitting room, stood there thinking awhile, and then went into the maids' room. There an old maidservant was grumbling at a young girl who stood panting, having just run in through the cold from the serfs' quarters.

"Stop playing—there's a time for everything," said the old woman.

"Let her alone, Kondrátevna," said Natásha. "Go, Mavrushka, go."

Having released Mavrushka, Natásha crossed the dancing-hall and went to the vestibule. There an old footman and two young ones were playing cards. They broke off and rose as she entered.

"What can I do with them?" thought Natásha.

"Oh, Nikíta, please go . . . where can I send him? . . . Yes, go to the yard and fetch a fowl, please, a cock, and you, Mísha, bring me some oats."

"Just a few oats?" said Mísha, cheerfully and readily.

"Go, go quickly," the old man urged him.

"And you, Theodore, get me a piece of chalk."

On her way past the butler's pantry she told them to set a samovar, though it was not at all the time for tea.

Fóka, the butler, was the most ill-tempered person in the house. Natásha liked to test her power over him. He distrusted the order and asked whether the samovar was really wanted.

"Oh dear, what a young lady!" said Fóka, pretending to frown at Natásha.

No one in the house sent people about or gave them as much trouble as Natásha did. She could not see people unconcernedly, but had to send them on some errand. She seemed to be trying whether any of them would get angry or sulky with her; but the serfs fulfilled no one's orders so readily as they did hers. "What can I do, where can I go?" thought she, as she went slowly along the passage.

"Nastásya Ivánovna, what sort of children shall I have?" she asked the buffoon, who was coming toward her in a woman's jacket.

"Why, fleas, crickets, grasshoppers," answered the buffoon.

"O Lord, O Lord, it's always the same! Oh, where am I to go? What am I to do with myself?" And tapping with her heels, she ran quickly upstairs to see Vogel and his wife who lived on the upper story.

Two governesses were sitting with the Vogels at a table, on which were plates of raisins, walnuts, and almonds. The governesses were discussing whether it was cheaper to live in Moscow or Odessa. Natásha sat down, listened to their talk with a serious and thoughtful air, and then got up again.

"The island of Madagascar," she said, "Ma-da-gas-car," she repeated, articulating each syllable distinctly, and not replying to Madame Schoss who asked her what she was saying, she went out of the room.

Her brother Pétya was upstairs too; with the man in attendance on him he was preparing fireworks to let off that night.

"Pétya! Pétya!" she called to him. "Carry me downstairs."

Pétya ran up and offered her his back. She jumped on it, putting her arms round his neck, and he pranced along with her.

"No, don't . . . the island of Madagascar!" she said, and jumping off his back she went downstairs.

Having as it were reviewed her kingdom, tested her power, and made sure that everyone was submissive, but that all the same it was dull, Natásha betook herself to the ballroom, picked up her guitar, sat down in a dark corner behind a bookcase and began to run her fingers over the strings in the bass, picking out a passage she recalled from an opera she had heard in Petersburg with Prince Andrew. What she drew from the guitar would have had no meaning for other listeners, but in her imagination a whole series of reminiscences arose from those sounds. She sat behind the bookcase with her eyes fixed on a streak of light escaping from the pantry door and listened to herself and pondered. She was in a mood for brooding on the past.

Sónya passed to the pantry with a glass in her hand. Natásha glanced at her and at the crack in the pantry door, and it seemed to her that she remembered the light failing through that crack once before and Sónya passing with a glass in her hand. "Yes, it was exactly the same," thought Natásha.

"Sónya, what is this?" she cried, twanging a thick string.

"Oh, you are there!" said Sónya with a start, and came near and listened. "I don't know. A storm?" she ventured timidly, afraid of being wrong.

"There! That's just how she started and just how she came up smiling timidly when all this happened before," thought Natásha, "and in just the same way I thought there was something lacking in her."

"No, it's the chorus from the *Water-Carrier,* listen!" and Natásha sang the air of the chorus so that Sónya should catch it. "Where were you going?" she asked.

"To change the water in this glass. I am just finishing the design."

"You always find something to do, but I can't," said Natásha. "And where's Nicholas?"

"Asleep, I think."

"Sónya, go and wake him," said Natásha. "Tell him I want him to come and sing."

She sat awhile, wondering what the meaning of it all having happened before could be, and without solving this problem, or at all regretting not having done so, she again passed in fancy to the time when she was with *him* and he was looking at her with a lover's eyes.

"Oh, if only he would come quicker! I am so afraid it will never be! And, worst of all, I am growing old—that's the thing! There won't then be in me what there is now. But perhaps he'll come today, will come immediately. Perhaps he has come and is sitting in the drawing room. Perhaps he came yesterday and I have forgotten it." She rose, put down the guitar, and went to the drawing room.

All the domestic circle, tutors, governesses, and guests, were already at the tea-table. The servants stood round the table—but Prince Andrew was not there and life was going on as before.

"Ah, here she is!" said the old count, when he saw Natásha enter. "Well, sit down by me." But Natásha stayed by her mother and glanced round as if looking for something.

"Mamma!" she muttered, "give him to me, give him, Mamma, quickly, quickly!" and she again had difficulty in repressing her sobs.

She sat down at the table and listened to the conversation between the elders and Nicholas, who had also come to the table. "My God, my God! The same faces, the same talk, Papa holding his cup and blowing in the same way!" thought Natásha, feeling with horror a sense of repulsion rising up in her for the whole household, because they were always the same.

After tea, Nicholas, Sónya, and Natásha went to the sitting room, to their favorite corner where their most intimate talks always began.

Chapter X

"DOES IT EVER HAPPEN TO YOU," SAID NATÁSHA TO HER BROTHER, WHEN THEY SETTLED DOWN in the sitting room, "does it ever happen to you to feel as if there were nothing more to come—nothing; that everything good is past? And to feel not exactly dull, but sad?"

"I should think so!" he replied. "I have felt like that when everything was all right and everyone was cheerful. The thought has come into my mind that I was already tired of it all, and that we must all die. Once in the regiment I had not gone to some merrymaking where there was music . . . and suddenly I felt so depressed . . ."

"Oh yes, I know, I know, I know!" Natásha interrupted him. "When I was quite little that used to be so with me. Do you remember when I was punished once about some plums? You were all dancing, and I sat sobbing in the schoolroom? I shall never forget it: I felt sad and sorry for everyone, for myself, and for everyone. And I was innocent—that was the chief thing," said Natásha. "Do you remember?"

"I remember," answered Nicholas. "I remember that I came to you afterward and wanted to comfort you, but do you know, I felt ashamed to. We were terribly absurd. I had a funny doll then and wanted to give it to you. Do you remember?"

"And do you remember," Natásha asked with a pensive smile, "how once, long long ago, when we were quite little, uncle called us into the study—that was in the old house—and it was dark—we went in and suddenly there stood . . ."

"A negro," chimed in Nicholas with a smile of delight. "Of course I remember. Even now I don't know whether there really was a negro, or if we only dreamed it or were told about him."

"He was gray, you remember, and had white teeth, and stood and looked at us. . . ."

"Sónya, do *you* remember?" asked Nicholas.

"Yes, yes, I do remember something too," Sónya answered timidly.

"You know I have asked Papa and Mamma about that negro," said Natásha, "and they say there was no negro at all. But you see, you remember!"

"Of course I do, I remember his teeth as if I had just seen them."

"How strange it is! It's as if it were a dream! I like that."

"And do you remember how we rolled hard-boiled eggs in the ballroom, and suddenly two old women began spinning round on the carpet? Was that real or not? Do you remember what fun it was?"

"Yes, and you remember how Papa in his blue overcoat fired a gun in the porch?"

So they went through their memories, smiling with pleasure: not the sad memories of old age, but poetic, youthful ones—those impressions of one's most distant past in which dreams and realities blend—and they laughed with quiet enjoyment.

Sónya, as always, did not quite keep pace with them, though they shared the same reminiscences.

Much that they remembered had slipped from her mind, and what she recalled did not arouse the same poetic feeling as they experienced. She simply enjoyed their pleasure and tried to fit in with it.

She only really took part when they recalled Sónya's first arrival. She told them how afraid she had been of Nicholas because he had on a corded jacket and her nurse had told her that she, too, would be sewn up with cords.

"And I remember their telling me that you had been born under a cabbage," said Natásha, "and I remember that I dared not disbelieve it then, but knew that it was not true, and I felt so uncomfortable."

While they were talking a maid thrust her head in at the other door of the sitting room.

"They have brought the cock, Miss," she said in a whisper.

"It isn't wanted, Pólya. Tell them to take it away," replied Natásha.

In the middle of their talk in the sitting room, Dimmler came in and went up to the harp that stood there in a corner. He took off its cloth covering, and the harp gave out a jarring sound.

"Mr. Dimmler, please play my favorite nocturne by Field," came the old countess's voice from the drawing room.

Dimmler struck a chord, and turning to Natásha, Nicholas, and Sónya, remarked: "How quiet you young people are!"

"Yes, we're philosophizing," said Natásha, glancing round for a moment and then continuing the conversation. They were now discussing dreams.

Dimmler began to play; Natásha went on tiptoe noiselessly to the table, took up a candle, carried it out and returned, seating herself quietly in her former place. It was dark in the room especially where they were sitting on the sofa, but through the big windows the silvery light of the full moon fell on the floor. Dimmler had finished the piece but still sat softly running his fingers over the strings, evidently uncertain whether to stop or to play something else.

"Do you know," said Natásha in a whisper, moving closer to Nicholas and Sónya, "that when one goes on and on recalling memories, one at last begins to remember what happened before one was in the world . . ."

"That is metempsychosis," said Sónya, who had always learned well, and remembered everything. "The Egyptians believed that our souls have lived in animals, and will go back into animals again."

"No, I don't believe we ever were in animals," said Natásha, still in a whisper though the music had ceased. "But I am certain that we were angels somewhere *there,* and have been here, and that is why we remember. . . ."

"May I join you?" said Dimmler who had come up quietly, and he sat down by them.

"If we have been angels, why have we fallen lower?" said Nicholas. "No, that can't be!"

"Not lower, who said we were lower? . . . How do I know what I was before?" Natásha rejoined with conviction. "The soul is immortal—well then, if I shall always live I must have lived before, lived for a whole eternity."

"Yes, but it is hard for us to imagine eternity," remarked Dimmler, who had joined the young folk with a mildly condescending smile, but now spoke as quietly and seriously as they.

"Why is it hard to imagine eternity?" said Natásha. "It is now today, and it will be tomorrow, and always; and there was yesterday, and the day before . . ."

"Natásha! Now it's your turn. Sing me something," they heard the countess say. "Why are you sitting there like conspirators?"

"Mamma, I don't at all want to," replied Natásha, but all the same she rose.

None of them, not even the middle-aged Dimmler, wanted to break off their conversation and quit that corner in the sitting room, but Natásha got up and Nicholas sat down at the clavichord. Standing as usual in the middle of the hall and choosing the place where the resonance was best, Natásha began to sing her mother's favorite song.

She had said she did not want to sing, but it was long since she had sung, and long before she again sang, as she did that evening. The count, from his study where he was talking to Mítenka, heard her, and like a schoolboy in a hurry to run out to play, blundered in his talk while giving orders to the steward, and at last stopped, while Mítenka stood in front of him also listening and smiling. Nicholas did not take his eyes off his sister and drew breath in time with her. Sónya, as she listened, thought of the immense difference there was between herself and her friend, and how impossible it was for her to be anything like as bewitching as her cousin. The old countess sat with a blissful yet sad smile and with tears in her eyes, occasionally shaking her head. She thought of Natásha and of her own youth, and of how there was something unnatural and dreadful in this impending marriage of Natásha and Prince Andrew.

Dimmler, who had seated himself beside the countess, listened with closed eyes.

"Ah, countess," he said at last, "that's a European talent, she has nothing to learn—what softness, tenderness, and strength. . . ."

"Ah, how afraid I am for her, how afraid I am!" said the countess, not realizing to whom she was speaking. Her maternal instinct told her that Natásha had too much of something, and that because of this she would not be happy. Before Natásha had finished singing, fourteen-year-old Pétya rushed in delightedly, to say that some mummers had arrived.

Natásha stopped abruptly.

"Idiot!" she screamed at her brother and running to a chair, threw herself on it, sobbing so violently that she could not stop for a long time.

"It's nothing, Mamma, really it's nothing; only Pétya startled me," she said, trying to smile, but her tears still flowed and sobs still choked her.

The mummers (some of the house serfs) dressed up as bears, Turks, innkeepers and ladies—frightening and funny—bringing in with them the cold from outside and a feeling of gaiety, crowded, at first timidly, into the anteroom, then hiding behind one another they pushed into the ballroom where, shyly at first and then more and more merrily and heartily, they started singing, dancing, and playing Christmas games. The countess, when she had identified them and laughed at their costumes, went into the drawing room. The count sat in the ballroom, smiling radiantly and applauding the players. The young people had disappeared.

Half an hour later there appeared among the other mummers in the ballroom an old lady in a hooped skirt—this was Nicholas. A Turkish girl was Pétya. A clown was Dimmler. A hussar was Natásha, and a Circassian was Sónya with burned-cork mustache and eyebrows.

After the condescending surprise, non-recognition, and praise, from those who were not themselves dressed up, the young people decided that their costumes were so good that they ought to be shown elsewhere.

Nicholas, who, as the roads were in splendid condition, wanted to take them all for a drive in his troyka, proposed to take with them about a dozen of the serf mummers and drive to "Uncle's."

"No, why disturb the old fellow?" said the countess, "besides, you wouldn't have room to turn round there. If you must go, go to the Melyukóvs'."

Melyukóva was a widow, who, with her family and their tutors and governesses, lived three miles from the Rostóvs.

"That's right, my dear," chimed in the old count, thoroughly aroused. "I'll dress up at once and go with them. I'll make Pashette open her eyes."

But the countess would not agree to his going; he had had a bad leg all these last days. It was decided that the count must not go, but that if Louisa Ivánovna (Madame Schoss) would go with them, the young ladies might go to the Melyukóvs', Sónya, generally so timid and shy, more urgently than anyone begging Louisa Ivánovna not to refuse.

Sónya's costume was the best of all. Her mustache and eyebrows were extraordinarily becoming. Everyone told her she looked very handsome, and she was in a spirited and energetic mood unusual with her. Some inner voice told her that now or never her fate would be decided, and in her male attire she seemed quite a different person. Louisa Ivánovna consented to go, and in half an hour four troika-sleighs with large and small bells, their runners squeaking and whistling over the frozen snow, drove up to the porch.

Natásha was foremost in setting a merry holiday tone, which, passing from one to another, grew stronger and reached its climax when they all came out into the frost and got into the sleighs, talking, calling to one another, laughing and shouting.

Two of the troykas were the usual household sleighs, the third was the old count's with a trotter from the Orlóv stud as shaft-horse, the fourth was Nicholas's own with a short shaggy black shaft-horse. Nicholas, in his old lady's dress over which he had belted his hussar overcoat, stood in the middle of the sleigh, reins in hand.

It was so light that he could see the moonlight reflected from the metal harness disks and from the eyes of the horses, who looked round in alarm at the noisy party under the shadow of the porch-roof.

Natásha, Sónya, Madame Schoss and two maids got into Nicholas's sleigh; Dimmler, his wife, and Pétya, into the old count's, and the rest of the mummers seated themselves in the other two sleighs.

"You go ahead, Zakhár!" shouted Nicholas to his father's coachman, wishing for a chance to race past him.

The old count's troyka, with Dimmler and his party, started forward, squeaking on its runners as though freezing to the snow, its deep-toned bell clanging. The side-horses, pressing against the shafts of the middle horse, sank in the snow which was dry and glittered like sugar, and threw it up.

Nicholas set off, following the first sleigh; behind him the others moved noisily, their runners squeaking. At first they drove at a steady trot along the narrow road. While they drove past the garden the shadows of the bare trees often fell across the road and hid the brilliant moonlight, but as soon as they were past the fence, the snowy plain bathed in moonlight and motionless spread out before them glittering like diamonds and dappled with bluish shadows. *Bang, bang!* went the first sleigh over a cradle-hole in the snow of the road, and each of the other sleighs jolted in the same way, and rudely breaking the frost-bound stillness, the troykas began to speed along the road, one after the other.

"A hare's track, a lot of tracks!" rang out Natásha's voice through the frost-bound air.

"How light it is, Nicholas!" came Sónya's voice.

Nicholas glanced round at Sónya, and bent down to see her face closer. Quite a new, sweet face with black eyebrows and mustaches peeped up at him from her sable furs—so close and yet so distant—in the moonlight.

"That used to be Sónya," thought he, and looked at her closer and smiled.

"What is it, Nicholas?"

"Nothing," said he and turned again to the horses.

When they came out onto the beaten highroad—polished by sleigh-runners and cut up by rough-shod hoofs, the marks of which were visible in the moonlight—the horses began to tug at the reins of their own accord and increased their pace. The near side-horse, arching his head and breaking into a short canter, tugged at his traces. The shaft-horse swayed from side to side, moving his ears as if asking: "Isn't it time to begin now?" In front, already far ahead the deep bell of the sleigh ringing farther and farther off, the black horses driven by Zakhár could be clearly seen against the white snow. From that sleigh one could hear the shouts, laughter, and voices of the mummers.

"Gee up, my darlings!" shouted Nicholas, pulling the reins to one side and flourishing the whip.

It was only by the keener wind that met them and the jerks given by the side-horses who pulled harder—ever increasing their gallop—that one noticed how fast the troyka was flying. Nicholas looked back. With screams, squeals, and waving of whips, that caused even the shaft-horses to gallop—the other sleighs followed. The shaft-horse swung steadily beneath the bow over its head, with no thought of slackening pace and ready to put on speed when required.

Nicholas overtook the first sleigh. They were driving downhill and coming out upon a broad trodden track across a meadow, near a river.

"Where are we?" thought he. "It's the Kosóy meadow, I suppose. But no—this is something new I've never seen before. This isn't the Kosóy meadow nor the Dëmkin hill, and heaven only knows what it is! It is something new and enchanted. Well, whatever it may be . . ." And shouting to his horses, he began to pass the first sleigh.

Zakhár held back his horses and turned his face, which was already covered with hoarfrost to his eyebrows.

Nicholas gave the horses the rein, and Zakhár, stretching out his arms, clucked his tongue and let his horses go.

"Now, look out, Master!" he cried.

Faster still the two troykas flew side by side, and faster moved the feet of the galloping side-horses. Nicholas began to draw ahead. Zakhár, while still keeping his arms extended, raised one hand with the reins.

"No you won't, Master!" he shouted.

Nicholas put all his horses to a gallop and passed Zakhár. The horses showered the fine snow on the faces of those in the sleigh—beside them sounded quick ringing bells and they caught confused glimpses of swiftly moving legs and the shadows of the troyka they were passing. The whistling sound of the runners on the snow and the voices of girls shrieking, were heard from different sides.

Again checking his horses, Nicholas looked around him. They were still surrounded by the magic plain bathed in moonlight and spangled with stars.

"Zakhár is shouting that I should turn to the left, but why to the left?" thought Nicholas. "Are we getting to the Melyukóvs'? Is this Melyukóvka? Heaven only knows where we are going, and heaven knows what is happening to us—but it is very strange and pleasant whatever it is." And he looked round in the sleigh.

"Look, his mustache and eyelashes are all white!" said one of the strange, pretty, unfamiliar people—the one with fine eyebrows and mustache.

"I think this used to be Natásha," thought Nicholas, "and that was Madame Schoss, but perhaps it's not, and this Circassian with the mustache I don't know, but I love her."

"Aren't you cold?" he asked.

They did not answer but began to laugh. Dimmler from the sleigh behind shouted something—probably something funny—but they could not make out what he said.

"Yes, yes!" some voices answered, laughing.

"But here was a fairy forest with black moving shadows, and a glitter of diamonds and a flight of marble steps and the silver roofs of fairy buildings and the shrill yells of some animals. And if this is really Melyukóvka, it is still stranger that we drove heaven knows where and have come to Melyukóvka," thought Nicholas.

It really was Melyukóvka, and maids and footmen with merry faces came running out to the porch carrying candles.

"Who is it?" asked someone in the porch.

"The mummers from the count's. I know by the horses," replied some voices.

Chapter XI

PELAGÉYA DANÍLOVNA MELYUKÓVA, A BROADLY BUILT, ENERGETIC WOMAN WEARING SPECTACLES, sat in the drawing room in a loose dress, surrounded by her daughters whom she was trying to keep from feeling dull. They were quietly dropping melted wax into snow and looking at the shadows the wax figures would throw on the wall, when they heard the steps and voices of new arrivals in the vestibule.

Hussars, ladies, witches, clowns and bears, after clearing their throats and wiping the hoarfrost from their faces in the vestibule, came into the ballroom where candles were hurriedly lit. The clown—Dimmler—and the lady—Nicholas—started a dance. Surrounded by the screaming children the mummers, covering their faces and disguising their voices, bowed to their hostess and arranged themselves about the room.

"Dear me! there's no recognizing them! And Natásha! See whom she looks like! She really reminds me of somebody. But Herr Dimmler—isn't he good! I didn't know him! And how he dances. Dear me, there's a Circassian. Really, how becoming it is to dear Sónya. And who is that? Well, you have cheered us up! Nikíta and Ványa—clear away the tables! And we were sitting so quietly. Ha, ha, ha! . . . The hussar, the hussar! Just like a boy! And the legs! . . . I can't look at him . . ." different voices were saying.

Natásha, the young Melyukóvs' favorite, disappeared with them into the back rooms where a cork and various dressing-gowns and male garments were called for, and received from the footman by bare girlish arms from behind the door. Ten minutes later, all the young Melyukóvs joined the mummers.

Pelagéya Danílovna, having given orders to clear the rooms for the visitors and arranged about refreshments for the gentry and the serfs, went about among the mummers without removing her spectacles, peering into their faces with a suppressed smile and failing to recognize any of them. It was not merely Dimmler and the Rostóvs she failed to recognize, she did not even recognize her own daughters, or her late husband's dressing-gowns and uniforms, which they had put on.

"And who is is this?" she asked her governess, peering into the face of her own daughter dressed up as a Kazán-Tartar. "I suppose it is one of the Rostóvs! Well, Mr. Hussar, and what regiment do you serve in?" she asked Natásha. "Here, hand some fruit-jelly to the Turk!" she ordered the butler who was handing things round. "That's not forbidden by his law."

Sometimes, as she looked at the strange but amusing capers cut by the dancers, who—having decided once for all that being disguised, no one would recognize them—were not at all shy, Pelagéya Danílovna hid her face in her handkerchief, and her whole stout body shook with irrepressible, kindly, elderly laughter.

"My little Sásha! Look at Sásha!" she said.

After Russian country-dances and chorus-dances, Pelagéya Danílovna made the serfs and gentry join in one large circle: a ring, a string, and a silver ruble, were fetched and they all played games together.

In an hour, all the costumes were crumpled and disordered. The corked eyebrows and mustaches were smeared over the perspiring, flushed and merry faces. Pelagéya Danílovna began to recognize the mummers, admired their cleverly contrived costumes, and particularly how they suited the young ladies, and she thanked them all for having entertained her so well. The visitors were invited to supper in the drawing room, and the serfs had something served to them in the ballroom.

"Now to tell one's fortune in the empty bathhouse is frightening!" said an old maid who lived with the Melyukóvs, during supper.

"Why?" said the eldest Melyukóv girl.

"You wouldn't go, it takes courage . . ."

"I'll go," said Sónya.

"Tell what happened to the young lady!" said the second Melyukóv girl.

"Well," began the old maid, "a young lady once went out, took a cock, laid the table for two, all properly, and sat down. After sitting a while, she suddenly hears someone coming . . . a sleigh drives up with harness bells; she hears him coming! He comes in, just in the shape of a man, like an officer—comes in and sits down to table with her."

"Ah! ah!" screamed Natásha, rolling her eyes with horror.

"Yes? And how . . . did he speak?"

"Yes, like a man. Everything quite all right, and he began persuading her; and she should have kept him talking till cock-crow, but she got frightened, just got frightened and hid her face in her hands. Then he caught her up. It was lucky the maids ran in just then . . ."

"Now, why frighten them?" said Pelagéya Danílovna.

"Mamma, you used to try your fate yourself . . ." said her daughter.

"And how does one do it in a barn?" inquired Sónya.

"Well, say you went to the barn now, and listened. It depends on what you hear; hammering and knocking—that's bad; but a sound of shifting grain is good and one sometimes hears that, too."

"Mamma, tell us what happened to you in the barn."

Pelagéya Danílovna smiled.

"Oh, I've forgotten . . ." she replied. "But none of you would go?"

"Yes, I will; Pelagéya Danílovna, let me! I'll go," said Sónya.

"Well, why not, if you're not afraid?"

"Louisa Ivánovna, may I?" asked Sónya.

Whether they were playing the ring and string game or the ruble game, or talking as now, Nicholas did not leave Sónya's side, and gazed at her with quite new eyes. It seemed to him that it was only today, thanks to that burned-cork mustache, that he had fully learned to know her. And really, that evening, Sónya was brighter, more animated, and prettier, than Nicholas had ever seen her before.

"So that's what she is like; what a fool I have been!" he thought gazing at her sparkling eyes, and under the mustache a happy rapturous smile dimpled her cheeks, a smile he had never seen before.

"I'm not afraid of anything," said Sónya. "May I go at once?" She got up.

They told her where the barn was and how she should stand and listen, and they handed her a fur cloak. She threw this over her head and shoulders and glanced at Nicholas.

"What a darling that girl is!" thought he. "And what have I been thinking of till now?"

Sónya went out into the passage to go to the barn. Nicholas went hastily to the front porch, saying he felt too hot. The crowd of people really had made the house stuffy.

Outside, there was the same cold stillness and the same moon, but even brighter than before. The light was so strong and the snow sparkled with so many stars, that one did not wish to look up at the sky and the real stars were unnoticed. The sky was black and dreary, while the earth was gay.

"I am a fool, a fool! what have I been waiting for?" thought Nicholas, and running out from the porch he went round the corner of the house and along the path that led to the back porch. He knew Sónya would pass that way. Halfway lay some snow-covered piles of firewood and across and along them a network of shadows from the bare old lime trees fell on the snow and on the path. This path led to the barn. The log walls of the barn and its snow-covered roof, that looked as if hewn out of some precious stone, sparkled in the moonlight. A tree in the garden snapped with the frost, and then all was again perfectly silent. His bosom seemed to inhale not air but the strength of eternal youth and gladness.

From the back porch came the sound of feet descending the steps, the bottom step upon which snow had fallen gave a ringing creak and he heard the voice of an old maidservant saying, "Straight, straight, along the path, Miss. Only, don't look back."

"I am not afraid," answered Sónya's voice, and along the path toward Nicholas came the crunching, whistling sound of Sónya's feet in her thin shoes.

Sónya came along, wrapped in her cloak. She was only a couple of paces away when she saw him, and to her too he was not the Nicholas she had known and always slightly feared. He was in a woman's dress, with tousled hair and a happy smile new to Sónya. She ran rapidly toward him.

"Quite different and yet the same," thought Nicholas, looking at her face all lit up by the moonlight. He slipped his arms under the cloak that covered her head, embraced her, pressed her to him, and kissed her on the lips that wore a mustache and had a smell of burned cork. Sónya kissed him full on the lips, and disengaging her little hands pressed them to his cheeks.

"Sónya!" . . . "Nicholas!" . . . was all they said. They ran to the barn and then back again, re-entering, he by the front and she by the back porch.

Chapter XII

When they all drove back from Pelagéya Danílovna's, Natásha, who always saw and noticed everything, arranged that she and Madame Schoss should go back in the sleigh with Dimmler, and Sónya with Nicholas and the maids.

On the way back Nicholas drove at a steady pace instead of racing, and kept peering by that fantastic all-transforming light into Sónya's face and searching beneath the eyebrows and mustache for his former and his present Sónya from whom he had resolved never to be parted again. He looked and recognizing in her both the old and the new Sónya, and being reminded by the smell of burned cork of the sensation of her kiss, inhaled the frosty air with a full breast and, looking at the ground flying beneath him and at the sparkling sky, felt himself again in fairyland.

"Sónya, is it well with *thee?*" he asked from time to time.

"Yes!" she replied. "And with *thee?*"

When halfway home Nicholas handed the reins to the coachman and ran for a moment to Natásha's sleigh and stood on its wing.

"Natásha!" he whispered in French, "do you know I have made up my mind about Sónya?"

"Have you told her?" asked Natásha, suddenly beaming all over with joy.

"Oh, how strange you are with that mustache and those eyebrows! . . . Natásha—are you glad?"

"I am so glad, so glad! I was beginning to be vexed with you. I did not tell you, but you have been treating her badly. What a heart she has, Nicholas! I am horrid sometimes, but I was ashamed to be happy while Sónya was not," continued Natásha. "Now I am so glad! Well, run back to her."

"No, wait a bit. . . . Oh, how funny you look!" cried Nicholas, peering into her face and finding in his sister too something new, unusual, and bewitchingly tender, that he had not seen in her before. "Natásha, it's magical, isn't it?"

"Yes," she replied. "You have done splendidly."

"Had I seen her before as she is now," thought Nicholas, "I should long ago have asked her what to do and have done whatever she told me, and all would have been well."

"So you are glad and I have done right?"

"Oh, quite right! I had a quarrel with Mamma some time ago about it. Mamma said she was angling for you. How could she say such a thing! I nearly stormed at Mamma. I will never let anyone say anything bad of Sónya, for there is nothing but good in her."

"Then it's all right?" said Nicholas, again scrutinizing the expression of his sister's face to see if she was in earnest. Then he jumped down and, his boots scrunching the snow, ran back to his sleigh. The same happy, smiling Circassian, with mustache and beaming eyes looking up from under a sable hood, was still sitting there, and that Circassian was Sónya, and that Sónya was certainly his future happy and loving wife.

When they reached home and had told their mother how they had spent the evening at the Melyukóvs', the girls went to their bedroom. When they had undressed, but without washing off the cork mustaches, they sat a long time talking of their happiness. They talked of how they would live when they were married, how their husbands would be friends, and how happy they would be. On Natásha's table stood two looking-glasses which Dunyásha had prepared beforehand.

"Only when will all that be? I am afraid never. . . . It would be too good!" said Natásha, rising and going to the looking-glasses.

"Sit down, Natásha; perhaps you'll see him," said Sónya.

Natásha lit the candles, one on each side of one of the looking-glasses, and sat down.

"I see someone with a mustache," said Natásha, seeing her own face.

"You mustn't laugh, Miss," said Dunyásha.

With Sónya's help and the maid's, Natásha got the glass she held into the right position opposite the other; her face assumed a serious expression and she sat silent. She sat a long time looking at the receding line of candles reflected in the glasses and expecting (from tales she had heard) to see a coffin, or *him,* Prince Andrew, in that last dim, indistinctly outlined square. But ready as she was to take the smallest speck for the image of a man or of a coffin, she saw nothing. She began blinking rapidly and moved away from the looking-glasses.

"Why is it others see things and I don't?" she said. "You sit down now, Sónya. You absolutely must, tonight! Do it for me. . . . Today I feel so frightened!"

Sónya sat down before the glasses, got the right position, and began looking.

"Now, Miss Sónya is sure to see something," whispered Dunyásha; "while you do nothing but laugh."

Sónya heard this and Natásha's whisper:

"I know she will. She saw something last year."

For about three minutes all were silent.

"Of course she will!" whispered Natásha, but did not finish . . . suddenly Sónya pushed away the glass she was holding and covered her eyes with her hand.

"Oh, Natásha!" she cried.

"Did you see? Did you? What was it?" exclaimed Natásha, holding up the looking-glass.

Sónya had not seen anything, she was just wanting to blink and to get up when she heard Natásha say, "Of course she will!" She did not wish to disappoint either Dunyásha or Natásha, but it was hard to sit still. She did not herself know how or why the exclamation escaped her when she covered her eyes.

"You saw him?" urged Natásha, seizing her hand.

"Yes. Wait a bit . . . I . . . saw him," Sónya could not help saying, not yet knowing whom Natásha meant by *him*, Nicholas or Prince Andrew.

"But why shouldn't I say I saw something? Others do see! Besides who can tell whether I saw anything or not?" flashed through Sónya's mind.

"Yes, I saw him," she said.

"How? Standing or lying?"

"No, I saw . . . At first there was nothing, then I saw him lying down."

"Andrew lying? Is he ill?" asked Natásha, her frightened eyes fixed on her friend.

"No, on the contrary, on the contrary! His face was cheerful, and he turned to me." And when saying this she herself fancied she had really seen what she described.

"Well, and then, Sónya? . . ."

"After that, I could not make out what there was; something blue and red . . ."

"Sónya! When will he come back? When shall I see him! Oh, God, how afraid I am for him and for myself and about everything! . . ." Natásha began, and without replying to Sónya's words of comfort she got into bed, and long after her candle was out lay open-eyed and motionless, gazing at the moonlight through the frosty window-panes.

Chapter XIII

SOON AFTER THE CHRISTMAS HOLIDAYS NICHOLAS TOLD HIS MOTHER OF HIS LOVE FOR SÓNYA AND of his firm resolve to marry her. The countess, who had long noticed what was going on between them and was expecting this declaration, listened to him in silence, and then told her son that he might marry whom he pleased, but that neither she nor his father would give their blessing to such a marriage. Nicholas, for the first time, felt that his mother was displeased with him and that, despite her love for him, she would not give way. Coldly, without looking at her son, she sent for her husband and, when he came, tried briefly and coldly to inform him of the facts, in her son's presence, but unable to restrain herself she burst into tears of vexation and left the room. The old count began irresolutely to admonish Nicholas and beg him to abandon his purpose. Nicholas replied that he could not go back on his word, and his father, sighing and evidently disconcerted, very soon became silent and went in to the countess. In all his encounters with his son, the count was always conscious of his own guilt toward him for having wasted the family fortune, and so he could not be angry with him for refusing to marry an heiress and choosing the dowerless Sónya. On this occasion, he was only more vividly conscious of the fact that if his affairs had not been in disorder, no better wife for Nicholas than Sónya could have been wished for, and that no one but himself with his Mítenka and his uncomfortable habits, was to blame for the condition of the family finances.

The father and mother did not speak of the matter to their son again, but a few days later the countess sent for Sónya and, with a cruelty neither of them expected, reproached her niece for trying to catch Nicholas and for ingratitude. Sónya listened silently with downcast eyes to the countess's cruel words, without understanding what was required of her. She was ready to sacrifice everything for her benefactors. Self-sacrifice was her most cherished idea; but in this case she could not see what she ought to sacrifice, or for whom. She could not help loving the countess and the whole Rostóv family, but neither could she help loving Nicholas and knowing that his happiness depended on that love. She was silent and sad, and did not reply. Nicholas felt the situation to be intolerable and went to have an explanation with his mother. He first implored her to forgive him and Sónya and consent to their marriage, then he threatened that if she molested Sónya he would at once marry her secretly.

The countess, with a coldness her son had never seen in her before, replied that he was of age, that Prince Andrew was marrying without his father's consent, and he could do the same, but that she would never receive that *intriguer* as her daughter.

Exploding at the word *intriguer,* Nicholas, raising his voice, told his mother he had never expected her to try to force him to sell his feelings, but if that were so, he would say for the last time. . . . But he had no time to utter the decisive word which the expression of his face caused his mother to await with terror, and which would perhaps have forever remained a cruel memory to them both. He had not time to say it, for Natásha, with a pale and set face, entered the room from the door at which she had been listening.

"Nicholas, you are talking nonsense! Be quiet, be quiet, be quiet, I tell you! . . ." she almost screamed, so as to drown his voice.

"Mamma darling, it's not at all so . . . my poor, sweet darling," she said to her mother, who conscious that they had been on the brink of a rupture gazed at her son with terror, but in the obstinacy and excitement of the conflict could not and would not give way.

"Nicholas, I'll explain to you. Go away! Listen, Mamma darling," said Natásha.

Her words were incoherent, but they attained the purpose at which she was aiming.

The countess, sobbing heavily, hid her face on her daughter's breast, while Nicholas rose, clutching his head, and left the room.

Natásha set to work to effect a reconciliation, and so far succeeded that Nicholas received a promise from his mother that Sónya should not be troubled, while he on his side promised not to undertake anything without his parents' knowledge.

Firmly resolved, after putting his affairs in order in the regiment, to retire from the army and return and marry Sónya, Nicholas, serious, sorrowful, and at variance with his parents, but, as it seemed to him, passionately in love, left at the beginning of January to rejoin his regiment.

After Nicholas had gone things in the Rostóv household were more depressing than ever, and the countess fell ill from mental agitation.

Sónya was unhappy at the separation from Nicholas, and still more so on account of the hostile tone the countess could not help adopting toward her. The count was more perturbed than ever by the condition of his affairs, which called for some decisive action. Their town house and estate near Moscow had inevitably to be sold, and for this they had to go to Moscow. But the countess's health obliged them to delay their departure from day to day.

Natásha, who had borne the first period of separation from her betrothed lightly and even cheerfully, now grew more agitated and impatient every day. The thought that her best days, which she would have employed in loving him, were being vainly wasted with no advantage to anyone, tormented her incessantly. His letters for the most part irritated her. It hurt her to think that while she lived only in the thought of him, he was living a real life, seeing new places and new people that interested him. The more interesting his letters were the more vexed she felt. Her letters to him, far from giving her any comfort, seemed to her a wearisome and artificial obligation. She could not write, because she could not conceive the possibility of expressing sincerely in a letter even a thousandth part of what she expressed by voice, smile, and glance. She wrote to him formal, monotonous, and dry letters, to which she attached no importance herself, and in the rough copies of which the countess corrected her mistakes in spelling.

There was still no improvement in the countess's health, but it was impossible to defer the journey to Moscow any longer. Natásha's trousseau had to be ordered and the house sold. Moreover, Prince Andrew was expected in Moscow, where old Prince Bolkónski was spending the winter, and Natásha felt sure he had already arrived.

So the countess remained in the country, and the count, taking Sónya and Natásha with him, went to Moscow at the end of January.

Part Eight

Chapter I

AFTER PRINCE ANDREWS ENGAGEMENT TO NATÁSHA, PIERRE WITHOUT ANY APPARENT CAUSE suddenly felt it impossible to go on living as before. Firmly convinced as he was of the truths revealed to him by his benefactor, and happy as he had been in perfecting his inner man, to which he had devoted himself with such ardor—all the zest of such a life vanished after the engagement of Andrew and Natásha and the death of Joseph Alexéevich, the news of which reached him almost at the same time. Only the skeleton of life remained: his house, a brilliant wife who now enjoyed the favors of a very important personage, acquaintance with all Petersburg, and his Court service with its dull formalities. And this life suddenly seemed to Pierre unexpectedly loathsome. He ceased keeping a diary, avoided the company of the Brothers, began going to the Club again, drank a great deal, and came once more in touch with the bachelor sets, leading such a life that the Countess Hélène thought it necessary to speak severely to him about it. Pierre felt that she right, and to avoid compromising her went away to Moscow.

In Moscow as soon as he entered his huge house in which the faded and fading princesses still lived, with its enormous retinue; as soon as, driving through the town, he saw the Iberian shrine with innumerable tapers burning before the golden covers of the icons, the Kremlin Square with its snow undisturbed by vehicles, the sleigh-drivers and hovels of the Sívtsev Vrazhók, those old Muscovites who desired nothing, hurried nowhere, and were ending their days leisurely; when he saw those old Moscow ladies, the Moscow balls and the English Club, he felt himself at home in a quiet haven. In Moscow he felt at peace, at home, warm and dirty as in an old dressing-gown.

Moscow society, from the old women down to the children, received Pierre like a long-expected guest whose place was always ready awaiting him. For Moscow society Pierre was the nicest, kindest, most intellectual, merriest and most magnanimous of cranks, a heedless, genial nobleman of the old Russian type. His purse was always empty because it was open to everyone.

Benefit performances, poor pictures, statues, benevolent societies, gypsy choirs, schools, subscription dinners, sprees, freemasons, churches and books—no one and nothing met with a refusal from him, and had it not been for two friends who had borrowed large sums from him and taken him under their protection, he would have given everything away. There was never a dinner or soirée at the Club without him. As soon as he sank into his place on the sofa after two bottles of Margaux he was surrounded, and talking, disputing and joking began. When there were quarrels, his kindly smile and well-timed jests reconciled the antagonists. The masonic dinners were dull and dreary when he was not there.

When after a bachelor supper he rose with his amiable and kindly smile, yielding to the entreaties of the festive company to drive off somewhere with them, shouts of delight and triumph arose among the young men. At balls he danced if a partner was needed. Young ladies, married and unmarried, liked him because without making love to any of them, he was equally amiable to all, especially after supper. *"Il est charmant; il n'a pas de sexe,"* they said of him.

Pierre was one of those retired gentlemen-in-waiting of whom there were hundreds good-humoredly ending their days in Moscow.

How horrified he would have been seven years before, when he first arrived from abroad, had he been told that there was no need for him to seek or plan anything, that his rut had long been shaped, eternally predetermined, and that wriggle as he might, he would be what all in his position were. He could not have believed it! Had he not at one time longed with all his heart to establish a republic in Russia; then himself to be a Napoleon; then to be a philosopher; and then a strategist and the conqueror of Napoleon? Had he not seen the possibility of, and passionately desired, the regeneration of the sinful human race, and his own progress to the highest degree of perfection? Had he not established schools and hospitals and liberated his serfs?

But instead of all that—here he was, the wealthy husband of an unfaithful wife, a retired gentleman-in-waiting, fond of eating and drinking and, as he unbuttoned his waistcoat, of abusing the government a bit, a member of the Moscow English Club and a universal favorite in Moscow society. For a long time he could not reconcile himself to the idea that he was one of those same retired Moscow gentlemen-in-waiting he had so despised seven years before.

Sometimes he consoled himself with the thought that he was only living this life temporarily; but then he was shocked by the thought of how many, like himself, had entered that life and that Club temporarily, with all their teeth and hair, and had only left it when not a single tooth or hair remained.

In moments of pride, when he thought of his position it seemed to him that he was quite different and distinct from those other retired gentlemen-in-waiting he had formerly despised: they were empty, stupid, contented fellows, satisfied with their position, "while I am still discontented and want to do something for mankind. But perhaps all these comrades of mine struggled just like me and sought something new, a path in life of their own, and like me were brought by force of circumstances, society, and race—by that elemental force against which man is powerless—to the condition I am in," said he to himself in moments of humility; and after living some time in Moscow he no longer despised, but began to grow fond of, to respect and to pity his comrades in destiny, as he pitied himself.

Pierre longer suffered moments of despair, hypochondria and disgust with life, but the malady that had formerly found expression in such acute attacks was driven inward and never left him for a moment. "What for? Why? What is going on in the world?" he would ask himself in perplexity several times a day, involuntarily beginning to reflect anew on the meaning of the phenomena of life; but knowing by experience that there were no answers to these questions he made haste to turn away from them, and took up a book, or hurried of to the Club or to Apollón Nikoláevich's, to exchange the gossip of the town.

"Hélène, who has never cared for anything but her own body and is one of the stupidest women in the world," thought Pierre, "is regarded by people as the acme of intelligence and refinement, and they pay homage to her. Napoleon Bonaparte was despised by all as long as he was great, but now that he has become a wretched comedian the Emperor Francis wants to offer him his daughter in an illegal marriage. The Spaniards, through the Catholic clergy, offer praise to God for their victory over the French on the 14th of June, and the French, also through the Catholic clergy, offer praise because on that same 14th of June they defeated the Spaniards. My brother masons swear by the blood that they are ready to sacrifice everything for their neighbor, but they do not give a ruble each to the collections for the poor, and they intrigue, the Astr'a Lodge against the Manna Seekers, and fuss about an authentic Scotch carpet and a charter that nobody needs, and the meaning of which the very man who wrote it does not understand. We all profess the Christian law of forgiveness of injuries and love of our neighbors, the law in honor of which we have built in Moscow forty times forty churches—but yesterday a deserter was knouted to death and a minister of that same law of love and forgiveness, a priest, gave the soldier a cross to kiss before his execution." So thought Pierre, and the whole of this general deception which everyone accepts, accustomed as he was to it, astonished him each time as if it were something new. "I understand the deception and confusion," he thought, "but how am I to tell them all that I see? I have tried, and have always found that they too in the depths of their souls understand it as I do, and only try not to see it. So it appears that it must be so! But I—what is to become of me?" thought he. He had the unfortunate capacity many men, especially Russians, have of seeing and believing in the possibility of goodness and truth, but of seeing the evil and falsehood of life too clearly to be able to take a serious part in it. Every sphere of work was connected, in his eyes, with evil and deception. Whatever he tried to be, whatever he engaged in, the evil and falsehood of it repulsed him and blocked every path of activity. Yet he had to live and to find occupation. It was too dreadful to be under the burden of these insoluble problems, so he abandoned himself to any distraction in order to forget them. He frequented every kind of society, drank much, bought pictures, engaged in building, and above all—read.

He read, and read everything that came to hand. On coming home, while his valets were still taking off his things, he picked up a book and began to read. From reading he passed to sleeping, from sleeping to gossip in drawing rooms of the Club, from gossip to carousals and women; from carousals back to gossip, reading and wine. Drinking became more and more a physical and also a moral necessity. Though the doctors warned him that with his corpulence wine was dangerous for him, he drank a great deal. He was only quite at ease when having poured several glasses of wine mechanically into his large mouth he felt a pleasant warmth in his body, an amiability toward all his fellows, and a readiness to respond superficially to every idea without probing it deeply. Only after emptying a bottle or two did he feel dimly that the terribly tangled skein of life which previously had terrified him was not as dreadful as he had thought. He was always conscious of some aspect of that skein, as with a buzzing in his head after dinner or supper he chatted or listened to conversation or read. But under the influence of wine he said to himself: "It doesn't matter. I'll get it unraveled. I have a solution ready, but have no time now—I'll think it all out later on!" but the *later on* never came.

In the morning, on an empty stomach, all the old questions appeared as insoluble and terrible as ever, and Pierre hastily picked up a book, and if anyone came to see him he was glad.

Sometimes he remembered how he had heard that soldiers in war when entrenched under the enemy's fire, if they have nothing to do, try hard to find some occupation the more easily to bear the danger. To Pierre all men seemed like those soldiers, seeking refuge from life: some in ambition, some in cards, some in framing laws, some in women, some in toys, some in horses, some in politics, some in sport, some in wine, and some in governmental affairs. "Nothing is trivial, and nothing is important, it's all the same—only to save oneself from it as best one can," thought Pierre. "Only not to see *it*, that dreadful *it!*"

Chapter II

AT THE BEGINNING OF WINTER PRINCE NICHOLAS BOLKÓNSKI AND HIS DAUGHTER MOVED TO Moscow. At that time enthusiasm for the Emperor Alexander's regime had weakened and a patriotic and anti-French tendency prevailed there, and this together with his past and his intellect and his originality, at once made Prince Nicholas Bolkónski an object of particular respect to the Muscovites and the center of the Moscow opposition to the government.

The prince had aged very much that year. He showed marked signs of senility by a tendency to fall asleep, forgetfulness of quite recent events, remembrance of remote ones and the childish vanity with which he accepted the rôle of head of the Moscow opposition. In spite of this the old man inspired in all his visitors alike a feeling of respectful veneration—especially of an evening when he came in to tea in his old-fashioned coat and powdered wig, and aroused by anyone, told his abrupt stories of the past, or uttered yet more abrupt and scathing criticisms of the present. For them all, that old-fashioned house with its gigantic mirrors, pre-Revolution furniture, powdered footmen, and the stern shrewd old man (himself a relic of the past century) with his gentle daughter and the pretty Frenchwoman who were reverently devoted to him presented a majestic and agreeable spectacle. But the visitors did not reflect that besides the couple of hours during which they saw their host, there were also twenty-two hours in the day during which the private and intimate life of the house continued.

Latterly that private life had become very trying for Princess Mary. There in Moscow she was deprived of her greatest pleasures—talks with the pilgrims and the solitude which refreshed her at Bald Hills—and she had none of the advantages and pleasures of city life. She did not go out into society; everyone knew that her father would not let her go anywhere without him, and his failing health prevented his going out himself, so that she was not invited to dinners and evening parties. She had quite abandoned the hope of getting married. She saw the coldness and malevolence with which the old prince received and dismissed the young men, possible suitors, who sometimes appeared at their house. She had no friends: during this visit to Moscow she had been disappointed in the two who had been nearest to her. Mademoiselle Bourienne, with whom she had never been able to be quite frank, had now become unpleasant to her, and for various reasons Princess Mary avoided her. Julie, with whom she had corresponded for the last five years, was in Moscow, but proved to be quite alien to her when they met. Just then Julie, who by the death of her brothers had become one of the richest heiresses in Moscow, was in the full whirl of society pleasures. She was surrounded by young men who, she fancied, had suddenly learned to appreciate her worth. Julie was at that stage in the life of a society woman when she feels that her last chance of marrying has come and that her fate must be decided now or never. On Thursday Princess Mary remembered with a mournful smile that she now had no one to write to, since Julie—whose presence gave her no pleasure—was here and they met every week. Like the old *émigré* who declined to marry the lady with whom he had spent his evenings for years, she regretted Julie's presence and having no one to write to. In Moscow Princess Mary had no one to talk to, no one to whom to confide her sorrow, and much sorrow fell to her lot just then. The time for Prince Andrew's return and marriage was approaching, but his request to her to prepare his father for it had not been carried out; in fact it seemed as if matters were quite hopeless, for at every mention of the young Countess Rostóva the old prince (who apart from that was usually in a bad temper) lost control of himself. Another lately added sorrow arose from the lessons she gave her six-year-old nephew. To her consternation she detected in herself in relation to little Nicholas some symptoms of her father's irritability. However often she told herself that she must not get irritable when teaching her nephew, almost every time that, pointer in hand, she sat down to show him the French alphabet, she so longed to pour her own knowledge quickly and easily into the child—who was already afraid that Auntie might at any moment get angry—that at his slightest inattention she trembled, became flustered and heated, raised her voice, and sometimes pulled him by the arm and put him in the corner. Having put him in the corner she would herself begin to cry over her cruel, evil nature, and little Nicholas, following her example, would sob, and without permission would leave the corner, come to her, pull her wet hands from her face and comfort her. But what distressed the princess most of all was her father's irritability, which was always directed against her and had of late amounted to cruelty. Had he forced her to prostrate herself to the ground all night, had he beaten her or made her fetch wood or water, it would never have entered her mind to think her position hard; but this loving despot—the more cruel because he loved her and for that reason tormented himself and her—knew how not merely to hurt and humiliate her deliberately, but to show her that she was always to blame for everything. Of late he had exhibited a new trait that tormented Princess Mary more than anything else; this was his ever-increasing intimacy with Mademoiselle Bourienne. The idea that at the first moment of receiving the news of his son's intentions had occurred to him in jest—that if Andrew got married he himself would marry Bourienne—had evidently pleased him, and latterly he had persistently, and as it seemed to Princess Mary merely to offend her, shown special endearments to the companion, and expressed his dissatisfaction with his daughter by demonstrations of love of Bourienne.

One day in Moscow in Princess Mary's presence (she thought her father did it purposely when she was there) the old prince kissed Mademoiselle Bourienne's hand and, drawing her to him, embraced her affectionately. Princess Mary flushed and ran out of the room. A few minutes later Mademoiselle Bourienne came into Princess Mary's rooms smiling and making cheerful remarks in her agreeable voice. Princess Mary hastily wiped away her tears, went resolutely up to Mademoiselle Bourienne, and evidently unconscious of what she was doing began shouting in angry haste at the Frenchwoman, her voice breaking: "It's horrible, vile, inhuman, to take advantage of the weakness . . ." she did not finish. "Leave my room," she exclaimed, and burst into sobs.

Next day the prince did not say a word to his daughter, but she noticed that at dinner he gave orders that Mademoiselle Bourienne should be served first. After dinner, when the footman handed coffee and from habit began with the princess, the prince suddenly grew furious, threw his stick at Philip, and instantly gave instructions to have him conscripted for the army.

"He doesn't obey . . . I said it twice . . . and he doesn't obey! She is the first person in this house; she's my best friend," cried the prince. "And if you allow yourself," he screamed in a fury, addressing Princess Mary for the first time, "to forget yourself again before her as you dared to do yesterday, I will show you who is master in this house. Go! Don't let me set eyes on you; beg her pardon!"

Princess Mary asked Mademoiselle Bourienne's pardon, and also her father's pardon for herself and for Philip the footman, who had begged for her intervention.

At such moments something like a pride of sacrifice gathered in her soul. And suddenly that father whom she had judged would look for his spectacles in her presence, fumbling near them and not seeing them, or would forget something that had just occurred, or take a false step with his failing legs and turn to see if anyone had noticed his feebleness, or, worst of all, at dinner when there were no visitors to excite him would suddenly fall asleep, letting his napkin drop and his shaking head sink over his plate. "He is old and feeble, and I dare to condemn him!" she thought at such moments, with a feeling of revulsion against herself.

Chapter III

IN 1811 THERE WAS LIVING IN MOSCOW A FRENCH DOCTOR—MÉTIVIER—WHO HAD RAPIDLY BEcome the fashion. He was enormously tall, handsome, amiable as Frenchmen are, and was, as all Moscow said, an extraordinarily clever doctor. He was received in the best houses not merely as a doctor, but as an equal.

Prince Nicholas had always ridiculed medicine, but latterly on Mademoiselle Bourienne's advice had allowed this doctor to visit him and had grown accustomed to him. Métivier came to see the prince about twice a week.

On December 6th—St. Nicholas's Day and the prince's name-day—all Moscow came to the prince's front door but he gave orders to admit no one, and to invite to dinner only a small number, a list of whom he gave to Princess Mary.

Métivier, who came in the morning with his felicitations, considered it proper in his quality of doctor *de forcer la consigne,* as he told Princess Mary, and went in to see the prince. It happened that on that morning of his name-day the prince was in one of his worst moods. He had been going about the house all the morning finding fault with everyone and pretending not to understand what was said to him and not to be understood himself. Princess Mary well knew this mood of quiet absorbed querulousness, which generally culminated in a burst of rage, and she went about all that morning as though facing a cocked and loaded gun and awaited the inevitable explosion. Until the doctor's arrival the morning had passed off safely. After admitting the doctor, Princess Mary sat down with a book in the drawing room near the door through which she could hear all that passed in the study.

At first she heard only Métivier's voice, then her father's, then both voices began speaking at the same time, the door was flung open, and on the threshold appeared the handsome figure of the terrified Métivier with his shock of black hair, and the prince in his dressing-gown and fez, his face distorted with fury and the pupils of his eyes rolled downward.

"You don't understand?" shouted the prince, "but I do! French spy, slave of Buonaparte, spy, get out of my house! Be off, I tell you . . ." and he slammed the door.

Métivier, shrugging his shoulders, went up to Mademoiselle Bourienne who at the sound of shouting had run in from an adjoining room.

"The prince is not very well: bile and rush of blood to the head. Keep calm, I will call again tomorrow," said Métivier; and putting his fingers to his lips he hastened away.

Through the study door came the sound of slippered feet and the cry: "Spies, traitors, traitors everywhere! Not a moment's peace in my own house!"

After Métivier's departure the old prince called his daughter in, and the whole weight of his wrath fell on her. She was to blame that a spy had been admitted. Had he not told her, yes, told her to make a list, and not to admit anyone who was not on that list? Then why was that scoundrel admitted? She was the cause of it all. With her, he said, he could not have a moment's peace, and could not die quietly.

"No, ma'am! We must part, we must part! Understand that, understand it! I cannot endure any more," he said, and left the room. Then, as if afraid she might find some means of consolation, he returned and trying to appear calm added: "And don't imagine I have said this in a moment of anger. I am calm. I have thought it over, and it will be carried out—we must part; so find some place for yourself! . . ." But he could not restrain himself and with the virulence of which only one who loves is capable, evidently suffering himself, he shook his fists at her and screamed:

"If only some fool would marry her!" Then he slammed the door, sent for Mademoiselle Bourienne and subsided into his study.

At two o'clock the six chosen guests assembled for dinner.

These guests—the famous Count Rostopchín, Prince Lopukhín with his nephew, General Chatróv an old war comrade of the prince's, and of the younger generation Pierre and Borís Drubetskóy—awaited the prince in the drawing room.

Borís, who had come to Moscow on leave a few days before, had been anxious to be presented to Prince Nicholas Bolkónski, and had contrived to ingratiate himself so well that the old prince in his case made an exception to the rule of not receiving bachelors in his house.

The prince's house did not belong to what is known as *fashionable society,* but his little circle—though not much talked about in town—was one it was more flattering to be received in than any other. Borís had realized this the week before when the commander-in-chief in his presence invited Rostopchín to dinner on St. Nicholas's Day, and Rostopchín had replied that he could not come:

"On that day I always go to pay my devotions to the relics of Prince Nicholas Bolkónski."

"Oh, yes, yes!" replied the commander-in-chief. "How is he? . . ."

The small group that assembled before dinner in the lofty old-fashioned drawing room with its old furniture, resembled the solemn gathering of a Court of Justice. All were silent or talked in low tones. Prince Nicholas came in serious and taciturn. Princess Mary seemed even quieter and more diffident than usual. The guests were reluctant to address her, feeling that she was in no mood for their conversation. Count Rostopchín alone kept the conversation going, now relating the latest town news, and now the latest political gossip.

Lopukhín and the old general occasionally took part in the conversation. Prince Bolkónski listened as a presiding judge receives a report, only now and then, silently or by a brief word, showing that he took heed of what was being reported to him. The tone of the conversation was such as indicated that no one approved of what was being done in the political world. Incidents were related evidently confirming the opinion that everything was going from bad to worse, but whether telling a story or giving an opinion the speaker always stopped, or was stopped, at the point beyond which his criticism might touch the sovereign himself.

At dinner the talk turned on the latest political news: Napoleon's seizure of the Duke of Oldenburg's territory, and the Russian Note, hostile to Napoleon, which had been sent to all the European courts.

"Bonaparte treats Europe as a pirate does a captured vessel," said Count Rostopchín, repeating a phrase he had uttered several times before. "One only wonders at the long-suffering or blindness of the crowned heads. Now the Pope's turn has come and Bonaparte doesn't scruple to depose the head of the Catholic Church—yet all keep silent! Our sovereign alone has protested against the seizure of the Duke of Oldenburg's territory, and even . . ." Count Rostopchín paused, feeling that he had reached the limit beyond which censure was impossible.

"Other territories have been offered in exchange for the Duchy of Oldenburg," said Prince Bolkónski. "He shifts the Dukes about as I might move my serfs from Bald Hills to Boguchárovo or my Ryazán estates."

"The Duke of Oldenburg bears his misfortunes with admirable strength of character and resignation," remarked Borís, joining in respectfully.

He said this because on his journey from Petersburg he had had the honor of being presented to the Duke. Prince Bolkónski glanced at the young man as if about to say something in reply, but changed his mind, evidently considering him too young.

"I have read our protests about the Oldenburg affair and was surprised how badly the Note was worded," remarked Count Rostopchín in the casual tone of a man dealing with a subject quite familiar to him.

Pierre looked at Rostopchín with naïve astonishment, not understanding why he should be disturbed by the bad composition of the Note.

"Does it matter, count, how the Note is worded," he asked, "so long as its substance is forcible?"

"My dear fellow, with our five hundred thousand troops it should be easy to have a good style," returned Count Rostopchín.

Pierre now understood the count's dissatisfaction with the wording of the Note.

"One would have thought quill-drivers enough had sprung up," remarked the old prince. "There in Petersburg they are always writing—not notes only but even new laws. My Andrew there has written a whole volume of laws for Russia. Nowadays they are always writing!" and he laughed unnaturally.

There was a momentary pause in the conversation; the old general cleared his throat to draw attention.

"Did you hear of the last event at the review in Petersburg? The figure cut by the new French ambassador."

"Eh? Yes, I heard something: he said something awkward in his Majesty's presence."

"His Majesty drew attention to the Grenadier division and to the march past," continued the general, "and it seems the ambassador took no notice and allowed himself to reply that: 'We in France pay no attention to such trifles!' The Emperor did not condescend to reply. At the next review, they say, the Emperor did not once deign to address him."

All were silent. On this fact relating to the Emperor personally, it was impossible to pass any judgment.

"Impudent fellows!" said the prince. "You know Métivier? I turned him out of my house this morning. He was here; they admitted him spite of my request that they should let no one in," he went on, glancing angrily at his daughter.

And he narrated his whole conversation with the French doctor and the reasons that convinced him that Métivier was a spy. Though these reasons were very insufficient and obscure, no one made any rejoinder.

After the roast, champagne was served. The guests rose to congratulate the old prince. Princess Mary, too, went round to him.

He gave her a cold, angry look, and offered her his wrinkled, clean-shaven cheek to kiss. The whole expression of his face told her that he had not forgotten the morning's talk, that his decision remained in force, and only the presence of visitors hindered his speaking of it to her now.

When they went into the drawing room where coffee was served, the old men sat together.

Prince Nicholas grew more animated and expressed his views on the impending war.

He said that our wars with Bonaparte would be disastrous so long as we sought alliances with the Germans and thrust ourselves into European affairs, into which we had been drawn by the Peace of Tilsit. "We ought not to fight either for or against Austria. Our political interests are all in the East, and in regard to Bonaparte the only thing is to have an armed frontier and a firm policy, and he will never dare to cross the Russian frontier, as was the case in 1807!"

"How can we fight the French, prince?" said Count Rostopchín. "Can we arm ourselves against our teachers and divinities? Look at our youths, look at our ladies! The French are our Gods: Paris is our Kingdom of Heaven."

He began speaking louder, evidently to be heard by everyone.

"French dresses, French ideas, French feelings! There now, you turned Métivier out by the scruff of his neck because he is a Frenchman and a scoundrel, but our ladies crawl after him on their knees. I went to a party last night, and there out of five ladies three were Roman Catholics and had the Pope's indulgence for doing woolwork on Sundays. And they themselves sit there nearly naked, like the sign-boards at our Public Baths if I may say so. Ah, when one looks at our young people, prince, one would like to take Peter the Great's old cudgel out of the museum and belabor them in the Russian way till all the nonsense jumps out of them."

All were silent. The old prince looked at Rostopchín with a smile and wagged his head approvingly.

"Well, good-bye, your excellency, keep well!" said Rostopchín, getting up with characteristic briskness and holding out his hand to the prince.

"Good-bye, my dear fellow. . . . His words are music, I never tire of hearing him!" said the old prince, keeping hold of the hand and offering his cheek to be kissed.

Following Rostopchín's example the others also rose.

Chapter IV

PRINCESS MARY, AS SHE SAT LISTENING TO THE OLD MEN'S TALK AND FAULT-FINDING, UNDERSTOOD nothing of what she heard; she only wondered whether the guests had all observed her father's hostile attitude toward her. She did not even notice the special attentions and amiabilities shown her during dinner by Borís Drubetskóy, who was visiting them for the third time already.

Princess Mary turned with an absent-minded questioning look to Pierre, who hat in hand and with a smile on his face was the last of the guests to approach her after the old prince had gone out and they were left alone in the drawing room.

"May I stay a little longer?" he said, letting his stout body sink into an arm-chair beside her.

"Oh, yes," she answered. "You noticed nothing?" her look asked.

Pierre was in an agreeable after-dinner mood. He looked straight before him and smiled quietly.

"Have you known that young man long, princess?" he asked.

"Who?"

"Drubetskóy."

"No, not long . . ."

"Do you like him?"

"Yes, he is an agreeable young man. . . . Why do you ask me that?" said Princess Mary, still thinking of that morning's conversation with her father.

"Because I have noticed that when a young man comes on leave from Petersburg to Moscow it is usually with the object of marrying an heiress."

"You have observed that?" said Princess Mary.

"Yes," returned Pierre with a smile, "and this young man now manages matters so that where there is a wealthy heiress there he is too. I can read him like a book. At present he is hesitating whom to lay siege to—you or Mademoiselle Julie Karágina. He is very attentive to her."

"He visits them?"

"Yes, very often. And do you know the new way of courting?" said Pierre with an amused smile, evidently in that cheerful mood of good-humored raillery for which he so often reproached himself in his diary.

"No," replied Princess Mary.

"To please Moscow girls nowadays one has to be melancholy. He is very melancholy with Mademoiselle Karágina," said Pierre.

"Really?" asked Princess Mary, looking into Pierre's kindly face and still thinking of her own sorrow. "It would be a relief," thought she, "if I ventured to confide what I am feeling to someone. I should like to tell everything to Pierre. He is kind and generous. It would be a relief. He would give me advice."

"Would you marry him?"

"Oh, my God, count, there are moments when I would marry anybody!" she cried suddenly to her own surprise and with tears in her voice. "Ah, how bitter it is to love someone near to you and to feel that . . ." she went on in a trembling voice, "that you can do nothing for him but grieve him, and to know that you cannot alter this. Then there is only one thing left—to go away, but where could I go?"

"What is wrong? What is it, princess?"

But without finishing what she was saying, Princess Mary burst into tears.

"I don't know what is the matter with me today. Don't take any notice—forget what I have said!"

Pierre's gaiety vanished completely. He anxiously questioned the princess, asked her to speak out fully and confide her grief to him; but she only repeated that she begged him to forget what she had said, that she did not remember what she had said, and that she had no trouble except the one he knew of—that Prince Andrew's marriage threatened to cause a rupture between father and son.

"Have you any news of the Rostóvs?" she asked, to change the subject. "I was told they are coming soon. I am also expecting Andrew any day. I should like them to meet here."

"And how does he now regard the matter?" asked Pierre, referring to the old prince.

Princess Mary shook her head.

"What is to be done? In a few months the year will be up. The thing is impossible. I only wish I could spare my brother the first moments. I wish they would come sooner. I hope to be friends with her. You have known them a long time," said Princess Mary. "Tell me honestly the whole truth: what sort of girl is she, and what do you think of her?—The real truth, because you know Andrew is risking so much doing this against his father's will, that I should like to know. . . ."

An undefined instinct told Pierre that these explanations, and repeated requests to be told the *whole truth*, expressed ill-will on the princess's part toward her future sister-in-law and a wish that he should disapprove of Andrew's choice; but in reply he said what he felt rather than what he thought.

"I don't know how to answer your question," he said, blushing without knowing why. "I really don't know what sort of girl she is; I can't analyze her at all. She is enchanting, but what makes her so I don't know. That is all one can say about her."

Princess Mary sighed, and the expression on her face said: "Yes, that's what I expected and feared."

"Is she clever?" she asked.

Pierre considered.

"I think not," he said, "and yet—yes. She does not deign to be clever. . . . Oh no, she is simply enchanting, and that is all."

Princess Mary again shook her head disapprovingly.

"Ah, I so long to like her! Tell her so if you see her before I do."

"I hear they are expected very soon," said Pierre.

Princess Mary told Pierre of her plan to become intimate with her future sister-in-law as soon as the Rostóvs arrived, and to try to accustom the old prince to her.

Chapter V

BORÍS HAD NOT SUCCEEDED IN MAKING A WEALTHY MATCH IN PETERSBURG, SO WITH THE SAME object in view he came to Moscow. There he wavered between the two richest heiresses, Julie and Princess Mary. Though Princess Mary despite her plainness seemed to him more attractive than Julie, he, without knowing why, felt awkward about paying court to her. When they had last met on the old prince's name-day, she had answered at random all his attempts to talk sentimentally, evidently not listening to what he was saying.

Julie on the contrary accepted his attentions readily, though in a manner peculiar to herself.

She was twenty-seven. After the death of her brothers she had become very wealthy. She was by now decidedly plain, but thought herself not merely as good-looking as before but even far more attractive. She was confirmed in this delusion by the fact that she had become a very wealthy heiress and also by the fact that the older she grew the less dangerous she became to men, and the more freely they could associate with her and avail themselves of her suppers, soireés, and the animated company that assembled at her house, without incurring any obligation. A man who would have been afraid ten years before of going every day to the house when there was a girl of seventeen there, for fear of compromising her and committing himself, would now go boldly every day and treat her not as a marriageable girl but as a sexless acquaintance.

That winter the Karagins' house was the most agreeable and hospitable in Moscow. In addition to the formal evening and dinner parties, a large company, chiefly of men, gathered there every day, supping at midnight and staying till three in the morning. Julie never missed a ball, a promenade or a play. Her dresses were always of the latest fashion. But in spite of that she seemed to be disillusioned about everything, and told everyone that she did not believe either in friendship or in love, or any of the joys of life, and expected peace only "yonder." She adopted the tone of one who has suffered a great disappointment, like a girl who has either lost the man she loved or been cruelly deceived by him. Though nothing of the kind had happened to her she was regarded in that light, and had even herself come to believe that she had suffered much in life. This melancholy, which did not prevent her amusing herself, did not hinder the young people who came to her house from passing the time pleasantly. Every visitor who came to the house paid his tribute to the melancholy mood of the hostess, and then amused himself with society gossip, dancing, intellectual games and *bouts rimés,* which were in vogue at the Karagins'. Only a few of these young men, among them Borís, entered more deeply into Julie's melancholy, and with these she had prolonged conversations in private on the vanity of all worldly things, and to them she showed her albums filled with mournful sketches, maxims and verses.

To Borís Julie was particularly gracious: she regretted his early disillusionment with life, offered him such consolation of friendship as she who had herself suffered so much could render, and showed him her album. Borís sketched two trees in the album and wrote: "Rustic trees, your dark branches shed gloom and melancholy upon me."

On another page he drew a tomb, and wrote:

La mort est secourable et la mort est tranquille.
Ah! contre les douleurs il n'y a pas d'autre asile.

Julia said this was charming

"There is something so enchanting in the smile of melancholy," she said to Borís, repeating word for word a passage she had copied from a book. "It is a ray of light in the darkness, a shade between sadness and despair, showing the possibility of consolation."

In reply Borís wrote these lines:

Aliment de poison d'une âme trop sensible,
Toi, sans qui le bonheur me serait impossible,
Tendre mélancholie, ah, viens me consoler,
Viens calmer les tourments de ma sombre retraite,
Et mêle une douceur secrète
A ces pleurs que je sens couler.

For Borís, Julie played most doleful nocturnes on her harp. Borís read *Poor Liza* aloud to her, and more than once interrupted the reading because of the emotions that choked him. Meeting at large gatherings Julie and Borís looked on one another as the only souls who understood one another in a world of indifferent people.

Anna Mikháylovna, who often visited the Karagins, while playing cards with the mother made careful inquiries as to Julie's dowry (she was to have two estates in Pénza and the Nizhegórod forests). Anna Mikháylovna regarded the refined sadness that united her son to the wealthy Julie with emotion, and resignation to the Divine will.

"You are always charming and melancholy, my dear Julie," she said to the daughter. "Borís says his soul finds repose at your house. He has suffered so many disappointments and is so sensitive," said she to the mother. "Ah, my dear, I can't tell you how fond I have grown of Julie latterly," she said to her son. "But who could help loving her? She is an angelic being! Ah, Borís, Borís!"—she paused. "And how I pity her mother," she went on; "today she showed me her accounts and letters from Pénza (they have enormous estates there), and she, poor thing, has no one to help her, and they do cheat her so!"

Borís smiled almost imperceptibly while listening to his mother. He laughed blandly at her naïve diplomacy but listened to what she had to say, and sometimes questioned her carefully about the Pénza and Nizhegórod estates.

Julie had long been expecting a proposal from her melancholy adorer and was ready to accept it; but some secret feeling of repulsion for her, for her passionate desire to get married, for her artificiality, and a feeling of horror at renouncing the possibility of real love, still restrained Borís. His leave was expiring. He spent every day and whole days at the Karagins', and every day on thinking the matter over told himself that he would propose tomorrow. But in Julie's presence, looking at her red face and chin (nearly always powdered), her moist eyes, and her expression of continual readiness to pass at once from melancholy to an unnatural rapture of married bliss, Borís could not utter the decisive words, though in imagination he had long regarded himself as the possessor of those Pénza and Nizhegórod estates and had apportioned the use of the income from them. Julie saw Borís's indecision, and sometimes the thought occurred to her that she was repulsive to him, but her feminine self-deception immediately supplied her with consolation, and she told herself that he was only shy from love. Her melancholy however began to turn to irritability, and not long before Borís's departure she formed a definite plan of action. Just as Borís's leave of absence was expiring Anatole Kurágin made his appearance in Moscow, and of course in the Karagins' drawing room, and Julie, suddenly abandoning her melancholy, became cheerful and very attentive to Kurágin.

"My dear," said Anna Mikháylovna to her son, "I know from a reliable source that Prince Vasíli has sent his son to Moscow to get him married to Julie. I am so fond of Julie that I should be sorry for her. What do you think of it, my dear?"

The idea of being made a fool of and of having thrown away that whole month of arduous melancholy service to Julie, and of seeing all the revenue from the Pénza estates which he had already mentally apportioned and put to proper use fall into the hands of another, and especially into the hands of that idiot Anatole, pained Borís. He drove to the Karagins' with the firm intention of proposing. Julie met him in a gay, careless manner, spoke casually of how she had enjoyed yesterday's ball, and asked when he was leaving. Though Borís had come intentionally to speak of his love and therefore meant to be tender, he began speaking irritably of feminine inconstancy, of how easily women can turn from sadness to joy, and how their moods depend solely on who happens to be paying court to them. Julie was offended, and replied that it was true that a woman needs variety, and the same thing over and over again would weary anyone.

"Then I should advise you . . ." Borís began, wishing to sting her; but at that instant the galling thought occurred to him that he might have to leave Moscow without having accomplished his aim, and have vainly wasted his efforts—which was a thing he never allowed to happen.

He checked himself in the middle of the sentence, lowered his eyes to avoid seeing her unpleasantly irritated and irresolute face, and said:

"I did not come here at all to quarrel with you. On the contrary . . ."

He glanced at her to make sure that he might go on. Her irritability had suddenly quite vanished, and her anxious, imploring eyes were fixed on him with greedy expectation. "I can always arrange so as not to see her often," thought Borís. "The affair has been begun and must be finished!" He blushed hotly, raised his eyes to hers, and said:

"You know my feelings for you!"

There was no need to say more: Julie's face shone with triumph and self-satisfaction; but she forced Borís to say all that is said on such occasions—that he loved her and had never loved any other woman more than her. She knew that for the Pénza estates and Nizhegórod forests she could demand this, and she received what she demanded.

The affianced couple, no longer alluding to trees that shed gloom and melancholy upon them, planned the arrangements of a splendid house in Petersburg, paid calls, and prepared everything for a brilliant wedding.

Chapter VI

AT THE END OF JANUARY OLD COUNT ROSTÓV WENT TO MOSCOW WITH NATÁSHA AND SÓNYA. The countess was still unwell and unable to travel but it was impossible to wait for her recovery. Prince Andrew was expected in Moscow any day, the trousseau had to be ordered and the estate near Moscow had to be sold, besides which the opportunity of presenting his future daughter-in-law to old Prince Bolkónski while he was in Moscow could not be missed. The Rostóvs' Moscow house had not been heated that winter and, as they had come only for a short time and the countess was not with them, the count decided to stay with Márya Dmítrievna Akhrosímova, who had long been pressing her hospitality on them.

Late one evening the Rostóvs' four sleighs drove into Márya Dmítrievna's courtyard in the old Konyusheny street. Márya Dmítrievna lived alone. She had already married off her daughter, and her sons were all in the service.

She held herself as erect, told everyone her opinion as candidly, loudly and bluntly as ever, and her whole bearing seemed a reproach to others for any weakness, passion, or temptation—the possibility of which she did not admit. From early in the morning, wearing a dressing-jacket, she attended to her household affairs, and then she drove out: on holy days to church, and after the service to jails and prisons on affairs of which she never spoke to anyone. On ordinary days, after dressing, she received petitioners of various classes, of whom there were always some. Then she had dinner, a substantial and appetizing meal at which there were always three or four guests; after dinner she played a game of boston, and at night she had the newspapers or a new book read to her while she knitted. She rarely made an exception and went out to pay visits, and then only to the most important persons in the town.

She had not yet gone to bed when the Rostóvs arrived and the pulley of the hall door squeaked from the cold as it let in the Rostóvs and their servants. Márya Dmítrievna, with her spectacles hanging down on her nose and her head flung back, stood in the hall doorway looking with a stern, grim face at the new arrivals. One might have thought she was angry with the travelers and would immediately turn them out, had she not at the same time been giving careful instructions to the servants for the accommodation of the visitors and their belongings.

"The count's things? Bring them here," she said, pointing to the portmanteaux and not greeting anyone. "The young ladies? There to the left. Now what are you dawdling for?" she cried to the maids. "Get the samovar ready! . . . You've grown plumper and prettier," she remarked, drawing Natásha (whose cheeks were glowing from the cold) to her by the hood. "Foo! You *are* cold! Now take off your things, quick!" she shouted to the count who was going to kiss her hand. "You're half frozen, I'm sure! Bring some rum for tea! . . . *Bonjour,* Sónya dear!" she added, turning to Sónya and indicating by this French greeting her slightly contemptuous though affectionate attitude toward her.

When they came in to tea, having taken off their outdoor things and tidied themselves up after their journey, Márya Dmítrievna kissed them all in due order.

"I'm heartily glad you have come and are staying with me. It was high time," she said, giving Natásha a significant look. "The old man is here and his son's expected any day. You'll have to make his acquaintance. But we'll speak of that later on," she added, glancing at Sónya with a look that showed she did not want to speak of it in her presence. "Now listen," she said to the count. "What do you want tomorrow? Whom will you send for? Shinshín?" She crooked one of her fingers. "The sniveling Anna Mikháylovna? That's two. She's here with her son. The son is getting married! Then Bezúkhov, eh? He is here too, with his wife. He ran away from her and she came galloping after him. He dined with me on Wednesday. As for them"—and she pointed to the girls—

"tomorrow I'll take them first to the Iberian shrine of the Mother of God, and then we'll drive to the Super-Rogue's. I suppose you'll have everything new. Don't judge by me: sleeves nowadays are this size! The other day young Princess Irína Vasílevna came to see me; she was an awful sight—looked as if she had put two barrels on her arms. You know not a day passes now without some new fashion. . . . And what have you to do yourself?" she asked the count sternly.

"One thing has come on top of another: her rags to buy, and now a purchaser has turned up for the Moscow estate and for the house. If you will be so kind, I'll fix a time and go down to the estate just for a day, and leave my lassies with you."

"All right. All right. They'll be safe with me, as safe as in Chancery! I'll take them where they must go, scold them a bit, and pet them a bit," said Márya Dmítrievna, touching her goddaughter and favorite, Natásha, on the cheek with her large hand.

Next morning Márya Dmítrievna took the young ladies to the Iberian shrine of the Mother of God and to Madame Suppert-Roguet, who was so afraid of Márya Dmítrievna that she always let her have costumes at a loss merely to get rid of her. Márya Dmítrievna ordered almost the whole trousseau. When they got home she turned everybody out of the room except Natásha, and then called her pet to her arm-chair.

"Well, now we'll talk. I congratulate you on your betrothed. You've hooked a fine fellow! I am glad for your sake and I've known him since he was so high." She held her hand a couple of feet from the ground. Natásha blushed happily. "I like him and all his family. Now listen! You know that old Prince Nicholas much dislikes his son's marrying. The old fellow's crotchety! Of course Prince Andrew is not a child and can shift without him, but it's not nice to enter a family against a father's will. One wants to do it peacefully and lovingly. You're a clever girl and you'll know how to manage. Be kind, and use your wits. Then all will be well."

Natásha remained silent, from shyness Márya Dmítrievna supposed, but really because she disliked anyone interfering in what touched her love of Prince Andrew, which seemed to her so apart from all human affairs that no one could understand it. She loved and knew Prince Andrew, he loved her only, and was to come one of these days and take her. She wanted nothing more.

"You see I have known him a long time and am also fond of Mary, your future sister-in-law. 'Husbands' sisters bring up blisters,' but this one wouldn't hurt a fly. She has asked me to bring you two together. Tomorrow you'll go with your father to see her. Be very nice and affectionate to her: you're younger than she. When *he* comes, he'll find you already know his sister and father and are liked by them. Am I right or not? Won't that be best?"

"Yes, it will," Natásha answered reluctantly.

Chapter VII

NEXT DAY, BY MÁRYA DMÍTRIEVNA'S ADVICE, COUNT ROSTÓV TOOK NATÁSHA TO CALL ON PRINCE Nicholas Bolkónski. The count did not set out cheerfully on this visit, at heart he felt afraid. He well remembered the last interview he had had with the old prince at the time of the enrollment, when in reply to an invitation to dinner he had had to listen to an angry reprimand for not having provided his full quota of men. Natásha, on the other hand, having put on her best gown was in the highest spirits. "They can't help liking me," she thought. "Everybody always has liked me, and I am so willing to do anything they wish, so ready to be fond of him—for being *his* father—and of her—for being *his* sister—that there is no reason for them not to like me. . . ."

They drove up to the gloomy old house on the Vozdvízhenka and entered the vestibule.

"Well, the Lord have mercy on us!" said the count, half in jest half in earnest; but Natásha noticed that her father was flurried on entering the anteroom, and inquired timidly and softly whether the prince and princess were at home.

When they had been announced a perturbation was noticeable among the servants. The footman who had gone to announce them was stopped by another in the large hall and they whispered to one another. Then a maidservant ran into the hall and hurriedly said something, mentioning the princess. At last an old, cross-looking footman came and announced to the Rostóvs that the prince was not receiving, but that the princess begged them to walk up. The first person who came to meet the visitors was Mademoiselle Bourienne. She greeted the father and daughter with special politeness, and showed them to the princess's room. The princess, looking excited and nervous, her face flushed in patches, ran in to meet the visitors, treading heavily, and vainly trying to appear cordial and at ease. From the first glance Princess Mary did not like Natásha. She thought her too fashionably dressed, frivolously gay and vain. She did not at all realize that before having seen her future sister-in-law she was prejudiced against her by involuntary envy of her beauty, youth, and happiness, as well as by jealousy of her brother's love for her. Apart from this insuperable antipathy to her, Princess Mary was agitated just then because on the Rostóvs' being announced, the old prince had shouted that he did not wish to see them, that Princess Mary might do so if she chose, but they were not to be admitted to him. She had decided to receive them, but feared lest the prince might at any moment indulge in some freak, as he seemed much upset by the Rostóvs' visit.

"There, my dear princess, I've brought you my songstress," said the count, bowing and looking round uneasily as if afraid the old prince might appear. "I am so glad you should get to know one another . . . very sorry the prince is still ailing," and after a few more commonplace remarks he rose. "If you'll allow me to leave my Natásha in your hands for a quarter of an hour, princess, I'll drive round to see Anna Semënovna, it's quite near in the Dogs' Square, and then I'll come back for her."

The count had devised this diplomatic ruse (as he afterward told his daughter) to give the future sisters-in-law an opportunity to talk to one another freely, but another motive was to avoid the danger of encountering the old prince, of whom he was afraid. He did not mention this to his daughter, but Natásha noticed her father's nervousness and anxiety and felt mortified by it. She blushed for him, grew still angrier at having blushed, and looked at the princess with a bold and defiant expression which said that she was not afraid of anybody. The princess told the count that she would be delighted, and only begged him to stay longer at Anna Semënovna's, and he departed.

Despite the uneasy glances thrown at her by Princess Mary—who wished to have a tête-à-tête with Natásha—Mademoiselle Bourienne remained in the room and persistently talked about Moscow amusements and theaters. Natásha felt offended by the hesitation she had noticed in the anteroom, by her father's nervousness, and by the unnatural manner of the princess who—she thought—was making a favor of receiving her, and so everything displeased her. She did not like Princess Mary, whom she thought very plain, affected and dry. Natásha suddenly shrank into herself, and involuntarily assumed an off-hand air which alienated Princess Mary still more. After five minutes of irksome, constrained conversation, they heard the sound of slippered feet rapidly approaching. Princess Mary looked frightened. The door opened and the old prince, in a dressing-gown and a white nightcap, came in.

"Ah, madam!" he began. "Madam, Countess . . . Countess Rostóv, if I am not mistaken . . . I beg you to excuse me, to excuse me . . . I did not know, madam. God is my witness, I did not know you had honored us with a visit, and I came in such a costume only to see my daughter. I beg you to excuse me . . . God is my witness, I didn't know—" he repeated, stressing the word "God" so unnaturally and so unpleasantly that Princess Mary stood with downcast eyes not daring to look either at her father or at Natásha.

Nor did the latter, having risen and curtsied, know what to do. Mademoiselle Bourienne alone smiled agreeably.

"I beg you to excuse me, excuse me! God is my witness, I did not know," muttered the old man, and after looking Natásha over from head to foot he went out.

Mademoiselle Bourienne was the first to recover herself after this apparition, and began speaking about the prince's indisposition. Natásha and Princess Mary looked at one another in silence, and the longer they did so without saying what they wanted to say, the greater grew their antipathy to one another.

When the count returned, Natásha was impolitely pleased, and hastened to get away: at that moment she hated the stiff, elderly princess, who could place her in such an embarrassing position and had spent half an hour with her without once mentioning Prince Andrew. "I couldn't begin talking about him in the presence of that Frenchwoman," thought Natásha. The same thought was meanwhile tormenting Princess Mary. She knew what she ought to have said to Natásha, but she had been unable to say it because Mademoiselle Bourienne was in the way, and because, without knowing why, she felt it very difficult to speak of the marriage. When the count was already leaving the room, Princess Mary went up hurriedly to Natásha, took her by the hand, and said with a deep sigh:

"Wait, I must . . ."

Natásha glanced at her ironically without knowing why.

"Dear Natalie," said Princess Mary, "I want you to know that I am glad my brother has found happiness. . . ."

She paused, feeling that she was not telling the truth. Natásha noticed this and guessed its reason.

"I think, princess, it is not convenient to speak of that now," she said with external dignity and coldness, though she felt the tears choking her.

"What have I said and what have I done?" thought she, as soon as she was out of the room.

They waited a long time for Natásha to come to dinner that day. She sat in her room crying like a child, blowing her nose and sobbing. Sónya stood beside her, kissing her hair.

"Natásha, what is it about?" she asked. "What do they matter to you? It will all pass, Natásha."

"But if you only knew how offensive it was . . . as if I . . ."

"Don't talk about it, Natásha. It wasn't your fault so why should you mind? Kiss me," said Sónya.

Natásha raised her head and, kissing her friend on the lips, pressed her wet face against her.

"I can't tell you, I don't know. No one's to blame," said Natásha—"It's my fault. But it all hurts terribly. Oh, why doesn't he come? . . ."

She came in to dinner with red eyes. Márya Dmítrievna who knew how the prince had received the Rostóvs, pretended not to notice how upset Natásha was, and jested resolutely and loudly at table with the count and the other guests.

Chapter VIII

THAT EVENING THE ROSTÓVS WENT TO THE OPERA, FOR WHICH MÁRYA DMÍTRIEVNA HAD TAKEN a box.

Natásha did not want to go, but could not refuse Márya Dmítrievna's kind offer which was intended expressly for her. When she came ready dressed into the ballroom to await her father, and looking in the large mirror there saw that she was pretty, very pretty, she felt even more sad, but it was a sweet, tender sadness.

"O, God, if he were here now I would not behave as I did then, but differently. I would not be silly and afraid of things, I would simply embrace him, cling to him, and make him look at me with those searching inquiring eyes with which he has so often looked at me, and then I would make him laugh as he used to laugh. And his eyes—how I see those eyes!" thought Natásha. "And what do his father and sister matter to me? I love him alone, him, him, with that face and those eyes, with his smile, manly and yet childlike. . . . No, I had better not think of him; not think of him but forget him, quite forget him for the present. I can't bear this waiting and I shall cry in a minute!" and she turned away from the glass, making an effort not to cry. "And how can Sónya love Nicholas so calmly and quietly and wait so long and so patiently?" thought she, looking at Sónya, who also came in quite ready, with a fan in her hand. "No, she's altogether different. I can't!"

Natásha at that moment felt so softened and tender that it was not enough for her to love and know she was beloved, she wanted now, at once, to embrace the man she loved, to speak and hear from him words of love such as filled her heart. While she sat in the carriage beside her father, pensively watching the lights of the street lamps flickering on the frozen window, she felt still sadder and more in love, and forgot where she was going and with whom. Having fallen into the line of carriages, the Rostóvs' carriage drove up to the theater its wheels squeaking over the snow. Natásha and Sónya, holding up their dresses, jumped out quickly. The count got out helped by the footmen, and, passing among men and women who were entering and the program sellers, they all three went along the corridor to the first row of boxes. Through the closed doors the music was already audible.

"Natásha, your hair! . . ." whispered Sónya.

An attendant deferentially and quickly slipped before the ladies and opened the door of their box. The music sounded louder and through the door rows of brightly lit boxes in which ladies sat with bare arms and shoulders, and noisy stalls brilliant with uniforms, glittered before their eyes. A lady entering the next box shot a glance of feminine envy at Natásha. The curtain had not yet risen and the overture was being played. Natásha, smoothing her gown, went in with Sónya and sat down, scanning the brilliant tiers of boxes opposite. A sensation she had not experienced for a long time—that of hundreds of eyes looking at her bare arms and neck—suddenly affected her both agreeably and disagreeably and called up a whole crowd of memories, desires and emotions associated with that feeling.

The two remarkably pretty girls, Natásha and Sónya, with Count Rostóv who had not been seen in Moscow for a long time, attracted general attention. Moreover, everybody knew vaguely of Natásha's engagement to Prince Andrew, and knew that the Rostóvs had lived in the country ever since, and all looked with curiosity at a fiancée who was making one of the best matches in Russia.

Natásha's looks, as everyone told her, had improved in the country, and that evening thanks to her agitation she was particularly pretty. She struck those who saw her by her fullness of life and beauty, combined with her indifference to everything about her. Her black eyes looked at the crowd without seeking anyone, and her delicate arm, bare to above the elbow, lay on the velvet edge of the box, while, evidently unconsciously, she opened and closed her hand in time to the music, crumpling her program.

"Look, there's Alénina," said Sónya, "with her mother, isn't it?"

"Dear me, Michael Kirílovich has grown still stouter!" remarked the count.

"Look at our Anna Mikháylovna—what a headdress she has on!"

"The Karagins, Julie—and Borís with them. One can see at once that they're engaged. . . ."

"Drubetskóy has proposed?"

"Oh yes, I heard it today," said Shinshín, coming into the Rostóvs' box.

Natásha looked in the direction in which her father's eyes were turned, and saw Julie sitting beside her mother with a happy look on her face and a string of pearls round her thick red neck—which Natásha knew was covered with powder. Behind them, wearing a smile and leaning over with an ear to Julie's mouth, was Borís's handsome smoothly brushed head. He looked the Rostóvs from under his brows and said something, smiling, to his betrothed.

"They are talking about us, about me and him!" thought Natásha. "And he no doubt is calming her jealousy of me. They needn't trouble themselves! If only they knew how little I am concerned about any of them."

Behind them sat Anna Mikháylovna wearing a green headdress and with a happy look of resignation to the will of God on her face. Their box was pervaded by that atmosphere of an affianced couple which Natásha knew so well and liked so much. She turned away and suddenly remembered all that had been so humiliating in her morning's visit.

"What right has he not to wish to receive me into his family? Oh, better not think of it—not till he comes back!" she told herself, and began looking at the faces, some strange and some familiar, in the stalls. In the front, in the very center, leaning back against the orchestra-rail, stood Dólokhov in a Persian dress, his curly hair brushed up into a huge shock. He stood in full view of the audience, well aware that he was attracting everyone's attention, yet as much at ease as though he were in his own room. Around him thronged Moscow's most brilliant young men, whom he evidently dominated.

The count, laughing, nudged the blushing Sónya and pointed to her former adorer.

"Do you recognize him?" said he. "And where has he sprung from?" he asked, turning to Shinshín. "Didn't he vanish somewhere?"

"He did," replied Shinshín. "He was in the Caucasus and ran away from there. They say he has been acting as minister to some ruling prince in Persia, where he killed the Shah's brother. Now all the Moscow ladies are mad about him! It's 'Dólokhov the Persian' that does it! We never hear a word but Dólokhov is mentioned. They swear by him, they offer him to you as they would a dish of choice sterlet. Dólokhov and Anatole Kurágin have turned all our ladies' heads."

A tall, beautiful woman with a mass of plaited hair and much exposed plump white shoulders and neck, round which she wore a double string of large pearls, entered the adjoining box rustling her heavy silk dress, and took a long time settling into her place.

Natásha involuntarily gazed at that neck, those shoulders and pearls and *coiffure*, and admired the beauty of the shoulders and the pearls. While Natásha was fixing her gaze on her for the second time the lady looked round, and meeting the count's eyes nodded to him and smiled. She was the Countess Bezúkhova, Pierre's wife, and the count who knew everyone in society, leaned over and spoke to her.

"Have you been here long, countess?" he inquired. "I'll call, I'll call to kiss your hand. I'm here on business and have brought my girls with me. They say Semënova acts marvelously. Count Pierre never used to forget us. Is he here?"

"Yes, he meant to look in," answered Hélène, and glanced attentively at Natásha.

Count Rostóv resumed his seat.

"Handsome, isn't she?" he whispered to Natásha.

"Wonderful!" answered Natásha. "She's a woman one could easily fall in love with."

Just then the last chords of the overture were heard and the conductor tapped with his stick. Some latecomers took their seats in the stalls, and the curtain rose.

As soon as it rose everyone in the boxes and stalls became silent, and all the men, old and young, in uniform and evening dress, and all the women with gems on their bare flesh, turned their whole attention with eager curiosity to the stage. Natásha too began to look at it.

Chapter IX

THE FLOOR OF THE STAGE CONSISTED OF SMOOTH BOARDS, AT THE SIDES WAS SOME PAINTED cardboard representing trees, and at the back was a cloth stretched over boards. In the center of the stage sat some girls in red bodices and white skirts. One very fat girl in a white silk dress sat apart on a low bench, to the back of which a piece of green cardboard was glued. They all sang something. When they had finished their song the girl in white went up to the prompter's box and a man with tight silk trousers over his stout legs, and holding a plume and a dagger, went up to her and began singing, waving his arms about.

First the man in the tight trousers sang alone, then she sang, then they both paused while the orchestra played and the man fingered the hand of the girl in white, obviously awaiting the beat to start singing with her. They sang together and everyone in the theater began clapping and shouting, while the man and woman on the stage—who represented lovers—began smiling, spreading out their arms and bowing.

After her life in the country, and in her present serious mood, all this seemed grotesque and amazing to Natásha. She could not follow the opera nor even listen to the music, she saw only the painted cardboard and the queerly dressed men and women who moved, spoke and sang so strangely in that brilliant light. She knew what it was all meant to represent, but it was so pretentiously false and unnatural that she first felt ashamed for the actors and then amused at them. She looked at the faces of the audience, seeking in them the same sense of ridicule and perplexity she herself experienced, but they all seemed attentive to what was happening on the stage, and expressed delight which to Natásha seemed feigned. "I suppose it has to be like this!" she thought. She kept looking round in turn at the rows of pomaded heads in the stalls and then at the semi-nude women in the boxes, especially at Hélène in the next box, who—apparently quite unclothed—sat with a quiet tranquil smile, not taking her eyes off the stage. And feeling the bright light that flooded the whole place and the warm air heated by the crowd, Natásha little by little began to pass into a state of intoxication she had not experienced for a long while. She did not realize who and where she was, nor what was going on before her. As she looked and thought, the strangest fancies unexpectedly and disconnectedly passed through her mind: the idea occurred to her of jumping onto the edge of the box and singing the air the actress was singing, then she wished to touch with her fan an old gentleman sitting not far from her, then to lean over to Hélène and tickle her.

At a moment when all was quiet before the commencement of a song, a door leading to the stalls on the side nearest the Rostóvs' box creaked, and the steps of a belated arrival were heard. "There's Kurágin!" whispered Shinshín. Countess Bezúkhova turned smiling to the newcomer, and Natásha, following the direction of that look, saw an exceptionally handsome adjutant approaching their box with a self-assured yet courteous bearing. This was Anatole Kurágin whom she had seen and noticed long ago at the ball in Petersburg. He was now in an adjutant's uniform with one epaulet and a shoulder-knot. He moved with a restrained swagger which would have been ridiculous had he not been so good-looking and had his handsome face not worn such an expression of good-humored complacency and gaiety. Though the performance was proceeding, he walked deliberately down the carpeted gangway, his sword and spurs slightly jingling and his handsome perfumed head held high. Having looked at Natásha he approached his sister, laid his well-gloved hand on the edge of her box, nodded to her, and leaning forward asked a question, with a motion toward Natásha.

"Mais charmante!" said he, evidently referring to Natásha, who did not exactly hear his words but understood them from the movement of his lips. Then he took his place in the first row of the stalls and sat down beside Dólokhov, nudging with his elbow in a friendly and off-hand way that

Dólokhov whom others treated so fawningly. He winked at him gaily, smiled, and rested his foot against the orchestra-screen.

"How like the brother is to the sister," remarked the count. "And how handsome they both are!"

Shinshín lowering his voice, began to tell the count of some intrigue of Kurágin's in Moscow, and Natásha tried to overhear it just because he had said she was *"charmante."*

The first act was over. In the stalls everyone began moving about, going out and coming in.

Borís came to the Rostóvs' box, received their congratulations very simply, and raising his eyebrows with an absent-minded smile conveyed to Natásha and Sónya his fiancée's invitation to her wedding, and went away. Natásha with a gay coquettish smile talked to him, and congratulated on his approaching wedding that same Borís with whom she had formerly been in love. In the state of intoxication she was in everything seemed simple and natural.

The scantily clad Hélène smiled at everyone in the same way, and Natásha gave Borís a similar smile.

Hélène's box was filled and surrounded from the stalls, by the most distinguished and intellectual men, who seemed to vie with one another in their wish to let everyone see that they knew her.

During the whole of that *entr'acte* Kurágin stood with Dólokhov in front of the orchestra partition looking at the Rostóvs' box. Natásha knew he was talking about her and this afforded her pleasure. She even turned so that he should see her profile in what she thought was its most becoming aspect. Before the beginning of the second act Pierre appeared in the stalls. The Rostóvs had not seen him since their arrival. His face looked sad, and he had grown still stouter since Natásha last saw him. He passed up to the front rows not noticing anyone. Anatole went up to him and began speaking to him, looking at and indicating the Rostóvs' box. On seeing Natásha Pierre grew animated and hastily passing between the rows, came toward their box. When he got there he leaned on his elbows and smiling, talked to her for a long time. While conversing with Pierre, Natásha heard a man's voice in Countess Bezúkhova's box and something told her it was Kurágin. She turned and their eyes met. Almost smiling, he gazed straight into her eyes with such an enraptured caressing look that it seemed strange to be so near him, to look at him like that, to be so sure he admired her, and not to be acquainted with him.

In the second act there was scenery representing tombstones, there was a round hole in the canvas to represent the moon, shades were raised over the footlights, and from horns and contrabass came deep notes while many people appeared from right and left wearing black cloaks and holding things like daggers in their hands. They began waving their arms. Then some other people ran in and began dragging away the maiden who had been in white and was now in light blue. They did not drag her away at once, but sang with her for a long time and then at last dragged her off, and behind the scenes something metallic was struck three times and everyone knelt down and sang a prayer. All these things were repeatedly interrupted by the enthusiastic shouts of the audience.

During this act every time Natásha looked toward the stalls she saw Anatole Kurágin with an arm thrown across the back of his chair, staring at her. She was pleased to see that he was captivated by her and it did not occur to her that there was anything wrong in it.

When the second act was over Countess Bezúkhova rose, turned to the Rostóvs' box—her whole bosom completely exposed—beckoned the old count with a gloved finger, and paying no attention to those who had entered her box began talking to him with an amiable smile.

"Do make me acquainted with your charming daughters," said she. "The whole town is singing their praises and I don't even know them!"

Natásha rose and curtsied to the splendid countess. She was so pleased by praise from this brilliant beauty that she blushed with pleasure.

"I want to become a Muscovite too, now," said Hélène. "How is it you're not ashamed to bury such pearls in the country?"

Countess Bezúkhova quite deserved her reputation of being a fascinating woman. She could say what she did not think—especially what was flattering—quite simply and naturally.

"Dear count, you must let me look after your daughters! Though I am not staying here long this time—nor are you—I will try to amuse them. I have already heard much of you in Petersburg and wanted to get to know you," said she to Natásha with her stereotyped and lovely smile. "I had heard about you from my page, Drubetskóy. Have you heard he is getting married? And also from my husband's friend Bolkónski, Prince Andrew Bolkónski," she went on with special emphasis, implying that she knew of his relation to Natásha. To get better acquainted she asked that one of the young ladies should come into her box for the rest of the performance, and Natásha moved over to it.

The scene of the third act represented a palace in which many candles were burning and pictures of knights with short beards hung on the walls. In the middle stood what were probably a king and a queen. The king waved his right arm and, evidently nervous, sang something badly and sat down on a crimson throne. The maiden who had been first in white and then in light blue, now wore only a smock, and stood beside the throne with her hair down. She sang something mournfully, addressing the queen, but the king waved his arm severely, and men and women with bare legs came in from both sides and began dancing all together. Then the violins played very shrilly and merrily and one of the women with thick bare legs and thin arms, separating from the others, went behind the wings, adjusted her bodice, returned to the middle of the stage, and began jumping and striking one foot rapidly against the other. In the stalls everyone clapped and shouted "bravo!" Then one of the men went into a corner of the stage. The cymbals and horns in the orchestra struck up more loudly, and this man with bare legs jumped very high and waved his feet about very rapidly. (He was Duport, who received sixty thousand rubles a year for this art.) Everybody in the stalls, boxes and galleries began clapping and shouting with all their might, and the man stopped and began smiling and bowing to all sides. Then other men and women danced with bare legs. Then the king again shouted to the sound of music, and they all began singing. But suddenly a storm came on, chromatic scales and diminished sevenths were heard in the orchestra, everyone ran off, again dragging one of their number away, and the curtain dropped. Once more there was a terrible noise and clatter among the audience, and with rapturous faces everyone began shouting: "Duport! Duport! Duport!" Natásha no longer thought this strange. She look about with pleasure, smiling joyfully.

"Isn't Duport delightful?" Hélène asked her.

"Oh yes," replied Natásha.

Chapter X

DURING THE ENTR'ACTE A WHIFF OF COLD AIR CAME INTO HÉLÈNE'S BOX, THE DOOR OPENED and Anatole entered, stooping and trying not to brush against anyone.

"Let me introduce my brother to you," said Hélène, her eyes shifting uneasily from Natásha to Anatole.

Natásha turned her pretty little head toward the elegant young officer, and smiled at him over her bare shoulder. Anatole, who was as handsome at close quarters as at a distance, sat down beside her and told her he had long wished to have this happiness—ever since the Naryshkins' ball in fact, at which he had had the well-remembered pleasure of seeing her. Kurágin was much more sensible and simple with women than among men. He talked boldly and naturally, and Natásha was strangely and agreeably struck by the fact that there was nothing formidable in this man about whom there was so much talk, but that on the contrary his smile was most naïve, cheerful and good-natured.

Kurágin asked her opinion of the performance, and told her how at a previous performance Semënova had fallen down on the stage.

"And do you know, countess," he said, suddenly addressing her as an old, familiar acquaintance, "we are getting up a costume-tournament; you ought to take part in it! It will be great fun. We shall all meet at the Karagins'! Please come! No! Really, eh?" said he.

While saying this he never removed his smiling eyes from her face, neck, and her bare arms. Natásha knew for certain that he was enraptured by her. This pleased her, yet his presence made her feel constrained and oppressed. When she was not looking at him she felt that he was looking at her shoulders, and she involuntarily caught his eye so that he should look into hers rather than this. But looking into his eyes she was frightened, realizing that there was not that barrier of modesty she had always felt between herself and other men. She did not know how it was that within five minutes she had come to feel herself terribly near to this man. When she turned away she feared he might seize her from behind by her bare arm and kiss her on the neck. They spoke of most ordinary things, yet she felt that they were closer to one another than she had ever been to any man. Natásha kept turning to Hélène and to her father, as if asking what it all meant, but Hélène was engaged in conversation with a general and did not answer her look, and her father's eyes said nothing but what they always said: "Having a good time? Well, I'm glad of it!"

During one of these moments of awkward silence when Anatole's prominent eyes were gazing calmly and fixedly at her, Natásha, to break the silence, asked him how he liked Moscow. She asked the question and blushed. She felt all the time that by talking to him she was doing something improper. Anatole smiled as though to encourage her.

"At first I did not like it much, because what makes a town pleasant *ce sont les jolies femmes,* isn't that so? But now I like it very much indeed," he said, looking at her significantly. "You'll come to the costume-tournament, countess? Do come!" and putting out his hand to her bouquet and dropping his voice, he added, "You will be the prettiest there. Do come, dear countess, and give me this flower as a pledge!"

Natásha did not understand what he was saying any more than he did himself, but she felt that his incomprehensible words had an improper intention. She did not know what to say, and turned away as if she had not heard his remark. But as soon as she had turned away she felt that he was there, behind, so close behind her.

"How is he now? Confused? Angry? Ought I to put it right?" she asked herself, and she could not refrain from turning round. She looked straight into his eyes, and his nearness, self-assurance, and the good-natured tenderness of his smile, vanquished her. She smiled just as he was doing, gazing straight into his eyes. And again she felt with horror that no barrier lay between him and her.

The curtain rose again. Anatole left the box, serene and gay. Natásha went back to her father in the other box, now quite submissive to the world she found herself in. All that was going on before her now seemed quite natural, but on the other hand all her previous thoughts of her betrothed, of Princess Mary, or of life in the country, did not once recur to her mind and were as if belonging to a remote past.

In the fourth act there was some sort of devil who sang waving his arm about, till the boards were withdrawn from under him and he disappeared down below. That was the only part of the fourth act that Natásha saw. She felt agitated and tormented, and the cause of this was Kurágin whom she could not help watching. As they were leaving the theater Anatole came up to them, called their carriage and helped them in. As he was putting Natásha in he pressed her arm above the elbow. Agitated and flushed she turned round. He was looking at her with glittering eyes, smiling tenderly.

Only after she had reached home was Natásha able clearly to think over what had happened to her, and suddenly remembering Prince Andrew she was horrified, and at tea to which all had sat down after the opera, she gave a loud exclamation, flushed and ran out of the room.

"O God! I am lost!" she said to herself. "How could I let him?" She sat for a long time hiding her flushed face in her hands trying to realize what had happened to her, but was unable either to understand what had happened or what she felt. Everything seemed dark, obscure and terrible. There in that enormous, illuminated theater where the bare-legged Duport, in a tinsel-decorated jacket, jumped about to the music on wet boards, and young girls and old men, and the nearly naked Hélène with her proud, calm smile, rapturously cried "bravo!"—there in the presence of that Hélène it had all seemed clear and simple; but now, alone by herself, it was incomprehensible. "What is it? What was that terror I felt of him? What is this gnawing of conscience I am feeling now?" she thought.

Only to the old countess at night in bed could Natásha have told all she was feeling. She knew that Sónya with her severe and simple views would either not understand it at all or would be horrified at such a confession. So Natásha tried to solve what was torturing her by herself.

"Am I spoiled for Andrew's love or not?" she asked herself, and with soothing irony replied: "What a fool I am to ask that! What did happen to me? Nothing! I have done nothing, I didn't lead him on at all. Nobody will know and I shall never see him again," she told herself. "So it is plain that nothing has happened and there is nothing to repent of, and Andrew can love me still. But why 'still'? O God, O God, why isn't he here?" Natásha quieted herself for a moment, but again some instinct told her that though all this was true, and though nothing had happened, yet the former purity of her love for Prince Andrew had perished. And again in imagination she went over her whole conversation with Kurágin, and again saw the face, gestures and tender smile of that bold handsome man when he pressed her arm.

Chapter XI

ANATOLE KURÁGIN WAS STAYING IN MOSCOW BECAUSE HIS FATHER HAD SENT HIM AWAY FROM PETERSBURG, where he had been spending twenty thousand rubles a year in cash, besides running up debts for as much more, which his creditors demanded from his father.

His father announced to him that he would now pay half his debts for the last time, but only on condition that he went to Moscow as adjutant to the commander-in-chief—a post his father had procured for him—and would at last try to make a good match there. He indicated to him Princess Mary and Julie Karágina.

Anatole consented and went to Moscow, where he put up at Pierre's house. Pierre received him unwillingly at first, but got used to him after a while, sometimes even accompanied him on his carousals, and gave him money under the guise of loans.

As Shinshín had remarked, from the time of his arrival Anatole had turned the heads of the Moscow ladies, especially by the fact that he slighted them and plainly preferred the gypsy girls and French actresses—with the chief of whom, Mademoiselle George, he was said to be on intimate relations. He had never missed a carousal at Danílov's or other Moscow revelers', drank whole nights through, outvying everyone else, and was at all the balls and parties of the best society. There was talk of his intrigues with some of the ladies, and he flirted with a few of them at the balls. But he did not run after the unmarried girls, especially the rich heiresses who were most of them plain. There was a special reason for this, as he had got married two years before—a fact known only to his most intimate friends. At that time while with his regiment in Poland, a Polish landowner of small means had forced him to marry his daughter. Anatole had very soon abandoned his wife, and for a payment which he agreed to send to his father-in-law, had arranged to be free to pass himself off as a bachelor.

Anatole was always content with his position, with himself and with others. He was instinctively and thoroughly convinced that was impossible for him to live otherwise than as he did, and that he had never in his life done anything base. He was incapable of considering how his actions might affect others or what the consequences of this or that action of his might be. He was convinced that, as a duck is so made that it must live in water, so God had made him such that he must spend thirty thousand rubles a year and always occupy a prominent position in society. He believed this so firmly that others, looking at him, were persuaded of it too, and did not refuse him either a leading place in society, or money, which he borrowed from anyone and everyone and evidently would not repay.

He was not a gambler, at any rate he did not care about winning. He was not vain. He did not mind what people thought of him. Still less could he be accused of ambition. More than once he had vexed his father by spoiling his own career, and he laughed at distinctions of all kinds. He was not mean, and did not refuse anyone who asked of him. All he cared about was gaiety and women, and as according to his ideas there was nothing dishonorable in these tastes, and he was incapable of considering what the gratification of his tastes entailed for others, he honestly considered himself irreproachable, sincerely despised rogues and bad people, and with a tranquil conscience carried his head high.

Rakes, those male Magdalenes, have a secret feeling of innocence similar to that which female Magdalenes have, based on the same hope of forgiveness. "All will be forgiven her, for she loved much; and all will be forgiven him, for he enjoyed much."

Dólokhov, who had reappeared that year in Moscow after his exile and his Persian adventures, and was leading a life of luxury, gambling and dissipation, associated with his old Petersburg comrade Kurágin and made use of him for his own ends.

Anatole was sincerely fond of Dólokhov for his cleverness and audacity. Dólokhov, who needed Anatole Kurágin's name, position and connections as a bait to draw rich young men into his gambling set, made use of him and amused himself at his expense without letting the other feel it. Apart from the advantage he derived from Anatole, the very process of dominating another's will was in itself a pleasure, a habit, and a necessity to Dólokhov.

Natásha had made a strong impression on Kurágin. At supper after the opera he described to Dólokhov with the air of a connoisseur the attractions of her arms, shoulders, feet and hair, and expressed his intention of making love to her. Anatole had no notion and was incapable of considering what might come of such love-making, as he never had any notion of the outcome of any of his actions.

"She's first rate, my dear fellow, but not for us," replied Dólokhov.

"I will tell my sister to ask her to dinner," said Anatole. "Eh?"

"You'd better wait till she's married. . . ."

"You know, I adore little girls, they lose their heads at once," pursued Anatole.

"You have been caught once already by a 'little girl,' " said Dólokhov who knew of Kurágin's marriage. "Take care!"

"Well, that can't happen twice! Eh?" said Anatole, with a good-humored laugh.

Chapter XII

The day after the opera the Rostóvs went nowhere and nobody came to see them. Márya Dmítrievna talked to the count about something which they concealed from Natásha. Natásha guessed they were talking about the old prince and planning something, and this disquieted and offended her. She was expecting Prince Andrew any moment and twice that day sent a manservant to the Vozdvízhenka to ascertain whether he had come. He had not arrived. She suffered more now than during her first days in Moscow. To her impatience and pining for him were now added the unpleasant recollection of her interview with Princess Mary and the old prince, and a fear and anxiety of which she did not understand the cause. She continually fancied that either he would never come or that something would happen to her before he came. She could no longer think of him by herself calmly and continuously as she had done before. As soon as she began to think of him, the recollection of the old prince, of Princess Mary, of the theater and of Kurágin, mingled with her thoughts. The question again presented itself whether she was not guilty, whether she had not already broken faith with Prince Andrew, and again she found herself recalling to the minutest detail every word, every gesture and every shade in the play of expression on the face of the man who had been able to arouse in her such an incomprehensible and terrifying feeling. To the family Natásha seemed livelier than usual, but she was far less tranquil and happy than before.

On Sunday morning Márya Dmítrievna invited her visitors to Mass at her parish church—the Church of the Assumption built over the graves of victims of the plague.

"I don't like those fashionable churches," she said, evidently priding herself on her independence of thought. "God is the same everywhere. We have an excellent priest, he conducts the service decently and with dignity, and the deacon is the same. What holiness is there in giving concerts in the choir? I don't like it, it's just self-indulgence!"

Márya Dmítrievna liked Sundays and knew how to keep them. Her whole house was scrubbed and cleaned on Saturdays; neither she nor the servants worked, and they all wore holiday dress and went to church. At her table there were extra dishes at dinner, and the servants had vodka and roast goose or sucking-pig. But in nothing in the house was the holiday so noticeable as in Márya Dmítrievna's broad, stern face, which on that day wore an invariable look of solemn festivity.

After Mass, when they had finished their coffee in the dining room where the loose covers had been removed from the furniture, a servant announced that the carriage was ready, and Márya Dmítrievna rose with a stern air. She wore her holiday shawl, in which she paid calls, and announced that she was going to see Prince Nicholas Bolkónski to have an explanation with him about Natásha.

After she had gone, a dressmaker from Madame Suppert-Roguet waited on the Rostóvs, and Natásha very glad of this diversion, having shut herself into a room adjoining the drawing room, occupied herself trying on the new dresses. Just as she had put on a bodice without sleeves and only tacked together, and was turning her head to see in the glass how the back fitted, she heard in the drawing room the animated sounds of her father's voice and another's—a woman's—that made her flush. It was Hélène. Natásha had not time to take off the bodice before the door opened and Countess Bezúkhova, dressed in a purple velvet gown with a high collar, came into the room beaming with good-humored amiable smiles.

"Oh, my enchantress!" she cried to the blushing Natásha. "Charming! No, this is really beyond anything, my dear count," said she to Count Rostóv who had followed her in. "How can you live in Moscow and go nowhere? No, I won't let you off! Mademoiselle George will recite at my house tonight and there'll be some people, and if you don't bring your lovely girls—who are prettier than

Mademoiselle George—I won't know you! My husband is away in Tver or I would send him to fetch you. You must come. You positively must! Between eight and nine."

She nodded to the dressmaker, whom she knew and who had curtsied respectfully to her, and seated herself in an arm-chair beside the looking-glass, draping the folds of her velvet dress picturesquely. She did not cease chattering good-naturedly and gaily, continually praising Natásha's beauty. She looked at Natásha's dresses and praised them, as well as a new dress of her own made of "metallic gauze," which she had received from Paris, and advised Natásha to have one like it.

"But anything suits you, my charmer!" she remarked.

A smile of pleasure never left Natásha's face. She felt happy and as if she were blossoming under the praise of this dear Countess Bezúkhova who had formerly seemed to her so unapproachable and important, and was now so kind to her. Natásha brightened up and felt almost in love with this woman, who was so beautiful and so kind. Hélène for her part was sincerely delighted with Natásha and wished to give her a good time. Anatole had asked her to bring him and Natásha together, and she was calling on the Rostóvs for that purpose. The idea of throwing her brother and Natásha together amused her.

Though at one time, in Petersburg, she had been annoyed with Natásha for drawing Borís away, she did not think of that now, and in her own way heartily wished Natásha well. As she was leaving the Rostóvs she called her protégée aside.

"My brother dined with me yesterday—we nearly died of laughter—he ate nothing and kept sighing for you, my charmer! He is madly, quite madly, in love with you, my dear."

Natásha blushed scarlet when she heard this.

"How she blushes, how she blushes, my pretty!" said Hélène. "You must certainly come. If you love somebody, my charmer, that is not a reason to shut yourself up. Even if you are engaged, I am sure your fiancé would wish you to go into society rather than be bored to death."

"So she knows I am engaged, and she and her husband Pierre—that good Pierre—have talked and laughed about this. So it's all right." And again, under Hélène's influence, what had seemed terrible now seemed simple and natural. "And she is such a *grande dame,* so kind, and evidently likes me so much. And why not enjoy myself?" thought Natásha, gazing at Hélène with wide-open, wondering eyes.

Márya Dmítrievna came back to dinner taciturn and serious, having evidently suffered a defeat at the old prince's. She was still too agitated by the encounter to be able to talk of the affair calmly. In answer to the count's inquiries she replied that things were all right and that she would tell about it next day. On hearing of Countess Bezúkhova's visit and the invitation for that evening, Márya Dmítrievna remarked:

"I don't care to have anything to do with Bezúkhova and don't advise you to; however, if you've promised—go. It will divert your thoughts," she added, addressing Natásha.

Chapter XIII

COUNT ROSTÓV TOOK THE GIRLS TO COUNTESS BEZÚKHOVA'S. THERE WERE A GOOD MANY PEOple there, but nearly all strangers to Natásha. Count Rostóv was displeased to see that the company consisted almost entirely of men and women known for the freedom of their conduct. Mademoiselle George was standing in a corner of the drawing room surrounded by young men. There were several Frenchmen present, among them Métivier who from the time Hélène reached Moscow had been an intimate in her house. The count decided not to sit down to cards or let his girls out of his sight, and to get away as soon as Mademoiselle George's performance was over.

Anatole was at the door, evidently on the look-out for the Rostóvs. Immediately after greeting the count he went up to Natásha and followed her. As soon as she saw him she was seized by the same feeling she had had at the opera—gratified vanity at his admiration of her, and fear at the absence of a moral barrier between them.

Hélène welcomed Natásha delightedly and was loud in admiration of her beauty and her dress. Soon after their arrival Mademoiselle George went out of the room to change her costume. In the drawing room people began arranging the chairs and taking their seats. Anatole moved a chair for Natásha and was about to sit down beside her, but the count, who never lost sight of her, took the seat himself. Anatole sat down behind her.

Mademoiselle George, with her bare, fat, dimpled arms, and a red shawl draped over one shoulder, came into the space left vacant for her, and assumed an unnatural pose. Enthusiastic whispering was audible.

Mademoiselle George looked sternly and gloomily at the audience and began reciting some French verses describing her guilty love for her son. In some places she raised her voice, in others she whispered, lifting her head triumphantly; sometimes she paused and uttered hoarse sounds, rolling her eyes.

"Adorable! divine! delicious!" was heard from every side.

Natásha looked at the fat actress, but neither saw nor heard nor understood anything of what went on before her. She only felt herself again completely borne away into this strange senseless world—so remote from her old world—a world in which it was impossible to know what was good or bad, reasonable or senseless. Behind her sat Anatole, and conscious of his proximity she experienced a frightened sense of expectancy.

After the first monologue the whole company rose and surrounded Mademoiselle George, expressing their enthusiasm.

"How beautiful she is!" Natásha remarked to her father who had also risen and was moving through the crowd toward the actress.

"I don't think so when I look at you!" said Anatole, following Natásha. He said this at a moment when she alone could hear him. "You are enchanting . . . from the moment I saw you I have never ceased . . ."

"Come, come, Natásha!" said the count, as he turned back for his daughter. "How beautiful she is!"

Natásha without saying anything stepped up to her father and looked at him with surprised inquiring eyes.

After giving several recitations, Mademoiselle George left, and Countess Bezúkhova asked her visitors into the ballroom.

The count wished to go home, but Hélène entreated him not to spoil her improvised ball, and the Rostóvs stayed on. Anatole asked Natásha for a valse and as they danced he pressed her waist and hand and told her she was bewitching and that he loved her. During the écossaise, which she also danced with him, Anatole said nothing when they happened to be by themselves, but merely gazed at her. Natásha lifted her frightened eyes to him, but there was such confident tenderness in his affectionate look and smile that she could not, whilst looking at him, say what she had to say. She lowered her eyes.

"Don't say such things to me. I am betrothed and love another," she said rapidly. . . . She glanced at him.

Anatole was not upset or pained by what she had said.

"Don't speak to me of that! What can I do?" said he. "I tell you I am madly, madly, in love with you! Is it my fault that you are enchanting? . . . It's our turn to begin."

Natásha, animated and excited, looked about her with wide-open frightened eyes and seemed merrier than usual. She understood hardly anything that went on that evening. They danced the écossaise and the *Grossvater*. Her father asked her to come home, but she begged to remain. Wherever she went and whomever she was speaking to, she felt *his* eyes upon her. Later on she recalled how she had asked her father to let her go to the dressing room to rearrange her dress, that Hélène had followed her and spoken laughingly of her brother's love, and that she again met Anatole in the little sitting room. Hélène had disappeared leaving them alone, and Anatole had taken her hand and said in a tender voice:

"I cannot come to visit you but is it possible that I shall never see you? I love you madly. Can I never . . . ?" and, blocking her path, he brought his face close to hers.

His large, glittering, masculine eyes were so close to hers that she saw nothing but them.

"Natalie?" he whispered inquiringly while she felt her hands being painfully pressed. "Natalie?"

"I don't understand. I have nothing to say," her eyes replied.

Burning lips were pressed to hers, and at the same instant she felt herself released, and Hélène's footsteps and the rustle of her dress were heard in the room. Natásha looked round at her, and then, red and trembling, threw a frightened look of inquiry at Anatole and moved toward the door.

"One word, just one, for God's sake!" cried Anatole.

She paused. She so wanted a word from him that would explain to her what had happened, and to which she could find no answer.

"Natalie, just a word, only one!" he kept repeating, evidently not knowing what to say—and he repeated it till Hélène came up to them.

Hélène returned with Natásha to the drawing room. The Rostóvs went away without staying for supper.

After reaching home Natásha did not sleep all night. She was tormented by the insoluble question whether she loved Anatole or Prince Andrew. She loved Prince Andrew—she remembered distinctly how deeply she loved him. But she also loved Anatole, of that there was no doubt. "Else how could all this have happened?" thought she. "If, after that, I could return his smile when saying good-bye, if I was able to let it come to that, it means that I loved him from the first. It means that he is kind, noble and splendid, and I could not help loving him. What am I to do if I love him and the other one too?" she asked herself, unable to find an answer to these terrible questions.

Chapter XIV

MORNING CAME WITH ITS CARES AND BUSTLE. EVERYONE GOT UP AND BEGAN TO MOVE ABOUT and talk, dressmakers came again. Márya Dmítrievna appeared, and they were called to breakfast. Natásha kept looking uneasily at everybody with wide-open eyes, as if wishing to intercept every glance directed toward her, and tried to appear the same as usual.

After breakfast, which was her best time, Márya Dmítrievna sat down in her arm-chair and called Natásha and the count to her.

"Well, friends, I have now thought the whole matter over and this is my advice," she began. "Yesterday, as you know, I went to see Prince Bolkónski. Well, I had a talk with him. . . . He took it into his head to begin shouting, but I am not one to be shouted down. I said what I had to say!"

"Well, and he?" asked the count.

"He? He's crazy . . . he did not want to listen. But what's the use of talking? As it is we have worn the poor girl out," said Márya Dmítrievna. "My advice to you is, finish your business and go back home to Otrádnoe . . . and wait there."

"Oh, no!" exclaimed Natásha.

"Yes, go back," said Márya Dmítrievna, "and wait there. If your betrothed comes here now—there will be no avoiding a quarrel; but alone with the old man he will talk things over and then come on to you."

Count Rostóv approved of this suggestion, appreciating its reasonableness. If the old man came round it would be all the better to visit him in Moscow or at Bald Hills later on; and if not, the wedding, against his wishes, could only be arranged at Otrádnoe.

"That is perfectly true. And I am sorry I went to see him and took her," said the old count.

"No, why be sorry? Being here, you had to pay your respects. But if he won't—that's his affair," said Márya Dmítrievna, looking for something in her reticule. "Besides, the trousseau is ready, so there is nothing to wait for; and what is not ready I'll send after you. Though I don't like letting you go, it is the best way. So go, with God's blessing!"

Having found what she was looking for in the reticule she handed it to Natásha. It was a letter from Princess Mary.

"She has written to you. How she torments herself, poor thing! She's afraid you might think that she does not like you."

"But she doesn't like me," said Natásha.

"Don't talk nonsense!" cried Márya Dmítrievna.

"I shan't believe anyone, I know she doesn't like me," replied Natásha boldly as she took the letter, and her face expressed a cold and angry resolution that caused Márya Dmítrievna to look at her more intently and to frown.

"Don't answer like that, my good girl!" she said. "What I say is true! Write an answer!"

Natásha did not reply, and went to her own room to read Princess Mary's letter.

Princess Mary wrote that she was in despair at the misunderstanding that had occurred between them. Whatever her father's feelings might be, she begged Natásha to believe that she could not help loving her as the one chosen by her brother, for whose happiness she was ready to sacrifice everything.

"Do not think, however," she wrote, "that my father is ill-disposed toward you. He is an invalid and an old man who must be forgiven; but he is good and magnanimous, and will love her who makes his son happy." Princess Mary went on to ask Natásha to fix a time when she could see her again.

After reading the letter Natásha sat down at the writing-table to answer it. "Dear Princess," she wrote in French quickly and mechanically, and then paused. What more could she write after all that had happened the evening before? "Yes, yes! All that has happened, and now all is changed," she thought as she sat with the letter she had begun before her. "Must I break off with him? Must I really? That's awful . . ." and to escape from these dreadful thoughts she went to Sónya and began sorting patterns with her.

After dinner Natásha went to her room and again took up Princess Mary's letter. "Can it be that it is all over?" she thought. "Can it be that all this has happened so quickly and has destroyed all that went before?" She recalled her love for Prince Andrew in all its former strength, and at the same time felt that she loved Kurágin. She vividly pictured herself as Prince Andrew's wife, and the scenes of happiness with him she had so often repeated in her imagination, and at the same time, aglow with excitement, recalled every detail of yesterday's interview with Anatole.

"Why could that not be as well?" she sometimes asked herself in complete bewilderment. "Only so could I be completely happy; but now I have to choose, and I can't be happy without either of them. Only," she thought, "to tell Prince Andrew what has happened or to hide it from him are both equally impossible. But with *that one* nothing is spoiled. But am I really to abandon forever the joy of Prince Andrew's love, in which I have lived so long?"

"Please, Miss!" whispered a maid entering the room with a mysterious air. "A man told me to give you this—" and she handed Natásha a letter.

"Only, for Christ's sake . . ." the girl went on, as Natásha, without thinking, mechanically broke the seal and read a love letter from Anatole, of which without taking in a word, she understood only that it was a letter from him—from the man she loved. Yes, she loved him, or else how could that have happened which had happened? And how could she have a love letter from him in her hand?

With trembling hands Natásha held that passionate love letter which Dólokhov had composed for Anatole, and as she read it she found in it an echo of all that she herself imagined she was feeling.

"Since yesterday evening my fate has been sealed; to be loved by you or to die. There is no other way for me," the letter began. Then he went on to say that he knew her parents would not give her to him—for this there were secret reasons he could reveal only to her—but that if she loved him she need only say the word *Yes,* and no human power could hinder their bliss. Love would conquer all. He would steal her away and carry her off to the ends of the earth.

"Yes, yes! I love him!" thought Natásha, reading the letter for the twentieth time and finding some peculiarly deep meaning in each word of it.

That evening Márya Dmítrievna was going to the Akhárovs' and proposed to take the girls with her. Natásha, pleading a headache, remained at home.

Chapter XV

On returning late in the evening Sónya went to Natásha's room, and to her surprise found her still dressed, and asleep on the sofa. Open on the table beside her lay Anatole's letter. Sónya picked it up and read it.

As she read she glanced at the sleeping Natásha, trying to find in her face an explanation of what she was reading, but did not find it. Her face was calm, gentle and happy. Clutching her breast to keep herself from choking, Sónya, pale and trembling with fear and agitation, sat down in an arm-chair and burst into tears.

"How was it I noticed nothing? How could it go so far? Can she have left off loving Prince Andrew? And how could she let Kurágin go to such lengths? He is a deceiver and a villain, that's plain! What will Nicholas, dear noble Nicholas, do when he hears of it? So this is the meaning of her excited, resolute, unnatural look the day before yesterday, yesterday, and today," thought Sónya. "But it can't be that she loves him! She probably opened the letter without knowing who it was from. Probably she is offended by it. She could not do such a thing!"

Sónya wiped away her tears and went up to Natásha, again scanning her face.

"Natásha!" she said, just audibly.

Natásha awoke and saw Sónya.

"Ah, you're back?"

And with the decision and tenderness that often come at the moment of awakening, she embraced her friend, but noticing Sónya's look of embarrassment, her own face expressed confusion and suspicion.

"Sónya, you've read that letter?" she demanded.

"Yes," answered Sónya softly.

Natásha smiled rapturously.

"No, Sónya, I can't any longer!" she said. "I can't hide it from you any longer. You know, we love one another! Sónya, darling, he writes . . . Sónya . . ."

Sónya stared open-eyed at Natásha, unable to believe her ears.

"And Bolkónski?" she asked.

"Ah, Sónya, if you only knew how happy I am!" cried Natásha. "You don't know what love is. . . ."

"But, Natásha, can *that* be all over?"

Natásha looked at Sónya with wide-open eyes as if she could not grasp the question.

"Well then, are you refusing Prince Andrew?" said Sónya.

"Oh, you don't understand anything! Don't talk nonsense, just listen!" said Natásha, with momentary vexation.

"But I can't believe it," insisted Sónya. "I don't understand. How is it you have loved a man for a whole year and suddenly . . . Why, you have only seen him three times! Natásha, I don't believe you, you're joking! In three days to forget everything and so . . ."

"Three days?" said Natásha. "It seems to me I've loved him a hundred years. It seems to me that I have never loved anyone before. You can't understand it. . . . Sónya, wait a bit, sit here," and Natásha embraced and kissed her.

"I had heard that it happens like this, and you must have heard it too, but it's only now that I feel such love. It's not the same as before. As soon as I saw him I felt he was my master and I his slave, and that I could not help loving him. Yes, his slave! Whatever he orders I shall do. You don't understand that. What can I do? What can I do, Sónya?" cried Natásha with a happy yet frightened expression.

"But think what you are doing," cried Sónya. "I can't leave it like this. This secret correspondence . . . How could you let him go so far?" she went on, with a horror and disgust she could hardly conceal.

"I told you that I have no will," Natásha replied. "Why can't you understand? I love him!"

"Then I won't let it come to that . . . I shall tell!" cried Sónya, bursting into tears.

"What do you mean? For God's sake . . . If you tell, you are my enemy!" declared Natásha. "You want me to be miserable, you want us to be separated. . . ."

When she saw Natásha's fright, Sónya shed tears of shame and pity for her friend.

"But what has happened between you?" she asked. "What has he said to you? Why doesn't he come to the house?"

Natásha did not answer her questions.

"For God's sake, Sónya, don't tell anyone, don't torture me," Natásha entreated. "Remember no one ought to interfere in such matters! I have confided in you. . . ."

"But why this secrecy? Why doesn't he come to the house?" asked Sónya. "Why doesn't he openly ask for your hand? You know Prince Andrew gave you complete freedom—if it is really so; but I don't believe it! Natásha, have you considered what these *secret reasons* can be?"

Natásha looked at Sónya with astonishment. Evidently this question presented itself to her mind for the first time and she did not know how to answer it.

"I don't know what the reasons are. But there must be reasons!"

Sónya sighed and shook her head incredulously.

"If there were reasons . . ." she began.

But Natásha, guessing her doubts, interrupted her in alarm.

"Sónya, one can't doubt him! One can't, one can't! Don't you understand?" she cried.

"Does he love you?"

"Does he love me?" Natásha repeated with a smile of pity at her friend's lack of comprehension. "Why, you have read his letter and you have seen him."

"But if he is dishonorable?"

"*He!* dishonorable? If you only knew!" exclaimed Natásha.

"If he is an honorable man he should either declare his intentions, or cease seeing you; and if you won't do this, I will. I will write to him, and I will tell Papa!" said Sónya resolutely.

"But I can't live without him!" cried Natásha.

"Natásha, I don't understand you. And what are you saying! Think of your father and of Nicholas."

"I don't want anyone, I don't love anyone but him. How dare you say he is dishonorable? Don't you know that I love him?" screamed Natásha. "Go away, Sónya! I don't want to quarrel with you, but go, for God's sake go! You see how I am suffering!" Natásha cried angrily, in a voice of despair and repressed irritation. Sónya burst into sobs and ran from the room.

Natásha went to the table and without a moment's reflection wrote that answer to Princess Mary which she had been unable to write all the morning. In this letter she said briefly that all their misunderstandings were at an end; that availing herself of the magnanimity of Prince Andrew who when he went abroad had given her her freedom, she begged Princess Mary to forget everything and forgive her if she had been to blame toward her, but that she could not be his wife. At that moment this all seemed quite easy, simple and clear to Natásha.

On Friday the Rostóvs were to return to the country, but on Wednesday the count went with the prospective purchaser to his estate near Moscow.

On the day the count left, Sónya and Natásha were invited to a big dinner party at the Karagins', and Márya Dmítrievna took them there. At that party Natásha again met Anatole, and Sónya noticed that she spoke to him, trying not to be overheard, and that all through dinner she was more agitated than ever. When they got home Natásha was the first to begin the explanation Sónya expected.

"There, Sónya, you were talking all sorts of nonsense about him," Natásha began in a mild voice such as children use when they wish to be praised. "We have had an explanation today."

"Well, what happened? What did he say? Natásha, how glad I am you're not angry with me! Tell me everything—the whole truth. What did he say?"

Natásha became thoughtful.

"Oh, Sónya, if you knew him as I do! He said . . . He asked me what I had promised Bolkónski. He was glad I was free to refuse him."

Sónya sighed sorrowfully.

"But you haven't refused Bolkónski?" said she.

"Perhaps I have. Perhaps all is over between me and Bolkónski. Why do you think so badly of me?"

"I don't think anything, only I don't understand this . . ."

"Wait a bit, Sónya, you'll understand everything. You'll see what a man he is! Now don't think badly of me or of him. I don't think badly of anyone: I love and pity everybody. But what am I to do?"

Sónya did not succumb to the tender tone Natásha used toward her. The more emotional and ingratiating the expression of Natásha's face became, the more serious and stern grew Sónya's.

"Natásha," said she, "you asked me not to speak to you, and I haven't spoken, but now you yourself have begun. I don't trust him, Natásha. Why this secrecy?"

"Again, again!" interrupted Natásha.

"Natásha, I am afraid for you!"

"Afraid of what?"

"I am afraid you're going to your ruin," said Sónya resolutely, and was herself horrified at what she had said.

Anger again showed in Natásha's face.

"And I'll go to my ruin, I will, as soon as possible! It's not your business! It won't be you, but I, who'll suffer. Leave me alone, leave me alone! I hate you!"

"Natásha!" moaned Sónya, aghast.

"I hate you, I hate you! You're my enemy forever!" And Natásha ran out of the room.

Natásha did not speak to Sónya again, and avoided her. With the same expression of agitated surprise and guilt she went about the house, taking up now one occupation now another, and at once abandoning them.

Hard as it was for Sónya, she watched her friend and did not let her out of her sight.

The day before the count was to return, Sónya noticed that Natásha sat by the drawing room window all the morning as if expecting something, and that she made a sign to an officer who drove past, whom Sónya took to be Anatole.

Sónya began watching her friend still more attentively, and noticed that at dinner and all that evening Natásha was in a strange and unnatural state. She answered questions at random, began sentences she did not finish, and laughed at everything.

After tea Sónya noticed a housemaid at Natásha's door timidly waiting to let her pass. She let the girl go in, and then listening at the door, learned that another letter had been delivered.

Then suddenly it became clear to Sónya that Natásha had some dreadful plan for that evening. Sónya knocked at her door. Natásha did not let her in.

"She will run away with him!" thought Sónya. "She is capable of anything. There was something particularly pathetic and resolute in her face today. She cried as she said good-bye to Uncle," Sónya remembered. "Yes, that's it, she means to elope with him, but what am I to do?" thought she, recalling all the signs that clearly indicated that Natásha had some terrible intention. "The count is away. What am I to do? Write to Kurágin demanding an explanation? But what is there to oblige him to reply? Write to Pierre, as Prince Andrew asked me to in case of some misfortune? . . . But perhaps she really has already refused Bolkónski—she sent a letter to Princess Mary yesterday. And Uncle is away. . . ." To tell Márya Dmítrievna who had such faith in Natásha, seemed to Sónya terrible. "Well, anyway," thought Sónya as she stood in the dark passage, "now or never I must prove that I remember the family's goodness to me and that I love Nicholas. Yes! If I don't sleep for three nights I'll not leave this passage, and will hold her back by force and not let the family be disgraced," thought she.

Chapter XVI

ANATOLE HAD LATELY MOVED TO DÓLOKHOV'S. THE PLAN FOR NATALIE ROSTÓVA'S ABDUCTION had been arranged and the preparations made by Dólokhov a few days before, and on the day that Sónya, after listening at Natásha's door, resolved to safeguard her, it was to have been put into execution. Natásha had promised to come out to Kurágin at the back porch at ten that evening. Kurágin was to put her into a troyka he would have ready, and to drive her forty miles to the village of Kámenka, where an unfrocked priest was in readiness to perform a marriage ceremony over them. At Kámenka a relay of horses was to wait which would take them to the Warsaw highroad, and from there they would hasten abroad with post-horses.

Anatole had a passport, an order for post-horses, ten thousand rubles he had taken from his sister and another ten thousand borrowed with Dólokhov's help.

Two witnesses for the mock marriage—Khvóstikov, a retired petty official whom Dólokhov made use of in his gambling transactions, and Makárin, a retired hussar, a kindly, weak fellow who had an unbounded affection for Kurágin—were sitting at tea in Dólokhov's front room.

In his large study, the walls of which were hung to the ceiling with Persian rugs, bearskins and weapons, sat Dólokhov in a traveling cloak and high boots, at an open desk on which lay an abacus and some bundles of paper money. Anatole, with uniform unbuttoned, walked to and fro from the room where the witnesses were sitting, through the study to the room behind, where his French valet and others were packing the last of his things. Dólokhov was counting the money and noting something down.

"Well," he said, "Khvóstikov must have two thousand."

"Give it to him, then," said Anatole.

"Makárka" (their name for Makárin) "will go through fire and water for you for nothing. So here are our accounts all settled," said Dólokhov, showing him the memorandum. "Is that right?"

"Yes, of course," returned Anatole, evidently not listening to Dólokhov and looking straight before him with a smile that did not leave his face.

Dólokhov banged down the lid of his desk and turned to Anatole with an ironic smile:

"Do you know? You'd really better drop it all. There's still time!"

"Fool," retorted Anatole. "Don't talk nonsense! If you only knew . . . it's the devil knows what!"

"No, really, give it up!" said Dólokhov. "I am speaking seriously. It's no joke, this plot you've hatched."

"What, teasing again? Go to the devil! Eh?" said Anatole, making a grimace. "Really it's no time for your stupid jokes," and he left the room.

Dólokhov smiled contemptuously and condescendingly when Anatole had gone out.

"You wait a bit," he called after him. "I'm not joking, I'm talking sense. Come here, come here!"

Anatole returned and looked at Dólokhov, trying to give him his attention and evidently submitting to him involuntarily.

"Now listen to me. I'm telling you this for the last time. Why should I joke about it? Did I hinder you? Who arranged everything for you? Who found the priest and got the passport? Who raised the money? I did it all."

"Well, thank you for it. Do you think I am not grateful?" And Anatole sighed and embraced Dólokhov.

"I helped you, but all the same I must tell you the truth; it is a dangerous business, and if you think about it—a stupid business. Well, you'll carry her off—all right! Will they let it stop at that? It will come out that you're already married. Why they'll have you in the criminal court. . . ."

"Oh, nonsense, nonsense!" Anatole ejaculated and again made a grimace. "Didn't I explain to you? What?" And Anatole, with the partiality dull-witted people have for any conclusion they have reached by their own reasoning, repeated the argument he had already put to Dólokhov a hundred times. "Didn't I explain to you that I have come to this conclusion: if this marriage is invalid," he went on, crooking one finger, "then I have nothing to answer for; but if it is valid, no matter! Abroad no one will know anything about it. Isn't that so? And don't talk to me, don't, don't!"

"Seriously, you'd better drop it! You'll only get yourself into a mess!"

"Go to the devil!" cried Anatole and clutching his hair left the room, but returned at once and dropped into an arm-chair in front of Dólokhov with his feet turned under him. "It's the very devil! What? Feel how it beats!" He took Dólokhov's hand and put it on his heart. "What a foot, my dear fellow! What a glance! A goddess!" he added in French. "What?"

Dólokhov with a cold smile and a gleam in his handsome insolent eyes looked at him—evidently wishing to get some more amusement out of him.

"Well and when the money's gone, what then?"

"What then? Eh?" repeated Anatole, sincerely perplexed by a thought of the future. "What then? . . . Then, I don't know . . . But why talk nonsense!" He glanced at his watch. "It's time!"

Anatole went into the back room.

"Now then! Nearly ready? You're dawdling!" he shouted to the servants.

Dólokhov put away the money, called a footman whom he ordered to bring something for them to eat and drink before the journey, and went into the room where Khvóstikov and Makárin were sitting.

Anatole lay on the sofa in the study leaning on his elbow and smiling pensively, while his handsome lips muttered tenderly to himself.

"Come and eat something. Have a drink!" Dólokhov shouted to him from the other room.

"I don't want to," answered Anatole continuing to smile.

"Come! Balagá is here."

Anatole rose and went into the dining room. Balagá was a famous troyka driver who had known Dólokhov and Anatole some six years and had given them good service with his troykas. More than once when Anatole's regiment was stationed at Tver he had taken him from Tver in the evening, brought him to Moscow by daybreak, and driven him back again the next night. More than once he had enabled Dólokhov to escape when pursued. More than once he had driven them through the town with gypsies and "ladykins" as he called the *cocottes.* More than once in their service he had run over pedestrians and upset vehicles in the streets of Moscow, and had always been protected from the consequences by "my gentlemen" as he called them. He had ruined more than one horse in their service. More than once they had beaten him, and more than once they had made him drunk on champagne and madeira, which he loved; and he knew more than one thing about each of them which would long ago have sent an ordinary man to Siberia. They often called Balagá into their orgies and made him drink and dance at the gypsies', and more than one thousand rubles of their money had passed through his hands. In their service he risked his skin and his life twenty times a year, and in their service he had lost more horses than the money he had from them would buy. But he liked them; liked that mad driving at twelve miles an hour, liked upsetting a driver or running down a pedestrian, and flying at full gallop through the Moscow streets. He liked to hear those wild, tipsy shouts behind him: "Get on! Get on!" when it was impossible to go any faster. He liked giving a painful lash on the neck to some peasant who, more dead than alive, was already hurrying out of his way. "Real gentlemen!" he considered them.

Anatole and Dólokhov liked Balagá too for his masterly driving and because he liked the things they liked. With others Balagá bargained, charging twenty-five rubles for a two-hours' drive, and rarely drove himself, generally letting his young men do so. But with "his gentlemen" he always drove himself and never demanded anything for his work. Only a couple of times a year—when he knew from their valets that they had money in hand—he would turn up of a morning quite sober, and with a deep bow would ask them to help him. The gentlemen always made him sit down.

"Do help me out, Theodore Iványch, sir," or "your excellency," he would say. "I am quite out of horses. Let me have what you can to go to the fair."

And Anatole and Dólokhov, when they had money, would give him a thousand or a couple of thousand rubles.

Balagá was a fair-haired, short, and snub-nosed peasant of about twenty-seven; red-faced, with a particularly red thick neck, glittering little eyes and a small beard. He wore a fine, dark-blue, silk-lined cloth coat over a sheepskin.

On entering the room now he crossed himself, turning toward the front corner of the room, and went up to Dólokhov holding out a small, black hand.

"Theodore Iványch!" he said, bowing.

"How d'you do, friend? Well, here he is!"

"Good day, your excellency!" he said, again holding out his hand to Anatole who had just come in.

"I say, Balagá," said Anatole, putting his hands on the man's shoulders, "do you care for me or not? Eh? Now, do me a service. . . . What horses have you come with? Eh?"

"As your messenger ordered, your special beasts," replied Balagá.

"Well, listen, Balagá! Drive all three to death but get me there in three hours. Eh?"

"When they are dead, what shall I drive?" said Balagá with a wink.

"Mind, I'll smash your face in! Don't make jokes!" cried Anatole, suddenly rolling his eyes.

"Why joke?" said the driver, laughing. "As if I'd grudge my gentlemen anything? As fast as ever the horses can gallop, so fast we'll go!"

"Ah!" said Anatole. "Well, sit down."

"Yes, sit down!" said Dólokhov.

"I'll stand, Theodore Iványch."

"Sit down; nonsense! Have a drink!" said Anatole, and filled a large glass of madeira for him.

The driver's eyes sparkled at the sight of the wine. After refusing it for manners' sake, he drank it and wiped his mouth with a red silk handkerchief he took out of his cap.

"And when are we to start, your excellency?"

"Well . . ." Anatole looked at his watch. "We'll start at once. Mind, Balagá! You'll get there in time? Eh?"

"That depends on our luck in starting, else why shouldn't we be there in time?" replied Balagá. "Didn't we get you to Tver in seven hours? I think you remember that, your excellency?"

"Do you know, one Christmas I drove from Tver," said Anatole, smilingly at the recollection and turning to Makárin who gazed rapturously at him with wide-open eyes. "Will you believe it, Makárka, it took one's breath away, the rate we flew. We came across a train of loaded sleighs, and drove right over two of them. Eh?"

"Those were horses!" Balagá continued the tale. "That time I'd harnessed two young side-horses with the bay in the shafts," he went on, turning to Dólokhov. "Will you believe it, Theodore Iványch, those animals flew forty miles? I couldn't hold them in, my hands grew numb in the sharp frost so that I threw down the reins—'Catch hold yourself, your excellency!' says I, and I just tumbled on the bottom of the sleigh and sprawled there. It wasn't a case of urging them on, there was no holding them in till we reached the place. The devils took us there in three hours! Only the near one died of it."

Chapter XVII

Anatole went out of the room and returned a few minutes later wearing a fur coat girt with a silver belt, and a sable cap jauntily set on one side and very becoming to his handsome face. Having looked in a mirror, and standing before Dólokhov in the same pose he had assumed before it, he lifted a glass of wine.

"Well, good-bye, Theodore. Thank you for everything and farewell!" said Anatole. "Well, comrades and friends . . ." he considered for a moment ". . . of my youth, farewell!" he said, turning to Makárin and the others.

Though they were all going with him, Anatole evidently wished to make something touching and solemn out of this address to his comrades. He spoke slowly in a loud voice, and throwing out his chest slightly swayed one leg.

"All take glasses; you too, Balagá. Well, comrades and friends of my youth, we've had our fling and lived and reveled. Eh? And now, when shall we meet again? I am going abroad. We have had a good time—now farewell lads! To our health! Hurrah! . . ." he cried, and emptying his glass flung it on the floor.

"To your health!" said Balagá who also emptied his glass, and wiped his mouth with his handkerchief.

Makárin embraced Anatole with tears in his eyes.

"Ah, prince, how sorry I am to part from you!

"Let's go. Let's go!" cried Anatole.

Balagá was about to leave the room.

"No, stop!" said Anatole. "Shut the door; we have first to sit down. That's the way."

They shut the door and all sat down.

"Now, quick march, lads!" said Anatole, rising.

Joseph, his valet, handed him his sabertache and saber, and they all went out into the vestibule.

"And where's the fur cloak?" asked Dólokhov. "Hey, Ignátka! Go to Matrëna Matrévna and ask her for the sable cloak. I have heard what elopements are like," continued Dólokhov with a wink. "Why, she'll rush out more dead than alive just in the things she is wearing; if you delay at all there'll be tears and 'Papa' and 'Mamma,' and she's frozen in a minute and must go back—but you wrap the fur cloak round her first thing and carry her to the sleigh."

The valet brought a woman's fox-lined cloak.

"Fool, I told you the sable one! Hey, Matrëna, the sable!" he shouted so that his voice rang far through the rooms.

A handsome, slim and pale-faced gypsy girl with glittering black eyes and curly-black hair, wearing a red shawl, ran out with a sable mantle on her arm.

"Here, I don't grudge it—take it!" she said, evidently afraid of her master and yet regretful of her cloak.

Dólokhov, without answering, took the cloak, threw it over Matrëna and wrapped her up in it.

"That's the way," said Dólokhov, "and then so!" and he turned the collar up round her head, leaving only a little of the face uncovered. "And then so, do you see?" and he pushed Anatole's head forward to meet the gap left by the collar, through which Matrëna's brilliant smile was seen.

"Well, good-bye, Matrëna," said Anatole, kissing her. "Ah, my revels here are over. Remember me to Stëshka. There, good-bye! Good-bye, Matrëna, wish me luck!"

"Well, prince, may God give you great luck!" said Matrëna in her gypsy accent.

Two troykas were standing before the porch and two young drivers were holding the horses. Balagá took his seat in the front one and holding his elbows high arranged the reins deliberately. Anatole and Dólokhov got in with him. Makárin, Khvóstikov and a valet seated themselves in the other sleigh.

"Well, are you ready?" asked Balagá.

"Go!" he cried, twisting the reins round his hands, and the troyka tore down the Nikítski Boulevard.

"Tproo! Get out of the way! Hi! . . . Tproo! . . ." The shouting of Balagá and of the sturdy young fellow seated on the box was all that could be heard. On the Arbát Square the troyka caught against a carriage; something cracked, shouts were heard and the troyka flew along the Arbát Street.

After taking a turn along the Podnovínski Boulevard, Balagá began to rein in, and turning back drew up at the crossing of the old Konyusheny Street.

The young fellow on the box jumped down to hold the horses and Anatole and Dólokhov went along the pavement. When they reached the gate Dólokhov whistled. The whistle was answered, and a maidservant ran out.

"Come into the courtyard or you'll be seen; she'll come out directly," said she.

Dólokhov stayed by the gate. Anatole followed the maid into the courtyard, turned the corner, and ran up into the porch.

He was met by Gabriel, Márya Dmítrievna's gigantic footman.

"Come to the mistress, please," said the footman in his deep bass, intercepting any retreat.

"To what mistress? Who are you?" asked Anatole in a breathless whisper.

"Kindly step in, my orders are to bring you in."

"Kurágin! Come back!" shouted Dólokhov. "Betrayed! Back!"

Dólokhov, after Anatole entered, had remained at the wicket-gate, and was struggling with the yard-porter who was trying to lock it. With a last desperate effort Dólokhov pushed the porter aside, and when Anatole ran back seized him by the arm, pulled him through the wicket, and ran back with him to the troyka.

Chapter XVIII

MÁRYA DMÍTRIEVNA, HAVING FOUND SÓNYA WEEPING IN THE CORRIDOR, MADE HER CONFESS everything, and intercepting the note to Natásha she read it and went into Natásha's room with it in her hand.

"You shameless good-for-nothing!" said she. "I won't hear a word."

Pushing back Natásha who looked at her with astonished but tearless eyes, she locked her in; and having given orders to the yard-porter to admit the persons who would be coming that evening, but not to let them out again, and having told the footman to bring them up to her, she seated herself in the drawing room to await the abductors.

When Gabriel came to inform her that the men who had come had run away again, she rose frowning, and clasping her hands behind her paced through the rooms a long time considering what she should do. Toward midnight she went to Natásha's room fingering the key in her pocket. Sónya was sitting sobbing in the corridor. "Márya Dmítrievna, for God's sake let me in to her!" she pleaded, but Márya Dmítrievna unlocked the door and went in without giving her an answer. . . . "Disgusting, abominable . . . In my house . . . horrid girl, hussy! I'm only sorry for her father!" thought she, trying to restrain her wrath. "Hard as it may be, I'll tell them all to hold their tongues and will hide it from the count." She entered the room with resolute steps. Natásha was lying on the sofa, her head hidden in her hands, and she did not stir. She was in just the same position in which Márya Dmítrievna had left her.

"A nice girl! Very nice!" said Márya Dmítrievna. "Arranging meetings with lovers in my house! It's no use pretending: you listen when I speak to you!" And Márya Dmítrievna touched her arm. "Listen when I speak! You've disgraced yourself like the lowest of hussies. I'd treat you differently, but I'm sorry for your father, so I will conceal it."

Natásha did not change her position, but her whole body heaved with noiseless, convulsive sobs which choked her. Márya Dmítrievna glanced round at Sónya and seated herself on the sofa beside Natásha.

"It's lucky for him that he escaped me; but I'll find him!" she said in her rough voice. "Do you hear what I am saying or not?" she added.

She put her large hand under Natásha's face and turned it toward her. Both Márya Dmítrievna and Sónya were amazed when they saw how Natásha looked. Her eyes were dry and glistening, her lips compressed, her cheeks sunken.

"Let me be! . . . What is it to me? . . . I shall die!" she muttered, wrenching herself from Márya Dmítrievna's hands with a vicious effort and sinking down again into her former position.

"Natalie!" said Márya Dmítrievna. "I wish for your good. Lie still, stay like that then, I won't touch you. But listen. I won't tell you how guilty you are. You know that yourself. But when your father comes back tomorrow—what am I to tell him? Eh?"

Again Natásha's body shook with sobs.

"Suppose he finds out, and your brother, and your betrothed?"

"I have no betrothed: I have refused him!" cried Natásha.

"That's all the same," continued Márya Dmítrievna. "If they hear of this will they let it pass? He, your father, I know him . . . if he challenges him to a duel will that be all right? Eh?"

"Oh, let me be! Why have you interfered at all? Why? Why? Who asked you to?" shouted Natásha, raising herself on the sofa and looking malignantly at Márya Dmítrievna.

"But what did you want?" cried Márya Dmítrievna, growing angry again. "Were you kept under lock and key? Who hindered his coming to the house? Why carry you off as if you were some gypsy singing-girl? . . . Well, if he had carried you off . . . do you think they wouldn't have found him? Your father, or brother, or your betrothed? And he's a scoundrel, a wretch—that's a fact!"

"He is better than any of you!" exclaimed Natásha getting up. "If you hadn't interfered . . . Oh, my God! What is it all? What is it? Sónya, why? . . . Go away!"

And she burst into sobs with the despairing vehemence with which people bewail disasters they feel they have themselves occasioned. Márya Dmítrievna was to speak again but Natásha cried out:

"Go away! Go away! You all hate and despise me!" and she threw herself back on the sofa.

Márya Dmítrievna went on admonishing her for some time, enjoining on her that it must all be kept from her father and assuring her that nobody would know anything about it if only Natásha herself would undertake to forget it all and not let anyone see that something had happened. Natásha did not reply, nor did she sob any longer, but she grew cold and had a shivering fit. Márya Dmítrievna put a pillow under her head, covered her with two quilts and herself brought her some lime-flower water, but Natásha did not respond to her.

"Well, let her sleep," said Márya Dmítrievna as she went of the room supposing Natásha to be asleep.

But Natásha was not asleep; with pale face and fixed wide-open eyes she looked straight before her. All that night she did not sleep or weep, and did not speak to Sónya who got up and went to her several times.

Next day Count Rostóv returned from his estate near Moscow in time for lunch as he had promised. He was in very good spirits; the affair with the purchaser was going on satisfactorily, and there was nothing to keep him any longer in Moscow, away from the countess whom he missed. Márya Dmítrievna met him and told him that Natásha had been very unwell the day before and that they had sent for the doctor, but that she was better now. Natásha had not left her room that morning. With compressed and parched lips, and dry fixed eyes, she sat at the window, uneasily watching the people who drove past, and hurriedly glancing round at anyone who entered the room. She was evidently expecting news of him and that he would come or would write to her.

When the count came to see her she turned anxiously round at the sound of a man's footstep, and then her face resumed its cold and malevolent expression. She did not even get up to greet him.

"What is the matter with you, my angel? Are you ill?" asked the count.

After a moment's silence Natásha answered: "Yes, ill."

In reply to the count's anxious inquiries as to why she was so dejected and whether anything had happened to her betrothed, she assured him that nothing had happened and asked him not to worry. Márya Dmítrievna confirmed Natásha's assurances that nothing had happened. From the pretense of illness, from his daughter's distress and by the embarrassed faces of Sónya and Márya Dmítrievna, the count saw clearly that something had gone wrong during his absence, but it was so terrible for him to think that anything disgraceful had happened to his beloved daughter, and he so prized his own cheerful tranquillity, that he avoided inquiries and tried to assure himself that nothing particular had happened; and he was only dissatisfied that her indisposition delayed their return to the country.

Chapter XIX

FROM THE DAY HIS WIFE ARRIVED IN MOSCOW PIERRE HAD BEEN INTENDING TO GO AWAY somewhere, so as not to be near her. Soon after the Rostóvs came to Moscow the effect Natásha had on him made him hasten to carry out his intention. He went to Tver to see Joseph Alexéevich's widow, who had long since promised to hand over to him some papers of her deceased husband's.

When he returned to Moscow Pierre was handed a letter from Márya Dmítrievna asking him to come and see her on a matter of great importance relating to Andrew Bolkónski and his betrothed. Pierre had been avoiding Natásha because it seemed to him that his feeling for her was stronger than a married man's should be for his friend's fiancée. Yet some fate constantly threw them together.

"What can have happened? And what can they want with me?" thought he as he dressed to go to Márya Dmítrievna's. "If only Prince Andrew would hurry up and come and marry her!" thought he on his way to the house.

On the Tverskóy Boulevard a familiar voice called to him.

"Pierre! Been back long?" someone shouted. Pierre raised his head. In a sleigh drawn by two gray trotting-horses that were bespattering the dashboard with snow, Anatole and his constant companion Makárin dashed past. Anatole was sitting upright in the classic pose of military dandies, the lower part of his face hidden by his beaver collar and his head slightly bent. His face was fresh and rosy, his white-plumed hat, tilted to one side, disclosed his curled and pomaded hair besprinkled with powdery snow.

"Yes, indeed, that's a true sage," thought Pierre. "He sees nothing beyond the pleasure of the moment, nothing troubles him and so he is always cheerful, satisfied and serene. What wouldn't I give to be like him!" he thought enviously.

In Márya Dmítrievna's anteroom the footman who helped him off with his fur coat said that the mistress asked him to come to her bedroom.

When he opened the ballroom door Pierre saw Natásha sitting at the window, with a thin, pale and spiteful face. She glanced round at him, frowned, and left the room with an expression of cold dignity.

"What has happened?" asked Pierre, entering Márya Dmítrievna's room.

"Fine doings!" answered Márya Dmítrievna. "For fifty-eight years have I lived in this world and never known anything so disgraceful!"

And having put him on his honor not to repeat anything she told him, Márya Dmítrievna informed him that Natásha had refused Prince Andrew without her parents' knowledge, and that the cause of this was Anatole Kurágin into whose society Pierre's wife had thrown her, and with whom Natásha had tried to elope during her father's absence, in order to be married secretly.

Pierre raised his shoulders and listened open-mouthed to what was told him, scarcely able to believe his own ears. That Prince Andrew's deeply loved affianced wife—the same Natásha Rostóva who used to be so charming—should give up Bolkónski for that fool Anatole who was already secretly married (as Pierre knew), and should be so in love with him as to agree to run away with him, was something Pierre could not conceive and could not imagine.

He could not reconcile the charming impression he had of Natásha, whom he had known from a child, with this new conception of her baseness, folly and cruelty. He thought of his wife. "They are all alike!" he said to himself, reflecting that he was not the only man unfortunate enough to be tied to a bad woman. But still he pitied Prince Andrew to the point of tears and sympathized with his wounded pride, and the more he pitied his friend the more did he think with contempt and even with disgust of that Natásha who had just passed him in the ballroom with such a look of cold dignity. He did not know that Natásha's soul was overflowing with despair, shame and humiliation, and that it was not her fault that her face happened to assume an expression of calm dignity and severity.

"But how get married?" said Pierre, in answer to Márya Dmítrievna. "He could not marry—he is married!"

"Things get worse from hour to hour!" ejaculated Márya Dmítrievna. "A nice youth! What a scoundrel! And she's expecting him—expecting him since yesterday. She must be told! Then at least she won't go on expecting him."

After hearing the details of Anatole's marriage from Pierre, and giving vent to her anger against Anatole in words of abuse, Márya Dmítrievna told Pierre why she had sent for him. She was afraid that the count or Bolkónski, who might arrive at any moment, if they knew of this affair (which she hoped to hide from them) might challenge Anatole to a duel, and she therefore asked Pierre to tell his brother-in-law in her name to leave Moscow and not dare to let her set eyes on him again. Pierre—only now realizing the danger to the old count, Nicholas, and Prince Andrew—promised to do as she wished. Having briefly and exactly explained her wishes to him, she let him go to the drawing room.

"Mind, the count knows nothing. Behave as if you know nothing either," she said. "And I will go and tell her it is no use expecting him! And stay to dinner if you care to!" she called after Pierre.

Pierre met the old count, who seemed nervous and upset. That morning Natásha had told him that she had rejected Bolkónski.

"Troubles, troubles, my dear fellow!" he said to Pierre. "What troubles one has with these girls without their mother! I do so regret having come here. . . . I will be frank with you. Have you heard she has broken off her engagement without consulting anybody? It's true this engagement never was much to my liking. Of course he is an excellent man, but still, with his father's disapproval they wouldn't have been happy, and Natásha won't lack suitors. Still, it has been going on so long, and to take such a step without father's or mother's consent! And now she's ill, and God knows what! It's hard, count, hard to manage daughters in their mother's absence. . . ."

Pierre saw that the count was much upset, and tried to change the subject, but the count returned to his troubles.

Sónya entered the room with an agitated face.

"Natásha is not quite well; she's in her room and would like to see you. Márya Dmítrievna is with her and she too asks you to come."

"Yes, you are a great friend of Bolkónski's, no doubt she wants to send him a message," said the count. "Oh dear! Oh dear! How happy it all was!"

And clutching the spare gray locks on his temples the count left the room.

When Márya Dmítrievna told Natásha that Anatole was married, Natásha did not wish to believe it and insisted on having it confirmed by Pierre himself. Sónya told Pierre this as she led him along the corridor to Natásha's room.

Natásha, pale and stern, was sitting beside Márya Dmítrievna, and her eyes, glittering feverishly, met Pierre with a questioning look the moment he entered. She did not smile or nod, but only gazed fixedly at him, and her look asked only one thing: was he a friend, or like the others an enemy in regard to Anatole? As for himself, Pierre evidently did not exist for her.

"He knows all about it," said Márya Dmítrievna pointing to Pierre and addressing Natásha. "Let him tell you whether I have told the truth."

Natásha looked from one to the other as a hunted and wounded animal looks at the approaching dogs and sportsmen.

"Natalya Ilyníchna," Pierre began, dropping his eyes with a feeling of pity for her and loathing for the thing he had to do, "whether it is true or not should make no difference to you, because . . ."

"Then it is not true that he's married!"

"Yes, it is true."

"Has he been married long?" she asked. "On your honor? . . ."

Pierre gave his word of honor.

"Is he still here?" she asked, quickly.

"Yes, I have just seen him."

She was evidently unable to speak, and made a sign with her hands that they should leave her alone.

Chapter XX

PIERRE DID NOT STAY FOR DINNER, BUT LEFT THE ROOM AND WENT AWAY AT ONCE. HE DROVE through the town seeking Anatole Kurágin, at the thought of whom now the blood rushed to his heart and he felt a difficulty in breathing. He was not at the ice-hills, nor at the gypsies', nor at Komoneno's. Pierre drove to the Club. In the Club all was going on as usual. The members who were assembling for dinner were sitting about in groups; they greeted Pierre and spoke of the town news. The footman having greeted him, knowing his habits and his acquaintances, told him there was a place left for him in the small dining room and that Prince Michael Zakhárych was in the library, but Paul Timoféevich had not yet arrived. One of Pierre's acquaintances, while they were talking about the weather, asked if he had heard of Kurágin's abduction of Rostóva which was talked of in the town, and was it true? Pierre laughed and said it was nonsense for he had just come from the Rostóvs'. He asked everyone about Anatole. One man told him he had not come yet, and another that he was coming to dinner. Pierre felt it strange to see this calm, indifferent crowd of people unaware of what was going on in his soul. He paced through the ballroom, waited till everyone had come, and as Anatole had not turned up, did not stay for dinner but drove home.

Anatole, for whom Pierre was looking, dined that day with Dólokhov, consulting him as to how to remedy this unfortunate affair. It seemed to him essential to see Natásha. In the evening he drove to his sister's to discuss with her how to arrange a meeting. When Pierre returned home after vainly hunting all over Moscow, his valet informed him that Prince Anatole was with the countess. The countess's drawing room was full of guests.

Pierre without greeting his wife whom he had not seen since his return—at that moment she was more repulsive to him than ever—entered the drawing room and seeing Anatole went up to him.

"Ah, Pierre," said the countess going up to her husband. "You don't know what a plight our Anatole . . ."

She stopped, seeing in the forward thrust of her husband's head, in his glowing eyes and his resolute gait, the terrible indications of that rage and strength which she knew, and had herself experienced after his duel with Dólokhov.

"Where you are, there is vice and evil!" said Pierre to his wife. "Anatole, come with me! I must speak to you," he added in French.

Anatole glanced round at his sister and rose submissively, ready to follow Pierre. Pierre, taking him by the arm, pulled him toward himself and was leading him from the room.

"If you allow yourself in my drawing room . . ." whispered Hélène, but Pierre did not reply and went out of the room.

Anatole followed him with his usual jaunty step but his face betrayed anxiety.

Having entered his study Pierre closed the door, and addressed Anatole without looking at him.

"You promised Countess Rostóva to marry her and were about to elope with her, is that so?"

"Mon cher," answered Anatole (their whole conversation was in French), "I don't consider myself bound to answer questions put to me in that tone."

Pierre's face, already pale, became distorted by fury. He seized Anatole by the collar of his uniform with his big hand, and shook him from side to side till Anatole's face showed a sufficient degree of terror.

"When I tell you that I must talk to you! . . ." repeated Pierre.

"Come now, this is stupid. What?" said Anatole, fingering a button of his collar that had been wrenched loose with a bit of the cloth.

"You're a scoundrel and a blackguard, and I don't know what deprives me from the pleasure of smashing your head with this!" said Pierre, expressing himself so artificially because he was talking French.

He took a heavy paper-weight and lifted it threateningly, but at once put it back in its place.

"Did you promise to marry her?"

"I . . . I . . . I didn't think of it. I never promised, because . . ."

Pierre interrupted him.

"Have you any letters of hers? Any letters?" he said, moving toward Anatole.

Anatole glanced at him and immediately thrust his hand into his pocket and drew out his pocketbook.

Pierre took the letter Anatole handed him, and pushing aside a table that stood in his way, threw himself on the sofa.

"I shan't be violent, don't be afraid!" said Pierre in answer to a frightened gesture of Anatole's. "First, the letters," said he, as if repeating a lesson to himself. "Secondly," he continued after a short pause, again rising and again pacing the room, "tomorrow you must get out of Moscow."

"But how can I? . . ."

"Thirdly," Pierre continued without listening to him, "you must never breathe a word of what has passed between you and Countess Rostóva. I know I can't prevent your doing so, but if you have a spark of conscience . . ." Pierre paced the room several times in silence.

Anatole sat at a table frowning and biting his lips.

"After all, you must understand that besides your pleasure there is such a thing as other people's happiness and peace, and that you are ruining a whole life for the sake of amusing yourself! Amuse yourself with women like my wife—with them you are within your rights, for they know what you want of them. They are armed against you by the same experience of debauchery; but to promise a *maid* to marry her . . . to deceive, to kidnap. . . . Don't you understand that it is as mean as beating an old man or a child? . . ."

Pierre paused and looked at Anatole no longer with an angry but with a questioning look.

"I don't know about that, eh?" said Anatole, growing more confident as Pierre mastered his wrath. "I don't know that and don't want to," he said, not looking at Pierre and with a slight tremor of his lower jaw, "but you have used such words to me—'mean' and so on, which as a man of honor I can't allow anyone to use."

Pierre glanced at him with amazement, unable to understand what he wanted.

"Though it was tête-à-tête," Anatole continued, "still I can't . . ."

"Is it satisfaction you want?" said Pierre ironically.

"You could at least take back your words. What? If you want me to do as you wish, eh?"

"I take them back, I take them back!" said Pierre, "and I ask you to forgive me." Pierre involuntarily glanced at the loose button. "And if you require money for your journey . . ."

Anatole smiled. The expression of that base and cringing smile, which Pierre knew so well in his wife, revolted him.

"Oh, vile and heartless brood!" he exclaimed, and left the room.

Next day Anatole left for Petersburg.

Chapter XXI

Pierre drove to Márya Dmítrievna's to tell her of the fulfillment of her wish that Kurágin should be banished from Moscow. The whole house was in a state of alarm and commotion. Natásha was very ill, having, as Márya Dmítrievna told him in secret, poisoned herself the night after she had been told that Anatole was married, with some arsenic she had stealthily procured. After swallowing a little she had been so frightened that she woke Sónya and told her what she had done. The necessary antidotes had been administered in time and she was now out of danger, though still so weak that it was out of the question to move her to the country, and so the countess had been sent for. Pierre saw the distracted count, and Sónya, who had a tear-stained face, but he could not see Natásha.

Pierre dined at the club that day and heard on all sides gossip about the attempted abduction of Rostóva. He resolutely denied these rumors, assuring everyone that nothing had happened except that his brother-in-law had proposed to her and been refused. It seemed to Pierre that it was his duty to conceal the whole affair and re-establish Natásha's reputation.

He was awaiting Prince Andrew's return with dread, and went every day to the old prince's for news of him.

Old Prince Bolkónski heard all the rumors current in the town from Mademoiselle Bourienne,and had read the note to Princess Mary in which Natásha had broken off her engagement. He seemed in better spirits than usual and awaited his son with great impatience.

Some days after Anatole's departure Pierre received a note from Prince Andrew, informing him of his arrival and asking him to come to see him.

Directly he reached Moscow Prince Andrew had received from his father Natásha's note to Princess Mary breaking off her engagement (Mademoiselle Bourienne had purloined it from Princess Mary and given it to the old prince), and he heard from him the story of Natásha's elopement, with additions.

Prince Andrew had arrived in the evening and Pierre came to see him next morning. Pierre expected to find Prince Andrew in almost the same state as Natásha, and was therefore surprised on entering the drawing room to hear him in the study talking in a loud animated voice about some intrigue going on in Petersburg. The old prince's voice and another now and then interrupted him. Princess Mary came out to meet Pierre. She sighed, looking toward the door of the room where Prince Andrew was, evidently intending to express her sympathy with his sorrow, but Pierre saw by her face that she was glad both at what had happened and at the way her brother had taken the news of Natásha's faithlessness.

"He says he expected it," she remarked. "I know his pride will not let him express his feelings, but still he has taken it better, far better, than I expected. Evidently it had to be. . . ."

"But is it possible that all is really ended?" asked Pierre.

Princess Mary looked at him with astonishment. She did not understand how he could ask such a question. Pierre went into the study. Prince Andrew, greatly changed and plainly in better health, but with a fresh horizontal wrinkle between his brows, stood in civilian dress facing his father and Prince Meshchérski, warmly disputing and vigorously gesticulating. The conversation was about Speránski—the news of whose sudden exile and alleged treachery had just reached Moscow.

"Now he is censured and accused by all who were enthusiastic about him a month ago," Prince Andrew was saying, "and by those who were unable to understand his aims. To judge a man who is in disfavor and to throw on him all the blame of other men's mistakes is very easy, but I maintain that if anything good has been accomplished in this reign it was done by him, by him alone."

He paused at the sight of Pierre. His face quivered and immediately assumed a vindictive expression.

"Posterity will do him justice," he concluded, and at once turned to Pierre.

"Well, how are you? Still getting stouter?" he said with animation, but the new wrinkle on his forehead deepened. "Yes, I am well," he said in answer to Pierre's question, and smiled.

To Pierre that smile said plainly: "I am well, but my health is now of no use to anyone."

After a few words to Pierre about the awful roads from the Polish frontier, about people he had met in Switzerland who knew Pierre, and about M. Dessalles, whom he had brought from abroad to be his son's tutor, Prince Andrew again joined warmly in the conversation about Speránski which was still going on between the two old men.

"If there were treason, or proofs of secret relations with Napoleon, they would have been made public," he said with warmth and haste. "I do not, and never did, like Speránski personally, but I like justice!"

Pierre now recognized in his friend a need with which he was only too familiar, to get excited and to have arguments about extraneous matters in order to stifle thoughts that were too oppressive and too intimate.

When Prince Meshchérski had left, Prince Andrew took Pierre's arm and asked him into the room that had been assigned him. A bed had been made up there, and some open portmanteaux and trunks stood about. Prince Andrew went to one and took out a small casket, from which he drew a packet wrapped in paper. He did it all silently and very quickly. He stood up and coughed. His face was gloomy and his lips compressed.

"Forgive me for troubling you . . ."

Pierre saw that Prince Andrew was going to speak of Natásha, and his broad face expressed pity and sympathy. This expression irritated Prince Andrew, and in a determined, ringing and unpleasant tone he continued:

"I have received a refusal from Countess Rostóva, and have heard reports of your brother-in-law having sought her hand, or something of that kind. Is that true?"

"Both true and untrue," Pierre began; but Prince Andrew interrupted him.

"Here are her letters and her portrait," said he.

He took the packet from the table and handed it to Pierre.

"Give this to the countess . . . if you see her."

"She is very ill," said Pierre.

"Then she is here still?" said Prince Andrew. "And Prince Kurágin?" he added quickly.

"He left long ago. She has been at death's door."

"I much regret her illness," said Prince Andrew; and he smiled like his father, coldly, maliciously and unpleasantly.

"So Monsieur Kurágin has not honored Countess Rostóva with his hand?" said Prince Andrew, and he snorted several times.

"He could not marry, for he was married already," said Pierre.

Prince Andrew laughed disagreeably, again reminding one of his father.

"And where is your brother-in-law now, if I may ask?" he said.

"He has gone to Peters . . . But I don't know," said Pierre.

"Well, it doesn't matter," said Prince Andrew. "Tell Countess Rostóva that she was and is perfectly free, and that I wish her all that is good."

Pierre took the packet. Prince Andrew, as if trying to remember whether he had something more to say, or waiting to see if Pierre would say anything, looked fixedly at him.

"I say, do you remember our discussion in Petersburg?" asked Pierre, "about . . ."

"Yes," returned Prince Andrew hastily. "I said that a fallen woman should be forgiven, but I didn't say I could forgive her. I can't."

"But can this be compared . . . ?" said Pierre.

Prince Andrew interrupted him and cried sharply:

"Yes, ask her hand again, be magnanimous, and so on? . . . Yes, that would be very noble, but I am unable to follow in that gentleman's footsteps. If you wish to be my friend never speak to me of that . . . of all that! Well, good-bye. So you'll give her the packet?"

Pierre left the room and went to the old prince and Princess Mary.

The old man seemed livelier than usual. Princess Mary was the same as always, but beneath her sympathy for her brother, Pierre noticed her satisfaction that the engagement had been broken off. Looking at them Pierre realized what contempt and animosity they all felt for the Rostóvs, and that it was impossible in their presence even to mention the name of her who could give up Prince Andrew for anyone else.

At dinner the talk turned on the war, the approach of which was becoming evident. Prince Andrew talked incessantly, arguing now with his father, now with the Swiss tutor Dessalles, and showing an unnatural animation, the cause of which Pierre so well understood.

Chapter XXII

THAT EVENING PIERRE WENT TO THE ROSTÓVS' TO FULFILL THE COMMISSION ENTRUSTED TO him. Natásha was in bed, the count at the club, and Pierre, after giving the letters to Sónya, went to Márya Dmítrievna who was interested to know how Prince Andrew had taken the news. Ten minutes later Sónya came to Márya Dmítrievna.

"Natásha insists on seeing Count Peter Kiríllovich," said she.

"But how? Are we to take him up to her? The room there has not been tidied up."

"No, she has dressed and gone into the drawing room," said Sónya.

Márya Dmítrievna only shrugged her shoulders.

"When will her mother come? She has worried me to death! Now mind, don't tell her everything!" said she to Pierre. "One hasn't the heart to scold her, she is so much to be pitied, so much to be pitied."

Natásha was standing in the middle of the drawing room, emaciated, with a pale set face, but not at all shamefaced as Pierre expected to find her. When he appeared at the door she grew flurried, evidently undecided whether to go to meet him or to wait till he came up.

Pierre hastened to her. He thought she would give him her hand as usual; but she, stepping up to him, stopped, breathing heavily, her arms hanging lifelessly just in the pose she used to stand in when she went to the middle of the ballroom to sing, but with quite a different expression of face.

"Peter Kiríllovich," she began rapidly, "Prince Bolkónski was your friend—is your friend," she corrected herself. (It seemed to her that everything that had once been, must now be different.) "He told me once to apply to you . . ."

Pierre sniffed as he looked at her, but did not speak. Till then he had reproached her in his heart and tried to despise her, but he now felt so sorry for her that there was no room in his soul for reproach.

"He is here now: tell him . . . to for . . . forgive me!"

She stopped and breathed still more quickly, but did not shed tears.

"Yes . . . I will tell him," answered Pierre; "but . . ."

He did not know what to say.

Natásha was evidently dismayed at the thought of what he might think she had meant.

"No, I know all is over," she said hurriedly. "No, that can never be. I'm only tormented by the wrong I have done him. Tell him only that I beg him to forgive, forgive, forgive me for everything. . . ."

She trembled all over and sat down on a chair.

A sense of pity he had never before known overflowed Pierre's heart.

"I will tell him, I will tell him everything once more," said Pierre. "But . . . I should like to know one thing. . . ."

"Know what?" Natásha's eyes asked.

"I should like to know, did you love . . ." Pierre did not know how to refer to Anatole and flushed at the thought of him—"did you love that bad man?"

"Don't call him bad!" said Natásha. "But I don't know, don't know at all. . . ."

She began to cry and a still greater sense of pity, tenderness and love welled up in Pierre. He felt the tears trickle under his spectacles and hoped they would not be noticed.

"We won't speak of it any more, my dear," said Pierre, and his gentle, cordial tone suddenly seemed very strange to Natásha.

"We won't speak of it, my dear—I'll tell him everything; but one thing I beg of you, consider me your friend and if you want help, advice, or simply to open your heart to someone—not now, but when your mind is clearer—think of me!" He took her hand and kissed it. "I shall be happy if it's in my power . . ."

Pierre grew confused.

"Don't speak to me like that. I am not worth it!" exclaimed Natásha and turned to leave the room, but Pierre held her hand.

He knew he had something more to say to her. But when he said it he was amazed at his own words.

"Stop, stop! You have your whole life before you," said he to her.

"Before me? No! All is over for me," she replied with shame and self-abasement.

"All over?" he repeated. "If I were not myself, but the handsomest, cleverest and best man in the world, and were free, I would this moment ask on my knees for your hand and your love!"

For the first time for many days Natásha wept tears of gratitude and tenderness, and glancing at Pierre she went out of the room.

Pierre too when she had gone almost ran into the anteroom, restraining tears of tenderness and joy that choked him, and without finding the sleeves of his fur cloak threw it on and got into his sleigh.

"Where to now, your excellency?" asked the coachman.

"Where to?" Pierre asked himself. "Where can I go now? Surely not to the club or to pay calls?" All men seemed so pitiful, so poor, in comparison with this feeling of tenderness and love he experienced: in comparison with that softened, grateful, last look she had given him through her tears.

"Home!" said Pierre, and despite twenty-two degrees of frost Fahrenheit he threw open the bearskin cloak from his broad chest and inhaled the air with joy.

It was clear and frosty. Above the dirty ill-lit streets, above the black roofs, stretched the dark starry sky. Only looking up at the sky did Pierre cease to feel how sordid and humiliating were all mundane things compared with the heights to which his soul had just been raised. At the entrance to the Arbát Square an immense expanse of dark starry sky presented itself to his eyes. Almost in the center of it, above the Prechístenka Boulevard, surrounded and sprinkled on all sides by stars but distinguished from them all by its nearness to the earth, its white light, and its long uplifted tail, shone the enormous and brilliant comet of 1812—the comet which was said to portend all kinds of woes and the end of the world. In Pierre however that comet with its long luminous tail aroused no feeling of fear. On the contrary he gazed joyfully, his eyes moist with tears, at this bright comet which, having traveled in its orbit with inconceivable velocity through immeasurable space, seemed suddenly—like an arrow piercing the earth—to remain fixed in a chosen spot, vigorously holding its tail erect, shining and displaying its white light amid countless other scintillating stars. It seemed to Pierre that this comet fully responded to what was passing in his own softened and uplifted soul, now blossoming into a new life.

Part Nine

Chapter I

FROM THE CLOSE OF THE YEAR 1811 AN INTENSIFIED ARMING AND CONCENTRATING OF THE forces of Western Europe began, and in 1812 these forces—millions of men, reckoning those transporting and feeding the army—moved from the west eastward to the Russian frontier, toward which since 1811 Russian forces had been similarly drawn. On the 12th of June, 1812, the forces of Western Europe crossed the Russian frontier and war began, that is, an event took place opposed to human reason and to human nature. Millions of men perpetrated against one another such innumerable crimes, frauds, treacheries, thefts, forgeries, issues of false money, burglaries, incendiarisms, and murders, as in whole centuries are not recorded in the annals of all the law-courts of the world, but which those who committed them did not at the time regard as being crimes.

What produced this extraordinary occurrence? What were its causes? The historians tell us with naïve assurance that its causes were the wrongs inflicted on the Duke of Oldenburg, the non-observance of the Continental System, the ambition of Napoleon, the firmness of Alexander, the mistakes of the diplomatists, and so on.

Consequently, it would only have been necessary for Metternich, Rumyántsev, or Talleyrand, between a levée and an evening party, to have taken proper pains and written a more adroit note, or for Napoleon to have written to Alexander: "My respected Brother, I consent to restore the duchy to the Duke of Oldenburg"—and there would have been no war.

We can understand that the matter seemed like that to contemporaries. It naturally seemed to Napoleon that the war was caused by England's intrigues (as in fact he said on the island of St. Helena). It naturally seemed to members of the English Parliament that the cause of the war was Napoleon's ambition; to the Duke of Oldenburg, that the cause of the war was the violence done to him; to business men that the cause of the war was the Continental System which was ruining Europe; to the generals and old soldiers that the chief reason for the war was the necessity of giving employment; to the legitimists of that day that it was the need of re-establishing *les bons principes*, and to the diplomatists of that time that it all resulted from the fact that the alliance between Russia and Austria in 1809 had not been sufficiently well concealed from Napoleon, and from the awkward wording of Memorandum No. 178. It is natural that these and a countless and infinite quantity of other reasons, the number depending on the endless diversity of points of view, presented themselves to the men of that day; but to us, to posterity who view the thing that happened in all its magnitude and perceive its plain and terrible meaning, these causes seem insufficient. To us it is incomprehensible that millions of Christian men killed and tortured each other either because Napoleon was ambitious or Alexander was firm, or because England's policy was astute or the Duke of Oldenburg was wronged. We cannot grasp what connection such circumstances have with the actual fact of slaughter and violence: why because the duke was wronged, thousands of men from the other side of Europe killed and ruined the people of Smolénsk and Moscow and were killed by them.

To us, their descendants, who are not historians and are not carried away by the process of research and can therefore regard the event with unclouded common sense, an incalculable number of causes present themselves. The deeper we delve in search of these causes the more of them we find; and each separate cause or whole series of causes appears to us equally valid in itself and equally false by its insignificance compared to the magnitude of the events, and by its impotence—apart from the cooperation of all the other coincident causes—to occasion the event. To us, the wish or objection of this or that French corporal to serve a second term appears as much a cause as Napoleon's refusal to withdraw his troops beyond the Vistula and to restore the duchy of Oldenburg; for had he not wished to serve, and had a second, a third, and a thousandth corporal and private also refused, there would have been so many less men in Napoleon's army and the war could not have occurred.

Had Napoleon not taken offense at the demand that he should withdraw beyond the Vistula, and not ordered his troops to advance, there would have been no war; but had all his sergeants objected to serving a second term then also there could have been no war. Nor could there have been a war had there been no English intrigues and no Duke of Oldenburg, and had Alexander not felt insulted, and had there not been an autocratic government in Russia, or a Revolution in France and a subsequent dictatorship and Empire, or all the things that produced the French Revolution, and so on. Without each of these causes nothing could have happened. So all these causes—myriads of causes—coincided to bring it about. And so there was no one cause for that occurrence, but it had to occur because it had to. Millions of men, renouncing their human feelings and reason, had to go from west to east to slay their fellows, just as some centuries previously hordes of men had come from the east to the west slaying their fellows.

The actions of Napoleon and Alexander, on whose words the event seemed to hang, were as little voluntary as the actions of any soldier who was drawn into the campaign by lot or by conscription. This could not be otherwise, for in order that the will of Napoleon and Alexander (on whom the event seemed to depend) should be carried out, the concurrence of innumerable circumstances was needed without any one of which the event could not have taken place. It was necessary that millions of men in whose hands lay the real power—the soldiers who fired, or transported provisions and guns—should consent to carry out the will of these weak individuals, and should have been induced to do so by an infinite number of diverse and complex causes.

We are forced to fall back on fatalism as an explanation of irrational events (that is to say, events the reasonableness of which we do not understand). The more we try to explain such events in history reasonably, the more unreasonable and incomprehensible do they become to us.

Each man lives for himself, using his freedom to attain his personal aims, and feels with his whole being that he can now do or abstain from doing this or that action; but as soon as he has done it, that action performed at a certain moment in time becomes irrevocable and belongs to history, in which it has not a free but a predestined significance.

There are two sides to the life of every man, his individual life which is the more free the more abstract its interests, and his elemental hive-life in which he inevitably obeys laws laid down for him.

Man lives consciously for himself, but is an unconscious instrument in the attainment of the historic, universal, aims of humanity. A deed done is irrevocable, and its result coinciding in time with the actions of millions of other men assumes an historic significance. The higher a man stands on the social ladder, the more people he is connected with and the more power he has over others, the more evident is the predestination and inevitability of his every action.

"The king's heart is in the hands of the Lord."

A king is history's slave.

History, that is, the unconscious, general, hive-life of mankind, uses every moment of the life of kings as a tool for its own purposes.

Though Napoleon at that time, in 1812, was more convinced than ever that it depended on him, *verser (ou ne pas verser) le sang de ses peuples*—as Alexander expressed it in the last letter he wrote him—he had never been so much in the grip of inevitable laws, which compelled him, while thinking that he was acting on his own volition, to perform for the hive-life—that is to say, for history—whatever had to be performed.

The people of the west moved eastward to slay their fellow-men, and by the law of coincidence thousands of minute causes fitted in and coordinated to produce that movement and war: reproaches for the non-observance of the Continental System, the Duke of Oldenburg's wrongs, the movement of troops into Prussia [undertaken, as it seemed to Napoleon, only for the purpose of securing an armed peace], the French Emperor's love and habit of war coinciding with his people's inclinations, allurement by the grandeur of the preparations, and the expenditure on those preparations and the need of obtaining advantages to compensate for that expenditure, the intoxicating honors he received in Dresden, the diplomatic negotiations which, in the opinion of contemporaries, were carried on with a sincere desire to attain peace, but which only wounded the self-love of both sides, and millions of other causes that adapted themselves to the event that was happening or coincided with it.

When an apple has ripened and falls, why does it fall? Because of its attraction to the earth, because its stalk withers, because it is dried by the sun, because it grows heavier, because the wind shakes it, or because the boy standing below wants to eat it?

Nothing is the cause. All this is only the coincidence of conditions in which all vital organic and elemental events occur. And the botanist who finds that the apple falls because the cellular tissue decays and so forth, is equally right with the child who stands under the tree and says the apple fell because he wanted to eat it and prayed for it. Equally right or wrong is he who says that Napoleon went to Moscow because he wanted it, and perished because Alexander desired his destruction, and he who says that an undermined hill weighing a million tons fell because the last navvy struck it for the last time with his mattock. In historic events the so-called great men are labels giving names to events, and like labels they have but the smallest connection with the event itself.

Every act of theirs, which appears to them an act of their own will, is in an historical sense involuntary and is related to the whole course of history and predestined from eternity.

Chapter II

On the 29th of May Napoleon left Dresden, where he had spent three weeks surrounded by a court that included princes, dukes, kings, and even an emperor. Before leaving, Napoleon showed favor to the emperor, kings and princes who had deserved it, reprimanded the kings and princes with whom he was dissatisfied, presented pearls and diamonds of his own—that is, which he had taken from other kings—to the Empress of Austria, and having, as his historian tells us, tenderly embraced the Empress Marie Louise—who regarded him as her husband, though he had left another wife in Paris—left her grieved by the parting which she seemed hardly able to bear. Though the diplomatists still firmly believed in the possibility of peace and worked zealously to that end, and though the Emperor Napoleon himself wrote a letter to Alexander, calling him *Monsieur mon frère*, and sincerely assured him that he did not want war and would always love and honor him—yet he set off to join his army, and at every station gave fresh orders to accelerate the movement of his troops from west to east. He went in a traveling coach with six horses, surrounded by pages, aides-de-camp, and an escort, along the road to Posen, Thorn, Danzig, and Königsberg. At each of these towns thousands of people met him with excitement and enthusiasm.

The army was moving from west to east, and relays of six horses carried him in the same direction. On the 10th of June, coming up with the army, he spent the night in apartments prepared for him on the estate of a Polish count in the Vilkavisski forest.

Next day, overtaking the army, he went in a carriage to the Niemen, and, changing into a Polish uniform, he drove to the riverbank in order to select a place for the crossing.

Seeing, on the other side, some Cossacks (*les Cosaques*) and the wide-spreading steppes in the midst of which lay the holy city of Moscow (*Moscou, la ville sainte*), the capital of a realm such as the Scythia into which Alexander the Great had marched—Napoleon unexpectedly, and contrary alike to strategic and diplomatic considerations, ordered an advance, and the next day his army began to cross the Niemen.

Early in the morning of the 12th of June he came out of his tent, which was pitched that day on the steep left bank of the Niemen, and looked through a spy-glass at the streams of his troops pouring out of the Vilkavisski forest and flowing over the three bridges thrown across the river. The troops, knowing of the Emperor's presence, were on the look-out for him, and when they caught sight of a figure in an overcoat and a cocked hat standing apart from his suite in front of his tent on the hill, they threw up their caps and shouted: *"Vive l'Empereur!"* and one after another poured in a ceaseless stream out of the vast forest that had concealed them and, separating, flowed on and on by the three bridges to the other side.

"Now we'll go into action. Oh, when he takes it in hand himself, things get hot . . . by heaven! . . . There he is! . . . *Vive l'Empereur!* So these are the steppes of Asia! It's a nasty country all the same. *Au revoir,* Beauché; I'll keep the best palace in Moscow for you! *Au revoir.* Good luck! . . . Did you see the Emperor? *Vive l'Empereur! . . . preur!*—If they make me Governor of India, Gérard, I'll make you Minister of Kashmir—that's settled. *Vive l'Empereur!* Hurrah! hurrah! hurrah! The Cossacks—those rascals—see how they run! *Vive l'Empereur!* There he is, do you see him? I've seen him twice, as I see you now. The little corporal . . . I saw him give the cross to one of the veterans. . . . *Vive l'Empereur!"* came the voices of men, old and young, of most diverse characters and social positions. On the faces of all was one common expression of joy at the commencement of the long-expected campaign and of rapture and devotion to the man in the gray coat who was standing on the hill.

On the 13th of June a rather small, thoroughbred Arab horse was brought to Napoleon. He mounted it and rode at a gallop to one of the bridges over the Niemen, deafened continually by incessant and rapturous acclamations which he evidently endured only because it was impossible to forbid the soldiers to express their love of him by such shouting, but the shouting which accompanied him everywhere disturbed him and distracted him from the military cares that had occupied him from the time he joined the army. He rode across one of the swaying pontoon bridges to the farther side, turned sharply to the left and galloped in the direction of Kóvno, preceded by enraptured, mounted chasseurs of the Guard who, breathless with delight, galloped ahead to clear a path for him through the troops. On reaching the broad river Víliya, he stopped near a regiment of Polish Uhlans stationed by the river.

"Vivat!" shouted the Poles, ecstatically, breaking their ranks and pressing against one another to see him.

Napoleon looked up and down the river, dismounted, and sat down on a log that lay on the bank. At a mute sign from him, a telescope was handed him which he rested on the back of a happy page who had run up to him, and he gazed at the opposite bank. Then he became absorbed in a map laid out on the logs. Without lifting his head he said something, and two of his aides-de-camp galloped off to the Polish Uhlans.

"What? What did he say?" was heard in the ranks of the Polish Uhlans when one of the aides-de-camp rode up to them.

The order was to find a ford and to cross the river. The colonel of the Polish Uhlans, a handsome old man, flushed, and fumbling in his speech from excitement, asked the aide-de-camp whether he would be permitted to swim the river with his Uhlans instead of seeking a ford. In evident fear of refusal, like a boy asking for permission to get on a horse, he begged to be allowed to swim across the river before the Emperor's eyes. The aide-de-camp replied that probably the Emperor would not be displeased at this excess of zeal.

As soon as the aide-de-camp had said this, the old mustached officer, with happy face and sparkling eyes, raised his saber, shouted *"Vivat!"* and, commanding the Uhlans to follow him, spurred his horse and galloped into the river. He gave an angry thrust to his horse, which had grown restive under him, and plunged into the water, heading for the deepest part where the current was swift. Hundreds of Uhlans galloped in after him. It was cold and uncanny in the rapid current in the middle of the stream, and the Uhlans caught hold of one another as they fell off their horses. Some of the horses were drowned and some of the men; the others tried to swim on, some in the saddle and some clinging to their horses' manes. They tried to make their way forward to the opposite bank and, though there was a ford half a verst away, were proud that they were swimming and drowning in this river under the eyes of the man who sat on the log and was not even looking at what they were doing. When the aide-de-camp, having returned and choosing an opportune moment, ventured to draw the Emperor's attention to the devotion of the Poles to his person, the little man in the gray overcoat got up and, having summoned Berthier, began pacing up and down the bank with him, giving him instructions and occasionally glancing disapprovingly at the drowning Uhlans who distracted his attention.

For him it was no new conviction that his presence in any part of the world, from Africa to the steppes of Muscovy alike, was enough to dumbfound people and impel them to insane self-oblivion. He called for his horse and rode to his quarters.

Some forty Uhlans were drowned in the river though boats were sent to their assistance. The majority struggled back to the bank from which they had started. The colonel and some of his men got across and with difficulty clambered out on the further bank. And as soon as they had got out, in their soaked and streaming clothes, they shouted *"Vivat!"* and looked ecstatically at the spot where Napoleon had been but where he no longer was, and at that moment considered themselves happy.

That evening, between issuing one order that the forged Russian paper money prepared for use in Russia should be delivered as quickly as possible, and another that a Saxon should be shot, on whom a letter containing information about the orders to the French army had been found, Napoleon also gave instructions that the Polish colonel who had needlessly plunged into the river should be enrolled in the *Legion d'honneur* of which Napoleon was himself the head.

Quos vult perdere dementat.

Chapter III

The Emperor of Russia had, meanwhile, been in Vílna for more than a month, reviewing troops and holding maneuvers. Nothing was ready for the war that everyone expected and to prepare for which the Emperor had come from Petersburg. There was no general plan of action. The vacillation between the various plans that were proposed had even increased after the Emperor had been at headquarters for a month. Each of the three armies had its own commander-in-chief, but there was no supreme commander of all the forces, and the Emperor did not assume that responsibility himself.

The longer the Emperor remained in Vílna the less did everybody—tired of waiting—prepare for the war. All the efforts of those who surrounded the sovereign seemed directed merely to making him spend his time pleasantly and forget that war was impending.

In June, after many balls and fêtes given by the Polish magnates, by the courtiers, and by the Emperor himself, it occurred to one of the Polish aides-de-camp in attendance that a dinner and ball should be given for the Emperor by his aides-de-camp. This idea was eagerly received. The Emperor gave his consent. The aides-de-camp collected money by subscription. The lady who was thought to be most pleasing to the Emperor was invited to act as hostess. Count Bennigsen, being a landowner in the Vílna province, offered his country house for the fête, and the 13th of June was fixed for a ball, dinner, regatta, and fireworks at Zakret, Count Bennigsen's country seat.

The very day that Napoleon issued the order to cross the Niemen, and his vanguard, driving off the Cossacks, crossed the Russian frontier, Alexander spent the evening at the entertainment given by his aides-de-camp at Bennigsen's country house.

It was a gay and brilliant fête. Connoisseurs of such matters declared that rarely had so many beautiful women been assembled in one place. Countess Bezúkhova was present among other Russian ladies who had followed the sovereign from Petersburg to Vílna, and eclipsed the refined Polish ladies by her massive, so-called Russian type of beauty. The Emperor noticed her, and honored her with a dance.

Borís Drubetskóy, having left his wife in Moscow and being for the present *en garçon* (as he phrased it), was also there and, though not an aide-de-camp, had subscribed a large sum toward the expenses. Borís was now a rich man who had risen to high honors and no longer sought patronage but stood on an equal footing with the highest of those of his own age. He was meeting Hélène in Vílna after not having seen her for a long time, and did not recall the past, but as Hélène was enjoying the favors of a very important personage and Borís had only recently married, they met as good friends of long standing.

At midnight dancing was still going on. Hélène, not having a suitable partner, herself offered to dance the mazurka with Borís. They were the third couple. Borís, coolly looking at Hélène's dazzling bare shoulders which emerged from a dark, gold-embroidered, gauze gown talked to her of old acquaintances, and at the same time, unaware of it himself and unnoticed by others, never for an instant ceased to observe the Emperor who was in the same room. The Emperor was not dancing, he stood in the doorway, stopping now one pair and now another with gracious words which he alone knew how to utter.

As the mazurka began, Borís saw that Adjutant-General Balashëv, one of those in closest attendance on the Emperor, went up to him and contrary to court etiquette stood near him while he was talking to a Polish lady. Having finished speaking to her, the Emperor looked inquiringly at Balashëv and, evidently understanding that he only acted thus because there were important reasons for so doing, nodded slightly to the lady and turned to him. Hardly had Balashëv begun to speak before a look of amazement appeared on the Emperor's face. He took Balashëv by the arm and crossed the room with him, unconsciously clearing a path seven yards wide as the people on both sides made way for him. Borís noticed Arakchéev's excited face when the sovereign went out with Balashëv. Arakchéev looked at the Emperor from under his brow and, sniffing with his red nose, stepped forward from the crowd as if expecting the Emperor to address him. (Borís understood that Arakchéev envied Balashëv and was displeased that evidently important news had reached the Emperor otherwise than through himself.)

But the Emperor and Balashëv passed out into the illuminated garden without noticing Arakchéev who, holding his sword and glancing wrathfully around, followed some twenty paces behind them.

All the time Borís was going through the figures of the mazurka, he was worried by the question of what news Balashëv had brought and how he could find it out before others.

In the figure in which he had to choose two ladies, he whispered to Hélène that he meant to choose Countess Potocka who he thought had gone out onto the veranda, and glided over the parquet to the door opening into the garden, where, seeing Balashëv and the Emperor returning to the veranda, he stood still. They were moving toward the door. Borís, fluttering as if he had not had time to withdraw, respectfully pressed close to the doorpost with bowed head.

The Emperor, with the agitation of one who has been personally affronted, was finishing with these words:

"To enter Russia without declaring war! I will not make peace as long as a single armed enemy remains in my country!"

It seemed to Borís that it gave the Emperor pleasure to utter these words. He was satisfied with the form in which he had expressed his thoughts, but displeased that Borís had overheard it.

"Let no one know of it!" the Emperor added with a frown.

Borís understood that this was meant for him and, closing his eyes, slightly bowed his head. The Emperor re-entered the ballroom and remained there about another half-hour.

Borís was thus the first to learn the news that the French army had crossed the Niemen and, thanks to this, was able to show certain important personages that much that was concealed from others was usually known to him, and by this means he rose higher in their estimation.

The unexpected news of the French having crossed the Niemen was particularly startling after a month of unfulfilled expectations, and at a ball. On first receiving the news, under the influence of indignation and resentment the Emperor had found a phrase that pleased him, fully expressed his feelings, and has since become famous. On returning home at two o'clock that night he sent for his secretary, Shishkóv, and told him to write an order to the troops and a rescript to Field Marshal Prince Saltykóv, in which he insisted on the words being inserted that he would not make peace so long as a single armed Frenchman remained on Russian soil.

Next day the following letter was sent to Napoleon:

MONSIEUR MON FRÈRE—Yesterday I learned that, despite the loyalty with which I have kept my engagements with your Majesty, your troops have crossed the Russian frontier, and I have this moment received from Petersburg a note, in which Count Lauriston informs me, as a reason for this aggression, that your Majesty has considered yourself to be in a state of war with me from the time Prince Kurákin asked for his passports. The reasons on which the Duc de Bassano based his refusal to deliver them to him would never have led me to suppose that that incident could serve as a pretext for aggression. In fact, the ambassador, as he himself has declared, was never authorized to make that demand, and as soon as I was informed of it I let him know how much I disapproved of it, and ordered him to remain at his post. If your Majesty does not intend to shed the blood of our peoples for such a misunderstanding, and consents to withdraw your troops from Russian territory, I will regard what has passed as not having occurred and an understanding between us will be possible. In the contrary case, your Majesty, I shall see myself forced to repel an attack that nothing on my part has provoked. It still depends on your Majesty to preserve humanity from the calamity of another war.

I am, etc.,
(signed) ALEXANDER

Chapter IV

AT TWO IN THE MORNING OF THE 14TH OF JUNE, THE EMPEROR, HAVING SENT FOR BALASHËV AND read him his letter to Napoleon, ordered him to take it and hand it personally to the French Emperor. When dispatching Balashëv, the Emperor repeated to him the words that he would not make peace so long as a single armed enemy remained on Russian soil, and told him to transmit those words to Napoleon. Alexander did not insert them in his letter to Napoleon, because with his characteristic tact he felt it would be injudicious to use them at a moment when a last attempt at reconciliation was being made, but he definitely instructed Balashëv to repeat them personally to Napoleon.

Having set off in the small hours of the 14th, accompanied by a bugler and two Cossacks, Balashëv reached the French outposts at the village of Rykónty, on the Russian side of the Niemen, by dawn. There he was stopped by French cavalry sentinels.

A French non-commissioned officer of hussars, in crimson uniform and a shaggy cap, shouted to the approaching Balashëv to halt. Balashëv did not do so at once, but continued to advance along the road at a walking pace.

The non-commissioned officer frowned, and muttering words of abuse, advanced his horse's chest against Balashëv, put his hand to his saber, and shouted rudely at the Russian general, asking: was he deaf that he did not do as he was told? Balashëv mentioned who he was. The non-commissioned officer began talking with his comrades about regimental matters without looking at the Russian general.

After living at the seat of the highest authority and power, after conversing with the Emperor less than three hours before, and in general being accustomed to the respect due to his rank in the service, Balashëv found it very strange here on Russian soil to encounter this hostile, and still more this disrespectful, application of brute force to himself.

The sun was only just appearing from behind the clouds, the air was fresh and dewy. A herd of cattle was being driven along the road from the village, and over the fields the larks rose trilling, one after another, like bubbles rising in water.

Balashëv looked around him, awaiting the arrival of an officer from the village. The Russian Cossacks and bugler and the French hussars looked silently at one another from time to time.

A French colonel of hussars, who had evidently just left his bed, came riding from the village on a handsome sleek gray horse, accompanied by two hussars. The officer, the soldiers and their horses, all looked smart and well-kept.

It was that first period of a campaign when troops are still in full trim, almost like that of peacetime maneuvers, but with a shade of martial swagger in their clothes, and a touch of the gaiety and spirit of enterprise which always accompany the opening of a campaign.

The French colonel with difficulty repressed a yawn, but was polite and evidently understood Balashëv's importance. He led him past his soldiers and behind the outposts and told him that his wish to be presented to the Emperor would most likely be satisfied immediately, as the Emperor's quarters were, he believed, not far off.

They rode through the village of Rykónty, past tethered French hussar horses, past sentinels and men who saluted their colonel and stared with curiosity at a Russian uniform, and came out at the other end of the village. The colonel said that the commander of the division was a mile and a quarter away and would receive Balashëv and conduct him to his destination.

The sun had by now risen, and shone gaily on the bright verdure.

They had hardly ridden up a hill, past a tavern, before they saw a group of horsemen coming toward them. In front of the group, on a black horse with trappings that glittered in the sun, rode a tall man with plumes in his hat and black hair curling down to his shoulders. He wore a red mantle, and stretched his long legs forward in French fashion. This man rode toward Balashëv at a gallop, his plumes flowing and his gems and gold lace glittering in the bright June sunshine.

Balashëv was only two horses' length from the equestrian with the bracelets, plumes, necklaces and gold embroidery, who was galloping toward him with a theatrically solemn countenance, when Julner, the French colonel, whispered respectfully: "The King of Naples!" It was, in fact, Murat, now called "King of Naples." Though it was quite incomprehensible why he should be King of Naples, he was called so, and was himself convinced that he was so, and therefore assumed a more solemn and important air than formerly. He was so sure that he really was the King of Naples that when, on the eve of his departure from that city, while walking through the streets with his wife, some Italians called out to him: *"Viva il re!"* he turned to his wife with a pensive smile and said: "Poor fellows, they don't know that I am leaving them tomorrow!"

But though he firmly believed himself to be King of Naples and pitied the grief felt by the subjects he was abandoning, latterly, after he had been ordered to return to military service—and especially since his last interview with Napoleon in Danzig, when his august brother-in-law had told him: "I made you King that you should reign in my way, but not in yours!"—he had cheerfully taken up his familiar business, and—like a well-fed but not over-fat horse that feels himself in harness and grows skittish between the shafts—he dressed up in clothes as variegated and expensive as possible, and gaily and contentedly galloped along the roads of Poland, without himself knowing why or whither.

On seeing the Russian general he threw back his head, with its long hair curling to his shoulders, in a majestically royal manner, and looked inquiringly at the French colonel. The colonel respectfully informed his Majesty of Balashëv's mission, whose name he could not pronounce.

"De Bal-machève!" said the King (overcoming by his assurance the difficulty that had presented itself to the colonel). "Charmed to make your acquaintance, general!" he added, with a gesture of kingly condescension.

As soon as the King began to speak loud and fast his royal dignity instantly forsook him, and without noticing it he passed into his natural tone of good-natured familiarity. He laid his hand on the withers of Balashëv's horse and said:

"Well, general, it all looks like war," as if regretting a circumstance of which he was unable to judge.

"Your Majesty," replied Balashëv, "my master, the Emperor, does not desire war and as your Majesty sees . . ." said Balashëv, using the words *your Majesty* at every opportunity, with the affectation unavoidable in frequently addressing one to whom the title was still a novelty.

Murat's face beamed with stupid satisfaction as he listened to "Monsieur de Bal-machève." But *royauté oblige!* and he felt it incumbent on him, as a king and an ally, to confer on state affairs with Alexander's envoy. He dismounted, took Balashëv's arm, and, moving a few steps away from his suite, which waited respectfully, began to pace up and down with him, trying to speak significantly. He referred to the fact that the Emperor Napoleon had resented the demand that he should withdraw his troops from Prussia, especially when that demand became generally known and the dignity of France was thereby offended.

Balashëv replied that there was nothing offensive in the demand, because . . . but Murat interrupted him.

"Then you don't consider the Emperor Alexander the aggressor?" he asked unexpectedly, with a kindly and foolish smile.

Balashëv told him why he considered Napoleon to be the originator of the war.

"Oh, my dear general!" Murat again interrupted him, "with all my heart I wish the Emperors may arrange the affair between them, and that the war begun by no wish of mine may finish as quickly as possible!" said he, in the tone of a servant who wants to remain good friends with another despite a quarrel between their masters.

And he went on to inquiries about the Grand Duke and the state of his health, and to reminiscences of the gay and amusing times he had spent with him in Naples. Then suddenly, as if remembering his royal dignity, Murat solemnly drew himself up, assumed the pose in which he had stood at his coronation and, waving his right arm, said:

"I won't detain you longer, general. I wish success to your mission," and with his embroidered red mantle, his flowing feathers, and his glittering ornaments, he rejoined his suite who were respectfully awaiting him.

Balashëv rode on, supposing from Murat's words that he would very soon be brought before Napoleon himself. But instead of that, at the next village the sentinels of Davout's infantry corps detained him as the pickets of the vanguard had done, and an adjutant of the corps-commander, who was fetched, conducted him into the village to Marshal Davout.

Chapter V

DAVOUT WAS TO NAPOLEON WHAT ARAKCHÉEV WAS TO ALEXANDER—THOUGH NOT A COWARD like Arakchéev, he was as precise, as cruel, and as unable to express his devotion to his monarch except by cruelty.

In the organism of States such men are necessary, as wolves are necessary in the organism of Nature, and they always exist, always appear and hold their own, however incongruous their presence and their proximity to the head of the government may be. This inevitability alone can explain how the cruel Arakchéev, who tore out a grenadier's mustache with his own hands, whose weak nerves rendered him unable to face danger, and who was neither an educated man nor a courtier, was able to maintain his powerful position with Alexander, whose own character was chivalrous, noble, and gentle.

Balashëv found Davout seated on a barrel in the shed of a peasant's hut, writing—he was auditing accounts. Better quarters could have been found him, but Marshal Davout was one of those men who purposely put themselves in most depressing conditions to have a justification for being gloomy. For the same reason they are always hard at work and in a hurry. "How can I think of the bright side of life when, as you see, I am sitting on a barrel and working in a dirty shed?" the expression of his face seemed to say. The chief pleasure and necessity of such men, when they encounter anyone who shows animation, is to flaunt their own dreary, persistent activity. Davout allowed himself that pleasure when Balashëv was brought in. He became still more absorbed in his task when the Russian general entered, and after glancing over his spectacles at Balashëv's face, which was animated by the beauty of the morning and by his talk with Murat, he did not rise or even stir, but scowled still more and sneered malevolently.

When he noticed in Balashëv's face the disagreeable impression this reception produced, Davout raised his head and coldly asked what he wanted.

Thinking he could have been received in such a manner only because Davout did not know that he was adjutant-general to the Emperor Alexander and even his envoy to Napoleon, Balashëv hastened to inform him of his rank and mission. Contrary to his expectation, Davout, after hearing him, became still surlier and ruder.

"Where is your dispatch?" he inquired. "Give it to me. I will send it to the Emperor."

Balashëv replied that he had been ordered to hand it personally to the Emperor.

"Your Emperor's orders are obeyed in your army, but here," said Davout, "you must do as you're told."

And, as if to make the Russian general still more conscious of his dependence on brute force, Davout sent an adjutant to call the officer on duty.

Balashëv took out the packet containing the Emperor's letter and laid it on the table (made of a door with its hinges still hanging on it, laid across two barrels). Davout took the packet and read the inscription.

"You are perfectly at liberty to treat me with respect or not," protested Balashëv, "but permit me to observe that I have the honor to be adjutant-general to his Majesty. . . ."

Davout glanced at him silently and plainly derived pleasure from the signs of agitation and confusion which appeared on Balashëv's face.

"You will be treated as is fitting," said he and, putting the packet in his pocket, left the shed.

A minute later the marshal's adjutant, de Castrès, came in and conducted Balashëv to the quarters assigned him.

That day he dined with the marshal, at the same board on the barrels.

Next day Davout rode out early, and after asking Balashëv to come to him, peremptorily requested him to remain there, to move on with the baggage-train should orders come for it to move, and to talk to no one except Monsieur de Castrès.

After four days of solitude, ennui, and consciousness of his impotence and insignificance—particularly acute by contrast with the sphere of power in which he had so lately moved—and after several marches with the marshal's baggage and the French army, which occupied the whole district, Balashëv was brought to Vílna—now occupied by the French—through the very gate by which he had left it four days previously.

Next day the imperial gentleman-in-waiting, the Comte de Turenne, came to Balashëv and informed him of the Emperor Napoleon's wish to honor him with an audience.

Four days before, sentinels of the Preobrazhénsk regiment had stood in front of the house to which Balashëv was conducted, and now two French grenadiers stood there in blue uniforms unfastened in front and with shaggy caps on their heads, and an escort of hussars and Uhlans and a brilliant suite of aides-de-camp, pages, and generals, who were waiting for Napoleon to come out, were standing at the porch, round his saddle-horse and his Mameluke, Rustan. Napoleon received Balashëv in the very house in Vílna from which Alexander had dispatched him on his mission.

Chapter VI

THOUGH BALASHËV WAS USED TO IMPERIAL POMP, HE WAS AMAZED AT THE LUXURY AND MAGNIFicence of Napoleon's court.

The Comte de Turenne showed him into a big reception room where many generals, gentlemen-in-waiting, and Polish magnates—several of whom Balashëv had seen at the court of the Emperor of Russia—were waiting. Duroc said that Napoleon would receive the Russian general before going for his ride.

After some minutes, the gentleman-in-waiting who was on duty came into the great reception room and, bowing politely, asked Balashëv to follow him.

Balashëv went into a small reception room, one door of which led into a study, the very one from which the Russian Emperor had dispatched him on his mission. He stood a minute or two, waiting. He heard hurried footsteps beyond the door, both halves of it were opened rapidly; all was silent and then from the study the sound was heard of other steps, firm and resolute—they were those of Napoleon. He had just finished dressing for his ride, and wore a blue uniform, opening in front over a white waistcoat so long that it covered his rotund stomach, white leather breeches tightly fitting the fat thighs of his short legs, and Hessian boots. His short hair had evidently just been brushed, but one lock hung down in the middle of his broad forehead. His plump white neck stood out sharply above the black collar of his uniform, and he smelled of eau-de-Cologne. His full face, rather young-looking, with its prominent chin, wore a gracious and majestic expression of imperial welcome.

He entered briskly, with a jerk at every step and his head slightly thrown back. His whole short corpulent figure with broad thick shoulders, and chest and stomach involuntarily protruding, had that imposing and stately appearance one sees in men of forty who live in comfort. It was evident, too, that he was in the best of spirits that day.

He nodded in answer to Balashëv's low and respectful bow, and coming up to him at once began speaking like a man who values every moment of his time and does not condescend to prepare what he has to say but is sure he will always say the right thing and say it well.

"Good day, general!" said he. "I have received the letter you brought from the Emperor Alexander and am very glad to see you." He glanced with his large eyes into Balashëv's face and immediately looked past him.

It was plain that Balashëv's personality did not interest him at all. Evidently only what took place within *his own* mind interested him. Nothing outside himself had any significance for him, because everything in the world, it seemed to him, depended entirely on his will.

"I do not, and did not, desire war," he continued, "but it has been forced on me. Even *now*" (he emphasized the word) "I am ready to receive any explanations you can give me."

And he began clearly and concisely to explain his reasons for dissatisfaction with the Russian government. Judging by the calmly moderate and amicable tone in which the French Emperor spoke, Balashëv was firmly persuaded that he wished for peace and intended to enter into negotiations.

When Napoleon, having finished speaking, looked inquiringly at the Russian envoy, Balashëv began a speech he had prepared long before: "Sire! The Emperor, my master . . ." but the sight of the Emperor's eyes bent on him confused him. "You are flurried—compose yourself!" Napoleon seemed to say, as with a scarcely perceptible smile he looked at Balashëv's uniform and sword.

Balashëv recovered himself and began to speak. He said that the Emperor Alexander did not consider Kurákin's demand for his passports a sufficient cause for war; that Kurákin had acted on his own initiative and without his sovereign's assent, that the Emperor Alexander did not desire war, and had no relations with England.

"Not *yet!*" interposed Napoleon, and, as if fearing to give vent to his feelings, he frowned and nodded slightly as a sign that Balashëv might proceed.

After saying all he had been instructed to say, Balashëv added that the Emperor Alexander wished for peace, but would not enter into negotiations except on condition that . . . Here Balashëv hesitated: he remembered the words the Emperor Alexander had not written in his letter, but had specially inserted in the rescript to Saltykóv and had told Balashëv to repeat to Napoleon. Balashëv remembered these words, "So long as a single armed foe remains on Russian soil," but some complex feeling restrained him. He could not utter them, though he wished to do so. He grew confused and said: "On condition that the French army retires beyond the Niemen."

Napoleon noticed Balashëv's embarrassment when uttering these last words; his face twitched and the calf of his left leg began to quiver rhythmically. Without moving from where he stood he began speaking in a louder tone and more hurriedly than before. During the speech that followed, Balashëv, who more than once lowered his eyes, involuntarily noticed the quivering of Napoleon's left leg which increased the more, the more Napoleon raised his voice.

"I desire peace, no less than the Emperor Alexander," he began. "Have I not for eighteen months been doing everything to obtain it? I have waited eighteen months for explanations. But in order to begin negotiations, what is demanded of me?" he said, frowning and making an energetic gesture of inquiry with his small white plump hand.

"The withdrawal of your army beyond the Niemen, sire," replied Balashëv.

"The Niemen?" repeated Napoleon. "So now you want me to retire beyond the Niemen—only the Niemen?" repeated Napoleon, looking straight at Balashëv.

The latter bowed his head respectfully.

Instead of the demand of four months earlier to withdraw from Pomerania, only a withdrawal beyond the Niemen was now demanded. Napoleon turned quickly and began to pace the room.

"You say the demand now is that I am to withdraw beyond the Niemen before commencing negotiations, but in just the same way two months ago the demand was that I should withdraw beyond the Vistula and the Oder, and yet you are willing to negotiate."

He went in silence from one corner of the room to the other and again stopped in front of Balashëv. Balashëv noticed that his left leg was quivering faster than before and his face seemed petrified in its stern expression. This quivering of his left leg was a thing Napoleon was conscious of. "The vibration of my left calf is a great sign with me," he remarked at a later date.

"Such demands as to retreat beyond the Vistula and Oder may be made to a Prince of Baden, but not to me!" Napoleon almost screamed, quite to his own surprise. "If you gave me Petersburg and Moscow I could not accept such conditions. You say I have begun this war! But who first joined his army? The Emperor Alexander, not I! And you offer me negotiations when I have expended millions, when you are in alliance with England, and when your position is a bad one. You offer me negotiations! But what is the aim of your alliance with England? What has she given you?" he continued hurriedly, evidently no longer trying to show the advantages of peace and discuss its possibility, but only to prove his own rectitude and power and Alexander's errors and duplicity.

The commencement of his speech had obviously been made with the intention of demonstrating the advantages of his position and showing that he was nevertheless willing to negotiate. But he had begun talking, and the more he talked the less could he control his words.

The whole purport of his remarks now was evidently to exalt himself and insult Alexander—just what he had least desired at the commencement of the interview.

"I hear you have made peace with Turkey?"

Balashëv bowed his head affirmatively.

"Peace has been concluded . . ." he began.

But Napoleon did not let him speak. He evidently wanted to do all the talking himself, and continued to talk with the sort of eloquence and unrestrained irritability to which spoiled people are so prone.

"Yes, I know you have made peace with the Turks without obtaining Moldavia and Wallachia; I would have given your sovereign those provinces as I gave him Finland. Yes," he went on, "I promised and would have given the Emperor Alexander Moldavia and Wallachia, and now he won't have those splendid provinces. Yet he might have united them to his empire and in a single reign would have extended Russia from the Gulf of Bothnia to the mouths of the Danube. Catherine the Great could not have done more," said Napoleon, growing more and more excited as he paced up and down the room, repeating to Balashëv almost the very words he had used to Alexander himself at Tilsit. "All that, he would have owed to my friendship. Oh, what a splendid reign!" he repeated several times, then paused, drew from his pocket a gold snuffbox, lifted it to his nose, and greedily sniffed at it.

"What a splendid reign the Emperor Alexander's *might have been!*"

He looked compassionately at Balashëv, and as soon as the latter tried to make some rejoinder hastily interrupted him.

"What could he wish or look for that he would not have obtained through my friendship?" demanded Napoleon, shrugging his shoulders in perplexity. "But no, he has preferred to surround himself with my enemies, and with whom? With Steins, Armfeldts, Bennigsens, and Wintzingerodes! Stein, a traitor expelled from his own country; Armfeldt, a rake and an intriguer; Wintzingerode, a fugitive French subject; Bennigsen, rather more of a soldier than the others, but all the same an incompetent who was unable to do anything in 1807 and who should awaken terrible memories in the Emperor Alexander's mind. . . . Granted that were they competent they might be made use of," continued Napoleon—hardly able to keep pace in words with the rush of thoughts that incessantly sprang up, proving how right and strong he was (in his perception the two were one and the same)—"but they are not even that! They are neither fit for war nor peace! Barclay is said to be the most capable of them all, but I cannot say so, judging by his first movements. And what are they doing, all these courtiers? Pfuel proposes, Armfeldt disputes, Bennigsen considers, and Barclay, called on to act, does not know what to decide on, and time passes bringing no result. Bagratión alone is a military man. He's stupid, but he has experience, a quick eye, and resolution. . . . And what rôle is your young monarch playing in that monstrous crowd? They compromise him and throw on him the responsibility for all that happens. A sovereign should not be with the army unless he is a general!" said Napoleon, evidently uttering these words as a direct challenge to the Emperor. He knew how Alexander desired to be a military commander.

"The campaign began only a week ago, and you haven't even been able to defend Vílna. You are cut in two and have been driven out of the Polish provinces. Your army is grumbling."

"On the contrary, your Majesty," said Balashëv, hardly able to remember what had been said to him and following these verbal fireworks with difficulty, "the troops are burning with eagerness . . ."

"I know everything!" Napoleon interrupted him. "I know everything. I know the number of your battalions as exactly as I know my own. You have not two hundred thousand men, and I have three times that number. I give you my word of honor," said Napoleon, forgetting that his word of honor could carry no weight—"I give you my word of honor that I have five hundred and thirty thousand men this side of the Vistula. The Turks will be of no use to you; they are worth nothing and have shown it by making peace with you. As for the Swedes—it is their fate to be governed by mad kings. Their king was insane and they changed him for another—Bernadotte, who promptly went mad—for no Swede would ally himself with Russia unless he were mad."

Napoleon grinned maliciously and again raised his snuffbox to his nose.

Balashëv knew how to reply to each of Napoleon's remarks, and would have done so; he continually made the gesture of a man wishing to say something, but Napoleon always interrupted him. To the alleged insanity of the Swedes, Balashëv wished to reply that when Russia is on her side Sweden is practically an island: but Napoleon gave an angry exclamation to drown his voice. Napoleon was in that state of irritability in which a man has to talk, talk, and talk, merely to convince himself that he is in the right. Balashëv began to feel uncomfortable: as envoy he feared to demean his dignity and felt the necessity of replying; but, as a man, he shrank before the transport of groundless wrath that had evidently seized Napoleon. He knew that none of the words now uttered by Napoleon had any significance, and that Napoleon himself would be ashamed of them when he came to his senses. Balashëv stood with downcast eyes, looking at the movements of Napoleon's stout legs and trying to avoid meeting his eyes.

"But what do I care about your allies?" said Napoleon. "I have allies—the Poles. There are eighty thousand of them and they fight like lions. And there will be two hundred thousand of them."

And probably still more perturbed by the fact that he had uttered this obvious falsehood, and that Balashëv still stood silently before him in the same attitude of submission to fate, Napoleon abruptly turned round, drew close to Balashëv's face, and gesticulating rapidly and energetically with his white hands, almost shouted:

"Know that if you stir up Prussia against me, I'll wipe it off the map of Europe!" he declared, his face pale and distorted by anger, and he struck one of his small hands energetically with the other. "Yes, I will throw you back beyond the Dvína and beyond the Dnieper, and will re-erect against you that barrier which it was criminal and blind of Europe to allow to be destroyed. Yes, that is what will happen to you. That is what you have gained by alienating me!" And he walked silently several times up and down the room, his fat shoulders twitching.

He put his snuffbox into his waistcoat pocket, took it out again, lifted it several times to his nose, and stopped in front of Balashëv. He paused, looked ironically straight into Balashëv's eyes, and said in a quiet voice:

"And yet what a splendid reign your master *might have had!*"

Balashëv, feeling it incumbent on him to reply, said that from the Russian side things did not appear in so gloomy a light. Napoleon was silent, still looking derisively at him and evidently not listening to him. Balashëv said that in Russia the best results were expected from the war. Napoleon nodded condescendingly, as if to say, "I know it's your duty to say that, but you don't believe it yourself. I have convinced you."

When Balashëv had ended, Napoleon again took out his snuffbox, sniffed at it and stamped his foot twice on the floor as a signal. The door opened, a gentleman-in-waiting, bending respectfully, handed the Emperor his hat and gloves; another brought him a pocket-handkerchief. Napoleon, without giving them a glance, turned to Balashëv:

"Assure the Emperor Alexander from me," said he, taking his hat, "that I am as devoted to him as before: I know him thoroughly and very highly esteem his lofty qualities. I will detain you no longer, general; you shall receive my letter to the Emperor."

And Napoleon went quickly to the door. Everyone in the reception room rushed forward and descended the staircase.

Chapter VII

AFTER ALL THAT NAPOLEON HAD SAID TO HIM—THOSE BURSTS OF ANGER AND THE LAST DRYLY spoken words: "I will detain you no longer, general; you shall receive my letter," Balashëv felt convinced that Napoleon would not wish to see him, and would even avoid another meeting with him—an insulted envoy—especially as he had witnessed his unseemly anger. But, to his surprise, Balashëv received, through Duroc, an invitation to dine with the Emperor that day.

Bessierès, Caulaincourt and Berthier were present at that dinner.

Napoleon met Balashëv cheerfully and amiably. He not only showed no sign of constraint or self-reproach on account of his outburst that morning, but, on the contrary, tried to reassure Balashëv. It was evident that he had long been convinced that it was impossible for him to make a mistake, and that in his perception whatever he did was right, not because it harmonized with any idea of right and wrong, but because *he* did it.

The Emperor was in very good spirits after his ride through Vílna, where crowds of people had rapturously greeted and followed him. From all the windows of the streets through which he rode, rugs, flags, and his monogram were displayed, and the Polish ladies welcoming him, waved their handkerchiefs to him.

At dinner, having placed Balashëv beside him, Napoleon not only treated him amiably but behaved as if Balashëv were one of his own courtiers, one of those who sympathized with his plans and ought to rejoice at his success. In the course of conversation he mentioned Moscow, and questioned Balashëv about the Russian capital, not merely as an interested traveler asks about a new city he intends to visit, but as if convinced that Balashëv, as a Russian, must be flattered by his curiosity.

"How many inhabitants are there in Moscow? How many houses? Is it true that Moscow is called 'Holy Moscow'? How many churches are there in Moscow?" he asked.

And receiving the reply that there were more than two hundred churches, he remarked:

"Why such a quantity of churches?"

"The Russians are very devout," replied Balashëv.

"But a large number of monasteries and churches is always a sign of the backwardness of a people," said Napoleon, turning to Caulaincourt for appreciation of this remark.

Balashëv respectfully ventured to disagree with the French Emperor.

"Every country has its own character," said he.

"But nowhere in Europe is there anything like that," said Napoleon.

"I beg your Majesty's pardon," returned Balashëv, "besides Russia there is Spain, where there are also many churches and monasteries."

This reply of Balashëv's, which hinted at the recent defeats of the French in Spain, was much appreciated when he related it at Alexander's court, but it was not much appreciated at Napoleon's dinner, where it passed unnoticed.

The uninterested and perplexed faces of the marshals showed that they were puzzled as to what Balashëv's tone suggested. "If there is a point we don't see it, or it is not at all witty," their expressions seemed to say. So little was his rejoinder appreciated that Napoleon did not notice it at all, and naïvely asked Balashëv through what towns the direct road from there to Moscow passed. Balashëv, who was on the alert all through the dinner, replied that just as "all roads lead to Rome," so all roads lead to Moscow: there were many roads, and "among them the road through *Poltáva,* which Charles XII chose." Balashëv involuntarily flushed with pleasure at the aptitude of this reply, but hardly had he uttered the word *Poltáva* before Caulaincourt began speaking of the badness of the road from Petersburg to Moscow and of his Petersburg reminiscences.

After dinner they went to drink coffee in Napoleon's study, which four days previously had been that of the Emperor Alexander. Napoleon sat down, toying with his Sèvres coffee cup, and motioned Balashëv to a chair beside him.

Napoleon was in that well-known after-dinner mood which, more than any reasoned cause, makes a man contented with himself and disposed to consider everyone his friend. It seemed to him that he was surrounded by men who adored him: and he felt convinced that, after his dinner, Balashëv too was his friend and worshiper. Napoleon turned to him with a pleasant, though slightly ironic, smile.

"They tell me this is the room the Emperor Alexander occupied? Strange, isn't it, general?" he said, evidently not doubting that this remark would be agreeable to his hearer since it went to prove his, Napoleon's, superiority to Alexander.

Balashëv made no reply and bowed his head in silence.

"Yes. Four days ago in this room, Wintzingerode and Stein were deliberating," continued Napoleon with the same derisive and self-confident smile. "What I can't understand," he went on, "is that the Emperor Alexander has surrounded himself with my personal enemies. That I do not . . . understand. Has he not thought that I may the same?" and he turned inquiringly to Balashëv, and evidently this thought turned him back on to the track of his morning's anger, which was still fresh in him.

"And let him know that I will do so!" said Napoleon, rising and pushing his cup away with his hand. "I'll drive all his Wrtemberg, Baden, and Weimar relations out of Germany . . . Yes. I'll drive them out. Let him prepare an asylum for them in Russia!"

Balashëv bowed his head with an air indicating that he would like to make his bow and leave, and only listened because he could not help hearing what was said to him. Napoleon did not notice this expression; he treated Balashëv not as an envoy from his enemy, but as a man now fully devoted to him, and who must rejoice at his former master's humiliation.

"And why has the Emperor Alexander taken command of the armies? What is the good of that? War is my profession, but his business is to reign and not to command armies! Why has he taken on himself such a responsibility?"

Again Napoleon brought out his snuffbox, paced several times up and down the room in silence, and then, suddenly and unexpectedly, went up to Balashëv and with a slight smile, as confidently, quickly, and simply as if he were doing something not merely important but pleasing to Balashëv, he raised his hand to the forty-year-old Russian general's face, and taking him by the ear, pulled it gently, smiling with his lips only.

To have one's ear pulled by the Emperor was considered the greatest honor and mark of favor at the French court.

"Well, adorer and courtier of the Emperor Alexander, why don't you say anything?" said he, as if it was ridiculous, in his presence, to be the adorer and courtier of anyone but himself, Napoleon. "Are the horses ready for the general?" he added, with a slight inclination of his head in reply to Balashëv's bow. "Let him have mine, he has a *long way to go!*"

The letter taken by Balashëv was the last Napoleon sent to Alexander. Every detail of the interview was communicated to the Russian monarch, and the war began. . . .

Chapter VIII

After his interview with Pierre in Moscow, Prince Andrew went to Petersburg, on business as he told his family, but really to meet Anatole Kurágin whom he felt it necessary to encounter. On reaching Petersburg he inquired for Kurágin but the latter had already left the city. Pierre had warned his brother-in-law that Prince Andrew was on his track. Anatole Kurágin promptly obtained an appointment from the Minister of War and went to join the army in Moldavia. While in Petersburg Prince Andrew met Kutúzov, his former commander who was always well disposed toward him, and Kutúzov suggested that he should accompany him to the army in Moldavia, to which the old general had been appointed commander-in-chief. So Prince Andrew, having received an appointment on the headquarters staff, left for Turkey.

Prince Andrew did not think it proper to write and challenge Kurágin. He thought that if he challenged him without some fresh cause it might compromise the young Countess Rostóva, and so he wanted to meet Kurágin personally in order to find a fresh pretext for a duel. But he again failed to meet Kurágin in Turkey, for soon after Prince Andrew arrived, the latter returned to Russia. In a new country, amid new conditions, Prince Andrew found life easier to bear. After his betrothed had broken faith with him—which he felt the more acutely the more he tried to conceal its effects—the surroundings in which he had been happy became trying to him, and the freedom and independence he had once prized so highly were still more so. Not only could he no longer think the thoughts that had first come to him as he lay gazing at the sky on the field of Austerlitz and had later enlarged upon with Pierre, and which had filled his solitude at Bogucharovo and then in Switzerland and Rome, but he even dreaded to recall them and the bright and boundless horizons they had revealed. He was now concerned only with the nearest practical matters unrelated to his past interests, and he seized on these the more eagerly the more those past interests were closed to him. It was as if that lofty infinite canopy of heaven that had once towered above him had suddenly turned into a low, solid vault that weighed him down, in which all was clear, but nothing eternal or mysterious.

Of the activities that presented themselves to him, army service was the simplest and most familiar. As a general on duty on Kutúzov's staff, he applied himself to business with zeal and perseverance, and surprised Kutúzov by his willingness and accuracy in work. Not having found Kurágin in Turkey, Prince Andrew did not think it necessary to rush back to Russia after him, but all the same he knew that however long it might be before he met Kurágin, despite his contempt for him and despite all the proofs he deduced to convince himself that it was not worth stooping to a conflict with him—he knew that when he did meet him he would not be able to resist calling him out, any more than a ravenous man can help snatching at food. And the consciousness that the insult was not yet avenged, that his rancor was still unspent, weighed on his heart and poisoned the artificial tranquillity which he managed to obtain in Turkey by means of restless, plodding, and rather vainglorious and ambitious activity.

In the year 1812, when news of the war with Napoleon reached Bucharest—where Kutúzov had been living for two months, passing his days and nights with a Wallachian woman—Prince Andrew asked Kutúzov to transfer him to the Western Army. Kutúzov, who was already weary of Bolkónski's activity which seemed to reproach his own idleness, very readily let him go, and gave him a mission to Barclay de Tolly.

Before joining the Western Army which was then, in May, encamped at Drissa, Prince Andrew visited Bald Hills which was directly on his way, being only three versts off the Smolénsk highroad. During the last three years there had been so many changes in his life, he had thought, felt, and seen so much (having traveled both in the east and the west) that on reaching Bald Hills it struck him as strange and unexpected to find the way of life there unchanged and still the same in every detail. He entered through the gates with their stone pillars and drove up the avenue leading to the house as if he were entering an enchanted, sleeping castle. The same old stateliness, the same cleanliness, the same stillness reigned there, and inside there was the same furniture, the same walls, sounds and smell, and the same timid faces, only somewhat older. Princess Mary was still the same timid, plain maiden getting on in years, uselessly and joylessly passing the best years of her life in fear and constant suffering. Mademoiselle Bourienne was the same coquettish, self-satisfied girl, enjoying every moment of her existence and full of joyous hopes for the future. She had merely become more self-confident, Prince Andrew thought. Dessalles, the tutor he had brought from Switzerland, was wearing a coat of Russian cut and talking broken Russian to the servants, but was still the same narrowly intelligent, conscientious, and pedantic preceptor. The old prince had changed in appearance only by the loss of a tooth, which left a noticeable gap on one side of his mouth; in character he was the same as ever, only showing still more irritability and skepticism as to what was happening in the world. Little Nicholas alone had changed. He had grown, become rosier, had curly dark hair, and when merry and laughing, quite unconsciously lifted the upper lip of his pretty little mouth just as the little princess used to do. He alone did not obey the law of immutability in the enchanted, sleeping castle. But though externally all remained as of old, the inner relations of all these people had changed since Prince Andrew had seen them last. The household was divided into two alien and hostile camps, who changed their habits for his sake and only met because he was there. To the one camp belonged the old prince, Madmoiselle Bourienne, and the architect; to the other Princess Mary, Dessalles, little Nicholas, and all the old nurses and maids.

During his stay at Bald Hills all the family dined together, but they were ill at ease and Prince Andrew felt that he was a visitor for whose sake an exception was being made, and that his presence made them all feel awkward. Involuntarily feeling this at dinner on the first day, he was taciturn, and the old prince noticing this also became morosely dumb, and retired to his apartments directly after dinner. In the evening, when Prince Andrew went to him, and, trying to rouse him, began to tell him of the young Count Kámensky's campaign, the old prince began unexpectedly to talk about Princess Mary, blaming her for her superstitions and her dislike of Mademoiselle Bourienne, who, he said, was the only person really attached to him.

The old prince said that if he was ill it was only because of Princess Mary: that she purposely worried and irritated him, and that by indulgence and silly talk she was spoiling little Prince Nicholas. The old prince knew very well that he tormented his daughter and that her life was very hard, but he also knew that he could not help tormenting her and that she deserved it. "Why does Prince Andrew, who sees this, say nothing to me about his sister? Does he think me a scoundrel, or an old fool who, without any reason, keeps his own daughter at a distance and attaches this Frenchwoman to himself? He doesn't understand, so I must explain it, and he must hear me out," thought the old prince. And he began explaining why he could not put up with his daughter's unreasonable character.

"If you ask me," said Prince Andrew, without looking up (he was censuring his father for the first time in his life), "I did not wish to speak about it, but as you ask me I will give you my frank opinion. If there is any misunderstanding and discord between you and Mary, I can't blame her for it at all. I know how she loves and respects you. Since you ask me," continued Prince Andrew, becoming irritable—as he was always liable to do of late—"I can only say that if there are any misunderstandings they are caused by that worthless woman, who is not fit to be my sister's companion."

The old man at first stared fixedly at his son, and an unnatural smile disclosed the fresh gap between his teeth to which Prince Andrew could not get accustomed.

"What companion, my dear boy? Eh? You've already been talking it over! Eh?"

"Father, I did not want to judge," said Prince Andrew, in a hard and bitter tone, "but you challenged me, and I have said, and always shall say, that Mary is not to blame, but those to blame—the one to blame—is that Frenchwoman."

"Ah, he has passed judgment . . . passed judgment!" said the old man in a low voice and, as it seemed to Prince Andrew, with some embarrassment, but then he suddenly jumped up and cried: "Be off, be off! Let not a trace of you remain here! . . ."

Prince Andrew wished to leave at once, but Princess Mary persuaded him to stay another day. That day he did not see his father, who did not leave his room and admitted no one but Mademoiselle Bourienne and Tíkhon, but asked several times whether his son had gone. Next day, before leaving, Prince Andrew went to his son's rooms. The boy, curly-headed like his mother and glowing with health, sat on his knee, and Prince Andrew began telling him the story of Bluebeard, but fell into a reverie without finishing the story. He thought not of this pretty child, his son whom he held on his knee, but of himself. He sought in himself either remorse for having angered his father, or regret at leaving home for the first time in his life on bad terms with him, and was horrified to find neither. What meant still more to him was, that he sought and did not find in himself the former tenderness for his son which he had hoped to reawaken by caressing the boy and taking him on his knee.

"Well, go on!" said his son.

Prince Andrew, without replying, put him down from his knee and went out of the room.

As soon as Prince Andrew had given up his daily occupations, and especially on returning to the old conditions of life amid which he had been happy, weariness of life overcame him with its former intensity, and he hastened to escape from these memories and to find some work as soon as possible.

"So you've decided to go, Andrew?" asked his sister.

"Thank God that I can," replied Prince Andrew. "I am very sorry you can't."

"Why do you say that?" replied Princess Mary. "Why do you say that, when you are going to this terrible war, and he is so old? Mademoiselle Bourienne says he has been asking about you. . . ."

As soon as she began to speak of that, her lips trembled and her tears began to fall. Prince Andrew turned away and began pacing the room.

"Ah, my God! my God! When one thinks who and what—what trash—can cause people misery!" he said with a malignity that alarmed Princess Mary.

She understood that when speaking of "trash" he referred not only to Mademoiselle Bourienne, the cause of her misery, but also to the man who had ruined his own happiness.

"Andrew! One thing I beg, I entreat of you!" she said, touching his elbow and looking at him with eyes that shone through her tears. "I understand you" (she looked down). "Don't imagine that sorrow is the work of *men*. Men are His tools." She looked a little above Prince Andrew's head with the confident, accustomed look with which one looks at the place where a familiar portrait hangs. "Sorrow is sent by *Him*, not by men. Men are His instruments, they are not to blame. If you think someone has wronged you, forget it and forgive! We have no right to punish. And then you will know the happiness of forgiving."

"If I were a woman I would do so, Mary. That is a woman's virtue. But a man should not and cannot forgive and forget," he replied, and though till that moment he had not been thinking of Kurágin, all his unexpended anger suddenly swelled up in his heart.

"If Mary is already persuading me forgive, it means that I ought long ago to have punished him," he thought. And giving her no further reply, he began thinking of the glad vindictive moment when he would meet Kurágin who he knew was now in the army.

Princess Mary begged him to stay one day more, saying that she knew how unhappy her father would be if Andrew left without being reconciled to him, but Prince Andrew replied that he would probably soon be back again from the army, and would certainly write to his father, but that the longer he stayed now the more embittered their differences would become.

"Good-bye, Andrew! Remember that misfortunes come from God, and men are never to blame," were the last words he heard from his sister when he took leave of her.

"Then it must be so!" thought Prince Andrew as he drove out of the avenue from the house at Bald Hills. "She, poor innocent creature, is left to be victimized by an old man who has outlived his wits. The old man feels he is guilty, but cannot change himself. My boy is growing up and rejoices in life, in which like everybody else he will deceive or be deceived. And I am off to the army. Why? I myself don't know. I want to meet that man whom I despise, so as to give him a chance to kill and laugh at me!"

These conditions of life had been the same before, but then they were all connected, while now they had all tumbled to pieces. Only senseless things, lacking coherence, presented themselves one after another to Prince Andrew's mind.

Chapter IX

PRINCE ANDREW REACHED THE GENERAL HEADQUARTERS OF THE ARMY AT THE END OF JUNE. The first army, with which was the Emperor, occupied the fortified camp at Drissa, the second army was retreating, trying to effect a junction with the first one from which it was said to be cut off by large French forces. Everyone was dissatisfied with the general course of affairs in the Russian army, but no one anticipated any danger of invasion of the Russian provinces, and no one thought the war would extend farther than the western, the Polish, provinces.

Prince Andrew found Barclay de Tolly, to whom he had been assigned, on the bank of the Drissa. As there was not a single town or large village in the vicinity of the camp, the immense number of generals and courtiers accompanying the army were living in the best houses of the villages on both sides of the river, over a radius of six miles. Barclay de Tolly was quartered nearly three miles from the Emperor. He received Bolkónski stiffly and coldly, and told him in his foreign accent that he would mention him to the Emperor for a decision as to his employment, but asked him meanwhile to remain on his staff. Anatole Kurágin, whom Prince Andrew had hoped to find with the army, was not there. He had gone to Petersburg, but Prince Andrew was glad to hear this. His mind was occupied by the interests of the center that was conducting a gigantic war, and he was glad to be free for a while from the distraction caused by the thought of Kurágin. During the first four days, while no duties were required of him, Prince Andrew rode round the whole fortified camp and, by the aid of his own knowledge and by talks with experts, tried to form a definite opinion about it. But the question whether the camp was advantageous or disadvantageous remained for him undecided. Already from his military experience and what he had seen in the Austrian campaign, he had come to the conclusion that in war the most deeply considered plans have no significance, and that all depends on the way unexpected movements of the enemy—that cannot be foreseen—are met, and on how and by whom the whole matter is handled. To clear up this last point for himself, Prince Andrew, utilizing his position and acquaintances, tried to fathom the character of the control of the army and of the men and parties engaged in it, and he deduced for himself the following of the state of affairs.

While the Emperor had still been at Vílna, the forces had been divided into three armies. First, the army under Barclay de Tolly, secondly, the army under Bagratión, and thirdly, the one commanded by Tormásov. The Emperor was with the first army, but not as commander-in-chief. In the orders issued it was stated, not that the Emperor would take command, but only that he would be with the army. The Emperor, moreover, had with him not a commander-in-chief's staff but the imperial headquarters staff. In attendance on him was the head of the imperial staff, Quartermaster-

General Prince Volkónski, as well as generals, imperial aides-de-camp, diplomatic officials, and a large number of foreigners, but not the army staff. Besides these, there were in attendance on the Emperor without any definite appointments: Arakchéev, the ex-Minister of War; Count Bennigsen, the senior general in rank; the Grand Duke Tsarévich Constantine Pávlovich; Count Rumyántsev, the Chancellor; Stein, a former Prussian minister; Armfeldt, a Swedish general; Pfuel, the chief author of the plan of campaign; Paulucci, an adjutant-general and Sardinian *émigré*; Wolzogen—and many others. Though these men had no military appointment in the army, their position gave them influence, and often a corps commander, or even the commander-in-chief, did not know in what capacity he was questioned by Bennigsen, the Grand Duke, Arakchéev, or Prince Volkónski, or was given this or that advice, and did not know whether a certain order received in the form of advice emanated from the man who gave it or from the Emperor, and whether it had to be executed or not. But this was only the external condition; the essential significance of the presence of the Emperor and of all these people, from a courtier's point of view (and in an Emperor's vicinity all became courtiers), was clear to everyone. It was this: the Emperor did not assume the title of commander-in-chief, but disposed of all the armies; the men around him were his assistants. Arakchéev was a faithful custodian to enforce order, and acted as the sovereign's bodyguard. Bennigsen was a landlord in the Vílna province who appeared to be doing the honors of the district, but was in reality a good general, useful as an adviser and ready at hand to replace Barclay. The Grand Duke was there because it suited him to be. The ex-Minister Stein was there because his advice was useful and the Emperor Alexander held him in high esteem personally. Armfeldt virulently hated Napoleon and was a general full of self-confidence, a quality that always influenced Alexander. Paulucci was there because he was bold and decided in speech. The adjutants-general were there because they always accompanied the Emperor, and lastly and chiefly Pfuel was there because he had drawn up the plan of campaign against Napoleon, and having induced Alexander to believe in the efficacy of that plan, was directing the whole business of the war. With Pfuel was Wolzogen, who expressed Pfuel's thoughts in a more comprehensible way than Pfuel himself (who was a harsh, bookish theorist, self-confident to the point of despising everyone else) was able to do.

Besides these Russians and foreigners who propounded new and unexpected ideas every day—especially the foreigners, who did so with a boldness characteristic of people employed in a country not their own—there were many secondary personages accompanying the army because their principals were there.

Among the opinions and voices in this immense, restless, brilliant, and proud sphere, Prince Andrew noticed the following sharply defined sub-divisions of tendencies and parties:

The first party consisted of Pfuel and his adherents—military theorists who believed in a science of war with immutable laws—laws of oblique movements, outflankings, and so forth. Pfuel and his adherents demanded a retirement into the depths of the country in accordance with precise laws defined by a pseudo-theory of war, and they saw only barbarism, ignorance, or evil intention, in every deviation from that theory. To this party belonged the foreign nobles, Wolzogen, Wintzingerode, and others, chiefly Germans.

The second party was directly opposed to the first; one extreme, as always happens, was met by representatives of the other. The members of this party were those who had demanded an advance from Vílna into Poland, and freedom from all prearranged plans. Besides being advocates of bold action, this section also represented nationalism, which made them still more one-sided in the dispute. They were Russians: Bagratión, Ermólov (who was beginning to come to the front) and others. At that time a famous joke of Ermólov's was being circulated, that as a great favor he had petitioned the Emperor to make him a German. The men of that party, remembering Suvórov, said that what one had to do was not to reason, or stick pins into maps, but to fight, beat the enemy, keep him out of Russia and not let the army get discouraged.

To the third party—in which the Emperor had most confidence—belonged the courtiers who tried to arrange compromises between the other two. The members of this party, chiefly civilians and to whom Arakchéev belonged, thought and said what men who have no convictions but wish to seem to have some, generally say. They said that undoubtedly war, particularly against such a genius as Bonaparte (they called him Bonaparte now), needs most deeply devised plans and profound scientific knowledge and in that respect Pfuel was a genius, but at the same time it had to be acknowledged that the theorists are often one-sided, and therefore one should not trust them absolutely, but should also listen to what Pfuel's opponents and practical men of experience in warfare had to say, and then choose a middle course. They insisted on the retention of the camp at Drissa, according to Pfuel's plan, but on changing the movements of the other armies. Though, by this course, neither one aim nor the other could be attained, yet it seemed best to the adherents of this third party.

Of a fourth opinion the most conspicuous representative was the Tsarévich, who could not forget his disillusionment at Austerlitz, where he had ridden out at the head of the Guards, in his casque and cavalry uniform as to a review, expecting to crush the French gallantly; but unexpectedly finding himself in the front line had narrowly escaped amid the general confusion. The men of this party had both the quality and the defect of frankness in their opinions. They feared Napoleon, recognized his strength and their own weakness, and frankly said so. They said: "Nothing but sorrow, shame, and ruin will come of all this! We have abandoned Vílna and Vítebsk and shall abandon Drissa. The only reasonable thing left to do is to conclude peace as soon as possible, before we are turned out of Petersburg."

This view was very general in the upper army circles and found support also in Petersburg and from the chancellor, Rumyántsev, who, for other reasons of state, was in favor of peace.

The fifth party consisted of those who were adherents of Barclay de Tolly, not so much as a man but as minister of war and commander-in-chief. "Be he what he may" (they always began like that), "he is an honest, practical man and we have nobody better. Give him real power, for war cannot be conducted successfully without unity of command, and he will show what he can do, as he did in Finland. If our army is well organized and strong and has withdrawn to Drissa without suffering any defeats, we owe this entirely to Barclay. If Barclay is now to be superseded by Bennigsen all will be lost, for Bennigsen showed his incapacity already in 1807."

The sixth party, the Bennigsenites, said, on the contrary, that at any rate there was no one more active and experienced than Bennigsen: "and twist about as you may, you will have to come to Bennigsen eventually. Let the others make mistakes now!" said they, arguing that our retirement to Drissa was a most shameful reverse and an unbroken series of blunders. "The more mistakes that are made the better. It will at any rate be understood all the sooner that things cannot go on like this. What is wanted is not some Barclay or other, but a man like Bennigsen, who made his mark in 1807, and to whom Napoleon himself did justice—a man whose authority would be willingly recognized, and Bennigsen is the only such man."

The seventh party consisted of the sort of people who are always to be found, especially around young sovereigns, and of whom there were particularly many round Alexander—generals and imperial aides-de-camp passionately devoted to the Emperor, not merely as a monarch but as a man, adoring him sincerely and disinterestedly, as Rostóv had done in 1805, and who saw in him not only all the virtues but all human capabilities as well. These men, though enchanted with the sovereign for refusing the command of the army, yet blamed him for such excessive modesty, and only desired and insisted that their adored sovereign should abandon his diffidence and openly announce that he would place himself at the head of the army, gather round him a commander-in-chief's staff and, consulting experienced theoreticians and practical men where necessary, would himself lead the troops, whose spirits would thereby be raised to the highest pitch.

The eighth and largest group, which in its enormous numbers was to the others as ninety-nine to one, consisted of men who desired neither peace nor war, neither an advance nor a defensive camp at the Drissa or anywhere else, neither Barclay nor the Emperor, neither Pfuel nor Bennigsen, but only the one most essential thing—as much advantage and pleasure for themselves as possible. In the troubled waters of conflicting and intersecting intrigues that eddied about the Emperor's headquarters, it was possible to succeed in many ways unthinkable at other times. A man who simply wished to retain his lucrative post would today agree with Pfuel, tomorrow with his opponent, and the day after, merely to avoid responsibility or to please the Emperor, would declare that he had no opinion at all on the matter. Another who wished to gain some advantage would attract the Emperor's attention by loudly advocating the very thing the Emperor had hinted at the day before, and would dispute and shout at the council, beating his breast and challenging those who did not agree with him to duels, thereby proving that he was prepared to sacrifice himself for the common good. A third, in the absence of opponents, between two councils would simply solicit a special gratuity for his faithful services, well knowing that at that moment people would be too busy to refuse him. A fourth while seemingly overwhelmed with work would often come accidentally under the Emperor's eye. A fifth, to achieve his long-cherished aim of dining with the Emperor, would stubbornly insist on the correctness or falsity of some newly emerging opinion, and for this object would produce arguments more or less forcible and correct.

All the men of this party were fishing for rubles, decorations and promotions, and in this pursuit watched only the weather-cock of imperial favor, and directly they noticed it turning in any direction, this whole drone-population of the army began blowing hard that way, so that it was all the harder for the Emperor to turn it elsewhere. Amid the uncertainties of the position, with the menace of serious danger giving a peculiarly threatening character to everything, amid this vortex of intrigue, egotism, conflict of views and feelings, and the diversity of race among these people—this eighth and largest party of those preoccupied with personal interests imparted great confusion and obscurity to the common task. Whatever question arose, a swarm of these drones, without having finished their buzzing on a previous theme, flew over to the new one and by their hum drowned and obscured the voices of those who were disputing honestly.

From among all these parties, just at the time Prince Andrew reached the army, another, a ninth party, was being formed and was beginning to raise its voice. This was the party of the elders, reasonable men experienced and capable in state affairs, who, without sharing any of those conflicting opinions, were able to take a detached view of what was going on at the staff at headquarters, and to consider means of escape from this muddle, indecision, intricacy, and weakness.

The men of this party said and thought that what was wrong resulted chiefly from the Emperor's presence in the army with his military court, and from the consequent presence there of an indefinite, conditional, and unsteady fluctuation of relations, which is in place at court but harmful in an army; that a sovereign should reign but not command the army, and that the only way out of the position would be for the Emperor and his court to leave the army; that the mere presence of the Emperor paralyzed the action of fifty thousand men required to secure his personal safety, and that the worst commander-in-chief if independent would be better than the very best one trammeled by the presence and authority of the monarch.

Just at the time Prince Andrew was living unoccupied at Drissa, Shishkóv, the Secretary of State and one of the chief representatives of this party, wrote a letter to the Emperor which Arakchéev and Balashëv agreed to sign. In this letter, availing himself of permission given him by the Emperor to discuss the general course of affairs, he respectfully suggested—on the plea that it was necessary for the sovereign to arouse a warlike spirit in the people of the capital—that the Emperor should leave the army.

That arousing of the people by their sovereign and his call to them to defend their country—the very incitement which was the chief cause of Russia's triumph in so far as it was produced by the Tsar's personal presence in Moscow—was suggested to the Emperor, and accepted by him, as a pretext for quitting the army.

Chapter X

THIS LETTER HAD NOT YET BEEN PRESENTED TO THE EMPEROR WHEN BARCLAY, ONE DAY AT DINner, informed Bolkónski that the sovereign wished to see him personally, to question him about Turkey, and that Prince Andrew was to present himself at Bennigsen's quarters at six that evening.

News was received at the Emperor's quarters that very day of a fresh movement by Napoleon which might endanger the army—news subsequently found to be false. And that morning Colonel Michaud had ridden round the Drissa fortifications with the Emperor and had pointed out to him that this fortified camp constructed by Pfuel and till then considered a *chef-d'oeuvre* of tactical science which would ensure Napoleon's destruction, was an absurdity, threatening the destruction of the Russian army.

Prince Andrew arrived at Bennigsen's quarters—a country gentleman's house of moderate size, situated on the very banks of the river. Neither Bennigsen nor the Emperor was there, but Chernýshev, the Emperor's aide-de-camp, received Bolkónski and informed him that the Emperor, accompanied by General Bennigsen and Marquis Paulucci, had gone a second time that day to inspect the fortifications of the Drissa camp, of the suitability of which serious doubts were beginning to be felt.

Chernýshev was sitting at a window in the first room with a French novel in his hand. This room had probably been a music room; there was still an organ in it on which some rugs were piled, and in one corner stood the folding bedstead of Bennigsen's adjutant. This adjutant was also there and sat dozing on the rolled-up bedding, evidently exhausted by work or by feasting. Two doors led from the room, one straight on into what had been the drawing room, and another, on the right, to the study. Through the first door came the sound of voices conversing in German and occasionally in French. In that drawing room were gathered, by the Emperor's wish, not a military council (the Emperor preferred indefiniteness) but certain persons whose opinions he wished to know in view of the impending difficulties. It was not a council of war, but, as it were, a council to elucidate certain questions for the Emperor personally. To this semi-council had been invited the Swedish General Armfeldt, Adjutant-General Wolzogen, Wintzingerode (whom Napoleon had referred to as a renegade French subject), Michaud, Toll, Count Stein who was not a military man at all, and Pfuel himself, who, as Prince Andrew had heard, was the mainspring of the whole affair. Prince Andrew had an opportunity of getting a good look at him, for Pfuel arrived soon after himself, and in passing through to the drawing room stopped a minute to speak to Chernýshev.

At first sight, Pfuel, in his ill-made uniform of a Russian general, which fitted him badly like a fancy costume, seemed familiar to Prince Andrew, though he saw him now for the first time. There was about him something of Weyrother, Mack, and Schmidt, and many other German theorist-generals whom Prince Andrew had seen in 1805, but he was more typical than any of them. Prince Andrew had never yet seen a German theorist in whom all the characteristics of those others were united to such an extent.

Pfuel was short and very thin but broad-boned, of coarse, robust build, broad in the hips and with prominent shoulder blades. His face was much wrinkled and his eyes deep set. His hair had evidently been hastily brushed smooth in front of the temples, but stuck up behind in quaint little tufts. He entered the room, looking restlessly and angrily around, as if afraid of everything in that large apartment. Awkwardly holding up his sword, he addressed Chernýshev and asked in German where the Emperor was. One could see that he wished to pass through the rooms as quickly as possible, finish with the bows and greetings, and sit down to business in front of a map, where he would feel at home. He nodded hurriedly in reply to Chernýshev, and smiled ironically on hearing that the sovereign was inspecting the fortifications that he, Pfuel, had planned in accord with his theory. He muttered something to himself abruptly and in a bass voice, as self-assured Germans do—it might have been "stupid fellow" . . . or "the whole affair will be ruined," or "something absurd will come of it" . . . Prince Andrew did not catch what he said and would have passed on, but Chernyshev introduced him to Pfuel, remarking that Prince Andrew was just back from Turkey where the war had terminated so fortunately. Pfuel barely glanced—not so much at Prince Andrew as past him—and said, with a laugh: "That must have been a fine tactical war"; and laughing contemptuously, went on into the room from which the sound of voices was heard.

Pfuel, always inclined to be irritably sarcastic, was particularly disturbed that day, evidently by the fact that they had dared to inspect and criticize his camp in his absence. From this short interview with Pfuel, Prince Andrew, thanks to his Austerlitz experiences, was able to form a clear conception of the man. Pfuel was one of those hopelessly and immutably self-confident men, self-confident to the point of martyrdom as only Germans are, because only Germans are self-confident on the basis of an abstract notion—science, that is, the supposed knowledge of absolute truth. A Frenchman is self-assured because he regards himself personally, both in mind and body, as irresistibly attractive to men and women. An Englishman is self-assured, as being a citizen of the best-organized state in the world, and therefore as an Englishman always knows what he should do and knows that all he does as an Englishman is undoubtedly correct. An Italian is self-assured because he is excitable and easily forgets himself and other people. A Russian is self-assured just because he knows nothing does not want to know anything, since he does not believe that anything can be known. The German's self-assurance is worst of all, stronger and more repulsive than any other, because he imagines that he knows the truth—science—which he himself has invented but which is for him the absolute truth.

Pfuel was evidently of that sort. He had a science—the theory of oblique movements deduced by him from the history of Frederick the Great's wars, and all he came across in the history of more recent warfare seemed to him absurd and barbarous—monstrous collisions in which so many blunders were committed by both sides that these wars could not be called wars, they did not accord with the theory, and therefore could not serve as material for science.

In 1806 Pfuel had been one of those responsible for the plan of campaign that ended in Jena and Auerstadt, but he did not see the least proof of the fallibility of his theory in the disasters of that war. On the contrary, the deviations made from his theory were, in his opinion, the sole cause of the whole disaster, and with characteristically gleeful sarcasm he would remark, "There, I said the whole affair would go to the devil!" Pfuel was one of those theoreticians who so love their theory that they lose sight of the theory's object—its practical application. His love of theory made him hate everything practical, and he would not listen to it. He was even pleased by failures, for failures resulting from deviations in practice from the theory, only proved to him the accuracy of his theory.

He said a few words to Prince Andrew and Chernýshev about the present war, with the air of a man who knows beforehand that all will go wrong, and who is not displeased that it should be so. The unbrushed tufts of hair sticking up behind and the hastily brushed hair on his temples expressed this most eloquently.

He passed into the next room, and the deep, querulous sounds of his voice were at once heard from there.

Chapter XI

PRINCE ANDREW'S EYES WERE STILL FOLLOWING PFUEL OUT OF THE ROOM WHEN COUNT BENNIGSEN entered hurriedly, and nodding to Bolkónski, but not pausing, went into the study, giving instructions to his adjutant as he went. The Emperor was following him, and Bennigsen had hastened on to make some preparations and to be ready to receive the sovereign. Chernýshev and Prince Andrew went out into the porch, where the Emperor, who looked fatigued, was dismounting. Marquis Paulucci was talking to him with particular warmth and the Emperor, with his head bent to the left, was listening with a dissatisfied air. The Emperor moved forward evidently wishing to end the conversation, but the flushed and excited Italian, oblivious of decorum, followed him and continued to speak.

"And as for the man who advised forming this camp—the Drissa camp," said Paulucci, as the Emperor mounted the steps and noticing Prince Andrew scanned his unfamiliar face, "as to that person, sire . . ." continued Paulucci, desperately, apparently unable to restrain himself, "the man who advised the Drissa camp—I see no alternative but the lunatic asylum or the gallows!"

Without heeding the end of the Italian's remarks, and as though not hearing them, the Emperor, recognizing Bolkónski, addressed him graciously:

"I am very glad to see you! Go in there where they are meeting, and wait for me."

The Emperor went into the study. He was followed by Prince Peter Mikháylovich Volkónski and Baron Stein, and the door closed behind them. Prince Andrew, taking advantage of the Emperor's permission, accompanied Paulucci, whom he had known in Turkey, into the drawing room where the council was assembled.

Prince Peter Mikháylovich Volkónski occupied the position, as it were, of chief of the Emperor's staff. He came out of the study into the drawing room with some maps which he spread on a table, and put questions on which he wished to hear the opinion of the gentlemen present. What had happened was that news (which afterward proved to be false) had been received during the night of a movement by the French to outflank the Drissa camp.

The first to speak was General Armfeldt who, to meet the difficulty that presented itself, unexpectedly proposed a perfectly new position away from the Petersburg and Moscow roads. The reason for this was inexplicable (unless he wished to show that he, too, could have an opinion), but he urged that at this point the army should unite and there await the enemy. It was plain that Armfeldt had thought out that plan long ago, and now expounded it not so much to answer the questions put—which, in fact, his plan did not answer—as to avail himself of the opportunity to air it. It was one of the millions of proposals, one as good as another, that could be made as long as it was quite unknown what character the war would take. Some disputed his arguments, others defended them. Young Count Toll objected to the Swedish general's views more warmly than anyone else, and in the course of the dispute drew from his side pocket a well-filled notebook, which he asked permission to read to them. In these voluminous notes Toll suggested another scheme, totally different from Armfeldt's or Pfuel's plan of campaign. In answer to Toll, Paulucci suggested an advance and an attack which, he urged, could alone extricate us from the present uncertainty and from the trap (as he called the Drissa camp) in which we were situated.

During all these discussions Pfuel and his interpreter, Wolzogen (his "bridge" in court relations), were silent. Pfuel only snorted contemptuously and turned away, to show that he would never demean himself by replying to such nonsense as he was now hearing. So when Prince Volkónski, who was in the chair, called on him to give his opinion, he merely said:

"Why ask me? General Armfeldt has proposed a splendid position with an exposed rear, or why not this Italian gentleman's attack—very fine, or a retreat, also good! Why ask me?" said he. "Why, you yourselves know everything better than I do."

But when Volkónski said, with a frown, that it was in the Emperor's name that he asked his opinion, Pfuel rose and, suddenly growing animated, began to speak:

"Everything has been spoiled, everything muddled, everybody thought they knew better than I did, and now you come to me! How mend matters? There is nothing to mend! The principles laid down by me must be strictly adhered to," said he, drumming on the table with his bony fingers. "What is the difficulty? Nonsense, childishness!"

He went up to the map, and speaking rapidly began proving that no eventuality could alter the efficiency of the Drissa camp, that everything had been foreseen, and that if the enemy were really going to outflank it, the enemy would inevitably be destroyed.

Paulucci, who did not know German, began questioning him in French. Wolzogen came to the assistance of his chief, who spoke French badly, and began translating for him, hardly able to keep pace with Pfuel, who was rapidly demonstrating that not only all that had happened, but all that could happen, had been foreseen in his scheme, and that if there were now any difficulties the whole fault lay in the fact that his plan had not been precisely executed. He kept laughing sarcastically, he demonstrated, and at last contemptuously ceased to demonstrate, like a mathematician who ceases to prove in various ways the accuracy of a problem that has already been proven. Wolzogen took his place and continued to explain his views in French, every now and then turning to Pfuel and saying, "Is it not so, your excellency?" But Pfuel, like a man heated in a fight who strikes those on his own side, shouted angrily at his own supporter, Wolzogen:

"Well, of course, what more is there to explain?"

Paulucci and Michaud both attacked Wolzogen simultaneously in French. Armfeldt addressed Pfuel in German. Toll explained to Volkónski in Russian. Prince Andrew listened and observed in silence.

Of all these men Prince Andrew sympathized most with Pfuel, angry, determined, and absurdly self-confident as he was. Of all those present, evidently he alone was not seeking anything for himself, nursed no hatred against anyone, and only desired that the plan, formed on a theory arrived at by years of toil, should be carried out. He was ridiculous, and unpleasantly sarcastic, but yet he inspired involuntary respect by his boundless devotion to an idea. Besides this, the remarks of all except Pfuel had one common trait that had not been noticeable at the council of war in 1805: there was now a panic fear of Napoleon's genius, which, though concealed, was noticeable in every rejoinder. Everything was assumed to be possible for Napoleon, they expected him from every side, and invoked his terrible name to shatter each other's proposals. Pfuel alone seemed to consider Napoleon a barbarian like everyone else who opposed his theory. But besides this feeling of respect, Pfuel evoked pity in Prince Andrew. From the tone in which the courtiers addressed him and the way Paulucci had allowed himself to speak of him to the Emperor, but above all from a certain desperation in Pfuel's own expressions, it was clear that the others knew, and Pfuel himself felt, that his fall was at hand. And despite his self-confidence and grumpy German sarcasm he was pitiable, with his hair smoothly brushed on the temples and sticking up in tufts behind. Though he concealed the fact under a show of irritation and contempt, he was evidently in despair that the sole remaining chance of verifying his theory by a huge experiment and proving its soundness to the whole world, was slipping away from him.

The discussions continued a long time, and the longer they lasted the more heated became the disputes, culminating in shouts and personalities, and the less was it possible to arrive at any general conclusion from all that had been said. Prince Andrew, listening to this polyglot talk and to these surmises, plans, refutations and shouts, felt nothing but amazement at what they were saying. A thought that had long since and often occurred to him during his military activities—the idea that there is not and cannot be any science of war, and that therefore there can be no such thing as a military genius—now appeared to him an obvious truth. "What theory and science is possible about a matter the conditions and circumstances of which are unknown and cannot be defined, especially when the strength of the acting forces cannot be ascertained? No one was or is able to foresee in what condition our or the enemy's armies will be in a day's time, and no one can gauge the force of this or that detachment. Sometimes—when there is not a coward at the front to shout 'We are cut off!' and start running, but a brave and jolly lad who shouts 'Hurrah!'—a detachment of five thousand is worth thirty thousand, as at Schön Grabern, while at times fifty thousand run from eight thousand, as at Austerlitz. What science can there be in a matter in which, as in all practical matters, nothing can be defined and everything depends on innumerable conditions, the significance of which is determined at a particular moment which arrives no one knows when? Armfeldt says our army is cut in half, and Paulucci says we have got the French army between two fires; Michaud says that the worthlessness of the Drissa camp lies in having the river behind it, and Pfuel says that is what constitutes its strength; Toll proposes one plan, Armfeldt another, and they are all good and all bad, and the advantages of any suggestions can be seen only at the moment of trial. And why do they all speak of a 'military genius'? Is a man a genius who can order bread to be brought up at the right time and say who is to go to the right and who to the left? It is only because military men are invested with pomp and power and crowds of sychophants flatter power, attributing to it qualities of genius it does not possess. The best generals I have known were, on the contrary, stupid or absent-minded men. Bagratión was the best, Napoleon himself admitted that. And of Bonaparte himself! I remember his limited, self-satisfied face on the field of Austerlitz. Not only does a good army commander not need any special qualities, on the contrary he needs the absence of the highest and best human attributes—love, poetry, tenderness, and philosophic inquiring doubt. He should be limited, firmly convinced that what he is doing is very important (otherwise he will not have sufficient patience), and only then will he be a brave leader. God forbid that he should be humane, should love, or pity, or think of what is just and unjust. It is understandable that a theory of their 'genius' was invented for them long ago because they have power! The success of a military action depends not on them, but on the man in the ranks who shouts 'We are lost!' or who shouts 'Hurrah!' And only in the ranks can one serve with assurance of being useful."

So thought Prince Andrew as he listened to the talking, and he roused himself only when Paulucci called him and everyone was leaving.

At the review next day the Emperor asked Prince Andrew where he would like to serve, and Prince Andrew lost his standing in court circles forever by not asking to remain attached to the sovereign's person, but for permission to serve in the army.

Chapter XII

BEFORE THE BEGINNING OF THE CAMPAIGN, ROSTÓV HAD RECEIVED A LETTER FROM HIS PARENTS in which they told him briefly of Natásha's illness and the breaking off of her engagement to Prince Andrew (which they explained by Natásha's having rejected him) and again asked Nicholas to retire from the army and return home. On receiving this letter, Nicholas did not even make any attempt to get leave of absence or to retire from the army, but wrote to his parents that he was sorry Natásha was ill and her engagement broken off, and that he would do all he could to meet their wishes. To Sónya he wrote separately.

"Adored friend of my soul!" he wrote. "Nothing but honor could keep me from returning to the country. But now, at the commencement of the campaign, I should feel dishonored, not only in my comrades' eyes but in my own, if I preferred my own happiness to my love and duty to the Fatherland. But this shall be our last separation. Believe me, directly the war is over, if I am still alive and still loved by you, I will throw up everything and fly to you, to press you forever to my ardent breast."

It was, in fact, only the commencement of the campaign that prevented Rostóv from returning home as he had promised and marrying Sónya. The autumn in Otrádnoe with the hunting, and the winter with the Christmas holidays and Sónya's love, had opened out to him a vista of tranquil rural joys and peace such as he had never known before, and which now allured him. "A splendid wife, children, a good pack of hounds, a dozen leashes of smart borzois, agriculture, neighbors, service by election . . ." thought he. But now the campaign was beginning, and he had to remain with his regiment. And since it had to be so, Nicholas Rostóv, as was natural to him, felt contented with the life he led in the regiment, and was able to find pleasure in that life.

On his return from his furlough Nicholas, having been joyfully welcomed by his comrades, was sent to obtain remounts and brought back from the Ukraine excellent horses which pleased him and earned him commendation from his commanders. During his absence he had been promoted captain, and when the regiment was put on war-footing with an increase in numbers, he was again allotted his old squadron.

The campaign began, the regiment was moved into Poland on double pay, new officers arrived, new men and horses, and above all everybody was infected with the merrily excited mood that goes with the commencement of a war, and Rostóv, conscious of his advantageous position in the regiment, devoted himself entirely to the pleasures and interests of military service, though he knew that sooner or later he would have to relinquish them.

The troops retired from Vílna for various complicated reasons of state, political and strategic. Each step of the retreat was accompanied by a complicated interplay of interests, arguments and passions at headquarters. For the Pávlograd Hussars, however, the whole of this retreat during the finest period of summer and with sufficient supplies, was a very simple and agreeable business.

It was only at headquarters that there was depression, uneasiness, and intriguing; in the body of the army they did not ask themselves where they were going or why. If they regretted having to retreat, it was only because they had to leave billets they had grown accustomed to, or some pretty young Polish lady. If the thought that things looked bad chanced to enter anyone's head, he tried to be as cheerful as befits a good soldier and not to think of the general trend of affairs, but only of the task nearest to hand. First they camped gaily before Vílna, making acquaintance with the Polish landowners, preparing for reviews and being reviewed by the Emperor and other high commanders. Then came an order to retreat to Sventsyáni and destroy any provisions they could not carry away with them. Sventsyáni was remembered by the hussars only as the *drunken camp*, a name the whole army gave to their encampment there, and because many complaints were made against the troops, who, taking advantage of the order to collect provisions, took also horses, carriages, and carpets from the Polish proprietors. Rostóv remembered Sventsyáni, because on the first day of their arrival at that small town he changed his sergeant-major, and was unable to manage all the drunken men of his squadron who, unknown to him, had appropriated five barrels of old beer. From Sventsyáni they retired farther and farther to Drissa, and thence again beyond Drissa, drawing near to the frontier of Russia proper.

On the 13th of July the Pávlograds took part in a serious action for the first time.

On the 12th of July, on the eve of that action, there was a heavy storm of rain and hail. In general, the summer of 1812 was remarkable for its storms.

The two Pávlograd squadrons were bivouacking on a field of rye, which was already in ear but had been completely trodden down by cattle and horses. The rain was descending in torrents, and Rostóv, with a young officer named Ilyín, his protégé, was sitting in a hastily constructed shelter. An officer of their regiment, with long mustaches extending onto his cheeks, who after riding to the staff had been overtaken by the rain, entered Rostóv's shelter.

"I have come from the staff, count. Have you heard of Raévski's exploit?"

And the officer gave them details of the Saltánov battle, which he had heard at the staff.

Rostóv, smoking his pipe and turning his head about as the water trickled down his neck, listened inattentively, with an occasional glance at Ilyín, who was pressing close to him. This officer, a lad of sixteen who had recently joined the regiment, was now in the same relation to Nicholas that Nicholas had been to Denísov seven years before. Ilyín tried to imitate Rostóv in everything, and adored him as a girl might have done.

Zdrzhinski, the officer with the long mustache, spoke grandiloquently of the Saltánov dam being "a Russian Thermopylae," and of how a deed worthy of antiquity had been performed by General Raévski. He recounted how Raévski had led his two sons onto the dam under terrific fire, and had charged with them beside him. Rostóv heard the story and not only said nothing to encourage Zdrzhinski's enthusiasm but, on the contrary, looked like a man ashamed of what he was hearing, though with no intention of contradicting it. Since the campaigns of Austerlitz and of 1807 Rostóv knew by experience that men always lie when describing military exploits, as he himself had done when recounting them; besides that, he had experience enough to know that nothing happens in war at all as we can imagine or relate it. And so he did not like Zdrzhinski's tale, nor did he like Zdrzhinski himself who, with his mustaches extending over his cheeks, bent low over the face of his hearer, as was his habit, and crowded Rostóv in the narrow shanty. Rostóv looked at him in silence. "In the first place, there must have been such a confusion and crowding on the dam that was being attacked, that if Raévski did lead his sons there, it could have had no effect except perhaps on some dozen men nearest to him," thought he, "the rest could not have seen how or with whom Raévski came onto the dam. And even those who did see it, would not have been much stimulated by it, for what had they to do with Raévski's tender paternal feelings when their own skins were in danger? And besides, the fate of the Fatherland did not depend on whether they took the Saltánov dam or not, as we are told was the case at Thermopylae. So why should he have made such a sacrifice? And why expose his own children in the battle? I would not have taken my brother Pétya there, or even Ilyín, who's a stranger to me but a nice lad, but would have tried to put them somewhere under cover," Nicholas continued to think, as he listened to Zdrzhinski. But he did not express his thoughts for in such matters, too, he had gained experience. He knew that this tale redounded to the glory of our arms and so one had to pretend not to doubt it. And he acted accordingly.

"I can't stand this any more," said Ilyín, noticing that Rostóv did not relish Zdrzhinski's conversation. "My stockings and shirt . . . and the water is running on my seat! I'll go and look for shelter. The rain seems less heavy."

Ilyín went out and Zdrzhinski rode away.

Five minutes later Ilyín, splashing through the mud, came running back to the shanty.

"Hurrah! Rostóv, come quick! I've found it! About two hundred yards away there's a tavern where *ours* have already gathered. We can at least get dry there, and Mary Hendríkhovna's there."

Mary Hendríkhovna was the wife of the regimental doctor, a pretty young German woman he had married in Poland. The doctor, whether from lack of means or because he did not like to part from his young wife in the early days of their marriage, took her about with him wherever the hussar regiment went, and his jealousy had become a standing joke among the hussar officers.

Rostóv threw his cloak over his shoulders, shouted to Lavrúshka to follow with the things, and—now slipping in the mud, now splashing right through it—set off with Ilyín in the lessening rain, and the darkness that was occasionally rent by distant lightning.

"Rostóv, where are you?"

"Here. What lightning!" they called to one another.

Chapter XIII

In the tavern, before which stood the doctor's covered cart, there were already some five officers. Mary Hendríkhovna, a plump little blonde German, in a dressing-jacket and nightcap, was sitting on a broad bench in the front corner. Her husband, the doctor, lay asleep behind her. Rostóv and Ilyín, on entering the room, were welcomed with merry shouts and laughter.

"Dear me, how jolly we are!" said Rostóv laughing.

"And why do you stand there gaping?"

"What swells they are! Why, the water streams from them! Don't make our drawing room so wet."

"Don't mess Mary Hendríkhovna's dress!" cried other voices.

Rostóv and Ilyín hastened to find a corner where they could change into dry clothes without offending Mary Hendríkhovna's modesty. They were going into a tiny recess behind a partition to change, but found it completely filled by three officers who sat playing cards by the light of a solitary candle on an empty box, and these officers would on no account yield their position. Mary Hendríkhovna obliged them with the loan of a petticoat to be used as a curtain, and behind that screen Rostóv and Ilyín, helped by Lavrúshka who had brought their kits, changed their wet things for dry ones.

A fire was made up in the dilapidated brick stove. A board was found, fixed on two saddles and covered with a horsecloth, a small samovar was produced and a cellaret and half a bottle of rum, and having asked Mary Hendríkhovna to preside, they all crowded round her. One offered her a clean handkerchief to wipe her charming hands, another spread a jacket under her little feet to keep them from the damp, another hung his coat over the window to keep out the draft, and yet another waved the flies off her husband's face, lest he should wake up.

"Leave him alone," said Mary Hendríkhovna, smiling timidly and happily. "He is sleeping well as it is, after a sleepless night."

"Oh, no, Mary Hendríkhovna," replied the officer, "one must look after the doctor. Perhaps he'll take pity on me someday, when it comes to cutting off a leg or an arm for me."

There were only three tumblers, the water was so muddy that one could not make out whether the tea was strong or weak, and the samovar held only six tumblers of water, but this made it all the pleasanter to take turns in order of seniority to receive one's tumbler from Mary Hendríkhovna's plump little hands with their short and not over-clean nails. All the officers appeared to be, and really were, in love with her that evening. Even those playing cards behind the partition soon left their game and came over to the samovar, yielding to the general mood of courting Mary Hendríkhovna. She, seeing herself surrounded by such brilliant and polite young men, beamed with satisfaction, try as she might to hide it, and perturbed as she evidently was each time her husband moved in his sleep behind her.

There was only one spoon, sugar was more plentiful than anything else, but it took too long to dissolve, so it was decided that Mary Hendríkhovna should stir the sugar for everyone in turn. Rostóv received his tumbler, and adding some rum to it asked Mary Hendríkhovna to stir it.

"But you take it without sugar?" she said, smiling all the time, as if everything she said and everything the others said was very amusing and had a double meaning.

"It is not the sugar I want, but only that your little hand should stir my tea."

Mary Hendríkhovna assented and began looking for the spoon which someone meanwhile had pounced on.

"Use your finger, Mary Hendríkhovna, it will be still nicer," said Rostóv.

"Too hot!" she replied, blushing with pleasure.

Ilyín put a few drops of rum into the bucket of water and brought it to Mary Hendríkhovna, asking her to stir it with her finger.

"This is my cup," said he. "Only dip your finger in it and I'll drink it all up."

When they had emptied the samovar, Rostóv took a pack of cards and proposed that they should play "Kings" with Mary Hendríkhovna. They drew lots to settle who should make up her set. At Rostóv's suggestion it was agreed that whoever became "King" should have the right to kiss Mary Hendríkhovna's hand, and that the "Booby" should go to refill and reheat the samovar for the doctor when the latter awoke.

"Well, but supposing Mary Hendríkhovna is 'King'?" asked Ilyín.

"As it is, she is Queen, and her word is law!"

They had hardly begun to play before the doctor's disheveled head suddenly appeared from behind Mary Hendríkhovna. He had been awake for some time, listening to what was being said, and evidently found nothing entertaining or amusing in what was going on. His face was sad and depressed. Without greeting the officers, he scratched himself and asked to be allowed to pass as they were blocking the way. As soon as he had left the room all the officers burst into loud laughter and Mary Hendríkhovna blushed till her eyes filled with tears, and thereby became still more attractive to them. Returning from the yard, the doctor told his wife (who had ceased to smile so happily, and looked at him in alarm, awaiting her sentence), that the rain had ceased and they must go to sleep in their covered cart, or everything in it would be stolen.

"But I'll send an orderly. . . . Two of them!" said Rostóv. "What an idea, doctor!"

"I'll stand guard on it myself!" said Ilyín.

"No, gentlemen, you have had your sleep, but I have not slept for two nights," replied the doctor, and he sat down morosely beside his wife, waiting for the game to end.

Seeing his gloomy face as he frowned at his wife, the officers grew still merrier, and some of them could not refrain from laughter, for which they hurriedly sought plausible pretexts. When he had gone, taking his wife with him, and had settled down with her in their covered cart, the officers lay down in the tavern, covering themselves with their wet cloaks, but they did not sleep for a long time; now they exchanged remarks, recalling the doctor's uneasiness and his wife's delight, now they ran out into the porch and reported what was taking place in the covered trap. Several times Rostóv, covering his head, tried to go to sleep, but some remark would arouse him and conversation would be resumed, to the accompaniment of unreasoning, merry, childlike laughter.

Chapter XIV

It was nearly three o'clock but no one was yet asleep, when the quartermaster appeared with an order to move on to the little town of Ostróvna.

Still laughing and talking, the officers began hurriedly getting ready, and again boiled some muddy water in the samovar. But Rostóv went off to his squadron without waiting for tea. Day was breaking, the rain had ceased and the clouds were dispersing. It felt damp and cold, especially in clothes that were still moist. As they left the tavern in the twilight of the dawn, Rostóv and Ilyín both glanced under the wet and glistening leather hood of the doctor's cart, from under the apron of which his feet were sticking out, and in the middle of which his wife's nightcap was visible and her sleepy breathing audible.

"She really is a dear little thing," said Rostóv to Ilyín, who was following him.

"A charming woman!" said Ilyín, with all the gravity of a boy of sixteen.

Half an hour later the squadron was lined up on the road. The command was heard to "mount" and the soldiers crossed themselves and mounted. Rostóv riding in front gave the order "Forward!" and the hussars, with clanking sabers and subdued talk, their horses' hoofs splashing in the mud, defiled in fours and moved along the broad road planted with birch trees on each side, following the infantry and a battery that had gone on in front.

Tattered, blue-purple clouds, reddening in the east, were scudding before the wind. It was growing lighter and lighter. That curly grass which always grows by country roadsides became clearly visible, still wet with the night's rain; the drooping branches of the birches, also wet, swayed in the wind and flung down bright drops of water to one side. The soldiers' faces were more and more clearly visible. Rostóv, always closely followed by Ilyín, rode along the side of the road between two rows of birch trees.

When campaigning, Rostóv allowed himself the indulgence of riding not a regimental but a Cossack horse. A judge of horses and a sportsman, he had lately procured himself a large, fine, mettlesome, Donéts horse, dun-colored, with light mane and tail, and when he rode it no one could out-gallop him. To ride this horse was a pleasure to him, and he thought of the horse, of the morning, of the doctor's wife, but not once of the impending danger.

Formerly, when going into action, Rostóv had felt afraid; now he had not the least feeling of fear. He was fearless, not because he had grown used to being under fire (one cannot grow used to danger), but because he had learned how to manage his thoughts when in danger. He had grown accustomed when going into action to think about anything but what would seem most likely to interest him—the impending danger. During the first period of his service, hard as he tried and much as he reproached himself with cowardice, he had not been able to do this, but with time it had come of itself. Now he rode beside Ilyín under the birch trees, occasionally plucking leaves from a branch that met his hand, sometimes touching his horse's side with his foot, or without turning round, handing a pipe he had finished to a hussar riding behind him, with as calm and careless an air as though he were merely out for a ride. He glanced with pity at the excited face of Ilyín, who talked much and in great agitation. He knew from experience the tormenting expectation of terror and death the cornet was suffering, and knew that only time could help him.

As soon as the sun appeared in a clear strip of sky beneath the clouds, the wind fell, as if it dared not spoil the beauty of the summer morning after the storm; drops still continued to fall, but vertically now, and all was still. The whole sun appeared on the horizon and disappeared behind a long narrow cloud that hung above it. A few minutes later it reappeared brighter still from behind the top of the cloud, tearing its edge. Everything grew bright and glittered. And with that light, and as if in reply to it, came the sound of guns ahead of them.

Before Rostóv had had time to consider and determine the distance of that firing, Count Ostermann-Tolstóy's adjutant came galloping from Vítebsk with orders to advance at a trot along the road.

The squadron overtook and passed the infantry and the battery—which had also quickened their pace—rode down a hill, and passing through an empty and deserted village again ascended. The horses began to lather and the men to flush.

"Halt! Dress your ranks!" the order of the regimental commander was heard ahead. "Forward by the left. Walk, march!" came the order from in front.

And the hussars, passing along the line of troops on the left flank of our position, halted behind our Uhlans who were in the front line. To the right stood our infantry in a dense column: they were the reserve. Higher up the hill, on the very horizon, our guns were visible through the wonderfully clear air, brightly illuminated by slanting morning sunbeams. In front, beyond a hollow dale, could be seen the enemy's columns and guns. Our advanced line, already in action, could be heard briskly exchanging shots with the enemy in the dale.

At these sounds, long unheard, Rostóv's spirits rose, as at the strains of the merriest music. *Trap-ta-ta-tap!* cracked the shots, now together, now several quickly one after another. Again all was silent and then again it sounded as if someone were walking on detonators and exploding them.

The hussars remained in the same place for about an hour. A cannonade began. Count Ostermann with his suite rode up behind the squadron, halted, spoke to the commander of the regiment, and rode up the hill to the guns.

After Ostermann had gone, a command rang out to the Uhlans.

"Form column! Prepare to charge!"

The infantry in front of them parted into platoons to allow the cavalry to pass. The Uhlans started, the streamers on their spears fluttering, and trotted downhill toward the French cavalry which was seen below to the left.

As soon as the Uhlans descended the hill, the hussars were ordered up the hill to support the battery. As they took the places vacated by the Uhlans, bullets came from the front, whining and whistling, but fell spent without taking effect.

The sounds, which he had not heard for so long, had an even more pleasurable and exhilarating effect on Rostóv than the previous sounds of firing. Drawing himself up, he viewed the field of battle opening out before him from the hill, and with his whole soul followed the movement of the Uhlans. They swooped down close to the French dragoons, something confused happened there amid the smoke, and five minutes later our Uhlans were galloping back, not to the place they had occupied but more to the left, and among the orange-colored Uhlans on chestnut horses and behind them in a large group, blue French dragoons on gray horses could be seen.

Chapter XV

ROSTÓV, WITH HIS KEEN SPORTSMAN'S EYE, WAS ONE OF THE FIRST TO CATCH SIGHT OF THESE blue French dragoons pursuing our Uhlans. Nearer and nearer in disorderly crowds came the Uhlans and the French dragoons pursuing them. He could already see how these men, who looked so small at the foot of the hill, jostled and overtook one another, waving their arms and their sabers in the air.

Rostóv gazed at what was happening before him as at a hunt. He felt instinctively that if the hussars struck at the French dragoons now, the latter could not withstand them, but if a charge was to be made it must be done now, at that very moment, or it would be too late. He looked around. A captain, standing beside him, was gazing like himself with eyes fixed on the cavalry below them.

"Andrew Sevastyánych!" said Rostóv. "You know, we could crush them. . . ."

"A fine thing too!" replied the captain, "and really . . ."

Rostóv without waiting to hear him out touched his horse, galloped to the front of his squadron, and before he had time to finish giving the word of command, the whole squadron, sharing his feeling, was following him. Rostóv himself did not know how or why he did it. He acted as he did when hunting, without reflecting or considering. He saw the dragoons near, and that they were galloping in disorder; he knew they could not withstand an attack—knew there was only that moment and that if he let it slip it would not return. The bullets were whining and whistling so stimulatingly around him and his horse was so eager to go, that he could not restrain himself. He touched his horse, gave the word of command, and immediately, hearing behind him the tramp of the horses of his deployed squadron, rode at full trot downhill toward the dragoons. Hardly had they reached the bottom of the hill before their pace instinctively changed to a gallop, which grew faster and faster as they drew nearer to our Uhlans and the French dragoons who galloped after them. The dragoons were now close at hand. On seeing the hussars, the foremost began to turn, while those behind began to halt. With the same feeling with which he had galloped across the path of a wolf, Rostóv gave rein to his Donéts horse and galloped to intersect the path of the dragoons' disordered lines. One Uhlan stopped, another who was on foot flung himself to the ground to avoid being knocked over, and a riderless horse fell in among the hussars. Nearly all the French dragoons were galloping back. Rostóv, picking out one on a gray horse, dashed after him. On the way he came upon a bush, his gallant horse cleared it, and almost before he had righted himself in his saddle he saw that he would immediately overtake the enemy he had selected. That Frenchman, by his uniform an officer, was going at a gallop, crouching on his gray horse and urging it on with his saber. In another moment Rostóv's horse dashed its breast against the hindquarters of the officer's horse, almost knocking it over, and at the same instant Rostóv, without knowing why, raised his saber and struck the Frenchman with it.

The instant he had done this, all Rostóv's animation vanished. The officer fell, not so much from the blow—which had but slightly cut his arm above the elbow—as from the shock to his horse and from fright. Rostóv reined in his horse, and his eyes sought his foe to see whom he had vanquished. The French dragoon officer was hopping with one foot on the ground, the other being caught in the stirrup. His eyes, screwed up with fear as if he every moment expected another blow, gazed up at Rostóv with shrinking terror. His pale and mud-stained face—fair and young, with a dimple in the chin and light blue eyes—was not an enemy's face at all suited to a battlefield, but a most ordinary, homelike face. Before Rostóv had decided what to do with him, the officer cried, "I surrender!" He hurriedly but vainly tried to get his foot out of the stirrup, and did not remove his frightened blue eyes from Rostóv's face. Some hussars who galloped up disengaged his foot and helped him into the saddle. On all sides, the hussars were busy with the dragoons; one was wounded, but though his face was bleeding, he would not give up his horse; another was perched up behind a hussar with his arms round him; a third was being helped by a hussar to mount his horse. In front, the French infantry were firing as they ran. The hussars galloped hastily back with their prisoners. Rostóv galloped back with the rest, aware of an unpleasant feeling of depression in his heart. Something vague and confused, which he could not at all account for, had come over him with the capture of that officer and the blow he had dealt him.

Count Ostermann-Tolstóy met the returning hussars, sent for Rostóv, thanked him, and said he would report his gallant deed to the Emperor and would recommend him for a St. George's Cross. When sent for by Count Ostermann, Rostóv, remembering that he had charged without orders, felt sure his commander was sending for him to punish him for breach of discipline. Ostermann's flattering words and promise of a reward should therefore have struck him all the more pleasantly, but he still felt that same vaguely disagreeable feeling of moral nausea. "But what on earth is worrying me?" he asked himself as he rode back from the general. "Ilyín? No, he's safe. Have I disgraced myself in any way? No, that's not it." Something else, resembling remorse, tormented him. "Yes, oh yes, that French officer with the dimple. And I remember how my arm paused when I raised it."

Rostóv saw the prisoners being led away, and galloped after them to have a look at his Frenchman with the dimple on his chin. He was sitting in his foreign uniform on a hussar pack-horse, and looked anxiously about him. The sword-cut on his arm could scarcely be called a wound. He glanced at Rostóv with a feigned smile, and waved his hand in greeting. Rostóv still had the same indefinite feeling, as of shame.

All that day and the next his friends and comrades noticed that Rostóv, without being dull or angry, was silent, thoughtful and preoccupied. He drank reluctantly, tried to remain alone, and kept turning something over in his mind.

Rostóv was always thinking about that brilliant exploit of his, which to his amazement had gained him the St. George's Cross and even given him a reputation for bravery, and there was something he could not at all understand. "So others are even more afraid than I am!" he thought.

"So that's all there is in what is called heroism! And did I do it for my country's sake? And how was he to blame, with his dimple and blue eyes? And how frightened he was! He thought that I should kill him. Why should I kill him? My hand trembled. And they have given me a St. George's Cross. . . . I can't make it out at all."

But while Nicholas was considering these questions and still could reach no clear solution of what puzzled him so, the wheel of fortune in the service, as often happens, turned in his favor. After the affair at Ostróvna he was brought into notice, received command of a hussar battalion, and when a brave officer was needed he was chosen.

Chapter XVI

On receiving news of Natásha's illness, the countess, though not quite well yet and still weak, went to Moscow with Pétya and the rest of the household, and the whole family moved from Márya Dmítrievna's house to their own and settled down in town.

Natásha's illness was so serious that, fortunately for her and for her parents, the consideration of all that had caused the illness, her conduct and the breaking off of her engagement, receded into the background. She was so ill that it was impossible for them to consider in how far she was to blame for what had happened. She could not eat or sleep, grew visibly thinner, coughed and, as the doctors made them feel, was in danger. They could not think of anything but how to help her. Doctors came to see her singly and in consultation, talked much in French, German, and Latin, blamed one another, and prescribed a great variety of medicines for all the diseases known to them, but the simple idea never occurred to any of them that they could not know the disease Natásha was suffering from, as no disease suffered by a live man can be known, for every living person has his own peculiarities and always has his own peculiar, personal novel, complicated disease, unknown to medicine—not a disease of the lungs, liver, skin, heart, nerves, and so on mentioned in medical books, but a disease consisting of one of the innumerable combinations of the maladies of those organs. This simple thought could not occur to the doctors (as it cannot occur to a wizard that he is unable to work his charms) because the business of their lives was to cure, and they received money for it and had spent the best years of their lives on that business. But, above all, that thought was kept out of their minds by the fact that they saw they were really useful, as in fact they were to the whole Rostóv family. Their usefulness did not depend on making the patient swallow substances for the most part harmful (the harm was scarcely perceptible, as they were given in small doses), but they were useful, necessary and indispensable, because they satisfied a mental need of the invalid and of those who loved her—and that is why there are, and always will be, pseudo-healers, wise women, homeopaths and allopaths. They satisfied that eternal human need for hope of relief, for sympathy, and that something should be done, which is felt by those who are suffering. They satisfied the need seen in its most elementary form in a child, when it wants to have a place rubbed that has been hurt. A child knocks itself and runs at once to the arms of its mother or nurse to have the aching spot rubbed or kissed, and it feels better when this is done. The child cannot believe that the strongest and wisest of its people have no remedy for its pain, and the hope of relief and the expression of its mother's sympathy while she rubs the bump comforts it. The doctors were of use to Natásha because they kissed and rubbed her bump, assuring her that it would soon pass if only the coachman went to the chemist's in the Arbát and got a powder and some pills in a pretty box for a ruble and seventy kopeks, and if she took those powders in boiled water at intervals of precisely two hours, neither more nor less.

What would Sónya and the count and countess have done, how would they have looked, if nothing had been done, if there had not been those pills to give by the clock, the warm drinks, the chicken cutlets, and all the other details of life ordered by the doctors, the carrying out of which supplied an occupation and consolation to the family circle? How would the count have borne his dearly loved daughter's illness had he not known that it was costing him a thousand rubles, and that he would not grudge thousands more to benefit her, or had he not known that if her illness continued he would not grudge yet other thousands and would take her abroad for consultations there, and had he not been able to explain the details of how Métivier and Feller had not understood the symptoms, but Frise had, and Mudrov had diagnosed them even better? What would the countess have done had she not been able sometimes to scold the invalid for not strictly obeying the doctor's orders?

"You'll never get well like that," she would say, forgetting her grief in her vexation, "if you won't obey the doctor and take your medicine at the right time! You mustn't trifle with it, you know, or it may turn to *pneumonia*," she would go on, deriving much comfort from the utterance of that foreign word, incomprehensible to others as well as to herself.

What would Sónya have done without the glad consciousness that she had not undressed during the first three nights, in order to be ready to carry out all the doctor's injunctions with precision, and that she still kept awake at night so as not to miss the proper time when the slightly harmful pills in the little gilt box had to be administered? Even to Natásha herself it was pleasant to see that so many sacrifices were being made for her sake, and to know that she had to take medicine at certain hours, though she declared that no medicine would cure her and that it was all nonsense. And it was even pleasant to be able to show, by disregarding the orders, that she did not believe in medical treatment and did not value her life.

The doctor came every day, felt her pulse, looked at her tongue, and regardless of her grief-stricken face joked with her. But when he had gone into another room, to which the countess hurriedly followed him, he assumed a grave air and thoughtfully shaking his head said that though there was danger, he had hopes of the effect of this last medicine and one must wait and see, that the malady was chiefly mental, but . . . And the countess, trying to conceal the action from herself and from him, slipped a gold coin into his hand, and always returned to the patient with a more tranquil mind.

The symptoms of Natásha's illness were that she ate little, slept little, coughed, and was always low-spirited. The doctors said that she could not get on without medical treatment, so they kept her in the stifling atmosphere of the town, and the Rostóvs did not move to the country that summer of 1812.

In spite of the many pills she swallowed and the drops and powders out of the little bottles and boxes of which Madame Schoss who was fond of such things made a large collection, and in spite of being deprived of the country life to which she was accustomed, youth prevailed. Natásha's grief began to be overlaid by the impressions of daily life, it ceased to press so painfully on her heart, it gradually faded into the past, and she began to recover physically.

Chapter XVII

NATÁSHA WAS CALMER BUT NO HAPPIER. SHE NOT MERELY AVOIDED ALL EXTERNAL FORMS OF pleasure—balls, promenades, concerts, and theaters—but she never laughed without a sound of tears in her laughter. She could not sing. As soon as she began to laugh, or tried to sing by herself, tears choked her: tears of remorse, tears at the recollection of those pure times which could never return, tears of vexation that she should so uselessly have ruined her young life which might have been so happy. Laughter and singing in particular seemed to her like a blasphemy, in face of her sorrow. Without any need of self-restraint, no wish to coquet ever entered her head. She said and felt at that time that no man was more to her than Nastásya Ivánovna, the buffoon. Something stood sentinel within her and forbade her every joy. Besides, she had lost all the old interests of her carefree girlish life that had been so full of hope. The previous autumn, the hunting, "Uncle," and the Christmas holidays spent with Nicholas at Otrádnoe were what she recalled oftenest and most painfully. What would she not have given to bring back even a single day of that time! But it was gone forever. Her presentiment at the time had not deceived her—that that state of freedom and readiness for any enjoyment would not return again. Yet it was necessary to live on.

It comforted her to reflect that she was not better as she had formerly imagined, but worse, much worse, than anybody else in the world. But this was not enough. She knew that, and asked herself, "What next?" But there was nothing to come. There was no joy in life, yet life was passing. Natásha apparently tried not to be a burden or a hindrance to anyone, but wanted nothing for herself. She kept away from everyone in the house, and felt at ease only with her brother Pétya. She liked to be with him better than with the others, and when alone with him she sometimes laughed. She hardly ever left the house and of those who came to see them was glad to see only one person, Pierre. It would have been impossible to treat her with more delicacy, greater care, and at the same time more seriously, than did Count Bezúkhov. Natásha unconsciously felt this delicacy, and so found great pleasure in his society. But she was not even grateful to him for it, nothing good on Pierre's part seemed to her to be an effort, it seemed so natural for him to be kind to everyone that there was no merit in his kindness. Sometimes Natásha noticed embarrassment and awkwardness on his part in her presence, especially when he wanted to do something to please her, or feared that something they spoke of would awaken memories distressing to her. She noticed this and attributed it to his general kindness and shyness, which she imagined must be the same toward everyone as it was to her. After those involuntary words—that if he were free he would have asked on his knees for her hand and her love—uttered at a moment when she was so strongly agitated, Pierre never spoke to Natásha of his feelings; and it seemed plain to her that those words, which had then so comforted her, were spoken as all sorts of meaningless words are spoken to comfort a crying child. It was not because Pierre was a married man, but because Natásha felt very strongly with him that moral barrier the absence of which she had experienced with Kurágin, that it never entered her head that the relations between him and herself could lead to love on her part, still less on his, or even to the kind of tender, self-conscious, romantic friendship between a man and a woman of which she had known several instances.

Before the end of the fast of St. Peter, Agraféna Ivánovna Belóva, a country neighbor of the Rostóvs, came to Moscow to pay her devotions at the shrines of the Moscow saints. She suggested that Natásha should fast and prepare for Holy Communion, and Natásha gladly welcomed the idea. Despite the doctor's orders that she should not go out early in the morning, Natásha insisted on fasting and preparing for the sacrament, not as they generally prepared for it in the Rostóv family by attending three services in their own house, but as Agraféna Ivánovna did, by going to church every day for a week and not once missing Vespers, Matins, or Mass.

The countess was pleased with Natásha's zeal; after the poor results of the medical treatment, in the depths of her heart she hoped that prayer might help her daughter more than medicines and, though not without fear and concealing it from the doctor, she agreed to Natásha's wish and entrusted her to Belóva. Agraféna Ivánovna used to come to wake Natásha at three in the morning, but generally found her already awake. She was afraid of being late for Matins. Hastily washing, and meekly putting on her shabbiest dress and an old mantilla, Natásha, shivering in the fresh air, went out into the deserted streets lit by the clear light of dawn. By Agraféna Ivánovna's advice Natásha prepared herself not in their own parish, but at a church where according to the devout Agraféna Ivánovna the priest was a man of very severe and lofty life. There were never many people in the church; Natásha always stood beside Belóva in the customary place before an icon of the Blessed Virgin, let into the screen before the choir on the left side, and a feeling, new to her, of humility before something great and incomprehensible, seized her when at that unusual morning hour, gazing at the dark face of the Virgin illuminated by the candles burning before it and by the morning light falling from the window, she listened to the words of the service which she tried to follow with understanding. When she understood them her personal feeling became interwoven in the prayers with shades of its own. When she did not understand, it was sweeter still to think that the wish to understand everything is pride, that it is impossible to understand all, that it is only necessary to believe and to commit oneself to God, whom she felt guiding her soul at those moments. She crossed herself, bowed low, and when she did not understand, in horror at her own vileness, simply asked God to forgive her everything, everything, to have mercy upon her. The prayers to which she surrendered herself most of all were those of repentance. On her way home at an early hour when she met no one but bricklayers going to work or men sweeping the street, and everybody within the houses was still asleep, Natásha experienced a feeling new to her, a sense of the possibility of correcting her faults, the possibility of a new, clean life, and of happiness.

During the whole week she spent in this way, that feeling grew every day. And the happiness of taking communion, or "communing" as Agraféna Ivánovna, joyously playing with the word, called it, seemed to Natásha so great that she felt she should never live till that blessed Sunday.

But the happy day came, and on that memorable Sunday, when, dressed in white muslin, she returned home after communion, for the first time for many months she felt calm and not oppressed by the thought of the life that lay before her.

The doctor who came to see her that day ordered her to continue the powders he had prescribed a fortnight previously.

"She must certainly go on taking them morning and evening," said he, evidently sincerely satisfied with his success. "Only, please be particular about it.

"Be quite easy," he continued playfully, as he adroitly took the gold coin in his palm. "She will soon be singing and frolicking about. The last medicine has done her a very great deal of good. She has freshened up very much."

The countess, with a cheerful expression on her face, looked down at her nails and spat a little for luck as she returned to the drawing room.

Chapter XVIII

At the beginning of July more and more disquieting reports about the war began to spread in Moscow; people spoke of an appeal by the Emperor to the people, and of his coming himself from the army to Moscow. And as up to the 11th of July no manifesto or appeal had been received, exaggerated reports became current about them and about the position of Russia. It was said that the Emperor was leaving the army because it was in danger, it was said that Smolénsk had surrendered, that Napoleon had an army of a million and only a miracle could save Russia.

On the 11th of July, which was Saturday, the manifesto was received but was not yet in print, and Pierre, who was at the Rostóvs', promised to come to dinner next day, Sunday, and bring a copy of the manifesto and appeal, which he would obtain from Count Rostopchín.

That Sunday, the Rostóvs went to Mass at the Razumóvskis' private chapel as usual. It was a hot July day. Even at ten o'clock, when the Rostóvs got out of their carriage at the chapel, the sultry air, the shouts of hawkers, the light and gay summer clothes of the crowd, the dusty leaves of the trees on the boulevard, the sounds of the band and the white trousers of a battalion marching to parade, the rattling of wheels on the cobblestones, and the brilliant, hot sunshine, were all full of that summer languor, that content and discontent with the present, which is most strongly felt on a bright hot day in town. All the Moscow notabilities, all the Rostóvs' acquaintances, were at the Razumóvskis' chapel, for, as if expecting something to happen, many wealthy families who usually left town for their country estates had not gone away that summer. As Natásha, at her mother's side, passed through the crowd behind a liveried footman who cleared the way for them, she heard a young man speaking about her in too loud a whisper.

"That's Rostóva, the one who . . ."

"She's much thinner, but all the same she's pretty!"

She heard, or thought she heard, the names of Kurágin and Bolkónski. But she was always imagining that. It always seemed to her that everyone who looked at her was thinking only of what had happened to her. With a sinking heart, wretched as she always was now when she found herself in a crowd, Natásha in her lilac silk dress trimmed with black lace walked—as women can walk—with the more repose and stateliness the greater the pain and shame in her soul. She knew for certain that she was pretty, but this no longer gave her satisfaction as it used to. On the contrary it tormented her more than anything else of late, and particularly so on this bright, hot summer day in town. "It's Sunday again—another week past," she thought, recalling that she had been here the Sunday before, "and always the same life that is no life, and the same surroundings in which it used to be so easy to live. I'm pretty, I'm young, and I know that now I am good. I used to be bad, but now I know I am good," she thought, "but yet my best years are slipping by and are no good to anyone." She stood by her mother's side and exchanged nods with acquaintances near her. From habit she scrutinized the ladies' dresses, condemned the bearing of a lady standing close by who was not crossing herself properly but in a cramped manner, and again she thought with vexation that she was herself being judged and was judging others, and suddenly, at the sound of the service, she felt horrified at her own vileness, horrified that the former purity of her soul was again lost to her.

A comely, fresh-looking old man was conducting the service with that mild solemnity which has so elevating and soothing an effect on the souls of the worshipers. The gates of the sanctuary-screen were closed, the curtain was slowly drawn, and from behind it a soft mysterious voice pronounced some words. Tears, the cause of which she herself did not understand, made Natásha's breast heave, and a joyous but oppressive feeling agitated her.

"Teach me what I should do, how to live my life, how I may grow good forever, forever!" she pleaded.

The deacon came out onto the raised space before the altar-screen, and holding his thumb extended, drew his long hair from under his dalmatic, and, making the sign of the cross on his breast, began in a loud and solemn voice to recite the words of the prayer. . . .

"In peace let us pray unto the Lord."

"As one community, without distinction of class, without enmity, united by brotherly love—let us pray!" thought Natásha.

"For the peace that is from above, and for the salvation of our souls."

"For the world of angels and all the spirits who dwell above us," prayed Natásha.

When they prayed for the warriors, she thought of her brother and Denísov. When they prayed for all traveling by land and sea she remembered Prince Andrew, prayed for him, and asked God to forgive her all the wrongs she had done him. When they prayed for those who love us, she prayed for the members of her own family, her father and mother and Sónya, realizing for the first time how wrongly she had acted toward them, and feeling all the strength of her love for them. When they prayed for those who hate us, she tried to think of her enemies and people who hated her, in order to pray for them. She included among her enemies the creditors and all who had business dealings with her father, and always at the thought of enemies and those who hated her she remembered Anatole who had done her so much harm—and though he did not hate her she gladly prayed for him as for an enemy. Only at prayer did she feel able to think clearly and calmly of Prince Andrew and Anatole, as men for whom her feelings were as nothing compared with her awe and devotion to God. When they prayed for the Imperial family and the Synod she bowed very low and made the sign of the cross, saying to herself that even if she did not understand, still she could not doubt, and at any rate loved the governing Synod and prayed for it.

When he had finished the Litany the deacon crossed the stole over his breast and said,

"Let us commit ourselves and our whole lives to Christ the Lord!"

"Commit ourselves to God," Natásha inwardly repeated. "Lord God, I submit myself to Thy will!" she thought. "I want nothing, wish for nothing; teach me what to do and how to use my will! Take me, take me!" prayed Natásha, with impatient emotion in her heart, not crossing herself but letting her slender arms hang down as if expecting some invisible power at any moment to take her and deliver her from herself, from her regrets, desires, remorse, hopes and sins.

The countess looked round several times at her daughter's softened face and shining eyes, and prayed God to help her.

Unexpectedly, in the middle of the service, and not in the usual order Natásha knew so well, the deacon brought out a small stool, the one he knelt on when praying on Trinity Sunday, and placed it before the doors of the sanctuary-screen. The priest came out with his purple velvet biretta on his head, adjusted his hair, and knelt down with an effort. Everybody followed his example and they looked at one another in surprise. Then came the prayer just received from the Synod—a prayer for the deliverance of Russia from hostile invasion.

"Lord God of might, God of our salvation!" began the priest in that voice, clear, not grandiloquent but mild, in which only the Slav clergy read and which acts so irresistibly on a Russian heart.

"Lord God of might, God of our salvation! Look this day in mercy and blessing on Thy humble people, and graciously hear us, spare us, and have mercy upon us! This foe confounding Thy land, desiring to lay waste the whole world, rises against us; these lawless men are gathered together to overthrow Thy kingdom, to destroy Thy dear Jerusalem, Thy beloved Russia; to defile Thy temples, to overthrow Thine altars and to desecrate our holy shrines. How long, O Lord, how long shall the wicked triumph? How long shall they wield unlawful power?

"Lord God! Hear us when we pray to Thee; strengthen with Thy might our most gracious sovereign lord, the Emperor Alexander Pávlovich; be mindful of his uprightness and meekness, reward him according to his righteousness, and let it preserve us, Thy chosen Israel! Bless his counsels, his undertakings, and his work; strengthen his kingdom by Thine almighty hand, and give him victory over his enemy, even as Thou gavest Moses the victory over Amalek, Gideon over Midian, and David over Goliath. Preserve his army, put a bow of brass in the hands of those who have armed themselves in Thy Name, and gird their loins with strength for the fight. Take up the spear and shield and arise to help us; confound and put to shame those who have devised evil against us, may they be before the faces of Thy faithful warriors as dust before the wind, and may Thy mighty Angel confound them and put them to flight; may they be ensnared when they know it not, and may the plots they have laid in secret be turned against them; let them fall before Thy servants' feet and be laid low by our hosts! Lord, Thou art able to save both great and small; Thou art God, and man cannot prevail against Thee!

"God of our fathers! Remember Thy bounteous mercy and loving-kindness which are from of old; turn not Thy face from us, but be gracious to our unworthiness, and in Thy great goodness and Thy many mercies regard not our transgressions and iniquities! Create in us a clean heart and renew a right spirit within us, strengthen us all in Thy faith, fortify our hope, inspire us with true love one for another, arm us with unity of spirit in the righteous defense of the heritage Thou gavest to us and to our fathers, and let not the scepter of the wicked be exalted against the destiny of those Thou hast sanctified.

"O Lord our God, in whom we believe and in whom we put our trust, let us not be confounded in our hope of Thy mercy, and give us a token of Thy blessing, that those who hate us and our Orthodox faith may see it, and be put to shame and perish, and may all the nations know that Thou art the Lord and we are Thy people. Show Thy mercy upon us this day, O Lord, and grant us Thy salvation; make the hearts of Thy servants to rejoice in Thy mercy; smite down our enemies and destroy them swiftly beneath the feet of Thy faithful servants! For Thou art the defense, the succor, and the victory of them that put their trust in Thee, and to Thee be all glory, to Father, Son, and Holy Ghost, now and forever, world without end. Amen."

In Natásha's receptive condition of soul this prayer affected her strongly. She listened to every word about the victory of Moses over Amalek, of Gideon over Midian, and of David over Goliath, and about the destruction of "Thy Jerusalem," and she prayed to God with the tenderness and emotion with which her heart was overflowing, but without fully understanding what she was asking of God in that prayer. She shared with all her heart in the prayer for the spirit of righteousness, for the strengthening of the heart by faith and hope, and its animation by love. But she could not pray that her enemies might be trampled under foot when but a few minutes before she had been wishing she had more of them that she might pray for them. But neither could she doubt the righteousness of the prayer that was being read on bended knees. She felt in her heart a devout and tremulous awe at the thought of the punishment that overtakes men for their sins, and especially of her own sins, and she prayed to God to forgive them all, and her too, and to give them all, and her too, peace and happiness. And it seemed to her that God heard her prayer.

Chapter XIX

FROM THE DAY WHEN PIERRE, AFTER LEAVING THE ROSTÓVS' WITH NATÁSHA'S GRATEFUL LOOK fresh in his mind, had gazed at the comet that seemed to be fixed in the sky and felt that something new was appearing on his own horizon—from that day the problem of the vanity and uselessness of all earthly things, that had incessantly tormented him, no longer presented itself. That terrible question "Why?" "Wherefore?" which had come to him amid every occupation, was now replaced, not by another question or by a reply to the former question, but by *her* image. When he listened to, or himself took part in, trivial conversations, when he read or heard of human baseness or folly, he was not horrified as formerly, and did not ask himself why men struggled so about these things when all is so transient and incomprehensible—but he remembered her as he had last seen her, and all his doubts vanished—not because she had answered the questions that had haunted him, but because his conception of her transferred him instantly to another, a brighter, realm of spiritual activity in which no one could be justified or guilty—a realm of beauty and love which it was worth living for. Whatever worldly baseness presented itself to him, he said to himself:

"Well, supposing N. N. swindled the country and the Tsar, and the country and the Tsar confer honors upon him, what does that matter? She smiled at me yesterday and asked me to come again, and I love her, and no one will ever know it." And his soul felt calm and peaceful.

Pierre still went into society, drank as much and led the same idle and dissipated life, because besides the hours he spent at the Rostóvs' there were other hours he had to spend somehow, and the habits and acquaintances he had made in Moscow formed a current that bore him along irresistibly. But latterly, when more and more disquieting reports came from the seat of war and Natásha's health began to improve and she no longer aroused in him the former feeling of careful pity, an ever-increasing restlessness, which he could not explain, took possession of him. He felt that the condition he was in could not continue long, that a catastrophe was coming which would change his whole life, and he impatiently sought everywhere for signs of that approaching catastrophe. One of his brother masons had revealed to Pierre the following prophecy concerning Napoleon, drawn from the Revelation of St. John.

In chapter 13, verse 18, of the Apocalypse, it is said:

Here is wisdom. Let him that hath understanding count the number of the beast: for it is the number of a man; and his number is Six hundred threescore and six.

And in the fifth verse of the same chapter:

And there was given unto him a mouth speaking great things and blasphemies; and power was given unto him to continue forty and two months.

The French alphabet, written out with the same numerical values as the Hebrew, in which the first nine letters denote units and the others tens, will have the following significance:

a	b	c	d	e	f	g	h	i	k	l	m	n	o	p	q
1	2	3	4	5	6	7	8	9	10	20	30	40	50	60	70

r	s	t	u	v	w	x	y	z
80	90	100	110	120	130	140	150	160

Writing the words *L'Empereur Napoléon* in numbers, it appears that the sum of them is 666, and that Napoleon therefore the beast foretold in the Apocalypse. Moreover, by applying the same system to the words *quarante-deux* (forty-two), which was the term allowed to the beast that "spoke great things and blasphemies," the same number 666 was obtained; from which it followed that the limit fixed for Napoleon's power had come in the year 1812 when the French emperor was forty-two. This prophecy pleased Pierre very much and he often asked himself what would put an end to the power of the beast, that is, of Napoleon, and tried by the same system of using letters as numbers and adding them up, to find an answer to the question that engrossed him. He wrote the words *L'Empereur Alexander, La nation russe* and added up their numbers, but the sums were either more or less than 666. Once when making such calculations he wrote down his own name in French, Comte Pierre Besouhoff, but the sum of the numbers did not come right. Then he changed the spelling, substituting a *z* for the *s* and adding *de* and the article *le*, still without obtaining the desired result. Then it occurred to him: if the answer to the question were contained in his name, his nationality would also be given in the answer. So he wrote *Le russe Besuhof* and adding up the numbers got 671. This was only five too much, and five was represented by *e*, the very letter elided from the article *le* before the word *Empereur*. By omitting the *e*, though incorrectly, Pierre got the answer he sought. *L'russe Besuhof* made 666. This discovery excited him. How, or by what means, he was connected with the great event foretold in the Apocalypse he did not know, but he did not doubt that connection for a moment. His love for Natásha, Antichrist, Napoleon, the invasion, the comet, 666, *L'Empereur Napoléon*, and *L'russe Besuhof*—all this had to mature and culminate, to lift him out of that spellbound, petty sphere of Moscow habits in which he felt himself held captive, and lead him to a great achievement and great happiness.

On the eve of the Sunday when the special prayer was read, Pierre had promised the Rostóvs to bring them, from Count Rostopchín whom he knew well, both the appeal to the people and the news from the army. In the morning, when he went to call at Rostopchín's he met there a courier fresh from the army, an acquaintance of his own, who often danced at Moscow balls.

"Do, please, for heaven's sake, relieve me of something!" said the courier. "I have a sackful of letters to parents."

Among these letters was one from Nicholas Rostóv to his father. Pierre took that letter, and Rostopchín also gave him the Emperor's appeal to Moscow, which had just been printed, the last army orders, and his own most recent bulletin. Glancing through the army orders, Pierre found in one of them, in the lists of killed, wounded and rewarded, the name of Nicholas Rostóv, awarded a St. George's Cross of the Fourth Class for courage shown in the Ostróvna affair, and in the same order the name of Prince Andrew Bolkónski, appointed to the command of a regiment of Chasseurs. Though he did not want to remind the Rostóvs of Bolkónski, Pierre could not refrain from making them happy by the news of their son's having received a decoration, so he sent that printed army order and Nicholas's letter to the Rostóvs, keeping the appeal, the bulletin, and the other orders, to take with him when he went to dinner.

His conversation with Count Rostopchín and the latter's tone of anxious hurry, the meeting with the courier who talked casually of how badly things were going in the army, the rumors of the discovery of spies in Moscow and of a leaflet in circulation stating that Napoleon promised to be in both the Russian capitals by the autumn, and the talk of the Emperor's being expected to arrive next day—all aroused with fresh force that feeling of agitation and expectation in Pierre which he had been conscious of ever since the appearance of the comet, and especially since the beginning of the war.

He had long been thinking of entering the army and would have done so had he not been hindered, first, by his membership of the Society of Freemasons to which he was bound by oath and which preached perpetual peace and the abolition of war, and secondly, by the fact that when he saw the great mass of Muscovites who had donned uniform and were talking patriotism, he somehow felt ashamed to take the step. But the chief reason for not carrying out his intention to enter the army lay in the vague idea that he was *L'russe Besuhof* who had the number of the beast, 666; that his part in the great affair of setting a limit to the power of the beast that spoke great and blasphemous things had been predestined from eternity, and that therefore he ought not to undertake anything, but wait for what was bound to come to pass.

Chapter XX

A FEW INTIMATE FRIENDS WERE DINING WITH THE ROSTÓVS THAT DAY, AS USUAL ON SUNDAYS. Pierre came early so as to find them alone.

He had grown so stout this year that he would have been abnormal had he not been so tall, so broad of limb, and so strong that he carried his bulk with evident ease.

He went up the stairs, puffing and muttering something. His coachman did not even ask whether he was to wait. He knew that when his master was at the Rostóvs' he stayed till midnight. The Rostóvs' footman rushed eagerly forward to help him off with his cloak and take his hat and stick. Pierre, from club habit, always left both hat and stick in the anteroom.

The first person he saw in the house was Natásha. Even before he saw her, while taking off his cloak, he heard her. She was practicing sol-fa exercises in the music room. He knew that she had not sung since her illness, and so the sound of her voice surprised and delighted him. He opened the door softly and saw her, in the lilac dress she had worn at church, walking about the room singing. She had her back to him when he opened the door, but when, turning quickly, she saw his broad, surprised face, she blushed and came rapidly up to him.

"I want to try to sing again," she said, adding as if by way of excuse, "it is, at least, something to do."

"That's capital!"

"How glad I am you've come! I am so happy today," she said, with the old animation Pierre had not seen in her for along time. "You know Nicholas has received a St. George's Cross? I am so proud of him."

"Oh yes, I sent that announcement. But I don't want to interrupt you," he added, and was about to go to the drawing room.

Natásha stopped him.

"Count, is it wrong of me to sing?" she said blushing, and fixing her eyes inquiringly on him.

"No . . . Why should it be? On the contrary . . . But why do you ask me?"

"I don't know myself," Natásha answered quickly, "but I should not like to do anything you disapproved of. I believe in you completely. You don't know how important you are to me, how much you've done for me. . . ." She spoke rapidly and did not notice how Pierre flushed at her words. "I saw in that same army order that *he, Bolkónski*" (she whispered the name hastily), "is in Russia, and in the army again. What do you think?"—she was speaking hurriedly, evidently afraid her strength might fail her—"Will he ever forgive me? Will he not always have a bitter feeling toward me? What do you think? What do you think?"

"I think . . ." Pierre replied, "that he has nothing to forgive. . . . If I were in his place . . ."

By association of ideas, Pierre was at once carried back to the day when, trying to comfort her, he had said that if he were not himself but the best man in the world and free, he would ask on his knees for her hand; and the same feeling of pity, tenderness and love took possession of him and the same words rose to his lips. But she did not give him time to say them.

"Yes, you . . . you . . ." she said, uttering the word *you* rapturously—"that's a different thing. I know no one kinder, more generous, or better than you; nobody could be! Had you not been there then, and now too, I don't know what would have become of me, because . . ."

Tears suddenly rose in her eyes, she turned away, lifted her music before her eyes, began singing again, and again began walking up and down the room.

Just then Pétya came running in from the drawing room.

Pétya was now a handsome rosy lad of fifteen with full red lips, and resembled Natásha. He was preparing to enter the university, but he and his friend Obolénski had lately, in secret, agreed to join the hussars.

Pétya had come rushing out to talk to his namesake about this affair. He had asked Pierre to find out whether he would be accepted in the hussars.

Pierre walked up and down the drawing room not listening to what Pétya was saying.

Pétya pulled him by the arm to attract his attention.

"Well, what about my plan? Peter Kirílych, for heaven's sake! You are my only hope!" said Pétya.

"Oh yes, your plan. To join the hussars? I'll mention it, I'll bring it all up today."

"Well, *mon cher,* have you got the manifesto?" asked the old count. "The countess has been to Mass at the Razumóvskis' and heard the new prayer. She says it's very fine."

"Yes, I've got it," said Pierre. "The Emperor is to be here tomorrow . . . there's to be an Extraordinary Meeting of the nobility, and they are talking of a levy of ten men per thousand. Oh yes, let me congratulate you!"

"Yes, yes, thank God! Well, and what news from the army?"

"We are again retreating. They say we're already near Smolénsk," replied Pierre.

"O Lord, O Lord!" exclaimed the count. "Where is the manifesto?"

"The Emperor's appeal? Oh yes!"

Pierre began feeling in his pockets for the papers, but could not find them. Still slapping his pockets, he kissed the hand of the countess who entered the room and glanced uneasily round evidently expecting Natásha, who had left off singing but had not yet come into the drawing room.

"On my word, I don't know what I've done with it," he said.

"There he is, always losing everything!" remarked the countess.

Natásha entered with a softened and agitated expression of face, and sat down looking silently at Pierre. As soon as she entered, Pierre's features, which had been gloomy, suddenly lit up, and while still searching for the papers he glanced at her several times.

"No, really! I'll drive home, I must have left them there. I'll certainly . . ."

"But you'll be late for dinner."

"Oh! And my coachman has gone."

But Sónya, who had gone to look for the papers in the anteroom, had found them in Pierre's hat, where he had carefully tucked them under the lining. Pierre was about to begin reading.

"No, after dinner," said the old count, evidently expecting much enjoyment from that reading.

At dinner, at which champagne was drunk to the health of the new chevalier of St. George, Shinshín told them the town news, of the illness of the old Georgian princess, of Métivier's disappearance from Moscow, and of how some German fellow had been brought to Rostopchín and accused of being a French "spyer" (so Count Rostopchín had told the story), and how Rostopchín let him go and assured the people that he was "not a spire at all, but only an old German ruin."

"People are being arrested . . ." said the count. "I've told the countess she should not speak French so much. It's not the time for it now."

"And have you heard?" Shinshín asked. "Prince Golítsyn has engaged a master to teach him Russian. It is becoming dangerous to speak French in the streets."

"And how about you, Count Peter Kirílych? If they call up the militia, you too will have to mount a horse," remarked the old count, addressing Pierre.

Pierre had been silent and preoccupied all through dinner, seeming not to grasp what was said. He looked at the count.

"Oh yes, the war," he said. "No! What sort of warrior should I make? And yet everything is so strange, so strange! I can't make it out. I don't know, I am very far from having military tastes, but in these times no one can answer for himself."

After dinner the count settled himself comfortably in an easy chair and with a serious face asked Sónya, who was considered an excellent reader, to read the appeal.

"To Moscow, our ancient Capital!

"The enemy has entered the borders of Russia with immense forces. He comes to despoil our beloved country," Sónya read painstakingly in her high-pitched voice. The count listened with closed eyes, heaving abrupt sighs at certain passages.

Natásha sat erect, gazing with a searching look now at her father and now at Pierre.

Pierre felt her eyes on him and tried not to look round. The countess shook her head disapprovingly and angrily at every solemn expression in the manifesto. In all these words she saw only that the danger threatening her son would not soon be over. Shinshín, with a sarcastic smile on his lips, was evidently preparing to make fun of anything that gave him the opportunity: Sónya's reading, any remark of the count's, or even the manifesto itself should no better pretext present itself.

After reading about the dangers that threatened Russia, the hopes the Emperor placed on Moscow and especially on its illustrious nobility, Sónya, with a quiver in her voice due chiefly to the attention that was being paid to her, read the last words: "We ourselves will not delay to appear among our people in that Capital and in others parts of our realm for consultation, and for the direction of all our levies, both those now barring the enemy's path and those freshly formed to defeat him wherever he may appear. May the ruin he hopes to bring upon us recoil on his own head, and may Europe delivered from bondage glorify the name of Russia!"

"Yes, that's it!" cried the count, opening his moist eyes and sniffing repeatedly, as if a strong vinaigrette had been held to his nose; and he added, "Let the Emperor but say the word and we'll sacrifice everything and begrudge nothing."

Before Shinshín had time to utter the joke he was ready to make on the count's patriotism, Natásha jumped up from her place and ran to her father.

"What a darling our Papa is!" she cried, kissing him, and she again looked at Pierre with the unconscious coquetry that had returned to her with her better spirits.

"There! Here's a patriot for you!" said Shinshín.

"Not a patriot at all, but simply . . ." Natásha replied in an injured tone. "Everything seems funny to you, but this isn't at all a joke. . . ."

"A joke indeed!" put in the count. "Let him but say the word and we'll all go. . . . We're not Germans!"

"But did you notice, it says, 'for consultation'?" said Pierre.

"Never mind what it's for. . . ."

At this moment, Pétya, to whom nobody was paying any attention, came up to his father with a very flushed face, and said in his breaking voice that was now deep and now shrill:

"Well, Papa, I tell you definitely, and Mamma too, it's as you please, but I say definitely that you must let me enter the army, because I can't . . . that's all. . . ."

The countess, in dismay, looked up to heaven, clasped her hands, and turned angrily to her husband.

"That comes of your talking!" said she.

But the count had already recovered from his excitement.

"Come, come!" said he. "Here's a fine warrior! No! Nonsense! You must study."

"It's not nonsense, Papa! Fédya Obolénski is younger than I, and he's going too. Besides, all the same I can't study now when . . ." Pétya stopped short, flushed till he perspired, but still got out the words, "when our Fatherland is in danger."

"That'll do, that'll do—nonsense. . . ."

"But you said yourself that we would sacrifice everything."

"Pétya! Be quiet, I tell you!" cried the count, with a glance at his wife, who had turned pale and was staring fixedly at her son.

"And I tell you—Peter Kirílych here will also tell you . . ."

"Nonsense, I tell you. Your mother's milk has hardly dried on your lips and you want to go into the army! There, there, I tell you," and the count moved to go out of the room, taking the papers, probably to reread them in his study before having a nap.

"Well, Peter Kirílych, let's go and have a smoke," he said.

Pierre was agitated and undecided. Natásha's unwontedly brilliant eyes, continually glancing at him with a more than cordial look, had reduced him to this condition.

"No, I think I'll go home."

"Home? Why, you meant to spend the evening with us. . . . You don't often come nowadays as it is, and this girl of mine," said the count good-naturedly, pointing to Natásha, "only brightens up when you're here."

"Yes, I had forgotten . . . I really must go home . . . business . . ." said Pierre hurriedly.

"Well, then, *au revoir!*" said the count, and went out of the room.

"Why are you going? Why are you upset?" asked Natásha, and she looked challengingly into Pierre's eyes.

"Because I love you!" was what he wanted to say, but he did not say it, and only blushed till the tears came, and lowered his eyes.

"Because it is better for me to come less often . . . because . . . No, simply I have business. . . ."

"Why? No, tell me!" Natásha began resolutely, and suddenly stopped.

They looked at each other with dismayed and embarrassed faces. He tried to smile but could not: his smile expressed suffering, and he silently kissed her hand and went out.

Pierre made up his mind not to go to the Rostóvs' any more.

Chapter XXI

AFTER THE DEFINITE REFUSAL HE HAD RECEIVED, PÉTYA WENT TO HIS ROOM AND THERE LOCKED himself in and wept bitterly. When he came in to tea, silent, morose, and with tear-stained face, everybody pretended not to notice anything.

Next day the Emperor arrived in Moscow, and several of the Rostóvs' domestic serfs begged permission to go to have a look at him. That morning Pétya was a long time dressing and arranging his hair and collar to look like a grown-up man. He frowned before his looking-glass, gesticulated, shrugged his shoulders, and finally, without saying a word to anyone, took his cap and left the house by the back door, trying to avoid notice. Pétya decided to go straight to where the Emperor was and to explain frankly to some gentleman-in-waiting (he imagined the Emperor to be always surrounded by gentlemen-in-waiting) that he, Count Rostóv, in spite of his youth wished to serve his country; that youth could be no hindrance to loyalty, and that he was ready to . . . While dressing, Pétya had prepared many fine things he meant to say to the gentleman-in-waiting.

It was on the very fact of being so young that Pétya counted for success in reaching the Emperor—he even thought how surprised everyone would be at his youthfulness—and yet in the arrangement of his collar and hair and by his sedate deliberate walk he wished to appear a grown-up man. But the farther he went and the more his attention was diverted by the ever-increasing crowds moving toward the Kremlin, the less he remembered to walk with the sedateness and deliberation of a man. As he approached the Kremlin he even began to avoid being crushed and resolutely stuck out his elbows in a menacing way. But within the Trinity Gateway he was so pressed to the wall by people who probably were unaware of the patriotic intentions with which he had come, that in spite of all his determination he had to give in, and stop while carriages passed in, rumbling beneath the archway. Beside Pétya stood a peasant woman, a footman, two tradesmen and a discharged soldier. After standing some time in the gateway, Pétya tried to move forward in front of the others without waiting for all the carriages to pass, and he began resolutely working his way with his elbows, but the woman just in front of him, who was the first against whom he directed his efforts, angrily shouted at him:

"What are you shoving for, young lordling? Don't you see we're all standing still? Then why push?"

"Anybody can shove," said the footman, and also began working his elbows to such effect that he pushed Pétya into a very filthy corner of the gateway.

Pétya wiped his perspiring face with his hands and pulled up the damp collar which he had arranged so well at home to seem like a man's.

He felt that he no longer looked presentable, and feared that if he were now to approach the gentlemen-in-waiting in that plight he would not be admitted to the Emperor. But it was impossible to smarten oneself up or move to another place, because of the crowd. One of the generals who drove past was an acquaintance of the Rostóvs' and Pétya thought of asking his help, but came to the conclusion that that would not be a manly thing to do. When the carriages had all passed in, the crowd, carrying Pétya with it, streamed forward into the Kremlin Square which was already full of people. There were people not only in the square, but everywhere—on the slopes and on the roofs. As soon as Pétya found himself in the square he clearly heard the sound of bells and the joyous voices of the crowd that filled the whole Kremlin.

For a while the crowd was less dense, but suddenly all heads were bared, and everyone rushed forward in one direction. Pétya was being pressed so that he could scarcely breathe, and everybody shouted "hurrah! hurrah! hurrah!" Pétya stood on tiptoe, and pushed and pinched, but could see nothing except the people about him.

All the faces bore the same expression of excitement and enthusiasm. A tradesman's wife standing beside Pétya sobbed, and the tears ran down her cheeks.

"Father! Angel! Dear one!" she kept repeating, wiping away her tears with her fingers.

"Hurrah!" was heard on all sides.

For a moment the crowd stood still, but then it made another rush forward.

Quite beside himself, Pétya, clinching his teeth and rolling his eyes ferociously, pushed forward, elbowing his way and shouting "hurrah!" as if he were prepared that instant to kill himself and everyone else, but on both sides of him other people with similarly ferocious faces pushed forward and everybody shouted "hurrah!"

"So this is what the Emperor is!" thought Pétya. "No, I can't petition him myself—that would be too bold." But in spite of this he continued to struggle desperately forward, and from between the backs of those in front he caught glimpses of an open space with a strip of red cloth spread out on it; but just then the crowd swayed back—the police in front were pushing back those who had pressed too close to the procession: the Emperor was passing from the palace to the Cathedral of the Assumption—and Pétya unexpectedly received such a blow on his side and ribs and was squeezed so hard, that suddenly everything grew dim before his eyes and he lost consciousness. When he came to himself, a man of clerical appearance with a tuft of gray hair at the back of his head and wearing a shabby blue cassock—probably a church clerk and chanter—was holding him under the arm with one hand while warding off the pressure of the crowd with the other.

"You've crushed the young gentleman!" said the clerk. "What are you up to? Gently! . . . They've crushed him, crushed him!"

The Emperor entered the Cathedral of the Assumption. The crowd spread out again more evenly, and the clerk led Pétya—pale and breathless—to the Tsar-cannon. Several people were sorry for Pétya, and suddenly a crowd turned toward him and pressed round him. Those who stood nearest him attended to him, unbuttoned his coat, seated him on the raised platform of the cannon, and reproached those others (whoever they might be) who had crushed him.

"One might easily get killed that way! What do they mean by it? Killing people! Poor dear, he's as white as a sheet!"—various voices were heard saying.

Pétya soon came to himself, the color returned to his face, the pain had passed, and at the cost of that temporary unpleasantness he had obtained a place by the cannon from where he hoped to see the Emperor who would be returning that way. Pétya no longer thought of presenting his petition. If he could only see the Emperor he would be happy!

While the service was proceeding in the Cathedral of the Assumption—it was a combined service of prayer on the occasion of the Emperor's arrival and of thanksgiving for the conclusion of peace with the Turks—the crowd outside spread out and hawkers appeared, selling kvas, gingerbread and poppy-seed sweets (of which Pétya was particularly fond), and ordinary conversation could again be heard. A tradesman's wife was showing a rent in her shawl and telling how much the shawl had cost; another was saying that all silk goods had now got dear. The clerk who had rescued Pétya was talking to a functionary about the priests who were officiating that day with the bishop. The clerk several times used the word "plenary" (of the service), a word Pétya did not understand. Two young citizens were joking with some serf girls who were cracking nuts. All these conversations, especially the joking with the girls, were such as might have had a particular charm for Pétya at his age, but they did not interest him now. He sat on his elevation—the pedestal of the cannon—still agitated as before by the thought of the Emperor and by his love for him. The feeling of pain and fear he had experienced when he was being crushed, together with that of rapture, still further intensified his sense of the importance of the occasion.

Suddenly the sound of a firing of cannon was heard from the embankment, to celebrate the signing of peace with the Turks, and the crowd rushed impetuously toward the embankment to watch the firing. Pétya too would have run there, but the clerk who had taken the young gentleman under his protection stopped him. The firing was still proceeding when officers, generals and gentlemen-in-waiting came running out of the cathedral, and after them others in a more leisurely manner: caps were again raised, and those who had run to look at the cannon ran back again. At last four men in uniforms and sashes emerged from the cathedral doors. "Hurrah! hurrah!" shouted the crowd again.

"Which is he? Which?" asked Pétya in a tearful voice, of those around him, but no one answered him, everybody was too excited; and Pétya, fixing on one of those four men, whom he could not clearly see for the tears of joy that filled his eyes, concentrated all his enthusiasm on him—though it happened not to be the Emperor—frantically shouted "Hurrah!" and resolved that tomorrow, come what might, he would join the army.

The crowd ran after the Emperor, followed him to the palace, and began to disperse. It was already late, and Pétya had not eaten anything and was drenched with perspiration, yet he did not go home but stood with that diminishing, but still considerable, crowd before the palace while the Emperor dined—looking in at the palace windows, expecting he knew not what, and envying alike the notables he saw arriving at the entrance to dine with the Emperor and the court footmen who served at table, glimpses of whom could be seen through the windows.

While the Emperor was dining, Valúev, looking out of the window, said:

"The people are still hoping to see your Majesty again."

The dinner was nearly over, and the Emperor, munching a biscuit, rose and went out onto the balcony. The people, with Pétya among them, rushed toward the balcony.

"Angel! Dear one! Hurrah! Father! . . ." cried the crowd, and Pétya with it, and again the women and men of weaker mold, Pétya among them, wept with joy.

A largish piece of the biscuit the Emperor was holding in his hand broke off, fell on the balcony parapet, and then to the ground. A coachman in a jerkin, who stood nearest, sprang forward and snatched it up. Several people in the crowd rushed at the coachman. Seeing this the Emperor had a plateful of biscuits brought him, and began throwing them down from the balcony. Pétya's eyes grew bloodshot, and still more excited by the danger of being crushed, he rushed at the biscuits. He did not know why, but he had to have a biscuit from the Tsar's hand and he felt that he must not give way. He sprang forward and upset an old woman who was catching at a biscuit; the old woman did not consider herself defeated though she was lying on the ground—she grabbed at some biscuits but her hand did not reach them. Pétya pushed her hand away with his knee, seized a biscuit, and as if fearing to be too late, again shouted "Hurrah!" with a voice already hoarse.

The Emperor went in, and after that the greater part of the crowd began to disperse.

"There! I said if only we waited—and so it was!" was being joyfully said by various people.

Happy as Pétya was, he felt sad at having to go home knowing that all the enjoyment of that day was over. He did not go straight home from the Kremlin, but called on his friend Obolénski, who was fifteen and was also entering the regiment. On returning home Pétya announced resolutely and firmly that if he was not allowed to enter the service he would run away. And next day, Count Ilyá Rostóv—though he had not yet quite yielded—went to inquire how he could arrange for Pétya to serve where there would be least danger.

Chapter XXII

TWO DAYS LATER, ON THE 15TH OF JULY, AN IMMENSE NUMBER OF CARRIAGES WERE STANDING outside the Slobóda Palace.

The great halls were full. In the first were the nobility and gentry in their uniforms, in the second bearded merchants in full-skirted coats of blue cloth and wearing medals. In the noblemen's hall there was an incessant movement and buzz of voices. The chief magnates sat on high-backed chairs at a large table under the portrait of the Emperor, but most of the gentry were strolling about the room.

All these nobles, whom Pierre met every day at the club or in their own houses, were in uniform—some in that of Catherine's day, others in that of Emperor Paul, others again in the new uniforms of Alexander's time or the ordinary uniform of the nobility, and the general characteristic of being in uniform imparted something strange and fantastic to these diverse and familiar personalities, both old and young. The old men, dim-eyed, toothless, bald, sallow and bloated, or gaunt and wrinkled, were especially striking. For the most part they sat quietly in their places and were silent, or if they walked about and talked, attached themselves to someone younger. On all these faces, as on the faces of the crowd Pétya had seen in the Square, there was a striking contradiction: the general expectation of a solemn event, and at the same time the everyday interests in a boston card party, Peter the cook, Zinaída Dmítrievna's health and so on.

Pierre was there too, buttoned up since early morning in a nobleman's uniform that had become too tight for him. He was agitated; this extraordinary gathering not only of nobles but also of the merchant-class—*les états généraux* (States-General)—evoked in him a whole series of ideas he had long laid aside but which were deeply graven in his soul: thoughts of the *Contrat Social* and the French Revolution. The words that had struck him in the Emperor's appeal—that the sovereign was coming to the capital for consultation with his people—strengthened this idea. And imagining that in this direction something important which he had long awaited was drawing near, he strolled about watching and listening to conversations, but nowhere finding any confirmation of the ideas that occupied him.

The Emperor's manifesto was read, evoking enthusiasm, and then all moved about discussing it. Besides the ordinary topics of conversation, Pierre heard questions of where the marshals of the nobility were to stand when the Emperor entered, when a ball should be given in the Emperor's honor, whether they should group themselves by districts or by whole provinces . . . and so on; but as soon as the war was touched on, or what the nobility had been convened for, the talk became undecided and indefinite. Then all preferred listening to speaking.

A middle-aged man, handsome and virile, in the uniform of a retired naval officer, was speaking in one of the rooms, and a small crowd was pressing round him. Pierre went up to the circle that had formed round the speaker and listened. Count Ilyá Rostóv, in a military uniform of Catherine's time, was sauntering with a pleasant smile among the crowd, with all of whom he was acquainted. He too approached that group and listened with a kindly smile and nods of approval, as he always did, to what the speaker was saying. The retired naval man was speaking very boldly, as was evident from the expression on the faces of the listeners and from the fact that some people Pierre knew as the meekest and quietest of men walked away disapprovingly or expressed disagreement with him. Pierre pushed his way into the middle of the group, listened, and convinced himself that the man was indeed a Liberal, but of views quite different from his own. The naval officer spoke in a particularly sonorous, musical and aristocratic baritone voice, pleasantly swallowing his r's and generally slurring his consonants: the voice of a man calling out to his servant, "Heah! Bwing me my pipe!" It was indicative of dissipation and the exercise of authority.

"What if the Smolénsk people have offahd to waise militia for the Emperwah? Ah we to take Smolénsk as our patte'n? If the noble awistocwacy of the pwovince of Moscow thinks fit, it can show its loyalty to our sov'weign the Empewah in other ways. Have we fo'gotten the waising of the militia in the yeah 'seven? All that did was to enwich the pwiests' sons and thieves and wobbahs. . . ."

Count Ilyá Rostóv smiled blandly and nodded approval.

"And was our militia of any use to the Empia? Not at all! It only wuined our farming! Bettah have another conscwiption . . . o' ou' men will wetu'n neithah soldiers no' peasants, and we'll get only depwavity fwom them. The nobility don't gwudge theah lives—evewy one of us will go and bwing in more wecwuits, and the sov'weign" (that was the way he referred to the Emperor) "need only say the word and we'll all die fo' him!" added the orator with animation.

Count Rostóv's mouth watered with pleasure and he nudged Pierre, but Pierre wanted to speak himself. He pushed forward, feeling stirred, but not yet sure what stirred him or what he would say. Scarcely had he opened his mouth when one of the senators, a man without a tooth in his head, with a shrewd though angry expression, standing near the first speaker, interrupted him. Evidently accustomed to managing debates and to maintaining an argument, he began in low but distinct tones:

"I imagine, sir," said he, mumbling with his toothless mouth, "that we have been summoned here not to discuss whether it's best for the empire at the present moment to adopt conscription or to call out the militia. We have been summoned to reply to the appeal with which our sovereign the Emperor has honored us. But to judge what is best—conscription or the militia—we can leave to the supreme authority. . . ."

Pierre suddenly saw an outlet for his excitement. He hardened his heart against the senator who was introducing this set and narrow attitude into the deliberations of the nobility. Pierre stepped forward and interrupted him. He himself did not yet know what he would say, but he began to speak eagerly, occasionally lapsing into French or expressing himself in bookish Russian.

"Excuse me, your excellency," he began. (He was well acquainted with the senator, but thought it necessary on this occasion to address him formally.) "Though I don't agree with the gentleman . . ." (He hesitated: he wished to say, *"Mon très honorable préopinant"*—"My very honorable opponent") "with the gentleman . . . whom I have not the honor of knowing, I suppose that the nobility have been summoned not merely to express their sympathy and enthusiasm but also to consider the means by which we can assist our Fatherland! I imagine," he went on, warming to his subject, "that the Emperor himself would not be satisfied to find in us merely owners of serfs whom we are willing to devote to his service, and *chair à canon* we are ready to make of ourselves—and not to obtain from us any co-co-counsel."

Many persons withdrew from the circle, noticing the senator's sarcastic smile and the freedom of Pierre's remarks. Only Count Rostóv was pleased with them as he had been pleased with those of the naval officer, the senator, and in general with whatever speech he had last heard.

"I think that before discussing these questions," Pierre continued, "we should ask the Emperor—most respectfully ask his Majesty—to let us know the number of our troops and the position in which our army and our forces now are, and then . . ."

But scarcely had Pierre uttered these words before he was attacked from three sides. The most vigorous attack came from an old acquaintance, a boston player who had always been well disposed toward him, Stepán Stepánovich Adráksin. Adráksin was in uniform, and whether as a result of the uniform or from some other cause Pierre saw before him quite a different man. With a sudden expression of malevolence on his aged face, Adráksin shouted at Pierre:

"In the first place, I tell you we have no right to question the Emperor about that, and secondly, if the Russian nobility had that right, the Emperor could not answer such a question. The troops are moved according to the enemy's movements and the number of men increases and decreases. . . ."

Another voice, that of a nobleman of medium height and about forty years of age, whom Pierre had formerly met at the gypsies' and knew as a bad card-player, and who, also transformed by his uniform, came up to Pierre, interrupted Adráksin.

"Yes, and this is not a time for discussing," he continued, "but for acting: there is war in Russia! The enemy is advancing to destroy Russia, to desecrate the tombs of our fathers, to carry off our wives and children." The nobleman smote his breast. "We will all arise, every one of us will go, for our father the Tsar!" he shouted, rolling his bloodshot eyes. Several approving voices were heard in the crowd. "We are Russians and will not grudge our blood in defense of our faith, the throne and the Fatherland. We must cease raving if we are sons of our Fatherland! We will show Europe how Russia rises to the defense of Russia!"

Pierre wished to reply, but could not get in a word. He felt that his words, apart from what meaning they conveyed, were less audible than the sound of his opponent's voice.

Count Rostóv at the back of the crowd was expressing approval; several persons, briskly turning a shoulder to the orator at the end of a phrase, said:

"That's right, quite right! Just so!"

Pierre wished to say that he was ready to sacrifice his money, his serfs, or himself, only one ought to know the state of affairs in order to be able to improve it, but he was unable to speak. Many voices shouted and talked at the same time, so that Count Rostóv had not time to signify his approval of them all, and the group increased, dispersed, re-formed, and then moved with a hum of talk into the largest hall and to the big table. Not only was Pierre's attempt to speak unsuccessful, but he was rudely interrupted, pushed aside, and people turned away from him as from a common enemy. This happened not because they were displeased by the substance of his speech, which had even been forgotten after the many subsequent speeches, but to animate it the crowd needed a tangible object to love and a tangible object to hate. Pierre became the latter. Many other orators spoke after the excited nobleman, and all in the same tone. Many spoke eloquently and with originality.

Glínka, the editor of the *Russian Messenger*, who was recognized (cries of "author! author!" were heard in the crowd), said that "hell must be repulsed by hell," and that he had seen a child smiling at lightning flashes and thunderclaps, but "we will not be that child."

"Yes, yes, at thunderclaps!" was repeated approvingly in the back rows of the crowd.

The crowd drew up to the large table, at which sat gray-haired or bald seventy-year-old magnates, uniformed and besashed, almost all of whom Pierre had seen in their own homes with their buffoons, or playing boston at the clubs. With an incessant hum of voices the crowd advanced to the table. Pressed by the throng against the high backs of the chairs, the orators spoke one after another and sometimes two together. Those standing behind noticed what a speaker omitted to say and hastened to supply it. Others in that heat and crush racked their brains to find some thought and hastened to utter it. The old magnates, whom Pierre knew, sat and turned to look first at one and then at another, and their faces for the most part only expressed the fact that they found it very hot. Pierre, however, felt excited, and the general desire to show that they were ready to go to all lengths—which found expression in the tones and looks more than in the substance of the speeches—infected him too. He did not renounce his opinions, but felt himself in some way to blame and wished to justify himself.

"I only said that it would be more to the purpose to make sacrifices when we know what is needed!" said he, trying to be heard above the other voices.

One of the old men nearest to him looked round, but his attention was immediately diverted by an exclamation at the other side of the table.

"Yes, Moscow will be surrendered! She will be our expiation!" shouted one man.

"He is the enemy of mankind!" cried another. "Allow me to speak. . . ." "Gentlemen, you are crushing me! . . ."

Chapter XXIII

AT THAT MOMENT COUNT ROSTOPCHÍN WITH HIS PROTRUDING CHIN AND ALERT EYES, WEARING the uniform of a general with sash over his shoulder, entered the room, stepping briskly to the front of the crowd of gentry.

"Our sovereign the Emperor will be here in a moment," said Rostopchín. "I am straight from the palace. Seeing the position we are in, I think there is little need for discussion. The Emperor has deigned to summon us and the merchants. Millions will pour forth from there"—he pointed to the merchants' hall—"but our business is to supply men and not spare ourselves . . . That is the least we can do!"

A conference took place confined to the magnates sitting at the table. The whole consultation passed more than quietly. After all the preceding noise the sound of their old voices saying one after another, "I agree," or for variety, "I too am of that opinion" and so on, had even a mournful effect.

The secretary was told to write down the resolution of the Moscow nobility and gentry, that they would furnish ten men, fully equipped, out of every thousand serfs, as the Smolénsk gentry had done. Their chairs made a scraping noise as the gentlemen who had conferred rose with apparent relief, and began walking up and down, arm in arm, to stretch their legs and converse in couples.

"The Emperor! The Emperor!" a sudden cry resounded through the halls and the whole throng hurried to the entrance.

The Emperor entered the hall through a broad path between two lines of nobles. Every face expressed respectful, awestruck curiosity. Pierre stood rather far off and could not hear all that the Emperor said. From what he did hear he understood that the Emperor spoke of the danger threatening the empire and of the hopes he placed on the Moscow nobility. He was answered by a voice which informed him of the resolution just arrived at.

"Gentlemen!" said the Emperor with a quivering voice.

There was a rustling among the crowd and it again subsided, so that Pierre distinctly heard the pleasantly human voice of the Emperor saying with emotion:

"I never doubted the devotion of the Russian nobles, but today it has surpassed my expectations. I thank you in the name of the Fatherland! Gentlemen, let us act! Time is most precious. . . ."

The Emperor ceased speaking, the crowd began pressing round him, and rapturous exclamations were heard from all sides.

"Yes, most precious . . . a royal word," said Count Rostóv, with a sob. He stood at the back, and though he had heard hardly anything, understood everything in his own way.

From the hall of the nobility the Emperor went to that of the merchants. There he remained about ten minutes. Pierre was among those who saw him come out from the merchants' hall with tears of emotion in his eyes. As became known later, he had scarcely begun to address the merchants before tears gushed from his eyes and he concluded in a trembling voice. When Pierre saw the Emperor he was coming out accompanied by two merchants, one of whom Pierre knew, a fat *otkupshchík*. The other was the mayor, a man with a thin sallow face and narrow beard. Both were weeping. Tears filled the thin man's eyes, and the fat *otkupshchík* sobbed outright like a child, and kept repeating:

"Our lives and property—take them, your Majesty!"

Pierre's one feeling at the moment was a desire to show that he was ready to go all lengths and was prepared to sacrifice everything. He now felt ashamed of his speech with its constitutional tendency and sought an opportunity of effacing it. Having heard that Count Mamónov was furnishing a regiment, Bezúkhov at once informed Rostopchín that he would give a thousand men and their maintenance.

Old Rostóv could not tell his wife of what had passed without tears, and at once consented to Pétya's request and went himself to enter his name.

Next day the Emperor left Moscow. The assembled nobles all took off their uniforms and settled down again in their homes and clubs, and not without some groans gave orders to their stewards about the enrollment, feeling amazed themselves at what they had done.

Part Ten

Chapter I

NAPOLEON BEGAN THE WAR WITH RUSSIA BECAUSE HE COULD NOT RESIST GOING TO DRESden, could not help having his head turned by the homage he received, could not help donning a Polish uniform and yielding to the stimulating influence of a June morning, and could not refrain from bursts of anger in the presence of Kurákin and then of Balashëv.

Alexander refused negotiations because he felt himself to be personally insulted. Barclay de Tolly tried to command the army in the best way, because he wished to fulfill his duty and earn fame as a great commander. Rostóv charged the French because he could not restrain his wish for a gallop across a level field; and in the same way the innumerable people who took part in the war acted in accord with their personal characteristics, habits, circumstances and aims. They were moved by fear or vanity, rejoiced or were indignant, reasoned, imagining that they knew what they were doing and did it of their own free will, but they all were involuntary tools of history, carrying on a work concealed from them but comprehensible to us. Such is the inevitable fate of men of action, and the higher they stand in the social hierarchy the less are they free.

The actors of 1812 have long since left the stage, their personal interests have vanished leaving no trace, and nothing remains of that time but its historic results.

Providence compelled all these men, striving to attain personal aims, to further the accomplishment of a stupendous result no one of them at all expected—neither Napoleon, nor Alexander, nor still less any of those who did the actual fighting.

The cause of the destruction of the French army in 1812 is clear to us now. No one will deny that that cause was, on the one hand its advance into the heart of Russia late in the season without any preparation for a winter campaign, and on the other the character given to the war by the burning of Russian towns and the hatred of the foe this aroused among the Russian people. But no one at the time foresaw (what now seems so evident) that this was the only way an army of eight hundred thousand men—the best in the world and led by the best general—could be destroyed in conflict with a raw army of half its numerical strength, and led by inexperienced commanders as the Russian army was. *Not only did no one see this,* but *on the Russian side* every effort was made to hinder the only thing that could save Russia, while *on the French side,* despite Napoleon's experience and so-called military genius, every effort was directed to pushing on to Moscow at the end of the summer, that is, to doing the very thing that was bound to lead to destruction.

In historical works on the year 1812 French writers are very fond of saying that Napoleon felt the danger of extending his line, that he sought a battle and that his marshals advised him to stop at Smolénsk, and of making similar statements to show that the danger of the campaign was even then understood. Russian authors are still fonder of telling us that from the commencement of the campaign a Scythian war-plan was adopted to lure Napoleon into the depths of Russia, and this plan some of them attribute to Pfuel, others to a certain Frenchman, others to Toll, and others again to Alexander himself—pointing to notes, projects and letters which contain hints of such a line of action. But all these hints at what happened, both from the French side and the Russian, are advanced only because they fit in with the event. Had that event not occurred these hints would have been forgotten, as we have forgotten the thousands and millions of hints and expectations to the contrary which were current then but have now been forgotten because the event falsified them. There are always so many conjectures as to the issue of any event, that however it may end there will always be people to say: "I said then that it would be so," quite forgetting that amid their innumerable conjectures many were to quite the contrary effect.

Conjectures as to Napoleon's awareness of the danger of extending his line, and (on the Russian side) as to luring the enemy into the depths of Russia, are evidently of that kind, and only by much straining can historians attribute such conceptions to Napoleon and his marshals, or such plans to the Russian commanders. All the facts are in flat contradiction to such conjectures. During the whole period of the war not only was there no wish on the Russian side to draw the French into the heart of the country, but from their first entry into Russia everything was done to stop them. And not only was Napoleon not afraid to extend his line, but he welcomed every step forward as a triumph and did not seek battle as eagerly as in former campaigns, but very lazily.

At the very beginning of the war our armies were divided, and our sole aim was to unite them, though uniting the armies was no advantage if we meant to retire and lure the enemy into the depths of the country. Our Emperor joined the army to encourage it to defend every inch of Russian soil and not to retreat. The enormous Drissa camp was formed on Pfuel's plan, and there was no intention of retiring farther. The Emperor reproached the commanders in chief for every step they retired. He could not bear the idea of letting the enemy even reach Smolénsk, still less could he contemplate the burning of Moscow, and when our armies did unite he was displeased that Smolénsk was abandoned and burned without a general engagement having been fought under its walls.

So thought the Emperor, and the Russian commanders and people were still more provoked at the thought that our forces were retreating into the depths of the country.

Napoleon having cut our armies apart advanced far into the country and missed several chances of forcing an engagement. In August he was at Smolénsk and thought only of how to advance farther, though as we now see that advance was evidently ruinous to him.

The facts clearly show that Napoleon did not foresee the danger of the advance on Moscow, nor did Alexander and the Russian commanders then think of luring Napoleon on, but quite the contrary. The luring of Napoleon into the depths of the country was not the result of any plan, for no one believed it to be possible; it resulted from a most complex interplay of intrigues, aims and wishes among those who took part in the war and had no perception whatever of the inevitable, or of the one way of saving Russia. Everything came about fortuitously. The armies were divided at the commencement of the campaign. We tried to unite them, with the evident intention of giving battle and checking the enemy's advance, and by this effort to unite them while avoiding battle with a much stronger enemy, and necessarily withdrawing the armies at an acute angle—we led the French on to Smolénsk. But we withdrew at an acute angle not only because the French advanced between our two armies; the angle became still more acute and we withdrew still farther, because Barclay de Tolly was an unpopular foreigner disliked by Bagratión (who would come his command), and Bagratión—being in command of the second army—tried to postpone joining up and coming under Barclay's command as long as he could. Bagratión was slow in effecting the junction—though that was the chief aim of all at headquarters—because, as he alleged, he exposed his army to danger on this march, and it was best for him to retire more to the left and more to the south, worrying the enemy from flank and rear and securing from the Ukraine recruits for his army; and it looks as if he planned this in order not to come under the command of the detested foreigner Barclay, whose rank was inferior to his own.

The Emperor was with the army to encourage it, but his presence and ignorance of what steps to take, and the enormous number of advisers and plans, destroyed the first army's energy and it retired.

The intention was to make a stand at the Drissa camp, but Paulucci, aiming at becoming commander-in-chief, unexpectedly employed his energy to influence Alexander, and Pfuel's whole plan was abandoned and the command entrusted to Barclay. But as Barclay did not inspire confidence his power was limited. The armies were divided, there was no unity of command, and Barclay was unpopular; but from this confusion, division, and the unpopularity of the foreign commander-in-chief, there resulted on the one hand indecision and the avoidance of a battle (which we could not have refrained from had the armies been united and had someone else, instead of Barclay, been in command) and on the other an ever-increasing indignation against the foreigners and an increase in patriotic zeal.

At last the Emperor left the army, and as the most convenient and indeed the only pretext for his departure it was decided that it was necessary for him to inspire the people in the capitals and arouse the nation in general to a patriotic war. And by this visit of the Emperor to Moscow the strength of the Russian army was trebled.

He left in order not to obstruct the commander-in-chief's undivided control of the army, and hoping that more decisive action would then be taken, but the command of the armies became still more confused and enfeebled. Bennigsen, the Tsarévich, and a swarm of adjutants-general remained with the army to keep the commander-in-chief under observation and arouse his energy, and Barclay, feeling less free than ever under the observation of all these "eyes of the Emperor," became still more cautious of undertaking any decisive action and avoided giving battle.

Barclay stood for caution. The Tsarévich hinted at treachery and demanded a general engagement. Lubomírski, Bronnítski, Wlocki and the others of that group, stirred up so much trouble that Barclay, under pretext of sending papers to the Emperor, dispatched these Polish adjutants-general to Petersburg, and plunged into an open struggle with Bennigsen and the Tsarévich.

At Smolénsk the armies at last reunited, much as Bagratión disliked it.

Bagratión drove up in a carriage to to the house occupied by Barclay. Barclay donned his sash and came out to meet and report to his senior officer Bagratión.

Despite his seniority in rank Bagratión, in this contest of magnanimity, took his orders from Barclay, but, having submitted, agreed with him less than ever. By the Emperor's orders Bagratión reported direct to him. He wrote to Arakchéev, the Emperor's confidant: "It must be as my Sovereign pleases, but I cannot work with the *Minister* (meaning Barclay). For God's sake send me somewhere else if only in command of a regiment. I cannot stand it here. Headquarters are so full of Germans that a Russian cannot exist and there is no sense in anything. I thought I was really serving my Sovereign and the Fatherland, but it turns out that I am serving Barclay. I confess I do not want to."

The swarm of Bronnítskis and Wintzingerodes and their like still further embittered the relations between the commanders in chief, and even less unity resulted. Preparations were made to fight the French before Smolénsk. A general was sent to survey the position. This general, hating Barclay, rode to visit a friend of his own, a corps-commander, and having spent the day with him, returned to Barclay and condemned, as unsuitable from every point of view, the battleground he had not seen.

While disputes and intrigues were going on about the future field of battle, and while we were looking for the French—having lost touch with them—the French stumbled upon Nevérovski's division and reached the walls of Smolénsk.

It was necessary to fight an unexpected battle at Smolénsk to save our lines of communication. The battle was fought and thousands were killed on both sides.

Smolénsk was abandoned contrary to the wishes of the Emperor and of the whole people. But Smolénsk was burned by its own inhabitants who had been misled by their governor. And these ruined inhabitants, setting an example to other Russians, went to Moscow thinking only of their own losses but kindling hatred of the foe. Napoleon advanced farther and we retired, thus arriving at the very result which caused his destruction.

Chapter II

THE DAY AFTER HIS SON HAD LEFT, PRINCE NICHOLAS SENT FOR PRINCESS MARY TO COME TO HIS study.

"Well? Are you satisfied now?" said he. "You've made me quarrel with my son! Satisfied, are you? That's all you wanted! Satisfied? . . . It hurts me, it hurts. I'm old and weak and this is what you wanted. Well then, gloat over it! Gloat over it!"

After that Princess Mary did not see her father for a whole week. He was ill and did not leave his study.

Princess Mary noticed to her surprise that during this illness the old prince not only excluded her from his room, but did not admit Mademoiselle Bourienne either. Tíkhon alone attended him.

At the end of the week the prince reappeared and resumed his former way of life, devoting himself with special activity to building operations and the arrangement of the gardens, and completely breaking off his relations with Mademoiselle Bourienne. His looks and cold tone to his daughter seemed to say: "There, you see? You plotted against me, you lied to Prince Andrew about my relations with that Frenchwoman and made me quarrel with him, but you see I need neither her nor you!"

Princess Mary spent half of every day with little Nicholas, watching his lessons, teaching him Russian and music herself, and talking to Dessalles; the rest of the day she spent over her books, with her old nurse, or with "God's folk" who sometimes came by the back door to see her.

Of the war Princess Mary thought as women do think about wars. She feared for her brother who was in it, was horrified by and amazed at the strange cruelty that impels men to kill one another, but she did not understand the significance of this war, which seemed to her like all previous wars. She did not realize the significance of this war, though Dessalles with whom she constantly conversed was passionately interested in its progress and tried to explain his own conception of it to her, and though the "God's folk" who came to see her reported, in their own way, the rumors current among the people of an invasion by Antichrist, and though Julie (now Princess Drubetskáya), who had resumed correspondence with her, wrote patriotic letters from Moscow.

"I write you in Russian, my good friend," wrote Julie in her Frenchified Russian, "because I have a detestation for all the French, and the same for their language which I cannot support to hear spoken. . . . We in Moscow are elated by enthusiasm for our adored Emperor.

"My poor husband is enduring pains and hunger in Jewish taverns, but the news which I have inspires me yet more.

"You heard probably of the heroic exploit of Raévski, embracing his two sons and saying: 'I will perish with them but we will not be shaken!' And truly though the enemy was twice stronger than we, we were unshakeable. We pass the time as we can, but in war as in war! The princesses Aline and Sophie sit whole days with me, and we, unhappy widows of live men, make beautiful conversations over our *charpie,* only you my friend are missing . . ." and so on.

The chief reason Princess Mary did not realize the full significance of this war was that the old prince never spoke of it, did not recognize it, and laughed at Dessalles when he mentioned it at dinner. The prince's tone was so calm and confident that Princess Mary unhesitatingly believed him.

All that July the old prince was exceedingly active and even animated. He planned another garden and began a new building for the domestic serfs. The only thing that made Princess Mary anxious about him was that he slept very little and, instead of sleeping in his study as usual, changed his sleeping place every day. One day he would order his camp-bed to be set up in the glass-gallery, another day he remained on the couch or on the lounge-chair in the drawing room and dozed there without undressing, while—instead of Mademoiselle Bourienne—a serf boy read to him. Then again he would spend a night in the dining room.

On August 1st a second letter was received from Prince Andrew. In his first letter which came soon after he had left home, Prince Andrew had dutifully asked his father's forgiveness for what he had allowed himself to say, and begged to be restored to his favor. To this letter the old prince had replied affectionately, and from that time had kept the Frenchwoman at a distance. Prince Andrew's second letter, written near Vítebsk after the French had occupied that town, gave a brief account of the whole campaign, enclosed for them a plan he had drawn and forecasts as to the further progress of the war. In this letter Prince Andrew pointed out to his father the danger of staying at Bald Hills, so near the theater of war and on the army's direct line of march, and advised him to move to Moscow.

At dinner that day, on Dessalles' mentioning that the French were said to have already entered Vítebsk, the old prince remembered his son's letter.

"There was a letter from Prince Andrew today," he said to Princess Mary—"Haven't you read it?"

"No, father," she replied in a frightened voice.

She could not have read the letter as she did not even know it had arrived.

"He writes about this war," said the prince, with the ironic smile that had become habitual to him in speaking of the present war.

"That must be very interesting," said Dessalles. "Prince Andrew is in a position to know . . ."

"Oh, very interesting!" said Mademoiselle Bourienne.

"Go and get it for me," said the old prince to Mademoiselle Bourienne. "You know—under the paper-weight on the little table."

Mademoiselle Bourienne jumped up eagerly.

"No, don't!" he exclaimed with a frown. "You go, Michael Ivánovich."

Michael Ivánovich rose and went to the study. But as soon as he had left the room the old prince, looking uneasily round, threw down his napkin and went himself.

"They can't do anything . . . always make some muddle," he muttered.

While he was away Princess Mary, Dessalles, Mademoiselle Bourienne, and even little Nicholas, exchanged looks in silence. The old prince returned with quick steps, accompanied by Michael Ivánovich, bringing the letter and a plan. These he put down beside him—not letting anyone read them at dinner.

On moving to the drawing room he handed the letter to Princess Mary and, spreading out before him the plan of the new building and fixing his eyes upon it, told her to read the letter aloud. When she had done so Princess Mary looked inquiringly at her father. He was examining the plan, evidently engrossed in his own ideas.

"What do you think of it, prince?" Dessalles ventured to ask.

"I? I? . . ." said the prince as if unpleasantly awakened, and not taking his eyes from the plan of the building.

"Very possibly the theater of war will move so near to us that . . ."

"Ha ha ha! The theater of war!" said the prince. "I have said and still say, that the theater of war is Poland and the enemy will never get beyond the Niemen."

Dessalles looked in amazement at the prince, who was talking of the Niemen when the enemy was already at the Dnieper, but Princess Mary, forgetting the geographical position of the Niemen, thought that what her father was saying was correct.

"When the snow melts they'll sink in the Polish swamps. Only they could fail to see it," the prince continued, evidently thinking of the campaign of 1807 which seemed to him so recent. "Bennigsen should have advanced into Prussia sooner, then things would have taken a different turn . . ."

"But, prince," Dessalles began timidly, "the letter mentions Vítebsk. . . ."

"Ah, the letter? Yes . . ." replied the prince, peevishly. "Yes . . . yes . . ." His face suddenly took on a morose expression. He paused. "Yes, he writes that the French were beaten at . . . at . . . what river is it?"

Dessalles dropped his eyes.

"The prince says nothing about that," he remarked gently.

"Doesn't he? But I didn't invent it myself."

No one spoke for a long time.

"Yes . . . yes . . . Well, Michael Ivánovich," he suddenly went on, raising his head and pointing to the plan of the building, "tell me how you mean to alter it. . . ."

Michael Ivánovich went up to the plan, and the prince after speaking to him about the building looked angrily at Princess Mary and Dessalles and went to his own room.

Princess Mary saw Dessalles' embarrassed and astonished look fixed on her father, noticed his silence, and was struck by the fact that her father had forgotten his son's letter on the drawing room table; but she was not only afraid to speak of it and ask Dessalles the reason of his confusion and silence, but was afraid even to think about it.

In the evening Michael Ivánovich, sent by the prince, came to Princess Mary for Prince Andrew's letter which had been forgotten in the drawing room. She gave it to him and, unpleasant as it was to her to do so, ventured to ask him what her father was doing.

"Always busy," replied Michael Ivánovich with a respectfully ironic smile which caused Princess Mary to turn pale. "He's worrying very much about the new building. He has been reading a little, but now"—Michael Ivánovich went on, lowering his voice—"now he's at his desk, busy with his will, I expect." (One of the prince's favorite occupations of late had been the preparation of some papers he meant to leave at his death and which he called his "will.")

"And Alpátych is being sent to Smolénsk?" asked Princess Mary.

"Oh, yes, he has been waiting to start for some time."

Chapter III

When Michael Ivánovich returned to the study with the letter, the old prince, with spectacles on and a shade over his eyes, was sitting at his open bureau with screened candles, holding a paper in his outstretched hand, and in a somewhat dramatic attitude was reading his manuscript—his "Remarks" as he termed it—which was to be transmitted to the Emperor after his death.

When Michael Ivánovich went in there were tears in the prince's eyes evoked by the memory of the time when the paper he was now reading had been written. He took the letter from Michael Ivánovich's hand, put it in his pocket, folded up his papers, and called in Alpátych who had long been waiting.

The prince had a list of things to be bought in Smolénsk, and walking up and down the room past Alpátych who stood by the door, he gave his instructions.

"First, notepaper—do you hear? Eight quires, like this sample, gilt-edged . . . it must be exactly like the sample. Varnish, sealing-wax, as in Michael Ivánovich's list."

He paced up and down for a while and glanced at his notes.

"Then hand to the governor in person a letter about the deed."

Next, bolts for the doors of the new building were wanted and had to be of a special shape the prince had himself designed, and a leather case had to be ordered to keep the "will" in.

The instructions to Alpátych took over two hours and still the prince did not let him go. He sat down, sank into thought, closed his eyes, and dozed off. Alpátych made a slight movement.

"Well, go, go! If anything more is wanted I'll send after you."

Alpátych went out. The prince again went to his bureau, glanced into it, fingered his papers, closed the bureau again, and sat down at the table to write to the governor.

It was already late when he rose after sealing the letter. He wished to sleep, but he knew he would not be able to, and that most depressing thoughts came to him in bed. So he called Tíkhon and went through the rooms with him to show him where to set up the bed for that night.

He went about looking at every corner. Every place seemed unsatisfactory, but worst of all was his customary couch in the study. That couch was dreadful to him, probably because of the oppressive thoughts he had had when lying there. It was unsatisfactory everywhere, but the corner behind the piano in the sitting room was better than other places; he had never slept there yet.

With the help of a footman Tíkhon brought in the bedstead and began putting it up.

"That's not right! That's not right!" cried the prince, and himself pushed it a few inches from the corner and then closer in again.

"Well, at last I've finished, now I'll rest," thought the prince, and let Tíkhon undress him.

Frowning with vexation at the effort necessary to divest himself of his coat and trousers, the prince undressed, sat down heavily on the bed, and appeared to be meditating as he looked contemptuously at his withered yellow legs. He was not meditating, but only deferring the moment of making the effort to lift those legs up and turn over on the bed. "Ugh, how hard it is! Oh, that this toil might end and *you* would release me!" thought he. Pressing his lips together he made that effort for the twenty-thousandth time and lay down. But hardly had he done so before he felt the bed rocking backward and forward beneath him as if it were breathing heavily and jolting. This happened to him almost every night. He opened his eyes as they were closing.

"No peace, damn them!" he muttered, angry he knew not with whom. "Ah yes, there was something else important, very important, that I was keeping till I should be in bed. The bolts? No, I told him about them. No, it was something, something in the drawing room. Princess Mary talked some nonsense. Dessalles, that fool, said something. Something in my pocket—can't remember. . . ."

"Tíkhon, what did we talk about at dinner?"

"About Prince Michael . . ."

"Be quiet, quiet!" The prince slapped his hand on the table. "Yes, I know, Prince Andrew's letter! Princess Mary read it. Dessalles said something about Vítebsk. Now I'll read it."

He had the letter taken from his pocket, and the table—on which stood a glass of lemonade and a spiral wax candle—moved close to the bed, and putting on his spectacles he began reading. Only now in the stillness of the night, reading it by the faint light under the green shade, did he grasp its meaning for a moment.

"The French at Vítebsk, in four days' march they may be at Smolénsk; perhaps are already there! Tíkhon!" Tíkhon jumped up. "No, no, I don't want anything!" he shouted.

He put the letter under the candlestick and closed his eyes. And there rose before him the Danube at bright noonday: reeds, the Russian camp, and himself a young general without a wrinkle on his ruddy face, vigorous and alert, entering Potëmkin's gaily-colored tent, and a burning sense of jealousy of "the favorite" agitated him now as strongly as it had done then. He recalled all the words spoken at that first meeting with Potëmkin. And he saw before him a plump, rather sallow-faced, short, stout woman, the Empress-Mother, with her smile and her words at her first gracious reception of him, and then that same face on the catafalque, and the encounter he had with Zúbov over her coffin about his right to kiss her hand.

"Oh, quicker, quicker! To get back to that time and have done with all the present! Quicker, quicker—and that they should leave me in peace!"

Chapter IV

BALD HILLS, PRINCE NICHOLAS BOLKÓNSKI'S ESTATE, LAY FORTY MILES EAST FROM SMOLÉNSK AND two miles from the main road to Moscow.

The same evening that the prince gave his instructions to Alpátych, Dessalles having asked to see Princess Mary, told her that, as the prince was not very well and was taking no steps to secure his safety, though from Prince Andrew's letter it was evident that to remain at Bald Hills might be dangerous, he respectfully advised her to send a letter by Alpátych to the Provincial Governor at Smolénsk, asking him to let her know the state of affairs and the extent of the danger to which Bald Hills was exposed. Dessalles wrote this letter to the Governor for Princess Mary, she signed it, and it was given to Alpátych with instructions to hand it to the Governor and to come back as quickly as possible if there was danger.

Having received all his orders Alpátych, wearing a white beaver hat—a present from the prince—and carrying a stick as the prince did, went out accompanied by his family. Three well-fed roans stood ready harnessed to a small conveyance with a leather hood.

The larger bell was muffled and the little bells on the harness stuffed with paper. The prince allowed no one at Bald Hills to drive with ringing bells, but on a long journey Alpátych liked to have them. His satellites—the senior clerk, a counting house clerk, a scullery maid, a cook, two old women, a little page boy, the coachman and various domestic serfs—were seeing him off.

His daughter placed chintz-covered down cushions for him to sit on and behind his back. His old sister-in-law popped in a small bundle, and one of the coachmen helped him into the vehicle.

"There! There! Women's fuss! Women, women!" said Alpátych, puffing and speaking rapidly just as the prince did, and he climbed into the trap.

After giving the clerk orders about the work to be done, Alpátych, not trying to imitate the prince now, lifted the hat from his bald head and crossed himself three times.

"If there is anything . . . come back, Yákov Alpátych! For Christ's sake think of us!" cried his wife, referring to the rumors of war and the enemy.

"Women, women! Women's fuss!" muttered Alpátych to himself and started on his journey, looking round at the fields of yellow rye and the still green, thickly growing oats, and at other quite black fields just being plowed a second time.

As he went along he looked with pleasure at the year's splendid crop of corn, scrutinized the strips of ryefield which here and there were already being reaped, made his calculations as to the sowing and the harvest, and asked himself whether he had not forgotten any of the prince's orders.

Having baited the horses twice on the way, he arrived at the town toward evening on the 4th of August.

Alpátych kept meeting and overtaking baggage-trains and troops on the road. As he approached Smolénsk he heard the sounds of distant firing, but these did not impress him. What struck him most was the sight of a splendid field of oats in which a camp had been pitched, and which was being mown down by the soldiers evidently for fodder. This fact impressed Alpátych, but in thinking about his own business he soon forgot it.

All the interests of his life for more than thirty years had been bounded by the will of the prince, and he never went beyond that limit. Everything not connected with the execution of the prince's orders did not interest and did not even exist for Alpátych.

On reaching Smolénsk on the evening of the 4th of August he put up in the Gáchina suburb across the Dnieper, at the inn kept by Ferapóntov, where he had been in the habit of putting up for the last thirty years. Some thirty years ago Ferapóntov, by Alpátych's advice, had bought a wood from the prince, had begun to trade, and now had a house, an inn and a corn-dealer's shop in that province. He was a stout, dark, red-faced peasant in the forties, with thick lips, a broad knob of a nose, similar knobs over his black frowning brows, and a round belly.

Wearing a waistcoat over his cotton shirt, Ferapóntov was standing before his shop which opened onto the street. On seeing Alpátych he went up to him.

"You're welcome, Yákov Alpátych. Folks are leaving the town, but you have come to it," said he.

"Why are they leaving the town?" asked Alpátych.

"That's what I say. Folks are foolish! Always afraid of the French."

"Women's fuss, women's fuss!" said Alpátych.

"Just what I think, Yákov Alpátych. What I say is: orders have been given not to let them in, so that must be right. And the peasants are asking three rubles for carting—it isn't Christian!"

Yákov Alpátych heard without heeding. He asked for a samovar and for hay for his horses, and when he had had his tea he went to bed.

All night long troops were moving past the inn. Next morning Alpátych donned a jacket he wore only in town, and went out on business. It was a sunny morning and by eight o'clock it was already hot. "A good day for harvesting," thought Alpátych.

From beyond the town firing had been heard since early morning. At eight o'clock the booming of cannon was added to the sound of musketry. Many people were hurrying through the streets and there were many soldiers, but cabs were still driving about, tradesmen stood at their shops, and service was being held in the churches as usual. Alpátych went to the shops, to government offices, to the post office and to the Governor's. In the offices and shops and at the post office everyone was talking about the army and about the enemy who was already attacking the town, everybody was asking what should be done, and all were trying to calm one another.

In front of the Governor's house Alpátych found a large number of people, Cossacks, and a traveling carriage of the Governor's. At the porch he met two of the landed gentry, one of whom he knew. This man, an ex-captain of police, was saying angrily:

"It's no joke, you know! It's all very well if you're single. 'One man though undone is but one,' as the proverb says, but with thirteen in your family and all the property . . . They've brought us to utter ruin! What sort of Governors are they to do that? They ought to be hanged—the brigands! . . ."

"Oh come, that's enough!" said the other.

"What do I care? Let him hear! We're not dogs," said the ex-captain of police, and looking round he noticed Alpátych.

"Oh, Yákov Alpátych! What have you come for?"

"To see the Governor by his excellency's order," answered Alpátych, lifting his head and proudly thrusting his hand into the bosom of his coat as he always did when he mentioned the prince. . . . "He has ordered me to inquire into the position of affairs," he added.

"Yes, go and find out!" shouted the angry gentleman. "They've brought things to such a pass that there are no carts or anything! . . . There it is again, do you hear?" said he, pointing in the direction whence came the sounds of firing.

"They've brought us all to ruin . . . the brigands!" he repeated, and descended the porch steps.

Alpátych swayed his head and went upstairs. In the waiting room were tradesmen, women and officials, looking silently at one another. The door of the Governor's room opened and they all rose and moved forward. An official ran out, said some words to a merchant, called a stout official with a cross hanging on his neck to follow him, and vanished again, evidently wishing to avoid the inquiring looks and questions addressed to him. Alpátych moved forward and next time the official came out addressed him, one hand placed in the breast of his buttoned coat, and handed him two letters.

"To his Honor Baron Asch, from General-in-Chief Prince Bolkónski," he announced with such solemnity and significance that the official turned to him and took the letters.

A few minutes later the Governor received Alpátych and hurriedly said to him:

"Inform the prince and princess that I knew nothing: I acted on the highest instructions—here . . ." and he handed a paper to Alpátych. "Still, as the prince is unwell my advice is that they should go to Moscow. I am just starting myself. Inform them . . ."

But the Governor did not finish: a dusty perspiring officer ran into the room and began to say something in French. The Governor's face expressed terror.

"Go," he said, nodding his head to Alpátych, and began questioning the officer.

Eager, frightened, helpless glances were turned on Alpátych when he came out of the Governor's room. Involuntarily listening now to the firing, which had drawn nearer and was increasing in strength, Alpátych hurried to his inn. The paper handed to him by the Governor said this:

"I assure you that the town of Smolénsk is not in the slightest danger as yet and it is unlikely that it will be threatened with any. I from the one side and Prince Bagratión from the other are marching to unite our forces before Smolénsk, which junction will be effected on the 22nd instant, and both armies with their united forces will defend our compatriots of the province entrusted to your care till our efforts shall have beaten back the enemies of our Fatherland, or till the last warrior in our valiant ranks has perished. From this you will see that you have a perfect right to reassure the inhabitants of Smolénsk, for those defended by two such brave armies may feel assured of victory." (Instructions from Barclay de Tolly to Baron Asch, the civil governor of Smolénsk, 1812.)

People were anxiously roaming about the streets.

Carts piled high with household utensils, chairs and cupboards, kept emerging from the gates of the yards and moving along the streets. Loaded carts stood at the house next to Ferapóntov's and women were wailing and lamenting as they said good-bye. A small watch-dog ran round barking in front of the harnessed horses.

Alpátych entered the inn yard at a quicker pace than usual and went straight to the shed where his horses and trap were. The coachman was asleep. He woke him up, told him to harness, and went into the passage. From the host's room came the sounds of a child crying, the despairing sobs of a woman, and the hoarse angry shouting of Ferapóntov. The cook began running hither and thither in the passage like a frightened hen, just as Alpátych entered.

"He's done her to death. Killed the mistress! . . . Beat her . . . dragged her about so! . . ."

"What for?" asked Alpátych.

"She kept begging to go away. She's a woman! 'Take me away,' says she, 'don't let me perish with my little children! Folks,' she says, 'are all gone, so why,' she says, 'don't we go?' And he began beating and pulling her about so!"

At these words Alpátych nodded as if in approval, and not wishing to hear more went to the door of the room opposite the inn-keeper's, where he had left his purchases.

"You brute, you murderer!" screamed a thin, pale woman who, with a baby in her arms and her kerchief torn from her head, burst through the door at that moment and down the steps into the yard.

Ferapóntov came out after her, but on seeing Alpátych adjusted his waistcoat, smoothed his hair, yawned and followed Alpátych into the opposite room.

"Going already?" said he.

Alpátych, without answering or looking at his host, sorted his packages and asked how much he owed.

"We'll reckon up! Well, have you been to the Governor's?" asked Ferapóntov. "What has been decided?"

Alpátych replied that the Governor had not told him anything definite.

"With our business, how can we get away?" said Ferapóntov. "We'd have to pay seven rubles a cartload to Dorogobúzh and I tell them they're not Christians to ask it! Selivánov, now, did a good stroke last Thursday—sold flour to the army at nine rubles a sack. Will you have some tea?" he added.

While the horses were being harnessed Alpátych and Ferapóntov over their tea talked of the price of corn, the crops and the good weather for harvesting.

"Well, it seems to be getting quieter," remarked Ferapóntov, finishing his third cup of tea and getting up. "Ours must have got the best of it. The orders were not to let them in. So we're in force, it seems. . . . They say the other day Matthew Iványch Plátov drove them into the river Márina and drowned some eighteen thousand in one day."

Alpátych collected his parcels, handed them to the coachman who had come in, and settled up with the innkeeper. The noise of wheels, hoofs and bells was heard from the gateway as a little trap passed out.

It was by now late in the afternoon. Half the street was in shadow, the other half brightly lit by the sun. Alpátych looked out of the window and went to the door. Suddenly the strange sound of a far-off whistling and thud was heard, followed by a boom of cannon blending into a dull roar that set the windows rattling.

He went out into the street: two men were running past toward the bridge. From different sides came whistling sounds and the thud of cannon-balls and bursting shells falling on the town. But these sounds were hardly heard in comparison with the noise of the firing outside the town, and attracted little attention from the inhabitants. The town was being bombarded by a hundred and thirty guns which Napoleon had ordered up after four o'clock. The people did not at once realize the meaning of this bombardment.

At first the noise of the falling bombs and shells only aroused curiosity. Ferapóntov's wife who till then had not ceased wailing under the shed, became quiet, and with the baby in her arms went to the gate listening to the sounds and looking in silence at the people.

The cook and a shop-assistant came to the gate. With lively curiosity everyone tried to get a glimpse of the projectiles as they flew over their heads. Several people came round the corner talking eagerly.

"What force!" remarked one. "Knocked the roof and ceiling all to splinters!"

"Routed up the earth like a pig," said another.

"That's grand, it bucks one up!" laughed the first. "Lucky you jumped aside, or it would have wiped you out!"

Others joined those men, and stopped and told how cannon-balls had fallen on a house close to them. Meanwhile still more projectiles, now with the swift sinister whistle of a cannon-ball, now with the agreeable, intermittent whistle of a shell, flew over people's heads incessantly, but not one fell close by, they all flew over. Alpátych was getting into his trap. The innkeeper stood at the gate.

"What are you staring at?" he shouted to the cook, who in her red skirt, with sleeves rolled up, swinging her bare elbows, had stepped to the corner to listen to what was being said.

"What marvels!" she exclaimed, but hearing her master's voice she turned back, pulling down her tucked-up skirt.

Once more something whistled, but this time quite close, swooping downward like a little bird; a flame flashed in the middle of the street, something exploded and the street was shrouded in smoke.

"Scoundrel, what are you doing?" shouted the innkeeper, rushing to the cook.

At that moment the pitiful wailing of women was heard from different sides, the frightened baby began to cry, and people crowded silently with pale faces round the cook. The loudest sound in that crowd was her wailing.

"Oh-h-h! Dear souls, dear kind souls! Don't let me die! My good souls! . . ."

Five minutes later no one remained in the street. The cook, with her thigh broken by a shell-splinter, had been carried into the kitchen. Alpátych, his coachman, Ferapóntov's wife and children and the house-porter were all sitting in the cellar listening. The roar of guns, the whistling of projectiles and the piteous moaning of the cook, which rose above the other sounds, did not cease for a moment. The mistress rocked and hushed her baby, and when anyone came into the cellar asked in a pathetic whisper what had become of her husband who had remained in the street. A shopman who entered told her that her husband had gone with others to the cathedral, whence they were fetching the wonder-working icon of Smolénsk.

Toward dusk the cannonade began to subside. Alpátych left the cellar and stopped in the doorway. The evening sky that had been so clear was clouded with smoke, through which, high up, the sickle of the new moon shone strangely. Now that the terrible din of the guns had ceased a hush seemed to reign over the town, broken only by the rustle of footsteps, the moaning, the distant cries and the crackle of fires which seemed widespread everywhere. The cook's moans had now subsided. On two sides black curling clouds of smoke rose and spread from the fires. Through the streets soldiers in various uniforms walked or ran confusedly in different directions like ants from a ruined ant-hill. Several of them ran into Ferapóntov's yard before Alpátych's eyes. Alpátych went out to the gate. A retreating regiment, thronging and hurrying, blocked the street.

Noticing him, an officer said: "The town is being abandoned. Get away, get away!" and then turning to the soldiers, shouted:

"I'll teach you to run into the yards!"

Alpátych went back to the house, called the coachman and told him to set off. Ferapóntov's whole household came out too, following Alpátych and the coachman. The women, who had been silent till then, suddenly began to wail as they looked at the fires—the smoke and even the flames of which could be seen in the failing twilight—and as if in reply the same kind of lamentation was heard from other parts of the street. Inside the shed Alpátych and the coachman arranged the tangled reins and traces of their horses with trembling hands.

As Alpátych was driving out of the gate he saw some ten soldiers in Ferapóntov's open shop, talking loudly and filling their bags and knapsacks with flour and sunflower seeds. Just then Ferapóntov returned and entered his shop. On seeing the soldiers he was about to shout at them, but suddenly stopped, and clutching at his hair burst into sobs and laughter:

"Loot everything, lads! Don't let those devils get it!" he cried, taking some bags of flour himself and throwing them into the street.

Some of the soldiers were frightened and ran away, others went on filling their bags. On seeing Alpátych, Ferapóntov turned to him:

"Russia is done for!" he cried. "Alpátych, I'll set the place on fire myself. We're done for! . . ." and Ferapóntov ran into the yard.

Soldiers were passing in a constant stream along the street blocking it completely, so that Alpátych could not pass out and had to wait. Ferapóntov's wife and children were also sitting in a cart waiting till it was possible to drive out.

Night had come. There were stars in the sky and the new moon shone out amid the smoke that screened it. On the sloping descent to the Dnieper Alpátych's cart and that of the innkeeper's wife, which were slowly moving amid the rows of soldiers and of other vehicles, had to stop. In a side street near the crossroads where the vehicles had stopped a house and some shops were on fire. This fire was already burning itself out. The flames now died down and were lost in the black smoke, now suddenly flared up again brightly, lighting up with strange distinctness the faces of the people crowding at the crossroads. Black figures flitted about before the fire, and through the incessant crackling of the flames talking and shouting could be heard. Seeing that his trap would not be able to move on for some time, Alpátych got down and turned into the side street to look at the fire. Soldiers were continually rushing backward and forward near it, and he saw two of them and a man in a frieze coat dragging burning beams into another yard across the street, while others carried bundles of hay.

Alpátych went up to a large crowd standing before a high barn which was blazing briskly. The walls were all on fire and the back wall had fallen in, the wooden roof was collapsing and the rafters were alight. The crowd was evidently watching for the roof to fall in, and Alpátych watched for it too.

"Alpátych!" a familiar voice suddenly hailed the old man.

"Mercy on us! Your excellency!" answered Alpátych, immediately recognizing the voice of his young prince.

Prince Andrew in his riding cloak, mounted on a black horse, was looking at Alpátych from the back of the crowd.

"Why are you here?" he asked.

"Your . . . your excellency," stammered Alpátych and broke into sobs. "Are we really lost? Master! . . ."

"Why are you here?" Prince Andrew repeated.

At that moment the flames flared up and showed his young master's pale worn face. Alpátych told how he had been sent there and how difficult it was to get away.

"Are we really quite lost, your excellency?" he asked again.

Prince Andrew without replying took out a notebook and raising his knee began writing in pencil on a page he tore out. He wrote to his sister:

"Smolénsk is being abandoned. Bald Hills will be occupied by the enemy within a week. Set off immediately for Moscow. Let me know at once when you will start. Send by special messenger to Usvyázh."

Having written this and given the paper to Alpátych, he told him how to arrange for departure of the prince, the princess, his son and the boy's tutor, and how and where to let him know immediately. Before he had had time to finish giving these instructions, a chief of staff followed by a suite galloped up to him.

"You are a colonel?" shouted the chief of staff with a German accent, in a voice familiar to Prince Andrew. "Houses are set on fire in your presence and you stand by! What does this mean? You will answer for it!" shouted Berg, who was now assistant to the chief of staff of the commander of the left flank of the infantry of the First Army, a place, as Berg said, "very agreeable and well *en évidence.*"

Prince Andrew looked at him and without replying went on speaking to Alpátych.

"So tell them that I shall await a reply till the 10th, and if by the 10th I don't receive news that they have all got away I shall have to throw up everything and come myself to Bald Hills."

"Prince," said Berg, recognizing Prince Andrew, "I only spoke because I have to obey orders, because I always do obey exactly. . . . You must please excuse me," he went on apologetically.

Something cracked in the flames. The fire died down for a moment and wreaths of black smoke rolled from under the roof. There was another terrible crash and something huge collapsed.

"Ou-rou-rou!" yelled the crowd, echoing the crash of the collapsing roof of the barn, the burning grain in which diffused a cakelike aroma all around. The flames flared up again, lighting the animated, delighted, exhausted faces of the spectators.

The man in the frieze coat raised his arms and shouted:

"It's fine, lads! Now it's raging . . . It's fine!"

"That's the owner himself," cried several voices.

"Well then," continued Prince Andrew to Alpátych, "report to them as I have told you"; and not replying a word to Berg who was now mute beside him, he touched his horse and rode down the side street.

Chapter V

From Smolénsk the troops continued to retreat, followed by the enemy. On the 10th of August the regiment Prince Andrew commanded was marching along the highroad past the avenue leading to Bald Hills. Heat and drought had continued for more than three weeks. Each day fleecy clouds floated across the sky and occasionally veiled the sun, but toward evening the sky cleared again and the sun set in reddish-brown mist. Heavy night-dews alone refreshed the earth. The unreaped corn was scorched and shed its grain. The marshes dried up. The cattle lowed from hunger, finding no food on the sun-parched meadows. Only at night and in the forests while the dew lasted was there any freshness. But on the road, the highroad along which the troops marched, there was no such freshness even at night or when the road passed through the forest; the dew was imperceptible on the sandy dust churned up more than six inches deep. As soon as day dawned the march began. The artillery and baggage-wagons moved noiselessly through the deep dust that rose to the very hubs of the wheels, and the infantry sank ankle-deep in that soft, choking, hot dust that never cooled even at night. Some of this dust was kneaded by the feet and wheels, while the rest rose and hung like a cloud over the troops, settling in eyes, ears, hair and nostrils, and worst of all in the lungs of the men and beasts as they moved along that road. The higher the sun rose the higher rose that cloud of dust, and through the screen of its hot fine particles one could look with naked eye at the sun, which showed like a huge crimson ball in the unclouded sky. There was no wind, and the men choked in that motionless atmosphere. They marched with handkerchiefs tied over their noses and mouths. When they passed through a village they all rushed to the wells and fought for the water, and drank it down to the mud.

Prince Andrew was in command of a regiment, and the management of that regiment, the welfare of the men and the necessity of receiving and giving orders, engrossed him. The burning of Smolénsk and its abandonment made an epoch in his life. A novel feeling of anger against the foe made him forget his own sorrow. He was entirely devoted to the affairs of his regiment and was considerate and kind to his men and officers. In the regiment they called him "our prince," were proud of him and loved him. But he was kind and gentle only to those of his regiment, to Timókhin and the like—people quite new to him, belonging to a different world and who could not know and understand his past. As soon as he came across a former acquaintance or anyone from the staff, he bristled up immediately and grew spiteful, ironical and contemptuous. Everything that reminded him of his past was repugnant to him, and so in his relations with that former circle he confined himself to trying to do his duty and not to be unfair.

In truth everything presented itself in a dark and gloomy light to Prince Andrew, especially after the abandonment of Smolénsk on the 6th of August (he considered that it could and should have been defended) and after his sick father had had to flee to Moscow, abandoning to pillage his dearly beloved Bald Hills which he had built and peopled. But despite this, thanks to his regiment, Prince Andrew had something to think about entirely apart from general questions. Two days previously he had received news that his father, son and sister had left for Moscow; and though there was nothing for him to do at Bald Hills, Prince Andrew with a characteristic desire to foment his own grief decided that he must ride there.

He ordered his horse to be saddled and, leaving his regiment on the march, rode to his father's estate where he had been born and spent his childhood. Riding past the pond where there used always to be dozens of women chattering as they rinsed their linen or beat it with wooden beetles, Prince Andrew noticed that there was not a soul about, and that the little washing-wharf, torn from its place and half submerged, was floating on its side in the middle of the pond. He rode to the keeper's lodge. No one at the stone entrance-gates of the drive and the door stood open. Grass had already begun to grow on the garden paths, and horses and calves were straying in the English park. Prince Andrew rode up to the hothouse; some of the glass panes were broken, and of the trees in tubs some were overturned and others dried up. He called for Tarás the gardener, but no one replied. Having gone round the corner of the hothouse to the ornamental garden, he saw that the carved garden fence was broken and branches of the plum trees had been torn off with the fruit. An old peasant whom Prince Andrew in his childhood had often seen at the gate, was sitting on a green garden seat, plaiting a bast shoe.

He was deaf and did not hear Prince Andrew ride up. He was sitting on the seat the old prince used to like to sit on, and beside him strips of bast were hanging on the broken and withered branch of a magnolia.

Prince Andrew rode up to the house. Several limes in the old garden had been cut down and a piebald mare and her foal were wandering in front of the house among the rose bushes. The shutters were all closed, except at one window which was open. A little serf boy, seeing Prince Andrew ran into the house. Alpátych, having sent his family away, was alone at Bald Hills and was sitting indoors reading the *Lives of the Saints.* On hearing that Prince Andrew had come, he went out with his spectacles on his nose, buttoning his coat, and hastily stepping up without a word began weeping and kissing Prince Andrew's knee.

Then, vexed at his own weakness, he turned away and began to report on the position of affairs. Everything precious and valuable had been removed to Boguchárovo. Seventy quarters of grain had also been carted away. The hay and the spring corn, of which Alpátych said there had been a remarkable crop that year, had been commandeered by the troops and mown down while still green. The peasants were ruined; some of them too had gone to Boguchárovo, only a few remained.

Without waiting to hear him out, Prince Andrew asked:

"When did my father and sister leave?" meaning when did they leave for Moscow.

Alpátych, understanding the question to refer to their departure for Boguchárovo, replied that they had left on the 7th, and again went into details concerning the estate management, asking for instructions.

"Am I to let the troops have the oats, and to take a receipt for them? We have still six hundred quarters left," he inquired.

"What am I to say to him?" thought Prince Andrew, looking down on the old man's bald head shining in the sun and seeing by the expression on his face that the old man himself understood how untimely such questions were, and only asked them to allay his grief.

"Yes, let them have it," replied Prince Andrew.

"If you noticed some disorder in the garden," said Alpátych, "it was impossible to prevent it. Three regiments have been here and spent the night, dragoons mostly. I took down the name and rank of their commanding officer, to hand in a complaint about it."

"Well, and what are you going to do? Will you stay here if the enemy occupies the place?" asked Prince Andrew.

Alpátych turned his face to Prince Andrew, looked at him, and suddenly with a solemn gesture raised his arm.

"He is my refuge! His will be done!" he exclaimed.

A group of bareheaded peasants was approaching across the meadow toward the prince.

"Well, good-bye!" said Prince Andrew, bending over to Alpátych. "You must go away too, take away what you can and tell the serfs to go to the Ryazán estate or to the one near Moscow."

Alpátych clung to Prince Andrew's leg and burst into sobs. Gently disengaging himself, the prince spurred his horse and rode down the avenue at a gallop.

The old man was still sitting in the ornamental garden, like a fly impassive on the face of a loved one who is dead, tapping the last on which he was making the bast shoe, and two little girls, running out from the hothouse carrying in their skirts plums they had plucked from the trees there, came upon Prince Andrew. On seeing the young master, the elder one with frightened look clutched her younger companion by the hand and hid with her behind a birch tree, not stopping to pick up some green plums they had dropped.

Prince Andrew turned away with startled haste, unwilling to let them see that they had been observed. He was sorry for the pretty frightened little girl, was afraid of looking at her, and yet felt an irresistible desire to do so. A new sensation of comfort and relief came over him when, seeing these girls, he realized the existence of other human interests entirely aloof from his own and just as legitimate as those that occupied him. Evidently these girls passionately desired one thing—to carry away and eat those green plums without being caught—and Prince Andrew shared their wish for the success of their enterprise. He could not resist looking at them once more. Believing their danger past, they sprang from their ambush and, chirruping something in their shrill little voices and holding up their skirts, their bare little sunburned feet scampered merrily and quickly across the meadow grass.

Prince Andrew was somewhat refreshed by having ridden off the dusty highroad along which the troops were moving. But not far from Bald Hills he again came out on the road and overtook his regiment at its halting place by the dam of a small pond. It was past one o'clock. The sun, a red ball through the dust, burned and scorched his back intolerably through his black coat. The dust always hung motionless above the buzz of talk that came from the resting troops. There was no wind. As he crossed the dam Prince Andrew smelled the ooze and freshness of the pond. He longed to get into that water however dirty it might be, and he glanced round at the pool from whence came sounds of shrieks and laughter. The small, muddy, green pond had risen visibly more than a foot, flooding the dam, because it was full of the naked white bodies of soldiers with brick-red hands, necks and faces, who were splashing about in it. All this naked white human flesh, laughing and shrieking, floundering about in that dirty pool like carp stuffed into a watering can, and the suggestion of merriment in that floundering mass rendered it specially pathetic.

One fair-haired young soldier of the third company, whom Prince Andrew knew and who had a strap round the calf of one leg, crossed himself, stepped back to get a good run, and plunged into the water; another, a dark non-commissioned officer who was always shaggy, stood up to his waist in the water joyfully wriggling his muscular figure and snorted with satisfaction as he poured the water over his head with hands blackened to the wrists. There were sounds of men slapping one another, yelling and puffing.

Everywhere on the bank, on the dam and in the pond, there was healthy, white, muscular flesh. The officer, Timókhin, with his red little nose, standing on the dam wiping himself with a towel, felt confused at seeing the prince, but made up his mind to address him nevertheless.

"It's very nice, your excellency! Wouldn't you like to?" said he.

"It's dirty," replied Prince Andrew making a grimace.

"We'll clear it out for you in a minute," said Timókhin, and, still undressed, ran off to clear the men out of the pond.

"The prince wants to bathe."

"What prince? Ours?" said many voices, and the men were in such haste to clear out that the prince could hardly stop them. He decided that he would rather souse himself with water in the barn.

"Flesh, bodies, cannon-fodder!" he thought, and he looked at his own naked body and shuddered, not from cold but from a sense of disgust and horror he did not himself understand, aroused by the sight of that immense number of bodies splashing about in the dirty pond.

On the 7th of August Prince Bagratión wrote as follows from his quarters at Mikháylovna on the Smolénsk road:

Dear Count Aléxis Andréevich—(He was writing to Arakchéev but knew that his letter would be read by the Emperor, and therefore weighed every word in it to the best of his ability.)

I expect the Minister (Barclay de Tolly) has already reported the abandonment of Smolénsk to the enemy. It is pitiable and sad, and the whole army is in despair that this most important place has been wantonly abandoned. I, for my part, begged him personally most urgently and finally wrote him, but nothing would induce him to consent. I swear to you on my honor that Napoleon was in such a fix as never before, and might have lost half his army but could not have taken Smolénsk. Our troops fought, and are fighting, as never before. With fifteen thousand men I held the enemy at bay for thirty-five hours and beat him; but *he* would not hold out even for fourteen hours. It is disgraceful, a stain on our army, and as for him, he ought, it seems to me, not to live. If he reports that our losses were great, it is not true; perhaps about four thousand, not more, and not even that; but even were they ten thousand, that's war! But the enemy has lost masses. . . .

What would it have cost him to hold out for another two days? They would have had to retire of their own accord, for they had no water for men or horses. He gave me his word he would not retreat, but suddenly sent instructions that he was retiring that night. We cannot fight in this way, or we may soon bring the enemy to Moscow. . . .

There is a rumor that you are thinking of peace. God forbid that you should make peace after all our sacrifices and such insane retreats! You would set all Russia against you and every one of us would feel ashamed to wear the uniform. If it has come to this—we must fight as long as Russia can and as long as there are men able to stand. . . .

One man ought to be in command, and not two. Your Minister may perhaps be good as a Minister, but as a general he is not merely bad but execrable, yet to him is entrusted the fate of our whole country. . . . I am really frantic with vexation; forgive my writing boldly. It is clear that the man who advocates the conclusion of a peace, and that the Minister should command the army, does not love our Sovereign and desires the ruin of us all. So I write you frankly: call out the militia. For the Minister is leading these visitors after him to Moscow in a most masterly way. The whole army feels great suspicion of the Imperial aide-de-camp Wolzogen. He is said to be more Napoleon's man than ours, and he is always advising the Minister. I am not merely civil to him but obey him like a corporal, though I am his senior. This is painful, but loving my benefactor and Sovereign I submit. Only I am sorry for the Emperor that he entrusts our fine army to such as he. Consider that on our retreat we have lost by fatigue and left in the hospital more than fifteen thousand men, and had we attacked this would not have happened. Tell me, for God's sake, what will Russia, our mother Russia, say to our being so frightened, and why are we abandoning our good and gallant Fatherland to such rabble, and implanting feelings of hatred and shame in all our subjects? What are we scared at and of whom are we afraid? I am not to blame that the Minister is vacillating, a coward, dense, dilatory and has all bad qualities. The whole army bewails it and calls down curses upon him. . . .

Chapter VI

Among the innumerable categories applicable to the phenomena of human life one may discriminate between those in which substance prevails and those in which form prevails. To the latter—as distinguished from village, country, provincial, or even Moscow life—we may allot Petersburg life, and especially the life of its salons. That life of the salons is unchanging. Since the year 1805 we had made peace and had again quarreled with Bonaparte and had made constitutions and unmade them again, but the salons of Anna Pávlovna and Hélène remained just as they had been—the one seven and the other five years before. At Anna Pávlovna's they talked with perplexity of Bonaparte's successes just as before, and saw in them and in the subservience shown to him by the European sovereigns a malicious conspiracy the sole object of which was to cause unpleasantness and anxiety to the court circle of which Anna Pávlovna was the representative. And in Hélène's salon, which Rumyántsev himself honored with his visits, regarding Hélène as a remarkably intelligent woman, they talked with the same ecstasy in 1812 as in 1808 of the "great nation" and the "great man," and regretted our rupture with France, a rupture which according to them ought to be promptly terminated by peace.

Of late, since the Emperor's return from the army, there had been some excitement in these conflicting salon-circles and some demonstrations of hostility to one another, but each camp retained its own tendency. In Anna Pávlovna's circle only those Frenchmen were admitted who were deep-rooted legitimists, and patriotic views were expressed to the effect that one ought not to go to the French theater, and that to maintain the French troupe was costing the government as much as a whole army corps. The progress of the war was eagerly followed, and only the reports most flattering to our army were circulated. In the French circle of Hélène and Rumyántsev the reports of the cruelty of the enemy and of the war were contradicted and all Napoleon's attempts at conciliation were discussed. In that circle they discountenanced those who advised hurried preparations for a removal to Kazán of the court and the girls' educational establishments under the patronage of the Dowager Empress. In Hélène's circle the war in general was regarded as a series of formal demonstrations which would very soon end in peace, and the view prevailed expressed by Bilíbin—who now in Petersburg was quite at home in Hélène's house, which every clever man was obliged to visit—that not by gunpowder but by those who invented it would matters be settled. In that circle the Moscow enthusiasm—news of which had reached Petersburg simultaneously with the Emperor's return—was ridiculed sarcastically and very cleverly, though with much caution.

Anna Pávlovna's circle on the contrary was enraptured by this enthusiasm, and spoke of it as Plutarch speaks of the deeds of the ancients. Prince Vasíli, who still occupied his former important posts, formed a connecting link between these two circles. He visited his "good friend Anna Pávlovna" as well as his daughter's "diplomatic salon," and often in his constant comings and goings between the two camps became confused, and said at Hélène's what he should have said at Anna Pávlovna's and vice versa.

Soon after the Emperor's return Prince Vasíli in a conversation about the war at Anna Pávlovna's severely condemned Barclay de Tolly, but was undecided as to who ought to be appointed commander-in-chief. One of the visitors, usually spoken of as "a man of great merit," having described how he had that day seen Kutúzov, the newly chosen chief of the Petersburg militia, presiding over the enrollment of recruits at the Treasury, cautiously ventured to suggest that Kutúzov would be the man to satisfy all requirements.

Anna Pávlovna remarked with a melancholy smile that Kutúzov had done nothing but cause the Emperor annoyance.

"I have talked and talked at the Assembly of the Nobility," Prince Vasíli interrupted, "but they did not listen to me. I told them his election as chief of the militia would not please the Emperor. They did not listen to me.

"It's all this mania for opposition," he went on. "And who for? It is all because we want to ape the foolish enthusiasm of those Muscovites," Prince Vasíli continued, forgetting for a moment that though at Hélène's one had to ridicule the Moscow enthusiasm, at Anna Pávlovna's one had to be ecstatic about it. But he retrieved his mistake at once. "Now, is it suitable that Count Kutúzov, the oldest general in Russia, should preside at that tribunal? He will get nothing for his pains! How could they make a man commander-in-chief who cannot mount a horse, who drops asleep at a council and has the very worst morals! A good reputation he made for himself at Bucharest! I don't speak of his capacity as a general, but at a time like this how can they appoint a decrepit, blind old man, positively blind? A fine idea to have a blind general! He can't see anything. To play blindman's bluff? He can't see at all!"

No one replied to his remarks.

This was quite correct on the 24th of July. But on the 29th of July Kutúzov received the title of Prince. This might indicate a wish to get rid of him, and therefore Prince Vasíli's opinion continued to be correct though he was not now in any hurry to express it. But on the 8th of August a committee, consisting of Field Marshal Saltykóv, Arakchéev, Vyazmítinov, Lopukhín and Kochubéy met to consider the progress of the war. This committee came to the conclusion that our failures were due to a want of unity in the command and though the members of the committee were aware of the Emperor's dislike of Kutúzov, after a short deliberation they agreed to advise his appointment as Commander-in-chief. That same-day Kutúzov was appointed Commander-in-chief with full powers over the armies and over the whole region occupied by them.

On the 9th of August Prince Vasíli at Anna Pávlovna's again met the "man of great merit." The latter was very attentive to Anna Pávlovna because he wanted to be appointed director of one of the educational establishments for young ladies. Prince Vasíli entered the room with the air of a happy conqueror who has attained the object of his desires.

"Well, have you heard the great news? Prince Kutúzov is field marshal! All dissensions are at an end! I am so glad, so delighted! At last we have a man!" said he, glancing sternly and significantly round at everyone in the drawing room.

The "man of great merit," despite his desire to obtain the post of director, could not refrain from reminding Prince Vasíli of his former opinion. Though this was impolite to Prince Vasíli in Anna Pávlovna's drawing room, and also to Anna Pávlovna herself who had received the news with delight, he could not resist the temptation.

"But, prince, they say he is blind!" said he, reminding Prince Vasíli of his own words.

"Eh? Nonsense! He sees well enough," said Prince Vasíli rapidly, in a deep voice and with a slight cough—the voice and cough with which he was wont to dispose of all difficulties.

"He sees well enough," he added. "And what I am so pleased about," he went on, "is that our Sovereign has given him full power over all the armies and the whole region—powers no commander-in-chief ever had before. He is a second autocrat," he concluded with a victorious smile.

"God grant it! God grant it!" said Anna Pávlovna.

The "man of great merit," who was still a novice in court circles, wishing to flatter Anna Pávlovna by defending her former position on this question observed:

"It is said that the Emperor was reluctant to give Kutúzov those powers. They say he blushed like a girl to whom *Joconde* is read, when he said to Kutúzov: 'Your Emperor and the Fatherland award you this honor.' "

"Perhaps the heart took no part in that speech," said Anna Pávlovna.

"Oh, no, no!" warmly rejoined Prince Vasíli, who would not now yield Kutúzov to anyone; in his opinion Kutúzov was not only admirable himself, but was adored by everybody. "No, that's impossible," said he, "for our Sovereign appreciated him so highly before."

"God grant only that Prince Kutúzov assumes real power and does not allow *anyone* to put a spoke in his wheel," observed Anna Pávlovna.

Understanding at once to whom she alluded, Prince Vasíli said in a whisper:

"I know for a fact that Kutúzov made it an absolute condition that the Tsarévich should not be with the army. Do you know what he said to the Emperor?"

And Prince Vasíli repeated the words supposed to have been spoken by Kutúzov to the Emperor. "I can neither punish him if he does wrong nor reward him if he does right."

"Oh, a very wise man is Prince Kutúzov! I have known him a long time!"

"They even say," remarked the "man of great merit" who did not yet possess courtly tact, "that his excellency made it an express condition that the Sovereign himself should not be with the army."

As soon as he said this both Prince Vasíli and Anna Pávlovna turned away from him and glanced sadly at one another with a sigh at his naïveté.

Chapter VII

WHILE THIS WAS TAKING PLACE IN PETERSBURG THE FRENCH HAD ALREADY PASSED SMOLÉNSK and were drawing nearer and nearer to Moscow. Napoleon's historian Thiers, like other of his historians, trying to justify his hero says that he was drawn to the walls of Moscow against his will. He is as right as other historians who look for the explanation of historic events in the will of one man; he is as right as the Russian historians who maintain that Napoleon was drawn to Moscow by the skill of the Russian commanders. Here besides the law of retrospection, which regards all the past as a preparation for events that subsequently occur, the law of reciprocity comes in, confusing the whole matter. A good chess-player having lost a game is sincerely convinced that his loss resulted from a mistake he made, and looks for that mistake in the opening, but forgets that at each stage of the game there were similar mistakes and that none of his moves were perfect. He only notices the mistake to which he pays attention, because his opponent took advantage of it. How much more complex than this is the game of war, which occurs under certain limits of time, and where it is not one will that manipulates lifeless objects, but everything results from innumerable conflicts of various wills!

After Smolénsk Napoleon sought a battle beyond Dorogobúzh at Vyázma, and then at Tsárevo-Zaymíshche, but it happened that owing to a conjunction of innumerable circumstances the Russians could not give battle till they reached Borodinó, seventy miles from Moscow. From Vyázma Napoleon ordered a direct advance on Moscow.

Moscou, la capitale asiatique de ce grand empire, la ville sacrée des peuples d'Alexandre, Moscou avec ses innombrables églises en forme de pagodes chinoises, this Moscow gave Napoleon's imagination no rest. On the march from Vyázma to Tsárevo-Zaymíshche he rode his light bay bob-tailed ambler accompanied by his Guards, his bodyguard, his pages and aides-de-camp. Berthier, his chief of staff, dropped behind to question a Russian prisoner captured by the cavalry. Followed by Lelorgne d'Ideville, an interpreter, he overtook Napoleon at a gallop and reined in his horse with an amused expression.

"Well?" asked Napoleon.

"One of Plátov's Cossacks says that Plátov's corps is joining up with the main army and that Kutúzov has been appointed commander-in-chief. He is a very shrewd and garrulous fellow."

Napoleon smiled and told them to give the Cossack a horse and bring the man to him. He wished to talk to him himself. Several adjutants galloped off, and an hour later, Lavrúshka, the serf Denísov had handed over to Rostóv, rode up to Napoleon in an orderly's jacket and on a French cavalry saddle, with a roguish, merry and tipsy face. Napoleon told him to ride by his side and began questioning him.

"You are a Cossack?"

"Yes, a Cossack, your Honor."

"The Cossack, not knowing in what company he was, for Napoleon's plain appearance had nothing about it that would reveal to an Oriental mind the presence of a monarch, talked with extreme familiarity of the incidents of the war," says Thiers, narrating this episode. In reality Lavrúshka having got drunk the day before and left his master dinnerless, had been whipped and sent to the village in quest of chickens, where he engaged in looting till the French took him prisoner. Lavrúshka was one of those coarse, bare-faced lackeys who have seen all sorts of things, consider it necessary to do everything in a mean and cunning way, are ready to render any sort of service to their master, and are keen at guessing their master's baser impulses, especially those prompted by vanity and pettiness.

Finding himself in the company of Napoleon, whose identity he had easily and surely recognized, Lavrúshka was not in the least abashed but merely did his utmost to gain his new master's favor.

He knew very well that this was Napoleon, but Napoleon's presence could no more intimidate him than Rostóv's, or a sergeant-major's with the rods, would have done, for he had nothing that either the sergeant-major or Napoleon could deprive him of.

So he rattled on, telling all the gossip he had heard among the orderlies. Much of it true. But when Napoleon asked him whether the Russians thought they would beat Bonaparte or not, Lavrúshka screwed up his eyes and considered.

In this question he saw subtle cunning, as men of his type see cunning in everything, so he frowned and did not answer immediately.

"It's like this," he said thoughtfully, "if there's a battle soon, yours will win. That's right. But if three days pass, then after that, well, then that same battle will not soon be over."

Lelorgne d'Ideville smilingly interpreted this speech to Napoleon thus: "If a battle takes place within the next three days the French will win, but if later, God knows what will happen." Napoleon did not smile, though he was evidently in high good humor, and he ordered these words to be repeated.

Lavrúshka noticed this and to entertain him further, pretending not to know who Napoleon was, added:

"We know that you have Bonaparte and that he has beaten everybody in the world, but we are a different matter . . ."—without knowing why or how this bit of boastful patriotism slipped out at the end.

The interpreter translated these words without the last phrase, and Bonaparte smiled. "The young Cossack made his mighty interlocutor smile," says Thiers. After riding a few paces in silence, Napoleon turned to Berthier and said he wished to see how the news that he was talking to the Emperor himself, to that very Emperor who had written his immortally victorious name on the Pyramids, would affect this *enfant du Don*.

The fact was accordingly conveyed to Lavrúshka.

Lavrúshka, understanding that this was done to perplex him and that Napoleon expected him to be frightened, to gratify his new masters promptly pretended to be astonished and awestruck, opened his eyes wide and assumed the expression he usually put on when taken to be whipped. "As soon as Napoleon's interpreter had spoken," says Thiers, "the Cossack, seized by amazement, did not utter another word, but rode on, his eyes fixed on the conqueror whose fame had reached him across the steppes of the East. All his loquacity was suddenly arrested and replaced by a naïve and silent feeling of admiration. Napoleon, after making the Cossack a present, had him set free like a bird restored to its native fields."

Napoleon rode on, dreaming of the Moscow that so appealed to his imagination, and "the bird restored to its native fields" galloped to our outposts, inventing on the way all that had not taken place but that he meant to relate to his comrades. What had really taken place he did not wish to relate because it seemed to him not worth telling. He found the Cossacks, inquired for the regiment operating with Plátov's detachment, and by evening found his master, Nicholas Rostóv, quartered at Yankóvo. Rostóv was just mounting to go for a ride round the neighboring villages with Ilyín; he let Lavrúshka have another horse and took him along with him.

Chapter VIII

PRINCESS MARY WAS NOT IN MOSCOW AND OUT OF DANGER AS PRINCE ANDREW SUPPOSED.

After the return of Alpátych from Smolénsk the old prince suddenly seemed to awake as from a dream. He ordered the militiamen to be called up from the villages and armed, and wrote a letter to the commander-in-chief informing him that he had resolved to remain at Bald Hills to the last extremity and to defend it, leaving to the commander-in-chief's discretion to take measures or not for the defense of Bald Hills, where one of Russia's oldest generals would be captured or killed, and he announced to his household that he would remain at Bald Hills.

But while himself remaining, he gave instructions for the departure of the princess and Dessalles with the little prince to Boguchárovo and thence to Moscow. Princess Mary, alarmed by her father's feverish and sleepless activity after his previous apathy, could not bring herself to leave him alone, and for the first time in her life ventured to disobey him. She refused to go away and her father's fury broke over her in a terrible storm. He repeated every injustice he had ever inflicted on her. Trying to convict her, he told her she had worn him out, had caused his quarrel with his son, had harbored nasty suspicions of him, making it the object of her life to poison his existence, and he drove her from his study telling her that if she did not go away it was all the same to him. He declared that he did not wish to remember her existence and warned her not to dare to let him see her. The fact that he did not, as she had feared, order her to be carried away by force but only told her not to let him see her, cheered Princess Mary. She knew it was a proof that in the depth of his soul he was glad she was remaining at home and had not gone away.

The morning after little Nicholas had left, the old prince donned his full uniform and prepared to visit the commander-in-chief. His calèche was already at the door. Princess Mary saw him walk out of the house in his uniform wearing all his Orders and go down the garden to review his armed peasants and domestic serfs. She sat by the window listening to his voice which reached her from the garden. Suddenly several men came running up the avenue with frightened faces.

Princess Mary ran out to the porch, down the flower-bordered path, and into the avenue. A large crowd of militiamen and domestics were moving toward her, and in their midst several men were supporting by the armpits and dragging along a little old man in a uniform and decorations. She ran up to him and, in the play of the sunlight that fell in small round spots through the shade of the lime-tree avenue, could not be sure what change there was in his face. All she could see was that his former stern and determined expression had altered to one of timidity and submission. On seeing his daughter he moved his helpless lips and made a hoarse sound. It was impossible to make out what he wanted. He was lifted up, carried to his study and laid on the very couch he had so feared of late.

The doctor, who was fetched that same night, bled him and said that the prince had had a seizure paralyzing his right side.

It was becoming more and more dangerous to remain at Bald Hills, and next day they moved the prince to Boguchárovo, the doctor accompanying him.

By the time they reached Boguchárovo, Dessalles and the little prince had already left for Moscow.

For three weeks the old prince lay stricken by paralysis in the new house Prince Andrew had built at Boguchárovo, ever in the same state, getting neither better nor worse. He was unconscious and lay like a distorted corpse. He muttered unceasingly, his eyebrows and lips twitching, and it was impossible to tell whether he understood what was going on around him or not. One thing was certain—that he was suffering and wished to say something. But what it was, no one could tell: it might be some caprice of a sick and half-crazy man, or it might relate to public affairs, or possibly to family concerns.

The doctor said this restlessness did not mean anything and was due to physical causes; but Princess Mary thought he wished to tell her something, and the fact that her presence always increased his restlessness confirmed her opinion.

He was evidently suffering both physically and mentally. There was no hope of recovery. It was impossible for him to travel, it would not do to let him die on the road. "Would it not be better if the end did come, the very end?" Princess Mary sometimes thought. Night and day, hardly sleeping at all, she watched him, and terrible to say, often watched him not with hope of finding signs of improvement but wishing to find symptoms of the approach of the end.

Strange as it was to her to acknowledge this feeling in herself, yet there it was. And what seemed still more terrible to her was that since her father's illness began (perhaps even sooner, when she stayed with him expecting something to happen), all the personal desires and hopes that had been forgotten or sleeping within her had awakened. Thoughts that had not entered her mind for years—thoughts of a life free from the fears of her father, and even the possibility of love and of family happiness—floated continually in her imagination like temptations of the devil. Thrust them aside as she would, questions continually recurred to her as to how she would order her life now, after *that*. These were temptations of the devil and Princess Mary knew it. She knew that the sole weapon against *him* was prayer, and she tried to pray. She assumed an attitude of prayer, looked at the icons, repeated the words of a prayer, but she could not pray. She felt that a different world had now taken possession of her—the life of a world of strenuous and free activity, quite opposed to the spiritual world in which till now she had been confined and in which her greatest comfort had been prayer. She could not pray, could not weep, and worldly cares took possession of her.

It was becoming dangerous to remain in Boguchárovo. News of the approach of the French came from all sides, and in one village, ten miles from Boguchárovo, a homestead had been looted by French marauders.

The doctor insisted on the necessity of moving the prince; the provincial Marshal of the Nobility sent an official to Princess Mary to persuade her to get away as quickly as possible, and the head of the rural police having come to Boguchárovo urged the same thing, saying that the French were only some twenty-five miles away, that French proclamations were circulating in the villages, and that if the princess did not take her father away before the 15th, he could not answer for the consequences.

The princess decided to leave on the 15th. The cares of preparation and giving orders, for which everyone came to her, occupied her all day. She spent the night of the 14th as usual, without undressing, in the room next to the one where the prince lay. Several times, waking up, she heard his groans and muttering, the creak of his bed, and the steps of Tíkhon and the doctor when they turned him over. Several times she listened at the door, and it seemed to her that his mutterings were louder than usual and that they turned him over oftener. She could not sleep, and several times went to the door and listened, wishing to enter but not deciding to do so. Though he did not speak, Princess Mary saw and knew how unpleasant every sign of anxiety on his account was to him. She had noticed with what dissatisfaction he turned from the look she sometimes involuntarily fixed on him. She knew that her going in during the night at an unusual hour would irritate him.

But never had she felt so grieved for him or so much afraid of losing him. She recalled all her life with him, and in every word and act of his found an expression of his love of her. Occasionally amid these memories temptations of the devil would surge into her imagination: thoughts of how things would be after his death, and how her new, liberated life would be ordered. But she drove these thoughts away with disgust. Toward morning he became quiet and she fell asleep.

She woke late. That sincerity which often comes with waking showed her clearly what chiefly concerned her about her father's illness. On waking she listened to what was going on behind the door and, hearing him groan, said to herself with a sigh that things were still the same.

"But what could have happened? What did I want? I want his death!" she cried with a feeling of loathing for herself.

She washed, dressed, said her prayers and went out to the porch. In front of it stood carriages without horses and things were being packed into the vehicles.

It was a warm, gray morning. Princess Mary stopped at the porch, still horrified by her spiritual baseness and trying to arrange her thoughts before going to her father.

The doctor came downstairs and went out to her.

"He is a little better today," said he. "I was looking for you. One can make out something of what he is saying. His head is clearer. Come in, he is asking for you. . . ."

Princess Mary's heart beat so violently at this news that she grew pale and leaned against the wall to keep from falling. To see him, talk to him, feel his eyes on her now that her whole soul was overflowing with those dreadful, wicked temptations—was a torment of joy and terror.

"Come," said the doctor.

Princess Mary entered her father's room and went up to his bed. He was lying on his back propped up high, and his small bony hands with their knotted purple veins were lying on the quilt; his left eye gazed straight before him, his right eye was awry and his brows and lips motionless. He seemed altogether so thin, small and pathetic. His face seemed to have shriveled or melted; his features had grown smaller. Princess Mary went up and kissed his hand. His left hand pressed hers so that she understood that he had long been waiting for her to come. He twitched her hand, and his brows and lips quivered angrily.

She looked at him in dismay trying to guess what he wanted of her. When she changed her position so that his left eye could see her face he calmed down, not taking his eyes off her for some seconds. Then his lips and tongue moved, sounds came and he began to speak, gazing timidly and imploringly at her, evidently afraid that she might not understand.

Straining all her faculties Princess Mary looked at him. The comic efforts with which he moved his tongue made her drop her eyes and with difficulty repress the sobs that rose to her throat. He said something, repeating the same words several times. She could not understand them, but tried to guess what he was saying and inquiringly repeated the words he uttered.

"Mmm . . . ar . . . ate . . . ate . . ." he repeated several times.

It was quite impossible to understand these sounds. The doctor thought he had guessed them, and inquiringly repeated: *"Mary, are you afraid?"* The prince shook his head, again repeated the same sounds.

"My mind, my mind aches?" questioned Princess Mary.

He made a mumbling sound in confirmation of this, took her hand and began pressing it to different parts of his breast as if trying to find the right place for it.

"Always thoughts . . . about you . . . thoughts . . ." he then uttered much more clearly than he had done before, now that he was sure of being understood.

Princess Mary pressed her head against his hand trying to hide her sobs and tears.

He moved his hand over her hair.

"I have been calling you all night . . ." he brought out.

"If only I had known . . ." she said through her tears. "I was afraid to come in."

He pressed her hand.

"Weren't you asleep?"

"No, I did not sleep," said Princess Mary, shaking her head.

Unconsciously imitating her father, she now tried to express herself as he did, as much as possible by signs, and her tongue too seemed to move with difficulty.

"Dear one . . . Dearest . . ." Princess Mary could not quite make out what he said, but from his look it was clear that he had uttered a tender caressing word such as he had never used to her before. "Why didn't you come in?"

"And I, I was wishing for his death!" thought Princess Mary.

He was silent awhile.

"Thank you . . . daughter dear! . . . for all, for all . . . forgive! . . . thank you! . . . forgive! . . . thank you! . . ." and tears began to flow from his eyes. "Call Andrew!" he said suddenly, and a childish, timid expression of doubt showed itself on his face as he spoke.

He himself seemed aware that his demand was meaningless. So at least it seemed to Princess Mary.

"I have a letter from him," she replied.

He glanced at her with timid surprise.

"Where is he?"

"He's with the army, father, at Smolénsk."

He closed his eyes and remained silent a long time. Then as if in answer to his doubts and to confirm the fact that now he understood and remembered everything, he nodded his head and reopened his eyes.

"Yes," he said, softly and distinctly. "Russia has perished. They've destroyed her."

And he began to sob, and again tears flowed from his eyes. Princess Mary could no longer restrain herself and wept while she gazed at his face.

Again he closed his eyes. His sobs ceased, he pointed to his eyes, and Tíkhon, understanding him, wiped away the tears.

Then he again opened his eyes and said something none of them could understand for a long time, till at last Tíkhon understood and repeated it. Princess Mary had sought the meaning of his words in the mood in which he had just been speaking. She thought he was speaking of Russia, or Prince Andrew, of herself, of his grandson, or of his own death, and so she could not guess his words.

"Put on your white dress. I like it," was what he said.

Having understood this Princess Mary sobbed still louder, and the doctor taking her arm led her out to the veranda, soothing her and trying to persuade her to prepare for her journey. When she had left the room the prince again began speaking about his son, about the war and about the Emperor, angrily twitching his brows and raising his hoarse voice, and then he had a second and final stroke.

Princess Mary stayed on the veranda. The day had cleared, it was hot and sunny. She could understand nothing, think of nothing and feel nothing, except passionate love for her father, love such as she thought she had never felt till that moment. She ran out sobbing into the garden and as far as the pond, along the avenues of young lime trees Prince Andrew had planted.

"Yes . . . I . . . I . . . I wished for his death! Yes, I wanted it to end quicker. . . . I wished to be at peace. . . . And what will become of me? What use will peace be when he is no longer here?" Princess Mary murmured, pacing the garden with hurried steps and pressing her hands to her bosom which heaved with convulsive sobs.

When she had completed the tour of the garden, which brought her again to the house, she saw Mademoiselle Bourienne—who had remained at Boguchárovo and did not wish to leave it—coming toward her with a stranger. This was the Marshal of the Nobility of the district, who had come personally to point out to the princess the necessity for her prompt departure. Princess Mary listened without understanding him; she led him to the house, offered him lunch and sat down with him. Then, excusing herself, she went to the door of the old prince's room. The doctor came out with an agitated face and said she could not enter.

"Go away, princess! Go away . . . go away!"

She returned to the garden and sat down on the grass at the foot of the slope by the pond, where no one could see her. She did not know how long she had been there when she was aroused by the sound of a woman's footsteps running along the path. She rose and saw Dunyásha her maid, who was evidently looking for her, and who stopped suddenly as if in alarm on seeing her mistress.

"Please come, princess . . . The prince . . ." said Dunyásha in a breaking voice.

"Immediately, I'm coming, I'm coming!" replied the princess hurriedly, not giving Dunyásha time to finish what she was saying, and trying to avoid seeing the girl she ran toward the house.

"Princess, it's God's will! You must be prepared for everything," said the Marshal, meeting her at the house door.

"Let me alone; it's not true!" she cried angrily to him.

The doctor tried to stop her. She pushed him aside and ran to her father's door. "Why are these people with frightened faces stopping me? I don't want any of them! And what are they doing here?" she thought. She opened the door and the bright daylight in that previously darkened room startled her. In the room were her nurse and other women. They all drew back from the bed, making way for her. He was still lying on the bed as before, but the stern expression of his quiet face made Princess Mary stop short on the threshold.

"No, he's not dead—it's impossible!" she told herself and approached him, and repressing the terror that seized her, she pressed her lips to his cheek. But she stepped back immediately. All the force of the tenderness she had been feeling for him vanished instantly and was replaced by a feeling of horror at what lay there before her. "No, he is no more! He is not, but here where he was, is something unfamiliar and hostile, some dreadful terrifying and repellent mystery!" And hiding her face in her hands, Princess Mary sank into the arms of the doctor, who held her up.

In the presence of Tíkhon and the doctor the women washed what had been the prince, tied his head up with a handkerchief that the mouth should not stiffen while open, and with another handkerchief tied together the legs that were already spreading apart. Then they dressed him in uniform with his decorations, and placed his shriveled little body on a table. Heaven only knows who arranged all this and when, but it all got done as if of its own accord. Toward night candles were burning round his coffin, a pall was spread over it, the floor was strewn with sprays of juniper, a printed band was tucked in under his shriveled head, and in a corner of the room sat a chanter reading the psalms.

Just as horses shy and snort and gather about a dead horse, so the inmates of the house and strangers crowded into the drawing room round the coffin—the Marshal, the village Elder, peasant women—and all with fixed and frightened eyes, crossing themselves, bowed and kissed the old prince's cold and stiffened hand.

Chapter IX

UNTIL PRINCE ANDREW SETTLED IN BOGUCHÁROVO ITS OWNERS HAD ALWAYS BEEN ABSENTEES, and its peasants were of quite a different character from those of Bald Hills. They differed from them in speech, dress and disposition. They were called Steppe-peasants. The old prince used to approve of them for their endurance at work when they came to Bald Hills to help with the harvest or to dig ponds and ditches, but he disliked them for their boorishness.

Prince Andrew's last stay at Boguchárovo, when he introduced hospitals and schools and reduced the quitrent the peasants had to pay, had not softened their disposition but had on the contrary strengthened in them the traits of character the old prince called boorishness. Various obscure rumors were always current among them: at one time a rumor that they would all be enrolled as Cossacks; at another of a new religion to which they were all to be converted; then of some proclamation of the Tsar's and of an oath to the Tsar Paul in 1797 (in connection with which it was rumored that freedom had been granted them but the landowners had stopped it), then of Peter Fëdorovich's return to the throne in seven years' time, when everything would be made free and so "simple" that there would be no restrictions. Rumors of the war with Bonaparte and his invasion were connected in their minds with the same sort of vague notions of Antichrist, the end of the world and "pure freedom."

In the vicinity of Boguchárovo were large villages belonging to the crown or to owners whose serfs paid quitrent and could work where they pleased. There were very few resident landlords in the neighborhood and also very few domestic or literate serfs, and in the lives of the peasantry of those parts the mysterious undercurrents in the life of the Russian people, the causes and meaning of which are so baffling to contemporaries, were more clearly and strongly noticeable than among others. One instance, which had occurred some twenty years before, was a movement among the peasants to emigrate to some unknown "warm rivers." Hundreds of peasants, among them the Boguchárovo folk, suddenly began selling their cattle and moving in whole families toward the southeast. As birds migrate to somewhere beyond the sea, so these men with their wives and children streamed to the southeast, to parts where none of them had ever been. They set off in caravans, bought their freedom one by one or ran away, and drove or walked toward the "warm rivers." Many of them were punished, some sent to Siberia, many died of cold and hunger on the road, many returned of their own accord, and the movement died down of itself as it had sprung up, without apparent reason. But such undercurrents still existed among the people and gathered new forces ready to manifest themselves just as strangely, unexpectedly and at the same time simply, naturally and forcibly. Now in 1812, to anyone living in close touch with these people it was apparent that these undercurrents were acting strongly and nearing an eruption.

Alpátych, who had reached Boguchárovo shortly before the old prince's death, noticed an agitation among the peasants, and that contrary to what was happening in the Bald Hills district, where over a radius of sixty miles all the peasants were moving away and leaving their villages to be devastated by the Cossacks, the peasants in the steppe region round Boguchárovo were, it was rumored, in touch with the French, received leaflets from them that passed from hand to hand, and did not migrate. He learned from domestic serfs loyal to him that the peasant Karp, who possessed great influence in the village commune and had recently been away driving a government transport, had returned with news that the Cossacks were destroying deserted villages, but that the French did not harm them. Alpátych also knew that on the previous day another peasant had even brought from the village of Visloúkhovo, which was occupied by the French, a proclamation by a French general that no harm would be done to the inhabitants, and if they remained they would be paid for anything taken from them. As proof of this the peasant had brought from Visloúkhovo a hundred rubles in notes (he did not know that they were false) paid to him in advance for hay.

More important still, Alpátych learned that on the morning of the very day he gave the village Elder orders to collect carts to move the princess's luggage from Boguchárovo, there had been a village meeting at which it had been decided not to move but to wait. Yet there was no time to waste. On the 15th, the day of the old prince's death, the Marshal had insisted on Princess Mary's leaving at once, as it was becoming dangerous. He had told her that after the 16th he could not be responsible for what might happen. On the evening of the day the old prince died the Marshal went away, promising to return next day for the funeral. But this he was unable to do, for he received tidings that the French had unexpectedly advanced, and had barely time to remove his own family and valuables from his estate.

For some thirty years Boguchárovo had been managed by the village Elder Dron, whom the old prince called by the diminutive "Drónushka."

Dron was one of those physically and mentally vigorous peasants who grow big beards as soon as they are of age, and go on unchanged till they are sixty or seventy, without a gray hair or the loss of a tooth, as straight and strong at sixty as at thirty.

Soon after the migration to the "warm rivers," in which he had taken part like the rest, Dron was made village Elder and overseer of Boguchárovo, and had since filled that post irreproachably for twenty-three years. The peasants feared him more than they did their master. The masters, both the old prince and the young, and the steward, respected him and jestingly called him "the Minister." During the whole time of his service Dron had never been drunk or ill, never after sleepless nights or the hardest tasks had he shown the least fatigue, and though he could not read he had never forgotten a single money account, or the number of quarters of flour in any of the endless cartloads he sold for the prince, nor a single shock of the whole corn crop on any single acre of the Bogucharovo fields.

Alpátych, arriving from the devastated Bald Hills estate, sent for his Dron on the day of the prince's funeral and told him to have twelve horses got ready for the princess's carriages and eighteen carts for the things to be removed from Bogucharovo. Though the peasants paid quitrent, Alpátych thought no difficulty would be made about complying with this order, for there were two hundred and thirty households at work in Bogucharovo and the peasants were well-to-do. But on hearing the order Dron lowered his eyes and remained silent. Alpátych named certain peasants he knew, from whom he told him to take the carts.

Dron replied that the horses of these peasants were away carting. Alpátych named others, but they too, according to Dron, had no horses available: some horses were carting for the government, others were too weak, and others had died for want of fodder. It seemed that no horses could be had even for the carriages, much less for the carting.

Alpátych looked intently at Dron and frowned. Just as Dron was a model village Elder, so Alpátych had not managed the prince's estates for twenty years in vain. He a model steward, possessing in the highest degree the faculty of divining the needs and instincts of those he dealt with. Having glanced at Dron he at once understood that his answers did not express his personal views but the general mood of the Bogucharovo commune, by which the Elder had already been carried away. But he also knew that Dron, who had acquired property and was hated by the commune, must be hesitating between the two camps: the masters' and the serfs'. He noticed this hesitation in Dron's look and therefore frowned and moved closer up to him.

"Now just listen, Drónushka," said he. "Don't talk nonsense to me. His excellency Prince Andrew himself gave me orders to move all the people away and not leave them with the enemy, and there is an order from the Tsar about it too. Anyone who stays is a traitor to the Tsar. Do you hear?"

"I hear," Dron answered without lifting his eyes.

Alpátych was not satisfied with this reply.

"Eh, Dron, it will turn out badly!" he said, shaking his head.

"The power is in your hands," Dron rejoined sadly.

"Eh, Dron, drop it!" Alpátych repeated, withdrawing his hand from his bosom and solemnly pointing to the floor at Dron's feet. "I can see through you and three yards into the ground under you," he continued, gazing at the floor in front of Dron.

Dron was disconcerted, glanced furtively at Alpátych and again lowered his eyes.

"You drop this nonsense and tell the people to get ready to leave their homes and go to Moscow, and to get carts ready for tomorrow morning for the princess's things. And don't go to any meeting yourself, do you hear?"

Dron suddenly fell on his knees.

"Yákov Alpátych, discharge me! Take the keys from me and discharge me, for Christ's sake!"

"Stop that!" cried Alpátych sternly. "I see through you and three yards under you," he repeated, knowing that his skill in beekeeping, his knowledge of the right time to sow the oats and the fact that he had been able to retain the old prince's favor for twenty years, had long since gained him the reputation of being a wizard, and that the power of seeing three yards under a man is considered an attribute of wizards.

Dron got up and was about to say something, but Alpátych interrupted him.

"What is it you have got into your heads, eh? . . . What are you thinking of, eh?"

"What am I to do with the people?" said Dron. "They're quite beside themselves; I have already told them . . ."

" 'Told them,' I dare say!" said Alpátych. "Are they drinking?" he asked abruptly.

"Quite beside themselves, Yákov Alpátych; they've fetched another barrel."

"Well, then, listen! I'll go to the police officer, and you tell them so, and that they must stop this and the carts must be got ready."

"I understand."

Alpátych did not insist further. He had managed people for a long time, and knew that the chief way to make them obey is to show no suspicion that they can possibly disobey. Having wrung a submissive "I understand" from Dron, Alpátych contented himself with that, though he not only doubted but felt almost certain that without the help of troops the carts would not be forthcoming.

And so it was, for when evening came no carts had been provided. In the village, outside the drink-shop, another meeting was being held, which decided that the horses should be driven out into the woods and the carts should not be provided. Without saying anything of this to the princess, Alpátych had his own belongings taken out of the carts which had arrived from Bald Hills, and had those horses got ready for the princess's carriages. Meanwhile he went himself to the police authorities.

Chapter X

After her father's funeral Princess Mary shut herself up in her room and did not admit anyone. A maid came to the door to say that Alpátych was asking for orders about their departure. (This was before his talk with Dron.) Princess Mary raised herself on the sofa on which she had been lying and replied through the closed door that she did not mean to go away and begged to be left in peace.

The windows of the room in which she was lying looked westward. She lay on the sofa with her face to the wall, fingering the buttons of the leather cushion and seeing nothing but that cushion, and her confused thoughts were centered on one subject—the irrevocability of death and her own spiritual baseness, which she had not suspected, but which had shown itself during her father's illness. She wished to pray but did not dare, dared not in her present state of mind address herself to God. She lay for a long time in that position.

The sun had reached the other side of the house, and its slanting rays shone into the open window, lighting up the room and part of the morocco cushion at which Princess Mary was looking. The flow of her thoughts suddenly stopped. Unconsciously she sat up, smoothed her hair, got up and went to the window, involuntarily inhaling the freshness of the clear but windy evening.

"Yes, you can well enjoy the evening now! He is gone and no one will hinder you," she said to herself, and sinking into a chair she let her head fall on the window sill.

Someone spoke her name in a soft and tender voice from the garden and kissed her head. She looked up. It was Mademoiselle Bourienne in a black dress and weepers. She softly approached Princess Mary, sighed, kissed her and immediately began to cry. The princess looked up at her. All their former disharmony and her own jealousy recurred to her mind. But she remembered too how *he* had changed of late toward Mademoiselle Bourienne and could not bear to see her, thereby showing how unjust were the reproaches Princess Mary had mentally addressed to her. "Besides, is it for me, for me who desired his death, to condemn anyone?" she thought.

Princess Mary vividly pictured to herself the position of Mademoiselle Bourienne, whom she had of late kept at a distance, but who yet was dependent on her and living in her house. She felt sorry for her, and held out her hand with a glance of gentle inquiry. Mademoiselle Bourienne at once began crying again and kissed that hand, speaking of the princess's sorrow and making herself a partner in it. She said her only consolation was the fact that the princess allowed her to share her sorrow, that all the old misunderstandings should sink into nothing but this great grief; that she felt herself blameless in regard to everyone, and that *he,* from above, saw her affection and gratitude. The princess heard her, not heeding her words but occasionally looking up at her and listening to the sound of her voice.

"Your position is doubly terrible, dear princess," said Mademoiselle Bourienne after a pause. "I understand that you could not, and cannot, think of yourself, but with my love for you I must do so. . . . Has Alpátych been to you? Has he spoken to you of going away?" she asked.

Princess Mary did not answer. She did not understand who was to go or where to. "Is it possible to plan or think of anything now? Is it not all the same?" she thought, and did not reply.

"You know, *chère Marie,*" said Mademoiselle Bourienne, "that we are in danger—are surrounded by the French. It would be dangerous to move now. If we go we are almost sure to be taken prisoners, and God knows . . ."

Princess Mary looked at her companion without understanding what she was talking about.

"Oh, if anyone knew how little anything matters to me now," she said. "Of course I would on no account wish to go away from him. . . . Alpátych did say something about going. . . . Speak to him; I can do nothing, nothing, and don't want to. . . ."

"I've spoken to him. He hopes we should be in time to get away tomorrow, but I think it would now be better to stay here," said Mademoiselle Bourienne. "Because, you will agree, *chère Marie,* to fall into the hands of the soldiers or of riotous peasants would be terrible."

Mademoiselle Bourienne took from her reticule a proclamation (not printed on ordinary Russian paper) of General Rameau's, telling people not to leave their homes and that the French authorities would afford them proper protection. She handed this to the princess.

"I think it would be best to appeal to that general," she continued, "and I am sure that all due respect would be shown you."

Princess Mary read the paper, and her face began to quiver with stifled sobs.

"From whom did you get this?" she asked.

"They probably recognized that I am French, by my name," replied Mademoiselle Bourienne blushing.

Princess Mary, with the paper in her hand, rose from the window and with a pale face went out of the room and into what had been Prince Andrew's study.

"Dunyásha, send Alpátych, or Drónushka, or somebody to me!" she said, "and tell Mademoiselle Bourienne not to come to me," she added, hearing Mademoiselle Bourienne's voice. "We must go at once, at once!" she said, appalled at the thought of being left in the hands of the French.

"If Prince Andrew heard that I was in the power of the French! That I, the daughter of Prince Nicholas Bolkónski, asked General Rameau for protection and accepted his favor!" This idea horrified her, made her shudder, blush, and feel such a rush of anger and pride as she had never experienced before. All that was distressing, and especially all that was humiliating, in her position rose vividly to her mind. "They, the French, would settle in this house: M. le Général Rameau would occupy Prince Andrew's study and amuse himself by looking through and reading his letters and papers. Mademoiselle Bourienne would do the honors of Boguchárovo for him. I should be given a small room as a favor, the soldiers would violate my father's newly dug grave to steal his crosses and stars, they would tell me of their victories over the Russians, and would pretend to sympathize with my sorrow . . ." thought Princess Mary, not thinking her own thoughts but feeling bound to think like her father and her brother. For herself she did not care where she remained or what happened to her, but she felt herself the representative of her dead father and of Prince Andrew. Involuntarily she thought their thoughts and felt their feelings. What they would have said and what they would have done she felt bound to say and do. She went into Prince Andrew's study trying to enter completely into his ideas, and considered her position.

The demands of life, which had seemed to her annihilated by her father's death, all at once rose before her with a new, previously unknown force and took possession of her.

Agitated and flushed she paced the room, sending now for Michael Ivánovich and now for Tíkhon or Dron. Dunyásha, the nurse, and the other maids, could not say in how far Mademoiselle Bourienne's statement was correct. Alpátych was not at home, he had gone to the police. Neither could the architect Michael Ivánovich, who on being sent for came in with sleepy eyes, tell Princess Mary anything. With just the same smile of agreement with which for fifteen years he had been accustomed to answer the old prince without expressing views of his own, he now replied to Princess Mary, so that nothing definite could be got from his answers. The old valet Tíkhon, with sunken, emaciated face that bore the stamp of inconsolable grief, replied: "Yes, princess" to all Princess Mary's questions, and hardly refrained from sobbing as he looked at her.

At length Dron, the village Elder, entered the room, and with a deep bow to Princess Mary came to a halt by the doorpost.

Princess Mary walked up and down the room and stopped in front of him.

"Drónushka," she said, regarding as a sure friend this Drónushka who always used to bring a special kind of gingerbread from his visit to the fair at Vyázma every year and smilingly offer it to her, "Drónushka, now since our misfortune . . ." she began, but could not go on.

"We are all in God's hands," said he, with a sigh.

They were silent for a while.

"Drónushka, Alpátych has gone off somewhere and I have no one to turn to. Is it true, as they tell me, that I can't even go away?"

"Why shouldn't you go away, your excellency? You can go," said Dron.

"I was told it would be dangerous because of the enemy. Dear friend, I can do nothing. I understand nothing. I have nobody! I want to go away tonight or early tomorrow morning."

Dron paused. He looked askance at Princess Mary and said:

"There are no horses; I told Yákov Alpátych so."

"Why are there none?" asked the princess.

"It's all God's scourge," said Dron. "What horses we had, have been taken for the army or have died—this is such a year! It's not a case of feeding horses—we may die of hunger ourselves! As it is, some go three days without eating. We've nothing, we've been ruined."

Princess Mary listened attentively to what he told her.

"The peasants are ruined? They have no bread?" she asked.

"They're dying of hunger," said Dron. "It's not a case of carting."

"But why didn't you tell me, Drónushka? Isn't it possible to help them? I'll do all I can. . . ."

To Princess Mary it was strange that now, at a moment when such sorrow was filling her soul, there could be rich people and poor, and the rich could refrain from helping the poor. She had heard vaguely that there was such a thing as "landlord's corn" which was sometimes given to the peasants. She also knew that neither her father nor her brother would refuse to help the peasants in need, she only feared to make some mistake in speaking about the distribution of the grain she wished to give. She was glad such cares presented themselves, enabling her without scruple to forget her own grief. She began asking Dron about the peasants' needs, and what there was in Boguchárovo that belonged to the landlord.

"But we have grain belonging to my brother?" she said.

"The landlord's grain is all safe," replied Dron proudly. "Our prince did not order it to be sold."

"Give it to the peasants, let them have all they need; I give you leave in my brother's name," said she.

Dron made no answer but sighed deeply.

"Give them that corn if there is enough of it. Distribute it all. I give this order in my brother's name; and tell them that what is ours is theirs. We do not grudge them anything. Tell them so."

Dron looked intently at the princess while she was speaking.

"Discharge me, little Mother, for God's sake! Order the keys to be taken from me," said he. "I have served twenty-three years and have done no wrong. Discharge me, for God's sake!"

Princess Mary did not understand what he wanted of her or why he was asking to be discharged. She replied that she had never doubted his devotion and that she was ready to do anything for him and for the peasants.

Chapter XI

AN HOUR LATER DUNYÁSHA CAME TO TELL THE PRINCESS THAT DRON HAD COME, AND ALL THE peasants had assembled at the barn by the princess's order and wished to have word with their mistress.

"But I never told them to come," said Princess Mary. "I only told Dron to let them have the grain."

"Only, for God's sake, princess dear, have them sent away and don't go out to them. It's all a trick," said Dunyásha, "and when Yákov Alpátych returns let us get away . . . and please don't . . ."

"What is a trick?" asked Princess Mary in surprise.

"I know it is, only listen to me for God's sake! Ask nurse too. They say they don't agree to leave Boguchárovo as you ordered."

"You're making some mistake. I never ordered them to go away," said Princess Mary. "Call Drónushka."

Dron came and confirmed Dunyásha's words; the peasants had come by the princess's order.

"But I never sent for them," declared the princess. "You must have given my message wrong. I only said that you were to give them the grain."

Dron only sighed in reply.

"If you order it they will go away," said he.

"No, no. I'll go out to them," said Princess Mary, and in spite of the nurse's and Dunyásha's protests she went out into the porch; Dron, Dunyásha, the nurse and Michael Ivánovich following her.

"They probably think I am offering them the grain to bribe them to remain here, while I myself go away leaving them to the mercy of the French," thought Princess Mary. "I will offer them monthly rations and housing at our Moscow estate. I am sure Andrew would do even more in my place," she thought as she went out in the twilight toward the crowd standing on the pasture by the barn.

The men crowded closer together, stirred, and rapidly took off their hats. Princess Mary lowered her eyes and, tripping over her skirt, came close up to them. So many different eyes, old and young, were fixed on her, and there were so many different faces, that she could not distinguish any of them, and feeling that she must speak to them all at once, did not know how to do it. But again the sense that she represented her father and her brother gave her courage, and she boldly began her speech.

"I am very glad you have come," she said without raising her eyes, and feeling her heart beating quickly and violently. "Drónushka tells me that the war has ruined you. That is our common misfortune, and I shall grudge nothing to help you. I am myself going away because it is dangerous here . . . the enemy is near . . . because . . . I am giving you everything, my friends, and I beg you to take everything, all our grain, so that you may not suffer want! And if you have been told that I am giving you the grain to keep you here—that is not true. On the contrary, I ask you to go with all your belongings to our estate near Moscow, and I promise you I will see to it that there you shall want for nothing. You shall be given food and lodging."

The princess stopped. Sighs were the only sound heard in the crowd.

"I am not doing this on my own account," she continued, "I do it in the name of my dead father, who was a good master to you, and of my brother and his son."

Again she paused. No one broke the silence.

"Ours is a common misfortune and we will share it together. All that is mine is yours," she concluded, scanning the faces before her.

All eyes were gazing at her with one and the same expression. She could not fathom whether it was curiosity, devotion, gratitude, or apprehension and distrust—but the expression on all the faces was identical.

"We are all very thankful for your bounty, but it won't do for us to take the landlord's grain," said a voice at the back of the crowd.

"But why not?" asked the princess.

No one replied and Princess Mary, looking round at the crowd, found that every eye she met now was immediately dropped.

"But why don't you want to take it?" she asked again.

No one answered.

The silence began to oppress the princess and she tried to catch someone's eye.

"Why don't you speak?" she inquired of a very old man who stood just in front of her leaning on his stick. "If you think something more is wanted, tell me! I will do anything," said she, catching his eye.

But as if this angered him, he bent his head quite low and muttered:

"Why should we agree? We don't want the grain."

"Why should we give up everything? We don't agree. Don't agree. . . . We are sorry for you, but we're not willing. Go away yourself, alone . . ." came from various sides of the crowd.

And again all the faces in that crowd bore an identical expression, though now it was certainly not an expression of curiosity or gratitude, but of angry resolve.

"But you can't have understood me," said Princess Mary with a sad smile. "Why don't you want to go? I promise to house and feed you, while here the enemy would ruin you. . . ."

But her voice was drowned by the voices of the crowd.

"We're not willing. Let them ruin us! We won't take your grain. We don't agree."

Again Princess Mary tried to catch someone's eye, but not a single eye in the crowd was turned to her; evidently they were all trying to avoid her look. She felt strange and awkward.

"Oh yes, an artful tale! Follow her into slavery! Pull down your houses and go into bondage! I dare say! 'I'll give you grain, indeed!' she says," voices in the crowd were heard saying.

With drooping head Princess Mary left the crowd and went back to the house. Having repeated her order to Dron to have horses ready for her departure next morning, she went to her room and remained alone with her own thoughts.

Chapter XII

For a long time that night Princess Mary sat by the open window of her room hearing the sound of the peasants' voices that reached her from the village, but it was not of them she was thinking. She felt that she could not understand them however much she might think about them. She thought only of one thing, her sorrow, which after the break caused by cares for the present, seemed already to belong to the past. Now she could remember it and weep or pray.

After sunset the wind had dropped. The night was calm and fresh. Toward midnight the voices began to subside, a cock crowed, the full moon began to show from behind the lime trees, a fresh white dewy mist began to rise, and stillness reigned over the village and the house.

Pictures of the near past—her father's illness and last moments—rose one after another to her memory. With mournful pleasure she now lingered over these images, repelling with horror only the last one, the picture of his death, which she felt she could not contemplate even in imagination at this still and mystic hour of night. And these pictures presented themselves to her so clearly and in such detail that they seemed now present, now past and now future.

She vividly recalled the moment when he had his first stroke and was being dragged along by his armpits through the garden at Bald Hills, muttering something with his helpless tongue, twitching his gray eyebrows and looking uneasily and timidly at her.

"Even then he wanted to tell me what he told me the day he died," she thought. "He had always thought what he said then." And she recalled in all its detail the night at Bald Hills before he had the last stroke, when with a foreboding of disaster she had remained at home against his will. She had not slept and had stolen downstairs on tiptoe, and going to the door of the conservatory where he slept that night had listened at the door. In a suffering and weary voice he was saying something to Tíkhon, speaking of the Crimea and its warm nights and of the Empress. Evidently he had wanted to talk. "And why didn't he call me? Why didn't he let me be there instead of Tíkhon?" Princess Mary had thought and thought again now. "Now he will never tell anyone what he had in his soul. Never will that moment return for him or for me when he might have said all he longed to say, and not Tíkhon but I might have heard and understood him. Why didn't I enter the room?" she thought. "Perhaps he would then have said to me what he said the day he died. While talking to Tíkhon he asked about me twice. He wanted to see me, and I was standing close by, outside the door. It was sad and painful for him to talk to Tíkhon who did not understand him. I remember how he began speaking to him about Lise as if she were alive—he had forgotten she was dead—and Tíkhon reminded him that she was no more, and he shouted, 'Fool!' He was greatly depressed. From behind the door I heard how he lay down on his bed groaning and loudly exclaimed, 'My God!' Why didn't I go in then? What could he have done to me? What could I have lost? And perhaps he would then have been comforted and would have said that word to me." And Princess Mary uttered aloud the caressing word he had said to her on the day of his death. "Dear-est!" she repeated, and began sobbing, with tears that relieved her soul. She now saw his face before her. And not the face she had known ever since she could remember and had always seen at a distance, but the timid feeble face she had seen for the first time quite closely, with all its wrinkles and details, when she stooped near to his mouth to catch what he said.

"Dear-est!" she repeated again.

"What was he thinking when he uttered that word? What is he thinking now?" This question suddenly presented itself to her, and in answer she saw him before her with the expression that was on his face as he lay in his coffin with his chin bound up with a white handkerchief. And the horror that had seized her when she touched him and convinced herself that *that* was not *he*, but something mysterious and horrible, seized her again. She tried to think of something else and to pray, but could do neither. With wide-open eyes she gazed at the moonlight and the shadows, expecting every moment to see his dead face, and she felt that the silence brooding over the house and within it held her fast.

"Dunyásha," she whispered. "Dunyásha!" she screamed wildly, and tearing herself out of this silence she ran to the servants' quarters to meet her old nurse and the maidservants who came running toward her.

Chapter XIII

On the 17th of August Rostóv and Ilyín, accompanied by Lavrúshka who had just returned from captivity and by a hussar orderly, left their quarters at Yankóvo, ten miles from Boguchárovo, and went for a ride—to try a new horse Ilyín had bought and to find out whether there was any hay to be had in the villages.

For the last three days Boguchárovo had lain between the two hostile armies, so that it was as easy for the Russian rearguard to get to it as for the French vanguard; so Rostóv, as a careful squadron-commander, wished to take such provisions as remained at Boguchárovo before the French could get them.

Rostóv and Ilyín were in the merriest of moods. On the way to Boguchárovo, a princely estate with a dwelling house and farm where they hoped to find many domestic serfs and pretty girls, they questioned Lavrúshka about Napoleon and laughed at his stories, and raced one another to try Ilyín's horse.

Rostóv had no idea that the village he was entering was the property of that very Bolkónski who had been engaged to his sister.

Rostóv and Ilyín gave rein to their horses for a last race along the incline before reaching Boguchárovo, and Rostóv, outstripping Ilyín, was the first to gallop into the village street.

"You're first!" cried Ilyín, flushed.

"Yes, always first both on the grass-land and here," answered Rostóv, stroking his heated Donéts horse.

"And I'd have won on my Frenchy, your excellency," said Lavrúshka from behind, alluding to his shabby cart-horse, "only I didn't wish to mortify you."

They rode at a footpace to the barn, where a large crowd of peasants was standing.

Some of the men bared their heads, others stared at the new arrivals without doffing their caps. Two tall old peasants with wrinkled faces and scanty beards emerged from the tavern, smiling, staggering and singing some incoherent song, and approached the officers.

"Fine fellows!" said Rostóv laughing. "Is there any hay here?"

"And how like one another," said Ilyín.

"A mo-o-st me-r-r-y co-o-m-pa . . . !" sang one of the peasants with a blissful smile.

One of the men came out of the crowd and went up to Rostóv.

"Who do you belong to?" he asked.

"The French," replied Ilyín jestingly, "and here is Napoleon himself"—and he pointed to Lavrúshka.

"Then you are Russians?" the peasant asked again.

"And is there a large force of you here?" said another, a short man, coming up.

"Very large," answered Rostóv. "But why have you collected here?" he added. "Is it a holiday?"

"The old men have met to talk over the business of the commune," replied the peasant moving away.

At that moment, on the road leading from the big house, two women and a man in a white hat were seen coming toward the officers.

"The one in pink is mine, so keep off!" said Ilyín on seeing Dunyásha running resolutely toward him.

"She'll be ours!" said Lavrúshka to Ilyín, winking.

"What do you want, my pretty?" said Ilyín with a smile.

"The princess ordered me to ask your regiment and your name."

"This is Count Rostóv, squadron-commander, and I am your humble servant."

"Co-o-om-pa-ny!" roared the tipsy peasant with a beatific smile as he looked at Ilyín talking to the girl. Following Dunyásha, Alpátych advanced to Rostóv, having bared his head while still at a distance.

"May I make bold to trouble your Honor?" said he respectfully, but with a shade of contempt for the youthfulness of this officer and with a hand thrust into his bosom. "My mistress, daughter of General-in-Chief Prince Nicholas Bolkónski who died on the 15th of this month, finding herself in difficulties owing to the boorishness of these people"—he pointed to the peasants—"asks you to come up to the house. . . . Won't you, please, ride on a little farther," said Alpátych with a melancholy smile, "as it is not convenient in the presence of . . . ?" He pointed to the two peasants who kept as close to him as horseflies to a horse.

"Ah! . . . Alpátych . . . Ah, Yákov Alpátych . . . Grand! Forgive us for Christ's sake, eh?" said the peasants, smiling joyfully at him.

Rostóv looked at the tipsy peasants and smiled.

"Or perhaps they amuse your Honor?" remarked Alpátych with a staid air, as he pointed at the old men with his free hand.

"No, there's not much to be amused at here," said Rostóv, and rode on a little way. "What's the matter?" he asked.

"I make bold to inform your Honor that the rude peasants here don't wish to let the mistress leave the estate, and threaten to unharness her horses, so that though everything has been packed up since morning, her excellency cannot get away."

"Impossible!" exclaimed Rostóv.

"I have the honor to report to you the actual truth," said Alpátych.

Rostóv dismounted, gave his horse to the orderly and followed Alpátych to the house, questioning him as to the state of affairs. It appeared that the princess's offer of corn to the peasants the previous day, and her talk with Dron and at the meeting, had actually had so bad an effect that Dron had finally given up the keys and joined the peasants, and had not appeared when Alpátych sent for him; and that in the morning when the princess gave orders to harness for her journey, the peasants had come in a large crowd to the barn and sent word that they would not let her leave the village: that there was an order not to move, and that they would unharness the horses. Alpátych had gone out to admonish them, but was told (it was chiefly Karp who did the talking, Dron not showing himself in the crowd) that they could not let the princess go, that there was an order to the contrary, but that if she stayed they would serve her as before and obey her in everything.

At the moment when Rostóv and Ilyín were galloping along the road, Princess Mary, despite the dissuasions of Alpátych, her nurse and the maids, had given orders to harness and intended to start, but when the cavalrymen were espied they were taken for Frenchmen, the coachman ran away and the women in the house began to wail.

"Father! Benefactor! God has sent you!" exclaimed deeply moved voices as Rostóv passed through the anteroom.

Princess Mary was sitting helpless and bewildered in the large sitting room, when Rostóv was shown in. She could not grasp who he was and why he had come, or what was happening to her. When she saw his Russian face, and by his walk and the first words he uttered recognized him as a man of her own class, she glanced at him with her deep radiant look and began speaking in a voice that faltered and trembled with emotion. This meeting immediately struck Rostóv as a romantic event. "A helpless girl overwhelmed with grief, left to the mercy of coarse rioting peasants! And what a strange fate sent me here! What gentleness and nobility there is in her features and expression!" thought he as he looked at her and listened to her timid story.

When she began to tell him that all this had happened the day after her father's funeral, her voiced trembled. She turned away, and then, as if fearing he might take her words as meant to move him to pity, looked at him with an apprehensive glance of inquiry. There were tears in Rostóv's eyes. Princess Mary noticed this, and glanced gratefully at him with that radiant look which caused the plainness of her face to be forgotten.

"I cannot express, princess, how glad I am that I happened to ride here and am able to show my readiness to serve you," said Rostóv, rising. "Go when you please, and I give you my word of honor that no one shall dare to cause you annoyance if only you will allow me to act as your escort." And bowing respectfully, as if to a lady of royal blood, he moved toward the door.

Rostóv's deferential tone seemed to indicate that though he would consider himself happy to be acquainted with her, he did not wish to take advantage of her misfortunes to intrude upon her.

Princess Mary understood this and appreciated his delicacy.

"I am very, very grateful to you," she said in French, "but I hope it was all a misunderstanding and that no one is to blame for it." She suddenly began to cry.

"Excuse me!" she said.

Rostóv, knitting his brows, left the room with another low bow.

Chapter XIV

WELL, IS SHE PRETTY? AH, FRIEND—MY PINK ONE IS DELICIOUS; HER NAME IS DUNYÁSHA. . . ." But on glancing at Rostóv's face Ilyín stopped short. He saw that his hero and commander was following quite a different train of thought.

Rostóv glanced angrily at Ilyín and without replying strode off with rapid steps to the village.

"I'll show them; I'll give it to them, the brigands!" said he to himself.

Alpátych at a gliding trot, only just managing not to run, kept up with him with difficulty.

"What decision have you been pleased to come to?" said he.

Rostóv stopped and, clenching his fists, suddenly and sternly turned on Alpátych.

"Decision? What decision? Old dotard! . . ." cried he. "What have you been about? Eh? The peasants are rioting, and you can't manage them? You're a traitor yourself! I know you. I'll flay you all alive! . . ." And as if afraid of wasting his store of anger, he left Alpátych and went rapidly forward. Alpátych, mastering his offended feelings, kept pace with Rostóv at a gliding gait and continued to impart his views. He said the peasants were obdurate and that at the present moment it would be imprudent to "over-resist" them without an armed force, and would it not be better first to send for the military?

"I'll give them armed force . . . I'll 'over-resist' them!" uttered Rostóv meaninglessly, breathless with irrational animal fury and the need to vent it.

Without considering what he would do he moved unconciously with quick resolute steps toward the crowd. And the nearer he drew to it the more Alpátych felt that this unreasonable action might produce good results. The peasants in the crowd were similarly impressed when they saw Rostóv's rapid firm steps and resolute frowning face.

After the hussars had come to the village and Rostóv had gone to see the princess, a certain confusion and dissension had arisen among the crowd. Some of the peasants said that these new arrivals were Russians and might take it amiss that the mistress was being detained. Dron was of this opinion, but as soon as he expressed it Karp and others attacked their ex-Elder.

"How many years have you been fattening on the commune?" Karp shouted at him. "It's all one to you! You'll dig up your pot of money and take it away with you. . . . What does it matter to you whether our homes are ruined or not?"

"We've been told to keep order, and that no one is to leave their homes or take away a single grain, and that's all about it!" cried another.

"It was your son's turn to be conscripted, but no fear! You begrudged your lump of a son," a little old man suddenly began attacking Dron—"and so they took my Vánka to be shaved for a soldier! But we all have to die."

"To be sure, we all have to die. I'm not against the commune," said Dron.

"That's it—not against it! You've filled your belly. . . ."

The two tall peasants had their say. As soon as Rostóv followed by Ilyín, Lavrúshka and Alpátych, came up to the crowd, Karp, thrusting his fingers into his belt and smiling a little, walked to the front. Dron on the contrary retired to the rear and the crowd drew closer together.

"Who is your Elder here? Hey?" shouted Rostóv, coming up to the crowd with quick steps.

"The Elder? What do you want with him? . . ." asked Karp.

But before the words were well out of his mouth, his cap flew off and a fierce blow jerked his head to one side.

"Caps off, traitors!" shouted Rostóv in a wrathful voice. "Where's the Elder?" he cried furiously.

"The Elder. . . . He wants the Elder! . . . Dron Zakhárych, you!" meek and flustered voices here and there were heard calling and caps began to come off their heads.

"We don't riot, we're following the orders," declared Karp, and at that moment several voices began speaking together.

"It's as the old men have decided—there's too many of you giving orders."

"Arguing? Mutiny! . . . Brigands! Traitors!" cried Rostóv unmeaningly in a voice not his own, gripping Karp by the collar. "Bind him, bind him!" he shouted, though there was no one to bind him but Lavrúshka and Alpátych.

Lavrúshka however ran up to Karp and seized him by the arms from behind.

"Shall I call up our men from beyond the hill?" he called out.

Alpátych turned to the peasants and ordered two of them by name to come and bind Karp. The men obediently came out of the crowd, and began taking off their belts.

"Where's the Elder?" demanded Rostóv in a loud voice.

With a pale and frowning face Dron stepped out of the crowd.

"Are you the Elder? Bind him, Lavrúshka!" shouted Rostóv, as if that order, too, could not possibly meet with any opposition.

And in fact two more peasants began binding Dron, who took off his own belt and handed it to them, as if to aid them.

"And you all listen to me!" said Rostóv to the peasants. "Be off to your houses at once, and don't let one of your voices be heard!"

"Why, we've not done any harm! We did it just out of foolishness. It's all nonsense. . . . I said then that it was not in order," voices were heard bickering with one another.

"There! What did I say?" said Alpátych, coming into his own again. "It's wrong, lads!"

"All our stupidity, Yákov Alpátych," came the answers, and the crowd began at once to disperse through the village.

The two bound men were led off to the master's house. The two drunken peasants followed them.

"Aye, when I look at you! . . ." said one of them to Karp.

"How can one talk to the masters like that? What were you thinking of, you fool?" added the other—"A real fool!"

Two hours later the carts were standing in the courtyard of the Bogucharovo house. The peasants were briskly carrying out the proprietor's goods and packing them on the carts, and Dron, liberated at Princess Mary's wish from the cupboard where he had been confined, was standing in the yard directing the men.

"Don't put it in so carelessly," said one of the peasants, a man with a round smiling face, taking a casket from a housemaid. "You know it has cost money! How can you chuck it in like that or shove it under the cord where it'll get rubbed? I don't like that way of doing things. Let it all be done properly, according to rule. Look here, put it under the bast-matting and cover it with hay—that's the way!"

"Eh, books, books!" said another peasant bringing out Prince Andrew's library cupboards. "Don't catch up against it! It's heavy, lads—solid books."

"Yes, they worked all day and didn't play!" remarked the tall, round-faced peasant gravely, pointing with a significant wink at the dictionaries that were on the top.

Unwilling to obtrude himself on the princess, Rostóv did not go back to the house but remained in the village awaiting her departure. When her carriage drove out of the house, he mounted and accompanied her eight miles from Bogucharovo to where the road was occupied by our troops. At the inn at Yankóvo he respectfully took leave of her, for the first time permitting himself to kiss her hand.

"How can you speak so!" he blushingly replied to Princess Mary's expressions of gratitude for her deliverance, as she termed what had occurred. "Any police officer would have done as much! If we had had only peasants to fight, we should not have let the enemy come so far," said he with a sense of shame and wishing to change the subject. "I am only happy to have had the opportunity of making your acquaintance. Good-bye, princess. I wish you happiness and consolation and hope to meet you again in happier circumstances. If you don't want to make me blush, please don't thank me!"

But the princess, if she did not again thank him in words, thanked him with the whole expression of her face, radiant with gratitude and tenderness. She could not believe that there was nothing to thank him for. On the contrary it seemed to her certain that had he not been there she would have perished at the hands of the mutineers and of the French, and that he had exposed himself to terrible and obvious danger to save her, and even more certain was it that he was a man of lofty and noble soul, able to understand her position and her sorrow. His kind, honest eyes, with the tears rising in them when she herself had begun to cry as she spoke of her loss, did leave her memory.

When she had taken leave of him and remained alone she suddenly felt her eyes filling with tears, and then not for the first time the strange question presented itself to her: did she love him?

On the rest of the way to Moscow, though the princess's position was not a cheerful one, Dunyásha, who went with her in the carriage, more than once noticed that her mistress leaned out of the window and smiled at something with an expression of mingled joy and sorrow.

"Well, supposing I do love him?" thought Princess Mary.

Ashamed as she was of acknowledging to herself that she had fallen in love with a man who would perhaps never love her, she comforted herself with the thought that no one would ever know it, and that she would not be to blame if, without ever speaking of it to anyone, she continued to the end of her life to love the man with whom she had fallen in love for the first and last time in her life.

Sometimes when she recalled his looks, his sympathy and his words, happiness did not appear impossible to her. It was at those moments that Dunyásha noticed her smiling as she looked out of the carriage window.

"Was it not fate that brought him to Bogucharovo, and at that very moment?" thought Princess Mary, "and that caused his sister to refuse my brother?" And in all this Princess Mary saw the hand of Providence.

The impression the princess made on Rostóv was a very agreeable one. To remember her gave him pleasure, and when his comrades, hearing of his adventure at Bogucharovo, rallied him on having gone to look for hay and having picked up one of the wealthiest heiresses in Russia, he grew angry. It made him angry just because the idea of marrying the gentle Princess Mary, who was attractive to him and had an enormous fortune, had against his will more than once entered his head. For himself personally Nicholas could not wish for a better wife: by marrying her he would make the countess his mother happy, would be able to put his father's affairs in order, and would even—he felt it—ensure Princess Mary's happiness.

But Sónya? And his plighted word? That was why Rostóv grew angry when he was rallied about Princess Bolkónskaya.

Chapter XV

On receiving command of the armies Kutúzov remembered Prince Andrew and sent an order for him to report at headquarters.

Prince Andrew arrived at Tsárevo-Zaymíshche on the very day and at the very hour that Kutúzov was reviewing the troops for the first time. He stopped in the village at the priest's house in front of which stood the commander-in-chief's carriage, and he sat down on the bench at the gate awaiting his Serene Highness, as everyone now called Kutúzov. From the field beyond the village came, now sounds of regimental music and now the roar of many voices shouting "Hurrah!" to the new commander-in-chief. Two orderlies, a courier and a major-domo, stood nearby, some ten paces from Prince Andrew, availing themselves of Kutúzov's absence and of the fine weather. A short, swarthy lieutenant colonel of hussars with thick mustaches and whiskers rode up to the gate and, glancing at Prince Andrew, inquired whether his Serene Highness was putting up there and whether he would soon be back.

Prince Andrew replied that he was not on his Serene Highness's staff but was himself a new arrival. The lieutenant-colonel turned to a smart orderly, who with the peculiar contempt with which a commander-in-chief's orderly speaks to officers, replied:

"What? His Serene Highness? I expect he'll be here soon. What do you want?"

The lieutenant-colonel of hussars smiled beneath his mustache at the orderly's tone, dismounted, gave his horse to a dispatch-runner and approached Bolkónski with a slight bow. Bolkónski made room for him on the bench and the lieutenant-colonel sat down beside him.

"You're also waiting for the commander-in-chief?" said he. "They say he weceives evewyone, thank God! . . . It's awful with those sausage-eaters! Ermólov had weason to ask to be pwomoted to be a German! Now p'waps Wussians will get a look in. As it was, devil only knows what was happening. We kept wetweating and wetweating. Did you take part in the campaign?" he asked.

"I had the pleasure," replied Prince Andrew, "not only of taking part in the retreat but of losing in that retreat all I held dear—not to mention the estate and home of my birth—my father, who died of grief. I belong to the province of Smolénsk."

"Ah? You're Pwince Bolkónski? Vewy glad to make your acquaintance! I'm Lieutenant-Colonel Denísov, better known as 'Váska,' " said Denísov, pressing Prince Andrew's hand and looking into his face with a particularly kindly attention. "Yes, I heard," said he sympathetically, and after a short pause added: "Yes, it's Scythian warfare. It's all vewy well—only not for those who get it in the neck. So you are Pwince Andwew Bolkónski?" He swayed his head. "Vewy pleased, pwince, to make your acquaintance!" he repeated again, smiling sadly, and he again pressed Prince Andrew's hand.

Prince Andrew knew Denísov from what Natásha had told him of her first suitor. This memory carried him sadly and sweetly back to those painful feelings of which he had not thought lately, but which still found place in his soul. Of late he had received so many new and very serious impressions—such as the retreat from Smolénsk, his visit to Bald Hills and the recent news of his father's death—and had experienced so many emotions, that for a long time past those memories had not entered his mind, and now that they did, they did not act on him with nearly their former strength. For Denísov, too, the memories awakened by the name of Bolkónski belonged to a distant, romantic past, when after supper and after Natásha's singing he had proposed to a little girl of fifteen without realizing what he was doing. He smiled at the recollection of that time and of his love for Natásha, and passed at once to what now interested him passionately and exclusively. This was a plan of campaign he had devised while serving at the outposts during the retreat. He had proposed that plan to Barclay de Tolly and now wished to propose it to Kutúzov. The plan was based on the fact that the French line of operation was too extended, and it proposed that instead of, or concurrently with, action on the front to bar the advance of the French, we should attack their line of communication. He began explaining his plan to Prince Andrew.

"They can't hold all that line. It's impossible. I will undertake to bweak thwough. Give me five hundwed men and I will bweak the line, that's certain! There's only one way—guewilla warfare!"

Denísov rose and began gesticulating as he explained his plan to Bolkónski. In the midst of his explanation shouts were heard from the army, growing more incoherent and more diffused, mingling with music and songs and coming from the field where the review was held. Sounds of hoofs and shouts were nearing the village.

"He's coming! He's coming!" shouted a Cossack standing at the gate.

Bolkónski and Denísov moved to the gate, at which a knot of soldiers (a guard of honor) was standing, and they saw Kutúzov coming down the street mounted on a rather small sorrel horse. A huge suite of generals rode behind him. Barclay was riding almost beside him, and a crowd of officers ran after and around them shouting, "Hurrah!"

His adjutants galloped into the yard before him. Kutúzov was impatiently urging on his horse, which ambled smoothly under his weight, and he raised his hand to his white horse-guard's cap with a red band and no peak, nodding his head continually. When he came up to the guard of honor, a fine set of Grenadiers mostly wearing decorations, who were giving him the salute, he looked at them silently and attentively for nearly a minute with the steady gaze of a commander and then turned to the crowd of generals and officers surrounding him. Suddenly his face assumed a subtle expression, he shrugged his shoulders with an air of perplexity.

"And with such fine fellows to retreat and retreat! Well, good-bye, general," he added, and rode into the yard past Prince Andrew and Denísov.

"Hurrah! hurrah! hurrah!" shouted those behind him.

Since Prince Andrew had last seen him Kutúzov had grown still more corpulent, flaccid and fat. But the bleached eyeball, the scar, and the familiar weariness of his expression were still the same. He was wearing the white horse-guard's cap and a military overcoat with a whip hanging over his shoulder by a thin strap. He sat heavily and swayed limply on his brisk little horse.

"Whew . . . whew . . . whew!" he whistled just audibly as he rode into the yard. His face expressed the relief of relaxed strain felt by a man who means to rest after a ceremony. He drew his left foot out of the stirrup and, lurching with his whole body and puckering his face with the effort, raised it with difficulty onto the saddle, leaned on his knee, groaned and slipped down into the arms of the Cossacks and adjutants who stood ready to assist him.

He pulled himself together, looked round screwing up his eyes, glanced at Prince Andrew and, evidently not recognizing him, moved with his waddling gait to the porch. "Whew . . . whew . . . whew!" he whistled, and again glanced at Prince Andrew. As often occurs with old men, it was only after some seconds that the impression produced by Prince Andrew's face linked itself up with Kutúzov's remembrance of his personality.

"Ah, how do you do, my dear prince? How do you do, my dear boy? Come along . . ." said he glancing wearily round, and he stepped onto the porch which creaked under his weight.

He unbuttoned his coat and sat down on a bench in the porch.

"And how's your father?"

"I received news of his death, yesterday," replied Prince Andrew abruptly.

Kutúzov looked at him with eyes wide-open with dismay, and then took off his cap and crossed himself:

"May the kingdom of Heaven be his! God's will be done to us all!" He sighed deeply, his whole chest heaving, and was silent for a while. "I loved him and respected him, and sympathize with you with all my heart."

He embraced Prince Andrew, pressing him to his fat breast, and for some time did not let him go. When he released him Prince Andrew saw that Kutúzov's flabby lips were trembling and that tears were in his eyes. He sighed and pressed on the bench with both hands to raise himself.

"Come! Come with me, we'll have a talk," said he.

But at that moment Denísov, no more intimidated by his superiors than by the enemy, came with jingling spurs up the steps of the porch, despite the angry whispers of the adjutants who tried to stop him. Kutúzov, his hands still pressed on the seat, glanced at him glumly. Denísov, having given his name, announced that he had to communicate to his Serene Highness a matter of great importance for their country's welfare. Kutúzov looked wearily at him, and lifting his hands with a gesture of annoyance folded them across his stomach repeating the words: "For our country's welfare? Well, what is it? Speak!" Denísov blushed like a girl (it was strange to see the color rise in that shaggy, bibulous, time-worn face) and boldly began to expound his plan of cutting the enemy's lines of communication between Smolénsk and Vyázma. Denísov came from those parts and knew the country well. His plan seemed decidedly a good one, especially from the strength of conviction with which he spoke. Kutúzov looked down at his own legs, occasionally glancing at the door of the adjoining hut as if expecting something unpleasant to emerge from it. And from that hut, while Denísov was speaking, a general with a portfolio under his arm really did appear.

"What?" said Kutúzov, in the midst of Denísov's explanations, "are you ready so soon?"

"Ready, your Serene Highness," replied the general.

Kutúzov swayed his head, as much as to say: "How is one man to deal with it all?" and again listened to Denísov.

"I give my word of honor as a Wussian officer," said Denísov, "that I can bweak Napoleon's line of communication!"

"What relation are you to Intendant-General Kiríl Andréevich Denísov?" asked Kutúzov, interrupting him.

"He is my uncle, your Serene Highness."

"Ah, we were friends," said Kutúzov cheerfully. "All right, all right, friend, stay here at the staff and tomorrow we'll have a talk."

With a nod to Denísov he turned away and put out his hand for the papers Konovnítsyn had brought him.

"Would not your Serene Highness like to come inside?" said the general on duty in a discontented voice, "the plans must be examined and several papers have to be signed."

An adjutant came out and announced that everything was in readiness within. But Kutúzov evidently did not wish to enter that room till he was disengaged. He made a grimace. . . .

"No, tell them to bring a small table out here, my dear boy. I'll look at them here," said he.

"Don't go away," he added, turning to Prince Andrew, who remained in the porch and listened to the general's report.

While this was being given, Prince Andrew heard the whisper of a woman's voice and the rustle of a silk dress behind the door. Several times on glancing that way he noticed behind that door a plump, rosy, handsome woman in a pink dress with a lilac silk kerchief on her head, holding a dish and evidently awaiting the entrance of the commander-in-chief. Kutúzov's adjutant whispered to Prince Andrew that this was the wife of the priest whose home it was, and that she intended to offer his Serene Highness bread and salt. "Her husband has welcomed his Serene Highness with the cross at the church, and she intends to welcome him in the house. . . . She's very pretty," added the adjutant with a smile. At those words Kutúzov looked round. He was listening to the general's report—which consisted chiefly of a criticism of the position at Tsárevo-Zaymíshche—as he had listened to Denísov, and seven years previously had listened to the discussion at the Austerlitz council of war. He evidently listened only because he had ears which, though there was a piece of tow in one of them, could not help hearing; but it was evident that nothing the general could say would surprise or even interest him, that he knew all that would be said beforehand, and heard it all only because he had to, as one has to listen to the chanting of a service of prayer. All that Denísov had said was clever and to the point. What the general was saying was even more clever and to the point, but it was evident that Kutúzov despised knowledge and cleverness, and knew of something else that would decide the matter—something independent of cleverness and knowledge. Prince Andrew watched the commander-in-chief's face attentively, and the only expression he could see there was one of boredom, curiosity as to the meaning of the feminine whispering behind the door, and a desire to observe propriety. It was evident that Kutúzov despised cleverness and learning and even the patriotic feeling shown by Denísov, but despised them not because of his own intellect, feelings or knowledge—he did not try to display any of these—but because of something else. He despised them because of his old age and experience of life. The only instruction Kutúzov gave of his own accord during that report referred to looting by the Russian troops. At the end of the report the general put before him for signature a paper relating to the recovery of payment from army commanders for green oats mown down by the soldiers, when landowners lodged petitions for compensation.

After hearing the matter, Kutúzov smacked his lips together and shook his head.

"Into the stove . . . into the fire with it! I tell you once for all, my dear fellow," said he, "into the fire with all such things! Let them cut the crops and burn wood to their hearts' content. I don't order it or allow it, but I don't exact compensation either. One can't get on without it. 'When wood is chopped the chips will fly.' " He looked at the paper again. "Oh, this German precision!" he muttered, shaking his head.

Chapter XVI

"WELL, THAT'S ALL!" SAID KUTÚZOV AS HE SIGNED THE LAST OF THE DOCUMENTS, AND RISING heavily and smoothing out the folds in his fat white neck he moved toward the door with a more cheerful expression.

The priest's wife, flushing rosy red, caught up the dish she had after all not managed to present at the right moment, though she had so long been preparing for it, and with a low bow offered it to Kutúzov.

He screwed up his eyes, smiled, lifted her chin with his hand and said:

"Ah, what a beauty! Thank you, sweetheart!"

He took some gold pieces from his trouser pocket and put them on the dish for her. "Well, my dear, and how are we getting on?" he asked, moving to the door of the room assigned to him. The priest's wife smiled, and with dimples in her rosy cheeks followed him into the room. The adjutant came out to the porch and asked Prince Andrew to lunch with him. Half an hour later Prince Andrew was again called to Kutúzov. He found him reclining in an arm-chair, still in the same unbuttoned overcoat. He had in his hand a French book which he closed as Prince Andrew entered, marking the place with a knife. Prince Andrew saw by the cover that it was *Les Chevaliers du Cygne* by Madame de Genlis.

"Well, sit down, sit down here. Let's have a talk," said Kutúzov. "It's sad, very sad. But remember, my dear fellow, that I am a father to you, a second father . . ."

Prince Andrew told Kutúzov all he knew of his father's death, and what he had seen at Bald Hills when he passed through it.

"What . . . what they have brought us to!" Kutúzov suddenly cried in an agitated voice, evidently picturing vividly to himself from Prince Andrew's story the condition Russia was in: "But give me time, give me time!" he said with a grim look evidently not wishing to continue this agitating conversation, and added: "I sent for you to keep you with me."

"I thank your Serene Highness, but I fear I am no longer fit for the staff," replied Prince Andrew with a smile which Kutúzov noticed.

Kutúzov glanced inquiringly at him.

"But above all," added Prince Andrew, "I have grown used to my regiment, am fond of the officers, and I fancy the men also like me. I should be sorry to leave the regiment. If I decline the honor of being with you, believe me . . ."

A shrewd, kindly, yet subtly derisive expression lit up Kutúzov's podgy face. He cut Bolkónski short.

"I am sorry, for I need you. But you're right, you're right! It's not here that men are needed. Advisers are always plentiful, but men are not. The regiments would not be what they are if the would-be advisers served there as you do. I remember you at Austerlitz. . . . I remember, yes, I remember you with the standard!" said Kutúzov, and a flush of pleasure suffused Prince Andrew's face at this recollection.

Taking his hand and drawing him downward, Kutúzov offered his cheek to be kissed, and again Prince Andrew noticed tears in the old man's eyes. Though Prince Andrew knew that Kutúzov's tears came easily, and that he was particularly tender to and considerate of him from a wish to show sympathy with his loss, yet this reminder of Austerlitz was both pleasant and flattering to him.

"Go your way and God be with you. I know your path is the path of honor!" He paused. "I missed you at Bucharest, but I needed someone to send." And changing the subject, Kutúzov began to speak of the Turkish war and the peace that had been concluded. "Yes, I have been much blamed," he said, "both for that war and the peace . . . but everything came at the right time. *Tout vient à point à celui qui sait attendre*. And there were as many advisers there as here . . ." he went on, returning to the subject of "advisers" which evidently occupied him. "Ah, those advisers!" said he. "If we had listened to them all we should not have made peace with Turkey and should not have been through with that war. Everything in haste, but more haste less speed. Kámenski would have been lost if he had not died. He stormed fortresses with thirty thousand men. It is not difficult to capture a fortress but it is difficult to win a campaign. For that, storming and attacking but *patience and time* are wanted. Kámenski sent soldiers to Rustchuk, but I only employed these two things and took more fortresses than Kámenski and made the Turks eat horseflesh!" He swayed his head. "And the French shall too, believe me," he went on, growing warmer and beating his chest, "I'll make them eat horseflesh!" And tears again dimmed his eyes.

"But shan't we have to accept battle?" remarked Prince Andrew.

"We shall if everybody wants it; it can't be helped. . . . But believe me, my dear boy, there is nothing stronger than those two: *patience and time*, they will do it all. But the advisers *n'entendent pas de cette oreille, voilà le mal*. Some want a thing—others don't. What's one to do?" he asked, evidently expecting an answer. "Well, what do you want us to do?" he repeated and his eye shone with a deep, shrewd look. "I'll tell you what to do," he continued, as Prince Andrew still did not reply: "I will tell you what to do, and what I do. *Dans le doute, mon cher,*" he paused, *"abstiens-toi"*—he articulated the French proverb deliberately.

"Well, good-bye, my dear fellow; remember that with all my heart I share your sorrow, and that for you I am not a Serene Highness, nor a prince, nor a commander-in-chief, but a father! If you want anything come straight to me. Good-bye, my dear boy."

Again he embraced and kissed Prince Andrew, but before the latter had left the room Kutúzov gave a sigh of relief and went on with his unfinished novel, *Les Chevaliers du Cygne* by Madame de Genlis.

Prince Andrew could not have explained how or why it was, but after that interview with Kutúzov he went back to his regiment reassured as to the general course of affairs and as to the man to whom it had been entrusted. The more he realized the absence of all personal motive in that old man—in whom there seemed to remain only the habit of passions, and in place of an intellect (grouping events and drawing conclusions) only the capacity calmly to contemplate the course of events—the more reassured he was that everything would be as it should. "He will not bring in any plan of his own. He will not devise or undertake anything," thought Prince Andrew, "but he will hear everything, remember everything and put everything in its place. He will not hinder anything useful nor allow anything harmful. He understands that there is something stronger and more important than his own will—the inevitable course of events, and he can see them and grasp their significance, and seeing that significance can refrain from meddling and renounce his personal wish directed to something else. And above all," thought Prince Andrew, "one believes in him because he's Russian, despite the novel by Genlis and the French proverbs, and because his voice shook when he said: 'What they have brought us to!' and had a sob in it when he said he would 'make them eat horseflesh!' "

On such feelings, more or less dimly shared by all, the unanimity and general approval were founded with which, despite court influences, the popular choice of Kutúzov as commander-in-chief was received.

Chapter XVII

After the Emperor had left Moscow, life flowed on there in its usual course, and its course was so very usual that it was difficult to remember the recent days of patriotic elation and ardor, hard to believe that Russia was really in danger and that the members of the English Club were also sons of the Fatherland ready to sacrifice everything for it. The one thing that recalled the patriotic fervor everyone had displayed during the Emperor's stay was the call for contributions of men and money, a necessity that as soon as the promises had been made, assumed a legal, official form and became unavoidable.

With the enemy's approach to Moscow, the Muscovites' view of their situation did not grow more serious but on the contrary became even more frivolous, as always happens with people who see a great danger approaching. At the approach of danger there are always two voices that speak with equal power in the human soul: one very reasonably tells a man to consider the nature of the danger and the means of escaping it; the other, still more reasonably, says that it is too depressing and painful to think of the danger, since it is not in man's power to foresee everything and avert the general course of events, and it is therefore better to disregard what is painful till it comes, and to think about what is pleasant. In solitude a man generally listens to the first voice, but in society to the second. So it was now with the inhabitants of Moscow. It was long since people had been as gay in Moscow as that year.

Rostopchín's broadsheets, headed by woodcuts of a drink-shop, a potman, and a Moscow burgher called Karpushka Chigírin, *"who—having been a militiaman and having had rather too much at the pub—heard that Napoleon wished to come to Moscow, grew angry, abused the French in very bad language, came out of the drink-shop and, under the sign of the eagle, began to address the assembled people,"* were read and discussed, together with the latest of Vasíli Lvóvich Púshkin's *bouts rimés.*

In the corner room at the Club members gathered to read these broadsheets, and some liked the way Karpushka jeered at the French, saying: *"They will swell up with Russian cabbage, burst with our buckwheat porridge, and choke themselves with cabbage-soup. They are all dwarfs and one peasant woman will toss three of them with a hay-fork."* Others did not like that tone and said it was stupid and vulgar. It was said that Rostopchín had expelled all Frenchmen and even all foreigners from Moscow, and that there had been some spies and agents of Napoleon among them; but this was told chiefly to introduce Rostopchín's witty remark on that occasion. The foreigners were deported to Nízhni by boat, and Rostopchín had said to them in French: *"Rentrez en vous-mêmes; entrez dans la barque, et n'en faites pas une barque de Charon."* There was talk of all the government offices having been already removed from Moscow, and to this Shinshín's witticism was added—that for that alone Moscow ought to be grateful to Napoleon. It was said that Mamónov's regiment would cost him eight hundred thousand rubles, and that Bezúkhov had spent even more on his, but that the best thing about Bezúkhov's action was that he himself was going to don a uniform and ride at the head of his regiment without charging anything for the show.

"You don't spare anyone," said Julie Drubetskáya as she collected and pressed together a bunch of raveled lint with her thin, beringed fingers.

Julie was preparing to leave Moscow next day and was giving a farewell soireé.

"Bezúkhov est ridicule, but he is so kind and good-natured. What pleasure is there to be so *caustique?"*

"A forfeit!" cried a young man in militia uniform whom Julie called *"mon chevalier,"* and who was going with her to Nízhni.

In Julie's set, as in many other circles in Moscow, it had been agreed that they would speak nothing but Russian, and that those who made a slip and spoke French should pay fines to the Committee of Voluntary Contributions.

"Another forfeit for a Gallicism," said a Russian writer who was present. " 'What pleasure is there to be' is not Russian!"

"You spare no one," continued Julie to the young man without heeding the author's remark.

"For *caustique*—I am guilty and will pay, and I am prepared to pay again for the pleasure of telling you the truth. For Gallicisms I won't be responsible," she remarked, turning to the author: "I have neither the money nor the time, like Prince Galítsyn, to engage a master to teach me Russian!"

"Ah, here he is!" she added. "*Quand on* . . . No, no," she said to the militia officer, "you won't catch me. Speak of the sun and you see its rays!" and she smiled amiably at Pierre. "We were just talking of you," she said with the facility in lying natural to a society woman. "We were saying that your regiment would be sure to be better than Mamónov's."

"Oh don't talk to me of my regiment," replied Pierre, kissing his hostess's hand and taking a seat beside her. "I am so sick of it."

"You will, of course, command it yourself?" said Julie, directing a sly, sarcastic glance toward the militia officer.

The latter in Pierre's presence had ceased to be caustic, and his face expressed perplexity as to what Julie's smile might mean. In spite of his absent-mindedness and good nature, Pierre's personality immediately checked any attempt to ridicule him to his face.

"No," said Pierre, with a laughing glance at his big, stout body. "I should make too good a target for the French, besides I am afraid I should hardly be able to climb onto a horse."

Among those whom Julie's guests happened to choose to gossip about were the Rostóvs.

"I hear that their affairs are in a very bad way," said Julie. "And he is so unreasonable, the count himself I mean. The Razumóvskis wanted to buy his house and his estate near Moscow, but it drags on and on. He asks too much."

"No, I think the sale will come off in a few days," said someone. "Though it is madness to buy anything in Moscow now."

"Why?" asked Julie. "You don't think Moscow is in danger?"

"Then why are you leaving?"

"I? What a question! I am going because . . . well, because everyone is going: and besides—I am not Joan of Arc or an Amazon."

"Well, of course, of course! Let me have some more strips of linen."

"If he manages the business properly he will be able to pay off all his debts," said the militia officer, speaking of Rostóv.

"A kindly old man but not up to much. And why do they stay on so long in Moscow? They meant to leave for the country long ago. Natalie is quite well again now, isn't she?" Julie asked Pierre with a knowing smile.

"They are waiting for their younger son," Pierre replied. "He joined Obolénski's Cossacks and went to Bélaya Tsérkov where the regiment is being formed. But now they have had him transferred to my regiment and are expecting him every day. The count wanted to leave long ago, but the countess won't on any account leave Moscow till her son returns."

"I met them the day before yesterday at the Arkhárovs'. Natalie has recovered her looks and is brighter. She sang a song. How easily some people get over everything!"

"Get over what?" inquired Pierre looking displeased.

Julie smiled.

"You know, count, such knights as you are only found in Madame de Souza's novels."

"What knights? What do you mean?" demanded Pierre blushing.

"Oh, come, my dear count! *C'est la fable de tout Moscou. Je vous admire, ma parole d'honneur!*"

"Forfeit, forfeit!" cried the militia officer.

"All right, one can't talk—how tiresome!"

"What is 'the talk of all Moscow'?" Pierre asked angrily, rising to his feet.

"Come now, count, you know!"

"I don't know anything about it," said Pierre.

"I know you were friendly with Natalie, and so . . . but I was always more friendly with Véra—that dear Véra."

"No, madame!" Pierre continued in a tone of displeasure, "I have not taken on myself the rôle of Natalie Rostóva's knight at all, and have not been their house for nearly a month. But I cannot understand the cruelty . . ."

"Qui s'excuse, s'accuse," said Julie, smiling and waving the lint triumphantly, and to have the last word she promptly changed the subject. "Do you know what I heard today? Poor Mary Bolkónskaya arrived in Moscow yesterday. Do you know that she has lost her father?"

"Really? Where is she? I should like very much to see her," said Pierre.

"I spent the evening with her yesterday. She is going to their estate near Moscow either today or tomorrow morning, with her nephew."

"Well, and how is she?" asked Pierre.

"She is well, but sad. But do you know who rescued her? It is quite a romance. Nicholas Rostóv! She was surrounded, and they wanted to kill her and had wounded some of her people. He rushed in and saved her . . ."

"Another romance," said the militia officer. "Really, this general flight has been arranged to get all the old maids married off. Catiche is one and Princess Bolkónskaya another."

"Do you know, I really believe she is *un petit peu amoureuse du jeune homme.*"

"Forfeit, forfeit, forfeit!"

"But how could one say that in Russian?"

Chapter XVIII

WHEN PIERRE RETURNED HOME HE WAS HANDED TWO OF ROSTOPCHÍN'S BROADSHEETS THAT had been brought that day.

The first declared that the report that Count Rostopchín had forbidden people to leave Moscow was false; on the contrary he was glad that ladies and tradesmen's wives were leaving the city. "There will be less panic and less gossip," ran the broadsheet, "but I will stake my life on it that that scoundrel will not enter Moscow." These words showed Pierre clearly for the first time that the French would enter Moscow. The second broadsheet stated that our headquarters were at Vyázma, that Count Wittgenstein had defeated the French, but that as many of the inhabitants of Moscow wished to be armed, weapons were ready for them at the arsenal: sabers, pistols, and muskets which could be had at a low price. The tone of the proclamation was not as jocose as in the former Chigírin talks. Pierre pondered over these broadsheets. Evidently the terrible stormcloud he had desired with the whole strength of his soul but which yet aroused involuntary horror in him, was drawing near.

"Shall I join the army and enter the service, or wait?" he asked himself for the hundredth time. He took a pack of cards that lay on the table and began to lay them out for a game of patience.

"If this patience comes out," he said to himself after shuffling the cards, holding them in his hand and lifting his head, "if it comes out, it means . . . what does it mean?"

He had not decided what it should mean when he heard the voice of the eldest princess at the door asking whether she might come in.

"Then it will mean that I must go to the army," said Pierre to himself. "Come in, come in!" he added to the princess.

Only the eldest princess, the one with the stony face and long waist, was still living in Pierre's house. The two younger ones had both married.

"Excuse my coming to you, cousin," she said in a reproachful and agitated voice. "You know some decision must be come to. What is going to happen? Everyone has left Moscow and the people are rioting. How is it that we are staying on?"

"On the contrary things seem satisfactory, *ma cousine,*" said Pierre in the bantering tone he habitually adopted toward her, always feeling uncomfortable in the rôle of her benefactor.

"Satisfactory, indeed! Very satisfactory! Barbara Ivánovna told me today how our troops are distinguishing themselves. It certainly does them credit! And the people too are quite mutinous—they no longer obey, even my maid has taken to being rude. At this rate they will soon begin beating us. One can't walk in the streets. But, above all, the French will be here any day now, so what are we waiting for? I ask just one thing of you, cousin," she went on, "arrange for me to be taken to Petersburg. Whatever I may be, I can't live under Bonaparte's rule."

"Oh, come, *ma cousine!* Where do you get your information from? On the contrary . . ."

"I won't submit to your Napoleon! Others may if they please. . . . If you don't want to do this . . ."

"But I will, I'll give the order at once."

The princess was apparently vexed at not having anyone to be angry with. Muttering to herself, she sat down on a chair.

"But you have been misinformed," said Pierre. "Everything is quiet in the city and there is not the slightest danger. See! I've just been reading . . ." He showed her the broadsheet. "Count Rostopchín writes that he will stake his life on it that the enemy will not enter Moscow."

"Oh, that count of yours!" said the princess malevolently. "He is a hypocrite, a rascal who has himself roused the people to riot. Didn't he write in those idiotic broadsheets that anyone 'whoever it might be, should be dragged to the lock-up by his hair'? (How silly!) 'And honor and glory to whoever captures him,' he says. This is what his cajolery has brought us to! Barbara Ivánovna told me the mob near killed her because she said something in French."

"Oh, but it's so . . . You take everything so to heart," said Pierre, and began laying out his cards for patience.

Although that patience did come out, Pierre did not join the army, but remained in deserted Moscow ever in the same state of agitation, irresolution and alarm, yet at the same time joyfully expecting something terrible.

Next day toward evening the princess set off, and Pierre's head steward came to inform him that the money needed for the equipment of his regiment could not be found without selling one of the estates. In general the head steward made out to Pierre that his project of raising a regiment would ruin him. Pierre listened to him, scarcely able to repress a smile.

"Well then, sell it," said he. "What's to be done? I can't draw back now!"

The worse everything became, especially his own affairs, the better was Pierre pleased and the more evident was it that the catastrophe he expected was approaching. Hardly anyone he knew was left in town. Julie had gone, and so had Princess Mary. Of his intimate friends only the Rostóvs remained, but he did not go to see them.

To distract his thoughts he drove that day to the village of Vorontsóvo to see the great balloon Leppich was constructing to destroy the foe, and a trial balloon that was to go up next day. The balloon was not yet ready, but Pierre learned that it was being constructed by the Emperor's desire. The Emperor had written to Count Rostopchín as follows:

As soon as Leppich is ready, get together a crew of reliable and intelligent men for his car and send a courier to General Kutúzov to let him know. I have informed him of the matter.

Please impress upon Leppich to be very careful where he descends for the first time, that he may not make a mistake and fall into the enemy's hands. It is essential for him to combine his movements with those of the commander-in-chief.

On his way home from Vorontsóvo, as he was passing the Bolótnoe Place, Pierre, seeing a large crowd round the Lóbnoe Place, stopped and got out of his trap. A French cook accused of being a spy was being flogged. The flogging was only just over, and the executioner was releasing from the flogging-bench a stout man with red whiskers, in blue stockings and a green jacket, who was moaning piteously. Another criminal, thin and pale, stood near. Judging by their faces they were both Frenchmen. With a frightened and suffering look resembling that on the thin Frenchman's face, Pierre pushed his way in through the crowd.

"What is it? Who is it? What is it for?" he kept asking.

But the attention of the crowd—officials, burghers, shopkeepers, peasants, and women in cloaks and in pelisses—was so eagerly centered on what was passing in Lóbnoe Place that no one answered him. The stout man rose, frowned, shrugged his shoulders, and evidently trying to appear firm began to pull on his jacket without looking about him, but suddenly his lips trembled and he began to cry, in the way full-blooded grown-up men cry, though angry with himself for doing so. In the crowd people began talking loudly, to stifle their feelings of pity as it seemed to Pierre.

"He's cook to some prince."

"Eh, mounseer, Russian sauce seems to be sour to a Frenchman . . . sets his teeth on edge!" said a wrinkled clerk who was standing behind Pierre, when the Frenchman began to cry.

The clerk glanced round, evidently hoping that his joke would be appreciated. Some people began to laugh, others continued to watch in dismay the executioner who was undressing the other man.

Pierre choked, his face puckered and he turned hastily away, went back to his trap muttering something to himself as he went, and took his seat. As they drove along he shuddered, and exclaimed several times so audibly that the coachman asked him:

"What is your pleasure?"

"Where are you going?" shouted Pierre to the man, who was driving to Lubyánka Street.

"To the Governor's, as you ordered," answered the coachman.

"Fool! Idiot!" shouted Pierre, abusing his coachman—a thing he rarely did. "Home, I told you! And drive faster, blockhead!" "I must get away this very day," he murmured to himself.

At the sight of the tortured Frenchman and the crowd surrounding the Lóbnoe Place, Pierre had so definitely made up his mind that he could no longer remain in Moscow and would leave for the army that very day, that it seemed to him that either he had told the coachman this or that the man ought to have known it for himself.

On reaching home Pierre gave orders to Evstáfey—his head coachman who knew everything, could do anything, and was known to all Moscow—that he would leave that night for the army at Mozháysk, and that his saddle-horses should be sent there. This could not all be arranged that day, so on Evstafey's representation Pierre had to put off his departure till next day to allow time for the relay horses to be sent on in advance.

On the 24th the weather cleared up after a spell of rain, and after dinner Pierre left Moscow. When changing horses that night in Perkhúshkovo, he learned that there had been a great battle that evening. (This was the battle of Shevárdino.) He was told that there in Perkhúshkovo the earth trembled from the firing, but nobody could answer his questions as to who had won. At dawn next day Pierre was approaching Mozháysk.

Every house in Mozháysk had soldiers quartered in it, and at the hostel where Pierre was met by his groom and coachman there was no room to be had. It was full of officers.

Everywhere in Mozháysk and beyond it, troops were stationed or on the march. Cossacks, foot and horse soldiers, wagons, caissons and cannon were everywhere. Pierre pushed forward as fast as he could, and the farther he left Moscow behind and the deeper he plunged into that sea of troops the more was he overcome by restless agitation and a new and joyful feeling he had not experienced before. It was a feeling akin to what he had felt at the Slobóda Palace during the Emperor's visit—a sense of the necessity of undertaking something and sacrificing something. He now experienced a glad consciousness that everything that constitutes men's happiness—the comforts of life, wealth, even life itself—is rubbish it is pleasant to throw away, compared with something . . . With what? Pierre could not say, and he did not try to determine for whom and for what he felt such particular delight in sacrificing everything. He was not occupied with the question of what to sacrifice for; the fact of sacrificing in itself afforded him a new and joyous sensation.

Chapter XIX

ON THE 24TH OF AUGUST THE BATTLE OF THE SHEVÁRDINO REDOUBT WAS FOUGHT, ON THE 25TH not a shot was fired by either side, and on the 26th the battle of Borodinó itself took place.

Why and how were the battles of Shevárdino and Borodinó given and accepted? Why was the battle of Borodinó fought? There was not the least sense in it for either the French or the Russians. Its immediate result for the Russians was, and was bound to be, that we were brought nearer to the destruction of Moscow—which we feared more than anything in the world; and for the French its immediate result was that they were brought nearer to the destruction of their whole army—which they feared more than anything in the world. What the result must be was quite obvious, and yet Napoleon offered and Kutúzov accepted that battle.

If the commanders had been guided by reason, it would seem that it must have been obvious to Napoleon that by advancing thirteen hundred miles and giving battle with a probability of losing a quarter of his army, he was advancing to certain destruction, and it must have been equally clear to Kutúzov that by accepting battle and risking the loss of a quarter of his army he would certainly lose Moscow. For Kutúzov this was mathematically clear, as it is that if when playing draughts I have one man less and go on exchanging, I shall certainly lose, and therefore should not exchange. When my opponent has sixteen men and I have fourteen, I am only one-eighth weaker than he, but when I have exchanged thirteen more men he will be three times as strong as I am.

Before the battle of Borodinó our strength in proportion to the French was about as five to six, but after that battle it was little more than one to two: previously we had a hundred thousand against a hundred and twenty thousand; afterward little more than fifty thousand against a hundred thousand. Yet the shrewd and experienced Kutúzov accepted the battle, while Napoleon, who was said to be a commander of genius, gave it, losing a quarter of his army and lengthening his lines of communication still more. If it is said that he expected to end the campaign by occupying Moscow as he had ended a previous campaign by occupying Vienna, there is much evidence to the contrary. Napoleon's historians themselves tell us that from Smolénsk onward he wished to stop, knew the danger of his extended position, and knew that the occupation of Moscow would not be the end of the campaign, for he had seen at Smolénsk the state in which Russian towns were left to him, and had not received a single reply to his repeated announcements of his wish to negotiate.

In giving and accepting battle at Borodinó, Kutúzov acted involuntarily and irrationally. But later on, to fit what had occurred the historians provided cunningly devised evidence of the foresight and genius the generals, who of all the blind tools of history were the most enslaved and involuntary.

The ancients have left us model heroic poems in which the heroes furnish the whole interest of the story, and we are still unable to accustom ourselves to the fact that for our epoch histories of that kind are meaningless.

On the other question, how the battle of Borodinó and the preceding battle of Shevárdino were fought, there also exists a definite and well-known, but quite false, conception. All the historians describe the affair as follows:

The Russian army, they say, *in its retreat from Smolénsk sought out for itself the best position for a general engagement and found such a position at Borodinó.*

The Russians, they say, *fortified this position in advance on the left of the highroad (from Moscow to Smolénsk) and almost at a right angle to it, from Borodinó to Utítsa, at the very place where the battle was fought.*

In front of this position, they say, *a fortified outpost was set up on the Shevárdino mound to observe the enemy. On the 24th,* we are told, *Napoleon attacked this advanced post and took it, and on the 26th, attacked the whole Russian army, which was in position on the field of Borodinó.*

So the histories say, and it is all quite wrong, as anyone who cares to look into the matter can easily convince himself.

The Russians did not seek out the best position but, on the contrary, during the retreat passed many positions better than Borodinó. They did not stop at any one of these positions because Kutúzov did not wish to occupy a position he had not himself chosen, because the popular demand for a battle had not yet expressed itself strongly enough, and because Milorádovich had not yet arrived with the militia, and for many other reasons. The fact is that other positions they had passed were stronger, and that the position at Borodinó (the one where the battle was fought), far from being strong, was no more a *position* than any other spot one might find in the Russian Empire by sticking a pin into the map at hazard.

Not only did the Russians not fortify the position on the field of Borodinó to the left of, and at a right angle to, the highroad (that is, the position on which the battle took place), but never till the 25th of August 1812 did they think that a battle might be fought there. This was shown first by the fact that there were no entrenchments there by the 25th and that those begun on the 25th and 26th were not completed, and secondly, by the position of the Shevárdino Redoubt. That redoubt was quite senseless in front of the position where the battle was accepted. Why was it more strongly fortified than any other post? And why were all efforts exhausted and six thousand men sacrificed to defend it till late at night on the 24th? A Cossack patrol would have sufficed to observe the enemy. Thirdly, as proof that the position on which the battle was fought had not been foreseen and that the Shevárdino Redoubt was not an advanced post of that position, we have the fact that up to the 25th, Barclay de Tolly and Bagratión were convinced that the Shevárdino Redoubt was the *left flank* of the position, and that Kutúzov himself in his report written in hot haste after the battle, speaks of the Shevárdino Redoubt as the *left flank* of the position. It was much later, when reports on the battle of Borodinó were written at leisure, that the incorrect and extraordinary statement was invented (probably to justify the mistakes of a commander-in-chief who had to be represented as infallible) that the Shevárdino Redoubt was an *advanced* post—whereas in reality it was simply a fortified point on the left flank—and that the battle of Borodinó was fought by us on an entrenched position previously selected, where as it was fought on a quite unexpected spot which was almost unentrenched.

The case was evidently this: a position was selected along the river Kolochá—which crosses the highroad not at a right angle but at an acute angle—so that the left flank was at Shevárdino, the right flank near the village of Nóvoe, and the center at Borodinó at the confluence of the rivers Kolochá and Vóyna.

To anyone who looks at the field of Borodinó without thinking of how the battle was actually fought, this position, protected by the river Kolochá, presents itself as obvious for an army whose object was to prevent an enemy from advancing along the Smolénsk road to Moscow.

Napoleon, riding to Valúevo on the 24th, did not see (as the history books say he did) the position of the Russians from Utítsa to Borodinó (he could not have seen that position because it did not exist), nor did he see an advanced post of the Russian army, but while pursuing the Russian rearguard he came upon the left flank of the Russian position—at the Shevárdino Redoubt—and unexpectedly for the Russians moved his army across the Kolochá. And the Russians, not having time to begin a general engagement, withdrew their left wing from the position they had intended to occupy and took up a new position which had not been foreseen and was not fortified. By crossing to the other side of the Kolochá to the left of the highroad, Napoleon shifted the whole forthcoming battle from right to left (looking from the Russian side) and transferred it to the plain between Utítsa, Semënovsk and Borodinó—a plain no more advantageous as a position than any other plain in Russia—and there the whole battle of the 26th of August took place.

Had Napoleon not ridden out on the evening of the 24th to the Kolochá, and had he not then ordered an immediate attack on the redoubt but had begun the attack next morning, no one would have doubted that the Shevárdino Redoubt was the left flank of our position, and the battle would have taken place where we expected it. In that case we should probably have defended the Shevárdino Redoubt—our left flank—still more obstinately. We should have attacked Napoleon in the center or on the right, and the engagement would have taken place on the 25th, in the position we intended and had fortified. But as the attack on our left flank took place in the evening after the retreat of our rearguard (that is, immediately after the fight at Gridnëva), and as the Russian commanders did not wish, or were not in time, to begin a general engagement then on the evening of the 24th, the first and chief action of the battle of Borodinó was already lost on the 24th, and obviously led to the loss of the one fought on the 26th.

After the loss of the Shevárdino Redoubt, we found ourselves on the morning of the 25th without a position for our left flank, and were forced to bend it back and hastily entrench it where it chanced to be.

Not only was the Russian army on the 26th defended by weak, unfinished entrenchments, but the disadvantage of that position was increased by the fact that the Russian commanders—not having fully realized what had happened, namely the loss of our position on the left flank and the shifting of the whole field of the forthcoming battle from right to left—maintained their extended position from the village of Nóvoe to Utítsa, and consequently had to move their forces from right to left during the battle. So it happened that throughout the whole battle the Russians opposed the entire French army launched against our left flank with but half as many men. (Poniatowski's action against Utítsa, and Uvárov's on the right flank against the French, were actions distinct from the main course of the battle.) So the battle of Borodinó did not take place at all as (in an effort to conceal our commanders' mistakes even at the cost of diminishing the glory due to the Russian army and people) it has been described. The battle of Borodinó was not fought on a chosen and entrenched position with forces only slightly weaker than those of the enemy, but, as a result of the loss of the Shevárdino Redoubt, the Russians fought the battle of Borodinó on an open and almost unentrenched position, with forces only half as numerous as the French; that is to say, under conditions in which it was not merely unthinkable to fight for ten hours and secure an indecisive result, but unthinkable to keep an army even from complete disintegration and flight.

Chapter XX

On the morning of the 25th Pierre was leaving Mozháysk. At the descent of the high steep hill, down which a winding road led out of the town past the cathedral on the right, where a service was being held and the bells were ringing, Pierre got out of his vehicle and proceeded on foot. Behind him a cavalry regiment was coming down the hill preceded by its singers. Coming up toward him was a train of carts carrying men who had been wounded in the engagement the day before. The peasant drivers, shouting and lashing their horses, kept crossing from side to side. The carts, in each of which three or four wounded soldiers were lying or sitting, jolted over the stones that had been thrown on the steep incline to make it something like a road. The wounded, bandaged with rags, with pale cheeks, compressed lips and knitted brows, held on to the sides of the carts as they were jolted against one another. Almost all of them stared with naïve, childlike curiosity at Pierre's white hat and green swallow-tail coat.

Pierre's coachman shouted angrily at the convoy of wounded to keep to one side of the road. The cavalry regiment, as it descended the hill with its singers, surrounded Pierre's carriage and blocked the road. Pierre stopped, being pressed against the side of the cutting in which the road ran. The sunshine from behind the hill did not penetrate into the cutting and there it was cold and damp, but above Pierre's head was the bright August sunshine and the bells sounded merrily. One of the carts with wounded stopped by the side of the road close to Pierre. The driver in his bast shoes ran panting up to it, placed a stone under one of its tireless hind wheels, and began arranging the breeching on his little horse, which had stopped.

One of the wounded, an old soldier with a bandaged arm who was following the cart on foot, caught hold of it with his sound hand and turned to look at Pierre.

"I say, fellow-countryman! Will they set us down here or take us on to Moscow?" he asked.

Pierre was so deep in thought that he did not hear the question. He was looking now at the cavalry regiment that had met the convoy of wounded, now at the cart by which he was standing, in which two wounded men were sitting and one was lying. One of those sitting up in the cart had probably been wounded in the cheek. His whole head was wrapped in rags and one cheek was swollen to the size of a baby's head. His nose and mouth were twisted to one side. This soldier was looking at the cathedral and crossing himself. Another, a young lad, a fair-haired recruit as white as though there was no blood in his thin face, looked at Pierre kindly, with a fixed smile. The third lay prone so that his face was not visible. The cavalry singers were passing close by:

Ah lost, quite lost . . . is my head so keen,
Living in a foreign land . . .

they sang their soldiers' dance-song.

As if responding to them but with a different sort of merriment, the metallic sound of the bells reverberated high above and the hot rays of the sun bathed the top of the opposite slope with yet another sort of merriment. But beneath the slope, by the cart with the wounded near the panting little nag where Pierre stood, it was damp, somber and sad.

The soldier with the swollen cheek looked angrily at the cavalry singers.

"Oh, the coxcombs!" he muttered reproachfully.

"It's not the soldiers only, but I've seen peasants today, too. . . . The peasants—even they had to go," said the soldier behind the cart, addressing Pierre with a sad smile. "No distinctions made nowadays. . . . They want the whole nation to fall on them—in a word, it's Moscow! They want to make an end of it."

In spite of the obscurity of the soldier's words Pierre understood what he wanted to say, and nodded approval.

The road was clear again; Pierre descended the hill and drove on.

He kept looking to either side of the road for familiar faces, but only saw everywhere the unfamiliar faces of various military men of different branches of the service, who all looked with astonishment at his white hat and green tail-coat.

Having gone nearly three miles he at last met an acquaintance and eagerly addressed him. This was one of the head army-doctors. He was driving toward Pierre in a covered gig, sitting beside a young surgeon, and on recognizing Pierre he told the Cossack who occupied the driver's seat to pull up.

"Count! Your excellency, how come you to be here?" asked the doctor.

"Well, you know, I wanted to see . . ."

"Yes, yes, there will be something to see. . . ."

Pierre got out and talked to the doctor, explaining his intention of taking part in a battle.

The doctor advised him to apply direct to Kutúzov.

"Why should you be God knows where out of sight, during the battle?" he said, exchanging glances with his young companion. "Anyhow his Serene Highness knows you and will receive you graciously. That's what you must do."

The doctor seemed tired and in a hurry.

"You think so? . . . Ah, I also wanted to ask you where our position is exactly?" said Pierre.

"The position?" repeated the doctor. "Well, that's not my line. Drive past Tatárinova, a lot of digging is going on there. Go up the hillock and you'll see."

"Can one see from there? . . . If you would . . ."

But the doctor interrupted him and moved toward his gig.

"I would go with you but on my honor I'm up to here"—and he pointed to his throat. "I'm galloping to the commander of the corps. How do matters stand? . . . You know, count, there'll be a battle tomorrow. Out of an army of a hundred thousand we must expect at least twenty thousand wounded, and we haven't stretchers, or bunks, or dressers, or doctors enough for six thousand. We have ten thousand carts, but we need other things as well—we must manage as best we can!"

The strange thought, that of the thousands of men, young and old, who had stared with merry surprise at his hat (perhaps the very men he had noticed), twenty thousand were inevitably doomed to wounds and death, amazed Pierre.

"They may die tomorrow; why are they thinking of anything but death?" And by some latent sequence of thought the descent of the Mozháysk hill, the carts with the wounded, the ringing bells, the slanting rays of the sun and the songs of the cavalrymen, vividly recurred to his mind.

"The cavalry ride to battle and meet the wounded and do not for a moment think of what awaits them, but pass by, winking at the wounded. Yet from among these men twenty thousand are doomed to die, and they wonder at my hat! Strange!" thought Pierre, continuing his way to Tatárinova.

In front of a landowner's house to the left of the road stood carriages, wagons and crowds of orderlies and sentinels. The commander-in-chief was putting up there, but just when Pierre arrived he was not in and hardly any of the staff were there—they had gone to the church service. Pierre drove on toward Górki.

When he had ascended the hill and reached the little village street, he saw for the first time peasant militiamen in their white shirts and with crosses on their caps, who talking and laughing loudly, animated and perspiring, were at work on a huge knoll overgrown with grass to the right of the road.

Some of them were digging, others were wheeling barrow-loads of earth along planks, while others stood about doing nothing.

Two officers were standing on the knoll, directing the men. On seeing these peasants, who were evidently still amused by the novelty of their position as soldiers, Pierre once more thought of the wounded men at Mozháysk and understood what the soldier had meant when he said: "They want the whole nation to fall on them." The sight of these bearded peasants at work on the battlefield, with their queer, clumsy boots and perspiring necks, and their shirts opening from the left toward the middle, unfastened, exposing their sunburned collar-bones, impressed Pierre more strongly with the solemnity and importance of the moment than anything he had yet seen or heard.

Chapter XXI

PIERRE STEPPED OUT OF HIS CARRIAGE AND PASSING THE TOILING MILITIAMEN ASCENDED THE knoll from which, according to the doctor, the battlefield could be seen.

It was about eleven o'clock. The sun shone somewhat to the left and behind him, and brightly lit up the enormous panorama which, rising like an amphitheater, extended before him in the clear rarefied atmosphere.

From above on the left, bisecting that amphitheater, wound the Smolénsk highroad, passing through a village with a white church some five hundred paces in front of the knoll and below it. This was Borodinó. Below the village the road crossed the river by a bridge, and winding down and up, rose higher and higher to the village of Valúevo visible about four miles away, where Napoleon was then stationed. Beyond Valúevo the road disappeared into a yellowing forest on the horizon. Far in the distance in that birch and fir forest to the right of the road, the cross and belfry of the Kolochá Monastery gleamed in the sun. Here and there over the whole of that blue expanse, to right and left of the forest and the road, smoking campfires could be seen and indefinite masses of troops—ours and the enemy's. The ground to the right—along the course of the Kolochá and Moskvá rivers—was broken and hilly. Between the hollows the villages of Bezzúbova and Zakhárino showed in the distance. On the left the ground was more level; there were fields of grain, and the smoking ruins of Semënovsk, which had been burned down, could be seen.

All that Pierre saw was so indefinite that neither the left nor the right side of the field fully satisfied his expectations. Nowhere could he see the battlefield he had expected to find, but only fields, meadows, troops, woods, the smoke of campfires, villages, mounds and streams; and try as he would he could descry no military "position" in this place which teemed with life, nor could he even distinguish our troops from the enemy's.

"I must ask someone who knows," he thought, and addressed an officer who was looking with curiosity at his huge unmilitary figure.

"May I ask you," said Pierre, "what village that is in front?"

"Burdino, isn't it?" said the officer, turning to his companion.

"Borodinó," the other corrected him.

The officer, evidently glad of an opportunity for a talk, moved up to Pierre.

"Are those our men there?" Pierre inquired.

"Yes, and there, further on, are the French," said the officer. "There they are, there . . . you can see them."

"Where? Where?" asked Pierre.

"One can see them with the naked eye. . . . Why, there!"

The officer pointed with his hand to the smoke visible on the left beyond the river, and the same stern and serious expression that Pierre had noticed on many of the faces he had met came into his face.

"Ah, those are the French! And over there? . . ." Pierre pointed to a knoll on the left, near which some troops could be seen.

"Those are ours."

"Ah, ours! And there? . . ." Pierre pointed to another knoll in the distance with a big tree on it, near a village that lay in a hollow where also some campfires were smoking, and something black was visible.

"That's *his* again," said the officer. (It was the Shevárdino Redoubt.) "It was ours yesterday, but now it is *his*."

"Then how about our position?"

"Our position?" replied the officer with a smile of satisfaction. "I can tell you quite clearly, because I constructed nearly all our entrenchments. There, you see? There's our center, at Borodinó, just there," and he pointed to the village in front of them with the white church. "That's where one crosses the Kolochá. You see down there where the rows of hay are lying in the hollow, there's the bridge. That's our center. Our right flank is over there"—he pointed sharply to the right, far away in the broken ground—"That's where the Moskvá River is, and we have thrown up three redoubts there, very strong ones. The left flank . . ." here the officer paused. "Well, you see, that's difficult to explain. . . . Yesterday our left flank was there at Shevárdino, you see, where the oak is, but now we have withdrawn our left wing—now it is over there, do you see that village and the smoke? That's Semënovsk, yes, there," he pointed to Raévski's knoll. "But the battle will hardly be there. *His* having moved his troops there is only a ruse; *he* will probably pass round to the right of the Moskvá. But wherever it may be, many a man will be missing tomorrow!" he remarked.

An elderly sergeant who had approached the officer while he was giving these explanations had waited in silence for him to finish speaking, but at this point, evidently not liking the officer's remark, interrupted him.

"Gabions must be sent for," said he sternly.

The officer appeared abashed, as though he understood that one might think of how many men would be missing tomorrow but ought not to speak to speak of it.

"Well, send number three company again," the officer replied hurriedly.

"And you, are you one of the doctors?"

"No, I've come on my own," answered Pierre, and he went down the hill again passing the militiamen.

"Oh, those damned fellows!" muttered the officer who followed him, holding his nose as he ran past the men at work.

"There they are . . . bringing her, coming . . . There they are . . . They'll be here in a minute . . ." voices were suddenly heard saying; and officers, soldiers and militiamen began running forward along the road.

A church procession was coming up the hill from Borodinó. First along the dusty road came the infantry in ranks, bareheaded and with arms reversed. From behind them came the sound of church singing.

Soldiers and militiamen ran bareheaded past Pierre toward the procession.

"They are bringing her, our Protectress! . . . The Iberian Mother of God!" someone cried.

"The Smolénsk Mother of God," another corrected him.

The militiamen, both those who had been in the village and those who had been at work on the battery, threw down their spades and ran to meet the church procession. Following the battalion that marched along the dusty road, came priests in their vestments—one little old man in a hood with attendants and singers. Behind them soldiers and officers bore a large, dark-faced icon with an embossed metal cover. This was the icon that had been brought from Smólensk and had since accompanied the army. Behind, before, and on both sides, crowds of militiamen with bared heads walked, ran, and bowed to the ground.

At the summit of the hill they stopped with the icon; the men who had been holding it up by the linen bands attached to it were relieved by others, the chanters relit their censers and service began. The hot rays of the sun beat down vertically and a fresh soft wind played with the hair of the bared heads and with the ribbons decorating the icon. The singing did not sound loud under the open sky. An immense crowd of bareheaded officers, soldiers and militiamen surrounded the icon. Behind the priest and a chanter stood the notabilities on a spot reserved for them. A bald general with a St. George's Cross on his neck stood just behind the priest's back, and without crossing himself (he was evidently a German) patiently awaited the end of the service, which he considered it necessary to hear to the end, probably to arouse the patriotism of the Russian people. Another general stood in a martial pose, crossing himself by shaking his hand in front of his chest while looking about him. Standing among the crowd of peasants, Pierre recognized several acquaintances among these notables, but did not look at them—his whole attention was absorbed in watching the serious expression on the faces of the crowd of soldiers and militiamen who were all gazing eagerly at the icon. As soon as the tired chanters, who were singing the service for the twentieth time that day, began lazily and mechanically to sing: "Save from calamity Thy servants, O Mother of God," and the priest and deacon chimed in: "For to Thee under God we all flee as to an inviolable bulwark and protection," there again kindled in all those faces the same expression of consciousness of the solemnity of the impending moment that Pierre had seen on the faces at the foot of the hill at Mozháysk, and momentarily on many and many faces he had met that morning; and heads were bowed more frequently and hair tossed back, and sighs and the sound men made as they crossed themselves were heard.

The crowd round the icon suddenly parted, and pressed against Pierre. Someone, a very important personage judging by the haste with which way was made for him, was approaching the icon.

It was Kutúzov, who had been riding round the position and on his way back to Tatárinova had stopped where the service was being held. Pierre recognized him at once by his peculiar figure, which distinguished him from everybody else.

With a long overcoat on his exceedingly stout, round-shouldered body, with uncovered white head and puffy face showing the white ball of the eye he had lost, Kutúzov walked with plunging, swaying gait into the crowd and stopped behind the priest. He crossed himself with an accustomed movement, bent till he touched the ground with his hand, and bowed his white head with a deep sigh. Behind Kutúzov was Bennigsen and the suite. Despite the presence of the commander-in-chief, who attracted the attention of all the superior officers, the militiamen and soldiers continued their prayers without looking at him.

When the service was over, Kutúzov stepped up to the icon, sank heavily to his knees, bowed to the ground, and for a long time tried vainly to rise, but could not do so on account of his weakness and weight. His white head twitched with the effort. At last he rose, kissed the icon as a child does with naïvely pouting lips, and again bowed till he touched the ground with his hand. The other generals followed his example, then the officers, and after them with excited faces, pressing on one another, crowding, panting and pushing, scrambled the soldiers and militiamen.

Chapter XXII

STAGGERING AMID THE CRUSH, PIERRE LOOKED ABOUT HIM.

"Count Peter Kirílovich! How did you get here?" said a voice.

Pierre looked round. Borís Drubetskóy, brushing his knees with his hand (he had probably soiled them when he, too, had knelt before the icon), came up to him smiling. Borís was elegantly dressed, with a slightly martial touch appropriate to a campaign. He wore a long coat, and like Kutúzov had a whip slung across his shoulder.

Meanwhile Kutúzov had reached the village and seated himself in the shade of the nearest house, on a bench which one Cossack had run to fetch and another had hastily covered with a rug. An immense and brilliant suite surrounded him.

The icon was carried further, accompanied by the throng. Pierre stopped some thirty paces from Kutúzov, talking to Borís.

He explained his wish to be present at the battle and to see the position.

"This is what you must do," said Borís. "I will do the honors of the camp to you. You will see everything best from where Count Bennigsen will be. I am in attendance on him, you know; I'll mention it to him. But if you want to ride round the position, come along with us. We are just going to the left flank. Then when we get back, do spend the night with me and we'll arrange a game of cards. Of course you know Dmítri Sergéevich? Those are his quarters," and he pointed to the third house in the village of Górki.

"But I should like to see the right flank. They say it's very strong," said Pierre. "I should like to start from the Moskvá River and ride round the whole position."

"Well, you can do that later, but the chief thing is the left flank."

"Yes, yes. But where is Prince Bolkónski's regiment? Can you point it out to me?"

"Prince Andrew's? We shall pass it and I'll take you to him."

"What about the left flank?" asked Pierre

"To tell you the truth, between ourselves, God only knows what state our left flank is in," said Borís confidentially lowering his voice. "It is not at all what Count Bennigsen intended. He meant to fortify that knoll quite differently, but . . ." Borís shrugged his shoulders, "his Serene Highness would not have it, or someone persuaded him. You see . . ." but Borís did not finish, for at that moment Kaysárov, Kutúzov's adjutant, came up to Pierre. "Ah, Kaysárov!" said Borís, addressing him with an unembarrassed smile, "I was just trying to explain our position to the count. It is amazing how his Serene Highness could so foresee the intentions of the French!"

"You mean the left flank?" asked Kaysárov.

"Yes, exactly; the left flank is now extremely strong."

Though Kutúzov had dismissed all unnecessary men from the staff, Borís had contrived to remain at headquarters after the changes. He had established himself with Count Bennigsen, who, like all on whom Borís had been in attendance, considered young Prince Drubetskóy an invaluable man.

In the higher command there were two sharply defined parties: Kutúzov's party and that of Bennigsen, the chief of staff. Borís belonged to the latter and no one else, while showing servile respect to Kutúzov, could so create an impression that the old fellow was not much good, and that Bennigsen managed everything. Now the decisive moment of battle had come when Kutúzov would be destroyed and the power pass to Bennigsen, or even if Kutúzov won the battle it would be felt that everything was done by Bennigsen. In any case many great rewards would have to be given for tomorrow's action, and new men would come to the front. So Borís was full of nervous vivacity all that day.

After Kaysárov, others whom Pierre knew came up to him, and he had not time to reply to all the questions about Moscow that were showered upon him, or to listen to all that was told him. The faces all expressed animation and apprehension, but it seemed to Pierre that the cause of the excitement shown in some of these faces lay chiefly in questions of personal success; his mind, however, was occupied by the different expression he saw on other faces—an expression that spoke not of personal matters but of the universal questions of life and death. Kutúzov noticed Pierre's figure and the group gathered round him.

"Call him to me," said Kutúzov.

An adjutant told Pierre of his Serene Highness' wish, and Pierre went toward Kutúzov's bench. But a militiaman got there before him. It was Dólokhov.

"How did that fellow get here?" asked Pierre.

"He's a creature that wriggles in anywhere!" was the answer. "He has been degraded, you know. Now he wants to bob up again. He's been proposing some scheme or other and has crawled into the enemy's piquet line at night. . . . He's a brave fellow."

Pierre took off his hat and bowed respectfully to Kutúzov.

"I concluded that if I reported to your Serene Highness you might send me away or say that you knew what I was reporting, but then I shouldn't lose anything . . ." Dólokhov was saying.

"Yes, yes."

"But if I were right, I should be rendering a service to my Fatherland for which I am ready to die."

"Yes, yes."

"And should your Serene Highness require a man who will not spare his skin, please think of me. . . . Perhaps I may prove useful to your Serene Highness."

"Yes . . . Yes . . ." Kutúzov repeated, his laughing eye narrowing more and more as he looked at Pierre.

Just then Borís, with his courtierlike adroitness, stepped up to Pierre's side near Kutúzov and in a most natural manner, without raising his voice, said to Pierre, as though continuing an interrupted conversation:

"The militia have put on clean white shirts to be ready to die. What heroism, count!"

Borís evidently said this to Pierre in order to be overheard by his Serene Highness. He knew Kutúzov's attention would be caught by those words, and so it was.

"What are you saying about the militia?" he asked Borís.

"Preparing for tomorrow, your Serene Highness—for death—they have put on clean shirts."

"Ah . . . a wonderful, a matchless people!" said Kutúzov; and he closed his eyes and swayed his head. "A matchless people!" he repeated with a sigh.

"So you want to smell gunpowder?" he said to Pierre. "Yes, it's a pleasant smell. I have the honor to be one of your wife's adorers. Is she well? My quarters are at your service."

And as often happens with old people, Kutúzov began looking about absent-mindedly as if forgetting all he wanted to say or do.

Then, evidently remembering what he wanted, he beckoned to Andrew Kaysárov, his adjutant's brother.

"Those verses . . . those verses of Márin's . . . how do they go, eh? Those he wrote about Gerákov: 'Lectures for the corps inditing' . . . Recite them, recite them!" said he, evidently preparing to laugh.

Kaysárov recited. . . . Kutúzov smilingly nodded his head to the rhythm of the verses.

When Pierre had left Kutúzov, Dólokhov came up to him and took his hand.

"I am very glad to meet you here, count," he said aloud, regardless of the presence of strangers and in a particularly resolute and solemn tone. "On the eve of a day when God alone knows who of us is fated to survive, I am glad of this opportunity to tell you that I regret the misunderstandings that occurred between us, and should wish you not to have any ill feeling for me. I beg you to forgive me."

Pierre looked at Dólokhov with a smile, not knowing what to say to him. With tears in his eyes Dólokhov embraced Pierre and kissed him.

Borís said a few words to his general, and Count Bennigsen turned to Pierre and proposed that he should ride with him along the line.

"It will interest you," said he.

"Yes, very much," replied Pierre.

Half an hour later Kutúzov left for Tatárinova, and Bennigsen and his suite, with Pierre among them, set out on their ride along the line.

Chapter XXIII

FROM GÓRKI, BENNIGSEN DESCENDED THE HIGHROAD TO THE BRIDGE WHICH, WHEN THEY HAD looked at it from the hill, the officer had pointed out as being the center of our position and where rows of fragrant new-mown hay lay by the riverside. They rode across that bridge into the village of Borodinó and thence turned to the left, passing an enormous number of troops and guns, and came to a high knoll where militiamen were digging. This was the redoubt, as yet unnamed, which afterward became known as the Raévski Redoubt, or the Knoll Battery, but Pierre paid no special attention to it. He did not know that it would become more memorable to him than any other spot on the plain of Borodinó.

They then crossed the hollow to Semënovsk, where the soldiers were dragging away the last logs from the huts and barns. Then they rode downhill and uphill, across a ryefield trodden and beaten down as if by hail, following a track freshly made by the artillery over the furrows of the plowed land, and reached some *flèches* which were still being dug.

At the *flèches* Bennigsen stopped and began looking at the Shevárdino Redoubt opposite, which had been ours the day before and where several horsemen could be descried. The officers said that either Napoleon or Murat was there, and they all gazed eagerly at this little group of horsemen. Pierre also looked at them, trying to guess which of the scarcely discernible figures was Napoleon. At last those mounted men rode away from the mound and disappeared.

Bennigsen spoke to a general who approached him, and began explaining the whole position of our troops. Pierre listened to him, straining each faculty to understand the essential points of the impending battle, but was mortified to feel that his mental capacity was inadequate for the task. He could make nothing of it. Bennigsen stopped speaking and, noticing that Pierre was listening, suddenly said to him:

"I don't think this interests you?"

"On the contrary it's very interesting!" replied Pierre not quite truthfully.

From the *flèches* they rode still farther to the left, along a road winding through a thick, low-growing birch wood. In the middle of the woods a brown hare with white feet sprang out and, scared by the tramp of the many horses, grew so confused that it leaped along the road in front of them for some time, arousing general attention and laughter, and only when several voices shouted at it did it dart to one side and disappear in the thicket. After going through the wood for about a mile and a half they came out on a glade where troops of Túchkov's corps were stationed to defend the left flank.

Here, at the extreme left flank, Bennigsen talked a great deal and with much heat, and, as it seemed to Pierre, gave orders of great military importance. In front of Túchkov's troops was some high ground not occupied by troops. Bennigsen loudly criticized this mistake, saying that it was madness to leave a height which commanded the country around unoccupied and to take troops below it. Some of the generals expressed the same opinion. One in particular declared with martial heat that they were put there to be slaughtered. Bennigsen on his own authority ordered the troops to occupy the high ground. This disposition on the left flank increased Pierre's doubt of his own capacity to understand military matters. Listening to Bennigsen and the generals criticizing the position of the troops behind the hill, he quite understood them and shared their opinion, but for that very reason he could not understand how the man who put them there behind the hill could have made so gross and palpable a blunder.

Pierre did not know that these troops were not, as Bennigsen supposed, put there to defend the position, but were in a concealed position as an ambush, that they should not be seen and might be able to strike an approaching enemy unexpectedly. Bennigsen did not know this, and moved the troops forward according to his own ideas without mentioning the matter to the commander-in-chief.

Chapter XXIV

On that bright evening of August the 25th, Prince Andrew lay leaning on his elbow in a broken-down shed in the village of Knyazkóvo at the further end of his regiment's encampment. Through a gap in the broken wall he could see, beside the wooden fence, a row of thirty-year-old birches with their lower branches lopped off, a field on which shocks of oats were standing, and some bushes near which rose the smoke of campfires—the soldiers' kitchens.

Narrow and burdensome and useless to anyone as his life now seemed to him, Prince Andrew on the eve of battle felt agitated and irritable as he had done seven years before at Austerlitz.

He had received and given the orders for next day's battle, and had nothing more to do. But his thoughts—the simplest, clearest, and therefore most terrible thoughts—would give him no peace. He knew that tomorrow's battle would be the most terrible of all he had taken part in, and for the first time in his life the possibility of death presented itself to him—not in relation to any worldly matter or with reference to its effect on others, but simply in relation to himself, to his own soul—vividly, plainly, terribly, and almost as a certainty. And from the height of this perception all that had previously tormented and preoccupied him suddenly became illumined by a cold white light without shadows, without perspective and without distinction of outline. All life appeared to him like magic-lantern pictures at which he had long been gazing by artificial light through a glass. Now he suddenly saw those badly daubed pictures in clear daylight and without a glass. "Yes, yes! There they are, those false images that agitated, enraptured and tormented me," said he to himself, passing in review the principal pictures of the magic lantern of life and regarding them now in the cold white daylight of his clear perception of death. "There they are, those rudely painted figures that once seemed splendid and mysterious. Glory, the good of society, love of a woman, the Fatherland itself—how important these pictures appeared to me, with what profound meaning they seemed to be filled! And it is all so simple, pale and crude in the cold white light of this morning which I feel is dawning for me." The three great sorrows of his life held his attention in particular: his love for a woman, his father's death, and the French invasion which had overrun half Russia. "Love! . . . that little girl who seemed to me brimming over with mystic forces! Yes, indeed I loved her. I made romantic plans of love and happiness with her! Oh, what a boy I was!" he said aloud bitterly. "Ah me! I believed in some ideal love which was to keep her faithful to me for the whole year of my absence! Like the gentle dove in the fable she was to pine apart from me. . . . But it was much simpler really. . . . It was all very simple and horrible.

"When my father built Bald Hills he thought the place was his: his land, his air, his peasants. But Napoleon came and swept him aside, unconscious of his existence, as he might brush a chip from his path, and his Bald Hills and his whole life fell to pieces. Princess Mary says it is a trial sent from above. What is the trial for, when he is not here and will never return? He is not here! For whom then is the trial intended? The Fatherland, the destruction of Moscow! And tomorrow I shall be killed, perhaps not even by a Frenchman but by one of our own men, by a soldier discharging a musket close to my ear as one of them did yesterday, and the French will come and take me by head and heels and fling me into a hole that I may not stink under their noses, and new conditions of life will arise, which will seem quite ordinary to others and about which I shall know nothing. I shall not exist. . . ."

He looked at the row of birches shining in the sunshine, with their motionless green and yellow foliage and white bark. "To die . . . to be killed tomorrow . . . That I should not exist . . . That all this should still be, but no me. . . ."

And the birches with their light and shade, the curly clouds, the smoke of the campfires, and all that was around him changed and seemed terrible and menacing. A cold shiver ran down his spine. He rose quickly, went out of the shed, and began to walk about.

After he had returned, voices were heard outside the shed. "Who's that?" he cried.

The red-nosed Captain Timókhin, formerly Dólokhov's squadron-commander, but now from lack of officers a battalion-commander, shyly entered the shed followed by an adjutant and the regimental paymaster.

Prince Andrew rose hastily, listened to the business they had come about, gave them some further instructions, and was about to dismiss them when he heard a familiar, lisping voice behind the shed.

"Devil take it!" said the voice of a man stumbling over something.

Prince Andrew looked out of the shed and saw Pierre, who had tripped over a pole on the ground and had nearly fallen, coming his way. It was unpleasant to Prince Andrew to meet people of his own set in general, and Pierre especially, for he reminded him of all the painful moments of his last visit to Moscow.

"You? What a surprise!" said he. "What brings you here? This is unexpected!"

As he said this his eyes and face expressed more than coldness—they expressed hostility, which Pierre noticed at once. He had approached the shed full of animation, but on seeing Prince Andrew's face he felt constrained and ill at ease.

"I have come . . . simply . . . you know . . . come . . . it interests me," said Pierre, who had so often that day senselessly repeated that word "interesting." "I wish to see the battle."

"Oh, yes, and what do the masonic brothers say about war? How would they stop it?" said Prince Andrew sarcastically. "Well, and how's Moscow? And my people? Have they reached Moscow at last?" he asked seriously.

"Yes, they have. Julie Drubetskáya told me so. I went to see them, but missed them. They have gone to your estate near Moscow."

Chapter XXV

THE OFFICERS WERE ABOUT TO TAKE LEAVE, BUT PRINCE ANDREW, APPARENTLY RELUCTANT TO be left alone with his friend, asked them to stay and have tea. Seats were brought in and so was the tea. The officers gazed with surprise at Pierre's huge stout figure, and listened to his talk of Moscow and the position of our army, round which he had ridden. Prince Andrew remained silent, and his expression was so forbidding that Pierre addressed his remarks chiefly to Timókhin, the good-natured battalion-commander.

"So you understand the whole position of our troops?" Prince Andrew interrupted him.

"Yes—that is, how do you mean?" said Pierre. "Not being a military man I can't say I have understood it fully, but I understand the general position."

"Well, then, you know more than anyone else, be it who it may," said Prince Andrew.

"Oh!" said Pierre, looking over his spectacles in perplexity at Prince Andrew. "Well, and what do think of Kutúzov's appointment?" he asked.

"I was very glad of his appointment, that's all I know," replied Prince Andrew.

"And tell me your opinion of Barclay de Tolly. In Moscow they are saying heaven knows what about him. . . . What do you think of him?"

"Ask them," replied Prince Andrew, indicating the officers.

Pierre looked at Timókhin with the condescendingly interrogative smile with which everybody involuntarily addressed that officer.

"We see light again, since his Serenity has been appointed, your excellency," said Timókhin timidly, and continually turning to glance at his colonel.

"Why so?" asked Pierre.

"Well, to mention only firewood and fodder, let me inform you. Why, when we were retreating from Sventsyáni we dare not touch a stick, or a wisp of hay or anything. You see, we were going away, so *he* would get it all; wasn't it so, your excellency?" and again Timókhin turned to the prince. "But we daren't. In our regiment two officers were court-martialed for that kind of thing. But when his Serenity took command everything became straight forward. Now we see light. . . ."

"Then why was it forbidden?"

Timókhin looked about in confusion, not knowing what or how to answer such a question. Pierre put the same question to Prince Andrew.

"Why, so as not to lay waste the country we were abandoning to the enemy," said Prince Andrew with venomous irony. "It is very sound: one can't permit the land to be pillaged and accustom the troops to marauding. At Smolénsk too he judged correctly that the French might outflank us, as they had larger forces. But he could not understand this," cried Prince Andrew in a shrill voice that seemed to escape him involuntarily: "he could not understand that there, for the first time, we were fighting for Russian soil, and that there was a spirit in the men such as I had never seen before, that we had held the French for two days and that that success had increased our strength tenfold. He ordered us to retreat, and all our efforts and losses went for nothing. He had no thought of betraying us, he tried to do the best he could, he thought out everything, and that is why he is unsuitable. He is unsuitable now, just because he plans out everything very thoroughly and accurately as every German has to. How can I explain? . . . Well, say your father has a German valet, and he is a splendid valet and satisfies your father's requirements better than you could, then it's all right to let him serve. But if your father is mortally sick you'll send the valet away and attend to your father with your own unpracticed, awkward hands, and will soothe him better than a skilled man who is a stranger could. So it has been with Barclay. While Russia was well, a foreigner could serve her and be a splendid Minister; but as soon as she is in danger she needs one of her own kin. But in your Club they have been making him out a traitor! They slander him as a traitor, and the only result will be that afterward, ashamed of their false accusations, they will make him out a hero or a genius instead of a traitor, and that will be still more unjust. He is an honest and very punctilious German."

"And they say he's a skillful commander," rejoined Pierre.

"I don't understand what is meant by 'a skillful commander,' " replied Prince Andrew ironically.

"A skillful commander?" replied Pierre. "Why, one who foresees all contingencies . . . and foresees the adversary's intentions."

"But that's impossible," said Prince Andrew as if it were a matter settled long ago.

Pierre looked at him in surprise.

"And yet they say that war is like a game of chess?" he remarked.

"Yes," replied Prince Andrew, "but with this little difference, that in chess you may think over each move as long as you please and are not limited for time, and with this difference too, that a knight is always stronger than a pawn, and two pawns are always stronger than one, while in war a battalion is sometimes stronger than a division and sometimes weaker than a company. The relative strength of bodies of troops can never be known to anyone. Believe me," he went on, "if things depended on arrangements made by the staff, I should be there making arrangements, but instead of that I have the honor to serve here in the regiment with these gentlemen, and I consider that on us tomorrow's battle will depend and not on those others. . . . Success never depends, and never will depend, on position, or equipment, or even on numbers, and least of all on position."

"But on what then?"

"On the feeling that is in me and in him," he pointed to Timókhin, "and in each soldier."

Prince Andrew glanced at Timókhin, who looked at his commander in alarm and bewilderment. In contrast to his former reticent taciturnity Prince Andrew now seemed excited. He could apparently not refrain from expressing the thoughts that had suddenly occurred to him.

"A battle is won by those who firmly resolve to win it! Why did we lose the battle at Austerlitz? The French losses were almost equal to ours, but very early we said to ourselves that we were losing the battle, and we did lose it. And we said so because we had nothing to fight for there, we wanted to get away from the battlefield as soon as we could. 'We've lost, so let us run,' and we ran. If we had not said that till the evening, heaven knows what might not have happened. But tomorrow we shan't say it! You talk about our position, the left flank weak and the right flank too extended," he went on. "That's all nonsense, there's nothing of the kind. But what awaits us tomorrow? A hundred million most diverse chances which will be decided on the instant by the fact that our men or theirs run or do not run, and that this man or that man is killed, but all that is being done at present is only play. The fact is that those men with whom you have ridden round the position not only do not help matters, but hinder. They are only concerned with their own petty interests."

"At such a moment?" said Pierre reproachfully.

"At such a moment!" Prince Andrew repeated. "To them it is only a moment affording opportunities to undermine a rival and obtain an extra cross or ribbon. For me tomorrow means this: A Russian army of a hundred thousand and a French army of a hundred thousand have met to fight, and the thing is that these two hundred thousand men *will* fight and the side that fights more fiercely and spares itself least will win. And if you like I will tell you that whatever happens and whatever muddles those at the top may make, we shall win tomorrow's battle. Tomorrow, happen what may, we shall win!"

"There now, your excellency! That's the truth, the real truth," said Timókhin. "Who would spare himself now? The soldiers in my battalion, believe me, wouldn't drink their vodka! 'It's not the day for that!' they say."

All were silent. The officers rose. Prince Andrew went out of the shed with them, giving final orders to the adjutant. After they had gone Pierre approached Prince Andrew and was about to start a conversation when they heard the clatter of three horses' hoofs on the road not far from the shed, and looking in that direction Prince Andrew recognized Wolzogen and Clausewitz accompanied by a Cossack. They rode close by continuing to converse, and Prince Andrew involuntarily heard these words:

"Der Krieg muss in Raum verlegt werden. Der Ansicht kann ich nicht genug Preis geben," said one of them.

"Oh, ja," said the other, *"der Zweck ist nur den Feind zu schwächen, so kann man gewiss nicht den Verlust der Privat-Personen in Achtung nehmen."*

"Oh, no," agreed the other.

"Extend widely!" said Prince Andrew with an angry snort, when they had ridden past. "In that 'extend' were my father, son and sister, at Bald Hills. That's all the same to him! That's what I was saying to you—those German gentlemen won't win the battle tomorrow but will only make all the mess they can, because they have nothing in their German heads but theories not worth an empty egg-shell, and haven't in their hearts the one thing needed tomorrow—that which Timókhin has. They have yielded up all Europe to *him*, and have now come to teach us. Fine teachers!" and again his voice grew shrill.

"So you think we shall win tomorrow's battle?" asked Pierre.

"Yes, yes," answered Prince Andrew absently. "One thing I would do if I had the power," he began again, "I would not take prisoners. Why take prisoners? It's chivalry! The French have destroyed my home and are on their way to destroy Moscow, they have outraged and are outraging me every moment. They are my enemies. In my opinion they are all criminals. And so thinks Timókhin and the whole army. They should be executed! Since they are my foes they cannot be my friends, whatever may have been said at Tilsit."

"Yes, yes," muttered Pierre, looking with shining eyes at Prince Andrew. "I quite agree with you!"

The question that had perturbed Pierre on the Mozháysk hill and all that day now seemed to him quite clear and completely solved. He now understood the whole meaning and importance of this war and of the impending battle. All he had seen that day, all the significant and stern expressions on the faces he had seen in passing, were lit up for him by a new light. He understood that latent heat (as they say in physics) of patriotism which was present in all these men he had seen, and this explained to him why they all prepared for death calmly, and as it were light-heartedly.

"Not take prisoners," Prince Andrew continued. "That by itself would quite change the whole war and make it less cruel. As it is we have played at war—that's what's vile! We play at magnanimity and all that stuff. Such magnanimity and sensibility are like the magnanimity and sensibility of a lady who faints when she sees a calf being killed: she is so kind-hearted that she can't look at blood, but enjoys eating the calf served up with sauce. They talk to us of the rules of war, of chivalry, of flags of truce, of mercy to the unfortunate and so on. It's all rubbish! I saw chivalry and flags of truce in 1805; they humbugged us and we humbugged them. They plunder other people's houses, issue false paper money, and worst of all they kill my children and my father, and then talk of rules of war and magnanimity to foes! Take no prisoners, but kill and be killed! He who has come to this as I have through the same sufferings . . ."

Prince Andrew, who had thought it was all the same to him whether or not Moscow was taken as Smolénsk had been, was suddenly checked in his speech by an unexpected cramp in his throat. He paced up and down a few times in silence, but his eyes glittered feverishly and his lips quivered as he began to speak again.

"If there was none of this magnanimity in war, we should go to war only when it was worthwhile going to certain death, as now. Then there would not be war because Paul Ivánovich had offended Michael Ivánovich. And when there was a war, like this one, it would be war! And then the determination of the troops would be quite different. Then all these Westphalians and Hessians whom Napoleon is leading would not follow him into Russia, and we should not go to fight in Austria and Prussia without knowing why. War is not courtesy but the most horrible thing in life; and we ought to understand that and not play at war. We ought to accept this terrible necessity sternly and seriously. It all lies in that: get rid of falsehood and let war be war and not a game. As it is now, war is the favorite pastime of the idle and frivolous. The military calling is the most highly honored.

"But what is war? What is needed for success in warfare? What are the habits of the military? The aim of war is murder; the methods of war are spying, treachery, and their encouragement, the ruin of a country's inhabitants, robbing them or stealing to provision the army, and fraud and falsehood termed military craft. The habits of the military class are the absence of freedom, that is, discipline, idleness, ignorance, cruelty, debauchery and drunkenness. And in spite of all this it is the highest class, respected by everyone. All the kings, except the Chinese, wear military uniforms, and he who kills most people receives the highest rewards.

"They meet, as we shall meet tomorrow, to murder one another; they kill and maim tens of thousands, and then have thanksgiving services for having killed so many people (they even exaggerate the number), and they announce a victory, supposing that the more people they have killed the greater their achievement. How does God above look at them and hear them?" exclaimed Prince Andrew in a shrill, piercing voice. "Ah, my friend, it has of late become hard for me to live. I see that I have begun to understand too much. And it doesn't do for man to taste of the tree of knowledge of good and evil. . . . Ah, well, it's not for long!" he added.

"However, you're sleepy, and it's time for me to sleep. Go back to Górki!" said Prince Andrew suddenly.

"Oh, no!" Pierre replied, looking at Prince Andrew with frightened, compassionate eyes.

"Go, go! Before a battle one must have one's sleep out," repeated Prince Andrew.

He came quickly up to Pierre and embraced and kissed him.

"Good-bye, be off!" he shouted. "Whether we meet again or not . . ." and turning away hurriedly he entered the shed.

It was already dark, and Pierre could not make out whether the expression of Prince Andrew's face was angry or tender.

For some time he stood in silence considering whether he should follow him or go away. "No, he does not want it!" Pierre concluded, "and I know that this is our last meeting!" He sighed deeply and rode back to Górki.

On re-entering the shed Prince Andrew lay down on a rug, but he could not sleep.

He closed his eyes. One picture succeeded another in his imagination. On one of them he dwelled long and joyfully. He vividly recalled an evening in Petersburg. Natásha with animated and excited face was telling him how she had gone to look for mushrooms the previous summer and had lost her way in the big forest. She incoherently described the depths of the forest, her feelings and a talk with a beekeeper she met, and constantly interrupted her story to say: "No, I can't! I'm not telling it right; no, you don't understand," though he encouraged her by saying that he did understand, and he really had understood all she wanted to say. But Natásha was not satisfied with her own words: she felt that they did not convey the passionately poetic feeling she had experienced that day and wished to convey. "He was such a delightful old man, and it was so dark in the forest . . . and he had such kind . . . No, I can't describe it," she had said, flushed and excited. Prince Andrew smiled now the same happy smile as then when he had looked into her eyes. "I understood her," he thought. "I not only understood her, but it was just that inner, spiritual force, that sincerity, that frankness of soul—that very soul of hers which seemed to be fettered by her body—it was that soul I loved in her—loved so strongly and happily . . ." and suddenly he remembered how his love had ended. "*He* did not need anything of that kind. *He* neither saw nor understood anything of the sort. He only saw in her a pretty and *fresh* young girl, with whom he did not deign to unite his fate. And I? . . . and he is still alive and gay!"

Prince Andrew jumped up as if someone had burned him, and again began pacing up and down in front of the shed.

Chapter XXVI

On August 25th, the eve of the battle of Borodinó, M. de Beausset, prefect of the French Emperor's palace, arrived at Napoleon's quarters at Valúevo with Colonel Fabvier, the former from Paris and the latter from Madrid.

Donning his court uniform, M. de Beausset ordered a box he had brought for the Emperor to be carried before him, and entered the first compartment of Napoleon's tent, where he began opening the box while conversing with Napoleon's aides-de-camp who surrounded him.

Fabvier, not entering the tent, remained at the entrance talking to some generals of his acquaintance.

The Emperor Napoleon had not yet left his bedroom and was finishing his toilet. Slightly snorting and grunting, he presented now his back and now his plump hairy chest to the brush with which his valet was rubbing him down. Another valet, with his finger over the mouth of a bottle, was sprinkling eau-de-Cologne on the Emperor's pampered body with an expression which seemed to say that he alone knew where and how much eau-de-Cologne should be sprinkled. Napoleon's short hair was wet and matted on the forehead, but his face, though puffy and yellow, expressed physical satisfaction. "Go on, harder, go on!" he muttered to the valet who was rubbing him, slightly twitching and grunting. An aide-de-camp, who had entered the bedroom to report to the Emperor the number of prisoners taken in yesterday's action, was standing by the door after delivering his message, awaiting permission to withdraw. Napoleon, frowning, looked at him from under his brows.

"No prisoners!" said he, repeating the aide-de-camp's words. "They are forcing us to exterminate them. So much the worse for the Russian army. . . . Go on . . . harder, harder!" he muttered, hunching his back and presenting his fat shoulders.

"All right. Let Monsieur de Beausset enter, and Fabvier too," he said, nodding to the aide-de-camp.

"Yes, sire," and the aide-de-camp disappeared through the door of the tent.

Two valets rapidly dressed his Majesty, and wearing the blue uniform of the Guards he went with firm quick steps to the reception room.

De Beausset's hands meanwhile were busily engaged arranging the present he had brought from the Empress, on two chairs directly in front of the entrance. But Napoleon had dressed and come out with such unexpected rapidity that he had not time to finish arranging the surprise.

Napoleon noticed at once what they were about and guessed that they were not ready. He did not wish to deprive them of the pleasure of giving him a surprise, so he pretended not to see de Beausset and called Fabvier to him, listening silently and with a stern frown to what Fabvier told him of the heroism and devotion of his troops fighting at Salamanca, at the other end of Europe, with but one thought—to be worthy of their Emperor, and but one fear—to fail to please him. The result of that battle had been deplorable. Napoleon made ironic remarks during Fabvier's account, as if he had not expected that matters could go otherwise in his absence.

"I must make up for that in Moscow," said Napoleon. "I'll see you later," he added, and summoned de Beausset, who by that time had prepared the surprise, having placed something on the chairs and covered it with a cloth.

De Beausset bowed low, with that courtly French bow which only the old retainers of the Bourbons knew how to make, and approached him, presenting an envelope.

Napoleon turned to him gaily and pulled his ear.

"You have hurried here. I am very glad. Well, what is Paris saying?" he asked, suddenly changing his former stern expression for a most cordial tone.

"Sire, all Paris regrets your absence," replied de Beausset as was proper.

But though Napoleon knew that de Beausset had to say something of this kind, and though in his lucid moments he knew it was untrue, he was pleased to hear it from him. Again he honored him by touching his ear.

"I am very sorry to have made you travel so far," said he.

"Sire, I expected nothing less than to find you at the gates of Moscow," replied de Beausset.

Napoleon smiled and lifting his head absent-mindedly, glanced to the right. An aide-de-camp approached with gliding steps and offered him a gold snuffbox, which he took.

"Yes, it has happened luckily for you," he said, raising the open snuffbox to his nose. "You are fond of travel, and in three days you will see Moscow. You surely did not expect to see that Asiatic capital. You will have a pleasant journey."

De Beausset bowed gratefully at this regard for his taste for travel (of which he had not till then been aware).

"Ha, what's this?" asked Napoleon, noticing that all the courtiers were looking at something concealed under a cloth.

With courtly adroitness de Beausset half turned, and without turning his back to the Emperor retired two steps, twitching off the cloth at the same time, and said:

"A present to your Majesty from the Empress."

It was a portrait, painted in bright colors by Gérard, of the son borne to Napoleon by the daughter of the Emperor of Austria, the boy whom for some reason everyone called "The King of Rome."

A very pretty curly-headed boy with a look of the Christ in the Sistine Madonna, was depicted playing at stick and ball. The ball represented the terrestrial globe and the stick in his other hand a scepter.

Though it was not clear what the artist meant to express by depicting the so-called King of Rome spiking the earth with a stick, the allegory apparently seemed to Napoleon, as it had done to all who had seen it in Paris, quite clear and very pleasing.

"The King of Rome!" he said, pointing to the portrait with a graceful gesture, "Admirable!"

With the natural capacity of an Italian for changing the expression of his face at will, he drew nearer to the portrait and assumed a look of pensive tenderness. He felt that what he now said and did would be historical, and it seemed to him that it would now be best for him—whose grandeur enabled his son to play stick and ball with the terrestrial globe—to show, in contrast to that grandeur, the simplest paternal tenderness. His eyes grew dim, he moved forward, glanced round at a chair (which seemed to place itself under him), and sat down on it before the portrait. At a single gesture from him everyone went out on tiptoe, leaving the great man to himself and his emotion.

Having sat still for a while he touched—himself not knowing why—the thick spot of paint representing the highest light in the portrait, rose, and recalled de Beausset and the officer on duty. He ordered the portrait to be carried outside his tent, that the Old Guard, stationed round it, might not be deprived of the pleasure of seeing the King of Rome, the son and heir of their adored monarch.

And while he was doing M. de Beausset the honor of breakfasting with him, they heard, as Napoleon had anticipated, the rapturous cries of the officers and men of the Old Guard who had run up to see the portrait.

"Vive l'Empereur! Vive le roi de Rome! Vive l'Empereur!" came those ecstatic cries.

After breakfast Napoleon in de Beausset's presence dictated his order of the day to the army.

"Short and energetic!" he remarked when he had read over the proclamation which he had dictated straight off without corrections. It ran:

> "Soldiers! This is the battle you have so longed for. Victory depends on you. It is essential for us; it will give us all we need: comfortable quarters and a speedy return to our country. Behave as you did at Austerlitz, Friedland, Vítebsk and Smolénsk. Let our remotest posterity recall your achievements this day with pride. Let it be said of each of you: 'He was in the great battle before Moscow!' "

"Before Moscow!" repeated Napoleon, and inviting M. de Beausset, who was so fond of travel, to accompany him on his ride, he went out of the tent to where the horses stood saddled.

"Your Majesty is too kind!" replied de Beausset to the invitation to accompany the Emperor; he wanted to sleep, did not know how to ride and was afraid of doing so.

But Napoleon nodded to the traveler, and de Beausset had to mount. When Napoleon came out of the tent the shouting of the Guards before his son's portrait grew still louder. Napoleon frowned.

"Take him away!" he said, pointing with a gracefully majestic gesture to the portrait. "It is too soon for him to see a field of battle."

De Beausset closed his eyes, bowed his head and sighed deeply, to indicate how profoundly he valued and comprehended the Emperor's words.

Chapter XXVII

On the 25th of August, so his historians tell us, Napoleon spent the whole day on horseback inspecting the locality, considering plans submitted to him by his marshals, and personally giving commands to his generals.

The original line of the Russian forces along the river Kolochá had been dislocated by the capture of the Shevárdino Redoubt on the 24th, and part of the line—the left flank—had been drawn back. That part of the line was not entrenched and in front of it the ground was more open and level than elsewhere. It was evident to anyone, military or not, that it was here the French should attack. It would seem that not much consideration was needed to reach this conclusion, nor any particular care or trouble on the part of the Emperor and his marshals, nor was there any need of that special and supreme quality called genius, that people are so apt to ascribe to Napoleon; yet the historians who described the event later and the men who then surrounded Napoleon, and he himself, thought otherwise.

Napoleon rode over the plain and surveyed the locality with a profound air and in silence, nodded with approval or shook his head dubiously, and without communicating to the generals around him the profound course of ideas which guided his decisions, merely gave them his final conclusions in the form of commands. Having listened to a suggestion from Davout, who was now called Prince d'Eckmhl, to turn the Russian left wing, Napoleon said it should not be done, without explaining why not. To a proposal made by General Campan (who was to attack the *flèches*) to lead his division through the woods, Napoleon agreed, though the so-called Duke of Elchingen (Ney) ventured to remark that a movement through the woods was dangerous and might disorder the division.

Having inspected the country opposite the Shevárdino Redoubt, Napoleon pondered a little in silence and then indicated the spots where two batteries should be set up by the morrow to act against the Russian entrenchments, and the places where, in line with them, the field artillery should be placed.

After giving these and other commands he returned to his tent, and the dispositions for the battle were written down from his dictation.

These dispositions, of which the French historians write with enthusiasm and other historians with profound respect, were as follows:

> At dawn the two new batteries established during the night on the plain occupied by the Prince d'Eckmhl will open fire on the two opposing batteries of the enemy.
>
> At the same time the commander of the artillery of the 1st Corps, General Pernetti, with thirty cannon of Campan's division and all the howitzers of Dessaix's and Friant's divisions, will move forward, open fire and overwhelm with shellfire the enemy's battery, against which will operate:
>
> 24 guns of the artillery of the Guards
> 30 guns of Campan's division
> and 8 guns of Friant's and Dessaix's divisions
>
> in all 62 guns.
>
> The commander of the artillery of the 3rd Corps, General Fouché, will place the howitzers of the 3rd and 8th Corps, sixteen in all, on the flanks of the battery that is to

bombard the entrenchment on the left, which will have forty guns in all directed against it.

General Sorbier must be ready at the first order to advance with all the howitzers of the Guard's artillery against either one or other of the entrenchments.

During the cannonade Prince Poniatowski is to advance through the wood on the village and turn the enemy's position.

General Campan will move through the wood to seize the first fortification.

After the advance has begun in this manner, orders will be given in accordance with the enemy's movements.

The cannonade on the left flank will begin as soon as the guns of the right wing are heard. The sharpshooters of Morand's division and of the vice-King's division will open a heavy fire on seeing the attack commence on the right wing.

The vice-King will occupy the village and cross by its three bridges, advancing to the same heights as Morand's and Gérard's divisions, which under his leadership will be directed against the redoubt and come into line with the rest of the forces.

All this must be done in good order (*le tout se fera avec ordre et méthode*) as far as possible retaining troops in reserve.

The Imperial Camp near Mozháysk,
September 6th, 1812.

These dispositions, which are very obscure and confused if one allows oneself to regard the arrangements without religious awe of his genius, related to Napoleon's orders to deal with four points—four different orders. Not one of these was, or could be, carried out.

In the disposition it is said first, *that the batteries placed on the spot chosen by Napoleon, with the guns of Pernetti and Fouché which were to come in line with them, 102 guns in all, were to open fire and shower shells on the Russian* flèches *and redoubts.* This could not be done, as from the spots selected by Napoleon the projectiles did not carry to the Russian works, and those 102 guns shot into the air until the nearest commander, contrary to Napoleon's instructions, moved them forward.

The second order was that *Poniatowski, moving to the village through the wood, should turn the Russian left flank.* This could not be done and was not done, because Poniatowski, advancing on the village through the wood, met Túchkov there barring his way, and could not and did not turn the Russian position.

The third order was: *General Campan will move through the wood to seize the first fortification.* General Campan's division did not seize the first fortification but was driven back, for on emerging from the wood it had to re-form under grapeshot, of which Napoleon was unaware.

The fourth order was: *The vice-King will occupy the village* (Borodinó) *and cross by its three bridges, advancing to the same heights as Morand's and Gérard's divisions* (for whose movements no directions are given), *which under his leadership will be directed against the redoubt and come into line with the rest of the forces.*

As far as one can make out, not so much from this unintelligible sentence as from the attempts the vice-King made to execute the orders given him, he was to advance from the left through Borodinó to the redoubt while the divisions of Morand and Gérard were to advance simultaneously from the front.

All this, like the other parts of the disposition, was not and could not be executed. After passing through Borodinó the vice-King was driven back to the Kolochá and could get no farther; while the divisions of Morand and Gérard did not take the redoubt but were driven back, and the redoubt was only taken at the end of the battle by the cavalry (a thing probably unforeseen and not heard of by Napoleon). So not one of the orders in the disposition was, or could be, executed. But in the disposition it is said that, *after the fight has commenced in this manner, orders will be given in accordance with the enemy's movements,* and so it might be supposed that all necessary arrangements would be made by Napoleon during the battle. But this was not and could not be done, for during the whole battle Napoleon was so far away that, as appeared later, he could not know the course of the battle and not one of his orders during the fight could be executed.

Chapter XXVIII

MANY HISTORIANS SAY THAT THE FRENCH DID NOT WIN THE BATTLE OF BORODINÓ BECAUSE Napoleon had a cold, and that if he had not had a cold the orders he gave before and during the battle would have been still more full of genius and Russia would have been lost and the face of the world would have been changed. To historians who believe that Russia was shaped by the will of one man—Peter the Great—and that France from a republic became an empire and French armies went to Russia at the will of one man—Napoleon—to say that Russia remained a power because Napoleon had a bad cold on the 24th of August may seem logical and convincing.

If it had depended on Napoleon's will to fight or not to fight the battle of Borodinó, and if this or that other arrangement depended on his will, then evidently a cold affecting the manifestation of his will might have saved Russia, and consequently the valet who omitted to bring Napoleon his waterproof-boots on the 24th would have been the savior of Russia. Along that line of thought such a deduction is indubitable, as indubitable as the deduction Voltaire made in jest (without knowing what he was jesting at) when he said that the Massacre of St. Bartholomew was due to Charles IX's stomach being deranged. But to men who do not admit that Russia was formed by the will of one man, Peter I, or that the French Empire was formed and the war with Russia begun by the will of one man, Napoleon, that argument seems not merely untrue and irrational, but contrary to all human reality. To the question of what causes historic events another answer presents itself, namely, that the course of human events is predetermined from on high—depends on the coincidence of the wills of all who take part in the events, and that a Napoleon's influence on the course of these events is purely external and fictitious.

Strange as at first glance it may seem to suppose that the Massacre of St. Bartholomew was not due to Charles IX's will, though he gave the order for it and thought it was done as a result of that order; and strange as it may seem to suppose that the slaughter of eighty thousand men at Borodinó was not due to Napoleon's will, though he ordered the commencement and conduct of the battle and thought it was done because he ordered it; strange as these suppositions appear, yet human dignity—which tells me that each of us is, if not more at least not less a man than the great Napoleon—demands the acceptance of that solution of the question, and historic investigation abundantly confirms it.

At the battle of Borodinó Napoleon shot at no one and killed no one. That was all done by the soldiers. Therefore it was not he who killed people.

The French soldiers went to kill and be killed at the battle of Borodinó not because of Napoleon's orders but by their own volition. The whole army—French, Italian, German, Polish and Dutch—hungry, ragged and weary of the campaign, felt at the sight of an army blocking their road to Moscow that the wine was drawn and must be drunk. Had Napoleon then forbidden them to fight the Russians, they would have killed him and have proceeded to fight the Russians because it was inevitable.

When they heard Napoleon's proclamation offering them, as compensation for mutilation and death, the words of posterity about their having been in the battle before Moscow, they cried *"Vive l'Empereur!"* just as they had cried *"Vive l'Empereur!"* at the sight of the portrait of the boy piercing the terrestrial globe with a toy stick, and just as they would have cried *"Vive l'Empereur!"* at any nonsense that might be told them. There was nothing left for them to do but cry *"Vive l'Empereur!"* and go to fight, in order to get food and rest as conquerors in Moscow. So it was not because of Napoleon's commands that they killed their fellow-men.

And it was not Napoleon who directed the course of the battle, for none of his orders were executed and during the battle he did not know what was going on before him. So the way in which these people killed one another was not decided by Napoleon's will but occurred independently of him, in accord with the will of hundreds of thousands of people who took part in the common action. It *only seemed* to Napoleon that it all took place by his will. And so the question whether he had or had not a cold has no more historic interest than the cold of the least of the transport soldiers.

Moreover, the assertion made by various writers that his cold was the cause of his dispositions not being as well planned as on former occasions, and of his orders during the battle not being as good as previously, is quite baseless, which again shows that Napoleon's cold on the 26th of August was unimportant.

The dispositions cited above are not at all worse, but are even better, than previous dispositions by which he had won victories. His pseudo-orders during the battle were also no worse than formerly, but much the same as usual. These dispositions and orders only seem worse than previous ones because the battle of Borodinó was the first Napoleon did not win. The profoundest and most excellent dispositions and orders seem very bad, and every learned militarist criticizes them with looks of importance, when they relate to a battle that has been lost, and the very worst dispositions and orders seem very good, and serious people fill whole volumes to demonstrate their merits, when they relate to a battle that has been won.

The dispositions drawn up by Weyrother for the battle of Austerlitz were a model of perfection for that kind of composition, but still they were criticized—criticized for their very perfection, for their excessive minuteness.

Napoleon at the battle of Borodinó fulfilled his office as representative of authority as well as, and even better than, at other battles. He did nothing harmful to the progress of the battle; he inclined to the most reasonable opinions, he made no confusion, did not contradict himself, did not get frightened or run away from the field of battle, but with his great tact and military experience carried out his rôle of appearing to command, calmly and with dignity.

Chapter XXIX

On returning from a second careful inspection of the lines, Napoleon remarked:

"The chessmen are set up, the game will begin tomorrow!"

Having ordered punch and summoned de Beausset, he began to talk to him about Paris and about some changes he meant to make the Empress's household, surprising the prefect by his memory of minute details relating to the Court.

He showed an interest in trifles, joked about de Beausset's love of travel, and chatted carelessly, as a famous, self-confident surgeon who knows his job does when turning up his sleeves and putting on his apron while a patient is being strapped to the operating-table. "The matter is in my hands and is clear and definite in my head. When the times comes to set to work I shall do it as no one else could, but now I can jest, and the more I jest and the calmer I am the more tranquil and confident you ought to be, and the more amazed at my genius."

Having finished his second glass of punch, Napoleon went to rest before the serious business which, he considered, awaited him next day. He was so much interested in that task that he was unable to sleep, and in spite of his cold which had grown worse from the dampness of the evening, he went into the large division of the tent at three o'clock in the morning, loudly blowing his nose. He asked whether the Russians had not withdrawn, and was told that the enemy's fires were still in the same places. He nodded approval.

The adjutant in attendance came into the tent.

"Well, Rapp, do you think we shall do good business today?" Napoleon asked him.

"Without doubt, sire," replied Rapp.

Napoleon looked at him.

"Do you remember, sire, what you did me the honor to say at Smolénsk?" continued Rapp. "The wine is drawn and must be drunk."

Napoleon frowned, and sat silent for a long time leaning his head on his hand.

"This poor army!" he suddenly remarked. "It has diminished greatly since Smolénsk. Fortune is frankly a courtesan, Rapp. I have always said so and I am beginning to experience it. But the Guards, Rapp, the Guards are intact?" he remarked interrogatively.

"Yes, sire," replied Rapp.

Napoleon took a lozenge, put it in his mouth and glanced at his watch. He was not sleepy and it was still not nearly morning. It was impossible to give further orders for the sake of killing time, for the orders had all been given and were now being executed.

"Have the biscuits and rice been served out to the regiments of the Guards?" asked Napoleon sternly.

"Yes, sire."

"The rice too?"

Rapp replied that he had given the Emperor's order about the rice, but Napoleon shook his head in dissatisfaction as if not believing that his order had been executed. An attendant came in with punch. Napoleon ordered another glass to be brought for Rapp, and silently sipped his own.

"I have neither taste nor smell," he remarked, sniffing at his glass. "This cold is tiresome. They talk about medicine—what is the good of medicine when it can't cure a cold! Corvisart gave me these lozenges but they don't help at all. What can doctors cure? One can't cure anything. Our body is a machine for living. It is organized for that, it is its nature. Let life go on in it unhindered and let it defend itself, it will do more than if you paralyze it by encumbering it with remedies. Our body is like a perfect watch that should go for a certain time; watchmaker cannot open it, he can only adjust it by fumbling, and that blindfold. . . . Yes, our body is just a machine for living, that is all."

And having entered on the path of definition, of which he was fond, Napoleon suddenly and unexpectedly gave a new one.

"Do you know, Rapp, what military art is?" asked he. "It is the art of being stronger than the enemy at a given moment. That's all."

Rapp made no reply.

"Tomorrow we shall have to deal with Kutúzov!" said Napoleon. "We shall see! Do you remember at Braunau he commanded an army for three weeks and did not once mount a horse to inspect his entrenchments. . . . We shall see!"

He looked at his watch. It was still only four o'clock. He did not feel sleepy. The punch was finished and there was still nothing to do. He rose, walked to and fro, put on a warm overcoat and a hat, and went out of the tent. The night was dark and damp, a scarcely perceptible moisture was descending from above. Nearby, the campfires were dimly burning among the French Guards, and in the distance those of the Russian line shone through the smoke. The weather was calm, and the rustle and tramp of the French troops already beginning to move to take up their positions was clearly audible.

Napoleon walked about in front of his tent, looked at the fires and listened to these sounds, and as he was passing a tall guardsman in a shaggy cap, who was standing sentinel before his tent and had drawn himself up like a black pillar at sight of the Emperor, Napoleon stopped in front of him.

"What year did you enter the service?" he asked with that affectation of military bluntness and geniality with which he always addressed the soldiers.

The man answered the question.

"Ah! One of the old ones! Has your regiment had its rice?"

"It has, your Majesty."

Napoleon nodded and walked away.

At half-past five Napoleon rode to the village of Shevárdino.

It was growing light, the sky was clearing, only a single cloud lay in the east. The abandoned campfires were burning themselves out in the faint morning light.

On the right a single deep report of a cannon resounded and died away in the prevailing silence. Some minutes passed. A second and a third report shook the air, then a fourth and a fifth boomed solemnly nearby on the right.

The first shots had not yet ceased to reverberate before others rang out and yet more were heard mingling with and overtaking one another.

Napoleon with his suite rode up to the Shevárdino Redoubt where he dismounted. The game had begun.

Chapter XXX

On returning to Górki after having seen Prince Andrew, Pierre ordered his groom to get the horses ready and to call him early in the morning, and then immediately fell asleep behind a partition in a corner Borís had given up to him.

Before he was thoroughly awake next morning everybody had already left the hut. The panes were rattling in the little windows and his groom was shaking him.

"Your excellency! Your excellency! Your excellency!" he kept repeating pertinaciously while he shook Pierre by the shoulder without looking at him, having apparently lost hope of getting him to wake up.

"What? Has it begun? Is it time?" Pierre asked, waking up.

"Hear the firing," said the groom, a discharged soldier. "All the gentlemen have gone out, and his Serene Highness himself rode past long ago."

Pierre dressed hastily and ran out to the porch. Outside all was bright, fresh, dewy and cheerful. The sun, just bursting forth from behind a cloud that had concealed it, was shining, with rays still half broken by the clouds, over the roofs of the street opposite, on the dew-besprinkled dust of the road, on the walls of the houses, on the windows, the fence, and on Pierre's horses standing before the hut. The roar of guns sounded more distinct outside. An adjutant accompanied by a Cossack passed by at a sharp trot.

"It's time, count; it's time!" cried the adjutant.

Telling the groom to follow him with the horses, Pierre went down the street to the knoll from which he had looked at the field of battle the day before. A crowd of military men was assembled there, members of the staff could be heard conversing in French, and Kutúzov's gray head in a white cap with a red band was visible, his gray nape sunk between his shoulders. He was looking through a field-glass down the highroad before him.

Mounting the steps to the knoll Pierre looked at the scene before him, spellbound by its beauty. It was the same panorama he had admired from that spot the day before, but now the whole place was full of troops and covered by smoke-clouds from the guns, and the slanting rays of the bright sun, rising slightly to the left behind Pierre, cast upon it through the clear morning air penetrating streaks of rosy, golden-tinted light and long dark shadows. The forest at the farthest extremity of the panorama seemed carved in some precious stone of a yellowish-green color, its undulating outline was silhouetted against the horizon and was pierced beyond Valúevo by the Smolénsk highroad crowded with troops. Nearer at hand glittered golden cornfields interspersed with copses. There were troops to be seen everywhere, in front and to the right and left. All this was vivid, majestic and unexpected; but what impressed Pierre most of all was the view of the battlefield itself, of Borodinó and the hollows on both sides of the Kolochá.

Above the Kolochá, in Borodinó and on both sides of it, especially to the left where the Vóyna flowing between its marshy banks falls into the Kolochá, a mist had spread which seemed to melt, to dissolve and to become translucent when the brilliant sun appeared and magically colored and outlined everything. The smoke of the guns mingled with this mist, and over the whole expanse and through that mist the rays of the morning sun were reflected, flashing back like lightning from the water, from the dew, and from the bayonets of the troops crowded together by the riverbanks and in Borodinó. A white church could be seen through the mist, and here and there the roofs of huts in Borodinó as well as dense masses of soldiers, or green ammunition-chests and ordnance. And all this moved, or seemed to move, as the smoke and mist spread out over the whole space. Just as in the mist-enveloped hollow near Borodinó, so along the entire line outside and above it and especially in the woods and fields to the left, in the valleys and on the summits of the high ground, clouds of powder-smoke seemed continually to spring up out of nothing, now singly now several at a time, some translucent others dense, which, swelling, growing, rolling and blending, extended over the whole expanse.

These puffs of smoke and (strange to say) the sound of the firing produced the chief beauty of the spectacle.

"Puff!"—suddenly a round compact cloud of smoke was seen merging from violet into gray and milky-white, and *"boom!"* came the report a second later.

"Puff! puff!"—and two clouds arose pushing one another and blending together; and *"boom, boom!"* came the sounds confirming what the eye had seen.

Pierre glanced round at the first cloud, which he had seen as a round compact ball, and in its place already were balloons of smoke floating to one side—*"puff"* (with a pause)—*"puff, puff!"* three and then four more appeared and then from each, with the same interval—*"boom—boom, boom!"* came the fine, firm, precise sounds in reply. It seemed as if those smoke-clouds sometimes ran, and sometimes stood still while woods, fields and glittering bayonets ran past them. From the left, over fields and bushes, those large balls of smoke were continually appearing followed by their solemn reports, while nearer still, in the hollows and woods, there burst from the muskets small cloudlets that had no time to become balls, but had their little echoes in just the same way. *"Trakh-ta-ta-takh!"* came the frequent crackle of musketry, but it was irregular and feeble in comparison with the reports of the cannon.

Pierre wished to be there with that smoke, those shining bayonets, that movement and those sounds. He turned to look at Kutúzov and his suite, to compare his impressions with those of others. They were all looking at the field of battle as he was, and, as it seemed to him, with the same feelings. All their faces were now shining with that latent warmth of feeling Pierre had noticed the day before, and had fully understood after his talk with Prince Andrew.

"Go, my dear fellow, go . . . and Christ be with you!" Kutúzov was saying to a general who stood beside him, not taking his eye from the battlefield.

Having received this order the general passed by Pierre on his way down the knoll.

"To the crossing!" said the general coldly and sternly in reply to one of the staff who asked where he was going.

"I'll go there too, I too!" thought Pierre, and followed the general.

The general mounted a horse a Cossack had brought him. Pierre went to his groom who was holding his horses, and asking which was the quietest, clambered onto it, seized it by the mane, and turning out his toes, pressed his heels against its sides and, feeling that his spectacles were slipping off but unable to let go of the mane and reins, he galloped after the general, causing the staff-officers to smile as they watched him from the knoll.

Chapter XXXI

HAVING DESCENDED THE HILL THE GENERAL AFTER WHOM PIERRE WAS GALLOPING TURNED sharply to the left, and Pierre, losing sight of him, galloped in among some ranks of infantry marching ahead of him. He tried to pass either in front of them or to the right or left, but there were soldiers everywhere, all with the same preoccupied expression and busy with some unseen but evidently important task. They all gazed with the same dissatisfied and inquiring expression at this stout man in a white hat, who for some unknown reason threatened to trample them under his horse's hoofs.

"Why ride into the middle of the battalion?" one of them shouted at him.

Another prodded his horse with the butt-end of a musket, and Pierre, bending over his saddle-bow and hardly able to control his shying horse, galloped ahead of the soldiers where there was a free space.

There was a bridge ahead of him, where other soldiers stood firing. Pierre rode up to them. Without being aware of it he had come to the bridge across the Kolochá between Górki and Borodinó, which the French (having occupied Borodinó) were attacking in the first phase of the battle. Pierre saw that there was a bridge in front of him and that soldiers were doing something on both sides of it and in the meadow, among the rows of new-mown hay which he had taken no notice of amid the smoke of the campfires the day before; but despite the incessant firing going on there he had no idea that this was the field of battle. He did not notice the sound of the bullets whistling from every side, or the projectiles that flew over him, did not see the enemy on the other side of the river, and for a long time did not notice the killed and wounded, though many fell near him. He looked about him with a smile which did not leave his face.

"Why's that fellow in front of the line?" shouted somebody at him again.

"To the left! . . . Keep to the right!" the men shouted to him.

Pierre went to the right, and unexpectedly encountered one of Raévski's adjutants whom he knew. The adjutant looked angrily at him, evidently also intending to shout at him, but on recognizing him he nodded.

"How have you got here?" he said, and galloped on.

Pierre feeling out of place there, having nothing to do, and afraid of getting in someone's way again, galloped after the adjutant.

"What's happening here? May I come with you?" he asked.

"One moment, one moment!" replied the adjutant, and riding up to a stout colonel who was standing in the meadow, he gave him some message and then addressed Pierre.

"Why have you come here, count?" he asked with a smile. "Still inquisitive?"

"Yes, yes," assented Pierre.

But the adjutant turned his horse about and rode on.

"Here it's tolerable," said he, "but with Bagratión on the left flank they're getting it frightfully hot."

"Really?" said Pierre. "Where is that?"

"Come along with me to our knoll. We can get a view from there and in our battery it is still bearable," said the adjutant. "Will you come?"

"Yes, I'll come with you," replied Pierre, looking round for his groom.

It was only now that he noticed wounded men staggering along or being carried on stretchers. On that very meadow he had ridden over the day before, a soldier was lying athwart the rows of scented hay, with his head thrown awkwardly back and his shako off.

"Why haven't they carried him away?" Pierre was about to ask, but seeing the stern expression of the adjutant who was also looking that way, he checked himself.

Pierre did not find his groom, and rode along the hollow with the adjutant to Raévski's Redoubt. His horse lagged behind the adjutant's and jolted him at every step.

"You don't seem to be used to riding, count?" remarked the adjutant.

"No it's not that, but her action seems so jerky," said Pierre in a puzzled tone.

"Why . . . she's wounded!" said the adjutant. "In the off foreleg above the knee. A bullet, no doubt. I congratulate you, count, on your baptism of fire!"

Having ridden in the smoke past the Sixth Corps, behind the artillery which had been moved forward and was in action, deafening them with the noise of firing, they came to a small wood. There it was cool and quiet, with a scent of autumn. Pierre and the adjutant dismounted and walked up the hill on foot.

"Is the general here?" asked the adjutant on reaching the knoll.

"He was here a minute ago but has just gone that way," someone told him, pointing to the right.

The adjutant looked at Pierre as if puzzled what to do with him now.

"Don't trouble about me," said Pierre. "I'll go up onto the knoll if I may?"

"Yes, do. You'll see everything from there and it's less dangerous, and I'll come for you."

Pierre went to the battery and the adjutant rode on. They did not meet again, and only much later did Pierre learn that he lost an arm that day.

The knoll to which Pierre ascended was that famous one afterward known to the Russians as the Knoll Battery or Raévski's Redoubt, and to the French as *la grande redoute, la fatale redoute, la redoute du centre,* around which tens of thousands fell, and which the French regarded as the key to the whole position.

This redoubt consisted of a knoll, on three sides of which trenches had been dug. Within the entrenchment stood ten guns that were being fired through openings in the earthwork.

In line with the knoll on both sides stood other guns which also fired incessantly. A little behind the guns, stood infantry. When ascending that knoll Pierre had no notion that this spot, on which small trenches had been dug and from which a few guns were firing, was the most important point of the battle.

On the contrary, just because he happened to be there he thought it one of the least significant parts of the field.

Having reached the knoll, Pierre sat down at one end of a trench surrounding the battery, and gazed at what was going on around him with an unconsciously happy smile. Occasionally he rose and walked about the battery still with that same smile, trying not to obstruct the soldiers who were loading, hauling the guns and continually running past him with bags and charges. The guns of that battery were being fired continually one after another with a deafening roar, enveloping the whole neighborhood in powder-smoke.

In contrast with the dread felt by the infantrymen placed in support, here in the battery where a small number of men busy at their work were separated from the rest by a trench, everyone experienced a common and as it were family feeling of animation.

The intrusion of Pierre's non-military figure in a white hat made an unpleasant impression at first. The soldiers looked askance at him with surprise and even alarm as they went past him. The senior artillery officer, a tall, long-legged, pockmarked man, moved over to Pierre as if to see the action of the farthest gun, and looked at him with curiosity.

A young round-faced officer, quite a boy still and evidently only just out of the Cadet College, who was zealously commanding the two guns entrusted to him, addressed Pierre sternly.

"Sir," he said, "permit me to ask you to stand aside. You must not be here."

The soldiers shook their heads disapprovingly as they looked at Pierre. But when they had convinced themselves that this man in the white hat was doing no harm, but either sat quietly on the slope of the trench with a shy smile, or, politely making way for the soldiers, paced up and down the battery under fire as calmly as if he were on a boulevard, their feeling of hostile distrust gradually began to change into a kindly and bantering sympathy, such as soldiers feel for their dogs, cocks, goats and in general for the animals that live with the regiment. The men soon accepted Pierre into their family, adopted him, gave him a nickname ("our gentleman"), and made kindly fun of him among themselves.

A shell tore up the earth two paces from Pierre and he looked around with a smile as he brushed from his clothes some earth it had thrown up.

"And how's it you're not afraid, sir, really now?" a red-faced, broad-shouldered soldier asked Pierre, with a grin that disclosed a set of sound, white teeth.

"Are you afraid, then?" said Pierre.

"What else do you expect?" answered the soldier. "She has no mercy, you know! When she comes spluttering down, out go your innards. One can't help being afraid," he said laughing.

Several of the men, with bright kindly faces, stopped beside Pierre. They seemed not to have expected him to talk like anybody else, and the discovery that he did so delighted them.

"It's the business of us soldiers. But in a gentleman it's wonderful! There's a gentleman for you!"

"To your places!" cried the young officer to the men gathered round Pierre.

The young officer was evidently exercising his duties for the first or second time, and therefore treated both his superiors and the men with great precision and formality.

The booming cannonade and the fusillade of musketry was growing more intense over the whole field, especially to the left where Bagratión's *flèches* were, but where Pierre was the smoke of the firing made it almost impossible to distinguish anything. Moreover his whole attention was engrossed by watching the family circle—separated from all else—formed by the men in the battery. His first unconscious feeling of joyful animation produced by the sights and sounds of the battlefield was now replaced by another, especially since he had seen that soldier lying alone in the hayfield. Now, seated on the slope of the trench, he observed the faces of those around him.

By ten o'clock some twenty men had already been carried away from the battery; two guns were smashed and cannon-balls fell more and more frequently on the battery, and spent bullets buzzed and whistled around. But the men in the battery seemed not to notice this, and merry voices and jokes were heard on all sides.

"A live one!" shouted a man as a whistling shell approached.

"Not this way! To the infantry!" added another with loud laughter, seeing the shell fly past and fall into the ranks of the supports.

"Are you bowing to a friend, eh?" remarked another, chaffing a peasant who ducked low as a cannon-ball flew over.

Several soldiers gathered by the wall of the trench, looking out to see what was happening in front.

"They've withdrawn the front line, it has retired," said they, pointing over the earthwork.

"Mind your own business," an old sergeant shouted at them. "If they've retired it's because there's work for them to do farther back."

And the sergeant, taking one of the men by the shoulders, gave him a shove with his knee. This was followed by a burst of laughter.

"To the fifth gun, wheel it up!" came shouts from one side.

"Now then, all together, like bargees!" rose the merry voices of those who were moving the gun.

"Oh, she nearly knocked our gentleman's hat off!" cried the red-faced humorist, showing his teeth and chaffing Pierre. "Awkward baggage!" he added reproachfully to a cannon-ball that struck a cannon-wheel and a man's leg.

"Now then, you foxes!" said another, laughing at some militiamen who, stooping low, entered the battery to carry away the wounded man.

"So this gruel isn't to your taste? Oh, you crows! You're scared!" they shouted at the militiamen who stood hesitating before the man whose leg had been torn off.

"There lads . . . oh, oh!" they mimicked the peasants, "they don't like it at all!"

Pierre noticed that after every ball that hit the redoubt, and after every loss, the liveliness increased more and more.

As the flames of the fire hidden within come more and more vividly and rapidly from an approaching thundercloud, so, as if in opposition to what was taking place, the lightning of hidden fire growing more and more intense glowed in the faces of these men.

Pierre did not look out at the battlefield and was not concerned to know what was happening there; he was entirely absorbed in watching this fire which burned ever more brightly and which he felt was flaming up in the same way in his own soul.

At ten o'clock the infantry that had been among the bushes in front of the battery and along the Kámenka streamlet retreated. From the battery they could be seen running back past it carrying their wounded on their muskets. A general with his suite came to the battery, and after speaking to the colonel gave Pierre an angry look and went away again having ordered the infantry supports behind the battery to lie down, so as to be less exposed to fire. After this from amid the ranks of infantry to the right of the battery came the sound of a drum and shouts of command, and from the battery one saw how those ranks of infantry moved forward.

Pierre looked over the wall of the trench, and was particularly struck by a pale young officer who, letting his sword hang down, was walking backward and kept glancing uneasily around.

The ranks of the infantry disappeared amid the smoke but their long-drawn shout and rapid musketry firing could still be heard. A few minutes later crowds of wounded men and stretcher-bearers came back from that direction. Projectiles began to fall still more frequently in the battery. Several men were lying about who had not been removed. Around the cannon the men moved still more briskly and busily. No one any longer took notice of Pierre. Once or twice he was shouted at for being in the way. The senior officer moved with big, rapid strides from one gun to another with a frowning face. The young officer, with his face still more flushed, commanded the men more scrupulously than ever. The soldiers handed up the charges, turned, loaded, and did their business with strained smartness. They gave little jumps as they walked, as though they were on springs.

The stormcloud had come upon them, and in every face the fire which Pierre had watched kindle, burned up brightly. Pierre standing beside the commanding officer. The young officer, his hand to his shako, ran up to his superior.

"I have the honor to report, sir, that only eight rounds are left. Are we to continue firing?" he asked.

"Grapeshot!" the senior shouted, without answering the question, looking over the wall of the trench.

Suddenly something happened: the young officer gave a gasp and bending double sat down on the ground like a bird shot on the wing. Everything became strange, confused and misty in Pierre's eyes.

One cannon-ball after another whistled by and struck the earthwork, a soldier or a gun. Pierre, who had not noticed these sounds before, now heard nothing else. On the right of the battery soldiers shouting "Hurrah!" were running not forward but backward, it seemed to Pierre.

A cannon-ball struck the very end of the earthwork by which he was standing, crumbling down the earth; a black ball flashed before his eyes and at the same instant plumped into something. Some militiamen who were entering the battery ran back.

"All with grapeshot!" shouted the officer.

The sergeant ran up to the officer and in a frightened whisper informed him (as a butler at dinner informs his master that there is no more of some wine asked for) that there were no more charges.

"The scoundrels! What are they doing?" shouted the officer, turning to Pierre.

The officer's face was red and perspiring and his eyes glittered under his frowning brow.

"Run to the reserves and bring up the ammunition-boxes!" he yelled, angrily avoiding Pierre with his eyes and speaking to his men.

"I'll go," said Pierre.

The officer, without answering him, strode across to the opposite side.

"Don't fire. . . . Wait!" he shouted.

The man who had been ordered to go for ammunition stumbled against Pierre.

"Eh, sir, this is no place for you," said he, and ran down the slope.

Pierre ran after him, avoiding the spot where the young officer was sitting.

One cannon-ball, another, and a third flew over him, falling in front, beside and behind him. Pierre ran down the slope. "Where am I going?" he suddenly asked himself when he was already near the green ammunition-wagons. He halted irresolutely, not knowing whether to return or go on. Suddenly a terrible concussion threw him backward to the ground. At the same instant he was dazzled by a great flash of flame, and immediately a deafening roar, crackling and whistling, made his ears tingle.

When he came to himself he was sitting on the ground leaning on his hands; the ammunition-wagons he had been approaching no longer existed, only charred green boards and rags littered the scorched grass, and a horse, dangling fragments of its shafts behind it, galloped past, while another horse lay, like Pierre, on the ground, uttering prolonged and piercing cries.

Chapter XXXII

BESIDE HIMSELF WITH TERROR PIERRE JUMPED UP AND RAN BACK TO THE BATTERY, AS TO THE only refuge from the horrors that surrounded him.

On entering the earthwork he noticed that there were men doing something there but that no shots were being fired from the battery. He had no time to realize who these men were. He saw the senior officer lying on the earth wall with his back turned as if he were examining something down below, and that one of the soldiers he had noticed before was struggling forward shouting "Brothers!" and trying to free himself from some men who were holding him by the arm. He also saw something else that was strange.

But he had not time to realize that the colonel had been killed, that the soldier shouting "Brothers!" was a prisoner, and that another man had been bayoneted in the back before his eyes, for hardly had he run into the redoubt before a thin, sallow-faced, perspiring man in a blue uniform rushed on him sword in hand, shouting something. Instinctively guarding against the shock—for they had been running together at full speed before they saw one another—Pierre put out his hand

and seized the man (a French officer) by the shoulder with one hand and by the throat with the other. The officer, dropping his sword, seized Pierre by his collar.

For some seconds they gazed with frightened eyes at one another's unfamiliar faces, and both were perplexed at what they had done and what they were to do next. "Am I taken prisoner or have I taken him prisoner?" each was thinking. But the French officer was evidently more inclined to think he had been taken prisoner because Pierre's strong hand, impelled by instinctive fear, squeezed his throat ever tighter and tighter. The Frenchman was about to say something, when just above their heads, terrible and low, a cannon-ball whistled, and it seemed to Pierre that the French officer's head had been torn off, so swiftly had he ducked it.

Pierre too bent his head and let his hands fall. Without further thought as to who had taken whom prisoner, the Frenchman ran back to the battery and Pierre ran down the slope stumbling over the dead and wounded who, it seemed to him, caught at his feet. But before he reached the foot of the knoll he was met by a dense crowd of Russian soldiers who, stumbling, tripping up, and shouting, ran merrily and wildly toward the battery. (This was the attack for which Ermólov claimed the credit, declaring that only his courage and good luck made such a feat possible: it was the attack in which he was said to have thrown some St. George's Crosses he had in his pocket into the battery for the first soldiers to take who got there.)

The French who had occupied the battery fled, and our troops shouting "Hurrah!" pursued them so far beyond the battery that it was difficult to call them back.

The prisoners were brought down from the battery and among them was a wounded French general, whom the officers surrounded. Crowds of wounded—some known to Pierre and some unknown—Russians and French, with faces distorted by suffering, walked, crawled, and were carried on stretchers, from the battery. Pierre again went up onto the knoll where he had spent over an hour, and of that family circle which had received him as a member he did not find a single one. There were many dead whom he did not know, but some he recognized. The young officer still sat in the same way, bent double, in a pool of blood at the edge of the earth wall. The red-faced man was still twitching, but they did not carry him away.

Pierre ran down the slope once more.

"Now they will stop it, now they will be horrified at what they have done!" he thought, aimlessly going toward a crowd of stretcher-bearers moving from the battlefield.

But behind the veil of smoke the sun was still high, and in front and especially to the left, near Semënovsk, something seemed to be seething in the smoke, and the roar of cannon and musketry did not diminish, but even increased to desperation like a man who, straining himself, shrieks with all his remaining strength.

Chapter XXXIII

THE CHIEF ACTION OF THE BATTLE OF BORODINÓ WAS FOUGHT WITHIN THE SEVEN THOUSAND feet between Borodinó and Bagratión's *flèches*. Beyond that space there was, on the one side a demonstration made by the Russians with Uvárov's cavalry at midday, and on the other side, beyond Utítsa, Poniatowski's collision with Túchkov; but these two were detached and feeble actions in comparison with what took place in the center of the battlefield. On the field between Borodinó and the *flèches*, beside the wood, the chief action of the day took place on an open space visible from both sides, and was fought in the simplest and most artless way.

The battle began on both sides with a cannonade from several hundred guns.

Then when the whole field was covered with smoke, two divisions, Campan's and Dessaix's, advanced from the French right, while Murat's troops advanced on Borodinó from their left.

From the Shevárdino Redoubt where Napoleon was standing the *flèches* were a verst away, and it was more than two versts as the crow flies to Borodinó, so that Napoleon could not see what was happening there, especially as the smoke mingling with the mist hid the whole locality. The soldiers of Dessaix's division advancing against the *flèches* could only be seen till they had entered the hollow that lay between them and the *flèches*. As soon as they had descended into that hollow, the smoke of the guns and musketry on the *flèches* grew so dense that it covered the whole approach on that side of it. Through the smoke glimpses could be caught of something black—probably men—and at times the glint of bayonets. But whether they were moving or stationary, whether they were French or Russian, could not be discovered from the Shevárdino Redoubt.

The sun had risen brightly and its slanting rays struck straight into Napoleon's face as, shading his eyes with his hand, he looked at the *flèches*. The smoke spread out before them, and at times it looked as if the smoke were moving, at times as if the troops moved. Sometimes shouts were heard through the firing, but it was impossible to tell what was being done there.

Napoleon, standing on the knoll, looked through a field-glass, and in its small circlet saw smoke and men, sometimes his own and sometimes Russians, but when he looked again with the naked eye, he could not tell where what he had seen was.

He descended the knoll and began walking up and down before it.

Occasionally he stopped, listened to the firing, and gazed intently at the battlefield.

But not only was it impossible to make out what was happening from where he was standing down below, or from the knoll above on which some of his generals had taken their stand, but even from the *flèches* themselves—in which by this time there were now Russian and now French soldiers, alternately or together, dead, wounded, alive, frightened or maddened—even at those *flèches* themselves it was impossible to make out what was taking place. There for several hours amid incessant cannon and musketry fire, now Russians were seen alone, now Frenchmen alone, now infantry and now cavalry: they appeared, fired, fell, collided not knowing what to do with one another, screamed and ran back again.

From the battlefield adjutants he had sent out, and orderlies from his marshals, kept galloping up to Napoleon with reports of the progress of the action, but all these reports were false, both because it was impossible in the heat of battle to say what was happening at any given moment, and because many of the adjutants did not go to the actual place of conflict but reported what they had heard from others; and also because while an adjutant was riding the couple of versts to Napoleon circumstances changed and the news he brought was already becoming false. Thus an adjutant galloped up from Murat with tidings that Borodinó had been occupied and the bridge over the Kolochá was in the hands of the French. The adjutant asked whether Napoleon wished the troops to cross it? Napoleon gave orders that the troops should form up on the farther side and wait. But before that order was given—almost as soon in fact as the adjutant had left Borodinó—the bridge had been retaken by the Russians and burned, in the very skirmish at which Pierre had been present at the beginning of the battle.

An adjutant galloped up from the *flèches* with a pale and frightened face and reported to Napoleon that their attack had been repulsed, Campan wounded, and Davout killed; yet at the very time the adjutant had been told that the French had been repulsed, the *flèches* had in fact been recaptured by other French troops, and Davout was alive and only slightly bruised. On the basis of these necessarily untrustworthy reports Napoleon gave his orders, which had either been executed before he gave them, or could not be and were not executed.

The marshals and generals, who were nearer to the field of battle but, like Napoleon, did not take part in the actual fighting and only occasionally went within musketry range, made their own arrangements without asking Napoleon and issued orders where and in what direction to fire and where cavalry should gallop and infantry should run. But even their orders, like Napoleon's, were seldom carried out, and then but partially. For the most part things happened contrary to their orders. Soldiers ordered to advance ran back on meeting grapeshot; soldiers ordered to remain where they were, suddenly, seeing Russians unexpectedly before them, sometimes rushed back and sometimes forward, and the cavalry dashed without orders in pursuit of the flying Russians. In this way two cavalry regiments galloped through the Semënovsk hollow and as soon as they reached the top of the incline, turned round and galloped full speed back again. The infantry moved in the same way, sometimes running to quite other places than those they were ordered to go to. All orders as to where and when to move the guns, when to send infantry to shoot or horsemen to ride down the Russian infantry—all such orders were given by the officers on the spot nearest to the units concerned, without asking either Ney, Davout, or Murat, much less Napoleon. They did not fear getting into trouble for not fulfilling orders or for acting on their own initiative, for in battle what is at stake is what is dearest to man—his own life, and it sometimes seems that safety lies in running back, sometimes in running forward; and these men who were right in the heat of the battle acted according to the mood of the moment. In reality, however, all these movements forward and backward did not improve or alter the position of the troops. All their rushing and galloping at one another did little harm, the harm of disablement and death was caused by the balls and bullets that flew over the fields on which these men were floundering about. As soon as they left the place where the balls and bullets were flying about, their superiors, located in the background, re-formed them and brought them under discipline, and under the influence of that discipline led them back to the zone of fire, where under the influence of fear of death they lost their discipline and rushed about according to the chance promptings of the throng.

Chapter XXXIV

NAPOLEON'S GENERALS—DAVOUT, NEY AND MURAT, WHO WERE NEAR THAT REGION OF FIRE AND sometimes even entered it—repeatedly led into it huge masses of well-ordered troops. But contrary to what had always happened in their former battles, instead of the news they expected of the enemy's flight, these orderly masses returned thence as disorganized and terrified mobs. The generals re-formed them, but their numbers constantly decreased. In the middle of the day Murat sent his adjutant to Napoleon to demand reinforcements.

Napoleon sat at the foot of the knoll, drinking punch, when Murat's adjutant galloped up with an assurance that the Russians would be routed if his Majesty would let him have another division.

"Reinforcements?" said Napoleon in a tone of stern surprise, looking at the adjutant—a handsome lad with long black curls arranged like Murat's own—as though he did not understand his words.

"Reinforcements!" thought Napoleon to himself. "How can they need reinforcements when they already have half the army directed against a weak, unentrenched Russian wing?"

"Tell the King of Naples," said he sternly, "that it is not noon yet, and I don't yet see my chessboard clearly. Go! . . ."

The handsome boy-adjutant with the long hair sighed deeply without removing his hand from his hat, and galloped back to where men were being slaughtered.

Napoleon rose and having summoned Caulaincourt and Berthier began talking to them about matters unconnected with the battle.

In the midst of this conversation, which was beginning to interest Napoleon, Berthier's eyes turned to look at a general with a suite, who was galloping toward the knoll on a lathering horse. It was Belliard. Having dismounted he went up to the Emperor with rapid strides, and in a loud voice began boldly demonstrating the necessity of sending reinforcements. He swore on his honor that the Russians were lost if the Emperor would give another division.

Napoleon shrugged his shoulders and continued to pace up and down without replying. Belliard began talking loudly and eagerly to the generals of the suite around him.

"You are very fiery, Belliard," said Napoleon, when he again came up to the general. "In the heat of a battle it is easy to make a mistake. Go and have another look and then come back to me."

Before Belliard was out of sight, a messenger from another part of the battlefield galloped up.

"Now then, what do you want?" asked Napoleon in the tone of a man irritated at being continually disturbed.

"Sire, the prince . . ." began the adjutant.

"Asks for reinforcements?" said Napoleon with an angry gesture.

The adjutant bent his head affirmatively and began to report, but the Emperor turned from him, took a couple of steps, stopped, came back, and called Berthier.

"We must give reserves," he said, moving his arms slightly apart. "Who do you think should be sent there?" he asked of Berthier (whom he subsequently termed "that gosling I have made an eagle").

"Send Claparède's division, sire," replied Berthier, who knew all the divisions and battalions by heart.

Napoleon nodded assent.

The adjutant galloped to Claparède's division and a few minutes later the Young Guards stationed behind the knoll moved forward. Napoleon gazed silently in that direction.

"No!" he suddenly said to Berthier. "I can't send Claparède. Send Friant's division."

Though there was no advantage in sending Friant's division instead of Claparède's, and even in obvious inconvenience and delay in stopping Claparède and sending Friant now, the order was carried out exactly. Napoleon did not notice that in regard to his army he was playing the part of a doctor who hinders by his medicines—a rôle he so justly understood and condemned.

Friant's division disappeared as the others had done, into the smoke of the battlefield. From all sides adjutants continued to arrive at a gallop and as if by agreement all said the same thing. They all asked for reinforcements and all said that the Russians were holding their positions and maintaining a hellish fire under which the French army was melting away.

Napoleon sat on a camp-stool, wrapped in thought.

M. de Beausset, the man so fond of travel, having fasted since morning, came up to the Emperor and ventured respectfully to suggest lunch to his Majesty.

"I hope I may now congratulate your Majesty on a victory?" said he.

Napoleon silently shook his head in negation. Assuming the negation to refer only to the victory and not to the lunch, M. de Beausset ventured with respectful jocularity to remark that there is no reason for not having lunch when one can get it.

"Go away . . ." exclaimed Napoleon suddenly and morosely, and turned aside.

A beatific smile of regret, repentance and ecstasy beamed on M. de Beausset's face and he glided away to the other generals.

Napoleon was experiencing a feeling of depression like that of an ever-lucky gambler who, after recklessly flinging money about and always winning, suddenly just when he has calculated all the chances of the game, finds that the more he considers his play the more surely he loses.

His troops were the same, his generals the same, the same preparations had been made, the same dispositions, and the same proclamation *courte et énergique*, he himself was still the same: he knew that and knew that he was now even more experienced and skillful than before. Even the enemy was the same as at Austerlitz and Friedland—yet the terrible stroke of his arm had supernaturally become impotent.

All the old methods that had been unfailingly crowned with success: the concentration of batteries on one point, an attack by reserves to break the enemy's line and a cavalry attack by "the men of iron," all these methods had already been employed, yet not only was there no victory, but from all sides came the same news of generals killed and wounded, of reinforcements needed, of the impossibility of driving back the Russians, and of disorganization among his own troops.

Formerly, after he had given two or three orders and uttered a few phrases, marshals and adjutants had come galloping up with congratulations and happy faces, announcing the trophies taken, the corps of prisoners, bundles of enemy eagles and standards, cannon and stores, and Murat had only begged leave to loose the cavalry to gather in the baggage-wagons. So it had been at Lodi, Marengo, Arcola, Jena, Austerlitz, Wagram and so on. But now something strange was happening to his troops.

Despite news of the capture of the *flèches,* Napoleon saw that this was not the same, not at all the same, as what had happened in his former battles. He saw that what he was feeling was felt by all the men about him experienced in the art of war. All their faces looked dejected, and they all shunned one another's eyes—only a de Beausset could fail to grasp the meaning of what was happening.

But Napoleon with his long experience of war well knew the meaning of a battle not gained by the attacking side in eight hours, after all efforts had been expended. He knew that it was a lost battle and that the least accident might now—with the fight balanced on such a strained center—destroy him and his army.

When he ran his mind over the whole of this strange Russian campaign in which not one battle had been won, and in which not a flag, or cannon, or army corps had been captured in two months, when he looked at the concealed depression on the faces around him and heard reports of the Russians still holding their ground—a terrible feeling like a nightmare took possession of him, and all the unlucky accidents that might destroy him occurred to his mind. The Russians might fall on his left wing, might break through his center, he himself might be killed by a stray cannon-ball. All this was possible. In former battles he had only considered the possibilities of success, but now innumerable unlucky chances presented themselves, and he expected them all. Yes, it was like a dream in which a man fancies that a ruffian is coming to attack him, and raises his arm to strike that ruffian a terrible blow which he knows should annihilate him, but then feels that his arm drops powerless and limp like a rag, and the horror of unavoidable destruction seizes him in his helplessness.

The news that the Russians were attacking the left flank of the French army aroused that horror in Napoleon. He sat silently on a camp-stool below the knoll, with head bowed and elbows on his knees. Berthier approached and suggested that they should ride along the line to ascertain the position of affairs.

"What? What do you say?" asked Napoleon. "Yes, tell them to bring me my horse."

He mounted and rode toward Semënovsk.

Amid the powder-smoke, slowly dispersing over the whole space through which Napoleon rode, horses and men were lying in pools of blood, singly or in heaps. Neither Napoleon nor any of his generals had ever before seen such horrors or so many slain in such a small area. The roar of guns, that had not ceased for ten hours, wearied the ear and gave a peculiar significance to the spectacle, as music does to *tableaux vivants.* Napoleon rode up the high ground at Semënovsk, and through the smoke saw ranks of men in uniforms of a color unfamiliar to him. They were Russians.

The Russians stood in serried ranks behind Semënovsk village and its knoll, and their guns boomed incessantly along their line and sent forth clouds of smoke. It was no longer a battle: it was a continuous slaughter which could be of no avail either to the French or the Russians. Napoleon stopped his horse and again fell into the reverie from which Berthier had aroused him. He could not stop what was going on before him and around him and was supposed to be directed by him and to depend on him, and from its lack of success this affair, for the first time, seemed to him unnecessary and horrible.

One of the generals rode up to Napoleon and ventured to offer to lead the Old Guard into action. Ney and Berthier, standing near Napoleon, exchanged looks and smiled contemptuously at this general's senseless offer.

Napoleon bowed his head and remained silent a long time.

"At eight hundred leagues from France, I will not have my Guard destroyed!" he said, and turning his horse rode back to Shevárdino.

Chapter XXXV

On the rug-covered bench where Pierre had seen him in the morning sat Kutúzov, his gray head hanging, his heavy body relaxed. He gave no orders, but only assented to or dissented from what others suggested.

"Yes, yes, do that," he replied to various proposals. "Yes, yes: go, dear boy, and have a look," he would say to one or another of those about him; or, "No, don't, we'd better wait!" He listened to the reports that were brought him, and gave directions when his subordinates demanded that of him; but when listening to the reports it seemed as if he were not interested in the import of the words spoken, but rather in something else—in the expression of face and tone of voice of those who were reporting. By long years of military experience he knew, and with the wisdom of age understood, that it is impossible for one man to direct hundreds of thousands of others struggling with death, and he knew that the result of a battle is decided not by the orders of a commander-in-chief, nor the place where the troops are stationed, nor by the number of cannon or of slaughtered men, but by that intangible force called the spirit of the army, and he watched this force and guided it in as far as that was in his power.

Kutúzov's general expression was one of concentrated quiet attention, and his face wore a strained look as if he found it difficult to master the fatigue of his old and feeble body.

At eleven o'clock they brought him news that the *flèches* captured by the French had been retaken, but that Prince Bagratión was wounded. Kutúzov groaned and swayed his head.

"Ride over to Prince Peter Ivánovich and find out about it exactly," he said to one of his adjutants, and then turned to the Duke of Wrtemberg who was standing behind him.

"Will Your Highness please take command of the First Army?"

Soon after the duke's departure—before he could possibly have reached Semënovsk—his adjutant came back from him and told Kutúzov that the duke asked for more troops.

Kutúzov made a grimace and sent an order to Dokhtúrov to take over the command of the First Army, and a request to the duke—whom he said he could not spare at such an important moment—to return to him. When they brought him news that Murat had been taken prisoner, and the staff-officers congratulated him, Kutúzov smiled.

"Wait a little, gentlemen," said he. "The battle is won, and there is nothing extraordinary in the capture of Murat. Still, it is better to wait before we rejoice."

But he sent an adjutant to take the news round the army.

When Scherbínin came galloping from the left flank with news that the French had captured the *flèches* and the village of Semënovsk, Kutúzov, guessing by the sounds of the battle and by Scherbínin's looks that the news was bad, rose as if to stretch his legs, and, taking Scherbínin's arm, led him aside.

"Go, my dear fellow," he said to Ermólov, "and see whether something can't be done."

Kutúzov was in Górki, near the center of the Russian position. The attack directed by Napoleon against our left flank had been several times repulsed. In the center the French had not got beyond Borodinó, and on their left flank Uvárov's cavalry had put the French to flight.

Toward three o'clock the French attacks ceased. On the faces of all who came from the field of battle, and of those who stood around him, Kutúzov noticed an expression of extreme tension. He was satisfied with the day's success—a success exceeding his expectations, but the old man's strength was failing him. Several times his head dropped low as if it were falling, and he dozed off. Dinner was brought him.

Adjutant-General Wolzogen, the man who when riding past Prince Andrew had said, "the war should be extended widely," and whom Bagratión so detested, rode up while Kutúzov was at dinner. Wolzogen had come from Barclay de Tolly to report on the progress of affairs on the left flank. The sagacious Barclay de Tolly, seeing crowds of wounded men running back and the disordered rear of the army, weighed all the circumstances, concluded that the battle was lost, and sent his favorite officer to the commander-in-chief with that news.

Kutúzov was chewing a piece of roast chicken with difficulty, and glanced at Wolzogen with eyes that brightened under their puckering lids.

Wolzogen nonchalantly stretching his legs, approached Kutúzov with a half-contemptuous smile on his lips, scarcely touching the peak of his cap.

He treated his Serene Highness with a somewhat affected nonchalance intended to show that, as a highly trained military man, he left it to Russians to make an idol of this useless old man, but that he knew whom he was dealing with. *"Der alte Herr"* (as in their own set the Germans called Kutúzov) "is making himself very comfortable," thought Wolzogen, and looking severely at the dishes in front of Kutúzov he began to report to "the old gentleman" the position of affairs on the left flank as Barclay had ordered him to and as he himself had seen and understood it.

"All the points of our position are in the enemy's hands and we cannot dislodge them for lack of troops, the men are running away and it is impossible to stop them," he reported.

Kutúzov ceased chewing and fixed an astonished gaze on Wolzogen, as if not understanding what was said to him. Wolzogen noticing "the old gentleman's" agitation, said with a smile:

"I have not considered it right to conceal from your Serene Highness what I have seen. The troops are in complete disorder . . ."

"You have seen? You have seen? . . ." Kutúzov shouted frowning, and rising quickly he went up to Wolzogen.

"How . . . how dare you! . . ." he shouted, choking and making a threatening gesture with his trembling arms: "How dare you, sir, say that to *me?* You know nothing about it. Tell General Barclay from me that his information is incorrect and that the real course of the battle is better known to me, the commander-in-chief, than to him."

Wolzogen was about to make a rejoinder, but Kutúzov interrupted him.

"The enemy has been repulsed on the left and defeated on the right flank. If you have seen amiss, sir, do not allow yourself to say what you don't know! Be so good as to ride to General Barclay and inform him of my firm intention to attack the enemy tomorrow," said Kutúzov sternly.

All were silent, and the only sound audible was the heavy breathing of the panting old general.

"They are repulsed everywhere, for which I thank God and our brave army! The enemy is beaten, and tomorrow we shall drive him from the sacred soil of Russia," said Kutúzov crossing himself, and he suddenly sobbed as his eyes filled with tears.

Wolzogen, shrugging his shoulders and curling his lips, stepped silently aside, marveling at "the old gentleman's" conceited stupidity.

"Ah, here he is, my hero!" said Kutúzov to a portly, handsome, dark-haired general who was just ascending the knoll.

This was Raévski, who had spent the whole day at the most important part of the field of Borodinó.

Raévski reported that the troops were firmly holding their ground and that the French no longer ventured to attack.

After hearing him, Kutúzov said in French:

"Then you do not think, *like some others,* that we must retreat?"

"On the contrary, your Highness, in indecisive actions it is always the most stubborn who remain victors," replied Raévski, "and in my opinion . . ."

"Kaysárov!" Kutúzov called to his adjutant. "Sit down and write out the order of the day for tomorrow. And you," he continued, addressing another, "ride along the line and announce that tomorrow we attack."

While Kutúzov was talking to Raévski and dictating the order of the day, Wolzogen returned from Barclay and said that General Barclay wished to have written confirmation of the order the field marshal had given.

Kutúzov, without looking at Wolzogen, gave directions for the order to be written out which the former commander-in-chief, to avoid personal responsibility, very judiciously wished to receive.

And by means of that mysterious indefinable bond which maintains throughout an army one and the same temper, known as "the spirit of the army," and which constitutes the sinew of war, Kutúzov's words, his order for a battle next day, immediately became known from one end of the army to the other.

It was far from being the same words or the same order that reached the farthest links of that chain. The tales passing from mouth to mouth at different ends of the army did not even resemble what Kutúzov had said, but the sense of his words spread everywhere because what he said was not the outcome of cunning calculations, but of a feeling that lay in the commander-in-chief's soul as in that of every Russian.

And on learning that tomorrow they were to attack the enemy, and hearing from the highest quarters a confirmation of what they wanted to believe, the exhausted, wavering men felt comforted and inspirited.

Chapter XXXVI

PRINCE ANDREW'S REGIMENT WAS AMONG THE RESERVES WHICH TILL AFTER ONE O'CLOCK WERE stationed inactive behind Semënovsk, under heavy artillery fire. Toward two o'clock the regiment, having already lost more than two hundred men, was moved forward into a trampled oatfield in the gap between Semënovsk and the Knoll Battery, where thousands of men perished that day and on which an intense, concentrated fire from several hundred enemy guns was directed between one and two o'clock.

Without moving from that spot or firing a single shot the regiment here lost another third of its men. From in front and especially from the right, in the unlifting smoke the guns boomed, and out of the mysterious domain of smoke that overlay the whole space in front, quick hissing cannon-balls and slow whistling shells flew unceasingly. At times, as if to allow them a respite, a quarter of an hour passed during which the cannon-balls and shells all flew overhead, but sometimes several men were torn from the regiment in a minute and the slain were continually being dragged away and the wounded carried off.

With each fresh blow less and less chance of life remained for those not yet killed. The regiment stood in columns of battalion, three hundred paces apart, but nevertheless the men were always in one and the same mood. All alike were taciturn and morose. Talk was rarely heard in the ranks, and it ceased altogether every time the thud of a successful shot and the cry of "stretchers!" was heard. Most of the time, by their officers' order, the men sat on the ground. One, having taken off his shako, carefully loosened the gathers of its lining and drew them tight again; another, rubbing some dry clay between his palms, polished his bayonet; another fingered the strap and pulled the buckle of his bandolier, while another smoothed and refolded his legbands and put his boots on again. Some built little houses of the tufts in the plowed ground, or plaited baskets from the straw in the cornfield. All seemed fully absorbed in their pursuits. When men were killed or wounded, when rows of stretchers went past, when some troops retreated, and when great masses of the enemy came into view through the smoke, no one paid any attention to these things. But when our artillery or cavalry advanced or some of our infantry were seen to move forward, words of approval were heard on all sides. But the liveliest attention was attracted by occurrences quite apart from, and unconnected with, the battle. It was as if the minds of these morally exhausted men found relief in everyday, commonplace occurrences. A battery of artillery was passing in front of the regiment. The horse of an ammunition cart put its leg over a trace. "Hey, look at the trace-horse! . . . Get her leg out! She'll fall. . . . Ah, they don't see it!" came identical shouts from the ranks all along the regiment. Another time, general attention was attracted by a small brown dog, coming heaven knows whence, which trotted in a preoccupied manner in front of the ranks with tail stiffly erect till suddenly a shell fell close by, when it yelped, tucked its tail between its legs, and darted aside. Yells and shrieks of laughter rose from the whole regiment. But such distractions lasted only a moment, and for eight hours the men had been inactive, without food, in constant fear of death, and their pale and gloomy faces grew ever paler and gloomier.

Prince Andrew, pale and gloomy like everyone in the regiment, paced up and down from the border of one patch to another, at the edge of the meadow beside an oatfield, with head bowed and arms behind his back. There was nothing for him to do and no orders to be given. Everything went on of itself. The killed were dragged from the front, the wounded carried away, and the ranks closed up. If any soldiers ran to the rear they returned immediately and hastily. At first Prince Andrew, considering it his duty to rouse the courage of the men and to set them an example, walked about among the ranks, but he soon became convinced that this was unnecessary and that there was nothing he could teach them. All the powers of his soul, as of every soldier there, were unconsciously bent on avoiding the contemplation of the horrors of their situation. He walked along the meadow, dragging his feet, rustling the grass, and gazing at the dust that covered his boots; now he took big strides trying to keep to the footprints left on the meadow by the mowers, then he counted his steps, calculating how often he must walk from one strip to another to walk a mile, then he stripped the flowers from the wormwood that grew along a boundary rut, rubbed them in his palms and smelled their pungent, sweetly bitter scent. Nothing remained of the previous day's thoughts. He thought of nothing. He listened with weary ears to the ever-recurring sounds, distinguishing the whistle of flying projectiles from the booming of the reports, glanced at the tiresomely familiar faces of the men of the first battalion, and waited. "Here it comes . . . this one is coming our way again!" he thought, listening to an approaching whistle in the hidden region of smoke. "One, another! Again! It has hit. . . ." He stopped and looked at the ranks. "No, it has gone over. But this one has hit!" And again he started trying to reach the boundary strip in sixteen paces. A whizz and a thud! Five paces from him, a cannon-ball tore up the dry earth and disappeared. A chill ran down his back. Again he glanced at the ranks. Probably many had been hit—a large crowd had gathered near the second battalion.

"Adjutant!" he shouted. "Order them not to crowd together."

The adjutant, having obeyed this instruction, approached Prince Andrew. From the other side a battalion commander rode up.

"Look out!" came a frightened cry from a soldier and, like a bird whirring in rapid flight and alighting on the ground, a shell dropped with little noise within two steps of Prince Andrew and close to the battalion commander's horse. The horse first, regardless of whether it was right or wrong to show fear, snorted, reared almost throwing the major, and galloped aside. The horse's terror infected the men.

"Lie down!" cried the adjutant, throwing himself flat on the ground.

Prince Andrew hesitated. The smoking shell spun like a top between him and the prostrate adjutant, near a wormwood plant between the field and the meadow.

"Can this be death?" thought Prince Andrew, looking with a quite new, envious glance at the grass, the wormwood, and the streamlet of smoke that curled up from the rotating black ball. "I cannot, I do not wish to die. I love life—I love this grass, this earth, this air. . . ." He thought this, and at the same time remembered that people were looking at him.

"It's shameful, sir!" he said to the adjutant. "What . . ."

He did not finish speaking. At one and the same moment came the sound of an explosion, a whistle of splinters as from a breaking window frame, a suffocating smell of powder, and Prince Andrew started to one side, raising his arm, and fell on his chest. Several officers ran up to him. From the right side of his abdomen, blood was welling out making a large stain on the grass.

The militiamen with stretchers who were called up, stood behind the officers. Prince Andrew lay on his chest with his face in the grass, breathing heavily and noisily.

"What are you waiting for? Come along!"

The peasants went up and took him by his shoulders and legs, but he moaned piteously and, exchanging looks, they set him down again.

"Pick him up, lift him, it's all the same!" cried someone.

They again took him by the shoulders and laid him on the stretcher.

"Ah God! My God! What is it? The stomach? That means death! My God!"—voices among the officers were heard saying.

"It flew a hair's breadth past my ear," said the adjutant.

The peasants, adjusting the stretcher to their shoulders, started hurriedly along the path they had trodden down, to the dressing-station.

"Keep in step! Ah . . . those peasants!" shouted an officer, seizing by their shoulders and checking the peasants, who were walking unevenly and jolting the stretcher.

"Get into step, Fëdor . . . I say, Fëdor!" said the foremost peasant.

"Now that's right!" said the one behind joyfully, when he had got into step.

"Your excellency! Eh, prince!" said the trembling voice of Timókhin, who had run up and was looking down on the stretcher.

Prince Andrew opened his eyes and looked up at the speaker from the stretcher into which his head had sunk deep and again his eyelids drooped.

The militiamen carried Prince Andrew to dressing-station by the wood, where wagons were stationed. The dressing-station consisted of three tents with flaps turned back, pitched at the edge of a birch wood. In the wood, wagons and horses were standing. The horses were eating oats from their movable troughs and sparrows flew down and pecked the grains that fell. Some crows, scenting blood, flew among the birch trees cawing impatiently. Around the tents, over more than five acres, bloodstained men in various garbs stood, sat or lay. Around the wounded stood crowds of soldier stretcher-bearers with dismal and attentive faces, whom the officers keeping order tried in vain to drive from the spot. Disregarding the officers' orders, the soldiers stood leaning against their stretchers and gazing intently, as if trying to comprehend the difficult problem of what was taking place before them. From the tents came now loud angry cries and now plaintive groans. Occasionally dressers ran out to fetch water, or to point out those who were to be brought in next. The wounded men awaiting their turn outside the tents groaned, sighed, wept, screamed, swore, or asked for vodka. Some were delirious. Prince Andrew's bearers, stepping over the wounded who had not yet been bandaged, took him, as a regimental commander, close up to one of the tents and there stopped, awaiting instructions. Prince Andrew opened his eyes and for a long time could not make out what was going on around him. He remembered the meadow, the wormwood, the field, the whirling black ball, and his sudden rush of passionate love of life. Two steps from him, leaning against a branch and talking loudly and attracting general attention, stood a tall, handsome, black-haired non-commissioned officer with a bandaged head. He had been wounded in the head and leg by bullets. Around him, eagerly listening to his talk, a crowd of wounded and stretcher-bearers was gathered.

"We kicked *him* out from there so that he chucked everything, we grabbed the King himself!" cried he, looking around him with eyes that glittered with fever. "If only reserves had come up just then, lads, there wouldn't have been nothing left of him! I tell you surely. . . ."

Like all the others near the speaker, Prince Andrew looked at him with shining eyes and experienced a sense of comfort. "But isn't it all the same now?" thought he. "And what will be there, and what has there been here? Why was I so reluctant to part with life? There was something in this life I did not and do not understand."

Chapter XXXVII

One of the doctors came out of the tent in a bloodstained apron, holding a cigar between the thumb and little finger of one of his small bloodstained hands, so as not to smear it. He raised his head and looked about him, but above the level of the wounded men. He evidently wanted a little respite. After turning his head from right to left for some time, he sighed and looked down.

"All right, immediately," he replied to a dresser who pointed Prince Andrew out to him, and he told them to carry him into the tent.

Murmurs arose among the wounded who were waiting.

"It seems that even in the next world only the gentry are to have a chance!" remarked one.

Prince Andrew was carried in and laid on a table that had only just been cleared and which a dresser was washing down. Prince Andrew could not make out distinctly what was in that tent. The pitiful groans from all sides and the torturing pain in his thigh, stomach and back distracted him. All he saw about him merged into a general impression of naked bleeding human bodies that seemed to fill the whole of the low tent, as a few weeks previously, on that hot August day, such bodies had filled the dirty pond beside the Smolénsk road. Yes, it was the same flesh, the same *chair à canon*, the sight of which had even then filled him with horror, as by a presentiment.

There were three operating tables in the tent. Two were occupied, and on the third they placed Prince Andrew. For a little while he was left alone and involuntarily witnessed what was taking place on the other two tables. On the nearest one sat a Tartar, probably a Cossack, judging by the uniform thrown down beside him. Four soldiers were holding him, and a spectacled doctor was cutting into his muscular brown back.

"Ooh, ooh, ooh!" grunted the Tartar, and suddenly lifting up his swarthy snub-nosed face with its high cheekbones, and baring his white teeth, he began to wriggle and twitch his body and utter piercing, ringing and prolonged yells. On the other table, round which many people were crowding, a tall, well-fed man lay on his back with his head thrown back. His curly hair, its color and the shape of his head seemed strangely familiar to Prince Andrew. Several dressers were pressing on his chest to hold him down. One large, white, plump leg twitched rapidly all the time with a feverish tremor. The man was sobbing and choking convulsively. Two doctors—one of whom was pale and trembling—were silently doing something to this man's other, gory leg. When he had finished with the Tartar, whom they covered with an overcoat, the spectacled doctor came up to Prince Andrew, wiping his hands.

He glanced at Prince Andrew's face and quickly turned away.

"Undress him! What are you waiting for?" he cried angrily to the dressers.

His very first, remotest recollections of childhood came back to Prince Andrew's mind when the dresser with sleeves rolled up began hastily to undo the buttons of his clothes and undressed him. The doctor bent down over the wound, felt it, and sighed deeply. Then he made a sign to someone, and the torturing pain in his abdomen caused Prince Andrew to lose consciousness. When he came to himself the splintered portions of his thigh-bone had been extracted, the torn flesh cut away, and the wound bandaged. Water was being sprinkled on his face. As soon as Prince Andrew opened his eyes, the doctor bent over, kissed him silently on the lips, and hurried away.

After the sufferings he had been enduring, Prince Andrew enjoyed a blissful feeling such as he had not experienced for a long time. All the best and happiest moments of his life—especially his earliest childhood, when he used to be undressed and put to bed, and when leaning over him his nurse sang him to sleep and he, burying his head in the pillow, felt happy in the mere consciousness of life—returned to his memory, not merely as something past but as something present.

The doctors were busily engaged with the wounded man the shape of whose head seemed familiar to Prince Andrew: they were lifting him up and trying to quiet him.

"Show it to me. . . . Oh, ooh . . . oh! Oh, ooh!" his frightened moans could be heard, subdued by suffering and broken by sobs.

Hearing those moans Prince Andrew wanted to weep. Whether because he was dying without glory, or because he was sorry to part with life, or because of those memories of a childhood that could not return, or because he was suffering and others were suffering and that man near him was groaning so piteously—he felt like weeping childlike, kindly and almost happy tears.

The wounded man was shown his amputated leg stained with clotted blood and with the boot still on.

"Oh! Oh, ooh!" he sobbed, like a woman.

The doctor who had been standing beside him, preventing Prince Andrew from seeing his face, moved away.

"My God! What is this? Why is he here?" said Prince Andrew to himself.

In the miserable, sobbing, enfeebled man whose leg had just been amputated, he recognized Anatole Kurágin. Men were supporting him in their arms and offering him a glass of water, but his trembling, swollen lips could not grasp its rim. Anatole was sobbing painfully. "Yes, it is he! Yes, that man is somehow closely and painfully connected with me," thought Prince Andrew, not yet clearly grasping what he saw before him. "What is the connection of that man with my childhood and life?" he asked himself without finding an answer. And suddenly a new unexpected memory from that realm of pure and loving childhood presented itself to him. He remembered Natásha as he had seen her for the first time at the ball in 1810, with her slender neck and arms and with a frightened happy face ready for rapture, and love and tenderness for her, stronger and more vivid than ever, awoke in his soul. He now remembered the connection that existed between himself and this man who was dimly gazing at him through tears that filled his swollen eyes. He remembered everything, and ecstatic pity and love for that man overflowed his happy heart.

Prince Andrew could no longer restrain himself, and wept tender loving tears for his fellow-men, for himself, and for his own and their errors.

"Compassion, love of our brothers, for those who love us and for those who hate us, love of our enemies; yes, that love which God preached on earth and which Princess Mary taught me and I did not understand—that is what made me sorry to part with life, that is what remained for me had I lived. But now it is too late. I know it!"

Chapter XXXVIII

THE TERRIBLE SPECTACLE OF THE BATTLEFIELD COVERED WITH DEAD AND WOUNDED, TOGETHER with the heaviness of his head and the news that some twenty generals he knew personally had been killed or wounded, and the consciousness of the impotence of his once mighty arm, produced an unexpected impression on Napoleon who usually liked to look at the killed and wounded, thereby, he considered, testing his strength of mind. This day the horrible appearance of the battlefield overcame that strength of mind which he thought constituted his merit and his greatness. He rode hurriedly from the battlefield and returned to the Shevárdino knoll, where he sat on his camp-stool, his sallow face swollen and heavy, his eyes dim, his nose red, and his voice hoarse, involuntarily listening, with downcast eyes, to the sounds of firing. With painful dejection he awaited the end of this action, in which he regarded himself as a participant and which he was unable to arrest. A personal, human feeling for a brief moment got the better of the artificial phantasm of life he had served so long. He felt in his own person the sufferings and death he had witnessed on the battlefield. The heaviness of his head and chest reminded him of the possibility of suffering and death for himself. At that moment he did not desire Moscow, or victory, or glory (what need had he for any more glory?). The one thing he wished for was rest, tranquillity and freedom. But when he had been on the Semënovsk heights the artillery commander had proposed to him to bring several batteries of artillery up to those heights to strengthen the fire on the Russian troops crowded in front of Knyazkóvo. Napoleon had assented and had given orders that news should be brought to him of the effect those batteries produced.

An adjutant came now to inform him that the fire of two hundred guns had been concentrated on the Russians, as he had ordered, but that they still held their ground.

"Our fire is mowing them down by rows, but still they hold on," said the adjutant.

"They want more! . . ." said Napoleon in a hoarse voice.

"Sire?" asked the adjutant who had not heard the remark.

"They want more!" croaked Napoleon frowning. "Let them have it!"

Even before he gave that order the thing he did not desire, and for which he gave the order only because he thought it was expected of him, was being done. And he fell back into that artificial realm of imaginary greatness, and again—as a horse walking a treadmill thinks it is doing something for itself—he submissively fulfilled the cruel, sad, gloomy and inhuman rôle predestined for him.

And not for that day and hour alone were the mind and conscience darkened of this man on whom the responsibility for what was happening lay more than on all the others who took part in it. Never to the end of his life could he understand goodness, beauty, or truth, or the significance of his actions which were too contrary to goodness and truth, too remote from everything human, for him ever to be able to grasp their meaning. He could not disavow his actions, belauded as they were by half the world, and so he had to repudiate truth, goodness and all humanity.

Not only on that day, as he rode over the battlefield strewn with men killed and maimed (by his will as he believed), did he reckon as he looked at them how many Russians there were for each Frenchman and, deceiving himself, find reason for rejoicing in the calculation that there were five Russians for every Frenchman. Not on that day alone did he write in a letter to Paris that "the battlefield was superb," because fifty thousand corpses lay there, but even on the island of St. Helena in the peaceful solitude where he said he intended to devote his leisure to an account of the great deeds he had done, he wrote:

"The Russian war should have been the most popular war of modern times: it was a war of good sense, for real interests, for the tranquillity and security of all; it was purely pacific and conservative.

"It was a war for a great cause, the end of uncertainties and the beginning of security. A new horizon and new labors were opening out, full of well-being and prosperity for all. The European system was already founded; all that remained was to organize it.

"Satisfied on these great points and with tranquility everywhere, I too should have had my *Congress* and my *Holy Alliance*. Those ideas were stolen from me. In that reunion of great Sovereigns we should have discussed our interests like one family, and have rendered account to the peoples as clerk to master.

"Europe would in this way soon have been, in fact, but one people, and anyone who traveled anywhere would have found himself always in the common fatherland. I should have demanded the freedom of all navigable rivers for everybody, that the seas should be common to all, and that the great standing armies should be reduced henceforth to mere guards for the Sovereigns.

"On returning to France, to the bosom of the great, strong, magnificent, peaceful and glorious fatherland, I should have proclaimed her frontiers immutable; all future wars purely *defensive*, all aggrandizement *anti-national*. I should have associated my son in the Empire; my *dictatorship* would have been finished, and his constitutional reign would have begun.

"Paris would have been the capital of the world, and the French the envy of the nations!

"My leisure then, and my old age, would have been devoted, in company with the Empress and during the royal apprenticeship of my son, to leisurely visiting, with our own horses and like a true country couple, every corner of the Empire, receiving complaints, redressing wrongs, and scattering public buildings and benefactions on all sides and everywhere."

Napoleon, predestined by Providence for the gloomy rôle of executioner of the peoples, assured himself that the aim of his actions had been the peoples' welfare and that he could control the fate of millions and by the employment of power confer benefactions.

"Of four hundred thousand who crossed the Vistula," he wrote further of the Russian war, "half were Austrians, Prussians, Saxons, Poles, Bavarians, Wrtembergers, Mecklenburgers, Spaniards, Italians and Neapolitans. The Imperial army, strictly speaking, was one third composed of Dutch, Belgians, men from the borders of the Rhine, Piedmontese, Swiss, Genevese, Tuscans, Romans, inhabitants of the Thirty-Second Military Division, of Bremen, of Hamburg, and so on: it included scarcely a hundred and forty thousand who spoke French. The Russian expedition actually cost France less than fifty thousand men; the Russian army in its retreat from Vílna to Moscow lost in the various battles four times more men than the French army; the burning of Moscow cost the lives of a hundred thousand Russians who died of cold and want in the woods; finally, in its march from Moscow to the Oder the Russian army also suffered from the severity of the season; so that by the the time it reached Vílna it numbered only fifty thousand, and at Kálisch less than eighteen thousand."

He imagined that the war with Russia came about by his will, and the horrors that occurred did not stagger his soul. He boldly took the whole responsibility for what happened, and his darkened mind found justification in the belief that among the hundreds of thousands who perished there were fewer Frenchmen than Hessians and Bavarians.

Chapter XXXIX

SEVERAL TENS OF THOUSANDS OF THE SLAIN LAY IN DIVERSE POSTURES AND VARIOUS UNIFORMS on the fields and meadows belonging to the Davydov family and to the Crown serfs—those fields and meadows where for hundreds of years the peasants of Borodinó, Górki, Shevárdino and Semënovsk had reaped their harvests and pastured their cattle. At the dressing-stations the grass and earth were soaked with blood for a space of some three acres around. Crowds of men of various arms, wounded and unwounded, with frightened faces, dragged themselves back to Mozháysk from the one army, and back to Valúevo from the other. Other crowds, exhausted and hungry, went forward led by their officers. Others held their ground and continued to fire.

Over the whole field, previously so gaily beautiful with the glitter of bayonets and cloudlets of smoke in the morning sun, there now spread a mist of damp and smoke and a strange acid smell of saltpeter and blood. Clouds gathered and drops of rain began to fall on the dead and wounded, on the frightened, exhausted and hesitating men, as if to say: "Enough, men! Enough! Cease . . . bethink yourselves! What are you doing?"

To the men of both sides alike, worn out by want of food and rest, it began equally to appear doubtful whether they should continue to slaughter one another; all the faces expressed hesitation, and the question arose in every soul: "For what, for whom, must I kill and be killed? . . . You may go and kill whom you please, but I don't want to do so anymore!" By evening this thought had ripened in every soul. At any moment these men might have been seized with horror at what they were doing and might have thrown up everything and run away anywhere.

But though toward the end of the battle the men felt all the horror of what they were doing, though they would have been glad to leave off, some incomprehensible, mysterious power continued to control them, and they still brought up the charges, loaded, aimed, and applied the match, though only one artilleryman survived out of every three, and though they stumbled and panted with fatigue, perspiring and stained with blood and powder. The cannon-balls flew just as swiftly and cruelly from both sides, crushing human bodies, and that terrible work which was not done by the will of a man but at the will of Him who governs men and worlds, continued.

Anyone looking at the disorganized rear of the Russian army would have said that, if only the French made one more slight effort, it would disappear; and anyone looking at the rear of the French army would have said that the Russians need only make one more slight effort and the French would be destroyed. But neither the French nor the Russians made that effort, and the flame of battle burned slowly out.

The Russians did not make that effort because they were not attacking the French. At the beginning of the battle they stood blocking the way to Moscow and they still did so at the end of the battle as at the beginning. But even had the aim of the Russians been to drive the French from their positions, they could not have made this last effort, for all the Russian troops had been broken up, there was no part of the Russian army that had not suffered in the battle, and though still holding their positions they had lost one-half of their army.

The French, with the memory of all their former victories during fifteen years, with the assurance of Napoleon's invincibility, with the consciousness that they had captured part of the battlefield and had lost only a quarter of their men and still had their Guards intact, twenty thousand strong, might easily have made that effort. The French had attacked the Russian army in order to drive it from its position ought to have made that effort, for as long as the Russians continued to block the road to Moscow as before, the aim of the French had not been attained and all their efforts and losses were in vain. But the French did not make that effort. Some historians say that Napoleon need only have used his Old Guards, who were intact, and the battle would have been won. To speak of what would have happened had Napoleon sent his Guards is like talking of what would happen if autumn became spring. It could not be. Napoleon did not give his Guards, not because he did not want to, but because it could not be done. All the generals, officers and soldiers of the French army knew it could not be done, because the flagging spirit of the troops would not permit it.

It was not Napoleon alone who had experienced that nightmare feeling of the mighty arm being stricken powerless, but all the generals and soldiers of his army whether they had taken part in the battle or not, after all their experience of previous battles—when after one-tenth of such efforts the enemy had fled—experienced a similar feeling of terror before an enemy who after losing half his men, stood as threateningly at the end as at the beginning of the battle. The moral force of the attacking French army was exhausted. Not that sort of victory which is defined by the capture of pieces of material fastened to sticks, called standards, and of the ground on which the troops had stood and were standing, but a moral victory that convinces the enemy of the moral superiority of his opponent and of his own impotence, was gained by the Russians at Borodinó. The French invaders, like an infuriated animal that has in its onslaught received a mortal wound, felt that they were perishing, but could not stop, any more than the Russian army, weaker by one-half, could help swerving. By impetus gained, the French army was still able to roll forward to Moscow, but there, without further effort on the part of the Russians, it had to perish, bleeding from the mortal wound it had received at Borodinó. The direct consequence of the battle of Borodinó was Napoleon's senseless flight from Moscow, his retreat along the old Smolénsk road, the destruction of the invading army of five hundred thousand men, and the downfall of Napoleonic France, on which at Borodinó for the first time the hand of an opponent of stronger spirit had been laid.

Part Eleven

Chapter I

Absolute continuity of motion is not comprehensible to the human mind. Laws of motion of any kind become comprehensible to man only when he examines arbitrarily selected elements of that motion; but at the same time, a large proportion of human error comes from the arbitrary division of continuous motion into discontinuous elements. There is a well-known, so-called sophism of the ancients consisting in this, that Achilles could never catch up with a tortoise he was following, in spite of the fact that he traveled ten times as fast as the tortoise. By the time Achilles has covered the distance that separated him from the tortoise, the tortoise has covered one-tenth of that distance ahead of him: when Achilles has covered that tenth, the tortoise has covered another one-hundredth, and so on forever. This problem seemed to the ancients insoluble. The absurd answer (that Achilles could never overtake the tortoise) resulted from this: that motion was arbitrarily divided into discontinuous elements, whereas the motion both of Achilles and of the tortoise was continuous.

By adopting smaller and smaller elements of motion we only approach a solution of the problem, but never reach it. Only when we have admitted the conception of the infinitely small, and the resulting geometrical progression with a common ratio of one-tenth, and have found the sum of this progression to infinity, do we reach a solution of the problem.

A modern branch of mathematics having achieved the art of dealing with the infinitely small, can now yield solutions in other more complex problems of motion which used to appear insoluble.

This modern branch of mathematics, unknown to the ancients, when dealing with problems of motion admits the conception of the infinitely small, and so conforms to the chief condition of motion (absolute continuity) and thereby corrects the inevitable error which the human mind cannot avoid when it deals with separate elements of motion instead of examining continuous motion.

In seeking the laws of historical movement just the same thing happens. The movement of humanity, arising as it does from innumerable arbitrary human wills, is continuous.

To understand the laws of this continuous movement is the aim of history. But to arrive at these laws, resulting from the sum of all those human wills, man's mind postulates arbitrary and disconnected units. The first method of history is to take an arbitrarily selected series of continuous events and examine it apart from others, though there is and can be no *beginning* to any event, for one event always flows uninterruptedly from another.

The second method is to consider the actions of some one man—a king or a commander—as equivalent to the sum of many individual wills; whereas the sum of individual wills is never expressed by the activity of a single historic personage.

Historical science in its endeavor to draw nearer to truth continually takes smaller and smaller units for examination. But however small the units it takes, we feel that to take any unit disconnected from others, or to assume a *beginning* of any phenomenon, or to say that the will of many men is expressed by the actions of any one historic personage, is in itself false.

It needs no critical exertion to reduce utterly to dust any deductions drawn from history. It is merely necessary to select some larger or smaller unit as the subject of observation—as criticism has every right to do, seeing that whatever unit history observes must always be arbitrarily selected.

Only by taking infinitesimally small units for observation (the differential of history, that is, the individual tendencies of men) and attaining to the art of integrating them (that is, finding the sum of these infinitesimals) can we hope to arrive at the laws of history.

The first fifteen years of the nineteenth century in Europe present an extraordinary movement of millions of people. Men leave their customary pursuits, hasten from one side of Europe to the other, plunder and slaughter one another, triumph and are plunged in despair, and for some years the whole course of life is altered and presents an intensive movement which first increases and then slackens. What was the cause of this movement, by what laws was it governed? asks the mind of man.

The historians, replying to this question, lay before us the sayings and doings of a few dozen men in a building in the city of Paris, calling these sayings and doings "the Revolution"; then they give a detailed biography of Napoleon, and of certain people favorable or hostile to him; tell of the influence some of these people had on others, and say: That is why this movement took place and those are its laws.

But the mind of man not only refuses to believe this explanation, but plainly says that this method of explanation is fallacious, because in it a weaker phenomenon is taken as the cause of a stronger. The sum of human wills produced the Revolution and Napoleon, and only the sum of those wills first tolerated and then destroyed them.

"But every time there have been conquests there have been conquerors; every time there has been a revolution in any state there have been great men," says history. And indeed human reason replies: every time conquerors appear there have been wars, but this does not prove that the conquerors caused the wars and that it is possible to find the laws of a war in the personal activity of a single man. Whenever I look at my watch and its hands point to ten, I hear the bells of the neighboring church; but because the bells begin to ring when the hands of the clock reach ten, I have no right to assume that the movement of the bells is caused by the position of the hands of the watch.

Whenever I see the movement of a locomotive I hear the whistle and see the valves opening and wheels turning; but I have no right to conclude that the whistling and the turning of wheels are the cause of the movement of the engine.

The peasants say that a cold wind blows in late spring because the oaks are budding, and really every spring cold winds do blow when the oak is budding. But though I do not know what causes the cold winds to blow when the oak buds unfold, I cannot agree with the peasants that the unfolding of the oak-buds is the cause of the cold wind, for the force of the wind is beyond the influence of the buds. I see only a coincidence of occurrences such as happens with all the phenomena of life, and I see that however much and however carefully I observe the hands of the watch, and the valves and wheels of the engine, and the oak, I shall not discover the cause of the bells ringing, the engine moving, or of the winds of spring. To do that I must entirely change my point of view and study the laws of the movement of steam, of the bells, and of the wind. History must do the same. And attempts in this direction have already been made.

To study the laws of history we must completely change the subject of our observation, must leave aside kings, ministers and generals, and study the common, infinitesimally small elements by which the masses are moved. No one can say in how far it is possible for man to advance in this way toward an understanding of the laws of history; but it is evident that only along that path does the possibility of discovering the laws of history lie, and that as yet not a millionth part as much mental effort has been applied in this direction by historians as has been devoted to describing the actions of various kings, commanders and ministers and propounding the historians' own reflections concerning these actions.

Chapter II

THE FORCES OF A DOZEN EUROPEAN NATIONS BURST INTO RUSSIA. THE RUSSIAN ARMY AND people avoided a collision till Smolénsk was reached, and again from Smolénsk to Borodinó. The French army pushed on to Moscow, its goal, its impetus ever increasing as it neared its aim, just as the velocity of a falling body increases as it approaches the earth. Behind it were a thousand versts of hunger-stricken, hostile country; ahead were a few dozen versts separating it from its goal. Every soldier in Napoleon's army felt this and the invasion moved on by its own momentum.

The more the Russian army retreated the more fiercely a spirit of hatred of the enemy flared up, and while it retreated the army increased and consolidated. At Borodinó a collision took place. Neither army was broken up, but the Russian army retreated immediately after the collision as inevitably as a ball recoils after colliding with another having a greater momentum, and with equal inevitability the ball of invasion that had advanced with such momentum rolled on for some distance, though the collision had deprived it of all its force.

The Russians retreated eighty miles—to beyond Moscow—and the French reached Moscow and there came to a standstill. For five weeks after that there was not a single battle. The French did not move. As a bleeding, mortally wounded animal licks its wounds, they remained inert in Moscow for five weeks, and then suddenly, with no fresh reason, fled back: they made a dash for the Kalúga road, and (after a victory—for at Málo-Yaroslávets the field of conflict again remained theirs) without undertaking a single serious battle, they fled still more rapidly back to Smolénsk, beyond Smolénsk, beyond the Berëzina, beyond Vílna, and farther still.

On the evening of the 26th of August, Kutúzov and the whole Russian army were convinced that the battle of Borodinó was a victory. Kutúzov reported so to the Emperor. He gave orders to prepare for a fresh conflict to finish the enemy, and did this not to deceive anyone, but because he knew that the enemy was beaten, as everyone who had taken part in the battle knew it.

But all that evening and next day reports came in one after another of unheard-of losses, of the loss of half the army, and a fresh battle proved physically impossible.

It was impossible to give battle before information had been collected, the wounded gathered in, the supplies of ammunition replenished, the slain reckoned up, new officers appointed to replace those who had been killed, and before the men had had food and sleep. And meanwhile, the very next morning after the battle, the French army advanced of itself upon the Russians, carried forward by the force of its own momentum now seemingly increased in inverse proportion to the square of the distance from its aim. Kutúzov's wish was to attack next day, and the whole army desired to do so. But to make an attack the wish to do so is not sufficient, there must also be a possibility of doing it, and that possibility did not exist. It was impossible not to retreat a day's march, and then in the same way it was impossible not to retreat another and a third day's march, and at last, on the 1st of September when the army drew near Moscow—despite the strength of the feeling that had arisen in all ranks—the force of circumstances compelled it to retire beyond Moscow. And the troops retired one more, last, day's march, and abandoned Moscow to the enemy.

For people accustomed to think that plans of campaign and battles are made by generals—as any one of us sitting over a map in his study may imagine how he would have arranged things in this or that battle—the questions present themselves: Why did Kutúzov during the retreat not do this or that? Why did he not take up a position before reaching Filí? Why did he not retire at once by the Kalúga road, abandoning Moscow? and so on. People accustomed to think in that way forget, or do not know, the inevitable conditions which always limit the activities of any commander-in-chief. The activity of a commander-in-chief does not at all resemble the activity we imagine to ourselves when we sit at ease in our studies examining some campaign on the map, with a certain number of troops on this and that side in a certain known locality, and begin our plans from some given moment. A commander-in-chief is never dealing with the *beginning* of any event—the position from which we always contemplate it. The commander-in-chief is always in the midst of a series of shifting events and so he never can at any moment consider the whole import of an event that is occurring. Moment by moment the event is imperceptibly shaping itself, and at every moment of this continuous, uninterrupted shaping of events the commander-in-chief is in the midst of a most complex play of intrigues, worries, contingencies, authorities, projects, counsels, threats and deceptions, and is continually obliged to reply to innumerable questions addressed to him, which constantly conflict with one another.

Learned military authorities quite seriously tell us that Kutúzov should have moved his army to the Kalúga road long before reaching Filí, and that somebody actually submitted such a proposal to him. But a commander-in-chief, especially at a difficult moment, has always before him not one proposal but dozens simultaneously. And all these proposals, based on strategics and tactics, contradict each other.

A commander-in-chief's business, it would seem, is simply to choose one of these projects. But even that he cannot do. Events and time do not wait. For instance, on the 28th it is suggested to him to cross to the Kalúga road, but just then an adjutant gallops up from Milorádovich asking whether he is to engage the French or retire. An order must be given him at once, that instant. And the order to retreat carries us past the turn to the Kalúga road. And after the adjutant comes the commissary-general asking where the stores are to be taken, and the chief of the hospitals asks where the wounded are to go, and a courier from Petersburg brings a letter from the sovereign which does not admit of the possibility of abandoning Moscow, and the commander-in-chief's rival, the man who is undermining him (and there are always not merely one but several such), presents a new project diametrically opposed to that of turning to the Kalúga road, and the commander-in-chief himself needs sleep and refreshment to maintain his energy, and a respectable general who has been overlooked in the distribution of rewards comes to complain, and the inhabitants of the district pray to be defended, and an officer sent to inspect the locality comes in and gives a report quite contrary to what was said by the officer previously sent; and a spy, a prisoner, and a general who has been on reconnaissance, all describe the position of the enemy's army differently. People accustomed to misunderstand or to forget these inevitable conditions of a commander-in-chief's actions describe to us, for instance, the position of the army at Filí and assume that the commander-in-chief could, on the 1st of September, quite freely decide whether to abandon Moscow or defend it; whereas, with the Russian army less than four miles from Moscow, no such question existed. When had that question been settled? At Províssa and at Smolénsk and most palpably of all on the 24th of August at Shevárdino and on the 26th at Borodinó, and each day and hour and minute of the retreat from Borodinó to Filí.

Chapter III

When Ermólov, having been sent by Kutúzov to inspect the position, told the field marshal that it was impossible to fight there before Moscow and that they must retreat, Kutúzov looked at him in silence.

"Give me your hand," said he and, turning it over so as to feel the pulse, added: "You are not well, my dear fellow. Think what you are saying!"

Kutúzov could not yet admit the possibility of retreating beyond Moscow without a battle.

On the Poklónny Hill, four miles from the Dorgomílov gate of Moscow, Kutúzov got out of his carriage and sat down on a bench by the roadside. A great crowd of generals gathered round him, and Count Rostopchín, who had come out from Moscow, joined them. This brilliant company separated into several groups who all discussed the advantages and disadvantages of the position, the state of the army, the plans suggested, the situation of Moscow, and military questions generally. Though they had not been summoned for the purpose, and though it was not so called, they all felt that this was really a council of war. The conversations all dealt with public questions. If anyone gave or asked for personal news, it was done in a whisper and they immediately reverted to general matters. No jokes, or laughter, or smiles even, were seen among all these men. They evidently all made an effort to hold themselves at the height the situation demanded. And all these groups, while talking among themselves, tried to keep near the commander-in-chief (whose bench formed the center of the gathering) and to speak so that he might overhear them. The commander-in-chief listened to what was being said and sometimes asked them to repeat their remarks, but did not himself take part in the conversations or express any opinion. After hearing what was being said by one or other of these groups he generally turned away with an air of disappointment, as though they were not speaking of anything he wished to hear. Some discussed the position that had been chosen, criticizing not the position itself so much as the mental capacity of those who had chosen it. Others argued that a mistake had been made earlier and that a battle should have been fought two days before. Others again spoke of the battle of Salamanca, which was described by Crosart, a newly arrived Frenchman in a Spanish uniform. (This Frenchman and one of the German princes serving with the Russian army were discussing the siege of Saragossa and considering the possibility of defending Moscow in a similar manner.) Count Rostopchín was telling a fourth group that he was prepared to die with the city train-bands under the walls of the capital, but that he still could not help regretting having been left in ignorance of what was happening, and that had he known it sooner things would have been different.... A fifth group, displaying the profundity of their strategic perceptions, discussed the direction the troops would now have to take. A sixth group was talking absolute nonsense. Kutúzov's expression grew more and more preoccupied and gloomy. From all this talk he saw only one thing: that to defend Moscow was a *physical impossibility* in the full meaning of those words, that is to say, so utterly impossible that if any senseless commander were to give orders to fight, confusion would result but the battle would still not take place. It would not take place because the commanders not merely all recognized the position to be impossible, but in their conversations were only discussing what would happen after its inevitable abandonment. How could the commanders lead their troops to a field of battle they considered impossible to hold? The lower-grade officers and even the soldiers (who too reason) also considered the position impossible and therefore could not go to fight, fully convinced as they were of defeat. If Bennigsen insisted on the position being defended and others still discussed it, the question was no longer important in itself but only as a pretext for disputes and intrigue. This Kutúzov knew well.

Bennigsen, who had chosen the position, warmly displayed his Russian patriotism (Kutúzov could not listen to this without wincing) by insisting that Moscow must be defended. His aim was as clear as daylight to Kutúzov: if the defense failed, to throw the blame on Kutúzov who had brought the army as far as the Sparrow Hills without giving battle; if it succeeded, to claim the success as his own; or if battle were not given, to clear himself of the crime of abandoning Moscow. But this intrigue did not now occupy the old man's mind. One terrible question absorbed him and to that question he heard no reply from anyone. The question for him now was: "Have I really allowed Napoleon to reach Moscow, and when did I do so? When was it decided? Can it have been yesterday when I ordered Plátov to retreat, or was it the evening before, when I had a nap and told Bennigsen to issue orders? Or was it earlier still? . . . When, when was this terrible affair decided? Moscow must be abandoned. The army must retreat and the order to do so must be given." To give that terrible order seemed to him equivalent to resigning the command of the army. And not only did he love power to which he was accustomed (the honors awarded to Prince Prozoróvski, under whom he had served in Turkey, galled him), but he was convinced that he was destined to save Russia and that that was why, against the Emperor's wish and by the will of the people, he had been chosen commander-in-chief. He was convinced that he alone could maintain command of the army in these difficult circumstances, and that in all the world he alone could encounter the invincible Napoleon without fear, and he was horrified at the thought of the order he had to issue. But something had to be decided, and these conversations around him which were assuming too free a character must be stopped.

He called the most important generals to him.

"My head, be it good or bad, must depend on itself," said he, rising from the bench, and he rode to Filí where his carriages were waiting.

Chapter IV

THE COUNCIL OF WAR BEGAN TO ASSEMBLE AT TWO IN THE AFTERNOON IN THE BETTER AND roomier part of Andrew Savostyánov's hut. The men, women and children of the large peasant family crowded into the back room across the passage. Only Malásha, Andrew's six-year-old granddaughter whom his Serene Highness had petted and to whom he had given a lump of sugar while drinking his tea, remained on the top of the brick oven in the larger room. Malásha looked down from the oven with shy delight at the faces, uniforms and decorations of the generals, who one after another came into the room and sat down on the broad benches in the corner under the icons. "Grandad" himself, as Malásha in her own mind called Kutúzov, sat apart in a dark corner behind the oven. He sat, sunk deep in a folding arm-chair, and continually cleared his throat and pulled at the collar of his coat which, though it was unbuttoned, still seemed to pinch his neck. Those who entered went up one by one to the field marshal; he pressed the hands of some and nodded to others. His adjutant Kaysárov was about to draw back the curtain of the window facing Kutúzov, but the latter moved his hand angrily and Kaysárov understood that his Serene Highness did not wish his face to be seen.

Round the peasant's deal table on which lay maps, plans, pencils and papers, so many people gathered that the orderlies brought in another bench and put it beside the table. Ermólov, Kaysárov and Toll, who had just arrived, sat down on this bench. In the foremost place, immediately under the icons, sat Barclay de Tolly, his high forehead merging into his bald crown. He had a St. George's Cross round his neck and looked pale and ill. He had been feverish for two days and was now shivering and in pain. Beside him sat Uvárov, who with rapid gesticulations was giving him some information, speaking in low tones as they all did. Chubby little Dokhtúrov was listening attentively with eyebrows raised and arms folded on his stomach. On the other side sat Count Ostermann-Tolstóy, seemingly absorbed in his own thoughts. His broad head with its bold features and glittering eyes was resting on his hand. Raévski, twitching forward the black hair on his temples as was his habit, glanced now at Kutúzov and now at the door with a look of impatience. Konovnítsyn's firm, handsome and kindly face was lit up by a tender, sly smile. His glance met Malásha's, and the expression of his eyes caused the little girl to smile.

They were all waiting for Bennigsen, who on the pretext of inspecting the position was finishing his savory dinner. They waited for him from four till six o'clock and did not begin their deliberations all that time but talked in low tones of other matters.

Only when Bennigsen had entered the hut did Kutúzov leave his corner and draw toward the table, but not near enough for the candles that had been placed there to light up his face.

Bennigsen opened the council with the question: "Are we to abandon Russia's ancient and sacred capital without a struggle, or are we to defend it?" A prolonged and general silence followed. There was a frown on every face and only Kutúzov's angry grunts and occasional cough broke the silence. All eyes were gazing at him. Malásha too looked at "Grandad." She was nearest to him and saw how his face puckered; he seemed about to cry, but this did not last long.

"Russia's ancient and sacred capital!" he suddenly said, repeating Bennigsen's words in an angry voice and thereby drawing attention to the false note in them. "Allow me to tell you, your excellency, that that question has no meaning for a Russian." (He lurched his heavy body forward.) "Such a question cannot be put, it is senseless! The question I have asked these gentlemen to meet to discuss is a military one. The question is that of saving Russia. Is it better to give up Moscow without a battle, or by accepting battle to risk losing the army as well as Moscow? That is the question on which I want your opinion," and he sank back in his chair.

The discussion began. Bennigsen did not yet consider his game lost. Admitting the view of Barclay and others that a defensive battle at Filí was impossible, but imbued with Russian patriotism and the love of Moscow, he proposed to move troops from the right to the left flank during the night, and attack the French right flank the following day. Opinions were divided, and arguments were advanced for and against that project. Ermólov, Dokhtúrov and Raévski agreed with Bennigsen. Whether feeling it necessary to make a sacrifice before abandoning the capital, or guided by other, personal, considerations, these generals seemed not to understand that this council could not alter the inevitable course of events, and that Moscow was in effect already abandoned. The other generals however understood it and, leaving aside the question of Moscow, spoke of the direction the army should take in its retreat. Malásha, who kept her eyes fixed on what was going on before her, understood the meaning of the council differently. It seemed to her that it was only a personal struggle between "Grandad" and "Long-coat" as she termed Bennigsen. She saw that they grew spiteful when they spoke to one another, and in her heart she sided with "Grandad." In the midst of the conversation she noticed "Grandad" give Bennigsen a quick, subtle glance, and then to her joy she saw that "Grandad" said something to "Long-coat" which settled him. Bennigsen suddenly reddened, and paced angrily up and down the room. What so affected him was Kutúzov's calm and quiet comment on the advantage or disadvantage of Bennigsen's proposal to move troops by night from the right to the left flank to attack the French right wing.

"Gentlemen," said Kutúzov, "I cannot approve of the count's plan. Moving troops in close proximity to an enemy is always dangerous, and military history supports that view. For instance . . ." Kutúzov seemed to reflect, searching for an example, then with a clear naïve look at Bennigsen he added: "Oh yes; take the battle of Friedland, which I think the count well remembers, and which was . . . not fully successful, only because our troops were rearranged too near the enemy. . . ."

There followed a momentary pause, which seemed very long to them all.

The discussion recommenced, but pauses frequently occurred and they all felt that there was no more to be said.

During one of these pauses Kutúzov heaved a deep sigh as if preparing to speak. They all looked at him.

"Well, gentlemen, I see that it is I who will have to pay for the broken crockery," said he, and rising slowly he moved to the table. "Gentlemen, I have heard your views. Some of you will not agree with me. But I," he paused, "by the authority entrusted to me by my Sovereign and country, order a retreat."

After that the generals began to disperse with the solemnity and circumspect silence of people who are leaving after a funeral.

Some of the generals, in low tones and in a strain very different from the way they had spoken during the council, communicated something to their commander-in-chief.

Malásha, who had long been expected for supper, climbed carefully backward down from the oven, her bare little feet catching at its projections, and slipping between the legs of the generals she darted out of the room.

When he had dismissed the generals Kutúzov sat a long time with his elbows on the table, thinking always of the same terrible question: "When, when did the abandonment of Moscow become inevitable? When was that done which settled the matter? And who was to blame for it?"

"I did not expect this," said he to his adjutant Schneider when the latter came in late that night. "I did not expect this! I did not think this would happen."

"You should take some rest, your Serene Highness," replied Schneider.

"But no! They shall eat horseflesh yet, like the Turks!" exclaimed Kutúzov without replying, striking the table with his podgy fist. "They shall too, if only . . ."

Chapter V

AT THAT VERY TIME, IN CIRCUMSTANCES EVEN MORE IMPORTANT THAN RETREATING WITHOUT A battle, namely the evacuation and burning of Moscow, Rostopchín, who is usually represented as being the instigator of that event, acted in an altogether different manner from Kutúzov.

After the battle of Borodinó the abandonment and burning of Moscow was as inevitable as the retreat of the army beyond Moscow without fighting.

Every Russian might have predicted it, not by reasoning but by the feeling implanted in each of us and in our fathers.

The same thing that took place in Moscow had happened in all the towns and villages on Russian soil beginning with Smolénsk, without the participation of Count Rostopchín and his broadsheets. The people awaited the enemy unconcernedly, did not riot or become excited or tear anyone to pieces, but faced its fate, feeling within it the strength to find what it should do at that most difficult moment. And as soon as the enemy drew near the wealthy classes went away abandoning their property, while the poorer remained and burned and destroyed what was left.

The consciousness that this would be so and would always be so, was and is present in the heart of every Russian. And a consciousness of this, and a foreboding that Moscow would be taken, was present in Russian Moscow society in 1812. Those who had quitted Moscow already in July and at the beginning of August showed that they expected this. Those who went away, taking what they could and abandoning their houses and half their belongings, did so from the latent patriotism which expresses itself not by phrases or by giving one's children to save the fatherland and similar unnatural exploits, but unobtrusively, simply, organically, and therefore in the way that always produces the most powerful results.

"It is disgraceful to run away from danger; only cowards are running away from Moscow," they were told. In his broadsheets Rostopchín impressed on them that to leave Moscow was shameful. They were ashamed to be called cowards, ashamed to leave, but still they left, knowing it had to be done. Why did they go? It is impossible to suppose that Rostopchín had scared them by his accounts of horrors Napoleon had committed in conquered countries. The first people to go away were the rich educated people who knew quite well that Vienna and Berlin had remained intact, and that during Napoleon's occupation the inhabitants had spent their time pleasantly in the company of the charming Frenchmen whom the Russians, and especially the Russian ladies, then liked so much.

They went away because for Russians there could be no question as to whether things would go well or ill under French rule in Moscow. It was out of the question to be under French rule, it would be the worst thing that could happen. They went away even before the battle of Borodinó and still more rapidly after it, despite Rostopchín's calls to defend Moscow or the announcement of his intention to take the wonder-working icon of the Iberian Mother of God and go to fight, or of the balloons that were to destroy the French, and despite all the nonsense Rostopchín wrote in his broadsheets. They knew that it was for the army to fight, and that if it could not succeed it would not do to take young ladies and house serfs to the Three Hills quarter of Moscow to fight Napoleon, and that they must go away, sorry as they were to abandon their property to destruction. They went away without thinking of the tremendous significance of that immense and wealthy city being given over to destruction, for a great city with wooden buildings was certain when abandoned by its inhabitants to be burned. They went away each on his own account, and yet it was only in consequence of their going away that the momentous event was accomplished that will always remain the greatest glory of the Russian people. The lady who, afraid of being stopped by Count Rostopchín's orders, had already in June moved with her negroes and her women-jesters from Moscow to her Sarátov estate with a vague consciousness that she was not Bonaparte's servant, was really, simply and truly carrying out the great work which saved Russia. But Count Rostopchín, who now taunted those who left Moscow and now had the Government offices removed; now distributed quite useless weapons to the drunken rabble; now had processions displaying the icons, and now forbade Father Augustin to remove icons or the relics of saints; now seized all the private carts in Moscow and on one hundred and thirty-six of them removed the balloon that was being constructed by Leppich; now hinted that he would burn Moscow and related how he had set fire to his own house; now wrote a proclamation to the French solemnly upbraiding them for having destroyed his Orphanage; now claimed the glory of having hinted that he would burn Moscow and now repudiated the deed; now ordered the people to catch all spies and bring them to him, and now reproached them for doing so; now expelled all the French residents from Moscow, and now allowed Madame Aubert-Chalmé (the center of the whole French colony in Moscow) to remain, but ordered the venerable old postmaster Klyucharëv to be arrested and exiled for no particular offense; now assembled the people at the Three Hills to fight the French and now, to get rid of them, handed over to them a man to be killed and himself drove away by a back gate; now declared that he would not survive the fall of Moscow, and now wrote French verses in albums concerning his share in the affair—this man did not understand the meaning of what was happening but merely wanted to do something himself that would astonish people, to perform some patriotically heroic feat; and like a child he made sport of the momentous and unavoidable event—the abandonment and burning of Moscow—and tried with his puny hand now to speed and now to stay the enormous, popular tide that bore him along with it.

Chapter VI

HÉLÈNE, HAVING RETURNED WITH THE COURT FROM VÍLNA TO PETERSBURG, FOUND HERSELF IN a difficult position.

In Petersburg she had enjoyed the special protection of a grandee who occupied one of the highest posts in the Empire. In Vílna she had formed an intimacy with a young foreign prince. When she returned to Petersburg both the magnate and the prince were there, and both claimed their rights. Hélène was faced by a new problem—how to preserve her intimacy with both without offending either.

What would have seemed difficult or even impossible to another woman did not cause the least embarrassment to Countess Bezúkhova, who evidently deserved her reputation of being a very clever woman. Had she attempted concealment, or tried to extricate herself from her awkward position by cunning, she would have spoiled her case by acknowledging herself guilty. But Hélène, like a really great man who can do whatever he pleases, at once assumed her own position to be correct, as she sincerely believed it to be, and that everyone else was to blame.

The first time the young foreigner allowed himself to reproach her, she lifted her beautiful head and, half turning to him, said firmly:

"That's just like a man—selfish and cruel! I expected nothing else. A woman sacrifices herself for you, she suffers, and this is her reward! What right have you, Monseigneur, to demand an account of my attachments and friendships? He is a man who has been more than a father to me!"

The prince was about to say something, but Hélène interrupted him.

"Well, yes," said she, "it may be that he has other sentiments for me than those of a father, but that is not a reason for me to shut my door on him. I am not a man, that I should repay kindness with ingratitude! Know, Monseigneur, that in all that relates to my intimate feelings I render account only to God and to my conscience," she concluded, laying her hand on her beautiful, fully expanded bosom and looking up to heaven.

"But for heaven's sake listen to me!"

"Marry me, and I will be your slave!"

"But that's impossible."

"You won't deign to demean yourself by marrying me, you . . ." said Hélène, beginning to cry.

The prince tried to comfort her, but Hélène, as if quite distraught, said through her tears that there was nothing to prevent her marrying, that there were precedents (there were up to that time very few, but she mentioned Napoleon and some other exalted personages), that she had never been her husband's wife, and that she had been sacrificed.

"But the law, religion . . ." said the prince, already yielding.

"The law, religion . . . What have they been invented for if they can't arrange that?" said Hélène.

The prince was surprised that so simple an idea had not occurred to him, and he applied for advice to the holy brethren of the Society of Jesus, with whom he was on intimate terms.

A few days later at one of those enchanting fêtes which Hélène gave at her country house on the Stone Island, the charming Monsieur de Jobert, a man no longer young, with snow-white hair and brilliant black eyes, a Jesuit *à robe courte,* was presented to her, and in the garden by the light of the illuminations and to the sound of music talked to her for a long time of the love of God, of Christ, of the Sacred Heart, and of the consolations the one true Catholic religion affords in this world and the next. Hélène was touched, and more than once tears rose to her eyes and to those of Monsieur de Jobert and their voices trembled. A dance, for which her partner came to seek her, put an end to her discourse with her future *directeur de conscience,* but the next evening Monsieur de Jobert came to see Hélène when she was alone, and after that often came again.

One day he took the countess to a Roman Catholic church, where she knelt down before the altar to which she was led. The enchanting, middle-aged Frenchman laid his hands on her head and, as she herself afterward described it, she felt something like a fresh breeze wafted into her soul. It was explained to her that this was *la grâce.*

After that a long-frocked abbé was brought to her. She confessed to him, and he absolved her from her sins. Next day she received a box containing the Sacred Host, which was left at her house for her to partake of. A few days later Hélène learned with pleasure that she had now been admitted to the true Catholic Church, and that in a few days the Pope himself would hear of her and would send her a certain document.

All that was done around her and to her at this time, all the attention devoted to her by so many clever men and expressed in such pleasant, refined ways, and the state of dovelike purity she was now in (she wore only white dresses and white ribbons all that time) gave her pleasure, but her pleasure did not cause her for a moment to forget her aim. And as it always happens in contests of cunning that a stupid person gets the better of cleverer ones, Hélène—having realized that the main object of all these words and all this trouble was, after converting her to Catholicism, to obtain money from her for Jesuit institutions (as to which she received indications)—before parting with her money insisted that the various operations necessary to free her from her husband should be performed. In her view the aim of every religion was merely to preserve certain proprieties while affording satisfaction to human desires. And with this aim, in one of her talks with her Father Confessor she insisted on an answer to the question, in how far was she bound by her marriage?

They were sitting in the twilight by a window in the drawing room. The scent of flowers came in at the window. Hélène was wearing a white dress, transparent over her shoulders and bosom. The abbé a well-fed man with a plump, clean-shaven chin, a pleasant firm mouth, and white hands meekly folded on his knees, sat close to Hélène and with a subtle smile on his lips and a peaceful look of delight at her beauty, occasionally glanced at her face as he explained his opinion on the subject. Hélène with an uneasy smile looked at his curly hair and his plump clean-shaven blackish cheeks, and every moment expected the conversation to take a fresh turn. But the abbé, though he evidently enjoyed the beauty of his companion, was absorbed in his mastery of the matter.

The course of the Father Confessor's arguments ran as follows: "Ignorant of the import of what you were undertaking, you made a vow of conjugal fidelity to a man on his part, by entering the married state without faith in the religious significance of marriage, committed an act of sacrilege. That marriage lacked the dual significance it should have had. Yet in spite of this your vow was binding. You swerved from it. What did you commit by so acting? A venial, or a mortal, sin? A venial sin, for you acted without evil intention. If now you married again with the object of bearing children, your sin might be forgiven. But the question is again a twofold one: firstly . . ."

But suddenly Hélène, who was getting bored, said with one of her bewitching smiles: "But I think that having espoused the true religion I cannot be bound by what a false religion laid upon me."

The director of her conscience was astounded at having the case presented to him thus with the simplicity of Columbus's egg. He was delighted at the unexpected rapidity of his pupil's progress, but could not abandon the edifice of argument he had laboriously constructed.

"Let us understand one another, countess," said he with a smile, and began refuting his spiritual daughter's arguments.

Chapter VII

HÉLÈNE UNDERSTOOD THAT THE QUESTION WAS VERY SIMPLE AND EASY FROM THE ECCLESIASTIcal point of view, and that her directors were making difficulties only because they were apprehensive as to how the matter would be regarded by the secular authorities.

So she decided that it was necessary to prepare the opinion of society. She provoked the jealousy of the elderly magnate and told him what she had told her other suitor, that is she put the matter so that the only way for him to obtain a right over her was to marry her. The elderly magnate was at first as much taken aback by this suggestion of marriage with a woman whose husband was alive, as the younger man had been, but Hélène's imperturbable conviction that it was as simple and natural as marrying a maiden had its effect on him too. Had Hélène herself shown the least sign of hesitation, shame or secrecy, her cause would certainly have been lost; but not only did she show no signs of secrecy or shame, on the contrary, with good-natured naïveté she told her intimate friends (and these were all Petersburg) that both the prince and the magnate had proposed to her, and that she loved both and was afraid of grieving either.

A rumor immediately spread in Petersburg, not that Hélène wanted to be divorced from her husband (had such a report spread many would have opposed so illegal an intention) but simply that the unfortunate and interesting Hélène was in doubt which of the two men she should marry. The question was no longer whether this was possible, but only which was the better match and how the matter would be regarded at court. There were it is true some rigid individuals unable to rise to the height of such a question, who saw in the project a desecration of the sacrament of marriage, but there were not many such and they remained silent, while the majority were interested in Hélène's good fortune and in the question which match would be the more advantageous. Whether it was right or wrong to remarry while one had a husband living they did not discuss, for that question had evidently been settled by people "wiser than you or me," as they said, and to doubt the correctness of that decision would be to risk exposing one's stupidity and incapacity to live in society.

Only Márya Dmítrievna Akhrosímova, who had come to Petersburg that summer to see one of her sons, allowed herself plainly to express an opinion contrary to the general one. Meeting Hélène at a ball she stopped her in the middle of the room and, amid general silence, said in her gruff voice: "So wives of living men have started marrying again! Perhaps you think you have invented a novelty? You have been forestalled, my dear! It was thought of long ago. It is done in all the brothels," and with these words Márya Dmítrievna, turning up her wide sleeves with her usual threatening gesture and glancing sternly round, moved across the room.

Though people were afraid of Márya Dmítrievna she was regarded in Petersburg as a buffoon, and so of what she had said they only noticed, and repeated in a whisper, the one coarse word she had used, supposing the whole sting of her remark to lie in that word.

Prince Vasíli, who of late very often forgot what he had said and repeated one and the same thing a hundred times, remarked to his daughter whenever he chanced to see her:

"Hélène, I have a word to say to you," and he would lead her aside, drawing her hand downward. "I have heard of certain projects concerning . . . you know. Well, my dear child, you know how your father's heart rejoices to know that you . . . You have suffered so much. . . . But my dear child, consult only your own heart. That is all I have to say," and concealing his unvarying emotion he would press his cheek against his daughter's and move away.

Bilíbin, who had not lost his reputation of an exceedingly clever man, and who was one of the disinterested friends so brilliant a woman as Hélène always has—men-friends who can never change into lovers—once gave her his view of the matter at a small and intimate gathering.

"Listen, Bilíbin," said Hélène (she always called friends of that sort by their surnames), and she touched his coat-sleeve with her white, beringed fingers. "Tell me, as you would a sister, what I ought to do. Which of the two?"

Bilíbin wrinkled up the skin over his eyebrows and pondered, with a smile on his lips.

"You are not taking me unawares, you know," said he. "As a true friend, I have thought and thought again about your affair. You see, if you marry the prince"—he meant the younger man—and he crooked one finger, "you forever lose the chance of marrying the other, and you will displease the court besides. (You know there is some kind of connection.) But if you marry the old count you will make his last days happy, and as widow of the Grand . . . the prince would no longer be making a mésalliance by marrying you," and Bilíbin smoothed out his forehead.

"That's a true friend!" said Hélène beaming, and again touching Bilíbin's sleeve. "But I love them, you know, and don't want to distress either of them. I would give my life for the happiness of them both."

Bilíbin shrugged his shoulders, as much as to say that not even he could help in that difficulty.

"*Une maîtresse-femme!* That's what is called putting things squarely. She would like to be married to all three at the same time," thought he.

"But tell me, how will your husband look at the matter?" Bilíbin asked, his reputation being so well-established that he did not fear to ask so naïve a question. "Will he agree?"

"Oh, he loves me so!" said Hélène, who for some reason imagined that Pierre too loved her. "He will do anything for me."

Bilíbin puckered his skin in preparation for something witty.

"Even divorce you?" said he.

Hélène laughed.

Among those who ventured to doubt the justifiability of the proposed marriage was Hélène's mother, Princess Kurágina. She was continually tormented by jealousy of her daughter, and now that jealousy concerned a subject near to her own heart, she could not reconcile herself to the idea. She consulted a Russian priest as to the possibility of divorce and remarriage during a husband's lifetime, and the priest told her that it was impossible, and to her delight showed her a text in the Gospel which (as it seemed to him) plainly forbids remarriage while the husband is alive.

Armed with these arguments, which appeared to her unanswerable, she drove to her daughter's early one morning so as to find her alone.

Having listened to her mother's objections, Hélène smiled blandly and ironically.

"But it says plainly: 'Whosoever shall marry her that is divorced . . .' " said the old princess.

"Ah, maman, ne dites pas de bêtises. Vous ne comprenez rein. Dans ma position j'ai des devoirs," said Hélène changing from Russian, in which language she always felt that her case did not sound quite clear, into French which suited it better.

"But, my dear . . ."

"Oh, Mamma, how is it you don't understand that the Holy Father, who has the right to grant dispensations . . ."

Just then the lady companion who lived with Hélène came in to announce that his Highness was in the ballroom and wished to see her.

"Non, dites-lui que je ne veux pas le voir, que je suis furieuse contre lui, parce qu'il m' a manqué parole."

"Comtesse, à tout peché miséricorde," said a fair-haired young man with a long face and nose, as he entered the room.

The old princess rose respectfully and curtsied. The young man who had entered took no notice of her. The princess nodded to her daughter and sidled out of the room.

"Yes, she is right," thought the old princess, all her convictions dissipated by the appearance of his Highness. "She is right, but how is it that we in our irrecoverable youth did not know it? Yet it is so simple," she thought as she got into her carriage.

By the beginning of August Hélène's affairs were clearly defined and she wrote a letter to her husband—who, as she imagined, loved her very much—informing him of her intention to marry N. N. and of her having embraced the one true faith, and asking him to carry out all the formalities necessary for a divorce, which would be explained to him by the bearer of the letter.

And so I pray God to have you, my friend, in His holy and powerful keeping—Your friend Hélène.

This letter was brought to Pierre's house when he was on the field of Borodinó.

Chapter VIII

TOWARD THE END OF THE BATTLE OF BORODINÓ, PIERRE, HAVING RUN DOWN FROM RAÉVSKI'S battery a second time, made his way through a gully to Knyazkóvo with a crowd of soldiers, reached the dressing-station, and seeing blood and hearing cries and groans hurried on, still entangled in the crowds of soldiers.

The one thing he now desired with his whole soul was to get away quickly from the terrible sensations amid which he had lived that day, and return to ordinary conditions of life and sleep quietly in a room in his own bed. He felt that only in the ordinary conditions of life would he be able to understand himself and all he had seen and felt. But such ordinary conditions of life were nowhere to be found.

Though shells and bullets did not whistle over the road along which he was going, still on all sides there was what there had been on the field of battle. There were still the same suffering, exhausted and sometimes strangely indifferent faces, the same blood, the same soldiers' overcoats, the same sounds of firing, which though distant now, still aroused terror, and besides this there were the foul air and the dust.

Having gone a couple of miles along the Mozháysk road, Pierre sat down by the roadside.

Dusk had fallen, and the roar of guns died away. Pierre lay leaning on his elbow for a long time, gazing at the shadows that moved past him in the darkness. He was continually imagining that a cannon-ball was flying toward him with a terrific whizz, and then he shuddered and sat up. He had no idea how long he had been there. In the middle of the night three soldiers, having brought some firewood, settled down near him and began lighting a fire.

The soldiers, who threw sidelong glances at Pierre, got the fire to burn and placed an iron pot on it into which they broke some dried bread and put a little dripping. The pleasant odor of greasy viands mingled with the smell of smoke. Pierre sat up and sighed. The three soldiers were eating and talking among themselves, taking no notice of him.

"And who may you be?" one of them suddenly asked Pierre, evidently meaning what Pierre himself had in mind, namely: "If you want to eat we'll give you some food, only let us know whether you are an honest man."

"I, I . . ." said Pierre, feeling it necessary to minimize his social position as much as possible so as to be nearer to the soldiers and better understood by them. "By rights I am a militia officer, but my men are not here. I came to the battle and have lost them."

"There now!" said one of the soldiers.

Another shook his head.

"Would you like a little mash?" the first soldier asked, and handed Pierre a wooden spoon after licking it clean.

Pierre sat down by the fire and began eating the mash, as they called the food in the cauldron, and he thought it more delicious than any food he had ever tasted. As he sat bending greedily over it, helping himself to large spoonfuls and chewing one after another, his was lit up by the fire and the soldiers looked at him in silence.

"Where have you to go to? Tell us!" said one of them.

"To Mozháysk."

"You're a gentleman, aren't you?"

"Yes."

"And what's your name?"

"Peter Kiríllych."

"Well then Peter Kiríllych, come along with us, we'll take you there."

In the total darkness the soldiers walked with Pierre to Mozháysk.

By the time they got near Mozháysk and began ascending the steep hill into the town, the cocks were already crowing. Pierre went on with the soldiers, quite forgetting that his inn was at the bottom of the hill and that he had already passed it. He would not soon have remembered this, such was his state of forgetfulness, had he not halfway up the hill stumbled upon his groom, who had been to look for him in the town and was returning to the inn. The groom recognized Pierre in the darkness by his white hat.

"Your excellency!" he said. "Why, we were beginning to despair! How is it you are on foot? And where are you going, please?"

"Oh, yes!" said Pierre.

The soldiers stopped.

"So you've found your folk?" said one of them. "Well, good-bye, Peter Kirílych—isn't it?"

"Good-bye, Peter Kirílych!" Pierre heard the other voices repeat.

"Good-bye!" he said and turned with his groom toward the inn.

"I ought to give them something!" he thought, and felt in his pocket. "No, better not!" said another, inner voice.

There was not a room to be had at the inn, they were all occupied. Pierre went out into the yard and, covering himself up head and all, lay down in his carriage.

Chapter IX

SCARCELY HAD PIERRE LAID HIS HEAD ON THE PILLOW BEFORE HE FELT HIMSELF FALLING ASLEEP, but suddenly, almost with the distinctness of reality, he heard the *boom, boom, boom* of firing, the thud of projectiles, groans and cries, and smelled blood and powder, and a feeling of horror and dread of death seized him. Filled with fright he opened his eyes and lifted his head from under his cloak. All was tranquil in the yard. Only someone's orderly passed through the gateway, splashing through the mud, and talked to the innkeeper. Above Pierre's head some pigeons, disturbed by the movement he had made in sitting up, fluttered under the dark roof of the penthouse. The whole courtyard was permeated by a strong peaceful smell of stable-yards, delightful to Pierre at that moment. He could see the clear starry sky between the dark roofs of two penthouses.

"Thank God, there is no more of that!" he thought, covering up his head again. "Oh, what a terrible thing is fear, and how shamefully I yielded to it! But they . . . *they* were steady and calm all the time, to the end . . ." thought he.

They, in Pierre's mind, were the soldiers, those who had been at the battery, those who had given him food, and those who had prayed before the icon. *They,* those strange men he had not previously known, stood out clearly and sharply from everyone else.

"To be a soldier, just a soldier!" thought Pierre as he fell asleep, "to enter communal life completely, to be imbued by what makes them what they are. But how cast off all the superfluous, devilish burden of my outer man? There was a time when I could have done it. I could have run away from my father, as I wanted to. Or I might have been sent to serve as a soldier after the duel with Dólokhov." And the memory of the dinner at the English Club when he had challenged Dólokhov flashed through Pierre's mind, and then he remembered his benefactor at Torzhók. And now a picture of a solemn meeting of the Lodge presented itself to his mind. It was taking place at the English Club and someone near and dear to him sat at the end of the table. "Yes, that is he! It is my benefactor. But he died!" thought Pierre. "Yes, he died, and I did not know he was alive. How sorry I am that he died, and how glad I am that he is alive again!" On one side of the table sat Anatole, Dólokhov, Nesvítski, Denísov, and others like them (in his dream the category to which these men belonged was as clearly defined in his mind as the category of those he termed *they*), and he heard those people, Anatole and Dólokhov, shouting and singing loudly; yet through their shouting the voice of his benefactor was heard speaking all the time and the sound of his words was as weighty and uninterrupted as the booming on the battlefield, but pleasant and comforting. Pierre did not understand what his benefactor was saying, but he knew (the categories of thoughts were also quite distinct in his dream) that he was talking of goodness and the possibility of being what *they* were. And *they* with their simple, kind, firm faces surrounded his benefactor on all sides. But though they were kindly they did not look at Pierre and did not know him. Wishing to speak and to attract their attention, he got up, but at that moment his legs grew cold and bare.

He felt ashamed, and with one arm covered his legs from which his cloak had in fact slipped. For a moment as he was rearranging his cloak Pierre opened his eyes and saw the same penthouse roofs, posts, and yard, but now they were all bluish, lit up, and glittering with frost or dew.

"It is dawn," thought Pierre. "But that's not what I want. I want to hear and understand my benefactor's words." Again he covered himself up with his cloak, but now neither the Lodge nor his benefactor was there. There were only thoughts clearly expressed in words, thoughts that someone was uttering or that he himself was formulating.

Afterward when he recalled those thoughts Pierre was convinced that someone outside himself had spoken them, though the impressions of that day had evoked them. He had never, it seemed to him, been able to think and express his thoughts like that when awake.

"To endure war is the most difficult subordination of man's freedom to the law of God," the voice had said. "Simplicity is submission to the will of God; you cannot escape from Him. And *they* are simple. *They* do not talk, but act. The spoken word is silver but the unspoken is golden. Man can be master of nothing while he fears death, but he who does not fear it possesses all. If there were no suffering, man would not know his limitations, would not know himself. The hardest thing (Pierre went on thinking, or hearing, in his dream) is to be able in your soul to unite the meaning of all. To unite all?" he asked himself. "No, not to unite. Thoughts cannot be united, but to *harness* all these thoughts together is what we need! Yes, one *must harness* them, *must harness* them!" he repeated to himself with inward rapture, feeling that these words and they alone expressed what he wanted to say and solved the question that tormented him.

"Yes, one must harness, it is time to harness."

"Time to harness, time to harness, your excellency! Your excellency!" some voice was repeating. "We must harness, it is time to harness. . . ."

It was the voice of the groom, trying to wake him. The sun shone straight into Pierre's face. He glanced at the dirty innyard in the middle of which soldiers were watering their lean horses at the pump while carts were passing out of the gate. Pierre turned away with repugnance, and closing his eyes quickly fell back on the carriage seat. "No, I don't want that, I don't want to see and understand that. I want to understand what was revealing itself to me in my dream. One second more and I should have understood it all! But what am I to do? Harness, but how can I harness everything?" and Pierre felt with horror that the meaning of all he had seen and thought in the dream had been destroyed.

The groom, the coachman, and the innkeeper told Pierre that an officer had come with news that the French were already near Mozháysk and that our men were leaving it.

Pierre got up and, having told them to harness and overtake him, went on foot through the town.

The troops were moving on, leaving about ten thousand wounded behind them. There were wounded in the yards, at the windows of the houses, and the streets were crowded with them. In the streets, around carts that were to take some of the wounded away, shouts, curses and blows could be heard. Pierre offered the use of his carriage, which had overtaken him, to a wounded general he knew, and drove with him to Moscow. On the way Pierre was told of the death of his brother-in-law Anatole, and of that of Prince Andrew.

Chapter X

On the 30th of August Pierre reached Moscow. Close to the gates of the city he was met by Count Rostopchín's adjutant.

"We have been looking for you everywhere," said the adjutant. "The count wants to see you particularly. He asks you to come to him at once on a very important matter."

Without going home, Pierre took a cab and drove to see the Moscow commander-in-chief.

Count Rostopchín had only that morning returned to town from his summer villa at Sokólniki. The anteroom and reception room of his house were full of officials who had been summoned or had come for orders. Vasílchikov and Plátov had already seen the count and explained to him that it was impossible to defend Moscow and that it would have to be surrendered. Though this news was being concealed from the inhabitants, the officials—the heads of the various Government departments—knew that Moscow would soon be in the enemy's hands, just as Count Rostopchín himself knew it, and to escape personal responsibility they had all come to the governor to ask how they were to deal with their various departments.

As Pierre was entering the reception room a courier from the army came out of Rostopchín's private room.

In answer to questions with which he was greeted, the courier made a despairing gesture with his hand and passed through the room.

While waiting in the reception room Pierre with weary eyes watched the various officials, old and young, military and civilian, who were there. They all seemed dissatisfied and uneasy. Pierre went up to a group of men, one of whom he knew. After greeting Pierre they continued their conversation.

"If they're sent out and brought back again later on it will do no harm, but as things are now one can't answer for anything."

"But you see what he writes . . ." said another, pointing to a printed sheet he held in his hand.

"That's another matter. That's necessary for the people," said the first.

"What is it?" asked Pierre.

"Oh, it's a fresh broadsheet."

Pierre took it and began reading.

> His Serene Highness has passed through Mozháysk in order to join up with the troops moving toward him, and has taken up a strong position where the enemy will not soon attack him. Forty-eight guns with ammunition have been sent him from here, and his Serene Highness says he will defend Moscow to the last drop of blood and is even ready to fight in the streets. Do not be upset, brothers, that the Law-Courts are closed; things have to be put in order, and we will deal with villains in our own way! When the time comes I shall want both town and peasant lads and will raise the cry a day or two beforehand, but they are not wanted yet so I hold my peace. An ax will be useful, a hunting-spear not bad, but a three-pronged fork will be best of all: a Frenchman is no heavier than a sheaf of rye. Tomorrow after dinner I shall take the Iberian icon of the Mother of God

to the wounded in the Catherine Hospital where we will have some water blessed. That will help them to get well quicker. I, too, am well now: one of my eyes was sore but now I am on the look-out with both.

"But military men have told me that it is impossible to fight in the town," said Pierre, "and that the position . . ."

"Well, of course! That's what we were saying," replied the first speaker.

"And what does he mean by 'One of my eyes was sore but now I am on the look-out with both'?" asked Pierre.

"The count had a sty," replied the adjutant smiling, "and was very much upset when I told him people had come to ask what was the matter with him. By the by, count," he added suddenly, addressing Pierre with a smile, "we heard that you have family troubles and that the countess your wife . . ."

"I have heard nothing," Pierre replied unconcernedly. "But what have you heard?"

"Oh, well, you know people often invent things. I only say what I heard."

"But what did you hear?"

"Well, they say," continued the adjutant with the same smile, "that the countess, your wife, is preparing to go abroad. I expect it's nonsense. . . ."

"Possibly," remarked Pierre, looking about him absent-mindedly. "And who is that?" he asked, indicating a short old man in a clean blue peasant overcoat, with a big snow-white beard and eyebrows and a ruddy face.

"He? That's a tradesman, that is to say, he's the restaurant-keeper, Vereshchágin. Perhaps you have heard of that affair with the proclamation."

"Oh, so that is Vereshchágin!" said Pierre, looking at the firm calm face of the old man and seeking any indication of his being a traitor.

"That's not he himself, that's the father of the fellow who wrote the proclamation," said the adjutant. "The young man is in prison and I expect it will go hard with him."

An old gentleman wearing a star and another official, a German wearing a cross round his neck, approached the speaker.

"It's a complicated story, you know," said the adjutant. "That proclamation appeared about two months ago. The count was informed of it. He gave orders to investigate the matter. Gabriel Ivánovich here made the inquiries. The proclamation had passed through exactly sixty-three hands. He asked one, 'From whom did you get it?' 'From so-and-so.' He went to the next one. 'From whom did you get it?' and so on till he reached Vereshchágin, a half-educated tradesman, you know, 'a pet of a trader,' " said the adjutant smiling. "They asked him, 'Who gave it you?' And the point is that we knew whom he had it from. He could only have had it from the Postmaster. But evidently they had come to some understanding. He replied: 'From no one; I made it up myself.' They threatened and questioned him, but he stuck to that: 'I made it up myself.' And so it was reported to the count, who sent for the man. 'From whom did you get the proclamation?' 'I wrote it myself.' Well, you know the count," said the adjutant cheerfully, with a smile of pride, "he flared up dreadfully—and just think of the fellow's audacity, lying and obstinacy!"

"And the count wanted him to say it was from Klyucharëv? I understand!" said Pierre.

"Not at all," rejoined the adjutant in dismay. "Klyucharëv had his own sins to answer for without that and that is why he has been banished. But the point is that the count was much annoyed. 'How could you have written it yourself?' said he, and he took up the Hamburg Gazette that was lying on the table. 'Here it is! You did not write it yourself but translated it, and translated it abominably, because you don't even know French, you fool.' And what do you think? 'No,' said he, 'I have not read any papers, I made it up myself.' 'If that's so, you're a traitor and I'll have you tried, and you'll be hanged! Say from whom you had it.' 'I have seen no papers, I made it up myself.' And that was the end of it. The count had the father fetched, but the fellow stuck to it. He was sent for trial and condemned to hard labor, I believe. Now the father has come to intercede for him. But he's a good-for-nothing lad! You know that sort of tradesman's son, a dandy and lady-killer. He attended some lectures somewhere and imagines that the devil is no match for him. That's the sort of fellow he is. His father keeps a cookshop here by the Stone Bridge, and you know there was a large icon of God Almighty painted with a scepter in one hand and an orb in the other. Well, he took that icon home with him for a few days and what did he do? He found some scoundrel of a painter . . ."

Chapter XI

IN THE MIDDLE OF THIS FRESH TALE PIERRE WAS SUMMONED TO THE COMMANDER-IN-CHIEF.

When he entered the private room Count Rostopchín, puckering his face, was rubbing his forehead and eyes with his hand. A short man was saying something, but when Pierre entered he stopped speaking and went out.

"Ah, how do you do, great warrior?" said Rostopchín as soon as the short man had left the room. "We have heard of your prowess. But that's not the point. Between ourselves, *mon cher,* do you belong to the masons?" he went on severely, as though there were something wrong about it which he nevertheless intended to pardon. Pierre remained silent. "I am well-informed, my friend, but I am aware that there are masons and masons and I hope that you are not one of those who on pretense of saving mankind wish to ruin Russia."

"Yes, I am a mason," Pierre replied.

"There, you see, *mon cher!* I expect you know that Messrs. Speránski and Magnítski have been deported to their proper place. Mr. Klyucharëv has been treated in the same way, and so have others who on the plea of building up the temple of Solomon have tried to destroy the temple of their fatherland. You can understand that there are reasons for this and that I could not have exiled the Postmaster had he not been a harmful person. It has now come to my knowledge that you lent him your carriage for his removal from town, and that you have even accepted papers from him for safe custody. I like you and don't wish you any harm and—as you are only half my age—I advise you as a father would, to cease all communication with men of that stamp and to leave here as soon as possible."

"But what did Klyucharëv do wrong, count?" asked Pierre.

"That is for me to know, but not for you to ask," shouted Rostopchín.

"If he is accused of circulating Napoleon's proclamation it is not proved that he did so," said Pierre without looking at Rostopchín, "and Vereshchágin . . ."

"There we are!" Rostopchín shouted at Pierre louder than before, frowning suddenly. "Vereshchágin is a renegade and a traitor who will be punished as he deserves," said he with the vindictive heat with which people speak when recalling an insult. "But I did not summon you to discuss my actions, but to give you advice—or an order if you prefer it. I beg you to leave the town and break off all communication with such men as Klyucharëv. And I will knock the nonsense out of anybody"—but probably realizing that he was shouting at Bezúkhov who so far was not guilty of anything, he added, taking Pierre's hand in a friendly manner, "We are on the eve of a public disaster and I haven't time to be polite to everybody who has business with me. My head is sometimes in a whirl. Well, *mon cher,* what are you doing personally?"

"Why, nothing," answered Pierre without raising his eyes or changing the thoughtful expression of his face.

The count frowned.

"A word of friendly advice, *mon cher.* Be off as soon as you can, that's all I have to tell you. Happy he who has ears to hear. Good-bye, my dear fellow. Oh, by the by!" he shouted through the doorway after Pierre, "is it true that the countess has fallen into the clutches of the holy fathers of the Society of Jesus?"

Pierre did not answer, and left Rostopchín's room more sullen and angry than he had ever before shown himself.

When he reached home it was already getting dark. Some eight people had come to see him that evening: the secretary of a committee, the colonel of his battalion, his steward, his major-domo, and various petitioners. They all had business with Pierre and wanted decisions from him. Pierre did not understand and was not interested in any of these questions, and only answered them in order to get rid of these people. When left alone at last he opened and read his wife's letter.

"*They,* the soldiers at the battery, Prince Andrew killed . . . that old man . . . Simplicity is submission to God. Suffering is necessary . . . the meaning of all . . . one must harness . . . my wife is getting married . . . One must forget and understand . . ." And going to his bed he threw himself on it without undressing and immediately fell asleep.

When he awoke next morning the major-domo came to inform him that a special messenger, a police officer, had come from Count Rostopchín to know whether Count Bezúkhov had left or was leaving the town.

A dozen persons who had business with Pierre were awaiting him in the drawing room. Pierre dressed hurriedly, and instead of going to see them went to the back porch and out through the gate.

From that time till the end of the destruction of Moscow no one of Bezúkhov's household, despite all the search they made, saw Pierre again or knew where he was.

Chapter XII

THE ROSTÓVS REMAINED IN MOSCOW TILL THE 1ST OF SEPTEMBER, THAT IS, TILL THE EVE OF THE enemy's entry into the city.

After Pétya had joined Obolénski's regiment of Cossacks and left for Bélaya Tsérkov where that regiment was forming, the countess was seized with terror. The thought that both her sons were at the war, had both gone from under her wing, that today or tomorrow either or both of them might be killed like the three sons of one of her acquaintances, struck her that summer for the first time with cruel clearness. She tried to get Nicholas back, and wished to go herself to join Pétya, or to get him an appointment somewhere in Petersburg, but neither of these proved possible. Pétya could not return unless his regiment did so or unless he was transferred to another regiment on active service. Nicholas was somewhere with the army and had not sent a word since his last letter, in which he had given a detailed account of his meeting with Princess Mary. The countess did not sleep at night, or when she did fall asleep dreamed that she saw her sons lying dead. After many consultations and conversations, the count at last devised means to tranquillize her. He got Pétya transferred from Obolénski's regiment to Bezúkhov's, which was in training near Moscow. Though Pétya would remain in the service, this transfer would give the countess the consolation of seeing at least one of her sons under her wing, and she hoped to arrange matters for her Pétya so as not to let him go again, but always get him appointed to places where he could not possibly take part in a battle. As long as Nicholas alone was in danger the countess imagined that she loved her first-born more than all her other children and even reproached herself for it; but when her youngest: the scapegrace who had been bad at lessons, was always breaking things in the house and making himself a nuisance to everybody, that snub-nosed Pétya with his merry black eyes and fresh rosy cheeks where soft down was just beginning to show—when he was thrown amid those big, dreadful, cruel men who were fighting somewhere about something and apparently finding pleasure in it—then his mother thought she loved him more, much more, than all her other children. The nearer the time came for Pétya to return, the more uneasy grew the countess. She began to think she would never live to see such happiness. The presence of Sónya, of her beloved Natásha, or even of her husband, irritated her. "What do I want with them? I want no one but Pétya," she thought.

At the end of August the Rostóvs received another letter from Nicholas. He wrote from the province of Vorónezh where he had been sent to procure remounts, but that letter did not set the countess at ease. Knowing that one son was out of danger she became the more anxious about Pétya.

Though by the 20th of August nearly all the Rostóvs' acquaintances had left Moscow, and though everybody tried to persuade the countess to get away as quickly as possible, she would not hear of leaving before her treasure, her adored Pétya, returned. On the 28th of August he arrived. The passionate tenderness with which his mother received him did not please the sixteen-year-old officer. Though she concealed from him her intention of keeping him under her wing, Pétya guessed her designs, and instinctively fearing that he might give way to emotion when with her—might "become womanish" as he termed it to himself—he treated her coldly, avoided her, and during his stay in Moscow attached himself exclusively to Natásha for whom he had always had a particularly brotherly tenderness, almost loverlike.

Owing to the count's customary carelessness nothing was ready for their departure by the 28th of August and the carts that were to come from their Ryazán and Moscow estates to remove their household belongings did not arrive till the 30th.

From the 28th till the 31st all Moscow was in a bustle and commotion. Every day thousands of men wounded at Borodinó were brought in by the Dorogomílov gate and taken to various parts of Moscow, and thousands of carts conveyed the inhabitants and their possessions out by the other gates. In spite of Rostopchín's broadsheets, or because of them or independently of them, the strangest and most contradictory rumors were current in the town. Some said that no one was to be allowed to leave the city, others on the contrary said that all the icons had been taken out of the churches and everybody was to be ordered to leave. Some said there had been another battle after Borodinó at which the French had been routed, while others on the contrary reported that the Russian army had been destroyed. Some talked about the Moscow militia which, preceded by the clergy, would go to the Three Hills; others whispered that Augustin had been forbidden to leave, that traitors had been seized, that the peasants were rioting and robbing people on their way from Moscow, and so on. But all this was only talk; in reality (though the Council of Filí, at which it was decided to abandon Moscow, had not yet been held) both those who went away and those who remained behind felt, though they did not show it, that Moscow would certainly be abandoned, and that they ought to get away as quickly as possible and save their belongings. It was felt that everything would suddenly break up and change, but up to the 1st of September nothing had done so. As a criminal who is being led to execution knows that he must die immediately, but yet looks about him and straightens the cap that is awry on his head, so Moscow involuntarily continued its wonted life, though it knew that the time of its destruction was near when the conditions of life to which its people were accustomed to submit would be completely upset.

During the three days preceding the occupation of Moscow the whole Rostóv family was absorbed in various activities. The head of the family, Count Ilyá Rostóv, continually drove about the city collecting the current rumors from all sides, and gave superficial and hasty orders at home about the preparations for their departure.

The countess watched the things being packed, was dissatisfied with everything, was constantly in pursuit of Pétya who was always running away from her, and was jealous of Natásha with whom he spent all his time. Sónya alone directed the practical side of matters by getting things packed. But of late Sónya had been particularly sad and silent. Nicholas's letter in which he mentioned Princess Mary had elicited, in her presence, joyous comments from the countess, who saw an intervention of Providence in this meeting of the princess and Nicholas.

"I was never pleased at Bolkónski's engagement to Natásha," said the countess, "but I always wanted Nicholas to marry the princess, and had a presentiment that it would happen. What a good thing it would be!"

Sónya felt that this was true: that the only possibility of retrieving the Rostóv affairs was by Nicholas marrying a rich woman, and that the princess was a good match. It was very bitter for her. But despite her grief, or perhaps just because of it, she took on herself all the difficult work of directing the storing and packing of their things and was busy for whole days. The count and countess turned to her when they had any orders to give. Pétya and Natásha on the contrary, far from helping their parents were generally a nuisance and a hindrance to everyone. Almost all day long the house resounded with their running feet, their cries and their spontaneous laughter. They laughed and were gay not because there was any reason to laugh, but because gaiety and mirth were in their hearts and so everything that happened was a cause for gaiety and laughter to them. Pétya was in high spirits because having left home a boy he had returned (as everybody told him) a fine young man, because he was at home, because he had left Bélaya Tsérkov where there was no hope of soon taking part in a battle and had come to Moscow where there was to be fighting in a few days, and chiefly because Natásha, whose lead he always followed, was in high spirits. Natásha was gay because she had been sad too long and now nothing reminded her of the cause of her sadness, and because she was feeling well. She was also happy because she had someone to adore her: the adoration of others was a lubricant the wheels of her machine needed to make them run freely—and Pétya adored her. Above all, they were gay because there was a war near Moscow, there would be fighting at the town gates, arms were being given out, everybody was escaping—going away somewhere, and in general something extraordinary was happening, and that is always exciting, especially to the young.

Chapter XIII

On Saturday the 31st of August everything in the Rostóvs' house seemed topsy-turvy. All the doors were open, all the furniture was being carried out or moved about, and the mirrors and pictures had been taken down. There were trunks in the rooms, and hay, wrapping-paper, and ropes were scattered about. The peasants and house serfs carrying out the things were treading heavily on the parquet floors. The yard was crowded with peasant carts, some loaded high and already corded up, others still empty.

The voices and footsteps of the many servants and of the peasants who had come with the carts, resounded as they shouted to one another in the yard and in the house. The count had been out since morning. The countess had a headache brought on by all the noise and turmoil and was lying down in the new sitting room with a vinegar compress on her head. Pétya was not at home, he had gone to visit a friend with whom he meant to obtain a transfer from the militia to the active army. Sónya was in the ballroom looking after the packing of the glass and china. Natásha was sitting on the floor of her dismantled room with dresses, ribbons and scarves strewn all about her, gazing fixedly at the floor and holding in her hands the old ball dress (already out of fashion) which she had worn at her first Petersburg ball.

Natásha was ashamed of doing nothing when everyone else was so busy, and several times that morning had tried to set to work, but her heart was not in it, and she could not and did not know how to do anything except with all her heart and all her might. For a while she had stood beside Sónya while the china was being packed, and tried to help, but soon gave it up and went to her room to pack her own things. At first she found it amusing to give away dresses and ribbons to the maids, but when that was done and what was left had still to be packed, she found it dull.

"Dunyásha, you pack! You will, won't you, dear?" And when Dunyásha willingly promised to do it all for her, Natásha sat down on the floor, took her old ball dress, and fell into a reverie quite unrelated to what ought to have occupied her thoughts now. She was roused from her reverie by the talk of the maids in the next room (which was theirs) and by the sound of their hurried footsteps going to the back porch. Natásha got up and looked out of the window. An enormously long row of carts full of wounded men had stopped in the street.

The housekeeper, the old nurse, the cooks, coachmen, maids, footmen, postilions and scullions, stood at the gate, staring at the wounded.

Natásha, throwing a clean pocket-handkerchief over her hair and holding an end of it in each hand, went out into the street.

The former housekeeper, old Mávra Kuzmínichna, had stepped out of the crowd by the gate, gone up to a cart with a hood constructed of bast mats, and was speaking to a pale young officer who lay inside. Natásha moved a few steps forward and stopped shyly, still holding her handkerchief, and listened to what the housekeeper was saying.

"Then you have nobody in Moscow?" she was saying. "You would be more comfortable somewhere in a house . . . in ours, for instance . . . the family are leaving."

"I don't know if it would be allowed," replied the officer in a weak voice. "Here is our commanding officer . . . ask him," and he pointed to a stout major who was walking back along the street past the row of carts.

Natásha glanced with frightened eyes at the face of the wounded officer and at once went to meet the major.

"May the wounded men stay in our house?" she asked.

The major raised his hand to his cap with a smile.

"Which one do you want, Ma'am'selle?" said he, screwing up his eyes and smiling.

Natásha quietly repeated her question, and her face and whole manner were so serious, though she was still holding the ends of her handkerchief, that the major ceased smiling and after some reflection—as if considering in how far the thing was possible—replied in the affirmative.

"Oh yes, why not? They may," he said.

With a slight inclination of her head, Natásha stepped back quickly to Mávra Kuzmínichna, who stood talking compassionately to the officer.

"They may. He says they may!" whispered Natásha.

The cart in which the officer lay was turned into the Rostóvs' yard, and dozens of carts with wounded men began at the invitation of the townsfolk to turn into the yards and to draw up at the entrances of the houses in Povarskáya Street. Natásha was evidently pleased to be dealing with new people outside the ordinary routine of her life. She and Mávra Kuzmínichna tried to get as many of the wounded as possible into their yard.

"Your Papa must be told, though," said Mávra Kuzmínichna.

"Never mind, never mind, what does it matter? For one day we can move into the drawing room. They can have all our half of the house."

"There now, young lady, you do take things into your head! Even if we put them into the wing, the men's room, or the nurse's room, we must ask permission."

"Well, I'll ask."

Natásha ran into the house and went on tiptoe through the half-open door into the sitting room, where there was a smell of vinegar and Hoffman's drops.

"Are you asleep, Mamma?"

"Oh, what sleep—?" said the countess, waking up just as she was dropping into a doze.

"Mamma darling!" said Natásha, kneeling by her mother and bringing her face close to her mother's, "I am sorry, forgive me, I'll never do it again; I woke you up! Mávra Kuzmínichna has sent me: they have brought some wounded here—officers. Will you let them come? They have nowhere to go. I knew you'd let them come . . ." she said quickly all in one breath.

"What officers? Whom have they brought? I don't understand anything about it," said the countess.

Natásha laughed, and the countess too smiled slightly.

"I knew you'd give permission . . . so I'll tell them," and, having kissed her mother, Natásha got up and went to the door.

In the hall she met her father, who had returned with bad news.

"We've stayed too long!" said the count with involuntary vexation. "The Club is closed and the police are leaving."

"Papa, is it all right—I've invited some of the wounded into the house?" said Natásha.

"Of course it is," he answered absently. "That's not the point. I beg you not to indulge in trifles now, but to help to pack, and tomorrow we must go, go, go!. . . ."

And the count gave a similar order to the major-domo and the servants.

At dinner Pétya having returned home told them the news he had heard. He said the people had been getting arms in the Kremlin, and that though Rostopchín's broadsheet had said that he would sound a call two or three days in advance, the order had certainly already been given for everyone to go armed to the Three Hills tomorrow, and that there would be a big battle there.

The countess looked with timid horror at her son's eager, excited face as he said this. She realized that if she said a word about his not going to the battle (she knew he enjoyed the thought of the impending engagement) he would say something about men, honor and the fatherland—something senseless, masculine, and obstinate which there would be no contradicting, and her plans would be spoiled; and so, hoping to arrange to leave before then and take Pétya with her as their protector and defender, she did not answer him, but after dinner called the count aside and implored him with tears to take her away quickly, that very night if possible. With a woman's involuntary loving cunning she, who till then had not shown any alarm, said that she would die of fright if they did not leave that very night. Without any pretense she was now afraid of everything.

Chapter XIV

MADAME SCHOSS, WHO HAD BEEN OUT TO VISIT HER DAUGHTER, INCREASED THE COUNTESS'S fears still more by telling what she had seen at a spirit-dealer's in Myasnítski Street. When returning by that street she had been unable to pass because of a drunken crowd rioting in front of the shop. She had taken a cab and driven home by a side street and the cabman had told her that the people were breaking open the barrels at the drink store, having received orders to do so.

After dinner the whole Rostóv household set to work with enthusiastic haste packing their belongings and preparing for their departure. The old count, suddenly setting to work, kept passing from the yard to the house and back again, shouting confused instructions to the hurrying people, and flurrying them still more. Pétya directed things in the yard. Sónya owing to the count's contradictory orders lost her head and did not know what to do. The servants ran noisily about the house and yard, shouting and disputing. Natásha with the ardor characteristic of all she did suddenly set to work too. At first her intervention in the business of packing was received skeptically.

Everybody expected some prank from her and did not wish to obey her; but she resolutely and passionately demanded obedience, grew angry and nearly cried because they did not heed her, and at last succeeded in making them believe her. Her first exploit, which cost her immense effort and established her authority, was the packing of the carpets. The count had valuable Gobelin tapestries and Persian carpets in the house. When Natásha set to work two cases were standing open in the ballroom, one almost full up with crockery, the other with carpets. There was also much china standing on the tables, and still more was being brought in from the storeroom. A third case was needed and servants had gone to fetch it.

"Sónya, wait a bit—we'll pack everything into these," said Natásha.

"You can't, Miss, we have tried to," said the butler's assistant.

"No, wait a minute, please."

And Natásha began rapidly taking out of the case dishes and plates wrapped in paper.

"The dishes must go in here among the carpets," said she.

"Why, it's a mercy if we can get the carpets alone into three cases," said the butler's assistant.

"Oh, wait, please!" And Natásha began rapidly and deftly sorting out the things. "These aren't needed," said she, putting aside some plates of Kiev ware. "These—yes, these must go among the carpets," she said, referring to the Saxony china dishes.

"Don't, Natásha! Leave it alone! We'll get it all packed," urged Sónya reproachfully.

"What a young lady she is!" remarked the major-domo.

But Natásha would not give in. She turned everything out and began quickly repacking, deciding that the inferior Russian carpets and unnecessary crockery should not be taken at all. When everything had been taken out of the cases, they recommenced packing, and it turned out that when the cheaper things not worth taking had nearly all been rejected, the valuable ones really did all go into the two cases. Only the lid of the case containing the carpets would not shut down. A few more things might have been taken out, but Natásha insisted on having her own way. She packed, repacked, pressed, made the butler's assistant and Pétya—whom she had drawn into the business of packing—press on the lid, and made desperate efforts herself.

"That's enough, Natásha," said Sónya. "I see you were right, but just take out the top one."

"I won't!" cried Natásha, with one hand holding back the hair that hung over her perspiring face, while with the other she pressed down the carpets. "Now press, Pétya! Press, Vasílich, press hard!" she cried.

The carpets yielded and the lid closed; Natásha, clapping her hands, screamed with delight and tears fell from her eyes. But this only lasted a moment. She at once set to work afresh and they now trusted her completely. The count was not angry even when they told him that Natásha had countermanded an order of his, and the servants now came to her to ask whether a cart was sufficiently loaded, and whether it might be corded up. Thanks to Natásha's directions the work now went on expeditiously, unnecessary things were left, and the most valuable packed as compactly as possible.

But hard as they all worked till quite late that night, they could not get everything packed. The countess had fallen asleep and the count, having put off their departure till next morning, went to bed.

Sónya and Natásha slept in the sitting room without undressing.

That night another wounded man was driven down the Povarskáya, and Mávra Kuzmínichna, who was standing at the gate, had him brought into the Rostóvs' yard. Mávra Kuzmínichna concluded that he was a very important man. He was being conveyed in a calèche with a raised hood, and was quite covered by an apron. On the box beside the driver sat a venerable old attendant. A doctor and two soldiers followed the carriage in a cart.

"Please come in here. The masters are going away and the whole house will be empty," said the old woman to the old attendant.

"Well, perhaps," said he with a sigh. "We don't expect to get him home alive! We have a house of our own in Moscow, but it's a long way from here, and there's nobody living in it."

"Do us the honor to come in, there's plenty of everything in the master's house. Come in," said Mávra Kuzmínichna. "Is he very ill?" she asked.

The attendant made a hopeless gesture.

"We don't expect to get him home! We must ask the doctor."

And the old servant got down from the box and went up to the cart.

"All right!" said the doctor.

The old servant returned to the calèche, looked into it, shook his head disconsolately, told the driver to turn into the yard, and stopped beside Mávra Kuzmínichna.

"O, Lord Jesus Christ!" she murmured.

She invited them to take the wounded man into the house.

"The masters won't object . . ." she said.

But they had to avoid carrying the man upstairs, and so they took him into the wing and put him in the room that had been Madame Schoss's.

This wounded man was Prince Andrew Bolkónski.

Chapter XV

MOSCOW'S LAST DAY HAD COME. IT WAS A CLEAR BRIGHT AUTUMN DAY, A SUNDAY. THE CHURCH bells everywhere were ringing for service, just as usual on Sundays. Nobody seemed yet to realize what awaited the city.

Only two things indicated the social condition of Moscow—the rabble, that is the poor people, and the price of commodities. An enormous crowd of factory-hands, house serfs and peasants, with whom some officials, seminarists and gentry were mingled, had gone early that morning to the Three Hills. Having waited there for Rostopchín who did not turn up, they became convinced that Moscow would be surrendered, and then dispersed all about the town to the public houses and cookshops. Prices too that day indicated the state of affairs. The price of weapons, of gold, of carts and horses, kept rising, but the value of paper money and city articles kept falling, so that by midday there were instances of carters removing valuable goods, such as cloth, and receiving in payment a half of what they carted, while peasant horses were fetching five hundred rubles each, and furniture, mirrors and bronzes were being given away for nothing.

In the Rostóvs' staid old-fashioned house the dissolution of former conditions of life was but little noticeable. As to the serfs the only indication was that three out of their huge retinue disappeared during the night, but nothing was stolen; and as to the value of their possessions, the thirty peasant carts that had come in from their estates and which many people envied, proved to be extremely valuable and they were offered enormous sums of money for them. Not only were huge sums offered for the horses and carts, but on the previous evening and early in the morning of the 1st of September, orderlies and servants sent by wounded officers came to the Rostóvs' yard, and wounded men dragged themselves there from the Rostóvs' and from neighboring houses where they were accommodated, entreating the servants to try to get them a lift out of Moscow. The major-domo to whom these entreaties were addressed, though he was sorry for the wounded, resolutely refused, saying that he dare not even mention the matter to the count. Pity these wounded men as one might, it was evident that if they were given one cart there would be no reason to refuse another, or all the carts and one's own carriages as well. Thirty carts could not save all the wounded and in the general catastrophe one could not disregard oneself and one's own family. So thought the major-domo on his master's behalf.

On waking up that morning Count Ilyá Rostóv left his bedroom softly, so as not to wake the countess who had fallen asleep only toward morning, and came out to the porch in his lilac silk dressing-gown. In the yard stood the carts ready corded. The carriages were at the front porch. The major-domo stood at the porch talking to an elderly orderly and to a pale young officer with a bandaged arm. On seeing the count the major-domo made a significant and stern gesture to them both to go away.

"Well, Vasílich, is everything ready?" asked the count, and stroking his bald head he looked good-naturedly at the officer and the orderly and nodded to them. (He liked to see new faces.)

"We can harness at once, your excellency."

"Well, that's right. As soon as the countess wakes we'll be off, God willing! What is it, gentlemen?" he added, turning to the officer. "Are you staying in my house?"

The officer came nearer and suddenly his face flushed crimson.

"Count, be so good as to allow me . . . for God's sake, to get into some corner of one of your carts! I have nothing here with me. . . . I shall be all right on a loaded cart. . . ."

Before the officer had finished speaking the orderly made the same request on behalf of his master.

"Oh yes, yes, yes!" said the count hastily. "I shall be very pleased, very pleased. Vasílich, you'll see to it. Just unload one or two carts. Well, what of it . . . do what's necessary . . ." said the count, muttering some indefinite order.

But at the same moment an expression of warm gratitude on the officer's face had already sealed the order. The count looked around him. In the yard, at the gates, at the window of the wings, wounded officers and their orderlies were to be seen. They were all looking at the count and moving toward the porch.

"Please step into the gallery, your excellency," said the major-domo. "What are your orders about the pictures?"

The count went into the house with him, repeating his order not to refuse the wounded who asked for a lift.

"Well, never mind, some of the things can be unloaded," he added in a soft, confidential voice, as though afraid of being overheard.

At nine o'clock the countess woke up, and Matrëna Timoféevna who had been her lady's maid before her marriage and now performed a sort of chief gendarme's duty for her, came to say that Madame Schoss was much offended and the young ladies' summer dresses could not be left behind. On inquiry, the countess learned that Madame Schoss was offended because her trunk had been taken down from its cart, and all the loads were being uncorded and the luggage taken out of the carts to make room for wounded men whom the count in the simplicity of his heart had ordered that they should take with them. The countess sent for her husband.

"What is this, my dear? I hear that the luggage is being unloaded."

"You know, love, I wanted to tell you . . . Countess dear . . . an officer came to me to ask for a few carts for the wounded. After all, ours are things that can be bought but think what being left behind means to them! . . . Really now, in our own yard—we asked them in ourselves and there are officers among them. . . . You know, I think, my dear . . . let them be taken . . . where's the hurry?"

The count spoke timidly, as he always did when talking of money matters. The countess was accustomed to this tone as a precursor of news of something detrimental to the children's interests, such as the building of a new gallery or conservatory, the inauguration of a private theater or an orchestra. She was accustomed always to oppose anything announced in that timid tone, and considered it her duty to do so.

She assumed her dolefully submissive manner and said to her husband:

"Listen to me, count, you have managed matters so that we are getting nothing for the house, and now you wish to throw away all our—all the *children's* property! You said yourself that we have a hundred thousand rubles' worth of things in the house. I don't consent, my dear, I don't! Do as you please! It's the government's business to look after the wounded; they know that. Look at the Lopukhíns opposite, they cleared out everything two days ago. That's what other people do. It's only we who are such fools. If you have no pity on me, have some for the children."

Flourishing his arms in despair the count left the room without replying.

"Papa, what are you doing that for?" asked Natásha, who had followed him into her mother's room.

"Nothing! What business is it of yours?" muttered the count angrily.

"But I heard," said Natásha. "Why does Mamma object?"

"What business is it of yours?" cried the count.

Natásha stepped up to the window and pondered.

"Papa! Here's Berg coming to see us," said she, looking out of the window.

Chapter XVI

BERG, THE ROSTÓVS' SON-IN-LAW, WAS ALREADY A COLONEL WEARING THE ORDERS OF VLADÍMIR and Anna, and he still filled the quiet and agreeable post of assistant to the head of the staff of the assistant-commander of the first division of the Second Army.

On the 1st of September he had come to Moscow from the army.

He had nothing to do in Moscow, but he had noticed that everyone in the army was asking for leave to visit Moscow and had something to do there. So he considered it necessary to ask for leave of absence for family and domestic reasons.

Berg drove up to his father-in-law's house in his spruce little trap with a pair of sleek roans, exactly like those of a certain prince. He looked attentively at the carts in the yard and while going up to the porch took out a clean pocket-handkerchief and tied a knot in it.

From the anteroom Berg ran with smooth though impatient steps into the drawing room, where he embraced the count, kissed the hands of Natásha and Sónya, and hastened to inquire after "Mamma's" health.

"Health, at a time like this?" said the count. "Come, tell us the news! Is the army retreating or will there be another battle?"

"God Almighty alone can decide the fate of our Fatherland, Papa," said Berg. "The army is burning with a spirit of heroism and the leaders, so to say, have now assembled in council. No one knows what is coming. But in general I can tell you, Papa, that such a heroic spirit, the truly antique valor of the Russian army, which they—which it" (he corrected himself) "has shown or displayed in the battle of the 26th—there are no words worthy to do it justice! I tell you, Papa" (he smote himself on the breast as a general he had heard speaking had done, but Berg did it a trifle late for he should have struck his breast at the words "Russian army"), "I tell you frankly that we, the commanders, far from having to urge the men on or anything of that kind, could hardly restrain those . . . those . . . yes, those exploits of antique valor," he went on rapidly. "General Barclay de Tolly risked his life everywhere at the head of the troops, I can assure you. Our corps was stationed on a hillside. You can imagine!"

And Berg related all that he remembered of the various tales he had heard those days. Natásha watched him with an intent gaze that confused him, as if she were trying to find in his face the answer to some question.

"Altogether such heroism as was displayed by the Russian warriors cannot be imagined or adequately praised!" said Berg, glancing round at Natásha, and as if anxious to conciliate her, replying to her intent look with a smile. " 'Russia is not in Moscow, she lives in the hearts of her sons!' Isn't it so, Papa?" said he.

Just then the countess came in from the sitting room with a weary and dissatisfied expression. Berg hurriedly jumped up, kissed her hand, asked about her health, and swaying his head from side to side to express sympathy, remained standing beside her.

"Yes, Mamma, I tell you sincerely that these are hard and sad times for every Russian. But why are you so anxious? You have still time to get away. . . ."

"I can't think what the servants are about," said the countess, turning to her husband. "I have just been told that nothing is ready yet. Somebody after all must see to things. One misses Mítenka at such times. There won't be any end to it."

The count was about to say something, but evidently restrained himself. He got up from his chair and went to the door.

At that moment Berg drew out his handkerchief as if to blow his nose, and seeing the knot in it pondered, shaking his head sadly and significantly.

"And I have a great favor to ask of you, Papa," said he.

"Hm . . ." said the count, and stopped.

"I was driving past Yusupov's house just now," said Berg with a laugh, "when the steward, a man I know, ran out and asked me whether I wouldn't buy something. I went in out of curiosity you know, and there is a small chiffonier and a dressing-table. You know how dear Véra wanted a chiffonier like that and how we had a dispute about it." (At the mention of the chiffonier and dressing-table Berg involuntarily changed his tone to one of pleasure at his admirable domestic arrangements.) "And it's such a beauty! It pulls out and has a secret English drawer, you know! And dear Véra has long wanted one. I wish to give her a surprise, you see. I saw so many of those peasant carts in your yard. Please let me have one, I will pay the man well, and . . ."

The count frowned and coughed.

"Ask the countess, I don't give orders."

"If it's inconvenient, please don't," said Berg. "Only I so wanted it, for dear Véra's sake."

"Oh, go to the devil, all of you! To the devil, the devil, the devil . . . !" cried the old count. "My head is in a whirl!"

And he left the room. The countess began to cry.

"Yes, Mamma! Yes, these are very hard times!" said Berg.

Natásha left the room with her father and, as if finding it difficult to reach some decision, first followed him and then ran downstairs.

Pétya was in the porch, engaged in giving out weapons to the servants who were to leave Moscow. The loaded carts were still standing in the yard. Two of them had been uncorded and a wounded officer was climbing into one of them helped by an orderly.

"Do you know what it's about?" Pétya asked Natásha.

She understood that he meant what were their parents quarreling about. She did not answer.

"It's because Papa wanted to give up all the carts to the wounded," said Pétya. "Vasílich told me. I consider . . ."

"I consider," Natásha suddenly almost shouted, turning her angry face to Pétya, "I consider it so horrid, so abominable, so . . . I don't know what. Are we despicable Germans?"

Her throat quivered with convulsive sobs and, afraid of weakening and letting the force of her anger run to waste, she turned and rushed headlong up the stairs.

Berg was sitting beside the countess consoling her with the respectful attention of a relative. The count, pipe in hand, was pacing up and down the room, when Natásha, her face distorted by anger, burst in like a tempest and approached her mother with rapid steps.

"It's horrid! It's abominable!" she screamed. "You can't possibly have ordered it!"

Berg and the countess looked at her, perplexed and frightened. The count stood still at the window and listened.

"Mamma, it's impossible: see what is going on in the yard!" she cried. "They will be left! . . ."

"What's the matter with you? Who are 'they'? What do you want?"

"Why, the wounded! It's impossible, Mamma. It's monstrous! . . . No, Mamma darling, it's not the thing. Please forgive me, darling. . . . Mamma, what does it matter what we take away? Only look what is going on in the yard . . . Mamma! . . . It's impossible!"

The count stood by the window and listened without turning round. Suddenly he sniffed and put his face closer to the window.

The countess glanced at her daughter, saw her face full of shame for her mother, saw her agitation, and understood why her husband did not turn to look at her now, and she glanced round quite disconcerted.

"Oh, do as you like! Am I hindering anyone?" she said, not surrendering at once.

"Mamma, darling, forgive me!"

But the countess pushed her daughter away and went up to her husband.

"My dear, you order what is right. . . . You know I don't understand about it," said she, dropping her eyes shamefacedly.

"The eggs . . . the eggs are teaching the hen . . ." muttered the count through tears of joy, and he embraced his wife who was glad to hide her look of shame on his breast.

"Papa! Mamma! May I see to it? May I? . . ." asked Natásha. "We will still take all the most necessary things."

The count nodded affirmatively, and Natásha, at the rapid pace at which she used to run when playing at tag, ran through the ballroom to the anteroom and downstairs into the yard.

The servants gathered round Natásha, but could not believe the strange order she brought them until the count himself, in his wife's name, confirmed the order to give up all the carts to the wounded and take the trunks to the storerooms. When they understood that order the servants set to work at this new task with pleasure and zeal. It no longer seemed strange to them but on the contrary it seemed the only thing that could be done, just as a quarter of an hour before it had not seemed strange to anyone that the wounded should be left behind and the goods carted away but that had seemed the only thing to do.

The whole household, as if to atone for not having done it sooner, set eagerly to work at the new task of placing the wounded in the carts. The wounded dragged themselves out of their rooms and stood with pale but happy faces round the carts. The news that carts were to be had spread to the neighboring houses, from which wounded men began to come into the Rostóvs' yard. Many of the wounded asked them not to unload the carts but only to let them sit on the top of the things. But the work of unloading, once started, could not be arrested. It seemed not to matter whether all or only half the things were left behind. Cases full of china, bronzes, pictures and mirrors that had been so carefully packed the night before, now lay about the yard, and still they went on searching for and finding possibilities of unloading this or that and letting the wounded have another and yet another cart.

"We can take four more men," said the steward. "They can have my trap, or else what is to become of them?"

"Let them have my wardrobe cart," said the countess. "Dunyásha can go with me in the carriage."

They unloaded the wardrobe cart and sent it to take wounded men from a house two doors off. The whole household, servants included, was bright and animated. Natásha was in a state of rapturous excitement such as she had not known for a long time.

"What could we fasten this onto?" asked the servants, trying to fix a trunk on the narrow footboard behind a carriage. "We must keep at least one cart."

"What's in it?" asked Natásha.

"The count's books."

"Leave it, Vasílich will put it away. It's not wanted."

The phaeton was full of people and there was a doubt as to where Count Peter could sit.

"On the box. You'll sit on the box, won't you, Pétya?" cried Natásha.

Sónya too was busy all this time, but the aim of her efforts was quite different from Natásha's. She was putting away the things that had to be left behind and making a list of them as the countess wished, and she tried to get as much taken away with them as possible.

Chapter XVII

Before two o'clock in the afternoon the Rostóvs' four carriages, packed full and with the horses harnessed, stood at the front door. One by one the carts with the wounded had moved out of the yard.

The calèche in which Prince Andrew was being taken attracted Sónya's attention as it passed the front porch. With the help of a maid she was arranging a seat for the countess in the huge high coach that stood at the entrance.

"Whose calèche is that?" she inquired, leaning out of the carriage window.

"Why, didn't you know, Miss?" replied the maid. "The wounded prince: he spent the night in our house and is going with us."

"But who is it? What's his name?"

"It's our intended that was—Prince Bolkónski himself! They say he is dying," replied the maid with a sigh.

Sónya jumped out of the coach and ran to the countess. The countess, tired out and already dressed in shawl and bonnet for her journey, was pacing up and down the drawing room, waiting for the household to assemble for the usual silent prayer with closed doors before starting. Natásha was not in the room.

"Mamma," said Sónya, "Prince Andrew is here, mortally wounded. He is going with us."

The countess opened her eyes in dismay, and seizing Sónya's arm glanced around.

"Natásha?" she murmured.

At that moment this news had only one significance for both of them. They knew their Natásha, and alarm as to what would happen if she heard this news stifled all sympathy for the man they both liked.

"Natásha does not know yet, but he is going with us," said Sónya.

"You say he is dying?"

Sónya nodded.

The countess put her arms around Sónya and began to cry.

"The ways of God are past finding out!" she thought, feeling that the Almighty Hand, hitherto unseen, was becoming manifest in all that was now taking place.

"Well, Mamma? Everything is ready. What's the matter?" asked Natásha, as with animated face she ran into the room.

"Nothing," answered the countess. "If everything is ready let us start."

And the countess bent over her reticule to hide her agitated face. Sónya embraced Natásha and kissed her.

Natásha looked at her inquiringly.

"What is it? What has happened?"

"Nothing . . . No . . ."

"Is it something very bad for me? What is it?" persisted Natásha with her quick intuition.

Sónya sighed and made no reply. The count, Pétya, Madame Schoss, Mávra Kuzmínichna and Vasílich came into the drawing room, and having closed the doors they all sat down and remained for some moments silently seated without looking at one another.

The count was the first to rise, and with a loud sigh crossed himself before the icon. All the others did the same. Then the count embraced Mávra Kuzmínichna and Vasílich, who were to remain in Moscow, and while they caught at his hand and kissed his shoulder he patted their backs lightly with some vaguely affectionate and comforting words. The countess went into the oratory and there Sónya found her on her knees before the icons that had been left here and there hanging on the wall. (The most precious ones, with which some family tradition was connected, were being taken with them.)

In the porch and in the yard the men whom Pétya had armed with swords and daggers, with trousers tucked inside their high boots and with belts and girdles tightened, were taking leave of those remaining behind.

As is always the case at a departure, much had been forgotten or put in the wrong place, and for a long time two menservants stood one on each side of the open door and the carriage steps waiting to help the countess in, while maids rushed with cushions and bundles from the house to the carriages, the calèche, the phaeton, and back again.

"They always will forget everything!" said the countess. "Don't you know I can't sit like that?"

And Dunyásha, with clenched teeth, without replying but with an aggrieved look on her face, hastily got into the coach to rearrange the seat.

"Oh, those servants!" said the count, swaying his head.

Efím, the old coachman, who was the only one the countess trusted to drive her, sat perched up high on the box and did not so much as glance round at what was going on behind him. From thirty years' experience he knew it would be some time yet before the order, "Be off, in God's name!" would be given him: and he knew that even when it was said he would be stopped once or twice more while they sent back to fetch something that had been forgotten, and even after that he would again be stopped and the countess herself would lean out of the window and beg him for the love of Heaven to drive carefully down the hill. He knew all this and therefore waited calmly for what would happen, with more patience than the horses, especially the near one, the chestnut Falcon, who was pawing the ground and champing his bit. At last all were seated, the carriage steps were folded and pulled up, the door was shut, somebody was sent for a traveling-case, and the countess leaned out and said what she had to say. Then Efím deliberately doffed his hat and began crossing himself. The postilion and all the other servants did the same. "Off, in God's name!" said Efím, putting on his hat. "Start!" The postilion started the horses, the off pole-horse tugged at his collar, the high springs creaked and the body of the coach swayed. The footman sprang onto the box of the moving coach which jolted as it passed out of the yard onto the uneven roadway; the other vehicles jolted in their turn, and the procession of carriages moved up the street. In the carriages, the calèche, and the phaeton, all crossed themselves as they passed the church opposite the house. Those who were to remain in Moscow walked on either side of the vehicles seeing the travelers off.

Rarely had Natásha experienced so joyful a feeling as now, sitting in the carriage beside the countess and gazing at the slowly receding walls of forsaken agitated Moscow. Occasionally she leaned out of the carriage window and looked back and then forward at the long train of wounded in front of them. Almost at the head of the line she could see the raised hood of Prince Andrew's calèche. She did not know who was in it, but each time she looked at the procession her eyes sought that calèche. She knew it was right in front.

In Kúdrino, from the Nikítski, Présnya and Podnovínsk Streets came several other trains of vehicles similar to the Rostóvs', and as they passed along the Sadóvaya Street the carriages and carts formed two rows abreast.

As they were going round the Súkharev water tower Natásha, who was inquisitively and alertly scrutinizing the people driving or walking past, suddenly cried out in joyful surprise:

"Dear me! Mamma, Sónya, look, it's he!"

"Who? Who?"

"Look! Yes, on my word, it's Bezúkhov!" said Natásha, putting her head out of the carriage and staring at a tall, stout man in a coachman's long coat, who from his manner of walking and moving was evidently a gentleman in disguise, and who was passing under the arch of the Súkharev tower accompanied by a small sallow-faced, beardless old man in a frieze coat.

"Yes, it really is Bezúkhov in a coachman's coat, with a queer-looking old boy. Really," said Natásha, "look, look!"

"No, it's not he. How can you talk such nonsense?"

"Mamma," screamed Natásha, "I'll stake my head it's he! I assure you! Stop, stop!" she cried to the coachman.

But the coachman could not stop, for from the Meshchánski Street came more carts and carriages, and the Rostóvs were being shouted at to move on and not block the way.

In fact however, though now much farther off than before, the Rostóvs all saw Pierre—or someone extraordinarily like him—in a coachman's coat, going down the street with head bent and a serious face beside a small, beardless old man who looked like a footman. That old man noticed a face thrust out of the carriage window gazing at them, and respectfully touching Pierre's elbow said something to him and pointed to the carriage. Pierre, evidently engrossed in thought, could not at first understand him. At length when he had understood and looked in the direction the old man indicated, he recognized Natásha, and following his first impulse stepped instantly and rapidly toward the coach. But having taken a dozen steps he seemed to remember something and stopped.

Natásha's face, leaning out of the window beamed with quizzical kindliness.

"Peter Kirílovich, come here! We have recognized you! This is wonderful!" she cried, holding out her hand to him. "What are you doing? Why are you like this?"

Pierre took her outstretched hand and kissed it awkwardly as he walked along beside her while the coach still moved on.

"What is the matter, count?" asked the countess in a surprised and commiserating tone.

"What? What? Why? Don't ask me," said Pierre, and looked round at Natásha whose radiant, happy expression—of which he was conscious without looking at her—filled him with enchantment.

"Are you remaining in Moscow, then?"

Pierre hesitated.

"In Moscow?" he said in a questioning tone. "Yes, in Moscow. Good-bye!"

"Ah, if only I were a man! I'd certainly stay with you. How splendid!" said Natásha. "Mamma, if you'll let me, I'll stay!"

Pierre glanced absently at Natásha and was about to say something, but the countess interrupted him.

"You were at the battle, we heard?"

"Yes, I was," Pierre answered. "There will be another battle tomorrow . . ." he began, but Natásha interrupted him.

"But what is the matter with you, count? You are not like yourself. . . ."

"Oh, don't ask me, don't ask me! I don't know myself. Tomorrow . . . But no! Good-bye, good-bye!" he muttered. "It's an awful time!" and dropping behind the carriage he stepped onto the pavement.

Natásha continued to lean out of the window for a long time, beaming at him with her kindly, slightly quizzical, happy smile.

Chapter XVIII

FOR THE LAST TWO DAYS, EVER SINCE LEAVING HOME, PIERRE HAD BEEN LIVING IN THE EMPTY house of his deceased benefactor, Bazdéev. This is how it happened.

When he woke up on the morning after his return to Moscow and his interview with Count Rostopchín, he could not for some time make out where he was and what was expected of him. When he was informed that among others awaiting him in his reception room there was a Frenchman who had brought a letter from his wife, the Countess Hélène, he felt suddenly overcome by that sense of confusion and hopelessness to which he was apt to succumb. He felt that everything was now at an end, all was in confusion and crumbling to pieces, that nobody was right or wrong, the future held nothing, and there was no escape from this position. Smiling unnaturally and muttering to himself, he first sat down on the sofa in an attitude of despair, then rose, went to the door of the reception room and peeped through the crack, returned flourishing his arms, and took up a book. His major-domo came in a second time to say that the Frenchman who had brought the letter from the countess was very anxious to see him if only for a minute, and that someone from Bazdéev's widow had called to ask Pierre to take charge of her husband's books, as she herself was leaving for the country.

"Oh, yes, in a minute; wait . . . or no! No, of course . . . go and say I will come directly," Pierre replied to the major-domo.

But as soon as the man had left the room Pierre took up his hat which was lying on the table and went out of his study by the other door. There was no one in the passage. He went along the whole length of this passage to the stairs and, frowning and rubbing his forehead with both hands, went down as far as the first landing. The hall-porter was standing at the front door. From the landing where Pierre stood there was a second staircase leading to the back entrance. He went down that staircase and out into the yard. No one had seen him. But there were some carriages waiting, and as soon as Pierre stepped out of the gate the coachmen and the yard-porter noticed him and raised their caps to him. When he felt he was being looked at he behaved like an ostrich which hides its head in a bush in order not to be seen; he hung his head and quickening his pace went down the street.

Of all the affairs awaiting Pierre that day the sorting of Joseph Bazdéev's books and papers appeared to him the most necessary.

He hired the first cab he met and told the driver to go to the Patriarch's Ponds, where the widow Bazdéev's house was.

Continually turning round to look at the rows of loaded carts that were making their way from all sides out of Moscow, and balancing his bulky body so as not to slip out of the ramshackle old vehicle, Pierre, experiencing the joyful feeling of a boy escaping from school, began to talk to his driver.

The man told him that arms were being distributed today at the Kremlin, and that tomorrow everyone would be sent out beyond the Three Hills gates, and a great battle would be fought there.

Having reached the Patriarch's Ponds Pierre found the Bazdéevs' house, where he had not been for a long time past. He went up to the gate. Gerásim, that sallow beardless old man Pierre had seen at Torzhók five years before with Joseph Bazdéev, came out in answer to his knock.

"At home?" asked Pierre.

"Owing to the present state of things Sophia Danílovna has gone to the Torzhók estate with the children, your excellency."

"I will come in all the same, I have to look through the books," said Pierre.

"Be so good as to step in. Makár Alexéevich, the brother of my late master—may the kingdom of heaven be his—has remained here, but he is in a weak state as you know," said the old servant.

Pierre knew that Makár Alexéevich was Joseph Bazdéev's half-brother, and a hard drinker.

"Yes, yes, I know. Let us go in . . ." said Pierre and entered the house.

A tall, bald-headed old man with a red nose, wearing a dressing-gown and with galoshes on his bare feet, stood in the anteroom. On seeing Pierre he muttered something angrily and went away along the passage.

"He was a very clever man but has now grown quite feeble, as your Honor sees," said Gerásim. "Will you step into the study?" Pierre nodded. "As it was sealed up so it has remained, but Sophia Danílovna gave orders that if anyone should come from you they were to have the books."

Pierre went into that gloomy study which he had entered with such trepidation in his benefactor's lifetime. The room, dusty and untouched since the death of Joseph Bazdéev, was now even gloomier.

Gerásim opened one of the shutters and left the room on tiptoe. Pierre went round the study, approached the cupboard in which the manuscripts were kept, and took out what had once been one of the most important, the holy of holies of the Order. This was the authentic Scotch Acts with Bazdéev's notes and explanations. He sat down at the dusty writing-table, and having laid the manuscripts before him, opened them out, closed them, finally pushed them away, and resting his head on his hand sank into meditation.

Gerásim looked cautiously into the study several times and saw Pierre always sitting in the same attitude.

More than two hours passed and Gerásim took the liberty of making a slight noise at the door to attract his attention, but Pierre did not hear him.

"Is the cabman to be discharged, your Honor?"

"Oh yes!" said Pierre, rousing himself and rising hurriedly. "Look here," he added, taking Gerásim by a button of his coat and looking down at the old man with moist, shining and ecstatic eyes, "I say, do you know that there is going to be a battle tomorrow?"

"We heard so," replied the man.

"I beg you not to tell anyone who I am, and to do what I ask you."

"Yes, your excellency," replied Gerásim. "Will you have something to eat?"

"No, but I want something else. I want peasant clothes and a pistol," said Pierre, unexpectedly blushing.

"Yes, your excellency," said Gerásim after thinking for a moment.

All the rest of that day Pierre spent alone in his benefactor's study, and Gerásim heard him pacing restlessly from one corner to another and talking to himself. And he spent the night on a bed made up for him there.

Gerásim, being a servant who in his time had seen many strange things, accepted Pierre's taking up his residence in the house without surprise, and seemed pleased to have someone to wait on. That same evening—without even asking himself what they were wanted for—he procured a coachman's coat and cap for Pierre, and promised to get him the pistol next day. Makár Alexéevich came twice that evening shuffling along in his galoshes as far as the door, and stopped and looked ingratiatingly at Pierre. But as soon as Pierre turned toward him he wrapped his dressing-gown around him with a shamefaced and angry look and hurried away. It was when Pierre (wearing the coachman's coat which Gerásim had procured for him and had disinfected by steam) was on his way with the old man to buy the pistol at the Súkharev market, that he met the Rostóvs.

Chapter XIX

KUTÚZOV'S ORDER TO RETREAT THROUGH MOSCOW TO THE RYAZÁN ROAD WAS ISSUED AT NIGHT on the 1st of September.

The first troops started at once, and during the night they marched slowly and steadily without hurry. At daybreak however, those nearing the town at the Dorogomílov bridge saw ahead of them masses of soldiers crowding and hurrying across the bridge, ascending on the opposite side and blocking the streets and alleys, while endless masses of troops were bearing down on them from behind, and an unreasoning hurry and alarm overcame them. They all rushed forward to the bridge, onto it, and to the fords and the boats. Kutúzov himself had driven round by side streets to the other side of Moscow.

By ten o'clock in the morning of the 2nd of September, only the rearguard remained in the Dorogomílov suburb, where they had ample room. The main army was on the other side of Moscow or beyond it.

At that very time, at ten in the morning of the 2nd of September, Napoleon was standing among his troops on the Poklónny Hill looking at the panorama spread out before him. From the 26th of August to the 2nd of September, that is from the battle of Borodinó to the entry of the French into Moscow, during the whole of that agitating, memorable week, there had been the extraordinary autumn weather that always comes as a surprise, when the sun hangs low and gives more heat than in spring, when everything shines so brightly in the rare clear atmosphere that the eyes smart, when the lungs are strengthened and refreshed by inhaling the aromatic autumn air, when even the nights are warm, and when in those dark warm nights, golden stars startle and delight us continually by falling from the sky.

At ten in the morning of the 2nd of September this weather still held.

The brightness of the morning was magical. Moscow seen from the Poklónny Hill lay spaciously spread out with her river, her gardens and her churches, and she seemed to be living her usual life, her cupolas glittering like stars in the sunlight.

The view of the strange city with its peculiar architecture, such as he had never seen before, filled Napoleon with the rather envious and uneasy curiosity men feel when they see an alien form of life that has no knowledge of them. This city was evidently living with the full force of its own life. By the indefinite signs which, even at a distance, distinguish a living body from a dead one, Napoleon from the Poklónny Hill perceived the throb of life in the town and felt, as it were, the breathing of that great and beautiful body.

Every Russian looking at Moscow feels her to be a mother; every foreigner who sees her, even if ignorant of her significance as the mother city, must feel her feminine character, and Napoleon felt it.

"Cette ville asiatique aux innombrables églises, Moscou la sainte. La voilà donc enfin, cette fameuse ville! Il était temps," said he, and dismounting he ordered a plan of Moscow to be spread out before him, and summoned Lelorgne d'Ideville, the interpreter.

"A town captured by the enemy is like a maid who has lost her honor," thought he (he had said so to Túchkov at Smolénsk). From that point of view he gazed at the Oriental beauty he had not seen before. It seemed strange to him that his long-felt wish, which had seemed unattainable, had at last been realized. In the clear morning light he gazed now at the city and now at the plan, considering its details, and the assurance of possessing it agitated and awed him.

"But could it be otherwise?" he thought. "Here is this capital at my feet. Where is Alexander now, and of what is he thinking? A strange, beautiful and majestic city; and a strange and majestic moment! In what light must I appear to them!" thought he, thinking of his troops. "Here she is, the reward for all those faint-hearted men," he reflected, glancing at those near him and at the troops who were approaching and forming up. "One word from me, one movement of my hand, and that ancient capital of the Tsars would perish. But my clemency is always ready to descend upon the vanquished. I must be magnanimous and truly great. But no, it can't be true that I am in Moscow," he suddenly thought. "Yet here she is lying at my feet, with her golden domes and crosses scintillating and twinkling in the sunshine. But I shall spare her. On the ancient monuments of barbarism and despotism I will inscribe great words of justice and mercy. . . . It is just this which Alexander will feel most painfully, I know him." (It seemed to Napoleon that the chief import of what was taking place lay in the personal struggle between himself and Alexander.) "From the height of the Kremlin—yes, there is the Kremlin, yes—I will give them just laws; I will teach them the meaning of true civilization, I will make generations of boyars remember their conqueror with love. I will tell the deputation that I did not, and do not, desire war, that I have waged war only against the false policy of their court; that I love and respect Alexander and that in Moscow I will accept terms of peace worthy of myself and of my people. I do not wish to utilize the fortunes of war to humiliate an honored monarch. 'Boyars,' I will say to them, 'I do not desire war, I desire the peace and welfare of all my subjects.' However, I know their presence will inspire me, and I shall speak to them as I always do: clearly, impressively and majestically. But can it be true that I am in Moscow? Yes, there she lies."

"Qu'on m'amène les boyars," said he to his suite.

A general with a brilliant suite galloped off at once to fetch the boyars.

Two hours passed. Napoleon had lunched and was again standing in the same place on the Poklónny Hill awaiting the deputation. His speech to the boyars had already taken definite shape in his imagination. That speech was full of dignity and greatness as Napoleon understood it.

He was himself carried away by the tone of magnanimity he intended to adopt toward Moscow. In his imagination he appointed days for assemblies at the palace of the Tsars, at which Russian notables and his own would mingle. He mentally appointed a governor, one who would win the hearts of the people. Having learned that there were many charitable institutions in Moscow he mentally decided that he would shower favors on them all. He thought that, as in Africa he had to put on a burnous and sit in a mosque, so in Moscow he must be beneficent like the Tsars. And in order finally to touch the hearts of the Russians—and being like all Frenchmen unable to imagine anything sentimental without a reference to *ma chère, ma tendre, ma pauvre mère*—he decided that he would place an inscription on all these establishments in large letters: "This establishment is dedicated to my dear mother." Or no, it should be simply: *Maison de ma Mère,* he concluded. "But am I really in Moscow? Yes, here it lies before me, but why is the deputation from the city so long in appearing?" he wondered.

Meanwhile an agitated consultation was being carried on in whispers among his generals and marshals at the rear of his suite. Those sent to fetch the deputation had returned with the news that Moscow was empty, that everyone had left it. The faces of those who were not conferring together were pale and perturbed. They were not alarmed by the fact that Moscow had been abandoned by its inhabitants (grave as that fact seemed), but by the question how to tell the Emperor—without putting him in the terrible position of appearing ridiculous—that he had been awaiting the boyars so long in vain: that there were drunken mobs left in Moscow but no one else. Some said that a deputation of some sort must be scraped together, others disputed that opinion and maintained that the Emperor should first be carefully and skillfully prepared, and then told the truth.

"He will have to be told, all the same," said some gentlemen of the suite. "But, gentlemen . . ."

The position was the more awkward because the Emperor, meditating upon his magnanimous plans, was pacing patiently up and down before the outspread map, occasionally glancing along the road to Moscow from under his lifted hand with a bright and proud smile.

"But it's impossible . . ." declared the gentlemen of the suite, shrugging their shoulders but not venturing to utter the implied word—*le ridicule. . . .*

At last the Emperor, tired of futile expectation, his actor's instinct suggesting to him that the sublime moment having been too long drawn out was beginning to lose its sublimity, gave a sign with his hand. A single report of a signaling-gun followed, and the troops, who were already spread out on different sides of Moscow, moved into the city through Tver, Kalúga and Dorogomílov gates. Faster and faster, vying with one another, they moved at the double or at a trot, vanishing amid the clouds of dust they raised and making the air ring with a deafening roar of mingling shouts.

Drawn on by the movement of his troops Napoleon rode with them as far as the Dorogomílov gate, but there again stopped and, dismounting from his horse, paced for a long time by the Kámmer-Kollézski rampart awaiting the deputation.

Chapter XX

MEANWHILE MOSCOW WAS EMPTY. THERE WERE STILL PEOPLE IN IT, PERHAPS A FIFTIETH PART of its former inhabitants had remained, but it was empty. It was empty in the sense that a dying queenless hive is empty.

In a queenless hive no life is left though to a superficial glance it seems as much alive as other hives.

The bees circle round a queenless hive in the hot beams of the midday sun as gaily as around the living hives; from a distance it smells of honey like the others, and bees fly in and out in the same way. But one has only to observe that hive to realize that there is no longer any life in it. The bees do not fly in the same way, the smell and the sound that meet the beekeeper are not the same. To the beekeeper's tap on the wall of the sick hive, instead of the former instant unanimous humming of tens of thousands of bees with their abdomens threateningly compressed, and producing by the rapid vibration of their wings an aerial living sound, the only reply is a disconnected buzzing from different parts of the deserted hive. From the alighting-board, instead of the former spirituous fragrant smell of honey and venom, and the warm whiffs of crowded life, comes an odor of emptiness and decay mingling with the smell of honey. There are no longer sentinels sounding the alarm with their abdomens raised, and ready to die in defense of the hive. There is no longer the measured quiet sound of throbbing activity, like the sound of boiling water, but diverse discordant sounds of disorder. In and out of the hive long black robber-bees smeared with honey fly timidly and shiftily. They do not sting, but crawl away from danger. Formerly only bees laden with honey flew into the hive, and they flew out empty; now they fly out laden. The beekeeper opens the lower part of the hive and peers in. Instead of black, glossy bees—tamed by toil, clinging to one another's legs and drawing out the wax, with a ceaseless hum of labor—that used to hang in long clusters down to the floor of the hive, drowsy shriveled bees crawl about separately in various directions on the floor and walls of the hive. Instead of a neatly glued floor, swept by the bees with the fanning of their wings, there is a floor littered with bits of wax, excrement, dying bees scarcely moving their legs, and dead ones that have not been cleared away.

The beekeeper opens the upper part of the hive and examines the super. Instead of serried rows of bees sealing up every gap in the combs and keeping the brood warm, he sees the skillful complex structures of the combs, but no longer in their former state of purity. All is neglected and foul. Black robber-bees are swiftly and stealthily prowling about the combs, and the short home-bees, shriveled and listless as if they were old, creep slowly about without trying to hinder the robbers, having lost all motive and all sense of life. Drones, bumble-bees, wasps and butterflies knock awkwardly against the walls of the hive in their flight. Here and there among the cells containing dead brood and honey an angry buzzing can sometimes be heard. Here and there a couple of bees, by force of habit and custom cleaning out the brood cells, with efforts beyond their strength laboriously drag away a dead bee or bumble-bee without knowing why they do it. In another corner two old bees are languidly fighting, or cleaning themselves, or feeding one another, without themselves knowing whether they do it with friendly or hostile intent. In a third place a crowd of bees, crushing one another, attack some victim and fight and smother it, and the victim, enfeebled or killed, drops from above slowly and lightly as a feather, among the heap of corpses. The keeper opens the two center partitions to examine the brood-cells. In place of the former close dark circles formed by thousands of bees sitting back to back and guarding the high mystery of generation, he sees hundreds of dull, listless, and sleepy shells of bees. They have almost all died unawares, sitting in the sanctuary they had guarded and which is now no more. They reek of decay and death. Only a few of them still move, rise, and feebly fly to settle on the enemy's hand, lacking the spirit to die stinging him; the rest are dead and fall as lightly as fish scales. The beekeeper closes the hive, chalks a mark on it, and when he has time tears out its contents and burns it clean.

So in the same way Moscow was empty when Napoleon, weary, uneasy and morose, paced up and down in front of the Kámmer-Kollézski rampart, awaiting what to his mind was a necessary, if but formal, observance of the proprieties—a deputation.

In various corners of Moscow there still remained a few people aimlessly moving about, following their old habits and hardly aware of what they were doing.

When with due circumspection Napoleon was informed that Moscow was empty, he looked angrily at his informant, turned away, and silently continued to walk to and fro.

"My carriage!" he said.

He took his seat beside the aide-de-camp on duty and drove into the suburb. "Moscow deserted!" he said to himself. "What an incredible event!"

He did not drive into the town, but put up at an inn in the Dorogomílov suburb.

The *coup de théâtre* had not come off.

Chapter XXI

THE RUSSIAN TROOPS WERE PASSING THROUGH MOSCOW FROM TWO O'CLOCK AT NIGHT TILL TWO in the afternoon, and bore away with them the wounded and the last of the inhabitants who were leaving.

The greatest crush during the movement of the troops took place at the Stone, Moskvá and Yaúza bridges.

While the troops, dividing into two parts when passing around the Kremlin, were thronging the Moskvá and the Stone bridges, a great many soldiers, taking advantage of the stoppage and congestion, turned back from the bridges and slipped stealthily and silently past the church of Vasíli the Beatified and under the Borovítski gate, back up the hill to the Red Square where some instinct told them they could easily take things not belonging to them. Crowds of the kind seen at cheap sales filled all the passages and alleys of the Bazaar. But there were no dealers with voices of ingratiating affability inviting customers to enter; there were no hawkers, nor the usual motley crowd of female purchasers—but only soldiers, in uniforms and overcoats though without muskets, entering the Bazaar empty-handed and silently making their way out through its passages with bundles. Tradesmen and their assistants (of whom there were but few) moved about among the soldiers quite bewildered. They unlocked their shops and locked them up again, and themselves carried goods away with the help of their assistants. On the square in front of the Bazaar were drummers beating the muster-call. But the roll of the drums did not make the looting soldiers run in the direction of the drum as formerly, but made them, on the contrary, run farther away. Among the soldiers in the shops and passages some men were to be seen in gray coats, with closely-shaven heads. Two officers, one with a scarf over his uniform and mounted on a lean dark-gray horse, the other in an overcoat and on foot, stood at the corner of Ilyínka Street, talking. A third officer galloped up to them.

"The general orders them all to be driven out at once, without fail. This is outrageous! Half the men have dispersed."

"Where are you off to? . . . Where? . . ." he shouted to three infantrymen without muskets who, holding up the skirts of their overcoats, were slipping past him into the Bazaar passage. "Stop, you rascals!"

"But how are you going to stop them?" replied another officer. "There is no getting them together. The army should push on before the rest bolt, that's all!"

"How can one push on? They are stuck there, wedged on the bridge, and don't move. Shouldn't we put a cordon round to prevent the rest from running away?"

"Come, go in there and drive them out!" shouted the senior officer.

The officer in the scarf dismounted, called up a drummer, and went with him into the arcade. Some soldiers started running away in a group. A shopkeeper with red pimples on his cheeks near the nose, and a calm, persistent, calculating expression on his plump face, hurriedly and ostentatiously approached the officer, swinging his arms.

"Your Honor!" said he. "Be so good as to protect us! We won't grudge trifles, you are welcome to anything—we shall be delighted! Pray! . . . I'll fetch a piece of cloth at once for such an honorable gentleman, or even two pieces with pleasure. For we feel how it is; but what's all this—sheer robbery! If you please, could not guards be placed if only to let us close the shop. . . ."

Several shopkeepers crowded round the officer.

"Eh, what twaddle!" said one of them, a thin, stern-looking man. "When one's head is gone one doesn't weep for one's hair! Take what any of you like!" And flourishing his arms energetically he turned sideways to the officer.

"It's all very well for you, Iván Sídorych, to talk," said the first tradesman angrily. "Please step inside, your Honor!"

"Talk indeed!" cried the thin one. "In my three shops here I have a hundred thousand rubles' worth of goods. Can they be saved when the army has gone? Eh, what people! 'Against God's might our hands can't fight.' "

"Come inside, your Honor!" repeated the tradesman, bowing.

The officer stood perplexed and his face showed indecision.

"It's not my business!" he exclaimed, and strode on quickly down one of the passages.

From one open shop came the sound of blows and vituperation, and just as the officer came up to it a man in a gray coat with a shaven head was flung out violently.

This man, bent double, rushed past the tradesman and the officer. The officer pounced on the soldiers who were in the shops, but at that moment fearful screams reached them from the huge crowd on the Moskvá bridge and the officer ran out into the square.

"What is it? What is it?" he asked, but his comrade was already galloping off past Vasíli the Beatified in the direction from which the screams came.

The officer mounted his horse and rode after him. When he reached the bridge he saw two unlimbered guns, the infantry crossing the bridge, several overturned carts, and frightened and laughing faces among the troops. Beside the cannon a cart was standing to which two horses were harnessed. Four borzois with collars were pressing close to the wheels. The cart was loaded high, and at the very top, beside a child's chair with its legs in the air, sat a peasant woman uttering piercing and desperate shrieks. He was told by his fellow-officers that the screams of the crowd and the shrieks of the woman were due to the fact that General Ermólov, coming up to the crowd and learning that soldiers were dispersing among the shops while crowds of civilians blocked the bridge, had ordered two guns to be unlimbered and made a show of firing at the bridge. The crowd, crushing one another, upsetting carts, and shouting and squeezing desperately, had cleared off the bridge and the troops were now moving forward.

Chapter XXII

MEANWHILE, THE CITY ITSELF WAS DESERTED. THERE WAS HARDLY ANYONE IN THE STREETS. The gates and shops were all closed, only here and there round the taverns solitary shouts or drunken songs could be heard. Nobody drove through the streets and footsteps were rarely heard. The Povarskáya was quite still and deserted. The huge courtyard of the Rostóvs' house was littered with wisps of hay and with dung from the horses, and not a soul was to be seen there. In the great drawing room of the house, which had been left with all it contained, were two people. They were the yard-porter Ignát, and the page boy Míshka, Vasílich's grandson who had stayed in Moscow with his grandfather. Míshka had opened the clavichord and was strumming on it with one finger. The yard-porter, his arms akimbo, stood smiling with satisfaction before the large mirror.

"Isn't it fine, eh, Uncle Ignát?" said the boy, suddenly beginning to strike the keyboard with both hands.

"Only fancy!" answered Ignát, surprised at the broadening grin on his face in the mirror.

"Impudence! Impudence!" they heard behind them the voice of Mávra Kuzmínichna who had entered silently. "How he's grinning, the fat mug! Is that what you're here for? Nothing's cleared away down there and Vasílich is worn out. Just you wait a bit!"

Ignát left off smiling, adjusted his belt, and went out of the room with meekly downcast eyes.

"Aunt, I did it gently," said the boy.

"I'll give you something gently, you monkey you!" cried Mávra Kuzmínichna, raising her arm threateningly. "Go and get the samovar to boil for your grandfather."

Mávra Kuzmínichna flicked the dust off the clavichord and closed it, and with a deep sigh left the drawing room and locked its main door.

Going out into the yard she paused to consider where she should go next—to drink tea in the servants' wing with Vasílich, or into the storeroom to put away what still lay about.

She heard the sound of quick footsteps in the quiet street. Someone stopped at the gate, and the latch rattled as someone tried to open it.

Mávra Kuzmínichna went to the gate.

"Who do you want?"

"The count—Count Ilyá Andréevich Rostóv."

"And who are you?"

"An officer, I have to see him," came the reply in a pleasant, well-bred Russian voice.

Mávra Kuzmínichna opened the gate and an officer of eighteen, with the round face of a Rostóv, entered the yard.

"They have gone away, sir. Went away yesterday at vespertime," said Mávra Kuzmínichna cordially.

The young officer standing in the gateway, as if hesitating whether to enter or not, clicked his tongue.

"Ah, how annoying!" he muttered. "I should have come yesterday. . . . Ah, what a pity."

Meanwhile, Mávra Kuzmínichna was attentively and sympathetically examining the familiar Rostóv features of the young man's face, his tattered coat and trodden-down boots.

"What did you want to see the count for?" she asked.

"Oh well . . . it can't be helped!" said he in a tone of vexation and placed his hand on the gate as if to leave.

He again paused in indecision.

"You see," he suddenly said, "I am a kinsman of the count's and he has been very kind to me. As you see" (he glanced with an amused air and good-natured smile at his coat and boots) "my things are worn out and I have no money, so I was going to ask the count . . ."

Mávra Kuzmínichna did not let him finish.

"Just wait a minute, sir. One little moment," said she.

And as soon as the officer let go of the gate-handle she turned, and hurrying away on her old legs went through the backyard to the servants' quarters.

While Mávra Kuzmínichna was running to her room the officer walked about the yard gazing at his worn-out boots with lowered head and a faint smile on his lips. "What a pity I've missed uncle! What a nice old woman! Where has she run off to? And how am I to find the nearest way to overtake my regiment, which must by now be getting near the Rogózhski gate?" thought he. Just then Mávra Kuzmínichna appeared from behind the corner of the house with a frightened yet resolute look, carrying a rolled-up check kerchief in her hand. While still a few steps from the officer she unfolded the kerchief and took out of it a white twenty-five ruble assignat and hastily handed it to him.

"If his excellency had been at home, as a kinsman he would of course . . . but as it is . . ."

Mávra Kuzmínichna grew abashed and confused. The officer did not decline, but took the note quietly and thanked her.

"If the count had been at home . . ." Mávra Kuzmínichna went on apologetically. "Christ be with you, sir! May God preserve you!" said she, bowing as she saw him out.

Swaying his head and smiling as if amused at himself, the officer ran almost at a trot through the deserted streets toward the Yaúza bridge to overtake his regiment.

But Mávra Kuzmínichna stood at the closed gate for some time with moist eyes, pensively swaying her head and feeling an unexpected flow of motherly tenderness and pity for the unknown young officer.

Chapter XXIII

FROM AN UNFINISHED HOUSE ON THE VARVÁRKA, THE GROUND-FLOOR OF WHICH WAS A dramshop, came drunken shouts and songs. On benches round the tables in a dirty little room sat some ten factory-hands. Tipsy and perspiring, with dim eyes and wide-open mouths, they were all laboriously singing some song or other. They were singing discordantly, arduously and with great effort, evidently not because they wished to sing, but because they wanted to show they were drunk and on a spree. One, a tall, fair-haired lad in a clean blue coat, was standing over the others. His face with its fine straight nose would have been handsome had it not been for his thin, compressed, twitching lips and dull, gloomy, fixed eyes. Evidently possessed by some idea, he stood over those who were singing, and solemnly and jerkily flourished above their heads his white arm with the sleeve turned up to the elbow, trying unnaturally to spread out his dirty fingers. The sleeve of his coat kept slipping down and he always carefully rolled it up again with his left hand, as if it were most important that the sinewy white arm he was flourishing should be bare. In the midst of the song cries were heard, and fighting and blows in the passage and porch. The tall lad waved his arm.

"Stop it!" he exclaimed peremptorily. "There's a fight, lads!" And, still rolling up his sleeve, he went out to the porch.

The factory-hands followed him. These men, who under the leadership of the tall lad were drinking in the dramshop that morning, had brought the publican some skins from the factory and for this had had drink served them. The blacksmiths from a neighboring smithy, hearing the sounds of revelry in the tavern and supposing it to have been broken into, wished to force their way in too and a fight in the porch had resulted.

The publican was fighting one of the smiths at the door, and when the workmen came out the smith, wrenching himself free from the tavern-keeper, fell face downward on the pavement.

Another smith tried to enter the doorway, pressing against the publican with his chest.

The lad with the turned-up sleeve gave the smith a blow in the face and cried wildly:

"They're fighting us, lads!"

At that moment the first smith got up and scratching his bruised face to make it bleed, shouted in a tearful voice:

"Police! Murder! . . . They've killed a man, lads!"

"Oh, gracious me, a man beaten to death—killed! . . ." screamed a woman coming out of a gate close by.

A crowd gathered round the bloodstained smith.

"Haven't you robbed people enough—taking their last shirts?" said a voice addressing the publican. "What have you killed a man for, you thief?"

The tall lad, standing in the porch, turned his bleared eyes from the publican to the smith and back again as if considering whom he ought to fight now.

"Murderer!" he shouted suddenly to the publican. "Bind him, lads!"

"I dare say you would like to bind me!" shouted the publican, pushing away the men advancing on him, and snatching his cap from his head he flung it on the ground.

As if this action had some mysterious and menacing significance, the workmen surrounding the publican paused in indecision.

"I know the law very well, mates! I'll take the matter to the captain of police. You think I won't get to him? Robbery is not permitted to anybody nowadays!" shouted the publican, picking up his cap.

"Come along then! Come along then!" the publican and the tall young fellow repeated one after the other, and they moved up the street together.

The bloodstained smith went beside them. The factory-hands and others followed behind, talking and shouting.

At the corner of the Moroséyka, opposite a large house with closed shutters and bearing a bootmaker's signboard, stood a score of thin, worn-out, gloomy-faced bootmakers, wearing overalls and long tattered coats.

"He should pay folks off properly," a thin working man, with frowning brows and a straggly beard, was saying.

"But he's sucked our blood and now he thinks he's quit of us. He's been misleading us all the week and now that he's brought us to this pass he's made off."

On seeing the crowd and the bloodstained man the workman ceased speaking, and with eager curiosity all the bootmakers joined the moving crowd.

"Where are all the folks going?"

"Why, to the police, of course!"

"I say, is it true that we have been beaten?"

"And what did you think? Look what folks are saying."

Questions and answers were heard. The publican, taking advantage of the increased crowd, dropped behind and returned to his tavern.

The tall youth, not noticing the disappearance of his foe, waved his bare arm and went on talking incessantly, attracting general attention to himself. It was around him that the people chiefly crowded, expecting answers from him to the questions that occupied all their minds.

"He must keep order, keep the law, that's what the government is there for. Am I not right, good Christians?" said the tall youth, with a scarcely perceptible smile. "He thinks there's no government! How can one do without government? Or else there would be plenty who'd rob us."

"Why talk nonsense?" rejoined voices in the crowd. "Will they give up Moscow like this? They told you that for fun, and you believed it! Aren't there plenty of troops on the march? Let *him* in, indeed! That's what the government is for. You'd better listen to what people are saying," said some of the mob pointing to the tall youth.

By the wall of China-Town a smaller group of people were gathered round a man in a frieze coat who held a paper in his hand.

"An ukáse, they are reading an ukáse! Reading an ukáse!" cried voices in the crowd, and the people rushed toward the reader.

The man in the frieze coat was reading the broadsheet of August 31st. When the crowd collected round him he seemed confused, but at the demand of the tall lad who had pushed his way up to him, he began in a rather tremulous voice to read the sheet from the beginning.

"Early tomorrow I shall go to his Serene Highness," he read ("*Sirin Highness,*" said the tall fellow with a triumphant smile on his lips and a frown on his brow) "to consult with him to act, and to aid the army to exterminate these scoundrels. We too will take part . . ." the reader went on, and then paused ("Do you see," shouted the youth victoriously, "he's going to clear up the whole affair for you. . . .") "in destroying them, and will send these visitors to the devil. I will come back to dinner, and we'll set to work. We will do, completely do, and undo these scoundrels."

The last words were read out in the midst of complete silence. The tall lad hung his head gloomily. It was evident that no one had understood the last part. In particular, the words "I will come back to dinner," evidently displeased both reader and audience. The people's minds were tuned to a high pitch and this was too simple and needlessly comprehensible—it was what any one of them might have said, and therefore was what an ukáse emanating from the highest authority should not say.

They all stood despondent and silent. The tall youth moved his lips and swayed from side to side.

"We should ask him . . . that's he himself!" . . . "Yes, ask him indeed!" . . . "Why not? He'll explain" . . . voices in the rear of the crowd were suddenly heard saying, and the general attention turned to the police-superintendent's trap which drove into the square attended by two mounted dragoons.

The superintendent of police who had that morning by Count Rostopchín's orders to burn the barges, and had in connection with that matter acquired a large sum of money which was at that moment in his pocket, on seeing a crowd bearing down upon him told his coachman to stop.

"What people are these?" he shouted to the men, who were moving singly and timidly in the direction of his trap.

"What people are these?" he shouted again, receiving no answer.

"Your Honor . . ." replied the shopman in the frieze coat, "your Honor, in accord with the proclamation of his Highest Excellency the count, they desire to serve, not sparing their lives, and it is not any kind of riot, but as his Highest Excellence said . . ."

"The count has not left, he is here, and an order will be issued concerning you," said the superintendent of police. "Go on!" he ordered his coachman.

The crowd halted, pressing around those who had heard what the superintendent had said, and looking at the departing trap.

The superintendent of police turned round at that moment with a scared look, said something to his coachman, and his horses increased their speed.

"It's a fraud, lads! Lead the way to him, himself!" shouted the tall youth. "Don't let him go, lads! Let him answer us! Keep him!" shouted different people, and the people dashed in pursuit of the trap.

Following the superintendent of police and talking loudly the crowd went in the direction of the Lubyánka Street.

"There now, the gentry and merchants have gone away and left us to perish. Do they think we're dogs?" voices in the crowd were heard saying more and more frequently.

Chapter XXIV

On the evening of the 1st of September, after his interview with Kutúzov, Count Rostopchín had returned to Moscow mortified and offended because he had not been invited to attend the council of war, and because Kutúzov had paid no attention to his offer to take part in the defense of the city; amazed also at the novel outlook revealed to him at the camp, which treated the tranquillity of the capital and its patriotic fervor as not merely secondary but quite irrelevant and unimportant matters. Distressed, offended and surprised by all this, Rostopchín had returned to Moscow. After supper he lay down on a sofa without undressing, and was awakened soon after midnight by a courier bringing him a letter from Kutúzov. This letter requested the count to send police officers to guide the troops through the town, as the army was retreating to the Ryazán road beyond Moscow. This was not news to Rostopchín. He had known that Moscow would be abandoned not merely since his interview the previous day with Kutúzov on the Poklónny Hill but ever since the battle of Borodinó, for all the generals who came to Moscow after that battle had said unanimously that it was impossible to fight another battle, and since then the government property had been removed every night, and half the inhabitants had left the city with Rostopchín's own permission. Yet all the same this information astonished and irritated the count, coming as it did in the form of a simple note with an order from Kutúzov, and received at night, breaking in on his beauty sleep.

When later on in his memoirs Count Rostopchín explained his actions at this time, he repeatedly says that he was then actuated by two important considerations: to maintain tranquillity in Moscow and expedite the departure of the inhabitants. If one accepts this twofold aim all Rostopchín's actions appear irreproachable. "Why were the holy relics, the arms, ammunition, gunpowder and stores of corn not removed? Why were thousands of inhabitants deceived into believing that Moscow would not be given up—and thereby ruined?" "To preserve the tranquillity of the city," explains Count Rostopchín. "Why were bundles of useless papers from the government offices, and Leppich's balloon and other articles removed?" "To leave the town empty," explains Count Rostopchín. One need only admit that public tranquillity is in danger and any action finds a justification.

All the horrors of the reign of terror were based only on solicitude for public tranquillity.

On what, then, was Count Rostopchín's fear for the tranquillity of Moscow based in 1812? What reason was there for assuming any probability of an uprising in the city? The inhabitants were leaving it and the retreating troops were filling it. Why should that cause the masses to riot?

Neither in Moscow nor anywhere in Russia did anything resembling an insurrection ever occur when the enemy entered a town. More than ten thousand people were still in Moscow on the 1st and 2nd of September, and except for a mob in the governor's courtyard, assembled there at his bidding, nothing happened. It is obvious that there would have been even less reason to expect a disturbance among the people if after the battle of Borodinó, when the surrender of Moscow became certain or at least probable, Rostopchín instead of exciting the people by distributing arms and broadsheets had taken steps to remove all the holy relics, the gunpowder, munitions and money, and had told the population plainly that the town would be abandoned.

Rostopchín, though he had patriotic sentiments, was a sanguine and impulsive man who had always moved in the highest administrative circles and had no understanding at all of the people he supposed himself to be guiding. Ever since the enemy's entry into Smolénsk he had in imagination been playing the rôle of director of the popular feeling of "the heart of Russia." Not only did it seem to him (as to all administrators) that he controlled the external actions of Moscow's inhabitants, but he also thought he controlled their mental attitude by means of his broadsheets and posters, written in a coarse tone which the people despise in their own class and do not understand from those in authority. Rostopchín was so pleased with the fine rôle of leader of popular feeling, and had grown so used to it, that the necessity of relinquishing that rôle and abandoning Moscow without any heroic display took him unawares and he suddenly felt the ground slip away from under his feet, so that he positively did not know what to do. Though he knew it was coming, he did not till the last moment whole-heartedly believe that Moscow would be abandoned, and did not prepare for it. The inhabitants left against his wishes. If the government offices were removed, this was only done on the demand of officials to whom the count yielded reluctantly. He was absorbed in the rôle he had created for himself. As is often the case with those gifted with an ardent imagination, though he had long known that Moscow would be abandoned he knew it only with his intellect, he did not believe it in his heart and did not adapt himself mentally to this new position of affairs.

All his painstaking and energetic activity (in how far it was useful and had any effect on the people is another question) had been simply directed toward arousing in the masses his own feeling of patriotic hatred of the French.

But when events assumed their true historical character, when expressing hatred for the French in words proved insufficient, when it was not even possible to express that hatred by fighting a battle, when self-confidence was of no avail in relation to the one question before Moscow, when the whole population streamed out of Moscow as one man, abandoning their belongings and proving by that negative action all the depth of their national feeling, then the rôle chosen by Rostopchín suddenly appeared senseless. He unexpectedly felt himself ridiculous, weak and alone, with no ground to stand on.

When, awakened from his sleep, he received that cold, peremptory note from Kutúzov, he felt the more irritated the more he felt himself to blame. All that he had been specially put in charge of, the state property which he should have removed, was still in Moscow and it was no longer possible to take the whole of it away.

"Who is to blame for it? Who has let things come to such a pass?" he ruminated. "Not I, of course. I had everything ready. I had Moscow firmly in hand. And this is what they have let it come to! Villains! Traitors!" he thought, without clearly defining who the villains and traitors were, but feeling it necessary to hate those traitors whoever they might be who were to blame for the false and ridiculous position in which he found himself.

All that night Count Rostopchín issued orders, for which people came to him from all parts of Moscow. Those about him had never seen the count so morose and irritable.

"Your excellency, the Director of the Registrar's Department has sent for instructions. . . . From the Consistory, from the Senate, from the University, from the Foundling Hospital, the Suffragan has sent . . . asking for information. . . . What are your orders about the Fire Brigade? From the governor of the prison . . . from the superintendent of the lunatic asylum . . ." All night long such announcements were continually being received by the count.

To all these inquiries he gave brief and angry replies indicating that orders from him were not now needed, that the whole affair, carefully prepared by him, had now been ruined by somebody, and that that somebody would have to bear the whole responsibility for all that might happen.

"Oh, tell that blockhead," he said in reply to the question from the Registrar's Department, "that he should remain to guard his documents. Now why are you asking silly questions about the Fire Brigade? They have horses, let them be off to Vladímir, and not leave them to the French."

"Your excellency, the superintendent of the lunatic asylum has come: what are your commands?"

"My commands? Let them go away, that's all. . . . And let the lunatics out into the town. When lunatics command our armies God evidently means these other madmen to be free."

In reply to an inquiry about the convicts in the prison, Count Rostopchín shouted angrily at the governor:

"Do you expect me to give you two battalions—which we have not got—for a convoy? Release them, that's all about it!"

"Your excellency, there are some political prisoners, Meshkóv, Vereshchágin . . ."

"Vereshchágin! Hasn't he been hanged yet?" shouted Rostopchín. "Bring him to me!"

Chapter XXV

TOWARD NINE O'CLOCK IN THE MORNING, WHEN THE TROOPS WERE ALREADY MOVING THROUGH Moscow, nobody came to the count any more for instructions. Those who were able to get away were going of their own accord, those who remained behind decided for themselves what they must do.

The count ordered his carriage that he might drive to Sokólniki, and sat in his study with folded hands, morose, sallow and taciturn.

In quiet and untroubled times it seems to every administrator that it is only by his efforts that the whole population under his rule is kept going, and in this consciousness of being indispensable every administrator finds the chief reward of his labor and efforts. While the sea of history remains calm the ruler-administrator in his frail bark, holding on with a boat-hook to the ship of the people and himself moving, naturally imagines that his efforts move the ship he is holding on to. But as soon as a storm arises and the sea begins to heave and the ship to move, such a delusion is no longer possible. The ship moves independently with its own enormous motion, the boat-hook no longer reaches the moving vessel, and suddenly the administrator, instead of appearing a ruler and a source of power, becomes an insignificant, useless, feeble man.

Rostopchín felt this, and it was this which exasperated him.

The superintendent of police, whom the crowd had stopped, went in to see him at the same time as an adjutant who informed the count that the horses were harnessed. They were both pale, and the superintendent of police after reporting that he had executed the instructions he had received, informed the count that an immense crowd had collected in the courtyard and wished to see him.

Without saying a word Rostopchín rose and walked hastily to his light, luxurious drawing room, went to the balcony door, took hold of the handle, let it go again, and went to the window from which he had a better view of the whole crowd. The tall lad was standing in front, flourishing his arm and saying something with a stern look. The blood stained smith stood beside him with a gloomy face. A drone of voices was audible through the closed window.

"Is my carriage ready?" asked Rostopchín, stepping back from the window.

"It is, your excellency," replied the adjutant.

Rostopchín went again to the balcony door.

"But what do they want?" he asked the superintendent of police.

"Your excellency, they say they have got ready, according to your orders, to go against the French, and they shouted something about treachery. But it is a turbulent crowd, your excellency—I hardly managed to get away from it. Your excellency, I venture to suggest . . ."

"You may go. I don't need you to tell me what to do!" exclaimed Rostopchín angrily.

He stood by the balcony door looking at the crowd.

"This is what they have done with Russia! This is what they have done with me!" thought he, full of an irrepressible fury that welled up within him against the someone to whom what was happening might be attributed. As often happens with passionate people, he was mastered by anger but was still seeking an object on which to vent it. "Here is that mob, the dregs of the people," he thought as he gazed at the crowd: "this rabble they have roused by their folly! They want a victim," he thought as he looked at the tall lad flourishing his arm. And this thought occurred to him just because he himself desired a victim, something on which to vent his rage.

"Is the carriage ready?" he asked again.

"Yes, your excellency. What are your orders about Vereshchágin? He is waiting at the porch," said the adjutant.

"Ah!" exclaimed Rostopchín, as if struck by an unexpected recollection.

And rapidly opening the door he went resolutely out onto the balcony. The talking instantly ceased, hats and caps were doffed and all eyes were raised to the count.

"Good morning, lads!" said the count briskly and loudly. "Thank you for coming. I'll come out to you in a moment, but we must first settle with the villain. We must punish the villain who has caused the ruin of Moscow. Wait for me!"

And the count stepped as briskly back into the room and slammed the door behind him.

A murmur of approbation and satisfaction ran through the crowd. "He'll settle with all the villains, you'll see! And you said the French . . . He'll show you what law is!" the mob were saying as if reproving one another for their lack of confidence.

A few minutes later an officer came hurriedly out of the front door, gave an order, and the dragoons formed up in line. The crowd moved eagerly from the balcony toward the porch. Rostopchín, coming out there with quick angry steps, looked hastily around as if seeking someone.

"Where is he?" he inquired. And as he spoke he saw a young man coming round the corner of the house between two dragoons. He had a long thin neck, and his head, that had been half shaved, was again covered by short hair. This young man was dressed in a threadbare blue cloth coat lined with fox fur, that had once been smart, and dirty hempen convict trousers, over which were pulled his thin, dirty, trodden-down boots. On his thin weak legs were heavy chains which hampered his irresolute movements.

"Ah!" said Rostopchín, hurriedly turning away his eyes from the young man in the fur-lined coat and pointing to the bottom step of the porch. "Put him there."

The young man in his clattering chains stepped clumsily to the spot indicated, holding away with one finger the coat collar which chafed his neck, turned his long neck twice this way and that, sighed, and submissively folded before him his thin hands, unused to work.

For several seconds while the young man was taking his place on the step the silence continued. Only among the back rows of the people, who were all pressing toward the one spot, could sighs, groans, and the shuffling of feet be heard.

While waiting for the young man to take his place on the step Rostopchín stood frowning and rubbing his face with his hand.

"Lads!" said he, with a metallic ring in his voice. "This man, Vereshchágin, is the scoundrel by whose doing Moscow is perishing."

The young man in the fur-lined coat, stooping a little, stood in a submissive attitude, his fingers clasped before him. His emaciated young face, disfigured by the half-shaven head, hung down hopelessly. At the count's first words he raised it slowly and looked up at him as if wishing to say something or at least to meet his eye. But Rostopchín did not look at him. A vein in the young man's long thin neck swelled like a cord and went blue behind the ear, and suddenly his face flushed.

All eyes were fixed on him. He looked at the crowd, and rendered more hopeful by the expression he read on the faces there, he smiled sadly and timidly, and lowering his head shifted his feet on the step.

"He has betrayed his Tsar and his country, he had gone over to Bonaparte. He alone of all the Russians has disgraced the Russian name, he has caused Moscow to perish," said Rostopchín in a sharp, even voice, but suddenly he glanced down at Vereshchágin who continued to stand in the same submissive attitude. As if inflamed by the sight, he raised his arm and addressed the people, almost shouting:

"Deal with him as you think fit! I hand him over to you."

The crowd remained silent and only pressed closer and closer to one another. To keep one another back, to breathe in that stifling atmosphere, to be unable to stir, and to await something unknown, uncomprehended and terrible, was becoming unbearable. Those standing in front, who had seen and heard what had taken place before them, all stood with wide-open eyes and mouths, straining with all their strength, and held back the crowd that was pushing behind them.

"Beat him! . . . Let the traitor perish and not disgrace the Russian name!" shouted Rostopchín. "Cut him down. I command it."

Hearing not so much the words as the angry tone of Rostopchín's voice, the crowd moaned and heaved forward, but again paused.

"Count!" exclaimed the timid yet theatrical voice of Vereshchágin in the midst of the momentary silence that ensued, "Count! One God is above us both. . . ." He lifted his head and again the thick vein in his thin neck filled with blood and the color rapidly came and went in his face.

He did not finish what he wished to say.

"Cut him down! I command it . . ." shouted Rostopchín, suddenly growing pale like Vereshchágin.

"Draw sabers!" cried the dragoon officer, drawing his own.

Another still stronger wave flowed through the crowd and reaching the front ranks carried it swaying to the very steps of the porch. The tall youth, with a stony look on his face, and rigid and uplifted arm, stood beside Vereshchágin.

"Saber him!" the dragoon officer almost whispered.

And one of the soldiers, his face all at once distorted with fury, struck Vereshchágin on the head with the blunt side of his saber.

"Ah!" cried Vereshchágin in meek surprise, looking round with a frightened glance as if not understanding why this was done to him. A similar moan of surprise and horror ran through the crowd. "O Lord!" exclaimed a sorrowful voice.

But after the exclamation of surprise that had escaped from Vereshchágin he uttered a plaintive cry of pain, and that cry was fatal. The barrier of human feeling, strained to the utmost, that had held the crowd in check, suddenly broke. The crime had begun and must now be completed. The plaintive moan of reproach was drowned by the threatening and angry roar of the crowd. Like the seventh and last wave that shatters a ship, that last irresistible wave burst from the rear and reached the front ranks, carrying them off their feet and engulfing them all. The dragoon was about to repeat his blow. Vereshchágin with a cry of horror, covering his head with his hands, rushed toward the crowd. The tall youth, against whom he stumbled, seized his thin neck with his hands and, yelling wildly, fell with him under the feet of the pressing struggling crowd.

Some beat and tore at Vereshchágin, others at the tall youth. And the screams of those that were being trampled on and of those who tried to rescue the tall lad, only increased the fury of the crowd. It was a long time before the dragoons could extricate the bleeding youth, beaten almost to death. And for a long time, despite the feverish haste with which the mob tried to end the work that had been begun, those who were hitting, throttling, and tearing at Vereshchágin were unable to kill him, for the crowd pressed from all sides, swaying as one mass with them in the center and rendering it impossible for them either to kill him or let him go.

"Hit him with an axe, eh! . . . Crushed? . . . Traitor, he sold Christ . . . Still alive . . . tenacious . . . serve him right! Torture serves a thief right. Use the hatchet! . . . What—still alive?"

Only when the victim ceased to struggle and his cries changed to a long-drawn, measured death-rattle, did the crowd around his prostrate, bleeding corpse begin rapidly to change places. Each one came up, glanced at what had been done, and with horror, reproach and astonishment, pushed back again.

"O Lord! The people are like wild beasts! How could he be alive?" voices in the crowd could be heard saying. "Quite a young fellow too . . . must have been a merchant's son. What men! . . . and they say he's not the right one. . . . How not the right one? . . . O Lord! And there's another has been beaten too—they say he's nearly done for. . . . Oh, the people . . . Aren't they afraid of sinning? . . ." said the same mob now, looking with pained distress at the dead body with its long thin half-severed neck and its livid face stained with blood and dust.

A painstaking police officer, considering the presence of a corpse in his excellency's courtyard unseemly, told the dragoons to take it away. Two dragoons took it by its distorted legs and dragged it along the ground. The gory, dust-stained, half-shaven head with its long neck, trailed twisting along the ground. The crowd shrank back from it.

At the moment when Vereshchágin fell and the crowd closed in with savage yells and swayed about him, Rostopchín suddenly turned pale and, instead of going to the back entrance where his carriage awaited him, went with hurried steps and bent head, not knowing where and why, along the passage leading to the rooms on the ground-floor. The count's face was white and he could not control the feverish twitching of his lower jaw.

"This way, your excellency . . . Where are you going? . . . This way, please . . ." said a trembling, frightened voice behind him.

Count Rostopchín was unable to reply and, turning obediently, went in the direction indicated. At the back entrance stood his calèche. The distant roar of the yelling crowd was audible even there. He hastily took his seat and told the coachman to drive him to his country house in Sokólniki.

When they reached the Myasnítski Street and could no longer hear the shouts of the mob, the count began to repent. He remembered with dissatisfaction the agitation and fear he had betrayed before his subordinates. "The mob is terrible—disgusting," he said to himself in French. "They are like wolves whom nothing but flesh can appease." "Count! One God is above us both!"—Vereshchágin's words suddenly recurred to him, and a disagreeable shiver ran down his back. But this was only a momentary feeling and Count Rostopchín smiled disdainfully at himself. "I had other duties," thought he. "The people had to be appeased. Many other victims have perished and are perishing for the public good"—and he began thinking of his social duties to his family and to the city entrusted to him, and of himself—not himself as Theodore Vasílyevich Rostopchín (he fancied that Theodore Vasílyevich Rostopchín was sacrificing himself for the public good) but himself as governor, the representative of authority and of the Tsar. "Had I been simply Theodore Vasílyevich my course of action would have been quite different, but it was my duty to safeguard my life and dignity as commander-in-chief."

Lightly swaying on the flexible springs of his carriage and no longer hearing the terrible sounds of the crowd, Rostopchín grew physically calm and, as always happens, as soon as he became physically tranquil his mind devised reasons why he should be mentally tranquil too. The thought which tranquillized Rostopchín was not a new one. Since the world began and men have killed one another no one has ever committed such a crime against his fellow-man without comforting himself with this same idea. This idea is *le bien public,* the hypothetical welfare of other people.

To a man not swayed by passion that welfare is never certain, but he who commits such a crime always knows just where that welfare lies. And Rostopchín now knew it.

Not only did his reason not reproach him for what he had done, but he even found cause for self-satisfaction in having so successfully contrived to avail himself of a convenient opportunity to punish a criminal and at the same time pacify the mob.

"Vereshchágin was tried and condemned to death," thought Rostopchín (though the Senate had only condemned Vereshchágin to hard labor), "he was a traitor and a spy. I could not let him go unpunished and so I have killed two birds with one stone: to appease the mob I gave them a victim, and at the same time punished a miscreant."

Having reached his country house and begun to give orders about domestic arrangements, the count grew quite tranquil.

Half an hour later he was driving with his fast horses across the Sokólniki field, no longer thinking of what had occurred but considering what was to come. He was driving to the Yaúza bridge where he had heard that Kutúzov was. Count Rostopchín was mentally preparing the angry and stinging reproaches he meant to address to Kutúzov for his deception. He would make that foxy old courtier feel that the responsibility for all the calamities that would follow the abandonment of the city and the ruin of Russia (as Rostopchín regarded it) would fall upon his doting old head. Planning beforehand what he would say to Kutúzov, Rostopchín turned angrily in his calèche and gazed sternly from side to side.

The Sokólniki field was deserted. Only at the end of it, in front of the almshouse and the lunatic asylum, could be seen some people in white, and others like them walking singly across the field shouting and gesticulating.

One of these was running to cross the path of Count Rostopchín's carriage, and the count himself, his coachman and his dragoons, looked with vague horror and curiosity at these released lunatics and especially at the one running toward them.

Swaying from side to side on his long thin legs in his fluttering dressing-gown, this lunatic was running impetuously, his gaze fixed on Rostopchín, shouting something in a hoarse voice and making signs to him to stop. The lunatic's solemn, gloomy face was thin and yellow, with its beard growing in uneven tufts. His black, agate pupils with saffron-yellow whites moved restlessly near the lower eyelids.

"Stop! Pull up, I tell you!" he cried in a piercing voice, and again shouted something breathlessly with emphatic intonations and gestures.

Coming abreast of the calèche he ran beside it.

"Thrice have they slain me, thrice have I risen from the dead. They stoned me, crucified me . . . I shall rise . . . shall rise . . . shall rise. They have torn my body. The kingdom of God will be overthrown . . . Thrice will I overthrow it and thrice re-establish it!" he cried, raising his voice higher and higher.

Count Rostopchín suddenly grew pale as he had done when the crowd closed in on Vereshchágin. He turned away. "Go fas . . . faster!" he cried in a trembling voice to his coachman. The calèche flew over the ground as fast as the horses could draw it, but for a long time Count Rostopchín still heard the insane despairing screams growing fainter in the distance, while his eyes saw nothing but the astonished, frightened, bloodstained face of "the traitor" in the fur-lined coat.

Recent as that mental picture was, Rostopchín already felt that it had cut deep into his heart and drawn blood. Even now he felt clearly that the gory trace of that recollection would not pass with time, but that the terrible memory would, on the contrary, dwell in his heart ever more cruelly and painfully to the end of his life. He seemed still to hear the sound of his own words: "Cut him down! I command it. . . ."

"Why did I utter those words? It was by some accident I said them. . . . I need not have said them," he thought. "And then nothing would have happened." He saw the frightened and then infuriated face of the dragoon who dealt the blow, the look of silent, timid reproach that boy in the fur-lined coat had turned upon him. "But I did not do it for my own sake. I was bound to act that way. . . . The mob, the traitor . . . the public welfare," thought he.

Troops were still crowding at the Yaúza bridge. It was hot. Kutúzov, dejected and frowning, sat on a bench by the bridge toying with his whip in the sand when a calèche dashed up noisily. A man in a general's uniform with plumes in his hat went up to Kutúzov and said something in French. It was Count Rostopchín. He told Kutúzov that he had come because Moscow, the capital, was no more and only the army remained.

"Things would have been different if your Serene Highness had not told me that you would not abandon Moscow without another battle; all this would not have happened," he said.

Kutúzov looked at Rostopchín as if, not grasping what was said to him, he was trying to read something peculiar written at that moment on the face of the man addressing him. Rostopchín grew confused and became silent. Kutúzov slightly shook his head and not taking his penetrating gaze from Rostopchín's face muttered softly:

"No! I shall not give up Moscow without a battle!"

Whether Kutúzov was thinking of something entirely different when he spoke those words, or uttered them purposely, knowing them to be meaningless, at any rate Rostopchín made no reply and hastily left him. And strange to say the Governor of Moscow, the proud Count Rostopchín, took up a Cossack whip and went to the bridge where he began with shouts to drive on the carts that blocked the way.

Chapter XXVI

TOWARD FOUR O'CLOCK IN THE AFTERNOON MURAT'S TROOPS WERE ENTERING MOSCOW. IN front rode a detachment of Wrtemberg hussars, and behind them rode the King of Naples himself accompanied by a numerous suite.

About the middle of the Arbát Street, near the Church of the Miraculous Icon of St. Nicholas, Murat halted to await news from the advanced detachment as to the condition in which they had found the citadel, *le Kremlin*.

Around Murat gathered a group of those who had remained in Moscow. They all stared in timid bewilderment at the strange, long-haired commander dressed up in feathers and gold.

"Is that their Tsar himself? He's not bad!" low voices could be heard saying.

An interpreter rode up to the group.

"Take off your cap . . . your caps!" These words went from one to another in the crowd. The interpreter addressed an old porter and asked if it was far to the Kremlin. The porter, listening in perplexity to the unfamiliar Polish accent and not realizing that the interpreter was speaking Russian, did not understand what was being said to him and slipped behind the others.

Murat approached the interpreter and told him to ask where the Russian army was. One of the Russians understood what was asked and several voices at once began answering the interpreter. A French officer, returning from the advanced detachment, rode up to Murat and reported that the gates of the citadel had been barricaded and that there was probably an ambuscade there.

"Good!" said Murat and, turning to one of the gentlemen in his suite, ordered four light guns to be moved forward to fire at the gates.

The guns emerged at a trot from the column following Murat, and advanced up the Arbát. When they reached the end of the Vozdvízhenka Street they halted and drew in the Square. Several French officers superintended the placing of the guns and looked at the Kremlin through field-glasses.

The bells in the Kremlin were ringing for vespers, and this sound troubled the French. They imagined it to be a call to arms. A few infantrymen ran to the Kutáfyev Gate. Beams and wooden screens had been put there, and two musket shots rang out from under the gate as soon as an officer and men began to run toward it. A general who was standing by the guns shouted some words of command to the officer, and the latter ran back again with his men.

The sound of three more shots came from the gate.

One shot struck a French soldier's foot, and from behind the screens came the strange sound of a few voices shouting. Instantly as at a word of command the expression of cheerful serenity on the faces of the French general, officers and men, changed to one of determined concentrated readiness for strife and suffering. To all of them from the marshal to the least soldier, that place was not the Vozdvízhenka, Mokhaváya or Kutáfyev Street, nor the Tróitsa Gate (places familiar in Moscow), but a new battlefield which would probably prove sanguinary. And all made ready for that battle. The cries from the gates ceased. The guns were advanced, the artillerymen blew the ash off their linstocks, and an officer gave the word "Fire!" This was followed by two whistling sounds of canister-shot, one after another. The shot rattled against the stone of the gate and upon the wooden beams and screens and two wavering clouds of smoke rose over the Square.

A few instants after the echo of the reports resounding over the stone-built Kremlin had died away the French heard a strange sound above their heads. Thousands of crows rose above the walls and circled in the air, cawing and noisily flapping their wings. Together with that sound came a solitary human cry from the gateway and amid the smoke appeared the figure of a bareheaded man in a peasant's coat. He grasped a musket and took aim at the French. "Fire!" repeated the officer once more, and the reports of a musket and of two cannon-shots were heard simultaneously. The gate was again hidden by smoke.

Nothing more stirred behind the screens and the French infantry soldiers and officers advanced to the gate. In the gateway lay three wounded and four dead. Two men in peasant coats ran away at the foot of the wall, toward the Známenka.

"Clear that away!" said the officer, pointing to the beams and the corpses, and the French soldiers, after dispatching the wounded, threw the corpses over the parapet.

Who these men were nobody knew. "Clear that away!" was all that was said of them, and they were thrown over the parapet, and removed later on that they might not stink. Thiers alone dedicates a few eloquent lines to their memory: "These wretches had occupied the sacred citadel, having supplied themselves with guns from the arsenal, and fired" (the wretches) "at the French. Some of them were sabered and the Kremlin was purged of their presence."

Murat was informed that the way had been cleared. The French entered the gates and began pitching their camp in the Senate Square. Out of the windows of the Senate House the soldiers threw chairs into the Square for fuel, and kindled fires there.

Other detachments passed through the Kremlin and encamped along the Moroséyka, the Lubyánka and Pokróvka Streets. Others quartered themselves along the Vozdvízhenka, the Nikólski and the Tverskóy Streets. No masters of the houses being found anywhere, the French were not billeted on the inhabitants as is usual in towns but lived in it as in a camp.

Though tattered, hungry, worn out, and reduced to a third of their original number, the French entered Moscow in good marching order. It was a weary and famished, but still a fighting and menacing army. But it remained an army only until its soldiers had dispersed into their different lodgings. As soon as the men of the various regiments began to disperse among the wealthy and deserted houses, the army was lost forever and there came into being something non-descript, neither citizens nor soldiers but what are known as marauders. When five weeks later these same men left Moscow, they no longer formed an army. They were a mob of marauders, each carrying a quantity of articles which seemed to him valuable or useful. The aim of each man when he left Moscow was no longer, as it had been, to conquer, but merely to keep what he had acquired. Like a monkey which puts its paw into the narrow neck of a jug, and having seized a handful of nuts will not open its fist for fear of losing what it holds, and therefore perishes, the French when they left Moscow had inevitably to perish because they carried their loot with them, yet to abandon what they had stolen was as impossible for them as it is for the monkey to open its paw and let go of its nuts. Ten minutes after each regiment had entered a Moscow district, not a soldier or officer was left. Men in military uniforms and Hessian boots could be seen through the windows laughing and walking through the rooms. In cellars and storerooms similar men were busy among the provisions, and in the yards unlocking or breaking open coach house and stable doors, lighting fires in kitchens and kneading and baking bread with rolled-up sleeves, and cooking; or frightening, amusing or caressing, women and children. There were many such men both in the shops and houses—but there was no army.

Order after order was issued by the French commanders that day forbidding the men to disperse about the town, sternly forbidding any violence to the inhabitants or any looting, and announcing a roll-call for that very evening. But despite all these measures the men, who had till then constituted an army, flowed all over the wealthy, deserted city with its comforts and plentiful supplies. As a hungry herd of cattle keeps well together when crossing a barren field, but gets out of hand and at once disperses uncontrollably as soon as it reaches rich pastures, so did the army disperse all over the wealthy city.

No residents were left in Moscow, and the soldiers—like water percolating through sand—spread irresistibly through the city in all directions from the Kremlin into which they had first marched. The cavalry, on entering a merchant's house that had been abandoned and finding there stabling more than sufficient for their horses, went on, all the same, to the next house which seemed to them better. Many of them appropriated several houses, chalked their names on them, and quarreled and even fought with other companies for them. Before they had had time to secure quarters the soldiers ran out into the streets to see the city, and hearing that everything had been abandoned, rushed to places where valuables were to be had for the taking. The officers followed to check the soldiers, and were involuntarily drawn into doing the same. In Carriage Row carriages had been left in the shops, and generals flocked there to select calèches and coaches for themselves. The few inhabitants who had remained invited commanding officers to their houses, hoping thereby to secure themselves from being plundered. There were masses of wealth and there seemed no end to it. All around the quarters occupied by the French were other regions still unexplored and unoccupied where, they thought, yet greater riches might be found. When water is spilled on dry ground both the dry ground and the water disappear and mud results; and in the same way the entry of the famished army into the rich and deserted city resulted in fires and looting and the destruction of both the army and the wealthy city.

The French attributed the Fire of Moscow *au patriotisme féroce de Rostopchíne*, the Russians to the barbarity of the French. In reality, however, it was not, and could not be, possible to explain the burning of Moscow by making any individual, or any group of people, responsible for it. Moscow was burned because it found itself in a position in which any town built of wood was bound to burn, quite apart from whether it had, or had not, a hundred and thirty inferior fire-engines. Deserted Moscow had to burn as inevitably as a heap of shavings has to burn on which sparks continually fall for several days. A town built of wood where scarcely a day passes without conflagrations when the house-owners are in residence and a police force is present, cannot help burning when its inhabitants have left it and it is occupied by soldiers who smoke pipes, make campfires of the Senate chairs in the Senate Square, and cook themselves meals twice a day. In peacetime it is only necessary to billet troops in the villages of any district and the number of fires in that district immediately increases. How much then must the probability of fire be increased in an abandoned, wooden town where foreign troops are quartered. *"Le patriotisme féroce de Rostopchíne"* and the barbarity of the French were not to blame in the matter. Moscow was set on fire by the soldiers' pipes, kitchens and campfires, and by the carelessness of enemy soldiers occupying houses they did not own. Even if there was any arson (which is very doubtful, for no one had any reason to burn the houses—in any case a troublesome and dangerous thing to do), arson cannot be regarded as the cause, for the same thing would have happened without any incendiarism.

However tempting it might be for the French to blame Rostopchín's ferocity and for Russians to blame the scoundrel Bonaparte, or later on to place an heroic torch in the hands of their own people, it is impossible not to see that there could be no such direct cause of the fire, for Moscow had to burn as every village, factory, or house must burn which is left by its owners and in which strangers are allowed to live and cook their porridge. Moscow was burned by its inhabitants it is true, but by those who had abandoned it and not by those who remained in it. Moscow when occupied by the enemy did not remain intact like Berlin, Vienna, and other towns, simply because its inhabitants abandoned it and did not welcome the French with bread and salt, nor bring them the keys of the city.

Chapter XXVII

THE ABSORPTION OF THE FRENCH BY MOSCOW, RADIATING STAR-WISE AS IT DID, ONLY REACHED the quarter where Pierre was staying by the evening of the 2nd of September.

After the last two days spent in solitude and unusual circumstances, Pierre was in a state bordering on insanity. He was completely obsessed by one persistent thought. He did not know how or when this thought had taken such possession of him, but he remembered nothing of the past, understood nothing of the present, and all he saw and heard appeared to him like a dream.

He had left home only to escape the intricate tangle of life's demands that enmeshed him, and which in his present condition he was unable to unravel. He had gone to Joseph Alexéevich's house, on the plea of sorting the deceased's books and papers, only in search of rest from life's turmoil, for in his mind the memory of Joseph Alexéevich was connected with a world of eternal, solemn and calm thoughts, quite contrary to the restless confusion into which he felt himself being drawn. He sought a quiet refuge, and in Joseph Alexéevich's study he really found it. When he sat with his elbows on the dusty writing-table in the deathlike stillness of the study, calm and significant memories of the last few days rose one after another in his imagination, particularly of the battle of Borodinó and of that vague sense of his own insignificance and insincerity compared with the truth, simplicity, and strength of the class of men he mentally classed as *they* When Gerásim roused him from his reverie the idea occurred to him of taking part in the popular defense of Moscow which he knew was projected. And with that object he had asked Gerásim to get him a peasant's coat and a pistol, confiding to him his intentions of remaining in Joseph Alexéevich's house and keeping his name secret. Then during the first day spent in inaction and solitude (he tried several times to fix his attention on the masonic manuscripts, but was unable to do so) the idea that had previously occurred to him of the cabalistic significance of his name in connection with Bonaparte's more than once vaguely presented itself. But the idea that he, *L'russe Besuhof,* was destined to set a limit to the power of *the Beast,* was as yet only one of the fancies that often passed through his mind and left no trace behind.

When, having bought the coat merely with the object of taking part among the people in the defense of Moscow, Pierre had met the Rostóvs and Natásha had said to him: "Are you remaining in Moscow? . . . How splendid!" the thought flashed into his mind that it really would be a good thing, even if Moscow were taken, for him to remain there and do what he was predestined to do.

Next day, with the sole idea of not sparing himself and not lagging in any way behind *them*, Pierre went to the Three Hills gate. But when he returned to the house convinced that Moscow would not be defended, he suddenly felt that what before had seemed to him merely a possibility had now become absolutely necessary and inevitable. He must remain in Moscow, concealing his name, and must meet Napoleon and kill him, and either perish or put an end to the misery of all Europe—which it seemed to him was solely due to Napoleon.

Pierre knew all the details of the attempt on Bonaparte's life in 1809 by a German student in Vienna, and knew that the student had been shot. And the risk to which he would expose his life by carrying out his design excited him still more.

Two equally strong feelings drew Pierre irresistibly to this purpose. The first was a feeling of the necessity of sacrifice and suffering in view of the common calamity, the same feeling that had caused him to go to Mozháysk on the 25th and to make his way to the very thick of the battle, and had now caused him to run away from his home and, in place of the luxury and comfort to which he was accustomed, to sleep on a hard sofa without undressing and eat the same food as Gerásim. The other was that vague and quite Russian feeling of contempt for everything conventional, artificial and human—for everything the majority of men regard as the greatest good in the world. Pierre had first experienced this strange and fascinating feeling at the Slobóda Palace, when he had suddenly felt that wealth, power and life—all that men so painstakingly acquire and guard—if it has any worth has so only by reason of the joy with which it can all be renounced.

It was the feeling that induces a volunteer-recruit to spend his last penny on drink, and a drunken man to smash mirrors or glasses for no apparent reason and knowing that it will cost him all the money he possesses: the feeling which causes a man to perform actions which from an ordinary point of view are insane, to test, as it were, his personal power and strength, affirming the existence of a higher, non-human criterion of life.

From the very day Pierre had experienced this feeling for the first time at the Slobóda Palace he had been continuously under its influence, but only now found full satisfaction for it. Moreover, at this moment Pierre was supported in his design and prevented from renouncing it by what he had already done in that direction. If he were now to leave Moscow like everyone else, his flight from home, the peasant coat, the pistol, and his announcement to the Rostóvs that he would remain in Moscow, would all become not merely meaningless but contemptible and ridiculous, and to this Pierre was very sensitive.

Pierre's physical condition, as is always the case, corresponded to his mental state. The unaccustomed coarse food, the vodka he drank during those days, the absence of wine and cigars, his dirty unchanged linen, two almost sleepless nights passed on a short sofa without bedding—all this kept him in a state of excitement bordering on insanity.

It was two o'clock in the afternoon. The French had already entered Moscow. Pierre knew this, but instead of acting he only thought about his undertaking, going over its minutest details in his mind. In his fancy he did not clearly picture to himself either the striking of the blow or the death of Napoleon, but with extraordinary vividness and melancholy enjoyment imagined his own destruction and heroic endurance.

"Yes, alone, for the sake of all, I must do it or perish!" he thought. "Yes, I will approach . . . and then suddenly . . . with pistol or dagger? But that is all the same! 'It is not I but the hand of Providence that punishes thee,' I shall say," thought he, imagining what he would say when killing

Napoleon. "Well then, take me and execute me!" he went on, speaking to himself and bowing his head with a sad but firm expression.

While Pierre, standing in the middle of the room, was talking to himself in this way, the study door opened and on the threshold appeared the figure of Makár Alexéevich, always so timid before but now quite transformed.

His dressing-gown was unfastened, his face red and distorted. He was obviously drunk. On seeing Pierre he grew confused at first, but noticing embarrassment on Pierre's face immediately grew bold and, staggering on his thin legs, advanced into the middle of the room.

"They're frightened," he said confidentially in a hoarse voice. "I say I won't surrender, I say . . . Am I not right, sir?"

He paused and then suddenly seeing the pistol on the table, seized it with unexpected rapidity and ran out into the corridor.

Gerásim and the porter, who had followed Makár Alexéevich, stopped him in the vestibule and tried to take the pistol from him. Pierre, coming out into the corridor, looked with pity and repulsion at the half-crazy old man. Makár Alexéevich, frowning with exertion, held on to the pistol and screamed hoarsely, evidently with some heroic fancy in his head.

"To arms! Board them! No, you shan't get it," he yelled.

"That will do, please, that will do. Have the goodness—please sir, to let go! Please, sir . . ." pleaded Gerásim, trying carefully to steer Makár Alexéevich by the elbows back to the door.

"Who are you? Bonaparte! . . ." shouted Makár Alexéevich.

"That's not right, sir. Come to your room, please, and rest. Allow me to have the pistol."

"Be off, thou base slave! Touch me not! See this?" shouted Makár Alexéevich, brandishing the pistol. "Board them!"

"Catch hold!" whispered Gerásim to the porter.

They seized Makár Alexéevich by the arms and dragged him to the door.

The vestibule was filled with the discordant sounds of a struggle and of a tipsy, hoarse voice.

Suddenly a fresh sound, a piercing feminine scream, reverberated from the porch and the cook came running into the vestibule.

"It's them? Gracious heavens! O Lord, four of them, horsemen!" she cried.

Gerásim and the porter let Makár Alexéevich go, and in the now silent corridor the sound of several hands knocking at the front door could be heard.

Chapter XXVIII

PIERRE, HAVING DECIDED THAT UNTIL HE HAD CARRIED OUT HIS DESIGN HE WOULD DISCLOSE neither his identity nor his knowledge of French, stood at the half-open door of the corridor, intending to conceal himself as soon as the French entered. But the French entered and still Pierre did not retire—an irresistible curiosity kept him there.

There were two of them. One was an officer—a tall, soldierly, handsome man—the other evidently a private or an orderly, sunburned, short, and thin, with sunken cheeks and a dull expression. The officer walked in front, leaning on a stick and slightly limping. When he had advanced a few steps he stopped, having apparently decided that these were good quarters, turned round to the soldiers standing at the entrance and in a loud voice of command ordered them to put up the horses. Having done that, the officer lifting his elbow with a smart gesture stroked his mustache and lightly touched his hat.

"Bonjour, la compagnie!" said he gaily, smiling and looking about him.

No one gave any reply.

"Vous êtes le bourgeois?" the officer asked Gerásim.

Gerásim gazed at the officer with an alarmed and inquiring look.

"Quartier, quartier, logement!" said the officer, looking down at the little man with a condescending and good-natured smile. *"Les Français sont de bons enfants. Que diable! Voyons! Ne nous fâchons pas, mon vieux!"* added he, clapping the scared and silent Gerásim on the shoulder. "Well, does no one speak French in this establishment?" he asked again in French, looking around and meeting Pierre's eyes. Pierre moved away from the door.

Again the officer turned to Gerásim and asked him to show him the rooms in the house.

"Master, not here—don't understand . . . me, you . . ." said Gerásim, trying to render his words more comprehensible by contorting them.

Still smiling, the French officer spread out his hands before Gerásim's nose, intimating that he did not understand him either, and moved, limping, to the door at which Pierre was standing. Pierre wished to go away and conceal himself, but at that moment he saw Makár Alexéevich appearing at the open kitchen door with the pistol in his hand. With a madman's cunning, Makár Alexéevich eyed the Frenchman, raised his pistol, and took aim.

"Board them!" yelled the tipsy man trying to press the trigger. Hearing the yell the officer turned round, and at the same moment, Pierre threw himself on the drunkard. Just when Pierre snatched at and struck up the pistol Makár Alexéevich at last got his fingers on the trigger, there was a deafening report, and all were enveloped in a cloud of smoke. The Frenchman turned pale and rushed to the door.

Forgetting his intention of concealing his knowledge of French, Pierre, snatching away the pistol and throwing it down, ran up to the officer and addressed him in French.

"You are not wounded?" he asked.

"I think not," answered the Frenchman feeling himself over. "But I have had a lucky escape this time," he added, pointing to the damaged plaster of the wall. "Who is that man?" said he, looking sternly at Pierre.

"Oh, I am really in despair at what has occurred," said Pierre rapidly, quite forgetting the part he had intended to play. "He is an unfortunate madman who did not know what he was doing."

The officer went up to Makár Alexéevich and took him by the collar.

Makár Alexéevich was standing with parted lips, swaying, as if about to fall asleep, as he leaned against the wall.

"Brigand! You shall pay for this," said the Frenchman, letting go of him. "We French are merciful after victory, but we do not pardon traitors," he added, with a look of gloomy dignity and a fine energetic gesture.

Pierre continued, in French, to persuade the officer not to hold that drunken imbecile to account. The Frenchman listened in silence with the same gloomy expression, but suddenly turned to Pierre with a smile. For a few seconds he looked at him in silence. His handsome face assumed a melodramatically gentle expression and he held out his hand.

"You have saved my life. You are French," said he.

For a Frenchman that deduction was indubitable. Only a Frenchman could perform a great deed, and to save his life—the life of M. Ramballe, captain of the 13th Light Regiment—was undoubtedly a very great deed.

But however indubitable that conclusion and the officer's conviction based upon it, Pierre felt it necessary to disillusion him.

"I am Russian," he said quickly.

"Tut, tut, tut! Tell that to others," said the officer, waving his finger before his nose and smiling. "You shall tell me all about that presently. I am delighted to meet a compatriot. Well, and what are we to do with this man?" he added, addressing himself to Pierre as to a brother.

Even if Pierre were not a Frenchman, having once received that loftiest of human appellations he could not renounce it, said the officer's look and tone. In reply to his last question Pierre again explained who Makár Alexéevich was, and how just before their arrival that drunken imbecile had seized the loaded pistol which they had not had time to recover from him, and begged the officer to let the deed go unpunished.

The Frenchman expanded his chest and made a majestic gesture with his arm.

"You have saved my life! You are French. You ask his pardon? I grant it you. Lead that man away!" said he quickly and energetically, and taking the arm of Pierre whom he had promoted to be a Frenchman for saving his life, he went with him into the room.

The soldiers in the yard, hearing the shot, came into the passage asking what had happened, and expressed their readiness to punish the culprits, but the officer sternly checked them.

"You will be called in when you are wanted," he said.

The soldiers went out again, and the orderly, who had meanwhile had time to visit the kitchen, came up to his officer.

"Captain, there is soup and a leg of mutton in the kitchen," said he. "Shall I serve them up?"

"Yes, and some wine," answered the captain.

Chapter XXIX

When the French officer went into the room with Pierre the latter again thought it his duty to assure him that he was not French, and wished to go away, but the officer would not hear of it. He was so very polite, amiable, good-natured, and genuinely grateful to Pierre for saving his life, that Pierre had not the heart to refuse, and sat down with him in the parlor—the first room they entered. To Pierre's assurances that he was not a Frenchman, the captain, evidently not understanding how anyone could decline so flattering an appellation, shrugged his shoulders and said that if Pierre absolutely insisted on passing for a Russian let it be so, but for all that he would be forever bound to Pierre by gratitude for saving his life.

Had this man been endowed with the slightest capacity for perceiving the feelings of others, and had he at all understood what Pierre's feelings were, the latter would probably have left him, but the man's animated obtuseness to everything other than himself disarmed Pierre.

"A Frenchman or a Russian prince incognito," said the officer, looking at Pierre's fine though dirty linen and at the ring on his finger. "I owe my life to you and offer you my friendship. A Frenchman never forgets either an insult or a service. I offer you my friendship. That is all I can say."

There was so much good-nature and nobility (in the French sense of the word) in the officer's voice, in the expression of his face and in his gestures, that Pierre unconsciously smiling in response to the Frenchman's smile, pressed the hand held out to him.

"Captain Ramballe, of the 13th Light Regiment, Chevalier of the Legion of Honor for the affair on the 7th of September," he introduced himself, a self-satisfied irrepressible smile puckering his lips under his mustache. "Will you now be so good as to tell me with whom I have the honor of conversing so pleasantly, instead of being in the ambulance with that maniac's bullet in my body?"

Pierre replied that he could not tell him his name and, blushing, began to try to invent a name and to say something about his reason for concealing it, but the Frenchman hastily interrupted him.

"Oh, please!" said he. "I understand your reasons. You are an officer . . . a superior officer perhaps. You have borne arms against us. That's not my business. I owe you my life. That is enough for me. I am quite at your service. You belong to the gentry?" he concluded with a shade of inquiry in his tone. Pierre bent his head. "Your baptismal name, if you please. That is all I ask. Monsieur Pierre, you say. . . . Excellent! That's all I want to know."

When the mutton and an omelette had been served and a samovar and vodka brought, with some wine which the French had taken from a Russian cellar and brought with them, Ramballe invited Pierre to share his dinner, and himself began to eat greedily and quickly like a healthy and hungry man, munching his food rapidly with his strong teeth, continually smacking his lips, and repeating—"Excellent! Delicious!" His face grew red and was covered with perspiration. Pierre was hungry and shared the dinner with pleasure. Morel, the orderly, brought some hot water in a saucepan and placed a bottle of claret in it. He also brought a bottle of kvas, taken from the kitchen for them to try. That beverage was already known to the French and had been given a special name. They called it *limonade de cochon* (pig's lemonade), and Morel spoke well of the *limonade de cochon* he had found in the kitchen. But as the captain had the wine they had taken while passing through Moscow, he left the kvas to Morel and applied himself to the bottle of Bordeaux. He wrapped the bottle up to its neck in a table napkin and poured out wine for himself and for Pierre. The satisfaction of his hunger and the wine rendered the captain still more lively and he chatted incessantly all through dinner.

"Yes, my dear Monsieur Pierre, I owe you a fine votive candle for saving me from that maniac. . . . You see, I have bullets enough in my body already. Here is one I got at Wagram" (he touched his side) "and a second at Smolénsk"—he showed a scar on his cheek—"and this leg which as you see does not want to march, I got that on the 7th at the great battle of la Moskowa. *Sacré Dieu!* It was splendid! That deluge of fire was worth seeing. It was a tough job you set us there, my word! You may be proud of it! And on my honor, in spite of the cough I caught there, I should be ready to begin again. I pity those who did not see it."

"I was there," said Pierre.

"Bah, really? So much the better! You are certainly brave foes. The great redoubt held out well, by my pipe!" continued the Frenchman. "And you made us pay dear for it. I was at it three times—sure as I sit here. Three times we reached the guns and three times we were thrown back like cardboard figures. Oh, it was beautiful, Monsieur Pierre! Your grenadiers were splendid, by heaven! I saw them close up their ranks six times in succession and march as if on parade. Fine fellows! Our King of Naples, who knows what's what, cried 'Bravo!' Ha, ha! So you are one of us soldiers!" he added, smiling, after a momentary pause. "So much the better, so much the better, Monsieur Pierre! Terrible in battle . . . gallant . . . with the fair" (he winked and smiled), "that's what the French are, Monsieur Pierre, aren't they?"

The captain was so naïvely and good-humoredly gay, so real, and so pleased with himself, that Pierre almost winked back as he looked merrily at him. Probably the word "gallant" turned the captain's thoughts to the state of Moscow.

"Apropos, tell me please, is it true that the women have all left Moscow? What a queer idea! What had they to be afraid of?"

"Would not the French ladies leave Paris if the Russians entered it?" asked Pierre.

"Ha, ha, ha!" The Frenchman emitted a merry, sanguine chuckle, patting Pierre on the shoulder. "What a thing to say!" he exclaimed. "Paris? . . . But Paris, Paris . . ."

"Paris—the capital of the world," Pierre finished his remark for him.

The captain looked at Pierre. He had a habit of stopping short in the middle of his talk and gazing intently with his laughing, kindly eyes.

"Well, if you hadn't told me you were Russian, I should have wagered that you were Parisian! You have that . . . I don't know what, that . . ." and having uttered this compliment, he again gazed at him in silence.

"I have been in Paris. I spent years there," said Pierre.

"Oh yes, one sees that plainly. Paris! . . . A man who doesn't know Paris is a savage. You can tell a Parisian two leagues off. Paris is Talma, la Duchénois, Potier, the Sorbonne, the boulevards," and noticing that his conclusion was weaker than what had gone before, he added quickly: "There is only one Paris in the world. You have been to Paris and have remained Russian. Well, I don't esteem you the less for it."

Under the influence of the wine he had drunk, and after the days he had spent alone with his depressing thoughts, Pierre involuntarily enjoyed talking with this cheerful and good-natured man.

"To return to your ladies—I hear they are lovely. What a wretched idea to go and bury themselves in the steppes when the French army is in Moscow. What a chance those girls have missed! Your peasants, now—that's another thing, but you civilized people, you ought to know us better than that. We took Vienna, Berlin, Madrid, Naples, Rome, Warsaw, all the world's capitals. . . . We are feared, but we are loved. We are nice to know. And then the Emperor . . ." he began, but Pierre interrupted him.

"The Emperor," Pierre repeated, and his face suddenly became sad and embarrassed, "Is the Emperor . . . ?"

"The Emperor? He is generosity, mercy, justice, order, genius—that's what the Emperor is! It is I, Ramballe, who tell you so. . . . I assure you I was his enemy eight years ago. My father was an emigrant count. . . . But that man has vanquished me. He has taken hold of me. I could not resist the sight of the grandeur and glory with which he has covered France. When I understood what he wanted—when I saw that he was preparing a bed of laurels for us, you know, I said to myself: 'That is a monarch,' and I devoted myself to him! So there! Oh yes, *mon cher,* he is the greatest man of the ages past or future."

"Is he in Moscow?" Pierre stammered with a guilty look.

The Frenchman looked at his guilty face, and smiled.

"No, he will make his entry tomorrow," he replied, and continued his talk.

Their conversation was interrupted by the cries of several voices at the gate and by Morel, who came to say that some Wrtemberg hussars had come and wanted to put up their horses in the yard where the captain's horses were. This difficulty had arisen chiefly because the hussars did not understand what was said to them in French.

The captain had their senior sergeant called in, and in a stern voice asked him to what regiment he belonged, who was his commanding officer, and by what right he allowed himself to claim quarters that were already occupied. The German who knew little French, answered the two first questions by giving the names of his regiment and of his commanding officer, but in reply to the third question which he did not understand, said, introducing broken French into his own German, that he was the quartermaster of the regiment and his commander had ordered him to occupy all the houses one after another. Pierre, who knew German, translated what the German said to the captain and gave the captain's reply to the Wrtemberg hussar in German. When he had understood what was said to him, the German submitted and took his men elsewhere. The captain went out into the porch and gave some orders in a loud voice.

When he returned to the room Pierre was sitting in the same place as before, with his head in his hands. His face expressed suffering. He really was suffering at that moment. When the captain went out and he was left alone, suddenly he came to himself and realized the position he was in. It was not that Moscow had been taken or that the happy conquerors were masters in it and were patronizing him. Painful as that was it was not that which tormented Pierre at the moment. He was tormented by the consciousness of his own weakness. The few glasses of wine he had drunk and the conversation with this good-natured man had destroyed the mood of concentrated gloom in which he had spent the last few days and which was essential for the execution of his design. The pistol, dagger, and peasant coat were ready. Napoleon was to enter the town next day. Pierre still considered that it would be a useful and worthy action to slay the evil-doer, but now he felt that he would not do it. He did not know why, but he felt a foreboding that he would not carry out his intention. He struggled against the confession of his weakness but dimly felt that he could not overcome it and that his former gloomy frame of mind, concerning vengeance, killing, and self-sacrifice, had been dispersed like dust by contact with the first man he met.

The captain returned to the room, limping slightly and whistling a tune.

The Frenchman's chatter which had previously amused Pierre, now repelled him. The tune he was whistling, his gait, and the gesture with which he twirled his mustache, all now seemed offensive. "I will go away immediately. I won't say another word to him," thought Pierre. He thought this, but still sat in the same place. A strange feeling of weakness tied him to the spot, he wished to get up and go away, but could not do so.

The captain, on the other hand, seemed very cheerful. He paced up and down the room twice. His eyes shone and his mustache twitched as if he were smiling to himself at some amusing thought.

"The colonel of those Wrtembergers is delightful," he suddenly said. "He's a German, but a nice fellow all the same. . . . But he's a German." He sat down facing Pierre. "By the way, you know German, then?"

Pierre looked at him in silence.

"What is the German for 'shelter'?"

"Shelter?" Pierre repeated. "The German for shelter is *Unterkunft*."

"How do you say it?" the captain asked quickly and doubtfully.

"*Unterkunft*," Pierre repeated.

"Onterkoff," said the captain and looked at Pierre for some seconds with laughing eyes. "These Germans are first rate fools, don't you think so, Monsieur Pierre?" he concluded.

"Well, let's have another bottle of this Moscow Bordeaux, shall we? Morel will warm us up another little bottle. Morel!" he called out gaily.

Morel brought candles and a bottle of wine. The captain looked at Pierre by the candlelight and was evidently struck by the troubled expression on his companion's face. Ramballe, with genuine distress and sympathy in his face, went up to Pierre and bent over him.

"There now, we're sad," said he, touching Pierre's hand. "Have I upset you? No, really, have you anything against me?" he asked Pierre. "Perhaps it's the state of affairs?"

Pierre did not answer, but looked cordially into the Frenchman's eyes whose expression of sympathy was pleasing to him.

"Honestly, without speaking of what I owe you, I feel friendship for you. Can I do anything for you? Dispose of me. It is for life and death. I say it with my hand on my heart!" said he, striking his chest.

"Thank you," said Pierre.

The captain gazed intently at him as he had done when he learned that "shelter" was *Unterkunft* in German, and his face suddenly brightened.

"Well, in that case, I drink to our friendship!" he cried gaily, filling two glasses with wine.

Pierre took one of the glasses and emptied it. Ramballe emptied his too, again pressed Pierre's hand, and leaned his elbows on the table in a pensive attitude.

"Yes, my dear friend," he began, "such is fortune's caprice. Who would have said that I should be a soldier and a captain of dragoons in the service of Bonaparte, as we used to call him? Yet here I am in Moscow with him. I must tell you, *mon cher*," he continued in the sad and measured tones of a man who intends to tell a long story, "that our name is one of the most ancient in France."

And with a Frenchman's easy and naïve frankness the captain told Pierre the story of his ancestors, his childhood, youth and manhood, and all about his relations and his financial and family affairs, "*ma pauvre mère*" playing of course an important part in the story.

"But all that is only life's setting, the real thing is love—love! Am I not right, Monsieur Pierre?" said he, growing animated. "Another glass?"

Pierre again emptied his glass and poured himself out a third.

"Oh, women, women!" and the captain, looking with glistening eyes at Pierre, began talking of love and of his love affairs.

There were very many of these, as one could easily believe, looking at the officer's handsome, self-satisfied face, and noting the eager enthusiasm with which he spoke of women. Though all Ramballe's love stories had the sensual character which Frenchmen regard as the special charm and poetry of love, yet he told his story with such sincere conviction that he alone had experienced and known all the charm of love, and he described women so alluringly that Pierre listened to him with curiosity.

It was plain that *l'amour* which the Frenchman was so fond of was not that low and simple kind that Pierre had once felt for his wife, nor was it the romantic love stimulated by himself, that he experienced for Natásha. (Ramballe despised both these kinds of love equally: the one he considered the "love of clod-hoppers" and the other the "love of simpletons.") *L'amour* which the Frenchman worshipped consisted principally in the unnaturalness of his relation to the woman and in a combination of incongruities giving the chief charm to the feeling.

Thus the captain touchingly recounted the story of his love for a fascinating Marquise of thirty-five and at the same time for a charming, innocent child of seventeen, daughter of the bewitching Marquise. The conflict of magnanimity between the mother and the daughter, ending in the mother's sacrificing herself and offering her daughter in marriage to her lover, even now agitated the captain, though it was the memory of a distant past. Then he recounted an episode in which the husband played the part of the lover, and he—the lover—assumed the rôle of the husband, as well as several droll incidents from his recollections of Germany, where "shelter" is called *Unterkunft*, and where the husbands eat sauerkraut and the young girls are "too blonde."

Finally, the latest episode in Poland still fresh in the captain's memory and which he narrated with rapid gestures and glowing face, was of how he had saved the life of a Pole (in general, the saving of life continually occurred in the captain's stories) and the Pole had entrusted to him his enchanting wife (*parisienne de coeur*) while himself entering the French service. The captain was happy, the enchanting Polish lady wished to elope with him, but, prompted by magnanimity, the captain restored the wife to the husband, saying as he did so: "I have saved your life, and I save your honor!" Having repeated these words the captain wiped his eyes and gave himself a shake, as if driving away the weakness which assailed him at this touching recollection.

Listening to the captain's tales, Pierre—as often happens late in the evening and under the influence of wine—followed all that was told him, understood it all, and at the same time followed a train of personal memories which, he knew not why, suddenly arose in his mind. While listening to these love stories his own love for Natásha unexpectedly rose to his mind, and going over the pictures of that love in his imagination he mentally compared them with Ramballe's tales. Listening to the story of the struggle between love and duty, Pierre saw before his eyes every minutest detail of his last meeting with the object of his love at the Súkharev water tower. At the time of that meeting it had not produced an effect upon him—he had not even once recalled it. But now it seemed to him that that meeting had had in it something very important and poetic.

"Peter Kirílovich, come here! We have recognized you," he now seemed to hear the words she had uttered and to see before him her eyes, her smile, her traveling hood, and a stray lock of her hair . . . and there seemed to him something pathetic and touching in all this.

Having finished his tale about the enchanting Polish lady, the captain asked Pierre if he had ever experienced a similar impulse to sacrifice himself for love and a feeling of envy of the legitimate husband.

Challenged by this question Pierre raised his head and felt a need to express the thoughts that filled his mind. He began to explain that he understood love for a woman somewhat differently. He said that in all his life he had loved and still loved only one woman, and that she could never be his.

"*Tiens!*" said the captain.

Pierre then explained that he had loved this woman from his earliest years, but that he had not dared to think of her because she was too young, and because he had been an illegitimate son without a name. Afterward when he had received a name and wealth he dared not think of her because he loved her too well, placing her far above everything in the world, and especially therefore above himself.

When he had reached this point, Pierre asked the captain whether he understood that.

The captain made a gesture signifying that even if he did not understand it he begged Pierre to continue.

"Platónic love, clouds . . ." he muttered.

Whether it was the wine he had drunk, or an impulse of frankness, or the thought that this man did not, and never would, know any of those who played a part in his story, or whether it was all these things together, something loosened Pierre's tongue. Speaking thickly and with a faraway look in his shining eyes, he told the whole story of his life: his marriage, Natásha's love for his best friend, her betrayal of him, and all his own simple relations with her. Urged on by Ramballe's questions he also told what he had at first concealed—his own position and even his name.

More than anything else in Pierre's story the captain was impressed by the fact that Pierre was very rich, had two mansions in Moscow, and that he had abandoned everything and not left the city, but remained there concealing his name and station.

When it was late at night they went out together into the street. The night was warm and light. To the left of the house on the Pokróvka a fire glowed—the first of those that were beginning in Moscow. To the right and high up in the sky, was the sickle of the waning moon and opposite to it hung that bright comet which was connected in Pierre's heart with his love. At the gate stood Gerásim, the cook and two Frenchmen. Their laughter and their mutually incomprehensible remarks in two languages could be heard. They were looking at the glow seen in the town.

There was nothing terrible in the one small, distant fire in the immense city.

Gazing at the high starry sky, at the moon, at the comet, and at the glow from the fire, Pierre experienced a joyful emotion. "There now, how good it is, what more does one need?" thought he. And suddenly remembering his intention he grew dizzy, and felt so faint that he leaned against the fence to save himself from falling.

Without taking leave of his new friend, Pierre left the gate with unsteady steps and returning to his room lay down on the sofa and immediately fell asleep.

Chapter XXX

THE GLOW OF THE FIRST FIRE THAT BEGAN ON THE 2ND OF SEPTEMBER WAS WATCHED FROM THE various roads by the fugitive Muscovites and by the retreating troops, with many different feelings.

The Rostóv party spent the night at Mytíshchi, fourteen miles from Moscow. They had started so late on the 1st of September, the road had been so blocked by vehicles and troops, so many things had been forgotten for which servants were sent back, that they had decided to spend that night at a place three miles out of Moscow. The next morning they woke late and were again delayed so often that they only got as far as Great Mytíshchi. At ten o'clock that evening the Rostóv family and the wounded traveling with them, were all distributed in the yards and huts of that large village. The Rostóvs' servants and coachmen and the orderlies of the wounded officers, after attending to their masters, had supper, fed the horses, and came out into the porches.

In a neighboring hut lay Raévski's adjutant with a fractured wrist. The awful pain he suffered made him moan incessantly and piteously, and his moaning sounded terrible in the darkness of the autumn night. He had spent the first night in the same yard as the Rostóvs. The countess said she had been unable to close her eyes on account of his moaning, and at Mytíshchi she moved into a worse hut simply to be farther away from the wounded man.

In the darkness of the night one of the servants noticed, above the high body of a coach standing before the porch, the small glow of another fire. One glow had long been visible and everybody knew that it was Little Mytíshchi burning—set on fire by Mamónov's Cossacks.

"But look here, brothers, there's another fire!" remarked an orderly.

All turned their attention to the glow.

"But they told us Little Mytíshchi had been set on fire by Mamónov's Cossacks."

"But that's not Mytíshchi, it's farther away."

"Look, it must be in Moscow!"

Two of the gazers went round to the other side of the coach and sat down on its steps.

"It's more to the left, why, Little Mytíshchi is over there, and this is right on the other side."

Several men joined the first two.

"See how it's flaring," said one. "That's a fire in Moscow: either in the Sushchévski or the Rogózhski quarter."

No one replied to this remark and for some time they all gazed silently at the spreading flames of the second fire in the distance.

Old Daniel Teréntich, the count's valet (as he was called), came up to the group and shouted at Míshka.

"What are you staring at, you good-for-nothing? . . . The count will be calling and there's nobody there; go and gather the clothes together."

"I only ran out to get some water," said Míshka.

"But what do you think, Daniel Teréntich? Doesn't it look as if that glow were in Moscow?" remarked one of the footmen.

Daniel Teréntich made no reply, and again for a long time they were all silent. The glow spread, rising and falling, farther and farther still.

"God have mercy. . . . It's windy and dry . . ." said another voice.

"Just look! See what it's doing now. O Lord! You can even see the crows flying. Lord have mercy on us sinners!"

"They'll put it out, no fear!"

"Who's to put it out?" Daniel Teréntich who had hitherto been silent, was heard to say. His voice was calm and deliberate. "Moscow it is, brothers," said he. "Mother Moscow, the white . . ." his voice faltered, and he gave way to an old man's sob.

And it was as if they had all only waited for this to realize the significance for them of the glow they were watching. Sighs were heard, words of prayer and the sobbing of the count's old valet.

Chapter XXXI

THE VALET, RETURNING TO THE COTTAGE, INFORMED THE COUNT THAT MOSCOW WAS BURNING. The count donned his dressing-gown and went out to look. Sónya and Madame Schoss who had not yet undressed, went out with him. Only Natásha and the countess remained in the room. Pétya was no longer with the family, he had gone on with his regiment which was making for Tróitsa.

The countess, on hearing that Moscow was on fire, began to cry. Natásha, pale, with a fixed look, was sitting on the bench under the icons just where she had sat down on arriving and paid no attention to her father's words. She was listening to the ceaseless moaning of the adjutant, three houses off.

"Oh, how terrible," said Sónya, returning from the yard chilled and frightened. "I believe the whole of Moscow will burn, there's an awful glow! Natásha, do look! You can see it from the window," she said to her cousin, evidently wishing to distract her mind.

But Natásha looked at her as if not understanding what was said to her, and again fixed her eyes on the corner of the stove. She had been in this condition of stupor since the morning, when Sónya, to the surprise and annoyance of the countess, had for some unaccountable reason found it necessary to tell Natásha of Prince Andrew's wound and of his being with their party. The countess had seldom been so angry with anyone as she was with Sónya. Sónya had cried and begged to be forgiven and now, as if trying to atone for her fault, paid unceasing attention to her cousin.

"Look, Natásha, how dreadfully it is burning!" said she.

"What's burning?" asked Natásha. "Oh, yes, Moscow."

And as if in order not to offend Sónya and to get rid of her, she turned her face to the window, looked out in such a way that it was evident that she could not see anything, and again settled down in her former attitude.

"But you didn't see it!"

"Yes, really I did," Natásha replied in a voice that pleaded to be left in peace.

Both the countess and Sónya understood that, naturally, neither Moscow nor the burning of Moscow, nor anything else, could seem of importance to Natásha.

The count returned and lay down behind the partition. The countess went up to her daughter and touched her head with the back of her hand as she was wont to do when Natásha was ill, then touched her forehead with her lips as if to feel whether she was feverish, and finally kissed her.

"You are cold. You are trembling all over. You'd better lie down," said the countess.

"Lie down? All right, I will. I'll lie down at once," said Natásha.

When Natásha had been told that morning that Prince Andrew was seriously wounded and was traveling with their party, she had at first asked many questions: Where was he going? How was he wounded? Was it serious? And could she see him? But after she had been told that she could not see him, that he was seriously wounded but that his life was not in danger, she ceased to ask questions or to speak at all, evidently disbelieving what they told her, and convinced that say what she might she would still be told the same. All the way she had sat motionless in a corner of the coach with wide-open eyes, and the expression in them which the countess knew so well and feared so much, and now she sat in the same way on the bench where she had seated herself on arriving. She was planning something, and either deciding or had already decided something in her mind. The countess knew this, but what it might be she did not know, and this alarmed and tormented her.

"Natásha, undress, darling; lie down on my bed."

A bed had been made on a bedstead for the countess only. Madame Schoss and the two girls were to sleep on some hay on the floor.

"No, Mamma, I will lie down here on the floor," Natásha replied irritably and she went to the window and opened it. Through the open window the moans of the adjutant could be heard more distinctly. She put her head out into the damp night air, and the countess saw her slim neck shaking with sobs and throbbing against the window-frame. Natásha knew it was not Prince Andrew who was moaning. She knew Prince Andrew was in the same yard as themselves and in a part of the hut across the passage; but this dreadful incessant moaning made her sob. The countess exchanged a look with Sónya.

"Lie down, darling; lie down, my pet," said the countess, softly touching Natásha's shoulders. "Come, lie down."

"Oh, yes . . . I'll lie down at once," said Natásha, and began hurriedly undressing, tugging at the tapes of her petticoat.

When she had thrown off her dress and put on a dressing-jacket, she sat down with her foot under her on the bed that had been made up on the floor, jerked her thin and rather short plait of hair to the front, and began replaiting it. Her long, thin, practiced fingers rapidly unplaited, replaited, and tied up her plait. Her head moved from side to side from habit, but her eyes, feverishly wide, looked fixedly before her. When her toilet for the night was finished she sank gently onto the sheet spread over the hay on the side nearest the door.

"Natásha, you'd better lie in the middle," said Sónya.

"I'll stay here," muttered Natásha. "Do lie down," she added crossly, and buried her face in the pillow.

The countess, Madame Schoss, and Sónya undressed hastily and lay down. The small lamp in front of the icons was the only light left in the room. But in the yard there was a light from the fire at Little Mytíshchi a mile and a half away, and through the night came the noise of people shouting at a tavern Mamónov's Cossacks had set up across the street, and the adjutant's unceasing moans could still be heard.

For a long time Natásha listened attentively to the sounds that reached her from inside and outside the room and did not move. First she heard her mother praying and sighing and the creaking of her bed under her, then Madame Schoss's familiar whistling snore and Sónya's gentle breathing. Then the countess called to Natásha. Natásha did not answer.

"I think she's asleep, Mamma," said Sónya softly.

After short silence the countess spoke again but this time no one replied.

Soon after that Natásha heard her mother's even breathing. Natásha did not move, though her little bare foot, thrust out from under the quilt, was growing cold on the bare floor.

As if to celebrate a victory over everybody, a cricket chirped in a crack in the wall. A cock crowed far off and another replied nearby. The shouting in the tavern had died down; only the moaning of the adjutant was heard. Natásha sat up.

"Sónya, are you asleep? Mamma?" she whispered.

No one replied. Natásha rose slowly and carefully, crossed herself, and stepped cautiously on the cold and dirty floor with her slim, supple, bare feet. The boards of the floor creaked. Stepping cautiously from one foot to the other she ran like a kitten the few steps to the door and grasped the cold door handle.

It seemed to her that something heavy was beating rhythmically against all the walls of the room: it was her own heart, sinking with alarm and terror and overflowing with love.

She opened the door and stepped across the threshold and onto the cold damp earthen floor of the passage. The cold she felt refreshed her. With her bare feet she touched a sleeping man, stepped over him, and opened the door into the part of the hut where Prince Andrew lay. It was dark in there. In the farthest corner, on a bench beside a bed on which something was lying, stood a tallow candle with a long, thick and smoldering wick.

From the moment she had been told that of Prince Andrew's wound and his presence there, Natásha had resolved to see him. She did not know why she had to, she knew the meeting would be painful, but felt the more convinced that it was necessary.

All day she had lived only in hope of seeing him that night. But now that the moment had come she was filled with dread of what she might see. How was he maimed? What was left of him? Was he like that incessant moaning of the adjutant's? Yes, he was altogether like that. In her imagination he was that terrible moaning personified. When she saw an indistinct shape in the corner, and mistook his knees raised under the quilt for his shoulders, she imagined a horrible body there, and stood still in terror. But an irresistible impulse drew her forward. She cautiously took one step and then another, and found herself in the middle of a small room containing baggage. Another man—Timókhin—was lying in a corner on the benches beneath the icons, and two others—the doctor and a valet—lay on the floor.

The valet sat up and whispered something. Timókhin, kept awake by the pain in his wounded leg, gazed with wide-open eyes at this strange apparition of a girl in a white chemise, dressing-jacket and nightcap. The valet's sleepy, frightened exclamation, "What do you want? What's the matter?" made Natásha approach more swiftly to what was lying in the corner. Horribly unlike a man as that body looked, she must see him. She passed the valet, the snuff fell from the candle wick, and she saw Prince Andrew clearly with his arms outside the quilt, and such as she had always seen him.

He was the same as ever, but the feverish color of his face, his glittering eyes rapturously turned toward her, and especially his neck, delicate as a child's, revealed by the turn-down collar of his shirt, gave him a peculiarly innocent, childlike look, such as she had never seen on him before. She went up to him and with a swift, flexible, youthful movement dropped on her knees.

He smiled and held out his hand to her.

Chapter XXXII

SEVEN DAYS HAD PASSED SINCE PRINCE ANDREW FOUND HIMSELF IN THE AMBULANCE STATION ON the field of Borodinó. His feverish state and the inflammation of his bowels, which were injured, were in the doctor's opinion sure to carry him off. But on the seventh day he ate with pleasure a piece of bread with some tea, and the doctor noticed that his temperature was lower. He had regained consciousness that morning. The first night after they left Moscow had been fairly warm and he had remained in the calèche, but at Mytíshchi the wounded man himself asked to be taken out and given some tea. The pain caused by his removal into the hut had made him groan aloud and again lose consciousness. When he had been placed on his camp-bed he lay for a long time motionless with closed eyes. Then he opened them and whispered softly: "And the tea?" His remembering such a small detail of everyday life astonished the doctor. He felt Prince Andrew's pulse, and to his surprise and dissatisfaction found it had improved. He was dissatisfied because he knew by experience that if his patient did not die now, he would do so a little later with greater suffering. Timókhin, the red-nosed major of Prince Andrew's regiment, had joined him in Moscow and was being taken along with him, having been wounded in the leg at the battle of Borodinó. They were accompanied by a doctor, Prince Andrew's valet, his coachman and two orderlies.

They gave Prince Andrew some tea. He drank it eagerly, looking with feverish eyes at the door in front of him as if trying to understand and remember something.

"I don't want any more. Is Timókhin here?" he asked.

Timókhin crept along the bench to him.

"I am here, your excellency."

"How's your wound?"

"Mine, sir? All right. But how about you?"

Prince Andrew again pondered as if trying to remember something.

"Couldn't one get a book?" he asked.

"What book?"

"The Gospels. I haven't one."

The doctor promised to procure it for him, and began to ask how he was feeling. Prince Andrew answered all his questions reluctantly but reasonably, and then said he wanted a bolster placed under him as he was uncomfortable and in great pain. The doctor and valet lifted the cloak with which he was covered, and making wry faces at the noisome smell of mortifying flesh that came from the wound, began examining that dreadful place. The doctor was very much displeased about something, and made a change in the dressings, turning the wounded man over so that he groaned again and grew unconscious and delirious from the agony. He kept asking them to get him the book and put it under him.

"What trouble would it be to you?" he said. "I have not got one. Please get it for me and put it under me for a moment," he pleaded in a piteous voice.

The doctor went into the passage to wash his hands.

"You fellows have no conscience," said he to the valet who was pouring water over his hands. "For just one moment I didn't look after you . . . It's such pain, you know, that I wonder how he can bear it."

"By the Lord Jesus Christ, I thought we had put something under him!" said the valet.

The first time Prince Andrew understood where he was and what was the matter with him and remembered being wounded and how, was when he asked to be carried into the hut after his calèche had stopped at Mytíshchi. After growing confused from pain while being carried into the hut he again regained consciousness, and while drinking tea once more recalled all that had happened to him, and above all vividly remembered the moment at the ambulance station when, at the sight of the sufferings of a man he disliked, those new thoughts had come to him which promised him happiness. And those thoughts though now vague and indefinite, again possessed his soul. He remembered that he had now a new source of happiness and that this happiness had something to do with the Gospels. That was why he asked for a copy of them. The uncomfortable position in which they had put him and turned him over, again confused his thoughts, and when he came to himself a third time it was in the complete stillness of the night. Everybody near him was sleeping. A cricket chirped from across the passage; someone was shouting and singing in the street; cockroaches rustled on the table, on the icons, and on the walls, and a big fly flopped at the head of the bed and around the candle beside him, the wick of which was charred and had shaped itself like a mushroom.

His mind was not in a normal state. A healthy man usually thinks of, feels, and remembers, innumerable things simultaneously, but has the power and will to select one sequence of thoughts or events on which to fix his whole attention. A healthy man can tear himself away from the deepest reflections to say a civil word to someone who comes in, and can then return again to his own thoughts. But Prince Andrew's mind was not in a normal state in that respect. All the powers of his mind were more active and clearer than ever, but they acted apart from his will. Most diverse thoughts and images occupied him simultaneously. At times his brain suddenly began to work with a vigor, clearness, and depth it had never reached when he was in health, but suddenly in the midst of its work it would turn to some unexpected idea and he had not the strength to turn it back again.

"Yes, a new happiness was revealed to me of which man cannot be deprived," he thought as he lay in the semi-darkness of the quiet hut gazing fixedly before him with feverish, wide-open eyes. "A happiness lying beyond material forces, outside the material influences that act on man—a happiness of the soul alone, the happiness of loving. Every man can understand it, but to conceive it and enjoin it was possible only for God. But how did God enjoin that law? And why was the Son . . . ?"

And suddenly the sequence of these thoughts broke off, and Prince Andrew heard (without knowing whether it was a delusion or reality) a soft whispering voice incessantly and rhythmically repeating "piti-piti-piti," and then "ti-ti," and then again "piti-piti-piti," and "ti-ti" once more. At the same time he felt that above his face, above the very middle of it, some strange airy structure was being erected out of slender needles or splinters, to the sound of this whispered music. He felt that he had to balance carefully (though it was difficult) so that this airy structure should not collapse; but nevertheless it kept collapsing and again slowly rising to the sound of whispered rhythmic music—"it stretches, stretches, spreading out and stretching," said Prince Andrew to himself. While listening to this whispering and feeling the sensation of this drawing out and the construction of this edifice of needles, he also saw by glimpses a red halo round the candle, and heard the rustle of the cockroaches and the buzzing of the fly that flopped against his pillow and his face. Each time the fly touched his face it gave him a burning sensation and yet to his surprise it did not destroy the structure, though it knocked against the very region of his face where it was rising. But besides this there was something else of importance. It was something white by the door—the statue of a sphinx, which also oppressed him.

"But perhaps that's my shirt on the table," he thought, "and that's my legs, and that is the door, but why is it always stretching and drawing itself out, and 'piti-piti-piti' and 'ti-ti' and 'piti-piti-piti' . . . ? That's enough, please leave off!" Prince Andrew painfully entreated someone. And suddenly thoughts and feelings again swam to the surface of his mind with peculiar clearness and force.

"Yes—love," he thought again quite clearly. "But not love which loves for something, for some quality, for some purpose, or for some reason, but the love which I—while dying—first experienced when I saw my enemy and yet loved him. I experienced that feeling of love which is the very essence of the soul and does not require an object. Now again I feel that bliss. To love one's neighbors, to love one's enemies, to love everything, to love God in all His manifestations. It is possible to love someone dear to you with human love, but an enemy can only be loved by divine love. That is why I experienced such joy when I felt that I loved that man. What has become of him? Is he alive? . . .

"When loving with human love one may pass from love to hatred, but divine love cannot change. No, neither death nor anything else can destroy it. It is the very essence of the soul. Yet how many people have I hated in my life? And of them all, I loved and hated none as I did her." And he vividly pictured to himself Natásha, not as he had done in the past with nothing but her charms which gave him delight, but for the first time picturing to himself her soul. And he understood her feelings, her sufferings, shame, and remorse. He now understood for the first time all the cruelty of his rejection of her, the cruelty of his rupture with her. "If only it were possible for me to see her once more! Just once, looking into those eyes to say . . ."

"Piti-piti-piti and ti-ti and piti-piti-piti boom!" flopped the fly. . . . And his attention was suddenly carried into another world, a world of reality and delirium in which something particular was happening. In that world some structure was still being erected and did not fall, something was still stretching out, and the candle with its red halo was still burning, and the same shirtlike sphinx lay near the door; but besides all this something creaked, there was a whiff of fresh air, and a new white sphinx appeared, standing at the door. And that sphinx had the pale face and shining eyes of the very Natásha of whom he had just been thinking.

"Oh, how oppressive this continual delirium is," thought Prince Andrew, trying to drive that face from his imagination. But the face remained before him with the force of reality and drew nearer. Prince Andrew wished to return to that former world of pure thought, but he could not, and delirium drew him back into its domain. The soft whispering voice continued its rhythmic murmur, something oppressed him and stretched out, and the strange face was before him. Prince Andrew collected all his strength in an effort to recover his senses, he moved a little, and suddenly there was a ringing in his ears, a dimness in his eyes, and like a man plunged into water he lost consciousness. When he came to himself, Natásha, that same living Natásha whom of all people he most longed to love with this new pure divine love that had been revealed to him, was kneeling before him. He realized that it was the real living Natásha, and he was not surprised but quietly happy. Natásha, motionless on her knees (she was unable to stir), with frightened eyes riveted on him, was restraining her sobs. Her face was pale and rigid. Only in the lower part of it something quivered.

Prince Andrew sighed with relief, smiled, and held out his hand.

"You?" he said. "How fortunate!"

With a rapid but careful movement Natásha drew nearer to him on her knees, and taking his hand carefully, bent her face over it and began kissing it, just touching it lightly with her lips.

"Forgive me!" she whispered, raising her head and glancing at him. "Forgive me!"

"I love you," said Prince Andrew.

"Forgive . . . !"

"Forgive what?" he asked.

"Forgive me for what I ha-ve do-ne!" faltered Natásha in a scarcely audible, broken whisper, and began kissing his hand more rapidly, just touching it with her lips.

"I love you more, better than before," said Prince Andrew, lifting her face with his hand so as to look into her eyes.

Those eyes, filled with happy tears, gazed at him timidly, compassionately and with joyous love. Natásha's thin pale face, with its swollen lips, was more than plain—it was dreadful. But Prince Andrew did not see that, he saw her shining eyes which were beautiful. They heard the sound of voices behind them.

Peter the valet, who was now wide awake, had roused the doctor. Timókhin, who had not slept at all because of the pain in his leg, had long been watching all that was going on, carefully covering his bare body with the sheet as he huddled up on his bench.

"What's this?" said the doctor, rising from his bed. "Please go away, madam!"

At that moment a maid sent by the countess, who had noticed her daughter's absence, knocked at the door.

Like a somnambulist aroused from her sleep Natásha went out of the room, and returning to her hut fell sobbing on her bed.

From that time, during all the rest of the Rostóvs' journey, at every halting place and wherever they spent a night, Natásha never left the wounded Bolkónski, and the doctor had to admit that he had not expected from a young girl either such firmness, or such skill in nursing a wounded man.

Dreadful as the countess imagined it would be should Prince Andrew die in her daughter's arms during the journey—as, judging by what the doctor said, it seemed might easily happen—she could not oppose Natásha. Though with the intimacy now established between the wounded man and Natásha the thought occurred that should he recover their former engagement would be renewed, no one—least of all Natásha and Prince Andrew—spoke of this: the unsettled question of life and death, which hung not only over Bolkónski but over all Russia, shut out all other considerations.

Chapter XXXIII

On the 3rd of September Pierre awoke late. His head was aching, the clothes in which he had slept without undressing felt uncomfortable on his body, and his mind had a dim consciousness of something shameful he had done the day before. That something shameful was his yesterday's conversation with Captain Ramballe.

It was eleven by the clock, but it seemed peculiarly dark out of doors. Pierre rose, rubbed his eyes, and seeing the pistol with an engraved stock which Gerásim had replaced on the writing-table, he remembered where he was and what lay before him that very day.

"Am I not too late?" he thought. "No, probably *he* won't make his entry into Moscow before noon."

Pierre did not allow himself to reflect on what lay before him, but hastened to act.

After arranging his clothes, he took the pistol and was about to go out. But it then occurred to him for the first time that he certainly could not carry the weapon in his hand through the streets. It was difficult to hide such a big pistol even under his wide coat. He could not carry it unnoticed in his belt, nor under his arm. Besides it had been discharged, and he had not had time to reload it. "No matter, the dagger will do," he said to himself, though when planning his design he had more than once come to the conclusion that the chief mistake made by the student in 1809 had been to try to kill Napoleon with a dagger. But as his chief aim consisted not in carrying out his design, but in proving to himself that he would not abandon his intention and was doing all he could to achieve it, Pierre hastily took the blunt jagged dagger in a green sheath which he had bought at the Súkharev market with the pistol, and hid it under his waistcoat.

Having tied a girdle over his coat and pulled his cap low on his head, Pierre went down the corridor trying to avoid making a noise or meeting the captain, and passed out into the street.

The conflagration, at which he had looked with so much indifference the evening before, had greatly increased during the night. Moscow was on fire in several places. The buildings in Carriage Row, across the river, in the Bazaar and the Povarskóy, as well as the barges on the Moskvá River and the timber yards by the Dorogomílov Bridge, were all ablaze.

Pierre's way led through side streets to the Povarskóy and from there to the church of St. Nicholas on the Arbát, where he had long before decided that the deed should be done. The gates of most of the houses were locked and the shutters up. The streets and lanes were deserted. The air was full of smoke and the smell of burning. Now and then he met Russians with anxious and timid faces, and Frenchmen with an air not of the city but of the camp, walking in the middle of the streets. Both the Russians and the French looked at Pierre with surprise. Besides his height and stoutness, and the strange morose look of suffering in his face and whole figure, the Russians stared at Pierre because they could not make out to what class he could belong. The French followed him with astonishment in their eyes chiefly because Pierre, unlike all the other Russians who gazed at the French with fear and curiosity, paid no attention to them. At the gate of one house three Frenchmen, who were explaining something to some Russians who did not understand them, stopped Pierre asking if he did not know French.

Pierre shook his head and went on. In another side street a sentinel standing beside a green caisson shouted at him, but only when the shout was threateningly repeated and he heard the click of the man's musket as he raised it did Pierre understand that he had to pass on the other side of the street. He heard nothing and saw nothing of what went on around him. He carried his resolution within himself in terror and haste, like something dreadful and alien to him, for, after the previous night's experience, he was afraid of losing it. But he was not destined to bring his mood safely to his destination. And even had he not been hindered by anything on the way, his intention could not now have been carried out, for Napoleon had passed the Arbát more than four hours previously on his way from the Dorogomílov suburb to the Kremlin, and was now sitting in a very gloomy frame of mind in a royal study in the Kremlin, giving detailed and exact orders as to measures to be taken immediately to extinguish the fire, to prevent looting, and to reassure the inhabitants. But Pierre did not know this; he was entirely absorbed in what lay before him, and was tortured—as those are who obstinately undertake a task that is impossible for them not because of its difficulty but because of its incompatibility with their natures—by the fear of weakening at the decisive moment and so losing his self-esteem.

Though he heard and saw nothing around him he found his way by instinct, and did not go wrong in the side streets that led to the Povarskóy.

As Pierre approached that street the smoke became denser and denser—he even felt the heat of the fire. Occasionally curly tongues of flame rose from under the roofs of the houses. He met more people in the streets and they were more excited. But Pierre, though he felt that something unusual was happening around him, did not realize that he was approaching the fire. As he was going along a footpath across a wide-open space adjoining the Povarskóy on one side and the gardens of Prince Gruzínski's house on the other, Pierre suddenly heard the desperate weeping of a woman close to him. He stopped as if awakening from a dream and lifted his head.

By the side of the path, on the dusty dry grass, all sorts of household goods lay in a heap: feather-beds, a samovar, icons and trunks. On the ground, beside the trunks, sat a thin woman no longer young, with long prominent upper teeth, and wearing a black cloak and cap. This woman, swaying to and fro and muttering something, was choking with sobs. Two girls of about ten and twelve, dressed in dirty short frocks and cloaks, were staring at their mother with a look of stupefaction on their pale frightened faces. The youngest child, a boy of about seven, who wore an overcoat and an immense cap evidently not his own, was crying in his old nurse's arms. A dirty, barefooted maid was sitting on a trunk, and having undone her pale-colored plait, was pulling it straight and sniffing at her singed hair. The woman's husband, a short, round-shouldered man in the undress uniform of a civilian official, with sausage-shaped whiskers and showing under his square set cap the hair smoothly brushed forward over his temples, with expressionless face was moving the trunks, which were placed one on another, and was dragging some garments from under them.

As soon as she saw Pierre, the woman almost threw herself at his feet.

"Dear people, good Christians, save me, help me, dear friends . . . help us, somebody," she muttered between her sobs. "My girl . . . My daughter! My youngest daughter is left behind. She's burned! Ooh! Was it for this I nursed you. . . . Ooh!"

"Don't, Mary Nikoláevna!" said her husband to her in a low voice, evidently only to justify himself before the stranger. "Sister must have taken her, or else where can she be?" he added.

"Monster! Villain!" shouted the woman angrily, suddenly ceasing to weep. "You have no heart, you don't feel for your own child! Another man would have rescued her from the fire. But this is a monster and neither a man nor a father! You, honored sir, are a noble man," she went on, addressing Pierre rapidly between her sobs. "The fire broke out alongside, and blew our way, the maid called out 'Fire!' and we rushed to collect our things. We ran out just as we were. . . . This is what we have brought away. . . . The icons, and my dowry bed, all the rest is lost. We seized the children. But not Katie! Ooh! O Lord! . . ." and again she began to sob. "My child, my dear one! Burned, burned!"

"But where was she left?" asked Pierre.

From the expression of his animated face the woman saw that this man might help her.

"Oh, dear sir!" she cried, seizing him by the legs. "My benefactor, set my heart at ease. . . . Aníska, go, you horrid girl, show him the way!" she cried to the maid, angrily opening her mouth and still farther exposing her long teeth.

"Show me the way, show me, I . . . I'll do it," gasped Pierre rapidly.

The dirty maidservant stepped from behind the trunk, put up her plait, sighed, and went on her short, bare feet along the path. Pierre felt as if he had come back to life after a heavy swoon. He held his head higher, his eyes shone with the light of life, and with swift steps he followed the maid, overtook her and came out on the Povarskóy. The whole street was full of clouds of black smoke. Tongues of flame here and there broke through that cloud. A great number of people crowded in front of the conflagration. In the middle of the street stood a French general saying something to those around him. Pierre, accompanied by the maid, was advancing to the spot where the general stood, but the French soldiers stopped him.

"On ne passe pas!" cried a voice.

"This way, uncle," cried the girl. "We'll pass through the side street, by the Nikúlins!"

Pierre turned back, giving a spring now and then to keep up with her. She ran across the street, turned down a side street to the left end, passing three houses, turned into a yard on the right.

"It's here, close by," said she, and running across the yard, opened a gate in a wooden fence and, stopping, pointed out to him a small wooden wing of the house, which was burning brightly and fiercely. One of its sides had fallen in, another was on fire, and bright flames issued from the openings of the windows and from under the roof.

As Pierre passed through the fence gate, he was enveloped by hot air, and involuntarily stopped.

"Which is it? Which is your house?" he asked.

"Ooh!" wailed the girl, pointing to the wing. "That's it, that was our lodging. You've burned to death, our treasure, Katie, my precious little missy! Ooh!" lamented Anı́ska, who at the sight of the fire felt that she too must give expression to her feelings.

Pierre rushed to the wing, but the heat was so great that he involuntarily passed round in a curve and came upon the large house that was as yet burning only at one end, just below the roof, and around which swarmed a crowd of Frenchmen. At first Pierre did not realize what these men, who were dragging something out, were about; but seeing before him a Frenchman hitting a peasant with a blunt saber and trying to take from him a fox-fur coat, he vaguely understood that looting was going on there, but he had no time to dwell on that idea.

The sounds of crackling and the din of falling walls and ceilings, the whistle and hiss of the flames, the excited shouts of the people and the sight of the swaying smoke, now gathering into thick black clouds and now soaring up with glittering sparks, with here and there dense sheaves of flame (now red and now like golden fish-scales creeping along the walls) and the heat and smoke and rapidity of motion, produced on Pierre the usual animating effects of a conflagration. It had a peculiarly strong effect on him because at the sight of the fire he felt himself suddenly freed from the ideas that had weighed him down. He felt young, bright, adroit and resolute. He ran round to the other side of the lodge and was about to dash into that part of it which was still standing, when just above his head he heard several voices shouting, and then a cracking sound and the ring of something heavy falling close beside him.

Pierre looked up and saw at a window of the large house, some Frenchmen who had just thrown out the drawer of a chest, filled with metal articles. Other French soldiers standing below went up to the drawer.

"What does this fellow want?" shouted one of them referring to Pierre.

"There's a child in that house. Haven't you seen a child?" cried Pierre.

"What's he talking about? Get along!" said several voices, and one of the soldiers, evidently afraid that Pierre might want to take from them some of the plate and bronzes that were in the drawer, moved threateningly toward him.

"A child?" shouted a Frenchman from above. "I did hear something squealing in the garden. Perhaps it's his brat that the fellow is looking for. After all one must be human, you know. . . ."

"Where is it? Where?" said Pierre.

"There! There!" shouted the Frenchman at the window, pointing to the garden at the back of the house. "Wait a bit—I'm coming down."

And a minute or two later the Frenchman, a black-eyed fellow with a spot on his cheek, in shirt-sleeves, really did jump out of a window on the ground-floor, and clapping Pierre on the shoulder ran with him into the garden.

"Hurry up, you others!" he called out to his comrades. "It's getting hot."

When they reached a gravel path behind the house the Frenchman pulled Pierre by the arm and pointed to a round, graveled space where a three-year-old girl in a pink dress was lying under a seat.

"There is your child! Oh, a girl, so much the better!" said the Frenchman. "Good-bye, Fatty. We must be human, we are all mortal you know!" and the Frenchman with the spot on his cheek ran back to his comrades.

Breathless with joy, Pierre ran to the little girl and was going to take her in his arms. But seeing a stranger the sickly, scrofulous-looking child, unattractively like her mother, began to yell and run away. Pierre, however, seized her and lifted her in his arms. She screamed desperately and angrily and tried with her little hands to pull Pierre's hands away, and to bite them with her slobbering mouth. Pierre was seized by a sense of horror and repulsion such as he had experienced when touching some nasty little animal. But he made an effort not to throw the child down, and ran with her to the large house. It was now, however, impossible to get back the way he had come; the maid, Aníska, was no longer there, and Pierre with a feeling of pity and disgust pressed the wet, painfully-sobbing child to himself as tenderly as he could and ran with her through the garden seeking another way out.

Chapter XXXIV

HAVING RUN THROUGH DIFFERENT YARDS AND SIDE STREETS, PIERRE GOT BACK WITH HIS LITTLE burden to the Gruzínski garden at the corner of the Povarskóy. He did not at first recognize the place from which he had set out to look for the child, so crowded was it now with people and goods that had been dragged out of the houses. Besides Russian families who had taken refuge here from the fire with their belongings, there were several French soldiers in a variety of clothing. Pierre took no notice of them. He hurried to find the family of that civil servant in order to restore the daughter to her mother and go to save someone else. Pierre felt that he had still much to do and to do quickly. Glowing with the heat and from running he felt at that moment more strongly than ever the sense of youth, animation and determination that had come on him when he ran to save the child. She had now become quiet and, clinging with her little hands to Pierre's coat, sat on his arm gazing about her like some little wild animal. He glanced at her occasionally with a slight smile. He fancied he saw something pathetically innocent in that frightened sickly little face.

He did not find the civil servant or his wife where he had left them. He walked among the crowd with rapid steps, scanning the various faces he met. Involuntarily he noticed a Georgian or Armenian family consisting of a very handsome old man of Oriental type, wearing a new, cloth-covered, sheepskin coat and new boots, an old woman of similar type and a young woman. That very young woman seemed to Pierre the perfection of Oriental beauty, with her sharply outlined, arched, black eyebrows and the extraordinarily soft bright color of her long, beautiful, expressionless face. Amid the scattered property and the crowd on the open space, she, in her rich satin cloak with a bright lilac shawl on her head, suggested a delicate exotic plant thrown out onto the snow. She was sitting on some bundles a little behind the old woman, and looked from under her long lashes with motionless, large almond-shaped eyes, at the ground before her. Evidently she was aware of her beauty and fearful because of it. Her face struck Pierre, and hurrying along by the fence he turned several times to look at her. When he had reached the fence, still without finding those he sought, he stopped and looked about him.

With the child in his arms his figure was now more conspicuous than before, and a group of Russians, both men and women, gathered about him.

"Have you lost anyone, my dear fellow? You're of the gentry yourself, aren't you? Whose child is it?" they asked him.

Pierre replied that the child belonged to a woman in a black coat who had been sitting there with her other children, and he asked whether anyone knew where she had gone.

"Why, that must be the Anférovs," said an old deacon, addressing a pockmarked peasant woman. "Lord have mercy, Lord have mercy!" he added in his customary bass.

"The Anférovs? No," said the woman. "They left in the morning. That must be either Mary Nikoláevna's or the Ivánovs'!"

"He says 'a woman,' and Mary Nikoláevna is a lady," remarked a house serf.

"Do you know her? She's thin, with long teeth," said Pierre.

"That's Mary Nikoláevna! They went inside the garden when these wolves swooped down," said the woman, pointing to the French soldiers.

"O Lord, have mercy!" added the deacon.

"Go over that way, they're there. It's she! She kept on lamenting and crying," continued the woman. "It's she. Here, this way!"

But Pierre was not listening to the woman. He had for some seconds been intently watching what was going on a few steps away. He was looking at the Armenian family and at two French soldiers who had gone up to them. One of these, a nimble little man, was wearing a blue coat tied round the waist with a rope. He had a nightcap on his head and his feet were bare. The other, whose appearance particularly struck Pierre, was a long, lank, round-shouldered, fair-haired man, slow in his movements and with an idiotic expression of face. He wore a woman's loose gown of frieze, blue trousers, and large torn Hessian boots. The little barefooted Frenchman in the blue coat went up to the Armenians, and saying something, immediately seized the old man by his legs and the old man at once began pulling off his boots. The other in the frieze gown stopped in front of the beautiful Armenian girl and with his hands in his pockets stood staring at her, motionless and silent.

"Here, take the child!" said Pierre peremptorily and hurriedly to the woman, handing the little girl to her. "Give her back to them, give her back!" he almost shouted, putting the child, who began screaming, on the ground, and again looking at the Frenchman and the Armenian family.

The old man was already sitting barefoot. The little Frenchman had secured his second boot and was slapping one boot against the other. The old man was saying something in a voice broken by sobs, but Pierre caught but a glimpse of this, his whole attention was directed to the Frenchman in the frieze gown who meanwhile, swaying slowly from side to side, had drawn nearer to the young woman and taking his hands from his pockets had seized her by the neck.

The beautiful Armenian still sat motionless and in the same attitude, with her long lashes drooping as if she did not see or feel what the soldier was doing to her.

While Pierre was running the few steps that separated him from the Frenchman, the tall marauder in the frieze gown was already tearing from her neck the necklace the young Armenian was wearing, and the young woman, clutching at her neck, screamed piercingly.

"Let that woman alone!" exclaimed Pierre hoarsely in a furious voice, seizing the soldier by his round shoulders and throwing him aside.

The soldier fell, got up, and ran away. But his comrade, throwing down the boots and drawing his sword, moved threateningly toward Pierre.

"Voyons, pas de bêtises!" he cried.

Pierre was in such a transport of rage that he remembered nothing and his strength increased tenfold. He rushed at the barefooted Frenchman and, before the latter had time to draw his sword, knocked him off his feet and hammered him with his fists. Shouts of approval were heard from the crowd around, and at the same moment a mounted patrol of French Uhlans appeared from round the corner. The Uhlans came up at a trot to Pierre and the Frenchman and surrounded them. Pierre remembered nothing of what happened after that. He only remembered beating someone and being beaten, and finally feeling that his hands were bound and that a crowd of French soldiers stood around him and were searching him.

"Lieutenant, he has a dagger," were the first words Pierre understood.

"Ah, a weapon?" said the officer and turned to the barefooted soldier who had been arrested with Pierre. "All right, you can tell all about it at the court-martial." Then he turned to Pierre. "Do you speak French?"

Pierre looked around him with bloodshot eyes and did not reply. His face probably looked very terrible, for the officer said something in a whisper and four more Uhlans left the ranks and placed themselves on both sides of Pierre.

"Do you speak French?" the officer asked again, keeping at a distance from Pierre. "Call the interpreter."

A little man in Russian civilian clothes rode out from the ranks, and by his clothes and manner of speaking Pierre at once knew him to be a French salesman from one of the Moscow shops.

"He does not look like a common man," said the interpreter, after a searching look at Pierre.

"Ah, he looks very much like an incendiary," remarked the officer. "And ask him who he is," he added.

"Who are you?" asked the interpreter in poor Russian. "You must answer the chief."

"I will not tell you who I am. I am your prisoner—take me!" Pierre suddenly replied in French.

"Ah, ah!" muttered the officer with a frown. "Well then, march!"

A crowd had collected round the Uhlans. Nearest to Pierre stood the pockmarked peasant woman with the little girl, and when the patrol started she moved forward.

"Where are they taking you to, you poor dear?" said she. "And the little girl, the little girl, what am I to do with her if she's not theirs?" said the woman.

"What does that woman want?" asked the officer.

Pierre was as if intoxicated. His elation increased at the sight of the little girl he had saved.

"What does she want?" he murmured. "She is bringing me my daughter whom I have just saved from the flames," said he. "Good-bye!" And without knowing how this aimless lie had escaped him, he went along with resolute and triumphant steps between the French soldiers.

The French patrol was one of those sent out through the various streets of Moscow by Durosnel's order to put a stop to the pillage, and especially to catch the incendiaries who, according to the general opinion which had that day originated among the higher French officers, were the cause of the conflagrations. After marching through a number of streets the patrol arrested five more Russian suspects: a small shopkeeper, two seminary students, a peasant and a house serf, besides several looters. But of all these various suspected characters, Pierre was considered to be the most suspicious of all. When they had all been brought for the night to a large house on the Zúbov Rampart that was being used as a guardhouse, Pierre was placed apart under strict guard.

"Do you speak French?" the officer asked again, keeping at a distance from Pierre. "Call the interpreter!"

A little man in Russian civilian clothes rode out from the ranks, and by his clothes and manner of speaking Pierre at once knew him to be a French salesman from one of the Moscow shops.

"He does not look like a common man," said the interpreter, after a searching look at Pierre.

"Ah, he looks very much like an incendiary," remarked the officer. "And ask him who he is," he added.

"Who are you?" asked the interpreter in poor Russian. "You must answer the chief!"

"I will not tell you who I am. I am your prisoner—take me!" Pierre suddenly replied in French.

"Ah, ah!" muttered the officer with a frown. "Well, march!"

A crowd had collected round the Uhlans. Nearest to Pierre stood the pockmarked peasant woman with the little girl, and when the patrol started she stepped forward.

"Where are they taking you to, you poor dear?" said she. "And the little girl, the little girl, what am I to do with her if she's not theirs?" said the woman.

"What does this woman want?" asked the officer.

Pierre was as if intoxicated. His elation increased at the sight of the little girl he had saved.

"What does she want?" he murmured. "She is bringing me my daughter whom I have just saved from the flames," said he. "Good-bye!" And without knowing how this aimless lie had escaped him, he went along resolutely and triumphantly between the French soldiers.

The French patrol was one of those sent out through the various streets of Moscow by Durosnel's order to put a stop to the pillage, and especially to catch the incendiaries who, according to the general opinion which had that day originated among the higher French officers, were the cause of the conflagrations. After marching through a number of streets the patrol arrested five more Russian suspects: a small shopkeeper, two seminary students, a peasant, and a house serf, besides several looters. But of all these various suspects Pierre was considered to be the most suspicious of all. When they had all been brought for the night to a large house on the Zúbov Rampart that was being used as a guardhouse, Pierre was placed apart under strict guard.

Part Twelve

Chapter I

IN PETERSBURG AT THAT TIME A COMPLICATED STRUGGLE WAS BEING CARRIED ON WITH GREATER heat than ever in the highest circles, between the parties of Rumyántsev, the French, Márya Fëdorovna, the Tsarévich and others, drowned as usual by the buzzing of the Court drones. But the calm, luxurious life of Petersburg, concerned only about phantoms and reflections of real life, went on in its old way and made it hard, except by a great effort, to realize the danger and the difficult position of the Russian people. There were the same receptions and balls, the same French theater, the same Court interests and service interests and intrigues as usual. Only in the very highest circles were attempts made to keep in mind the difficulties of the actual position. Stories were whispered of how differently the two Empresses behaved in these difficult circumstances. The Empress Márya, concerned for the welfare of the charitable and educational institutions under her patronage, had given directions that they should all be removed to Kazán, and the things belonging to these institutions had already been packed up. The Empress Elisabeth, however, when asked what instructions she would be pleased to give—with her characteristic Russian patriotism had replied that she could give no directions about State institutions for that was the affair of the Sovereign, but as far as she personally was concerned she would be the last to quit Petersburg.

At Anna Pávlovna's on the 26th of August, the very day of the battle of Borodinó, there was a soireé, the chief feature of which was to be the reading of a letter from his Lordship the Bishop when sending the Emperor an icon of the Venerable Sergius. It was regarded as a model of ecclesiastical, patriotic eloquence. Prince Vasíli himself, famed for his elocution, was to read it. (He used to read at the Empress's.) The art of his reading was supposed to lie in rolling out the words, quite independently of their meaning, in a loud and sing-song voice alternating between a despairing wail and a tender murmur, so that the wail fell quite at random on one word and the murmur on another. This reading, as was always the case at Anna Pávlovna's soireés, had a political significance. That evening she expected several important personages who had to be made ashamed of their visits to the French theater and aroused to a patriotic temper. A good many people had already arrived, but Anna Pávlovna, not yet seeing all those whom she wanted in her drawing room, did not let the reading begin but wound up the springs of a general conversation.

The news of the day in Petersburg was the illness of Countess Bezúkhova. She had fallen ill unexpectedly a few days previously, had missed several gatherings of which she was usually the ornament, and was said to be receiving no one, and instead of the celebrated Petersburg doctors who usually attended her, had entrusted herself to some Italian doctor who was treating her in some new and unusual way.

They all knew very well that the enchanting countess's illness arose from an inconvenience resulting from marrying two husbands at the same time, and that the Italian's cure consisted in removing such inconvenience; but in Anna Pávlovna's presence no one dared to think of this or even appear to know it.

"They say the poor countess is very ill. The doctor says it is angina pectoris."

"Angina? Oh, that's a terrible illness!"

"They say that the rivals are reconciled, thanks to the angina . . ." and the word *angina* was repeated with great satisfaction.

"The count is pathetic, they say. He cried like a child when the doctor told him the case was dangerous."

"Oh, it would be a terrible loss, she is an enchanting woman."

"You are speaking of the poor countess?" said Anna Pávlovna, coming up just then. "I sent to ask for news, and hear that she is a little better. Oh, she is certainly the most charming woman in the world," she went on, with a smile at her own enthusiasm. "We belong to different camps, but that does not prevent my esteeming her as she deserves. She is very unfortunate!" added Anna Pávlovna.

Supposing that by these words Anna Pávlovna was somewhat lifting the veil from the secret of the countess's malady, an unwary young man ventured to express surprise that well-known doctors had not been called in and that the countess was being attended by a charlatan who might employ dangerous remedies.

"Your information may be better than mine," Anna Pávlovna suddenly and venomously retorted on the inexperienced young man, "but I know on good authority that this doctor is a very learned and able man. He is private physician to the Queen of Spain."

And having thus demolished the young man, Anna Pávlovna turned to another group where Bilíbin was talking about the Austrians: having wrinkled up his face he was evidently preparing to smooth it out again and utter one of his *mots.*

"I think it is delightful," he said, referring to a diplomatic note that had been sent to Vienna with some Austrian banners captured from the French by Wittgenstein, "the hero of Petropol" as he was then called in Petersburg.

"What? What's that?" asked Anna Pávlovna, securing silence for the *mot,* which she had heard before.

And Bilíbin repeated the actual words of the diplomatic dispatch, which he had himself composed.

"The Emperor returns these Austrian banners," said Bilíbin, "friendly banners gone astray and found on a wrong path," and his brow became smooth again.

"Charming, charming!" observed Prince Vasíli.

"The path to Warsaw, perhaps," Prince Hippolyte remarked loudly and unexpectedly. Everybody looked at him, not understanding what he meant. Prince Hippolyte himself glanced around with amused surprise. He knew no more than the others what his words meant. During his diplomatic career he had more than once noticed that such utterances were received as very witty, and at every opportunity he uttered in that way the first words that entered his head. "It may turn out very well," he thought, "but if not, they'll know how to arrange matters." And really, during the awkward silence that ensued, that insufficiently patriotic person entered whom Anna Pávlovna had been waiting for and wished to convert, and she, smiling, and shaking a finger at Hippolyte, invited Prince Vasíli to the table and bringing him two candles and the manuscript begged him to begin. Everyone became silent.

"Most Gracious Sovereign and Emperor!" Prince Vasíli sternly declaimed, looking round at his audience as if to inquire whether anyone had anything to say to the contrary. But no one said anything. "Moscow, our ancient Capital, the New Jerusalem, receives *her* Christ"—he placed a sudden emphasis on the word *her*—"as a mother receives her zealous sons into her arms, and through the gathering mists, foreseeing the brilliant glory of thy rule, sings in exultation, 'Hosanna, blessed is he that cometh!' "

Prince Vasíli pronounced these last words in a tearful voice.

Bilíbin attentively examined his nails, and many of those present appeared intimidated, as if asking in what they were to blame. Anna Pávlovna whispered the next words in advance, like an old woman muttering the prayer at Communion: "Let the bold and insolent Goliath . . ." she whispered.

Prince Vasíli continued.

"Let the bold and insolent Goliath from the borders of France encompass the realms of Russia with death-bearing terrors; humble Faith, the sling of the Russian David, shall suddenly smite his head in his bloodthirsty pride. This icon of the Venerable Sergius, the servant of God and zealous champion of old of our country's weal, is offered to your Imperial Majesty. I grieve that my waning strength prevents my rejoicing in the sight of your most gracious presence. I raise fervent prayers to Heaven that the Almighty may exalt the race of the just, and mercifully fulfill the desires of your Majesty."

"What force! What a style!" was uttered in approval both of reader and of author.

Animated by that address Anna Pávlovna's guests talked for a long time of the state of the fatherland, and offered various conjectures as to the result of the battle to be fought in a few days.

"You will see," said Anna Pávlovna, "that tomorrow on the Emperor's birthday, we shall receive news. I have a favorable presentiment!"

Chapter II

Anna Pávlovna's presentiment was in fact fulfilled. Next day during the service at the Palace church in honor of the Emperor's birthday, Prince Volkónski was called out of the church and received a dispatch from Prince Kutúzov. It was Kutúzov's report, written from Tatárinova on the day of the battle. Kutúzov wrote that the Russians had not retreated a step, that the French losses were much heavier than ours, and that he was writing in haste from the field of battle before collecting full information. It followed that there must have been a victory. And at once, without leaving the church, thanks were rendered to the Creator for His help, and for the victory.

Anna Pávlovna's presentiment was justified, and all that morning a joyously festive mood reigned in the city. Everyone believed the victory to have been complete, and some even spoke of Napoleon's having been captured, of his deposition, and of the choice of a new ruler for France.

It is very difficult for events to be reflected in their real strength and completeness amid the conditions of Court life and far from the scene of action. General events involuntarily group themselves around some particular incident. So now the courtiers' pleasure was based as much on the fact that the news had arrived on the Emperor's birthday, as on the fact of the victory itself. It was like a successfully arranged surprise. Mention was made in Kutúzov's report of the Russian losses, among which figured the names of Túchkov, Bagratión, and Kutáysov. In the Petersburg world this sad side of the affair again involuntarily centered round a single incident: Kutáysov's death. Everybody knew him, the Emperor liked him, and he was young and interesting. That day everyone met with the words:

"What a wonderful coincidence! Just during the service. But what a loss Kutáysov is! How sorry I am!"

"What did I tell about Kutúzov?" Prince Vasíli now said with a prophet's pride. "I always said he was the only man capable of defeating Napoleon."

But next day no news arrived from the army and the public mood grew anxious. The courtiers suffered because of the suffering the suspense occasioned the Emperor.

"Fancy the Emperor's position!" said they, and instead of extolling Kutúzov as they had done the day before, they condemned him as the cause of the Emperor's anxiety. That day Prince Vasíli no longer boasted of his protégé Kutúzov, but remained silent when the commander-in-chief was mentioned. Moreover toward evening, as if everything conspired to make Petersburg society anxious and uneasy, a terrible piece of news was added. Countess Hélène Bezúkhova had suddenly died of that terrible malady it had been so agreeable to mention. Officially, at large gatherings, everyone said that Countess Bezúkhova had died of a terrible attack of angina pectoris, but in intimate circles details were mentioned of how the private physician of the Queen of Spain had prescribed small doses of a certain drug to produce a certain effect; but Hélène, tortured by the fact that the old count suspected her and that her husband to whom she had written (that wretched, profligate

Pierre) had not replied, had suddenly taken a very large dose of the drug, and had died in agony before assistance could be rendered her. It was said that Prince Vasíli and the old count had turned upon the Italian, but the latter had produced such letters from the unfortunate deceased that they had immediately let the matter drop.

Talk in general centered round three melancholy facts: the Emperor's lack of news, the loss of Kutúzov, and the death of Hélène.

On the third day after Kutúzov's report a country gentleman arrived from Moscow, and news of the surrender of Moscow to the French spread through the whole town. This was terrible! What a position for the Emperor to be in! Kutúzov was a traitor, and Prince Vasíli during the visits of condolence paid to him on the occasion of his daughter's death said of Kutúzov, whom he had formerly praised (it was excusable for him in his grief to forget what he had said) that it was impossible to expect anything else from a blind and depraved old man.

"I only wonder that the fate of Russia could have been entrusted to such a man."

As long as this news remained unofficial it was possible to doubt it, but the next day the following communication was received from Count Rostopchín:

> Prince Kutúzov's adjutant has brought me a letter in which he demands police officers to guide the army to the Ryazán road. He writes that he is regretfully abandoning Moscow. Sire! Kutúzov's action decides the fate of the capital and of your empire! Russia will shudder to learn of the abandonment of the city in which her greatness is centered, and in which lie the ashes of your ancestors! I shall follow the army. I have had everything removed, and it only remains for me to weep over the fate of my fatherland.

On receiving this dispatch the Emperor sent Prince Volkónski to Kutúzov with the following rescript:

> Prince Michael Ilariónovich! Since the 29th of August I have received no communication from you, yet on the 1st of September I received from the commander-in-chief of Moscow, via Yaroslávl, the sad news that you, with the army, have decided to abandon Moscow. You can yourself imagine the effect this news has had on me, and your silence increases my astonishment. I am sending this by Adjutant-General Prince Volkónski, to hear from you the situation of the army and the reasons that have induced you to take this melancholy decision.

Chapter III

Nine days after the abandonment of Moscow, a messenger from Kutúzov reached Petersburg with the official announcement of that event. This messenger was Michaud, a Frenchman who did not know Russian, but who was *quoique étranger, russe de coeur et d'âme,* as he said of himself.

The Emperor at once received this messenger in his study at the palace on Stone Island. Michaud, who had never seen Moscow before the campaign and who did not know Russian, yet felt deeply moved (as he wrote) when he appeared before *notre très gracieux souverain* with the news of the burning of Moscow, *dont les flammes éclairaient sa route.*

Though the source of M. Michaud's chagrin must have been different from that which caused

Russians to grieve, he had such a sad face when shown into the Emperor's study that the latter at once asked:

"Have you brought me sad news, colonel?"

"Very sad, sire," replied Michaud, lowering his eyes with a sigh. "The abandonment of Moscow."

"Have they surrendered my ancient capital without a battle?" asked the Emperor quickly, his face suddenly flushing.

Michaud respectfully delivered the message Kutúzov had entrusted to him, which was that it had been impossible to fight before Moscow, and that as the only remaining choice was between losing the army as well as Moscow, or losing Moscow alone, the field marshal had to choose the latter.

The Emperor listened in silence not looking at Michaud.

"Has the enemy entered the city?" he asked.

"Yes, sire, and Moscow is now in ashes. I left it all in flames," replied Michaud in a decided tone, but glancing at the Emperor he was frightened by what he had done.

The Emperor began to breathe heavily and rapidly, his lower lip trembled and tears instantly appeared in his fine blue eyes.

But this lasted only a moment. He suddenly frowned as if blaming himself for his weakness, and raising his head addressed Michaud in a firm voice:

"I see, colonel, from all that is happening, that Providence requires great sacrifices of us. . . . I am ready to submit myself in all things to His will; but tell me, Michaud, how did you leave the army when it saw my ancient capital abandoned without a battle? Did you not notice discouragement? . . ."

Seeing that his most gracious ruler was calm once more, Michaud also grew calm, but was not immediately ready to reply to the Emperor's direct and relevant question which required a direct answer.

"Sire, will you allow me to speak frankly as befits a loyal soldier?" he asked to gain time.

"Colonel, I always require it," replied the Emperor. "Conceal nothing from me, I wish to know absolutely how things are."

"Sire!" said Michaud with a subtle, scarcely perceptible smile on his lips, having now prepared a well-phrased reply, "Sire, I left the whole army, from its chiefs to the lowest soldier, without exception in desperate and agonized terror . . ."

"How is that?" the Emperor interrupted him, frowning sternly. "Would misfortune make my Russians lose heart? . . . Never!"

Michaud had only waited for this to bring out the phrase he had prepared.

"Sire," he said, with respectful playfulness, "they are only afraid lest your Majesty, in the goodness of your heart, should allow yourself to be persuaded to make peace. They are burning for the combat," declared this representative of the Russian nation, "and to prove to your Majesty by the sacrifice of their lives how devoted they are. . . ."

"Ah!" said the Emperor reassured, and with a kindly gleam in his eyes, he patted Michaud on the shoulder. "You set me at ease, colonel."

He bent his head and was silent for some time.

"Well then, go back to the army," he said drawing himself up to his full height and addressing Michaud with a gracious and majestic gesture, "and tell our brave men and all my good subjects wherever you go that when I have not a soldier left I shall put myself at the head of my beloved nobility and my good peasants and so use the last resources of my empire. It still offers me more than my enemies suppose," said the Emperor growing more and more animated; "but should it ever be ordained by Divine Providence," he continued, raising to heaven his fine eyes shining with emotion, "that my dynasty should cease to reign on the throne of my ancestors, then after exhausting all the means at my command, I shall let my beard grow to here" (he pointed halfway down his chest) "and go and eat potatoes with the meanest of my peasants, rather than sign the disgrace of my country and of my beloved people whose sacrifices I know how to appreciate."

Having uttered these words in an agitated voice the Emperor suddenly turned away as if to hide from Michaud the tears that rose to his eyes, and went to the further end of his study. Having stood there a few moments, he strode back to Michaud and pressed his arm below the elbow with a vigorous movement. The Emperor's mild and handsome face was flushed and his eyes gleamed with resolution and anger.

"Colonel Michaud, do not forget what I say to you here, perhaps we may recall it with pleasure some day . . . Napoleon or I," said the Emperor, touching his breast. "We can no longer both reign together. I have learned to know him, and he will not deceive me any more. . . ."

And the Emperor paused, with a frown.

When he heard these words and saw the expression of firm resolution in the Emperor's eyes, Michaud—*quoique étranger, russe de coeur et d'âme*—at that solemn moment felt himself enraptured by all that he had heard (as he used afterward to say), and gave expression to his own feelings and those of the Russian people whose representative he considered himself to be, in the following words:

"Sire!" said he, "your Majesty is at this moment signing the glory of the nation and the salvation of Europe!"

With an inclination of the head the Emperor dismissed him.

Chapter IV

It is natural for us who were not living in those days to imagine that when half Russia had been conquered and the inhabitants were fleeing to distant provinces, and one levy after another was being raised for the defense of the fatherland, all Russians from the greatest to the least were solely engaged in sacrificing themselves, saving their fatherland, or weeping over its downfall. The tales and descriptions of that time without exception speak only of the self-sacrifice, patriotic devotion, despair, grief, and the heroism of the Russians. But it was not really so. It appears so to us because we see only the general historic interest of that time and do not see all the personal human interests that people had. Yet in reality those personal interests of the moment so much transcend the general interests that they always prevent the public interest from being felt or even noticed. Most of the people at that time paid no attention to the general progress of events but were guided only by their private interests, and they were the very people whose activities at that period were most useful.

Those who tried to understand the general course of events and to take part in it by self-sacrifice and heroism, were the most useless members of society, they saw everything upside down, and all they did for the common good turned out to be useless and foolish—like Pierre's and Mamónov's regiments which looted Russian villages, and the lint the young ladies prepared and that never reached the wounded, and so on. Even those, fond of intellectual talk and of expressing their feelings, who discussed Russia's position at the time, involuntarily introduced into their conversation either a shade of pretense and falsehood, or useless condemnation and anger directed against people accused of actions no one could possibly be guilty of. In historic events the rule forbidding us to eat of the fruit of the Tree of Knowledge is specially applicable. Only unconscious action bears fruit, and he who plays a part in an historic event never understands its significance. If he tries to realize it his efforts are fruitless.

The more closely a man was engaged in the events then taking place in Russia the less did he realize their significance. In Petersburg and in the provinces at a distance from Moscow, ladies, and gentlemen in militia uniforms, wept for Russia and its ancient capital and talked of self-sacrifice and so on; but in the army which retired beyond Moscow there was little talk or thought of Moscow, and when they caught sight of its burned ruins no one swore to be avenged on the French, but they thought about their next pay, their next quarters, of Matrëshka the vivandière, and like matters.

As the war had caught him in the service, Nicholas Rostóv took a close and prolonged part in the defense of his country, but did so casually, without any aim at self-sacrifice, and he therefore looked at what was going on in Russia without despair and without dismally racking his brains over it. Had he been asked what he thought of the state of Russia, he would have said that it was not his business to think about it, that Kutúzov and others were there for that purpose, but that he had heard that the regiments were to be made up to their full strength, that fighting would probably go on for a long time yet, and that things being so it was quite likely he might be in command of a regiment in a couple of years' time.

As he looked at the matter in this way, he learned that he was being sent to Vorónezh to buy remounts for his division, not only without regret as being prevented from taking part in the coming battle, but with the greatest pleasure—which he did not conceal and which his comrades fully understood.

A few days before the battle of Borodinó, Nicholas received the necessary money and warrants, and having sent some hussars on in advance, he set out with post-horses for Vorónezh.

Only a man who has experienced it—that is, has passed some months continuously in an atmosphere of campaigning and war—can understand the delight Nicholas felt when he escaped from the region covered by the army's foraging operations, provision-trains, and hospitals. When—free from soldiers, wagons, and the filthy traces of a camp—he saw villages with peasants and peasant-women, gentlemen's country houses, fields where cattle were grazing, post houses with stationmasters asleep in them, he rejoiced as though seeing all this for the first time. What for a long while specially surprised and delighted him were the women, young and healthy, without a dozen officers making up to each of them; women, too, who were pleased and flattered that a passing officer should joke with them.

In the highest spirits Nicholas arrived at night at a hotel in Vorónezh, ordered things he had long been deprived of in camp, and next day, very clean-shaven and in a full-dress uniform he had not worn for a long time, went to present himself to the authorities.

The commander of the militia was a civilian general, an old man who was evidently pleased with his military designation and rank. He received Nicholas brusquely (imagining this to be characteristically military) and questioned him with an important air, as if considering the general progress of affairs and approving and disapproving with full right to do so. Nicholas was in such good spirits that this merely amused him.

From the commander of the militia he drove to the governor. The governor was a brisk little man, very simple and affable. He indicated the stud-farms at which Nicholas might procure horses, recommended to him a horse dealer in the town and a landowner fourteen miles out of town who had the best horses, and promised to assist him in every way.

"You are Count Ilyá Rostóv's son? My wife was a great friend of your mother's. We are at home on Thursdays—today is Thursday, so please come and see us quite informally," said the governor, taking leave of him.

Immediately on leaving the governor's, Nicholas hired post-horses and taking his squadron quartermaster with him, drove at a gallop to the landowner, fourteen miles away, who had the stud. Everything seemed to him pleasant and easy during that first part of his stay in Vorónezh, and as usually happens when a man is in a pleasant state of mind, everything went well and easily.

The landowner to whom Nicholas went was a bachelor, an old cavalryman, a horse-fancier, a sportsman, the possessor of some century-old brandy and some old Hungarian wine, who had a snuggery where he smoked, and who owned some splendid horses.

In very few words Nicholas bought seventeen picked stallions for six thousand rubles—to serve as he said as samples of his remounts. After dining and taking rather too much of the Hungarian wine, Nicholas—having exchanged kisses with the landowner, with whom he was already on the friendliest terms—galloped back over abominable roads, in the brightest frame of mind, continually urging on the driver so as to be in time for the governor's party.

When he had changed, poured water over his head and scented himself, Nicholas arrived at the governor's rather late, but with the phrase "better late than never" on his lips.

It was not a ball, nor had dancing been announced, but everyone knew that Catherine Petróvna would play valses and the écossaise on the clavichord and that there would be dancing, and so everyone had come as to a ball.

Provincial life in 1812 went on very much as usual, but with this difference, that it was livelier in the towns in consequence of the arrival of many wealthy families from Moscow, and as in everything that went on in Russia at that time a special recklessness was noticeable, an "in for a penny, in for a pound—who cares?" spirit, and the inevitable small talk, instead of turning on the weather and mutual acquaintances, now turned on Moscow, the army, and Napoleon.

The society gathered together at the governor's was the best in Vorónezh.

There were a great many ladies and some of Nicholas's Moscow acquaintances, but there were no men who could at all vie with the cavalier of St. George, the hussar remount-officer, the good-natured and well-bred Count Rostóv. Among the men was an Italian prisoner, an officer of the French army; and Nicholas felt that the presence of that prisoner enhanced his own importance as a Russian hero. The Italian was, as it were, a war trophy. Nicholas felt this, it seemed to him that everyone regarded the Italian in the same light, and he treated him cordially though with dignity and restraint.

As soon as Nicholas entered in his hussar uniform, diffusing around him a fragrance of perfume and wine, and had uttered the words "better late than never" and heard them repeated several times by others, people clustered around him; all eyes turned on him, and he felt at once that he had entered into his proper position in the province—that of a universal favorite: a very pleasant position, and intoxicatingly so after his long privations. At posting-stations, at inns, and in the landowner's snuggery, maidservants had been flattered by his notice, and here too at the governor's party there were (as it seemed to Nicholas) an inexhaustible number of pretty young women, married and unmarried, impatiently awaiting his notice. The women and girls flirted with him and, from the first day the old people concerned themselves to get this fine young dare-devil of a hussar married and settled down. Among these was the governor's wife herself, who welcomed Rostóv as a near relative and called him "Nicholas."

Catherine Petróvna did actually play valses and the écossaise, and dancing began in which Nicholas still further captivated the provincial society by his agility. His particularly free manner of dancing even surprised them all. Nicholas was himself rather surprised at the way he danced that evening. He had never danced like that in Moscow and would even have considered such a very free and easy manner improper and in bad form, but here he felt it incumbent on him to astonish them all by something unusual, something they would have to accept as the regular thing in the capital though new to them in the provinces.

All the evening Nicholas paid attention to a blue-eyed, plump and pleasing little blonde, the wife of one of the provincial officials. With the naïve conviction of young men in a merry mood that other men's wives were created for them, Rostóv did not leave the lady's side and treated her husband in a friendly and conspiratorial style, as if, without speaking of it, they knew how capitally Nicholas and the lady would get on together. The husband, however, did not seem to share that conviction and tried to behave morosely with Rostóv. But the latter's good-natured naïveté was so boundless that sometimes even he involuntarily yielded to Nicholas's good-humor. Toward the end of the evening, however, as the wife's face grew more flushed and animated, the husband's became more and more melancholy and solemn, as though there were but a given amount of animation between them and as the wife's share increased the husband's diminished.

Chapter V

Nicholas sat leaning slightly forward in an arm-chair, bending closely over the blonde lady and paying her mythological compliments with a smile that never left his face.

Jauntily shifting the position of his legs in their tight riding-breeches, diffusing an odor of perfume, and admiring his partner, himself, and the fine outlines of his legs in their well-fitting Hessian boots, Nicholas told the blonde lady that he wished to run away with a certain lady here in Vorónezh.

"Which lady?"

"A charming lady, a divine one. Her eyes" (Nicholas looked at his partner) "are blue, her mouth coral and ivory; her figure" (he glanced at her shoulders) "like Diana's. . . ."

The husband came up and sullenly asked his wife what she was talking about.

"Ah, Nikíta Iványch!" cried Nicholas rising politely, and as if wishing Nikíta Iványch to share his joke, he began to tell him of his intention to elope with a blonde lady.

The husband smiled gloomily, the wife gaily. The governor's good-natured wife came up with a look of disapproval.

"Anna Ignátyevna wants to see you, Nicholas," said she, pronouncing the name so that Nicholas at once understood that Anna Ignátyevna was a very important person. "Come, Nicholas! You know you let me call you so?"

"Oh, yes, Aunt. Who is she?"

"Anna Ignátyevna Malvíntseva. She has heard from her niece how you rescued her. . . . Can you guess?"

"I rescued such a lot of them!" said Nicholas.

"Her niece, Princess Bolkónskaya. She is here in Vorónezh with her aunt. Oho! How you blush. Why, are . . . ?"

"Not a bit! Please don't, Aunt!"

"Very well, very well! . . . Oh, what a fellow you are!"

The governor's wife led him up to a tall and very stout old lady with a blue headdress, who had just finished her game of cards with the most important personages of the town. This was Malvíntseva, Princess Mary's aunt on her mother's side, a rich, childless widow who always lived in Vorónezh. When Rostóv approached her she was standing settling up for the game. She looked at him, and screwing up her eyes sternly, continued to upbraid the general who had won from her.

"Very pleased, *mon cher,*" she then said, holding out her hand to Nicholas. "Pray come and see me."

After a few words about Princess Mary and her late father, whom Malvíntseva had evidently not liked, and having asked what Nicholas knew of Prince Andrew, who also was evidently no favorite of hers, the important old lady dismissed Nicholas after repeating her invitation to come to see her.

Nicholas promised to come and blushed again as he bowed. At the mention of Princess Mary he experienced a feeling of shyness and even of fear, which he himself did not understand.

When he had parted from Malvíntseva Nicholas wished to return to the dancing, but the governor's little wife placed her plump hand on his sleeve and, saying that she wanted to have a talk with him, led him to her sitting room, from which those who were there immediately withdrew so as not to be in her way.

"Do you know, dear boy," began the governor's wife with a serious expression on her kind little face, "that really would be the match for you: would you like me to arrange it?"

"Whom do you mean, Aunt?" asked Nicholas.

"I will make a match for you with the princess. Catherine Petróvna speaks of Lily, but I say, no—the princess! Do you want me to do it? I am sure your mother will be grateful to me. What a charming girl she is, really! And she is not at all so plain, either."

"Not at all," replied Nicholas as if offended at the idea. "As befits a soldier, Aunt, I don't force myself on anyone or refuse anything," he said before he had time to consider what he was saying.

"Well then, remember, this is not a joke!"

"Of course not!"

"Yes, yes," the governor's wife said as if talking to herself. "But, my dear boy, among other things you are too attentive to the other, the blonde. One is sorry for the husband, really. . . ."

"Oh no, we are good friends with him," said Nicholas in the simplicity of his heart; it did not enter his head that a pastime so pleasant to himself might not be pleasant to someone else.

"But what nonsense I have been saying to the governor's wife!" thought Nicholas suddenly at supper. "She will really begin to arrange a match . . . and Soyna . . . ?" And on taking leave of the governor's wife, when she again smilingly said to him, "Well then, remember!" he drew her aside.

"But see here, to tell the truth, Aunt . . ."

"What is it, my dear? Come, let's sit down here," said she.

Nicholas suddenly felt a desire and need to tell his most intimate thoughts (which he would not have told to his mother, his sister, or his friend) to this woman who was almost a stranger. When he afterward recalled that impulse to unsolicited and inexplicable frankness which had very important results for him, it seemed to him—as it seems to everyone in such cases—that it was merely some silly whim that seized him: yet that burst of frankness, together with other trifling events, had immense consequences for him and for all his family.

"You see, Aunt, Mamma has long wanted me to marry an heiress, but the very idea of marrying for money is repugnant to me."

"Oh yes, I understand," said the governor's wife.

"But Princess Bolkónskaya—that's another matter. I will tell you the truth. In the first place I like her very much, I feel drawn to her; and then, after I met her under such circumstances—so strangely, the idea often occurred to me: 'This is fate.' Especially if you remember that Mamma had long been thinking of it; but I had never happened to meet her before, somehow it had always happened that we did not meet. And as long as my sister Natásha was engaged to her brother it was of course out of the question for me to think of marrying her. And it must needs happen that I should meet her just when Natásha's engagement had been broken off . . . and then everything . . . So you see . . . I never told this to anyone and never will, only to you."

The governor's wife pressed his elbow gratefully.

"You know Sónya, my cousin? I love her, and promised to marry her, and will do so. . . . So you see there can be no question about—" said Nicholas incoherently and blushing.

"My dear boy, what a way to look at it! You know Sónya has nothing and you yourself say your Papa's affairs are in a very bad way. And what about your mother? It would kill her, that's one thing. And what sort of a life would it be for Sónya—if she's a girl with a heart? Your mother in despair, and you all ruined. . . . No, my dear, you and Sónya ought to understand that."

Nicholas remained silent. It comforted him to hear these arguments.

"All the same, Aunt, it is impossible," he rejoined with a sigh, after a short pause. "Besides, would the princess have me? And besides, she is now in mourning. How can one think of it!"

"But you don't suppose I'm going to get you married at once? There is always a right way of doing things," replied the governor's wife.

"What a matchmaker you are, Aunt . . ." said Nicholas, kissing her plump little hand.

Chapter VI

On reaching Moscow after her meeting with Rostóv, Princess Mary had found her nephew there with his tutor, and a letter from Prince Andrew giving her instructions how to get to her Aunt Malvíntseva at Vorónezh. That feeling akin to temptation which had tormented her during her father's illness, since his death, and especially since her meeting with Rostóv, was smothered by arrangements for the journey, anxiety about her brother, settling in a new house, meeting new people, and attending to her nephew's education. She was sad. Now, after a month passed in quiet surroundings, she felt more and more deeply the loss of her father which was associated in her mind with the ruin of Russia. She was agitated and incessantly tortured by the thought of the dangers to which her brother, the only intimate person now remaining to her, was exposed. She was worried too about her nephew's education for which she had always felt herself incompetent, but in the depths of her soul she felt at peace—a peace arising from consciousness of having stifled those personal dreams and hopes that had been on the point of awakening within her and were related to her meeting with Rostóv.

The day after her party the governor's wife came to see Malvíntseva and, after discussing her plan with the aunt, remarked that though under present circumstances a formal betrothal was, of course, not to be thought of, all the same the young people might be brought together and could get to know one another. Malvíntseva expressed approval, and the governor's wife began to speak of Rostóv in Mary's presence, praising him and telling how he had blushed when Princess Mary's name was mentioned. But Princess Mary experienced a painful rather than a joyful feeling—her mental tranquillity was destroyed, and desires, doubts, self-reproach and hopes reawoke.

During the two days that elapsed before Rostóv called, Princess Mary continually thought of how she ought to behave to him. First she decided not to come to the drawing room when he called to see her aunt—that it would not be proper for her, in her deep mourning, to receive visitors; then she thought this would be rude after what he had done for her; then it occurred to her that her aunt and the governor's wife had intentions concerning herself and Rostóv—their looks and words at times seemed to confirm this supposition—then she told herself that only she, with her sinful nature, could think this of them: they could not forget that situated as she was, while still wearing deep mourning, such matchmaking would be an insult to her and to her father's memory. Assuming that she did go down to see him, Princess Mary imagined the words he would say to her and what she would say to him, and these words sometimes seemed undeservedly cold, and then to mean too much. More than anything she feared lest the confusion she felt might overwhelm her and betray her as soon as she saw him.

But when on Sunday after church the footman announced in the drawing room that Count Rostóv had called, the princess showed no confusion, only a slight blush suffused her cheeks and her eyes lit up with a new and radiant light.

"You have met him, Aunt?" said she in a calm voice, unable herself to understand that she could be outwardly so calm and natural.

When Rostóv entered the room the princess dropped her eyes for an instant, as if to give the visitor time to greet her aunt, and then just as Nicholas turned to her she raised her head and met his look with shining eyes. With a movement full of dignity and grace she half rose with a smile of pleasure, held out her slender delicate hand to him, and began to speak in a voice in which for the first time new deep womanly notes vibrated. Mademoiselle Bourienne, who was in the drawing room, looked at Princess Mary in bewildered surprise. Herself a consummate coquette, she could not have maneuvered better on meeting a man she wished to attract.

"Either black is particularly becoming to her or she really has greatly improved without my having noticed it. And above all, what tact and grace!" thought Mademoiselle Bourienne.

Had Princess Mary been capable of reflection at that moment, she would have been more surprised than Mademoiselle Bourienne at the change that had taken place in herself. From the moment she recognized that dear, loved face, a new life-force took possession of her and compelled her to speak and act apart from her own will. From the time Rostóv entered her face became suddenly transformed. It was as if a light had been kindled in a carved and painted lantern and the intricate, skillful, artistic work on its sides, that previously seemed dark, coarse, and meaningless, was suddenly shown up in unexpected and striking beauty. For the first time all that pure, spiritual, inward travail through which she had lived appeared on the surface. All her inward labor, her dissatisfaction with herself, her sufferings, her strivings after goodness, her meekness, love, and self-sacrifice—all this now shone in those radiant eyes, in her delicate smile, and in every trait of her gentle face.

Rostóv saw all this as clearly as if he had known her whole life. He felt that the being before him was quite different from, and better than, anyone he had met before, and above all better than himself.

Their conversation was very simple and unimportant. They spoke of the war, and like everyone else unconsciously exaggerated their sorrow about it; they spoke of their last meeting—Nicholas trying to change the subject—they talked of the governor's kind wife, of Nicholas's relations, and of Princess Mary's.

She did not talk about her brother, diverting the conversation as soon as her aunt mentioned Andrew. Evidently she could speak of Russia's misfortunes with a certain artificiality, but her brother was too near her heart and she neither could nor would speak lightly of him. Nicholas noticed this, as he noticed every shade of Princess Mary's character with an observation unusual to him, and everything confirmed his conviction that she was a quite unusual and extraordinary being. Nicholas blushed and was confused when people spoke to him about the princess (as she did when he was mentioned) and even when he thought of her, but in her presence he felt quite at ease, and said not at all what he had prepared, but what, quite appropriately, occurred to him at the moment.

When a pause occurred during his short visit, Nicholas, as is usual when there are children, turned to Prince Andrew's little son, caressing him and asking whether he would like to be a hussar. He took the boy on his knee, played with him, and looked round at Princess Mary. With a softened, happy, and timid look she watched the boy she loved in the arms of the man she loved. Nicholas also noticed that look and, as if understanding it, flushed with pleasure and began to kiss the boy with good-natured playfulness.

As she was in mourning Princess Mary did not go out into society, and Nicholas did not think it the proper thing to visit her again; but all the same the governor's wife went on with her matchmaking, passing on to Nicholas the flattering things Princess Mary said of him and vice versa, and insisting on his declaring himself to Princess Mary. For this purpose she arranged a meeting between the young people at the bishop's house before Mass.

Though Rostóv told the governeor's wife that he would not make any declaration to Princess Mary, he promised to go.

As at Tilsit Rostóv had not allowed himself to doubt that what everybody considered right was right, so now, after a short but sincere struggle between his effort to arrange his life by his own sense of justice, and in obedient submission to circumstances, he chose the latter and yielded to the power he felt irresistibly carrying him he knew not where. He knew that after his promise to Sónya it would be what he deemed base to declare his feelings to Princess Mary. And he knew that he would never act basely. But he also knew (or rather felt at the bottom of his heart) that by resigning himself now to the force of circumstances and to those who were guiding him, he was not only doing nothing wrong, but was doing something very very important—more important than anything he had ever done in his life.

After meeting Princess Mary, though the course of his life went on externally as before, all his former amusements lost their charm for him and he often thought about her. But he never thought about her as he had thought of all the young ladies without exception whom he had met in society, nor as he had for a long time, and at one time rapturously, thought about Sónya. He had pictured each of those young ladies as almost all honest-hearted young men do, that is as a possible wife, adapting her in his imagination to all the conditions of married life: a white dressing-gown, his wife at the tea-table, his wife's carriage, little ones, Mamma and Papa, their relations to her, and so on—and these pictures of the future had given him pleasure. But with Princess Mary, to whom they were trying to get him engaged, he could never picture anything of future married life. If he tried, his pictures seemed incongruous and false. It made him afraid.

Chapter VII

THE DREADFUL NEWS OF THE BATTLE OF BORODINÓ, OF OUR LOSSES IN KILLED AND WOUNDED, and the still more terrible news of the loss of Moscow, reached Vorónezh in the middle of September. Princess Mary having learned of her brother's wound only from the Gazette and having no definite news of him, prepared (so Nicholas heard, he had not seen her again himself) to set off in search of Prince Andrew.

When he received the news of the battle of Borodinó and the abandonment of Moscow, Rostóv was not seized with despair, anger, the desire for vengeance, or any feeling of that kind, but everything in Vorónezh suddenly seemed to him dull and tiresome, and he experienced an indefinite feeling of shame and awkwardness. The conversations he heard seemed to him insincere; he did not know how to judge all these affairs and felt that only in the regiment would everything again become clear to him. He made haste to finish buying the horses, and often became unreasonably angry with his servant and squadron quartermaster.

A few days before his departure a special thanksgiving, at which Nicholas was present, was held in the cathedral for the Russian victory. He stood a little behind the governor and held himself with military decorum through the service, meditating on a great variety of subjects. When the service was over the governor's wife beckoned him to her.

"Have you seen the princess?" she asked, indicating with a movement of her head a lady standing on the opposite side, beyond the choir.

Nicholas immediately recognized Princess Mary not so much by the profile he saw under her bonnet as by the feeling of solicitude, timidity and pity that immediately overcame him. Princess Mary, evidently engrossed by her thoughts, was crossing herself for the last time before leaving the church.

Nicholas looked at her face with surprise. It was the same face he had seen before, there was the same general expression of refined, inner, spiritual labor, but now it was quite differently lit up. There was a pathetic expression of sorrow, prayer and hope in it. As had occurred before when she was present, Nicholas went up to her without waiting to be prompted by the governor's wife and not asking himself whether or not it was right and proper to address her here in church, and told her he had heard of her trouble and sympathized with his whole soul. As soon as she heard his voice a vivid glow kindled in her face, lighting up both her sorrow and her joy.

"There is one thing I wanted to tell you, princess," said Rostóv. "It is that if your brother, Prince Andrew Nikoláevich, were not living, it would have been at once announced in the Gazette, as he is a colonel."

The princess looked at him, not grasping what he was saying, but cheered by the expression of regretful sympathy on his face.

"And I have known so many cases of a splinter-wound" (the Gazette said it was a shell) "either proving fatal at once or being very slight," continued Nicholas. "We must hope for the best, and I am sure . . ."

Princess Mary interrupted him.

"Oh, that would be so dread . . ." she began and, prevented by agitation from finishing, she bent her head with a movement as graceful as everything she did in his presence and looking up at him gratefully, went out, following her aunt.

That evening Nicholas did not go out, but stayed at home to settle some accounts with the horse dealers. When he had finished that business it was already too late to go anywhere but still too early to go to bed, and for a long time he paced up and down the room, reflecting on his life, a thing he rarely did.

Princess Mary had made an agreeable impression on him when he had met her in Smolénsk Province. His having encountered her in such exceptional circumstances, and his mother having at one time mentioned her to him as a good match, had drawn his particular attention to her. When he met her again in Vorónezh the impression she made on him was not merely pleasing but powerful. Nicholas had been struck by the peculiar moral beauty he observed in her at this time. He was, however, preparing to go away and it had not entered his head to regret that he was thus depriving himself of chances of meeting her. But that day's encounter in church had, he felt, sunk deeper than was desirable for his peace of mind. That pale, sad, refined face, that radiant look, those gentle graceful gestures, and especially the deep and tender sorrow expressed in all her features, agitated him and evoked his sympathy. In men Rostóv could not bear to see the expression of a higher spiritual life (that was why he did not like Prince Andrew) and he referred to it contemptuously as philosophy and dreaminess, but in Princess Mary that very sorrow which revealed the depth of a whole spiritual world foreign to him was an irresistible attraction.

"She must be a wonderful woman. A real angel!" he said to himself. "Why am I not free? Why was I in such a hurry with Sónya?" And he involuntarily compared the two: the lack of spirituality in the one and the abundance of it in the other—a spirituality he himself lacked and therefore valued most highly. He tried to picture what would happen were he free. How he would propose to her and how she would become his wife. But no, he could not imagine that. He felt awed, and no clear picture presented itself to his mind. He had long ago pictured to himself a future with Sónya, and that was all clear and simple just because it had all been thought out and he knew all there was in Sónya, but it was impossible to picture a future with Princess Mary, because he did not understand her but simply loved her.

Reveries about Sónya had had something merry and playful in them, but to dream of Princess Mary was always difficult and a little frightening.

"How she prayed!" he thought. "It was plain that her whole soul was in her prayer. Yes, that was the prayer that moves mountains, and I am sure her prayer will be answered. Why don't I pray for what I want?" he suddenly thought. "What do I want? To be free, released from Sónya . . . She was right," he thought, remembering what the governor's wife had said: "Nothing but misfortune can come of marrying Sónya. Muddles, grief for Mamma . . . business difficulties . . . muddles, terrible muddles! Besides, I don't love her—not as I should. O God! release me from this dreadful, inextricable position!" he suddenly began to pray. "Yes, prayer can move mountains, but one must have faith and not pray as Natásha and I used to as children, that the snow might turn into sugar—and then run out into the yard to see whether it had done so. No, but I am not praying for trifles now," he thought as he put his pipe down in a corner, and folding his hands placed himself before the icon. Softened by memories of Princess Mary he began to pray as he had not done for a long time. Tears were in his eyes and in his throat when the door opened and Lavrúshka came in with some papers.

"Blockhead! Why do you come in without being called?" cried Nicholas, quickly changing his attitude.

"From the governor," said Lavrúshka in a sleepy voice. "A courier has arrived and there's a letter for you."

"Well, all right, thanks. You can go!"

Nicholas took the two letters, one of which was from his mother and the other from Sónya. He recognized them by the handwriting and opened Sónya's first. He had read only a few lines when he turned pale and his eyes opened wide with fear and joy.

"No, it's not possible!" he cried aloud.

Unable to sit still he paced up and down the room holding the letter and reading it. He glanced through it, then read it again, and then again, and standing still in the middle of the room he raised his shoulders, stretching out his hands, with his mouth wide-open and his eyes fixed. What he had just been praying for with confidence that God would hear him had come to pass; but Nicholas was as much astonished as if it were something extraordinary and unexpected, and as if the very fact that it had happened so quickly proved that it had not come from God to whom he had prayed, but by some ordinary coincidence.

This unexpected and as it seemed to Nicholas quite voluntary letter from Sónya, freed him from the knot that fettered him and from which there had seemed no escape. She wrote that the last unfortunate events—the loss of almost the whole of the Rostóvs' Moscow property—and the countess's repeatedly expressed wish that Nicholas should marry Princess Bolkónskaya, together with his silence and coldness of late, had all combined to make her decide to release him from his promise and set him completely free.

"It would be too painful to me to think that I might be a cause of sorrow or discord in the family that has been so good to me," she wrote, "and my love has no aim but the happiness of those I love; so, Nicholas, I beg you to consider yourself free, and to be assured that, in spite of everything, no one can love you more than does

YOUR SÓNYA"

Both letters were written from Tróitsa. The other, from the countess, described their last days in Moscow, their departure, the fire, and the destruction of all their property. In this letter the countess also mentioned that Prince Andrew was among the wounded traveling with them; his state was very critical, but the doctor said there was now more hope. Sónya and Natásha were nursing him.

Next day Nicholas took his mother's letter and went to see Princess Mary. Neither he nor she said a word about what "Natásha nursing him" might mean, but thanks to this letter Nicholas suddenly became almost as intimate with the princess as if they were relations.

The following day he saw Princess Mary off on her journey to Yaroslávl, and a few days later left to rejoin his regiment.

Chapter VIII

SÓNYA'S LETTER WRITTEN FROM TRÓITSA, WHICH HAD COME AS AN ANSWER TO NICHOLAS'S prayer, was prompted by this: the thought of getting Nicholas married to an heiress occupied the old countess's mind more and more. She knew that Sónya was the chief obstacle to this happening, and Sónya's life in the countess's house had grown harder and harder, especially after they had received a letter from Nicholas telling of his meeting with Princess Mary in Boguchárovo. The countess let no occasion slip of making humiliating or cruel allusions to Sónya.

But a few days before they left Moscow, moved and excited by all that was going on she called Sónya to her and, instead of reproaching and making demands on her, tearfully implored her to sacrifice herself and repay all that the family had done for her by breaking off her engagement with Nicholas.

"I shall not be at peace till you promise me this."

Sónya burst into hysterical tears and replied through her sobs that she would do anything and was prepared for anything, but gave no actual promise and could not bring herself to decide to do what was demanded of her. She must sacrifice herself for the family that had reared and brought her up. To sacrifice herself for others was Sónya's habit. Her position in the house was such that only by sacrifice could she show her worth, and she was accustomed to this and loved doing it. But in all her former acts of self-sacrifice she had been happily conscious that they raised her in her own esteem and in that of others, and so made her more worthy of Nicholas whom she loved more than anything in the world. But now they wanted her to sacrifice the very thing that constituted the whole reward for her self-sacrifice and the whole meaning of her life. And for the first time she felt bitterness against those who had been her benefactors only to torture her the more painfully; she felt jealous of Natásha who had never experienced anything of this sort, had never needed to sacrifice herself, but made others sacrifice themselves for her and yet was beloved by everybody. And for the first time Sónya felt that out of her pure, quiet love for Nicholas a passionate feeling was beginning to grow up which was stronger than principle, virtue or religion. Under the influence of this feeling Sónya, whose life of dependence had taught her involuntarily to be secretive, having answered the countess in vague general terms, avoided talking with her and resolved to wait till she should see Nicholas, not in order to set him free but on the contrary at that meeting to bind him to her forever.

The bustle and terror of the Rostóvs' last days in Moscow stifled the gloomy thoughts that oppressed Sónya. She was glad to find escape from them in practical activity. But when she heard of Prince Andrew's presence in their house, despite her sincere pity for him and for Natásha, she was seized by a joyful and superstitious feeling that God did not intend her to be separated from Nicholas. She knew that Natásha loved no one but Prince Andrew and had never ceased to love him. She knew that being thrown together again under such terrible circumstances they would again fall in love with one another, and that Nicholas would then not be able to marry Princess Mary as they would be within the prohibited degrees of affinity. Despite all the terror of what had happened during those last days and during the first days of their journey, this feeling that Providence was intervening in her personal affairs cheered Sónya.

At the Tróitsa monastery the Rostóvs first broke their journey for a whole day.

Three large rooms were assigned to them in the monastery hostelry, one of which was occupied by Prince Andrew. The wounded man was much better that day and Natásha was sitting with him. In the next room sat the count and countess respectfully conversing with the Prior, who was calling on them as old acquaintances and benefactors of the monastery. Sónya was there too, tormented by curiosity as to what Prince Andrew and Natásha were talking about. She heard the sound of their voices through the door. That door opened and Natásha came out, looking excited. Not noticing the monk, who had risen to greet her and was drawing back the wide sleeve on his right arm, she went up to Sónya and took her hand.

"Natásha, what are you about? Come here!" said the countess.

Natásha went up to the monk for his blessing, and he advised her to pray for aid to God and His saint.

As soon as the Prior withdrew Natásha took her friend by the hand and went with her into the unoccupied room.

"Sónya, will he live?" she asked. "Sónya, how happy I am, and how unhappy! . . . Sónya, dovey, everything is as it used to be. If only he lives! He cannot . . . because . . . because . . . of . . ." and Natásha burst into tears.

"Yes, I knew it! Thank God!" murmured Sónya. "He will live."

Sónya was not less agitated than her friend by the latter's fear and grief and by her own personal feelings which she shared with no one. Sobbing, she kissed and comforted Natásha. "If only he lives!" she thought. Having wept, talked, and wiped away her tears, the two friends went together to Prince Andrew's door. Natásha opened it cautiously and glanced into the room, Sónya standing beside her at the half-open door.

Prince Andrew was lying raised high on three pillows. His pale face was calm, his eyes closed, and they could see his regular breathing.

"Oh Natásha!" Sónya suddenly almost screamed, catching her companion's arm, and stepping back from the door.

"What? What is it?" asked Natásha.

"It's that, that . . ." said Sónya, with a white face and trembling lips.

Natásha softly closed the door and went with Sónya to the window, not yet understanding what the latter was telling her.

"You remember," said Sónya with a solemn and frightened expression. "You remember when I looked in the mirror for you . . . at Otrádnoe at Christmas? Do you remember what I saw?"

"Yes, yes!" cried Natásha opening her eyes wide, and vaguely recalling that Sónya had told her something about Prince Andrew whom she had seen lying down.

"You remember?" Sónya went on. "I saw it then and told everybody, you and Dunyásha. I saw him lying on a bed," said she, making a gesture with her hand and a lifted finger at each detail, "and that he had his eyes closed and was covered just with a pink quilt, and that his hands were folded," she concluded, convincing herself that the details she had just seen were exactly what she had seen in the mirror.

She had in fact seen nothing then but had mentioned the first thing that came into her head, but what she had invented then seemed to her now as real as any other recollection. She not only remembered what she had then said—that he turned to look at her and smiled and was covered with something red, but was firmly convinced that she had then seen and said that he was covered with a pink quilt and that his eyes were closed.

"Yes, yes, it really was pink!" cried Natásha, who now thought she too remembered the word pink being used, and saw in this the most extraordinary and mysterious part of the prediction.

"But what does it mean?" she added meditatively.

"Oh I don't know, it is all so strange," replied Sónya, clutching at her head.

A few minutes later Prince Andrew rang and Natásha went to him, but Sónya, feeling unusually excited and touched, remained at the window thinking about the strangeness of what had occurred.

They had an opportunity that day to send letters to the army, and the countess was writing to her son.

"Sónya!" said the countess, raising her eyes from her letter as her niece passed, "Sónya, won't you write to Nicholas?" She spoke in a soft tremulous voice, and in the weary eyes that looked over her spectacles Sónya read all that the countess meant to convey with these words. Those eyes expressed entreaty, shame at having to ask, fear of a refusal, and readiness for relentless hatred in case of such refusal.

Sónya went up to the countess and, kneeling down, kissed her hand.

"Yes, Mamma, I will write," said she.

Sónya was softened, excited, and touched by all that had occurred that day, especially by the mysterious fulfillment she had just seen of her vision. Now that she knew that the renewal of Natásha's relations with Prince Andrew would prevent Nicholas from marrying Princess Mary, she was joyfully conscious of a return of that self-sacrificing spirit in which she was accustomed to live and loved to live. So with a joyful consciousness of performing a magnanimous deed—interrupted several times by the tears that dimmed her velvety black eyes—she wrote that touching letter the arrival of which had so amazed Nicholas.

Chapter IX

THE OFFICER AND SOLDIERS WHO HAD ARRESTED PIERRE TREATED HIM WITH HOSTILITY BUT YET with respect, in the guardhouse to which he was taken. In their attitude toward him could still be felt both uncertainty as to who he might be—perhaps a very important person—and hostility as a result of their recent personal conflict with him.

But when the guard was relieved next morning, Pierre felt that for the new guard—both officers and men—he was not as interesting as he had been to his captors; and in fact the guard of the second day did not recognize in this big, stout man in a peasant coat the vigorous person who had fought so desperately with the marauder and the convoy and had uttered those solemn words about saving a child; they saw in him only No. 17 of the captured Russians, arrested and detained for some reason by order of the Higher Command. If they noticed anything remarkable about Pierre, it was only his unabashed, meditative concentration and thoughtfulness, and the way he spoke French, which struck them as surprisingly good. In spite of this he was placed that day with the other arrested suspects, as the separate room he had occupied was required by an officer.

All the Russians confined with Pierre were men of the lowest class and, recognizing him as a gentleman, they all avoided him, more especially as he spoke French. Pierre felt sad at hearing them making fun of him.

That evening he learned that all these prisoners (he, probably, among them) were to be tried for incendiarism. On the third day he was taken with the others to a house where a French general with a white mustache sat with two colonels and other Frenchmen with scarves on their arms. With the precision and definiteness customary in addressing prisoners, and which is supposed to preclude human frailty, Pierre like the others was questioned as to who he was, where he had been, with what object, and so on.

These questions, like questions put at trials generally, left the essence of the matter aside, shut out the possibility of that essence's being revealed, and were designed only to form a channel through which the judges wished the answers of the accused to flow so as to lead to the desired result, namely a conviction. As soon as Pierre began to say anything that did not fit in with that aim, the channel was removed and the water could flow to waste. Pierre felt, moreover, what the accused always feel at their trial, perplexity as to why these questions were put to him. He had a feeling that it was only out of condescension or a kind of civility, that this device of placing a channel was employed. He knew he was in these men's power, that only by force had they brought him there, that force alone gave them the right to demand answers to their questions, and that the sole object of that assembly was to inculpate him. And so, as they had the power and wish to inculpate him, this expedient of an inquiry and trial seemed unnecessary. It was evident that any answer would lead to conviction. When asked what he was doing when he was arrested, Pierre replied in a rather tragic manner that he was restoring to its parents a child he had saved from the flames. Why had he fought the marauder? Pierre answered that he "was protecting a woman," and that "to protect a woman who was being insulted, was the duty of every man; that . . ." They interrupted him, for this was not to the point. Why was he in the yard of a burning house where witnesses had seen him? He replied that he had gone out to see what was happening in Moscow. Again they interrupted him: they had not asked where he was going, but why he was found near the fire? Who was he? they asked, repeating their first question, which he had declined to answer. Again he replied that he could not answer it.

"Put that down, that's bad . . . very bad," sternly remarked the general with the white mustache and red flushed face.

On the fourth day fires broke out on the Zúbovski rampart.

Pierre and thirteen others were moved to the coach house of a merchant's house near the Crimean Bridge. On his way through the streets Pierre felt stifled by the smoke which seemed to hang over the whole city. Fires were visible on all sides. He did not then realize the significance of the burning of Moscow, and looked at the fires with horror.

He passed four days in the coach house near the Crimean Bridge and during that time learned, from the talk of the French soldiers, that all those confined there were awaiting a decision which might come any day from the marshal. What marshal this was, Pierre could not learn from the soldiers. Evidently for them "the marshal" represented a very high and rather mysterious power.

These first days, before the 8th of September when the prisoners were had up for a second examination, were the hardest of all for Pierre.

Chapter X

On the 8th of September an officer—a very important one judging by the respect the guards showed him—entered the coach house where the prisoners were. This officer, probably someone on the staff, was holding a paper in his hand, and called over all the Russians there, naming Pierre as "the man who does not give his name." Glancing indolently and indifferently at all the prisoners, he ordered the officer in charge to have them decently dressed and tidied up before taking them to the marshal. An hour later a squad of soldiers arrived and Pierre with thirteen others was led to the Virgin's Field. It was a fine day, sunny after rain, and the air was unusually pure. The smoke did not hang low as on the day when Pierre had been taken from the guardhouse on the Zúbovski rampart, but rose through the pure air in columns. No flames were seen, but columns of smoke rose on all sides, and all Moscow as far as Pierre could see was one vast charred ruin. On all sides there were waste spaces with only stoves and chimney stacks still standing, and here and there the blackened walls of some brick houses. Pierre gazed at the ruins and did not recognize districts he had known well. Here and there he could see churches that had not been burned. The Kremlin, which was not destroyed, gleamed white in the distance with its towers and the belfry of Iván the Great. The domes of the New Convent of the Virgin glittered brightly and its bells were ringing particularly clearly. These bells reminded Pierre that it was Sunday, and the feast of the Nativity of the Virgin. But there seemed to be no one to celebrate this holiday: everywhere were blackened ruins, and the few Russians to be seen were tattered and frightened people who tried to hide when they saw the French.

It was plain that the Russian nest was ruined and destroyed, but in place of the Russian order of life that had been destroyed, Pierre unconsciously felt that a quite different, firm, French order had been established over this ruined nest. He felt this in the looks of the soldiers who, marching in regular ranks briskly and gaily, were escorting him and the other criminals; he felt it in the looks of an important French official in a carriage and pair driven by a soldier, whom they met on the way.

He felt it in the merry sounds of regimental music he heard from the left side of the field, and felt and realized it especially from the list of prisoners the French officer had read out when he came that morning. Pierre had been taken by one set of soldiers and led first to one and then to another place with dozens of other men, and it seemed that they might have forgotten him, or confused him with the others. But no: the answers he had given when questioned had come back to him in his designation as "the man who does not give his name," and under that appellation, which to Pierre seemed terrible, they were now leading him somewhere with unhesitating assurance on their faces that he and all the other prisoners were exactly the ones they wanted and that they were being taken to the proper place. Pierre felt himself to be an insignificant chip fallen among the wheels of a machine whose action he did not understand but which was working well.

He and the other prisoners were taken to the right side of the Virgin's Field, to a large white house with an immense garden not far from the convent. This was Prince Shcherbátov's house, where Pierre had often been in other days, and which, as he learned from the talk of the soldiers, was now occupied by the marshal, the Duke of Eckmhl (Davout).

They were taken to the entrance, and led into the house one by one. Pierre was the sixth to enter. He was conducted through a glass gallery, an anteroom and a hall, which were familiar to him, into a long low study at the door of which stood an adjutant.

Davout, spectacles on nose, sat bent over a table at the further end of the room. Pierre went close up to him, but Davout, evidently consulting a paper that lay before him, did not look up. Without raising his eyes, he said in a low voice:

"Who are you?"

Pierre was silent because he was incapable of uttering a word. To him Davout was not merely a French general, but a man notorious for his cruelty. Looking at his cold face, as he sat like a stern schoolmaster who was prepared to wait a while for an answer, Pierre felt that every instant of delay might cost him his life; but he did not know what to say. He did not venture to repeat what he had said at his first examination, yet to disclose his rank and position was dangerous and embarrassing. So he was silent. But before he had decided what to do, Davout raised his head, pushed his spectacles back on his forehead, screwed up his eyes, and looked intently at him.

"I know that man," he said in a cold, measured tone, evidently calculated to frighten Pierre.

The chill that had been running down Pierre's back now seized his head as in a vise.

"You cannot know me, general, I have never seen you . . ."

"He is a Russian spy," Davout interrupted, addressing another general who was present, but whom Pierre had not noticed.

Davout turned away. With an unexpected reverberation in his voice Pierre rapidly began:

"No, monseigneur," he said, suddenly remembering that Davout was a duke. "No, monseigneur, you cannot have known me. I am a militia officer and have not quitted Moscow."

"Your name?" asked Davout.

"Bezúkhov."

"What proof have I that you are not lying?"

"Monseigneur!" exclaimed Pierre not in an offended but in a pleading voice.

Davout looked up and gazed intently at him. For some seconds they looked at one another, and that look saved Pierre. Apart from conditions of war and law, that look established human relations between the two men. At that moment an immense number of things passed dimly through both their minds, and they realized that they were both children of humanity and were brothers.

At the first glance, when Davout had only raised his head from the papers where human affairs and lives were indicated by numbers, Pierre was merely a circumstance, and Davout could have shot him without burdening his conscience with an evil deed, but now he saw in him a human being. He reflected for a moment.

"How can you show me that you are telling the truth?" said Davout coldly.

Pierre remembered Ramballe, and named him and his regiment and the street where the house was.

"You are not what you say," returned Davout.

In a trembling, faltering voice Pierre began adducing proofs of the truth of his statements.

But at that moment an adjutant entered and reported something to Davout.

Davout brightened up at the news the adjutant brought, and began buttoning up his uniform. It seemed that he had quite forgotten Pierre.

When the adjutant reminded him of the prisoner, he jerked his head in Pierre's direction with a frown and ordered him to be led away. But where they were to take him Pierre did not know: back to the coach house or to the place of execution his companions had pointed out to him as they crossed the Virgin's Field.

He turned his head and saw that the adjutant was putting another question to Davout.

"Yes, of course!" replied Davout, but what this *"yes"* meant, Pierre did not know.

Pierre could not afterward remember how he went, whether it was far, or in which direction. His faculties were quite numbed, he was stupefied, and noticing nothing around him went on moving his legs as the others did till they all stopped and he stopped too. The only thought in his mind at that time was: Who was it that had really sentenced him to death? Not the men on the Commission that had first examined him—not one of them wished to or, evidently, could have done it. It was not Davout, who had looked at him in so human a way. In another moment Davout would have realized that he was doing wrong, but just then the adjutant had come in and interrupted him. The adjutant, also, had evidently had no evil intent though he might have refrained from coming in. Then who was executing him, killing him, depriving him of life—him, Pierre, with all his memories, aspirations, hopes and thoughts? Who was doing this? And Pierre felt that it was no one.

It was a system—a concurrence of circumstances.

A system of some sort was killing me—Pierre—depriving him of life, of everything, annihilating him.

Chapter XI

FROM PRINCE SHCHERBÁTOV'S HOUSE THE PRISONERS WERE LED STRAIGHT DOWN THE VIRGIN'S Field, to the left of the nunnery, as far as a kitchen-garden in which a post had been set up. Beyond that post a fresh pit had been dug in the ground, and near the post and the pit a large crowd stood in a semicircle. The crowd consisted of a few Russians and many of Napoleon's soldiers who were not on duty—Germans, Italians and Frenchmen, in a variety of uniforms. To the right and left of the post stood rows of French troops in blue uniforms with red epaulets and high boots and shakos.

The prisoners were placed in a certain order, according to the list (Pierre was sixth), and were led to the post. Several drums suddenly began to beat on both sides of them, and at that sound Pierre felt as if part of his soul had been torn away. He lost the power of thinking or understanding. He could only hear and see. And he had only one wish—that the frightful thing that had to happen should happen quickly. Pierre looked round at his fellow-prisoners and scrutinized them.

The two first were convicts with shaven heads. One was tall and thin, the other dark, shaggy and sinewy, with a flat nose. The third was a domestic serf, about forty-five years old, with grizzled hair and a plump, well-nourished body. The fourth was a peasant, a very handsome man with a broad light-brown beard and black eyes. The fifth was a factory-hand, a thin, sallow-faced lad of eighteen in a loose cloak.

Pierre heard the French consulting whether to shoot them separately or two at a time. "In couples," replied the officer in command in a calm voice. There was a stir in the ranks of the soldiers and it was evident that they were all hurrying—not as men hurry to do something they understand, but as people hurry to finish a necessary but unpleasant and incomprehensible task.

A French official wearing a scarf came up to the right of the row of prisoners, and read out the sentence in Russian and in French.

Then two pairs of Frenchmen approached the criminals, and at the officer's command took the two convicts who stood first in the row. The convicts stopped when they reached the post and, while sacks were being brought, looked dumbly around as a wounded beast looks at an approaching huntsman. One crossed himself continually, the other scratched his back and made a movement of the lips resembling a smile. With hurried hands the soldiers blindfolded them, drawing the sacks over their heads, and bound them to the post.

Twelve sharpshooters with muskets stepped out of the ranks with a firm regular tread, and halted eight paces from the post. Pierre turned away to avoid seeing what was going to happen. Suddenly a crackling rolling noise was heard which seemed to him louder than the most terrific thunder, and he looked round. There was some smoke, and the Frenchmen were doing something near the pit, with pale faces and trembling hands. Two more prisoners were led up. In the same way and with similar looks, these two glanced vainly at the onlookers with only a silent appeal for protection in their eyes, evidently unable to understand or believe what was going to happen to them. They could not believe it because they alone knew what their life meant to them, and so they neither understood nor believed that it could be taken from them.

Again Pierre did not wish to look, and again turned away; but again the sound as of a frightful explosion struck his ear, and at the same moment he saw smoke, blood, and the pale, scared faces of the Frenchmen who were again doing something by the post, their trembling hands impeding one another. Pierre, breathing heavily, looked around as if asking what it meant. The same question was expressed in all the looks that met his.

On the faces of all the Russians and of the French soldiers and officers without exception, he read the same dismay, horror and conflict that were in his own heart. "But who, after all, is doing this? They are all suffering as I am. Who then is it? Who?" flashed for an instant through his mind.

"Sharpshooters of the 86th, forward!" shouted someone. The fifth prisoner, the one next to Pierre, was led away—alone. Pierre did not understand that he was saved, that he and the rest had been brought there only to witness the execution. With ever-growing horror, and no sense of joy or relief, he gazed at what was taking place. The fifth man was the factory lad in the loose cloak. The moment they laid hands on him he sprang aside in terror and clutched at Pierre. (Pierre shuddered and shook himself free.) The lad was unable to walk. They dragged him along holding him up under the arms, and he screamed. When they got him to the post he grew quiet, as if he suddenly understood something. Whether he understood that screaming was useless, or whether he thought it incredible that men should kill him, at any rate he took his stand at the post, waiting to be blindfolded like the others, and like a wounded animal looked around him with glittering eyes.

Pierre was no longer able to turn away and close his eyes. His curiosity and agitation, like that of the whole crowd, reached the highest pitch at this fifth murder. Like the others this fifth man seemed calm; he wrapped his loose cloak closer and rubbed one bare foot with the other.

When they began to blindfold him he himself adjusted the knot which hurt the back of his head; then when they propped him against the bloodstained post, he leaned back and, not being comfortable in that position, straightened himself, adjusted his feet, and leaned back again more comfortably. Pierre did not take his eyes from him and did not miss his slightest movement.

Probably a word of command was given and was followed by the reports of eight muskets; but try as he would Pierre could not afterward remember having heard the slightest sound of the shots. He only saw how the workman suddenly sank down on the cord that held him, how blood showed itself in two places, how the ropes slackened under the weight of the hanging body, and how the workman sat down, his head hanging unnaturally and one leg bent under him. Pierre ran up to the post. No one hindered him. Pale, frightened people were doing something around the workman. The lower jaw of an old Frenchman with a thick mustache trembled as he untied the ropes. The body collapsed. The soldiers dragged it awkwardly from the post and began pushing it into the pit.

They all plainly and certainly knew that they were criminals who must hide the traces of their guilt as quickly as possible.

Pierre glanced into the pit, and saw that the factory lad was lying with his knees close up to his head and one shoulder higher than the other. That shoulder rose and fell rhythmically and convulsively, but spadefuls of earth were already being thrown over the whole body. One of the soldiers, evidently suffering, shouted gruffly and angrily at Pierre to go back. But Pierre did not understand him and remained near the post, and no one drove him away.

When the pit had been filled up a command was given. Pierre was taken back to his place, and the rows of troops on both sides of the post made a half-turn and went past it at a measured pace. The twenty-four sharpshooters with discharged muskets, standing in the center of the circle, ran back to their places as the companies passed by.

Pierre gazed now with dazed eyes at these sharpshooters who ran in couples out of the circle. All but one rejoined their companies. This one, a young soldier, his face deadly pale, his shako pushed back, and his musket resting on the ground, still stood near the pit at the spot from which he had fired. He swayed like a drunken man, taking some steps forward and back to save himself from falling. An old, non-commissioned officer ran out of the ranks and taking him by the elbow dragged him to his company. The crowd of Russians and Frenchmen began to disperse. They all went away silently and with drooping heads.

"That will teach them to start fires," said one of the Frenchmen.

Pierre glanced round at the speaker and saw that it was a soldier who was trying to find some relief after what had been done, but was not able to do so. Without finishing what he had begun to say he made a hopeless movement with his arm and went away.

Chapter XII

After the execution Pierre was separated from the rest of the prisoners and placed alone in a small, ruined and befouled church.

Toward evening a non-commissioned officer entered with two soldiers and told him that he had been pardoned and would now go to the barracks for the prisoners-of-war. Without understanding what was said to him, Pierre got up and went with the soldiers. They took him to the upper end of the field, where there were some sheds built of charred planks, beams and battens, and led him into one of them. In the darkness some twenty different men surrounded Pierre. He looked at them without understanding who they were, why they were there, or what they wanted of him. He heard what they said, but did not understand the meaning of the words and made no kind of deduction from or application of them. He replied to questions they put to him, but did not consider who was listening to his replies, nor how they would understand them. He looked at their faces and figures, but they all seemed to him equally meaningless.

From the moment Pierre had witnessed those terrible murders committed by men who did not wish to commit them, it was as if the mainspring of his life, on which everything depended and which made everything appear alive, had suddenly been wrenched out and everything had collapsed into a heap of meaningless rubbish. Though he did not acknowledge it to himself, his faith in the right ordering of the universe, in humanity, in his own soul and in God, had been destroyed. He had experienced this before, but never so strongly as now. When similar doubts had assailed him before, they had been the result of his own wrongdoing, and at the bottom of his heart he had felt that relief from his despair and from those doubts was to be found within himself. But now he felt that the universe had crumbled before his eyes and only meaningless ruins remained, and this not by any fault of his own. He felt that it was not in his power to regain faith in the meaning of life.

Around him in the darkness men were standing and evidently something about him interested them greatly. They were telling him something and asking him something. Then they led him away somewhere, and at last he found himself in a corner of the shed among men who were laughing and talking on all sides.

"Well, then, mates . . . that very prince *who* . . ." some voice at the other end of the shed was saying, with a strong emphasis on the word *who*.

Sitting silent and motionless on a heap of straw against the wall, Pierre sometimes opened and sometimes closed his eyes. But as soon as he closed them he saw before him the dreadful face of the factory lad—especially dreadful because of its simplicity—and the faces of the murderers, even more dreadful because of their disquiet. And he opened his eyes again and stared vacantly into the darkness around him.

Beside him in a stooping position sat a small man of whose presence he was first made aware by a strong smell of perspiration which came from him every time he moved. This man was doing something to his legs in the darkness, and though Pierre could not see his face he felt that the man continually glanced at him. On growing used to the darkness Pierre saw that the man was taking off his legbands, and the way he did it aroused Pierre's interest.

Having unwound the string that tied the band on one leg, he carefully coiled it up and immediately set to work on the other leg, glancing up at Pierre. While one hand hung up the first string the other was already unwinding the band on the second leg. In this way, having carefully removed the legbands by deft circular motions of his arm following one another uninterruptedly, the man hung the legbands up on some pegs fixed above his head. Then he took out a knife, cut something, closed the knife, placed it under the head of his bed, and seating himself comfortably, clasped his arms round his lifted knees and fixed his eyes on Pierre. The latter was conscious of something pleasant, comforting and well-rounded in these deft movements, in the man's well-ordered arrangements in his corner, and even in his very smell, and he looked at the man without taking his eyes from him.

"You've seen a lot of trouble, sir, eh?" the little man suddenly said.

And there was so much kindliness and simplicity in his sing-song voice that Pierre tried to reply, but his jaw trembled and he felt tears rising to his eyes. The little fellow, giving Pierre no time to betray his confusion, instantly continued in the same pleasant tones:

"Eh, lad, don't fret!" said he, in the tender sing-song caressing voice old Russian peasant women employ. "Don't fret, friend—'suffer an hour, live for an age!' that's how it is, my dear fellow. And here we live, thank Heaven, without offense. Among these folk, too, there are good men as well as bad," said he, and still speaking, he turned on his knees with a supple movement, got up, coughed, and went off to another part of the shed.

"Eh, you rascal!" Pierre heard the same kind voice saying at the other end of the shed. "So you've come, you rascal? She remembers. . . . Now, now, that'll do!"

And the soldier, pushing away a little dog that was jumping up at him, returned to his place and sat down. In his hands he had something wrapped in a rag.

"Here, eat a bit, sir," said he, resuming his former respectful tone as he unwrapped and offered Pierre some baked potatoes. "We had soup for dinner and the potatoes are grand!"

Pierre had not eaten all day and the smell of the potatoes seemed extremely pleasant to him. He thanked the soldier and began to eat.

"Well, are they all right?" said the soldier with a smile. "You should do like this."

He took a potato, drew out his clasp knife, cut the potato into two equal halves on the palm of his hand, sprinkled some salt on it from the rag, and handed it to Pierre.

"The potatoes are grand!" he said once more. "Eat some like that!"

Pierre thought he had never eaten anything that tasted better.

"Oh, I'm all right," said he, "but why did they shoot those poor fellows? The last one was hardly twenty."

"Tss, tt . . . !" said the little man. "Ah, what a sin . . . what a sin!" he added quickly, and as if his words were always waiting ready in his mouth and flew out involuntarily he went on: "How was it, sir, that you stayed in Moscow?"

"I didn't think they would come so soon. I stayed accidentally," replied Pierre.

"And how did they arrest you, dear lad? At your house?"

"No, I went to look at the fire, and they arrested me there, and tried me as an incendiary."

"Where there's law there's injustice," put in the little man.

"And have you been here long?" Pierre asked as he munched the last of the potato.

"I? It was last Sunday they took me, out of a hospital in Moscow."

"Why, are you a soldier then?"

"Yes, we are soldiers of the œpsheron regiment. I was dying of fever. We weren't told anything. There were some twenty of us lying there. We had no idea, never guessed at all."

"And do you feel sad here?" Pierre inquired.

"How can one help it, lad? My name is Platón, and the surname is Karatáev," he added, evidently wishing to make it easier for Pierre to address him. "They call me 'little falcon' in the regiment. How is one to help feeling sad? Moscow—she's the mother of cities. How can one see all this and not feel sad? But 'the maggot gnaws the cabbage, yet dies first'; that's what the old folks used to tell us," he added rapidly.

"What? What did you say?" asked Pierre.

"Who? I?" said Karatáev. "I say things happen not as we plan but as God judges," he replied, thinking that he was repeating what he had said before, and immediately continued:

"Well, and you, have you a family estate, sir? And a house? So you have abundance, then? And a housewife? And your old parents, are they still living?" he asked.

And though it was too dark for Pierre to see, he felt that a suppressed smile of kindliness puckered the soldier's lips as he put these questions. He seemed grieved that Pierre had no parents, especially that he had no mother.

"A wife for counsel, a mother-in-law for welcome, but there's none as dear as one's own mother!" said he. "Well, and have you little ones?" he went on asking.

Again Pierre's negative answer seemed to distress him, and he hastened to add:

"Never mind! You're young folks yet, and please God may still have some. The great thing is to live in harmony. . . ."

"But it's all the same now," Pierre could not help saying.

"Ah, my dear fellow!" rejoined Karatáev, "never decline a prison or a beggar's sack!"

He seated himself more comfortably and coughed, evidently preparing to tell a long story.

"Well, my dear fellow, I was still living at home," he began. "We had a well-to-do homestead, plenty of land, we peasants lived well and our house was one to thank God for. When father and we went out mowing there were seven of us. We lived well. We were real peasants. It so happened . . ."

And Platón Karatáev told a long story of how he had gone into someone's copse to take wood, how he had been caught by the keeper, had been tried, flogged, and sent to serve as a soldier.

"Well, lad," and a smile changed the tone of his voice, "we thought it was a misfortune but it turned out a blessing! If it had not been for my sin, my brother would have had to go as a soldier.

But he, my younger brother, had five little ones, while I, you see, only left a wife behind. We had a little girl, but God took her before I went as a soldier. I came home on leave and I'll tell you how it was, I look and see that they are living better than before. The yard full of cattle, the women at home, two brothers away earning wages, and only Michael, the youngest, at home. Father, he says, 'All my children are the same to me: it hurts the same whichever finger gets bitten. But if Platón hadn't been shaved for a soldier, Michael would have had to go.' He calls us all to him and, will you believe it, placed us in front of the icons. 'Michael,' he says, 'come here and bow down to his feet; and you, young woman, you bow down too; and you, grandchildren, also bow down before him! Do you understand?' he says. That's how it is, dear fellow. Fate looks for a head. But we are always judging, 'that's not well—that's not right!' Our luck is like water in a drag-net: you pull at it and it bulges, but when you've drawn it out it's empty! That's how it is."

And Platón shifted his seat on the straw.

After a short silence he rose.

"Well, I think you must be sleepy," said he, and began rapidly crossing himself and repeating:

"Lord Jesus Christ, holy Saint Nicholas, Frola and Lavra! Lord Jesus Christ, holy Saint Nicholas, Frola and Lavra! Lord Jesus Christ, have mercy on us and save us!" he concluded, then bowed to the ground, got up, sighed, and sat down again on his heap of straw. "That's the way. Lay me down like a stone, O God, and raise me up like a loaf," he muttered as he lay down, pulling his coat over him.

"What prayer was that you were saying?" asked Pierre.

"Eh?" murmured Platón, who had almost fallen asleep. "What was I saying? I was praying. Don't you pray?"

"Yes, I do," said Pierre. "But what was that you said: Frola and Lavra?"

"Well, of course," replied Platón quickly, "the horses' saints. One must pity the animals too. Eh, the rascal! Now you've curled up and got warm, you daughter of a bitch!" said Karatáev, touching the dog that lay at his feet, and again turning over he fell asleep immediately.

Sounds of crying and screaming came from somewhere in the distance outside, and flames were visible through the cracks of the shed, but inside it was quiet and dark. For a long time Pierre did not sleep, but lay with eyes open in the darkness, listening to the regular snoring of Platón who lay beside him, and he felt that the world that had been shattered was once more stirring in his soul with a new beauty and on new and unshakable foundations.

Chapter XIII

TWENTY-THREE SOLDIERS, THREE OFFICERS AND TWO OFFICIALS WERE CONFINED IN THE SHED in which Pierre had been placed and where he remained for four weeks.

When Pierre remembered them afterward they all seemed misty figures to him except Platón Karatáev, who always remained in his mind a most vivid and precious memory and the personification of everything Russian, kindly and round. When Pierre saw his neighbor next morning at dawn the first impression of him, as of something round, was fully confirmed: Platón's whole figure—in a French overcoat girdled with a cord, a soldier's cap, and bast shoes—was round. His head was quite round, his back, chest, shoulders, and even his arms, which he held as if ever ready to embrace something, were rounded, his pleasant smile and his large gentle brown eyes were also round.

Platón Karatáev must have been fifty judging by his stories of campaigns he had been in, told as by an old soldier. He did not himself know his age and was quite unable to determine it. But his brilliantly white, strong teeth which showed in two unbroken semicircles when he laughed—as he often did—were all sound and good, there was not a gray hair in his beard or on his head, and his whole body gave an impression of suppleness and especially of firmness and endurance.

His face, despite its fine, rounded wrinkles, had an expression of innocence and youth, his voice was pleasant and musical. But the chief peculiarity of his speech was its directness and appositeness. It was evident that he never considered what he had said or was going to say, and consequently the rapidity and justice of his intonation had an irresistible persuasiveness.

His physical strength and agility during the first days of his imprisonment were such that he seemed not to know what fatigue and sickness meant. Every night before lying down, he said: "Lord, lay me down as a stone and raise me up as a loaf!" and every morning on getting up, he said: "I lay down and curled up, I get up and shake myself." And indeed he only had to lie down, to fall asleep like a stone, and he only had to shake himself, to be ready without a moment's delay for some work, just as children are ready to play directly they awake. He could do everything, not very well but not badly. He baked, cooked, sewed, planed, and mended boots. He was always busy, and only at night allowed himself conversation—of which he was fond—and songs. He did not sing like a trained singer who knows he is listened to, but like the birds, evidently giving vent to the sounds in the same way that one stretches oneself or walks about to get rid of stiffness, and the sounds were always high-pitched, mournful, delicate, and almost feminine, and his face at such times was very serious.

Having been taken prisoner and allowed his beard to grow, he seemed to have thrown off all that had been forced upon him—everything military and alien to himself—and had returned to his former peasant habits.

"A soldier on leave—a shirt outside breeches," he would say.

He did not like talking about his life as a soldier, though he did not complain, and often mentioned that he had not been flogged once during the whole of his army service. When he related anything it was generally some old and evidently precious memory of his "Christian" life, as he called his peasant existence. The proverbs, of which his talk was full, were for the most part not the coarse and indecent saws soldiers employ, but those folk-sayings which taken without a context seem so insignificant, but when used appositely suddenly acquire a significance of profound wisdom.

He would often say the exact opposite of what he had said on a previous occasion, yet both would be right. He liked to talk and he talked well, adorning his speech with terms of endearment and with folk-sayings which Pierre thought he invented himself, but the chief charm of his talk lay in the fact that the commonest events—sometimes just such as Pierre had witnessed without taking notice of them—assumed in Karatáev's speech a character of solemn fitness. He liked to hear the folk-tales one of the soldiers used to tell of an evening (they were always the same), but most of all he liked to hear stories of real life. He would smile joyfully when listening to such stories, now and then putting in a word or asking a question to make the moral beauty of what he was told clear to himself. Karatáev had no attachments, friendships, or love, as Pierre understood them, but loved and lived affectionately with everything life brought him in contact with, particularly with man—not any particular man, but those with whom he happened to be. He loved his dog, his comrades, the French, and Pierre who was his neighbor, but Pierre felt that in spite of Karatáev's affectionate tenderness for him (by which he unconsciously gave Pierre's spiritual life its due) he would not have grieved for a moment at parting from him. And Pierre began to feel in the same way toward Karatáev.

To all the other prisoners Platón Karatáev seemed a most ordinary soldier. They called him "little falcon" or "Platósha," chaffed him good-naturedly, and sent him on errands. But to Pierre he always remained what he had seemed that first night: an unfathomable, rounded, eternal personification of the spirit of simplicity and truth.

Platón Karatáev knew nothing by heart except his prayers. When he began to speak he seemed not to know how he would conclude.

Sometimes Pierre, struck by the meaning of his words, would ask him to repeat them, but Platón could never recall what he had said a moment before, just as he never could repeat to Pierre the words of his favorite song: *Native* and *birch tree* and *my heart is sick* occurred in it, but when spoken and not sung, no meaning could be got out of it. He did not, and could not, understand the meaning of words apart from their context. Every word and action of his was the manifestation of an activity unknown to him, which was his life. But his life, as he regarded it, had no meaning as a separate thing. It had meaning only as part of a whole of which he was always conscious. His words and actions flowed from him as evenly, inevitably and spontaneously, as fragrance exhales from a flower. He could not understand the value or significance of any word or deed taken separately.

Chapter XIV

WHEN PRINCESS MARY HEARD FROM NICHOLAS THAT HER BROTHER WAS WITH THE ROSTÓVS AT Yaroslávl she at once prepared to go there, in spite of her aunt's efforts to dissuade her—and not merely to go herself but to take her nephew with her. Whether it were difficult or easy, possible or impossible, she did not ask and did not want to know: it was her duty not only herself to be near her brother who was perhaps dying, but to do everything possible to take his son to him, and so she prepared to set off. That she had not heard from Prince Andrew himself, Princess Mary attributed to his being too weak to write or to his considering the long journey too hard and too dangerous for her and his son.

In a few days Princess Mary was ready to start. Her equipages were the huge family coach in which she had traveled to Vorónezh, a semi-open trap, and a baggage-cart. With her traveled Mademoiselle Bourienne, little Nicholas and his tutor, her old nurse, three maids, Tíkhon, and a young footman and courier her aunt had sent to accompany her.

The usual route through Moscow could not be thought of, and the roundabout way Princess Mary was obliged to take through Lípetsk, Ryazán, Vladímir and Shuya was very long, and as post-horses were not everywhere obtainable, very difficult, and near Ryazán where the French were said to have shown themselves, was even dangerous.

During this difficult journey Mademoiselle Bourienne, Dessalles and Princess Mary's servants were astonished at her energy and firmness of spirit. She went to bed later and rose earlier than any of them, and no difficulties daunted her. Thanks to her activity and energy, which infected her fellow-travelers, they approached Yaroslávl by the end of the second week.

The last days of her stay in Vorónezh had been the happiest of her life. Her love for Rostóv no longer tormented or agitated her. It filled her whole soul, had become an integral part of herself, and she no longer struggled against it. Latterly she had become convinced that she loved and was beloved, though she never said this definitely to herself in words. She had become convinced of it at her interview with Nicholas, when he had come to tell her that her brother was with the Rostóvs. Not by a single word had Nicholas alluded to the fact that Prince Andrew's relations with Natásha might, if he recovered, be renewed, but Princess Mary saw by his face that he knew and thought of this.

Yet in spite of that, his relation to her—considerate, delicate and loving—not only remained unchanged, but it sometimes seemed to Princess Mary that he was even glad that the family connection between them allowed him to express his friendship more freely. She knew that she loved for the first and only time in her life, and felt that she was beloved, and was happy in regard to it.

But this happiness on one side of her spiritual nature did not prevent her feeling grief for her brother with full force; on the contrary that spiritual tranquility on the one side made it the more possible for her to give full play to her feeling for her brother. That feeling was so strong at the moment of leaving Voronezh that those who saw her off, as they looked at her careworn despairing face, felt sure she would fall ill on the journey. But the very difficulties and preoccupations of the journey, which she took so actively in hand, saved her for a while from her grief and gave her strength.

As always happens when traveling, Princess Mary thought only of the journey itself, forgetting its object. But as she approached Yaroslávl the thought of what might await her there—not after many days, but that very evening—again presented itself to her and her agitation increased to its utmost limit.

The courier who had been sent on in advance to find out where the Rostóvs were staying in Yaroslávl and in what condition Prince Andrew was, when he met the big coach just entering the town gates was appalled by the terrible pallor of the princess's face that looked out at him from the window.

"I have found out everything, your excellency: the Rostóvs are staying at the merchant Brónnikov's house, in the Square not far from here, right above the Vólga," said the courier.

Princess Mary looked at him with frightened inquiry, not understanding why he did not reply to what she chiefly wanted to know: How was her brother? Mademoiselle Bourienne put that question for her.

"How is the prince?" she asked.

"His excellency is staying in the same house with them."

"Then he is alive," thought Princess Mary, and asked in a low voice: "How is he?"

"The servants say he is still the same."

What "still the same" might mean Princess Mary did not ask, but with an unnoticed glance at little seven-year-old Nicholas, who was sitting in front of her looking with pleasure at the town, she bowed her head and did not raise it again till the heavy coach, rumbling, shaking and swaying, came to a stop. The carriage steps clattered as they were let down.

The carriage door was opened. On the left there was water—a great river—and on the right a porch. There were people at the entrance: servants, and a rosy girl with a large plait of black hair, smiling as it seemed to Princess Mary in an unpleasantly affected way. (This was Sónya.) Princess Mary ran up the steps. "This way, this way!" said the girl, with the same artificial smile, and the princess found herself in the hall facing an elderly woman of Oriental type, who came rapidly to meet her with a look of emotion. This was the countess. She embraced Princess Mary and kissed her.

"Mon enfant!" she muttered, *"je vous aime et vous connais depuis longtemps."*

Despite her excitement, Princess Mary realized that this was the countess and that it was necessary to say something to her. Hardly knowing how she did it, she contrived to utter a few polite phrases in French in the same tone as those that had been addressed to her, and asked: "How is he?"

"The doctor says that he is not in danger," said the countess, but as she spoke she raised her eyes with a sigh, and her gesture conveyed a contradiction of her words.

"Where is he? Can I see him—can I?" asked the princess.

"One moment, princess, one moment, my dear! Is this his son?" said the countess, turning to little Nicholas who was coming in with Dessalles. "There will be room for everybody, this is a big house. Oh, what a lovely boy!"

The countess took Princess Mary into the drawing room, where Sónya was talking to Mademoiselle Bourienne. The countess caressed the boy, and the old count came in and welcomed the princess. He had changed very much since Princess Mary had last seen him. Then he had been a brisk, cheerful, self-assured old man, now he seemed a pitiful, bewildered person. While talking to Princess Mary he continually looked round as if asking everyone whether he was doing the right thing. After the destruction of Moscow and of his property, thrown out of his accustomed groove he seemed to have lost the sense of his own significance and to feel that there was no longer a place for him in life.

In spite of her one desire to see her brother as soon as possible, and her vexation that at the moment when all she wanted was to see him they should be trying to entertain her and pretending to admire her nephew, the princess noted all that was going on around her and felt the necessity of submitting, for a time, to this new order of things which she had entered. She knew it to be necessary, and though it was hard for her she was not vexed with these people.

"This is my niece," said the count, introducing Sónya—"You don't know her, princess?"

Princess Mary turned to Sónya, and trying to stifle the hostile feeling that arose in her toward the girl, she kissed her. But she felt oppressed by the fact that the mood of everyone around her was so far from what was in her own heart.

"Where is he?" she asked again, addressing them all.

"He is downstairs. Natásha is with him," answered Sónya flushing. "We have sent to ask. I think you must be tired, princess."

Tears of vexation showed themselves in Princess Mary's eyes. She turned away and was about to ask the countess again how to go to him, when light, impetuous, and seemingly buoyant steps were heard at the door. The princess looked round and saw Natásha coming in, almost running—that Natásha whom she had liked so little at their meeting in Moscow long since.

But hardly had the princess looked at Natásha's face before she realized that here was a real comrade in her grief, and consequently a friend. She ran to meet her, embraced her, and began to cry on her shoulder.

As soon as Natásha, sitting at the head of Prince Andrew's bed, heard of Princess Mary's arrival, she softly left his room, and hastened to her with those swift steps that had sounded buoyant to Princess Mary.

There was only one expression on her agitated face when she ran into the drawing room—that of love—boundless love for him, for her, and for all that was near to the man she loved; and of pity, suffering for others, and passionate desire to give herself entirely to helping them. It was plain that at that moment there was in Natásha's heart no thought of herself or of her own relations with Prince Andrew.

Princess Mary, with her acute sensibility, understood all this at the first glance at Natásha's face, and wept on her shoulder with sorrowful pleasure.

"Come, come to him, Mary," said Natásha, leading her into the other room.

Princess Mary raised her head, dried her eyes, and turned to Natásha. She felt that from her she would be able to understand and learn everything.

"How . . ." she began her question but stopped short.

She felt that it was impossible to ask, or to answer, in words. Natásha's face eyes would have to tell her all more clearly and profoundly.

Natásha was gazing at her, but seemed afraid and in doubt whether to say all she knew or not; she seemed to feel that before those luminous eyes which penetrated into the very depths of her heart, it was impossible not to tell the whole truth which she saw. And suddenly, Natásha's lips twitched, ugly wrinkles gathered round her mouth, and covering her face with her hands she burst into sobs.

Princess Mary understood.

But she still hoped, and asked, in words she herself did not trust:

"But how is his wound? What is his general condition?"

"You, you . . . will see," was all Natásha could say.

They sat a little while downstairs near his room till they had left off crying and were able to go to him with calm faces.

"How has his whole illness gone? Is it long since he grew worse? When did this happen?" Princess Mary inquired.

Natásha told her that at first there had been danger from his feverish condition and the pain he suffered, but at Tróitsa that had passed and the doctor had only been afraid of gangrene. That danger had also passed. When they reached Yaroslávl the wound had begun to fester (Natásha knew all about such things as festering) and the doctor had said that the festering might take a normal course. Then fever set in, but the doctor had said the fever was not very serious.

"But two days ago *this* suddenly happened," said Natásha, struggling with her sobs. "I don't know why, but you will see what he is like."

"Is he weaker? Thinner?" asked the princess.

"No, it's not that, but worse. You will see. O, Mary, he is too good, he cannot, cannot live, because . . ."

Chapter XV

When Natásha opened Prince Andrew's door with a familiar movement and let Princess Mary pass into the room before her, the princess felt the sobs rising in her throat. Hard as she had tried to prepare herself, and now tried to remain tranquil, she knew that she would be unable to look at him without tears.

The princess understood what Natásha had meant by the words: "two days ago *this* suddenly happened." She understood those words to mean that he had suddenly softened and that this softening and gentleness were signs of approaching death. As she stepped to the door she already saw in imagination Andrew's face as she remembered it in childhood, a gentle, mild, sympathetic face which he had rarely shown, and which therefore affected her very strongly. She was sure he would speak soft, tender words to her such as her father had uttered before his death, and that she would not be able to bear it and would burst into sobs in his presence. Yet sooner or later it had to be, and she went in. The sobs rose higher and higher in her throat as she more and more clearly distinguished his form and her short-sighted eyes tried to make out his features, and then she saw his face and met his gaze.

He was lying in a squirrel-fur dressing-gown on a divan, surrounded by pillows. He was thin and pale. In one thin, translucently white hand he held a handkerchief, while with the other he stroked the delicate mustache he had grown, moving his fingers slowly. His eyes gazed at them as they entered.

On seeing his face and meeting his eyes Princess Mary's pace suddenly slackened, she felt her tears dry up and her sobs ceased. She suddenly felt guilty and grew timid on catching the expression of his face and eyes.

"But in what am I to blame?" she asked herself. And his cold stern look replied: "Because you are alive and thinking of the living, while I . . ."

In the deep gaze that seemed to look not outward but inward there was an almost hostile expression as he slowly regarded his sister and Natásha.

He kissed his sister, holding her hand in his as was their wont.

"How are you, Mary? How did you manage to get here?" said he in a voice as calm and aloof as his look.

Had he screamed in agony, that scream would not have struck such horror into Princess Mary's heart as the tone of his voice.

"And have you brought little Nicholas?" he asked in the same slow, quiet manner and with an obvious effort to remember.

"How are you now?" said Princess Mary, herself surprised at what she was saying.

"That, my dear, you must ask the doctor," he replied, and again making an evident effort to be affectionate, he said with his lips only (his words clearly did not correspond to his thoughts):

"Merci, chère amie, d'être venue."

Princess Mary pressed his hand. The pressure made him wince just perceptibly. He was silent, and she did not know what to say. She now understood what had happened to him two days before. In his words, his tone, and especially in that calm, almost antagonistic look could be felt an estrangement from everything belonging to this world, terrible in one who is alive. Evidently only with an effort did he understand anything living; but it was obvious that he failed to understand, not because he lacked the power to do so but because he understood something else—something the living did not and could not understand—and which wholly occupied his mind.

"There, you see how strangely fate has brought us together," said he, breaking the silence and pointing to Natásha. "She looks after me all the time."

Princess Mary heard him and did not understand how he could say such a thing. He, the sensitive, tender Prince Andrew, how could he say that, before her whom he loved and who loved him? Had he expected to live he could not have said those words in that offensively cold tone. If he had not known that he was dying, how could he have failed to pity her and how could he speak like that in her presence? The only explanation was that he was indifferent, because something else, much more important, had been revealed to him.

The conversation was cold and disconnected, and continually broke off.

"Mary came by way of Ryazán," said Natásha.

Prince Andrew did not notice that she called his sister *Mary*, and only after calling her so in his presence did Natásha notice it herself.

"Really?" he asked.

"They told her that all Moscow has been burned down, and that . . ."

Natásha stopped. It was impossible to talk. It was plain that he was making an effort to listen, but could not do so.

"Yes, they say it's burned," he said. "It's a great pity," and he gazed straight before him absently stroking his mustache with his fingers.

"And so you have met Count Nicholas, Mary?" Prince Andrew suddenly said, evidently wishing to speak pleasantly to them. "He wrote here that he took a great liking to you," he went on simply and calmly, evidently unable to understand all the complex significance his words had for living people. "If you liked him too, it would be a good thing for you to get married," he added rather more quickly, as if pleased at having found words he had long been seeking.

Princess Mary heard his words but they had no meaning for her, except as a proof of how far away he now was from everything living.

"Why talk of me?" she said quietly and glanced at Natásha.

Natásha, who felt her glance, did not look at her. All three were again silent.

"Andrew, would you like . . ." Princess Mary suddenly said in a trembling voice, "would you like to see little Nicholas? He is always talking about you!"

Prince Andrew smiled just perceptibly and for the first time, but Princess Mary, who knew his face so well, saw with horror that he did not smile with pleasure or affection for his son, but with quiet gentle irony because he thought she was trying what she believed to be the last means of arousing him.

"Yes, I shall be very glad to see him. Is he quite well?"

When little Nicholas was brought into Prince Andrew's room he looked at his father with frightened eyes, but did not cry, because no one else was crying. Prince Andrew kissed him and evidently did not know what to say to him.

When Nicholas had been led away, Princess Mary again went up to her brother, kissed him, and unable to restrain her tears any longer, began to cry.

He looked at her attentively.

"Is it about Nicholas?" he asked.

Princess Mary nodded her head, weeping.

"Mary, you know the Gosp . . ." but he broke off.

"What did you say?"

"Nothing. You mustn't cry here," he said, looking at her with the same cold expression.

When Princess Mary began to cry, he understood that she was crying at the thought that little Nicholas would be left without a father. With a great effort he tried to return to life and to see things from their point of view.

"Yes, to them it must seem sad!" he thought. "But how simple it is.

"The fowls of the air sow not, neither do they reap, yet your Father feedeth them," he said to himself and wished to say to Princess Mary; "but no, they will take it their own way, they won't understand! They can't understand that all those feelings they prize so—all our feelings, all those ideas that seem so important to us, are *unnecessary*. We cannot understand one another," and he remained silent.

Prince Andrew's little son was seven. He could scarcely read, and knew nothing. After that day he lived through many things, gaining knowledge, observation and experience, but had he possessed all the faculties he afterward acquired, he could not have had a better or more profound understanding of the meaning of the scene he had witnessed between his father, Mary and Natásha, than he had then. He understood it completely, and leaving the room without crying, went silently up to Natásha who had come out with him and looked shyly at her with his beautiful, thoughtful eyes, then his uplifted, rosy upper lip trembled and leaning his head against her he began to cry.

After that he avoided Dessalles and the countess who caressed him, and either sat alone, or came timidly to Princess Mary, or to Natásha of whom he seemed even fonder than of his aunt, and clung to them quietly and shyly.

When Princess Mary had left Prince Andrew she fully understood what Natásha's face had told her. She did not speak any more to Natásha of hopes of saving his life. She took turns with her beside his sofa, and did not cry any more, but prayed continually, turning in soul to that Eternal and Unfathomable, whose presence above the dying man was now so evident.

Chapter XVI

Not only did Prince Andrew know he would die, but he felt that he was dying and was already half dead. He was conscious of an aloofness from everything earthly and a strange and joyous lightness of existence. Without haste or agitation he awaited what was coming. That inexorable, eternal, distant, and unknown—the presence of which he had felt continually all his life—was now near to him, and, by the strange lightness he experienced, almost comprehensible and palpable. . . .

Formerly he had feared the end. He had twice experienced that terribly tormenting fear of death—the end—but now he no longer understood that fear.

He had felt it for the first time when the shell spun like a top before him, and he looked at the fallow field, the bushes and the sky, and knew that he was face to face with death. When he came to himself after being wounded and the flower of eternal, unfettered love had instantly unfolded itself in his soul as if freed from the bondage of life that had restrained it, he no longer feared death, and ceased to think about it.

During the hours of solitude, suffering and partial delirium he spent after he was wounded, the more deeply he penetrated into the new principle of eternal love revealed to him, the more he unconsciously detached himself from earthly life. To love everything and everybody and always to sacrifice oneself for love, meant not to love anyone, not to live this earthly life. And the more imbued he became with that principle of love, the more he renounced life and the more completely he destroyed that dreadful barrier which—in the absence of such love—stands between life and death. When during those first days he remembered that he would have to die, he said to himself: "Well, what of it? So much the better!"

But after the night in Mytíshchi when, half delirious, he had seen her for whom he longed appear before him, and having pressed her hand to his lips, had shed gentle happy tears, love for a particular woman again crept unobserved into his heart and once more bound him to life. And joyful and agitating thoughts began to occupy his mind. Recalling the moment at the ambulance station when he had seen Kurágin, he could not now regain the feeling he then had, but was tormented by the question whether Kurágin was alive. And he dared not inquire.

His illness pursued its normal physical course, but what Natásha referred to when she said: "*This* suddenly happened," had occurred two days before Princess Mary arrived. It was the last spiritual struggle between life and death, in which death gained the victory. It was the unexpected realization of the fact that he still valued life as presented to him in the form of his love for Natásha, and a last, though ultimately vanquished, attack of terror before the unknown.

It was evening. As usual after dinner he was slightly feverish, and his thoughts were preternaturally clear. Sónya was sitting by the table. He began to doze. Suddenly a feeling of happiness seized him.

"Ah, she has come!" thought he.

And so it was: in Sónya's place sat Natásha who had just come in noiselessly.

Since she had begun looking after him, he had always experienced this physical consciousness of her nearness. She was sitting in an arm-chair placed sideways, screening the light of the candle from him, and was knitting a stocking. She had learned to knit stockings since Prince Andrew had casually mentioned that no one nursed the sick so well as old nurses who knit stockings, and that there is something soothing in the knitting of stockings. The needles clicked lightly in her slender, rapidly moving hands, and he could clearly see the thoughtful profile of her drooping face. She moved, and the ball rolled off her knees. She started, glanced round at him, and screening the candle with her hand, stooped carefully with a supple and exact movement, picked up the ball, and regained her former position.

He looked at her without moving and saw that she wanted to draw a deep breath after stooping, but refrained from doing so and breathed cautiously.

At the Tróitsa monastery they had spoken of the past, and he had told her that if he lived he would always thank God for his wound which had brought them together again, but after that they never spoke of the future.

"Can it or can it not be?" he now thought as he looked at her and listened to the light click of the steel needles. "Can fate have brought me to her so strangely only for me to die? . . . Is it possible that the truth of life has been revealed to me only to show me that I have spent my life in falsity? I love her more than anything in the world! But what am I to do if I love her?" he thought, and he involuntarily groaned, from a habit acquired during his sufferings.

On hearing that sound Natásha put down the stocking, leaned nearer to him, and suddenly, noticing his shining eyes, stepped lightly up to him and bent over him.

"You are not asleep?"

"No, I have been looking at you a long time. I felt you come in. No one else gives me that sense of soft tranquillity that you do . . . that light. I want to weep for joy."

Natásha drew closer to him. Her face shone with rapturous joy.

"Natásha, I love you too much! More than anything in the world."

"And I!"—She turned away for an instant. "Why too much?" she asked.

"Why too much? . . . Well, what do you think, what do you feel in your soul, your whole soul—shall I live? What do you think?"

"I am sure of it, sure!" Natásha almost shouted, taking hold of both his hands with a passionate movement.

He remained silent awhile.

"How good it would be!" and taking her hand he kissed it.

Natásha felt happy and agitated, but at once remembered that this would not do and that he had to be quiet.

"But you have not slept," she said, repressing her joy. "Try to sleep . . . please!"

He pressed her hand and released it, and she went back to the candle and sat down again in her former position. Twice she turned and looked at him, and her eyes met his beaming at her. She set herself a task on her stocking and resolved not to turn round till it was finished.

Soon he really shut his eyes and fell asleep. He did not sleep long, and suddenly awoke with a start and in a cold perspiration.

As he fell asleep he had still been thinking of the subject that now always occupied his mind—about life and death, and chiefly about death. He felt himself nearer to it.

"Love? What is love?" he thought.

"Love hinders death. Love is life. All, everything that I understand, I understand only because I love. Everything is, everything exists, only because I love. Everything is united by it alone. Love is God, and to die means that I, a particle of love, shall return to the general and eternal source." These thoughts seemed to him comforting. But they were only thoughts. Something was lacking in them, they were not clear, they were too one-sidedly personal and brain-spun. And there was the former agitation and obscurity. He fell asleep.

He dreamed that he was lying in the room he really was in, but that he was quite well and unwounded. Many various indifferent and insignificant people appeared before him. He talked to them, and discussed something trivial. They were preparing to go away somewhere. Prince Andrew dimly realized that all this was trivial and that he had more important cares, but he continued to speak, surprising them by empty witticisms. Gradually, unnoticed, all these persons began to disappear and a single question, that of the closed door, superseded all else. He rose and went to the door to bolt and lock it. Everything depended on whether he was, or was not, in time to lock it. He went, and tried to hurry, but his legs refused to move and he knew he would not be in time to lock the door though he painfully strained all his powers. He was seized by an agonizing fear. And that fear was the fear of death. *It* stood behind the door. But just when he was clumsily creeping toward the door, that dreadful something on the other side was already pressing against it and forcing its way in. Something not human—death—was breaking in through that door, and had to be kept out. He seized the door, making a final effort to hold it back—to lock it was no longer possible—but his efforts were weak and clumsy and the door, pushed from behind by that terror, opened and closed again.

Once again *it* pushed from outside. His last superhuman efforts were vain and both halves of the door noiselessly opened. *It* entered, and it was *death,* and Prince Andrew died.

But at the instant he died, Prince Andrew remembered that he was asleep, and at the very instant he died, having made an effort, he awoke.

"Yes, it was death! I died—and woke up. Yes, death is an awakening!" And all at once it grew light in his soul and the veil that had till then concealed the unknown was lifted from his spiritual vision. He felt as if powers till then confined within him had been liberated, and that strange lightness did not again leave him.

When, waking in a cold perspiration, he moved on the divan, Natásha went up and asked him what was the matter. He did not answer and looked at her strangely, not understanding.

That was what had happened to him two days before Princess Mary's arrival. From that day, as the doctor expressed it, the wasting fever assumed a malignant character, but what the doctor said did not interest Natásha, she saw the terrible moral symptoms which to her were more convincing.

From that day an awakening from life came to Prince Andrew together with his awakening from sleep. And compared to the duration of life it did not seem to him slower than an awakening from sleep compared to the duration of a dream.

There was nothing terrible or violent in this comparatively slow awakening.

His last days and hours passed in an ordinary and simple way. Both Princess Mary and Natásha, who did not leave him, felt this. They did not weep or shudder and during these last days they themselves felt that they were not attending on him (he was no longer there, he had left them) but on what reminded them most closely of him—his body. Both felt this so strongly that the outward and terrible side of death did not affect them and they did not feel it necessary to foment their grief. Neither in his presence nor out of it did they weep, nor did they ever talk to one another about him. They felt that they could not express in words what they understood.

They both saw that he was sinking slowly and quietly, deeper and deeper, away from them, and they both knew that this had to be so and that it was right.

He confessed, and received communion: everyone came to take leave of him. When they brought his son to him, he pressed his lips to the boy's and turned away, not because he felt it hard and sad (Princess Mary and Natásha understood that) but simply because he thought it was all that was required of him, but when they told him to bless the boy, he did what was demanded and looked round as if asking whether there was anything else he should do.

When the last convulsions of the body, which the spirit was leaving, occurred, Princess Mary and Natásha were present.

"Is it over?" said Princess Mary when his body had for a few minutes lain motionless, growing cold before them. Natásha went up, looked at the dead eyes, and hastened to close them. She closed them but did not kiss them, but clung to that which reminded her most nearly of him—his body.

"Where has he gone? Where is he now? . . ."

When the body, washed and dressed, lay in the coffin on a table, everyone came to take leave of him and they all wept.

Little Nicholas cried because his heart was rent by painful perplexity. The countess and Sónya cried from pity for Natásha and because he was no more. The old count cried because he felt that before long, he, too, must take the same terrible step.

Natásha and Princess Mary also wept now, but not because of their own personal grief; they wept with a reverent and softening emotion which had taken possession of their souls at the consciousness of the simple and solemn mystery of death, that had been accomplished in their presence.

Part Thirteen

Chapter I

MAN'S MIND CANNOT GRASP THE CAUSES OF EVENTS IN THEIR COMPLETENESS, BUT THE desire to find those causes is implanted in man's soul. And without considering the multiplicity and complexity of the conditions any one of which taken separately may seem to be the cause, he snatches at the first approximation to a cause that seems to him intelligible, and says: "This is the cause!" In historical events (where the actions of men are the subject of observation) the first and most primitive approximation to present itself was the will of the gods, and after that, the will of those who stood in the most prominent position—the heroes of history. But we need only penetrate to the essence of any historic event—which lies in the activity of the general mass of men who take part in it—to be convinced that the will of the historic hero does not control the actions of the mass but is itself continually controlled. It may seem to be a matter of indifference whether we understand the meaning of historical events this way or that; yet there is the same difference between a man who says that the people of the West moved on the East because Napoleon wished it, and a man who says that this happened because it had to happen, as there is between those who declared that the earth was stationary and that the planets moved round it, and those who admitted that they did not know what upheld the earth, but knew there were laws directing its movement and that of the other planets. There is, and can be, no cause of an historical event except the one cause of all causes. But there are laws directing events, and some of these laws are known to us while we are conscious of others we cannot comprehend. The discovery of these laws is only possible when we have quite abandoned the attempt to find the cause in the will of some one man, just as the discovery of the laws of the motion of the planets was possible only when men abandoned the conception of the fixity of the earth.

The historians consider that, next to the battle of Borodinó and the occupation of Moscow by the enemy and its destruction by fire, the most important episode of the war of 1812 was the movement of the Russian army from the Ryazán to the Kalúga road and to the Tarútino camp—the so-called flank march across the Krásnaya Pakhrá River. They ascribe the glory of that achievement of genius to different men, and dispute as to whom the honor is due. Even foreign historians, including the French, acknowledge the genius of the Russian commanders when they speak of that flank march. But it is hard to understand why military writers, and following them others, consider this flank march to be the profound conception of some one man who saved Russia and destroyed Napoleon. In the first place it is hard to understand where the profundity and genius of this movement lay, for not much mental effort was needed to see that the best position for an army when it is not being attacked, is where there are most provisions; and even a dull boy of thirteen could have guessed that the best position for an army after its retreat from Moscow in 1812 was on the Kalúga road. So it is impossible to understand by what reasoning the historians reach the conclusion that this maneuver was a profound one. And it is even more difficult to understand just why they think that this maneuver was calculated to save Russia and destroy the French; for this flank march, had it been preceded, accompanied, or followed by other circumstances, might have proved ruinous to the Russians and salutary for the French. If the position of the Russian army really began to improve from the time of that march, it does not at all follow that the march was the cause of it.

That flank march might not only have failed to give any advantage to the Russian army, but might in other circumstances have led to its destruction. What would have happened had Moscow not burned down? If Murat had not lost sight of the Russians? If Napoleon had not remained inactive? If the Russian army at Krásnaya Pakhrá had given battle as Bennigsen and Barclay advised? What would have happened had the French attacked the Russians while they were marching beyond the Pakhrá? What would have happened if on approaching Tarútino, Napoleon had attacked the

Russians with but a tenth of the energy he had shown when he attacked them at Smolénsk? What would have happened had the French moved on Petersburg? . . . In any of these eventualities the flank march that brought salvation might have proved disastrous.

The third and most incomprehensible thing is that people studying history deliberately avoid seeing that this flank march cannot be attributed to any one man, that no one ever foresaw it, and that in reality, like the retreat from Filí, it did not suggest itself to anyone in its entirety, but resulted—moment by moment, step by step, event by event—from an endless number of most diverse circumstances and was only seen in its entirety when it had been accomplished and belonged to the past.

At the council at Filí the prevailing thought in the minds of the Russian commanders was the one naturally suggesting itself, namely, a direct retreat by the Nízhni road. In proof of this there is the fact that the majority of the council voted for such a retreat, and above all there is the well-known conversation after the council, between the commander-in-chief and Lanskóy, who was in charge of the commissariat department. Lanskoy informed the commander-in-chief that the army supplies were for the most part stored along the Oká in the Túla and Ryazán provinces, and that if they retreated on Nízhni the army would be separated from its supplies by the broad river Oká, which cannot be crossed early in winter. This was the first indication of the necessity of deviating from what had previously seemed the most natural course—a direct retreat on Nízhni-Nóvgorod. The army turned more to the south, along the Ryazán road and nearer to its supplies. Subsequently the inactivity of the French (who even lost sight of the Russian army), concern for the safety of the arsenal at Túla, and especially the advantages of drawing nearer to its supplies, caused the army to turn still further south to the Túla road. Having crossed over, by a forced march, to the Túla road beyond the Pakhrá, the Russian commanders intended to remain at Podólsk and had no thought of the Tarútino position; but innumerable circumstances and the reappearance of French troops who had for a time lost touch with the Russians, and projects of giving battle, and above all the abundance of provisions in Kalúga province, obliged our army to turn still more to the south and to cross from the Túla to the Kalúga road and go to Tarútino, which was between the roads along which those supplies lay. Just as it is impossible to say when it was decided to abandon Moscow, so it is impossible to say precisely when, or by whom, it was decided to move to Tarútino. Only when the army had got there, as the result of innumerable and varying forces, did people begin to assure themselves that they had desired this movement and long ago foreseen its result.

Chapter II

THE FAMOUS FLANK MOVEMENT MERELY CONSISTED IN THIS: AFTER THE ADVANCE OF THE FRENCH had ceased, the Russian army, which had been continually retreating straight back from the invaders, deviated from that direct course and, not finding itself pursued, was naturally drawn toward the district where supplies were abundant.

If instead of imagining to ourselves commanders of genius leading the Russian army, we picture that army without any leaders, it could not have done anything but make a return movement toward Moscow, describing an arc in the direction where most provisions were to be found and where the country was richest.

That movement from the Nízhni to the Ryazán, Túla, and Kalúga roads was so natural that even the Russian marauders moved in that direction, and demands were sent from Petersburg for Kutúzov to take his army that way. At Tarútino Kutúzov received what was almost a reprimand from the Emperor for having moved his army along the Ryazán road, and the Emperor's letter indicated to him the very position he had already occupied near Kalúga.

Having rolled like a ball in the direction of the impetus given by the whole campaign and by the battle of Borodinó, the Russian army—when the strength of that impetus was exhausted and no fresh push was received—assumed the position natural to it.

Kutúzov's merit lay, not in any strategic maneuver of genius, as it is called, but in the fact that he alone understood the significance of what had happened. He alone then understood the meaning of the French army's inactivity, he alone continued to assert that the battle of Borodinó had been a victory, he alone—who as commander-in-chief might have been expected to be eager to attack—employed his whole strength to restrain the Russian army from useless engagements.

The beast wounded at Borodinó was lying where the fleeing hunter had left him; but whether he was still alive, whether he was strong and merely lying low, the hunter did not know. Suddenly the beast was heard to moan.

The moan of that wounded beast (the French army) which betrayed its calamitous condition, was the sending of Lauriston to Kutúzov's camp with overtures for peace.

Napoleon, with his usual assurance that whatever entered his head was right, wrote to Kutúzov the first words that occurred to him, though they were meaningless.

"Monsieur le prince Koutouzov," he wrote, "I am sending one of my adjutants-general to discuss several interesting questions with you. I beg your Highness to credit what he says to you, *especially when he expresses the sentiment of esteem and special regard I have long entertained for your person. This letter having no other object, I pray God, monsieur le Prince Koutouzov, to keep you in His holy and gracious protection!*

NAPOLEON"

Moscow, October 30th, 1812

Kutúzov replied: "I should be cursed by posterity were I looked on as the initiator of a settlement of any sort. *Such is the present spirit of my nation.*" But he continued to exert all his powers to restrain his troops from attacking.

During the month that the French troops were pillaging in Moscow and the Russian troops were quietly encamped at Tarútino, a change had taken place in the relative strength of the two armies—both in spirit and in number—as a result of which the superiority had passed to the Russian side. Though the condition and numbers of the French army were unknown to the Russians, as soon as that change occurred the need of attacking at once showed itself by countless signs. These signs were: Lauriston's mission; the abundance of provisions at Tarútino; the reports coming in from all sides of the inactivity and disorder of the French; the flow of recruits to our regiments; the fine weather; the long rest the Russian soldiers had enjoyed, and the impatience to do what they had been assembled for, which usually shows itself in an army that has been resting; curiosity as to what the French army, so long lost sight of, was doing; the boldness with which our outposts now scouted close up to the French stationed at Tarútino; the news of easy successes gained by peasants and guerrilla troops over the French, the envy aroused by this; the desire for revenge that lay in the heart of every Russian as long as the French were in Moscow, and (above all) a dim consciousness in every soldier's mind that the relative strength of the armies had changed and that the advantage was now on our side. There was a substantial change in the relative strength, and an advance had become inevitable. And at once, as a clock begins to strike and chime as soon as the minute hand has completed a full circle, this change was shown by an increased activity, whirring and chiming in the higher spheres.

Chapter III

THE RUSSIAN ARMY WAS COMMANDED BY KUTÚZOV AND HIS STAFF, AND ALSO BY THE EMPEROR from Petersburg. Before the news of the abandonment of Moscow had been received in Petersburg, a detailed plan of the whole campaign had been drawn up and sent to Kutúzov for his guidance. Though this plan had been drawn up on the supposition that Moscow was still in our hands, it was approved by the staff and accepted as a basis for action. Kutúzov only replied that movements arranged from a distance were always difficult to execute. So fresh instructions were sent for the solution of difficulties that might be encountered, as well as fresh people who were to watch Kutúzov's actions and report upon them.

Besides this, the whole staff of the Russian army was now reorganized. The posts left vacant by Bagratión who had been killed, and by Barclay who had gone away in dudgeon, had to be filled. Very serious consideration was given to the question whether it would be better to put A in B's place and B in D's, or on the contrary to put D in A's place, and so on—as if anything more than A's or B's satisfaction depended on this.

As a result of the hostility between Kutúzov and Bennigsen his Chief of Staff, the presence of confidential representatives of the Emperor, and these transfers, a more than usually complicated play of parties was going on among the staff of the army. A was undermining B, D was undermining C, and so on in all possible combinations and permutations. In all these plottings the subject of intrigue was generally the conduct of the war, which all these men believed they were directing; but this affair of the war went on independently of them, as it had to go: that is, never in the way people devised, but flowing always from the essential attitude of the masses. Only in the highest spheres did all these schemes, crossings and interminglings appear to be a true reflection of what had to happen.

"Prince Michael Ilariónovich!" wrote the Emperor on the 2nd of October in a letter that reached Kutúzov after the battle at Tarútino, "Since September 2nd Moscow has been in the hands of the enemy. Your last reports were written on the 20th, and during all this time not only has no action been taken against the enemy or for the relief of the ancient capital, but according to your last report you have even retreated farther. Sérpukhov is already occupied by an enemy detachment and Túla with its famous arsenal, so indispensable to the army, is in danger. From General Wintzingerode's reports, I see that an enemy corps of ten thousand men is moving on the Petersburg road. Another corps of several thousand men is moving on Dmítrov. A third has advanced along the Vladímir road, and a fourth, rather considerable detachment, is stationed between Rúza and Mozháysk. Napoleon himself was in Moscow as late as the 25th. In view of all this information, when the enemy has scattered his forces in large detachments, and with Napoleon and his Guards in Moscow, is it possible that the enemy's forces confronting you are so considerable as not to allow of your taking the offensive? On the contrary, he is probably pursuing you with detachments, or at most with an army corps much weaker than the army entrusted to you. It would seem that, availing yourself of these circumstances, you might advantageously attack a weaker enemy and annihilate him, or at least oblige him to retreat, retaining in our hands an important part of the provinces now occupied by the enemy, and thereby averting danger from Túla and other towns in the interior. You will be responsible if the enemy is able to direct a force of any size against Petersburg to threaten this capital in which it has not been possible to retain many troops; for with the army entrusted to you, and acting with resolution and energy, you have ample means to avert this fresh calamity. Remember that you have still to answer to our offended country for the loss of Moscow. You have experienced my readiness to reward you. That readiness will not weaken in me, but I and Russia have a right to expect from you all the zeal, firmness and success which your intellect, military talent, and the courage of the troops you command, justify us in expecting."

But by the time this letter, which proved that the real relation of the forces had already made itself felt in Petersburg, was dispatched, Kutúzov had found himself unable any longer to restrain the army he commanded from attacking and a battle had taken place.

On the 2nd of October a Cossack, Shapoválov, who was out scouting, killed one hare and wounded another. Following the wounded hare he made his way far into the forest and came upon the left flank of Murat's army, encamped there without any precautions. The Cossack laughingly told his comrades how he had almost fallen into the hands of the French. A cornet, hearing the story, informed his commander.

The Cossack was sent for and questioned. The Cossack officers wished to take advantage of this chance to capture some horses, but one of the superior officers who was acquainted with the higher authorities, reported the incident to a general on the staff. The state of things on the staff had of late been exceedingly strained. Ermólov had been to see Bennigsen a few days previously and had entreated him to use his influence with the commander-in-chief to induce him to take the offensive.

"If I did not know you I should think you did not want what you are asking for. I need only advise anything and his Highness is sure to do the opposite," replied Bennigsen.

The Cossack's report, confirmed by horse patrols who were sent out, was the final proof that events had matured. The tightly coiled spring was released, the clock began to whirr and the chimes to play. Despite all his supposed power, his intellect, his experience and his knowledge of men, Kutúzov—having taken into consideration the Cossack's report, a note from Bennigsen who sent personal reports to the Emperor, the wishes he supposed the Emperor to hold, and the fact that all the generals expressed the same wish—could no longer check the inevitable movement, and gave the order to do what he regarded as useless and harmful—gave his approval, that is, to the accomplished fact.

Chapter IV

Bennigsen's note and the Cossack's information that the left flank of the French was unguarded were merely final indications that it was necessary to order an attack, and it was fixed for the 5th of October.

On the morning of the 4th of October Kutúzov signed the dispositions. Toll read them to Ermólov, asking him to attend to the further arrangements.

"All right—all right. I haven't time just now," replied Ermólov, and left the hut.

The dispositions drawn up by Toll were very good. As in the Austerlitz dispositions, it was written—though not in German this time:

"The First Column will march here and here," "the Second Column will march there and there," and so on; and on paper, all these columns arrived at their places at the appointed time and destroyed the enemy. Everything had been admirably thought out as is usual in dispositions, and as is always the case, not a single column reached its place at the appointed time.

When the necessary number of copies of the dispositions had been prepared, an officer was summoned and sent to deliver them to Ermólov to deal with. A young officer of the Horse-Guards, Kutúzov's orderly, pleased at the importance of the mission entrusted to him, went to Ermólov's quarters.

"Gone away," said Ermólov's orderly.

The officer of the Horse-Guards went to a general with whom Ermólov was often to be found.

"No, and the general's out too."

The officer, mounting his horse, rode off to someone else.

"No, he's gone out."

"If only they don't make me responsible for this delay! What a nuisance it is!" thought the officer, and he rode round the whole camp. One man said he had seen Ermólov ride past with some other generals, others said he must have returned home. The officer searched till six o'clock in the evening without even stopping to eat. Ermólov was nowhere to be found and no one knew where he was. The officer snatched a little food at a comrade's, and rode again to the vanguard to find Milorádovich. Milorádovich too was away, but here he was told that he had gone to a ball at General Kíkin's and that Ermólov was probably there too.

"But where is it?"

"Why, there, over at

chkino," said a Cossack officer, pointing to a country house in the far distance.

"What, outside our line?"

"They've put two regiments as outposts, and they're having such a spree there, it's awful! Two bands and three sets of singers!"

The officer rode out beyond our lines to Échkino. While still at a distance he heard as he rode the merry sounds of a soldier's dance-song proceeding from the house.

"In the meadows . . . in the meadows!" he heard, accompanied by whistling and the sound of a *torban*, drowned every now and then by shouts. These sounds made his spirits rise, but at the same time he was afraid that he would be blamed for not having executed sooner the important order entrusted to him. It was already past eight o'clock. He dismounted, and went up into the porch of a large country house which had remained intact between the Russian and French forces. In the refreshment room and the hall, footmen were bustling about with wine and viands. Groups of singers stood outside the windows. The officer was admitted and immediately saw all the chief generals of the army together, and among them Ermólov's big imposing figure. They all had their coats unbuttoned and were standing in a semicircle with flushed and animated faces, laughing loudly. In the middle of the room a short handsome general with a red face was dancing the *trepák* with much spirit and agility.

"Ha, ha, ha! Bravo, Nicholas Iványch! Ha, ha, ha!"

The officer felt that by arriving with important orders at such a moment he was doubly to blame, and he would have preferred to wait; but one of the generals espied him and, hearing what he had come about, informed Ermólov.

Ermólov came forward with a frown on his face and, hearing what the officer had to say, took the papers from him without a word.

"You think he went off just by chance?" said a comrade, who was on the staff that evening to the officer of the Horse-Guards, referring to Ermólov. "It was a trick. It was done on purpose to get Konovnítsyn into trouble. You'll see what a mess there'll be tomorrow."

Chapter V

NEXT DAY THE DECREPIT KUTÚZOV, HAVING GIVEN ORDERS TO BE CALLED EARLY, SAID HIS prayers, dressed, and, with an unpleasant consciousness of having to direct a battle he did not approve of, got into his calèche and drove from Letashóvka (a village three and a half miles from Tarútino) to the place where the attacking columns were to meet. He sat in the calèche, dozing and waking up by turns, and listening for any sound of firing on the right as an indication that the action had begun. But all was still quiet. A damp dull autumn morning was just dawning. On approaching Tarútino Kutúzov noticed cavalrymen leading their horses to water across the road along which he was driving. Kutúzov looked at them searchingly, stopped his carriage, and inquired what regiment they belonged to. They belonged to a column that should have been far in front and in ambush long before then. "It may be a mistake," thought the old commander-in-chief. But a little further on he saw infantry regiments with their arms piled and the soldiers, only partly dressed, eating their rye-porridge, and carrying fuel. He sent for an officer. The officer reported that no order to advance had been received.

"How! Not rec . . ." Kutúzov began, but checked himself immediately and sent for a senior officer. Getting out of his calèche, he waited with drooping head and breathing heavily, pacing silently up and down. When ykhen, the officer of the general staff whom he had summoned, appeared, Kutúzov went purple in the face, not because that officer was to blame for the mistake, but because he was an object of sufficient importance for him to vent his wrath on. Trembling and panting the old man fell into that state of fury in which he sometimes used to roll on the ground, and he fell upon ykhen, threatening him with his hands, shouting and loading him with gross abuse. Another man, Captain Brózin, who happened to turn up and who was not at all to blame, suffered the same fate.

"What sort of another blackguard are you? I'll have you shot! Scoundrels!" yelled Kutúzov in a hoarse voice, waving his arms and reeling.

He was suffering physically. He, the commander-in-chief, a Serene Highness who everybody said possessed powers such as no man had ever had in Russia, to be placed in this position—made the laughing stock of the whole army! "I needn't have been in such a hurry to pray about today, or have kept awake thinking everything over all night," thought he to himself. "When I was a chit of an officer no one would have dared to mock me so . . . and now!" He was in a state of physical suffering as if from corporal punishment, and could not avoid expressing it by cries of anger and distress. But his strength soon began to fail him, and looking about him, conscious of having said much that was amiss, he again got into his calèche and drove back in silence.

His wrath, once expended, did not return, and blinking feebly he listened to excuses and self-justifications (Ermólov did not come to see him till the next day) and to the insistence of Bennigsen, Konovnítsyn and Toll that the movement that had miscarried should be executed next day. And once more Kutúzov had to consent.

Chapter VI

NEXT DAY THE TROOPS ASSEMBLED IN THEIR APPOINTED PLACES IN THE EVENING AND ADVANCED during the night. It was an autumn night with dark purple clouds, but no rain. The ground was damp but not muddy, and the troops advanced noiselessly, only occasionally a jingling of the artillery could be faintly heard. The men were forbidden to talk out loud, to smoke their pipes, or to strike a light, and they tried to prevent their horses neighing. The secrecy of the undertaking heightened its charm and they marched gaily. Some columns, supposing they had reached their destination, halted, piled arms, and settled down on the cold ground, but the majority marched all night and arrived at places where they evidently should not have been.

Only Count Orlóv-Denísov with his Cossacks (the least important detachment of all) got to his appointed place at the right time. This detachment halted at the outskirts of a forest, on the path leading from the village of Stromílova to Dmítrovsk.

Toward dawn, Count Orlóv-Denísov, who had dozed off, was awakened by a deserter from the French army being brought to him. This was a Polish sergeant of Poniatowski's corps, who explained in Polish that he had come over because he had been slighted in the service: that he ought long ago to have been made an officer, that he was braver than any of them, and so he had left them and wished to pay them out. He said that Murat was spending the night only a verst from where they were, and that if they would let him have a convoy of a hundred men he would capture him alive. Count Orlóv-Denísov consulted his fellow-officers.

The offer was too tempting to be refused. Everyone volunteered to go and everybody advised making the attempt. After much disputing and arguing, Major-General Grékov with two Cossack regiments decided to go with the Polish sergeant.

"Now, remember," said Count Orlóv-Denísov to the sergeant at parting, "if you have been lying I'll have you hanged like a dog; but if it's true you shall have a hundred gold pieces!"

Without replying the sergeant, with a resolute air, mounted and rode away with Grékov whose men had quickly assembled. They disappeared into the forest, and Count Orlóv-Denísov, having seen Grékov off, returned, shivering from the freshness of the early dawn and excited by what he had undertaken on his own responsibility, and began looking at the enemy camp, now just visible in the deceptive light of dawn and the dying campfires. Our columns ought to have begun to appear on an open declivity to his right. He looked in that direction, but though the columns would have been visible quite far off, they were not to be seen. It seemed to the count that things were beginning to stir in the French camp, and his keen-sighted adjutant confirmed this.

"Oh, it is really too late," said Count Orlóv, looking at the camp.

As often happens when someone we have trusted is no longer before our eyes, it suddenly seemed quite clear and obvious to him that the sergeant was an impostor, that he had lied, and that the whole Russian attack would be ruined by the absence of those two regiments, which he would lead away heaven only knew where. How could one capture a commander-in-chief from among such a mass of troops!

"I am sure that rascal was lying," said the count.

"They can still be called back," said one of his suite, who like Count Orlóv felt distrustful of the adventure when he looked at the enemy's camp.

"Eh? Really . . . what do you think? Should we let them go on or not?"

"Will you have them fetched back?"

"Fetch them back, fetch them back!" said Count Orlóv with sudden determination, looking at his watch. "It will be too late. It is quite light."

And the adjutant galloped through the forest after Grékov. When Grékov returned, Count Orlóv-Denísov, excited both by the abandoned attempt and by vainly awaiting the infantry columns that still did not appear, as well as by the proximity of the enemy, resolved to advance. All his men felt the same excitement.

"Mount!" he commanded in a whisper. The men took their places and crossed themselves. . . . "Forward, with God's aid!"

"Hurrah-ah-ah!" reverberated in the forest, and the Cossack companies, trailing their lances and advancing one after another as if poured out of a sack, dashed gaily across the brook toward the camp.

One desperate frightened yell from the first French soldier who saw the Cossacks, and all who were in the camp, undressed and only just waking up, ran off in all directions, abandoning cannons, muskets and horses.

Had the Cossacks pursued the French, without heeding what was behind and around them, they would have captured Murat and everything there. That was what the officers desired. But it was impossible to make the Cossacks budge when once they had got booty and prisoners. None of them listened to orders. Fifteen hundred prisoners and thirty-eight guns were taken on the spot, besides standards and (what seemed most important to the Cossacks) horses, saddles, horsecloths, and the like. All this had to be dealt with, the prisoners and guns secured, the booty divided—not without some shouting and even a little fighting among themselves—and it was on this that the Cossacks all busied themselves.

The French, not being farther pursued, began to recover themselves: they formed into detachments and began firing. Orlóv-Denísov, still waiting for the other columns to arrive, advanced no further.

Meantime, according to the dispositions which said that "the First Column will march" and so on, the infantry of the belated columns, commanded by Bennigsen and directed by Toll, had started in due order and, as always happens, had got somewhere, but not to their appointed places. As always happens the men, starting cheerfully, began to halt; murmurs were heard, there was a sense of confusion, and finally a backward movement. Adjutants and generals galloped about, shouted, grew angry, quarreled, said they had come quite wrong and were late, gave vent to a little abuse, and at last gave it all up and went forward, simply to get somewhere. "We shall get somewhere or other!" And they did indeed get somewhere, though not to their right places; a few eventually even got to their right place, but too late to be of any use and only in time to be fired at. Toll, who in this battle played the part of Weyrother at Austerlitz, galloped assiduously from place to place, finding everything upside down everywhere. Thus he stumbled on Bagovút's corps in a wood when it was already broad daylight, though the corps should long before have joined Orlóv-Denísov. Excited and vexed by the failure and supposing that someone must be responsible for it, Toll galloped up to the commander of the corps and began upbraiding him severely, saying that he ought to be shot. General Bagovút, a fighting old soldier of placid temperament, being also upset by all the delay, confusion and cross-purposes, fell into a rage to everybody's surprise and quite contrary to his usual character, and said disagreeable things to Toll.

"I prefer not to take lessons from anyone, but I can die with my men as well as anybody," he said, and advanced with a single division.

Coming out onto a field under the enemy's fire, this brave general went straight ahead, leading his men under fire, without considering in his agitation whether going into action now, with a single division, would be of any use or no. Danger, cannon-balls and bullets were just what he needed in his angry mood. One of the first bullets killed him, and other bullets killed many of his men. And his division remained under fire for some time quite uselessly.

Chapter VII

MEANWHILE ANOTHER COLUMN WAS TO HAVE ATTACKED THE FRENCH FROM THE FRONT, BUT Kutúzov accompanied that column. He well knew that nothing but confusion would come of this battle undertaken against his will, and as far as was in his power held the troops back. He did not advance.

He rode silently on his small gray horse, indolently answering suggestions that they should attack.

"The word *attack* is always on your tongue, but you don't see that we are unable to execute complicated maneuvers," said he to Milorádovich who asked permission to advance.

"We couldn't take Murat prisoner this morning or get to the place in time, and nothing can be done now!" he replied to someone else.

When Kutúzov was informed that at the French rear—where according to the reports of the Cossacks there had previously been nobody—there were now two battalions of Poles, he gave a side-long glance at Ermólov who was behind him and to whom he had not spoken since the previous day.

"You see! They are asking to attack and making plans of all kinds, but as soon as one gets to business nothing is ready, and the enemy, forewarned, takes measures accordingly."

Ermólov screwed up his eyes and smiled faintly on hearing these words. He understood that for him the storm had blown over, and that Kutúzov would content himself with that hint.

"He's having a little fun at my expense," said Ermólov softly, nudging with his knee Raévski who was at his side.

Soon after this, Ermólov moved up to Kutúzov and respectfully remarked:

"It is not too late yet, your Highness—the enemy has not gone away—if you were to order an attack! If not, the Guards will not so much as see a little smoke."

Kutúzov did not reply, but when they reported to him that Murat's troops were in retreat he ordered an advance, though at every hundred paces he halted for three-quarters of an hour.

The whole battle consisted in what Orlóv-Denísov's Cossacks had done: the rest of the army merely lost some hundreds of men uselessly.

In consequence of this battle Kutúzov received a diamond decoration, and Bennigsen some diamonds and a hundred thousand rubles, others also received pleasant recognitions corresponding to their various grades, and following the battle fresh changes were made in the staff.

"That's how everything is done with us, all topsy-turvy!" said the Russian officers and generals after the Tarútino battle, letting it be understood that some fool there is doing things all wrong but that we ourselves should not have done so, just as people speak today. But people who talk like that either do not know what they are talking about, or deliberately deceive themselves. No battle—Tarútino, Borodinó, or Austerlitz—takes place as those who planned it anticipated. That is an essential condition.

A countless number of free forces (for nowhere is man freer than during a battle, where it is a question of life and death) influence the course taken by the fight, and that course never can be known in advance and never coincides with the direction of any one force.

If many simultaneously and variously directed forces act on a given body, the direction of its motion cannot coincide with any one of those forces, but will always be a mean—what in mechanics is represented by the diagonal of a parallelogram of forces.

If in the descriptions given by historians, especially French ones, we find their wars and battles carried out in accordance with previously formed plans, the only conclusion to be drawn is that those descriptions are false.

The battle of Tarútino obviously did not attain the aim Toll had in view—to lead the troops into action in the order prescribed by the dispositions; nor that which Count Orlóv-Denísov may have had in view—to take Murat prisoner; nor the result of immediately destroying the whole corps, which Bennigsen and others may have had in view; nor the aim of the officer who wished to go into action to distinguish himself; nor that of the Cossack who wanted more booty than he got, and so on. But if the aim of the battle was what actually resulted and what all the Russians of that day desired—to drive the French out of Russia and destroy their army—it is quite clear that the battle of Tarútino, just because of its incongruities, was exactly what was wanted at that stage of the campaign. It would be difficult and even impossible to imagine any result more opportune than the actual outcome of this battle. With a minimum of effort and insignificant losses, despite the greatest confusion, the most important results of the whole campaign were attained: the transition from retreat to advance, an exposure of the weakness of the French, and the administration of that shock which Napoleon's army had only awaited to begin its flight.

Chapter VIII

NAPOLEON ENTERS MOSCOW AFTER THE BRILLIANT VICTORY *DE LA MOSKOWA*; THERE CAN BE NO doubt about the victory for the battlefield remains in the hands of the French. The Russians retreat and abandon their ancient capital. Moscow, abounding in provisions, arms, munitions and incalculable wealth, is in Napoleon's hands. The Russian army, only half the strength of the French, does not make a single attempt to attack for a whole month. Napoleon's position is most brilliant. He can either fall on the Russian army with double its strength and destroy it; negotiate an advantageous peace, or in case of a refusal make a menacing move on Petersburg or even, in the case of a reverse, return to Smolénsk or Vílna; or remain in Moscow; in short, no special genius would seem to be required to retain the brilliant position the French held at that time. For that, only very simple and easy steps were necessary: not to allow the troops to loot, to prepare winter clothing—of which there was sufficient in Moscow for the whole army, and methodically to collect the provisions, of which (according to the French historians) there were enough in Moscow to supply the whole army for six months. Yet Napoleon, that greatest of all geniuses, who the historians declare had control of the army, took none of these steps.

He not merely did nothing of the kind, but on the contrary he used his power to select the most foolish and ruinous of all the courses open to him. Of all that Napoleon might have done: wintering in Moscow, advancing on Petersburg or on Nízhni-Nóvgorod, or retiring by a more northerly or more southerly route (say by the road Kutúzov afterward took) nothing more stupid or disastrous can be imagined than what he actually did. He remained in Moscow till October, letting the troops plunder the city; then, hesitating whether to leave a garrison behind him, he quitted Moscow, approached Kutúzov without joining battle, turned to the right and reached Málo-Yaroslávets, again without attempting to break through and take the road Kutúzov took, but retiring instead to Mozháysk along the devastated Smolénsk road. Nothing more stupid than that could have been devised, or more disastrous for the army, as the sequel showed. Had Napoleon's aim been to destroy his army, the most skillful strategist could hardly have devised any series of actions that would so completely have accomplished that purpose, independently of anything the Russian army might do.

Napoleon, the man of genius, did this! But to say that he destroyed his army because he wished to, or because he was very stupid, would be as unjust as to say that he had brought his troops to Moscow because he wished to and because he was very clever and a genius.

In both cases his personal activity, having no more force than the personal activity of any soldier, merely coincided with the laws that guided the event.

The historians quite falsely represent Napoleon's faculties as having weakened in Moscow, and do so only because the results did not justify his actions. He employed all his ability and strength to do the best he could for himself and his army, as he had done previously and as he did subsequently in 1813. His activity at that time was no less astounding than it was in Egypt, in Italy, in Austria and in Prussia. We do not know for certain in how far his genius was genuine in Egypt—where forty centuries looked down upon his grandeur—for his great exploits there are all told us by Frenchmen. We cannot accurately estimate his genius in Austria or Prussia, for we have to draw our information from French or German sources, and the incomprehensible surrender of whole corps without fighting and of fortresses without a siege, must incline Germans to recognize his genius as the only explanation of the war carried on in Germany. But we, thank God, have no need to recognize his genius in order to hide our shame. We have paid for the right to look at the matter plainly and simply, and we will not abandon that right.

His activity in Moscow was as amazing and as full of genius as elsewhere. Order after order and plan after plan was issued by him from the time he entered Moscow till the time he left it. The absence of citizens and of a deputation, and even the burning of Moscow, did not disconcert him. He did not lose sight either of the welfare of his army or of the doings of the enemy, or of the welfare of the people of Russia, or of the direction of affairs in Paris, or of diplomatic considerations concerning the terms of the anticipated peace.

Chapter IX

WITH REGARD TO MILITARY MATTERS, NAPOLEON IMMEDIATELY ON HIS ENTRY INTO MOSCOW gave General Sabastiani strict orders to observe the movements of the Russian army, sent army corps out along the different roads, and charged Murat to find Kutúzov. Then he gave careful directions about the fortification of the Kremlin, and drew up a brilliant plan for a future campaign over the whole map of Russia.

With regard to diplomatic questions, Napoleon summoned Captain Yákovlev, who had been robbed and was in rags and did not know how to get out of Moscow, minutely explained to him his whole policy and his magnanimity, and having written a letter to the Emperor Alexander in which he considered it his duty to inform his Friend and Brother that Rostopchín had managed affairs badly in Moscow, he dispatched Yákovlev to Petersburg.

Having similarly explained his views and his magnanimity to Tutólmin, he dispatched that old man also to Petersburg to negotiate.

With regard to legal matters, immediately after the fires he gave orders to find and execute the incendiaries. And the scoundrel Rostopchín was punished by an order to burn down his houses.

With regard to administrative matters, Moscow was granted a constitution. A municipality was established and the following announcement issued:

INHABITANTS OF MOSCOW!

Your misfortunes are cruel, but his Majesty the Emperor and King desires to arrest their course. Terrible examples have taught you how he punishes disobedience and crime. Strict measures have been taken to put an end to disorder and to re-establish public security. A paternal administration, chosen from among yourselves, will form your municipality or city government. It will take care of you, of your needs, and of your welfare. Its members will be distinguished by a red ribbon worn across the shoulder, and the mayor of the city will wear a white belt as well. But when not on duty they will only wear a red ribbon round the left arm.

The city police is established on its former footing, and better order already prevails in consequence of its activity. The government has appointed two commissaries-general, or chiefs of police, and twenty commissaries or captains of wards have been appointed to the different wards of the city. You will recognize them by the white ribbon they will wear on the left arm. Several churches of different denominations are open, and divine service is performed in them unhindered. Your fellow-citizens are returning every day to their homes. and orders have been given that they should find in them the help and protection due to their misfortunes. These are the measures the government has adopted to re-establish order and relieve your condition. But to achieve this aim it is necessary that you should add your efforts and should, if possible, forget the misfortunes you have suffered, should entertain the hope of a less cruel fate, should be certain that inevitable and ignominious death awaits those who make any attempt on your persons or on what remains of your property, and finally that you should not doubt that these will be safeguarded, since such is the will of the greatest and most just of monarchs. Soldiers and citizens, of whatever nation you may be, re-establish public confidence, the source of the welfare of a state, live like brothers, render mutual aid and protection one to another, unite to defeat the intentions of the evil-minded, obey the military and civil authorities, and your tears will soon cease to flow!

With regard to supplies for the army, Napoleon decreed that all the troops in turn should enter Moscow *à la maraude* to obtain provisions for themselves, so that the army might have its future provided for.

With regard to religion, Napoleon ordered the priests to be brought back and services to be again performed in the churches.

With regard to commerce and to provisioning the army, the following was placarded everywhere:

PROCLAMATION!

You, peaceful inhabitants of Moscow, artisans and workmen whom misfortune has driven from the city, and you scattered tillers of the soil, still kept out in the fields by groundless fear, listen! Tranquillity is returning to this capital and order is being restored in it. Your fellow-countrymen are emerging boldly from their hiding-places on finding that they are respected. Any violence to them or to their property is promptly punished. His Majesty the Emperor and King protects them, and considers no one among you his enemy except those who disobey his orders. He desires to end your misfortunes and restore you to your homes and families. Respond therefore to his benevolent intentions and come to us without fear. Inhabitants, return with confidence to your abodes! You will soon find means of satisfying your needs. Craftsmen and industrious artisans, return to your work, your houses, your shops, where the protection of guards awaits you! You shall receive proper pay for your work. And lastly you too, peasants, come from the forests where you are hiding in terror, return to your huts without fear, in full assurance that you will find protection! Markets are established in the city where peasants can bring their surplus supplies and the products of the soil. The government has taken the following steps to ensure freedom of sale for them: (1) From today, peasants, husbandmen, and those living in the neighborhood of Moscow, may without any danger bring their supplies of all kinds to two appointed markets, of which one is on the Mokhováya Street and the other at the Provision Market. (2) Such supplies will be bought from them at such prices as seller and buyer may agree on, and if a seller is unable to obtain a fair price he will be free to take his goods back to his village and no one may hinder him under any pretense. (3) Sunday and Wednesday of each week are appointed as the chief market-days and to that end a sufficient number of troops will be stationed along the highroads on Tuesdays and Saturdays at such distances from the town as to protect the carts. (4) Similar measures will be taken that peasants with their carts and horses may meet with no hindrance on their return journey. (5) Steps will immediately be taken to re-establish ordinary trading.

Inhabitants of the city and villages, and you, working men and artisans, to whatever nation you belong, you are called on to carry out the paternal intentions of his Majesty the Emperor and King and to cooperate with him for the public welfare! Lay your respect and confidence at his feet and do not delay to unite with us!

With the object of raising the spirits of the troops and of the people, reviews were constantly held and rewards distributed. The Emperor rode through the streets to comfort the inhabitants, and, despite his preoccupation with state affairs, himself visited the theaters that were established by his order.

In regard to philanthropy, the greatest virtue of crowned heads, Napoleon also did all in his power. He caused the words *Maison de ma Mère* to be inscribed on the charitable institutions, thereby combining tender filial affection with the majestic benevolence of a monarch. He visited the Foundling Hospital and, allowing the orphans saved by him to kiss his white hands, graciously conversed with Tutólmin. Then, as Thiers eloquently recounts, he ordered his soldiers to be paid in forged Russian money which he had prepared: "Raising the use of these means by an act worthy of himself and of the French army, he let relief be distributed to those who had been burned out. But as food was too precious to be given to foreigners, who were for the most part enemies, Napoleon preferred to supply them with money with which to purchase food from outside, and had paper rubles distributed to them."

With reference to army discipline, orders were continually being issued to inflict severe punishment for the non-performance of military duties and to suppress robbery.

Chapter X

But strange to say, all these measures, efforts and plans—which were not at all worse than others issued in similar circumstances—did not affect the essence of the matter but, like the hands of a clock detached from the mechanism, swung about in an arbitrary and aimless way without engaging the cogwheels.

With reference to the military side—the plan of campaign—that work of genius of which Thiers remarks that, "His genius never devised anything more profound, more skillful, or more admirable," and enters into a polemic with M. Fain to prove that this work of genius must be referred not to the 4th but to the 15th of October—that plan never was or could be executed, for it was quite out of touch with the facts of the case. The fortifying of the Kremlin, for which *la Mosquée* (as Napoleon termed the church of Basil the Beatified) was to have been razed to the ground, proved quite useless. The mining of the Kremlin only helped toward fulfilling Napoleon's wish that it should be blown up when he left Moscow—as a child wants the floor on which he has hurt himself to be beaten. The pursuit of the Russian army, about which Napoleon was so concerned, produced an unheard-of result. The French generals lost touch with the Russian army of sixty thousand men, and according to Thiers it was only eventually found, like a lost pin, by the skill—and apparently the genius—of Murat.

With reference to diplomacy, all Napoleon's arguments as to his magnanimity and justice both to Tutólmin and to Yákovlev (whose chief concern was to obtain a greatcoat and a conveyance), proved useless; Alexander did not receive these envoys and did not reply to their embassage.

With regard to legal matters, after the execution of the supposed incendiaries the rest of Moscow burned down.

With regard to administrative matters, the establishment of a municipality did not stop the robberies and was only of use to certain people who formed part of that municipality and under pretext of preserving order looted Moscow or saved their own property from being looted.

With regard to religion, as to which in Egypt matters had so easily been settled by Napoleon's visit to a mosque, no results were achieved. Two or three priests who were found in Moscow did try to carry out Napoleon's wish, but one of them was slapped in the face by a French soldier while conducting service, and a French official reported of another that: "The priest whom I found and invited to say Mass, cleaned and locked up the church. That night the doors were again broken open, the padlocks smashed, the books mutilated, and other disorders perpetrated."

With reference to commerce, the proclamation to industrious workmen and to peasants evoked no response. There were no industrious workmen, and the peasants caught the commissaries who ventured too far out of town with the proclamation and killed them.

As to the theaters for the entertainment of the people and the troops, these did not meet with success either. The theaters set up in the Kremlin and in Posnyakóv's house were closed again at once because the actors and actresses were robbed.

Even philanthropy did not have the desired effect. The genuine as well as the false paper money which flooded Moscow lost its value. The French, collecting booty, cared only for gold. Not only was the paper money valueless which Napoleon so graciously distributed to the unfortunate, but even silver lost its value in relation to gold.

But the most amazing example of the ineffectiveness of the orders given by the authorities at that time was Napoleon's attempt to stop the looting and re-establish discipline.

This is what the army authorities were reporting:

"Looting continues in the city despite the decrees against it. Order is not yet restored and not a single merchant is carrying on trade in a lawful manner. The sutlers alone venture to trade, and they sell stolen goods."

"The neighborhood of my ward continues to be pillaged by soldiers of the 3rd Corps, who not satisfied with taking from the unfortunate inhabitants hiding in the cellars the little they have left, even have the ferocity to wound them with their sabers, as I have repeatedly witnessed."

"Nothing new, except that the soldiers are robbing and pillaging—9th October."

"Robbery and pillaging continue. There is a band of thieves in our district who ought to be arrested by a strong force—11th October."

"The Emperor is extremely displeased that despite the strict orders to stop pillage, parties of marauding Guards are continually seen returning to the Kremlin. Among the Old Guard disorder and pillage were renewed more violently than ever yesterday evening, last night and today. The Emperor sees with regret that the picked soldiers appointed to guard his person, who should set an example of discipline, carry disobedience to such a point that they break into the cellars and stores containing army supplies. Others have disgraced themselves to the extent of disobeying sentinels and officers, and have abused and beaten them."

"The Grand Marshal of the palace," wrote the governor, "complains bitterly that in spite of repeated orders, the soldiers continue to commit nuisances in all the courtyards and even under the very windows of the Emperor."

That army, like a herd of cattle run wild and trampling underfoot the provender which might have saved it from starvation, disintegrated and perished with each additional day it remained in Moscow. But it did not go away.

It began to run away only when suddenly seized by a panic caused by the capture of transport trains on the Smolénsk road, and by the battle of Tarútino. The news of that battle of Tarútino, unexpectedly received by Napoleon at a review, evoked in him a desire to punish the Russians (Thiers says), and he issued the order for departure which the whole army was demanding.

Fleeing from Moscow the soldiers took with them everything they had stolen. Napoleon, too, carried away his own personal *trésor*, but on seeing the baggage-trains that impeded the army, he was (Thiers says) horror-struck. And yet with his experience of war he did not order all the superfluous vehicles to be burned, as he had done with those of a certain marshal when approaching Moscow. He gazed at the calèches and carriages in which soldiers were riding and remarked that it was a very good thing, as those vehicles could be used to carry provisions, the sick and the wounded.

The plight of the whole army resembled that of a wounded animal which feels it is perishing and does not know what it is doing. To study the skillful tactics and aims of Napoleon and his army from the time it entered Moscow till it was destroyed, is like studying the dying leaps and shudders of a mortally wounded animal. Very often a wounded animal, hearing a rustle, rushes straight at the hunter's gun, runs forward and back again, and hastens its own end. Napoleon, under pressure from his whole army, did the same thing. The rustle of the battle of Tarútino frightened the beast, and it rushed forward onto the hunter's gun, reached him, turned back, and finally—like any wild beast—ran back along the most disadvantageous and dangerous path, where the old scent was familiar.

During the whole of that period Napoleon, who seems to us to have been the leader of all these movements—as the figurehead of a ship may seem to a savage to guide the vessel—acted like a child who, holding a couple of strings inside a carriage, thinks he is driving it.

Chapter XI

EARLY IN THE MORNING OF THE 6TH OF OCTOBER PIERRE WENT OUT OF THE SHED, AND ON RE-turning stopped by the door to play with a little blue-gray dog with a long body and short bandy legs, that jumped about him. This little dog lived in their shed, sleeping beside Karatáev at night; it sometimes made excursions into the town but always returned again. Probably it had never had an owner, and it still belonged to nobody and had no name. The French called it Azor; the soldier who told stories called it Femgálka; Karatáev and others called it Gray, or sometimes Flabby. Its lack of a master, a name, or even of a breed or any definite color, did not seem to trouble the blue-gray dog in the least. Its furry tail stood up firm and round as a plume, its bandy legs served it so well that it would often gracefully lift a hind leg and run very easily and quickly on three legs, as if disdaining to use all four. Everything pleased it. Now it would roll on its back, yelping with delight, now bask in the sun with a thoughtful air of importance, and now frolic about playing with a chip of wood or a straw.

Pierre's attire by now consisted of a dirty torn shirt (the only remnant of his former clothing), a pair of soldier's trousers which by Karatáev's advice he tied with string round the ankles for warmth, and a peasant coat and cap. Physically he had changed much during this time. He no longer seemed stout, though he still had the appearance of solidity and strength hereditary in his family. A beard and mustache covered the lower part of his face, and a tangle of hair, infested with lice, curled round his head like a cap. The look of his eyes was resolute, calm, and animatedly alert, as never before. The former slackness which had shown itself even in his eyes was now replaced by an energetic readiness for action and resistance. His feet were bare.

Pierre first looked down the field across which vehicles and horsemen were passing that morning, then into the distance across the river, then at the dog who was pretending to be in earnest about biting him, and then at his bare feet which he placed with pleasure in various positions, moving his dirty thick big toes. Every time he looked at his bare feet a smile of animated self-satisfaction flitted across his face. The sight of them reminded him of all he had experienced and learned during these weeks and this recollection was pleasant to him.

For some days the weather had been calm and clear with slight frosts in the mornings—what is called an "old wives' summer."

In the sunshine the air was warm, and that warmth was particularly pleasant with the invigorating freshness of the morning frost still in the air.

On everything—far and near—lay the magic crystal glitter seen only at that time of autumn.

The Sparrow Hills were visible in the distance, with the village, the church and the large white house. The bare trees, the sand, the bricks and roofs of the houses, the green church spire and the corners of the white house in the distance, all stood out in the transparent air in most delicate outline and with unnatural clearness. Nearby could be seen the familiar ruins of a half-burned mansion occupied by the French, with lilac bushes still showing dark green beside the fence. And even that ruined and befouled house—which in dull weather was repulsively ugly—seemed quietly beautiful now, in the clear motionless brilliance.

A French corporal with coat unbuttoned in a homely way, a skull-cap on his head and a short pipe in his mouth, came from behind a corner of the shed and approached Pierre with a friendly wink.

"What sunshine, Monsieur Kiríl!" (their name for Pierre). "Eh? Just like spring!"

And the corporal leaned against the door and offered Pierre his pipe, though whenever he offered it Pierre always declined it.

"To be on the march in such weather . . ." he began.

Pierre inquired what was being said about leaving, and the corporal told him that nearly all the troops were starting and there ought to be an order about the prisoners that day. Sokolóv, one of the soldiers in the shed with Pierre, was dying, and Pierre told the corporal that something should be done about him. The corporal replied that Pierre need not worry about that as they had an ambulance and a permanent hospital and arrangements would be made for the sick, and that in general everything that could happen had been foreseen by the authorities.

"Besides, Monsieur Kiríl, you have only to say a word to the captain, you know. He is a man who never forgets anything. Speak to the captain when he makes his round, he will do anything for you."

(The captain of whom the corporal spoke often had long chats with Pierre and showed him all sorts of favors.)

" 'You see, St. Thomas,' he said to me the other day. 'Monsieur Kiríl is a man of education, who speaks French. He is a Russian seigneur who has had misfortunes, but he is a man. He knows what's what. . . . If he wants anything and asks me, he won't get a refusal. When one has studied, you see, one likes education and well-bred people.' It is for your sake I mention it, Monsieur Kiríl. The other day if it had not been for you that affair would have ended ill."

And after chatting a while longer, the corporal went away. (The affair he had alluded to had happened a few days before—a fight between the prisoners and the French soldiers, in which Pierre had succeeded in pacifying his comrades.) Some of the prisoners who had heard Pierre talking to the corporal, immediately asked what the Frenchman had said. While Pierre was repeating what he had been told about the army leaving Moscow, a thin, sallow, tattered French soldier came up to the door of the shed. Rapidly and timidly raising his fingers to his forehead by way of greeting, he asked Pierre whether the soldier Platoche to whom he had given a shirt to sew, was in that shed.

A week before the French had had boot-leather and linen issued to them, which they had given out to the prisoners to make up into boots and shirts for them.

"Ready, ready, dear fellow!" said Karatáev, coming out with a neatly folded shirt.

Karatáev, on account of the warm weather and for convenience at work, was wearing only trousers and a tattered shirt as black as soot. His hair was bound round, workman-fashion, with a wisp of lime-tree bast, and his round face seemed rounder and pleasanter than ever.

"A promise is own brother to performance! I said Friday and here it is, ready," said Platón, smiling and unfolding the shirt he had sewn.

The Frenchman glanced round uneasily and then, as if overcoming his hesitation, rapidly threw off his uniform and put on the shirt. He had a long, greasy, flowered silk waistcoat next to his sallow thin bare body, but no shirt. He was evidently afraid the prisoners looking on would laugh at him, and thrust his head into the shirt hurriedly. None of the prisoners said a word.

"See, it fits well!" Platón kept repeating, pulling the shirt straight.

The Frenchman having pushed his head and hands through, without raising his eyes, looked down at the shirt and examined the seams.

"You see, dear man, this is not a sewing shop, and I had no proper tools; and, as they say, one needs a tool even to kill a louse," said Platón with one of his round smiles, obviously pleased with his work.

"It's good, quite good, thank you," said the Frenchman, in French, "but there must be some linen left over."

"It will fit better still when it sets to your body," said Karatáev, still admiring his handiwork. "You'll be nice and comfortable. . . ."

"Thanks, thanks, old fellow. . . . But the bits left over?" said the Frenchman again and smiled. He took out an assignation ruble note and gave it to Karatáev. "But give me the pieces that are over."

Pierre saw that Platón did not want to understand what the Frenchman was saying, and he looked on without interfering. Karatáev thanked the Frenchman for the money and went on admiring his own work. The Frenchman insisted on having the pieces returned that were left over and asked Pierre to translate what he said.

"What does he want the bits for?" said Karatáev. "They'd make fine legbands for us. Well, never mind."

And Karatáev with a suddenly changed and saddened expression, took a small bundle of scraps from inside his shirt and gave it to the Frenchman without looking at him. "Oh dear!" muttered Karatáev and went away. The Frenchman looked at the linen, considered for a moment, then looked inquiringly at Pierre and as if Pierre's look had told him something, suddenly blushed and shouted in a squeaky voice:

"Platoche! Eh, Platoche! Keep them yourself!" And handing back the odd bits he turned and went out.

"There, look at that," said Karatáev, swaying his head. "People said they were not Christians, but they too have souls. It's what the old folk used to say: 'A sweating hand's an open hand, a dry hand's close.' He's naked, but yet he's given it back."

Karatáev smiled thoughtfully, and was silent awhile looking at the pieces.

"But they'll make grand legbands, dear friend," he said, and went back into the shed.

Chapter XII

FOUR WEEKS HAD PASSED SINCE PIERRE HAD BEEN TAKEN PRISONER AND THOUGH THE FRENCH had offered to move him from the men's to the officers' shed, he had stayed in the shed where he was first put.

In burned and devastated Moscow Pierre experienced almost the extreme limits of privation a man can endure; but thanks to his physical strength and health, of which he had till then been unconscious, and thanks especially to the fact that the privations came so gradually that it was impossible to say when they began, he endured his position not only lightly but joyfully. And just at this time he obtained the tranquillity and ease of mind he had formerly striven in vain to reach. He had long sought in different ways that tranquillity of mind, that inner harmony which had so impressed him in the soldiers at the battle of Borodinó. He had sought it in philanthropy, in freemasonry, in the dissipations of town life, in wine, in heroic feats of self-sacrifice, and in romantic love for Natásha; he had sought it by reasoning—and all these quests and experiments had failed him. And now without thinking about it he had found that peace and inner harmony only through the horror of death, through privation, and through what he recognized in Karatáev.

Those dreadful moments he had lived through at the executions had as it were forever washed away from his imagination and memory the agitating thoughts and feelings that had formerly seemed so important. It did not now occur to him to think of Russia, or the war, or politics, or Napoleon. It was plain to him that all these things were no business of his, and that he was not called on to judge concerning them and therefore could not do so. "Russia and summer weather are not bound together," he thought, repeating words of Karatáev's which he found strangely consoling. His intention of killing Napoleon and his calculations of the cabalistic number of the beast of the Apocalypse, now seemed to him meaningless and even ridiculous. His anger with his wife and anxiety that his name should not be smirched, now seemed not merely trivial but even amusing. What concern was it of his that somewhere or other that woman was leading the life she preferred? What did it matter to anybody, and especially to him, whether or not they found out that their prisoner's name was Count Bezúkhov?

He now often remembered his conversation with Prince Andrew and quite agreed with him, though he understood Prince Andrew's thoughts somewhat differently. Prince Andrew had thought and said that happiness could only be negative, but had said it with a shade of bitterness and irony as though he was really saying that all desire for positive happiness is implanted in us merely to torment us and never be satisfied. But Pierre believed it without any mental reservation. The absence of suffering, the satisfaction of one's needs and consequent freedom in the choice of one's occupation, that is of one's way of life, now seemed to Pierre to be indubitably man's highest happiness. Here and now for the first time he fully appreciated the enjoyment of eating when he wanted to eat, drinking when he wanted to drink, sleeping when he wanted to sleep, of warmth when he was cold, of talking to a fellow-man when he wished to talk and to hear a human voice. The satisfaction of one's needs—good food, cleanliness and freedom—now that he was deprived of all this, seemed to Pierre to constitute perfect happiness; and the choice of occupation, that is, of his way of life—now that that was so restricted—seemed to him such an easy matter that he forgot that a superfluity of the comforts of life destroys all joy in satisfying one's needs, while great freedom in the choice of occupation—such freedom as his wealth, his education and his social position had given him in his own life—is just what makes the choice of occupation insolubly difficult, and destroys the desire and possibility of having an occupation.

All Pierre's daydreams now turned on the time when he would be free. Yet subsequently, and for the rest of his life, he thought and spoke with enthusiasm of that month of captivity, of those irrecoverable, strong, joyful sensations, and chiefly of the complete peace of mind and inner freedom which he experienced only during those weeks.

When on the first day he got up early, went out of the shed at dawn and saw the cupolas and crosses of the New Convent of the Virgin still dark at first, the hoarfrost on the dusty grass, the Sparrow Hills, and the wooded banks above the winding river vanishing in the purple distance, when he felt the contact of the fresh air and heard the noise of the crows flying from Moscow across the field, and when afterward light gleamed from the east and the sun's rim appeared solemnly from behind a cloud, and the cupolas and crosses, the hoarfrost, the distance and the river, all began to sparkle in the glad light—Pierre felt a new joy and strength in life such as he had never before known. And this not only stayed with him during the whole of his imprisonment, but even grew in strength as the hardships of his position increased.

That feeling of alertness and of readiness for anything was still further strengthened in him by the high opinion his fellow-prisoners formed of him soon after his arrival at the shed. With his knowledge of languages, the respect shown him by the French, his simplicity, his readiness to give anything asked of him (he received the allowance of three rubles a week made to officers); with his strength, which he showed to the soldiers by pressing nails into the walls of the hut; his gentleness to his companions, and his capacity for sitting still and thinking without doing anything (which seemed to them incomprehensible), he appeared to them a rather mysterious and superior being. The very qualities that had been a hindrance, if not actually harmful to him in the world he had lived in—his strength, his disdain for the comforts of life, his absent-mindedness and simplicity—here among these people gave him almost the status of a hero. And Pierre felt that their opinion placed responsibilities upon him.

Chapter XIII

THE FRENCH EVACUATION BEGAN ON THE NIGHT BETWEEN THE 6TH and 7TH OF OCTOBER: kitchens and sheds were dismantled, carts loaded and troops and baggage-trains started.

At seven in the morning a French convoy in marching trim, wearing shakos and carrying muskets, knapsacks and enormous sacks, stood in front of the sheds, and animated French talk mingled with curses sounded all along the lines.

In the shed everyone was ready, dressed, belted, shod, and only awaited the order to start. The sick soldier, Sokolóv, pale and thin with dark shadows round his eyes, alone sat in his place barefoot and not dressed. His eyes, prominent from the emaciation of his face, gazed inquiringly at his comrades who were paying no attention to him, and he moaned regularly and quietly. It was evidently not so much his sufferings that caused him to moan (he had dysentery) as his fear and grief at being left alone.

Pierre, girt with a rope round his waist and wearing shoes Karatáev had made for him from some leather a French soldier had torn off a tea-chest and brought to have his boots mended with, went up to the sick man and squatted down beside him.

"You know, Sokolóv, they are not all going away! They have a hospital here. You may be better off than we others," said Pierre.

"O Lord! Oh, it will be the death of me! O Lord!" moaned the man in a louder voice.

"I'll go and ask them again directly," said Pierre, rising and going to the door of the shed.

Just as Pierre reached the door, the corporal who had offered him a pipe the day before came up to it with two soldiers. The corporal and soldiers were in marching kit with knapsacks and shakos that had metal straps, and these changed their familiar faces.

The corporal came, according to orders, to shut the door. The prisoners had to be counted before being let out.

"Corporal, what will they do with the sick man? . . ." Pierre began.

But even as he spoke he began to doubt whether this was the corporal he knew or a stranger, so unlike himself did the corporal seem at that moment. Moreover, just as Pierre was speaking a sharp rattle of drums was suddenly heard from both sides. The corporal frowned at Pierre's words, and uttering some meaningless oaths slammed the door. The shed became semi-dark, and the sharp rattle of the drums on two sides drowned the sick man's groans.

"There it is! . . . *It* again! . . ." said Pierre to himself, and an involuntary shudder ran down his spine. In the corporal's changed face, in the sound of his voice, in the stirring and deafening noise of the drums, he recognized that mysterious, callous force which compelled people against their will to kill their fellow-men—that force the effect of which he had witnessed during the executions. To fear or to try to escape that force, to address entreaties or exhortations to those who served as its tools, was useless. Pierre knew this now. One had to wait and endure. He did not again go to the sick man, nor turn to look at him, but stood frowning by the door of the hut.

When that door was opened and the prisoners, crowding against one another like a flock of sheep, squeezed into the exit, Pierre pushed his way forward and approached that very captain who as the corporal had assured him was ready to do anything for him. The captain was also in marching kit, and on his cold face appeared that same *it* which Pierre had recognized in the corporal's words and in the roll of the drums.

"Pass on, pass on!" the captain reiterated, frowning sternly, and looking at the prisoners who thronged past him.

Pierre went up to him, though he knew his attempt would be vain.

"What now?" the officer asked with a cold look as if not recognizing Pierre.

Pierre told him about the sick man.

"He'll manage to walk, devil take him!" said the captain. "Pass on, pass on!" he continued without looking at Pierre.

"But he is dying," Pierre again began.

"Be so good . . ." shouted the captain, frowning angrily.

"Dram-da-da-dam, dam-dam . . ." rattled the drums, and Pierre understood that this mysterious force completely controlled these men and that it was now useless to say any more.

The officer-prisoners were separated from the soldiers and told to march in front. There were about thirty officers, with Pierre among them, and about three hundred men.

The officers, who had come from the other sheds, were all strangers to Pierre and much better dressed than he. They looked at him and at his shoes mistrustfully, as at an alien. Not far from him walked a fat major with a sallow, bloated, angry face, who was wearing a Kazán dressing-gown tied round with a towel, and who evidently enjoyed the respect of his fellow-prisoners. He kept one hand, in which he clasped his tobacco-pouch, inside the bosom of his dressing gown and held the stem of his pipe firmly with the other. Panting and puffing, the major grumbled and growled at everybody because he thought he was being pushed and that they were all hurrying when they had nowhere to hurry to, and were all surprised at something when there was nothing to be surprised at. Another, a thin little officer, was speaking to everyone, conjecturing where they were now being taken and how far they would get that day. An official in felt boots and wearing a commissariat uniform ran round from side to side and gazed at the ruins of Moscow, loudly announcing his observations as to what had been burned down, and what this or that part of the city was that they could see. A third officer, who by his accent was a Pole, disputed with the commissariat officer, arguing that he was mistaken in his identification of the different wards of Moscow.

"What are you disputing about?" said the major angrily. "What does it matter whether it is St. Nicholas or St. Blasius? You see it's burned down, and there's an end of it. . . . What are you pushing for? Isn't the road wide enough?" said he, turning to a man behind him who was not pushing him at all.

"Oh, oh, oh! What have they done?" the prisoners on one side and another were heard saying as they gazed on the charred ruins. "All beyond the river, and Zúbova, and in the Kremlin. . . . Just look! There's not half of it left. Yes, I told you—the whole quarter beyond the river, and so it is."

"Well, you know it's burned, so what's the use of talking?" said the major.

As they passed near a church in the Khamóvniki (one of the few unburned quarters of Moscow) the whole mass of prisoners suddenly started to one side and exclamations of horror and disgust were heard.

"Ah, the villains! What heathens! Yes; dead, dead, so he is. . . . And smeared with something!"

Pierre too drew near the church where the thing was that evoked these exclamations, and dimly made out something leaning against the palings surrounding the church. From the words of his comrades who saw better than he did, he found that this was the body of a man, set upright against the palings with its face smeared with soot.

"Go on! What the devil . . . Go on! Thirty thousand devils! . . ." the convoy guards began cursing and the French soldiers, with fresh virulence, drove away with their swords the crowd of prisoners who were gazing at the dead man.

Chapter XIV

THROUGH THE CROSS-STREETS OF THE KHAMÓVNIKI QUARTER THE PRISONERS MARCHED, followed only by their escort and the vehicles and wagons belonging to that escort, but when they reached the supply-stores they came among a huge and closely packed train of artillery mingled with private vehicles.

At the bridge they all halted, waiting for those in front to get across. From the bridge they had a view of endless lines of moving baggage-trains before and behind them. To the right, where the Kalúga road turns near Neskúchny, endless rows of troops and carts stretched away into the distance. These were troops of Beauharnais' corps which had started before any of the others. Behind, along the riverside and across the Stone Bridge, were Ney's troops and transport.

Davout's troops, in whose charge were the prisoners, were crossing the Crimean Bridge and some were already debouching into the Kalúga road. But the baggage-trains stretched out so that the last of Beauharnais' train had not yet got out of Moscow and reached the Kalúga road when the vanguard of Ney's army was already emerging from the Great Ordynka street.

When they had crossed the Crimean Bridge the prisoners moved a few steps forward, halted, and again moved on, and from all sides vehicles and men crowded closer and closer together. They advanced the few hundred paces that separated the bridge from the Kalúga road, taking more than an hour to do so, and came out upon the square where the streets of the Transmoskvá ward and the Kalúga road converge, and the prisoners jammed close together had to stand for some hours at that cross-way. From all sides, like the roar of the sea was heard the rattle of wheels, the tramp of feet, and incessant shouts of anger and abuse. Pierre stood pressed against the wall of a charred house, listening to that noise which mingled in his imagination with the roll of the drums.

To get a better view, several officer-prisoners climbed onto the wall of the half-burned house against which Pierre was leaning.

"What crowds! Just look at the crowds! . . . They've loaded goods even on the cannon! Look there, those are furs!" they exclaimed. "Just see what the blackguards have looted. . . . There! See what that one has behind in the cart. . . . Why those are settings taken from some icons, by heaven! . . . Oh, the rascals! . . . See how that fellow has loaded himself up, he can hardly walk! Good lord, they've even grabbed those chaises! . . . See that fellow there sitting on the trunks. . . . Heavens! They're fighting."

"That's right, hit him on the snout—on his snout! Like this, we shan't get away before evening. Look, look there. . . . Why, that must be Napoleon's own. See what horses! And the monograms with a crown! It's like a portable house. . . . That fellow's dropped his sack and doesn't see it. Fighting again . . . A woman with a baby, and not bad-looking either! Yes, I dare say, that's the way they'll let you pass . . . Just look, there's no end to it. Russian wenches, by heaven, so they are! In carriages—see how comfortably they've settled themselves!"

Again, as at the church in Khamóvniki, a wave of general curiosity bore all the prisoners forward onto the road, and Pierre thanks to his stature saw over the heads of the others what so attracted their curiosity. In three carriages involved among the munition carts, closely squeezed together, sat women with rouged faces, dressed in glaring colors, who were shouting something in shrill voices.

From the moment Pierre had recognized the appearance of the mysterious force nothing had seemed to him strange or dreadful: neither the corpse smeared with soot for fun, nor these women hurrying away nor the burned ruins of Moscow. All that he now witnessed scarcely made an impression on him—as if his soul, making ready for a hard struggle, refused to receive impressions that might weaken it.

The women's vehicles drove by. Behind them came more carts, soldiers, wagons, soldiers, gun-carriages, carriages, soldiers, ammunition carts, more soldiers, and now and then women.

Pierre did not see the people as individuals but saw their movement.

All these people and horses seemed driven forward by some invisible power. During the hour Pierre watched them they all came flowing from the different streets with one and the same desire to get on quickly; they all jostled one another, began to grow angry and to fight, white teeth gleamed, brows frowned, ever the same words of abuse flew from side to side, and all the faces bore the same swaggeringly resolute and coldly cruel expression that had struck Pierre that morning on the corporal's face when the drums were beating.

It was not till nearly evening that the officer commanding the escort collected his men and with shouts and quarrels forced his way in among the baggage-trains, and the prisoners hemmed in on all sides, emerged onto the Kalúga road.

They marched very quickly, without resting, and halted only when the sun began to set. The baggage-carts drew up close together and the men began to prepare for their night's rest. They all appeared angry and dissatisfied. For a long time, oaths, angry shouts, and fighting could be heard from all sides. A carriage that followed the escort ran into one of the carts and knocked a hole in it with its pole. Several soldiers ran toward the cart from different sides: some beat the carriage horses on their heads, turning them aside, others fought among themselves, and Pierre saw that one German was badly wounded on the head by a sword.

It seemed that all these men, now that they had stopped amid fields in the chill dusk of the autumn evening, experienced one and the same feeling of unpleasant awakening from the hurry and eagerness to push on that had seized them at the start. Once at a standstill they all seemed to understand that they did not yet know where they were going, and that much that was painful and difficult awaited them on this journey.

During this halt the escort treated the prisoners even worse than they had done at the start. It was here that the prisoners for the first time received horseflesh for their meat-ration.

From the officer down to the lowest soldier they showed what seemed like personal spite against each of the prisoners, in unexpected contrast to their former friendly relations.

This spite increased still more when, on calling over the roll of prisoners, it was found that in the bustle of leaving Moscow one Russian soldier, who had pretended to suffer from colic, had escaped. Pierre saw a Frenchman beat a Russian soldier cruelly for straying too far from the road, and heard his friend the captain reprimand and threaten to court-martial a non-commissioned officer on account of the escape of the Russian. To the non-commissioned officer's excuse that the prisoner was ill and could not walk, the officer replied that the order was to shoot those who lagged behind. Pierre felt that that fatal force which had crushed him during the executions, but which he had not felt during his imprisonment, now again controlled his existence. It was terrible, but he felt that in proportion to the efforts of that fatal force to crush him, there grew and strengthened in his soul a power of life independent of it.

He ate his supper of buckwheat soup with horseflesh, and chatted with his comrades.

Neither Pierre nor any of the others spoke of what they had seen in Moscow, or of the roughness of their treatment by the French, or of the order to shoot them which had been announced to them. As if in reaction against the worsening of their position they were all particularly animated and gay. They spoke of personal reminiscences, of amusing scenes they had witnessed during the campaign, and avoided all talk of their present situation.

The sun had set long since. Bright stars shone out here and there in the sky. A red glow as of a conflagration spread above the horizon from the rising full moon, and that vast red ball swayed strangely in the gray haze. It grew light. The evening was ending, but the night had not yet come. Pierre got up and left his new companions, crossing between the campfires to the other side of the road where he had been told the common soldier-prisoners were stationed. He wanted to talk to them. On the road he was stopped by a French sentinel who ordered him back.

Pierre turned back, not to his companions by the campfire, but to an unharnessed cart where there was nobody. Tucking his legs under him and dropping his head he sat down on the cold ground by the wheel of the cart and remained motionless a long while sunk in thought. Suddenly he burst out into a fit of his broad, good-natured laughter, so loud that men from various sides turned with surprise to see what this strange and evidently solitary laughter could mean.

"Ha-ha-ha!" laughed Pierre. And he said aloud to himself: "The soldier did not let me pass. They took me and shut me up. They hold me captive. What, me? My immortal soul? Ha-ha-ha! Ha-ha-ha! . . ." and he laughed till tears started to his eyes.

A man got up and came to see what this queer big fellow was laughing at all by himself. Pierre stopped laughing, got up, went farther away from the inquisitive man, and looked around him.

The huge, endless bivouac that had previously resounded with the crackling of campfires and the voices of many men had grown quiet, the red campfires were growing paler and dying down. High up in the light sky hung the full moon. Forests and fields beyond the camp, unseen before, were now visible in the distance. And farther still, beyond those forests and fields the bright, oscillating, limitless distance lured one to itself. Pierre glanced up at the sky and the twinkling stars in its far-away depths. "And all that is me, all that is within me, and it is all I!" thought Pierre. "And they caught all that and put it into a shed boarded up with planks!" He smiled, and went and lay down to sleep beside his companions.

Chapter XV

In the early days of October another envoy came to Kutúzov with a letter from Napoleon proposing peace and falsely dated from Moscow, though Napoleon was already not far from Kutúzov on the old Kalúga road. Kutúzov replied to this letter as he had done to the one formerly brought by Lauriston, saying that there could be no question of peace.

Soon after that a report was received from Dórokhov's guerrilla detachment operating to the left of Tarútino, that troops of Broussier's division had been seen at Formínsk, and that being separated from the rest of the French army they might easily be destroyed. The soldiers and officers again demanded action. Generals on the staff, excited by the memory of the easy victory at Tarútino, urged Kutúzov to carry out Dórokhov's suggestion. Kutúzov did not consider any offensive necessary. The result was a compromise which was inevitable: a small detachment was sent to Formínsk to attack Broussier.

By a strange coincidence, this task, which turned out to be a most difficult and important one, was entrusted to Dokhtúrov—that same modest little Dokhtúrov whom no one had described to us as drawing up plans of battles, dashing about in front of regiments, showering crosses on batteries, and so on, and who was thought to be and was spoken of as undecided and undiscerning—but whom we find commanding wherever the position was most difficult all through the Russo-French wars from Austerlitz to the year 1813. At Austerlitz he remained last at the Augezd dam, rallying the regiments, saving what was possible when all were flying and perishing and not a single general was left in the rearguard. Ill with fever he went to Smolénsk with twenty thousand men to defend the town against Napoleon's whole army. In Smolénsk, at the Malákhov Gate, he had hardly dozed off in a paroxysm of fever before he was awakened by the bombardment of the town—and Smolénsk held out all day long. At the battle of Borodinó, when Bagratión was killed and nine-tenths of the men of our left flank had fallen and the full force of the French artillery fire was directed against it, the man sent there was this same irresolute and undiscerning Dokhtúrov—Kutúzov hastening to rectify a mistake he had made by sending someone else there first. And the quiet little Dokhtúrov rode thither, and Borodinó became the greatest glory of the Russian army. Many heroes have been described to us in verse and prose, but of Dokhtúrov scarcely a word has been said.

It was Dokhtúrov again whom they sent to Formínsk and from there to Málo-Yaroslávets, the place where the last battle with the French was fought and where the obvious disintegration of the French army began; and we are told of many geniuses and heroes of that period of the campaign, but of Dokhtúrov nothing or very little is said and that dubiously. And this silence about Dokhtúrov is the clearest testimony to his merit.

It is natural for a man who does not understand the workings of a machine to imagine that a shaving that has fallen into it by chance and is interfering with its action and tossing about in it, is its most important part. The man who does not understand the construction of the machine cannot conceive that the small connecting cogwheel which revolves quietly is one of the most essential parts of the machine, and not the shaving which merely harms and hinders the working.

On the 10th of October when Dokhtúrov had gone halfway to Formínsk and stopped at the village of Aristóvo preparing faithfully to execute the orders he had received, the whole French army having, in its convulsive movement, reached Murat's position apparently in order to give battle—suddenly without any reason turned off to the left onto the new Kalúga road and began to enter Formínsk, where only Broussier had been till then. At that time Dokhtúrov had under his command, besides Dórokhov's detachment, the two small guerrilla detachments of Figner and Seslávin.

On the evening of October the 11th Seslávin came to the Aristóvo headquarters with a French guardsman he had captured. The prisoner said that the troops that had entered Formínsk that day were the vanguard of the whole army, that Napoleon was there and the whole army had left Moscow four days previously. That same evening a house serf who had come from Bórovsk, said he had seen an immense army entering the town. Some Cossacks of Dokhtúrov's detachment reported having sighted the French Guards marching along the road to Bórovsk. From all these reports it was evident that where they had expected to meet a single division there was now the whole French army marching from Moscow in an unexpected direction—along the Kalúga road. Dokhtúrov was unwilling to undertake any action, as it was not clear to him now what he ought to do. He had been ordered to attack Formínsk. But only Broussier had been there at that time and now the whole French army was there. Ermólov wished to act on his own judgment, but Dokhtúrov insisted that he must have Kutúzov's instructions. So it was decided to send a dispatch to the staff.

For this purpose a capable officer, Bolkhovítinov, was chosen, who was to explain the whole affair by word of mouth, besides delivering a written report. Toward midnight Bolkhovítinov, having received the dispatch and verbal instructions, galloped off to the General Staff accompanied by a Cossack with spare horses.

Chapter XVI

IT WAS A WARM, DARK, AUTUMN NIGHT. IT HAD BEEN RAINING FOR FOUR DAYS. HAVING CHANGED horses twice and galloped twenty miles in an hour and a half over a sticky muddy road, Bolkhovítinov reached Litashëvka after one o'clock at night. Dismounting at a cottage on whose wattle fence hung a signboard, "General Staff," and throwing down his reins, he entered a dark passage.

"The general on duty, quick! It's very important!" said he to someone who had risen and was sniffing in the dark passage.

"He has been very unwell since the evening and this is the third night he has not slept," said the orderly pleadingly in a whisper. "You should wake the captain first."

"But this is very important, from General Dokhtúrov," said Bolkhovítinov, entering the open door which he had found by feeling in the dark.

The orderly had gone in before him and began waking somebody.

"Your Honor, your Honor! A courier."

"What? What's that? From whom?" came a sleepy voice.

"From Dokhtúrov and from Alexéy Petróvich. Napoleon is at Formínsk," said Bolkhovítinov, unable to see in the dark who was speaking but guessing by the voice that it was not Konovnítsyn.

The man who had wakened yawned and stretched himself.

"I don't like waking him," he said, fumbling for something. "He is very ill. Perhaps this is only a rumor."

"Here is the dispatch," said Bolkhovítinov. "My orders are to give it at once to the general on duty."

"Wait a moment, I'll light a candle. You damned rascal, where do you always hide it?" said the voice of the man who was stretching himself, to the orderly. (This was Shcherbínin, Konovnítsyn's adjutant.) "I've found it, I've found it!" he added.

The orderly was striking a light and Shcherbínin was fumbling for something on the candlestick.

"Oh, the nasty beasts!" said he with disgust.

By the light of the sparks Bolkhovítinov saw Shcherbínin's youthful face as he held the candle, and the face of another man who was still asleep. This was Konovnítsyn.

When the flame of the sulfur-splinters kindled by the tinder burned up, first blue and then red, Shcherbínin lit the tallow candle, from the candlestick of which the cockroaches that had been gnawing it were running away, and looked at the messenger. Bolkhovítinov was bespattered all over with mud, and had smeared his face by wiping it with his sleeve.

"Who gave the report?" inquired Shcherbínin, taking the envelope.

"The news is reliable," said Bolkhovítinov. "Prisoners, Cossacks and the scouts all say the same thing."

"There's nothing to be done, we'll have to wake him," said Shcherbínin, rising and going up to the man in the nightcap who lay covered by a greatcoat. "Peter Petróvich!" said he. (Konovnítsyn did not stir.) "To the General Staff!" he said with a smile, knowing that those words would be sure to arouse him.

And in fact the head in the nightcap was lifted at once. On Konovnítsyn's handsome, resolute face with cheeks flushed by fever, there still remained for an instant a far-away dreamy expression remote from present affairs, but then he suddenly started and his face assumed its habitual calm and firm appearance.

"Well, what is it? From whom?" he asked immediately but without hurry, blinking at the light.

While listening to the officer's report Konovnítsyn broke the seal and read the dispatch. Hardly had he done so before he lowered his legs in their woolen stockings to the earthen floor and began putting on his boots. Then he took off his nightcap, combed his hair over his temples, and donned his cap.

"Did you get here quickly? Let us go to his Highness."

Konovnítsyn had understood at once that the news brought was of great importance and that no time must be lost. He did not consider or ask himself whether the news was good or bad. That did not interest him. He regarded the whole business of the war not with his intelligence or his reason but by something else. There was within him a deep unexpressed conviction that all would be well, but that one must not trust to this and still less speak about it, but must only attend to one's own work. And he did his work, giving his whole strength to the task.

Peter Petróvich Konovnítsyn, like Dokhtúrov, seems to have been included merely for propriety's sake in the list of the so-called heroes of 1812—the Barclays, Raévskis, Ermólovs, Plátovs and Milorádoviches. Like Dokhtúrov he had the reputation of being a man of very limited capacity and information, and like Dokhtúrov he never made plans of battle but was always found where the situation was most difficult. Since his appointment as general on duty he had always slept with his door open, giving orders that every messenger should be allowed to wake him up. In battle he was always under fire, so that Kutúzov reproved him for it and feared to send him to the front, and like Dokhtúrov he was one of those unnoticed cogwheels that, without clatter or noise, constitute the most essential part of the machine.

Coming out of the hut into the damp, dark night Konovnítsyn frowned—partly from an increased pain in his head and partly at the unpleasant thought that occurred to him, of how all that nest of influential men on the staff would be stirred up by this news, especially Bennigsen, who ever since Tarútino had been at daggers drawn with Kutúzov; and how they would make suggestions, quarrel, issue orders, and rescind them. And this premonition was disagreeable to him though he knew it could not be helped.

And in fact Toll, to whom he went to communicate the news, immediately began to expound his plans to a general sharing his quarters, until Konovnítsyn, who listened in weary silence, reminded him that they must go to see his Highness.

Chapter XVII

KUTÚZOV LIKE ALL OLD PEOPLE DID NOT SLEEP MUCH AT NIGHT. HE OFTEN FELL ASLEEP UNEXpectedly in the daytime, but at night, lying on his bed without undressing, he generally remained awake thinking.

So he lay now on his bed, supporting his large, heavy, scarred head on his plump hand, with his one eye open, meditating and peering into the darkness.

Since Bennigsen, who corresponded with the Emperor and had more influence than anyone else on the staff, had begun to avoid him, Kutúzov was more at ease as to the possibility of himself and his troops being obliged to take part in useless aggressive movements. The lesson of the Tarútino battle and of the day before it, which Kutúzov remembered with pain, must he thought have some effect on others too.

"They must understand that we can only lose by taking the offensive. Patience and time are my warriors, my champions," thought Kutúzov. He knew that an apple should not be plucked while it is green. It will fall of itself when ripe, but if picked unripe the apple is spoiled, the tree is harmed, and your teeth are set on edge. Like an experienced sportsman he knew that the beast was wounded, and wounded as only the whole strength of Russia could have wounded it, but whether it was mortally wounded or not was still an undecided question. Now by the fact of Lauriston and Barthélemi having been sent, and by the reports of the guerrillas, Kutúzov was almost sure that the wound was mortal. But he needed further proofs and it was necessary to wait.

"They want to run to see how they have wounded it. Wait and we shall see! Continual maneuvers, continual advances!" thought he. "What for? Only to distinguish themselves! As if fighting were fun. They are like children from whom one can't get any sensible account of what has happened because they all want to show how well they can fight. But that's not what is needed now.

"And what ingenious maneuvers they all propose to me! It seems to them that when they have thought of two or three contingencies" (he remembered the general plan sent him from Petersburg) "they have foreseen everything. But the contingencies are endless."

The undecided question as to whether the wound inflicted at Borodinó was mortal or not, had hung over Kutúzov's head for a whole month. On the one hand the French had occupied Moscow. On the other Kutúzov felt assured with all his being that the terrible blow into which he and all the Russians had put their whole strength must have been mortal. But in any case proofs were needed; he had waited a whole month for them and grew more impatient the longer he waited. Lying on his bed during those sleepless nights he did just what he reproached those younger generals for doing. He imagined all sorts of possible contingencies, just like the younger men, but with this difference, that he saw thousands of contingencies instead of two or three and based nothing on them. The longer he thought the more contingencies presented themselves. He imagined all sorts of movements of the Napoleonic army as a whole or in sections—against Petersburg, or against him, or to outflank him. He thought too of the possibility (which he feared most of all) that Napoleon might fight him with his own weapon and remain in Moscow awaiting him. Kutúzov even imagined that Napoleon's army might turn back through Medyn and Yukhnóv, but the one thing he could not foresee was what happened—the insane, convulsive stampede of Napoleon's army during its first eleven days after leaving Moscow: a stampede which made possible what Kutúzov had not yet even dared to think of—the complete extermination of the French. Dórokhov's report about Broussier's division, the guerrillas' reports of distress in Napoleon's army, rumors of preparations for leaving Moscow, all confirmed the supposition that the French army was beaten and preparing for flight. But these were only suppositions, which seemed important to the younger men but not to Kutúzov. With his sixty years' experience he knew what value to attach to rumors, knew how apt people who desire anything are to group all news so that it appears to confirm what they desire, and he knew how readily in such cases they omit all that makes for the contrary. And the more he desired it the less he allowed himself to believe it. This question absorbed all his mental powers. All else was to him only life's customary routine. To such customary routine belonged his conversations with the staff, the letters he wrote from Tarútino to Madame de Staël, the reading of novels, the distribution of awards, his correspondence with Petersburg, and so on. But the destruction of the French, which he alone foresaw, was his heart's one desire.

On the night of the 11th of October he lay leaning on his arm and thinking of that.

There was a stir in the next room and he heard the steps of Toll, Konovnítsyn and Bolkhovítinov.

"Eh, who's there? Come in, come in! What news?" the Field Marshal called out to them.

While a footman was lighting a candle, Toll communicated the substance of the news.

"Who brought it?" asked Kutúzov with a look which, when the candle was lit, struck Toll by its cold severity.

"There can be no doubt about it, your Highness."

"Call him in, call him here."

Kutúzov sat up with one leg hanging down from the bed and his big paunch resting against the other which was doubled under him. He screwed up his seeing eye to scrutinize the messenger more carefully, as if wishing to read in his face what preoccupied his own mind.

"Tell me, tell me, friend," said he to Bolkhovítinov in his low, aged voice, as he pulled together the shirt which gaped open on his chest, "come nearer—nearer. What news have you brought me? Eh? That Napoleon has left Moscow? Are you sure? Eh?"

Bolkhovítinov gave a detailed account from the beginning of all he had been told to report.

"Speak quicker, quicker! Don't torture me!" Kutúzov interrupted him.

Bolkhovítinov told him everything and was then silent, awaiting instructions. Toll was beginning to say something but Kutúzov checked him. He tried to say something, but his face suddenly puckered and wrinkled; he waved his arm at Toll and turned to the opposite side of the room, to the corner darkened by the icons that hung there.

"O Lord, my Creator, Thou has heard our prayer . . ." said he in a tremulous voice with folded hands. "Russia is saved. I thank Thee, O Lord!" and he wept.

Chapter XVIII

FROM THE TIME HE RECEIVED THIS NEWS TO THE END OF THE CAMPAIGN ALL KUTÚZOV'S ACTIVITY WAS directed toward restraining his troops, by authority, by guile and by entreaty, from useless attacks, maneuvers, or encounters with the perishing enemy. Dokhtúrov went to Málo-Yaroslávets, but Kutúzov lingered with the main army and gave orders for the evacuation of Kalúga—a retreat beyond which town seemed to him quite possible.

Everywhere Kutúzov retreated, but the enemy without waiting for his retreat fled in the opposite direction.

Napoleon's historians describe to us his skilled maneuvers at Tarútino and Málo-Yaroslávets, and make conjectures as to what would have happened had Napoleon been in time to penetrate into the rich southern provinces.

But not to speak of the fact that nothing prevented him from advancing into those southern provinces (for the Russian army did not bar his way), the historians forget that nothing could have saved his army, for then already it bore within itself the germs of inevitable ruin. How could that army—which had found abundant supplies in Moscow and had trampled them underfoot instead of keeping them, and on arriving at Smolénsk had looted provisions instead of storing them—how could that army recuperate in Kalúga province, which was inhabited by Russians such as those who lived in Moscow, and where fire had the same property of consuming what was set ablaze?

That army could not recover anywhere. Since the battle of Borodinó and the pillage of Moscow it had borne within itself, as it were, the chemical elements of dissolution.

The members of what had once been an army—Napoleon himself and all his soldiers—fled without knowing whither, each concerned only to make his escape as quickly as possible from this position, of the hopelessness of which they were all more or less vaguely conscious.

So it came about that at the council at Málo-Yaroslávets, when the generals pretending to confer together expressed various opinions, all mouths were closed by the opinion uttered by the simple-minded soldier Mouton who, speaking last, said what they all felt: that the one thing needful was to get away as quickly as possible; and no one, not even Napoleon, could say anything against that truth which they all recognized.

But though they all realized that it was necessary to get away, there still remained a feeling of shame at admitting that they must flee. An external shock was needed to overcome that shame, and this shock came in due time. It was what the French called *"le hourra de l'Empereur."*

The day after the council at Málo-Yaroslávets Napoleon rode out early in the morning amid the lines of his army with his suite of marshals and an escort, on the pretext of inspecting the army and the scene of the previous and of the impending battle. Some Cossacks on the prowl for booty fell in with the Emperor and very nearly captured him. If the Cossacks did not capture Napoleon then, what saved him was the very thing that was destroying the French army, the booty on which the Cossacks fell. Here as at Tarútino they went after plunder, leaving the men. Disregarding Napoleon they rushed after the plunder and Napoleon managed to escape.

When *les enfants du Don* might so easily have taken the Emperor himself in the midst of his army, it was clear that there was nothing for it but to fly as fast as possible along the nearest, familiar road. Napoleon with his forty-year-old stomach understood that hint, not feeling his former agility and boldness, and under the influence of the fright the Cossacks had given him he at once agreed with Mouton and issued orders—as the historians tell us—to retreat by the Smolénsk road.

That Napoleon agreed with Mouton, and that the army retreated, does not prove that Napoleon caused it to retreat, but that the forces which influenced the whole army and directed it along the Mozháysk (that is, the Smolénsk) road acted simultaneously on him also.

Chapter XIX

A MAN IN MOTION ALWAYS DEVISES AN AIM FOR THAT MOTION. TO BE ABLE TO GO A THOUSAND versts he must imagine that something good awaits him at the end of those thousand versts. One must have the prospect of a promised land to have the strength to move.

The promised land for the French during their advance had been Moscow, during their retreat it was their native land. But that native land was too far off, and for a man going a thousand versts it is absolutely necessary to set aside his final goal and to say to himself: "Today I shall get to a place forty versts off where I shall rest and spend the night," and during the first day's journey that resting-place eclipses his ultimate goal and attracts all his hopes and desires. And the impulses felt by a single person are always magnified in a crowd.

For the French retreating along the old Smolénsk road, the final goal—their native land—was too remote, and their immediate goal was Smolénsk, toward which all their desires and hopes, enormously intensified in the mass, urged them on. It was not that they knew that much food and fresh troops awaited them in Smolénsk, nor that they were told so (on the contrary their superior officers, and Napoleon himself, knew that provisions were scarce there) but because this alone could give them strength to move on and endure their present privations. So both those who knew and those who did not know, deceived themselves, and pushed on to Smolénsk as to a promised land.

Coming out onto the highroad the French fled with surprising energy and unheard-of rapidity toward the goal they had fixed on. Besides the common impulse which bound the whole crowd of French into one mass and supplied them with a certain energy, there was another cause binding them together—their great numbers. As with the physical law of gravity, their enormous mass drew the individual human atoms to itself. In their hundreds of thousands they moved like a whole nation.

Each of them desired nothing more than to give himself up as a prisoner to escape from all this horror and misery; but on the one hand the force of this common attraction to Smolénsk, their goal, drew each of them in the same direction; on the other hand an army corps could not surrender to a company, and though the French availed themselves of every convenient opportunity to detach themselves and to surrender on the slightest decent pretext, such pretexts did not always occur. Their very numbers and their crowded and swift movement deprived them of that possibility and rendered it not only difficult but impossible for the Russians to stop this movement, to which the French were directing all their energies. Beyond a certain limit no mechanical disruption of the body could hasten the process of decomposition.

A lump of snow cannot be melted instantaneously. There is a certain limit of time in less than which no amount of heat can melt the snow. On the contrary the greater the heat the more solidified the remaining snow becomes.

Of the Russian commanders Kutúzov alone understood this. When the flight of the French army along the Smolénsk road became well defined, what Konovnítsyn had foreseen on the night of the 11th of October began to occur. The superior officers all wanted to distinguish themselves, to cut off, to seize, to capture and to overthrow the French, and all clamored for action.

Kutúzov alone used all his power (and such power is very limited in the case of any commander-in-chief) to prevent an attack.

He could not tell them what we say now: "Why fight, why block the road, losing our own men and inhumanly slaughtering unfortunate wretches? What is the use of that, when a third of their army has melted away on the road from Moscow to Vyázma without any battle?" But drawing from his aged wisdom what they could understand, he told them of the golden bridge, and they laughed at and slandered him, flinging themselves on, rending and exulting over the dying beast.

Ermólov, Milorádovich, Plátov, and others in proximity to the French near Vyázma, could not resist their desire to cut off and break up two French corps, and by way of reporting their intention to Kutúzov they sent him a blank sheet of paper in an envelope.

And try as Kutúzov might to restrain the troops, our men attacked, trying to bar the road. Infantry regiments, we are told, advanced to the attack with music and with drums beating, and killed and lost thousands of men.

But they did not cut off or overthrow anybody and the French army, closing up more firmly at the danger, continued, while steadily melting away, to pursue its fatal path to Smolénsk.

Part Fourteen

Chapter I

THE BATTLE OF BORODINÓ, WITH THE OCCUPATION OF MOSCOW THAT FOLLOWED IT AND THE flight of the French without further conflicts, is one of the most instructive phenomena in history.

All historians agree that the external activity of states and nations in their conflicts with one another is expressed in wars, and that as a direct result of greater or less success in war the political strength of states and nations increases or decreases.

Strange as may be the historical account of how some king or emperor, having quarreled with another, collects an army, fights his enemy's army, gains a victory by killing three, five, or ten thousand men, and subjugates a kingdom and an entire nation of several millions, all the facts of history (as far as we know it) confirm the truth of the statement that the greater or lesser success of one army against another is the cause, or at least an essential indication, of an increase or decrease in the strength of the nation—even though it is unintelligible why the defeat of an army—a hundredth part of a nation—should oblige that whole nation to submit. An army gains a victory, and at once the rights of the conquering nation have increased to the detriment of the defeated. An army has suffered defeat, and at once a people loses its rights in proportion to the severity of the reverse, and if its army suffers a complete defeat the nation is quite subjugated.

So according to history it has been found from the most ancient times, and so it is to our own day. All Napoleon's wars serve to confirm this rule. In proportion to the defeat of the Austrian army Austria loses its rights, and the rights and the strength of France increase. The victories of the French at Jena and Auerstädt destroy the independent existence of Prussia.

But then, in 1812 the French gain a victory near Moscow. Moscow is taken and after that, with no further battles, it is not Russia that ceases to exist, but the French army of six hundred thousand, and then Napoleonic France itself. To strain the facts to fit the rules of history: to say that the field of battle at Borodinó remained in the hands of the Russians, or that after Moscow there were other battles that destroyed Napoleon's army, is impossible.

After the French victory at Borodinó there was no general engagement nor any that were at all serious, yet the French army ceased to exist. What does this mean? If it were an example taken from the history of China, we might say that it was not an historic phenomenon (which is the historians' usual expedient when anything does not fit their standards); if the matter concerned some brief conflict in which only a small number of troops took part, we might treat it as an exception; but this event occurred before our fathers' eyes, and for them it was a question of the life or death of their fatherland, and it happened in the greatest of all known wars.

The period of the campaign of 1812 from the battle of Borodinó to the expulsion of the French, proved that the winning of a battle does not produce a conquest and is not even an invariable indication of conquest; it proved that the force which decides the fate of peoples lies not in the conquerors, nor even in armies and battles, but in something else.

The French historians, describing the condition of the French army before it left Moscow, affirm that all was in order in the Grand Army, except the cavalry, the artillery and the transport—there was no forage for the horses or the cattle. That was a misfortune no one could remedy, for the peasants of the district burned their hay rather than let the French have it.

The victory gained did not bring the usual results because the peasants Karp and Vlas (who after the French had evacuated Moscow drove in their carts to pillage the town, and in general personally failed to manifest any heroic feelings), and the whole innumerable multitude of such peasants, did not bring their hay to Moscow for the high price offered them, but burned it instead.

Let us imagine two men who have come out to fight a duel with rapiers according to all the rules of the art of fencing. The fencing has gone on for some time; suddenly one of the combatants, feeling himself wounded and understanding that the matter is no joke but concerns his life, throws down his rapier, and seizing the first cudgel that comes to hand begins to brandish it. Then let us imagine that the combatant who so sensibly employed the best and simplest means to attain his end, was at the same time influenced by traditions of chivalry and, desiring to conceal the facts of the case, insisted that he had gained his victory with the rapier according to all the rules of art. One can imagine what confusion and obscurity would result from such an account of the duel.

The fencer who demanded a contest according to the rules of fencing was the French army; his opponent who threw away the rapier and snatched up the cudgel was the Russian people; those who try to explain the matter according to the rules of fencing are the historians who have described the event.

After the burning of Smolénsk a war began which did not follow any previous traditions of war. The burning of towns and villages, the retreats after battles, the blow dealt at Borodinó and the renewed retreat, the burning of Moscow, the capture of marauders, the seizure of transports, and the guerrilla war—were all departures from the rules.

Napoleon felt this, and from the time he took up the correct fencing attitude in Moscow and instead of his opponent's rapier saw a cudgel raised above his head, he did not cease to complain to Kutúzov and to the Emperor Alexander that the war was being carried on contrary to all the rules—as if there were any rules for killing people. In spite of the complaints of the French as to the non-observance of the rules, in spite of the fact that to some highly placed Russians it seemed rather disgraceful to fight with a cudgel and they wanted to assume a pose *en quarte* or *en tierce* according to all the rules, and to make an adroit thrust *en prime*, and so on—the cudgel of the people's war was lifted with all its menacing and majestic strength, and without consulting anyone's tastes or rules and regardless of anything else, it rose and fell with stupid simplicity, but consistently, and belabored the French till the whole invasion had perished.

And it is well for a people who do not—as the French did in 1813—salute according to all the rules of art, and presenting the hilt of their rapier gracefully and politely, hand it to their magnanimous conqueror, but at the moment of trial, without asking what rules others have adopted in similar cases, simply and easily pick up the first cudgel that comes to hand, and strike with it till the feeling of resentment and revenge in their soul yields to a feeling of contempt and compassion.

Chapter II

One of the most obvious and advantageous departures from the so-called laws of war is the action of scattered groups against men pressed together in a mass. Such action always occurs in wars that take on a national character. In such actions, instead of two crowds opposing each other, the men disperse, attack singly, run away when attacked by stronger forces, but again attack when opportunity offers. This was done by the guerrillas in Spain, by the mountain tribes in the Caucasus, and by the Russians in 1812.

People have called this kind of war "guerrilla warfare" and assume that by so calling it they have explained its meaning. But such a war does not fit in under any rule and is directly opposed to a well-known rule of tactics which is accepted as infallible. That rule says that an attacker should concentrate his forces in order to be stronger than his opponent at the moment of conflict.

Guerrilla war (always successful, as history shows) directly infringes that rule.

This contradiction arises from the fact that military science assumes the strength of an army to be identical with its numbers. Military science says that the more troops the greater the strength. *Les gros bataillons ont toujours raison.*

For military science to say this, is like defining momentum in mechanics by reference to the mass only: stating that momenta are equal or unequal to each other simply because the masses involved are equal or unequal.

Momentum (quantity of motion) is the product of mass and velocity.

In military affairs the strength of an army is the product of its mass and some unknown x.

Military science, seeing in history innumerable instances of the fact that the size of any army does not coincide with its strength and that small detachments defeat larger ones, obscurely admits the existence of this unknown factor and tries to discover it—now in a geometric formation, now in the equipment employed, now, and most usually, in the genius of the commanders. But the assignment of these various meanings to the factor does not yield results which accord with the historic facts.

Yet it is only necessary to abandon the false view (adopted to gratify the "heroes") of the efficacy of the directions issued in wartime by commanders, in order to find this unknown quantity.

That unknown quantity is the spirit of the army, that is to say, the greater or lesser readiness to fight and face danger felt by all the men composing an army, quite independently of whether they are, or are not, fighting under the command of a genius, in two or three-line formation, with cudgels or with rifles that repeat thirty times a minute. Men who want to fight will always put themselves in the most advantageous conditions for fighting.

The spirit of an army is the factor which multiplied by the mass gives the resulting force. To define and express the significance of this unknown factor—the spirit of an army—is a problem for science.

This problem is only solvable if we cease arbitrarily to substitute for the unknown x itself, the conditions under which that force becomes apparent—such as the commands of the general, the equipment employed, and so on—mistaking these for the real significance of the factor, and if we recognize this unknown quantity in its entirety as being the greater or lesser desire to fight and to face danger. Only then, expressing known historic facts by equations and comparing the relative significance of this factor, can we hope to define the unknown.

Ten men, battalions, or divisions, fighting fifteen men, battalions, or divisions, conquer—that is, kill or take captive—all the others, while themselves losing four, so that on the one side four and on the other fifteen were lost. Consequently the four were equal to the fifteen, and therefore $4x = 15y$. Consequently $x/y = 15/4$. This equation does not give us the value of the unknown factor but gives us a ratio between two unknowns. And by bringing variously selected historic units (battles, campaigns, periods of war) into such equations, a series of numbers could be obtained in which certain laws should exist and might be discovered.

The tactical rule that an army should act in masses when attacking and in smaller groups in retreat, unconsciously confirms the truth that the strength of an army depends on its spirit. To lead men forward under fire more discipline (obtainable only by movement in masses) is needed than is needed to resist attacks. But this rule which leaves out of account the spirit of the army continually proves incorrect, and is in particularly striking contrast to the facts when some strong rise or fall in the spirit of the troops occurs, as in all national wars.

The French, retreating in 1812—though according to tactics they should have separated into detachments to defend themselves—congregated into a mass because the spirit of the army had so fallen that only the mass held the army together. The Russians, on the contrary, ought according to tactics to have attacked in mass, but in fact they split up into small units, because their spirit had so risen that separate individuals, without orders, dealt blows at the French without needing any compulsion to induce them to expose themselves to hardships and dangers.

Chapter III

THE SO-CALLED PARTISAN WAR BEGAN WITH THE ENTRY OF THE FRENCH INTO SMOLÉNSK.

Before partisan warfare had been officially recognized by the government, thousands of enemy stragglers, marauders and foragers had been destroyed by the Cossacks and the peasants, who killed them off as instinctively as dogs worry a stray mad dog to death. Denís Davydov, with his Russian instinct, was the first to recognize the value of this terrible cudgel which regardless of the rules of military science destroyed the French, and to him belongs the credit for taking the first steps toward regularizing this method of warfare.

On August 24th Davydov's first partisan detachment was formed and then others were recognized. The further the campaign progressed the more numerous these detachments became.

The irregulars destroyed the great army piecemeal. They gathered the fallen leaves that dropped of themselves from that withered tree—the French army—and sometimes shook that tree itself. By October, when the French were fleeing toward Smolénsk, there were hundreds of such companies, of various sizes and characters. There were some that adopted all the army methods and had infantry, artillery, staffs, and the comforts of life. Others consisted solely of Cossack cavalry. There were also small scratch groups of foot and horse, and groups of peasants and landowners that remained unknown. A sacristan commanded one party which captured several hundred prisoners in the course of a month; and there was Vasilísa, the wife of a village elder, who slew hundreds of the French.

The partisan warfare flamed up most fiercely in the latter days of October. Its first period had passed: when the partisans themselves, amazed at their own boldness, feared every minute to be surrounded and captured by the French, and hid in the forests without unsaddling, hardly daring to dismount and always expecting to be pursued. By the end of October this kind of warfare had taken definite shape: it had become clear to all what could be ventured against the French and what could not. Now only the commanders of detachments with staffs, and moving according to rules at a distance from the French, still regarded many things as impossible. The small bands that had started their activities long before and had already observed the French closely, considered things possible which the commanders of the big detachments did not dare to contemplate. The Cossacks and peasants who crept in among the French now considered everything possible.

On October 22nd, Denísov (who was one of the irregulars) was with his group at the height of the guerrilla enthusiasm. Since early morning he and his party had been on the move. All day long he had been watching from the forest that skirted the highroad, a large French convoy of cavalry baggage and Russian prisoners separated from the rest of the army, which—as was learned from spies and prisoners—was moving under a strong escort to Smolénsk. Besides Denísov and Dólokhov (who also led a small party and moved in Denísov's vicinity), the commanders of some large divisions with staffs also knew of this convoy and, as Denísov expressed it, were sharpening their teeth for it. Two of the commanders of large parties—one a Pole and the other a German—sent invitations to Denísov almost simultaneously, requesting him to join up with their divisions to attack the convoy.

"No, bwother, I have gwown mustaches myself," said Denísov on reading these documents, and he wrote to the German that, despite his heartfelt desire to serve under so valiant and renowned a general, he had to forgo that pleasure because he was already under the command of the Polish general. To the Polish general he replied to the same effect, informing him that he was already under the command of the German.

Having arranged matters thus, Denísov and Dólokhov intended, without reporting matters to the higher command, to attack and seize that convoy with their own small forces. On October 22nd it was moving from the village of Mikulino to that of Shámshevo. To the left of the road between Mikulino and Shámshevo there were large forests, extending in some places up to the road itself though in others a verst or more back from it. Through these forests Denísov and his party rode all day, sometimes keeping well back in them and sometimes coming to the very edge, but never losing sight of the moving French. That morning, Cossacks of Denísov's party had seized and carried off into the forest two wagons loaded with cavalry saddles, which had stuck in the mud not far from Mikulino where the forest ran close to the road. Since then, and until evening, the party had watched the movements of the French without attacking. It was necessary to let the French reach Shámshevo quietly without alarming them and then, after joining Dólokhov who was to come that evening to a consultation at a watchman's hut in the forest a verst from Shámshevo, to surprise the French at dawn, falling like an avalanche on their heads from two sides, and rout and capture them all at one blow.

In their rear, two versts from Mikulino where the forest came right up to the road, six Cossacks were posted to report if any fresh columns of French should show themselves.

Beyond Shámshevo, Dólokhov was to observe the road in the same way, to find out at what distance there were other French troops. They reckoned that the convoy had fifteen hundred men. Denísov had two hundred, and Dólokhov might have as many more, but the disparity of numbers did not deter Denísov. All that he now wanted to know was what troops these were, and to learn that, he had to capture a "tongue"—that is a man from the enemy column. That morning's attack on the wagons had been made so hastily that the Frenchmen with the wagons had all been killed; only a little drummer boy had been taken alive, and as he was a straggler he could tell them nothing definite about the troops in that column.

Denísov considered it dangerous to make a second attack for fear of putting the whole column on the alert, so he sent Tíkhon Shcherbáty, a peasant of his party, to Shámshevo to try and seize at least one of the French quartermasters who had been sent on in advance.

Chapter IV

It was a warm rainy autumn day. The sky and the horizon were both the color of muddy water. At times a sort of mist descended, and then suddenly heavy slanting rain came down.

Denísov in a felt cloak and a sheepskin cap from which the rain ran down, was riding a thin thoroughbred horse with sunken sides. Like his horse, which turned its head and laid its ears back, he shrank from the driving rain and gazed anxiously before him. His thin face with its short thick black beard looked angry.

Beside Denísov rode an esaul, Denísov's fellow-worker, also in felt cloak and sheepskin cap, and riding a large sleek Don horse.

Esaul Lováyski the Third was a tall man as straight as an arrow, pale-faced, fair-haired, with narrow light eyes and with calm self-satisfaction in his face and bearing. Though it was impossible to say in what the peculiarity of the horse and rider lay, yet at first glance at the esaul and Denísov one saw that the latter was wet and uncomfortable and was a man mounted on a horse, while looking at the esaul one saw that he was as comfortable and as much at ease as always, and that he was not a man who had mounted a horse, but a man who was one with his horse, a being consequently possessed of twofold strength.

A little ahead of them walked a peasant guide, wet to the skin and wearing a gray peasant coat and a white knitted cap.

A little behind, on a poor, small, lean Kirghíz mount with an enormous tail and mane and a bleeding mouth, rode a young officer in a blue French overcoat.

Beside him rode a hussar, with a boy in a tattered French uniform and blue cap behind him on the crupper of his horse. The boy held on to the hussar with cold, red hands, and raising his eyebrows gazed about him with surprise. This was the French drummer boy captured that morning.

Behind them along the narrow, sodden, cut-up forest road came hussars in threes and fours, and then Cossacks: some in felt cloaks, some in French greatcoats, and some with horsecloths over their heads. The horses, being drenched by the rain, all looked black whether chestnut or bay. Their necks, with their wet close-clinging manes, looked strangely thin. Steam rose from them. Clothes, saddles, reins, were all wet, slippery and sodden, like the ground and the fallen leaves that strewed the road. The men sat huddled up trying not to stir, so as to warm the water that had trickled to their bodies and not admit the fresh cold water that was leaking in under their seats, their knees, and at the back of their necks. In the midst of the outspread line of Cossacks two wagons, drawn by French horses and by saddled Cossack horses that had been hitched on in front, rumbled over the tree-stumps and branches and splashed through the water that lay in the ruts.

Denísov's horse swerved aside to avoid a pool in the track and bumped his rider's knee against a tree.

"Oh, the devil!" exclaimed Denísov angrily, and showing his teeth he struck his horse three times with his whip, splashing himself and his comrades with mud.

Denísov was out of sorts both because of the rain and also from hunger (none of them had eaten anything since morning), and yet more because he still had no news from Dólokhov and the man sent to capture a "tongue" had not returned.

"There'll hardly be another such chance to fall on a transport as today. It's too risky to attack them by oneself, and if we put it off till another day one of the big guerrilla detachments will snatch the prey from under our noses," thought Denísov, continually peering forward, hoping to see a messenger from Dólokhov.

On coming to a path in the forest along which he could see far to the right, Denísov stopped.

"There's someone coming," said he.

The esaul looked in the direction Denísov indicated.

"There are two, an officer and a Cossack. But it is not *presupposable* that it is the lieutenant-colonel himself," said the esaul, who was fond of using words the Cossacks did not know.

The approaching riders having descended a decline were no longer visible, but they reappeared a few minutes later. In front, at a weary gallop and using his leather whip, rode an officer, disheveled and drenched, whose trousers had worked up to above his knees. Behind him, standing in the stirrups, trotted a Cossack. The officer, a very young lad with a broad rosy face and keen merry eyes, galloped up to Denísov and handed him a sodden envelope.

"From the general," said the officer. "Please excuse its not being quite dry."

Denísov, frowning, took the envelope and opened it.

"There, they kept telling us: 'It's dangerous, it's dangerous,' " said the officer, addressing the esaul while Denísov was reading the dispatch. "But Komaróv and I"—he pointed to the Cossack—"were prepared. We have each of us two pistols. . . . But what's this?" he asked, noticing the French drummer boy. "A prisoner? You've already been in action? May I speak to him?"

"Wostóv! Pétya!" exclaimed Denísov, having run through the dispatch. "Why didn't you say who you were?" and turning with a smile he held out his hand to the lad.

The officer was Pétya Rostóv.

All the way Pétya had been preparing himself to behave with Denísov as befitted a grown-up man and an officer—without hinting at their previous acquaintance. But as soon as Denísov smiled at him Pétya brightened up, blushed with pleasure, forgot the official manner he had been rehearsing, and began telling him how he had already been in a battle near Vyázma, and how a certain hussar had distinguished himself there.

"Well, I am glad to see you," Denísov interrupted him, and his face again assumed its anxious expression.

"Michael Feoklítych," said he to the esaul, "this is again fwom that German, you know. He"—he indicated Pétya—"is serving under him."

And Denísov told the esaul that the dispatch just delivered was a repetition of the German general's demand that he should join forces with him for an attack on the transport.

"If we don't take it tomowwow, he'll snatch it fwom under our noses," he added.

While Denísov was talking to the esaul, Pétya—abashed by Denísov's cold tone and supposing that it was due to the condition of his trousers—furtively tried to pull them down under his greatcoat so that no one should notice it, while maintaining as martial an air as possible.

"Will there be any orders, your Honor?" he asked Denísov, holding his hand at the salute and resuming the game of adjutant and general for which he had prepared himself, "or shall I remain with your Honor?"

"Orders?" Denísov repeated thoughtfully. "But can you stay till tomowwow?"

"Oh, please . . . May I stay with you?" cried Pétya.

"But, just what did the genewal tell you? To weturn at once?" asked Denísov.

Pétya blushed.

"He gave me no instructions. I think I could?" he returned, inquiringly.

"Well, all wight," said Denísov.

And turning to his men he directed a party to go on to the halting place arranged near the watchman's hut in the forest, and told the officer on the Kirghíz horse (who performed the duties of an adjutant) to go and find out where Dólokhov was and whether he would come that evening. Denísov himself intended going with the esaul and Pétya to the edge of the forest where it reached out to Shámshevo, to have a look at the part of the French bivouac they were to attack next day.

"Well, old fellow," said he to the peasant guide, "lead us to Shámshevo."

Denísov, Pétya and the esaul, accompanied by some Cossacks and the hussar who had the prisoner, rode to the left across a ravine to the edge of the forest.

Chapter V

THE RAIN HAD STOPPED, AND ONLY THE MIST WAS FALLING AND DROPS FROM THE TREES. Denísov, the esaul and Pétya rode silently, following the peasant in the knitted cap who, stepping lightly with out-turned toes and moving noiselessly in his bast shoes over the roots and wet leaves, silently led them to the edge of the forest.

He ascended an incline, stopped, looked about him, and advanced to where the screen of trees was less dense. On reaching a large oak tree that had not yet shed its leaves, he stopped and beckoned mysteriously to them with his hand.

Denísov and Pétya rode up to him. From the spot where the peasant was standing they could see the French. Immediately beyond the forest, on a downward slope, lay a field of spring rye. To the right, beyond a steep ravine, was a small village and a landowner's house with a broken roof. In the village, in the house, in the garden, by the well, by the pond, over all the rising ground, and all along the road uphill from the bridge leading to the village, not more than five hundred yards away, crowds of men could be seen through the shimmering mist. Their un-Russian shouting at their horses which were straining uphill with the carts, and their calls to one another, could be clearly heard.

"Bwing the prisoner here," said Denísov in a low voice, not taking his eyes off the French.

A Cossack dismounted, lifted the boy down, and took him to Denísov. Pointing to the French troops, Denísov asked him what these and those of them were. The boy, thrusting his cold hands into his pockets and lifting his eyebrows, looked at Denísov in affright, but in spite of an evident desire to say all he knew, gave confused answers, merely assenting to everything Denísov asked him. Denísov turned away from him frowning, and addressed the esaul, conveying his own conjectures to him.

Pétya, rapidly turning his head, looked now at the drummer boy, now at Denísov, now at the esaul, and now at the French in the village and along the road, trying not to miss anything of importance.

"Whether Dólokhov comes or not, we must seize it, eh?" said Denísov with a merry sparkle in his eyes.

"It is a very suitable spot," said the esaul.

"We'll send the infantwy down by the swamps," Denísov continued. "They'll cweep up to the garden; you'll wide up fwom there with the Cossacks"—he pointed to a spot in the forest beyond the village—"and I with my hussars from here. And at the signal shot . . ."

"The hollow is impassable—there's a swamp there," said the esaul. "The horses would sink. We must ride round more to the left. . . ."

While they were talking in undertones the crack of a shot sounded from the low ground by the pond, a puff of white smoke appeared, then another, and the sound of hundreds of seemingly merry French voices shouting together came up from the slope. For a moment Denísov and the esaul drew back. They were so near that they thought they were the cause of the firing and shouting. But the firing and shouting did not relate to them. Down below, a man wearing something red was running through the marsh. The French were evidently firing and shouting at him.

"Why, that's our Tíkhon," said the esaul.

"So it is! It is!"

"The wascal!" said Denísov.

"He'll get away!" said the esaul, screwing up his eyes.

The man whom they called Tíkhon having run to the stream, plunged in so that the water splashed in the air, and having disappeared for an instant, scrambled out on all fours, all black with the wet, and ran on. The French who had been pursuing him stopped.

"Smart, that!" said the esaul.

"What a beast!" said Denísov with his former look of vexation. "What has he been doing all this time?"

"Who is he?" asked Pétya.

"He's our *plastun*. I sent him to capture a 'tongue.' "

"Oh, yes," said Pétya, nodding at the first words Denísov uttered as if he understood it all, though he really did not understand anything of it.

Tíkhon Shcherbáty was one of the most indispensable men in their band. He was a peasant from Pokróvsk, near the river Gzhat. When Denísov had come to Pokróvsk at the beginning of his operations and had as usual summoned the village Elder and asked him what he knew about the French, the Elder, as though shielding himself, had replied as all village Elders did, that he had neither seen nor heard anything of them. But when Denísov explained that his purpose was to kill the French, and asked if no French had strayed that way, the Elder replied that some "more-orderers" had really been at their village, but that Tíkhon Shcherbáty was the only man who dealt with such matters. Denísov had Tíkhon called, and having praised him for his activity, said a few words in the Elder's presence about loyalty to the Tsar and the country and the hatred of the French that all sons of the fatherland should cherish.

"We don't do the French any harm," said Tíkhon, evidently frightened by Denísov's words. "We only fooled about with the lads for fun, you know! We killed a score or so of 'more-orderers,' but we did no harm else. . . ."

Next day when Denísov had left Pokróvsk, having quite forgotten about this peasant, it was reported to him that Tíkhon had attached himself to their party and asked to be allowed to remain with it. Denísov gave orders to let him do so.

Tíkhon who at first did rough work, laying campfires, fetching water, flaying dead horses, and so on, soon showed a great liking and aptitude for partisan warfare. At night he would go out for booty and always brought back French clothing and weapons, and when told to would bring in French captives also. Denísov then relieved him from drudgery and began taking him with him when he went out on expeditions, and had him enrolled among the Cossacks.

Tíkhon did not like riding, and always went on foot, never lagging behind the cavalry. He was armed with a musketoon (which he carried rather as a joke), a pike and an axe, which latter he used as a wolf uses its teeth, with equal ease picking fleas out of its fur or crunching thick bones. Tíkhon with equal accuracy would split logs with blows at arm's length, or holding the head of the ax would cut thin little pegs or carve spoons. In Denísov's party he held a peculiar and exceptional position. When anything particularly difficult or nasty had to be done—to push a cart out of the mud with one's shoulders, pull a horse out of a swamp by its tail, skin it, slink in among the French, or walk more than thirty miles in a day—everybody pointed laughingly at Tíkhon.

"It won't hurt that devil—he's as strong as a horse," they said of him.

Once a Frenchman Tíkhon was trying to capture fired a pistol at him and shot him in the fleshy part of the back. That wound (which Tíkhon treated only with internal and external applications of vodka) was the subject of the liveliest jokes by the whole detachment—jokes in which Tíkhon readily joined.

"Hallo, mate! Never again? Gave you a twist?" the Cossacks would banter him. And Tíkhon, purposely writhing and making faces, pretended to be angry and swore at the French with the funniest curses. The only effect of this incident on Tíkhon was that after being wounded he seldom brought in prisoners.

He was the bravest and most useful man in the party. No one found more opportunities for attacking, no one captured or killed more Frenchmen, and consequently he was made the buffoon of all the Cossacks and hussars and willingly accepted that rôle. Now he had been sent by Denísov overnight to Shámshevo to capture a "tongue." But whether because he had not been content to take only one Frenchman or because he had slept through the night, he had crept by day into some bushes right among the French and, as Denísov had witnessed from above, had been detected by them.

Chapter VI

After talking for some time with the esaul about next day's attack, which now, seeing how near they were to the French, he seemed to have definitely decided on, Denísov turned his horse and rode back.

"Now, my lad, we'll go and get dwy," he said to Pétya.

As they approached the watchhouse Denísov stopped, peering into the forest. Among the trees a man with long legs and long, swinging arms, wearing a short jacket, bast shoes and a Kazán hat, was approaching with long light steps. He had a musketoon over his shoulder and an ax stuck in his girdle. When he espied Denísov he hastily threw something into the bushes, removed his sodden hat by its floppy brim, and approached his commander. It was Tíkhon. His wrinkled and pockmarked face and narrow little eyes beamed with self-satisfied merriment. He lifted his head high and gazed at Denísov as if repressing a laugh.

"Well, where did you disappear to?" inquired Denísov.

"Where did I disappear to? I went to get Frenchmen," answered Tíkhon boldly and hurriedly, in a husky but melodious bass voice.

"Why did you push yourself in there by daylight? You ass! Well, why haven't you taken one?"

"Oh, I took one all right," said Tíkhon.

"Where is he?"

"You see, I took him first thing at dawn," Tíkhon continued, spreading out his flat feet with out-turned toes in their bast shoes. "I took him into the forest. Then I see he's no good and think I'll go and fetch a likelier one."

"You see? . . . What a wogue—it's just as I thought," said Denísov to the esaul. "Why didn't you bwing that one?"

"What was the good of bringing him?" Tíkhon interrupted hastily and angrily—"that one wouldn't have done for you. As if I don't know what sort you want!"

"What a bwute you are! . . . Well?"

"I went for another one," Tíkhon continued, "and I crept like this through the wood and lay down." (He suddenly lay down on his stomach with a supple movement to show how he had done it.) "One turned up and I grabbed him, like this." (He jumped up quickly and lightly.) " 'Come along to the colonel,' I said. He starts yelling, and suddenly there were four of them. They rushed at me with their little swords. So I went for them with my axe, this way: 'What are you up to?' says I. 'Christ be with you!' " shouted Tíkhon, waving his arms with an angry scowl and throwing out his chest.

"Yes, we saw from the hill how you took to your heels through the puddles!" said the esaul, screwing up his glittering eyes.

Pétya badly wanted to laugh, but noticed that they all refrained from laughing. He turned his eyes rapidly from Tíkhon's face to the esaul's and Denísov's, unable to make out what it all meant.

"Don't play the fool!" said Denísov, coughing angrily. "Why didn't you bwing the first one?"

Tíkhon scratched his back with one hand and his head with the other, then suddenly his whole face expanded into a beaming, foolish grin, disclosing a gap where he had lost a tooth (that was why he was called Shcherbáty—the gap-toothed). Denísov smiled, and Pétya burst into a peal of merry laughter in which Tíkhon himself joined.

"Oh, but he was a regular good-for-nothing," said Tíkhon. "The clothes on him—poor stuff! How could I bring him? And so rude, your Honor! Why, he says: 'I'm a general's son myself, I won't go!' he says."

"You are a bwute!" said Denísov. "I wanted to question . . ."

"But I questioned him," said Tíkhon. "He said he didn't know much. 'There are a lot of us,' he says, 'but all poor stuff—only soldiers in name,' he says. 'Shout loud at them,' he says, 'and you'll take them all,' " Tíkhon concluded, looking cheerfully and resolutely into Denísov's eyes.

"I'll give you a hundwed sharp lashes—that'll teach you to play the fool!" said Denísov severely.

"But why are you angry?" remonstrated Tíkhon, "just as if I'd never seen your Frenchmen! Only wait till it gets dark and I'll fetch you any of them you want—three if you like."

"Well, let's go," said Denísov, and rode all the way to the watchhouse in silence and frowning angrily.

Tíkhon followed behind and Pétya heard the Cossacks laughing with him and at him, about some pair of boots he had thrown into the bushes.

When the fit of laughter that had seized him at Tíkhon's words and smile had passed and Pétya realized for a moment that this Tíkhon had killed a man, he felt uneasy. He looked round at the captive drummer boy and felt a pang in his heart. But this uneasiness lasted only a moment. He felt it necessary to hold his head higher, to brace himself, and to question the esaul with an air of importance about tomorrow's undertaking, that he might not be unworthy of the company in which he found himself.

The officer who had been sent to inquire, met Denísov on the way with the news that Dólokhov was soon coming and that all was well with him.

Denísov at once cheered up and calling Pétya to him, said: "Well, tell me about yourself."

Chapter VII

PÉTYA HAVING LEFT HIS PEOPLE AFTER THEIR DEPARTURE FROM MOSCOW, JOINED HIS REGIMENT and was soon taken as orderly by a general commanding a large guerrilla detachment. From the time he received his commission, and especially since he had joined the active army and taken part in the battle of Vyázma, Pétya had been in a constant state of blissful excitement at being grown-up, and in a perpetual ecstatic hurry not to miss any chance to do something really heroic. He was highly delighted with what he saw and experienced in the army, but at the same time it always seemed to him that the really heroic exploits were being performed just where he did not happen to be. And he was always in a hurry to get where he was not.

When on the 21st of October his general expressed a wish to send somebody to Denísov's detachment, Pétya begged so piteously to be sent, that the general could not refuse. But when dispatching him he recalled Pétya's mad action at the battle of Vyázma, where instead of riding by the road to the place to which he had been sent, he had galloped to the advanced line under the fire of the French and had there twice fired his pistol. So now the general explicitly forbade his taking part in any action whatever of Denísov's. That was why Pétya had blushed and grown confused when Denísov asked him whether he could stay. Before they had ridden to the outskirts of the forest Pétya had considered that he must carry out his instructions strictly and return at once. But when he saw the French and saw Tíkhon, and learned that there would certainly be an attack that night, he decided, with the rapidity with which young people change their views, that the general, whom he had greatly respected till then, was a rubbishy German, that Denísov was a hero, the esaul a hero, and Tíkhon a hero too, and that it would be shameful for him to leave them at a moment of difficulty.

It was already growing dusk when Denísov, Pétya and the esaul rode up to the watchhouse. In the twilight saddled horses could be seen, and Cossacks and hussars who had rigged up rough shelters in the glade and were kindling glowing fires in a hollow of the forest where the French could not see the smoke. In the passage of the small watchhouse a Cossack with sleeves rolled up was chopping some mutton. In the room three officers of Denísov's band were converting a door into a tabletop. Pétya took off his wet clothes, gave them to be dried, and at once began helping the officers to fix up the dinner-table.

In ten minutes the table was ready and a napkin spread on it. On the table were vodka, a flask of rum, white bread, roast mutton and salt.

Sitting at table with the officers and tearing the fat savory mutton with his hands, down which the grease trickled, Pétya was in an ecstatic childish state of love for all men, and consequently of confidence that others loved him in the same way.

"So then what do you think, Vasíli Dmítrich?" said he to Denísov, "it's all right my staying a day with you?" And not waiting for a reply he answered his own question: "You see I was told to find out—well, I am finding out. . . . Only do let me into the very . . . into the chief . . . I don't want a reward. . . . But I want . . ."

Pétya clenched his teeth and looked around, throwing back his head and flourishing his arms.

"Into the very chief . . ." Denísov repeated with a smile.

"Only, please let me command something, so that I may really command . . ." Pétya went on. "What would it be to you? . . . Oh, you want a knife?" he said, turning to an officer who wished to cut himself a piece of mutton.

And he handed him his clasp-knife. The officer admired it.

"Please keep it. I have several like it," said Pétya, blushing. "Heavens! I was quite forgetting!" he suddenly cried. "I have some raisins, fine ones; you know, seedless ones. We have a new sutler and he has such capital things. I bought ten pounds. I am used to something sweet. Would you like some? . . ." and Pétya ran out into the passage to his Cossack and brought back some bags which contained about five pounds of raisins. "Have some, gentlemen, have some!"

"You want a coffee pot, don't you?" he asked the esaul. "I bought a capital one from our sutler! He has splendid things. And he's very honest, that's the chief thing. I'll be sure to send it to you. Or perhaps your flints are giving out, or are worn out—that happens sometimes, you know. I have brought some with me, here they are"—and he showed a bag—"a hundred flints. I bought them very cheap. Please take as many as you want, or all if you like. . . ."

Then suddenly, dismayed lest he had said too much, Pétya stopped and blushed.

He tried to remember whether he had not done anything else that was foolish. And running over the events of the day he remembered the French drummer boy. "It's capital for us here, but what of him? Where have they put him? Have they fed him? Haven't they hurt his feelings?" he thought. But having caught himself saying too much about the flints, he was now afraid to speak out.

"I might ask," he thought, "but they'll say: 'He's a boy himself and so he pities the boy.' I'll show them tomorrow whether I'm a boy. Will it seem odd if I ask?" Pétya thought. "Well, never mind!" and immediately, blushing and looking anxiously at the officers to see if they appeared ironical, he said:

"May I call in that boy who was taken prisoner and give him something to eat? . . . Perhaps . . ."

"Yes, he's a poor little fellow," said Denísov, who evidently saw nothing shameful in this reminder. "Call him in. His name is Vincent Bosse. Have him fetched."

"I'll call him," said Pétya.

"Yes, yes, call him. A poor little fellow," Denísov repeated.

Pétya was standing at the door when Denísov said this. He slipped in between the officers, came close to Denísov, and said:

"Let me kiss you, dear old fellow! Oh, how fine, how splendid!"

And having kissed Denísov he ran out of the hut.

"Bosse! Vincent!" Pétya cried, stopping outside the door.

"Who do you want, sir?" asked a voice in the darkness.

Pétya replied that he wanted the French lad who had been captured that day.

"Ah, Vesénny?" said a Cossack.

Vincent, the boy's name, had already been changed by the Cossacks into Vesénny (vernal) and into Vesénya by the peasants and soldiers. In both these adaptations the reference to spring (*vesná*) matched the impression made by the young lad.

"He is warming himself there by the bonfire. Ho, Vesénya! Vesénya!—Vesénny!" laughing voices were heard calling to one another in the darkness.

"He's a smart lad," said a hussar standing near Pétya. "We gave him something to eat a while ago. He was awfully hungry!"

The sound of bare feet splashing through the mud was heard in the darkness, and the drummer boy came to the door.

"Ah, c'est vous!" said Pétya. *"Voulez-vous manger? N'ayez pas peur, on ne vous fera pas de mal,"* he added shyly and affectionately, touching the boy's hand. *"Entrez, entrez."*

"Merci, monsieur," said the drummer boy in a trembling almost childish voice, and he began scraping his dirty feet on the threshold.

There were many things Pétya wanted to say to the drummer boy, but did not dare to. He stood irresolutely beside him in the passage. Then in the darkness he took the boy's hand and pressed it.

"Come in, come in!" he repeated in a gentle whisper. "Oh, what can I do for him?" he thought, and opening the door he let the boy pass in first.

When the boy had entered the hut, Pétya sat down at a distance from him, considering it beneath his dignity to pay attention to him. But he fingered the money in his pocket and wondered whether it would seem ridiculous to give some to the drummer boy.

Chapter VIII

THE ARRIVAL OF DÓLOKHOV DIVERTED PÉTYA'S ATTENTION FROM THE DRUMMER BOY, TO WHOM Denísov had had some mutton and vodka given, and whom he had had dressed in a Russian coat so that he might be kept with their band and not sent away with the other prisoners. Pétya had heard in the army many stories of Dólokhov's extraordinary bravery and of his cruelty to the French, so from the moment he entered the hut Pétya did not take his eyes from him, but braced himself up more and more and held his head high, that he might not be unworthy even of such company.

Dólokhov's appearance amazed Pétya by its simplicity.

Denísov wore a Cossack coat, had a beard, had an icon of Nicholas the Wonder-Worker on his breast, and his way of speaking and everything he did indicated his unusual position. But Dólokhov, who in Moscow had worn a Persian costume, had now the appearance of a most correct officer of the Guards. He was clean-shaven and wore a Guardsman's padded coat with an Order of St. George at his buttonhole and a plain forage-cap set straight on his head. He took off his wet felt cloak in a corner of the room, and without greeting anyone went up to Denísov and began questioning him about the matter in hand. Denísov told him of the designs the large detachments had on the transport, of the message Pétya had brought, and his own replies to both generals. Then he told him all he knew of the French detachment.

"That's so. But we must know what troops they are and their numbers," said Dólokhov. "It will be necessary to go there. We can't start the affair without knowing for certain how many of them there are. I like to work accurately. Here now—wouldn't one of these gentlemen like to ride over to the French camp with me? I have brought a spare uniform."

"I, I . . . I'll go with you!" cried Pétya.

"There's no need for you to go at all," said Denísov, addressing Dólokhov, "and as for him, I won't let him go on any account."

"I like that!" exclaimed Pétya. "Why shouldn't I go?"

"Because it's useless."

"Well, you must excuse me, because . . . because . . . I shall go, and that's all. You'll take me, won't you?" he said, turning to Dólokhov.

"Why not?" Dólokhov answered absently, scrutinizing the face of the French drummer boy. "Have you had that youngster with you long?" he asked Denísov.

"He was taken today but he knows nothing. I'm keeping him with me."

"Yes, and where do you put the others?" inquired Dólokhov.

"Where? I send them away and take a weceipt for them," shouted Denísov, suddenly flushing.

"And I say boldly that I have not a single man's life on my conscience. Would it be difficult for you to send thirty or thwee-hundwed men to town under escort, instead of staining—I speak bluntly—staining the honor of a soldier?"

"That kind of amiable talk would be suitable from this young count of sixteen," said Dólokhov with cold irony, "but it's time for you to drop it."

"Why, I've not said anything! I only say that I'll certainly go with you," said Pétya shyly.

"But for you and me, old fellow, it's time to drop these amenities," continued Dólokhov, as if he found particular pleasure in speaking of this subject which irritated Denísov. "Now, why have you kept this lad?" he went on, swaying his head. "Because you are sorry for him! Don't we know those 'receipts' of yours? You send a hundred men away, and thirty get there. The rest either starve or get killed. So isn't it all the same not to send them?"

The esaul, screwing up his light-colored eyes, nodded approvingly.

"That's not the point. I'm not going to discuss the matter. I do not wish to take it on my conscience. You say they'll die. All wight. Only not by my fault!"

Dólokhov began laughing.

"Who has told them not to capture me these twenty times over? But if they did catch me they'd string me up to an aspen tree, and you with all your chivalry just the same." He paused. "However, we must get to work. Tell the Cossack to fetch my kit. I have two French uniforms in it. Well, are you coming with me?" he asked Pétya.

"I? Yes, yes, certainly!" cried Pétya, blushing almost to tears and glancing at Denísov.

While Dólokhov had been disputing with Denísov what should be done with prisoners, Pétya had once more felt awkward and restless; but again he had no time to grasp fully what they were talking about. "If grown-up, distinguished men think so, it must be necessary and right," thought he. "But above all Denísov must not dare to imagine that I'll obey him and that he can order me about. I will certainly go to the French camp with Dólokhov. If he can, so can I!"

And to all Denísov's persuasions, Pétya replied that he too was accustomed to do everything accurately and not just anyhow, and that he never considered personal danger.

"For you'll admit that if we don't know for sure how many of them there are . . . hundreds of lives may depend on it, while there are only two of us. Besides, I want to go very much and certainly will go, so don't hinder me," said he. "It will only make things worse. . . ."

Chapter IX

HAVING PUT ON FRENCH GREATCOATS AND SHAKOS, PÉTYA AND DÓLOKHOV RODE TO THE CLEARing from which Denísov had reconnoitered the French camp, and emerging from the forest in pitch darkness they descended into the hollow. On reaching the bottom, Dólokhov told the Cossacks accompanying him to await him there and rode on at a quick trot along the road to the bridge. Pétya, his heart in his mouth with excitement, rode by his side.

"If we're caught, I won't be taken alive! I have a pistol," whispered he.

"Don't talk Russian," said Dólokhov in a hurried whisper, and at that very moment they heard through the darkness the challenge: *"Qui vive?"* and the click of a musket.

The blood rushed to Pétya's face and he grasped his pistol.

"Lanciers du 6-me," replied Dólokhov, neither hastening nor slackening his horse's pace.

The black figure of a sentinel stood on the bridge.

"Mot d'ordre."

Dólokhov reined in his horse and advanced at a walk.

"Dites donc, le colonel Gérard est ici?" he asked.

"Mot d'ordre," repeated the sentinel, barring the way and not replying.

"Quand un officier fait sa ronde, les sentinelles ne demandent pas le mot d'ordre . . ." cried Dólokhov suddenly flaring up and riding straight at the sentinel. *"Je vous demande si le colonel est ici."*

And without waiting for an answer from the sentinel, who had stepped aside, Dólokhov rode up the incline at a walk.

Noticing the black outline of a man crossing the road, Dólokhov stopped him and inquired where the commander and officers were. The man, a soldier with a sack over his shoulder, stopped, came close up to Dólokhov's horse, touched it with his hand, and explained simply and in a friendly way that the commander and the officers were higher up the hill to the right in the courtyard of the farm, as he called the landowner's house.

Having ridden up the road, on both sides of which French talk could be heard around the campfires, Dólokhov turned into the courtyard of the landowner's house. Having ridden in, he dismounted and approached a big blazing campfire, around which sat several men talking noisily. Something was boiling in a small cauldron at the edge of the fire and a soldier in a peaked cap and blue overcoat, lit up by the fire, was kneeling beside it stirring its contents with a ramrod.

"Oh, he's a hard nut to crack," said one of the officers who was sitting in the shadow at the other side of the fire.

"He'll make them get a move on, those fellows!" said another, laughing.

Both fell silent, peering out through the darkness at the sound of Dólokhov's and Pétya's steps as they advanced to the fire leading their horses.

"Bonjour, messieurs!" said Dólokhov loudly and clearly.

There was a stir among the officers in the shadow beyond the fire, and one tall long-necked officer, walking round the fire, came up to Dólokhov.

"Is that you, Clément?" he asked. "Where the devil . . . ?" But, noticing his mistake he broke off short and, with a frown, greeted Dólokhov as a stranger, asking what he could do for him.

Dólokhov said that he and his companion were trying to overtake their regiment, and addressing the company in general asked whether they knew anything of the 6th Regiment. None of them knew anything, and Pétya thought the officers were beginning to look at him and Dólokhov with hostility and suspicion. For some seconds all were silent.

"If you were counting on the evening soup, you have come too late," said a voice from behind the fire with a repressed laugh.

Dólokhov replied that they were not hungry and must push on farther that night.

He handed the horses over to the soldier who was stirring the pot, and squatted down on his heels by the fire beside the officer with the long neck. That officer did not take his eyes from Dólokhov and again asked to what regiment he belonged. Dólokhov, as if he had not heard the question, did not reply, but lighting a short French pipe which he took from his pocket, began asking the officer in how far the road before them was safe from Cossacks.

"Those brigands are everywhere," replied an officer from behind the fire.

Dólokhov remarked that the Cossacks were a danger only to stragglers such as his companion and himself, "but probably they would not dare to attack large detachments?" he added inquiringly. No one replied.

"Well, now he'll come away," Pétya thought every moment as he stood by the campfire listening to the talk.

But Dólokhov restarted the conversation which had dropped, and began putting direct questions as to how many men there were in the battalion, how many battalions, and how many prisoners. Asking about the Russian prisoners with that detachment, Dólokhov said:

"A horrid business dragging these corpses about with one! It would be better to shoot such rabble," and burst into loud laughter, so strange that Pétya thought the French would immediately detect their disguise, and involuntarily took a step back from the campfire.

No one replied a word to Dólokhov's laughter, and a French officer whom they could not see (he lay wrapped in a greatcoat) rose and whispered something to a companion. Dólokhov got up and called to the soldier who was holding their horses.

"Will they bring our horses or not?" thought Pétya, instinctively drawing nearer to Dólokhov.

The horses were brought.

"Good evening, gentlemen," said Dólokhov.

Pétya wished to say "Good night" but could not utter a word. The officers were whispering together. Dólokhov was a long time mounting his horse which would not stand still, then he rode out of the yard at a footpace. Pétya rode beside him, longing to look round to see whether or no the French were running after them, but not daring to.

Coming out onto the road Dólokhov did not ride back across the open country, but through the village. At one spot he stopped and listened. "Do you hear?" he asked. Pétya recognized the sound of Russian voices and saw the dark figures of Russian prisoners round their campfires. When they had descended to the bridge Pétya and Dólokhov rode past the sentinel, who without saying a word paced morosely up and down it, then they descended into the hollow where the Cossacks awaited them.

"Well now, good-bye. Tell Denísov, 'at the first shot at daybreak,' " said Dólokhov and was about to ride away, but Pétya seized hold of him.

"Really!" he cried, "you are such a hero! Oh, how fine, how splendid! How I love you!"

"All right, all right!" said Dólokhov. But Pétya did not let go of him and Dólokhov saw through the gloom that Pétya was bending toward him and wanted to kiss him. Dólokhov kissed him, laughed, turned his horse, and vanished into the darkness.

Chapter X

Having returned to the watchman's hut, Pétya found Denísov in the passage. He was awaiting Pétya's return in a state of agitation, anxiety and self-reproach for having let him go.

"Thank God!" he exclaimed. "Yes, thank God!" he repeated, listening to Pétya's rapturous account. "But, devil take you, I haven't slept because of you! Well, thank God. Now lie down. We can still get a nap before morning."

"But . . . no," said Pétya, "I don't want to sleep yet. Besides I know myself, if I fall asleep it's finished. And then I am used to not sleeping before a battle."

He sat awhile in the hut joyfully recalling the details of his expedition and vividly picturing to himself what would happen next day. Then, noticing that Denísov was asleep, he rose and went out of doors.

It was still quite dark outside. The rain was over, but drops were still falling from the trees. Near the watchman's hut the black shapes of the Cossacks' shanties and of horses tethered together could be seen. Behind the hut the dark shapes of the two wagons with their horses beside them were discernible, and in the hollow the dying campfire gleamed red. Not all the Cossacks and hussars were asleep; here and there, amid the sounds of falling drops and the munching of the horses nearby, could be heard low voices which seemed to be whispering.

Pétya came out, peered into the darkness, and went up to the wagons. Someone was snoring under them, and around them stood saddled horses munching their oats. In the dark Pétya recognized his own horse, which he called "Karabákh" though it was of Ukranian breed, and went up to it.

"Well, Karabákh! We'll do some service tomorrow," said he, sniffing its nostrils and kissing it.

"Why aren't you asleep, sir?" said a Cossack who was sitting under a wagon.

"No, ah . . . Likhachëv—isn't that your name? Do you know I have only just come back! We've been into the French camp."

And Pétya gave the Cossack a detailed account not only of his ride but also of his object, and why he considered it better to risk his life than to act "just anyhow."

"Well, you should get some sleep now," said the Cossack.

"No, I am used to this," said Pétya. "I say, aren't the flints in your pistols worn out? I brought some with me. Don't you want any? You can have some."

The Cossack bent forward from under the wagon to get a closer look at Pétya.

"Because I am accustomed to doing everything accurately," said Pétya. "Some fellows do things just anyhow, without preparation, and then they're sorry for it afterward. I don't like that."

"Just so," said the Cossack.

"Oh yes, another thing! Please, my dear fellow, will you sharpen my saber for me? It's got bl . . ." (Pétya feared to tell a lie, and the saber never had been sharpened.) "Can you do it?"

"Of course I can."

Likhachëv got up, rummaged in his pack, and soon Pétya heard the warlike sound of steel on whetstone. He climbed onto the wagon and sat on its edge. The Cossack was sharpening the saber under the wagon.

"I say! Are the lads asleep?" asked Pétya.

"Some are, and some aren't—like us."

"Well, and that boy?"

"Vesénny? Oh, he's thrown himself down there in the passage. Fast asleep after his fright. He was that glad!"

After that Pétya remained silent for a long time, listening to the sounds. He heard footsteps in the darkness and a black figure appeared.

"What are you sharpening?" asked a man coming up to the wagon.

"Why, this gentleman's saber."

"That's right," said the man, whom Pétya took to be a hussar. "Was the cup left here?"

"There, by the wheel!"

The hussar took the cup.

"It must be daylight soon," said he yawning, and went away.

Pétya ought to have known that he was in a forest with Denísov's guerrilla band, a verst from the road, sitting on a wagon captured from the French beside which horses were tethered, that under it Likhachëv was sitting sharpening a saber for him, that the big dark blotch to the right was the watchman's hut, and the red blotch below to the left was the dying embers of a campfire, that the man who had come for the cup was a hussar who wanted a drink; but he neither knew nor waited to know anything of all this. He was in a fairy kingdom where nothing resembled reality. The big dark blotch might really be the watchman's hut or it might be a cavern leading to the very depths of the earth. Perhaps the red spot was a fire, or it might be the eye of an enormous monster. Perhaps he was really sitting on a wagon, but it might very well be that he was not sitting on a wagon but on a terribly high tower from which, if he fell, he would have to fall for a whole day or a whole month, or go on falling and never reach the bottom. Perhaps it was just the Cossack, Likhachëv, who was sitting under the wagon, but it might be the kindest, bravest, most wonderful, most splendid man in the world, whom no one knew of. It might really have been that the hussar came for water and went back into the hollow, but perhaps he had simply vanished—disappeared altogether and dissolved into nothingness.

Nothing Pétya could have seen now would have surprised him. He was in a fairy kingdom where everything was possible.

He looked up at the sky. And the sky was a fairy realm like the earth. It was clearing, and over the tops of the trees clouds were swiftly sailing as if unveiling the stars. Sometimes it looked as if the clouds were passing, and a clear black sky appeared. Sometimes it seemed as if the black spaces were clouds. Sometimes the sky seemed to be rising high, high overhead, and then it seemed to sink so low that one could touch it with one's hand.

Pétya's eyes began to close and he swayed a little.

The trees were dripping. Quiet talking was heard. The horses neighed and jostled one another. Someone snored.

"Ozheg-zheg, Ozheg-zheg . . ." hissed the saber against the whetstone, and suddenly Pétya heard an harmonious orchestra playing some unknown, sweetly solemn hymn. Pétya was as musical as Natásha and more so than Nicholas, but had never learned music or thought about it, and so the melody that unexpectedly came to his mind seemed to him particularly fresh and attractive. The music became more and more audible. The melody grew and passed from one instrument to another. And what was played was a fugue—though Pétya had not the least conception of what a fugue is. Each instrument—now resembling a violin and now a horn, but better and clearer than violin or horn—played its own part, and before it had finished the melody merged with another instrument that began almost the same air, and then with a third and a fourth; and they all blended into one and again became separate and again blended, now into solemn church music, now into something dazzlingly brilliant and triumphant.

"Oh—why, that was in a dream!" Pétya said to himself, as he lurched forward. "It's in my ears. But perhaps it's music of my own. Well, go on, my music! Now! . . ."

He closed his eyes, and from all sides as if from a distance, sounds fluttered, grew into harmonies, separated, blended, and again all mingled into the same sweet and solemn hymn. "Oh, this is delightful! As much as I like and as I like!" said Pétya to himself. He tried to conduct that enormous orchestra.

"Now softly, softly die away!" and the sounds obeyed him. "Now fuller, more joyful. Still more and more joyful!" And from an unknown depth rose increasingly triumphant sounds. "Now voices join in!" ordered Pétya. And at first from afar he heard men's voices and then women's. The voices grew in harmonious triumphant strength, and Pétya listened to their surpassing beauty in awe and joy.

With a solemn triumphal march there mingled a song, the drip from the trees, and the hissing of the saber, *"Ozheg-zheg-zheg . . ."* and again the horses jostled one another and neighed, not disturbing the choir but joining in it.

Pétya did not know how long this lasted: he enjoyed himself all the time, wondered at his enjoyment and regretted that there was no one to share it. He was awakened by Likhachëv's kindly voice.

"It's ready, your Honor; you can split a Frenchman in half with it!"

Pétya woke up.

"It's getting light, it's really getting light!" he exclaimed.

The horses that had previously been invisible could now be seen to their very tails, and a watery light showed itself through the bare branches. Pétya shook himself, jumped up, took a ruble from his pocket and gave it to Likhachëv; then he flourished the saber, tested it, and sheathed it. The Cossacks were untying their horses and tightening their saddlegirths.

"And here's the commander," said Likhachëv.

Denísov came out of the watchman's hut and, having called Pétya, gave orders to get ready.

Chapter XI

The men rapidly picked out their horses in the semi-darkness, tightened their saddlegirths, and formed companies. Denísov stood by the watchman's hut giving final orders. The infantry of the detachment passed along the road and quickly disappeared amid the trees in the mist of early dawn, hundreds of feet splashing through the mud. The esaul gave some orders to his men. Pétya held his horse by the bridle, impatiently awaiting the order to mount. His face, having been bathed in cold water, was all aglow, and his eyes were particularly brilliant. Cold shivers ran down his spine and his whole body pulsed rhythmically.

"Well, is ev'wything weady?" asked Denísov. "Bwing the horses."

The horses were brought. Denísov was angry with the Cossack because the saddlegirths were too slack, reproved him, and mounted. Pétya put his foot in the stirrup. His horse by habit made as if to nip his leg, but Pétya leaped quickly into the saddle unconscious of his own weight and, turning to look at the hussars starting in the darkness behind him, rode up to Denísov.

"Vasíli Dmítrich, entrust me with some commission! Please . . . for God's sake . . . !" said he.

Denísov seemed to have forgotten Pétya's very existence. He turned to glance at him.

"I ask one thing of you," he said sternly, "to obey me and not shove yourself fo'ward anywhere."

He did not say another word to Pétya but rode in silence all the way. When they had come to the edge of the forest it was noticeably growing light over the field. Denísov talked in whispers with the esaul and the Cossacks rode past Pétya and Denísov. When they had all ridden by, Denísov touched his horse and rode down the hill. Slipping onto their haunches and sliding, the horses descended with their riders into the ravine. Pétya rode beside Denísov, the pulsation of his body constantly increasing. It was getting lighter and lighter, but the mist still hid distant objects. Having reached the valley, Denísov looked back and nodded to a Cossack beside him.

"The signal!" said he.

The Cossack raised his arm and a shot rang out. In an instant the tramp of horses galloping forward was heard, shouts came from various sides, and then more shots.

At the first sound of trampling hoofs and shouting, Pétya lashed his horse and loosening his rein galloped forward, not heeding Denísov who shouted at him. It seemed to Pétya that at the moment the shot was fired it suddenly became as bright as noon. He galloped to the bridge. Cossacks were galloping along the road in front of him. On the bridge he collided with a Cossack who had fallen behind, but he galloped on. In front of him soldiers, probably Frenchmen, were running from right to left across the road. One of them fell in the mud under his horse's feet.

Cossacks were crowding about a hut, busy with something. From the midst of that crowd terrible screams arose. Pétya galloped up, and the first thing he saw was the pale face and trembling jaw of a Frenchman, clutching the handle of a lance that had been aimed at him.

"Hurrah! . . . Lads! . . . ours!" shouted Pétya, and giving rein to his excited horse he galloped forward along the village street.

He could hear shooting ahead of him. Cossacks, hussars, and ragged Russian prisoners, who had come running from both sides of the road, were shouting something loudly and incoherently. A gallant-looking Frenchman in a blue overcoat, capless, and with a frowning red face, had been defending himself against the hussars. When Pétya galloped up the Frenchman had already fallen. "Too late again!" flashed through Pétya's mind and he galloped on to the place from which the rapid firing could be heard. The shots came from the yard of the landowner's house he had visited the night before with Dólokhov. The French were making a stand there behind a wattle fence in a garden thickly overgrown with bushes, and were firing at the Cossacks who crowded at the gateway. Through the smoke, as he approached the gate, Pétya saw Dólokhov, whose face was of a pale greenish tint, shouting to his men. "Go round! Wait for the infantry!" he exclaimed as Pétya rode up to him.

"Wait? . . . Hurrah-ah-ah!" shouted Pétya, and without pausing a moment, galloped to the place whence came the sounds of firing and where the smoke was thickest.

A volley was heard, and some bullets whistled past, while others plashed against something. The Cossacks and Dólokhov galloped after Pétya into the gateway of the courtyard. In the dense wavering smoke some of the French threw down their arms and ran out of the bushes to meet the Cossacks, while others ran down the hill toward the pond. Pétya was galloping along the courtyard, but instead of holding the reins he waved both his arms about rapidly and strangely, slipping farther and farther to one side in his saddle. His horse, having galloped up to a campfire that was smoldering in the morning light, stopped suddenly, and Pétya fell heavily on to the wet ground. The Cossacks saw that his arms and legs jerked rapidly though his head was quite motionless. A bullet had pierced his skull.

After speaking to the senior French officer, who came out of the house with a white handkerchief tied to his sword and announced that they surrendered, Dólokhov dismounted and went up to Pétya, who lay motionless with outstretched arms.

"Done for!" he said with a frown, and went to the gate to meet Denísov who was riding toward him.

"Killed?" cried Denísov, recognizing from a distance the unmistakably lifeless attitude—very familiar to him—in which Pétya's body was lying.

"Done for!" repeated Dólokhov as if the utterance of these words afforded him pleasure, and he went quickly up to the prisoners, who were surrounded by Cossacks who had hurried up. "We won't take them!" he called out to Denísov.

Denísov did not reply; he rode up to Pétya, dismounted, and with trembling hands turned toward himself the bloodstained, mud-bespattered face which had already gone white.

"I am used to something sweet. Raisins, fine ones . . . take them all!" he recalled Pétya's words. And the Cossacks looked round in surprise at the sound, like the yelp of a dog, with which Denísov turned away, walked to the wattle fence, and seized hold of it.

Among the Russian prisoners rescued by Denísov and Dólokhov was Pierre Bezúkhov.

Chapter XII

DURING THE WHOLE OF THEIR MARCH FROM MOSCOW NO FRESH ORDERS HAD BEEN ISSUED BY the French authorities concerning the party of prisoners among whom was Pierre. On the 22nd of October that party was no longer with the same troops and baggage-trains with which it had left Moscow. Half the wagons laden with hard-tack that had traveled the first stages with them had been captured by Cossacks, the other half had gone on ahead. Not one of those dismounted cavalrymen who had marched in front of the prisoners was left; they had all disappeared. The artillery the prisoners had seen in front of them during the first days was now replaced by Marshal Junot's enormous baggage-train, convoyed by Westphalians. Behind the prisoners came a cavalry baggage-train.

From Vyázma onward the French army, which had till then moved in three columns, went on as a single group. The symptoms of disorder that Pierre had noticed at their first halting place after leaving Moscow, had now reached the utmost limit.

The road along which they moved was bordered on both sides by dead horses; ragged men who had fallen behind from various regiments continually changed about, now joining the moving column, now again lagging behind it.

Several times during the march false alarms had been given and the soldiers of the escort had raised their muskets, fired, and run headlong, crushing one another, but had afterward reassembled and abused each other for their causeless panic.

These three groups traveling together—the cavalry stores, the convoy of prisoners, and Junot's baggage-train—still constituted a separate and united whole, though each of the groups was rapidly melting away.

Of the artillery baggage-train which had consisted of a hundred and twenty wagons, not more than sixty now remained; the rest had been captured or left behind. Some of Junot's wagons also had been captured or abandoned. Three wagons had been raided and robbed by stragglers from Davout's corps. From the talk of the Germans Pierre learned that a larger guard had been allotted to that baggage-train than to the prisoners, and that one of their comrades, a German soldier, had been shot by the marshal's own order because a silver spoon belonging to the marshal had been found in his possession.

The group of prisoners had melted away most of all. Of the three hundred and thirty men who had set out from Moscow less than a hundred now remained. The prisoners were more burdensome to the escort than even the cavalry-saddles, or Junot's baggage. They understood that the saddles and Junot's spoon might be of some use, but that cold and hungry soldiers should have to stand and guard equally cold and hungry Russians who froze and lagged behind on the road (in which case the order was to shoot them) was not merely incomprehensible but revolting. And the escort, as if afraid in the grievous condition they themselves were in, of giving way to the pity they felt for the prisoners and so rendering their own plight still worse, treated them with particular moroseness and severity.

At Dorogobúzh while the soldiers of the convoy, after locking the prisoners in a stable, had gone off to pillage their own stores, several of the soldier-prisoners tunneled under the wall and ran away, but were recaptured by the French and shot.

The arrangement adopted when they started, that the officer-prisoners should be kept separate from the rest, had long since been abandoned. All who could walk went together, and after the third stage Pierre had rejoined Karatáev and the gray-blue bandy-legged dog that had chosen Karatáev for its master.

On the third day after leaving Moscow Karatáev again fell ill with the fever he had suffered from in the hospital in Moscow, and as he grew gradually weaker Pierre kept away from him. Pierre did not know why, but since Karatáev had begun to grow weaker it had cost him an effort to go near him. When he did so and heard the subdued moaning with which Karatáev generally lay down at the halting places, and when he smelled the odor emanating from him which was now stronger than before, Pierre moved further away and did not think about him.

While imprisoned in the shed Pierre had learned not with his intellect but with his whole being, by life itself, that man is created for happiness, that happiness is within him, in the satisfaction of simple human needs, and that all unhappiness arises not from privation but from superfluity. And now during these last three weeks of the march he had learned still another new, consolatory truth—that nothing in this world is terrible. He had learned that as there is no condition in which man can be happy and entirely free, so there is no condition in which he need be unhappy and lack freedom. He learned that suffering and freedom have their limits and that those limits are very near together; that the person in a bed of roses with one crumpled petal suffered as keenly as he now, sleeping on the bare damp earth with one side growing chilled while the other was warming; and that when he had put on tight dancing-shoes he had suffered just as he did now when he walked with bare feet that were covered with sores—his footgear having long since fallen to pieces. He discovered that when he had married his wife—of his own free will as it had seemed to him—he had been no more free than now when they locked him up at night in a stable. Of all that he himself subsequently termed his sufferings, but which at the time he scarcely felt, the worst was the state of his bare, raw, and scab-covered feet. (The horseflesh was appetizing and nourishing, the saltpeter flavor of the gunpowder they used instead of salt was even pleasant; there was no great cold, it was always warm walking in the daytime, and at night there were the campfires; the lice that devoured him warmed his body.) The one thing that was at first hard to bear was his feet.

After the second day's march Pierre having examined his feet by the campfire, thought it would be impossible to walk on them; but when everybody got up he went along, limping, and when he had warmed up, walked without feeling the pain, though at night his feet were more terrible to look at than before. However he did not look at them now, but thought of other things.

Only now did Pierre realize the full strength of life in man and the saving power he has of transferring his attention from one thing to another, which is like the safety valve of a boiler that allows superfluous steam to blow off when the pressure exceeds a certain limit.

He did not see and did not hear how they shot the prisoners who lagged behind, though more than a hundred perished in that way. He did not think of Karatáev who grew weaker every day and evidently would soon have to share that fate. Still less did Pierre think about himself. The harder his position became and the more terrible the future, the more independent of that position in which he found himself were the joyful and comforting thoughts, memories and imaginings that came to him.

Chapter XIII

AT MIDDAY ON THE 22ND OF OCTOBER PIERRE WAS GOING UPHILL ALONG THE MUDDY SLIPPERY road, looking at his feet and at the roughness of the way. Occasionally he glanced at the familiar crowd around him and then again at his feet. The former and the latter were alike familiar and his own. The blue-gray bandy-legged dog ran merrily along the side of the road, sometimes in proof of its agility and self-satisfaction lifting one hind leg and hopping along on three, and then again going on all four and rushing to bark at the crows that sat on the carrion. The dog was merrier and sleeker than it had been in Moscow. All around lay the flesh of different animals—from men to horses—in various stages of decomposition; and as the wolves were kept off by the passing men the dog could eat all it wanted.

It had been raining since morning and had seemed as if at any moment it might cease and the sky clear, but after a short break it began raining harder than before. The saturated road no longer absorbed the water, which ran along the ruts in streams.

Pierre walked along, looking from side to side, counting his steps in threes, and reckoning them off on his fingers. Mentally addressing the rain, he repeated: "Now then, now then, go on! Pelt harder!"

It seemed to him that he was thinking of nothing, but far down and deep within him his soul was occupied with something important and comforting. This something was a most subtle spiritual deduction from a conversation with Karatáev the day before.

At their yesterday's halting place, feeling chilly by a dying campfire, Pierre had got up and gone to the next one, which was burning better. There Platón Karatáev was sitting covered up—head and all—with his greatcoat as if it were a vestment, telling the soldiers in his effective and pleasant though now feeble voice a story Pierre knew. It was already past midnight, the hour when Karatáev was usually free of his fever and particularly lively. When Pierre reached the fire and heard Platón's voice enfeebled by illness, and saw his pathetic face brightly lit up by the blaze, he felt a painful prick at his heart. His feeling of pity for this man frightened him and he wished to go away, but there was no other fire, and Pierre sat down, trying not to look at Platón.

"Well, how are you?" he asked.

"How am I? If we grumble at sickness, God won't grant us death," replied Platón, and at once resumed the story he had begun.

"And so, brother," he continued, with a smile on his pale emaciated face and a particularly happy light in his eyes, "you see, brother . . ."

Pierre had long been familiar with that story. Karatáev had told it to him alone some half dozen times and always with a specially joyful emotion. But well as he knew it, Pierre now listened to that tale as to something new, and the quiet rapture Karatáev evidently felt as he told it communicated itself also to Pierre. The story was of an old merchant who lived a good and God-fearing life with his family, and who went once to the Nízhni fair with a companion—a rich merchant.

Having put up at an inn they both went to sleep, and next morning his companion was found robbed and with his throat cut. A bloodstained knife was found under the old merchant's pillow. He was tried, knouted, and his nostrils having been torn off, "all in due form" as Karatáev put it, he was sent to hard labor in Siberia.

"And so, brother" (it was at this point that Pierre came up), "ten years or more passed by. The old man was living as a convict, submitting as he should and doing no wrong. Only he prayed to God for death. Well, one night the convicts were gathered just as we are, with the old man among them. And they began telling what each was suffering for, and how they had sinned against God. One told how he had taken a life, another had taken two, a third had set a house on fire, while another had simply been a vagrant and had done nothing. So they asked the old man: 'What are you being punished for, Daddy?'—'I, my dear brothers,' said he, 'am being punished for my own and other men's sins. But I have not killed anyone or taken anything that was not mine, but have only helped my poorer brothers. I was a merchant, my dear brothers, and had much property.' And he went on to tell them all about it in due order. 'I don't grieve for myself,' he says, 'God it seems has chastened me. Only I am sorry for my old wife and the children,' and the old man began to weep. Now it happened that in the group was the very man who had killed the other merchant. 'Where did it happen, Daddy?' he said. 'When, and in what month?' He asked all about it and his heart began to ache. So he comes up to the old man like this, and falls down at his feet! 'You are perishing because of me, Daddy,' he says. 'It's quite true, lads, that this man,' he says, 'is being tortured innocently and for nothing! I,' he says, 'did that deed, and I put the knife under your head while you were asleep. Forgive me, Daddy,' he says, 'for Christ's sake!' "

Karatáev paused, smiling joyously as he gazed into the fire, and he drew the logs together.

"And the old man said, 'God will forgive you, we are all sinners in His sight. I suffer for my own sins,' and he wept bitter tears. Well, and what do you think, dear friends?" Karatáev continued, his face brightening more and more with a rapturous smile as if what he now had to tell contained the chief charm and the whole meaning of his story: "What do you think, dear fellows? That murderer confessed to the authorities. 'I have taken six lives,' he says (he was a great sinner), 'but what I am most sorry for is this old man. Don't let him suffer because of me.' So he confessed and it was all written down and the papers sent off in due form. The place was a long way off, and while they were judging, what with one thing and another, filling in the papers all in due form—the authorities I mean—time passed. The affair reached the Tsar. After a while the Tsar's decree came: to set the merchant free and give him a compensation that had been awarded. The paper arrived and they began to look for the old man. 'Where is the old man who has been suffering innocently and in vain? A paper has come from the Tsar!' So they began looking for him," here Karatáev's lower jaw trembled, "but God had already forgiven him—he was dead! That's how it was, dear fellows!" Karatáev concluded and sat for a long time silent, gazing before him with a smile.

And Pierre's soul was dimly but joyfully filled not by the story itself but by its mysterious significance: by the rapturous joy that lit up Karatáev's face as he told it, and the mystic significance of that joy.

Chapter XIV

"*A VOS PLACES!*" SUDDENLY CRIED A VOICE.

A pleasant feeling of excitement and an expectation of something joyful and solemn was aroused among the soldiers of the convoy and the prisoners. From all sides came shouts of command, and from the left came smartly-dressed cavalrymen on good horses, passing the prisoners at a trot. The expression on all faces showed the tension people feel at the approach of those in authority. The prisoners thronged together and were pushed off the road. The convoy formed up.

"The Emperor! The Emperor! The Marshal! The Duke!" and hardly had the sleek cavalry passed, before a carriage drawn by six gray horses rattled by. Pierre caught a glimpse of a man in a three-cornered hat with a tranquil look on his handsome, plump, white face. It was one of the marshals. His eye fell on Pierre's large and striking figure, and in the expression with which he frowned and looked away Pierre thought he detected sympathy and a desire to conceal that sympathy.

The general in charge of the stores galloped after the carriage with a red and frightened face, whipping up his skinny horse. Several officers formed a group and some soldiers crowded round them. Their faces all looked excited and worried.

"What did he say? What did he say?" Pierre heard them ask.

While the marshal was passing the prisoners had huddled together in a crowd, and Pierre saw Karatáev whom he had not yet seen that morning. He sat in his short overcoat leaning against a birch tree. On his face, besides the look of joyful emotion it had worn yesterday while telling the tale of the merchant who suffered innocently, there was now an expression of quiet solemnity.

Karatáev looked at Pierre with his kindly round eyes now filled with tears, evidently wishing him to come near that he might say something to him. But Pierre was not sufficiently sure of himself. He made as if he did not notice that look and moved hastily away.

When the prisoners again went forward Pierre looked round. Karatáev was still sitting at the side of the road under the birch tree and two Frenchmen were talking over his head. Pierre did not look round again but went limping up the hill.

From behind, where Karatáev had been sitting, came the sound of a shot. Pierre heard it plainly, but at that moment he remembered that he had not yet finished reckoning up how many stages still remained to Smolénsk—a calculation he had begun before the marshal went by. And he again started reckoning. Two French soldiers ran past Pierre, one of whom carried a lowered and smoking gun. They both looked pale, and in the expression on their faces—one of them glanced timidly at Pierre—there was something resembling what he had seen on the face of the young soldier at the execution. Pierre looked at the soldier and remembered that, two days before, that man had burned his shirt while drying it at the fire and how they had laughed at him.

Behind him, where Karatáev had been sitting, the dog began to howl. "What a stupid beast! Why is it howling?" thought Pierre.

His comrades, the prisoner-soldiers walking beside him, avoided looking back at the place where the shot had been fired and the dog was howling, just as Pierre did, but there was a set look on all their faces.

Chapter XV

The stores, the prisoners, and the marshal's baggage-train stopped at the village of Shámshevo. The men crowded together round the campfires. Pierre went up to the fire, ate some roast horseflesh, lay down with his back to the fire and immediately fell asleep. He again slept as he had done at Mozháysk after the battle of Borodinó.

Again real events mingled with dreams and again someone, he or another, gave expression to his thoughts, and even to the same thoughts that had been expressed in his dream at Mozháysk.

"Life is everything. Life is God. Everything changes and moves and that movement is God. And while there is life there is joy in consciousness of the divine. To love life is to love God. Harder and more blessed than all else is to love this life in one's sufferings, in innocent sufferings."

"Karatáev!" came to Pierre's mind.

And suddenly he saw vividly before him a long-forgotten, kindly old man who had given him geography lessons in Switzerland. "Wait a bit," said the old man, and showed Pierre a globe. This globe was alive—a vibrating ball without fixed dimensions. Its whole surface consisted of drops closely pressed together, and all these drops moved and changed places, sometimes several of them merging into one, sometimes one dividing into many. Each drop tried to spread out and occupy as much space as possible, but others striving to do the same compressed it, sometimes destroyed it, and sometimes merged with it.

"That is life," said the old teacher.

"How simple and clear it is," thought Pierre. "How is it I did not know it before?"

"God is in the midst, and each drop tries to expand so as to reflect Him to the greatest extent. And it grows, merges, disappears from the surface, sinks to the depth and again emerges. There now, Karatáev has spread out and disappeared. Do you understand, my child?" said the teacher.

"Do you understand, damn you?" shouted a voice, and Pierre woke up.

He lifted himself and sat up. A Frenchman who had just pushed a Russian soldier away was squatting by the fire, engaged in roasting a piece of meat stuck on a ramrod. His sleeves were rolled up and his sinewy, hairy, red hands with their short fingers deftly turned the ramrod. His brown morose face with frowning brows was clearly visible by the glow of the charcoal.

"It's all the same to him," he muttered, turning quickly to a soldier who stood behind him. "Brigand! Get away!"

And twisting the ramrod he looked gloomily at Pierre, who turned away and gazed into the darkness. A prisoner, the Russian soldier the Frenchman had pushed away, was sitting near the fire patting something with his hand. Looking more closely Pierre recognized the blue-gray dog, sitting beside the soldier wagging its tail.

"Ah, he's come?" said Pierre. "And Plat—" he began, but did not finish.

Suddenly and simultaneously a crowd of memories awoke in his fancy—of the look Platón had given him as he sat under the tree, of the shot heard from that spot, of the dog's howl, of the guilty faces of the two Frenchmen as they ran past him, of the lowered and smoking gun, and of Karatáev's absence at this halt—and he was on the point of realizing that Karatáev had been killed, but just at that instant, he knew not why, the recollection came to his mind of a summer evening he had spent with a beautiful Polish lady on the veranda of his house in Kiev. And without linking up the events of the day or drawing a conclusion from them, Pierre closed his eyes, seeing a vision of the country in summertime mingled with memories of bathing and of the liquid, vibrating globe, and he sank into water so that it closed over his head.

Before sunrise he was awakened by shouts and loud and rapid firing. French soldiers were running past him.

"The Cossacks!" one of them shouted, and a moment later a crowd of Russians surrounded Pierre.

For a long time he could not understand what was happening to him. All around he heard his comrades sobbing with joy.

"Brothers! Dear fellows! Darlings!" old soldiers exclaimed, weeping, as they embraced Cossacks and hussars.

The hussars and Cossacks crowded round the prisoners; one offered them clothes, another boots, and a third bread. Pierre sobbed as he sat among them and could not utter a word. He hugged the first soldier who approached him, and kissed him, weeping.

Dólokhov stood at the gate of the ruined house, letting a crowd of disarmed Frenchmen pass by. The French excited by all that had happened, were talking loudly among themselves, but as they passed Dólokhov who gently switched his boots with his whip and watched them with cold glassy eyes that boded no good, they became silent. On the opposite side stood Dólokhov's Cossack, counting the prisoners and marking off each hundred with a chalk line on the gate.

"How many?" Dólokhov asked the Cossack.

"The second hundred," replied the Cossack.

"Filez, filez!" Dólokhov kept saying, having adopted this expression from the French, and when his eyes met those of the prisoners they flashed with a cruel light.

Denísov, bareheaded and with a gloomy face, walked behind some Cossacks who were carrying the body of Pétya Rostóv to a hole that had been dug in the garden.

Chapter XVI

AFTER THE 28TH OF OCTOBER WHEN THE FROSTS BEGAN, THE FLIGHT OF THE FRENCH ASSUMED a still more tragic character, with men freezing, or roasting themselves to death at the campfires, while carriages with people dressed in furs continued to drive past, carrying away the property that had been stolen by the Emperor, kings and dukes; but the process of the flight and disintegration of the French army went on essentially as before.

From Moscow to Vyázma the French army of seventy-three thousand men not reckoning the Guards (who did nothing during the whole war but pillage) was reduced to thirty-six thousand, though not more than five thousand had fallen in battle. From this beginning the succeeding terms of the progression could be determined mathematically. The French army melted away and perished at the same rate from Moscow to Vyázma, from Vyázma to Smolénsk, from Smolénsk to the Berëzina, and from the Berëzina to Vílna—independently of the greater or lesser intensity of the cold, the pursuit, the barring of the way, or any other particular conditions. Beyond Vyázma the French army instead of moving in three columns huddled together into one mass, and so went on to the end. Berthier wrote to his Emperor (we know how far commanding officers allow themselves to diverge from the truth in describing the condition of an army) and this is what he said:

> I deem it my duty to report to your Majesty the condition of the various corps I have had occasion to observe during different stages of the last two or three days' march. They are almost disbanded. Scarcely a quarter of the soldiers remain with the standards of their regiments, the others go off by themselves in different directions hoping to find food and escape discipline. In general they regard Smolénsk as the place where they hope to recover. During the last few days many of the men have been seen to throw away their car-

tridges and their arms. In such a state of affairs, whatever your ultimate plans may be, the interest of your Majesty's service demands that the army should be rallied at Smolénsk and should first of all be freed from ineffectives, such as dismounted cavalry, unnecessary baggage, and artillery material that is no longer in proportion to the present forces. The soldiers, who are worn out with hunger and fatigue, need supplies as well as a few days' rest. Many have died these last days on the road or at the bivouacs. This state of things is continually becoming worse and makes one fear that unless a prompt remedy is applied the troops will no longer be under control in case of an engagement.

9th of November: thirty versts from Smolénsk.

After staggering into Smolénsk which seemed to them a promised land, the French, searching for food, killed one another, sacked their own stores, and when everything had been plundered fled farther.

They all went without knowing whither or why they were going. Still less did that genius, Napoleon, know it, for no one issued any orders to him. But still he and those about him retained their old habits: wrote commands, letters, reports, and orders of the day; called one another *sire, mon cousin, prince d'Eckmhl, roi de Naples,* and so on. But these orders and reports were only on paper, nothing in them was acted upon for they could not be carried out, and though they entitled one another Majesties, Highnesses, or Cousins, they all felt that they were miserable wretches who had done much evil for which they had now to pay. And though they pretended to be concerned about the army, each was thinking only of himself and of how to get away quickly and save himself.

Chapter XVII

THE MOVEMENTS OF THE RUSSIAN AND FRENCH ARMIES DURING THE CAMPAIGN FROM MOSCOW back to the Niemen were like those in a game of Russian blindman's buff, in which two players are blindfolded and one of them occasionally rings a little bell to inform the catcher of his whereabouts. First he rings his bell fearlessly, but when he gets into a tight place he runs away as quietly as he can, and often thinking to escape runs straight into his opponent's arms.

At first while they were still moving along the Kalúga road, Napoleon's armies made their presence known, but later when they reached the Smolénsk road they ran holding the clapper of their bell tight—and often thinking they were escaping ran right into the Russians.

Owing to the rapidity of the French flight and the Russian pursuit and the consequent exhaustion of the horses, the chief means of approximately ascertaining the enemy's position—by cavalry scouting—was not available. Besides, as a result of the frequent and rapid change of position by each army, even what information was obtained could not be delivered in time. If news was received one day that the enemy had been in a certain position the day before, by the third day when something could have been done, that army was already two days' march further on and in quite another position.

One army fled and the other pursued. Beyond Smolénsk there were several different roads available for the French, and one would have thought that during their stay of four days they might have learned where the enemy was, might have arranged some more advantageous plan and undertaken something new. But after a four days' halt the mob, with no maneuvers or plans, again began running along the beaten track, neither to the right nor to the left but along the old—the worst—road, through Krásnoe and Orshá.

Expecting the enemy from behind and not in front, the French separated in their flight and spread out over a distance of twenty-four hours. In front of them all fled the Emperor, then the kings, then the dukes. The Russian army, expecting Napoleon to take the road to the right beyond the Dnieper—which was the only reasonable thing for him to do—themselves turned to the right and came out onto the highroad at Krásnoe. And here as in a game of blindman's buff the French ran into our vanguard. Seeing their enemy unexpectedly the French fell into confusion and stopped short from the sudden fright, but then they resumed their flight, abandoning their comrades who were further behind. Then for three days separate portions of the French army—first Murat's (the vice-king's), then Davout's, and then Ney's—ran, as it were, the gauntlet of the Russian army. They abandoned one another, abandoned all their heavy baggage, their artillery, and half their men, and fled, getting past the Russians by night by making semicircles to the right.

Ney who came last, had been busying himself blowing up the walls of Smolénsk which were in nobody's way, because despite the unfortunate plight of the French or because of it, they wished to punish the floor against which they had hurt themselves. Ney who had had a corps of ten thousand men, reached Napoleon at Orshá with only one thousand men left, having abandoned all the rest and all his cannon, and having crossed the Dnieper at night by stealth at a wooded spot.

From Orshá they fled farther along the road to Vílna, still playing at blindman's buff with the pursuing army. At the Berëzina they again became disorganized, many were drowned and many surrendered, but those who got across the river fled farther. Their supreme chief donned a fur coat and having seated himself in a sleigh, galloped on alone, abandoning his companions. The others who could do so drove away too, leaving those who could not to surrender or die.

Chapter XVIII

THIS CAMPAIGN CONSISTED IN A FLIGHT OF THE FRENCH DURING WHICH THEY DID ALL THEY could to destroy themselves. From the time they turned onto the Kalúga road to the day their leader fled from the army, none of the movements of the crowd had any sense. So one might have thought that regarding this period of the campaign the historians, who attributed the actions of the mass to the will of one man, would have found it impossible to make the story of the retreat fit their theory. But no! Mountains of books have been written by the historians about this campaign, and everywhere are described Napoleon's arrangements, the maneuvers, and his profound plans which guided the army, as well as the military genius shown by his marshals.

The retreat from Málo-Yaroslávets when he had a free road into a well-supplied district and the parallel road was open to him along which Kutúzov afterward pursued him—this unnecessary retreat along a devastated road—is explained to us as being due to profound considerations. Similarly profound considerations are given for his retreat from Smolénsk to Orshá. Then his heroism at Krásnoe is described, where he is reported to have been prepared to accept battle and take personal command, and to have walked about with a birch stick and said:

"J'ai assez fait l'empereur; il est temps de faire le général," but nevertheless immediately ran away again, abandoning to its fate the scattered fragments of the army he left behind.

Then we are told of the greatness of soul of the marshals, especially of Ney—a greatness of soul consisting in this: that he made his way by night around through the forest and across the Dnieper and escaped to Orshá, abandoning standards, artillery, and nine-tenths of his men.

And lastly, the final departure of the great Emperor from his heroic army is presented to us by the historians as something great and characteristic of genius. Even that final running away, described in ordinary language as the lowest depth of baseness which every child is taught to be ashamed of—even that act finds justification in the historians' language.

When it is impossible to stretch the very elastic threads of historical ratiocination any farther, when actions are clearly contrary to all that humanity calls right or even just, the historians produce a saving conception of "greatness." "Greatness," it seems, excludes the standards of right and wrong. For the "great" man nothing is wrong, there is no atrocity for which a "great" man can be blamed.

"C'est grand!" say the historians, and there no longer exists either good or evil but only *"grand"* and *"not grand." Grand* is good, not *grand* is bad. *Grand* is the characteristic, in their conception, of some special animals called "heroes." And Napoleon escaping home in a warm fur coat and leaving to perish those who were not merely his comrades but were (in his opinion) men he had brought there, feels *que c'est grand,* and his soul is tranquil.

"*Du sublime* (he saw something sublime in himself) *au ridicule il n'y a qu'un pas,*" said he. And the whole world for fifty years has been repeating: *"Sublime! Grand! Napoléon le Grand!" Du sublime au ridicule il n'y a qu'un pas.*

And it occurs to no one that to admit a greatness not commensurable with the standard of right and wrong is merely to admit one's own nothingness and immeasurable meanness.

For us with the standard of good and evil given us by Christ, no human actions are incommensurable. And there is no greatness where simplicity, goodness and truth are absent.

Chapter XIX

WHAT RUSSIAN, READING THE ACCOUNT OF THE LAST PART OF THE CAMPAIGN OF 1812, HAS NOT experienced an uncomfortable feeling of regret, dissatisfaction and perplexity? Who has not asked himself how it is that the French were not all captured or destroyed when our three armies surrounded them in superior numbers, when the disordered French, hungry and freezing, surrendered in crowds, and when (as the historians relate) the aim of the Russians was to stop the French, to cut them off and capture them all?

How was it that the Russian army, which when numerically weaker than the French had given battle at Borodinó, did not achieve its purpose when it had surrounded the French on three sides and when its aim was to capture them? Can the French be so enormously superior to us that when we had surrounded them with superior forces we could not beat them? How could that happen?

History (or what is called by that name) replying to these questions says that this occurred because Kutúzov and Tormásov and Chichagóv, and this man and that man, did not execute such and such maneuvers. . . .

But why did they not execute those maneuvers? And why if they were guilty of not carrying out a prearranged plan were they not tried and punished? But even if we admitted that Kutúzov, Chichagóv, and others were the cause of the Russian failures, it is still incomprehensible why, the position of the Russian army being what it was at Krásnoe and at the Berëzina (in both cases we had superior forces), the French army with its marshals, kings, and Emperor was not captured, if that was what the Russians aimed at.

The explanation of this strange fact given by Russian military historians (to the effect that Kutúzov hindered an attack) is unfounded, for we know that he could not restrain the troops from attacking at Vyázma and Tarútino.

Why was the Russian army—which with inferior forces had withstood the enemy in full strength at Borodinó—defeated at Krásnoe and the Berëzina by the disorganized crowds of the French when it was numerically superior?

If the aim of the Russians consisted in cutting off and capturing Napoleon and his marshals—

and that aim was not merely frustrated but all attempts to attain it were most shamefully baffled—then this last period of the campaign is quite rightly considered by the French to be a series of victories, and quite wrongly considered victorious by Russian historians.

The Russian military historians in so far as they submit to claims of logic must admit that conclusion, and in spite of their lyrical rhapsodies about valor, devotion and so forth, must reluctantly admit that the French retreat from Moscow was a series of victories for Napoleon and defeats for Kutúzov.

But putting national vanity entirely aside one feels that such a conclusion involves a contradiction, since the series of French victories brought the French complete destruction, while the series of Russian defeats led to the total destruction of their enemy and the liberation of their country.

The source of this contradiction lies in the fact that the historians studying the events from the letters of the sovereigns and the generals, from memoirs, reports, projects and so forth, have attributed to this last period of the war of 1812 an aim that never existed, namely that of cutting off and capturing Napoleon with his marshals and his army.

There never was or could have been such an aim, for it would have been senseless and its attainment quite impossible.

It would have been senseless, first because Napoleon's disorganized army was flying from Russia with all possible speed, that is to say was doing just what every Russian desired. So what was the use of performing various operations on the French who were running away as fast as they possibly could?

Secondly, it would have been senseless to block the passage of men whose whole energy was directed to flight.

Thirdly, it would have been senseless to sacrifice one's own troops in order to destroy the French army, which without external interference was destroying itself at such a rate that, though its path was not blocked, it could not carry across the frontier more than it actually did in December, namely a hundredth part of the original army.

Fourthly, it would have been senseless to wish to take captive the Emperor, kings and dukes—whose capture would have been in the highest degree embarrassing for the Russians, as the most adroit diplomatists of the time (Joseph de Maistre and others) recognized. Still more senseless would have been the wish to capture army corps of the French, when our own army had melted away to half before reaching Krásnoe and a whole division would have been needed to convoy the corps of prisoners, and when our men were not always getting full rations, and the prisoners already taken were perishing of hunger.

All the profound plans about cutting off and capturing Napoleon and his army were like the plan of a market-gardener, who when driving out of his garden a cow that had trampled down the beds he had planted, should run to the gate and hit the cow on the head. The only thing to be said in excuse of that gardener would be that he was very angry. But not even that could be said for those who drew up this project, for it was not they who had suffered from the trampled beds.

But besides the fact that cutting off Napoleon with his army would have been senseless, it was impossible.

It was impossible first because—as experience shows that a three-mile movement of columns on a battlefield never coincides with the plans—the probability of Chichagóv, Kutúzov and Wittgenstein effecting a junction on time at an appointed place was so remote as to be tantamount to impossibility, as in fact thought Kutúzov, who when he received the plan remarked that diversions planned over great distances do not yield the desired results.

Secondly it was impossible, because to paralyze the momentum with which Napoleon's army was retiring, incomparably greater forces than the Russians possessed would have been required.

Thirdly it was impossible, because the military term "to cut off" has no meaning. One can cut off a slice of bread, but not an army. To cut off an army—to bar its road—is quite impossible, for there is always plenty of room to avoid capture and there is the night when nothing can be seen, as the military scientists might convince themselves by the example of Krásnoe and of the Berëzina. It is only possible to capture prisoners if they agree to be captured, just as it is only possible to catch a swallow if it settles on one's hand. Men can only be taken prisoners if they surrender according to the rules of strategy and tactics, as the Germans did. But the French troops quite rightly did not consider that this suited them, since death by hunger and cold awaited them in flight or captivity alike.

Fourthly and chiefly it was impossible, because never since the world began has a war been fought under such conditions as those that obtained in 1812, and the Russian army in its pursuit of the French strained its strength to the utmost and could not have done more without destroying itself.

During the movement of the Russian army from Tarútino to Krásnoe it lost fifty thousand sick or stragglers, that is a number equal to the population of a large provincial town. Half the men fell out of the army without a battle.

And it is of this period of the campaign—when the army lacked boots and sheepskin coats, was short of provisions and without vodka, and was camping out at night for months in the snow with fifteen degrees of frost, when there were only seven or eight hours of daylight and the rest was night in which the influence of discipline cannot be maintained, when men were taken into that region of death where discipline fails, not for a few hours only as in a battle, but for months, where they were every moment fighting death from hunger and cold, when half the army perished in a single month—it is of this period of the campaign that the historians tell us how Milorádovich should have made a flank march to such and such a place, Tormásov to another place, and Chichagóv should have crossed (more than knee-deep in snow) to somewhere else, and how so-and-so "routed" and "cut off" the French and so on and so on.

The Russians, half of whom died, did all that could and should have been done to attain an end worthy of the nation, and they are not to blame because other Russians, sitting in warm rooms, proposed that they should do what was impossible.

All that strange contradiction now difficult to understand between the facts and the historical accounts, only arises because the historians dealing with the matter have written the history of the beautiful words and sentiments of various generals, and not the history of the events.

To them the words of Milorádovich seem very interesting, and so do their surmises and the rewards this or that general received; but the question of those fifty thousand men who were left in hospitals and in graves does not even interest them, for it does not come within the range of their investigation.

Yet one need only discard the study of the reports and general plans and consider the movement of those hundreds of thousands of men who took a direct part in the events, and all the questions that seemed insoluble, easily and simply receive an immediate and certain solution.

The aim of cutting off Napoleon and his army never existed except in the imaginations of a dozen people. It could not exist because it was senseless and unattainable.

The people had a single aim: to free their land from invasion. That aim was attained in the first place of itself, as the French ran away and so it was only necessary not to stop their flight. Secondly it was attained by the guerrilla warfare which was destroying the French, and thirdly by the fact that a large Russian army was following the French, ready to use its strength in case their movement stopped.

The Russian army had to act like a whip to a running animal. And the experienced driver knew it was better to hold the whip raised as a menace than to strike the running animal on the head.

Part Fifteen

Chapter I

When seeing a dying animal a man feels a sense of horror: substance similar to his own is perishing before his eyes. But when it is a beloved and intimate human being that is dying, besides this horror at the extinction of life there is a severance, a spiritual wound, which like a physical wound is sometimes fatal and sometimes heals, but always aches and shrinks at any external irritating touch.

After Prince Andrew's death Natásha and Princess Mary alike felt this. Drooping in spirit and closing their eyes before the menacing cloud of death that overhung them, they dared not look life in the face. They carefully guarded their open wounds from any rough and painful contact. Everything: a carriage passing rapidly in the street, a summons to dinner, the maid's inquiry what dress to prepare, or worse still any word of insincere or feeble sympathy, seemed an insult, painfully irritated the wound, interrupting that necessary quiet in which they both tried to listen to the stern and dreadful choir that still resounded in their imagination, and hindered their gazing into those mysterious limitless vistas that for an instant had opened out before them.

Only when alone together were they free from such outrage and pain. They spoke little even to one another, and when they did it was of very unimportant matters.

Both avoided any allusion to the future. To admit the possibility of a future seemed to them to insult his memory. Still more carefully did they avoid anything relating to him who was dead. It seemed to them that what they had lived through and experienced could not be expressed in words, and that any reference to the details of his life infringed the majesty and sacredness of the mystery that had been accomplished before their eyes.

Continued abstention from speech, and constant avoidance of everything that might lead up to the subject—this halting on all sides at the boundary of what they might not mention—brought before their minds with still greater purity and clearness what they were both feeling.

But pure and complete sorrow is as impossible as pure and complete joy. Princess Mary in her position as absolute and independent arbiter of her own fate and guardian and instructor of her nephew, was the first to be called back to life from that realm of sorrow in which she had dwelled for the first fortnight. She received letters from her relations to which she had to reply; the room in which little Nicholas had been put was damp and he began to cough; Alpátych came to Yaroslávl with reports on the state of their affairs and with advice and suggestions that they should return to Moscow to the house on the Vozdvízhenka Street, which had remained uninjured and needed only slight repairs. Life did not stand still and it was necessary to live. Hard as it was for Princess Mary to emerge from the realm of secluded contemplation in which she had lived till then, and sorry and almost ashamed as she felt to leave Natásha alone, yet the cares of life demanded her attention and she involuntarily yielded to them. She went through the accounts with Alpátych, conferred with Dessalles about her nephew, and gave orders and made preparations for the journey to Moscow.

Natásha remained alone, and from the time Princess Mary began making preparations for departure, held aloof from her too.

Princess Mary asked the countess to let Natásha go with her to Moscow, and both parents gladly accepted this offer, for they saw their daughter losing strength every day and thought that a change of scene and the advice of Moscow doctors would be good for her.

"I am not going anywhere," Natásha replied when this was proposed to her. "Do please just leave me alone!" And she ran out of the room, with difficulty refraining from tears of vexation and irritation rather than of sorrow.

After she felt herself deserted by Princes Mary and alone in her grief, Natásha spent most of the time in her room by herself, sitting huddled up feet and all in the corner of the sofa, tearing and twisting something with her slender nervous fingers and gazing intently and fixedly at whatever her eyes chanced to fall on. This solitude exhausted and tormented her but she was in absolute need of it. As soon as anyone entered she got up quickly, changed her position and expression, and picked up a book or some sewing, evidently waiting impatiently for the intruder to go.

She felt all the time as if she might at any moment penetrate that on which—with a terrible questioning too great for her strength—her spiritual gaze was fixed.

One day toward the end of December Natásha, pale and thin, dressed in a black woolen gown, her plaited hair negligently twisted into a knot, was crouched feet and all in the corner of her sofa, nervously crumpling and smoothing out the end of her sash while she looked at a corner of the door.

She was gazing in the direction in which he had gone—to the other side of life. And that other side of life, of which she had never before thought and which had formerly seemed to her so far away and improbable, was now nearer and more akin and more comprehensible than this side of life, where everything was either emptiness and desolation or suffering and indignity.

She was gazing where she knew him to be; but she could not imagine him otherwise than as he had been here. She now saw him again as he had been at Mytíshchi, at Tróitsa, and at Yaroslávl.

She saw his face, heard his voice, repeated his words and her own, and sometimes devised other words they might have spoken.

There he is lying back in an arm-chair in his velvet cloak, leaning his head on his thin pale hand. His chest is dreadfully hollow and his shoulders raised. His lips are firmly closed, his eyes glitter, and a wrinkle comes and goes on his pale forehead. One of his legs twitches just perceptibly, but rapidly. Natásha knows that he is struggling with terrible pain. "What is that pain like? Why does he have that pain? What does he feel? How does it hurt him?" thought Natásha. He noticed her watching him, raised his eyes, and began to speak seriously:

"One thing would be terrible," said he: "to bind oneself forever to a suffering man. It would be continual torture." And he looked searchingly at her. Natásha as usual answered before she had time to think what she would say. She said: "This can't go on—it won't. You will get well—quite well."

She now saw him from the commencement of that scene and relived what she had then felt. She recalled his long sad and severe look at those words, and understood the meaning of the rebuke and despair in that protracted gaze.

"I agreed," Natásha now said to herself, "that it would be dreadful if he always continued to suffer. I said it then only because it would have been dreadful for him, but he understood it differently. He thought it would be dreadful for me. He then still wished to live and feared death. And I said it so awkwardly and stupidly! I did not say what I meant. I thought quite differently. Had I said what I thought, I should have said: even if he had to go on dying, to die continually before my eyes, I should have been happy compared with what I am now. Now there is nothing . . . nobody. Did he know that? No, he did not and never will know it. And now it will never, never, be possible to put it right." And now he again seemed to be saying the same words to her, only in her imagination Natásha this time gave him a different answer. She stopped him and said: "Terrible for you, but not for me! You know that for me there is nothing in life but you, and to suffer with you is the greatest happiness for me," and he took her hand and pressed it as he had pressed it that terrible evening four days before his death. And in her imagination she said other tender and loving words which she might have said then but only spoke now: "I love thee! . . . thee! I love, love . . ." she said, convulsively pressing her hands and setting her teeth with a desperate effort. . . .

She was overcome by sweet sorrow and tears were already rising in her eyes; then she suddenly asked herself to whom she was saying this? Again everything was shrouded in hard dry perplexity, and again with a strained frown she peered toward the world where he was. And now, now it seemed to her she was penetrating the mystery. . . . But at the instant when it seemed that the incomprehensible was revealing itself to her a loud rattle of the door handle struck painfully on her ears. Dunyásha, her maid, entered the room quickly and abruptly with a frightened look on her face and showing no concern for her mistress.

"Come to your Papa at once, please!" said she with a strange, excited look. "A misfortune . . . about Peter Ilynich . . . a letter," she finished with a sob.

Chapter II

BESIDES A FEELING OF ALOOFNESS FROM EVERYBODY NATÁSHA WAS FEELING A SPECIAL ESTRANGEment from the members of her own family. All of them—her father, mother and Sónya—were so near to her, so familiar, so commonplace, that all their words and feelings seemed an insult to the world in which she had been living of late, and she felt not merely indifferent to them but regarded them with hostility. She heard Dunyásha's words about Peter Ilynich and a misfortune, but did not grasp them.

"What misfortune? What misfortune can happen to them? They just live their own old quiet and commonplace life," thought Natásha.

As she entered the ballroom her father was hurriedly coming out of her mother's room. His face was puckered up and wet with tears. He had evidently run out of that room to give vent to the sobs that were choking him. When he saw Natásha he waved his arms despairingly and burst into convulsively painful sobs that distorted his soft round face.

"Pe . . . Pétya . . . Go, go, she . . . is calling . . ." and weeping like a child and quickly shuffling on his feeble legs to a chair, he almost fell into it, covering his face with his hands.

Suddenly an electric shock seemed to run through Natásha's whole being. Terrible anguish struck her heart, she felt a dreadful ache as if something was being torn inside her and she were dying. But the pain was immediately followed by a feeling of release from the oppressive constraint that had prevented her taking part in life. The sight of her father, the terribly wild cries of her mother that she heard through the door, made her immediately forget herself and her own grief.

She ran to her father, but he feebly waved his arm pointing to her mother's door. Princess Mary, pale and with quivering chin, came out from that room and taking Natásha by the arm said something to her. Natásha neither saw nor heard her. She went in with rapid steps, pausing at the door for an instant as if struggling with herself, and then ran to her mother.

The countess was lying in an arm-chair in a strange and awkward position, stretching out and beating her head against the wall. Sónya and the maids were holding her arms.

"Natásha! Natásha! . . ." cried the countess. "It's not true . . . it's not true . . . He's lying . . . Natásha!" she shrieked, pushing those around her away. "Go away all of you; it's not true! Killed! . . . ha, ha, ha! . . . It's not true!"

Natásha put one knee on the arm-chair, stooped over her mother, embraced her, and with unexpected strength raised her, turned her face toward herself, and clung to her.

"Mummy . . . darling . . . ! I am here, my dearest Mummy," she kept on whispering, not pausing an instant.

She did not let go of her mother but struggled tenderly with her, demanded a pillow and hot water, and unfastened and tore open her mother's dress.

"My dearest darling . . . Mummy, my precious! . . ." she whispered incessantly, kissing her head, her hands, her face, and feeling her own irrepressible and streaming tears tickling her nose and cheeks.

The countess pressed her daughter's hand, closed her eyes, and became quiet for a moment.

Suddenly she sat up with unaccustomed swiftness, glanced vacantly around her, and seeing Natásha began to press her daughter's head with all her strength. Then she turned toward her daughter's face which was wincing with pain, and gazed long at it.

"Natásha, you love me?" she said in a soft trustful whisper. "Natásha, you would not deceive me? You'll tell me the whole truth?"

Natásha looked at her with eyes full of tears and in her look there was nothing but love and an entreaty for forgiveness.

"My darling Mummy!" she repeated, straining all the power of her love to find some way of taking on herself the excess of grief that crushed her mother.

And again in a futile struggle with reality her mother, refusing to believe that she could live when her beloved boy was killed in the bloom of life, escaped from reality into a world of delirium.

Natásha did not remember how that day passed nor that night, nor the next day and night. She did not sleep and did not leave her mother. Her persevering and patient love seemed completely to surround the countess every moment, not explaining or consoling, but recalling her to life.

During the third night the countess kept very quiet for a few minutes, and Natásha rested her head on the arm of her chair and closed her eyes, but opened them again on hearing the bedstead creak. The countess was sitting up in bed and speaking softly.

"How glad I am you have come. You are tired. Won't you have some tea?" Natásha went up to her. "You have improved in looks and grown more manly," continued the countess, taking her daughter's hand.

"Mamma! What are you saying? . . ."

"Natásha, he is no more, no more!"

And embracing her daughter, the countess began to weep for the first time.

Chapter III

PRINCESS MARY POSTPONED HER DEPARTURE. SÓNYA AND THE COUNT TRIED TO REPLACE Natásha but could not. They saw that she alone was able to restrain her mother from unreasoning despair. For three weeks Natásha remained constantly at her mother's side, sleeping on a lounge chair in her room, making her eat and drink, and talking to her incessantly because the mere sound of her tender caressing tones soothed her mother.

The mother's wounded spirit could not heal. Pétya's death had torn from her half her life. When the news of Pétya's death had come she had been a fresh and vigorous woman of fifty, but a month later she left her room a listless old woman taking no interest in life. But the same blow that almost killed the countess, this second blow, restored Natásha to life.

A spiritual wound produced by a rending of the spiritual body is like a physical wound and, strange as it may seem, just as a deep wound may heal and its edges join, physical and spiritual wounds alike can yet heal completely only as the result of a vital force from within.

Natásha's wound healed in that way. She thought her life was ended, but her love for her mother unexpectedly showed her that the essence of life—love—was still active within her. Love awoke and so did life.

Prince Andrew's last days had bound Princess Mary and Natásha together; this new sorrow brought them still closer to one another. Princess Mary put off her departure, and for three weeks looked after Natásha as if she had been a sick child. The last weeks passed in her mother's bedroom had strained Natásha's physical strength.

One afternoon noticing Natásha shivering with fever, Princess Mary took her to her own room and made her lie down on the bed. Natásha lay down, but when Princess Mary had drawn the blinds and was going away she called her back.

"I don't want to sleep, Mary, sit by me a little."

"You are tired—try to sleep."

"No, no. Why did you bring me away? She will be asking for me."

"She is much better. She spoke so well today," said Princess Mary.

Natásha lay on the bed and in the semi-darkness of the room scanned Princess Mary's face.

"Is she like him?" thought Natásha. "Yes, like and yet not like. But she is quite original, strange, new and unknown. And she loves me. What is in her heart? All that is good. But how? What is her mind like? What does she think about me? Yes, she is splendid!"

"Mary," she said timidly, drawing Princess Mary's hand to herself, "Mary, you mustn't think me wicked. No? Mary darling, how I love you! Let us be quite, quite friends."

And Natásha embracing her, began kissing her face and hands, making Princess Mary feel shy but happy by this demonstration of her feelings.

From that day a tender and passionate friendship such as exists only between women, was established between Princess Mary and Natásha. They were continually kissing and saying tender things to one another and spent most of their time together. When one went out the other became restless and hastened to rejoin her. Together they felt more in harmony with one another than either of them felt with herself when alone. A feeling stronger than friendship sprang up between them; an exclusive feeling of life being possible only in each other's presence.

Sometimes they were silent for hours; sometimes after they were already in bed they would begin talking and go on till morning. They spoke most of what was long past. Princess Mary spoke of her childhood, of her mother, her father, and her daydreams; and Natásha, who with a passive lack of understanding had formerly turned away from that life of devotion, submission, and the poetry of Christian self-sacrifice, now feeling herself bound to Princess Mary by affection, learned to love her past too and to understand a side of life previously incomprehensible to her. She did not think of applying submission and self-abnegation to her own life, for she was accustomed to seek other joys, but she understood and loved in another those previously incomprehensible virtues. For Princess Mary, listening to Natásha's tales of childhood and early youth, there also opened out a new and hitherto uncomprehended side of life: belief in life and its enjoyment.

Just as before, they never mentioned *him* so as not to lower (as they thought) their exalted feelings by words; but this silence about him had the effect of making them gradually begin to forget him without being conscious of it.

Natásha had grown thin and pale and physically so weak that they all talked about her health, and this pleased her. But sometimes she was suddenly overcome by fear not only of death but of sickness, weakness, and loss of good looks, and involuntarily she examined her bare arm carefully, surprised at its thinness, and in the morning noticed her drawn and as it seemed to her piteous face in her glass. It seemed to her that things must be so, and yet it was dreadfully sad.

One day she went quickly upstairs and found herself out of breath. Unconsciously she immediately invented a reason for going down, and then, testing her strength, ran upstairs again, observing the result.

Another time when she called Dunyásha her voice trembled, so she called again—though she could hear Dunyásha coming—called her in the deep chest tones in which she had been wont to sing, sing, and listened attentively to herself.

She did not know and would not have believed it, but beneath the layer of slime that covered her soul and seemed to her impenetrable, delicate young shoots of grass were already sprouting, which taking root would so cover with their living verdure the grief that weighed her down that it would soon no longer be seen or noticed. The wound had begun to heal from within.

At the end of January Princess Mary left for Moscow, and the count insisted on Natásha's going with her to consult the doctors.

Chapter IV

After the encounter at Vyázma, where Kutúzov had been unable to hold back his troops in their anxiety to overwhelm and cut off the enemy and so on, the farther movement of the fleeing French, and of the Russians who pursued them, continued as far as Krásnoe without a battle. The flight was so rapid that the Russian army pursuing the French could not keep up with them; cavalry and artillery horses broke down, and the information received of the movements of the French was never reliable.

The men in the Russian army were so worn out by this continuous marching at the rate of twenty-seven miles a day that they could not go any faster.

To realize the degree of exhaustion of the Russian army it is only necessary to grasp clearly the meaning of the fact, that while not losing more than five thousand killed and wounded after Tarútino and less than a hundred prisoners, the Russian army which left that place a hundred thousand strong, reached Krásnoe with only fifty thousand.

The rapidity of the Russian pursuit was just as destructive to our army as the flight of the French was to theirs. The only difference was that the Russian army moved voluntarily, with no such threat of destruction as hung over the French, and that the sick Frenchmen were left behind in enemy hands while the sick Russians left behind were among their own people. The chief cause of the wastage of Napoleon's army was the rapidity of its movement, and a convincing proof of this is the corresponding decrease of the Russian army.

Kutúzov as far as was in his power, instead of trying to check the movement of the French as was desired in Petersburg and by the Russian army generals, directed his whole activity here as he had done at Tarútino and Vyázma, to hastening it on while easing the movement of our army.

But besides this, since the exhaustion and enormous diminution of the army caused by the rapidity of the advance had become evident, another reason for slackening the pace and delaying presented itself to Kutúzov. The aim of the Russian army was to pursue the French. The road the French would take was unknown, and so the closer our troops trod on their heels the greater distance they had to cover. Only by following at some distance could one cut across the zigzag path of the French. All the artful maneuvers suggested by our generals meant fresh movements of the army and a lengthening of its marches, whereas the only reasonable aim was to shorten those marches. To that end Kutúzov's activity was directed during the whole campaign from Moscow to Vílna—not casually or intermittently but so consistently that he never once deviated from it.

Kutúzov felt and knew—not by reasoning or science but with the whole of his Russian being—what every Russian soldier felt: that the French were beaten, that the enemy was flying and must be driven out; but at the same time he like the soldiers realized all the hardship of this march, the rapidity of which was unparalleled for such a time of year.

But to the generals, especially the foreign ones in the Russian army, who wished to distinguish themselves, to astonish somebody, and for some reason to capture a king or a duke—it seemed that now—when any battle must be horrible and senseless—was the very time to fight and conquer somebody. Kutúzov merely shrugged his shoulders when one after another they presented projects of maneuvers to be made with those soldiers—ill-shod, insufficiently clad, and half-starved—who within a month and without fighting a battle had dwindled to half their number, and who at the best if the flight continued would have to go a greater distance than they had already traversed, before they reached the frontier.

This longing to distinguish themselves, to maneuver, to overthrow and to cut off, showed itself particularly whenever the Russians stumbled on the French army.

So it was at Krásnoe, where they expected to find one of the three French columns and stumbled instead on Napoleon himself with sixteen thousand men. Despite all Kutúzov's efforts to avoid that ruinous encounter and to preserve his troops, the massacre of the broken mob of French soldiers by worn-out Russians continued at Krásnoe for three days.

Toll wrote a disposition: "The first column will march to so-and-so," etc. And as usual nothing happened in accord with the disposition. Prince Eugène of Wrtemberg fired from a hill over the French crowds that were running past, and demanded reinforcements which did not arrive. The French, avoiding the Russians, dispersed and hid themselves in the forest by night, making their way round as best they could, and continued their flight.

Milorádovich, who said he did not want to know anything about the commissariat affairs of his detachment, and could never be found when he was wanted—that *chevalier sans peur et sans reproche* as he styled himself—who was fond of parleys with the French, sent envoys demanding their surrender, wasted time, and did not do what he was ordered to do.

"I give you that column, lads," he said, riding up to the troops and pointing out the French to the cavalry.

And the cavalry, with spurs and sabers urging on horses that could scarcely move, trotted with much effort to the column presented to them—that is to say, to a crowd of Frenchmen stark with cold, frost-bitten and starving—and the column that had been presented to them threw down its arms and surrendered as it had long been anxious to do.

At Krásnoe they took twenty-six thousand prisoners, several hundred cannon, and a stick called a "marshal's staff," and disputed as to who had distinguished himself and were pleased with their achievement—though they much regretted not having taken Napoleon, or at least a marshal or a hero of some sort, and reproached one another and especially Kutúzov for having failed to do so.

These men, carried away by their passions, were but blind tools of the most melancholy law of necessity, but considered themselves heroes and imagined that they were accomplishing a most noble and honorable deed. They blamed Kutúzov and said that from the very beginning of the campaign he had prevented their vanquishing Napoleon, that he thought nothing but satisfying his passions and would not advance from the Linen Factories because he was comfortable there, that at Krásnoe he checked the advance because on learning that Napoleon was there he had quite lost his head, and that it was probable that he had an understanding with Napoleon and had been bribed by him, and so on, and so on.

Not only did his contemporaries, carried away by their passions, talk in this way, but posterity and history have acclaimed Napoleon as *grand,* while Kutúzov is described by foreigners as a crafty, dissolute, weak old courtier, and by Russians as something indefinite—a sort of puppet useful only because he had a Russian name.

Chapter V

IN 1812 AND 1813 KUTÚZOV WAS OPENLY ACCUSED OF BLUNDERING. THE EMPEROR WAS DISSATISFIED with him. And in a history recently written by order of the Highest Authorities it is said that Kutúzov was a cunning court liar, frightened of the name of Napoleon, and that by his blunders at Krásnoe and the Berëzina he deprived the Russian army of the glory of complete victory over the French.

Such is the fate not of great men (*grands hommes*) whom the Russian mind does not acknowledge, but of those rare and always solitary individuals who discerning the will of Providence submit their personal will to it. The hatred and contempt of the crowd punish such men for discerning the higher laws.

For Russian historians, strange and terrible to say, Napoleon—that most insignificant tool of history who never anywhere, even in exile, showed human dignity—Napoleon is the object of adulation and enthusiasm; he is *grand*. But Kutúzov—the man who from the beginning to the end of his activity in 1812, never once swerving by word or deed from Borodinó to Vílna, presented an example exceptional in history of self-sacrifice and a present consciousness of the future importance of what was happening—Kutúzov seems to them something indefinite and pitiful, and when speaking of him and of the year 1812 they always seem a little ashamed.

And yet it is difficult to imagine an historical character whose activity was so unswervingly directed to a single aim; and it would be difficult to imagine any aim more worthy or more consonant with the will of the whole people. Still more difficult would it be to find an instance in history of the aim of an historical personage being so completely accomplished as that to which all Kutúzov's efforts were directed in 1812.

Kutúzov never talked of "forty centuries looking down from the Pyramids," of the sacrifices he offered for the fatherland, or of what he intended to accomplish or had accomplished; in general he said nothing about himself, adopted no pose, always appeared to be the simplest and most ordinary of men, and said the simplest and most ordinary things. He wrote letters to his daughters and to Madame de Staël, read novels, liked the society of pretty women, jested with generals, officers, and soldiers, and never contradicted those who tried to prove anything to him. When Count Rostopchín at the Yaúza Bridge galloped up to Kutúzov with personal reproaches for having caused the destruction of Moscow, and said: "How was it you promised not to abandon Moscow without a battle?" Kutúzov replied: "And I shall not abandon Moscow without a battle," though Moscow was then already abandoned. When Arakchéev, coming to him from the Emperor, said that Ermólov ought to be appointed chief of the artillery, Kutúzov replied: "Yes, I was just saying so myself," though a moment before he had said quite the contrary. What did it matter to him—who then alone amid a senseless crowd understood the whole tremendous significance of what was happening—what did it matter to him whether Rostopchín attributed the calamities of Moscow to him or to himself? Still less could it matter to him who was appointed chief of the artillery.

Not merely in these cases but continually did that old man—who by experience of life had reached the conviction that thoughts and the words serving as their expression are not what move people—use quite meaningless words that happened to enter his head.

But that man, so heedless of his words, did not once during the whole time of his activity utter one word inconsistent with the single aim toward which he moved throughout the whole war. Obviously in spite of himself, in very diverse circumstances, he repeatedly expressed his real thoughts with the bitter conviction that he would not be understood. Beginning with the battle of Borodinó, from which time his disagreement with those about him began, he alone said that *the battle of Borodinó was a victory,* and repeated this both verbally and in his dispatches and reports up to the time of his death. He alone said that the *loss of Moscow is not the loss of Russia.* In reply to Lauriston's proposal of peace, he said: *There can be no peace, for such is the people's will.* He alone during the retreat of the French said that *all our maneuvers are useless, everything is being accomplished of itself better than we could desire*; that *the enemy must be offered "a golden bridge"*; *that neither the Tarútino, the Vyázma, nor the Krásnoe battles were necessary*; that *we must keep some force to reach the frontier with,* and that *he would not sacrifice a single Russian for ten Frenchmen.*

And this courtier, as he is described to us, who lies to Arakchéev to please the Emperor, he alone—incurring thereby the Emperor's displeasure—said in Vílna that to *carry the war beyond the frontier is useless and harmful.*

Nor do words alone prove that only he understood the meaning of the events. His actions—without the smallest deviation—were all directed to one and the same threefold end: (1) to brace all his strength for conflict with the French, (2) to defeat them, and (3) to drive them out of Russia, minimizing as far as possible the sufferings of our people and of our army.

This procrastinator Kutúzov, whose motto was "Patience and Time," this enemy of decisive action, gave battle at Borodinó, investing the preparations for it with unparalleled solemnity. This Kutúzov who before the battle of Austerlitz began said that it would be lost, he alone, in contradiction to everyone else, declared till his death that Borodinó was a victory, despite the assurance of generals that the battle was lost and despite the fact that for an army to have to retire after winning a battle was unprecedented. He alone during the whole retreat insisted that battles, which were useless then, should not be fought, and that a new war should not be begun nor the frontiers of Russia crossed.

It is easy now to understand the significance of these events—if only we abstain from attributing to the activity of the mass aims that existed only in the heads of a dozen individuals—for the events and their results now lie before us.

But how did that old man, alone, in opposition to the general opinion, so truly discern the importance of the people's view of the events that in all his activity he was never once untrue to it?

The source of that extraordinary power of penetrating the meaning of the events then occurring, lay in the national feeling which he possessed in full purity and strength.

Only the recognition of the fact that he possessed this feeling caused the people in so strange a manner, contrary to the Tsar's wish, to select him—an old man in disfavor—to be their representative in the national war. And only that feeling placed him on that highest human pedestal from which he, the commander-in-chief, devoted all his powers not to slaying and destroying men but to saving and showing pity on them.

That simple, modest, and therefore truly great, figure could not be cast in the false mold of a European hero—the supposed ruler of men—that history has invented.

To a lackey no man can be great, for a lackey has his own conception of greatness.

Chapter VI

THE 5TH OF NOVEMBER WAS THE FIRST DAY OF WHAT IS CALLED THE BATTLE OF KRÁSNOE. Toward evening—after much disputing and many mistakes made by generals who did not go to their proper places, and after adjutants had been sent about with counter orders—when it had become plain that the enemy was everywhere in flight and that there could and would be no battle, Kutúzov left Krásnoe and went to Dóbroe whither his headquarters had that day been transferred.

The day was clear and frosty. Kutúzov rode to Dóbroe on his plump little white horse, followed by an enormous suite of discontented generals who whispered among themselves behind his back. All along the road groups of French prisoners captured that day (there were seven thousand of them) were crowding to warm themselves at campfires. Near Dóbroe an immense crowd of tattered prisoners buzzing with talk and wrapped and bandaged in anything they had been able to get hold of, were standing in the road beside a long row of unharnessed French guns. At the approach of the commander-in-chief the buzz of talk ceased and all eyes were fixed on Kutúzov who, wearing a white cap with a red band and a padded overcoat that bulged on his round shoulders, moved slowly along the road on his white horse. One of the generals was reporting to him where the guns and prisoners had been captured.

Kutúzov seemed preoccupied and did not listen to what the general was saying. He screwed up his eyes with a dissatisfied look as he gazed attentively and fixedly at these prisoners, who presented a specially wretched appearance. Most of them were disfigured by frost-bitten noses and cheeks, and nearly all had red, swollen and festering eyes.

One group of the French stood close to the road, and two of them, one of whom had his face covered with sores, were tearing a piece of raw flesh with their hands. There was something horrible and bestial in the fleeting glance they threw at the riders and in the malevolent expression with which, after a glance at Kutúzov, the soldier with the sores immediately turned away and went on with what he was doing.

Kutúzov looked long and intently at these two soldiers. He puckered his face, screwed up his eyes and pensively swayed his head. At another spot he noticed a Russian soldier laughingly patting a Frenchman on the shoulder, saying something to him in a friendly manner, and Kutúzov with the same expression on his face again swayed his head.

"What were you saying?" he asked the general, who continuing his report directed the commander-in-chief's attention to some standards captured from the French and standing in front of the Preobrazhénsk regiment.

"Ah, the standards!" said Kutúzov, evidently detaching himself with difficulty from the thoughts that preoccupied him.

He looked about him absently. Thousands of eyes were looking at him from all sides awaiting a word from him.

He stopped in front of the Preobrazhénsk regiment, sighed deeply and closed his eyes. One of his suite beckoned to the soldiers carrying the standards to advance and surround the commander-in-chief with them. Kutúzov was silent for a few seconds and then, submitting with evident reluctance to the duty imposed by his position, raised his head and began to speak. A throng of officers surrounded him. He looked attentively around at the circle of officers, recognizing several of them.

"I thank you all!" he said, addressing the soldiers and then again the officers. In the stillness around him his slowly uttered words were distinctly heard. "I thank you all for your hard and faithful service. The victory is complete and Russia will not forget you! Honor to you forever."

He paused and looked around.

"Lower its head, lower it!" he said to a soldier who had accidentally lowered the French eagle he was holding before the Preobrazhénsk standards. "Lower, lower, that's it. Hurrah lads!" he added, addressing the men with a rapid movement of his chin.

"Hur-r-rah!" roared thousands of voices.

While the soldiers were shouting Kutúzov leaned forward in his saddle and bowed his head, and his eye lit up with a mild and apparently ironic gleam.

"You see, brothers . . ." said he when the shouts had ceased . . . and all at once his voice and the expression of his face changed. It was no longer the commander-in-chief speaking but an ordinary old man who wanted to tell his comrades something very important.

There was a stir among the throng of officers and in the ranks of the soldiers, who moved that they might hear better what he was going to say.

"You see, brothers, I know it's hard for you, but it can't be helped! Bear up; it won't be for long now! We'll see our visitors off and then we'll rest. The Tsar won't forget your service. It is hard for you, but still you are at home while they—you see what they have come to," said he, pointing to the prisoners. "Worse off than our poorest beggars. While they were strong we didn't spare ourselves, but now we may even pity them. They are human beings too. Isn't it so, lads?"

He looked around, and in the direct, respectful, wondering gaze fixed upon him he read sympathy with what he had said. His face grew brighter and brighter with an old man's mild smile, which drew the corners of his lips and eyes into a cluster of wrinkles. He ceased speaking and bowed his head as if in perplexity.

"But after all who asked them here? Serves them right, the b . . . b . . . ! . . ." he cried, suddenly lifting his head.

And flourishing his whip he rode off at a gallop for the first time during the whole campaign, and left the broken ranks of the soldiers laughing joyfully and shouting "hurrah!"

Kutúzov's words were hardly understood by the troops. No one could have repeated the field marshal's address, begun solemnly and then changing into an old man's simple-hearted talk; but the hearty sincerity of that speech, the feeling of majestic triumph combined with pity for the foe and consciousness of the justice of our cause, exactly expressed by that old man's good-natured expletives, was not merely understood but lay in the soul of every soldier and found expression in their joyous and long-sustained shouts. Afterward when one of the generals addressed Kutúzov asking whether he wished his calèche to be sent for, Kutúzov in answering unexpectedly gave a sob, being evidently greatly moved.

Chapter VII

When the troops reached their night's halting place on the 8th of November, the last day of the Krásnoe battles, it was already growing dusk. All day it had been calm and frosty with occasional lightly falling snow, and toward evening it began to clear. Through the falling snow a purple-black and starry sky showed itself and the frost grew keener.

An infantry regiment which had left Tarútino three thousand strong but now numbered only nine hundred, was one of the first to arrive that night at its halting place—a village on the highroad. The quartermasters who met the regiment announced that all the huts were full of sick and dead Frenchmen, cavalrymen and members of the staff. There was only one hut available for the regimental commander.

The commander rode up to his hut. The regiment passed through the village and stacked its arms in front of the last huts.

Like some huge many-limbed animal, the regiment began to prepare its lair and its food. One part of it dispersed and waded knee-deep through the snow into a birch forest to the right of the village, and immediately the sound of axes and swords, the crashing of branches, and merry voices, could be heard from there. Another section amid the regimental wagons and horses which were standing in a group, was busy getting out caldrons and rye biscuit, and feeding the horses. A third section scattered through the village arranging quarters for the staff-officers, carrying out the French corpses that were in the huts, and dragging away boards, dry wood, and thatch from the roofs, for the campfires, or wattle fences to serve for shelter.

Some fifteen men with merry shouts were shaking down the high wattle wall of a shed, the roof of which had already been removed.

"Now then, all together—shove!" cried the voices, and the huge surface of the wall, sprinkled with snow and creaking with frost, was seen swaying in the gloom of the night. The lower stakes cracked more and more and at last the wall fell, and with it the men who had been pushing it. Loud coarse laughter and joyous shouts ensued.

"Now then, catch hold in twos! Hand up the lever! That's it. . . . Where are you shoving to?"

"Now, all together! But wait a moment boys . . . With a song!"

All stood silent, and a soft, pleasant velvety voice began to sing. At the end of the third verse as the last note died away, twenty voices roared out at once: "Oo-oo-oo-oo! That's it. All together! Heave away, boys! . . ." but despite their united efforts the wattle hardly moved, and in the silence that followed the heavy breathing of the men was audible.

"Here, you of the Sixth Company! Devils that you are! Lend a hand . . . will you? You may want us one of these days."

Some twenty men of the Sixth Company who were on their way into the village joined the haulers, and the wattle wall which was about thirty-five feet long and seven feet high, moved forward along the village street, swaying, pressing upon and cutting the shoulders of the gasping men.

"Get along . . . Falling? What are you stopping for? There now. . . ."

Merry senseless words of abuse flowed freely.

"What are you up to?" suddenly came the authoritative voice of a sergeant-major who came upon the men who were hauling their burden. "There are gentry here; the general himself is in that hut, and you foul-mouthed devils, you brutes, I'll give it to you!" shouted he, hitting the first man who came in his way a swinging blow on the back. "Can't you make less noise?"

The men became silent. The soldier who had been struck groaned and wiped his face, which had been scratched till it bled by his falling against the wattle.

"There, how that devil hits out! He's made my face all bloody," said he in a frightened whisper when the sergeant-major had passed on.

"Don't you like it?" said a laughing voice, and moderating their tones the men moved forward.

When they were out of the village they began talking again as loud as before, interlarding their talk with the same aimless expletives.

In the hut which the men had passed, the chief officers had gathered and were in animated talk over their tea about the events of the day and the maneuvers suggested for tomorrow. It was proposed to make a flank march to the left, cut off the Vice-King (Murat) and capture him.

By the time the soldiers had dragged the wattle fence to its place the campfires were blazing on all sides ready for cooking, the wood crackled, the snow was melting, and black shadows of soldiers flitted to and fro all over the occupied space where the snow had been trodden down.

Axes and choppers were plied all around. Everything was done without any orders being given. Stores of wood were brought for the night, shelters were rigged up for the officers, cauldrons were being boiled, and muskets and accouterments put in order.

The wattle wall the men had brought was set up in a semicircle by the Eighth Company as a shelter from the north, propped up by musket-rests, and a campfire was built before it. They beat the tattoo, called the roll, had supper, and settled down round the fires for the night—some repairing their footgear, some smoking pipes, and some stripping themselves naked to steam the lice out of their shirts.

Chapter VIII

One would have thought that under the almost incredibly wretched conditions the Russian soldiers were in at that time—lacking warm boots and sheepskin coats, without a roof over their heads, in the snow with eighteen degrees of frost, and without even full rations (the commissariat did not always keep up with the troops)—they would have presented a very sad and depressing spectacle.

On the contrary the army had never under the best material conditions presented a more cheerful and animated aspect. This was because all who began to grow depressed or who lost strength were sifted out of the army day by day. All the physically or morally weak had long since been left behind and only the flower of the army—physically and mentally—remained.

More men collected behind the wattle fence of the Eighth Company than anywhere else. Two sergeant-majors were sitting with them and their campfires blazed brighter than the others. For leave to sit by their wattle they demanded contributions of fuel.

"Eh, Makéev! What has become of you, you son of a bitch? Are you lost or have the wolves eaten you? Fetch some more wood!" shouted a red-haired and red-faced man, screwing up his eyes and blinking because of the smoke but not moving back from the fire. "And you, Jackdaw, go and fetch some wood!" said he to another soldier.

This red-haired man was neither a sergeant nor a corporal, but being robust he ordered about those weaker than himself. The soldier they called "Jackdaw," a thin little fellow with a sharp nose, rose obediently and was about to go but at that instant there came into the light of the fire the slender, handsome figure of a young soldier carrying a load of wood.

"Bring it here—that's fine!"

They split up the wood, pressed it down on the fire, blew at it with their mouths and fanned it with the skirts of their greatcoats, making the flames hiss and crackle. The men drew nearer and lit their pipes. The handsome young soldier who had brought the wood, setting his arms akimbo began stamping his cold feet rapidly and deftly on the spot where he stood.

"Mother! The dew is cold but clear. . . . It's well that I'm a musketeer . . ." he sang, pretending to hiccough after each syllable.

"Look out, your soles will fly off!" shouted the red-haired man, noticing that the sole of the dancer's boot was hanging loose. "What a fellow you are for dancing!"

The dancer stopped, pulled off the loose piece of leather, and threw it on the fire.

"Right enough, friend," said he, and having sat down, took out of his knapsack a scrap of blue French cloth and wrapped it round his foot. "It's the steam that spoils them," he added, stretching out his feet toward the fire.

"They'll soon be issuing us new ones. They say that when we've finished hammering them, we're to receive double kits!"

"And that son of a bitch Petróv has lagged behind after all, it seems," said one sergeant-major.

"I've had an eye on him this long while," said the other.

"Well, he's a poor sort of soldier. . . ."

"But in the Third Company they say nine men were missing yesterday."

"Yes, it's all very well, but when a man's feet are frozen how can he walk?"

"Eh? Don't talk nonsense!" said a sergeant-major.

"Do you want to be doing the same?" said an old soldier, turning reproachfully to the man who had spoken of frozen feet.

"Well, you know," said the sharp-nosed man they called Jackdaw, in a squeaky and unsteady voice, raising himself at the other side of the fire, "a plump man gets thin, but for a thin one it's death.

Take me, now! I've got no strength left," he added with sudden resolution turning to the sergeant-major. "Tell them to send me to hospital; I'm aching all over! anyway I shan't be able to keep up."

"That'll do, that'll do!" replied the sergeant-major quietly.

The soldier said no more and the talk went on.

"What a lot of those Frenchies were taken today, and the fact is that not one of them had what you might call real boots on," said a soldier, starting a new theme. "They were no more than make-believes."

"The Cossacks have taken their boots. They were clearing the hut for the colonel and carried them out. It was pitiful to see them, boys," put in the dancer. "As they turned them over one seemed still alive and, would you believe it, he jabbered something in their lingo."

"But they're a clean folk, lads," the first man went on; "he was white—as white as birch-bark—and some of them are such fine fellows, you might think they were nobles."

"Well, what do you think? They make soldiers of all classes there."

"But they don't understand our talk at all," said the dancer with a puzzled smile. "I asked him whose subject he was, and he jabbered in his own way. A queer lot!"

"But it's strange, friends," continued the man who had wondered at their whiteness, "the peasants at Mozháysk were saying that when they began burying the dead—where the battle was you know—well, those dead had been lying there for nearly a month, and says the peasant, 'they lie as white as paper, clean and not as much smell as a puff of powder smoke.' "

"Was it from the cold?" asked someone.

"You're a clever fellow! From the cold indeed! Why, it was hot. If it had been from the cold, ours would not have rotted either. 'But,' he says, 'go up to ours and they are all rotten and maggoty. So,' he says, 'we tie our faces up with kerchiefs and turn our heads away as we dragged them off: we can hardly do it. But theirs,' he says, 'are white as paper and not so much smell as a whiff of gunpowder.' "

All were silent.

"It must be from their food," said the sergeant-major. "They used to gobble the same food as the gentry."

No one contradicted him.

"That peasant near Mozháysk where the battle was, said the men were all called up from ten villages around and they carted for twenty days and still didn't finish carting the dead away. And as for the wolves, he says . . ."

"That was a real battle," said an old soldier. "It's the only one worth remembering; but since that . . . it's only been tormenting folk."

"And do you know, Daddy, the day before yesterday we ran at them and, my word, they didn't let us get near before they just threw down their muskets and went on their knees. 'Pardon!' they say. That's only one case. They say Plátov took 'Poleon himself twice. But he didn't know the right charm. He catches him and catches him—no good! He turns into a bird in his hands and flies away. And there's no way of killing him either."

"You're a first-class liar, Kiselëv, when I come to look at you!"

"Liar, indeed! It's the real truth."

"If he fell into my hands, when I'd caught him I'd bury him in the ground with an aspen-stake to fix him down. What a lot of men he's ruined!"

"Well, anyhow we're going to end it. He won't come here again," remarked the old soldier yawning.

The conversation flagged, and the soldiers began settling down to sleep.

"Look at the stars. It's wonderful how they shine! You would think the women had spread out their linen," said one of the men, gazing with admiration at the Milky Way.

"That's a sign of a good harvest next year."

"We shall want some more wood."

"You warm your back and your belly gets frozen. That's queer."

"O Lord!"

"What are you pushing for? Is the fire only for you? Look how he's sprawling!"

In the silence that ensued, the snoring of those who had fallen asleep could be heard. Others turned over and warmed themselves, now and again exchanging a few words. From a campfire a hundred paces off came a sound of general, merry laughter.

"Hark at them roaring there in the Fifth Company!" said one of the soldiers, "and what a lot of them there are!"

One of the men got up and went over to the Fifth Company.

"They're having such fun," said he coming back. "Two Frenchies have turned up. One's quite frozen and the other's an awful swaggerer. He's singing songs. . . ."

"Oh, I'll go across and have a look. . . ."

And several of the men went over to the Fifth Company.

Chapter IX

THE FIFTH COMPANY WAS BIVOUACKING AT THE VERY EDGE OF THE FOREST. A HUGE CAMPFIRE was blazing brightly in the midst of the snow, lighting up the branches of trees heavy with hoarfrost.

About midnight they heard the sound of steps in the snow of the forest, and the crackling of dry branches.

"A bear, lads," said one of the men.

They all raised their heads to listen, and out of the forest into the bright firelight stepped two strangely clad human figures clinging to one another.

These were two Frenchmen who had been hiding in the forest. They came up to the fire, hoarsely uttering something in a language our soldiers did not understand. One was taller than the other; he wore an officer's hat and seemed quite exhausted. On approaching the fire he had been going to sit down, but fell. The other, a short, sturdy soldier with a shawl tied round his head, was stronger. He raised his companion and said something, pointing to his mouth. The soldiers surrounded the Frenchmen, spread a greatcoat on the ground for the sick man, and brought some buckwheat porridge and vodka for both of them.

The exhausted French officer was Ramballe and the man with his head wrapped in the shawl was Morel, his orderly.

When Morel had drunk some vodka and finished his bowl of porridge he suddenly became unnaturally merry and chattered incessantly to the soldiers, who could not understand him. Ramballe refused food and resting his head on his elbow lay silent beside the campfire, looking at the Russian soldiers with red and vacant eyes. Occasionally he emitted a long-drawn groan and then again became silent. Morel, pointing to his shoulders, tried to impress on the soldiers the fact that Ramballe was an officer and ought to be warmed. A Russian officer who had come up to the fire sent to ask his colonel whether he would not take a French officer into his hut to warm him, and when the messenger returned and said that the colonel wished the officer to be brought to him, Ramballe was told to go. He rose and tried to walk, but staggered and would have fallen had not a soldier standing by held him up.

"You won't do it again, eh?" said one of the soldiers, winking and turning mockingly to Ramballe.

"Oh, you fool! Why talk rubbish, lout that you are—a real peasant!" came rebukes from all sides addressed to the jesting soldier.

They surrounded Ramballe, lifted him on the crossed arms of two soldiers and carried him to the hut. Ramballe put his arms around their necks while they carried him and began wailing plaintively:

"Oh, you fine fellows, my kind, kind friends! These are men! Oh, my brave, kind friends," and he leaned his head against the shoulder of one of the men like a child.

Meanwhile Morel was sitting in the best place by the fire, surrounded by the soldiers.

Morel, a short sturdy Frenchman with inflamed and streaming eyes, was wearing a woman's cloak and had a shawl tied woman-fashion round his head over his cap. He was evidently tipsy, and was singing a French song in a hoarse broken voice, with an arm thrown round the nearest soldier. The soldiers simply held their sides as they watched him.

"Now then, now then, teach us how it goes! I'll soon pick it up. How is it?" said the man—a singer and a wag—whom Morel was embracing.

"Vive Henri Quatre! Vive ce roi vaillant!" sang Morel, winking. *"Ce diable à quatre . . ."*

"Vivarika! Vif-seruvaru! Sedyablyaka!" repeated the soldier, flourishing his arm and really catching the tune.

"Bravo! Ha, ha, ha!" rose their rough joyous laughter from all sides.

Morel, wrinkling up his face, laughed too.

"Well, go on, go on!"

"Qui eut le triple talent,
De boire, de battre,
Et d'être un vert gallant . . ."

"It goes smoothly, too. Well, now Zaletáev!"

"Ke . . ." Zaletáev brought out with effort: "ke-e-e-e," he drawled, laboriously pursing his lips, "le-trip-ta-la-de-bu-de-ba, e de-tra-va-ga-la!" he sang.

"Fine! Just like the Frenchie! Oh, ho ho! Do you want some more to eat?"

"Give him some porridge: it takes a long time to get filled up after starving."

They gave him some more porridge and Morel with a laugh set to work on his third bowl. All the young soldiers smiled gaily as they watched him. The older men, who thought it undignified to amuse themselves with such nonsense, continued to lie at the opposite side of the fire, but one would occasionally raise himself on an elbow and glance at Morel with a smile.

"They are men too," said one of them as he wrapped himself up in his coat. "Even wormwood grows on its own root."

"O Lord, O Lord! How starry it is! Tremendous! That means a hard frost. . . ."

They all grew silent. The stars, as if knowing that no one was looking at them, began to disport themselves in the dark sky: now flaring up, now vanishing, now trembling, they were busy whispering something gladsome and mysterious to one another.

Chapter X

THE FRENCH ARMY MELTED AWAY AT THE UNIFORM RATE OF A MATHEMATICAL PROGRESSION; AND that crossing of the Berëzina about which so much has been written, was only one intermediate stage in its destruction, and not at all the decisive episode of the campaign. If so much has been and still is written about the Berëzina, on the French side this is only because at the broken bridge across that river the calamities their army had been previously enduring were suddenly concentrated at one moment into a tragic spectacle that remained in every memory, and on the Russian side merely because in Petersburg—far from the seat of war—a plan (again one of Pfuel's) had been devised to catch Napoleon in a strategic trap at the Berëzina River. Everyone assured himself that all would happen according to plan, and therefore insisted that it was just the crossing of the Berëzina that destroyed the French army. In reality the results of the crossing were much less disastrous to the French—in guns and men lost—than Krásnoe had been, as the figures show.

The sole importance of the crossing of the Berëzina lies in the fact that it plainly and indubitably proved the fallacy of all the plans for cutting off the enemy's retreat, and the soundness of the only possible line of action—the one Kutúzov and the general mass of the army demanded—namely, simply to follow the enemy up. The French crowd fled at a continually increasing speed and all its energy was directed to reaching its goal. It fled like a wounded animal and it was impossible to block its path. This was shown not so much by the arrangements it made for crossing, as by what took place at the bridges. When the bridges broke down, unarmed soldiers, people from Moscow and women with children who were with the French transport, all—carried on by *vis inertiae*—pressed forward into boats and into the ice-covered water and did not surrender.

That impulse was reasonable. The condition of fugitives and of pursuers was equally bad. As long as they remained with their own people each might hope for help from his fellows and the definite place he held among them. But those who surrendered, while remaining in the same pitiful plight, would be on a lower level to claim a share in the necessities of life. The French did not need to be informed of the fact that half the prisoners—with whom the Russians did not know what to do—perished of cold and hunger despite their captors' desire to save them; they felt that it could not be otherwise. The most compassionate Russian commanders, those favorable to the French—and even the Frenchmen in the Russian service—could do nothing for the prisoners. The French perished from the conditions to which the Russian army was itself exposed. It was impossible to take bread and clothes from our hungry and indispensable soldiers to give to the French who though not harmful, or hated, or guilty, were simply unnecessary. Some Russians even did that, but they were exceptions.

Certain destruction lay behind the French but in front there was hope. Their ships had been burned, there was no salvation save in collective flight, and on that the whole strength of the French was concentrated.

The farther they fled the more wretched became the plight of the remnant, especially after the Berëzina, on which (in consequence of the Petersburg plan) special hopes had been placed by the Russians, and the keener grew the passions of the Russian commanders, who blamed one another and Kutúzov most of all. Anticipation that the failure of the Petersburg Berëzina plan would be attributed to Kutúzov, led to dissatisfaction, contempt and ridicule, more and more strongly expressed. The ridicule and contempt were of course expressed in a respectful form, making it impossible for him to ask wherein he was to blame. They did not talk seriously to him; when reporting to him or asking for his sanction they appeared to be fulfilling a regrettable formality, but they winked behind his back and tried to mislead him at every turn.

Because they could not understand him all these people assumed that it was useless to talk to the old man; that he would never grasp the profundity of their plans, that he would answer with his phrases (which they thought were mere phrases) about a "golden bridge," about the impossibility of crossing the frontier with a crowd of tatterdemalions, and so forth. They had heard all that before. And all he said—that it was necessary to await provisions, or that the men had no boots—was so simple, while what they proposed was so complicated and clever, that it was evident that he was old and stupid and that they, though not in power, were commanders of genius.

After the junction with the army of the brilliant admiral and Petersburg hero Wittgenstein, this mood and the gossip of the staff reached their maximum. Kutúzov saw this and merely sighed and shrugged his shoulders. Only once, after the affair of the Berëzina, did he get angry and write to Bennigsen (who reported separately to the Emperor) the following letter:

"On account of your spells of ill health, will your excellency please be so good as to set off for Kalúga on receipt of this, and there await further commands and appointments from his Imperial Majesty."

But after Bennigsen's departure, the Grand Duke Tsarévich Constantine Pávlovich joined the army. He had taken part in the beginning of the campaign but had subsequently been removed from the army by Kutúzov. Now having come to the army, he informed Kutúzov of the Emperor's displeasure at the poor success of our forces and the slowness of their advance. The Emperor intended to join the army personally in a few days' time.

The old man, experienced in court as well as in military affairs—this same Kutúzov who in August had been chosen commander-in-chief against the Sovereign's wishes and who had removed the Grand Duke and heir-apparent from the army—who on his own authority and contrary to the Emperor's will had decided on the abandonment of Moscow, now realized at once that his day was over, that his part was played, and that the power he was supposed to hold was no longer his. And he understood this not merely from the attitude of the court. He saw on the one hand that the military business in which he had played his part was ended and felt that his mission was accomplished; and at the same time he began to be conscious of the physical weariness of his aged body and of the necessity of physical rest.

On the 29th of November Kutúzov entered Vílna—his "dear Vílna" as he called it. Twice during his career Kutúzov had been Governor of Vílna. In that wealthy town, which had not been injured, he found old friends and associations, besides the comforts of life of which he had so long been deprived. And he suddenly turned from the cares of army and state and, as far as the passions that seethed around him allowed, immersed himself in the quiet life to which he had formerly been accustomed, as if all that was taking place and all that had still to be done in the realm of history did not concern him at all.

Chichagóv, one of the most zealous "cutters-off" and "breakers-up," who had first wanted to effect a diversion in Greece and then in Warsaw but never wished to go where he was sent: Chichagóv, noted for the boldness with which he spoke to the Emperor, and who considered Kutúzov to be under an obligation to him because when he was sent to make peace with Turkey in 1811 independently of Kutúzov, and found that peace had already been concluded, he admitted to the Emperor that the merit of securing that peace was really Kutúzov's; this Chichagóv was the first to meet Kutúzov at the castle where the latter was to stay. In undress naval uniform, with a dirk, and holding his cap under his arm, he handed Kutúzov a garrison-report and the keys of the town. The contemptuously respectful attitude of the younger men to the old man in his dotage was expressed in the highest degree by the behavior of Chichagóv, who knew of the accusations that were being directed against Kutúzov.

When speaking to Chichagóv, Kutúzov incidentally mentioned that the vehicles packed with china that had been captured from him at Borísov had been recovered and would be restored to him.

"You mean to imply that I have nothing to eat out of. . . . On the contrary, I can supply you with everything even if you want to give dinner parties," warmly replied Chichagóv, who tried by every word he spoke to prove his own rectitude and therefore imagined Kutúzov to be animated by the same desire.

Kutúzov, shrugging his shoulders, replied with his subtle penetrating smile: "I meant merely to say what I said."

Contrary to the Emperor's wish Kutúzov detained the greater part of the army at Vílna. Those about him said that he became extraordinarily slack and physically feeble during his stay in that town. He attended to army affairs reluctantly, left everything to his generals, and while awaiting the Emperor's arrival led a dissipated life.

Having left Petersburg on the 7th of December with his suite—Count Tolstóy, Prince Volkónski, Arakchéev, and others—the Emperor reached Vílna on the 11th, and in his traveling sleigh drove straight to the castle. In spite of the severe frost some hundred generals and staff-officers in full parade uniform stood in front of the castle, as well as a guard of honor of the Semënov regiment.

A courier who galloped to the castle in advance in a troyka with three foam-flecked horses, shouted "Coming!" and Konovnítsyn rushed into the vestibule to inform Kutúzov, who was waiting in the hall-porter's little lodge.

A minute later the old man's large stout figure in full dress uniform, his chest covered with Orders and a scarf drawn round his stomach, waddled out into the porch. He put on his hat with its peaks to the sides, and holding his gloves in his hand and walking with an effort sideways down the steps to the level of the street, took in his hand the report he had prepared for the Emperor.

There was running to and fro and whispering; another troyka flew furiously up, and then all eyes were turned on an approaching sleigh in which the figures of the Emperor and Volkónski could already be descried.

From the habit of fifty years all this had a physically agitating effect on the old general. He carefully and hastily felt himself all over, readjusted his hat, and pulling himself together drew himself up, and at the very moment when the Emperor, having alighted from the sleigh lifted his eyes to him, handed him the report and began speaking in his smooth, ingratiating voice.

The Emperor with a rapid glance scanned Kutúzov from head to foot, frowned for an instant, but immediately mastering himself went up to the old man, extended his arms and embraced him. And this embrace too, owing to a long-standing impression related to his innermost feeling, had its usual effect on Kutúzov and he gave a sob.

The Emperor greeted the officers and the Semënov guard, and again pressing the old man's hand went with him into the castle.

When alone with the field marshal the Emperor expressed his dissatisfaction at the slowness of the pursuit and at the mistakes made at Krásnoe and the Berëzina, and informed him of his intentions for a future campaign abroad. Kutúzov made no rejoinder or remark. The same submissive, expressionless look with which he had listened to the Emperor's commands on the field of Austerlitz seven years before, settled on his face now.

When Kutúzov came out of the study and with lowered head was crossing the ballroom with his heavy waddling gait, he was arrested by someone's voice saying:

"Your Serene Highness!"

Kutúzov raised his head and looked for a long while into the eyes of Count Tolstóy, who stood before him holding a silver salver on which lay a small object. Kutúzov seemed not to understand what was expected of him.

Suddenly he seemed to remember; a scarcely perceptible smile flashed across his puffy face, and bowing low and respectfully he took the object that lay on the salver. It was the Order of St. George of the First Class.

Chapter XI

NEXT DAY THE FIELD MARSHAL GAVE A DINNER AND BALL WHICH THE EMPEROR HONORED BY HIS presence. Kutúzov had received the Order of St. George of the First Class and the Emperor showed him the highest honors, but everyone knew of the Imperial dissatisfaction with him. The proprieties were observed and the Emperor was the first to set that example, but everybody understood that the old man was blameworthy and good-for-nothing. When Kutúzov, conforming to a custom of Catherine's day, ordered the standards that had been captured to be lowered at the Emperor's feet on his entering the ballroom, the Emperor made a wry face and muttered something in which some people caught the words, "the old comedian."

The Emperor's displeasure with Kutúzov was specially increased at Vílna by the fact that Kutúzov evidently could not or would not understand the importance of the coming campaign.

When on the following morning the Emperor said to the officers assembled about him: "You have not only saved Russia, you have saved Europe!" they all understood that the war was not ended.

Kutúzov alone would not see this and openly expressed his opinion that no fresh war could improve the position or add to the glory of Russia, but could only spoil and lower the glorious position that Russia had gained. He tried to prove to the Emperor the impossibility of levying fresh troops, spoke of the hardships already endured by the people, of the possibility of failure and so forth.

This being the field marshal's frame of mind he was naturally regarded as merely a hindrance and obstacle to the impending war.

To avoid unpleasant encounters with the old man, the natural method was to do what had been done with him at Austerlitz and with Barclay at the beginning of the Russian campaign—to transfer the authority to the Emperor himself, thus cutting the ground from under the commander-in-chief's feet without upsetting the old man by informing him of the change.

With this object his Staff was gradually reconstructed and its real strength removed and transferred to the Emperor. Toll, Konovnítsyn, and Ermólov received fresh appointments. Everyone spoke loudly of the field marshal's great weakness and failing health.

His health had to be bad for his place to be taken away and given to another. And in fact his health was poor.

So naturally, simply and gradually—just as he had come from Turkey to the Treasury in Petersburg to recruit the militia, and then to the army when he was needed there—now when his part was played out, Kutúzov's place was taken by a new and necessary performer.

The war 1812, besides its national significance dear to every Russian heart, was now to assume another, a European, significance.

The movement of peoples from west to east was to be succeeded by a movement of peoples from east to west, and for this fresh war another leader was necessary, having qualities and views differing from Kutúzov's and animated by different motives.

Alexander I was as necessary for the movement of the peoples from east to west and for the refixing of national frontiers as Kutúzov had been for the salvation and glory of Russia.

Kutúzov did not understand what Europe, the balance of power, or Napoleon meant. He could not understand it. For the representative of the Russian people, after the enemy had been destroyed and Russia had been liberated and raised to the summit of her glory, there was nothing left to do as a Russian. Nothing remained for the representative of the national war but to die, and Kutúzov died.

Chapter XII

As generally happens, Pierre did not feel the full effects of the physical privation and strain he had suffered as prisoner until after they were over. After his liberation he reached Orël, and on the third day there, when preparing to go to Kiev, he fell ill and was laid up for three months. He had what the doctors termed "bilious fever." But despite the fact that the doctors treated him, bled him, and gave him medicines to drink—he recovered.

Scarcely any impression was left on Pierre's mind by all that happened to him from the time of his rescue till his illness. He remembered only the dull gray weather now rainy and now snowy, internal physical distress, and pains in his feet and side. He remembered a general impression of the misfortunes and sufferings of people and of being worried by the curiosity of officers and generals who questioned him, he also remembered his difficulty in procuring a conveyance and horses, and above all he remembered his incapacity to think and feel all that time. On the day of his rescue he had seen the body of Pétya Rostóv. That same-day he had learned that Prince Andrew after surviving the battle of Borodinó for more than a month, had recently died in the Rostóvs' house at Yaroslávl, and Denísov who told him this news also mentioned Hélène's death, supposing that Pierre had heard of it long before. All this at the time seemed merely strange to Pierre: he felt he could not grasp its significance. Just then he was only anxious to get away as quickly as possible from places where people were killing one another, to some peaceful refuge where he could recover himself, rest, and think over all the strange new facts he had learned; but on reaching Orël he immediately fell ill. When he came to himself after his illness he saw in attendance on him two of his servants, Terénty and Váska, who had come from Moscow; and also his cousin the eldest princess, who had been living on his estate at Eléts and hearing of his rescue and illness had come to look after him.

It was only gradually during his convalescence that Pierre lost the impressions he had become accustomed to during the last few months and got used to the idea that no one would oblige him to go anywhere tomorrow, that no one would deprive him of his warm bed, and that he would be sure to get his dinner, tea and supper. But for a long time in his dreams he still saw himself in the conditions of captivity. In the same way little by little he came to understand the news he had been told after his rescue, about the death of Prince Andrew, the death of his wife, and the destruction of the French.

A joyous feeling of freedom—that complete inalienable freedom natural to man which he had first experienced at the first halt outside Moscow—filled Pierre's soul during his convalescence. He was surprised to find that this inner freedom which was independent of external conditions, now had as it were an additional setting of external liberty. He was alone in a strange town, without acquaintances. No one demanded anything of him or sent him anywhere. He had all he wanted: the thought of his wife which had been a continual torment to him was no longer there, since she was no more.

"Oh, how good! How splendid!" said he to himself when a cleanly-laid table was moved up to him with savory beef-tea, or when he lay down for the night on a soft clean bed, or when he remembered that the French had gone and that his wife was no more. "Oh, how good, how splendid!"

And by old habit he asked himself the question: "Well, and what then? What am I going to do?" And he immediately gave himself the answer: "Well, I shall live. Ah, how splendid!"

The very question that had formerly tormented him, the thing he had continually sought to find—the aim of life—no longer existed for him now. That search for the aim of life had not merely disappeared temporarily—he felt that it no longer existed for him and could not present itself again. And this very absence of an aim gave him the complete, joyous sense of freedom which constituted his happiness at this time.

He could not see an aim, for he now had faith—not faith in any kind of rule, or words, or ideas, but faith in an ever-living ever-manifest God. Formerly he had sought Him in aims he set himself. That search for an aim had been simply a search for God, and suddenly in his captivity he had learned not by words or reasoning but by direct feeling, what his nurse had told him long ago: that God is here and everywhere. In his captivity he had learned that in Karatáev God was greater, more infinite and unfathomable, than in the Architect of the Universe recognized by the freemasons. He felt like a man who after straining his eyes to see into the far distance finds what he sought at his very feet. All his life he had looked over the heads of the men around him, when he should have merely looked in front of him without straining his eyes.

In the past he had never been able to find that great inscrutable infinite *something.* He had only felt that it must exist somewhere and had looked for it. In everything near and comprehensible he had seen only what was limited, petty, commonplace and senseless. He had equipped himself with a mental telescope and looked into remote space, where petty worldliness hiding itself in misty distance had seemed to him great and infinite merely because it was not clearly seen. And such had European life, politics, freemasonry, philosophy and philanthropy, seemed to him. But even then, at moments of weakness as he had accounted them, his mind had penetrated to those distances and he had there seen the same pettiness, worldliness and senselessness. Now however he had learned to see the great, eternal and infinite in everything, and therefore—to see it and enjoy its contemplation—he naturally threw away the telescope through which he had till now gazed over men's heads, and gladly regarded the ever-changing, eternally great, unfathomable and infinite life around him. And the closer he looked the more tranquil and happy he became. That dreadful question, What for? which had formerly destroyed all his mental edifices, no longer existed for him. To that question, What for? a simple answer was now always ready in his soul: "Because there is a God, that God, without whose will not one hair falls from a man's head."

Chapter XIII

IN EXTERNAL WAYS PIERRE HAD HARDLY CHANGED AT ALL. IN APPEARANCE HE WAS JUST WHAT HE used to be. As before he was absent-minded and seemed occupied not with what was before his eyes but with something special of his own. The difference between his former and present self was that formerly when he did not grasp what lay before him or was said to him, he had puckered his forehead painfully as if vainly seeking to distinguish something at a distance. At present he still forgot what was said to him and still did not see what was before his eyes, but he now looked with a scarcely perceptible and seemingly ironic smile at what was before him and listened to what was said, though evidently seeing and hearing something quite different. Formerly he had appeared to be a kind-hearted but unhappy man, and so people had been inclined to avoid him. Now a smile at the joy of life always played round his lips, and sympathy for others shone in his eyes with a questioning look as to whether they were as contented as he was, and people felt pleased by his presence.

Previously he had talked a great deal, grew excited when he talked, and seldom listened; now he was seldom carried away in conversation and knew how to listen so that people readily told him their most intimate secrets.

The princess, who had never liked Pierre and had been particularly hostile to him since she had felt herself under obligations to him after the old count's death, now after staying a short time in Orël—where she had come intending to show Pierre that in spite of his ingratitude she considered it her duty to nurse him—felt to her surprise and vexation that she had become fond of him. Pierre did not in any way seek her approval, he merely studied her with interest. Formerly she had felt that he regarded her with indifference and irony, and so had shrunk into herself as she did with others and had shown him only the combative side of her nature; but now he seemed to be trying to understand the most intimate places of her heart, and mistrustfully at first but afterward gratefully, she let him see the hidden, kindly sides of her character.

The most cunning man could not have crept into her confidence more successfully, evoking memories of the best times of her youth and showing sympathy with them. Yet Pierre's cunning consisted simply in finding pleasure in drawing out the human qualities of the embittered, hard, and (in her own way) proud princess.

"Yes, he is a very, very kind man when he is not under the influence of bad people but of people such as myself," thought she.

His servants too—Terénty and Váska—in their own way noticed the change that had taken place in Pierre. They considered that he had become much "simpler." Terénty, when he had helped him undress and wished him good night, often lingered with his master's boots in his hands and clothes over his arm, to see whether he would not start a talk. And Pierre, noticing that Terénty wanted a chat, generally kept him there.

"Well, tell me . . . now, how did you get food?" he would ask.

And Terénty would begin talking of the destruction of Moscow, and of the old count, and would stand for a long time holding the clothes and talking, or sometimes listening to Pierre's stories, and then would go out into the hall with a pleasant sense of intimacy with his master and affection for him.

The doctor who attended Pierre and visited him every day, though he considered it his duty as a doctor to pose as a man whose every moment was of value to suffering humanity, would sit for hours with Pierre telling him his favorite anecdotes and his observations on the characters of his patients in general, and especially of the ladies.

"It's a pleasure to talk to a man like that; he is not like our provincials," he would say.

There were several prisoners from the French army in Orël, and the doctor brought one of them, a young Italian, to see Pierre.

This officer began visiting Pierre, and the princess used to make fun of the tenderness the Italian expressed for him.

The Italian seemed happy only when he could come to see Pierre, talk with him, tell him about his past, his life at home, and his love, and pour out to him his indignation against the French and especially against Napoleon.

"If all Russians are in the least like you, it is sacrilege to fight such a nation," he said to Pierre. "You, who have suffered so from the French, do not even feel animosity toward them."

Pierre had evoked the passionate affection of the Italian merely by evoking the best side of his nature and taking a pleasure in so doing.

During the last days of Pierre's stay in Orël his old masonic acquaintance Count Willarski, who had introduced him to the Lodge in 1807, came to see him. Willarski was married to a Russian heiress who had a large estate in Orël province, and he occupied a temporary post in the commissariat department in that town.

Hearing that Bezúkhov was in Orël, Willarski though they had never been intimate came to him with the professions of friendship and intimacy that people who meet in a desert generally express for one another. Willarski felt dull in Orël and was pleased to meet a man of his own circle and, as he supposed, of similar interests.

But to his surprise Willarski soon noticed that Pierre had lagged much behind the times, and had sunk, as he expressed it to himself, into apathy and egotism.

"You are letting yourself go, my dear fellow," he said.

But for all that Willarski found it pleasanter now than it had been formerly to be with Pierre, and came to see him every day. To Pierre as he looked at and listened to Willarski, it seemed strange to think that he had been like that himself but a short time before.

Willarski was a married man with a family, busy with his family affairs, his wife's affairs, and his official duties. He regarded all these occupations as hindrances to life, and considered that they were all contemptible because their aim was the welfare of himself and his family. Military, administrative, political and masonic interests continually absorbed his attention. And Pierre, without trying to change the other's views and without condemning him, but with the quiet joyful and amused smile now habitual to him, was interested in this strange though very familiar phenomenon.

There was a new feature in Pierre's relations with Willarski, with the princess, with the doctor, and with all the people he now met, which gained for him the general good-will. This was his acknowledgment of the impossibility of changing a man's convictions by words, and his recognition of the possibility of everyone thinking, feeling and seeing things each from his own point of view. This legitimate peculiarity of each individual which used to excite and irritate Pierre, now became a basis of the sympathy he felt for, and the interest he took in, other people. The difference, and sometimes complete contradiction, between men's opinions and their lives, and between one man and another, pleased him and drew from him an amused and gentle smile.

In practical matters Pierre unexpectedly felt within himself a center of gravity he had previously lacked. Formerly all pecuniary questions, especially requests for money to which, as an extremely wealthy man, he was very frequently exposed, produced in him a state of hopeless agitation and perplexity. "To give or not to give?" he had asked himself. "I have it and he needs it. But someone else needs it still more. Who needs it most? And perhaps they are both impostors?" In the old days he had been unable to find a way out of all these surmises and had given to all who asked as long as he had anything to give. Formerly he had been in a similar state of perplexity with regard to every question concerning his property, when one person advised one thing and another something else.

Now to his surprise he found that he no longer felt either doubt or perplexity about these questions. There was now within him a judge who by some rule unknown to him decided what should or should not be done.

He was as indifferent as heretofore to money matters, but now he felt certain of what ought and what ought not to be done. The first time he had recourse to his new judge was when a French prisoner, a colonel, came to him and after talking a great deal about his exploits, concluded by making what amounted to a demand that Pierre should give him four thousand francs to send to his wife and children. Pierre refused without the least difficulty or effort, and was afterward surprised how simple and easy had been what used to appear so insurmountably difficult. At the same time that he refused the colonel's demand he made up his mind that he must have recourse to artifice when leaving Orël, to induce the Italian officer to accept some money of which he was evidently in need. A further proof to Pierre of his own more settled outlook on practical matters was furnished by his decision with regard to his wife's debts and to the rebuilding of his houses in and near Moscow.

His head steward came to him at Orël and Pierre reckoned up with him his diminished income. The burning of Moscow had cost him, according to the head steward's calculation, about two million rubles.

To console Pierre for these losses the head steward gave him an estimate showing that despite these losses his income would not be diminished but would even be increased if he refused to pay his wife's debts which he was under no obligation to meet, and did not rebuild his Moscow house and the country house on his Moscow estate, which had cost him eighty thousand rubles a year and brought in nothing.

"Yes, of course that's true," said Pierre with a cheerful smile. "I don't need all that at all. By being ruined I have become much richer."

But in January Savélich came from Moscow and gave him an account of the state of things there, and spoke of the estimate an architect had made of the cost of rebuilding the town and country houses, speaking of this as of a settled matter. About the same time he received letters from Prince Vasíli and other Petersburg acquaintances speaking of his wife's debts. And Pierre decided that the steward's proposals which had so pleased him were wrong, and that he must go to Petersburg and settle his wife's affairs, and must rebuild in Moscow. Why this was necessary he did not know, but he knew for certain that it was necessary. His income would be reduced by three-fourths, but he felt it must be done.

Willarski was going to Moscow and they agreed to travel together.

During the whole time of his convalescence in Orël Pierre had experienced a feeling of joy, freedom, and life; but when during his journey he found himself in the open world and saw hundreds of new faces, that feeling was intensified. Throughout his journey he felt like a schoolboy on holiday. Everyone—the stage-coach driver, the post house overseers, the peasants on the roads and in the villages—had a new significance for him. The presence and remarks of Willarski who continually deplored the ignorance and poverty of Russia and its backwardness compared with Europe, only heightened Pierre's pleasure. Where Willarski saw deadness Pierre saw an extraordinary strength and vitality—the strength which in that vast space amid the snows maintained the life of this original, peculiar and unique people. He did not contradict Willarski and even seemed to agree with him—an apparent agreement being the simplest way to avoid discussions that could lead to nothing—and he smiled joyfully as he listened to him.

Chapter XIV

It would be difficult to explain why and whither ants whose heap has been destroyed are hurrying: some from the heap dragging bits of rubbish, larvae and corpses, others back to the heap, or why they jostle, overtake one another, and fight, and it would be equally difficult to explain what caused the Russians after the departure of the French to throng to the place that had formerly been Moscow. But when we watch the ants round their ruined heap, the tenacity, energy, and immense number of the delving insects prove that despite the destruction of the heap, something indestructible which though intangible is the real strength of the colony, still exists; and similarly, though in Moscow in the month of October there was no government no churches, shrines, riches or houses—it was still the Moscow it had been in August. All was destroyed, except something intangible yet powerful and indestructible.

The motives of those who thronged from all sides to Moscow after it had been cleared of the enemy were most diverse and personal, and at first for the most part savage and brutal. One motive only they all had in common: a desire to get to the place that had been called Moscow, to apply their activities there.

Within a week Moscow already had fifteen thousand inhabitants, in a fortnight twenty-five thousand, and so on. By the autumn of 1813 the number, ever increasing and increasing, exceeded what it had been in 1812.

The first Russians to enter Moscow were the Cossacks of Wintzingerode's detachment, peasants from the adjacent villages, and residents who had fled from Moscow and had been hiding in its vicinity. The Russians who entered Moscow, finding it plundered, plundered it in their turn. They continued what the French had begun. Trains of peasant carts came to Moscow to carry off to the villages what had been abandoned in the ruined houses and the streets. The Cossacks carried off what they could to their camps, and the householders seized all they could find in other houses and moved it to their own, pretending that it was their property.

But the first plunderers were followed by a second and a third contingent, and with increasing numbers plundering became more and more difficult and assumed more definite forms.

The French found Moscow abandoned but with all the organizations of regular life, with diverse branches of commerce and craftsmanship, with luxury, and governmental and religious institutions. These forms were lifeless but still existed. There were bazaars, shops, warehouses, market-stalls, granaries—for the most part still stocked with goods—and there were factories and workshops, palaces and wealthy houses filled with luxuries, hospitals, prisons, government offices, churches and cathedrals. The longer the French remained the more these forms of town life perished, until finally all was merged into one confused, lifeless scene of plunder.

The more the plundering by the French continued, the more both the wealth of Moscow and the strength of its plunderers was destroyed. But plundering by the Russians, with which the reoccupation of the city began, had an opposite effect: the longer it continued and the greater the number of people taking part in it the more rapidly was the wealth of the city and its regular life restored.

Besides the plunderers, very various people, some drawn by curiosity, some by official duties, some by self-interest—house owners, clergy, officials of all kinds, tradesmen, artisans and peasants—streamed into Moscow as blood flows to the heart.

Within a week the peasants who came with empty carts to carry off plunder were stopped by the authorities and made to cart the corpses out of the town. Other peasants, having heard of their comrades' discomfiture, came to town bringing rye, oats and hay, and beat down one another's prices to below what they had been in former days. Gangs of carpenters hoping for high pay arrived in Moscow every day, and on all sides logs were being hewn, new houses built, and old, charred ones repaired. Tradesmen began trading in booths. Cookshops and taverns were opened in partially burned houses. The clergy resumed the services in many churches that had not been burned. Donors contributed Church property that had been stolen. Government clerks set up their baize-covered tables and their pigeon-holes of documents in small rooms. The higher authorities and the police organized the distribution of goods left behind by the French. The owners of houses in which much property had been left, brought there from other houses, complained of the injustice of taking everything to the Faceted Palace in the Kremlin; others insisted that as the French had gathered things from different houses into this or that house, it would be unfair to allow its owner to keep all that was found there. They abused the police and bribed them, made out estimates at ten times their value for government stores that had perished in the fire, and demanded relief. And Count Rostopchín wrote proclamations.

Chapter XV

AT THE END OF JANUARY PIERRE WENT TO MOSCOW AND STAYED IN AN ANNEX OF HIS HOUSE which had not been burned. He called on Count Rostopchín and on some acquaintances who were back in Moscow, and he intended to leave for Petersburg two days later. Everybody was celebrating the victory, everything was bubbling with life in the ruined but reviving city. Everyone was pleased to see Pierre, everyone wished to meet him and everyone questioned him about what he had seen. Pierre felt particularly well disposed toward them all, but was now instinctively on his guard for fear of binding himself in any way. To all questions put to him—whether important or quite trifling—such as: Where would he live? Was he going to rebuild? When was he going to Petersburg and would he mind taking a parcel for someone?—he replied: "Yes, perhaps," or, "I think so," and so on.

He had heard that the Rostóvs were at Kostromá but the thought of Natásha seldom occurred to him. If it did it was only as a pleasant memory of the distant past. He felt himself not only free from social obligations but also from that feeling which, it seemed to him, he had aroused in himself.

On the third day after his arrival he heard from the Drubetskóys that Princess Mary was in Moscow. The death, sufferings and last days of Prince Andrew had often occupied Pierre's thoughts and now recurred to him with fresh vividness. Having heard at dinner that Princess Mary was in Moscow and living in her house—which had not been burned—in Vozdvízhenka Street, he drove that same evening to see her.

On his way to the house Pierre kept thinking of Prince Andrew, of their friendship, of his various meetings with him, and especially of the last one at Borodinó.

"Is it possible that he died in the bitter frame of mind he was then in? Is it possible that the meaning of life was not disclosed to him before he died?" thought Pierre. He recalled Karatáev and his death, and involuntarily began to compare these two men, so different, and yet so similar in that they had both lived and both died, and in the love he felt for both of them.

Pierre drove up to the house of the old prince in a most serious mood. The house had escaped the fire; it showed signs of damage but its general aspect was unchanged. The old footman, who met Pierre with a stern face as if wishing to make the visitor feel that the absence of the old prince had not disturbed the order of things in the house, informed him that the princess had gone to her own apartments, and that she received on Sundays.

"Announce me. Perhaps she will see me," said Pierre.

"Yes, sir," said the man. "Please step into the portrait-gallery."

A few minutes later the footman returned with Dessalles, who brought word from the princess that she would be very glad to see Pierre if he would excuse her want of ceremony and come upstairs to her apartment.

In a rather low room lit by one candle sat the princess, and with her another person dressed in black. Pierre remembered that the princess always had lady companions, but who they were and what they were like he never knew or remembered. "This must be one of her companions," he thought, glancing at the lady in the black dress.

The princess rose quickly to meet him and held out her hand.

"Yes," she said, looking at his altered face after he had kissed her hand, "so this is how we meet again. He often spoke of you even at the very last," she went on, turning her eyes from Pierre to her companion with a shyness that surprised him for an instant.

"I was so glad to hear of your safety. It was the first piece of good news we had received for a long time."

Again the princess glanced round at her companion with even more uneasiness in her manner and was about to add something, but Pierre interrupted her.

"Just imagine—I knew nothing about him!" said he. "I thought he had been killed. All I know I heard at second-hand from others. I only know that he fell in with the Rostóvs. . . . What a strange coincidence!"

Pierre spoke rapidly and with animation. He glanced once at the companion's face, saw her attentive and kindly gaze fixed on him and, as often happens when one is talking, felt somehow that this companion in the black dress was a good, kind, excellent creature who would not hinder his conversing freely with Princess Mary.

But when he mentioned the Rostóvs, Princess Mary's face expressed still greater embarrassment. She again glanced rapidly from Pierre's face to that of the lady in the black dress and said:

"Do you really not recognize her?"

Pierre looked again at the companion's pale delicate face with its black eyes and peculiar mouth, and something near to him, long forgotten and more than sweet, looked at him from those attentive eyes.

"But no, it can't be!" he thought. "This stern, thin, pale face that looks so much older! It cannot be she. It merely reminds me of her." But at that moment Princess Mary said "Natásha!" And with difficulty, effort and stress, like the opening of a door grown rusty on its hinges, a smile appeared on the face with the attentive eyes, and from that opening door came a breath of fragrance which suffused Pierre with a happiness he had long forgotten and of which he had not even been thinking—especially at that moment. It suffused him, seized him and enveloped him completely. When she smiled doubt was no longer possible, it was Natásha and he loved her.

At that moment Pierre involuntarily betrayed to her, to Princess Mary, and above all to himself, a secret of which he himself had been unaware. He flushed joyfully yet with painful distress. He tried to hide his agitation. But the more he tried to hide it the more clearly—clearer than any words could have done—did he betray to himself, to her, and to Princess Mary, that he loved her.

"No, it's only the unexpectedness of it," thought Pierre. But as soon as he tried to continue the conversation he had begun with Princess Mary he again glanced at Natásha, and a still deeper flush suffused his face and a still stronger agitation of mingled joy and fear seized his soul. He became confused in his speech and stopped in the middle of what he was saying.

Pierre had failed to notice Natásha because he did not at all expect to see her there, but he had failed to recognize her because the change in her since he last saw her was immense. She had grown thin and pale, but that was not what made her unrecognizable; she was unrecognizable at the moment he entered because on that face whose eyes had always shone with a suppressed smile of the joy of life, now when he first entered and glanced at her there was not the least shadow of a smile: only her eyes were kindly attentive and sadly interrogative.

Pierre's confusion was not reflected by any confusion on Natásha's part, but only by the pleasure that just perceptibly lit up her whole face.

Chapter XVI

SHE HAS COME TO STAY WITH ME," SAID PRINCESS MARY. "THE COUNT AND COUNTESS WILL BE here in a few days. The countess is in a dreadful state; but it was necessary for Natásha herself to see a doctor. They insisted on her coming with me."

"Yes, is there a family free from sorrow now?" said Pierre, addressing Natásha. "You know it happened the very day we were rescued. I saw him. What a delightful boy he was!"

Natásha looked at him, and by way of answer to his words her eyes widened and lit up.

"What can one say or think of as a consolation?" said Pierre. "Nothing! Why had such a splendid boy, so full of life, to die?"

"Yes, in these days it would be hard to live without faith . . ." remarked Princess Mary.

"Yes, yes, that is really true," Pierre hastily interrupted her.

"Why is it true?" Natásha asked, looking attentively into Pierre's eyes.

"How can you ask why?" said Princess Mary. "The thought alone of what awaits . . ."

Natásha without waiting for Princess Mary to finish again looked inquiringly at Pierre.

"And because," Pierre continued, "only one who believes that there is a God ruling us can bear a loss such as hers and . . . yours."

Natásha had already opened her mouth to speak but suddenly stopped. Pierre hurriedly turned away from her and again addressed Princess Mary, asking about his friend's last days.

Pierre's confusion had now almost vanished, but at the same time he felt that his freedom had also completely gone. He felt that there was now a judge of his every word and action whose judgment mattered more to him than that of all the rest of the world. As he spoke now he was considering what impression his words would make on Natásha. He did not purposely say things to please her, but whatever he was saying he regarded from her standpoint.

Princess Mary—reluctantly as is usual in such cases—began telling of the condition in which she had found Prince Andrew. But Pierre's face quivering with emotion, his questions and his eager restless expression, gradually compelled her to go into details which she feared to recall for her own sake.

"Yes, yes, and so . . . ?" Pierre kept saying as he leaned toward her with his whole body and eagerly listened to her story. "Yes, yes . . . so he grew tranquil and softened? With all his soul he had always sought one thing—to be perfectly good—so he could not be afraid of death. The faults he had—if he had any—were not of his making. So he did soften? . . . What a happy thing that he saw you again," he added, suddenly turning to Natásha and looking at her with eyes full of tears.

Natásha's face twitched. She frowned and lowered her eyes for a moment. She hesitated for an instant whether to speak or not.

"Yes, that was happiness," she then said in her quiet voice with its deep chest notes. "For me it certainly was happiness." She paused. "And he . . . he . . . he said he was wishing for it at the very moment I entered the room. . . ."

Natásha's voice broke. She blushed, pressed her clasped hands on her knees, and then controlling herself with an evident effort, lifted her head and began to speak rapidly.

"We knew nothing of it when we started from Moscow. I did not dare to ask about him. Then suddenly Sónya told me he was traveling with us. I had no idea and could not imagine what state he was in, all I wanted was to see him and be with him," she said trembling, and breathing quickly.

And not letting them interrupt her she went on to tell what she had never yet mentioned to anyone—all she had lived through during those three weeks of their journey and life at Yaroslávl.

Pierre listened to her with lips parted and eyes fixed upon her full of tears. As he listened he did not think of Prince Andrew, nor of death, nor of what she was telling. He listened to her and felt only pity for her, for what she was suffering now while she was speaking.

Princess Mary, frowning in her effort to hold back her tears, sat beside Natásha, and heard for the first time the story of those last days of her brother's and Natásha's love.

Evidently Natásha needed to tell that painful yet joyful tale.

She spoke, mingling most trifling details with the intimate secrets of her soul, and it seemed as if she could never finish. Several times she repeated the same thing twice.

Dessalles' voice was heard outside the door asking whether little Nicholas might come in to say good night.

"Well, that's all—everything," said Natásha.

She got up quickly just as Nicholas entered, almost ran to the door which was hidden by curtains, struck her head against it and rushed from the room with a moan either of pain or sorrow.

Pierre gazed at the door through which she had disappeared and did not understand why he suddenly felt all alone in the world.

Princess Mary roused him from his abstraction by drawing his attention to her nephew who had entered the room.

At that moment of emotional tenderness young Nicholas's face, which resembled his father's, affected Pierre so much that when he had kissed the boy he got up quickly, took out his handkerchief and went to the window. He wished to take leave of Princess Mary, but she would not let him go.

"No, Natásha and I sometimes don't go to sleep till after two, so please don't go. I will order supper. Go downstairs, we will come immediately."

Before Pierre left the room Princess Mary told him: "This is the first time she has talked of him like that."

Chapter XVII

PIERRE WAS SHOWN INTO THE LARGE, BRIGHTLY-LIT DINING ROOM; A FEW MINUTES LATER HE heard footsteps and Princess Mary entered with Natásha. Natásha was calm, though a severe and grave expression had again settled on her face. They all three of them now experienced that feeling of awkwardness which usually follows after a serious and heartfelt talk. It is impossible to go back to the same conversation, to talk of trifles is awkward, and yet the desire to speak is there and silence seems like affectation. They went silently to table. The footmen drew back the chairs and pushed them up again. Pierre unfolded his cold table napkin and, resolving to break the silence, looked at Natásha and at Princess Mary. They had evidently both formed the same resolution; the eyes of both shone with satisfaction and a confession that besides sorrow life also has joy.

"Do you take vodka, count?" asked Princess Mary, and those words suddenly banished the shadows of the past. "Now tell us about yourself," said she. "One hears such improbable wonders about you."

"Yes," replied Pierre with the smile of mild irony now habitual to him. "They even tell me wonders I myself never dreamed of! Mary Abrámovna invited me to her house and kept telling me what had happened, or ought to have happened, to me. Stepán Stepánych also instructed me how I ought to tell of my experiences. In general I have noticed that it is very easy to be an interesting man (I am an interesting man now); people invite me out and tell me all about myself."

Natásha smiled and was on the point of speaking.

"We have been told," Princess Mary interrupted her, "that you lost two millions in Moscow. Is that true?"

"But I am three times as rich as before," returned Pierre.

Though the position was now altered by his decision to pay his wife's debts and to rebuild his houses, Pierre still maintained that he had become three times as rich as before.

"What I have certainly gained is freedom," he began seriously, but did not continue, noticing that this theme was too egotistic.

"And are you building?"

"Yes. Savélich says I must!"

"Tell me, you did not know of the countess's death when you decided to remain in Moscow?" asked Princess Mary and immediately blushed, noticing that her question, following his mention of freedom, ascribed to his words a meaning he had perhaps not intended.

"No," answered Pierre, evidently not considering awkward the meaning Princess Mary had given to his words. "I heard of it in Orël and you cannot imagine how it shocked me. We were not an exemplary couple," he added quickly, glancing at Natásha and noticing on her face curiosity as to how he would speak of his wife, "but her death shocked me terribly. When two people quarrel they are always both in fault, and one's own guilt suddenly becomes terribly serious when the other is no longer alive. And then such a death . . . without friends and without consolation! I am very, very sorry for her," he concluded, and was pleased to notice a look of glad approval on Natásha's face.

"Yes, and so you are once more an eligible bachelor," said Princess Mary.

Pierre suddenly flushed crimson and for a long time tried not to look at Natásha. When he ventured to glance her way again her face was cold, stern, and he fancied even contemptuous.

"And did you really see and speak to Napoleon, as we have been told?" said Princess Mary.

Pierre laughed.

"No, not once! Everybody seems to imagine that being taken prisoner means being Napoleon's guest. Not only did I never see him but I heard nothing about him—I was in much lower company!"

Supper was over, and Pierre who at first declined to speak about his captivity, was gradually led on to do so.

"But it's true that you remained in Moscow to kill Napoleon?" Natásha asked with a slight smile. "I guessed it then when we met at the Súkharev Tower, do you remember?"

Pierre admitted that it was true, and from that was gradually led by Princess Mary's questions and especially by Natásha's into giving a detailed account of his adventures.

At first he spoke with the amused and mild irony now customary with him toward everybody and especially toward himself, but when he came to describe the horrors and sufferings he had witnessed he was unconsciously carried away and began speaking with the suppressed emotion of a man re-experiencing in recollection strong impressions he has lived through.

Princess Mary with a gentle smile looked now at Pierre and now at Natásha. In the whole narrative she saw only Pierre and his goodness. Natásha, leaning on her elbow, the expression of her face constantly changing with the narrative, watched Pierre with an attention that never wandered—evidently herself experiencing all that he described. Not only her look but her exclamations and the brief questions she put, showed Pierre that she understood just what he wished to convey. It was clear that she understood not only what he said but also what he wished to, but could not, express in words. The account Pierre gave of the incident with the child and the woman for protecting whom he was arrested, was this: "It was an awful sight—children abandoned, some in the flames . . . One was snatched out before my eyes . . . and there were women who had their things snatched off and their ear-rings torn out . . ." he flushed and grew confused. "Then a patrol arrived and all the men—all those who were not looting, that is—were arrested, and I among them."

"I am sure you're not telling us everything; I am sure you did something . . ." said Natásha and pausing added, "something fine?"

Pierre continued. When he spoke of the execution he wanted to pass over the horrible details, but Natásha insisted that he should not omit anything.

Pierre began to tell about Karatáev, but paused. By this time he had risen from the table and was pacing the room, Natásha following him with her eyes. Then he added:

"No, you can't understand what I learned from that illiterate man—that simple fellow."

"Yes, yes, go on!" said Natásha. "Where is he?"

"They killed him almost before my eyes."

And Pierre, his voice trembling continually, went on to tell of the last days of their retreat, of Karatáev's illness and his death.

He told of his adventures as he had never yet recalled them. He now, as it were, saw a new meaning in all he had gone through. Now that he was telling it all to Natásha he experienced that pleasure which a man has when women listen to him—not clever women who when listening either try to remember what they hear to enrich their minds and when opportunity offers to retell it, or who wish to adapt it to some thought of their own and promptly contribute their own clever comments prepared in their own little mental workshop—but the pleasure given by real women gifted with a capacity to select and absorb the very best a man shows of himself. Natásha without knowing it was all attention: she did not lose a word, no single quiver in Pierre's voice, no look, no twitch of a muscle in his face, nor a single gesture. She caught the unfinished word in its flight and took it straight into her open heart, divining the secret meaning of all Pierre's mental travail.

Princess Mary understood his story and sympathized with him, but she now saw something else that absorbed all her attention. She saw the possibility of love and happiness between Natásha and Pierre, and the first thought of this filled her heart with gladness.

It was three o'clock in the morning. The footmen came in with sad and stern faces to change the candles, but no one noticed them.

Pierre finished his story. Natásha continued to look at him intently with bright, attentive and animated eyes, as if trying to understand something more which he had perhaps left untold. Pierre in shamefaced and happy confusion glanced occasionally at her, and tried to think what to say next to introduce a fresh subject. Princess Mary was silent. It occurred to none of them that it was three o'clock and time to go to bed.

"People speak of misfortunes and sufferings," remarked Pierre, "but if at this moment I were asked: 'Would you rather be what you were before you were taken prisoner, or go through all this again?' then for heaven's sake let me again have captivity and horseflesh! We imagine that when we are thrown out of our usual ruts all is lost, but it is only then that what is new and good begins.

While there is life there is happiness. There is much, much before us. I say this to you," he added, turning to Natásha.

"Yes, yes," she said, answering something quite different. "I too should wish nothing but to relive it all from the beginning."

Pierre looked intently at her.

"Yes, and nothing more," said Natásha.

"It's not true, not true!" cried Pierre. "I am not to blame for being alive and wishing to live—nor you either."

Suddenly Natásha bent her head, covered her face with her hands and began to cry.

"What is it, Natásha?" said Princess Mary.

"Nothing, nothing." She smiled at Pierre through her tears. "Good night! It is time for bed."

Pierre rose and took his leave.

Princess Mary and Natásha met as usual in the bedroom. They talked of what Pierre had told them. Princess Mary did not express her opinion of Pierre nor did Natásha speak of him.

"Well, good night, Mary!" said Natásha. "Do you know, I am often afraid that by not speaking of him" (she meant Prince Andrew) "for fear of not doing justice to our feelings, we forget him."

Princess Mary sighed deeply and thereby acknowledged the justice of Natásha's remark, but she did not express agreement in words.

"Is it possible to forget?" said she.

"It did me so much good to tell all about it today. It was hard and painful, but good, very good!" said Natásha. "I am sure he really loved him. That is why I told him . . . Was it all right?" she added, suddenly blushing.

"To tell Pierre? Oh, yes. What a splendid man he is!" said Princess Mary.

"Do you know, Mary . . ." Natásha suddenly said with a mischievous smile such as Princess Mary had not seen on her face for a long time, "he has somehow grown so clean, smooth and fresh—as if he had just come out of a Russian bath; do you understand? Out of a moral bath. Isn't it true?"

"Yes," replied Princess Mary. "He has greatly improved."

"With a short coat and his hair cropped; just as if, well, just as if he had come straight from the bath . . . Papa used to . . ."

"I understand why *he*" (Prince Andrew) "liked no one so much as him," said Princess Mary.

"Yes, and yet he is quite different. They say men are friends when they are quite different. That must be true. Really he is quite unlike him—in everything."

"Yes, but he's wonderful."

"Well, good night," said Natásha.

And the same mischievous smile lingered for a long time on her face as if it had been forgotten there.

Chapter XVIII

IT WAS A LONG TIME BEFORE PIERRE COULD FALL ASLEEP THAT NIGHT. HE PACED UP AND DOWN HIS room, now turning his thoughts on a difficult problem and frowning, now suddenly shrugging his shoulders and wincing, and now smiling happily.

He was thinking of Prince Andrew, of Natásha, and of their love, at one moment jealous of her past, then reproaching himself for that feeling. It was already six in the morning and he still paced up and down the room.

"Well, what's to be done if it cannot be avoided? What's to be done? Evidently it has to be so," said he to himself, and hastily undressing he got into bed, happy and agitated but free from hesitation or indecision.

"Strange and impossible as such happiness seems, I must do everything that she and I may be man and wife," he told himself.

A few days previously Pierre had decided to go to Petersburg on the Friday. When he awoke on the Thursday, Savélich came to ask him about packing for the journey.

"What, to Petersburg? What is Petersburg? Who is there in Petersburg?" he asked involuntarily, though only to himself. "Oh, yes, long ago before this happened I did for some reason mean to go to Petersburg," he reflected. "Why? But perhaps I shall go. What a good fellow he is and how attentive, and how he remembers everything," he thought, looking at Savélich's old face, "and what a pleasant smile he has!"

"Well, Savélich, do you still not wish to accept your freedom?" Pierre asked him.

"What's the good of freedom to me, your excellency? We lived under the late count—the Kingdom of Heaven be his!—and we have lived under you too, without ever being wronged."

"And your children?"

"The children will live just the same. With such masters one can live."

"But what about my heirs?" said Pierre. "Supposing I suddenly marry . . . it might happen," he added with an involuntary smile.

"If I may take the liberty, your excellency, it would be a good thing."

"How easy he thinks it," thought Pierre. "He doesn't know how terrible it is and how dangerous. Too soon or too late . . . it is terrible!"

"So what are your orders? Are you starting tomorrow?" asked Savélich.

"No, I'll put it off for a bit. I'll tell you later. You must forgive the trouble I have put you to," said Pierre, and seeing Savélich smile, he thought: "But how strange it is that he should not know that now there is no Petersburg for me, and that *that* must be settled first of all! But probably he knows it well enough and is only pretending. Shall I have a talk with him and see what he thinks?" Pierre reflected. "No, another time."

At breakfast Pierre told the princess, his cousin, that he had been to see Princess Mary the day before and had there met—"Whom do you think? Natásha Rostóva!"

The princess seemed to see nothing more extraordinary in that than if he had seen Anna Semënovna.

"Do you know her?" asked Pierre.

"I have seen the princess," she replied. "I heard that they were arranging a match for her with young Rostóv. It would be a very good thing for the Rostóvs, they are said to be utterly ruined."

"No; I mean do you know Natásha Rostóva?"

"I heard about that affair of hers at the time. It was a great pity."

"No, she either doesn't understand or is pretending," thought Pierre. "Better not say anything to her either."

The princess too had prepared provisions for Pierre's journey.

"How kind they all are," thought Pierre. "What is surprising is that they should trouble about these things now when it can no longer be of interest to them. And all for me!"

On the same-day the Chief of Police came to Pierre, inviting him to send a representative to the Faceted Palace to recover things that were to be returned to their owners that day.

"And this man too," thought Pierre, looking into the face of the Chief of Police. "What a fine, good-looking officer and how kind. Fancy bothering about such trifles *now!* And they actually say he is not honest and takes bribes. What nonsense! Besides, why shouldn't he take bribes? That's the way he was brought up, and everybody does it. But what a kind, pleasant face and how he smiles as he looks at me."

Pierre went to Princess Mary's to dinner.

As he drove through the streets past the houses that had been burned down, he was surprised by the beauty of those ruins. The picturesqueness of the chimney-stacks and tumble-down walls of the burned-out quarters of the town, stretching out and concealing one another, reminded him of the Rhine and the Colosseum. The cabmen he met and their passengers, the carpenters cutting the timber for new houses with their axes, the women hawkers and the shopkeepers, all looked at him with cheerful beaming eyes that seemed to say: "Ah, there he is! Let's see what will come of it!"

At the entrance to Princess Mary's house Pierre felt doubtful whether he had really been there the night before and really seen Natásha and talked to her. "Perhaps I imagined it; perhaps I shall go in and find no one there." But he had hardly entered the room before he felt her presence with his whole being by the loss of his sense of freedom. She was in the same black dress with soft folds and her hair was done the same way as the day before, yet she was quite different. Had she been like this when he entered the day before he could not for a moment have failed to recognize her.

She was as he had known her almost as a child and later on as Prince Andrew's fiancée. A bright questioning light shone in her eyes, and on her face was a friendly and strangely roguish expression.

Pierre dined with them and would have spent the whole evening there, but Princess Mary was going to vespers and Pierre left the house with her.

Next day he came early, dined, and stayed the whole evening. Though Princess Mary and Natásha were evidently glad to see their visitor and though all Pierre's interest was now centered in that house, by the evening they had talked over everything and the conversation passed from one trivial topic to another and repeatedly broke off. He stayed so long that Princess Mary and Natásha exchanged glances, evidently wondering when he would go. Pierre noticed this but could not go. He felt uneasy and embarrassed, but sat on because he simply could not get up and take his leave.

Princess Mary foreseeing no end to this, rose first, and complaining of a headache began to say good night.

"So you are going to Petersburg tomorrow?" she asked.

"No, I am not going," Pierre replied hastily, in a surprised tone and as though offended. "Yes . . . no . . . to Petersburg? Tomorrow—but I won't say good-bye yet. I will call round in case you have any commissions for me," said he, standing before Princess Mary and turning red, but not taking his departure.

Natásha gave him her hand and went out. Princess Mary on the other hand instead of going away sank into an arm-chair, and looked sternly and intently at him with her deep, radiant eyes. The weariness she had plainly shown before had now quite passed off. With a deep and long-drawn sigh she seemed to be prepared for a lengthy talk.

When Natásha left the room Pierre's confusion and awkwardness immediately vanished and were replaced by eager excitement. He quickly moved an arm-chair toward Princess Mary.

"Yes, I wanted to tell you," said he, answering her look as if she had spoken. "Princess, help me! What am I to do? Can I hope? Princess, my dear friend, listen! I know it all. I know I am not worthy of her, I know it's impossible to speak of it now. But I want to be a brother to her. No, not that, I don't, I can't . . ."

He paused and rubbed his face and eyes with his hands.

"Well," he went on with an evident effort at self-control and coherence. "I don't know when I began to love her, but I have loved her and her alone all my life, and I love her so that I cannot imagine life without her. I cannot propose to her at present, but the thought that perhaps she might some day be my wife and that I may be missing that possibility . . . that possibility . . . is terrible.

Tell me, can I hope? Tell me what I am to do, dear princess!" he added after a pause, and touched her hand as she did not reply.

"I am thinking of what you have told me," answered Princess Mary. "This is what I will say. You are right that to speak to her of love at present . . ."

Princess Mary stopped. She was going to say that to speak of love was impossible, but she stopped because she had seen by the sudden change in Natásha two days before that she would not only not be hurt if Pierre spoke of his love, but that it was the very thing she wished for.

"To speak to her now wouldn't do," said the Princess all the same.

"But what am I to do?"

"Leave it to me," said Princess Mary. "I know . . ."

Pierre was looking into Princess Mary's eyes.

"Well? . . . Well? . . ." he said.

"I know that she loves . . . will love you," Princess Mary corrected herself.

Before her words were out, Pierre had sprung up and with a frightened expression seized Princess Mary's hand.

"What makes you think so? You think I may hope? You think . . . ?"

"Yes, I think so," said Princess Mary with a smile. "Write to her parents, and leave it to me. I will tell her when I can. I wish it to happen and my heart tells me it will."

"No, it cannot be! How happy I am! But it can't be. . . . How happy I am! No, it can't be!" Pierre kept saying as he kissed Princess Mary's hands.

"Go to Petersburg, that will be best. And I will write to you," she said.

"To Petersburg? Go there? Very well, I'll go. But I may come again tomorrow?"

Next day Pierre came to say good-bye. Natásha was less animated than she had been the day before; but that day as he looked at her Pierre sometimes felt as if he was vanishing and that neither he nor she existed any longer, that nothing existed but happiness. "Is it possible? No, it can't be," he told himself at every look, gesture and word that filled his soul with joy.

When on saying good-bye he took her thin slender hand, he could not help holding it a little longer in his own.

"Is it possible that this hand, that face, those eyes, all this treasure of feminine charm so strange to me now, is it possible that it will one day be mine forever, as familiar to me as I am to myself? . . . No, that's impossible . . . !"

"Good-bye, count," she said aloud. "I shall look forward very much to your return," she added in a whisper.

And these simple words, her look, and the expression on her face which accompanied them, formed for two months the subject of inexhaustible memories, interpretations, and happy meditations for Pierre. " 'I shall look forward very much to your return. . . . ' Yes, yes, how did she say it? Yes, 'I shall look forward very much to your return.' Oh, how happy I am! What is happening to me? How happy I am!" said Pierre to himself.

Chapter XIX

THERE WAS NOTHING IN PIERRE'S SOUL NOW AT ALL LIKE WHAT HAD TROUBLED IT DURING HIS courtship of Hélène.

He did not repeat to himself with a sickening feeling of shame the words he had spoken, or say: "Oh, why did I not say that?" and, "whatever made me say *'Je vous aime'*?" On the contrary, he now repeated in imagination every word that he or Natásha had spoken and pictured every detail of her face and smile, and did not wish to diminish or add anything, but only to repeat it again and again. There was now not a shadow of doubt in his mind as to whether what he had undertaken was right or wrong. Only one terrible doubt sometimes crossed his mind: "Wasn't it all a dream? Isn't Princess Mary mistaken? Am I not too conceited and self-confident? I believe all this—and suddenly Princess Mary will tell her, and she will be sure to smile and say: 'How strange! He must be deluding himself. Doesn't he know that he is a man, just a man, while I . . . ? I am something altogether different and higher.' "

That was the only doubt often troubling Pierre. He did not now make any plans. The happiness before him appeared so inconceivable that if only he could attain it, it would be the end of all things. Everything ended with that.

A joyful, unexpected frenzy of which he had thought himself incapable, possessed him. The whole meaning of life—not for him alone but for the whole world—seemed to him centered in his love and the possibility of being loved by her. At times everybody seemed to him to be occupied with one thing only—his future happiness. Sometimes it seemed to him that other people were all as pleased as he was himself, and merely tried to hide that pleasure by pretending to be busy with other interests. In every word and gesture he saw allusions to his happiness. He often surprised those he met by his significantly happy looks and smiles which seemed to express a secret understanding between him and them. And when he realized that people might not be aware of his happiness, he pitied them with his whole heart and felt a desire somehow to explain to them that all that occupied them was a mere frivolous trifle unworthy of attention.

When it was suggested to him that he should enter the civil service, or when the war or any general political affairs were discussed on the assumption that everybody's welfare depended on this or that issue of events, he would listen with a mild and pitying smile and surprise people by his strange comments. But at this time he saw everybody—both those who as he imagined understood the real meaning of life (that is, what he was feeling) and those unfortunates who evidently did not understand it—in the bright light of the emotion that shone within himself, and at once without any effort saw in everyone he met everything that was good and worthy of being loved.

When dealing with the affairs and papers of his dead wife, her memory aroused in him no feeling but pity that she had not known the bliss he now knew. Prince Vasíli who having obtained a new post and some fresh decorations was particularly proud at this time, seemed to him a pathetic, kindly old man much to be pitied.

Often in after-life Pierre recalled this period of blissful insanity. All the views he formed of men and circumstances at this time remained true for him always. He not only did not renounce them subsequently, but when he was in doubt or inwardly at variance, he referred to the views he had held at this time of his madness and they always proved correct.

"I may have appeared strange and queer then," he thought, "but I was not so mad as I seemed. On the contrary I was then wiser and had more insight than at any other time, and understood all that is worth understanding in life, because . . . because I was happy."

Pierre's insanity consisted in not waiting, as he used to do, to discover personal attributes which he termed "good qualities" in people before loving them; his heart was now overflowing with love, and by loving people without cause he discovered indubitable causes for loving them.

Chapter XX

After Pierre's departure that first evening, when Natásha had said to Princess Mary with a gaily mocking smile: "He looks just, yes, just as if he had come out of a Russian bath—in a short coat and with his hair cropped," something hidden and unknown to herself but irrepressible, awoke in Natásha's soul.

Everything: her face, walk, look and voice, was suddenly altered. To her own surprise a power of life and hope of happiness rose to the surface and demanded satisfaction. From that evening she seemed to have forgotten all that had happened to her. She no longer complained of her position, did not say a word about the past, and no longer feared to make happy plans for the future. She spoke little of Pierre, but when Princess Mary mentioned him a long-extinguished light once more kindled in her eyes and her lips curved with a strange smile.

The change that took place in Natásha at first surprised Princess Mary; but when she understood its meaning it grieved her. "Can she have loved my brother so little as to be able to forget him so soon?" she thought when she reflected on the change. But when she was with Natásha she was not vexed with her and did not reproach her. The reawakened power of life that had seized Natásha was so evidently irrepressible and unexpected by her, that in her presence Princess Mary felt that she had no right to reproach her even in her heart.

Natásha gave herself up so fully and frankly to this new feeling that she did not try to hide the fact that she was no longer sad, but bright and cheerful.

When Princess Mary returned to her room after her nocturnal talk with Pierre, Natásha met her on the threshold.

"He has spoken? Yes? He has spoken?" she repeated.

And a joyful yet pathetic expression which seemed to beg forgiveness for her joy, settled on Natásha's face.

"I wanted to listen at the door, but I knew you would tell me."

Understandable and touching as the look with which Natásha gazed at her seemed to Princess Mary, and sorry as she was to see her agitation, these words pained her for a moment. She remembered her brother and his love.

"But what's to be done? She can't help it," thought the princess.

And with a sad and rather stern look she told Natásha all that Pierre had said. On hearing that he was going to Petersburg Natásha was astounded.

"To Petersburg!" she repeated as if unable to understand.

But noticing the grieved expression on Princess Mary's face she guessed the reason of that sadness and suddenly began to cry.

"Mary," said she, "tell me what I should do! I am afraid of being bad. Whatever you tell me, I will do. Tell me. . . ."

"You love him?"

"Yes," whispered Natásha.

"Then why are you crying? I am happy for your sake," said Princess Mary, who because of those tears quite forgave Natásha's joy.

"It won't be just yet—some day. Think what fun it will be when I am his wife and you marry Nicholas!"

"Natásha, I have asked you not to speak of that. Let us talk about you."

They were silent awhile.

"But why go to Petersburg?" Natásha suddenly asked, and hastily replied to her own question. "But no, no, he must . . . Yes, Mary, He must. . . ."

First Epilogue

Chapter I

SEVEN YEARS HAD PASSED. THE STORM-TOSSED SEA OF EUROPEAN HISTORY HAD SUBSIDED within its shores and seemed to have become calm. But the mysterious forces that move humanity (mysterious because the laws of their motion are unknown to us) continued to operate.

Though the surface of the sea of history seemed motionless the movement of humanity went on as unceasingly as the flow of time. Various groups of people formed and dissolved, the coming formation and dissolution of kingdoms and displacement of peoples was in course of preparation.

The sea of history was not driven spasmodically from shore to shore as previously. It was seething in its depths. Historic figures were not borne by the waves from one shore to another as before. They now seemed to rotate on one spot. The historical figures at the head of armies, who formerly reflected the movement of the masses by ordering wars, campaigns and battles, now reflected the restless movement by political and diplomatic combinations, laws and treaties.

The historians call this activity of the historical figures "the reaction."

In dealing with this period they sternly condemn the historical personages who, in their opinion, caused what they describe as *the reaction*. All the well-known people of that period, from Alexander and Napoleon to Madame de Staël, Photius, Schelling, Fichte, Chateaubriand and the rest, pass before their stern judgment seat and are acquitted or condemned according to whether they conduced to *progress* or to *reaction*.

According to their accounts a reaction took place at that time in Russia also, and the chief culprit was Alexander I, the same man who according to them was the chief cause of the Liberal movement at the commencement of his reign, being the savior of Russia.

There is no one in Russian literature now, from schoolboy essayist to learned historian, who does not throw his little stone at Alexander for things he did wrong at this period of his reign.

"He ought to have acted in this way and in that way. In this case he did well and in that case badly. He behaved admirably at the beginning of his reign and during 1812, but acted badly by giving a constitution to Poland, forming the Holy Alliance, entrusting power to Arakchéev, favoring Golítsyn and mysticism, and afterward Shishkóv and Photius. He also acted badly by concerning himself with the active army and disbanding the Semënov regiment."

It would take a dozen pages to enumerate all the reproaches the historians address to him, based on their knowledge of what is good for humanity.

What do these reproaches mean?

Do not the very actions for which the historians praise Alexander I (the liberal attempts at the beginning of his reign, his struggle with Napoleon, the firmness he displayed in 1812 and the campaign of 1813) flow from the same sources—the circumstances of his birth, education and life—that made his personality what it was and from which the actions for which they blame him (the Holy Alliance, the restoration of Poland, and the reaction of 1820 and later) also flowed?

In what does the substance of those reproaches lie?

It lies in the fact that an historic character like Alexander I, standing on the highest possible pinnacle of human power with the blinding light of history focused upon him; a character exposed to those strongest of all influences: the intrigues, flattery and self-deception inseparable from power; a character who at every moment of his life felt a responsibility for all that was happening in Europe; and not a fictitious but a live character who like every man had his personal habits, passions, and impulses toward goodness, beauty and truth—that this character—though not lacking in virtue (the historians do not accuse him of that)—had not the same conception of the welfare of humanity fifty years ago as a present-day professor who from his youth upward has been occupied with learning: that is with books and lectures and with taking notes from them.

But even if we assume that fifty years ago Alexander I was mistaken in his view of what was good for the people, we must inevitably assume that the historian who judges Alexander will also after the lapse of some time turn out to be mistaken in his view of what is good for humanity. This assumption is all the more natural and inevitable because, watching the movement of history, we see that every year and with each new writer, opinion as to what is good for mankind changes; so that what once seemed good, ten years later seems bad, and vice versa. And what is more, we find at one and the same time quite contradictory views as to what is bad and what is good in history: some people regard giving a constitution to Poland and forming the Holy Alliance as praiseworthy in Alexander, while others regard it as blameworthy.

The activity of Alexander or of Napoleon cannot be called useful or harmful, for it is impossible to say for what it was useful or harmful. If that activity displeases somebody, this is only because it does not agree with his limited understanding of what is good. Whether the preservation of my father's house in Moscow, or the glory of the Russian arms, or the prosperity of the Petersburg and other Universities, or the freedom of Poland or the greatness of Russia, or the balance of power in Europe, or a certain kind of European culture called "progress," appear to me to be good or bad, I must admit that besides these things the action of every historic character has other more general purposes inaccessible to me.

But let us assume that what is called science can harmonize all contradictions and possesses an unchanging standard of good and bad by which to try historic characters and events; let us say that Alexander could have done everything differently; let us say that with guidance from those who blame him and who profess to know the ultimate aim of the movement of humanity, he might have arranged matters according to the program his present accusers would have given him—of nationality, freedom, equality and progress (these I think cover the ground). Let us assume that this program was possible and had then been formulated, and that Alexander had acted on it. What would then have become of the activity of all those who opposed the tendency that then prevailed in the government—an activity that in the opinion of the historians was good and beneficent? Their activity would not have existed: there would have been no life, there would have been nothing.

If we admit that human life can be ruled by reason, the possibility of life is destroyed.

Chapter II

If we assume as the historians do that great men lead humanity to the attainment of certain ends—the greatness of Russia or of France, the balance of power in Europe, the diffusion of the ideas of the Revolution, general progress, or anything else—then it is impossible to explain the facts of history without introducing the conceptions of *chance* and *genius.*

If the aim of the European wars at the beginning of the nineteenth century had been the aggrandizement of Russia, that aim might have been accomplished without all the preceding wars and without the invasion. If the aim was the aggrandizement of France, that might have been attained without the Revolution and without the Empire. If the aim was the dissemination of ideas, the printing-press could have accomplished that much better than warfare. If the aim was the progress of civilization, it is easy to see that there are other ways of diffusing civilization more expedient than by the destruction of wealth and of human lives.

Why did it happen in this and not in some other way?

Because it happened so! "*Chance* created the situation; *genius* utilized it," says history.

But what is *chance?* What is *genius?*

The words *chance* and *genius* do not denote any really existing thing and therefore cannot be defined. Those words only denote a certain stage of understanding of phenomena. I do not know why a certain event occurs; I think that I cannot know it; so I do not try to know it and I talk about *chance*. I see a force producing effects beyond the scope of ordinary human agencies; I do not understand why this occurs and I talk of *genius*.

To a herd of rams, the ram the herdsman drives each evening into a special enclosure to feed and that becomes twice as fat as the others, must seem to be a genius. And it must appear an astonishing conjunction of genius with a whole series of extraordinary chances that this ram, who instead of getting into the general fold every evening goes into a special enclosure where there are oats—that this very ram, swelling with fat, is killed for meat.

But the rams need only cease to suppose that all that happens to them happens solely for the attainment of their sheepish aims, they need only admit that what happens to them may also have purposes beyond their ken, and they will at once perceive a unity and coherence in what happened to the ram that was fattened. Even if they do not know for what purpose they are fattened, they will at least know that all that happened to the ram did not happen accidentally, and will no longer need the conceptions of *chance* or *genius*.

Only by renouncing our claim to discern a purpose immediately intelligible to us, and admitting the ultimate purpose to be beyond our ken, may we discern the sequence of experiences in the lives of historic characters and perceive the cause of the effect they produce (incommensurable with ordinary human capabilities) and then the words *chance* and *genius* become superfluous.

We need only confess that we do not know the purpose of the European convulsions and that we know only the facts—that is the murders, first in France, then in Italy, in Africa, in Prussia, in Austria, in Spain, and in Russia—and that the movements from the west to the east and from the east to the west form the essence and purpose of these events, and not only shall we have no need to see exceptional ability and genius in Napoleon and Alexander, but we shall be unable to consider them to be anything but like other men, and we shall not be obliged to have recourse to *chance* for an explanation of those small events which made these people what they were, but it will be clear that all those small events were inevitable.

By discarding a claim to knowledge of the ultimate purpose, we shall clearly perceive that just as one cannot imagine a blossom or seed for any single plant better suited to it than those it produces, so it is impossible to imagine any two people more completely adapted down to the smallest detail for the purpose they had to fulfill, than Napoleon and Alexander with all their antecedents.

Chapter III

THE FUNDAMENTAL AND ESSENTIAL SIGNIFICANCE OF THE EUROPEAN EVENTS OF THE BEGINNING of the nineteenth century lies in the movement of the mass of the European peoples from west to east and afterward from east to west. The commencement of that movement was the movement from west to east. For the peoples of the west to be able to make their warlike movement to Moscow it was necessary: (1) that they should form themselves into a military group of a size able to endure a collision with the warlike military group of the east, (2) that they should abandon all established traditions and customs, and (3) that during their military movement they should have at their head a man who could justify to himself and to them the deceptions, robberies and murders which would have to be committed during that movement.

And beginning with the French Revolution the old inadequately large group was destroyed, as well as the old habits and traditions, and step by step a group was formed of larger dimensions with new customs and traditions, and a man was produced who would stand at the head of the coming movement and bear the responsibility for all that had to be done.

A man without convictions, without habits, without traditions, without a name, and not even a Frenchman, emerges—by what seem the strangest chances—from among all the seething French parties, and without joining any one of them, is borne forward to a prominent position.

The ignorance of his colleagues, the weakness and insignificance of his opponents, the frankness of his falsehoods and the dazzling and self-confident limitations of this man, raise him to the head of the army. The brilliant qualities of the soldiers of the army sent to Italy, his opponents' reluctance to fight and his own childish audacity and self-confidence, secure him military fame. Innumerable so-called *chances* accompany him everywhere. The disfavor into which he falls with the rulers of France turns to his advantage. His attempts to avoid his predestined path are unsuccessful: he is not received into the Russian service, and the appointment he seeks in Turkey comes to nothing. During the war in Italy he is several times on the verge of destruction and each time is saved in an unexpected manner. Owing to various diplomatic considerations the Russian armies—just those which might have destroyed his prestige—do not appear upon the scene till he is no longer there.

On his return from Italy he finds the government in Paris in a process of dissolution in which all those who are in it are inevitably wiped out and destroyed. And by chance an escape from this dangerous position presents itself in the form of an aimless and senseless expedition to Africa. Again so-called *chance* accompanies him. Impregnable Malta surrenders without a shot; his most reckless schemes are crowned with success. The enemy's fleet which subsequently did not let a single boat pass, allows his entire army to elude it. In Africa a whole series of outrages are committed against the almost unarmed inhabitants. And the men who commit these crimes, especially their leader, assure themselves that this is admirable, this is glory—it resembles Caesar and Alexander the Great and is therefore good.

This ideal of *glory* and *grandeur*—which consists not merely in considering nothing wrong that one does but in priding oneself on every crime one commits, ascribing to it an incomprehensible supernatural significance—that ideal, destined to guide this man and his associates, had scope for its development in Africa. Whatever he does succeeds. The plague does not touch him. The cruelty of murdering prisoners is not imputed to him as a fault. His childishly rash, uncalled for and ignoble departure from Africa, leaving his comrades in distress, is set down to his credit, and again the enemy's fleet twice lets him slip past. When, intoxicated by the crimes he has committed so successfully, he reaches Paris, the dissolution of the Republican government, which a year earlier might have ruined him, has reached its extreme limit, and his presence there now as a newcomer free from party entanglements can only serve to exalt him—and though he himself has no plan, he is quite ready for his new rôle.

He had no plan, he was afraid of everything, but the parties snatched at him and demanded his participation.

He alone—with his ideal of glory and grandeur developed in Italy and Egypt, his insane self-adulation, his boldness in crime and frankness in lying—he alone could justify what had to be done.

He is needed for the place that awaits him, and so almost apart from his will and despite his indecision, his lack of a plan and all his mistakes, he is drawn into a conspiracy that aims at seizing power and the conspiracy is crowned with success.

He is pushed into a meeting of the legislature. In alarm he wishes to flee, considering himself lost. He pretends to fall into a swoon and says senseless things that should have ruined him. But the once proud and shrewd rulers of France, feeling that their part is played out, are even more bewildered than he, and do not say the words they should have said to destroy him and retain their power.

Chance, millions of *chances,* give him power, and all men as if by agreement cooperate to confirm that power. *Chance* forms the characters of the rulers of France, who submit to him; *chance* forms the character of Paul I of Russia who recognizes his government; *chance* contrives a plot against him which not only fails to harm him but confirms his power. *Chance* puts the duc d'Enghien in his hands and unexpectedly causes him to kill him—thereby convincing the mob more forcibly than in any other way that he had the right, since he had the might. *Chance* contrives that though he directs all his efforts to prepare an expedition against England (which would inevitably have ruined him) he never carries out that intention, but unexpectedly falls upon Mack and the Austrians, who surrender without a battle. *Chance* and *genius* give him the victory at Austerlitz; and by *chance* all men, not only the French but all Europe—except England which does not take part in the events about to happen—despite their former horror and detestation of his crimes, now recognize his authority, the title he has given himself, and his ideal of grandeur and glory, which seems excellent and reasonable to them all.

As if measuring themselves and preparing for the coming movement, the western forces push toward the east several times in 1805, 1806, 1807 and 1809, gaining strength and growing. In 1811 the group of people that had formed in France unites into one group with the peoples of Central Europe. The strength of the justification of the man who stands at the head of the movement grows with the increased size of the group. During the ten-year preparatory period this man had formed relations with all the crowned heads of Europe. The discredited rulers of the world can oppose no reasonable ideal to the insensate Napoleonic ideal of *glory* and *grandeur.* One after another they hasten to display their insignificance before him. The King of Prussia sends his wife to seek the great man's mercy; the Emperor of Austria considers it a favor that this man receives a daughter the Caesars into his bed; the Pope, the guardian of all that the nations hold sacred, utilizes religion for the aggrandizement of the great man. It is not Napoleon who prepares himself for the accomplishment of his rôle, so much as all those round him who prepare him to take on himself the whole responsibility for what is happening and has to happen. There is no step, no crime or petty fraud he commits, which in the mouths of those around him is not at once represented as a great deed. The most suitable fête the Germans can devise for him is a celebration of Jena and Auerstädt. Not only is he great, but so are his ancestors, his brothers, his stepsons, and his brothers-in-law. Everything is done to deprive him of the remains of his reason and to prepare him for his terrible part. And when he is ready so too are the forces.

The invasion pushes eastward and reaches its final goal—Moscow. That city is taken; the Russian army suffers heavier losses than the opposing armies had suffered in the former war from Austerlitz to Wagram. But suddenly instead of those *chances* and that *genius* which hitherto had so consistently led him by an uninterrupted series of successes to the predestined goal, an innumerable sequence of inverse *chances* occur—from the cold in his head at Borodinó to the sparks which set Moscow on fire, and the frosts—and instead of *genius,* stupidity and immeasurable baseness become evident.

The invaders flee, turn back, flee again, and all the chances are now not for Napoleon but always against him.

A counter-movement is then accomplished from east to west with a remarkable resemblance to the preceding movement from west to east. Attempted drives from east to west—similar to the contrary movements of 1805, 1807 and 1809—precede the great westward movement; there is the same coalescence into a group of enormous dimensions; the same adhesion of the people of Central Europe to the movement; the same hesitation midway, and the same increasing rapidity as the goal is approached.

Paris, the ultimate goal, is reached. The Napoleonic government and army are destroyed. Napoleon himself is no longer of any account; all his actions are evidently pitiful and mean, but again an inexplicable *chance* occurs. The allies detest Napoleon whom they regard as the cause of their sufferings. Deprived of power and authority, his crimes and his craft exposed, he should have appeared to them what he appeared ten years previously and one year later—an outlawed brigand.

But by some strange chance no one perceives this. His part is not yet ended. The man who ten years before and a year later was considered an outlawed brigand is sent to an island two days' sail from France, which for some reason is presented to him as his dominion, and guards are given to him and millions of money are paid him.

Chapter IV

THE FLOOD OF NATIONS BEGINS TO SUBSIDE INTO ITS NORMAL CHANNELS. THE WAVES OF THE great movement abate, and on the calm surface eddies are formed in which float the diplomatists, who imagine that they have caused the floods to abate.

But the smooth sea again suddenly becomes disturbed. The diplomatists think that their disagreements are the cause of this fresh pressure of natural forces; they anticipate war between their sovereigns; the position seems to them insoluble. But the wave they feel to be rising does not come from the quarter they expect. It rises again from the same point as before—Paris. The last backwash of the movement from the west occurs: a backwash which serves to solve the apparently insuperable diplomatic difficulties and ends the military movement of that period of history.

The man who had devastated France returns to France alone, without any conspiracy and without soldiers. Any guard might arrest him, but by strange chance no one does so and all rapturously greet the man they cursed the day before and will curse again a month later.

This man is still needed to justify the final collective act.

That act is performed.

The last rôle is played. The actor is bidden to disrobe and wash off his powder and paint: he will not be wanted any more.

And some years pass during which he plays a pitiful comedy to himself in solitude on his island, justifying his actions by intrigues and lies when the justification is no longer needed, and displaying to the whole world what it was that people had mistaken for strength as long as an unseen hand directed his actions.

The manager having brought the drama to a close and stripped the actor, shows him to us.

"See what you believed in! This is he! Do you now see that it was not he, but I who moved you?"

But dazed by the force of the movement, it was long before people understood this.

Still greater coherence and inevitability is seen in the life of Alexander I, the man who stood at the head of the counter-movement from east to west.

What was needed for him who, overshadowing others, stood at the head of that movement from east to west?

What was needed was a sense of justice and a sympathy with European affairs, but a remote sympathy not dulled by petty interests; a moral superiority over those sovereigns of the day who cooperated with him; a mild and attractive personality; and a personal grievance against Napoleon. And all this was found in Alexander I; all this had been prepared by innumerable so-called *chances* in his life: his education, his early liberalism, the advisers who surrounded him, and by Austerlitz, and Tilsit, and Erfurt.

During the national war he was inactive because he was not needed. But as soon as the necessity for a general European war presented itself he appeared in his place at the given moment and, uniting the nations of Europe, led them to the goal.

The goal is reached. After the final war of 1815 Alexander possesses all possible power. How does he use it?

Alexander I—the pacifier of Europe, the man who from his early years had striven only for his people's welfare, the originator of the liberal innovations in his fatherland—now that he seemed to possess the utmost power and therefore to have the possibility of bringing about the welfare of his peoples—at the time when Napoleon in exile was drawing up childish and mendacious plans of how he would have made mankind happy had he retained power—Alexander I, having fulfilled his mission and feeling the hand of God upon him, suddenly recognizes the insignificance of that supposed power, turns away from it, and gives it into the hands of contemptible men whom he despises, saying only:

"Not unto us, not unto us, but unto Thy Name! . . . I too am a man like the rest of you. Let me live like a man and think of my soul and of God."

As the sun and each atom of ether is a sphere complete in itself, and yet at the same time only a part of a whole too immense for man to comprehend, so each individual has within himself his own aims and yet has them to serve a general purpose incomprehensible to man.

A bee settling on a flower has stung a child. And the child is afraid of bees and declares that bees exist to sting people. A poet admires the bee sucking from the chalice of a flower and says it exists to suck the fragrance of flowers. A beekeeper, seeing the bee collect pollen from flowers and carry it to the hive, says that it exists to gather honey. Another beekeeper who has studied the life of the hive more closely, says that the bee gathers pollen-dust to feed the young bees and rear a queen, and that it exists to perpetuate its race. A botanist notices that the bee flying with the pollen of a male flower to a pistil fertilizes the latter, and sees in this the purpose of the bee's existence. Another, observing the migration of plants, notices that the bee helps in this work, and may say that in this lies the purpose of the bee. But the ultimate purpose of the bee is not exhausted by the first, the second, or any of the processes the human mind can discern. The higher the human intellect rises in the discovery of these purposes, the more obvious it becomes that the ultimate purpose is beyond our comprehension.

All that is accessible to man, is the relation of the life of the bee to other manifestations of life. And so it is with the purpose of historic characters and nations.

Chapter V

NATÁSHA'S WEDDING TO BEZÚKHOV, WHICH TOOK PLACE IN 1813, WAS THE LAST HAPPY EVENT IN the family of the old Rostóvs. Count Ilyá Rostóv died that same year and, as always happens, after the father's death the family group broke up.

The events of the previous year: the burning of Moscow and the flight from it, the death of Prince Andrew, Natásha's despair, Pétya's death, and the old countess's grief, fell blow after blow on the old count's head. He seemed to be unable to understand the meaning of all these events, and bowed his old head in a spiritual sense as if expecting and inviting further blows which would finish him. He seemed now frightened and distraught and now unnaturally animated and enterprising.

The arrangements for Natásha's marriage occupied him for a while. He ordered dinners and suppers and obviously tried to appear cheerful, but his cheerfulness was not infectious as it used to be: on the contrary it evoked the compassion of those who knew and liked him.

When Pierre and his wife had left, he grew very quiet and began to complain of depression. A few days later he fell ill and took to his bed. He realized from the first that he would not get up again, despite the doctor's encouragement. The countess passed a fortnight in an arm-chair by his pillow without undressing. Every time she gave him his medicine he sobbed, and silently kissed her hand. On his last day, sobbing, he asked her and his absent son to forgive him for having dissipated their property—that being the chief fault of which he was conscious. After receiving communion and unction he quietly died; and next day a throng of acquaintances who came to pay their last respects to the deceased filled the house rented by the Rostóvs. All these acquaintances, who had so often dined and danced at his house and had so often laughed at him, now said, with a common feeling of self-reproach and emotion, as if justifying themselves: "Well, whatever he may have been he was a most worthy man. You don't meet such men nowadays. . . . And which of us has not weaknesses of his own?"

It was just when the count's affairs had become so involved that it was impossible to say what would happen if he lived another year, that he unexpectedly died.

Nicholas was with the Russian army in Paris when the news of his father's death reached him. He at once resigned his commission, and without waiting for it to be accepted took leave of absence and went to Moscow. The state of the count's affairs became quite obvious a month after his death, surprising everyone by the immense total of small debts the existence of which no one had suspected. The debts amounted to double the value of the property.

Friends and relations advised Nicholas to decline the inheritance. But he regarded such a refusal as a slur on his father's memory, which he held sacred, and therefore would not hear of refusing and accepted the inheritance together with the obligation to pay the debts.

The creditors who had so long been silent, restrained by a vague but powerful influence exerted on them while he lived by the count's careless good nature, all proceeded to enforce their claims at once. As always happens in such cases rivalry sprang up as to which should get paid first, and those who like Mítenka held promissory notes given them as presents, now became the most exacting of the creditors. Nicholas was allowed no respite and no peace, and those who had seemed to pity the old man—the cause of their losses (if they were losses)—now remorselessly pursued the young heir who had voluntarily undertaken the debts and was obviously not guilty of contracting them.

Not one of the plans Nicholas tried succeeded; the estate was sold by auction for half its value, and half the debts still remained unpaid. Nicholas accepted thirty thousand rubles offered him by his brother-in-law Bezúkhov to pay off debts he regarded as genuinely due for value received. And to avoid being imprisoned for the remainder, as the creditors threatened, he re-entered the government service.

He could not rejoin the army where he would have been made colonel at the next vacancy, for his mother now clung to him as her one hold on life; and so despite his reluctance to remain in Moscow among people who had known him before, and despite his abhorrence of the civil service, he accepted a post in Moscow in that service, doffed the uniform of which he was so fond and moved with his mother and Sónya to a small house on the Sívtsev Vrazhëk.

Natásha and Pierre were living in Petersburg at the time and had no clear idea of Nicholas's circumstances. Having borrowed money from his brother-in-law, Nicholas tried to hide his wretched condition from him. His position was the more difficult because with his salary of twelve hundred rubles he had not only to keep himself, his mother and Sónya, but had to shield his mother from knowledge of their poverty. The countess could not conceive of life without the luxurious conditions she had been used to from childhood and, unable to realize how hard it was for her son, kept demanding now a carriage (which they did not keep) to send for a friend, now some expensive article of food for herself, or wine for her son, or money to buy a present as a surprise for Natásha or Sónya, or for Nicholas himself.

Sónya kept house, attended on her aunt, read to her, put up with her whims and secret ill-will, and helped Nicholas to conceal their poverty from the old countess. Nicholas felt himself irredeemably indebted to Sónya for all she was doing for his mother, and greatly admired her patience and devotion, but tried to keep aloof from her.

He seemed in his heart to reproach her for being too perfect, and because there was nothing to reproach her with. She had all that people are valued for, but little that could have made him love her. He felt that the more he valued her the less he loved her. He had taken her at her word when she wrote giving him his freedom, and now behaved as if all that had passed between them had been long forgotten and could never in any case be renewed.

Nicholas's position became worse and worse. The idea of putting something aside out of his salary proved a dream. Not only did he not save anything, but to comply with his mother's demands he even incurred some small debts. He could see no way out of this situation. The idea of marrying some rich woman, which was suggested to him by his female relations, was repugnant to him. The other way out—his mother's death—never entered his head. He wished for nothing and hoped for nothing, and deep in his heart experienced a gloomy and stern satisfaction in an uncomplaining endurance of his position. He tried to avoid his old acquaintances with their commiseration and offensive offers of assistance; he avoided all distraction and recreation, and even at home did nothing but play cards with his mother, pace silently up and down the room, and smoke one pipe after another. He seemed carefully to cherish within himself the gloomy mood which alone enabled him to endure his position.

Chapter VI

AT THE BEGINNING OF WINTER PRINCESS MARY CAME TO MOSCOW. FROM REPORTS CURRENT IN town she learned how the Rostóvs were situated, and how "the son has sacrificed himself for his mother," as people were saying.

"I never expected anything else of him," said Princess Mary to herself, feeling a joyous sense of her love for him. Remembering her friendly relations with all the Rostóvs which had made her almost a member of the family, she thought it her duty to go to see them. But remembering her relations with Nicholas in Vorónezh she was shy about doing so. Making a great effort she did however go to call on them a few weeks after her arrival in Moscow.

Nicholas was the first to meet her, as the countess's room could only be reached through his. But instead of being greeted with pleasure as she had expected, at his first glance at her his face assumed a cold, stiff, proud expression she had not seen on it before. He inquired about her health, led the way to his mother, and having sat there for five minutes left the room.

When the princess came out of the countess's room Nicholas met her again, and with marked solemnity and stiffness accompanied her to the anteroom. To her remarks about his mother's health he made no reply. "What's that to you? Leave me in peace," his looks seemed to say.

"Why does she come prowling here? What does she want? I can't bear these ladies and all these civilities!" said he aloud in Sónya's presence, evidently unable to repress his vexation, after the princess's carriage had disappeared.

"O Nicholas, how can you talk like that?" cried Sónya, hardly able to conceal her delight. "She is so kind and Mamma is so fond of her!"

Nicholas did not reply and tried to avoid speaking of the princess any more. But after her visit the old countess spoke of her several times a day.

She sang her praises, insisted that her son must call on her, expressed a wish to see her often, but yet always became ill-humored when she began to talk about her.

Nicholas tried to keep silence when his mother spoke of the princess, but his silence irritated her.

"She is a very admirable and excellent young woman," said she, "and you must go and call on her. You would at least be seeing somebody, and I think it must be dull for you only seeing us."

"But I don't in the least want to, Mamma."

"You used to want to, and now you don't. Really I don't understand you, my dear. One day you are dull, and the next you refuse to see anyone."

"But I never said I was dull."

"Why, you said yourself you don't want even to see her. She is a very admirable young woman and you always liked her, but now suddenly you have got some notion or other in your head. You hide everything from me."

"Not at all, Mamma."

"If I were asking you to do something disagreeable now—but I only ask you to return a call. One would think mere politeness required it. . . . Well, I have asked you, and now I won't interfere any more since you have secrets from your mother."

"Well, then, I'll go if you wish it."

"It doesn't matter to me. I only wish it for your sake."

Nicholas sighed, bit his mustache, and laid out the cards for a patience, trying to divert his mother's attention to another topic.

The same conversation was repeated next day and the day after, and the day after that.

After her visit to the Rostóvs and her unexpectedly chilly reception by Nicholas, Princess Mary confessed to herself that she had been right in not wishing to be the first to call.

"I expected nothing else," she told herself, calling her pride to her aid. "I have nothing to do with him and I only wanted to see the old lady, who was always kind to me and to whom I am under many obligations."

But she could not pacify herself with these reflections; a feeling akin to remorse troubled her when she thought of her visit. Though she had firmly resolved not to call on the Rostóvs again and to forget the whole matter, she felt herself all the time in an awkward position. And when she asked herself what distressed her, she had to admit that it was her relation to Rostóv. His cold, polite manner did not express his feeling for her (she knew that) but it concealed something, and until she could discover what that something was, she felt that she could not be at ease.

One day in midwinter when sitting in the schoolroom attending to her nephew's lessons, she was informed that Rostóv had called. With a firm resolution not to betray herself and not show her agitation, she sent for Mademoiselle Bourienne and went with her to the drawing room.

Her first glance at Nicholas's face told her that he had only come to fulfill the demands of politeness, and she firmly resolved to maintain the tone in which he addressed her.

They spoke of the countess's health, of their mutual friends, of the latest war news, and when the ten minutes required by propriety had elapsed after which a visitor may rise, Nicholas got up to say good-bye.

With Mademoiselle Bourienne's help the princess had maintained the conversation very well, but at the very last moment, just when he rose, she was so tired of talking of what did not interest her, and her mind was so full of the question why she alone was granted so little happiness in life, that in a fit of absent-mindedness she sat still, her luminous eyes gazing fixedly before her, not noticing that he had risen.

Nicholas glanced at her and, wishing to appear not to notice her abstraction, made some remark to Mademoiselle Bourienne and then again looked at the princess. She still sat motionless with a look of suffering on her gentle face. He suddenly felt sorry for her and was vaguely conscious that he might be the cause of the sadness her face expressed. He wished to help her and say something pleasant, but could think of nothing to say.

"Good-bye, princess!" said he.

She started, flushed, and sighed deeply.

"Oh, I beg your pardon," she said as if waking up. "Are you going already, count? Well then, good-bye! Oh, but the cushion for the countess!"

"Wait a moment, I'll fetch it," said Mademoiselle Bourienne, and she left the room.

They both sat silent, with an occasional glance at one another.

"Yes, princess," said Nicholas at last with a sad smile, "it doesn't seem long ago since we first met at Boguchárovo, but how much water has flowed since then! In what distress we all seemed to be then, yet I would give much to bring back that time . . . but there's no bringing it back."

Princess Mary gazed intently into his eyes with her own luminous ones as he said this. She seemed to be trying to fathom the hidden meaning of his words which would explain his feeling for her.

"Yes, yes," said she, "but you have no reason to regret the past, count. As I understand your present life, I think you will always recall it with satisfaction, because the self-sacrifice that fills it now . . ."

"I cannot accept your praise," he interrupted her hurriedly. "On the contrary I continually reproach myself. . . . But this is not at all an interesting or cheerful subject."

His face again resumed its former stiff and cold expression. But the princess had caught a glimpse of the man she had known and loved, and it was to him that she now spoke.

"I thought you would allow me to tell you this," she said. "I had come so near to you . . . and to all your family, that I thought you would not consider my sympathy misplaced, but I was mistaken," and suddenly her voice trembled. "I don't know why," she continued, recovering herself, "but you used to be different, and . . ."

"There are a thousand reasons *why,*" laying special emphasis on the *why.* "Thank you, princess," he added softly. "Sometimes it is hard."

"So that's why! That's why!" a voice whispered in Princess Mary's soul. "No, it was not only that gay, kind and frank look, not only that handsome exterior, that I loved in him. I divined his noble, resolute, self-sacrificing spirit too," she said to herself. "Yes, he is poor now and I am rich. . . . Yes, that's the only reason. . . . Yes, were it not for that . . ." And remembering his former tenderness, and looking now at his kind sorrowful face, she suddenly understood the cause of his coldness.

"But why, count, why?" she almost cried, unconsciously moving closer to him. "Why? Tell me. You must tell me!"

He was silent.

"I don't understand your *why,* count," she continued, "but it's hard for me . . . I confess it. For some reason you wish to deprive me of our former friendship. And that hurts me." There were tears in her eyes and in her voice. "I have had so little happiness in life that every loss is hard for me to bear. . . . Excuse me, good-bye!" and suddenly she began to cry and was hurrying from the room.

"Princess, for God's sake!" he exclaimed, trying to stop her. "Princess!"

She turned round. For a few seconds they gazed silently into one another's eyes—and what had seemed impossible and remote suddenly became possible, inevitable and very near.

Chapter VII

IN THE WINTER OF 1813 NICHOLAS MARRIED PRINCESS MARY AND MOVED TO BALD HILLS WITH HIS wife, his mother and Sónya.

Within four years he had paid off all his remaining debts without selling any of his wife's property, and having received a small inheritance on the death of a cousin he paid his debt to Pierre as well.

In another three years, by 1820, he had so managed his affairs that he was able to buy a small estate adjoining Bald Hills, and was negotiating to buy back Otrádnoe—that being his pet dream.

Having started farming from necessity, he soon grew so devoted to it that it became his favorite and almost his sole occupation. Nicholas was a plain farmer: he did not like innovations, especially the English ones then coming into vogue. He laughed at theoretical treatises on estate management, disliked factories, the raising of expensive products and the buying of expensive seed corn, and did not make a hobby of any particular part of the work on his estate. He always had before his mind's eye *the estate* as a whole and not any particular part of it. The chief thing in his eyes was not the nitrogen in the soil, nor the oxygen in the air, nor manures, nor special plows, but that most important agent by which nitrogen, oxygen, manure and plow were made effective—the peasant laborer. When Nicholas first began farming and began to understand its different branches, it was the serf who especially attracted his attention. The peasant seemed to him not merely a tool, but also a judge of farming and an end in himself. At first he watched the serfs, trying to understand their aims and what they considered good and bad, and only pretended to direct them and give orders while in reality learning from them their methods, their manner of speech, and their judgment of what was good and bad. Only when he had understood the peasants' tastes and aspirations, had learned to talk their language, to grasp the hidden meaning of their words and felt akin to them, did he begin boldly to manage his serfs, that is, to perform toward them the duties demanded of him. And Nicholas's management produced very brilliant results.

Guided by some gift of insight, on taking up the management of the estates he at once unerringly appointed as bailiff, village Elder, and delegate, the very men the serfs would themselves have chosen had they had the right to choose, and these posts never changed hands. Before analyzing the properties of manure, before entering into the *debit* and *credit* (as he ironically called it) he found out how many cattle the peasants had, and increased the number by all possible means. He kept the peasant families together in the largest groups possible, not allowing the family groups to divide into separate households. He was hard alike on the lazy, the depraved, and the weak, and tried to get them expelled from the Commune.

He was as careful of the sowing and reaping of the peasants' hay and corn as of his own, and few landowners had their crops sown and harvested so early and so well, or got so good a return, as did Nicholas.

He disliked having anything to do with the domestic serfs—the "drones" as he called them—and everyone said he spoiled them by his laxity. When a decision had to be taken regarding a domestic serf, especially if one had to be punished, he always felt undecided and consulted everybody in the house; but when it was possible to have a domestic serf conscripted instead of a land worker he did so without the least hesitation. He never felt any hesitation in dealing with the peasants. He knew that his every decision would be approved by them all with very few exceptions.

He did not allow himself either to be hard on or punish a man, or to make things easy for or reward anyone, merely because he felt inclined to do so. He could not have said by what standard he judged what he should or should not do, but the standard was quite firm and definite in his own mind.

Often, speaking with vexation of some failure or irregularity, he would say: "What can one do with our Russian peasants?" and imagined that he could not bear them.

Yet he loved "our Russian peasants" and their way of life with his whole soul, and for that very reason had understood and assimilated the one way and manner of farming which produced good results.

Countess Mary was jealous of this passion of her husband's, and regretted that she could not share it; but she could not understand the joys and vexations he derived from that world, to her so remote and alien. She could not understand why he was so particularly animated and happy when, after getting up at daybreak and spending the whole morning in the fields or on the threshing floor, he returned from the sowing or mowing or reaping to have tea with her. She did not understand why he spoke with such admiration and delight of the farming of the thrifty and well-to-do peasant Matthew Ermíshin, who with his family had carted corn all night; or of the fact that his (Nicholas') sheaves were already stacked before anyone else had his harvest in. She did not understand why he stepped out from the window to the veranda and smiled under his mustache and winked so joyfully, when warm steady rain began to fall on the dry and thirsty shoots of the young oats, or why when the wind carried away a threatening cloud during the hay harvest he would return from the barn, flushed, sunburned, and perspiring, with a smell of wormwood and gentian in his hair and, gleefully rubbing his hands, would say: "Well, one more day and my grain and the peasants' will all be under cover."

Still less did she understand why he, kind-hearted and always ready to anticipate her wishes, should become almost desperate when she brought him a petition from some peasant man or woman who had appealed to her to be excused some work; why he, that kind Nicholas, should obstinately refuse her, angrily asking her not to interfere in what was not her business. She felt he had a world apart, which he loved passionately and which had laws she had not fathomed.

Sometimes when, trying to understand him, she spoke of the good work he was doing for his serfs, he would be vexed and reply: "Not in the least; it never entered my head and I wouldn't do *that* for their good! That's all poetry and old wives' talk—all that doing good to one's neighbor! What I want is that our children should not have to go begging. I must put our affairs in order while I am alive, that's all. And to do that, order and strictness are essential. . . . That's all about it!" said he, clenching his vigorous fist. "And fairness, of course," he added, "for if the peasant is naked and hungry and has only one miserable horse, he can do no good either for himself or for me."

And all Nicholas did was fruitful—probably just because he refused to allow himself to think that he was doing good to others for virtue's sake. His means increased rapidly; serfs from neighboring estates came to beg him to buy them, and long after his death the memory of his administration was devoutly preserved among the serfs. "He was a master . . . the peasants' affairs first and then his own. Of course he was not to be trifled with either—in a word, he was a real master!"

Chapter VIII

One matter connected with his management sometimes worried Nicholas, and that was his quick temper together with his old hussar habit of making free use of his fists. At first he saw nothing reprehensible in this, but in the second year of his marriage his view of that form of punishment suddenly changed.

Once in summer he had sent for the village Elder from Boguchárovo, a man who had succeeded to the post when Dron died and who was accused of dishonesty and various irregularities. Nicholas went out into the porch to question him, and immediately after the Elder had given a few replies the sound of cries and blows were heard. On returning to lunch Nicholas went up to his wife, who sat with her head bent low over her embroidery frame, and as usual began to tell her what he had been doing that morning. Among other things he spoke of the Boguchárovo Elder. Countess Mary turned red and then pale, but continued to sit with head bowed and lips compressed and gave her husband no reply.

"Such an insolent scoundrel!" he cried, growing hot again at the mere recollection of him. "If he had told me he was drunk and did not see . . . But what is the matter with you, Mary?" he suddenly asked.

Countess Mary raised her head and tried to speak, but hastily looked down again and her lips puckered.

"Why, whatever is the matter, my dearest?"

The looks of the plain Countess Mary always improved when she was in tears. She never cried from pain or vexation, but always from sorrow or pity, and when she wept her radiant eyes acquired an irresistible charm.

The moment Nicholas took her hand she could no longer restrain herself and began to cry.

"Nicholas, I saw it . . . he was to blame, but why do you . . . Nicholas!" and she covered her face with her hands.

Nicholas said nothing. He flushed crimson, left her side, and paced up and down the room. He understood what she was weeping about, but could not in his heart at once agree with her that what he had regarded from childhood as quite an everyday event was wrong. "Is it just sentimentality, old wives' tales, or is she right?" he asked himself. Before he had solved that point he glanced again at her face filled with love and pain, and he suddenly realized that she was right and that he had long been sinning against himself.

"Mary," he said softly, going up to her, "it will never happen again; I give you my word. Never," he repeated in a trembling voice like a boy asking for forgiveness.

The tears flowed faster still from the countess's eyes. She took his hand and kissed it.

"Nicholas, when did you break your cameo?" she asked to change the subject, looking at his finger on which he wore a ring with a cameo of Laocoon's head.

"Today—it was the same affair. O Mary, don't remind me of it!" and again he flushed. "I give you my word of honor it shan't occur again, and let this always be a reminder to me," and he pointed to the broken ring.

After that, when in discussions with his village Elders or stewards the blood rushed to his face and his fists began to clench, Nicholas would turn the broken ring on his finger and would drop his eyes before the man who was making him angry. But he did forget himself once or twice within a twelvemonth, and then he would go and confess to his wife, and would again promise that this should really be the very last time.

"Mary, you must despise me!" he would say. "I deserve it."

"You should go, go away at once, if you don't feel strong enough to control yourself," she would reply sadly, trying to comfort her husband.

Among the gentry of the province Nicholas was respected but not liked. He did not concern himself with the interests of his own class, and consequently some thought him proud and others thought him stupid. The whole summer, from spring sowing to harvest, he was busy with the work on his farm. In autumn he gave himself up to hunting with the same businesslike seriousness—leaving home for a month, or even two, with his hunt. In winter he visited his other villages or spent his time reading. The books he read were chiefly historical, and on these he spent a certain sum every year. He was collecting, as he said, a serious library, and he made it a rule to read through all the books he bought. He would sit in his study with a grave air, reading—a task he first imposed upon himself as a duty, but which afterward became a habit affording him a special kind of pleasure and a consciousness of being occupied with serious matters. In winter, except for business excursions, he spent most of his time at home making himself one with his family and entering into all the details of his children's relations with their mother. The harmony between him and his wife grew closer and closer and he daily discovered fresh spiritual treasures in her.

From the time of his marriage Sónya had lived in his house. Before that, Nicholas had told his wife all that had passed between himself and Sónya, blaming himself and commending her. He had asked Princess Mary to be gentle and kind to his cousin. She thoroughly realized the wrong he had done Sónya, felt herself to blame toward her, and imagined that her wealth had influenced Nicholas's choice. She could not find fault with Sónya in any way and tried to be fond of her, but often felt ill-will toward her which she could not overcome.

Once she had a talk with her friend Natásha about Sónya and about her own injustice toward her.

"You know," said Natásha, "you have read the Gospels a great deal—there is a passage in them that just fits Sónya."

"What?" asked Countess Mary, surprised.

" 'To him that hath shall be given, and from him that hath not shall be taken away.' You remember? She is one that hath not; why, I don't know. Perhaps she lacks egotism, I don't know, but from her is taken away, and everything has been taken away. Sometimes I am dreadfully sorry for her. Formerly I very much wanted Nicholas to marry her, but I always had a sort of presentiment that it would not come off. She is a *sterile flower,* you know—like some strawberry blossoms. Sometimes I am sorry for her, and sometimes I think she doesn't feel it as you or I would."

Though Countess Mary told Natásha that those words in the Gospel must be understood differently, yet looking at Sónya she agreed with Natásha's explanation. It really seemed that Sónya did not feel her position trying, and had grown quite reconciled to her lot as a *sterile flower.* She seemed to be fond not so much of individuals as of the family as a whole. Like a cat, she had attached herself not to the people but to the home. She waited on the old countess, petted and spoiled the children, was always ready to render the small services for which she had a gift, and all this was unconsciously accepted from her with insufficient gratitude.

The country seat at Bald Hills had been rebuilt, though not on the same scale as under the old prince.

The buildings, begun under straitened circumstances, were more than simple. The immense house on the old stone foundations was of wood, plastered only inside. It had bare deal floors and was furnished with very simple hard sofas, arm-chairs, tables and chairs, made by their own serf carpenters out of their own birchwood. The house was spacious and had rooms for the house serfs and apartments for visitors. Whole families of the Rostóvs' and Bolkónskis' relations sometimes came to Bald Hills with sixteen horses and dozens of servants and stayed for months. Besides that, four times a year, on the name-days and birthdays of the hosts, as many as a hundred visitors would gather there for a day or two. The rest of the year life pursued its unbroken routine with its ordinary occupations, and its breakfasts, lunches, dinners and suppers, provided out of the produce of the estate.

Chapter IX

IT WAS THE EVE OF ST. NICHOLAS, THE 5TH OF DECEMBER 1820. NATÁSHA HAD BEEN STAYING AT HER brother's with her husband and children since early autumn. Pierre had gone to Petersburg on business of his own for three weeks as he said, but had remained there nearly seven weeks and was expected back every minute.

Besides the Bezúkhov family, Nicholas's old friend the retired General Vasíli Dmítrich Denísov was staying with the Rostóvs this 5th of December.

On the 6th, which was his name-day when the house would be full of visitors, Nicholas knew he would have to exchange his Tartar tunic for a tail-coat, and put on narrow boots with pointed toes, and drive to the new church he had built, and then receive visitors who would come to congratulate him, offer them refreshments, and talk about the elections of the nobility; but he considered himself entitled to spend the eve of that day in his usual way. He examined the bailiff's accounts of the village in Ryazán which belonged to his wife's nephew, wrote two business letters, and walked over to the granaries, cattle yards and stables before dinner. Having taken precautions against the general drunkenness to be expected on the morrow because it was a great saint's day, he returned to dinner, and without having time for a private talk with his wife sat down at the long table laid for twenty persons, at which the whole household had assembled. At that table were his mother, his mother's old lady-companion Belóva, his wife, their three children with their governess and tutor, his wife's nephew with his tutor, Sónya, Denísov, Natásha, her three children, their governess, and old Michael Ivánovich, the late prince's architect, who was living on in retirement at Bald Hills.

Countess Mary sat at the other end of the table. When her husband took his place she concluded, from the rapid manner in which after taking up his table napkin he pushed back the tumbler and wine glass standing before him, that he was out of humor, as was sometimes the case when he came in to dinner straight from the farm—especially before the soup. Countess Mary well knew that mood of his, and when she herself was in a good frame of mind quietly waited till he had had his soup and then began to talk to him and make him admit that there was no cause for his ill-humor. But today she quite forgot that, and was hurt that he should be angry with her without any reason, and she felt unhappy. She asked him where he had been. He replied. She again inquired whether everything was going well on the farm. Her unnatural tone made him wince unpleasantly and he replied hastily.

"Then I'm not mistaken," thought Countess Mary. "Why is he cross with me?" She concluded from his tone that he was vexed with her and wished to end the conversation. She knew her remarks sounded unnatural, but could not refrain from asking some more questions.

Thanks to Denísov the conversation at table soon became general and lively, and she did not talk to her husband. When they left the table and went as usual to thank the old countess, Countess Mary held out her hand and kissed her husband, and asked him why he was angry with her.

"You always have such strange fancies! I didn't even think of being angry," he replied.

But the word *always* seemed to her to imply: "Yes, I am angry but I won't tell you why."

Nicholas and his wife lived together so happily that even Sónya and the old countess, who felt jealous and would have liked them to disagree, could find nothing to reproach them with; but even they had their moments of antagonism. Occasionally, and it was always just after they had been happiest together, they suddenly had a feeling of estrangement and hostility, which occurred most frequently during Countess Mary's pregnancies, and this was such a time.

"Well, *messieurs et mesdames,*" said Nicholas loudly and with apparent cheerfulness (it seemed to Countess Mary that he did it on purpose to vex her), "I have been on my feet since six this morning. Tomorrow I shall have to suffer, so today I'll go and rest."

And without a word to his wife he went to the little sitting room and lay down on the sofa.

"That's always the way," thought Countess Mary. "He talks to everyone except me. I see . . . I see that I am repulsive to him, especially when I am in this condition." She looked down at her expanded figure and in the glass at her pale, sallow, emaciated face in which her eyes now looked larger than ever.

And everything annoyed her—Denísov's shouting and laughter, Natásha's talk, and especially a quick glance Sónya gave her.

Sónya was always the first excuse Countess Mary found for feeling irritated.

Having sat awhile with her visitors without understanding anything of what they were saying, she softly left the room and went to the nursery.

The children were playing at "going to Moscow" in a carriage made of chairs and invited her to go with them. She sat down and played with them a little, but the thought of her husband and his unreasonable crossness worried her. She got up, and walking on tiptoe with difficulty went to the small sitting room.

"Perhaps he is not asleep; I'll have an explanation with him," she said to herself. Little Andrew, her eldest boy, imitating his mother, followed her on tiptoe. She did not notice him.

"Mary, dear, I think he is asleep—he was so tired," said Sónya, meeting her in the large sitting room (it seemed to Countess Mary that she crossed her path everywhere). "Andrew may wake him."

Countess Mary looked round, saw little Andrew following her, felt that Sónya was right, and for that very reason flushed and with evident difficulty refrained from saying something harsh. She made no reply, but to avoid obeying Sónya beckoned to Andrew to follow her quietly and went to the door. Sónya went away by another door. From the room in which Nicholas was sleeping came the sound of his even breathing, every slightest tone of which was familiar to his wife. As she listened to it she saw before her his smooth handsome forehead, his mustache and his whole face, as she had so often seen it in the stillness of the night when he slept. Nicholas suddenly moved and cleared his throat. And at that moment little Andrew shouted from outside the door: "Papa! Mamma's standing here!" Countess Mary turned pale with fright and made signs to the boy. He grew silent, and quiet ensued for a moment, terrible to Countess Mary. She knew how Nicholas disliked being waked. Then through the door she heard Nicholas clearing his throat again and stirring, and his voice said crossly:

"I can't get a moment's peace. . . . Mary, is that you? Why did you bring him here?"

"I only came in to look and did not notice . . . forgive me. . . ."

Nicholas coughed and said no more. Countess Mary moved away from the door and took the boy back to the nursery. Five minutes later little black-eyed three-year-old Natásha, her father's pet, having learned from her brother that Papa was asleep and Mamma was in the sitting room, ran to her father unobserved by her mother. The dark-eyed little girl boldly opened the creaking door, went up to the sofa with energetic steps of her sturdy little legs, and having examined the position of her father, who was asleep with his back to her, rose on tiptoe and kissed the hand which lay under his head. Nicholas turned with a tender smile on his face.

"Natásha, Natásha!" came Countess Mary's frightened whisper from the door. "Papa wants to sleep."

"No, Mamma, he doesn't want to sleep," said little Natásha with conviction. "He's laughing."

Nicholas lowered his legs, rose, and took his daughter in his arms.

"Come in, Mary," he said to his wife.

She went in and sat down by her husband.

"I did not notice him following me," she said timidly. "I just looked in."

Holding his little girl with one arm, Nicholas glanced at his wife and seeing her guilty expression, put his other arm around her and kissed her hair.

"May I kiss Mamma?" he asked Natásha.

Natásha smiled bashfully.

"Again!" she commanded, pointing with a peremptory gesture to the spot where Nicholas had placed the kiss.

"I don't know why you think I am cross," said Nicholas, replying to the question he knew was in his wife's mind.

"You have no idea how unhappy, how lonely, I feel when you are like that. It always seems to me . . ."

"Mary, don't talk nonsense. You ought to be ashamed of yourself!" he said gaily.

"It seems to be that you can't love me, that I am so plain . . . always . . . and now . . . in this cond . . ."

"Oh, how absurd you are! It is not beauty that endears, it's love that makes us see beauty. It is only Malvínas and women of that kind who are loved for their beauty. But do I love my wife? I don't love her, but . . . I don't know how to put it. Without you, or when something comes between us like this, I seem lost and can't do anything. Now do I love my finger? I don't love it, but just try to cut it off!"

"I'm not like that myself, but I understand. So you're not angry with me?"

"Awfully angry!" he said, smiling and getting up. And smoothing his hair he began to pace the room.

"Do you know, Mary, what I've been thinking?" he began, immediately thinking aloud in his wife's presence now that they had made it up.

He did not ask if she was ready to listen to him. He did not care. A thought had occurred to him and so it belonged to her also. And he told her of his intention to persuade Pierre to stay with them till spring.

Countess Mary listened till he had finished, made some remark, and in her turn began thinking aloud. Her thoughts were about the children.

"You can see the woman in her already," she said in French, pointing to little Natásha. "You reproach us women with being illogical. Here is our logic. I say: 'Papa wants to sleep!' but she says, 'No, he's laughing.' And she was right," said Countess Mary with a happy smile.

"Yes, yes." And Nicholas, taking his little daughter in his strong hand lifted her high, placed her on his shoulder, held her by the legs and paced the room with her. There was an expression of carefree happiness on the faces of both father and daughter.

"But you know you may be unfair. You are too fond of this one," his wife whispered in French.

"Yes, but what am I to do? . . . I try not to show . . ."

At that moment they heard the sound of the door-pulley and footsteps in the hall and anteroom, as if someone had arrived.

"Somebody has come."

"I am sure it is Pierre. I will go and see," said Countess Mary and left the room.

In her absence Nicholas allowed himself to give his little daughter a gallop round the room. Out of breath, he took the laughing child quickly from his shoulder and pressed her to his heart. His capers reminded him of dancing, and looking at the child's round happy little face he thought of what she would be like when he was an old man, taking her into society and dancing the mazurka with her as his old father had danced *Daniel Cooper* with his daughter.

"It is he, it is he, Nicholas!" said Countess Mary re-entering the room a few minutes later. "Now our Natásha has come to life. You should have seen her ecstasy, and how he caught it for having stayed away so long. Well, come along now, quick, quick! It's time you two were parted," she added, looking smilingly at the little girl who clung to her father.

Nicholas went out holding the child by the hand.

Countess Mary remained in the sitting room.

"I should never, never have believed that one could be so happy," she whispered to herself. A smile lit up her face but at the same time she sighed, and her deep eyes expressed a quiet sadness as though she felt, through her happiness, that there is another sort of happiness unattainable in this life and of which she involuntarily thought at that instant.

Chapter X

NATÁSHA HAD MARRIED IN THE EARLY SPRING OF 1813, AND IN 1820 ALREADY HAD THREE DAUGHTERS besides a son for whom she had longed and whom she was now nursing. She had grown stouter and broader, so that it was difficult to recognize in this robust motherly woman the slim lively Natásha of former days. Her features were more defined and had a calm, soft and serene expression. In her face there was none of the ever-glowing animation that had formerly burned there and constituted its charm. Now her face and body were often all that one saw, and her soul was not visible at all. All that struck the eye was a strong, handsome and fertile woman. The old fire very rarely kindled in her face now. That happened only when, as was the case that day, her husband returned home, or a sick child was convalescent, or when she and Countess Mary spoke of Prince Andrew (she never mentioned him to her husband, who she imagined was jealous of Prince Andrew's memory), or on the rare occasions when something happened to induce her to sing, a practice she had quite abandoned since her marriage. At the rare moments when the old fire did kindle in her handsome fully-developed body she was even more attractive than in former days.

Since their marriage Natásha and her husband had lived in Moscow, in Petersburg, on their estate near Moscow, or with her mother, that is to say, in Nicholas's house. The young Countess Bezúkhova was not often seen in society, and those who met her there were not pleased with her and found her neither attractive nor amiable. Not that Natásha liked solitude—she did not know whether she liked it or not, she even thought that she did not—but with her pregnancies, her confinements, the nursing of her children, and sharing every moment of her husband's life, she had demands on her time which could be satisfied only by renouncing society. All who had known Natásha before her marriage wondered at the change in her as at something extraordinary. Only the old countess with her maternal instinct had realized that all Natásha's outbursts had been due to her need of children and a husband—as she herself had once exclaimed at Otrádnoe not so much in fun as in earnest—and her mother was now surprised at the surprise expressed by those who had never understood Natásha, and she kept saying that she had always known that Natásha would make an exemplary wife and mother.

"Only she lets her love of her husband and children overflow all bounds," said the countess, "so that it even becomes absurd."

Natásha did not follow the golden rule advocated by clever folk, especially by the French, which says that a girl should not let herself go when she marries, should not neglect her accomplishments, should be even more careful of her appearance than when she was unmarried, and should fascinate her husband as much as she did before he became her husband. Natásha on the contrary had at once abandoned all her witchery, of which her singing had been an unusually powerful part. She gave it up just because it was so powerfully seductive. She took no pains with her manners or with delicacy of speech, or with her toilet, or to show herself to her husband in her most becoming attitudes, or to avoid inconveniencing him by being too exacting. She acted in contradiction to all those rules. She felt that the allurements instinct had formerly taught her to use would now be merely ridiculous in the eyes of her husband, to whom she had from the first moment given herself up entirely—that is, with her whole soul, leaving no corner of it hidden from him. She felt that her unity with her husband was not maintained by the poetic feelings that had attracted him to her, but by something else—indefinite but firm as the bond between her own body and soul.

To fluff out her curls, put on fashionable dresses and sing romantic songs to fascinate her husband, would have seemed as strange as to adorn herself to attract herself. To adorn herself for others might perhaps have been agreeable—she did not know—but she had no time at all for it. The chief reason for devoting no time either to singing, to dress, or to choosing her words, was that she really had no time to spare for these things.

We know that man has the faculty of becoming completely absorbed in a subject however trivial it may be, and that there is no subject so trivial that it will not grow to infinite proportions if one's entire attention is devoted to it.

The subject which wholly engrossed Natásha's attention was her family: that is, her husband whom she had to keep so that he should belong entirely to her and to the home, and the children whom she had to bear, bring into the world, nurse and bring up.

And the deeper she penetrated, not with her mind only but with her whole soul, her whole being, into the subject that absorbed her, the larger did that subject grow and the weaker and more inadequate did her powers appear, so that she concentrated them wholly on that one thing and yet was unable to accomplish all that she considered necessary.

There were then as now conversations and discussions about women's rights, the relations of husband and wife and their freedom and rights, though these themes were not yet termed *questions* as they are now; but these topics were not merely uninteresting to Natásha, she positively did not understand them.

These questions, then as now, existed only for those who see nothing in marriage but the pleasure married people get from one another, that is, only the beginnings of marriage and not its whole significance, which lies in the family.

Discussions and questions of that kind, which are like the question of how to get the greatest gratification from one's dinner, did not then and do not now exist for those for whom the purpose of a dinner is the nourishment it affords; and the purpose of marriage is the family.

If the purpose of dinner is to nourish the body, a man who eats two dinners at once may perhaps get more enjoyment but will not attain his purpose, for his stomach will not digest the two dinners.

If the purpose of marriage is the family, the person who wishes to have many wives or husbands may perhaps obtain much pleasure, but in that case will not have a family.

If the purpose of food is nourishment and the purpose of marriage is the family, the whole question resolves itself into not eating more than one can digest, and not having more wives or husbands than are needed for the family—that is, one wife or one husband. Natásha needed a husband. A husband was given her and he gave her a family. And she not only saw no need of any other or better husband, but as all the powers of her soul were intent on serving that husband and family, she could not imagine and saw no interest in imagining, how it would be if things were different.

Natásha did not care for society in general, but prized the more the society of her relatives—Countess Mary, and her brother, her mother and Sónya. She valued the company of those to whom she could come striding disheveled from the nursery in her dressing-gown, and with joyful face show a yellow instead of a green stain on baby's napkin, and from whom she could hear reassuring words to the effect that baby was much better.

To such an extent had Natásha let herself go, that the way she dressed and did her hair, her ill-chosen words, and her jealousy—she was jealous of Sónya, of the governess, and of every woman, pretty or plain—were habitual subjects of jest to those about her. The general opinion was that Pierre was under his wife's thumb, which was really true. From the very first days of their married life Natásha had announced her demands. Pierre was greatly surprised by his wife's view, to him a perfectly novel one, that every moment of his life belonged to her and to the family. His wife's demands astonished him, but they also flattered him, and he submitted to them.

Pierre's subjection consisted in the fact that he not only dared not flirt with, but dared not even speak smilingly to, any other woman; did not dare dine at the Club as a pastime, did not dare spend money on a whim, and did not dare absent himself for any length of time, except on business—in which his wife included his intellectual pursuits, which she did not in the least understand but to which she attributed great importance. To make up for this, at home Pierre had the right to regulate his life and that of the whole family exactly as he chose. At home Natásha placed herself in the position of a slave to her husband, and the whole household went on tiptoe when he was occupied—that is, was reading or writing in his study. Pierre had but to show a partiality for anything to get just what he liked done always. He had only to express a wish and Natásha would jump up and run to fulfill it.

The entire household was governed according to Pierre's supposed orders, that is, by his wishes which Natásha tried to guess. Their way of life and place of residence, their acquaintances and ties, Natásha's occupations, the children's upbringing, were all selected not merely with regard to Pierre's expressed wishes, but to what Natásha from the thoughts he expressed in conversation supposed his wishes to be. And she deduced the essentials of his wishes quite correctly, and having once arrived at them clung to them tenaciously. When Pierre himself wanted to change his mind she would fight him with his own weapons.

Thus in a time of trouble ever memorable to him after the birth of their first child who was delicate, when they had to change the wet-nurse three times and Natásha fell ill from despair, Pierre one day told her of Rousseau's view, with which he quite agreed, that to have a wet-nurse is unnatural and harmful. When her next baby was born, despite the opposition of her mother, the doctors, and even of her husband himself—who were all vigorously opposed to her nursing her baby herself, a thing then unheard of and considered injurious—she insisted on having her own way, and after that nursed all her babies herself.

It very often happened that in a moment of irritation husband and wife would have a dispute, but long afterward Pierre to his surprise and delight would find in his wife's ideas and actions the very thought against which she had argued, but divested of everything superfluous that in the excitement of the dispute he had added when expressing his opinion.

After seven years of marriage Pierre had the joyous and firm consciousness that he was not a bad man, and he felt this because he saw himself reflected in his wife. He felt the good and bad within himself inextricably mingled and overlapping. But only what was really good in him was reflected in his wife, all that was not quite good was rejected. And this was not the result of logical reasoning but was a direct and mysterious reflection.

Chapter XI

Two months previously when Pierre was already staying with the Rostóvs he had received a letter from Prince Theodore, asking him to come to Petersburg to confer on some important questions that were being discussed there by a Society of which Pierre was one of the principal founders.

On reading that letter (she always read her husband's letters) Natásha herself suggested that he should go to Petersburg, though she would feel his absence very acutely. She attributed immense importance to all her husband's intellectual and abstract interests though she did not understand them, and she always dreaded being a hindrance to him in such matters. To Pierre's timid look of inquiry after reading the letter she replied by asking him to go, but to fix a definite date for his return. He was given four weeks' leave of absence.

Ever since that leave of absence had expired, more than a fortnight before, Natásha had been in a constant state of alarm, depression and irritability.

Denísov, now a general on the retired list and much dissatisfied with the present state of affairs, had arrived during that fortnight. He looked at Natásha with sorrow and surprise as at a bad likeness of a person once dear. A dull dejected look, random replies and talk about the nursery, was all he saw and heard from his former enchantress.

Natásha was sad and irritable all that time, especially when her mother, her brother, Sónya, or Countess Mary in their efforts to console her tried to excuse Pierre and suggested reasons for his delay in returning.

"It's all nonsense, all rubbish—those discussions which lead to nothing and all those idiotic societies!" Natásha declared of the very affairs in the immense importance of which she firmly believed.

And she would go to the nursery to nurse Pétya her only boy. No one else could tell her anything so comforting or so reasonable as this little three-month-old creature when he lay at her breast and she was conscious of the movement of his lips and the snuffling of his little nose. That creature said: "You are angry—you are jealous, you would like to pay him out, you are afraid—but here am I! And I am he . . ." and that was unanswerable. It was more than true.

During that fortnight of anxiety Natásha resorted to the baby for comfort so often, and fussed over him so much, that she overfed him and he fell ill. She was terrified by his illness, and yet that was just what she needed. While attending to him she bore the anxiety about her husband more easily.

She was nursing her boy when the sound of Pierre's sleigh was heard at the front door, and the old nurse—knowing how to please her mistress—entered the room inaudibly but hurriedly and with a beaming face.

"Has he come?" Natásha asked quickly in a whisper, afraid to move lest she should rouse the dozing baby.

"He's come, ma'am," whispered the nurse.

The blood rushed to Natásha's face and her feet involuntarily moved, but she could not jump up and run out. The baby again opened his eyes and looked at her. "You're here?" he seemed to be saying, and again lazily smacked his lips.

Cautiously withdrawing her breast, Natásha rocked him a little, handed him to the nurse and went with rapid steps toward the door. But at the door she stopped as if her conscience reproached her for having in her joy left the child too soon, and she glanced round. The nurse with raised elbows was lifting the infant over the rail of his cot.

"Go, ma'am! Don't worry, go!" she whispered smiling, with the kind of familiarity that grows up between a nurse and her mistress.

Natásha ran with light footsteps to the anteroom.

Denísov who had come out of the study into the dancing room with his pipe, now for the first time recognized the old Natásha. A flood of brilliant, joyful light poured from her transfigured face.

"He's come!" she exclaimed as she ran past, and Denísov felt that he too was delighted that Pierre, whom he did not much care for, had returned.

On reaching the vestibule Natásha saw a tall figure in a fur coat unwinding his scarf. "It's he! It's really he! He has come!" she said to herself, and rushing at him embraced him, pressed his head to her breast, and then pushed him back and gazed at his ruddy, happy face, covered with hoarfrost. "Yes, it is he, happy and contented. . . ."

Then all at once she remembered the tortures of suspense she had experienced for the last fortnight, and the joy that had lit up her face vanished; she frowned and overwhelmed Pierre with a torrent of reproaches and angry words.

"Yes, it's all very well for you. You are pleased, you've had a good time. . . . But what about me? You might at least have shown consideration for the children. I am nursing and my milk was spoiled. . . . Pétya was at death's door. But you were enjoying yourself. Yes, enjoying . . ."

Pierre knew he was not to blame for he could not have come sooner; he knew this outburst was unseemly and would blow over in a minute or two; above all he knew that he himself was bright and happy. He wanted to smile but dared not even think of doing so. He made a piteous, frightened face and bent down.

"I could not, on my honor. But how is Pétya?"

"All right now. Come along! I wonder you're not ashamed! If only you could see what I was like without you, how I suffered!"

"You are well?"

"Come, come!" she said, not letting go of his arm. And they went to their rooms.

When Nicholas and his wife came to look for Pierre he was in the nursery holding his baby son, who was again awake, on his huge right palm and dandling him. A blissful bright smile was fixed on the baby's broad face with its toothless open mouth. The storm was long since over and there was bright, joyous sunshine on Natásha's face as she gazed tenderly at her husband and child.

"And have you talked everything well over with Prince Theodore?" she asked.

"Yes, capitally."

"You see, he holds it up." (She meant the baby's head.) "But how he did frighten me . . . You've seen the princess? Is it true she's in love with that . . ."

"Yes, just fancy . . ."

At that moment Nicholas and Countess Mary came in. Pierre with the baby on his hand stooped, kissed them, and replied to their inquiries. But in spite of much that was interesting and had to be discussed, the baby with the little cap on its unsteady head evidently absorbed all his attention.

"How sweet!" said Countess Mary, looking at and playing with the baby. "Now, Nicholas," she added turning to her husband, "I can't understand how it is you don't see the charm of these delicious marvels."

"I don't and can't," replied Nicholas, looking coldly at the baby. "A lump of flesh. Come along, Pierre!"

"And yet he's such an affectionate father," said Countess Mary, vindicating her husband, "but only after they are a year old or so . . ."

"Now Pierre nurses them splendidly," said Natásha. "He says his hand is just made for a baby's seat. Just look!"

"Only not for this . . ." Pierre suddenly exclaimed with a laugh, and shifting the baby he gave him to the nurse.

Chapter XII

As in every large household, there were at Bald Hills several perfectly distinct worlds which merged into one harmonious whole, though each retained its own peculiarities and made concessions to the others. Every event, joyful or sad, that took place in that house was important to all these worlds, but each had its own special reasons to rejoice or grieve over that occurrence independently of the others.

For instance, Pierre's return was a joyful and important event and they all felt it to be so.

The servants—the most reliable judges of their masters because they judge not by their conversation or expressions of feeling but by their acts and way of life—were glad of Pierre's return because they knew that when he was there Count Nicholas would cease going every day to attend to the estate, and would be in better spirits and temper, and also because they would all receive handsome presents for the holidays.

The children and their governesses were glad of Pierre's return because no one else drew them into the social life of the household as he did. He alone could play on the clavichord that *écossaise* (his only piece) to which as he said all possible dances could be danced, and they felt sure he had brought presents for them all.

Young Nicholas, now a slim lad of fifteen, delicate and intelligent, with curly light-brown hair and beautiful eyes, was delighted because Uncle Pierre as he called him was the object of his rapturous and passionate affection. No one had instilled into him this love for Pierre whom he saw only occasionally. Countess Mary who had brought him up had done her utmost to make him love her husband as she loved him, and little Nicholas did love his uncle, but loved him with just a shade of contempt. Pierre however he adored. He did not want to be a hussar or a Knight of St. George like his uncle Nicholas; he wanted to be learned, wise and kind like Pierre. In Pierre's presence his face always shone with pleasure and he flushed and was breathless when Pierre spoke to him. He did not miss a single word he uttered, and would afterward, with Dessalles or by himself, recall and reconsider the meaning of everything Pierre had said. Pierre's past life and his unhappiness prior to 1812 (of which young Nicholas had formed a vague poetic picture from some words he had overheard), his adventures in Moscow, his captivity, Platón Karatáev (of whom he had heard from Pierre), his love for Natásha (of whom the lad was also particularly fond) and especially Pierre's friendship with the father whom Nicholas could not remember—all this made Pierre in his eyes a hero and a saint.

From broken remarks about Natásha and his father, from the emotion with which Pierre spoke of that dead father, and from the careful reverent tenderness with which Natásha spoke of him, the boy, who was only just beginning to guess what love is, derived the notion that his father had loved Natásha and when dying had left her to his friend. But the father whom the boy did not remember appeared to him a divinity who could not be pictured, and of whom he never thought without a swelling heart and tears of sadness and rapture. So the boy also was happy that Pierre had arrived.

The guests welcomed Pierre because he always helped to enliven and unite any company he was in.

The grown-up members of the family not to mention his wife, were pleased to have back a friend whose presence made life run more smoothly and peacefully.

The old ladies were pleased with the presents he brought them, and especially that Natásha would now be herself again.

Pierre felt the different outlooks of these various worlds and made haste to satisfy all their expectations.

Though the most absent-minded and forgetful of men, Pierre with the aid of a list his wife drew up, had now bought everything, not forgetting his mother-and brother-in-law's commissions, nor the dress material for a present to Belóva, nor toys for his wife's nephews. In the early days of his marriage it had seemed strange to him that his wife should expect him not to forget to procure all the things he undertook to buy, and he had been taken aback by her serious annoyance when on his first trip he forgot everything. But in time he grew used to this demand. Knowing that Natásha asked nothing for herself, and gave him commissions for others only when he himself had offered to undertake them, he now found an unexpected and childlike pleasure in this purchase of presents for everyone in the house, and never forgot anything. If he now incurred Natásha's censure it was only for buying too many and too expensive things. To her other defects (as most people thought them, but which to Pierre were qualities) of untidiness and neglect of herself, she now added stinginess.

From the time that Pierre began life as a family man on a footing entailing heavy expenditure, he had noticed to his surprise that he spent only half as much as before, and that his affairs—which had been in disorder of late, chiefly because of his first wife's debts—had begun to improve.

Life was cheaper because it was circumscribed: that most expensive luxury, the kind of life that can be changed at any moment, was no longer his nor did he wish for it. He felt that his way of life had now been settled once for all till death and that to change it was not in his power, and so that way of life proved economical.

With a merry, smiling face Pierre was sorting his purchases.

"What do you think of this?" said he, unrolling a piece of stuff like a shopman.

Natásha who was sitting opposite to him with her eldest daughter on her lap, turned her sparkling eyes swiftly from her husband to the things he showed her.

"That's for Belóva? Excellent!" She felt the quality of the material. "It was a ruble an arshín, I suppose?"

Pierre told her the price.

"Too dear!" Natásha remarked. "How pleased the children will be and Mamma too! Only you need not have bought me this," she added, unable to suppress a smile as she gazed admiringly at a gold comb set with pearls, of a kind then just coming into fashion.

"Adèle tempted me: she kept on telling me to buy it," returned Pierre.

"When am I to wear it?" and Natásha stuck it in her coil of hair. "When I take little Másha into society? Perhaps they will be fashionable again by then. Well, let's go now."

And collecting the presents they went first to the nursery and then to the old countess's rooms.

The countess was sitting with her companion Belóva, playing grand-patience as usual, when Pierre and Natásha came into the drawing room with parcels under their arms.

The countess was now over sixty, was quite gray, and wore a cap with a frill that surrounded her face. Her face had shriveled, her upper lip had sunk in and her eyes were dim.

After the deaths of her son and husband in such rapid succession, she felt herself a being accidentally forgotten in this world and left without aim or object for her existence. She ate, drank, slept or kept awake, but did not *live*. Life gave her no new impressions. She wanted nothing from life but tranquillity, and that tranquillity only death could give her. But until death came she had to go on living, that is, to use her vital forces. A peculiarity one sees in very young children and very old people was particularly evident in her. Her life had no external aims—only a need to exercise her various functions and inclinations was apparent. She had to eat, sleep, think, speak, weep, work, give vent to her anger, and so on, merely because she had a stomach, a brain, muscles, nerves and a liver. She did these things not under any external impulse as people in the full vigor of life do, when behind the purpose for which they strive that of exercising their functions remains unnoticed. She talked only because she physically needed to exercise her tongue and lungs. She cried as a child does, because her nose had to be cleared, and so on. What for people in their full vigor is an aim was for her evidently merely a pretext.

Thus in the morning—especially if she had eaten anything rich the day before—she felt a need of being angry and would choose as the handiest pretext Belóva's deafness.

She would begin to say something to her in a low tone from the other end of the room.

"It seems a little warmer today, my dear," she would murmur.

And when Belóva replied: "Oh yes, they've come," she would mutter angrily: "O Lord! How stupid and deaf she is!"

Another pretext would be her snuff, which would seem too dry or too damp, or not rubbed fine enough. After these fits of irritability her face would grow yellow, and her maids knew by infallible symptoms when Belóva would again be deaf, the snuff damp, and the countess's face yellow. Just as she needed to work off her spleen so she had sometimes to exercise her still existing faculty of thinking—and the pretext for that was a game of patience. When she needed to cry, the deceased count would be the pretext. When she wanted to be agitated, Nicholas and his health would be the pretext, and when she felt a need to speak spitefully, the pretext would be Countess Mary. When her vocal organs needed exercise, which was usually toward seven o'clock when she had had an after-dinner rest in a darkened room, the pretext would be the retelling of the same stories over and over again to the same audience.

The old lady's condition was understood by the whole household though no one ever spoke of it, and they all made every possible effort to satisfy her needs. Only by a rare glance exchanged with a sad smile between Nicholas, Pierre, Natásha, and Countess Mary, was the common understanding of her condition expressed.

But those glances expressed something more: they said that she had played her part in life, that what they now saw was not her whole self, that we must all become like her, and that they were glad to yield to her, to restrain themselves for this once precious being formerly as full of life as themselves, but now so much to be pitied. *"Memento mori,"* said these glances.

Only the really heartless, the stupid ones of that household and the little children, failed to understand this and avoided her.

Chapter XIII

WHEN PIERRE AND HIS WIFE ENTERED THE DRAWING ROOM THE COUNTESS WAS IN ONE OF HER customary states in which she needed the mental exertion of playing patience, and so—though by force of habit she greeted him with the words she always used when Pierre or her son returned after an absence: "High time, my dear, high time! We were all weary of waiting for you. Well, thank God!" and received her presents with another customary remark: "It's not the gift that's precious, my dear, but that you give it to me, an old woman . . ."—yet it was evident that she was not pleased by Pierre's arrival at that moment when it diverted her attention from the unfinished game.

She finished her game of patience and only then examined the presents. They consisted of a box for cards, of splendid workmanship, a bright blue Sèvres tea-cup with shepherdesses depicted on it and with a lid, and a gold snuffbox with the count's portrait on the lid which Pierre had had done by a miniaturist in Petersburg. The countess had long wished for such a box, but as she did not want to cry just then she glanced indifferently at the portrait and gave her attention chiefly to the box for cards.

"Thank you, my dear, you have cheered me up," said she as she always did. "But best of all you have brought yourself back—for I never saw anything like it, you ought to give your wife a scolding! What are we to do with her? She is like a mad woman when you are away. Doesn't see anything, doesn't remember anything" she went on, repeating her usual phrases. "Look, Anna Timoféevna," she added to her companion, "see what a box for cards my son has brought us!"

Belóva admired the presents and was delighted with her dress material.

Though Pierre, Natásha, Nicholas, Countess Mary and Denísov had much to talk about that they could not discuss before the old countess—not that anything was hidden from her, but because she had dropped so far behindhand in many things that had they begun to converse in her presence they would have had to answer inopportune questions and to repeat what they had already told her many times: that so-and-so was dead and so-and-so was married, which she would again be unable to remember—yet they sat at tea round the samovar in the drawing room from habit, and Pierre answered the countess's questions as to whether Prince Vasíli had aged and whether Countess Mary Alexéevna had sent greetings and still thought of them, and other matters that interested no one and to which she herself was indifferent.

Conversation of this kind, interesting to no one yet unavoidable, continued all through teatime. All the grown-up members of the family were assembled near the round tea-table at which Sónya presided beside the samovar. The children with their tutors and governesses had had tea and their voices were audible from the next room. At tea all sat in their accustomed places: Nicholas beside the stove at a small table where his tea was handed to him; Mílka, the old gray borzoi bitch (daughter of the first Mílka) with a quite gray face and large black eyes that seemed more prominent than ever, lay on the arm-chair beside him; Denísov whose curly hair, mustache and whiskers had turned half gray, sat beside countess Mary with his general's tunic unbuttoned; Pierre sat between his wife and the old countess. He spoke of what he knew might interest the old lady and that she could understand. He told her of external social events and of the people who had formed the circle of her contemporaries and had once been a real, living and distinct group, but who were now for the most part scattered about the world and like herself were garnering the last ears of the harvests they had sown in earlier years. But to the old countess those contemporaries of hers seemed to be the only serious and real society. Natásha saw by Pierre's animation that his visit had been interesting and that he had much to tell them but dare not say it before the old countess. Denísov not being a member of the family did not understand Pierre's caution and being, as a malcontent, much interested in what was occurring in Petersburg, kept urging Pierre to tell them about what had happened in the Semënovsk regiment, then about Arakchéev, and then about the Bible Society. Once or twice Pierre was carried away and began to speak of these things, but Nicholas and Natásha always brought him back to the health of Prince Iván and Countess Mary Alexéevna.

"Well, and all this idiocy—Gossner and Tatáwinova?" Denísov asked. "Is that weally still going on?"

"Going on?" Pierre exclaimed. "Why more than ever! The Bible Society is the whole government now!"

"What is that, *mon cher ami?*" asked the countess, who had finished her tea and evidently needed a pretext for being angry after her meal. "What are you saying about the government? I don't understand."

"Well, you know, *Maman,*" Nicholas interposed, knowing how to translate things into his mother's language, "Prince Alexander Golítsyn has founded a society and in consequence has great influence, they say."

"Arakchéev and Golítsyn," incautiously remarked Pierre, "are now the whole government! And what a government! They see treason everywhere and are afraid of everything."

"Well, and how is Prince Alexander to blame? He is a most estimable man. I used to meet him at Mary Antónovna's," said the countess in an offended tone; and still more offended that they all remained silent, she went on: "Nowadays everyone finds fault. A Gospel Society! Well, and what harm is there in that?" and she rose (everybody else got up too) and with a severe expression sailed back to her table in the sitting room.

The melancholy silence that followed was broken by the sounds of the children's voices and laughter from the next room. Evidently some jolly excitement was going on there.

"Finished, finished!" little Natásha's gleeful yell rose above them all.

Pierre exchanged glances with Countess Mary and Nicholas (Natásha he never lost sight of) and smiled happily.

"That's delightful music!" said he.

"It means that Anna Makárovna has finished her stocking," said Countess Mary.

"Oh, I'll go and see," said Pierre, jumping up. "You know," he added, stopping at the door, "why I'm especially fond of that music? It is always the first thing that tells me all is well. When I was driving here today, the nearer I got to the house the more anxious I grew. As I entered the anteroom I heard Andrúsha's peals of laughter and that meant that all was well."

"I know! I know that feeling," said Nicholas. "But I mustn't go there—those stockings are to be a surprise for me."

Pierre went to the children, and the shouting and laughter grew still louder.

"Come, Anna Makárovna," Pierre's voice was heard saying, "come here into the middle of the room and at the word of command, 'One, two,' and when I say 'three' . . . You stand here, and you in my arms—well now! One, two! . . ." said Pierre, and a silence followed: "three!"—and a rapturously breathless cry of children's voices filled the room. "Two, two!" they shouted.

This meant two stockings, which by a secret process known only to herself Anna Makárovna used to knit at the same time on the same needles, and which, when they were ready, she always triumphantly drew, one out of the other, in the children's presence.

Chapter XIV

SOON AFTER THIS THE CHILDREN CAME IN TO SAY GOOD NIGHT. THEY KISSED EVERYONE, THE TUtors and governesses made their bows, and they went out. Only young Nicholas and his tutor remained. Dessalles whispered to the boy to come downstairs.

"No, Monsieur Dessalles, I will ask my aunt to let me stay," replied Nicholas Bolkónski also in a whisper.

"*Ma tante,* please let me stay," said he, going up to his aunt.

His face expressed entreaty, agitation and ecstasy. Countess Mary glanced at him and turned to Pierre.

"When you are here he can't tear himself away," she said.

"I will bring him to you directly, Monsieur Dessalles. Good night!" said Pierre, giving his hand to the Swiss tutor, and he turned to young Nicholas with a smile. "You and I haven't seen anything of one another yet. . . . How like he is growing, Mary!" he added, addressing Countess Mary.

"Like my father?" asked the boy, flushing crimson and looking up at Pierre with bright, ecstatic eyes.

Pierre nodded, and went on with what he had been saying when the children had interrupted. Countess Mary sat down doing wool-work; Natásha did not take her eyes off her husband. Nicholas and Denísov rose, asked for their pipes, smoked, went to fetch more tea from Sónya—who sat weary but resolute at the samovar—and questioned Pierre. The curly-headed, delicate boy sat with shining eyes unnoticed in a corner, starting every now and then and muttering something to himself, and evidently experiencing a new and powerful emotion as he turned his curly head with his thin neck exposed by his turn-down collar, toward the place where Pierre sat.

The conversation turned on the contemporary gossip about those in power, in which most people see the chief interest of home politics. Denísov dissatisfied with the government on account of his own disappointments in the service, heard with pleasure of the things done in Petersburg which seemed to him stupid, and made forcible and sharp comments on what Pierre told them.

"One used to have to be a German—now one must dance with Tatáwinova and Madame Kwdener, and wead Ecka'tshausen and the bwethwen. Oh, they should let that fine fellow Bonaparte loose—he'd knock all this nonsense out of them! Fancy giving the command of the Semënov wegiment to a fellow like that Schwa'tz!" he cried.

Nicholas though free from Denísov's readiness to find fault with everything, also thought that discussion of the government was a very serious and weighty matter, and the fact that *A* had been appointed Minister of This and *B* Governor General of That, and that the Emperor had said so-and-so and this Minister so-and-so, seemed to him very important. And so he thought it necessary to take an interest in these things and to question Pierre. The questions put by these two kept the conversation from changing its ordinary character of gossip about the higher government circles.

But Natásha knowing all her husband's ways and ideas, saw that he had long been wishing but had been unable, to divert the conversation to another channel and express his own deeply-felt idea for the sake of which he had gone to Petersburg to consult with his new friend Prince Theodore, and she helped him by asking how his affairs with Prince Theodore had gone.

"What was it about?" asked Nicholas.

"Always the same thing," said Pierre, looking round at his listeners. "Everybody sees that things are going so badly that they cannot be allowed to go on so and that it is the duty of all decent men to counteract it as far as they can."

"What can decent men do?" Nicholas inquired, frowning slightly. "What can be done?"

"Why, this . . ."

"Come into my study," said Nicholas.

Natásha who had long expected to be fetched to nurse her baby, now heard the nurse calling her and went to the nursery. Countess Mary followed her. The men went into the study and little Nicholas Bolkónski followed them unnoticed by his uncle, and sat down at the writing-table in a shady corner by the window.

"Well, what would you do?" asked Denísov.

"Always some fantastic schemes," said Nicholas.

"Why this," began Pierre not sitting down but pacing the room, sometimes stopping short, gesticulating and lisping: "the position in Petersburg is this: the Emperor does not look into anything. He has abandoned himself altogether to this mysticism" (Pierre could not tolerate mysticism in anyone now). "He seeks only for peace, and only these people *sans foi ni loi* can give it him—people who recklessly hack at and strangle everything—Magnítski, Arakchéev, and *tutti quanti*. . . . You will agree that if you did not look after your estates yourself but only wanted a quiet life, the harsher your steward was the more readily your object might be attained," he said to Nicholas.

"Well, what does that lead up to?" said Nicholas.

"Well, everything is going to ruin! Robbery in the law-courts, in the army nothing but flogging, drilling and Military Settlements; the people are tortured, enlightenment is suppressed. All that is young and honest is crushed! Everyone sees that this cannot go on. Everything is strained to such a degree that it will certainly break," said Pierre (as those who examine the actions of any government have always said since governments began). "I told them just one thing in Petersburg."

"Told whom?"

"Well, you know whom," said Pierre, with a meaning glance from under his brows. "Prince Theodore and all those. To encourage culture and philanthropy is all very well of course. The aim is excellent but in the present circumstances something else is needed."

At that moment Nicholas noticed the presence of his nephew. His face darkened and he went up to the boy.

"Why are you here?"

"Why? Let him be," said Pierre taking Nicholas by the arm and continuing. "That is not enough, I told them. Something else is needed. When you stand expecting the overstrained string to snap at any moment, when everyone is expecting the inevitable catastrophe, as many as possible must join hands as closely as they can to withstand the general calamity. Everything that is young and strong is being enticed away and depraved. One is lured by women, another by honors, a third by ambition or money, and they go over to that camp. No independent men, such as you or I, are left. What I say is, widen the scope of our Society, let the *mot d'ordre* be not virtue alone but independence and action as well!"

Nicholas, who had left his nephew, irritably pushed up an arm-chair, sat down in it, and listened to Pierre, coughing discontentedly and frowning more and more.

"But action with what aim?" he cried. "And what position will you adopt toward the government?"

"Why, the position of assistants. The Society need not be secret if the government allows it. Not merely is it not hostile to government, but it is a society of true conservatives—a society of gentlemen in the full meaning of that word. It is only to prevent some Pugachëv or other from killing my children and yours, and Arakchéev from sending me off to some Military Settlement. We join hands only for the public welfare and the general safety."

"Yes, but it's a secret society and therefore a hostile and harmful one which can only cause harm."

"Why? Did the Tugendbund which saved Europe" (they did not then venture to suggest that Russia had saved Europe) "do any harm? The Tugendbund is an alliance of virtue: it is love, mutual help . . . it is what Christ preached on the Cross."

Natásha who had come in during the conversation, looked joyfully at her husband. It was not what he was saying that pleased her—that did not even interest her for it seemed to her that was all extremely simple and that she had known it a long time (it seemed so to her because she knew that it sprang from Pierre's whole soul), but it was his animated and enthusiastic appearance that made her glad.

The boy with the thin neck stretching out from the turn-down collar—whom everyone had forgotten—gazed at Pierre with even greater and more rapturous joy. Every word of Pierre's burned into his heart, and with a nervous movement of his fingers he unconsciously broke the sealing-wax and quill pens his hands came upon on his uncle's table.

"It is not at all what you suppose; but that is what the German Tugendbund was, and what I am proposing."

"No, my fwiend! The Tugendbund is all vewy well for the sausage-eaters, but I don't understand it and can't even pwonounce it," interposed Denísov in a loud and resolute voice. "I agwee that evewything here is wotten and howwible, but the *Tugendbund* I don't understand. If we're not satisfied, let us have a *bunt* of our own. That's all wight. *Je suis votre homme!*"

Pierre smiled. Natásha began to laugh, but Nicholas knitted his brows still more and began proving to Pierre that there was no prospect of any great change and that all the danger he spoke of existed only in his imagination. Pierre maintained the contrary, and as his mental faculties were greater and more resourceful, Nicholas felt himself cornered. This made him still angrier for he was fully convinced, not by reasoning but by something within him stronger than reason, of the justice of his opinion.

"I will tell you this," he said, rising and trying with nervously twitching fingers to prop up his pipe in a corner, but finally abandoning the attempt. "I can't prove it to you. You say that everything here is rotten and that an overthrow is coming: I don't see it. But you also say that our oath of allegiance is a conditional matter, and to that I reply: 'You are my best friend, as you know, but if you formed a secret society and began working against the government—be it what it may—I know it is my duty to obey the government. And if Arakchéev ordered me to lead a squadron against you and cut you down, I should not hesitate an instant, but should do it.' And you may argue about that as you like!"

An awkward silence followed these words. Natásha was the first to speak, defending her husband and attacking her brother. Her defense was weak and inapt but she attained her object. The conversation was resumed, and no longer in the unpleasantly hostile tone of Nicholas's last remark.

When they all got up to go in to supper, little Nicholas Bolkónski went up to Pierre, pale and with shining, radiant eyes.

"Uncle Pierre, you . . . no . . . If Papa were alive . . . would he agree with you?" he asked.

And Pierre suddenly realized what a special, independent, complex and powerful process of thought and feeling must have been going on in this boy during that conversation, and remembering all he had said he regretted that the lad should have heard him. He had however to give him an answer.

"Yes, I think so," he said reluctantly, and left the study.

The lad looked down and seemed now for the first time to notice what he had done to the things on the table. He flushed and went up to Nicholas.

"Uncle, forgive me, I did that . . . unintentionally," he said, pointing to the broken sealing-wax and pens.

Nicholas started angrily.

"All right, all right," he said, throwing the bits under the table.

And evidently suppressing his vexation with difficulty, he turned away from the boy.

"You ought not to have been here at all," he said.

Chapter XV

THE CONVERSATION AT SUPPER WAS NOT ABOUT POLITICS OR SOCIETIES, BUT TURNED ON THE subject Nicholas liked best—recollections of 1812. Denísov started these and Pierre was particularly agreeable and amusing about them. The family separated on the most friendly terms.

After supper Nicholas having undressed in his study and given instructions to the steward who had been waiting for him, went to the bedroom in his dressing-gown, where he found his wife still at her table, writing.

"What are you writing, Mary?" Nicholas asked.

Countess Mary blushed. She was afraid that what she was writing would not be understood or approved by her husband.

She had wanted to conceal what she was writing from him but at the same time was glad he had surprised her at it and that she would now have to tell him.

"A diary, Nicholas," she replied, handing him a blue exercise-book filled with her firm, bold writing.

"A diary?" Nicholas repeated with a shade of irony, and he took up the book.

It was in French.

> "4th December. Today when Andrúsha" (her eldest boy) "woke up he did not wish to dress and Mademoiselle Louise sent for me. He was naughty and obstinate. I tried threats, but he only grew angrier. Then I took the matter in hand: I left him alone and began with nurse's help to get the other children up, telling him that I did not love him. For a long time he was silent, as if astonished, then he jumped out of bed, ran to me in his shirt, and sobbed so that I could not calm him for a long time. It was plain that what troubled him most was that he had grieved me. Afterward in the evening when I gave him his ticket, he again began crying piteously and kissing me. One can do anything with him by tenderness."

"What is a 'ticket'?" Nicholas inquired.

"I have begun giving the elder ones marks every evening, showing how they have behaved."

Nicholas looked into the radiant eyes that were gazing at him, and continued to turn over the pages and read. In the diary was set down everything in the children's lives that seemed noteworthy to their mother as showing their characters or suggesting general reflections on educational methods. They were for the most part quite insignificant trifles, but did not seem so to the mother or to the father either, now that he read this diary about his children for the first time.

Under the date "5th" was entered:

> Mítya was naughty at table. Papa said he was to have no pudding. He had none, but looked so unhappily and greedily at the others while they were eating! I think that punishment by depriving children of sweets only develops their greediness. Must tell Nicholas this.

Nicholas put down the book and looked at his wife. The radiant eyes gazed at him questioningly: would he approve or disapprove of her diary? There could be no doubt not only of his approval but also of his admiration for his wife.

Perhaps it need not be done so pedantically, thought Nicholas, or even done at all, but this untiring continual spiritual effort of which the sole aim was the children's moral welfare, delighted him. Had Nicholas been able to analyze his feelings he would have found that his steady, tender and proud love of his wife rested on his feeling of wonder at her spirituality and at the lofty moral world, almost beyond his reach, in which she had her being.

He was proud of her intelligence and goodness, recognized his own insignificance beside her in the spiritual world, and rejoiced all the more that she with such a soul not only belonged to him but was part of himself.

"I quite, quite approve, my dearest!" said he with a significant look, and after a short pause he added: "And I behaved badly today. You weren't in the study. We began disputing—Pierre and I—and I lost my temper. But he is impossible: such a child! I don't know what would become of him if Natásha didn't keep him in hand. . . . Have you any idea why he went to Petersburg? They have formed . . ."

"Yes, I know," said Countess Mary. "Natásha told me."

"Well, then, you know," Nicholas went on, growing hot at the mere recollection of their discussion, "he wanted to convince me that it is every honest man's duty to go against the government, and that the oath of allegiance and duty . . . I am sorry you weren't there. They all fell on me—Denísov and Natásha . . . Natásha is absurd. How she rules over him! And yet there need only be a discussion and she has no words of her own but only repeats his sayings . . ." added Nicholas, yielding to that irresistible inclination which tempts us to judge those nearest and dearest to us. He forgot that what he was saying about Natásha could have been applied word for word to himself in relation to his wife.

"Yes, I have noticed that," said Countess Mary.

"When I told him that duty and the oath were above everything, he started proving goodness knows what! A pity you were not there—what would you have said?"

"As I see it you were quite right, and I told Natásha so. Pierre says everybody is suffering, tortured, and being corrupted, and that it is our duty to help our neighbor. Of course he is right there," said Countess Mary, "but he forgets that we have other duties nearer to us, duties indicated to us by God Himself, and that though we might expose ourselves to risks we must not risk our children."

"Yes, that's it! That's just what I said to him," put in Nicholas, who fancied he really had said it. "But they insisted on their own view: love of one's neighbor and Christianity—and all this in the presence of young Nicholas, who had gone into my study and broke all my things."

"Ah, Nicholas, do you know I am often troubled about little Nicholas," said Countess Mary. "He is such an exceptional boy. I am afraid I neglect him in favor of my own: we all have children and relations while he has no one. He is constantly alone with his thoughts."

"Well, I don't think you need reproach yourself on his account. All that the fondest mother could do for her son you have done and are doing for him, and of course I am glad of it. He is a fine lad, a fine lad! This evening he listened to Pierre in a sort of trance, and fancy—as we were going in to supper I looked and he had broken everything on my table to bits, and he told me of it himself at once! I never knew him to tell an untruth. A fine lad, a fine lad!" repeated Nicholas, who at heart was not fond of Nicholas Bolkónski but was always anxious to recognize that he was a fine lad.

"Still, I am not the same as his own mother," said Countess Mary. "I feel I am not the same and it troubles me. A wonderful boy, but I am dreadfully afraid for him. It would be good for him to have companions."

"Well it won't be for long. Next summer I'll take him to Petersburg," said Nicholas. "Yes, Pierre always was a dreamer and always will be," he continued, returning to the talk in the study which had evidently disturbed him. "Well, what business is it of mine what goes on there—whether Arakchéev is bad, and all that? What business was it of mine when I married and was so deep in debt that I was threatened with prison, and had a mother who could not see or understand it? And then there are you and the children and our affairs. Is it for my own pleasure that I am at the farm or in the office from morning to night? No, but I know I must work to comfort my mother, to repay you, and not to leave the children such beggars as I was."

Countess Mary wanted to tell him that man does not live by bread alone and that he attached too much importance to these matters. But she knew she must not say this and that it would be useless to do so. She only took his hand and kissed it. He took this as a sign of approval and a confirmation of his thoughts, and after a few minutes' reflection continued to think aloud.

"You know, Mary, today Elias Mitrofánych" (this was his overseer) "came back from the Tambóv estate and told me they are already offering eighty thousand rubles for the forest."

And with an eager face Nicholas began to speak of the possibility of repurchasing Otrádnoe before long, and added: "Another ten years of life and I shall leave the children . . . in an excellent position."

Countess Mary listened to her husband and understood all that he told her. She knew that when he thought aloud in this way he would sometimes ask her what he had been saying, and be vexed if he noticed that she had been thinking about something else. But she had to force herself to attend, for what he was saying did not interest her at all. She looked at him and did not think, but felt, about something different. She felt a submissive tender love for this man who would never understand all that she understood, and this seemed to make her love for him still stronger and added a touch of passionate tenderness. Besides this feeling which absorbed her altogether and hindered her from following the details of her husband's plans, thoughts that had no connection with what he was saying flitted through her mind. She thought of her nephew. Her husband's account of the boy's agitation while Pierre was speaking struck her forcibly, and various traits of his gentle sensitive character recurred to her mind; and while thinking of her nephew she thought also of her own children. She did not compare them with him, but compared her feeling for them with her feeling for him, and felt with regret that there was something lacking in her feeling for young Nicholas.

Sometimes it seemed to her that this difference arose from the difference in their ages, but she felt herself to blame toward him and promised in her heart to do better and to accomplish the impossible—in this life to love her husband, her children, little Nicholas, and all her neighbors, as Christ loved mankind. Countess Mary's soul always strove toward the infinite, the eternal and the absolute, and could therefore never be at peace. A stern expression of the lofty, secret suffering of a soul burdened by the body appeared on her face. Nicholas gazed at her. "O God! What will become of us if she dies, as I always fear when her face is like that?" thought he, and placing himself before the icon he began to say his evening prayers.

Chapter XVI

NATÁSHA AND PIERRE, LEFT ALONE, ALSO BEGAN TO TALK AS ONLY A HUSBAND AND WIFE CAN talk, that is, with extraordinary clearness and rapidity, understanding and expressing each other's thoughts in ways contrary to all rules of logic, without premises, deductions, or conclusions, and in a quite peculiar way. Natásha was so used to this kind of talk with her husband that for her it was the surest sign of something being wrong between them if Pierre followed a line of logical reasoning. When he began proving anything, or talking argumentatively and calmly and she led on by his example began to do the same, she knew that they were on the verge of a quarrel.

From the moment they were alone and Natásha came up to him with wide-open happy eyes, and quickly seizing his head pressed it to her bosom, saying: "Now you are all mine, mine! You won't escape!"—from that moment this conversation began, contrary to all the laws of logic and contrary to them because quite different subjects were talked about at one and the same time. This simultaneous discussion of many topics did not prevent a clear understanding but on the contrary was the surest sign that they fully understood one another.

Just as in a dream when all is uncertain, unreasoning and contradictory, except the feeling that guides the dream, so in this intercourse contrary to all laws of reason, the words themselves were not consecutive and clear but only the feeling that prompted them.

Natásha spoke to Pierre about her brother's life and doings, of how she had suffered and lacked life during his own absence, and of how she was fonder than ever of Mary, and how Mary was in every way better than herself. In saying this Natásha was sincere in acknowledging Mary's superiority, but at the same time by saying it she made a demand on Pierre that he should, all the same, prefer her to Mary and to all other women, and that now, especially after having seen many women in Petersburg, he should tell her so afresh.

Pierre, answering Natásha's words, told her how intolerable it had been for him to meet ladies at dinners and balls in Petersburg.

"I have quite lost the knack of talking to ladies," he said. "It was simply dull. Besides, I was very busy."

Natásha looked intently at him and went on:

"Mary is so splendid," she said. "How she understands children! It is as if she saw straight into their souls. Yesterday, for instance, Mítya was naughty . . ."

"How like his father he is," Pierre interjected.

Natásha knew why he mentioned Mítya's likeness to Nicholas: the recollection of his dispute with his brother-in-law was unpleasant and he wanted to know what Natásha thought of it.

"Nicholas has the weakness of never agreeing with anything not generally accepted. But I understand that you value what opens up a fresh line," said she, repeating words Pierre had once uttered.

"No, the chief point is that to Nicholas ideas and discussions are an amusement—almost a pastime," said Pierre. "For instance he is collecting a library and has made it a rule not to buy a new book till he has read what he had already bought—Sismondi and Rousseau and Montesquieu," he added with a smile. "You know how much I . . ." he began, to soften down what he had said; but Natásha interrupted him to show that this was unnecessary.

"So you say ideas are an amusement to him. . . ."

"Yes, and for me nothing else is serious. All the time in Petersburg I saw everyone as in a dream. When I am taken up by a thought, all else is mere amusement."

"Ah, I'm so sorry I wasn't there when you met the children," said Natásha. "Which was most delighted? Lisa, I'm sure."

"Yes," Pierre replied, and went on with what was in his mind. "Nicholas says we ought not to think. But I can't help it. Besides, when I was in Petersburg I felt (I can say this to you) that the whole affair would go to pieces without me—everyone was pulling his own way. But I succeeded in uniting them all; and then my idea is so clear and simple. You see, I don't say that we ought to oppose this and that. We may be mistaken. What I say is: 'Join hands, you who love the right, and let there be but one banner—that of active virtue.' Prince Sergéy is a fine fellow and clever."

Natásha would have had no doubt as to the greatness of Pierre's idea, but one thing disconcerted her. "Can a man so important and necessary to society be also my husband? How did this happen?" She wished to express this doubt to him. "Now who could decide whether he is really cleverer than all the others?" she asked herself, and passed in review all those whom Pierre most respected. Judging by what he had said there was no one he had respected so highly as Platón Karatáev.

"Do you know what I am thinking about?" she asked. "About Platón Karatáev. Would he have approved of you now, do you think?"

Pierre was not at all surprised at this question. He understood his wife's line of thought.

"Platón Karatáev?" he repeated, and pondered, evidently sincerely trying to imagine Karatáev's opinion on the subject. "He would not have understood . . . yet perhaps he would."

"I love you awfully!" Natásha suddenly said. "Awfully, awfully!"

"No, he would not have approved," said Pierre, after reflection. "What he would have approved of is our family life. He was always so anxious to find seemliness, happiness, and peace in everything, and I should have been proud to let him see us. There now—you talk of my absence, but you wouldn't believe what a special feeling I have for you after a separation. . . ."

"Yes, I should think . . ." Natásha began.

"No, it's not that. I never leave off loving you. And one couldn't love more, but this is something special. . . . Yes, of course—" he did not finish because their eyes meeting said the rest.

"What nonsense it is," Natásha suddenly exclaimed, "about honeymoons, and that the greatest happiness is at first! On the contrary, now is the best of all. If only you did not go away! Do you remember how we quarreled? And it was always my fault. Always mine. And what we quarreled about—I don't even remember!"

"Always about the same thing," said Pierre with a smile. "Jealo . . ."

"Don't say it! I can't bear it!" Natásha cried, and her eyes glittered coldly and vindictively. "Did you see her?" she added, after a pause.

"No, and if I had I shouldn't have recognized her."

They were silent for a while.

"Oh, do you know? While you were talking in the study I was looking at you," Natásha began, evidently anxious to disperse the cloud that had come over them. "You are as like him as two peas—like the boy." (She meant her little son.) "Oh, it's time to go to him. . . . The milk's come. . . . But I'm sorry to leave you."

They were silent for a few seconds. Then suddenly turning to one another at the same time they both began to speak. Pierre began with self-satisfaction and enthusiasm, Natásha with a quiet happy smile. Having interrupted one another they both stopped to let the other continue.

"No. What did you say? Go on, go on."

"No, you go on, I was talking nonsense," said Natásha.

Pierre finished what he had begun. It was the sequel to his complacent reflections on his success in Petersburg. At that moment it seemed to him that he was chosen to give a new direction to the whole of Russian society and to the whole world.

"I only wished to say that ideas that have great results are always simple ones. My whole idea is that if vicious people are united and constitute a power, then honest folk must do the same. Now that's simple enough."

"Yes."

"And what were you going to say?"

"I? Only nonsense."

"But all the same?"

"Oh nothing, only a trifle," said Natásha, smilingly still more brightly. "I only wanted to tell you about Pétya: today nurse was coming to take him from me, and he laughed, shut his eyes and clung to me. I'm sure he thought he was hiding. Awfully sweet! There, now he's crying. Well, good-bye!" and she left the room.

Meanwhile downstairs in young Nicholas Bolkónski's bedroom a little lamp was burning as usual. (The boy was afraid of the dark and they could not cure him of it.) Dessalles slept propped up on four pillows and his Roman nose emitted sounds of rhythmic snoring. Little Nicholas, who had just waked up in a cold perspiration, sat up in bed and gazed before him with wide-open eyes. He had awaked from a terrible dream. He had dreamed that he and Uncle Pierre, wearing helmets such as were depicted in his Plutarch, were leading a huge army. The army was made up of white slanting lines that filled the air like the cobwebs that float about in autumn and which Dessalles called *les fils de la Vierge*. In front was Glory, which was similar to those threads but rather thicker. He and Pierre were borne along lightly and joyously, nearer and nearer to their goal. Suddenly the threads that moved them began to slacken and become entangled and it grew difficult to move. And Uncle Nicholas stood before them in a stern and threatening attitude.

"Have you done this?" he said, pointing to some broken sealing-wax and pens. "I loved you, but I have orders from Arakchéev and will kill the first of you who moves forward." Little Nicholas turned to look at Pierre but Pierre was no longer there. In his place was his father—Prince Andrew—and his father had neither shape nor form, but he existed, and when little Nicholas perceived him he grew faint with love: he felt himself powerless, limp and formless. His father caressed and pitied him. But Uncle Nicholas came nearer and nearer to them. Terror seized young Nicholas and he awoke.

"My father!" he thought. (Though there were two good portraits of Prince Andrew in the house, Nicholas never imagined him in human form.) "My father has been with me and caressed me. He approved of me and of Uncle Pierre. Whatever he may tell me, I will do it. Mucius Scaevola burned his hand. Why should not the same sort of thing happen to me? I know they want me to learn. And I will learn. But someday I shall have finished learning, and then I will do something. I only pray God that something may happen to me such as happened to Plutarch's men, and I will act as they did. I will do better. Everyone shall know me, love me, and be delighted with me!" And suddenly his bosom heaved with sobs and he began to cry.

"Are you ill?" he heard Dessalles' voice asking.

"No," answered Nicholas, and lay back on his pillow.

"He is good and kind and I am fond of him!" he thought of Dessalles. "But Uncle Pierre! Oh, what a wonderful man he is! And my father? Oh, father, father! Yes, I will do something with which even *he* would be satisfied. . . ."

Second Epilogue

Chapter I

History is the life of nations and of humanity. To seize and put into words, to describe directly the life of humanity or even of a single nation, appears impossible.

The ancient historians all employed one and the same method to describe and seize the apparently elusive—the life of a people. They described the activity of individuals who ruled the people, and regarded the activity of those men as representing the activity of the whole nation.

The question: how did individuals make nations act as they wished and by what was the will of these individuals themselves guided? the ancients met by recognizing a divinity which subjected the nations to the will of a chosen man, and guided the will of that chosen man so as to accomplish ends that were predestined.

For the ancients these questions were solved by a belief in the direct participation of the Deity in human affairs.

Modern history, in theory, rejects both these principles.

It would seem that having rejected the belief of the ancients in man's subjection to the Deity and in a predetermined aim toward which nations are led, modern history should study not the manifestations of power but the causes that produce it. But modern history has not done this. Having in theory rejected the view held by the ancients, it still follows them in practice.

Instead of men endowed with divine authority and directly guided by the will of God, modern history has given us either heroes endowed with extraordinary, superhuman capacities, or simply men of very various kinds, from monarchs to journalists, who lead the masses. Instead of the former divinely appointed aims of the Jewish, Greek, or Roman nations, which ancient historians regarded as representing the progress of humanity, modern history has postulated its own aims—the welfare of the French, German, or English people, or in its highest abstraction, the welfare and civilization of humanity in general, by which is usually meant that of the peoples occupying a small northwesterly portion of a large continent.

Modern history has rejected the beliefs of the ancients without replacing them by a new conception, and the logic of the situation has obliged the historians, after they had apparently rejected the divine authority of the kings and the "fate" of the ancients, to reach the same conclusion by another road, that is, to recognize (1) nations guided by individual men, and (2) the existence of a known aim to which these nations and humanity at large are tending.

At the basis of the works of all the modern historians from Gibbon to Buckle, despite their seeming disagreements and the apparent novelty of their outlooks, lie those two old, unavoidable assumptions.

In the first place the historian describes the activity of individuals who in his opinion have directed humanity (one historian considers only monarchs, generals, and ministers as being such men, while another includes also orators, learned men, reformers, philosophers and poets). Secondly, it is assumed that the goal toward which humanity is being led is known to the historians: to one of them this goal is the greatness of the Roman, Spanish, or French realm; to another it is liberty, equality, and a certain kind of civilization of a small corner of the world called Europe.

In 1789 a ferment arises in Paris; it grows, spreads, and is expressed by a movement of peoples from west to east. Several times it moves eastward and collides with a counter-movement from the east westwards. In 1812 it reaches its extreme limit, Moscow, and then with remarkable symmetry, a counter-movement occurs from east to west, attracting to it as the first movement had done, the nations of middle Europe. The counter-movement reaches the starting point of the first movement in the west—Paris—and subsides.

During that twenty-year period an immense number of fields were left untilled, houses were burned, trade changed its direction, millions of men migrated, were impoverished or were enriched, and millions of Christian men professing the law of love of their fellows slew one another.

What does all this mean? Why did it happen? What made those people burn houses and slay their fellow-men? What were the causes of these events? What force made men act so? These are the instinctive, plain and most legitimate questions humanity asks itself when it encounters the monuments and tradition of that period.

For a reply to these questions the common sense of mankind turns to the science of history, whose aim is to enable nations and humanity to know themselves.

If history had retained the conception of the ancients it would have said that God, to reward or punish his people, gave Napoleon power and directed his will to the fulfillment of the divine ends, and that reply, would have been clear and complete. One might believe or disbelieve in the divine significance of Napoleon, but for anyone believing in it there would have been nothing unintelligible in the history of that period, nor would there have been any contradictions.

But modern history cannot give that reply. Science does not admit the conception of the ancients as to the direct participation of the Deity in human affairs, and therefore history ought to give other answers.

Modern history replying to these questions says: You want to know what this movement means, what caused it, and what force produced these events? Then listen:

"Louis XIV was a very proud and self-confident man; he had such and such mistresses and such and such ministers and he ruled France badly. His descendants were weak men and they too ruled France badly. And they had such and such favorites and such and such mistresses. Moreover certain men wrote some books at that time. At the end of the eighteenth century there were a couple of dozen men in Paris who began to talk about all men being free and equal. This caused people all over France to begin to slash at and down one another. They killed the king and many other people. At that time there was in France a man of genius—Napoleon. He conquered everybody everywhere—that is, he killed many people because he was a great genius. And for some reason he went to kill Africans, and killed them so well and was so cunning and wise that when he returned to France he ordered everybody to obey him, and they all obeyed him. Having become an Emperor he again went out to kill people in Italy, Austria and Prussia. And there too he killed a great many. In Russia there was an Emperor, Alexander, who decided to restore order in Europe and therefore fought against Napoleon. In 1807 he suddenly made friends with him, but in 1811 they again quarreled and again began killing many people. Napoleon led six hundred thousand men into Russia and captured Moscow; then he suddenly ran away from Moscow, and the Emperor Alexander, helped by the advice of Stein and others, united Europe to arm against the disturber of its peace. All Napoleon's allies suddenly became his enemies and their forces advanced against the fresh forces he raised. The Allies defeated Napoleon, entered Paris, forced Napoleon to abdicate and sent him to the island of Elba, not depriving him of the title of Emperor and showing him every respect, though five years before and one year later they all regarded him as an outlaw and a brigand. Then Louis XVIII who till then had been the laughing-stock both of the French and the Allies, began to reign. And Napoleon shedding tears before his Old Guards, renounced the throne and went into exile. Then the skillful statesmen and diplomatists (especially Talleyrand, who managed to sit down in a particular chair before anyone else and thereby extended the frontiers of France) talked in Vienna and by these conversations made the nations happy or unhappy. Suddenly the diplomatists and monarchs nearly quarreled and were on the point of again ordering their armies to kill one another, but just then Napoleon arrived in France with a battalion, and the French, who had been hating him, immediately all submitted to him. But the Allied monarchs were angry at this and went to fight the French once more. And they defeated the genius Napoleon and, suddenly recognizing him as a brigand, sent him to the island of St. Helena. And the exile, separated from the beloved France so dear to his heart, died a lingering death on that rock and bequeathed his great deeds to posterity.

But in Europe a reaction occurred and the sovereigns once again all began to oppress their subjects."

It would be a mistake to think that this is ironic—a caricature of the historical accounts. On the contrary it is a very mild expression of the contradictory replies, not meeting the questions, which *all* the historians give, from the compilers of memoirs and the histories of separate States to the writers of general histories and the new histories of the *culture* of that period.

The strangeness and absurdity of these replies arise from the fact that modern history, like a deaf man, answers questions no one has asked.

If the purpose of history be to give a description of the movement of humanity and of the peoples, the first question—in the absence of a reply to which all the rest will be incomprehensible—is: What is the power that moves peoples? To this, modern history laboriously replies either that Napoleon was a great genius, or that Louis XIV was very proud, or that certain writers wrote certain books.

All that may be so and mankind is ready to agree with it, but it is not what was asked. All *that* would be interesting if we recognized a divine power based on itself and always consistently directing its nations through Napoleons, Louis-es, and writers; but we do not acknowledge such a power, and therefore before speaking about Napoleons, Louis-es and authors, we ought to be shown the connection existing between these men and the movement of the nations.

If instead of a divine power some other force has appeared, it should be explained in what this new force consists, for the whole interest of history lies precisely in that force.

History seems to assume that this force is self-evident and known to everyone. But in spite of every desire to regard it as known, anyone reading many historical works cannot help doubting whether this new force, so variously understood by the historians themselves, is really quite well known to everybody.

Chapter II

WHAT FORCE MOVES THE NATIONS?

Biographical historians and historians of separate nations understand this force as a power inherent in heroes and rulers. In their narration events occur solely by the will of a Napoleon, an Alexander, or in general of the persons they describe. The answers given by this kind of historian to the question of what force causes events to happen, are satisfactory only as long as there is but one historian to each event. As soon as historians of different nationalities and tendencies begin to describe the same event, the replies they give immediately lose all meaning, for this force is understood by them all not only differently but often in quite contradictory ways. One historian says that an event was produced by Napoleon's power, another that it was produced by Alexander's, a third that it was due to the power of some other person. Besides this, historians of that kind contradict each other even in their statement as to the force on which the authority of some particular person was based. Thiers, a Bonapartist, says that Napoleon's power was based on his virtue and genius. Lanfrey, a Republican, says it was based on his trickery and deception of the people. So the historians of this class, by mutually destroying one another's positions, destroy the understanding of the force which produces events, and furnish no reply to history's essential question.

Writers of universal history who deal with all the nations, seem to recognize how erroneous is the specialist historians' view of the force which produces events. They do not recognize it as a power inherent in heroes and rulers, but as the resultant of a multiplicity of variously directed forces. In describing a war or the subjugation of a people, a general historian looks for the cause of the event not in the power of one man, but in the interaction of many persons connected with the event.

According to this view the power of historical personages, represented as the product of many forces, can no longer it would seem be regarded as a force that itself produces events. Yet in most cases universal historians still employ the conception of power as a force that itself produces events, and treat it as their cause. In their exposition, an historic character is first the product of his time, and his power only the resultant of various forces, and then his power is itself a force producing events. Gervinus, Schlosser and others, for instance, at one time prove Napoleon to be a product of the Revolution, of the ideas of 1789 and so forth, and at another plainly say that the campaign of 1812 and other things they do not like were simply the product of Napoleon's misdirected will, and that the very ideas of 1789 were arrested in their development by Napoleon's caprice. The ideas of the Revolution and the general temper of the age produced Napoleon's power. But Napoleon's power suppressed the ideas of the Revolution and the general temper of the age.

This curious contradiction is not accidental. Not only does it occur at every step, but the universal historians' accounts are all made up of a chain of such contradictions. This contradiction occurs because after entering the field of analysis the universal historians stop halfway.

To find component forces equal to the composite or resultant force, the sum of the components must equal the resultant. This condition is never observed by the universal historians, and so to explain the resultant forces they are obliged to admit, in addition to the insufficient components, another unexplained force affecting the resultant action.

Specialist historians describing the campaign of 1813 or the restoration of the Bourbons, plainly assert that these events were produced by the will of Alexander. But the universal historian Gervinus, refuting this opinion of the specialist historian, tries to prove that the campaign of 1813 and the restoration of the Bourbons were due to other things beside Alexander's will—such as the activity of Stein, Metternich, Madame de Staël, Talleyrand, Fichte, Chateaubriand, and others. The historian evidently decomposes Alexander's power into the components: Talleyrand, Chateaubriand, and the rest—but the sum of the components, that is, the interactions of Chateaubriand, Talleyrand, Madame de Staël and the others, evidently does not equal the resultant, namely the phenomenon of millions of Frenchmen submitting to the Bourbons. That Chateaubriand, Madame de Staël and others spoke certain words to one another, only affected their mutual relations but does not account for the submission of millions. And therefore to explain how from these relations of theirs the submission of millions of people resulted—that is, how component forces equal to one A gave a resultant equal to a thousand times *A*—the historian is again obliged to fall back on power—the force he had denied—and to recognize it as the resultant of the forces, that is, he has to admit an unexplained force acting on the resultant. And that is just what the universal historians do, and consequently they not only contradict the specialist historians but contradict themselves.

Peasants having no clear idea of the cause of rain, say, according to whether they want rain or fine weather: "The wind has blown the clouds away," or, "The wind has brought up the clouds." And in the same way the universal historians sometimes, when it pleases them and fits in with their theory, say that power is the result of events, and sometimes, when they want to prove something else, say that power produces events.

A third class of historians—the so-called historians of culture—following the path laid down by the universal historians who sometimes accept writers and ladies as forces producing events—again take that force to be something quite different. They see it in what is called culture—in mental activity.

The historians of culture are quite consistent in regard to their progenitors the writers of universal histories, for if historical events may be explained by the fact that certain persons treated one another in such and such ways, why not explain them by the fact that such and such people wrote such and such books? Of the immense number of indications accompanying every vital phenomenon, these historians select the indication of intellectual activity and say that this indication is the cause. But despite their endeavors to prove that the cause of events lies in intellectual activity, only by a great stretch can one admit that there is any connection between intellectual activity and the movement of peoples, and in no case can one admit that intellectual activity controls people's actions, for that view is not confirmed by such facts as the very cruel murders of the French Revolution resulting from the doctrine of the equality of man, or the very cruel wars and executions resulting from the preaching of love.

But even admitting as correct all the cunningly devised arguments with which these histories are filled—admitting that nations are governed by some undefined force called an *idea*—history's essential question still remains unanswered, and to the former power of monarchs and to the influence of advisers and other people introduced by the universal historians, another, newer force—the *idea*—is added, the connection of which with the masses needs explanation. It is possible to understand that Napoleon had power and so events occurred; with some effort one may even conceive that Napoleon together with other influences was the cause of an event; but how a book, *Le Contrat Social,* had the effect of making Frenchmen begin to drown one another, cannot be understood without an explanation of the causal nexus of this new force with the event.

Undoubtedly some relation exists between all who live contemporaneously, and so it is possible to find some connection between the intellectual activity of men and their historical movements, just as such a connection may be found between the movements of humanity and commerce, handicraft, gardening, or anything else you please. But why intellectual activity is considered by the historians of culture to be the cause or expression of the whole historical movement is hard to understand. Only the following considerations can have led the historians to such a conclusion: (1) that history is written by learned men, and so it is natural and agreeable for them to think that the activity of their class supplies the basis of the movement of all humanity, just as a similar belief is natural and agreeable to traders, agriculturists and soldiers (if they do not express it, that is merely because traders and soldiers do not write history) and (2) that spiritual activity, enlightenment, civilization, culture, ideas, are all indistinct, indefinite conceptions under whose banner it is very easy to use words having a still less definite meaning, and which can therefore be readily introduced into any theory.

But not to speak of the intrinsic quality of histories of this kind (which may possibly even be of use to someone for something) the histories of culture, to which all general histories tend more and more to approximate, are significant from the fact that after seriously and minutely examining various religious, philosophic and political doctrines as causes of events, as soon as they have to describe an actual historic event such as the campaign of 1812 for instance, they involuntarily describe it as resulting from an exercise of power—and say plainly that that was the result of Napoleon's will. Speaking so, the historians of culture involuntarily contradict themselves, and show that the new force they have devised does not account for what happens in history, and that history can only be explained by introducing a power which they apparently do not recognize.

Chapter III

A LOCOMOTIVE IS MOVING. SOMEONE ASKS: WHAT MOVES IT? A PEASANT SAYS THE DEVIL MOVES it. Another man says the locomotive moves because its wheels go round. A third asserts that the cause of its movement lies in the smoke which the wind carries away.

The peasant is irrefutable. He has devised a complete explanation. To refute him someone would have to prove to him that there is no devil, or another peasant would have to explain to him that it is not the devil but a German, who moves the locomotive. Only then, as a result of the contradiction, will they see that they are both wrong. But the man who says that the movement of the wheels is the cause refutes himself, for having once begun to analyze he ought to go on and explain further why the wheels go round; and till he has reached the ultimate cause of the movement of the locomotive in the pressure of steam in the boiler, he has no right to stop in his search for the cause. The man who explains the movement of the locomotive by the smoke that is carried back, has noticed that the wheels do not supply an explanation, and has taken the first sign that occurs to him and in his turn has offered that as an explanation.

The only conception that can explain the movement of the locomotive is that of a force commensurate with the movement observed.

The only conception that can explain the movement of the peoples is that of some force commensurate with the whole movement of the peoples.

Yet to supply this conception various historians take forces of different kinds, all of which are incommensurate with the movement observed. Some see it as a force directly inherent in heroes, as the peasant sees the devil in the locomotive; others as a force resulting from several other forces, like the movement of the wheels; others again as an intellectual influence, like the smoke that is blown away.

So long as histories are written of separate individuals, whether Caesars, Alexanders, Luthers or Voltaires, and not the histories of *all*, absolutely *all* those who take part in an event, it is quite impossible to describe the movement of humanity without the conception of a force compelling men to direct their activity toward a certain end. And the only such conception known to historians is that of power.

This conception is the one handle by means of which the material of history, as at present expounded, can be dealt with, and anyone who breaks that handle off, as Buckle did, without finding some other method of treating historical material, merely deprives himself of the one possible way of dealing with it. The necessity of the conception of power as an explanation of historical events is best demonstrated by the universal historians and historians of culture themselves, for they professedly reject that conception but inevitably have recourse to it at every step.

In dealing with humanity's inquiry, the science of history up to now is like money in circulation—paper money and coin. The biographies and special national histories are like paper money. They can be used and can circulate and fulfill their purpose without harm to anyone and even advantageously, as long as no one asks what is the security behind them. You need only forget to ask how the will of heroes produces events, and such histories as Thiers' will be interesting and instructive and may perhaps even possess a tinge of poetry. But just as doubts of the real value of paper money arise either because, being easy to make, too much of it gets made, or because people try to exchange it for gold; so also doubts concerning the real value of such histories arise either because too many of them are written, or because in his simplicity of heart someone inquires: By what force did Napoleon do this?—that is, wants to exchange the current paper money for the real gold of actual comprehension.

The writers of universal histories and of the history of culture are like people who, recognizing the defects of paper money, decide to substitute for it money made of metal that has not the specific gravity of gold. It may indeed make jingling coin, but will do no more than that. Paper money may deceive the ignorant, but nobody is deceived by tokens of base metal that have no value but merely jingle. As gold is gold only if it is serviceable not merely for exchange but also for use, so universal historians will be valuable only when they can reply to history's essential question: What is power? The universal historians give contradictory replies to that question, while the historians of culture evade it and answer something quite different. And as counters of imitation gold can be used only among a group of people who agree to accept them as gold, or among those who do not know the nature of gold, so universal historians and historians of culture, not answering humanity's essential question, serve as currency for some purposes of their own, only in Universities and among the mass of readers who have a taste for what they call "serious reading."

Chapter IV

HAVING ABANDONED THE CONCEPTION OF THE ANCIENTS AS TO THE DIVINE SUBJECTION OF THE will of a nation to some chosen man and the subjection of that man's will to the Deity, history cannot without contradictions take a single step till it has chosen one of two things: either a return to the former belief in the direct intervention of the Deity in human affairs, or a definite explanation of the meaning of the force producing historical events and termed "power."

A return to the first is impossible, the belief has been destroyed; and so it is essential to explain what is meant by power.

Napoleon ordered an army to be raised and go to war. We are so accustomed to that idea and have become so used to it, that the question: Why did six hundred thousand men go to fight when Napoleon uttered certain words, seems to us senseless. He had the power and so what he ordered was done.

This reply is quite satisfactory if we believe that the power was given him by God. But as soon as we do not admit that, it becomes essential to determine what is this power of one man over others.

It cannot be the direct physical power of a strong man over a weak one—a domination based on the application or threat of physical force, like the power of Hercules; nor can it be based on the effect of moral force, as in their simplicity some historians think who say that the leading figures in history are heroes, that is, men gifted with a special strength of soul and mind called genius. This power cannot be based on the predominance of moral strength for, not to mention heroes such as Napoleon about whose moral qualities opinions differ widely, history shows us that neither a Louis XI nor a Metternich, who ruled over millions of people, had any particular moral qualities, but on the contrary were generally morally weaker than any of the millions they ruled over.

If the source of power lies neither in the physical nor in the moral qualities of him who possesses it, it must evidently be looked for elsewhere—in the relation to the people of the man who wields the power.

And that is how power is understood by the science of jurisprudence, that exchange-bank of history which offers to exchange history's understanding of power for true gold.

Power is the collective will of the people transferred, by expressed or tacit consent, to their chosen rulers.

In the domain of jurisprudence, which consists of discussions of how a State and power might be arranged were it possible for all that to be arranged, it is all very clear; but when applied to history that definition of power needs explanation.

The science of jurisprudence regards the State and power as the ancients regarded fire—namely, as something existing absolutely. But for history, the State and power are merely phenomena, just as for modern physics fire is not an element but a phenomenon.

From this fundamental difference between the view held by history and that held by jurisprudence, it follows that jurisprudence can tell minutely how in its opinion power should be constituted and what power—existing immutably outside time—is, but to history's questions about the meaning of the mutations of power *in* time it can answer nothing.

If power be the collective will of the people transferred to their ruler, was Pugachëv a representative of the will of the people? If not, then why was Napoleon I? Why was Napoleon III a criminal when he was taken prisoner at Boulogne, and why, later on, were those criminals whom he arrested?

Do palace revolutions—in which sometimes only two or three people take part—transfer the will of the people to a new ruler? In international relations, is the will of the people also transferred to their conqueror? Was the will of the Confederation of the Rhine transferred to Napoleon in 1808? Was the will of the Russian people transferred to Napoleon in 1809, when our army in alliance with the French went to fight the Austrians?

To these questions three answers are possible:

Either to assume (1) that the will of the people is always unconditionally transferred to the ruler or rulers they have chosen, and that therefore every emergence of a new power, every struggle against the power once appointed, should be absolutely regarded as an infringement of the real power; or (2) that the will of the people is transferred to the rulers conditionally, under definite and known conditions, and to show that all limitations, conflicts, and even destructions of power, result from a non-observance by the rulers of the conditions under which their power was entrusted to them; or (3) that the will of the people is delegated to the rulers conditionally, but that the conditions are unknown and indefinite, and that the appearance of several authorities, their struggles and their falls, result solely from the greater or lesser fulfillment by the rulers of these unknown conditions on which the will of the people is transferred from some people to others.

And these are the three ways in which the historians do explain the relation of the people to their rulers.

Some historians—those biographical and specialist historians already referred to—in their simplicity failing to understand the question of the meaning of power, seem to consider that the collective will of the people is unconditionally transferred to historical persons, and therefore when describing some single State they assume that particular power to be the one absolute and real power, and that any other force opposing this is not a power but a violation of power—mere violence.

Their theory, suitable for primitive and peaceful periods of history, has the inconvenience—in application to complex and stormy periods in the life of nations during which various powers arise simultaneously and struggle with one another—that a Legitimist historian will prove that the National Convention, the Directory, and Bonaparte, were mere infringers of the true power, while a Republican and a Bonapartist will prove: the one that the Convention and the other that the Empire was the real power, and that all the others were violations of power. Evidently the explanations furnished by these historians being mutually contradictory can only satisfy young children.

Recognizing the falsity of this view of history, another set of historians say that power rests on a conditional delegation of the will of the people to their rulers, and that historical leaders have power only conditionally on carrying out the program that the will of the people has by tacit agreement prescribed to them. But what this program consists in these historians do not say, or if they do they continually contradict one another.

Each historian, according to his view of what constitutes a nation's progress, looks for these conditions in the greatness, wealth, freedom, or enlightenment of the citizens of France or some other country. But not to mention the historians' contradictions as to the nature of this program—or even admitting that some one general program of these conditions exists—the facts of history almost always contradict that theory. If the conditions under which power is entrusted consist in the wealth, freedom, and enlightenment of the people, how is it that Louis XIV and Iván the Terrible end their reigns tranquilly, while Louis XVI and Charles I are executed by their people? To this question the historians reply that Louis XIV's activity contrary to the program, reacted on Louis XVI. But why did it not react on Louis XIV or on Louis XV—why should it react just on Louis XVI? And what is the time limit for such reactions? To these questions there are and can be no answers. Equally little does this view explain why for several centuries the collective will is not withdrawn from certain rulers and their heirs, and then suddenly during a period of fifty years is transferred to the Convention, to the Directory, to Napoleon, to Alexander, to Louis XVIII, to Napoleon again, to Charles X, to Louis Philippe, to a Republican government, and to Napoleon III. When explaining these rapid transfers of the people's will from one individual to another, especially in view of international relations, conquests and alliances, the historians are obliged to admit that some of these transfers are not normal delegations of the people's will but are accidents dependent on cunning, on mistakes, on craft, or on the weakness of a diplomatist, a ruler, or a party leader. So that the greater part of the events of history—civil wars, revolutions and conquests—are presented by these historians not as the results of free transferences of the people's will, but as results of the ill-directed will of one or more individuals, that is, once again, as usurpations of power. And so these historians also see and admit historical events which are exceptions to the theory.

These historians resemble a botanist who having noticed that some plants grow from seeds producing two cotyledons, should insist that all that grows does so by sprouting into two leaves, and that the palm, the mushroom, and even the oak which blossom into full growth and no longer resemble two leaves, are deviations from the theory.

Historians of the third class assume that the will of the people is transferred to historic personages conditionally, but that the conditions are unknown to us. They say that historical personages have power only because they fulfill the will of the people which has been delegated to them.

But in that case, if the force that moves nations lies not in the historic leaders but in the nations themselves, what significance have those leaders?

The leaders, these historians tell us, express the will of the people: the activity of the leaders represents the activity of the people.

But in that case the question arises whether all the activity of the leaders serves as an expression of the people's will or only some part of it? If the whole activity of the leaders serves as the expression of the people's will, as some historians suppose, then all the details of the court scandals contained in the biographies of a Napoleon or a Catherine serve to express the life of the nation, which is evident nonsense; but if it is only some particular side of the activity of an historical leader which serves to express the people's life, as other so-called "philosophical" historians believe, then to determine which side of the activity of a leader expresses the nation's life, we have first of all to know in what the nation's life consists.

Met by this difficulty historians of that class devise some most obscure, impalpable and general abstraction which can cover all conceivable occurrences, and declare this abstraction to be the aim of humanity's movement. The most usual generalizations adopted by almost all the historians are: freedom, equality, enlightenment, progress, civilization and culture. Postulating some generalization as the goal of the movement of humanity, the historians study the men of whom the greatest number of monuments have remained: kings, ministers, generals, authors, reformers, popes and journalists, to the extent to which in their opinion these persons have promoted or hindered that abstraction. But as it is in no way proved that the aim of humanity does consist in freedom, equality, enlightenment, or civilization, and as the connection of the people with the rulers and enlighteners of humanity is only based on the arbitrary assumption that the collective will of the people is always transferred to the men whom we have noticed, it happens that the activity of the millions who migrate, burn houses, abandon agriculture, and destroy one another, never is expressed in the account of the activity of some dozen people who did not burn houses, practice agriculture, or slay their fellow-creatures.

History proves this at every turn. Is the ferment of the peoples of the west at the end of the XVIIIth century and their drive eastward explained by the activity of Louis XIV, XV, and XVI, their mistresses and ministers, and by the lives of Napoleon, Rousseau, Diderot, Beaumarchais and others?

Is the movement of the Russian people eastward to Kazán and Siberia expressed by details of the morbid character of Iván the Terrible and by his correspondence with Kurbski?

Is the movement of the peoples at the time of the Crusades explained by the life and activity of the Godfreys and the Louis-es and their ladies? For us that movement of the peoples from west to east, without leaders, with a crowd of vagrants, and with Peter the Hermit, remains incomprehensible. And yet more incomprehensible is the cessation of that movement when a rational and sacred aim for the Crusade—the deliverance of Jerusalem—had been clearly defined by historic leaders. Popes, kings and knights incited the peoples to free the Holy Land; but the people did not go, for the unknown cause which had previously impelled them to go no longer existed. The history of the Godfreys and the Minnesingers can evidently not cover the life of the peoples. And the history of the Godfreys and the Minnesingers has remained the history of Godfreys and Minnesingers, but the history of the life of the peoples and their impulses has remained unknown.

Still less does the history of authors and reformers explain to us the life of the peoples.

The history of culture explains to us the impulses and conditions of life and thought of a writer or a reformer. We learn that Luther had a hot temper and said such and such things; we learn that Rousseau was suspicious and wrote such and such books; but we do not learn why after the Reformation the peoples massacred one another, nor why during the French Revolution they guillotined one another.

If we unite both these kinds of history, as is done by the newest historians, we shall have the history of monarchs and writers, but not the history of the life of the peoples.

Chapter V

THE LIFE OF THE NATIONS IS NOT CONTAINED IN THE LIVES OF A FEW MEN, FOR THE CONNECTION between those men and the nations has not been found. The theory that this connection is based on the transference of the collective will of a people to certain historical personages, is an hypothesis unconfirmed by the experience of history.

The theory of the transference of the collective will of the people to historic persons may perhaps explain much in the domain of jurisprudence and be essential for its purposes, but in its application to history, as soon as revolutions, conquests, or civil wars occur—that is, as soon as history begins—that theory explains nothing.

The theory seems irrefutable just because the act of transference of the people's will cannot be verified, for it never occurred.

Whatever happens and whoever may stand at the head of affairs, the theory can always say that such and such a person took the lead because the collective will was transferred to him.

The replies this theory gives to historical questions are like the replies of a man who, watching the movements of a herd of cattle and paying no attention to the varying quality of the pasturage in different parts of the field, or to the driving of the herdsman, should attribute the direction the herd takes to what animal happens to be at its head.

"The herd goes in that direction because the animal in front leads it and the collective will of all the other animals is vested in that leader." This is what historians of the first class say—those who assume the unconditional transference of the people's will.

"If the animals leading the herd change, this happens because the collective will of all the animals is transferred from one leader to another, according to whether the animal is or is not leading them in the direction selected by the whole herd." Such is the reply historians who assume that the collective will of the people is delegated to rulers under conditions which they regard as known. (With this method of observation it often happens that the observer, influenced by the direction he himself prefers, regards those as leaders who owing to the people's change of direction are no longer in front, but on one side, or even in the rear.)

"If the animals in front are continually changing and the direction of the whole herd is constantly altered, this is because in order to follow a given direction the animals transfer their will to the animals that have attracted our attention, and to study the movements of the herd we must watch the movements of all the prominent animals moving on all sides of the herd." So say the third class of historians who regard all historical persons, from monarchs to journalists, as the expression of their age.

The theory of the transference of the will of the people to historic persons is merely a paraphrase—a restatement of the question in other words.

What causes historical events? Power. What is power? Power is the collective will of the people transferred to one person. Under what condition is the will of the people delegated to one person? On condition that that person expresses the will of the whole people. That is, power is power: in other words, power is a word the meaning of which we do not understand.

If the realm of human knowledge were confined to abstract reasoning, then having subjected to criticism the explanation of "power" that juridical science gives us, humanity would conclude that power is merely a word and has no real existence. But to understand phenomena man has, besides abstract reasoning, experience by which he verifies his reflections. And experience tells us that power is not merely a word but an actually existing phenomenon.

Not to speak of the fact that no description of the collective activity of men can do without the conception of power, the existence of power is proved both by history and by observing contemporary events.

Whenever an event occurs a man appears or men appear, by whose will the event seems to have taken place. Napoleon III issues a decree and the French go to Mexico. The King of Prussia and Bismarck issue decrees and an army enters Bohemia. Napoleon I issues a decree and an army enters Russia. Alexander I gives a command and the French submit to the Bourbons. Experience shows us that whatever event occurs it is always related to the will of one or of several men who have decreed it.

The historians, in accord with the old habit of acknowledging divine intervention in human affairs, want to see the cause of events in the expression of the will of someone endowed with power, but that supposition is not confirmed either by reason or by experience.

On the one side reflection shows that the expression of a man's will—his words—are only part of the general activity expressed in an event, as for instance in a war or a revolution, and so without assuming an incomprehensible, supernatural force—a miracle—one cannot admit that words can be the immediate cause of the movements of millions of men. On the other hand, even if we admitted that words could be the cause of events, history shows that the expression of the will of historical personages does not in most cases produce any effect, that is to say, their commands are often not executed, and sometimes the very opposite of what they order occurs.

Without admitting divine intervention in the affairs of humanity we cannot regard "power" as the cause of events.

Power, from the standpoint of experience, is merely the relation that exists between the expression of someone's will and the execution of that will by others.

To explain the conditions of that relationship we must first establish a conception of the expression of will, referring it to man and not to the Deity.

If the Deity issues a command, expresses His will, as ancient history tells us, the expression of that will is independent of time and is not caused by anything, for the Divinity is not controlled by an event. But speaking of commands that are the expression of the will of men acting in time and in relation to one another, to explain the connection of commands with events we must restore: (1) the condition of all that takes place: the continuity of movement in time both of the events and of the person who commands, and (2) the inevitability of the connection between the person commanding and those who execute his command.

Chapter VI

ONLY THE EXPRESSION OF THE WILL OF THE DEITY, NOT DEPENDENT ON TIME, CAN RELATE TO a whole series of events occurring over a period of years or centuries, and only the Deity, independent of everything, can by His sole will determine the direction of humanity's movement; but man acts in time and himself takes part in what occurs.

Reinstating the first condition omitted, that of time, we see that no command can be executed without some preceding order having been given rendering the execution of the last command possible.

No command ever appears spontaneously, or itself covers a whole series of occurrences; but each command follows from another, and never refers to a whole series of events but always to one moment only of an event.

When, for instance, we say that Napoleon ordered armies to go to war, we combine in one simultaneous expression a whole series of consecutive commands dependent one on another. Napoleon could not have commanded an invasion of Russia and never did so. Today he ordered such and such papers to be written to Vienna, to Berlin, and to Petersburg; tomorrow such and such decrees and orders to the army, the fleet, the commissariat, and so on and so on—millions of commands, which formed a whole series corresponding to a series of events which brought the French armies into Russia.

If throughout his reign Napoleon gave commands concerning an invasion of England and expended on no other undertaking so much time and effort, and yet during his whole reign never once attempted to execute that design but undertook an expedition into Russia, with which country he considered it desirable to be in alliance (a conviction he repeatedly expressed)—this came about because his commands did not correspond to the course of events in the first case, but did so correspond in the latter.

For an order to be certainly executed, it is necessary that a man should order what can be executed. But to know what can and what cannot be executed is impossible, not only in the case of Napoleon's invasion of Russia in which millions participated, but even in the simplest event, for in either case millions of obstacles may arise to prevent its execution. Every order executed is always one of an immense number unexecuted. All the impossible orders inconsistent with the course of events remain unexecuted. Only the possible ones get linked up with a consecutive series of commands corresponding to a series of events, and are executed.

Our false conception that an event is caused by a command which precedes it, is due to the fact that when the event has taken place and out of thousands of others those few commands which were consistent with that event have been executed, we forget about the others that were not executed because they could not be. Apart from that, the chief source of our error in this matter is due to the fact that in the historical accounts a whole series of innumerable, diverse and petty events, such for instance as all those which led the French armies to Russia, is generalized into one event in accord with the result produced by that series of events, and corresponding with this generalization the whole series of commands is also generalized into a single expression of will.

We say that Napoleon wished to invade Russia and invaded it. In reality in all Napoleon's activity we never find anything resembling an expression of that wish, but find a series of orders, or expressions of his will, very variously and indefinitely directed. Amid a long series of unexecuted orders of Napoleon's one series, for the campaign of 1812, was carried out—not because those orders differed in any way from the other, unexecuted orders but because they coincided with the course of events that led the French army into Russia; just as in stencil work this or that figure comes out not because the color was laid on from this side or in that way, but because it was laid on from all sides over the figure cut in the stencil.

So that examining the relation in time of the commands to the events, we find that a command can never be the cause of the event, but that a certain definite dependence exists between the two.

To understand in what this dependence consists it is necessary to reinstate another omitted condition of every command proceeding not from the Deity but from a man, which is, that the man who gives the command himself takes part in the event.

This relation of the commander to those he commands is just what is called power. This relation consists in the following:

For common action people always unite in certain combinations, in which regardless of the difference of the aims set for the common action, the relation between those taking part in it is always the same.

Men uniting in these combinations always assume such relations toward one another that the larger number take a more direct share, and the smaller number a less direct share, in the collective action for which they have combined.

Of all the combinations in which men unite for collective action one of the most striking and definite examples is an army.

Every army is composed of lower grades of the service—the rank and file—of whom there are always the greatest number; of the next higher military rank—corporals and noncommissioned officers of whom there are fewer, and of still higher officers of whom there are still fewer, and so on to the highest military command which is concentrated in one person.

A military organization may be quite correctly compared to a cone, of which the base with the largest diameter consists of the rank and file; the next higher and smaller section of the cone consists of the next higher grades of the army, and so on to the apex, the point of which will represent the commander-in-chief.

The soldiers, of whom there are the most, form the lower section of the cone and its base. The soldier himself does the stabbing, hacking, burning and pillaging, and always receives orders for these actions from men above him; he himself never gives an order. The non-commissioned officers (of whom there are fewer) perform the action itself less frequently than the soldiers, but they already give commands. An officer still less often acts directly himself, but commands still more frequently. A general does nothing but command the troops, indicates the objective, and hardly ever uses a weapon himself. The commander-in-chief never takes direct part in the action itself, but only gives general orders concerning the movement of the mass of the troops. A similar relation of people to one another is seen in every combination of men for common activity—in agriculture, trade, and every administration.

And so without particularly analyzing all the contiguous sections of a cone and of the ranks of an army, or the ranks and positions in any administrative or public business whatever from the lowest to the highest, we see a law by which men, to take associated action, combine in such relations that the more directly they participate in performing the action the less they can command and the more numerous they are, while the less their direct participation in the action itself, the more they command and the fewer of them there are; rising in this way from the lowest ranks to the man at the top, who takes the least direct share in the action and directs his activity chiefly to commanding.

This relation of the men who command to those they command is what constitutes the essence of the conception called power.

Having restored the condition of time under which all events occur, we find that a command is executed only when it is related to a corresponding series of events. Restoring the essential condition of relation between those who command and those who execute, we find that by the very nature of the case those who command take the smallest part in the action itself and that their activity is exclusively directed to commanding.

Chapter VII

When an event is taking place people express their opinions and wishes about it, and as the event results from the collective activity of many people, some one of the opinions or wishes expressed is sure to be fulfilled if but approximately. When one of the opinions expressed is fulfilled, that opinion gets connected with the event as a command preceding it.

Men are hauling a log. Each of them expresses his opinion as to how and where to haul it. They haul the log away, and it happens that this is done as one of them said. He *ordered* it. There we have command and power in their primary form. The man who worked most with his hands could not think so much about what he was doing, or reflect on or command what would result from the common activity; while the man who commanded more would evidently work less with his hands on account of his greater verbal activity.

When some larger concourse of men direct their activity to a common aim there is a yet sharper division of those who, because their activity is given to directing and commanding, take less less part in the direct work.

When a man works alone he always has a certain set of reflections which as it seems to him directed his past activity, justify his present activity, and guide him in planning his future actions. Just the same is done by a concourse of people, allowing those who do not take a direct part in the activity to devise considerations, justifications and surmises concerning their collective activity.

For reasons known or unknown to us the French began to drown and kill one another. And corresponding to the event its justification appears in people's belief that this was necessary for the welfare of France, for liberty, and for equality. People ceased to kill one another, and this event was accompanied by its justification in the necessity for a centralization of power, resistance to Europe, and so on. Men went from the west to the east killing their fellow-men, and the event was accompanied by phrases about the glory of France, the baseness of England, and so on. History shows us that these justifications of the events have no common sense and are all contradictory, as in the case of killing a man as the result of recognizing his rights, and the killing of millions in Russia for the humiliation of England. But these justifications have a very necessary significance in their own day.

These justifications release those who produce the events from moral responsibility. These temporary aims are like the broom fixed in front of a locomotive to clear the snow from the rails in front: they clear men's moral responsibilities from their path.

Without such justification there would be no reply to the simplest question that presents itself when examining each historical event. How is it that millions of men commit collective crimes—make war, commit murder, and so on?

With the present complex forms of political and social life in Europe can any event that is not prescribed, decreed, or ordered by monarchs, ministers, parliaments, or newspapers, be imagined? Is there any collective action which cannot find its justification in political unity, in patriotism, in the balance-of-power, or in civilization? So that every event that occurs inevitably coincides with some expressed wish, and receiving a justification, presents itself as the result of the will of one man or of several men.

In whatever direction a ship moves, the flow of the waves it cuts will always be noticeable ahead of it. To those on board the ship the movement of those waves will be the only perceptible motion.

Only by watching closely moment by moment the movement of that flow and comparing it with the movement of the ship, do we convince ourselves that every bit of it is occasioned by the forward movement of the ship, and that we were led into error by the fact that we ourselves were imperceptibly moving.

We see the same if we watch moment by moment the movement of historical characters (that is, re-establish the inevitable condition of all that occurs—the continuity of movement in time) and do not lose sight of the essential connection of historical persons with the masses.

When the ship moves in one direction there is one and the same wave ahead of it, when it turns frequently the wave ahead of it also turns frequently. But wherever it may turn there always will be the wave anticipating its movement.

Whatever happens it always appears that just that event was foreseen and decreed. Wherever the ship may go, the rush of water which neither directs nor increases its movement foams ahead of it, and at a distance seems to us not merely to move of itself but to govern the ship's movement also.

Examining only those expressions of the will of historical persons which, as commands, were related to events, historians have assumed that the events depended on those commands. But examining the events themselves and the connection in which the historical persons stood to the people, we have found that they and their orders were dependent on events. The incontestable proof of this deduction is that however many commands were issued the event does not take place unless there are other causes for it, but as soon as an event occurs—be it what it may—then out of all the continually expressed wishes of different people some will always be found which by their meaning and their time of utterance are related as commands to the events.

Arriving at this conclusion we can reply directly and positively to these two essential questions of history:

(1) What is power?

(2) What force produces the movement of the nations?

(1) Power is the relation of a given person to other individuals, in which the more this person expresses opinions, predictions and justifications of the collective action that is performed, the less is his participation in that action.

(2) The movement of nations is caused not by power, nor by intellectual activity, nor even by a combination of the two as historians have supposed, but by the activity of *all* the people who participate in the events, and who always combine in such a way that those taking the largest direct share in the event take on themselves the least responsibility and vice versa.

Morally the wielder of power appears to cause the event; physically it is those who submit to the power. But as the moral activity is inconceivable without the physical, the cause of the event is neither in the one nor in the other but in the union of the two.

Or in other words, the conception of a cause is inapplicable to the phenomena we are examining.

In the last analysis we reach the circle of infinity—that final limit to which in every domain of thought man's reason arrives if it is not playing with the subject. Electricity produces heat, heat produces electricity. Atoms attract each other and atoms repel one another.

Speaking of the interaction of heat and electricity and of atoms, we cannot say why this occurs, and we say that it is so because it is inconceivable otherwise, because it must be so and that it is a law. The same applies to historical events. Why war and revolution occur we do not know. We only know that to produce the one or the other action, people combine in a certain formation in which they all take part, and we say that this is so because it is unthinkable otherwise, or in other words that it is a law.

Chapter VIII

IF HISTORY DEALT ONLY WITH EXTERNAL PHENOMENA, THE ESTABLISHMENT OF THIS SIMPLE AND obvious law would suffice and we should have finished our argument. But the law of history relates to man. A particle of matter cannot tell us that it does not feel the law of attraction or repulsion and that that law is untrue, but man, who is the subject of history, says plainly: I am free, and am therefore not subject to the law.

The presence of the problem of man's free will, though unexpressed, is felt at every step of history.

All seriously thinking historians have involuntarily encountered this question. All the contradictions and obscurities of history and the false path historical science has followed, are due solely to the lack of a solution of that question.

If the will of every man were free, that is, if each man could act as he pleased, all history would be a series of disconnected incidents.

If in a thousand years even one man in a million could act freely, that is, as he chose, it is evident that one single free act of that man's in violation of the laws governing human action would destroy the possibility of the existence of any laws for the whole of humanity.

If there be a single law governing the actions of men free will cannot exist, for then man's will is subject to that law.

In this contradiction lies the problem of free will, which from most ancient times has occupied the best human minds and from most ancient times has been presented in its whole tremendous significance.

The problem is, that regarding man as a subject of observation from whatever point of view—theological, historical, ethical, or philosophic—we find a general law of necessity to which he (like all that exists) is subject. But regarding him from within ourselves as what we are conscious of, we feel ourselves to be free.

This consciousness is a source of self-cognition quite apart from and independent of reason. Through his reason man observes himself, but only through consciousness does he know himself.

Apart from consciousness of self no observation or application of reason is conceivable.

To understand, observe, and draw conclusions, man must first of all be conscious of himself as living. A man is only conscious of himself as a living being by the fact that he wills, that is, is conscious of his volition. But his will—which forms the essence of his life—man recognizes (and can but recognize) as free.

If, observing himself, man sees that his will is always directed by one and the same law (whether he observes the necessity of taking food, using his brain, or anything else) he cannot recognize this never-varying direction of his will otherwise than as a limitation of it. Were it not free it could not be limited. A man's will seems to him to be limited just because he is not conscious of it except as free.

You say: I am not free. But I have lifted my hand and let it fall. Everyone understands that this illogical reply is an irrefutable demonstration of freedom.

That reply is the expression of a consciousness that is not subject to reason.

If the consciousness of freedom were not a separate and independent source of self-consciousness it would be subject to reasoning and to experience, but in fact such subjection does not exist and is inconceivable.

A series of experiments and arguments proves to every man that he, as an object of observation, is subject to certain laws, and man submits to them and never resists the laws of gravity or impermeability once he has become acquainted with them. But the same series of experiments and arguments proves to him that the complete freedom of which he is conscious in himself is impossible, and that his every action depends on his organization, his character, and the motives acting upon him; yet man never submits to the deductions of these experiments and arguments. Having learned from experiment and argument that a stone falls downward, a man indubitably believes this and always expects the law that he has learned to be fulfilled.

But learning just as certainly that his will is subject to laws, he does not and cannot believe this.

However often experiment and reasoning may show a man that under the same conditions and with the same character he will do the same thing as before, yet when under the same conditions and with the same character he approaches for the thousandth time the action that always ends in the same way, he feels as certainly convinced as before the experiment that he can act as he pleases. Every man, savage or sage, however incontestably reason and experiment may prove to him that it is impossible to imagine two different courses of action in precisely the same conditions, feels that without this irrational conception (which constitutes the essence of freedom) he cannot imagine life. He feels that however impossible it may be, it is so, for without this conception of freedom not only would he be unable to understand life, but he would be unable to live for a single moment.

He could not live, because all man's efforts, all his impulses to life, are only efforts to increase freedom. Wealth and poverty, fame and obscurity, power and subordination, strength and weakness, health and disease, culture and ignorance, work and leisure, repletion and hunger, virtue and vice, are only greater or lesser degrees of freedom.

A man having no freedom cannot be conceived of except as deprived of life.

If the conception of freedom appears to reason to be a senseless contradiction like the possibility of performing two actions at one and the same instant of time, or of an effect without a cause, that only proves that consciousness is not subject to reason.

This unshakable, irrefutable consciousness of freedom, uncontrolled by experiment or argument, recognized by all thinkers and felt by everyone without exception, this consciousness without which no conception of man is possible, constitutes the other side of the question.

Man is the creation of an all-powerful, all-good, and all-seeing God. What is sin, the conception of which arises from the consciousness of man's freedom? That is a question for theology.

The actions of men are subject to general immutable laws expressed in statistics. What is man's responsibility to society, the conception of which results from the conception of freedom? That is a question for jurisprudence.

Man's actions proceed from his innate character and the motives acting upon him. What is conscience and the perception of right and wrong in actions, that follows from the consciousness of freedom? That is a question for ethics.

Man in connection with the general life of humanity appears subject to laws which determine that life. But the same man apart from that connection appears to be free. How should the past life of nations and of humanity be regarded—as the result of the free, or as the result of the constrained, activity of man? That is a question for history.

Only in our self-confident day of the popularization of knowledge—thanks to that most powerful engine of ignorance the diffusion of printed matter—has the question of the freedom of will been put on a level on which the question itself cannot exist. In our time the majority of so-called advanced people—that is, the crowd of ignoramuses—have taken the work of the naturalists who deal with one side of the question for a solution of the whole problem.

They say and write and print that the soul and freedom do not exist, for the life of man is expressed by muscular movements and muscular movements are conditioned by the activity of the nerves; the soul and free will do not exist because at an unknown period of time we sprang from the apes. They say this, not at all suspecting that thousands of years ago that same law of necessity which with such ardor they are now trying to prove by physiology and comparative zoology, was not merely acknowledged by all the religions and all the thinkers, but has never been denied. They do not see that the rôle of the natural sciences in this matter is merely to serve as an instrument for the illumination of one side of it. For the fact that, from the point of view of observation, reason and the will are merely secretions of the brain, and that man following the general law may have developed from lower animals at some unknown period of time, only explains from a fresh side the truth admitted thousands of years ago by all the religious and philosophic theories—that from the point of view of reason man is subject to the law of necessity; but it does not advance by a hair's breadth the solution of the question, which has another, opposite, side, based on the consciousness of freedom.

If men descended from the apes at an unknown period of time, that is as comprehensible as that they were made from a handful of earth at a certain period of time (in the first case the unknown quantity is the time, in the second case it is the origin); and the question of how man's consciousness of freedom is to be reconciled with the law of necessity to which he is subject, cannot be solved by comparative physiology and zoology, for in a frog, a rabbit, or an ape, we can observe only the muscular nervous activity, but in man we observe consciousness as well as the muscular and nervous activity.

The naturalists and their followers, thinking they can solve this question, are like plasterers set to plaster one side of the walls of a church who, availing themselves of the absence of the chief superintendent of the work, should in an access of zeal plaster over the windows, icons, woodwork, and still unbuttressed walls, and should be delighted that from their point of view as plasterers, everything is now so smooth and regular.

Chapter IX

For the solution of the question of free will or inevitability, history has this advantage over other branches of knowledge in which the question is dealt with, that for history this question does not refer to the essence of man's free will but its manifestation in the past and under certain conditions.

In regard to this question, history stands to the other sciences as experimental science stands to abstract science.

The subject for history is not man's will itself but our presentation of it.

And so for history, the insoluble mystery presented by the incompatibility of free will and inevitability does not exist as it does for theology, ethics and philosophy. History surveys a presentation of man's life in which the union of these two contradictions has already taken place.

In actual life each historic event, each human action, is very clearly and definitely understood without any sense of contradiction, although each event presents itself as partly free and partly compulsory.

To solve the question of how freedom and necessity are combined and what constitutes the essence of these two conceptions, the philosophy of history can and should follow a path contrary to that taken by other sciences. Instead of first defining the conceptions of freedom and inevitability in themselves, and then ranging the phenomena of life under those definitions, history should deduce a definition of the conception of freedom and inevitability themselves from the immense quantity of phenomena of which it is cognizant and that always appear dependent on these two elements.

Whatever presentation of the activity of many men or of an individual we may consider, we always regard it as the result partly of man's free will and partly of the law of inevitability.

Whether we speak of the migration of the peoples and the incursions of the barbarians, or of the decrees of Napoleon III, or of someone's action an hour ago in choosing one direction out of several for his walk, we are unconscious of any contradiction. The degree of freedom and inevitability governing the actions of these people is clearly defined for us.

Our conception of the degree of freedom often varies according to differences in the point of view from which we regard the event, but every human action appears to us as a certain combination of freedom and inevitability. In every action we examine we see a certain measure of freedom and a certain measure of inevitability. And always the more freedom we see in any action the less inevitability do we perceive, and the more inevitability the less freedom.

The proportion of freedom to inevitability decreases and increases according to the point of view from which the action is regarded, but their relation is always one of inverse proportion.

A sinking man who clutches at another and drowns him; or a hungry mother exhausted by feeding her baby, who steals some food; or a man trained to discipline who on duty at the word of command kills a defenseless man—seem less guilty, that is less free and more subject to the law of necessity to one who knows the circumstances in which these people were placed, and more free to one who does not know that the man was himself drowning, that the mother was hungry, that the soldier was in the ranks, and so on. Similarly a man who committed a murder twenty years ago and has since lived peaceably and harmlessly in society, seems less guilty and his action more due to the law of inevitability, to someone who considers his action after twenty years have elapsed, than to one who examined it the day after it was committed. And in the same way every action of an insane, intoxicated, or highly excited man, appears less free and more inevitable to one who knows the mental condition of him who committed the action, and seems more free and less inevitable to one who does not know it. In all these cases the conception of freedom is increased or diminished and the conception of compulsion is correspondingly decreased or increased, according to the point of view from which the action is regarded. So that the greater the conception of necessity the smaller the conception of freedom and vice versa.

Religion, the common sense of mankind, the science of jurisprudence, and history itself, understand alike this relation between necessity and freedom.

All cases without exception in which our conception of freedom and necessity is increased and diminished, depend on three considerations:

(1) The relation to the external world of the man who commits the deeds.

(2) His relation to time.

(3) His relation to the causes leading to the action.

The first consideration is the clearness of our perception of the man's relation to the external world and the greater or lesser clearness of our understanding of the definite position occupied by the man in relation to everything co-existing with him. This is what makes it evident that a drowning man is less free and more subject to necessity than one standing on dry ground, and that makes the actions of a man closely connected with others in a thickly populated district, or of one bound by family, official, or business duties, seem certainly less free and more subject to necessity than those of a man living in solitude and seclusion.

If we consider a man alone, apart from his relation to everything around him, each action of his seems to us free. But if we see his relation to anything around him, if we see his connection with anything whatever—with a man who speaks to him, a book he reads, the work on which he is engaged, even with the air he breathes or the light that falls on the things about him—we see that each of these circumstances has an influence on him and controls at least some side of his activity. And the more we perceive of these influences the more our conception of his freedom diminishes and the more our conception of the necessity that weighs on him increases.

The second consideration is the more or less evident time relation of the man to the world and the clearness of our perception of the place the man's action occupies in time. That is the ground which makes the fall of the first man, resulting in the production of the human race, appear evidently less free than a man's entry into marriage today. It is the reason why the life and activity of people who lived centuries ago and are connected with me in time, cannot seem to me as free as the life of a contemporary, the consequences of which are still unknown to me.

The degree of our conception of freedom or inevitability depends in this respect on the greater or lesser lapse of time between the performance of the action and our judgment of it.

If I examine an act I performed a moment ago in approximately the same circumstances as those I am in now, my action appears to me undoubtedly free. But if I examine an act performed a month ago, then being in different circumstances, I cannot help recognizing that if that act had not been committed much that resulted from it—good, agreeable, and even essential—would not have taken place. If I reflect on an action still more remote, ten years ago or more, then the consequences of my action are still plainer to me and I find it hard to imagine what would have happened had that action not been performed. The farther I go back in memory, or what is the same thing the farther I go forward in my judgment, the more doubtful becomes my belief in the freedom of my action.

In history we find a very similar progress of conviction concerning the part played by free will in the general affairs of humanity. A contemporary event seems to us to be indubitably the doing of all the known participants, but with a more remote event we already see its inevitable results which prevent our considering anything else possible. And the farther we go back in examining events the less arbitrary do they appear.

The Austro-Prussian war appears to us undoubtedly the result of the crafty conduct of Bismarck, and so on. The Napoleonic wars still seem to us, though already questionably, to be the outcome of their heroes' will. But in the Crusades we already see an event occupying its definite place in history and without which we cannot imagine the modern history of Europe, though to the chroniclers of the Crusades that event appeared as merely due to the will of certain people. In regard to the migration of the peoples it does not enter anyone's head today to suppose that the renovation of the European world depended on Attila's caprice. The farther back in history the object of our observation lies, the more doubtful does the free will of those concerned in the event become and the more manifest the law of inevitability.

The third consideration is the degree to which we apprehend that endless chain of causation inevitably demanded by reason, in which each phenomenon comprehended, and therefore man's every action, must have its definite place as a result of what has gone before and as a cause of what will follow.

The better we are acquainted with the physiological, psychological, and historical laws deduced by observation and by which man is controlled, and the more correctly we perceive the physiological, psychological, and historical causes of the action, and the simpler the action we are observing and the less complex the character and mind of the man in question, the more subject to inevitability and the less free do our actions and those of others appear.

When we do not at all understand the cause of an action, whether a crime, a good action, or even one that is simply non-moral, we ascribe a greater amount of freedom to it. In the case of a crime we most urgently demand the punishment for such an act; in the case of a virtuous act we rate its merit most highly. In an indifferent case we recognize in it more individuality, originality and independence. But if even one of the innumerable causes of the act is known to us we recognize a certain element of necessity and are less insistent on punishment for the crime, or the acknowledgment of the merit of the virtuous act, or the freedom of the apparently original action. That a criminal was reared among malefactors mitigates his fault in our eyes. The self-sacrifice of a father or mother, or self-sacrifice with the possibility of a reward, is more comprehensible than gratuitous self-sacrifice, and therefore seems less deserving of sympathy and less the result of free will. The founder of a sect or party, or an inventor, impresses us less when we know how or by what the way was prepared for his activity. If we have a large range of examples, if our observation is constantly directed to seeking the correlation of cause and effect in people's actions, their actions appear to us more under compulsion and less free the more correctly we connect the effects with the causes. If we examined simple actions and had a vast number of such actions under observation, our conception of their inevitability would be still greater. The dishonest conduct of the son of a dishonest father, the misconduct of a woman who had fallen into bad company, a drunkard's relapse into drunkenness, and so on, are actions that seem to us less free the better we understand their cause. If the man whose actions we are considering is on a very low stage of mental development, like a child, a madman, or a simpleton—then, knowing the causes of the act and the simplicity of the character and intelligence in question, we see so large an element of necessity and so little free will that as soon as we know the cause prompting the action we can foretell the result.

On these three considerations alone is based the conception of irresponsibility for crimes, and the extenuating circumstances admitted by all legislative codes. The responsibility appears greater or less according to our greater or lesser knowledge of the circumstances in which the man was placed whose action is being judged, and according to the greater or lesser interval of time between the commission of the action and its investigation, and according to the greater or lesser understanding of the causes that led to the action.

Chapter X

THUS OUR CONCEPTION OF FREE WILL AND INEVITABILITY GRADUALLY DIMINISHES OR INCREASES according to the greater or lesser connection with the external world, the greater or lesser remoteness of time, and the greater or lesser dependence on the causes in relation to which we contemplate a man's life.

So that if we examine the case of a man whose connection with the external world is well known, where the time between the action and its examination is great, and where the causes of the action are most accessible, we get the conception of a maximum of inevitability and a minimum of free will. If we examine a man little dependent on external conditions, whose action was performed very recently, and the causes of whose action are beyond our ken, we get the conception of a minimum of inevitability and a maximum of freedom.

In neither case—however we may change our point of view, however plain we may make to ourselves the connection between the man and the external world, however inaccessible it may be to us, however long or short the period of time, however intelligible or incomprehensible the causes of the action may be—can we ever conceive either complete freedom or complete necessity.

(1) To whatever degree we may imagine a man to be exempt from the influence of the external world, we never get a conception of freedom in space. Every human action is inevitably conditioned by what surrounds him and by his own body. I lift my arm and let it fall. My action seems to me free; but asking myself whether I could raise my arm in every direction, I see that I raised it in the direc-

tion in which there was least obstruction to that action either from things around me or from the construction of my own body. I chose one out of all the possible directions because in it there were fewest obstacles. For my action to be free it was necessary that it should encounter no obstacles. To conceive of a man being free we must imagine him outside space, which is evidently impossible.

(2) However much we approximate the time of judgment to the time of the deed, we never get a conception of freedom in time. For if I examine an action committed a second ago I must still recognize it as not being free, for it is irrevocably linked to the moment at which it was committed. Can I lift my arm? I lift it, but ask myself: Could I have abstained from lifting my arm at the moment that has already passed? To convince myself of this I do not lift it the next moment. But I am not now abstaining from doing so at the first moment when I asked the question. Time has gone by which I could not detain, the arm I then lifted is no longer the same as the arm I now refrain from lifting, nor is the air in which I lifted it the same that now surrounds me. The moment in which the first movement was made is irrevocable, and at that moment I could make only one movement, and whatever movement I made would be the only one. That I did not lift my arm a moment later does not prove that I could have abstained from lifting it then. And since I could make only one movement at that single moment of time, it could not have been any other. To imagine it as free, it is necessary to imagine it in the present, on the boundary between the past and the future—that is, outside time, which is impossible.

(3) However much the difficulty of understanding the causes may be increased, we never reach a conception of complete freedom, that is, an absence of cause. However inaccessible to us may be the cause of the expression of will in any action, our own or another's, the first demand of reason is the assumption of and search for a cause, for without a cause no phenomenon is conceivable. I raise my arm to perform an action independently of any cause, but my wish to perform an action without a cause is the cause of my action.

But even if—imagining a man quite exempt from all influences, examining only his momentary action in the present, unevoked by any cause—we were to admit so infinitely small a remainder of inevitability as equaled zero, we should even then not have arrived at the conception of complete freedom in man, for a being uninfluenced by the external world, standing outside of time and independent of cause, is no longer a man.

In the same way we can never imagine the action of a man quite devoid of freedom and entirely subject to the law of inevitability.

(1) However we may increase our knowledge of the conditions of space in which man is situated, that knowledge can never be complete, for the number of those conditions is as infinite as the infinity of space. And therefore so long as not *all* the conditions influencing men are defined, there is no complete inevitability but a certain measure of freedom remains.

(2) However we may prolong the period of time between the action we are examining and the judgment upon it, that period will be finite, while time is infinite, and so in this respect too there can never be absolute inevitability.

(3) However accessible may be the chain of causation of any action, we shall never know the whole chain since it is endless, and so again we never reach absolute inevitability.

But besides this, even if, admitting the remaining minimum of freedom to equal zero, we assumed in some given case—as for instance in that of a dying man, an unborn babe, or an idiot—complete absence of freedom, by so doing we should destroy the very conception of man in the case we are examining, for as soon as there is no freedom there is also no man. And so the conception of the action of a man subject solely to the law of inevitability without any element of freedom, is just as impossible as the conception of a man's completely free action.

And so to imagine the action of a man entirely subject to the law of inevitability without any freedom, we must assume the knowledge of an *infinite* number of space relations, an *infinitely* long period of time, and an *infinite* series of causes.

To imagine a man perfectly free and not subject to the law of inevitability, we must imagine him all alone, *beyond space, beyond time,* and *free from dependence on cause.*

In the first case, if inevitability were possible without freedom we should have reached a definition of inevitability by the laws of inevitability itself, that is, a mere form without content.

In the second case, if freedom were possible without inevitability we should have arrived at unconditioned freedom beyond space, time and cause, which by the fact of its being unconditioned and unlimited would be nothing, or mere content without form.

We should in fact have reached those two fundamentals of which man's whole outlook on the universe is constructed—the incomprehensible essence of life, and the laws defining that essence.

Reason says: (1) Space with all the forms of matter that give it visibility is infinite, and cannot be imagined otherwise. (2) Time is infinite motion without a moment of rest and is unthinkable otherwise. (3) The connection between cause and effect has no beginning and can have no end.

Consciousness says: (1) I alone am, and all that exists is but me, consequently I include space. (2) I measure flowing time by the fixed moment of the present in which alone I am conscious of myself as living, consequently I am outside time. (3) I am beyond cause, for I feel myself to be the cause of every manifestation of my life.

Reason gives expression to the laws of inevitability. Consciousness gives expression to the essence of freedom.

Freedom not limited by anything is the essence of life, in man's consciousness. Inevitability without content is man's reason in its three forms.

Freedom is the thing examined. Inevitability is what examines. Freedom is the content. Inevitability is the form.

Only by separating the two sources of cognition, related to one another as form to content, do we get the mutually exclusive and separately incomprehensible conceptions of freedom and inevitability.

Only by uniting them do we get a clear conception of man's life.

Apart from these two concepts which in their union mutually define one another as form and content, no conception of life is possible.

All that we know of the life of man is merely a certain relation of free will to inevitability, that is, of consciousness to the laws of reason.

All that we know of the external world of nature is only a certain relation of the forces of nature to inevitability, or of the essence of life to the laws of reason.

The great natural forces lie outside us and we are not conscious of them; we call those forces gravitation, inertia, electricity, animal force, and so on, but we are conscious of the force of life in man and we call that freedom.

But just as the force of gravitation, incomprehensible in itself but felt by every man, is understood by us only to the extent to which we know the laws of inevitability to which it is subject (from the first knowledge that all bodies have weight, up to Newton's law), so too the force of free will, incomprehensible in itself but of which everyone is conscious, is intelligible to us only in as far as we know the laws of inevitability to which it is subject (from the fact that every man dies, up to the knowledge of the most complex economic and historic laws).

All knowledge is merely a bringing of this essence of life under the laws of reason.

Man's free will differs from every other force in that man is directly conscious of it, but in the eyes of reason it in no way differs from any other force. The forces of gravitation, electricity, or chemical affinity, are only distinguished from one another in that they are differently defined by reason. Just so the force of man's free will is distinguished by reason from the other forces of nature only by the definition reason gives it. Freedom apart from necessity, that is, apart from the laws of reason that define it, differs in no way from gravitation, or heat, or the force that makes things grow; for reason, it is only a momentary undefinable sensation of life.

And as the undefinable essence of the force moving the heavenly bodies, the undefinable essence of the forces of heat and electricity, or of chemical affinity, or of the vital force, forms the content of astronomy, physics, chemistry, botany, zoology and so on, just in the same way does the force of free will form the content of history. But just as the subject of every science is the manifestation of this unknown essence of life while that essence itself can only be the subject of metaphysics, even so the manifestation of the force of free will in human beings in space, in time, and in dependence on cause, forms the subject of history, while free will itself is the subject of metaphysics.

In the experimental sciences what we know we call the laws of inevitability, what is unknown to us we call vital force. Vital force is only an expression for the unknown remainder over and above what we know of the essence of life.

So also in history what is known to us we call laws of inevitability, what is unknown we call free will. Free will is for history only an expression for the unknown remainder of what we know about the laws of human life.

Chapter XI

HISTORY EXAMINES THE MANIFESTATIONS OF MAN'S FREE WILL IN CONNECTION WITH THE EXternal world in time and in dependence on cause, that is, it defines this freedom by the laws of reason, and so history is a science only in so far as this free will is defined by those laws.

The recognition of man's free will as something capable of influencing historical events, that is, as not subject to laws, is the same for history as the recognition of a free force moving the heavenly bodies would be for astronomy.

That assumption would destroy the possibility of the existence of laws, that is, of any science whatever. If there is even a single body moving freely, then the laws of Kepler and Newton are negatived and no conception of the movement of the heavenly bodies any longer exists. If any single action is due to free will, then not a single historical law can exist, nor any conception of historical events.

For history, lines exist of the movement of human wills, one end of which is hidden in the unknown but at the other end of which a consciousness of man's will in the present moves in space, time, and dependence on cause.

The more this field of motion spreads out before our eyes, the more evident are the laws of that movement. To discover and define those laws is the problem of history.

From the standpoint from which the science of history now regards its subject on the path it now follows, seeking the causes of events in man's free will, a scientific enunciation of those laws is impossible, for however man's free will may be restricted, as soon as we recognize it as a force not subject to law, the existence of law becomes impossible.

Only by reducing this element of free will to the infinitesimal, that is, by regarding it as an infinitely small quantity, can we convince ourselves of the absolute inaccessibility of the causes, and then instead of seeking causes, history will take the discovery of laws as its problem.

The search for these laws has long been begun and the new methods of thought which history must adopt are being worked out simultaneously with the self-destruction toward which—ever dissecting and dissecting the causes of phenomena—the old method of history is moving.

All human sciences have traveled along that path. Arriving at infinitesimals, mathematics, the most exact of sciences, abandons the process of analysis and enters on the new process of the integration of unknown, infinitely small, quantities. Abandoning the conception of cause, mathematics seeks law, that is, the property common to all unknown, infinitely small, elements.

In another form but along the same path of reflection the other sciences have proceeded. When Newton enunciated the law of gravity he did not say that the sun or the earth had a property of attraction; he said that all bodies from the largest to the smallest have the property of attracting one another, that is, leaving aside the question of the cause of the movement of the bodies, he expressed the property common to all bodies from the infinitely large to the infinitely small. The same is done by the natural sciences: leaving aside the question of cause, they seek for laws. History stands on the same path. And if history has for its object the study of the movement of the nations and of humanity and not the narration of episodes in the lives of individuals, it too, setting aside the conception of cause, should seek the laws common to all the inseparably interconnected infinitesimal elements of free will.

Chapter XII

FROM THE TIME THE LAW OF COPERNICUS WAS DISCOVERED AND PROVED, THE MERE RECOGNITION of the fact that it was not the sun but the earth that moves sufficed to destroy the whole cosmography of the ancients. By disproving that law it might have been possible to retain the old conception of the movements of the bodies, but without disproving it, it would seem impossible to continue studying the Ptolemaic worlds. But even after the discovery of the law of Copernicus the Ptolemaic worlds were still studied for a long time.

From the time the first person said and proved that the number of births or of crimes is subject to mathematical laws, and that this or that mode of government is determined by certain geographical and economic conditions, and that certain relations of population to soil produce migrations of peoples, the foundations on which history had been built were destroyed in their essence.

By refuting these new laws the former view of history might have been retained; but without refuting them it would seem impossible to continue studying historic events as the results of man's free will. For if a certain mode of government was established or certain migrations of peoples took place in consequence of such and such geographic, ethnographic, or economic conditions, then the free will of those individuals who appear to us to have established that mode of government or occasioned the migrations can no longer be regarded as the cause.

And yet the former history continues to be studied side by side with the laws of statistics, geography, political economy, comparative philology, and geology, which directly contradict its assumptions.

The struggle between the old views and the new was long and stubbornly fought out in physical philosophy. Theology stood on guard for the old views and accused the new of violating revelation. But when truth conquered, theology established itself just as firmly on the new foundation.

Just as prolonged and stubborn is the struggle now proceeding between the old and the new conception of history, and theology in the same way stands on guard for the old view, and accuses the new view of subverting revelation.

In the one case as in the other, on both sides the struggle provokes passion and stifles truth. On the one hand there is fear and regret for the loss of the whole edifice constructed through the ages, on the other is the passion for destruction.

To the men who fought against the rising truths of physical philosophy, it seemed that if they admitted that truth it would destroy faith in God, in the creation of the firmament, and in the miracle of Joshua the son of Nun. To the defenders of the laws of Copernicus and Newton, to Voltaire for example, it seemed that the laws of astronomy destroyed religion, and he utilized the law of gravitation as a weapon against religion.

Just so it now seems as if we have only to admit the law of inevitability, to destroy the conception of the soul, of good and evil, and all the institutions of State and Church that have been built up on those conceptions.

So too, like Voltaire in his time, uninvited defenders of the law of inevitability today use that law as a weapon against religion, though the law of inevitability in history, like the law of Copernicus in astronomy, far from destroying, even strengthens the foundation on which the institutions of State and Church are erected.

As in the question of astronomy then, so in the question of history now, the whole difference of opinion is based on the recognition or non-recognition of something absolute, serving as the measure of visible phenomena. In astronomy it was the immovability of the earth, in history it is the independence of personality—free will.

As with astronomy the difficulty of recognizing the motion of the earth lay in abandoning the immediate sensation of the earth's fixity and of the motion of the planets, so in history the difficulty of recognizing the subjection of personality to the laws of space, time and cause, lies in renouncing the direct feeling of the independence of one's own personality. But as in astronomy the new view said: "It is true that we do not feel the movement of the earth, but by admitting its immobility we arrive at absurdity, while by admitting its motion (which we do not feel) we arrive at laws," so also in history the new view says: "It is true that we are not conscious of our dependence, but by admitting our free will we arrive at absurdity, while by admitting our dependence on the external world, on time, and on cause, we arrive at laws."

In the first case it was necessary to renounce the consciousness of an unreal immobility in space and to recognize a motion we did not feel; in the present case it is similarly necessary to renounce a freedom that does not exist, and to recognize a dependence of which we are not conscious.

ANNA KARENINA

Contents

PART ONE

Chapter I

HAPPY FAMILIES ARE ALL ALIKE; EVERY UNHAPPY FAMILY IS UNHAPPY IN ITS OWN WAY.

Everything was in confusion in the Oblonskys' house. The wife had discovered that the husband was carrying on an intrigue with a French girl, who had been a governess in their family, and she had announced to her husband that she could not go on living in the same house with him. This position of affairs had now lasted three days, and not only the husband and wife themselves, but all the members of their family and household, were painfully conscious of it. Every person in the house felt that there was no sense in their living together, and that the stray people brought together by chance in any inn had more in common with one another than they, the members of the family and household of the Oblonskys. The wife did not leave her own room, the husband had not been at home for three days. The children ran wild all over the house; the English governess quarreled with the housekeeper, and wrote to a friend asking her to look out for a new situation for her; the man-cook had walked off the day before just at dinnertime; the kitchenmaid and the coachman had given warning.

Three days after the quarrel, Prince Stepan Arkadyevitch Oblonsky—Stiva, as he was called in the fashionable world—woke up at his usual hour, that is, at eight o'clock in the morning, not in his wife's bedroom, but on the leather-covered sofa in his study. He turned over his stout, well-cared-for person on the springy sofa, as though he would sink into a long sleep again; he vigorously embraced the pillow on the other side and buried his face in it; but all at once he jumped up, sat up on the sofa, and opened his eyes.

"Yes, yes, how was it now?" he thought, going over his dream. "Now, how was it? To be sure! Alabin was giving a dinner at Darmstadt; no, not Darmstadt, but something American. Yes, but then, Darmstadt was in America. Yes, Alabin was giving a dinner on glass tables, and the tables sang, *Il mio tesoro*—not *Il mio tesoro* though, but something better, and there were some sort of little decanters on the table, and they were women, too," he remembered.

Stepan Arkadyevitch's eyes twinkled gaily, and he pondered with a smile. "Yes, it was nice, very nice. There was a great deal more that was delightful, only there's no putting it into words, or even expressing it in one's thoughts awake." And noticing a gleam of light peeping in beside one of the serge curtains, he cheerfully dropped his feet over the edge of the sofa, and felt about with them for his slippers, a present on his last birthday, worked for him by his wife on gold-colored morocco. And, as he had done every day for the last nine years, he stretched out his hand, without getting up, towards the place where his dressing-gown always hung in his bedroom. And thereupon he suddenly remembered that he was not sleeping in his wife's room, but in his study, and why: the smile vanished from his face, he knitted his brows.

"Ah, ah, ah! Oo! . . ." he muttered, recalling everything that had happened. And again every detail of his quarrel with his wife was present to his imagination, all the hopelessness of his position, and worst of all, his own fault.

"Yes, she won't forgive me, and she can't forgive me. And the most awful thing about it is that it's all my fault—all my fault, though I'm not to blame. That's the point of the whole situation," he reflected. "Oh, oh, oh!" he kept repeating in despair, as he remembered the acutely painful sensations caused him by this quarrel.

Most unpleasant of all was the first minute when, on coming, happy and good-humored, from the theater, with a huge pear in his hand for his wife, he had not found his wife in the drawing room, to his surprise had not found her in the study either, and saw her at last in her bedroom with the unlucky letter that revealed everything in her hand.

She, his Dolly, forever fussing and worrying over household details, and limited in her ideas, as he considered, was sitting perfectly still with the letter in her hand, looking at him with an expression of horror, despair, and indignation.

"What's this? this?" she asked, pointing to the letter.

And at this recollection, Stepan Arkadyevitch, as is so often the case, was not so much annoyed at the fact itself as at the way in which he had met his wife's words.

There happened to him at that instant what does happen to people when they are unexpectedly caught in something very disgraceful. He did not succeed in adapting his face to the position in which he was placed towards his wife by the discovery of his fault. Instead of being hurt, denying, defending himself, begging forgiveness, instead of remaining indifferent even—anything would have been better than what he did do—his face utterly involuntarily (reflex spinal action, reflected Stepan Arkadyevitch, who was fond of physiology)—utterly involuntarily assumed its habitual, good-humored, and therefore idiotic smile.

This idiotic smile he could not forgive himself. Catching sight of that smile, Dolly shuddered as though at physical pain, broke out with her characteristic heat into a flood of cruel words, and rushed out of the room. Since then she had refused to see her husband.

"It's that idiotic smile that's to blame for it all," thought Stepan Arkadyevitch.

"But what's to be done? What's to be done?" he said to himself in despair, and found no answer.

Chapter II

STEPAN ARKADYEVITCH WAS A TRUTHFUL MAN IN HIS RELATIONS WITH HIMSELF. HE WAS INCApable of deceiving himself and persuading himself that he repented of his conduct. He could not at this date repent of the fact that he, a handsome, susceptible man of thirty-four, was not in love with his wife, the mother of five living and two dead children, and only a year younger than himself. All he repented of was that he had not succeeded better in hiding it from his wife. But he felt all the difficulty of his position and was sorry for his wife, his children, and himself. Possibly he might have managed to conceal his sins better from his wife if he had anticipated that the knowledge of them would have had such an effect on her. He had never clearly thought out the subject, but he had vaguely conceived that his wife must long ago have suspected him of being unfaithful to her, and shut her eyes to the fact. He had even supposed that she, a worn-out woman no longer young or good-looking, and in no way remarkable or interesting, merely a good mother, ought from a sense of fairness to take an indulgent view. It had turned out quite the other way.

"Oh, it's awful! oh dear, oh dear! awful!" Stepan Arkadyevitch kept repeating to himself, and he could think of nothing to be done. "And how well things were going up till now! how well we got on! She was contented and happy in her children; I never interfered with her in anything; I let her manage the children and the house just as she liked. It's true it's bad *her* having been a governess in our house. That's bad! There's something common, vulgar, in flirting with one's governess. But what a governess!" (He vividly recalled the roguish black eyes of Mlle. Roland and her smile.) "But after all, while she was in the house, I kept myself in hand. And the worst of it all is that she's already . . . it seems as if ill-luck would have it so! Oh, oh! But what, what is to be done?"

There was no solution, but that universal solution which life gives to all questions, even the most complex and insoluble. That answer is: one must live in the needs of the day—that is, forget oneself. To forget himself in sleep was impossible now, at least till nighttime; he could not go back now to the music sung by the decanter-women; so he must forget himself in the dream of daily life.

"Then we shall see," Stepan Arkadyevitch said to himself, and getting up he put on a gray dressing-gown lined with blue silk, tied the tassels in a knot, and, drawing a deep breath of air into his broad, bare chest, he walked to the window with his usual confident step, turning out his feet that carried his full frame so easily. He pulled up the blind and rang the bell loudly. It was at once answered by the appearance of an old friend, his valet, Matvey, carrying his clothes, his boots, and a telegram. Matvey was followed by the barber with all the necessaries for shaving.

"Are there any papers from the office?" asked Stepan Arkadyevitch, taking the telegram and seating himself at the looking-glass.

"On the table," replied Matvey, glancing with inquiring sympathy at his master; and, after a short pause, he added with a sly smile, "They've sent from the carriage-jobbers."

Stepan Arkadyevitch made no reply, he merely glanced at Matvey in the looking-glass. In the glance, in which their eyes met in the looking-glass, it was clear that they understood one another. Stepan Arkadyevitch's eyes asked: "Why do you tell me that? don't you know?"

Matvey put his hands in his jacket pockets, thrust out one leg, and gazed silently, good-humoredly, with a faint smile, at his master.

"I told them to come on Sunday, and till then not to trouble you or themselves for nothing," he said. He had obviously prepared the sentence beforehand.

Stepan Arkadyevitch saw Matvey wanted to make a joke and attract attention to himself. Tearing open the telegram, he read it through, guessing at the words, misspelled as they always are in telegrams, and his face brightened.

"Matvey, my sister Anna Arkadyevna will be here tomorrow," he said, checking for a minute the sleek, plump hand of the barber, cutting a pink path through his long, curly whiskers.

"Thank God!" said Matvey, showing by this response that he, like his master, realized the significance of this arrival—that is, that Anna Arkadyevna, the sister he was so fond of, might bring about a reconciliation between husband and wife.

"Alone, or with her husband?" inquired Matvey.

Stepan Arkadyevitch could not answer, as the barber was at work on his upper lip, and he raised one finger. Matvey nodded at the looking-glass.

"Alone. Is the room to be got ready upstairs?"

"Inform Darya Alexandrovna: where she orders."

"Darya Alexandrovna?" Matvey repeated, as though in doubt.

"Yes, inform her. Here, take the telegram; give it to her, and then do what she tells you."

"You want to try it on," Matvey understood, but he only said, "Yes sir."

Stepan Arkadyevitch was already washed and combed and ready to be dressed, when Matvey, stepping deliberately in his creaky boots, came back into the room with the telegram in his hand. The barber had gone.

"Darya Alexandrovna told me to inform you that she is going away. Let him do—that is you—as he likes," he said, laughing only with his eyes, and putting his hands in his pockets, he watched his master with his head on one side. Stepan Arkadyevitch was silent a minute. Then a good-humored and rather pitiful smile showed itself on his handsome face.

"Eh, Matvey?" he said, shaking his head.

"It's all right, sir; things will come round," said Matvey.

"Come round?"

"Yes, sir."

"Do you think so? Who's there?" asked Stepan Arkadyevitch, hearing the rustle of a woman's dress at the door.

"It's I," said a firm, pleasant, woman's voice, and the stern, pockmarked face of Matrona Philimonovna, the nurse, was thrust in at the doorway.

"Well, what is it, Matrona?" queried Stepan Arkadyevitch, going up to her at the door.

Although Stepan Arkadyevitch was completely in the wrong as regards his wife, and was conscious of this himself, almost everyone in the house (even the nurse, Darya Alexandrovna's chief ally) was on his side.

"Well, what now?" he asked disconsolately.

"Go to her, sir; own your fault again. Maybe God will aid you. She is suffering so, it's sad to see her; and besides, everything in the house is topsy-turvy. You must have pity, sir, on the children. Beg her forgiveness, sir. There's no help for it! One must take the consequences. . . ."

"But she won't see me."

"You do your part. God is merciful; pray to God, sir, pray to God."

"Come, that'll do, you can go," said Stepan Arkadyevitch, blushing suddenly. "Well now, do dress me." He turned to Matvey and threw off his dressing-gown decisively.

Matvey was already holding up the shirt like a horse's collar, and, blowing off some invisible speck, he slipped it with obvious pleasure over the well-groomed body of his master.

Chapter III

WHEN HE WAS DRESSED, STEPAN ARKADYEVITCH SPRINKLED SOME SCENT ON HIMSELF, PULLED down his shirt-cuffs, distributed into his pockets his cigarettes, pocketbook, matches, and watch with its double chain and seals, and shaking out his handkerchief, feeling himself clean, fragrant, healthy, and physically at ease, in spite of his unhappiness, he walked with a slight swing on each leg into the dining room, where coffee was already waiting for him, and beside the coffee, letters and papers from the office.

He read the letters. One was very unpleasant, from a merchant who was buying a forest on his wife's property. To sell this forest was absolutely essential; but at present, until he was reconciled with his wife, the subject could not be discussed. The most unpleasant thing of all was that his pecuniary interests should in this way enter into the question of his reconciliation with his wife. And the idea that he might be led on by his interests, that he might seek a reconciliation with his wife on account of the sale of the forest—that idea hurt him.

When he had finished his letters, Stepan Arkadyevitch moved the office-papers close to him, rapidly looked through two pieces of business, made a few notes with a big pencil, and pushing away the papers, turned to his coffee. As he sipped his coffee, he opened a still damp morning paper, and began reading it.

Stepan Arkadyevitch took in and read a liberal paper, not an extreme one, but one advocating the views held by the majority. And in spite of the fact that science, art, and politics had no special interest for him, he firmly held those views on all these subjects which were held by the majority and by his paper, and he only changed them when the majority changed them—or, more strictly speaking, he did not change them, but they imperceptibly changed of themselves within him.

Stepan Arkadyevitch had not chosen his political opinions or his views; these political opinions and views had come to him of themselves, just as he did not choose the shapes of his hat and coat, but simply took those that were being worn. And for him, living in a certain society—owing to the need, ordinarily developed at years of discretion, for some degree of mental activity—to have views was just as indispensable as to have a hat. If there was a reason for his preferring liberal to conservative views, which were held also by many of his circle, it arose not from his considering liberalism more rational, but from its being in closer accordance with his manner of life. The liberal party said that in Russia everything is wrong, and certainly Stepan Arkadyevitch had many debts and was decidedly short of money. The liberal party said that marriage is an institution quite out of date, and that it needs reconstruction; and family life certainly afforded Stepan Arkadyevitch little gratification, and forced him into lying and hypocrisy, which was so repulsive to his nature. The liberal party said, or rather allowed it to be understood, that religion is only a curb to keep in check the barbarous classes of the people; and Stepan Arkadyevitch could not get through even a short service without his legs aching from standing up, and could never make out what was the object of all the terrible and high-flown language about another world when life might be so very amusing in this world. And with all this, Stepan Arkadyevitch, who liked a joke, was fond of puzzling a plain man by saying that if he prided himself on his origin, he ought not to stop at Rurik and disown the first founder of his family—the monkey. And so Liberalism had become a habit of Stepan Arkadyevitch's, and he liked his newspaper, as he did his cigar after dinner, for the slight fog it diffused in his brain. He read the leading article, in which it was maintained that it was quite senseless in our day to raise an outcry that radicalism was threatening to swallow up all conservative elements, and that the government ought to take measures to crush the revolutionary hydra; that, on the contrary, "in our opinion the danger lies not in that fantastic revolutionary hydra, but in the obstinacy of traditionalism clogging progress," etc., etc. He read another article, too, a financial one, which alluded to Bentham and Mill, and dropped some innuendoes reflecting on the ministry. With his characteristic quick-wittedness he caught the drift of each innuendo, divined whence it came, at whom and on what ground it was aimed, and that afforded him, as it always did, a certain satisfaction. But today that satisfaction was embittered by Matrona Philimonovna's advice and the unsatisfactory state of the household. He read, too, that Count Beist was rumored to have left for Wiesbaden, and that one need have no more gray hair, and of the sale of a light carriage, and of a young person seeking a situation; but these items of information did not give him, as usual, a quiet, ironical gratification. Having finished the paper, a second cup of coffee and a roll and butter, he got up, shaking the crumbs of the roll off his waistcoat; and, squaring his broad chest, he smiled joyously: not because there was anything particularly agreeable in his mind—the joyous smile was evoked by a good digestion.

But this joyous smile at once recalled everything to him, and he grew thoughtful.

Two childish voices (Stepan Arkadyevitch recognized the voices of Grisha, his youngest boy, and Tanya, his eldest girl) were heard outside the door. They were carrying something, and dropped it.

"I told you not to sit passengers on the roof," said the little girl in English; "there, pick them up!"

"Everything's in confusion," thought Stepan Arkadyevitch; "there are the children running about by themselves." And going to the door, he called them. They threw down the box, that represented a train, and came in to their father.

The little girl, her father's favorite, ran up boldly, embraced him, and hung laughingly on his neck, enjoying as she always did the smell of scent that came from his whiskers. At last the little girl kissed his face, which was flushed from his stooping posture and beaming with tenderness, loosed her hands, and was about to run away again; but her father held her back.

"How is mamma?" he asked, passing his hand over his daughter's smooth, soft little neck. "Good morning," he said, smiling to the boy, who had come up to greet him. He was conscious that he loved the boy less, and always tried to be fair; but the boy felt it, and did not respond with a smile to his father's chilly smile.

"Mamma? She is up," answered the girl.

Stepan Arkadyevitch sighed. "That means that she's not slept again all night," he thought.

"Well, is she cheerful?"

The little girl knew that there was a quarrel between her father and mother, and that her mother could not be cheerful, and that her father must be aware of this, and that he was pretending when he asked about it so lightly. And she blushed for her father. He at once perceived it, and blushed too.

"I don't know," she said. "She did not say we must do our lessons, but she said we were to go for a walk with Miss Hoole to grandmamma's."

"Well, go, Tanya, my darling. Oh, wait a minute, though," he said, still holding her and stroking her soft little hand.

He took off the mantelpiece, where he had put it yesterday, a little box of sweets, and gave her two, picking out her favorites, a chocolate and a fondant.

"For Grisha?" said the little girl, pointing to the chocolate.

"Yes, yes." And still stroking her little shoulder, he kissed her on the roots of her hair and neck, and let her go.

"The carriage is ready," said Matvey; "but there's someone to see you with a petition."

"Been here long?" asked Stepan Arkadyevitch.

"Half an hour."

"How many times have I told you to tell me at once?"

"One must let you drink your coffee in peace, at least," said Matvey, in the affectionately gruff tone with which it was impossible to be angry.

"Well, show the person up at once," said Oblonsky, frowning with vexation.

The petitioner, the widow of a staff captain Kalinin, came with a request impossible and unreasonable; but Stepan Arkadyevitch, as he generally did, made her sit down, heard her to the end attentively without interrupting her, and gave her detailed advice as to how and to whom to apply, and even wrote her, in his large, sprawling, good and legible hand, a confident and fluent little note to a personage who might be of use to her. Having got rid of the staff captain's widow, Stepan Arkadyevitch took his hat and stopped to recollect whether he had forgotten anything. It appeared that he had forgotten nothing except what he wanted to forget—his wife.

"Ah, yes!" He bowed his head, and his handsome face assumed a harassed expression. "To go, or not to go!" he said to himself; and an inner voice told him he must not go, that nothing could come of it but falsity; that to amend, to set right their relations was impossible, because it was impossible to make her attractive again and able to inspire love, or to make him an old man, not susceptible to love. Except deceit and lying nothing could come of it now; and deceit and lying were opposed to his nature.

"It must be some time, though: it can't go on like this," he said, trying to give himself courage. He squared his chest, took out a cigarette, took two whiffs at it, flung it into a mother-of-pearl ashtray, and with rapid steps walked through the drawing room, and opened the other door into his wife's bedroom.

Chapter IV

DARYA ALEXANDROVNA, IN A DRESSING-JACKET, AND WITH HER NOW SCANTY, ONCE LUXURIANT and beautiful hair fastened up with hairpins on the nape of her neck, with a sunken, thin face and large, startled eyes, which looked prominent from the thinness of her face, was standing among a litter of all sorts of things scattered all over the room, before an open bureau, from which she was taking something. Hearing her husband's steps, she stopped, looking towards the door, and trying assiduously to give her features a severe and contemptuous expression. She felt she was afraid of him, and afraid of the coming interview. She was just attempting to do what she had attempted to do ten times already in these last three days—to sort out the children's things and her own, so as to take them to her mother's—and again she could not bring herself to do this; but now again, as each time before, she kept saying to herself, "that things cannot go on like this, that she must take some step" to punish him, put him to shame, avenge on him some little part at least of the suffering he had caused her. She still continued to tell herself that she should leave him, but she was conscious that this was impossible; it was impossible because she could not get out of the habit of regarding him as her husband and loving him. Besides this, she realized that if even here in her own house she could hardly manage to look after her five children properly, they would be still worse off where she was going with them all. As it was, even in the course of these three days, the youngest was unwell from being given unwholesome soup, and the others had almost gone without their dinner the day before. She was conscious that it was impossible to go away; but, cheating herself, she went on all the same sorting out her things and pretending she was going.

Seeing her husband, she dropped her hands into the drawer of the bureau as though looking for something, and only looked round at him when he had come quite up to her. But her face, to which she tried to give a severe and resolute expression, betrayed bewilderment and suffering.

"Dolly!" he said in a subdued and timid voice. He bent his head towards his shoulder and tried to look pitiful and humble, but for all that he was radiant with freshness and health. In a rapid glance she scanned his figure that beamed with health and freshness. "Yes, he is happy and content!" she thought; "while I . . . And that disgusting good-nature, which everyone likes him for and praises—I hate that good-nature of his," she thought. Her mouth stiffened, the muscles of the cheek contracted on the right side of her pale, nervous face.

"What do you want?" she said in a rapid, deep, unnatural voice.

"Dolly!" he repeated, with a quiver in his voice. "Anna is coming today."

"Well, what is that to me? I can't see her!" she cried.

"But you must, really, Dolly. . . ."

"Go away, go away, go away!" she shrieked, not looking at him, as though this shriek were called up by physical pain.

Stepan Arkadyevitch could be calm when he thought of his wife, he could hope that she would *come round*, as Matvey expressed it, and could quietly go on reading his paper and drinking his coffee; but when he saw her tortured, suffering face, heard the tone of her voice, submissive to fate and full of despair, there was a catch in his breath and a lump in his throat, and his eyes began to shine with tears.

"My God! what have I done? Dolly! For God's sake! . . . You know . . ." He could not go on; there was a sob in his throat.

She shut the bureau with a slam, and glanced at him.

"Dolly, what can I say? . . . One thing: forgive . . . Remember, cannot nine years of my life atone for an instant . . ."

She dropped her eyes and listened, expecting what he would say, as it were beseeching him in some way or other to make her believe differently.

"—instant of passion?" he said, and would have gone on, but at that word, as at a pang of physical pain, her lips stiffened again, and again the muscles of her right cheek worked.

"Go away, go out of the room!" she shrieked still more shrilly, "and don't talk to me of your passion and your loathsomeness."

She tried to go out, but tottered, and clung to the back of a chair to support herself. His face relaxed, his lips swelled, his eyes were swimming with tears.

"Dolly!" he said, sobbing now; "for mercy's sake, think of the children; they are not to blame! I am to blame, and punish me, make me expiate my fault. Anything I can do, I am ready to do anything! I am to blame, no words can express how much I am to blame! But, Dolly, forgive me!"

She sat down. He listened to her hard, heavy breathing, and he was unutterably sorry for her. She tried several times to begin to speak, but could not. He waited.

"You remember the children, Stiva, to play with them; but I remember them, and know that this means their ruin," she said—obviously one of the phrases she had more than once repeated to herself in the course of the last few days.

She had called him "Stiva," and he glanced at her with gratitude, and moved to take her hand, but she drew back from him with aversion.

"I think of the children, and for that reason I would do anything in the world to save them, but I don't myself know how to save them. By taking them away from their father, or by leaving them with a vicious father—yes, a vicious father. . . . Tell me, after what . . . has happened, can we live together? Is that possible? Tell me, eh, is it possible?" she repeated, raising her voice, "after my husband, the father of my children, enters into a love affair with his own children's governess?"

"But what could I do? what could I do?" he kept saying in a pitiful voice, not knowing what he was saying, as his head sank lower and lower.

"You are loathsome to me, repulsive!" she shrieked, getting more and more heated. "Your tears mean nothing! You have never loved me; you have neither heart nor honorable feeling! You are hateful to me, disgusting, a stranger—yes, a complete stranger!" With pain and wrath she uttered the word so terrible to herself—*stranger.*

He looked at her, and the fury expressed in her face alarmed and amazed him. He did not understand how his pity for her exasperated her. She saw in him sympathy for her, but not love. "No, she hates me. She will not forgive me," he thought.

"It is awful! awful!" he said.

At that moment in the next room a child began to cry; probably it had fallen down. Darya Alexandrovna listened, and her face suddenly softened.

She seemed to be pulling herself together for a few seconds, as though she did not know where she was, and what she was doing, and getting up rapidly, she moved towards the door.

"Well, she loves my child," he thought, noticing the change of her face at the child's cry, "my child: how can she hate me?"

"Dolly, one word more," he said, following her.

"If you come near me, I will call in the servants, the children! They may all know you are a scoundrel! I am going away at once, and you may live here with your mistress!"

And she went out, slamming the door.

Stepan Arkadyevitch sighed, wiped his face, and with a subdued tread walked out of the room. "Matvey says she will look up; but how? I don't see the least chance of it. Ah, oh, how horrible it is! And how vulgarly she shouted," he said to himself, remembering her shriek and the words—"scoundrel" and "mistress." "And very likely the maids were listening! Horribly vulgar! horrible!" Stepan Arkadyevitch stood a few seconds alone, wiped his face, squared his chest, and walked out of the room.

It was Friday, and in the dining room the German watchmaker was winding up the clock. Stepan Arkadyevitch remembered his joke about this punctual, bald watchmaker, "that the German was wound up for a whole lifetime himself, to wind up watches," and he smiled. Stepan Arkadyevitch was fond of a joke. "And maybe she will look up! That's a good expression, '*come round,*'" he thought. "I must repeat that."

"Matvey!" he shouted. "Arrange everything with Darya in the sitting room for Anna Arkadyevna," he said to Matvey when he came in.

"Yes, sir."

Stepan Arkadyevitch put on his fur coat and went out onto the steps.

"You won't dine at home?" said Matvey, seeing him off.

"That's as it happens. But here's for the housekeeping," he said, taking ten roubles from his pocketbook. "That'll be enough."

"Enough or not enough, we must make it do," said Matvey, slamming the carriage door and stepping back onto the steps.

Darya Alexandrovna meanwhile having pacified the child, and knowing from the sound of the carriage that he had gone off, went back again to her bedroom. It was her solitary refuge from the household cares which crowded upon her directly she went out from it. Even now, in the short time she had been in the nursery, the English governess and Matrona Philimonovna had succeeded in putting several questions to her, which did not admit of delay, and which only she could answer: "What were the children to put on for their walk? Should they have any milk? Should not a new cook be sent for?"

"Ah, let me alone, let me alone!" she said, and going back to her bedroom she sat down in the same place as she had sat when talking to her husband, clasping tightly her thin hands with the rings that slipped down on her bony fingers, and fell to going over in her memory all the conversation. "He has gone! But has he broken it off with her?" she thought. "Can it be he sees her? Why didn't I ask him! No, no, reconciliation is impossible. Even if we remain in the same house, we are strangers—strangers forever!" She repeated again with special significance the word so dreadful to her. "And how I loved him! my God, how I loved him!. . . . How I loved him! And now don't I love him? Don't I love him more than before? The most horrible thing is," she began, but did not finish her thought, because Matrona Philimonovna put her head in at the door.

"Let us send for my brother," she said; "he can get a dinner anyway, or we shall have the children getting nothing to eat till six again, like yesterday."

"Very well, I will come directly and see about it. But did you send for some new milk?"

And Darya Alexandrovna plunged into the duties of the day, and drowned her grief in them for a time.

Chapter V

STEPAN ARKADYEVITCH HAD LEARNED EASILY AT SCHOOL, THANKS TO HIS EXCELLENT ABILITIES, but he had been idle and mischievous, and therefore was one of the lowest in his class. But in spite of his habitually dissipated mode of life, his inferior grade in the service, and his comparative youth, he occupied the honorable and lucrative position of president of one of the government boards at Moscow. This post he had received through his sister Anna's husband, Alexey Alexandrovitch Karenin, who held one of the most important positions in the ministry to whose department the Moscow office belonged. But if Karenin had not got his brother-in-law this berth, then through a hundred other personages—brothers, sisters, cousins, uncles, and aunts—Stiva Oblonsky would have received this post, or some other similar one, together with the salary of six thousand absolutely needful for him, as his affairs, in spite of his wife's considerable property, were in an embarrassed condition.

Half Moscow and Petersburg were friends and relations of Stepan Arkadyevitch. He was born in the midst of those who had been and are the powerful ones of this world. One-third of the men in the government, the older men, had been friends of his father's, and had known him in petticoats; another third were his intimate chums, and the remainder were friendly acquaintances. Consequently the distributors of earthly blessings in the shape of places, rents, shares, and such, were all his friends, and could not overlook one of their own set; and Oblonsky had no need to make any special exertion to get a lucrative post. He had only not to refuse things, not to show jealousy, not to be quarrelsome or take offense, all of which from his characteristic good-nature he never did. It would have struck him as absurd if he had been told that he would not get a position with the salary he required, especially as he expected nothing out of the way; he only wanted what the men of his own age and standing did get, and he was no worse qualified for performing duties of the kind than any other man.

Stepan Arkadyevitch was not merely liked by all who knew him for his good-humor, but for his bright disposition, and his unquestionable honesty. In him, in his handsome, radiant figure, his sparkling eyes, black hair and eyebrows, and the white and red of his face, there was something which produced a physical effect of kindliness and good-humor on the people who met him. "Aha! Stiva! Oblonsky! Here he is!" was almost always said with a smile of delight on meeting him. Even though it happened at times that after a conversation with him it seemed that nothing particularly delightful had happened, the next day, and the next, everyone was just as delighted at meeting him again.

After filling for three years the post of president of one of the government boards at Moscow, Stepan Arkadyevitch had won the respect, as well as the liking, of his fellow-officials, subordinates, and superiors, and all who had had business with him. The principal qualities in Stepan Arkadyevitch which had gained him this universal respect in the service consisted, in the first place, of his extreme indulgence for others, founded on a consciousness of his own shortcomings; secondly, of his perfect liberalism—not the liberalism he read of in the papers, but the liberalism that was in his blood, in virtue of which he treated all men perfectly equally and exactly the same, whatever their fortune or calling might be; and thirdly—the most important point—his complete indifference to the business in which he was engaged, in consequence of which he was never carried away, and never made mistakes.

On reaching the offices of the board, Stepan Arkadyevitch, escorted by a deferential porter with a portfolio, went into his little private room, put on his uniform, and went into the board room. The clerks and copyists all rose, greeting him with good-humored deference. Stepan Arkadyevitch moved quickly, as ever, to his place, shook hands with his colleagues, and sat down. He made a joke or two, and talked just as much as was consistent with due decorum, and began work. No one knew better than Stepan Arkadyevitch how to hit on the exact line between freedom, simplicity, and official stiffness necessary for the agreeable conduct of business. A secretary, with the good-humored deference common to everyone in Stepan Arkadyevitch's office, came up with papers, and began to speak in the familiar and easy tone which had been introduced by Stepan Arkadyevitch.

"We have succeeded in getting the information from the government department of Penza. Here, would you care? . . ."

"You've got them at last?" said Stepan Arkadyevitch, laying his finger on the paper. "Now, gentlemen. . . ."

And the sitting of the board began.

"If they knew," he thought, bending his head with a significant air as he listened to the report, "what a guilty little boy their president was half an hour ago." And his eyes were laughing during the reading of the report. Till two o'clock the sitting would go on without a break, and at two o'clock there would be an interval and luncheon.

It was not yet two, when the large glass doors of the board room suddenly opened and someone came in.

All the officials sitting on the farther side under the portrait of the Tsar and the eagle, delighted at any distraction, looked round at the door; but the doorkeeper standing at the door at once drove out the intruder, and closed the glass door after him.

When the case had been read through, Stepan Arkadyevitch got up and stretched, and by way of tribute to the liberalism of the times took out a cigarette in the board room and went into his private room. Two of the members of the board, the old veteran in the service, Nikitin, and the *Kammerjunker* Grinevitch, went in with him.

"We shall have time to finish after lunch," said Stepan Arkadyevitch.

"To be sure we shall!" said Nikitin.

"A pretty sharp fellow this Fomin must be," said Grinevitch of one of the persons taking part in the case they were examining.

Stepan Arkadyevitch frowned at Grinevitch's words, giving him thereby to understand that it was improper to pass judgment prematurely, and made him no reply.

"Who was that came in?" he asked the doorkeeper.

"Someone, your excellency, crept in without permission directly my back was turned. He was asking for you. I told him: when the members come out, then . . ."

"Where is he?"

"Maybe he's gone into the passage, but here he comes anyway. That is he," said the doorkeeper, pointing to a strongly built, broad-shouldered man with a curly beard, who, without taking off his sheepskin cap, was running lightly and rapidly up the worn steps of the stone staircase. One of the members going down—a lean official with a portfolio—stood out of his way and looked disapprovingly at the legs of the stranger, then glanced inquiringly at Oblonsky.

Stepan Arkadyevitch was standing at the top of the stairs. His good-naturedly beaming face above the embroidered collar of his uniform beamed more than ever when he recognized the man coming up.

"Why, it's actually you, Levin, at last!" he said with a friendly mocking smile, scanning Levin as he approached. "How is it you have deigned to look me up in this den?" said Stepan Arkadyevitch, and not content with shaking hands, he kissed his friend. "Have you been here long?"

"I have just come, and very much wanted to see you," said Levin, looking shyly and at the same time angrily and uneasily around.

"Well, let's go into my room," said Stepan Arkadyevitch, who knew his friend's sensitive and irritable shyness, and, taking his arm, he drew him along, as though guiding him through dangers.

Stepan Arkadyevitch was on familiar terms with almost all his acquaintances, and called almost all of them by their Christian names: old men of sixty, boys of twenty, actors, ministers, merchants, and adjutant-generals, so that many of his intimate chums were to be found at the extreme ends of the social ladder, and would have been very much surprised to learn that they had, through the medium of Oblonsky, something in common. He was the familiar friend of everyone with whom he took a glass of champagne, and he took a glass of champagne with everyone, and when in consequence he met any of his *disreputable* chums, as he used in joke to call many of his friends, in the presence of his subordinates, he well knew how, with his characteristic tact, to diminish the disagreeable impression made on them. Levin was not a disreputable chum, but Oblonsky, with his ready tact, felt that Levin fancied he might not care to show his intimacy with him before his subordinates, and so he made haste to take him off into his room.

Levin was almost of the same age as Oblonsky; their intimacy did not rest merely on champagne. Levin had been the friend and companion of his early youth. They were fond of one another in spite of the difference of their characters and tastes, as friends are fond of one another who have been together in early youth. But in spite of this, each of them—as is often the way with men who have selected careers of different kinds—though in discussion he would even justify the other's career, in his heart despised it. It seemed to each of them that the life he led himself was the only real life, and the life led by his friend was a mere phantasm. Oblonsky could not restrain a slight mocking smile at the sight of Levin. How often he had seen him come up to Moscow from the country where he was doing something, but what precisely Stepan Arkadyevitch could never quite make out, and indeed he took no interest in the matter. Levin arrived in Moscow always excited and in a hurry, rather ill at ease and irritated by his own want of ease, and for the most part with a perfectly new, unexpected view of things. Stepan Arkadyevitch laughed at this, and liked it. In the same way Levin in his heart despised the town mode of life of his friend, and his official duties, which he laughed at, and regarded as trifling. But the difference was that Oblonsky, as he was doing the same as everyone did, laughed complacently and good-humoredly, while Levin laughed without complacency and sometimes angrily.

"We have long been expecting you," said Stepan Arkadyevitch, going into his room and letting Levin's hand go as though to show that here all danger was over. "I am very, very glad to see you," he went on. "Well, how are you? Eh? When did you come?"

Levin was silent, looking at the unknown faces of Oblonsky's two companions, and especially at the hand of the elegant Grinevitch, which had such long white fingers, such long yellow filbert-shaped nails, and such huge shining studs on the shirt-cuff, that apparently they absorbed all his attention, and allowed him no freedom of thought. Oblonsky noticed this at once, and smiled.

"Ah, to be sure, let me introduce you," he said. "My colleagues: Philip Ivanitch Nikitin, Mihail Stanislavitch Grinevitch"—and turning to Levin—"a district councilor, a modern district councilman, a gymnast who lifts thirteen stone with one hand, a cattle-breeder and sportsman, and my friend, Konstantin Dmitrievitch Levin, the brother of Sergey Ivanovitch Koznishev."

"Delighted," said the veteran.

"I have the honor of knowing your brother, Sergey Ivanovitch," said Grinevitch, holding out his slender hand with its long nails.

Levin frowned, shook hands coldly, and at once turned to Oblonsky. Though he had a great respect for his half-brother, an author well-known to all Russia, he could not endure it when people treated him not as Konstantin Levin, but as the brother of the celebrated Koznishev.

"No, I am no longer a district councilor. I have quarreled with them all, and don't go to the meetings anymore," he said, turning to Oblonsky.

"You've been quick about it!" said Oblonsky with a smile. "But how? why?"

"It's a long story. I will tell you some time," said Levin, but he began telling him at once. "Well, to put it shortly, I was convinced that nothing was really done by the district councils, or ever could be," he began, as though someone had just insulted him. "On one side it's a plaything; they play at being a parliament, and I'm neither young enough nor old enough to find amusement in playthings: and on the other side" (he stammered) "it's a means for the coterie of the district to make money. Formerly they had wardships, courts of justice, now they have the district council—not in the form of bribes, but in the form of unearned salary," he said, as hotly as though someone of those present had opposed his opinion.

"Aha! You're in a new phase again, I see—a conservative," said Stepan Arkadyevitch. "However, we can go into that later."

"Yes, later. But I wanted to see you," said Levin, looking with hatred at Grinevitch's hand.

Stepan Arkadyevitch gave a scarcely perceptible smile.

"How was it you used to say you would never wear European dress again?" he said, scanning his new suit, obviously cut by a French tailor. "Ah! I see: a new phase."

Levin suddenly blushed, not as grown men blush, slightly, without being themselves aware of it, but as boys blush, feeling that they are ridiculous through their shyness, and consequently ashamed of it and blushing still more, almost to the point of tears. And it was so strange to see this sensible, manly face in such a childish plight, that Oblonsky left off looking at him.

"Oh, where shall we meet? You know I want very much to talk to you," said Levin.

Oblonsky seemed to ponder.

"I'll tell you what: let's go to Gurin's to lunch, and there we can talk. I am free till three."

"No," answered Levin, after an instant's thought, "I have got to go on somewhere else."

"All right, then, let's dine together."

"Dine together? But I have nothing very particular, only a few words to say, and a question I want to ask you, and we can have a talk afterwards."

"Well, say the few words, then, at once, and we'll gossip after dinner."

"Well, it's this," said Levin; "but it's of no importance, however."

His face all at once took an expression of anger from the effort he was making to surmount his shyness.

"What are the Shtcherbatskys doing? Everything as it used to be?" he said.

Stepan Arkadyevitch, who had long known that Levin was in love with his sister-in-law, Kitty, gave a hardly perceptible smile, and his eyes sparkled merrily.

"You said a few words, but I can't answer in a few words, because . . . Excuse me a minute. . . ."

A secretary came in, with respectful familiarity and the modest consciousness, characteristic of every secretary, of superiority to his chief in the knowledge of their business; he went up to Oblonsky with some papers, and began, under pretense of asking a question, to explain some objection. Stepan Arkadyevitch, without hearing him out, laid his hand genially on the secretary's sleeve.

"No, you do as I told you," he said, softening his words with a smile, and with a brief explanation of his view of the matter he turned away from the papers, and said: "So do it that way, if you please, Zahar Nikititch."

The secretary retired in confusion. During the consultation with the secretary Levin had completely recovered from his embarrassment. He was standing with his elbows on the back of a chair, and on his face was a look of ironical attention.

"I don't understand it, I don't understand it," he said.

"What don't you understand?" said Oblonsky, smiling as brightly as ever, and picking up a cigarette. He expected some queer outburst from Levin.

"I don't understand what you are doing," said Levin, shrugging his shoulders. "How can you do it seriously?"

"Why not?"

"Why, because there's nothing in it."

"You think so, but we're overwhelmed with work."

"On paper. But, there, you've a gift for it," added Levin.

"That's to say, you think there's a lack of something in me?"

"Perhaps so," said Levin. "But all the same I admire your grandeur, and am proud that I've a friend in such a great person. You've not answered my question, though," he went on, with a desperate effort looking Oblonsky straight in the face.

"Oh, that's all very well. You wait a bit, and you'll come to this yourself. It's very nice for you to have over six thousand acres in the Karazinsky district, and such muscles, and the freshness of a girl of twelve; still you'll be one of us one day. Yes, as to your question, there is no change, but it's a pity you've been away so long."

"Oh, why so?" Levin queried, panic-stricken.

"Oh, nothing," responded Oblonsky. "We'll talk it over. But what's brought you up to town?"

"Oh, we'll talk about that, too, later on," said Levin, reddening again up to his ears.

"All right. I see," said Stepan Arkadyevitch. "I should ask you to come to us, you know, but my wife's not quite the thing. But I tell you what; if you want to see them, they're sure now to be at the Zoological Gardens from four to five. Kitty skates. You drive along there, and I'll come and fetch you, and we'll go and dine somewhere together."

"Capital. So good-bye till then."

"Now mind, you'll forget, I know you, or rush off home to the country!" Stepan Arkadyevitch called out laughing.

"No, truly!"

And Levin went out of the room, only when he was in the doorway remembering that he had forgotten to take leave of Oblonsky's colleagues.

"That gentleman must be a man of great energy," said Grinevitch, when Levin had gone away.

"Yes, my dear boy," said Stepan Arkadyevitch, nodding his head, "he's a lucky fellow! Over six thousand acres in the Karazinsky district; everything before him; and what youth and vigor! Not like some of us."

"You have a great deal to complain of, haven't you, Stepan Arkadyevitch?"

"Ah, yes, I'm in a poor way, a bad way," said Stepan Arkadyevitch with a heavy sigh.

Chapter VI

WHEN OBLONSKY ASKED LEVIN WHAT HAD BROUGHT HIM TO TOWN, LEVIN BLUSHED, AND WAS furious with himself for blushing, because he could not answer, "I have come to make your sister-in-law an offer," though that was precisely what he had come for.

The families of the Levins and the Shtcherbatskys were old, noble Moscow families, and had always been on intimate and friendly terms. This intimacy had grown still closer during Levin's student-days. He had both prepared for the university with the young Prince Shtcherbatsky, the brother of Kitty and Dolly, and had entered at the same time with him. In those days Levin used often to be in the Shtcherbatskys' house, and he was in love with the Shtcherbatsky household. Strange as it may appear, it was with the household, the family, that Konstantin Levin was in love, especially with the feminine half of the household. Levin did not remember his own mother, and his only sister was older than he was, so that it was in the Shtcherbatskys' house that he saw for the first time that inner life of an old, noble, cultivated, and honorable family of which he had been deprived by the death of his father and mother. All the members of that family, especially the feminine half, were pictured by him, as it were, wrapped about with a mysterious poetical veil, and he not only perceived no defects whatever in them, but under the poetical veil that shrouded them he assumed the existence of the loftiest sentiments and every possible perfection. Why it was the three young ladies had one day to speak French, and the next English; why it was that at certain hours they played by turns on the piano, the sounds of which were audible in their brother's room above, where the students used to work; why they were visited by those professors of French literature, of music, of drawing, of dancing; why at certain hours all the three young ladies, with Mademoiselle Linon, drove in the coach to the Tversky boulevard, dressed in their satin cloaks, Dolly in a long one, Natalia in a half-long one, and Kitty in one so short that her shapely legs in tightly-drawn red stockings were visible to all beholders; why it was they had to walk about the Tversky boulevard escorted by a footman with a gold cockade in his hat—all this and much more that was done in their mysterious world he did not understand, but he was sure that everything that was done there was very good, and he was in love precisely with the mystery of the proceedings.

In his student-days he had all but been in love with the eldest, Dolly, but she was soon married to Oblonsky. Then he began being in love with the second. He felt, as it were, that he had to be in love with one of the sisters, only he could not quite make out which. But Natalia, too, had hardly made her appearance in the world when she married the diplomat Lvov. Kitty was still a child when Levin left the university. Young Shtcherbatsky went into the navy, was drowned in the Baltic, and Levin's relations with the Shtcherbatskys, in spite of his friendship with Oblonsky, became less intimate. But when early in the winter of this year Levin came to Moscow, after a year in the country, and saw the Shtcherbatskys, he realized which of the three sisters he was indeed destined to love.

One would have thought that nothing could be simpler than for him, a man of good family, rather rich than poor, and thirty-two years old, to make the young Princess Shtcherbatskaya an offer of marriage; in all likelihood he would at once have been looked upon as a good match. But Levin was in love, and so it seemed to him that Kitty was so perfect in every respect that she was a creature far above everything earthly; and that he was a creature so low and so earthly that it could not even be conceived that other people and she herself could regard him as worthy of her.

After spending two months in Moscow in a state of enchantment, seeing Kitty almost every day in society, into which he went so as to meet her, he abruptly decided that it could not be, and went back to the country.

Levin's conviction that it could not be was founded on the idea that in the eyes of her family he was a disadvantageous and worthless match for the charming Kitty, and that Kitty herself could not love him. In her family's eyes he had no ordinary, definite career and position in society, while his contemporaries by this time, when he was thirty-two, were already, one a colonel, and another a professor, another director of a bank and railways, or president of a board like Oblonsky. But he (he knew very well how he must appear to others) was a country gentleman, occupied in breeding cattle, shooting game, and building barns; in other words, a fellow of no ability, who had not turned out well, and who was doing just what, according to the ideas of the world, is done by people fit for nothing else.

The mysterious, enchanting Kitty herself could not love such an ugly person as he conceived himself to be, and, above all, such an ordinary, in no way striking person. Moreover, his attitude to Kitty in the past—the attitude of a grown-up person to a child, arising from his friendship with her brother—seemed to him yet another obstacle to love. An ugly, good-natured man, as he considered himself, might, he supposed, be liked as a friend; but to be loved with such a love as that with which he loved Kitty, one would need to be a handsome and, still more, a distinguished man.

He had heard that women often did care for ugly and ordinary men, but he did not believe it, for he judged by himself, and he could not himself have loved any but beautiful, mysterious, and exceptional women.

But after spending two months alone in the country, he was convinced that this was not one of those passions of which he had had experience in his early youth; that this feeling gave him not an instant's rest; that he could not live without deciding the question, would she or would she not be his wife, and that his despair had arisen only from his own imaginings, that he had no sort of proof that he would be rejected. And he had now come to Moscow with a firm determination to make an offer, and get married if he were accepted. Or . . . he could not conceive what would become of him if he were rejected.

Chapter VII

ON ARRIVING IN MOSCOW BY A MORNING TRAIN, LEVIN HAD PUT UP AT THE HOUSE OF HIS ELDER half-brother, Koznishev. After changing his clothes he went down to his brother's study, intending to talk to him at once about the object of his visit, and to ask his advice; but his brother was not alone. With him there was a well-known professor of philosophy, who had come from Harkov expressly to clear up a difference that had arisen between them on a very important philosophical question. The professor was carrying on a hot crusade against materialists. Sergey Koznishev had been following this crusade with interest, and after reading the professor's last article, he had written him a letter stating his objections. He accused the professor of making too great concessions to the materialists. And the professor had promptly appeared to argue the matter out. The point in discussion was the question then in vogue: Is there a line to be drawn between psychological and physiological phenomena in man? and if so, where?

Sergey Ivanovitch met his brother with the smile of chilly friendliness he always had for everyone, and introducing him to the professor, went on with the conversation.

A little man in spectacles, with a narrow forehead, tore himself from the discussion for an instant to greet Levin, and then went on talking without paying any further attention to him. Levin sat down to wait till the professor should go, but he soon began to get interested in the subject under discussion.

Levin had come across the magazine articles about which they were disputing, and had read them, interested in them as a development of the first principles of science, familiar to him as a natural science student at the university. But he had never connected these scientific deductions as to the origin of man as an animal, as to reflex action, biology, and sociology, with those questions as to the meaning of life and death to himself, which had of late been more and more often in his mind.

As he listened to his brother's argument with the professor, he noticed that they connected these scientific questions with those spiritual problems, that at times they almost touched on the latter; but every time they were close upon what seemed to him the chief point, they promptly beat a hasty retreat, and plunged again into a sea of subtle distinctions, reservations, quotations, allusions, and appeals to authorities, and it was with difficulty that he understood what they were talking about.

"I cannot admit it," said Sergey Ivanovitch, with his habitual clearness, precision of expression, and elegance of phrase. "I cannot in any case agree with Keiss that my whole conception of the external world has been derived from perceptions. The most fundamental idea, the idea of existence, has not been received by me through sensation; indeed, there is no special sense-organ for the transmission of such an idea."

"Yes, but they—Wurt, and Knaust, and Pripasov—would answer that your consciousness of existence is derived from the conjunction of all your sensations, that that consciousness of existence is the result of your sensations. Wurt, indeed, says plainly that, assuming there are no sensations, it follows that there is no idea of existence."

"I maintain the contrary," began Sergey Ivanovitch.

But here it seemed to Levin that just as they were close upon the real point of the matter, they were again retreating, and he made up his mind to put a question to the professor.

"According to that, if my senses are annihilated, if my body is dead, I can have no existence of any sort?" he queried.

The professor, in annoyance, and, as it were, mental suffering at the interruption, looked round at the strange inquirer, more like a bargeman than a philosopher, and turned his eyes upon Sergey Ivanovitch, as though to ask: What's one to say to him? But Sergey Ivanovitch, who had been talking with far less heat and one-sidedness than the professor, and who had sufficient breadth of mind to answer the professor, and at the same time to comprehend the simple and natural point of view from which the question was put, smiled and said:

"That question we have no right to answer as yet."

"We have not the requisite data," chimed in the professor, and he went back to his argument. "No," he said; "I would point out the fact that if, as Pripasov directly asserts, perception is based on sensation, then we are bound to distinguish sharply between these two conceptions."

Levin listened no more, and simply waited for the professor to go.

Chapter VIII

WHEN THE PROFESSOR HAD GONE, SERGEY IVANOVITCH TURNED TO HIS BROTHER.

"Delighted that you've come. For some time, is it? How's your farming getting on?"

Levin knew that his elder brother took little interest in farming, and only put the question in deference to him, and so he only told him about the sale of his wheat and money matters.

Levin had meant to tell his brother of his determination to get married, and to ask his advice; he had indeed firmly resolved to do so. But after seeing his brother, listening to his conversation with the professor, hearing afterwards the unconsciously patronizing tone in which his brother questioned him about agricultural matters (their mother's property had not been divided, and Levin took charge of both their shares), Levin felt that he could not for some reason begin to talk to him of his intention of marrying. He felt that his brother would not look at it as he would have wished him to.

"Well, how is your district council doing?" asked Sergey Ivanovitch, who was greatly interested in these local boards and attached great importance to them.

"I really don't know."

"What! Why, surely you're a member of the board?"

"No, I'm not a member now; I've resigned," answered Levin, "and I no longer attend the meetings."

"What a pity!" commented Sergey Ivanovitch, frowning.

Levin in self-defense began to describe what took place in the meetings in his district.

"That's how it always is!" Sergey Ivanovitch interrupted him. "We Russians are always like that. Perhaps it's our strong point, really, the faculty of seeing our own shortcomings; but we overdo it, we comfort ourselves with irony which we always have on the tip of our tongues. All I say is, give such rights as our local self-government to any other European people—why, the Germans or the English would have worked their way to freedom from them, while we simply turn them into ridicule."

"But how can it be helped?" said Levin penitently. "It was my last effort. And I did try with all my soul. I can't. I'm no good at it."

"It's not that you're no good at it," said Sergey Ivanovitch; "it is that you don't look at it as you should."

"Perhaps not," Levin answered dejectedly.

"Oh! do you know brother Nikolay's turned up again?"

This brother Nikolay was the elder brother of Konstantin Levin, and half-brother of Sergey Ivanovitch; a man utterly ruined, who had dissipated the greater part of his fortune, was living in the strangest and lowest company, and had quarreled with his brothers.

"What did you say?" Levin cried with horror. "How do you know?"

"Prokofy saw him in the street."

"Here in Moscow? Where is he? Do you know?" Levin got up from his chair, as though on the point of starting off at once.

"I am sorry I told you," said Sergey Ivanovitch, shaking his head at his younger brother's excitement. "I sent to find out where he is living, and sent him his IOU to Trubin, which I paid. This is the answer he sent me."

And Sergey Ivanovitch took a note from under a paperweight and handed it to his brother.

Levin read in the queer, familiar handwriting: "I humbly beg you to leave me in peace. That's the only favor I ask of my gracious brothers.—NIKOLAY LEVIN."

Levin read it, and without raising his head stood with the note in his hands opposite Sergey Ivanovitch.

There was a struggle in his heart between the desire to forget his unhappy brother for the time, and the consciousness that it would be base to do so.

"He obviously wants to offend me," pursued Sergey Ivanovitch; "but he cannot offend me, and I should have wished with all my heart to assist him, but I know it's impossible to do that."

"Yes, yes," repeated Levin. "I understand and appreciate your attitude to him; but I shall go and see him."

"If you want to, do; but I shouldn't advise it," said Sergey Ivanovitch. "As regards myself, I have no fear of your doing so; he will not make you quarrel with me; but for your own sake, I should say you would do better not to go. You can't do him any good; still, do as you please."

"Very likely I can't do any good, but I feel—especially at such a moment—but that's another thing—I feel I could not be at peace."

"Well, that I don't understand," said Sergey Ivanovitch. "One thing I do understand," he added; "it's a lesson in humility. I have come to look very differently and more charitably on what is called infamous since brother Nikolay has become what he is . . . you know what he did. . . ."

"Oh, it's awful, awful!" repeated Levin.

After obtaining his brother's address from Sergey Ivanovitch's footman, Levin was on the point of setting off at once to see him, but on second thought he decided to put off his visit till the evening. The first thing to do to set his heart at rest was to accomplish what he had come to Moscow for. From his brother's Levin went to Oblonsky's office, and on getting news of the Shtcherbatskys from him, he drove to the place where he had been told he might find Kitty.

Chapter IX

At four o'clock, conscious of his throbbing heart, Levin stepped out of a hired sleigh at the Zoological Gardens, and turned along the path to the frozen mounds and the skating-ground, knowing that he would certainly find her there, as he had seen the Shtcherbatskys' carriage at the entrance.

It was a bright, frosty day. Rows of carriages, sleighs, drivers, and policemen were standing in the approach. Crowds of well-dressed people, with hats bright in the sun, swarmed about the entrance and along the well-swept little paths between the little houses adorned with carving in the Russian style. The old curly birches of the gardens, all their twigs laden with snow, looked as though freshly decked in sacred vestments.

He walked along the path towards the skating-ground, and kept saying to himself—"You mustn't be excited, you must be calm. What's the matter with you? What do you want? Be quiet, stupid," he conjured his heart. And the more he tried to compose himself, the more breathless he found himself. An acquaintance met him and called him by his name, but Levin did not even recognize him. He went towards the mounds, whence came the clank of the chains of sleighs as they slipped down or were dragged up, the rumble of the sliding sleighs, and the sounds of merry voices. He walked on a few steps, and the skating-ground lay open before his eyes, and at once, amidst all the skaters, he knew her.

He knew she was there by the rapture and the terror that seized on his heart. She was standing talking to a lady at the opposite end of the ground. There was apparently nothing striking either in her dress or her attitude. But for Levin she was as easy to find in that crowd as a rose among nettles. Everything was made bright by her. She was the smile that shed light on all round her. "Is it possible I can go over there on the ice, go up to her?" he thought. The place where she stood seemed to him a holy shrine, unapproachable, and there was one moment when he was almost retreating, so overwhelmed was he with terror. He had to make an effort to master himself, and to remind himself that people of all sorts were moving about her, and that he too might come there to skate. He walked down, for a long while avoiding looking at her as at the sun, but seeing her, as one does the sun, without looking.

On that day of the week and at that time of day people of one set, all acquainted with one another, used to meet on the ice. There were crack skaters there, showing off their skill, and learners clinging to chairs with timid, awkward movements, boys, and elderly people skating with hygienic motives. They seemed to Levin an elect band of blissful beings because they were here, near her. All the skaters, it seemed, with perfect self-possession, skated towards her, skated by her, even spoke to her, and were happy, quite apart from her, enjoying the capital ice and the fine weather.

Nikolay Shtcherbatsky, Kitty's cousin, in a short jacket and tight trousers, was sitting on a garden seat with his skates on. Seeing Levin, he shouted to him:

"Ah, the first skater in Russia! Been here long? First rate ice—do put your skates on."

"I haven't got my skates," Levin answered, marveling at this boldness and ease in her presence, and not for one second losing sight of her, though he did not look at her. He felt as though the sun were coming near him. She was in a corner, and turning out her slender feet in their high boots with obvious timidity, she skated towards him. A boy in Russian dress, desperately waving his arms and bowed down to the ground, overtook her. She skated a little uncertainly; taking her hands out of the little muff that hung on a cord, she held them ready for emergency, and looking towards Levin, whom she had recognized, she smiled at him, and at her own fears. When she had got round the turn, she gave herself a push off with one foot, and skated straight up to Shtcherbatsky. Clutching at his arm, she nodded smiling to Levin. She was more splendid than he had imagined her.

When he thought of her, he could call up a vivid picture of her to himself, especially the charm of that little fair head, so freely set on the shapely girlish shoulders, and so full of childish brightness and good-humor. The childishness of her expression, together with the delicate beauty of her figure, made up her special charm, and that he fully realized. But what always struck him in her as something unlooked for, was the expression of her eyes, soft, serene, and truthful, and above all, her smile, which always transported Levin to an enchanted world, where he felt himself softened and tender, as he remembered himself in some days of his early childhood.

"Have you been here long?" she said, giving him her hand. "Thank you," she added, as he picked up the handkerchief that had fallen out of her muff.

"I? I've not long . . . yesterday . . . I mean today . . . I arrived," answered Levin, in his emotion not at once understanding her question. "I was meaning to come and see you," he said; and then, recollecting with what intention he was trying to see her, he was promptly overcome with confusion and blushed.

"I didn't know you could skate, and skate so well."

She looked at him earnestly, as though wishing to make out the cause of his confusion.

"Your praise is worth having. The tradition is kept up here that you are the best of skaters," she said, with her little black-gloved hand brushing a grain of hoarfrost off her muff.

"Yes, I used once to skate with passion; I wanted to reach perfection."

"You do everything with passion, I think," she said smiling. "I should so like to see how you skate. Put on skates, and let us skate together."

"Skate together! Can that be possible?" thought Levin, gazing at her.

"I'll put them on directly," he said.

And he went off to get skates.

"It's a long while since we've seen you here, sir," said the attendant, supporting his foot, and screwing on the heel of the skate. "Except you, there's none of the gentlemen first rate skaters. Will that be all right?" said he, tightening the strap.

"Oh, yes, yes; make haste, please," answered Levin, with difficulty restraining the smile of rapture which would overspread his face. "Yes," he thought, "this now is life, this is happiness! *Together*, she said; *let us skate together!* Speak to her now? But that's just why I'm afraid to speak—because I'm happy now, happy in hope, anyway. . . . And then? . . . . But I must! I must! I must! Away with weakness!"

Levin rose to his feet, took off his overcoat, and scurrying over the rough ice round the hut, came out on the smooth ice and skated without effort, as it were, by simple exercise of will, increasing and slackening speed and turning his course. He approached with timidity, but again her smile reassured him.

She gave him her hand, and they set off side by side, going faster and faster, and the more rapidly they moved the more tightly she grasped his hand.

"With you I should soon learn; I somehow feel confidence in you," she said to him.

"And I have confidence in myself when you are leaning on me," he said, but was at once panic-stricken at what he had said, and blushed. And indeed, no sooner had he uttered these words, when all at once, like the sun going behind a cloud, her face lost all its friendliness, and Levin detected the familiar change in her expression that denoted the working of thought; a crease showed on her smooth brow.

"Is there anything troubling you?—though I've no right to ask such a question," he added hurriedly.

"Oh, why so? . . . No, I have nothing to trouble me," she responded coldly; and she added immediately: "You haven't seen Mlle. Linon, have you?"

"Not yet."

"Go and speak to her, she likes you so much."

"What's wrong? I have offended her. Lord help me!" thought Levin, and he flew towards the old Frenchwoman with the gray ringlets, who was sitting on a bench. Smiling and showing her false teeth, she greeted him as an old friend.

"Yes, you see we're growing up," she said to him, glancing towards Kitty, "and growing old. *Tiny bear* has grown big now!" pursued the Frenchwoman, laughing, and she reminded him of his joke about the three young ladies whom he had compared to the three bears in the English nursery tale. "Do you remember that's what you used to call them?"

He remembered absolutely nothing, but she had been laughing at the joke for ten years now, and was fond of it.

"Now, go and skate, go and skate. Our Kitty has learned to skate nicely, hasn't she?"

When Levin darted up to Kitty her face was no longer stern; her eyes looked at him with the same sincerity and friendliness, but Levin fancied that in her friendliness there was a certain note of deliberate composure. And he felt depressed. After talking a little of her old governess and her peculiarities, she questioned him about his life.

"Surely you must be dull in the country in the winter, aren't you?" she said.

"No, I'm not dull, I am very busy," he said, feeling that she was holding him in check by her composed tone, which he would not have the force to break through, just as it had been at the beginning of the winter.

"Are you going to stay in town long?" Kitty questioned him.

"I don't know," he answered, not thinking of what he was saying. The thought that if he were held in check by her tone of quiet friendliness he would end by going back again without deciding anything came into his mind, and he resolved to make a struggle against it.

"How is it you don't know?"

"I don't know. It depends upon you," he said, and was immediately horror-stricken at his own words.

Whether it was that she had heard his words, or that she did not want to hear them, she made a sort of stumble, twice struck out, and hurriedly skated away from him. She skated up to Mlle. Linon, said something to her, and went towards the pavilion where the ladies took off their skates.

"My God! what have I done! Merciful God! help me, guide me," said Levin, praying inwardly, and at the same time, feeling a need of violent exercise, he skated about describing inner and outer circles.

At that moment one of the young men, the best of the skaters of the day, came out of the coffee-house in his skates, with a cigarette in his mouth. Taking a run, he dashed down the steps in his skates, crashing and bounding up and down. He flew down, and without even changing the position of his hands, skated away over the ice.

"Ah, that's a new trick!" said Levin, and he promptly ran up to the top to do this new trick.

"Don't break your neck! it needs practice!" Nikolay Shtcherbatsky shouted after him.

Levin went to the steps, took a run from above as best he could, and dashed down, preserving his balance in this unwonted movement with his hands. On the last step he stumbled, but barely touching the ice with his hand, with a violent effort recovered himself, and skated off, laughing.

"How splendid, how nice he is!" Kitty was thinking at that time, as she came out of the pavilion with Mlle Linon, and looked towards him with a smile of quiet affection, as though he were a favorite brother. "And can it be my fault, can I have done anything wrong? They talk of flirtation. I know it's not he that I love; but still I am happy with him, and he's so jolly. Only, why did he say that? . . ." she mused.

Catching sight of Kitty going away, and her mother meeting her at the steps, Levin, flushed from his rapid exercise, stood still and pondered a minute. He took off his skates, and overtook the mother and daughter at the entrance of the gardens.

"Delighted to see you," said Princess Shtcherbatskaya. "On Thursdays we are home, as always."

"Today, then?"

"We shall be pleased to see you," the princess said stiffly.

This stiffness hurt Kitty, and she could not resist the desire to smooth over her mother's coldness. She turned her head, and with a smile said:

"Good-bye till this evening."

At that moment Stepan Arkadyevitch, his hat cocked on one side, with beaming face and eyes, strode into the garden like a conquering hero. But as he approached his mother-in-law, he responded in a mournful and crestfallen tone to her inquiries about Dolly's health. After a little subdued and dejected conversation with his mother-in-law, he threw out his chest again, and put his arm in Levin's.

"Well, shall we set off?" he asked. "I've been thinking about you all this time, and I'm very, very glad you've come," he said, looking him in the face with a significant air.

"Yes, come along," answered Levin in ecstasy, hearing unceasingly the sound of that voice saying, "Good-bye till this evening," and seeing the smile with which it was said.

"To the England or the Hermitage?"

"I don't mind which."

"All right, then, the England," said Stepan Arkadyevitch, selecting that restaurant because he owed more there than at the Hermitage, and consequently considered it mean to avoid it. "Have you got a sleigh? That's first rate, for I sent my carriage home."

The friends hardly spoke all the way. Levin was wondering what that change in Kitty's expression had meant, and alternately assuring himself that there was hope, and falling into despair, seeing clearly that his hopes were insane, and yet all the while he felt himself quite another man, utterly unlike what he had been before her smile and those words, "Good-bye till this evening."

Stepan Arkadyevitch was absorbed during the drive in composing the menu of the dinner.

"You like turbot, don't you?" he said to Levin as they were arriving.

"Eh?" responded Levin. "Turbot? Yes, I'm *awfully* fond of turbot."

Chapter X

WHEN LEVIN WENT INTO THE RESTAURANT WITH OBLONSKY, HE COULD NOT HELP NOTICING A certain peculiarity of expression, as it were, a restrained radiance, about the face and whole figure of Stepan Arkadyevitch. Oblonsky took off his overcoat, and with his hat over one ear walked into the dining room, giving directions to the Tatar waiters, who were clustered about him in evening coats, bearing napkins. Bowing to right and left to the people he met, and here as everywhere joyously greeting acquaintances, he went up to the sideboard for a preliminary appetizer of fish and vodka, and said to the painted Frenchwoman decked in ribbons, lace, and ringlets, behind the counter, something so amusing that even that Frenchwoman was moved to genuine laughter. Levin for his part refrained from taking any vodka simply because he felt such a loathing of that Frenchwoman, all made up, it seemed, of false hair, *poudre de riz*, and *vinaigre de toilette*. He made haste to move away from her, as from a dirty place. His whole soul was filled with memories of Kitty, and there was a smile of triumph and happiness shining in his eyes.

"This way, your excellency, please. Your excellency won't be disturbed here," said a particularly pertinacious, white-headed old Tatar with immense hips and coat-tails gaping widely behind. "Walk in, your excellency," he said to Levin; by way of showing his respect to Stepan Arkadyevitch, being attentive to his guest as well.

Instantly flinging a fresh cloth over the round table under the bronze chandelier, though it already had a tablecloth on it, he pushed up velvet chairs, and came to a standstill before Stepan Arkadyevitch with a napkin and a bill of fare in his hands, awaiting his commands.

"If you prefer it, your excellency, a private room will be free directly; Prince Golistin with a lady. Fresh oysters have come in."

"Ah! oysters."

Stepan Arkadyevitch became thoughtful.

"How if we were to change our program, Levin?" he said, keeping his finger on the bill of fare. And his face expressed serious hesitation. "Are the oysters good? Mind now."

"They're Flensburg, your excellency. We've no Ostend."

"Flensburg will do, but are they fresh?"

"Only arrived yesterday."

"Well, then, how if we were to begin with oysters, and so change the whole program? Eh?"

"It's all the same to me. I should like cabbage soup and porridge better than anything; but of course there's nothing like that here."

"*Porridge à la Russe*, your honor would like?" said the Tatar, bending down to Levin, like a nurse speaking to a child.

"No, joking apart, whatever you choose is sure to be good. I've been skating, and I'm hungry. And don't imagine," he added, detecting a look of dissatisfaction on Oblonsky's face, "that I shan't appreciate your choice. I am fond of good things."

"I should hope so! After all, it's one of the pleasures of life," said Stepan Arkadyevitch. "Well, then, my friend, you give us two—or better say three—dozen oysters, clear soup with vegetables. . . ."

"*Printanière*," prompted the Tatar. But Stepan Arkadyevitch apparently did not care to allow him the satisfaction of giving the French names of the dishes.

"With vegetables in it, you know. Then turbot with thick sauce, then . . . roast beef; and mind it's good. Yes, and capons, perhaps, and then sweets."

The Tatar, recollecting that it was Stepan Arkadyevitch's way not to call the dishes by the names in the French bill of fare, did not repeat them after him, but could not resist rehearsing the whole menu to himself according to the bill—"*Soupe printanière, turbot, sauce Beaumarchais, poulard à l'estragon, macédoine de fruits* . . . etc.," and then instantly, as though worked by springs, laying down one bound bill of fare, he took up another, the list of wines, and submitted it to Stepan Arkadyevitch.

"What shall we drink?"

"What you like, only not too much. Champagne," said Levin.

"What! to start with? You're right though, I dare say. Do you like the white seal?"

"*Cachet blanc*," prompted the Tatar.

"Very well, then, give us that brand with the oysters, and then we'll see."

"Yes, sir. And what table wine?"

"You can give us Nuits. Oh, no, better the classic Chablis."

"Yes, sir. And *your* cheese, your excellency?"

"Oh, yes, Parmesan. Or would you like another?"

"No, it's all the same to me," said Levin, unable to suppress a smile.

And the Tatar ran off with flying coat-tails, and in five minutes darted in with a dish of opened oysters on mother-of-pearl shells, and a bottle between his fingers.

Stepan Arkadyevitch crushed the starchy napkin, tucked it into his waistcoat, and settling his arms comfortably, started on the oysters.

"Not bad," he said, stripping the oysters from the pearly shell with a silver fork, and swallowing them one after another. "Not bad," he repeated, turning his dewy, brilliant eyes from Levin to the Tatar.

Levin ate the oysters indeed, though white bread and cheese would have pleased him better. But he was admiring Oblonsky. Even the Tatar, uncorking the bottle and pouring the sparkling wine into the delicate glasses, glanced at Stepan Arkadyevitch, and settled his white cravat with a perceptible smile of satisfaction.

"You don't care much for oysters, do you?" said Stepan Arkadyevitch, emptying his wine glass, "or you're worried about something. Eh?"

He wanted Levin to be in good spirits. But it was not that Levin was not in good spirits; he was ill at ease. With what he had in his soul, he felt sore and uncomfortable in the restaurant, in the midst of private rooms where men were dining with ladies, in all this fuss and bustle; the surroundings of bronzes, looking-glasses, gas, and waiters—all of it was offensive to him. He was afraid of sullying what his soul was brimful of.

"I? Yes, I am; but besides, all this bothers me," he said. "You can't conceive how queer it all seems to a country person like me, as queer as that gentleman's nails I saw at your place. . . ."

"Yes, I saw how much interested you were in poor Grinevitch's nails," said Stepan Arkadyevitch, laughing.

"It's too much for me," responded Levin. "Do try, now, and put yourself in my place, take the point of view of a country person. We in the country try to bring our hands into such a state as will be most convenient for working with. So we cut our nails; sometimes we turn up our sleeves. And here people purposely let their nails grow as long as they will, and link on small saucers by way of studs, so that they can do nothing with their hands."

Stepan Arkadyevitch smiled gaily.

"Oh, yes, that's just a sign that he has no need to do coarse work. His work is with the mind. . . ."

"Maybe. But still it's queer to me, just as at this moment it seems queer to me that we country folks try to get our meals over as soon as we can, so as to be ready for our work, while here are we trying to drag out our meal as long as possible, and with that object eating oysters. . . ."

"Why, of course," objected Stepan Arkadyevitch. "But that's just the aim of civilization—to make everything a source of enjoyment."

"Well, if that's its aim, I'd rather be a savage."

"And so you are a savage. All you Levins are savages."

Levin sighed. He remembered his brother Nikolay, and felt ashamed and sore, and he scowled; but Oblonsky began speaking of a subject which at once drew his attention.

"Oh, I say, are you going tonight to our people, the Shtcherbatskys', I mean?" he said, his eyes sparkling significantly as he pushed away the empty rough shells, and drew the cheese towards him.

"Yes, I shall certainly go," replied Levin; "though I fancied the princess was not very warm in her invitation."

"What nonsense! That's her manner. . . . Come, boy, the soup!. . . . That's her manner—

grande dame," said Stepan Arkadyevitch. "I'm coming, too, but I have to go to the Countess Bonina's rehearsal. Come, isn't it true that you're a savage? How do you explain the sudden way in which you vanished from Moscow? The Shtcherbatskys were continually asking me about you, as though I ought to know. The only thing I know is that you always do what no one else does."

"Yes," said Levin, slowly and with emotion, "you're right. I am a savage. Only, my savageness is not in having gone away, but in coming now. Now I have come . . ."

"Oh, what a lucky fellow you are!" broke in Stepan Arkadyevitch, looking into Levin's eyes.

"Why?"

"I know a gallant steed by tokens sure,
And by his eyes I know a youth in love,"

declaimed Stepan Arkadyevitch. "Everything is before you."

"Why, is it over for you already?"

"No; not over exactly, but the future is yours, and the present is mine, and the present—well, it's not all that it might be."

"How so?"

"Oh, things go wrong. But I don't want to talk of myself, and besides I can't explain it all," said Stepan Arkadyevitch. "Well, why have you come to Moscow, then? . . . Hi! take away!" he called to the Tatar.

"You guess?" responded Levin, his eyes like deep wells of light fixed on Stepan Arkadyevitch.

"I guess, but I can't be the first to talk about it. You can see by that whether I guess right or wrong," said Stepan Arkadyevitch, gazing at Levin with a subtle smile.

"Well, and what have you to say to me?" said Levin in a quivering voice, feeling that all the muscles of his face were quivering too. "How do you look at the question?"

Stepan Arkadyevitch slowly emptied his glass of Chablis, never taking his eyes off Levin.

"I?" said Stepan Arkadyevitch, "there's nothing I desire so much as that—nothing! It would be the best thing that could be."

"But you're not making a mistake? You know what we're speaking of?" said Levin, piercing him with his eyes. "You think it's possible?"

"I think it's possible. Why not possible?"

"No! do you really think it's possible? No, tell me all you think! Oh, but if . . . if refusal's in store for me! . . . Indeed I feel sure . . ."

"Why should you think that?" said Stepan Arkadyevitch, smiling at his excitement.

"It seems so to me sometimes. That will be awful for me, and for her too."

"Oh, well, anyway there's nothing awful in it for a girl. Every girl's proud of an offer."

"Yes, every girl, but not she."

Stepan Arkadyevitch smiled. He so well knew that feeling of Levin's, that for him all the girls in the world were divided into two classes: one class—all the girls in the world except her, and those girls with all sorts of human weaknesses, and very ordinary girls: the other class—she alone, having no weaknesses of any sort and higher than all humanity.

"Stay, take some sauce," he said, holding back Levin's hand as it pushed away the sauce.

Levin obediently helped himself to sauce, but would not let Stepan Arkadyevitch go on with his dinner.

"No, stop a minute, stop a minute," he said. "You must understand that it's a question of life and death for me. I have never spoken to anyone of this. And there's no one I could speak of it to, except you. You know we're utterly unlike each other, different tastes and views and everything; but I know you're fond of me and understand me, and that's why I like you awfully. But for God's sake, be quite straight-forward with me."

"I tell you what I think," said Stepan Arkadyevitch, smiling. "But I'll say more: my wife is a wonderful woman . . ." Stepan Arkadyevitch sighed, remembering his position with his wife, and, after a moment's silence, resumed—"She has a gift of foreseeing things. She sees right through people; but that's not all; she knows what will come to pass, especially in the way of marriages. She foretold, for instance, that Princess Shahovskaya would marry Brenteln. No one would believe it, but it came to pass. And she's on your side."

"How do you mean?"

"It's not only that she likes you—she says that Kitty is certain to be your wife."

At these words Levin's face suddenly lit up with a smile, a smile not far from tears of emotion.

"She says that!" cried Levin. "I always said she was exquisite, your wife. There, that's enough, enough said about it," he said, getting up from his seat.

"All right, but do sit down."

But Levin could not sit down. He walked with his firm tread twice up and down the little cage of a room, blinked his eyelids that his tears might not fall, and only then sat down to the table.

"You must understand," said he, "it's not love. I've been in love, but it's not that. It's not my feeling, but a sort of force outside me has taken possession of me. I went away, you see, because I made up my mind that it could never be, you understand, as a happiness that does not come on earth; but I've struggled with myself, I see there's no living without it. And it must be settled."

"What did you go away for?"

"Ah, stop a minute! Ah, the thoughts that come crowding on one! The questions one must ask oneself! Listen. You can't imagine what you've done for me by what you said. I'm so happy that I've become positively hateful; I've forgotten everything. I heard today that my brother Nikolay . . . you know, he's here . . . I had even forgotten him. It seems to me that he's happy too. It's a sort of madness. But one thing's awful. . . . Here, you've been married, you know the feeling . . . it's awful that we—old—with a past . . . not of love, but of sins . . . are brought all at once so near to a creature pure and innocent; it's loathsome, and that's why one can't help feeling oneself unworthy."

"Oh, well, you've not many sins on your conscience."

"Alas! all the same," said Levin, "when with loathing I go over my life, I shudder and curse and bitterly regret it . . . Yes."

"What would you have? The world's made so," said Stepan Arkadyevitch.

"The one comfort is like that prayer, which I always liked: 'Forgive me not according to my unworthiness, but according to Thy lovingkindness.' That's the only way she can forgive me."

Chapter XI

LEVIN EMPTIED HIS GLASS, AND THEY WERE SILENT FOR A WHILE.

"There's one other thing I ought to tell you. Do you know Vronsky?" Stepan Arkadyevitch asked Levin.

"No, I don't. Why do you ask?"

"Give us another bottle," Stepan Arkadyevitch directed the Tatar, who was filling up their glasses and fidgeting round them just when he was not wanted.

"Why you ought to know Vronsky is that he's one of your rivals."

"Who's Vronsky?" said Levin, and his face was suddenly transformed from the look of childlike ecstasy which Oblonsky had just been admiring to an angry and unpleasant expression.

"Vronsky is one of the sons of Count Kirill Ivanovitch Vronsky, and one of the finest specimens of the gilded youth of Petersburg. I made his acquaintance in Tver when I was there on official business, and he came there for the levy of recruits. Fearfully rich, handsome, great connections, an aide-de-camp, and with all that a very nice, good-natured fellow. But he's more than simply a good-natured fellow, as I've found out here—he's a cultivated man, too, and very intelligent; he's a man who'll make his mark."

Levin scowled and was dumb.

"Well, he turned up here soon after you'd gone, and as I can see, he's over head and ears in love with Kitty, and you know that her mother . . ."

"Excuse me, but I know nothing," said Levin, frowning gloomily. And immediately he recollected his brother Nikolay and how hateful he was to have been able to forget him.

"You wait a bit, wait a bit," said Stepan Arkadyevitch, smiling and touching his hand. "I've told you what I know, and I repeat that in this delicate and tender matter, as far as one can conjecture, I believe the chances are in your favor."

Levin dropped back in his chair; his face was pale.

"But I would advise you to settle the thing as soon as may be," pursued Oblonsky, filling up his glass.

"No, thanks, I can't drink anymore," said Levin, pushing away his glass. "I shall be drunk. . . . Come, tell me how are you getting on?" he went on, obviously anxious to change the conversation.

"One word more: in any case I advise you to settle the question soon. Tonight I don't advise you to speak," said Stepan Arkadyevitch. "Go round tomorrow morning, make an offer in due form, and God bless you. . . ."

"Oh, do you still think of coming to me for some shooting? Come next spring, do," said Levin.

Now his whole soul was full of remorse that he had begun this conversation with Stepan Arkadyevitch. A feeling such as his was profaned by talk of the rivalry of some Petersburg officer, of the suppositions and the counsels of Stepan Arkadyevitch.

Stepan Arkadyevitch smiled. He knew what was passing in Levin's soul.

"I'll come someday," he said. "But women, my boy, they're the pivot everything turns upon. Things are in a bad way with me, very bad. And it's all through women. Tell me frankly now," he pursued, picking up a cigar and keeping one hand on his glass; "give me your advice."

"Why, what is it?"

"I'll tell you. Suppose you're married, you love your wife, but you're fascinated by another woman. . . ."

"Excuse me, but I'm absolutely unable to comprehend how . . . just as I can't comprehend how I could now, after my dinner, go straight to a baker's shop and steal a roll."

Stepan Arkadyevitch's eyes sparkled more than usual.

"Why not? A roll will sometimes smell so good one can't resist it."

"Himmlisch ist's, wenn ich bezwungen
Meine irdische Begier;
Aber doch wenn's nicht gelungen
Hatt' ich auch recht hübsch Plaisir!"

As he said this, Stepan Arkadyevitch smiled subtly. Levin, too, could not help smiling.

"Yes, but joking apart," resumed Stepan Arkadyevitch, "you must understand that the woman is a sweet, gentle loving creature, poor and lonely, and has sacrificed everything. Now, when the thing's done, don't you see, can one possibly cast her off? Even supposing one parts from her, so as not to break up one's family life, still, can one help feeling for her, setting her on her feet, softening her lot?"

"Well, you must excuse me there. You know to me all women are divided into two classes . . . at least no . . . truer to say: there are women and there are . . . I've never seen exquisite fallen beings, and I never shall see them, but such creatures as that painted Frenchwoman at the counter with the ringlets are vermin to my mind, and all fallen women are the same."

"But the Magdalen?"

"Ah, drop that! Christ would never have said those words if He had known how they would be abused. Of all the Gospel those words are the only ones remembered. However, I'm not saying so much what I think, as what I feel. I have a loathing for fallen women. You're afraid of spiders, and I of these vermin. Most likely you've not made a study of spiders and don't know their character; and so it is with me."

"It's very well for you to talk like that; it's very much like that gentleman in Dickens who used to fling all difficult questions over his right shoulder. But to deny the facts is no answer. What's to be done—you tell me that, what's to be done? Your wife gets older, while you're full of life. Before you've time to look round, you feel that you can't love your wife with love, however much you may esteem her. And then all at once love turns up, and you're done for, done for," Stepan Arkadyevitch said with weary despair.

Levin half smiled.

"Yes, you're done for," resumed Oblonsky. "But what's to be done?"

"Don't steal rolls."

Stepan Arkadyevitch laughed outright.

"Oh, moralist! But you must understand, there are two women; one insists only on her rights, and those rights are your love, which you can't give her; and the other sacrifices everything for you and asks for nothing. What are you to do? How are you to act? There's a fearful tragedy in it."

"If you care for my profession of faith as regards that, I'll tell you that I don't believe there was any tragedy about it. And this is why. To my mind, love . . . both the sorts of love, which you remember Plato defines in his Banquet, served as the test of men. Some men only understand one sort, and some only the other. And those who only know the non-platonic love have no need to talk of tragedy. In such love there can be no sort of tragedy. 'I'm much obliged for the gratification, my humble respects'—that's all the tragedy. And in platonic love there can be no tragedy, because in that love all is clear and pure, because . . ."

At that instant Levin recollected his own sins and the inner conflict he had lived through. And he added unexpectedly:

"But perhaps you are right. Very likely. . . . I don't know, I don't know."

"It's this, don't you see," said Stepan Arkadyevitch, "you're very much all of a piece. That's your strong point and your failing. You have a character that's all of a piece, and you want the whole of life to be of a piece too—but that's not how it is. You despise public official work because you want the reality to be invariably corresponding all the while with the aim—and that's not how it is. You want a man's work, too, always to have a defined aim, and love and family life always to be undivided—and that's not how it is. All the variety, all the charm, all the beauty of life is made up of light and shadow."

Levin sighed and made no reply. He was thinking of his own affairs, and did not hear Oblonsky.

And suddenly both of them felt that though they were friends, though they had been dining and drinking together, which should have drawn them closer, yet each was thinking only of his own affairs, and they had nothing to do with one another. Oblonsky had more than once experienced this extreme sense of aloofness, instead of intimacy, coming on after dinner, and he knew what to do in such cases.

"Bill!" he called, and he went into the next room, where he promptly came across an aide-de-camp of his acquaintance and dropped into conversation with him about an actress and her protector. And at once in the conversation with the aide-de-camp Oblonsky had a sense of relaxation and relief after the conversation with Levin, which always put him to too great a mental and spiritual strain.

When the Tatar appeared with a bill for twenty-six roubles and odd kopecks, besides a tip for himself, Levin, who would another time have been horrified, like anyone from the country, at his share of fourteen roubles, did not notice it, paid, and set off homewards to dress and go to the Shtcherbatskys' there to decide his fate.

Chapter XII

THE YOUNG PRINCESS KITTY SHTCHERBATSKAYA WAS EIGHTEEN. IT WAS THE FIRST WINTER THAT she had been out in the world. Her success in society had been greater than that of either of her elder sisters, and greater even than her mother had anticipated. To say nothing of the young men who danced at the Moscow balls being almost all in love with Kitty, two serious suitors had already this first winter made their appearance: Levin, and immediately after his departure, Count Vronsky.

Levin's appearance at the beginning of the winter, his frequent visits, and evident love for Kitty, had led to the first serious conversations between Kitty's parents as to her future, and to disputes between them. The prince was on Levin's side; he said he wished for nothing better for Kitty. The princess for her part, going round the question in the manner peculiar to women, maintained that Kitty was too young, that Levin had done nothing to prove that he had serious intentions, that Kitty felt no great attraction to him, and other side issues; but she did not state the principal point, which was that she looked for a better match for her daughter, and that Levin was not to her liking, and she did not understand him. When Levin had abruptly departed, the princess was delighted, and said to her husband triumphantly: "You see I was right." When Vronsky appeared on the scene, she was still more delighted, confirmed in her opinion that Kitty was to make not simply a good, but a brilliant match.

In the mother's eyes there could be no comparison between Vronsky and Levin. She disliked in Levin his strange and uncompromising opinions and his shyness in society, founded, as she supposed, on his pride and his queer sort of life, as she considered it, absorbed in cattle and peasants. She did not very much like it that he, who was in love with her daughter, had kept coming to the house for six weeks, as though he were waiting for something, inspecting, as though he were afraid he might be doing them too great an honor by making an offer, and did not realize that a man, who continually visits at a house where there is a young unmarried girl, is bound to make his intentions clear. And suddenly, without doing so, he disappeared. "It's as well he's not attractive enough for Kitty to have fallen in love with him," thought the mother.

Vronsky satisfied all the mother's desires. Very wealthy, clever, of aristocratic family, on the highroad to a brilliant career in the army and at court, and a fascinating man. Nothing better could be wished for.

Vronsky openly flirted with Kitty at balls, danced with her, and came continually to the house; consequently there could be no doubt of the seriousness of his intentions. But, in spite of that, the mother had spent the whole of that winter in a state of terrible anxiety and agitation.

Princess Shtcherbatskaya had herself been married thirty years ago, her aunt arranging the match. Her husband, about whom everything was well-known before hand, had come, looked at his future bride, and been looked at. The matchmaking aunt had ascertained and communicated their mutual impression. That impression had been favorable. Afterwards, on a day fixed beforehand, the expected offer was made to her parents, and accepted. All had passed very simply and easily. So it seemed, at least, to the princess. But over her own daughters she had felt how far from simple and easy is the business, apparently so commonplace, of marrying off one's daughters. The panics that had been lived through, the thoughts that had been brooded over, the money that had been wasted, and the disputes with her husband over marrying the two elder girls, Darya and Natalia! Now, since the youngest had come out, she was going through the same terrors, the same doubts, and still more violent quarrels with her husband than she had over the elder girls. The old prince, like all fathers indeed, was exceedingly punctilious on the score of the honor and reputation of his daughters. He was irrationally jealous over his daughters, especially over Kitty, who was his favorite. At every turn he had scenes with the princess for compromising her daughter. The princess had grown accustomed to this already with her other daughters, but now she felt that there was more ground for the prince's touchiness. She saw that of late years much was changed in the manners of society, that a mother's duties had become still more difficult. She saw that girls of Kitty's age formed some sort of clubs, went to some sort of lectures, mixed freely in men's society; drove about the streets alone, many of them did not curtsey, and, what was the most important thing, all the girls were firmly convinced that to choose their husbands was their own affair, and not their parents'. "Marriages aren't made nowadays as they used to be," was thought and said by all these young girls, and even by their elders. But how marriages were made now, the princess could not learn from anyone. The French fashion—of the parents arranging their children's future—was not accepted; it was condemned. The English fashion of the complete independence of girls was also not accepted, and not possible in Russian society. The Russian fashion of matchmaking by the offices of intermediate persons was for some reason considered unseemly; it was ridiculed by everyone, and by the princess herself. But how girls were to be married, and how parents were to marry them, no one knew. Everyone with whom the princess had chanced to discuss the matter said the same thing: "Mercy on us, it's high time in our day to cast off all that old-fashioned business. It's the young people have to marry, and not their parents; and so we ought to leave the young people to arrange it as they choose." It was very easy for anyone to say that who had no daughters, but the princess realized that in the process of getting to know each other, her daughter might fall in love, and fall in love with someone who did not care to marry her or who was quite unfit to be her husband. And, however much it was instilled into the princess that in our times young people ought to arrange their lives for themselves, she was unable to believe it, just as she would have been unable to believe that, at any time whatever, the most suitable playthings for children five years old ought to be loaded pistols. And so the princess was more uneasy over Kitty than she had been over her elder sisters.

Now she was afraid that Vronsky might confine himself to simply flirting with her daughter. She saw that her daughter was in love with him, but tried to comfort herself with the thought that he was an honorable man, and would not do this. But at the same time she knew how easy it is, with the freedom of manners of today, to turn a girl's head, and how lightly men generally regard such a crime. The week before, Kitty had told her mother of a conversation she had with Vronsky during a mazurka. This conversation had partly reassured the princess; but perfectly at ease she could not be. Vronsky had told Kitty that both he and his brother were so used to obeying their mother that they never made up their minds to any important undertaking without consulting her. "And just now, I am impatiently awaiting my mother's arrival from Petersburg, as peculiarly fortunate," he told her.

Kitty had repeated this without attaching any significance to the words. But her mother saw them in a different light. She knew that the old lady was expected from day to day, that she would be pleased at her son's choice, and she felt it strange that he should not make his offer through fear of vexing his mother. However, she was so anxious for the marriage itself, and still more for relief from her fears, that she believed it was so. Bitter as it was for the princess to see the unhappiness of her eldest daughter, Dolly, on the point of leaving her husband, her anxiety over the decision of her youngest daughter's fate engrossed all her feelings. Today, with Levin's reappearance, a fresh source of anxiety arose. She was afraid that her daughter, who had at one time, as she fancied, a feeling for Levin, might, from extreme sense of honor, refuse Vronsky, and that Levin's arrival might generally complicate and delay the affair so near being concluded.

"Why, has he been here long?" the princess asked about Levin, as they returned home.

"He came today, mamma."

"There's one thing I want to say . . ." began the princess, and from her serious and alert face, Kitty guessed what it would be.

"Mamma," she said, flushing hotly and turning quickly to her, "please, please don't say anything about that. I know, I know all about it."

She wished for what her mother wished for, but the motives of her mother's wishes wounded her.

"I only want to say that to raise hopes . . ."

"Mamma, darling, for goodness' sake, don't talk about it. It's so horrible to talk about it."

"I won't," said her mother, seeing the tears in her daughter's eyes; "but one thing, my love; you promised me you would have no secrets from me. You won't?"

"Never, mamma, none," answered Kitty, flushing a little, and looking her mother straight in the face, "but there's no use in my telling you anything, and I . . . I . . . if I wanted to, I don't know what to say or how . . . I don't know . . ."

"No, she could not tell an untruth with those eyes," thought the mother, smiling at her agitation and happiness. The princess smiled that what was taking place just now in her soul seemed to the poor child so immense and so important.

Chapter XIII

AFTER DINNER, AND TILL THE BEGINNING OF THE EVENING, KITTY WAS FEELING A SENSATION akin to the sensation of a young man before a battle. Her heart throbbed violently, and her thoughts would not rest on anything.

She felt that this evening, when they would both meet for the first time, would be a turning-point in her life. And she was continually picturing them to herself, at one moment each separately, and then both together. When she mused on the past, she dwelled with pleasure, with tenderness, on the memories of her relations with Levin. The memories of childhood and of Levin's friendship with her dead brother gave a special poetic charm to her relations with him. His love for her, of which she felt certain, was flattering and delightful to her; and it was pleasant for her to think of Levin. In her memories of Vronsky there always entered a certain element of awkwardness, though he was in the highest degree well-bred and at ease, as though there were some false note—not in Vronsky, he was very simple and nice, but in herself, while with Levin she felt perfectly simple and clear. But, on the other hand, directly she thought of the future with Vronsky, there arose before her a perspective of brilliant happiness; with Levin the future seemed misty.

When she went upstairs to dress, and looked into the looking-glass, she noticed with joy that it was one of her good days, and that she was in complete possession of all her forces—she needed this so for what lay before her: she was conscious of external composure and free grace in her movements.

At half-past seven she had only just gone down into the drawing room, when the footman announced, "Konstantin Dmitrievitch Levin." The princess was still in her room, and the prince had not come in. "So it is to be," thought Kitty, and all the blood seemed to rush to her heart. She was horrified at her paleness, as she glanced into the looking-glass. At that moment she knew beyond doubt that he had come early on purpose to find her alone and to make her an offer. And only then for the first time the whole thing presented itself in a new, different aspect; only then she realized that the question did not affect her only—with whom she would be happy, and whom she loved—but that she would have that moment to wound a man whom she liked. And to wound him cruelly.

What for? Because he, dear fellow, loved her, was in love with her. But there was no help for it, so it must be, so it would have to be.

"My God! shall I myself really have to say it to him?" she thought. "Can I tell him I don't love him? That will be a lie. What am I to say to him? That I love someone else? No, that's impossible. I'm going away, I'm going away."

She had reached the door, when she heard his step. "No! it's not honest. What have I to be afraid of? I have done nothing wrong. What is to be, will be! I'll tell the truth. And with him one can't be ill at ease. Here he is," she said to herself, seeing his powerful, shy figure, with his shining eyes fixed on her. She looked straight into his face, as though imploring him to spare her, and gave her hand.

"It's not time yet; I think I'm too early," he said glancing round the empty drawing room. When he saw that his expectations were realized, that there was nothing to prevent him from speaking, his face became gloomy.

"Oh, no," said Kitty, and sat down at the table.

"But this was just what I wanted, to find you alone," he began, not sitting down, and not looking at her, so as not to lose courage.

"Mamma will be down directly. She was very much tired . . . Yesterday . . ."

She talked on, not knowing what her lips were uttering, and not taking her supplicating and caressing eyes off him.

He glanced at her; she blushed, and ceased speaking.

"I told you I did not know whether I should be here long . . . that it depended on you . . ."

She dropped her head lower and lower, not knowing herself what answer she should make to what was coming.

"That it depended on you," he repeated. "I meant to say . . . I meant to say . . . I came for this . . . to be my wife!" he brought out, not knowing what he was saying; but feeling that the most terrible thing was said, he stopped short and looked at her. . . .

She was breathing heavily, not looking at him. She was feeling ecstasy. Her soul was flooded with happiness. She had never anticipated that the utterance of love would produce such a powerful effect on her. But it lasted only an instant. She remembered Vronsky. She lifted her clear, truthful eyes, and seeing his desperate face, she answered hastily:

"That cannot be . . . forgive me."

A moment ago, and how close she had been to him, of what importance in his life! And how aloof and remote from him she had become now!

"It was bound to be so," he said, not looking at her.

He bowed, and was meaning to retreat.

Chapter XIV

BUT AT THAT VERY MOMENT THE PRINCESS CAME IN. THERE WAS A LOOK OF HORROR ON HER FACE when she saw them alone, and their disturbed faces. Levin bowed to her, and said nothing. Kitty did not speak nor lift her eyes. "Thank God, she has refused him," thought the mother, and her face lit up with the habitual smile with which she greeted her guests on Thursdays. She sat down and began questioning Levin about his life in the country. He sat down again, waiting for other visitors to arrive, in order to retreat unnoticed.

Five minutes later there came in a friend of Kitty's, married the preceding winter, Countess Nordston.

She was a thin, sallow, sickly, and nervous woman, with brilliant black eyes. She was fond of Kitty, and her affection for her showed itself, as the affection of married women for girls always does, in the desire to make a match for Kitty after her own ideal of married happiness; she wanted her to marry Vronsky. Levin she had often met at the Shtcherbatskys' early in the winter, and she had always disliked him. Her invariable and favorite pursuit, when they met, consisted in making fun of him.

"I do like it when he looks down at me from the height of his grandeur, or breaks off his learned conversation with me because I'm a fool, or is condescending to me. I like that so; to see him condescending! I am so glad he can't bear me," she used to say of him.

She was right, for Levin actually could not bear her, and despised her for what she was proud of and regarded as a fine characteristic—her nervousness, her delicate contempt and indifference for everything coarse and earthly.

The Countess Nordston and Levin got into that relation with one another not seldom seen in society, when two persons, who remain externally on friendly terms, despise each other to such a degree that they cannot even take each other seriously, and cannot even be offended by each other.

The Countess Nordston pounced upon Levin at once.

"Ah, Konstantin Dmitrievitch! So you've come back to our corrupt Babylon," she said, giving him her tiny, yellow hand, and recalling what he had chanced to say early in the winter, that Moscow was a Babylon. "Come, is Babylon reformed, or have you degenerated?" she added, glancing with a simper at Kitty.

"It's very flattering for me, countess, that you remember my words so well," responded Levin, who had succeeded in recovering his composure, and at once from habit dropped into his tone of joking hostility to the Countess Nordston. "They must certainly make a great impression on you."

"Oh, I should think so! I always note them all down. Well, Kitty, have you been skating again? . . ."

And she began talking to Kitty. Awkward as it was for Levin to withdraw now, it would still have been easier for him to perpetrate this awkwardness than to remain all the evening and see Kitty, who glanced at him now and then and avoided his eyes. He was on the point of getting up, when the princess, noticing that he was silent, addressed him.

"Shall you be long in Moscow? You're busy with the district council, though, aren't you, and can't be away for long?"

"No, princess, I'm no longer a member of the council," he said. "I have come up for a few days."

"There's something the matter with him," thought Countess Nordston, glancing at his stern, serious face. "He isn't in his old argumentative mood. But I'll draw him out. I do love making a fool of him before Kitty, and I'll do it."

"Konstantin Dmitrievitch," she said to him, "do explain to me, please, what's the meaning of it. You know all about such things. At home in our village of Kaluga all the peasants and all the women have drunk up all they possessed, and now they can't pay us any rent. What's the meaning of that? You always praise the peasants so."

At that instant another lady came into the room, and Levin got up.

"Excuse me, countess, but I really know nothing about it, and can't tell you anything," he said, and looked round at the officer who came in behind the lady.

"That must be Vronsky," thought Levin, and, to be sure of it, glanced at Kitty. She had already had time to look at Vronsky, and looked round at Levin. And simply from the look in her eyes, that grew unconsciously brighter, Levin knew that she loved that man, knew it as surely as if she had told him so in words. But what sort of a man was he? Now, whether for good or for ill, Levin could not choose but remain; he must find out what the man was like whom she loved.

There are people who, on meeting a successful rival, no matter in what, are at once disposed to turn their backs on everything good in him, and to see only what is bad. There are people, on the other hand, who desire above all to find in that lucky rival the qualities by which he has outstripped them, and seek with a throbbing ache at heart only what is good. Levin belonged to the second class. But he had no difficulty in finding what was good and attractive in Vronsky. It was apparent at the first glance. Vronsky was a squarely built, dark man, not very tall, with a good-humored, handsome, and exceedingly calm and resolute face. Everything about his face and figure, from his short-cropped black hair and freshly shaven chin down to his loosely fitting, brand-new uniform, was simple and at the same time elegant. Making way for the lady who had come in, Vronsky went up to the princess and then to Kitty.

As he approached her, his beautiful eyes shone with a specially tender light, and with a faint, happy, and modestly triumphant smile (so it seemed to Levin), bowing carefully and respectfully over her, he held out his small broad hand to her.

Greeting and saying a few words to everyone, he sat down without once glancing at Levin, who had never taken his eyes off him.

"Let me introduce you," said the princess, indicating Levin. "Konstantin Dmitrievitch Levin, Count Alexey Kirillovitch Vronsky."

Vronsky got up and, looking cordially at Levin, shook hands with him.

"I believe I was to have dined with you this winter," he said, smiling his simple and open smile; "but you had unexpectedly left for the country."

"Konstantin Dmitrievitch despises and hates town and us townspeople," said Countess Nordston.

"My words must make a deep impression on you, since you remember them so well," said Levin, and, suddenly conscious that he had said just the same thing before, he reddened.

Vronsky looked at Levin and Countess Nordston, and smiled.

"Are you always in the country?" he inquired. "I should think it must be dull in the winter."

"It's not dull if one has work to do; besides, one's not dull by oneself," Levin replied abruptly.

"I am fond of the country," said Vronsky, noticing, and affecting not to notice, Levin's tone.

"But I hope, count, you would not consent to live in the country always," said Countess Nordston.

"I don't know; I have never tried for long. I experienced a queer feeling once," he went on. "I never longed so for the country, Russian country, with bast shoes and peasants, as when I was spending a winter with my mother in Nice. Nice itself is dull enough, you know. And indeed, Naples and Sorrento are only pleasant for a short time. And it's just there that Russia comes back to me most vividly, and especially the country. It's as though . . ."

He talked on, addressing both Kitty and Levin, turning his serene, friendly eyes from one to the other, and saying obviously just what came into his head.

Noticing that Countess Nordston wanted to say something, he stopped short without finishing what he had begun, and listened attentively to her.

The conversation did not flag for an instant, so that the princess, who always kept in reserve, in case a subject should be lacking, two heavy guns—the relative advantages of classical and of modern education, and universal military service—had not to move out either of them, while Countess Nordston had not a chance of chaffing Levin.

Levin wanted to, and could not, take part in the general conversation; saying to himself every instant, "Now go," he still did not go, as though waiting for something.

The conversation fell upon table-turning and spirits, and Countess Nordston, who believed in spiritualism, began to describe the marvels she had seen.

"Ah, countess, you really must take me, for pity's sake do take me to see them! I have never seen anything extraordinary, though I am always on the lookout for it everywhere," said Vronsky, smiling.

"Very well, next Saturday," answered Countess Nordston. "But you, Konstantin Dmitrievitch, do you believe in it?" she asked Levin.

"Why do you ask me? You know what I shall say."

"But I want to hear your opinion."

"My opinion," answered Levin, "is only that this table-turning simply proves that educated society—so called—is no higher than the peasants. They believe in the evil eye, and in witchcraft and omens, while we . . ."

"Oh, then you don't believe in it?"

"I can't believe in it, countess."

"But if I've seen it myself?"

"The peasant women too tell us they have seen goblins."

"Then you think I tell a lie?"

And she laughed a mirthless laugh.

"Oh, no, Masha, Konstantin Dmitrievitch said he could not believe in it," said Kitty, blushing for Levin, and Levin saw this, and, still more exasperated, would have answered, but Vronsky with his bright frank smile rushed to the support of the conversation, which was threatening to become disagreeable.

"You do not admit the conceivability at all?" he queried. "But why not? We admit the existence of electricity, of which we know nothing. Why should there not be some new force, still unknown to us, which . . ."

"When electricity was discovered," Levin interrupted hurriedly, "it was only the phenomenon that was discovered, and it was unknown from what it proceeded and what were its effects, and ages passed before its applications were conceived. But the spiritualists have begun with tables writing for them, and spirits appearing to them, and have only later started saying that it is an unknown force."

Vronsky listened attentively to Levin, as he always did listen, obviously interested in his words.

"Yes, but the spiritualists say we don't know at present what this force is, but there is a force, and these are the conditions in which it acts. Let the scientific men find out what the force consists in. No, I don't see why there should not be a new force, if it . . ."

"Why, because with electricity," Levin interrupted again, "every time you rub tar against wool, a recognized phenomenon is manifested, but in this case it does not happen every time, and so it follows it is not a natural phenomenon."

Feeling probably that the conversation was taking a tone too serious for a drawing room, Vronsky made no rejoinder, but by way of trying to change the conversation, he smiled brightly, and turned to the ladies.

"Do let us try at once, countess," he said; but Levin would finish saying what he thought.

"I think," he went on, "that this attempt of the spiritualists to explain their marvels as some sort of new natural force is most futile. They boldly talk of spiritual force, and then try to subject it to material experiment."

Everyone was waiting for him to finish, and he felt it.

"And I think you would be a first rate medium," said Countess Nordston; "there's something enthusiastic in you."

Levin opened his mouth, was about to say something, reddened, and said nothing.

"Do let us try table-turning at once, please," said Vronsky. "Princess, will you allow it?"

And Vronsky stood up, looking about for a little table.

Kitty got up to fetch a table, and as she passed, her eyes met Levin's. She felt for him with her whole heart, the more because she was pitying him for suffering of which she was herself the cause. "If you can forgive me, forgive me," said her eyes, "I am so happy."

"I hate them all, and you, and myself," his eyes responded, and he took up his hat. But he was not destined to escape. Just as they were arranging themselves round the table, and Levin was on the point of retiring, the old prince came in, and after greeting the ladies, addressed Levin.

"Ah!" he began joyously. "Been here long, my boy? I didn't even know you were in town. Very glad to see you." The old prince embraced Levin, and talking to him did not observe Vronsky, who had risen, and was serenely waiting till the prince should turn to him.

Kitty felt how distasteful her father's warmth was to Levin after what had happened. She saw, too, how coldly her father responded at last to Vronsky's bow, and how Vronsky looked with amiable perplexity at her father, as though trying and failing to understand how and why anyone could be hostilely disposed towards him, and she flushed.

"Prince, let us have Konstantin Dmitrievitch," said Countess Nordston; "we want to try an experiment."

"What experiment? Table-turning? Well, you must excuse me, ladies and gentlemen, but to my mind it is better fun to play the ring game," said the old prince, looking at Vronsky, and guessing that it had been his suggestion. "There's some sense in that, anyway."

Vronsky looked wonderingly at the prince with his resolute eyes, and, with a faint smile, began immediately talking to Countess Nordston of the great ball that was to come off next week.

"I hope you will be there?" he said to Kitty. As soon as the old prince turned away from him, Levin went out unnoticed, and the last impression he carried away with him of that evening was the smiling, happy face of Kitty answering Vronsky's inquiry about the ball.

Chapter XV

AT THE END OF THE EVENING KITTY TOLD HER MOTHER OF HER CONVERSATION WITH LEVIN, AND in spite of all the pity she felt for Levin, she was glad at the thought that she had received an *offer*. She had no doubt that she had acted rightly. But after she had gone to bed, for a long while she could not sleep. One impression pursued her relentlessly. It was Levin's face, with his scowling brows, and his kind eyes looking out in dark dejection below them, as he stood listening to her father, and glancing at her and at Vronsky. And she felt so sorry for him that tears came into her eyes. But immediately she thought of the man for whom she had given him up. She vividly recalled his manly, resolute face, his noble self-possession, and the good-nature conspicuous in everything towards everyone. She remembered the love for her of the man she loved, and once more all was gladness in her soul, and she lay on the pillow, smiling with happiness. "I'm sorry, I'm sorry; but what could I do? It's not my fault," she said to herself; but an inner voice told her something else. Whether she felt remorse at having won Levin's love, or at having refused him, she did not know. But her happiness was poisoned by doubts. "Lord, have pity on us; Lord, have pity on us; Lord, have pity on us!" she repeated to herself, till she fell asleep.

Meanwhile there took place below, in the prince's little library, one of the scenes so often repeated between the parents on account of their favorite daughter.

"What? I'll tell you what!" shouted the prince, waving his arms, and at once wrapping his squirrel-lined dressing-gown round him again. "That you've no pride, no dignity; that you're disgracing, ruining your daughter by this vulgar, stupid matchmaking!"

"But, really, for mercy's sake, prince, what have I done?" said the princess, almost crying.

She, pleased and happy after her conversation with her daughter, had gone to the prince to say good night as usual, and though she had no intention of telling him of Levin's offer and Kitty's refusal, still she hinted to her husband that she fancied things were practically settled with Vronsky, and that he would declare himself so soon as his mother arrived. And thereupon, at those words, the prince had all at once flown into a passion, and began to use unseemly language.

"What have you done? I'll tell you what. First of all, you're trying to catch an eligible gentleman, and all Moscow will be talking of it, and with good reason. If you have evening parties, invite everyone, don't pick out the possible suitors. Invite all the young bucks. Engage a piano player, and let them dance, and not as you do things nowadays, hunting up good matches. It makes me sick, sick to see it, and you've gone on till you've turned the poor wench's head. Levin's a thousand times the better man. As for this little Petersburg swell, they're turned out by machinery, all on one pattern, and all precious rubbish. But if he were a prince of the blood, my daughter need not run after anyone."

"But what have I done?"

"Why, you've . . ." The prince was crying wrathfully.

"I know if one were to listen to you," interrupted the princess, "we should never marry our daughter. If it's to be so, we'd better go into the country."

"Well, and we had better."

"But do wait a minute. Do I try and catch them? I don't try to catch them in the least. A young man, and a very nice one, has fallen in love with her, and she, I fancy . . ."

"Oh, yes, you fancy! And how if she really is in love, and he's no more thinking of marriage than I am! . . . Oh, that I should live to see it! Ah! spiritualism! Ah! Nice! Ah! the ball!" And the prince, imagining that he was mimicking his wife, made a mincing curtsey at each word. "And this is how we're preparing wretchedness for Kitty; and she's really got the notion into her head . . ."

"But what makes you suppose so?"

"I don't suppose; I know. We have eyes for such things, though womenfolk haven't. I see a man who has serious intentions, that's Levin: and I see a peacock, like this feather-head, who's only amusing himself."

"Oh, well, when once you get an idea into your head! . . ."

"Well, you'll remember my words, but too late, just as with Dolly."

"Well, well, we won't talk of it," the princess stopped him, recollecting her unlucky Dolly.

"By all means, and good night!"

And signing each other with the cross, the husband and wife parted with a kiss, feeling that they each remained of their own opinion.

The princess had at first been quite certain that that evening had settled Kitty's future, and that there could be no doubt of Vronsky's intentions, but her husband's words had disturbed her. And returning to her own room, in terror before the unknown future, she, too, like Kitty, repeated several times in her heart, "Lord, have pity; Lord, have pity; Lord, have pity."

Chapter XVI

VRONSKY HAD NEVER HAD A REAL HOME LIFE. HIS MOTHER HAD BEEN IN HER YOUTH A BRILLIANT society woman, who had had during her married life, and still more afterwards, many love affairs notorious in the whole fashionable world. His father he scarcely remembered, and he had been educated in the Corps of Pages.

Leaving the school very young as a brilliant officer, he had at once got into the circle of wealthy Petersburg army men. Although he did go more or less into Petersburg society, his love affairs had always hitherto been outside it.

In Moscow he had for the first time felt, after his luxurious and coarse life at Petersburg, all the charm of intimacy with a sweet and innocent girl of his own rank, who cared for him. It never even entered his head that there could be any harm in his relations with Kitty. At balls he danced principally with her. He was a constant visitor at their house. He talked to her as people commonly do talk in society—all sorts of nonsense, but nonsense to which he could not help attaching a special meaning in her case. Although he said nothing to her that he could not have said before everybody, he felt that she was becoming more and more dependent upon him, and the more he felt this, the better he liked it, and the tenderer was his feeling for her. He did not know that his mode of behavior in relation to Kitty had a definite character, that it is courting young girls with no intention of marriage, and that such courting is one of the evil actions common among brilliant young men such as he was. It seemed to him that he was the first who had discovered this pleasure, and he was enjoying his discovery.

If he could have heard what her parents were saying that evening, if he could have put himself at the point ov view of the family and have heard that Kitty would be unhappy if he did not marry her, he would have been greatly astonished, and would not have believed it. He could not believe that what gave such great and delicate pleasure to him, and above all to her, could be wrong. Still less could he have believed that he ought to marry.

Marriage had never presented itself to him as a possibility. He not only disliked family life, but a family, and especially a husband was, in accordance with the views general in the bachelor world in which he lived, conceived as something alien, repellant, and, above all, ridiculous.

But though Vronsky had not the least suspicion what the parents were saying, he felt on coming away from the Shtcherbatskys' that the secret spiritual bond which existed between him and Kitty had grown so much stronger that evening that some step must be taken. But what step could and ought to be taken he could not imagine.

"What is so exquisite," he thought, as he returned from the Shtcherbatskys', carrying away with him, as he always did, a delicious feeling of purity and freshness, arising partly from the fact that he had not been smoking for a whole evening, and with it a new feeling of tenderness at her love for him—"what is so exquisite is that not a word has been said by me or by her, but we understand each other so well in this unseen language of looks and tones, that this evening more clearly than ever she told me she loves me. And how secretly, simply, and most of all, how trustfully! I feel myself better, purer. I feel that I have a heart, and that there is a great deal of good in me. Those sweet, loving eyes! When she said: 'Indeed I do. . . . '

"Well, what then? Oh, nothing. It's good for me, and good for her." And he began wondering where to finish the evening.

He passed in review of the places he might go to. "Club? a game of bezique, champagne with Ignatov? No, I'm not going. Château des Fleurs; there I shall find Oblonsky, songs, the cancan. No, I'm sick of it. That's why I like the Shtcherbatskys', that I'm growing better. I'll go home." He went straight to his room at Dussot's Hotel, ordered supper, and then undressed, and as soon as his head touched the pillow, fell into a sound sleep.

Chapter XVII

NEXT DAY AT ELEVEN O'CLOCK IN THE MORNING VRONSKY DROVE TO THE STATION OF THE PETERSburg railway to meet his mother, and the first person he came across on the great flight of steps was Oblonsky, who was expecting his sister by the same train.

"Ah! your excellency!" cried Oblonsky, "whom are you meeting?"

"My mother," Vronsky responded, smiling, as everyone did who met Oblonsky. He shook hands with him, and together they ascended the steps. "She is to be here from Petersburg today."

"I was looking out for you till two o'clock last night. Where did you go after the Shtcherbatskys'?"

"Home," answered Vronsky. "I must own I felt so well content yesterday after the Shtcherbatskys' that I didn't care to go anywhere."

"I know a gallant steed by tokens sure,
And by his eyes I know a youth in love,"

declaimed Stepan Arkadyevitch, just as he had done before to Levin.

Vronsky smiled with a look that seemed to say that he did not deny it, but he promptly changed the subject.

"And whom are you meeting?" he asked.

"I? I've come to meet a pretty woman," said Oblonsky.

"You don't say so!"

"*Honi soit qui mal y pense!* My sister Anna."

"Ah! that's Madame Karenina," said Vronsky.

"You know her, no doubt?"

"I think I do. Or perhaps not . . . I really am not sure," Vronsky answered heedlessly, with a vague recollection of something stiff and tedious evoked by the name Karenina.

"But Alexey Alexandrovitch, my celebrated brother-in-law, you surely must know. All the world knows him."

"I know him by reputation and by sight. I know that he's clever, learned, religious somewhat . . . But you know that's not . . . *not in my line,*" said Vronsky in English.

"Yes, he's a very remarkable man; rather a conservative, but a splendid man," observed Stepan Arkadyevitch, "a splendid man."

"Oh, well, so much the better for him," said Vronsky smiling. "Oh, you've come," he said, addressing a tall old footman of his mother's, standing at the door; "come here."

Besides the charm Oblonsky had in general for everyone, Vronsky had felt of late specially drawn to him by the fact that in his imagination he was associated with Kitty.

"Well, what do you say? Shall we give a supper on Sunday for the diva?" he said to him with a smile, taking his arm.

"Of course. I'm collecting subscriptions. Oh, did you make the acquaintance of my friend Levin?" asked Stepan Arkadyevitch.

"Yes; but he left rather early."

"He's a capital fellow," pursued Oblonsky. "Isn't he?"

"I don't know why it is," responded Vronsky, "in all Moscow people—present company of course excepted," he put in jestingly, "there's something uncompromising. They are all on the defensive, lose their tempers, as though they all want to make one feel something. . . ."

"Yes, that's true, it is so," said Stepan Arkadyevitch, laughing good-humoredly.

"Will the train soon be in?" Vronsky asked a railway official.

"The train's signaled," answered the man.

The approach of the train was more and more evident by the preparatory bustle in the station, the rush of porters, the movement of policemen and attendants, and people meeting the train. Through the frosty vapor could be seen workmen in short sheepskins and soft felt boots crossing the rails of the curving line. The hiss of the boiler could be heard on the distant rails, and the rumble of something heavy.

"No," said Stepan Arkadyevitch, who felt a great inclination to tell Vronsky of Levin's intentions in regard to Kitty. "No, you've not got a true impression of Levin. He's a very nervous man, and is sometimes out of humor, it's true, but then he is often very nice. He's such a true, honest nature, and a heart of gold. But yesterday there were special reasons," pursued Stepan Arkadyevitch, with a meaning smile, totally oblivious of the genuine sympathy he had felt the day before for his friend, and feeling the same sympathy now, only for Vronsky. "Yes, there were reasons why he could not help being either particularly happy or particularly unhappy."

Vronsky stood still and asked directly: "How so? Do you mean he made your *belle-soeur* an offer yesterday?"

"Maybe," said Stepan Arkadyevitch. "I fancied something of the sort yesterday. Yes, if he went away early, and was out of humor too, it must mean it . . . He's been so long in love, and I'm very sorry for him."

"So that's it! . . . I should imagine, though, she might reckon on a better match," said Vronsky, drawing himself up and walking about again, "though I don't know him, of course," he added. "Yes, that is a hateful position! That's why most fellows prefer to have to do with Klaras. If you don't succeed with them it only proves that you've not enough cash, but in this case one's dignity's at stake. But here's the train."

The engine had already whistled in the distance. A few instants later the platform was quivering, and with puffs of steam hanging low in the air from the frost, the engine rolled up, with the lever of the middle wheel rhythmically moving up and down, and the stooping figure of the engine-driver covered with frost. Behind the tender, setting the platform more and more slowly swaying, came the luggage-van with a dog whining in it. At last the passenger carriages rolled in, oscillating before coming to a standstill.

A smart guard jumped out, giving a whistle, and after him one by one the impatient passengers began to get down: an officer of the guards, holding himself erect, and looking severely about him; a nimble little merchant with a satchel, smiling gaily; a peasant with a sack over his shoulder.

Vronsky, standing beside Oblonsky, watched the carriages and the passengers, totally oblivious of his mother. What he had just heard about Kitty excited and delighted him. Unconsciously he arched his chest, and his eyes flashed. He felt himself a conqueror.

"Countess Vronskaya is in that compartment," said the smart guard, going up to Vronsky.

The guard's words roused him, and forced him to think of his mother and his approaching meeting with her. He did not in his heart respect his mother, and without acknowledging it to himself, he did not love her, though in accordance with the ideas of the set in which he lived, and with his own education, he could not have conceived of any behavior to his mother not in the highest degree respectful and obedient, and the more externally obedient and respectful his behavior, the less in his heart he respected and loved her.

Chapter XVIII

VRONSKY FOLLOWED THE GUARD TO THE CARRIAGE, AND AT THE DOOR OF THE COMPARTMENT he stopped short to make room for a lady who was getting out.

With the insight of a man of the world, from one glance at this lady's appearance Vronsky classified her as belonging to the best society. He begged pardon, and was getting into the carriage, but felt he must glance at her once more; not that she was very beautiful, not on account of the elegance and modest grace which were apparent in her whole figure, but because in the expression of her charming face, as she passed close by him, there was something peculiarly caressing and soft. As he looked round, she too turned her head. Her shining gray eyes, that looked dark from the thick lashes, rested with friendly attention on his face, as though she were recognizing him, and then promptly turned away to the passing crowd, as though seeking someone. In that brief look Vronsky had time to notice the suppressed eagerness which played over her face, and flitted between the brilliant eyes and the faint smile that curved her red lips. It was as though her nature were so brimming over with something that against her will it showed itself now in the flash of her eyes, and now in her smile. Deliberately she shrouded the light in her eyes, but it shone against her will in the faintly perceptible smile.

Vronsky stepped into the carriage. His mother, a dried-up old lady with black eyes and ringlets, screwed up her eyes, scanning her son, and smiled slightly with her thin lips. Getting up from the seat and handing her maid a bag, she gave her little wrinkled hand to her son to kiss, and lifting his head from her hand, kissed him on the cheek.

"You got my telegram? Quite well? Thank God."

"You had a good journey?" said her son, sitting down beside her, and involuntarily listening to a woman's voice outside the door. He knew it was the voice of the lady he had met at the door.

"All the same I don't agree with you," said the lady's voice.

"It's the Petersburg view, madame."

"Not Petersburg, but simply feminine," she responded.

"Well, well, allow me to kiss your hand."

"Good-bye, Ivan Petrovitch. And would you see if my brother is here, and send him to me?" said the lady in the doorway, and stepped back again into the compartment.

"Well, have you found your brother?" said Countess Vronskaya, addressing the lady.

Vronsky understood now that this was Madame Karenina.

"Your brother is here," he said, standing up. "Excuse me, I did not know you, and, indeed, our acquaintance was so slight," said Vronsky, bowing, "that no doubt you do not remember me."

"Oh, no," said she, "I should have known you because your mother and I have been talking, I think, of nothing but you all the way." As she spoke she let the eagerness that would insist on coming out show itself in her smile. "And still no sign of my brother."

"Do call him, Alexey," said the old countess. Vronsky stepped out onto the platform and shouted:

"Oblonsky! Here!"

Madame Karenina, however, did not wait for her brother, but catching sight of him she stepped out with her light, resolute step. And as soon as her brother had reached her, with a gesture that struck Vronsky by its decision and its grace, she flung her left arm around his neck, drew him rapidly to her, and kissed him warmly. Vronsky gazed, never taking his eyes from her, and smiled, he could not have said why. But recollecting that his mother was waiting for him, he went back again into the carriage.

"She's very sweet, isn't she?" said the countess of Madame Karenina. "Her husband put her with me, and I was delighted to have her. We've been talking all the way. And so you, I hear . . . *vous filez le parfait amour. Tant mieux, mon cher, tant mieux.*"

"I don't know what you are referring to, maman," he answered coldly. "Come, maman, let us go."

Madame Karenina entered the carriage again to say good-bye to the countess.

"Well, countess, you have met your son, and I my brother," she said. "And all my gossip is exhausted. I should have nothing more to tell you."

"Oh, no," said the countess, taking her hand. "I could go all around the world with you and never be dull. You are one of those delightful women in whose company it's sweet to be silent as well as to talk. Now please don't fret over your son; you can't expect never to be parted."

Madame Karenina stood quite still, holding herself very erect, and her eyes were smiling.

"Anna Arkadyevna," the countess said in explanation to her son, "has a little son eight years old, I believe, and she has never been parted from him before, and she keeps fretting over leaving him."

"Yes, the countess and I have been talking all the time, I of my son and she of hers," said Madame Karenina, and again a smile lit up her face, a caressing smile intended for him.

"I am afraid that you must have been dreadfully bored," he said, promptly catching the ball of coquetry she had flung him. But apparently she did not care to pursue the conversation in that strain, and she turned to the old countess.

"Thank you so much. The time has passed so quickly. Good-bye, countess."

"Good-bye, my love," answered the countess. "Let me have a kiss of your pretty face. I speak plainly, at my age, and I tell you simply that I've lost my heart to you."

Stereotyped as the phrase was, Madame Karenina obviously believed it and was delighted by it. She flushed, bent down slightly, and put her cheek to the countess's lips, drew herself up again, and with the same smile fluttering between her lips and her eyes, she gave her hand to Vronsky. He pressed the little hand she gave him, and was delighted, as though at something special, by the energetic squeeze with which she freely and vigorously shook his hand. She went out with the rapid step which bore her rather fully-developed figure with such strange lightness.

"Very charming," said the countess.

That was just what her son was thinking. His eyes followed her till her graceful figure was out of sight, and then the smile remained on his face. He saw out of the window how she went up to her brother, put her arm in his, and began telling him something eagerly, obviously something that had nothing to do with him, Vronsky, and at that he felt annoyed.

"Well, maman, are you perfectly well?" he repeated, turning to his mother.

"Everything has been delightful. Alexander has been very good, and Marie has grown very pretty. She's very interesting."

And she began telling him again of what interested her most—the christening of her grandson, for which she had been staying in Petersburg, and the special favor shown her elder son by the Tsar.

"Here's Lavrenty," said Vronsky, looking out of the window; "now we can go, if you like."

The old butler who had traveled with the countess, came to the carriage to announce that everything was ready, and the countess got up to go.

"Come; there's not such a crowd now," said Vronsky.

The maid took a hand-bag and the lap-dog, the butler and a porter the other baggage. Vronsky gave his mother his arm; but just as they were getting out of the carriage several men ran suddenly by with panic-stricken faces. The stationmaster, too, ran by in his extraordinary colored cap. Obviously something unusual had happened. The crowd who had left the train were running back again.

"What? . . . What? . . . Where? . . . Flung—himself! . . . Crushed! . . ." was heard among the crowd. Stepan Arkadyevitch, with his sister on his arm, turned back. They too looked scared, and stopped at the carriage door to avoid the crowd.

The ladies got in, while Vronsky and Stepan Arkadyevitch followed the crowd to find out details of the disaster.

A guard, either drunk or too much muffled up in the bitter frost, had not heard the train moving back, and had been crushed.

Before Vronsky and Oblonsky came back the ladies heard the facts from the butler.

Oblonsky and Vronsky had both seen the mutilated corpse. Oblonsky was evidently upset. He frowned and seemed ready to cry.

"Ah, how awful! Ah, Anna, if you had seen it! Ah, how awful!" he said.

Vronsky did not speak; his handsome face was serious, but perfectly composed.

"Oh, if you had seen it, countess," said Stepan Arkadyevitch. "And his wife was there. . . . It was awful to see her!. . . . She flung herself on the body. They say he was the only support of an immense family. How awful!"

"Couldn't one do anything for her?" said Madame Karenina in an agitated whisper.

Vronsky glanced at her, and immediately got out of the carriage.

"I'll be back directly, maman," he remarked, turning round in the doorway.

When he came back a few minutes later, Stepan Arkadyevitch was already in conversation with the countess about the new singer, while the countess was impatiently looking towards the door, waiting for her son.

"Now let us be off," said Vronsky, coming in. They went out together. Vronsky was in front with his mother. Behind walked Madame Karenina with her brother. Just as they were going out of the station the stationmaster overtook Vronsky.

"You gave my assistant two hundred roubles. Would you kindly explain for whose benefit you intend them?"

"For the widow," said Vronsky, shrugging his shoulders. "I should have thought there was no need to ask."

"You gave that?" cried Oblonsky, behind, and, pressing his sister's hand, he added: "Very nice, very nice! Isn't he a splendid fellow? Good-bye, countess."

And he and his sister stood still, looking for her maid.

When they went out the Vronsky's carriage had already driven away. People coming in were still talking of what happened.

"What a horrible death!" said a gentleman, passing by. "They say he was cut in two pieces."

"On the contrary, I think it's the easiest—instantaneous," observed another.

"How is it they don't take proper precautions?" said a third.

Madame Karenina seated herself in the carriage, and Stepan Arkadyevitch saw with surprise that her lips were quivering, and she was with difficulty restraining her tears.

"What is it, Anna?" he asked, when they had driven a few hundred yards.

"It's an omen of evil," she said.

"What nonsense!" said Stepan Arkadyevitch. "You've come, that's the chief thing. You can't conceive how I'm resting my hopes on you."

"Have you known Vronsky long?" she asked.

"Yes. You know we're hoping he will marry Kitty."

"Yes?" said Anna softly. "Come now, let us talk of you," she added, tossing her head, as though she would physically shake off something superfluous oppressing her. "Let us talk of your affairs. I got your letter, and here I am."

"Yes, all my hopes are in you," said Stepan Arkadyevitch.

"Well, tell me all about it."

And Stepan Arkadyevitch began to tell his story.

On reaching home Oblonsky helped his sister out, sighed, pressed her hand, and set off to his office.

Chapter XIX

WHEN ANNA WENT INTO THE ROOM, DOLLY WAS SITTING IN THE LITTLE DRAWING ROOM WITH a white-headed fat little boy, already like his father, giving him a lesson in French reading. As the boy read, he kept twisting and trying to tear off a button that was nearly off his jacket. His mother had several times taken his hand from it, but the fat little hand went back to the button again. His mother pulled the button off and put it in her pocket.

"Keep your hands still, Grisha," she said, and she took up her work, a coverlet she had long been making. She always set to work on it at depressed moments, and now she knitted at it nervously, twitching her fingers and counting the stitches. Though she had sent word the day before to her husband that it was nothing to her whether his sister came or not, she had made everything ready for her arrival, and was expecting her sister-in-law with emotion.

Dolly was crushed by her sorrow, utterly swallowed up by it. Still she did not forget that Anna, her sister-in-law, was the wife of one of the most important personages in Petersburg, and was a Petersburg *grande dame*. And, thanks to this circumstance, she did not carry out her threat to her husband—that is to say, she remembered that her sister-in-law was coming. "And, after all, Anna is in no wise to blame," thought Dolly. "I know nothing of her except the very best, and I have seen nothing but kindness and affection from her towards myself." It was true that as far as she could recall her impressions at Petersburg at the Karenins', she did not like their household itself; there was something artificial in the whole framework of their family life. "But why should I not receive her? If only she doesn't take it into her head to console me!" thought Dolly. "All consolation and counsel and Christian forgiveness, all that I have thought over a thousand times, and it's all no use."

All these days Dolly had been alone with her children. She did not want to talk of her sorrow, but with that sorrow in her heart she could not talk of outside matters. She knew that in one way or another she would tell Anna everything, and she was alternately glad at the thought of speaking freely, and angry at the necessity of speaking of her humiliation with her, his sister, and of hearing her ready-made phrases of good advice and comfort. She had been on the lookout for her, glancing at her watch every minute, and, as often happens, let slip just that minute when her visitor arrived, so that she did not hear the bell.

Catching a sound of skirts and light steps at the door, she looked round, and her care-worn face unconsciously expressed not gladness, but wonder. She got up and embraced her sister-in-law.

"What, here already!" she said as she kissed her.

"Dolly, how glad I am to see you!"

"I am glad, too," said Dolly, faintly smiling, and trying by the expression of Anna's face to find out whether she knew. "Most likely she knows," she thought, noticing the sympathy in Anna's face. "Well, come along, I'll take you to your room," she went on, trying to defer as long as possible the moment of confidences.

"Is this Grisha? Heavens, how he's grown!" said Anna; and kissing him, never taking her eyes off Dolly, she stood still and flushed a little. "No, please, let us stay here."

She took off her kerchief and her hat, and catching it in a lock of her black hair, which was a mass of curls, she tossed her head and shook her hair down.

"You are radiant with health and happiness!" said Dolly, almost with envy.

"I? . . . Yes," said Anna. "Merciful heavens, Tanya! You're the same age as my Seryozha," she added, addressing the little girl as she ran in. She took her in her arms and kissed her. "Delightful child, delightful! Show me them all."

She mentioned them, not only remembering the names, but the years, months, characters, illnesses of all the children, and Dolly could not but appreciate that.

"Very well, we will go to them," she said. "It's a pity Vassya's asleep."

After seeing the children, they sat down, alone now, in the drawing room, to coffee. Anna took the tray, and then pushed it away from her.

"Dolly," she said, "he has told me."

Dolly looked coldly at Anna; she was waiting now for phrases of conventional sympathy, but Anna said nothing of the sort.

"Dolly, dear," she said, "I don't want to speak for him to you, nor to try to comfort you; that's impossible. But, darling, I'm simply sorry, sorry from my heart for you!"

Under the thick lashes of her shining eyes tears suddenly glittered. She moved nearer to her sister-in-law and took her hand in her vigorous little hand. Dolly did not shrink away, but her face did not lose its frigid expression. She said:

"To comfort me's impossible. Everything's lost after what has happened, everything's over!"

And directly she had said this, her face suddenly softened. Anna lifted the wasted, thin hand of Dolly, kissed it and said:

"But, Dolly, what's to be done, what's to be done? How is it best to act in this awful position—that's what you must think of."

"All's over, and there's nothing more," said Dolly. "And the worst of it all is, you see, that I can't cast him off: there are the children, I am tied. And I can't live with him! It's a torture to me to see him."

"Dolly, darling, he has spoken to me, but I want to hear it from you: tell me about it."

Dolly looked at her inquiringly.

Sympathy and love unfeigned were visible on Anna's face.

"Very well," she said all at once. "But I will tell you it from the beginning. You know how I was married. With the education mamma gave us I was more than innocent, I was stupid. I knew nothing. I know they say men tell their wives of their former lives, but Stiva"—she corrected herself—"Stepan Arkadyevitch told me nothing. You'll hardly believe it, but till now I imagined that I was the only woman he had known. So I lived eight years. You must understand that I was so far from suspecting infidelity, I regarded it as impossible, and then—try to imagine it—with such ideas, to find out suddenly all the horror, all the loathsomeness. . . . You must try and understand me. To be fully convinced of one's happiness, and all at once . . ." continued Dolly, holding back her sobs, "to get a letter . . . his letter to his mistress, my governess. No, it's too awful!" She hastily pulled out her handkerchief and hid her face in it. "I can understand being carried away by feeling," she went on after a brief silence, "but deliberately, slyly deceiving me . . . and with whom? . . . To go on being my husband together with her . . . it's awful! You can't understand . . ."

"Oh, yes, I understand! I understand! Dolly, dearest, I do understand," said Anna, pressing her hand.

"And do you imagine he realizes all the awfulness of my position?" Dolly resumed. "Not the slightest! He's happy and contented."

"Oh, no!" Anna interposed quickly. "He's to be pitied, he's weighed down by remorse . . ."

"Is he capable of remorse?" Dolly interrupted, gazing intently into her sister-in-law's face.

"Yes. I know him. I could not look at him without feeling sorry for him. We both know him. He's good-hearted, but he's proud, and now he's so humiliated. What touched me most . . ." (and here Anna guessed what would touch Dolly most) "he's tortured by two things: that he's ashamed for the children's sake, and that, loving you—yes, yes, loving you beyond everything on earth," she hurriedly interrupted Dolly, who would have answered—"he has hurt you, pierced you to the heart. 'No, no, she cannot forgive me,' he keeps saying."

Dolly looked dreamily away beyond her sister-in-law as she listened to her words.

"Yes, I can see that his position is awful; it's worse for the guilty than the innocent," she said, "if he feels that all the misery comes from his fault. But how am I to forgive him, how am I to be his wife again after her? For me to live with him now would be torture, just because I love my past love for him. . . ."

And sobs cut short her words. But as though of set design, each time she was softened she began to speak again of what exasperated her.

"She's young, you see, she's pretty," she went on. "Do you know, Anna, my youth and my beauty are gone, taken by whom? By him and his children. I have worked for him, and all I had has gone in his service, and now of course any fresh, vulgar creature has more charm for him. No doubt they talked of me together, or, worse still, they were silent. Do you understand?"

Again her eyes glowed with hatred.

"And after that he will tell me. . . . What! can I believe him? Never! No, everything is over, everything that once made my comfort, the reward of my work, and my sufferings. . . . Would you believe it, I was teaching Grisha just now: once this was a joy to me, now it is a torture. What have I to strive and toil for? Why are the children here? What's so awful is that all at once my heart's turned, and instead of love and tenderness, I have nothing but hatred for him; yes, hatred. I could kill him."

"Darling Dolly, I understand, but don't torture yourself. You are so distressed, so overwrought, that you look at many things mistakenly."

Dolly grew calmer, and for two minutes both were silent.

"What's to be done? Think for me, Anna, help me. I have thought over everything, and I see nothing."

Anna could think of nothing, but her heart responded instantly to each word, to each change of expression of her sister-in-law.

"One thing I would say," began Anna. "I am his sister, I know his character, that faculty of forgetting everything, everything" (she waved her hand before her forehead), "that faculty for being completely carried away, but for completely repenting too. He cannot believe it, he cannot comprehend now how he can have acted as he did."

"No; he understands, he understood!" Dolly broke in. "But I . . . you are forgetting me . . . does it make it easier for me?"

"Wait a minute. When he told me, I will own I did not realize all the awfulness of your position. I saw nothing but him, and that the family was broken up. I felt sorry for him, but after talking to you, I see it, as a woman, quite differently. I see your agony, and I can't tell you how sorry I am for you! But, Dolly, darling, I fully realize your sufferings, only there is one thing I don't know; I don't know . . . I don't know how much love there is still in your heart for him. That you know—whether there is enough for you to be able to forgive him. If there is, forgive him!"

"No," Dolly was beginning, but Anna cut her short, kissing her hand once more.

"I know more of the world than you do," she said. "I know how men like Stiva look at it. You speak of his talking of you with her. That never happened. Such men are unfaithful, but their home and wife are sacred to them. Somehow or other these women are still looked on with contempt by them, and do not touch on their feeling for their family. They draw a sort of line that can't be crossed between them and their families. I don't understand it, but it is so."

"Yes, but he has kissed her . . ."

"Dolly, hush, darling. I saw Stiva when he was in love with you. I remember the time when he came to me and cried, talking of you, and all the poetry and loftiness of his feeling for you, and I know that the longer he has lived with you the loftier you have been in his eyes. You know we have sometimes laughed at him for putting in at every word: 'Dolly's a marvelous woman.' You have always been a divinity for him, and you are that still, and this has not been an infidelity of the heart. . . ."

"But if it is repeated?"

"It cannot be, as I understand it. . . ."

"Yes, but could you forgive it?"

"I don't know, I can't judge. . . . Yes, I can," said Anna, thinking a moment; and grasping the position in her thought and weighing it in her inner balance, she added: "Yes, I can, I can, I can. Yes, I could forgive it. I could not be the same, no; but I could forgive it, and forgive it as though it had never been, never been at all. . . ."

"Oh, of course," Dolly interposed quickly, as though saying what she had more than once thought, "else it would not be forgiveness. If one forgives, it must be completely, completely. Come, let us go; I'll take you to your room," she said, getting up, and on the way she embraced Anna. "My dear, how glad I am you came. It has made things better, ever so much better."

Chapter XX

THE WHOLE OF THAT DAY ANNA SPENT AT HOME, THAT'S TO SAY AT THE OBLONSKYS', AND received no one, though some of her acquaintances had already heard of her arrival, and came to call the same day. Anna spent the whole morning with Dolly and the children. She merely sent a brief note to her brother to tell him that he must not fail to dine at home. "Come, God is merciful," she wrote.

Oblonsky did dine at home: the conversation was general, and his wife, speaking to him, addressed him as "Stiva," as she had not done before. In the relations of the husband and wife the same estrangement still remained, but there was no talk now of separation, and Stepan Arkadyevitch saw the possibility of explanation and reconciliation.

Immediately after dinner Kitty came in. She knew Anna Arkadyevna, but only very slightly, and she came now to her sister's with some trepidation at the prospect of meeting this fashionable Petersburg lady, whom everyone spoke so highly of. But she made a favorable impression on Anna Arkadyevna—she saw that at once. Anna was unmistakably admiring her loveliness and her youth: before Kitty knew where she was she found herself not merely under Anna's sway, but in love with her, as young girls do fall in love with older and married women. Anna was not like a fashionable lady, nor the mother of a boy of eight years old. In the elasticity of her movements, the freshness and the unflagging eagerness which persisted in her face and broke out in her smile and her glance, she would rather have passed for a girl of twenty, had it not been for a serious and at times mournful look in her eyes, which struck and attracted Kitty. Kitty felt that Anna was perfectly simple and was concealing nothing, but that she had another higher world of interests inaccessible to her, complex and poetic.

After dinner, when Dolly went away to her own room, Anna rose quickly and went up to her brother, who was just lighting a cigar.

"Stiva," she said to him, winking gaily, crossing him, and glancing towards the door, "go, and God help you."

He threw down the cigar, understanding her, and departed through the doorway.

When Stepan Arkadyevitch had disappeared, she went back to the sofa where she had been sitting, surrounded by the children. Either because the children saw that their mother was fond of this aunt, or that they felt a special charm in her themselves, the two elder ones, and the younger following their lead, as children so often do, had clung about their new aunt since before dinner, and would not leave her side. And it had become a sort of game among them to sit a close as possible to their aunt, to touch her, hold her little hand, kiss it, play with her ring, or even touch the flounce of her skirt.

"Come, come, as we were sitting before," said Anna Arkadyevna, sitting down in her place.

And again Grisha poked his little face under her arm, and nestled with his head on her gown, beaming with pride and happiness.

"And when is your next ball?" she asked Kitty.

"Next week, and a splendid ball. One of those balls where one always enjoys oneself."

"Why, are there balls where one always enjoys oneself?" Anna said, with tender irony.

"It's strange, but there are. At the Bobrishtchevs' one always enjoys oneself, and at the Nikitins' too, while at the Mezhkovs' it's always dull. Haven't you noticed it?"

"No, my dear, for me there are no balls now where one enjoys oneself," said Anna, and Kitty detected in her eyes that mysterious world which was not open to her. "For me there are some less dull and tiresome."

"How can *you* be dull at a ball?"

"Why should not *I* be dull at a ball?" inquired Anna.

Kitty perceived that Anna knew what answer would follow.

"Because you always look nicer than anyone."

Anna had the faculty of blushing. She blushed a little, and said:

"In the first place it's never so; and secondly, if it were, what difference would it make to me?"

"Are you coming to this ball?" asked Kitty.

"I imagine it won't be possible to avoid going. Here, take it," she said to Tanya, who was pulling the loosely-fitting ring off her white, slender-tipped finger.

"I shall be so glad if you go. I should so like to see you at a ball."

"Anyway, if I do go, I shall comfort myself with the thought that it's a pleasure to you . . . . Grisha, don't pull my hair. It's untidy enough without that," she said, putting up a straying lock, which Grisha had been playing with.

"I imagine you at the ball in lilac."

"And why in lilac precisely?" asked Anna, smiling. "Now, children, run along, run along. Do you hear? Miss Hoole is calling you to tea," she said, tearing the children from her, and sending them off to the dining room.

"I know why you press me to come to the ball. You expect a great deal of this ball, and you want everyone to be there to take part in it."

"How do you know? Yes."

"Oh! what a happy time you are at," pursued Anna. "I remember, and I know that blue haze like the mist on the mountains in Switzerland. That mist which covers everything in that blissful time when childhood is just ending, and out of that vast circle, happy and gay, there is a path growing narrower and narrower, and it is delightful and alarming to enter the ballroom, bright and splendid as it is. . . . Who has not been through it?"

Kitty smiled without speaking. "But how did she go through it? How I should like to know all her love story!" thought Kitty, recalling the unromantic appearance of Alexey Alexandrovitch, her husband.

"I know something. Stiva told me, and I congratulate you. I liked him so much," Anna continued. "I met Vronsky at the railway station."

"Oh, was he there?" asked Kitty, blushing. "What was it Stiva told you?"

"Stiva gossiped about it all. And I should be so glad . . . I traveled yesterday with Vronsky's mother," she went on; "and his mother talked without a pause of him, he's her favorite. I know mothers are partial, but . . ."

"What did his mother tell you?"

"Oh, a great deal! And I know that he's her favorite; still one can see how chivalrous he is . . . Well, for instance, she told me that he had wanted to give up all his property to his brother, that he had done something extraordinary when he was quite a child, saved a woman out of the water. He's a hero, in fact," said Anna, smiling and recollecting the two hundred roubles he had given at the station.

But she did not tell Kitty about the two hundred roubles. For some reason it was disagreeable to her to think of it. She felt that there was something that had to do with her in it, and something that ought not to have been.

"She pressed me very much to go and see her," Anna went on; "and I shall be glad to go to see her tomorrow. Stiva is staying a long while in Dolly's room, thank God," Anna added, changing the subject, and getting up, Kitty fancied, displeased with something.

"No, I'm first! No, I!" screamed the children, who had finished tea, running up to their Aunt Anna.

"All together," said Anna, and she ran laughing to meet them, and embraced and swung round all the throng of swarming children, shrieking with delight.

Chapter XXI

DOLLY CAME OUT OF HER ROOM TO THE TEA OF THE GROWN-UP PEOPLE. STEPAN ARKADYEVITCH did not come out. He must have left his wife's room by the other door.

"I am afraid you'll be cold upstairs," observed Dolly, addressing Anna; "I want to move you downstairs, and we shall be nearer."

"Oh, please, don't trouble about me," answered Anna, looking intently into Dolly's face, trying to make out whether there had been a reconciliation or not.

"It will be lighter for you here," answered her sister-in-law.

"I assure you that I sleep everywhere, and always like a marmot."

"What's the question?" inquired Stepan Arkadyevitch, coming out of his room and addressing his wife.

From his tone both Kitty and Anna knew that a reconciliation had taken place.

"I want to move Anna downstairs, but we must hang up blinds. No one knows how to do it; I must see to it myself," answered Dolly addressing him.

"God knows whether they are fully reconciled," thought Anna, hearing her tone, cold and composed.

"Oh, nonsense, Dolly, always making difficulties," answered her husband. "Come, I'll do it all, if you like . . ."

"Yes, they must be reconciled," thought Anna.

"I know how you do everything," answered Dolly. "You tell Matvey to do what can't be done, and go away yourself, leaving him to make a muddle of everything," and her habitual, mocking smile curved the corners of Dolly's lips as she spoke.

"Full, full reconciliation, full," thought Anna; "thank God!" and rejoicing that she was the cause of it, she went up to Dolly and kissed her.

"Not at all. Why do you always look down on me and Matvey?" said Stepan Arkadyevitch, smiling hardly perceptibly, and addressing his wife.

The whole evening Dolly was, as always, a little mocking in her tone to her husband, while Stepan Arkadyevitch was happy and cheerful, but not so as to seem as though, having been forgiven, he had forgotten his offense.

At half-past nine o'clock a particularly joyful and pleasant family conversation over the tea-table at the Oblonskys' was broken up by an apparently simple incident. But this simple incident for some reason struck everyone as strange. Talking about common acquaintances in Petersburg, Anna got up quickly.

"She is in my album," she said; "and, by the way, I'll show you my Seryozha," she added, with a mother's smile of pride.

Towards ten o'clock, when she usually said good night to her son, and often before going to a ball put him to bed herself, she felt depressed at being so far from him; and whatever she was talking about, she kept coming back in thought to her curly-headed Seryozha. She longed to look at his photograph and talk of him. Seizing the first pretext, she got up, and with her light, resolute step went for her album. The stairs up to her room came out on the landing of the great warm main staircase.

Just as she was leaving the drawing room, a ring was heard in the hall.

"Who can that be?" said Dolly.

"It's early for me to be fetched, and for anyone else it's late," observed Kitty.

"Sure to be someone with papers for me," put in Stepan Arkadyevitch. When Anna was passing the top of the staircase, a servant was running up to announce the visitor, while the visitor himself was standing under a lamp. Anna glancing down at once recognized Vronsky, and a strange feeling of pleasure and at the same time of dread of something stirred in her heart. He was standing still, not taking off his coat, pulling something out of his pocket. At the instant when she was just facing the stairs, he raised his eyes, caught sight of her, and into the expression of his face there passed a shade of embarrassment and dismay. With a slight inclination of her head she passed, hearing behind her Stepan Arkadyevitch's loud voice calling him to come up, and the quiet, soft, and composed voice of Vronsky refusing.

When Anna returned with the album, he was already gone, and Stepan Arkadyevitch was telling them that he had called to inquire about the dinner they were giving next day to a celebrity who had just arrived. "And nothing would induce him to come up. What a queer fellow he is!" added Stepan Arkadyevitch.

Kitty blushed. She thought that she was the only person who knew why he had come, and why he would not come up. "He has been at home," she thought, "and didn't find me, and thought I should be here, but he did not come up because he thought it late, and Anna's here."

All of them looked at each other, saying nothing, and began to look at Anna's album.

There was nothing either exceptional or strange in a man's calling at half-past nine on a friend to inquire details of a proposed dinner party and not coming in, but it seemed strange to all of them. Above all, it seemed strange and not right to Anna.

Chapter XXII

THE BALL WAS ONLY JUST BEGINNING AS KITTY AND HER MOTHER WALKED UP THE GREAT STAIRcase, flooded with light, and lined with flowers and footmen in powder and red coats. From the rooms came a constant, steady hum, as from a hive, and the rustle of movement; and while on the landing between plants they gave last touches to their hair and dresses before the mirror, they heard from the ballroom the careful, distinct notes of the fiddles of the orchestra beginning the first waltz. A little old man in civilian dress, arranging his gray curls before another mirror, and diffusing an odor of scent, stumbled against them on the stairs, and stood aside, evidently admiring Kitty, whom he did not know. A beardless youth, one of those society youths whom the old Prince Shtcherbatsky called "young bucks," in an exceedingly open waistcoat, straightening his white tie as he went, bowed to them, and after running by, came back to ask Kitty for a quadrille. As the first quadrille had already been given to Vronsky, she had to promise this youth the second. An officer, buttoning his glove, stood aside in the doorway, and, stroking his mustache, admired rosy Kitty.

Although her dress, her coiffure, and all the preparations for the ball had cost Kitty great trouble and consideration, at this moment she walked into the ballroom in her elaborate tulle dress over a pink slip as easily and simply as though all the rosettes and lace, all the minute details of her attire, had not cost her or her family a moment's attention, as though she had been born in that tulle and lace, with her hair done up high on her head, and a rose and two leaves on the top of it.

When, just before entering the ballroom, the princess, her mother, tried to turn right side out of the ribbon of her sash, Kitty had drawn back a little. She felt that everything must be right of itself, and graceful, and nothing could need setting straight.

It was one of Kitty's best days. Her dress was not uncomfortable anywhere; her lace berthe did not droop anywhere; her rosettes were not crushed nor torn off; her pink slippers with high, hollowed-out heels did not pinch, but gladdened her feet; and the thick rolls of fair chignon kept up on her head as if they were her own hair. All the three buttons buttoned up without tearing on the long glove that covered her hand without concealing its lines. The black velvet of her locket nestled with special softness round her neck. That velvet was delicious; at home, looking at her neck in the looking-glass, Kitty had felt that that velvet was speaking. About all the rest there might be a doubt, but the velvet was delicious. Kitty smiled here too, at the ball, when she glanced at it in the glass. Her bare shoulders and arms gave Kitty a sense of chill marble, a feeling she particularly liked. Her eyes sparkled, and her rosy lips could not keep from smiling from the consciousness of her own attractiveness. She had scarcely entered the ballroom and reached the throng of ladies, all tulle, ribbons, lace, and flowers, waiting to be asked to dance—Kitty was never one of that throng—when she was asked for a waltz, and asked by the best partner, the first star in the hierarchy of the ballroom, a renowned director of dances, a married man, handsome and well-built, Yegorushka Korsunsky. He had only just left the Countess Bonina, with whom he had danced the first half of the waltz, and, scanning his kingdom—that is to say, a few couples who had started dancing—he caught sight of Kitty, entering, and flew up to her with that peculiar, easy amble which is confined to directors of balls. Without even asking her if she cared to dance, he put out his arm to encircle her slender waist. She looked round for someone to give her fan to, and their hostess, smiling to her, took it.

"How nice you've come in good time," he said to her, embracing her waist; "such a bad habit to be late." Bending her left hand, she laid it on his shoulder, and her little feet in their pink slippers began swiftly, lightly, and rhythmically moving over the slippery floor in time to the music.

"It's a rest to waltz with you," he said to her, as they fell into the first slow steps of the waltz. "It's exquisite—such lightness, precision." He said to her the same thing he said to almost all his partners whom he knew well.

She smiled at his praise, and continued to look about the room over his shoulder. She was not like a girl at her first ball, for whom all faces in the ballroom melt into one vision of fairyland. And she was not a girl who had gone the stale round of balls till every face in the ballroom was familiar and tiresome. But she was in the middle stage between these two; she was excited, and at the same time she had sufficient self-possession to be able to observe. In the left corner of the ballroom she saw the cream of society gathered together. There—incredibly naked—was the beauty Lidi, Korsunsky's wife; there was the lady of the house; there shone the bald head of Krivin, always to be found where the best people were. In that direction gazed the young men, not venturing to approach. There, too, she descried Stiva, and there she saw the exquisite figure and head of Anna in a black velvet gown. And *he* was there. Kitty had not seen him since the evening she refused Levin. With her long-sighted eyes, she knew him at once, and was even aware that he was looking at her.

"Another turn, eh? You're not tired?" said Korsunsky, a little out of breath.

"No, thank you!"

"Where shall I take you?"

"Madame Karenina's here, I think . . . take me to her."

"Wherever you command."

And Korsunsky began waltzing with measured steps straight towards the group in the left corner, continually saying, "Pardon, mesdames, pardon, pardon, mesdames"; and steering his course through the sea of lace, tulle, and ribbon, and not disarranging a feather, he turned his partner sharply round, so that her slim ankles, in light transparent stockings, were exposed to view, and her train floated out in fan shape and covered Krivin's knees. Korsunsky bowed, set straight his open shirt front, and gave her his arm to conduct her to Anna Arkadyevna. Kitty, flushed, took her train from Krivin's knees, and, a little giddy, looked round, seeking Anna. Anna was not in lilac, as Kitty had so urgently wished, but in a black, low-cut, velvet gown, showing her full throat and shoulders, that looked as though carved in old ivory, and her rounded arms, with tiny, slender wrists. The whole gown was trimmed with Venetian guipure. On her head, among her black hair—her own, with no false additions—was a little wreath of pansies, and a bouquet of the same in the black ribbon of her sash among white lace. Her coiffure was not striking. All that was noticeable was the little willful tendrils of her curly hair that would always break free about her neck and temples. Round her well-cut, strong neck was a thread of pearls.

Kitty had been seeing Anna every day; she adored her, and had pictured her invariably in lilac. But now seeing her in black, she felt that she had not fully seen her charm. She saw her now as someone quite new and surprising to her. Now she understood that Anna could not have been in lilac, and that her charm was just that she always stood out against her attire, that her dress could never be noticeable on her. And her black dress, with its sumptuous lace, was not noticeable on her; it was only the frame, and all that was seen was she—simple, natural, elegant, and at the same time gay and eager.

She was standing holding herself, as always, very erect, and when Kitty drew near the group she was speaking to the master of the house, her head slightly turned towards him.

"No, I don't throw stones," she was saying, in answer to something, "though I can't understand it," she went on, shrugging her shoulders, and she turned at once with a soft smile of protection towards Kitty. With a flying, feminine glance she scanned her attire, and made a movement of her head, hardly perceptible, but understood by Kitty, signifying approval of her dress and her looks. "You came into the room dancing," she added.

"This is one of my most faithful supporters," said Korsunsky, bowing to Anna Arkadyevna, whom he had not yet seen. "The princess helps to make balls happy and successful. Anna Arkadyevna, a waltz?" he said, bending down to her.

"Why, have you met?" inquired their host.

"Is there anyone we have not met? My wife and I are like white wolves—everyone knows us," answered Korsunsky. "A waltz, Anna Arkadyevna?"

"I don't dance when it's possible not to dance," she said.

"But tonight it's impossible," answered Korsunsky.

At that instant Vronsky came up.

"Well, since it's impossible tonight, let us start," she said, not noticing Vronsky's bow, and she hastily put her hand on Korsunsky's shoulder.

"What is she vexed with him about?" thought Kitty, discerning that Anna had intentionally not responded to Vronsky's bow. Vronsky went up to Kitty reminding her of the first quadrille, and expressing his regret that he had not seen her all this time. Kitty gazed in admiration at Anna waltzing, and listened to him. She expected him to ask her for a waltz, but he did not, and she glanced wonderingly at him. He flushed slightly, and hurriedly asked her to waltz, but he had only just put his arm round her waist and taken the first step when the music suddenly stopped. Kitty looked into his face, which was so close to her own, and long afterwards—for several years after—that look, full of love, to which he made no response, cut her to the heart with an agony of shame.

"*Pardon! pardon!* Waltz! waltz!" shouted Korsunsky from the other side of the room, and seizing the first young lady he came across he began dancing himself.

Chapter XXIII

VRONSKY AND KITTY WALTZED SEVERAL TIMES ROUND THE ROOM. AFTER THE FIRST WALTZ KITTY went to her mother, and she had hardly time to say a few words to Countess Nordston when Vronsky came up again for the first quadrille. During the quadrille nothing of any significance was said: there was disjointed talk between them of the Korsunskys, husband and wife, whom he described very amusingly, as delightful children at forty, and of the future town theater; and only once the conversation touched her to the quick, when he asked her about Levin, whether he was here, and added that he liked him so much. But Kitty did not expect much from the quadrille. She looked forward with a thrill at her heart to the mazurka. She fancied that in the mazurka everything must be decided. The fact that he did not during the quadrille ask her for the mazurka did not trouble her. She felt sure she would dance the mazurka with him as she had done at former balls, and refused five young men, saying she was engaged for the mazurka. The whole ball up to the last quadrille was for Kitty an enchanted vision of delightful colors, sounds, and motions. She only sat down when she felt too tired and begged for a rest. But as she was dancing the last quadrille with one of the tiresome young men whom she could not refuse, she chanced to be *vis-à-vis* with Vronsky and Anna. She had not been near Anna again since the beginning of the evening, and now again she saw her suddenly quite new and surprising. She saw in her the signs of that excitement of success she knew so well in herself; she saw that she was intoxicated with the delighted admiration she was exciting. She knew that feeling and knew its signs, and saw them in Anna; saw the quivering, flashing light in her eyes, and the smile of happiness and excitement unconsciously playing on her lips, and the deliberate grace, precision, and lightness of her movements.

"Who?" she asked herself. "All or one?" And not assisting the harassed young man she was dancing with in the conversation, the thread of which he had lost and could not pick up again, she obeyed with external liveliness the peremptory shouts of Korsunsky starting them all into the *grand rond*, and then into the *chaîne*, and at the same time she kept watch with a growing pang at her heart. "No, it's not the admiration of the crowd has intoxicated her, but the adoration of one. And that one? can it be he?" Every time he spoke to Anna the joyous light flashed into her eyes, and the smile of happiness curved her red lips. She seemed to make an effort to control herself, to try not to show these signs of delight, but they came out on her face of themselves. "But what of him?" Kitty looked at him and was filled with terror. What was pictured so clearly to Kitty in the mirror of Anna's face she saw in him. What had become of his always self-possessed resolute manner, and the carelessly serene expression of his face? Now every time he turned to her, he bent his head, as though he would have fallen at her feet, and in his eyes there was nothing but humble submission and dread. "I would not offend you," his eyes seemed every time to be saying, "but I want to save myself, and I don't know how." On his face was a look such as Kitty had never seen before.

They were speaking of common acquaintances, keeping up the most trivial conversation, but to Kitty it seemed that every word they said was determining their fate and hers. And strange it was that they were actually talking of how absurd Ivan Ivanovitch was with his French, and how the Eletsky girl might have made a better match, yet these words had all the while consequence for them, and they were feeling just as Kitty did. The whole ball, the whole world, everything seemed lost in fog in Kitty's soul. Nothing but the stern discipline of her bringing-up supported her and forced her to do what was expected of her, that is, to dance, to answer questions, to talk, even to smile. But before the mazurka, when they were beginning to rearrange the chairs and a few couples moved out of the smaller rooms into the big room, a moment of despair and horror came for Kitty. She had refused five partners, and now she was not dancing the mazurka. She had not even a hope of being asked for it, because she was so successful in society that the idea would never occur to anyone that she had remained disengaged till now. She would have to tell her mother she felt ill and go home, but she had not the strength to do this. She felt crushed. She went to the furthest end of the little drawing room and sank into a low chair. Her light, transparent skirts rose like a cloud about her slender waist; one bare, thin, soft, girlish arm, hanging listlessly, was lost in the folds of her pink tunic; in the other she held her fan, and with rapid, short strokes fanned her burning face. But while she looked like a butterfly, clinging to a blade of grass, and just about to open its rainbow wings for fresh flight, her heart ached with a horrible despair.

"But perhaps I am wrong, perhaps it was not so?" And again she recalled all she had seen.

"Kitty, what is it?" said Countess Nordston, stepping noiselessly over the carpet towards her. "I don't understand it."

Kitty's lower lip began to quiver; she got up quickly.

"Kitty, you're not dancing the mazurka?"

"No, no," said Kitty in a voice shaking with tears.

"He asked her for the mazurka before me," said Countess Nordston, knowing Kitty would understand who were "he" and "her." "She said: 'Why, aren't you going to dance it with Princess Shtcherbatskaya?' "

"Oh, I don't care!" answered Kitty.

No one but she herself understood her position; no one knew that she had just refused the man whom perhaps she loved, and refused him because she had put her faith in another.

Countess Nordston found Korsunsky, with whom she was to dance the mazurka, and told him to ask Kitty.

Kitty danced in the first couple, and luckily for her she had not to talk, because Korsunsky was all the time running about directing the figure. Vronsky and Anna sat almost opposite her. She saw them with her long-sighted eyes, and saw them, too, close by, when they met in the figures, and the more she saw of them the more convinced was she that her unhappiness was complete. She saw that they felt themselves alone in that crowded room. And on Vronsky's face, always so firm and independent, she saw that look that had struck her, of bewilderment and humble submissiveness, like the expression of an intelligent dog when it has done wrong.

Anna smiled, and her smile was reflected by him. She grew thoughtful, and he became serious. Some supernatural force drew Kitty's eyes to Anna's face. She was fascinating in her simple black dress, fascinating were her round arms with their bracelets, fascinating was her firm neck with its thread of pearls, fascinating the straying curls of her loose hair, fascinating the graceful, light movements of her little feet and hands, fascinating was that lovely face in its eagerness, but there was something terrible and cruel in her fascination.

Kitty admired her more than ever, and more and more acute was her suffering. Kitty felt overwhelmed, and her face showed it. When Vronsky saw her, coming across her in the mazurka, he did not at once recognize her, she was so changed.

"Delightful ball!" he said to her, for the sake of saying something.

"Yes," she answered.

In the middle of the mazurka, repeating a complicated figure, newly invented by Korsunsky, Anna came forward into the center of the circle, chose two gentlemen, and summoned a lady and Kitty. Kitty gazed at her in dismay as she went up. Anna looked at her with drooping eyelids, and smiled, pressing her hand. But, noticing that Kitty only responded to her smile by a look of despair and amazement, she turned away from her, and began gaily talking to the other lady.

"Yes, there is something uncanny, devilish and fascinating in her," Kitty said to herself.

Anna did not mean to stay to supper, but the master of the house began to press her to do so.

"Nonsense, Anna Arkadyevna," said Korsunsky, drawing her bare arm under the sleeve of his dress-coat, "I've such an idea for a *cotillion! Un bijou!*"

And he moved gradually on, trying to draw her along with him. Their host smiled approvingly.

"No, I am not going to stay," answered Anna, smiling, but in spite of her smile, both Korsunsky and the master of the house saw from her resolute tone that she would not stay.

"No; why, as it is, I have danced more at your ball in Moscow than I have all the winter in Petersburg," said Anna, looking round at Vronsky, who stood near her. "I must rest a little before my journey."

"Are you certainly going tomorrow then?" asked Vronsky.

"Yes, I suppose so," answered Anna, as it were wondering at the boldness of his question; but the irrepressible, quivering brilliance of her eyes and her smile set him on fire as she said it.

Anna Arkadyevna did not stay to supper, but went home.

Chapter XXIV

"YES, THERE IS SOMETHING IN ME HATEFUL, REPULSIVE," THOUGHT LEVIN, AS HE CAME AWAY FROM the Shtcherbatskys', and walked in the direction of his brother's lodgings. "And I don't get on with other people. Pride, they say. No, I have no pride. If I had any pride, I should not have put myself in such a position." And he pictured to himself Vronsky, happy, good-natured, clever, and self-possessed, certainly never placed in the awful position in which he had been that evening. "Yes, she was bound to choose him. So it had to be, and I cannot complain of anyone or anything. I am myself to blame. What right had I to imagine she would care to join her life to mine? Who am I and what am I? A nobody, not wanted by anyone, nor of use to anybody." And he recalled his brother Nikolay, and dwelled with pleasure on the thought of him. "Isn't he right that everything in the world is base and loathsome? And are we fair in our judgment of brother Nikolay? Of course, from the point of view of Prokofy, seeing him in a torn cloak and tipsy, he's a despicable person. But I know him differently. I know his soul, and know that we are like him. And I, instead of going to seek him out, went out to dinner, and came here." Levin walked up to a lamppost, read his brother's address, which was in his pocketbook, and called a sleigh. All the long way to his brother's, Levin vividly recalled all the facts familiar to him of his brother Nikolay's life. He remembered how his brother, while at the university, and for a year afterwards, had, in spite of the jeers of his companions, lived like a monk, strictly observing all religious rites, services, and fasts, and avoiding every sort of pleasure, especially women. And afterwards, how he had all at once broken out: he had associated with the most horrible people, and rushed into the most senseless debauchery. He remembered later the scandal over a boy, whom he had taken from the country to bring up, and, in a fit of rage, had so violently beaten that proceedings were brought against him for unlawfully wounding. Then he recalled the scandal with a sharper, to whom he had lost money, and given a promissory note, and against whom he had himself lodged a complaint, asserting that he had cheated him. (This was the money Sergey Ivanovitch had paid.) Then he remembered how he had spent a night in the lockup for disorderly conduct in the street. He remembered the shameful proceedings he had tried to get up against his brother Sergey Ivanovitch, accusing him of not having paid him his share of his mother's fortune, and the last scandal, when he had gone to a western province in an official capacity, and there had got into trouble for assaulting a village elder. . . . It was all horribly disgusting, yet to Levin it appeared not at all in the same disgusting light as it inevitably would to those who did not know Nikolay, did not know all his story, did not know his heart.

Levin remembered that when Nikolay had been in the devout stage, the period of fasts and monks and church services, when he was seeking in religion a support and a curb for his passionate temperament, everyone, far from encouraging him, had jeered at him, and he, too, with the others. They had teased him, called him Noah and Monk; and, when he had broken out, no one had helped him, but everyone had turned away from him with horror and disgust.

Levin felt that, in spite of all the ugliness of his life, his brother Nikolay, in his soul, in the very depths of his soul, was no more in the wrong than the people who despised him. He was not to blame for having been born with his unbridled temperament and his somehow limited intelligence. But he had always wanted to be good. "I will tell him everything, without reserve, and I will make him speak without reserve, too, and I'll show him that I love him, and so understand him," Levin resolved to himself, as, towards eleven o'clock, he reached the hotel of which he had the address.

"At the top, 12 and 13," the porter answered Levin's inquiry.

"At home?"

"Sure to be at home."

The door of No. 12 was half-open, and there came out into the streak of light thick fumes of cheap, poor tobacco, and the sound of a voice, unknown to Levin; but he knew at once that his brother was there; he heard his cough.

As he went in the door, the unknown voice was saying:

"It all depends with how much judgment and knowledge the thing's done."

Konstantin Levin looked in at the door, and saw that the speaker was a young man with an immense shock of hair, wearing a Russian jerkin, and that a pockmarked woman in a woolen gown, without collar or cuffs, was sitting on the sofa. His brother was not to be seen. Konstantin felt a sharp pang at his heart at the thought of the strange company in which his brother spent his life. No one had heard him, and Konstantin, taking off his galoshes, listened to what the gentleman in the jerkin was saying. He was speaking of some enterprise.

"Well, the devil flay them, the privileged classes," his brother's voice responded, with a cough. "Masha! get us some supper and some wine if there's any left; or else go and get some."

The woman rose, came out from behind the screen, and saw Konstantin.

"There's some gentleman, Nikolay Dmitrievitch," she said.

"Whom do you want?" said the voice of Nikolay Levin, angrily.

"It's I," answered Konstantin Levin, coming forward into the light.

"Who's *I?*" Nikolay's voice said again, still more angrily. He could be heard getting up hurriedly, stumbling against something, and Levin saw, facing him in the doorway, the big, scared eyes, and the huge, thin, stooping figure of his brother, so familiar, and yet astonishing in its weirdness and sickliness.

He was even thinner than three years before, when Konstantin Levin had seen him last. He was wearing a short coat, and his hands and big bones seemed huger than ever. His hair had grown thinner, the same straight mustaches hid his lips, the same eyes gazed strangely and naïvely at his visitor.

"Ah, Kostya!" he exclaimed suddenly, recognizing his brother, and his eyes lit up with joy. But the same second he looked round at the young man, and gave the nervous jerk of his head and neck that Konstantin knew so well, as if his neckband hurt him; and a quite different expression, wild, suffering, and cruel, rested on his emaciated face.

"I wrote to you and Sergey Ivanovitch both that I don't know you and don't want to know you. What is it you want?"

He was not at all the same as Konstantin had been fancying him. The worst and most tiresome part of his character, what made all relations with him so difficult, had been forgotten by Konstantin Levin when he thought of him, and now, when he saw his face, and especially that nervous twitching of his head, he remembered it all.

"I didn't want to see you for anything," he answered timidly. "I've simply come to see you."

His brother's timidity obviously softened Nikolay. His lips twitched.

"Oh, so that's it?" he said. "Well, come in; sit down. Like some supper? Masha, bring supper for three. No, stop a minute. Do you know who this is?" he said, addressing his brother, and indicating the gentleman in the jerkin: "This is Mr. Kritsky, my friend from Kiev, a very remarkable man. He's persecuted by the police, of course, because he's not a scoundrel."

And he looked round in the way he always did at everyone in the room. Seeing that the woman standing in the doorway was moving to go, he shouted to her, "Wait a minute, I said." And with the inability to express himself, the incoherence that Konstantin knew so well, he began, with another look round at everyone, to tell his brother Kritsky's story: how he had been expelled from the university for starting a benefit society for the poor students and Sunday-schools; and how he had afterwards been a teacher in a peasant school, and how he had been driven out of that too, and had afterwards been condemned for something.

"You're of the Kiev university?" said Konstantin Levin to Kritsky, to break the awkward silence that followed.

"Yes, I was of Kiev," Kritsky replied angrily, his face darkening.

"And this woman," Nikolay Levin interrupted him, pointing to her, "is the partner of my life, Marya Nikolaevna. I took her out of a bad house," and he jerked his neck saying this; "but I love her and respect her, and anyone who wants to know me," he added, raising his voice and knitting his brows, "I beg to love her and respect her. She's just the same as my wife, just the same. So now you know whom you've got to do with. And if you think you're lowering yourself, well, here's the floor, there's the door."

And again his eyes traveled inquiringly over all of them.

"Why I should be lowering myself, I don't understand."

"Then, Masha, tell them to bring supper; three portions, spirits and wine. . . . No, wait a minute. . . . No, it doesn't matter. . . . Go along."

Chapter XXV

SO YOU SEE," PURSUED NIKOLAY LEVIN, PAINFULLY WRINKLING HIS FOREHEAD AND TWITCHING. It was obviously difficult for him to think of what to say and do.

"Here, do you see?" . . . He pointed to some sort of iron bars, fastened together with strings, lying in a corner of the room. "Do you see that? That's the beginning of a new thing we're going into. It's a productive association. . . ."

Konstantin scarcely heard him. He looked into his sickly, consumptive face, and he was more and more sorry for him, and he could not force himself to listen to what his brother was telling him about the association. He saw that this association was a mere anchor to save him from self-contempt. Nikolay Levin went on talking:

"You know that capital oppresses the laborer. The laborers with us, the peasants, bear all the burden of labor, and are so placed that however much they work they can't escape from their position of beasts of burden. All the profits of labor, on which they might improve their position, and gain leisure for themselves, and after that education, all the surplus values are taken from them by the capitalists. And society's so constituted that the harder they work, the greater the profit of the merchants and landowners, while they stay beasts of burden to the end. And that state of things must be changed," he finished up, and he looked questioningly at his brother.

"Yes, of course," said Konstantin, looking at the patch of red that had come out on his brother's projecting cheekbones.

"And so we're founding a locksmiths' association, where all the production and profit and the chief instruments of production will be in common."

"Where is the association to be?" asked Konstantin Levin.

"In the village of Vozdrem, Kazan government."

"But why in a village? In the villages, I think, there is plenty of work as it is. Why a locksmiths' association in a village?"

"Why? Because the peasants are just as much slaves as they ever were, and that's why you and Sergey Ivanovitch don't like people to try and get them out of their slavery," said Nikolay Levin, exasperated by the objection.

Konstantin Levin sighed, looking meanwhile about the cheerless and dirty room. This sigh seemed to exasperate Nikolay still more.

"I know your and Sergey Ivanovitch's aristocratic views. I know that he applies all the power of his intellect to justify existing evils."

"No; and what do you talk of Sergey Ivanovitch for?" said Levin, smiling.

"Sergey Ivanovitch? I'll tell you what for!" Nikolay Levin shrieked suddenly at the name of

Sergey Ivanovitch. "I'll tell you what for. . . . But what's the use of talking? There's only one thing. . . . What did you come to me for? You look down on this, and you're welcome to—and go away, in God's name go away!" he shrieked, getting up from his chair. "And go away, and go away!"

"I don't look down on it at all," said Konstantin Levin timidly. "I don't even dispute it."

At that instant Marya Nikolaevna came back. Nikolay Levin looked round angrily at her. She went quickly to him, and whispered something.

"I'm not well; I've grown irritable," said Nikolay Levin, getting calmer and breathing painfully; "and then you talk to me of Sergey Ivanovitch and his article. It's such rubbish, such lying, such self-deception. What can a man write of justice who knows nothing of it? Have you read his article?" he asked Kritsky, sitting down again at the table, and moving back off half of it the scattered cigarettes, so as to clear a space.

"I've not read it," Kritsky responded gloomily, obviously not desiring to enter into the conversation.

"Why not?" said Nikolay Levin, now turning with exasperation upon Kritsky.

"Because I didn't see the use of wasting my time over it."

"Oh, but excuse me, how did you know it would be wasting your time? That article's too deep for many people—that's to say it's over their heads. But with me, it's another thing; I see through his ideas, and I know where its weakness lies."

Everyone was mute. Kritsky got up deliberately and reached his cap.

"Won't you have supper? All right, good-bye! Come round tomorrow with the locksmith."

Kritsky had hardly gone out when Nikolay Levin smiled and winked.

"He's no good either," he said. "I see, of course . . ."

But at that instant Kritsky, at the door, called him. . . .

"What do you want now?" he said, and went out to him in the passage. Left alone with Marya Nikolaevna, Levin turned to her.

"Have you been long with my brother?" he said to her.

"Yes, more than a year. Nikolay Dmitrievitch's health has become very poor. Nikolay Dmitrievitch drinks a great deal," she said.

"That is . . . how does he drink?"

"Drinks vodka, and it's bad for him."

"And a great deal?" whispered Levin.

"Yes," she said, looking timidly towards the doorway, where Nikolay Levin had reappeared.

"What were you talking about?" he said, knitting his brows, and turning his scared eyes from one to the other. "What was it?"

"Oh, nothing," Konstantin answered in confusion.

"Oh, if you don't want to say, don't. Only it's no good your talking to her. She's a wench, and you're a gentleman," he said with a jerk of the neck. "You understand everything, I see, and have taken stock of everything, and look with commiseration on my shortcomings," he began again, raising his voice.

"Nikolay Dmitrievitch, Nikolay Dmitrievitch," whispered Marya Nikolaevna, again going up to him.

"Oh, very well, very well! . . . But where's the supper? Ah, here it is," he said, seeing a waiter with a tray. "Here, set it here," he added angrily, and promptly seizing the vodka, he poured out a glassful and drank it greedily. "Like a drink?" he turned to his brother, and at once became better humored.

"Well, enough of Sergey Ivanovitch. I'm glad to see you, anyway. After all's said and done, we're not strangers. Come, have a drink. Tell me what you're doing," he went on, greedily munching a piece of bread, and pouring out another glassful. "How are you living?"

"I live alone in the country, as I used to. I'm busy looking after the land," answered Konstantin, watching with horror the greediness with which his brother ate and drank, and trying to conceal that he noticed it.

"Why don't you get married?"

"It hasn't happened so," Konstantin answered, reddening a little.

"Why not? For me now . . . everything's at an end! I've made a mess of my life. But this I've said, and I say still, that if my share had been given me when I needed it, my whole life would have been different."

Konstantin made haste to change the conversation.

"Do you know your little Vanya's with me, a clerk in the counting house at Pokrovskoe?"

Nikolay jerked his neck, and sank into thought.

"Yes, tell me what's going on at Pokrovskoe. Is the house standing still, and the birch trees, and our schoolroom? And Philip the gardener, is he living? How I remember the arbor and the seat! Now mind and don't alter anything in the house, but make haste and get married, and make everything as it used to be again. Then I'll come and see you, if your wife is nice."

"But come to me now," said Levin. "How nicely we would arrange it!"

"I'd come and see you if I were sure I should not find Sergey Ivanovitch."

"You wouldn't find him there. I live quite independently of him."

"Yes, but say what you like, you will have to choose between me and him," he said, looking timidly into his brother's face.

This timidity touched Konstantin.

"If you want to hear my confession of faith on the subject, I tell you that in your quarrel with Sergey Ivanovitch I take neither side. You're both wrong. You're more wrong externally, and he inwardly."

"Ah, ah! You see that, you see that!" Nikolay shouted joyfully.

"But I personally value friendly relations with you more because . . ."

"Why, why?"

Konstantin could not say that he valued it more because Nikolay was unhappy, and needed affection. But Nikolay knew that this was just what he meant to say, and scowling he took up the vodka again.

"Enough, Nikolay Dmitrievitch!" said Marya Nikolaevna, stretching out her plump, bare arm towards the decanter.

"Let it be! Don't insist! I'll beat you!" he shouted.

Marya Nikolaevna smiled a sweet and good-humored smile, which was at once reflected on Nikolay's face, and she took the bottle.

"And do you suppose she understands nothing?" said Nikolay. "She understands it all better than any of us. Isn't it true there's something good and sweet in her?"

"Were you never before in Moscow?" Konstantin said to her, for the sake of saying something.

"Only you mustn't be polite and stiff with her. It frightens her. No one ever spoke to her so but the justices of the peace who tried her for trying to get out of a house of ill-fame. Mercy on us, the senselessness in the world!" he cried suddenly. "These new institutions, these justices of the peace, rural councils, what hideousness it all is!"

And he began to enlarge on his encounters with the new institutions.

Konstantin Levin heard him, and the disbelief in the sense of all public institutions, which he shared with him, and often expressed, was distasteful to him now from his brother's lips.

"In another world we shall understand it all," he said lightly.

"In another world! Ah, I don't like that other world! I don't like it," he said, letting his scared eyes rest on his brother's eyes. "Here one would think that to get out of all the baseness and the mess, one's own and other people's, would be a good thing, and yet I'm afraid of death, awfully afraid of death." He shuddered. "But do drink something. Would you like some champagne? Or shall we go somewhere? Let's go to the Gypsies! Do you know I have got so fond of the Gypsies and Russian songs."

His speech had begun to falter, and he passed abruptly from one subject to another. Konstantin with the help of Masha persuaded him not to go out anywhere, and got him to bed hopelessly drunk.

Masha promised to write to Konstantin in case of need, and to persuade Nikolay Levin to go and stay with his brother.

Chapter XXVI

IN THE MORNING KONSTANTIN LEVIN LEFT MOSCOW, AND TOWARD EVENING HE REACHED HOME. On the journey in the train he talked to his neighbors about politics and the new railways, and, just as in Moscow, he was overcome by a sense of confusion of ideas, dissatisfaction with himself, shame of something or other. But when he got out at his own station, when he saw his one-eyed coachman, Ignat, with the collar of his coat turned up; when, in the dim light reflected by the station fires, he saw his own sleigh, his own horses with their tails tied up, in their harness trimmed with rings and tassels; when the coachman Ignat, as he put in his luggage, told him the village news, that the contractor had arrived, and that Pava had calved—he felt that little by little the confusion was clearing up, and the shame and self-dissatisfaction were passing away. He felt this at the mere sight of Ignat and the horses; but when he had put on the sheepskin brought for him, had sat down wrapped up in the sleigh, and had driven off pondering on the work that lay before him in the village, and staring at the side-horse, that had been his saddle-horse, past his prime now, but a spirited beast from the Don, he began to see what had happened to him in quite a different light. He felt himself, and did not want to be anyone else. All he wanted now was to be better than before. In the first place he resolved that from that day he would give up hoping for any extraordinary happiness, such as marriage must have given him, and consequently he would not so disdain what he really had. Secondly, he would never again let himself give way to low passion, the memory of which had so tortured him when he had been making up his mind to make an offer. Then remembering his brother Nikolay, he resolved to himself that he would never allow himself to forget him, that he would follow him up, and not lose sight of him, so as to be ready to help when things should go ill with him. And that would be soon, he felt. Then, too, his brother's talk of communism, which he had treated so lightly at the time, now made him think. He considered a revolution in economic conditions nonsense. But he always felt the injustice of his own abundance in comparison with the poverty of the peasants, and now he determined that so as to feel quite in the right, though he had worked hard and lived by no means luxuriously before, he would now work still harder, and would allow himself even less luxury. And all this seemed to him so easy a conquest over himself that he spent the whole drive in the pleasantest daydreams. With a resolute feeling of hope in a new, better life, he reached home before nine o'clock at night.

The snow of the little quadrangle before the house was lit up by a light in the bedroom windows of his old nurse, Agafea Mihalovna, who performed the duties of housekeeper in his house. She was not yet asleep. Kouzma, waked up by her, came sidling sleepily out onto the steps. A setter bitch, Laska, ran out too, almost upsetting Kouzma, and whining, turned round about Levin's knees, jumping up and longing, but not daring, to put her forepaws on his chest.

"You're soon back again, sir," said Agafea Mihalovna.

"I got tired of it, Agafea Mihalovna. With friends, one is well; but at home, one is well," he answered, and went into his study.

The study was slowly lit up as the candle was brought in. The familiar details came out: the stag's horns, the bookshelves, the looking-glass, the stove with its ventilator, which had long wanted mending, his father's sofa, a large table, on the table an open book, a broken ashtray, a manuscript-book with his handwriting. As he saw all this, there came over him for an instant a doubt of the possibility of arranging the new life, of which he had been dreaming on the road. All these traces of his life seemed to clutch him, and to say to him: "No, you're not going to get away from us, and you're not going to be different, but you're going to be the same as you've always been; with doubts, everlasting dissatisfaction with yourself, vain efforts to amend, and falls, and everlasting expectation, of a happiness which you won't get, and which isn't possible for you."

This the things said to him, but another voice in his heart was telling him that he must not fall under the sway of the past, and that one can do anything with oneself. And hearing that voice, he went into the corner where stood his two heavy dumb-bells, and began brandishing them like a gymnast, trying to restore his confident temper. There was a creak of steps at the door. He hastily put down the dumb-bells.

The bailiff came in, and said everything, thank God, was doing well; but informed him that the buckwheat in the new drying machine had been a little scorched. This piece of news irritated Levin. The new drying machine had been constructed and partly invented by Levin. The bailiff had always been against the drying machine, and now it was with suppressed triumph that he announced that the buckwheat had been scorched. Levin was firmly convinced that if the buckwheat had been scorched, it was only because the precautions had not been taken, for which he had hundreds of times given orders. He was annoyed, and reprimanded the bailiff. But there had been an important and joyful event: Pava, his best cow, an expensive beast, bought at a show, had calved.

"Kouzma, give me my sheepskin. And you tell them to take a lantern. I'll come and look at her," he said to the bailiff.

The cowhouse for the more valuable cows was just behind the house. Walking across the yard, passing a snowdrift by the lilac tree, he went into the cowhouse. There was the warm, steamy smell of dung when the frozen door was opened, and the cows, astonished at the unfamiliar light of the lantern, stirred on the fresh straw. He caught a glimpse of the broad, smooth, black and piebald back of Hollandka. Berkoot, the bull, was lying down with his ring in his lip, and seemed about to get up, but thought better of it, and only gave two snorts as they passed by him. Pava, a perfect beauty, huge as a hippopotamus, with her back turned to them, prevented their seeing the calf, as she sniffed her all over.

Levin went into the pen, looked Pava over, and lifted the red and spotted calf onto her long, tottering legs. Pava, uneasy, began lowing, but when Levin put the calf close to her she was soothed, and, sighing heavily, began licking her with her rough tongue. The calf, fumbling, poked her nose under her mother's udder, and stiffened her tail out straight.

"Here, bring the light, Fyodor, this way," said Levin, examining the calf. "Like the mother! though the color takes after the father; but that's nothing. Very good. Long and broad in the haunch. Vassily Fedorovitch, isn't she splendid?" he said to the bailiff, quite forgiving him for the buckwheat under the influence of his delight in the calf.

"How could she fail to be? Oh, Semyon the contractor came the day after you left. You must settle with him, Konstantin Dmitrievitch," said the bailiff, "I did inform you about the machine."

This question was enough to take Levin back to all the details of his work on the estate, which was on a large scale, and complicated. He went straight from the cowhouse to the counting house, and after a little conversation with the bailiff and Semyon the contractor, he went back to the house and straight upstairs to the drawing room.

Chapter XXVII

THE HOUSE WAS BIG AND OLD-FASHIONED, AND LEVIN, THOUGH HE LIVED ALONE, HAD THE whole house heated and used. He knew that this was stupid, he knew that it was positively not right, and contrary to his present new plans, but this house was a whole world to Levin. It was the world in which his father and mother had lived and died. They had lived just the life that to Levin seemed the ideal of perfection, and that he had dreamed of beginning with his wife, his family.

Levin scarcely remembered his mother. His conception of her was for him a sacred memory, and his future wife was bound to be in his imagination a repetition of that exquisite, holy ideal of a woman that his mother had been.

He was so far from conceiving of love for woman apart from marriage that he positively pictured to himself first the family, and only secondarily the woman who would give him a family. His ideas of marriage were, consequently, quite unlike those of the great majority of his acquaintances, for whom getting married was one of the numerous facts of social life. For Levin it was the chief affair of life, on which its whole happiness turned. And now he had to give up that.

When he had gone into the little drawing room, where he always had tea, and had settled himself in his arm-chair with a book, and Agafea Mihalovna had brought him tea, and with her usual, "Well, I'll stay a while, sir," had taken a chair in the window, he felt that, however strange it might be, he had not parted from his daydreams, and that he could not live without them. Whether with her, or with another, still it would be. He was reading a book, and thinking of what he was reading, and stopping to listen to Agafea Mihalovna, who gossiped away without flagging, and yet with all that, all sorts of pictures of family life and work in the future rose disconnectedly before his imagination. He felt that in the depth of his soul something had been put in its place, settled down, and laid to rest.

He heard Agafea Mihalovna talking of how Prohor had forgotten his duty to God, and with the money Levin had given him to buy a horse, had been drinking without stopping, and had beaten his wife till he'd half killed her. He listened, and read his book, and recalled the whole train of ideas suggested by his reading. It was Tyndall's *Treatise on Heat*. He recalled his own criticisms of Tyndall for his complacent satisfaction in the cleverness of his experiments, and for his lack of philosophic insight. And suddenly there floated into his mind the joyful thought: "In two years' time I shall have two Dutch cows; Pava herself will perhaps still be alive, a dozen young daughters of Berkoot and the three others—how lovely!"

He took up his book again. "Very good, electricity and heat are the same thing; but is it possible to substitute the one quantity for the other in the equation for the solution of any problem? No. Well, then what of it? The connection between all the forces of nature is felt instinctively. . . . It's particulary nice if Pava's daughter should be a red-spotted cow, and all the herd will take after her, and the other three, too! Splendid! To go out with my wife and visitors to meet the herd. . . . My wife says, 'Kostya and I looked after that calf like a child.' 'How can it interest you so much?' says a visitor. 'Everything that interests him, interests me.' But who will she be?" And he remembered what had happened at Moscow. . . . "Well, there's nothing to be done. . . . It's not my fault. But now everything shall go on in a new way. It's nonsense to pretend that life won't let one, that the past won't let one. One must struggle to live better, much better." . . . He raised his head, and fell to dreaming. Old Laska, who had not yet fully digested her delight at his return, and had run out into the yard to bark, came back wagging her tail, and crept up to him, bringing in the scent of the fresh air, put her head under his hand, and whined plaintively, asking to be stroked.

"There, who'd have thought it?" said Agafea Mihalovna. "The dog now . . . why, she understands that her master's come home, and that he's low-spirited."

"Why low-spirited?"

"Do you suppose I don't see it, sir? It's high time I should know the gentry. Why, I've grown up from a little thing with them. It's nothing, sir, so long as there's health and a clear conscience."

Levin looked intently at her, surprised at how well she knew his thought.

"Shall I fetch you another cup?" said she, and taking his cup she went out.

Laska kept poking her head under his hand. He stroked her, and she promptly curled up at his feet, laying her head on a hind-paw. And in token of all now being well and satisfactory, she opened her mouth a little, smacked her lips, and settling her sticky lips more comfortably about her old teeth, she sank into blissful repose. Levin watched all her movements attentively.

"That's what I'll do," he said to himself; "that's what I'll do! Nothing's amiss. . . . All's well."

Chapter XXVIII

AFTER THE BALL, EARLY NEXT MORNING, ANNA ARKADYEVNA SENT HER HUSBAND A TELEGRAM that she was leaving Moscow the same day.

"No, I must go, I must go"; she explained to her sister-in-law the change in her plans in a tone that suggested that she had to remember so many things that there was no enumerating them: "no, it had really better be today!"

Stepan Arkadyevitch was not dining at home, but he promised to come and see his sister off at seven o'clock.

Kitty, too, did not come, sending a note that she had a headache. Dolly and Anna dined alone with the children and the English governess. Whether it was that the children were fickle, or that they had acute senses, and felt that Anna was quite different that day from what she had been when they had taken such a fancy to her, that she was not now interested in them—but they had abruptly dropped their play with their aunt, and their love for her, and were quite indifferent that she was going away. Anna was absorbed the whole morning in preparations for her departure. She wrote notes to her Moscow acquaintances, put down her accounts, and packed. Altogether Dolly fancied she was not in a placid state of mind, but in that worried mood, which Dolly knew well with herself, and which does not come without cause, and for the most part covers dissatisfaction with self. After dinner, Anna went up to her room to dress, and Dolly followed her.

"How queer you are today!" Dolly said to her.

"I? Do you think so? I'm not queer, but I'm nasty. I am like that sometimes. I keep feeling as if I could cry. It's very stupid, but it'll pass off," said Anna quickly, and she bent her flushed face over a tiny bag in which she was packing a nightcap and some cambric handkerchiefs. Her eyes were particularly bright, and were continually swimming with tears. "In the same way I didn't want to leave Petersburg, and now I don't want to go away from here."

"You came here and did a good deed," said Dolly, looking intently at her.

Anna looked at her with eyes wet with tears.

"Don't say that, Dolly. I've done nothing, and could do nothing. I often wonder why people are all in league to spoil me. What have I done, and what could I do? In your heart there was found love enough to forgive. . . ."

"If it had not been for you, God knows what would have happened! How happy you are, Anna!" said Dolly. "Everything is clear and good in your heart."

"Every heart has its own *skeletons*, as the English say."

"You have no sort of *skeleton*, have you? Everything is so clear in you."

"I have!" said Anna suddenly, and, unexpectedly after her tears, a sly, ironical smile curved her lips.

"Come, he's amusing, anyway, your *skeleton*, and not depressing," said Dolly, smiling.

"No, he's depressing. Do you know why I'm going today instead of tomorrow? It's a confession that weighs on me; I want to make it to you," said Anna, letting herself drop definitely into an arm-chair, and looking straight into Dolly's face.

And to her surprise Dolly saw that Anna was blushing up to her ears, up to the curly black ringlets on her neck.

"Yes," Anna went on. "Do you know why Kitty didn't come to dinner? She's jealous of me. I have spoiled . . . I've been the cause of that ball being a torture to her instead of a pleasure. But truly, truly, it's not my fault, or only my fault a little bit," she said, daintily drawling the words "a little bit."

"Oh, how like Stiva you said that!" said Dolly, laughing.

Anna was hurt.

"Oh no, oh no! I'm not Stiva," she said, knitting her brows. "That's why I'm telling you, just because I could never let myself doubt myself for an instant," said Anna.

But at the very moment she was uttering the words, she felt that they were not true. She was not merely doubting herself, she felt emotion at the thought of Vronsky, and was going away sooner than she had meant, simply to avoid meeting him.

"Yes, Stiva told me you danced the mazurka with him, and that he . . ."

"You can't imagine how absurdly it all came about. I only meant to be matchmaking, and all at once it turned out quite differently. Possibly against my own will . . ."

She crimsoned and stopped.

"Oh, they feel it directly!" said Dolly.

"But I should be in despair if there were anything serious in it on his side," Anna interrupted her. "And I am certain it will all be forgotten, and Kitty will leave off hating me."

"All the same, Anna, to tell you the truth, I'm not very anxious for this marriage for Kitty. And it's better it should come to nothing, if he, Vronsky, is capable of falling in love with you in a single day."

"Oh, heavens, that would be too silly!" said Anna, and again a deep flush of pleasure came out on her face, when she heard the idea, that absorbed her, put into words. "And so here I am going away, having made an enemy of Kitty, whom I liked so much! Ah, how sweet she is! But you'll make it right, Dolly? Eh?"

Dolly could scarcely suppress a smile. She loved Anna, but she enjoyed seeing that she too had her weaknesses.

"An enemy? That can't be."

"I did so want you all to care for me, as I do for you, and now I care for you more than ever," said Anna, with tears in her eyes. "Ah, how silly I am today!"

She passed her handkerchief over her face and began dressing.

At the very moment of starting Stepan Arkadyevitch arrived, late, rosy and good-humored, smelling of wine and cigars.

Anna's emotionalism infected Dolly, and when she embraced her sister-in-law for the last time, she whispered: "Remember, Anna, what you've done for me—I shall never forget. And remember that I love you, and shall always love you as my dearest friend!"

"I don't know why," said Anna, kissing her and hiding her tears.

"You understood me, and you understand. Good-bye, my darling!"

Chapter XXIX

"COME, IT'S ALL OVER, AND THANK GOD!" WAS THE FIRST THOUGHT THAT CAME TO ANNA Arkadyevna, when she had said good-bye for the last time to her brother, who had stood blocking up the entrance to the carriage till the third bell rang. She sat down on her lounge beside Annushka, and looked about her in the twilight of the sleeping-carriage. "Thank God! tomorrow I shall see Seryozha and Alexey Alexandrovitch, and my life will go on in the old way, all nice and as usual."

Still in the same anxious frame of mind, as she had been all that day, Anna took pleasure in arranging herself for the journey with great care. With her little deft hands she opened and shut her little red bag, took out a cushion, laid it on her knees, and carefully wrapping up her feet, settled herself comfortably. An invalid lady had already lain down to sleep. Two other ladies began talking to Anna, and a stout elderly lady tucked up her feet, and made observations about the heating of the train. Anna answered a few words, but not foreseeing any entertainment from the conversation, she asked Annushka to get a lamp, hooked it onto the arm of her seat, and took from her bag a paper-knife and an English novel. At first her reading made no progress. The fuss and bustle were disturbing; then when the train had started, she could not help listening to the noises; then the snow beating on the left window and sticking to the pane, and the sight of the muffled guard passing by, covered with snow on one side, and the conversations about the terrible snowstorm raging outside, distracted her attention. Farther on, it was continually the same again and again: the same shaking and rattling, the same snow on the window, the same rapid transitions from steaming heat to cold, and back again to heat, the same passing glimpses of the same figures in the twilight, and the same voices, and Anna began to read and to understand what she read. Annushka was already dozing, the red bag on her lap, clutched by her broad hands, in gloves, of which one was torn. Anna Arkadyevna read and understood, but it was distasteful to her to read, that is, to follow the reflection of other people's lives. She had too great a desire to live herself. If she read that the heroine of the novel was nursing a sick man, she longed to move with noiseless steps about the room of a sick man; if she read of a member of Parliament making a speech, she longed to be delivering the speech; if she read of how Lady Mary had ridden after the hounds, and had provoked her sister-in-law, and had surprised everyone by her boldness, she too wished to be doing the same. But there was no chance of doing anything; and twisting the smooth paper-knife in her little hands, she forced herself to read.

The hero of the novel was already almost reaching his English happiness, a baronetcy and an estate, and Anna was feeling a desire to go with him to the estate, when she suddenly felt that *he* ought to feel ashamed, and that she was ashamed of the same thing. But what had he to be ashamed of? "What have I to be ashamed of?" she asked herself in injured surprise. She laid down the book and sank against the back of the chair, tightly gripping the paper-cutter in both hands. There was nothing. She went over all her Moscow recollections. All were good, pleasant. She remembered the ball, remembered Vronsky and his face of slavish adoration, remembered all her conduct with him: there was nothing shameful. And for all that, at the same point in her memories, the feeling of shame was intensified, as though some inner voice, just at the point when she thought of Vronsky, were saying to her, "Warm, very warm, hot." "Well, what is it?" she said to herself resolutely, shifting her seat in the lounge. "What does it mean? Am I afraid to look it straight in the face? Why, what is it? Can it be that between me and this officer boy there exist, or can exist, any other relations than such as are common with every acquaintance?" She laughed contemptuously and took up her book again; but now she was definitely unable to follow what she read. She passed the paper-knife over the window pane, then laid its smooth, cool surface to her cheek, and almost laughed aloud at the feeling of delight that all at once without cause came over her. She felt as though her nerves were strings being strained tighter and tighter on some sort of screwing peg. She felt her eyes opening wider and wider, her fingers and toes twitching nervously, something within oppressing her breathing, while all shapes and sounds seemed in the uncertain half-light to strike her with unaccustomed vividness. Moments of doubt were continually coming upon her, when she was uncertain whether the train were going forwards or backwards, or were standing still altogether; whether it were Annushka at her side or a stranger. "What's that on the arm of the chair, a fur cloak or some beast? And what am I myself? Myself or some other woman?" She was afraid of giving way to this delirium. But something drew her towards it, and she could yield to it or resist it at will. She got up to rouse herself, and slipped off her plaid and the cape of her warm dress. For a moment she regained her self-possession, and realized that the thin peasant who had come in wearing a long overcoat, with buttons missing from it, was the stoveheater, that he was looking at the thermometer, that it was the wind and snow bursting in after him at the door; but then everything grew blurred again. . . . That peasant with the long waist seemed to be gnawing something on the wall, the old lady began stretching her legs the whole length of the carriage, and filling it with a black cloud; then there was a fearful shrieking and banging, as though someone were being torn to pieces; then there was a blinding dazzle of red fire before her eyes and a wall seemed to rise up and hide everything. Anna felt as though she were sinking down. But it was not terrible, but delightful. The voice of a man muffled up and covered with snow shouted something in her ear. She got up and pulled herself together; she realized that they had reached a station and that this was the guard. She asked Annushka to hand her the cape she had taken off and her shawl, put them on and moved towards the door.

"Do you wish to get out?" asked Annushka.

"Yes, I want a little air. It's very hot in here." And she opened the door. The driving snow and the wind rushed to meet her and struggled with her over the door. But she enjoyed the struggle.

She opened the door and went out. The wind seemed as though lying in wait for her; with gleeful whistle it tried to snatch her up and bear her off, but she clung to the cold doorpost, and holding her skirt got down onto the platform and under the shelter of the carriages. The wind had been powerful on the steps, but on the platform, under the lee of the carriages, there was a lull. With enjoyment she drew deep breaths of the frozen, snowy air, and standing near the carriage looked about the platform and the lit station.

Chapter XXX

THE RAGING TEMPEST RUSHED WHISTLING BETWEEN THE WHEELS OF THE CARRIAGES, ABOUT THE scaffolding, and round the corner of the station. The carriages, posts, people, everything that was to be seen was covered with snow on one side, and was getting more and more thickly covered. For a moment there would come a lull in the storm, but then it would swoop down again with such onslaughts that it seemed impossible to stand against it. Meanwhile men ran to and fro, talking merrily together, their steps crackling on the platform as they continually opened and closed the big doors. The bent shadow of a man glided by at her feet, and she heard sounds of a hammer upon iron. "Hand over that telegram!" came an angry voice out of the stormy darkness on the other side. "This way! No. 28!" several different voices shouted again, and muffled figures ran by covered with snow. Two gentlemen with lit cigarettes passed by her. She drew one more deep breath of the fresh air, and had just put her hand out of her muff to take hold of the doorpost and get back into the carriage, when another man in a military overcoat, quite close beside her, stepped between her and the flickering light of the lamp post. She looked round, and the same instant recognized Vronsky's face. Putting his hand to the peak of his cap, he bowed to her and asked, Was there anything she wanted? Could he be of any service to her? She gazed rather a long while at him without answering, and, in spite of the shadow in which he was standing, she saw, or fancied she saw, both the expression of his face and his eyes. It was again that expression of reverential ecstasy which had so worked upon her the day before. More than once she had told herself during the past few days, and again only a few moments before, that Vronsky was for her only one of the hundreds of young men, forever exactly the same, that are met everywhere, that she would never allow herself to bestow a thought upon him. But now at the first instant of meeting him, she was seized by a feeling of joyful pride. She had no need to ask why he had come. She knew as certainly as if he had told her that he was here to be where she was.

"I didn't know you were going. What are you coming for?" she said, letting fall the hand with which she had grasped the doorpost. And irrepressible delight and eagerness shone in her face.

"What am I coming for?" he repeated, looking straight into her eyes. "You know that I have come to be where you are," he said; "I can't help it."

At that moment the wind, as it were, surmounting all obstacles, sent the snow flying from the carriage roofs, and clanked some sheet of iron it had torn off, while the hoarse whistle of the engine roared in front, plaintively and gloomily. All the awfulness of the storm seemed to her more splendid now. He had said what her soul longed to hear, though she feared it with her reason. She made no answer, and in her face he saw conflict.

"Forgive me, if you dislike what I said," he said humbly.

He had spoken courteously, deferentially, yet so firmly, so stubbornly, that for a long while she could make no answer.

"It's wrong, what you say, and I beg you, if you're a good man, to forget what you've said, as I forget it," she said at last.

"Not one word, not one gesture of yours shall I, could I, ever forget. . . ."

"Enough, enough!" she cried trying assiduously to give a stern expression to her face, into which he was gazing greedily. And clutching at the cold doorpost, she clambered up the steps and got rapidly into the corridor of the carriage. But in the little corridor she paused, going over in her imagination what had happened. Though she could not recall her own words or his, she realized instinctively that the momentary conversation had brought them fearfully closer; and she was panic-stricken and blissful at it. After standing still a few seconds, she went into the carriage and sat down in her place. The overstrained condition which had tormented her before did not only come back, but was intensified, and reached such a pitch that she was afraid every minute that something would snap within her from the excessive tension. She did not sleep all night. But in that nervous tension, and in the visions that filled her imagination, there was nothing disagreeable or gloomy: on the contrary there was something blissful, glowing, and exhilarating. Towards morning Anna sank into a doze, sitting in her place, and when she waked it was daylight and the train was near Petersburg. At once thoughts of home, of husband and of son, and the details of that day and the following came upon her.

At Petersburg, as soon as the train stopped and she got out, the first person that attracted her attention was her husband. "Oh, mercy! why do his ears look like that?" she thought, looking at his frigid and imposing figure, and especially the ears that struck her at the moment as propping up the brim of his round hat. Catching sight of her, he came to meet her, his lips falling into their habitual sarcastic smile, and his big, tired eyes looking straight at her. An unpleasant sensation gripped at her heart when she met his obstinate and weary glance, as though she had expected to see him different. She was especially struck by the feeling of dissatisfaction with herself that she experienced on meeting him. That feeling was an intimate, familiar feeling, like a consciousness of hypocrisy, which she experienced in her relations with her husband. But hitherto she had not taken note of the feeling, now she was clearly and painfully aware of it.

"Yes, as you see, your tender spouse, as devoted as the first year after marriage, burned with impatience to see you," he said in his deliberate, high-pitched voice, and in that tone which he almost always took with her, a tone of jeering at anyone who should say in earnest what he said.

"Is Seryozha quite well?" she asked.

"And is this all the reward," said he, "for my ardor? He's quite well. . . ."

Chapter XXXI

VRONSKY HAD NOT EVEN TRIED TO SLEEP ALL THAT NIGHT. HE SAT IN HIS ARM-CHAIR, LOOKING straight before him or scanning the people who got in and out. If he had indeed on previous occasions struck and impressed people who did not know him by his air of unhesitating composure, he seemed now more haughty and self-possessed than ever. He looked at people as if they were things. A nervous young man, a clerk in a law-court, sitting opposite him, hated him for that look. The young man asked him for a light, and entered into conversation with him, and even pushed against him, to make him feel that he was not a thing, but a person. But Vronsky gazed at him exactly as he did at the lamp, and the young man made a wry face, feeling that he was losing his self-possession under the oppression of this refusal to recognize him as a person.

Vronsky saw nothing and no one. He felt himself a king, not because he believed that he had made an impression on Anna—he did not yet believe that—but because the impression she had made on him gave him happiness and pride.

What would come of it all he did not know, he did not even think. He felt that all his forces, hitherto dissipated, wasted, were centered on one thing, and bent with fearful energy on one blissful goal. And he was happy at it. He knew only that he had told her the truth, that he had come where she was, that all the happiness of his life, the only meaning in life for him, now lay in seeing and hearing her. And when he got out of the carriage at Bologova to get some seltzer water, and caught sight of Anna, involuntarily his first word had told her just what he thought. And he was glad he had told her it, that she knew it now and was thinking of it. He did not sleep all night. When he was back in the carriage, he kept unceasingly going over every position in which he had seen her, every word she had uttered, and before his fancy, making his heart faint with emotion, floated pictures of a possible future.

When he got out of the train at Petersburg, he felt after his sleepless night as keen and fresh as after a cold bath. He paused near his compartment, waiting for her to get out. "Once more," he said to himself, smiling unconsciously, "once more I shall see her walk, her face; she will say something, turn her head, glance, smile, maybe." But before he caught sight of her, he saw her husband, whom the stationmaster was deferentially escorting through the crowd. "Ah, yes! The husband." Only now for the first time did Vronsky realize clearly the fact that there was a person attached to her, a husband. He knew that she had a husband, but had hardly believed in his existence, and only now fully believed in him, with his head and shoulders, and his legs clad in black trousers; especially when he saw this husband calmly take her arm with a sense of property.

Seeing Alexey Alexandrovitch with his Petersburg face and severely self-confident figure, in his round hat, with his rather prominent spine, he believed in him, and was aware of a disagreeable sensation, such as a man might feel tortured by thirst, who, on reaching a spring, should find a dog, a sheep, or a pig, who has drunk of it and muddied the water. Alexey Alexandrovitch's manner of walking, with a swing of the hips and flat feet, particularly annoyed Vronsky. He could recognize in no one but himself an indubitable right to love her. But she was still the same, and the sight of her affected him the same way, physically reviving him, stirring him, and filling his soul with rapture. He told his German valet, who ran up to him from the second class, to take his things and go on, and he himself went up to her. He saw the first meeting between the husband and wife, and noted with a lover's insight the signs of slight reserve with which she spoke to her husband. "No, she does not love him and cannot love him," he decided to himself.

At the moment when he was approaching Anna Arkadyevna he noticed too with joy that she was conscious of his being near, and looked round, and seeing him, turned again to her husband.

"Have you passed a good night?" he asked, bowing to her and her husband together, and leaving it up to Alexey Alexandrovitch to accept the bow on his own account, and to recognize it or not, as he might see fit.

"Thank you, very good," she answered.

Her face looked weary, and there was not that play of eagerness in it, peeping out in her smile and her eyes; but for a single instant, as she glanced at him, there was a flash of something in her eyes, and although the flash died away at once, he was happy for that moment. She glanced at her husband to find out whether he knew Vronsky. Alexey Alexandrovitch looked at Vronsky with displeasure, vaguely recalling who this was. Vronsky's composure and self-confidence here struck, like a scythe against a stone, upon the cold self-confidence of Alexey Alexandrovitch.

"Count Vronsky," said Anna.

"Ah! We are acquainted, I believe," said Alexey Alexandrovitch indifferently, giving his hand.

"You set off with the mother and you return with the son," he said, articulating each syllable, as though each were a separate favor he was bestowing.

"You're back from leave, I suppose?" he said, and without waiting for a reply, he turned to his wife in his jesting tone: "Well, were a great many tears shed at Moscow at parting?"

By addressing his wife like this he gave Vronsky to understand that he wished to be left alone, and, turning slightly towards him, he touched his hat; but Vronsky turned to Anna Arkadyevna.

"I hope I may have the honor of calling on you," he said.

Alexey Alexandrovitch glanced with his weary eyes at Vronsky.

"Delighted," he said coldly. "On Mondays we're at home. Most fortunate," he said to his wife, dismissing Vronsky altogether, "that I should just have half an hour to meet you, so that I can prove my devotion," he went on in the same jesting tone.

"You lay too much stress on your devotion for me to value it much," she responded in the same jesting tone, involuntarily listening to the sound of Vronsky's steps behind them. "But what has it to do with me?" she said to herself, and she began asking her husband how Seryozha had got on without her.

"Oh, capitally! Mariette says he has been very good, and . . . I must disappoint you . . . but he has not missed you as your husband has. But once more *merci*, my dear, for giving me a day. Our dear *Samovar* will be delighted." (He used to call the Countess Lidia Ivanovna, well-known in society, a samovar, because she was always bubbling over with excitement.) "She has been continually asking after you. And, do you know, if I may venture to advise you, you should go and see her today. You know how she takes everything to heart. Just now, with all her own cares, she's anxious about the Oblonskys being brought together."

The Countess Lidia Ivanovna was a friend of her husband's, and the center of that one of the coteries of the Petersburg world with which Anna was, through her husband, in the closest relations.

"But you know I wrote to her?"

"Still she'll want to hear details. Go and see her, if you're not too tired, my dear. Well, Kondraty will take you in the carriage, while I go to my committee. I shall not be alone at dinner again," Alexey Alexandrovitch went on, no longer in a sarcastic tone. "You wouldn't believe how I've missed . . ." And with a long pressure of her hand and a meaning smile, he put her in her carriage.

Chapter XXXII

THE FIRST PERSON TO MEET ANNA AT HOME WAS HER SON. HE DASHED DOWN THE STAIRS TO HER, in spite of the governess's call, and with desperate joy shrieked: "Mother! mother!" Running up to her, he hung on her neck.

"I told you it was mother!" he shouted to the governess. "I knew!"

And her son, like her husband, aroused in Anna a feeling akin to disappointment. She had imagined him better than he was in reality. She had to let herself drop down to the reality to enjoy him as he really was. But even as he was, he was charming, with his fair curls, his blue eyes, and his plump, graceful little legs in tightly pulled-up stockings. Anna experienced almost physical pleasure in the sensation of his nearness, and his caresses, and moral soothing, when she met his simple, confiding, and loving glance, and heard his naïve questions. Anna took out the presents Dolly's children had sent him, and told her son what sort of little girl was Tanya at Moscow, and how Tanya could read, and even taught the other children.

"Why, am I not so nice as she?" asked Seryozha.

"To me you're nicer than anyone in the world."

"I know that," said Seryozha, smiling.

Anna had not had time to drink her coffee when the Countess Lidia Ivanovna was announced. The Countess Lidia Ivanovna was a tall, stout woman, with an unhealthily sallow face and splendid, pensive black eyes. Anna liked her, but today she seemed to be seeing her for the first time with all her defects.

"Well, my dear, so you took the olive branch?" inquired Countess Lidia Ivanovna, as soon as she came into the room.

"Yes, it's all over, but it was all much less serious than we had supposed," answered Anna. "My *belle-soeur* is in general too hasty."

But Countess Lidia Ivanovna, though she was interested in everything that did not concern her, had a habit of never listening to what interested her; she interrupted Anna:

"Yes, there's plenty of sorrow and evil in the world. I am so worried today."

"Oh, why?" asked Anna, trying to suppress a smile.

"I'm beginning to be weary of fruitlessly championing the truth, and sometimes I'm quite unhinged by it. The Society of the Little Sisters" (this was a religiously-patriotic, philanthropic institution) "was going splendidly, but with these gentlemen it's impossible to do anything," added Countess Lidia Ivanovna in a tone of ironical submission to destiny. "They pounce on the idea, and distort it, and then work it out so pettily and unworthily. Two or three people, your husband among them, understand all the importance of the thing, but the others simply drag it down. Yesterday Pravdin wrote to me . . ."

Pravdin was a well-known Panslavist abroad, and Countess Lidia Ivanovna described the purport of his letter.

Then the countess told her of more disagreements and intrigues against the work of the unification of the churches, and departed in haste, as she had that day to be at the meeting of some society and also at the Slavonic committee.

"It was all the same before, of course; but why was it I didn't notice it before?" Anna asked herself. "Or has she been very much irritated today? It's really ludicrous; her object is doing good; she a Christian, yet she's always angry; and she always has enemies, and always enemies in the name of Christianity and doing good."

After Countess Lidia Ivanovna another friend came, the wife of a chief secretary, who told her all the news of the town. At three o'clock she too went away, promising to come to dinner. Alexey

Alexandrovitch was at the ministry. Anna, left alone, spent the time till dinner in assisting at her son's dinner (he dined apart from his parents) and in putting her things in order, and in reading and answering the notes and letters which had accumulated on her table.

The feeling of causeless shame, which she had felt on the journey, and her excitement, too, had completely vanished. In the habitual conditions of her life she felt again resolute and irreproachable.

She recalled with wonder her state of mind on the previous day. "What was it? Nothing. Vronsky said something silly, which it was easy to put a stop to, and I answered as I ought to have done. To speak of it to my husband would be unnecessary and out of the question. To speak of it would be to attach importance to what has no importance." She remembered how she had told her husband of what was almost a declaration made her at Petersburg by a young man, one of her husband's subordinates, and how Alexey Alexandrovitch had answered that every woman living in the world was exposed to such incidents, but that he had the fullest confidence in her tact, and could never lower her and himself by jealousy. "So then there's no reason to speak of it? And indeed, thank God, there's nothing to speak of," she told herself.

Chapter XXXIII

ALEXEY ALEXANDROVITCH CAME BACK FROM THE MEETING OF THE MINISTERS AT FOUR O'CLOCK, but as often happened, he had not time to come in to her. He went into his study to see the people waiting for him with petitions, and to sign some papers brought him by his chief secretary. At dinnertime (there were always a few people dining with the Karenins) there arrived an old lady, a cousin of Alexey Alexandrovitch, the chief secretary of the department and his wife, and a young man who had been recommended to Alexey Alexandrovitch for the service. Anna went into the drawing room to receive these guests. Precisely at five o'clock, before the bronze Peter the First clock had struck the fifth stroke, Alexey Alexandrovitch came in, wearing a white tie and evening-coat with two stars, as he had to go out directly after dinner. Every minute of Alexey Alexandrovitch's life was portioned out and occupied. And to make time to get through all that lay before him everyday, he adhered to the strictest punctuality. "Unhasting and unresting," was his motto. He came into the dining hall, greeted everyone, and hurriedly sat down, smiling to his wife.

"Yes, my solitude is over. You wouldn't believe how uncomfortable" (he laid stress on the word *uncomfortable*) "it is to dine alone."

At dinner he talked a little to his wife about Moscow matters, and, with a sarcastic smile, asked her after Stepan Arkadyevitch; but the conversation was for the most part general, dealing with Petersburg official and public news. After dinner he spent half an hour with his guests, and again, with a smile, pressed his wife's hand, withdrew, and drove off to the council. Anna did not go out that evening either to the Princess Betsy Tverskaya, who, hearing of her return, had invited her, nor to the theater, where she had a box for that evening. She did not go out principally because the dress she had reckoned upon was not ready. Altogether, Anna, on turning, after the departure of her guests, to the consideration of her attire, was very much annoyed. She was generally a mistress of the art of dressing well without great expense, and before leaving Moscow she had given her dressmaker three dresses to transform. The dresses had to be altered so that they could not be recognized, and they ought to have been ready three days before. It appeared that two dresses had not been done at all, while the other one had not been altered as Anna had intended. The dressmaker came to explain, declaring that it would be better as she had done it, and Anna was so furious that she felt ashamed when she thought of it afterwards. To regain her serenity completely she went into the nursery, and spent the whole evening with her son, put him to bed herself, signed him with the cross, and tucked him up. She was glad she had not gone out anywhere, and had spent the evening so well. She felt so light-hearted and serene, she saw so clearly that all that had seemed to her so important on her railway journey was only one of the common trivial incidents of fashionable life, and that she had no reason to feel ashamed before anyone else or before herself. Anna sat down at the hearth with an English novel and waited for her husband. Exactly at half-past nine she heard his ring, and he came into the room.

"Here you are at last!" she observed, holding out her hand to him.

He kissed her hand and sat down beside her.

"Altogether then, I see your visit was a success," he said to her.

"Oh, yes," she said, and she began telling him about everything from the beginning: her journey with Countess Vronskaya, her arrival, the accident at the station. Then she described the pity she had felt, first for her brother, and afterwards for Dolly.

"I imagine one cannot exonerate such a man from blame, though he is your brother," said Alexey Alexandrovitch severely.

Anna smiled. She knew that he said that simply to show that family considerations could not prevent him from expressing his genuine opinion. She knew that characteristic in her husband, and liked it.

"I am glad it has all ended so satisfactorily, and that you are back again," he went on. "Come, what do they say about the new act I have got passed in the council?"

Anna had heard nothing of this act, And she felt conscience-stricken at having been able so readily to forget what was to him of such importance.

"Here, on the other hand, it has made a great sensation," he said, with a complacent smile.

She saw that Alexey Alexandrovitch wanted to tell her something pleasant to him about it, and she brought him by questions to telling it. With the same complacent smile he told her of the ovations he had received in consequence of the act he had passed.

"I was very, very glad. It shows that at last a reasonable and steady view of the matter is becoming prevalent among us."

Having drunk his second cup of tea with cream, and bread, Alexey Alexandrovitch got up, and was going towards his study.

"And you've not been anywhere this evening? You've been dull, I expect?" he said.

"Oh, no!" she answered, getting up after him and accompanying him across the room to his study. "What are you reading now?" she asked.

"Just now I'm reading Duc de Lille, *Poésie des Enfers,*" he answered. "A very remarkable book."

Anna smiled, as people smile at the weaknesses of those they love, and, putting her hand under his, she escorted him to the door of the study. She knew his habit, that had grown into a necessity, of reading in the evening. She knew, too, that in spite of his official duties, which swallowed up almost the whole of his time, he considered it his duty to keep up with everything of note that appeared in the intellectual world. She knew, too, that he was really interested in books dealing with politics, philosophy, and theology, that art was utterly foreign to his nature; but, in spite of this, or rather, in consequence of it, Alexey Alexandrovitch never passed over anything in the world of art, but made it his duty to read everything. She knew that in politics, in philosophy, in theology, Alexey Alexandrovitch often had doubts, and made investigations; but on questions of art and poetry, and, above all, of music, of which he was totally devoid of understanding, he had the most distinct and decided opinions. He was fond of talking about Shakespeare, Raphael, Beethoven, of the significance of new schools of poetry and music, all of which were classified by him with very conspicuous consistency.

"Well, God be with you," she said at the door of the study, where a shaded candle and a decanter of water were already put by his arm-chair. "And I'll write to Moscow."

He pressed her hand, and again kissed it.

"All the same he's a good man; truthful, good-hearted, and remarkable in his own line," Anna said to herself going back to her room, as though she were defending him to someone who had attacked him and said that one could not love him. "But why is it his ears stick out so strangely? Or has he had his hair cut?"

Precisely at twelve o'clock, when Anna was still sitting at her writing-table, finishing a letter to Dolly, she heard the sound of measured steps in slippers, and Alexey Alexandrovitch, freshly washed and combed, with a book under his arm, came in to her.

"It's time, it's time," said he, with a meaning smile, and he went into their bedroom.

"And what right had he to look at him like that?" thought Anna, recalling Vronsky's glance at Alexey Alexandrovitch.

Undressing, she went into the bedroom; but her face had none of the eagerness which, during her stay in Moscow, had fairly flashed from her eyes and her smile; on the contrary, now the fire seemed quenched in her, hidden somewhere far away.

Chapter XXXIV

WHEN VRONSKY WENT TO MOSCOW FROM PETERSBURG, HE HAD LEFT HIS LARGE SET OF ROOMS in Morskaia to his friend and favorite comrade Petritsky.

Petritsky was a young lieutenant, not particularly well-connected, and not merely not wealthy, but always hopelessly in debt. Towards evening he was always drunk, and he had often been locked up after all sorts of ludicrous and disgraceful scandals, but he was a favorite both of his comrades and his superior officers. On arriving at twelve o'clock from the station at his flat, Vronsky saw, at the outer door, a hired carriage familiar to him. While still outside his own door, as he rang, he heard masculine laughter, the lisp of a feminine voice, and Petritsky's voice. "If that's one of the villains, don't let him in!" Vronsky told the servant not to announce him, and slipped quietly into the first room, Baroness Shilton, a friend of Petritsky's, with a rosy little face and flaxen hair, resplendent in a lilac satin gown, and filling the whole room, like a canary, with her Parisian chatter, sat at the round table making coffee. Petritsky, in his overcoat, and the cavalry captain Kamerovsky, in full uniform, probably just come from duty, were sitting each side of her.

"Bravo! Vronsky!" shouted Petritsky, jumping up, scraping his chair. "Our host himself! Baroness, some coffee for him out of the new coffee pot. Why, we didn't expect you! Hope you're satisfied with the ornament of your study," he said, indicating the baroness. "You know each other, of course?"

"I should think so," said Vronsky, with a bright smile, pressing the baroness's little hand. "What next! I'm an old friend."

"You're home after a journey," said the baroness, "so I'm flying. Oh, I'll be off this minute, if I'm in the way."

"You're home, wherever you are, baroness," said Vronsky. "How do you do, Kamerovsky?" he added, coldly shaking hands with Kamerovsky.

"There, you never know how to say such pretty things," said the baroness, turning to Petritsky.

"No; what's that for? After dinner I say things quite as good."

"After dinner there's no credit in them! Well, then, I'll make you some coffee, so go and wash and get ready," said the baroness, sitting down again, and anxiously turning the screw in the new coffee pot. "Pierre, give me the coffee," she said, addressing Petritsky, whom she called Pierre as a contraction of his surname, making no secret of her relations with him. "I'll put it in."

"You'll spoil it!"

"No, I won't spoil it! Well, and your wife?" said the baroness suddenly, interrupting Vronsky's conversation with his comrade. "We've been marrying you here. Have you brought your wife?"

"No, baroness. I was born a Bohemian, and a Bohemian I shall die."

"So much the better, so much the better. Shake hands on it."

And the baroness, detaining Vronsky, began telling him, with many jokes, about her last new plans of life, asking his advice.

"He persists in refusing to give me a divorce! Well, what am I to do?" (*He* was her husband.) "Now I want to begin a suit against him. What do you advise? Kamerovsky, look after the coffee; it's boiling over. You see, I'm engrossed with business! I want a lawsuit, because I must have my property. Do you understand the folly of it, that on the pretext of my being unfaithful to him," she said contemptuously, "he wants to get the benefit of my fortune."

Vronsky heard with pleasure this light-hearted prattle of a pretty woman, agreed with her, gave her half-joking counsel, and altogether dropped at once into the tone habitual to him in talking to such women. In his Petersburg world all people were divided into utterly opposed classes. One, the lower class, vulgar, stupid, and, above all, ridiculous people, who believe that one husband ought to live with the one wife whom he has lawfully married; that a girl should be innocent, a woman modest, and a man manly, self-controlled, and strong; that one ought to bring up one's children, earn one's bread, and pay one's debts; and various similar absurdities. This was the class of old-fashioned and ridiculous people. But there was another class of people, the real people. To this class they all belonged, and in it the great thing was to be elegant, generous, plucky, gay, to abandon oneself without a blush to every passion, and to laugh at everything else.

For the first moment only, Vronsky was startled after the impressions of a quite different world that he had brought with him from Moscow. But immediately as though slipping his feet into old slippers, he dropped back into the light-hearted, pleasant world he had always lived in.

The coffee was never really made, but spluttered over everyone, and boiled away, doing just what was required of it—that is, providing cause for much noise and laughter, and spoiling a costly rug and the baroness's gown.

"Well now, good-bye, or you'll never get washed, and I shall have on my conscience the worst sin a gentleman can commit. So you would advise a knife to his throat?"

"To be sure, and manage that your hand may not be far from his lips. He'll kiss your hand, and all will end satisfactorily," answered Vronsky.

"So at the Français!" and, with a rustle of her skirts, she vanished.

Kamerovsky got up too, and Vronsky, not waiting for him to go, shook hands and went off to his dressing room.

While he was washing, Petritsky described to him in brief outlines his position, as far as it had changed since Vronsky had left Petersburg. No money at all. His father said he wouldn't give him any and pay his debts. His tailor was trying to get him locked up, and another fellow, too, was threatening to get him locked up. The colonel of the regiment had announced that if these scandals did not cease he would have to leave. As for the baroness, he was sick to death of her, especially since she'd taken to offering continually to lend him money. But he had found a girl—he'd show her to Vronsky—a marvel, exquisite, in the strict Oriental style, "genre of the slave Rebecca, don't you know." He'd had a row, too, with Berkoshov, and was going to send seconds to him, but of course it would come to nothing. Altogether everything was supremely amusing and jolly. And, not letting his comrade enter into further details of his position, Petritsky proceeded to tell him all the interesting news. As he listened to Petritsky's familiar stories in the familiar setting of the rooms he had spent the last three years in, Vronsky felt a delightful sense of coming back to the careless Petersburg life that he was used to.

"Impossible!" he cried, letting down the pedal of the washing basin in which he had been sousing his healthy red neck. "Impossible!" he cried, at the news that Laura had flung over Fertinghof and had made up to Mileev. "And is he as stupid and pleased as ever? Well, and how's Buzulukov?"

"Oh, there is a tale about Buzulukov—simply lovely!" cried Petritsky. "You know his weakness for balls, and he never misses a single court ball. He went to a big ball in a new helmet. Have you seen the new helmets? Very nice, lighter. Well, so he's standing . . . No, I say, do listen."

"I am listening," answered Vronsky, rubbing himself with a rough towel.

"Up comes the Grand-Duchess with some ambassador or other, and, as ill-luck would have it, she begins talking to him about the new helmets. The Grand-Duchess positively wanted to show the new helmet to the ambassador. They see our friend standing there." (Petritsky mimicked how he was standing with the helmet.) "The Grand-Duchess asked him to give her the helmet; he doesn't give it to her. What do you think of that? Well, everyone's winking at him, nodding, frowning—give it to her, do! He doesn't give it to her. He's mute as a fish. Only picture it! . . . Well, the . . . what's his name, whatever he was . . . tries to take the helmet from him . . . he won't give it up! . . . He pulls it from him, and hands it to the Grand-Duchess. 'Here, your Highness,' says he, 'is the new helmet.' She turned the helmet the other side up, and—just picture it!—plop went a pear and sweetmeats out of it, two pounds of sweetmeats! . . . He'd been storing them up, the darling!"

Vronsky burst into roars of laughter. And long afterwards, when he was talking of other things, he broke out into his healthy laugh, showing his strong, close rows of teeth, when he thought of the helmet.

Having heard all the news, Vronsky, with the assistance of his valet, got into his uniform, and went off to report himself. He intended, when he had done that, to drive to his brother's, and to Betsy's and to pay several visits with a view to beginning to go into that society where he might meet Madame Karenina. As he always did in Petersburg, he left home not meaning to return till late at night.

Part Two

Chapter I

At the end of the winter, in the Shtcherbatskys' house, a consultation was being held, which was to pronounce on the state of Kitty's health and the measures to be taken to restore her failing strength. She had been ill, and as spring came on she grew worse. The family doctor gave her cod-liver oil, then iron, then nitrate of silver, but as the first and the second and the third were alike in doing no good, and as his advice when spring came was to go abroad, a celebrated physician was called in. The celebrated physician, a very handsome man, still youngish, asked to examine the patient. He maintained, with peculiar satisfaction, it seemed, that maiden modesty is a mere relic of barbarism, and that nothing could be more natural than for a man still youngish to handle a young girl naked. He thought it natural because he did it everyday, and felt and thought, as it seemed to him, no harm as he did it and consequently he considered modesty in the girl not merely as a relic of barbarism, but also as an insult to himself.

There was nothing for it but to submit, since, although all the doctors had studied in the same school, had read the same books, and learned the same science, and though some people said this celebrated doctor was a bad doctor, in the princess's household and circle it was for some reason accepted that this celebrated doctor alone had some special knowledge, and that he alone could save Kitty. After a careful examination and sounding of the bewildered patient, dazed with shame, the celebrated doctor, having scrupulously washed his hands, was standing in the drawing room talking to the prince. The prince frowned and coughed, listening to the doctor. As a man who had seen something of life, and neither a fool nor an invalid, he had no faith in medicine, and in his heart was furious at the whole farce, specially as he was perhaps the only one who fully comprehended the cause of Kitty's illness. "Conceited blockhead!" he thought, as he listened to the celebrated doctor's chatter about his daughter's symptoms. The doctor was meantime with difficulty restraining the expression of his contempt for this old gentleman, and with difficulty condescending to the level of his intelligence. He perceived that it was no good talking to the old man, and that the principal person in the house was the mother. Before her he decided to scatter his pearls. At that instant the princess came into the drawing room with the family doctor. The prince withdrew, trying not to show how ridiculous he thought the whole performance. The princess was distracted, and did not know what to do. She felt she had sinned against Kitty.

"Well, doctor, decide our fate," said the princess. "Tell me everything."

"Is there hope?" she meant to say, but her lips quivered, and she could not utter the question. "Well, doctor?"

"Immediately, princess. I will talk it over with my colleague, and then I will have the honor of laying my opinion before you."

"So we had better leave you?"

"As you please."

The princess went out with a sigh.

When the doctors were left alone, the family doctor began timidly explaining his opinion, that there was a commencement of tuberculous trouble, but . . . and so on. The celebrated doctor listened to him, and in the middle of his sentence looked at his big gold watch.

"Yes," said he. "But . . ."

The family doctor respectfully ceased in the middle of his observations.

"The commencement of the tuberculous process we are not, as you are aware, able to define; till there are cavities, there is nothing definite. But we may suspect it. And there are indications; malnutrition, nervous excitability, and so on. The question stands thus: in presence of indications of tuberculous process, what is to be done to maintain nutrition?"

"But, you know, there are always moral, spiritual causes at the back in these cases," the family doctor permitted himself to interpolate with a subtle smile.

"Yes, that's an understood thing," responded the celebrated physician, again glancing at his watch. "Beg pardon, is the Yausky bridge done yet, or shall I have to drive around?" he asked. "Ah! it is. Oh, well, then I can do it in twenty minutes. So we were saying the problem may be put thus: to maintain nutrition and to give tone to the nerves. The one is in close connection with the other, one must attack both sides at once."

"And how about a tour abroad?" asked the family doctor.

"I've no liking for foreign tours. And take note: if there is an early stage of tuberculous process, of which we cannot be certain, a foreign tour will be of no use. What is wanted is means of improving nutrition, and not for lowering it." And the celebrated doctor expounded his plan of treatment with Soden waters, a remedy obviously prescribed primarily on the ground that they could do no harm.

The family doctor listened attentively and respectfully.

"But in favor of foreign travel I would urge the change of habits, the removal from conditions calling up reminiscences. And then the mother wishes it," he added.

"Ah! Well, in that case, to be sure, let them go. Only, those German quacks are mischievous. . . . They ought to be persuaded. . . . Well, let them go then."

He glanced once more at his watch.

"Oh! time's up already," and he went to the door. The celebrated doctor announced to the princess (a feeling of what was due from him dictated his doing so) that he ought to see the patient once more.

"What! another examination!" cried the mother, with horror.

"Oh, no, only a few details, princess."

"Come this way."

And the mother, accompanied by the doctor, went into the drawing room to Kitty. Wasted and flushed, with a peculiar glitter in her eyes, left there by the agony of shame she had been put through, Kitty stood in the middle of the room. When the doctor came in she flushed crimson, and her eyes filled with tears. All her illness and treatment struck her as a thing so stupid, ludicrous even! Doctoring her seemed to her as absurd as putting together the pieces of a broken vase. Her heart was broken. Why would they try to cure her with pills and powders? But she could not grieve her mother, especially as her mother considered herself to blame.

"May I trouble you to sit down, princess?" the celebrated doctor said to her.

He sat down with a smile, facing her, felt her pulse, and again began asking her tiresome questions. She answered him, and all at once got up, furious.

"Excuse me, doctor, but there is really no object in this. This is the third time you've asked me the same thing."

The celebrated doctor did not take offense.

"Nervous irritability," he said to the princess, when Kitty had left the room. "However, I had finished. . . ."

And the doctor began scientifically explaining to the princess, as an exceptionally intelligent woman, the condition of the young princess, and concluded by insisting on the drinking of the waters, which were certainly harmless. At the question: Should they go abroad? the doctor plunged into deep meditation, as though resolving a weighty problem. Finally his decision was pronounced: they were to go abroad, but to put no faith in foreign quacks, and to apply to him in any need.

It seemed as though some piece of good fortune had come to pass after the doctor had gone. The mother was much more cheerful when she went back to her daughter, and Kitty pretended to be more cheerful. She had often, almost always, to be pretending now.

"Really, I'm quite well, mamma. But if you want to go abroad, let's go!" she said, and trying to appear interested in the proposed tour, she began talking of the preparations for the journey.

Chapter II

SOON AFTER THE DOCTOR, DOLLY HAD ARRIVED. SHE KNEW THAT THERE WAS TO BE A CONSULTAtion that day, and though she was only just up after her confinement (she had another baby, a little girl, born at the end of the winter), though she had trouble and anxiety enough of her own, she had left her tiny baby and a sick child, to come and hear Kitty's fate, which was to be decided that day.

"Well, well?" she said, coming into the drawing room, without taking off her hat. "You're all in good spirits. Good news, then?"

They tried to tell her what the doctor had said, but it appeared that though the doctor had talked distinctly enough and at great length, it was utterly impossible to report what he had said. The only point of interest was that it was settled they should go abroad.

Dolly could not help sighing. Her dearest friend, her sister, was going away. And her life was not a cheerful one. Her relations with Stepan Arkadyevitch after their reconciliation had become humiliating. The union Anna had cemented turned out to be of no solid character, and family harmony was breaking down again at the same point. There had been nothing definite, but Stepan Arkadyevitch was hardly ever at home; money, too, was hardly ever forthcoming, and Dolly was continually tortured by suspicions of infidelity, which she tried to dismiss, dreading the agonies of jealousy she had been through already. The first onslaught of jealousy, once lived through, could never come back again, and even the discovery of infidelities could never now affect her as it had the first time. Such a discovery now would only mean breaking up family habits, and she let herself be deceived, despising him and still more herself, for the weakness. Besides this, the care of her large family was a constant worry to her: first, the nursing of her young baby did not go well, then the nurse had gone away, now one of the children had fallen ill.

"Well, how are all of you?" asked her mother.

"Ah, mamma, we have plenty of troubles of our own. Lili is ill, and I'm afraid it's scarlatina. I have come here now to hear about Kitty, and then I shall shut myself up entirely, if—God forbid—it should be scarlatina."

The old prince too had come in from his study after the doctor's departure, and after presenting his cheek to Dolly, and saying a few words to her, he turned to his wife:

"How have you settled it? you're going? Well, and what do you mean to do with me?"

"I suppose you had better stay here, Alexander," said his wife.

"That's as you like."

"Mamma, why shouldn't father come with us?" said Kitty. "It would be nicer for him and for us as well."

The old prince got up and stroked Kitty's hair. She lifted her head and looked at him with a forced smile. It always seemed to her that he understood her better than anyone in the family, though he did not say much about her.

Being the youngest, she was her father's favorite, and she fancied that his love gave him insight. When now her glance met his blue kindly eyes looking intently at her, it seemed to her that he saw right through her, and understood all that was not good that was passing within her. Reddening, she stretched out towards him expecting a kiss, but he only patted her hair and said:

"These stupid chignons! There's no getting at the real daughter. One simply strokes the bristles of dead women. Well, Dolinka," he turned to his elder daughter, "what's your young buck about, hey?"

"Nothing, father," answered Dolly, understanding that her husband was meant. "He's always out; I scarcely ever see him," she could not resist adding with a sarcastic smile.

"Why, hasn't he gone into the country yet—to see about selling that forest?"

"No, he's still getting ready for the journey."

"Oh, that's it!" said the prince. "And so am I to be getting ready for a journey too? At your service," he said to his wife, sitting down. "And I tell you what, Katia," he went on to his younger daughter, "you must wake up one fine day and say to yourself: Why, I'm quite well, and merry, and going out again with father for an early morning walk in the frost. Hey?"

What her father said seemed simple enough, yet at these words Kitty became confused and overcome like a detected criminal. "Yes, he sees it all, he understands it all, and in these words he's telling me that though I'm ashamed, I must get over my shame." She could not pluck up spirit to make any answer. She tried to begin, and all at once burst into tears, and rushed out of the room.

"See what comes of your jokes!" the princess pounced down on her husband. "You're always . . ." she began a string of reproaches.

The prince listened to the princess's scolding rather a long while without speaking, but his face was more and more frowning.

"She's so much to be pitied, poor child, so much to be pitied, and you don't feel how it hurts her to hear the slightest reference to the cause of it. Ah! to be so mistaken in people!" said the princess, and by the change in her tone both Dolly and the prince knew she was speaking of Vronsky. "I don't know why there aren't laws against such base, dishonorable people."

"Ah, I can't bear to hear you!" said the prince gloomily, getting up from his low chair, and seeming anxious to get away, yet stopping in the doorway. "There are laws, madam, and since you've challenged me to it, I'll tell you who's to blame for it all: you and you, you and nobody else. Laws against such young gallants there have always been, and there still are! Yes, if there has been nothing that ought not to have been, old as I am, I'd have called him out to the barrier, the young dandy. Yes, and now you physic her and call in these quacks."

The prince apparently had plenty more to say, but as soon as the princess heard his tone she subsided at once, and became penitent, as she always did on serious occasions.

"Alexander, Alexander," she whispered, moving to him and beginning to weep.

As soon as she began to cry the prince too calmed down. He went up to her.

"There, that's enough, that's enough! You're wretched too, I know. It can't be helped. There's no great harm done. God is merciful . . . thanks . . ." he said, not knowing what he was saying, as he responded to the tearful kiss of the princess that he felt on his hand. And the prince went out of the room.

Before this, as soon as Kitty went out of the room in tears, Dolly, with her motherly, family instincts, had promptly perceived that here a woman's work lay before her, and she prepared to do it. She took off her hat, and, morally speaking, tucked up her sleeves and prepared for action. While her mother was attacking her father, she tried to restrain her mother, so far as filial reverence would allow. During the prince's outburst she was silent; she felt ashamed for her mother, and tender towards her father for so quickly being kind again. But when her father left them she made ready for what was the chief thing needful—to go to Kitty and console her.

"I'd been meaning to tell you something for a long while, mamma: did you know that Levin meant to make Kitty an offer when he was here the last time? He told Stiva so."

"Well, what then? I don't understand . . ."

"So did Kitty perhaps refuse him? . . . She didn't tell you so?"

"No, she has said nothing to me either of one or the other; she's too proud. But I know it's all on account of the other."

"Yes, but suppose she has refused Levin, and she wouldn't have refused him if it hadn't been for the other, I know. And then, he has deceived her so horribly."

It was too terrible for the princess to think how she had sinned against her daughter, and she broke out angrily.

"Oh, I really don't understand! Nowadays they will all go their own way, and mothers haven't a word to say in anything, and then . . ."

"Mamma, I'll go up to her."

"Well, do. Did I tell you not to?" said her mother.

Chapter III

WHEN SHE WENT INTO KITTY'S LITTLE ROOM, A PRETTY, PINK LITTLE ROOM, FULL OF KNICK-knacks in *vieux saxe,* as fresh, and pink, and white, and gay as Kitty herself had been two months ago, Dolly remembered how they had decorated the room the year before together, with what love and gaiety. Her heart turned cold when she saw Kitty sitting on a low chair near the door, her eyes fixed immovably on a corner of the rug. Kitty glanced at her sister, and the cold, rather ill-tempered expression of her face did not change.

"I'm just going now, and I shall have to keep in and you won't be able to come to see me," said Dolly, sitting down beside her. "I want to talk to you."

"What about?" Kitty asked swiftly, lifting her head in dismay.

"What should it be, but your trouble?"

"I have no trouble."

"Nonsense, Kitty. Do you suppose I could help knowing? I know all about it. And believe me, it's of so little consequence. . . . We've all been through it."

Kitty did not speak, and her face had a stern expression.

"He's not worth your grieving over him," pursued Darya Alexandrovna, coming straight to the point.

"No, because he has treated me with contempt," said Kitty, in a breaking voice. "Don't talk of it! Please, don't talk of it!"

"But who can have told you so? No one has said that. I'm certain he was in love with you, and would still be in love with you, if it hadn't . . ."

"Oh, the most awful thing of all for me is this sympathizing!" shrieked Kitty, suddenly flying into a passion. She turned round on her chair, flushed crimson, and rapidly moving her fingers, pinched the clasp of her belt first with one hand and then with the other. Dolly knew this trick her sister had of clenching her hands when she was much excited; she knew, too, that in moments of excitement Kitty was capable of forgetting herself and saying a great deal too much, and Dolly would have soothed her, but it was too late.

"What, what is it you want to make me feel, eh?" said Kitty quickly. "That I've been in love with a man who didn't care a straw for me, and that I'm dying of love for him? And this is said to me by my own sister, who imagines that . . . that . . . that she's sympathizing with me! . . . I don't want these condolences and this humbug!"

"Kitty, you're unjust."

"Why are you tormenting me?"

"But I . . . quite the contrary . . . I see you're unhappy. . . ."

But Kitty in her fury did not hear her.

"I've nothing to grieve over and be comforted about. I am too proud ever to allow myself to care for a man who does not love me."

"Yes, I don't say so either. . . . Only one thing. Tell me the truth," said Darya Alexandrovna, taking her by the hand: "tell me, did Levin speak to you? . . ."

The mention of Levin's name seemed to deprive Kitty of the last vestige of self-control. She leaped up from her chair, and flinging her clasp on the ground, she gesticulated rapidly with her hands and said:

"Why bring Levin in too? I can't understand what you want to torment me for. I've told you, and I say it again, that I have some pride, and never, *never* would I do as you're doing—go back to a man who's deceived you, who has cared for another woman. I can't understand it! You may, but I can't!"

And saying these words she glanced at her sister, and seeing that Dolly sat silent, her head mournfully bowed, Kitty, instead of running out of the room as she had meant to do, sat down near the door, and hid her face in her handkerchief.

The silence lasted for two minutes: Dolly was thinking of herself. That humiliation of which she was always conscious came back to her with a peculiar bitterness when her sister reminded her of it. She had not looked for such cruelty in her sister, and she was angry with her. But suddenly she heard the rustle of a skirt, and with it the sound of heart-rending, smothered sobbing, and felt arms about her neck. Kitty was on her knees before her.

"Dolinka, I am so, so wretched!" she whispered penitently. And the sweet face covered with tears hid itself in Darya Alexandrovna's skirt.

As though tears were the indispensable oil, without which the machinery of mutual confidence could not run smoothly between the two sisters, the sisters after their tears talked, not of what was uppermost in their minds, but, though they talked of outside matters, they understood each other. Kitty knew that the words she had uttered in anger about her husband's infidelity and her humiliating position had cut her poor sister to the heart, but that she had forgiven her. Dolly for her part knew all she had wanted to find out. She felt certain that her surmises were correct; that Kitty's misery, her inconsolable misery, was due precisely to the fact that Levin had made her an offer and she had refused him, and Vronsky had deceived her, and that she was fully prepared to love Levin and to detest Vronsky. Kitty said not a word of that; she talked of nothing but her spiritual condition.

"I have nothing to make me miserable," she said, getting calmer; "but can you understand that everything has become hateful, loathsome, coarse to me, and I myself most of all? You can't imagine what loathsome thoughts I have about everything."

"Why, whatever loathsome thoughts can you have?" asked Dolly, smiling.

"The most utterly loathsome and coarse: I can't tell you. It's not unhappiness, or low spirits, but much worse. As though everything that was good in me was all hidden away, and nothing was left but the most loathsome. Come, how am I to tell you?" she went on, seeing the puzzled look in her sister's eyes. "Father began saying something to me just now. . . . It seems to me he thinks all I want is to be married. Mother takes me to a ball: it seems to me she only takes me to get me married off as soon as may be, and be rid of me. I know it's not the truth, but I can't drive away such thoughts. Eligible suitors, as they call them—I can't bear to see them. It seems to me they're taking stock of me and summing me up. In old days to go anywhere in a ball dress was a simple joy to me, I admired myself; now I feel ashamed and awkward. And then! The doctor . . . Then . . ." Kitty hesitated; she wanted to say further that ever since this change had taken place in her, Stepan Arkadyevitch had become insufferably repulsive to her, and that she could not see him without the grossest and most hideous conceptions rising before her imagination.

"Oh, well, everything presents itself to me, in the coarsest, most loathsome light," she went on. "That's my illness. Perhaps it will pass off."

"But you mustn't think about it."

"I can't help it. I'm never happy except with the children at your house."

"What a pity you can't be with me!"

"Oh, yes, I'm coming. I've had scarlatina, and I'll persuade mamma to let me."

Kitty insisted on having her way, and went to stay at her sister's and nursed the children all through the scarlatina, for scarlatina it turned out to be. The two sisters brought all the six children successfully through it, but Kitty was no better in health, and in Lent the Shtcherbatskys went abroad.

Chapter IV

THE HIGHEST PETERSBURG SOCIETY IS ESSENTIALLY ONE: IN IT EVERYONE KNOWS EVERYONE ELSE, everyone even visits everyone else. But this great set has its subdivisions. Anna Arkadyevna Karenina had friends and close ties in three different circles of this highest society. One circle was her husband's government official set, consisting of his colleagues and subordinates, brought together in the most various and capricious manner, and belonging to different social strata. Anna found it difficult now to recall the feeling of almost awe-stricken reverence which she had at first entertained for these persons. Now she knew all of them as people know one another in a country town; she knew their habits and weaknesses, and where the shoe pinched each one of them. She knew their relations with one another and with the head authorities, knew who was for whom, and how each one maintained his position, and where they agreed and disagreed. But that circle of political, masculine interests had never interested her, in spite of Countess Lidia Ivanovna's influence, and she avoided it.

Another little set with which Anna was in close relations was the one by means of which Alexey Alexandrovitch had made his career. The center of this circle was the Countess Lidia Ivanovna. It was a set made up of elderly, ugly, benevolent, and godly women, and clever, learned, and ambitious men. One of the clever people belonging to the set had called it "the conscience of Petersburg society." Alexey Alexandrovitch had the highest esteem for this circle, and Anna with her special gift for getting on with everyone, had in the early days of her life in Petersburg made friends in this circle also. Now, since her return from Moscow, she had come to feel this set insufferable. It seemed to her that both she and all of them were insincere, and she felt so bored and ill at ease in that world that she went to see the Countess Lidia Ivanovna as little as possible.

The third circle with which Anna had ties was pre-eminently the fashionable world—the world of balls, of dinners, of sumptuous dresses, the world that hung on to the court with one hand, so as to avoid sinking to the level of the demi-monde. For the demi-monde the members of that fashionable world believed that they despised, though their tastes were not merely similar, but in fact identical. Her connection with this circle was kept up through Princess Betsy Tverskaya, her cousin's wife, who had an income of a hundred and twenty thousand roubles, and who had taken a great fancy to Anna ever since she first came out, showed her much attention, and drew her into her set, making fun of Countess Lidia Ivanovna's coterie.

"When I'm old and ugly I'll be the same," Betsy used to say; "but for a pretty young woman like you it's early days for that house of charity."

Anna had at first avoided as far as she could Princess Tverskaya's world, because it necessitated an expenditure beyond her means, and besides in her heart she preferred the first circle. But since her visit to Moscow she had done quite the contrary. She avoided her serious-minded friends, and went out into the fashionable world. There she met Vronsky, and experienced an agitating joy at those meetings. She met Vronsky specially often at Betsy's, for Betsy was a Vronsky by birth and his cousin. Vronsky was everywhere where he had any chance of meeting Anna, and speaking to her, when he could, of his love. She gave him no encouragement, but every time she met him there surged up in her heart that same feeling of quickened life that had come upon her that day in the railway carriage when she saw him for the first time. She was conscious herself that her delight sparkled in her eyes and curved her lips into a smile, and she could not quench the expression of this delight.

At first Anna sincerely believed that she was displeased with him for daring to pursue her. Soon after her return from Moscow, on arriving at a soirée where she had expected to meet him, and not finding him there, she realized distinctly from the rush of disappointment that she had been deceiving herself, and that this pursuit was not merely not distasteful to her, but that it made the whole interest of her life.

The celebrated singer was singing for the second time, and all the fashionable world was in the theater. Vronsky, seeing his cousin from his stall in the front row, did not wait till the *entr'acte,* but went to her box.

"Why didn't you come to dinner?" she said to him. "I marvel at the second sight of lovers," she added with a smile, so that no one but he could hear; "*she wasn't there.* But come after the opera."

Vronsky looked inquiringly at her. She nodded. He thanked her by a smile, and sat down beside her.

"But how I remember your jeers!" continued Princess Betsy, who took a peculiar pleasure in following up this passion to a successful issue. "What's become of all that? You're caught, my dear boy."

"That's my one desire, to be caught," answered Vronsky, with his serene, good-humored smile. "If I complain of anything it's only that I'm not caught enough, to tell the truth. I begin to lose hope."

"Why, whatever hope can you have?" said Betsy, offended on behalf of her friend. "*Entendons nous.* . . ." But in her eyes there were gleams of light that betrayed that she understood perfectly and precisely as he did what hope he might have.

"None whatever," said Vronsky, laughing and showing his even rows of teeth. "Excuse me," he added, taking an opera glass out of her hand, and proceeding to scrutinize, over her bare shoulder, the row of boxes facing them. "I'm afraid I'm becoming ridiculous."

He was very well aware that he ran no risk of being ridiculous in the eyes of Betsy or any other fashionable people. He was very well aware that in their eyes the position of an unsuccessful lover of a girl, or of any woman free to marry, might be ridiculous. But the position of a man pursuing a married woman, and, regardless of everything, staking his life on drawing her into adultery, has something fine and grand about it, and can never be ridiculous; and so it was with a proud and gay smile under his mustaches that he lowered the opera glass and looked at his cousin.

"But why was it you didn't come to dinner?" she said, admiring him.

"I must tell you about that. I was busily employed, and doing what, do you suppose? I'll give you a hundred guesses, a thousand . . . you'd never guess. I've been reconciling a husband with a man who'd insulted his wife. Yes, really!"

"Well, did you succeed?"

"Almost."

"You really must tell me about it," she said, getting up. "Come to me in the next *entr'acte.*"

"I can't; I'm going to the French theater."

"From Nilsson?" Betsy queried in horror, though she could not herself have distinguished Nilsson's voice from any chorus girl's.

"Can't help it. I've an appointment there, all to do with my mission of peace."

" 'Blessed are the peacemakers; theirs is the kingdom of heaven,' " said Betsy, vaguely recollecting she had heard some similar saying from someone. "Very well, then, sit down, and tell me what it's all about."

And she sat down again.

Chapter V

"THIS IS RATHER INDISCREET, BUT IT'S SO GOOD IT'S AN AWFUL TEMPTATION TO TELL THE STORY," said Vronsky, looking at her with his laughing eyes. "I'm not going to mention any names."

"But I shall guess, so much the better."

"Well, listen: two festive young men were driving . . ."

"Officers of your regiment, of course?"

"I didn't say they were officers—two young men who had been lunching."

"In other words, drinking."

"Possibly. They were driving on their way to dinner with a friend in the most festive state of mind. And they beheld a pretty woman in a hired sleigh; she overtakes them, looks round at them, and, so they fancy anyway, nods to them and laughs. They, of course, follow her. They gallop at full speed. To their amazement, the fair one alights at the entrance of the very house to which they were going. The fair one darts upstairs to the top story. They get a glimpse of red lips under a short veil, and exquisite little feet."

"You describe it with such feeling that I fancy you must be one of the two."

"And after what you said, just now! Well, the young men go in to their comrade's; he was giving a farewell dinner. There they certainly did drink a little too much, as one always does at farewell dinners. And at dinner they inquire who lives at the top in that house. No one knows; only their host's valet, in answer to their inquiry whether any 'young ladies' are living on the top floor, answered that there were a great many of them about there. After dinner the two young men go into their host's study, and write a letter to the unknown fair one. They compose an ardent epistle, a declaration in fact, and they carry the letter upstairs themselves, so as to elucidate whatever might appear not perfectly intelligible in the letter."

"Why are you telling me these horrible stories? Well?"

"They ring. A maidservant opens the door, they hand her the letter, and assure the maid that they're both so in love that they'll die on the spot at the door. The maid, stupefied, carries in their messages. All at once a gentleman appears with whiskers like sausages, as red as a lobster, announces that there is no one living in the flat except his wife, and sends them both about their business."

"How do you know he had whiskers like sausages, as you say?"

"Ah, you shall hear. I've just been to make peace between them."

"Well, and what then?"

"That's the most interesting part of the story. It appears that it's a happy couple, a government clerk and his lady. The government clerk lodges a complaint, and I became a mediator, and such a mediator! . . . I assure you Talleyrand couldn't hold a candle to me."

"Why, where was the difficulty?"

"Ah, you shall hear. . . . We apologize in due form: we are in despair, we entreat forgiveness for the unfortunate misunderstanding. The government clerk with the sausages begins to melt, but he, too, desires to express his sentiments, and as soon as ever he begins to express them, he begins to get hot and say nasty things, and again I'm obliged to trot out all my diplomatic talents. I allowed that their conduct was bad, but I urged him to take into consideration their heedlessness, their youth; then, too, the young men had only just been lunching together. 'You understand. They regret it deeply, and beg you to overlook their misbehavior.' The government clerk was softened once more. 'I consent, count, and am ready to overlook it; but you perceive that my wife—my wife's a respectable woman—has been exposed to the persecution, and insults, and effrontery of young upstarts, scoundrels. . . .' And you must understand, the young upstarts are present all the while, and I have to keep the peace between them. Again I call out all my diplomacy, and again as soon as the thing was about at an end, our friend the government clerk gets hot and red, and his sausages stand on end with wrath, and once more I launch out into diplomatic wiles."

"Ah, he must tell you this story!" said Betsy, laughing, to a lady who came into her box. "He has been making me laugh so."

"Well, *bonne chance!*" she added, giving Vronsky one finger of the hand in which she held her fan, and with a shrug of her shoulders she twitched down the bodice of her gown that had worked up, so as to be duly naked as she moved forward towards the footlights into the light of the gas, and the sight of all eyes.

Vronsky drove to the French theater, where he really had to see the colonel of his regiment, who never missed a single performance there. He wanted to see him, to report on the result of his mediation, which had occupied and amused him for the last three days. Petritsky, whom he liked, was implicated in the affair, and the other culprit was a capital fellow and first rate comrade, who had lately joined the regiment, the young Prince Kedrov. And what was most important, the interests of the regiment were involved in it too.

Both the young men were in Vronsky's company. The colonel of the regiment was waited upon by the government clerk, Venden, with a complaint against his officers, who had insulted his wife. His young wife, so Venden told the story—he had been married half a year—was at church with her mother, and suddenly overcome by indisposition, arising from her interesting condition, she could not remain standing, she drove home in the first sleigh, a smart-looking one, she came across. On the spot the officers set off in pursuit of her; she was alarmed, and feeling still more unwell, ran up the staircase home. Venden himself, on returning from his office, heard a ring at their bell and voices, went out, and seeing the intoxicated officers with a letter, he had turned them out. He asked for exemplary punishment.

"Yes, it's all very well," said the colonel to Vronsky, whom he had invited to come and see him. "Petritsky's becoming impossible. Not a week goes by without some scandal. This government clerk won't let it drop, he'll go on with the thing."

Vronsky saw all the thanklessness of the business, and that there could be no question of a duel in it, that everything must be done to soften the government clerk, and hush the matter up. The colonel had called in Vronsky just because he knew him to be an honorable and intelligent man, and, more than all, a man who cared for the honor of the regiment. They talked it over, and decided that Petritsky and Kedrov must go with Vronsky to Venden's to apologize. The colonel and Vronsky were both fully aware that Vronsky's name and rank would be sure to contribute greatly to the softening of the injured husband's feelings.

And these two influences were not in fact without effect; though the result remained, as Vronsky had described, uncertain.

On reaching the French theater, Vronsky retired to the foyer with the colonel, and reported to him his success, or non-success. The colonel, thinking it all over, made up his mind not to pursue the matter further, but then for his own satisfaction proceeded to cross-examine Vronsky about his interview; and it was a long while before he could restrain his laughter, as Vronsky described how the government clerk, after subsiding for a while, would suddenly flare up again, as he recalled the details, and how Vronsky, at the last half word of conciliation, skillfully maneuvered a retreat, shoving Petritsky out before him.

"It's a disgraceful story, but killing. Kedrov really can't fight the gentleman! Was he so awfully hot?" he commented, laughing. "But what do you say to Claire today? She's marvelous," he went on, speaking of a new French actress. "However often you see her, everyday she's different. It's only the French who can do that."

Chapter VI

Princess Betsy drove home from the theater, without waiting for the end of the last act. She had only just time to go into her dressing room, sprinkle her long, pale face with powder, rub it, set her dress to rights, and order tea in the big drawing room, when one after another carriages drove up to her huge house in Bolshaia Morskaia. Her guests stepped out at the wide entrance, and the stout porter, who used to read the newspapers in the mornings behind the glass door, to the edification of the passers-by, noiselessly opened the immense door, letting the visitors pass by him into the house.

Almost at the same instant the hostess, with freshly arranged coiffure and freshened face, walked in at one door and her guests at the other door of the drawing room, a large room with dark walls, downy rugs, and a brightly lit table, gleaming with the light of candles, white cloth, silver samovar, and transparent china tea-things.

The hostess sat down at the table and took off her gloves. Chairs were set with the aid of footmen, moving almost imperceptibly about the room; the party settled itself, divided into two groups: one round the samovar near the hostess, the other at the opposite end of the drawing room, round the handsome wife of an ambassador, in black velvet, with sharply defined black eyebrows. In both groups conversation wavered, as it always does, for the first few minutes, broken up by meetings, greetings, offers of tea, and as it were, feeling about for something to rest upon.

"She's exceptionally good as an actress; one can see she's studied Kaulbach," said a diplomatic attaché in the group round the ambassador's wife. "Did you notice how she fell down? . . ."

"Oh, please, don't let us talk about Nilsson! No one can possibly say anything new about her," said a fat, red-faced, flaxen-headed lady, without eyebrows and chignon, wearing an old silk dress. This was Princess Myakaya, noted for her simplicity and the roughness of her manners, and nicknamed *enfant terrible.* Princess Myakaya, sitting in the middle between the two groups, and listening to both, took part in the conversation first of one and then of the other. "Three people have used that very phrase about Kaulbach to me today already, just as though they had made a compact about it. And I can't see why they liked that remark so."

The conversation was cut short by this observation, and a new subject had to be thought of again.

"Do tell me something amusing but not spiteful," said the ambassador's wife, a great proficient in the art of that elegant conversation called by the English, *small-talk.* She addressed the attaché, who was at a loss now what to begin upon.

"They say that that's a difficult task, that nothing's amusing that isn't spiteful," he began with a smile. "But I'll try. Get me a subject. It all lies in the subject. If a subject's given me, it's easy to spin something round it. I often think that the celebrated talkers of the last century would have found it difficult to talk cleverly now. Everything clever is so stale . . ."

"That has been said long ago," the ambassador's wife interrupted him, laughing.

The conversation began amiably, but just because it was too amiable, it came to a stop again. They had to have recourse to the sure, never-failing topic—gossip.

"Don't you think there's something Louis Quinze about Tushkevitch?" he said, glancing towards a handsome, fair-haired young man, standing at the table.

"Oh, yes! He's in the same style as the drawing room, and that's why it is he's so often here."

This conversation was maintained, since it rested on allusions to what could not be talked of in that room—that is to say, of the relations of Tushkevitch with their hostess.

Round the samovar and the hostess the conversation had been meanwhile vacillating in just the same way between three inevitable topics: the latest piece of public news, the theater, and scandal. It, too, came finally to rest on the last topic, that is, ill-natured gossip.

"Have you heard the Maltishtcheva woman—the mother, not the daughter—has ordered a costume in *diable rose* color?"

"Nonsense! No, that's too lovely!"

"I wonder that with her sense—for she's not a fool, you know—that she doesn't see how funny she is."

Everyone had something to say in censure or ridicule of the luckless Madame Maltishtcheva, and the conversation crackled merrily, like a burning fagot-stack.

The husband of Princess Betsy, a good-natured fat man, an ardent collector of engravings, hearing that his wife had visitors, came into the drawing room before going to his club. Stepping noiselessly over the thick rugs, he went up to Princess Myakaya.

"How did you like Nilsson?" he asked.

"Oh, how can you steal upon anyone like that! How you startled me!" she responded. "Please don't talk to me about the opera; you know nothing about music. I'd better meet you on your own ground, and talk about your majolica and engravings. Come now, what treasure have you been buying lately at the old curiosity shops?"

"Would you like me to show you? But you don't understand such things."

"Oh, do show me! I've been learning about them at those—what's their names? . . . the bankers . . . they've some splendid engravings. They showed them to us."

"Why, have you been at the Schützburgs?" asked the hostess from the samovar.

"Yes, *ma chère*. They asked my husband and me to dinner, and told us the sauce at that dinner cost a hundred pounds," Princess Myakaya said, speaking loudly, and conscious everyone was listening; "and very nasty sauce it was, some green mess. We had to ask them, and I made them sauce for eighteenpence, and everybody was very much pleased with it. I can't run to hundred-pound sauces."

"She's unique!" said the lady of the house.

"Marvelous!" said someone.

The sensation produced by Princess Myakaya's speeches was always unique, and the secret of the sensation she produced lay in the fact that though she spoke not always appropriately, as now, she said simple things with some sense in them. In the society in which she lived such plain statements produced the effect of the wittiest epigram. Princess Myakaya could never see why it had that effect, but she knew it had, and took advantage of it.

As everyone had been listening while Princess Myakaya spoke, and so the conversation around the ambassador's wife had dropped, Princess Betsy tried to bring the whole party together, and turned to the ambassador's wife.

"Will you really not have tea? You should come over here by us."

"No, we're very happy here," the ambassador's wife responded with a smile, and she went on with the conversation that had been begun.

"It was a very agreeable conversation. They were criticizing the Karenins, husband and wife.

"Anna is quite changed since her stay in Moscow. There's something strange about her," said her friend.

"The great change is that she brought back with her the shadow of Alexey Vronsky," said the ambassador's wife.

"Well, what of it? There's a fable of Grimm's about a man without a shadow, a man who's lost his shadow. And that's his punishment for something. I never could understand how it was a punishment. But a woman must dislike being without a shadow."

"Yes, but women with a shadow usually come to a bad end," said Anna's friend.

"Bad luck to your tongue!" said Princess Myakaya suddenly. "Madame Karenina's a splendid woman. I don't like her husband, but I like her very much."

"Why don't you like her husband? He's such a remarkable man," said the ambassador's wife. "My husband says there are few statesmen like him in Europe."

"And my husband tells me just the same, but I don't believe it," said Princess Myakaya. "If our husbands didn't talk to us, we should see the facts as they are. Alexey Alexandrovitch, to my thinking, is simply a fool. I say it in a whisper . . . but doesn't it really make everything clear? Before, when I was told to consider him clever, I kept looking for his ability, and thought myself a fool for not seeing it; but directly I said, *he's a fool,* though only in a whisper, everything's explained, isn't it?"

"How spiteful you are today!"

"Not a bit. I'd no other way out of it. One of the two had to be a fool. And, well, you know one can't say that of oneself."

" 'No one is satisfied with his fortune, and everyone is satisfied with his wit.' " The attaché repeated the French saying.

"That's just it, just it," Princess Myakaya turned to him. "But the point is that I won't abandon Anna to your mercies. She's so nice, so charming. How can she help it if they're all in love with her, and follow her about like shadows?"

"Oh, I had no idea of blaming her for it," Anna's friend said in self-defense.

"If no one follows us about like a shadow, that's no proof that we've any right to blame her."

And having duly disposed of Anna's friend, the Princess Myakaya got up, and together with the ambassador's wife, joined the group at the table, where the conversation was dealing with the king of Prussia.

"What wicked gossip were you talking over there?" asked Betsy.

"About the Karenins. The princess gave us a sketch of Alexey Alexandrovitch," said the ambassador's wife with a smile, as she sat down at the table.

"Pity we didn't hear it!" said Princess Betsy, glancing towards the door. "Ah, here you are at last!" she said, turning with a smile to Vronsky, as he came in.

Vronsky was not merely acquainted with all the persons whom he was meeting here; he saw them all everyday; and so he came in with the quiet manner with which one enters a room full of people from whom one has only just parted.

"Where do I come from?" he said, in answer to a question from the ambassador's wife. "Well, there's no help for it, I must confess. From the *opéra bouffe.* I do believe I've seen it a hundred times, and always with fresh enjoyment. It's exquisite! I know it's disgraceful, but I go to sleep at the opera, and I sit out the *opéra bouffe* to the last minute, and enjoy it. This evening . . ."

He mentioned a French actress, and was going to tell something about her; but the ambassador's wife, with playful horror, cut him short.

"Please don't tell us about that horror."

"All right, I won't especially as everyone knows those horrors."

"And we should all go to see them if it were accepted as the correct thing, like the opera," chimed in Princess Myakaya.

Chapter VII

STEPS WERE HEARD AT THE DOOR, AND PRINCESS BETSY, KNOWING IT WAS MADAME KARENINA, glanced at Vronsky. He was looking towards the door, and his face wore a strange new expression. Joyfully, intently, and at the same time timidly, he gazed at the approaching figure, and slowly he rose to his feet. Anna walked into the drawing room. Holding herself extremely erect, as always, looking straight before her, and moving with her swift, resolute, and light step, that distinguished her from all other society women, she crossed the short space to her hostess, shook hands with her, smiled, and with the same smile looked around at Vronsky. Vronsky bowed low and pushed a chair up for her.

She acknowledged this only by a slight nod, flushed a little, and frowned. But immediately, while rapidly greeting her acquaintances, and shaking the hands proffered to her, she addressed Princess Betsy:

"I have been at Countess Lidia's, and meant to have come here earlier, but I stayed on. Sir John was there. He's very interesting."

"Oh, that's this missionary?"

"Yes; he told us about the life in India, most interesting things."

The conversation, interrupted by her coming in, flickered up again like the light of a lamp being blown out.

"Sir John! Yes, Sir John; I've seen him. He speaks well. The Vlassieva girl's quite in love with him."

"And is it true the younger Vlassieva girl's to marry Topov?"

"Yes, they say it's quite a settled thing."

"I wonder at the parents! They say it's a marriage for love."

"For love? What antediluvian notions you have! Can one talk of love in these days?" said the ambassador's wife.

"What's to be done? It's a foolish old fashion that's kept up still," said Vronsky.

"So much the worse for those who keep up the fashion. The only happy marriages I know are marriages of prudence."

"Yes, but then how often the happiness of these prudent marriages flies away like dust just because that passion turns up that they have refused to recognize," said Vronsky.

"But by marriages of prudence we mean those in which both parties have sown their wild oats already. That's like scarlatina—one has to go through it and get it over."

"Then they ought to find out how to vaccinate for love, like smallpox."

"I was in love in my young days with a deacon," said the Princess Myakaya. "I don't know that it did me any good."

"No; I imagine, joking apart, that to know love, one must make mistakes and then correct them," said Princess Betsy.

"Even after marriage?" said the ambassador's wife playfully.

" 'It's never too late to mend.' " The attaché repeated the English proverb.

"Just so," Betsy agreed; "one must make mistakes and correct them. What do you think about it?" she turned to Anna, who, with a faintly perceptible resolute smile on her lips, was listening in silence to the conversation.

"I think," said Anna, playing with the glove she had taken off, "I think . . . of so many men, so many minds, certainly so many hearts, so many kinds of love."

Vronsky was gazing at Anna, and with a fainting heart waiting for what she would say. He sighed as after a danger escaped when she uttered these words.

Anna suddenly turned to him.

"Oh, I have had a letter from Moscow. They write me that Kitty Shtcherbatskaya's very ill."

"Really?" said Vronsky, knitting his brows.

Anna looked sternly at him.

"That doesn't interest you?"

"On the contrary, it does, very much. What was it exactly they told you, if I may know?" he questioned.

Anna got up and went to Betsy.

"Give me a cup of tea," she said, standing at her table.

While Betsy was pouring out the tea, Vronsky went up to Anna.

"What is it they write to you?" he repeated.

"I often think men have no understanding of what's not honorable though they're always talking of it," said Anna, without answering him. "I've wanted to tell you so a long while," she added, and moving a few steps away, she sat down at a table in a corner covered with albums.

"I don't quite understand the meaning of your words," he said, handing her the cup.

She glanced towards the sofa beside her, and he instantly sat down.

"Yes, I have been wanting to tell you," she said, not looking at him. "You behaved wrongly, very wrongly."

"Do you suppose I don't know that I've acted wrongly? But who was the cause of my doing so?"

"What do you say that to me for?" she said, glancing severely at him.

"You know what for," he answered boldly and joyfully, meeting her glance and not dropping his eyes.

Not he, but she, was confused.

"That only shows you have no heart," she said. But her eyes said that she knew he had a heart, and that was why she was afraid of him.

"What you spoke of just now was a mistake, and not love."

"Remember that I have forbidden you to utter that word, that hateful word," said Anna, with a shudder. But at once she felt that by that very word "forbidden" she had shown that she acknowledged certain rights over him, and by that very fact was encouraging him to speak of love. "I have long meant to tell you this," she went on, looking resolutely into his eyes, and hot all over from the burning flush on her cheeks. "I've come on purpose this evening, knowing I should meet you. I have come to tell you that this must end. I have never blushed before anyone, and you force me to feel to blame for something."

He looked at her and was struck by a new spiritual beauty in her face.

"What do you wish of me?" he said simply and seriously.

"I want you to go to Moscow and ask for Kitty's forgiveness," she said.

"You don't wish that?" he said.

He saw she was saying what she forced herself to say, not what she wanted to say.

"If you love me, as you say," she whispered, "do so that I may be at peace."

His face grew radiant.

"Don't you know that you're all my life to me? But I know no peace, and I can't give it to you; all myself—and love . . . yes. I can't think of you and myself apart. You and I are one to me. And I see no chance before us of peace for me or for you. I see a chance of despair, of wretchedness . . . or I see a chance of bliss, what bliss! . . . Can it be there's no chance of it?" he murmured with his lips; but she heard.

She strained every effort of her mind to say what ought to be said. But instead of that she let her eyes rest on him, full of love, and made no answer.

"It's come!" he thought in ecstasy. "When I was beginning to despair, and it seemed there would be no end—it's come! She loves me! She owns it!"

"Then do this for me: never say such things to me, and let us be friends," she said in words; but her eyes spoke quite differently.

"Friends we shall never be, you know that yourself. Whether we shall be the happiest or the wretchedest of people—that's in your hands."

She would have said something, but he interrupted her.

"I ask one thing only: I ask for the right to hope, to suffer as I do. But if even that cannot be, command me to disappear, and I disappear. You shall not see me if my presence is distasteful to you."

"I don't want to drive you away."

"Only don't change anything, leave everything as it is," he said in a shaky voice. "Here's your husband."

At that instant Alexey Alexandrovitch did in fact walk into the room with his calm, awkward gait.

Glancing at his wife and Vronsky, he went up to the lady of the house, and sitting down for a cup of tea, began talking in his deliberate, always audible voice, in his habitual tone of banter, ridiculing someone.

"Your Rambouillet is in full conclave," he said, looking round at all the party; "the graces and the muses."

But Princess Betsy could not endure that tone of his—"sneering," as she called it, using the English word, and like a skillful hostess she at once brought him into a serious conversation on the subject of universal conscription. Alexey Alexandrovitch was immediately interested in the subject, and began seriously defending the new imperial decree against Princess Betsy, who had attacked it.

Vronsky and Anna still sat at the little table.

"This is getting indecorous," whispered one lady, with an expressive glance at Madame Karenina, Vronsky, and her husband.

"What did I tell you?" said Anna's friend.

But not only those ladies, almost everyone in the room, even the Princess Myakaya and Betsy herself, looked several times in the direction of the two who had withdrawn from the general circle, as though that were a disturbing fact. Alexey Alexandrovitch was the only person who did not once look in that direction, and was not diverted from the interesting discussion he had entered upon.

Noticing the disagreeable impression that was being made on everyone, Princess Betsy slipped someone else into her place to listen to Alexey Alexandrovitch, and went up to Anna.

"I'm always amazed at the clearness and precision of your husband's language," she said. "The most transcendental ideas seem to be within my grasp when he's speaking."

"Oh, yes!" said Anna, radiant with a smile of happiness, and not understanding a word of what Betsy had said. She crossed over to the big table and took part in the general conversation.

Alexey Alexandrovitch, after staying half an hour, went up to his wife and suggested that they should go home together. But she answered, not looking at him, that she was staying to supper. Alexey Alexandrovitch made his bows and withdrew.

The fat old Tatar, Madame Karenina's coachman, was with difficulty holding one of her pair of grays, chilled with the cold and rearing at the entrance. A footman stood opening the carriage door. The hall-porter stood holding open the great door of the house. Anna Arkadyevna, with her quick little hand, was unfastening the lace of her sleeve, caught in the hook of her fur cloak, and with bent head listening to the words Vronsky murmured as he escorted her down.

"You've said nothing, of course, and I ask nothing," he was saying; "but you know that friendship's not what I want: that there's only one happiness in life for me, that word that you dislike so . . . yes, love! . . ."

"Love," she repeated slowly, in an inner voice, and suddenly, at the very instant she unhooked the lace, she added, "Why I don't like the word is that it means too much to me, far more than you can understand," and she glanced into his face. *"Au revoir!"*

She gave him her hand, and with her rapid, springy step she passed by the porter and vanished into the carriage.

Her glance, the touch of her hand, set him aflame. He kissed the palm of his hand where she had touched it, and went home, happy in the sense that he had got nearer to the attainment of his aims that evening than during the last two months.

Chapter VIII

ALEXEY ALEXANDROVITCH HAD SEEN NOTHING STRIKING OR IMPROPER IN THE FACT THAT HIS wife was sitting with Vronsky at a table apart, in eager conversation with him about something. But he noticed that to the rest of the party this appeared something striking and improper, and for that reason it seemed to him too to be improper. He made up his mind that he must speak of it to his wife.

On reaching home Alexey Alexandrovitch went to his study, as he usually did, seated himself in his low chair, opened a book on the Papacy at the place where he had laid the paper-knife in it, and read till one o'clock, just as he usually did. But from time to time he rubbed his high forehead and shook his head, as though to drive away something. At his usual time he got up and made his toilet for the night. Anna Arkadyevna had not yet come in. With a book under his arm he went upstairs. But this evening, instead of his usual thoughts and meditations upon official details, his thoughts were absorbed by his wife and something disagreeable connected with her. Contrary to his usual habit, he did not get into bed, but fell to walking up and down the rooms with his hands clasped behind his back. He could not go to bed, feeling that it was absolutely needful for him first to think thoroughly over the position that had just arisen.

When Alexey Alexandrovitch had made up his mind that he must talk to his wife about it, it had seemed a very easy and simple matter. But now, when he began to think over the question that had just presented itself, it seemed to him very complicated and difficult.

Alexey Alexandrovitch was not jealous. Jealousy according to his notions was an insult to one's wife, and one ought to have confidence in one's wife. Why one ought to have confidence—that is to say, complete conviction that his young wife would always love him—he did not ask himself. But he had no experience of lack of confidence, because he had confidence in her, and told himself that he ought to have it. Now, though his conviction that jealousy was a shameful feeling and that one ought to feel confidence, had not broken down, he felt that he was standing face to face with something illogical and irrational, and did not know what was to be done. Alexey Alexandrovitch was standing face to face with life, with the possibility of his wife's loving someone other than himself, and this seemed to him very irrational and incomprehensible because it was life itself. All his life Alexey Alexandrovitch had lived and worked in official spheres, having to do with the reflection of life. And every time he had stumbled against life itself he had shrunk away from it. Now he experienced a feeling akin to that of a man who, while calmly crossing a precipice by a bridge, should suddenly discover that the bridge is broken, and that there is a chasm below. That chasm was life itself, the bridge that artificial life in which Alexey Alexandrovitch had lived. For the first time the question presented itself to him of the possibility of his wife's loving someone else, and he was horrified at it.

He did not undress, but walked up and down with his regular tread over the resounding parquet of the dining room, where one lamp was burning, over the carpet of the dark drawing room, in which the light was reflected on the big new portrait of himself hanging over the sofa, and across her boudoir, where two candles burned, lighting up the portraits of her parents and woman friends, and the pretty knick-knacks of her writing-table, that he knew so well. He walked across her boudoir to the bedroom door, and turned back again. At each turn in his walk, especially at the parquet of the lit dining room, he halted and said to himself, "Yes, this I must decide and put a stop to; I must express my view of it and my decision." And he turned back again. "But express what—what decision?" he said to himself in the drawing room, and he found no reply. "But after all," he asked himself before turning into the boudoir, "what has occurred? Nothing. She was talking a long while with him. But what of that? Surely women in society can talk to whom they please. And then, jealousy means lowering both myself and her," he told himself as he went into her boudoir; but this dictum, which had always had such weight with him before, had now no weight and no meaning at all. And from the bedroom door he turned back again; but as he entered the dark drawing room some inner voice told him that it was not so, and that if others noticed it that showed that there was something. And he said to himself again in the dining room, "Yes, I must decide and put a stop to it, and express my view of it . . ." And again at the turn in the drawing room he asked himself, "Decide how?" And again he asked himself, "What had occurred?" and answered, "Nothing," and recollected that jealousy was a feeling insulting to his wife; but again in the drawing room he was convinced that something had happened. His thoughts, like his body, went round a complete circle, without coming upon anything new. He noticed this, rubbed his forehead, and sat down in her boudoir.

There, looking at her table, with the malachite blotting-case lying at the top and an unfinished letter, his thoughts suddenly changed. He began to think of her, of what she was thinking and feeling. For the first time he pictured vividly to himself her personal life, her ideas, her desires, and the idea that she could and should have a separate life of her own seemed to him so alarming that he made haste to dispel it. It was the chasm which he was afraid to peep into. To put himself in thought and feeling in another person's place was a spiritual exercise not natural to Alexey Alexandrovitch. He looked on this spiritual exercise as a harmful and dangerous abuse of the fancy.

"And the worst of it all," thought he, "is that just now, at the very moment when my great work is approaching completion" (he was thinking of the project he was bringing forward at the time), "when I stand in need of all my mental peace and all my energies, just now this stupid worry should fall foul of me. But what's to be done? I'm not one of those men who submit to uneasiness and worry without having the force of character to face them.

"I must think it over, come to a decision, and put it out of my mind," he said aloud.

"The question of her feelings, of what has passed and may be passing in her soul, that's not my affair; that's the affair of her conscience, and falls under the head of religion," he said to himself, feeling consolation in the sense that he had found to which division of regulating principles this new circumstance could be properly referred.

"And so," Alexey Alexandrovitch said to himself, "questions as to her feelings, and so on, are questions for her conscience, with which I can have nothing to do. My duty is clearly defined. As the head of the family, I am a person bound in duty to guide her, and consequently, in part the person responsible; I am bound to point out the danger I perceive, to warn her, even to use my authority. I ought to speak plainly to her." And everything that he would say tonight to his wife took clear shape in Alexey Alexandrovitch's head. Thinking over what he would say, he somewhat regretted that he should have to use his time and mental powers for domestic consumption, with so little to show for it, but, in spite of that, the form and contents of the speech before him shaped itself as clearly and distinctly in his head as a ministerial report.

"I must say and express fully the following points: first, exposition of the value to be attached to public opinion and to decorum; secondly, exposition of religious significance of marriage; thirdly, if need be, reference to the calamity possibly ensuing to our son; fourthly, reference to the unhappiness likely to result to herself." And, interlacing his fingers, Alexey Alexandrovitch stretched them, and the joints of the fingers cracked. This trick, a bad habit, the cracking of his fingers, always soothed him, and gave precision to his thoughts, so needful to him at this juncture.

There was the sound of a carriage driving up to the front door. Alexey Alexandrovitch halted in the middle of the room.

A woman's step was heard mounting the stairs. Alexey Alexandrovitch, ready for his speech, stood compressing his crossed fingers, waiting to see if the crack would not come again. One joint cracked.

Already, from the sound of light steps on the stairs, he was aware that she was close, and though he was satisfied with his speech, he felt frightened of the explanation confronting him.

Chapter IX

ANNA CAME IN WITH HANGING HEAD, PLAYING WITH THE TASSELS OF HER HOOD. HER FACE WAS brilliant and glowing; but this glow was not one of brightness; it suggested the fearful glow of a conflagration in the midst of a dark night. On seeing her husband, Anna raised her head and smiled, as though she had just waked up.

"You're not in bed? What a wonder!" she said, letting fall her hood, and, without stopping, she went on into the dressing room. "It's late, Alexey Alexandrovitch," she said, when she had gone through the doorway.

"Anna, it's necessary for me to have a talk with you."

"With me?" she said, wonderingly. She came out from behind the door of the dressing room, and looked at him. "Why, what is it? What about?" she asked, sitting down. "Well, let's talk, if it's so necessary. But it would be better to get to sleep."

Anna said what came to her lips, and marveled, hearing herself, at her own capacity for lying. How simple and natural were her words, and how likely that she was simply sleepy! She felt herself clad in an impenetrable armor of falsehood. She felt that some unseen force had come to her aid and was supporting her.

"Anna, I must warn you," he began.

"Warn me?" she said. "Of what?"

She looked at him so simply, so brightly, that anyone who did not know her as her husband knew her could not have noticed anything unnatural, either in the sound or the sense of her words. But to him, knowing her, knowing that whenever he went to bed five minutes later than usual, she noticed it, and asked him the reason; to him, knowing that every joy, every pleasure and pain that she felt she communicated to him at once; to him, now to see that she did not care to notice his state of mind, that she did not care to say a word about herself, meant a great deal. He saw that the inmost recesses of her soul, that had always hitherto lain open before him, were closed against him. More than that, he saw from her tone that she was not even perturbed at that, but as it were said straight out to him: "Yes, it's shut up, and so it must be, and will be in future." Now he experienced a feeling such as a man might have, returning home and finding his own house locked up. "But perhaps the key may yet be found," thought Alexey Alexandrovitch.

"I want to warn you," he said in a low voice, "that through thoughtlessness and lack of caution you may cause yourself to be talked about in society. Your too animated conversation this evening with Count Vronsky" (he enunciated the name firmly and with deliberate emphasis) "attracted attention."

He talked and looked at her laughing eyes, which frightened him now with their impenetrable look, and, as he talked, he felt all the uselessness and idleness of his words.

"You're always like that," she answered as though completely misapprehending him, and of all he had said only taking in the last phrase. "One time you don't like my being dull, and another time you don't like my being lively. I wasn't dull. Does that offend you?"

Alexey Alexandrovitch shivered, and bent his hands to make the joints crack.

"Oh, please, don't do that, I do so dislike it," she said.

"Anna, is this you?" said Alexey Alexandrovitch, quietly making an effort over himself, and restraining the motion of his fingers.

"But what is it all about?" she said, with such genuine and droll wonder. "What do you want of me?"

Alexey Alexandrovitch paused, and rubbed his forehead and his eyes. He saw that instead of doing as he had intended—that is to say, warning his wife against a mistake in the eyes of the world—he had unconsciously become agitated over what was the affair of her conscience, and was struggling against the barrier he fancied between them.

"This is what I meant to say to you," he went on coldly and composedly, "and I beg you to listen to it. I consider jealousy, as you know, a humiliating and degrading feeling, and I shall never allow myself to be influenced by it; but there are certain rules of decorum which cannot be disregarded with impunity. This evening it was not I observed it, but judging by the impression made on the company, everyone observed that your conduct and deportment were not altogether what could be desired."

"I positively don't understand," said Anna, shrugging her shoulders.—"He doesn't care," she thought. "But other people noticed it, and that's what upsets him."—"You're not well, Alexey Alexandrovitch," she added, and she got up, and would have gone towards the door; but he moved forward as though he would stop her.

His face was ugly and forbidding, as Anna had never seen him. She stopped, and bending her head back and on one side, began with her rapid hand taking out her hairpins.

"Well, I'm listening to what's to come," she said, calmly and ironically; "and indeed I listen with interest, for I should like to understand what's the matter."

She spoke, and marveled at the confident, calm, and natural tone in which she was speaking, and the choice of the words she used.

"To enter into all the details of your feelings I have no right, and besides, I regard that as useless and even harmful," began Alexey Alexandrovitch. "Ferreting in one's soul, one often ferrets out something that might have lain there unnoticed. Your feelings are an affair of your own conscience; but I am in duty bound to you, to myself, and to God, to point out to you your duties. Our life has been joined, not by man, but by God. That union can only be severed by a crime, and a crime of that nature brings its own chastisement."

"I don't understand a word. And, oh dear! how sleepy I am, unluckily," she said, rapidly passing her hand through her hair, feeling for the remaining hairpins.

"Anna, for God's sake don't speak like that!" he said gently. "Perhaps I am mistaken, but believe me, what I say, I say as much for myself as for you. I am your husband, and I love you."

For an instant her face fell, and the mocking gleam in her eyes died away; but the word love threw her into revolt again. She thought: "Love? Can he love? If he hadn't heard there was such a thing as love, he would never have used the word. He doesn't even know what love is."

"Alexey Alexandrovitch, really I don't understand," she said. "Define what it is you find . . ."

"Pardon, let me say all I have to say. I love you. But I am not speaking of myself; the most important persons in this matter are our son and yourself. It may very well be, I repeat, that my words seem to you utterly unnecessary and out of place; it may be that they are called forth by my mistaken impression. In that case, I beg you to forgive me. But if you are conscious yourself of even the smallest foundation for them, then I beg you to think a little, and if your heart prompts you, to speak out to me . . ."

Alexey Alexandrovitch was unconsciously saying something utterly unlike what he had prepared.

"I have nothing to say. And besides," she said hurriedly, with difficulty repressing a smile, "it's really time to be in bed."

Alexey Alexandrovitch sighed, and, without saying more, went into the bedroom.

When she came into the bedroom, he was already in bed. His lips were sternly compressed, and his eyes looked away from her. Anna got into her bed, and lay expecting every minute that he would begin to speak to her again. She both feared his speaking and wished for it. But he was silent. She waited for a long while without moving, and had forgotten about him. She thought of that other; she pictured him, and felt how her heart was flooded with emotion and guilty delight at the thought of him. Suddenly she heard an even, tranquil snore. For the first instant Alexey Alexandrovitch seemed, as it were, appalled at his own snoring, and ceased; but after an interval of two breathings the snore sounded again, with a new tranquil rhythm.

"It's late, it's late," she whispered with a smile. A long while she lay, not moving, with open eyes, whose brilliance she almost fancied she could herself see in the darkness.

Chapter X

FROM THAT TIME A NEW LIFE BEGAN FOR ALEXEY ALEXANDROVITCH AND FOR HIS WIFE. NOTHING special happened. Anna went out into society, as she had always done, was particularly often at Princess Betsy's, and met Vronsky everywhere. Alexey Alexandrovitch saw this, but could do nothing. All his efforts to draw her into open discussion she confronted with a barrier which he could not penetrate, made up of a sort of amused perplexity. Outwardly everything was the same, but their inner relations were completely changed. Alexey Alexandrovitch, a man of great power in the world of politics, felt himself helpless in this. Like an ox with head bent, submissively he awaited the blow which he felt was lifted over him. Every time he began to think about it, he felt that he must try once more, that by kindness, tenderness, and persuasion there was still hope of saving her, of bringing her back to herself, and everyday he made ready to talk to her. But every time he began talking to her, he felt that the spirit of evil and deceit, which had taken possession of her, had possession of him too, and he talked to her in a tone quite unlike that in which he had meant to talk. Involuntarily he talked to her in his habitual tone of jeering at anyone who should say what he was saying. And in that tone it was impossible to say what needed to be said to her.

Chapter XI

THAT WHICH FOR VRONSKY HAD BEEN ALMOST A WHOLE YEAR THE ONE ABSORBING DESIRE OF his life, replacing all his old desires; that which for Anna had been an impossible, terrible, and even for that reason more entrancing dream of bliss, that desire had been fulfilled. He stood before her, pale, his lower jaw quivering, and besought her to be calm, not knowing how or why.

"Anna! Anna!" he said with a choking voice, "Anna, for pity's sake! . . ."

But the louder he spoke, the lower she dropped her once proud and gay, now shame-stricken head, and she bowed down and sank from the sofa where she was sitting, down on the floor, at his feet; she would have fallen on the carpet if he had not held her.

"My God! Forgive me!" she said, sobbing, pressing his hands to her bosom.

She felt so sinful, so guilty, that nothing was left her but to humiliate herself and beg forgiveness; and as now there was no one in her life but him, to him she addressed her prayer for forgiveness. Looking at him, she had a physical sense of her humiliation, and she could say nothing more. He felt what a murderer must feel, when he sees the body he has robbed of life. That body, robbed by him of life, was their love, the first stage of their love. There was something awful and revolting in the memory of what had been bought at this fearful price of shame. Shame at their spiritual nakedness crushed her and infected him. But in spite of all the murderer's horror before the body of his victim, he must hack it to pieces, hide the body, must use what he has gained by his murder.

And with fury, as it were with passion, the murderer falls on the body, and drags it and hacks at it; so he covered her face and shoulders with kisses. She held his hand, and did not stir. "Yes, these kisses—that is what has been bought by this shame. Yes, and one hand, which will always be mine—the hand of my accomplice." She lifted up that hand and kissed it. He sank on his knees and tried to see her face; but she hid it, and said nothing. At last, as though making an effort over herself, she got up and pushed him away. Her face was still as beautiful, but it was only the more pitiful for that.

"All is over," she said; "I have nothing but you. Remember that."

"I can never forget what is my whole life. For one instant of this happiness . . ."

"Happiness!" she said with horror and loathing and her horror unconsciously infected him. "For pity's sake, not a word, not a word more."

She rose quickly and moved away from him.

"Not a word more," she repeated, and with a look of chill despair, incomprehensible to him, she parted from him. She felt that at that moment she could not put into words the sense of shame, of rapture, and of horror at this stepping into a new life, and she did not want to speak of it, to vulgarize this feeling by inappropriate words. But later too, and the next day and the third day, she still found no words in which she could express the complexity of her feelings; indeed, she could not even find thoughts in which she could clearly think out all that was in her soul.

She said to herself: "No, just now I can't think of it, later on, when I am calmer." But this calm for thought never came; every time the thought rose of what she had done and what would happen to her, and what she ought to do, a horror came over her and she drove those thoughts away.

"Later, later," she said—"when I am calmer."

But in dreams, when she had no control over her thoughts, her position presented itself to her in all its hideous nakedness. One dream haunted her almost every night. She dreamed that both were her husbands at once, that both were lavishing caresses on her. Alexey Alexandrovitch was weeping, kissing her hands, and saying, "How happy we are now!" And Alexey Vronsky was there too, and he too was her husband. And she was marveling that it had once seemed impossible to her, was explaining to them, laughing, that this was ever so much simpler, and that now both of them were happy and contented. But this dream weighed on her like a nightmare, and she awoke from it in terror.

Chapter XII

In the early days after his return from Moscow, whenever Levin shuddered and grew red, remembering the disgrace of his rejection, he said to himself: "This was just how I used to shudder and blush, thinking myself utterly lost, when I was plucked in physics and did not get my remove; and how I thought myself utterly ruined after I had mismanaged that affair of my sister's that was entrusted to me. And yet, now that years have passed, I recall it and wonder that it could distress me so much. It will be the same thing too with this trouble. Time will go by and I shall not mind about this either."

But three months had passed and he had not left off minding about it; and it was as painful for him to think of it as it had been those first days. He could not be at peace because after dreaming so long of family life, and feeling himself so ripe for it, he was still not married, and was further than ever from marriage. He was painfully conscious himself, as were all about him, that at his years it is not well for man to be alone. He remembered how before starting for Moscow he had once said to his cowman Nikolay, a simple-hearted peasant, whom he liked talking to: "Well, Nikolay! I mean to get married," and how Nikolay had promptly answered, as of a matter on which there could be no possible doubt: "And high time too, Konstantin Demitrievitch." But marriage had now become further off than ever. The place was taken, and whenever he tried to imagine any of the girls he knew in that place, he felt that it was utterly impossible. Moreover, the recollection of the rejection and the part he had played in the affair tortured him with shame. However often he told himself that he was in no way to blame in it, that recollection, like other humiliating reminiscences of a similar kind, made him twinge and blush. There had been in his past, as in every man's, actions, recognized by him as bad, for which his conscience ought to have tormented him; but the memory of these evil actions was far from causing him so much suffering as those trivial but humiliating reminiscences. These wounds never healed. And with these memories was now ranged his rejection and the pitiful position in which he must have appeared to others that evening. But time and work did their part. Bitter memories were more and more covered up by the incidents—paltry in his eyes, but really important—of his country life. Every week he thought less often of Kitty. He was impatiently looking forward to the news that she was married, or just going to be married, hoping that such news would, like having a tooth out, completely cure him.

Meanwhile spring came on, beautiful and kindly, without the delays and treacheries of spring—one of those rare springs in which plants, beasts, and man rejoice alike. This lovely spring roused Levin still more, and strengthened him in his resolution of renouncing all his past and building up his lonely life firmly and independently. Though many of the plans with which he had returned to the country had not been carried out, still his most important resolution—that of purity—had been kept by him. He was free from that shame, which had usually harassed him after a fall; and he could look everyone straight in the face. In February he had received a letter from Marya Nikolaevna telling him that his brother Nikolay's health was getting worse, but that he would not take advice, and in consequence of this letter Levin went to Moscow to his brother's, and succeeded in persuading him to see a doctor and to go to a watering place abroad. He succeeded so well in persuading his brother, and in lending him money for the journey without irritating him, that he was satisfied with himself in that matter. In addition to his farming, which called for special attention in spring, and in addition to reading, Levin had begun that winter a work on agriculture, the plan of which turned on taking into account the character of the laborer on the land as one of the unalterable data of the question, like the climate and the soil, and consequently deducing all the principles of scientific culture, not simply from the data of soil and climate, but from the data of soil, climate, and a certain unalterable character of the laborer. Thus, in spite of his solitude, or in consequence of his solitude, his life was exceedingly full. Only rarely he suffered from an unsatisfied desire to communicate his stray ideas to someone besides Agafea Mihalovna. With her indeed he not infrequently fell into discussions upon physics, the theory of agriculture, and especially philosophy; philosophy was Agafea Mihalovna's favorite subject.

Spring was slow in unfolding. For the last few weeks it had been steadily fine frosty weather. In the daytime it thawed in the sun, but at night there were even seven degrees of frost. There was such a frozen surface on the snow that they drove the wagons anywhere off the roads. Easter came in the snow. Then all of a sudden, on Easter Monday, a warm wind sprang up, storm clouds swooped down, and for three days and three nights the warm, driving rain fell in streams. On Thursday the wind dropped, and a thick gray fog brooded over the land as though hiding the mysteries of the transformations that were being wrought in nature. Behind the fog there was the flowing of water, the cracking and floating of ice, the swift rush of turbid, foaming torrents; and on the following Monday, in the evening, the fog parted, the storm clouds split up into little curling crests of cloud, the sky cleared, and the real spring had come. In the morning the sun rose brilliant and quickly wore away the thin layer of ice that covered the water, and all the warm air was quivering with the steam that rose up from the quickened earth. The old grass looked greener, and the young grass thrust up its tiny blades; the buds of the guelder-rose and of the currant and the sticky birch-buds were swollen with sap, and an exploring bee was humming about the golden blossoms that studded the willow. Larks trilled unseen above the velvety green fields and the ice-covered stubble-land; peewits wailed over the low lands and marshes flooded by the pools; cranes and wild geese flew high across the sky uttering their spring calls. The cattle, bald in patches where the new hair had not grown yet, lowed in the pastures; the bowlegged lambs frisked round their bleating mothers. Nimble children ran about the drying paths, covered with the prints of bare feet. There was a merry chatter of peasant women over their linen at the pond, and the ring of axes in the yard, where the peasants were repairing ploughs and harrows. The real spring had come.

Chapter XIII

LEVIN PUT ON HIS BIG BOOTS, AND, FOR THE FIRST TIME, A CLOTH JACKET, INSTEAD OF HIS FUR cloak, and went out to look after his farm, stepping over streams of water that flashed in the sunshine and dazzled his eyes, and treading one minute on ice and the next into sticky mud.

Spring is the time of plans and projects. And, as he came out into the farmyard, Levin, like a tree in spring that knows not what form will be taken by the young shoots and twigs imprisoned in its swelling buds, hardly knew what undertakings he was going to begin upon now in the farm-work that was so dear to him. But he felt that he was full of the most splendid plans and projects. First of all he went to the cattle. The cows had been let out into their paddock, and their smooth sides were already shining with their new, sleek, spring coats; they basked in the sunshine and lowed to go to the meadow. Levin gazed admiringly at the cows he knew so intimately to the minutest detail of their condition, and gave orders for them to be driven out into the meadow, and the calves to be let into the paddock. The herdsman ran gaily to get ready for the meadow. The cowherd girls, picking up their petticoats, ran splashing through the mud with bare legs, still white, not yet brown from the sun, waving brush wood in their hands, chasing the calves that frolicked in the mirth of spring.

After admiring the young ones of that year, who were particularly fine—the early calves were the size of a peasant's cow, and Pava's daughter, at three months old, was as big as a yearling—Levin gave orders for a trough to be brought out and for them to be fed in the paddock. But it appeared that as the paddock had not been used during the winter, the hurdles made in the autumn for it were broken. He sent for the carpenter, who, according to his orders, ought to have been at work at the threshing machine. But it appeared that the carpenter was repairing the harrows, which ought to have been repaired before Lent. This was very annoying to Levin. It was annoying to come upon that everlasting slovenliness in the farm-work against which he had been striving with all his might for so many years. The hurdles, as he ascertained, being not wanted in winter, had been carried to the cart-horses' stable, and there broken, as they were of light construction, only meant for folding calves. Moreover, it was apparent also that the harrows and all the agricultural implements, which he had directed to be looked over and repaired in the winter, for which very purpose he had hired three carpenters, had not been put into repair, and the harrows were being repaired when they ought to have been harrowing the field. Levin sent for his bailiff, but immediately went off himself to look for him. The bailiff, beaming all over, like everyone that day, in a sheepskin bordered with astrachan, came out of the barn, twisting a bit of straw in his hands.

"Why isn't the carpenter at the threshing machine?"

"Oh, I meant to tell you yesterday, the harrows want repairing. Here it's time they got to work in the fields."

"But what were they doing in the winter, then?"

"But what did you want the carpenter for?"

"Where are the hurdles for the calves' paddock?"

"I ordered them to be got ready. What would you have with those peasants!" said the bailiff, with a wave of his hand.

"It's not those peasants but this bailiff!" said Levin, getting angry. "Why, what do I keep you for?" he cried. But, bethinking himself that this would not help matters, he stopped short in the middle of a sentence, and merely sighed. "Well, what do you say? Can sowing begin?" he asked, after a pause.

"Behind Turkin tomorrow or the next day they might begin."

"And the clover?"

"I've sent Vassily and Mishka; they're sowing. Only I don't know if they'll manage to get through; it's so slushy."

"How many acres?"

"About fifteen."

"Why not sow all?" cried Levin.

That they were only sowing the clover on fifteen acres, not on all the forty-five, was still more annoying to him. Clover, as he knew, both from books and from his own experience, never did well except when it was sown as early as possible, almost in the snow. And yet Levin could never get this done.

"There's no one to send. What would you have with such a set of peasants? Three haven't turned up. And there's Semyon . . ."

"Well, you should have taken some men from the thatching."

"And so I have, as it is."

"Where are the peasants, then?"

"Five are making *compôte*" (which meant compost), "four are shifting the oats for fear of a touch of mildew, Konstantin Dmitrievitch."

Levin knew very well that "a touch of mildew" meant that his English seed oats were already ruined. Again they had not done as he had ordered.

"Why, but I told you during Lent to put in pipes," he cried.

"Don't put yourself out; we shall get it all done in time."

Levin waved his hand angrily, went into the granary to glance at the oats, and then to the stable. The oats were not yet spoiled. But the peasants were carrying the oats in spades when they might simply let them slide down into the lower granary; and arranging for this to be done, and taking two workmen from there for sowing clover, Levin got over his vexation with the bailiff. Indeed, it was such a lovely day that one could not be angry.

"Ignat!" he called to the coachman, who, with his sleeves tucked up, was washing the carriage wheels, "saddle me . . ."

"Which, sir?"

"Well, let it be Kolpik."

"Yes, sir."

While they were saddling his horse, Levin again called up the bailiff, who was hanging about in sight, to make it up with him, and began talking to him about the spring operations before them, and his plans for the farm.

The wagons were to begin carting manure earlier, so as to get all done before the early mowing. And the ploughing of the further land to go on without a break so as to let it ripen lying fallow. And the mowing to be all done by hired labor, not on half-profits. The bailiff listened attentively, and obviously made an effort to approve of his employer's projects. But still he had that look Levin knew so well that always irritated him, a look of hopelessness and despondency. That look said: "That's all very well, but as God wills."

Nothing mortified Levin so much as that tone. But it was the tone common to all the bailiffs he had ever had. They had all taken up that attitude to his plans, and so now he was not angered by it, but mortified, and felt all the more roused to struggle against this, as it seemed, elemental force continually ranged against him, for which he could find no other expression than "as God wills."

"If we can manage it, Konstantin Dmitrievitch," said the bailiff.

"Why ever shouldn't you manage it?"

"We positively must have another fifteen laborers. And they don't turn up. There were some here today asking seventy roubles for the summer."

Levin was silent. Again he was brought face to face with that opposing force. He knew that however much they tried, they could not hire more than forty—thirty-seven perhaps or thirty-eight—laborers for a reasonable sum. Some forty had been taken on, and there were no more. But still he could not help struggling against it.

"Send to Sury, to Tchefirovka; if they don't come we must look for them."

"Oh, I'll send, to be sure," said Vassily Fedorovitch despondently. "But there are the horses, too, they're not good for much."

"We'll get some more. I know, of course," Levin added laughing, "you always want to do with as little and as poor quality as possible; but this year I'm not going to let you have things your own way. I'll see to everything myself."

"Why, I don't think you take much rest as it is. It cheers us up to work under the master's eye . . ."

"So they're sowing clover behind the Birch Dale? I'll go and have a look at them," he said, getting on to the little bay cob, Kolpik, who was led up by the coachman.

"You can't get across the streams, Konstantin Dmitrievitch," the coachman shouted.

"All right, I'll go by the forest."

And Levin rode through the slush of the farmyard to the gate and out into the open country, his good little horse, after his long inactivity, stepping out gallantly, snorting over the pools, and asking, as it were, for guidance. If Levin had felt happy before in the cattle pens and farmyard, he felt happier yet in the open country. Swaying rhythmically with the ambling paces of his good little cob, drinking in the warm yet fresh scent of the snow and the air, as he rode through his forest over the crumbling, wasted snow, still left in parts, and covered with dissolving tracks, he rejoiced over every tree, with the moss reviving on its bark and the buds swelling on its shoots. When he came out of the forest, in the immense plain before him, his grass fields stretched in an unbroken carpet of green, without one bare place or swamp, only spotted here and there in the hollows with patches of melting snow. He was not put out of temper even by the sight of the peasants' horses and colts trampling down his young grass (he told a peasant he met to drive them out), nor by the sarcastic and stupid reply of the peasant Ipat, whom he met on the way, and asked, "Well, Ipat, shall we soon be sowing?" "We must get the ploughing done first, Konstantin Dmitrievitch," answered Ipat. The further he rode, the happier he became, and plans for the land rose to his mind each better than the last; to plant all his fields with hedges along the southern borders, so that the snow should not lie under them; to divide them up into six fields of arable and three of pasture and hay; to build a cattle yard at the further end of the estate, and to dig a pond and to construct movable pens for the cattle as a means of manuring the land. And then eight hundred acres of wheat, three hundred of potatoes, and four hundred of clover, and not one acre exhausted.

Absorbed in such dreams, carefully keeping his horse by the hedges, so as not to trample his young crops, he rode up to the laborers who had been sent to sow clover. A cart with the seed in it was standing, not at the edge, but in the middle of the crop, and the winter corn had been torn up by the wheels and trampled by the horse. Both the laborers were sitting in the hedge, probably smoking a pipe together. The earth in the cart, with which the seed was mixed, was not crushed to powder, but crusted together or adhering in clods. Seeing the master, the laborer, Vassily, went towards the cart, while Mishka set to work sowing. This was not as it should be, but with the laborers Levin seldom lost his temper. When Vassily came up, Levin told him to lead the horse to the hedge.

"It's all right, sir, it'll spring up again," responded Vassily.

"Please don't argue," said Levin, "but do as you're told."

"Yes, sir," answered Vassily, and he took the horse's head. "What a sowing, Konstantin Dmitrievitch," he said, hesitating; "first rate. Only it's a work to get about! You drag a ton of earth on your shoes."

"Why is it you have earth that's not sifted?" said Levin.

"Well, we crumble it up," answered Vassily, taking up some seed and rolling the earth in his palms.

Vassily was not to blame for their having filled up his cart with unsifted earth, but still it was annoying.

Levin had more than once already tried a way he knew for stifling his anger, and turning all that seemed dark right again, and he tried that way now. He watched how Mishka strode along, swinging the huge clods of earth that clung to each foot; and getting off his horse, he took the sieve from Vassily and started sowing himself.

"Where did you stop?"

Vassily pointed to the mark with his foot, and Levin went forward as best he could, scattering the seed on the land. Walking was as difficult as on a bog, and by the time Levin had ended the row he was in a great heat, and he stopped and gave up the sieve to Vassily.

"Well, master, when summer's here, mind you don't scold me for these rows," said Vassily.

"Eh?" said Levin cheerily, already feeling the effect of his method.

"Why, you'll see in the summertime. It'll look different. Look you where I sowed last spring. How I did work at it! I do my best, Konstantin Dmitrievitch, d'ye see, as I would for my own father. I don't like bad work myself, nor would I let another man do it. What's good for the master's good for us too. To look out yonder now," said Vassily, pointing, "it does one's heart good."

"It's a lovely spring, Vassily."

"Why, it's a spring such as the old men don't remember the like of. I was up home; an old man up there has sown wheat too, about an acre of it. He was saying you wouldn't know it from rye."

"Have you been sowing wheat long?"

"Why, sir, it was you taught us the year before last. You gave me two measures. We sold about eight bushels and sowed a rood."

"Well, mind you crumble up the clods," said Levin, going towards his horse, "and keep an eye on Mishka. And if there's a good crop you shall have half a ruble for every acre."

"Humbly thankful. We are very well content, sir, as it is."

Levin got on his horse and rode towards the field where was last year's clover, and the one which was ploughed ready for the spring corn.

The crop of clover coming up in the stubble was magnificent. It had survived everything, and stood up vividly green through the broken stalks of last year's wheat. The horse sank in up to the pasterns, and he drew each hoof with a sucking sound out of the half-thawed ground. Over the ploughland riding was utterly impossible; the horse could only keep a foothold where there was ice, and in the thawing furrows he sank deep in at each step. The ploughland was in splendid condition; in a couple of days it would be fit for harrowing and sowing. Everything was capital, everything was cheering. Levin rode back across the streams, hoping the water would have gone down. And he did in fact get across, and startled two ducks. "There must be snipe too," he thought, and just as he reached the turning homewards he met the forest-keeper, who confirmed his theory about the snipe.

Levin went home at a trot, so as to have time to eat his dinner and get his gun ready for the evening.

Chapter XIV

AS HE RODE UP TO THE HOUSE IN THE HAPPIEST FRAME OF MIND, LEVIN HEARD THE BELL RING AT the side of the principal entrance of the house.

"Yes, that's someone from the railway station," he thought, "just the time to be here from the Moscow train. . . . Who could it be? What if it's brother Nikolay? He did say: 'Maybe I'll go to the waters, or maybe I'll come down to you.' " He felt dismayed and vexed for the first minute, that his brother Nikolay's presence should come to disturb his happy mood of spring. But he felt ashamed of the feeling, and at once he opened, as it were, the arms of his soul, and with a softened feeling of joy and expectation, now he hoped with all his heart that it was his brother. He pricked up his horse, and riding out from behind the acacias he saw a hired three-horse sleigh from the railway station, and a gentleman in a fur coat. It was not his brother. "Oh, if it were only some nice person one could talk to a little!" he thought.

"Ah," cried Levin joyfully, flinging up both his hands. "Here's a delightful visitor! Ah, how glad I am to see you!" he shouted, recognizing Stepan Arkadyevitch.

"I shall find out for certain whether she's married, or when she's going to be married," he thought. And on that delicious spring day he felt that the thought of her did not hurt him at all.

"Well, you didn't expect me, eh?" said Stepan Arkadyevitch, getting out of the sleigh, splashed with mud on the bridge of his nose, on his cheek, and on his eyebrows, but radiant with health and good spirits. "I've come to see you in the first place," he said, embracing and kissing him, "to have some stand-shooting second, and to sell the forest at Ergushovo third."

"Delightful! What a spring we're having! How ever did you get along in a sleigh?"

"In a cart it would have been worse still, Konstantin Dmitrievitch," answered the driver, who knew him.

"Well, I'm very, very glad to see you," said Levin, with a genuine smile of childlike delight.

Levin led his friend to the room set apart for visitors, where Stepan Arkadyevitch's things were carried also—a bag, a gun in a case, a satchel for cigars. Leaving him there to wash and change his clothes, Levin went off to the counting house to speak about the ploughing and clover. Agafea Mihalovna, always very anxious for the credit of the house, met him in the hall with inquiries about dinner.

"Do just as you like, only let it be as soon as possible," he said, and went to the bailiff.

When he came back, Stepan Arkadyevitch, washed and combed, came out of his room with a beaming smile, and they went upstairs together.

"Well, I am glad I managed to get away to you! Now I shall understand what the mysterious business is that you are always absorbed in here. No, really, I envy you. What a house, how nice it all is! So bright, so cheerful!" said Stepan Arkadyevitch, forgetting that it was not always spring and fine weather like that day. "And your nurse is simply charming! A pretty maid in an apron might be even more agreeable, perhaps; but for your severe monastic style it does very well."

Stepan Arkadyevitch told him many interesting pieces of news; especially interesting to Levin was the news that his brother, Sergey Ivanovitch, was intending to pay him a visit in the summer.

Not one word did Stepan Arkadyevitch say in reference to Kitty and the Shtcherbatskys; he merely gave him greetings from his wife. Levin was grateful to him for his delicacy and was very glad of his visitor. As always happened with him during his solitude, a mass of ideas and feelings had been accumulating within him, which he could not communicate to those about him. And now he poured out upon Stepan Arkadyevitch his poetic joy in the spring, and his failures and plans for the land, and his thoughts and criticisms on the books he had been reading, and the idea of his own book, the basis of which really was, though he was unaware of it himself, a criticism of all the old books on agriculture. Stepan Arkadyevitch, always charming, understanding everything at the slightest reference, was particularly charming on this visit, and Levin noticed in him a special tenderness, as it were, and a new tone of respect that flattered him.

The efforts of Agafea Mihalovna and the cook, that the dinner should be particularly good, only ended in the two famished friends attacking the preliminary course, eating a great deal of bread-and-butter, salt goose and salted mushrooms, and in Levin's finally ordering the soup to be served without the accompaniment of little pies, with which the cook had particularly meant to impress their visitor. But though Stepan Arkadyevitch was accustomed to very different dinners, he thought everything excellent: the herb brandy, and the bread, and the butter, and above all the salt goose and the mushrooms, and the nettle soup, and the chicken in white sauce, and the white Crimean wine—everything was superb and delicious.

"Splendid, splendid!" he said, lighting a fat cigar after the roast. "I feel as if, coming to you, I had landed on a peaceful shore after the noise and jolting of a steamer. And so you maintain that the laborer himself is an element to be studied and to regulate the choice of methods in agriculture. Of course, I'm an ignorant outsider; but I should fancy theory and its application will have its influence on the laborer too."

"Yes, but wait a bit. I'm not talking of political economy, I'm talking of the science of agriculture. It ought to be like the natural sciences, and to observe given phenomena and the laborer in his economic, ethnographical . . ."

At that instant Agafea Mihalovna came in with jam.

"Oh, Agafea Mihalovna," said Stepan Arkadyevitch, kissing the tips of his plump fingers, "what salt goose, what herb brandy! . . . What do you think, isn't it time to start, Kostya?" he added.

Levin looked out of the window at the sun sinking behind the bare tree-tops of the forest.

"Yes, it's time," he said. "Kouzma, get ready the trap," and he ran downstairs.

Stepan Arkadyevitch, going down, carefully took the canvas cover off his varnished gun case with his own hands, and opening it, began to get ready his expensive new-fashioned gun. Kouzma, who already scented a big tip, never left Stepan Arkadyevitch's side, and put on him both his stockings and boots, a task which Stepan Arkadyevitch readily left him.

"Kostya, give orders that if the merchant Ryabinin comes . . . I told him to come today, he's to be brought in and to wait for me . . ."

"Why, do you mean to say you're selling the forest to Ryabinin?"

"Yes. Do you know him?"

"To be sure I do. I have had to do business with him, 'positively and conclusively.' "

Stepan Arkadyevitch laughed. "Positively and conclusively" were the merchant's favorite words.

"Yes, it's wonderfully funny the way he talks. She knows where her master's going!" he added, patting Laska, who hung about Levin, whining and licking his hands, his boots, and his gun.

The trap was already at the steps when they went out.

"I told them to bring the trap round; or would you rather walk?"

"No, we'd better drive," said Stepan Arkadyevitch, getting into the trap. He sat down, tucked the tiger-skin rug round him, and lit a cigar. "How is it you don't smoke? A cigar is a sort of thing, not exactly a pleasure, but the crown and outward sign of pleasure. Come, this is life! How splendid it is! This is how I should like to live!"

"Why, who prevents you?" said Levin, smiling.

"No, you're a lucky man! You've got everything you like. You like horses—and you have them; dogs—you have them; shooting—you have it; farming—you have it."

"Perhaps because I rejoice in what I have, and don't fret for what I haven't," said Levin, thinking of Kitty.

Stepan Arkadyevitch comprehended, looked at him, but said nothing.

Levin was grateful to Oblonsky for noticing, with his never-failing tact, that he dreaded conversation about the Shtcherbatskys, and so saying nothing about them. But now Levin was longing to find out what was tormenting him so, yet he had not the courage to begin.

"Come, tell me how things are going with you," said Levin, bethinking himself that it was not nice of him to think only of himself.

Stepan Arkadyevitch's eyes sparkled merrily.

"You don't admit, I know, that one can be fond of new rolls when one has had one's rations of bread—to your mind it's a crime; but I don't count life as life without love," he said, taking Levin's question in his own way. "What am I to do? I'm made that way. And really, one does so little harm to anyone, and gives oneself so much pleasure . . ."

"What! is there something new, then?" queried Levin.

"Yes, my boy, there is! There, do you see, you know the type of Ossian's women. . . . Women, such as one sees in dreams . . . Well, these women are sometimes to be met in reality . . . and these women are terrible. Woman, don't you know, is such a subject that however much you study it, it's always perfectly new."

"Well, then, it would be better not to study it."

"No. Some mathematician has said that enjoyment lies in the search for truth, not in the finding it."

Levin listened in silence, and in spite of all the efforts he made, he could not in the least enter into the feelings of his friend and understand his sentiments and the charm of studying such women.

Chapter XV

THE PLACE FIXED ON FOR THE STAND-SHOOTING WAS NOT FAR ABOVE A STREAM IN A LITTLE aspen copse. On reaching the copse, Levin got out of the trap and led Oblonsky to a corner of a mossy, swampy glade, already quite free from snow. He went back himself to a double birch tree on the other side, and leaning his gun on the fork of a dead lower branch, he took off his full overcoat, fastened his belt again, and worked his arms to see if they were free.

Gray old Laska, who had followed them, sat down warily opposite him and pricked up her ears. The sun was setting behind a thick forest, and in the glow of sunset the birch trees, dotted about in the aspen copse, stood out clearly with their hanging twigs, and their buds swollen almost to bursting.

From the thickest parts of the copse, where the snow still remained, came the faint sound of narrow winding threads of water running away. Tiny birds twittered, and now and then fluttered from tree to tree.

In the pauses of complete stillness there came the rustle of last year's leaves, stirred by the thawing of the earth and the growth of the grass.

"Imagine! One can hear and see the grass growing!" Levin said to himself, noticing a wet, slate-colored aspen leaf moving beside a blade of young grass. He stood, listened, and gazed sometimes down at the wet mossy ground, sometimes at Laska listening all alert, sometimes at the sea of bare treetops that stretched on the slope below him, sometimes at the darkening sky, covered with white streaks of cloud.

A hawk flew high over a forest far away with slow sweep of its wings; another flew with exactly the same motion in the same direction and vanished. The birds twittered more and more loudly and busily in the thicket. An owl hooted not far off, and Laska, starting, stepped cautiously a few steps forward, and putting her head on one side, began to listen intently. Beyond the stream was heard the cuckoo. Twice she uttered her usual cuckoo-call, and then gave a hoarse, hurried call and broke down.

"Imagine! the cuckoo already!" said Stepan Arkadyevitch, coming out from behind a bush.

"Yes, I hear it," answered Levin, reluctantly breaking the stillness with his voice, which sounded disagreeable to himself. "Now it's coming!"

Stepan Arkadyevitch's figure again went behind the bush, and Levin saw nothing but the bright flash of a match, followed by the red glow and blue smoke of a cigarette.

"Tchk! tchk!" came the snapping sound of Stepan Arkadyevitch cocking his gun.

"What's that cry?" asked Oblonsky, drawing Levin's attention to a prolonged cry, as though a colt were whinnying in a high voice, in play.

"Oh, don't you know it? That's the hare. But enough talking! Listen, it's flying!" almost shrieked Levin, cocking his gun.

They heard a shrill whistle in the distance, and in the exact time, so well-known to the sportsman, two seconds later—another, a third, and after the third whistle the hoarse, guttural cry could be heard.

Levin looked about him to right and to left, and there, just facing him against the dusky blue sky above the confused mass of tender shoots of the aspens, he saw the flying bird. It was flying straight towards him; the guttural cry, like the even tearing of some strong stuff, sounded close to his ear; the long beak and neck of the bird could be seen, and at the very instant when Levin was taking aim, behind the bush where Oblonsky stood, there was a flash of red lightning: the bird dropped like an arrow, and darted upwards again. Again came the red flash and the sound of a blow, and fluttering its wings as though trying to keep up in the air, the bird halted, stopped still an instant, and fell with a heavy splash on the slushy ground.

"Can I have missed it?" shouted Stepan Arkadyevitch, who could not see for the smoke.

"Here it is!" said Levin, pointing to Laska, who with one ear raised, wagging the end of her shaggy tail, came slowly back as though she would prolong the pleasure, and as it were smiling, brought the dead bird to her master. "Well, I'm glad you were successful," said Levin, who, at the same time, had a sense of envy that he had not succeeded in shooting the snipe.

"It was a bad shot from the right barrel," responded Stepan Arkadyevitch, loading his gun. "Sh . . . it's flying!"

The shrill whistles rapidly following one another were heard again. Two snipe, playing and chasing one another, and only whistling, not crying, flew straight at the very heads of the sportsmen. There was the report of four shots, and like swallows the snipe turned swift somersaults in the air and vanished from sight.

The stand-shooting was capital. Stepan Arkadyevitch shot two more birds and Levin two, of which one was not found. It began to get dark. Venus, bright and silvery, shone with her soft light low down in the west behind the birch trees, and high up in the east twinkled the red lights of Arcturus. Over his head Levin made out the stars of the Great Bear and lost them again. The snipe had ceased flying; but Levin resolved to stay a little longer, till Venus, which he saw below a branch of birch, should be above it, and the stars of the Great Bear should be perfectly plain. Venus had risen above the branch, and the car of the Great Bear with its shaft was now all plainly visible against the dark blue sky, yet still he waited.

"Isn't it time to go home?" said Stepan Arkadyevitch.

It was quite still now in the copse, and not a bird was stirring.

"Let's stay a little while," answered Levin.

"As you like."

They were standing now about fifteen paces from one another.

"Stiva!" said Levin unexpectedly; "how is it you don't tell me whether your sister-in-law's married yet, or when she's going to be?"

Levin felt so resolute and serene that no answer, he fancied, could affect him. But he had never dreamed of what Stepan Arkadyevitch replied.

"She's never thought of being married, and isn't thinking of it; but she's very ill, and the doctors have sent her abroad. They're positively afraid she may not live."

"What!" cried Levin. "Very ill? What is wrong with her? How has she . . . ?"

While they were saying this, Laska, with ears pricked up, was looking upwards at the sky, and reproachfully at them.

"They have chosen a time to talk," she was thinking. "It's on the wing . . . Here it is, yes, it is. They'll miss it," thought Laska.

But at that very instant both suddenly heard a shrill whistle which, as it were, smote on their ears, and both suddenly seized their guns and two flashes gleamed, and two gangs sounded at the very same instant. The snipe flying high above instantly folded its wings and fell into a thicket, bending down the delicate shoots.

"Splendid! Together!" cried Levin, and he ran with Laska into the thicket to look for the snipe.

"Oh, yes, what was it that was unpleasant?" he wondered. "Yes, Kitty's ill. . . . Well, it can't be helped; I'm very sorry," he thought.

"She's found it! Isn't she a clever thing?" he said, taking the warm bird from Laska's mouth and packing it into the almost full game bag. "I've got it, Stiva!" he shouted.

Chapter XVI

On the way home Levin asked all details of Kitty's illness and the Shtcherbatskys' plans, and though he would have been ashamed to admit it, he was pleased at what he heard. He was pleased that there was still hope, and still more pleased that she should be suffering who had made him suffer so much. But when Stepan Arkadyevitch began to speak of the causes of Kitty's illness, and mentioned Vronsky's name, Levin cut him short.

"I have no right whatever to know family matters, and, to tell the truth, no interest in them either."

Stepan Arkadyevitch smiled hardly perceptibly, catching the instantaneous change he knew so well in Levin's face, which had become as gloomy as it had been bright a minute before.

"Have you quite settled about the forest with Ryabinin?" asked Levin.

"Yes, it's settled. The price is magnificent; thirty-eight thousand. Eight straight away, and the rest in six years. I've been bothering about it forever so long. No one would give more."

"Then you've as good as given away your forest for nothing," said Levin gloomily.

"How do you mean for nothing?" said Stepan Arkadyevitch with a good-humored smile, knowing that nothing would be right in Levin's eyes now.

"Because the forest is worth at least a hundred and fifty roubles the acre," answered Levin.

"Oh, these farmers!" said Stepan Arkadyevitch playfully. "Your tone of contempt for us poor townsfolk! . . . But when it comes to business, we do it better than anyone. I assure you I have reckoned it all out," he said, "and the forest is fetching a very good price—so much so that I'm afraid of this fellow's crying off, in fact. You know it's not 'timber,' " said Stepan Arkadyevitch, hoping by this distinction to convince Levin completely of the unfairness of his doubts. "And it won't run to more than twenty-five yards of fagots per acre, and he's giving me at the rate of seventy roubles the acre."

Levin smiled contemptuously. "I know," he thought, "that fashion not only in him, but in all city people, who, after being twice in ten years in the country, pick up two or three phrases and use them in season and out of season, firmly persuaded that they know all about it. '*Timber, run to so many yards the acre.*' He says those words without understanding them himself."

"I wouldn't attempt to teach you what you write about in your office," said he, "and if need arose, I should come to you to ask about it. But you're so positive you know all the lore of the forest. It's difficult. Have you counted the trees?"

"How count the trees?" said Stepan Arkadyevitch, laughing, still trying to draw his friend out of his ill-temper. "Count the sands of the sea, number the stars. Some higher power might do it."

"Oh, well, the higher power of Ryabinin can. Not a single merchant ever buys a forest without counting the trees, unless they get it given them for nothing, as you're doing now. I know your forest. I go there every year shooting, and your forest's worth a hundred and fifty roubles an acre paid down, while he's giving you sixty by installments. So that in fact you're making him a present of thirty thousand."

"Come, don't let your imagination run away with you," said Stepan Arkadyevitch piteously. "Why was it none would give it, then?"

"Why, because he has an understanding with the merchants; he's bought them off. I've had to do with all of them; I know them. They're not merchants, you know: they're speculators. He wouldn't look at a bargain that gave him ten, fifteen per cent profit, but holds back to buy a ruble's worth for twenty kopecks."

"Well, enough of it! You're out of temper."

"Not the least," said Levin gloomily, as they drove up to the house.

At the steps there stood a trap tightly covered with iron and leather, with a sleek horse tightly harnessed with broad collar-straps. In the trap sat the chubby, tightly belted clerk who served Ryabinin as coachman. Ryabinin himself was already in the house, and met the friends in the hall. Ryabinin was a tall, thinnish, middle-aged man, with mustache and a projecting clean-shaven chin, and prominent muddy-looking eyes. He was dressed in a long-skirted blue coat, with buttons below the waist at the back, and wore high boots wrinkled over the ankles and straight over the calf, with big galoshes drawn over them. He rubbed his face with his handkerchief, and wrapping round him his coat, which sat extremely well as it was, he greeted them with a smile, holding out his hand to Stepan Arkadyevitch, as though he wanted to catch something.

"So here you are," said Stepan Arkadyevitch, giving him his hand. "That's capital."

"I did not venture to disregard your excellency's commands, though the road was extremely bad. I positively walked the whole way, but I am here at my time. Konstantin Dmitrievitch, my respects"; he turned to Levin, trying to seize his hand too. But Levin, scowling, made as though he did not notice his hand, and took out the snipe. "Your honors have been diverting yourselves with the chase? What kind of bird may it be, pray?" added Ryabinin, looking contemptuously at the snipe: "a great delicacy, I suppose." And he shook his head disapprovingly, as though he had grave doubts whether this game were worth the candle.

"Would you like to go into my study?" Levin said in French to Stepan Arkadyevitch, scowling morosely. "Go into my study; you can talk there."

"Quite so, where you please," said Ryabinin with contemptuous dignity, as though wishing to make it felt that others might be in difficulties as to how to behave, but that he could never be in any difficulty about anything.

On entering the study Ryabinin looked about, as his habit was, as though seeking the holy picture, but when he had found it, he did not cross himself. He scanned the bookcases and bookshelves, and with the same dubious air with which he had regarded the snipe, he smiled contemptuously and shook his head disapprovingly, as though by no means willing to allow that this game were worth the candle.

"Well, have you brought the money?" asked Oblonsky. "Sit down."

"Oh, don't trouble about the money. I've come to see you to talk it over."

"What is there to talk over? But do sit down."

"I don't mind if I do," said Ryabinin, sitting down and leaning his elbows on the back of his chair in a position of the most intense discomfort to himself. "You must knock it down a bit, prince. It would be too bad. The money is ready conclusively to the last farthing. As to paying the money down, there'll be no hitch there."

Levin, who had meanwhile been putting his gun away in the cupboard, was just going out of the door, but catching the merchant's words, he stopped.

"Why, you've got the forest for nothing as it is," he said. "He came to me too late, or I'd have fixed the price for him."

Ryabinin got up, and in silence, with a smile, he looked Levin down and up.

"Very close about money is Konstantin Dmitrievitch," he said with a smile, turning to Stepan Arkadyevitch; "there's positively no dealing with him. I was bargaining for some wheat of him, and a pretty price I offered too."

"Why should I give you my goods for nothing? I didn't pick it up on the ground, nor steal it either."

"Mercy on us! nowadays there's no chance at all of stealing. With the open courts and everything done in style, nowadays there's no question of stealing. We are just talking things over like gentlemen. His excellency's asking too much for the forest. I can't make both ends meet over it. I must ask for a little concession."

"But is the thing settled between you or not? If it's settled, it's useless haggling; but if it's not," said Levin, "I'll buy the forest."

The smile vanished at once from Ryabinin's face. A hawklike, greedy, cruel expression was left upon it. With rapid, bony fingers he unbuttoned his coat, revealing a shirt, bronze waistcoat buttons, and a watch-chain, and quickly pulled out a fat old pocketbook.

"Here you are, the forest is mine," he said, crossing himself quickly, and holding out his hand. "Take the money; it's my forest. That's Ryabinin's way of doing business; he doesn't haggle over every half-penny," he added, scowling and waving the pocketbook.

"I wouldn't be in a hurry if I were you," said Levin.

"Come, really," said Oblonsky in surprise. "I've given my word, you know."

Levin went out of the room, slamming the door. Ryabinin looked towards the door and shook his head with a smile.

"It's all youthfulness—positively nothing but boyishness. Why, I'm buying it, upon my honor, simply, believe me, for the glory of it, that Ryabinin, and no one else, should have bought the copse of Oblonsky. And as to the profits, why, I must make what God gives. In God's name. If you would kindly sign the title-deed . . ."

Within an hour the merchant, stroking his big overcoat neatly down, and hooking up his jacket, with the agreement in his pocket, seated himself in his tightly covered trap, and drove homewards.

"Ugh, these gentlefolks!" he said to the clerk. "They—they're a nice lot!"

"That's so," responded the clerk, handing him the reins and buttoning the leather apron. "But I can congratulate you on the purchase, Mihail Ignatitch?"

"Well, well. . . ."

Chapter XVII

STEPAN ARKADYEVITCH WENT UPSTAIRS WITH HIS POCKET BULGING WITH NOTES, WHICH THE merchant had paid him for three months in advance. The business of the forest was over, the money in his pocket; their shooting had been excellent, and Stepan Arkadyevitch was in the happiest frame of mind, and so he felt specially anxious to dissipate the ill-humor that had come upon Levin. He wanted to finish the day at supper as pleasantly as it had been begun.

Levin certainly was out of humor, and in spite of all his desire to be affectionate and cordial to his charming visitor, he could not control his mood. The intoxication of the news that Kitty was not married had gradually begun to work upon him.

Kitty was not married, but ill, and ill from love for a man who had slighted her. This slight, as it were, rebounded upon him. Vronsky had slighted her, and she had slighted him, Levin. Consequently Vronsky had the right to despise Levin, and therefore he was his enemy. But all this Levin did not think out. He vaguely felt that there was something in it insulting to him, and he was not angry now at what had disturbed him, but he fell foul of everything that presented itself. The stupid sale of the forest, the fraud practiced upon Oblonsky and concluded in his house, exasperated him.

"Well, finished?" he said, meeting Stepan Arkadyevitch upstairs. "Would you like supper?"

"Well, I wouldn't say no to it. What an appetite I get in the country! Wonderful! Why didn't you offer Ryabinin something?"

"Oh, damn him!"

"Still, how you do treat him!" said Oblonsky. "You didn't even shake hands with him. Why not shake hands with him?"

"Because I don't shake hands with a waiter, and a waiter's a hundred times better than he is."

"What a reactionist you are, really! What about the amalgamation of classes?" said Oblonsky.

"Anyone who likes amalgamating is welcome to it, but it sickens me."

"You're a regular reactionist, I see."

"Really, I have never considered what I am. I am Konstantin Levin, and nothing else."

"And Konstantin Levin very much out of temper," said Stepan Arkadyevitch, smiling.

"Yes, I am out of temper, and do you know why? Because—excuse me—of your stupid sale. . . ."

Stepan Arkadyevitch frowned good-humoredly, like one who feels himself teased and attacked for no fault of his own.

"Come, enough about it!" he said. "When did anybody ever sell anything without being told immediately after the sale, 'It was worth much more'? But when one wants to sell, no one will give anything. . . . No, I see you've a grudge against that unlucky Ryabinin."

"Maybe I have. And do you know why? You'll say again that I'm a reactionist, or some other terrible word; but all the same it does annoy and anger me to see on all sides the impoverishing of the nobility to which I belong, and, in spite of the amalgamation of classes, I'm glad to belong. And their impoverishment is not due to extravagance—that would be nothing; living in good style—that's the proper thing for noblemen; it's only the nobles who know how to do it. Now the peasants about us buy land, and I don't mind that. The gentleman does nothing, while the peasant works and supplants the idle man. That's as it ought to be. And I'm very glad for the peasant. But I do mind seeing the process of impoverishment from a sort of—I don't know what to call it—innocence. Here a Polish speculator bought for half its value a magnificent estate from a young lady who lives in Nice. And there a merchant will get three acres of land, worth ten roubles, as security for the loan of one ruble. Here, for no kind of reason, you've made that rascal a present of thirty thousand roubles."

"Well, what should I have done? Counted every tree?"

"Of course, they must be counted. You didn't count them, but Ryabinin did. Ryabinin's children will have means of livelihood and education, while yours maybe will not!"

"Well, you must excuse me, but there's something mean in this counting. We have our business and they have theirs, and they must make their profit. Anyway, the thing's done, and there's an end of it. And here come some poached eggs, my favorite dish. And Agafea Mihalovna will give us that marvelous herb brandy. . . ."

Stepan Arkadyevitch sat down at the table and began joking with Agafea Mihalovna, assuring her that it was long since he had tasted such a dinner and such a supper.

"Well, you do praise it, anyway," said Agafea Mihalovna, "but Konstantin Dmitrievitch, give him what you will—a crust of bread—he'll eat it and walk away."

Though Levin tried to control himself, he was gloomy and silent. He wanted to put one question to Stepan Arkadyevitch, but he could not bring himself to the point, and could not find the words or the moment in which to put it. Stepan Arkadyevitch had gone down to his room, undressed, again washed, and attired in a nightshirt with goffered frills, he had got into bed, but Levin still lingered in his room, talking of various trifling matters, and not daring to ask what he wanted to know.

"How wonderfully they make this soap," he said gazing at a piece of soap he was handling, which Agafea Mihalovna had put ready for the visitor but Oblonsky had not used. "Only look; why, it's a work of art."

"Yes, everything's brought to such a pitch of perfection nowadays," said Stepan Arkadyevitch, with a moist and blissful yawn. "The theater, for instance, and the entertainments . . . a-a-a!" he yawned. "The electric light everywhere . . . a-a-a!"

"Yes, the electric light," said Levin. "Yes. Oh, and where's Vronsky now?" he asked suddenly, laying down the soap.

"Vronsky?" said Stepan Arkadyevitch, checking his yawn; "he's in Petersburg. He left soon after you did, and he's not once been in Moscow since. And do you know, Kostya, I'll tell you the truth," he went on, leaning his elbow on the table, and propping on his hand his handsome ruddy face, in which his moist, good-natured, sleepy eyes shone like stars. "It's your own fault. You took fright at the sight of your rival. But, as I told you at the time, I couldn't say which had the better chance. Why didn't you fight it out? I told you at the time that . . ." He yawned inwardly, without opening his mouth.

"Does he know, or doesn't he, that I did make an offer?" Levin wondered, gazing at him. "Yes, there's something humbugging, diplomatic in his face," and feeling he was blushing, he looked Stepan Arkadyevitch straight in the face without speaking.

"If there was anything on her side at the time, it was nothing but a superficial attraction," pursued Oblonsky. "His being such a perfect aristocrat, don't you know, and his future position in society, had an influence not with her, but with her mother."

Levin scowled. The humiliation of his rejection stung him to the heart, as though it were a fresh wound he had only just received. But he was at home, and the walls of home are a support.

"Stay, stay," he began, interrupting Oblonsky. "You talk of his being an aristocrat. But allow me to ask what it consists in, that aristocracy of Vronsky or of anybody else, beside which I can be looked down upon? You consider Vronsky an aristocrat, but I don't. A man whose father crawled up from nothing at all by intrigue, and whose mother—God knows whom she wasn't mixed up with. . . . No, excuse me, but I consider myself aristocratic, and people like me, who can point back in the past to three or four honorable generations of their family, of the highest degree of breeding (talent and intellect, of course that's another matter), and have never curried favor with anyone, never depended on anyone for anything, like my father and my grandfather. And I know many such. You think it mean of me to count the trees in my forest, while you make Ryabinin a present-of thirty thousand; but you get rents from your lands and I don't know what, while I don't, and so I prize what's come to me from my ancestors or been won by hard work. . . . We are aristocrats, and not those who can only exist by favor of the powerful of this world, and who can be bought for twopence halfpenny."

"Well, but whom are you attacking? I agree with you," said Stepan Arkadyevitch, sincerely and genially; though he was aware that in the class of those who could be bought for twopence halfpenny Levin was reckoning him too. Levin's warmth gave him genuine pleasure. "Whom are you attacking? Though a good deal is not true that you say about Vronsky, but I won't talk about that. I tell you straight out, if I were you, I should go back with me to Moscow, and . . ."

"No; I don't know whether you know it or not, but I don't care. And I tell you—I did make an offer and was rejected, and Katerina Alexandrovna is nothing now to me but a painful and humiliating reminiscence."

"What ever for? What nonsense!"

"But we won't talk about it. Please forgive me, if I've been nasty," said Levin. Now that he had opened his heart, he became as he had been in the morning. "You're not angry with me, Stiva? Please don't be angry," he said, and smiling, he took his hand.

"Of course not; not a bit, and no reason to be. I'm glad we've spoken openly. And do you know, stand-shooting in the morning is unusually good—why not go? I couldn't sleep the night anyway, but I might go straight from shooting to the station."

"Capital."

Chapter XVIII

ALTHOUGH ALL VRONSKY'S INNER LIFE WAS ABSORBED IN HIS PASSION, HIS EXTERNAL LIFE UNALterably and inevitably followed along the old accustomed lines of his social and regimental ties and interests. The interests of his regiment took an important place in Vronsky's life, both because he was fond of the regiment, and because the regiment was fond of him. They were not only fond of Vronsky in his regiment, they respected him too, and were proud of him; proud that this man, with his immense wealth, his brilliant education and abilities, and the path open before him to every kind of success, distinction, and ambition, had disregarded all that, and of all the interests of life had the interests of his regiment and his comrades nearest to his heart. Vronsky was aware of his comrades' view of him, and in addition to his liking for the life, he felt bound to keep up that reputation.

It need not be said that he did not speak of his love to any of his comrades, nor did he betray his secret even in the wildest drinking bouts (though indeed he was never so drunk as to lose all control of himself). And he shut up any of his thoughtless comrades who attempted to allude to his connection. But in spite of that, his love was known to all the town; everyone guessed with more or less confidence at his relations with Madame Karenina. The majority of the younger men envied him for just what was the most irksome factor in his love—the exalted position of Karenin, and the consequent publicity of their connection in society.

The greater number of the young women, who envied Anna and had long been weary of hearing her called *virtuous*, rejoiced at the fulfillment of their predictions, and were only waiting for a decisive turn in public opinion to fall upon her with all the weight of their scorn. They were already making ready their handfuls of mud to fling at her when the right moment arrived. The greater number of the middle-aged people and certain great personages were displeased at the prospect of the impending scandal in society.

Vronsky's mother, on hearing of his connection, was at first pleased at it, because nothing to her mind gave such a finishing touch to a brilliant young man as a *liaison* in the highest society; she was pleased, too, that Madame Karenina, who had so taken her fancy, and had talked so much of her son, was, after all, just like all other pretty and well-bred women—at least according to the Countess Vronskaya's ideas. But she had heard of late that her son had refused a position offered him of great importance to his career, simply in order to remain in the regiment, where he could be constantly seeing Madame Karenina. She learned that great personages were displeased with him on this account, and she changed her opinion. She was vexed, too, that from all she could learn of this connection it was not that brilliant, graceful, worldly *liaison* which she would have welcomed, but a sort of Wertherish, desperate passion, so she was told, which might well lead him into imprudence. She had not seen him since his abrupt departure from Moscow, and she sent her elder son to bid him come to see her.

This elder son, too, was displeased with his younger brother. He did not distinguish what sort of love his might be, big or little, passionate or passionless, lasting or passing (he kept a ballet girl himself, though he was the father of a family, so he was lenient in these matters), but he knew that this love affair was viewed with displeasure by those whom it was necessary to please, and therefore he did not approve of his brother's conduct.

Besides the service and society, Vronsky had another great interest—horses; he was passionately fond of horses.

That year races and a steeplechase had been arranged for the officers. Vronsky had put his name down, bought a thoroughbred English mare, and in spite of his love affair, he was looking forward to the races with intense, though reserved, excitement. . . .

These two passions did not interfere with one another. On the contrary, he needed occupation and distraction quite apart from his love, so as to recruit and rest himself from the violent emotions that agitated him.

Chapter XIX

On the day of the races at Krasnoe Selo, Vronsky had come earlier than usually to eat beef-steak in the common messroom of the regiment. He had no need to be strict with himself, as he had very quickly been brought down to the required light weight; but still he had to avoid gaining flesh, and so he eschewed farinaceous and sweet dishes. He sat with his coat unbuttoned over a white waistcoat, resting both elbows on the table, and while waiting for the steak he had ordered he looked at a French novel that lay open on his plate. He was only looking at the book to avoid conversation with the officers coming in and out; he was thinking.

He was thinking of Anna's promise to see him that day after the races. But he had not seen her for three days, and as her husband had just returned from abroad, he did not know whether she would be able to meet him today or not, and he did not know how to find out. He had had his last interview with her at his cousin Betsy's summer villa. He visited the Karenins' summer villa as rarely as possible. Now he wanted to go there, and he pondered the question how to do it.

"Of course I shall say Betsy has sent me to ask whether she's coming to the races. Of course, I'll go," he decided, lifting his head from the book. And as he vividly pictured the happiness of seeing her, his face lit up.

"Send to my house, and tell them to have out the carriage and three horses as quick as they can," he said to the servant, who handed him the steak on a hot silver dish, and moving the dish up he began eating.

From the billiard room next door came the sound of balls knocking, of talk and laughter. Two officers appeared at the entrance-door: one, a young fellow, with a feeble, delicate face, who had lately joined the regiment from the Corps of Pages; the other, a plump, elderly officer, with a bracelet on his wrist, and little eyes, lost in fat.

Vronsky glanced at them, frowned, and looking down at his book as though he had not noticed them, he proceeded to eat and read at the same time.

"What? Fortifying yourself for your work?" said the plump officer, sitting down beside him.

"As you see," responded Vronsky, knitting his brows, wiping his mouth, and not looking at the officer.

"So you're not afraid of getting fat?" said the latter, turning a chair round for the young officer.

"What?" said Vronsky angrily, making a wry face of disgust, and showing his even teeth.

"You're not afraid of getting fat?"

"Waiter, sherry!" said Vronsky, without replying, and moving the book to the other side of him, he went on reading.

The plump officer took up the list of wines and turned to the young officer.

"You choose what we're to drink," he said, handing him the card, and looking at him.

"Rhine wine, please," said the young officer, stealing a timid glance at Vronsky, and trying to pull his scarcely visible mustache. Seeing that Vronsky did not turn round, the young officer got up.

"Let's go into the billiard room," he said.

The plump officer rose submissively, and they moved towards the door.

At that moment there walked into the room the tall and well-built Captain Yashvin. Nodding with an air of lofty contempt to the two officers, he went up to Vronsky.

"Ah! here he is!" he cried, bringing his big hand down heavily on his epaulet. Vronsky looked round angrily, but his face lit up immediately with his characteristic expression of genial and manly serenity.

"That's it, Alexey," said the captain, in his loud baritone. "You must just eat a mouthful, now, and drink only one tiny glass."

"Oh, I'm not hungry."

"There go the inseparables," Yashvin dropped, glancing sarcastically at the two officers who were at that instant leaving the room. And he bent his long legs, swathed in tight riding breeches, and sat down in the chair, too low for him, so that his knees were cramped up in a sharp angle.

"Why didn't you turn up at the Red Theater yesterday? Numerova wasn't at all bad. Where were you?"

"I was late at the Tverskoys'," said Vronsky.

"Ah!" responded Yashvin.

Yashvin, a gambler and a rake, a man not merely without moral principles, but of immoral principles, Yashvin was Vronsky's greatest friend in the regiment. Vronsky liked him both for his exceptional physical strength, which he showed for the most part by being able to drink like a fish, and do without sleep without being in the slightest degree affected by it; and for his great strength of character, which he showed in his relations with his comrades and superior officers, commanding both fear and respect, and also at cards, when he would play for tens of thousands and however much he might have drunk, always with such skill and decision that he was reckoned the best player in the English Club. Vronsky respected and liked Yashvin particularly because he felt Yashvin liked him, not for his name and his money, but for himself. And of all men he was the only one with whom Vronsky would have liked to speak of his love. He felt that Yashvin, in spite of his apparent contempt for every sort of feeling, was the only man who could, so he fancied, comprehend the intense passion which now filled his whole life. Moreover, he felt certain that Yashvin, as it was, took no delight in gossip and scandal, and interpreted his feeling rightly, that is to say, knew and believed that this passion was not a jest, not a pastime, but something more serious and important.

Vronsky had never spoken to him of his passion, but he was aware that he knew all about it, and that he put the right interpretation on it, and he was glad to see that in his eyes.

"Ah! yes," he said, to the announcement that Vronsky had been at the Tverskoys'; and his black eyes shining, he plucked at his left mustache, and began twisting it into his mouth, a bad habit he had.

"Well, and what did you do yesterday? Win anything?" asked Vronsky.

"Eight thousand. But three don't count; he won't pay up."

"Oh, then you can afford to lose over me," said Vronsky, laughing. (Yashvin had bet heavily on Vronsky in the races.)

"No chance of my losing. Mahotin's the only one that's risky."

And the conversation passed to forecasts of the coming race, the only thing Vronsky could think of just now.

"Come along, I've finished," said Vronsky, and getting up he went to the door. Yashvin got up too, stretching his long legs and his long back.

"It's too early for me to dine, but I must have a drink. I'll come along directly. Hi, wine!" he shouted, in his rich voice, that always rang out so loudly at drill, and set the windows shaking now.

"No, all right," he shouted again immediately after. "You're going home, so I'll go with you."

And he walked out with Vronsky.

Chapter XX

VRONSKY WAS STAYING IN A ROOMY, CLEAN, FINNISH HUT, DIVIDED INTO TWO BY A PARTITION. Petritsky lived with him in camp too. Petritsky was asleep when Vronsky and Yashvin came into the hut.

"Get up, don't go on sleeping," said Yashvin, going behind the partition and giving Petritsky, who was lying with ruffled hair and with his nose in the pillow, a prod on the shoulder.

Petritsky jumped up suddenly onto his knees and looked round.

"Your brother's been here," he said to Vronsky. "He waked me up, damn him, and said he'd look in again." And pulling up the rug he flung himself back on the pillow. "Oh, do shut up, Yashvin!" he said, getting furious with Yashvin, who was pulling the rug off him. "Shut up!" He turned over and opened his eyes. "You'd better tell me what to drink; such a nasty taste in my mouth, that . . ."

"Brandy's better than anything," boomed Yashvin. "Tereshtchenko! brandy for your master and cucumbers," he shouted, obviously taking pleasure in the sound of his own voice.

"Brandy, do you think? Eh?" queried Petritsky, blinking and rubbing his eyes. "And you'll drink something? All right then, we'll have a drink together! Vronsky, have a drink?" said Petritsky, getting up and wrapping the tiger-skin rug round him. He went to the door of the partition wall, raised his hands, and hummed in French, "There was a king in Thule." "Vronsky, will you have a drink?"

"Go along," said Vronsky, putting on the coat his valet handed to him.

"Where are you off to?" asked Yashvin. "Oh, here are your three horses," he added, seeing the carriage drive up.

"To the stables, and I've got to see Bryansky, too, about the horses," said Vronsky.

Vronsky had as a fact promised to call at Bryansky's, some eight miles from Peterhof, and to bring him some money owing for some horses; and he hoped to have time to get that in too. But his comrades were at once aware that he was not only going there.

Petritsky, still humming, winked and made a pout with his lips, as though he would say: "Oh, yes, we know your Bryansky."

"Mind you're not late!" was Yashvin's only comment; and to change the conversation: "How's my roan? is he doing all right?" he inquired, looking out of the window at the middle one of the three horses, which he had sold Vronsky.

"Stop!" cried Petritsky to Vronsky as he was just going out. "Your brother left a letter and a note for you. Wait a bit; where are they?"

Vronsky stopped.

"Well, where are they?"

"Where are they? That's just the question!" said Petritsky solemnly, moving his forefinger upwards from his nose.

"Come, tell me; this is silly!" said Vronsky smiling.

"I have not lit the fire. Here somewhere about."

"Come, enough fooling! Where is the letter?"

"No, I've forgotten really. Or was it a dream? Wait a bit, wait a bit! But what's the use of getting in a rage. If you'd drunk four bottles yesterday as I did you'd forget where you were lying. Wait a bit, I'll remember!"

Petritsky went behind the partition and lay down on his bed.

"Wait a bit! This was how I was lying, and this was how he was standing. Yes—yes—yes. . . . Here it is!"—and Petritsky pulled a letter out from under the mattress, where he had hidden it.

Vronsky took the letter and his brother's note. It was the letter he was expecting—from his mother, reproaching him for not having been to see her—and the note was from his brother to say that he must have a little talk with him. Vronsky knew that it was all about the same thing. "What business is it of theirs!" thought Vronsky, and crumpling up the letters he thrust them between the buttons of his coat so as to read them carefully on the road. In the porch of the hut he was met by two officers; one of his regiment and one of another.

Vronsky's quarters were always a meeting place for all the officers.

"Where are you off to?"

"I must go to Peterhof."

"Has the mare come from Tsarskoe?"

"Yes, but I've not seen her yet."

"They say Mahotin's Gladiator's lame."

"Nonsense! But however are you going to race in this mud?" said the other.

"Here are my saviors!" cried Petritsky, seeing them come in. Before him stood the orderly with a tray of brandy and salted cucumbers. "Here's Yashvin ordering me to drink a pick-me-up."

"Well, you did give it to us yesterday," said one of those who had come in; "you didn't let us get a wink of sleep all night."

"Oh, didn't we make a pretty finish!" said Petritsky. "Volkov climbed onto the roof and began telling us how sad he was. I said: 'Let's have music, the funeral march!' He fairly dropped asleep on the roof over the funeral march."

"Drink it up; you positively must drink the brandy, and then seltzer water and a lot of lemon," said Yashvin, standing over Petritsky like a mother making a child take medicine, "and then a little champagne—just a small bottle."

"Come, there's some sense in that. Stop a bit, Vronsky. We'll all have a drink."

"No; good-bye all of you. I'm not going to drink today."

"Why, are you gaining weight? All right, then we must have it alone. Give us the seltzer water and lemon."

"Vronsky!" shouted someone when he was already outside.

"Well?"

"You'd better get your hair cut, it'll weigh you down, especially at the top."

Vronsky was in fact beginning, prematurely, to get a little bald. He laughed gaily, showing his even teeth, and pulling his cap over the thin place, went out and got into his carriage.

"To the stables!" he said, and was just pulling out the letters to read them through, but he thought better of it, and put off reading them so as not to distract his attention before looking at the mare. "Later!"

Chapter XXI

THE TEMPORARY STABLE, A WOODEN SHED, HAD BEEN PUT UP CLOSE TO THE RACE COURSE, AND there his mare was to have been taken the previous day. He had not yet seen her there.

During the last few days he had not ridden her out for exercise himself, but had put her in the charge of the trainer, and so now he positively did not know in what condition his mare had arrived yesterday and was today. He had scarcely got out of his carriage when his groom, the so-called "stable boy," recognizing the carriage some way off, called the trainer. A dry-looking Englishman, in high boots and a short jacket, clean-shaven, except for a tuft below his chin, came to meet him, walking with the uncouth gait of jockey, turning his elbows out and swaying from side to side.

"Well, how's Frou-Frou?" Vronsky asked in English.

"All right, sir," the Englishman's voice responded somewhere in the inside of his throat. "Better not go in," he added, touching his hat. "I've put a muzzle on her, and the mare's fidgety. Better not go in, it'll excite the mare."

"No, I'm going in. I want to look at her."

"Come along, then," said the Englishman, frowning, and speaking with his mouth shut, and with swinging elbows, he went on in front with his disjointed gait.

They went into the little yard in front of the shed. A stable boy, spruce and smart in his holiday attire, met them with a broom in his hand, and followed them. In the shed there were five horses in their separate stalls, and Vronsky knew that his chief rival, Gladiator, a very tall chestnut horse, had been brought there, and must be standing among them. Even more than his mare, Vronsky longed to see Gladiator, whom he had never seen. But he knew that by the etiquette of the race course it was not merely impossible for him to see the horse, but improper even to ask questions about him. Just as he was passing along the passage, the boy opened the door into the second horse-box on the left, and Vronsky caught a glimpse of a big chestnut horse with white legs. He knew that this was Gladiator, but, with the feeling of a man turning away from the sight of another man's open letter, he turned round and went into Frou-Frou's stall.

"The horse is here belonging to Mak . . . Mak . . . I never can say the name," said the Englishman, over his shoulder, pointing his big finger and dirty nail towards Gladiator's stall.

"Mahotin? Yes, he's my most serious rival," said Vronsky.

"If you were riding him," said the Englishman, "I'd bet on you."

"Frou-Frou's more nervous; he's stronger," said Vronsky, smiling at the compliment to his riding.

"In a steeplechase it all depends on riding and on pluck," said the Englishman.

Of pluck—that is, energy and courage—Vronsky did not merely feel that he had enough; what was of far more importance, he was firmly convinced that no one in the world could have more of this "pluck" than he had.

"Don't you think I want more thinning down?"

"Oh, no," answered the Englishman. "Please, don't speak loud. The mare's fidgety," he added, nodding towards the horse-box, before which they were standing, and from which came the sound of restless stamping in the straw.

He opened the door, and Vronsky went into the horse-box, dimly lit by one little window. In the horse-box stood a dark bay mare, with a muzzle on, picking at the fresh straw with her hoofs. Looking round him in the twilight of the horse-box, Vronsky unconsciously took in once more in a comprehensive glance all the points of his favorite mare. Frou-Frou was a beast of medium size, not altogether free from reproach, from a breeder's point of view. She was small-boned all over; though her chest was extremely prominent in front, it was narrow. Her hind-quarters were a little drooping, and in her fore-legs, and still more in her hind-legs, there was a noticeable curvature. The muscles of both hind-and fore-legs were not very thick; but across her shoulders the mare was exceptionally broad, a peculiarity specially striking now that she was lean from training. The bones of her legs below the knees looked no thicker than a finger from in front, but were extraordinarily thick seen from the side. She looked altogether, except across the shoulders, as it were, pinched in at the sides and pressed out in depth. But she had in the highest degree the quality that makes all defects forgotten: that quality was *blood,* the blood *that tells,* as the English expression has it. The muscles stood up sharply under the network of sinews, covered with the delicate, mobile skin, soft as satin, and they were hard as bone. Her clean-cut head, with prominent, bright, spirited eyes, broadened out at the open nostrils, that showed the red blood in the cartilage within. About all her figure, and especially her head, there was a certain expression of energy, and, at the same time, of softness. She was one of those creatures which seem only not to speak because the mechanism of their mouth does not allow them to.

To Vronsky, at any rate, it seemed that she understood all he felt at that moment, looking at her.

Directly Vronsky went towards her, she drew in a deep breath, and, turning back her prominent eye till the white looked bloodshot, she started at the approaching figures from the opposite side, shaking her muzzle, and shifting lightly from one leg to the other.

"There, you see how fidgety she is," said the Englishman.

"There, darling! There!" said Vronsky, going up to the mare and speaking soothingly to her.

But the nearer he came, the more excited she grew. Only when he stood by her head, she was suddenly quieter, while the muscles quivered under her soft, delicate coat. Vronsky patted her strong neck, straightened over her sharp withers a stray lock of her mane that had fallen on the other side, and moved his face near her dilated nostrils, transparent as a bat's wing. She drew a loud breath and snorted out through her tense nostrils, started, pricked up her sharp ear, and put out her strong, black lip towards Vronsky, as though she would nip hold of his sleeve. But remembering the muzzle, she shook it and again began restlessly stamping one after the other her shapely legs.

"Quiet, darling, quiet!" he said, patting her again over her hind-quarters; and with a glad sense that his mare was in the best possible condition, he went out of the horse-box.

The mare's excitement had infected Vronsky. He felt that his heart was throbbing, and that he, too, like the mare, longed to move, to bite; it was both dreadful and delicious.

"Well, I rely on you, then," he said to the Englishman; "half-past six on the ground."

"All right," said the Englishman. "Oh, where are you going, my lord?" he asked suddenly, using the title "my lord," which he had scarcely ever used before.

Vronsky in amazement raised his head, and stared, as he knew how to stare, not into the Englishman's eyes, but at his forehead, astounded at the impertinence of his question. But realizing that in asking this the Englishman had been looking at him not as an employer, but as a jockey, he answered:

"I've got to go to Bryansky's; I shall be home within an hour."

"How often I'm asked that question today!" he said to himself, and he blushed, a thing which rarely happened to him. The Englishman looked gravely at him; and, as though he, too, knew where Vronsky was going, he added:

"The great thing's to keep quiet before a race," said he; "don't get out of temper or upset about anything."

"All right," answered Vronsky, smiling; and jumping into his carriage, he told the man to drive to Peterhof.

Before he had driven many paces away, the dark clouds that had been threatening rain all day broke, and there was a heavy downpour of rain.

"What a pity!" thought Vronsky, putting up the roof of the carriage. "It was muddy before, now it will be a perfect swamp." As he sat in solitude in the closed carriage, he took out his mother's letter and his brother's note, and read them through.

Yes, it was the same thing over and over again. Everyone, his mother, his brother, everyone thought fit to interfere in the affairs of his heart. This interference aroused in him a feeling of angry hatred—a feeling he had rarely known before. "What business is it of theirs? Why does everybody feel called upon to concern himself about me? And why do they worry me so? Just because they see that this is something they can't understand. If it were a common, vulgar, worldly intrigue, they would have left me alone. They feel that this is something different, that this is not a mere pastime, that this woman is dearer to me than life. And this is incomprehensible, and that's why it annoys them. Whatever our destiny is or may be, we have made it ourselves, and we do not complain of it," he said, in the word *we* linking himself with Anna. "No, they must needs teach us how to live. They haven't an idea of what happiness is; they don't know that without our love, for us there is neither happiness nor unhappiness—no life at all," he thought.

He was angry with all of them for their interference just because he felt in his soul that they, all these people, were right. He felt that the love that bound him to Anna was not a momentary impulse, which would pass, as worldly intrigues do pass, leaving no other traces in the life of either but pleasant or unpleasant memories. He felt all the torture of his own and her position, all the difficulty there was for them, conspicuous as they were in the eye of all the world, in concealing their love, in lying and deceiving; and in lying, deceiving, feigning, and continually thinking of others, when the passion that united them was so intense that they were both oblivious of everything else but their love.

He vividly recalled all the constantly recurring instances of inevitable necessity for lying and deceit, which were so against his natural bent. He recalled particularly vividly the shame he had more than once detected in her at this necessity for lying and deceit. And he experienced the strange feeling that had sometimes come upon him since his secret love for Anna. This was a feeling of loathing for something—whether for Alexey Alexandrovitch, or for himself, or for the whole world, he could not have said. But he always drove away this strange feeling. Now, too, he shook it off and continued the thread of his thoughts.

"Yes, she was unhappy before, but proud and at peace; and now she cannot be at peace and feel secure in her dignity, though she does not show it. Yes, we must put an end to it," he decided.

And for the first time the idea clearly presented itself that it was essential to put an end to this false position, and the sooner the better. "Throw up everything, she and I, and hide ourselves somewhere alone with our love," he said to himself.

Chapter XXII

THE RAIN DID NOT LAST LONG, AND BY THE TIME VRONSKY ARRIVED, HIS SHAFT-HORSE TROTTING at full speed and dragging the trace-horses galloping through the mud, with their reins hanging loose, the sun had peeped out again, the roofs of the summer villas and the old limetrees in the gardens on both sides of the principal streets sparkled with wet brilliance, and from the twigs came a pleasant drip and from the roofs rushing streams of water. He thought no more of the shower spoiling the race course, but was rejoicing now that—thanks to the rain—he would be sure to find her at home and alone, as he knew that Alexey Alexandrovitch, who had lately returned from a foreign watering place, had not moved from Petersburg.

Hoping to find her alone, Vronsky alighted, as he always did, to avoid attracting attention, before crossing the bridge, and walked to the house. He did not go up the steps to the street door, but went into the court.

"Has your master come?" he asked a gardener.

"No, sir. The mistress is at home. But will you please go to the front door; there are servants there," the gardener answered. "They'll open the door."

"No, I'll go in from the garden."

And feeling satisfied that she was alone, and wanting to take her by surprise, since he had not promised to be there today, and she would certainly not expect him to come before the races, he walked, holding his sword and stepping cautiously over the sandy path, bordered with flowers, to the terrace that looked out upon the garden. Vronsky forgot now all that he had thought on the way of the hardships and difficulties of their position. He thought of nothing but that he would see her directly, not in imagination, but living, all of her, as she was in reality. He was just going in, stepping on his whole foot so as not to creak, up the worn steps of the terrace, when he suddenly remembered what he always forgot, and what caused the most torturing side of his relations with her, her son with his questioning—hostile, as he fancied—eyes.

This boy was more often than anyone else a check upon their freedom. When he was present, both Vronsky and Anna did not merely avoid speaking of anything that they could not have repeated before everyone; they did not even allow themselves to refer by hints to anything the boy did not understand. They had made no agreement about this, it had settled itself. They would have felt it wounding themselves to deceive the child. In his presence they talked like acquaintances. But in spite of this caution, Vronsky often saw the child's intent, bewildered glance fixed upon him, and a strange shyness, uncertainty, at one time friendliness, at another, coldness and reserve, in the boy's manner to him; as though the child felt that between this man and his mother there existed some important bond, the significance of which he could not understand.

As a fact, the boy did feel that he could not understand this relation, and he tried painfully, and was not able to make clear to himself what feeling he ought to have for this man. With a child's keen instinct for every manifestation of feeling, he saw distinctly that his father, his governess, his nurse—all did not merely dislike Vronsky, but looked on him with horror and aversion, though they never said anything about him, while his mother looked on him as her greatest friend.

"What does it mean? Who is he? How ought I to love him? If I don't know, it's my fault; either I'm stupid or a naughty boy," thought the child. And this was what caused his dubious, inquiring, sometimes hostile, expression, and the shyness and uncertainty which Vronsky found so irksome. This child's presence always and infallibly called up in Vronsky that strange feeling of inexplicable loathing which he had experienced of late. This child's presence called up both in Vronsky and in Anna a feeling akin to the feeling of a sailor who sees by the compass that the direction in which he is swiftly moving is far from the right one, but that to arrest his motion is not in his power, that every instant is carrying him further and further away, and that to admit to himself his deviation from the right direction is the same as admitting his certain ruin.

This child, with his innocent outlook upon life, was the compass that showed them the point to which they had departed from what they knew, but did not want to know.

This time Seryozha was not at home, and she was completely alone. She was sitting on the terrace waiting for the return of her son, who had gone out for his walk and been caught in the rain. She had sent a manservant and a maid out to look for him. Dressed in a white gown, deeply embroidered, she was sitting in a corner of the terrace behind some flowers, and did not hear him. Bending her curly black head, she pressed her forehead against a cool watering pot that stood on the parapet, and both her lovely hands, with the rings he knew so well, clasped the pot. The beauty of her whole figure, her head, her neck, her hands, struck Vronsky every time as something new and unexpected. He stood still, gazing at her in ecstasy. But, directly he would have made a step to come nearer to her, she was aware of his presence, pushed away the watering pot, and turned her flushed face towards him.

"What's the matter? You are ill?" he said to her in French, going up to her. He would have run to her, but remembering that there might be spectators, he looked round towards the balcony door, and reddened a little, as he always reddened, feeling that he had to be afraid and be on his guard.

"No, I'm quite well," she said, getting up and pressing his outstretched hand tightly. "I did not expect . . . thee."

"Mercy! what cold hands!" he said.

"You startled me," she said. "I'm alone, and expecting Seryozha; he's out for a walk; they'll come in from this side."

But, in spite of her efforts to be calm, her lips were quivering.

"Forgive me for coming, but I couldn't pass the day without seeing you," he went on, speaking French, as he always did to avoid using the stiff Russian plural form, so impossibly frigid between them, and the dangerously intimate singular.

"Forgive you? I'm so glad!"

"But you're ill or worried," he went on, not letting go her hands and bending over her. "What were you thinking of?"

"Always the same thing," she said, with a smile.

She spoke the truth. If ever at any moment she had been asked what she was thinking of, she could have answered truly: of the same thing, of her happiness and her unhappiness. She was thinking, just when he came upon her, of this: why was it, she wondered, that to others, to Betsy (she knew of her secret connection with Tushkevitch) it was all easy, while to her it was such torture? Today this thought gained special poignancy from certain other considerations. She asked him about the races. He answered her questions, and, seeing that she was agitated, trying to calm her, he began telling her in the simplest tone the details of his preparations for the races.

"Tell him or not tell him?" she thought, looking into his quiet, affectionate eyes. "He is so happy, so absorbed in his races that he won't understand as he ought, he won't understand all the gravity of this fact to us."

"But you haven't told me what you were thinking of when I came in," he said, interrupting his narrative; "please tell me!"

She did not answer, and, bending her head a little, she looked inquiringly at him from under her brows, her eyes shining under their long lashes. Her hand shook as it played with a leaf she had picked. He saw it, and his face expressed that utter subjection, that slavish devotion, which had done so much to win her.

"I see something has happened. Do you suppose I can be at peace, knowing you have a trouble I am not sharing? Tell me, for God's sake," he repeated imploringly.

"Yes, I shan't be able to forgive him if he does not realize all the gravity of it. Better not tell;

why put him to the proof?" she thought, still staring at him in the same way, and feeling the hand that held the leaf was trembling more and more.

"For God's sake!" he repeated, taking her hand.

"Shall I tell you?"

"Yes, yes, yes . . ."

"I'm with child," she said, softly and deliberately. The leaf in her hand shook more violently, but she did not take her eyes off him, watching how he would take it. He turned white, would have said something, but stopped; he dropped her hand, and his head sank on his breast. "Yes, he realizes all the gravity of it," she thought, and gratefully she pressed his hand.

But she was mistaken in thinking he realized the gravity of the fact as she, a woman, realized it. On hearing it, he felt come upon him with tenfold intensity that strange feeling of loathing of someone. But at the same time, he felt that the turning point he had been longing for had come now; that it was impossible to go on concealing things from her husband, and it was inevitable in one way or another that they should soon put an end to their unnatural position. But, besides that, her emotion physically affected him in the same way. He looked at her with a look of submissive tenderness, kissed her hand, got up, and, in silence, paced up and down the terrace.

"Yes," he said, going up to her resolutely. "Neither you nor I have looked on our relations as a passing amusement, and now our fate is sealed. It is absolutely necessary to put an end"—he looked round as he spoke—"to the deception in which we are living."

"Put an end? How put an end, Alexey?" she said softly.

She was calmer now, and her face lit up with a tender smile.

"Leave your husband and make our life one."

"It is one as it is," she answered, scarcely audibly.

"Yes, but altogether; altogether."

"But how, Alexey, tell me how?" she said in melancholy mockery at the hopelessness of her own position. "Is there any way out of such a position? Am I not the wife of my husband?"

"There is a way out of every position. We must take our line," he said. "Anything's better than the position in which you're living. Of course, I see how you torture yourself over everything—the world and your son and your husband."

"Oh, not over my husband," she said, with a quiet smile. "I don't know him, I don't think of him. He doesn't exist."

"You're not speaking sincerely. I know you. You worry about him too."

"Oh, he doesn't even know," she said, and suddenly a hot flush came over her face; her cheeks, her brow, her neck crimsoned, and tears of shame came into her eyes. "But we won't talk of him."

Chapter XXIII

VRONSKY HAD SEVERAL TIMES ALREADY, THOUGH NOT SO RESOLUTELY AS NOW, TRIED TO BRING her to consider their position, and every time he had been confronted by the same superficiality and triviality with which she met his appeal now. It was as though there were something in this which she could not or would not face, as though directly she began to speak of this, she, the real Anna, retreated somehow into herself, and another strange and unaccountable woman came out, whom he did not love, and whom he feared, and who was in opposition to him. But today he was resolved to have it out.

"Whether he knows or not," said Vronsky, in his usual quiet and resolute tone, "that's nothing to do with us. We cannot . . . you cannot stay like this, especially now."

"What's to be done, according to you?" she asked with the same frivolous irony. She who had so feared he would take her condition too lightly was now vexed with him for deducing from it the necessity of taking some step.

"Tell him everything, and leave him."

"Very well, let us suppose I do that," she said. "Do you know what the result of that would be? I can tell you it all beforehand," and a wicked light gleamed in her eyes, that had been so soft a minute before. " 'Eh, you love another man, and have entered into criminal intrigues with him?' " (Mimicking her husband, she threw an emphasis on the word "criminal," as Alexey Alexandrovitch did.) " 'I warned you of the results in the religious, the civil, and the domestic relation. You have not listened to me. Now I cannot let you disgrace my name—' " and my son, she had meant to say, but about her son she could not jest—" 'disgrace my name, and'—and more in the same style," she added. "In general terms, he'll say in his official manner, and with all distinctness and precision, that he cannot let me go, but will take all measures in his power to prevent scandal. And he will calmly and punctually act in accordance with his words. That's what will happen. He's not a man, but a machine, and a spiteful machine when he's angry," she added, recalling Alexey Alexandrovitch as she spoke, with all the peculiarities of his figure and manner of speaking, and reckoning against him every defect she could find in him, softening nothing for the great wrong she herself was doing him.

"But, Anna," said Vronsky, in a soft and persuasive voice, trying to soothe her, "we absolutely must, anyway, tell him, and then be guided by the line he takes."

"What, run away?"

"And why not run away? I don't see how we can keep on like this. And not for my sake—I see that you suffer."

"Yes, run away, and become your mistress," she said angrily.

"Anna," he said, with reproachful tenderness.

"Yes," she went on, "become your mistress, and complete the ruin of . . ."

Again she would have said "my son," but she could not utter that word.

Vronsky could not understand how she, with her strong and truthful nature, could endure this state of deceit, and not long to get out of it. But he did not suspect that the chief cause of it was the word—*son,* which she could not bring herself to pronounce. When she thought of her son, and his future attitude to his mother, who had abandoned his father, she felt such terror at what she had done, that she could not face it; but, like a woman, could only try to comfort herself with lying assurances that everything would remain as it always had been, and that it was possible to forget the fearful question of how it would be with her son.

"I beg you, I entreat you," she said suddenly, taking his hand, and speaking in quite a different tone, sincere and tender, "never speak to me of that!"

"But, Anna . . ."

"Never. Leave it to me. I know all the baseness, all the horror of my position; but it's not so easy to arrange as you think. And leave it to me, and do what I say. Never speak to me of it. Do you promise me? . . . No, no, promise! . . ."

"I promise everything, but I can't be at peace, especially after what you have told me. I can't be at peace, when you can't be at peace. . . ."

"I?" she repeated. "Yes, I am worried sometimes; but that will pass, if you will never talk about this. When you talk about it—it's only then it worries me."

"I don't understand," he said.

"I know," she interrupted him, "how hard it is for your truthful nature to lie, and I grieve for you. I often think that you have ruined your whole life for me."

"I was just thinking the very same thing," he said; "how could you sacrifice everything for my sake? I can't forgive myself that you're unhappy."

"I unhappy?" she said, coming closer to him, and looking at him with an ecstatic smile of love. "I am like a hungry man who has been given food. He may be cold, and dressed in rags, and ashamed, but he is not unhappy. I unhappy? No, this is my unhappiness. . . ."

She could hear the sound of her son's voice coming towards them, and glancing swiftly round the terrace, she got up impulsively. Her eyes glowed with the fire he knew so well; with a rapid movement she raised her lovely hands, covered with rings, took his head, looked a long look into his face, and, putting up her face with smiling, parted lips, swiftly kissed his mouth and both eyes, and pushed him away. She would have gone, but he held her back.

"When?" he murmured in a whisper, gazing in ecstasy at her.

"Tonight, at one o'clock," she whispered, and, with a heavy sigh, she walked with her light, swift step to meet her son.

Seryozha had been caught by the rain in the big garden, and he and his nurse had taken shelter in an arbor.

"Well, *au revoir,*" she said to Vronsky. "I must soon be getting ready for the races. Betsy promised to fetch me."

Vronsky, looking at his watch, went away hurriedly.

Chapter XXIV

WHEN VRONSKY LOOKED AT HIS WATCH ON THE KARENINS' BALCONY, HE WAS SO GREATLY AGitated and lost in his thoughts that he saw the figures on the watch's face, but could not take in what time it was. He came out on to the highroad and walked, picking his way carefully through the mud, to his carriage. He was so completely absorbed in his feeling for Anna, that he did not even think what o'clock it was, and whether he had time to go to Bryansky's. He had left him, as often happens, only the external faculty of memory, that points out each step one has to take, one after the other. He went up to his coachman, who was dozing on the box in the shadow, already lengthening, of a thick limetree; he admired the shifting clouds of midges circling over the hot horses, and, waking the coachman, he jumped into the carriage, and told him to drive to Bryansky's. It was only after driving nearly five miles that he had sufficiently recovered himself to look at his watch, and realize that it was half-past five, and he was late.

There were several races fixed for that day: the Mounted Guards' race, then the officers' mile-and-a-half race, then the three-mile race, and then the race for which he was entered. He could still be in time for his race, but if he went to Bryansky's he could only just be in time, and he would arrive when the whole of the court would be in their places. That would be a pity. But he had promised Bryansky to come, and so he decided to drive on, telling the coachman not to spare the horses.

He reached Bryansky's, spent five minutes there, and galloped back. This rapid drive calmed him. All that was painful in his relations with Anna, all the feeling of indefiniteness left by their conversation, had slipped out of his mind. He was thinking now with pleasure and excitement of the race, of his being anyhow, in time, and now and then the thought of the blissful interview awaiting him that night flashed across his imagination like a flaming light.

The excitement of the approaching race gained upon him as he drove farther and farther into the atmosphere of the races, overtaking carriages driving up from the summer villas or out of Petersburg.

At his quarters no one was left at home; all were at the races, and his valet was looking out for him at the gate. While he was changing his clothes, his valet told him that the second race had begun already, that a lot of gentlemen had been to ask for him, and a boy had twice run up from the stables. Dressing without hurry (he never hurried himself, and never lost his self-possession), Vronsky drove to the sheds. From the sheds he could see a perfect sea of carriages, and people on foot, soldiers surrounding the race course, and pavilions swarming with people. The second race was apparently going on, for just as he went into the sheds he heard a bell ringing. Going towards the stable, he met the white-legged chestnut, Mahotin's Gladiator, being led to the race course in a blue forage horsecloth, with what looked like huge ears edged with blue.

"Where's Cord?" he asked the stable-boy.

"In the stable, putting on the saddle."

In the open horse-box stood Frou-Frou, saddled ready. They were just going to lead her out.

"I'm not too late?"

"All right! All right!" said the Englishman; "don't upset yourself!"

Vronsky once more took in in one glance the exquisite lines of his favorite mare, who was quivering all over, and with an effort he tore himself from the sight of her, and went out of the stable. He went towards the pavilions at the most favorable moment for escaping attention. The mile-and-a-half race was just finishing, and all eyes were fixed on the horse-guard in front and the light hussar behind, urging their horses on with a last effort close to the winning post. From the center and outside of the ring all were crowding to the winning post, and a group of soldiers and officers of the horse-guards were shouting loudly their delight at the expected triumph of their officer and comrade. Vronsky moved into the middle of the crowd unnoticed, almost at the very moment when the bell rang at the finish of the race, and the tall, mudspattered horse-guard who came in first, bending over the saddle, let go the reins of his panting gray horse that looked dark with sweat.

The horse, stiffening out its legs, with an effort stopped its rapid course, and the officer of the horse-guards looked round him like a man waking up from a heavy sleep, and just managed to smile. A crowd of friends and outsiders pressed round him.

Vronsky intentionally avoided that select crowd of the upper world, which was moving and talking with discreet freedom before the pavilions. He knew that Madame Karenina was there, and Betsy, and his brother's wife, and he purposely did not go near them for fear of something distracting his attention. But he was continually met and stopped by acquaintances, who told him about the previous races, and kept asking him why he was so late.

At the time when the racers had to go to the pavilion to receive the prizes, and all attention was directed to that point, Vronsky's elder brother, Alexander, a colonel with heavy fringed epaulets, came up to him. He was not tall, though as broadly built as Alexey, and handsomer and rosier than he; he had a red nose, and an open, drunken-looking face.

"Did you get my note?" he said. "There's never any finding you."

Alexander Vronsky, in spite of the dissolute life, and in especial the drunken habits, for which he was notorious, was quite one of the court circle.

Now, as he talked to his brother of a matter bound to be exceedingly disagreeable to him, knowing that the eyes of many people might be fixed upon him, he kept a smiling countenance, as though he were jesting with his brother about something of little moment.

"I got it, and I really can't make out what *you* are worrying yourself about," said Alexey.

"I'm worrying myself because the remark has just been made to me that you weren't here, and that you were seen in Peterhof on Monday."

"There are matters which only concern those directly interested in them, and the matter you are so worried about is . . ."

"Yes, but if so, you may as well cut the service. . . ."

"I beg you not to meddle, and that's all I have to say."

Alexey Vronsky's frowning face turned white, and his prominent lower jaw quivered, which happened rarely with him. Being a man of very warm heart, he was seldom angry; but when he was angry, and when his chin quivered, then, as Alexander Vronsky knew, he was dangerous. Alexander Vronsky smiled gaily.

"I only wanted to give you Mother's letter. Answer it and don't worry about anything just before the race. *Bonne chance,*" he added, smiling and he moved away from him. But after him another friendly greeting brought Vronsky to a standstill.

"So you won't recognize your friends! How are you, *mon cher?*" said Stepan Arkadyevitch, as conspicuously brilliant in the midst of all the Petersburg brilliance as he was in Moscow, his face rosy, and his whiskers sleek and glossy. "I came up yesterday, and I'm delighted that I shall see your triumph. When shall we meet?"

"Come tomorrow to the mess room," said Vronsky, and squeezing him by the sleeve of his coat, with apologies, he moved away to the center of the race course, where the horses were being led for the great steeplechase.

The horses who had run in the last race were being led home, steaming and exhausted, by the stable-boys, and one after another the fresh horses for the coming race made their appearance, for the most part English racers, wearing horsecloths, and looking with their drawn-up bellies like strange, huge birds. On the right was led in Frou-Frou, lean and beautiful, lifting up her elastic, rather long pasterns, as though moved by springs. Not far from her they were taking the rug off the lop-eared Gladiator. The strong, exquisite, perfectly correct lines of the stallion, with his superb hind-quarters and excessively short pasterns almost over his hoofs, attracted Vronsky's attention in spite of himself. He would have gone up to his mare, but he was again detained by an acquaintance.

"Oh, there's Karenin!" said the acquaintance with whom he was chatting. "He's looking for his wife, and she's in the middle of the pavilion. Didn't you see her?"

"No," answered Vronsky, and without even glancing round towards the pavilion where his friend was pointing out Madame Karenina, he went up to his mare.

Vronsky had not had time to look at the saddle, about which he had to give some direction, when the competitors were summoned to the pavilion to receive their numbers and places in the row at starting. Seventeen officers, looking serious and severe, many with pale faces, met together in the pavilion and drew the numbers. Vronsky drew the number seven. The cry was heard: "Mount!"

Feeling that with the others riding in the race, he was the center upon which all eyes were fastened, Vronsky walked up to his mare in that state of nervous tension in which he usually became deliberate and composed in his movements. Cord, in honor of the races, had put on his best clothes, a black coat buttoned up, a stiffly starched collar, which propped up his cheeks, a round black hat, and top boots. He was calm and dignified as ever, and was with his own hands holding Frou-Frou by both reins, standing straight in front of her. Frou-Frou was still trembling as though in a fever. Her eye, full of fire, glanced sideways at Vronsky. Vronsky slipped his finger under the saddle-girth. The mare glanced aslant at him, drew up her lip, and twitched her ear. The Englishman puckered up his lips, intending to indicate a smile that anyone should verify his saddling.

"Get up; you won't feel so excited."

Vronsky looked round for the last time at his rivals. He knew that he would not see them during the race. Two were already riding forward to the point from which they were to start. Galtsin, a friend of Vronsky's and one of his more formidable rivals, was moving round a bay horse that would not let him mount. A little light hussar in tight riding breeches rode off at a gallop, crouched up like a cat on the saddle, in imitation of English jockeys. Prince Kuzovlev sat with a white face on his thoroughbred mare from the Grabovsky stud, while an English groom led her by the bridle. Vronsky and all his comrades knew Kuzovlev and his peculiarity of "weak nerves" and terrible vanity. They knew that he was afraid of everything, afraid of riding a spirited horse. But now, just because it was terrible, because people broke their necks, and there was a doctor standing at each obstacle, and an ambulance with a cross on it, and a sister of mercy, he had made up his mind to take part in the race. Their eyes met, and Vronsky gave him a friendly and encouraging nod. Only one he did not see, his chief rival, Mahotin on Gladiator.

"Don't be in a hurry," said Cord to Vronsky, "and remember one thing: don't hold her in at the fences, and don't urge her on; let her go as she likes."

"All right, all right," said Vronsky, taking the reins.

"If you can, lead the race; but don't lose heart till the last minute, even if you're behind."

Before the mare had time to move, Vronsky stepped with an agile, vigorous movement into the steel-toothed stirrup, and lightly and firmly seated himself on the creaking leather of the saddle. Getting his right foot in the stirrup, he smoothed the double reins, as he always did, between his fingers, and Cord let go.

As though she did not know which foot to put first, Frou-Frou started, dragging at the reins with her long neck, and as though she were on springs, shaking her rider from side to side. Cord quickened his step, following him. The excited mare, trying to shake off her rider first on one side and then the other, pulled at the reins, and Vronsky tried in vain with voice and hand to soothe her.

They were just reaching the dammed-up stream on their way to the starting point. Several of the riders were in front and several behind, when suddenly Vronsky heard the sound of a horse galloping in the mud behind him, and he was overtaken by Mahotin on his white-legged, lop-eared Gladiator. Mahotin smiled, showing his long teeth, but Vronsky looked angrily at him. He did not like him, and regarded him now as his most formidable rival. He was angry with him for galloping past and exciting his mare. Frou-Frou started into a gallop, her left foot forward, made two bounds, and fretting at the tightened reins, passed into a jolting trot, bumping her rider up and down. Cord, too, scowled, and followed Vronsky almost at a trot.

Chapter XXV

THERE WERE SEVENTEEN OFFICERS IN ALL RIDING IN THIS RACE. THE RACE COURSE WAS A LARGE three-mile ring of the form of an ellipse in front of the pavilion. On this course nine obstacles had been arranged: the stream, a big and solid barrier five feet high, just before the pavilion, a dry ditch, a ditch full of water, a precipitous slope, an Irish barricade (one of the most difficult obstacles, consisting of a mound fenced with brushwood, beyond which was a ditch out of sight for the horses, so that the horse had to clear both obstacles or might be killed); then two more ditches filled with water, and one dry one; and the end of the race was just facing the pavilion. But the race began not in the ring, but two hundred yards away from it, and in that part of the course was the first obstacle, a dammed-up stream, seven feet in breadth, which the racers could leap or wade through as they preferred.

Three times they were ranged ready to start, but each time some horse thrust itself out of line, and they had to begin again. The umpire who was starting them, Colonel Sestrin, was beginning to lose his temper, when at last for the fourth time he shouted "Away!" and the racers started.

Every eye, every opera glass, was turned on the brightly colored group of riders at the moment they were in line to start.

"They're off! They're starting!" was heard on all sides after the hush of expectation.

And little groups and solitary figures among the public began running from place to place to get a better view. In the very first minute the close group of horsemen drew out, and it could be seen that they were approaching the stream in two's and three's and one behind another. To the spectators it seemed as though they had all started simultaneously, but to the racers there were seconds of difference that had great value to them.

Frou-Frou, excited and over-nervous, had lost the first moment, and several horses had started before her, but before reaching the stream, Vronsky, who was holding in the mare with all his force as she tugged at the bridle, easily overtook three, and there were left in front of him Mahotin's chestnut Gladiator, whose hind-quarters were moving lightly and rhythmically up and down exactly in front of Vronsky, and in front of all, the dainty mare Diana bearing Kuzovlev more dead than alive.

For the first instant Vronsky was not master either of himself or his mare. Up to the first obstacle, the stream, he could not guide the motions of his mare.

Gladiator and Diana came up to it together and almost at the same instant; simultaneously they rose above the stream and flew across to the other side; Frou-Frou darted after them, as if flying; but at the very moment when Vronsky felt himself in the air, he suddenly saw almost under his mare's hoofs Kuzovlev, who was floundering with Diana on the further side of the stream. (Kuzovlev had let go the reins as he took the leap, and the mare had sent him flying over her head.) Those details Vronsky learned later; at the moment all he saw was that just under him, where Frou-Frou must alight, Diana's legs or head might be in the way. But Frou-Frou drew up her legs and back in the very act of leaping, like a falling cat, and, clearing the other mare, alighted beyond her.

"O the darling!" thought Vronsky.

After crossing the stream Vronsky had complete control of his mare, and began holding her in, intending to cross the great barrier behind Mahotin, and to try to overtake him in the clear ground of about five hundred yards that followed it.

The great barrier stood just in front of the imperial pavilion. The Tsar and the whole court and crowds of people were all gazing at them—at him, and Mahotin a length ahead of him, as they drew near the "devil," as the solid barrier was called. Vronsky was aware of those eyes fastened upon him from all sides, but he saw nothing except the ears and neck of his own mare, the ground racing to meet him, and the back and white legs of Gladiator beating time swiftly before him, and keeping always the same distance ahead. Gladiator rose, with no sound of knocking against anything. With a wave of his short tail he disappeared from Vronsky's sight.

"Bravo!" cried a voice.

At the same instant, under Vronsky's eyes, right before him flashed the palings of the barrier. Without the slightest change in her action his mare flew over it; the palings vanished, and he heard only a crash behind him. The mare, excited by Gladiator's keeping ahead, had risen too soon before the barrier, and grazed it with her hind hoofs. But her pace never changed, and Vronsky, feeling a spatter of mud in his face, realized that he was once more the same distance from Gladiator. Once more he perceived in front of him the same back and short tail, and again the same swiftly moving white legs that got no further away.

At the very moment when Vronsky thought that now was the time to overtake Mahotin, Frou-Frou herself, understanding his thoughts, without any incitement on his part, gained ground considerably, and began getting alongside of Mahotin on the most favorable side, close to the inner cord. Mahotin would not let her pass that side. Vronsky had hardly formed the thought that he could perhaps pass on the outer side, when Frou-Frou shifted her pace and began overtaking him on the other side. Frou-Frou's shoulder, beginning by now to be dark with sweat, was even with Gladiator's back. For a few lengths they moved evenly. But before the obstacle they were approaching, Vronsky began working at the reins, anxious to avoid having to take the outer circle, and swiftly passed Mahotin just upon the declivity. He caught a glimpse of his mud-stained face as he flashed by. He even fancied that he smiled. Vronsky passed Mahotin, but he was immediately aware of him close upon him, and he never ceased hearing the even-thudding hoofs and the rapid and still quite fresh breathing of Gladiator.

The next two obstacles, the water course and the barrier, were easily crossed, but Vronsky began to hear the snorting and thud of Gladiator closer upon him. He urged on his mare, and to his delight felt that she easily quickened her pace, and the thud of Gladiator's hoofs was again heard at the same distance away.

Vronsky was at the head of the race, just as he wanted to be and as Cord had advised, and now he felt sure of being the winner. His excitement, his delight, and his tenderness for Frou-Frou grew keener and keener. He longed to look round again, but he did not dare do this, and tried to be cool and not to urge on his mare so to keep the same reserve of force in her as he felt that Gladiator still kept. There remained only one obstacle, the most difficult; if he could cross it ahead of the others he would come in first. He was flying towards the Irish barricade, Frou-Frou and he both together saw the barricade in the distance, and both the man and the mare had a moment's hesitation. He saw the uncertainty in the mare's ears and lifted the whip, but at the same time felt that his fears were groundless; the mare knew what was wanted. She quickened her pace and rose smoothly, just as he had fancied she would, and as she left the ground gave herself up to the force of her rush, which carried her far beyond the ditch; and with the same rhythm, without effort, with the same leg forward, Frou-Frou fell back into her pace again.

"Bravo, Vronsky!" he heard shouts from a knot of men—he knew they were his friends in the regiment—who were standing at the obstacle. He could not fail to recognize Yashvin's voice though he did not see him.

"O my sweet!" he said inwardly to Frou-Frou, as he listened for what was happening behind. "He's cleared it!" he thought, catching the thud of Gladiator's hoofs behind him. There remained only the last ditch, filled with water and five feet wide. Vronsky did not even look at it, but anxious to get in a long way first began sawing away at the reins, lifting the mare's head and letting it go in time with her paces. He felt that the mare was at her very last reserve of strength; not her neck and shoulders merely were wet, but the sweat was standing in drops on her mane, her head, her sharp ears, and her breath came in short, sharp gasps. But he knew that she had strength left more than enough for the remaining five hundred yards. It was only from feeling himself nearer the ground and from the peculiar smoothness of his motion that Vronsky knew how greatly the mare had quickened her pace. She flew over the ditch as though not noticing it. She flew over it like a bird; but at the same instant Vronsky, to his horror, felt that he had failed to keep up with the mare's pace, that he had, he did not know how, made a fearful, unpardonable mistake, in recovering his seat in the saddle. All at once his position had shifted and he knew that something awful had happened. He could not yet make out what had happened, when the white legs of a chestnut horse flashed by close to him, and Mahotin passed at a swift gallop. Vronsky was touching the ground with one foot, and his mare was sinking on that foot. He just had time to free his leg when she fell on one side, gasping painfully, and, making vain efforts to rise with her delicate, soaking neck, she fluttered on the ground at his feet like a shot bird. The clumsy movement made by Vronsky had broken her back. But that he only knew much later. At that moment he knew only that Mahotin had flown swiftly by, while he stood staggering alone on the muddy, motionless ground, and Frou-Frou lay gasping before him, bending her head back and gazing at him with her exquisite eyes. Still unable to realize what had happened, Vronsky tugged at his mare's reins. Again she struggled all over like a fish, and her shoulders setting the saddle heaving, she rose on her front legs but unable to lift her back, she quivered all over and again fell on her side. With a face hideous with passion, his lower jaw trembling, and his cheeks white, Vronsky kicked her with his heel in the stomach and again fell to tugging at the rein. She did not stir, but thrusting her nose into the ground, she simply gazed at her master with her speaking eyes.

"A—a—a!" groaned Vronsky, clutching at his head. "Ah! what have I done!" he cried. "The race lost! And my fault! shameful, unpardonable! And the poor darling, ruined mare! Ah! what have I done!"

A crowd of men, a doctor and his assistant, the officers of his regiment, ran up to him. To his misery he felt that he was whole and unhurt. The mare had broken her back, and it was decided to shoot her. Vronsky could not answer questions, could not speak to anyone. He turned, and without picking up his cap that had fallen off, walked away from the race course, not knowing where he was going. He felt utterly wretched. For the first time in his life he knew the bitterest sort of misfortune, misfortune beyond remedy, and caused by his own fault.

Yashvin overtook him with his cap, and led him home, and half an hour later Vronsky had regained his self-possession. But the memory of that race remained for long in his heart, the cruelest and bitterest memory of his life.

Chapter XXVI

The external relations of Alexey Alexandrovitch and his wife had remained unchanged. The sole difference lay in the fact that he was more busily occupied than ever. As in former years, at the beginning of the spring he had gone to a foreign watering place for the sake of his health, deranged by the winter's work that every year grew heavier. And just as always he returned in July and at once fell to work as usual with increased energy. As usual, too, his wife had moved for the summer to a villa out of town, while he remained in Petersburg. From the date of their conversation after the party at Princess Tverskaya's he had never spoken again to Anna of his suspicions and his jealousies, and that habitual tone of his bantering mimicry was the most convenient tone possible for his present attitude to his wife. He was a little colder to his wife. He simply seemed to be slightly displeased with her for that first midnight conversation, which she had repelled. In his attitude to her there was a shade of vexation, but nothing more. "You would not be open with me," he seemed to say, mentally addressing her; "so much the worse for you. Now you may beg as you please, but I won't be open with you. So much the worse for you!" he said mentally, like a man who, after vainly attempting to extinguish a fire, should fly in a rage with his vain efforts and say, "Oh, very well then! you shall burn for this!" This man, so subtle and astute in official life, did not realize all the senselessness of such an attitude to his wife. He did not realize it, because it was too terrible to him to realize his actual position, and he shut down and locked and sealed up in his heart that secret place where lay hid his feelings towards his family, that is, his wife and son. He who had been such a careful father, had from the end of that winter become peculiarly frigid to his son, and adopted to him just the same bantering tone he used with his wife. "Aha, young man!" was the greeting with which he met him.

Alexey Alexandrovitch asserted and believed that he had never in any previous year had so much official business as that year. But he was not aware that he sought work for himself that year, that this was one of the means for keeping shut that secret place where lay hid his feelings towards his wife and son and his thoughts about them, which became more terrible the longer they lay there. If anyone had had the right to ask Alexey Alexandrovitch what he thought of his wife's behavior, the mild and peaceable Alexey Alexandrovitch would have made no answer, but he would have been greatly angered with any man who should question him on that subject. For this reason there positively came into Alexey Alexandrovitch's face a look of haughtiness and severity whenever anyone inquired after his wife's health. Alexey Alexandrovitch did not want to think at all about his wife's behavior, and he actually succeeded in not thinking about it at all.

Alexey Alexandrovitch's permanent summer villa was in Peterhof, and the Countess Lidia Ivanovna used as a rule to spend the summer there, close to Anna, and constantly seeing her. That year Countess Lidia Ivanovna declined to settle in Peterhof, was not once at Anna Arkadyevna's, and in conversation with Alexey Alexandrovitch hinted at the unsuitability of Anna's close intimacy with Betsy and Vronsky. Alexey Alexandrovitch sternly cut her short, roundly declaring his wife to be above suspicion, and from that time began to avoid Countess Lidia Ivanovna. He did not want to see, and did not see, that many people in society cast dubious glances on his wife; he did not want to understand, and did not understand, why his wife had so particularly insisted on staying at Tsarskoe, where Betsy was staying, and not far from the camp of Vronsky's regiment. He did not allow himself to think about it, and he did not think about it; but all the same though he never admitted it to himself, and had no proofs, not even suspicious evidence, in the bottom of his heart he knew beyond all doubt that he was a deceived husband, and he was profoundly miserable about it.

How often during those eight years of happy life with his wife Alexey Alexandrovitch had looked at other men's faithless wives and other deceived husbands and asked himself: "How can people descend to that? How is it they don't put an end to such a hideous position?" But now, when the misfortune had come upon himself, he was so far from thinking of putting an end to the position that he would not recognize it at all, would not recognize it just because it was too awful, too unnatural.

Since his return from abroad Alexey Alexandrovitch had twice been at their country villa. Once he dined there, another time he spent the evening there with a party of friends, but he had not once stayed the night there, as it had been his habit to do in previous years.

The day of the races had been a very busy day for Alexey Alexandrovitch; but when mentally sketching out the day in the morning, he made up his mind to go to their country house to see his wife immediately after dinner, and from there to the races, which all the Court were to witness, and at which he was bound to be present. He was going to see his wife, because he had determined to see her once a week to keep up appearances. And besides, on that day, as it was the fifteenth, he had to give his wife some money for her expenses, according to their usual arrangement.

With his habitual control over his thoughts, though he thought all this about his wife, he did not let his thoughts stray further in regard to her.

That morning was a very full one for Alexey Alexandrovitch. The evening before, Countess Lidia Ivanovna had sent him a pamphlet by a celebrated traveler in China, who was staying in Petersburg, and with it she enclosed a note begging him to see the traveler himself, as he was an extremely interesting person from various points of view, and likely to be useful. Alexey Alexandrovitch had not had time to read the pamphlet through in the evening, and finished it in the morning. Then people began arriving with petitions, and there came the reports, interviews, appointments, dismissals, apportionment of rewards, pensions, grants, notes, the workaday round, as Alexey Alexandrovitch called it, that always took up so much time. Then there was private business of his own, a visit from the doctor and the steward who managed his property. The steward did not take up much time. He simply gave Alexey Alexandrovitch the money he needed together with a brief statement of the position of his affairs, which was not altogether satisfactory, as it had happened that during that year, owing to increased expenses, more had been paid out than usual, and there was a deficit. But the doctor, a celebrated Petersburg doctor, who was an intimate acquaintance of Alexey Alexandrovitch, took up a great deal of time. Alexey Alexandrovitch had not expected him that day, and was surprised at his visit, and still more so when the doctor questioned him very carefully about his health, listened to his breathing, and tapped at his liver. Alexey Alexandrovitch did not know that his friend Lidia Ivanovna, noticing that he was not as well as usual that year, had begged the doctor to go and examine him. "Do this for my sake," the Countess Lidia Ivanovna had said to him.

"I will do it for the sake of Russia, countess," replied the doctor.

"A priceless man!" said the Countess Lidia Ivanovna.

The doctor was extremely dissatisfied with Alexey Alexandrovitch. He found the liver considerably enlarged, and the digestive powers weakened, while the course of mineral waters had been quite without effect. He prescribed more physical exercise as far as possible, and as far as possible less mental strain, and above all no worry—in other words, just what was as much out of

Alexey Alexandrovitch's power as abstaining from breathing. Then he withdrew, leaving in Alexey Alexandrovitch an unpleasant sense that something was wrong with him, and that there was no chance of curing it.

As he was coming away, the doctor chanced to meet on the staircase an acquaintance of his, Sludin, who was secretary of Alexey Alexandrovitch's department. They had been comrades at the university, and though they rarely met, they thought highly of each other and were excellent friends, and so there was no one to whom the doctor would have given his opinion of a patient so freely as to Sludin.

"How glad I am you've been seeing him!" said Sludin. "He's not well, and I fancy . . . Well, what do you think of him?"

"I'll tell you," said the doctor, beckoning over Sludin's head to his coachman to bring the carriage round. "It's just this," said the doctor, taking a finger of his kid glove in his white hands and pulling it, "if you don't strain the strings, and then try to break them, you'll find it a difficult job; but strain a string to its very utmost, and the mere weight of one finger on the strained string will snap it. And with his close assiduity, his conscientious devotion to his work, he's strained to the utmost; and there's some outside burden weighing on him, and not a light one," concluded the doctor, raising his eyebrows significantly. "Will you be at the races?" he added, as he sank into his seat in the carriage.

"Yes, yes, to be sure; it does waste a lot of time," the doctor responded vaguely to some reply of Sludin's he had not caught.

Directly after the doctor, who had taken up so much time, came the celebrated traveler, and Alexey Alexandrovitch, by means of the pamphlet he had only just finished reading and his previous acquaintance with the subject, impressed the traveler by the depth of his knowledge of the subject and the breadth and enlightenment of his view of it.

At the same time as the traveler there was announced a provincial marshal of nobility on a visit to Petersburg, with whom Alexey Alexandrovitch had to have some conversation. After his departure, he had to finish the daily routine of business with his secretary, and then he still had to drive round to call on a certain great personage on a matter of grave and serious import. Alexey Alexandrovitch only just managed to be back by five o'clock, his dinner-hour, and after dining with his secretary, he invited him to drive with him to his country villa and to the races.

Though he did not acknowledge it to himself, Alexey Alexandrovitch always tried nowadays to secure the presence of a third person in his interviews with his wife.

Chapter XXVII

ANNA WAS UPSTAIRS, STANDING BEFORE THE LOOKING-GLASS, AND, WITH ANNUSHKA'S ASSIStance, pinning the last ribbon on her gown when she heard carriage wheels crunching the gravel at the entrance.

"It's too early for Betsy," she thought, and glancing out of the window she caught sight of the carriage and the black hat of Alexey Alexandrovitch, and the ears that she knew so well sticking up each side of it. "How unlucky! Can he be going to stay the night?" she wondered, and the thought of all that might come of such a chance struck her as so awful and terrible that, without dwelling on it for a moment, she went down to meet him with a bright and radiant face; and conscious of the presence of that spirit of falsehood and deceit in herself that she had come to know of late, she abandoned herself to that spirit and began talking, hardly knowing what she was saying.

"Ah, how nice of you!" she said, giving her husband her hand, and greeting Sludin, who was like one of the family, with a smile. "You're staying the night, I hope?" was the first word the spirit of falsehood prompted her to utter; "and now we'll go together. Only it's a pity I've promised Betsy. She's coming for me."

Alexey Alexandrovitch knit his brows at Betsy's name.

"Oh, I'm not going to separate the inseparables," he said in his usual bantering tone. "I'm going with Mihail Vassilievitch. I'm ordered exercise by the doctors too. I'll walk, and fancy myself at the springs again."

"There's no hurry," said Anna. "Would you like tea?"

She rang.

"Bring in tea, and tell Seryozha that Alexey Alexandrovitch is here. Well, tell me, how have you been? Mihail Vassilievitch, you've not been to see me before. Look how lovely it is out on the terrace," she said, turning first to one and then to the other.

She spoke very simply and naturally, but too much and too fast. She was the more aware of this from noticing in the inquisitive look Mihail Vassilievitch turned on her that he was, as it were, keeping watch on her.

Mihail Vassilievitch promptly went out on the terrace.

She sat down beside her husband.

"You don't look quite well," she said.

"Yes," he said; "the doctor's been with me today and wasted an hour of my time. I feel that some one of our friends must have sent him: my health's so precious, it seems."

"No; what did he say?"

She questioned him about his health and what he had been doing, and tried to persuade him to take a rest and come out to her.

All this she said brightly, rapidly, and with a peculiar brilliance in her eyes. But Alexey Alexandrovitch did not now attach any special significance to this tone of hers. He heard only her words and gave them only the direct sense they bore. And he answered simply, though jestingly. There was nothing remarkable in all this conversation, but never after could Anna recall this brief scene without an agonizing pang of shame.

Seryozha came in preceded by his governess. If Alexey Alexandrovitch had allowed himself to observe he would have noticed the timid and bewildered eyes with which Seryozha glanced first at his father and then at his mother. But he would not see anything, and he did not see it.

"Ah, the young man! He's grown. Really, he's getting quite a man. How are you, young man?"

And he gave his hand to the scared child. Seryozha had been shy of his father before, and now, ever since Alexey Alexandrovitch had taken to calling him young man, and since that insoluble question had occurred to him whether Vronsky were a friend or a foe, he avoided his father. He looked round towards his mother as though seeking shelter. It was only with his mother that he was at ease. Meanwhile, Alexey Alexandrovitch was holding his son by the shoulder while he was speaking to the governess, and Seryozha was so miserably uncomfortable that Anna saw he was on the point of tears.

Anna, who had flushed a little the instant her son came in, noticing that Seryozha was uncomfortable, got up hurriedly, took Alexey Alexandrovitch's hand from her son's shoulder, and kissing the boy, led him out onto the terrace, and quickly came back.

"It's time to start, though," said she, glancing at her watch. "How is it Betsy doesn't come? . . ."

"Yes," said Alexey Alexandrovitch, and getting up, he folded his hands and cracked his fingers. "I've come to bring you some money, too, for nightingales, we know, can't live on fairy tales," he said. "You want it, I expect?"

"No, I don't . . . yes, I do," she said, not looking at him, and crimsoning to the roots of her hair. "But you'll come back here after the races, I suppose?"

"Oh, yes!" answered Alexey Alexandrovitch. "And here's the glory of Peterhof, Princess Tverskaya," he added, looking out of the window at the elegant English carriage with the tiny seats placed extremely high. "What elegance! Charming! Well, let us be starting too, then."

Princess Tverskaya did not get out of her carriage, but her groom, in high boots, a cape, and block hat, darted out at the entrance.

"I'm going; good-bye!" said Anna, and kissing her son, she went up to Alexey Alexandrovitch and held out her hand to him. "It was ever so nice of you to come."

Alexey Alexandrovitch kissed her hand.

"Well, *au revoir*, then! You'll come back for some tea; that's delightful!" she said, and went out, gay and radiant. But as soon as she no longer saw him, she was aware of the spot on her hand that his lips had touched, and she shuddered with repulsion.

Chapter XXVIII

When Alexey Alexandrovitch reached the race course, Anna was already sitting in the pavilion beside Betsy, in that pavilion where all the highest society had gathered. She caught sight of her husband in the distance. Two men, her husband and her lover, were the two centers of her existence, and unaided by her external senses she was aware of their nearness. She was aware of her husband approaching a long way off, and she could not help following him in the surging crowd in the midst of which he was moving. She watched his progress towards the pavilion, saw him now responding condescendingly to an ingratiating bow, now exchanging friendly, nonchalant greetings with his equals, now assiduously trying to catch the eye of some great one of this world, and taking off his big round hat that squeezed the tips of his ears. All these ways of his she knew, and all were hateful to her. "Nothing but ambition, nothing but the desire to get on, that's all there is in his soul," she thought; "as for these lofty ideals, love of culture, religion, they are only so many tools for getting on."

From his glances towards the ladies' pavilion (he was staring straight at her, but did not distinguish his wife in the sea of muslin, ribbons, feathers, parasols and flowers) she saw that he was looking for her, but she purposely avoided noticing him.

"Alexey Alexandrovitch!" Princess Betsy called to him; "I'm sure you don't see your wife: here she is."

He smiled his chilly smile.

"There's so much splendor here that one's eyes are dazzled," he said, and he went into the pavilion. He smiled to his wife as a man should smile on meeting his wife after only just parting from her, and greeted the princess and other acquaintances, giving to each what was due—that is to say, jesting with the ladies and dealing out friendly greetings among the men. Below, near the pavilion, was standing an adjutant-general of whom Alexey Alexandrovitch had a high opinion, noted for his intelligence and culture. Alexey Alexandrovitch entered into conversation with him.

There was an interval between the races, and so nothing hindered conversation. The adjutant-general expressed his disapproval of races. Alexey Alexandrovitch replied defending them. Anna heard his high, measured tones, not losing one word, and every word struck her as false, and stabbed her ears with pain.

When the three-mile steeplechase was beginning, she bent forward and gazed with fixed eyes at Vronsky as he went up to his horse and mounted, and at the same time she heard that loathsome, never-ceasing voice of her husband. She was in an agony of terror for Vronsky, but a still greater agony was the never-ceasing, as it seemed to her, stream of her husband's shrill voice with its familiar intonations.

"I'm a wicked woman, a lost woman," she thought; "but I don't like lying, I can't endure falsehood, while as for *him* (her husband) it's the breath of his life—falsehood. He knows all about it, he sees it all; what does he care if he can talk so calmly? If he were to kill me, if he were to kill Vronsky, I might respect him. No, all he wants is falsehood and propriety," Anna said to herself, not considering exactly what it was she wanted of her husband, and how she would have liked to see him behave. She did not understand either that Alexey Alexandrovitch's peculiar loquacity that day, so exasperating to her, was merely the expression of his inward distress and uneasiness. As a child that has been hurt skips about, putting all his muscles into movement to drown the pain, in the same way Alexey Alexandrovitch needed mental exercise to drown the thoughts of his wife that in her presence and in Vronsky's, and with the continual iteration of his name, would force themselves on his attention. And it was as natural for him to talk well and cleverly, as it is natural for a child to skip about. He was saying:

"Danger in the races of officers, of cavalry men, is an essential element in the race. If England can point to the most brilliant feats of cavalry in military history, it is simply owing to the fact that she has historically developed this force both in beasts and in men. Sport has, in my opinion, a great value, and as is always the case, we see nothing but what is most superficial."

"It's not superficial," said Princess Tverskaya. "One of the officers, they say, has broken two ribs."

Alexey Alexandrovitch smiled his smile, which uncovered his teeth, but revealed nothing more.

"We'll admit, princess, that that's not superficial," he said, "but internal. But that's not the point," and he turned again to the general with whom he was talking seriously; "we mustn't forget that those who are taking part in the race are military men, who have chosen that career, and one must allow that every calling has its disagreeable side. It forms an integral part of the duties of an officer. Low sports, such as prize-fighting or Spanish bull-fights, are a sign of barbarity. But specialized trials of skill are a sign of development."

"No, I shan't come another time; it's too upsetting," said Princess Betsy. "Isn't it, Anna?"

"It is upsetting, but one can't tear oneself away," said another lady. "If I'd been a Roman woman I should never have missed a single circus."

Anna said nothing, and keeping her opera glass up, gazed always at the same spot.

At that moment a tall general walked through the pavilion. Breaking off what he was saying, Alexey Alexandrovitch got up hurriedly, though with dignity, and bowed low to the general.

"You're not racing?" the officer asked, chaffing him.

"My race is a harder one," Alexey Alexandrovitch responded deferentially.

And though the answer meant nothing, the general looked as though he had heard a witty remark from a witty man, and fully relished *la pointe de la sauce*.

"There are two aspects," Alexey Alexandrovitch resumed: "those who take part and those who look on; and love for such spectacles is an unmistakable proof of a low degree of development in the spectator, I admit, but . . ."

"Princess, bets!" sounded Stepan Arkadyevitch's voice from below, addressing Betsy. "Who's your favorite?"

"Anna and I are for Kuzovlev," replied Betsy.

"I'm for Vronsky. A pair of gloves?"

"Done!"

"But it is a pretty sight, isn't it?"

Alexey Alexandrovitch paused while there was talking about him, but he began again directly.

"I admit that manly sports do not . . ." he was continuing.

But at that moment the racers started, and all conversation ceased. Alexey Alexandrovitch too was silent, and everyone stood up and turned towards the stream. Alexey Alexandrovitch took no interest in the race, and so he did not watch the racers, but fell listlessly to scanning the spectators with his weary eyes. His eyes rested upon Anna.

Her face was white and set. She was obviously seeing nothing and no one but one man. Her hand had convulsively clutched her fan, and she held her breath. He looked at her and hastily turned away, scrutinizing other faces.

"But here's this lady too, and others very much moved as well; it's very natural," Alexey Alexandrovitch told himself. He tried not to look at her, but unconsciously his eyes were drawn to her. He examined that face again, trying not to read what was so plainly written on it, and against his own will, with horror read on it what he did not want to know.

The first fall—Kuzovlev's, at the stream—agitated everyone, but Alexey Alexandrovitch saw distinctly on Anna's pale, triumphant face that the man she was watching had not fallen. When, after Mahotin and Vronsky had cleared the worst barrier, the next officer had been thrown straight on his head at it and fatally injured, and a shudder of horror passed over the whole public, Alexey Alexandrovitch saw that Anna did not even notice it, and had some difficulty in realizing what they were talking of about her. But more and more often, and with greater persistence, he watched her. Anna, wholly engrossed as she was with the race, became aware of her husband's cold eyes fixed upon her from one side.

She glanced round for an instant, looked inquiringly at him, and with a slight frown turned away again.

"Ah, I don't care!" she seemed to say to him, and she did not once glance at him again.

The race was an unlucky one, and of the seventeen officers who rode in it more than half were thrown and hurt. Towards the end of the race everyone was in a state of agitation, which was intensified by the fact that the Tsar was displeased.

Chapter XXIX

EVERYONE WAS LOUDLY EXPRESSING DISAPPROBATION, EVERYONE WAS REPEATING A PHRASE someone had uttered—"The lions and gladiators will be the next thing," and everyone was feeling horrified; so that when Vronsky fell to the ground, and Anna moaned aloud, there was nothing very out of the way in it. But afterwards a change came over Anna's face which really was beyond decorum. She utterly lost her head. She began fluttering like a caged bird, at one moment would have got up and moved away, at the next turned to Betsy.

"Let us go, let us go!" she said.

But Betsy did not hear her. She was bending down, talking to a general who had come up to her.

Alexey Alexandrovitch went up to Anna and courteously offered her his arm.

"Let us go, if you like," he said in French, but Anna was listening to the general and did not notice her husband.

"He's broken his leg too, so they say," the general was saying. "This is beyond everything."

Without answering her husband, Anna lifted her opera glass and gazed towards the place where Vronsky had fallen; but it was so far off, and there was such a crowd of people about it, that she could make out nothing. She laid down the opera glass, and would have moved away, but at that moment an officer galloped up and made some announcement to the Tsar. Anna craned forward, listening.

"Stiva! Stiva!" she cried to her brother.

But her brother did not hear her. Again she would have moved away.

"Once more I offer you my arm if you want to be going," said Alexey Alexandrovitch, reaching towards her hand.

She drew back from him with aversion, and without looking in his face answered:

"No, no, let me be, I'll stay."

She saw now that from the place of Vronsky's accident an officer was running across the course towards the pavilion. Betsy waved her handkerchief to him. The officer brought the news that the rider was not killed, but the horse had broken its back.

On hearing this Anna sat down hurriedly, and hid her face in her fan. Alexey Alexandrovitch saw that she was weeping, and could not control her tears, nor even the sobs that were shaking her bosom. Alexey Alexandrovitch stood so as to screen her, giving her time to recover herself.

"For the third time I offer you my arm," he said to her after a little time, turning to her. Anna gazed at him and did not know what to say. Princess Betsy came to her rescue.

"No, Alexey Alexandrovitch; I brought Anna and I promised to take her home," put in Betsy.

"Excuse me, princess," he said, smiling courteously but looking her very firmly in the face, "but I see that Anna's not very well, and I wish her to come home with me."

Anna looked about her in a frightened way, got up submissively, and laid her hand on her husband's arm.

"I'll send to him and find out, and let you know," Betsy whispered to her.

As they left the pavilion, Alexey Alexandrovitch, as always, talked to those he met, and Anna had, as always, to talk and answer; but she was utterly beside herself, and moved hanging on her husband's arm as though in a dream.

"Is he killed or not? Is it true? Will he come or not? Shall I see him today?" she was thinking.

She took her seat in her husband's carriage in silence, and in silence drove out of the crowd of carriages. In spite of all he had seen, Alexey Alexandrovitch still did not allow himself to consider his wife's real condition. He merely saw the outward symptoms. He saw that she was behaving unbecomingly, and considered it his duty to tell her so. But it was very difficult for him not to say more, to tell her nothing but that. He opened his mouth to tell her she had behaved unbecomingly, but he could not help saying something utterly different.

"What an inclination we all have, though, for these cruel spectacles," he said. "I observe . . ."

"Eh? I don't understand," said Anna contemptuously.

He was offended, and at once began to say what he had meant to say.

"I am obliged to tell you," he began.

"So now we are to have it out," she thought, and she felt frightened.

"I am obliged to tell you that your behavior has been unbecoming today," he said to her in French.

"In what way has my behavior been unbecoming?" she said aloud, turning her head swiftly and looking him straight in the face, not with the bright expression that seemed covering something, but with a look of determination, under which she concealed with difficulty the dismay she was feeling.

"Mind," he said, pointing to the open window opposite the coachman.

He got up and pulled up the window.

"What did you consider unbecoming?" she repeated.

"The despair you were unable to conceal at the accident to one of the riders."

He waited for her to answer, but she was silent, looking straight before her.

"I have already begged you so to conduct yourself in society that even malicious tongues can find nothing to say against you. There was a time when I spoke of your inward attitude, but I am not speaking of that now. Now I speak only of your external attitude. You have behaved improperly, and I would wish it not to occur again."

She did not hear half of what he was saying; she felt panic-stricken before him, and was thinking whether it was true that Vronsky was not killed. Was it of him they were speaking when they said the rider was unhurt, but the horse had broken its back? She merely smiled with a pretense of irony when he finished, and made no reply, because she had not heard what he said. Alexey Alexandrovitch had begun to speak boldly, but as he realized plainly what he was speaking of, the dismay she was feeling infected him too. He saw the smile, and a strange misapprehension came over him.

"She is smiling at my suspicions. Yes, she will tell me directly what she told me before; that there is no foundation for my suspicions, that it's absurd."

At that moment, when the revelation of everything was hanging over him, there was nothing he expected so much as that she would answer mockingly as before that his suspicions were absurd and utterly groundless. So terrible to him was what he knew that now he was ready to believe anything. But the expression of her face, scared and gloomy, did not now promise even deception.

"Possibly I was mistaken," said he. "If so, I beg your pardon."

"No, you were not mistaken," she said deliberately, looking desperately into his cold face. "You were not mistaken. I was, and I could not help being in despair. I hear you, but I am thinking of him. I love him, I am his mistress; I can't bear you; I'm afraid of you, and I hate you. . . . You can do what you like to me."

And dropping back into the corner of the carriage, she broke into sobs, hiding her face in her hands. Alexey Alexandrovitch did not stir, and kept looking straight before him. But his whole face suddenly bore the solemn rigidity of the dead, and his expression did not change during the whole time of the drive home. On reaching the house he turned his head to her, still with the same expression.

"Very well! But I expect a strict observance of the external forms of propriety till such time"—his voice shook—"as I may take measures to secure my honor and communicate them to you."

He got out first and helped her to get out. Before the servants he pressed her hand, took his seat in the carriage, and drove back to Petersburg. Immediately afterwards a footman came from Princess Betsy and brought Anna a note.

"I sent to Alexey to find out how he is, and he writes me he is quite well and unhurt, but in despair."

"So *he* will be here," she thought. "What a good thing I told him all!"

She glanced at her watch. She had still three hours to wait, and the memories of their last meeting set her blood in flame.

"My God, how light it is! It's dreadful, but I do love to see his face, and I do love this fantastic light. . . . My husband! Oh! Yes . . . Well, thank God! everything's over with him."

Chapter XXX

IN THE LITTLE GERMAN WATERING-PLACE TO WHICH THE SHTCHERBATSKYS HAD BETAKEN THEMselves, as in all places indeed where people are gathered together, the usual process, as it were, of the crystallization of society went on, assigning to each member of that society a definite and unalterable place. Just as the particle of water in frost, definitely and unalterably, takes the special form of the crystal of snow, so each new person that arrived at the springs was at once placed in his special place.

Fürst Shtcherbatsky, *sammt Gemahlin und Tochter,* by the apartments they took, and from their name and from the friends they made, were immediately crystallized into a definite place marked out for them.

There was visiting the watering place that year a real German Frstin, in consequence of which the crystallizing process went on more vigorously than ever. Princess Shtcherbatskaya wished, above everything, to present her daughter to this German princess, and the day after their arrival she duly performed this rite. Kitty made a low and graceful curtsey in the *very simple,* that is to say, very elegant frock that had been ordered her from Paris. The German princess said, "I hope the roses will soon come back to this pretty little face," and for the Shtcherbatskys certain definite lines of existence were at once laid down from which there was no departing. The Shtcherbatskys made the acquaintance too of the family of an English Lady Somebody, and of a German countess and her son, wounded in the last war, and of a learned Swede, and of M. Canut and his sister. But yet inevitably the Shtcherbatskys were thrown most into the society of a Moscow lady, Marya Yevgenyevna Rtishtcheva and her daughter, whom Kitty disliked, because she had fallen ill, like herself, over a love affair, and a Moscow colonel, whom Kitty had known from childhood, and always seen in uniform and epaulets, and who now, with his little eyes and his open neck and flowered cravat, was uncommonly ridiculous and tedious, because there was no getting rid of him. When all this was so firmly established, Kitty began to be very much bored, especially as the prince went away to Carlsbad and she was left alone with her mother. She took no interest in the people she knew, feeling that nothing fresh would come of them. Her chief mental interest in the watering place consisted in watching and making theories about the people she did not know. It was characteristic of Kitty that she always imagined everything in people in the most favorable light possible, especially so in those she did not know. And now as she made surmises as to who people were, what were their relations to one another, and what they were like, Kitty endowed them with the most marvelous and noble characters, and found confirmation of her idea in her observations.

Of these people the one that attracted her most was a Russian girl who had come to the watering place with an invalid Russian lady, Madame Stahl, as everyone called her. Madame Stahl belonged to the highest society, but she was so ill that she could not walk, and only on exceptionally fine days made her appearance at the springs in an invalid carriage. But it was not so much from ill-health as from pride—so Princess Shtcherbatskaya interpreted it—that Madame Stahl had not made the acquaintance of anyone among the Russians there. The Russian girl looked after Madame Stahl, and besides that, she was, as Kitty observed, on friendly terms with all the invalids who were seriously ill, and there were many of them at the springs, and looked after them in the most natural way. This Russian girl was not, as Kitty gathered, related to Madame Stahl, nor was she a paid attendant. Madame Stahl called her Varenka, and other people called her "Mademoiselle Varenka." Apart from the interest Kitty took in this girl's relations with Madame Stahl and with other unknown persons, Kitty, as often happened, felt an inexplicable attraction to Mademoiselle Varenka, and was aware when their eyes met that she too liked her.

Of Mademoiselle Varenka one would not say that she had passed her first youth, but she was, as it were, a creature without youth; she might have been taken for nineteen or for thirty. If her features were criticized separately, she was handsome rather than plain, in spite of the sickly hue of her face. She would have been a good figure, too, if it had not been for her extreme thinness and the size of her head, which was too large for her medium height. But she was not likely to be attractive to men. She was like a fine flower, already past its bloom and without fragrance, though the petals were still unwithered. Moreover, she would have been unattractive to men also from the lack of just what Kitty had too much of—of the suppressed fire of vitality, and the consciousness of her own attractiveness.

She always seemed absorbed in work about which there could be no doubt, and so it seemed she could not take interest in anything outside it. It was just this contrast with her own position that was for Kitty the great attraction of Mademoiselle Varenka. Kitty felt that in her, in her manner of life, she would find an example of what she was now so painfully seeking: interest in life, a dignity in life—apart from the worldly relations of girls with men, which so revolted Kitty, and appeared to her now as a shameful hawking about of goods in search of a purchaser. The more attentively Kitty watched her unknown friend, the more convinced she was this girl was the perfect creature she fancied her, and the more eagerly she wished to make her acquaintance.

The two girls used to meet several times a day, and every time they met, Kitty's eyes said: "Who are you? What are you? Are you really the exquisite creature I imagine you to be? But for goodness' sake don't suppose," her eyes added, "that I would force my acquaintance on you, I simply admire you and like you." "I like you too, and you're very, very sweet. And I should like you better still, if I had time," answered the eyes of the unknown girl. Kitty saw indeed, that she was always busy. Either she was taking the children of a Russian family home from the springs, or fetching a shawl for a sick lady, and wrapping her up in it, or trying to interest an irritable invalid, or selecting and buying cakes for tea for someone.

Soon after the arrival of the Shtcherbatskys there appeared in the morning crowd at the springs two persons who attracted universal and unfavorable attention. These were a tall man with a stooping figure, and huge hands, in an old coat too short for him, with black, simple, and yet terrible eyes, and a pockmarked, kind-looking woman, very badly and tastelessly dressed. Recognizing these persons as Russians, Kitty had already in her imagination begun constructing a delightful and touching romance about them. But the princess, having ascertained from the visitors' list that this was Nikolay Levin and Marya Nikolaevna, explained to Kitty what a bad man this Levin was, and all her fancies about these two people vanished. Not so much from what her mother told her, as from the fact that it was Konstantin's brother, this pair suddenly seemed to Kitty intensely unpleasant. This Levin, with his continual twitching of his head, aroused in her now an irrepressible feeling of disgust.

It seemed to her that his big, terrible eyes, which persistently pursued her, expressed a feeling of hatred and contempt, and she tried to avoid meeting him.

Chapter XXXI

IT WAS A WET DAY; IT HAD BEEN RAINING ALL THE MORNING, AND THE INVALIDS, WITH THEIR PARAsols, had flocked into the arcades.

Kitty was walking there with her mother and the Moscow colonel, smart and jaunty in his European coat, bought ready-made at Frankfort. They were walking on one side of the arcade, trying to avoid Levin, who was walking on the other side. Varenka, in her dark dress, in a black hat with a turn-down brim, was walking up and down the whole length of the arcade with a blind Frenchwoman, and, every time she met Kitty, they exchanged friendly glances.

"Mamma, couldn't I speak to her?" said Kitty, watching her unknown friend, and noticing that she was going up to the spring, and that they might come there together.

"Oh, if you want to so much, I'll find out about her first and make her acquaintance myself," answered her mother. "What do you see in her out of the way? A companion, she must be. If you like, I'll make acquaintance with Madame Stahl; I used to know her *belle-soeur*," added the princess, lifting her head haughtily.

Kitty knew that the princess was offended that Madame Stahl had seemed to avoid making her acquaintance. Kitty did not insist.

"How wonderfully sweet she is!" she said, gazing at Varenka just as she handed a glass to the Frenchwoman. "Look how natural and sweet it all is."

"It's so funny to see your *engouements*," said the princess. "No, we'd better go back," she added, noticing Levin coming towards them with his companion and a German doctor, to whom he was talking very noisily and angrily.

They turned to go back, when suddenly they heard, not noisy talk, but shouting. Levin, stopping short, was shouting at the doctor, and the doctor, too, was excited. A crowd gathered about them. The princess and Kitty beat a hasty retreat, while the colonel joined the crowd to find out what was the matter.

A few minutes later the colonel overtook them.

"What was it?" inquired the princess.

"Scandalous and disgraceful!" answered the colonel. "The one thing to be dreaded is meeting Russians abroad. That tall gentleman was abusing the doctor, flinging all sorts of insults at him because he wasn't treating him quite as he liked, and he began waving his stick at him. It's simply a scandal!"

"Oh, how unpleasant!" said the princess. "Well, and how did it end?"

"Luckily at that point that . . . the one in the mushroom hat . . . intervened. A Russian lady, I think she is," said the colonel.

"Mademoiselle Varenka?" asked Kitty.

"Yes, yes. She came to the rescue before anyone; she took the man by the arm and led him away."

"There, mamma," said Kitty; "you wonder that I'm enthusiastic about her."

The next day, as she watched her unknown friend, Kitty noticed that Mademoiselle Varenka was already on the same terms with Levin and his companion as with her other protégés. She went up to them, entered into conversation with them, and served as interpreter for the woman, who could not speak any foreign language.

Kitty began to entreat her mother still more urgently to let her make friends with Varenka. And, disagreeable as it was to the princess to seem to take the first step in wishing to make the acquaintance of Madame Stahl, who thought fit to give herself airs, she made inquiries about Varenka, and, having ascertained particulars about her tending to prove that there could be no harm though little good in the acquaintance, she herself approached Varenka and made acquaintance with her.

Choosing a time when her daughter had gone to the spring, while Varenka had stopped outside the baker's, the princess went up to her.

"Allow me to make your acquaintance," she said, with her dignified smile. "My daughter has lost her heart to you," she said. "Possibly you do not know me. I am . . ."

"That feeling is more than reciprocal, princess," Varenka answered hurriedly.

"What a good deed you did yesterday to our poor compatriot!" said the princess.

Varenka flushed a little. "I don't remember. I don't think I did anything," she said.

"Why, you saved that Levin from disagreeable consequences."

"Yes, *sa compagne* called me, and I tried to pacify him; he's very ill, and was dissatisfied with the doctor. I'm used to looking after such invalids."

"Yes, I've heard you live at Mentone with your aunt—I think—Madame Stahl: I used to know her *belle-soeur*."

"No, she's not my aunt. I call her mamma, but I am not related to her; I was brought up by her," answered Varenka, flushing a little again.

This was so simply said, and so sweet was the truthful and candid expression of her face, that the princess saw why Kitty had taken such a fancy to Varenka.

"Well, and what's this Levin going to do?" asked the princess.

"He's going away," answered Varenka.

At that instant Kitty came up from the spring beaming with delight that her mother had become acquainted with her unknown friend.

"Well, see, Kitty, your intense desire to make friends with Mademoiselle . . ."

"Varenka," Varenka put in smiling, "that's what everyone calls me."

Kitty blushed with pleasure, and slowly, without speaking, pressed her new friend's hand, which did not respond to her pressure, but lay motionless in her hand. The hand did not respond to her pressure, but the face of Mademoiselle Varenka glowed with a soft, glad, though rather mournful smile, that showed large but handsome teeth.

"I have long wished for this too," she said.

"But you are so busy."

"Oh, no, I'm not at all busy," answered Varenka, but at that moment she had to leave her new friends because two little Russian girls, children of an invalid, ran up to her.

"Varenka, mamma's calling!" they cried.

And Varenka went after them.

Chapter XXXII

The particulars which the princess had learned in regard to Varenka's past and her relations with Madame Stahl were as follows:

Madame Stahl, of whom some people said that she had worried her husband out of his life, while others said it was he who had made her wretched by his immoral behavior, had always been a woman of weak health and enthusiastic temperament. When, after her separation from her husband, she gave birth to her only child, the child had died almost immediately, and the family of Madame Stahl, knowing her sensibility, and fearing the news would kill her, had substituted another child, a baby born the same night and in the same house in Petersburg, the daughter of the chief cook of the Imperial Household. This was Varenka. Madame Stahl learned later on that Varenka was not her own child, but she went on bringing her up, especially as very soon afterwards Varenka had not a relation of her own living. Madame Stahl had now been living more than ten years continuously abroad, in the south, never leaving her couch. And some people said that Madame Stahl had made her social position as a philanthropic, highly religious woman; other people said she really was at heart the highly ethical being, living for nothing but the good of her fellow-creatures, which she represented herself to be. No one knew what her faith was—Catholic, Protestant, or Orthodox. But one fact was indubitable—she was in amicable relations with the highest dignitaries of all the churches and sects.

Varenka lived with her all the while abroad, and everyone who knew Madame Stahl knew and liked Mademoiselle Varenka, as everyone called her.

Having learned all these facts, the princess found nothing to object to in her daughter's intimacy with Varenka, more especially as Varenka's breeding and education were of the best—she spoke French and English extremely well—and what was of the most weight, brought a message from Madame Stahl expressing her regret that she was prevented by her ill-health from making the acquaintance of the princess.

After getting to know Varenka, Kitty became more and more fascinated by her friend, and everyday she discovered new virtues in her.

The princess, hearing that Varenka had a good voice, asked her to come and sing to them in the evening.

"Kitty plays, and we have a piano; not a good one, it's true, but you will give us so much pleasure," said the princess with her affected smile, which Kitty disliked particularly just then, because she noticed that Varenka had no inclination to sing. Varenka came, however, in the evening and brought a roll of music with her. The princess had invited Marya Yevgenyevna and her daughter and the colonel.

Varenka seemed quite unaffected by there being persons present she did not know, and she went directly to the piano. She could not accompany herself, but she could sing music at sight very well. Kitty, who played well, accompanied her.

"You have an extraordinary talent," the princess said to her after Varenka had sung the first song extremely well.

Marya Yevgenyevna and her daughter expressed their thanks and admiration.

"Look," said the colonel, looking out of the window, "what an audience has collected to listen to you." There actually was quite a considerable crowd under the windows.

"I am very glad it gives you pleasure," Varenka answered simply.

Kitty looked with pride at her friend. She was enchanted by her talent, and her voice, and her face, but most of all by her manner, by the way Varenka obviously thought nothing of her singing and was quite unmoved by their praises. She seemed only to be asking: "Am I to sing again, or is that enough?"

"If it had been I," thought Kitty, "how proud I should have been! How delighted I should have been to see that crowd under the windows! But she's utterly unmoved by it. Her only motive is to avoid refusing and to please mamma. What is there in her? What is it gives her the power to look down on everything, to be calm independently of everything? How I should like to know it and to learn it of her!" thought Kitty, gazing into her serene face. The princess asked Varenka to sing again, and Varenka sang another song, also smoothly, distinctly, and well, standing erect at the piano and beating time on it with her thin, dark-skinned hand.

The next song in the book was an Italian one. Kitty played the opening bars, and looked round at Varenka.

"Let's skip that," said Varenka, flushing a little. Kitty let her eyes rest on Varenka's face, with a look of dismay and inquiry.

"Very well, the next one," she said hurriedly, turning over the pages, and at once feeling that there was something connected with the song.

"No," answered Varenka with a smile, laying her hand on the music, "no, let's have that one." And she sang it just as quietly, as coolly, and as well as the others.

When she had finished, they all thanked her again, and went off to tea. Kitty and Varenka went out into the little garden that adjoined the house.

"Am I right, that you have some reminiscences connected with that song?" said Kitty. "Don't tell me," she added hastily, "only say if I'm right."

"No, why not? I'll tell you simply," said Varenka, and, without waiting for a reply, she went on: "Yes, it brings up memories, once painful ones. I cared for someone once, and I used to sing him that song."

Kitty with big, wide-open eyes gazed silently, sympathetically at Varenka.

"I cared for him, and he cared for me; but his mother did not wish it, and he married another girl. He's living now not far from us, and I see him sometimes. You didn't think I had a love story too," she said, and there was a faint gleam in her handsome face of that fire which Kitty felt must once have glowed all over her.

"I didn't think so? Why, if I were a man, I could never care for anyone else after knowing you. Only I can't understand how he could, to please his mother, forget you and make you unhappy; he had no heart."

"Oh, no, he's a very good man, and I'm not unhappy; quite the contrary, I'm very happy. Well, so we shan't be singing anymore now," she added, turning towards the house.

"How good you are! how good you are!" cried Kitty, and stopping her, she kissed her. "If I could only be even a little like you!"

"Why should you be like anyone? You're nice as you are," said Varenka, smiling her gentle, weary smile.

"No, I'm not nice at all . . . Come, tell me. Stop a minute, let's sit down," said Kitty, making her sit down again beside her. "Tell me, isn't it humiliating to think that a man has disdained your love, that he hasn't cared for it? . . ."

"But he didn't disdain it; I believe he cared for me, but he was a dutiful son . . ."

"Yes, but if it hadn't been on account of his mother, if it had been his own doing? . . ." said Kitty, feeling she was giving away her secret, and that her face, burning with the flush of shame, had betrayed her already.

"In that case he would have done wrong, and I should not have regretted him," answered Varenka, evidently realizing that they were now talking not of her, but of Kitty.

"But the humiliation," said Kitty, "the humiliation one can never forget, can never forget," she said, remembering her look at the last ball during the pause in the music.

"Where is the humiliation? Why, you did nothing wrong?"

"Worse than wrong—shameful."

Varenka shook her head and laid her hand on Kitty's hand.

"Why, what is there shameful?" she said. "You didn't tell a man, who didn't care for you, that you loved him, did you?"

"Of course not; I never said a word, but he knew it. No, no, there are looks, there are ways; I can't forget it, if I live a hundred years."

"Why so? I don't understand. The whole point is whether you love him now or not," said Varenka, who called everything by its name.

"I hate him; I can't forgive myself."

"Why, what for?"

"The shame, the humiliation!"

"Oh! if everyone were as sensitive as you are!" said Varenka. "There isn't a girl who hasn't been through the same. And it's all so unimportant."

"Why, what is important?" said Kitty, looking into her face with inquisitive wonder.

"Oh, there's so much that's important," said Varenka, smiling.

"Why, what?"

"Oh, so much that's more important," answered Varenka, not knowing what to say. But at that instant they heard the princess's voice from the window. "Kitty, it's cold! Either get a shawl, or come indoors."

"It really is time to go in!" said Varenka, getting up. "I have to go on to Madame Berthe's; she asked me to."

Kitty held her by the hand, and with passionate curiosity and entreaty her eyes asked her: "What is it, what is this of such importance that gives you such tranquillity? You know, tell me!" But Varenka did not even know what Kitty's eyes were asking her. She merely thought that she had to go to see Madame Berthe too that evening, and to make haste home in time for *maman's* tea at twelve o'clock. She went indoors, collected her music, and saying good-bye to everyone, was about to go.

"Allow me to see you home," said the colonel.

"Yes, how can you go alone at night like this?" chimed in the princess. "Anyway, I'll send Parasha."

Kitty saw that Varenka could hardly restrain a smile at the idea that she needed an escort.

"No, I always go about alone and nothing ever happens to me," she said, taking her hat. And kissing Kitty once more, without saying what was important, she stepped out courageously with the music under her arm and vanished into the twilight of the summer night, bearing away with her her secret of what was important and what gave her the calm and dignity so much to be envied.

Chapter XXXIII

KITTY MADE THE ACQUAINTANCE OF MADAME STAHL TOO, AND THIS ACQUAINTANCE, TOGETHER with her friendship with Varenka, did not merely exercise a great influence on her, it also comforted her in her mental distress. She found this comfort through a completely new world being opened to her by means of this acquaintance, a world having nothing in common with her past, an exalted, noble world, from the height of which she could contemplate her past calmly. It was revealed to her that besides the instinctive life to which Kitty had given herself up hitherto there was a spiritual life. This life was disclosed in religion, but a religion having nothing in common with that one which Kitty had known from childhood, and which found expression in litanies and all-night services at the Widow's Home, where one might meet one's friends, and in learning by heart Slavonic texts with the priest. This was a lofty, mysterious religion connected with a whole series of noble thoughts and feelings, which one could do more than merely believe because one was told to, which one could love.

Kitty found all this out not from words. Madame Stahl talked to Kitty as to a charming child that one looks on with pleasure as on the memory of one's youth, and only once she said in passing that in all human sorrows nothing gives comfort but love and faith, and that in the sight of Christ's compassion for us no sorrow is trifling—and immediately talked of other things. But in every gesture of Madame Stahl, in every word, in every heavenly—as Kitty called it—look, and above all in the whole story of her life, which she heard from Varenka, Kitty recognized that something "that was important," of which, till then, she had known nothing.

Yet, elevated as Madame Stahl's character was, touching as was her story, and exalted and moving as was her speech, Kitty could not help detecting in her some traits which perplexed her. She noticed that when questioning her about her family, Madame Stahl had smiled contemptuously, which was not in accord with Christian meekness. She noticed, too, that when she had found a Catholic priest with her, Madame Stahl had studiously kept her face in the shadow of the lamp-shade and had smiled in a peculiar way. Trivial as these two observations were, they perplexed her, and she had her doubts as to Madame Stahl. But on the other hand Varenka, alone in the world, without friends or relations, with a melancholy disappointment in the past, desiring nothing, regretting nothing, was just that perfection of which Kitty dared hardly dream. In Varenka she realized that one has but to forget oneself and love others, and one will be calm, happy, and noble. And that was what Kitty longed to be. Seeing now clearly what was *the most important,* Kitty was not satisfied with being enthusiastic over it; she at once gave herself up with her whole soul to the new life that was opening to her. From Varenka's accounts of the doings of Madame Stahl and other people whom she mentioned, Kitty had already constructed the plan of her own future life. She would, like Madame Stahl's niece, Aline, of whom Varenka had talked to her a great deal, seek out those who were in trouble, wherever she might be living, help them as far as she could, give them the Gospel, read the Gospel to the sick, to criminals, to the dying. The idea of reading the Gospel to criminals, as Aline did, particularly fascinated Kitty. But all these were secret dreams, of which Kitty did not talk either to her mother or to Varenka.

While awaiting the time for carrying out her plans on a large scale, however, Kitty, even then at the springs, where there were so many people ill and unhappy, readily found a chance for practicing her new principles in imitation of Varenka.

At first the princess noticed nothing but that Kitty was much under the influence of her *engouement*, as she called it, for Madame Stahl, and still more for Varenka. She saw that Kitty did not merely imitate Varenka in her conduct, but unconsciously imitated her in her manner of walking, of talking, of blinking her eyes. But later on the princess noticed that, apart from this adoration, some kind of serious spiritual change was taking place in her daughter.

The princess saw that in the evenings Kitty read a French testament that Madame Stahl had given her—a thing she had never done before; that she avoided society acquaintances and associated with the sick people who were under Varenka's protection, and especially one poor family, that of a sick painter, Petrov. Kitty was unmistakably proud of playing the part of a sister of mercy in that family. All this was well enough, and the princess had nothing to say against it, especially as Petrov's wife was a perfectly nice sort of woman, and that the German princess, noticing Kitty's devotion, praised her, calling her an angel of consolation. All this would have been very well, if there had been no exaggeration. But the princess saw that her daughter was rushing into extremes, and so indeed she told her.

"Il ne faut jamais rien outrer," she said to her.

Her daughter made her no reply, only in her heart she thought that one could not talk about exaggeration where Christianity was concerned. What exaggeration could there be in the practice of a doctrine wherein one was bidden to turn the other cheek when one was smitten, and give one's cloak if one's coat were taken? But the princess disliked this exaggeration, and disliked even more the fact that she felt her daughter did not care to show her all her heart. Kitty did in fact conceal her new views and feelings from her mother. She concealed them not because she did not respect or did not love her mother, but simply because she was her mother. She would have revealed them to anyone sooner than to her mother.

"How is it Anna Pavlovna's not been to see us for so long?" the princess said one day of Madame Petrova. "I've asked her, but she seems put out about something."

"No, I've not noticed it, maman," said Kitty, flushing hotly.

"Is it long since you went to see them?"

"We're meaning to make an expedition to the mountains tomorrow," answered Kitty,

"Well, you can go," answered the princess, gazing at her daughter's embarrassed face and trying to guess the cause of her embarrassment.

That day Varenka came to dinner and told them that Anna Pavlovna had changed her mind and given up the expedition for the morrow. And the princess noticed again that Kitty reddened.

"Kitty, haven't you had some misunderstanding with the Petrovs?" said the princess, when they were left alone. "Why has she given up sending the children and coming to see us?"

Kitty answered that nothing had happened between them, and that she could not tell why Anna Pavlovna seemed displeased with her. Kitty answered perfectly truly. She did not know the reason Anna Pavlovna had changed to her, but she guessed it. She guessed at something which she could not tell her mother, which she did not put into words to herself. It was one of those things which one knows but which one can never speak of even to oneself so terrible and shameful would it be to be mistaken.

Again and again she went over in her memory all her relations with the family. She remembered the simple delight expressed on the round, good-humored face of Anna Pavlovna at their meetings; she remembered their secret confabulations about the invalid, their plots to draw him away from the work which was forbidden him, and to get him out-of-doors; the devotion of the youngest boy, who used to call her "my Kitty," and would not go to bed without her. How nice it all was! Then she recalled the thin, terribly thin figure of Petrov, with his long neck, in his brown coat, his scant, curly hair, his questioning blue eyes that were so terrible to Kitty at first, and his painful attempts to seem hearty and lively in her presence. She recalled the efforts she had made at first to overcome the repugnance she felt for him, as for all consumptive people, and the pains it had cost her to think of things to say to him. She recalled the timid, softened look with which he gazed at her, and the strange feeling of compassion and awkwardness, and later of a sense of her own goodness, which she had felt at it. How nice it all was! But all that was at first. Now, a few days ago, everything was suddenly spoiled. Anna Pavlovna had met Kitty with affected cordiality, and had kept continual watch on her and on her husband.

Could that touching pleasure he showed when she came near be the cause of Anna Pavlovna's coolness?

"Yes," she mused, "there was something unnatural about Anna Pavlovna, and utterly unlike her good-nature, when she said angrily the day before yesterday: 'There, he will keep waiting for you; he wouldn't drink his coffee without you, though he's grown so dreadfully weak.' "

"Yes, perhaps, too, she didn't like it when I gave him the rug. It was all so simple, but he took it so awkwardly, and was so long thanking me, that I felt awkward too. And then that portrait of me he did so well. And most of all that look of confusion and tenderness! Yes, yes, that's it!" Kitty repeated to herself with horror. "No, it can't be, it oughtn't to be! He's so much to be pitied!" she said to herself directly after.

This doubt poisoned the charm of her new life.

Chapter XXXIV

BEFORE THE END OF THE COURSE OF DRINKING THE WATERS, PRINCE SHTCHERBATSKY, WHO HAD gone on from Carlsbad to Baden and Kissingen to Russian friends—to get a breath of Russian air, as he said—came back to his wife and daughter.

The views of the prince and of the princess on life abroad were completely opposed. The princess thought everything delightful, and in spite of her established position in Russian society, she tried abroad to be like a European fashionable lady, which she was not—for the simple reason that she was a typical Russian gentlewoman; and so she was affected, which did not altogether suit her. The prince, on the contrary, thought everything foreign detestable, got sick of European life, kept to his Russian habits, and purposely tried to show himself abroad less European than he was in reality.

The prince returned thinner, with the skin hanging in loose bags on his cheeks, but in the most cheerful frame of mind. His good-humor was even greater when he saw Kitty completely recovered. The news of Kitty's friendship with Madame Stahl and Varenka, and the reports the princess gave him of some kind of change she had noticed in Kitty, troubled the prince and aroused his habitual feeling of jealousy of everything that drew his daughter away from him, and a dread that his daughter might have got out of the reach of his influence into regions inaccessible to him. But these unpleasant matters were all drowned in the sea of kindliness and good-humor which was always within him, and more so than ever since his course of Carlsbad waters.

The day after his arrival the prince, in his long overcoat, with his Russian wrinkles and baggy cheeks propped up by a starched collar, set off with his daughter to the spring in the greatest good-humor.

It was a lovely morning: the bright, cheerful houses with their little gardens, the sight of the red-faced, red-armed, beer-drinking German waitresses, working away merrily, did the heart good. But the nearer they got to the springs the oftener they met sick people; and their appearance seemed more pitiable than ever among the everyday conditions of prosperous German life. Kitty was no longer struck by this contrast. The bright sun, the brilliant green of the foliage, the strains of the music were for her the natural setting of all these familiar faces, with their changes to greater emaciation or to convalescence, for which she watched. But to the prince the brightness and gaiety of the June morning, and the sound of the orchestra playing a gay waltz then in fashion, and above all, the appearance of the healthy attendants, seemed something unseemly and monstrous, in conjunction with these slowly moving, dying figures gathered together from all parts of Europe. In spite of his feeling of pride and, as it were, of the return of youth, with his favorite daughter on his arm, he felt awkward, and almost ashamed of his vigorous step and his sturdy, stout limbs. He felt almost like a man not dressed in a crowd.

"Present me to your new friends," he said to his daughter, squeezing her hand with his elbow. "I like even your horrid Soden for making you so well again. Only it's melancholy, very melancholy here. Who's that?"

Kitty mentioned the names of all the people they met, with some of whom she was acquainted and some not. At the entrance of the garden they met the blind lady, Madame Berthe, with her guide, and the prince was delighted to see the old Frenchwoman's face light up when she heard Kitty's voice. She at once began talking to him with French exaggerated politeness, applauding him for having such a delightful daughter, extolling Kitty to the skies before her face, and calling her a treasure, a pearl, and a consoling angel.

"Well, she's the second angel, then," said the prince, smiling. "she calls Mademoiselle Varenka angel number one."

"Oh! Mademoiselle Varenka, she's a real angel, allez," Madame Berthe assented.

In the arcade they met Varenka herself. She was walking rapidly towards them carrying an elegant red bag.

"Here is papa come," Kitty said to her.

Varenka made—simply and naturally as she did everything—a movement between a bow and a curtsey, and immediately began talking to the prince, without shyness, naturally, as she talked to everyone.

"Of course I know you; I know you very well," the prince said to her with a smile, in which Kitty detected with joy that her father liked her friend. "Where are you off to in such haste?"

"Maman's here," she said, turning to Kitty. "She has not slept all night, and the doctor advised her to go out. I'm taking her her work."

"So that's angel number one?" said the prince when Varenka had gone on.

Kitty saw that her father had meant to make fun of Varenka, but that he could not do it because he liked her.

"Come, so we shall see all your friends," he went on, "even Madame Stahl, if she deigns to recognize me."

"Why, did you know her, papa?" Kitty asked apprehensively, catching the gleam of irony that kindled in the prince's eyes at the mention of Madame Stahl.

"I used to know her husband, and her too a little, before she'd joined the Pietists."

"What is a Pietist, papa?" asked Kitty, dismayed to find that what she prized so highly in Madame Stahl had a name.

"I don't quite know myself. I only know that she thanks God for everything, for every misfortune, and thanks God too that her husband died. And that's rather droll, as they didn't get on together."

"Who's that? What a piteous face!" he asked, noticing a sick man of medium height sitting on a bench, wearing a brown overcoat and white trousers that fell in strange folds about his long, fleshless legs. This man lifted his straw hat, showed his scanty curly hair and high forehead, painfully reddened by the pressure of the hat.

"That's Petrov, an artist," answered Kitty, blushing. "And that's his wife," she added, indicating Anna Pavlovna, who, as though on purpose, at the very instant they approached walked away after a child that had run off along a path.

"Poor fellow! and what a nice face he has!" said the prince. "Why don't you go up to him? He wanted to speak to you."

"Well, let us go, then," said Kitty, turning round resolutely. "How are you feeling today?" she asked Petrov.

Petrov got up, leaning on his stick, and looked shyly at the prince.

"This is my daughter," said the prince. "Let me introduce myself."

The painter bowed and smiled, showing his strangely dazzling white teeth.

"We expected you yesterday, princess," he said to Kitty. He staggered as he said this, and then repeated the motion, trying to make it seem as if it had been intentional.

"I meant to come, but Varenka said that Anna Pavlovna sent word you were not going."

"Not going!" said Petrov, blushing, and immediately beginning to cough, and his eyes sought his wife. "Anita! Anita!" he said loudly, and the swollen veins stood out like cords on his thin white neck.

Anna Pavlovna came up.

"So you sent word to the princess that we weren't going!" he whispered to her angrily, losing his voice.

"Good morning, princess," said Anna Pavlovna, with an assumed smile utterly unlike her former manner. "Very glad to make your acquaintance," she said to the prince. "You've long been expected, prince."

"What did you send word to the princess that we weren't going for?" the artist whispered hoarsely once more, still more angrily, obviously exasperated that his voice failed him so that he could not give his words the expression he would have liked to.

"Oh, mercy on us! I thought we weren't going," his wife answered crossly.

"What, when . . ." He coughed and waved his hand. The prince took off his hat and moved away with his daughter.

"Ah! ah!" he sighed deeply. "Oh, poor things!"

"Yes, papa," answered Kitty. "And you must know they've three children, no servant, and scarcely any means. He gets something from the Academy," she went on briskly, trying to drown the distress that the queer change in Anna Pavlovna's manner to her had aroused in her.

"Oh, here's Madame Stahl," said Kitty, indicating an invalid carriage, where, propped on pillows, something in gray and blue was lying under a sunshade. This was Madame Stahl. Behind her stood the gloomy healthy-looking German workman who pushed the carriage. Close by was standing a flaxen-headed Swedish count, whom Kitty knew by name. Several invalids were lingering near the low carriage, staring at the lady as though she were some curiosity.

The prince went up to her, and Kitty detected that disconcerting gleam of irony in his eyes. He went up to Madame Stahl, and addressed her with extreme courtesy and affability in that excellent French that so few speak nowadays.

"I don't know if you remember me, but I must recall myself to thank you for your kindness to my daughter," he said, taking off his hat and not putting it on again.

"Prince Alexander Shtcherbatsky," said Madame Stahl, lifting upon him her heavenly eyes, in which Kitty discerned a look of annoyance. "Delighted! I have taken a great fancy to your daughter."

"You are still in weak health?"

"Yes; I'm used to it," said Madame Stahl, and she introduced the prince to the Swedish count.

"You are scarcely changed at all," the prince said to her. "It's ten or eleven years since I had the honor of seeing you."

"Yes; God sends the cross and sends the strength to bear it. Often one wonders what is the goal of this life? . . . The other side!" she said angrily to Varenka, who had rearranged the rug over her feet not to her satisfaction.

"To do good, probably," said the prince with a twinkle in his eye.

"That is not for us to judge," said Madame Stahl, perceiving the shade of expression on the prince's face. "So you will send me that book, dear count? I'm very grateful to you," she said to the young Swede.

"Ah!" cried the prince, catching sight of the Moscow colonel standing near, and with a bow to Madame Stahl he walked away with his daughter and the Moscow colonel, who joined them.

"That's our aristocracy, prince!" the Moscow colonel said with ironical intention. He cherished a grudge against Madame Stahl for not making his acquaintance.

"She's just the same," replied the prince.

"Did you know her before her illness, prince—that's to say before she took to her bed?"

"Yes. She took to her bed before my eyes," said the prince.

"They say it's ten years since she has stood on her feet."

"She doesn't stand up because her legs are too short. She's a very bad figure."

"Papa, it's not possible!" cried Kitty.

"That's what wicked tongues say, my darling. And your Varenka catches it too," he added. "Oh, these invalid ladies!"

"Oh, no, papa!" Kitty objected warmly. "Varenka worships her. And then she does so much good! Ask anyone! Everyone knows her and Aline Stahl."

"Perhaps so," said the prince, squeezing her hand with his elbow; "but it's better when one does good so that you may ask everyone and no one knows."

Kitty did not answer, not because she had nothing to say, but because she did not care to reveal her secret thoughts even to her father. But, strange to say, although she had so made up her mind not to be influenced by her father's views, not to let him into her inmost sanctuary, she felt that the heavenly image of Madame Stahl, which she had carried for a whole month in her heart, had vanished, never to return, just as the fantastic figure made up of some clothes thrown down at random vanishes when one sees that it is only some garment lying there. All that was left was a woman with short legs, who lay down because she had a bad figure, and worried patient Varenka for not arranging her rug to her liking. And by no effort of the imagination could Kitty bring back the former Madame Stahl.

Chapter XXXV

The prince communicated his good-humor to his own family and his friends, and even to the German landlord in whose rooms the Shtcherbatskys were staying.

On coming back with Kitty from the springs, the prince, who had asked the colonel, and Marya Yevgenyevna, and Varenka all to come and have coffee with them, gave orders for a table and chairs to be taken into the garden under the chestnut tree, and lunch to be laid there. The landlord and the servants, too, grew brisker under the influence of his good spirits. They knew his open-handedness; and half an hour later the invalid doctor from Hamburg, who lived on the top floor, looked enviously out of the window at the merry party of healthy Russians assembled under the chestnut tree. In the trembling circles of shadow cast by the leaves, at a table, covered with a white cloth, and set with coffee pot, bread-and-butter, cheese, and cold game, sat the princess in a high cap with lilac ribbons, distributing cups and bread-and-butter. At the other end sat the prince, eating heartily, and talking loudly and merrily. The prince had spread out near him his purchases, carved boxes, and knick-knacks, paper-knives of all sorts, of which he bought a heap at every watering place, and bestowed them upon everyone, including Lieschen, the servant girl, and the landlord, with whom he jested in his comically bad German, assuring him that it was not the water had cured Kitty, but his splendid cookery, especially his plum soup. The princess laughed at her husband for his Russian ways, but she was more lively and good-humored than she had been all the while she had been at the waters. The colonel smiled, as he always did, at the prince's jokes, but as far as regards Europe, of which he believed himself to be making a careful study, he took the princess's side. The simple-hearted Marya Yevgenyevna simply roared with laughter at everything absurd the prince said, and his jokes made Varenka helpless with feeble but infectious laughter, which was something Kitty had never seen before.

Kitty was glad of all this, but she could not be light-hearted. She could not solve the problem her father had unconsciously set her by his good-humored view of her friends, and of the life that had so attracted her. To this doubt there was joined the change in her relations with the Petrovs, which had been so conspicuously and unpleasantly marked that morning. Everyone was good-humored, but Kitty could not feel good-humored, and this increased her distress. She felt a feeling such as she had known in childhood, when she had been shut in her room as a punishment, and had heard her sisters' merry laughter outside.

"Well, but what did you buy this mass of things for?" said the princess, smiling, and handing her husband a cup of coffee.

"One goes for a walk, one looks in a shop, and they ask you to buy. '*Erlaucht, Durchlaucht?*' Directly they say '*Durchlaucht,*' I can't hold out. I lose ten thalers."

"It's simply from boredom," said the princess.

"Of course it is. Such boredom, my dear, that one doesn't know what to do with oneself."

"How can you be bored, prince? There's so much that's interesting now in Germany," said Marya Yevgenyevna.

"But I know everything that's interesting: the plum soup I know, and the pea sausages I know. I know everything."

"No, you may say what you like, prince, there's the interest of their institutions," said the colonel.

"But what is there interesting about it? They're all as pleased as brass halfpence. They've conquered everybody, and why am I to be pleased at that? I haven't conquered anyone; and I'm obliged to take off my own boots, yes, and put them away too; in the morning, get up and dress at once, and go to the dining room to drink bad tea! How different it is at home! You get up in no haste, you get cross, grumble a little, and come round again. You've time to think things over, and no hurry."

"But time's money, you forget that," said the colonel.

"Time, indeed, that depends! Why, there's time one would give a month of for sixpence, and time you wouldn't give half an hour of for any money. Isn't that so, Katinka? What is it? why are you so depressed?"

"I'm not depressed."

"Where are you off to? Stay a little longer," he said to Varenka.

"I must be going home," said Varenka, getting up, and again she went off into a giggle. When she had recovered, she said good-bye, and went into the house to get her hat.

Kitty followed her. Even Varenka struck her as different. She was not worse, but different from what she had fancied her before.

"Oh, dear! it's a long while since I've laughed so much!" said Varenka, gathering up her parasol and her bag. "How nice he is, your father!"

Kitty did not speak.

"When shall I see you again?" asked Varenka.

"Mamma meant to go and see the Petrovs. Won't you be there?" said Kitty, to try Varenka.

"Yes," answered Varenka. "They're getting ready to go away, so I promised to help them pack."

"Well, I'll come too, then."

"No, why should you?"

"Why not? why not? why not?" said Kitty, opening her eyes wide, and clutching at Varenka's parasol, so as not to let her go. "No, wait a minute; why not?"

"Oh, nothing; your father has come, and besides, they will feel awkward at your helping."

"No, tell me why you don't want me to be often at the Petrovs. You don't want me to—why not?"

"I didn't say that," said Varenka quietly.

"No, please tell me!"

"Tell you everything?" asked Varenka.

"Everything, everything!" Kitty assented.

"Well, there's really nothing of any consequence; only that Mihail Alexeyevitch" (that was the artist's name) "had meant to leave earlier, and now he doesn't want to go away," said Varenka, smiling.

"Well, well!" Kitty urged impatiently, looking darkly at Varenka.

"Well, and for some reason Anna Pavlovna told him that he didn't want to go because you are here. Of course, that was nonsense; but there was a dispute over it—over you. You know how irritable these sick people are."

Kitty, scowling more than ever, kept silent, and Varenka went on speaking alone, trying to soften or soothe her, and seeing a storm coming—she did not know whether of tears or of words.

"So you'd better not go. . . . You understand; you won't be offended? . . ."

"And it serves me right! And it serves me right!" Kitty cried quickly, snatching the parasol out of Varenka's hand, and looking past her friend's face.

Varenka felt inclined to smile, looking at her childish fury, but she was afraid of wounding her.

"How does it serve you right? I don't understand," she said.

"It serves me right, because it was all sham; because it was all done on purpose, and not from the heart. What business had I to interfere with outsiders? And so it's come about that I'm a cause of quarrel, and that I've done what nobody asked me to do. Because it was all a sham! a sham! a sham! . . ."

"A sham! with what object?" said Varenka gently.

"Oh, it's so idiotic! so hateful! There was no need whatever for me. . . . Nothing but sham!" she said, opening and shutting the parasol.

"But with what object?"

"To seem better to people, to myself, to God; to deceive everyone. No! now I won't descend to that. I'll be bad; but anyway not a liar, a cheat."

"But who is a cheat?" said Varenka reproachfully. "You speak as if . . ."

But Kitty was in one of her gusts of fury, and she would not let her finish.

"I don't talk about you, not about you at all. You're perfection. Yes, yes, I know you're all perfection; but what am I to do if I'm bad? This would never have been if I weren't bad. So let me be what I am. I won't be a sham. What have I to do with Anna Pavlovna? Let them go their way, and me go mine. I can't be different. . . . And yet it's not that, it's not that."

"What is not that?" asked Varenka in bewilderment.

"Everything. I can't act except from the heart, and you act from principle. I liked you simply, but you most likely only wanted to save me, to improve me."

"You are unjust," said Varenka.

"But I'm not speaking of other people, I'm speaking of myself."

"Kitty," they heard her mother's voice, "come here, show papa your necklace."

Kitty, with a haughty air, without making peace with her friend, took the necklace in a little box from the table and went to her mother.

"What's the matter? Why are you so red?" her mother and father said to her with one voice.

"Nothing," she answered. "I'll be back directly," and she ran back.

"She's still here," she thought. "What am I to say to her? Oh, dear! what have I done, what have I said? Why was I rude to her? What am I to do? What am I to say to her?" thought Kitty, and she stopped in the doorway.

Varenka in her hat and with the parasol in her hands was sitting at the table examining the spring which Kitty had broken. She lifted her head.

"Varenka, forgive me, do forgive me," whispered Kitty, going up to her. "I don't remember what I said. I . . ."

"I really didn't mean to hurt you," said Varenka, smiling.

Peace was made. But with her father's coming all the world in which she had been living was transformed for Kitty. She did not give up everything she had learned, but she became aware that she had deceived herself in supposing she could be what she wanted to be. Her eyes were, it seemed, opened; she felt all the difficulty of maintaining herself without hypocrisy and self-conceit on the pinnacle to which she had wished to mount. Moreover she became aware of all the dreariness of the world of sorrow, of sick and dying people, in which she had been living. The efforts she had made to like it seemed to her intolerable, and she felt a longing to get back quickly into the fresh air, to Russia, to Ergushovo, where, as she knew from letters, her sister Dolly had already gone with her children.

But her affection for Varenka did not wane. As she said good-bye, Kitty begged her to come to them in Russia.

"I'll come when you get married," said Varenka.

"I shall never marry."

"Well, then, I shall never come."

"Well, then, I shall be married simply for that. Mind now, remember your promise," said Kitty.

The doctor's prediction was fulfilled. Kitty returned home to Russia cured. She was not so gay and thoughtless as before, but she was serene. Her Moscow troubles had become a memory to her.

Part Three

Chapter I

Sergey Ivanovitch Koznishev wanted a rest from mental work, and instead of going abroad as he usually did, he came towards the end of May to stay in the country with his brother. In his judgment the best sort of life was a country life. He had come now to enjoy such a life at his brother's. Konstantin Levin was very glad to have him, especially as he did not expect his brother Nikolay that summer. But in spite of his affection and respect for Sergey Ivanovitch, Konstantin Levin was uncomfortable with his brother in the country. It made him uncomfortable, and it positively annoyed him to see his brother's attitude to the country. To Konstantin Levin the country was the background of life, that is of pleasures, endeavors, labor. To Sergey Ivanovitch the country meant on one hand rest from work, on the other a valuable antidote to the corrupt influences of town, which he took with satisfaction and a sense of its utility. To Konstantin Levin the country was good first because it afforded a field for labor, of the usefulness of which there could be no doubt. To Sergey Ivanovitch the country was particularly good, because there it was possible and fitting to do nothing. Moreover, Sergey Ivanovitch's attitude to the peasants rather piqued Konstantin. Sergey Ivanovitch used to say that he knew and liked the peasantry, and he often talked to the peasants, which he knew how to do without affectation or condescension, and from every such conversation he would deduce general conclusions in favor of the peasantry and in confirmation of his knowing them. Konstantin Levin did not like such an attitude to the peasants. To Konstantin the peasant was simply the chief partner in their common labor, and in spite of all the respect and the love, almost like that of kinship, he had for the peasant—sucked in probably, as he said himself, with the milk of his peasant nurse—still as a fellow-worker with him, while sometimes enthusiastic over the vigor, gentleness, and justice of these men, he was very often, when their common labors called for other qualities, exasperated with the peasant for his carelessness, lack of method, drunkenness, and lying. If he had been asked whether he liked or didn't like the peasants, Konstantin Levin would have been absolutely at a loss what to reply. He liked and did not like the peasants, just as he liked and did not like men in general. Of course, being a good-hearted man, he liked men rather than he disliked them, and so too with the peasants. But like or dislike "the people" as something apart he could not, not only because he lived with "the people," and all his interests were bound up with theirs, but also because he regarded himself as a part of "the people," did not see any special qualities or failings distinguishing himself and "the people," and could not contrast himself with them. Moreover, although he had lived so long in the closest relations with the peasants, as farmer and arbitrator, and what was more, as adviser (the peasants trusted him, and for thirty miles round they would come to ask his advice), he had no definite views of "the people," and would have been as much at a loss to answer the question whether he knew "the people" as the question whether he liked them. For him to say he knew the peasantry would have been the same as to say he knew men. He was continually watching and getting to know people of all sorts, and among them peasants, whom he regarded as good and interesting people, and he was continually observing new points in them, altering his former views of them and forming new ones. With Sergey Ivanovitch it was quite the contrary. Just as he liked and praised a country life in comparison with the life he did not like, so too he liked the peasantry in contradistinction to the class of men he did not like, and so too he knew the peasantry as something distinct from and opposed to men generally. In his methodical brain there were distinctly formulated certain aspects of peasant life, deduced partly from that life itself, but chiefly from contrast with other modes of life. He never changed his opinion of the peasantry and his sympathetic attitude towards them.

In the discussions that arose between the brothers on their views of the peasantry, Sergey Ivanovitch always got the better of his brother, precisely because Sergey Ivanovitch had definite ideas about the peasant—his character, his qualities, and his tastes. Konstantin Levin had no definite and unalterable idea on the subject, and so in their arguments Konstantin was readily convicted of contradicting himself.

In Sergey Ivanovitch's eyes his younger brother was a capital fellow, *with his heart in the right place* (as he expressed it in French), but with a mind which, though fairly quick, was too much influenced by the impressions of the moment, and consequently filled with contradictions. With all the condescension of an elder brother he sometimes explained to him the true import of things, but he derived little satisfaction from arguing with him because he got the better of him too easily.

Konstantin Levin regarded his brother as a man of immense intellect and culture, as generous in the highest sense of the word, and possessed of a special faculty for working for the public good. But in the depths of his heart, the older he became, and the more intimately he knew his brother, the more and more frequently the thought struck him that this faculty of working for the public good, of which he felt himself utterly devoid, was possibly not so much a quality as a lack of something—not a lack of good, honest, noble desires and tastes, but a lack of vital force, of what is called heart, of that impulse which drives a man to choose someone out of the innumerable paths of life, and to care only for that one. The better he knew his brother, the more he noticed that Sergey Ivanovitch, and many other people who worked for the public welfare, were not led by an impulse of the heart to care for the public good, but reasoned from intellectual considerations that it was a right thing to take interest in public affairs, and consequently took interest in them. Levin was confirmed in this generalization by observing that his brother did not take questions affecting the public welfare or the question of the immortality of the soul a bit more to heart than he did chess problems, or the ingenious construction of a new machine.

Besides this, Konstantin Levin was not at his ease with his brother, because in summer in the country Levin was continually busy with work on the land, and the long summer day was not long enough for him to get through all he had to do, while Sergey Ivanovitch was taking a holiday. But though he was taking a holiday now, that is to say, he was doing no writing, he was so used to intellectual activity that he liked to put into concise and eloquent shape the ideas that occurred to him, and liked to have someone to listen to him. His most usual and natural listener was his brother. And so in spite of the friendliness and directness of their relations, Konstantin felt an awkwardness in leaving him alone. Sergey Ivanovitch liked to stretch himself on the grass in the sun, and to lie so, basking and chatting lazily.

"You wouldn't believe," he would say to his brother, "what a pleasure this rural laziness is to me. Not an idea in one's brain, as empty as a drum!"

But Konstantin Levin found it dull sitting and listening to him, especially when he knew that while he was away they would be carting dung onto the fields not ploughed ready for it, and heaping it all up anyhow; and would not screw the shares in the ploughs, but would let them come off and then say that the new ploughs were a silly invention, and there was nothing like the old Andreevna plough, and so on.

"Come, you've done enough trudging about in the heat," Sergey Ivanovitch would say to him.

"No, I must just run round to the counting house for a minute," Levin would answer, and he would run off to the fields.

Chapter II

EARLY IN JUNE IT HAPPENED THAT AGAFEA MIHALOVNA, THE OLD NURSE AND HOUSEKEEPER, IN carrying to the cellar a jar of mushrooms she had just pickled, slipped, fell, and sprained her wrist. The district doctor, a talkative young medical student, who had just finished his studies, came to see her. He examined the wrist, said it was not broken, was delighted at a chance of talking to the celebrated Sergey Ivanovitch Koznishev, and to show his advanced views of things told him all the scandal of the district, complaining of the poor state into which the district council had fallen. Sergey Ivanovitch listened attentively, asked him questions, and, roused by a new listener, he talked fluently, uttered a few keen and weighty observations, respectfully appreciated by the young doctor, and was soon in that eager frame of mind his brother knew so well, which always, with him, followed a brilliant and eager conversation. After the departure of the doctor, he wanted to go with a fishing rod to the river. Sergey Ivanovitch was fond of angling, and was, it seemed, proud of being able to care for such a stupid occupation.

Konstantin Levin, whose presence was needed in the ploughland and meadows, had come to take his brother in the trap.

It was that time of the year, the turning point of summer, when the crops of the present year are a certainty, when one begins to think of the sowing for next year, and the mowing is at hand; when the rye is all in ear, though its ears are still light, not yet full, and it waves in gray-green billows in the wind; when the green oats, with tufts of yellow grass scattered here and there among it, droop irregularly over the late-sown fields; when the early buckwheat is already out and hiding the ground; when the fallow lands, trodden hard as stone by the cattle, are half-ploughed over, with paths left untouched by the plough; when from the dry dung-heaps carted onto the fields there comes at sunset a smell of manure mixed with meadow-sweet, and on the low-lying lands the riverside meadows are a thick sea of grass waiting for the mowing, with blackened heaps of the stalks of sorrel among it.

It was the time when there comes a brief pause in the toil of the fields before the beginning of the labors of harvest—every year recurring, every year straining every nerve of the peasants. The crop was a splendid one, and bright, hot summer days had set in with short, dewy nights.

The brothers had to drive through the woods to reach the meadows. Sergey Ivanovitch was all the while admiring the beauty of the woods, which were a tangled mass of leaves, pointing out to his brother now an old lime tree on the point of flowering, dark on the shady side, and brightly spotted with yellow stipules, now the young shoots of this year's saplings brilliant with emerald. Konstantin Levin did not like talking and hearing about the beauty of nature. Words for him took away the beauty of what he saw. He assented to what his brother said, but he could not help beginning to think of other things. When they came out of the woods, all his attention was engrossed by the view of the fallow land on the upland, in parts yellow with grass, in parts trampled and checkered with furrows, in parts dotted with ridges of dung, and in parts even ploughed. A string of carts was moving across it. Levin counted the carts, and was pleased that all that were wanted had been brought, and at the sight of the meadows his thoughts passed to the mowing. He always felt something special moving him to the quick at the hay-making. On reaching the meadow Levin stopped the horse.

The morning dew was still lying on the thick undergrowth of the grass, and that he might not get his feet wet, Sergey Ivanovitch asked his brother to drive him in the trap up to the willow tree from which the carp was caught. Sorry as Konstantin Levin was to crush down his mowing-grass, he drove him into the meadow. The high grass softly turned about the wheels and the horse's legs, leaving its seeds clinging to the wet axles and spokes of the wheels. His brother seated himself under a bush, arranging his tackle, while Levin led the horse away, fastened him up, and walked into the vast gray-green sea of grass unstirred by the wind. The silky grass with its ripe seeds came almost to his waist in the dampest spots.

Crossing the meadow, Konstantin Levin came out onto the road, and met an old man with a swollen eye, carrying a skep on his shoulder.

"What? taken a stray swarm, Fomitch?" he asked.

"No, indeed, Konstantin Dmitrich! All we can do to keep our own! This is the second swarm that has flown away. . . . Luckily the lads caught them. They were ploughing your field. They unyoked the horses and galloped after them."

"Well, what do you say, Fomitch—start mowing or wait a bit?"

"Eh, well. Our way's to wait till St. Peter's Day. But you always mow sooner. Well, to be sure, please God, the hay's good. There'll be plenty for the beasts."

"What do you think about the weather?"

"That's in God's hands. Maybe it will be fine."

Levin went up to his brother.

Sergey Ivanovitch had caught nothing, but he was not bored, and seemed in the most cheerful frame of mind. Levin saw that, stimulated by his conversation with the doctor, he wanted to talk. Levin, on the other hand, would have liked to get home as soon as possible to give orders about getting together the mowers for next day, and to set at rest his doubts about the mowing, which greatly absorbed him.

"Well, let's be going," he said.

"Why be in such a hurry? Let's stay a little. But how wet you are! Even though one catches nothing, it's nice. That's the best thing about every part of sport, that one has to do with nature. How exquisite this steely water is!" said Sergey Ivanovitch. "These riverside banks always remind me of the riddle—do you know it? 'The grass says to the water: we quiver and we quiver.' "

"I don't know the riddle," answered Levin wearily.

Chapter III

"DO YOU KNOW I'VE BEEN THINKING ABOUT YOU," SAID SERGEY IVANOVITCH. "IT'S BEYOND everything what's being done in the district, according to what this doctor tells me. He's a very intelligent fellow. And as I've told you before, I tell you again: it's not right for you not to go to the meetings, and altogether to keep out of the district business. If decent people won't go into it, of course it's bound to go all wrong. We pay the money, and it all goes in salaries, and there are no schools, nor district nurses, nor midwives, nor drugstores—nothing."

"Well, I did try, you know," Levin said slowly and unwillingly. "I can't! and so there's no help for it."

"But why can't you? I must own I can't make it out. Indifference, incapacity—I won't admit; surely it's not simply laziness?"

"None of those things. I've tried, and I see I can do nothing," said Levin.

He had hardly grasped what his brother was saying. Looking towards the ploughland across the river, he made out something black, but he could not distinguish whether it was a horse or the bailiff on horseback.

"Why is it you can do nothing? You made an attempt and didn't succeed, as you think, and you give in. How can you have so little self-respect?"

"Self-respect!" said Levin, stung to the quick by his brother's words; "I don't understand. If they'd told me at college that other people understood the integral calculus, and I didn't, then pride would have come in. But in this case one wants first to be convinced that one has certain qualifications for this sort of business, and especially that all this business is of great importance."

"What! do you mean to say it's not of importance?" said Sergey Ivanovitch, stung to the quick too at his brother's considering anything of no importance that interested him, and still more at his obviously paying little attention to what he was saying.

"I don't think it important; it does not take hold of me, I can't help it," answered Levin, making out that what he saw was the bailiff, and that the bailiff seemed to be letting the peasants go off the ploughed land. They were turning the plough over. "Can they have finished ploughing?" he wondered.

"Come, really though," said the elder brother, with a frown on his handsome, clever face, "there's a limit to everything. It's very well to be original and genuine, and to dislike everything conventional—I know all about that; but really, what you're saying either has no meaning, or it has a very wrong meaning. How can you think it a matter of no importance whether the peasant, whom you love as you assert, . . ."

"I never did assert it," thought Konstantin Levin.

"—dies without help? The ignorant peasant-women starve the children, and the people stagnate in darkness, and are helpless in the hands of every village clerk, while you have at your disposal a means of helping them, and don't help them because to your mind it's of no importance."

And Sergey Ivanovitch put before him the alternative: either you are so undeveloped that you can't see all that you can do, or you won't sacrifice your ease, your vanity, or whatever it is, to do it.

Konstantin Levin felt that there was no course open to him but to submit, or to confess to a lack of zeal for the public good. And this mortified him and hurt his feelings.

"It's both," he said resolutely; "I don't see that it was possible . . ."

"What! was it impossible, if the money were properly laid out, to provide medical aid?"

"Impossible, as it seems to me. . . . For the three thousand square miles of our district, what with our thaws, and the storms, and the work in the fields, I don't see how it is possible to provide medical aid all over. And besides, I don't believe in medicine."

"Oh, well, that's unfair. . . . I can quote to you thousands of instances. . . . But the schools, anyway."

"Why have schools?"

"What do you mean? Can there be two opinions of the advantage of education? If it's a good thing for you, it's a good thing for everyone."

Konstantin Levin felt himself morally pinned against a wall, and so he got hot, and unconsciously blurted out the chief cause of his indifference to public business.

"Perhaps it may all be very good; but why should I worry myself about establishing dispensaries which I shall never make use of, and schools to which I shall never send my children, to which even the peasants don't want to send their children, and to which I've no very firm faith that they ought to send them?" said he.

Sergey Ivanovitch was for a minute surprised at this unexpected view of the subject; but he promptly made a new plan of attack. He was silent for a little, drew out a hook, threw it in again, and turned to his brother smiling.

"Come, now. . . . In the first place, the dispensary is needed. We ourselves sent for the district doctor for Agafea Mihalovna."

"Oh, well, but I fancy her wrist will never be straight again."

"That remains to be proved. . . . Next, the peasant who can read and write is as a workman of more use and value to you."

"No, you can ask anyone you like," Konstantin Levin answered with decision, "the man that can read and write is much inferior as a workman. And mending the highroads is an impossibility; and as soon as they put up bridges they're stolen."

"Still, that's not the point," said Sergey Ivanovitch, frowning. He disliked contradiction, and still more, arguments that were continually skipping from one thing to another, introducing new and disconnected points, so that there was no knowing to which to reply. "Do you admit that education is a benefit for the people?"

"Yes, I admit it," said Levin without thinking, and he was conscious immediately that he had said what he did not think. He felt that if he admitted that, it would be proved that he had been talking meaningless rubbish. How it would be proved he could not tell, but he knew that this would inevitably be logically proved to him, and he awaited the proofs.

The argument turned out to be far simpler than he had expected.

"If you admit that it is a benefit," said Sergey Ivanovitch, "then, as an honest man, you cannot help caring about it and sympathizing with the movement, and so wishing to work for it."

"But I still do not admit this movement to be just," said Konstantin Levin, reddening a little.

"What! But you said just now . . ."

"That's to say, I don't admit it's being either good or possible."

"That you can't tell without making the trial."

"Well, supposing that's so," said Levin, though he did not suppose so at all, "supposing that is so, still I don't see, all the same, what I'm to worry myself about it for."

"How so?"

"No; since we are talking, explain it to me from the philosophical point of view," said Levin.

"I can't see where philosophy comes in," said Sergey Ivanovitch, in a tone, Levin fancied, as though he did not admit his brother's right to talk about philosophy. And that irritated Levin.

"I'll tell you, then," he said with heat, "I imagine the mainspring of all our actions is, after all, self-interest. Now in the local institutions I, as a nobleman, see nothing that could conduce to my prosperity, and the roads are not better and could not be better; my horses carry me well enough over bad ones. Doctors and dispensaries are no use to me. An arbitrator of disputes is no use to me. I never appeal to him, and never shall appeal to him. The schools are no good to me, but positively harmful, as I told you. For me the district institutions simply mean the liability to pay fourpence halfpenny for every three acres, to drive into the town, sleep with bugs, and listen to all sorts of idiocy and loathsomeness, and self-interest offers me no inducement."

"Excuse me," Sergey Ivanovitch interposed with a smile, "self-interest did not induce us to work for the emancipation of the serfs, but we did work for it."

"No!" Konstantin Levin broke in with still greater heat; "the emancipation of the serfs was a different matter. There self-interest did come in. One longed to throw off that yoke that crushed us, all decent people among us. But to be a town councilor and discuss how many dustmen are needed, and how chimneys shall be constructed in the town in which I don't live—to serve on a jury and try a peasant who's stolen a flitch of bacon, and listen for six hours at a stretch to all sorts of jabber from the counsel for the defense and the prosecution, and the president cross-examining my old half-witted Alioshka, 'Do you admit, prisoner in the dock, the fact of the removal of the bacon?' 'Eh?' "

Konstantin Levin had warmed to his subject, and began mimicking the president and the half-witted Alioshka: it seemed to him that it was all to the point.

But Sergey Ivanovitch shrugged his shoulders.

"Well, what do you mean to say, then?"

"I simply mean to say that those rights that touch me . . . my interest, I shall always defend to the best of my ability; that when they made raids on us students, and the police read our letters, I was ready to defend those rights to the utmost, to defend my rights to education and freedom. I can understand compulsory military service, which affects my children, my brothers, and myself, I am ready to deliberate on what concerns me; but deliberating on how to spend forty thousand roubles of district council money, or judging the half-witted Alioshka—I don't understand, and I can't do it."

Konstantin Levin spoke as though the floodgates of his speech had burst open. Sergey Ivanovitch smiled.

"But tomorrow it'll be your turn to be tried; would it have suited your tastes better to be tried in the old criminal tribunal?"

"I'm not going to be tried. I shan't murder anybody, and I've no need of it. Well, I tell you what," he went on, flying off again to a subject quite beside the point, "our district self-government and all the rest of it—it's just like the birch branches we stick in the ground on Trinity Day, for instance, to look like a copse which has grown up of itself in Europe, and I can't gush over these birch branches and believe in them."

Sergey Ivanovitch merely shrugged his shoulders, as though to express his wonder how the birch branches had come into their argument at that point, though he did really understand at once what his brother meant.

"Excuse me, but you know one really can't argue in that way," he observed.

But Konstantin Levin wanted to justify himself for the failing, of which he was conscious, of lack of zeal for the public welfare, and he went on.

"I imagine," he said, "that no sort of activity is likely to be lasting if it is not founded on self-interest, that's a universal principle, a philosophical principle," he said, repeating the word "philosophical" with determination, as though wishing to show that he had as much right as anyone else to talk of philosophy.

Sergey Ivanovitch smiled. "He too has a philosophy of his own at the service of his natural tendencies," he thought.

"Come, you'd better let philosophy alone," he said. "The chief problem of the philosophy of all ages consists just in finding the indispensable connection which exists between individual and social interests. But that's not to the point; what is to the point is a correction I must make in your comparison. The birches are not simply stuck in, but some are sown and some are planted, and one must deal carefully with them. It's only those peoples that have an intuitive sense of what's of importance and significance in their institutions, and know how to value them, that have a future before them—it's only those peoples that one can truly call historical."

And Sergey Ivanovitch carried the subject into the regions of philosophical history where Konstantin Levin could not follow him, and showed him all the incorrectness of his view.

"As for your dislike of it, excuse my saying so, that's simply our Russian sloth and old serf-owner's ways, and I'm convinced that in you it's a temporary error and will pass."

Konstantin was silent. He felt himself vanquished on all sides, but he felt at the same time that what he wanted to say was unintelligible to his brother. Only he could not make up his mind whether it was unintelligible because he was not capable of expressing his meaning clearly, or because his brother would not or could not understand him. But he did not pursue the speculation, and without replying, he fell to musing on a quite different and personal matter.

Sergey Ivanovitch wound up the last line, untied the horse, and they drove off.

Chapter IV

THE PERSONAL MATTER THAT ABSORBED LEVIN DURING HIS CONVERSATION WITH HIS BROTHER was this. Once in a previous year he had gone to look at the mowing, and being made very angry by the bailiff he had recourse to his favorite means for regaining his temper—he took a scythe from a peasant and began mowing.

He liked the work so much that he had several times tried his hand at mowing since. He had cut the whole of the meadow in front of his house, and this year ever since the early spring he had cherished a plan for mowing for whole days together with the peasants. Ever since his brother's arrival, he had been in doubt whether to mow or not. He was loathe to leave his brother alone all day long, and he was afraid his brother would laugh at him about it. But as he drove into the meadow, and recalled the sensations of mowing, he came near deciding that he would go mowing. After the irritating discussion with his brother, he pondered over this intention again.

"I must have physical exercise, or my temper'll certainly be ruined," he thought, and he determined he would go mowing, however awkward he might feel about it with his brother or the peasants.

Towards evening Konstantin Levin went to his counting house, gave directions as to the work to be done, and sent about the village to summon the mowers for the morrow, to cut the hay in Kalinov meadow, the largest and best of his grass lands.

"And send my scythe, please, to Tit, for him to set it, and bring it round tomorrow. I shall maybe do some mowing myself too," he said, trying not to be embarrassed.

The bailiff smiled and said: "Yes, sir."

At tea the same evening Levin said to his brother:

"I fancy the fine weather will last. Tomorrow I shall start mowing."

"I'm so fond of that form of field labor," said Sergey Ivanovitch.

"I'm awfully fond of it. I sometimes mow myself with the peasants, and tomorrow I want to try mowing the whole day."

Sergey Ivanovitch lifted his head, and looked with interest at his brother.

"How do you mean? Just like one of the peasants, all day long?"

"Yes, it's very pleasant," said Levin.

"It's splendid as exercise, only you'll hardly be able to stand it," said Sergey Ivanovitch, without a shade of irony.

"I've tried it. It's hard work at first, but you get into it. I dare say I shall manage to keep it up. . . ."

"Really! what an idea! But tell me, how do the peasants look at it? I suppose they laugh in their sleeves at their master's being such a queer fish?"

"No, I don't think so; but it's so delightful, and at the same time such hard work, that one has no time to think about it."

"But how will you do about dining with them? To send you a bottle of Lafitte and roast turkey out there would be a little awkward."

"No, I'll simply come home at the time of their noonday rest."

Next morning Konstantin Levin got up earlier than usual, but he was detained giving directions on the farm, and when he reached the mowing-grass the mowers were already at their second row.

From the uplands he could get a view of the shaded cut part of the meadow below, with its grayish ridges of cut grass, and the black heaps of coats, taken off by the mowers at the place from which they had started cutting.

Gradually, as he rode towards the meadow, the peasants came into sight, some in coats, some in their shirts, mowing, one behind another in a long string, swinging their scythes differently. He counted forty-two of them.

They were mowing slowly over the uneven, low-lying parts of the meadow, where there had been an old dam. Levin recognized some of his own men. Here was old Yermil in a very long white smock, bending forward to swing a scythe; there was a young fellow, Vaska, who had been a coachman of Levin's, taking every row with a wide sweep. Here, too, was Tit, Levin's preceptor in the art of mowing, a thin little peasant. He was in front of all, and cut his wide row without bending, as though playing with the scythe.

Levin got off his mare, and fastening her up by the roadside went to meet Tit, who took a second scythe out of a bush and gave it to him.

"It's ready, sir; it's like a razor, cuts of itself," said Tit, taking off his cap with a smile and giving him the scythe.

Levin took the scythe, and began trying it. As they finished their rows, the mowers, hot and good-humored, came out into the road one after another, and, laughing a little, greeted the master. They all stared at him, but no one made any remark, till a tall old man, with a wrinkled, beardless face, wearing a short sheepskin jacket, came out into the road and accosted him.

"Look'ee now, master, once take hold of the rope there's no letting it go!" he said, and Levin heard smothered laughter among the mowers.

"I'll try not to let it go," he said, taking his stand behind Tit, and waiting for the time to begin.

"Mind'ee," repeated the old man.

Tit made room, and Levin started behind him. The grass was short close to the road, and Levin, who had not done any mowing for a long while, and was disconcerted by the eyes fastened upon him, cut badly for the first moments, though he swung his scythe vigorously. Behind him he heard voices:

"It's not set right; handle's too high; see how he has to stoop to it," said one.

"Press more on the heel," said another.

"Never mind, he'll get on all right," the old man resumed.

"He's made a start. . . . You swing it too wide, you'll tire yourself out. . . . The master, sure, does his best for himself! But see the grass missed out! For such work us fellows would catch it!"

The grass became softer, and Levin, listening without answering, followed Tit, trying to do the best he could. They moved a hundred paces. Tit kept moving on, without stopping, not showing the slightest weariness, but Levin was already beginning to be afraid he would not be able to keep it up: he was so tired.

He felt as he swung his scythe that he was at the very end of his strength, and was making up his mind to ask Tit to stop. But at that very moment Tit stopped of his own accord, and stooping down picked up some grass, rubbed his scythe, and began whetting it. Levin straightened himself, and drawing a deep breath looked round. Behind him came a peasant, and he too was evidently tired, for he stopped at once without waiting to mow up to Levin, and began whetting his scythe. Tit sharpened his scythe and Levin's, and they went on. The next time it was just the same. Tit moved on with sweep after sweep of his scythe, not stopping nor showing signs of weariness. Levin followed him, trying not to get left behind, and he found it harder and harder: the moment came when he felt he had no strength left, but at that very moment Tit stopped and whetted the scythes.

So they mowed the first row. And this long row seemed particularly hard work to Levin; but when the end was reached and Tit, shouldering his scythe, began with deliberate stride returning on the tracks left by his heels in the cut grass, and Levin walked back in the same way over the space he had cut, in spite of the sweat that ran in streams over his face and fell in drops down his nose, and drenched his back as though he had been soaked in water, he felt very happy. What delighted him particularly was that now he knew he would be able to hold out.

His pleasure was only disturbed by his row not being well cut. "I will swing less with my arm and more with my whole body," he thought, comparing Tit's row, which looked as if it had been cut with a line, with his own unevenly and irregularly lying grass.

The first row, as Levin noticed, Tit had mowed specially quickly, probably wishing to put his master to the test, and the row happened to be a long one. The next rows were easier, but still Levin had to strain every nerve not to drop behind the peasants.

He thought of nothing, wished for nothing, but not to be left behind the peasants, and to do his work as well as possible. He heard nothing but the swish of scythes, and saw before him Tit's upright figure mowing away, the crescent-shaped curve of the cut grass, the grass and flower heads slowly and rhythmically falling before the blade of his scythe, and ahead of him the end of the row, where would come the rest.

Suddenly, in the midst of his toil, without understanding what it was or whence it came, he felt a pleasant sensation of chill on his hot, moist shoulders. He glanced at the sky in the interval for whetting the scythes. A heavy, lowering storm cloud had blown up, and big raindrops were falling. Some of the peasants went to their coats and put them on; others—just like Levin himself—merely shrugged their shoulders, enjoying the pleasant coolness of it.

Another row, and yet another row, followed—long rows and short rows, with good grass and with poor grass. Levin lost all sense of time, and could not have told whether it was late or early now. A change began to come over his work, which gave him immense satisfaction. In the midst of his toil there were moments during which he forgot what he was doing, and it came all easy to him, and at those same moments his row was almost as smooth and well cut as Tit's. But so soon as he recollected what he was doing, and began trying to do better, he was at once conscious of all the difficulty of his task, and the row was badly mown.

On finishing yet another row he would have gone back to the top of the meadow again to begin the next, but Tit stopped, and going up to the old man said something in a low voice to him. They both looked at the sun. "What are they talking about, and why doesn't he go back?" thought Levin, not guessing that the peasants had been mowing no less than four hours without stopping, and it was time for their lunch.

"Lunch, sir," said the old man.

"Is it really time? That's right; lunch, then."

Levin gave his scythe to Tit, and together with the peasants, who were crossing the long stretch of mown grass, slightly sprinkled with rain, to get their bread from the heap of coats, he went towards his house. Only then he suddenly awoke to the fact that he had been wrong about the weather and the rain was drenching his hay.

"The hay will be spoiled," he said.

"Not a bit of it, sir; mow in the rain, and you'll rake in fine weather!" said the old man.

Levin untied his horse and rode home to his coffee. Sergey Ivanovitch was only just getting up. When he had drunk his coffee, Levin rode back again to the mowing before Sergey Ivanovitch had had time to dress and come down to the dining room.

Chapter V

AFTER LUNCH LEVIN WAS NOT IN THE SAME PLACE IN THE STRING OF MOWERS AS BEFORE, BUT stood between the old man who had accosted him jocosely, and now invited him to be his neighbor, and a young peasant, who had only been married in the autumn, and who was mowing this summer for the first time.

The old man, holding himself erect, moved in front, with his feet turned out, taking long, regular strides, and with a precise and regular action which seemed to cost him no more effort than swinging one's arms in walking, as though it were in play, he laid down the high, even row of grass. It was as though it were not he but the sharp scythe of itself swishing through the juicy grass.

Behind Levin came the lad Mishka. His pretty, boyish face, with a twist of fresh grass bound round his hair, was all working with effort; but whenever anyone looked at him he smiled. He would clearly have died sooner than own it was hard work for him.

Levin kept between them. In the very heat of the day the mowing did not seem such hard work to him. The perspiration with which he was drenched cooled him, while the sun, that burned his back, his head, and his arms, bare to the elbow, gave a vigor and dogged energy to his labor; and more and more often now came those moments of unconsciousness, when it was possible not to think what one was doing. The scythe cut of itself. These were happy moments. Still more delightful were the moments when they reached the stream where the rows ended, and the old man rubbed his scythe with the wet, thick grass, rinsed its blade in the fresh water of the stream, ladled out a little in a tin dipper, and offered Levin a drink.

"What do you say to my home-brew, eh? Good, eh?" said he, winking.

And truly Levin had never drunk any liquor so good as this warm water with green bits floating in it, and a taste of rust from the tin dipper. And immediately after this came the delicious, slow saunter, with his hand on the scythe, during which he could wipe away the streaming sweat, take deep breaths of air, and look about at the long string of mowers and at what was happening around in the forest and the country.

The longer Levin mowed, the oftener he felt the moments of unconsciousness in which it seemed not his hands that swung the scythe, but the scythe mowing of itself, a body full of life and consciousness of its own, and as though by magic, without thinking of it, the work turned out regular and well-finished of itself. These were the most blissful moments.

It was only hard work when he had to break off the motion, which had become unconscious, and to think; when he had to mow round a hillock or a tuft of sorrel. The old man did this easily. When a hillock came he changed his action, and at one time with the heel, and at another with the tip of his scythe, clipped the hillock round both sides with short strokes. And while he did this he kept looking about and watching what came into his view: at one moment he picked a wild berry and ate it or offered it to Levin, then he flung away a twig with the blade of the scythe, then he looked at a quail's nest, from which the bird flew just under the scythe, or caught a snake that crossed his path, and lifting it on the scythe as though on a fork showed it to Levin and threw it away.

For both Levin and the young peasant behind him, such changes of position were difficult. Both of them, repeating over and over again the same strained movement, were in a perfect frenzy of toil, and were incapable of shifting their position and at the same time watching what was before them.

Levin did not notice how time was passing. If he had been asked how long he had been working he would have said half an hour—and it was getting on for dinnertime. As they were walking back over the cut grass, the old man called Levin's attention to the little girls and boys who were coming from different directions, hardly visible through the long grass, and along the road towards the mowers, carrying sacks of bread dragging at their little hands and pitchers of the sour rye-beer, with cloths wrapped round them.

"Look'ee, the little emmets crawling!" he said, pointing to them, and he shaded his eyes with his hand to look at the sun. They mowed two more rows; the old man stopped.

"Come, master, dinnertime!" he said briskly. And on reaching the stream the mowers moved off across the lines of cut grass towards their pile of coats, where the children who had brought their dinners were sitting waiting for them. The peasants gathered into groups—those further away under a cart, those nearer under a willow bush.

Levin sat down by them; he felt disinclined to go away.

All constraint with the master had disappeared long ago. The peasants got ready for dinner. Some washed, the young lads bathed in the stream, others made a place comfortable for a rest, untied their sacks of bread, and uncovered the pitchers of rye-beer. The old man crumbled up some bread in a cup, stirred it with the handle of a spoon, poured water on it from the dipper, broke up some more bread, and having seasoned it with salt, he turned to the east to say his prayer.

"Come, master, taste my sop," said he, kneeling down before the cup.

The sop was so good that Levin gave up the idea of going home. He dined with the old man, and talked to him about his family affairs, taking the keenest interest in them, and told him about his own affairs and all the circumstances that could be of interest to the old man. He felt much nearer to him than to his brother, and could not help smiling at the affection he felt for this man. When the old man got up again, said his prayer, and lay down under a bush, putting some grass under his head for a pillow, Levin did the same, and in spite of the clinging flies that were so persistent in the sunshine, and the midges that tickled his hot face and body, he fell asleep at once and only waked when the sun had passed to the other side of the bush and reached him. The old man had been awake a long while, and was sitting up whetting the scythes of the younger lads.

Levin looked about him and hardly recognized the place, everything was so changed. The immense stretch of meadow had been mown and was sparkling with a peculiar fresh brilliance, with its lines of already sweet-smelling grass in the slanting rays of the evening sun. And the bushes about the river had been cut down, and the river itself, not visible before, now gleaming like steel in its bends, and the moving, ascending peasants, and the sharp wall of grass of the unmown part of the meadow, and the hawks hovering over the stripped meadow—all was perfectly new. Raising himself, Levin began considering how much had been cut and how much more could still be done that day.

The work done was exceptionally much for forty-two men. They had cut the whole of the big meadow, which had, in the years of serf labor, taken thirty scythes two days to mow. Only the corners remained to do, where the rows were short. But Levin felt a longing to get as much mowing done that day as possible, and was vexed with the sun sinking so quickly in the sky. He felt no weariness; all he wanted was to get his work done more and more quickly and as much done as possible.

"Could you cut Mashkin Upland too?—what do you think?" he said to the old man.

"As God wills, the sun's not high. A little vodka for the lads?"

At the afternoon rest, when they were sitting down again, and those who smoked had lit their pipes, the old man told the men that "Mashkin Upland's to be cut—there'll be some vodka."

"Why not cut it? Come on, Tit! We'll look sharp! We can eat at night. Come on!" cried voices, and eating up their bread, the mowers went back to work.

"Come, lads, keep it up!" said Tit, and ran on ahead almost at a trot.

"Get along, get along!" said the old man, hurrying after him and easily overtaking him, "I'll mow you down, look out!"

And young and old mowed away, as though they were racing with one another. But however fast they worked, they did not spoil the grass, and the rows were laid just as neatly and exactly. The little piece left uncut in the corner was mown in five minutes. The last of the mowers were just ending their rows while the foremost snatched up their coats onto their shoulders, and crossed the road towards Mashkin Upland.

The sun was already sinking into the trees when they went with their jingling dippers into the wooded ravine of Mashkin Upland. The grass was up to their waists in the middle of the hollow, soft, tender, and feathery, spotted here and there among the trees with wild heart's-ease.

After a brief consultation—whether to take the rows lengthwise or diagonally—Prohor Yermilin, also a renowned mower, a huge, black-haired peasant, went on ahead. He went up to the top, turned back again and started mowing, and they all proceeded to form in line behind him, going downhill through the hollow and uphill right up to the edge of the forest. The sun sank behind the forest. The dew was falling by now; the mowers were in the sun only on the hillside, but below, where a mist was rising, and on the opposite side, they mowed into the fresh, dewy shade. The work went rapidly. The grass cut with a juicy sound, and was at once laid in high, fragrant rows. The mowers from all sides, brought closer together in the short row, kept urging one another on to the sound of jingling dippers and clanging scythes, and the hiss of the whetstones sharpening them, and good-humored shouts.

Levin still kept between the young peasant and the old man. The old man, who had put on his short sheepskin jacket, was just as good-humored, jocose, and free in his movements. Among the trees they were continually cutting with their scythes the so-called "birch mushrooms," swollen fat in the succulent grass. But the old man bent down every time he came across a mushroom, picked it up and put it in his bosom. "Another present for my old woman," he said as he did so.

Easy as it was to mow the wet, soft grass, it was hard work going up and down the steep sides of the ravine. But this did not trouble the old man. Swinging his scythe just as ever, and moving his feet in their big, plaited shoes with firm, little steps, he climbed slowly up the steep place, and though his breeches hanging out below his smock, and his whole frame trembled with effort, he did not miss one blade of grass or one mushroom on his way, and kept making jokes with the peasants and Levin. Levin walked after him and often thought he must fall, as he climbed with a scythe up a steep cliff where it would have been hard work to clamber without anything. But he climbed up and did what he had to do. He felt as though some external force were moving him.

Chapter VI

MASHKIN UPLAND WAS MOWN, THE LAST ROW FINISHED, THE PEASANTS HAD PUT ON THEIR COATS and were gaily trudging home. Levin got on his horse and, parting regretfully from the peasants, rode homewards. On the hillside he looked back; he could not see them in the mist that had risen from the valley; he could only hear rough, good-humored voices, laughter, and the sound of clanking scythes.

Sergey Ivanovitch had long ago finished dinner, and was drinking iced lemon and water in his own room, looking through the reviews and papers which he had only just received by post, when Levin rushed into the room, talking merrily, with his wet and matted hair sticking to his forehead, and his back and chest grimed and moist.

"We mowed the whole meadow! Oh, it is nice, delicious! And how have you been getting on?" said Levin, completely forgetting the disagreeable conversation of the previous day.

"Mercy! what do you look like!" said Sergey Ivanovitch, for the first moment looking round with some dissatisfaction. "And the door, do shut the door!" he cried. "You must have let in a dozen at least."

Sergey Ivanovitch could not endure flies, and in his own room he never opened the window except at night, and carefully kept the door shut.

"Not one, on my honor. But if I have, I'll catch them. You wouldn't believe what a pleasure it is! How have you spent the day?"

"Very well. But have you really been mowing the whole day? I expect you're as hungry as a wolf. Kouzma has got everything ready for you."

"No, I don't feel hungry even. I had something to eat there. But I'll go and wash."

"Yes, go along, go along, and I'll come to you directly," said Sergey Ivanovitch, shaking his head as he looked at his brother. "Go along, make haste," he added smiling, and gathering up his books, he prepared to go too. He, too, felt suddenly good-humored and disinclined to leave his brother's side. "But what did you do while it was raining?"

"Rain? Why, there was scarcely a drop. I'll come directly. So you had a nice day too? That's first rate." And Levin went off to change his clothes.

Five minutes later the brothers met in the dining room. Although it seemed to Levin that he was not hungry, and he sat down to dinner simply so as not to hurt Kouzma's feelings, yet when he began to eat the dinner struck him as extraordinarily good. Sergey Ivanovitch watched him with a smile.

"Oh, by the way, there's a letter for you," said he. "Kouzma, bring it down, please. And mind you shut the doors."

The letter was from Oblonsky. Levin read it aloud. Oblonsky wrote to him from Petersburg: "I have had a letter from Dolly; she's at Ergushovo, and everything seems going wrong there. Do ride over and see her, please; help her with advice; you know all about it. She will be so glad to see you. She's quite alone, poor thing. My mother-in-law and all of them are still abroad."

"That's capital! I will certainly ride over to her," said Levin. "Or we'll go together. She's such a splendid woman, isn't she?"

"They're not far from here, then?"

"Twenty-five miles. Or perhaps it is thirty. But a capital road. Capital, we'll drive over."

"I shall be delighted," said Sergey Ivanovitch, still smiling. The sight of his younger brother's appearance had immediately put him in a good-humor.

"Well, you have an appetite!" he said, looking at his dark-red, sunburned face and neck bent over the plate.

"Splendid! You can't imagine what an effectual remedy it is for every sort of foolishness. I want to enrich medicine with a new word: *Arbeitskur.*"

"Well, but you don't need it, I should fancy."

"No, but for all sorts of nervous invalids."

"Yes, it ought to be tried. I had meant to come to the mowing to look at you, but it was so unbearably hot that I got no further than the forest. I sat there a little, and went on by the forest to the village, met your old nurse, and sounded her as to the peasants' view of you. As far as I can make out, they don't approve of this. She said: 'It's not a gentleman's work.' Altogether, I fancy that in the people's ideas there are very clear and definite notions of certain, as they call it, 'gentlemanly' lines of action. And they don't sanction the gentry's moving outside bounds clearly laid down in their ideas."

"Maybe so; but anyway it's a pleasure such as I have never known in my life. And there's no harm in it, you know. Is there?" answered Levin. "I can't help it if they don't like it. Though I do believe it's all right. Eh?"

"Altogether," pursued Sergey Ivanovitch, "you're satisfied with your day?"

"Quite satisfied. We cut the whole meadow. And such a splendid old man I made friends with there! You can't fancy how delightful he was!"

"Well, so you're content with your day. And so am I. First, I solved two chess problems, and one a very pretty one—a pawn opening. I'll show it you. And then—I thought over our conversation yesterday."

"Eh! our conversation yesterday?" said Levin, blissfully dropping his eyelids and drawing deep breaths after finishing his dinner, and absolutely incapable of recalling what their conversation yesterday was about.

"I think you are partly right. Our difference of opinion amounts to this, that you make the mainspring self-interest, while I suppose that interest in the common weal is bound to exist in every man of a certain degree of advancement. Possibly you are right too, that action founded on material interest would be more desirable. You are altogether, as the French say, too *primesautière* a nature; you must have intense, energetic action, or nothing."

Levin listened to his brother and did not understand a single word, and did not want to understand. He was only afraid his brother might ask him some question which would make it evident he had not heard.

"So that's what I think it is, my dear boy," said Sergey Ivanovitch, touching him on the shoulder.

"Yes, of course. But, do you know? I won't stand up for my view," answered Levin, with a guilty, childlike smile. "Whatever was it I was disputing about?" he wondered. "Of course, I'm right, and he's right, and it's all first rate. Only I must go round to the counting house and see to things." He got up, stretching and smiling. Sergey Ivanovitch smiled too.

"If you want to go out, let's go together," he said, disinclined to be parted from his brother, who seemed positively breathing out freshness and energy. "Come, we'll go to the counting house, if you have to go there."

"Oh, heavens!" shouted Levin, so loudly that Sergey Ivanovitch was quite frightened.

"What, what is the matter?"

"How's Agafea Mihalovna's hand?" said Levin, slapping himself on the head. "I'd positively forgotten her even."

"It's much better."

"Well, anyway I'll run down to her. Before you've time to get your hat on, I'll be back."

And he ran downstairs, clattering with his heels like a spring-rattle.

Chapter VII

STEPHAN ARKADYEVITCH HAD GONE TO PETERSBURG TO PERFORM THE MOST NATURAL AND ESsential official duty—so familiar to everyone in the government service, though incomprehensible to outsiders—that duty, but for which one could hardly be in government service, of reminding the ministry of his existence—and having, for the due performance of this rite, taken all the available cash from home, was gaily and agreeably spending his days at the races and in the summer villas. Meanwhile Dolly and the children had moved into the country, to cut down expenses as much as possible. She had gone to Ergushovo, the estate that had been her dowry, and the one where in spring the forest had been sold. It was nearly forty miles from Levin's Pokrovskoe. The big, old house at Ergushovo had been pulled down long ago, and the old prince had had the lodge done up and built on to. Twenty years before, when Dolly was a child, the lodge had been roomy and comfortable, though, like all lodges, it stood sideways to the entrance avenue, and faced the south. But by now this lodge was old and dilapidated. When Stepan Arkadyevitch had gone down in the spring to sell the forest, Dolly had begged him to look over the house and order what repairs might be needed. Stepan Arkadyevitch, like all unfaithful husbands indeed, was very solicitous for his wife's comfort, and he had himself looked over the house, and given instructions about everything that he considered necessary. What he considered necessary was to cover all the furniture with cretonne, to put up curtains, to weed the garden, to make a little bridge on the pond, and to plant flowers. But he forgot many other essential matters, the want of which greatly distressed Darya Alexandrovna later on.

In spite of Stepan Arkadyevitch's efforts to be an attentive father and husband, he never could keep in his mind that he had a wife and children. He had bachelor tastes, and it was in accordance with them that he shaped his life. On his return to Moscow he informed his wife with pride that everything was ready, that the house would be a little paradise, and that he advised her most certainly to go. His wife's staying away in the country was very agreeable to Stepan Arkadyevitch from every point of view: it did the children good, it decreased expenses, and it left him more at liberty. Darya Alexandrovna regarded staying in the country for the summer as essential for the children, especially for the little girl, who had not succeeded in regaining her strength after the scarlatina, and also as a means of escaping the petty humiliations, the little bills owing to the wood-merchant, the fishmonger, the shoemaker, which made her miserable. Besides this, she was pleased to go away to the country because she was dreaming of getting her sister Kitty to stay with her there. Kitty was to be back from abroad in the middle of the summer, and bathing had been prescribed for her. Kitty wrote that no prospect was so alluring as to spend the summer with Dolly at Ergushovo, full of childish associations for both of them.

The first days of her existence in the country were very hard for Dolly. She used to stay in the country as a child, and the impression she had retained of it was that the country was a refuge from all the unpleasantness of the town, that life there, though not luxurious—Dolly could easily make up her mind to that—was cheap and comfortable; that there was plenty of everything, everything was cheap, everything could be got, and children were happy. But now coming to the country as the head of a family, she perceived that it was all utterly unlike what she had fancied.

The day after their arrival there was a heavy fall of rain and in the night the water came through in the corridor and in the nursery, so that the beds had to be carried into the drawing room. There was no kitchenmaid to be found; of the nine cows, it appeared from the words of the cowherd-woman that some were about to calve, others had just calved, others were old, and others again hard-uddered; there was not butter nor milk enough even for the children. There were no eggs. They could get no fowls; old, purplish, stringy cocks were all they had for roasting and boiling. Impossible to get women to scrub the floors—all were potato-hoeing. Driving was out of the question, because one of the horses was restive, and bolted in the shafts. There was no place where they could bathe; the whole of the riverbank was trampled by the cattle and open to the road; even walks were impossible, for the cattle strayed into the garden through a gap in the hedge, and there was one terrible bull, who bellowed, and therefore might be expected to gore somebody. There were no proper cupboards for their clothes; what cupboards there were either would not close at all, or burst open whenever anyone passed by them. There were no pots and pans; there was no copper in the wash house, nor even an ironing-board in the maids' room.

Finding instead of peace and rest all these, from her point of view, fearful calamities, Darya Alexandrovna was at first in despair. She exerted herself to the utmost, felt the hopelessness of the position, and was every instant suppressing the tears that started into her eyes. The bailiff, a retired quartermaster, whom Stepan Arkadyevitch had taken a fancy to and had appointed bailiff on account of his handsome and respectful appearance as a hall-porter, showed no sympathy for Darya Alexandrovna's woes. He said respectfully, "nothing can be done, the peasants are such a wretched lot," and did nothing to help her.

The position seemed hopeless. But in the Oblonskys' household, as in all families indeed, there was one inconspicuous but most valuable and useful person, Marya Philimonovna. She soothed her mistress, assured her that everything would *come round* (it was her expression, and Matvey had borrowed it from her), and without fuss or hurry proceeded to set to work herself. She had immediately made friends with the bailiff's wife, and on the very first day she drank tea with her and the bailiff under the acacias, and reviewed all the circumstances of the position. Very soon Marya Philimonovna had established her club, so to say, under the acacias, and there it was, in this club consisting of the bailiff's wife, the village elder, and the counting house clerk, that the difficulties of existence were gradually smoothed away, and in a week's time everything actually had come round. The roof was mended, a kitchenmaid was found—a crony of the village elder's—hens were bought, the cows began giving milk, the garden hedge was stopped up with stakes, the carpenter made a mangle, hooks were put in the cupboards, and they ceased to burst open spontaneously, and an ironing-board covered with army cloth was placed across from the arm of a chair to the chest of drawers, and there was a smell of flatirons in the maids' room.

"Just see, now, and you were quite in despair," said Marya Philimonovna, pointing to the ironing-board. They even rigged up a bathing-shed of straw hurdles. Lily began to bathe, and Darya Alexandrovna began to realize, if only in part, her expectations, if not of a peaceful, at least of a comfortable, life in the country. Peaceful with six children Darya Alexandrovna could not be. One would fall ill, another might easily become so, a third would be without something necessary, a fourth would show symptoms of a bad disposition, and so on. Rare indeed were the brief periods of peace. But these cares and anxieties were for Darya Alexandrovna the sole happiness possible. Had it not been for them, she would have been left alone to brood over her husband who did not love her.

And besides, hard though it was for the mother to bear the dread of illness, the illnesses themselves, and the grief of seeing signs of evil propensities in her children—the children themselves were even now repaying her in small joys for her sufferings. Those joys were so small that they passed unnoticed, like gold in sand, and at bad moments she could see nothing but the pain, nothing but sand; but there were good moments too when she saw nothing but the joy, nothing but gold.

Now in the solitude of the country, she began to be more and more frequently aware of those joys. Often, looking at them, she would make every possible effort to persuade herself that she was mistaken, that she as a mother was partial to her children. All the same, she could not help saying to herself that she had charming children, all six of them in different ways, but a set of children such as is not often to be met with, and she was happy in them, and proud of them.

Chapter VIII

TOWARDS THE END OF MAY, WHEN EVERYTHING HAD BEEN MORE OR LESS SATISFACTORILY arranged, she received her husband's answer to her complaints of the disorganized state of things in the country. He wrote begging her forgiveness for not having thought of everything before, and promised to come down at the first chance. This chance did not present itself, and till the beginning of June Darya Alexandrovna stayed alone in the country.

On the Sunday in St. Peter's week Darya Alexandrovna drove to mass for all her children to take the sacrament. Darya Alexandrovna in her intimate, philosophical talks with her sister, her mother, and her friends very often astonished them by the freedom of her views in regard to religion. She had a strange religion of transmigration of souls all her own, in which she had firm faith, troubling herself little about the dogmas of the Church. But in her family she was strict in carrying out all that was required by the Church—and not merely in order to set an example, but with all her heart in it. The fact that the children had not been at the sacrament for nearly a year worried her extremely, and with the full approval and sympathy of Marya Philimonovna she decided that this should take place now in the summer.

For several days before, Darya Alexandrovna was busily deliberating on how to dress all the children. Frocks were made or altered and washed, seams and flounces were let out, buttons were sewn on, and ribbons got ready. One dress, Tanya's, which the English governess had undertaken, cost Darya Alexandrovna much loss of temper. The English governess in altering it had made the seams in the wrong place, had taken up the sleeves too much, and altogether spoiled the dress. It was so narrow on Tanya's shoulders that it was quite painful to look at her. But Marya Philimonovna had the happy thought of putting in gussets, and adding a little shoulder-cape. The dress was set right, but there was nearly a quarrel with the English governess. On the morning, however, all was happily arranged, and towards ten o'clock—the time at which they had asked the priest to wait for them for the mass—the children in their new dresses, with beaming faces, stood on the step before the carriage waiting for their mother.

To the carriage, instead of the restive Raven, they had harnessed, thanks to the representations of Marya Philimonovna, the bailiff's horse, Brownie, and Darya Alexandrovna, delayed by anxiety over her own attire, came out and got in, dressed in a white muslin gown.

Darya Alexandrovna had done her hair, and dressed with care and excitement. In the old days she had dressed for her own sake to look pretty and be admired. Later on, as she got older, dress became more and more distasteful to her. She saw that she was losing her good looks. But now she began to feel pleasure and interest in dress again. Now she did not dress for her own sake, not for the sake of her own beauty, but simply that as the mother of those exquisite creatures she might not spoil the general effect. And looking at herself for the last time in the looking-glass she was satisfied with herself. She looked nice. Not nice as she would have wished to look nice in old days at a ball, but nice for the object which she now had in view.

In the church there was no one but the peasants, the servants and their womenfolk. But Darya Alexandrovna saw, or fancied she saw, the sensation produced by her children and her. The children were not only beautiful to look at in their smart little dresses, but they were charming in the way they behaved. Aliosha, it is true, did not stand quite correctly; he kept turning round, trying to look at his little jacket from behind; but all the same he was wonderfully sweet. Tanya behaved like a grown-up person, and looked after the little ones. And the smallest, Lily, was bewitching in her naïve astonishment at everything, and it was difficult not to smile when, after taking the sacrament, she said in English, "Please, some more."

On the way home the children felt that something solemn had happened, and were very sedate.

Everything went happily at home too; but at lunch Grisha began whistling, and, what was worse, was disobedient to the English governess, and was forbidden to have any tart. Darya Alexandrovna would not have let things go so far on such a day had she been present; but she had to support the English governess's authority, and she upheld her decision that Grisha should have no tart. This rather spoiled the general good-humor. Grisha cried, declaring that Nikolinka had whistled too, and he was not punished, and that he wasn't crying for the tart—he didn't care—but at being unjustly treated. This was really too tragic, and Darya Alexandrovna made up her mind to persuade the English governess to forgive Grisha, and she went to speak to her. But on the way, as she passed the drawing room, she beheld a scene, filling her heart with such pleasure that the tears came into her eyes, and she forgave the delinquent herself.

The culprit was sitting at the window in the corner of the drawing room; beside him was standing Tanya with a plate. On the pretext of wanting to give some dinner to her dolls, she had asked the governess's permission to take her share of tart to the nursery, and had taken it instead to her brother. While still weeping over the injustice of his punishment, he was eating the tart, and kept saying through his sobs, "Eat yourself; let's eat it together . . . together."

Tanya had at first been under the influence of her pity for Grisha, then of a sense of her noble action, and tears were standing in her eyes too; but she did not refuse, and ate her share.

On catching sight of their mother they were dismayed, but, looking into her face, they saw they were not doing wrong. They burst out laughing, and, with their mouths full of tart, they began wiping their smiling lips with their hands, and smearing their radiant faces all over with tears and jam.

"Mercy! Your new white frock; Tanya! Grisha!" said their mother, trying to save the frock, but with tears in her eyes, smiling a blissful, rapturous smile.

The new frocks were taken off, and orders were given for the little girls to have their blouses put on, and the boys their old jackets, and the wagonette to be harnessed; with Brownie, to the bailiff's annoyance, again in the shafts, to drive out for mushroom-picking and bathing. A roar of delighted shrieks arose in the nursery, and never ceased till they had set off for the bathing-place.

They gathered a whole basketful of mushrooms; even Lily found a birch mushroom. It had always happened before that Miss Hoole found them and pointed them out to her; but this time she found a big one quite of herself, and there was a general scream of delight, "Lily has found a mushroom!"

Then they reached the river, put the horses under the birch trees, and went to the bathing-place. The coachman, Terenty, fastened the horses, who kept whisking away the flies, to a tree, and, treading down the grass, lay down in the shade of a birch and smoked his shag, while the never-ceasing shrieks of delight of the children floated across to him from the bathing-place.

Though it was hard work to look after all the children and restrain their wild pranks, though it was difficult too to keep in one's head and not mix up all the stockings, little breeches, and shoes for the different legs, and to undo and to do up again all the tapes and buttons, Darya Alexandrovna, who had always liked bathing herself, and believed it to be very good for the children, enjoyed nothing so much as bathing with all the children. To go over all those fat little legs, pulling on their stockings, to take in her arms and dip those little naked bodies, and to hear their screams of delight and alarm, to see the breathless faces with wide-open, scared, and happy eyes of all her splashing cherubs, was a great pleasure to her.

When half the children had been dressed, some peasant women in holiday dress, out picking herbs, came up to the bathing-shed and stopped shyly. Marya Philimonovna called one of them and handed her a sheet and a shirt that had dropped into the water for her to dry them, and Darya Alexandrovna began to talk to the women. At first they laughed behind their hands and did not understand her questions, but soon they grew bolder and began to talk, winning Darya Alexandrovna's heart at once by the genuine admiration of the children that they showed.

"My, what a beauty! as white as sugar," said one, admiring Tanitchka, and shaking her head; "but thin . . ."

"Yes, she has been ill."

"And so they've been bathing you too," said another to the baby.

"No; he's only three months old," answered Darya Alexandrovna with pride.

"You don't say so!"

"And have you any children?"

"I've had four; I've two living—a boy and a girl. I weaned her last carnival."

"How old is she?"

"Why, two years old."

"Why did you nurse her so long?"

"It's our custom; for three fasts. . . ."

And the conversation became most interesting to Darya Alexandrovna. What sort of time did she have? What was the matter with the boy? Where was her husband? Did it often happen?

Darya Alexandrovna felt disinclined to leave the peasant women, so interesting to her was their conversation, so completely identical were all their interests. What pleased her most of all was that she saw clearly what all the women admired more than anything was her having so many children, and such fine ones. The peasant women even made Darya Alexandrovna laugh, and offended the English governess, because she was the cause of the laughter she did not understand. One of the younger women kept staring at the Englishwoman, who was dressing after all the rest, and when she put on her third petticoat she could not refrain from the remark, "My, she keeps putting on and putting on, and she'll never have done!" she said, and they all went off into roars.

Chapter IX

On the drive home, as Darya Alexandrovna, with all her children round her, their heads still wet from their bath, and a kerchief tied over her own head, was getting near the house, the coachman said, "There's some gentleman coming: the master of Pokrovskoe, I do believe."

Darya Alexandrovna peeped out in front, and was delighted when she recognized in the gray hat and gray coat the familiar figure of Levin walking to meet them. She was glad to see him at any time, but at this moment she was specially glad he should see her in all her glory. No one was better able to appreciate her grandeur than Levin.

Seeing her, he found himself face to face with one of the pictures of his daydream of family life.

"You're like a hen with your chickens, Darya Alexandrovna."

"Ah, how glad I am to see you!" she said, holding out her hand to him.

"Glad to see me, but you didn't let me know. My brother's staying with me. I got a note from Stiva that you were here."

"From Stiva?" Darya Alexandrovna asked with surprise.

"Yes; he writes that you are here, and that he thinks you might allow me to be of use to you," said Levin, and as he said it he became suddenly embarrassed, and, stopping abruptly, he walked on in silence by the wagonette, snapping off the buds of the lime trees and nibbling them. He was embarrassed through a sense that Darya Alexandrovna would be annoyed by receiving from an outsider help that should by rights have come from her own husband. Darya Alexandrovna certainly did not like this little way of Stepan Arkadyevitch's of foisting his domestic duties on others. And she was at once aware that Levin was aware of this. It was just for this fineness of perception, for this delicacy, that Darya Alexandrovna liked Levin.

"I know, of course," said Levin, "that that simply means that you would like to see me, and I'm exceedingly glad. Though I can fancy that, used to town housekeeping as you are, you must feel in the wilds here, and if there's anything wanted, I'm altogether at your disposal."

"Oh, no!" said Dolly. "At first things were rather uncomfortable, but now we've settled everything capitally—thanks to my old nurse," she said, indicating Marya Philimonovna, who, seeing that they were speaking of her, smiled brightly and cordially to Levin. She knew him, and knew that he would be a good match for her young lady, and was very keen to see the matter settled.

"Won't you get in, sir, we'll make room this side!" she said to him.

"No, I'll walk. Children, who'd like to race the horses with me?" The children knew Levin very little, and could not remember when they had seen him, but they experienced in regard to him none of that strange feeling of shyness and hostility which children so often experience towards hypocritical, grown-up people, and for which they are so often and miserably punished. Hypocrisy in anything whatever may deceive the cleverest and most penetrating man, but the least wide-awake of children recognizes it, and is revolted by it, however ingeniously it may be disguised. Whatever faults Levin had, there was not a trace of hypocrisy in him, and so the children showed him the same friendliness that they saw in their mother's face. On his invitation, the two elder ones at once jumped out to him and ran with him as simply as they would have done with their nurse or Miss Hoole or their mother. Lily, too, began begging to go to him, and her mother handed her to him; he sat her on his shoulder and ran along with her.

"Don't be afraid, don't be afraid, Darya Alexandrovna!" he said, smiling good-humoredly to the mother; "there's no chance of my hurting or dropping her."

And, looking at his strong, agile, assiduously careful and needlessly wary movements, the mother felt her mind at rest, and smiled gaily and approvingly as she watched him.

Here, in the country, with children, and with Darya Alexandrovna, with whom he was in sympathy, Levin was in a mood not infrequent with him, of childlike light-heartedness that she particularly liked in him. As he ran with the children, he taught them gymnastic feats, set Miss Hoole laughing with his queer English accent, and talked to Darya Alexandrovna of his pursuits in the country.

After dinner, Darya Alexandrovna, sitting alone with him on the balcony, began to speak of Kitty.

"You know, Kitty's coming here, and is going to spend the summer with me."

"Really," he said, flushing and at once, to change the conversation, he said: "Then I'll send you two cows, shall I? If you insist on a bill you shall pay me five roubles a month; but it's really too bad of you."

"No, thank you. We can manage very well now."

"Oh, well, then, I'll have a look at your cows, and if you'll allow me, I'll give directions about their food. Everything depends on their food."

And Levin, to turn the conversation, explained to Darya Alexandrovna the theory of cow-keeping, based on the principle that the cow is simply a machine for the transformation of food into milk, and so on.

He talked of this, and passionately longed to hear more of Kitty, and, at the same time, was afraid of hearing it. He dreaded the breaking up of the inward peace he had gained with such effort.

"Yes, but still all this has to be looked after, and who is there to look after it?" Darya Alexandrovna responded, without interest.

She had by now got her household matters so satisfactorily arranged, thanks to Marya Philimonovna, that she was disinclined to make any change in them; besides, she had no faith in Levin's knowledge of farming. General principles, as to the cow being a machine for the production of milk, she looked on with suspicion. It seemed to her that such principles could only be a hindrance in farm management. It all seemed to her a far simpler matter: all that was needed, as Marya Philimonovna had explained, was to give Brindle and Whitebreast more food and drink, and not to let the cook carry all the kitchen slops to the laundry-maid's cow. That was clear. But general propositions as to feeding on meal and on grass were doubtful and obscure. And, what was most important, she wanted to talk about Kitty.

Chapter X

"KITTY WRITES TO ME THAT THERE'S NOTHING SHE LONGS FOR SO MUCH AS QUIET AND SOLITUDE," Dolly said after the silence that had followed.

"And how is she—better?" Levin asked in agitation.

"Thank God, she's quite well again. I never believed her lungs were affected."

"Oh, I'm very glad!" said Levin, and Dolly fancied she saw something touching, helpless, in his face as he said this and looked silently into her face.

"Let me ask you, Konstantin Dmitrievitch," said Darya Alexandrovna, smiling her kindly and rather mocking smile, "why is it you are angry with Kitty?"

"I? I'm not angry with her," said Levin.

"Yes, you are angry. Why was it you did not come to see us nor them when you were in Moscow?"

"Darya Alexandrovna," he said, blushing up to the roots of his hair, "I wonder really that with your kind heart you don't feel this. How it is you feel no pity for me, if nothing else, when you know . . ."

"What do I know?"

"You know I made an offer and that I was refused," said Levin, and all the tenderness he had been feeling for Kitty a minute before was replaced by a feeling of anger for the slight he had suffered.

"What makes you suppose I know?"

"Because everybody knows it . . ."

"That's just where you are mistaken; I did not know it, though I had guessed it was so."

"Well, now you know it."

"All I knew was that something had happened that made her dreadfully miserable, and that she begged me never to speak of it. And if she would not tell me, she would certainly not speak of it to anyone else. But what did pass between you? Tell me."

"I have told you."

"When was it?"

"When I was at their house the last time."

"Do you know that," said Darya Alexandrovna, "I am awfully, awfully sorry for her. You suffer only from pride. . . ."

"Perhaps so," said Levin, "but . . ."

She interrupted him.

"But she, poor girl . . . I am awfully, awfully sorry for her. Now I see it all."

"Well, Darya Alexandrovna, you must excuse me," he said, getting up. "Good-bye, Darya Alexandrovna, till we meet again."

"No, wait a minute," she said, clutching him by the sleeve. "Wait a minute, sit down."

"Please, please, don't let us talk of this," he said, sitting down, and at the same time feeling rise up and stir within his heart a hope he had believed to be buried.

"If I did not like you," she said, and tears came into her eyes; "if I did not know you, as I do know you . . ."

The feeling that had seemed dead revived more and more, rose up and took possession of Levin's heart.

"Yes, I understand it all now," said Darya Alexandrovna. "You can't understand it; for you men, who are free and make your own choice, it's always clear whom you love. But a girl's in a position of suspense, with all a woman's or maiden's modesty, a girl who sees you men from afar, who takes everything on trust—a girl may have, and often has, such a feeling that she cannot tell what to say."

"Yes, if the heart does not speak . . ."

"No, the heart does speak; but just consider: you men have views about a girl, you come to the house, you make friends, you criticize, you wait to see if you have found what you love, and then, when you are sure you love her, you make an offer . . ."

"Well, that's not quite it."

"Anyway you make an offer, when your love is ripe or when the balance has completely turned between the two you are choosing from. But a girl is not asked. She is expected to make her choice, and yet she cannot choose, she can only answer 'yes' or 'no.' "

"Yes, to choose between me and Vronsky," thought Levin, and the dead thing that had come to life within him died again, and only weighed on his heart and set it aching.

"Darya Alexandrovna," he said, "that's how one chooses a new dress, or some purchase or other, not love. The choice has been made, and so much the better . . . And there can be no repeating it."

"Ah, pride, pride!" said Darya Alexandrovna, as though despising him for the baseness of this feeling in comparison with that other feeling which only women know. "At the time when you made Kitty an offer she was just in a position in which she could not answer. She was in doubt. Doubt between you and Vronsky. Him she was seeing everyday, and you she had not seen for a long while. Supposing she had been older . . . I, for instance, in her place could have felt no doubt. I always disliked him, and so it has turned out."

Levin recalled Kitty's answer. She had said: *"No, that cannot be . . ."*

"Darya Alexandrovna," he said dryly, "I appreciate your confidence in me; I believe you are making a mistake. But whether I am right or wrong, that pride you so despise makes any thought of Katerina Alexandrovna out of the question for me—you understand, utterly out of the question."

"I will only say one thing more: you know that I am speaking of my sister, whom I love as I love my own children. I don't say she cared for you, all I meant to say is that her refusal at that moment proves nothing."

"I don't know!" said Levin, jumping up. "If you only knew how you are hurting me. It's just as if a child of yours were dead, and they were to say to you: He would have been like this and like that, and he might have lived, and how happy you would have been in him. But he's dead, dead, dead! . . ."

"How absurd you are!" said Darya Alexandrovna, looking with mournful tenderness at Levin's excitement. "Yes, I see it all more and more clearly," she went on musingly. "So you won't come to see us, then, when Kitty's here?"

"No, I shan't come. Of course I won't avoid meeting Katerina Alexandrovna, but as far as I can, I will try to save her the annoyance of my presence."

"You are very, very absurd," repeated Darya Alexandrovna, looking with tenderness into his face. "Very well then, let it be as though we had not spoken of this. What have you come for, Tanya?" she said in French to the little girl who had come in.

"Where's my spade, mamma?"

"I speak French, and you must too."

The little girl tried to say it in French, but could not remember the French for spade; the mother prompted her, and then told her in French where to look for the spade. And this made a disagreeable impression on Levin.

Everything in Darya Alexandrovna's house and children struck him now as by no means so charming as a little while before. "And what does she talk French with the children for?" he thought; "how unnatural and false it is! And the children feel it so: Learning French and unlearning sincerity," he thought to himself, unaware that Darya Alexandrovna had thought all that over twenty times already, and yet, even at the cost of some loss of sincerity, believed it necessary to teach her children French in that way.

"But why are you going? Do stay a little."

Levin stayed to tea; but his good-humor had vanished, and he felt ill at ease.

After tea he went out into the hall to order his horses to be put in, and, when he came back, he found Darya Alexandrovna greatly disturbed, with a troubled face, and tears in her eyes. While Levin had been outside, an incident had occurred which had utterly shattered all the happiness she had been feeling that day, and her pride in her children. Grisha and Tanya had been fighting over a ball. Darya Alexandrovna, hearing a scream in the nursery, ran in and saw a terrible sight. Tanya was pulling Grisha's hair, while he, with a face hideous with rage, was beating her with his fists wherever he could get at her. Something snapped in Darya Alexandrovna's heart when she saw this. It was as if darkness had swooped down upon her life; she felt that these children of hers, that she was so proud of, were not merely most ordinary, but positively bad, ill-bred children, with coarse, brutal propensities—wicked children.

She could not talk or think of anything else, and she could not speak to Levin of her misery.

Levin saw she was unhappy and tried to comfort her, saying that it showed nothing bad, that all children fight; but, even as he said it, he was thinking in his heart: "No, I won't be artificial and talk French with my children; but my children won't be like that. All one has to do is not spoil children, not to distort their nature, and they'll be delightful. No, my children won't be like that."

He said good-bye and drove away, and she did not try to keep him.

Chapter XI

IN THE MIDDLE OF JULY THE ELDER OF THE VILLAGE ON LEVIN'S SISTER'S ESTATE, ABOUT FIFTEEN miles from Pokrovskoe, came to Levin to report on how things were going there and on the hay. The chief source of income on his sister's estate was from the riverside meadows. In former years the hay had been bought by the peasants for twenty roubles the three acres. When Levin took over the management of the estate, he thought on examining the grasslands that they were worth more, and he fixed the price at twenty-five roubles the three acres. The peasants would not give that price, and, as Levin suspected, kept off other purchasers. Then Levin had driven over himself, and arranged to have the grass cut, partly by hired labor, partly at a payment of a certain proportion of the crop. His own peasants put every hindrance they could in the way of this new arrangement, but it was carried out, and the first year the meadows had yielded a profit almost double. The previous year—which was the third year—the peasants had maintained the same opposition to the arrangement, and the hay had been cut on the same system. This year the peasants were doing all the mowing for a third of the hay crop, and the village elder had come now to announce that the hay had been cut, and that, fearing rain, they had invited the counting house clerk over, had divided the crop in his presence, and had raked together eleven stacks as the owner's share. From the vague answers to his question how much hay had been cut on the principal meadow, from the hurry of the village elder who had made the division, not asking leave, from the whole tone of the peasant, Levin perceived that there was something wrong in the division of the hay, and made up his mind to drive over himself to look into the matter.

Arriving to dinner at the village, and leaving his horse at the cottage of an old friend of his, the husband of his brother's wet-nurse, Levin went to see the old man in his bee house, wanting to find out from him the truth about the hay. Parmenitch, a talkative, comely old man, gave Levin a very warm welcome, showed him all he was doing, told him everything about his bees and the swarms of that year; but gave vague and unwilling answers to Levin's inquiries about the mowing. This confirmed Levin still more in his suspicions. He went to the hayfields and examined the stacks. The haystacks could not possibly contain fifty wagon-loads each, and to convict the peasants Levin ordered the wagons that had carried the hay to be brought up directly, to lift one stack, and carry it into the barn. There turned out to be only thirty-two loads in the stack. In spite of the village elder's assertions about the compressibility of hay, and its having settled down in the stacks, and his swearing that everything had been done in the fear of God, Levin stuck to his point that the hay had been divided without his orders, and that, therefore, he would not accept that hay as fifty loads to a stack. After a prolonged dispute the matter was decided by the peasants taking these eleven stacks, reckoning them as fifty loads each. The arguments and the division of the haycocks lasted the whole afternoon. When the last of the hay had been divided, Levin, entrusting the superintendence of the rest to the counting house clerk, sat down on a haycock marked off by a stake of willow, and looked admiringly at the meadow swarming with peasants.

In front of him, in the bend of the river beyond the marsh, moved a bright-colored line of peasant women, and the scattered hay was being rapidly formed into gray winding rows over the pale green stubble. After the women came the men with pitchforks, and from the gray rows there were growing up broad, high, soft haycocks. To the left, carts were rumbling over the meadow that had been already cleared, and one after another the haycocks vanished, flung up in huge forkfuls, and in their place there were rising heavy cartloads of fragrant hay hanging over the horses' hind-quarters.

"What weather for haying! What hay it'll be!" said an old man, squatting down beside Levin. "It's tea, not hay! It's like scattering grain to the ducks, the way they pick it up!" he added, pointing to the growing haycocks. "Since dinnertime they've carried a good half of it."

"The last load, eh?" he shouted to a young peasant, who drove by, standing in the front of an empty cart, shaking the cord reins.

"The last, dad!" the lad shouted back, pulling in the horse, and, smiling, he looked round at a bright, rosy-checked peasant girl who sat in the cart smiling too, and drove on.

"Who's that? Your son?" asked Levin.

"My baby," said the old man with a tender smile.

"What a fine fellow!"

"The lad's all right."

"Married already?"

"Yes, it's two years last St. Philip's day."

"Any children?"

"Children indeed! Why, for over a year he was innocent as a babe himself, and bashful too," answered the old man. "Well, the hay! It's as fragrant as tea!" he repeated, wishing to change the subject.

Levin looked more attentively at Ivan Parmenov and his wife. They were loading a haycock onto the cart not far from him. Ivan Parmenov was standing on the cart, taking, laying in place, and stamping down the huge bundles of hay, which his pretty young wife deftly handed up to him, at first in armfuls, and then on the pitchforks. The young wife worked easily, merrily, and dexterously. The close-packed hay did not once break away off her fork. First she gathered it together, stuck the fork into it, then with a rapid, supple movement leaned the whole weight of her body on it, and at once with a bend of her back under the red belt she drew herself up, and arching her full bosom under the white smock, with a smart turn swung the fork in her arms, and flung the bundle of hay high onto the cart. Ivan, obviously doing his best to save her every minute of unnecessary labor, made haste, opening his arms to clutch the bundle and lay it in the cart. As she raked together what was left of the hay, the young wife shook off the bits of hay that had fallen on her neck, and straightening the red kerchief that had dropped forward over her white brow, not browned like her face by the sun, she crept under the cart to tie up the load. Ivan directed her how to fasten the cord to the cross-piece, and at something she said he laughed aloud. In the expressions of both faces was to be seen vigorous, young, freshly awakened love.

Chapter XII

The load was tied on. Ivan jumped down and took the quiet, sleek horse by the bridle. The young wife flung the rake up on the load, and with a bold step, swinging her arms, she went to join the women, who were forming a ring for the haymakers' dance. Ivan drove off to the road and fell into line with the other loaded carts. The peasant women, with their rakes on their shoulders, gay with bright flowers, and chattering with ringing, merry voices, walked behind the hay cart. One wild untrained female voice broke into a song, and sang it alone through a verse, and then the same verse was taken up and repeated by half a hundred strong healthy voices, of all sorts, coarse and fine, singing in unison.

The women, all singing, began to come close to Levin, and he felt as though a storm were swooping down upon him with a thunder of merriment. The storm swooped down, enveloped him and the haycock on which he was lying, and the other haycocks, and the wagon-loads, and the whole meadow and distant fields all seemed to be shaking and singing to the measures of this wild merry song with its shouts and whistles and clapping. Levin felt envious of this health and mirthfulness; he longed to take part in the expression of this joy of life. But he could do nothing, and had to lie and look on and listen. When the peasants, with their singing, had vanished out of sight and hearing, a weary feeling of despondency at his own isolation, his physical inactivity, his alienation from this world, came over Levin.

Some of the very peasants who had been most active in wrangling with him over the hay, some whom he had treated with contumely, and who had tried to cheat him, those very peasants had greeted him good-humoredly, and evidently had not, were incapable of having any feeling of rancor against him, any regret, any recollection even of having tried to deceive him. All that was drowned in a sea of merry common labor. God gave the day, God gave the strength. And the day and the strength were consecrated to labor, and that labor was its own reward. For whom the labor? What would be its fruits? These were idle considerations—beside the point.

Often Levin had admired this life, often he had a sense of envy of the men who led this life; but today for the first time, especially under the influence of what he had seen in the attitude of Ivan Parmenov to his young wife, the idea presented itself definitely to his mind that it was in his power to exchange the dreary, artificial, idle, and individualistic life he was leading for this laborious, pure, and social delightful life.

The old man who had been sitting beside him had long ago gone home; the people had all separated. Those who lived near had gone home, while those who came from far were gathered into a group for supper, and to spend the night in the meadow. Levin, unobserved by the peasants, still lay on the haycock, and still looked on and listened and mused. The peasants who remained for the night in the meadow scarcely slept all the short summer night. At first there was the sound of merry talk and laughing all together over the supper, then singing again and laughter.

All the long day of toil had left no trace in them but lightness of heart. Before the early dawn all was hushed. Nothing was to be heard but the night sounds of the frogs that never ceased in the marsh, and the horses snorting in the mist that rose over the meadow before the morning. Rousing himself, Levin got up from the haycock, and looking at the stars, he saw that the night was over.

"Well, what am I going to do? How am I to set about it?" he said to himself, trying to express to himself all the thoughts and feelings he had passed through in that brief night. All the thoughts and feelings he had passed through fell into three separate trains of thought. One was the renunciation of his old life, of his utterly useless education. This renunciation gave him satisfaction, and was easy and simple. Another series of thoughts and mental images related to the life he longed to live now. The simplicity, the purity, the sanity of this life he felt clearly, and he was convinced he would find in it the content, the peace, and the dignity, of the lack of which he was so miserably conscious. But a third series of ideas turned upon the question how to effect this transition from the old life to the new. And there nothing took clear shape for him. "Have a wife? Have work and the necessity of work? Leave Pokrovskoe? Buy land? Become a member of a peasant community? Marry a peasant girl? How am I to set about it?" he asked himself again, and could not find an answer. "I haven't slept all night, though, and I can't think it out clearly," he said to himself. "I'll work it out later. One thing's certain, this night has decided my fate. All my old dreams of home life were absurd, not the real thing," he told himself. "It's all ever so much simpler and better. . . ."

"How beautiful!" he thought, looking at the strange, as it were, mother-of-pearl shell of white fleecy cloudlets resting right over his head in the middle of the sky. "How exquisite it all is in this exquisite night! And when was there time for that cloud-shell to form? Just now I looked at the sky, and there was nothing in it—only two white streaks. Yes, and so imperceptibly too my views of life changed!"

He went out of the meadow and walked along the highroad towards the village. A slight wind arose, and the sky looked gray and sullen. The gloomy moment had come that usually precedes the dawn, the full triumph of light over darkness.

Shrinking from the cold, Levin walked rapidly, looking at the ground. "What's that? Someone coming," he thought, catching the tinkle of bells, and lifting his head. Forty paces from him a carriage with four horses harnessed abreast was driving towards him along the grassy highroad on which he was walking. The shaft-horses were tilted against the shafts by the ruts, but the dexterous driver sitting on the box held the shaft over the ruts, so that the wheels ran on the smooth part of the road.

This was all Levin noticed, and without wondering who it could be, he gazed absently at the coach.

In the coach was an old lady dozing in one corner, and at the window, evidently only just awake, sat a young girl holding in both hands the ribbons of a white cap. With a face full of light and thought, full of a subtle, complex inner life, that was remote from Levin, she was gazing beyond him at the glow of the sunrise.

At the very instant when this apparition was vanishing, the truthful eyes glanced at him. She recognized him, and her face lit up with wondering delight.

He could not be mistaken. There were no other eyes like those in the world. There was only one creature in the world that could concentrate for him all the brightness and meaning of life. It was she. It was Kitty. He understood that she was driving to Ergushovo from the railway station. And everything that had been stirring Levin during that sleepless night, all the resolutions he had made, all vanished at once. He recalled with horror his dreams of marrying a peasant girl. There only, in the carriage that had crossed over to the other side of the road, and was rapidly disappearing, there only could he find the solution of the riddle of his life, which had weighed so agonizingly upon him of late.

She did not look out again. The sound of the carriage-springs was no longer audible, the bells could scarcely be heard. The barking of dogs showed the carriage had reached the village, and all that was left was the empty fields all round, the village in front, and he himself isolated and apart from it all, wandering lonely along the deserted highroad.

He glanced at the sky, expecting to find there the cloudshell he had been admiring and taking as the symbol of the ideas and feelings of that night. There was nothing in the sky in the least like a shell. There, in the remote heights above, a mysterious change had been accomplished. There was no trace of shell, and there was stretched over fully half the sky an even cover of tiny and ever tinier cloudlets. The sky had grown blue and bright; and with the same softness, but with the same remoteness, it met his questioning gaze.

"No," he said to himself, "however good that life of simplicity and toil may be, I cannot go back to it. I love *her*."

Chapter XIII

NONE BUT THOSE WHO WERE MOST INTIMATE WITH ALEXEY ALEXANDROVITCH KNEW THAT, while on the surface the coldest and most reasonable of men, he had one weakness quite opposed to the general trend of his character. Alexey Alexandrovitch could not hear or see a child or woman crying without being moved. The sight of tears threw him into a state of nervous agitation, and he utterly lost all power of reflection. The chief secretary of his department and his private secretary were aware of this, and used to warn women who came with petitions on no account to give way to tears, if they did not want to ruin their chances. "He will get angry, and will not listen to you," they used to say. And as a fact, in such cases the emotional disturbance set up in Alexey Alexandrovitch by the sight of tears found expression in hasty anger. "I can do nothing. Kindly leave the room!" he would commonly cry in such cases.

When returning from the races Anna had informed him of her relations with Vronsky, and immediately afterwards had burst into tears, hiding her face in her hands, Alexey Alexandrovitch, for all the fury aroused in him against her, was aware at the same time of a rush of that emotional disturbance always produced in him by tears. Conscious of it, and conscious that any expression of his feelings at that minute would be out of keeping with the position, he tried to suppress every manifestation of life in himself, and so neither stirred nor looked at her. This was what had caused that strange expression of deathlike rigidity in his face which had so impressed Anna.

When they reached the house he helped her to get out of the carriage, and making an effort to master himself, took leave of her with his usual urbanity, and uttered that phrase that bound him to nothing; he said that tomorrow he would let her know his decision.

His wife's words, confirming his worst suspicions, had sent a cruel pang to the heart of Alexey

Alexandrovitch. That pang was intensified by the strange feeling of physical pity for her set up by her tears. But when he was all alone in the carriage Alexey Alexandrovitch, to his surprise and delight, felt complete relief both from this pity and from the doubts and agonies of jealousy.

He experienced the sensations of a man who has had a tooth out after suffering long from toothache. After a fearful agony and a sense of something huge, bigger than the head itself, being torn out of his jaw, the sufferer, hardly able to believe in his own good luck, feels all at once that what has so long poisoned his existence and enchained his attention, exists no longer, and that he can live and think again, and take interest in other things besides his tooth. This feeling Alexey Alexandrovitch was experiencing. The agony had been strange and terrible, but now it was over; he felt that he could live again and think of something other than his wife.

"No honor, no heart, no religion; a corrupt woman. I always knew it and always saw it, though I tried to deceive myself to spare her," he said to himself. And it actually seemed to him that he always had seen it: he recalled incidents of their past life, in which he had never seen anything wrong before—now these incidents proved clearly that she had always been a corrupt woman. "I made a mistake in linking my life to hers; but there was nothing wrong in my mistake, and so I cannot be unhappy. It's not I that am to blame," he told himself, "but she. But I have nothing to do with her. She does not exist for me. . . ."

Everything relating to her and her son, towards whom his sentiments were as much changed as towards her, ceased to interest him. The only thing that interested him now was the question of in what way he could best, with most propriety and comfort for himself, and thus with most justice, extricate himself from the mud with which she had spattered him in her fall, and then proceed along his path of active, honorable, and useful existence.

"I cannot be made unhappy by the fact that a contemptible woman has committed a crime. I have only to find the best way out of the difficult position in which she has placed me. And I shall find it," he said to himself, frowning more and more. "I'm not the first nor the last." And to say nothing of historical instances dating from the "Fair Helen" of Menelaus, recently revived in the memory of all, a whole list of contemporary examples of husbands with unfaithful wives in the highest society rose before Alexey Alexandrovitch's imagination. "Daryalov, Poltavsky, Prince Karibanov, Count Paskudin, Dram . . . Yes, even Dram, such an honest, capable fellow. . . . Semyonov, Tchagin, Sigonin," Alexey Alexandrovitch remembered. "Admitting that a certain quite irrational *ridicule* falls to the lot of these men, yet I never saw anything but a misfortune in it, and always felt sympathy for it," Alexey Alexandrovitch said to himself, though indeed this was not the fact, and he had never felt sympathy for misfortunes of that kind, but the more frequently he had heard of instances of unfaithful wives betraying their husbands, the more highly he had thought of himself. "It is a misfortune which may befall anyone. And this misfortune has befallen me. The only thing to be done is to make the best of the position."

And he began passing in review the methods of proceeding of men who had been in the same position that he was in.

"Daryalov fought a duel. . . ."

The duel had particularly fascinated the thoughts of Alexey Alexandrovitch in his youth, just because he was physically a coward, and was himself well aware of the fact. Alexey Alexandrovitch could not without horror contemplate the idea of a pistol aimed at himself, and had never made use of any weapon in his life. This horror had in his youth set him pondering on dueling, and picturing himself in a position in which he would have to expose his life to danger. Having attained success and an established position in the world, he had long ago forgotten this feeling; but the habitual bent of feeling reasserted itself, and dread of his own cowardice proved even now so strong that Alexey Alexandrovitch spent a long while thinking over the question of dueling in all its aspects, and hugging the idea of a duel, though he was fully aware beforehand that he would never under any circumstances fight one.

"There's no doubt our society is still so barbarous (it's not the same in England) that very many"—and among these were those whose opinion Alexey Alexandrovitch particularly valued—"look favorably on the duel; but what result is attained by it? Suppose I call him out," Alexey Alexandrovitch went on to himself, and vividly pictured the night he would spend after the challenge, and the pistol aimed at him, he shuddered, and knew that he never would do it—"suppose I call him out. Suppose I am taught," he went on musing, "to shoot; I press the trigger," he said to himself, closing his eyes, "and it turns out I have killed him," Alexey Alexandrovitch said to himself, and he shook his head as though to dispel such silly ideas. "What sense is there in murdering a man in order to define one's relation to a guilty wife and son? I should still just as much have to decide what I ought to do with her. But what is more probable and what would doubtless occur—I should be killed or wounded. I, the innocent person, should be the victim—killed or wounded. It's even more senseless. But apart from that, a challenge to fight would be an act hardly honest on my side. Don't I know perfectly well that my friends would never allow me to fight a duel—would never allow the life of a statesman, needed by Russia, to be exposed to danger? Knowing perfectly well beforehand that the matter would never come to real danger, it would amount to my simply trying to gain a certain sham reputation by such a challenge. That would be dishonest, that would be false, that would be deceiving myself and others. A duel is quite irrational, and no one expects it of me. My aim is simply to safeguard my reputation, which is essential for the uninterrupted pursuit of my public duties." Official duties, which had always been of great consequence in Alexey Alexandrovitch's eyes, seemed of special importance to his mind at this moment. Considering and rejecting the duel, Alexey Alexandrovitch turned to divorce—another solution selected by several of the husbands he remembered. Passing in mental review all the instances he knew of divorces (there were plenty of them in the very highest society with which he was very familiar), Alexey Alexandrovitch could not find a single example in which the object of divorce was that which he had in view. In all these instances the husband had practically ceded or sold his unfaithful wife, and the very party which, being in fault, had not the right to contract a fresh marriage, had formed counterfeit, pseudo-matrimonial ties with a self-styled husband. In his own case, Alexey Alexandrovitch saw that a legal divorce, that is to say, one in which only the guilty wife would be repudiated, was impossible of attainment. He saw that the complex conditions of the life they led made the coarse proofs of his wife's guilt, required by the law, out of the question; he saw that a certain refinement in that life would not admit of such proofs being brought forward, even if he had them, and that to bring forward such proofs would damage him in the public estimation more than it would her.

An attempt at divorce could lead to nothing but a public scandal, which would be a perfect godsend to his enemies for calumny and attacks on his high position in society. His chief object, to define the position with the least amount of disturbance possible, would not be attained by divorce either. Moreover, in the event of divorce, or even of an attempt to obtain a divorce, it was obvious that the wife broke off all relations with the husband and threw in her lot with the lover. And in spite of the complete, as he supposed, contempt and indifference he now felt for his wife, at the bottom of his heart Alexey Alexandrovitch still had one feeling left in regard to her—a disinclination to see her free to throw in her lot with Vronsky, so that her crime would be to her advantage. The mere notion of this so exasperated Alexey Alexandrovitch, that directly it rose to his mind he groaned with inward agony, and got up and changed his place in the carriage, and for a long while after, he sat with scowling brows, wrapping his numbed and bony legs in the fleecy rug.

"Apart from formal divorce, One might still do like Karibanov, Paskudin, and that good fellow Dram—that is, separate from one's wife," he went on thinking, when he had regained his composure. But this step too presented the same drawback of public scandal as a divorce, and what was more, a separation, quite as much as a regular divorce, flung his wife into the arms of Vronsky. "No, it's out of the question, out of the question!" he said again, twisting his rug about him again. "I cannot be unhappy, but neither she nor he ought to be happy."

The feeling of jealousy, which had tortured him during the period of uncertainty, had passed away at the instant when the tooth had been with agony extracted by his wife's words. But that feeling had been replaced by another, the desire, not merely that she should not be triumphant, but that she should get due punishment for her crime. He did not acknowledge this feeling, but at the bottom of his heart he longed for her to suffer for having destroyed his peace of mind—his honor. And going once again over the conditions inseparable from a duel, a divorce, a separation, and once again rejecting them, Alexey Alexandrovitch felt convinced that there was only one solution—to keep her with him, concealing what had happened from the world, and using every measure in his power to break off the intrigue, and still more—though this he did not admit to himself—to punish her. "I must inform her of my conclusion, that thinking over the terrible position in which she has placed her family, all other solutions will be worse for both sides than an external *status quo,* and that such I agree to retain, on the strict condition of obedience on her part to my wishes, that is to say, cessation of all intercourse with her lover." When this decision had been finally adopted, another weighty consideration occurred to Alexey Alexandrovitch in support of it. "By such a course only shall I be acting in accordance with the dictates of religion," he told himself. "In adopting this course, I am not casting off a guilty wife, but giving her a chance of amendment; and, indeed, difficult as the task will be to me, I shall devote part of my energies to her reformation and salvation."

Though Alexey Alexandrovitch was perfectly aware that he could not exert any moral influence over his wife, that such an attempt at reformation could lead to nothing but falsity; though in passing through these difficult moments he had not once thought of seeking guidance in religion, yet now, when his conclusion corresponded, as it seemed to him, with the requirements of religion, this religious sanction to his decision gave him complete satisfaction, and to some extent restored his peace of mind. He was pleased to think that, even in such an important crisis in life, no one would be able to say that he had not acted in accordance with the principles of that religion whose banner he had always held aloft amid the general coolness and indifference. As he pondered over subsequent developments, Alexey Alexandrovitch did not see, indeed, why his relations with his wife should not remain practically the same as before. No doubt, she could never regain his esteem, but there was not, and there could not be, any sort of reason that his existence should be troubled, and that he should suffer because she was a bad and faithless wife. "Yes, time will pass; time, which arranges all things, and the old relations will be re-established," Alexey Alexandrovitch told himself; "so far re-established, that is, that I shall not be sensible of a break in the continuity of my life. She is bound to be unhappy, but I am not to blame, and so I cannot be unhappy."

Chapter XIV

As he neared Petersburg, Alexey Alexandrovitch not only adhered entirely to his decision, but was even composing in his head the letter he would write to his wife. Going into the porter's room, Alexey Alexandrovitch glanced at the letters and papers brought from his office, and directed that they should be brought to him in his study.

"The horses can be taken out and I will see no one," he said in answer to the porter, with a certain pleasure, indicative of his agreeable frame of mind, emphasizing the words, "see no one."

In his study Alexey Alexandrovitch walked up and down twice, and stopped at an immense writing-table, on which six candles had already been lit by the valet who had preceded him. He cracked his knuckles, and sat down, sorting out his writing appurtenances. Putting his elbows on the table, he bent his head on one side, thought a minute, and began to write, without pausing for a second. He wrote without using any form of address to her, and wrote in French, making use of the plural *"vous,"* which has not the same note of coldness as the corresponding Russian form.

At our last conversation, I notified you of my intention to communicate to you my decision in regard to the subject of that conversation. Having carefully considered everything, I am writing now with the object of fulfilling that promise. My decision is as follows. Whatever your conduct may have been, I do not consider myself justified in breaking the ties in which we are bound by a Higher Power. The family cannot be broken up by a whim, a caprice, or even by the sin of one of the partners in the marriage, and our life must go on as it has done in the past. This is essential for me, for you, and for our son. I am fully persuaded that you have repented and do repent of what has called forth the present letter, and that you will cooperate with me in eradicating the cause of our estrangement, and forgetting the past. In the contrary event, you can conjecture what awaits you and your son. All this I hope to discuss more in detail in a personal interview. As the season is drawing to a close, I would beg you to return to Petersburg as quickly as possible, not later than Tuesday. All necessary preparations shall be made for your arrival here. I beg you to note that I attach particular significance to compliance with this request.

A. KARENIN

P.S.—I enclose the money which may be needed for your expenses."

He read the letter through and felt pleased with it, and especially that he had remembered to enclose money: there was not a harsh word, not a reproach in it, nor was there undue indulgence. Most of all, it was a golden bridge for return. Folding the letter and smoothing it with a massive ivory knife, and putting it in an envelope with the money, he rang the bell with the gratification it always afforded him to use the well arranged appointments of his writing-table.

"Give this to the courier to be delivered to Anna Arkadyevna tomorrow at the summer villa," he said, getting up.

"Certainly, your excellency; tea to be served in the study?"

Alexey Alexandrovitch ordered tea to be brought to the study, and playing with the massive paper-knife, he moved to his easy chair, near which there had been placed ready for him a lamp and the French work on Egyptian hieroglyphics that he had begun. Over the easy chair there hung in a gold frame an oval portrait of Anna, a fine painting by a celebrated artist. Alexey Alexandrovitch glanced at it. The unfathomable eyes gazed ironically and insolently at him. Insufferably insolent and challenging was the effect in Alexey Alexandrovitch's eyes of the black lace about the head, admirably touched in by the painter, the black hair and handsome white hand with one finger lifted, covered with rings. After looking at the portrait for a minute, Alexey Alexandrovitch shuddered so that his lips quivered and he uttered the sound "brrr," and turned away. He made haste to sit down in his easy chair and opened the book. He tried to read, but he could not revive the very vivid interest he had felt before in Egyptian hieroglyphics. He looked at the book and thought of something else. He thought not of his wife, but of a complication that had arisen in his official life, which at the time constituted the chief interest of it. He felt that he had penetrated more deeply than ever before into this intricate affair, and that he had originated a leading idea—he could say it without self-flattery—calculated to clear up the whole business, to strengthen him in his official career, to discomfit his enemies, and thereby to be of the greatest benefit to the government. Directly the servant had set the tea and left the room, Alexey Alexandrovitch got up and went to the writing-table. Moving into the middle of the table a portfolio of papers, with a scarcely perceptible smile of self-satisfaction, he took a pencil from a rack and plunged into the perusal of a complex report relating to the present complication. The complication was of this nature: Alexey Alexandrovitch's characteristic quality as a politician, that special individual qualification that every rising functionary possesses, the qualification that with his unflagging ambition, his reserve, his honesty, and with his self-confidence had made his career, was his contempt for red tape, his cutting down of correspondence, his direct contact, wherever possible, with the living fact, and his economy. It happened that the famous Commission of the 2nd of June had set on foot an inquiry into the irrigation of lands in the Zaraisky province, which fell under Alexey Alexandrovitch's department, and was a glaring example of fruitless expenditure and paper reforms. Alexey Alexandrovitch was aware of the truth of this. The irrigation of these lands in the Zaraisky province had been initiated by the predecessor of Alexey Alexandrovitch's predecessor. And vast sums of money had actually been spent and were still being spent on this business, and utterly unproductively, and the whole business could obviously lead to nothing whatever. Alexey Alexandrovitch had perceived this at once on entering office, and would have liked to lay hands on the Board of Irrigation. But at first, when he did not yet feel secure in his position, he knew it would affect too many interests, and would be injudicious. Later on he had been engrossed in other questions, and had simply forgotten the Board of Irrigation. It went of itself, like all such boards, by the mere force of inertia. (Many people gained their livelihood by the Board of Irrigation, especially one highly conscientious and musical family: all the daughters played on stringed instruments, and Alexey Alexandrovitch knew the family and had stood godfather to one of the elder daughters.) The raising of this question by a hostile department was in Alexey Alexandrovitch's opinion a dishonorable proceeding, seeing that in every department there were things similar and worse, which no one inquired into, for well-known reasons of official etiquette. However, now that the glove had been thrown down to him, he had boldly picked it up and demanded the appointment of a special commission to investigate and verify the working of the Board of Irrigation of the lands in the Zaraisky province. But in compensation he gave no quarter to the enemy either. He demanded the appointment of another special commission to inquire into the question of the Native Tribes Organization Committee. The question of the Native Tribes had been brought up incidentally in the Commission of the 2nd of June, and had been pressed forward actively by Alexey Alexandrovitch as one admitting of no delay on account of the deplorable condition of the native tribes. In the commission this question had been a ground of contention between several departments. The department hostile to Alexey Alexandrovitch proved that the condition of the native tribes was exceedingly flourishing, that the proposed reconstruction might be the ruin of their prosperity, and that if there were anything wrong, it arose mainly from the failure on the part of Alexey Alexandrovitch's department to carry out the measures prescribed by law. Now Alexey Alexandrovitch intended to demand: First, that a new commission should be formed which should be empowered to investigate the condition of the native tribes on the spot, secondly, if it should appear that the condition of the native tribes actually was such as it appeared to be from the official documents in the hands of the committee, that another new scientific commission should be appointed to investigate the deplorable condition of the native tribes from the—(1) political, (2) administrative, (3) economic, (4) ethnographical, (5) material, and (6) religious points of view; thirdly, that evidence should be required from the rival department of the measures that had been taken during the last ten years by that department for averting the disastrous conditions in which the native tribes were now placed; and fourthly and finally, that that department be asked to explain why it had, as appeared from the evidence before the committee, from No. 17,015 and 18,038, from December 5, 1863, and June 7, 1864, acted in direct contravention of the intention of the law T . . . Act 18, and the note to Act 36. A flash of eagerness suffused the face of Alexey Alexandrovitch as he rapidly wrote out a synopsis of these ideas for his own benefit. Having filled a sheet of paper, he got up, rang, and sent a note to the chief secretary of his department to look up certain necessary facts for him. Getting up and walking about the room, he glanced again at the portrait, frowned, and smiled contemptuously. After reading a little more of the book on Egyptian hieroglyphics, and renewing his interest in it, Alexey Alexandrovitch went to bed at eleven o'clock, and recollecting as he lay in bed the incident with his wife, he saw it now in by no means such a gloomy light.

Chapter XV

THOUGH ANNA HAD OBSTINATELY AND WITH EXASPERATION CONTRADICTED VRONSKY WHEN HE told her their position was impossible, at the bottom of her heart she regarded her own position as false and dishonorable, and she longed with her whole soul to change it. On the way home from the races she had told her husband the truth in a moment of excitement, and in spite of the agony she had suffered in doing so, she was glad of it. After her husband had left her, she told herself that she was glad, that now everything was made clear, and at least there would be no more lying and deception. It seemed to her beyond doubt that her position was now made clear forever. It might be bad, this new position, but it would be clear; there would be no indefiniteness or falsehood about it. The pain she had caused herself and her husband in uttering those words would be rewarded now by everything being made clear, she thought. That evening she saw Vronsky, but she did not tell him of what had passed between her and her husband, though, to make the position definite, it was necessary to tell him.

When she woke up next morning the first thing that rose to her mind was what she had said to her husband, and those words seemed to her so awful that she could not conceive now how she could have brought herself to utter those strange, coarse words, and could not imagine what would come of it. But the words were spoken, and Alexey Alexandrovitch had gone away without saying anything. "I saw Vronsky and did not tell him. At the very instant he was going away I would have turned him back and told him, but I changed my mind, because it was strange that I had not told him the first minute. Why was it I wanted to tell him and did not tell him?" And in answer to this question a burning blush of shame spread over her face. She knew what had kept her from it, she knew that she had been ashamed. Her position, which had seemed to her simplified the night before, suddenly struck her now as not only not simple, but as absolutely hopeless. She felt terrified at the disgrace, of which she had not ever thought before. Directly she thought of what her husband would do, the most terrible ideas came to her mind. She had a vision of being turned out of the house, of her shame being proclaimed to all the world. She asked herself where she should go when she was turned out of the house, and she could not find an answer.

When she thought of Vronsky, it seemed to her that he did not love her, that he was already beginning to be tired of her, that she could not offer herself to him, and she felt bitter against him for it. It seemed to her that the words that she had spoken to her husband, and had continually repeated in her imagination, she had said to everyone, and everyone had heard them. She could not bring herself to look those of her own household in the face. She could not bring herself to call her maid, and still less go downstairs and see her son and his governess.

The maid, who had been listening at her door for a long while, came into her room of her own accord. Anna glanced inquiringly into her face, and blushed with a scared look. The maid begged her pardon for coming in, saying that she had fancied the bell rang. She brought her clothes and a note. The note was from Betsy. Betsy reminded her that Liza Merkalova and Baroness Shtoltz were coming to play croquet with her that morning with their adorers, Kaluzhsky and old Stremov. "Come, if only as a study in morals. I shall expect you," she finished.

Anna read the note and heaved a deep sigh.

"Nothing, I need nothing," she said to Annushka, who was rearranging the bottles and brushes on the dressing-table. "You can go. I'll dress at once and come down. I need nothing."

Annushka went out, but Anna did not begin dressing, and sat in the same position, her head and hands hanging listlessly, and every now and then she shivered all over, seemed as though she would make some gesture, utter some word, and sank back into lifelessness again. She repeated continually, "My God! my God!" But neither "God" nor "my" had any meaning to her. The idea of seeking help in her difficulty in religion was as remote from her as seeking help from Alexey Alexandrovitch himself, although she had never had doubts of the faith in which she had been brought up. She knew that the support of religion was possible only upon condition of renouncing what made up for her the whole meaning of life. She was not simply miserable, she began to feel alarm at the new spiritual condition, never experienced before, in which she found herself. She felt as though everything were beginning to be double in her soul, just as objects sometimes appear double to over-tired eyes. She hardly knew at times what it was she feared, and what she hoped for. Whether she feared or desired what had happened, or what was going to happen, and exactly what she longed for, she could not have said.

"Ah, what am I doing!" she said to herself, feeling a sudden thrill of pain in both sides of her head. When she came to herself, she saw that she was holding her hair in both hands, each side of her temples, and pulling it. She jumped up, and began walking about.

"The coffee is ready, and mademoiselle and Seryozha are waiting," said Annushka, coming back again and finding Anna in the same position.

"Seryozha? What about Seryozha?" Anna asked, with sudden eagerness, recollecting her son's existence for the first time that morning.

"He's been naughty, I think," answered Annushka with a smile.

"In what way?"

"Some peaches were lying on the table in the corner room. I think he slipped in and ate one of them on the sly."

The recollection of her son suddenly roused Anna from the helpless condition in which she found herself. She recalled the partly sincere, though greatly exaggerated, rôle of the mother living for her child, which she had taken up of late years, and she felt with joy that in the plight in which she found herself she had a support, quite apart from her relation to her husband or to Vronsky. This support was her son. In whatever position she might be placed, she could not lose her son. Her husband might put her to shame and turn her out, Vronsky might grow cold to her and go on living his own life apart (she thought of him again with bitterness and reproach); she could not leave her son. She had an aim in life. And she must act; act to secure this relation to her son, so that he might not be taken from her. Quickly indeed, as quickly as possible, she must take action before he was taken from her. She must take her son and go away. Here was the one thing she had to do now. She needed consolation. She must be calm, and get out of this insufferable position. The thought of immediate action binding her to her son, of going away somewhere with him, gave her this consolation.

She dressed quickly, went downstairs, and with resolute steps walked into the drawing room, where she found, as usual, waiting for her, the coffee, Seryozha, and his governess. Seryozha, all in white, with his back and head bent, was standing at a table under a looking-glass, and with an expression of intense concentration which she knew well, and in which he resembled his father, he was doing something to the flowers he carried.

The governess had a particularly severe expression. Seryozha screamed shrilly, as he often did, "Ah, mamma!" and stopped, hesitating whether to go to greet his mother and put down the flowers, or to finish making the wreath and go with the flowers.

The governess, after saying good-morning, began a long and detailed account of Seryozha's naughtiness, but Anna did not hear her; she was considering whether she would take her with her or not. "No, I won't take her," she decided. "I'll go alone with my child."

"Yes, it's very wrong," said Anna, and taking her son by the shoulder she looked at him, not severely, but with a timid glance that bewildered and delighted the boy, and she kissed him. "Leave him to me," she said to the astonished governess, and not letting go of her son, she sat down at the table, where coffee was set ready for her.

"Mamma! I . . . I . . . didn't . . ." he said, trying to make out from her expression what was in store for him in regard to the peaches.

"Seryozha," she said, as soon as the governess had left the room, "that was wrong, but you'll never do it again, will you? . . . You love me?"

She felt that the tears were coming into her eyes. "Can I help loving him?" she said to herself, looking deeply into his scared and at the same time delighted eyes. "And can he ever join his father in punishing me? Is it possible he will not feel for me?" Tears were already flowing down her face, and to hide them she got up abruptly and almost ran out on to the terrace.

After the tundershowers of the last few days, cold, bright weather had set in. The air was cold in the bright sun that filtered through the freshly washed leaves.

She shivered, both from the cold and from the inward horror which had clutched her with fresh force in the open air.

"Run along, run along to Mariette," she said to Seryozha, who had followed her out, and she began walking up and down on the straw matting of the terrace. "Can it be that they won't forgive me, won't understand how it all couldn't be helped?" she said to herself.

Standing still, and looking at the tops of the aspen trees waving in the wind, with their freshly washed, brightly shining leaves in the cold sunshine, she knew that they would not forgive her, that everyone and everything would be merciless to her now as was that sky, that green. And again she felt that everything was split in two in her soul. "I mustn't, mustn't think," she said to herself. "I must get ready. To go where? When? Whom to take with me? Yes, to Moscow by the evening train. Annushka and Seryozha, and only the most necessary things. But first I must write to them both." She went quickly indoors into her boudoir, sat down at the table, and wrote to her husband:—"After what has happened, I cannot remain any longer in your house. I am going away, and taking my son with me. I don't know the law, and so I don't know with which of the parents the son should remain; but I take him with me because I cannot live without him. Be generous, leave him to me."

Up to this point she wrote rapidly and naturally, but the appeal to his generosity, a quality she did not recognize in him, and the necessity of winding up the letter with something touching, pulled her up. "Of my fault and my remorse I cannot speak, because . . ."

She stopped again, finding no connection in her ideas. "No," she said to herself, "there's no need of anything," and tearing up the letter, she wrote it again, leaving out the allusion to generosity, and sealed it up.

Another letter had to be written to Vronsky. "I have told my husband," she wrote, and she sat a long while unable to write more. It was so coarse, so unfeminine. "And what more am I to write to him?" she said to herself. Again a flush of shame spread over her face; she recalled his composure, and a feeling of anger against him impelled her to tear the sheet with the phrase she had written into tiny bits. "No need of anything," she said to herself, and closing her blotting-case she went upstairs, told the governess and the servants that she was going that day to Moscow, and at once set to work to pack up her things.

Chapter XVI

ALL THE ROOMS OF THE SUMMER VILLA WERE FULL OF PORTERS, GARDENERS, AND FOOTMEN going to and fro carrying out things. Cupboards and chests were open; twice they had sent to the shop for cord; pieces of newspaper were tossing about on the floor. Two trunks, some bags and strapped-up rugs, had been carried down into the hall. The carriage and two hired cabs were waiting at the steps. Anna, forgetting her inward agitation in the work of packing, was standing at a table in her boudoir, packing her traveling bag, when Annushka called her attention to the rattle of some carriage driving up. Anna looked out of the window and saw Alexey Alexandrovitch's courier on the steps, ringing at the front door bell.

"Run and find out what it is," she said, and with a calm sense of being prepared for anything, she sat down in a low chair, folding her hands on her knees. A footman brought in a thick packet directed in Alexey Alexandrovitch's hand.

"The courier has orders to wait for an answer," he said.

"Very well," she said, and as soon as he had left the room she tore open the letter with trembling fingers. A roll of unfolded notes done up in a wrapper fell out of it. She disengaged the letter and began reading it at the end. "Preparations shall be made for your arrival here . . . I attach particular significance to compliance . . ." she read. She ran on, then back, read it all through, and once more read the letter all through again from the beginning. When she had finished, she felt that she was cold all over, and that a fearful calamity, such as she had not expected, had burst upon her.

In the morning she had regretted that she had spoken to her husband, and wished for nothing so much as that those words could be unspoken. And here this letter regarded them as unspoken, and gave her what she had wanted. But now this letter seemed to her more awful than anything she had been able to conceive.

"He's right!" she said; "of course, he's always right; he's a Christian, he's generous! Yes, vile, base creature! And no one understands it except me, and no one ever will; and I can't explain it. They say he's so religious, so high-principled, so upright, so clever; but they don't see what I've seen. They don't know how he has crushed my life for eight years, crushed everything that was living in me—he has not once even thought that I'm a live woman who must have love. They don't know how at every step he's humiliated me, and been just as pleased with himself. Haven't I striven, striven with all my strength, to find something to give meaning to my life? Haven't I struggled to love him, to love my son when I could not love my husband? But the time came when I knew that I couldn't cheat myself any longer, that I was alive, that I was not to blame, that God has made me so that I must love and live. And now what does he do? If he'd killed me, if he'd killed him, I could have borne anything, I could have forgiven anything; but, no, he . . . How was it I didn't guess what he would do? He's doing just what's characteristic of his mean character. He'll keep himself in the right, while me, in my ruin, he'll drive still lower to worse ruin yet. . . ."

She recalled the words from the letter. "You can conjecture what awaits you and your son. . . ." "That's a threat to take away my child, and most likely by their stupid law he can. But I know very well why he says it. He doesn't believe even in my love for my child, or he despises it (just as he always used to ridicule it). He despises that feeling in me, but he knows that I won't abandon my child, that I can't abandon my child, that there could be no life for me without my child, even with him whom I love; but that if I abandoned my child and ran away from him, I should be acting like the most infamous, basest of women. He knows that, and knows that I am incapable of doing that."

She recalled another sentence in the letter. "Our life must go on as it has done in the past. . . ." "That life was miserable enough in the old days; it has been awful of late. What will it be now? And he knows all that; he knows that I can't repent that I breathe, that I love; he knows that it can lead to nothing but lying and deceit; but he wants to go on torturing me. I know him; I know that he's at home and is happy in deceit, like a fish swimming in the water. No, I won't give him that happiness. I'll break through the spiderweb of lies in which he wants to catch me, come what may. Anything's better than lying and deceit.

"But how? My God! my God! Was ever a woman so miserable as I am? . . ."

"No; I will break through it, I will break through it!" she cried, jumping up and keeping back her tears. And she went to the writing-table to write him another letter. But at the bottom of her heart she felt that she was not strong enough to break through anything, that she was not strong enough to get out of her old position, however false and dishonorable it might be.

She sat down at the writing-table, but instead of writing she clasped her hands on the table, and, laying her head on them, burst into tears, with sobs and heaving breast like a child crying. She was weeping that her dream of her position being made clear and definite had been annihilated forever. She knew beforehand that everything would go on in the old way, and far worse, indeed, than in the old way. She felt that the position in the world that she enjoyed, and that had seemed to her of so little consequence in the morning, that this position was precious to her, that she would not have the strength to exchange it for the shameful position of a woman who has abandoned husband and child to join her lover; that however much she might struggle, she could not be stronger than herself. She would never know freedom in love, but would remain forever a guilty wife, with the menace of detection hanging over her at every instant; deceiving her husband for the sake of a shameful connection with a man living apart and away from her, whose life she could never share. She knew that this was how it would be, and at the same time it was so awful that she could not even conceive what it would end in. And she cried without restraint, as children cry when they are punished.

The sound of the footman's steps forced her to rouse herself, and, hiding her face from him, she pretended to be writing.

"The courier asks if there's an answer," the footman announced.

"An answer? Yes," said Anna. "Let him wait. I'll ring."

"What can I write?" she thought. "What can I decide upon alone? What do I know? What do I want? What is there I care for?" Again she felt that her soul was beginning to be split in two. She was terrified again at this feeling, and clutched at the first pretext for doing something which might divert her thoughts from herself. "I ought to see Alexey" (so she called Vronsky in her thoughts); "no one but he can tell me what I ought to do. I'll go to Betsy's, perhaps I shall see him there," she said to herself, completely forgetting that when she had told him the day before that she was not going to Princess Tverskaya's, he had said that in that case he should not go either. She went up to the table, wrote to her husband, "I have received your letter.—A."; and, ringing the bell, gave it to the footman.

"We are not going," she said to Annushka, as she came in.

"Not going at all?"

"No; don't unpack till tomorrow, and let the carriage wait. I'm going to the princess's."

"Which dress am I to get ready?"

Chapter XVII

THE CROQUET PARTY TO WHICH THE PRINCESS TVERSKAYA HAD INVITED ANNA WAS TO CONSIST of two ladies and their adorers. These two ladies were the chief representatives of a select new Petersburg circle, nicknamed, in imitation of some imitation, *les sept merveilles du monde.* These ladies belonged to a circle which, though of the highest society, was utterly hostile to that in which Anna moved. Moreover, Stremov, one of the most influential people in Petersburg, and the elderly admirer of Liza Merkalova, was Alexey Alexandrovitch's enemy in the political world. From all these considerations Anna had not meant to go, and the hints in Princess Tverskaya's note referred to her refusal. But now Anna was eager to go, in the hope of seeing Vronsky.

Anna arrived at Princess Tverskaya's earlier than the other guests.

At the same moment as she entered, Vronsky's footman, with side-whiskers combed out like a *Kammerjunker,* went in too. He stopped at the door, and, taking off his cap, let her pass. Anna recognized him, and only then recalled that Vronsky had told her the day before that he would not come. Most likely he was sending a note to say so.

As she took off her outer garment in the hall, she heard the footman, pronouncing his *"r's"* even like a *Kammerjunker,* say, "From the count for the princess," and hand the note.

She longed to question him as to where his master was. She longed to turn back and send him a letter to come and see her, or to go herself to see him. But neither the first nor the second nor the third course was possible. Already she heard bells ringing to announce her arrival ahead of her, and Princess Tverskaya's footman was standing at the open door waiting for her to go forward into the inner rooms.

"The princess is in the garden; they will inform her immediately. Would you be pleased to walk into the garden?" announced another footman in another room.

The position of uncertainty, of indecision, was still the same as at home—worse, in fact, since it was impossible to take any step, impossible to see Vronsky, and she had to remain here among outsiders, in company so uncongenial to her present mood. But she was wearing a dress that she knew suited her. She was not alone; all around was that luxurious setting of idleness that she was used to, and she felt less wretched than at home. She was not forced to think what she was to do. Everything would be done of itself. On meeting Betsy coming towards her in a white gown that struck her by its elegance, Anna smiled at her just as she always did. Princess Tverskaya was walking with Tushkevitch and a young lady, a relation, who, to the great joy of her parents in the provinces, was spending the summer with the fashionable princess.

There was probably something unusual about Anna, for Betsy noticed it at once.

"I slept badly," answered Anna, looking intently at the footman who came to meet them, and, as she supposed, brought Vronsky's note.

"How glad I am you've come!" said Betsy. "I'm tired, and was just longing to have some tea before they come. You might go"—she turned to Tushkevitch—"with Masha, and try the croquet ground over there where they've been cutting it. We shall have time to talk a little over tea; we'll have a cozy chat, eh?" she said in English to Anna, with a smile, pressing the hand with which she held a parasol.

"Yes, especially as I can't stay very long with you. I'm forced to go on to old Madame Vrede. I've been promising to go for a century," said Anna, to whom lying, alien as it was to her nature, had become not merely simple and natural in society, but a positive source of satisfaction. Why she said this, which she had not thought of a second before, she could not have explained. She had said it simply from the reflection that as Vronsky would not be here, she had better secure her own freedom, and try to see him somehow. But why she had spoken of old Madame Vrede, whom she had to go and see, as she had to see many other people, she could not have explained; and yet, as it afterwards turned out, had she contrived the most cunning devices to meet Vronsky, she could have thought of nothing better.

"No. I'm not going to let you go for anything," answered Betsy, looking intently into Anna's face. "Really, if I were not fond of you, I should feel offended. One would think you were afraid my society would compromise you. Tea in the little dining room, please," she said, half closing her eyes, as she always did when addressing the footman.

Taking the note from him, she read it.

"Alexey's playing us false," she said in French; "he writes that he can't come," she added in a tone as simple and natural as though it could never enter her head that Vronsky could mean anything more to Anna than a game of croquet. Anna knew that Betsy knew everything, but, hearing how she spoke of Vronsky before her, she almost felt persuaded for a minute that she knew nothing.

"Ah!" said Anna indifferently, as though not greatly interested in the matter, and she went on smiling: "How can you or your friends compromise anyone?"

This playing with words, this hiding of a secret, had a great fascination for Anna, as, indeed, it has for all women. And it was not the necessity of concealment, not the aim with which the concealment was contrived, but the process of concealment itself attracted her.

"I can't be more Catholic than the Pope," she said. "Stremov and Liza Merkalova, why, they're the cream of the cream of society. Besides, they're received everywhere, and *I*"—she laid special stress on the I—"have never been strict and intolerant. It's simply that I haven't the time."

"No; you don't care, perhaps, to meet Stremov? Let him and Alexey Alexandrovitch tilt at each other in the committee—that's no affair of ours. But in the world, he's the most amiable man I know, and a devoted croquet player. You shall see. And, in spite of his absurd position as Liza's lovesick swain at his age, you ought to see how he carries off the absurd position. He's very nice. Sappho Shtoltz you don't know? Oh, that's a new type, quite new."

Betsy said all this, and, at the same time, from her good-humored, shrewd glance, Anna felt that she partly guessed her plight, and was hatching something for her benefit. They were in the little boudoir.

"I must write to Alexey though," and Betsy sat down to the table, scribbled a few lines, and put the note in an envelope.

"I'm telling him to come to dinner. I've one lady extra to dinner with me, and no man to take her in. Look what I've said, will that persuade him? Excuse me, I must leave you for a minute. Would you seal it up, please, and send it off?" she said from the door; "I have to give some directions."

Without a moment's thought, Anna sat down to the table with Betsy's letter, and, without reading it, wrote below: "It's essential for me to see you. Come to the Vrede garden. I shall be there at six o'clock." She sealed it up, and, Betsy coming back, in her presence handed the note to be taken.

At tea, which was brought them on a little tea-table in the cool little drawing room, the cozy chat promised by Princess Tverskaya before the arrival of her visitors really did come off between the two women. They criticized the people they were expecting, and the conversation fell upon Liza Merkalova.

"She's very sweet, and I always liked her," said Anna.

"You ought to like her. She raves about you. Yesterday she came up to me after the races and was in despair at not finding you. She says you're a real heroine of romance, and that if she were a man she would do all sorts of mad things for your sake. Stremov says she does that as it is."

"But do tell me, please, I never could make it out," said Anna, after being silent for some time, speaking in a tone that showed she was not asking an idle question, but that what she was asking was of more importance to her than it should have been; "do tell me, please, what are her relations with Prince Kaluzhsky, Mishka, as he's called? I've met them so little. What does it mean?"

Betsy smiled with her eyes, and looked intently at Anna.

"It's a new manner," she said. "They've all adopted that manner. They've flung their caps over the windmills. But there are ways and ways of flinging them."

"Yes, but what are her relations precisely with Kaluzhsky?"

Betsy broke into unexpectedly mirthful and irrepressible laughter, a thing which rarely happened with her.

"You're encroaching on Princess Myakaya's special domain now. That's the question of an *enfant terrible*," and Betsy obviously tried to restrain herself, but could not, and went off into peals of that infectious laughter that people laugh who do not laugh often. "You'd better ask them," she brought out, between tears of laughter.

"No; you laugh," said Anna, laughing too in spite of herself, "but I never could understand it. I can't understand the husband's rôle in it."

"The husband? Liza Merkalova's husband carries her shawl, and is always ready to be of use. But anything more than that in reality, no one cares to inquire. You know in decent society one doesn't talk or think even of certain details of the toilet. That's how it is with this."

"Will you be at Madame Rolandak's fête?" asked Anna, to change the conversation.

"I don't think so," answered Betsy, and, without looking at her friend, she began filling the little transparent cups with fragrant tea. Putting a cup before Anna, she took out a cigarette, and, fitting it into a silver holder, she lit it.

"It's like this, you see: I'm in a fortunate position," she began, quite serious now, as she took up her cup. "I understand you, and I understand Liza. Liza now is one of those naïve natures that, like children, don't know what's good and what's bad. Anyway, she didn't comprehend it when she was very young. And now she's aware that the lack of comprehension suits her. Now, perhaps, she doesn't know on purpose," said Betsy, with a subtle smile. "But, anyway, it suits her. The very same thing, don't you see, may be looked at tragically, and turned into a misery, or it may be looked at simply and even humorously. Possibly you are inclined to look at things too tragically."

"How I should like to know other people just as I know myself!" said Anna, seriously and dreamily. "Am I worse than other people, or better? I think I'm worse."

"Enfant terrible, enfant terrible!" repeated Betsy. "But here they are."

Chapter XVIII

THEY HEARD THE SOUND OF STEPS AND A MAN'S VOICE, THEN A WOMAN'S VOICE AND LAUGHTER, and immediately thereafter there walked in the expected guests: Sappho Shtoltz, and a young man beaming with excess of health, the so-called Vaska. It was evident that ample supplies of beefsteak, truffles, and Burgundy never failed to reach him at the fitting hour. Vaska bowed to the two ladies, and glanced at them, but only for one second. He walked after Sappho into the drawing room, and followed her about as though he were chained to her, keeping his sparkling eyes fixed on her as though he wanted to eat her. Sappho Shtoltz was a blonde beauty with black eyes. She walked with smart little steps in high-heeled shoes, and shook hands with the ladies vigorously like a man.

Anna had never met this new star of fashion, and was struck by her beauty, the exaggerated extreme to which her dress was carried, and the boldness of her manners. On her head there was such a superstructure of soft, golden hair—her own and false mixed—that her head was equal in size to the elegantly rounded bust, of which so much was exposed in front. The impulsive abruptness of her movements was such that at every step the lines of her knees and the upper part of her legs were distinctly marked under her dress, and the question involuntarily rose to the mind where in the undulating, piled-up mountain of material at the back the real body of the woman, so small and slender, so naked in front, and so hidden behind and below, really came to an end.

Betsy made haste to introduce her to Anna.

"Only fancy, we all but ran over two soldiers," she began telling them at once, using her eyes, smiling and twitching away her tail, which she flung back at one stroke all on one side. "I drove here with Vaska. . . . Ah, to be sure, you don't know each other." And mentioning his surname she introduced the young man, and reddening a little, broke into a ringing laugh at her mistake—that is, at her having called him Vaska to a stranger. Vaska bowed once more to Anna, but he said nothing to her. He addressed Sappho: "You've lost your bet. We got here first. Pay up," said he, smiling.

Sappho laughed still more festively.

"Not just now," said she.

"Oh, all right, I'll have it later."

"Very well, very well. Oh, yes." She turned suddenly to Princess Betsy: "I am a nice person . . . I positively forgot it . . . I've brought you a visitor. And here he comes." The unexpected visitor whom Sappho had invited, and whom she had forgotten, was, however, a personage of such consequence that, in spite of his youth, both the ladies rose on his entrance.

He was a new admirer of Sappho's. He now dogged her footsteps, like Vaska.

Soon after Prince Kaluzhsky arrived, and Liza Merkalova with Stremov. Liza Merkalova was a thin brunette, with an Oriental, languid type of face, and—as everyone used to say—exquisite enigmatic eyes. The tone of her dark dress (Anna immediately observed and appreciated the fact) was in perfect harmony with her style of beauty. Liza was as soft and enervated as Sappho was smart and abrupt.

But to Anna's taste Liza was far more attractive. Betsy had said to Anna that she had adopted the pose of an innocent child, but when Anna saw her, she felt that this was not the truth. She really was both innocent and corrupt, but a sweet and passive woman. It is true that her tone was the same as Sappho's; that like Sappho, she had two men, one young and one old, tacked onto her, and devouring her with their eyes. But there was something in her higher than what surrounded her. There was in her the glow of the real diamond among glass imitations. This glow shone out in her exquisite, truly enigmatic eyes. The weary, and at the same time passionate, glance of those eyes, encircled by dark rings, impressed one by its perfect sincerity. Everyone looking into those eyes fancied he knew her wholly, and knowing her, could not but love her. At the sight of Anna, her whole face lit up at once with a smile of delight.

"Ah, how glad I am to see you!" she said, going up to her. "Yesterday at the races all I wanted was to get to you, but you'd gone away. I did so want to see you, yesterday especially. Wasn't it awful?" she said, looking at Anna with eyes that seemed to lay bare all her soul.

"Yes; I had no idea it would be so thrilling," said Anna, blushing.

The company got up at this moment to go into the garden.

"I'm not going," said Liza, smiling and settling herself close to Anna. "You won't go either, will you? Who wants to play croquet?"

"Oh, I like it," said Anna.

"There, how do you manage never to be bored by things? It's delightful to look at you. You're alive, but I'm bored."

"How can you be bored? Why, you live in the liveliest set in Petersburg," said Anna.

"Possibly the people who are not of our set are even more bored; but we—I certainly—are not happy, but awfully, awfully bored."

Sappho smoking a cigarette went off into the garden with the two young men. Betsy and Stremov remained at the tea-table.

"What, bored!" said Betsy. "Sappho says they did enjoy themselves tremendously at your house last night."

"Ah, how dreary it all was!" said Liza Merkalova. "We all drove back to my place after the races. And always the same people, always the same. Always the same thing. We lounged about on sofas all the evening. What is there to enjoy in that? No; do tell me how you manage never to be bored?" she said, addressing Anna again. "One has but to look at you and one sees, here's a woman who may be happy or unhappy, but isn't bored. Tell me how you do it?"

"I do nothing," answered Anna, blushing at these searching questions.

"That's the best way," Stremov put in. Stremov was a man of fifty, partly gray, but still vigorous-looking, very ugly, but with a characteristic and intelligent face. Liza Merkalova was his wife's niece, and he spent all his leisure hours with her. On meeting Anna Karenina, as he was Alexey Alexandrovitch's enemy in the government, he tried, like a shrewd man and a man of the world, to be particularly cordial with her, the wife of his enemy.

" 'Nothing,' " he put in with a subtle smile, "that's the very best way. I told you long ago," he said, turning to Liza Merkalova, "that if you don't want to be bored, you mustn't think you're going to be bored. It's just as you mustn't be afraid of not being able to fall asleep, if you're afraid of sleeplessness. That's just what Anna Arkadyevna has just said."

"I should be very glad if I had said it, for it's not only clever but true," said Anna, smiling.

"No, do tell me why it is one can't go to sleep, and one can't help being bored?"

"To sleep well one ought to work, and to enjoy oneself one ought to work too."

"What am I to work for when my work is no use to anybody? And I can't and won't knowingly make a pretense about it."

"You're incorrigible," said Stremov, not looking at her, and he spoke again to Anna. As he rarely met Anna, he could say nothing but commonplaces to her, but he said those commonplaces as to when she was returning to Petersburg, and how fond Countess Lidia Ivanovna was of her, with an expression which suggested that he longed with his whole soul to please her and show his regard for her and even more than that.

Tushkevitch came in, announcing that the party were awaiting the other players to begin croquet.

"No, don't go away, please don't," pleaded Liza Merkalova, hearing that Anna was going. Stremov joined in her entreaties.

"It's too violent a transition," he said, "to go from such company to old Madame Vrede. And besides, you will only give her a chance for talking scandal, while here you arouse none but such different feelings of the highest and most opposite kind," he said to her.

Anna pondered for an instant in uncertainty. This shrewd man's flattering words, the naïve, childlike affection shown her by Liza Merkalova, and all the social atmosphere she was used to—it was all so easy, and what was in store for her was so difficult, that she was for a minute in uncertainty whether to remain, whether to put off a little longer the painful moment of explanation. But remembering what was in store for her alone at home, if she did not come to some decision, remembering that gesture—terrible even in memory—when she had clutched her hair in both hands—she said good-bye and went away.

Chapter XIX

IN SPITE OF VRONSKY'S APPARENTLY FRIVOLOUS LIFE IN SOCIETY, HE WAS A MAN WHO HATED IRregularity. In early youth in the Corps of Pages, he had experienced the humiliation of a refusal, when he had tried, being in difficulties, to borrow money, and since then he had never once put himself in the same position again.

In order to keep his affairs in some sort of order, he used about five times a year (more or less frequently, according to circumstances) to shut himself up alone and put all his affairs into definite shape. This he used to call his day of reckoning or *faire la lessive.*

On waking up the day after the races, Vronsky put on a white linen coat, and without shaving or taking his bath, he distributed about the table moneys, bills, and letters, and set to work. Petritsky, who knew he was ill-tempered on such occasions, on waking up and seeing his comrade at the writing-table, quietly dressed and went out without getting in his way.

Every man who knows to the minutest details all the complexity of the conditions surrounding him, cannot help imagining that the complexity of these conditions, and the difficulty of making them clear, is something exceptional and personal, peculiar to himself, and never supposes that others are surrounded by just as complicated an array of personal affairs as he is. So indeed it seemed to Vronsky. And not without inward pride, and not without reason, he thought that any other man would long ago have been in difficulties, would have been forced to some dishonorable course, if he had found himself in such a difficult position. But Vronsky felt that now especially it was essential for him to clear up and define his position if he were to avoid getting into difficulties.

What Vronsky attacked first as being the easiest was his pecuniary position. Writing out on notepaper in his minute hand all that he owed, he added up the amount and found that his debts amounted to seventeen thousand and some odd hundreds, which he left out for the sake of clearness. Reckoning up his money and his bank-book, he found that he had left one thousand eight hundred roubles, and nothing coming in before the New Year. Reckoning over again his list of debts, Vronsky copied it, dividing it into three classes. In the first class he put the debts which he would have to pay at once, or for which he must in any case have the money ready so that on demand for payment there could not be a moment's delay in paying. Such debts amounted to about four thousand: one thousand five hundred for a horse, and two thousand five hundred as surety for a young comrade, Venovsky, who had lost that sum to a cardsharper in Vronsky's presence. Vronsky had wanted to pay the money at the time (he had that amount then), but Venovsky and Yashvin had insisted that they would pay and not Vronsky, who had not played. That was so far well, but Vronsky knew that in this dirty business, though his only share in it was undertaking by word of mouth to be surety for Venovsky, it was absolutely necessary for him to have the two thousand five hundred roubles so as to be able to fling it at the swindler, and have no more words with him. And so for this first and most important division he must have four thousand roubles. The second class—eight thousand roubles—consisted of less important debts. These were principally accounts owing in connection with his race-horses, to the purveyor of oats and hay, the English saddler, and so on. He would have to pay some two thousand roubles on these debts too, in order to be quite free from anxiety. The last class of debts—to shops, to hotels, to his tailor—were such as need not be considered. So that he needed at least six thousand roubles for current expenses, and he only had one thousand eight hundred. For a man with one hundred thousand roubles of revenue, which was what everyone fixed as Vronsky's income, such debts, one would suppose, could hardly be embarrassing; but the fact was that he was far from having one hundred thousand. His father's immense property, which alone yielded a yearly income of two hundred thousand, was left undivided between the brothers. At the time when the elder brother, with a mass of debts, married Princess Varya Tchirkova, the daughter of a Decembrist without any fortune whatever, Alexey had given up to his elder brother almost the whole income from his father's estate, reserving for himself only twenty-five thousand a year from it. Alexey had said at the time to his brother that that sum would be sufficient for him until he married, which he probably never would do. And his brother, who was in command of one of the most expensive regiments, and was only just married, could not decline the gift. His mother, who had her own separate property, had allowed Alexey every year twenty thousand in addition to the twenty-five thousand he had reserved, and Alexey had spent it all. Of late his mother, incensed with him on account of his love affair and his leaving Moscow, had given up sending him the money. And in consequence of this, Vronsky, who had been in the habit of living on the scale of forty-five thousand a year, having only received twenty thousand that year, found himself now in difficulties. To get out of these difficulties, he could not apply to his mother for money. Her last letter, which he had received the day before, had particularly exasperated him by the hints in it that she was quite ready to help him to succeed in the world and in the army, but not to lead a life which was a scandal to all good society. His mother's attempt to buy him stung him to the quick and made him feel colder than ever to her. But he could not draw back from the generous word when it was once uttered, even though he felt now, vaguely foreseeing certain eventualities in his intrigue with Madame Karenina, that this generous word had been spoken thoughtlessly, and that even though he were not married he might need all the hundred thousand of income. But it was impossible to draw back. He had only to recall his brother's wife, to remember how that sweet, delightful Varya sought, at every convenient opportunity, to remind him that she remembered his generosity and appreciated it, to grasp the impossibility of taking back his gift. It was as impossible as beating a woman, stealing, or lying. One thing only could and ought to be done, and Vronsky determined upon it without an instant's hesitation: to borrow money from a money-lender, ten thousand roubles, a proceeding which presented no difficulty, to cut down his expenses generally, and to sell his race-horses. Resolving on this, he promptly wrote a note to Rolandak, who had more than once sent to him with offers to buy horses from him. Then he sent for the Englishman and the money-lender, and divided what money he had according to the accounts he intended to pay. Having finished this business, he wrote a cold and cutting answer to his mother. Then he took out of his notebook three notes of Anna's, read them again, burned them, and remembering their conversation on the previous day, he sank into meditation.

Chapter XX

VRONSKY'S LIFE WAS PARTICULARLY HAPPY IN THAT HE HAD A CODE OF PRINCIPLES, WHICH DEfined with unfailing certitude what he ought and what he ought not to do. This code of principles covered only a very small circle of contingencies, but then the principles were never doubtful, and Vronsky, as he never went outside that circle, had never had a moment's hesitation about doing what he ought to do. These principles laid down as invariable rules: that one must pay a cardsharper, but need not pay a tailor; that one must never tell a lie to a man, but one may to a woman; that one must never cheat anyone, but one may a husband; that one must never pardon an insult, but one may give one and so on. These principles were possibly not reasonable and not good, but they were of unfailing certainty, and so long as he adhered to them, Vronsky felt that his heart was at peace and he could hold his head up. Only quite lately in regard to his relations with Anna, Vronsky had begun to feel that his code of principles did not fully cover all possible contingencies, and to foresee in the future difficulties and perplexities for which he could find no guiding clue.

His present relation to Anna and to her husband was to his mind clear and simple. It was clearly and precisely defined in the code of principles by which he was guided.

She was an honorable woman who had bestowed her love upon him, and he loved her, and therefore she was in his eyes a woman who had a right to the same, or even more, respect than a lawful wife. He would have had his hand chopped off before he would have allowed himself by a word, by a hint, to humiliate her, or even to fall short of the fullest respect a woman could look for.

His attitude to society, too, was clear. Everyone might know, might suspect it, but no one might dare to speak of it. If any did so, he was ready to force all who might speak to be silent and to respect the non-existent honor of the woman he loved.

His attitude to the husband was the clearest of all. From the moment that Anna loved Vronsky, he had regarded his own right over her as the one thing unassailable. Her husband was simply a superfluous and tiresome person. No doubt he was in a pitiable position, but how could that be helped? The one thing the husband had a right to was to demand satisfaction with a weapon in his hand, and Vronsky was prepared for this at any minute.

But of late new inner relations had arisen between him and her, which frightened Vronsky by their indefiniteness. Only the day before she had told him that she was with child. And he felt that this fact and what she expected of him called for something not fully defined in that code of principles by which he had hitherto steered his course in life. And he had been indeed caught unawares, and at the first moment when she spoke to him of her position, his heart had prompted him to beg her to leave her husband. He had said that, but now thinking things over he saw clearly that it would be better to manage to avoid that; and at the same time, as he told himself so, he was afraid whether it was not wrong.

"If I told her to leave her husband, that must mean uniting her life with mine; am I prepared for that? How can I take her away now, when I have no money? Supposing I could arrange . . . But how can I take her away while I'm in the service? If I say that—I ought to be prepared to do it, that is, I ought to have the money and to retire from the army."

And he grew thoughtful. The question whether to retire from the service or not brought him to the other and perhaps the chief though hidden interest of his life, of which none knew but he.

Ambition was the old dream of his youth and childhood, a dream which he did not confess even to himself, though it was so strong that now this passion was even doing battle with his love. His first steps in the world and in the service had been successful, but two years before he had made a great mistake. Anxious to show his independence and to advance, he had refused a post that had been offered him, hoping that this refusal would heighten his value; but it turned out that he had been too bold, and he was passed over. And having, whether he liked or not, taken up for himself the position of an independent man, he carried it off with great tact and good sense, behaving as though he bore no grudge against anyone, did not regard himself as injured in any way, and cared for nothing but to be left alone since he was enjoying himself. In reality he had ceased to enjoy himself as long ago as the year before, when he went away to Moscow. He felt that this independent attitude of a man who might have done anything, but cared to do nothing, was already beginning to pall, that many people were beginning to fancy that he was not really capable of anything but being a straightforward, good-natured fellow. His connection with Madame Karenina, by creating so much sensation and attracting general attention, had given him a fresh distinction which soothed his gnawing worm of ambition for a while, but a week before that worm had been roused up again with fresh force. The friend of his childhood, a man of the same set, of the same coterie, his comrade in the Corps of Pages, Serpuhovskoy, who had left school with him and had been his rival in class, in gymnastics, in their scrapes and their dreams of glory, had come back a few days before from Central Asia, where he had gained two steps up in rank, and an order rarely bestowed upon generals so young.

As soon as he arrived in Petersburg, people began to talk about him as a newly risen star of the first magnitude. A schoolfellow of Vronsky's and of the same age, he was a general and was expecting a command, which might have influence on the course of political events; while Vronsky, independent and brilliant and beloved by a charming woman though he was, was simply a cavalry captain who was readily allowed to be as independent as ever he liked. "Of course I don't envy Serpuhovskoy and never could envy him; but his advancement shows me that one has only to watch one's opportunity, and the career of a man like me may be very rapidly made. Three years ago he was in just the same position as I am. If I retire, I burn my ships. If I remain in the army, I lose nothing. She said herself she did not wish to change her position. And with her love I cannot feel envious of Serpuhovskoy." And slowly twirling his mustaches, he got up from the table and walked about the room. His eyes shone particularly brightly, and he felt in that confident, calm, and happy frame of mind which always came after he had thoroughly faced his position. Everything was straight and clear, just as after former days of reckoning. He shaved, took a cold bath, dressed and went out.

Chapter XXI

I'VE COME TO FETCH YOU. YOUR *LESSIVE* LASTED A GOOD TIME TODAY," SAID PETRITSKY. "WELL, is it over?"

"It is over," answered Vronsky, smiling with his eyes only, and twirling the tips of his mustaches as circumspectly as though after the perfect order into which his affairs had been brought any over-bold or rapid movement might disturb it.

"You're always just as if you'd come out of a bath after it," said Petritsky. "I've come from Gritsky's" (that was what they called the colonel); "they're expecting you."

Vronsky, without answering, looked at his comrade, thinking of something else.

"Yes; is that music at his place?" he said, listening to the familiar sounds of polkas and waltzes floating across to him. "What's the fête?"

"Serpuhovskoy's come."

"Aha!" said Vronsky, "why, I didn't know."

The smile in his eyes gleamed more brightly than ever.

Having once made up his mind that he was happy in his love, that he sacrificed his ambition to it—having anyway taken up this position, Vronsky was incapable of feeling either envious of Serpuhovskoy or hurt with him for not coming first to him when he came to the regiment. Serpuhovskoy was a good friend, and he was delighted he had come.

"Ah, I'm very glad!"

The colonel, Demin, had taken a large country house. The whole party were in the wide lower balcony. In the courtyard the first objects that met Vronsky's eyes were a band of singers in white linen coats, standing near a barrel of vodka, and the robust, good-humored figure of the colonel surrounded by officers. He had gone out as far as the first step of the balcony and was loudly shouting across the band that played Offenbach's quadrille, waving his arms and giving some orders to a few soldiers standing on one side. A group of soldiers, a quartermaster, and several subalterns came up to the balcony with Vronsky. The colonel returned to the table, went out again onto the steps with a tumbler in his hand, and proposed the toast, "To the health of our former comrade, the gallant general, Prince Serpuhovskoy. Hurrah!"

The colonel was followed by Serpuhovskoy, who came out onto the steps smiling, with a glass in his hand.

"You always get younger, Bondarenko," he said to the rosy-checked, smart-looking quartermaster standing just before him, still youngish-looking though doing his second term of service.

It was three years since Vronsky had seen Serpuhovskoy. He looked more robust, had let his whiskers grow, but was still the same graceful creature, whose face and figure were even more striking from their softness and nobility than their beauty. The only change Vronsky detected in him was that subdued, continual radiance of beaming content which settles on the faces of men who are successful and are sure of the recognition of their success by everyone. Vronsky knew that radiant air, and immediately observed it in Serpuhovskoy.

As Serpuhovskoy came down the steps he saw Vronsky. A smile of pleasure lit up his face. He tossed his head upwards and waved the glass in his hand, greeting Vronsky, and showing him by the gesture that he could not come to him before the quartermaster, who stood craning forward his lips ready to be kissed.

"Here he is!" shouted the colonel. "Yashvin told me you were in one of your gloomy tempers."

Serpuhovskoy kissed the moist, fresh lips of the gallant-looking quartermaster, and wiping his mouth with his handkerchief, went up to Vronsky.

"How glad I am!" he said, squeezing his hand and drawing him on one side.

"You look after him," the colonel shouted to Yashvin, pointing to Vronsky; and he went down below to the soldiers.

"Why weren't you at the races yesterday? I expected to see you there," said Vronsky, scrutinizing Serpuhovskoy.

"I did go, but late. I beg your pardon," he added, and he turned to the adjutant: "Please have this divided from me, each man as much as it runs to." And he hurriedly took notes for three hundred roubles from his pocketbook, blushing a little.

"Vronsky! Have anything to eat or drink?" asked Yashvin. "Hi, something for the count to eat! Ah, here it is: have a glass!"

The fête at the colonel's lasted a long while. There was a great deal of drinking. They tossed Serpuhovskoy in the air and caught him again several times. Then they did the same to the colonel. Then, to the accompaniment of the band, the colonel himself danced with Petritsky. Then the colonel, who began to show signs of feebleness, sat down on a bench in the courtyard and began demonstrating to Yashvin the superiority of Russia over Poland, especially in cavalry attack, and there was a lull in the revelry for a moment. Serpuhovskoy went into the house to the bathroom to wash his hands and found Vronsky there; Vronsky was drenching his head with water. He had taken off his coat and put his sunburned, hairy neck under the tap, and was rubbing it and his head with his hands. When he had finished, Vronsky sat down by Serpuhovskoy. They both sat down in the bathroom on a lounge, and a conversation began which was very interesting to both of them.

"I've always been hearing about you through my wife," said Serpuhovskoy. "I'm glad you've been seeing her pretty often."

"She's friendly with Varya, and they're the only women in Petersburg I care about seeing," answered Vronsky, smiling. He smiled because he foresaw the topic the conversation would turn on, and he was glad of it.

"The only ones?" Serpuhovskoy queried, smiling.

"Yes; and I heard news of you, but not only through your wife," said Vronsky, checking his hint by a stern expression of face. "I was greatly delighted to hear of your success, but not a bit surprised. I expected even more."

Serpuhovskoy smiled. Such an opinion of him was obviously agreeable to him, and he did not think it necessary to conceal it.

"Well, I on the contrary expected less—I'll own frankly. But I'm glad, very glad. I'm ambitious; that's my weakness, and I confess to it."

"Perhaps you wouldn't confess to it if you hadn't been successful," said Vronsky.

"I don't suppose so," said Serpuhovskoy, smiling again. "I won't say life wouldn't be worth living without it, but it would be dull. Of course I may be mistaken, but I fancy I have a certain capacity for the line I've chosen, and that power of any sort in my hands, if it is to be, will be better than in the hands of a good many people I know," said Serpuhovskoy, with beaming consciousness of success; "and so the nearer I get to it, the better pleased I am."

"Perhaps that is true for you, but not for everyone. I used to think so too, but here I live and think life worth living not only for that."

"There it's out! here it comes!" said Serpuhovskoy laughing. "Ever since I heard about you, about your refusal, I began . . . Of course, I approved of what you did. But there are ways of doing everything. And I think your action was good in itself, but you didn't do it quite in the way you ought to have done."

"What's done can't be undone, and you know I never go back on what I've done. And besides, I'm very well off."

"Very well off—for the time. But you're not satisfied with that. I wouldn't say this to your brother. He's a nice child, like our host here. There he goes!" he added, listening to the roar of "hurrah!"—"and he's happy, but that does not satisfy you."

"I didn't say it did satisfy me."

"Yes, but that's not the only thing. Such men as you are wanted."

"By whom?"

"By whom? By society, by Russia. Russia needs men; she needs a party, or else everything goes and will go to the dogs."

"How do you mean? Bertenev's party against the Russian communists?"

"No," said Serpuhovskoy, frowning with vexation at being suspected of such an absurdity. "*Tout ça est une blague.* That's always been and always will be. There are no communists. But intriguing people have to invent a noxious, dangerous party. It's an old trick. No, what's wanted is a powerful party of independent men like you and me."

"But why so?" Vronsky mentioned a few men who were in power. "Why aren't they independent men?"

"Simply because they have not, or have not had from birth, an independent fortune; they've not had a name, they've not been close to the sun and center as we have. They can be bought either by money or by favor. And they have to find a support for themselves in inventing a policy. And they bring forward some notion, some policy that they don't believe in, that does harm; and the whole policy is really only a means to a government house and so much income. *Cela n'est pas plus fin que ça,* when you get a peep at their cards. I may be inferior to them, stupider perhaps, though I don't see why I should be inferior to them. But you and I have one important advantage over them for certain, in being more difficult to buy. And such men are more needed than ever."

Vronsky listened attentively, but he was not so much interested by the meaning of the words as by the attitude of Serpuhovskoy who was already contemplating a struggle with the existing powers, and already had his likes and dislikes in that higher world, while his own interest in the governing world did not go beyond the interests of his regiment. Vronsky felt, too, how powerful Serpuhovskoy might become through his unmistakable faculty for thinking things out and for taking things in, through his intelligence and gift of words, so rarely met with in the world in which he moved. And, ashamed as he was of the feeling, he felt envious.

"Still I haven't the one thing of most importance for that," he answered; "I haven't the desire for power. I had it once, but it's gone."

"Excuse me, that's not true," said Serpuhovskoy smiling.

"Yes, it is true, it is true . . . now!" Vronsky added, to be truthful.

"Yes, it's true now, that's another thing; but that *now* won't last forever."

"Perhaps," answered Vronsky.

"You say *perhaps,*" Serpuhovskoy went on, as though guessing his thoughts, "but I say *for certain.* And that's what I wanted to see you for. Your action was just what it should have been. I see that, but you ought not to keep it up. I only ask you to give me *carte blanche.* I'm not going to offer you my protection . . . though, indeed, why shouldn't I protect you?—you've protected me often enough! I should hope our friendship rises above all that sort of thing. Yes," he said, smiling to him as tenderly as a woman, "give me *carte blanche,* retire from the regiment, and I'll draw you upwards imperceptibly."

"But you must understand that I want nothing," said Vronsky, "except that all should be as it is."

Serpuhovskoy got up and stood facing him.

"You say that all should be as it is. I understand what that means. But listen: we're the same age, you've known a greater number of women perhaps than I have." Serpohovskoy's smile and gestures told Vronsky that he mustn't be afraid, that he would be tender and careful in touching the sore place. "But I'm married, and believe me, in getting to know thoroughly one's wife, if one loves her, as someone has said, one gets to know all women better than if one knew thousands of them."

"We're coming directly!" Vronsky shouted to an officer, who looked into the room and called them to the colonel.

Vronsky was longing now to hear to the end and know what Serpuhovskey would say to him.

"And here's my opinion for you. Women are the chief stumbling block in a man's career. It's hard to love a woman and do anything. There's only one way of having love conveniently without its being a hindrance—that's marriage. How, how am I to tell you what I mean?" said Serpuhovskoy, who liked similes. "Wait a minute, wait a minute! Yes, just as you can only carry a *fardeau* and do something with your hands, when the fardeau is tied on your back, and that's marriage. And that's what I felt when I was married. My hands were suddenly set free. But to drag that *fardeau* about with you without marriage, your hands will always be so full that you can do nothing. Look at Mazankov, at Krupov. They've ruined their careers for the sake of women."

"What women!" said Vronsky, recalling the Frenchwoman and the actress with whom the two men he had mentioned were connected.

"The firmer the woman's footing in society, the worse it is. That's much the same as—not merely carrying the *fardeau* in your arms—but tearing it away from someone else."

"You have never loved," Vronsky said softly, looking straight before him and thinking of Anna.

"Perhaps. But you remember what I've said to you. And another thing, women are all more materialistic than men. We make something immense out of love, but they are always *terre-à-terre.*"

"Directly, directly!" he cried to a footman who came in. But the footman had not come to call them again, as he supposed. The footman brought Vronsky a note.

"A man brought it from Princess Tverskaya."

Vronsky opened the letter, and flushed crimson.

"My head's begun to ache; I'm going home," he said to Serpuhovskoy.

"Oh, good-bye then. You give me *carte blanche!*"

"We'll talk about it later on; I'll look you up in Petersburg."

Chapter XXII

IT WAS SIX O'CLOCK ALREADY, AND SO, IN ORDER TO BE THERE QUICKLY, AND AT THE SAME TIME not to drive with his own horses, known to everyone, Vronsky got into Yashvin's hired fly, and told the driver to drive as quickly as possible. It was a roomy, old-fashioned fly, with seats for four. He sat in one corner, stretched his legs out on the front seat, and sank into meditation.

A vague sense of the order into which his affairs had been brought, a vague recollection of the friendliness and flattery of Serpuhovskoy, who had considered him a man that was needed, and most of all, the anticipation of the interview before him—all blended into a general, joyous sense of life. This feeling was so strong that he could not help smiling. He dropped his legs, crossed one leg over the other knee, and taking it in his hand, felt the springy muscle of the calf, where it had been grazed the day before by his fall, and leaning back he drew several deep breaths.

"I'm happy, very happy!" he said to himself. He had often before had this sense of physical joy in his own body, but he had never felt so fond of himself, of his own body, as at that moment. He enjoyed the slight ache in his strong leg, he enjoyed the muscular sensation of movement in his chest as he breathed. The bright, cold August day, which had made Anna feel so hopeless, seemed to him keenly stimulating, and refreshed his face and neck that still tingled from the cold water. The scent of brilliantine on his whiskers struck him as particularly pleasant in the fresh air. Everything he saw from the carriage window, everything in that cold pure air, in the pale light of the sunset, was as fresh, and gay, and strong as he was himself: the roofs of the houses shining in the rays of the setting sun, the sharp outlines of fences and angles of buildings, the figures of passers-by, the carriages that met him now and then, the motionless green of the trees and grass, the fields with evenly drawn furrows of potatoes, and the slanting shadows that fell from the houses, and trees, and bushes, and even from the rows of potatoes—everything was bright like a pretty landscape just finished and freshly varnished.

"Get on, get on!" he said to the driver, putting his head out of the window, and pulling a three-ruble note out of his pocket he handed it to the man as he looked round. The driver's hand fumbled with something at the lamp, the whip cracked, and the carriage rolled rapidly along the smooth highroad.

"I want nothing, nothing but this happiness," he thought, staring at the bone button of the bell in the space between the windows, and picturing to himself Anna just as he had seen her last time. "And as I go on, I love her more and more. Here's the garden of the Vrede Villa. Whereabouts will she be? Where? How? Why did she fix on this place to meet me, and why does she write in Betsy's letter?" he thought, wondering now for the first time at it. But there was now no time for wonder. He called to the driver to stop before reaching the avenue, and opening the door, jumped out of the carriage as it was moving, and went into the avenue that led up to the house. There was no one in the avenue; but looking round to the right he caught sight of her. Her face was hidden by a veil, but he drank in with glad eyes the special movement in walking, peculiar to her alone, the slope of the shoulders, and the setting of the head, and at once a sort of electric shock ran all over him. With fresh force, he felt conscious of himself from the springy motions of his legs to the movements of his lungs as he breathed, and something set his lips twitching.

Joining him, she pressed his hand tightly.

"You're not angry that I sent for you? I absolutely had to see you," she said; and the serious and set line of her lips, which he saw under the veil, transformed his mood at once.

"I angry! But how have you come, where from?"

"Never mind," she said, laying her hand on his, "come along, I must talk to you."

He saw that something had happened, and that the interview would not be a joyous one. In her presence he had no will of his own: without knowing the grounds of her distress, he already felt the same distress unconsciously passing over him.

"What is it? what?" he asked her, squeezing her hand with his elbow, and trying to read her thoughts in her face.

She walked on a few steps in silence, gathering up her courage; then suddenly she stopped.

"I did not tell you yesterday," she began, breathing quickly and painfully, "that coming home with Alexey Alexandrovitch I told him everything . . . told him I could not be his wife, that . . . and told him everything."

He heard her, unconsciously bending his whole figure down to her as though hoping in this way to soften the hardness of her position for her. But directly she had said this he suddenly drew himself up, and a proud and hard expression came over his face.

"Yes, yes, that's better, a thousand times better! I know how painful it was," he said. But she was not listening to his words, she was reading his thoughts from the expression of his face. She could not guess that that expression arose from the first idea that presented itself to Vronsky—that a duel was now inevitable. The idea of a duel had never crossed her mind, and so she put a different interpretation on this passing expression of hardness.

When she got her husband's letter, she knew then at the bottom of her heart that everything would go on in the old way, that she would not have the strength of will to forego her position, to abandon her son, and to join her lover. The morning spent at Princess Tverskaya's had confirmed her still more in this. But this interview was still of the utmost gravity for her. She hoped that this interview would transform her position, and save her. If on hearing this news he were to say to her resolutely, passionately, without an instant's wavering: "Throw up everything and come with me!" she would give up her son and go away with him. But this news had not produced what she had expected in him; he simply seemed as though he were resenting some affront.

"It was not in the least painful to me. It happened of itself," she said irritably; "and see . . ." she pulled her husband's letter out of her glove.

"I understand, I understand," he interrupted her, taking the letter, but not reading it, and trying to soothe her. "The one thing I longed for, the one thing I prayed for, was to cut short this position, so as to devote my life to your happiness."

"Why do you tell me that?" she said. "Do you suppose I can doubt it? If I doubted . . ."

"Who's that coming?" said Vronsky suddenly, pointing to two ladies walking towards them. "Perhaps they know us!" and he hurriedly turned off, drawing her after him into a side path.

"Oh, I don't care!" she said. Her lips were quivering. And he fancied that her eyes looked with strange fury at him from under the veil. "I tell you that's not the point—I can't doubt that; but see what he writes to me. Read it." She stood still again.

Again, just as at the first moment of hearing of her rupture with her husband, Vronsky, on reading the letter, was unconsciously carried away by the natural sensation aroused in him by his own relation to the betrayed husband. Now while he held his letter in his hands, he could not help picturing the challenge, which he would most likely find at home today or tomorrow, and the duel itself, in which, with the same cold and haughty expression that his face was assuming at this moment he would await the injured husband's shot, after having himself fired into the air. And at that instant there flashed across his mind the thought of what Serpuhovskoy had just said to him, and what he had himself been thinking in the morning—that it was better not to bind himself—and he knew that this thought he could not tell her.

Having read the letter, he raised his eyes to her, and there was no determination in them. She saw at once that he had been thinking about it before by himself. She knew that whatever he might say to her, he would not say all he thought. And she knew that her last hope had failed her. This was not what she had been reckoning on.

"You see the sort of man he is," she said, with a shaking voice; "he . . ."

"Forgive me, but I rejoice at it," Vronsky interrupted. "For God's sake, let me finish!" he added, his eyes imploring her to give him time to explain his words. "I rejoice, because things cannot, cannot possibly remain as he supposes."

"Why can't they?" Anna said, restraining her tears, and obviously attaching no sort of consequence to what he said. She felt that her fate was sealed.

Vronsky meant that after the duel—inevitable, he thought—things could not go on as before, but he said something different.

"It can't go on. I hope that now you will leave him. I hope"—he was confused, and reddened—"that you will let me arrange and plan our life. Tomorrow . . ." he was beginning.

She did not let him go on.

"But my child!" she shrieked. "You see what he writes! I should have to leave him, and I can't and won't do that."

"But, for God's sake, which is better?—leave your child, or keep up this degrading position?"

"To whom is it degrading?"

"To all, and most of all to you."

"You say degrading . . . don't say that. Those words have no meaning for me," she said in a shaking voice. She did not want him now to say what was untrue. She had nothing left her but his love, and she wanted to love him. "Don't you understand that from the day I loved you everything has changed for me? For me there is one thing, and one thing only—your love. If that's mine, I feel so exalted, so strong, that nothing can be humiliating to me. I am proud of my position, because . . . proud of being . . . proud. . . ." She could not say what she was proud of. Tears of shame and despair choked her utterance. She stood still and sobbed.

He felt, too, something swelling in his throat and twitching in his nose, and for the first time in his life he felt on the point of weeping. He could not have said exactly what it was touched him so. He felt sorry for her, and he felt he could not help her, and with that he knew that he was to blame for her wretchedness, and that he had done something wrong.

"Is not a divorce possible?" he said feebly. She shook her head, not answering. "Couldn't you take your son, and still leave him?"

"Yes; but it all depends on him. Now I must go to him," she said shortly. Her presentiment that all would again go on in the old way had not deceived her.

"On Tuesday I shall be in Petersburg, and everything can be settled."

"Yes," she said. "But don't let us talk anymore of it."

Anna's carriage, which she had sent away, and ordered to come back to the little gate of the Vrede garden, drove up. Anna said good-bye to Vronsky, and drove home.

Chapter XXIII

ON MONDAY THERE WAS THE USUAL SITTING OF THE COMMISSION OF THE 2ND OF JUNE. ALEXEY Alexandrovitch walked into the hall where the sitting was held, greeted the members and the president, as usual, and sat down in his place, putting his hand on the papers laid ready before him. Among these papers lay the necessary evidence and a rough outline of the speech he intended to make. But he did not really need these documents. He remembered every point, and did not think it necessary to go over in his memory what he would say. He knew that when the time came, and when he saw his enemy facing him, and studiously endeavoring to assume an expression of indifference, his speech would flow of itself better than he could prepare it now. He felt that the import of his speech was of such magnitude that every word of it would have weight. Meantime, as he listened to the usual report, he had the most innocent and inoffensive air. No one, looking at his white hands, with their swollen veins and long fingers, so softly stroking the edges of the white paper that lay before him, and at the air of weariness with which his head drooped on one side, would have suspected that in a few minutes a torrent of words would flow from his lips that would arouse a fearful storm, set the members shouting and attacking one another, and force the president to call for order. When the report was over, Alexey Alexandrovitch announced in his subdued, delicate voice that he had several points to bring before the meeting in regard to the Commission for the Reorganization of the Native Tribes. All attention was turned upon him. Alexey Alexandrovitch cleared his throat, and not looking at his opponent, but selecting, as he always did while he was delivering his speeches, the first person sitting opposite him, an inoffensive little old man, who never had an opinion of any sort in the Commission, began to expound his views. When he reached the point about the fundamental and radical law, his opponent jumped up and began to protest. Stremov, who was also a member of the Commission, and also stung to the quick, began defending himself, and altogether a stormy sitting followed; but Alexey Alexandrovitch triumphed, and his motion was carried, three new commissions were appointed, and the next day in a certain Petersburg circle nothing else was talked of but this sitting. Alexey Alexandrovitch's success had been even greater than he had anticipated.

Next morning, Tuesday, Alexey Alexandrovitch, on waking up, recollected with pleasure his triumph of the previous day, and he could not help smiling, though he tried to appear indifferent, when the chief secretary of his department, anxious to flatter him, informed him of the rumors that had reached him concerning what had happened in the Commission.

Absorbed in business with the chief secretary, Alexey Alexandrovitch had completely forgotten that it was Tuesday, the day fixed by him for the return of Anna Arkadyevna, and he was surprised and received a shock of annoyance when a servant came in to inform him of her arrival.

Anna had arrived in Petersburg early in the morning; the carriage had been sent to meet her in accordance with her telegram, and so Alexey Alexandrovitch might have known of her arrival. But when she arrived, he did not meet her. She was told that he had not yet gone out, but was busy with his secretary. She sent word to her husband that she had come, went to her own room, and occupied herself in sorting out her things, expecting he would come to her. But an hour passed; he did not come. She went into the dining room on the pretext of giving some directions, and spoke loudly on purpose, expecting him to come out there; but he did not come, though she heard him go to the door of his study as he parted from the chief secretary. She knew that he usually went out quickly to his office, and she wanted to see him before that, so that their attitude to one another might be defined.

She walked across the drawing room and went resolutely to him. When she went into his study he was in official uniform, obviously ready to go out, sitting at a little table on which he rested his elbows, looking dejectedly before him. She saw him before he saw her, and she saw that he was thinking of her.

On seeing her, he would have risen, but changed his mind, then his face flushed hotly—a thing Anna had never seen before, and he got up quickly and went to meet her, looking not at her eyes, but above them at her forehead and hair. He went up to her, took her by the hand, and asked her to sit down.

"I am very glad you have come," he said, sitting down beside her, and obviously wishing to say something, he stuttered. Several times he tried to begin to speak, but stopped. In spite of the fact that, preparing herself for meeting him, she had schooled herself to despise and reproach him, she did not know what to say to him, and she felt sorry for him. And so the silence lasted for some time. "Is Seryozha quite well?" he said, and not waiting for an answer, he added: "I shan't be dining at home today, and I have got to go out directly."

"I had thought of going to Moscow," she said.

"No, you did quite, quite right to come," he said, and was silent again.

Seeing that he was powerless to begin the conversation, she began herself.

"Alexey Alexandrovitch," she said, looking at him and not dropping her eyes under his persistent gaze at her hair, "I'm a guilty woman, I'm a bad woman, but I am the same as I was, as I told you then, and I have come to tell you that I can change nothing."

"I have asked you no question about that," he said, all at once, resolutely and with hatred looking her straight in the face; "that was as I had supposed." Under the influence of anger he apparently regained complete possession of all his faculties. "But as I told you then, and have written to you," he said in a thin, shrill voice, "I repeat now, that I am not bound to know this. I ignore it. Not all wives are so kind as you, to be in such a hurry to communicate such agreeable news to their husbands." He laid special emphasis on the word "agreeable." "I shall ignore it so long as the world knows nothing of it, so long as my name is not disgraced. And so I simply inform you that our relations must be just as they have always been, and that only in the event of your compromising me I shall be obliged to take steps to secure my honor."

"But our relations cannot be the same as always," Anna began in a timid voice, looking at him with dismay.

When she saw once more those composed gestures, heard that shrill, childish, and sarcastic voice, her aversion for him extinguished her pity for him, and she felt only afraid, but at all costs she wanted to make clear her position.

"I cannot be your wife while I . . ." she began.

He laughed a cold and malignant laugh.

"The manner of life you have chosen is reflected, I suppose, in your ideas. I have too much respect or contempt, or both . . . I respect your past and despise your present . . . that I was far from the interpretation you put on my words."

Anna sighed and bowed her head.

"Though indeed I fail to comprehend how, with the independence you show," he went on, getting hot, "—announcing your infidelity to your husband and seeing nothing reprehensible in it, apparently—you can see anything reprehensible in performing a wife's duties in relation to your husband."

"Alexey Alexandrovitch! What is it you want of me?"

"I want you not to meet that man here, and to conduct yourself so that neither the world nor the servants can reproach you . . . not to see him. That's not much, I think. And in return you will enjoy all the privileges of a faithful wife without fulfilling her duties. That's all I have to say to you. Now it's time for me to go. I'm not dining at home." He got up and moved towards the door.

Anna got up too. Bowing in silence, he let her pass before him.

Chapter XXIV

THE NIGHT SPENT BY LEVIN ON THE HAYCOCK DID NOT PASS WITHOUT RESULT FOR HIM. THE WAY in which he had been managing his land revolted him and had lost all attraction for him. In spite of the magnificent harvest, never had there been, or, at least, never it seemed to him, had there been so many hindrances and so many quarrels between him and the peasants as that year, and the origin of these failures and this hostility was now perfectly comprehensible to him. The delight he had experienced in the work itself, and the consequent greater intimacy with the peasants, the envy he felt of them, of their life, the desire to adopt that life, which had been to him that night not a dream but an intention, the execution of which he had thought out in detail—all this had so transformed his view of the farming of the land as he had managed it, that he could not take his former interest in it, and could not help seeing that unpleasant relation between him and the workpeople which was the foundation of it all. The herd of improved cows such as Pava, the whole land ploughed over and enriched, the nine level fields surrounded with hedges, the two hundred and forty acres heavily manured, the seed sown in drills, and all the rest of it—it was all splendid if only the work had been done for themselves, or for themselves and comrades—people in sympathy with them. But he saw clearly now (his work on a book of agriculture, in which the chief element in husbandry was to have been the laborer, greatly assisted him in this) that the sort of farming he was carrying on was nothing but a cruel and stubborn struggle between him and the laborers, in which there was on one side—his side—a continual intense effort to change everything to a pattern he considered better; on the other side, the natural order of things. And in this struggle he saw that with immense expenditure of force on his side, and with no effort or even intention on the other side, all that was attained was that the work did not go to the liking of either side, and that splendid tools, splendid cattle and land were spoiled with no good to anyone. Worst of all, the energy expended on this work was not simply wasted. He could not help feeling now, since the meaning of this system had become clear to him, that the aim of his energy was a most unworthy one. In reality, what was the struggle about? He was struggling for every farthing of his share (and he could not help it, for he had only to relax his efforts, and he would not have had the money to pay his laborers' wages), while they were only struggling to be able to do their work easily and agreeably, that is to say, as they were used to doing it. It was for his interests that every laborer should work as hard as possible, and that while doing so he should keep his wits about him, so as to try not to break the winnowing machines, the horse rakes, the threshing machines, that he should attend to what he was doing. What the laborer wanted was to work as pleasantly as possible, with rests, and above all, carelessly and heedlessly, without thinking. That summer Levin saw this at every step. He sent the men to mow some clover for hay, picking out the worst patches where the clover was overgrown with grass and weeds and of no use for seed; again and again they mowed the best acres of clover, justifying themselves by the pretense that the bailiff had told them to, and trying to pacify him with the assurance that it would be splendid hay; but he knew that it was owing to those acres being so much easier to mow. He sent out a hay machine for pitching the hay—it was broken at the first row because it was dull work for a peasant to sit on the seat in front with the great wings waving above him. And he was told, "Don't trouble, your honor, sure, the womenfolks will pitch it quick enough." The ploughs were practically useless, because it never occurred to the laborer to raise the share when he turned the plough, and forcing it round, he strained the horses and tore up the ground, and Levin was begged not to mind about it. The horses were allowed to stray into the wheat because not a single laborer would consent to be night-watchman, and in spite of orders to the contrary, the laborers insisted on taking turns for night duty, and Ivan, after working all day long, fell asleep, and was very penitent for his fault, saying, "Do what you will to me, your honor."

They killed three of the best calves by letting them into the clover aftermath without care as to their drinking, and nothing would make the men believe that they had been blown out by the clover, but they told him, by way of consolation, that one of his neighbors had lost a hundred and twelve head of cattle in three days. All this happened, not because anyone felt ill-will to Levin or his farm; on the contrary, he knew that they liked him, thought him a simple gentleman (their highest praise); but it happened simply because all they wanted was to work merrily and carelessly, and his interests were not only remote and incomprehensible to them, but fatally opposed to their most just claims. Long before, Levin had felt dissatisfaction with his own position in regard to the land. He saw where his boat leaked, but he did not look for the leak, perhaps purposely deceiving himself. (Nothing would be left him if he lost faith in it.) But now he could deceive himself no longer. The farming of the land, as he was managing it, had become not merely unattractive but revolting to him, and he could take no further interest in it.

To this now was joined the presence, only twenty-five miles off, of Kitty Shtcherbatskaya, whom he longed to see and could not see. Darya Alexandrovna Oblonskaya had invited him, when he was over there, to come; to come with the object of renewing his offer to her sister, who would, so she gave him to understand, accept him now. Levin himself had felt on seeing Kitty Shtcherbatskaya that he had never ceased to love her; but he could not go over to the Oblonskys', knowing she was there. The fact that he had made her an offer, and she had refused him, had placed an insuperable barrier between her and him. "I can't ask her to be my wife merely because she can't be the wife of the man she wanted to marry," he said to himself. The thought of this made him cold and hostile to her. "I should not be able to speak to her without a feeling of reproach; I could not look at her without resentment; and she will only hate me all the more, as she's bound to. And besides, how can I now, after what Darya Alexandrovna told me, go to see them? Can I help showing that I know what she told me? And me to go magnanimously to forgive her, and have pity on her! Me go through a performance before her of forgiving, and deigning to bestow my love on her! . . . What induced Darya Alexandrovna to tell me that? By chance I might have seen her, then everything would have happened of itself; but, as it is, it's out of the question, out of the question!"

Darya Alexandrovna sent him a letter, asking him for a side-saddle for Kitty's use. "I'm told you have a side-saddle," she wrote to him; "I hope you will bring it over yourself."

This was more than he could stand. How could a woman of any intelligence, of any delicacy, put her sister in such a humiliating position! He wrote ten notes, and tore them all up, and sent the saddle without any reply. To write that he would go was impossible, because he could not go; to write that he could not come because something prevented him, or that he would be away, that was still worse. He sent the saddle without an answer, and with a sense of having done something shameful; he handed over all the now revolting business of the estate to the bailiff, and set off next day to a remote district to see his friend Sviazhsky, who had splendid marshes for grouse in his neighborhood, and had lately written to ask him to keep a long-standing promise to stay with him. The grouse-marsh, in the Surovsky district, had long tempted Levin, but he had continually put off this visit on account of his work on the estate. Now he was glad to get away from the neighborhood of the Shtcherbatskys, and still more from his farm-work, especially on a shooting expedition, which always in trouble served as the best consolation.

Chapter XXV

In the Surovsky district there was no railway nor service of post-horses, and Levin drove there with his own horses in his big, old-fashioned carriage.

He stopped halfway at a well-to-do peasant's to feed his horses. A bald, well-preserved old man, with a broad, red beard, gray on his cheeks, opened the gate, squeezing against the gatepost to let the three horses pass. Directing the coachman to a place under the shed in the big, clean, tidy yard, with charred, old-fashioned ploughs in it, the old man asked Levin to come into the parlor. A cleanly dressed young woman, with clogs on her bare feet, was scrubbing the floor in the new outer room. She was frightened of the dog, that ran in after Levin, and uttered a shriek, but began laughing at her own fright at once when she was told the dog would not hurt her. Pointing Levin with her bare arm to the door into the parlor, she bent down again, hiding her handsome face, and went on scrubbing.

"Would you like the samovar?" she asked.

"Yes, please."

The parlor was a big room, with a Dutch stove, and a screen dividing it into two. Under the holy pictures stood a table painted in patterns, a bench, and two chairs. Near the entrance was a dresser full of crockery. The shutters were closed, there were few flies, and it was so clean that Levin was anxious that Laska, who had been running along the road and bathing in puddles, should not muddy the floor, and ordered her to a place in the corner by the door. After looking round the parlor, Levin went out in the backyard. The good-looking young woman in clogs, swinging the empty pails on the yoke, ran on before him to the well for water.

"Look sharp, my girl!" the old man shouted after her, good-humoredly, and he went up to Levin. "Well, sir, are you going to Nikolay Ivanovitch Sviazhsky? His honor comes to us too," he began, chatting, leaning his elbows on the railing of the steps. In the middle of the old man's account of his acquaintance with Sviazhsky, the gates creaked again, and laborers came into the yard from the fields, with wooden ploughs and harrows. The horses harnessed to the ploughs and harrows were sleek and fat. The laborers were obviously of the household: two were young men in cotton shirts and caps, the two others were hired laborers in homespun shirts, one an old man, the other a young fellow. Moving off from the steps, the old man went up to the horses and began unharnessing them.

"What have they been ploughing?" asked Levin.

"Ploughing up the potatoes. We rent a bit of land too. Fedot, don't let out the gelding, but take it to the trough, and we'll put the other in harness."

"Oh, father, the ploughshares I ordered, has he brought them along?" asked the big, healthy-looking fellow, obviously the old man's son.

"There . . . in the outer room," answered the old man, bundling together the harness he had taken off, and flinging it on the ground. "You can put them on, while they have dinner."

The good-looking young woman came into the outer room with the full pails dragging at her shoulders. More women came on the scene from somewhere, young and handsome, middle-aged, old and ugly, with children and without children.

The samovar was beginning to sing; the laborers and the family, having disposed of the horses, came in to dinner. Levin, getting his provisions out of his carriage, invited the old man to take tea with him.

"Well, I have had some today already," said the old man, obviously accepting the invitation with pleasure. "But just a glass for company."

Over their tea Levin heard all about the old man's farming. Ten years before, the old man had rented three hundred acres from the lady who owned them, and a year ago he had bought them and rented another three hundred from a neighboring landowner. A small part of the land—the worst part—he let out for rent, while a hundred acres of arable land he cultivated himself with his family and two hired laborers. The old man complained that things were doing badly. But Levin saw that he simply did so from a feeling of propriety, and that his farm was in a flourishing condition. If it had been unsuccessful he would not have bought land at thirty-five roubles the acre, he would not have married his three sons and a nephew, he would not have rebuilt twice after fires, and each time on a larger scale. In spite of the old man's complaints, it was evident that he was proud, and justly proud, of his prosperity, proud of his sons, his nephew, his sons' wives, his horses and his cows, and especially of the fact that he was keeping all this farming going. From his conversation with the old man, Levin thought he was not averse to new methods either. He had planted a great many potatoes, and his potatoes, as Levin had seen driving past, were already past flowering and beginning to die down, while Levin's were only just coming into flower. He earthed up his potatoes with a modern plough borrowed from a neighboring landowner. He sowed wheat. The trifling fact that, thinning out his rye, the old man used the rye he thinned out for his horses, specially struck Levin. How many times had Levin seen this splendid fodder wasted, and tried to get it saved; but always it had turned out to be impossible. The peasant got this done, and he could not say enough in praise of it as food for the beasts.

"What have the wenches to do? They carry it out in bundles to the roadside, and the cart brings it away."

"Well, we landowners can't manage well with our laborers," said Levin, handing him a glass of tea.

"Thank you," said the old man, and he took the glass, but refused sugar, pointing to a lump he had left. "They're simple destruction," said he. "Look at Sviazhsky's, for instance. We know what the land's like—first rate, yet there's not much of a crop to boast of. It's not looked after enough—that's all it is!"

"But you work your land with hired laborers?"

"We're all peasants together. We go into everything ourselves. If a man's no use, he can go, and we can manage by ourselves."

"Father, Finogen wants some tar," said the young woman in the clogs, coming in.

"Yes, yes, that's how it is, sir!" said the old man, getting up, and crossing himself deliberately, he thanked Levin and went out.

When Levin went into the kitchen to call his coachman he saw the whole family at dinner. The women were standing up waiting on them. The young, sturdy-looking son was telling something funny with his mouth full of pudding, and they were all laughing, the woman in the clogs, who was pouring cabbage soup into a bowl, laughing most merrily of all.

Very probably the good-looking face of the young woman in the clogs had a good deal to do with the impression of well-being this peasant household made upon Levin, but the impression was so strong that Levin could never get rid of it. And all the way from the old peasant's to Sviazhsky's he kept recalling this peasant farm as though there were something in this impression that demanded his special attention.

Chapter XXVI

SVIAZHSKY WAS THE MARSHAL OF HIS DISTRICT. HE WAS FIVE YEARS OLDER THAN LEVIN, AND HAD long been married. His sister-in-law, a young girl Levin liked very much, lived in his house; and Levin knew that Sviazhsky and his wife would have greatly liked to marry the girl to him. He knew this with certainty, as so-called eligible young men always know it, though he could never have brought himself to speak of it to anyone; and he knew too that, although he wanted to get married, and although by every token this very attractive girl would make an excellent wife, he could no more have married her, even if he had not been in love with Kitty Shtcherbatskaya, than he could have flown up to the sky. And this knowledge poisoned the pleasure he had hoped to find in the visit to Sviazhsky.

On getting Sviazhsky's letter with the invitation for shooting, Levin had immediately thought of this; but in spite of it he had made up his mind that Sviazhsky's having such views for him was simply his own groundless supposition, and so he would go, all the same. Besides, at the bottom of his heart he had a desire to try himself, put himself to the test in regard to this girl. The Sviazhskys' home life was exceedingly pleasant, and Sviazhsky himself, the best type of man taking part in local affairs that Levin knew, was very interesting to him.

Sviazhsky was one of those people, always a source of wonder to Levin, whose convictions, very logical though never original, go one way by themselves, while their life, exceedingly definite and firm in its direction, goes its way quite apart and almost always in direct contradiction to their convictions. Sviazhsky was an extremely advanced man. He despised the nobility, and believed the mass of the nobility to be secretly in favor of serfdom, and only concealing their views from cowardice. He regarded Russia as a ruined country, rather after the style of Turkey, and the government of Russia as so bad that he never permitted himself to criticize its doings seriously, and yet he was a functionary of that government and a model marshal of nobility, and when he drove about he always wore the cockade of office and the cap with the red band. He considered human life only tolerable abroad, and went abroad to stay at every opportunity, and at the same time he carried on a complex and improved system of agriculture in Russia, and with extreme interest followed everything and knew everything that was being done in Russia. He considered the Russian peasant as occupying a stage of development intermediate between the ape and the man, and at the same time in the local assemblies no one was readier to shake hands with the peasants and listen to their opinion. He believed neither in God nor the devil, but was much concerned about the question of the improvement of the clergy and the maintenance of their revenues, and took special trouble to keep up the church in his village.

On the woman question he was on the side of the extreme advocates of complete liberty for women, and especially their right to labor. But he lived with his wife on such terms that their affectionate childless home life was the admiration of everyone, and arranged his wife's life so that she did nothing and could do nothing but share her husband's efforts that her time should pass as happily and as agreeably as possible.

If it had not been a characteristic of Levin's to put the most favorable interpretation on people, Sviazhsky's character would have presented no doubt or difficulty to him: he would have said to himself, "a fool or a knave," and everything would have seemed clear. But he could not say "a fool," because Sviazhsky was unmistakably clever, and moreover, a highly cultivated man, who was exceptionally modest over his culture. There was not a subject he knew nothing of. But he did not display his knowledge except when he was compelled to do so. Still less could Levin say that he was a knave, as Sviazhsky was unmistakably an honest, good-hearted, sensible man, who worked good-humoredly, keenly, and perseveringly at his work; he was held in high honor by everyone about him, and certainly he had never consciously done, and was indeed incapable of doing, anything base.

Levin tried to understand him, and could not understand him, and looked at him and his life as at a living enigma.

Levin and he were very friendly, and so Levin used to venture to sound Sviazhsky, to try to get at the very foundation of his view of life; but it was always in vain. Every time Levin tried to penetrate beyond the outer chambers of Sviazhsky's mind, which were hospitably open to all, he noticed that Sviazhsky was slightly disconcerted; faint signs of alarm were visible in his eyes, as though he were afraid Levin would understand him, and he would give him a kindly, good-humored repulse.

Just now, since his disenchantment with farming, Levin was particularly glad to stay with Sviazhsky. Apart from the fact that the sight of this happy and affectionate couple, so pleased with themselves and everyone else, and their well-ordered home had always a cheering effect on Levin, he felt a longing, now that he was so dissatisfied with his own life, to get at that secret in Sviazhsky that gave him such clearness, definiteness, and good courage in life. Moreover, Levin knew that at Sviazhsky's he should meet the landowners of the neighborhood, and it was particularly interesting for him just now to hear and take part in those rural conversations concerning crops, laborers' wages, and so on, which, he was aware, are conventionally regarded as something very low, but which seemed to him just now to constitute the one subject of importance. "It was not, perhaps, of importance in the days of serfdom, and it may not be of importance in England. In both cases the conditions of agriculture are firmly established; but among us now, when everything has been turned upside down and is only just taking shape, the question what form these conditions will take is the one question of importance in Russia," thought Levin.

The shooting turned out to be worse than Levin had expected. The marsh was dry and there were no grouse at all. He walked about the whole day and only brought back three birds, but to make up for that—he brought back, as he always did from shooting, an excellent appetite, excellent spirits, and that keen, intellectual mood which with him always accompanied violent physical exertion. And while out shooting, when he seemed to be thinking of nothing at all, suddenly the old man and his family kept coming back to his mind, and the impression of them seemed to claim not merely his attention, but the solution of some question connected with them.

In the evening at tea, two landowners who had come about some business connected with a wardship were of the party, and the interesting conversation Levin had been looking forward to sprang up.

Levin was sitting beside his hostess at the tea-table, and was obliged to keep up a conversation with her and her sister, who was sitting opposite him. Madame Sviazhskaya was a round-faced, fair-haired, rather short woman, all smiles and dimples. Levin tried through her to get a solution of the weighty enigma her husband presented to his mind; but he had not complete freedom of ideas, because he was in an agony of embarrassment. This agony of embarrassment was due to the fact that the sister-in-law was sitting opposite to him, in a dress, specially put on, as he fancied, for his benefit, cut particularly open, in the shape of a trapeze, on her white bosom. This quadrangular opening, in spite of the bosom's being very white, or just because it was very white, deprived Levin of the full use of his faculties. He imagined, probably mistakenly, that this low-necked bodice had been made on his account, and felt that he had no right to look at it, and tried not to look at it; but he felt that he was to blame for the very fact of the low-necked bodice having been made. It seemed to Levin that he had deceived someone, that he ought to explain something, but that to explain it was impossible, and for that reason he was continually blushing, was ill at ease and awkward. His awkwardness infected the pretty sister-in-law too. But their hostess appeared not to observe this, and kept purposely drawing her into the conversation.

"You say," she said, pursuing the subject that had been started, "that my husband cannot be interested in what's Russian. It's quite the contrary; he is always in cheerful spirits abroad, but not as he is here. Here, he feels in his proper place. He has so much to do, and he has the faculty of interesting himself in everything. Oh, you've not been to see our school, have you?"

"I've seen it. . . . The little house covered with ivy, isn't it?"

"Yes; that's Nastia's work," she said, indicating her sister.

"You teach in it yourself?" asked Levin, trying to look above the open neck, but feeling that wherever he looked in that direction he should see it.

"Yes; I used to teach in it myself, and do teach still, but we have a first rate schoolmistress now. And we've started gymnastic exercises."

"No, thank you, I won't have anymore tea," said Levin, and conscious of doing a rude thing, but incapable of continuing the conversation, he got up, blushing. "I hear a very interesting conversation," he added, and walked to the other end of the table, where Sviazhsky was sitting with the two gentlemen of the neighborhood. Sviazhsky was sitting sideways, with one elbow on the table, and a cup in one hand, while with the other hand he gathered up his beard, held it to his nose and let it drop again, as though he were smelling it. His brilliant black eyes were looking straight at the excited country gentleman with gray whiskers, and apparently he derived amusement from his remarks. The gentleman was complaining of the peasants. It was evident to Levin that Sviazhsky knew an answer to this gentleman's complaints, which would at once demolish his whole contention, but that in his position he could not give utterance to this answer, and listened, not without pleasure, to the landowner's comic speeches.

The gentleman with the gray whiskers was obviously an inveterate adherent of serfdom and a devoted agriculturist, who had lived all his life in the country. Levin saw proofs of this in his dress, in the old-fashioned threadbare coat, obviously not his everyday attire, in his shrewd, deep-set eyes, in his idiomatic, fluent Russian, in the imperious tone that had become habitual from long use, and in the resolute gestures of his large, red, sunburned hands, with an old betrothal ring on the little finger.

Chapter XXVII

"IF I'D ONLY THE HEART TO THROW UP WHAT'S BEEN SET GOING . . . SUCH A LOT OF TROUBLE wasted . . . I'd turn my back on the whole business, sell up, go off like Nikolay Ivanovitch . . . to hear *La Belle Hélène*," said the landowner, a pleasant smile lighting up his shrewd old face.

"But you see you don't throw it up," said Nikolay Ivanovitch Sviazhsky; "so there must be something gained."

"The only gain is that I live in my own house, neither bought nor hired. Besides, one keeps hoping the people will learn sense. Though, instead of that, you'd never believe it—the drunkenness, the immorality! They keep chopping and changing their bits of land. Not a sight of a horse or a cow. The peasant's dying of hunger, but just go and take him on as a laborer, he'll do his best to do you a mischief, and then bring you up before the justice of the peace."

"But then you make complaints to the justice too," said Sviazhsky.

"I lodge complaints? Not for anything in the world! Such a talking, and such a to-do, that one would have cause to regret it. At the works, for instance, they pocketed the advance-money and made off. What did the justice do? Why, acquitted them. Nothing keeps them in order but their own communal court and their village elder. He'll flog them in the good old style! But for that there'd be nothing for it but to give it all up and run away."

Obviously the landowner was chaffing Sviazhsky, who, far from resenting it, was apparently amused by it.

"But you see we manage our land without such extreme measures," said he, smiling: "Levin and I and this gentleman."

He indicated the other landowner.

"Yes, the thing's done at Mihail Petrovitch's, but ask him how it's done. Do you call that a rational system?" said the landowner, obviously rather proud of the word "rational."

"My system's very simple," said Mihail Petrovitch, "thank God. All my management rests on getting the money ready for the autumn taxes, and the peasants come to me, 'Father, master, help us!' Well, the peasants are all one's neighbors; one feels for them. So one advances them a third, but one says: 'Remember, lads, I have helped you, and you must help me when I need it—whether it's the sowing of the oats, or the haycutting, or the harvest'; and well, one agrees, so much for each taxpayer—though there are dishonest ones among them too, it's true."

Levin, who had long been familiar with these patriarchal methods, exchanged glances with Sviazhsky and interrupted Mihail Petrovitch, turning again to the gentleman with the gray whiskers.

"Then what do you think?" he asked; "what system is one to adopt nowadays?"

"Why, manage like Mihail Petrovitch, or let the land for half the crop or for rent to the peasants; that one can do—only that's just how the general prosperity of the country is being ruined. Where the land with serf-labor and good management gave a yield of nine to one, on the half-crop system it yields three to one. Russia has been ruined by the emancipation!"

Sviazhsky looked with smiling eyes at Levin, and even made a faint gesture of irony to him; but Levin did not think the landowner's words absurd, he understood them better than he did Sviazhsky. A great deal more of what the gentleman with the gray whiskers said to show in what way Russia was ruined by the emancipation struck him indeed as very true, new to him, and quite incontestable. The landowner unmistakably spoke his own individual thought—a thing that very rarely happens—and a thought to which he had been brought not by a desire of finding some exercise for an idle brain, but a thought which had grown up out of the conditions of his life, which he had brooded over in the solitude of his village, and had considered in every aspect.

"The point is, don't you see, that progress of every sort is only made by use of authority," he said, evidently wishing to show he was not without culture. "Take the reforms of Peter, of Catherine, of Alexander. Take European history. And progress in agriculture more than anything else—the potato, for instance, that was introduced among us by force. The wooden plough too wasn't always used. It was introduced maybe in the days before the Empire, but it was probably brought in by force. Now, in our own day, we landowners in the serf times used various improvements in our husbandry: drying machines and threshing machines, and carting manure and all the modern implements—all that we brought into use by our authority, and the peasants opposed it at first, and ended by imitating us. Now, by the abolition of serfdom we have been deprived of our authority; and so our husbandry, where it had been raised to a high level, is bound to sink to the most savage primitive condition. That's how I see it."

"But why so? If it's rational, you'll be able to keep up the same system with hired labor," said Sviazhsky.

"We've no power over them. With whom am I going to work the system, allow me to ask?"

"There it is—the labor force—the chief element in agriculture," thought Levin.

"With laborers."

"The laborers won't work well, and won't work with good implements. Our laborer can do nothing but get drunk like a pig, and when he's drunk he ruins everything you give him. He makes the horses ill with too much water, cuts good harness, barters the tires of the wheels for drink, drops bits of iron into the threshing machine, so as to break it. He loathes the sight of anything that's not after his fashion. And that's how it is the whole level of husbandry has fallen. Lands gone out of cultivation, overgrown with weeds, or divided among the peasants, and where millions of bushels were raised you get a hundred thousand; the wealth of the country has decreased. If the same thing had been done, but with care that . . ."

And he proceeded to unfold his own scheme of emancipation by means of which these drawbacks might have been avoided.

This did not interest Levin, but when he had finished, Levin went back to his first position, and, addressing Sviazhsky, and trying to draw him into expressing his serious opinion—

"That the standard of culture is falling, and that with our present relations to the peasants there is no possibility of farming on a rational system to yield a profit—that's perfectly true," said he.

"I don't believe it," Sviazhsky replied quite seriously; "all I see is that we don't know how to cultivate the land, and that our system of agriculture in the serf days was by no means too high, but too low. We have no machines, no good stock, no efficient supervision; we don't even know how to keep accounts. Ask any landowner; he won't be able to tell you what crop's profitable, and what's not."

"Italian bookkeeping," said the gentleman of the gray whiskers ironically. "You may keep your books as you like, but if they spoil everything for you, there won't be any profit."

"Why do they spoil things? A poor threshing machine, or your Russian presser, they will break, but my steam press they don't break. A wretched Russian nag they'll ruin, but keep good dray-horses or cart-horses—they won't ruin them. And so it is all round. We must raise our farming to a higher level."

"Oh, if one only had the means to do it, Nikolay Ivanovitch! It's all very well for you; but for me, with a son to keep at the university, lads to be educated at the high school—how am I going to buy these dray-horses?"

"Well, that's what the land banks are for."

"To get what's left me sold by auction? No, thank you."

"I don't agree that it's necessary or possible to raise the level of agriculture still higher," said Levin. "I devote myself to it, and I have means, but I can do nothing. As to the banks, I don't know to whom they're any good. For my part, anyway, whatever I've spent money on in the way of husbandry, it has been a loss: stock—a loss, machinery—a loss."

"That's true enough," the gentleman with the gray whiskers chimed in, positively laughing with satisfaction.

"And I'm not the only one," pursued Levin. "I mix with all the neighboring landowners, who are cultivating their land on a rational system; they all, with rare exceptions, are doing so at a loss. Come, tell us how does your land do—does it pay?" said Levin, and at once in Sviazhsky's eyes he detected that fleeting expression of alarm which he had noticed whenever he had tried to penetrate beyond the outer chambers of Sviazhsky's mind.

Moreover, this question on Levin's part was not quite in good faith. Madame Sviazhskaya had just told him at tea that they had that summer invited a German expert in bookkeeping from Moscow, who for a consideration of five hundred roubles had investigated the management of their property, and found that it was costing them a loss of three thousand odd roubles. She did not remember the precise sum, but it appeared that the German had worked it out to the fraction of a farthing.

The gray-whiskered landowner smiled at the mention of the profits of Sviazhsky's farming, obviously aware how much gain his neighbor and marshal was likely to be making.

"Possibly it does not pay," answered Sviazhsky. "That merely proves either that I'm a bad manager, or that I've sunk my capital for the increase of my rents."

"Oh, rent!" Levin cried with horror. "Rent there may be in Europe, where land has been improved by the labor put into it; but with us all the land is deteriorating from the labor put into it—in other words they're working it out; so there's no question of rent."

"How no rent? It's a law."

"Then we're outside the law; rent explains nothing for us, but simply muddles us. No, tell me how there can be a theory of rent? . . ."

"Will you have some junket? Masha, pass us some junket or raspberries." He turned to his wife. "Extraordinarily late the raspberries are lasting this year."

And in the happiest frame of mind Sviazhsky got up and walked off, apparently supposing the conversation to have ended at the very point when to Levin it seemed that it was only just beginning.

Having lost his antagonist, Levin continued the conversation with the gray-whiskered landowner, trying to prove to him that all the difficulty arises from the fact that we don't find out the peculiarities and habits of our laborer; but the landowner, like all men who think independently and in isolation, was slow in taking in any other person's idea, and particularly partial to his own. He stuck to it that the Russian peasant is a swine and likes swinishness, and that to get him out of his swinishness one must have authority, and there is none; one must have the stick, and we have become so liberal that we have all of a sudden replaced the stick that served us for a thousand years by lawyers and model prisons, where the worthless, stinking peasant is fed on good soup and has a fixed allowance of cubic feet of air.

"What makes you think," said Levin, trying to get back to the question, "that it's impossible to find some relation to the laborer in which the labor would become productive?"

"That never could be so with the Russian peasantry; we've no power over them," answered the landowner.

"How can new conditions be found?" said Sviazhsky. Having eaten some junket and lit a cigarette, he came back to the discussion. "All possible relations to the labor force have been defined and studied," he said. "The relic of barbarism, the primitive commune with each guarantee for all, will disappear of itself; serfdom has been abolished—there remains nothing but free labor, and its forms are fixed and ready made, and must be adopted. Permanent hands, day-laborers, farmers—you can't get out of those forms."

"But Europe is dissatisfied with these forms."

"Dissatisfied, and seeking new ones. And will find them, in all probability."

"That's just what I was meaning," answered Levin. "Why shouldn't we seek them for ourselves?"

"Because it would be just like inventing afresh the means for constructing railways. They are ready, invented."

"But if they don't do for us, if they're stupid?" said Levin.

And again he detected the expression of alarm in the eyes of Sviazhsky.

"Oh, yes; we'll bury the world under our caps! We've found the secret Europe was seeking for! I've heard all that; but, excuse me, do you know all that's been done in Europe on the question of the organization of labor?"

"No, very little."

"That question is now absorbing the best minds in Europe. The Schulze-Delitsch movement. . . . And then all this enormous literature of the labor question, the most liberal Lassalle movement . . . the Mulhausen experiment? That's a fact by now, as you're probably aware."

"I have some idea of it, but very vague."

"No, you only say that; no doubt you know all about it as well as I do. I'm not a professor of sociology, of course, but it interested me, and really, if it interests you, you ought to study it."

"But what conclusion have they come to?"

"Excuse me . . ."

The two neighbors had risen, and Sviazhsky, once more checking Levin in his inconvenient habit of peeping into what was beyond the outer chambers of his mind, went to see his guests out.

Chapter XXVIII

LEVIN WAS INSUFFERABLY BORED THAT EVENING WITH THE LADIES; HE WAS STIRRED AS HE HAD never been before by the idea that the dissatisfaction he was feeling with his system of managing his land was not an exceptional case, but the general condition of things in Russia; that the organization of some relation of the laborers to the soil in which they would work, as with the peasant he had met halfway to the Sviazhskys', was not a dream, but a problem which must be solved. And it seemed to him that the problem could be solved, and that he ought to try and solve it.

After saying good night to the ladies, and promising to stay the whole of the next day, so as to make an expedition on horseback with them to see an interesting ruin in the crown forest, Levin went, before going to bed, into his host's study to get the books on the labor question that Sviazhsky had offered him. Sviazhsky's study was a huge room, surrounded by bookcases and with two tables in it—one a massive writing-table, standing in the middle of the room, and the other a round table, covered with recent numbers of reviews and journals in different languages, ranged like the rays of a star round the lamp. On the writing-table was a stand of drawers marked with gold lettering, and full of papers of various sorts.

Sviazhsky took out the books, and sat down in a rocking-chair.

"What are you looking at there?" he said to Levin, who was standing at the round table looking through the reviews.

"Oh, yes, there's a very interesting article here," said Sviazhsky of the review Levin was holding in his hand. "It appears," he went on, with eager interest, "that Friedrich was not, after all, the person chiefly responsible for the partition of Poland. It is proved . . ."

And with his characteristic clearness, he summed up those new, very important, and interesting revelations. Although Levin was engrossed at the moment by his ideas about the problem of the land, he wondered, as he heard Sviazhsky: "What is there inside of him? And why, why is he interested in the partition of Poland?" When Sviazhsky had finished, Levin could not help asking: "Well, and what then?" But there was nothing to follow. It was simply interesting that it had been proved to be so and so. But Sviazhsky did not explain, and saw no need to explain why it was interesting to him.

"Yes, but I was very much interested by your irritable neighbor," said Levin, sighing. "He's a clever fellow, and said a lot that was true."

"Oh, get along with you! An inveterate supporter of serfdom at heart, like all of them!" said Sviazhsky.

"Whose marshal you are."

"Yes, only I marshal them in the other direction," said Sviazhsky, laughing.

"I'll tell you what interests me very much," said Levin. "He's right that our system, that's to say of rational farming, doesn't answer, that the only thing that answers is the money-lender system, like that meek-looking gentleman's, or else the very simplest. . . . Whose fault is it?"

"Our own, of course. Besides, it's not true that it doesn't answer. It answers with Vassiltchikov."

"A factory . . ."

"But I really don't know what it is you are surprised at. The people are at such a low stage of rational and moral development, that it's obvious they're bound to oppose everything that's strange to them. In Europe, a rational system answers because the people are educated; it follows that we must educate the people—that's all."

"But how are we to educate the people?"

"To educate the people three things are needed: schools, and schools, and schools.

"But you said yourself the people are at such a low stage of material development: what help are schools for that?"

"Do you know, you remind me of the story of the advice given to the sick man—You should try purgative medicine. Taken: worse. Try leeches. Tried them: worse. Well, then, there's nothing left but to pray to God. Tried it: worse. That's just how it is with us. I say political economy; you say—worse. I say socialism: worse. Education: worse."

"But how do schools help matters?"

"They give the peasant fresh wants."

"Well, that's a thing I've never understood." Levin replied with heat. "In what way are schools going to help the people to improve their material position? You say schools, education, will give them fresh wants. So much the worse, since they won't be capable of satisfying them. And in what way a knowledge of addition and subtraction and the catechism is going to improve their material condition, I never could make out. The day before yesterday, I met a peasant woman in the evening with a little baby, and asked her where she was going. She said 'she was going to the wise woman; her boy had screaming fits, so she was taking him to be doctored.' I asked, 'Why, how does the wise woman cure screaming fits?' 'She puts the child on the hen-roost and repeats some charm. . . .' "

"Well, you're saying it yourself! What's wanted to prevent her taking her child to the hen-roost to cure it of screaming fits is just . . ." Sviazhsky said, smiling good-humoredly.

"Oh, no!" said Levin with annoyance; "that method of doctoring I merely meant as a simile for doctoring the people with schools. The people are poor and ignorant—that we see as surely as the peasant woman sees the baby is ill because it screams. But in what way this trouble of poverty and ignorance is to be cured by schools is as incomprehensible as how the hen-roost affects the screaming. What has to be cured is what makes him poor."

"Well, in that, at least, you're in agreement with Spencer, whom you dislike so much. He says, too, that education may be the consequence of greater prosperity and comfort, of more frequent washing, as he says, but not of being able to read and write . . ."

"Well, then, I'm very glad—or the contrary, very sorry, that I'm in agreement with Spencer; only I've known it a long while. Schools can do no good; what will do good is an economic organization in which the people will become richer, will have more leisure—and then there will be schools."

"Still, all over Europe now schools are obligatory."

"And how far do you agree with Spencer yourself about it?" asked Levin.

But there was a gleam of alarm in Sviazhsky's eyes, and he said smiling:

"No; that screaming story is positively capital! Did you really hear it yourself?"

Levin saw that he was not to discover the connection between this man's life and his thoughts. Obviously he did not care in the least what his reasoning led him to; all he wanted was the process of reasoning. And he did not like it when the process of reasoning brought him into a blind alley. That was the only thing he disliked, and avoided by changing the conversation to something agreeable and amusing.

All the impressions of the day, beginning with the impression made by the old peasant, which served, as it were, as the fundamental basis of all the conceptions and ideas of the day, threw Levin into violent excitement. This dear good Sviazhsky, keeping a stock of ideas simply for social purposes, and obviously having some other principles hidden from Levin, while with the crowd, whose name is legion, he guided public opinion by ideas he did not share; that irascible country gentleman, perfectly correct in the conclusions that he had been worried into by life, but wrong in his exasperation against a whole class, and that the best class in Russia; his own dissatisfaction with the work he had been doing, and the vague hope of finding a remedy for all this—all was blended in a sense of inward turmoil, and anticipation of some solution near at hand.

Left alone in the room assigned him, lying on a spring mattress that yielded unexpectedly at every movement of his arm or his leg, Levin did not fall asleep for a long while. Not one conversation with Sviazhsky, though he had said a great deal that was clever, had interested Levin; but the conclusions of the irascible landowner required consideration. Levin could not help recalling every word he had said, and in imagination amending his own replies.

"Yes, I ought to have said to him: You say that our husbandry does not answer because the peasant hates improvements, and that they must be forced on him by authority. If no system of husbandry answered at all without these improvements, you would be quite right. But the only system that does answer is whenlaborer is working in accordance with his habits, just as on the old peasant's land halfway here. Your and our general dissatisfaction with the system shows that either we are to blame or the laborers. We have gone our way—the European way—a long while, without asking ourselves about the qualities of our labor force. Let us try to look upon the labor force not as an abstract force, but as the *Russian peasant* with his instincts, and we shall arrange our system of culture in accordance with that. Imagine, I ought to have said to him, that you have the same system as the old peasant has, that you have found means of making your laborers take an interest in the success of the work, and have found the happy mean in the way of improvements which they will admit, and you will, without exhausting the soil, get twice or three times the yield you got before. Divide it in halves, give half as the share of labor, the surplus left you will be greater, and the share of labor will be greater too. And to do this one must lower the standard of husbandry and interest the laborers in its success. How to do this?—that's a matter of detail; but undoubtedly it can be done."

This idea threw Levin into a great excitement. He did not sleep half the night, thinking over in detail the putting of his idea into practice. He had not intended to go away next day, but he now determined to go home early in the morning. Besides, the sister-in-law with her low-necked bodice aroused in him a feeling akin to shame and remorse for some utterly base action. Most important of all—he must get back without delay: he would have to make haste to put his new project to the peasants before the sowing of the winter wheat, so that the sowing might be undertaken on a new basis. He had made up his mind to revolutionize his whole system.

Chapter XXIX

THE CARRYING OUT OF LEVIN'S PLAN PRESENTED MANY DIFFICULTIES; BUT HE STRUGGLED ON, doing his utmost, and attained a result which, though not what he desired, was enough to enable him, without self-deception, to believe that the attempt was worth the trouble. One of the chief difficulties was that the process of cultivating the land was in full swing, that it was impossible to stop everything and begin it all again from the beginning, and the machine had to be mended while in motion.

When on the evening that he arrived home he informed the bailiff of his plans, the latter with visible pleasure agreed with what he said so long as he was pointing out that all that had been done up to that time was stupid and useless. The bailiff said that he had said so a long while ago, but no heed had been paid him. But as for the proposal made by Levin—to take a part as shareholder with his laborers in each agricultural undertaking—at this the bailiff simply expressed a profound despondency, and offered no definite opinion, but began immediately talking of the urgent necessity of carrying the remaining sheaves of rye the next day, and of sending the men out for the second ploughing, so that Levin felt that this was not the time for discussing it.

On beginning to talk to the peasants about it, and making a proposition to cede them the land on new terms, he came into collision with the same great difficulty that they were so much absorbed by the current work of the day, that they had not time to consider the advantages and disadvantages of the proposed scheme.

The simple-hearted Ivan, the cowherd, seemed completely to grasp Levin's proposal—that he should with his family take a share of the profits of the cattle yard—and he was in complete sympathy with the plan. But when Levin hinted at the future advantages, Ivan's face expressed alarm and regret that he could not hear all he had to say, and he made haste to find himself some task that would admit of no delay: he either snatched up the fork to pitch the hay out of the pens, or ran to get water or to clear out the dung.

Another difficulty lay in the invincible disbelief of the peasant that a landowner's object could be anything else than a desire to squeeze all he could out of them. They were firmly convinced that his real aim (whatever he might say to them) would always be in what he did not say to them. And they themselves, in giving their opinion, said a great deal but never said what was their real object. Moreover (Levin felt that the irascible landowner had been right) the peasants made their first and unalterable condition of any agreement whatever that they should not be forced to any new methods of tillage of any kind, nor to use new implements. They agreed that the modern plough ploughed better, that the scarifier did the work more quickly, but they found thousands of reasons that made it out of the question for them to use either of them; and though he had accepted the conviction that he would have to lower the standard of cultivation, he felt sorry to give up improved methods, the advantages of which were so obvious. But in spite of all these difficulties he got his way, and by autumn the system was working, or at least so it seemed to him.

At first Levin had thought of giving up the whole farming of the land just as it was to the peasants, the laborers, and the bailiff on new conditions of partnership; but he was very soon convinced that this was impossible, and determined to divide it up. The cattle yard, the garden, hayfields, and arable land, divided into several parts, had to be made into separate lots. The simple-hearted cowherd, Ivan, who, Levin fancied, understood the matter better than any of them, collecting together a gang of workers to help him, principally of his own family, became a partner in the cattle yard. A distant part of the estate, a tract of waste land that had lain fallow for eight years, was with the help of the clever carpenter, Fyodor Ryezunov, taken by six families of peasants on new conditions of partnership, and the peasant Shuraev took the management of all the vegetable gardens on the same terms. The remainder of the land was still worked on the old system, but these three associated partnerships were the first step to a new organization of the whole, and they completely took up Levin's time.

It is true that in the cattle yard things went no better than before, and Ivan strenuously opposed warm housing for the cows and butter made of fresh cream, affirming that cows require less food if kept cold, and that butter is more profitable made from sour cream, and he asked for wages just as under the old system, and took not the slightest interest in the fact that the money he received was not wages but an advance out of his future share in the profits.

It is true that Fyodor Ryezunov's company did not plough over the ground twice before sowing, as had been agreed, justifying themselves on the plea that the time was too short. It is true that the peasants of the same company, though they had agreed to work the land on new conditions, always spoke of the land, not as held in partnership, but as rented for half the crop, and more than once the peasants and Ryezunov himself said to Levin, "If you would take a rent for the land, it would save you trouble, and we should be more free." Moreover the same peasants kept putting off, on various excuses, the building of a cattle yard and barn on the land as agreed upon, and delayed doing it till the winter.

It is true that Shuraev would have liked to let out the kitchen gardens he had undertaken in small lots to the peasants. He evidently quite misunderstood, and apparently intentionally misunderstood, the conditions upon which the land had been given to him.

Often, too, talking to the peasants and explaining to them all the advantages of the plan, Levin felt that the peasants heard nothing but the sound of his voice, and were firmly resolved, whatever he might say, not to let themselves be taken in. He felt this especially when he talked to the cleverest of the peasants, Ryezunov, and detected the gleam in Ryezunov's eyes which showed so plainly both ironical amusement at Levin, and the firm conviction that, if anyone were to be taken in, it would not be he, Ryezunov. But in spite of all this Levin thought the system worked, and that by keeping accounts strictly and insisting on his own way, he would prove to them in the future the advantages of the arrangement, and then the system would go of itself.

These matters, together with the management of the land still left on his hands, and the indoor work over his book, so engrossed Levin the whole summer that he scarcely ever went out shooting. At the end of August he heard that the Oblonskys had gone away to Moscow, from their servant who brought back the side-saddle. He felt that in not answering Darya Alexandrovna's letter he had by his rudeness, of which he could not think without a flush of shame, burned his ships, and that he would never go and see them again. He had been just as rude with the Sviazhskys, leaving them without saying good-bye. But he would never go to see them again either. He did not care about that now. The business of reorganizing the farming of his land absorbed him as completely as though there would never be anything else in his life. He read the books lent him by Sviazhsky, and copying out what he had not got, he read both the economic and socialistic books on the subject, but, as he had anticipated, found nothing bearing on the scheme he had undertaken. In the books on political economy—in Mill, for instance—whom he studied first with great ardor, hoping every minute to find an answer to the questions that were engrossing him, found laws deduced from the condition of land culture in Europe; but he did not see why these laws, which did not apply in Russia, must be general. He saw just the same thing in the socialistic books: either they were the beautiful but impracticable fantasies which had fascinated him when he was a student, or they were attempts at improving, rectifying the economic position in which Europe was placed, with which the system of land tenure in Russia had nothing in common. Political economy told him that the laws by which the wealth of Europe had been developed, and was developing, were universal and unvarying. Socialism told him that development along these lines leads to ruin. And neither of them gave an answer, or even a hint, in reply to the question what he, Levin, and all the Russian peasants and landowners, were to do with their millions of hands and millions of acres, to make them as productive as possible for the common weal.

Having once taken the subject up, he read conscientiously everything bearing on it, and intended in the autumn to go abroad to study land systems on the spot, in order that he might not on this question be confronted with what so often met him on various subjects. Often, just as he was beginning to understand the idea in the mind of anyone he was talking to, and was beginning to explain his own, he would suddenly be told: "But Kauffmann, but Jones, but Dubois, but Michelli? You haven't read them: they've thrashed that question out thoroughly."

He saw now distinctly that Kauffmann and Michelli had nothing to tell him. He knew what he wanted. He saw that Russia has splendid land, splendid laborers, and that in certain cases, as at the peasant's on the way to Sviazhsky's, the produce raised by the laborers and the land is great—in the majority of cases when capital is applied in the European way the produce is small, and that this simply arises from the fact that the laborers want to work and work well only in their own peculiar way, and that this antagonism is not incidental but invariable, and has its roots in the national spirit. He thought that the Russian people whose task it was to colonize and cultivate vast tracts of unoccupied land, consciously adhered, till all their land was occupied, to the methods suitable to their purpose, and that their methods were by no means so bad as was generally supposed. And he wanted to prove this theoretically in his book and practically on his land.

Chapter XXX

At the end of September the timber had been carted for building the cattle yard on the land that had been allotted to the association of peasants, and the butter from the cows was sold and the profits divided. In practice the system worked capitally, or, at least, so it seemed to Levin. In order to work out the whole subject theoretically and to complete his book, which, in Levin's daydreams, was not merely to effect a revolution in political economy, but to annihilate that science entirely and to lay the foundation of a new science of the relation of the people to the soil, all that was left to do was to make a tour abroad, and to study on the spot all that had been done in the same direction, and to collect conclusive evidence that all that had been done there was not what was wanted. Levin was only waiting for the delivery of his wheat to receive the money for it and go abroad. But the rains began, preventing the harvesting of the corn and potatoes left in the fields, and putting a stop to all work, even to the delivery of the wheat.

The mud was impassable along the roads; two mills were carried away, and the weather got worse and worse.

On the 30th of September the sun came out in the morning, and hoping for fine weather, Levin began making final preparations for his journey. He gave orders for the wheat to be delivered, sent the bailiff to the merchant to get the money owing him, and went out himself to give some final directions on the estate before setting off.

Having finished all his business, soaked through with the streams of water which kept running down the leather behind his neck and his gaiters, but in the keenest and most confident temper, Levin returned homewards in the evening. The weather had become worse than ever towards evening; the hail lashed the drenched mare so cruelly that she went along sideways, shaking her head and ears; but Levin was all right under his hood, and he looked cheerfully about him at the muddy streams running under the wheels, at the drops hanging on every bare twig, at the whiteness of the patch of unmelted hailstones on the planks of the bridge, at the thick layer of still juicy, fleshy leaves that lay heaped up about the stripped elm tree. In spite of the gloominess of nature around him, he felt peculiarly eager. The talks he had been having with the peasants in the further village had shown that they were beginning to get used to their new position. The old servant to whose hut he had gone to get dry evidently approved of Levin's plan, and of his own accord proposed to enter the partnership by the purchase of cattle.

"I have only to go stubbornly on towards my aim, and I shall attain my end," thought Levin; "and it's something to work and take trouble for. This is not a matter of myself individually; the question of the public welfare comes into it. The whole system of culture, the chief element in the condition of the people, must be completely transformed. Instead of poverty, general prosperity and content; instead of hostility, harmony and unity of interests. In short, a bloodless revolution, but a revolution of the greatest magnitude, beginning in the little circle of our district, then the province, then Russia, the whole world. Because a just idea cannot but be fruitful. Yes, it's an aim worth working for. And its being me, Kostya Levin, who went to a ball in a black tie, and was refused by the Shtcherbatskaya girl, and who was intrinsically such a pitiful, worthless creature—that proves nothing; I feel sure Franklin felt just as worthless, and he too had no faith in himself, thinking of himself as a whole. That means nothing. And he too, most likely, had an Agafea Mihalovna to whom he confided his secrets."

Musing on such thoughts Levin reached home in the darkness.

The bailiff, who had been to the merchant, had come back and brought part of the money for the wheat. An agreement had been made with the old servant, and on the road the bailiff had learned that everywhere the corn was still standing in the fields, so that his one hundred and sixty shocks that had not been carried were nothing in comparison with the losses of others.

After dinner Levin was sitting, as he usually did, in an easy chair with a book, and as he read he went on thinking of the journey before him in connection with his book. Today all the significance of his book rose before him with special distinctness, and whole periods ranged themselves in his mind in illustration of his theories. "I must write that down," he thought. "That ought to form a brief introduction, which I thought unnecessary before." He got up to go to his writing-table, and Laska, lying at his feet, got up too, stretching and looking at him as though to inquire where to go. But he had not time to write it down, for the head peasants had come round, and Levin went out into the hall to them.

After his levee, that is to say, giving directions about the labors of the next day, and seeing all the peasants who had business with him, Levin went back to his study and sat down to work.

Laska lay under the table; Agafea Mihalovna settled herself in her place with her stocking.

After writing for a little while, Levin suddenly thought with exceptional vividness of Kitty, her refusal, and their last meeting. He got up and began walking about the room.

"What's the use of being dreary?" said Agafea Mihalovna. "Come, why do you stay on at home? You ought to go to some warm springs, especially now you're ready for the journey."

"Well, I am going away the day after tomorrow, Agafea Mihalovna; I must finish my work."

"There, there, your work, you say! As if you hadn't done enough for the peasants! Why, as 'tis, they're saying, 'Your master will be getting some honor from the Tsar for it.' Indeed and it is a strange thing; why need you worry about the peasants?"

"I'm not worrying about them; I'm doing it for my own good."

Agafea Mihalovna knew every detail of Levin's plans for his land. Levin often put his views before her in all their complexity, and not uncommonly he argued with her and did not agree with her comments. But on this occasion she entirely misinterpreted what he had said.

"Of one's soul's salvation we all know and must think before all else," she said with a sigh. "Parfen Denisitch now, for all he was no scholar, he died a death that God grant every one of us the like," she said, referring to a servant who had died recently. "Took the sacrament and all."

"That's not what I mean," said he. "I mean that I'm acting for my own advantage. It's all the better for me if the peasants do their work better."

"Well, whatever you do, if he's a lazy good-for-nought, everything'll be at sixes and sevens. If he has a conscience, he'll work, and if not, there's no doing anything."

"Oh, come, you say yourself Ivan has begun looking after the cattle better."

"All I say is," answered Agafea Mihalovna, evidently not speaking at random, but in strict sequence of idea, "that you ought to get married, that's what I say."

Agafea Mihalovna's allusion to the very subject he had only just been thinking about, hurt and stung him. Levin scowled, and without answering her, he sat down again to his work, repeating to himself all that he had been thinking of the real significance of that work. Only at intervals he listened in the stillness to the click of Agafea Mihalovna's needles, and recollecting what he did not want to remember, he frowned again.

At nine o'clock they heard the bell and the faint vibration of a carriage over the mud.

"Well, here's visitors come to us, and you won't be dull," said Agafea Mihalovna, getting up and going to the door. But Levin overtook her. His work was not going well now, and he was glad of a visitor, whoever it might be.

Chapter XXXI

RUNNING HALFWAY DOWN THE STAIRCASE, LEVIN CAUGHT A SOUND HE KNEW, A FAMILIAR COUGH in the hall. But he heard it indistinctly through the sound of his own footsteps, and hoped he was mistaken. Then he caught sight of a long, bony, familiar figure, and now it seemed there was no possibility of mistake; and yet he still went on hoping that this tall man taking off his fur cloak and coughing was not his brother Nikolay.

Levin loved his brother, but being with him was always a torture. Just now, when Levin, under the influence of the thoughts that had come to him, and Agafea Mihalovna's hint, was in a troubled and uncertain humor, the meeting with his brother that he had to face seemed particularly difficult. Instead of a lively, healthy visitor, some outsider who would, he hoped, cheer him up in his uncertain humor, he had to see his brother, who knew him through and through, who would call forth all the thoughts nearest his heart, would force him to show himself fully. And that he was not disposed to do.

Angry with himself for so base a feeling, Levin ran into the hall; as soon as he had seen his brother close, this feeling of selfish disappointment vanished instantly and was replaced by pity. Terrible as his brother Nikolay had been before in his emaciation and sickliness, now he looked still more emaciated, still more wasted. He was a skeleton covered with skin.

He stood in the hall, jerking his long thin neck, and pulling the scarf off it, and smiled a strange and pitiful smile. When he saw that smile, submissive and humble, Levin felt something clutching at his throat.

"You see, I've come to you," said Nikolay in a thick voice, never for one second taking his eyes off his brother's face. "I've been meaning to a long while, but I've been unwell all the time. Now I'm ever so much better," he said, rubbing his beard with his big thin hands.

"Yes, yes!" answered Levin. And he felt still more frightened when, kissing him, he felt with his lips the dryness of his brother's skin and saw close to him his big eyes, full of a strange light.

A few weeks before, Konstantin Levin had written to his brother that through the sale of the small part of the property, that had remained undivided, there was a sum of about two thousand roubles to come to him as his share.

Nikolay said that he had come now to take this money and, what was more important, to stay a while in the old nest, to get in touch with the earth, so as to renew his strength like the heroes of old for the work that lay before him. In spite of his exaggerated stoop, and the emaciation that was so striking from his height, his movements were as rapid and abrupt as ever. Levin led him into his study.

His brother dressed with particular care—a thing he never used to do—combed his scanty, lank hair, and, smiling, went upstairs.

He was in the most affectionate and good-humored mood, just as Levin often remembered him in childhood. He even referred to Sergey Ivanovitch without rancor. When he saw Agafea Mihalovna, he made jokes with her and asked after the old servants. The news of the death of Parfen Denisitch made a painful impression on him. A look of fear crossed his face, but he regained his serenity immediately.

"Of course he was quite old," he said, and changed the subject. "Well, I'll spend a month or two with you, and then I'm off to Moscow. Do you know, Myakov has promised me a place there, and I'm going into the service. Now I'm going to arrange my life quite differently," he went on. "You know I got rid of that woman."

"Marya Nikolaevna? Why, what for?"

"Oh, she was a horrid woman! She caused me all sorts of worries." But he did not say what the annoyances were. He could not say that he had cast off Marya Nikolaevna because the tea was weak, and, above all, because she would look after him, as though he were an invalid.

"Besides, I want to turn over a new leaf completely now. I've done silly things, of course, like everyone else, but money's the last consideration; I don't regret it. So long as there's health, and my health, thank God, is quite restored."

Levin listened and racked his brains, but could think of nothing to say. Nikolay probably felt the same; he began questioning his brother about his affairs; and Levin was glad to talk about himself, because then he could speak without hypocrisy. He told his brother of his plans and his doings.

His brother listened, but evidently he was not interested by it.

These two men were so akin, so near each other, that the slightest gesture, the tone of voice, told both more than could be said in words.

Both of them now had only one thought—the illness of Nikolay and the nearness of his death—which stifled all else. But neither of them dared to speak of it, and so whatever they said—not uttering the one thought that filled their minds—was all falsehood. Never had Levin been so glad when the evening was over and it was time to go to bed. Never with any outside person, never on any official visit had he been so unnatural and false as he was that evening. And the consciousness of this unnaturalness, and the remorse he felt at it, made him even more unnatural. He wanted to weep over his dying, dearly loved brother, and he had to listen and keep on talking of how he meant to live.

As the house was damp, and only one bedroom had been kept heated, Levin put his brother to sleep in his own bedroom behind a screen.

His brother got into bed, and whether he slept or did not sleep, tossed about like a sick man, coughed, and when he could not get his throat clear, mumbled something. Sometimes when his breathing was painful, he said, "Oh, my God!" Sometimes when he was choking he muttered angrily, "Ah, the devil!" Levin could not sleep for a long while, hearing him. His thoughts were of the most various, but the end of all his thoughts was the same—death. Death, the inevitable end of all, for the first time presented itself to him with irresistible force. And death, which was here in this loved brother, groaning half asleep and from habit calling without distinction on God and the devil, was not so remote as it had hitherto seemed to him. It was in himself too he felt that. If not today, tomorrow, if not tomorrow, in thirty years, wasn't it all the same! And what was this inevitable death—he did not know, had never thought about it, and what was more, had not the power, had not the courage to think about it.

"I work, I want to do something, but I had forgotten it must all end; I had forgotten—death."

He sat on his bed in the darkness, crouched up, hugging his knees, and holding his breath from the strain of thought, he pondered. But the more intensely he thought, the clearer it became to him that it was indubitably so, that in reality, looking upon life, he had forgotten one little fact—that death will come, and all ends; that nothing was even worth beginning, and that there was no helping it anyway. Yes, it was awful, but it was so.

"But I am alive still. Now what's to be done? what's to be done?" he said in despair. He lit a candle, got up cautiously and went to the looking-glass, and began looking at his face and hair. Yes, there were gray hairs about his temples. He opened his mouth. His back teeth were beginning to decay. He bared his muscular arms. Yes, there was strength in them. But Nikolay, who lay there breathing with what was left of lungs, had had a strong, healthy body too. And suddenly he recalled how they used to go to bed together as children, and how they only waited till Fyodor Bogdanitch was out of the room to fling pillows at each other and laugh, laugh irrepressibly, so that even their awe of Fyodor Bogdanitch could not check the effervescing, overbrimming sense of life and happiness. "And now that bent, hollow chest . . . and I, not knowing what will become of me, or wherefore . . ."

"K . . . ha! K . . . ha! Damnation! Why do you keep fidgeting, why don't you go to sleep?" his brother's voice called to him.

"Oh, I don't know, I'm not sleepy."

"I have had a good sleep, I'm not in a sweat now. Just see, feel my shirt; it's not wet, is it?"

Levin felt, withdrew behind the screen, and put out the candle, but for a long while he could not sleep. The question how to live had hardly begun to grow a little clearer to him, when a new, insoluble question presented itself—death.

"Why, he's dying—yes, he'll die in the spring, and how help him? What can I say to him? What do I know about it? I'd even forgotten that it was at all."

Chapter XXXII

LEVIN HAD LONG BEFORE MADE THE OBSERVATION THAT WHEN ONE IS UNCOMFORTABLE WITH people from their being excessively amenable and meek, one is apt very soon after to find things intolerable from their touchiness and irritability. He felt that this was how it would be with his brother. And his brother Nikolay's gentleness did in fact not last out for long. The very next morning he began to be irritable, and seemed doing his best to find fault with his brother, attacking him on his tenderest points.

Levin felt himself to blame, and could not set things right. He felt that if they had both not kept up appearances, but had spoken, as it is called, from the heart—that is to say, had said only just what they were thinking and feeling—they would simply have looked into each other's faces, and Konstantin could only have said, "You're dying, you're dying!" and Nikolay could only have answered, "I know I'm dying, but I'm afraid, I'm afraid, I'm afraid!" And they could have said nothing more, if they had said only what was in their hearts. But life like that was impossible, and so Konstantin tried to do what he had been trying to do all his life, and never could learn to do, though, as far as he could observe, many people knew so well how to do it, and without it there was no living at all. He tried to say what he was not thinking, but he felt continually that it had a ring of falsehood, that his brother detected him in it, and was exasperated at it.

The third day Nikolay induced his brother to explain his plan to him again, and began not merely attacking it, but intentionally confounding it with communism.

"You've simply borrowed an idea that's not your own, but you've distorted it, and are trying to apply it where it's not applicable."

"But I tell you it's nothing to do with it. They deny the justice of property, of capital, of inheritance, while I do not deny this chief stimulus." (Levin felt disgusted himself at using such expressions, but ever since he had been engrossed by his work, he had unconsciously come more and more frequently to use words not Russian.) "All I want is to regulate labor."

"Which means, you've borrowed an idea, stripped it of all that gave it its force, and want to make believe that it's something new," said Nikolay, angrily tugging at his necktie.

"But my idea has nothing in common . . ."

"That, anyway," said Nikolay Levin, with an ironical smile, his eyes flashing malignantly, "has the charm of—what's one to call it?—geometrical symmetry, of clearness, of definiteness. It may be a Utopia. But if once one allows the possibility of making of all the past a *tabula rasa*—no property, no family—then labor would organize itself. But you gain nothing . . ."

"Why do you mix things up? I've never been a communist."

"But I have, and I consider it's premature, but rational, and it has a future, just like Christianity in its first ages."

"All that I maintain is that the labor force ought to be investigated from the point of view of natural science; that is to say, it ought to be studied, its qualities ascertained . . ."

"But that's utter waste of time. That force finds a certain form of activity of itself, according to the stage of its development. There have been slaves first everywhere, then metayers; and we have the half-crop system, rent, and day-laborers. What are you trying to find?"

Levin suddenly lost his temper at these words, because at the bottom of his heart he was afraid that it was true—true that he was trying to hold the balance even between communism and the familiar forms, and that this was hardly possible.

"I am trying to find means of working productively for myself and for the laborers. I want to organize . . ." he answered hotly.

"You don't want to organize anything; it's simply just as you've been all your life, that you want to be original to pose as not exploiting the peasants simply, but with some idea in view."

"Oh, all right, that's what you think—and let me alone!" answered Levin, feeling the muscles of his left cheek twitching uncontrollably.

"You've never had, and never have, convictions; all you want is to please your vanity."

"Oh, very well; then let me alone!"

"And I will let you alone! and it's high time I did, and go to the devil with you! and I'm very sorry I ever came!"

In spite of all Levin's efforts to soothe his brother afterwards, Nikolay would listen to nothing he said, declaring that it was better to part, and Konstantin saw that it simply was that life was unbearable to him.

Nikolay was just getting ready to go, when Konstantin went in to him again and begged him, rather unnaturally, to forgive him if he had hurt his feelings in any way.

"Ah, generosity!" said Nikolay, and he smiled. "If you want to be right, I can give you that satisfaction. You're in the right; but I'm going all the same."

It was only just at parting that Nikolay kissed him, and said, looking with sudden strangeness and seriousness at his brother:

"Anyway, don't remember evil against me, Kostya!" and his voice quivered. These were the only words that had been spoken sincerely between them. Levin knew that those words meant, "You see, and you know, that I'm in a bad way, and maybe we shall not see each other again." Levin knew this, and the tears gushed from his eyes. He kissed his brother once more, but he could not speak, and knew not what to say.

Three days after his brother's departure, Levin too set off for his foreign tour. Happening to meet Shtcherbatsky, Kitty's cousin, in the railway train, Levin greatly astonished him by his depression.

"What's the matter with you?" Shtcherbatsky asked him.

"Oh, nothing; there's not much happiness in life."

"Not much? You come with me to Paris instead of to Mulhausen. You shall see how to be happy."

"No, I've done with it all. It's time I was dead."

"Well, that's a good one!" said Shtcherbatsky, laughing; "why, I'm only just getting ready to begin."

"Yes, I thought the same not long ago, but now I know I shall soon be dead."

Levin said what he had genuinely been thinking of late. He saw nothing but death or the advance towards death in everything. But his cherished scheme only engrossed him the more. Life had to be got through somehow till death did come. Darkness had fallen upon everything for him; but just because of this darkness he felt that the one guiding clue in the darkness was his work, and he clutched it and clung to it with all his strength.

Part Four

Chapter I

THE KARENINS, HUSBAND AND WIFE, CONTINUED LIVING IN THE SAME HOUSE, MET EVERY-day, but were complete strangers to one another. Alexey Alexandrovitch made it a rule to see his wife everyday, so that the servants might have no grounds for suppositions, but avoided dining at home. Vronsky was never at Alexey Alexandrovitch's house, but Anna saw him away from home, and her husband was aware of it.

The position was one of misery for all three; and not one of them would have been equal to enduring this position for a single day, if it had not been for the expectation that it would change, that it was merely a temporary painful ordeal which would pass over. Alexey Alexandrovitch hoped that this passion would pass, as everything does pass, that everyone would forget about it, and his name would remain unsullied. Anna, on whom the position depended, and for whom it was more miserable than for anyone, endured it because she not merely hoped, but firmly believed, that it would all very soon be settled and come right. She had not the least idea what would settle the position, but she firmly believed that something would very soon turn up now. Vronsky, against his own will or wishes, followed her lead, hoped too that something, apart from his own action, would be sure to solve all difficulties.

In the middle of the winter Vronsky spent a very tiresome week. A foreign prince, who had come on a visit to Petersburg, was put under his charge, and he had to show him the sights worth seeing. Vronsky was of distinguished appearance; he possessed, moreover, the art of behaving with respectful dignity, and was used to having to do with such grand personages—that was how he came to be put in charge of the prince. But he felt his duties very irksome. The prince was anxious to miss nothing of which he would be asked at home, had he seen that in Russia? And on his own account he was anxious to enjoy to the utmost all Russian forms of amusement. Vronsky was obliged to be his guide in satisfying both these inclinations. The mornings they spent driving to look at places of interest; the evenings they passed enjoying the national entertainments. The prince rejoiced in health exceptional even among princes. By gymnastics and careful attention to his health he had brought himself to such a point that in spite of his excess in pleasure he looked as fresh as a big glossy green Dutch cucumber. The prince had traveled a great deal, and considered one of the chief advantages of modern facilities of communication was the accessibility of the pleasures of all nations.

He had been in Spain, and there had indulged in serenades and had made friends with a Spanish girl who played the mandolin. In Switzerland he had killed chamois. In England he had galloped in a red coat over hedges and killed two hundred pheasants for a bet. In Turkey he had got into a harem; in India he had hunted on an elephant, and now in Russia he wished to taste all the specially Russian forms of pleasure.

Vronsky, who was, as it were, chief master of the ceremonies to him, was at great pains to arrange all the Russian amusements suggested by various persons to the prince. They had race-horses, and Russian pancakes and bear hunts and three-horse sleighs, and gypsies and drinking feasts, with the Russian accompaniment of broken crockery. And the prince with surprising ease fell in with the Russian spirit, smashed trays full of crockery, sat with a gypsy girl on his knee, and seemed to be asking—what more, and does the whole Russian spirit consist in just this?

In reality, of all the Russian entertainments the prince liked best French actresses and ballet dancers and white-seal champagne. Vronsky was used to princes, but, either because he had himself changed of late, or that he was in too close proximity to the prince, that week seemed fearfully wearisome to him. The whole of that week he experienced a sensation such as a man might have set in charge of a dangerous madman, afraid of the madman, and at the same time, from being with him, fearing for his own reason. Vronsky was continually conscious of the necessity of never for a second relaxing the tone of stern official respectfulness, that he might not himself be insulted. The prince's manner of treating the very people who, to Vronsky's surprise, were ready to descend to any depths to provide him with Russian amusements, was contemptuous. His criticisms of Russian women, whom he wished to study, more than once made Vronsky crimson with indignation. The chief reason why the prince was so particularly disagreeable to Vronsky was that he could not help seeing himself in him. And what he saw in this mirror did not gratify his self-esteem. He was a very stupid and very self-satisfied and very healthy and very well-washed man, and nothing else. He was a gentleman—that was true, and Vronsky could not deny it. He was equable and not cringing with his superiors, was free and ingratiating in his behavior with his equals, and was contemptuously indulgent with his inferiors. Vronsky was himself the same, and regarded it as a great merit to be so. But for this prince he was an inferior, and his contemptuous and indulgent attitude to him revolted him.

"Brainless beef! can I be like that?" he thought.

Be that as it might, when, on the seventh day, he parted from the prince, who was starting for Moscow, and received his thanks, he was happy to be rid of his uncomfortable position and the unpleasant reflection of himself. He said good-bye to him at the station on their return from a bear hunt, at which they had had a display of Russian prowess kept up all night.

Chapter II

WHEN HE GOT HOME, VRONSKY FOUND THERE A NOTE FROM ANNA. SHE WROTE, "I AM ILL AND unhappy. I cannot come out, but I cannot go on longer without seeing you. Come in this evening. Alexey Alexandrovitch goes to the council at seven and will be there till ten." Thinking for an instant of the strangeness of her bidding him come straight to her, in spite of her husband's insisting on her not receiving him, he decided to go.

Vronsky had that winter got his promotion, was now a colonel, had left the regimental quarters, and was living alone. After having some lunch, he lay down on the sofa immediately, and in five minutes memories of the hideous scenes he had witnessed during the last few days were confused together and joined on to a mental image of Anna and of the peasant who had played an important part in the bear hunt, and Vronsky fell asleep. He waked up in the dark, trembling with horror, and made haste to light a candle. "What was it? What? What was the dreadful thing I dreamed? Yes, yes; I think a little dirty man with a disheveled beard was stooping down doing something, and all of a sudden he began saying some strange words in French. Yes, there was nothing else in the dream," he said to himself. "But why was it so awful?" He vividly recalled the peasant again and those incomprehensible French words the peasant had uttered, and a chill of horror ran down his spine.

"What nonsense!" thought Vronsky, and glanced at his watch.

It was half-past eight already. He rang up his servant, dressed in haste, and went out onto the steps, completely forgetting the dream and only worried at being late. As he drove up to the Karenins' entrance he looked at his watch and saw it was ten minutes to nine. A high, narrow carriage with a pair of grays was standing at the entrance. He recognized Anna's carriage. "She is coming to me," thought Vronsky, "and better she should. I don't like going into that house. But no matter; I can't hide myself," he thought, and with that manner peculiar to him from childhood, as of a man who has nothing to be ashamed of, Vronsky got out of his sleigh and went to the door. The door opened, and the hall-porter with a rug on his arm called the carriage. Vronsky, though he did not usually notice details, noticed at this moment the amazed expression with which the porter glanced at him. In the very doorway Vronsky almost ran up against Alexey Alexandrovitch. The gas jet threw its full light on the bloodless, sunken face under the black hat and on the white cravat, brilliant against the beaver of the coat. Karenin's fixed, dull eyes were fastened upon Vronsky's face. Vronsky bowed, and Alexey Alexandrovitch, chewing his lips, lifted his hand to his hat and went on. Vronsky saw him without looking round get into the carriage, pick up the rug and the opera glass at the window and disappear. Vronsky went into the hall. His brows were scowling, and his eyes gleamed with a proud and angry light in them.

"What a position!" he thought. "If he would fight, would stand up for his honor, I could act, could express my feelings; but this weakness or baseness . . . He puts me in the position of playing false, which I never meant and never mean to do."

Vronsky's ideas had changed since the day of his conversation with Anna in the Vrede garden. Unconsciously yielding to the weakness of Anna—who had surrendered herself up to him utterly, and simply looked to him to decide her fate, ready to submit to anything—he had long ceased to think that their tie might end as he had thought then. His ambitious plans had retreated into the background again, and feeling that he had got out of that circle of activity in which everything was definite, he had given himself entirely to his passion, and that passion was binding him more and more closely to her.

He was still in the hall when he caught the sound of her retreating footsteps. He knew she had been expecting him, had listened for him, and was now going back to the drawing room.

"No," she cried, on seeing him, and at the first sound of her voice the tears came into her eyes. "No; if things are to go on like this, the end will come much, much too soon."

"What is it, dear one?"

"What? I've been waiting in agony for an hour, two hours. . . . No, I won't . . . I can't quarrel with you. Of course you couldn't come. No, I won't." She laid her two hands on his shoulders, and looked a long while at him with a profound, passionate, and at the same time searching look. She was studying his face to make up for the time she had not seen him. She was, every time she saw him, making the picture of him in her imagination (incomparably superior, impossible in reality) fit with him as he really was.

Chapter III

"YOU MET HIM?" SHE ASKED, WHEN THEY HAD SAT DOWN AT THE TABLE IN THE LAMPLIGHT. "You're punished, you see, for being late."

"Yes; but how was it? Wasn't he to be at the council?"

"He had been and come back, and was going out somewhere again. But that's no matter. Don't talk about it. Where have you been? With the prince still?"

She knew every detail of his existence. He was going to say that he had been up all night and had dropped asleep, but looking at her thrilled and rapturous face, he was ashamed. And he said he had had to go to report on the prince's departure.

"But it's over now? He is gone!"

"Thank God it's over! You wouldn't believe how insufferable it's been for me."

"Why so? Isn't it the life all of you, all young men, always lead?" she said, knitting her brows; and taking up the crochet-work that was lying on the table, she began drawing the hook out of it, without looking at Vronsky.

"I gave that life up long ago," said he, wondering at the change in her face, and trying to divine its meaning. "And I confess," he said, with a smile, showing his thick, white teeth, "this week I've been, as it were, looking at myself in a glass, seeing that life, and I didn't like it."

She held the work in her hands, but did not crochet, and looked at him with strange, shining, and hostile eyes.

"This morning Liza came to see me—they're not afraid to call on me, in spite of the Countess Lidia Ivanovna," she put in—"and she told me about your Athenian evening. How loathsome!"

"I was just going to say . . ."

She interrupted him.

"It was that Thérèse you used to know?"

"I was just saying . . ."

"How disgusting you are, you men! How is it you can't understand that a woman can never forget that," she said, getting more and more angry, and so letting him see the cause of her irritation, "especially a woman who cannot know your life? What do I know? What have I ever known?" she said, "what you tell me. And how do I know whether you tell me the truth? . . ."

"Anna, you hurt me. Don't you trust me? Haven't I told you that I haven't a thought I wouldn't lay bare to you?"

"Yes, yes," she said, evidently trying to suppress her jealous thoughts. "But if only you knew how wretched I am! I believe you, I believe you. . . . What were you saying?"

But he could not at once recall what he had been going to say. These fits of jealousy, which of late had been more and more frequent with her, horrified him, and however much he tried to disguise the fact, made him feel cold to her, although he knew the cause of her jealousy was her love for him. How often he had told himself that her love was happiness; and now she loved him as a woman can love when love has outweighed for her all the good things of life—and he was much further from happiness than when he had followed her from Moscow. Then he had thought himself unhappy, but happiness was before him; now he felt that the best happiness was already left behind. She was utterly unlike what she had been when he first saw her. Both morally and physically she had changed for the worse. She had broadened out all over, and in her face at the time when she was speaking of the actress there was an evil expression of hatred that distorted it. He looked at her as a man looks at a faded flower he has gathered, with difficulty recognizing in it the beauty for which he picked and ruined it. And in spite of this he felt that then, when his love was stronger, he could, if he had greatly wished it, have torn that love out of his heart; but now, when as at that moment it seemed to him he felt no love for her, he knew that what bound him to her could not be broken.

"Well, well, what was it you were going to say about the prince? I have driven away the fiend," she added. The fiend was the name they had given her jealousy. "What did you begin to tell me about the prince? Why did you find it so tiresome?"

"Oh, it was intolerable!" he said, trying to pick up the thread of his interrupted thought. "He does not improve on closer acquaintance. If you want him defined, here he is: a prime, well-fed beast such as takes medals at the cattle shows, and nothing more," he said, with a tone of vexation that interested her.

"No; how so?" she replied. "He's seen a great deal, anyway; he's cultured?"

"It's an utterly different culture—their culture. He's cultivated, one sees, simply to be able to despise culture, as they despise everything but animal pleasures."

"But don't you all care for these animal pleasures?" she said, and again he noticed a dark look in her eyes that avoided him.

"How is it you're defending him?" he said, smiling.

"I'm not defending him, it's nothing to me; but I imagine, if you had not cared for those pleasures yourself, you might have got out of them. But if it affords you satisfaction to gaze at Therese in the attire of Eve . . ."

"Again, the devil again," Vronsky said, taking the hand she had laid on the table and kissing it.

"Yes; but I can't help it. You don't know what I have suffered waiting for you. I believe I'm not jealous. I'm not jealous: I believe you when you're here; but when you're away somewhere leading your life, so incomprehensible to me . . ."

She turned away from him, pulled the hook at last out of the crochet-work, and rapidly, with the help of her forefinger, began working loop after loop of the wool that was dazzling white in the lamplight, while the slender wrist moved swiftly, nervously in the embroidered cuff.

"How was it, then? Where did you meet Alexey Alexandrovitch?" Her voice sounded in an unnatural and jarring tone.

"We ran up against each other in the doorway."

"And he bowed to you like this?"

She drew a long face, and half-closing her eyes, quickly transformed her expression, folded her hands, and Vronsky suddenly saw in her beautiful face the very expression with which Alexey Alexandrovitch had bowed to him. He smiled, while she laughed gaily, with that sweet, deep laugh, which was one of her greatest charms.

"I don't understand him in the least," said Vronsky. "If after your avowal to him at your country house he had broken with you, if he had called me out—but this I can't understand. How can he put up with such a position? He feels it, that's evident."

"He?" she said sneeringly. "He's perfectly satisfied."

"What are we all miserable for, when everything might be so happy?"

"Only not he. Don't I know him, the falsity in which he's utterly steeped? . . . Could one, with any feeling, live as he is living with me? He understands nothing, and feels nothing. Could a man of any feeling live in the same house with his unfaithful wife? Could he talk to her, call her 'my dear'?"

And again she could not help mimicking him: " 'Anna, *ma chère!*"

"He's not a man, not a human being—he's a doll! No one knows him; but I know him. Oh, if I'd been in his place, I'd long ago have killed, have torn to pieces a wife like me. I wouldn't have said, 'Anna, *ma chère*'! He's not a man, he's an official machine. He doesn't understand that I'm your wife, that he's outside, that he's superfluous. . . . Don't let's talk of him! . . ."

"You're unfair, very unfair, dearest," said Vronsky, trying to soothe her. "But never mind, don't let's talk of him. Tell me what you've been doing? What is the matter? What has been wrong with you, and what did the doctor say?"

She looked at him with mocking amusement. Evidently she had hit on other absurd and grotesque aspects in her husband and was awaiting the moment to give expression to them.

But he went on:

"I imagine that it's not illness, but your condition. When will it be?"

The ironical light died away in her eyes, but a different smile, a consciousness of something, he did not know what, and of quiet melancholy, came over her face.

"Soon, soon. You say that our position is miserable, that we must put an end to it. If you knew how terrible it is to me, what I would give to be able to love you freely and boldly! I should not torture myself and torture you with my jealousy. . . . And it will come soon, but not as we expect."

And at the thought of how it would come, she seemed so pitiable to herself that tears came into her eyes, and she could not go on. She laid her hand on his sleeve, dazzling and white with its rings in the lamplight.

"It won't come as we suppose. I didn't mean to say this to you, but you've made me. Soon, soon, all will be over, and we shall all, all be at peace, and suffer no more."

"I don't understand," he said, understanding her.

"You asked when? Soon. And I shan't live through it. Don't interrupt me!" and she made haste to speak. "I know it; I know for certain. I shall die; and I'm very glad I shall die, and release myself and you."

Tears dropped from her eyes; he bent down over her hand and began kissing it, trying to hide his emotion, which, he knew, had no sort of grounds, though he could not control it.

"Yes, it's better so," she said, tightly gripping his hand. "That's the only way, the only way left us."

He had recovered himself, and lifted his head.

"How absurd! What absurd nonsense you are talking!"

"No, it's the truth."

"What, what's the truth?"

"That I shall die. I have had a dream."

"A dream?" repeated Vronsky, and instantly he recalled the peasant of his dream.

"Yes, a dream," she said. "It's a long while since I dreamed it. I dreamed that I ran into my bedroom, that I had to get something there, to find out something; you know how it is in dreams," she said, her eyes wide with horror; "and in the bedroom, in the corner, stood something."

"Oh, what nonsense! How can you believe . . ."

But she would not let him interrupt her. What she was saying was too important to her.

"And the something turned round, and I saw it was a peasant with a disheveled beard, little, and dreadful-looking. I wanted to run away, but he bent down over a sack, and was fumbling there with his hands . . ."

She showed how he had moved his hands. There was terror in her face. And Vronsky, remembering his dream, felt the same terror filling his soul.

"He was fumbling and kept talking quickly, quickly in French, you know: *Il faut le battre, le fer, le brayer, le pétrir*. . . . And in my horror I tried to wake up, and woke up . . . but woke up in the dream. And I began asking myself what it meant. And Korney said to me: 'In childbirth you'll die, ma'am, you'll die. . . .' And I woke up."

"What nonsense, what nonsense!" said Vronsky; but he felt himself that there was no conviction in his voice.

"But don't let's talk of it. Ring the bell, I'll have tea. And stay a little now; it's not long I shall . . ."

But all at once she stopped. The expression of her face instantaneously changed. Horror and excitement were suddenly replaced by a look of soft, solemn, blissful attention. He could not comprehend the meaning of the change. She was listening to the stirring of the new life within her.

Chapter IV

ALEXEY ALEXANDROVITCH, AFTER MEETING VRONSKY ON HIS OWN STEPS, DROVE, AS HE HAD intended, to the Italian opera. He sat through two acts there, and saw everyone he had wanted to see. On returning home, he carefully scrutinized the hat-stand, and noticing that there was not a military overcoat there, he went, as usual, to his own room. But, contrary to his usual habit, he did not go to bed, he walked up and down his study till three o'clock in the morning. The feeling of furious anger with his wife, who would not observe the proprieties and keep to the one stipulation he had laid on her, not to receive her lover in her own home, gave him no peace. She had not complied with his request, and he was bound to punish her and carry out his threat—obtain a divorce and take away his son. He knew all the difficulties connected with this course, but he had said he would do it, and now he must carry out his threat. Countess Lidia Ivanovna had hinted that this was the best way out of his position, and of late the obtaining of divorces had been brought to such perfection that Alexey Alexandrovitch saw a possibility of overcoming the formal difficulties. Misfortunes never come singly, and the affairs of the reorganization of the native tribes, and of the irrigation of the lands of the Zaraisky province, had brought such official worries upon Alexey Alexandrovitch that he had been of late in a continual condition of extreme irritability.

He did not sleep the whole night, and his fury growing in a sort of vast, arithmetical progression, reached its highest limits in the morning. He dressed in haste, and as though carrying his cup full of wrath, and fearing to spill any over, fearing to lose with his wrath the energy necessary for the interview with his wife, he went into her room directly he heard she was up.

Anna, who had thought she knew her husband so well, was amazed at his appearance when he went in to her. His brow was lowering, and his eyes stared darkly before him, avoiding her eyes; his mouth was tightly and contemptuously shut. In his walk, in his gestures, in the sound of his voice there was a determination and firmness such as his wife had never seen in him. He went into her room, and without greeting her, walked straight up to her writing-table, and taking her keys, opened a drawer.

"What do you want?" she cried.

"Your lover's letters," he said.

"They're not here," she said, shutting the drawer; but from that action he saw he had guessed right, and roughly pushing away her hand, he quickly snatched a portfolio in which he knew she used to put her most important papers. She tried to pull the portfolio away, but he pushed her back.

"Sit down! I have to speak to you," he said, putting the portfolio under his arm, and squeezing it so tightly with his elbow that his shoulder stood up. Amazed and intimidated, she gazed at him in silence.

"I told you that I would not allow you to receive your lover in this house."

"I had to see him to . . ."

She stopped, not finding a reason.

"I do not enter into the details of why a woman wants to see her lover."

"I meant, I only . . ." she said, flushing hotly. This coarseness of his angered her, and gave her courage. "Surely you must feel how easy it is for you to insult me?" she said.

"An honest man and an honest woman may be insulted, but to tell a thief he's a thief is simply *la constatation d'un fait.*"

"This cruelty is something new I did not know in you."

"You call it cruelty for a husband to give his wife liberty, giving her the honorable protection of his name, simply on the condition of observing the proprieties: is that cruelty?"

"It's worse than cruel—it's base, if you want to know!" Anna cried, in a rush of hatred, and getting up, she was going away.

"No!" he shrieked, in his shrill voice, which pitched a note higher than usual even, and his big hands clutching her by the arm so violently that red marks were left from the bracelet he was squeezing, he forcibly sat her down in her place.

"Base! If you care to use that word, what is base is to forsake husband and child for a lover, while you eat your husband's bread!"

She bowed her head. She did not say what she had said the evening before to her lover, that *he* was her husband, and her husband was superfluous; she did not even think that. She felt all the justice of his words, and only said softly:

"You cannot describe my position as worse than I feel it to be myself; but what are you saying all this for?"

"What am I saying it for? what for?" he went on, as angrily. "That you may know that since you have not carried out my wishes in regard to observing outward decorum, I will take measures to put an end to this state of things."

"Soon, very soon, it will end, anyway," she said; and again, at the thought of death near at hand and now desired, tears came into her eyes.

"It will end sooner than you and your lover have planned! If you must have the satisfaction of animal passion . . ."

"Alexey Alexandrovitch! I won't say it's not generous, but it's not like a gentleman to strike anyone who's down."

"Yes, you only think of yourself! But the sufferings of a man who was your husband have no interest for you. You don't care that his whole life is ruined, that he is thuff . . . thuff . . ."

Alexey Alexandrovitch was speaking so quickly that he stammered, and was utterly unable to articulate the word "suffering." In the end he pronounced it "suffering." She wanted to laugh, and was immediately ashamed that anything could amuse her at such a moment. And for the first time, for an instant, she felt for him, put herself in his place, and was sorry for him. But what could she say or do? Her head sank, and she sat silent. He too was silent for some time, and then began speaking in a frigid, less shrill voice, emphasizing random words that had no special significance.

"I came to tell you . . ." he said.

She glanced at him. "No, it was my fancy," she thought, recalling the expression of his face when he stumbled over the word "suffering." "No; can a man with those dull eyes, with that self-satisfied complacency, feel anything?"

"I cannot change anything," she whispered.

"I have come to tell you that I am going tomorrow to Moscow, and shall not return again to this house, and you will receive notice of what I decide through the lawyer into whose hands I shall entrust the task of getting a divorce. My son is going to my sister's," said Alexey Alexandrovitch, with an effort recalling what he had meant to say about his son.

"You take Seryozha to hurt me," she said, looking at him from under her brows. "You do not love him. . . . Leave me Seryozha!"

"Yes, I have lost even my affection for my son, because he is associated with the repulsion I feel for you. But still I shall take him. Good-bye!"

And he was going away, but now she detained him.

"Alexey Alexandrovitch, leave me Seryozha!" she whispered once more. "I have nothing else to say. Leave Seryozha till my . . . I shall soon be confined; leave him!"

Alexey Alexandrovitch flew into a rage, and, snatching his hand from her, he went out of the room without a word.

Chapter V

THE WAITING ROOM OF THE CELEBRATED PETERSBURG LAWYER WAS FULL WHEN ALEXEY ALEXANDROVITCH entered it. Three ladies—an old lady, a young lady, and a merchant's wife—and three gentlemen—one a German banker with a ring on his finger, the second a merchant with a beard, and the third a wrathful-looking government clerk in official uniform, with a cross on his neck—had obviously been waiting a long while already. Two clerks were writing at tables with scratching pens. The appurtenances of the writing-tables, about which Alexey Alexandrovitch was himself very fastidious, were exceptionally good. He could not help observing this. One of the clerks, without getting up, turned wrathfully to Alexey Alexandrovitch, half closing his eyes.

"What are you wanting?"

He replied that he had to see the lawyer on some business.

"He is engaged," the clerk responded severely, and he pointed with his pen at the persons waiting, and went on writing.

"Can't he spare time to see me?" said Alexey Alexandrovitch.

"He has no time free; he is always busy. Kindly wait your turn."

"Then I must trouble you to give him my card," Alexey Alexandrovitch said with dignity, seeing the impossibility of preserving his incognito.

The clerk took the card and, obviously not approving of what he read on it, went to the door.

Alexey Alexandrovitch was in principle in favor of the publicity of legal proceedings, though for some higher official considerations he disliked the application of the principle in Russia, and disapproved of it, as far as he could disapprove of anything instituted by authority of the Emperor. His whole life had been spent in administrative work, and consequently, when he did not approve of anything, his disapproval was softened by the recognition of the inevitability of mistakes and the possibility of reform in every department. In the new public law-courts he disliked the restrictions laid on the lawyers conducting cases. But till then he had had nothing to do with the law-courts, and so had disapproved of their publicity simply in theory; now his disapprobation was strengthened by the unpleasant impression made on him in the lawyer's waiting room.

"Coming immediately," said the clerk; and two minutes later there did actually appear in the doorway the large figure of an old solicitor who had been consulting with the lawyer himself.

The lawyer was a little, squat, bald man, with a dark, reddish beard, light-colored long eyebrows, and an overhanging brow. He was attired as though for a wedding, from his cravat to his double watch-chain and varnished boots. His face was clever and manly, but his dress was dandified and in bad taste.

"Pray walk in," said the lawyer, addressing Alexey Alexandrovitch; and, gloomily ushering Karenin in before him, he closed the door.

"Won't you sit down?" He indicated an arm-chair at a writing-table covered with papers. He sat down himself, and, rubbing his little hands with short fingers covered with white hairs, he bent his head on one side. But as soon as he was settled in this position a moth flew over the table. The lawyer, with a swiftness that could never have been expected of him, opened his hands, caught the moth, and resumed his former attitude.

"Before beginning to speak of my business," said Alexey Alexandrovitch, following the lawyer's movements with wondering eyes, "I ought to observe that the business about which I have to speak to you is to be strictly private."

The lawyer's overhanging reddish mustaches were parted in a scarcely perceptible smile.

"I should not be a lawyer if I could not keep the secrets confided to me. But if you would like proof . . ."

Alexey Alexandrovitch glanced at his face, and saw that the shrewd, gray eyes were laughing, and seemed to know all about it already.

"You know my name?" Alexey Alexandrovitch resumed.

"I know you and the good"—again he caught a moth—"work you are doing, like every Russian," said the lawyer, bowing.

Alexey Alexandrovitch sighed, plucking up his courage. But having once made up his mind he went on in his shrill voice, without timidity or hesitation, accentuating here and there a word.

"I have the misfortune," Alexey Alexandrovitch began, "to have been deceived in my married life, and I desire to break off all relations with my wife by legal means—that is, to be divorced, but to do this so that my son may not remain with his mother."

The lawyer's gray eyes tried not to laugh, but they were dancing with irrepressible glee, and Alexey Alexandrovitch saw that it was not simply the delight of a man who has just got a profitable job: there was triumph and joy, there was a gleam like the malignant gleam he saw in his wife's eyes.

"You desire my assistance in securing a divorce?"

"Yes, precisely so; but I ought to warn you that I may be wasting your time and attention. I have come simply to consult you as a preliminary step. I want a divorce, but the form in which it is possible is of great consequence to me. It is very possible that if that form does not correspond with my requirements I may give up a legal divorce."

"Oh, that's always the case," said the lawyer, "and that's always for you to decide."

He let his eyes rest on Alexey Alexandrovitch's feet, feeling that he might offend his client by the sight of his irrepressible amusement. He looked at a moth that flew before his nose, and moved his hands, but did not catch it from regard for Alexey Alexandrovitch's position.

"Though in their general features our laws on this subject are known to me," pursued Alexey Alexandrovitch, "I should be glad to have an idea of the forms in which such things are done in practice."

"You would be glad," the lawyer, without lifting his eyes, responded, adopting, with a certain satisfaction, the tone of his client's remarks, "for me to lay before you all the methods by which you could secure what you desire?"

And on receiving an assuring nod from Alexey Alexandrovitch, he went on, stealing a glance now and then at Alexey Alexandrovitch's face, which was growing red in patches.

"Divorce by our laws," he said, with a slight shade of disapprobation of our laws, "is possible, as you are aware, in the following cases . . . Wait a little!" he called to a clerk who put his head in at the door, but he got up all the same, said a few words to him, and sat down again. ". . . In the following cases: physical defect in the married parties, desertion without communication for five years," he said, crooking a short finger covered with hair, "adultery" (this word he pronounced with obvious satisfaction), "subdivided as follows" (he continued to crook his fat fingers, though the three cases and their subdivisions could obviously not be classified together): "physical defect of the husband or of the wife, adultery of the husband or of the wife." As by now all his fingers were used up, he uncrooked all his fingers and went on: "This is the theoretical view; but I imagine you have done me the honor to apply to me in order to learn its application in practice. And therefore, guided by precedents, I must inform you that in practice cases of divorce may all be reduced to the following—there's no physical defect, I may assume, nor desertion? . . ."

Alexey Alexandrovitch bowed his head in assent.

"—May be reduced to the following: adultery of one of the married parties, and the detection in the fact of the guilty party by mutual agreement, and failing such agreement, accidental detection. It must be admitted that the latter case is rarely met with in practice," said the lawyer, and stealing a glance at Alexey Alexandrovitch he paused, as a man selling pistols, after enlarging on the advantages of each weapon, might await his customer's choice. But Alexey Alexandrovitch said nothing, and therefore the lawyer went on: "The most usual and simple, the sensible course, I consider, is adultery by mutual consent. I should not permit myself to express it so, speaking with a man of no education," he said, "but I imagine that to you this is comprehensible."

Alexey Alexandrovitch was, however, so perturbed that he did not immediately comprehend all the good sense of adultery by mutual consent, and his eyes expressed this uncertainty, but the lawyer promptly came to his assistance.

"People cannot go on living together—here you have a fact. And if both are agreed about it, the details and formalities become a matter of no importance. And at the same time this is the simplest and most certain method."

Alexey Alexandrovitch fully understood now. But he had religious scruples, which hindered the execution of such a plan.

"That is out of the question in the present case," he said. "Only one alternative is possible: undesigned detection, supported by letters which I have."

At the mention of letters the lawyer pursed up his lips, and gave utterance to a thin little compassionate and contemptuous sound.

"Kindly consider," he began, "cases of that kind are, as you are aware, under ecclesiastical jurisdiction; the reverend fathers are fond of going into the minutest details in cases of that kind," he said with a smile, which betrayed his sympathy with the reverend fathers' taste. "Letters may, of course, be a partial confirmation; but detection in the fact there must be of the most direct kind, that is, by eyewitnesses. In fact, if you do me the honor to entrust your confidence to me, you will do well to leave me the choice of the measures to be employed. If one wants the result, one must admit the means."

"If it is so . . ." Alexey Alexandrovitch began, suddenly turning white; but at that moment the lawyer rose and again went to the door to speak to the intruding clerk.

"Tell her we don't haggle over fees!" he said, and returned to Alexey Alexandrovitch.

On his way back he caught unobserved another moth. "Nice state my rep curtains will be in by the summer!" he thought, frowning.

"And so you were saying? . . ." he said.

"I will communicate my decision to you by letter," said Alexey Alexandrovitch, getting up, and he clutched at the table. After standing a moment in silence, he said: "From your words I may consequently conclude that a divorce may be obtained? I would ask you to let me know what are your terms."

"It may be obtained if you give me complete liberty of action," said the lawyer, not answering his question. "When can I reckon on receiving information from you?" he asked, moving towards the door, his eyes and his varnished boots shining.

"In a week's time. Your answer as to whether you will undertake to conduct the case, and on what terms, you will be so good as to communicate to me."

"Very good."

The lawyer bowed respectfully, let his client out of the door, and, left alone, gave himself up to his sense of amusement. He felt so mirthful that, contrary to his rules, he made a reduction in his terms to the haggling lady, and gave up catching moths, finally deciding that next winter he must have the furniture covered with velvet, like Sigonin's.

Chapter VI

ALEXEY ALEXANDROVITCH HAD GAINED A BRILLIANT VICTORY AT THE SITTING OF THE COMMISsion of the 17th of August, but in the sequel this victory cut the ground from under his feet. The new commission for the inquiry into the condition of the native tribes in all its branches had been formed and despatched to its destination with an unusual speed and energy inspired by Alexey Alexandrovitch. Within three months a report was presented. The condition of the native tribes was investigated in its political, administrative, economic, ethnographic, material, and religious aspects. To all these questions there were answers admirably stated, and answers admitting no shade of doubt, since they were not a product of human thought, always liable to error, but were all the product of official activity. The answers were all based on official data furnished by governors and heads of churches, and founded on the reports of district magistrates and ecclesiastical superintendents, founded in their turn on the reports of parochial overseers and parish priests; and so all of these answers were unhesitating and certain. All such questions as, for instance, of the cause of failure of crops, of the adherence of certain tribes to their ancient beliefs, etc.—questions which, but for the convenient intervention of the official machine, are not, and cannot be solved for ages—received full, unhesitating solution. And this solution was in favor of Alexey Alexandrovitch's contention. But Stremov, who had felt stung to the quick at the last sitting, had, on the reception of the commission's report, resorted to tactics which Alexey Alexandrovitch had not anticipated. Stremov, carrying with him several other members, went over to Alexey Alexandrovitch's side, and not contenting himself with warmly defending the measure proposed by Karenin, proposed other more extreme measures in the same direction. These measures, still further exaggerated in opposition to what was Alexey Alexandrovitch's fundamental idea, were passed by the commission, and then the aim of Stremov's tactics became apparent. Carried to an extreme, the measures seemed at once to be so absurd that the highest authorities, and public opinion, and intellectual ladies, and the newspapers, all at the same time fell foul of them, expressing their indignation both with the measures and their nominal father, Alexey Alexandrovitch. Stremov drew back, affecting to have blindly followed Karenin, and to be astounded and distressed at what had been done. This meant the defeat of Alexey Alexandrovitch. But in spite of failing health, in spite of his domestic griefs, he did not give in. There was a split in the commission. Some members, with Stremov at their head, justified their mistake on the ground that they had put faith in the commission of revision, instituted by Alexey Alexandrovitch, and maintained that the report of the commission was rubbish, and simply so much waste paper. Alexey Alexandrovitch, with a following of those who saw the danger of so revolutionary an attitude to official documents, persisted in upholding the statements obtained by the revising commission. In consequence of this, in the higher spheres, and even in society, all was chaos, and although everyone was interested, no one could tell whether the native tribes really were becoming impoverished and ruined, or whether they were in a flourishing condition. The position of Alexey Alexandrovitch, owing to this, and partly owing to the contempt lavished on him for his wife's infidelity, became very precarious. And in this position he took an important resolution. To the astonishment of the commission, he announced that he should ask permission to go himself to investigate the question on the spot. And having obtained permission, Alexey Alexandrovitch prepared to set off to these remote provinces.

Alexey Alexandrovitch's departure made a great sensation, the more so as just before he started he officially returned the posting-fares allowed him for twelve horses, to drive to his destination.

"I think it very noble," Betsy said about this to the Princess Myakaya. "Why take money for posting-horses when everyone knows that there are railways everywhere now?"

But Princess Myakaya did not agree, and the Princess Tverskaya's opinion annoyed her indeed.

"It's all very well for you to talk," said she, "when you have I don't know how many millions; but I am very glad when my husband goes on a revising tour in the summer. It's very good for him and pleasant traveling about, and it's a settled arrangement for me to keep a carriage and coachman on the money."

On his way to the remote provinces Alexey Alexandrovitch stopped for three days at Moscow.

The day after his arrival he was driving back from calling on the governor-general. At the crossroads by Gazetny Place, where there are always crowds of carriages and sleighs, Alexey Alexandrovitch suddenly heard his name called out in such a loud and cheerful voice that he could not help looking round. At the corner of the pavement, in a short, stylish overcoat and a low-crowned fashionable hat, jauntily askew, with a smile that showed a gleam of white teeth and red lips, stood Stepan Arkadyevitch, radiant, young, and beaming. He called him vigorously and urgently, and insisted on his stopping. He had one arm on the window of a carriage that was stopping at the corner, and out of the window were thrust the heads of a lady in a velvet hat, and two children. Stepan Arkadyevitch was smiling and beckoning to his brother-in-law. The lady smiled a kindly smile too, and she too waved her hand to Alexey Alexandrovitch. It was Dolly with her children.

Alexey Alexandrovitch did not want to see anyone in Moscow, and least of all his wife's brother. He raised his hat and would have driven on, but Stepan Arkadyevitch told his coachman to stop, and ran across the snow to him.

"Well, what a shame not to have let us know! Been here long? I was at Dussot's yesterday and saw 'Karenin' on the visitors' list, but it never entered my head that it was you," said Stepan Arkadyevitch, sticking his head in at the window of the carriage, "or I should have looked you up. I am glad to see you!" he said, knocking one foot against the other to shake the snow off. "What a shame of you not to let us know!" he repeated.

"I had no time; I am very busy," Alexey Alexandrovitch responded dryly.

"Come to my wife, she does so want to see you."

Alexey Alexandrovitch unfolded the rug in which his frozen feet were wrapped, and getting out of his carriage made his way over the snow to Darya Alexandrovna.

"Why, Alexey Alexandrovitch, what are you cutting us like this for?" said Dolly, smiling.

"I was very busy. Delighted to see you!" he said in a tone clearly indicating that he was annoyed by it. "How are you?"

"Tell me, how is my darling Anna?"

Alexey Alexandrovitch mumbled something and would have gone on. But Stepan Arkadyevitch stopped him.

"I tell you what we'll do tomorrow. Dolly, ask him to dinner. We'll ask Koznishev and Pestsov, so as to entertain him with our Moscow celebrities."

"Yes, please, do come," said Dolly; "we will expect you at five, or six o'clock, if you like. How is my darling Anna? How long . . ."

"She is quite well," Alexey Alexandrovitch mumbled, frowning. "Delighted!" and he moved away towards his carriage.

"You will come?" Dolly called after him.

Alexey Alexandrovitch said something which Dolly could not catch in the noise of the moving carriages.

"I shall come round tomorrow!" Stepan Arkadyevitch shouted to him.

Alexey Alexandrovitch got into his carriage, and buried himself in it so as neither to see nor be seen.

"Queer fish!" said Stepan Arkadyevitch to his wife, and glancing at his watch, he made a motion of his hand before his face, indicating a caress to his wife and children, and walked jauntily along the pavement.

"Stiva! Stiva!" Dolly called, reddening.

He turned round.

"I must get coats, you know, for Grisha and Tanya. Give me the money."

"Never mind; you tell them I'll pay the bill!" and he vanished, nodding genially to an acquaintance who drove by.

Chapter VII

THE NEXT DAY WAS SUNDAY. STEPAN ARKADYEVITCH WENT TO THE GRAND THEATER TO A REhearsal of the ballet, and gave Masha Tchibisova, a pretty dancing-girl whom he had just taken under his protection, the coral necklace he had promised her the evening before, and behind the scenes in the dim daylight of the theater, managed to kiss her pretty little face, radiant over her present. Besides the gift of the necklace he wanted to arrange with her about meeting after the ballet. After explaining that he could not come at the beginning of the ballet, he promised he would come for the last act and take her to supper. From the theater Stepan Arkadyevitch drove to Ohotny Row, selected himself the fish and asparagus for dinner, and by twelve o'clock was at Dussot's, where he had to see three people, luckily all staying at the same hotel: Levin, who had recently come back from abroad and was staying there; the new head of his department, who had just been promoted to that position, and had come on a tour of revision to Moscow; and his brother-in-law, Karenin, whom he must see, so as to be sure of bringing him to dinner.

Stepan Arkadyevitch liked dining, but still better he liked to give a dinner, small, but very choice, both as regards the food and drink and as regards the selection of guests. He particularly liked the program of that day's dinner. There would be fresh perch, asparagus, and *la pièce de résistance*—first rate, but quite plain, roast beef, and wines to suit: so much for the eating and drinking. Kitty and Levin would be of the party, and that this might not be obtrusively evident, there would be a girl cousin too, and young Shtcherbatsky, and *la pièce de résistance* among the guests—Sergey Koznishev and Alexey Alexandrovitch. Sergey Ivanovitch was a Moscow man, and a philosopher; Alexey Alexandrovitch a Petersburger, and a practical politician. He was asking, too, the well-known eccentric enthusiast, Pestsov, a liberal, a great talker, a musician, an historian, and the most delightfully youthful person of fifty, who would be a sauce or garnish for Koznishev and Karenin. He would provoke them and set them off.

The second installment for the forest had been received from the merchant and was not yet exhausted; Dolly had been very amiable and good-humored of late, and the idea of the dinner pleased Stepan Arkadyevitch from every point of view. He was in the most light-hearted mood. There were two circumstances a little unpleasant, but these two circumstances were drowned in the sea of good-humored gaiety which flooded the soul of Stepan Arkadyevitch. These two circumstances were: first, that on meeting Alexey Alexandrovitch the day before in the street he had noticed that he was cold and reserved with him, and putting the expression of Alexey Alexandrovitch's face and the fact that he had not come to see them or let them know of his arrival with the rumors he had heard about Anna and Vronsky, Stepan Arkadyevitch guessed that something was wrong between the husband and wife.

That was one disagreeable thing. The other slightly disagreeable fact was that the new head of his department, like all new heads, had the reputation already of a terrible person, who got up at six o'clock in the morning, worked like a horse, and insisted on his subordinates working in the same way. Moreover, this new head had the further reputation of being a bear in his manners, and was, according to all reports, a man of a class in all respects the opposite of that to which his predecessor had belonged, and to which Stepan Arkadyevitch had hitherto belonged himself. On the previous day Stepan Arkadyevitch had appeared at the office in a uniform, and the new chief had been very affable and had talked to him as to an acquaintance. Consequently Stepan Arkadyevitch deemed it his duty to call upon him in his non-official dress. The thought that the new chief might not give him a warm reception was the other unpleasant thing. But Stepan Arkadyevitch instinctively felt that everything would *come round* all right. "They're all people, all men, like us poor sinners; why be nasty and quarrelsome?" he thought as he went into the hotel.

"Good day, Vassily," he said, walking into the corridor with his hat cocked on one side, and addressing a footman he knew; "why, you've let your whiskers grow! Levin, number seven, eh? Take me up, please. And find out whether Count Anitchkin" (this was the new head) "is receiving."

"Yes, sir," Vassily responded, smiling. "You've not been to see us for a long while."

"I was here yesterday, but at the other entrance. Is this number seven?"

Levin was standing with a peasant from Tver in the middle of the room, measuring a fresh bearskin, when Stepan Arkadyevitch went in.

"What! you killed him?" cried Stepan Arkadyevitch. "Well done! A she-bear? How are you, Arhip!"

He shook hands with the peasant and sat down on the edge of a chair, without taking off his coat and hat.

"Come, take off your coat and stay a little," said Levin, taking his hat.

"No, I haven't time; I've only looked in for a tiny second," answered Stepan Arkadyevitch. He threw open his coat, but afterwards did take it off, and sat on for a whole hour, talking to Levin about hunting and the most intimate subjects.

"Come, tell me, please, what you did abroad? Where have you been?" said Stepan Arkadyevitch, when the peasant had gone.

"Oh, I stayed in Germany, in Prussia, in France, and in England—not in the capitals, but in the manufacturing towns, and saw a great deal that was new to me. And I'm glad I went."

"Yes, I knew your idea of the solution of the labor question."

"Not a bit: in Russia there can be no labor question. In Russia the question is that of the relation of the working people to the land; though the question exists there too—but there it's a matter of repairing what's been ruined, while with us . . ."

Stepan Arkadyevitch listened attentively to Levin.

"Yes, yes!" he said, "it's very possible you're right. But I'm glad you're in good spirits, and are hunting bears, and working, and interested. Shtcherbatsky told me another story—he met you—that you were in such a depressed state, talking of nothing but death. . . ."

"Well, what of it? I've not given up thinking of death," said Levin. "It's true that it's high time I was dead; and that all this is nonsense. It's the truth I'm telling you. I do value my idea and my work awfully; but in reality only consider this: all this world of ours is nothing but a speck of mildew, which has grown up on a tiny planet. And for us to suppose we can have something great—ideas, work—it's all dust and ashes."

"But all that's as old as the hills, my boy!"

"It is old; but do you know, when you grasp this fully, then somehow everything becomes of no consequence. When you understand that you will die tomorrow, if not today, and nothing will be left, then everything is so unimportant! And I consider my idea very important, but it turns out really to be as unimportant too, even if it were carried out, as doing for that bear. So one goes on living, amusing oneself with hunting, with work—anything so as not to think of death!"

Stepan Arkadyevitch smiled a subtle affectionate smile as he listened to Levin.

"Well, of course! Here you've come round to my point. Do you remember you attacked me for seeking enjoyment in life? Don't be so severe, O moralist!"

"No; all the same, what's fine in life is . . ." Levin hesitated—"oh, I don't know. All I know is that we shall soon be dead."

"Why so soon?"

"And do you know, there's less charm in life, when one thinks of death, but there's more peace."

"On the contrary, the finish is always the best. But I must be going," said Stepan Arkadyevitch, getting up for the tenth time.

"Oh, no, stay a bit!" said Levin, keeping him. "Now, when shall we see each other again? I'm going tomorrow."

"I'm a nice person! Why, that's just what I came for! You simply must come to dinner with us today. Your brother's coming, and Karenin, my brother-in-law."

"You don't mean to say he's here?" said Levin, and he wanted to inquire about Kitty. He had heard at the beginning of the winter that she was at Petersburg with her sister, the wife of the diplomat, and he did not know whether she had come back or not; but he changed his mind and did not ask. "Whether she's coming or not, I don't care," he said to himself.

"So you'll come?"

"Of course."

"At five o'clock, then, and not evening dress."

And Stepan Arkadyevitch got up and went down below to the new head of his department. Instinct had not misled Stepan Arkadyevitch. The terrible new head turned out to be an extremely amenable person, and Stepan Arkadyevitch lunched with him and stayed on, so that it was four o'clock before he got to Alexey Alexandrovitch.

Chapter VIII

ALEXEY ALEXANDROVITCH, ON COMING BACK FROM CHURCH SERVICE, HAD SPENT THE WHOLE morning indoors. He had two pieces of business before him that morning; first, to receive and send on a deputation from the native tribes which was on its way to Petersburg, and now at Moscow; secondly, to write the promised letter to the lawyer. The deputation, though it had been summoned at Alexey Alexandrovitch's instigation, was not without its discomforting and even dangerous aspect, and he was glad he had found it in Moscow. The members of this deputation had not the slightest conception of their duty and the part they were to play. They naïvely believed that it was their business to lay before the commission their needs and the actual condition of things, and to ask assistance of the government, and utterly failed to grasp that some of their statements and requests supported the contention of the enemy's side, and so spoiled the whole business. Alexey Alexandrovitch was busily engaged with them for a long while, drew up a program for them from which they were not to depart, and on dismissing them wrote a letter to Petersburg for the guidance of the deputation. He had his chief support in this affair in the Countess Lidia Ivanovna. She was a specialist in the matter of deputations, and no one knew better than she how to manage them, and put them in the way they should go. Having completed this task, Alexey Alexandrovitch wrote the letter to the lawyer. Without the slightest hesitation he gave him permission to act as he might judge best. In the letter he enclosed three of Vronsky's notes to Anna, which were in the portfolio he had taken away.

Since Alexey Alexandrovitch had left home with the intention of not returning to his family again, and since he had been at the lawyer's and had spoken, though only to one man, of his intention, since especially he had translated the matter from the world of real life to the world of ink and paper, he had grown more and more used to his own intention, and by now distinctly perceived the feasibility of its execution.

He was sealing the envelope to the lawyer, when he heard the loud tones of Stepan Arkadyevitch's voice. Stepan Arkadyevitch was disputing with Alexey Alexandrovitch's servant, and insisting on being announced.

"No matter," thought Alexey Alexandrovitch, "so much the better. I will inform him at once of my position in regard to his sister, and explain why it is I can't dine with him."

"Come in!" he said aloud, collecting his papers, and putting them in the blotting-paper.

"There, you see, you're talking nonsense, and he's at home!" responded Stepan Arkadyevitch's voice, addressing the servant, who had refused to let him in, and taking off his coat as he went, Oblonsky walked into the room. "Well, I'm awfully glad I've found you! So I hope . . ." Stepan Arkadyevitch began cheerfully.

"I cannot come," Alexey Alexandrovitch said coldly, standing and not asking his visitor to sit down.

Alexey Alexandrovitch had thought to pass at once into those frigid relations in which he ought to stand with the brother of a wife against whom he was beginning a suit for divorce. But he had not taken into account the ocean of kindliness brimming over in the heart of Stepan Arkadyevitch.

Stepan Arkadyevitch opened wide his clear, shining eyes.

"Why can't you? What do you mean?" he asked in perplexity, speaking in French. "Oh, but it's a promise. And we're all counting on you."

"I want to tell you that I can't dine at your house, because the terms of relationship which have existed between us must cease."

"How? How do you mean? What for?" said Stepan Arkadyevitch with a smile.

"Because I am beginning an action for divorce against your sister, my wife. I ought to have . . ."

But, before Alexey Alexandrovitch had time to finish his sentence, Stepan Arkadyevitch was behaving not at all as he had expected. He groaned and sank into an arm-chair.

"No, Alexey Alexandrovitch! What are you saying?" cried Oblonsky, and his suffering was apparent in his face.

"It is so."

"Excuse me, I can't, I can't believe it!"

Alexey Alexandrovitch sat down, feeling that his words had not had the effect he anticipated, and that it would be unavoidable for him to explain his position, and that, whatever explanations he might make, his relations with his brother-in-law would remain unchanged.

"Yes, I am brought to the painful necessity of seeking a divorce," he said.

"I will say one thing, Alexey Alexandrovitch. I know you for an excellent, upright man; I know Anna—excuse me, I can't change my opinion of her—for a good, an excellent woman; and so, excuse me, I cannot believe it. There is some misunderstanding," said he.

"Oh, if it were merely a misunderstanding! . . ."

"Pardon, I understand," interposed Stepan Arkadyevitch. "But of course . . . One thing: you must not act in haste. You must not, you must not act in haste!"

"I am not acting in haste," Alexey Alexandrovitch said coldly, "but one cannot ask advice of anyone in such a matter. I have quite made up my mind."

"This is awful!" said Stepan Arkadyevitch. "I would do one thing, Alexey Alexandrovitch. I beseech you, do it!" he said. "No action has yet been taken, if I understand rightly. Before you take advice, see my wife, talk to her. She loves Anna like a sister, she loves you, and she's a wonderful woman. For God's sake, talk to her! Do me that favor, I beseech you!"

Alexey Alexandrovitch pondered, and Stepan Arkadyevitch looked at him sympathetically, without interrupting his silence.

"You will go to see her?"

"I don't know. That was just why I have not been to see you. I imagine our relations must change."

"Why so? I don't see that. Allow me to believe that apart from our connection you have for me, at least in part, the same friendly feeling I have always had for you . . . and sincere esteem," said Stepan Arkadyevitch, pressing his hand. "Even if your worst suppositions were correct, I don't—and never would—take on myself to judge either side, and I see no reason why our relations should be affected. But now, do this, come and see my wife."

"Well, we look at the matter differently," said Alexey Alexandrovitch coldly. "However, we won't discuss it."

"No; why shouldn't you come today to dine, anyway? My wife's expecting you. Please, do come. And, above all, talk it over with her. She's a wonderful woman. For God's sake, on my knees, I implore you!"

"If you so much wish it, I will come," said Alexey Alexandrovitch, sighing.

And, anxious to change the conversation, he inquired about what interested them both—the new head of Stepan Arkadyevitch's department, a man not yet old, who had suddenly been promoted to so high a position.

Alexey Alexandrovitch had previously felt no liking for Count Anitchkin, and had always differed from him in his opinions. But now, from a feeling readily comprehensible to officials—that hatred felt by one who has suffered a defeat in the service for one who has received a promotion, he could not endure him.

"Well, have you seen him?" said Alexey Alexandrovitch with a malignant smile.

"Of course; he was at our sitting yesterday. He seems to know his work capitally, and to be very energetic."

"Yes, but what is his energy directed to?" said Alexey Alexandrovitch. "Is he aiming at doing anything, or simply undoing what's been done? It's the great misfortune of our government—this paper administration, of which he's a worthy representative."

"Really, I don't know what fault one could find with him. His policy I don't know, but one thing—he's a very nice fellow," answered Stepan Arkadyevitch. "I've just been seeing him, and he's really a capital fellow. We lunched together, and I taught him how to make, you know that drink, wine and oranges. It's so cooling. And it's a wonder he didn't know it. He liked it awfully. No, really he's a capital fellow."

Stepan Arkadyevitch glanced at his watch.

"Why, good heavens, it's four already, and I've still to go to Dolgovushin's! So please come round to dinner. You can't imagine how you will grieve my wife and me."

The way in which Alexey Alexandrovitch saw his brother-in-law out was very different from the manner in which he had met him.

"I've promised, and I'll come," he answered wearily.

"Believe me, I appreciate it, and I hope you won't regret it," answered Stepan Arkadyevitch, smiling.

And, putting on his coat as he went, he patted the footman on the head, chuckled, and went out.

"At five o'clock, and not evening dress, please," he shouted once more, turning at the door.

Chapter IX

IT WAS PAST FIVE, AND SEVERAL GUESTS HAD ALREADY ARRIVED, BEFORE THE HOST HIMSELF GOT home. He went in together with Sergey Ivanovitch Koznishev and Pestsov, who had reached the street door at the same moment. These were the two leading representatives of the Moscow intellectuals, as Oblonsky had called them. Both were men respected for their character and their intelligence. They respected each other, but were in complete and hopeless disagreement upon almost every subject, not because they belonged to opposite parties, but precisely because they were of the same party (their enemies refused to see any distinction between their views); but, in that party, each had his own special shade of opinion. And since no difference is less easily overcome than the difference of opinion about semi-abstract questions, they never agreed in any opinion, and had long, indeed, been accustomed to jeer without anger, each at the other's incorrigible aberrations.

They were just going in at the door, talking of the weather, when Stepan Arkadyevitch overtook them. In the drawing room there were already sitting Prince Alexander Dmitrievitch Shtcherbatsky, young Shtcherbatsky, Turovtsin, Kitty, and Karenin.

Stepan Arkadyevitch saw immediately that things were not going well in the drawing room without him. Darya Alexandrovna, in her best gray silk gown, obviously worried about the children, who were to have their dinner by themselves in the nursery, and by her husband's absence, was not equal to the task of making the party mix without him. All were sitting like so many priests' wives on a visit (so the old prince expressed it), obviously wondering why they were there, and pumping up remarks simply to avoid being silent. Turovtsin—good, simple man—felt unmistakably a fish out of water, and the smile with which his thick lips greeted Stepan Arkadyevitch said, as plainly as words: "Well, old boy, you have popped me down in a learned set! A drinking party now, or the Château des Fleurs, would be more in my line!" The old prince sat in silence, his bright little eyes watching Karenin from one side, and Stepan Arkadyevitch saw that he had already formed a phrase to sum up that politician of whom guests were invited to partake as though he were a sturgeon. Kitty was looking at the door, calling up all her energies to keep her from blushing at the entrance of Konstantin Levin. Young Shtcherbatsky, who had not been introduced to Karenin, was trying to look as though he were not in the least conscious of it. Karenin himself had followed the Petersburg fashion for a dinner with ladies and was wearing evening dress and a white tie. Stepan Arkadyevitch saw by his face that he had come simply to keep his promise, and was performing a disagreeable duty in being present at this gathering. He was indeed the person chiefly responsible for the chill benumbing all the guests before Stepan Arkadyevitch came in.

On entering the drawing room Stepan Arkadyevitch apologized, explaining that he had been detained by that prince, who was always the scapegoat for all his absences and unpunctualities, and in one moment he had made all the guests acquainted with each other, and, bringing together Alexey Alexandrovitch and Sergey Koznishev, started them on a discussion of the Russification of Poland, into which they immediately plunged with Pestsov. Slapping Turovtsin on the shoulder, he whispered something comic in his ear, and set him down by his wife and the old prince. Then he told Kitty she was looking very pretty that evening, and presented Shtcherbatsky to Karenin. In a moment he had so kneaded together the social dough that the drawing room became very lively, and there was a merry buzz of voices. Konstantin Levin was the only person who had not arrived. But this was so much the better, as going into the dining room, Stepan Arkadyevitch found to his horror that the port and sherry had been procured from Depré, and not from Levy, and, directing that the coachman should be sent off as speedily as possible to Levy's, he was going back to the drawing room.

In the dining room he was met by Konstantin Levin.

"I'm not late?"

"You can never help being late!" said Stepan Arkadyevitch, taking his arm.

"Have you a lot of people? Who's here?" asked Levin, unable to help blushing, as he knocked the snow off his cap with his glove.

"All our own set. Kitty's here. Come along, I'll introduce you to Karenin."

Stepan Arkadyevitch, for all his liberal views, was well aware that to meet Karenin was sure to be felt a flattering distinction, and so treated his best friends to this honor. But at that instant Konstantin Levin was not in a condition to feel all the gratification of making such an acquaintance. He had not seen Kitty since that memorable evening when he met Vronsky, not counting, that is, the moment when he had had a glimpse of her on the highroad. He had known at the bottom of his heart that he would see her here today. But to keep his thoughts free, he had tried to persuade himself that he did not know it. Now when he heard that she was here, he was suddenly conscious of such delight, and at the same time of such dread, that his breath failed him and he could not utter what he wanted to say.

"What is she like, what is she like? Like what she used to be, or like what she was in the carriage? What if Darya Alexandrovna told the truth? Why shouldn't it be the truth?" he thought.

"Oh, please, introduce me to Karenin," he brought out with an effort, and with a desperately determined step he walked into the drawing room and beheld her.

She was not the same as she used to be, nor was she as she had been in the carriage; she was quite different.

She was scared, shy, shame-faced, and still more charming from it. She saw him the very instant he walked into the room. She had been expecting him. She was delighted, and so confused at her own delight that there was a moment, the moment when he went up to her sister and glanced again at her, when she, and he, and Dolly, who saw it all, thought she would break down and would begin to cry. She crimsoned, turned white, crimsoned again, and grew faint, waiting with quivering lips for him to come to her. He went up to her, bowed, and held out his hand without speaking. Except for the slight quiver of her lips and the moisture in her eyes that made them brighter, her smile was almost calm as she said:

"How long it is since we've seen each other!" and with desperate determination she pressed his hand with her cold hand.

"You've not seen me, but I've seen you," said Levin, with a radiant smile of happiness. "I saw you when you were driving from the railway station to Ergushovo."

"When?" she asked, wondering.

"You were driving to Ergushovo," said Levin, feeling as if he would sob with the rapture that was flooding his heart. "And how dared I associate a thought of anything not innocent with this touching creature? And, yes, I do believe it's true what Darya Alexandrovna told me," he thought.

Stepan Arkadyevitch took him by the arm and led him away to Karenin.

"Let me introduce you." He mentioned their names.

"Very glad to meet you again," said Alexey Alexandrovitch coldly, shaking hands with Levin.

"You are acquainted?" Stepan Arkadyevitch asked in surprise.

"We spent three hours together in the train," said Levin smiling, "but got out, just as in a masquerade, quite mystified—at least I was."

"Nonsense! Come along, please," said Stepan Arkadyevitch, pointing in the direction of the dining room.

The men went into the dining room and went up to a table, laid with six sorts of spirits and as many kinds of cheese, some with little silver spades and some without, caviar, herrings, preserves of various kinds, and plates with slices of French bread.

The men stood round the strong-smelling spirits and salt delicacies, and the discussion of the Russification of Poland between Koznishev, Karenin, and Pestsov died down in anticipation of dinner.

Sergey Ivanovitch was unequaled in his skill in winding up the most heated and serious argument by some unexpected pinch of Attic salt that changed the disposition of his opponent. He did this now.

Alexey Alexandrovitch had been maintaining that the Russification of Poland could only be accomplished as a result of larger measures which ought to be introduced by the Russian government.

Pestsov insisted that one country can only absorb another when it is the more densely populated.

Koznishev admitted both points, but with limitations. As they were going out of the drawing room to conclude the argument, Koznishev said, smiling:

"So, then, for the Russification of our foreign populations there is but one method—to bring up as many children as one can. My brother and I are terribly in fault, I see. You married men, especially you, Stepan Arkadyevitch, are the real patriots: what number have you reached?" he said, smiling genially at their host and holding out a tiny wine glass to him.

Everyone laughed, and Stepan Arkadyevitch with particular good-humor.

"Oh, yes, that's the best method!" he said, munching cheese and filling the wine glass with a special sort of spirit. The conversation dropped at the jest.

"This cheese is not bad. Shall I give you some?" said the master of the house. "Why, have you been going in for gymnastics again?" he asked Levin, pinching his muscle with his left hand. Levin smiled, bent his arm, and under Stepan Arkadyevitch's fingers the muscles swelled up like a sound cheese, hard as a knob of iron, through the fine cloth of the coat.

"What biceps! A perfect Samson!"

"I imagine great strength is needed for hunting bears," observed Alexey Alexandrovitch, who had the mistiest notions about the chase. He cut off and spread with cheese a wafer of bread fine as a spider-web.

Levin smiled.

"Not at all. Quite the contrary; a child can kill a bear," he said, with a slight bow moving aside for the ladies, who were approaching the table.

"You have killed a bear, I've been told!" said Kitty, trying assiduously to catch with her fork a perverse mushroom that would slip away, and setting the lace quivering over her white arm. "Are there bears on your place?" she added, turning her charming little head to him and smiling.

There was apparently nothing extraordinary in what she said, but what unutterable meaning there was for him in every sound, in every turn of her lips, her eyes, her hand as she said it! There was entreaty for forgiveness, and trust in him, and tenderness—soft, timid tenderness—and promise and hope and love for him, which he could not but believe in and which choked him with happiness.

"No, we've been hunting in the Tver province. It was coming back from there that I met your *beau-frère* in the train, or your *beau-frère's* brother-in-law," he said with a smile. "It was an amusing meeting."

And he began telling with droll good-humor how, after not sleeping all night, he had, wearing an old fur-lined, full-skirted coat, got into Alexey Alexandrovitch's compartment.

"The conductor, forgetting the proverb, would have chucked me out on account of my attire; but thereupon I began expressing my feelings in elevated language, and . . . you, too," he said, addressing Karenin and forgetting his name, "at first would have ejected me on the ground of the old coat, but afterwards you took my part, for which I am extremely grateful."

"The rights of passengers generally to choose their seats are too ill-defined," said Alexey Alexandrovitch, rubbing the tips of his fingers on his handkerchief.

"I saw you were in uncertainty about me," said Levin, smiling good-naturedly, "but I made haste to plunge into intellectual conversation to smooth over the defects of my attire."

Sergey Ivanovitch, while he kept up a conversation with their hostess, had one ear for his brother, and he glanced askance at him. "What is the matter with him today? Why such a conquering hero?" he thought. He did not know that Levin was feeling as though he had grown wings. Levin knew she was listening to his words and that she was glad to listen to him. And this was the only thing that interested him. Not in that room only, but in the whole world, there existed for him only himself, with enormously increased importance and dignity in his own eyes, and she. He felt himself on a pinnacle that made him giddy, and far away down below were all those nice excellent Karenins, Oblonskys, and all the world.

Quite without attracting notice, without glancing at them, as though there were no other places left, Stepan Arkadyevitch put Levin and Kitty side by side.

"Oh, you may as well sit there," he said to Levin.

The dinner was as choice as the china, in which Stepan Arkadyevitch was a connoisseur. The *soupe Marie-Louise* was a splendid success; the tiny pies eaten with it melted in the mouth and were irreproachable. The two footmen and Matvey, in white cravats, did their duty with the dishes and wines unobtrusively, quietly, and swiftly. On the material side the dinner was a success; it was no less so on the immaterial. The conversation, at times general and at times between individuals, never paused, and towards the end the company was so lively that the men rose from the table, without stopping speaking, and even Alexey Alexandrovitch thawed.

Chapter X

PESTSOV LIKED THRASHING AN ARGUMENT OUT TO THE END, AND WAS NOT SATISFIED WITH Sergey Ivanovitch's words, especially as he felt the injustice of his view.

"I did not mean," he said over the soup, addressing Alexey Alexandrovitch, "mere density of population alone, but in conjunction with fundamental ideas, and not by means of principles."

"It seems to me," Alexey Alexandrovitch said languidly, and with no haste, "that that's the same thing. In my opinion, influence over another people is only possible to the people which has the higher development, which . . ."

"But that's just the question," Pestsov broke in in his bass.

He was always in a hurry to speak, and seemed always to put his whole soul into what he was saying: "In what are we to make higher development consist? The English, the French, the Germans, which is at the highest stage of development? Which of them will nationalize the other? We see the Rhine provinces have been turned French, but the Germans are not at a lower stage!" he shouted. "There is another law at work there."

"I fancy that the greater influence is always on the side of true civilization," said Alexey Alexandrovitch, slightly lifting his eyebrows.

"But what are we to lay down as the outward signs of true civilization?" said Pestsov.

"I imagine such signs are generally very well-known," said Alexey Alexandrovitch.

"But are they fully known?" Sergey Ivanovitch put in with a subtle smile. "It is the accepted view now that real culture must be purely classical; but we see most intense disputes on each side of the question, and there is no denying that the opposite camp has strong points in its favor."

"You are for classics, Sergey Ivanovitch. Will you take red wine?" said Stepan Arkadyevitch.

"I am not expressing my own opinion of either form of culture," Sergey Ivanovitch said, holding out his glass with a smile of condescension, as to a child. "I only say that both sides have strong arguments to support them," he went on, addressing Alexey Alexandrovitch. "My sympathies are classical from education, but in this discussion I am personally unable to arrive at a conclusion. I see no distinct grounds for classical studies being given a pre-eminence over scientific studies."

"The natural sciences have just as great an educational value," put in Pestsov. "Take astronomy, take botany, or zoology with its system of general principles."

"I cannot quite agree with that," responded Alexey Alexandrovitch "It seems to me that one must admit that the very process of studying the forms of language has a peculiarly favorable influence on intellectual development. Moreover, it cannot be denied that the influence of the classical authors is in the highest degree moral, while, unfortunately, with the study of the natural sciences are associated the false and noxious doctrines which are the curse of our day."

Sergey Ivanovitch would have said something, but Pestsov interrupted him in his rich bass. He began warmly contesting the justice of this view. Sergey Ivanovitch waited serenely to speak, obviously with a convincing reply ready.

"But," said Sergey Ivanovitch, smiling subtly, and addressing Karenin, "One must allow that to weigh all the advantages and disadvantages of classical and scientific studies is a difficult task, and the question which form of education was to be preferred would not have been so quickly and conclusively decided if there had not been in favor of classical education, as you expressed it just now, its moral—*disons le mot*—anti-nihilist influence."

"Undoubtedly."

"If it had not been for the distinctive property of anti-nihilistic influence on the side of classical studies, we should have considered the subject more, have weighed the arguments on both sides," said Sergey Ivanovitch with a subtle smile, "we should have given elbow-room to both tendencies. But now we know that these little pills of classical learning possess the medicinal property of anti-nihilism, and we boldly prescribe them to our patients . . . But what if they had no such medicinal property?" he wound up humorously.

At Sergey Ivanovitch's little pills, everyone laughed; Turovtsin in especial roared loudly and jovially, glad at last to have found something to laugh at, all he ever looked for in listening to conversation.

Stepan Arkadyevitch had not made a mistake in inviting Pestsov. With Pestsov intellectual conversation never flagged for an instant. Directly Sergey Ivanovitch had concluded the conversation with his jest, Pestsov promptly started a new one.

"I can't agree even," said he, "that the government had that aim. The government obviously is guided by abstract considerations, and remains indifferent to the influence its measures may exercise. The education of women, for instance, would naturally be regarded as likely to be harmful, but the government opens schools and universities for women."

And the conversation at once passed to the new subject of the education of women.

Alexey Alexandrovitch expressed the idea that the education of women is apt to be confounded with the emancipation of women, and that it is only so that it can be considered dangerous.

"I consider, on the contrary, that the two questions are inseparably connected together," said Pestsov; "it is a vicious circle. Woman is deprived of rights from lack of education, and the lack of education results from the absence of rights. We must not forget that the subjection of women is so complete, and dates from such ages back that we are often unwilling to recognize the gulf that separates them from us," said he.

"You said rights," said Sergey Ivanovitch, waiting till Pestsov had finished, "meaning the right of sitting on juries, of voting, of presiding at official meetings, the right of entering the civil service, of sitting in parliament . . ."

"Undoubtedly."

"But if women, as a rare exception, can occupy such positions, it seems to me you are wrong in using the expression 'rights.' It would be more correct to say duties. Every man will agree that in doing the duty of a juryman, a witness, a telegraph clerk, we feel we are performing duties. And therefore it would be correct to say that women are seeking duties, and quite legitimately. And one can but sympathize with this desire to assist in the general labor of man."

"Quite so," Alexey Alexandrovitch assented. "The question, I imagine, is simply whether they are fitted for such duties."

"They will most likely be perfectly fitted," said Stepan Arkadyevitch, "when education has become general among them. We see this . . ."

"How about the proverb?" said the prince, who had a long while been intent on the conversation, his little comical eyes twinkling. "I can say it before my daughters: her hair is long, because her wit is . . ."

"Just what they thought of the negroes before their emancipation!" said Pestsov angrily.

"What seems strange to me is that women should seek fresh duties," said Sergey Ivanovitch, "while we see, unhappily, that men usually try to avoid them."

"Duties are bound up with rights—power, money, honor; those are what women are seeking," said Pestsov.

"Just as though I should seek the right to be a wet-nurse and feel injured because women are paid for the work, while no one will take me," said the old prince.

Turovtsin exploded in a loud roar of laughter and Sergey Ivanovitch regretted that he had not made this comparison. Even Alexey Alexandrovitch smiled.

"Yes, but a man can't nurse a baby," said Pestsov, "while a woman . . ."

"No, there was an Englishman who did suckle his baby on board ship," said the old prince, feeling this freedom in conversation permissible before his own daughters.

"There are as many such Englishmen as there would be women officials," said Sergey Ivanovitch.

"Yes, but what is a girl to do who has no family?" put in Stepan Arkadyevitch, thinking of Masha Tchibisova, whom he had had in his mind all along, in sympathizing with Pestsov and supporting him.

"If the story of such a girl were thoroughly sifted, you would find she had abandoned a family—her own or a sister's, where she might have found a woman's duties," Darya Alexandrovna broke in unexpectedly in a tone of exasperation, probably suspecting what sort of girl Stepan Arkadyevitch was thinking of.

"But we take our stand on principle as the ideal," replied Pestsov in his mellow bass. "Woman desires to have rights, to be independent, educated. She is oppressed, humiliated by the consciousness of her disabilities."

"And I'm oppressed and humiliated that they won't engage me at the Foundling," the old prince said again, to the huge delight of Turovtsin, who in his mirth dropped his asparagus with the thick end in the sauce.

Chapter XI

EVERYONE TOOK PART IN THE CONVERSATION EXCEPT KITTY AND LEVIN. AT FIRST, WHEN THEY were talking of the influence that one people has on another, there rose to Levin's mind what he had to say on the subject. But these ideas, once of such importance in his eyes, seemed to come into his brain as in a dream, and had now not the slightest interest for him. It even struck him as strange that they should be so eager to talk of what was of no use to anyone. Kitty, too, should, one would have supposed, have been interested in what they were saying of the rights and education of women. How often she had mused on the subject, thinking of her friend abroad, Varenka, of her painful state of dependence, how often she had wondered about herself what would become of her if she did not marry, and how often she had argued with her sister about it! But it did not interest her at all. She and Levin had a conversation of their own, yet not a conversation, but some sort of mysterious communication, which brought them every moment nearer, and stirred in both a sense of glad terror before the unknown into which they were entering.

At first Levin, in answer to Kitty's question how he could have seen her last year in the carriage, told her how he had been coming home from the mowing along the highroad and had met her.

"It was very, very early in the morning. You were probably only just awake. Your mother was asleep in the corner. It was an exquisite morning. I was walking along wondering who it could be in a four-in-hand? It was a splendid set of four horses with bells, and in a second you flashed by, and I saw you at the window—you were sitting like this, holding the strings of your cap in both hands, and thinking awfully deeply about something," he said, smiling. "How I should like to know what you were thinking about then! Something important?"

"Wasn't I dreadfully untidy?" she wondered, but seeing the smile of ecstasy these reminiscences called up, she felt that the impression she had made had been very good. She blushed and laughed with delight: "Really I don't remember."

"How nicely Turovtsin laughs!" said Levin, admiring his moist eyes and shaking chest.

"Have you known him long?" asked Kitty.

"Oh, everyone knows him!"

"And I see you think he's a horrid man?"

"Not horrid, but nothing in him."

"Oh, you're wrong! And you must give up thinking so directly!" said Kitty. "I used to have a very poor opinion of him too, but he, he's an awfully nice and wonderfully good-hearted man. He has a heart of gold."

"How could you find out what sort of heart he has?"

"We are great friends. I know him very well. Last winter, soon after . . . you came to see us," she said, with a guilty and at the same time confiding smile, "all Dolly's children had scarlet fever, and he happened to come and see her. And only fancy," she said in a whisper, "he felt so sorry for her that he stayed and began to help her look after the children. Yes, and for three weeks he stopped with them, and looked after the children like a nurse."

"I am telling Konstantin Dmitrievitch about Turovtsin in the scarlet fever," she said, bending over to her sister.

"Yes, it was wonderful, noble!" said Dolly, glancing towards Turovtsin, who had become aware they were talking of him, and smiling gently to him. Levin glanced once more at Turovtsin, and wondered how it was he had not realized all this man's goodness before.

"I'm sorry, I'm sorry, and I'll never think ill of people again!" he said gaily, genuinely expressing what he felt at the moment.

Chapter XII

CONNECTED WITH THE CONVERSATION THAT HAD SPRUNG UP ON THE RIGHTS OF WOMEN THERE were certain questions as to the inequality of rights in marriage improper to discuss before the ladies. Pestsov had several times during dinner touched upon these questions, but Sergey Ivanovitch and Stepan Arkadyevitch carefully drew him off them.

When they rose from the table and the ladies had gone out, Pestsov did not follow them, but addressing Alexey Alexandrovitch, began to expound the chief ground of inequality. The inequality in marriage, in his opinion, lay in the fact that the infidelity of the wife and the infidelity of the husband are punished unequally, both by the law and by public opinion. Stepan Arkadyevitch went hurriedly up to Alexey Alexandrovitch and offered him a cigar.

"No, I don't smoke," Alexey Alexandrovitch answered calmly, and as though purposely wishing to show that he was not afraid of the subject, he turned to Pestsov with a chilly smile.

"I imagine that such a view has a foundation in the very nature of things," he said, and would have gone on to the drawing room. But at this point Turovtsin broke suddenly and unexpectedly into the conversation, addressing Alexey Alexandrovitch.

"You heard, perhaps, about Pryatchnikov?" said Turovtsin, warmed up by the champagne he had drunk, and long waiting for an opportunity to break the silence that had weighed on him. "Vasya Pryatchnikov," he said, with a good-natured smile on his damp, red lips, addressing himself principally to the most important guest, Alexey Alexandrovitch, "they told me today he fought a duel with Kvitsky at Tver, and has killed him."

Just as it always seems that one bruises oneself on a sore place, so Stepan Arkadyevitch felt now that the conversation would by ill luck fall every moment on Alexey Alexandrovitch's sore spot. He would again have got his brother-in-law away, but Alexey Alexandrovitch himself inquired, with curiosity:

"What did Pryatchnikov fight about?"

"His wife. Acted like a man, he did! Called him out and shot him!"

"Ah!" said Alexey Alexandrovitch indifferently, and lifting his eyebrows, he went into the drawing room.

"How glad I am you have come," Dolly said with a frightened smile, meeting him in the outer drawing room. "I must talk to you. Let's sit here."

Alexey Alexandrovitch, with the same expression of indifference, given him by his lifted eyebrows, sat down beside Darya Alexandrovna, and smiled affectedly.

"It's fortunate," said he, "especially as I was meaning to ask you to excuse me, and to be taking leave. I have to start tomorrow."

Darya Alexandrovna was firmly convinced of Anna's innocence, and she felt herself growing pale and her lips quivering with anger at this frigid, unfeeling man, who was so calmly intending to ruin her innocent friend.

"Alexey Alexandrovitch," she said, with desperate resolution looking him in the face, "I asked you about Anna; you made me no answer. How is she?"

"She is, I believe, quite well, Darya Alexandrovna," replied Alexey Alexandrovitch, not looking at her.

"Alexey Alexandrovitch, forgive me, I have no right . . . but I love Anna as a sister, and esteem her; I beg, I beseech you to tell me what is wrong between you? what fault do you find with her?"

Alexey Alexandrovitch frowned, and almost closing his eyes, dropped his head.

"I presume that your husband has told you the grounds on which I consider it necessary to change my attitude to Anna Arkadyevna?" he said, not looking her in the face, but eyeing with displeasure Shtcherbatsky, who was walking across the drawing room.

"I don't believe it, I don't believe it, I can't believe it!" Dolly said, clasping her bony hands before her with a vigorous gesture. She rose quickly, and laid her hand on Alexey Alexandrovitch's sleeve. "We shall be disturbed here. Come this way, please."

Dolly's agitation had an effect on Alexey Alexandrovitch. He got up and submissively followed her to the schoolroom. They sat down to a table covered with an oilcloth cut in slits by penknives.

"I don't, I don't believe it!" Dolly said, trying to catch his glance that avoided her.

"One cannot disbelieve facts, Darya Alexandrovna," said he, with an emphasis on the word "facts."

"But what has she done?" said Darya Alexandrovna. "What precisely has she done?"

"She has forsaken her duty, and deceived her husband. That's what she has done," said he.

"No, no, it can't be! No, for God's sake, you are mistaken," said Dolly, putting her hands to her temples and closing her eyes.

Alexey Alexandrovitch smiled coldly, with his lips alone, meaning to signify to her and to himself the firmness of his conviction; but this warm defense, though it could not shake him, reopened his wound. He began to speak with greater heat.

"It is extremely difficult to be mistaken when a wife herself informs her husband of the fact—informs him that eight years of her life, and a son, all that's a mistake, and that she wants to begin life again," he said angrily, with a snort.

"Anna and sin—I cannot connect them, I cannot believe it!"

"Darya Alexandrovna," he said, now looking straight into Dolly's kindly, troubled face, and feeling that his tongue was being loosened in spite of himself, "I would give a great deal for doubt to be still possible. When I doubted, I was miserable, but it was better than now. When I doubted, I had hope; but now there is no hope, and still I doubt of everything. I am in such doubt of everything that I even hate my son, and sometimes do not believe he is my son. I am very unhappy."

He had no need to say that. Darya Alexandrovna had seen that as soon as he glanced into her face; and she felt sorry for him, and her faith in the innocence of her friend began to totter.

"Oh, this is awful, awful! But can it be true that you are resolved on a divorce?"

"I am resolved on extreme measures. There is nothing else for me to do."

"Nothing else to do, nothing else to do . . ." she replied, with tears in her eyes. "Oh no, don't say nothing else to do!" she said.

"What is horrible in a trouble of this kind is that one cannot, as in any other—in loss, in death—bear one's trouble in peace, but that one must act," said he, as though guessing her thought. "One must get out of the humiliating position in which one is placed; one can't live *à trois*."

"I understand, I quite understand that," said Dolly, and her head sank. She was silent for a little, thinking of herself, of her own grief in her family, and all at once, with an impulsive movement, she raised her head and clasped her hands with an imploring gesture. "But wait a little! You are a Christian. Think of her! What will become of her, if you cast her off?"

"I have thought, Darya Alexandrovna, I have thought a great deal," said Alexey Alexandrovitch. His face turned red in patches, and his dim eyes looked straight before him. Darya Alexandrovna at that moment pitied him with all her heart. "That was what I did indeed when she herself made known to me my humiliation; I left everything as of old. I gave her a chance to reform, I tried to save her. And with what result? She would not regard the slightest request—that she should observe decorum," he said, getting heated. "One may save anyone who does not want to be ruined; but if the whole nature is so corrupt, so depraved, that ruin itself seems to her salvation, what's to be done?"

"Anything, only not divorce!" answered Darya Alexandrovna

"But what is anything?"

"No, it is awful! She will be no one's wife; she will be lost!"

"What can I do?" said Alexey Alexandrovitch, raising his shoulders and his eyebrows. The recollection of his wife's last act had so incensed him that he had become frigid, as at the beginning of the conversation. "I am very grateful for your sympathy, but I must be going," he said, getting up.

"No, wait a minute. You must not ruin her. Wait a little; I will tell you about myself. I was married, and my husband deceived me; in anger and jealousy, I would have thrown up everything, I would myself. . . . But I came to myself again; and who did it? Anna saved me. And here I am living on. The children are growing up, my husband has come back to his family, and feels his fault, is growing purer, better, and I live on. . . . I have forgiven it, and you ought to forgive!"

Alexey Alexandrovitch heard her, but her words had no effect on him now. All the hatred of that day when he had resolved on a divorce had sprung up again in his soul. He shook himself, and said in a shrill, loud voice:

"Forgive I cannot, and do not wish to, and I regard it as wrong. I have done everything for this woman, and she has trodden it all in the mud to which she is akin. I am not a spiteful man, I have never hated anyone, but I hate her with my whole soul, and I cannot even forgive her, because I hate her too much for all the wrong she has done me!" he said, with tones of hatred in his voice.

"Love those that hate you . . ." Darya Alexandrovna whispered timorously.

Alexey Alexandrovitch smiled contemptuously. That he knew long ago, but it could not be applied to his case.

"Love those that hate you, but to love those one hates is impossible. Forgive me for having troubled you. Everyone has enough to bear in his own grief!" And regaining his self-possession, Alexey Alexandrovitch quietly took leave and went away.

Chapter XIII

WHEN THEY ROSE FROM TABLE, LEVIN WOULD HAVE LIKED TO FOLLOW KITTY INTO THE DRAWing room; but he was afraid she might dislike this, as too obviously paying her attention. He remained in the little ring of men, taking part in the general conversation, and without looking at Kitty, he was aware of her movements, her looks, and the place where she was in the drawing room.

He did at once, and without the smallest effort, keep the promise he had made her—always to think well of all men, and to like everyone always. The conversation fell on the village commune, in which Pestsov saw a sort of special principle, called by him the choral principle. Levin did not agree with Pestsov, nor with his brother, who had a special attitude of his own, both admitting and not admitting the significance of the Russian commune. But he talked to them, simply trying to reconcile and soften their differences. He was not in the least interested in what he said himself, and even less so in what they said; all he wanted was that they and everyone should be happy and contented. He knew now the one thing of importance; and that one thing was at first there, in the drawing room, and then began moving across and came to a standstill at the door. Without turning round he felt the eyes fixed on him, and the smile, and he could not help turning round. She was standing in the doorway with Shtcherbatsky, looking at him.

"I thought you were going towards the piano," said he, going up to her. "That's something I miss in the country—music."

"No; we only came to fetch you and thank you," she said, rewarding him with a smile that was like a gift, "for coming. What do they want to argue for? No one ever convinces anyone, you know."

"Yes; that's true," said Levin; "it generally happens that one argues warmly simply because one can't make out what one's opponent wants to prove."

Levin had often noticed in discussions between the most intelligent people that after enormous efforts, and an enormous expenditure of logical subtleties and words, the disputants finally arrived at being aware that what they had so long been struggling to prove to one another had long ago, from the beginning of the argument, been known to both, but that they liked different things, and would not define what they liked for fear of its being attacked. He had often had the experience of suddenly in a discussion grasping what it was his opponent liked and at once liking it too, and immediately he found himself agreeing, and then all arguments fell away as useless. Sometimes, too, he had experienced the opposite, expressing at last what he liked himself, which he was devising arguments to defend, and, chancing to express it well and genuinely, he had found his opponent at once agreeing and ceasing to dispute his position. He tried to say this.

She knitted her brow, trying to understand. But directly he began to illustrate his meaning, she understood at once.

"I know: one must find out what he is arguing for, what is precious to him, then one can . . ."

She had completely guessed and expressed his badly expressed idea. Levin smiled joyfully; he was struck by this transition from the confused, verbose discussion with Pestsov and his brother to this laconic, clear, almost wordless communication of the most complex ideas.

Shtcherbatsky moved away from them, and Kitty, going up to a card-table, sat down, and, taking up the chalk, began drawing diverging circles over the new green cloth.

They began again on the subject that had been started at dinner—the liberty and occupations of women. Levin was of the opinion of Darya Alexandrovna that a girl who did not marry should find a woman's duties in a family. He supported this view by the fact that no family can get on without women to help; that in every family, poor or rich, there are and must be nurses, either relations or hired.

"No," said Kitty, blushing, but looking at him all the more boldly with her truthful eyes; "a girl may be so circumstanced that she cannot live in the family without humiliation, while she herself . . ."

At the hint he understood her.

"Oh, yes," he said. "Yes, yes, yes—you're right; you're right!"

And he saw all that Pestsov had been maintaining at dinner of the liberty of woman, simply from getting a glimpse of the terror of an old maid's existence and its humiliation in Kitty's heart; and loving her, he felt that terror and humiliation, and at once gave up his arguments.

A silence followed. She was still drawing with the chalk on the table. Her eyes were shining with a soft light. Under the influence of her mood he felt in all his being a continually growing tension of happiness.

"Ah! I've scribbled all over the table!" she said, and laying down the chalk, she made a movement as though to get up.

"What! shall I be left alone—without her?" he thought with horror, and he took the chalk. "Wait a minute," he said, sitting down to the table. "I've long wanted to ask you one thing."

He looked straight into her caressing, though frightened eyes.

"Please, ask it."

"Here," he said; and he wrote the initial letters, *w, y, t, m, i, c, n, b, d, t, m, n, o, t.* These letters meant, "When you told me it could never be, did that mean never, or then?" There seemed no likelihood that she could make out this complicated sentence; but he looked at her as though his life depended on her understanding the words. She glanced at him seriously, then leaned her puckered brow on her hands and began to read. Once or twice she stole a look at him, as though asking him, "Is it what I think?"

"I understand," she said, flushing a little.

"What is this word?" he said, pointing to the *n* that stood for *never.*

"It means *never,*" she said; "but that's not true!"

He quickly rubbed out what he had written, gave her the chalk, and stood up. She wrote, *t, i, c, n, a, d.*

Dolly was completely comforted in the depression caused by her conversation with Alexey Alexandrovitch when she caught sight of the two figures: Kitty with the chalk in her hand, with a shy and happy smile looking upwards at Levin, and his handsome figure bending over the table with glowing eyes fastened one minute on the table and the next on her. He was suddenly radiant: he had understood. It meant, "Then I could not answer differently."

He glanced at her questioningly, timidly.

"Only then?"

"Yes," her smile answered.

"And n . . . and now?" he asked.

"Well, read this. I'll tell you what I should like—should like so much!" she wrote the initial letters, *i, y, c, f, a, f, w, h.* This meant, "If you could forget and forgive what happened."

He snatched the chalk with nervous, trembling fingers, and breaking it, wrote the initial letters of the following phrase, "I have nothing to forget and to forgive; I have never ceased to love you."

She glanced at him with a smile that did not waver.

"I understand," she said in a whisper.

He sat down and wrote a long phrase. She understood it all, and without asking him, "Is it this?" took the chalk and at once answered.

For a long while he could not understand what she had written, and often looked into her eyes. He was stupefied with happiness. He could not supply the words she had meant; but in her charming eyes, beaming with happiness, he saw all he needed to know. And he wrote three letters. But he had hardly finished writing when she read them over her arm, and herself finished and wrote the answer, "Yes."

"You're playing secrétaire?" said the old prince. "But we must really be getting along if you want to be in time at the theater."

Levin got up and escorted Kitty to the door.

In their conversation everything had been said; it had been said that she loved him, and that she would tell her father and mother that he would come tomorrow morning.

Chapter XIV

WHEN KITTY HAD GONE AND LEVIN WAS LEFT ALONE, HE FELT SUCH UNEASINESS WITHOUT HER and such an impatient longing to get as quickly, as quickly as possible, to tomorrow morning, when he would see her again and be plighted to her forever, that he felt afraid, as though of death, of those fourteen hours that he had to get through without her. It was essential for him to be with someone to talk to, so as not to be left alone, to kill time. Stepan Arkadyevitch would have been the companion most congenial to him, but he was going out, he said, to a *soirée,* in reality to the ballet. Levin only had time to tell him he was happy, and that he loved him, and would never, never forget what he had done for him. The eyes and the smile of Stepan Arkadyevitch showed Levin that he comprehended that feeling fittingly.

"Oh, so it's not time to die yet?" said Stepan Arkadyevitch, pressing Levin's hand with emotion.

"N-n-no!" said Levin.

Darya Alexandrovna too, as she said good-bye to him, gave him a sort of congratulation, saying, "How glad I am you have met Kitty again! One must value old friends." Levin did not like these words of Darya Alexandrovna's. She could not understand how lofty and beyond her it all was, and she ought not to have dared to allude to it. Levin said good-bye to them, but, not to be left alone, he attached himself to his brother.

"Where are you going?"

"I'm going to a meeting."

"Well, I'll come with you. Can I?"

"What for? Yes, come along," said Sergey Ivanovitch, smiling. "What is the matter with you today?"

"With me? Happiness is the matter with me!" said Levin, letting down the window of the carriage they were driving in. "You don't mind?—it's so stifling. It's happiness is the matter with me! Why is it you have never married?"

Sergey Ivanovitch smiled.

"I am very glad, she seems a nice gi . . ." Sergey Ivanovitch was beginning.

"Don't say it! don't say it!" shouted Levin, clutching at the collar of his fur coat with both hands, and muffling him up in it. "She's a nice girl" were such simple, humble words, so out of harmony with his feeling.

Sergey Ivanovitch laughed outright a merry laugh, which was rare with him.

"Well, anyway, I may say that I'm very glad of it."

"That you may do tomorrow, tomorrow and nothing more! Nothing, nothing, silence," said Levin, and muffling him once more in his fur coat, he added: "I do like you so! Well, is it possible for me to be present at the meeting?"

"Of course it is."

"What is your discussion about today?" asked Levin, never ceasing smiling.

They arrived at the meeting. Levin heard the secretary hesitatingly read the minutes which he obviously did not himself understand; but Levin saw from this secretary's face what a good, nice, kind-hearted person he was. This was evident from his confusion and embarrassment in reading the minutes. Then the discussion began. They were disputing about the misappropriation of certain sums and the laying of certain pipes, and Sergey Ivanovitch was very cutting to two members, and said something at great length with an air of triumph; and another member, scribbling something on a bit of paper, began timidly at first, but afterwards answered him very viciously and delightfully. And then Sviazhsky (he was there too) said something too, very handsomely and nobly. Levin listened to them, and saw clearly that these missing sums and these pipes were not anything real, and that they were not at all angry, but were all the nicest, kindest people, and everything was as happy and charming as possible among them. They did no harm to anyone, and were all enjoying it. What struck Levin was that he could see through them all today, and from little, almost imperceptible signs knew the soul of each, and saw distinctly that they were all good at heart. And Levin himself in particular they were all extremely fond of that day. That was evident from the way they spoke to him, from the friendly, affectionate way even those he did not know looked at him.

"Well, did you like it?" Sergey Ivanovitch asked him.

"Very much. I never supposed it was so interesting! Capital! Splendid!"

Sviazhsky went up to Levin and invited him to come round to tea with him. Levin was utterly at a loss to comprehend or recall what it was he had disliked in Sviazhsky, what he had failed to find in him. He was a clever and wonderfully good-hearted man.

"Most delighted," he said, and asked after his wife and sister-in-law. And from a queer association of ideas, because in his imagination the idea of Sviazhsky's sister-in-law was connected with marriage, it occurred to him that there was no one to whom he could more suitably speak of his happiness and he was very glad to go and see them.

Sviazhsky questioned him about his improvements on his estate, presupposing, as he always did, that there was no possibility of doing anything not done already in Europe, and now this did not in the least annoy Levin. On the contrary, he felt that Sviazhsky was right, that the whole business was of little value, and he saw the wonderful softness and consideration with which Sviazhsky avoided fully expressing his correct view. The ladies of the Sviazhsky household were particularly delightful. It seemed to Levin that they knew all about it already and sympathized with him, saying nothing merely from delicacy. He stayed with them one hour, two, three, talking of all sorts of subjects but the one thing that filled his heart, and did not observe that he was boring them dreadfully, and that it was long past their bedtime.

Sviazhsky went with him into the hall, yawning and wondering at the strange humor his friend was in. It was past one o'clock. Levin went back to his hotel, and was dismayed at the thought that all alone now with his impatience he had ten hours still left to get through. The servant, whose turn it was to be up all night, lit his candles, and would have gone away, but Levin stopped him. This servant, Yegor, whom Levin had noticed before, struck him as a very intelligent, excellent, and, above all, good-hearted man.

"Well, Yegor, it's hard work not sleeping, isn't it?"

"One's got to put up with it! It's part of our work, you see. In a gentleman's house it's easier; but then here one makes more."

It appeared that Yegor had a family, three boys and a daughter, a sempstress, whom he wanted to marry to a cashier in a saddler's shop.

Levin, on hearing this, informed Yegor that, in his opinion, in marriage the great thing was love, and that with love one would always be happy, for happiness rests only on oneself.

Yegor listened attentively, and obviously quite took in Levin's idea, but by way of assent to it he enunciated, greatly to Levin's surprise, the observation that when he had lived with good masters he had always been satisfied with his masters, and now was perfectly satisfied with his employer, though he was a Frenchman.

"Wonderfully good-hearted fellow!" thought Levin.

"Well, but you yourself, Yegor, when you got married, did you love your wife?"

"Ay! and why not?" responded Yegor.

And Levin saw that Yegor too was in an excited state and intending to express all his most heartfelt emotions.

"My life, too, has been a wonderful one. From a child up . . ." he was beginning with flashing eyes, apparently catching Levin's enthusiasm, just as people catch yawning.

But at that moment a ring was heard. Yegor departed, and Levin was left alone. He had eaten scarcely anything at dinner, had refused tea and supper at Sviazhsky's, but he was incapable of thinking of supper. He had not slept the previous night, but was incapable of thinking of sleep either. His room was cold, but he was oppressed by heat. He opened both the movable panes in his window and sat down to the table opposite the open panes. Over the snow-covered roofs could be seen a decorated cross with chains, and above it the rising triangle of Charles's Wain with the yellowish light of Capella. He gazed at the cross, then at the stars, drank in the fresh freezing air that flowed evenly into the room, and followed as though in a dream the images and memories that rose in his imagination. At four o'clock he heard steps in the passage and peeped out at the door. It was the gambler Myaskin, whom he knew, coming from the club. He walked gloomily, frowning and coughing. "Poor, unlucky fellow!" thought Levin, and tears came into his eyes from love and pity for this man. He would have talked with him, and tried to comfort him, but remembering that he had nothing but his shirt on, he changed his mind and sat down again at the open pane to bathe in the cold air and gaze at the exquisite lines of the cross, silent, but full of meaning for him, and the mounting lurid yellow star. At seven o'clock there was a noise of people polishing the floors, and bells ringing in some servants' department, and Levin felt that he was beginning to get frozen. He closed the pane, washed, dressed, and went out into the street.

Chapter XV

THE STREETS WERE STILL EMPTY. LEVIN WENT TO THE HOUSE OF THE SHTCHERBATSKYS. THE VISitors' doors were closed and everything was asleep. He walked back, went into his room again, and asked for coffee. The day servant, not Yegor this time, brought it to him. Levin would have entered into conversation with him, but a bell rang for the servant, and he went out. Levin tried to drink coffee and put some roll in his mouth, but his mouth was quite at a loss what to do with the roll. Levin, rejecting the roll, put on his coat and went out again for a walk. It was nine o'clock when he reached the Shtcherbatskys' steps the second time. In the house they were only just up, and the cook came out to go marketing. He had to get through at least two hours more.

All that night and morning Levin lived perfectly unconsciously, and felt perfectly lifted out of the conditions of material life. He had eaten nothing for a whole day, he had not slept for two nights, had spent several hours undressed in the frozen air, and felt not simply fresher and stronger than ever, but felt utterly independent of his body; he moved without muscular effort, and felt as if he could do anything. He was convinced he could fly upwards or lift the corner of the house, if need be. He spent the remainder of the time in the street, incessantly looking at his watch and gazing about him.

And what he saw then, he never saw again after. The children especially going to school, the bluish doves flying down from the roofs to the pavement, and the little loaves covered with flour, thrust out by an unseen hand, touched him. Those loaves, those doves, and those two boys were not earthly creatures. It all happened at the same time: a boy ran towards a dove and glanced smiling at Levin; the dove, with a whir of her wings, darted away, flashing in the sun, amid grains of snow that quivered in the air, while from a little window there came a smell of fresh-baked bread, and the loaves were put out. All of this together was so extraordinarily nice that Levin laughed and cried with delight. Going a long way round by Gazetny Place and Kislovka, he went back again to the hotel, and putting his watch before him, he sat down to wait for twelve o'clock. In the next room they were talking about some sort of machines, and swindling, and coughing their morning coughs. They did not realize that the hand was near twelve. The hand reached it. Levin went out onto the steps. The sleigh-drivers clearly knew all about it. They crowded round Levin with happy faces, quarreling among themselves, and offering their services. Trying not to offend the other sleigh-drivers, and promising to drive with them too, Levin took one and told him to drive to the Shtcherbatskys'. The sleigh-driver was splendid in a white shirt-collar sticking out over his over-coat and into his strong, full-blooded red neck. The sleigh was high and comfortable, and altogether such a one as Levin never drove in after, and the horse was a good one, and tried to gallop but didn't seem to move. The driver knew the Shtcherbatskys' house, and drew up at the entrance with a curve of his arm and a "Wo!" especially indicative of respect for his fare. The Shtcherbatskys' hall-porter certainly knew all about it. This was evident from the smile in his eyes and the way he said:

"Well, it's a long while since you've been to see us, Konstantin Demitrievitch!"

Not only he knew all about it, but he was unmistakably delighted and making efforts to conceal his joy. Looking into his kindly old eyes, Levin realized even something new in his happiness.

"Are they up?"

"Pray walk in! Leave it here," said he, smiling, as Levin would have come back to take his hat. That meant something.

"To whom shall I announce your honor?" asked the footman.

The footman, though a young man, and one of the new school of footmen, a dandy, was a very kind-hearted, good fellow, and he too knew all about it.

"The princess . . . the prince . . . the young princess . . ." said Levin.

The first person he saw was Mademoiselle Linon. She walked across the room, and her ringlets and her face were beaming. He had only just spoken to her, when suddenly he heard the rustle of a skirt at the door, and Mademoiselle Linon vanished from Levin's eyes, and a joyful terror came over him at the nearness of his happiness. Mademoiselle Linon was in great haste, and leaving him, went out at the other door. Directly she had gone out, swift, swift light steps sounded on the parquet, and his bliss, his life, himself—what was best in himself, what he had so long sought and longed for—was quickly, so quickly approaching him. She did not walk, but seemed, by some unseen force, to float to him. He saw nothing but her clear, truthful eyes, frightened by the same bliss of love that flooded his heart. Those eyes were shining nearer and nearer, blinding him with their light of love. She stopped still close to him, touching him. Her hands rose and dropped onto his shoulders.

She had done all she could—she had run up to him and given herself up entirely, shy and happy. He put his arms round her and pressed his lips to her mouth that sought his kiss.

She too had not slept all night, and had been expecting him all the morning.

Her mother and father had consented without demur, and were happy in her happiness. She had been waiting for him. She wanted to be the first to tell him her happiness and his. She had got ready to see him alone, and had been delighted at the idea, and had been shy and ashamed, and did not know herself what she was doing. She had heard his steps and voice and had waited at the door for Mademoiselle Linon to go. Mademoiselle Linon had gone away. Without thinking, without asking herself how and what, she had gone up to him, and did as she was doing.

"Let us go to mamma!" she said, taking him by the hand. For a long while he could say nothing, not so much because he was afraid of desecrating the loftiness of his emotion by a word, as that every time he tried to say something, instead of words he felt that tears of happiness were welling up. He took her hand and kissed it.

"Can it be true?" he said at last in a choked voice. "I can't believe you love me, dear!"

She smiled at that "dear," and at the timidity with which he glanced at her.

"Yes!" she said significantly, deliberately. "I am so happy!"

Not letting go his hands, she went into the drawing room. The princess, seeing them, breathed quickly, and immediately began to cry and then immediately began to laugh and with a vigorous step Levin had not expected, ran up to him, and hugging his head, kissed him, wetting his cheeks with her tears.

"So it is all settled! I am glad. Love her. I am glad . . . Kitty!"

"You've not been long settling things," said the old prince, trying to seem unmoved; but Levin noticed that his eyes were wet when he turned to him.

"I've long, always wished for this!" said the prince, taking Levin by the arm and drawing him towards himself. "Even when this little feather-head fancied . . ."

"Papa!" shrieked Kitty, and shut his mouth with her hands.

"Well, I won't!" he said. "I'm very, very . . . plea . . . Oh, what a fool I am . . ."

He embraced Kitty, kissed her face, her hand, her face again and made the sign of the cross over her.

And there came over Levin a new feeling of love for this man, till then so little known to him, when he saw how slowly and tenderly Kitty kissed his muscular hand.

Chapter XVI

THE PRINCESS SAT IN HER ARM-CHAIR, SILENT AND SMILING; THE PRINCE SAT DOWN BESIDE HER. Kitty stood by her father's chair, still holding his hand. All were silent.

The princess was the first to put everything into words, and to translate all thoughts and feelings into practical questions. And all equally felt this strange and painful for the first minute.

"When is it to be? We must have the benediction and announcement. And when's the wedding to be? What do you think, Alexander?"

"Here he is," said the old prince, pointing to Levin—"he's the principal person in the matter."

"When?" said Levin blushing. "Tomorrow. If you ask me, I should say, the benediction today and the wedding tomorrow."

"Come, *mon cher,* that's nonsense!"

"Well, in a week."

"He's quite mad."

"No, why so?"

"Well, upon my word!" said the mother, smiling, delighted at this haste. "How about the trousseau?"

"Will there really be a trousseau and all that?" Levin thought with horror. "But can the trousseau and the benediction and all that—can it spoil my happiness? Nothing can spoil it!" He glanced at Kitty, and noticed that she was not in the least, not in the very least, disturbed by the idea of the trousseau. "Then it must be all right," he thought.

"Oh, I know nothing about it; I only said what I should like," he said apologetically.

"We'll talk it over, then. The benediction and announcement can take place now. That's very well."

The princess went up to her husband, kissed him, and would have gone away, but he kept her, embraced her, and, tenderly as a young lover, kissed her several times, smiling. The old people were obviously muddled for a moment, and did not quite know whether it was they who were in love again or their daughter. When the prince and the princess had gone, Levin went up to his betrothed and took her hand. He was self-possessed now and could speak, and he had a great deal he wanted to tell her. But he said not at all what he had to say.

"How I knew it would be so! I never hoped for it; and yet in my heart I was always sure," he said. "I believe that it was ordained."

"And I!" she said. "Even when. . . ." She stopped and went on again, looking at him resolutely with her truthful eyes, "Even when I thrust from me my happiness. I always loved you alone, but I was carried away. I ought to tell you . . . Can you forgive that?"

"Perhaps it was for the best. You will have to forgive me so much. I ought to tell you . . ."

This was one of the things he had meant to speak about. He had resolved from the first to tell her two things—that he was not chaste as she was, and that he was not a believer. It was agonizing, but he considered he ought to tell her both these facts.

"No, not now, later!" he said.

"Very well, later, but you must certainly tell me. I'm not afraid of anything. I want to know everything. Now it is settled."

He added: "Settled that you'll take me whatever I may be—you won't give me up? Yes?"

"Yes, yes."

Their conversation was interrupted by Mademoiselle Linon, who with an affected but tender smile came to congratulate her favorite pupil. Before she had gone, the servants came in with their congratulations. Then relations arrived, and there began that state of blissful absurdity from which Levin did not emerge till the day after his wedding. Levin was in a continual state of awkwardness and discomfort, but the intensity of his happiness went on all the while increasing. He felt continually that a great deal was being expected of him—what, he did not know; and he did everything he was told, and it all gave him happiness. He had thought his engagement would have nothing about it like others, that the ordinary conditions of engaged couples would spoil his special happiness; but it ended in his doing exactly as other people did, and his happiness being only increased thereby and becoming more and more special, more and more unlike anything that had ever happened.

"Now we shall have sweetmeats to eat," said Mademoiselle Linon—and Levin drove off to buy sweetmeats.

"Well, I'm very glad," said Sviazhsky. "I advise you to get the bouquets from Fomin's."

"Oh, are they wanted?" And he drove to Fomin's.

His brother offered to lend him money, as he would have so many expenses, presents to give. . . .

"Oh, are presents wanted?" And he galloped to Foulde's.

And at the confectioner's, and at Fomin's, and at Foulde's he saw that he was expected; that they were pleased to see him, and prided themselves on his happiness, just as everyone whom he had to do with during those days. What was extraordinary was that everyone not only liked him, but even people previously unsympathetic, cold, and callous, were enthusiastic over him, gave way to him in everything, treated his feeling with tenderness and delicacy, and shared his conviction that he was the happiest man in the world because his betrothed was beyond perfection. Kitty too felt the same thing. When Countess Nordston ventured to hint that she had hoped for something better, Kitty was so angry and proved so conclusively that nothing in the world could be better than Levin, that Countess Nordston had to admit it, and in Kitty's presence never met Levin without a smile of ecstatic admiration.

The confession he had promised was the one painful incident of this time. He consulted the old prince, and with his sanction gave Kitty his diary, in which there was written the confession that tortured him. He had written this diary at the time with a view to his future wife. Two things caused him anguish: his lack of purity and his lack of faith. His confession of unbelief passed unnoticed. She was religious, had never doubted the truths of religion, but his external unbelief did not affect her in the least. Through love she knew all his soul, and in his soul she saw what she wanted, and that such a state of soul should be called unbelieving was to her a matter of no account. The other confession set her weeping bitterly.

Levin, not without an inner struggle, handed her his diary. He knew that between him and her there could not be, and should not be, secrets, and so he had decided that so it must be. But he had not realized what an effect it would have on her, he had not put himself in her place. It was only when the same evening he came to their house before the theater, went into her room and saw her tear-stained, pitiful, sweet face, miserable with suffering he had caused and nothing could undo, he felt the abyss that separated his shameful past from her dovelike purity, and was appalled at what he had done.

"Take them, take these dreadful books!" she said, pushing away the notebooks lying before her on the table. "Why did you give them me? No, it was better anyway," she added, touched by his despairing face. "But it's awful, awful!"

His head sank, and he was silent. He could say nothing.

"You can't forgive me," he whispered.

"Yes, I forgive you; but it's terrible!"

But his happiness was so immense that this confession did not shatter it, it only added another shade to it. She forgave him; but from that time more than ever he considered himself unworthy of her, morally bowed down lower than ever before her, and prized more highly than ever his undeserved happiness.

Chapter XVII

UNCONSCIOUSLY GOING OVER IN HIS MEMORY THE CONVERSATIONS THAT HAD TAKEN PLACE during and after dinner, Alexey Alexandrovitch returned to his solitary room. Darya Alexandrovna's words about forgiveness had aroused in him nothing but annoyance. The applicability or non-applicability of the Christian precept to his own case was too difficult a question to be discussed lightly, and this question had long ago been answered by Alexey Alexandrovitch in the negative. Of all that had been said, what stuck most in his memory was the phrase of stupid, good-natured Turovtsin—*"Acted like a man, he did! Called him out and shot him!"* Everyone had apparently shared this feeling, though from politeness they had not expressed it.

"But the matter is settled, it's useless thinking about it," Alexey Alexandrovitch told himself. And thinking of nothing but the journey before him, and the revision work he had to do, went into his room and asked the porter who escorted him where his man was. The porter said that the man had only just gone out. Alexey Alexandrovitch ordered tea to be sent him, sat down to the table, and taking the guide-book, began considering the route of his journey.

"Two telegrams," said his manservant, coming into the room. "I beg your pardon, your excellency; I'd only just that minute gone out."

Alexey Alexandrovitch took the telegrams and opened them. The first telegram was the announcement of Stremov's appointment to the very post Karenin had coveted. Alexey Alexandrovitch flung the telegram down, and flushing a little, got up and began to pace up and down the room. *"Quos vult perdere dementat,"* he said, meaning by *quos* the persons responsible for this appointment. He was not so much annoyed that he had not received the post, that he had been conspicuously passed over; but it was incomprehensible, amazing to him that they did not see that the wordy phrase-monger Stremov was the last man fit for it. How could they fail to see how they were ruining themselves, lowering their *prestige* by this appointment?

"Something else in the same line," he said to himself bitterly, opening the second telegram. The telegram was from his wife. Her name, written in blue pencil, "Anna," was the first thing that caught his eye. "I am dying; I beg, I implore you to come. I shall die easier with your forgiveness," he read. He smiled contemptuously, and flung down the telegram. That this was a trick and a fraud, of that, he thought for the first minute, there could be no doubt.

"There is no deceit she would stick at. She was near her confinement. Perhaps it is the confinement. But what can be their aim? To legitimize the child, to compromise me, and prevent a divorce," he thought. "But something was said in it: I am dying . . ." He read the telegram again, and suddenly the plain meaning of what was said in it struck him.

"And if it is true?" he said to himself. "If it is true that in the moment of agony and nearness to death she is genuinely penitent, and I, taking it for a trick, refuse to go? That would not only be cruel, and everyone would blame me, but it would be stupid on my part."

"Piotr, call a coach; I am going to Petersburg," he said to his servant.

Alexey Alexandrovitch decided that he would go to Petersburg and see his wife. If her illness was a trick, he would say nothing and go away again. If she was really in danger, and wished to see him before her death, he would forgive her if he found her alive, and pay her the last duties if he came too late.

All the way he thought no more of what he ought to do.

With a sense of weariness and uncleanness from the night spent in the train, in the early fog of Petersburg Alexey Alexandrovitch drove through the deserted Nevsky and stared straight before him, not thinking of what was awaiting him. He could not think about it, because in picturing what would happen, he could not drive away the reflection that her death would at once remove all the difficulty of his position. Bakers, closed shops, night-cabmen, porters sweeping the pavements flashed past his eyes, and he watched it all, trying to smother the thought of what was awaiting him, and what he dared not hope for, and yet was hoping for. He drove up to the steps. A sleigh and a carriage with the coachman asleep stood at the entrance. As he went into the entry, Alexey Alexandrovitch, as it were, got out his resolution from the remotest corner of his brain, and mastered it thoroughly. Its meaning ran: "If it's a trick, then calm contempt and departure. If truth, do what is proper."

The porter opened the door before Alexey Alexandrovitch rang. The porter, Kapitonitch, looked queer in an old coat, without a tie, and in slippers.

"How is your mistress?"

"A successful confinement yesterday."

Alexey Alexandrovitch stopped short and turned white. He felt distinctly now how intensely he had longed for her death.

"And how is she?"

Korney in his morning apron ran downstairs.

"Very ill," he answered. "There was a consultation yesterday, and the doctor's here now."

"Take my things," said Alexey Alexandrovitch, and feeling some relief at the news that there was still hope of her death, he went into the hall.

On the hat-stand there was a military overcoat. Alexey Alexandrovitch noticed it and asked:

"Who is here?"

"The doctor, the midwife, and Count Vronsky."

Alexey Alexandrovitch went into the inner rooms.

In the drawing room there was no one; at the sound of his steps there came out of her boudoir the midwife in a cap with lilac ribbons.

She went up to Alexey Alexandrovitch, and with the familiarity given by the approach of death took him by the arm and drew him towards the bedroom.

"Thank God you've come! She keeps on about you and nothing but you," she said.

"Make haste with the ice!" the doctor's peremptory voice said from the bedroom.

Alexey Alexandrovitch went into her boudoir.

At the table, sitting sideways in a low chair, was Vronsky, his face hidden in his hands, weeping. He jumped up at the doctor's voice, took his hands from his face, and saw Alexey Alexandrovitch. Seeing the husband, he was so overwhelmed that he sat down again, drawing his head down to his shoulders, as if he wanted to disappear; but he made an effort over himself, got up and said:

"She is dying. The doctors say there is no hope. I am entirely in your power, only let me be here . . . though I am at your disposal. I . . ."

Alexey Alexandrovitch, seeing Vronsky's tears, felt a rush of that nervous emotion always produced in him by the sight of other people's suffering, and turning away his face, he moved hurriedly to the door, without hearing the rest of his words. From the bedroom came the sound of Anna's voice saying something. Her voice was lively, eager, with exceedingly distinct intonations. Alexey Alexandrovitch went into the bedroom, and went up to the bed. She was lying turned with her face towards him. Her cheeks were flushed crimson, her eyes glittered, her little white hands thrust out from the sleeves of her dressing-gown were playing with the quilt, twisting it about. It seemed as though she were not only well and blooming, but in the happiest frame of mind. She was talking rapidly, musically, and with exceptionally correct articulation and expressive intonation.

"For Alexey—I am speaking of Alexey Alexandrovitch (what a strange and awful thing that both are Alexey, isn't it?)—Alexey would not refuse me. I should forget, he would forgive. . . . But why doesn't he come? He's so good he doesn't know himself how good he is. Ah, my God, what agony! Give me some water, quick! Oh, that will be bad for her, my little girl! Oh, very well then, give her to a nurse. Yes, I agree, it's better in fact. He'll be coming; it will hurt him to see her. Give her to the nurse."

"Anna Arkadyevna, he has come. Here he is!" said the midwife, trying to attract her attention to Alexey Alexandrovitch.

"Oh, what nonsense!" Anna went on, not seeing her husband. "No, give her to me; give me my little one! He has not come yet. You say he won't forgive me, because you don't know him. No one knows him. I'm the only one, and it was hard for me even. His eyes I ought to know—Seryozha has just the same eyes—and I can't bear to see them because of it. Has Seryozha had his dinner? I know everyone will forget him. He would not forget. Seryozha must be moved into the corner room, and Mariette must be asked to sleep with him."

All of a sudden she shrank back, was silent; and in terror, as though expecting a blow, as though to defend herself, she raised her hands to her face. She had seen her husband.

"No, no!" she began. "I am not afraid of him; I am afraid of death. Alexey, come here. I am in a hurry, because I've no time, I've not long left to live; the fever will begin directly and I shall understand nothing more. Now I understand, I understand it all, I see it all!"

Alexey Alexandrovitch's wrinkled face wore an expression of agony; he took her by the hand and tried to say something, but he could not utter it; his lower lip quivered, but he still went on struggling with his emotion, and only now and then glanced at her. And each time he glanced at her, he saw her eyes gazing at him with such passionate and triumphant tenderness as he had never seen in them.

"Wait a minute, you don't know . . . stay a little, stay! . . ." She stopped, as though collecting her ideas. "Yes," she began; "yes, yes, yes. This is what I wanted to say. Don't be surprised at me. I'm still the same. . . . But there is another woman in me, I'm afraid of her: she loved that man, and I tried to hate you, and could not forget about her that used to be. I'm not that woman. Now I'm my real self, all myself. I'm dying now, I know I shall die, ask him. Even now I feel—see here, the weights on my feet, on my hands, on my fingers. My fingers—see how huge they are! But this will soon all be over . . . Only one thing I want: forgive me, forgive me quite. I'm terrible, but my nurse used to tell me; the holy martyr—what was her name? She was worse. And I'll go to Rome; there's a wilderness, and there I shall be no trouble to anyone, only I'll take Seryozha and the little one . . . No, you can't forgive me! I know, it can't be forgiven! No, no, go away, you're too good!" She held his hand in one burning hand, while she pushed him away with the other.

The nervous agitation of Alexey Alexandrovitch kept increasing, and had by now reached such a point that he ceased to struggle with it. He suddenly felt that what he had regarded as nervous agitation was on the contrary a blissful spiritual condition that gave him all at once a new happiness he had never known. He did not think that the Christian law that he had been all his life trying to follow, enjoined on him to forgive and love his enemies; but a glad feeling of love and forgiveness for his enemies filled his heart. He knelt down, and laying his head in the curve of her arm, which burned him as with fire through the sleeve, he sobbed like a little child. She put her arm around his head, moved towards him, and with defiant pride lifted up her eyes.

"That is he. I knew him! Now, forgive me, everyone, forgive me! . . . They've come again; why don't they go away? . . . Oh, take these cloaks off me!"

The doctor unloosed her hands, carefully laying her on the pillow, and covered her up to the shoulders. She lay back submissively, and looked before her with beaming eyes.

"Remember one thing, that I needed nothing but forgiveness, and I want nothing more. . . . Why doesn't *he* come?" she said, turning to the door towards Vronsky. "Do come, do come! Give him your hand."

Vronsky came to the side of the bed, and seeing Anna, again hid his face in his hands.

"Uncover your face—look at him! He's a saint," she said. "Oh! uncover your face, do uncover it!" she said angrily. "Alexey Alexandrovitch, do uncover his face! I want to see him."

Alexey Alexandrovitch took Vronsky's hands and drew them away from his face, which was awful with the expression of agony and shame upon it.

"Give him your hand. Forgive him."

Alexey Alexandrovitch gave him his hand, not attempting to restrain the tears that streamed from his eyes.

"Thank God, thank God!" she said, "now everything is ready. Only to stretch my legs a little. There, that's capital. How badly these flowers are done—not a bit like a violet," she said, pointing to the hangings. "My God, my God! when will it end? Give me some morphine. Doctor, give me some morphine! Oh, my God, my God!"

And she tossed about on the bed.

The doctors said that it was puerperal fever, and that it was ninety-nine chances in a hundred it would end in death. The whole day long there was fever, delirium, and unconsciousness. At midnight the patient lay without consciousness, and almost without pulse.

The end was expected every minute.

Vronsky had gone home, but in the morning he came to inquire, and Alexey Alexandrovitch meeting him in the hall, said: "Better stay, she might ask for you," and himself led him to his wife's boudoir. Towards morning, there was a return again of excitement, rapid thought and talk, and again it ended in unconsciousness. On the third day it was the same thing, and the doctors said there was hope. That day Alexey Alexandrovitch went into the boudoir where Vronsky was sitting, and closing the door sat down opposite him.

"Alexey Alexandrovitch," said Vronsky, feeling that a statement of the position was coming, "I can't speak, I can't understand. Spare me! However hard it is for you, believe me, it is more terrible for me."

He would have risen; but Alexey Alexandrovitch took him by the hand and said:

"I beg you to hear me out; it is necessary. I must explain my feelings, the feelings that have guided me and will guide me, so that you may not be in error regarding me. You know I had resolved on a divorce, and had even begun to take proceedings. I won't conceal from you that in beginning this I was in uncertainty, I was in misery; I will confess that I was pursued by a desire to revenge myself on you and on her. When I got the telegram, I came here with the same feelings; I will say more, I longed for her death. But . . ." He paused, pondering whether to disclose or not to disclose his feeling to him. "But I saw her and forgave her. And the happiness of forgiveness has revealed to me my duty. I forgive completely. I would offer the other cheek, I would give my cloak if my coat be taken. I pray to God only not to take from me the bliss of forgiveness!"

Tears stood in his eyes, and the luminous, serene look in them impressed Vronsky.

"This is my position: you can trample me in the mud, make me the laughing-stock of the world, I will not abandon her, and I will never utter a word of reproach to you," Alexey Alexandrovitch went on. "My duty is clearly marked for me; I ought to be with her, and I will be. If she wishes to see you, I will let you know, but now I suppose it would be better for you to go away."

He got up, and sobs cut short his words. Vronsky too was getting up, and in a stooping, not yet erect posture, looked up at him from under his brows. He did not understand Alexey Alexandrovitch's feeling, but he felt that it was something higher and even unattainable for him with his view of life.

Chapter XVIII

AFTER THE CONVERSATION WITH ALEXEY ALEXANDROVITCH, VRONSKY WENT OUT ONTO THE steps of the Karenins' house and stood still, with difficulty remembering where he was, and where he ought to walk or drive. He felt disgraced, humiliated, guilty, and deprived of all possibility of washing away his humiliation. He felt thrust out of the beaten track along which he had so proudly and lightly walked till then. All the habits and rules of his life that had seemed so firm, had turned out suddenly false and inapplicable. The betrayed husband, who had figured till that time as a pitiful creature, an incidental and somewhat ludicrous obstacle to his happiness, had suddenly been summoned by her herself, elevated to an awe-inspiring pinnacle, and on the pinnacle that husband had shown himself, not malignant, not false, not ludicrous, but kind and straightforward and large. Vronsky could not but feel this, and the parts were suddenly reversed. Vronsky felt his elevation and his own abasement, his truth and his own falsehood. He felt that the husband was magnanimous even in his sorrow, while he had been base and petty in his deceit. But this sense of his own humiliation before the man he had unjustly despised made up only a small part of his misery. He felt unutterably wretched now, for his passion for Anna, which had seemed to him of late to be growing cooler, now that he knew he had lost her forever, was stronger than ever it had been. He had seen all of her in her illness, had come to know her very soul, and it seemed to him that he had never loved her till then. And now when he had learned to know her, to love her as she should be loved, he had been humiliated before her, and had lost her forever, leaving with her nothing of himself but a shameful memory. Most terrible of all had been his ludicrous, shameful position when Alexey Alexandrovitch had pulled his hands away from his humiliated face. He stood on the steps of the Karenins' house like one distraught, and did not know what to do.

"A sleigh, sir?" asked the porter.

"Yes, a sleigh."

On getting home, after three sleepless nights, Vronsky, without undressing, lay down flat on the sofa, clasping his hands and laying his head on them. His head was heavy. Images, memories, and ideas of the strangest description followed one another with extraordinary rapidity and vividness. First it was the medicine he had poured out for the patient and spilt over the spoon, then the midwife's white hands, then the queer posture of Alexey Alexandrovitch on the floor beside the bed.

"To sleep! To forget!" he said to himself with the serene confidence of a healthy man that if he is tired and sleepy, he will go to sleep at once. And the same instant his head did begin to feel drowsy and he began to drop off into forgetfulness. The waves of the sea of unconsciousness had begun to meet over his head, when all at once—it was as though a violent shock of electricity had passed over him. He started so that he leaped up on the springs of the sofa, and leaning on his arms got in a panic onto his knees. His eyes were wide open as though he had never been asleep. The heaviness in his head and the weariness in his limbs that he had felt a minute before had suddenly gone.

"You may trample me in the mud," he heard Alexey Alexandrovitch's words and saw him standing before him, and saw Anna's face with its burning flush and glittering eyes, gazing with love and tenderness not at him but at Alexey Alexandrovitch; he saw his own, as he fancied, foolish and ludicrous figure when Alexey Alexandrovitch took his hands away from his face. He stretched out his legs again and flung himself on the sofa in the same position and shut his eyes.

"To sleep! To forget!" he repeated to himself. But with his eyes shut he saw more distinctly than ever Anna's face as it had been on the memorable evening before the races.

"That is not and will not be, and she wants to wipe it out of her memory. But I cannot live without it. How can we be reconciled? how can we be reconciled?" he said aloud, and unconsciously began to repeat these words. This repetition checked the rising up of fresh images and memories, which he felt were thronging in his brain. But repeating words did not check his imagination for long. Again in extraordinarily rapid succession his best moments rose before his mind, and then his recent humiliation. "Take away his hands," Anna's voice says. He takes away his hands and feels the shame-struck and idiotic expression of his face.

He still lay down, trying to sleep, though he felt there was not the smallest hope of it, and kept repeating stray words from some chain of thought, trying by this to check the rising flood of fresh images. He listened, and heard in a strange, mad whisper words repeated: "I did not appreciate it, did not make enough of it. I did not appreciate it, did not make enough of it."

"What's this? Am I going out of my mind?" he said to himself. "Perhaps. What makes men go out of their minds; what makes men shoot themselves?" he answered himself, and opening his eyes, he saw with wonder an embroidered cushion beside him, worked by Varya, his brother's wife. He touched the tassel of the cushion, and tried to think of Varya, of when he had seen her last. But to think of anything extraneous was an agonizing effort. "No, I must sleep!" He moved the cushion up, and pressed his head into it, but he had to make an effort to keep his eyes shut. He jumped up and sat down. "That's all over for me," he said to himself. "I must think what to do. What is left?" His mind rapidly ran through his life apart from his love of Anna.

"Ambition? Serpuhovskoy? Society? The court?" He could not come to a pause anywhere. All of it had had meaning before, but now there was no reality in it. He got up from the sofa, took off his coat, undid his belt, and uncovering his hairy chest to breathe more freely, walked up and down the room. "This is how people go mad," he repeated, "and how they shoot themselves . . . to escape humiliation," he added slowly.

He went to the door and closed it, then with fixed eyes and clenched teeth he went up to the table, took a revolver, looked round him, turned it to a loaded barrel, and sank into thought. For two minutes, his head bent forward with an expression of an intense effort of thought, he stood with the revolver in his hand, motionless, thinking.

"Of course," he said to himself, as though a logical, continuous, and clear chain of reasoning had brought him to an indubitable conclusion. In reality this "of course," that seemed convincing to him, was simply the result of exactly the same circle of memories and images through which he had passed ten times already during the last hour—memories of happiness lost forever. There was the same conception of the senselessness of everything to come in life, the same consciousness of humiliation. Even the sequence of these images and emotions was the same.

"Of course," he repeated, when for the third time his thought passed again round the same spellbound circle of memories and images, and pulling the revolver to the left side of his chest, and clutching it vigorously with his whole hand, as it were, squeezing it in his fist, he pulled the trigger. He did not hear the sound of the shot, but a violent blow on his chest sent him reeling. He tried to clutch at the edge of the table, dropped the revolver, staggered, and sat down on the ground, looking about him in astonishment. He did not recognize his room, looking up from the ground, at the bent legs of the table, at the wastepaper basket, and the tiger-skin rug. The hurried, creaking steps of his servant coming through the drawing room brought him to his senses. He made an effort at thought, and was aware that he was on the floor; and seeing blood on the tiger-skin rug and on his arm, he knew he had shot himself.

"Idiotic! Missed!" he said, fumbling after the revolver. The revolver was close beside him—he sought further off. Still feeling for it, he stretched out to the other side, and not being strong enough to keep his balance, fell over, streaming with blood.

The elegant, whiskered manservant, who used to be continually complaining to his acquaintances of the delicacy of his nerves, was so panic-stricken on seeing his master lying on the floor, that he left him losing blood while he ran for assistance. An hour later Varya, his brother's wife, had arrived, and with the assistance of three doctors, whom she had sent for in all directions, and who all appeared at the same moment, she got the wounded man to bed, and remained to nurse him.

Chapter XIX

THE MISTAKE MADE BY ALEXEY ALEXANDROVITCH IN THAT, WHEN PREPARING FOR SEEING HIS wife, he had overlooked the possibility that her repentance might be sincere, and he might forgive her, and she might not die—this mistake was two months after his return from Moscow brought home to him in all its significance. But the mistake made by him had arisen not simply from his having overlooked that contingency, but also from the fact that until that day of his interview with his dying wife, he had not known his own heart. At his sick wife's bedside he had for the first time in his life given way to that feeling of sympathetic suffering always roused in him by the sufferings of others, and hitherto looked on by him with shame as a harmful weakness. And pity for her, and remorse for having desired her death, and most of all, the joy of forgiveness, made him at once conscious, not simply of the relief of his own sufferings, but of a spiritual peace he had never experienced before. He suddenly felt that the very thing that was the source of his sufferings had become the source of his spiritual joy; that what had seemed insoluble while he was judging, blaming, and hating, had become clear and simple when he forgave and loved.

He forgave his wife and pitied her for her sufferings and her remorse. He forgave Vronsky, and pitied him, especially after reports reached him of his despairing action. He felt more for his son than before. And he blamed himself now for having taken too little interest in him. But for the little newborn baby he felt a quite peculiar sentiment, not of pity, only, but of tenderness. At first, from a feeling of compassion alone, he had been interested in the delicate little creature, who was not his child, and who was cast on one side during her mother's illness, and would certainly have died if he had not troubled about her, and he did not himself observe how fond he became of her. He would go into the nursery several times a day, and sit there for a long while, so that the nurses, who were at first afraid of him, got quite used to his presence. Sometimes for half an hour at a stretch he would sit silently gazing at the saffron-red, downy, wrinkled face of the sleeping baby, watching the movements of the frowning brows, and the fat little hands, with clenched fingers, that rubbed the little eyes and nose. At such moments particularly Alexey Alexandrovitch had a sense of perfect peace and inward harmony, and saw nothing extraordinary in his position, nothing that ought to be changed.

But as time went on, he saw more and more distinctly that however natural the position now seemed to him, he would not long be allowed to remain in it. He felt that besides the blessed spiritual force controlling his soul, there was another, a brutal force, as powerful, or more powerful, which controlled his life, and that this force would not allow him that humble peace he longed for. He felt that everyone was looking at him with inquiring wonder, that he was not understood, and that something was expected of him. Above all, he felt the instability and unnaturalness of his relations with his wife.

When the softening effect of the near approach of death had passed away, Alexey Alexandrovitch began to notice that Anna was afraid of him, ill at ease with him, and could not look him straight in the face. She seemed to be wanting, and not daring, to tell him something; and as though foreseeing their present relations could not continue, she seemed to be expecting something from him.

Towards the end of February it happened that Anna's baby daughter, who had been named Anna too, fell ill. Alexey Alexandrovitch was in the nursery in the morning, and leaving orders for the doctor to be sent for, he went to his office. On finishing his work, he returned home at four. Going into the hall he saw a handsome groom, in a braided livery and a bear fur cape, holding a white fur cloak.

"Who is here?" asked Alexey Alexandrovitch.

"Princess Elizaveta Federovna Tverskaya," the groom answered, and it seemed to Alexey Alexandrovitch that he grinned.

During all this difficult time Alexey Alexandrovitch had noticed that his worldly acquaintances, especially women, took a peculiar interest in him and his wife. All these acquaintances he observed with difficulty concealing their mirth at something; the same mirth that he had perceived in the lawyer's eyes, and just now in the eyes of this groom. Everyone seemed, somehow, hugely delighted, as though they had just been at a wedding. When they met him, with ill-disguised enjoyment they inquired after his wife's health. The presence of Princess Tverskaya was unpleasant to Alexey Alexandrovitch from the memories associated with her, and also because he disliked her, and he went straight to the nursery. In the day-nursery Seryozha, leaning on the table with his legs on a chair, was drawing and chatting away merrily. The English governess, who had during Anna's illness replaced the French one, was sitting near the boy knitting a shawl. She hurriedly got up, curtseyed, and pulled Seryozha.

Alexey Alexandrovitch stroked his son's hair, answered the governess's inquiries about his wife, and asked what the doctor had said of the baby.

"The doctor said it was nothing serious, and he ordered a bath, sir."

"But she is still in pain," said Alexey Alexandrovitch, listening to the baby's screaming in the next room.

"I think it's the wet-nurse, sir," the Englishwoman said firmly.

"What makes you think so?" he asked, stopping short.

"It's just as it was at Countess Paul's, sir. They gave the baby medicine, and it turned out that the baby was simply hungry: the nurse had no milk, sir."

Alexey Alexandrovitch pondered, and after standing still a few seconds he went in at the other door. The baby was lying with its head thrown back, stiffening itself in the nurse's arms, and would not take the plump breast offered it; and it never ceased screaming in spite of the double hushing of the wet-nurse and the other nurse, who was bending over her.

"Still no better?" said Alexey Alexandrovitch.

"She's very restless," answered the nurse in a whisper.

"Miss Edwarde says that perhaps the wet-nurse has no milk," he said.

"I think so too, Alexey Alexandrovitch."

"Then why didn't you say so?"

"Who's one to say it to? Anna Arkadyevna still ill . . ." said the nurse discontentedly.

The nurse was an old servant of the family. And in her simple words there seemed to Alexey Alexandrovitch an allusion to his position.

The baby screamed louder than ever, struggling and sobbing. The nurse, with a gesture of despair, went to it, took it from the wet-nurse's arms, and began walking up and down, rocking it.

"You must ask the doctor to examine the wet-nurse," said Alexey Alexandrovitch. The smartly dressed and healthy-looking nurse, frightened at the idea of losing her place, muttered something to herself, and covering her bosom, smiled contemptuously at the idea of doubts being cast on her abundance of milk. In that smile, too, Alexey Alexandrovitch saw a sneer at his position.

"Luckless child!" said the nurse, hushing the baby, and still walking up and down with it.

Alexey Alexandrovitch sat down, and with a despondent and suffering face watched the nurse walking to and fro.

When the child at last was still, and had been put in a deep bed, and the nurse, after smoothing the little pillow, had left her, Alexey Alexandrovitch got up, and walking awkwardly on tiptoe, approached the baby. For a minute he was still, and with the same despondent face gazed at the baby; but all at once a smile, that moved his hair and the skin of his forehead, came out on his face, and he went as softly out of the room.

In the dining room he rang the bell, and told the servant who came in to send again for the doctor. He felt vexed with his wife for not being anxious about this exquisite baby, and in this vexed humor he had no wish to go to her; he had no wish, either, to see Princess Betsy. But his wife might wonder why he did not go to her as usual; and so, overcoming his disinclination, he went towards the bedroom. As he walked over the soft rug towards the door, he could not help overhearing a conversation he did not want to hear.

"If he hadn't been going away, I could have understood your answer and his too. But your husband ought to be above that," Betsy was saying.

"It's not for my husband; for myself I don't wish it. Don't say that!" answered Anna's excited voice.

"Yes, but you must care to say good-bye to a man who has shot himself on your account. . . ."

"That's just why I don't want to."

With a dismayed and guilty expression, Alexey Alexandrovitch stopped and would have gone back unobserved. But reflecting that this would be undignified, he turned back again, and clearing his throat, he went up to the bedroom. The voices were silent, and he went in.

Anna, in a gray dressing-gown, with a crop of short clustering black curls on her round head, was sitting on a settee. The eagerness died out of her face, as it always did, at the sight of her husband; she dropped her head and looked round uneasily at Betsy. Betsy, dressed in the height of the latest fashion, in a hat that towered somewhere over her head like a shade on a lamp, in a blue dress with violet crossway stripes slanting one way on the bodice and the other way on the skirt, was sitting beside Anna, her tall flat figure held erect. Bowing her head, she greeted Alexey Alexandrovitch with an ironical smile.

"Ah!" she said, as though surprised. "I'm very glad you're at home. You never put in an appearance anywhere, and I haven't seen you ever since Anna has been ill. I have heard all about it—your anxiety. Yes, you're a wonderful husband!" she said, with a meaning and affable air, as though she were bestowing an order of magnanimity on him for his conduct to his wife.

Alexey Alexandrovitch bowed frigidly, and kissing his wife's hand, asked how she was.

"Better, I think," she said, avoiding his eyes.

"But you've rather a feverish-looking color," he said, laying stress on the word "feverish."

"We've been talking too much," said Betsy. "I feel it's selfishness on my part, and I am going away."

She got up, but Anna, suddenly flushing, quickly caught at her hand.

"No, wait a minute, please. I must tell you . . . no, you." She turned to Alexey Alexandrovitch, and her neck and brow were suffused with crimson. "I won't and can't keep anything secret from you," she said.

Alexey Alexandrovitch cracked his fingers and bowed his head.

"Betsy's been telling me that Count Vronsky wants to come here to say good-bye before his departure for Tashkend." She did not look at her husband, and was evidently in haste to have everything out, however hard it might be for her. "I told her I could not receive him."

"You said, my dear, that it would depend on Alexey Alexandrovitch," Betsy corrected her.

"Oh, no, I can't receive him; and what object would there . . ." She stopped suddenly, and glanced inquiringly at her husband (he did not look at her). "In short, I don't wish it . . ."

Alexey Alexandrovitch advanced and would have taken her hand.

Her first impulse was to jerk back her hand from the damp hand with big swollen veins that sought hers, but with an obvious effort to control herself she pressed his hand.

"I am very grateful to you for your confidence, but . . ." he said, feeling with confusion and annoyance that what he could decide easily and clearly by himself, he could not discuss before Princess Tverskaya, who to him stood for the incarnation of that brute force which would inevitably control him in the life he led in the eyes of the world, and hinder him from giving way to his feeling of love and forgiveness. He stopped short, looking at Princess Tverskaya.

"Well, good-bye, my darling," said Betsy, getting up. She kissed Anna, and went out. Alexey Alexandrovitch escorted her out.

"Alexey Alexandrovitch! I know you are a truly magnanimous man," said Betsy, stopping in the little drawing room, and with special warmth shaking hands with him once more. "I am an outsider, but I so love her and respect you that I venture to advise. Receive him. Alexey Vronsky is the soul of honor, and he is going away to Tashkend."

"Thank you, princess, for your sympathy and advice. But the question of whether my wife can or cannot see anyone she must decide herself."

He said this from habit, lifting his brows with dignity, and reflected immediately that whatever his words might be, there could be no dignity in his position. And he saw this by the suppressed, malicious, and ironical smile with which Betsy glanced at him after this phrase.

Chapter XX

ALEXEY ALEXANDROVITCH TOOK LEAVE OF BETSY IN THE DRAWING ROOM, AND WENT TO HIS wife. She was lying down, but hearing his steps she sat up hastily in her former attitude, and looked in a scared way at him. He saw she had been crying.

"I am very grateful for your confidence in me." He repeated gently in Russian the phrase he had said in Betsy's presence in French, and sat down beside her. When he spoke to her in Russian, using the Russian "thou" of intimacy and affection, it was insufferably irritating to Anna. "And I am very grateful for your decision. I, too, imagine that since he is going away, there is no sort of necessity for Count Vronsky to come here. However, if . . ."

"But I've said so already, so why repeat it?" Anna suddenly interrupted him with an irritation she could not succeed in repressing. "No sort of necessity," she thought, "for a man to come and say good-bye to the woman he loves, for whom he was ready to ruin himself, and has ruined himself, and who cannot live without him. No sort of necessity!" she compressed her lips, and dropped her burning eyes to his hands with their swollen veins. They were rubbing each other.

"Let us never speak of it," she added more calmly.

"I have left this question to you to decide, and I am very glad to see . . ." Alexey Alexandrovitch was beginning.

"That my wish coincides with your own," she finished quickly, exasperated at his talking so slowly while she knew beforehand all he would say.

"Yes," he assented; "and Princess Tverskaya's interference in the most difficult private affairs is utterly uncalled for. She especially . . ."

"I don't believe a word of what's said about her," said Anna quickly. "I know she really cares for me."

Alexey Alexandrovitch sighed and said nothing. She played nervously with the tassel of her dressing-gown, glancing at him with that torturing sensation of physical repulsion for which she blamed herself, though she could not control it. Her only desire now was to be rid of his oppressive presence.

"I have just sent for the doctor," said Alexey Alexandrovitch.

"I am very well; what do I want the doctor for?"

"No, the little one cries, and they say the nurse hasn't enough milk."

"Why didn't you let me nurse her, when I begged to? Anyway" (Alexey Alexandrovitch knew what was meant by that "anyway"), "she's a baby, and they're killing her." She rang the bell and ordered the baby to be brought her. "I begged to nurse her, I wasn't allowed to, and now I'm blamed for it."

"I don't blame . . ."

"Yes, you do blame me! My God! why didn't I die!" And she broke into sobs. "Forgive me, I'm nervous, I'm unjust," she said, controlling herself, "but do go away . . ."

"No, it can't go on like this," Alexey Alexandrovitch said to himself decidedly as he left his wife's room.

Never had the impossibility of his position in the world's eyes, and his wife's hatred of him, and altogether the might of that mysterious brutal force that guided his life against his spiritual inclinations, and exacted conformity with its decrees and change in his attitude to his wife, been presented to him with such distinctness as that day. He saw clearly that all the world and his wife expected of him something, but what exactly, he could not make out. He felt that this was rousing in his soul a feeling of anger destructive of his peace of mind and of all the good of his achievement. He believed that for Anna herself it would be better to break off all relations with Vronsky; but if they all thought this out of the question, he was even ready to allow these relations to be renewed, so long as the children were not disgraced, and he was not deprived of them nor forced to change his position. Bad as this might be, it was anyway better than a rupture, which would put her in a hopeless and shameful position, and deprive him of everything he cared for. But he felt helpless; he knew beforehand that everyone was against him, and that he would not be allowed to do what seemed to him now so natural and right, but would be forced to do what was wrong, though it seemed the proper thing to them.

Chapter XXI

BEFORE BETSY HAD TIME TO WALK OUT OF THE DRAWING ROOM, SHE WAS MET IN THE DOORWAY by Stepan Arkadyevitch, who had just come from Yeliseev's, where a consignment of fresh oysters had been received.

"Ah! princess! what a delightful meeting!" he began. "I've been to see you."

"A meeting for one minute, for I'm going," said Betsy, smiling and putting on her glove.

"Don't put on your glove yet, princess; let me kiss your hand. There's nothing I'm so thankful to the revival of the old fashions for as the kissing the hand." He kissed Betsy's hand. "When shall we see each other?"

"You don't deserve it," answered Betsy, smiling.

"Oh, yes, I deserve a great deal, for I've become a most serious person. I don't only manage my own affairs, but other people's too," he said, with a significant expression.

"Oh, I'm so glad!" answered Betsy, at once understanding that he was speaking of Anna. And going back into the drawing room, they stood in a corner. "He's killing her," said Betsy in a whisper full of meaning. "It's impossible, impossible . . ."

"I'm so glad you think so," said Stepan Arkadyevitch, shaking his head with a serious and sympathetically distressed expression, "that's what I've come to Petersburg for."

"The whole town's talking of it," she said. "It's an impossible position. She pines and pines away. He doesn't understand that she's one of those women who can't trifle with their feelings. One of two things: either let him take her away, act with energy, or give her a divorce. This is stifling her."

"Yes, yes . . . just so . . ." Oblonsky said, sighing. "That's what I've come for. At least not solely for that . . . I've been made a *Kammerherr*; of course, one has to say thank you. But the chief thing was having to settle this."

"Well, God help you!" said Betsy.

After accompanying Betsy to the outside hall, once more kissing her hand above the glove, at the point where the pulse beats, and murmuring to her such unseemly nonsense that she did not know whether to laugh or be angry, Stepan Arkadyevitch went to his sister. He found her in tears.

Although he happened to be bubbling over with good spirits, Stepan Arkadyevitch immediately and quite naturally fell into the sympathetic, poetically emotional tone which harmonized with her mood. He asked her how she was, and how she had spent the morning.

"Very, very miserably. Today and this morning and all past days and days to come," she said.

"I think you're giving way to pessimism. You must rouse yourself, you must look life in the face. I know it's hard, but . . ."

"I have heard it said that women love men even for their vices," Anna began suddenly, "but I hate him for his virtues. I can't live with him. Do you understand? the sight of him has a physical effect on me, it makes me beside myself. I can't, I can't live with him. What am I to do? I have been unhappy, and used to think one couldn't be more unhappy, but the awful state of things I am going through now, I could never have conceived. Would you believe it, that knowing he's a good man, a splendid man, that I'm not worth his little finger, still I hate him. I hate him for his generosity. And there's nothing left for me but . . ."

She would have said death, but Stepan Arkadyevitch would not let her finish.

"You are ill and overwrought," he said; "believe me, you're exaggerating dreadfully. There's nothing so terrible in it."

And Stepan Arkadyevitch smiled. No one else in Stepan Arkadyevitch's place, having to do with such despair, would have ventured to smile (the smile would have seemed brutal); but in his smile there was so much of sweetness and almost feminine tenderness that his smile did not wound, but softened and soothed. His gentle, soothing words and smiles were as soothing and softening as almond oil. And Anna soon felt this.

"No, Stiva," she said, "I'm lost, lost! worse than lost! I can't say yet that all is over; on the contrary, I feel that it's not over. I'm an overstrained string that must snap. But it's not ended yet . . . and it will have a fearful end."

"No matter, we must let the string be loosened, little by little. There's no position from which there is no way of escape."

"I have thought, and thought. Only one . . ."

Again he knew from her terrified eyes that this one way of escape in her thought was death, and he would not let her say it.

"Not at all," he said. "Listen to me. You can't see your own position as I can. Let me tell you candidly my opinion." Again he smiled discreetly his almond-oil smile. "I'll begin from the beginning. You married a man twenty years older than yourself. You married him without love and not knowing what love was. It was a mistake, let's admit."

"A fearful mistake!" said Anna.

"But I repeat, it's an accomplished fact. Then you had, let us say, the misfortune to love a man not your husband. That was a misfortune; but that, too, is an accomplished fact. And your husband knew it and forgave it." He stopped at each sentence, waiting for her to object, but she made no answer. "That's so. Now the question is: can you go on living with your husband? Do you wish it? Does he wish it?"

"I know nothing, nothing."

"But you said yourself that you can't endure him."

"No, I didn't say so. I deny it. I can't tell, I don't know anything about it."

"Yes, but let . . ."

"You can't understand. I feel I'm lying head downwards in a sort of pit, but I ought not to save myself. And I can't . . ."

"Never mind, we'll slip something under and pull you out. I understand you: I understand that you can't take it on yourself to express your wishes, your feelings."

"There's nothing, nothing I wish . . . except for it to be all over."

"But he sees this and knows it. And do you suppose it weighs on him any less than on you? You're wretched, he's wretched, and what good can come of it? while divorce would solve the difficulty completely." With some effort Stepan Arkadyevitch brought out his central idea, and looked significantly at her.

She said nothing, and shook her cropped head in dissent. But from the look in her face, that suddenly brightened into its old beauty, he saw that if she did not desire this, it was simply because it seemed to her unattainable happiness.

"I'm awfully sorry for you! And how happy I should be if I could arrange things!" said Stepan Arkadyevitch, smiling more boldly. "Don't speak, don't say a word! God grant only that I may speak as I feel. I'm going to him."

Anna looked at him with dreamy, shining eyes, and said nothing.

Chapter XXII

STEPAN ARKADYEVITCH, WITH THE SAME SOMEWHAT SOLEMN EXPRESSION WITH WHICH HE USED to take his presidential chair at his board, walked into Alexey Alexandrovitch's room. Alexey Alexandrovitch was walking about his room with his hands behind his back, thinking of just what Stepan Arkadyevitch had been discussing with his wife.

"I'm not interrupting you?" said Stepan Arkadyevitch, on the sight of his brother-in-law becoming suddenly aware of a sense of embarrassment unusual with him. To conceal this embarrassment he took out a cigarette-case he had just bought that opened in a new way, and sniffing the leather, took a cigarette out of it.

"No. Do you want anything?" Alexey Alexandrovitch asked without eagerness.

"Yes, I wished . . . I wanted . . . yes, I wanted to talk to you," said Stepan Arkadyevitch, with surprise aware of an unaccustomed timidity.

This feeling was so unexpected and so strange that he did not believe it was the voice of conscience telling him that what he was meaning to do was wrong.

Stepan Arkadyevitch made an effort and struggled with the timidity that had come over him.

"I hope you believe in my love for my sister and my sincere affection and respect for you," he said, reddening.

Alexey Alexandrovitch stood still and said nothing, but his face struck Stepan Arkadyevitch by its expression of an unresisting sacrifice.

"I intended . . . I wanted to have a little talk with you about my sister and your mutual position," he said, still struggling with an unaccustomed constraint.

Alexey Alexandrovitch smiled mournfully, looked at his brother-in-law, and without answering went up to the table, took from it an unfinished letter, and handed it to his brother-in-law.

"I think unceasingly of the same thing. And here is what I had begun writing, thinking I could say it better by letter, and that my presence irritates her," he said, as he gave him the letter.

Stepan Arkadyevitch took the letter, looked with incredulous surprise at the lusterless eyes fixed so immovably on him, and began to read.

"I see that my presence is irksome to you. Painful as it is to me to believe it, I see that it is so, and cannot be otherwise. I don't blame you, and God is my witness that on seeing you at the time of your illness I resolved with my whole heart to forget all that had passed between us and to begin a new life. I do not regret, and shall never regret, what I have done; but I have desired one thing—your good, the good of your soul—and now I see I have not attained that. Tell me yourself what will give you true happiness and peace to your soul. I put myself entirely in your hands, and trust to your feeling of what's right."

Stepan Arkadyevitch handed back the letter, and with the same surprise continued looking at his brother-in-law, not knowing what to say. This silence was so awkward for both of them that Stepan Arkadyevitch's lips began twitching nervously, while he still gazed without speaking at Karenin's face.

"That's what I wanted to say to her," said Alexey Alexandrovitch, turning away.

"Yes, yes . . ." said Stepan Arkadyevitch, not able to answer for the tears that were choking him.

"Yes, yes, I understand you," he brought out at last.

"I want to know what she would like," said Alexey Alexandrovitch.

"I am afraid she does not understand her own position. She is not a judge," said Stepan Arkadyevitch, recovering himself. "She is crushed, simply crushed by your generosity. If she were to read this letter, she would be incapable of saying anything, she would only hang her head lower than ever."

"Yes, but what's to be done in that case? how explain, how find out her wishes?"

"If you will allow me to give my opinion, I think that it lies with you to point out directly the steps you consider necessary to end the position."

"So you consider it must be ended?" Alexey Alexandrovitch interrupted him. "But how?" he added, with a gesture of his hands before his eyes not usual with him. "I see no possible way out of it."

"There is some way of getting out of every position," said Stepan Arkadyevitch, standing up and becoming more cheerful. "There was a time when you thought of breaking off . . . If you are convinced now that you cannot make each other happy . . ."

"Happiness may be variously understood. But suppose that I agree to everything, that I want nothing: what way is there of getting out of our position?"

"If you care to know my opinion," said Stepan Arkadyevitch with the same smile of softening, almond-oil tenderness with which he had been talking to Anna. His kindly smile was so winning that Alexey Alexandrovitch, feeling his own weakness and unconsciously swayed by it, was ready to believe what Stepan Arkadyevitch was saying.

"She will never speak out about it. But one thing is possible, one thing she might desire," he went on, "that is the cessation of your relations and all memories associated with them. To my thinking, in your position what's essential is the formation of a new attitude to one another. And that can only rest on a basis of freedom on both sides."

"Divorce," Alexey Alexandrovitch interrupted, in a tone of aversion.

"Yes, I imagine that divorce—yes, divorce," Stepan Arkadyevitch repeated, reddening. "That is from every point of view the most rational course for married people who find themselves in the position you are in. What can be done if married people find that life is impossible for them together? That may always happen."

Alexey Alexandrovitch sighed heavily and closed his eyes.

"There's only one point to be considered: is either of the parties desirous of forming new ties? If not, it is very simple," said Stepan Arkadyevitch, feeling more and more free from constraint.

Alexey Alexandrovitch, scowling with emotion, muttered something to himself, and made no answer. All that seemed so simple to Stepan Arkadyevitch, Alexey Alexandrovitch had thought over thousands of times. And, so far from being simple, it all seemed to him utterly impossible: Divorce, the details of which he knew by this time, seemed to him now out of the question, because the sense of his own dignity and respect for religion forbade his taking upon himself a fictitious charge of adultery, and still more suffering his wife, pardoned and beloved by him, to be caught in the fact and put to public shame. Divorce appeared to him impossible also on other still more weighty grounds.

What would become of his son in case of a divorce? To leave him with his mother was out of the question. The divorced mother would have her own illegitimate family, in which his position as a stepson and his education would not be good. Keep him with him? He knew that would be an act of vengeance on his part, and that he did not want. But apart from this, what more than all made divorce seem impossible to Alexey Alexandrovitch was, that by consenting to a divorce he would be completely ruining Anna. The saying of Darya Alexandrovna at Moscow, that in deciding on a divorce he was thinking of himself, and not considering that by this he would be ruining her irrevocably, had sunk into his heart. And connecting this saying with his forgiveness of her, with his devotion to the children, he understood it now in his own way. To consent to a divorce, to give her her freedom, meant in his thoughts to take from himself the last tie that bound him to life—the children whom he loved; and to take from her the last prop that stayed her on the path of right, to thrust her down to her ruin. If she were divorced, he knew she would join her life to Vronsky's, and their tie would be an illegitimate and criminal one, since a wife, by the interpretation of the ecclesiastical law, could not marry while her husband was living. "She will join him, and in a year or two he will throw her over, or she will form a new tie," thought Alexey Alexandrovitch. "And I, by agreeing to an unlawful divorce, shall be to blame for her ruin." He had thought it all over hundreds of times, and was convinced that a divorce was not at all simple, as Stepan Arkadyevitch had said, but was utterly impossible. He did not believe a single word Stepan Arkadyevitch said to him; to every word he had a thousand objections to make, but he listened to him, feeling that his words were the expression of that mighty brutal force which controlled his life and to which he would have to submit.

"The only question is on what terms you agree to give her a divorce. She does not want anything, does not dare ask you for anything, she leaves it all to your generosity."

"My God, my God! what for?" thought Alexey Alexandrovitch, remembering the details of divorce proceedings in which the husband took the blame on himself, and with just the same gesture with which Vronsky had done the same, he hid his face for shame in his hands.

"You are distressed, I understand that. But if you think it over . . ."

"Whosoever shall smite thee on thy right cheek, turn to him the other also; and if any man take away thy coat, let him have thy cloak also," thought Alexey Alexandrovitch.

"Yes, yes!" he cried in a shrill voice. "I will take the disgrace on myself, I will give up even my son, but . . . but wouldn't it be better to let it alone? Still you may do as you like . . ."

And turning away so that his brother-in-law could not see him, he sat down on a chair at the window. There was bitterness, there was shame in his heart, but with bitterness and shame he felt joy and emotion at the height of his own meekness.

Stepan Arkadyevitch was touched. He was silent for a space.

"Alexey Alexandrovitch, believe me, she appreciates your generosity," he said. "But it seems it was the will of God," he added, and as he said it felt how foolish a remark it was, and with difficulty repressed a smile at his own foolishness.

Alexey Alexandrovitch would have made some reply, but tears stopped him.

"This is an unhappy fatality, and one must accept it as such. I accept the calamity as an accomplished fact, and am doing my best to help both her and you," said Stepan Arkadyevitch.

When he went out of his brother-in-law's room he was touched, but that did not prevent him from being glad he had successfully brought the matter to a conclusion, for he felt certain Alexey Alexandrovitch would not go back on his words. To this satisfaction was added the fact that an idea had just struck him for a riddle turning on his successful achievement, that when the affair was over he would ask his wife and most intimate friends. He put this riddle into two or three different ways. "But I'll work it out better than that," he said to himself with a smile.

Chapter XXIII

VRONSKY'S WOUND HAD BEEN A DANGEROUS ONE, THOUGH IT DID NOT TOUCH THE HEART, AND for several days he had lain between life and death. The first time he was able to speak, Varya, his brother's wife, was alone in the room.

"Varya," he said, looking sternly at her, "I shot myself by accident. And please never speak of it, and tell everyone so. Or else it's too ridiculous."

Without answering his words, Varya bent over him, and with a delighted smile gazed into his face. His eyes were clear, not feverish; but their expression was stern.

"Thank God!" she said. "You're not in pain?"

"A little here." He pointed to his breast.

"Then let me change your bandages."

In silence, stiffening his broad jaws, he looked at her while she bandaged him up. When she had finished he said:

"I'm not delirious. Please manage that there may be no talk of my having shot myself on purpose."

"No one does say so. Only I hope you won't shoot yourself by accident anymore," she said, with a questioning smile.

"Of course I won't, but it would have been better . . ."

And he smiled gloomily.

In spite of these words and this smile, which so frightened Varya, when the inflammation was over and he began to recover, he felt that he was completely free from one part of his misery. By his action he had, as it were, washed away the shame and humiliation he had felt before. He could now think calmly of Alexey Alexandrovitch. He recognized all his magnanimity, but he did not now feel himself humiliated by it. Besides, he got back again into the beaten track of his life. He saw the possibility of looking men in the face again without shame, and he could live in accordance with his own habits. One thing he could not pluck out of his heart, though he never ceased struggling with it, was the regret, amounting to despair, that he had lost her forever. That now, having expiated his sin against the husband, he was bound to renounce her, and never in future to stand between her with her repentance and her husband, he had firmly decided in his heart; but he could not tear out of his heart his regret at the loss of her love, he could not erase from his memory those moments of happiness that he had so little prized at the time, and that haunted him in all their charm.

Serpuhovskoy had planned his appointment at Tashkend, and Vronsky agreed to the proposition without the slightest hesitation. But the nearer the time of departure came, the bitterer was the sacrifice he was making to what he thought his duty.

His wound had healed, and he was driving about making preparations for his departure for Tashkend.

"To see her once and then to bury myself, to die," he thought, and as he was paying farewell visits, he uttered this thought to Betsy. Charged with this commission, Betsy had gone to Anna, and brought him back a negative reply.

"So much the better," thought Vronsky, when he received the news. "It was a weakness, which would have shattered what strength I have left."

Next day Betsy herself came to him in the morning, and announced that she had heard through Oblonsky as a positive fact that Alexey Alexandrovitch had agreed to a divorce, and that therefore Vronsky could see Anna.

Without even troubling himself to see Betsy out of his flat, forgetting all his resolutions, without asking when he could see her, where her husband was, Vronsky drove straight to the Karenins'. He ran up the stairs seeing no one and nothing, and with a rapid step, almost breaking into a run, he went into her room. And without considering, without noticing whether there was anyone in the room or not, he flung his arms round her, and began to cover her face, her hands, her neck with kisses.

Anna had been preparing herself for this meeting, had thought what she would say to him, but she did not succeed in saying anything of it; his passion mastered her. She tried to calm him, to calm herself, but it was too late. His feeling infected her. Her lips trembled so that for a long while she could say nothing.

"Yes, you have conquered me, and I am yours," she said at last, pressing his hands to her bosom.

"So it had to be," he said. "So long as we live, it must be so. I know it now."

"That's true," she said, getting whiter and whiter, and embracing his head. "Still there is something terrible in it after all that has happened."

"It will all pass, it will all pass; we shall be so happy. Our love, if it could be stronger, will be strengthened by there being something terrible in it," he said, lifting his head and parting his strong teeth in a smile.

And she could not but respond with a smile—not to his words, but to the love in his eyes. She took his hand and stroked her chilled cheeks and cropped head with it.

"I don't know you with this short hair. You've grown so pretty. A boy. But how pale you are!"

"Yes, I'm very weak," she said, smiling. And her lips began trembling again.

"We'll go to Italy; you will get strong," he said.

"Can it be possible we could be like husband and wife, alone, your family with you?" she said, looking close into his eyes.

"It only seems strange to me that it can ever have been otherwise."

"Stiva says that *he* has agreed to everything, but I can't accept *his* generosity," she said, looking dreamily past Vronsky's face. "I don't want a divorce; it's all the same to me now. Only I don't know what he will decide about Seryozha."

He could not conceive how at this moment of their meeting she could remember and think of her son, of divorce. What did it all matter?

"Don't speak of that, don't think of it," he said, turning her hand in his, and trying to draw her attention to him; but still she did not look at him.

"Oh, why didn't I die! it would have been better," she said, and silent tears flowed down both her cheeks; but she tried to smile, so as not to wound him.

To decline the flattering and dangerous appointment at Tashkend would have been, Vronsky had till then considered, disgraceful and impossible. But now, without an instant's consideration, he declined it, and observing dissatisfaction in the most exalted quarters at this step, he immediately retired from the army.

A month later Alexey Alexandrovitch was left alone with his son in his house at Petersburg, while Anna and Vronsky had gone abroad, not having obtained a divorce, but having absolutely declined all idea of one.

PART FIVE

Chapter I

PRINCESS SHTCHERBATSKAYA CONSIDERED THAT IT WAS OUT OF THE QUESTION FOR THE wedding to take place before Lent, just five weeks off, since not half the trousseau could possibly be ready by that time. But she could not but agree with Levin that to fix it for after Lent would be putting it off too late, as an old aunt of Prince Shtcherbatsky's was seriously ill and might die, and then the mourning would delay the wedding still longer. And therefore, deciding to divide the trousseau into two parts—a larger and smaller trousseau—the princess consented to have the wedding before Lent. She determined that she would get the smaller part of the trousseau all ready now, and the larger part should be made later, and she was much vexed with Levin because he was incapable of giving her a serious answer to the question whether he agreed to this arrangement or not. The arrangement was the more suitable as, immediately after the wedding, the young people were to go to the country, where the more important part of the trousseau would not be wanted.

Levin still continued in the same delirious condition in which it seemed to him that he and his happiness constituted the chief and sole aim of all existence, and that he need not now think or care about anything, that everything was being done and would be done for him by others. He had not even plans and aims for the future, he left its arrangement to others, knowing that everything would be delightful. His brother Sergey Ivanovitch, Stepan Arkadyevitch, and the princess guided him in doing what he had to do. All he did was to agree entirely with everything suggested to him. His brother raised money for him, the princess advised him to leave Moscow after the wedding. Stepan Arkadyevitch advised him to go abroad. He agreed to everything. "Do what you choose, if it amuses you. I'm happy, and my happiness can be no greater and no less for anything you do," he thought. When he told Kitty of Stepan Arkadyevitch's advice that they should go abroad, he was much surprised that she did not agree to this, and had some definite requirements of her own in regard to their future. She knew Levin had work he loved in the country. She did not, as he saw, understand this work, she did not even care to understand it. But that did not prevent her from regarding it as a matter of great importance. And then she knew their home would be in the country, and she wanted to go, not abroad where she was not going to live, but to the place where their home would be. This definitely expressed purpose astonished Levin. But since he did not care either way, he immediately asked Stepan Arkadyevitch, as though it were his duty, to go down to the country and to arrange everything there to the best of his ability with the taste of which he had so much.

"But I say," Stepan Arkadyevitch said to him one day after he had come back from the country, where he had got everything ready for the young people's arrival, "have you a certificate of having been at confession?"

"No. But what of it?"

"You can't be married without it."

"Aïe, aïe, aïe!" cried Levin. "Why, I believe it's nine years since I've taken the sacrament! I never thought of it."

"You're a pretty fellow!" said Stepan Arkadyevitch laughing, "and you call me a Nihilist! But this won't do, you know. You must take the sacrament."

"When? There are four days left now."

Stepan Arkadyevitch arranged this also, and Levin had to go to confession. To Levin, as to any unbeliever who respects the beliefs of others, it was exceedingly disagreeable to be present at and take part in church ceremonies. At this moment, in his present softened state of feeling, sensitive to everything, this inevitable act of hypocrisy was not merely painful to Levin, it seemed to him utterly impossible. Now, in the heyday of his highest glory, his fullest flower, he would have to be a liar or a scoffer. He felt incapable of being either. But though he repeatedly plied Stepan Arkadyevitch with questions as to the possibility of obtaining a certificate without actually communicating, Stepan Arkadyevitch maintained that it was out of the question.

"Besides, what is it to you—two days? And he's an awfully nice clever old fellow. He'll pull the tooth out for you so gently, you won't notice it."

Standing at the first litany, Levin attempted to revive in himself his youthful recollections of the intense religious emotion he had passed through between the ages of sixteen and seventeen.

But he was at once convinced that it was utterly impossible to him. He attempted to look at it all as an empty custom, having no sort of meaning, like the custom of paying calls. But he felt that he could not do that either. Levin found himself, like the majority of his contemporaries, in the vaguest position in regard to religion. Believe he could not, and at the same time he had no firm conviction that it was all wrong. And consequently, not being able to believe in the significance of what he was doing nor to regard it with indifference as an empty formality, during the whole period of preparing for the sacrament he was conscious of a feeling of discomfort and shame at doing what he did not himself understand, and what, as an inner voice told him, was therefore false and wrong.

During the service he would first listen to the prayers, trying to attach some meaning to them not discordant with his own views; then feeling that he could not understand and must condemn them, he tried not to listen to them, but to attend to the thoughts, observations, and memories which floated through his brain with extreme vividness during this idle time of standing in church.

He had stood through the litany, the evening service and the midnight service, and the next day he got up earlier than usual, and without having tea went at eight o'clock in the morning to the church for the morning service and the confession.

There was no one in the church but a beggar soldier, two old women, and the church officials. A young deacon, whose long back showed in two distinct halves through his thin undercassock, met him, and at once going to a little table at the wall read the exhortation. During the reading, especially at the frequent and rapid repetition of the same words, "Lord, have mercy on us!" which resounded with an echo, Levin felt that thought was shut and sealed up, and that it must not be touched or stirred now or confusion would be the result; and so standing behind the deacon he went on thinking of his own affairs, neither listening nor examining what was said. "It's wonderful what expression there is in her hand," he thought, remembering how they had been sitting the day before at a corner table. They had nothing to talk about, as was almost always the case at this time, and laying her hand on the table she kept opening and shutting it, and laughed herself as she watched her action. He remembered how he had kissed it and then had examined the lines on the pink palm. "Have mercy on us again!" thought Levin, crossing himself, bowing, and looking at the supple spring of the deacon's back bowing before him. "She took my hand then and examined the lines 'You've got a splendid hand,' she said." And he looked at his own hand and the short hand of the deacon. "Yes, now it will soon be over," he thought. "No, it seems to be beginning again," he thought, listening to the prayers. "No, it's just ending: there he is bowing down to the ground. That's always at the end."

The deacon's hand in a plush cuff unobtrusively accepted a three-ruble note, and the deacon said he would put it down in the register, and his new boots creaking jauntily over the flagstones of the empty church, he went to the altar. A moment later he peeped out thence and beckoned to Levin. Thought, till then locked up, began to stir in Levin's head, but he made haste to drive it away. "It will come right somehow," he thought, and went towards the altar-rails. He went up the steps, and turning to the right saw the priest. The priest, a little old man with a scanty grizzled beard and weary, good-natured eyes, was standing at the altar-rails, turning over the pages of a missal. With a slight bow to Levin he began immediately reading prayers in the official voice. When he had finished them he bowed down to the ground and turned, facing Levin.

"Christ is present here unseen, receiving your confession," he said, pointing to the crucifix. "Do you believe in all the doctrines of the Holy Apostolic Church?" the priest went on, turning his eyes away from Levin's face and folding his hands under his stole.

"I have doubted, I doubt everything," said Levin in a voice that jarred on himself, and he ceased speaking.

The priest waited a few seconds to see if he would not say more, and closing his eyes he said quickly, with a broad, Vladimirsky accent:

"Doubt is natural to the weakness of mankind, but we must pray that God in His mercy will strengthen us. What are your special sins?" he added, without the slightest interval, as though anxious not to waste time.

"My chief sin is doubt. I have doubts of everything, and for the most part I am in doubt."

"Doubt is natural to the weakness of mankind," the priest repeated the same words. "What do you doubt about principally?"

"I doubt of everything. I sometimes even have doubts of the existence of God," Levin could not help saying, and he was horrified at the impropriety of what he was saying. But Levin's words did not, it seemed, make much impression on the priest.

"What sort of doubt can there be of the existence of God?" he said hurriedly, with a just perceptible smile.

Levin did not speak.

"What doubt can you have of the Creator when you behold His creation?" the priest went on in the rapid customary jargon. "Who has decked the heavenly firmament with its lights? Who has clothed the earth in its beauty? How explain it without the Creator?" he said, looking inquiringly at Levin.

Levin felt that it would be improper to enter upon a metaphysical discussion with the priest, and so he said in reply merely what was a direct answer to the question.

"I don't know," he said.

"You don't know! Then how can you doubt that God created all?" the priest said, with good-humored perplexity.

"I don't understand it at all," said Levin, blushing, and feeling that his words were stupid, and that they could not be anything but stupid in such a position.

"Pray to God and beseech Him. Even the holy fathers had doubts, and prayed to God to strengthen their faith. The devil has great power, and we must resist him. Pray to God, beseech Him. Pray to God," he repeated hurriedly.

The priest paused for some time, as though meditating.

"You're about, I hear, to marry the daughter of my parishioner and son in the spirit, Prince Shtcherbatsky?" he resumed, with a smile. "An excellent young lady."

"Yes," answered Levin, blushing for the priest. "What does he want to ask me about this at confession for?" he thought.

And, as though answering his thought, the priest said to him:

"You are about to enter into holy matrimony, and God may bless you with offspring. Well, what sort of bringing-up can you give your babes if you do not overcome the temptation of the devil, enticing you to infidelity?" he said, with gentle reproachfulness. "If you love your child as a good father, you will not desire only wealth, luxury, honor for your infant; you will be anxious for his salvation, his spiritual enlightenment with the light of truth. Eh? What answer will you make him when the innocent babe asks you: 'Papa! who made all that enchants me in this world—the earth, the waters, the sun, the flowers, the grass?' Can you say to him: 'I don't know'? You cannot but know, since the Lord God in His infinite mercy has revealed it to us. Or your child will ask you: 'What awaits me in the life beyond the tomb?' What will you say to him when you know nothing? How will you answer him? Will you leave him to the allurements of the world and the devil? That's not right," he said, and he stopped, putting his head on one side and looking at Levin with his kindly, gentle eyes.

Levin made no answer this time, not because he did not want to enter upon a discussion with the priest, but because, so far, no one had ever asked him such questions, and when his babes did ask him those questions, it would be time enough to think about answering them.

"You are entering upon a time of life," pursued the priest, "when you must choose your path and keep to it. Pray to God that He may in His mercy aid you and have mercy on you!" he concluded. "Our Lord and God, Jesus Christ, in the abundance and riches of His lovingkindness, forgives this child . . ." and, finishing the prayer of absolution, the priest blessed him and dismissed him.

On getting home that day, Levin had a delightful sense of relief at the awkward position being over and having been got through without his having to tell a lie. Apart from this, there remained a vague memory that what the kind, nice old fellow had said had not been at all so stupid as he had fancied at first, and that there was something in it that must be cleared up.

"Of course, not now," thought Levin, "but some day later on." Levin felt more than ever now that there was something not clear and not clean in his soul, and that, in regard to religion, he was in the same position which he perceived so clearly and disliked in others, and for which he blamed his friend Sviazhsky.

Levin spent that evening with his betrothed at Dolly's, and was in very high spirits. To explain to Stepan Arkadyevitch the state of excitement in which he found himself, he said that he was happy like a dog being trained to jump through a hoop, who, having at last caught the idea, and done what was required of him, whines and wags its tail, and jumps up to the table and the windows in its delight.

Chapter II

ON THE DAY OF THE WEDDING, ACCORDING TO THE RUSSIAN CUSTOM (THE PRINCESS AND DARYA Alexandrovna insisted on strictly keeping all the customs), Levin did not see his betrothed, and dined at his hotel with three bachelor friends, casually brought together at his rooms. These were Sergey Ivanovitch, Katavasov, a university friend, now professor of natural science, whom Levin had met in the street and insisted on taking home with him, and Tchirikov, his best man, a Moscow conciliation-board judge, Levin's companion in his bear hunts. The dinner was a very merry one: Sergey Ivanovitch was in his happiest mood, and was much amused by Katavasov's originality. Katavasov, feeling his originality was appreciated and understood, made the most of it. Tchirikov always gave a lively and good-humored support to conversation of any sort.

"See, now," said Katavasov, drawling his words from a habit acquired in the lecture-room, "what a capable fellow was our friend Konstantin Dmitrievitch. I'm not speaking of present company, for he's absent. At the time he left the university he was fond of science, took an interest in humanity; now one-half of his abilities is devoted to deceiving himself, and the other to justifying the deceit."

"A more determined enemy of matrimony than you I never saw," said Sergey Ivanovitch.

"Oh, no, I'm not an enemy of matrimony. I'm in favor of division of labor. People who can do nothing else ought to rear people while the rest work for their happiness and enlightenment. That's how I look at it. To muddle up two trades is the error of the amateur; I'm not one of their number."

"How happy I shall be when I hear that you're in love!" said Levin. "Please invite me to the wedding."

"I'm in love now."

"Yes, with a cuttlefish! You know," Levin turned to his brother, "Mihail Semyonovitch is writing a work on the digestive organs of the . . ."

"Now, make a muddle of it! It doesn't matter what about. And the fact is, I certainly do love cuttlefish."

"But that's no hindrance to your loving your wife."

"The cuttlefish is no hindrance. The wife is the hindrance."

"Why so?"

"Oh, you'll see! You care about farming, hunting—well, you'd better look out!"

"Arship was here today; he said there were a lot of elks in Prudno, and two bears," said Tchirikov.

"Well, you must go and get them without me."

"Ah, that's the truth," said Sergey Ivanovitch. "And you may say good-bye to bear hunting for the future—your wife won't allow it!"

Levin smiled. The picture of his wife not letting him go was so pleasant that he was ready to renounce the delights of looking upon bears forever.

"Still, it's a pity they should get those two bears without you. Do you remember last time at Hapilovo? That was a delightful hunt!" said Tchirikov.

Levin had not the heart to disillusion him of the notion that there could be something delightful apart from her, and so said nothing.

"There's some sense in this custom of saying good-bye to bachelor life," said Sergey Ivanovitch. "However happy you may be, you must regret your freedom."

"And confess there is a feeling that you want to jump out of the window, like Gogol's bridegroom?"

"Of course there is, but it isn't confessed," said Katavasov, and he broke into loud laughter.

"Oh, well, the window's open. Let's start off this instant to Tver! There's a big she-bear; one can go right up to the lair. Seriously, let's go by the five o'clock! And here let them do what they like," said Tchirikov, smiling.

"Well, now, on my honor," said Levin, smiling, "I can't find in my heart that feeling of regret for my freedom."

"Yes, there's such a chaos in your heart just now that you can't find anything there," said Katavasov. "Wait a bit, when you set it to rights a little, you'll find it!"

"No; if so, I should have felt a little, apart from my feeling" (he could not say love before them) "and happiness, a certain regret at losing my freedom. . . . On the contrary, I am glad at the very loss of my freedom."

"Awful! It's a hopeless case!" said Katavasov. "Well, let's drink to his recovery, or wish that a hundredth part of his dreams may be realized—and that would be happiness such as never has been seen on earth!"

Soon after dinner the guests went away to be in time to be dressed for the wedding.

When he was left alone, and recalled the conversation of these bachelor friends, Levin asked himself: had he in his heart that regret for his freedom of which they had spoken? He smiled at the question. "Freedom! What is freedom for? Happiness is only in loving and wishing her wishes, thinking her thoughts, that is to say, not freedom at all—that's happiness!"

"But do I know her ideas, her wishes, her feelings?" some voice suddenly whispered to him. The smile died away from his face, and he grew thoughtful. And suddenly a strange feeling came upon him. There came over him a dread and doubt—doubt of everything.

"What if she does not love me? What if she's marrying me simply to be married? What if she doesn't see herself what she's doing?" he asked himself. "She may come to her senses, and only when she is being married realize that she does not and cannot love me." And strange, most evil thoughts of her began to come to him. He was jealous of Vronsky, as he had been a year ago, as though the evening he had seen her with Vronsky had been yesterday. He suspected she had not told him everything.

He jumped up quickly. "No, this can't go on!" he said to himself in despair. "I'll go to her; I'll ask her; I'll say for the last time: we are free, and hadn't we better stay so? Anything's better than endless misery, disgrace, unfaithfulness!" With despair in his heart and bitter anger against all men, against himself, against her, he went out of the hotel and drove to her house.

He found her in one of the back rooms. She was sitting on a chest and making some arrangements with her maid, sorting over heaps of dresses of different colors, spread on the backs of chairs and on the floor.

"Ah!" she cried, seeing him, and beaming with delight. "Kostya! Konstantin Dmitrievitch!" (These latter days she used these names almost alternately.) "I didn't expect you! I'm going through my wardrobe to see what's for whom . . ."

"Oh! that's very nice!" he said gloomily, looking at the maid.

"You can go, Dunyasha, I'll call you presently," said Kitty. "Kostya, what's the matter?" she asked, definitely adopting this familiar name as soon as the maid had gone out. She noticed his strange face, agitated and gloomy, and a panic came over her.

"Kitty! I'm in torture. I can't suffer alone," he said with despair in his voice, standing before her and looking imploringly into her eyes. He saw already from her loving, truthful face, that nothing could come of what he had meant to say, but yet he wanted her to reassure him herself. "I've come to say that there's still time. This can all be stopped and set right."

"What? I don't understand. What is the matter?"

"What I have said a thousand times over, and can't help thinking . . . that I'm not worthy of you. You couldn't consent to marry me. Think a little. You've made a mistake. Think it over thoroughly. You can't love me. . . . If . . . better say so," he said, not looking at her. "I shall be wretched. Let people say what they like; anything's better than misery. . . . Far better now while there's still time. . . ."

"I don't understand," she answered, panic-stricken; "you mean you want to give it up . . . don't want it?"

"Yes, if you don't love me."

"You're out of your mind!" she cried, turning crimson with vexation. But his face was so piteous, that she restrained her vexation, and flinging some clothes off an arm-chair, she sat down beside him. "What are you thinking? tell me all."

"I am thinking you can't love me. What can you love me for?"

"My God! what can I do? . . ." she said, and burst into tears.

"Oh! what have I done?" he cried, and kneeling before her, he fell to kissing her hands.

When the princess came into the room five minutes later, she found them completely reconciled. Kitty had not simply assured him that she loved him, but had gone so far—in answer to his question, what she loved him for—as to explain what for. She told him that she loved him because she understood him completely, because she knew what he would like, and because everything he liked was good. And this seemed to him perfectly clear. When the princess came to them, they were sitting side by side on the chest, sorting the dresses and disputing over Kitty's wanting to give Dunyasha the brown dress she had been wearing when Levin proposed to her, while he insisted that that dress must never be given away, but Dunyasha must have the blue one.

"How is it you don't see? She's a brunette, and it won't suit her. . . . I've worked it all out."

Hearing why he had come, the princess was half humorously, half seriously angry with him, and sent him home to dress and not to hinder Kitty's hair-dressing, as Charles the hair-dresser was just coming.

"As it is, she's been eating nothing lately and is losing her looks, and then you must come and upset her with your nonsense," she said to him. "Get along with you, my dear!"

Levin, guilty and shamefaced, but pacified, went back to his hotel. His brother, Darya Alexandrovna, and Stepan Arkadyevitch, all in full dress, were waiting for him to bless him with the holy picture. There was no time to lose. Darya Alexandrovna had to drive home again to fetch her curled and pomaded son, who was to carry the holy pictures after the bride. Then a carriage had to be sent for the best man, and another that would take Sergey Ivanovitch away would have to be sent back. . . . Altogether there were a great many most complicated matters to be considered and arranged. One thing was unmistakable, that there must be no delay, as it was already half-past six.

Nothing special happened at the ceremony of benediction with the holy picture. Stepan Arkadyevitch stood in a comically solemn pose beside his wife, took the holy picture, and telling Levin to bow down to the ground, he blessed him with his kindly, ironical smile, and kissed him three times; Darya Alexandrovna did the same, and immediately was in a hurry to get off, and again plunged into the intricate question of the destinations of the various carriages.

"Come, I'll tell you how we'll manage: you drive in our carriage to fetch him, and Sergey Ivanovitch, if he'll be so good, will drive there and then send his carriage."

"Of course; I shall be delighted."

"We'll come on directly with him. Are your things sent off?" said Stepan Arkadyevitch.

"Yes," answered Levin, and he told Kouzma to put out his clothes for him to dress.

Chapter III

A CROWD OF PEOPLE, PRINCIPALLY WOMEN, WAS THRONGING ROUND THE CHURCH LIT UP FOR THE wedding. Those who had not succeeded in getting into the main entrance were crowding about the windows, pushing, wrangling, and peeping through the gratings.

More than twenty carriages had already been drawn up in ranks along the street by the police. A police officer, regardless of the frost, stood at the entrance, gorgeous in his uniform. More carriages were continually driving up, and ladies wearing flowers and carrying their trains, and men taking off their helmets or black hats kept walking into the church. Inside the church both lusters were already lit, and all the candles before the holy pictures. The gilt on the red ground of the holy picture-stand, and the gilt relief on the pictures, and the silver of the lusters and candlesticks, and the stones of the floor, and the rugs, and the banners above in the choir, and the steps of the altar, and the old blackened books, and the cassocks and surplices—all were flooded with light. On the right side of the warm church, in the crowd of frock-coats and white ties, uniforms and broadcloth, velvet, satin, hair and flowers, bare shoulders and arms and long gloves, there was discreet but lively conversation that echoed strangely in the high cupola. Every time there was heard the creak of the opened door the conversation in the crowd died away, and everybody looked round expecting to see the bride and bridegroom come in. But the door had opened more than ten times, and each time it was either a belated guest or guests, who joined the circle of the invited on the right, or a spectator, who had eluded or softened the police officer, and went to join the crowd of outsiders on the left. Both the guests and the outside public had by now passed through all the phases of anticipation.

At first they imagined that the bride and bridegroom would arrive immediately, and attached no importance at all to their being late. Then they began to look more and more often towards the door, and to talk of whether anything could have happened. Then the long delay began to be positively discomforting, and relations and guests tried to look as if they were not thinking of the bridegroom but were engrossed in conversation.

The head deacon, as though to remind them of the value of his time, coughed impatiently, making the window-panes quiver in their frames. In the choir the bored choristers could be heard trying their voices and blowing their noses. The priest was continually sending first the beadle and then the deacon to find out whether the bridegroom had not come, more and more often he went himself, in a lilac vestment and an embroidered sash, to the side door, expecting to see the bridegroom. At last one of the ladies, glancing at her watch, said, "It really is strange, though!" and all the guests became uneasy and began loudly expressing their wonder and dissatisfaction. One of the bridegroom's best men went to find out what had happened. Kitty meanwhile had long ago been quite ready, and in her white dress and long veil and wreath of orange blossoms she was standing in the drawing room of the Shtcherbatskys' house with her sister, Madame Lvova, who was her bridal-mother. She was looking out of the window, and had been for over half an hour anxiously expecting to hear from the best man that her bridegroom was at the church.

Levin meanwhile, in his trousers, but without his coat and waistcoat, was walking to and fro in his room at the hotel, continually putting his head out of the door and looking up and down the corridor. But in the corridor there was no sign of the person he was looking for and he came back in despair, and frantically waving his hands addressed Stepan Arkadyevitch, who was smoking serenely.

"Was ever a man in such a fearful fool's position?" he said.

"Yes, it is stupid," Stepan Arkadyevitch assented, smiling soothingly. "But don't worry, it'll be brought directly."

"No, what is to be done!" said Levin, with smothered fury. "And these fools of open waistcoats! Out of the question!" he said, looking at the crumpled front of his shirt. "And what if the things have been taken on to the railway station!" he roared in desperation.

"Then you must put on mine."

"I ought to have done so long ago, if at all."

"It's not nice to look ridiculous. . . . Wait a bit! it will *come round.*"

The point was that when Levin asked for his evening suit, Kouzma, his old servant, had brought him the coat, waistcoat, and everything that was wanted.

"But the shirt!" cried Levin.

"You've got a shirt on," Kouzma answered, with a placid smile.

Kouzma had not thought of leaving out a clean shirt, and on receiving instructions to pack up everything and send it round to the Shtcherbatskys' house, from which the young people were to set out the same evening, he had done so, packing everything but the dress suit. The shirt worn since the morning was crumpled and out of the question with the fashionable open waistcoat. It was a long way to send to the Shtcherbatskys'. They sent out to buy a shirt. The servant came back; everything was shut up—it was Sunday. They sent to Stepan Arkadyevitch's and brought a shirt—it was impossibly wide and short. They sent finally to the Shtcherbatskys' to unpack the things. The bridegroom was expected at the church while he was pacing up and down his room like a wild beast in a cage, peeping out into the corridor, and with horror and despair recalling what absurd things he had said to Kitty and what she might be thinking now.

At last the guilty Kouzma flew panting into the room with the shirt.

"Only just in time. They were just lifting it into the van," said Kouzma.

Three minutes later Levin ran full speed into the corridor, not looking at his watch for fear of aggravating his sufferings.

"You won't help matters like this," said Stepan Arkadyevitch with a smile, hurrying with more deliberation after him. *"It will come round, it will come round* . . . I tell you."

Chapter IV

"THEY'VE COME!" "HERE HE IS!" "WHICH ONE?" "RATHER YOUNG, EH?" "WHY, MY DEAR SOUL, SHE looks more dead than alive!" were the comments in the crowd, when Levin, meeting his bride in the entrance, walked with her into the church.

Stepan Arkadyevitch told his wife the cause of the delay, and the guests were whispering it with smiles to one another. Levin saw nothing and no one; he did not take his eyes off his bride.

Everyone said she had lost her looks dreadfully of late, and was not nearly so pretty on her wedding day as usual; but Levin did not think so. He looked at her hair done up high, with the long white veil and white flowers and the high, stand-up, scalloped collar, that in such a maidenly fashion hid her long neck at the sides and only showed it in front, her strikingly slender figure, and it seemed to him that she looked better than ever—not because these flowers, this veil, this gown from Paris added anything to her beauty; but because, in spite of the elaborate sumptuousness of her attire, the expression of her sweet face, of her eyes, of her lips was still her own characteristic expression of guileless truthfulness.

"I was beginning to think you meant to run away," she said, and smiled to him.

"It's so stupid, what happened to me, I'm ashamed to speak of it!" he said, reddening, and he was obliged to turn to Sergey Ivanovitch, who came up to him.

"This is a pretty story of yours about the shirt!" said Sergey Ivanovitch, shaking his head and smiling.

"Yes, yes!" answered Levin, without an idea of what they were talking about.

"Now, Kostya, you have to decide," said Stepan Arkadyevitch with an air of mock dismay, "a weighty question. You are at this moment just in the humor to appreciate all its gravity. They ask me, are they to light the candles that have been lit before or candles that have never been lit? It's a matter of ten roubles," he added, relaxing his lips into a smile. "I have decided, but I was afraid you might not agree."

Levin saw it was a joke, but he could not smile.

"Well, how's it to be then?—unlighted or lit candles? that's the question."

"Yes, yes, unlighted."

"Oh, I'm very glad. The question's decided!" said Stepan Arkadyevitch, smiling. "How silly men are, though, in this position," he said to Tchirikov, when Levin, after looking absently at him, had moved back to his bride.

"Kitty, mind you're the first to step on the carpet," said Countess Nordston, coming up. "You're a nice person!" she said to Levin.

"Aren't you frightened, eh?" said Marya Dmitrievna, an old aunt.

"Are you cold? You're pale. Stop a minute, stoop down," said Kitty's sister, Madame Lvova, and with her plump, handsome arms she smilingly set straight the flowers on her head.

Dolly came up, tried to say something, but could not speak, cried, and then laughed unnaturally.

Kitty looked at all of them with the same absent eyes as Levin.

Meanwhile the officiating clergy had got into their vestments, and the priest and deacon came out to the lectern, which stood in the forepart of the church. The priest turned to Levin, saying something. Levin did not hear what the priest said.

"Take the bride's hand and lead her up," the best man said to Levin.

It was a long while before Levin could make out what was expected of him. For a long time they tried to set him right and made him begin again—because he kept taking Kitty by the wrong arm or with the wrong arm—till he understood at last that what he had to do was, without changing his position, to take her right hand in his right hand. When at last he had taken the bride's hand in the correct way, the priest walked a few paces in front of them and stopped at the lectern. The crowd of friends and relations moved after them, with a buzz of talk and a rustle of skirts. Someone stooped down and pulled out the bride's train. The church became so still that the drops of wax could be heard falling from the candles.

The little old priest in his ecclesiastical cap, with his long silvery-gray locks of hair parted behind his ears, was fumbling with something at the lectern, putting out his little old hands from under the heavy silver vestment with the gold cross on the back of it.

Stepan Arkadyevitch approached him cautiously, whispered something, and making a sign to Levin, walked back again.

The priest lit two candles, wreathed with flowers, and holding them sideways so that the wax dropped slowly from them he turned, facing the bridal pair. The priest was the same old man that had confessed Levin. He looked with weary and melancholy eyes at the bride and bridegroom, sighed, and putting his right hand out from his vestment, blessed the bridegroom with it, and also with a shade of solicitous tenderness laid the crossed fingers on the bowed head of Kitty. Then he gave them the candles, and taking the censer, moved slowly away from them.

"Can it be true?" thought Levin, and he looked round at his bride. Looking down at her he saw her face in profile, and from the scarcely perceptible quiver of her lips and eyelashes he knew she was aware of his eyes upon her. She did not look round, but the high scalloped collar, that reached her little pink ear, trembled faintly. He saw that a sigh was held back in her throat, and the little hand in the long glove shook as it held the candle.

All the fuss of the shirt, of being late, all the talk of friends and relations, their annoyance, his ludicrous position—all suddenly passed away and he was filled with joy and dread.

The handsome, stately head deacon wearing a silver robe and his curly locks standing out at each side of his head, stepped smartly forward, and lifting his stole on two fingers, stood opposite the priest.

"Blessed be the name of the Lord," the solemn syllables rang out slowly one after another, setting the air quivering with waves of sound.

"Blessed is the name of our God, from the beginning, is now, and ever shall be," the little old priest answered in a submissive, piping voice, still fingering something at the lectern. And the full chorus of the unseen choir rose up, filling the whole church, from the windows to the vaulted roof, with broad waves of melody. It grew stronger, rested for an instant, and slowly died away.

They prayed, as they always do, for peace from on high and for salvation, for the Holy Synod, and for the Tsar; they prayed, too, for the servants of God, Konstantin and Ekaterina, now plighting their troth.

"Vouchsafe to them love made perfect, peace and help, O Lord, we beseech Thee," the whole church seemed to breathe with the voice of the head deacon.

Levin heard the words, and they impressed him. "How did they guess that it is help, just help that one wants?" he thought, recalling all his fears and doubts of late. "What do I know? what can I do in this fearful business," he thought, "without help? Yes, it is help I want now."

When the deacon had finished the prayer for the Imperial family, the priest turned to the bridal pair with a book: "Eternal God, that joinest together in love them that were separate," he read in a gentle, piping voice: "who hast ordained the union of holy wedlock that cannot be set asunder, Thou who didst bless Isaac and Rebecca and their descendants, according to Thy Holy Covenant; bless Thy servants, Konstantin and Ekaterina, leading them in the path of all good works. For gracious and merciful art Thou, our Lord, and glory be to Thee, the Father, the Son, and the Holy Ghost, now and ever shall be."

"Amen!" the unseen choir sent rolling again upon the air.

" 'Joinest together in love them that were separate.' What deep meaning in those words, and how they correspond with what one feels at this moment," thought Levin. "Is she feeling the same as I?"

And looking round, he met her eyes, and from their expression he concluded that she was understanding it just as he was. But this was a mistake; she almost completely missed the meaning of the words of the service; she had not heard them, in fact. She could not listen to them and take them in, so strong was the one feeling that filled her breast and grew stronger and stronger. That feeling was joy at the completion of the process that for the last month and a half had been going on in her soul, and had during those six weeks been a joy and a torture to her. On the day when in the drawing room of the house in Arbaty Street she had gone up to him in her brown dress, and given herself to him without a word—on that day, at that hour, there took place in her heart a complete severance from all her old life, and a quite different, new, utterly strange life had begun for her, while the old life was actually going on as before. Those six weeks had for her been a time of the utmost bliss and the utmost misery. All her life, all her desires and hopes were concentrated on this one man, still uncomprehended by her, to whom she was bound by a feeling of alternate attraction and repulsion, even less comprehended than the man himself, and all the while she was going on living in the outward conditions of her old life. Living the old life, she was horrified at herself, at her utter insurmountable callousness to all her own past, to things, to habits, to the people she had loved, who loved her—to her mother, who was wounded by her indifference, to her kind, tender father, till then dearer than all the world. At one moment she was horrified at this indifference, at another she rejoiced at what had brought her to this indifference. She could not frame a thought, not a wish apart from life with this man; but this new life was not yet, and she could not even picture it clearly to herself. There was only anticipation, the dread and joy of the new and the unknown. And now behold—anticipation and uncertainty and remorse at the abandonment of the old life —all was ending, and the new was beginning. This new life could not but have terrors for her inexperience; but, terrible or not, the change had been wrought six weeks before in her soul, and this was merely the final sanction of what had long been completed in her heart.

Turning again to the lectern, the priest with some difficulty took Kitty's little ring, and asking Levin for his hand, put it on the first joint of his finger. "The servant of God, Konstantin, plights his troth to the servant of God, Ekaterina." And putting his big ring on Kitty's touchingly weak, pink little finger, the priest said the same thing.

And the bridal pair tried several times to understand what they had to do, and each time made some mistake and were corrected by the priest in a whisper. At last, having duly performed the ceremony, having signed the rings with the cross, the priest handed Kitty the big ring, and Levin the little one. Again they were puzzled, and passed the rings from hand to hand, still without doing what was expected.

Dolly, Tchirikov, and Stepan Arkadyevitch stepped forward to set them right. There was an interval of hesitation, whispering, and smiles; but the expression of solemn emotion on the faces of the betrothed pair did not change: on the contrary, in their perplexity over their hands they looked more grave and deeply moved than before, and the smile with which Stepan Arkadyevitch whispered to them that now they would each put on their own ring died away on his lips. He had a feeling that any smile would jar on them.

"Thou who didst from the beginning create male and female," the priest read after the exchange of rings, "from Thee woman was given to man to be a helpmeet to him, and for the procreation of children. O Lord, our God, who hast poured down the blessings of Thy Truth according to Thy Holy Covenant upon Thy chosen servants, our fathers, from generation to generation, bless Thy servants Konstantin and Ekaterina, and make their troth fast in faith, and union of hearts, and truth, and love. . . ."

Levin felt more and more that all his ideas of marriage, all his dreams of how he would order his life, were mere childishness, and that it was something he had not understood hitherto, and now understood less than ever, though it was being performed upon him. The lump in his throat rose higher and higher, tears that would not be checked came into his eyes.

Chapter V

IN THE CHURCH THERE WAS ALL MOSCOW, ALL THE FRIENDS AND RELATIONS; AND DURING THE CEREMONY of plighting troth, in the brilliantly lit church, there was an incessant flow of discreetly subdued talk in the circle of gaily dressed women and girls, and men in white ties, frock-coats, and uniforms. The talk was principally kept up by the men, while the women were absorbed in watching every detail of the ceremony, which always means so much to them.

In the little group nearest to the bride were her two sisters: Dolly, and the other one, the self-possessed beauty, Madame Lvova, who had just arrived from abroad.

"Why is it Marie's in lilac, as bad as black, at a wedding?" said Madame Korsunskaya.

"With her complexion, it's the one salvation," responded Madame Trubetskaya. "I wonder why they had the wedding in the evening? It's like shop-people . . ."

"So much prettier. I was married in the evening too . . ." answered Madame Korsunskaya, and she sighed, remembering how charming she had been that day, and how absurdly in love her husband was, and how different it all was now.

"They say if anyone's best man more than ten times, he'll never be married. I wanted to be for the tenth time, but the post was taken," said Count Siniavin to the pretty Princess Tcharskaya, who had designs on him.

Princess Tcharskaya only answered with a smile. She looked at Kitty, thinking how and when she would stand with Count Siniavin in Kitty's place, and how she would remind him then of his joke today.

Shtcherbatsky told the old maid of honor, Madame Nikolaeva, that he meant to put the crown on Kitty's chignon for luck.

"She ought not to have worn a chignon," answered Madame Nikolaeva, who had long ago made up her mind that if the elderly widower she was angling for married her, the wedding should be of the simplest. "I don't like such grandeur."

Sergey Ivanovitch was talking to Darya Dmitrievna, jestingly assuring her that the custom of going away after the wedding was becoming common because newly married people always felt a little ashamed of themselves.

"Your brother may feel proud of himself. She's a marvel of sweetness. I believe you're envious."

"Oh, I've got over that, Darya Dmitrievna," he answered, and a melancholy and serious expression suddenly came over his face.

Stepan Arkadyevitch was telling his sister-in-law his joke about divorce.

"The wreath wants setting straight," she answered, not hearing him.

"What a pity she's lost her looks so," Countess Nordston said to Madame Lvova. "Still he's not worth her little finger, is he?"

"Oh, I like him so—not because he's my future *beau-frère*," answered Madame Lvova. "And how well he's behaving! It's so difficult, too, to look well in such a position, not to be ridiculous. And he's not ridiculous, and not affected; one can see he's moved."

"You expected it, I suppose?"

"Almost. She always cared for him."

"Well, we shall see which of them will step on the rug first. I warned Kitty."

"It will make no difference," said Madame Lvova; "we're all obedient wives; it's in our family."

"Oh, I stepped on the rug before Vassily on purpose. And you, Dolly?"

Dolly stood beside them; she heard them, but she did not answer. She was deeply moved. The tears stood in her eyes, and she could not have spoken without crying. She was rejoicing over Kitty and Levin; going back in thought to her own wedding, she glanced at the radiant figure of Stepan Arkadyevitch, forgot all the present, and remembered only her own innocent love. She recalled not herself only, but all her women-friends and acquaintances. She thought of them on the one day of their triumph, when they had stood like Kitty under the wedding crown, with love and hope and dread in their hearts, renouncing the past, and stepping forward into the mysterious future. Among the brides that came back to her memory, she thought too of her darling Anna, of whose proposed divorce she had just been hearing. And she had stood just as innocent in orange flowers and bridal veil. And now? "It's terribly strange," she said to herself. It was not merely the sisters, the women-friends and female relations of the bride who were following every detail of the ceremony. Women who were quite strangers, mere spectators, were watching it excitedly, holding their breath, in fear of losing a single movement or expression of the bride and bridegroom, and angrily not answering, often not hearing, the remarks of the callous men, who kept making joking or irrelevant observations.

"Why has she been crying? Is she being married against her will?"

"Against her will to a fine fellow like that? A prince, isn't he?"

"Is that her sister in the white satin? Just listen how the deacon booms out, 'and fearing her husband.' "

"Are the choristers from Tchudovo?"

"No, from the Synod."

"I asked the footman. He says he's going to take her home to his country place at once. Awfully rich, they say. That's why she's being married to him."

"No, they're a well-matched pair."

"I say, Marya Vassilievna, you were making out those fly-away crinolines were not being worn. Just look at her in the puce dress—an ambassador's wife they say she is—how her skirt bounces out from side to side!"

"What a pretty dear the bride is—like a lamb decked with flowers! Well, say what you will, we women feel for our sister."

Such were the comments in the crowd of gazing women who had succeeded in slipping in at the church doors.

Chapter VI

WHEN THE CEREMONY OF PLIGHTING TROTH WAS OVER, THE BEADLE SPREAD BEFORE THE lectern in the middle of the church a piece of pink silken stuff, the choir sang a complicated and elaborate psalm, in which the bass and tenor sang responses to one another, and the priest turning round pointed the bridal pair to the pink silk rug. Though both had often heard a great deal about the saying that the one who steps first on the rug will be the head of the house, neither Levin nor Kitty were capable of recollecting it, as they took the few steps towards it. They did not hear the loud remarks and disputes that followed, some maintaining he had stepped on first, and others that both had stepped on together.

After the customary questions, whether they desired to enter upon matrimony, and whether they were pledged to anyone else, and their answers, which sounded strange to themselves, a new ceremony began. Kitty listened to the words of the prayer, trying to make out their meaning, but she could not. The feeling of triumph and radiant happiness flooded her soul more and more as the ceremony went on, and deprived her of all power of attention.

They prayed: "Endow them with continence and fruitfulness, and vouchsafe that their hearts may rejoice looking upon their sons and daughters." They alluded to God's creation of a wife from Adam's rib "and for this cause a man shall leave father and mother, and cleave unto his wife, and they two shall be one flesh," and that "this is a great mystery"; they prayed that God would make them fruitful and bless them, like Isaac and Rebecca, Joseph, Moses and Zipporah, and that they might look upon their children's children. "That's all splendid," thought Kitty, catching the words, "all that's just as it should be," and a smile of happiness, unconsciously reflected in everyone who looked at her, beamed on her radiant face.

"Put it on quite," voices were heard urging when the priest had put on the wedding crowns, and Shtcherbatsky, his hand shaking in its three-button glove, held the crown high above her head.

"Put it on!" she whispered, smiling.

Levin looked round at her, and was struck by the joyful radiance on her face, and unconsciously her feeling infected him. He too, like her felt glad and happy.

They enjoyed hearing the epistle read, and the roll of the head deacon's voice at the last verse, awaited with such impatience by the outside public. They enjoyed drinking out of the shallow cup of warm red wine and water, and they were still more pleased when the priest, flinging back his stole and taking both their hands in his, led them round the lectern to the accompaniment of bass voices chanting "Glory to God."

Shtcherbatsky and Tchirikov, supporting the crowns and stumbling over the bride's train, smiling too and seeming delighted at something, were at one moment left behind, at the next treading on the bridal pair as the priest came to a halt. The spark of joy kindled in Kitty seemed to have infected everyone in the church. It seemed to Levin that the priest and the deacon too wanted to smile just as he did.

Taking the crowns off their heads the priest read the last prayer and congratulated the young people. Levin looked at Kitty, and he had never before seen her look as she did. She was charming with the new radiance of happiness in her face. Levin longed to say something to her, but he did not know whether it was all over. The priest got him out of his difficulty. He smiled his kindly smile and said gently, "Kiss your wife, and you kiss your husband," and took the candles out of their hands.

Levin kissed her smiling lips with timid care, gave her his arm, and with a new strange sense of closeness, walked out of the church. He did not believe, he could not believe, that it was true. It was only when their wondering and timid eyes met that he believed in it, because he felt that they were one.

After supper, the same night, the young people left for the country.

Chapter VII

VRONSKY AND ANNA HAD BEEN TRAVELING FOR THREE MONTHS TOGETHER IN EUROPE. THEY HAD visited Venice, Rome, and Naples, and had just arrived at a small Italian town where they meant to stay some time. A handsome head waiter, with thick pomaded hair parted from the neck upwards, an evening coat, a broad white cambric shirt front, and a bunch of trinkets hanging above his rounded stomach, stood with his hands in the full curve of his pockets, looking contemptuously from under his eyelids while he gave some frigid reply to a gentleman who had stopped him. Catching the sound of footsteps coming from the other side of the entry towards the staircase, the head waiter turned round, and seeing the Russian count, who had taken their best rooms, he took his hands out of his pockets deferentially, and with a bow informed him that a courier had been, and that the business about the palazzo had been arranged. The steward was prepared to sign the agreement.

"Ah! I'm glad to hear it," said Vronsky. "Is madame at home or not?"

"Madame has been out for a walk but has returned now," answered the waiter.

Vronsky took off his soft, wide-brimmed hat and passed his handkerchief over his heated brow and hair, which had grown half over his ears, and was brushed back covering the bald patch on his head. And glancing casually at the gentleman, who still stood there gazing intently at him, he would have gone on.

"This gentleman is a Russian, and was inquiring after you," said the head waiter.

With mingled feelings of annoyance at never being able to get away from acquaintances anywhere, and longing to find some sort of diversion from the monotony of his life, Vronsky looked once more at the gentleman, who had retreated and stood still again, and at the same moment a light came into the eyes of both.

"Golenishtchev!"

"Vronsky!"

It really was Golenishtchev, a comrade of Vronsky's in the Corps of Pages. In the corps Golenishtchev had belonged to the liberal party; he left the corps without entering the army, and had never taken office under the government. Vronsky and he had gone completely different ways on leaving the corps, and had only met once since.

At that meeting Vronsky perceived that Golenishtchev had taken up a sort of lofty, intellectually liberal line, and was consequently disposed to look down upon Vronsky's interests and calling in life. Hence Vronsky had met him with the chilling and haughty manner he so well knew how to assume, the meaning of which was: "You may like or dislike my way of life, that's a matter of the most perfect indifference to me; you will have to treat me with respect if you want to know me." Golenishtchev had been contemptuously indifferent to the tone taken by Vronsky. This second meeting might have been expected, one would have supposed, to estrange them still more. But now they beamed and exclaimed with delight on recognizing one another. Vronsky would never have expected to be so pleased to see Golenishtchev, but probably he was not himself aware how bored he was. He forgot the disagreeable impression of their last meeting, and with a face of frank delight held out his hand to his old comrade. The same expression of delight replaced the look of uneasiness on Golenishtchev's face.

"How glad I am to meet you!" said Vronsky, showing his strong white teeth in a friendly smile.

"I heard the name Vronsky, but I didn't know which one. I'm very, very glad!"

"Let's go in. Come, tell me what you're doing."

"I've been living here for two years. I'm working."

"Ah!" said Vronsky, with sympathy; "let's go in." And with the habit common with Russians, instead of saying in Russian what he wanted to keep from the servants, he began to speak in French.

"Do you know Madame Karenina? We are traveling together. I am going to see her now," he said in French, carefully scrutinizing Golenishtchev's face.

"Ah! I did not know" (though he did know), Golenishtchev answered carelessly. "Have you been here long?" he added.

"Four days," Vronsky answered, once more scrutinizing his friend's face intently.

"Yes, he's a decent fellow, and will look at the thing properly," Vronsky said to himself, catching the significance of Golenishtchev's face and the change of subject. "I can introduce him to Anna, he looks at it properly."

During those three months that Vronsky had spent abroad with Anna, he had always on meeting new people asked himself how the new person would look at his relations with Anna, and for the most part, in men, he had met with the "proper" way of looking at it. But if he had been asked, and those who looked at it "properly" had been asked, exactly how they did look at it, both he and they would have been greatly puzzled to answer.

In reality, those who in Vronsky's opinion had the "proper" view had no sort of view at all, but behaved in general as well-bred persons do behave in regard to all the complex and insoluble problems with which life is encompassed on all sides; they behaved with propriety, avoiding allusions and unpleasant questions. They assumed an air of fully comprehending the import and force of the situation, of accepting and even approving of it, but of considering it superfluous and uncalled for to put all this into words.

Vronsky at once divined that Golenishtchev was of this class, and therefore was doubly pleased to see him. And in fact, Golenishtchev's manner to Madame Karenina, when he was taken to call on her, was all that Vronsky could have desired. Obviously without the slightest effort he steered clear of all subjects which might lead to embarrassment.

He had never met Anna before, and was struck by her beauty, and still more by the frankness with which she accepted her position. She blushed when Vronsky brought in Golenishtchev, and he was extremely charmed by this childish blush overspreading her candid and handsome face. But what he liked particularly was the way in which at once, as though on purpose that there might be no misunderstanding with an outsider, she called Vronsky simply Alexey, and said they were moving into a house they had just taken, what was here called a palazzo. Golenishtchev liked this direct and simple attitude to her own position. Looking at Anna's manner of simple-hearted, spirited gaiety, and knowing Alexey Alexandrovitch and Vronsky, Golenishtchev fancied that he understood her perfectly. He fancied that he understood what she was utterly unable to understand: how it was that, having made her husband wretched, having abandoned him and her son and lost her good name, she yet felt full of spirits, gaiety, and happiness.

"It's in the guide-book," said Golenishtchev, referring to the palazzo Vronsky had taken. "There's a first rate Tintoretto there. One of his latest period."

"I tell you what: it's a lovely day, let's go and have another look at it," said Vronsky, addressing Anna.

"I shall be very glad to; I'll go and put on my hat. Would you say it's hot?" she said, stopping short in the doorway and looking inquiringly at Vronsky. And again a vivid flush overspread her face.

Vronsky saw from her eyes that she did not know on what terms he cared to be with Golenishtchev, and so was afraid of not behaving as he would wish.

He looked a long, tender look at her.

"No, not very," he said.

And it seemed to her that she understood everything, most of all, that he was pleased with her; and smiling to him, she walked with her rapid step out at the door.

The friends glanced at one another, and a look of hesitation came into both faces, as though Golenishtchev, unmistakably admiring her, would have liked to say something about her, and could not find the right thing to say, while Vronsky desired and dreaded his doing so.

"Well then," Vronsky began to start a conversation of some sort; "so you're settled here? You're still at the same work, then?" he went on, recalling that he had been told Golenishtchev was writing something.

"Yes, I'm writing the second part of the *Two Elements,*" said Golenishtchev, coloring with pleasure at the question—"that is, to be exact, I am not writing it yet; I am preparing, collecting materials. It will be of far wider scope, and will touch on almost all questions. We in Russia refuse to see that we are the heirs of Byzantium," and he launched into a long and heated explanation of his views.

Vronsky at the first moment felt embarrassed at not even knowing of the first part of the *Two Elements,* of which the author spoke as something well-known. But as Golenishtchev began to lay down his opinions and Vronsky was able to follow them even without knowing the *Two Elements,* he listened to him with some interest, for Golenishtchev spoke well. But Vronsky was startled and annoyed by the nervous irascibility with which Golenishtchev talked of the subject that engrossed him. As he went on talking, his eyes glittered more and more angrily; he was more and more hurried in his replies to imaginary opponents, and his face grew more and more excited and worried. Remembering Golenishtchev, a thin, lively, good-natured and well-bred boy, always at the head of the class, Vronsky could not make out the reason of his irritability, and he did not like it. What he particularly disliked was that Golenishtchev, a man belonging to a good set, should put himself on a level with some scribbling fellows, with whom he was irritated and angry. Was it worth it? Vronsky disliked it, yet he felt that Golenishtchev was unhappy, and was sorry for him. Unhappiness, almost mental derangement, was visible on his mobile, rather handsome face, while without even noticing Anna's coming in, he went on hurriedly and hotly expressing his views.

When Anna came in in her hat and cape, and her lovely hand rapidly swinging her parasol, and stood beside him, it was with a feeling of relief that Vronsky broke away from the plaintive eyes of Golenishtchev which fastened persistently upon him, and with a fresh rush of love looked at his charming companion, full of life and happiness. Golenishtchev recovered himself with an effort, and at first was dejected and gloomy, but Anna, disposed to feel friendly with everyone as she was at that time, soon revived his spirits by her direct and lively manner. After trying various subjects of conversation, she got him upon painting, of which he talked very well, and she listened to him attentively. They walked to the house they had taken, and looked over it.

"I am very glad of one thing," said Anna to Golenishtchev when they were on their way back, "Alexey will have a capital *atelier.* You must certainly take that room," she said to Vronsky in Russian, using the affectionately familiar form as though she saw that Golenishtchev would become intimate with them in their isolation, and that there was no need of reserve before him.

"Do you paint?" said Golenishtchev, turning round quickly to Vronsky.

"Yes, I used to study long ago, and now I have begun to do a little," said Vronsky, reddening.

"He has great talent," said Anna with a delighted smile. "I'm no judge, of course. But good judges have said the same."

Chapter VIII

ANNA, IN THAT FIRST PERIOD OF HER EMANCIPATION AND RAPID RETURN TO HEALTH, FELT HERself unpardonably happy and full of the joy of life. The thought of her husband's unhappiness did not poison her happiness. On one side that memory was too awful to be thought of. On the other side her husband's unhappiness had given her too much happiness to be regretted. The memory of all that had happened after her illness: her reconciliation with her husband, its breakdown, the news of Vronsky's wound, his visit, the preparations for divorce, the departure from her husband's house, the parting from her son—all that seemed to her like a delirious dream, from which she had waked up alone with Vronsky abroad. The thought of the harm caused to her husband aroused in her a feeling like repulsion, and akin to what a drowning man might feel who has shaken off another man clinging to him. That man did drown. It was an evil action, of course, but it was the sole means of escape, and better not to brood over these fearful facts.

One consolatory reflection upon her conduct had occurred to her at the first moment of the final rupture, and when now she recalled all the past, she remembered that one reflection. "I have inevitably made that man wretched," she thought; "but I don't want to profit by his misery. I too am suffering, and shall suffer; I am losing what I prized above everything—I am losing my good name and my son. I have done wrong, and so I don't want happiness, I don't want a divorce, and shall suffer from my shame and the separation from my child." But, however sincerely Anna had meant to suffer, she was not suffering. Shame there was not. With the tact of which both had such a large share, they had succeeded in avoiding Russian ladies abroad, and so had never placed themselves in a false position, and everywhere they had met people who pretended that they perfectly understood their position, far better indeed than they did themselves. Separation from the son she loved—even that did not cause her anguish in these early days. The baby girl—*his* child—was so sweet, and had so won Anna's heart, since she was all that was left her, that Anna rarely thought of her son.

The desire for life, waxing stronger with recovered health, was so intense, and the conditions of life were so new and pleasant, that Anna felt unpardonably happy. The more she got to know Vronsky, the more she loved him. She loved him for himself, and for his love for her. Her complete ownership of him was a continual joy to her. His presence was always sweet to her. All the traits of his character, which she learned to know better and better, were unutterably dear to her. His appearance, changed by his civilian dress, was as fascinating to her as though she were some young girl in love. In everything he said, thought, and did, she saw something particularly noble and elevated. Her adoration of him alarmed her indeed; she sought and could not find in him anything not fine. She dared not show him her sense of her own insignificance beside him. It seemed to her that, knowing this, he might sooner cease to love her; and she dreaded nothing now so much as losing his love, though she had no grounds for fearing it. But she could not help being grateful to him for his attitude to her, and showing that she appreciated it. He, who had in her opinion such a marked aptitude for a political career, in which he would have been certain to play a leading part—he had sacrificed his ambition for her sake, and never betrayed the slightest regret. He was more lovingly respectful to her than ever, and the constant care that she should not feel the awkwardness of her position never deserted him for a single instant. He, so manly a man, never opposed her, had indeed, with her, no will of his own, and was anxious, it seemed, for nothing but to anticipate her wishes. And she could not but appreciate this, even though the very intensity of his solicitude for her, the atmosphere of care with which he surrounded her, sometimes weighed upon her.

Vronsky, meanwhile, in spite of the complete realization of what he had so long desired, was not perfectly happy. He soon felt that the realization of his desires gave him no more than a grain of sand out of the mountain of happiness he had expected. It showed him the mistake men make in picturing to themselves happiness as the realization of their desires. For a time after joining his life to hers, and putting on civilian dress, he had felt all the delight of freedom in general, of which he had known nothing before, and of freedom in his love—and he was content, but not for long. He was soon aware that there was springing up in his heart a desire for desires—*ennui*. Without conscious intention he began to clutch at every passing caprice, taking it for a desire and an object. Sixteen hours of the day must be occupied in some way, since they were living abroad in complete freedom, outside the conditions of social life which filled up time in Petersburg. As for the amusements of bachelor existence, which had provided Vronsky with entertainment on previous tours abroad, they could not be thought of, since the sole attempt of the sort had led to a sudden attack of depression in Anna, quite out of proportion with the cause—a late supper with bachelor friends. Relations with the society of the place—foreign and Russian—were equally out of the question owing to the irregularity of their position. The inspection of objects of interest, apart from the fact that everything had been seen already, had not for Vronsky, a Russian and a sensible man, the immense significance Englishmen are able to attach to that pursuit.

And just as the hungry stomach eagerly accepts every object it can get, hoping to find nourishment in it, Vronsky quite unconsciously clutched first at politics, then at new books, and then at pictures.

As he had from a child a taste for painting, and as, not knowing what to spend his money on, he had begun collecting engravings, he came to a stop at painting, began to take interest in it, and concentrated upon it the unoccupied mass of desires which demanded satisfaction.

He had a ready appreciation of art, and probably, with a taste for imitating art, he supposed himself to have the real thing essential for an artist, and after hesitating for some time which style of painting to select—religious, historical, realistic, or genre painting—he set to work to paint. He appreciated all kinds, and could have felt inspired by anyone of them; but he had no conception of the possibility of knowing nothing at all of any school of painting, and of being inspired directly by what is within the soul, without caring whether what is painted will belong to any recognized school. Since he knew nothing of this, and drew his inspiration, not directly from life, but indirectly from life embodied in art, his inspiration came very quickly and easily, and as quickly and easily came his success in painting something very similar to the sort of painting he was trying to imitate.

More than any other style he liked the French—graceful and effective—and in that style he began to paint Anna's portrait in Italian costume, and the portrait seemed to him, and to everyone who saw it, extremely successful.

Chapter IX

THE OLD NEGLECTED PALAZZO, WITH ITS LOFTY CARVED CEILINGS AND FRESCOES ON THE WALLS, with its floors of mosaic, with its heavy yellow stuff curtains on the windows, with its vases on pedestals, and its open fireplaces, its carved doors and gloomy reception rooms, hung with pictures—this palazzo did much, by its very appearance after they had moved into it, to confirm in Vronsky the agreeable illusion that he was not so much a Russian country gentleman, a retired army officer, as an enlightened amateur and patron of the arts, himself a modest artist who had renounced the world, his connections, and his ambition for the sake of the woman he loved.

The pose chosen by Vronsky with their removal into the palazzo was completely successful, and having, through Golenishtchev, made acquaintance with a few interesting people, for a time he was satisfied. He painted studies from nature under the guidance of an Italian professor of painting, and studied mediaeval Italian life. Mediaeval Italian life so fascinated Vronsky that he even wore a hat and flung a cloak over his shoulder in the mediaeval style, which, indeed, was extremely becoming to him.

"Here we live, and know nothing of what's going on," Vronsky said to Golenishtchev as he came to see him one morning. "Have you seen Mihailov's picture?" he said, handing him a Russian gazette he had received that morning, and pointing to an article on a Russian artist, living in the very same town, and just finishing a picture which had long been talked about, and had been bought beforehand. The article reproached the government and the academy for letting so remarkable an artist be left without encouragement and support.

"I've seen it," answered Golenishtchev. "Of course, he's not without talent, but it's all in a wrong direction. It's all the Ivanov-Strauss-Renan attitude to Christ and to religious painting."

"What is the subject of the picture?" asked Anna.

"Christ before Pilate. Christ is represented as a Jew with all the realism of the new school."

And the question of the subject of the picture having brought him to one of his favorite theories, Golenishtchev launched forth into a disquisition on it.

"I can't understand how they can fall into such a gross mistake. Christ always has His definite embodiment in the art of the great masters. And therefore, if they want to depict, not God, but a revolutionist or a sage, let them take from history a Socrates, a Franklin, a Charlotte Corday, but not Christ. They take the very figure which cannot be taken for their art, and then . . ."

"And is it true that this Mihailov is in such poverty?" asked Vronsky, thinking that, as a Russian Maecenas, it was his duty to assist the artist regardless of whether the picture were good or bad.

"I should say not. He's a remarkable portrait-painter. Have you ever seen his portrait of

Madame Vassiltchikova? But I believe he doesn't care about painting anymore portraits, and so very likely he is in want. I maintain that . . ."

"Couldn't we ask him to paint a portrait of Anna Arkadyevna?" said Vronsky.

"Why mine?" said Anna. "After yours I don't want another portrait. Better have one of Annie" (so she called her baby girl). "Here she is," she added, looking out of the window at the handsome Italian nurse, who was carrying the child out into the garden, and immediately glancing unnoticed at Vronsky. The handsome nurse, from whom Vronsky was painting a head for his picture, was the one hidden grief in Anna's life. He painted with her as his model, admired her beauty and mediaevalism, and Anna dared not confess to herself that she was afraid of becoming jealous of this nurse, and was for that reason particularly gracious and condescending both to her and her little son. Vronsky, too, glanced out of the window and into Anna's eyes, and, turning at once to Golenishtchev, he said:

"Do you know this Mihailov?"

"I have met him. But he's a queer fish, and quite without breeding. You know, one of those uncouth new people one's so often coming across nowadays, one of those free-thinkers you know, who are reared *d'emblée* in theories of atheism, scepticism, and materialism. In former days," said Golenishtchev, not observing, or not willing to observe, that both Anna and Vronsky wanted to speak, "in former days the free-thinker was a man who had been brought up in ideas of religion, law, and morality, and only through conflict and struggle came to free-thought; but now there has sprung up a new type of born free-thinkers who grow up without even having heard of principles of morality or of religion, of the existence of authorities, who grow up directly in ideas of negation in everything, that is to say, savages. Well, he's of that class. He's the son, it appears, of some Moscow butler, and has never had any sort of bringing-up. When he got into the academy and made his reputation he tried, as he's no fool, to educate himself. And he turned to what seemed to him the very source of culture—the magazines. In old times, you see, a man who wanted to educate himself—a Frenchman, for instance—would have set to work to study all the classics and theologians and tragedians and historiaris and philosophers, and, you know, all the intellectual work that came in his way. But in our day he goes straight for the literature of negation, very quickly assimilates all the extracts of the science of negation, and he's ready. And that's not all—twenty years ago he would have found in that literature traces of conflict with authorities, with the creeds of the ages; he would have perceived from this conflict that there was something else; but now he comes at once upon a literature in which the old creeds do not even furnish matter for discussion, but it is stated baldly that there is nothing else—evolution, natural selection, struggle for existence—and that's all. In my article I've . . ."

"I tell you what," said Anna, who had for a long while been exchanging wary glances with Vronsky, and knew that he was not in the least interested in the education of this artist, but was simply absorbed by the idea of assisting him, and ordering a portrait of him; "I tell you what," she said, resolutely interrupting Golenishtchev, who was still talking away, "let's go and see him!"

Golenishtchev recovered his self-possession and readily agreed. But as the artist lived in a remote suburb, it was decided to take the carriage.

An hour later Anna, with Golenishtchev by her side and Vronsky on the front seat of the carriage, facing them, drove up to a new ugly house in the remote suburb. On learning from the porter's wife, who came out to them, that Mihailov saw visitors at his studio, but that at that moment he was in his lodging only a couple of steps off, they sent her to him with their cards, asking permission to see his picture.

Chapter X

THE ARTIST MIHAILOV WAS, AS ALWAYS, AT WORK WHEN THE CARDS OF COUNT VRONSKY AND Golenishtchev were brought to him. In the morning he had been working in his studio at his big picture. On getting home he flew into a rage with his wife for not having managed to put off the landlady, who had been asking for money.

"I've said it to you twenty times, don't enter into details. You're fool enough at all times, and when you start explaining things in Italian you're a fool three times as foolish," he said after a long dispute.

"Don't let it run so long; it's not my fault. If I had the money . . ."

"Leave me in peace, for God's sake!" Mihailov shrieked, with tears in his voice, and, stopping his ears, he went off into his working room, the other side of a partition wall, and closed the door after him. "Idiotic woman!" he said to himself, sat down to the table, and, opening a portfolio, he set to work at once with peculiar fervor at a sketch he had begun.

Never did he work with such fervor and success as when things went ill with him, and especially when he quarreled with his wife. "Oh! damn them all!" he thought as he went on working. He was making a sketch for the figure of a man in a violent rage. A sketch had been made before, but he was dissatisfied with it. "No, that one was better . . . where is it?" He went back to his wife, and scowling, and not looking at her, asked his eldest little girl, where was that piece of paper he had given them? The paper with the discarded sketch on it was found, but it was dirty, and spotted with candle-grease. Still, he took the sketch, laid it on his table, and, moving a little away, screwing up his eyes, he fell to gazing at it. All at once he smiled and gesticulated gleefully.

"That's it! that's it!" he said, and, at once picking up the pencil, he began rapidly drawing. The spot of tallow had given the man a new pose.

He had sketched this new pose, when all at once he recalled the face of a shopkeeper of whom he had bought cigars, a vigorous face with a prominent chin, and he sketched this very face, this chin on to the figure of the man. He laughed aloud with delight. The figure from a lifeless imagined thing had become living, and such that it could never be changed. That figure lived, and was clearly and unmistakably defined. The sketch might be corrected in accordance with the requirements of the figure, the legs, indeed, could and must be put differently, and the position of the left hand must be quite altered; the hair too might be thrown back. But in making these corrections he was not altering the figure but simply getting rid of what concealed the figure. He was, as it were, stripping off the wrappings which hindered it from being distinctly seen. Each new feature only brought out the whole figure in all its force and vigor, as it had suddenly come to him from the spot of tallow. He was carefully finishing the figure when the cards were brought him.

"Coming, coming!"

He went in to his wife.

"Come, Sasha, don't be cross!" he said, smiling timidly and affectionately at her. "You were to blame. I was to blame. I'll make it all right." And having made peace with his wife he put on an olive-green overcoat with a velvet collar and a hat, and went towards his studio. The successful figure he had already forgotten. Now he was delighted and excited at the visit of these people of consequence, Russians, who had come in their carriage.

Of his picture, the one that stood now on his easel, he had at the bottom of his heart one conviction—that no one had ever painted a picture like it. He did not believe that his picture was better than all the pictures of Raphael, but he knew that what he tried to convey in that picture, no one ever had conveyed. This he knew positively, and had known a long while, ever since he had begun to paint it. But other people's criticisms, whatever they might be, had yet immense consequence in his eyes, and they agitated him to the depths of his soul. Any remark, the most insignificant, that showed that the critic saw even the tiniest part of what he saw in the picture, agitated him to the depths of his soul. He always attributed to his critics a more profound comprehension than he had himself, and always expected from them something he did not himself see in the picture. And often in their criticisms he fancied that he had found this.

He walked rapidly to the door of his studio, and in spite of his excitement he was struck by the soft light on Anna's figure as she stood in the shade of the entrance listening to Golenishtchev, who was eagerly telling her something, while she evidently wanted to look round at the artist. He was himself unconscious how, as he approached them, he seized on this impression and absorbed it, as he had the chin of the shopkeeper who had sold him the cigars, and put it away somewhere to be brought out when he wanted it. The visitors, not agreeably impressed beforehand by Golenishtchev's account of the artist, were still less so by his personal appearance. Thick-set and of middle height, with nimble movements, with his brown hat, olive-green coat and narrow trousers—though wide trousers had been a long while in fashion—most of all, with the ordinariness of his broad face, and the combined expression of timidity and anxiety to keep up his dignity, Mihailov made an unpleasant impression.

"Please step in," he said, trying to look indifferent, and going into the passage he took a key out of his pocket and opened the door.

Chapter XI

On entering the studio, Mihailov once more scanned his visitors and noted down in his imagination Vronsky's expression too, and especially his jaws. Although his artistic sense was unceasingly at work collecting materials, although he felt a continually increasing excitement as the moment of criticizing his work drew nearer, he rapidly and subtly formed, from imperceptible signs, a mental image of these three persons.

That fellow (Golenishtchev) was a Russian living here. Mihailov did not remember his surname nor where he had met him, nor what he had said to him. He only remembered his face as he remembered all the faces he had ever seen; but he remembered, too, that it was one of the faces laid by in his memory in the immense class of the falsely consequential and poor in expression. The abundant hair and very open forehead gave an appearance of consequence to the face, which had only one expression—a petty, childish, peevish expression, concentrated just above the bridge of the narrow nose. Vronsky and Madame Karenina must be, Mihailov supposed, distinguished and wealthy Russians, knowing nothing about art, like all those wealthy Russians, but posing as amateurs and connoisseurs. "Most likely they've already looked at all the antiques, and now they're making the round of the studios of the new people, the German humbug, and the cracked Pre-Raphaelite English fellow, and have only come to me to make the point of view complete," he thought. He was well acquainted with the way dilettanti have (the cleverer they were the worse he found them) of looking at the works of contemporary artists with the sole object of being in a position to say that art is a thing of the past, and that the more one sees of the new men the more one sees how inimitable the works of the great old masters have remained. He expected all this; he saw it all in their faces, he saw it in the careless indifference with which they talked among themselves, stared at the lay figures and busts, and walked about in leisurely fashion, waiting for him to uncover his picture. But in spite of this, while he was turning over his studies, pulling up the blinds and taking off the sheet, he was in intense excitement, especially as, in spite of his conviction that all distinguished and wealthy Russians were certain to be beasts and fools, he liked Vronsky, and still more Anna.

"Here, if you please," he said, moving on one side with his nimble gait and pointing to his picture, "it's the exhortation to Pilate. Matthew, chapter xxvii," he said, feeling his lips were beginning to tremble with emotion. He moved away and stood behind them.

For the few seconds during which the visitors were gazing at the picture in silence Mihailov too gazed at it with the indifferent eye of an outsider. For those few seconds he was sure in anticipation that a higher, juster criticism would be uttered by them, by those very visitors whom he had been so despising a moment before. He forgot all he had thought about his picture before during the three years he had been painting it; he forgot all its qualities which had been absolutely certain to him—he saw the picture with their indifferent, new, outside eyes, and saw nothing good in it. He saw in the foreground Pilate's irritated face and the serene face of Christ, and in the background the figures of Pilate's retinue and the face of John watching what was happening. Every face that, with such agony, such blunders and corrections had grown up within him with its special character, every face that had given him such torments and such raptures, and all these faces so many times transposed for the sake of the harmony of the whole, all the shades of color and tones that he had attained with such labor—all of this together seemed to him now, looking at it with their eyes, the merest vulgarity, something that had been done a thousand times over. The face dearest to him, the face of Christ, the center of the picture, which had given him such ecstasy as it unfolded itself to him, was utterly lost to him when he glanced at the picture with their eyes. He saw a well-painted (no, not even that—he distinctly saw now a mass of defects) repetition of those endless Christs of Titian, Raphael, Rubens, and the same soldiers and Pilate. It was all common, poor, and stale, and positively badly painted—weak and unequal. They would be justified in repeating hypocritically civil speeches in the presence of the painter, and pitying him and laughing at him when they were alone again.

The silence (though it lasted no more than a minute) became too intolerable to him. To break it, and to show he was not agitated, he made an effort and addressed Golenishtchev.

"I think I've had the pleasure of meeting you," he said, looking uneasily first at Anna, then at Vronsky, in fear of losing any shade of their expression.

"To be sure! We met at Rossi's, do you remember, at that *soirée* when that Italian lady recited—the new Rachel?" Golenishtchev answered easily, removing his eyes without the slightest regret from the picture and turning to the artist.

Noticing, however, that Mihailov was expecting a criticism of the picture, he said:

"Your picture has got on a great deal since I saw it last time; and what strikes me particularly now, as it did then, is the figure of Pilate. One so knows the man: a good-natured, capital fellow, but an official through and through, who does not know what it is he's doing. But I fancy . . ."

All Mihailov's mobile face beamed at once; his eyes sparkled. He tried to say something, but he could not speak for excitement, and pretended to be coughing. Low as was his opinion of Golenishtchev's capacity for understanding art, trifling as was the true remark upon the fidelity of the expression of Pilate as an official, and offensive as might have seemed the utterance of so unimportant an observation while nothing was said of more serious points, Mihailov was in an ecstasy of delight at this observation. He had himself thought about Pilate's figure just what Golenishtchev said. The fact that this reflection was but one of millions of reflections, which as Mihailov knew for certain would be true, did not diminish for him the significance of Golenishtchev's remark. His heart warmed to Golenishtchev for this remark, and from a state of depression he suddenly passed to ecstasy. At once the whole of his picture lived before him in all the indescribable complexity of everything living. Mihailov again tried to say that that was how he understood Pilate, but his lips quivered intractably, and he could not pronounce the words. Vronsky and Anna too said something in that subdued voice in which, partly to avoid hurting the artist's feelings and partly to avoid saying out loud something silly—so easily said when talking of art—people usually speak at exhibitions of pictures. Mihailov fancied that the picture had made an impression on them too. He went up to them.

"How marvelous Christ's expression is!" said Anna. Of all she saw she liked that expression most of all, and she felt that it was the center of the picture, and so praise of it would be pleasant to the artist. "One can see that He is pitying Pilate."

This again was one of the million true reflections that could be found in his picture and in the figure of Christ. She said that He was pitying Pilate. In Christ's expression there ought to be indeed an expression of pity, since there is an expression of love, of heavenly peace, of readiness for death, and a sense of the vanity of words. Of course there is the expression of an official in Pilate and of pity in Christ, seeing that one is the incarnation of the fleshly and the other of the spiritual life. All this and much more flashed into Mihailov's thoughts.

"Yes, and how that figure is done—what atmosphere! One can walk round it," said Golenishtchev, unmistakably betraying by this remark that he did not approve of the meaning and idea of the figure.

"Yes, there's a wonderful mastery!" said Vronsky. "How those figures in the background stand out! There you have technique," he said, addressing Golenishtchev, alluding to a conversation between them about Vronsky's despair of attaining this technique.

"Yes, yes, marvelous!" Golenishtchev and Anna assented. In spite of the excited condition in which he was, the sentence about technique had sent a pang to Mihailov's heart, and looking angrily at Vronsky he suddenly scowled. He had often heard this word technique, and was utterly unable to understand what was understood by it. He knew that by this term was understood a mechanical facility for painting or drawing, entirely apart from its subject. He had noticed often that even in actual praise technique was opposed to essential quality, as though one could paint well something that was bad. He knew that a great deal of attention and care was necessary in taking off the coverings, to avoid injuring the creation itself, and to take off all the coverings; but there was no art of painting—no technique of any sort—about it. If to a little child or to his cook were revealed what he saw, it or she would have been able to peel the wrappings off what was seen. And the most experienced and adroit painter could not by mere mechanical facility paint anything if the lines of the subject were not revealed to him first. Besides, he saw that if it came to talking about technique, it was impossible to praise him for it. In all he had painted and repainted he saw faults that hurt his eyes, coming from want of care in taking off the wrappings—faults he could not correct now without spoiling the whole. And in almost all the figures and faces he saw, too, remnants of the wrappings not perfectly removed that spoiled the picture.

"One thing might be said, if you will allow me to make the remark . . ." observed Golenishtchev.

"Oh, I shall be delighted, I beg you," said Mihailov with a forced smile.

"That is, that you make Him the man-god, and not the God-man. But I know that was what you meant to do."

"I cannot paint a Christ that is not in my heart," said Mihailov gloomily.

"Yes; but in that case, if you will allow me to say what I think. . . . Your picture is so fine that my observation cannot detract from it, and, besides, it is only my personal opinion. With you it is different. Your very motive is different. But let us take Ivanov. I imagine that if Christ is brought down to the level of an historical character, it would have been better for Ivanov to select some other historical subject, fresh, untouched."

"But if this is the greatest subject presented to art?"

"If one looked one would find others. But the point is that art cannot suffer doubt and discussion. And before the picture of Ivanov the question arises for the believer and the unbeliever alike, 'Is it God, or is it not God?' and the unity of the impression is destroyed."

"Why so? I think that for educated people," said Mihailov, "the question cannot exist."

Golenishtchev did not agree with this, and confounded Mihailov by his support of his first idea of the unity of the impression being essential to art.

Mihailov was greatly perturbed, but he could say nothing in defense of his own idea.

Chapter XII

Anna and Vronsky had long been exchanging glances, regretting their friend's flow of cleverness. At last Vronsky, without waiting for the artist, walked away to another small picture.

"Oh, how exquisite! What a lovely thing! A gem! How exquisite!" they cried with one voice.

"What is it they're so pleased with?" thought Mihailov. He had positively forgotten that picture he had painted three years ago. He had forgotten all the agonies and the ecstasies he had lived through with that picture when for several months it had been the one thought haunting him day and night. He had forgotten, as he always forgot, the pictures he had finished. He did not even like to look at it, and had only brought it out because he was expecting an Englishman who wanted to buy it.

"Oh, that's only an old study," he said.

"How fine!" said Golenishtchev, he too, with unmistakable sincerity, falling under the spell of the picture.

Two boys were angling in the shade of a willow tree. The elder had just dropped in the hook, and was carefully pulling the float from behind a bush, entirely absorbed in what he was doing. The other, a little younger, was lying in the grass leaning on his elbows, with his tangled, flaxen head in his hands, staring at the water with his dreamy blue eyes. What was he thinking of?

The enthusiasm over this picture stirred some of the old feeling for it in Mihailov, but he feared and disliked this waste of feeling for things past, and so, even though this praise was grateful to him, he tried to draw his visitors away to a third picture.

But Vronsky asked whether the picture was for sale. To Mihailov at that moment, excited by visitors, it was extremely distasteful to speak of money matters.

"It is put up there to be sold," he answered, scowling gloomily.

When the visitors had gone, Mihailov sat down opposite the picture of Pilate and Christ, and in his mind went over what had been said, and what, though not said, had been implied by those visitors. And, strange to say, what had had such weight with him, while they were there and while he mentally put himself at their point of view, suddenly lost all importance for him. He began to look at his picture with all his own full artist vision, and was soon in that mood of conviction of the perfectibility, and so of the significance, of his picture—a conviction essential to the intensest fervor, excluding all other interests—in which alone he could work.

Christ's foreshortened leg was not right, though. He took his palette and began to work. As he corrected the leg he looked continually at the figure of John in the background, which his visitors had not even noticed, but which he knew was beyond perfection. When he had finished the leg he wanted to touch that figure, but he felt too much excited for it. He was equally unable to work when he was cold and when he was too much affected and saw everything too much. There was only one stage in the transition from coldness to inspiration, at which work was possible. Today he was too much agitated. He would have covered the picture, but he stopped, holding the cloth in his hand, and, smiling blissfully, gazed a long while at the figure of John. At last, as it were regretfully tearing himself away, he dropped the cloth, and, exhausted but happy, went home.

Vronsky, Anna, and Golenishtchev, on their way home, were particularly lively and cheerful. They talked of Mihailov and his pictures. The word *talent,* by which they meant an inborn, almost physical, aptitude apart from brain and heart, and in which they tried to find an expression for all the artist had gained from life, recurred particularly often in their talk, as though it were necessary for them to sum up what they had no conception of, though they wanted to talk of it. They said that there was no denying his talent, but that his talent could not develop for want of education—the common defect of our Russian artists. But the picture of the boys had imprinted itself on their memories, and they were continually coming back to it. "What an exquisite thing! How he has succeeded in it, and how simply! He doesn't even comprehend how good it is. Yes, I mustn't let it slip; I must buy it," said Vronsky.

Chapter XIII

MIHAILOV SOLD VRONSKY HIS PICTURE, AND AGREED TO PAINT A PORTRAIT OF ANNA. ON THE day fixed he came and began the work.

From the fifth sitting the portrait impressed everyone, especially Vronsky, not only by its resemblance, but by its characteristic beauty. It was strange how Mihailov could have discovered just her characteristic beauty. "One needs to know and love her as I have loved her to discover the very sweetest expression of her soul," Vronsky thought, though it was only from this portrait that he had himself learned this sweetest expression of her soul. But the expression was so true that he, and others too, fancied they had long known it.

"I have been struggling on forever so long without doing anything," he said of his own portrait of her, "and he just looked and painted it. That's where technique comes in."

"That will come," was the consoling reassurance given him by Golenishtchev, in whose view Vronsky had both talent, and what was most important, culture, giving him a wider outlook on art. Golenishtchev's faith in Vronsky's talent was propped up by his own need of Vronsky's sympathy and approval for his own articles and ideas, and he felt that the praise and support must be mutual.

In another man's house, and especially in Vronsky's palazzo, Mihailov was quite a different man from what he was in his studio. He behaved with hostile courtesy, as though he were afraid of coming closer to people he did not respect. He called Vronsky "your excellency," and notwithstanding Anna's and Vronsky's invitations, he would never stay to dinner, nor come except for the sittings. Anna was even more friendly to him than to other people, and was very grateful for her portrait. Vronsky was more than cordial with him, and was obviously interested to know the artist's opinion of his picture. Golenishtchev never let slip an opportunity of instilling sound ideas about art into Mihailov. But Mihailov remained equally chilly to all of them. Anna was aware from his eyes that he liked looking at her, but he avoided conversation with her. Vronsky's talk about his painting he met with stubborn silence, and he was as stubbornly silent when he was shown Vronsky's picture. He was unmistakably bored by Golenishtchev's conversation, and he did not attempt to oppose him.

Altogether Mihailov, with his reserved and disagreeable, as it were, hostile attitude, was quite disliked by them as they got to know him better; and they were glad when the sittings were over, and they were left with a magnificent portrait in their possession, and he gave up coming. Golenishtchev was the first to give expression to an idea that had occurred to all of them, which was that Mihailov was simply jealous of Vronsky.

"Not envious, let us say, since he has *talent*; but it annoys him that a wealthy man of the highest society, and a count, too (you know they all detest a title), can, without any particular trouble, do as well, if not better, than he who has devoted all his life to it. And more than all, it's a question of culture, which he is without."

Vronsky defended Mihailov, but at the bottom of his heart he believed it, because in his view a man of a different, lower world would be sure to be envious.

Anna's portrait—the same subject painted from nature both by him and by Mihailov—ought to have shown Vronsky the difference between him and Mihailov; but he did not see it. Only after

Mihailov's portrait was painted he left off painting his portrait of Anna, deciding that it was now not needed. His picture of mediaeval life he went on with. And he himself, and Golenishtchev, and still more Anna, thought it very good, because it was far more like the celebrated pictures they knew than Mihailov's picture.

Mihailov meanwhile, although Anna's portrait greatly fascinated him, was even more glad than they were when the sittings were over, and he had no longer to listen to Golenishtchev's disquisitions upon art, and could forget about Vronsky's painting. He knew that Vronsky could not be prevented from amusing himself with painting; he knew that he and all dilettanti had a perfect right to paint what they liked, but it was distasteful to him. A man could not be prevented from making himself a big wax doll, and kissing it. But if the man were to come with the doll and sit before a man in love, and begin caressing his doll as the lover caressed the woman he loved, it would be distasteful to the lover. Just such a distasteful sensation was what Mihailov felt at the sight of Vronsky's paintings: he felt it both ludicrous and irritating, both pitiable and offensive.

Vronsky's interest in painting and the Middle Ages did not last long. He had enough taste for painting to be unable to finish his picture. The picture came to a standstill. He was vaguely aware that its defects, inconspicuous at first, would be glaring if he were to go on with it. The same experience befell him as Golenishtchev, who felt that he had nothing to say, and continually deceived himself with the theory that his idea was not yet mature, that he was working it out and collecting materials. This exasperated and tortured Golenishtchev, but Vronsky was incapable of deceiving and torturing himself, and even more incapable of exasperation. With his characteristic decision, without explanation or apology, he simply ceased working at painting.

But without this occupation, the life of Vronsky and of Anna, who wondered at his loss of interest in it, struck them as intolerably tedious in an Italian town. The palazzo suddenly seemed so obtrusively old and dirty, the spots on the curtains, the cracks in the floors, the broken plaster on the cornices became so disagreeably obvious, and the everlasting sameness of Golenishtchev, and the Italian professor and the German traveler became so wearisome, that they had to make some change. They resolved to go to Russia, to the country. In Petersburg Vronsky intended to arrange a partition of the land with his brother, while Anna meant to see her son. The summer they intended to spend on Vronsky's great family estate.

Chapter XIV

LEVIN HAD BEEN MARRIED THREE MONTHS. HE WAS HAPPY, BUT NOT AT ALL IN THE WAY HE HAD expected to be. At every step he found his former dreams disappointed, and new, unexpected surprises of happiness. He was happy; but on entering upon family life he saw at every step that it was utterly different from what he had imagined. At every step he experienced what a man would experience who, after admiring the smooth, happy course of a little boat on a lake, should get himself into that little boat. He saw that it was not all sitting still, floating smoothly; that one had to think too, not for an instant to forget where one was floating; and that there was water under one, and that one must row; and that his unaccustomed hands would be sore; and that it was only to look at it that was easy; but that doing it, though very delightful, was very difficult.

As a bachelor, when he had watched other people's married life, seen the petty cares, the squabbles, the jealousy, he had only smiled contemptuously in his heart. In his future married life there could be, he was convinced, nothing of that sort; even the external forms, indeed, he fancied, must be utterly unlike the life of others in everything. And all of a sudden, instead of his life with his wife being made on an individual pattern, it was, on the contrary, entirely made up of the pettiest details, which he had so despised before, but which now, by no will of his own, had gained an extraordinary importance that it was useless to contend against. And Levin saw that the organization of all these details was by no means so easy as he had fancied before. Although Levin believed himself to have the most exact conceptions of domestic life, unconsciously, like all men, he pictured domestic life as the happiest enjoyment of love, with nothing to hinder and no petty cares to distract. He ought, as he conceived the position, to do his work, and to find repose from it in the happiness of love. She ought to be beloved, and nothing more. But, like all men, he forgot that she too would want work. And he was surprised that she, his poetic, exquisite Kitty, could, not merely in the first weeks, but even in the first days of their married life, think, remember, and busy herself about tablecloths, and furniture, about mattresses for visitors, about a tray, about the cook, and the dinner, and so on. While they were still engaged, he had been struck by the definiteness with which she had declined the tour abroad and decided to go into the country, as though she knew of something she wanted, and could still think of something outside her love. This had jarred upon him then, and now her trivial cares and anxieties jarred upon him several times. But he saw that this was essential for her. And, loving her as he did, though he did not understand the reason of them, and jeered at these domestic pursuits, he could not help admiring them. He jeered at the way in which she arranged the furniture they had brought from Moscow; rearranged their room; hung up curtains; prepared rooms for visitors; a room for Dolly; saw after an abode for her new maid; ordered dinner of the old cook; came into collision with Agafea Mihalovna, taking from her the charge of the stores. He saw how the old cook smiled, admiring her, and listening to her inexperienced, impossible orders, how mournfully and tenderly Agafea Mihalovna shook her head over the young mistress's new arrangements. He saw that Kitty was extraordinarily sweet when, laughing and crying, she came to tell him that her maid, Masha, was used to looking upon her as her young lady, and so no one obeyed her. It seemed to him sweet, but strange, and he thought it would have been better without this.

He did not know how great a sense of change she was experiencing; she, who at home had sometimes wanted some favorite dish, or sweets, without the possibility of getting either, now could order what she liked, buy pounds of sweets, spend as much money as she liked, and order any puddings she pleased.

She was dreaming with delight now of Dolly's coming to them with her children, especially because she would order for the children their favorite puddings and Dolly would appreciate all her new housekeeping. She did not know herself why and wherefore, but the arranging of her house had an irresistible attraction for her. Instinctively feeling the approach of spring, and knowing that there would be days of rough weather too, she built her nest as best she could, and was in haste at the same time to build it and to learn how to do it.

This care for domestic details in Kitty, so opposed to Levin's ideal of exalted happiness, was at first one of the disappointments; and this sweet care of her household, the aim of which he did not understand, but could not help loving, was one of the new happy surprises.

Another disappointment and happy surprise came in their quarrels. Levin could never have conceived that between him and his wife any relations could arise other than tender, respectful and loving, and all at once in the very early days they quarreled, so that she said he did not care for her, that he cared for no one but himself, burst into tears, and wrung her arms.

This first quarrel arose from Levin's having gone out to a new farmhouse and having been away half an hour too long, because he had tried to get home by a short cut and had lost his way. He drove home thinking of nothing but her, of her love, of his own happiness, and the nearer he drew to home, the warmer was his tenderness for her. He ran into the room with the same feeling, with an even stronger feeling than he had had when he reached the Shtcherbatskys' house to make his offer. And suddenly he was met by a lowering expression he had never seen in her. He would have kissed her; she pushed him away.

"What is it?"

"You've been enjoying yourself," she began, trying to be calm and spiteful. But as soon as she opened her mouth, a stream of reproach, of senseless jealousy, of all that had been torturing her during that half-hour which she had spent sitting motionless at the window, burst from her. It was only then, for the first time, that he clearly understood what he had not understood when he led her out of the church after the wedding. He felt now that he was not simply close to her, but that he did not know where he ended and she began. He felt this from the agonizing sensation of division that he experienced at that instant. He was offended for the first instant, but the very same second he felt that he could not be offended by her, that she was himself. He felt for the first moment as a man feels when, having suddenly received a violent blow from behind, turns round, angry and eager to avenge himself, to look for his antagonist, and finds that it is he himself who has accidentally struck himself, that there is no one to be angry with, and that he must put up with and try to soothe the pain.

Never afterwards did he feel it with such intensity, but this first time he could not for a long while get over it. His natural feeling urged him to defend himself, to prove to her she was wrong; but to prove her wrong would mean irritating her still more and making the rupture greater that was the cause of all his suffering. One habitual feeling impelled him to get rid of the blame and to pass it on her. Another feeling, even stronger, impelled him as quickly as possible to smooth over the rupture without letting it grow greater. To remain under such undeserved reproach was wretched, but to make her suffer by justifying himself was worse still. Like a man half-awake in an agony of pain, he wanted to tear out, to fling away the aching place, and coming to his senses, he felt that the aching place was himself. He could do nothing but try to help the aching place to bear it, and this he tried to do.

They made peace. She, recognizing that she was wrong, though she did not say so, became tenderer to him, and they experienced new, redoubled happiness in their love. But that did not prevent such quarrels from happening again, and exceedingly often too, on the most unexpected and trivial grounds. These quarrels frequently arose from the fact that they did not yet know what was of importance to each other, and that all this early period they were both often in a bad temper. When one was in a good temper, and the other in a bad temper, the peace was not broken; but when both happened to be in an ill-humor, quarrels sprang up from such incomprehensibly trifling causes, that they could never remember afterwards what they had quarreled about. It is true that when they were both in a good temper their enjoyment of life was redoubled. But still this first period of their married life was a difficult time for them.

During all this early time they had a peculiarly vivid sense of tension, as it were, a tugging in opposite directions of the chain by which they were bound. Altogether their honeymoon—that is to say, the month after their wedding—from which from tradition Levin expected so much, was not merely not a time of sweetness, but remained in the memories of both as the bitterest and most humiliating period in their lives. They both alike tried in later life to blot out from their memories all the monstrous, shameful incidents of that morbid period, when both were rarely in a normal frame of mind, both were rarely quite themselves.

It was only in the third month of their married life, after their return from Moscow, where they had been staying for a month, that their life began to go more smoothly.

Chapter XV

THEY HAD JUST COME BACK FROM MOSCOW, AND WERE GLAD TO BE ALONE. HE WAS SITTING AT the writing-table in his study, writing. She, wearing the dark lilac dress she had worn during the first days of their married life, and put on again today, a dress particularly remembered and loved by him, was sitting on the sofa, the same old-fashioned leather sofa which had always stood in the study in Levin's father's and grandfather's days. She was sewing at *broderie anglaise.* He thought and wrote, never losing the happy consciousness of her presence. His work, both on the land and on the book, in which the principles of the new land system were to be laid down, had not been abandoned; but just as formerly these pursuits and ideas had seemed to him petty and trivial in comparison with the darkness that overspread all life, now they seemed as unimportant and petty in comparison with the life that lay before him suffused with the brilliant light of happiness. He went on with his work, but he felt now that the center of gravity of his attention had passed to something else, and that consequently he looked at his work quite differently and more clearly. Formerly this work had been for him an escape from life. Formerly he had felt that without this work his life would be too gloomy. Now these pursuits were necessary for him that life might not be too uniformly bright. Taking up his manuscript, reading through what he had written, he found with pleasure that the work was worth his working at. Many of his old ideas seemed to him superfluous and extreme, but many blanks became distinct to him when he reviewed the whole thing in his memory. He was writing now a new chapter on the causes of the present disastrous condition of agriculture in Russia. He maintained that the poverty of Russia arises not merely from the anomalous distribution of landed property and misdirected reforms, but that what had contributed of late years to this result was the civilization from without abnormally grafted upon Russia, especially facilities of communication, as railways, leading to centralization in towns, the development of luxury, and the consequent development of manufactures, credit and its accompaniment of speculation—all to the detriment of agriculture. It seemed to him that in a normal development of wealth in a state all these phenomena would arise only when a considerable amount of labor had been put into agriculture, when it had come under regular, or at least definite, conditions; that the wealth of a country ought to increase proportionally, and especially in such a way that other sources of wealth should not outstrip agriculture; that in harmony with a certain stage of agriculture there should be means of communication corresponding to it, and that in our unsettled condition of the land, railways, called into being by political and not by economic needs, were premature, and instead of promoting agriculture, as was expected of them, they were competing with agriculture and promoting the development of manufactures and credit, and so arresting its progress; and that just as the one-sided and premature development of one organ in an animal would hinder its general development, so in the general development of wealth in Russia, credit, facilities of communication, manufacturing activity, indubitably necessary in Europe, where they had arisen in their proper time, had with us only done harm, by throwing into the background the chief question calling for settlement—the question of the organization of agriculture.

While he was writing his ideas she was thinking how unnaturally cordial her husband had been to young Prince Tcharsky, who had, with great want of tact, flirted with her the day before they left Moscow. "He's jealous," she thought. "Goodness! how sweet and silly he is! He's jealous of me! If he knew that I think no more of them than of Piotr the cook," she thought, looking at his head and red neck with a feeling of possession strange to herself. "Though it's a pity to take him from his work (but he has plenty of time!), I must look at his face; will he feel I'm looking at him? I wish he'd turn round . . . I'll *will* him to!" and she opened her eyes wide, as though to intensify the influence of her gaze.

"Yes, they draw away all the sap and give a false appearance of prosperity," he muttered, stopping to write, and, feeling that she was looking at him and smiling, he looked round.

"Well?" he queried, smiling, and getting up.

"He looked round," she thought.

"It's nothing; I wanted you to look round," she said, watching him, and trying to guess whether he was vexed at being interrupted or not.

"How happy we are alone together!—I am, that is," he said, going up to her with a radiant smile of happiness.

"I'm just as happy. I'll never go anywhere, especially not to Moscow."

"And what were you thinking about?"

"I? I was thinking . . . No, no, go along, go on writing; don't break off," she said, pursing up her lips, "and I must cut out these little holes now, do you see?"

She took up her scissors and began cutting them out.

"No; tell me, what was it?" he said, sitting down beside her and watching the tiny scissors moving round.

"Oh! what was I thinking about? I was thinking about Moscow, about the back of your head."

"Why should I, of all people, have such happiness! It's unnatural, too good," he said, kissing her hand.

"I feel quite the opposite; the better things are, the more natural it seems to me."

"And you've got a little curl loose," he said, carefully turning her head round.

"A little curl, oh yes. No, no, we are busy at our work!"

Work did not progress further, and they darted apart from one another like culprits when Kouzma came in to announce that tea was ready.

"Have they come from the town?" Levin asked Kouzma.

"They've just come; they're unpacking the things."

"Come quickly," she said to him as she went out of the study, "or else I shall read your letters without you."

Left alone, after putting his manuscripts together in the new portfolio bought by her, he washed his hands at the new washstand with the elegant fittings, that had all made their appearance with her. Levin smiled at his own thoughts, and shook his head disapprovingly at those thoughts; a feeling akin to remorse fretted him. There was something shameful, effeminate, Capuan, as he called it to himself, in his present mode of life. "It's not right to go on like this," he thought. "It'll soon be three months, and I'm doing next to nothing. Today, almost for the first time, I set to work seriously, and what happened? I did nothing but begin and throw it aside. Even my ordinary pursuits I have almost given up. On the land I scarcely walk or drive about at all to look after things. Either I am loath to leave her, or I see she's dull alone. And I used to think that, before marriage, life was nothing much, somehow didn't count, but that after marriage, life began in earnest. And here almost three months have passed, and I have spent my time so idly and unprofitably. No, this won't do; I must begin. Of course, it's not her fault. She's not to blame in any way. I ought myself to be firmer, to maintain my masculine independence of action; or else I shall get into such ways, and she'll get used to them too. . . . Of course she's not to blame," he told himself.

But it is hard for anyone who is dissatisfied not to blame someone else, and especially the person nearest of all to him, for the ground of his dissatisfaction. And it vaguely came into Levin's mind that she herself was not to blame (she could not be to blame for anything), but what was to blame was her education, too superficial and frivolous. ("That fool Tcharsky: she wanted, I know, to stop him, but didn't know how to.") "Yes, apart from her interest in the house (that she has), apart from dress and *broderie anglaise,* she has no serious interests. No interest in her work, in the estate, in the peasants, nor in music, though she's rather good at it, nor in reading. She does nothing, and is perfectly satisfied." Levin, in his heart, censured this, and did not as yet understand that she was preparing for that period of activity which was to come for her when she would at once be the wife of her husband and mistress of the house, and would bear, and nurse, and bring up children. He knew not that she was instinctively aware of this, and preparing herself for this time of terrible toil, did not reproach herself for the moments of carelessness and happiness in her love that she enjoyed now while gaily building her nest for the future.

Chapter XVI

When Levin went upstairs, his wife was sitting near the new silver samovar behind the new tea service, and, having settled old Agafea Mihalovna at a little table with a full cup of tea, was reading a letter from Dolly, with whom they were in continual and frequent correspondence.

"You see, your good lady's settled me here, told me to sit a bit with her," said Agafea Mihalovna, smiling affectionately at Kitty.

In these words of Agafea Mihalovna, Levin read the final act of the drama which had been enacted of late between her and Kitty. He saw that, in spite of Agafea Mihalovna's feelings being hurt by a new mistress taking the reins of government out of her hands, Kitty had yet conquered her and made her love her.

"Here, I opened your letter too," said Kitty, handing him an illiterate letter. "It's from that woman, I think, your brother's . . ." she said. "I did not read it through. This is from my people and from Dolly. Fancy! Dolly took Tanya and Grisha to a children's ball at the Sarmatskys': Tanya was a French marquise."

But Levin did not hear her. Flushing, he took the letter from Marya Nikolaevna, his brother's former mistress, and began to read it. This was the second letter he had received from Marya Nikolaevna. In the first letter, Marya Nikolaevna wrote that his brother had sent her away for no fault of hers, and, with touching simplicity, added that though she was in want again, she asked for nothing, and wished for nothing, but was only tormented by the thought that Nikolay Dmitrievitch would come to grief without her, owing to the weak state of his health, and begged his brother to look after him. Now she wrote quite differently. She had found Nikolay Dmitrievitch, had again made it up with him in Moscow, and had moved with him to a provincial town, where he had received a post in the government service. But that he had quarreled with the head official, and was on his way back to Moscow, only he had been taken so ill on the road that it was doubtful if he would ever leave his bed again, she wrote. "It's always of you he has talked, and, besides, he has no more money left."

"Read this; Dolly writes about you," Kitty was beginning, with a smile; but she stopped suddenly, noticing the changed expression on her husband's face.

"What is it? What's the matter?"

"She writes to me that Nikolay, my brother, is at death's door. I shall go to him."

Kitty's face changed at once. Thoughts of Tanya as a marquise, of Dolly, all had vanished.

"When are you going?" she said.

"Tomorrow."

"And I will go with you, can I?" she said.

"Kitty! What are you thinking of?" he said reproachfully.

"How do you mean?" offended that he should seem to take her suggestion unwillingly and with vexation. "Why shouldn't I go? I shan't be in your way. I . . ."

"I'm going because my brother is dying," said Levin. "Why should you . . ."

"Why? For the same reason as you."

"And, at a moment of such gravity for me, she only thinks of her being dull by herself," thought Levin. And this lack of candor in a matter of such gravity infuriated him.

"It's out of the question," he said sternly.

Agafea Mihalovna, seeing that it was coming to a quarrel, gently put down her cup and withdrew. Kitty did not even notice her. The tone in which her husband had said the last words wounded her, especially because he evidently did not believe what she had said.

"I tell you, that if you go, I shall come with you; I shall certainly come," she said hastily and wrathfully. "Why out of the question? Why do you say it's out of the question?"

"Because it'll be going God knows where, by all sorts of roads and to all sorts of hotels. You would be a hindrance to me," said Levin, trying to be cool.

"Not at all. I don't want anything. Where you can go, I can. . . ."

"Well, for one thing then, because this woman's there whom you can't meet."

"I don't know and don't care to know who's there and what. I know that my husband's brother is dying and my husband is going to him, and I go with my husband too. . . ."

"Kitty! Don't get angry. But just think a little: this is a matter of such importance that I can't bear to think that you should bring in a feeling of weakness, of dislike to being left alone. Come, you'll be dull alone, so go and stay at Moscow a little."

"There, you always ascribe base, vile motives to me," she said with tears of wounded pride and fury. "I didn't mean, it wasn't weakness, it wasn't . . . I feel that it's my duty to be with my husband when he's in trouble, but you try on purpose to hurt me, you try on purpose not to understand. . . ."

"No; this is awful! To be such a slave!" cried Levin, getting up, and unable to restrain his anger any longer. But at the same second he felt that he was beating himself.

"Then why did you marry? You could have been free. Why did you, if you regret it?" she said, getting up and running away into the drawing room.

When he went to her, she was sobbing.

He began to speak, trying to find words not to dissuade but simply to soothe her. But she did not heed him, and would not agree to anything. He bent down to her and took her hand, which resisted him. He kissed her hand, kissed her hair, kissed her hand again—still she was silent. But when he took her face in both his hands and said "Kitty!" she suddenly recovered herself, and began to cry, and they were reconciled.

It was decided that they should go together the next day. Levin told his wife that he believed she wanted to go simply in order to be of use, agreed that Marya Nikolaevna's being with his brother did not make her going improper, but he set off at the bottom of his heart dissatisfied both with her and with himself. He was dissatisfied with her for being unable to make up her mind to let him go when it was necessary (and how strange it was for him to think that he, so lately hardly daring to believe in such happiness as that she could love him—now was unhappy because she loved him too much!), and he was dissatisfied with himself for not showing more strength of will. Even greater was the feeling of disagreement at the bottom of his heart as to her not needing to consider the woman who was with his brother, and he thought with horror of all the contingencies they might meet with. The mere idea of his wife, his Kitty, being in the same room with a common wench, set him shuddering with horror and loathing.

Chapter XVII

THE HOTEL OF THE PROVINCIAL TOWN WHERE NIKOLAY LEVIN WAS LYING ILL WAS ONE OF THOSE provincial hotels which are constructed on the newest model of modern improvements, with the best intentions of cleanliness, comfort, and even elegance, but owing to the public that patronizes them, are with astounding rapidity transformed into filthy taverns with a pretension of modern improvement that only makes them worse than the old-fashioned, honestly filthy hotels. This hotel had already reached that stage, and the soldier in a filthy uniform smoking in the entry, supposed to stand for a hall-porter, and the cast-iron, slippery, dark, and disagreeable staircase, and the free and easy waiter in a filthy frock-coat, and the common dining room with a dusty bouquet of wax flowers adorning the table, and filth, dust, and disorder everywhere, and at the same time the sort of modern up-to-date self-complacent railway uneasiness of this hotel, aroused a most painful feeling in Levin after their fresh young life, especially because the impression of falsity made by the hotel was so out of keeping with what awaited them.

As is invariably the case, after they had been asked at what price they wanted rooms, it appeared that there was not one decent room for them; one decent room had been taken by the inspector of railroads, another by a lawyer from Moscow, a third by Princess Astafieva from the country. There remained only one filthy room, next to which they promised that another should be empty by the evening. Feeling angry with his wife because what he had expected had come to pass, which was that at the moment of arrival, when his heart throbbed with emotion and anxiety to know how his brother was getting on, he should have to be seeing after her, instead of rushing straight to his brother, Levin conducted her to the room assigned them.

"Go, do go!" she said, looking at him with timid and guilty eyes.

He went out of the door without a word, and at once stumbled over Marya Nikolaevna, who had heard of his arrival and had not dared to go in to see him. She was just the same as when he saw her in Moscow; the same woolen gown, and bare arms and neck, and the same good-naturedly stupid, pockmarked face, only a little plumper.

"Well, how is he? how is he?"

"Very bad. He can't get up. He has kept expecting you. He. . . . Are you . . . with your wife?"

Levin did not for the first moment understand what it was confused her, but she immediately enlightened him.

"I'll go away. I'll go down to the kitchen," she brought out. "Nikolay Dmitrievitch will be delighted. He heard about it, and knows your lady, and remembers her abroad."

Levin realized that she meant his wife, and did not know what answer to make.

"Come along, come along to him!" he said.

But as soon as he moved, the door of his room opened and Kitty peeped out. Levin crimsoned both from shame and anger with his wife, who had put herself and him in such a difficult position; but Marya Nikolaevna crimsoned still more. She positively shrank together and flushed to the point of tears, and clutching the ends of her apron in both hands, twisted them in her red fingers without knowing what to say and what to do.

For the first instant Levin saw an expression of eager curiosity in the eyes with which Kitty looked at this awful woman, so incomprehensible to her; but it lasted only a single instant.

"Well! how is he?" she turned to her husband and then to her.

"But one can't go on talking in the passage like this!" Levin said, looking angrily at a gentleman who walked jauntily at that instant across the corridor, as though about his affairs.

"Well then, come in," said Kitty, turning to Marya Nikolaevna, who had recovered herself, but noticing her husband's face of dismay; "or go on; go, and then come for me," she said, and went back into the room.

Levin went to his brother's room. He had not in the least expected what he saw and felt in his brother's room. He had expected to find him in the same state of self-deception which he had heard was so frequent with the consumptive, and which had struck him so much during his brother's visit in the autumn. He had expected to find the physical signs of the approach of death more marked—greater weakness, greater emaciation, but still almost the same condition of things. He had expected himself to feel the same distress at the loss of the brother he loved and the same horror in face of death as he had felt then, only in a greater degree. And he had prepared himself for this; but he found something utterly different.

In a little dirty room with the painted panels of its walls filthy with spittle, and conversation audible through the thin partition from the next room, in a stifling atmosphere saturated with impurities, on a bedstead moved away from the wall, there lay covered with a quilt, a body. One arm of this body was above the quilt, and the wrist, huge as a rake-handle, was attached, inconceivably it seemed, to the thin, long bone of the arm smooth from the beginning to the middle. The head lay sideways on the pillow. Levin could see the scanty locks wet with sweat on the temples and tense, transparent-looking forehead.

"It cannot be that that fearful body was my brother Nikolay?" thought Levin. But he went closer, saw the face, and doubt became impossible. In spite of the terrible change in the face, Levin had only to glance at those eager eyes raised at his approach, only to catch the faint movement of the mouth under the sticky mustache, to realize the terrible truth that this deathlike body was his living brother.

The glittering eyes looked sternly and reproachfully at his brother as he drew near. And immediately this glance established a living relationship between living men. Levin immediately felt the reproach in the eyes fixed on him, and felt remorse at his own happiness.

When Konstantin took him by the hand, Nikolay smiled. The smile was faint, scarcely perceptible, and in spite of the smile the stern expression of the eyes was unchanged.

"You did not expect to find me like this," he articulated with effort.

"Yes . . . no," said Levin, hesitating over his words. "How was it you didn't let me know before, that is, at the time of my wedding? I made inquiries in all directions."

He had to talk so as not to be silent, and he did not know what to say, especially as his brother made no reply, and simply stared without dropping his eyes, and evidently penetrated to the inner meaning of each word. Levin told his brother that his wife had come with him. Nikolay expressed pleasure, but said he was afraid of frightening her by his condition. A silence followed. Suddenly Nikolay stirred, and began to say something. Levin expected something of peculiar gravity and importance from the expression of his face, but Nikolay began speaking of his health. He found fault with the doctor, regretting he had not a celebrated Moscow doctor. Levin saw that he still hoped.

Seizing the first moment of silence, Levin got up, anxious to escape, if only for an instant, from his agonizing emotion, and said that he would go and fetch his wife.

"Very well, and I'll tell her to tidy up here. It's dirty and stinking here, I expect. Marya! clear up the room," the sick man said with effort. "Oh, and when you've cleared up, go away yourself," he added, looking inquiringly at his brother.

Levin made no answer. Going out into the corridor, he stopped short. He had said he would fetch his wife, but now, taking stock of the emotion he was feeling, he decided that he would try on the contrary to persuade her not to go in to the sick man. "Why should she suffer as I am suffering?" he thought.

"Well, how is he?" Kitty asked with a frightened face.

"Oh, it's awful, it's awful! What did you come for?" said Levin.

Kitty was silent for a few seconds, looking timidly and ruefully at her husband; then she went up and took him by the elbow with both hands.

"Kostya! take me to him; it will be easier for us to bear it together. You only take me, take me to him, please, and go away," she said. "You must understand that for me to see you, and not to see him, is far more painful. There I might be a help to you and to him. Please, let me!" she besought her husband, as though the happiness of her life depended on it.

Levin was obliged to agree, and regaining his composure, and completely forgetting about Marya Nikolaevna by now, he went again in to his brother with Kitty.

Stepping lightly, and continually glancing at her husband, showing him a valorous and sympathetic face, Kitty went into the sickroom, and, turning without haste, noiselessly closed the door. With inaudible steps she went quickly to the sick man's bedside, and going up so that he had not to turn his head, she immediately clasped in her fresh young hand the skeleton of his huge hand, pressed it, and began speaking with that soft eagerness, sympathetic and not jarring, which is peculiar to women.

"We have met, though we were not acquainted, at Soden," she said. "You never thought I was to be your sister?"

"You would not have recognized me?" he said, with a radiant smile at her entrance.

"Yes, I should. What a good thing you let us know! Not a day has passed that Kostya has not mentioned you, and been anxious."

But the sick man's interest did not last long.

Before she had finished speaking, there had come back into his face the stern, reproachful expression of the dying man's envy of the living.

"I am afraid you are not quite comfortable here," she said, turning away from his fixed stare, and looking about the room. "We must ask about another room," she said to her husband, "so that we might be nearer."

Chapter XVIII

LEVIN COULD NOT LOOK CALMLY AT HIS BROTHER; HE COULD NOT HIMSELF BE NATURAL AND CALM in his presence. When he went in to the sick man, his eyes and his attention were unconsciously dimmed, and he did not see and did not distinguish the details of his brother's position. He smelled the awful odor, saw the dirt, disorder, and miserable condition, and heard the groans, and felt that nothing could be done to help. It never entered his head to analyze the details of the sick man's situation, to consider how that body was lying under the quilt, how those emaciated legs and thighs and spine were lying huddled up, and whether they could not be made more comfortable, whether anything could not be done to make things, if not better, at least less bad. It made his blood run cold when he began to think of all these details. He was absolutely convinced that nothing could be done to prolong his brother's life or to relieve his suffering. But a sense of his regarding all aid as out of the question was felt by the sick man, and exasperated him. And this made it still more painful for Levin. To be in the sickroom was agony to him, not to be there still worse. And he was continually, on various pretexts, going out of the room, and coming in again, because he was unable to remain alone.

But Kitty thought, and felt, and acted quite differently. On seeing the sick man, she pitied him. And pity in her womanly heart did not arouse at all that feeling of horror and loathing that it aroused in her husband, but a desire to act, to find out all the details of his state, and to remedy them. And since she had not the slightest doubt that it was her duty to help him, she had no doubt either that it was possible, and immediately set to work. The very details, the mere thought of which reduced her husband to terror, immediately engaged her attention. She sent for the doctor, sent to the chemist's, set the maid who had come with her and Marya Nikolaevna to sweep and dust and scrub; she herself washed up something, washed out something else, laid something under the quilt. Something was by her directions brought into the sickroom, something else was carried out. She herself went several times to her room, regardless of the men she met in the corridor, got out and brought in sheets, pillowcases, towels, and shirts.

The waiter, who was busy with a party of engineers dining in the dining hall, came several times with an irate countenance in answer to her summons, and could not avoid carrying out her orders, as she gave them with such gracious insistence that there was no evading her. Levin did not approve of all this; he did not believe it would be of any good to the patient. Above all, he was afraid the patient would be angry at it. But the sick man, though he seemed and was indifferent about it, was not angry, but only abashed, and on the whole as it were interested in what she was doing with him. Coming back from the doctor to whom Kitty had sent him, Levin, on opening the door, came upon the sick man at the instant when, by Kitty's directions, they were changing his linen. The long white ridge of his spine, with the huge, prominent shoulder blades and jutting ribs and vertebrae, was bare, and Marya Nikolaevna and the waiter were struggling with the sleeve of the nightshirt, and could not get the long, limp arm into it. Kitty, hurriedly closing the door after Levin, was not looking that way; but the sick man groaned, and she moved rapidly towards him.

"Make haste," she said.

"Oh, don't you come," said the sick man angrily. "I'll do it my myself. . . ."

"What say?" queried Marya Nikolaevna. But Kitty heard and saw he was ashamed and uncomfortable at being naked before her.

"I'm not looking, I'm not looking!" she said, putting the arm in. "Marya Nikolaevna, you come this side, you do it," she added.

"Please go for me, there's a little bottle in my small bag," she said, turning to her husband, "you know, in the side pocket; bring it, please, and meanwhile they'll finish clearing up here."

Returning with the bottle, Levin found the sick man settled comfortably and everything about him completely changed. The heavy smell was replaced by the smell of aromatic vinegar, which Kitty with pouting lips and puffed-out, rosy cheeks was squirting through a little pipe. There was no dust visible anywhere, a rug was laid by the bedside. On the table stood medicine bottles and decanters tidily arranged, and the linen needed was folded up there, and Kitty's *broderie anglaise*. On the other table by the patient's bed there were candles and drink and powders. The sick man himself, washed and combed, lay in clean sheets on high raised pillows, in a clean nightshirt with a white collar about his astoundingly thin neck, and with a new expression of hope looked fixedly at Kitty.

The doctor brought by Levin, and found by him at the club, was not the one who had been attending Nikolay Levin, as the patient was dissatisfied with him. The new doctor took up a stethoscope and sounded the patient, shook his head, prescribed medicine, and with extreme minuteness explained first how to take the medicine and then what diet was to be kept to. He advised eggs, raw or hardly cooked, and seltzer water, with warm milk at a certain temperature. When the doctor had gone away the sick man said something to his brother, of which Levin could distinguish only the last words: "Your Katya." By the expression with which he gazed at her, Levin saw that he was praising her. He called indeed to Katya, as he called her.

"I'm much better already," he said. "Why, with you I should have got well long ago. How nice it is!" he took her hand and drew it towards his lips, but as though afraid she would dislike it he changed his mind, let it go, and only stroked it. Kitty took his hand in both hers and pressed it.

"Now turn me over on the left side and go to bed," he said.

No one could make out what he said but Kitty; she alone understood. She understood because she was all the while mentally keeping watch on what he needed.

"On the other side," she said to her husband, "he always sleeps on that side. Turn him over, it's so disagreeable calling the servants. I'm not strong enough. Can you?" she said to Marya Nikolaevna.

"I'm afraid not," answered Marya Nikolaevna.

Terrible as it was to Levin to put his arms round that terrible body, to take hold of that under the quilt, of which he preferred to know nothing, under his wife's influence he made his resolute face that she knew so well, and putting his arms into the bed took hold of the body, but in spite of his own strength he was struck by the strange heaviness of those powerless limbs. While he was turning him over, conscious of the huge emaciated arm about his neck, Kitty swiftly and noiselessly turned the pillow, beat it up and settled in it the sick man's head, smoothing back his hair, which was sticking again to his moist brow.

The sick man kept his brother's hand in his own. Levin felt that he meant to do something with his hand and was pulling it somewhere. Levin yielded with a sinking heart: yet, he drew it to his mouth and kissed it. Levin, shaking with sobs and unable to articulate a word, went out of the room.

Chapter XIX

"THOU HAST HID THESE THINGS FROM THE WISE AND PRUDENT, AND HAST REVEALED THEM UNTO babes." So Levin thought about his wife as he talked to her that evening.

Levin thought of the text, not because he considered himself "wise and prudent." He did not so consider himself, but he could not help knowing that he had more intellect than his wife and Agafea Mihalovna, and he could not help knowing that when he thought of death, he thought with all the force of his intellect. He knew too that the brains of many great men, whose thoughts he had read, had brooded over death and yet knew not a hundredth part of what his wife and Agafea Mihalovna knew about it. Different as those two women were, Agafea Mihalovna and Katya, as his brother Nikolay had called her, and as Levin particularly liked to call her now, they were quite alike in this. Both knew, without a shade of doubt, what sort of thing life was and what was death, and though neither of them could have answered, and would even not have understood the questions that presented themselves to Levin, both had no doubt of the significance of this event, and were precisely alike in their way of looking at it, which they shared with millions of people. The proof that they knew for a certainty the nature of death lay in the fact that they knew without a second of hesitation how to deal with the dying, and were not frightened of them. Levin and other men like him, though they could have said a great deal about death, obviously did not know this since they were afraid of death, and were absolutely at a loss what to do when people were dying. If Levin had been alone now with his brother Nikolay, he would have looked at him with terror, and with still greater terror waited, and would not have known what else to do.

More than that, he did not know what to say, how to look, how to move. To talk of outside things seemed to him shocking, impossible, to talk of death and depressing subjects—also impossible. To be silent, also impossible. "If I look at him he will think I am studying him, I am afraid; if I don't look at him, he'll think I'm thinking of other things. If I walk on tiptoe, he will be vexed; to tread firmly, I'm ashamed." Kitty evidently did not think of herself, and had no time to think about herself: she was thinking about him because she knew something, and all went well. She told him about herself even and about her wedding, and smiled and sympathized with him and petted him, and talked of cases of recovery and all went well; so then she must know. The proof that her behavior and Agafea Mihalovna's was not instinctive, animal, irrational, was that apart from the physical treatment, the relief of suffering, both Agafea Mihalovna and Kitty required for the dying man something else more important than the physical treatment, and something which had nothing in common with physical conditions. Agafea Mihalovna, speaking of the man just dead, had said: "Well, thank God, he took the sacrament and received absolution; God grant each one of us such a death." Katya in just the same way, besides all her care about linen, bedsores, drink, found time the very first day to persuade the sick man of the necessity of taking the sacrament and receiving absolution.

On getting back from the sickroom to their own two rooms for the night, Levin sat with hanging head not knowing what to do. Not to speak of supper, of preparing for bed, of considering what they were going to do, he could not even talk to his wife; he was ashamed to. Kitty, on the contrary, was more active than usual. She was even livelier than usual. She ordered supper to be brought, herself unpacked their things, and herself helped to make the beds, and did not even forget to sprinkle them with Persian powder. She showed that alertness, that swiftness of reflection comes out in men before a battle, in conflict, in the dangerous and decisive moments of life—those moments when a man shows once and for all his value, and that all his past has not been wasted but has been a preparation for these moments.

Everything went rapidly in her hands, and before it was twelve o'clock all their things were arranged cleanly and tidily in her rooms, in such a way that the hotel rooms seemed like home: the beds were made, brushes, combs, looking-glasses were put out, table napkins were spread.

Levin felt that it was unpardonable to eat, to sleep, to talk even now, and it seemed to him that every movement he made was unseemly. She arranged the brushes, but she did it all so that there was nothing shocking in it.

They could neither of them eat, however, and for a long while they could not sleep, and did not even go to bed.

"I am very glad I persuaded him to receive extreme unction tomorrow," she said, sitting in her dressing-jacket before her folding looking-glass, combing her soft, fragrant hair with a fine comb. "I have never seen it, but I know, mamma has told me, there are prayers said for recovery."

"Do you suppose he can possibly recover?" said Levin, watching a slender tress at the back of her round little head that was continually hidden when she passed the comb through the front.

"I asked the doctor; he said he couldn't live more than three days. But can they be sure? I'm very glad, anyway, that I persuaded him," she said, looking askance at her husband through her hair. "Anything is possible," she added with that peculiar, rather sly expression that was always in her face when she spoke of religion.

Since their conversation about religion when they were engaged neither of them had ever started a discussion of the subject, but she performed all the ceremonies of going to church, saying her prayers, and so on, always with the unvarying conviction that this ought to be so. In spite of his assertion to the contrary, she was firmly persuaded that he was as much a Christian as she, and indeed a far better one; and all that he said about it was simply one of his absurd masculine freaks, just as he would say about her *broderie anglaise*, that good people patch holes, but that she cut them on purpose, and so on.

"Yes, you see this woman, Marya Nikolaevna, did not know how to manage all this," said Levin. "And . . . I must own I'm very, very glad you came. You are such purity that. . . ." He took her hand and did not kiss it (to kiss her hand in such closeness to death seemed to him improper); he merely squeezed it with a penitent air, looking at her brightening eyes.

"It would have been miserable for you to be alone," she said, and lifting her hands which hid her cheeks, flushing with pleasure, twisted her coil of hair on the nape of her neck and pinned it there. "No," she went on, "she did not know how. . . . Luckily, I learned a lot at Soden."

"Surely there are not people there so ill?"

"Worse."

"What's so awful to me is that I can't see him as he was when he was young. You would not believe how charming he was as a youth, but I did not understand him then."

"I can quite, quite believe it. How I feel that we might have been friends!" she said; and, distressed at what she had said, she looked round at her husband, and tears came into her eyes.

"Yes, *might have been*," he said mournfully. "He's just one of those people of whom they say they're not for this world."

"But we have many days before us; we must go to bed," said Kitty, glancing at her tiny watch.

Chapter XX

THE NEXT DAY THE SICK MAN RECEIVED THE SACRAMENT AND EXTREME UNCTION. DURING THE ceremony Nikolay Levin prayed fervently. His great eyes, fastened on the holy image that was set out on a card-table covered with a colored napkin, expressed such passionate prayer and hope that it was awful to Levin to see it. Levin knew that this passionate prayer and hope would only make him feel more bitterly parting from the life he so loved. Levin knew his brother and the workings of his intellect: he knew that his unbelief came not from life being easier for him without faith, but had grown up because step by step the contemporary scientific interpretation of natural phenomena crushed out the possibility of faith; and so he knew that his present return was not a legitimate one, brought about by way of the same working of his intellect, but simply a temporary, interested return to faith in a desperate hope of recovery. Levin knew too that Kitty had strengthened his hope by accounts of the marvelous recoveries she had heard of. Levin knew all this; and it was agonizingly painful to him to behold the supplicating, hopeful eyes and the emaciated wrist, lifted with difficulty, making the sign of the cross on the tense brow, and the prominent shoulders and hollow, gasping chest, which one could not feel consistent with the life the sick man was praying for. During the sacrament Levin did what he, an unbeliever, had done a thousand times. He said, addressing God, "If Thou dost exist, make this man to recover" (of course this same thing has been repeated many times), "and Thou wilt save him and me."

After extreme unction the sick man became suddenly much better. He did not cough once in the course of an hour, smiled, kissed Kitty's hand, thanking her with tears, and said he was comfortable, free from pain, and that he felt strong and had an appetite. He even raised himself when his soup was brought, and asked for a cutlet as well. Hopelessly ill as he was, obvious as it was at the first glance that he could not recover, Levin and Kitty were for that hour both in the same state of excitement, happy, though fearful of being mistaken.

"Is he better?"

"Yes, much."

"It's wonderful."

"There's nothing wonderful in it."

"Anyway, he's better," they said in a whisper, smiling to one another.

This self-deception was not of long duration. The sick man fell into a quiet sleep, but he was waked up half an hour later by his cough. And all at once every hope vanished in those about him and in himself. The reality of his suffering crushed all hopes in Levin and Kitty and in the sick man himself, leaving no doubt, no memory even of past hopes.

Without referring to what he had believed in half an hour before, as though ashamed even to recall it, he asked for iodine to inhale in a bottle covered with perforated paper. Levin gave him the bottle, and the same look of passionate hope with which he had taken the sacrament was now fastened on his brother, demanding from him the confirmation of the doctor's words that inhaling iodine worked wonders.

"Is Katya not here?" he gasped, looking round while Levin reluctantly assented to the doctor's words. "No; so I can say it. . . . It was for her sake I went through that farce. She's so sweet; but you and I can't deceive ourselves. This is what I believe in," he said, and, squeezing the bottle in his bony hand, he began breathing over it.

At eight o'clock in the evening Levin and his wife were drinking tea in their room when Marya Nikolaevna ran in to them breathlessly. She was pale, and her lips were quivering. "He is dying!" she whispered. "I'm afraid will die this minute."

Both of them ran to him. He was sitting raised up with one elbow on the bed, his long back bent, and his head hanging low.

"How do you feel?" Levin asked in a whisper, after a silence.

"I feel I'm setting off," Nikolay said with difficulty, but with extreme distinctness, screwing the words out of himself. He did not raise his head, but simply turned his eyes upwards, without their reaching his brother's face. "Katya, go away!" he added.

Levin jumped up, and with a peremptory whisper made her go out.

"I'm setting off," he said again.

"Why do you think so?" said Levin, so as to say something.

"Because I'm setting off," he repeated, as though he had a liking for the phrase. "It's the end."

Marya Nikolaevna went up to him.

"You had better lie down; you'd be easier," she said.

"I shall lie down soon enough," he pronounced slowly, "when I'm dead," he said sarcastically, wrathfully. "Well, you can lay me down if you like."

Levin laid his brother on his back, sat down beside him, and gazed at his face, holding his breath. The dying man lay with closed eyes, but the muscles twitched from time to time on his forehead, as with one thinking deeply and intensely. Levin involuntarily thought with him of what it was that was happening to him now, but in spite of all his mental efforts to go along with him he saw by the expression of that calm, stern face that for the dying man all was growing clearer and clearer that was still as dark as ever for Levin.

"Yes, yes, so," the dying man articulated slowly at intervals. "Wait a little." He was silent. "Right!" he pronounced all at once reassuringly, as though all were solved for him. "O Lord!" he murmured, and sighed deeply.

Marya Nikolaevna felt his feet. "They're getting cold," she whispered.

For a long while, a very long while it seemed to Levin, the sick man lay motionless. But he was still alive, and from time to time he sighed. Levin by now was exhausted from mental strain. He felt that, with no mental effort, could he understand what it was that was *right*. He could not even think of the problem of death itself, but with no will of his own thoughts kept coming to him of what he had to do next; closing the dead man's eyes, dressing him, ordering the coffin. And, strange to say, he felt utterly cold, and was not conscious of sorrow nor of loss, less still of pity for his brother. If he had any feeling for his brother at that moment, it was envy for the knowledge the dying man had now that he could not have.

A long time more he sat over him so, continually expecting the end. But the end did not come. The door opened and Kitty appeared. Levin got up to stop her. But at the moment he was getting up, he caught the sound of the dying man stirring.

"Don't go away," said Nikolay and held out his hand. Levin gave him his, and angrily waved to his wife to go away.

With the dying man's hand in his hand, he sat for half an hour, an hour, another hour. He did not think of death at all now. He wondered what Kitty was doing; who lived in the next room; whether the doctor lived in a house of his own. He longed for food and for sleep. He cautiously drew away his hand and felt the feet. The feet were cold, but the sick man was still breathing. Levin tried again to move away on tiptoe, but the sick man stirred again and said: "Don't go."

* * *

The dawn came; the sick man's condition was unchanged. Levin stealthily withdrew his hand, and without looking at the dying man, went off to his own room and went to sleep. When he woke up, instead of news of his brother's death which he expected, he learned that the sick man had returned to his earlier condition. He had begun sitting up again, coughing, had begun eating again, talking again, and again had ceased to talk of death, again had begun to express hope of his recovery, and had become more irritable and more gloomy than ever. No one, neither his brother nor Kitty, could soothe him. He was angry with everyone, and said nasty things to everyone, reproached everyone for his sufferings, and insisted that they should get him a celebrated doctor from Moscow. To all inquiries made him as to how he felt, he made the same answer with an expression of vindictive reproachfulness, "I'm suffering horribly, intolerably!"

The sick man was suffering more and more, especially from bedsores, which it was impossible now to remedy, and grew more and more angry with everyone about him, blaming them for everything, and especially for not having brought him a doctor from Moscow. Kitty tried in every possible way to relieve him, to soothe him; but it was all in vain, and Levin saw that she herself was exhausted both physically and morally, though she would not admit it. The sense of death, which had been evoked in all by his taking leave of life on the night when he had sent for his brother, was broken up. Everyone knew that he must inevitably die soon, that he was half dead already. Everyone wished for nothing but that he should die as soon as possible, and everyone, concealing this, gave him medicines, tried to find remedies, and doctors, and deceived him and themselves and each other. All this was falsehood, disgusting, irreverent deceit. And owing to the bent of his character, and because he loved the dying man more than anyone else did, Levin was most painfully conscious of this deceit.

Levin, who had long been possessed by the idea of reconciling his brothers, at least in face of death, had written to his brother, Sergey Ivanovitch, and having received an answer from him, he read this letter to the sick man. Sergey Ivanovitch wrote that he could not come himself, and in touching terms he begged his brother's forgiveness.

The sick man said nothing.

"What am I to write to him?" said Levin. "I hope you are not angry with him?"

"No, not the least!" Nikolay answered, vexed at the question. "Tell him to send me a doctor."

Three more days of agony followed; the sick man was still in the same condition. The sense of longing for his death was felt by everyone now at the mere sight of him, by the waiters and the hotel-keeper and all the people staying in the hotel, and the doctor and Marya Nikolaevna and Levin and Kitty. The sick man alone did not express this feeling, but on the contrary was furious at their not getting him doctors, and went on taking medicine and talking of life. Only at rare moments, when the opium gave him an instant's relief from the never-ceasing pain, he would sometimes, half asleep, utter what was ever more intense in his heart than in all the others: "Oh, if it were only the end!" or: "When will it be over?"

His sufferings, steadily growing more intense, did their work and prepared him for death. There was no position in which he was not in pain, there was not a minute in which he was unconscious of it, not a limb, not a part of his body that did not ache and cause him agony. Even the memories, the impressions, the thoughts of this body awakened in him now the same aversion as the body itself. The sight of other people, their remarks, his own reminiscences, everything was for him a source of agony. Those about him felt this, and instinctively did not allow themselves to move freely, to talk, to express their wishes before him. All his life was merged in the one feeling of suffering and desire to be rid of it.

There was evidently coming over him that revulsion that would make him look upon death as the goal of his desires, as happiness. Hitherto each individual desire, aroused by suffering or privation, such as hunger, fatigue, thirst, had been satisfied by some bodily function giving pleasure. But now no physical craving or suffering received relief, and the effort to relieve them only caused fresh suffering. And so all desires were merged in one—the desire to be rid of all his sufferings and their source, the body. But he had no words to express this desire of deliverance, and so he did not speak of it, and from habit asked for the satisfaction of desires which could not now be satisfied. "Turn me over on the other side," he would say, and immediately after he would ask to be turned back again as before. "Give me some broth. Take away the broth. Talk of something: why are you silent?" And directly they began to talk he would close his eyes, and would show weariness, indifference, and loathing.

On the tenth day from their arrival at the town, Kitty was unwell. She suffered from headache and sickness, and she could not get up all the morning.

The doctor opined that the indisposition arose from fatigue and excitement, and prescribed rest.

After dinner, however, Kitty got up and went as usual with her work to the sick man. He looked at her sternly when she came in, and smiled contemptuously when she said she had been unwell. That day he was continually blowing his nose, and groaning piteously.

"How do you feel?" she asked him.

"Worse," he articulated with difficulty. "In pain!"

"In pain, where?"

"Everywhere."

"It will be over today, you will see," said Marya Nikolaevna. Though it was said in a whisper, the sick man, whose hearing Levin had noticed was very keen, must have heard. Levin said hush to her, and looked round at the sick man. Nikolay had heard; but these words produced no effect on him. His eyes had still the same intense, reproachful look.

"Why do you think so?" Levin asked her, when she had followed him into the corridor.

"He has begun picking at himself," said Marya Nikolaevna.

"How do you mean?"

"Like this," she said, tugging at the folds of her woolen skirt. Levin noticed, indeed, that all that day the patient pulled at himself, as it were, trying to snatch something away.

Marya Nikolaevna's prediction came true. Towards night the sick man was not able to lift his hands, and could only gaze before him with the same intensely concentrated expression in his eyes. Even when his brother or Kitty bent over him, so that he could see them, he looked just the same. Kitty sent for the priest to read the prayer for the dying.

While the priest was reading it, the dying man did not show any sign of life; his eyes were closed. Levin, Kitty, and Marya Nikolaevna stood at the bedside. The priest had not quite finished reading the prayer when the dying man stretched, sighed, and opened his eyes. The priest, on finishing the prayer, put the cross to the cold forehead, then slowly returned it to the stand, and after standing for two minutes more in silence, he touched the huge, bloodless hand that was turning cold.

"He is gone," said the priest, and would have moved away; but suddenly there was a faint stir in the mustaches of the dead man that seemed glued together, and quite distinctly in the hush they heard from the bottom of the chest the sharply defined sounds:

"Not quite . . . soon."

And a minute later the face brightened, a smile came out under the mustaches, and the women who had gathered round began carefully laying out the corpse.

The sight of his brother, and the nearness of death, revived in Levin that sense of horror in face of the insoluble enigma, together with the nearness and inevitability of death, that had come upon him that autumn evening when his brother had come to him. This feeling was now even stronger than before; even less than before did he feel capable of apprehending the meaning of death, and its inevitability rose up before him more terrible than ever. But now, thanks to his wife's presence, that feeling did not reduce him to despair. In spite of death, he felt the need of life and love. He felt that love saved him from despair, and that this love, under the menace of despair, had become still stronger and purer. The one mystery of death, still unsolved, had scarcely passed before his eyes, when another mystery had arisen, as insoluble, urging him to love and to life.

The doctor confirmed his suppositions in regard to Kitty. Her indisposition was a symptom that she was with child.

Chapter XXI

FROM THE MOMENT WHEN ALEXEY ALEXANDROVITCH UNDERSTOOD FROM HIS INTERVIEWS WITH Betsy and with Stepan Arkadyevitch that all that was expected of him was to leave his wife in peace, without burdening her with his presence, and that his wife herself desired this, he felt so distraught that he could come to no decision of himself; he did not know himself what he wanted now, and putting himself in the hands of those who were so pleased to interest themselves in his affairs, he met everything with unqualified assent. It was only when Anna had left his house, and the English governess sent to ask him whether she should dine with him or separately, that for the first time he clearly comprehended his position, and was appalled by it. Most difficult of all in this position was the fact that he could not in any way connect and reconcile his past with what was now. It was not the past when he had lived happily with his wife that troubled him. The transition from that past to a knowledge of his wife's unfaithfulness he had lived through miserably already; that state was painful, but he could understand it. If his wife had then, on declaring to him her unfaithfulness, left him, he would have been wounded, unhappy, but he would not have been in the hopeless position—incomprehensible to himself—in which he felt himself now. He could not now reconcile his immediate past, his tenderness, his love for his sick wife, and for the other man's child with what was now the case, that is with the fact that, as it were, in return for all this he now found himself alone, put to shame, a laughing-stock, needed by no one, and despised by everyone.

For the first two days after his wife's departure Alexey Alexandrovitch received applicants for assistance and his chief secretary, drove to the committee, and went down to dinner in the dining room as usual. Without giving himself a reason for what he was doing, he strained every nerve of his being for those two days, simply to preserve an appearance of composure, and even of indifference. Answering inquiries about the disposition of Anna Arkadyevna's rooms and belongings, he had exercised immense self-control to appear like a man in whose eyes what had occurred was not unforeseen nor out of the ordinary course of events, and he attained his aim: no one could have detected in him signs of despair. But on the second day after her departure, when Korney gave him a bill from a fashionable draper's shop, which Anna had forgotten to pay, and announced that the clerk from the shop was waiting, Alexey Alexandrovitch told him to show the clerk up.

"Excuse me, your excellency, for venturing to trouble you. But if you direct us to apply to her excellency, would you graciously oblige us with her address?"

Alexey Alexandrovitch pondered, as it seemed to the clerk, and all at once, turning round, he sat down at the table. Letting his head sink into his hands, he sat for a long while in that position, several times attempted to speak and stopped short. Korney, perceiving his master's emotion, asked the clerk to call another time. Left alone, Alexey Alexandrovitch recognized that he had not the strength to keep up the line of firmness and composure any longer. He gave orders for the carriage that was awaiting him to be taken back, and for no one to be admitted, and he did not go down to dinner.

He felt that he could not endure the weight of universal contempt and exasperation, which he had distinctly seen in the face of the clerk and of Korney, and of everyone, without exception, whom he had met during those two days. He felt that he could not turn aside from himself the hatred of men, because that hatred did not come from his being bad (in that case he could have tried to be better), but from his being shamefully and repulsively unhappy. He knew that for this, for the very fact that his heart was torn with grief, they would be merciless to him. He felt that men would crush him as dogs strangle a torn dog yelping with pain. He knew that his sole means of security against people was to hide his wounds from them, and instinctively he tried to do this for two days, but now he felt incapable of keeping up the unequal struggle.

His despair was even intensified by the consciousness that he was utterly alone in his sorrow. In all Petersburg there was not a human being to whom he could express what he was feeling, who would feel for him, not as a high official, not as a member of society, but simply as a suffering man; indeed he had not such a one in the whole world.

Alexey Alexandrovitch grew up an orphan. There were two brothers. They did not remember their father, and their mother died when Alexey Alexandrovitch was ten years old. The property was a small one. Their uncle, Karenin, a government official of high standing, at one time a favorite of the late Tsar, had brought them up.

On completing his high school and university courses with medals, Alexey Alexandrovitch had, with his uncle's aid, immediately started in a prominent position in the service, and from that time forward he had devoted himself exclusively to political ambition. In the high school and the university, and afterwards in the service, Alexey Alexandrovitch had never formed a close friendship with anyone. His brother had been the person nearest to his heart, but he had a post in the Ministry of Foreign Affairs, and was always abroad, where he had died shortly after Alexey Alexandrovitch's marriage.

While he was governor of a province, Anna's aunt, a wealthy provincial lady, had thrown him—middle-aged as he was, though young for a governor—with her niece, and had succeeded in putting him in such a position that he had either to declare himself or to leave the town. Alexey Alexandrovitch was not long in hesitation. There were at the time as many reasons for the step as against it, and there was no overbalancing consideration to outweigh his invariable rule of abstaining when in doubt. But Anna's aunt had through a common acquaintance insinuated that he had already compromised the girl, and that he was in honor bound to make her an offer. He made the offer, and concentrated on his betrothed and his wife all the feeling of which he was capable.

The attachment he felt to Anna precluded in his heart every need of intimate relations with others. And now among all his acquaintances he had not one friend. He had plenty of so-called connections, but no friendships. Alexey Alexandrovitch had plenty of people whom he could invite to dinner, to whose sympathy he could appeal in any public affair he was concerned about, whose interest he could reckon upon for anyone he wished to help, with whom he could candidly discuss other people's business and affairs of state. But his relations with these people were confined to one clearly defined channel, and had a certain routine from which it was impossible to depart. There was one man, a comrade of his at the university, with whom he had made friends later, and with whom he could have spoken of a personal sorrow; but this friend had a post in the Department of Education in a remote part of Russia. Of the people in Petersburg the most intimate and most possible were his chief secretary and his doctor.

Mihail Vassilievitch Sludin, the chief secretary, was a straightforward, intelligent, goodhearted, and conscientious man, and Alexey Alexandrovitch was aware of his personal goodwill. But their five years of official work together seemed to have put a barrier between them that cut off warmer relations.

After signing the papers brought him, Alexey Alexandrovitch had sat for a long while in silence, glancing at Mihail Vassilievitch, and several times he attempted to speak, but could not. He had already prepared the phrase: "You have heard of my trouble?" But he ended by saying, as usual: "So you'll get this ready for me?" and with that dismissed him.

The other person was the doctor, who had also a kindly feeling for him; but there had long existed a taciturn understanding between them that both were weighed down by work, and always in a hurry.

Of his women-friends, foremost among them Countess Lidia Ivanovna, Alexey Alexandrovitch never thought. All women, simply as women, were terrible and distasteful to him.

Chapter XXII

ALEXEY ALEXANDROVITCH HAD FORGOTTEN THE COUNTESS LIDIA IVANOVNA, BUT SHE HAD NOT forgotten him. At the bitterest moment of his lonely despair she came to him, and without waiting to be announced, walked straight into his study. She found him as he was sitting with his head in both hands.

"J'ai forcé la consigne," she said, walking in with rapid steps and breathing hard with excitement and rapid exercise. "I have heard all! Alexey Alexandrovitch! Dear friend!" she went on, warmly squeezing his hand in both of hers and gazing with her fine pensive eyes into his.

Alexey Alexandrovitch, frowning, got up, and disengaging his hand, moved her a chair.

"Won't you sit down, countess? I'm seeing no one because I'm unwell, countess," he said, and his lips twitched.

"Dear friend!" repeated Countess Lidia Ivanovna, never taking her eyes off his, and suddenly her eyebrows rose at the inner corners, describing a triangle on her forehead, her ugly yellow face became still uglier, but Alexey Alexandrovitch felt that she was sorry for him and was preparing to cry. And he too was softened; he snatched her plump hand and proceeded to kiss it.

"Dear friend!" she said in a voice breaking with emotion. "You ought not to give way to grief. Your sorrow is a great one, but you ought to find consolation."

"I am crushed, I am annihilated, I am no longer a man!" said Alexey Alexandrovitch, letting go her hand, but still gazing into her brimming eyes. "My position is so awful because I can find nowhere, I cannot find within me strength to support me."

"You will find support; seek it—not in me, though I beseech you to believe in my friendship," she said, with a sigh. "Our support is love, that love that He has vouchsafed us. His burden is light," she said, with the look of ecstasy Alexey Alexandrovitch knew so well. "He will be your support and your succor."

Although there was in these words a flavor of that sentimental emotion at her own lofty feelings, and that new mystical fervor which had lately gained ground in Petersburg, and which seemed to Alexey Alexandrovitch disproportionate, still it was pleasant to him to hear this now.

"I am weak. I am crushed. I foresaw nothing, and now I understand nothing."

"Dear friend," repeated Lidia Ivanovna.

"It's not the loss of what I have not now, it's not that!" pursued Alexey Alexandrovitch. "I do not grieve for that. But I cannot help feeling humiliated before other people for the position I am placed in. It is wrong, but I can't help it, I can't help it."

"Not you it was performed that noble act of forgiveness, at which I was moved to ecstasy, and everyone else too, but He, working within your heart," said Countess Lidia Ivanovna, raising her eyes rapturously, "and so you cannot be ashamed of your act."

Alexey Alexandrovitch knitted his brows, and crooking his hands, he cracked his fingers.

"One must know all the facts," he said in his thin voice. "A man's strength has its limits, countess, and I have reached my limits. The whole day I have had to be making arrangements, arrangements about household matters arising" (he emphasized the word *arising*) "from my new, solitary position. The servants, the governess, the accounts. . . . These pinpricks have stabbed me to the heart, and I have not the strength to bear it. At dinner . . . yesterday, I was almost getting up from the dinner-table. I could not bear the way my son looked at me. He did not ask me the meaning of it all, but he wanted to ask, and I could not bear the look in his eyes. He was afraid to look at me, but that is not all. . . ." Alexey Alexandrovitch would have referred to the bill that had been brought him, but his voice shook, and he stopped. That bill on blue paper, for a hat and ribbons, he could not recall without a rush of self-pity.

"I understand, dear friend," said Lidia Ivanovna. "I understand it all. Succor and comfort you will find not in me, though I have come only to aid you if I can. If I could take from off you all these petty, humiliating cares . . . I understand that a woman's word, a woman's superintendence is needed. You will entrust it to me?"

Silently and gratefully Alexey Alexandrovitch pressed her hand.

"Together we will take care of Seryozha. Practical affairs are not my strong point. But I will set to work. I will be your housekeeper. Don't thank me. I do it not from myself . . ."

"I cannot help thanking you."

"But, dear friend, do not give way to the feeling of which you spoke—being ashamed of what is the Christian's highest glory: *he who humbles himself shall be exalted*. And you cannot thank me. You must thank Him, and pray to Him for succor. In Him alone we find peace, consolation, salvation, and love," she said, and turning her eyes heavenwards, she began praying, as Alexey Alexandrovitch gathered from her silence.

Alexey Alexandrovitch listened to her now, and those expressions which had seemed to him, if not distasteful, at least exaggerated, now seemed to him natural and consolatory. Alexey Alexandrovitch had disliked this new enthusiastic fervor. He was a believer, who was interested in religion primarily in its political aspect, and the new doctrine which ventured upon several new interpretations, just because it paved the way to discussion and analysis, was in principle disagreeable to him. He had hitherto taken up a cold and even antagonistic attitude to this new doctrine, and with Countess Lidia Ivanovna, who had been carried away by it, he had never argued, but by silence had assiduously parried her attempts to provoke him into argument. Now for the first time he heard her words with pleasure, and did not inwardly oppose them.

"I am very, very grateful to you, both for your deeds and for your words," he said, when she had finished praying.

Countess Lidia Ivanovna once more pressed both her friend's hands.

"Now I will enter upon my duties," she said with a smile after a pause, as she wiped away the traces of tears. "I am going to Seryozha. Only in the last extremity shall I apply to you." And she got up and went out.

Countess Lidia Ivanovna went into Seryozha's part of the house, and dropping tears on the scared child's cheeks, she told him that his father was a saint and his mother was dead.

Countess Lidia Ivanovna kept her promise. She did actually take upon herself the care of the organization and management of Alexey Alexandrovitch's household. But she had not overstated the case when saying that practical affairs were not her strong point. All her arrangements had to be modified because they could not be carried out, and they were modified by Korney, Alexey Alexandrovitch's valet, who, though no one was aware of the fact, now managed Karenin's household, and quietly and discreetly reported to his master while he was dressing all it was necessary for him to know. But Lidia Ivanovna's help was none the less real; she gave Alexey Alexandrovitch moral support in the consciousness of her love and respect for him, and still more, as it was soothing to her to believe, in that she almost turned him to Christianity—that is, from an indifferent and apathetic believer she turned him into an ardent and steadfast adherent of the new interpretation of Christian doctrine, which had been gaining ground of late in Petersburg. It was easy for Alexey Alexandrovitch to believe in this teaching. Alexey Alexandrovitch, like Lidia Ivanovna indeed, and others who shared their views, was completely devoid of vividness of imagination, that spiritual faculty in virtue of which the conceptions evoked by the imagination become so vivid that they must needs be in harmony with other conceptions, and with actual fact. He saw nothing impossible and inconceivable in the idea that death, though existing for unbelievers, did not exist for him, and that, as he was possessed of the most perfect faith, of the measure of which he was himself the judge, therefore there was no sin in his soul, and he was experiencing complete salvation here on earth.

It is true that the erroneousness and shallowness of this conception of his faith was dimly perceptible to Alexey Alexandrovitch, and he knew that when, without the slightest idea that his forgiveness was the action of a higher power, he had surrendered directly to the feeling of forgiveness, he had felt more happiness than now when he was thinking every instant that Christ was in his heart, and that in signing official papers he was doing His will. But for Alexey Alexandrovitch it was a necessity to think in that way; it was such a necessity for him in his humiliation to have some elevated standpoint, however imaginary, from which, looked down upon by all, he could look down on others, that he clung, as to his one salvation, to his delusion of salvation.

Chapter XXIII

THE COUNTESS LIDIA IVANOVNA HAD, AS A VERY YOUNG AND SENTIMENTAL GIRL, BEEN MARRIED to a wealthy man of high rank, very good-natured, jovial, and extremely dissipated rake. Two months after marriage her husband abandoned her, and her impassioned protestations of affection he met with a sarcasm and even hostility that people knowing the count's good heart, and seeing no defects in the sentimental Lidia, were at a loss to explain. Though they were divorced and lived apart, yet whenever the husband met the wife, he invariably behaved to her with the same malignant irony, the cause of which was incomprehensible.

Countess Lidia Ivanovna had long given up being in love with her husband, but from that time she had never given up being in love with someone. She was in love with several people at once, both men and women; she had been in love with almost everyone who had been particularly distinguished in any way. She was in love with all the new princes and princesses who married into the imperial family; she had been in love with a high dignitary of the Church, a vicar, and a parish priest; she had been in love with a journalist, three Slavophiles, with Komissarov, with a minister, a doctor, an English missionary and Karenin. All these passions constantly waning or growing more ardent, did not prevent her from keeping up the most extended and complicated relations with the court and fashionable society. But from the time that after Karenin's trouble she took him under her special protection, from the time that she set to work in Karenin's household looking after his welfare, she felt that all her other attachments were not the real thing, and that she was now genuinely in love, and with no one but Karenin. The feeling she now experienced for him seemed to her stronger than any of her former feelings. Analyzing her feeling, and comparing it with former passions, she distinctly perceived that she would not have been in love with Komissarov if he had not saved the life of the Tsar, that she would not have been in love with Ristitch-Kudzhitsky if there had been no Slavonic question, but that she loved Karenin for himself, for his lofty, uncomprehended soul, for the sweet—to her—high notes of his voice, for his drawling intonation, his weary eyes, his character, and his soft white hands with their swollen veins. She was not simply overjoyed at meeting him, but she sought in his face signs of the impression she was making on him. She tried to please him, not by her words only, but in her whole person. For his sake it was that she now lavished more care on her dress than before. She caught herself in reveries on what might have been, if she had not been married and he had been free. She blushed with emotion when he came into the room, she could not repress a smile of rapture when he said anything amiable to her.

For several days now Countess Lidia Ivanovna had been in a state of intense excitement. She had learned that Anna and Vronsky were in Petersburg. Alexey Alexandrovitch must be saved from seeing her, he must be saved even from the torturing knowledge that that awful woman was in the same town with him, and that he might meet her any minute.

Lidia Ivanovna made inquiries through her friends as to what those *infamous people,* as she called Anna and Vronsky, intended doing, and she endeavored so to guide every movement of her friend during those days that he could not come across them. The young adjutant, an acquaintance of Vronsky, through whom she obtained her information, and who hoped through Countess Lidia Ivanovna to obtain a concession, told her that they had finished their business and were going away next day. Lidia Ivanovna had already begun to calm down, when the next morning a note was brought her, the handwriting of which she recognized with horror. It was the handwriting of Anna Karenina. The envelope was of paper as thick as bark; on the oblong yellow paper there was a huge monogram, and the letter smelled of agreeable scent.

"Who brought it?"

"A commissionaire from the hotel."

It was some time before Countess Lidia Ivanovna could sit down to read the letter. Her excitement brought on an attack of asthma, to which she was subject. When she had recovered her composure, she read the following letter in French:

MADAME LA COMTESSE—The Christian feelings with which your heart is filled give me the, I feel, unpardonable boldness to write to you. I am miserable at being separated from my son. I entreat permission to see him once before my departure. Forgive me for recalling myself to your memory. I apply to you and not to Alexey Alexandrovitch, simply because I do not wish to cause that generous man to suffer in remembering me. Knowing your friendship for him, I know you will understand me. Could you send Seryozha to me, or should I come to the house at some fixed hour, or will you let me know when and where I could see him away from home? I do not anticipate a refusal, knowing the magnanimity of him with whom it rests. You cannot conceive the craving I have to see him, and so cannot conceive the gratitude your help will arouse in me.

ANNA

Everything in this letter exasperated Countess Lidia Ivanovna: its contents and the allusion to magnanimity, and especially its free and easy—as she considered—tone.

"Say that there is no answer," said Countess Lidia Ivanovna, and immediately opening her blotting-book, she wrote to Alexey Alexandrovitch that she hoped to see him at one o'clock at the levee.

"I must talk with you of a grave and painful subject. There we will arrange where to meet. Best of all at my house, where I will order tea *as you like it.* Urgent. He lays the cross, but He gives the strength to bear it," she added, so as to give him some slight preparation. Countess Lidia Ivanovna usually wrote some two or three letters a day to Alexey Alexandrovitch. She enjoyed that form of communication, which gave opportunity for a refinement and air of mystery not afforded by their personal interviews.

Chapter XXIV

THE LEVEE WAS DRAWING TO A CLOSE. PEOPLE MET AS THEY WERE GOING AWAY, AND GOSSIPED of the latest news, of the newly bestowed honors and the changes in the positions of the higher functionaries.

"If only Countess Marya Borissovna were Minister of War, and Princess Vatkovskaya were Commander-in-Chief," said a gray-headed, little old man in a gold-embroidered uniform, addressing a tall, handsome maid of honor who had questioned him about the new appointments.

"And me among the adjutants," said the maid of honor, smiling.

"You have an appointment already. You're over the ecclesiastical department. And your assistant's Karenina."

"Good day, prince!" said the little old man to a man who came up to him.

"What were you saying of Karenin?" said the prince.

"He and Putyatov have received the Alexander Nevsky."

"I thought he had it already."

"No. Just look at him," said the little old man, pointing with his embroidered hat to Karenin in a court uniform with the new red ribbon across his shoulders, standing in the doorway of the hall with an influential member of the Imperial Council. "Pleased and happy as a brass farthing," he added, stopping to shake hands with a handsome gentleman of the bedchamber of colossal proportions.

"No; he's looking older," said the gentleman of the bedchamber.

"From overwork. He's always drawing up projects nowadays. He won't let a poor devil go nowadays till he's explained it all to him under heads."

"Looking older, did you say? *Il fait des passions.* I believe Countess Lidia Ivanovna's jealous now of his wife."

"Oh, come now, please don't say any harm of Countess Lidia Ivanovna."

"Why, is there any harm in her being in love with Karenin?"

"But is it true Madame Karenina's here?"

"Well, not here in the palace, but in Petersburg. I met her yesterday with Alexey Vronsky, *bras dessus, bras dessous,* in the Morsky."

"C'est un homme qui n'a pas, . . ." the gentleman of the bedchamber was beginning, but he stopped to make room, bowing, for a member of the Imperial family to pass.

Thus people talked incessantly of Alexey Alexandrovitch, finding fault with him and laughing at him, while he, blocking up the way of the member of the Imperial Council he had captured, was explaining to him point by point his new financial project, never interrupting his discourse for an instant for fear he should escape.

Almost at the same time that his wife left Alexey Alexandrovitch there had come to him that bitterest moment in the life of an official—the moment when his upward career comes to a full stop. This full stop had arrived and everyone perceived it, but Alexey Alexandrovitch himself was not yet aware that his career was over. Whether it was due to his feud with Stremov, or his misfortune with his wife, or simply that Alexey Alexandrovitch had reached his destined limits, it had become evident to everyone in the course of that year that his career was at an end. He still filled a position of consequence, he sat on many commissions and committees, but he was a man whose day was over, and from whom nothing was expected. Whatever he said, whatever he proposed, was heard as though it were something long familiar, and the very thing that was not needed. But Alexey Alexandrovitch was not aware of this, and, on the contrary, being cut off from direct participation in governmental activity, he saw more clearly than ever the errors and defects in the action of others, and thought it his duty to point out means for their correction. Shortly after his separation from his wife, he began writing his first note on the new judicial procedure, the first of the endless series of notes he was destined to write in the future.

Alexey Alexandrovitch did not merely fail to observe his hopeless position in the official world, he was not merely free from anxiety on this head, he was positively more satisfied than ever with his own activity.

"He that is unmarried careth for the things that belong to the Lord, how he may please the Lord: But he that is married careth for the things that are of the world, how he may please his wife," says the Apostle Paul, and Alexey Alexandrovitch, who was now guided in every action by Scripture, often recalled this text. It seemed to him that ever since he had been left without a wife, he had in these very projects of reform been serving the Lord more zealously than before.

The unmistakable impatience of the member of the Council trying to get away from him did not trouble Alexey Alexandrovitch; he gave up his exposition only when the member of the Council, seizing his chance when one of the Imperial family was passing, slipped away from him.

Left alone, Alexey Alexandrovitch looked down, collecting his thoughts, then looked casually about him and walked towards the door, where he hoped to meet Countess Lidia Ivanovna.

"And how strong they all are, how sound physically," thought Alexey Alexandrovitch, looking at the powerfully built gentleman of the bedchamber with his well-combed, perfumed whiskers, and at the red neck of the prince, pinched by his tight uniform. He had to pass them on his way. "Truly is it said that all the world is evil," he thought, with another sidelong glance at the calves of the gentleman of the bedchamber.

Moving forward deliberately, Alexey Alexandrovitch bowed with his customary air of weariness and dignity to the gentleman who had been talking about him, and looking towards the door, his eyes sought Countess Lidia Ivanovna.

"Ah! Alexey Alexandrovitch!" said the little old man, with a malicious light in his eyes, at the moment when Karenin was on a level with them, and was nodding with a frigid gesture, "I haven't congratulated you yet," said the old man, pointing to his newly received ribbon.

"Thank you," answered Alexey Alexandrovitch. "What an *exquisite* day to day," he added, laying emphasis in his peculiar way on the word *exquisite.*

That they laughed at him he was well aware, but he did not expect anything but hostility from them; he was used to that by now.

Catching sight of the yellow shoulders of Lidia Ivanovna jutting out above her corset, and her fine pensive eyes bidding him to her, Alexey Alexandrovitch smiled, revealing untarnished white teeth, and went towards her.

Lidia Ivanovna's dress had cost her great pains, as indeed all her dresses had done of late. Her aim in dress was now quite the reverse of that she had pursued thirty years before. Then her desire had been to adorn herself with something, and the more adorned the better. Now, on the contrary, she was perforce decked out in a way so inconsistent with her age and her figure, that her one anxiety was to contrive that the contrast between these adornments and her own exterior should not be too appalling. And as far as Alexey Alexandrovitch was concerned she succeeded, and was in his eyes attractive. For him she was the one island not only of goodwill to him, but of love in the midst of the sea of hostility and jeering that surrounded him.

Passing through rows of ironical eyes, he was drawn as naturally to her loving glance as a plant to the sun.

"I congratulate you," she said to him, her eyes on his ribbon.

Suppressing a smile of pleasure, he shrugged his shoulders, closing his eyes, as though to say that that could not be a source of joy to him. Countess Lidia Ivanovna was very well aware that it was one of his chief sources of satisfaction, though he never admitted it.

"How is our angel?" said Countess Lidia Ivanovna, meaning Seryozha.

"I can't say I was quite pleased with him," said Alexey Alexandrovitch, raising his eyebrows and opening his eyes. "And Sitnikov is not satisfied with him." (Sitnikov was the tutor to whom Seryozha's secular education had been entrusted.) "As I have mentioned to you, there's a sort of coldness in him towards the most important questions which ought to touch the heart of every man and every child. . . ." Alexey Alexandrovitch began expounding his views on the sole question that interested him besides the service—the education of his son.

When Alexey Alexandrovitch with Lidia Ivanovna's help had been brought back anew to life and activity, he felt it his duty to undertake the education of the son left on his hands. Having never before taken any interest in educational questions, Alexey Alexandrovitch devoted some time to the theoretical study of the subject. After reading several books on anthropology, education, and didactics, Alexey Alexandrovitch drew up a plan of education, and engaging the best tutor in Petersburg to superintend it, he set to work, and the subject continually absorbed him.

"Yes, but the heart. I see in him his father's heart, and with such a heart a child cannot go far wrong," said Lidia Ivanovna with enthusiasm.

"Yes, perhaps . . . As for me, I do my duty. It's all I can do."

"You're coming to me," said Countess Lidia Ivanovna, after a pause; "we have to speak of a subject painful for you. I would give anything to have spared you certain memories, but others are not of the same mind. I have received a letter from *her. She* is here in Petersburg."

Alexey Alexandrovitch shuddered at the allusion to his wife, but immediately his face assumed the deathlike rigidity which expressed utter helplessness in the matter.

"I was expecting it," he said.

Countess Lidia Ivanovna looked at him ecstatically, and tears of rapture at the greatness of his soul came into her eyes.

Chapter XXV

When Alexey Alexandrovitch came into the Countess Lidia Ivanovna's snug little boudoir, decorated with old china and hung with portraits, the lady herself had not yet made her appearance.

She was changing her dress.

A cloth was laid on a round table, and on it stood a china tea service and a silver spirit-lamp and tea kettle. Alexey Alexandrovitch looked idly about at the endless familiar portraits which adorned the room, and sitting down to the table, he opened a New Testament lying upon it. The rustle of the countess's silk skirt drew his attention off.

"Well now, we can sit quietly," said Countess Lidia Ivanovna, slipping hurriedly with an agitated smile between the table and the sofa, "and talk over our tea."

After some words of preparation, Countess Lidia Ivanovna, breathing hard and flushing crimson, gave into Alexey Alexandrovitch's hands the letter she had received.

After reading the letter, he sat a long while in silence.

"I don't think I have the right to refuse her," he said, timidly lifting his eyes.

"Dear friend, you never see evil in anyone!"

"On the contrary, I see that all is evil. But whether it is just . . ."

His face showed irresolution, and a seeking for counsel, support, and guidance in a matter he did not understand.

"No," Countess Lidia Ivanovna interrupted him; "there are limits to everything. I can understand immorality," she said, not quite truthfully, since she never could understand that which leads women to immorality; "but I don't understand cruelty: to whom? to you! How can she stay in the town where you are? No, the longer one lives the more one learns. And I'm learning to understand your loftiness and her baseness."

"Who is to throw a stone?" said Alexey Alexandrovitch, unmistakably pleased with the part he had to play. "I have forgiven all, and so I cannot deprive her of what is exacted by love in her—by her love for her son . . ."

"But is that love, my friend? Is it sincere? Admitting that you have forgiven—that you forgive—have we the right to work on the feelings of that angel? He looks on her as dead. He prays for her, and beseeches God to have mercy on her sins. And it is better so. But now what will he think?"

"I had not thought of that," said Alexey Alexandrovitch, evidently agreeing.

Countess Lidia Ivanovna hid her face in her hands and was silent. She was praying.

"If you ask my advice," she said, having finished her prayer and uncovered her face, "I do not advise you to do this. Do you suppose I don't see how you are suffering, how this has torn open your wounds? But supposing that, as always, you don't think of yourself, what can it lead to?—to fresh suffering for you, to torture for the child. If there were a trace of humanity left in her, she ought not to wish for it herself. No, I have no hesitation in saying I advise not, and if you will entrust it to me, I will write to her."

And Alexey Alexandrovitch consented, and Countess Lidia Ivanovna sent the following letter in French:

DEAR MADAME—To be reminded of you might have results for your son in leading to questions on his part which could not be answered without implanting in the child's soul a spirit of censure towards what should be for him sacred, and therefore I beg you to interpret your husband's refusal in the spirit of Christian love. I pray to Almighty God to have mercy on you.

COUNTESS LIDIA

This letter attained the secret object which Countess Lidia Ivanovna had concealed from herself. It wounded Anna to the quick.

For his part, Alexey Alexandrovitch, on returning home from Lidia Ivanovna's, could not all that day concentrate himself on his usual pursuits, and find that spiritual peace of one saved and believing which he had felt of late.

The thought of his wife, who had so greatly sinned against him, and towards whom he had been so saintly, as Countess Lidia Ivanovna had so justly told him, ought not to have troubled him; but he was not easy; he could not understand the book he was reading; he could not drive away harassing recollections of his relations with her, of the mistake which, as it now seemed, he had made in regard to her. The memory of how he had received her confession of infidelity on their way home from the races (especially that he had insisted only on the observance of external decorum, and had not sent a challenge) tortured him like a remorse. He was tortured too by the thought of the letter he had written her; and most of all, his forgiveness, which nobody wanted, and his care of the other man's child made his heart burn with shame and remorse.

And just the same feeling of shame and regret he felt now, as he reviewed all his past with her, recalling the awkward words in which, after long wavering, he had made her an offer.

"But how have I been to blame?" he said to himself. And this question always excited another question in him—whether they felt differently, did their loving and marrying differently, these Vronskys and Oblonskys . . . these gentlemen of the bedchamber, with their fine calves. And there passed before his mind a whole series of these mettlesome, vigorous, self-confident men, who always and everywhere drew his inquisitive attention in spite of himself. He tried to dispel these thoughts, he tried to persuade himself that he was not living for this transient life, but for the life of eternity, and that there was peace and love in his heart.

But the fact that he had in this transient, trivial life made, as it seemed to him, a few trivial mistakes tortured him as though the eternal salvation in which he believed had no existence. But this temptation did not last long, and soon there was re-established once more in Alexey Alexandrovitch's soul the peace and the elevation by virtue of which he could forget what he did not want to remember.

Chapter XXVI

WELL, KAPITONITCH? SAID SERYOZHA, COMING BACK ROSY AND GOOD-HUMORED FROM HIS walk the day before his birthday, and giving his overcoat to the tall old hall-porter, who smiled down at the little person from the height of his long figure. "Well, has the bandaged clerk been here today? Did papa see him?"

"He saw him. The minute the chief secretary came out, I announced him," said the hall-porter with a good-humored wink. "Here, I'll take it off."

"Seryozha!" said the tutor, stopping in the doorway leading to the inner rooms. "Take it off yourself." But Seryozha, though he heard his tutor's feeble voice, did not pay attention to it. He stood keeping hold of the hall-porter's belt, and gazing into his face.

"Well, and did papa do what he wanted for him?"

The hall-porter nodded his head affirmatively. The clerk with his face tied up, who had already been seven times to ask some favor of Alexey Alexandrovitch, interested both Seryozha and the hall-porter. Seryozha had come upon him in the hall, and had heard him plaintively beg the hall-porter to announce him, saying that he and his children had death staring them in the face.

Since then Seryozha, having met him a second time in the hall, took great interest in him.

"Well, was he very glad?" he asked.

"Glad? I should think so! Almost dancing as he walked away."

"And has anything been left?" asked Seryozha, after a pause.

"Come, sir," said the hall-porter; then with a shake of his head he whispered, "Something from the countess."

Seryozha understood at once that what the hall-porter was speaking of was a present from Countess Lidia Ivanovna for his birthday.

"What do you say? Where?"

"Korney took it to your papa. A fine plaything it must be too!"

"How big? Like this?"

"Rather small, but a fine thing."

"A book."

"No, a thing. Run along, run along, Vassily Lukitch is calling you," said the porter, hearing the tutor's steps approaching, and carefully taking away from his belt the little hand in the glove half pulled off, he signed with his head towards the tutor.

"Vassily Lukitch, in a tiny minute!" answered Seryozha with that gay and loving smile which always won over the conscientious Vassily Lukitch.

Seryozha was too happy, everything was too delightful for him to be able to help sharing with his friend the porter the family good fortune of which he had heard during his walk in the public gardens from Lidia Ivanovna's niece. This piece of good news seemed to him particularly important from its coming at the same time with the gladness of the bandaged clerk and his own gladness at toys having come for him. It seemed to Seryozha that this was a day on which everyone ought to be glad and happy.

"You know papa's received the Alexander Nevsky today?"

"To be sure I do! People have been already to congratulate him."

"And is he glad?"

"Glad at the Tsar's gracious favor! I should think so! It's a proof he's deserved it," said the porter severely and seriously.

Seryozha fell to dreaming, gazing up at the face of the porter, which he had thoroughly studied in every detail, especially the chin that hung down between the gray whiskers, never seen by anyone but Seryozha, who saw him only from below.

"Well, and has your daughter been to see you lately?"

The porter's daughter was a ballet dancer.

"When is she to come on weekdays? They've their lessons to learn too. And you've your lesson, sir; run along."

On coming into the room, Seryozha, instead of sitting down to his lessons, told his tutor of his supposition that what had been brought him must be a machine. "What do you think?" he inquired.

But Vassily Lukitch was thinking of nothing but the necessity of learning the grammar lesson for the teacher, who was coming at two.

"No, do just tell me, Vassily Lukitch," he asked suddenly, when he was seated at their worktable with the book in his hands, "what is greater than the Alexander Nevsky? You know papa's received the Alexander Nevsky?"

Vassily Lukitch replied that the Vladimir was greater than the Alexander Nevsky.

"And higher still?"

"Well, highest of all is the Andrey Pervozvanny."

"And higher than the Andrey?"

"I don't know."

"What, you don't know?" and Seryozha, leaning on his elbows, sank into deep meditation.

His meditations were of the most complex and diverse character. He imagined his father's having suddenly been presented with both the Vladimir and the Andrey today, and in consequence being much better tempered at his lesson, and dreamed how, when he was grown-up, he would himself receive all the orders, and what they might invent higher than the Andrey. Directly any higher order were invented, he would win it. They would make a higher one still, and he would immediately win that too.

The time passed in such meditations, and when the teacher came, the lesson about the adverbs of place and time and manner of action was not ready, and the teacher was not only displeased, but hurt. This touched Seryozha. He felt he was not to blame for not having learned the lesson; however much he tried, he was utterly unable to do that. As long as the teacher was explaining to him, he believed him and seemed to comprehend, but as soon as he was left alone, he was positively unable to recollect and to understand that the short and familiar word "suddenly" is an adverb of manner of action. Still he was sorry that he had disappointed the teacher.

He chose a moment when the teacher was looking in silence at the book.

"Mihail Ivanitch, when is your birthday?" he asked all, of a sudden.

"You'd much better be thinking about your work. Birthdays are of no importance to a rational being. It's a day like any other on which one has to do one's work."

Seryozha looked intently at the teacher, at his scanty beard, at his spectacles, which had slipped down below the ridge on his nose, and fell into so deep a reverie that he heard nothing of what the teacher was explaining to him. He knew that the teacher did not think what he said, he felt it from the tone in which it was said. "But why have they all agreed to speak just in the same manner always the dreariest and most useless stuff? Why does he keep me off; why doesn't he love me?" he asked himself mournfully, and could not think of an answer.

Chapter XXVII

AFTER THE LESSON WITH THE GRAMMAR TEACHER CAME HIS FATHER'S LESSON. WHILE WAITING for his father, Seryozha sat at the table playing with a penknife, and fell to dreaming. Among Seryozha's favorite occupations was searching for his mother during his walks. He did not believe in death generally, and in her death in particular, in spite of what Lidia Ivanovna had told him and his father had confirmed, and it was just because of that, and after he had been told she was dead, that he had begun looking for her when out for a walk. Every woman of full, graceful figure with dark hair was his mother. At the sight of such a woman such a feeling of tenderness was stirred within him that his breath failed him, and tears came into his eyes. And he was on the tiptoe of expectation that she would come up to him, would lift her veil. All her face would be visible, she would smile, she would hug him, he would sniff her fragrance, feel the softness of her arms, and cry with happiness, just as he had one evening lain on her lap while she tickled him, and he laughed and bit her white, ring-covered fingers. Later, when he accidentally learned from his old nurse that his mother was not dead, and his father and Lidia Ivanovna had explained to him that she was dead to him because she was wicked (which he could not possibly believe, because he loved her), he went on seeking her and expecting her in the same way. That day in the public gardens there had been a lady in a lilac veil, whom he had watched with a throbbing heart, believing it to be she as she came towards them along the path. The lady had not come up to them, but had disappeared somewhere. That day, more intensely than ever, Seryozha felt a rush of love for her, and now, waiting for his father, he forgot everything, and cut all round the edge of the table with his penknife, staring straight before him with sparkling eyes and dreaming of her.

"Here is your papa!" said Vassily Lukitch, rousing him.

Seryozha jumped up and went up to his father, and kissing his hand, looked at him intently, trying to discover signs of his joy at receiving the Alexander Nevsky.

"Did you have a nice walk?" said Alexey Alexandrovitch, sitting down in his easy chair, pulling the volume of the Old Testament to him and opening it. Although Alexey Alexandrovitch had more than once told Seryozha that every Christian ought to know Scripture history thoroughly, he often referred to the Bible himself during the lesson, and Seryozha observed this.

"Yes, it was very nice indeed, papa," said Seryozha, sitting sideways on his chair and rocking it, which was forbidden. "I saw Nadinka" (Nadinka was a niece of Lidia Ivanovna's who was being brought up in her house). "She told me you'd been given a new star. Are you glad, papa?"

"First of all, don't rock your chair, please," said Alexey Alexandrovitch. "And secondly, it's not the reward that's precious, but the work itself. And I could have wished you understood that. If you now are going to work, to study in order to win a reward, then the work will seem hard to you; but when you work" (Alexey Alexandrovitch, as he spoke, thought of how he had been sustained by a sense of duty through the wearisome labor of the morning, consisting of signing one hundred and eighty papers), "loving your work, you will find your reward in it."

Seryozha's eyes, that had been shining with gaiety and tenderness, grew dull and dropped before his father's gaze. This was the same long-familiar tone his father always took with him, and Seryozha had learned by now to fall in with it. His father always talked to him—so Seryozha felt—as though he were addressing some boy of his own imagination, one of those boys that exist in books, utterly unlike himself. And Seryozha always tried with his father to act being the storybook boy.

"You understand that, I hope?" said his father.

"Yes, papa," answered Seryozha, acting the part of the imaginary boy.

The lesson consisted of learning by heart several verses out of the Gospel and the repetition of the beginning of the Old Testament. The verses from the Gospel Seryozha knew fairly well, but at the moment when he was saying them he became so absorbed in watching the sharply protruding, bony knobbiness of his father's forehead, that he lost the thread, and he transposed the end of one verse and the beginning of another. So it was evident to Alexey Alexandrovitch that he did not understand what he was saying, and that irritated him.

He frowned, and began explaining what Seryozha had heard many times before and never could remember, because he understood it too well, just as that "suddenly" is an adverb of manner of action. Seryozha looked with scared eyes at his father, and could think of nothing but whether his father would make him repeat what he had said, as he sometimes did. And this thought so alarmed Seryozha that he now understood nothing. But his father did not make him repeat it, and passed on to the lesson out of the Old Testament. Seryozha recounted the events themselves well enough, but when he had to answer questions as to what certain events prefigured, he knew nothing, though he had already been punished over this lesson. The passage at which he was utterly unable to say anything, and began fidgeting and cutting the table and swinging his chair, was where he had to repeat the patriarchs before the Flood. He did not know one of them, except Enoch, who had been taken up alive to heaven. Last time he had remembered their names, but now he had forgotten them utterly, chiefly because Enoch was the personage he liked best in the whole of the Old Testament, and Enoch's translation to heaven was connected in his mind with a whole long train of thought, in which he became absorbed now while he gazed with fascinated eyes at his father's watch-chain and a half-unbuttoned button on his waistcoat.

In death, of which they talked to him so often, Seryozha disbelieved entirely. He did not believe that those he loved could die, above all that he himself would die. That was to him something utterly inconceivable and impossible. But he had been told that all men die; he had asked people, indeed, whom he trusted, and they too, had confirmed it; his old nurse, too, said the same, though reluctantly. But Enoch had not died, and so it followed that everyone did not die. "And why cannot anyone else so serve God and be taken alive to heaven?" thought Seryozha. Bad people, that is those Seryozha did not like, they might die, but the good might all be like Enoch.

"Well, what are the names of the patriarchs?"

"Enoch, Enos—"

"But you have said that already. This is bad, Seryozha, very bad. If you don't try to learn what is more necessary than anything for a Christian," said his father, getting up, "whatever can interest you? I am displeased with you, and Piotr Ignatitch" (this was the most important of his teachers) "is displeased with you. . . . I shall have to punish you."

His father and his teacher were both displeased with Seryozha, and he certainly did learn his lessons very badly. But still it could not be said he was a stupid boy. On the contrary, he was far cleverer than the boys his teacher held up as examples to Seryozha. In his father's opinion, he did not want to learn what he was taught. In reality he could not learn that. He could not, because the claims of his own soul were more binding on him than those claims his father and his teacher made upon him. Those claims were in opposition, and he was in direct conflict with his education. He was nine years old; he was a child; but he knew his own soul, it was precious to him, he guarded it as the eyelid guards the eye, and without the key of love he let no one into his soul. His teachers complained that he would not learn, while his soul was brimming over with thirst for knowledge. And he learned from Kapitonitch, from his nurse, from Nadinka, from Vassily Lukitch, but not from his teachers. The spring his father and his teachers reckoned upon to turn their mill-wheels had long dried up at the source, but its waters did their work in another channel.

His father punished Seryozha by not letting him go to see Nadinka, Lidia Ivanovna's niece; but this punishment turned out happily for Seryozha. Vassily Lukitch was in a good-humor, and showed him how to make windmills. The whole evening passed over this work and in dreaming how to make a windmill on which he could turn himself—clutching at the sails or tying himself on and whirling round. Of his mother Seryozha did not think all the evening, but when he had gone to bed, he suddenly remembered her, and prayed in his own words that his mother tomorrow for his birthday might leave off hiding herself and come to him.

"Vassily Lukitch, do you know what I prayed for tonight extra besides the regular things?"

"That you might learn your lessons better?"

"No."

"Toys?"

"No. You'll never guess. A splendid thing; but it's a secret! When it comes to pass I'll tell you. Can't you guess!"

"No, I can't guess. You tell me," said Vassily Lukitch with a smile, which was rare with him. "Come, lie down, I'm putting out the candle."

"Without the candle I can see better what I see and what I prayed for. There! I was almost telling the secret!" said Seryozha, laughing gaily.

When the candle was taken away, Seryozha heard and felt his mother. She stood over him, and with loving eyes caressed him. But then came windmills, a knife, everything began to be mixed up, and he fell asleep.

Chapter XXVIII

On arriving in Petersburg, Vronsky and Anna stayed at one of the best hotels; Vronsky apart in a lower story, Anna above with her child, its nurse, and her maid, in a large suite of four rooms.

On the day of his arrival Vronsky went to his brother's. There he found his mother, who had come from Moscow on business. His mother and sister-in-law greeted him as usual: they asked him about his stay abroad, and talked of their common acquaintances, but did not let drop a single word in allusion to his connection with Anna. His brother came the next morning to see Vronsky, and of his own accord asked him about her, and Alexey Vronsky told him directly that he looked upon his connection with Madame Karenina as marriage; that he hoped to arrange a divorce, and then to marry her, and until then he considered her as much a wife as any other wife, and he begged him to tell their mother and his wife so.

"If the world disapproves, I don't care," said Vronsky; "but if my relations want to be on terms of relationship with me, they will have to be on the same terms with my wife."

The elder brother, who had always a respect for his younger brother's judgment, could not well tell whether he was right or not till the world had decided the question; for his part he had nothing against it, and with Alexey he went up to see Anna.

Before his brother, as before everyone, Vronsky addressed Anna with a certain formality, treating her as he might a very intimate friend, but it was understood that his brother knew their real relations, and they talked about Anna's going to Vronsky's estate.

In spite of all his social experience Vronsky was, in consequence of the new position in which he was placed, laboring under a strange misapprehension. One would have thought he must have understood that society was closed for him and Anna; but now some vague ideas had sprung up in his brain that this was only the case in old-fashioned days, and that now with the rapidity of modern progress (he had unconsciously become by now a partisan of every sort of progress) the views of society had changed, and that the question whether they would be received in society was not a foregone conclusion. "Of course," he thought, "she would not be received at court, but intimate friends can and must look at it in the proper light." One may sit for several hours at a stretch with one's legs crossed in the same position, if one knows that there's nothing to prevent one's changing one's position; but if a man knows that he must remain sitting so with crossed legs, then cramps come on, the legs begin to twitch and to strain towards the spot to which one would like to draw them. This was what Vronsky was experiencing in regard to the world. Though at the bottom of his heart he knew that the world was shut on them, he put it to the test whether the world had not changed by now and would not receive them. But he very quickly perceived that though the world was open for him personally, it was closed for Anna. Just as in the game of cat and mouse, the hands raised for him were dropped to bar the way for Anna.

One of the first ladies of Petersburg society whom Vronsky saw was his cousin Betsy.

"At last!" she greeted him joyfully. "And Anna? How glad I am! Where are you stopping? I can fancy after your delightful travels you must find our poor Petersburg horrid. I can fancy your honeymoon in Rome. How about the divorce? Is that all over?"

Vronsky noticed that Betsy's enthusiasm waned when she learned that no divorce had as yet taken place.

"People will throw stones at me, I know," she said, "but I shall come and see Anna; yes, I shall certainly come. You won't be here long, I suppose?"

And she did certainly come to see Anna the same day, but her tone was not at all the same as in former days. She unmistakably prided herself on her courage, and wished Anna to appreciate the fidelity of her friendship. She only stayed ten minutes, talking of society gossip, and on leaving she said:

"You've never told me when the divorce is to be? Supposing I'm ready to fling my cap over the mill, other starchy people will give you the cold shoulder until you're married. And that's so simple nowadays. *Ça se fait*. So you're going on Friday? Sorry we shan't see each other again."

From Betsy's tone Vronsky might have grasped what he had to expect from the world; but he made another effort in his own family. His mother he did not reckon upon. He knew that his mother, who had been so enthusiastic over Anna at their first acquaintance, would have no mercy on her now for having ruined her son's career. But he had more hope of Varya, his brother's wife. He fancied she would not throw stones, and would go simply and directly to see Anna, and would receive her in her own house.

The day after his arrival Vronsky went to her, and finding her alone, expressed his wishes directly.

"You know, Alexey," she said after hearing him, "how fond I am of you, and how ready I am to do anything for you; but I have not spoken, because I knew I could be of no use to you and to Anna Arkadyevna," she said, articulating the name "Anna Arkadyevna" with particular care. "Don't suppose, please, that I judge her. Never; perhaps in her place I should have done the same. I don't and can't enter into that," she said, glancing timidly at his gloomy face. "But one must call things by their names. You want me to go and see her, to ask her here, and to rehabilitate her in society; but do understand that I *cannot* do so. I have daughters growing up, and I must live in the world for my husband's sake. Well, I'm ready to come and see Anna Arkadyevna: she will understand that I can't ask her here, or I should have to do so in such a way that she would not meet people who look at things differently; that would offend her. I can't raise her . . ."

"Oh, I don't regard her as fallen more than hundreds of women you do receive!" Vronsky interrupted her still more gloomily, and he got up in silence, understanding that his sister-in-law's decision was not to be shaken.

"Alexey! don't be angry with me. Please understand that I'm not to blame," began Varya, looking at him with a timid smile.

"I'm not angry with you," he said still as gloomily; "but I'm sorry in two ways. I'm sorry, too, that this means breaking up our friendship—if not breaking up, at least weakening it. You will understand that for me, too, it cannot be otherwise."

And with that he left her.

Vronsky knew that further efforts were useless, and that he had to spend these few days in Petersburg as though in a strange town, avoiding every sort of relation with his own old circle in order not to be exposed to the annoyances and humiliations which were so intolerable to him. One of the most unpleasant features of his position in Petersburg was that Alexey Alexandrovitch and his name seemed to meet him everywhere. He could not begin to talk of anything without the conversation turning on Alexey Alexandrovitch, he could not go anywhere without risk of meeting him. So at least it seemed to Vronsky, just as it seems to a man with a sore finger that he is continually, as though on purpose, grazing his sore finger on everything.

Their stay in Petersburg was the more painful to Vronsky that he perceived all the time a sort of new mood that he could not understand in Anna. At one time she would seem in love with him, and then she would become cold, irritable, and impenetrable. She was worrying over something, and keeping something back from him, and did not seem to notice the humiliations which poisoned his existence, and for her, with her delicate intuition, must have been still more unbearable.

Chapter XXIX

ONE OF ANNA'S OBJECTS IN COMING BACK TO RUSSIA HAD BEEN TO SEE HER SON. FROM THE DAY she left Italy the thought of it had never ceased to agitate her. And as she got nearer to Petersburg, the delight and importance of this meeting grew ever greater in her imagination. She did not even put to herself the question how to arrange it. It seemed to her natural and simple to see her son when she should be in the same town with him. But on her arrival in Petersburg she was suddenly made distinctly aware of her present position in society, and she grasped the fact that to arrange this meeting was no easy matter.

She had now been two days in Petersburg. The thought of her son never left her for a single instant, but she had not yet seen him. To go straight to the house, where she might meet Alexey Alexandrovitch, that she felt she had no right to do. She might be refused admittance and insulted. To write and so enter into relations with her husband—that it made her miserable to think of doing; she could only be at peace when she did not think of her husband. To get a glimpse of her son out walking, finding out where and when he went out, was not enough for her; she had so looked forward to this meeting, she had so much she must say to him, she so longed to embrace him, to kiss him. Seryozha's old nurse might be a help to her and show her what to do. But the nurse was not now living in Alexey Alexandrovitch's house. In this uncertainty, and in efforts to find the nurse, two days had slipped by.

Hearing of the close intimacy between Alexey Alexandrovitch and Countess Lidia Ivanovna, Anna decided on the third day to write to her a letter, which cost her great pains, and in which she intentionally said that permission to see her son must depend on her husband's generosity. She knew that if the letter were shown to her husband, he would keep up his character of magnanimity, and would not refuse her request.

The commissionaire who took the letter had brought her back the most cruel and unexpected answer, that there was no answer. She had never felt so humiliated as at the moment when, sending for the commissionaire, she heard from him the exact account of how he had waited, and how afterwards he had been told there was no answer. Anna felt humiliated, insulted, but she saw that from her point of view Countess Lidia Ivanovna was right. Her suffering was the more poignant that she had to bear it in solitude. She could not and would not share it with Vronsky. She knew that to him, although he was the primary cause of her distress, the question of her seeing her son would seem a matter of very little consequence. She knew that he would never be capable of understanding all the depth of her suffering, that for his cool tone at any allusion to it she would begin to hate him. And she dreaded that more than anything in the world, and so she hid from him everything that related to her son. Spending the whole day at home she considered ways of seeing her son, and had reached a decision to write to her husband. She was just composing this letter when she was handed the letter from Lidia Ivanovna. The countess's silence had subdued and depressed her, but the letter, all that she read between the lines in it, so exasperated her, this malice was so revolting beside her passionate, legitimate tenderness for her son, that she turned against other people and left off blaming herself.

"This coldness—this pretense of feeling!" she said to herself. "They must needs insult me and torture the child, and I am to submit to it! Not on any consideration! She is worse than I am. I don't lie, anyway." And she decided on the spot that next day, Seryozha's birthday, she would go straight to her husband's house, bribe or deceive the servants, but at any cost see her son and overturn the hideous deception with which they were encompassing the unhappy child.

She went to a toy shop, bought toys and thought over a plan of action. She would go early in the morning at eight o'clock, when Alexey Alexandrovitch would be certain not to be up. She would have money in her hand to give the hall-porter and the footman, so that they should let her in, and not raising her veil, she would say that she had come from Seryozha's godfather to congratulate him, and that she had been charged to leave the toys at his bedside. She had prepared everything but the words she should say to her son. Often as she had dreamed of it, she could never think of anything.

The next day, at eight o'clock in the morning, Anna got out of a hired sleigh and rang at the front entrance of her former home.

"Run and see what's wanted. Some lady," said Kapitonitch, who, not yet dressed, in his overcoat and galoshes, had peeped out of the window and seen a lady in a veil standing close up to the door. His assistant, a lad Anna did not know, had no sooner opened the door to her than she came in, and pulling a three-ruble note out of her muff put it hurriedly into his hand.

"Seryozha—Sergey Alexeitch," she said, and was going on. Scrutinizing the note, the porter's assistant stopped her at the second glass door.

"Whom do you want?" he asked.

She did not hear his words and made no answer.

Noticing the embarrassment of the unknown lady, Kapitonitch went out to her, opened the second door for her, and asked her what she was pleased to want.

"From Prince Skorodumov for Sergey Alexeitch," she said.

"His honor's not up yet," said the porter, looking at her attentively.

Anna had not anticipated that the absolutely unchanged hall of the house where she had lived for nine years would so greatly affect her. Memories sweet and painful rose one after another in her heart, and for a moment she forgot what she was here for.

"Would you kindly wait?" said Kapitonitch, taking off her fur cloak.

As he took off the cloak, Kapitonitch glanced at her face, recognized her, and made her a low bow in silence.

"Please walk in, your excellency," he said to her.

She tried to say something, but her voice refused to utter any sound; with a guilty and imploring glance at the old man she went with light, swift steps up the stairs. Bent double, and his galoshes catching in the steps, Kapitonitch ran after her, trying to overtake her.

"The tutor's there; maybe he's not dressed. I'll let him know."

Anna still mounted the familiar staircase, not understanding what the old man was saying.

"This way, to the left, if you please. Excuse its not being tidy. His honor's in the old parlor now," the hall-porter said, panting. "Excuse me, wait a little, your excellency; I'll just see," he said, and overtaking her, he opened the high door and disappeared behind it. Anna stood still waiting. "He's only just awake," said the hall-porter, coming out. And at the very instant the porter said this, Anna caught the sound of a childish yawn. From the sound of this yawn alone she knew her son and seemed to see him living before her eyes.

"Let me in; go away!" she said, and went in through the high doorway. On the right of the door stood a bed, and sitting up in the bed was the boy. His little body bent forward with his nightshirt unbuttoned, he was stretching and still yawning. The instant his lips came together they curved into a blissfully sleepy smile, and with that smile he slowly and deliciously rolled back again.

"Seryozha!" she whispered, going noiselessly up to him.

When she was parted from him, and all this latter time when she had been feeling a fresh rush of love for him, she had pictured him as he was at four years old, when she had loved him most of all. Now he was not even the same as when she had left him; he was still further from the four-year-old baby, more grown and thinner. How thin his face was, how short his hair was! What long hands! How he had changed since she left him! But it was he with his head, his lips, his soft neck and broad little shoulders.

"Seryozha!" she repeated just in the child's ear.

He raised himself again on his elbow, turned his tangled head from side to side as though looking for something, and opened his eyes. Slowly and inquiringly he looked for several seconds at his mother standing motionless before him, then all at once he smiled a blissful smile, and shutting his eyes, rolled not backwards but towards her into her arms.

"Seryozha! my darling boy!" she said, breathing hard and putting her arms round his plump little body. "Mother!" he said, wriggling about in her arms so as to touch her hands with different parts of him.

Smiling sleepily still with closed eyes, he flung fat little arms round her shoulders, rolled towards her, with the delicious sleepy warmth and fragrance that is only found in children, and began rubbing his face against her neck and shoulders.

"I know," he said, opening his eyes; "it's my birthday today. I knew you'd come. I'll get up directly."

And saying that he dropped asleep.

Anna looked at him hungrily; she saw how he had grown and changed in her absence. She knew, and did not know, the bare legs so long now, that were thrust out below the quilt, those short-cropped curls on his neck in which she had so often kissed him. She touched all this and could say nothing; tears choked her.

"What are you crying for, mother?" he said, waking completely up. "Mother, what are you crying for?" he cried in a tearful voice.

"I won't cry . . . I'm crying for joy. It's so long since I've seen you. I won't, I won't," she said, gulping down her tears and turning away. "Come, it's time for you to dress now," she added, after a pause, and, never letting go his hands, she sat down by his bedside on the chair, where his clothes were put ready for him.

"How do you dress without me? How . . ." she tried to begin talking simply and cheerfully, but she could not, and again she turned away.

"I don't have a cold bath, papa didn't order it. And you've not seen Vassily Lukitch? He'll come in soon. Why, you're sitting on my clothes!"

And Seryozha went off into a peal of laughter. She looked at him and smiled.

"Mother, darling, sweet one!" he shouted, flinging himself on her again and hugging her. It was as though only now, on seeing her smile, he fully grasped what had happened.

"I don't want that on," he said, taking off her hat. And as it were, seeing her afresh without her hat, he fell to kissing her again.

"But what did you think about me? You didn't think I was dead?"

"I never believed it."

"You didn't believe it, my sweet?"

"I knew, I knew!" he repeated his favorite phrase, and snatching the hand that was stroking his hair, he pressed the open palm to his mouth and kissed it.

Chapter XXX

MEANWHILE VASSILY LUKITCH HAD NOT AT FIRST UNDERSTOOD WHO THIS LADY WAS, AND HAD learned from their conversation that it was no other person than the mother who had left her husband, and whom he had not seen, as he had entered the house after her departure. He was in doubt whether to go in or not, or whether to communicate with Alexey Alexandrovitch. Reflecting finally that his duty was to get Seryozha up at the hour fixed, and that it was therefore not his business to consider who was there, the mother or anyone else, but simply to do his duty, he finished dressing, went to the door and opened it.

But the embraces of the mother and child, the sound of their voices, and what they were saying, made him change his mind.

He shook his head, and with a sigh he closed the door. "I'll wait another ten minutes," he said to himself, clearing his throat and wiping away tears.

Among the servants of the household there was intense excitement all this time. All had heard that their mistress had come, and that Kapitonitch had let her in, and that she was even now in the nursery, and that their master always went in person to the nursery at nine o'clock, and everyone fully comprehended that it was impossible for the husband and wife to meet, and that they must prevent it. Korney, the valet, going down to the hall-porter's room, asked who had let her in, and how it was he had done so, and ascertaining that Kapitonitch had admitted her and shown her up, he gave the old man a talking-to. The hall-porter was doggedly silent, but when Korney told him he ought to be sent away, Kapitonitch darted up to him, and waving his hands in Korney's face, began:

"Oh yes, to be sure you'd not have let her in! After ten years' service, and never a word but of kindness, and there you'd up and say, 'Be off, go along, get away with you!' Oh yes, you're a shrewd one at politics, I dare say! You don't need to be taught how to swindle the master, and to filch fur coats!"

"Soldier!" said Korney contemptuously, and he turned to the nurse who was coming in. "Here, what do you think, Marya Efimovna: he let her in without a word to anyone," Korney said addressing her. "Alexey Alexandrovitch will be down immediately—and go into the nursery!"

"A pretty business, a pretty business!" said the nurse. "You, Korney Vassilievitch, you'd best keep him some way or other, the master, while I'll run and get her away somehow. A pretty business!"

When the nurse went into the nursery, Seryozha was telling his mother how he and Nadinka had had a fall in sledging downhill, and had turned over three times. She was listening to the sound of his voice, watching his face and the play of expression on it, touching his hand, but she did not follow what he was saying. She must go, she must leave him—this was the only thing she was thinking and feeling. She heard the steps of Vassily Lukitch coming up to the door and coughing; she heard, too, the steps of the nurse as she came near; but she sat like one turned to stone, incapable of beginning to speak or to get up.

"Mistress, darling!" began the nurse, going up to Anna and kissing her hands and shoulders. "God has brought joy indeed to our boy on his birthday. You aren't changed one bit."

"Oh, nurse dear, I didn't know you were in the house," said Anna, rousing herself for a moment.

"I'm not living here, I'm living with my daughter. I came for the birthday, Anna Arkadyevna, darling!"

The nurse suddenly burst into tears, and began kissing her hand again.

Seryozha, with radiant eyes and smiles, holding his mother by one hand and his nurse by the other, pattered on the rug with his fat little bare feet. The tenderness shown by his beloved nurse to his mother threw him into an ecstasy.

"Mother! She often comes to see me, and when she comes . . ." he was beginning, but he stopped, noticing that the nurse was saying something in a whisper to his mother, and that in his mother's face there was a look of dread and something like shame, which was so strangely unbecoming to her.

She went up to him.

"My sweet!" she said.

She could not say *good-bye,* but the expression on her face said it, and he understood. "Darling, darling Kootik!" she used the name by which she had called him when he was little, "you won't forget me? You . . ." but she could not say more.

How often afterwards she thought of words she might have said. But now she did not know how to say it, and could say nothing. But Seryozha knew all she wanted to say to him. He understood that she was unhappy and loved him. He understood even what the nurse had whispered. He had caught the words "always at nine o'clock," and he knew that this was said of his father, and that his father and mother could not meet. That he understood, but one thing he could not understand—why there should be a look of dread and shame in her face? . . . She was not in fault, but she was afraid of him and ashamed of something. He would have liked to put a question that would have set at rest this doubt, but he did not dare; he saw that she was miserable, and he felt for her. Silently he pressed close to her and whispered, "Don't go yet. He won't come just yet."

The mother held him away from her to see what he was thinking, what to say to him, and in his frightened face she read not only that he was speaking of his father, but, as it were, asking her what he ought to think about his father.

"Seryozha, my darling," she said, "love him; he's better and kinder than I am, and I have done him wrong. When you grow up you will judge."

"There's no one better than you! . . ." he cried in despair through his tears, and, clutching her by the shoulders, he began squeezing her with all his force to him, his arms trembling with the strain.

"My sweet, my little one!" said Anna, and she cried as weakly and childishly as he.

At that moment the door opened. Vassily Lukitch came in.

At the other door there was the sound of steps, and the nurse in a scared whisper said, "He's coming," and gave Anna her hat.

Seryozha sank onto the bed and sobbed, hiding his face in his hands. Anna removed his hands, once more kissed his wet face, and with rapid steps went to the door. Alexey Alexandrovitch walked in, meeting her. Seeing her, he stopped short and bowed his head.

Although she had just said he was better and kinder than she, in the rapid glance she flung at him, taking in his whole figure in all its details, feelings of repulsion and hatred for him and jealousy over her son took possession of her. With a swift gesture she put down her veil, and, quickening her pace, almost ran out of the room.

She had not time to undo, and so carried back with her, the parcel of toys she had chosen the day before in a toy shop with such love and sorrow.

Chapter XXXI

Intensely as Anna had longed to see her son, and long as she had been thinking of it and preparing herself for it, she had not in the least expected that seeing him would affect her so deeply. On getting back to her lonely rooms in the hotel she could not for a long while understand why she was there. "Yes, it's all over, and I am again alone," she said to herself, and without taking off her hat she sat down in a low chair by the hearth. Fixing her eyes on a bronze clock standing on a table between the windows, she tried to think.

The French maid brought from abroad came in to suggest she should dress. She gazed at her wonderingly and said, "Presently." A footman offered her coffee. "Later on," she said.

The Italian nurse, after taking the baby out in her best, came in with her, and brought her to Anna. The plump, well-fed little baby, on seeing her mother, as she always did, held out her fat little hands, and with a smile on her toothless mouth, began, like a fish with a float, bobbing her fingers up and down the starched folds of her embroidered skirt, making them rustle. It was impossible not to smile, not to kiss the baby, impossible not to hold out a finger for her to clutch, crowing and prancing all over; impossible not to offer her a lip which she sucked into her little mouth by way of a kiss. And all this Anna did, and took her in her arms and made her dance, and kissed her fresh little cheek and bare little elbows; but at the sight of this child it was plainer than ever to her that the feeling she had for her could not be called love in comparison with what she felt for Seryozha. Everything in this baby was charming, but for some reason all this did not go deep to her heart. On her first child, though the child of an unloved father, had been concentrated all the love that had never found satisfaction. Her baby girl had been born in the most painful circumstances and had not had a hundredth part of the care and thought which had been concentrated on her first child. Besides, in the little girl everything was still in the future, while Seryozha was by now almost a personality, and a personality dearly loved. In him there was a conflict of thought and feeling; he understood her, he loved her, he judged her, she thought, recalling his words and his eyes. And she was forever—not physically only but spiritually—divided from him, and it was impossible to set this right.

She gave the baby back to the nurse, let her go, and opened the locket in which there was Seryozha's portrait when he was almost of the same age as the girl. She got up, and, taking off her hat, took up from a little table an album in which there were photographs of her son at different ages. She wanted to compare them, and began taking them out of the album. She took them all out except one, the latest and best photograph. In it he was in a white smock, sitting astride a chair, with frowning eyes and smiling lips. It was his best, most characteristic expression. With her little supple hands, her white, delicate fingers, that moved with a peculiar intensity today, she pulled at a corner of the photograph, but the photograph had caught somewhere, and she could not get it out. There was no paper-knife on the table, and so, pulling out the photograph that was next to her son's (it was a photograph of Vronsky taken at Rome in a round hat and with long hair), she used it to push out her son's photograph. "Oh, here is he!" she said, glancing at the portrait of Vronsky, and she suddenly recalled that he was the cause of her present misery. She had not once thought of him all the morning. But now, coming all at once upon that manly, noble face, so familiar and so dear to her, she felt a sudden rush of love for him.

"But where is he? How is it he leaves me alone in my misery?" she thought all at once with a feeling of reproach, forgetting she had herself kept from him everything concerning her son. She sent to ask him to come to her immediately; with a throbbing heart she awaited him, rehearsing to herself the words in which she would tell him all, and the expressions of love with which he would console her. The messenger returned with the answer that he had a visitor with him, but that he would come immediately, and that he asked whether she would let him bring with him Prince Yashvin, who had just arrived in Petersburg. "He's not coming alone, and since dinner yesterday he has not seen me," she thought; "he's not coming so that I could tell him everything, but coming with Yashvin." And all at once a strange idea came to her: what if he had ceased to love her?

And going over the events of the last few days, it seemed to her that she saw in everything a confirmation of this terrible idea. The fact that he had not dined at home yesterday, and the fact that he had insisted on their taking separate sets of rooms in Petersburg, and that even now he was not coming to her alone, as though he were trying to avoid meeting her face to face.

"But he ought to tell me so. I must know that it is so. If I knew it, then I know what I should do," she said to herself, utterly unable to picture to herself the position she would be in if she were convinced of his not caring for her. She thought he had ceased to love her, she felt close upon despair, and consequently she felt exceptionally alert. She rang for her maid and went to her dressing room. As she dressed, she took more care over her appearance than she had done all those days, as though he might, if he had grown cold to her, fall in love with her again because she had dressed and arranged her hair in the way most becoming to her.

She heard the bell ring before she was ready. When she went into the drawing room it was not he, but Yashvin, who met her eyes. Vronsky was looking through the photographs of her son, which she had forgotten on the table, and he made no haste to look round at her.

"We have met already," she said, putting her little hand into the huge hand of Yashvin, whose bashfulness was so queerly out of keeping with his immense frame and coarse face. "We met last year at the races. Give them to me," she said, with a rapid movement snatching from Vronsky the photographs of her son, and glancing significantly at him with flashing eyes. "Were the races good this year? Instead of them I saw the races in the Corso in Rome. But you don't care for life abroad," she said with a cordial smile. "I know you and all your tastes, though I have seen so little of you."

"I'm awfully sorry for that, for my tastes are mostly bad," said Yashvin, gnawing at his left mustache.

Having talked a little while, and noticing that Vronsky glanced at the clock, Yashvin asked her whether she would be staying much longer in Petersburg, and unbending his huge figure reached after his cap.

"Not long, I think," she said hesitatingly, glancing at Vronsky.

"So then we shan't meet again?"

"Come and dine with me," said Anna resolutely, angry it seemed with herself for her embarrassment, but flushing as she always did when she defined her position before a fresh person. "The dinner here is not good, but at least you will see him. There is no one of his old friends in the regiment Alexey cares for as he does for you."

"Delighted," said Yashvin with a smile, from which Vronsky could see that he liked Anna very much.

Yashvin said good-bye and went away; Vronsky stayed behind.

"Are you going too?" she said to him.

"I'm late already," he answered. "Run along! I'll catch you up in a moment," he called to Yashvin.

She took him by the hand, and without taking her eyes off him, gazed at him while she ransacked her mind for the words to say that would keep him.

"Wait a minute, there's something I want to say to you," and taking his broad hand she pressed it on her neck. "Oh, was it right my asking him to dinner?"

"You did quite right," he said with a serene smile that showed his even teeth, and he kissed her hand.

"Alexey, you have not changed to me?" she said, pressing his hand in both of hers. "Alexey, I am miserable here. When are we going away?"

"Soon, soon. You wouldn't believe how disagreeable our way of living here is to me too," he said, and he drew away his hand.

"Well, go, go!" she said in a tone of offense, and she walked quickly away from him.

Chapter XXXII

WHEN VRONSKY RETURNED HOME, ANNA WAS NOT YET HOME. SOON AFTER HE HAD LEFT, SOME lady, so they told him, had come to see her, and she had gone out with her. That she had gone out without leaving word where she was going, that she had not yet come back, and that all the morning she had been going about somewhere without a word to him—all this, together with the strange look of excitement in her face in the morning, and the recollection of the hostile tone with which she had before Yashvin almost snatched her son's photographs out of his hands, made him serious. He decided he absolutely must speak openly with her. And he waited for her in her drawing room. But Anna did not return alone, but brought with her old unmarried aunt, Princess Oblonskaya. This was the lady who had come in the morning, and with whom Anna had gone out shopping. Anna appeared not to notice Vronsky's worried and inquiring expression, and began a lively account of her morning's shopping. He saw that there was something working within her; in her flashing eyes, when they rested for a moment on him, there was an intense concentration, and in her words and movements there was that nervous rapidity and grace which, during the early period of their intimacy, had so fascinated him, but which now so disturbed and alarmed him.

The dinner was laid for four. All were gathered together and about to go into the little dining room when Tushkevitch made his appearance with a message from Princess Betsy. Princess Betsy begged her to excuse her not having come to say good-bye; she had been indisposed, but begged Anna to come to her between half-past six and nine o'clock. Vronsky glanced at Anna at the precise limit of time, so suggestive of steps having been taken that she should meet no one; but Anna appeared not to notice it.

"Very sorry that I can't come just between half-past six and nine," she said with a faint smile.

"The princess will be very sorry."

"And so am I."

"You're going, no doubt, to hear Patti?" said Tushkevitch.

"Patti? You suggest the idea to me. I would go if it were possible to get a box."

"I can get one," Tushkevitch offered his services.

"I should be very, very grateful to you," said Anna. "But won't you dine with us?"

Vronsky gave a hardly perceptible shrug. He was at a complete loss to understand what Anna was about. What had she brought the old Princess Oblonskaya home for, what had she made Tushkevitch stay to dinner for, and, most amazing of all, why was she sending him for a box? Could she possibly think in her position of going to Patti's benefit, where all the circle of her acquaintances would be? He looked at her with serious eyes, but she responded with that defiant, half-mirthful, half-desperate look, the meaning of which he could not comprehend. At dinner Anna was in aggressively high spirits—she almost flirted both with Tushkevitch and with Yashvin. When they got up from dinner and Tushkevitch had gone to get a box at the opera, Yashvin went to smoke, and Vronsky went down with him to his own rooms. After sitting there for some time he ran upstairs. Anna was already dressed in a low-necked gown of light silk and velvet that she had had made in Paris, and with costly white lace on her head, framing her face, and particularly becoming, showing up her dazzling beauty.

"Are you really going to the theater?" he said, trying not to look at her.

"Why do you ask with such alarm?" she said, wounded again at his not looking at her. "Why shouldn't I go?"

She appeared not to understand the motive of his words.

"Oh, of course, there's no reason whatever," he said, frowning.

"That's just what I say," she said, willfully refusing to see the irony of his tone, and quietly turning back her long, perfumed glove.

"Anna, for God's sake! what is the matter with you?" he said, appealing to her exactly as once her husband had done.

"I don't understand what you are asking."

"You know that it's out of the question to go."

"Why so? I'm not going alone. Princess Varvara has gone to dress, she is going with me."

He shrugged his shoulders with an air of perplexity and despair.

"But do you mean to say you don't know? . . ." he began.

"But I don't care to know!" she almost shrieked. "I don't care to. Do I regret what I have done? No, no, no! If it were all to do again from the beginning, it would be the same. For us, for you and for me, there is only one thing that matters, whether we love each other. Other people we need not consider. Why are we living here apart and not seeing each other? Why can't I go? I love you, and I don't care for anything," she said in Russian, glancing at him with a peculiar gleam in her eyes that he could not understand. "If you have not changed to me, why don't you look at me?"

He looked at her. He saw all the beauty of her face and full dress, always so becoming to her. But now her beauty and elegance were just what irritated him.

"My feeling cannot change, you know, but I beg you, I entreat you," he said again in French, with a note of tender supplication in his voice, but with coldness in his eyes.

She did not hear his words, but she saw the coldness of his eyes, and answered with irritation: "And I beg you to explain why I should not go."

"Because it might cause you . . ." He hesitated.

"I don't understand. Yashvin *n'est pas compromettant,* and Princess Varvara is no worse than others. Oh, here she is!"

Chapter XXXIII

VRONSKY FOR THE FIRST TIME EXPERIENCED A FEELING OF ANGER AGAINST ANNA, ALMOST A HAtred for her willfully refusing to understand her own position. This feeling was aggravated by his being unable to tell her plainly the cause of his anger. If he had told her directly what he was thinking, he would have said:

"In that dress, with a princess only too well-known to everyone, to show yourself at the theater is equivalent not merely to acknowledging your position as a fallen woman, but is flinging down a challenge to society, that is to say, cutting yourself off from it forever."

He could not say that to her. "But how can she fail to see it, and what is going on in her?" he said to himself. He felt at the same time that his respect for her was diminished while his sense of her beauty was intensified.

He went back scowling to his rooms, and sitting down beside Yashvin, who, with his long legs stretched out on a chair, was drinking brandy and seltzer water, he ordered a glass of the same for himself.

"You were talking of Lankovsky's Powerful. That's a fine horse, and I would advise you to buy him," said Yashvin, glancing at his comrade's gloomy face. "His hind-quarters aren't quite first rate, but the legs and head—one couldn't wish for anything better."

"I think I will take him," answered Vronsky.

Their conversation about horses interested him, but he did not for an instant forget Anna, and could not help listening to the sound of steps in the corridor and looking at the clock on the chimney piece.

"Anna Arkadyevna gave orders to announce that she has gone to the theater."

Yashvin, tipping another glass of brandy into the bubbling water, drank it and got up, buttoning his coat.

"Well, let's go," he said, faintly smiling under his mustache, and showing by this smile that he knew the cause of Vronsky's gloominess, and did not attach any significance to it.

"I'm not going," Vronsky answered gloomily.

"Well, I must, I promised to. Good-bye, then. If you do, come to the stalls; you can take Kruzin's stall," added Yashvin as he went out.

"No, I'm busy."

"A wife is a care, but it's worse when she's not a wife," thought Yashvin, as he walked out of the hotel.

Vronsky, left alone, got up from his chair and began pacing up and down the room.

"And what's today? The fourth night. . . . Yegor and his wife are there, and my mother, most likely. Of course all Petersburg's there. Now she's gone in, taken off her cloak and come into the light. Tushkevitch, Yashvin, Princess Varvara," he pictured them to himself. . . . "What about me? Either that I'm frightened or have given up to Tushkevitch the right to protect her? From every point of view—stupid, stupid! . . . And why is she putting me in such a position?" he said with a gesture of despair.

With that gesture he knocked against the table, on which there was standing the seltzer water and the decanter of brandy, and almost upset it. He tried to catch it, let it slip, and angrily kicked the table over and rang.

"If you care to be in my service," he said to the valet who came in, "you had better remember your duties. This shouldn't be here. You ought to have cleared away."

The valet, conscious of his own innocence, would have defended himself, but glancing at his master, he saw from his face that the only thing to do was to be silent, and hurriedly threading his way in and out, dropped down on the carpet and began gathering up the whole and broken glasses and bottles.

"That's not your duty; send the waiter to clear away, and get my dress-coat out."

Vronsky went into the theater at half-past eight. The performance was in full swing. The little old box-keeper, recognizing Vronsky as he helped him off with his fur coat, called him "Your Excellency," and suggested he should not take a number but should simply call Fyodor. In the brightly lit corridor there was no one but the box-opener and two attendants with fur cloaks on their arms listening at the doors. Through the closed doors came the sounds of the discreet *staccato* accompaniment of the orchestra, and a single female voice rendering distinctly a musical phrase. The door opened to let the box-opener slip through, and the phrase drawing to the end reached Vronsky's hearing clearly. But the doors were closed again at once, and Vronsky did not hear the end of the phrase and the cadence of the accompaniment, though he knew from the thunder of applause that it was over. When he entered the hall, brilliantly lit with chandeliers and gas jets, the noise was still going on. On the stage the singer, bowing and smiling, with bare shoulders flashing with diamonds, was, with the help of the tenor who had given her his arm, gathering up the bouquets that were flying awkwardly over the footlights. Then she went up to a gentleman with glossy pomaded hair parted down the center, who was stretching across the footlights holding out something to her, and all the public in the stalls as well as in the boxes was in excitement, craning forward, shouting and clapping. The conductor in his high chair assisted in passing the offering, and straightened his white tie. Vronsky walked into the middle of the stalls, and, standing still, began looking about him. That day less than ever was his attention turned upon the familiar, habitual surroundings, the stage, the noise, all the familiar, uninteresting, particolored herd of spectators in the packed theater.

There were, as always, the same ladies of some sort with officers of some sort in the back of the boxes; the same gaily dressed women—God knows who—and uniforms and black coats; the same dirty crowd in the upper gallery; and among the crowd, in the boxes and in the front rows, were some forty of the *real* people. And to those oases Vronsky at once directed his attention, and with them he entered at once into relation.

The act was over when he went in, and so he did not go straight to his brother's box, but going up to the first row of stalls stopped at the footlights with Serpuhovskoy, who, standing with one knee raised and his heel on the footlights, caught sight of him in the distance and beckoned to him, smiling.

Vronsky had not yet seen Anna. He purposely avoided looking in her direction. But he knew by the direction of people's eyes where she was. He looked round discreetly, but he was not seeking her; expecting the worst, his eyes sought for Alexey Alexandrovitch. To his relief Alexey Alexandrovitch was not in the theater that evening.

"How little of the military man there is left in you!" Serpuhovskoy was saying to him. "A diplomat, an artist, something of that sort, one would say."

"Yes, it was like going back home when I put on a black coat," answered Vronsky, smiling and slowly taking out his opera glass.

"Well, I'll own I envy you there. When I come back from abroad and put on this," he touched his epaulets, "I regret my freedom."

Serpuhovskoy had long given up all hope of Vronsky's career, but he liked him as before, and was now particularly cordial to him.

"What a pity you were not in time for the first act!"

Vronsky, listening with one ear, moved his opera glass from the stalls and scanned the boxes. Near a lady in a turban and a bald old man, who seemed to wave angrily in the moving opera glass, Vronsky suddenly caught sight of Anna's head, proud, strikingly beautiful, and smiling in the frame of lace. She was in the fifth box, twenty paces from him. She was sitting in front, and slightly turning, was saying something to Yashvin. The setting of her head on her handsome, broad shoulders, and the restrained excitement and brilliance of her eyes and her whole face reminded him of her just as he had seen her at the ball in Moscow. But he felt utterly different towards her beauty now. In his feeling for her now there was no element of mystery, and so her beauty, though it attracted him even more intensely than before, gave him now a sense of injury. She was not looking in his direction, but Vronsky felt that she had seen him already.

When Vronsky turned the opera glass again in that direction, he noticed that Princess Varvara was particularly red, and kept laughing unnaturally and looking round at the next box. Anna, folding her fan and tapping it on the red velvet, was gazing away and did not see, and obviously did not wish to see, what was taking place in the next box. Yashvin's face wore the expression which was common when he was losing at cards. Scowling, he sucked the left end of his mustache further and further into his mouth, and cast sidelong glances at the next box.

In that box on the left were the Kartasovs. Vronsky knew them, and knew that Anna was acquainted with them. Madame Kartasova, a thin little woman, was standing up in her box, and, her back turned upon Anna, she was putting on a mantle that her husband was holding for her. Her face was pale and angry, and she was talking excitedly. Kartasov, a fat, bald man, was continually looking round at Anna, while he attempted to soothe his wife. When the wife had gone out, the husband lingered a long while, and tried to catch Anna's eye, obviously anxious to bow to her. But Anna, with unmistakable intention, avoided noticing him, and talked to Yashvin, whose cropped head was bent down to her. Kartasov went out without making his salutation, and the box was left empty.

Vronsky could not understand exactly what had passed between the Kartasovs and Anna, but he saw that something humiliating for Anna had happened. He knew this both from what he had seen, and most of all from the face of Anna, who, he could see, was taxing every nerve to carry through the part she had taken up. And in maintaining this attitude of external composure she was completely successful. Anyone who did not know her and her circle, who had not heard all the utterances of the women expressive of commiseration, indignation, and amazement, that she should show herself in society, and show herself so conspicuously with her lace and her beauty, would have admired the serenity and loveliness of this woman without a suspicion that she was undergoing the sensations of a man in the stocks.

Knowing that something had happened, but not knowing precisely what, Vronsky felt a thrill of agonizing anxiety, and hoping to find out something, he went towards his brother's box. Purposely choosing the way round furthest from Anna's box, he jostled as he came out against the colonel of his old regiment talking to two acquaintances. Vronsky heard the name of Madame Karenina, and noticed how the colonel hastened to address Vronsky loudly by name, with a meaning glance at his companions.

"Ah, Vronsky! When are you coming to the regiment? We can't let you off without a supper. You're one of the old set," said the colonel of his regiment.

"I can't stop, awfully sorry, another time," said Vronsky, and he ran upstairs towards his brother's box.

The old countess, Vronsky's mother, with her steel-gray curls, was in his brother's box. Varya with the young Princess Sorokina met him in the corridor.

Leaving the Princess Sorokina with her mother, Varya held out her hand to her brother-in-law, and began immediately to speak of what interested him. She was more excited than he had ever seen her.

"I think it's mean and hateful, and Madame Kartasova had no right to do it. Madame Karenina . . ." she began.

"But what is it? I don't know."

"What? you've not heard?"

"You know I should be the last person to hear of it."

"There isn't a more spiteful creature than that Madame Kartasova!"

"But what did she do?"

"My husband told me. . . . She has insulted Madame Karenina. Her husband began talking to her across the box, and Madame Kartasova made a scene. She said something aloud, he says, something insulting, and went away."

"Count, your maman is asking for you," said the young Princess Sorokina, peeping out of the door of the box.

"I've been expecting you all the while," said his mother, smiling sarcastically. "You were nowhere to be seen."

Her son saw that she could not suppress a smile of delight.

"Good evening, maman. I have come to you," he said coldly.

"Why aren't you going to *faire la cour à Madame Karenina?*" she went on, when Princess Sorokina had moved away. *"Elle fait sensation. On oublie la Patti pour elle."*

"Maman, I have asked you not to say anything to me of that," he answered, scowling.

"I'm only saying what everyone's saying."

Vronsky made no reply, and saying a few words to Princess Sorokina, he went away. At the door he met his brother.

"Ah, Alexey!" said his brother. "How disgusting! Idiot of a woman, nothing else. . . . I wanted to go straight to her. Let's go together."

Vronsky did not hear him. With rapid steps he went downstairs; he felt that he must do something, but he did not know what. Anger with her for having put herself and him in such a false position, together with pity for her suffering, filled his heart. He went down, and made straight for Anna's box. At her box stood Stremov, talking to her.

"There are no more tenors. *Le moule en est brisé!*"

Vronsky bowed to her and stopped to greet Stremov.

"You came in late, I think, and have missed the best song," Anna said to Vronsky, glancing ironically, he thought, at him.

"I am a poor judge of music," he said, looking sternly at her.

"Like Prince Yashvin," she said smiling, "who considers that Patti sings too loud."

"Thank you," she said, her little hand in its long glove taking the playbill Vronsky picked up, and suddenly at that instant her lovely face quivered. She got up and went into the interior of the box.

Noticing in the next act that her box was empty, Vronsky, rousing indignant "hushes" in the silent audience, went out in the middle of a solo and drove home.

Anna was already at home. When Vronsky went up to her, she was in the same dress as she had worn at the theater. She was sitting in the first arm-chair against the wall, looking straight before her. She looked at him, and at once resumed her former position.

"Anna," he said.

"You, you are to blame for everything!" she cried, with tears of despair and hatred in her voice, getting up.

"I begged, I implored you not to go, I knew it would be unpleasant . . ."

"Unpleasant!" she cried—"hideous! As long as I live I shall never forget it. She said it was a disgrace to sit beside me."

"A silly woman's chatter," he said: "but why risk it, why provoke? . . ."

"I hate your calm. You ought not to have brought me to this. If you had loved me . . ."

"Anna! How does the question of my love come in?"

"Oh, if you loved me, as I love, if you were tortured as I am! . . ." she said, looking at him with an expression of terror.

He was sorry for her, and angry notwithstanding. He assured her of his love because he saw that this was the only means of soothing her, and he did not reproach her in words, but in his heart he reproached her.

And the asseverations of his love, which seemed to him so vulgar that he was ashamed to utter them, she drank in eagerly, and gradually became calmer. The next day, completely reconciled, they left for the country.

Part Six

Chapter I

DARYA ALEXANDROVNA SPENT THE SUMMER WITH HER CHILDREN AT POKROVSKOE, AT HER sister Kitty Levin's. The house on her own estate was quite in ruins, and Levin and his wife had persuaded her to spend the summer with them. Stepan Arkadyevitch greatly approved of the arrangement. He said he was very sorry his official duties prevented him from spending the summer in the country with his family, which would have been the greatest happiness for him; and remaining in Moscow, he came down to the country from time to time for a day or two. Besides the Oblonskys, with all their children and their governess, the old princess too came to stay that summer with the Levins, as she considered it her duty to watch over her inexperienced daughter in her *interesting condition*. Moreover, Varenka, Kitty's friend abroad, kept her promise to come to Kitty when she was married, and stayed with her friend. All of these were friends or relations of Levin's wife. And though he liked them all, he rather regretted his own Levin world and ways, which was smothered by this influx of the "Shtcherbatsky element," as he called it to himself. Of his own relations there stayed with him only Sergey Ivanovitch, but he too was a man of the Koznishev and not the Levin stamp, so that the Levin spirit was utterly obliterated.

In the Levins' house, so long deserted, there were now so many people that almost all the rooms were occupied, and almost everyday it happened that the old princess, sitting down to table, counted them all over, and put the thirteenth grandson or granddaughter at a separate table. And Kitty, with her careful housekeeping, had no little trouble to get all the chickens, turkeys, and geese, of which so many were needed to satisfy the summer appetites of the visitors and children.

The whole family were sitting at dinner. Dolly's children, with their governess and Varenka, were making plans for going to look for mushrooms. Sergey Ivanovitch, who was looked up to by all the party for his intellect and learning, with a respect that almost amounted to awe, surprised everyone by joining in the conversation about mushrooms.

"Take me with you. I am very fond of picking mushrooms," he said, looking at Varenka; "I think it's a very nice occupation."

"Oh, we shall be delighted," answered Varenka, coloring a little. Kitty exchanged meaningful glances with Dolly. The proposal of the learned and intellectual Sergey Ivanovitch to go looking for mushrooms with Varenka confirmed certain theories of Kitty's with which her mind had been very busy of late. She made haste to address some remark to her mother, so that her look should not be noticed. After dinner Sergey Ivanovitch sat with his cup of coffee at the drawing room window, and while he took part in a conversation he had begun with his brother, he watched the door through which the children would start on the mushroom-picking expedition. Levin was sitting in the window near his brother.

Kitty stood beside her husband, evidently awaiting the end of a conversation that had no interest for her, in order to tell him something.

"You have changed in many respects since your marriage, and for the better," said Sergey Ivanovitch, smiling to Kitty, and obviously little interested in the conversation, "but you have remained true to your passion for defending the most paradoxical theories."

"Katya, it's not good for you to stand," her husband said to her, putting a chair for her and looking significantly at her.

"Oh, and there's no time either," added Sergey Ivanovitch, seeing the children running out.

At the head of them all Tanya galloped sideways, in her tightly-drawn stockings, and waving a basket and Sergey Ivanovitch's hat, she ran straight up to him.

Boldly running up to Sergey Ivanovitch with shining eyes, so like her father's fine eyes, she handed him his hat and made as though she would put it on for him, softening her freedom by a shy and friendly smile.

"Varenka's waiting," she said, carefully putting his hat on, seeing from Sergey Ivanovitch's smile that she might do so.

Varenka was standing at the door, dressed in a yellow print gown, with a white kerchief on her head.

"I'm coming, I'm coming, Varvara Andreevna," said Sergey Ivanovitch, finishing his cup of coffee, and putting into their separate pockets his handkerchief and cigar-case.

"And how sweet my Varenka is! eh?" said Kitty to her husband, as soon as Sergey Ivanovitch rose. She spoke so that Sergey Ivanovitch could hear, and it was clear that she meant him to do so. "And how good-looking she is—such a refined beauty! Varenka!" Kitty shouted. "Shall you be in the mill copse? We'll come out to you."

"You certainly forget your condition, Kitty," said the old princess, hurriedly coming out at the door. "You mustn't shout like that."

Varenka, hearing Kitty's voice and her mother's reprimand, went with light, rapid steps up to Kitty. The rapidity of her movement, her flushed and eager face, everything betrayed that something out of the common was going on in her. Kitty knew what this was, and had been watching her intently. She called Varenka at that moment merely in order mentally to give her a blessing for the important event which, as Kitty fancied, was bound to come to pass that day after dinner in the wood.

"Varenka, I should be very happy if a certain something were to happen," she whispered as she kissed her.

"And are you coming with us?" Varenka said to Levin in confusion, pretending not to have heard what had been said.

"I am coming, but only as far as the threshing-floor, and there I shall stop."

"Why, what do you want there?" said Kitty.

"I must go to have a look at the new wagons, and to check the invoice," said Levin; "and where will you be?"

"On the terrace."

Chapter II

On the terrace were assembled all the ladies of the party. They always liked sitting there after dinner, and that day they had work to do there too. Besides the sewing and knitting of baby clothes, with which all of them were busy, that afternoon jam was being made on the terrace by a method new to Agafea Mihalovna, without the addition of water. Kitty had introduced this new method, which had been in use in her home. Agafea Mihalovna, to whom the task of jam-making had always been entrusted, considering that what had been done in the Levin household could not be amiss, had nevertheless put water with the strawberries, maintaining that the jam could not be made without it. She had been caught in the act, and was now making jam before everyone, and it was to be proved to her conclusively that jam could be very well made without water.

Agafea Mihalovna, her face heated and angry, her hair untidy, and her thin arms bare to the elbows, was turning the preserving-pan over the charcoal stove, looking darkly at the raspberries and devoutly hoping they would stick and not cook properly. The princess, conscious that Agafea Mihalovna's wrath must be chiefly directed against her, as the person responsible for the raspberry jam-making, tried to appear to be absorbed in other things and not interested in the jam, talked of other matters, but cast stealthy glances in the direction of the stove.

"I always buy my maids' dresses myself, of some cheap material," the princess said, continuing the previous conversation. "Isn't it time to skim it, my dear?" she added, addressing Agafea Mihalovna. "There's not the slightest need for you to do it, and it's hot for you," she said, stopping Kitty.

"I'll do it," said Dolly, and getting up, she carefully passed the spoon over the frothing sugar, and from time to time shook off the clinging jam from the spoon by knocking it on a plate that was covered with yellow-red scum and blood-colored syrup. "How they'll enjoy this at teatime!" she thought of her children, remembering how she herself as a child had wondered how it was the grown-up people did not eat what was best of all—the scum of the jam.

"Stiva says it's much better to give money." Dolly took up meanwhile the weighty subject under discussion, what presents should be made to servants. "But . . ."

"Money's out of the question!" the princess and Kitty exclaimed with one voice. "They appreciate a present . . ."

"Well, last year, for instance, I bought our Matrona Semyenovna, not a poplin, but something of that sort," said the princess.

"I remember she was wearing it on your nameday."

"A charming pattern—so simple and refined—I should have liked it myself, if she hadn't had it. Something like Varenka's. So pretty and inexpensive."

"Well, now I think it's done," said Dolly, dropping the syrup from the spoon.

"When it sets as it drops, it's ready. Cook it a little longer, Agafea Mihalovna."

"The flies!" said Agafea Mihalovna angrily. "It'll be just the same," she added.

"Ah! how sweet it is! don't frighten it!" Kitty said suddenly, looking at a sparrow that had settled on the step and was pecking at the center of a raspberry.

"Yes, but you keep a little further from the stove," said her mother.

"*A propos de Varenka,*" said Kitty, speaking in French, as they had been doing all the while, so that Agafea Mihalovna should not understand them, "you know, mamma, I somehow expect things to be settled today. You know what I mean. How splendid it would be!"

"But what a famous matchmaker she is!" said Dolly. "How carefully and cleverly she throws them together! . . ."

"No; tell me, mamma, what do you think?"

"Why, what is one to think? He" (*he* meant Sergey Ivanovitch) "might at any time have been a match for anyone in Russia; now, of course, he's not quite a young man, still I know ever so many girls would be glad to marry him even now. . . . She's a very nice girl, but he might . . ."

"Oh, no, mamma, do understand why, for him and for her too, nothing better could be imagined. In the first place, she's charming!" said Kitty, crooking one of her fingers.

"He thinks her very attractive, that's certain," assented Dolly.

"Then he occupies such a position in society that he has no need to look for either fortune or position in his wife. All he needs is a good, sweet wife—a restful one."

"Well, with her he would certainly be restful," Dolly assented.

"Thirdly, that she should love him. And so it is . . . that is, it would be so splendid! . . . I look forward to seeing them coming out of the forest—and everything settled. I shall see at once by their eyes. I should be so delighted! What do you think, Dolly?"

"But don't excite yourself. It's not at all the thing for you to be excited," said her mother.

"Oh, I'm not excited, mamma. I fancy he will make her an offer today."

"Ah, that's so strange, how and when a man makes an offer! . . . There is a sort of barrier, and all at once it's broken down," said Dolly, smiling pensively and recalling her past with Stepan Arkadyevitch.

"Mamma, how did papa make you an offer?" Kitty asked suddenly.

"There was nothing out of the way, it was very simple," answered the princess, but her face beamed all over at the recollection.

"Oh, but how was it? You loved him, anyway, before you were allowed to speak?"

Kitty felt a peculiar pleasure in being able now to talk to her mother on equal terms about those questions of such paramount interest in a woman's life.

"Of course I did; he had come to stay with us in the country."

"But how was it settled between you, mamma?"

"You imagine, I dare say, that you invented something quite new? It's always just the same: it was settled by the eyes, by smiles . . ."

"How nicely you said that, mamma! It's just by the eyes, by smiles that it's done," Dolly assented.

"But what words did he say?"

"What did Kostya say to you?"

"He wrote it in chalk. It was wonderful. . . . How long ago it seems!" she said.

And the three women all fell to musing on the same thing. Kitty was the first to break the silence. She remembered all that last winter before her marriage, and her passion for Vronsky.

"There's one thing . . . that old love affair of Varenka's," she said, a natural chain of ideas bringing her to this point. "I should have liked to say something to Sergey Ivanovitch, to prepare him. They're all—all men, I mean," she added, "awfully jealous over our past."

"Not all," said Dolly. "You judge by your own husband. It makes him miserable even now to remember Vronsky. Eh? that's true, isn't it?"

"Yes," Kitty answered, a pensive smile in her eyes.

"But I really don't know," the mother put in in defense of her motherly care of her daughter, "what there was in your past that could worry him? That Vronsky paid you attentions—that happens to every girl."

"Oh, yes, but we didn't mean that," Kitty said, flushing a little.

"No, let me speak," her mother went on, "why, you yourself would not let me have a talk to Vronsky. Don't you remember?"

"Oh, mamma!" said Kitty, with an expression of suffering.

"There's no keeping you young people in check nowadays. . . . Your friendship could not have gone beyond what was suitable. I should myself have called upon him to explain himself. But, my darling, it's not right for you to be agitated. Please remember that, and calm yourself."

"I'm perfectly calm, maman."

"How happy it was for Kitty that Anna came then," said Dolly, "and how unhappy for her. It turned out quite the opposite," she said, struck by her own ideas. "Then Anna was so happy, and Kitty thought herself unhappy. Now it is just the opposite. I often think of her."

"A nice person to think about! Horrid, repulsive woman—no heart," said her mother, who could not forget that Kitty had married not Vronsky, but Levin.

"What do you want to talk of it for?" Kitty said with annoyance. "I never think about it, and I don't want to think of it. . . . And I don't want to think of it," she said, catching the sound of her husband's well-known step on the steps of the terrace.

"What's that you don't want to think about?" inquired Levin, coming onto the terrace.

But no one answered him, and he did not repeat the question.

"I'm sorry I've broken in on your feminine parliament," he said, looking round on everyone discontentedly, and perceiving that they had been talking of something which they would not talk about before him.

For a second he felt that he was sharing the feeling of Agafea Mihalovna, vexation at their making jam without water, and altogether at the outside Shtcherbatsky element. He smiled, however, and went up to Kitty.

"Well, how are you?" he asked her, looking at her with the expression with which everyone looked at her now.

"Oh, very well," said Kitty, smiling, "and how have things gone with you?"

"The wagon held three times as much as the old carts did. Well, are we going for the children? I've ordered the horses to be put in."

"What! you want to take Kitty in the wagonette?" her mother said reproachfully.

"Yes, at a walking pace, princess."

Levin never called the princess "maman" as men often do call their mothers-in-law, and the princess disliked his not doing so. But though he liked and respected the princess, Levin could not call her so without a sense of profaning his feeling for his dead mother.

"Come with us, maman," said Kitty.

"I don't like to see such imprudence."

"Well, I'll walk then, I'm so well." Kitty got up and went to her husband and took his hand.

"You may be well, but everything in moderation," said the princess.

"Well, Agafea Mihalovna, is the jam done?" said Levin, smiling to Agafea Mihalovna, and trying to cheer her up. "Is it all right in the new way?"

"I suppose it's all right. For our notions it's boiled too long."

"It'll be all the better, Agafea Mihalovna, it won't mildew, even though our ice has begun to thaw already, so that we've no cool cellar to store it," said Kitty, at once divining her husband's motive, and addressing the old housekeeper with the same feeling; "but your pickle's so good, that mamma says she never tasted any like it," she added, smiling, and putting her kerchief straight.

Agafea Mihalovna looked angrily at Kitty.

"You needn't try to console me, mistress. I need only to look at you with him, and I feel happy," she said, and something in the rough familiarity of that *with him* touched Kitty.

"Come along with us to look for mushrooms, you will show us the best places." Agafea Mihalovna smiled and shook her head, as though to say: "I should like to be angry with you too, but I can't."

"Do it, please, by my receipt," said the princess; "put some paper over the jam, and moisten it with a little rum, and without even ice, it will never go mildewy."

Chapter III

KITTY WAS PARTICULARLY GLAD OF A CHANCE OF BEING ALONE WITH HER HUSBAND, FOR SHE had noticed the shade of mortification that had passed over his face—always so quick to reflect every feeling—at the moment when he had come onto the terrace and asked what they were talking of, and had got no answer.

When they had set off on foot ahead of the others, and had come out of sight of the house onto the beaten dusty road, marked with rusty wheels and sprinkled with grains of corn, she clung faster to his arm and pressed it closer to her. He had quite forgotten the momentary unpleasant impression, and alone with her he felt, now that the thought of her approaching motherhood was never for a moment absent from his mind, a new and delicious bliss, quite pure from all alloy of sense, in the being near to the woman he loved. There was no need of speech, yet he longed to hear the sound of her voice, which like her eyes had changed since she had been with child. In her voice, as in her eyes, there was that softness and gravity which is found in people continually concentrated on some cherished pursuit.

"So you're not tired? Lean more on me," said he.

"No, I'm so glad of a chance of being alone with you, and I must own, though I'm happy with them, I do regret our winter evenings alone."

"That was good, but this is even better. Both are better," he said, squeezing her hand.

"Do you know what we were talking about when you came in?"

"About jam?"

"Oh, yes, about jam too; but afterwards, about how men make offers."

"Ah!" said Levin, listening more to the sound of her voice than to the words she was saying, and all the while paying attention to the road, which passed now through the forest, and avoiding places where she might make a false step.

"And about Sergey Ivanovitch and Varenka. You've noticed? . . . I'm very anxious for it," she went on. "What do you think about it?" And she peeped into his face.

"I don't know what to think," Levin answered, smiling. "Sergey seems very strange to me in that way. I told you, you know . . ."

"Yes, that he was in love with that girl who died. . . ."

"That was when I was a child; I know about it from hearsay and tradition. I remember him then. He was wonderfully sweet. But I've watched him since with women; he is friendly, some of them he likes, but one feels that to him they're simply people, not women."

"Yes, but now with Varenka . . . I fancy there's something . . ."

"Perhaps there is. . . . But one has to know him. . . . He's a peculiar, wonderful person. He lives a spiritual life only. He's too pure, too exalted a nature."

"Why? Would this lower him, then?"

"No, but he's so used to a spiritual life that he can't reconcile himself with actual fact, and Varenka is after all fact."

Levin had grown used by now to uttering his thought boldly, without taking the trouble of clothing it in exact language. He knew that his wife, in such moments of loving tenderness as now, would understand what he meant to say from a hint, and she did understand him.

"Yes, but there's not so much of that actual fact about her as about me. I can see that he would never have cared for me. She is altogether spiritual."

"Oh, no, he is so fond of you, and I am always so glad when my people like you. . . ."

"Yes, he's very nice to me; but . . ."

"It's not as it was with poor Nikolay . . . you really cared for each other," Levin finished. "Why not speak of him?" he added. "I sometimes blame myself for not; it ends in one's forgetting. Ah, how terrible and dear he was! . . . Yes, what were we talking about?" Levin said, after a pause.

"You think he can't fall in love," said Kitty, translating into her own language.

"It's not so much that he can't fall in love," Levin said, smiling, "but he has not the weakness necessary. . . . I've always envied him, and even now, when I'm so happy, I still envy him."

"You envy him for not being able to fall in love?"

"I envy him for being better than me," said Levin. "He does not live for himself. His whole life is subordinated to his duty. And that's why he can be calm and contented."

"And you?" Kitty asked, with an ironical and loving smile.

She could never have explained the chain of thought that made her smile; but the last link in it was that her husband, in exalting his brother and abasing himself, was not quite sincere. Kitty knew that this insincerity came from his love for his brother, from his sense of shame at being too happy, and above all from his unflagging craving to be better—she loved it in him, and so she smiled.

"And you? What are you dissatisfied with?" she asked, with the same smile.

Her disbelief in his self-dissatisfaction delighted him, and unconsciously he tried to draw her into giving utterance to the grounds of her disbelief.

"I am happy, but dissatisfied with myself . . ." he said.

"Why, how can you be dissatisfied with yourself if you are happy?"

"Well, how shall I say? . . . In my heart I really care for nothing whatever but that you should not stumble—see? Oh, but really you mustn't skip about like that!" he cried, breaking off to scold her for too agile a movement in stepping over a branch that lay in the path. "But when I think about myself, and compare myself with others, especially with my brother, I feel I'm a poor creature."

"But in what way?" Kitty pursued with the same smile. "Don't you too work for others? What about your cooperative settlement, and your work on the estate, and your book? . . ."

"Oh, but I feel, and particularly just now—it's your fault," he said, pressing her hand—"that all that doesn't count. I do it in a way half-heartedly. If I could care for all that as I care for you! . . . Instead of that, I do it in these days like a task that is set me."

"Well, what would you say about papa?" asked Kitty. "Is he a poor creature then, as he does nothing for the public good?"

"He?—no! But then one must have the simplicity, the straightforwardness, the goodness of your father: and I haven't got that. I do nothing, and I fret about it. It's all your doing. Before there was you—and *this* too," he added with a glance towards her waist that she understood—"I put all my energies into work; now I can't, and I'm ashamed; I do it just as though it were a task set me, I'm pretending. . . ."

"Well, but would you like to change this minute with Sergey Ivanovitch?" said Kitty. "Would you like to do this work for the general good, and to love the task set you, as he does, and nothing else?"

"Of course not," said Levin. "But I'm so happy that I don't understand anything. So you think he'll make her an offer today?" he added after a brief silence.

"I think so, and I don't think so. Only, I'm awfully anxious for it. Here, wait a minute." She stooped down and picked a wild camomile at the edge of the path. "Come, count: he does propose, he doesn't," she said, giving him the flower.

"He does, he doesn't," said Levin, tearing off the white petals.

"No, no!" Kitty, snatching at his hand, stopped him. She had been watching his fingers with interest. "You picked off two."

"Oh, but see, this little one shan't count to make up," said Levin, tearing off a little half-grown petal. "Here's the wagonette overtaking us."

"Aren't you tired, Kitty?" called the princess.

"Not in the least."

"If you are you can get in, as the horses are quiet and walking."

But it was not worthwhile to get in, they were quite near the place, and all walked on together.

Chapter IV

VARENKA WITH HER WHITE KERCHIEF ON HER BLACK HAIR, SURROUNDED BY THE CHILDREN, gaily and good-humoredly looking after them, and at the same time visibly excited at the possibility of receiving a declaration from the man she cared for, was very attractive. Sergey Ivanovitch walked beside her, and never left off admiring her. Looking at her, he recalled all the delightful things he had heard from her lips, all the good he knew about her, and became more and more conscious that the feeling he had for her was something special that he had felt long, long ago, and only once, in his early youth. The feeling of happiness in being near her continually grew, and at last reached such a point that, as he put a huge, slender-stalked agaric fungus in her basket, he looked straight into her face, and noticing the flush of glad and alarmed excitement that overspread her face, he was confused himself, and smiled to her in silence a smile that said too much.

"If so," he said to himself, "I ought to think it over and make up my mind, and not give way like a boy to the impulse of a moment."

"I'm going to pick by myself apart from all the rest, or else my efforts will make no show," he said, and he left the edge of the forest where they were walking on low silky grass between old birch trees standing far apart, and went more into the heart of the wood, where between the white birch trunks there were gray trunks of aspen and dark bushes of hazel. Walking some forty paces away, Sergey Ivanovitch, knowing he was out of sight, stood still behind a bushy spindle tree in full flower with its rosy red catkins. It was perfectly still all round him. Only overhead in the birches under which he stood, the flies, like a swarm of bees, buzzed unceasingly, and from time to time the children's voices were floated across to him. All at once he heard, not far from the edge of the wood, the sound of Varenka's contralto voice, calling Grisha, and a smile of delight passed over Sergey Ivanovitch's face. Conscious of this smile, he shook his head disapprovingly at his own condition, and taking out a cigar, he began lighting it. For a long while he could not get a match to light against the trunk of a birch tree. The soft scales of the white bark rubbed off the phosphorus, and the light went out. At last one of the matches burned, and the fragrant cigar smoke, hovering uncertainly in flat, wide coils, stretched away forwards and upwards over a bush under the overhanging branches of a birch tree. Watching the streak of smoke, Sergey Ivanovitch walked gently on, deliberating on his position.

"Why not?" he thought. "If it were only a passing fancy or a passion, if it were only this attraction—this mutual attraction (I can call it a *mutual* attraction), but I felt that it was in contradiction with the whole bent of my life—if I felt that in giving way to this attraction I should be false to my vocation and my duty . . . but it's not so. The only thing I can say against it is that, when I lost Marie, I said to myself that I would remain faithful to her memory. That's the only thing I can say against my feeling. . . . That's a great thing," Sergey Ivanovitch said to himself, feeling at the same time that this consideration had not the slightest importance for him personally, but would only perhaps detract from his romantic character in the eyes of others. "But apart from that, however much I searched, I should never find anything to say against my feeling. If I were choosing by considerations of suitability alone, I could not have found anything better."

However many women and girls he thought of whom he knew, he could not think of a girl who united to such a degree all, positively all, the qualities he would wish to see in his wife. She had all the charm and freshness of youth, but she was not a child; and if she loved him, she loved him consciously as a woman ought to love; that was one thing. Another point: she was not only far from being worldly, but had an unmistakable distaste for worldly society, and at the same time she knew the world, and had all the ways of a woman of the best society, which were absolutely essential to Sergey Ivanovitch's conception of the woman who was to share his life. Thirdly: she was religious, and not like a child, unconsciously religious and good, as Kitty, for example, was, but her life was founded on religious principles. Even in trifling matters, Sergey Ivanovitch found in her all that he wanted in his wife: she was poor and alone in the world, so she would not bring with her a mass of relations and their influence into her husband's house, as he saw now in Kitty's case. She would owe everything to her husband, which was what he had always desired too for his future family life. And this girl, who united all these qualities, loved him. He was a modest man, but he could not help seeing it. And he loved her. There was one consideration against it—his age. But he came of a long-lived family, he had not a single gray hair, no one would have taken him for forty, and he remembered Varenka's saying that it was only in Russia that men of fifty thought themselves old, and that in France a man of fifty considers himself *dans la force de l'age,* while a man of forty is *un jeune homme*. But what did the mere reckoning of years matter when he felt as young in heart as he had been twenty years ago? Was it not youth to feel as he felt now, when coming from the other side to the edge of the wood he saw in the glowing light of the slanting sunbeams the gracious figure of Varenka in her yellow gown with her basket, walking lightly by the trunk of an old birch tree, and when this impression of the sight of Varenka blended so harmoniously with the beauty of the view, of the yellow oatfield lying bathed in the slanting sunshine, and beyond it the distant ancient forest flecked with yellow and melting into the blue of the distance? His heart throbbed joyously. A softened feeling came over him. He felt that he had made up his mind. Varenka, who had just crouched down to pick a mushroom, rose with a supple movement and looked round. Flinging away the cigar, Sergey Ivanovitch advanced with resolute steps towards her.

Chapter V

VARVARA ANDREEVNA, WHEN I WAS VERY YOUNG, I SET BEFORE MYSELF THE IDEAL OF THE woman I loved and should be happy to call my wife. I have lived through a long life, and now for the first time I have met what I sought—in you. I love you, and offer you my hand.

Sergey Ivanovitch was saying this to himself while he was ten paces from Varvara. Kneeling down, with her hands over the mushrooms to guard them from Grisha, she was calling little Masha.

"Come here, little ones! There are so many!" she was saying in her sweet, deep voice.

Seeing Sergey Ivanovitch approaching, she did not get up and did not change her position, but everything told him that she felt his presence and was glad of it.

"Well, did you find some?" she asked from under the white kerchief, turning her handsome, gently smiling face to him.

"Not one," said Sergey Ivanovitch. "Did you?"

She did not answer, busy with the children who thronged about her.

"That one too, near the twig," she pointed out to little Masha a little fungus, split in half across its rosy cap by the dry grass from under which it thrust itself. Varenka got up while Masha picked the fungus, breaking it into two white halves. "This brings back my childhood," she added, moving apart from the children beside Sergey Ivanovitch.

They walked on for some steps in silence. Varenka saw that he wanted to speak; she guessed of what, and felt faint with joy and panic. They had walked so far away that no one could hear them now, but still he did not begin to speak. It would have been better for Varenka to be silent. After a silence it would have been easier for them to say what they wanted to say than after talking about mushrooms. But against her own will, as it were accidentally, Varenka said:

"So you found nothing? In the middle of the wood there are always fewer, though." Sergey Ivanovitch sighed and made no answer. He was annoyed that she had spoken about the mushrooms. He wanted to bring her back to the first words she had uttered about her childhood; but after a pause of some length, as though against his own will, he made an observation in response to her last words.

"I have heard that the white edible funguses are found principally at the edge of the wood, though I can't tell them apart."

Some minutes more passed, they moved still further away from the children, and were quite alone. Varenka's heart throbbed so that she heard it beating, and felt that she was turning red and pale and red again.

To be the wife of a man like Koznishev, after her position with Madame Stahl, was to her imagination the height of happiness. Besides, she was almost certain that she was in love with him. And this moment it would have to be decided. She felt frightened. She dreaded both his speaking and his not speaking.

Now or never it must be said—that Sergey Ivanovitch felt too. Everything in the expression, the flushed cheeks and the downcast eyes of Varenka betrayed a painful suspense. Sergey Ivanovitch saw it and felt sorry for her. He felt even that to say nothing now would be a slight to her. Rapidly in his own mind he ran over all the arguments in support of his decision. He even said over to himself the words in which he meant to put his offer, but instead of those words, some utterly unexpected reflection that occurred to him made him ask:

"What is the difference between the 'birch' mushroom and the 'white' mushroom?"

Varenka's lips quivered with emotion as she answered:

"In the top part there is scarcely any difference, it's in the stalk."

And as soon as these words were uttered, both he and she felt that it was over, that what was to have been said would not be said; and their emotion, which had up to then been continually growing more intense, began to subside.

"The birch mushroom's stalk suggests a dark man's chin after two days without shaving," said Sergey Ivanovitch, speaking quite calmly now.

"Yes, that's true," answered Varenka smiling, and unconsciously the direction of their walk changed. They began to turn towards the children. Varenka felt both sore and ashamed; at the same time she had a sense of relief.

When he had got home again and went over the whole subject, Sergey Ivanovitch thought his previous decision had been a mistaken one. He could not be false to the memory of Marie.

"Gently, children, gently!" Levin shouted quite angrily to the children, standing before his wife to protect her when the crowd of children flew with shrieks of delight to meet them.

Behind the children Sergey Ivanovitch and Varenka walked out of the wood. Kitty had no need to ask Varenka; she saw from the calm and somewhat crestfallen faces of both that her plans had not come off.

"Well?" her husband questioned her as they were going home again.

"It doesn't bite," said Kitty, her smile and manner of speaking recalling her father, a likeness Levin often noticed with pleasure.

"How doesn't bite?"

"I'll show you," she said, taking her husband's hand, lifting it to her mouth, and just faintly brushing it with closed lips. "Like a kiss on a priest's hand."

"Which didn't it bite with?" he said, laughing.

"Both. But it should have been like this . . ."

"There are some peasants coming . . ."

"Oh, they didn't see."

Chapter VI

During the time of the children's tea the grown-up people sat in the balcony and talked as though nothing had happened, though they all, especially Sergey Ivanovitch and Varenka, were very well aware that there had happened an event which, though negative, was of very great importance. They both had the same feeling, rather like that of a schoolboy after an examination, which has left him in the same class or shut him out of the school forever. Everyone present, feeling too that something had happened, talked eagerly about extraneous subjects. Levin and Kitty were particularly happy and conscious of their love that evening. And their happiness in their love seemed to imply a disagreeable slur on those who would have liked to feel the same and could not—and they felt a prick of conscience.

"Mark my words, Alexander will not come," said the old princess.

That evening they were expecting Stepan Arkadyevitch to come down by train, and the old prince had written that possibly he might come too.

"And I know why," the princess went on; "he says that young people ought to be left alone for a while at first."

"But papa has left us alone. We've never seen him," said Kitty. "Besides, we're not young people!—we're old, married people by now."

"Only if he doesn't come, I shall say good-bye to you children," said the princess, sighing mournfully.

"What nonsense, mamma!" both the daughters fell upon her at once.

"How do you suppose he is feeling? Why, now . . ."

And suddenly there was an unexpected quiver in the princess's voice. Her daughters were silent, and looked at one another. "Maman always finds something to be miserable about," they said in that glance. They did not know that happy as the princess was in her daughter's house, and useful as she felt herself to be there, she had been extremely miserable, both on her own account and her husband's, ever since they had married their last and favorite daughter, and the old home had been left empty.

"What is it, Agafea Mihalovna?" Kitty asked suddenly of Agafea Mihalovna, who was standing with a mysterious air, and a face full of meaning.

"About supper."

"Well, that's right," said Dolly; "you go and arrange about it, and I'll go and hear Grisha repeat his lesson, or else he will have nothing done all day."

"That's my lesson! No, Dolly, I'm going," said Levin, jumping up.

Grisha, who was by now at a high school, had to go over the lessons of the term in the summer holidays. Darya Alexandrovna, who had been studying Latin with her son in Moscow before, had made it a rule on coming to the Levins' to go over with him, at least once a day, the most difficult lessons of Latin and arithmetic. Levin had offered to take her place, but the mother, having once overheard Levin's lesson, and noticing that it was not given exactly as the teacher in Moscow had given it, said resolutely, though with much embarrassment and anxiety not to mortify Levin, that they must keep strictly to the book as the teacher had done, and that she had better undertake it again herself. Levin was amazed both at Stepan Arkadyevitch, who, by neglecting his duty, threw upon the mother the supervision of studies of which she had no comprehension, and at the teachers for teaching the children so badly. But he promised his sister-in-law to give the lessons exactly as she wished. And he went on teaching Grisha, not in his own way, but by the book, and so took little interest in it, and often forgot the hour of the lesson. So it had been today.

"No, I'm going, Dolly, you sit still," he said. "We'll do it all properly, like the book. Only when Stiva comes, and we go out shooting, then we shall have to miss it."

And Levin went to Grisha.

Varenka was saying the same thing to Kitty. Even in the happy, well-ordered household of the Levins Varenka had succeeded in making herself useful.

"I'll see to the supper, you sit still," she said, and got up to go to Agafea Mihalovna.

"Yes, yes, most likely they've not been able to get chickens. If so, ours . . ."

"Agafea Mihalovna and I will see about it," and Varenka vanished with her.

"What a nice girl!" said the princess.

"Not nice, maman; she's an exquisite girl; there's no one else like her."

"So you are expecting Stepan Arkadyevitch today?" said Sergey Ivanovitch, evidently not disposed to pursue the conversation about Varenka. "It would be difficult to find two sons-in-law more unlike than yours," he said with a subtle smile. "One all movement, only living in society, like a fish in water; the other our Kostya, lively, alert, quick in everything, but as soon as he is in society, he either sinks into apathy, or struggles helplessly like a fish on land."

"Yes, he's very heedless," said the princess, addressing Sergey Ivanovitch. "I've been meaning, indeed, to ask you to tell him that it's out of the question for her" (she indicated Kitty) "to stay here; that she positively must come to Moscow. He talks of getting a doctor down . . ."

"Maman, he'll do everything; he has agreed to everything," Kitty said, angry with her mother for appealing to Sergey Ivanovitch to judge in such a matter.

In the middle of their conversation they heard the snorting of horses and the sound of wheels on the gravel. Dolly had not time to get up to go and meet her husband, when from the window of the room below, where Grisha was having his lesson, Levin leaped out and helped Grisha out after him.

"It's Stiva!" Levin shouted from under the balcony. "We've finished, Dolly, don't be afraid!" he added, and started running like a boy to meet the carriage.

"Is ea id, ejus, ejus, ejus!" shouted Grisha, skipping along the avenue.

"And someone else too! Papa, of course!" cried Levin, stopping at the entrance of the avenue. "Kitty, don't come down the steep staircase, go round."

But Levin had been mistaken in taking the person sitting in the carriage for the old prince. As he got nearer to the carriage he saw beside Stepan Arkadyevitch not the prince but a handsome, stout young man in a Scotch cap, with long ends of ribbon behind. This was Vassenka Veslovsky, a distant cousin of the Shtcherbatskys, a brilliant young gentleman in Petersburg and Moscow society. "A capital fellow, and a keen sportsman," as Stepan Arkadyevitch said, introducing him.

Not a whit abashed by the disappointment caused by his having come in place of the old prince, Veslovsky greeted Levin gaily, claiming acquaintance with him in the past, and snatching up Grisha into the carriage, lifted him over the pointer that Stepan Arkadyevitch had brought with him.

Levin did not get into the carriage, but walked behind. He was rather vexed at the non-arrival of the old prince, whom he liked more and more the more he saw of him, and also at the arrival of this Vassenka Veslovsky, a quite uncongenial and superfluous person. He seemed to him still more uncongenial and superfluous when, on approaching the steps where the whole party, children and grown-up, were gathered together in much excitement, Levin saw Vassenka Veslovsky, with a particularly warm and gallant air, kissing Kitty's hand.

"Your wife and I are cousins and very old friends," said Vassenka Veslovsky, once more shaking Levin's hand with great warmth.

"Well, are there plenty of birds?" Stepan Arkadyevitch said to Levin, hardly leaving time for everyone to utter their greetings. "We've come with the most savage intentions. Why, maman, they've not been in Moscow since! Look, Tanya, here's something for you! Get it, please, it's in the carriage, behind!" he talked in all directions. "How pretty you've grown, Dolly," he said to his wife, once more kissing her hand, holding it in one of his, and patting it with the other.

Levin, who a minute before had been in the happiest frame of mind, now looked darkly at everyone, and everything displeased him.

"Who was it he kissed yesterday with those lips?" he thought, looking at Stepan Arkadyevitch's tender demonstrations to his wife. He looked at Dolly, and he did not like her either.

"She doesn't believe in his love. So what is she so pleased about? Revolting!" thought Levin.

He looked at the princess, who had been so dear to him a minute before, and he did not like the manner in which she welcomed this Vassenka, with his ribbons, just as though she were in her own house.

Even Sergey Ivanovitch, who had come out too onto the steps, seemed to him unpleasant with the show of cordiality with which he met Stepan Arkadyevitch, though Levin knew that his brother neither liked nor respected Oblonsky.

And Varenka, even she seemed hateful, with her air *sainte nitouche* making the acquaintance of this gentleman, while all the while she was thinking of nothing but getting married.

And more hateful than anyone was Kitty for falling in with the tone of gaiety with which this gentleman regarded his visit in the country, as though it were a holiday for himself and everyone else. And, above all, unpleasant was that particular smile with which she responded to his smile.

Noisily talking, they all went into the house; but as soon as they were all seated, Levin turned and went out.

Kitty saw something was wrong with her husband. She tried to seize a moment to speak to him alone, but he made haste to get away from her, saying he was wanted at the counting house. It was long since his own work on the estate had seemed to him so important as at that moment. "It's all holiday for them," he thought; "but these are no holiday matters, they won't wait, and there's no living without them."

Chapter VII

Levin came back to the house only when they sent to summon him to supper. On the stairs were standing Kitty and Agafea Mihalovna, consulting about wines for supper.

"But why are you making all this fuss? Have what we usually do."

"No, Stiva doesn't drink . . . Kostya, stop, what's the matter?" Kitty began, hurrying after him, but he strode ruthlessly away to the dining room without waiting for her, and at once joined in the lively general conversation which was being maintained there by Vassenka Veslovsky and Stepan Arkadyevitch.

"Well, what do you say, are we going shooting tomorrow?" said Stepan Arkadyevitch.

"Please, do let's go," said Veslovsky, moving to another chair, where he sat down sideways, with one fat leg crossed under him.

"I shall be delighted, we will go. And have you had any shooting yet this year?" said Levin to Veslovsky, looking intently at his leg, but speaking with that forced amiability that Kitty knew so well in him, and that was so out of keeping with him. "I can't answer for our finding grouse, but there are plenty of snipe. Only we ought to start early. You're not tired? Aren't you tired, Stiva?"

"Me tired? I've never been tired yet. Suppose we stay up all night. Let's go for a walk!"

"Yes, really, let's not go to bed at all! Capital!" Veslovsky chimed in.

"Oh, we all know you can do without sleep, and keep other people up too," Dolly said to her husband, with that faint note of irony in her voice which she almost always had now with her husband. "But to my thinking, it's time for bed now . . . I'm going, I don't want supper."

"No, do stay a little, Dolly," said Stepan Arkadyevitch, going round to her side behind the table where they were having supper. "I've so much still to tell you."

"Nothing really, I suppose."

"Do you know Veslovsky has been at Anna's, and he's going to them again? You know they're hardly fifty miles from you, and I too must certainly go over there. Veslovsky, come here!"

Vassenka crossed over to the ladies, and sat down beside Kitty.

"Ah, do tell me, please; you have stayed with her? How was she?" Darya Alexandrovna appealed to him.

Levin was left at the other end of the table, and though never pausing in his conversation with the princess and Varenka, he saw that there was an eager and mysterious conversation going on between Stepan Arkadyevitch, Dolly, Kitty, and Veslovsky. And that was not all. He saw on his wife's face an expression of real feeling as she gazed with fixed eyes on the handsome face of Vassenka, who was telling them something with great animation.

"It's exceedingly nice at their place," Veslovsky was telling them about Vronsky and Anna. "I can't, of course, take it upon myself to judge, but in their house you feel the real feeling of home."

"What do they intend doing?"

"I believe they think of going to Moscow."

"How jolly it would be for us all to go over to them together! When are you going there?" Stepan Arkadyevitch asked Vassenka.

"I'm spending July there."

"Will you go?" Stepan Arkadyevitch said to his wife.

"I've been wanting to a long while; I shall certainly go," said Dolly. "I am sorry for her, and I know her. She's a splendid woman. I will go alone, when you go back, and then I shall be in no one's way. And it will be better indeed without you."

"To be sure," said Stepan Arkadyevitch. "And you, Kitty?"

"I? Why should I go?" Kitty said, flushing all over, and she glanced round at her husband.

"Do you know Anna Arkadyevna, then?" Veslovsky asked her. "She's a very fascinating woman."

"Yes," she answered Veslovsky, crimsoning still more. She got up and walked across to her husband.

"Are you going shooting, then, tomorrow?" she said.

His jealousy had in these few moments, especially at the flush that had overspread her cheeks while she was talking to Veslovsky, gone far indeed. Now as he heard her words, he construed them in his own fashion. Strange as it was to him afterwards to recall it, it seemed to him at the moment clear that in asking whether he was going shooting, all she cared to know was whether he would give that pleasure to Vassenka Veslovsky, with whom, as he fancied, she was in love.

"Yes, I'm going," he answered her in an unnatural voice, disagreeable to himself.

"No, better spend the day here tomorrow, or Dolly won't see anything of her husband, and set off the day after," said Kitty.

The motive of Kitty's words was interpreted by Levin thus: "Don't separate me from *him*. I don't care about *your* going, but do let me enjoy the society of this delightful young man."

"Oh, if you wish, we'll stay here tomorrow," Levin answered, with peculiar amiability.

Vassenka meanwhile, utterly unsuspecting the misery his presence had occasioned, got up from the table after Kitty, and watching her with smiling and admiring eyes, he followed her.

Levin saw that look. He turned white, and for a minute he could hardly breathe. "How dare he look at my wife like that!" was the feeling that boiled within him.

"Tomorrow, then? Do, please, let us go," said Vassenka, sitting down on a chair, and again crossing his leg as his habit was.

Levin's jealousy went further still. Already he saw himself a deceived husband, looked upon by his wife and her lover as simply necessary to provide them with the conveniences and pleasures of life. . . . But in spite of that he made polite and hospitable inquiries of Vassenka about his shooting, his gun, and his boots, and agreed to go shooting next day.

Happily for Levin, the old princess cut short his agonies by getting up herself and advising Kitty to go to bed. But even at this point Levin could not escape another agony. As he said good night to his hostess, Vassenka would again have kissed her hand, but Kitty, reddening, drew back her hand and said with a naïve bluntness, for which the old princess scolded her afterwards:

"We don't like that fashion."

In Levin's eyes she was to blame for having allowed such relations to arise, and still more to blame for showing so awkwardly that she did not like them.

"Why, how can one want to go to bed!" said Stepan Arkadyevitch, who, after drinking several glasses of wine at supper, was now in his most charming and sentimental humor. "Look, Kitty," he said, pointing to the moon, which had just risen behind the lime trees—"how exquisite! Veslovsky, this is the time for a serenade. You know, he has a splendid voice; we practiced songs together along the road. He has brought some lovely songs with him, two new ones. Varvara Andreevna and he must sing some duets."

When the party had broken up, Stepan Arkadyevitch walked a long while about the avenue with Veslovsky; their voices could be heard singing one of the new songs.

Levin hearing these voices sat scowling in an easy chair in his wife's bedroom, and maintained an obstinate silence when she asked him what was wrong. But when at last with a timid glance she hazarded the question: "Was there perhaps something you disliked about Veslovsky?"—it all burst out, and he told her all. He was humiliated himself at what he was saying, and that exasperated him all the more.

He stood facing her with his eyes glittering menacingly under his scowling brows, and he squeezed his strong arms across his chest, as though he were straining every nerve to hold himself in. The expression of his face would have been grim, and even cruel, if it had not at the same time had a look of suffering which touched her. His jaws were twitching, and his voice kept breaking.

"You must understand that I'm not jealous, that's a nasty word. I can't be jealous, and believe that. . . . I can't say what I feel, but this is awful. . . . I'm not jealous, but I'm wounded, humiliated that anybody dare think, that anybody dare look at you with eyes like that."

"Eyes like what?" said Kitty, trying as conscientiously as possible to recall every word and gesture of that evening and every shade implied in them.

At the very bottom of her heart she did think there had been something precisely at the moment when he had crossed over after her to the other end of the table; but she dared not own it even to herself, and would have been even more unable to bring herself to say so to him, and so increase his suffering.

"And what can there possibly be attractive about me as I am now? . . ."

"Ah!" he cried, clutching at his head, "you shouldn't say that! . . . If you had been attractive then . . ."

"Oh, no, Kostya, oh, wait a minute, oh, do listen!" she said, looking at him with an expression of pained commiseration. "Why, what can you be thinking about! When for me there's no one in the world, no one, no one! . . . Would you like me never to see anyone?"

For the first minute she had been offended at his jealousy; she was angry that the slightest amusement, even the most innocent, should be forbidden her; but now she would readily have sacrificed, not merely such trifles, but everything, for his peace of mind, to save him from the agony he was suffering.

"You must understand the horror and comedy of my position," he went on in a desperate whisper; "that he's in my house, that he's done nothing improper positively except his free and easy airs and the way he sits on his legs. He thinks it's the best possible form, and so I'm obliged to be civil to him."

"But, Kostya, you're exaggerating," said Kitty, at the bottom of her heart rejoicing at the depth of his love for her, shown now in his jealousy.

"The most awful part of it all is that you're just as you always are, and especially now when to me you're something sacred, and we're so happy, so particularly happy—and all of a sudden a little wretch. . . . He's not a little wretch; why should I abuse him? I have nothing to do with him. But why should my, and your, happiness . . ."

"Do you know, I understand now what it's all come from," Kitty was beginning.

"Well, what? what?"

"I saw how you looked while we were talking at supper."

"Well, well!" Levin said in dismay.

She told him what they had been talking about. And as she told him, she was breathless with emotion. Levin was silent for a space, then he scanned her pale and distressed face, and suddenly he clutched at his head.

"Katya, I've been worrying you! Darling, forgive me! It's madness! Katya, I'm a criminal. And how could you be so distressed at such idiocy?"

"Oh, I was sorry for you."

"For me? for me? How mad I am! . . . But why make you miserable? It's awful to think that any outsider can shatter our happiness."

"It's humiliating too, of course."

"Oh, then I'll keep him here all the summer, and will overwhelm him with civility," said Levin, kissing her hands. "You shall see. Tomorrow . . . Oh, yes, we are going tomorrow."

Chapter VIII

NEXT DAY, BEFORE THE LADIES WERE UP, THE WAGONETTE AND A TRAP FOR THE SHOOTING party were at the door, and Laska, aware since early morning that they were going shooting, after much whining and darting to and fro, had sat herself down in the wagonette beside the coachman, and, disapproving of the delay, was excitedly watching the door from which the sportsmen still did not come out. The first to come out was Vassenka Veslovsky, in new high boots that reached halfway up his thick thighs, in a green blouse, with a new Russian leather cartridge-belt, and in his Scotch cap with ribbons, with a brand-new English gun without a sling. Laska flew up to him, welcomed him, and jumping up, asked him in her own way whether the others were coming soon, but getting no answer from him, she returned to her post of observation and sank into repose again, her head on one side, and one ear pricked up to listen. At last the door opened with a creak, and Stepan Arkadyevitch's spot-and-tan pointer Krak flew out, running round and round and turning over in the air. Stepan Arkadyevitch himself followed with a gun in his hand and a cigar in his mouth.

"Good dog, good dog, Krak!" he cried encouragingly to the dog, who put his paws up on his chest, catching at his game bag. Stepan Arkadyevitch was dressed in rough leggings and spats, in torn trousers and a short coat. On his head there was a wreck of a hat of indefinite form, but his gun of a new patent was a perfect gem, and his game bag and cartridge-belt, though worn, were of the very best quality.

Vassenka Veslovsky had had no notion before that it was truly *chic* for a sportsman to be in tatters, but to have his shooting outfit of the best quality. He saw it now as he looked at Stepan Arkadyevitch, radiant in his rags, graceful, well-fed, and joyous, a typical Russian nobleman. And he made up his mind that next time he went shooting he would certainly adopt the same get-up.

"Well, and what about our host?" he asked.

"A young wife," said Stepan Arkadyevitch, smiling.

"Yes, and such a charming one!"

"He came down dressed. No doubt he's run up to her again."

Stepan Arkadyevitch guessed right. Levin had run up again to his wife to ask her once more if she forgave him for his idiocy yesterday, and, moreover, to beg her for Christ's sake to be more careful. The great thing was for her to keep away from the children—they might any minute push against her. Then he had once more to hear her declare that she was not angry with him for going away for two days, and to beg her to be sure to send him a note next morning by a servant on horseback, to write him, if it were but two words only, to let him know that all was well with her.

Kitty was distressed, as she always was, at parting for a couple of days from her husband, but when she saw his eager figure, looking big and strong in his shooting-boots and his white blouse, and a sort of sportsman elation and excitement incomprehensible to her, she forgot her own chagrin for the sake of his pleasure, and said good-bye to him cheerfully.

"Pardon, gentlemen!" he said, running out onto the steps. "Have you put the lunch in? Why is the chestnut on the right? Well, it doesn't matter. Laska, down; go and lie down!"

"Put it with the herd of oxen," he said to the herdsman, who was waiting for him at the steps with some question. "Excuse me, here comes another villain."

Levin jumped out of the wagonette, in which he had already taken his seat, to meet the carpenter, who came towards the steps with a rule in his hand.

"You didn't come to the counting house yesterday, and now you're detaining me. Well, what is it?"

"Would your honor let me make another turning? It's only three steps to add. And we make it just fit at the same time. It will be much more convenient."

"You should have listened to me," Levin answered with annoyance. "I said: Put the lines and then fit in the steps. Now there's no setting it right. Do as I told you, and make a new staircase."

The point was that in the lodge that was being built the carpenter had spoiled the staircase, fitting it together without calculating the space it was to fill, so that the steps were all sloping when it was put in place. Now the carpenter wanted keeping the same staircase, to add three steps.

"It will be much better."

"But where's your staircase coming out with its three steps?"

"Why, upon my word, sir," the carpenter said with a contemptuous smile. "It comes out right at the very spot. It starts, so to speak," he said, with a persuasive gesture; "it comes down, and comes down, and comes out."

"But three steps will add to the length too . . . where is it to come out?"

"Why, to be sure, it'll start from the bottom and go up and go up, and come out so," the carpenter said obstinately and convincingly.

"It'll reach the ceiling and the wall."

"Upon my word! Why, it'll go up, and up, and come out like this."

Levin took out a ramrod and began sketching him the staircase in the dust.

"There, do you see?"

"As your honor likes," said the carpenter, with a sudden gleam in his eyes, obviously understanding the thing at last. "It seems it'll be best to make a new one."

"Well, then, do it as you're told," Levin shouted, seating himself in the wagonette. "Down! Hold the dogs, Philip!"

Levin felt now at leaving behind all his family and household cares such an eager sense of joy in life and expectation that he was not disposed to talk. Besides that, he had that feeling of concentrated excitement that every sportsman experiences as he approaches the scene of action. If he had anything on his mind at that moment, it was only the doubt whether they would start anything in the Kolpensky marsh, whether Laska would show to advantage in comparison with Krak, and whether he would shoot well that day himself. Not to disgrace himself before a new spectator—not to be outdone by Oblonsky—that too was a thought that crossed his brain.

Oblonsky was feeling the same, and he too was not talkative. Vassenka Veslovsky kept up alone a ceaseless flow of cheerful chatter. As he listened to him now, Levin felt ashamed to think how unfair he had been to him the day before. Vassenka was really a nice fellow, simple, good-hearted, and very good-humored. If Levin had met him before he was married, he would have made friends with him. Levin rather disliked his holiday attitude to life and a sort of free and easy assumption of elegance. It was as though he assumed a high degree of importance in himself that could not be disputed, because he had long nails and a stylish cap, and everything else to correspond; but this could be forgiven for the sake of his good-nature and good breeding. Levin liked him for his good education, for speaking French and English with such an excellent accent, and for being a man of his world.

Vassenka was extremely delighted with the left horse, a horse of the Don Steppes. He kept praising him enthusiastically. "How fine it must be galloping over the steppes on a steppe horse! Eh? isn't it?" he said. He had imagined riding on a steppe horse as something wild and romantic, and it turned out nothing of the sort. But his simplicity, particularly in conjunction with his good looks, his amiable smile, and the grace of his movements, was very attractive. Either because his nature was sympathetic to Levin, or because Levin was trying to atone for his sins of the previous evening by seeing nothing but what was good in him, anyway he liked his society.

After they had driven over two miles from home, Veslovsky all at once felt for a cigar and his pocketbook, and did not know whether he had lost them or left them on the table. In the pocketbook there were thirty-seven pounds, and so the matter could not be left in uncertainty.

"Do you know what, Levin, I'll gallop home on that left trace-horse. That will be splendid. Eh?" he said, preparing to get out.

"No, why should you?" answered Levin, calculating that Vassenka could hardly weigh less than seventeen stone. "I'll send the coachman."

The coachman rode back on the trace-horse, and Levin himself drove the remaining pair.

Chapter IX

WELL, NOW WHAT'S OUR PLAN OF CAMPAIGN? TELL US ALL ABOUT IT, SAID STEPAN ARKADYEvitch.

"Our plan is this. Now we're driving to Gvozdyov. In Gvozdyov there's a grouse marsh on this side, and beyond Gvozdyov come some magnificent snipe marshes where there are grouse too. It's hot now, and we'll get there—it's fifteen miles or so—towards evening and have some evening shooting; we'll spend the night there and go on tomorrow to the bigger moors."

"And is there nothing on the way?"

"Yes; but we'll reserve ourselves; besides it's hot. There are two nice little places, but I doubt there being anything to shoot."

Levin would himself have liked to go into these little places, but they were near home; he could shoot them over any time, and they were only little places—there would hardly be room for three to shoot. And so, with some insincerity, he said that he doubted there being anything to shoot. When they reached a little marsh Levin would have driven by, but Stepan Arkadyevitch, with the experienced eye of a sportsman, at once detected reeds visible from the road.

"Shan't we try that?" he said, pointing to the little marsh.

"Levin, do, please! how delightful!" Vassenka Veslovsky began begging, and Levin could but consent.

Before they had time to stop, the dogs had flown one before the other into the marsh.

"Krak! Laska! . . ."

The dogs came back.

"There won't be room for three. I'll stay here," said Levin, hoping they would find nothing but peewits, who had been startled by the dogs, and turning over in their flight, were plaintively wailing over the marsh.

"No! Come along, Levin, let's go together!" Veslovsky called.

"Really, there's not room. Laska, back, Laska! You won't want another dog, will you?"

Levin remained with the wagonette, and looked enviously at the sportsmen. They walked right across the marsh. Except little birds and peewits, of which Vassenka killed one, there was nothing in the marsh.

"Come, you see now that it was not that I grudged the marsh," said Levin, "only it's wasting time."

"Oh, no, it was jolly all the same. Did you see us?" said Vassenka Veslovsky, clambering awkwardly into the wagonette with his gun and his peewit in his hands. "How splendidly I shot this bird! Didn't I? Well, shall we soon be getting to the real place?"

The horses started off suddenly, Levin knocked his head against the stock of someone's gun, and there was the report of a shot. The gun did actually go off first, but that was how it seemed to Levin. It appeared that Vassenka Veslovsky had pulled only one trigger, and had left the other hammer still cocked. The charge flew into the ground without doing harm to anyone. Stepan Arkadyevitch shook his head and laughed reprovingly at Veslovsky. But Levin had not the heart to reprove him. In the first place, any reproach would have seemed to be called forth by the danger he had incurred and the bump that had come up on Levin's forehead. And besides, Veslovsky was at first so naïvely distressed, and then laughed so good-humoredly and infectiously at their general dismay, that one could not but laugh with him.

When they reached the second marsh, which was fairly large, and would inevitably take some time to shoot over, Levin tried to persuade them to pass it by. But Veslovsky again overpersuaded him. Again, as the marsh was narrow, Levin, like a good host, remained with the carriage.

Krak made straight for some clumps of sedge. Vassenka Veslovsky was the first to run after the dog. Before Stepan Arkadyevitch had time to come up, a grouse flew out. Veslovsky missed it and it flew into an unmown meadow. This grouse was left for Veslovsky to follow up. Krak found it again and pointed, and Veslovsky shot it and went back to the carriage. "Now you go and I'll stay with the horses," he said.

Levin had begun to feel the pangs of a sportsman's envy. He handed the reins to Veslovsky and walked into the marsh.

Laska, who had been plaintively whining and fretting against the injustice of her treatment, flew straight ahead to a hopeful place that Levin knew well, and that Krak had not yet come upon.

"Why don't you stop her?" shouted Stepan Arkadyevitch.

"She won't scare them," answered Levin, sympathizing with his bitch's pleasure and hurrying after her.

As she came nearer and nearer to the familiar breeding-places there was more and more earnestness in Laska's exploration. A little marsh bird did not divert her attention for more than an instant. She made one circuit round the clump of reeds, was beginning a second, and suddenly quivered with excitement and became motionless.

"Come, come, Stiva!" shouted Levin, feeling his heart beginning to beat more violently; and all of a sudden, as though some sort of shutter had been drawn back from his straining ears, all sounds, confused but loud, began to beat on his hearing, losing all sense of distance. He heard the steps of Stepan Arkadyevitch, mistaking them for the tramp of the horses in the distance; he heard the brittle sound of the twigs on which he had trodden, taking this sound for the flying of a grouse. He heard too, not far behind him, a splashing in the water, which he could not explain to himself.

Picking his steps, he moved up to the dog.

"Fetch it!"

Not a grouse but a snipe flew up from beside the dog. Levin had lifted his gun, but at the very instant when he was taking aim, the sound of splashing grew louder, came closer, and was joined with the sound of Veslovsky's voice, shouting something with strange loudness. Levin saw he had his gun pointed behind the snipe, but still he fired.

When he had made sure he had missed, Levin looked round and saw the horses and the wagonette not on the road but in the marsh.

Veslovsky, eager to see the shooting, had driven into the marsh, and got the horses stuck in the mud.

"Damn the fellow!" Levin said to himself, as he went back to the carriage that had sunk in the mire. "What did you drive in for?" he said to him dryly, and calling the coachman, he began pulling the horses out.

Levin was vexed both at being hindered from shooting and at his horses getting stuck in the mud, and still more at the fact that neither Stepan Arkadyevitch nor Veslovsky helped him and the coachman to unharness the horses and get them out, since neither of them had the slightest notion of harnessing. Without vouchsafing a syllable in reply to Vassenka's protestations that it had been quite dry there, Levin worked in silence with the coachman at extricating the horses. But then, as he got warm at the work and saw how assiduously Veslovsky was tugging at the wagonette by one of the mud-guards, so that he broke it indeed, Levin blamed himself for having under the influence of yesterday's feelings been too cold to Veslovsky, and tried to be particularly genial so as to smooth over his chilliness. When everything had been put right, and the carriage had been brought back to the road, Levin had the lunch served.

"Bon appétit—bonne conscience! Ce poulet va tomber jusqu'au fond de mes bottes," Vassenka, who had recovered his spirits, quoted the French saying as he finished his second chicken. "Well, now our troubles are over, now everything's going to go well. Only, to atone for my sins, I'm bound to sit on the box. That's so? eh? No, no! I'll be your Automedon. You shall see how I'll get you along," he answered, not letting go the rein, when Levin begged him to let the coachman drive. "No, I must atone for my sins, and I'm very comfortable on the box." And he drove.

Levin was a little afraid he would exhaust the horses, especially the chestnut, whom he did not know how to hold in; but unconsciously he fell under the influence of his gaiety and listened to the songs he sang all the way on the box, or the descriptions and representations he gave of driving in the English fashion, four-in-hand; and it was in the very best of spirits that after lunch they drove to the Gvozdyov marsh.

Chapter X

VASSENKA DROVE THE HORSES SO SMARTLY THAT THEY REACHED THE MARSH TOO EARLY, WHILE it was still hot.

As they drew near this more important marsh, the chief aim of their expedition, Levin could not help considering how he could get rid of Vassenka and be free in his movements. Stepan Arkadyevitch evidently had the same desire, and on his face Levin saw the look of anxiety always present in a true sportsman when beginning shooting, together with a certain good-humored slyness peculiar to him.

"How shall we go? It's a splendid marsh, I see, and there are hawks," said Stepan Arkadyevitch, pointing to two great birds hovering over the reeds. "Where there are hawks, there is sure to be game."

"Now, gentlemen," said Levin, pulling up his boots and examining the lock of his gun with rather a gloomy expression, "do you see those reeds?" He pointed to an oasis of blackish green in the huge half-mown wet meadow that stretched along the right bank of the river. "The marsh begins here, straight in front of us, do you see—where it is greener? From here it runs to the right where the horses are; there are breeding-places there, and grouse, and all round those reeds as far as that alder, and right up to the mill. Over there, do you see, where the pools are? That's the best place. There I once shot seventeen snipe. We'll separate with the dogs and go in different directions, and then meet over there at the mill."

"Well, which shall go to left and which to right?" asked Stepan Arkadyevitch. "It's wider to the right; you two go that way and I'll take the left," he said with apparent carelessness.

"Capital! we'll make the bigger bag! Yes, come along, come along!" Vassenka exclaimed.

Levin could do nothing but agree, and they divided.

As soon as they entered the marsh, the two dogs began hunting about together and made towards the green, slime-covered pool. Levin knew Laska's method, wary and indefinite; he knew the place too and expected a whole covey of snipe.

"Veslovsky, beside me, walk beside me!" he said in a faint voice to his companion splashing in the water behind him. Levin could not help feeling an interest in the direction his gun was pointed, after that casual shot near the Kolpensky marsh.

"Oh, I won't get in your way, don't trouble about me."

But Levin could not help troubling, and recalled Kitty's words at parting: "Mind you don't shoot one another." The dogs came nearer and nearer, passed each other, each pursuing its own scent. The expectation of snipe was so intense that to Levin the squelching sound of his own heel, as he drew it up out of the mire, seemed to be the call of a snipe, and he clutched and pressed the lock of his gun.

"Bang! bang!" sounded almost in his ear. Vassenka had fired at a flock of ducks which was hovering over the marsh and flying at that moment towards the sportsmen, far out of range. Before Levin had time to look round, there was the whir of one snipe, another, a third, and some eight more rose one after another.

Stepan Arkadyevitch hit one at the very moment when it was beginning its zigzag movements, and the snipe fell in a heap into the mud. Oblonsky aimed deliberately at another, still flying low in the reeds, and together with the report of the shot, that snipe too fell, and it could be seen fluttering out where the sedge had been cut, its unhurt wing showing white beneath.

Levin was not so lucky: he aimed at his first bird too low, and missed; he aimed at it again, just as it was rising, but at that instant another snipe flew up at his very feet, distracting him so that he missed again.

While they were loading their guns, another snipe rose, and Veslovsky, who had had time to load again, sent two charges of small-shot into the water. Stepan Arkadyevitch picked up his snipe, and with sparkling eyes looked at Levin.

"Well, now let us separate," said Stepan Arkadyevitch, and limping on his left foot, holding his gun in readiness and whistling to his dog, he walked off in one direction. Levin and Veslovsky walked in the other.

It always happened with Levin that when his first shots were a failure he got hot and out of temper, and shot badly the whole day. So it was that day. The snipe showed themselves in numbers. They kept flying up from just under the dogs, from under the sportsmen's legs, and Levin might have retrieved his ill luck. But the more he shot, the more he felt disgraced in the eyes of Veslovsky, who kept popping away merrily and indiscriminately, killing nothing, and not in the slightest abashed by his ill success. Levin, in feverish haste, could not restrain himself, got more and more out of temper, and ended by shooting almost without a hope of hitting. Laska, indeed, seemed to understand this. She began looking more languidly, and gazed back at the sportsmen, as it were, with perplexity or reproach in her eyes. Shots followed shots in rapid succession. The smoke of the powder hung about the sportsmen, while in the great roomy net of the game bag there were only three light little snipe. And of these one had been killed by Veslovsky alone, and one by both of them together. Meanwhile from the other side of the marsh came the sound of Stepan Arkadyevitch's shots, not frequent, but, as Levin fancied, well-directed, for almost after each they heard "Krak, Krak, *apporte!*"

This excited Levin still more. The snipe were floating continually in the air over the reeds. Their whirring wings close to the earth, and their harsh cries high in the air, could be heard on all sides; the snipe that had risen first and flown up into the air, settled again before the sportsmen. Instead of two hawks there were now dozens of them hovering with shrill cries over the marsh.

After walking through the larger half of the marsh, Levin and Veslovsky reached the place where the peasants' mowing-grass was divided into long strips reaching to the reeds, marked off in one place by the trampled grass, in another by a path mown through it. Half of these strips had already been mown.

Though there was not so much hope of finding birds in the uncut part as the cut part, Levin had promised Stepan Arkadyevitch to meet him, and so he walked on with his companion through the cut and uncut patches.

"Hi, sportsmen!" shouted one of a group of peasants, sitting on an unharnessed cart; "come and have some lunch with us! Have a drop of wine!"

Levin looked round.

"Come along, it's all right!" shouted a good-humored-looking bearded peasant with a red face, showing his white teeth in a grin, and holding up a greenish bottle that flashed in the sunlight.

"Qu'est-ce qu'ils disent?" asked Veslovsky.

"They invite you to have some vodka. Most likely they've been dividing the meadow into lots. I should have some," said Levin, not without some guile, hoping Veslovsky would be tempted by the vodka, and would go away to them.

"Why do they offer it?"

"Oh, they're merry-making. Really, you should join them. You would be interested."

"Allons, c'est curieux."

"You go, you go, you'll find the way to the mill!" cried Levin, and looking round he perceived with satisfaction that Veslovsky, bent and stumbling with weariness, holding his gun out at arm's length, was making his way out of the marsh towards the peasants.

"You come too!" the peasants shouted to Levin. "Never fear! You taste our cake!"

Levin felt a strong inclination to drink a little vodka and to eat some bread. He was exhausted, and felt it a great effort to drag his staggering legs out of the mire, and for a minute he hesitated. But Laska was setting. And immediately all his weariness vanished, and he walked lightly through the swamp towards the dog. A snipe flew up at his feet; he fired and killed it. Laska still pointed.—"Fetch it!" Another bird flew up close to the dog. Levin fired. But it was an unlucky day for him; he missed it, and when he went to look for the one he had shot, he could not find that either. He wandered all about the reeds, but Laska did not believe he had shot it, and when he sent her to find it, she pretended to hunt for it, but did not really. And in the absence of Vassenka, on whom Levin threw the blame of his failure, things went no better. There were plenty of snipe still, but Levin made one miss after another.

The slanting rays of the sun were still hot; his clothes, soaked through with perspiration, stuck to his body; his left boot full of water weighed heavily on his leg and squeaked at every step; the sweat ran in drops down his powder-grimed face, his mouth was full of the bitter taste, his nose of the smell of powder and stagnant water, his ears were ringing with the incessant whir of the snipe; he could not touch the stock of his gun, it was so hot; his heart beat with short, rapid throbs; his hands shook with excitement, and his weary legs stumbled and staggered over the hillocks and in the swamp, but still he walked on and still he shot. At last, after a disgraceful miss, he flung his gun and his hat on the ground.

"No, I must control myself," he said to himself. Picking up his gun and his hat, he called Laska, and went out of the swamp. When he got on to dry ground he sat down, pulled off his boot and emptied it, then walked to the marsh, drank some stagnant-tasting water, moistened his burning hot gun, and washed his face and hands. Feeling refreshed, he went back to the spot where a snipe had settled, firmly resolved to keep cool.

He tried to be calm, but it was the same again. His finger pressed the cock before he had taken a good aim at the bird. It got worse and worse.

He had only five birds in his game bag when he walked out of the marsh towards the alders where he was to rejoin Stepan Arkadyevitch.

Before he caught sight of Stepan Arkadyevitch he saw his dog. Krak darted out from behind the twisted root of an alder, black all over with the stinking mire of the marsh, and with the air of a conqueror sniffed at Laska. Behind Krak there came into view in the shade of the alder tree the shapely figure of Stepan Arkadyevitch. He came to meet him, red and perspiring, with unbuttoned neckband, still limping in the same way.

"Well? You have been popping away!" he said, smiling good-humoredly.

"How have you got on?" queried Levin. But there was no need to ask, for he had already seen the full game bag.

"Oh, pretty fair."

He had fourteen birds.

"A splendid marsh! I've no doubt Veslovsky got in your way. It's awkward too, shooting with one dog," said Stepan Arkadyevitch, to soften his triumph.

Chapter XI

WHEN LEVIN AND STEPAN ARKADYEVITCH REACHED THE PEASANT'S HUT WHERE LEVIN ALWAYS used to stay, Veslovsky was already there. He was sitting in the middle of the hut, clinging with both hands to the bench from which he was being pulled by a soldier, the brother of the peasant's wife, who was helping him off with his miry boots. Veslovsky was laughing his infectious, good-humored laugh.

"I've only just come. *Ils ont été charmants*. Just fancy, they gave me drink, fed me! Such bread, it was exquisite! *Délicieux!* And the vodka, I never tasted any better. And they would not take a penny for anything. And they kept saying: 'Excuse our homely ways.' "

"What should they take anything for? They were entertaining you, to be sure. Do you suppose they keep vodka for sale?" said the soldier, succeeding at last in pulling the soaked boot off the blackened stocking.

In spite of the dirtiness of the hut, which was all muddied by their boots and the filthy dogs licking themselves clean, and the smell of marsh mud and powder that filled the room, and the absence of knives and forks, the party drank their tea and ate their supper with a relish only known to sportsmen. Washed and clean, they went into a hay-barn swept ready for them, where the coachman had been making up beds for the gentlemen.

Though it was dusk, not one of them wanted to go to sleep.

After wavering among reminiscences and anecdotes of guns, of dogs, and of former shooting parties, the conversation rested on a topic that interested all of them. After Vassenka had several times over expressed his appreciation of this delightful sleeping place among the fragrant hay, this delightful broken cart (he supposed it to be broken because the shafts had been taken out), of the good-nature of the peasants that had treated him to vodka, of the dogs who lay at the feet of their respective masters, Oblonsky began telling them of a delightful shooting party at Malthus's, where he had stayed the previous summer.

Malthus was a well-known capitalist, who had made his money by speculation in railway shares. Stepan Arkadyevitch described what grouse moors this Malthus had bought in the Tver province, and how they were preserved, and of the carriages and dogcarts in which the shooting party had been driven, and the luncheon pavilion that had been rigged up at the marsh.

"I don't understand you," said Levin, sitting up in the hay; "how is it such people don't disgust you? I can understand a lunch with Lafitte is all very pleasant, but don't you dislike just that very sumptuousness? All these people, just like our spirit monopolists in old days, get their money in a way that gains them the contempt of everyone. They don't care for their contempt, and then they use their dishonest gains to buy off the contempt they have deserved."

"Perfectly true!" chimed in Vassenka Veslovsky. "Perfectly! Oblonsky, of course, goes out of *bonhomie,* but other people say: 'Well, Oblonsky stays with them.' . . ."

"Not a bit of it." Levin could hear that Oblonsky was smiling as he spoke. "I simply don't consider him more dishonest than any other wealthy merchant or nobleman. They've all made their money alike—by their work and their intelligence."

"Oh, by what work? Do you call it work to get hold of concessions and speculate with them?"

"Of course it's work. Work in this sense, that if it were not for him and others like him, there would have been no railways."

"But that's not work, like the work of a peasant or a learned profession."

"Granted, but it's work in the sense that his activity produces a result—the railways. But of course you think the railways useless."

"No, that's another question; I am prepared to admit that they're useful. But all profit that is out of proportion to the labor expended is dishonest."

"But who is to define what is proportionate?"

"Making profit by dishonest means, by trickery," said Levin, conscious that he could not draw a distinct line between honesty and dishonesty. "Such as banking, for instance," he went on. "It's an evil—the amassing of huge fortunes without labor, just the same thing as with the spirit monopolies, it's only the form that's changed. *Le roi est mort, vive le roi.* No sooner were the spirit monopolies abolished than the railways came up, and banking companies; that, too, is profit without work."

"Yes, that may all be very true and clever. . . . Lie down, Krak!" Stepan Arkadyevitch called to his dog, who was scratching and turning over all the hay. He was obviously convinced of the correctness of his position, and so talked serenely and without haste. "But you have not drawn the line between honest and dishonest work. That I receive a bigger salary than my chief clerk, though he knows more about the work than I do—that's dishonest, I suppose?"

"I can't say."

"Well, but I can tell you: your receiving some five thousand, let's say, for your work on the land, while our host, the peasant here, however hard he works, can never get more than fifty roubles, is just as dishonest as my earning more than my chief clerk, and Malthus getting more than a stationmaster. No, quite the contrary; I see that society takes up a sort of antagonistic attitude to these people, which is utterly baseless, and I fancy there's envy at the bottom of it. . . ."

"No, that's unfair," said Veslovsky; "how could envy come in? There is something not nice about that sort of business."

"You say," Levin went on, "that it's unjust for me to receive five thousand, while the peasant has fifty; that's true. It is unfair, and I feel it, but . . ."

"It really is. Why is it we spend our time riding, drinking, shooting, doing nothing, while they are forever at work?" said Vassenka Veslovsky, obviously for the first time in his life reflecting on the question, and consequently considering it with perfect sincerity.

"Yes, you feel it, but you don't give him your property," said Stepan Arkadyevitch, intentionally, as it seemed, provoking Levin.

There had arisen of late something like a secret antagonism between the two brothers-in-law; as though, since they had married sisters, a kind of rivalry had sprung up between them as to which was ordering his life best, and now this hostility showed itself in the conversation, as it began to take a personal note.

"I don't give it away, because no one demands that from me, and if I wanted to, I could not give it away," answered Levin, "and have no one to give it to."

"Give it to this peasant, he would not refuse it."

"Yes, but how am I to give it up? Am I to go to him and make a deed of conveyance?"

"I don't know; but if you are convinced that you have no right . . ."

"I'm not at all convinced. On the contrary, I feel I have no right to give it up, that I have duties both to the land and to my family."

"No, excuse me, but if you consider this inequality is unjust, why is it you don't act accordingly? . . ."

"Well, I do act negatively on that idea, so far as not trying to increase the difference of position existing between him and me."

"No, excuse me, that's a paradox."

"Yes, there's something of a sophistry about that," Veslovsky agreed. "Ah! our host; so you're not asleep yet?" he said to the peasant who came into the barn, opening the creaking door. "How is it you're not asleep?"

"No, how's one to sleep! I thought our gentlemen would be asleep, but I heard them chattering. I want to get a hook from here. She won't bite?" he added, stepping cautiously with his bare feet.

"And where are you going to sleep?"

"We are going out for the night with the beasts."

"Ah, what a night!" said Veslovsky, looking out at the edge of the hut and the unharnessed wagonette that could be seen in the faint light of the evening glow in the great frame of the open doors. "But listen, there are women's voices singing, and, on my word, not badly too. Who's that singing, my friend?"

"That's the maids from hard by here."

"Let's go, let's have a walk! We shan't go to sleep, you know. Oblonsky, come along!"

"If one could only do both, lie here and go," answered Oblonsky, stretching. "It's capital lying here."

"Well, I shall go by myself," said Veslovsky, getting up eagerly, and putting on his shoes and stockings. "Good-bye, gentlemen. If it's fun, I'll fetch you. You've treated me to some good sport, and I won't forget you."

"He really is a capital fellow, isn't he?" said Stepan Arkadyevitch, when Veslovsky had gone out and the peasant had closed the door after him.

"Yes, capital," answered Levin, still thinking of the subject of their conversation just before. It seemed to him that he had clearly expressed his thoughts and feelings to the best of his capacity, and yet both of them, straightforward men and not fools, had said with one voice that he was comforting himself with sophistries. This disconcerted him.

"It's just this, my dear boy. One must do one of two things: either admit that the existing order of society is just, and then stick up for one's rights in it; or acknowledge that you are enjoying unjust privileges, as I do, and then enjoy them and be satisfied."

"No, if it were unjust, you could not enjoy these advantages and be satisfied—at least I could not. The great thing for me is to feel that I'm not to blame."

"What do you say, why not go after all?" said Stepan Arkadyevitch, evidently weary of the strain of thought. "We shan't go to sleep, you know. Come, let's go!"

Levin did not answer. What they had said in the conversation, that he acted justly only in a negative sense, absorbed his thoughts. "Can it be that it's only possible to be just negatively?" he was asking himself.

"How strong the smell of the fresh hay is, though," said Stepan Arkadyevitch, getting up. "There's not a chance of sleeping. Vassenka has been getting up some fun there. Do you hear the laughing and his voice? Hadn't we better go? Come along!"

"No, I'm not coming," answered Levin.

"Surely that's not a matter of principle too," said Stepan Arkadyevitch, smiling, as he felt about in the dark for his cap.

"It's not a matter of principle, but why should I go?"

"But do you know you are preparing trouble for yourself," said Stepan Arkadyevitch, finding his cap and getting up.

"How so?"

"Do you suppose I don't see the line you've taken up with your wife? I heard how it's a question of the greatest consequence, whether or not you're to be away for a couple of days' shooting. That's all very well as an idyllic episode, but for your whole life that won't answer. A man must be independent; he has his masculine interests. A man has to be manly," said Oblonsky, opening the door.

"In what way? To go running after servant girls?" said Levin.

"Why not, if it amuses him? *Ça ne tire pas à conséquence.* It won't do my wife any harm, and it'll amuse me. The great thing is to respect the sanctity of the home. There should be nothing in the home. But don't tie your own hands."

"Perhaps so," said Levin dryly, and he turned on his side. "Tomorrow, early, I want to go shooting, and I won't wake anyone, and shall set off at daybreak."

"Messieurs, venez vite!" they heard the voice of Veslovsky coming back. "*Charmante!* I've made such a discovery. *Charmante!* a perfect Gretchen, and I've already made friends with her. Really, exceedingly pretty," he declared in a tone of approval, as though she had been made pretty entirely on his account, and he was expressing his satisfaction with the entertainment that had been provided for him.

Levin pretended to be asleep, while Oblonsky, putting on his slippers, and lighting a cigar, walked out of the barn, and soon their voices were lost.

For a long while Levin could not get to sleep. He heard the horses munching hay, then he heard the peasant and his elder boy getting ready for the night, and going off for the night watch with the beasts, then he heard the soldier arranging his bed on the other side of the barn, with his nephew, the younger son of their peasant host. He heard the boy in his shrill little voice telling his uncle what he thought about the dogs, who seemed to him huge and terrible creatures, and asking what the dogs were going to hunt next day, and the soldier in a husky, sleepy voice, telling him the sportsmen were going in the morning to the marsh, and would shoot with their guns; and then, to check the boy's questions, he said, "Go to sleep, Vaska; go to sleep, or you'll catch it," and soon after he began snoring himself, and everything was still. He could only hear the snort of the horses, and the guttural cry of a snipe.

"Is it really only negative?" he repeated to himself. "Well, what of it? It's not my fault." And he began thinking about the next day.

"Tomorrow I'll go out early, and I'll make a point of keeping cool. There are lots of snipe; and there are grouse too. When I come back there'll be the note from Kitty. Yes, Stiva may be right, I'm not manly with her, I'm tied to her apron-strings. . . . Well, it can't be helped! Negative again. . . ."

Half asleep, he heard the laughter and mirthful talk of Veslovsky and Stepan Arkadyevitch. For an instant he opened his eyes: the moon was up, and in the open doorway, brightly lit up by the moonlight, they were standing talking. Stepan Arkadyevitch was saying something of the freshness of one girl, comparing her to a freshly peeled nut, and Veslovsky with his infectious laugh was repeating some words, probably said to him by a peasant: "Ah, you do your best to get round her!" Levin, half asleep, said:

"Gentlemen, tomorrow before daylight!" and fell asleep.

Chapter XII

WAKING UP AT EARLIEST DAWN, LEVIN TRIED TO WAKE HIS COMPANIONS. VASSENKA, LYING ON his stomach, with one leg in a stocking thrust out, was sleeping so soundly that he could elicit no response. Oblonsky, half asleep, declined to get up so early. Even Laska, who was asleep, curled up in the hay, got up unwillingly, and lazily stretched out and straightened her hind legs one after the other. Getting on his boots and stockings, taking his gun, and carefully opening the creaking door of the barn, Levin went out into the road. The coachmen were sleeping in their carriages, the horses were dozing. Only one was lazily eating oats, dipping its nose into the manger. It was still gray out-of-doors.

"Why are you up so early, my dear?" the old woman, their hostess, said, coming out of the hut and addressing him affectionately as an old friend.

"Going shooting, granny. Do I go this way to the marsh?"

"Straight out at the back; by our threshing floor, my dear, and hemp patches; there's a little footpath." Stepping carefully with her sunburned, bare feet, the old woman conducted Levin, and moved back the fence for him by the threshing floor.

"Straight on and you'll come to the marsh. Our lads drove the cattle there yesterday evening."

Laska ran eagerly forward along the little path. Levin followed her with a light, rapid step, continually looking at the sky. He hoped the sun would not be up before he reached the marsh. But the sun did not delay. The moon, which had been bright when he went out, by now shone only like a crescent of quicksilver. The pink flush of dawn, which one could not help seeing before, now had to be sought to be discerned at all. What were before undefined, vague blurs in the distant countryside could now be distinctly seen. They were sheaves of rye. The dew, not visible till the sun was up, wetted Levin's legs and his blouse above his belt in the high growing, fragrant hemp patch, from which the pollen had already fallen out. In the transparent stillness of morning the smallest sounds were audible. A bee flew by Levin's ear with the whizzing sound of a bullet. He looked carefully, and saw a second and a third. They were all flying from the beehives behind the hedge, and they disappeared over the hemp patch in the direction of the marsh. The path led straight to the marsh. The marsh could be recognized by the mist which rose from it, thicker in one place and thinner in another, so that the reeds and willow bushes swayed like islands in this mist. At the edge of the marsh and the road, peasant boys and men, who had been herding for the night, were lying, and in the dawn all were asleep under their coats. Not far from them were three hobbled horses. One of them clanked a chain. Laska walked beside her master, pressing a little forward and looking round. Passing the sleeping peasants and reaching the first reeds, Levin examined his pistols and let his dog off. One of the horses, a sleek, dark-brown three-year-old, seeing the dog, started away, switched its tail and snorted. The other horses too were frightened, and splashing through the water with their hobbled legs, and drawing their hoofs out of the thick mud with a squelching sound, they bounded out of the marsh. Laska stopped, looking ironically at the horses and inquiringly at Levin. Levin patted Laska, and whistled as a sign that she might begin.

Laska ran joyfully and anxiously through the slush that swayed under her.

Running into the marsh among the familiar scents of roots, marsh plants, and slime, and the extraneous smell of horse dung, Laska detected at once a smell that pervaded the whole marsh, the scent of that strong-smelling bird that always excited her more than any other. Here and there among the moss and marsh plants this scent was very strong, but it was impossible to determine in which direction it grew stronger or fainter. To find the direction, she had to go farther away from the wind. Not feeling the motion of her legs, Laska bounded with a stiff gallop, so that at each bound she could stop short, to the right, away from the wind that blew from the east before sunrise, and turned facing the wind. Sniffing in the air with dilated nostrils, she felt at once that not their tracks only but they themselves were here before her, and not one, but many. Laska slackened her speed. They were here, but where precisely she could not yet determine. To find the very spot, she began to make a circle, when suddenly her master's voice drew her off. "Laska! here?" he asked, pointing her to a different direction. She stopped, asking him if she had better not go on doing as she had begun. But he repeated his command in an angry voice, pointing to a spot covered with water, where there could not be anything. She obeyed him, pretending she was looking, so as to please him, went round it, and went back to her former position, and was at once aware of the scent again. Now when he was not hindering her, she knew what to do, and without looking at what was under her feet, and to her vexation stumbling over a high stump into the water, but righting herself with her strong, supple legs, she began making the circle which was to make all clear to her. The scent of them reached her, stronger and stronger, and more and more defined, and all at once it became perfectly clear to her that one of them was here, behind this tuft of reeds, five paces in front of her; she stopped, and her whole body was still and rigid. On her short legs she could see nothing in front of her, but by the scent she knew it was sitting not more than five paces off. She stood still, feeling more and more conscious of it, and enjoying it in anticipation. Her tail was stretched straight and tense, and only wagging at the extreme end. Her mouth was slightly open, her ears raised. One ear had been turned wrong side out as she ran up, and she breathed heavily but warily, and still more warily looked round, but more with her eyes than her head, to her master. He was coming along with the face she knew so well, though the eyes were always terrible to her. He stumbled over the stump as he came, and moved, as she thought, extraordinarily slowly. She thought he came slowly, but he was running.

Noticing Laska's special attitude as she crouched on the ground, as it were, scratching big prints with her hind paws, and with her mouth slightly open, Levin knew she was pointing at grouse, and with an inward prayer for luck, especially with the first bird, he ran up to her. Coming quite close up to her, he could from his height look beyond her, and he saw with his eyes what she was seeing with her nose. In a space between two little thickets, at a couple of yards' distance, he could see a grouse. Turning its head, it was listening. Then lightly preening and folding its wings, it disappeared round a corner with a clumsy wag of its tail.

"Fetch it, fetch it!" shouted Levin, giving Laska a shove from behind.

"But I can't go," thought Laska. "Where am I to go? From here I feel them, but if I move forward I shall know nothing of where they are or who they are." But then he shoved her with his knee, and in an excited whisper said, "Fetch it, Laska."

"Well, if that's what he wishes, I'll do it, but I can't answer for myself now," she thought, and darted forward as fast as her legs would carry her between the thick bushes. She scented nothing now; she could only see and hear, without understanding anything.

Ten paces from her former place a grouse rose with a guttural cry and the peculiar round sound of its wings. And immediately after the shot it splashed heavily with its white breast on the wet mire. Another bird did not linger, but rose behind Levin without the dog. When Levin turned towards it, it was already some way off. But his shot caught it. Flying twenty paces further, the second grouse rose upwards, and whirling round like a ball, dropped heavily on a dry place.

"Come, this is going to be some good!" thought Levin, packing the warm and fat grouse into his game bag. "Eh, Laska, will it be good?"

When Levin, after loading his gun, moved on, the sun had fully risen, though unseen behind the storm clouds. The moon had lost all of its luster, and was like a white cloud in the sky. Not a single star could be seen. The sedge, silvery with dew before, now shone like gold. The stagnant pools were all like amber. The blue of the grass had changed to yellow-green. The marsh birds twittered and swarmed about the brook and upon the bushes that glittered with dew and cast long shadows. A hawk woke up and settled on a haycock, turning its head from side to side and looking discontentedly at the marsh. Crows were flying about the field, and a bare-legged boy was driving the horses to an old man, who had got up from under his long coat and was combing his hair. The smoke from the gun was white as milk over the green of the grass.

One of the boys ran up to Levin.

"Uncle, there were ducks here yesterday!" he shouted to him, and he walked a little way off behind him.

And Levin was doubly pleased, in sight of the boy, who expressed his approval, at killing three snipe, one after another, straight off.

Chapter XIII

The sportsman's saying, that if the first beast or the first bird is not missed, the day will be lucky, turned out correct.

At ten o'clock Levin, weary, hungry, and happy after a tramp of twenty miles, returned to his night's lodging with nineteen head of fine game and one duck, which he tied to his belt, as it would not go into the game bag. His companions had long been awake, and had had time to get hungry and have breakfast.

"Wait a bit, wait a bit, I know there are nineteen," said Levin, counting a second time over the grouse and snipe, that looked so much less important now, bent and dry and bloodstained, with heads crooked aside, than they did when they were flying.

The number was verified, and Stepan Arkadyevitch's envy pleased Levin. He was pleased too on returning to find the man sent by Kitty with a note was already there.

"I am perfectly well and happy. If you were uneasy about me, you can feel easier than ever. I've a new bodyguard, Marya Vlasyevna,"—this was the midwife, a new and important personage in Levin's domestic life. "She has come to have a look at me. She found me perfectly well, and we have kept her till you are back. All are happy and well, and please, don't be in a hurry to come back, but, if the sport is good, stay another day."

These two pleasures, his lucky shooting and the letter from his wife, were so great that two slightly disagreeable incidents passed lightly over Levin. One was that the chestnut trace horse, who had been unmistakably overworked on the previous day, was off his feed and out of sorts. The coachman said he was "Overdriven yesterday, Konstantin Dmitrievitch. Yes, indeed! driven ten miles with no sense!"

The other unpleasant incident, which for the first minute destroyed his good-humor, though later he laughed at it a great deal, was to find that of all the provisions Kitty had provided in such abundance that one would have thought there was enough for a week, nothing was left. On his way back, tired and hungry from shooting, Levin had so distinct a vision of meat-pies that as he approached the hut he seemed to smell and taste them, as Laska had smelled the game, and he immediately told Philip to give him some. It appeared that there were no pies left, nor even any chicken.

"Well, this fellow's appetite!" said Stepan Arkadyevitch, laughing and pointing at Vassenka Veslovsky. "I never suffer from loss of appetite, but he's really marvelous! . . ."

"Well, it can't be helped," said Levin, looking gloomily at Veslovsky. "Well, Philip, give me some beef, then."

"The beef's been eaten, and the bones given to the dogs," answered Philip.

Levin was so hurt that he said, in a tone of vexation, "You might have left me something!" and he felt ready to cry.

"Then put away the game," he said in a shaking voice to Philip, trying not to look at Vassenka, "and cover them with some nettles. And you might at least ask for some milk for me."

But when he had drunk some milk, he felt ashamed immediately at having shown his annoyance to a stranger, and he began to laugh at his hungry mortification.

In the evening they went shooting again, and Veslovsky had several successful shots, and in the night they drove home.

Their homeward journey was as lively as their drive out had been. Veslovsky sang songs and related with enjoyment his adventures with the peasants, who had regaled him with vodka, and said to him, "Excuse our homely ways," and his night's adventures with kiss-in-the-ring and the servant girl and the peasant, who had asked him was he married, and on learning that he was not, said to him, "Well, mind you don't run after other men's wives—you'd better get one of your own." These words had particularly amused Veslovsky.

"Altogether, I've enjoyed our outing awfully. And you, Levin?"

"I have, very much," Levin said quite sincerely. It was particularly delightful to him to have got rid of the hostility he had been feeling towards Vassenka Veslovsky at home, and to feel instead the most friendly disposition to him.

Chapter XIV

NEXT DAY AT TEN O'CLOCK LEVIN, WHO HAD ALREADY GONE HIS ROUNDS, KNOCKED AT THE room where Vassenka had been put for the night.

"Entrez!" Veslovsky called to him. "Excuse me, I've only just finished my ablutions," he said, smiling, standing before him in his underclothes only.

"Don't mind me, please." Levin sat down in the window. "Have you slept well?"

"Like the dead. What sort of day is it for shooting?"

"What will you take, tea or coffee?"

"Neither. I'll wait till lunch. I'm really ashamed. I suppose the ladies are down? A walk now would be capital. You show me your horses."

After walking about the garden, visiting the stable, and even doing some gymnastic exercises together on the parallel bars, Levin returned to the house with his guest, and went with him into the drawing room.

"We had splendid shooting, and so many delightful experiences!" said Veslovsky, going up to Kitty, who was sitting at the samovar. "What a pity ladies are cut off from these delights!"

"Well, I suppose he must say something to the lady of the house," Levin said to himself. Again he fancied something in the smile, in the all-conquering air with which their guest addressed Kitty. . . .

The princess, sitting on the other side of the table with Marya Vlasyevna and Stepan Arkadyevitch, called Levin to her side, and began to talk to him about moving to Moscow for Kitty's confinement, and getting ready rooms for them. Just as Levin had disliked all the trivial preparations for his wedding, as derogatory to the grandeur of the event, now he felt still more offensive the preparations for the approaching birth, the date of which they reckoned, it seemed, on their fingers. He tried to turn a deaf ear to these discussions of the best patterns of long clothes for the coming baby; tried to turn away and avoid seeing the mysterious, endless strips of knitting, the triangles of linen, and so on, to which Dolly attached special importance. The birth of a son (he was certain it would be a son) which was promised him, but which he still could not believe in—so marvelous it seemed—presented itself to his mind, on one hand, as a happiness so immense, and therefore so incredible; on the other, as an event so mysterious, that this assumption of a definite knowledge of what would be, and consequent preparation for it, as for something ordinary that did happen to people, jarred on him as confusing and humiliating.

But the princess did not understand his feelings, and put down his reluctance to think and talk about it to carelessness and indifference, and so she gave him no peace. She had commissioned Stepan Arkadyevitch to look at a flat, and now she called Levin up.

"I know nothing about it, princess. Do as you think fit," he said.

"You must decide when you will move."

"I really don't know. I know millions of children are born away from Moscow, and doctors . . . why . . ."

"But if so . . ."

"Oh, no, as Kitty wishes."

"We can't talk to Kitty about it! Do you want me to frighten her? Why, this spring Natalia Golitzina died from having an ignorant doctor."

"I will do just what you say," he said gloomily.

The princess began talking to him, but he did not hear her. Though the conversation with the princess had indeed jarred upon him, he was gloomy, not on account of that conversation, but from what he saw at the samovar.

"No, it's impossible," he thought, glancing now and then at Vassenka bending over Kitty, telling her something with his charming smile, and at her, flushed and disturbed.

There was something not nice in Vassenka's attitude, in his eyes, in his smile. Levin even saw something not nice in Kitty's attitude and look. And again the light died away in his eyes. Again, as before, all of a sudden, without the slightest transition, he felt cast down from a pinnacle of happiness, peace, and dignity, into an abyss of despair, rage, and humiliation. Again everything and everyone had become hateful to him.

"You do just as you think best, princess," he said again, looking round.

"Heavy is the cap of Monomach," Stepan Arkadyevitch said playfully, hinting, evidently, not simply at the princess's conversation, but at the cause of Levin's agitation, which he had noticed. "How late you are today, Dolly!"

Everyone got up to greet Darya Alexandrovna. Vassenka only rose for an instant, and with the lack of courtesy to ladies characteristic of the modern young man, he scarcely bowed, and resumed his conversation again, laughing at something.

"I've been worried about Masha. She did not sleep well, and is dreadfully tiresome today," said Dolly.

The conversation Vassenka had started with Kitty was running on the same lines as on the previous evening, discussing Anna, and whether love is to be put higher than worldly considerations. Kitty disliked the conversation, and she was disturbed both by the subject and the tone in which it was conducted, and also by the knowledge of the effect it would have on her husband. But she was too simple and innocent to know how to cut short this conversation, or even to conceal the superficial pleasure afforded her by the young man's very obvious admiration. She wanted to stop it, but she did not know what to do. Whatever she did she knew would be observed by her husband, and the worst interpretation put on it. And, in fact, when she asked Dolly what was wrong with Masha, and Vassenka, waiting till this uninteresting conversation was over, began to gaze indifferently at Dolly, the question struck Levin as an unnatural and disgusting piece of hypocrisy.

"What do you say, shall we go and look for mushrooms today?" said Dolly.

"By all means, please, and I shall come too," said Kitty, and she blushed. She wanted from politeness to ask Vassenka whether he would come, and she did not ask him. "Where are you going, Kostya?" she asked her husband with a guilty face, as he passed by her with a resolute step. This guilty air confirmed all his suspicions.

"The mechanician came when I was away; I haven't seen him yet," he said, not looking at her.

He went downstairs, but before he had time to leave his study he heard his wife's familiar footsteps running with reckless speed to him.

"What do you want?" he said to her shortly. "We are busy."

"I beg your pardon," she said to the German mechanician; "I want a few words with my husband."

The German would have left the room, but Levin said to him:

"Don't disturb yourself."

"The train is at three?" queried the German. "I mustn't be late."

Levin did not answer him, but walked out himself with his wife.

"Well, what have you to say to me?" he said to her in French.

He did not look her in the face, and did not care to see that she in her condition was trembling all over, and had a piteous, crushed look.

"I . . . I want to say that we can't go on like this; that this is misery . . ." she said.

"The servants are here at the sideboard," he said angrily; "don't make a scene."

"Well, let's go in here!"

They were standing in the passage. Kitty would have gone into the next room, but there the English governess was giving Tanya a lesson.

"Well, come into the garden."

In the garden they came upon a peasant weeding the path. And no longer considering that the peasant could see her tear-stained and his agitated face, that they looked like people fleeing from some disaster, they went on with rapid steps, feeling that they must speak out and clear up misunderstandings, must be alone together, and so get rid of the misery they were both feeling.

"We can't go on like this! It's misery! I am wretched; you are wretched. What for?" she said, when they had at last reached a solitary garden seat at a turn in the lime tree avenue.

"But tell me one thing: was there in his tone anything unseemly, not nice, humiliatingly horrible?" he said, standing before her again in the same position with his clenched fists on his chest, as he had stood before her that night.

"Yes," she said in a shaking voice; "but, Kostya, surely you see I'm not to blame? All the morning I've been trying to take a tone . . . but such people . . . Why did he come? How happy we were!" she said, breathless with the sobs that shook her.

Although nothing had been pursuing them, and there was nothing to run away from, and they could not possibly have found anything very delightful on that garden seat, the gardener saw with astonishment that they passed him on their way home with comforted and radiant faces.

Chapter XV

After escorting his wife upstairs, Levin went to Dolly's part of the house. Darya Alexandrovna, for her part, was in great distress too that day. She was walking about the room, talking angrily to a little girl, who stood in the corner roaring.

"And you shall stand all day in the corner, and have your dinner all alone, and not see one of your dolls, and I won't make you a new frock," she said, not knowing how to punish her.

"Oh, she is a disgusting child!" she turned to Levin. "Where does she get such wicked propensities?"

"Why, what has she done?" Levin said without much interest, for he had wanted to ask her advice, and so was annoyed that he had come at an unlucky moment.

"Grisha and she went into the raspberries, and there . . . I can't tell you really what she did. It's a thousand pities Miss Elliot's not with us. This one sees to nothing—she's a machine. . . . *Figurez-vous que la petite? . . .*"

And Darya Alexandrovna described Masha's crime.

"That proves nothing; it's not a question of evil propensities at all, it's simply mischief," Levin assured her.

"But you are upset about something? What have you come for?" asked Dolly. "What's going on there?"

And in the tone of her question Levin heard that it would be easy for him to say what he had meant to say.

"I've not been in there, I've been alone in the garden with Kitty. We've had a quarrel for the second time since . . . Stiva came."

Dolly looked at him with her shrewd, comprehending eyes.

"Come, tell me, honor bright, has there been . . . not in Kitty, but in that gentleman's behavior, a tone which might be unpleasant—not unpleasant, but horrible, offensive to a husband?"

"You mean, how shall I say . . . Stay, stay in the corner!" she said to Masha, who, detecting a faint smile in her mother's face, had been turning round. "The opinion of the world would be that he is behaving as young men do behave. *Il fait la cour à une jeune et jolie femme,* and a husband who's a man of the world should only be flattered by it."

"Yes, yes," said Levin gloomily; "but you noticed it?"

"Not only I, but Stiva noticed it. Just after breakfast he said to me in so many words, *Je crois que Veslovsky fait un petit brin de cour à Kitty.*"

"Well, that's all right then; now I'm satisfied. I'll send him away," said Levin.

"What do you mean! Are you crazy?" Dolly cried in horror; "nonsense, Kostya, only think!" she said, laughing. "You can go now to Fanny," she said to Masha. "No, if you wish it, I'll speak to Stiva. He'll take him away. He can say you're expecting visitors. Altogether he doesn't fit into the house."

"No, no, I'll do it myself."

"But you'll quarrel with him?"

"Not a bit. I shall so enjoy it," Levin said, his eyes flashing with real enjoyment. "Come, forgive her, Dolly, she won't do it again," he said of the little sinner, who had not gone to Fanny, but was standing irresolutely before her mother, waiting and looking up from under her brows to catch her mother's eye.

The mother glanced at her. The child broke into sobs, hid her face on her mother's lap, and Dolly laid her thin, tender hand on her head.

"And what is there in common between us and him?" thought Levin, and he went off to look for Veslovsky.

As he passed through the passage he gave orders for the carriage to be got ready to drive to the station.

"The spring was broken yesterday," said the footman.

"Well, the covered trap, then, and make haste. Where's the visitor?"

"The gentleman's gone to his room."

Levin came upon Veslovsky at the moment when the latter, having unpacked his things from his trunk, and laid out some new songs, was putting on his gaiters to go out riding.

Whether there was something exceptional in Levin's face, or that Vassenka was himself conscious that *ce petit brin de cour* he was making was out of place in this family, but he was somewhat (as much as a young man in society can be) disconcerted at Levin's entrance.

"You ride in gaiters?"

"Yes, it's much cleaner," said Vassenka, putting his fat leg on a chair, fastening the bottom hook, and smiling with simple-hearted good-humor.

He was undoubtedly a good-natured fellow, and Levin felt sorry for him and ashamed of himself, as his host, when he saw the shy look on Vassenka's face.

On the table lay a piece of stick which they had broken together that morning, trying their strength. Levin took the fragment in his hands and began smashing it up, breaking bits off the stick, not knowing how to begin.

"I wanted . . ." He paused, but suddenly, remembering Kitty and everything that had happened, he said, looking him resolutely in the face: "I have ordered the horses to be put-to for you."

"How so?" Vassenka began in surprise. "To drive where?"

"For you to drive to the station," Levin said gloomily.

"Are you going away, or has something happened?"

"It happens that I expect visitors," said Levin, his strong fingers more and more rapidly breaking off the ends of the split stick. "And I'm not expecting visitors, and nothing has happened, but I beg you to go away. You can explain my rudeness as you like."

Vassenka drew himself up.

"I beg you to explain . . ." he said with dignity, understanding at last.

"I can't explain," Levin said softly and deliberately, trying to control the trembling of his jaw; "and you'd better not ask."

And as the split ends were all broken off, Levin clutched the thick ends in his finger, broke the stick in two, and carefully caught the end as it fell.

Probably the sight of those nervous fingers, of the muscles he had proved that morning at gymnastics, of the glittering eyes, the soft voice, and quivering jaws, convinced Vassenka better than any words. He bowed, shrugging his shoulders, and smiling contemptuously.

"Can I not see Oblonsky?"

The shrug and the smile did not irritate Levin.

"What else was there for him to do?" he thought.

"I'll send him to you at once."

"What madness is this?" Stepan Arkadyevitch said when, after hearing from his friend that he was being turned out of the house, he found Levin in the garden, where he was walking about waiting for his guest's departure. "*Mais c'est ridicule!* What fly has stung you? *Mais c'est du dernier ridicule!* What did you think, if a young man . . ."

But the place where Levin had been stung was evidently still sore, for he turned pale again, when Stepan Arkadyevitch would have enlarged on the reason, and he himself cut him short.

"Please don't go into it! I can't help it. I feel ashamed of how I'm treating you and him. But it won't be, I imagine, a great grief to him to go, and his presence was distasteful to me and to my wife."

"But it's insulting to him! *Et puis c'est ridicule.*"

"And to me it's both insulting and distressing! And I'm not at fault in any way, and there's no need for me to suffer."

"Well, this I didn't expect of you! *On peut etre jaloux, mais a ce point, c'est du dernier ridicule!*"

Levin turned quickly, and walked away from him into the depths of the avenue, and he went on walking up and down alone. Soon he heard the rumble of the trap, and saw from behind the trees how Vassenka, sitting in the hay (unluckily there was no seat in the trap) in his Scotch cap, was driven along the avenue, jolting up and down over the ruts.

"What's this?" Levin thought, when a footman ran out of the house and stopped the trap. It was the mechanician, whom Levin had totally forgotten. The mechanician, bowing low, said something to Veslovsky, then clambered into the trap, and they drove off together.

Stepan Arkadyevitch and the princess were much upset by Levin's action. And he himself felt not only in the highest degree *ridicule*, but also utterly guilty and disgraced. But remembering what sufferings he and his wife had been through, when he asked himself how he should act another time, he answered that he should do just the same again.

In spite of all this, towards the end of that day, everyone except the princess, who could not pardon Levin's action, became extraordinarily lively and good-humored, like children after a punishment or grown-up people after a dreary, ceremonious reception, so that by the evening Vassenka's dismissal was spoken of, in the absence of the princess, as though it were some remote event. And Dolly, who had inherited her father's gift of humorous storytelling, made Varenka helpless with laughter as she related for the third and fourth time, always with fresh humorous additions, how she had only just put on her new shoes for the benefit of the visitor, and on going into the drawing room, heard suddenly the rumble of the trap. And who should be in the trap but Vassenka himself, with his Scotch cap, and his songs and his gaiters, and all, sitting in the hay.

"If only you'd ordered out the carriage! But no! and then I hear: 'Stop!' Oh, I thought they've relented. I look out, and behold a fat German being sat down by him and driving away . . . And my new shoes all for nothing! . . ."

Chapter XVI

DARYA ALEXANDROVNA CARRIED OUT HER INTENTION AND WENT TO SEE ANNA. SHE WAS SORRY to annoy her sister and to do anything Levin disliked. She quite understood how right the Levins were in not wishing to have anything to do with Vronsky. But she felt she must go and see Anna, and show her that her feelings could not be changed, in spite of the change in her position. That she might be independent of the Levins in this expedition, Darya Alexandrovna sent to the village to hire horses for the drive; but Levin learning of it went to her to protest.

"What makes you suppose that I dislike your going? But, even if I did dislike it, I should still more dislike your not taking my horses," he said. "You never told me that you were going for certain. Hiring horses in the village is disagreeable to me, and, what's of more importance, they'll undertake the job and never get you there. I have horses. And if you don't want to wound me, you'll take mine."

Darya Alexandrovna had to consent, and on the day fixed Levin had ready for his sister-in-law a set of four horses and relays, getting them together from the farm-and saddle-horses—not at all a smart-looking set, but capable of taking Darya Alexandrovna the whole distance in a single day. At that moment, when horses were wanted for the princess, who was going, and for the midwife, it was a difficult matter for Levin to make up the number, but the duties of hospitality would not let him allow Darya Alexandrovna to hire horses when staying in his house. Moreover, he was well aware that the twenty roubles that would be asked for the journey were a serious matter for her; Darya Alexandrovna's pecuniary affairs, which were in a very unsatisfactory state, were taken to heart by the Levins as if they were their own.

Darya Alexandrovna, by Levin's advice, started before daybreak. The road was good, the carriage comfortable, the horses trotted along merrily, and on the box, besides the coachman, sat the counting house clerk, whom Levin was sending instead of a groom for greater security. Darya Alexandrovna dozed and waked up only on reaching the inn where the horses were to be changed.

After drinking tea at the same well-to-do peasant's with whom Levin had stayed on the way to Sviazhsky's, and chatting with the women about their children, and with the old man about Count Vronsky, whom the latter praised very highly, Darya Alexandrovna, at ten o'clock, went on again. At home, looking after her children, she had no time to think. So now, after this journey of four hours, all the thoughts she had suppressed before rushed swarming into her brain, and she thought over all her life as she never had before, and from the most different points of view. Her thoughts seemed strange even to herself. At first she thought about the children, about whom she was uneasy, although the princess and Kitty (she reckoned more upon her) had promised to look after them. "If only Masha does not begin her naughty tricks, if Grisha isn't kicked by a horse, and Lily's stomach isn't upset again!" she thought. But these questions of the present were succeeded by questions of the immediate future. She began thinking how she had to get a new flat in Moscow for the coming winter, to renew the drawing room furniture, and to make her elder girl a cloak. Then questions of the more remote future occurred to her: how she was to place her children in the world. "The girls are all right," she thought; "but the boys?"

"It's very well that I'm teaching Grisha, but of course that's only because I am free myself now, I'm not with child. Stiva, of course, there's no counting on. And with the help of good-natured friends I can bring them up; but if there's another baby coming? . . ." And the thought struck her how untruly it was said that the curse laid on woman was that in sorrow she should bring forth children.

"The birth itself, that's nothing; but the months of carrying the child—that's what's so intolerable," she thought, picturing to herself her last pregnancy, and the death of the last baby. And she recalled the conversation she had just had with the young woman at the inn. On being asked whether she had any children, the handsome young woman had answered cheerfully:

"I had a girl baby, but God set me free; I buried her last Lent."

"Well, did you grieve very much for her?" asked Darya Alexandrovna.

"Why grieve? The old man has grandchildren enough as it is. It was only a trouble. No working, nor nothing. Only a tie."

This answer had struck Darya Alexandrovna as revolting in spite of the good-natured and pleasing face of the young woman; but now she could not help recalling these words. In those cynical words there was indeed a grain of truth.

"Yes, altogether," thought Darya Alexandrovna, looking back over her whole existence during those fifteen years of her married life, "pregnancy, sickness, mental incapacity, indifference to everything, and most of all—hideousness. Kitty, young and pretty as she is, even Kitty has lost her looks; and I when I'm with child become hideous, I know it. The birth, the agony, the hideous agonies, that last moment . . . then the nursing, the sleepless nights, the fearful pains. . . ."

Darya Alexandrovna shuddered at the mere recollection of the pain from sore breasts which she had suffered with almost every child. "Then the children's illnesses, that everlasting apprehension; then bringing them up; evil propensities" (she thought of little Masha's crime among the raspberries), "education, Latin—it's all so incomprehensible and difficult. And on the top of it all, the death of these children." And there rose again before her imagination the cruel memory, that always tore her mother's heart, of the death of her last little baby, who had died of croup; his funeral, the callous indifference of all at the little pink coffin, and her own torn heart, and her lonely anguish at the sight of the pale little brow with its projecting temples, and the open, wondering little mouth seen in the coffin at the moment when it was being covered with the little pink lid with a cross braided on it.

"And all this, what's it for? What is to come of it all? That I'm wasting my life, never having a moment's peace, either with child, or nursing a child, forever irritable, peevish, wretched myself and worrying others, repulsive to my husband, while the children are growing up unhappy, badly educated, and penniless. Even now, if it weren't for spending the summer at the Levins', I don't know how we should be managing to live. Of course Kostya and Kitty have so much tact that we don't feel it; but it can't go on. They'll have children, they won't be able to keep us; it's a drag on them as it is. How is papa, who has hardly anything left for himself, to help us? So that I can't even bring the children up by myself, and may find it hard with the help of other people, at the cost of humiliation. Why, even if we suppose the greatest good luck, that the children don't die, and I bring them up somehow. At the very best they'll simply be decent people. That's all I can hope for. And to gain simply that—what agonies, what toil! . . . One's whole life ruined!" Again she recalled what the young peasant woman had said, and again she was revolted at the thought; but she could not help admitting that there was a grain of brutal truth in the words.

"Is it far now, Mihail?" Darya Alexandrovna asked the counting house clerk, to turn her mind from thoughts that were frightening her.

"From this village, they say, it's five miles." The carriage drove along the village street and onto a bridge. On the bridge was a crowd of peasant women with coils of ties for the sheaves on their shoulders, gaily and noisily chattering. They stood still on the bridge, staring inquisitively at the carriage. All the faces turned to Darya Alexandrovna looked to her healthy and happy, making her envious of their enjoyment of life. "They're all living, they're all enjoying life," Darya Alexandrovna still mused when she had passed the peasant women and was driving uphill again at a trot, seated comfortably on the soft springs of the old carriage, "while I, let out, as it were from prison, from the world of worries that fret me to death, am only looking about me now for an instant. They all live; those peasant women and my sister Natalia and Varenka and Anna, whom I am going to see—all, but not I.

"And they attack Anna. What for? am I any better? I have, anyway, a husband I love—not as I should like to love him, still I do love him, while Anna never loved hers. How is she to blame? She wants to live. God has put that in our hearts. Very likely I should have done the same. Even to this day I don't feel sure I did right in listening to her at that terrible time when she came to me in Moscow. I ought then to have cast off my husband and have begun my life fresh. I might have loved and have been loved in reality. And is it any better as it is? I don't respect him. He's necessary to me," she thought about her husband, "and I put up with him. Is that any better? At that time I could still have been admired, I had beauty left me still," Darya Alexandrovna pursued her thoughts, and she would have liked to look at herself in the looking-glass. She had a traveling looking-glass in her handbag, and she wanted to take it out; but looking at the backs of the coachman and the swaying counting house clerk, she felt that she would be ashamed if either of them were to look round, and she did not take out the glass.

But without looking in the glass, she thought that even now it was not too late; and she thought of Sergey Ivanovitch, who was always particularly attentive to her, of Stiva's good-hearted friend, Turovtsin, who had helped her nurse her children through the scarlatina, and was in love with her. And there was someone else, a quite young man, who—her husband had told her it as a joke—thought her more beautiful than either of her sisters. And the most passionate and impossible romances rose before Darya Alexandrovna's imagination. "Anna did quite right, and certainly I shall never reproach her for it. She is happy, she makes another person happy, and she's not broken down as I am, but most likely just as she always was, bright, clever, open to every impression," thought Darya Alexandrovna—and a sly smile curved her lips, for, as she pondered on Anna's love affair, Darya Alexandrovna constructed on parallel lines an almost identical love affair for herself, with an imaginary composite figure, the ideal man who was in love with her. She, like Anna, confessed the whole affair to her husband. And the amazement and perplexity of Stepan Arkadyevitch at this avowal made her smile.

In such daydreams she reached the turning of the highroad that led to Vozdvizhenskoe.

Chapter XVII

THE COACHMAN PULLED UP HIS FOUR HORSES AND LOOKED ROUND TO THE RIGHT, TO A FIELD of rye, where some peasants were sitting on a cart. The counting house clerk was just going to jump down, but on second thoughts he shouted peremptorily to the peasants instead, and beckoned to them to come up. The wind, that seemed to blow as they drove, dropped when the carriage stood still; gadflies settled on the steaming horses that angrily shook them off. The metallic clank of a whetstone against a scythe, that came to them from the cart, ceased. One of the peasants got up and came towards the carriage.

"Well, you are slow!" the counting house clerk shouted angrily to the peasant who was stepping slowly with his bare feet over the ruts of the rough dry road. "Come along, do!"

A curly-headed old man with a bit of bast tied round his hair, and his bent back dark with perspiration, came towards the carriage, quickening his steps, and took hold of the mud-guard with his sunburned hand.

"Vozdvizhenskoe, the manor house? the count's?" he repeated; "go on to the end of this track. Then turn to the left. Straight along the avenue and you'll come right upon it. But whom do you want? The count himself?"

"Well, are they at home, my good man?" Darya Alexandrovna said vaguely, not knowing how to ask about Anna, even of this peasant.

"At home for sure," said the peasant, shifting from one barefoot to the other, and leaving a distinct print of five toes and a heel in the dust. "Sure to be at home," he repeated, evidently eager to talk. "Only yesterday visitors arrived. There's a sight of visitors come. What do you want?" He turned round and called to a lad, who was shouting something to him from the cart. "Oh! They all rode by here not long since, to look at a reaping machine. They'll be home by now. And who will you be belonging to? . . ."

"We've come a long way," said the coachman, climbing onto the box. "So it's not far?"

"I tell you, it's just here. As soon as you get out . . ." he said, keeping hold all the while of the carriage.

A healthy-looking, broad-shouldered young fellow came up too.

"What, is it laborers they want for the harvest?" he asked.

"I don't know, my boy."

"So you keep to the left, and you'll come right on it," said the peasant, unmistakably loathe to let the travelers go, and eager to converse.

The coachman started the horses, but they were only just turning off when the peasant shouted: "Stop! Hi, friend! Stop!" called the two voices. The coachman stopped.

"They're coming! They're yonder!" shouted the peasant. "See what a turn-out!" he said, pointing to four persons on horseback, and two in a *char-à-banc,* coming along the road.

They were Vronsky with a jockey, Veslovsky and Anna on horseback, and Princess Varvara and Sviazhsky in the *char-à-banc.* They had gone out to look at the working of a new reaping machine.

When the carriage stopped, the party on horseback were coming at a walking pace. Anna was in front beside Veslovsky. Anna, quietly walking her horse, a sturdy English cob with cropped mane and short tail, her beautiful head with her black hair straying loose under her high hat, her full shoulders, her slender waist in her black riding habit, and all the ease and grace of her deportment, impressed Dolly.

For the first minute it seemed to her unsuitable for Anna to be on horseback. The conception of riding on horseback for a lady was, in Darya Alexandrovna's mind, associated with ideas of youthful flirtation and frivolity, which, in her opinion, was unbecoming in Anna's position. But when she had scrutinized her, seeing her closer, she was at once reconciled to her riding. In spite of her elegance, everything was so simple, quiet, and dignified in the attitude, the dress and the movements of Anna, that nothing could have been more natural.

Beside Anna, on a hot-looking gray cavalry-horse, was Vassenka Veslovsky in his Scotch cap with floating ribbons, his stout legs stretched out in front, obviously pleased with his own appearance. Darya Alexandrovna could not suppress a good-humored smile as she recognized him. Behind rode Vronsky on a dark bay mare, obviously heated from galloping. He was holding her in, pulling at the reins.

After him rode a little man in the dress of a jockey. Sviazhsky and Princess Varvara in a new *char-à-banc* with a big, raven-black trotting horse, overtook the party on horseback.

Anna's face suddenly beamed with a joyful smile at the instant when, in the little figure huddled in a corner of the old carriage, she recognized Dolly. She uttered a cry, started in the saddle, and set her horse into a gallop. On reaching the carriage she jumped off without assistance, and holding up her riding habit, she ran up to greet Dolly.

"I thought it was you and dared not think it. How delightful! You can't fancy how glad I am!" she said, at one moment pressing her face against Dolly and kissing her, and at the next holding her off and examining her with a smile.

"Here's a delightful surprise, Alexey!" she said, looking round at Vronsky, who had dismounted, and was walking towards them.

Vronsky, taking off his tall gray hat, went up to Dolly.

"You wouldn't believe how glad we are to see you," he said, giving peculiar significance to the words, and showing his strong white teeth in a smile.

Vassenka Veslovsky, without getting off his horse, took off his cap and greeted the visitor by gleefully waving the ribbons over his head.

"That's Princess Varvara," Anna said in reply to a glance of inquiry from Dolly as the *char-à-banc* drove up.

"Ah!" said Darya Alexandrovna, and unconsciously her face betrayed her dissatisfaction.

Princess Varvara was her husband's aunt, and she had long known her, and did not respect her. She knew that Princess Varvara had passed her whole life toadying on her rich relations, but that she should now be sponging on Vronsky, a man who was nothing to her, mortified Dolly on account of her kinship with her husband. Anna noticed Dolly's expression, and was disconcerted by it. She blushed, dropped her riding habit, and stumbled over it.

Darya Alexandrovna went up to the *char-à-banc* and coldly greeted Princess Varvara. Sviazhsky too she knew. He inquired how his queer friend with the young wife was, and running his eyes over the ill-matched horses and the carriage with its patched mud-guards, proposed to the ladies that they should get into the *char-à-banc*.

"And I'll get into this vehicle," he said. "The horse is quiet, and the princess drives capitally."

"No, stay as you were," said Anna, coming up, "and we'll go in the carriage," and taking Dolly's arm, she drew her away.

Darya Alexandrovna's eyes were fairly dazzled by the elegant carriage of a pattern she had never seen before, the splendid horses, and the elegant and gorgeous people surrounding her. But what struck her most of all was the change that had taken place in Anna, whom she knew so well and loved. Any other woman, a less close observer, not knowing Anna before, or not having thought as Darya Alexandrovna had been thinking on the road, would not have noticed anything special in Anna. But now Dolly was struck by that temporary beauty, which is only found in women during the moments of love, and which she saw now in Anna's face. Everything in her face, the clearly marked dimples in her cheeks and chin, the line of her lips, the smile which, as it were, fluttered about her face, the brilliance of her eyes, the grace and rapidity of her movements, the fulness of the notes of her voice, even the manner in which, with a sort of angry friendliness, she answered Veslovsky when he asked permission to get on her cob, so as to teach it to gallop with the right leg foremost—it was all peculiarly fascinating, and it seemed as if she were herself aware of it, and rejoicing in it.

When both the women were seated in the carriage, a sudden embarrassment came over both of them. Anna was disconcerted by the intent look of inquiry Dolly fixed upon her. Dolly was embarrassed because after Sviazhsky's phrase about "this vehicle," she could not help feeling ashamed of the dirty old carriage in which Anna was sitting with her. The coachman Philip and the counting house clerk were experiencing the same sensation. The counting house clerk, to conceal his confusion, busied himself settling the ladies, but Philip the coachman became sullen, and was bracing himself not to be overawed in future by this external superiority. He smiled ironically, looking at the raven horse, and was already deciding in his own mind that this smart trotter in the *char-à-banc* was only good for *promenage*, and wouldn't do thirty miles straight off in the heat.

The peasants had all got up from the cart and were inquisitively and mirthfully staring at the meeting of the friends, making their comments on it.

"They're pleased, too; haven't seen each other for a long while," said the curly-headed old man with the bast round his hair.

"I say, Uncle Gerasim, if we could take that raven horse now, to cart the corn, that 'ud be quick work!"

"Look-ee! Is that a woman in breeches?" said one of them, pointing to Vassenka Veslovsky sitting in a side saddle.

"Nay, a man! See how smartly he's going it!"

"Eh, lads! seems we're not going to sleep, then?"

"What chance of sleep today!" said the old man, with a sidelong look at the sun. "Midday's past, look-ee! Get your hooks, and come along!"

Chapter XVIII

ANNA LOOKED AT DOLLY'S THIN, CARE-WORN FACE, WITH ITS WRINKLES FILLED WITH DUST FROM the road, and she was on the point of saying what she was thinking, that is, that Dolly had got thinner. But, conscious that she herself had grown handsomer, and that Dolly's eyes were telling her so, she sighed and began to speak about herself.

"You are looking at me," she said, "and wondering how I can be happy in my position? Well! it's shameful to confess, but I . . . I'm inexcusably happy. Something magical has happened to me, like a dream, when you're frightened, panic-stricken, and all of a sudden you wake up and all the horrors are no more. I have waked up. I have lived through the misery, the dread, and now for a long while past, especially since we've been here, I've been so happy! . . ." she said, with a timid smile of inquiry looking at Dolly.

"How glad I am!" said Dolly smiling, involuntarily speaking more coldly than she wanted to. "I'm very glad for you. Why haven't you written to me?"

"Why? . . . Because I hadn't the courage. . . . You forget my position . . ."

"To me? Hadn't the courage? If you knew how I . . . I look at . . ."

Darya Alexandrovna wanted to express her thoughts of the morning, but for some reason it seemed to her now out of place to do so.

"But of that we'll talk later. What's this, what are all these buildings?" she asked, wanting to change the conversation and pointing to the red and green roofs that came into view behind the green hedges of acacia and lilac. "Quite a little town."

But Anna did not answer.

"No, no! How do you look at my position, what do you think of it?" she asked.

"I consider . . ." Darya Alexandrovna was beginning, but at that instant Vassenka Veslovsky, having brought the cob to gallop with the right leg foremost, galloped past them, bumping heavily up and down in his short jacket on the chamois leather of the side saddle. "He's doing it, Anna Arkadyevna!" he shouted.

Anna did not even glance at him; but again it seemed to Darya Alexandrovna out of place to enter upon such a long conversation in the carriage, and so she cut short her thought.

"I don't think anything," she said, "but I always loved you, and if one loves anyone, one loves the whole person, just as they are and not as one would like them to be. . . ."

Anna, taking her eyes off her friend's face and dropping her eyelids (this was a new habit Dolly had not seen in her before), pondered, trying to penetrate the full significance of the words. And obviously interpreting them as she would have wished, she glanced at Dolly.

"If you had any sins," she said, "they would all be forgiven you for your coming to see me and these words."

And Dolly saw that tears stood in her eyes. She pressed Anna's hand in silence.

"Well, what are these buildings? How many there are of them!" After a moment's silence she repeated her question.

"These are the servants' houses, barns, and stables," answered Anna. "And there the park begins. It had all gone to ruin, but Alexey had everything renewed. He is very fond of this place, and, what I never expected, he has become intensely interested in looking after it. But his is such a rich nature! Whatever he takes up, he does splendidly. So far from being bored by it, he works with passionate interest. He—with his temperament as I know it—he has become careful and businesslike, a first rate manager, he positively reckons every penny in his management of the land. But only in that. When it's a question of tens of thousands, he doesn't think of money." She spoke with that gleefully sly smile with which women often talk of the secret characteristics only known to them—of those they love. "Do you see that big building? that's the new hospital. I believe it will cost over a hundred thousand; that's his hobby just now. And do you know how it all came about? The peasants asked him for some meadowland, I think it was, at a cheaper rate, and he refused, and I accused him of being miserly. Of course it was not really because of that, but everything together, he began this hospital to prove, do you see, that he was not miserly about money. *C'est une petitesse*, if you like, but I love him all the more for it. And now you'll see the house in a moment. It was his grandfather's house, and he has had nothing changed outside."

"How beautiful!" said Dolly, looking with involuntary admiration at the handsome house with columns, standing out among the different-colored greens of the old trees in the garden.

"Isn't it fine? And from the house, from the top, the view is wonderful."

They drove into a courtyard strewn with gravel and bright with flowers, in which two laborers were at work putting an edging of stones round the light mould of a flowerbed, and drew up in a covered entry.

"Ah, they're here already!" said Anna, looking at the saddle horses, which were just being led away from the steps. "It is a nice horse, isn't it? It's my cob; my favorite. Lead him here and bring me some sugar. Where is the count?" she inquired of two smart footmen who darted out. "Ah, there he is!" she said, seeing Vronsky coming to meet her with Veslovsky.

"Where are you going to put the princess?" said Vronsky in French, addressing Anna, and without waiting for a reply, he once more greeted Darya Alexandrovna, and this time he kissed her hand. "I think the big balcony room."

"Oh, no, that's too far off! Better in the corner room, we shall see each other more. Come, let's go up," said Anna, as she gave her favorite horse the sugar the footman had brought her.

"Et vous oubliez votre devoir," she said to Veslovsky, who came out too on the steps.

"Pardon, j'en ai tout plein les poches," he answered, smiling, putting his fingers in his waistcoat pocket.

"Mais vous venez trop tard," she said, rubbing her handkerchief on her hand, which the horse had made wet in taking the sugar.

Anna turned to Dolly. "You can stay some time? For one day only? That's impossible!"

"I promised to be back, and the children . . ." said Dolly, feeling embarrassed both because she had to get her bag out of the carriage, and because she knew her face must be covered with dust.

"No, Dolly, darling! . . . Well, we'll see. Come along, come along!" and Anna led Dolly to her room.

That room was not the smart guest chamber Vronsky had suggested, but the one of which Anna had said that Dolly would excuse it. And this room, for which excuse was needed, was more full of luxury than any in which Dolly had ever stayed, a luxury that reminded her of the best hotels abroad.

"Well, darling, how happy I am!" Anna said, sitting down in her riding habit for a moment beside Dolly. "Tell me about all of you. Stiva I had only a glimpse of, and he cannot tell one about the children. How is my favorite, Tanya? Quite a big girl, I expect?"

"Yes, she's very tall," Darya Alexandrovna answered shortly, surprised herself that she should respond so coolly about her children. "We are having a delightful stay at the Levins'," she added.

"Oh, if I had known," said Anna, "that you do not despise me! . . . You might have all come to us. Stiva's an old friend and a great friend of Alexey's, you know," she added, and suddenly she blushed.

"Yes, but we are all . . ." Dolly answered in confusion.

"But in my delight I'm talking nonsense. The one thing, darling, is that I am so glad to have you!" said Anna, kissing her again. "You haven't told me yet how and what you think about me, and I keep wanting to know. But I'm glad you will see me as I am. The chief thing I shouldn't like would be for people to imagine I want to prove anything. I don't want to prove anything; I merely want to live, to do no one harm but myself. I have the right to do that, haven't I? But it is a big subject, and we'll talk over everything properly later. Now I'll go and dress and send a maid to you."

Chapter XIX

LEFT ALONE, DARYA ALEXANDROVNA, WITH A GOOD HOUSEWIFE'S EYE, SCANNED HER ROOM. ALL she had seen in entering the house and walking through it, and all she saw now in her room, gave her an impression of wealth and sumptuousness and of that modern European luxury of which she had only read in English novels, but had never seen in Russia and in the country. Everything was new from the new French hangings on the walls to the carpet which covered the whole floor. The bed had a spring mattress, and a special sort of bolster and silk pillowcases on the little pillows. The marble washstand, the dressing-table, the little sofa, the tables, the bronze clock on the chimney piece, the window curtains, and the portières were all new and expensive.

The smart maid, who came in to offer her services, with her hair done up high, and a gown more fashionable than Dolly's, was as new and expensive as the whole room. Darya Alexandrovna liked her neatness, her deferential and obliging manners, but she felt ill at ease with her. She felt ashamed of her seeing the patched dressing-jacket that had unluckily been packed by mistake for her. She was ashamed of the very patches and darned places of which she had been so proud at home. At home it had been so clear that for six dressing-jackets there would be needed twenty-four yards of nainsook at sixteen pence the yard, which was a matter of thirty shillings besides the cutting-out and making, and these thirty shillings had been saved. But before the maid she felt, if not exactly ashamed, at least uncomfortable.

Darya Alexandrovna had a great sense of relief when Annushka, whom she had known for years, walked in. The smart maid was sent for to go to her mistress, and Annushka remained with Darya Alexandrovna.

Annushka was obviously much pleased at that lady's arrival, and began to chatter away without a pause. Dolly observed that she was longing to express her opinion in regard to her mistress's position, especially as to the love and devotion of the count to Anna Arkadyevna, but Dolly carefully interrupted her whenever she began to speak about this.

"I grew up with Anna Arkadyevna; my lady's dearer to me than anything. Well, it's not for us to judge. And, to be sure, there seems so much love . . ."

"Kindly pour out the water for me to wash now, please," Darya Alexandrovna cut her short.

"Certainly. We've two women kept specially for washing small things, but most of the linen's done by machinery. The count goes into everything himself. Ah, what a husband! . . ."

Dolly was glad when Anna came in, and by her entrance put a stop to Annushka's gossip.

Anna had put on a very simple batiste gown. Dolly scrutinized that simple gown attentively. She knew what it meant, and the price at which such simplicity was obtained.

"An old friend," said Anna of Annushka.

Anna was not embarrassed now. She was perfectly composed and at ease. Dolly saw that she had now completely recovered from the impression her arrival had made on her, and had assumed that superficial, careless tone which, as it were, closed the door on that compartment in which her deeper feelings and ideas were kept.

"Well, Anna, and how is your little girl?" asked Dolly.

"Annie?" (This was what she called her little daughter Anna.) "Very well. She has got on wonderfully. Would you like to see her? Come, I'll show her to you. We had a terrible bother," she began telling her, "over nurses. We had an Italian wet-nurse. A good creature, but so stupid! We wanted to get rid of her, but the baby is so used to her that we've gone on keeping her still."

"But how have you managed? . . ." Dolly was beginning a question as to what name the little girl would have; but noticing a sudden frown on Anna's face, she changed the drift of her question.

"How did you manage? have you weaned her yet?"

But Anna had understood.

"You didn't mean to ask that? You meant to ask about her surname. Yes? That worries Alexey. She has no name—that is, she's a Karenina," said Anna, dropping her eyelids till nothing could be seen but the eyelashes meeting. "But we'll talk about all that later," her face suddenly brightening. "Come, I'll show you her. *Elle est très gentille.* She crawls now."

In the nursery the luxury which had impressed Dolly in the whole house struck her still more. There were little go-carts ordered from England, and appliances for learning to walk, and a sofa after the fashion of a billiard table, purposely constructed for crawling, and swings and baths, all of special pattern, and modern. They were all English, solid, and of good make, and obviously very expensive. The room was large, and very light and lofty.

When they went in, the baby, with nothing on but her little smock, was sitting in a little elbow-chair at the table, having her dinner of broth, which she was spilling all over her little chest. The baby was being fed, and the Russian nursery maid was evidently sharing her meal. Neither the wet-nurse nor the head nurse were there; they were in the next room, from which came the sound of their conversation in the queer French, which was their only means of communication.

Hearing Anna's voice, a smart, tall, English nurse with a disagreeable face and a dissolute expression walked in at the door, hurriedly shaking her fair curls, and immediately began to defend herself though Anna had not found fault with her. At every word Anna said, the English nurse said hurriedly several times, "Yes, my lady."

The rosy baby with her black eyebrows and hair, her sturdy red little body with tight goose-flesh skin, delighted Darya Alexandrovna in spite of the cross expression with which she stared at the stranger. She positively envied the baby's healthy appearance. She was delighted, too, at the baby's crawling. Not one of her own children had crawled like that. When the baby was put on the carpet and its little dress tucked up behind, it was wonderfully charming. Looking round like some little wild animal at the grown-up big people with her bright black eyes, she smiled, unmistakably pleased at their admiring her, and holding her legs sideways, she pressed vigorously on her arms, and rapidly drew her whole back up after, and then made another step forward with her little arms.

But the whole atmosphere of the nursery, and especially the English nurse, Darya Alexandrovna did not like at all. It was only on the supposition that no good nurse would have entered so irregular a household as Anna's that Darya Alexandrovna could explain to herself how Anna with her insight into people could take such an unprepossessing, disreputable-looking woman as nurse to her child.

Besides, from a few words that were dropped, Darya Alexandrovna saw at once that Anna, the two nurses, and the child had no common existence, and that the mother's visit was something exceptional. Anna wanted to get the baby her plaything, and could not find it.

Most amazing of all was the fact that on being asked how many teeth the baby had, Anna answered wrong, and knew nothing about the two last teeth.

"I sometimes feel sorry I'm so superfluous here," said Anna, going out of the nursery and holding up her skirt so as to escape the plaything standing in the doorway. "It was very different with my first child."

"I expected it to be the other way," said Darya Alexandrovna shyly.

"Oh, no! By the way, do you know I saw Seryozha?" said Anna, screwing up her eyes, as though looking at something far away. "But we'll talk about that later. You wouldn't believe it, I'm like a hungry beggar woman when a full dinner is set before her, and she does not know what to begin on first. The dinner is you, and the talks I have before me with you, which I could never have with anyone else; and I don't know which subject to begin upon first. *Mais je ne vous ferai grâce de rien.* I must have everything out with you."

"Oh, I ought to give you a sketch of the company you will meet with us," she went on. "I'll begin with the ladies. Princess Varvara—you know her, and I know your opinion and Stiva's about her. Stiva says the whole aim of her existence is to prove her superiority over Auntie Katerina Pavlovna: that's all true; but she's a good-natured woman, and I am so grateful to her. In Petersburg there was a moment when a chaperon was absolutely essential for me. Then she turned up. But really she is good-natured. She did a great deal to alleviate my position. I see you don't understand all the difficulty of my position . . . there in Petersburg," she added. "Here I'm perfectly at ease and happy. Well, of that later on, though. Then Sviazhsky—he's the marshal of the district, and he's a very good sort of a man, but he wants to get something out of Alexey. You understand, with his property, now that we are settled in the country, Alexey can exercise great influence. Then there's Tushkevitch—you have seen him, you know—Betsy's admirer. Now he's been thrown over and he's come to see us. As Alexey says, he's one of those people who are very pleasant if one accepts them for what they try to appear to be, *et puis il est comme il faut,* as Princess Varvara says. Then Veslovsky . . . you know him. A very nice boy," she said, and a sly smile curved her lips. "What's this wild story about him and the Levins? Veslovsky told Alexey about it, and we don't believe it. *Il est très gentil et naïf,*" she said again with the same smile. "Men need occupation, and Alexey needs a circle, so I value all these people. We have to have the house lively and gay, so that Alexey may not long for any novelty. Then you'll see the steward—a German, a very good fellow, and he understands his work. Alexey has a very high opinion of him. Then the doctor, a young man, not quite a Nihilist perhaps, but you know, eats with his knife . . . but a very good doctor. Then the architect . . . *Une petite cour!*"

Chapter XX

"Here's Dolly for you, Princess, you were so anxious to see her, said Anna, coming out with Darya Alexandrovna onto the stone terrace where Princess Varvara was sitting in the shade at an embroidery frame, working at a cover for Count Alexey Kirillovitch's easy chair. "She says she doesn't want anything before dinner, but please order some lunch for her, and I'll go and look for Alexey and bring them all in."

Princess Varvara gave Dolly a cordial and rather patronizing reception, and began at once explaining to her that she was living with Anna because she had always cared more for her than her sister Katerina Pavlovna, the aunt that had brought Anna up, and that now, when everyone had abandoned Anna, she thought it her duty to help her in this most difficult period of transition.

"Her husband will give her a divorce, and then I shall go back to my solitude; but now I can be of use, and I am doing my duty, however difficult it may be for me—not like some other people. And how sweet it is of you, how right of you to have come! They live like the best of married couples; it's for God to judge them, not for us. And didn't Biryuzovsky and Madame Avenieva . . . and Sam Nikandrov, and Vassiliev and Madame Mamonova, and Liza Neptunova. . . . Did no one say anything about them? And it has ended by their being received by everyone. And then, *c'est un intérieur si joli, si comme il faut. Tout-à-fait à l'anglaise. On se rèunit le matin au breakfast, et puis on se sèpare.* Everyone does as he pleases till dinnertime. Dinner at seven o'clock. Stiva did very rightly to send you. He needs their support. You know that through his mother and brother he can do anything. And then they do so much good. He didn't tell you about his hospital? *Ce sera admirable*—everything from Paris."

Their conversation was interrupted by Anna, who had found the men of the party in the billiard room, and returned with them to the terrace. There was still a long time before the dinner-hour, it was exquisite weather, and so several different methods of spending the next two hours were proposed. There were very many methods of passing the time at Vozdvizhenskoe, and these were all unlike those in use at Pokrovskoe.

"*Une partie de lawn-tennis,*" Veslovsky proposed, with his handsome smile. "We'll be partners again, Anna Arkadyevna."

"No, it's too hot; better stroll about the garden and have a row in the boat, show Darya Alexandrovna the river banks." Vronsky proposed.

"I agree to anything," said Sviazhsky.

"I imagine that what Dolly would like best would be a stroll—wouldn't you? And then the boat, perhaps," said Anna.

So it was decided. Veslovsky and Tushkevitch went off to the bathing-place, promising to get the boat ready and to wait there for them.

They walked along the path in two couples, Anna with Sviazhsky, and Dolly with Vronsky. Dolly was a little embarrassed and anxious in the new surroundings in which she found herself. Abstractly, theoretically, she did not merely justify, she positively approved of Anna's conduct. As is indeed not unfrequent with women of unimpeachable virtue, weary of the monotony of respectable existence, at a distance she not only excused illicit love, she positively envied it. Besides, she loved Anna with all her heart. But seeing Anna in actual life among these strangers, with this fashionable tone that was so new to Darya Alexandrovna, she felt ill at ease. What she disliked particularly was seeing Princess Varvara ready to overlook everything for the sake of the comforts she enjoyed.

As a general principle, abstractly, Dolly approved of Anna's action; but to see the man for whose sake her action had been taken was disagreeable to her. Moreover, she had never liked Vronsky. She thought him very proud, and saw nothing in him of which he could be proud except his wealth. But against her own will, here in his own house, he overawed her more than ever, and she could not be at ease with him. She felt with him the same feeling she had had with the maid about her dressing-jacket. Just as with the maid she had felt not exactly ashamed, but embarrassed at her darns, so she felt with him not exactly ashamed, but embarrassed at herself.

Dolly was ill at ease, and tried to find a subject of conversation. Even though she supposed that, through his pride, praise of his house and garden would be sure to be disagreeable to him, she did all the same tell him how much she liked his house.

"Yes, it's a very fine building, and in the good old-fashioned style," he said.

"I like so much the court in front of the steps. Was that always so?"

"Oh, no!" he said, and his face beamed with pleasure. "If you could only have seen that court last spring!"

And he began, at first rather diffidently, but more and more carried away by the subject as he went on, to draw her attention to the various details of the decoration of his house and garden. It was evident that, having devoted a great deal of trouble to improve and beautify his home, Vronsky felt a need to show off the improvements to a new person, and was genuinely delighted at Darya Alexandrovna's praise.

"If you would care to look at the hospital, and are not tired, indeed, it's not far. Shall we go?" he said, glancing into her face to convince himself that she was not bored. "Are you coming, Anna?" he turned to her.

"We will come, won't we?" she said, addressing Sviazhsky. "*Mais il ne faut pas laisser le pauvre Veslovski et Tushkevitch se morfondre là dans le bateau.* We must send and tell them."

"Yes, this is a monument he is setting up here," said Anna, turning to Dolly with that sly smile of comprehension with which she had previously talked about the hospital.

"Oh, it's a work of real importance!" said Sviazhsky. But to show he was not trying to ingratiate himself with Vronsky, he promptly added some slightly critical remarks.

"I wonder, though, count," he said, "that while you do so much for the health of the peasants, you take so little interest in the schools."

"*C'est devenu tellement commun les écoles,*" said Vronsky. "You understand it's not on that account, but it just happens so, my interest has been diverted elsewhere. This way then to the hospital," he said to Darya Alexandrovna, pointing to a turning out of the avenue.

The ladies put up their parasols and turned into the side path. After going down several turnings, and going through a little gate, Darya Alexandrovna saw standing on rising ground before her a large pretentious-looking red building, almost finished. The iron roof, which was not yet painted, shone with dazzling brightness in the sunshine. Beside the finished building another had been begun, surrounded by scaffolding. Workmen in aprons, standing on scaffolds, were laying bricks, pouring mortar out of vats, and smoothing it with trowels.

"How quickly work gets done with you!" said Sviazhsky. "When I was here last time the roof was not on."

"By the autumn it will all be ready. Inside almost everything is done," said Anna.

"And what's this new building?"

"That's the house for the doctor and the dispensary," answered Vronsky, seeing the architect in a short jacket coming towards him; and excusing himself to the ladies, he went to meet him.

Going round a hole where the workmen were slaking lime, he stood still with the architect and began talking rather warmly.

"The front is still too low," he said to Anna, who had asked what was the matter.

"I said the foundation ought to be raised," said Anna.

"Yes, of course it would have been much better, Anna Arkadyevna," said the architect, "but now it's too late."

"Yes, I take a great interest in it," Anna answered Sviazhsky, who was expressing his surprise at her knowledge of architecture. "This new building ought to have been in harmony with the hospital. It was an afterthought, and was begun without a plan."

Vronsky, having finished his talk with the architect, joined the ladies, and led them inside the hospital.

Although they were still at work on the cornices outside and were painting on the ground-floor, upstairs almost all the rooms were finished. Going up the broad cast-iron staircase to the landing, they walked into the first large room. The walls were stuccoed to look like marble, the huge plate-glass windows were already in, only the parquet floor was not yet finished, and the carpenters, who were planing a block of it, left their work, taking off the bands that fastened their hair, to greet the gentry.

"This is the reception room," said Vronsky. "Here there will be a desk, tables, and benches, and nothing more."

"This way; let us go in here. Don't go near the window," said Anna, trying the paint to see if it were dry. "Alexey, the paint's dry already," she added.

From the reception room they went into the corridor. Here Vronsky showed them the mechanism for ventilation on a novel system. Then he showed them marble baths, and beds with extraordinary springs. Then he showed them the wards one after another, the storeroom, the linen room, then the heating-stove of a new pattern, then the trolleys, which would make no noise as they carried everything needed along the corridors, and many other things. Sviazhsky, as a connoisseur in the latest mechanical improvements, appreciated everything fully. Dolly simply wondered at all she had not seen before, and, anxious to understand it all, made minute inquiries about everything, which gave Vronsky great satisfaction.

"Yes, I imagine that this will be the solitary example of a properly fitted hospital in Russia," said Sviazhsky.

"And won't you have a lying-in ward?" asked Dolly. "That's so much needed in the country. I have often . . ."

In spite of his usual courtesy, Vronsky interrupted her.

"This is not a lying-in home, but a hospital for the sick, and is intended for all diseases, except infectious complaints," he said. "Ah! look at this," and he rolled up to Darya Alexandrovna an invalid chair that had just been ordered for the convalescents. "Look." He sat down in the chair and began moving it. "The patient can't walk—still too weak, perhaps, or something wrong with his legs, but he must have air, and he moves, rolls himself along. . . ."

Darya Alexandrovna was interested by everything. She liked everything very much, but most of all she liked Vronsky himself with his natural, simple-hearted eagerness. "Yes, he's a very nice, good man," she thought several times, not hearing what he said, but looking at him and penetrating into his expression, while she mentally put herself in Anna's place. She liked him so much just now with his eager interest that she saw how Anna could be in love with him.

Chapter XXI

NO, I THINK THE PRINCESS IS TIRED, AND HORSES DON'T INTEREST HER, VRONSKY SAID TO ANNA, who wanted to go on to the stables, where Sviazhsky wished to see the new stallion. "You go on, while I escort the princess home, and we'll have a little talk," he said, "if you would like that?" he added, turning to her.

"I know nothing about horses, and I shall be delighted," answered Darya Alexandrovna, rather astonished.

She saw by Vronsky's face that he wanted something from her. She was not mistaken. As soon as they had passed through the little gate back into the garden, he looked in the direction Anna had taken, and having made sure that she could neither hear nor see them, he began:

"You guess that I have something I want to say to you," he said, looking at her with laughing eyes. "I am not wrong in believing you to be a friend of Anna's." He took off his hat, and taking out his handkerchief, wiped his head, which was growing bald.

Darya Alexandrovna made no answer, and merely stared at him with dismay. When she was left alone with him, she suddenly felt afraid; his laughing eyes and stern expression scared her.

The most diverse suppositions as to what he was about to speak of to her flashed into her brain. "He is going to beg me to come to stay with them with the children, and I shall have to refuse; or to create a set that will receive Anna in Moscow. . . . Or isn't it Vassenka Veslovsky and his relations with Anna? Or perhaps about Kitty, that he feels he was to blame?" All her conjectures were unpleasant, but she did not guess what he really wanted to talk about to her.

"You have so much influence with Anna, she is so fond of you," he said; "do help me."

Darya Alexandrovna looked with timid inquiry into his energetic face, which under the lime trees was continually being lit up in patches by the sunshine, and then passing into complete shadow again. She waited for him to say more, but he walked in silence beside her, scratching with his cane in the gravel.

"You have come to see us, you, the only woman of Anna's former friends—I don't count Princess Varvara—but I know that you have done this not because you regard our position as normal, but because, understanding all the difficulty of the position, you still love her and want to be a help to her. Have I understood you rightly?" he asked, looking round at her.

"Oh, yes," answered Darya Alexandrovna, putting down her sunshade, "but . . ."

"No," he broke in, and unconsciously, oblivious of the awkward position into which he was putting his companion, he stopped abruptly, so that she had to stop short too. "No one feels more deeply and intensely than I do all the difficulty of Anna's position; and that you may well understand, if you do me the honor of supposing I have any heart. I am to blame for that position, and that is why I feel it."

"I understand," said Darya Alexandrovna, involuntarily admiring the sincerity and firmness with which he said this. "But just because you feel yourself responsible, you exaggerate it, I am afraid," she said. "Her position in the world is difficult, I can well understand."

"In the world it is hell!" he brought out quickly, frowning darkly. "You can't imagine moral sufferings greater than what she went through in Petersburg in that fortnight . . . and I beg you to believe it."

"Yes, but here, so long as neither Anna . . . nor you miss society . . ."

"Society!" he said contemptuously, "how could I miss society?"

"So far—and it may be so always—you are happy and at peace. I see in Anna that she is happy, perfectly happy, she has had time to tell me so much already," said Darya Alexandrovna, smiling;

and involuntarily, as she said this, at the same moment a doubt entered her mind whether Anna really were happy.

But Vronsky, it appeared, had no doubts on that score.

"Yes, yes," he said, "I know that she has revived after all her sufferings; she is happy. She is happy in the present. But I? . . . I am afraid of what is before us . . . I beg your pardon, you would like to walk on?"

"No, I don't mind."

"Well, then, let us sit here."

Darya Alexandrovna sat down on a garden seat in a corner of the avenue. He stood up facing her.

"I see that she is happy," he repeated, and the doubt whether she were happy sank more deeply into Darya Alexandrovna's mind. "But can it last? Whether we have acted rightly or wrongly is another question, but the die is cast," he said, passing from Russian to French, "and we are bound together for life. We are united by all the ties of love that we hold most sacred. We have a child, we may have other children. But the law and all the conditions of our position are such that thousands of complications arise which she does not see and does not want to see. And that one can well understand. But I can't help seeing them. My daughter is by law not my daughter, but Karenin's. I cannot bear this falsity!" he said, with a vigorous gesture of refusal, and he looked with gloomy inquiry towards Darya Alexandrovna.

She made no answer, but simply gazed at him. He went on:

"One day a son may be born, my son, and he will be legally a Karenin; he will not be the heir of my name nor of my property, and however happy we may be in our home life and however many children we may have, there will be no real tie between us. They will be Karenins. You can understand the bitterness and horror of this position! I have tried to speak of this to Anna. It irritates her. She does not understand, and to her I cannot speak plainly of all this. Now look at another side. I am happy, happy in her love, but I must have occupation. I have found occupation, and am proud of what I am doing and consider it nobler than the pursuits of my former companions at court and in the army. And most certainly I would not change the work I am doing for theirs. I am working here, settled in my own place, and I am happy and contented, and we need nothing more to make us happy. I love my work here. *Ce n'est pas un pis-aller,* on the contrary . . ."

Darya Alexandrovna noticed that at this point in his explanation he grew confused, and she did not quite understand this digression, but she felt that having once begun to speak of matters near his heart, of which he could not speak to Anna, he was now making a clean breast of everything, and that the question of his pursuits in the country fell into the same category of matters near his heart, as the question of his relations with Anna.

"Well, I will go on," he said, collecting himself. "The great thing is that as I work I want to have a conviction that what I am doing will not die with me, that I shall have heirs to come after me—and this I have not. Conceive the position of a man who knows that his children, the children of the woman he loves, will not be his, but will belong to someone who hates them and cares nothing about them! It is awful!"

He paused, evidently much moved.

"Yes, indeed, I see that. But what can Anna do?" queried Darya Alexandrovna.

"Yes, that brings me to the object of my conversation," he said, calming himself with an effort. "Anna can, it depends on her. . . . Even to petition the Tsar for legitimization, a divorce is essential. And that depends on Anna. Her husband agreed to a divorce—at that time your husband had arranged it completely. And now, I know, he would not refuse it. It is only a matter of writing to him. He said plainly at that time that if she expressed the desire, he would not refuse. Of course," he said gloomily, "it is one of those Pharisaical cruelties of which only such heartless men are capable. He knows what agony any recollection of him must give her, and knowing her, he must have a letter from her. I can understand that it is agony to her. But the matter is of such importance, that one must *passer par-dessus toutes ces finesses de sentiment. Il y va du bonheur et de l'existence d'Anne et de ses enfants.* I won't speak of myself, though it's hard for me, very hard," he said, with an expression as though he were threatening someone for its being hard for him. "And so it is, princess, that I am shamelessly clutching at you as an anchor of salvation. Help me to persuade her to write to him and ask for a divorce."

"Yes, of course," Darya Alexandrovna said dreamily, as she vividly recalled her last interview with Alexey Alexandrovitch. "Yes, of course," she repeated with decision, thinking of Anna.

"Use your influence with her, make her write. I don't like—I'm almost unable to speak about this to her."

"Very well, I will talk to her. But how is it she does not think of it herself?" said Darya Alexandrovna, and for some reason she suddenly at that point recalled Anna's strange new habit of half-closing her eyes. And she remembered that Anna drooped her eyelids just when the deeper questions of life were touched upon. "Just as though she half-shut her eyes to her own life, so as not to see everything," thought Dolly. "Yes, indeed, for my own sake and for hers I will talk to her," Dolly said in reply to his look of gratitude.

They got up and walked to the house.

Chapter XXII

When Anna found Dolly at home before her, she looked intently in her eyes, as though questioning her about the talk she had had with Vronsky, but she made no inquiry in words.

"I believe it's dinnertime," she said. "We've not seen each other at all yet. I am reckoning on the evening. Now I want to go and dress. I expect you do too; we all got splashed at the buildings."

Dolly went to her room and she felt amused. To change her dress was impossible, for she had already put on her best dress. But in order to signify in some way her preparation for dinner, she asked the maid to brush her dress, changed her cuffs and tie, and put some lace on her head.

"This is all I can do," she said with a smile to Anna, who came in to her in a third dress, again of extreme simplicity.

"Yes, we are too formal here," she said, as it were apologizing for her magnificence. "Alexey is delighted at your visit, as he rarely is at anything. He has completely lost his heart to you," she added. "You're not tired?"

There was no time for talking about anything before dinner. Going into the drawing room they found Princess Varvara already there, and the gentlemen of the party in black frock-coats. The architect wore a swallow-tail coat. Vronsky presented the doctor and the steward to his guest. The architect he had already introduced to her at the hospital.

A stout butler, resplendent with a smoothly shaven round chin and a starched white cravat, announced that dinner was ready, and the ladies got up. Vronsky asked Sviazhsky to take in Anna Arkadyevna, and himself offered his arm to Dolly. Veslovsky was before Tushkevitch in offering his arm to Princess Varvara, so that Tushkevitch with the steward and the doctor walked in alone.

The dinner, the dining room, the service, the waiting at table, the wine, and the food, were not simply in keeping with the general tone of modern luxury throughout all the house, but seemed even more sumptuous and modern. Darya Alexandrovna watched this luxury which was novel to her, and as a good housekeeper used to managing a household—although she never dreamed of adapting anything she saw to her own household, as it was all in a style of luxury far above her own manner of living—she could not help scrutinizing every detail, and wondering how and by whom it was all done. Vassenka Veslovsky, her husband, and even Sviazhsky, and many other people she knew, would never have considered this question, and would have readily believed what every well-bred host tries to make his guests feel, that is, that all that is well-ordered in his house has cost him, the host, no trouble whatever, but comes of itself. Darya Alexandrovna was well aware that even porridge for the children's breakfast does not come of itself, and that therefore, where so complicated and magnificent a style of luxury was maintained, someone must give earnest attention to its organization. And from the glance with which Alexey Kirillovitch scanned the table, from the way he nodded to the butler, and offered Darya Alexandrovna her choice between cold soup and hot soup, she saw that it was all organized and maintained by the care of the master of the house himself. It was evident that it all rested no more upon Anna than upon Veslovsky. She, Sviazhsky, the princess, and Veslovsky, were equally guests, with light hearts enjoying what had been arranged for them.

Anna was the hostess only in conducting the conversation. The conversation was a difficult one for the lady of the house at a small table with persons present, like the steward and the architect, belonging to a completely different world, struggling not to be overawed by an elegance to which they were unaccustomed, and unable to sustain a large share in the general conversation. But this difficult conversation Anna directed with her usual tact and naturalness, and indeed she did so with actual enjoyment, as Darya Alexandrovna observed. The conversation began about the row Tushkevitch and Veslovsky had taken alone together in the boat, and Tushkevitch began describing the last boat races in Petersburg at the Yacht Club. But Anna, seizing the first pause, at once turned to the architect to draw him out of his silence.

"Nikolay Ivanitch was struck," she said, meaning Sviazhsky, "at the progress the new building had made since he was here last; but I am there everyday, and everyday I wonder at the rate at which it grows."

"It's first rate working with his excellency," said the architect with a smile (he was respectful and composed, though with a sense of his own dignity). "It's a very different matter to have to do with the district authorities. Where one would have to write out sheaves of papers, here I call upon the count, and in three words we settle the business."

"The American way of doing business," said Sviazhsky, with a smile.

"Yes, there they build in a rational fashion . . ."

The conversation passed to the misuse of political power in the United States, but Anna quickly brought it round to another topic, so as to draw the steward into talk.

"Have you ever seen a reaping machine?" she said, addressing Darya Alexandrovna. "We had just ridden over to look at one when we met. It's the first time I ever saw one."

"How do they work?" asked Dolly.

"Exactly like little scissors. A plank and a lot of little scissors. Like this."

Anna took a knife and fork in her beautiful white hands covered with rings, and began showing how the machine worked. It was clear that she saw nothing would be understood from her explanation; but aware that her talk was pleasant and her hands beautiful she went on explaining.

"More like little penknives," Veslovsky said playfully, never taking his eyes off her.

Anna gave a just perceptible smile, but made no answer. "Isn't it true, Karl Fedoritch, that it's just like little scissors?" she said to the steward.

"Oh, ja," answered the German. *"Es it ein ganz einfaches Ding,"* and he began to explain the construction of the machine.

"It's a pity it doesn't bind too. I saw one at the Vienna exhibition, which binds with a wire," said Sviazhsky. "They would be more profitable in use."

"Es kommt drauf an . . . Der Preis vom Draht muss zusgerechnet werden." And the German,

roused from his taciturnity, turned to Vronsky. *"Das lässt sich ausrechnen, Erlaucht."* The German was just feeling in the pocket where were his pencil and the notebook he always wrote in, but recollecting that he was at a dinner, and observing Vronsky's chilly glance, he checked himself. *"Zu compliziert, macht zu viel Klopot,"* he concluded.

"Wnscht man Dochots, so hat man auch Klopots," said Vassenka Veslovsky, mimicking the German. *"J'adore l'allemand,"* he addressed Anna again with the same smile.

"Cessez," she said with playful severity.

"We expected to find you in the fields, Vassily Semyonitch," she said to the doctor, a sickly-looking man; "have you been there?"

"I went there, but I had taken flight," the doctor answered with gloomy jocoseness.

"Then you've taken a good constitutional?"

"Splendid!"

"Well, and how was the old woman? I hope it's not typhus?"

"Typhus it is not, but it's taking a bad turn."

"What a pity!" said Anna, and having thus paid the dues of civility to her domestic circle, she turned to her own friends.

"It would be a hard task, though, to construct a machine from your description, Anna Arkadyevna," Sviazhsky said jestingly.

"Oh, no, why so?" said Anna with a smile that betrayed that she knew there was something charming in her disquisitions upon the machine that had been noticed by Sviazhsky. This new trait of girlish coquettishness made an unpleasant impression on Dolly.

"But Anna Arkadyevna's knowledge of architecture is marvelous," said Tushkevitch.

"To be sure, I heard Anna Arkadyevna talking yesterday about plinths and damp-courses," said Veslovsky. "Have I got it right?"

"There's nothing marvelous about it, when one sees and hears so much of it," said Anna. "But, I dare say, you don't even know what houses are made of?"

Darya Alexandrovna saw that Anna disliked the tone of raillery that existed between her and Veslovsky, but fell in with it against her will.

Vronsky acted in this matter quite differently from Levin. He obviously attached no significance to Veslovsky's chattering; on the contrary, he encouraged his jests.

"Come now, tell us, Veslovsky, how are the stones held together?"

"By cement, of course."

"Bravo! And what is cement?"

"Oh, some sort of paste . . . no, putty," said Veslovsky, raising a general laugh.

The company at dinner, with the exception of the doctor, the architect, and the steward, who remained plunged in gloomy silence, kept up a conversation that never paused, glancing off one subject, fastening on another, and at times stinging one or the other to the quick. Once Darya Alexandrovna felt wounded to the quick, and got so hot that she positively flushed and wondered afterwards whether she had said anything extreme or unpleasant. Sviazhsky began talking of Levin, describing his strange view that machinery is simply pernicious in its effects on Russian agriculture.

"I have not the pleasure of knowing this M. Levin," Vronsky said, smiling, "but most likely he has never seen the machines he condemns; or if he has seen and tried any, it must have been after a queer fashion, some Russian imitation, not a machine from abroad. What sort of views can anyone have on such a subject?"

"Turkish views, in general," Veslovsky said, turning to Anna with a smile.

"I can't defend his opinions," Darya Alexandrovna said, firing up; "but I can say that he's a highly cultivated man, and if he were here he would know very well how to answer you, though I am not capable of doing so."

"I like him extremely, and we are great friends," Sviazhsky said, smiling good-naturedly.

"*Mais pardon, il est un petit peu touqué*; he maintains, for instance, that district councils and arbitration boards are all of no use, and he is unwilling to take part in anything."

"It's our Russian apathy," said Vronsky, pouring water from an iced decanter into a delicate glass on a high stem; "we've no sense of the duties our privileges impose upon us, and so we refuse to recognize these duties."

"I know no man more strict in the performance of his duties," said Darya Alexandrovna, irritated by Vronsky's tone of superiority.

"For my part," pursued Vronsky, who was evidently for some reason or other keenly affected by this conversation, "such as I am, I am, on the contrary, extremely grateful for the honor they have done me, thanks to Nikolay Ivanitch" (he indicated Sviazhsky), "in electing me a justice of the peace. I consider that for me the duty of being present at the session, of judging some peasants' quarrel about a horse, is as important as anything I can do. And I shall regard it as an honor if they elect me for the district council. It's only in that way I can pay for the advantages I enjoy as a landowner. Unluckily they don't understand the weight that the big landowners ought to have in the state."

It was strange to Darya Alexandrovna to hear how serenely confident he was of being right at his own table. She thought how Levin, who believed the opposite, was just as positive in his opinions at his own table. But she loved Levin, and so she was on his side.

"So we can reckon upon you, count, for the coming elections?" said Sviazhsky. "But you must come a little beforehand, so as to be on the spot by the eighth. If you would do me the honor to stop with me."

"I rather agree with your *beau-frère*," said Anna, "though not quite on the same ground as he," she added with a smile. "I'm afraid that we have too many of these public duties in these latter days. Just as in old days there were so many government functionaries that one had to call in a functionary for every single thing, so now everyone's doing some sort of public duty. Alexey has been here now six months, and he's a member, I do believe, of five or six different public bodies. *Du train que cela va*, the whole time will be wasted on it. And I'm afraid that with such a multiplicity of these bodies, they'll end in being a mere form. How many are you a member of, Nikolay Ivanitch?" she turned to Sviazhsky—"over twenty, I fancy."

Anna spoke lightly, but irritation could be discerned in her tone. Darya Alexandrovna, watching Anna and Vronsky attentively, detected it instantly. She noticed, too, that as she spoke Vronsky's face had immediately taken a serious and obstinate expression. Noticing this, and that Princess Varvara at once made haste to change the conversation by talking of Petersburg acquaintances, and remembering what Vronsky had without apparent connection said in the garden of his work in the country, Dolly surmised that this question of public activity was connected with some deep private disagreement between Anna and Vronsky.

The dinner, the wine, the decoration of the table were all very good; but it was all like what Darya Alexandrovna had seen at formal dinners and balls which of late years had become quite unfamiliar to her; it all had the same impersonal and constrained character, and so on an ordinary day and in a little circle of friends it made a disagreeable impression on her.

After dinner they sat on the terrace, then they proceeded to play lawn tennis. The players, divided into two parties, stood on opposite sides of a tightly drawn net with gilt poles on the carefully leveled and rolled croquet-ground. Darya Alexandrovna made an attempt to play, but it was a long time before she could understand the game, and by the time she did understand it, she was so tired that she sat down with Princess Varvara and simply looked on at the players. Her partner, Tushkevitch, gave up playing too, but the others kept the game up for a long time. Sviazhsky and Vronsky both played very well and seriously. They kept a sharp lookout on the balls served to them, and without haste or getting in each other's way, they ran adroitly up to them, waited for the rebound, and neatly and accurately returned them over the net. Veslovsky played worse than the others. He was too eager, but he kept the players lively with his high spirits. His laughter and outcries never paused. Like the other men of the party, with the ladies' permission, he took off his coat, and his solid, comely figure in his white shirt-sleeves, with his red perspiring face and his impulsive movements, made a picture that imprinted itself vividly on the memory.

When Darya Alexandrovna lay in bed that night, as soon as she closed her eyes, she saw Vassenka Veslovsky flying about the croquet ground.

During the game Darya Alexandrovna was not enjoying herself. She did not like the light tone of raillery that was kept up all the time between Vassenka Veslovsky and Anna, and the unnaturalness altogether of grown-up people, all alone without children, playing at a child's game. But to avoid breaking up the party and to get through the time somehow, after a rest she joined the game again, and pretended to be enjoying it. All that day it seemed to her as though she were acting in a theater with actors cleverer than she, and that her bad acting was spoiling the whole performance. She had come with the intention of staying two days, if all went well. But in the evening, during the game, she made up her mind that she would go home next day. The maternal cares and worries, which she had so hated on the way, now, after a day spent without them, struck her in quite another light, and tempted her back to them.

When, after evening tea and a row by night in the boat, Darya Alexandrovna went alone to her room, took off her dress, and began arranging her thin hair for the night, she had a great sense of relief.

It was positively disagreeable to her to think that Anna was coming to see her immediately. She longed to be alone with her own thoughts.

Chapter XXIII

DOLLY WAS WANTING TO GO TO BED WHEN ANNA CAME IN TO SEE HER, ATTIRED FOR THE NIGHT. In the course of the day Anna had several times begun to speak of matters near her heart, and every time after a few words she had stopped: "Afterwards, by ourselves, we'll talk about everything. I've got so much I want to tell you," she said.

Now they were by themselves, and Anna did not know what to talk about. She sat in the window looking at Dolly, and going over in her own mind all the stores of intimate talk which had seemed so inexhaustible beforehand, and she found nothing. At that moment it seemed to her that everything had been said already.

"Well, what of Kitty?" she said with a heavy sigh, looking penitently at Dolly. "Tell me the truth, Dolly: isn't she angry with me?"

"Angry? Oh, no!" said Darya Alexandrovna, smiling.

"But she hates me, despises me?"

"Oh, no! But you know that sort of thing isn't forgiven."

"Yes, yes," said Anna, turning away and looking out of the open window. "But I was not to blame. And who is to blame? What's the meaning of being to blame? Could it have been otherwise? What do you think? Could it possibly have happened that you didn't become the wife of Stiva?"

"Really, I don't know. But this is what I want you to tell me . . ."

"Yes, yes, but we've not finished about Kitty. Is she happy? He's a very nice man, they say."

"He's much more than very nice. I don't know a better man."

"Ah, how glad I am! I'm so glad! Much more than very nice," she repeated.

Dolly smiled.

"But tell me about yourself. We've a great deal to talk about. And I've had a talk with . . ."

Dolly did not know what to call him. She felt it awkward to call him either the count or Alexey Kirillovitch.

"With Alexey," said Anna, "I know what you talked about. But I wanted to ask you directly what you think of me, of my life?"

"How am I to say like that straight off? I really don't know."

"No, tell me all the same. . . . You see my life. But you mustn't forget that you're seeing us in the summer, when you have come to us and we are not alone. . . . But we came here early in the spring, lived quite alone, and shall be alone again, and I desire nothing better. But imagine me living alone without him, alone, and that will be . . . I see by everything that it will often be repeated, that he will be half the time away from home," she said, getting up and sitting down close by Dolly.

"Of course," she interrupted Dolly, who would have answered, "of course I won't try to keep him by force. I don't keep him indeed. The races are just coming, his horses are running, he will go. I'm very glad. But think of me, fancy my position. . . . But what's the use of talking about it?" She smiled. "Well, what did he talk about with you?"

"He spoke of what I want to speak about of myself, and it's easy for me to be his advocate; of whether there is not a possibility . . . whether you could not. . . ." (Darya Alexandrovna hesitated) "correct, improve your position. . . . You know how I look at it. . . . But all the same, if possible, you should get married. . . ."

"Divorce, you mean?" said Anna. "Do you know, the only woman who came to see me in Petersburg was Betsy Tverskaya? You know her, of course? *Au fond, c'est la femme la plus depravèe qui existe.* She had an intrigue with Tushkevitch, deceiving her husband in the basest way. And she told me that she did not care to know me so long as my position was irregular. Don't imagine I would compare . . . I know you, darling. But I could not help remembering. . . . Well, so what did he say to you?" she repeated.

"He said that he was unhappy on your account and his own. Perhaps you will say that it's egoism, but what a legitimate and noble egoism. He wants first of all to legitimize his daughter, and to be your husband, to have a legal right to you."

"What wife, what slave can be so utterly a slave as I, in my position?" she put in gloomily.

"The chief thing he desires . . . he desires that you should not suffer."

"That's impossible. Well?"

"Well, and the most legitimate desire—he wishes that your children should have a name."

"What children?" Anna said, not looking at Dolly, and half closing her eyes.

"Annie and those to come . . ."

"He need not trouble on that score; I shall have no more children."

"How can you tell that you won't?"

"I shall not, because I don't wish it." And, in spite of all her emotion, Anna smiled, as she caught the naïve expression of curiosity, wonder, and horror on Dolly's face.

"The doctor told me after my illness . . ."

"Impossible!" said Dolly, opening her eyes wide.

For her this was one of those discoveries the consequences and deductions from which are so immense that all that one feels for the first instant is that it is impossible to take it all in, and that one will have to reflect a great, great deal upon it.

This discovery, suddenly throwing light on all those families of one or two children, which had hitherto been so incomprehensible to her, aroused so many ideas, reflections, and contradictory emotions, that she had nothing to say, and simply gazed with wide-open eyes of wonder at Anna. This was the very thing she had been dreaming of, but now learning that it was possible, she was horrified. She felt that it was too simple a solution of too complicated a problem.

"N'est-ce pas immoral?" was all she said, after a brief pause.

"Why so? Think, I have a choice between two alternatives: either to be with child, that is an invalid, or to be the friend and companion of my husband—practically my husband," Anna said in a tone intentionally superficial and frivolous.

"Yes, yes," said Darya Alexandrovna, hearing the very arguments she had used to herself, and not finding the same force in them as before.

"For you, for other people," said Anna, as though divining her thoughts, "there may be reason to hesitate; but for me . . . You must consider, I am not his wife; he loves me as long as he loves me. And how am I to keep his love? Not like this!"

She moved her white hands in a curve before her waist with extraordinary rapidity, as happens during moments of excitement; ideas and memories rushed into Darya Alexandrovna's head. "I," she thought, "did not keep my attraction for Stiva; he left me for others, and the first woman for whom he betrayed me did not keep him by being always pretty and lively. He deserted her and took another. And can Anna attract and keep Count Vronsky in that way? If that is what he looks for, he will find dresses and manners still more attractive and charming. And however white and beautiful her bare arms are, however beautiful her full figure and her eager face under her black curls, he will find something better still, just as my disgusting, pitiful, and charming husband does."

Dolly made no answer, she merely sighed. Anna noticed this sigh, indicating dissent, and she went on. In her armory she had other arguments so strong that no answer could be made to them.

"Do you say that it's not right? But you must consider," she went on; "you forget my position. How can I desire children? I'm not speaking of the suffering, I'm not afraid of that. Think only, what are my children to be? Ill-fated children, who will have to bear a stranger's name. For the very fact of their birth they will be forced to be ashamed of their mother, their father, their birth."

"But that is just why a divorce is necessary." But Anna did not hear her. She longed to give utterance to all the arguments with which she had so many times convinced herself.

"What is reason given me for, if I am not to use it to avoid bringing unhappy beings into the world!" She looked at Dolly, but without waiting for a reply she went on:

"I should always feel I had wronged these unhappy children," she said. "If they are not, at any rate they are not unhappy; while if they are unhappy, I alone should be to blame for it."

These were the very arguments Darya Alexandrovna had used in her own reflections; but she heard them without understanding them. "How can one wrong creatures that don't exist?" she thought. And all at once the idea struck her: could it possibly, under any circumstances, have been better for her favorite Grisha if he had never existed? And this seemed to her so wild, so strange, that she shook her head to drive away this tangle of whirling, mad ideas.

"No, I don't know; it's not right," was all she said, with an expression of disgust on her face.

"Yes, but you mustn't forget that you and I. . . . And besides that," added Anna, in spite of the wealth of her arguments and the poverty of Dolly's objections, seeming still to admit that it was not right, "don't forget the chief point, that I am not now in the same position as you. For you the question is: do you desire not to have anymore children; while for me it is: do I desire to have them? And that's a great difference. You must see that I can't desire it in my position."

Darya Alexandrovna made no reply. She suddenly felt that she had got far away from Anna; that there lay between them a barrier of questions on which they could never agree, and about which it was better not to speak.

Chapter XXIV

"THEN THERE IS ALL THE MORE REASON FOR YOU TO LEGALIZE YOUR POSITION, IF POSSIBLE," SAID Dolly.

"Yes, if possible," said Anna, speaking all at once in an utterly different tone, subdued and mournful.

"Surely you don't mean a divorce is impossible? I was told your husband had consented to it."

"Dolly, I don't want to talk about that."

"Oh, we won't then," Darya Alexandrovna hastened to say, noticing the expression of suffering on Anna's face. "All I see is that you take too gloomy a view of things."

"I? Not at all! I'm always bright and happy. You see, *je fais des passions.* Veslovsky . . ."

"Yes, to tell the truth, I don't like Veslovsky's tone," said Darya Alexandrovna, anxious to change the subject.

"Oh, that's nonsense! It amuses Alexey, and that's all; but he's a boy, and quite under my control. You know, I turn him as I please. It's just as it might be with your Grisha. . . . Dolly!"—she suddenly changed the subject—"you say I take too gloomy a view of things. You can't understand. It's too awful! I try not to take any view of it at all."

"But I think you ought to. You ought to do all you can."

"But what can I do? Nothing. You tell me to marry Alexey, and say I don't think about it. I don't think about it!" she repeated, and a flush rose into her face. She got up, straightening her chest, and sighed heavily. With her light step she began pacing up and down the room, stopping now and then. "I don't think of it? Not a day, not an hour passes that I don't think of it, and blame myself for thinking of it . . . because thinking of that may drive me mad. Drive me mad!" she repeated. "When I think of it, I can't sleep without morphine. But never mind. Let us talk quietly. They tell me, divorce. In the first place, he won't give me a divorce. He's under the influence of Countess Lidia Ivanovna now."

Darya Alexandrovna, sitting erect on a chair, turned her head, following Anna with a face of sympathetic suffering.

"You ought to make the attempt," she said softly.

"Suppose I make the attempt. What does it mean?" she said, evidently giving utterance to a thought, a thousand times thought over and learned by heart. "It means that I, hating him, but still recognizing that I have wronged him—and I consider him magnanimous—that I humiliate myself to write to him. . . . Well, suppose I make the effort; I do it. Either I receive a humiliating refusal or consent. . . . Well, I have received his consent, say . . ." Anna was at that moment at the furthest end of the room, and she stopped there, doing something to the curtain at the window. "I receive his consent, but my . . . my son? They won't give him up to me. He will grow up despising me, with his father, whom I've abandoned. Do you see, I love . . . equally, I think, but both more than myself—two creatures, Seryozha and Alexey."

She came out into the middle of the room and stood facing Dolly, with her arms pressed tightly across her chest. In her white dressing gown her figure seemed more than usually grand and broad. She bent her head, and with shining, wet eyes looked from under her brows at Dolly, a thin little pitiful figure in her patched dressing-jacket and nightcap, shaking all over with emotion.

"It is only those two creatures that I love, and one excludes the other. I can't have them together, and that's the only thing I want. And since I can't have that, I don't care about the rest. I don't care about anything, anything. And it will end one way or another, and so I can't, I don't like to talk of it. So don't blame me, don't judge me for anything. You can't with your pure heart understand all that I'm suffering." She went up, sat down beside Dolly, and with a guilty look, peeped into her face and took her hand.

"What are you thinking? What are you thinking about me? Don't despise me. I don't deserve contempt. I'm simply unhappy. If anyone is unhappy, I am," she articulated, and turning away, she burst into tears.

Left alone, Darya Alexandrovna said her prayers and went to bed. She had felt for Anna with all her heart while she was speaking to her, but now she could not force herself to think of her. The memories of home and of her children rose up in her imagination with a peculiar charm quite new to her, with a sort of new brilliance. That world of her own seemed to her now so sweet and precious that she would not on any account spend an extra day outside it, and she made up her mind that she would certainly go back next day.

Anna meantime went back to her boudoir, took a wine glass and dropped into it several drops of a medicine, of which the principal ingredient was morphine. After drinking it off and sitting still a little while, she went into her bedroom in a soothed and more cheerful frame of mind.

When she went into the bedroom, Vronsky looked intently at her. He was looking for traces of the conversation which he knew that, staying so long in Dolly's room, she must have had with her. But in her expression of restrained excitement, and of a sort of reserve, he could find nothing but the beauty that always bewitched him afresh though he was used to it, the consciousness of it, and the desire that it should affect him. He did not want to ask her what they had been talking of, but he hoped that she would tell him something of her own accord. But she only said:

"I am so glad you like Dolly. You do, don't you?"

"Oh, I've known her a long while, you know. She's very good-hearted, I suppose, *mais excessivement terre-à-terre*. Still, I'm very glad to see her."

He took Anna's hand and looked inquiringly into her eyes.

Misinterpreting the look, she smiled to him. Next morning, in spite of the protests of her hosts, Darya Alexandrovna prepared for her homeward journey. Levin's coachman, in his by no means new coat and shabby hat, with his ill-matched horses and his coach with the patched mud-guards, drove with gloomy determination into the covered gravel approach.

Darya Alexandrovna disliked taking leave of Princess Varvara and the gentlemen of the party. After a day spent together, both she and her hosts were distinctly aware that they did not get on together, and that it was better for them not to meet. Only Anna was sad. She knew that now, from Dolly's departure, no one again would stir up within her soul the feelings that had been roused by their conversation. It hurt her to stir up these feelings, but yet she knew that that was the best part of her soul, and that that part of her soul would quickly be smothered in the life she was leading.

As she drove out into the open country, Darya Alexandrovna had a delightful sense of relief, and she felt tempted to ask the two men how they had liked being at Vronsky's, when suddenly the coachman, Philip, expressed himself unasked:

"Rolling in wealth they may be, but three pots of oats was all they gave us. Everything cleared up till there wasn't a grain left by cockcrow. What are three pots? A mere mouthful! And oats now down to forty-five kopecks. At our place, no fear, all comers may have as much as they can eat."

"The master's a screw," put in the counting house clerk.

"Well, did you like their horses?" asked Dolly.

"The horses!—there's no two opinions about them. And the food was good. But it seemed to me sort of dreary there, Darya Alexandrovna. I don't know what you thought," he said, turning his handsome, good-natured face to her.

"I thought so too. Well, shall we get home by evening?"

"Eh, we must!"

On reaching home and finding everyone entirely satisfactory and particularly charming, Darya Alexandrovna began with great liveliness telling them how she had arrived, how warmly they had received her, of the luxury and good taste in which the Vronskys lived, and of their recreations, and she would not allow a word to be said against them.

"One has to know Anna and Vronsky—I have got to know him better now—to see how nice they are, and how touching," she said, speaking now with perfect sincerity, and forgetting the vague feeling of dissatisfaction and awkwardness she had experienced there.

Chapter XXV

VRONSKY AND ANNA SPENT THE WHOLE SUMMER AND PART OF THE WINTER IN THE COUNTRY, living in just the same condition, and still taking no steps to obtain a divorce. It was an understood thing between them that they should not go away anywhere; but both felt, the longer they lived alone, especially in the autumn, without guests in the house, that they could not stand this existence, and that they would have to alter it.

Their life was apparently such that nothing better could be desired. They had the fullest abundance of everything; they had a child, and both had occupation. Anna devoted just as much care to her appearance when they had no visitors, and she did a great deal of reading, both of novels and of what serious literature was in fashion. She ordered all the books that were praised in the foreign papers and reviews she received, and read them with that concentrated attention which is only given to what is read in seclusion. Moreover, every subject that was of interest to Vronsky, she studied in books and special journals, so that he often went straight to her with questions relating to agriculture or architecture, sometimes even with questions relating to horse-breeding or sport. He was amazed at her knowledge, her memory, and at first was disposed to doubt it, to ask for confirmation of her facts; and she would find what he asked for in some book, and show it to him.

The building of the hospital, too, interested her. She did not merely assist, but planned and suggested a great deal herself. But her chief thought was still of herself—how far she was dear to Vronsky, how far she could make up to him for all he had given up. Vronsky appreciated this desire not only to please, but to serve him, which had become the sole aim of her existence, but at the same time he wearied of the loving snares in which she tried to hold him fast. As time went on, and he saw himself more and more often held fast in these snares, he had an ever growing desire, not so much to escape from them, as to try whether they hindered his freedom. Had it not been for this growing desire to be free, not to have scenes every time he wanted to go to the town to a meeting or a race, Vronsky would have been perfectly satisfied with his life. The rôle he had taken up, the rôle of a wealthy landowner, one of that class which ought to be the very heart of the Russian aristocracy, was entirely to his taste; and now, after spending six months in that character, he derived even greater satisfaction from it. And his management of his estate, which occupied and absorbed him more and more, was most successful. In spite of the immense sums cost him by the hospital, by machinery, by cows ordered from Switzerland, and many other things, he was convinced that he was not wasting, but increasing his substance. In all matters affecting income, the sales of timber, wheat, and wool, the letting of lands, Vronsky was hard as a rock, and knew well how to keep up prices. In all operations on a large scale on this and his other estates, he kept to the simplest methods involving no risk, and in trifling details he was careful and exacting to an extreme degree. In spite of all the cunning and ingenuity of the German steward, who would try to tempt him into purchases by making his original estimate always far larger than really required, and then representing to Vronsky that he might get the thing cheaper, and so make a profit, Vronsky did not give in. He listened to his steward, cross-examined him, and only agreed to his suggestions when the implement to be ordered or constructed was the very newest, not yet known in Russia, and likely to excite wonder. Apart from such exceptions, he resolved upon an increased outlay only where there was a surplus, and in making such an outlay he went into the minutest details, and insisted on getting the very best for his money; so that by the method on which he managed his affairs, it was clear that he was not wasting, but increasing his substance.

In October there were the provincial elections in the Kashinsky province, where were the estates of Vronsky, Sviazhsky, Koznishev, Oblonsky, and a small part of Levin's land.

These elections were attracting public attention from several circumstances connected with them, and also from the people taking part in them. There had been a great deal of talk about them, and great preparations were being made for them. Persons who never attended the elections were coming from Moscow, from Petersburg, and from abroad to attend these. Vronsky had long before promised Sviazhsky to go to them. Before the elections Sviazhsky, who often visited Vozdvizhenskoe, drove over to fetch Vronsky. On the day before there had been almost a quarrel between Vronsky and Anna over this proposed expedition. It was the very dullest autumn weather, which is so dreary in the country, and so, preparing himself for a struggle, Vronsky, with a hard and cold expression, informed Anna of his departure as he had never spoken to her before. But, to his surprise, Anna accepted the information with great composure, and merely asked when he would be back. He looked intently at her, at a loss to explain this composure. She smiled at his look. He knew that way she had of withdrawing into herself, and knew that it only happened when she had determined upon something without letting him know her plans. He was afraid of this; but he was so anxious to avoid a scene that he kept up appearances, and half sincerely believed in what he longed to believe in—her reasonableness.

"I hope you won't be dull?"

"I hope not," said Anna. "I got a box of books yesterday from Gautier's. No, I shan't be dull."

"She's trying to take that tone, and so much the better," he thought, "or else it would be the same thing over and over again."

And he set off for the elections without appealing to her for a candid explanation. It was the first time since the beginning of their intimacy that he had parted from her without a full explanation. From one point of view this troubled him, but on the other side he felt that it was better so. "At first there will be, as this time, something undefined kept back, and then she will get used to it. In any case I can give up anything for her, but not my masculine independence," he thought.

Chapter XXVI

IN SEPTEMBER LEVIN MOVED TO MOSCOW FOR KITTY'S CONFINEMENT. HE HAD SPENT A WHOLE month in Moscow with nothing to do, when Sergey Ivanovitch, who had property in the Kashinsky province, and took great interest in the question of the approaching elections, made ready to set off to the elections. He invited his brother, who had a vote in the Seleznevsky district, to come with him. Levin had, moreover, to transact in Kashin some extremely important business relating to the wardship of land and to the receiving of certain redemption money for his sister, who was abroad.

Levin still hesitated, but Kitty, who saw that he was bored in Moscow, and urged him to go, on her own authority ordered him the proper nobleman's uniform, costing seven pounds. And that seven pounds paid for the uniform was the chief cause that finally decided Levin to go. He went to Kashin. . . .

Levin had been six days in Kashin, visiting the assembly each day, and busily engaged about his sister's business, which still dragged on. The district marshals of nobility were all occupied with the elections, and it was impossible to get the simplest thing done that depended upon the court of wardship. The other matter, the payment of the sums due, was met too by difficulties. After long negotiations over the legal details, the money was at last ready to be paid; but the notary, a most obliging person, could not hand over the order, because it must have the signature of the president, and the president, though he had not given over his duties to a deputy, was at the elections. All these worrying negotiations, this endless going from place to place, and talking with pleasant and excellent people, who quite saw the unpleasantness of the petitioner's position, but were powerless to assist him—all these efforts that yielded no result, led to a feeling of misery in Levin akin to the mortifying helplessness one experiences in dreams when one tries to use physical force. He felt this frequently as he talked to his most good-natured solicitor. This solicitor did, it seemed, everything possible, and strained every nerve to get him out of his difficulties. "I tell you what you might try," he said more than once; "go to so-and-so and so-and-so," and the solicitor drew up a regular plan for getting round the fatal point that hindered everything. But he would add immediately, "It'll mean some delay, anyway, but you might try it." And Levin did try, and did go. Everyone was kind and civil, but the point evaded seemed to crop up again in the end, and again to bar the way. What was particularly trying, was that Levin could not make out with whom he was struggling, to whose interest it was that his business should not be done. That no one seemed to know; the solicitor certainly did not know. If Levin could have understood why, just as he saw why one can only approach the booking office of a railway station in single file, it would not have been so vexatious and tiresome to him. But with the hindrances that confronted him in his business, no one could explain why they existed.

But Levin had changed a good deal since his marriage; he was patient, and if he could not see why it was all arranged like this, he told himself that he could not judge without knowing all about it, and that most likely it must be so, and he tried not to fret.

In attending the elections, too, and taking part in them, he tried now not to judge, not to fall foul of them, but to comprehend as fully as he could the question which was so earnestly and ardently absorbing honest and excellent men whom he respected. Since his marriage there had been revealed to Levin so many new and serious aspects of life that had previously, through his frivolous attitude to them, seemed of no importance, that in the question of the elections too he assumed and tried to find some serious significance.

Sergey Ivanovitch explained to him the meaning and object of the proposed revolution at the elections. The marshal of the province in whose hands the law had placed the control of so many important public functions—the guardianship of wards (the very department which was giving Levin so much trouble just now), the disposal of large sums subscribed by the nobility of the province, the high schools, female, male, and military, and popular instruction on the new model, and finally, the district council—the marshal of the province, Snetkov, was a nobleman of the old school—dissipating an immense fortune, a good-hearted man, honest after his own fashion, but utterly without any comprehension of the needs of modern days. He always took, in every question, the side of the nobility; he was positively antagonistic to the spread of popular education, and he succeeded in giving a purely party character to the district council which ought by rights to be of such an immense importance. What was needed was to put in his place a fresh, capable, perfectly modern man, of contemporary ideas, and to frame their policy so as from the rights conferred upon the nobles, not as the nobility, but as an element of the district council, to extract all the powers of self-government that could possibly be derived from them. In the wealthy Kashinsky province, which always took the lead of other provinces in everything, there was now such a preponderance of forces that this policy, once carried through properly there, might serve as a model for other provinces for all Russia. And hence the whole question was of the greatest importance. It was proposed to elect as marshal in place of Snetkov either Sviazhsky, or, better still, Nevyedovsky, a former university professor, a man of remarkable intelligence and a great friend of Sergey Ivanovitch.

The meeting was opened by the governor, who made a speech to the nobles, urging them to elect the public functionaries, not from regard for persons, but for the service and welfare of their fatherland, and hoping that the honorable nobility of the Kashinsky province would, as at all former elections, hold their duty as sacred, and vindicate the exalted confidence of the monarch.

When he had finished with his speech, the governor walked out of the hall, and the noblemen noisily and eagerly—some even enthusiastically—followed him and thronged round him while he put on his fur coat and conversed amicably with the marshal of the province. Levin, anxious to see into everything and not to miss anything, stood there too in the crowd, and heard the governor say: "Please tell Marya Ivanovna my wife is very sorry she couldn't come to the Home." And thereupon the nobles in high good-humor sorted out their fur coats and all drove off to the cathedral.

In the cathedral Levin, lifting his hand like the rest and repeating the words of the archdeacon, swore with most terrible oaths to do all the governor had hoped they would do. Church services always affected Levin, and as he uttered the words "I kiss the cross," and glanced round at the crowd of young and old men repeating the same, he felt touched.

On the second and third days there was business relating to the finances of the nobility and the female high school, of no importance whatever, as Sergey Ivanovitch explained, and Levin, busy seeing after his own affairs, did not attend the meetings. On the fourth day the auditing of the marshal's accounts took place at the high table of the marshal of the province. And then there occurred the first skirmish between the new party and the old. The committee who had been deputed to verify the accounts reported to the meeting that all was in order. The marshal of the province got up, thanked the nobility for their confidence, and shed tears. The nobles gave him a loud welcome, and shook hands with him. But at that instant a nobleman of Sergey Ivanovitch's party said that he had heard that the committee had not verified the accounts, considering such a verification an insult to the marshal of the province. One of the members of the committee incautiously admitted this. Then a small gentleman, very young-looking but very malignant, began to say that it would probably be agreeable to the marshal of the province to give an account of his expenditures of the public moneys, and that the misplaced delicacy of the members of the committee was depriving him of this moral satisfaction. Then the members of the committee tried to withdraw their admission, and Sergey Ivanovitch began to prove that they must logically admit either that they had verified the accounts or that they had not, and he developed this dilemma in detail. Sergey Ivanovitch was answered by the spokesman of the opposite party. Then Sviazhsky spoke, and then the malignant gentleman again. The discussion lasted a long time and ended in nothing. Levin was surprised that they should dispute upon this subject so long, especially as, when he asked Sergey Ivanovitch whether he supposed that money had been misappropriated, Sergey Ivanovitch answered:

"Oh, no! He's an honest man. But those old-fashioned methods of paternal family arrangements in the management of provincial affairs must be broken down."

On the fifth day came the elections of the district marshals. It was rather a stormy day in several districts. In the Seleznevsky district Sviazhsky was elected unanimously without a ballot, and he gave a dinner that evening.

Chapter XXVII

THE SIXTH DAY WAS FIXED FOR THE ELECTION OF THE MARSHAL OF THE PROVINCE.

The rooms, large and small, were full of noblemen in all sorts of uniforms. Many had come only for that day. Men who had not seen each other for years, some from the Crimea, some from Petersburg, some from abroad, met in the rooms of the Hall of Nobility. There was much discussion around the governor's table under the portrait of the Tsar.

The nobles, both in the larger and the smaller rooms, grouped themselves in camps, and from their hostile and suspicious glances, from the silence that fell upon them when outsiders approached a group, and from the way that some, whispering together, retreated to the farther corridor, it was evident that each side had secrets from the other. In appearance the noblemen were sharply divided into two classes: the old and the new. The old were for the most part either in old uniforms of the nobility, buttoned up closely, with spurs and hats, or in their own special naval, cavalry, infantry, or official uniforms. The uniforms of the older men were embroidered in the old-fashioned way with epaulets on their shoulders; they were unmistakably tight and short in the waist, as though their wearers had grown out of them. The younger men wore the uniform of the nobility with long waists and broad shoulders, unbuttoned over white waistcoats, or uniforms with black collars and with the embroidered badges of justices of the peace. To the younger men belonged the court uniforms that here and there brightened up the crowd.

But the division into young and old did not correspond with the division of parties. Some of the young men, as Levin observed, belonged to the old party; and some of the very oldest noblemen, on the contrary, were whispering with Sviazhsky, and were evidently ardent partisans of the new party.

Levin stood in the smaller room, where they were smoking and taking light refreshments, close to his own friends, and listening to what they were saying, he conscientiously exerted all his intelligence trying to understand what was said. Sergey Ivanovitch was the center round which the others grouped themselves. He was listening at that moment to Sviazhsky and Hliustov, the marshal of another district, who belonged to their party. Hliustov would not agree to go with his district to ask Snetkov to stand, while Sviazhsky was persuading him to do so, and Sergey Ivanovitch was approving of the plan. Levin could not make out why the opposition was to ask the marshal to stand whom they wanted to supersede.

Stepan Arkadyevitch, who had just been drinking and taking some lunch, came up to them in his uniform of a gentleman of the bedchamber, wiping his lips with a perfumed handkerchief of bordered batiste.

"We are placing our forces," he said, pulling out his whiskers, "Sergey Ivanovitch!"

And listening to the conversation, he supported Sviazhsky's contention.

"One district's enough, and Sviazhsky's obviously of the opposition," he said, words evidently intelligible to all except Levin.

"Why, Kostya, you here too! I suppose you're converted, eh?" he added, turning to Levin and drawing his arm through his. Levin would have been glad indeed to be converted, but could not make out what the point was, and retreating a few steps from the speakers, he explained to Stepan Arkadyevitch his inability to understand why the marshal of the province should be asked to stand.

"*O sancta simplicitas!*" said Stepan Arkadyevitch, and briefly and clearly he explained it to Levin. If, as at previous elections, all the districts asked the marshal of the province to stand, then he would be elected without a ballot. That must not be. Now eight districts had agreed to call upon him: if two refused to do so, Snetkov might decline to stand at all; and then the old party might choose another of their party, which would throw them completely out in their reckoning. But if only one district, Sviazhsky's, did not call upon him to stand, Snetkov would let himself be balloted for. They were even, some of them, going to vote for him, and purposely to let him get a good many votes, so that the enemy might be thrown off the scent, and when a candidate of the other side was put up, they too might give him some votes. Levin understood to some extent, but not fully, and would have put a few more questions, when suddenly everyone began talking and making a noise and they moved towards the big room.

"What is it? eh? whom?" "No guarantee? whose? what?" "They won't pass him?" "No guarantee?" "They won't let Flerov in?" "Eh, because of the charge against him?" "Why, at this rate, they won't admit anyone. It's a swindle!" "The law!" Levin heard exclamations on all sides, and he moved into the big room together with the others, all hurrying somewhere and afraid of missing something. Squeezed by the crowding noblemen, he drew near the high table where the marshal of the province, Sviazhsky, and the other leaders were hotly disputing about something.

Chapter XXVIII

LEVIN WAS STANDING RATHER FAR OFF. A NOBLEMAN BREATHING HEAVILY AND HOARSELY AT HIS side, and another whose thick boots were creaking, prevented him from hearing distinctly. He could only hear the soft voice of the marshal faintly, then the shrill voice of the malignant gentleman, and then the voice of Sviazhsky. They were disputing, as far as he could make out, as to the interpretation to be put on the act and the exact meaning of the words: "liable to be called up for trial."

The crowd parted to make way for Sergey Ivanovitch approaching the table. Sergey Ivanovitch, waiting till the malignant gentleman had finished speaking, said that he thought the best solution would be to refer to the act itself, and asked the secretary to find the act. The act said that in case of difference of opinion, there must be a ballot.

Sergey Ivanovitch read the act and began to explain its meaning, but at that point a tall, stout, round-shouldered landowner, with dyed whiskers, in a tight uniform that cut the back of his neck, interrupted him. He went up to the table, and striking it with his finger ring, he shouted loudly: "A ballot! Put it to the vote! No need for more talking!" Then several voices began to talk all at once, and the tall nobleman with the ring, getting more and more exasperated, shouted more and more loudly. But it was impossible to make out what he said.

He was shouting for the very course Sergey Ivanovitch had proposed; but it was evident that he hated him and all his party, and this feeling of hatred spread through the whole party and roused in opposition to it the same vindictiveness, though in a more seemly form, on the other side. Shouts were raised, and for a moment all was confusion, so that the marshal of the province had to call for order.

"A ballot! A ballot! Every nobleman sees it! We shed our blood for our country! . . . The confidence of the monarch. . . . No checking the accounts of the marshal; he's not a cashier. . . . But that's not the point. . . . Votes, please! Beastly! . . ." shouted furious and violent voices on all sides. Looks and faces were even more violent and furious than their words. They expressed the most implacable hatred. Levin did not in the least understand what was the matter, and he marveled at the passion with which it was disputed whether or not the decision about Flerov should be put to the vote. He forgot, as Sergey Ivanovitch explained to him afterwards, this syllogism: that it was necessary for the public good to get rid of the marshal of the province; that to get rid of the marshal it was necessary to have a majority of votes; that to get a majority of votes it was necessary to secure Flerov's right to vote; that to secure the recognition of Flerov's right to vote they must decide on the interpretation to be put on the act.

"And one vote may decide the whole question, and one must be serious and consecutive, if one wants to be of use in public life," concluded Sergey Ivanovitch. But Levin forgot all that, and it was painful to him to see all these excellent persons, for whom he had a respect, in such an unpleasant and vicious state of excitement. To escape from this painful feeling he went away into the other room where there was nobody except the waiters at the refreshment bar. Seeing the waiters busy over washing up the crockery and setting in order their plates and wine glasses, seeing their calm and cheerful faces, Levin felt an unexpected sense of relief as though he had come out of a stuffy room into the fresh air. He began walking up and down, looking with pleasure at the waiters. He particularly liked the way one gray-whiskered waiter, who showed his scorn for the other younger ones and was jeered at by them, was teaching them how to fold up napkins properly. Levin was just about to enter into conversation with the old waiter, when the secretary of the court of wardship, a little old man whose specialty it was to know all the noblemen of the province by name and patronymic, drew him away.

"Please come, Konstantin Dmitrievitch," he said, "your brother's looking for you. They are voting on the legal point."

Levin walked into the room, received a white ball, and followed his brother, Sergey Ivanovitch, to the table where Sviazhsky was standing with a significant and ironical face, holding his beard in his fist and sniffing at it. Sergey Ivanovitch put his hand into the box, put the ball somewhere, and making room for Levin, stopped. Levin advanced, but utterly forgetting what he was to do, and much embarrassed, he turned to Sergey Ivanovitch with the question, "Where am I to put it?" He asked this softly, at a moment when there was talking going on near, so that he had hoped his question would not be overheard. But the persons speaking paused, and his improper question was overheard. Sergey Ivanovitch frowned.

"That is a matter for each man's own decision," he said severely.

Several people smiled. Levin crimsoned, hurriedly thrust his hand under the cloth, and put the ball to the right as it was in his right hand. Having put it in, he recollected that he ought to have thrust his left hand too, and so he thrust it in though too late, and, still more overcome with confusion, he beat a hasty retreat into the background.

"A hundred and twenty-six for admission! Ninety-eight against!" sang out the voice of the secretary, who could not pronounce the letter *r*. Then there was a laugh; a button and two nuts were found in the box. The nobleman was allowed the right to vote, and the new party had conquered.

But the old party did not consider themselves conquered. Levin heard that they were asking Snetkov to stand, and he saw that a crowd of noblemen was surrounding the marshal, who was saying something. Levin went nearer. In reply Snetkov spoke of the trust the noblemen of the province had placed in him, the affection they had shown him, which he did not deserve, as his only merit had been his attachment to the nobility, to whom he had devoted twelve years of service. Several times he repeated the words: "I have served to the best of my powers with truth and good faith, I value your goodness and thank you," and suddenly he stopped short from the tears that choked him, and went out of the room. Whether these tears came from a sense of the injustice being done him, from his love for the nobility, or from the strain of the position he was placed in, feeling himself surrounded by enemies, his emotion infected the assembly, the majority were touched, and Levin felt a tenderness for Snetkov.

In the doorway the marshal of the province jostled against Levin.

"Beg pardon, excuse me, please," he said as to a stranger, but recognizing Levin, he smiled timidly. It seemed to Levin that he would have liked to say something, but could not speak for emotion. His face and his whole figure in his uniform with the crosses, and white trousers striped with braid, as he moved hurriedly along, reminded Levin of some hunted beast who sees that he is in evil case. This expression in the marshal's face was particularly touching to Levin, because, only the day before, he had been at his house about his trustee business and had seen him in all his grandeur, a kind-hearted, fatherly man. The big house with the old family furniture; the rather dirty, far from stylish, but respectful footmen, unmistakably old house serfs who had stuck to their master; the stout, good-natured wife in a cap with lace and a Turkish shawl, petting her pretty grandchild, her daughter's daughter; the young son, a sixth form high school boy, coming home from school, and greeting his father, kissing his big hand; the genuine, cordial words and gestures of the old man—all this had the day before roused an instinctive feeling of respect and sympathy in Levin. This old man was a touching and pathetic figure to Levin now, and he longed to say something pleasant to him.

"So you're sure to be our marshal again," he said.

"It's not likely," said the marshal, looking round with a scared expression. "I'm worn out, I'm old. If there are men younger and more deserving than I, let them serve."

And the marshal disappeared through a side door.

The most solemn moment was at hand. They were to proceed immediately to the election. The leaders of both parties were reckoning white and black on their fingers.

The discussion upon Flerov had given the new party not only Flerov's vote, but had also gained time for them, so that they could send to fetch three noblemen who had been rendered unable to take part in the elections by the wiles of the other party. Two noble gentlemen, who had a weakness for strong drink, had been made drunk by the partisans of Snetkov, and a third had been robbed of his uniform.

On learning this, the new party had made haste, during the dispute about Flerov, to send some of their men in a sleigh to clothe the stripped gentleman, and to bring along one of the intoxicated to the meeting.

"I've brought one, drenched him with water," said the landowner, who had gone on this errand, to Sviazhsky. "He's all right? he'll do."

"Not too drunk, he won't fall down?" said Sviazhsky, shaking his head.

"No, he's first rate. If only they don't give him anymore here. . . . I've told the waiter not to give him anything on any account."

Chapter XXIX

THE NARROW ROOM, IN WHICH THEY WERE SMOKING AND TAKING REFRESHMENTS, WAS FULL OF noblemen. The excitement grew more intense, and every face betrayed some uneasiness. The excitement was specially keen for the leaders of each party, who knew every detail, and had reckoned up every vote. They were the generals organizing the approaching battle. The rest, like the rank and file before an engagement, though they were getting ready for the fight, sought for other distractions in the interval. Some were lunching, standing at the bar, or sitting at the table; others were walking up and down the long room, smoking cigarettes, and talking with friends whom they had not seen for a long while.

Levin did not care to eat, and he was not smoking; he did not want to join his own friends, that is Sergey Ivanovitch, Stepan Arkadyevitch, Sviazhsky and the rest, because Vronsky in his equerry's uniform was standing with them in eager conversation. Levin had seen him already at the meeting on the previous day, and he had studiously avoided him, not caring to greet him. He went to the window and sat down, scanning the groups, and listening to what was being said around him. He felt depressed, especially because everyone else was, as he saw, eager, anxious, and interested, and he alone, with an old, toothless little man with mumbling lips wearing a naval uniform, sitting beside him, had no interest in it and nothing to do.

"He's such a blackguard! I have told him so, but it makes no difference. Only think of it! He couldn't collect it in three years!" he heard vigorously uttered by a round-shouldered, short, country gentleman, who had pomaded hair hanging on his embroidered collar, and new boots obviously put on for the occasion, with heels that tapped energetically as he spoke. Casting a displeased glance at Levin, this gentleman sharply turned his back.

"Yes, it's a dirty business, there's no denying," a small gentleman assented in a high voice.

Next, a whole crowd of country gentlemen, surrounding a stout general, hurriedly came near Levin. These persons were unmistakably seeking a place where they could talk without being overheard.

"How dare he say I had his breeches stolen! Pawned them for drink, I expect. Damn the fellow, prince indeed! He'd better not say it, the beast!"

"But excuse me! They take their stand on the act," was being said in another group; "the wife must be registered as noble."

"Oh, damn your acts! I speak from my heart. We're all gentlemen, aren't we? Above suspicion."

"Shall we go on, your excellency, *fine champagne?*"

Another group was following a nobleman, who was shouting something in a loud voice; it was one of the three intoxicated gentlemen.

"I always advised Marya Semyonovna to let for a fair rent, for she can never save a profit," he heard a pleasant voice say. The speaker was a country gentleman with gray whiskers, wearing the regimental uniform of an old general staff-officer. It was the very landowner Levin had met at Sviazhsky's. He knew him at once. The landowner too stared at Levin, and they exchanged greetings.

"Very glad to see you! To be sure! I remember you very well. Last year at our district marshal, Nikolay Ivanovitch's."

"Well, and how is your land doing?" asked Levin.

"Oh, still just the same, always at a loss," the landowner answered with a resigned smile, but with an expression of serenity and conviction that so it must be. "And how do you come to be in our province?" he asked. "Come to take part in our *coup d'etat?*" he said, confidently pronouncing the French words with a bad accent. "All Russia's here—gentlemen of the bedchamber, and everything short of the ministry." He pointed to the imposing figure of Stepan Arkadyevitch in white trousers and his court uniform, walking by with a general.

"I ought to own that I don't very well understand the drift of the provincial elections," said Levin.

The landowner looked at him.

"Why, what is there to understand? There's no meaning in it at all. It's a decaying institution that goes on running only by the force of inertia. Just look, the very uniforms tell you that it's an assembly of justices of the peace, permanent members of the court, and so on, but not of noblemen."

"Then why do you come?" asked Levin.

"From habit, nothing else. Then, too, one must keep up connections. It's a moral obligation of a sort. And then, to tell the truth, there's one's own interests. My son-in-law wants to stand as a permanent member; they're not rich people, and he must be brought forward. These gentlemen, now, what do they come for?" he said, pointing to the malignant gentleman, who was talking at the high table.

"That's the new generation of nobility."

"New it may be, but nobility it isn't. They're proprietors of a sort, but we're the landowners. As noblemen, they're cutting their own throats."

"But you say it's an institution that's served its time."

"That it may be, but still it ought to be treated a little more respectfully. Snetkov, now . . . We may be of use, or we may not, but we're the growth of a thousand years. If we're laying out a garden, planning one before the house, you know, and there you've a tree that's stood for centuries in the very spot. . . . Old and gnarled it may be, and yet you don't cut down the old fellow to make room for the flowerbeds, but lay out your beds so as to take advantage of the tree. You won't grow him again in a year," he said cautiously, and he immediately changed the conversation. "Well, and how is your land doing?"

"Oh, not very well. I make five per cent."

"Yes, but you don't reckon your own work. Aren't you worth something too? I'll tell you my own case. Before I took to seeing after the land, I had a salary of three hundred pounds from the service. Now I do more work than I did in the service, and like you I get five per cent. on the land, and thank God for that. But one's work is thrown in for nothing."

"Then why do you do it, if it's a clear loss?"

"Oh, well, one does it! What would you have? It's habit, and one knows it's how it should be. And what's more," the landowner went on, leaning his elbows on the window and chatting on, "my son, I must tell you, has no taste for it. There's no doubt he'll be a scientific man. So there'll be no one to keep it up. And yet one does it. Here this year I've planted an orchard."

"Yes, yes," said Levin, "that's perfectly true. I always feel there's no real balance of gain in my work on the land, and yet one does it. . . . It's a sort of duty one feels to the land."

"But I tell you what," the landowner pursued; "a neighbor of mine, a merchant, was at my place. We walked about the fields and the garden. 'No,' said he, 'Stepan Vassilievitch, everything's well looked after, but your garden's neglected.' But, as a fact, it's well kept up. 'To my thinking, I'd cut down that lime tree. Here you've thousands of limes, and each would make two good bundles of bark. And nowadays that bark's worth something. I'd cut down the lot.' "

"And with what he made he'd increase his stock, or buy some land for a trifle, and let it out in lots to the peasants," Levin added, smiling. He had evidently more than once come across those commercial calculations. "And he'd make his fortune. But you and I must thank God if we keep what we've got and leave it to our children."

"You're married, I've heard?" said the landowner.

"Yes," Levin answered, with proud satisfaction. "Yes, it's rather strange," he went on. "So we live without making anything, as though we were ancient vestals set to keep in a fire."

The landowner chuckled under his white mustaches.

"There are some among us, too, like our friend Nikolay Ivanovitch, or Count Vronsky, that's settled here lately, who try to carry on their husbandry as though it were a factory; but so far it leads to nothing but making away with capital on it."

"But why is it we don't do like the merchants? Why don't we cut down our parks for timber?" said Levin, returning to a thought that had struck him.

"Why, as you said, to keep the fire in. Besides that's not work for a nobleman. And our work as noblemen isn't done here at the elections, but yonder, each in our corner. There's a class instinct, too, of what one ought and oughtn't to do. There's the peasants, too, I wonder at them sometimes; any good peasant tries to take all the land he can. However bad the land is, he'll work it. Without a return too. At a simple loss."

"Just as we do," said Levin. "Very, very glad to have met you," he added, seeing Sviazhsky approaching him.

"And here we've met for the first time since we met at your place," said the landowner to Sviazhsky, "and we've had a good talk too."

"Well, have you been attacking the new order of things?" said Sviazhsky with a smile.

"That we're bound to do."

"You've relieved your feelings?"

Chapter XXX

SVIAZHSKY TOOK LEVIN'S ARM, AND WENT WITH HIM TO HIS OWN FRIENDS. THIS TIME THERE WAS no avoiding Vronsky. He was standing with Stepan Arkadyevitch and Sergey Ivanovitch, and looking straight at Levin as he drew near.

"Delighted! I believe I've had the pleasure of meeting you . . . at Princess Shtcherbatskaya's," he said, giving Levin his hand.

"Yes, I quite remember our meeting," said Levin, and blushing crimson, he turned away immediately, and began talking to his brother.

With a slight smile Vronsky went on talking to Sviazhsky, obviously without the slightest inclination to enter into conversation with Levin. But Levin, as he talked to his brother, was continually looking round at Vronsky, trying to think of something to say to him to gloss over his rudeness.

"What are we waiting for now?" asked Levin, looking at Sviazhsky and Vronsky.

"For Snetkov. He has to refuse or to consent to stand," answered Sviazhsky.

"Well, and what has he done, consented or not?"

"That's the point, that he's done neither," said Vronsky.

"And if he refuses, who will stand then?" asked Levin, looking at Vronsky.

"Whoever chooses to," said Sviazhsky.

"Shall you?" asked Levin.

"Certainly not I," said Sviazhsky, looking confused, and turning an alarmed glance at the malignant gentleman, who was standing beside Sergey Ivanovitch.

"Who then? Nevyedovsky?" said Levin, feeling he was putting his foot into it.

But this was worse still. Nevyedovsky and Sviazhsky were the two candidates.

"I certainly shall not, under any circumstances," answered the malignant gentleman.

This was Nevyedovsky himself. Sviazhsky introduced him to Levin.

"Well, you find it exciting too?" said Stepan Arkadyevitch, winking at Vronsky. "It's something like a race. One might bet on it."

"Yes, it is keenly exciting," said Vronsky. "And once taking the thing up, one's eager to see it through. It's a fight!" he said, scowling and setting his powerful jaws.

"What a capable fellow Sviazhsky is! Sees it all so clearly."

"Oh, yes!" Vronsky assented indifferently.

A silence followed, during which Vronsky—since he had to look at something—looked at Levin, at his feet, at his uniform, then at his face, and noticing his gloomy eyes fixed upon him, he said, in order to say something:

"How is it that you, living constantly in the country, are not a justice of the peace? You are not in the uniform of one."

"It's because I consider that the justice of the peace is a silly institution," Levin answered gloomily. He had been all the time looking for an opportunity to enter into conversation with Vronsky, so as to smooth over his rudeness at their first meeting.

"I don't think so, quite the contrary," Vronsky said, with quiet surprise.

"It's a plaything," Levin cut him short. "We don't want justices of the peace. I've never had a single thing to do with them during eight years. And what I have had was decided wrongly by them. The justice of the peace is over thirty miles from me. For some matter of two roubles I should have to send a lawyer, who costs me fifteen."

And he related how a peasant had stolen some flour from the miller, and when the miller told him of it, had lodged a complaint for slander. All this was utterly uncalled for and stupid, and Levin felt it himself as he said it.

"Oh, this is such an original fellow!" said Stepan Arkadyevitch with his most soothing, almond-oil smile. "But come along; I think they're voting. . . ."

And they separated.

"I can't understand," said Sergey Ivanovitch, who had observed his brother's clumsiness, "I can't understand how anyone can be so absolutely devoid of political tact. That's where we Russians are so deficient. The marshal of the province is our opponent, and with him you're *ami cochon*, and you beg him to stand. Count Vronsky, now . . . I'm not making a friend of him; he's asked me to dinner, and I'm not going; but he's one of our side—why make an enemy of him? Then you ask Nevyedovsky if he's going to stand. That's not a thing to do."

"Oh, I don't understand it at all! And it's all such nonsense," Levin answered gloomily.

"You say it's all such nonsense, but as soon as you have anything to do with it, you make a muddle."

Levin did not answer, and they walked together into the big room.

The marshal of the province, though he was vaguely conscious in the air of some trap being prepared for him, and though he had not been called upon by all to stand, had still made up his mind to stand. All was silence in the room. The secretary announced in a loud voice that the captain of the guards, Mihail Stepanovitch Snetkov, would now be balloted for as marshal of the province.

The district marshals walked carrying plates, on which were balls, from their tables to the high table, and the election began.

"Put it in the right side," whispered Stepan Arkadyevitch, as with his brother Levin followed the marshal of his district to the table. But Levin had forgotten by now the calculations that had been explained to him, and was afraid Stepan Arkadyevitch might be mistaken in saying "the right side." Surely Snetkov was the enemy. As he went up, he held the ball in his right hand, but thinking he was wrong, just at the box he changed to the left hand, and undoubtedly put the ball to the left. An adept in the business, standing at the box and seeing by the mere action of the elbow where each put his ball, scowled with annoyance. It was no good for him to use his insight.

Everything was still, and the counting of the balls was heard. Then a single voice rose and proclaimed the numbers for and against. The marshal had been voted for by a considerable majority. All was noise and eager movement towards the doors. Snetkov came in, and the nobles thronged round him, congratulating him.

"Well, now is it over?" Levin asked Sergey Ivanovitch.

"It's only just beginning," Sviazhsky said, replying for Sergey Ivanovitch with a smile. "Some other candidate may receive more votes than the marshal."

Levin had quite forgotten about that. Now he could only remember that there was some sort of trickery in it, but he was too bored to think what it was exactly. He felt depressed, and longed to get out of the crowd.

As no one was paying any attention to him, and no one apparently needed him, he quietly slipped away into the little room where the refreshments were, and again had a great sense of comfort when he saw the waiters. The little old waiter pressed him to have something, and Levin agreed. After eating a cutlet with beans and talking to the waiters of their former masters, Levin, not wishing to go back to the hall, where it was all so distasteful to him, proceeded to walk through the galleries. The galleries were full of fashionably dressed ladies, leaning over the balustrade and trying not to lose a single word of what was being said below. With the ladies were sitting and standing smart lawyers, high school teachers in spectacles, and officers. Everywhere they were talking of the election, and of how worried the marshal was, and how splendid the discussions had been. In one group Levin heard his brother's praises. One lady was telling a lawyer:

"How glad I am I heard Koznishev! It's worth losing one's dinner. He's exquisite! So clear and distinct all of it! There's not one of you in the law-courts that speaks like that. The only one is Meidel, and he's not so eloquent by a long way."

Finding a free place, Levin leaned over the balustrade and began looking and listening.

All the noblemen were sitting railed off behind barriers according to their districts. In the middle of the room stood a man in a uniform, who shouted in a loud high voice:

"As a candidate for the marshalship of the nobility of the province we call upon staff-captain Yevgeney Ivanovitch Apuhtin!" A dead silence followed, and then a weak old voice was heard: "Declined!"

"We call upon the privy councilor Pyotr Petrovitch Bol," the voice began again.

"Declined!" a high boyish voice replied.

Again it began, and again "Declined." And so it went on for about an hour. Levin, with his elbows on the balustrade, looked and listened. At first he wondered and wanted to know what it meant; then feeling sure that he could not make it out he began to be bored. Then recalling all the excitement and vindictiveness he had seen on all the faces, he felt sad; he made up his mind to go, and went downstairs. As he passed through the entry to the galleries he met a dejected high school boy walking up and down with tired-looking eyes. On the stairs he met a couple—a lady running quickly on her high heels and the jaunty deputy prosecutor.

"I told you you weren't late," the deputy prosecutor was saying at the moment when Levin moved aside to let the lady pass.

Levin was on the stairs to the way out, and was just feeling in his waistcoat pocket for the number of his overcoat, when the secretary overtook him.

"This way, please, Konstantin Dmitrievitch; they are voting."

The candidate who was being voted on was Nevyedovsky, who had so stoutly denied all idea of standing. Levin went up to the door of the room; it was locked. The secretary knocked, the door opened, and Levin was met by two red-faced gentlemen, who darted out.

"I can't stand anymore of it," said one red-faced gentleman.

After them the face of the marshal of the province was poked out. His face was dreadful-looking from exhaustion and dismay.

"I told you not to let anyone out!" he cried to the doorkeeper.

"I let someone in, your excellency!"

"Mercy on us!" and with a heavy sigh the marshal of the province walked with downcast head to the high table in the middle of the room, his legs staggering in his white trousers.

Nevyedovsky had scored a higher majority, as they had planned, and he was the new marshal of the province. Many people were amused, many were pleased and happy, many were in ecstasies, many were disgusted and unhappy. The former marshal of the province was in a state of despair, which he could not conceal. When Nevyedovsky went out of the room, the crowd thronged round him and followed him enthusiastically, just as they had followed the governor who had opened the meetings, and just as they had followed Snetkov when he was elected.

Chapter XXXI

The newly elected marshal and many of the successful party dined that day with Vronsky.

Vronsky had come to the elections partly because he was bored in the country and wanted to show Anna his right to independence, and also to repay Sviazhsky by his support at the election for all the trouble he had taken for Vronsky at the district council election, but chiefly in order strictly to perform all those duties of a nobleman and landowner which he had taken upon himself. But he had not in the least expected that the election would so interest him, so keenly excite him, and that he would be so good at this kind of thing. He was quite a new man in the circle of the nobility of the province, but his success was unmistakable, and he was not wrong in supposing that he had already obtained a certain influence. This influence was due to his wealth and reputation, the capital house in the town lent him by his old friend Shirkov, who had a post in the department of finances and was director of a flourishing bank in Kashin; the excellent cook Vronsky had brought from the country, and his friendship with the governor, who was a schoolfellow of Vronsky's—a schoolfellow he had patronized and protected indeed. But what contributed more than all to his success was his direct, equable manner with everyone, which very quickly made the majority of the noblemen reverse the current opinion of his supposed haughtiness. He was himself conscious that, except that whimsical gentleman married to Kitty Shtcherbatskaya, who had *a propos de bottes* poured out a stream of irrelevant absurdities with such spiteful fury, every nobleman with whom he had made acquaintance had become his adherent. He saw clearly, and other people recognized it, too, that he had done a great deal to secure the success of Nevyedovsky. And now at his own table, celebrating Nevyedovsky's election, he was experiencing an agreeable sense of triumph over the success of his candidate. The election itself had so fascinated him that, if he could succeed in getting married during the next three years, he began to think of standing himself—much as after winning a race ridden by a jockey, he had longed to ride a race himself.

Today he was celebrating the success of his jockey. Vronsky sat at the head of the table, on his right hand sat the young governor, a general of high rank. To all the rest he was the chief man in the province, who had solemnly opened the elections with his speech, and aroused a feeling of respect and even of awe in many people, as Vronsky saw; to Vronsky he was little Katka Maslov—that had been his nickname in the Pages' Corps—whom he felt to be shy and tried to *mettre à son aise.* On the left hand sat Nevyedovsky with his youthful, stubborn, and malignant face. With him Vronsky was simple and deferential.

Sviazhsky took his failure very light-heartedly. It was indeed no failure in his eyes, as he said himself, turning, glass in hand, to Nevyedovsky; they could not have found a better representative of the new movement, which the nobility ought to follow. And so every honest person, as he said, was on the side of today's success and was rejoicing over it.

Stepan Arkadyevitch was glad, too, that he was having a good time, and that everyone was pleased. The episode of the elections served as a good occasion for a capital dinner. Sviazhsky comically imitated the tearful discourse of the marshal, and observed, addressing Nevyedovsky, that his excellency would have to select another more complicated method of auditing the accounts than tears. Another nobleman jocosely described how footmen in stockings had been ordered for the marshal's ball, and how now they would have to be sent back unless the new marshal would give a ball with footmen in stockings.

Continually during dinner they said of Nevyedovsky: "Our marshal," and "your excellency."

This was said with the same pleasure with which a bride is called "Madame" and her husband's name. Nevyedovsky affected to be not merely indifferent but scornful of this appellation, but it was obvious that he was highly delighted, and had to keep a curb on himself not to betray the triumph which was unsuitable to their new liberal tone.

After dinner several telegrams were sent to people interested in the result of the election. And Stepan Arkadyevitch, who was in high good-humor, sent Darya Alexandrovna a telegram: "Nevyedovsky elected by twenty votes. Congratulations. Tell people." He dictated it aloud, saying: "We must let them share our rejoicing." Darya Alexandrovna, getting the message, simply sighed over the ruble wasted on it, and understood that it was an after-dinner affair. She knew Stiva had a weakness after dining for *faire jouer le télégraphe.*

Everything, together with the excellent dinner and the wine, not from Russian merchants, but imported direct from abroad, was extremely dignified, simple, and enjoyable. The party—some twenty—had been selected by Sviazhsky from among the more active new liberals, all of the same way of thinking, who were at the same time clever and well bred. They drank, also half in jest, to the health of the new marshal of the province, of the governor, of the bank director, and of "our amiable host."

Vronsky was satisfied. He had never expected to find so pleasant a tone in the provinces.

Towards the end of dinner it was still more lively. The governor asked Vronsky to come to a concert for the benefit of the Servians which his wife, who was anxious to make his acquaintance, had been getting up.

"There'll be a ball, and you'll see the belle of the province. Worth seeing, really."

"Not in my line," Vronsky answered. He liked that English phrase. But he smiled, and promised to come.

Before they rose from the table, when all of them were smoking, Vronsky's valet went up to him with a letter on a tray.

"From Vozdvizhenskoe by special messenger," he said with a significant expression.

"Astonishing! how like he is to the deputy prosecutor Sventitsky," said one of the guests in French of the valet, while Vronsky, frowning, read the letter.

The letter was from Anna. Before he read the letter, he knew its contents. Expecting the elections to be over in five days, he had promised to be back on Friday. Today was Saturday, and he knew that the letter contained reproaches for not being back at the time fixed. The letter he had sent the previous evening had probably not reached her yet.

The letter was what he had expected, but the form of it was unexpected, and particularly disagreeable to him. "Annie is very ill, the doctor says it may be inflammation. I am losing my head all alone. Princess Varvara is no help, but a hindrance. I expected you the day before yesterday, and yesterday, and now I am sending to find out where you are and what you are doing. I wanted to come myself, but thought better of it, knowing you would dislike it. Send some answer, that I may know what to do."

The child ill, yet she had thought of coming herself. Their daughter ill, and this hostile tone.

The innocent festivities over the election, and this gloomy, burdensome love to which he had to return struck Vronsky by their contrast. But he had to go, and by the first train that night he set off home.

Chapter XXXII

BEFORE VRONSKY'S DEPARTURE FOR THE ELECTIONS, ANNA HAD REFLECTED THAT THE SCENES constantly repeated between them each time he left home, might only make him cold to her instead of attaching him to her, and resolved to do all she could to control herself so as to bear the parting with composure. But the cold, severe glance with which he had looked at her when he came to tell her he was going had wounded her, and before he had started her peace of mind was destroyed.

In solitude afterwards, thinking over that glance which had expressed his right to freedom, she came, as she always did, to the same point—the sense of her own humiliation. "He has the right to go away when and where he chooses. Not simply to go away, but to leave me. He has every right, and I have none. But knowing that, he ought not to do it. What has he done, though? . . . He looked at me with a cold, severe expression. Of course that is something indefinable, impalpable, but it has never been so before, and that glance means a great deal," she thought. "That glance shows the beginning of indifference."

And though she felt sure that a coldness was beginning, there was nothing she could do, she could not in any way alter her relations to him. Just as before, only by love and by charm could she keep him. And so, just as before, only by occupation in the day, by morphine at night, could she stifle the fearful thought of what would be if he ceased to love her. It is true there was still one means; not to keep him—for that she wanted nothing more than his love—but to be nearer to him, to be in such a position that he would not leave her. That means was divorce and marriage. And she began to long for that, and made up her mind to agree to it the first time he or Stiva approached her on the subject.

Absorbed in such thoughts, she passed five days without him, the five days that he was to be at the elections.

Walks, conversation with Princess Varvara, visits to the hospital, and, most of all, reading—reading of one book after another—filled up her time. But on the sixth day, when the coachman came back without him, she felt that now she was utterly incapable of stifling the thought of him and of what he was doing there, just at that time her little girl was taken ill. Anna began to look after her, but even that did not distract her mind, especially as the illness was not serious. However hard she tried, she could not love this little child, and to feign love was beyond her powers. Towards the evening of that day, still alone, Anna was in such a panic about him that she decided to start for the town, but on second thoughts wrote him the contradictory letter that Vronsky received, and without reading it through, sent it off by a special messenger. The next morning she received his letter and regretted her own. She dreaded a repetition of the severe look he had flung at her at parting, especially when he knew that the baby was not dangerously ill. But still she was glad she had written to him. At this moment Anna was positively admitting to herself that she was a burden to him, that he would relinquish his freedom regretfully to return to her, and in spite of that she was glad he was coming. Let him weary of her, but he would be here with her, so that she would see him, would know of every action he took.

She was sitting in the drawing room near a lamp, with a new volume of Taine, and as she read, listening to the sound of the wind outside, and every minute expecting the carriage to arrive. Several times she had fancied she heard the sound of wheels, but she had been mistaken. At last she heard not the sound of wheels, but the coachman's shout and the dull rumble in the covered entry. Even Princess Varvara, playing patience, confirmed this, and Anna, flushing hotly, got up; but instead of going down, as she had done twice before, she stood still. She suddenly felt ashamed of her duplicity, but even more she dreaded how he might meet her. All feeling of wounded pride had passed now; she was only afraid of the expression of his displeasure. She remembered that her child had been perfectly well again for the last two days. She felt positively vexed with her for getting better from the very moment her letter was sent off. Then she thought of him, that he was here, all of him, with his hands, his eyes. She heard his voice. And forgetting everything, she ran joyfully to meet him.

"Well, how is Annie?" he said timidly from below, looking up to Anna as she ran down to him.

He was sitting on a chair, and a footman was pulling off his warm over-boot.

"Oh, she is better."

"And you?" he said, shaking himself.

She took his hand in both of hers, and drew it to her waist, never taking her eyes off him.

"Well, I'm glad," he said, coldly scanning her, her hair, her dress, which he knew she had put on for him. All was charming, but how many times it had charmed him! And the stern, stony expression that she so dreaded settled upon his face.

"Well, I'm glad. And are you well?" he said, wiping his damp beard with his handkerchief and kissing her hand.

"Never mind," she thought, "only let him be here, and so long as he's here he cannot, he dare not, cease to love me."

The evening was spent happily and gaily in the presence of Princess Varvara, who complained to him that Anna had been taking morphine in his absence.

"What am I to do? I couldn't sleep. . . . My thoughts prevented me. When he's here I never take it—hardly ever."

He told her about the election, and Anna knew how by adroit questions to bring him to what gave him most pleasure—his own success. She told him of everything that interested him at home; and all that she told him was of the most cheerful description.

But late in the evening, when they were alone, Anna, seeing that she had regained complete possession of him, wanted to erase the painful impression of the glance he had given her for her letter. She said:

"Tell me frankly, you were vexed at getting my letter, and you didn't believe me?"

As soon as she had said it, she felt that however warm his feelings were to her, he had not forgiven her for that.

"Yes," he said, "the letter was so strange. First, Annie ill, and then you thought of coming yourself."

"It was all the truth."

"Oh, I don't doubt it."

"Yes, you do doubt it. You are vexed, I see."

"Not for one moment. I'm only vexed, that's true, that you seem somehow unwilling to admit that there are duties . . ."

"The duty of going to a concert . . ."

"But we won't talk about it," he said.

"Why not talk about it?" she said.

"I only meant to say that matters of real importance may turn up. Now, for instance, I shall have to go to Moscow to arrange about the house. . . . Oh, Anna, why are you so irritable? Don't you know that I can't live without you?"

"If so," said Anna, her voice suddenly changing, "it means that you are sick of this life . . . Yes, you will come for a day and go away, as men do . . ."

"Anna, that's cruel. I am ready to give up my whole life."

But she did not hear him.

"If you go to Moscow, I will go too. I will not stay here. Either we must separate or else live together."

"Why, you know, that's my one desire. But for that . . ."

"We must get a divorce. I will write to him. I see I cannot go on like this . . . But I will come with you to Moscow."

"You talk as if you were threatening me. But I desire nothing so much as never to be parted from you," said Vronsky, smiling.

But as he said these words there gleamed in his eyes not merely a cold look, but the vindictive look of a man persecuted and made cruel.

She saw the look and correctly divined its meaning.

"If so, it's a calamity!" that glance told her. It was a moment's impression, but she never forgot it.

Anna wrote to her husband asking him about a divorce, and towards the end of November, taking leave of Princess Varvara, who wanted to go to Petersburg, she went with Vronsky to Moscow. Expecting everyday an answer from Alexey Alexandrovitch, and after that the divorce, they now established themselves together like married people.

"[illegible] don't care [illegible]

[illegible] you do [illegible] you [illegible] vexed [illegible]

[illegible] I'm only vexed [illegible] true, that you seem somehow unwilling to accept [illegible]

[illegible] are there.

"[illegible] the duty [illegible] going to a concert [illegible]"

"[illegible] we [illegible]," he said.

"[illegible] not all about?" she [illegible].

"[illegible] no importance [illegible] of real importance [illegible] Now for instance. [illegible] [illegible] about the [illegible] why are you so irritable? Don't you know [illegible] can't live without you?"

"[illegible]," said Anna [illegible] means that you are sick of [illegible] life [illegible] Yes, you [illegible] [illegible] as used to [illegible]

[illegible] that [illegible] ready to give up my whole life [illegible]

But she did not [illegible]

"[illegible] you go to Moscow, I will go too; I will not stay here. Either we must separate or else live together."

"Why, you know [illegible] one desire. But for that [illegible]

"[illegible] you write to [illegible] I cannot go on like this [illegible] I will come [illegible] with you to Moscow."

"[illegible] talk as if you were threatening me. [illegible] desire nothing so much as never to be parted [illegible] you," said Vronsky, smiling.

But [illegible] there gleamed in his eyes [illegible] would look [illegible]

[illegible] can be [illegible] and [illegible]

She saw the look [illegible] divined its meaning.

"If [illegible] that glance told her it was a [illegible] impression, but she never forgot it.

Anna wrote to [illegible] about a divorce, and towards the end of November, taking [illegible] to go to Petersburg [illegible] with [illegible] to Moscow. Expecting [illegible] day an answer from Alexey Alexandrovitch, and after that the divorce, they now established themselves together like married people.

Part Seven

Chapter I

THE LEVINS HAD BEEN THREE MONTHS IN MOSCOW. THE DATE HAD LONG PASSED ON WHICH, according to the most trustworthy calculations of people learned in such matters, Kitty should have been confined. But she was still about, and there was nothing to show that her time was any nearer than two months ago. The doctor, the monthly nurse, and Dolly and her mother, and most of all Levin, who could not think of the approaching event without terror, began to be impatient and uneasy. Kitty was the only person who felt perfectly calm and happy.

She was distinctly conscious now of the birth of a new feeling of love for the future child, for her to some extent actually existing already, and she brooded blissfully over this feeling. He was not by now altogether a part of herself, but sometimes lived his own life independently of her. Often this separate being gave her pain, but at the same time she wanted to laugh with a strange new joy.

All the people she loved were with her, and all were so good to her, so attentively caring for her, so entirely pleasant was everything presented to her, that if she had not known and felt that it must all soon be over, she could not have wished for a better and pleasanter life. The only thing that spoiled the charm of this manner of life was that her husband was not here as she loved him to be, and as he was in the country.

She liked his serene, friendly, and hospitable manner in the country. In the town he seemed continually uneasy and on his guard, as though he were afraid someone would be rude to him, and still more to her. At home in the country, knowing himself distinctly to be in his right place, he was never in haste to be off elsewhere. He was never unoccupied. Here in town he was in a continual hurry, as though afraid of missing something, and yet he had nothing to do. And she felt sorry for him. To others, she knew, he did not appear an object of pity. On the contrary, when Kitty looked at him in society, as one sometimes looks at those one loves, trying to see him as if he were a stranger, so as to catch the impression he must make on others, she saw with a panic even of jealous fear that he was far indeed from being a pitiable figure, that he was very attractive with his fine breeding, his rather old-fashioned, reserved courtesy with women, his powerful figure, and striking, as she thought, and expressive face. But she saw him not from without, but from within; she saw that here he was not himself; that was the only way she could define his condition to herself. Sometimes she inwardly reproached him for his inability to live in the town; sometimes she recognized that it was really hard for him to order his life here so that he could be satisfied with it.

What had he to do, indeed? He did not care for cards; he did not go to a club. Spending the time with jovial gentlemen of Oblonsky's type—she knew now what that meant . . . it meant drinking and going somewhere after drinking. She could not think without horror of where men went on such occasions. Was he to go into society? But she knew he could only find satisfaction in that if he took pleasure in the society of young women, and that she could not wish for. Should he stay at home with her, her mother and her sisters? But much as she liked and enjoyed their conversations forever on the same subjects—"Aline-Nodine," as the old prince called the sisters' talks—she knew it must bore him. What was there left for him to do? To go on writing at his book he had indeed attempted, and at first he used to go to the library and make extracts and look up references for his book. But, as he told her, the more he did nothing, the less time he had to do anything. And besides, he complained that he had talked too much about his book here, and that consequently all his ideas about it were muddled and had lost their interest for him.

One advantage in this town life was that quarrels hardly ever happened between them here in town. Whether it was that their conditions were different, or that they had both become more careful and sensible in that respect, they had no quarrels in Moscow from jealousy, which they had so dreaded when they moved from the country.

One event, an event of great importance to both from that point of view, did indeed happen—that was Kitty's meeting with Vronsky.

The old Princess Marya Borissovna, Kitty's godmother, who had always been very fond of her, had insisted on seeing her. Kitty, though she did not go into society at all on account of her condition, went with her father to see the venerable old lady, and there met Vronsky.

The only thing Kitty could reproach herself for at this meeting was that at the instant when she recognized in his civilian dress the features once so familiar to her, her breath failed her, the blood rushed to her heart, and a vivid blush—she felt it—overspread her face. But this lasted only a few seconds. Before her father, who purposely began talking in a loud voice to Vronsky, had finished, she was perfectly ready to look at Vronsky, to speak to him, if necessary, exactly as she spoke to Princess Marya Borissovna, and more than that, to do so in such a way that everything to the faintest intonation and smile would have been approved by her husband, whose unseen presence she seemed to feel about her at that instant.

She said a few words to him, even smiled serenely at his joke about the elections, which he called "our parliament." (She had to smile to show she saw the joke.) But she turned away immediately to Princess Marya Borissovna, and did not once glance at him till he got up to go; then she looked at him, but evidently only because it would be uncivil not to look at a man when he is saying good-bye.

She was grateful to her father for saying nothing to her about their meeting Vronsky, but she saw by his special warmth to her after the visit during their usual walk that he was pleased with her. She was pleased with herself. She had not expected she would have had the power, while keeping somewhere in the bottom of her heart all the memories of her old feeling for Vronsky, not only to seem but to be perfectly indifferent and composed with him.

Levin flushed a great deal more than she when she told him she had met Vronsky at Princess Marya Borissovna's. It was very hard for her to tell him this, but still harder to go on speaking of the details of the meeting, as he did not question her, but simply gazed at her with a frown.

"I am very sorry you weren't there," she said. "Not that you weren't in the room . . . I couldn't have been so natural in your presence . . . I am blushing now much more, much, much more," she said, blushing till the tears came into her eyes. "But that you couldn't see through a crack."

The truthful eyes told Levin that she was satisfied with herself, and in spite of her blushing he was quickly reassured and began questioning her, which was all she wanted. When he had heard everything, even to the detail that for the first second she could not help flushing, but that afterwards she was just as direct and as much at her ease as with any chance acquaintance, Levin was quite happy again and said he was glad of it, and would not now behave as stupidly as he had done at the election, but would try the first time he met Vronsky to be as friendly as possible.

"It's so wretched to feel that there's a man almost an enemy whom it's painful to meet," said Levin. "I'm very, very glad."

Chapter II

DO, PLEASE, GO THEN AND CALL ON THE BOLS, KITTY SAID TO HER HUSBAND, WHEN HE CAME IN to see her at eleven o'clock before going out. "I know you are dining at the club; papa put down your name. But what are you going to do in the morning?"

"I am only going to Katavasov," answered Levin.

"Why so early?"

"He promised to introduce me to Metrov. I wanted to talk to him about my work. He's a distinguished scientific man from Petersburg," said Levin.

"Yes; wasn't it his article you were praising so? Well, and after that?" said Kitty.

"I shall go to the court, perhaps, about my sister's business."

"And the concert?" she queried.

"I shan't go there all alone."

"No? do go; there are going to be some new things. . . . That interested you so. I should certainly go."

"Well, anyway, I shall come home before dinner," he said, looking at his watch.

"Put on your frock-coat, so that you can go straight to call on Countess Bola."

"But is it absolutely necessary?"

"Oh, absolutely! He has been to see us. Come, what is it? You go in, sit down, talk for five minutes of the weather, get up and go away."

"Oh, you wouldn't believe it! I've got so out of the way of all this that it makes me feel positively ashamed. It's such a horrible thing to do! A complete outsider walks in, sits down, stays on with nothing to do, wastes their time and worries himself, and walks away!"

Kitty laughed.

"Why, I suppose you used to pay calls before you were married, didn't you?"

"Yes, I did, but I always felt ashamed, and now I'm so out of the way of it that, by Jove! I'd sooner go two days running without my dinner than pay this call! One's so ashamed! I feel all the while that they're annoyed, that they're saying, 'What has he come for?' "

"No, they won't. I'll answer for that," said Kitty, looking into his face with a laugh. She took his hand. "Well, good-bye. . . . Do go, please."

He was just going out after kissing his wife's hand, when she stopped him.

"Kostya, do you know I've only fifty roubles left?"

"Oh, all right, I'll go to the bank and get some. How much?" he said, with the expression of dissatisfaction she knew so well.

"No, wait a minute." She held his hand. "Let's talk about it, it worries me. I seem to spend nothing unnecessary, but money seems to fly away simply. We don't manage well, somehow."

"Oh, it's all right," he said with a little cough, looking at her from under his brows.

That cough she knew well. It was a sign of intense dissatisfaction, not with her, but with himself. He certainly was displeased not at so much money being spent, but at being reminded of what he, knowing something was unsatisfactory, wanted to forget.

"I have told Sokolov to sell the wheat, and to borrow an advance on the mill. We shall have money enough in any case."

"Yes, but I'm afraid that altogether . . ."

"Oh, it's all right, all right," he repeated. "Well, good-bye, darling."

"No, I'm really sorry sometimes that I listened to mamma. How nice it would have been in the country! As it is, I'm worrying you all, and we're wasting our money."

"Not at all, not at all. Not once since I've been married have I said that things could have been better than they are. . . ."

"Truly?" she said, looking into his eyes.

He had said it without thinking, simply to console her. But when he glanced at her and saw those sweet truthful eyes fastened questioningly on him, he repeated it with his whole heart. "I was positively forgetting her," he thought. And he remembered what was before them, so soon to come.

"Will it be soon? How do you feel?" he whispered, taking her two hands.

"I have so often thought so, that now I don't think about it or know anything about it."

"And you're not frightened?"

She smiled contemptuously.

"Not the least little bit," she said.

"Well, if anything happens, I shall be at Katavasov's."

"No, nothing will happen, and don't think about it. I'm going for a walk on the boulevard with papa. We're going to see Dolly. I shall expect you before dinner. Oh, yes! Do you know that Dolly's position is becoming utterly impossible? She's in debt all round; she hasn't a penny. We were talking yesterday with mamma and Arseny" (this was her sister's husband Lvov), "and we determined to send you with him to talk to Stiva. It's really unbearable. One can't speak to papa about it. . . . But if you and he . . ."

"Why, what can we do?" said Levin.

"You'll be at Arseny's, anyway; talk to him, he will tell what we decided."

"Oh, I agree to everything Arseny thinks beforehand. I'll go and see him. By the way, if I do go to the concert, I'll go with Natalia. Well, good-bye."

On the steps Levin was stopped by his old servant Kouzma, who had been with him before his marriage, and now looked after their household in town.

"Beauty" (that was the left shaft-horse brought up from the country) "has been badly shod and is quite lame," he said. "What does your honor wish to be done?"

During the first part of their stay in Moscow, Levin had used his own horses brought up from the country. He had tried to arrange this part of their expenses in the best and cheapest way possible; but it appeared that their own horses came dearer than hired horses, and they still hired too.

"Send for the veterinary, there may be a bruise."

"And for Katerina Alexandrovna?" asked Kouzma.

Levin was not by now struck as he had been at first by the fact that to get from one end of Moscow to the other he had to have two powerful horses put into a heavy carriage, to take the carriage three miles through the snowy slush and to keep it standing there four hours, paying five roubles every time.

Now it seemed quite natural.

"Hire a pair for our carriage from the jobmaster," said he.

"Yes, sir."

And so, simply and easily, thanks to the facilities of town life, Levin settled a question which, in the country, would have called for so much personal trouble and exertion, and going out onto the steps, he called a sleigh, sat down, and drove to Nikitsky. On the way he thought no more of money, but mused on the introduction that awaited him to the Petersburg savant, a writer on sociology, and what he would say to him about his book.

Only during the first days of his stay in Moscow Levin had been struck by the expenditure, strange to one living in the country, unproductive but inevitable, that was expected of him on every side. But by now he had grown used to it. That had happened to him in this matter which is said to happen to drunkards—the first glass sticks in the throat, the second flies down like a hawk, but after the third they're like tiny little birds. When Levin had changed his first hundred-ruble note to pay for liveries for his footmen and hall-porter he could not help reflecting that these liveries were of no use to anyone—but they were indubitably necessary, to judge by the amazement of the princess and Kitty when he suggested that they might do without liveries—that these liveries would cost the wages of two laborers for the summer, that is, would pay for about three hundred working days from Easter to Ash Wednesday, and each a day of hard work from early morning to late evening—and that hundred-ruble note did stick in his throat. But the next note, changed to pay for providing a dinner for their relations, that cost twenty-eight roubles, though it did excite in Levin the reflection that twenty-eight roubles meant nine measures of oats, which men would with groans and sweat have reaped and bound and thrashed and winnowed and sifted and sown—this next one he parted with more easily. And now the notes he changed no longer aroused such reflections, and they flew off like little birds. Whether the labor devoted to obtaining the money corresponded to the pleasure given by what was bought with it, was a consideration he had long ago dismissed. His business calculation that there was a certain price below which he could not sell certain grain was forgotten too. The rye, for the price of which he had so long held out, had been sold for fifty kopecks a measure cheaper than it had been fetching a month ago. Even the consideration that with such an expenditure he could not go on living for a year without debt, that even had no force. Only one thing was essential: to have money in the bank, without inquiring where it came from, so as to know that one had the wherewithal to buy meat for tomorrow. And this condition had hitherto been fulfilled; he had always had the money in the bank. But now the money in the bank had gone, and he could not quite tell where to get the next installment. And this it was which, at the moment when Kitty had mentioned money, had disturbed him; but he had no time to think about it. He drove off, thinking of Katavasov and the meeting with Metrov that was before him.

Chapter III

LEVIN HAD ON THIS VISIT TO TOWN SEEN A GREAT DEAL OF HIS OLD FRIEND AT THE UNIVERSITY, Professor Katavasov, whom he had not seen since his marriage. He liked in Katavasov the clearness and simplicity of his conception of life. Levin thought that the clearness of Katavasov's conception of life was due to the poverty of his nature; Katavasov thought that the disconnectedness of Levin's ideas was due to his lack of intellectual discipline; but Levin enjoyed Katavasov's clearness, and Katavasov enjoyed the abundance of Levin's untrained ideas, and they liked to meet and to discuss.

Levin had read Katavasov some parts of his book, and he had liked them. On the previous day Katavasov had met Levin at a public lecture and told him that the celebrated Metrov, whose article Levin had so much liked, was in Moscow, that he had been much interested by what Katavasov had told him about Levin's work, and that he was coming to see him tomorrow at eleven, and would be very glad to make Levin's acquaintance.

"You're positively a reformed character, I'm glad to see," said Katavasov, meeting Levin in the little drawing room. "I heard the bell and thought: Impossible that it can be he at the exact time! . . . Well, what do you say to the Montenegrins now? They're a race of warriors."

"Why, what's happened?" asked Levin.

Katavasov in a few words told him the last piece of news from the war, and going into his study, introduced Levin to a short, thick-set man of pleasant appearance. This was Metrov. The conversation touched for a brief space on politics and on how recent events were looked at in the higher spheres in Petersburg. Metrov repeated a saying that had reached him through a most trustworthy source, reported as having been uttered on this subject by the Tsar and one of the ministers. Katavasov had heard also on excellent authority that the Tsar had said something quite different. Levin tried to imagine circumstances in which both sayings might have been uttered, and the conversation on that topic dropped.

"Yes, here he's written almost a book on the natural conditions of the laborer in relation to the land," said Katavasov; "I'm not a specialist, but I, as a natural science man, was pleased at his not taking mankind as something outside biological laws; but, on the contrary, seeing his dependence on his surroundings, and in that dependence seeking the laws of his development."

"That's very interesting," said Metrov.

"What I began precisely was to write a book on agriculture; but studying the chief instrument of agriculture, the laborer," said Levin, reddening, "I could not help coming to quite unexpected results."

And Levin began carefully, as it were, feeling his ground, to expound his views. He knew Metrov had written an article against the generally accepted theory of political economy, but to what extent he could reckon on his sympathy with his own new views he did not know and could not guess from the clever and serene face of the learned man.

"But in what do you see the special characteristics of the Russian laborer?" said Metrov; "in his biological characteristics, so to speak, or in the condition in which he is placed?"

Levin saw that there was an idea underlying this question with which he did not agree. But he went on explaining his own idea that the Russian laborer has a quite special view of the land, different from that of other people; and to support this proposition he made haste to add that in his opinion this attitude of the Russian peasant was due to the consciousness of his vocation to people vast unoccupied expanses in the East.

"One may easily be led into error in basing any conclusion on the general vocation of a people," said Metrov, interrupting Levin. "The condition of the laborer will always depend on his relation to the land and to capital."

And without letting Levin finish explaining his idea, Metrov began expounding to him the special point of his own theory.

In what the point of his theory lay, Levin did not understand, because he did not take the trouble to understand. He saw that Metrov, like other people, in spite of his own article, in which he had attacked the current theory of political economy, looked at the position of the Russian peasant simply from the point of view of capital, wages, and rent. He would indeed have been obliged to admit that in the eastern—much the larger—part of Russia rent was as yet nil, that for nine-tenths of the eighty millions of the Russian peasants wages took the form simply of food provided for themselves, and that capital does not so far exist except in the form of the most primitive tools. Yet it was only from that point of view that he considered every laborer, though in many points he differed from the economists and had his own theory of the wage-fund, which he expounded to Levin.

Levin listened reluctantly, and at first made objections. He would have liked to interrupt Metrov, to explain his own thought, which in his opinion would have rendered further exposition of Metrov's theories superfluous. But later on, feeling convinced that they looked at the matter so differently, that they could never understand one another, he did not even oppose his statements, but simply listened. Although what Metrov was saying was by now utterly devoid of interest for him, he yet experienced a certain satisfaction in listening to him. It flattered his vanity that such a learned man should explain his ideas to him so eagerly, with such intensity and confidence in Levin's understanding of the subject, sometimes with a mere hint referring him to a whole aspect of the subject. He put this down to his own credit, unaware that Metrov, who had already discussed his theory over and over again with all his intimate friends, talked of it with special eagerness to every new person, and in general was eager to talk to anyone of any subject that interested him, even if still obscure to himself.

"We are late though," said Katavasov, looking at his watch directly Metrov had finished his discourse.

"Yes, there's a meeting of the Society of Amateurs today in commemoration of the jubilee of Svintitch," said Katavasov in answer to Levin's inquiry. "Pyotr Ivanovitch and I were going. I've promised to deliver an address on his labors in zoology. Come along with us, it's very interesting."

"Yes, and indeed it's time to start," said Metrov. "Come with us, and from there, if you care to, come to my place. I should very much like to hear your work."

"Oh, no! It's no good yet, it's unfinished. But I shall be very glad to go to the meeting."

"I say, friends, have you heard? He has handed in the separate report," Katavasov called from the other room, where he was putting on his frock-coat.

And a conversation sprang up upon the university question, which was a very important event that winter in Moscow. Three old professors in the council had not accepted the opinion of the younger professors. The young ones had registered a separate resolution. This, in the judgment of some people, was monstrous, in the judgment of others it was the simplest and most just thing to do, and the professors were split up into two parties.

One party, to which Katavasov belonged, saw in the opposite party a scoundrelly betrayal and treachery, while the opposite party saw in them childishness and lack of respect for the authorities. Levin, though he did not belong to the university, had several times already during his stay in Moscow heard and talked about this matter, and had his own opinion on the subject. He took part in the conversation that was continued in the street, as they all three walked to the buildings of the old university.

The meeting had already begun. Round the cloth-covered table, at which Katavasov and Metrov seated themselves, there were some half-dozen persons, and one of these was bending close over a manuscript, reading something aloud. Levin sat down in one of the empty chairs that were standing round the table, and in a whisper asked a student sitting near what was being read. The student, eyeing Levin with displeasure, said:

"Biography."

Though Levin was not interested in the biography, he could not help listening, and learned some new and interesting facts about the life of the distinguished man of science.

When the reader had finished, the chairman thanked him and read some verses of the poet Ment sent him on the jubilee, and said a few words by way of thanks to the poet. Then Katavasov in his loud, ringing voice read his address on the scientific labors of the man whose jubilee was being kept.

When Katavasov had finished, Levin looked at his watch, saw it was past one, and thought that there would not be time before the concert to read Metrov his book, and indeed, he did not now care to do so. During the reading he had thought over their conversation. He saw distinctly now that though Metrov's ideas might perhaps have value, his own ideas had a value too, and their ideas could only be made clear and lead to something if each worked separately in his chosen path, and that nothing would be gained by putting their ideas together. And having made up his mind to refuse Metrov's invitation, Levin went up to him at the end of the meeting. Metrov introduced Levin to the chairman, with whom he was talking of the political news. Metrov told the chairman what he had already told Levin, and Levin made the same remarks on his news that he had already made that morning, but for the sake of variety he expressed also a new opinion which had only just struck him. After that the conversation turned again on the university question. As Levin had already heard it all, he made haste to tell Metrov that he was sorry he could not take advantage of his invitation, took leave, and drove to Lvov's.

Chapter IV

LVOV, THE HUSBAND OF NATALIA, KITTY'S SISTER, HAD SPENT ALL HIS LIFE IN FOREIGN CAPITALS, where he had been educated, and had been in the diplomatic service.

During the previous year he had left the diplomatic service, not owing to any "unpleasantness" (he never had any "unpleasantness" with anyone), and was transferred to the department of the court of the palace in Moscow, in order to give his two boys the best education possible.

In spite of the striking contrast in their habits and views and the fact that Lvov was older than Levin, they had seen a great deal of one another that winter, and had taken a great liking to each other.

Lvov was at home, and Levin went in to him unannounced.

Lvov, in a house coat with a belt and in chamois leather shoes, was sitting in an arm-chair, and with a pince-nez with blue glasses he was reading a book that stood on a reading desk, while in his beautiful hand he held a half-burned cigarette daintily away from him.

His handsome, delicate, and still youthful-looking face, to which his curly, glistening silvery hair gave a still more aristocratic air, lit up with a smile when he saw Levin.

"Capital! I was meaning to send to you. How's Kitty? Sit here, it's more comfortable." He got up and pushed up a rocking chair. "Have you read the last circular in the *Journal de St. Pétersbourg?* I think it's excellent," he said, with a slight French accent.

Levin told him what he had heard from Katavasov was being said in Petersburg, and after talking a little about politics, he told him of his interview with Metrov, and the learned society's meeting. To Lvov it was very interesting.

"That's what I envy you, that you are able to mix in these interesting scientific circles," he said. And as he talked, he passed as usual into French, which was easier to him. "It's true I haven't the time for it. My official work and the children leave me no time; and then I'm not ashamed to own that my education has been too defective."

"That I don't believe," said Levin with a smile, feeling, as he always did, touched at Lvov's low opinion of himself, which was not in the least put on from a desire to seem or to be modest, but was absolutely sincere.

"Oh, yes, indeed! I feel now how badly educated I am. To educate my children I positively have to look up a great deal, and in fact simply to study myself. For it's not enough to have teachers, there must be someone to look after them, just as on your land you want laborers and an overseer. See what I'm reading"—he pointed to Buslaev's *Grammar* on the desk—"it's expected of Misha, and it's so difficult. . . . Come, explain to me. . . . Here he says . . ."

Levin tried to explain to him that it couldn't be understood, but that it had to be taught; but Lvov would not agree with him.

"Oh, you're laughing at it!"

"On the contrary, you can't imagine how, when I look at you, I'm always learning the task that lies before me, that is the education of one's children."

"Well, there's nothing for you to learn," said Lvov.

"All I know," said Levin, "is that I have never seen better brought-up children than yours, and I wouldn't wish for children better than yours."

Lvov visibly tried to restrain the expression of his delight, but he was positively radiant with smiles.

"If only they're better than me! That's all I desire. You don't know yet all the work," he said, "with boys who've been left like mine to run wild abroad."

"You'll catch all that up. They're such clever children. The great thing is the education of character. That's what I learn when I look at your children."

"You talk of the education of character. You can't imagine how difficult that is! You have hardly succeeded in combating one tendency when others crop up, and the struggle begins again. If one had not a support in religion—you remember we talked about that—no father could bring children up relying on his own strength alone without that help."

This subject, which always interested Levin, was cut short by the entrance of the beauty Natalia Alexandrovna, dressed to go out.

"I didn't know you were here," she said, unmistakably feeling no regret, but a positive pleasure, in interrupting this conversation on a topic she had heard so much of that she was by now weary of it. "Well, how is Kitty? I am dining with you today. I tell you what, Arseny," she turned to her husband, "you take the carriage."

And the husband and wife began to discuss their arrangements for the day. As the husband had to drive to meet someone on official business, while the wife had to go to the concert and some public meeting of a committee on the Eastern Question, there was a great deal to consider and settle. Levin had to take part in their plans as one of themselves. It was settled that Levin should go with Natalia to the concert and the meeting, and that from there they should send the carriage to the office for Arseny, and he should call for her and take her to Kitty's; or that, if he had not finished his work, he should send the carriage back and Levin would go with her.

"He's spoiling me," Lvov said to his wife: "he assures me that our children are splendid, when I know how much that's bad there is in them."

"Arseny goes to extremes, I always say," said his wife. "If you look for perfection, you will never be satisfied. And it's true, as papa says—that when we were brought up there was one extreme—we were kept in the basement, while our parents lived in the best rooms; now it's just the other way—the parents are in the wash house, while the children are in the best rooms. Parents now are not expected to live at all, but to exist altogether for their children."

"Well, what if they like it better?" Lvov said, with his beautiful smile, touching her hand. "Anyone who didn't know you would think you were a stepmother, not a true mother."

"No, extremes are not good in anything," Natalia said serenely, putting his paper-knife straight in its proper place on the table.

"Well, come here, you perfect children," Lvov said to the two handsome boys who came in, and after bowing to Levin, went up to their father, obviously wishing to ask him about something.

Levin would have liked to talk to them, to hear what they would say to their father, but Natalia began talking to him, and then Lvov's colleague in the service, Mahotin, walked in, wearing his court uniform, to go with him to meet someone, and a conversation was kept up without a break upon Herzegovina, Princess Korzinskaya, the town council, and the sudden death of Madame Apraksina.

Levin even forgot the commission entrusted to him. He recollected it as he was going into the hall.

"Oh, Kitty told me to talk to you about Oblonsky," he said, as Lvov was standing on the stairs, seeing his wife and Levin off.

"Yes, yes, maman wants us, *les beaux-frères,* to attack him," he said, blushing. "But why should I?"

"Well, then, I will attack him," said Madame Lvova, with a smile, standing in her white sheepskin cape, waiting till they had finished speaking. "Come, let us go."

Chapter V

AT THE CONCERT IN THE AFTERNOON TWO VERY INTERESTING THINGS WERE PERFORMED. ONE was a fantasia, *King Lear;* the other was a quartette dedicated to the memory of Bach. Both were new and in the new style, and Levin was eager to form an opinion of them. After escorting his sister-in-law to her stall, he stood against a column and tried to listen as attentively and conscientiously as possible. He tried not to let his attention be distracted, and not to spoil his impression by looking at the conductor in a white tie, waving his arms, which always disturbed his enjoyment of music so much, or the ladies in bonnets, with strings carefully tied over their ears, and all these people either thinking of nothing at all or thinking of all sorts of things except the music. He tried to avoid meeting musical connoisseurs or talkative acquaintances, and stood looking at the floor straight before him, listening.

But the more he listened to the fantasia of *King Lear* the further he felt from forming any definite opinion of it. There was, as it were, a continual beginning, a preparation of the musical expression of some feeling, but it fell to pieces again directly, breaking into new musical motives, or simply nothing but the whims of the composer, exceedingly complex but disconnected sounds. And these fragmentary musical expressions, though sometimes beautiful, were disagreeable, because they were utterly unexpected and not led up to by anything. Gaiety and grief and despair and tenderness and triumph followed one another without any connection, like the emotions of a madman. And those emotions, like a madman's, sprang up quite unexpectedly.

During the whole of the performance Levin felt like a deaf man watching people dancing, and was in a state of complete bewilderment when the fantasia was over, and felt a great weariness from the fruitless strain on his attention. Loud applause resounded on all sides. Everyone got up, moved about, and began talking. Anxious to throw some light on his own perplexity from the impressions of others, Levin began to walk about, looking for connoisseurs, and was glad to see a well-known musical amateur in conversation with Pestsov, whom he knew.

"Marvelous!" Pestsov was saying in his mellow bass. "How are you, Konstantin Dmitrievitch? Particularly sculpturesque and plastic, so to say, and richly colored is that passage where you feel Cordelia's approach, where woman, *das ewig Weibliche,* enters into conflict with fate. Isn't it?"

"You mean . . . what has Cordelia to do with it?" Levin asked timidly, forgetting that the fantasia was supposed to represent King Lear.

"Cordelia comes in . . . see here!" said Pestsov, tapping his finger on the satiny surface of the f he held in his hand and passing it to Levin.

Only then Levin recollected the title of the fantasia, and made haste to read in the Russian translation the lines from Shakespeare that were printed on the back of the program.

"You can't follow it without that," said Pestsov, addressing Levin, as the person he had been speaking to had gone away, and he had no one to talk to.

In the *entr'acte* Levin and Pestsov fell into an argument upon the merits and defects of music of the Wagner school. Levin maintained that the mistake of Wagner and all his followers lay in their trying to take music into the sphere of another art, just as poetry goes wrong when it tries to paint a face as the art of painting ought to do, and as an instance of this mistake he cited the sculptor who carved in marble certain poetic phantasms flitting round the figure of the poet on the pedestal. "These phantoms were so far from being phantoms that they were positively clinging on the ladder," said Levin. The comparison pleased him, but he could not remember whether he had not used the same phrase before, and to Pestsov, too, and as he said it he felt confused.

Pestsov maintained that art is one, and that it can attain its highest manifestations only by conjunction with all kinds of art.

The second piece that was performed Levin could not hear. Pestsov, who was standing beside him, was talking to him almost all the time, condemning the music for its excessive affected assumption of simplicity, and comparing it with the simplicity of the Pre-Raphaelites in painting. As he went out Levin met manymore acquaintances, with whom he talked of politics, of music, and of common acquaintances. Among others he met Count Bol, whom he had utterly forgotten to call upon.

"Well, go at once then," Madame Lvova said, when he told her; "perhaps they'll not be at home, and then you can come to the meeting to fetch me. You'll find me still there."

Chapter VI

"PERHAPS THEY'RE NOT AT HOME? SAID LEVIN, AS HE WENT INTO THE HALL OF COUNTESS BOLA'S house.

"At home; please walk in," said the porter, resolutely removing his overcoat.

"How annoying!" thought Levin with a sigh, taking off one glove and stroking his hat. "What did I come for? What have I to say to them?"

As he passed through the first drawing room Levin met in the doorway Countess Bola, giving some order to a servant with a care-worn and severe face. On seeing Levin she smiled, and asked him to come into the little drawing room, where he heard voices. In this room there were sitting in arm-chairs the two daughters of the countess, and a Moscow colonel, whom Levin knew. Levin went up, greeted them, and sat down beside the sofa with his hat on his knees.

"How is your wife? Have you been at the concert? We couldn't go. Mamma had to be at the funeral service."

"Yes, I heard . . . What a sudden death!" said Levin.

The countess came in, sat down on the sofa, and she too asked after his wife and inquired about the concert.

Levin answered, and repeated an inquiry about Madame Apraksina's sudden death.

"But she was always in weak health."

"Were you at the opera yesterday?"

"Yes, I was."

"Lucca was very good."

"Yes, very good," he said, and as it was utterly of no consequence to him what they thought of him, he began repeating what they had heard a hundred times about the characteristics of the singer's talent. Countess Bola pretended to be listening. Then, when he had said enough and paused, the colonel, who had been silent till then, began to talk. The colonel too talked of the opera, and about culture. At last, after speaking of the proposed *folle journée* at Turin's, the colonel laughed, got up noisily, and went away. Levin too rose, but he saw by the face of the countess that it was not yet time for him to go. He must stay two minutes longer. He sat down.

But as he was thinking all the while how stupid it was, he could not find a subject for conversation, and sat silent.

"You are not going to the public meeting? They say it will be very interesting," began the countess.

"No, I promised my belle-soeur to fetch her from it," said Levin.

A silence followed. The mother once more exchanged glances with a daughter.

"Well, now I think the time has come," thought Levin, and he got up. The ladies shook hands with him, and begged him to say *mille choses* to his wife for them.

The porter asked him, as he gave him his coat, "Where is your honor staying?" and immediately wrote down his address in a big handsomely bound book.

"Of course I don't care, but still I feel ashamed and awfully stupid," thought Levin, consoling himself with the reflection that everyone does it. He drove to the public meeting, where he was to find his sister-in-law, so as to drive home with her.

At the public meeting of the committee there were a great many people, and almost all the highest society. Levin was in time for the report which, as everyone said, was very interesting. When the reading of the report was over, people moved about, and Levin met Sviazhsky, who invited him very pressingly to come that evening to a meeting of the Society of Agriculture, where a celebrated lecture was to be delivered, and Stepan Arkadyevitch, who had only just come from the races, and many other acquaintances; and Levin heard and uttered various criticisms on the meeting, on the new fantasia, and on a public trial. But, probably from the mental fatigue he was beginning to feel, he made a blunder in speaking of the trial, and this blunder he recalled several times with vexation. Speaking of the sentence upon a foreigner who had been condemned in Russia, and of how unfair it would be to punish him by exile abroad, Levin repeated what he had heard the day before in conversation from an acquaintance.

"I think sending him abroad is much the same as punishing a carp by putting it into the water," said Levin. Then he recollected that this idea, which he had heard from an acquaintance and uttered as his own, came from a fable of Krilov's, and that the acquaintance had picked it up from a newspaper article.

After driving home with his sister-in-law, and finding Kitty in good spirits and quite well, Levin drove to the club.

Chapter VII

LEVIN REACHED THE CLUB JUST AT THE RIGHT TIME. MEMBERS AND VISITORS WERE DRIVING UP AS he arrived. Levin had not been at the club for a very long while—not since he lived in Moscow, when he was leaving the university and going into society. He remembered the club, the external details of its arrangement, but he had completely forgotten the impression it had made on him in old days. But as soon as, driving into the wide semicircular court and getting out of the sleigh, he mounted the steps, and the hall-porter, adorned with a crossway scarf, noiselessly opened the door to him with a bow; as soon as he saw in the porter's room the cloaks and galoshes of members who thought it less trouble to take them off downstairs; as soon as he heard the mysterious ringing bell that preceded him as he ascended the easy, carpeted staircase, and saw the statue on the landing, and the third porter at the top doors, a familiar figure grown older, in the club livery, opening the door without haste or delay, and scanning the visitors as they passed in—Levin felt the old impression of the club come back in a rush, an impression of repose, comfort, and propriety.

"Your hat, please," the porter said to Levin, who forgot the club rule to leave his hat in the porter's room. "Long time since you've been. The prince put your name down yesterday. Prince Stepan Arkadyevitch is not here yet."

The porter did not only know Levin, but also all his ties and relationships, and so immediately mentioned his intimate friends.

Passing through the outer hall, divided up by screens, and the room partitioned on the right, where a man sits at the fruit buffet, Levin overtook an old man walking slowly in, and entered the dining room full of noise and people.

He walked along the tables, almost all full, and looked at the visitors. He saw people of all sorts, old and young; some he knew a little, some intimate friends. There was not a single cross or worried-looking face. All seemed to have left their cares and anxieties in the porter's room with their hats, and were all deliberately getting ready to enjoy the material blessings of life. Sviazhsky was here and Shtcherbatsky, Nevyedovsky and the old prince, and Vronsky and Sergey Ivanovitch.

"Ah! why are you late?" the prince said smiling, and giving him his hand over his own shoulder. "How's Kitty?" he added, smoothing out the napkin he had tucked in at his waistcoat buttons.

"All right; they are dining at home, all the three of them."

"Ah, 'Aline-Nadine,' to be sure! There's no room with us. Go to that table, and make haste and take a seat," said the prince, and turning away he carefully took a plate of eel soup.

"Levin, this way!" a good-natured voice shouted a little further on. It was Turovtsin. He was sitting with a young officer, and beside them were two chairs turned upside down. Levin gladly went up to them. He had always liked the good-hearted rake, Turovtsin—he was associated in his mind with memories of his courtship—and at that moment, after the strain of intellectual conversation, the sight of Turovtsin's good-natured face was particularly welcome.

"For you and Oblonsky. He'll be here directly."

The young man, holding himself very erect, with eyes forever twinkling with enjoyment, was an officer from Petersburg, Gagin. Turovtsin introduced them.

"Oblonsky's always late."

"Ah, here he is!"

"Have you only just come?" said Oblonsky, coming quickly towards them. "Good day. Had some vodka? Well, come along then."

Levin got up and went with him to the big table spread with spirits and appetizers of the most various kinds. One would have thought that out of two dozen delicacies one might find something to one's taste, but Stepan Arkadyevitch asked for something special, and one of the liveried waiters standing by immediately brought what was required. They drank a wine glassful and returned to their table.

At once, while they were still at the soup, Gagin was served with champagne, and told the waiter to fill four glasses. Levin did not refuse the wine, and asked for a second bottle. He was very hungry, and ate and drank with great enjoyment, and with still greater enjoyment took part in the lively and simple conversation of his companions. Gagin, dropping his voice, told the last good story from Petersburg, and the story, though improper and stupid, was so ludicrous that Levin broke into roars of laughter so loud that those near looked round.

"That's in the same style as, 'that's a thing I can't endure!' You know the story?" said Stepan Arkadyevitch. "Ah, that's exquisite! Another bottle," he said to the waiter, and he began to relate his good story.

"Pyotr Illyitch Vinovsky invites you to drink with him," a little old waiter interrupted Stepan Arkadyevitch, bringing two delicate glasses of sparkling champagne, and addressing Stepan Arkadyevitch and Levin. Stepan Arkadyevitch took the glass, and looking towards a bald man with red mustaches at the other end of the table, he nodded to him, smiling.

"Who's that?" asked Levin.

"You met him once at my place, don't you remember? A good-natured fellow."

Levin did the same as Stepan Arkadyevitch and took the glass.

Stepan Arkadyevitch's anecdote too was very amusing. Levin told his story, and that too was successful. Then they talked of horses, of the races, of what they had been doing that day, and of how smartly Vronsky's Atlas had won the first prize. Levin did not notice how the time passed at dinner.

"Ah! and here they are!" Stepan Arkadyevitch said towards the end of dinner, leaning over the back of his chair and holding out his hand to Vronsky, who came up with a tall officer of the Guards. Vronsky's face too beamed with the look of good-humored enjoyment that was general in the club. He propped his elbow playfully on Stepan Arkadyevitch's shoulder, whispering something to him, and he held out his hand to Levin with the same good-humored smile.

"Very glad to meet you," he said. "I looked out for you at the election, but I was told you had gone away."

"Yes, I left the same day. We've just been talking of your horse. I congratulate you," said Levin. "It was very rapidly run."

"Yes; you've race-horses too, haven't you?"

"No, my father had; but I remember and know something about it."

"Where have you dined?" asked Stepan Arkadyevitch.

"We were at the second table, behind the columns."

"We've been celebrating his success," said the tall colonel. "It's his second Imperial prize. I wish I might have the luck at cards he has with horses. Well, why waste the precious time? I'm going to the 'infernal regions,' " added the colonel, and he walked away.

"That's Yashvin," Vronsky said in answer to Turovtsin, and he sat down in the vacated seat beside them. He drank the glass offered him, and ordered a bottle of wine. Under the influence of the club atmosphere or the wine he had drunk, Levin chatted away to Vronsky of the best breeds of cattle, and was very glad not to feel the slightest hostility to this man. He even told him, among other things, that he had heard from his wife that she had met him at Princess Marya Borissovna's.

"Ah, Princess Marya Borissovna, she's exquisite!" said Stepan Arkadyevitch, and he told an anecdote about her which set them all laughing. Vronsky particularly laughed with such simple-hearted amusement that Levin felt quite reconciled to him.

"Well, have we finished?" said Stepan Arkadyevitch, getting up with a smile. "Let us go."

Chapter VIII

GETTING UP FROM THE TABLE, LEVIN WALKED WITH GAGIN THROUGH THE LOFTY ROOM TO THE billiard room, feeling his arms swing as he walked with a peculiar lightness and ease. As he crossed the big room, he came upon his father-in-law.

"Well, how do you like our Temple of Indolence?" said the prince, taking his arm. "Come along, come along!"

"Yes, I wanted to walk about and look at everything. It's interesting."

"Yes, it's interesting for you. But its interest for me is quite different. You look at those little old men now," he said, pointing to a club member with bent back and projecting lip, shuffling towards them in his soft boots, "and imagine that they were *shlupiks* like that from their birth up."

"How *shlupiks?*"

"I see you don't know that name. That's our club designation. You know the game of rolling eggs: when one's rolled a long while it becomes a *shlupik*. So it is with us; one goes on coming and coming to the club, and ends by becoming a *shlupik*. Ah, you laugh! but we look out, for fear of dropping into it ourselves. You know Prince Tchetchensky?" inquired the prince; and Levin saw by his face that he was just going to relate something funny.

"No, I don't know him."

"You don't say so! Well, Prince Tchetchensky is a well-known figure. No matter, though. He's always playing billiards here. Only three years ago he was not a *shlupik* and kept up his spirits and even used to call other people *shlupiks*. But one day he turns up, and our porter . . . you know Vassily? Why, that fat one; he's famous for his *bon mots*. And so Prince Tchetchensky asks him, 'Come, Vassily, who's here? Any *shlupiks* here yet?' And he says, 'You're the third.' Yes, my dear boy, that he did!"

Talking and greeting the friends they met, Levin and the prince walked through all the rooms: the great room where tables had already been set, and the usual partners were playing for small stakes; the divan room, where they were playing chess, and Sergey Ivanovitch was sitting talking to somebody; the billiard room, where, about a sofa in a recess, there was a lively party drinking champagne—Gagin was one of them. They peeped into the "infernal regions," where a good many men were crowding round one table, at which Yashvin was sitting. Trying not to make a noise, they walked into the dark reading room, where under the shaded lamps there sat a young man with a wrathful countenance, turning over one journal after another, and a bald general buried in a book. They went, too, into what the prince called the intellectual room, where three gentlemen were engaged in a heated discussion of the latest political news.

"Prince, please come, we're ready," said one of his card party, who had come to look for him, and the prince went off. Levin sat down and listened, but recalling all the conversation of the morning he felt all of a sudden fearfully bored. He got up hurriedly, and went to look for Oblonsky and Turovtsin, with whom it had been so pleasant.

Turovtsin was one of the circle drinking in the billiard room, and Stepan Arkadyevitch was talking with Vronsky near the door at the farther corner of the room.

"It's not that she's dull; but this undefined, this unsettled position," Levin caught, and he was hurrying away, but Stepan Arkadyevitch called to him.

"Levin," said Stepan Arkadyevitch; and Levin noticed that his eyes were not full of tears exactly, but moist, which always happened when he had been drinking, or when he was touched. Just now it was due to both causes. "Levin, don't go," he said, and he warmly squeezed his arm above the elbow, obviously not at all wishing to let him go.

"This is a true friend of mine—almost my greatest friend," he said to Vronsky. "You have become even closer and dearer to me. And I want you, and I know you ought, to be friends, and great friends, because you're both splendid fellows."

"Well, there's nothing for us now but to kiss and be friends," Vronsky said, with good-natured playfulness, holding out his hand.

Levin quickly took the offered hand, and pressed it warmly.

"I'm very, very glad," said Levin.

"Waiter, a bottle of champagne," said Stepan Arkadyevitch.

"And I'm very glad," said Vronsky.

But in spite of Stepan Arkadyevitch's desire, and their own desire, they had nothing to talk about, and both felt it.

"Do you know, he has never met Anna?" Stepan Arkadyevitch said to Vronsky. "And I want above everything to take him to see her. Let us go, Levin!"

"Really?" said Vronsky. "She will be very glad to see you. I should be going home at once," he added, "but I'm worried about Yashvin, and I want to stay on till he finishes."

"Why, is he losing?"

"He keeps losing, and I'm the only friend that can restrain him."

"Well, what do you say to pyramids? Levin, will you play? Capital!" said Stepan Arkadyevitch. "Get the table ready," he said to the marker.

"It has been ready a long while," answered the marker, who had already set the balls in a triangle, and was knocking the red one about for his own diversion.

"Well, let us begin."

After the game Vronsky and Levin sat down at Gagin's table, and at Stepan Arkadyevitch's suggestion Levin took a hand in the game.

Vronsky sat down at the table, surrounded by friends, who were incessantly coming up to him. Every now and then he went to the "infernal" to keep an eye on Yashvin. Levin was enjoying a delightful sense of repose after the mental fatigue of the morning. He was glad that all hostility was at an end with Vronsky, and the sense of peace, decorum, and comfort never left him.

When the game was over, Stepan Arkadyevitch took Levin's arm.

"Well, let us go to Anna's, then. At once? Eh? She is at home. I promised her long ago to bring you. Where were you meaning to spend the evening?"

"Oh, nowhere specially. I promised Sviazhsky to go to the Society of Agriculture. By all means, let us go," said Levin.

"Very good; come along. Find out if my carriage is here," Stepan Arkadyevitch said to the waiter.

Levin went up to the table, paid the forty roubles he had lost; paid his bill, the amount of which was in some mysterious way ascertained by the little old waiter who stood at the counter, and swinging his arms he walked through all the rooms to the way out.

Chapter IX

"OBLONSKY'S CARRIAGE!" THE PORTER SHOUTED IN AN ANGRY BASS. THE CARRIAGE DROVE UP and both got in. It was only for the first few moments, while the carriage was driving out of the clubhouse gates, that Levin was still under the influence of the club atmosphere of repose, comfort, and unimpeachable good form. But as soon as the carriage drove out into the street, and he felt it jolting over the uneven road, heard the angry shout of a sleigh-driver coming towards them, saw in the uncertain light the red blind of a tavern and the shops, this impression was dissipated, and he began to think over his actions, and to wonder whether he was doing right in going to see Anna. What would Kitty say? But Stepan Arkadyevitch gave him no time for reflection, and, as though divining his doubts, he scattered them.

"How glad I am," he said, "that you should know her! You know Dolly has long wished for it. And Lvov's been to see her, and often goes. Though she is my sister," Stepan Arkadyevitch pursued, "I don't hesitate to say that she's a remarkable woman. But you will see. Her position is very painful, especially now."

"Why especially now?"

"We are carrying on negotiations with her husband about a divorce. And he's agreed; but there are difficulties in regard to the son, and the business, which ought to have been arranged long ago, has been dragging on for three months past. As soon as the divorce is over, she will marry Vronsky. How stupid these old ceremonies are, that no one believes in, and which only prevent people being comfortable!" Stepan Arkadyevitch put in. "Well, then their position will be as regular as mine, as yours."

"What is the difficulty?" said Levin.

"Oh, it's a long and tedious story! The whole business is in such an anomalous position with us. But the point is she has been for three months in Moscow, where everyone knows her, waiting for the divorce; she goes out nowhere, sees no woman except Dolly, because, do you understand, she doesn't care to have people come as a favor. That fool Princess Varvara, even she has left her, considering this a breach of propriety. Well, you see, in such a position any other woman would not have found resources in herself. But you'll see how she has arranged her life—how calm, how dignified she is. To the left, in the crescent opposite the church!" shouted Stepan Arkadyevitch, leaning out of the window. "Phew! how hot it is!" he said, in spite of twelve degrees of frost, flinging his open overcoat still wider open.

"But she has a daughter: no doubt she's busy looking after her?" said Levin.

"I believe you picture every woman simply as a female, *une couveuse,*" said Stepan Arkadyevitch. "If she's occupied, it must be with her children. No, she brings her up capitally, I believe, but one doesn't hear about her. She's busy, in the first place, with what she writes. I see you're smiling ironically, but you're wrong. She's writing a children's book, and doesn't talk about it to anyone, but she read it to me and I gave the manuscript to Vorkuev . . . you know the publisher . . . and he's an author himself too, I fancy. He understands those things, and he says it's a remarkable piece of work. But are you fancying she's an authoress?—not a bit of it. She's a woman with a heart, before everything, but you'll see. Now she has a little English girl with her, and a whole family she's looking after."

"Oh, something in a philanthropic way?"

"Why, you will look at everything in the worst light. It's not from philanthropy, it's from the heart. They—that is, Vronsky—had a trainer, an Englishman, first rate in his own line, but a drunkard. He's completely given up to drink—delirium tremens—and the family were cast on the world. She saw them, helped them, got more and more interested in them, and now the whole family is on her hands. But not by way of patronage, you know, helping with money; she's herself preparing the boys in Russian for the high school, and she's taken the little girl to live with her. But you'll see her for yourself."

The carriage drove into the courtyard, and Stepan Arkadyevitch rang loudly at the entrance where sleighs were standing.

And without asking the servant who opened the door whether the lady were at home, Stepan Arkadyevitch walked into the hall. Levin followed him, more and more doubtful whether he was doing right or wrong.

Looking at himself in the glass, Levin noticed that he was red in the face, but he felt certain he was not drunk, and he followed Stepan Arkadyevitch up the carpeted stairs. At the top Stepan Arkadyevitch inquired of the footman, who bowed to him as to an intimate friend, who was with Anna Arkadyevna, and received the answer that it was M. Vorkuev.

"Where are they?"

"In the study."

Passing through the dining room, a room not very large, with dark paneled walls, Stepan Arkadyevitch and Levin walked over the soft carpet to the half-dark study, lit up by a single lamp with a big dark shade. Another lamp with a reflector was hanging on the wall, lighting up a big full-length portrait of a woman, which Levin could not help looking at. It was the portrait of Anna, painted in Italy by Mihailov. While Stepan Arkadyevitch went behind the *treillage,* and the man's voice which had been speaking paused, Levin gazed at the portrait, which stood out from the frame in the brilliant light thrown on it, and he could not tear himself away from it. He positively forgot where he was, and not even hearing what was said, he could not take his eyes off the marvelous portrait. It was not a picture, but a living, charming woman, with black curling hair, with bare arms and shoulders, with a pensive smile on the lips, covered with soft down; triumphantly and softly she looked at him with eyes that baffled him. She was not living only because she was more beautiful than a living woman can be.

"I am delighted!" He heard suddenly near him a voice, unmistakably addressing him, the voice of the very woman he had been admiring in the portrait. Anna had come from behind the *treillage* to meet him, and Levin saw in the dim light of the study the very woman of the portrait, in a dark blue shot gown, not in the same position nor with the same expression, but with the same perfection of beauty which the artist had caught in the portrait. She was less dazzling in reality, but, on the other hand, there was something fresh and seductive in the living woman which was not in the portrait.

Chapter X

SHE HAD RISEN TO MEET HIM, NOT CONCEALING HER PLEASURE AT SEEING HIM; AND IN THE QUIET ease with which she held out her little vigorous hand, introduced him to Vorkuev and indicated a red-haired, pretty little girl who was sitting at work, calling her her pupil, Levin recognized and liked the manners of a woman of the great world, always self-possessed and natural.

"I am delighted, delighted," she repeated, and on her lips these simple words took for Levin's ears a special significance. "I have known you and liked you for a long while, both from your friendship with Stiva and for your wife's sake. . . . I knew her for a very short time, but she left on me the impression of an exquisite flower, simply a flower. And to think she will soon be a mother!"

She spoke easily and without haste, looking now and then from Levin to her brother, and Levin felt that the impression he was making was good, and he felt immediately at home, simple and happy with her, as though he had known her from childhood.

"Ivan Petrovitch and I settled in Alexey's study," she said in answer to Stepan Arkadyevitch's question whether he might smoke, "just so as to be able to smoke"—and glancing at Levin, instead of asking whether he would smoke, she pulled closer a tortoise-shell cigar-case and took a cigarette.

"How are you feeling today?" her brother asked her.

"Oh, nothing. Nerves, as usual."

"Yes, isn't it extraordinarily fine?" said Stepan Arkadyevitch, noticing that Levin was scrutinizing the picture.

"I have never seen a better portrait."

"And extraordinarily like, isn't it?" said Vorkuev.

Levin looked from the portrait to the original. A peculiar brilliance lit up Anna's face when she felt his eyes on her. Levin flushed, and to cover his confusion would have asked whether she had seen Darya Alexandrovna lately; but at that moment Anna spoke. "We were just talking, Ivan Petrovitch and I, of Vashtchenkov's last pictures. Have you seen them?"

"Yes, I have seen them," answered Levin.

"But, I beg your pardon, I interrupted you . . . you were saying? . . ."

Levin asked if she had seen Dolly lately.

"She was here yesterday. She was very indignant with the high school people on Grisha's account. The Latin teacher, it seems, had been unfair to him."

"Yes, I have seen his pictures. I didn't care for them very much," Levin went back to the subject she had started.

Levin talked now not at all with that purely businesslike attitude to the subject with which he had been talking all the morning. Every word in his conversation with her had a special significance. And talking to her was pleasant; still pleasanter it was to listen to her.

Anna talked not merely naturally and cleverly, but cleverly and carelessly, attaching no value to her own ideas and giving great weight to the ideas of the person she was talking to.

The conversation turned on the new movement in art, on the new illustrations of the Bible by a French artist. Vorkuev attacked the artist for a realism carried to the point of coarseness.

Levin said that the French had carried conventionality further than anyone, and that consequently they see a great merit in the return to realism. In the fact of not lying they see poetry.

Never had anything clever said by Levin given him so much pleasure as this remark. Anna's face lit up at once, as at once she appreciated the thought. She laughed.

"I laugh," she said, "as one laughs when one sees a very true portrait. What you said so perfectly hits off French art now, painting and literature too, indeed—Zola, Daudet. But perhaps it is always so, that men form their conceptions from fictitious, conventional types, and then—all the *combinaisons* made—they are tired of the fictitious figures and begin to invent more natural, true figures."

"That's perfectly true," said Vorknuev.

"So you've been at the club?" she said to her brother.

"Yes, yes, this is a woman!" Levin thought, forgetting himself and staring persistently at her lovely, mobile face, which at that moment was all at once completely transformed. Levin did not hear what she was talking of as she leaned over to her brother, but he was struck by the change of her expression. Her face—so handsome a moment before in its repose—suddenly wore a look of strange curiosity, anger, and pride. But this lasted only an instant. She dropped her eyelids, as though recollecting something.

"Oh, well, but that's of no interest to anyone," she said, and she turned to the English girl.

"Please order the tea in the drawing room," she said in English.

The girl got up and went out.

"Well, how did she get through her examination?" asked Stepan Arkadyevitch.

"Splendidly! She's a very gifted child and a sweet character."

"It will end in your loving her more than your own."

"There a man speaks. In love there's no more nor less. I love my daughter with one love, and her with another."

"I was just telling Anna Arkadyevna," said Vorkuev, "that if she were to put a hundredth part of the energy she devotes to this English girl to the public question of the education of Russian children, she would be doing a great and useful work."

"Yes, but I can't help it; I couldn't do it. Count Alexey Kirillovitch urged me very much" (as she uttered the words *Count Alexey Kirillovitch* she glanced with appealing timidity at Levin, and he unconsciously responded with a respectful and reassuring look), "he urged me to take up the school in the village. I visited it several times. The children were very nice, but I could not feel drawn to the work. You speak of energy. Energy rests upon love; and come as it will, there's no forcing it. I took to this child—I could not myself say why."

And she glanced again at Levin. And her smile and her glance—all told him that it was to him only she was addressing her words, valuing his good opinion, and at the same time sure beforehand that they understood each other.

"I quite understand that," Levin answered. "It's impossible to give one's heart to a school or such institutions in general, and I believe that's just why philanthropic institutions always give such poor results."

She was silent for a while, then she smiled.

"Yes, yes," she agreed; "I never could. *Je n'ai pas le coeur assez large* to love a whole asylum of horrid little girls. *Cela ne m'a jamais reussi.* There are so many women who have made themselves une position sociale in that way. And now more than ever," she said with a mournful, confiding expression, ostensibly addressing her brother, but unmistakably intending her words only for Levin, "now when I have such need of some occupation, I cannot." And suddenly frowning (Levin saw that she was frowning at herself for talking about herself) she changed the subject. "I know about you," she said to Levin; "that you're not a public-spirited citizen, and I have defended you to the best of my ability."

"How have you defended me?"

"Oh, according to the attacks made on you. But won't you have some tea?" She rose and took up a book bound in morocco.

"Give it to me, Anna Arkadyevna," said Vorkuev, indicating the book. "It's well worth taking up."

"Oh, no, it's all so sketchy."

"I told him about it," Stepan Arkadyevitch said to his sister, nodding at Levin.

"You shouldn't have. My writing is something after the fashion of those little baskets and carving which Liza Mertsalova used to sell me from the prisons. She had the direction of the prison department in that society," she turned to Levin; "and they were miracles of patience, the work of those poor wretches."

And Levin saw a new trait in this woman, who attracted him so extraordinarily. Besides wit, grace, and beauty, she had truth. She had no wish to hide from him all the bitterness of her position. As she said that she sighed, and her face suddenly taking a hard expression, looked as it were turned to stone. With that expression on her face she was more beautiful than ever; but the expression was new; it was utterly unlike that expression, radiant with happiness and creating happiness, which had been caught by the painter in her portrait. Levin looked more than once at the portrait and at her figure, as taking her brother's arm she walked with him to the high doors and he felt for her a tenderness and pity at which he wondered himself.

She asked Levin and Vorkuev to go into the drawing room, while she stayed behind to say a few words to her brother. "About her divorce, about Vronsky, and what he's doing at the club, about me?" wondered Levin. And he was so keenly interested by the question of what she was saying to Stepan Arkadyevitch, that he scarcely heard what Vorkuev was telling him of the qualities of the story for children Anna Arkadyevna had written.

At tea the same pleasant sort of talk, full of interesting matter, continued. There was not a single instant when a subject for conversation was to seek; on the contrary, it was felt that one had hardly time to say what one had to say, and eagerly held back to hear what the others were saying. And all that was said, not only by her, but by Vorkuev and Stepan Arkadyevitch—all, so it seemed to Levin, gained peculiar significance from her appreciation and her criticism. While he followed this interesting conversation, Levin was all the time admiring her—her beauty, her intelligence, her culture, and at the same time her directness and genuine depth of feeling. He listened and talked, and all the while he was thinking of her inner life, trying to divine her feelings. And though he had judged her so severely hitherto, now by some strange chain of reasoning he was justifying her and was also sorry for her, and afraid that Vronsky did not fully understand her. At eleven o'clock, when Stepan Arkadyevitch got up to go (Vorkuev had left earlier), it seemed to Levin that he had only just come. Regretfully Levin too rose.

"Good-bye," she said, holding his hand and glancing into his face with a winning look. "I am very glad *que la glace est rompue*."

She dropped his hand, and half closed her eyes.

"Tell your wife that I love her as before, and that if she cannot pardon me my position, then my wish for her is that she may never pardon it. To pardon it, one must go through what I have gone through, and may God spare her that."

"Certainly, yes, I will tell her . . ." Levin said, blushing.

Chapter XI

WHAT A MARVELOUS, SWEET AND UNHAPPY WOMAN!" HE WAS THINKING, AS HE STEPPED OUT into the frosty air with Stepan Arkadyevitch.

"Well, didn't I tell you?" said Stepan Arkadyevitch, seeing that Levin had been completely won over.

"Yes," said Levin dreamily, "an extraordinary woman! It's not her cleverness, but she has such wonderful depth of feeling. I'm awfully sorry for her!"

"Now, please God everything will soon be settled. Well, well, don't be hard on people in future," said Stepan Arkadyevitch, opening the carriage door. "Good-bye; we don't go the same way."

Still thinking of Anna, of everything, even the simplest phrase in their conversation with her, and recalling the minutest changes in her expression, entering more and more into her position, and feeling sympathy for her, Levin reached home.

At home Kouzma told Levin that Katerina Alexandrovna was quite well, and that her sisters had not long been gone, and he handed him two letters. Levin read them at once in the hall, that he might not overlook them later. One was from Sokolov, his bailiff. Sokolov wrote that the corn could not be sold, that it was fetching only five and a half roubles, and that more than that could not be got for it. The other letter was from his sister. She scolded him for her business being still unsettled.

"Well, we must sell it at five and a half if we can't get more," Levin decided the first question, which had always before seemed such a weighty one, with extraordinary facility on the spot. "It's extraordinary how all one's time is taken up here," he thought, considering the second letter. He felt himself to blame for not having got done what his sister had asked him to do for her. "Today, again, I've not been to the court, but today I've certainly not had time." And resolving that he would not fail to do it next day, he went up to his wife. As he went in, Levin rapidly ran through mentally the day he had spent. All the events of the day were conversations, conversations he had heard and taken part in. All the conversations were upon subjects which, if he had been alone at home, he would never have taken up, but here they were very interesting. And all these conversations were right enough, only in two places there was something not quite right. One was what he had said about the carp, the other was something not "quite the thing" in the tender sympathy he was feeling for Anna.

Levin found his wife low-spirited and dull. The dinner of the three sisters had gone off very well, but then they had waited and waited for him, all of them had felt dull, the sisters had departed, and she had been left alone.

"Well, and what have you been doing?" she asked him, looking straight into his eyes, which shone with rather a suspicious brightness. But that she might not prevent his telling her everything, she concealed her close scrutiny of him, and with an approving smile listened to his account of how he had spent the evening.

"Well, I'm very glad I met Vronsky. I felt quite at ease and natural with him. You understand, I shall try not to see him, but I'm glad that this awkwardness is all over," he said, and remembering that by way of trying not to see him, he had immediately gone to call on Anna, he blushed. "We talk about the peasants drinking; I don't know which drinks most, the peasantry or our own class; the peasants do on holidays, but . . ."

But Kitty took not the slightest interest in discussing the drinking habits of the peasants. She saw that he blushed, and she wanted to know why.

"Well, and then where did you go?"

"Stiva urged me awfully to go and see Anna Arkadyevna."

And as he said this, Levin blushed even more, and his doubts as to whether he had done right in going to see Anna were settled once for all. He knew now that he ought not to have done so.

Kitty's eyes opened in a curious way and gleamed at Anna's name, but controlling herself with an effort, she concealed her emotion and deceived him.

"Oh!" was all she said.

"I'm sure you won't be angry at my going. Stiva begged me to, and Dolly wished it," Levin went on.

"Oh, no!" she said, but he saw in her eyes a constraint that boded him no good.

"She is a very sweet, very, very unhappy, good woman," he said, telling her about Anna, her occupations, and what she had told him to say to her.

"Yes, of course, she is very much to be pitied," said Kitty, when he had finished. "Whom was your letter from?"

He told her, and believing in her calm tone, he went to change his coat.

Coming back, he found Kitty in the same easy chair. When he went up to her, she glanced at him and broke into sobs.

"What? what is it?" he asked, knowing beforehand what.

"You're in love with that hateful woman; she has bewitched you! I saw it in your eyes. Yes, yes! What can it all lead to? You were drinking at the club, drinking and gambling, and then you went . . . to her of all people! No, we must go away. . . . I shall go away tomorrow."

It was a long while before Levin could soothe his wife. At last he succeeded in calming her, only by confessing that a feeling of pity, in conjunction with the wine he had drunk, had been too much for him, that he had succumbed to Anna's artful influence, and that he would avoid her. One thing he did with more sincerity confess to was that living so long in Moscow, a life of nothing but conversation, eating and drinking, he was degenerating. They talked till three o'clock in the morning. Only at three o'clock were they sufficiently reconciled to be able to go to sleep.

Chapter XII

After taking leave of her guests, Anna did not sit down, but began walking up and down the room. She had unconsciously the whole evening done her utmost to arouse in Levin a feeling of love—as of late she had fallen into doing with all young men—and she knew she had attained her aim, as far as was possible in one evening, with a married and conscientious man. She liked him indeed extremely, and, in spite of the striking difference, from the masculine point of view, between Vronsky and Levin, as a woman she saw something they had in common, which had made Kitty able to love both. Yet as soon as he was out of the room, she ceased to think of him.

One thought, and one only, pursued her in different forms, and refused to be shaken off. "If I have so much effect on others, on this man, who loves his home and his wife, why is it *he* is so cold to me? . . . not cold exactly, he loves me, I know that! But something new is drawing us apart now. Why wasn't he here all the evening? He told Stiva to say he could not leave Yashvin, and must watch over his play. Is Yashvin a child? But supposing it's true. He never tells a lie. But there's something else in it if it's true. He is glad of an opportunity of showing me that he has other duties; I know that, I submit to that. But why prove that to me? He wants to show me that his love for me is not to interfere with his freedom. But I need no proofs, I need love. He ought to understand all the bitterness of this life for me here in Moscow. Is this life? I am not living, but waiting for an event, which is continually put off and put off. No answer again! And Stiva says he cannot go to Alexey Alexandrovitch. And I can't write again. I can do nothing, can begin nothing, can alter nothing; I hold myself in, I wait, inventing amusements for myself—the English family, writing, reading—but it's all nothing but a sham, it's all the same as morphine. He ought to feel for me," she said, feeling tears of self-pity coming into her eyes.

She heard Vronsky's abrupt ring and hurriedly dried her tears—not only dried her tears, but sat down by a lamp and opened a book, affecting composure. She wanted to show him that she was displeased that he had not come home as he had promised—displeased only, and not on any account to let him see her distress, and least of all, her self-pity. She might pity herself, but he must not pity her. She did not want strife, she blamed him for wanting to quarrel, but unconsciously put herself into an attitude of antagonism.

"Well, you've not been dull?" he said, eagerly and good-humoredly, going up to her. "What a terrible passion it is—gambling!"

"No, I've not been dull; I've learned long ago not to be dull. Stiva has been here and Levin."

"Yes, they meant to come and see you. Well, how did you like Levin?" he said, sitting down beside her.

"Very much. They have not long been gone. What was Yashvin doing?"

"He was winning—seventeen thousand. I got him away. He had really started home, but he went back again, and now he's losing."

"Then what did you stay for?" she asked, suddenly lifting her eyes to him. The expression of her face was cold and ungracious. "You told Stiva you were staying on to get Yashvin away. And you have left him there."

The same expression of cold readiness for the conflict appeared on his face too.

"In the first place, I did not ask him to give you any message; and secondly, I never tell lies. But what's the chief point, I wanted to stay, and I stayed," he said, frowning. "Anna, what is it for, why will you?" he said after a moment's silence, bending over towards her, and he opened his hand, hoping she would lay hers in it.

She was glad of this appeal for tenderness. But some strange force of evil would not let her give herself up to her feelings, as though the rules of warfare would not permit her to surrender.

"Of course you wanted to stay, and you stayed. You do everything you want to. But what do you tell me that for? With what object?" she said, getting more and more excited. "Does anyone contest your rights? But you want to be right, and you're welcome to be right."

His hand closed, he turned away, and his face wore a still more obstinate expression.

"For you it's a matter of obstinacy," she said, watching him intently and suddenly finding the right word for that expression that irritated her, "simply obstinacy. For you it's a question of whether you keep the upper hand of me, while for me . . ." Again she felt sorry for herself, and she almost burst into tears. "If you knew what it is for me! When I feel as I do now that you are hostile, yes, hostile to me, if you knew what this means for me! If you knew how I feel on the brink of calamity at this instant, how afraid I am of myself!" And she turned away, hiding her sobs.

"But what are you talking about?" he said, horrified at her expression of despair, and again bending over her, he took her hand and kissed it. "What is it for? Do I seek amusements outside our home? Don't I avoid the society of women?"

"Well, yes! If that were all!" she said.

"Come, tell me what I ought to do to give you peace of mind? I am ready to do anything to make you happy," he said, touched by her expression of despair; "what wouldn't I do to save you from distress of any sort, as now, Anna!" he said.

"It's nothing, nothing!" she said. "I don't know myself whether it's the solitary life, my nerves . . . Come, don't let us talk of it. What about the race? You haven't told me!" she inquired, trying to conceal her triumph at the victory, which had anyway been on her side.

He asked for supper, and began telling her about the races; but in his tone, in his eyes, which became more and more cold, she saw that he did not forgive her for her victory, that the feeling of obstinacy with which she had been struggling had asserted itself again in him. He was colder to her than before, as though he were regretting his surrender. And she, remembering the words that had given her the victory, "how I feel on the brink of calamity, how afraid I am of myself," saw that this weapon was a dangerous one, and that it could not be used a second time. And she felt that beside the love that bound them together there had grown up between them some evil spirit of strife, which she could not exorcise from his, and still less from her own heart.

Chapter XIII

THERE ARE NO CONDITIONS TO WHICH A MAN CANNOT BECOME USED, ESPECIALLY IF HE SEES THAT all around him are living in the same way. Levin could not have believed three months before that he could have gone quietly to sleep in the condition in which he was that day, that leading an aimless, irrational life, living too beyond his means, after drinking to excess (he could not call what happened at the club anything else), forming inappropriately friendly relations with a man with whom his wife had once been in love, and a still more inappropriate call upon a woman who could only be called a lost woman, after being fascinated by that woman and causing his wife distress—he could still go quietly to sleep. But under the influence of fatigue, a sleepless night, and the wine he had drunk, his sleep was sound and untroubled.

At five o'clock the creak of a door opening waked him. He jumped up and looked round. Kitty was not in bed beside him. But there was a light moving behind the screen, and he heard her steps.

"What is it? . . . what is it?" he said, half-asleep. "Kitty! What is it?"

"Nothing," she said, coming from behind the screen with a candle in her hand. "I felt unwell," she said, smiling a particularly sweet and meaning smile.

"What? has it begun?" he said in terror. "We ought to send . . ." and hurriedly he reached after his clothes.

"No, no," she said, smiling and holding his hand. "It's sure to be nothing. I was rather unwell, only a little. It's all over now."

And getting into bed, she blew out the candle, lay down and was still. Though he thought her stillness suspicious, as though she were holding her breath, and still more suspicious the expression of peculiar tenderness and excitement with which, as she came from behind the screen, she said "nothing," he was so sleepy that he fell asleep at once. Only later he remembered the stillness of her breathing, and understood all that must have been passing in her sweet, precious heart while she lay beside him, not stirring, in anticipation of the greatest event in a woman's life. At seven o'clock he was waked by the touch of her hand on his shoulder, and a gentle whisper. She seemed struggling between regret at waking him, and the desire to talk to him.

"Kostya, don't be frightened. It's all right. But I fancy . . . We ought to send for Lizaveta Petrovna."

The candle was lit again. She was sitting up in bed, holding some knitting, which she had been busy upon during the last few days.

"Please, don't be frightened, it's all right. I'm not a bit afraid," she said, seeing his scared face, and she pressed his hand to her bosom and then to her lips.

He hurriedly jumped up, hardly awake, and kept his eyes fixed on her, as he put on his dressing-gown; then he stopped, still looking at her. He had to go, but he could not tear himself from her eyes. He thought he loved her face, knew her expression, her eyes, but never had he seen it like this. How hateful and horrible he seemed to himself, thinking of the distress he had caused her yesterday. Her flushed face, fringed with soft curling hair under her nightcap, was radiant with joy and courage.

Though there was so little that was complex or artificial in Kitty's character in general, Levin was struck by what was revealed now, when suddenly all disguises were thrown off and the very kernel of her soul shone in her eyes. And in this simplicity and nakedness of her soul, she, the very woman he loved in her, was more manifest than ever. She looked at him, smiling; but all at once her brows twitched, she threw up her head, and going quickly up to him, clutched his hand and pressed close up to him, breathing her hot breath upon him. She was in pain and was, as it were, complaining to him of her suffering. And for the first minute, from habit, it seemed to him that he was to blame. But in her eyes there was a tenderness that told him that she was far from reproaching him, that she loved him for her sufferings. "If not I, who is to blame for it?" he thought unconsciously, seeking someone responsible for this suffering for him to punish; but there was no one responsible. She was suffering, complaining, and triumphing in her sufferings, and rejoicing in them, and loving them. He saw that something sublime was being accomplished in her soul, but what? He could not make it out. It was beyond his understanding.

"I have sent to mamma. You go quickly to fetch Lizaveta Petrovna . . . Kostya! . . . Nothing, it's over."

She moved away from him and rang the bell.

"Well, go now; Pasha's coming. I am all right."

And Levin saw with astonishment that she had taken up the knitting she had brought in in the night and begun working at it again.

As Levin was going out of one door, he heard the maidservant come in at the other. He stood at the door and heard Kitty giving exact directions to the maid, and beginning to help her move the bedstead.

He dressed, and while they were putting in his horses, as a hired sleigh was not to be seen yet, he ran again up to the bedroom, not on tiptoe, it seemed to him, but on wings. Two maidservants were carefully moving something in the bedroom.

Kitty was walking about knitting rapidly and giving directions.

"I'm going for the doctor. They have sent for Lizaveta Petrovna, but I'll go on there too. Isn't there anything wanted? Yes, shall I go to Dolly's?"

She looked at him, obviously not hearing what he was saying.

"Yes, yes. Do go," she said quickly, frowning and waving her hand to him.

He had just gone into the drawing room, when suddenly a plaintive moan sounded from the bedroom, smothered instantly. He stood still, and for a long while he could not understand.

"Yes, that is she," he said to himself, and clutching at his head he ran downstairs.

"Lord have mercy on us! pardon us! aid us!" he repeated the words that for some reason came suddenly to his lips. And he, an unbeliever, repeated these words not with his lips only. At that instant he knew that all his doubts, even the impossibility of believing with his reason, of which he was aware in himself, did not in the least hinder his turning to God. All of that now floated out of his soul like dust. To whom was he to turn if not to Him in whose hands he felt himself, his soul, and his love?

The horse was not yet ready, but feeling a peculiar concentration of his physical forces and his intellect on what he had to do, he started off on foot without waiting for the horse, and told Kouzma to overtake him.

At the corner he met a night cabman driving hurriedly. In the little sleigh, wrapped in a velvet cloak, sat Lizaveta Petrovna with a kerchief round her head. "Thank God! thank God!" he said, overjoyed to recognize her little fair face which wore a peculiarly serious, even stern expression. Telling the driver not to stop, he ran along beside her.

"For two hours, then? Not more?" she inquired. "You should let Pyotr Dmitrievitch know, but don't hurry him. And get some opium at the chemist's."

"So you think that it may go on well? Lord have mercy on us and help us!" Levin said, seeing his own horse driving out of the gate. Jumping into the sleigh beside Kouzma, he told him to drive to the doctor's.

Chapter XIV

THE DOCTOR WAS NOT YET UP, AND THE FOOTMAN SAID THAT "HE HAD BEEN UP LATE, AND HAD given orders not to be waked, but would get up soon." The footman was cleaning the lamp-chimneys, and seemed very busy about them. This concentration of the footman upon his lamps, and his indifference to what was passing in Levin, at first astounded him, but immediately on considering the question he realized that no one knew or was bound to know his feelings, and that it was all the more necessary to act calmly, sensibly, and resolutely to get through this wall of indifference and attain his aim.

"Don't be in a hurry or let anything slip," Levin said to himself, feeling a greater and greater flow of physical energy and attention to all that lay before him to do.

Having ascertained that the doctor was not getting up, Levin considered various plans, and decided on the following one; that Kouzma should go for another doctor, while he himself should go to the chemist's for opium, and if when he came back the doctor had not yet begun to get up, he would either by tipping the footman, or by force, wake the doctor at all hazards.

At the chemist's the lank shopman sealed up a packet of powders for a coachman who stood waiting, and refused him opium with the same callousness with which the doctor's footman had cleaned his lamp-chimneys. Trying not to get flurried or out of temper, Levin mentioned the names of the doctor and midwife, and explaining what the opium was needed for, tried to persuade him.

The assistant inquired in German whether he should give it, and receiving an affirmative reply from behind the partition, he took out a bottle and a funnel, deliberately poured the opium from a bigger bottle into a little one, stuck on a label, sealed it up, in spite of Levin's request that he would not do so, and was about to wrap it up too. This was more than Levin could stand; he took the bottle firmly out of his hands, and ran to the big glass doors. The doctor was not even now getting up, and the footman, busy now in putting down the rugs, refused to wake him. Levin deliberately took out a ten-ruble note, and, careful to speak slowly, though losing no time over the business, he handed him the note, and explained that Pyotr Dmitrievitch (what a great and important personage he seemed to Levin now, this Pyotr Dmitrievitch, who had been of so little consequence in his eyes before!) had promised to come at any time; that he would certainly not be angry! and that he must therefore wake him at once.

The footman agreed, and went upstairs, taking Levin into the waiting room.

Levin could hear through the door the doctor coughing, moving about, washing, and saying something. Three minutes passed; it seemed to Levin that more than an hour had gone by. He could not wait any longer.

"Pyotr Dmitrievitch, Pyotr Dmitrievitch!" he said in an imploring voice at the open door. "For God's sake, forgive me! See me as you are. It's been going on more than two hours already."

"In a minute; in a minute!" answered a voice, and to his amazement Levin heard that the doctor was smiling as he spoke.

"For one instant."

"In a minute."

Two minutes more passed while the doctor was putting on his boots, and two minutes more while the doctor put on his coat and combed his hair.

"Pyotr Dmitrievitch!" Levin was beginning again in a plaintive voice, just as the doctor came in dressed and ready. "These people have no conscience," thought Levin. "Combing his hair, while we're dying!"

"Good morning!" the doctor said to him, shaking hands, and, as it were, teasing him with his composure. "There's no hurry. Well now?"

Trying to be as accurate as possible Levin began to tell him every unnecessary detail of his wife's condition, interrupting his account repeatedly with entreaties that the doctor would come with him at once.

"Oh, you needn't be in any hurry. You don't understand, you know. I'm certain I'm not wanted, still I've promised, and if you like, I'll come. But there's no hurry. Please sit down; won't you have some coffee?"

Levin stared at him with eyes that asked whether he was laughing at him; but the doctor had no notion of making fun of him.

"I know, I know," the doctor said, smiling; "I'm a married man myself; and at these moments we husbands are very much to be pitied. I've a patient whose husband always takes refuge in the stables on such occasions."

"But what do you think, Pyotr Dmitrievitch? Do you suppose it may go all right?"

"Everything points to a favorable issue."

"So you'll come immediately?" said Levin, looking wrathfully at the servant who was bringing in the coffee.

"In an hour's time."

"Oh, for mercy's sake!"

"Well, let me drink my coffee, anyway."

The doctor started upon his coffee. Both were silent.

"The Turks are really getting beaten, though. Did you read yesterday's telegrams?" said the doctor, munching some roll.

"No, I can't stand it!" said Levin, jumping up. "So you'll be with us in a quarter of an hour."

"In half an hour."

"On your honor?"

When Levin got home, he drove up at the same time as the princess, and they went up to the bedroom door together. The princess had tears in her eyes, and her hands were shaking. Seeing Levin, she embraced him, and burst into tears.

"Well, my dear Lizaveta Petrovna?" she queried, clasping the hand of the midwife, who came out to meet them with a beaming and anxious face.

"She's going on well," she said; "persuade her to lie down. She will be easier so."

From the moment when he had waked up and understood what was going on, Levin had prepared his mind to bear resolutely what was before him, and without considering or anticipating anything, to avoid upsetting his wife, and on the contrary to soothe her and keep up her courage. Without allowing himself even to think of what was to come, of how it would end, judging from his inquiries as to the usual duration of these ordeals, Levin had in his imagination braced himself to bear up and to keep a tight rein on his feelings for five hours, and it had seemed to him he could do this. But when he came back from the doctor's and saw her sufferings again, he fell to repeating more and more frequently: "Lord, have mercy on us, and succor us!" He sighed, and flung his head up, and began to feel afraid he could not bear it, that he would burst into tears or run away. Such agony it was to him. And only one hour had passed.

But after that hour there passed another hour, two hours, three, the full five hours he had fixed as the furthest limit of his sufferings, and the position was still unchanged; and he was still bearing it because there was nothing to be done but bear it; every instant feeling that he had reached the utmost limits of his endurance, and that his heart would break with sympathy and pain.

But still the minutes passed by and the hours, and still hours more, and his misery and horror grew and were more and more intense.

All the ordinary conditions of life, without which one can form no conception of anything, had ceased to exist for Levin. He lost all sense of time. Minutes—those minutes when she sent for him and he held her moist hand, that would squeeze his hand with extraordinary violence and then push it away—seemed to him hours, and hours seemed to him minutes. He was surprised when Lizaveta Petrovna asked him to light a candle behind a screen, and he found that it was five o'clock in the afternoon. If he had been told it was only ten o'clock in the morning, he would not have been more surprised. Where he was all this time, he knew as little as the time of anything. He saw her swollen face, sometimes bewildered and in agony, sometimes smiling and trying to reassure him. He saw the old princess too, flushed and overwrought, with her gray curls in disorder, forcing herself to gulp down her tears, biting her lips; he saw Dolly too and the doctor, smoking fat cigarettes, and Lizaveta Petrovna with a firm, resolute, reassuring face, and the old prince walking up and down the hall with a frowning face. But why they came in and went out, where they were, he did not know. The princess was with the doctor in the bedroom, then in the study, where a table set for dinner suddenly appeared; then she was not there, but Dolly was. Then Levin remembered he had been sent somewhere. Once he had been sent to move a table and sofa. He had done this eagerly, thinking it had to be done for her sake, and only later on he found it was his own bed he had been getting ready. Then he had been sent to the study to ask the doctor something. The doctor had answered and then had said something about the irregularities in the municipal council. Then he had been sent to the bedroom to help the old princess to move the holy picture in its silver and gold setting, and with the princess's old waiting maid he had clambered on a shelf to reach it and had broken the little lamp, and the old servant had tried to reassure him about the lamp and about his wife, and he carried the holy picture and set it at Kitty's head, carefully tucking it in behind the pillow. But where, when, and why all this had happened, he could not tell. He did not understand why the old princess took his hand, and looking compassionately at him, begged him not to worry himself, and Dolly persuaded him to eat something and led him out of the room, and even the doctor looked seriously and with commiseration at him and offered him a drop of something.

All he knew and felt was that what was happening was what had happened nearly a year before in the hotel of the country town at the deathbed of his brother Nikolay. But that had been grief—this was joy. Yet that grief and this joy were alike outside all the ordinary conditions of life; they were loop-holes, as it were, in that ordinary life through which there came glimpses of something sublime. And in the contemplation of this sublime something the soul was exalted to inconceivable heights of which it had before had no conception, while reason lagged behind, unable to keep up with it.

"Lord, have mercy on us, and succor us!" he repeated to himself incessantly, feeling, in spite of his long and, as it seemed, complete alienation from religion, that he turned to God just as trustfully and simply as he had in his childhood and first youth.

All this time he had two distinct spiritual conditions. One was away from her, with the doctor, who kept smoking one fat cigarette after another and extinguishing them on the edge of a full ashtray, with Dolly, and with the old prince, where there was talk about dinner, about politics, about Marya Petrovna's illness, and where Levin suddenly forgot for a minute what was happening, and felt as though he had waked up from sleep; the other was in her presence, at her pillow, where his heart seemed breaking and still did not break from sympathetic suffering, and he prayed to God without ceasing. And every time he was brought back from a moment of oblivion by a scream reaching him from the bedroom, he fell into the same strange terror that had come upon him the first minute. Every time he heard a shriek, he jumped up, ran to justify himself, remembered on the way that he was not to blame, and he longed to defend her, to help her. But as he looked at her, he saw again that help was impossible, and he was filled with terror and prayed: "Lord, have mercy on us, and help us!" And as time went on, both these conditions became more intense; the calmer he became away from her, completely forgetting her, the more agonizing became both her sufferings and his feeling of helplessness before them. He jumped up, would have liked to run away, but ran to her.

Sometimes, when again and again she called upon him, he blamed her; but seeing her patient, smiling face, and hearing the words, "I am worrying you," he threw the blame on God; but thinking of God, at once he fell to beseeching God to forgive him and have mercy.

Chapter XV

HE DID NOT KNOW WHETHER IT WAS LATE OR EARLY. THE CANDLES HAD ALL BURNED OUT. DOLLY had just been in the study and had suggested to the doctor that he should lie down. Levin sat listening to the doctor's stories of a quack mesmerizer and looking at the ashes of his cigarette. There had been a period of repose, and he had sunk into oblivion. He had completely forgotten what was going on now. He heard the doctor's chat and understood it. Suddenly there came an unearthly shriek. The shriek was so awful that Levin did not even jump up, but holding his breath, gazed in terrified inquiry at the doctor. The doctor put his head on one side, listened, and smiled approvingly. Everything was so extraordinary that nothing could strike Levin as strange. "I suppose it must be so," he thought, and still sat where he was. Whose scream was this? He jumped up, ran on tiptoe to the bedroom, edged round Lizaveta Petrovna and the princess, and took up his position at Kitty's pillow. The scream had subsided, but there was some change now. What it was he did not see and did not comprehend, and he had no wish to see or comprehend. But he saw it by the face of Lizaveta Petrovna. Lizaveta Petrovna's face was stern and pale, and still as resolute, though her jaws were twitching, and her eyes were fixed intently on Kitty. Kitty's swollen and agonized face, a tress of hair clinging to her moist brow, was turned to him and sought his eyes. Her lifted hands asked for his hands. Clutching his chill hands in her moist ones, she began squeezing them to her face.

"Don't go, don't go! I'm not afraid, I'm not afraid!" she said rapidly. "Mamma, take my earrings. They bother me. You're not afraid? Quick, quick, Lizaveta Petrovna . . ."

She spoke quickly, very quickly, and tried to smile. But suddenly her face was drawn, she pushed him away.

"Oh, this is awful! I'm dying, I'm dying! Go away!" she shrieked, and again he heard that unearthly scream.

Levin clutched at his head and ran out of the room.

"It's nothing, it's nothing, it's all right," Dolly called after him.

But they might say what they liked, he knew now that all was over. He stood in the next room, his head leaning against the doorpost, and heard shrieks, howls such as he had never heard before, and he knew that what had been Kitty was uttering these shrieks. He had long ago ceased to wish for the child. By now he loathed this child. He did not even wish for her life now, all he longed for was the end of this awful anguish.

"Doctor! What is it? What is it? By God!" he said, snatching at the doctor's hand as he came up.

"It's the end," said the doctor. And the doctor's face was so grave as he said it that Levin took *the end* as meaning her death.

Beside himself, he ran into the bedroom. The first thing he saw was the face of Lizaveta Petrovna. It was even more frowning and stern. Kitty's face he did not know. In the place where it had been was something that was fearful in its strained distortion and in the sounds that came from it. He fell down with his head on the wooden framework of the bed, feeling that his heart was bursting. The awful scream never paused, it became still more awful, and as though it had reached the utmost limit of terror, suddenly it ceased. Levin could not believe his ears, but there could be no doubt; the scream had ceased and he heard a subdued stir and bustle, and hurried breathing, and her voice, gasping, alive, tender, and blissful, uttered softly, "It's over!"

He lifted his head. With her hands hanging exhausted on the quilt, looking extraordinarily lovely and serene, she looked at him in silence and tried to smile, and could not.

And suddenly, from the mysterious and awful far-away world in which he had been living for the last twenty-two hours, Levin felt himself all in an instant borne back to the old every-day world, glorified though now, by such a radiance of happiness that he could not bear it. The strained chords snapped, sobs and tears of joy which he had never foreseen rose up with such violence that his whole body shook, that for long they prevented him from speaking.

Falling on his knees before the bed, he held his wife's hand before his lips and kissed it, and the hand, with a weak movement of the fingers, responded to his kiss. And meanwhile, there at the foot of the bed, in the deft hands of Lizaveta Petrovna, like a flickering light in a lamp, lay the life of a human creature, which had never existed before, and which would now with the same right, with the same importance to itself, live and create in its own image.

"Alive! alive! And a boy too! Set your mind at rest!" Levin heard Lizaveta Petrovna saying, as she slapped the baby's back with a shaking hand.

"Mamma, is it true?" said Kitty's voice.

The princess's sobs were all the answers she could make. And in the midst of the silence there came in unmistakable reply to the mother's question, a voice quite unlike the subdued voices speaking in the room. It was the bold, clamorous, self-assertive squall of the new human being, who had so incomprehensibly appeared.

If Levin had been told before that Kitty was dead, and that he had died with her, and that their children were angels, and that God was standing before him, he would have been surprised at nothing. But now, coming back to the world of reality, he had to make great mental efforts to take in that she was alive and well, and that the creature squalling so desperately was his son. Kitty was alive, her agony was over. And he was unutterably happy. That he understood; he was completely happy in it. But the baby? Whence, why, who was he? . . . He could not get used to the idea. It seemed to him something extraneous, superfluous, to which he could not accustom himself.

Chapter XVI

AT TEN O'CLOCK THE OLD PRINCE, SERGEY IVANOVITCH, AND STEPAN ARKADYEVITCH WERE SITting at Levin's. Having inquired after Kitty, they had dropped into conversation upon other subjects. Levin heard them, and unconsciously, as they talked, going over the past, over what had been up to that morning, he thought of himself as he had been yesterday till that point. It was as though a hundred years had passed since then. He felt himself exalted to unattainable heights, from which he studiously lowered himself so as not to wound the people he was talking to. He talked, and was all the time thinking of his wife, of her condition now, of his son, in whose existence he tried to school himself into believing. The whole world of woman, which had taken for him since his marriage a new value he had never suspected before, was now so exalted that he could not take it in in his imagination. He heard them talk of yesterday's dinner at the club, and thought: "What is happening with her now? Is she asleep? How is she? What is she thinking of? Is he crying, my son Dmitri?" And in the middle of the conversation, in the middle of a sentence, he jumped up and went out of the room.

"Send me word if I can see her," said the prince.

"Very well, in a minute," answered Levin, and without stopping, he went to her room.

She was not asleep, she was talking gently with her mother, making plans about the christening.

Carefully set to rights, with hair well-brushed, in a smart little cap with some blue in it, her arms out on the quilt, she was lying on her back. Meeting his eyes, her eyes drew him to her. Her face, bright before, brightened still more as he drew near her. There was the same change in it from earthly to unearthly that is seen in the face of the dead. But then it means farewell, here it meant welcome. Again a rush of emotion, such as he had felt at the moment of the child's birth, flooded his heart. She took his hand and asked him if he had slept. He could not answer, and turned away, struggling with his weakness.

"I have had a nap, Kostya!" she said to him; "and I am so comfortable now."

She looked at him, but suddenly her expression changed.

"Give him to me," she said, hearing the baby's cry. "Give him to me, Lizaveta Petrovna, and he shall look at him."

"To be sure, his papa shall look at him," said Lizaveta Petrovna, getting up and bringing something red, and queer, and wriggling. "Wait a minute, we'll make him tidy first," and Lizaveta Petrovna laid the red wobbling thing on the bed, began untrussing and trussing up the baby, lifting it up and turning it over with one finger and powdering it with something.

Levin, looking at the tiny, pitiful creature, made strenuous efforts to discover in his heart some traces of fatherly feeling for it. He felt nothing towards it but disgust. But when it was undressed and he caught a glimpse of wee, wee, little hands, little feet, saffron-colored, with little toes, too, and positively with a little big toe different from the rest, and when he saw Lizaveta Petrovna closing the wide-open little hands, as though they were soft springs, and putting them into linen garments, such pity for the little creature came upon him, and such terror that she would hurt it, that he held her hand back.

Lizaveta Petrovna laughed.

"Don't be frightened, don't be frightened!"

When the baby had been put to rights and transformed into a firm doll, Lizaveta Petrovna dandled it as though proud of her handiwork, and stood a little away so that Levin might see his son in all his glory.

Kitty looked sideways in the same direction, never taking her eyes off the baby. "Give him to me! give him to me!" she said, and even made as though she would sit up.

"What are you thinking of, Katerina Alexandrovna, you mustn't move like that! Wait a minute. I'll give him to you. Here we're showing papa what a fine fellow we are!"

And Lizaveta Petrovna, with one hand supporting the wobbling head, lifted up on the other arm the strange, limp, red creature, whose head was lost in its swaddling clothes. But it had a nose, too, and slanting eyes and smacking lips.

"A splendid baby!" said Lizaveta Petrovna.

Levin sighed with mortification. This splendid baby excited in him no feeling but disgust and compassion. It was not at all the feeling he had looked forward to.

He turned away while Lizaveta Petrovna put the baby to the unaccustomed breast.

Suddenly laughter made him look round. The baby had taken the breast.

"Come, that's enough, that's enough!" said Lizaveta Petrovna, but Kitty would not let the baby go. He fell asleep in her arms.

"Look, now," said Kitty, turning the baby so that he could see it. The aged-looking little face suddenly puckered up still more and the baby sneezed.

Smiling, hardly able to restrain his tears, Levin kissed his wife and went out of the dark room. What he felt towards this little creature was utterly unlike what he had expected. There was nothing cheerful and joyous in the feeling; on the contrary, it was a new torture of apprehension. It was the consciousness of a new sphere of liability to pain. And this sense was so painful at first, the apprehension lest this helpless creature should suffer was so intense, that it prevented him from noticing the strange thrill of senseless joy and even pride that he had felt when the baby sneezed.

Chapter XVII

STEPAN ARKADYEVITCH'S AFFAIRS WERE IN A VERY BAD WAY.

The money for two-thirds of the forest had all been spent already, and he had borrowed from the merchant in advance at ten per cent discount, almost all the remaining third. The merchant would not give more, especially as Darya Alexandrovna, for the first time that winter insisting on her right to her own property, had refused to sign the receipt for the payment of the last third of the forest. All his salary went on household expenses and in payment of petty debts that could not be put off. There was positively no money.

This was unpleasant and awkward, and in Stepan Arkadyevitch's opinion things could not go on like this. The explanation of the position was, in his view, to be found in the fact that his salary was too small. The post he filled had been unmistakably very good five years ago, but it was so no longer.

Petrov, the bank director, had twelve thousand; Sventitsky, a company director, had seventeen thousand; Mitin, who had founded a bank, received fifty thousand.

"Clearly I've been napping, and they've overlooked me," Stepan Arkadyevitch thought about himself. And he began keeping his eyes and ears open, and towards the end of the winter he had discovered a very good berth and had formed a plan of attack upon it, at first from Moscow through aunts, uncles, and friends, and then, when the matter was well advanced, in the spring, he went himself to Petersburg. It was one of those snug, lucrative berths of which there are so manymore nowadays than there used to be, with incomes ranging from one thousand to fifty thousand roubles. It was the post of secretary of the committee of the amalgamated agency of the southern railways, and of certain banking companies. This position, like all such appointments, called for such immense energy and such varied qualifications, that it was difficult for them to be found united in any one man. And since a man combining all the qualifications was not to be found, it was at least better that the post be filled by an honest than by a dishonest man. And Stepan Arkadyevitch was not merely an honest man—unemphatically—in the common acceptation of the words, he was an honest man—emphatically—in that special sense which the word has in Moscow, when they talk of an "honest" politician, an "honest" writer, an "honest" newspaper, an "honest" institution, an "honest" tendency, meaning not simply that the man or the institution is not dishonest, but that they are capable on occasion of taking a line of their own in opposition to the authorities.

Stepan Arkadyevitch moved in those circles in Moscow in which that expression had come into use, was regarded there as an honest man, and so had more right to this appointment than others.

The appointment yielded an income of from seven to ten thousand a year, and Oblonsky could fill it without giving up his government position. It was in the hands of two ministers, one lady, and two Jews, and all these people, though the way had been paved already with them, Stepan Arkadyevitch had to see in Petersburg. Besides this business, Stepan Arkadyevitch had promised his sister Anna to obtain from Karenin a definite answer on the question of divorce. And begging fifty roubles from Dolly, he set off for Petersburg.

Stepan Arkadyevitch sat in Karenin's study listening to his report on the causes of the unsatisfactory position of Russian finance, and only waiting for the moment when he would finish to speak about his own business or about Anna.

"Yes, that's very true," he said, when Alexey Alexandrovitch took off the pince-nez, without which he could not read now, and looked inquiringly at his former brother-in-law, "that's very true in particular cases, but still the principle of our day is freedom."

"Yes, but I lay down another principle, embracing the principle of freedom," said Alexey Alexandrovitch, with emphasis on the word "embracing," and he put on his pince-nez again, so as to read the passage in which this statement was made. And turning over the beautifully written, wide-margined manuscript, Alexey Alexandrovitch read aloud over again the conclusive passage.

"I don't advocate protection for the sake of private interests, but for the public weal, and for the lower and upper classes equally," he said, looking over his pince-nez at Oblonsky. "But *they* cannot grasp that, *they* are taken up now with personal interests, and carried away by phrases."

Stepan Arkadyevitch knew that when Karenin began to talk of what *they* were doing and thinking, the persons who would not accept his report and were the cause of everything wrong in Russia, that it was coming near the end. And so now he eagerly abandoned the principle of free-trade, and fully agreed. Alexey Alexandrovitch paused, thoughtfully turning over the pages of his manuscript.

"Oh, by the way," said Stepan Arkadyevitch, "I wanted to ask you, some time when you see Pomorsky, to drop him a hint that I should be very glad to get that new appointment of secretary of the committee of the amalgamated agency of the southern railways and banking companies." Stepan Arkadyevitch was familiar by now with the title of the post he coveted, and he brought it out rapidly without mistake.

Alexey Alexandrovitch questioned him as to the duties of this new committee, and pondered. He was considering whether the new committee would not be acting in some way contrary to the views he had been advocating. But as the influence of the new committee was of a very complex nature, and his views were of very wide application, he could not decide this straight off, and taking off his pince-nez, he said:

"Of course, I can mention it to him; but what is your reason precisely for wishing to obtain the appointment?"

"It's a good salary, rising to nine thousand, and my means . . ."

"Nine thousand!" repeated Alexey Alexandrovitch, and he frowned. The high figure of the salary made him reflect that on that side Stepan Arkadyevitch's proposed position ran counter to the main tendency of his own projects of reform, which always leaned towards economy.

"I consider, and I have embodied my views in a note on the subject, that in our day these immense salaries are evidence of the unsound economic *assiette* of our finances."

"But what's to be done?" said Stepan Arkadyevitch. "Suppose a bank director gets ten thousand—well, he's worth it; or an engineer gets twenty thousand—after all, it's a growing thing, you know!"

"I assume that a salary is the price paid for a commodity, and it ought to conform with the law of supply and demand. If the salary is fixed without any regard for that law, as, for instance, when I see two engineers leaving college together, both equally well trained and efficient, and one getting forty thousand while the other is satisfied with two; or when I see lawyers and hussars, having no special qualifications, appointed directors of banking companies with immense salaries, I conclude that the salary is not fixed in accordance with the law of supply and demand, but simply through personal interest. And this is an abuse of great gravity in itself, and one that reacts injuriously on the government service. I consider . . ."

Stepan Arkadyevitch made haste to interrupt his brother-in-law.

"Yes; but you must agree that it's a new institution of undoubted utility that's being started. After all, you know, it's a growing thing! What they lay particular stress on is the thing being carried on honestly," said Stepan Arkadyevitch with emphasis.

But the Moscow significance of the word "honest" was lost on Alexey Alexandrovitch.

"Honesty is only a negative qualification," he said.

"Well, you'll do me a great service, anyway," said Stepan Arkadyevitch, "by putting in a word to Pomorsky—just in the way of conversation. . . ."

"But I fancy it's more in Volgarinov's hands," said Alexey Alexandrovitch.

"Volgarinov has fully assented, as far as he's concerned," said Stepan Arkadyevitch, turning red. Stepan Arkadyevitch reddened at the mention of that name, because he had been that morning at the Jew Volgarinov's, and the visit had left an unpleasant recollection.

Stepan Arkadyevitch believed most positively that the committee in which he was trying to get an appointment was a new, genuine, and honest public body, but that morning when Volgarinov had—intentionally, beyond a doubt—kept him two hours waiting with other petitioners in his waiting room, he had suddenly felt uneasy.

Whether he was uncomfortable that he, a descendant of Rurik, Prince Oblonsky, had been kept for two hours waiting to see a Jew, or that for the first time in his life he was not following the example of his ancestors in serving the government, but was turning off into a new career, anyway he was very uncomfortable. During those two hours in Volgarinov's waiting room Stepan Arkadyevitch, stepping jauntily about the room, pulling his whiskers, entering into conversation with the other petitioners, and inventing an epigram on his position, assiduously concealed from others, and even from himself, the feeling he was experiencing.

But all the time he was uncomfortable and angry, he could not have said why—whether because he could not get his epigram just right, or from some other reason. When at last Volgarinov had received him with exaggerated politeness and unmistakable triumph at his humiliation, and had all but refused the favor asked of him, Stepan Arkadyevitch had made haste to forget it all as soon as possible. And now, at the mere recollection, he blushed.

Chapter XVIII

"NOW THERE IS SOMETHING I WANT TO TALK ABOUT, AND YOU KNOW WHAT IT IS. ABOUT ANNA," Stepan Arkadyevitch said, pausing for a brief space, and shaking off the unpleasant impression.

As soon as Oblonsky uttered Anna's name, the face of Alexey Alexandrovitch was completely transformed; all the life was gone out of it, and it looked weary and dead.

"What is it exactly that you want from me?" he said, moving in his chair and snapping his pince-nez.

"A definite settlement, Alexey Alexandrovitch, some settlement of the position. I'm appealing to you" ("not as an injured husband," Stepan Arkadyevitch was going to say, but afraid of wrecking his negotiation by this, he changed the words) "not as a statesman" (which did not sound *à propos*), "but simply as a man, and a good-hearted man and a Christian. You must have pity on her," he said.

"That is, in what way precisely?" Karenin said softly.

"Yes, pity on her. If you had seen her as I have!—I have been spending all the winter with her—you would have pity on her. Her position is awful, simply awful!"

"I had imagined," answered Alexey Alexandrovitch in a higher, almost shrill voice, "that Anna Arkadyevna had everything she had desired for herself."

"Oh, Alexey Alexandrovitch, for heaven's sake, don't let us indulge in recriminations! What is past is past, and you know what she wants and is waiting for—divorce."

"But I believe Anna Arkadyevna refuses a divorce, if I make it a condition to leave me my son. I replied in that sense, and supposed that the matter was ended. I consider it at an end," shrieked Alexey Alexandrovitch.

"But, for heaven's sake, don't get hot!" said Stepan Arkadyevitch, touching his brother-in-law's knee. "The matter is not ended. If you will allow me to recapitulate, it was like this: when you parted, you were as magnanimous as could possibly be; you were ready to give her everything—freedom, divorce even. She appreciated that. No, don't think that. She did appreciate it—to such a degree that at the first moment, feeling how she had wronged you, she did not consider and could not consider everything. She gave up everything. But experience, time, have shown that her position is unbearable, impossible."

"The life of Anna Arkadyevna can have no interest for me," Alexey Alexandrovitch put in, lifting his eyebrows.

"Allow me to disbelieve that," Stepan Arkadyevitch replied gently. "Her position is intolerable for her, and of no benefit to anyone whatever. She has deserved it, you will say. She knows that and asks you for nothing; she says plainly that she dare not ask you. But I, all of us, her relatives, all who love her, beg you, entreat you. Why should she suffer? Who is any the better for it?"

"Excuse me, you seem to put me in the position of the guilty party," observed Alexey Alexandrovitch.

"Oh, no, oh, no, not at all! please understand me," said Stepan Arkadyevitch, touching his hand again, as though feeling sure this physical contact would soften his brother-in-law. "All I say is this: her position is intolerable, and it might be alleviated by you, and you will lose nothing by it. I will arrange it all for you, so that you'll not notice it. You did promise it, you know."

"The promise was given before. And I had supposed that the question of my son had settled the matter. Besides, I had hoped that Anna Arkadyevna had enough generosity . . ." Alexey Alexandrovitch articulated with difficulty, his lips twitching and his face white.

"She leaves it all to your generosity. She begs, she implores one thing of you—to extricate her from the impossible position in which she is placed. She does not ask for her son now. Alexey Alexandrovitch, you are a good man. Put yourself in her position for a minute. The question of divorce for her in her position is a question of life and death. If you had not promised it once, she would have reconciled herself to her position, she would have gone on living in the country. But you promised it, and she wrote to you, and moved to Moscow. And here she's been for six months in Moscow, where every chance meeting cuts her to the heart, everyday expecting an answer. Why, it's like keeping a condemned criminal for six months with the rope round his neck, promising him perhaps death, perhaps mercy. Have pity on her, and I will undertake to arrange everything. *Vos scrupules* . . . "

"I am not talking about that, about that . . ." Alexey Alexandrovitch interrupted with disgust. "But, perhaps, I promised what I had no right to promise."

"So you go back from your promise?"

"I have never refused to do all that is possible, but I want time to consider how much of what I promised is possible."

"No, Alexey Alexandrovitch!" cried Oblonsky, jumping up, "I won't believe that! She's unhappy as only an unhappy woman can be, and you cannot refuse in such . . ."

"As much of what I promised as is possible. *Vous professez d'être libre penseur.* But I as a believer cannot, in a matter of such gravity, act in opposition to the Christian law."

"But in Christian societies and among us, as far as I'm aware, divorce is allowed," said Stepan Arkadyevitch. "Divorce is sanctioned even by our church. And we see . . ."

"It is allowed, but not in the sense . . ."

"Alexey Alexandrovitch, you are not like yourself," said Oblonsky, after a brief pause. "Wasn't it you (and didn't we all appreciate it in you?) who forgave everything, and moved simply by Christian feeling was ready to make any sacrifice? You said yourself: if a man take thy coat, give him thy cloak also, and now . . ."

"I beg," said Alexey Alexandrovitch shrilly, getting suddenly onto his feet, his face white and his jaws twitching, "I beg you to drop this . . . to drop . . . this subject!"

"Oh, no! Oh, forgive me, forgive me if I have wounded you," said Stepan Arkadyevitch, holding out his hand with a smile of embarrassment; "but like a messenger I have simply performed the commission given me."

Alexey Alexandrovitch gave him his hand, pondered a little, and said:

"I must think it over and seek for guidance. The day after tomorrow I will give you a final answer," he said, after considering a moment.

Chapter XIX

STEPAN ARKADYEVITCH WAS ABOUT TO GO AWAY WHEN KORNEY CAME IN TO ANNOUNCE: "Sergey Alexyevitch!"

"Who's Sergey Alexyevitch?" Stepan Arkadyevitch was beginning, but he remembered immediately.

"Ah, Seryozha!" he said aloud. "Sergey Alexyevitch! I thought it was the director of a department. Anna asked me to see him too," he thought.

And he recalled the timid, piteous expression with which Anna had said to him at parting: "Anyway, you will see him. Find out exactly where he is, who is looking after him. And Stiva . . . if it were possible! Could it be possible?" Stepan Arkadyevitch knew what was meant by that "if it were possible,"—if it were possible to arrange the divorce so as to let her have her son . . . Stepan Arkadyevitch saw now that it was no good to dream of that, but still he was glad to see his nephew.

Alexey Alexandrovitch reminded his brother-in-law that they never spoke to the boy of his mother, and he begged him not to mention a single word about her.

"He was very ill after that interview with his mother, which we had not foreseen," said Alexey Alexandrovitch. "Indeed, we feared for his life. But with rational treatment, and sea-bathing in the summer, he regained his strength, and now, by the doctor's advice, I have let him go to school. And certainly the companionship of school has had a good effect on him, and he is perfectly well, and making good progress."

"What a fine fellow he's grown! He's not Seryozha now, but quite full-fledged Sergey Alexyevitch!" said Stepan Arkadyevitch, smiling, as he looked at the handsome, broad-shouldered lad in blue coat and long trousers, who walked in alertly and confidently. The boy looked healthy and good-humored. He bowed to his uncle as to a stranger, but recognizing him, he blushed and turned hurriedly away from him, as though offended and irritated at something. The boy went up to his father and handed him a note of the marks he had gained in school.

"Well, that's very fair," said his father, "you can go."

"He's thinner and taller, and has grown out of being a child into a boy; I like that," said Stepan Arkadyevitch. "Do you remember me?"

The boy looked back quickly at his uncle.

"Yes, *mon oncle,*" he answered, glancing at his father, and again he looked downcast.

His uncle called him to him, and took his hand.

"Well, and how are you getting on?" he said, wanting to talk to him, and not knowing what to say.

The boy, blushing and making no answer, cautiously drew his hand away. As soon as Stepan Arkadyevitch let go his hand, he glanced doubtfully at his father, and like a bird set free, he darted out of the room.

A year had passed since the last time Seryozha had seen his mother. Since then he had heard nothing more of her. And in the course of that year he had gone to school, and made friends among his schoolfellows. The dreams and memories of his mother, which had made him ill after seeing her, did not occupy his thoughts now. When they came back to him, he studiously drove them away, regarding them as shameful and girlish, below the dignity of a boy and a schoolboy. He knew that his father and mother were separated by some quarrel, he knew that he had to remain with his father, and he tried to get used to that idea.

He disliked seeing his uncle, so like his mother, for it called up those memories of which he was ashamed. He disliked it all the more as from some words he had caught as he waited at the study door, and still more from the faces of his father and uncle, he guessed that they must have been talking of his mother. And to avoid condemning the father with whom he lived and on whom he was dependent, and, above all, to avoid giving way to sentimentality, which he considered so degrading, Seryozha tried not to look at his uncle who had come to disturb his peace of mind, and not to think of what he recalled to him.

But when Stepan Arkadyevitch, going out after him, saw him on the stairs, and calling to him, asked him how he spent his playtime at school, Seryozha talked more freely to him away from his father's presence.

"We have a railway now," he said in answer to his uncle's question. "It's like this, do you see: two sit on a bench—they're the passengers; and one stands up straight on the bench. And all are harnessed to it by their arms or by their belts, and they run through all the rooms—the doors are left open beforehand. Well, and it's pretty hard work being the conductor!"

"That's the one that stands?" Stepan Arkadyevitch inquired, smiling.

"Yes, you want pluck for it, and cleverness too, especially when they stop all of a sudden, or someone falls down."

"Yes, that must be a serious matter," said Stepan Arkadyevitch, watching with mournful interest the eager eyes, like his mother's; not childish now—no longer fully innocent. And though he had promised Alexey Alexandrovitch not to speak of Anna, he could not restrain himself.

"Do you remember your mother?" he asked suddenly.

"No, I don't," Seryozha said quickly. He blushed crimson, and his face clouded over. And his uncle could get nothing more out of him. His tutor found his pupil on the staircase half an hour later, and for a long while he could not make out whether he was ill-tempered or crying.

"What is it? I expect you hurt yourself when you fell down?" said the tutor. "I told you it was a dangerous game. And we shall have to speak to the director."

"If I had hurt myself, nobody should have found it out, that's certain."

"Well, what is it, then?"

"Leave me alone! If I remember, or if I don't remember? . . . what business is it of his? Why should I remember? Leave me in peace!" he said, addressing not his tutor, but the whole world.

Chapter XX

STEPAN ARKADYEVITCH, AS USUAL, DID NOT WASTE HIS TIME IN PETERSBURG. IN PETERSBURG, BEsides business, his sister's divorce, and his coveted appointment, he wanted, as he always did, to freshen himself up, as he said, after the mustiness of Moscow.

In spite of its *cafés chantants* and its omnibuses, Moscow was yet a stagnant bog. Stepan Arkadyevitch always felt it. After living for some time in Moscow, especially in close relations with his family, he was conscious of a depression of spirits. After being a long time in Moscow without a change, he reached a point when he positively began to be worrying himself over his wife's ill-humor and reproaches, over his children's health and education, and the petty details of his official work; even the fact of being in debt worried him. But he had only to go and stay a little while in Petersburg, in the circle there in which he moved, where people lived—really lived—instead of vegetating as in Moscow, and all such ideas vanished and melted away at once, like wax before the fire. His wife? . . . Only that day he had been talking to Prince Tchetchensky. Prince Tchetchensky had a wife and family, grown-up pages in the corps, . . . and he had another illegitimate family of children also. Though the first family was very nice too, Prince Tchetchensky felt happier in his second family; and he used to take his eldest son with him to his second family, and told Stepan Arkadyevitch that he thought it good for his son, enlarging his ideas. What would have been said to that in Moscow?

His children? In Petersburg children did not prevent their parents from enjoying life. The children were brought up in schools, and there was no trace of the wild idea that prevailed in Moscow, in Lvov's household, for instance, that all the luxuries of life were for the children, while the parents have nothing but work and anxiety. Here people understood that a man is in duty bound to live for himself, as every man of culture should live.

His official duties? Official work here was not the stiff, hopeless drudgery that it was in Moscow. Here there was some interest in official life. A chance meeting, a service rendered, a happy phrase, a knack of facetious mimicry, and a man's career might be made in a trice. So it had been with Bryantsev, whom Stepan Arkadyevitch had met the previous day, and who was one of the highest functionaries in government now. There was some interest in official work like that.

The Petersburg attitude on pecuniary matters had an especially soothing effect on Stepan Arkadyevitch. Bartnyansky, who must spend at least fifty thousand to judge by the style he lived in, had made an interesting comment the day before on that subject.

As they were talking before dinner, Stepan Arkadyevitch said to Bartnyansky:

"You're friendly, I fancy, with Mordvinsky; you might do me a favor: say a word to him, please, for me. There's an appointment I should like to get—secretary of the agency . . ."

"Oh, I shan't remember all that, if you tell it to me . . . But what possesses you to have to do with railways and Jews? . . . Take it as you will, it's a low business."

Stepan Arkadyevitch did not say to Bartnyansky that it was a "growing thing"—Bartnyansky would not have understood that.

"I want the money, I've nothing to live on."

"You're living, aren't you?"

"Yes, but in debt."

"Are you, though? Heavily?" said Bartnyansky sympathetically.

"Very heavily: twenty thousand."

Bartnyansky broke into good-humored laughter.

"Oh, lucky fellow!" said he. "My debts mount up to a million and a half, and I've nothing, and still I can live, as you see!"

And Stepan Arkadyevitch saw the correctness of this view not in words only but in actual fact. Zhivahov owed three hundred thousand, and hadn't a farthing to bless himself with, and he lived, and in style too! Count Krivtsov was considered a hopeless case by everyone, and yet he kept two mistresses. Petrovsky had run through five millions, and still lived in just the same style, and was even a manager in the financial department with a salary of twenty thousand. But besides this, Petersburg had physically an agreeable effect on Stepan Arkadyevitch. It made him younger. In Moscow he sometimes found a gray hair in his head, dropped asleep after dinner, stretched, walked slowly upstairs, breathing heavily, was bored by the society of young women, and did not dance at balls. In Petersburg he always felt ten years younger.

His experience in Petersburg was exactly what had been described to him on the previous day by Prince Pyotr Oblonsky, a man of sixty, who had just come back from abroad:

"We don't know the way to live here," said Pyotr Oblonsky. "I spent the summer in Baden, and you wouldn't believe it, I felt quite a young man. At a glimpse of a pretty woman, my thoughts. . . . One dines and drinks a glass of wine, and feels strong and ready for anything. I came home to Russia—had to see my wife, and, what's more, go to my country place; and there, you'd hardly believe it, in a fortnight I'd got into a dressing-gown and given up dressing for dinner. Needn't say I had no thoughts left for pretty women. I became quite an old gentleman. There was nothing left for me but to think of my eternal salvation. I went off to Paris—I was as right as could be at once."

Stepan Arkadyevitch felt exactly the difference that Pyotr Oblonsky described. In Moscow he degenerated so much that if he had had to be there for long together, he might in good earnest have come to considering his salvation; in Petersburg he felt himself a man of the world again.

Between Princess Betsy Tverskaya and Stepan Arkadyevitch there had long existed rather curious relations. Stepan Arkadyevitch always flirted with her in jest, and used to say to her, also in jest, the most unseemly things, knowing that nothing delighted her so much. The day after his conversation with Karenin, Stepan Arkadyevitch went to see her, and felt so youthful that in this jesting flirtation and nonsense he recklessly went so far that he did not know how to extricate himself, as unluckily he was so far from being attracted by her that he thought her positively disagreeable. What made it hard to change the conversation was the fact that he was very attractive to her. So that he was considerably relieved at the arrival of Princess Myakaya, which cut short their *tête-à-tête*.

"Ah, so you're here!" said she when she saw him. "Well, and what news of your poor sister? You needn't look at me like that," she added. "Ever since they've all turned against her, all those who're a thousand times worse than she, I've thought she did a very fine thing. I can't forgive Vronsky for not letting me know when she was in Petersburg. I'd have gone to see her and gone about with her everywhere. Please give her my love. Come, tell me about her."

"Yes, her position is very difficult; she . . ." began Stepan Arkadyevitch, in the simplicity of his heart accepting as sterling coin Princess Myakaya's words "tell me about her." Princess Myakaya interrupted him immediately, as she always did, and began talking herself.

"She's done what they all do, except me—only they hide it. But she wouldn't be deceitful, and she did a fine thing. And she did better still in throwing up that crazy brother-in-law of yours. You must excuse me. Everybody used to say he was so clever, so very clever; I was the only one that said he was a fool. Now that he's so thick with Lidia Ivanovna and Landau, they all say he's crazy, and I should prefer not to agree with everybody, but this time I can't help it."

"Oh, do please explain," said Stepan Arkadyevitch; "what does it mean? Yesterday I was seeing him on my sister's behalf, and I asked him to give me a final answer. He gave me no answer, and said he would think it over. But this morning, instead of an answer, I received an invitation from Countess Lidia Ivanovna for this evening."

"Ah, so that's it, that's it!" said Princess Myakaya gleefully, "they're going to ask Landau what he's to say."

"Ask Landau? What for? Who or what's Landau?"

"What! you don't know Jules Landau, *le fameux Jules Landau, le clairvoyant?* He's crazy too, but on him your sister's fate depends. See what comes of living in the provinces—you know nothing about anything. Landau, do you see, was a *commis* in a shop in Paris, and he went to a doctor's; and in the doctor's waiting room he fell asleep, and in his sleep he began giving advice to all the patients. And wonderful advice it was! Then the wife of Yury Meledinsky—you know, the invalid?—heard of this Landau, and had him to see her husband. And he cured her husband, though I can't say that I see he did him much good, for he's just as feeble a creature as ever he was, but they believed in him, and took him along with them and brought him to Russia. Here there's been a general rush to him, and he's begun doctoring everyone. He cured Countess Bezzubova, and she took such a fancy to him that she adopted him."

"Adopted him?"

"Yes, as her son. He's not Landau anymore now, but Count Bezzubov. That's neither here nor there, though; but Lidia—I'm very fond of her, but she has a screw loose somewhere—has lost her heart to this Landau now, and nothing is settled now in her house or Alexey Alexandrovitch's without him, and so your sister's fate is now in the hands of Landau, *alias* Count Bezzubov."

Chapter XXI

AFTER A CAPITAL DINNER AND A GREAT DEAL OF COGNAC DRUNK AT BARTNYANSKY'S, STEPAN Arkadyevitch, only a little later than the appointed time, went in to Countess Lidia Ivanovna's.

"Who else is with the countess?—a Frenchman?" Stepan Arkadyevitch asked the hall-porter, as he glanced at the familiar overcoat of Alexey Alexandrovitch and a queer, rather artless-looking overcoat with clasps.

"Alexey Alexandrovitch Karenin and Count Bezzubov," the porter answered severely.

"Princess Myakaya guessed right," thought Stepan Arkadyevitch, as he went upstairs. "Curious! It would be quite as well, though, to get on friendly terms with her. She has immense influence. If she would say a word to Pomorsky, the thing would be a certainty."

It was still quite light out-of-doors, but in Countess Lidia Ivanovna's little drawing room the blinds were drawn and the lamps lit. At a round table under a lamp sat the countess and Alexey Alexandrovitch, talking softly. A short, thinnish man, very pale and handsome, with feminine hips and knock-kneed legs, with fine brilliant eyes and long hair lying on the collar of his coat, was standing at the end of the room gazing at the portraits on the wall. After greeting the lady of the house and Alexey Alexandrovitch, Stepan Arkadyevitch could not resist glancing once more at the unknown man.

"Monsieur Landau!" the countess addressed him with a softness and caution that impressed Oblonsky. And she introduced them.

Landau looked round hurriedly, came up, and smiling, laid his moist, lifeless hand in Stepan Arkadyevitch's outstretched hand and immediately walked away and fell to gazing at the portraits again. The countess and Alexey Alexandrovitch looked at each other significantly.

"I am very glad to see you, particularly today," said Countess Lidia Ivanovna, pointing Stepan Arkadyevitch to a seat beside Karenin.

"I introduced you to him as Landau," she said in a soft voice, glancing at the Frenchman and again immediately after at Alexey Alexandrovitch, "but he is really Count Bezzubov, as you're probably aware. Only he does not like the title."

"Yes, I heard so," answered Stepan Arkadyevitch; "they say he completely cured Countess Bezzubova."

"She was here today, poor thing!" the countess said, turning to Alexey Alexandrovitch. "This separation is awful for her. It's such a blow to her!"

"And he positively is going?" queried Alexey Alexandrovitch.

"Yes, he's going to Paris. He heard a voice yesterday," said Countess Lidia Ivanovna, looking at Stepan Arkadyevitch.

"Ah, a voice!" repeated Oblonsky, feeling that he must be as circumspect as he possibly could in this society, where something peculiar was going on, or was to go on, to which he had not the key.

A moment's silence followed, after which Countess Lidia Ivanovna, as though approaching the main topic of conversation, said with a fine smile to Oblonsky:

"I've known you for a long while, and am very glad to make a closer acquaintance with you. *Les amis de nos amis sont nos amis.* But to be a true friend, one must enter into the spiritual state of one's friend, and I fear that you are not doing so in the case of Alexey Alexandrovitch. You understand what I mean?" she said, lifting her fine pensive eyes.

"In part, countess, I understand the position of Alexey Alexandrovitch . . ." said Oblonsky. Having no clear idea what they were talking about, he wanted to confine himself to generalities.

"The change is not in his external position," Countess Lidia Ivanovna said sternly, following with eyes of love the figure of Alexey Alexandrovitch as he got up and crossed over to Landau; "his heart is changed, a new heart has been vouchsafed him, and I fear you don't fully apprehend the change that has taken place in him."

"Oh, well, in general outlines I can conceive the change. We have always been friendly, and now . . ." said Stepan Arkadyevitch, responding with a sympathetic glance to the expression of the countess, and mentally balancing the question with which of the two ministers she was most intimate, so as to know about which to ask her to speak for him.

"The change that has taken place in him cannot lessen his love for his neighbors; on the contrary, that change can only intensify love in his heart. But I am afraid you do not understand me. Won't you have some tea?" she said, with her eyes indicating the footman, who was handing round tea on a tray.

"Not quite, countess. Of course, his misfortune . . ."

"Yes, a misfortune which has proved the highest happiness, when his heart was made new, was filled full of it," she said, gazing with eyes full of love at Stepan Arkadyevitch.

"I do believe I might ask her to speak to both of them," thought Stepan Arkadyevitch.

"Oh, of course, countess," he said; "but I imagine such changes are a matter so private that no one, even the most intimate friend, would care to speak of them."

"On the contrary! We ought to speak freely and help one another."

"Yes, undoubtedly so, but there is such a difference of convictions, and besides . . ." said Oblonsky with a soft smile.

"There can be no difference where it is a question of holy truth."

"Oh, no, of course; but . . ." and Stepan Arkadyevitch paused in confusion. He understood at last that they were talking of religion.

"I fancy he will fall asleep immediately," said Alexey Alexandrovitch in a whisper full of meaning, going up to Lidia Ivanovna.

Stepan Arkadyevitch looked round. Landau was sitting at the window, leaning on his elbow and the back of his chair, his head drooping. Noticing that all eyes were turned on him he raised his head and smiled a smile of childlike artlessness.

"Don't take any notice," said Lidia Ivanovna, and she lightly moved a chair up for Alexey Alexandrovitch. "I have observed . . ." she was beginning, when a footman came into the room with a letter. Lidia Ivanovna rapidly ran her eyes over the note, and excusing herself, wrote an answer with extraordinary rapidity, handed it to the man, and came back to the table. "I have observed," she went on, "that Moscow people, especially the men, are more indifferent to religion than anyone."

"Oh, no, countess, I thought Moscow people had the reputation of being the firmest in the faith," answered Stepan Arkadyevitch.

"But as far as I can make out, you are unfortunately one of the indifferent ones," said Alexey Alexandrovitch, turning to him with a weary smile.

"How anyone can be indifferent!" said Lidia Ivanovna.

"I am not so much indifferent on that subject as I am waiting in suspense," said Stepan Arkadyevitch, with his most deprecating smile. "I hardly think that the time for such questions has come yet for me."

Alexey Alexandrovitch and Lidia Ivanovna looked at each other.

"We can never tell whether the time has come for us or not," said Alexey Alexandrovitch severely. "We ought not to think whether we are ready or not ready. God's grace is not guided by human considerations: sometimes it comes not to those that strive for it, and comes to those that are unprepared, like Saul."

"No, I believe it won't be just yet," said Lidia Ivanovna, who had been meanwhile watching the movements of the Frenchman. Landau got up and came to them.

"Do you allow me to listen?" he asked.

"Oh, yes; I did not want to disturb you," said Lidia Ivanovna, gazing tenderly at him; "sit here with us."

"One has only not to close one's eyes to shut out the light," Alexey Alexandrovitch went on.

"Ah, if you knew the happiness we know, feeling His presence ever in our hearts!" said Countess Lidia Ivanovna with a rapturous smile.

"But a man may feel himself unworthy sometimes to rise to that height," said Stepan Arkadyevitch, conscious of hypocrisy in admitting this religious height, but at the same time unable to bring himself to acknowledge his free-thinking views before a person who, by a single word to Pomorsky, might procure him the coveted appointment.

"That is, you mean that sin keeps him back?" said Lidia Ivanovna. "But that is a false idea. There is no sin for believers, their sin has been atoned for. *Pardon*," she added, looking at the footman, who came in again with another letter. She read it and gave a verbal answer: "Tomorrow at the Grand Duchess's, say." "For the believer sin is not," she went on.

"Yes, but faith without works is dead," said Stepan Arkadyevitch, recalling the phrase from the catechism, and only by his smile clinging to his independence.

"There you have it—from the epistle of St. James," said Alexey Alexandrovitch, addressing

Lidia Ivanovna, with a certain reproachfulness in his tone. It was unmistakably a subject they had discussed more than once before. "What harm has been done by the false interpretation of that passage! Nothing holds men back from belief like that misinterpretation. 'I have not works, so I cannot believe,' though all the while that is not said. But the very opposite is said."

"Striving for God, saving the soul by fasting," said Countess Lidia Ivanovna, with disgusted contempt, "those are the crude ideas of our monks. . . . Yet that is nowhere said. It is far simpler and easier," she added, looking at Oblonsky with the same encouraging smile with which at court she encouraged youthful maids of honor, disconcerted by the new surroundings of the court.

"We are saved by Christ who suffered for us. We are saved by faith," Alexey Alexandrovitch chimed in, with a glance of approval at her words.

"Vous comprenez l'anglais?" asked Lidia Ivanovna, and receiving a reply in the affirmative, she got up and began looking through a shelf of books.

"I want to read him 'Safe and Happy,' or 'Under the Wing,' " she said, looking inquiringly at Karenin. And finding the book, and sitting down again in her place, she opened it. "It's very short. In it is described the way by which faith can be reached, and the happiness, above all earthly bliss, with which it fills the soul. The believer cannot be unhappy because he is not alone. But you will see." She was just settling herself to read when the footman came in again. "Madame Borozdina? Tell her, tomorrow at two o'clock. Yes," she said, putting her finger in the place in the book, and gazing before her with her fine pensive eyes, "that is how true faith acts. You know Marie Sanina? You know about her trouble? She lost her only child. She was in despair. And what happened? She found this comforter, and she thanks God now for the death of her child. Such is the happiness faith brings!"

"Oh, yes, that is most . . ." said Stepan Arkadyevitch, glad they were going to read, and let him have a chance to collect his faculties. "No, I see I'd better not ask her about anything today," he thought. "If only I can get out of this without putting my foot in it!"

"It will be dull for you," said Countess Lidia Ivanovna, addressing Landau; "you don't know English, but it's short."

"Oh, I shall understand," said Landau, with the same smile, and he closed his eyes. Alexey Alexandrovitch and Lidia Ivanovna exchanged meaningful glances, and the reading began.

Chapter XXII

STEPAN ARKADYEVITCH FELT COMPLETELY NONPLUSSED BY THE STRANGE TALK WHICH HE WAS hearing for the first time. The complexity of Petersburg, as a rule, had a stimulating effect on him, rousing him out of his Moscow stagnation. But he liked these complications, and understood them only in the circles he knew and was at home in. In these unfamiliar surroundings he was puzzled and disconcerted, and could not get his bearings. As he listened to Countess Lidia Ivanovna, aware of the beautiful, artless—or perhaps artful, he could not decide which—eyes of Landau fixed upon him, Stepan Arkadyevitch began to be conscious of a peculiar heaviness in his head.

The most incongruous ideas were in confusion in his head. "Marie Sanina is glad her child's dead. . . . How good a smoke would be now! . . . To be saved, one need only believe, and the monks don't know how the thing's to be done, but Countess Lidia Ivanovna does know. . . . And why is my head so heavy? Is it the cognac, or all this being so queer? Anyway, I fancy I've done nothing unsuitable so far. But anyway, it won't do to ask her now. They say they make one say one's prayers. I only hope they won't make me! That'll be too imbecile. And what stuff it is she's reading! but she has a good accent. Landau—Bezzubov—what's he Bezzubov for?" All at once Stepan

Arkadyevitch became aware that his lower jaw was uncontrollably forming a yawn. He pulled his whiskers to cover the yawn, and shook himself together. But soon after he became aware that he was dropping asleep and on the very point of snoring. He recovered himself at the very moment when the voice of Countess Lidia Ivanovna was saying "he's asleep." Stepan Arkadyevitch started with dismay, feeling guilty and caught. But he was reassured at once by seeing that the words "he's asleep" referred not to him, but to Landau. The Frenchman was asleep as well as Stepan Arkadyevitch. But Stepan Arkadyevitch's being asleep would have offended them, as he thought (though even this, he thought, might not be so, as everything seemed so queer), while Landau's being asleep delighted them extremely, especially Countess Lidia Ivanovna.

"Mon ami," said Lidia Ivanovna, carefully holding the folds of her silk gown so as not to rustle, and in her excitement calling Karenin not Alexey Alexandrovitch, but *"mon ami," "donnez-lui la main. Vous voyez?* Sh!" she hissed at the footman as he came in again. "Not at home."

The Frenchman was asleep, or pretending to be asleep, with his head on the back of his chair, and his moist hand, as it lay on his knee, made faint movements, as though trying to catch something. Alexey Alexandrovitch got up, tried to move carefully, but stumbled against the table, went up and laid his hand in the Frenchman's hand. Stepan Arkadyevitch got up too, and opening his eyes wide, trying to wake himself up if he were asleep, he looked first at one and then at the other. It was all real. Stepan Arkadyevitch felt that his head was getting worse and worse.

"Que la personne qui est arrivée la dernière, celle qui demande, qu'elle sorte! Qu'elle sorte!" articulated the Frenchman, without opening his eyes.

"Vous m'excuserez, mais vous voyez . . . Revenez virs dix heures, encore mieux demain."

"Qu'elle sorte!" repeated the Frenchman impatiently.

"C'est moi, n'est-ce pas?" And receiving an answer in the affirmative, Stepan Arkadyevitch, forgetting the favor he had meant to ask of Lidia Ivanovna, and forgetting his sister's affairs, caring for nothing, but filled with the sole desire to get away as soon as possible, went out on tiptoe and ran out into the street as though from a plague-stricken house. For a long while he chatted and joked with his cab-driver, trying to recover his spirits.

At the French theater where he arrived for the last act, and afterwards at the Tatar restaurant after his champagne, Stepan Arkadyevitch felt a little refreshed in the atmosphere he was used to. But still he felt quite unlike himself all that evening.

On getting home to Pyotr Oblonsky's, where he was staying, Stepan Arkadyevitch found a note from Betsy. She wrote to him that she was very anxious to finish their interrupted conversation, and begged him to come next day. He had scarcely read this note, and frowned at its contents, when he heard below the ponderous tramp of the servants, carrying something heavy.

Stepan Arkadyevitch went out to look. It was the rejuvenated Pyotr Oblonsky. He was so drunk that he could not walk upstairs; but he told them to set him on his legs when he saw Stepan Arkadyevitch, and clinging to him, walked with him into his room and there began telling him how he had spent the evening, and fell asleep doing so.

Stepan Arkadyevitch was in very low spirits, which happened rarely with him, and for a long while he could not go to sleep. Everything he could recall to his mind, everything was disgusting; but most disgusting of all, as if it were something shameful, was the memory of the evening he had spent at Countess Lidia Ivanovna's.

Next day he received from Alexey Alexandrovitch a final answer, refusing to grant Anna's divorce, and he understood that this decision was based on what the Frenchman had said in his real or pretended trance.

Chapter XXIII

In order to carry through any undertaking in family life, there must necessarily be either complete division between the husband and wife, or loving agreement. When the relations of a couple are vacillating and neither one thing nor the other, no sort of enterprise can be undertaken.

Many families remain for years in the same place, though both husband and wife are sick of it, simply because there is neither complete division nor agreement between them.

Both Vronsky and Anna felt life in Moscow insupportable in the heat and dust, when the spring sunshine was followed by the glare of summer, and all the trees in the boulevards had long since been in full leaf, and the leaves were covered with dust. But they did not go back to Vozdvizhenskoe, as they had arranged to do long before; they went on staying in Moscow, though they both loathed it, because of late there had been no agreement between them.

The irritability that kept them apart had no external cause, and all efforts to come to an understanding intensified it, instead of removing it. It was an inner irritation, grounded in her mind on the conviction that his love had grown less; in his, on regret that he had put himself for her sake in a difficult position, which she, instead of lightening, made still more difficult. Neither of them gave full utterance to their sense of grievance, but they considered each other in the wrong, and tried on every pretext to prove this to one another.

In her eyes the whole of him, with all his habits, ideas, desires, with all his spiritual and physical temperament, was one thing—love for women, and that love, she felt, ought to be entirely concentrated on her alone. That love was less; consequently, as she reasoned, he must have transferred part of his love to other women or to another woman—and she was jealous. She was jealous not of any particular woman but of the decrease of his love. Not having got an object for her jealousy, she was on the lookout for it. At the slightest hint she transferred her jealousy from one object to another. At one time she was jealous of those low women with whom he might so easily renew his old bachelor ties; then she was jealous of the society women he might meet; then she was jealous of the imaginary girl whom he might want to marry, for whose sake he would break with her. And this last form of jealousy tortured her most of all, especially as he had unwarily told her, in a moment of frankness, that his mother knew him so little that she had had the audacity to try and persuade him to marry the young Princess Sorokina.

And being jealous of him, Anna was indignant against him and found grounds for indignation in everything. For everything that was difficult in her position she blamed him. The agonizing condition of suspense she had passed in Moscow, the tardiness and indecision of Alexey Alexandrovitch, her solitude—she put it all down to him. If he had loved her he would have seen all the bitterness of her position, and would have rescued her from it. For her being in Moscow and not in the country, he was to blame too. He could not live buried in the country as she would have liked to do. He must have society, and he had put her in this awful position, the bitterness of which he would not see. And again, it was his fault that she was forever separated from her son.

Even the rare moments of tenderness that came from time to time did not soothe her; in his tenderness now she saw a shade of complacency, of self-confidence, which had not been of old, and which exasperated her.

It was dusk. Anna was alone, and waiting for him to come back from a bachelor dinner. She walked up and down in his study (the room where the noise from the street was least heard), and thought over every detail of their yesterday's quarrel. Going back from the well-remembered, offensive words of the quarrel to what had been the ground of it, she arrived at last at its origin. For a long while she could hardly believe that their dissension had arisen from a conversation so inoffensive, of so little moment to either. But so it actually had been. It all arose from his laughing at the girls' high schools, declaring they were useless, while she defended them. He had spoken slightingly of women's education in general, and had said that Hannah, Anna's English protégé, had not the slightest need to know anything of physics.

This irritated Anna. She saw in this a contemptuous reference to her occupations. And she bethought her of a phrase to pay him back for the pain he had given her. "I don't expect you to understand me, my feelings, as anyone who loved me might, but simple delicacy I did expect," she said.

And he had actually flushed with vexation, and had said something unpleasant. She could not recall her answer, but at that point, with an unmistakable desire to wound her too, he had said:

"I feel no interest in your infatuation over this girl, that's true, because I see it's unnatural."

The cruelty with which he shattered the world she had built up for herself so laboriously to enable her to endure her hard life, the injustice with which he had accused her of affectation, of artificiality, aroused her.

"I am very sorry that nothing but what's coarse and material is comprehensible and natural to you," she said and walked out of the room.

When he had come in to her yesterday evening, they had not referred to the quarrel, but both felt that the quarrel had been smoothed over, but was not at an end.

Today he had not been at home all day, and she felt so lonely and wretched in being on bad terms with him that she wanted to forget it all, to forgive him, and be reconciled with him; she wanted to throw the blame on herself and to justify him.

"I am myself to blame. I'm irritable, I'm insanely jealous. I will make it up with him, and we'll go away to the country; there I shall be more at peace."

"Unnatural!" She suddenly recalled the word that had stung her most of all, not so much the word itself as the intent to wound her with which it was said. "I know what he meant; he meant—unnatural, not loving my own daughter, to love another person's child. What does he know of love for children, of my love for Seryozha, whom I've sacrificed for him? But that wish to wound me! No, he loves another woman, it must be so."

And perceiving that, while trying to regain her peace of mind, she had gone round the same circle that she had been round so often before, and had come back to her former state of exasperation, she was horrified at herself. "Can it be impossible? Can it be beyond me to control myself?" she said to herself, and began again from the beginning. "He's truthful, he's honest, he loves me. I love him, and in a few days the divorce will come. What more do I want? I want peace of mind and trust, and I will take the blame on myself. Yes, now when he comes in, I will tell him I was wrong, though I was not wrong, and we will go away tomorrow."

And to escape thinking anymore, and being overcome by irritability, she rang, and ordered the boxes to be brought up for packing their things for the country.

At ten o'clock Vronsky came in.

Chapter XXIV

"WELL, WAS IT NICE?" SHE ASKED, COMING OUT TO MEET HIM WITH A PENITENT AND MEEK expression.

"Just as usual," he answered, seeing at a glance that she was in one of her good moods. He was used by now to these transitions, and he was particularly glad to see it today, as he was in a specially good-humor himself.

"What do I see? Come, that's good!" he said, pointing to the boxes in the passage.

"Yes, we must go. I went out for a drive, and it was so fine I longed to be in the country. There's nothing to keep you, is there?"

"It's the one thing I desire. I'll be back directly, and we'll talk it over; I only want to change my coat. Order some tea."

And he went into his room.

There was something mortifying in the way he had said "Come, that's good," as one says to a child when it leaves off being naughty, and still more mortifying was the contrast between her penitent and his self-confident tone; and for one instant she felt the lust of strife rising up in her again, but making an effort she conquered it, and met Vronsky as good-humoredly as before.

When he came in she told him, partly repeating phrases she had prepared beforehand, how she had spent the day, and her plans for going away.

"You know it came to me almost like an inspiration," she said. "Why wait here for the divorce? Won't it be just the same in the country? I can't wait any longer! I don't want to go on hoping, I don't want to hear anything about the divorce. I have made up my mind it shall not have anymore influence on my life. Do you agree?"

"Oh, yes!" he said, glancing uneasily at her excited face.

"What did you do? Who was there?" she said, after a pause.

Vronsky mentioned the names of the guests. "The dinner was first rate, and the boat race, and it was all pleasant enough, but in Moscow they can never do anything without something *ridicule.* A lady of a sort appeared on the scene, teacher of swimming to the Queen of Sweden, and gave us an exhibition of her skill."

"How? did she swim?" asked Anna, frowning.

"In an absurd red *costume de natation*; she was old and hideous too. So when shall we go?"

"What an absurd fancy! Why, did she swim in some special way, then?" said Anna, not answering.

"There was absolutely nothing in it. That's just what I say, it was awfully stupid. Well, then, when do you think of going?"

Anna shook her head as though trying to drive away some unpleasant idea.

"When? Why, the sooner the better! By tomorrow we shan't be ready. The day after tomorrow."

"Yes . . . oh, no, wait a minute! The day after tomorrow's Sunday, I have to be at maman's," said Vronsky, embarrassed, because as soon as he uttered his mother's name he was aware of her intent, suspicious eyes. His embarrassment confirmed her suspicion. She flushed hotly and drew away from him. It was now not the Queen of Sweden's swimming-mistress who filled Anna's imagination, but the young Princess Sorokina. She was staying in a village near Moscow with Countess Vronskaya.

"Can't you go tomorrow?" she said.

"Well, no! The deeds and the money for the business I'm going there for I can't get by tomorrow," he answered.

"If so, we won't go at all."

"But why so?"

"I shall not go later. Monday or never!"

"What for?" said Vronsky, as though in amazement. "Why, there's no meaning in it!"

"There's no meaning in it to you, because you care nothing for me. You don't care to understand my life. The one thing that I cared for here was Hannah. You say it's affectation. Why, you said yesterday that I don't love my daughter, that I love this English girl, that it's unnatural. I should like to know what life there is for me that could be natural!"

For an instant she had a clear vision of what she was doing, and was horrified at how she had fallen away from her resolution. But even though she knew it was her own ruin, she could not restrain herself, could not keep herself from proving to him that he was wrong, could not give way to him.

"I never said that; I said I did not sympathize with this sudden passion."

"How is it, though you boast of your straightforwardness, you don't tell the truth?"

"I never boast, and I never tell lies," he said slowly, restraining his rising anger. "It's a great pity if you can't respect . . ."

"Respect was invented to cover the empty place where love should be. And if you don't love me anymore, it would be better and more honest to say so."

"No, this is becoming unbearable!" cried Vronsky, getting up from his chair; and stopping short, facing her, he said, speaking deliberately: "What do you try my patience for?" looking as though he might have said much more, but was restraining himself. "It has limits."

"What do you mean by that?" she cried, looking with terror at the undisguised hatred in his whole face, and especially in his cruel, menacing eyes.

"I mean to say . . ." he was beginning, but he checked himself. "I must ask what it is you want of me?"

"What can I want? All I can want is that you should not desert me, as you think of doing," she said, understanding all he had not uttered. "But that I don't want; that's secondary. I want love, and there is none. So then all is over."

She turned towards the door.

"Stop! sto-op!" said Vronsky, with no change in the gloomy lines of his brows, though he held her by the hand. "What is it all about? I said that we must put off going for three days, and on that you told me I was lying, that I was not an honorable man."

"Yes, and I repeat that the man who reproaches me with having sacrificed everything for me," she said, recalling the words of a still earlier quarrel, "that he's worse than a dishonorable man—he's a heartless man."

"Oh, there are limits to endurance!" he cried, and hastily let go her hand.

"He hates me, that's clear," she thought, and in silence, without looking round, she walked with faltering steps out of the room. "He loves another woman, that's even clearer," she said to herself as she went into her own room. "I want love, and there is none. So, then, all is over." She repeated the words she had said, "and it must be ended."

"But how?" she asked herself, and she sat down in a low chair before the looking-glass.

Thoughts of where she would go now, whether to the aunt who had brought her up, to Dolly, or simply alone abroad, and of what *he* was doing now alone in his study; whether this was the final quarrel, or whether reconciliation were still possible; and of what all her old friends at Petersburg would say of her now; and of how Alexey Alexandrovitch would look at it, and many other ideas of what would happen now after this rupture, came into her head; but she did not give herself up to them with all her heart. At the bottom of her heart was some obscure idea that alone interested her, but she could not get clear sight of it. Thinking once more of Alexey Alexandrovitch, she recalled the time of her illness after her confinement, and the feeling which never left her at that time. "Why didn't I die?" and the words and the feeling of that time came back to her. And all at once she knew what was in her soul. Yes, it was that idea which alone solved all. "Yes, to die! . . . And the shame and disgrace of Alexey Alexandrovitch and of Seryozha, and my awful shame, it will all be saved by death. To die! and he will feel remorse; will be sorry; will love me; he will suffer on my account." With the trace of a smile of commiseration for herself she sat down in the arm-chair, taking off and putting on the rings on her left hand, vividly picturing from different sides his feelings after her death.

Approaching footsteps—his steps—distracted her attention. As though absorbed in the arrangement of her rings, she did not even turn to him.

He went up to her, and taking her by the hand, said softly:

"Anna, we'll go the day after tomorrow, if you like. I agree to everything."

She did not speak.

"What is it?" he urged.

"You know," she said, and at the same instant, unable to restrain herself any longer, she burst into sobs.

"Cast me off!" she articulated between her sobs. "I'll go away tomorrow . . . I'll do more. What am I? An immoral woman! A stone round your neck. I don't want to make you wretched, I don't want to! I'll set you free. You don't love me; you love someone else!"

Vronsky besought her to be calm, and declared that there was no trace of foundation for her jealousy; that he had never ceased, and never would cease, to love her; that he loved her more than ever.

"Anna, why distress yourself and me so?" he said to her, kissing her hands. There was tenderness now in his face, and she fancied she caught the sound of tears in his voice, and she felt them wet on her hand. And instantly Anna's despairing jealousy changed to a despairing passion of tenderness. She put her arms round him, and covered with kisses his head, his neck, his hands.

Chapter XXV

FEELING THAT THE RECONCILIATION WAS COMPLETE, ANNA SET EAGERLY TO WORK IN THE MORNING preparing for their departure. Though it was not settled whether they should go on Monday or Tuesday, as they had each given way to the other, Anna packed busily, feeling absolutely indifferent whether they went a day earlier or later. She was standing in her room over an open box, taking things out of it, when he came in to see her earlier than usual, dressed to go out.

"I'm going off at once to see maman; she can send me the money by Yegorov. And I shall be ready to go tomorrow," he said.

Though she was in such a good mood, the thought of his visit to his mother's gave her a pang.

"No, I shan't be ready by then myself," she said; and at once reflected, "so then it was possible to arrange to do as I wished." "No, do as you meant to do. Go into the dining room, I'm coming directly. It's only to turn out those things that aren't wanted," she said, putting something more on the heap of frippery that lay in Annushka's arms.

Vronsky was eating his beef-steak when she came into the dining-room.

"You wouldn't believe how distasteful these rooms have become to me," she said, sitting down beside him to her coffee. "There's nothing more awful than these *chambres garnies*. There's no individuality in them, no soul. These clocks, and curtains, and, worst of all, the wallpapers—they're a nightmare. I think of Vozdvizhenskoe as the promised land. You're not sending the horses off yet?"

"No, they will come after us. Where are you going to?"

"I wanted to go to Wilson's to take some dresses to her. So it's really to be tomorrow?" she said in a cheerful voice; but suddenly her face changed.

Vronsky's valet came in to ask him to sign a receipt for a telegram from Petersburg. There was nothing out of the way in Vronsky's getting a telegram, but he said, as though anxious to conceal something from her, that the receipt was in his study, and he turned hurriedly to her.

"By tomorrow, without fail, I will finish it all."

"From whom is the telegram?" she asked, not hearing him.

"From Stiva," he answered reluctantly.

"Why didn't you show it to me? What secret can there be between Stiva and me?"

Vronsky called the valet back, and told him to bring the telegram.

"I didn't want to show it to you, because Stiva has such a passion for telegraphing: why telegraph when nothing is settled?"

"About the divorce?"

"Yes; but he says he has not been able to come at anything yet. He has promised a decisive answer in a day or two. But here it is; read it."

With trembling hands Anna took the telegram, and read what Vronsky had told her. At the end was added: "Little hope; but I will do everything possible and impossible."

"I said yesterday that it's absolutely nothing to me when I get, or whether I never get, a divorce," she said, flushing crimson. "There was not the slightest necessity to hide it from me." "So he may hide and does hide his correspondence with women from me," she thought.

"Yashvin meant to come this morning with Voytov," said Vronsky; "I believe he's won from Pyevtsov all and more than he can pay, about sixty thousand."

"No," she said, irritated by his so obviously showing by this change of subject that he was irritated, "why did you suppose that this news would affect me so, that you must even try to hide it? I said I don't want to consider it, and I should have liked you to care as little about it as I do."

"I care about it because I like definiteness," he said.

"Definiteness is not in the form but the love," she said, more and more irritated, not by his words, but by the tone of cool composure in which he spoke. "What do you want it for?"

"My God! love again," he thought, frowning.

"Oh, you know what for; for your sake and your children's in the future."

"There won't be children in the future."

"That's a great pity," he said.

"You want it for the children's sake, but you don't think of me?" she said, quite forgetting or not having heard that he had said, "*For your sake* and the children's."

The question of the possibility of having children had long been a subject of dispute and irritation to her. His desire to have children she interpreted as a proof he did not prize her beauty.

"Oh, I said: for your sake. Above all for your sake," he repeated, frowning as though in pain, "because I am certain that the greater part of your irritability comes from the indefiniteness of the position."

"Yes, now he has laid aside all pretense, and all his cold hatred for me is apparent," she thought, not hearing his words, but watching with terror the cold, cruel judge who looked mocking her out of his eyes.

"The cause is not that," she said, "and, indeed, I don't see how the cause of my irritability, as you call it, can be that I am completely in your power. What indefiniteness is there in the position? on the contrary . . ."

"I am very sorry that you don't care to understand," he interrupted, obstinately anxious to give utterance to his thought. "The indefiniteness consists in your imagining that I am free."

"On that score you can set your mind quite at rest," she said, and turning away from him, she began drinking her coffee.

She lifted her cup, with her little finger held apart, and put it to her lips. After drinking a few sips she glanced at him, and by his expression, she saw clearly that he was repelled by her hand, and her gesture, and the sound made by her lips.

"I don't care in the least what your mother thinks, and what match she wants to make for you," she said, putting the cup down with a shaking hand.

"But we are not talking about that."

"Yes, that's just what we are talking about. And let me tell you that a heartless woman, whether she's old or not old, your mother or anyone else, is of no consequence to me, and I would not consent to know her."

"Anna, I beg you not to speak disrespectfully of my mother."

"A woman whose heart does not tell her where her son's happiness and honor lie has no heart."

"I repeat my request that you will not speak disrespectfully of my mother, whom I respect," he said, raising his voice and looking sternly at her.

She did not answer. Looking intently at him, at his face, his hands, she recalled all the details of their reconciliation the previous day, and his passionate caresses. "There, just such caresses he has lavished, and will lavish, and longs to lavish on other women!" she thought.

"You don't love your mother. That's all talk, and talk, and talk!" she said, looking at him with hatred in her eyes.

"Even if so, you must . . ."

"Must decide, and I have decided," she said, and she would have gone away, but at that moment Yashvin walked into the room. Anna greeted him and remained.

Why, when there was a tempest in her soul, and she felt she was standing at a turning point in her life, which might have fearful consequences—why, at that minute, she had to keep up appearances before an outsider, who sooner or later must know it all—she did not know. But at once quelling the storm within her, she sat down and began talking to their guest.

"Well, how are you getting on? Has your debt been paid you?" she asked Yashvin.

"Oh, pretty fair; I fancy I shan't get it all, but I shall get a good half. And when are you off?" said Yashvin, looking at Vronsky, and unmistakably guessing at a quarrel.

"The day after tomorrow, I think," said Vronsky.

"You've been meaning to go so long, though."

"But now it's quite decided," said Anna, looking Vronsky straight in the face with a look which told him not to dream of the possibility of reconciliation.

"Don't you feel sorry for that unlucky Pyevtsov?" she went on, talking to Yashvin.

"I've never asked myself the question, Anna Arkadyevna, whether I'm sorry for him or not. You see, all my fortune's here"—he touched his breast-pocket—"and just now I'm a wealthy man. But today I'm going to the club, and I may come out a beggar. You see, whoever sits down to play with me—he wants to leave me without a shirt to my back, and so do I him. And so we fight it out, and that's the pleasure of it."

"Well, but suppose you were married," said Anna, "how would it be for your wife?"

Yashvin laughed.

"That's why I'm not married, and never mean to be."

"And Helsingfors?" said Vronsky, entering into the conversation and glancing at Anna's smiling face. Meeting his eyes, Anna's face instantly took a coldly severe expression as though she were saying to him: "It's not forgotten. It's all the same."

"Were you really in love?" she said to Yashvin.

"Oh heavens! ever so many times! But you see, some men can play but only so that they can always lay down their cards when the hour of a *rendezvous* comes, while I can take up love, but only so as not to be late for my cards in the evening. That's how I manage things."

"No, I didn't mean that, but the real thing." She would have said *Helsingfors,* but would not repeat the word used by Vronsky.

Voytov, who was buying the horse, came in. Anna got up and went out of the room.

Before leaving the house, Vronsky went into her room. She would have pretended to be looking for something on the table, but ashamed of making a pretense, she looked straight in his face with cold eyes.

"What do you want?" she asked in French.

"To get the guarantee for Gambetta, I've sold him," he said, in a tone which said more clearly than words, "I've no time for discussing things, and it would lead to nothing."

"I'm not to blame in any way," he thought. "If she will punish herself, *tant pis pour elle.*" But as he was going he fancied that she said something, and his heart suddenly ached with pity for her.

"Eh, Anna?" he queried.

"I said nothing," she answered just as coldly and calmly.

"Oh, nothing, *tant pis* then," he thought, feeling cold again, and he turned and went out. As he was going out he caught a glimpse in the looking-glass of her face, white, with quivering lips. He even wanted to stop and to say some comforting word to her, but his legs carried him out of the room before he could think what to say. The whole of that day he spent away from home, and when he came in late in the evening the maid told him that Anna Arkadyevna had a headache and begged him not to go in to her.

Chapter XXVI

NEVER BEFORE HAD A DAY BEEN PASSED IN QUARREL. TODAY WAS THE FIRST TIME. AND THIS WAS not a quarrel. It was the open acknowledgment of complete coldness. Was it possible to glance at her as he had glanced when he came into the room for the guarantee?—to look at her, see her heart was breaking with despair, and go out without a word with that face of callous composure? He was not merely cold to her, he hated her because he loved another woman—that was clear.

And remembering all the cruel words he had said, Anna supplied, too, the words that he had unmistakably wished to say and could have said to her, and she grew more and more exasperated.

"I won't prevent you," he might say. "You can go where you like. You were unwilling to be divorced from your husband, no doubt so that you might go back to him. Go back to him. If you want money, I'll give it to you. How many roubles do you want?"

All the most cruel words that a brutal man could say, he said to her in her imagination, and she could not forgive him for them, as though he had actually said them.

"But didn't he only yesterday swear he loved me, he, a truthful and sincere man? Haven't I despaired for nothing many times already?" she said to herself afterwards.

All that day, except for the visit to Wilson's, which occupied two hours, Anna spent in doubts whether everything were over or whether there were still hope of reconciliation, whether she should go away at once or see him once more. She was expecting him the whole day, and in the evening, as she went to her own room, leaving a message for him that her head ached, she said to herself, "If he comes in spite of what the maid says, it means that he loves me still. If not, it means that all is over, and then I will decide what I'm to do! . . ."

In the evening she heard the rumbling of his carriage stop at the entrance, his ring, his steps and his conversation with the servant; he believed what was told him, did not care to find out more, and went to his own room. So then everything was over.

And death rose clearly and vividly before her mind as the sole means of bringing back love for her in his heart, of punishing him and of gaining the victory in that strife which the evil spirit in possession of her heart was waging with him.

Now nothing mattered: going or not going to Vozdvizhenskoe, getting or not getting a divorce from her husband—all that did not matter. The one thing that mattered was punishing him. When she poured herself out her usual dose of opium, and thought that she had only to drink off the whole bottle to die, it seemed to her so simple and easy, that she began musing with enjoyment on how he would suffer, and repent and love her memory when it would be too late. She lay in bed with open eyes, by the light of a single burned-down candle, gazing at the carved cornice of the ceiling and at the shadow of the screen that covered part of it, while she vividly pictured to herself how he would feel when she would be no more, when she would be only a memory to him. "How could I say such cruel things to her?" he would say. "How could I go out of the room without saying anything to her? But now she is no more. She has gone away from us forever. She is. . . ." Suddenly the shadow of the screen wavered, pounced on the whole cornice, the whole ceiling; other shadows from the other side swooped to meet it, for an instant the shadows flitted back, but then with fresh swiftness they darted forward, wavered, commingled, and all was darkness. "Death!" she thought. And such horror came upon her that for a long while she could not realize where she was, and for a long while her trembling hands could not find the matches and light another candle, instead of the one that had burned down and gone out. "No, anything—only to live! Why, I love him! Why, he loves me! This has been before and will pass," she said, feeling that tears of joy at the return to life were trickling down her cheeks. And to escape from her panic she went hurriedly to his room.

He was asleep there, and sleeping soundly. She went up to him, and holding the light above his face, she gazed a long while at him. Now when he was asleep, she loved him so that at the sight of him she could not keep back tears of tenderness. But she knew that if he waked up he would look at her with cold eyes, convinced that he was right, and that before telling him of her love, she would have to prove to him that he had been wrong in his treatment of her. Without waking him, she went back, and after a second dose of opium she fell towards morning into a heavy, incomplete sleep, during which she never quite lost consciousness.

In the morning she was waked by a horrible nightmare, which had recurred several times in her dreams, even before her connection with Vronsky. A little old man with unkempt beard was doing something bent down over some iron, muttering meaningless French words, and she, as she always did in this nightmare (it was what made the horror of it), felt that this peasant was taking no notice of her, but was doing something horrible with the iron—over her. And she waked up in a cold sweat.

When she got up, the previous day came back to her as though veiled in mist.

"There was a quarrel. Just what has happened several times. I said I had a headache, and he did not come in to see me. Tomorrow we're going away; I must see him and get ready for the journey," she said to herself. And learning that he was in his study, she went down to him. As she passed through the drawing room she heard a carriage stop at the entrance, and looking out of the window she saw the carriage, from which a young girl in a lilac hat was leaning out giving some direction to the footman ringing the bell. After a parley in the hall, someone came upstairs, and Vronsky's steps could be heard passing the drawing room. He went rapidly downstairs. Anna went again to the window. She saw him come out onto the steps without his hat and go up to the carriage. The young girl in the lilac hat handed him a parcel. Vronsky, smiling, said something to her. The carriage drove away, he ran rapidly upstairs again.

The mists that had shrouded everything in her soul parted suddenly. The feelings of yesterday pierced the sick heart with a fresh pang. She could not understand now how she could have lowered herself by spending a whole day with him in his house. She went into his room to announce her determination.

"That was Madame Sorokina and her daughter. They came and brought me the money and the deeds from maman. I couldn't get them yesterday. How is your head, better?" he said quietly, not wishing to see and to understand the gloomy and solemn expression of her face.

She looked silently, intently at him, standing in the middle of the room. He glanced at her, frowned for a moment, and went on reading a letter. She turned, and went deliberately out of the room. He still might have turned her back, but she had reached the door, he was still silent, and the only sound audible was the rustling of the notepaper as he turned it.

"Oh, by the way," he said at the very moment she was in the doorway, "we're going tomorrow for certain, aren't we?"

"You, but not I," she said, turning round to him.

"Anna, we can't go on like this . . ."

"You, but not I," she repeated.

"This is getting unbearable!"

"You . . . you will be sorry for this," she said, and went out.

Frightened by the desperate expression with which these words were uttered, he jumped up and would have run after her, but on second thoughts he sat down and scowled, setting his teeth. This vulgar—as he thought it—threat of something vague exasperated him. "I've tried everything," he thought; "the only thing left is not to pay attention," and he began to get ready to drive into town, and again to his mother's to get her signature to the deeds.

She heard the sound of his steps about the study and the dining room. At the drawing room he stood still. But he did not turn in to see her, he merely gave an order that the horse should be given to Voytov if he came while he was away. Then she heard the carriage brought round, the door opened, and he came out again. But he went back into the porch again, and someone was running upstairs. It was the valet running up for his gloves that had been forgotten. She went to the window and saw him take the gloves without looking, and touching the coachman on the back he said something to him. Then without looking up at the window he settled himself in his usual attitude in the carriage, with his legs crossed, and drawing on his gloves he vanished round the corner.

Chapter XXVII

He has gone! It is over!" Anna said to herself, standing at the window; and in answer to this statement the impression of the darkness when the candle had flickered out, and of her fearful dream mingling into one, filled her heart with cold terror.

"No, that cannot be!" she cried, and crossing the room she rang the bell. She was so afraid now of being alone, that without waiting for the servant to come in, she went out to meet him.

"Inquire where the count has gone," she said. The servant answered that the count had gone to the stable.

"His honor left word that if you cared to drive out, the carriage would be back immediately."

"Very good. Wait a minute. I'll write a note at once. Send Mihail with the note to the stables. Make haste."

She sat down and wrote:

"I was wrong. Come back home; I must explain. For God's sake come! I'm afraid."

She sealed it up and gave it to the servant.

She was afraid of being left alone now; she followed the servant out of the room, and went to the nursery.

"Why, this isn't it, this isn't he! Where are his blue eyes, his sweet, shy smile?" was her first thought when she saw her chubby, rosy little girl with her black, curly hair instead of Seryozha, whom in the tangle of her ideas she had expected to see in the nursery. The little girl sitting at the table was obstinately and violently battering on it with a cork, and staring aimlessly at her mother with her pitch-black eyes. Answering the English nurse that she was quite well, and that she was going to the country tomorrow, Anna sat down by the little girl and began spinning the cork to show her. But the child's loud, ringing laugh, and the motion of her eyebrows, recalled Vronsky so vividly that she got up hurriedly, restraining her sobs, and went away. "Can it be all over? No, it cannot be!" she thought. "He will come back. But how can he explain that smile, that excitement after he had been talking to her? But even if he doesn't explain, I will believe. If I don't believe, there's only one thing left for me, and I can't."

She looked at her watch. Twenty minutes had passed. "By now he has received the note and is coming back. Not long, ten minutes more. . . . But what if he doesn't come? No, that cannot be. He mustn't see me with tear-stained eyes. I'll go and wash. Yes, yes; did I do my hair or not?" she asked herself. And she could not remember. She felt her head with her hand. "Yes, my hair has been done, but when I did it I can't in the least remember." She could not believe the evidence of her hand, and went up to the pier glass to see whether she really had done her hair. She certainly had, but she could not think when she had done it. "Who's that?" she thought, looking in the looking-glass at the swollen face with strangely glittering eyes, that looked in a scared way at her. "Why, it's I!" she suddenly understood, and looking round, she seemed all at once to feel his kisses on her, and twitched her shoulders, shuddering. Then she lifted her hand to her lips and kissed it.

"What is it? Why, I'm going out of my mind!" and she went into her bedroom, where Annushka was tidying the room.

"Annushka," she said, coming to a standstill before her, and she stared at the maid, not knowing what to say to her.

"You meant to go and see Darya Alexandrovna," said the girl, as though she understood.

"Darya Alexandrovna? Yes, I'll go."

"Fifteen minutes there, fifteen minutes back. He's coming, he'll be here soon." She took out her watch and looked at it. "But how could he go away, leaving me in such a state? How can he live, without making it up with me?" She went to the window and began looking into the street. Judging by the time, he might be back now. But her calculations might be wrong, and she began once more to recall when he had started and to count the minutes.

At the moment when she had moved away to the big clock to compare it with her watch, someone drove up. Glancing out of the window, she saw his carriage. But no one came upstairs, and voices could be heard below. It was the messenger who had come back in the carriage. She went down to him.

"We didn't catch the count. The count had driven off on the lower city road."

"What do you say? What! . . ." she said to the rosy, good-humored Mihail, as he handed her back her note.

"Why, then, he has never received it!" she thought.

"Go with this note to Countess Vronskaya's place, you know? and bring an answer back immediately," she said to the messenger.

"And I, what am I going to do?" she thought. "Yes, I'm going to Dolly's, that's true or else I shall go out of my mind. Yes, and I can telegraph, too." And she wrote a telegram. "I absolutely must talk to you; come at once." After sending off the telegram, she went to dress. When she was dressed and in her hat, she glanced again into the eyes of the plump, comfortable-looking Annushka. There was unmistakable sympathy in those good-natured little gray eyes.

"Annushka, dear, what am I to do?" said Anna, sobbing and sinking helplessly into a chair.

"Why fret yourself so, Anna Arkadyevna? Why, there's nothing out of the way. You drive out a little, and it'll cheer you up," said the maid.

"Yes, I'm going," said Anna, rousing herself and getting up. "And if there's a telegram while I'm away, send it on to Darya Alexandrovna's . . . but no, I shall be back myself."

"Yes, I mustn't think, I must do something, drive somewhere, and most of all, get out of this house," she said, feeling with terror the strange turmoil going on in her own heart, and she made haste to go out and get into the carriage.

"Where to?" asked Pyotr before getting onto the box.

"To Znamenka, the Oblonskys'."

Chapter XXVIII

It was bright and sunny. A fine rain had been falling all the morning, and now it had not long cleared up. The iron roofs, the flags of the roads, the flints of the pavements, the wheels and leather, the brass and the tinplate of the carriages—all glistened brightly in the May sunshine. It was three o'clock, and the very liveliest time in the streets.

As she sat in a corner of the comfortable carriage, that hardly swayed on its supple springs, while the grays trotted swiftly, in the midst of the unceasing rattle of wheels and the changing impressions in the pure air, Anna ran over the events of the last days, and she saw her position quite differently from how it had seemed at home. Now the thought of death seemed no longer so terrible and so clear to her, and death itself no longer seemed so inevitable. Now she blamed herself for the humiliation to which she had lowered herself. "I entreat him to forgive me. I have given in to him. I have owned myself in fault. What for? Can't I live without him?" And leaving unanswered the question how she was going to live without him, she fell to reading the signs on the shops. "Office and warehouse. Dental surgeon. Yes, I'll tell Dolly all about it. She doesn't like Vronsky. I shall be sick and ashamed, but I'll tell her. She loves me, and I'll follow her advice. I won't give in to him; I won't let him train me as he pleases. Filippov, bun shop. They say they send their dough to Petersburg. The Moscow water is so good for it. Ah, the springs at Mitishtchen, and the pancakes!"

And she remembered how, long, long ago, when she was a girl of seventeen, she had gone with her aunt to Troitsa. "Riding, too. Was that really me, with red hands? How much that seemed to me then splendid and out of reach has become worthless, while what I had then has gone out of my reach forever! Could I ever have believed then that I could come to such humiliation? How conceited and self-satisfied he will be when he gets my note! But I will show him. . . . How horrid that paint smells! Why is it they're always painting and building? *Modes et robes,*" she read. A man bowed to her. It was Annushka's husband. "Our parasites"; she remembered how Vronsky had said that. "Our? Why our? What's so awful is that one can't tear up the past by its roots. One can't tear it out, but one can hide one's memory of it. And I'll hide it." And then she thought of her past with Alexey Alexandrovitch, of how she had blotted the memory of it out of her life. "Dolly will think I'm leaving my second husband, and so I certainly must be in the wrong. As if I cared to be right! I can't help it!" she said, and she wanted to cry. But at once she fell to wondering what those two girls could be smiling about. "Love, most likely. They don't know how dreary it is, how low. . . . The boulevard and the children. Three boys running, playing at horses. Seryozha! And I'm losing everything and not getting him back. Yes, I'm losing everything, if he doesn't return. Perhaps he was late for the train and has come back by now. Longing for humiliation again!" she said to herself. "No, I'll go to Dolly, and say straight out to her, I'm unhappy, I deserve this, I'm to blame, but still I'm unhappy, help me. These horses, this carriage—how loathsome I am to myself in this carriage—all his; but I won't see them again."

Thinking over the words in which she would tell Dolly, and mentally working her heart up to great bitterness, Anna went upstairs.

"Is there anyone with her?" she asked in the hall.

"Katerina Alexandrovna Levin," answered the footman.

"Kitty! Kitty, whom Vronsky was in love with!" thought Anna, "the girl he thinks of with love. He's sorry he didn't marry her. But me he thinks of with hatred, and is sorry he had anything to do with me."

The sisters were having a consultation about nursing when Anna called. Dolly went down alone to see the visitor who had interrupted their conversation.

"Well, so you've not gone away yet? I meant to have come to you," she said; "I had a letter from Stiva today."

"We had a telegram too," answered Anna, looking round for Kitty.

"He writes that he can't make out quite what Alexey Alexandrovitch wants, but he won't go away without a decisive answer."

"I thought you had someone with you. Can I see the letter?"

"Yes; Kitty," said Dolly, embarrassed. "She stayed in the nursery. She has been very ill."

"So I heard. May I see the letter?"

"I'll get it directly. But he doesn't refuse; on the contrary, Stiva has hopes," said Dolly, stopping in the doorway.

"I haven't, and indeed I don't wish it," said Anna.

"What's this? Does Kitty consider it degrading to meet me?" thought Anna when she was alone. "Perhaps she's right, too. But it's not for her, the girl who was in love with Vronsky, it's not for her to show me that, even if it is true. I know that in my position I can't be received by any decent woman. I knew that from the first moment I sacrificed everything to him. And this is my reward! Oh, how I hate him! And what did I come here for? I'm worse here, more miserable." She heard from the next room the sisters' voices in consultation. "And what am I going to say to Dolly now? Amuse Kitty by the sight of my wretchedness, submit to her patronizing? No; and besides, Dolly wouldn't understand. And it would be no good my telling her. It would only be interesting to see Kitty, to show her how I despise everyone and everything, how nothing matters to me now."

Dolly came in with the letter. Anna read it and handed it back in silence.

"I knew all that," she said, "and it doesn't interest me in the least."

"Oh, why so? On the contrary, I have hopes," said Dolly, looking inquisitively at Anna. She had never seen her in such a strangely irritable condition. "When are you going away?" she asked.

Anna, half-closing her eyes, looked straight before her and did not answer.

"Why does Kitty shrink from me?" she said, looking at the door and flushing red.

"Oh, what nonsense! She's nursing, and things aren't going right with her, and I've been advising her. . . . She's delighted. She'll be here in a minute," said Dolly awkwardly, not clever at lying. "Yes, here she is."

Hearing that Anna had called, Kitty had wanted not to appear, but Dolly persuaded her. Rallying her forces, Kitty went in, walked up to her, blushing, and shook hands.

"I am so glad to see you," she said with a trembling voice.

Kitty had been thrown into confusion by the inward conflict between her antagonism to this bad woman and her desire to be nice to her. But as soon as she saw Anna's lovely and attractive face, all feeling of antagonism disappeared.

"I should not have been surprised if you had not cared to meet me. I'm used to everything. You have been ill? Yes, you are changed," said Anna.

Kitty felt that Anna was looking at her with hostile eyes. She ascribed this hostility to the awkward position in which Anna, who had once patronized her, must feel with her now, and she felt sorry for her.

They talked of Kitty's illness, of the baby, of Stiva, but it was obvious that nothing interested Anna.

"I came to say good-bye to you," she said, getting up.

"Oh, when are you going?"

But again not answering, Anna turned to Kitty.

"Yes, I am very glad to have seen you," she said with a smile. "I have heard so much of you from everyone, even from your husband. He came to see me, and I liked him exceedingly," she said, unmistakably with malicious intent. "Where is he?"

"He has gone back to the country," said Kitty, blushing.

"Remember me to him, be sure you do."

"I'll be sure to!" Kitty said naïvely, looking compassionately into her eyes.

"So good-bye, Dolly." And kissing Dolly and shaking hands with Kitty, Anna went out hurriedly.

"She's just the same and just as charming! She's very lovely!" said Kitty, when she was alone with her sister. "But there's something piteous about her. Awfully piteous!"

"Yes, there's something unusual about her today," said Dolly. "When I went with her into the hall, I fancied she was almost crying."

Chapter XXIX

ANNA GOT INTO THE CARRIAGE AGAIN IN AN EVEN WORSE FRAME OF MIND THAN WHEN SHE SET out from home. To her previous tortures was added now that sense of mortification and of being an outcast which she had felt so distinctly on meeting Kitty.

"Where to? Home?" asked Pyotr.

"Yes, home," she said, not even thinking now where she was going.

"How they looked at me as something dreadful, incomprehensible, and curious! What can he be telling the other with such warmth?" she thought, staring at two men who walked by. "Can one ever tell anyone what one is feeling? I meant to tell Dolly, and it's a good thing I didn't tell her. How pleased she would have been at my misery! She would have concealed it, but her chief feeling would have been delight at my being punished for the happiness she envied me for. Kitty, she would have been even more pleased. How I can see through her! She knows I was more than usually sweet to her husband. And she's jealous and hates me. And she despises me. In her eyes I'm an immoral woman. If I were an immoral woman I could have made her husband fall in love with me . . . if I'd cared to. And, indeed, I did care to. There's someone who's pleased with himself," she thought, as she saw a fat, rubicund gentleman coming towards her. He took her for an acquaintance, and lifted his glossy hat above his bald, glossy head, and then perceived his mistake. "He thought he knew me. Well, he knows me as well as anyone in the world knows me. I don't know myself. I know my appetites, as the French say. They want that dirty ice cream, that they do know for certain," she thought, looking at two boys stopping an ice cream seller, who took a barrel off his head and began wiping his perspiring face with a towel. "We all want what is sweet and nice. If not sweetmeats, then a dirty ice. And Kitty's the same—if not Vronsky, then Levin. And she envies me, and hates me. And we all hate each other. I Kitty, Kitty me. Yes, that's the truth. *'Tiutkin, coiffeur.' Je me fais coiffer par Tiutkin.* . . . I'll tell him that when he comes," she thought and smiled. But the same instant she remembered that she had no one now to tell anything amusing to. "And there's nothing amusing, nothing mirthful, really. It's all hateful. They're singing for vespers, and how carefully that merchant crosses himself! as if he were afraid of missing something. Why these churches and this singing and this humbug? Simply to conceal that we all hate each other like these cab drivers who are abusing each other so angrily. Yashvin says, 'He wants to strip me of my shirt, and I him of his.' Yes, that's the truth!"

She was plunged in these thoughts, which so engrossed her that she left off thinking of her own position, when the carriage drew up at the steps of her house. It was only when she saw the porter running out to meet her that she remembered she had sent the note and the telegram.

"Is there an answer?" she inquired.

"I'll see this minute," answered the porter, and glancing into his room, he took out and gave her the thin square envelope of a telegram. "I can't come before ten o'clock.—Vronsky," she read.

"And hasn't the messenger come back?"

"No," answered the porter.

"Then, since it's so, I know what I must do," she said, and feeling a vague fury and craving for revenge rising up within her, she ran upstairs. "I'll go to him myself. Before going away forever, I'll tell him all. Never have I hated anyone as I hate that man!" she thought. Seeing his hat on the rack, she shuddered with aversion. She did not consider that his telegram was an answer to her telegram and that he had not yet received her note. She pictured him to herself as talking calmly to his mother and Princess Sorokina and rejoicing at her sufferings. "Yes, I must go quickly," she said, not knowing yet where she was going. She longed to get away as quickly as possible from the feelings she had gone through in that awful house. The servants, the walls, the things in that house—all aroused repulsion and hatred in her and lay like a weight upon her.

"Yes, I must go to the railway station, and if he's not there, then go there and catch him." Anna looked at the railway timetable in the newspapers. An evening train went at two minutes past eight. "Yes, I shall be in time." She gave orders for the other horses to be put in the carriage, and packed in a traveling bag the things needed for a few days. She knew she would never come back here again.

Among the plans that came into her head she vaguely determined that after what would happen at the station or at the countess's house, she would go as far as the first town on the Nizhni road and stop there.

Dinner was on the table; she went up, but the smell of the bread and cheese was enough to make her feel that all food was disgusting. She ordered the carriage and went out. The house threw a shadow now right across the street, but it was a bright evening and still warm in the sunshine. Annushka, who came down with her things, and Pyotr, who put the things in the carriage, and the coachman, evidently out of humor, were all hateful to her, and irritated her by their words and actions.

"I don't want you, Pyotr."

"But how about the ticket?"

"Well, as you like, it doesn't matter," she said crossly.

Pyotr jumped on the box, and putting his arms akimbo, told the coachman to drive to the booking-office.

Chapter XXX

"HERE IT IS AGAIN! AGAIN I UNDERSTAND IT ALL!" ANNA SAID TO HERSELF, AS SOON AS THE CARriage had started and swaying lightly, rumbled over the tiny cobbles of the paved road, and again one impression followed rapidly upon another.

"Yes; what was the last thing I thought of so clearly?" she tried to recall it. " *'Tiutkin, coiffeur?'*—no, not that. Yes, of what Yashvin says, the struggle for existence and hatred is the one thing that holds men together. No, it's a useless journey you're making," she said, mentally addressing a party in a coach and four, evidently going for an excursion into the country. "And the dog you're taking with you will be no help to you. You can't get away from yourselves." Turning her eyes in the direction Pyotr had turned to look, she saw a factory-hand almost dead-drunk, with hanging head, being led away by a policeman. "Come, he's found a quicker way," she thought. "Count Vronsky and I did not find that happiness either, though we expected so much from it." And now for the first time Anna turned that glaring light in which she was seeing everything on to her relations with him, which she had hitherto avoided thinking about. "What was it he sought in me? Not love so much as the satisfaction of vanity." She remembered his words, the expression of his face, that recalled an abject setter-dog, in the early days of their connection. And everything now confirmed this. "Yes, there was the triumph of success in him. Of course there was love too, but the chief element was the pride of success. He boasted of me. Now that's over. There's nothing to be proud of. Not to be proud of, but to be ashamed of. He has taken from me all he could, and now I am no use to him. He is weary of me and is trying not to be dishonorable in his behavior to me. He let that out yesterday—he wants divorce and marriage so as to burn his ships. He loves me, but how? The zest is gone, as the English say. That fellow wants everyone to admire him and is very much pleased with himself," she thought, looking at a red-faced clerk, riding on a riding school horse. "Yes, there's not the same flavor about me for him now. If I go away from him, at the bottom of his heart he will be glad."

This was not mere supposition, she saw it distinctly in the piercing light, which revealed to her now the meaning of life and human relations.

"My love keeps growing more passionate and egoistic, while his is waning and waning, and that's why we're drifting apart." She went on musing. "And there's no help for it. He is everything for me, and I want him more and more to give himself up to me entirely. And he wants more and more to get away from me. We walked to meet each other up to the time of our love, and then we have been irresistibly drifting in different directions. And there's no altering that. He tells me I'm insanely jealous, and I have told myself that I am insanely jealous; but it's not true. I'm not jealous, but I'm unsatisfied. But . . ." she opened her lips, and shifted her place in the carriage in the excitement, aroused by the thought that suddenly struck her. "If I could be anything but a mistress, passionately caring for nothing but his caresses; but I can't and I don't care to be anything else. And by that desire I rouse aversion in him, and he rouses fury in me, and it cannot be different. Don't I know that he wouldn't deceive me, that he has no schemes about Princess Sorokina, that he's not in love with Kitty, that he won't desert me! I know all that, but it makes it no better for me. If without loving me, from *duty* he'll be good and kind to me, without what I want, that's a thousand times worse than unkindness! That's—hell! And that's just how it is. For a long while now he hasn't loved me. And where love ends, hate begins. I don't know these streets at all. Hills it seems, and still houses, and houses. . . . And in the houses always people and people. . . . How many of them, no end, and all hating each other! Come, let me try and think what I want, to make me happy. Well? Suppose I am divorced, and Alexey Alexandrovitch lets me have Seryozha, and I marry Vronsky." Thinking of Alexey Alexandrovitch, she at once pictured him with extraordinary vividness as though he were alive before her, with his mild, lifeless, dull eyes, the blue veins in his white hands, his intonations and the cracking of his fingers, and remembering the feeling which had existed between them, and which was also called love, she shuddered with loathing. "Well, I'm divorced, and become Vronsky's wife. Well, will Kitty cease looking at me as she looked at me today? No. And will Seryozha leave off asking and wondering about my two husbands? And is there any new feeling I can awaken between Vronsky and me? Is there possible, if not happiness, some sort of ease from misery? No, no!" she answered now without the slightest hesitation. "Impossible! We are drawn apart by life, and I make his unhappiness, and he mine, and there's no altering him or me. Every attempt has been made, the screw has come unscrewed. Oh, a beggar woman with a baby. She thinks I'm sorry for her. Aren't we all flung into the world only to hate each other, and so to torture ourselves and each other? Schoolboys coming—laughing Seryozha?" she thought. "I thought, too, that I loved him, and used to be touched by my own tenderness. But I have lived without him, I gave him up for another love, and did not regret the exchange till that love was satisfied." And with loathing she thought of what she meant by that love. And the clearness with which she saw life now, her own and all men's, was a pleasure to her. "It's so with me and Pyotr, and the coachman, Fyodor, and that merchant, and all the people living along the Volga, where those placards invite one to go, and everywhere and always," she thought when she had driven under the low-pitched roof of the Nizhigorod station, and the porters ran to meet her.

"A ticket to Obiralovka?" said Pyotr.

She had utterly forgotten where and why she was going, and only by a great effort she understood the question.

"Yes," she said, handing him her purse, and taking a little red bag in her hand, she got out of the carriage.

Making her way through the crowd to the first-class waiting room, she gradually recollected all the details of her position, and the plans between which she was hesitating. And again at the old sore places, hope and then despair poisoned the wounds of her tortured, fearfully throbbing heart. As she sat on the star-shaped sofa waiting for the train, she gazed with aversion at the people coming and going (they were all hateful to her), and thought how she would arrive at the station, would write him a note, and what she would write to him, and how he was at this moment complaining to his mother of his position, not understanding her sufferings, and how she would go into the room, and what she would say to him. Then she thought that life might still be happy, and how miserably she loved and hated him, and how fearfully her heart was beating.

Chapter XXXI

A BELL RANG, SOME YOUNG MEN, UGLY AND IMPUDENT, AND AT THE SAME TIME CAREFUL OF THE impression they were making, hurried by. Pyotr, too, crossed the room in his livery and top-boots, with his dull, animal face, and came up to her to take her to the train. Some noisy men were quiet as she passed them on the platform, and one whispered something about her to another—something vile, no doubt. She stepped up on the high step, and sat down in a carriage by herself on a dirty seat that had been white. Her bag lay beside her, shaken up and down by the springiness of the seat. With a foolish smile Pyotr raised his hat, with its colored band, at the window, in token of farewell; an impudent conductor slammed the door and the latch. A grotesque-looking lady wearing a bustle (Anna mentally undressed the woman, and was appalled at her hideousness), and a little girl laughing affectedly ran down the platform.

"Katerina Andreevna, she's got them all, *ma tante!*" cried the girl.

"Even the child's hideous and affected," thought Anna. To avoid seeing anyone, she got up quickly and seated herself at the opposite window of the empty carriage. A misshapen-looking peasant covered with dirt, in a cap from which his tangled hair stuck out all round, passed by that window, stooping down to the carriage wheels. "There's something familiar about that hideous peasant," thought Anna. And remembering her dream, she moved away to the opposite door, shaking with terror. The conductor opened the door and let in a man and his wife.

"Do you wish to get out?"

Anna made no answer. The conductor and her two fellow-passengers did not notice under her veil her panic-stricken face. She went back to her corner and sat down. The couple seated themselves on the opposite side, and intently but surreptitiously scrutinized her clothes. Both husband and wife seemed repulsive to Anna. The husband asked, would she allow him to smoke, obviously not with a view to smoking but to getting into conversation with her. Receiving her assent, he said to his wife in French something about caring less to smoke than to talk. They made inane and affected remarks to one another, entirely for her benefit. Anna saw clearly that they were sick of each other, and hated each other. And no one could have helped hating such miserable monstrosities.

A second bell sounded, and was followed by moving of luggage, noise, shouting and laughter. It was so clear to Anna that there was nothing for anyone to be glad of, that this laughter irritated her agonizingly, and she would have liked to stop up her ears not to hear it. At last the third bell rang, there was a whistle and a hiss of steam, and a clank of chains, and the man in her carriage crossed himself. "It would be interesting to ask him what meaning he attaches to that," thought Anna, looking angrily at him. She looked past the lady out of the window at the people who seemed whirling by as they ran beside the train or stood on the platform. The train, jerking at regular intervals at the junctions of the rails, rolled by the platform, past a stone wall, a signal-box, past other trains; the wheels, moving more smoothly and evenly, resounded with a slight clang on the rails. The window was lit up by the bright evening sun, and a slight breeze fluttered the curtain. Anna forgot her fellow-passengers, and to the light swaying of the train she fell to thinking again, as she breathed the fresh air.

"Yes, what did I stop at? That I couldn't conceive a position in which life would not be a misery, that we are all created to be miserable, and that we all know it, and all invent means of deceiving each other. And when one sees the truth, what is one to do?"

"That's what reason is given man for, to escape from what worries him," said the lady in French, lisping affectedly, and obviously pleased with her phrase.

The words seemed an answer to Anna's thoughts.

"To escape from what worries him," repeated Anna. And glancing at the red-cheeked husband and the thin wife, she saw that the sickly wife considered herself misunderstood, and the husband deceived her and encouraged her in that idea of herself. Anna seemed to see all their history and all the crannies of their souls, as it were turning a light upon them. But there was nothing interesting in them, and she pursued her thought.

"Yes, I'm very much worried, and that's what reason was given me for, to escape; so then one must escape: why not put out the light when there's nothing more to look at, when it's sickening to look at it all? But how? Why did the conductor run along the footboard, why are they shrieking, those young men in that train? why are they talking, why are they laughing? It's all falsehood, all lying, all humbug, all cruelty! . . ."

When the train came into the station, Anna got out into the crowd of passengers, and moving apart from them as if they were lepers, she stood on the platform, trying to think what she had come here for, and what she meant to do. Everything that had seemed to her possible before was now so difficult to consider, especially in this noisy crowd of hideous people who would not leave her alone. One moment porters ran up to her proffering their services, then young men, clacking their heels on the planks of the platform and talking loudly, stared at her; people meeting her dodged past on the wrong side. Remembering that she had meant to go on further if there were no answer, she stopped a porter and asked if her coachman were not here with a note from Count Vronsky.

"Count Vronsky? They sent up here from the Vronskys just this minute, to meet Princess Sorokina and her daughter. And what is the coachman like?"

Just as she was talking to the porter, the coachman Mihail, red and cheerful in his smart blue coat and chain, evidently proud of having so successfully performed his commission, came up to her and gave her a letter. She broke it open, and her heart ached before she had read it.

"I am very sorry your note did not reach me. I will be home at ten," Vronsky had written carelessly. . . .

"Yes, that's what I expected!" she said to herself with an evil smile.

"Very good, you can go home then," she said softly, addressing Mihail. She spoke softly because the rapidity of her heart's beating hindered her breathing. "No, I won't let you make me miserable," she thought menacingly, addressing not him, not herself, but the power that made her suffer, and she walked along the platform.

Two maidservants walking along the platform turned their heads, staring at her and making some remarks about her dress. "Real," they said of the lace she was wearing. The young men would not leave her in peace. Again they passed by, peering into her face, and with a laugh shouting something in an unnatural voice. The stationmaster coming up asked her whether she was going by train.

A boy selling kvas never took his eyes off her. "My God! where am I to go?" she thought, going farther and farther along the platform. At the end she stopped. Some ladies and children, who had come to meet a gentleman in spectacles, paused in their loud laughter and talking, and stared at her as she reached them. She quickened her pace and walked away from them to the edge of the platform. A luggage train was coming in. The platform began to sway, and she fancied she was in the train again.

And all at once she thought of the man crushed by the train the day she had first met Vronsky, and she knew what she had to do. With a rapid, light step she went down the steps that led from the tank to the rails and stopped quite near the approaching train.

She looked at the lower part of the carriages, at the screws and chains and the tall cast-iron wheel of the first carriage slowly moving up, and trying to measure the middle between the front and back wheels, and the very minute when that middle point would be opposite her.

"There," she said to herself, looking into the shadow of the carriage, at the sand and coal dust which covered the sleepers—"there, in the very middle, and I will punish him and escape from everyone and from myself."

She tried to fling herself below the wheels of the first carriage as it reached her; but the red bag which she tried to drop out of her hand delayed her, and she was too late; she missed the moment. She had to wait for the next carriage. A feeling such as she had known when about to take the first plunge in bathing came upon her, and she crossed herself. That familiar gesture brought back into her soul a whole series of girlish and childish memories, and suddenly the darkness that had covered everything for her was torn apart, and life rose up before her for an instant with all its bright past joys. But she did not take her eyes from the wheels of the second carriage. And exactly at the moment when the space between the wheels came opposite her, she dropped the red bag, and drawing her head back into her shoulders, fell on her hands under the carriage, and lightly, as though she would rise again at once, dropped on to her knees. And at the same instant she was terror-stricken at what she was doing. "Where am I? What am I doing? What for?" She tried to get up, to drop backwards; but something huge and merciless struck her on the head and rolled her on her back. "Lord, forgive me all!" she said, feeling it impossible to struggle. A peasant muttering something was working at the iron above her. And the light by which she had read the book filled with troubles, falsehoods, sorrow, and evil, flared up more brightly than ever before, lit up for her all that had been in darkness, flickered, began to grow dim, and was quenched forever.

Part Eight

Chapter I

ALMOST TWO MONTHS HAD PASSED. THE HOT SUMMER WAS HALF OVER, BUT SERGEY Ivanovitch was only just preparing to leave Moscow.

Sergey Ivanovitch's life had not been uneventful during this time. A year ago he had finished his book, the fruit of six years' labor, *Sketch of a Survey of the Principles and Forms of Government in Europe and Russia.* Several sections of this book and its introduction had appeared in periodical publications, and other parts had been read by Sergey Ivanovitch to persons of his circle, so that the leading ideas of the work could not be completely novel to the public. But still Sergey Ivanovitch had expected that on its appearance his book would be sure to make a serious impression on society, and if it did not cause a revolution in social science it would, at any rate, make a great stir in the scientific world.

After the most conscientious revision the book had last year been published, and had been distributed among the booksellers.

Though he asked no one about it, reluctantly and with feigned indifference answered his friends' inquiries as to how the book was going, and did not even inquire of the booksellers how the book was selling, Sergey Ivanovitch was all on the alert, with strained attention, watching for the first impression his book would make in the world and in literature.

But a week passed, a second, a third, and in society no impression whatever could be detected. His friends who were specialists and savants, occasionally—unmistakably from politeness—alluded to it. The rest of his acquaintances, not interested in a book on a learned subject, did not talk of it at all. And society generally—just now especially absorbed in other things—was absolutely indifferent. In the press, too, for a whole month there was not a word about his book.

Sergey Ivanovitch had calculated to a nicety the time necessary for writing a review, but a month passed, and a second, and still there was silence.

Only in the *Northern Beetle,* in a comic article on the singer Drabanti, who had lost his voice, there was a contemptuous allusion to Koznishev's book, suggesting that the book had been long ago seen through by everyone, and was a subject of general ridicule.

At last in the third month a critical article appeared in a serious review. Sergey Ivanovitch knew the author of the article. He had met him once at Golubtsov's.

The author of the article was a young man, an invalid, very bold as a writer, but extremely deficient in breeding and shy in personal relations.

In spite of his absolute contempt for the author, it was with complete respect that Sergey Ivanovitch set about reading the article. The article was awful.

The critic had undoubtedly put an interpretation upon the book which could not possibly be put on it. But he had selected quotations so adroitly that for people who had not read the book (and obviously scarcely anyone had read it) it seemed absolutely clear that the whole book was nothing but a medley of high-flown phrases, not even—as suggested by marks of interrogation—used appropriately, and that the author of the book was a person absolutely without knowledge of the subject. And all this was so wittily done that Sergey Ivanovitch would not have disowned such wit himself. But that was just what was so awful.

In spite of the scrupulous conscientiousness with which Sergey Ivanovitch verified the correctness of the critic's arguments, he did not for a minute stop to ponder over the faults and mistakes which were ridiculed; but unconsciously he began immediately trying to recall every detail of his meeting and conversation with the author of the article.

"Didn't I offend him in some way?" Sergey Ivanovitch wondered.

And remembering that when they met he had corrected the young man about something he had said that betrayed ignorance, Sergey Ivanovitch found the clue to explain the article.

This article was followed by a deadly silence about the book both in the press and in conversation, and Sergey Ivanovitch saw that his six years' task, toiled at with such love and labor, had gone, leaving no trace.

Sergey Ivanovitch's position was still more difficult from the fact that, since he had finished his book, he had had no more literary work to do, such as had hitherto occupied the greater part of his time.

Sergey Ivanovitch was clever, cultivated, healthy, and energetic, and he did not know what use to make of his energy. Conversations in drawing rooms, in meetings, assemblies, and committees—everywhere where talk was possible—took up part of his time. But being used for years to town life, he did not waste all his energies in talk, as his less experienced younger brother did, when he was in Moscow. He had a great deal of leisure and intellectual energy still to dispose of.

Fortunately for him, at this period so difficult for him from the failure of his book, the various public questions of the dissenting sects, of the American alliance, of the Samara famine, of exhibitions, and of spiritualism, were definitely replaced in public interest by the Slavonic question, which had hitherto rather languidly interested society, and Sergey Ivanovitch, who had been one of the first to raise this subject, threw himself into it heart and soul.

In the circle to which Sergey Ivanovitch belonged, nothing was talked of or written about just now but the Servian War. Everything that the idle crowd usually does to kill time was done now for the benefit of the Slavonic States. Balls, concerts, dinners, matchboxes, ladies' dresses, beer, restaurants—everything testified to sympathy with the Slavonic peoples.

From much of what was spoken and written on the subject, Sergey Ivanovitch differed on various points. He saw that the Slavonic question had become one of those fashionable distractions which succeed one another in providing society with an object and an occupation. He saw, too, that a great many people were taking up the subject from motives of self-interest and self-advertisement. He recognized that the newspapers published a great deal that was superfluous and exaggerated, with the sole aim of attracting attention and outbidding one another. He saw that in this general movement those who thrust themselves most forward and shouted the loudest were men who had failed and were smarting under a sense of injury—generals without armies, ministers not in the ministry, journalists not on any paper, party leaders without followers. He saw that there was a great deal in it that was frivolous and absurd. But he saw and recognized an unmistakable growing enthusiasm, uniting all classes, with which it was impossible not to sympathize. The massacre of men who were fellow Christians, and of the same Slavonic race, excited sympathy for the sufferers and indignation against the oppressors. And the heroism of the Servians and Montenegrins struggling for a great cause begot in the whole people a longing to help their brothers not in word but in deed.

But in this there was another aspect that rejoiced Sergey Ivanovitch. That was the manifestation of public opinion. The public had definitely expressed its desire. The soul of the people had, as Sergey Ivanovitch said, found expression. And the more he worked in this cause, the more incontestable it seemed to him that it was a cause destined to assume vast dimensions, to create an epoch.

He threw himself heart and soul into the service of this great cause, and forgot to think about his book. His whole time now was engrossed by it, so that he could scarcely manage to answer all the letters and appeals addressed to him. He worked the whole spring and part of the summer, and it was only in July that he prepared to go away to his brother's in the country.

He was going both to rest for a fortnight, and in the very heart of the people, in the farthest wilds of the country, to enjoy the sight of that uplifting of the spirit of the people, of which, like all residents in the capital and big towns, he was fully persuaded. Katavasov had long been meaning to carry out his promise to stay with Levin, and so he was going with him.

Chapter II

SERGEY IVANOVITCH AND KATAVASOV HAD ONLY JUST REACHED THE STATION OF THE KURSK LINE, which was particularly busy and full of people that day, when, looking round for the groom who was following with their things, they saw a party of volunteers driving up in four cabs. Ladies met them with bouquets of flowers, and followed by the rushing crowd they went into the station.

One of the ladies, who had met the volunteers, came out of the hall and addressed Sergey Ivanovitch.

"You too come to see them off?" she asked in French.

"No, I'm going away myself, princess. To my brother's for a holiday. Do you always see them off?" said Sergey Ivanovitch with a hardly perceptible smile.

"Oh, that would be impossible!" answered the princess. "Is it true that eight hundred have been sent from us already? Malvinsky wouldn't believe me."

"More than eight hundred. If you reckon those who have been sent not directly from Moscow, over a thousand," answered Sergey Ivanovitch.

"There! That's just what I said!" exclaimed the lady. "And it's true too, I suppose, that more than a million has been subscribed?"

"Yes, princess."

"What do you say to today's telegram? Beaten the Turks again."

"Yes, so I saw," answered Sergey Ivanovitch. They were speaking of the last telegram stating that the Turks had been for three days in succession beaten at all points and put to flight, and that tomorrow a decisive engagement was expected.

"Ah, by the way, a splendid young fellow has asked leave to go, and they've made some difficulty, I don't know why. I meant to ask you; I know him; please write a note about his case. He's being sent by Countess Lidia Ivanovna."

Sergey Ivanovitch asked for all the details the princess knew about the young man, and going into the first-class waiting room, wrote a note to the person on whom the granting of leave of absence depended, and handed it to the princess.

"You know Count Vronsky, the notorious one . . . is going by this train?" said the princess with a smile full of triumph and meaning, when he found her again and gave her the letter.

"I had heard he was going, but I did not know when. By this train?"

"I've seen him. He's here: there's only his mother seeing him off. It's the best thing, anyway, that he could do."

"Oh, yes, of course."

While they were talking the crowd streamed by them into the dining room. They went forward too, and heard a gentleman with a glass in his hand delivering a loud discourse to the volunteers. "In the service of religion, humanity, and our brothers," the gentleman said, his voice growing louder and louder; "to this great cause mother Moscow dedicates you with her blessing. *Jivio!*" he concluded, loudly and tearfully.

Everyone shouted *Jivio!* and a fresh crowd dashed into the hall, almost carrying the princess off her legs.

"Ah, princess! that was something like!" said Stepan Arkadyevitch, suddenly appearing in the middle of the crowd and beaming upon them with a delighted smile. "Capitally, warmly said, wasn't it? Bravo! And Sergey Ivanovitch! Why, you ought to have said something—just a few words, you know, to encourage them; you do that so well," he added with a soft, respectful, and discreet smile, moving Sergey Ivanovitch forward a little by the arm.

"No, I'm just off."

"Where to?"

"To the country, to my brother's," answered Sergey Ivanovitch.

"Then you'll see my wife. I've written to her, but you'll see her first. Please tell her that they've seen me and that it's 'all right,' as the English say. She'll understand. Oh, and be so good as to tell her I'm appointed secretary of the committee. . . . But she'll understand! You know, *les petites misères de la vie humaine,*" he said, as it were apologizing to the princess. "And Princess Myakaya—not Liza, but Bibish—is sending a thousand guns and twelve nurses. Did I tell you?"

"Yes, I heard so," answered Koznishev indifferently.

"It's a pity you're going away," said Stepan Arkadyevitch. "Tomorrow we're giving a dinner to two who're setting off—Dimer-Bartnyansky from Petersburg and our Veslovsky, Grisha. They're both going. Veslovsky's only lately married. There's a fine fellow for you! Eh, princess?" he turned to the lady.

The princess looked at Koznishev without replying. But the fact that Sergey Ivanovitch and the princess seemed anxious to get rid of him did not in the least disconcert Stepan Arkadyevitch. Smiling, he stared at the feather in the princess's hat, and then about him as though he were going to pick something up. Seeing a lady approaching with a collecting-box, he beckoned her up and put in a five-ruble note.

"I can never see these collecting-boxes unmoved while I've money in my pocket," he said. "And how about today's telegram? Fine chaps those Montenegrins!"

"You don't say so!" he cried, when the princess told him that Vronsky was going by this train. For an instant Stepan Arkadyevitch's face looked sad, but a minute later, when, stroking his mustaches and swinging as he walked, he went into the hall where Vronsky was, he had completely forgotten his own despairing sobs over his sister's corpse, and he saw in Vronsky only a hero and an old friend.

"With all his faults one can't refuse to do him justice," said the princess to Sergey Ivanovitch as soon as Stepan Arkadyevitch had left them. "What a typically Russian, Slav nature! Only, I'm afraid it won't be pleasant for Vronsky to see him. Say what you will, I'm touched by that man's fate. Do talk to him a little on the way," said the princess.

"Yes, perhaps, if it happens so."

"I never liked him. But this atones for a great deal. He's not merely going himself, he's taking a squadron at his own expense."

"Yes, so I heard."

A bell sounded. Everyone crowded to the doors. "Here he is!" said the princess, indicating Vronsky, who with his mother on his arm walked by, wearing a long overcoat and wide-brimmed black hat. Oblonsky was walking beside him, talking eagerly of something.

Vronsky was frowning and looking straight before him, as though he did not hear what Stepan Arkadyevitch was saying.

Probably on Oblonsky's pointing them out, he looked round in the direction where the princess and Sergey Ivanovitch were standing, and without speaking lifted his hat. His face, aged and worn by suffering, looked stony.

Going onto the platform, Vronsky left his mother and disappeared into a compartment.

On the platform there rang out "God save the Tsar," then shouts of "hurrah!" and *"jivio!"* One of the volunteers, a tall, very young man with a hollow chest, was particularly conspicuous, bowing and waving his felt hat and a nosegay over his head. Then two officers emerged, bowing too, and a stout man with a big beard, wearing a greasy forage-cap.

Chapter III

SAYING GOOD-BYE TO THE PRINCESS, SERGEY IVANOVITCH WAS JOINED BY KATAVASOV; TOGETHER they got into a carriage full to overflowing, and the train started.

At Tsaritsino station the train was met by a chorus of young men singing "Hail to Thee!" Again the volunteers bowed and poked their heads out, but Sergey Ivanovitch paid no attention to them. He had had so much to do with the volunteers that the type was familiar to him and did not interest him. Katavasov, whose scientific work had prevented his having a chance of observing them hitherto, was very much interested in them and questioned Sergey Ivanovitch.

Sergey Ivanovitch advised him to go into the second class and talk to them himself. At the next station Katavasov acted on this suggestion.

At the first stop he moved into the second class and made the acquaintance of the volunteers. They were sitting in a corner of the carriage, talking loudly and obviously aware that the attention of the passengers and Katavasov as he got in was concentrated upon them. More loudly than all talked the tall, hollow-chested young man. He was unmistakably tipsy, and was relating some story that had occurred at his school. Facing him sat a middle-aged officer in the Austrian military jacket of the Guards uniform. He was listening with a smile to the hollow-chested youth, and occasionally pulling him up. The third, in an artillery uniform, was sitting on a box beside them. A fourth was asleep.

Entering into conversation with the youth, Katavasov learned that he was a wealthy Moscow merchant who had run through a large fortune before he was two-and-twenty. Katavasov did not like him, because he was unmanly and effeminate and sickly. He was obviously convinced, especially now after drinking, that he was performing a heroic action, and he bragged of it in the most unpleasant way.

The second, the retired officer, made an unpleasant impression too upon Katavasov. He was, it seemed, a man who had tried everything. He had been on a railway, had been a land-steward, and had started factories, and he talked, quite without necessity, of all he had done, and used learned expressions quite inappropriately.

The third, the artilleryman, on the contrary, struck Katavasov very favorably. He was a quiet, modest fellow, unmistakably impressed by the knowledge of the officer and the heroic self-sacrifice of the merchant and saying nothing about himself. When Katavasov asked him what had impelled him to go to Servia, he answered modestly:

"Oh, well, everyone's going. The Servians want help, too. I'm sorry for them."

"Yes, you artillerymen especially are scarce there," said Katavasov.

"Oh, I wasn't long in the artillery; maybe they'll put me into the infantry or the cavalry."

"Into the infantry when they need artillery more than anything?" said Katavasov, fancying from the artilleryman's apparent age that he must have reached a fairly high grade.

"I wasn't long in the artillery; I'm a cadet retired," he said, and he began to explain how he had failed in his examination.

All of this together made a disagreeable impression on Katavasov, and when the volunteers got out at a station for a drink, Katavasov would have liked to compare his unfavorable impression in conversation with someone. There was an old man in the carriage, wearing a military overcoat, who had been listening all the while to Katavasov's conversation with the volunteers. When they were left alone, Katavasov addressed him.

"What different positions they come from, all those fellows who are going off there," Katavasov said vaguely, not wishing to express his own opinion, and at the same time anxious to find out the old man's views.

The old man was an officer who had served on two campaigns. He knew what makes a soldier, and judging by the appearance and the talk of those persons, by the swagger with which they had recourse to the bottle on the journey, he considered them poor soldiers. Moreover, he lived in a district town, and he was longing to tell how one soldier had volunteered from his town, a drunkard and a thief whom no one would employ as a laborer. But knowing by experience that in the present condition of the public temper it was dangerous to express an opinion opposed to the general one, and especially to criticize the volunteers unfavorably, he too watched Katavasov without committing himself.

"Well, men are wanted there," he said, laughing with his eyes. And they fell to talking of the last war news, and each concealed from the other his perplexity as to the engagement expected next day, since the Turks had been beaten, according to the latest news, at all points. And so they parted, neither giving expression to his opinion.

Katavasov went back to his own carriage, and with reluctant hypocrisy reported to Sergey Ivanovitch his observations of the volunteers, from which it would appear that they were capital fellows.

At a big station at a town the volunteers were again greeted with shouts and singing, again men and women with collecting-boxes appeared, and provincial ladies brought bouquets to the volunteers and followed them into the refreshment room; but all this was on a much smaller and feebler scale than in Moscow.

Chapter IV

WHILE THE TRAIN WAS STOPPING AT THE PROVINCIAL TOWN, SERGEY IVANOVITCH DID NOT GO to the refreshment room, but walked up and down the platform.

The first time he passed Vronsky's compartment he noticed that the curtain was drawn over the window; but as he passed it the second time he saw the old countess at the window. She beckoned to Koznishev.

"I'm going, you see, taking him as far as Kursk," she said.

"Yes, so I heard," said Sergey Ivanovitch, standing at her window and peeping in. "What a noble act on his part!" he added, noticing that Vronsky was not in the compartment.

"Yes, after his misfortune, what was there for him to do?"

"What a terrible thing it was!" said Sergey Ivanovitch.

"Ah, what I have been through! But do get in. . . . Ah, what I have been through!" she repeated, when Sergey Ivanovitch had got in and sat down beside her. "You can't conceive it! For six weeks he did not speak to anyone, and would not touch food except when I implored him. And not for one minute could we leave him alone. We took away everything he could have used against himself. We lived on the ground-floor, but there was no reckoning on anything. You know, of course, that he had shot himself once already on her account," she said, and the old lady's eyelashes twitched at the recollection. "Yes, hers was the fitting end for such a woman. Even the death she chose was low and vulgar."

"It's not for us to judge, countess," said Sergey Ivanovitch; "but I can understand that it has been very hard for you."

"Ah, don't speak of it! I was staying on my estate, and he was with me. A note was brought him. He wrote an answer and sent it off. We hadn't an idea that she was close by at the station. In the evening I had only just gone to my room, when my Mary told me a lady had thrown herself under the train. Something seemed to strike me at once. I knew it was she. The first thing I said was, he was not to be told. But they'd told him already. His coachman was there and saw it all. When I ran into his room, he was beside himself—it was fearful to see him. He didn't say a word, but galloped off there. I don't know to this day what happened there, but he was brought back at death's door. I shouldn't have known him. *Prostration complète,* the doctor said. And that was followed almost by madness. Oh, why talk of it!" said the countess with a wave of her hand. "It was an awful time! No, say what you will, she was a bad woman. Why, what is the meaning of such desperate passions? It was all to show herself something out of the way. Well, and that she did do. She brought herself to ruin and two good men—her husband and my unhappy son."

"And what did her husband do?" asked Sergey Ivanovitch.

"He has taken her daughter. Alexey was ready to agree to anything at first. Now it worries him terribly that he should have given his own child away to another man. But he can't take back his word. Karenin came to the funeral. But we tried to prevent his meeting Alexey. For him, for her husband, it was easier, anyway. She had set him free. But my poor son was utterly given up to her. He had thrown up everything, his career, me, and even then she had no mercy on him, but of set purpose she made his ruin complete. No, say what you will, her very death was the death of a vile woman, of no religious feeling. God forgive me, but I can't help hating the memory of her, when I look at my son's misery!"

"But how is he now?"

"It was a blessing from Providence for us—this Servian war. I'm old, and I don't understand the rights and wrongs of it, but it's come as a providential blessing to him. Of course for me, as his mother, it's terrible; and what's worse, they say, *ce n'est pas très bien vu à Pétersbourg.* But it can't be helped! It was the one thing that could rouse him. Yashvin—a friend of his—he had lost all he had at cards and he was going to Servia. He came to see him and persuaded him to go. Now it's an interest for him. Do please talk to him a little. I want to distract his mind. He's so low-spirited. And as bad luck would have it, he has toothache too. But he'll be delighted to see you. Please do talk to him; he's walking up and down on that side."

Sergey Ivanovitch said he would be very glad to, and crossed over to the other side of the station.

Chapter V

IN THE SLANTING EVENING SHADOWS CAST BY THE BAGGAGE PILED UP ON THE PLATFORM, VRONSKY in his long overcoat and slouch hat, with his hands in his pockets, strode up and down, like a wild beast in a cage, turning sharply after twenty paces. Sergey Ivanovitch fancied, as he approached him, that Vronsky saw him but was pretending not to see. This did not affect Sergey Ivanovitch in the slightest. He was above all personal considerations with Vronsky.

At that moment Sergey Ivanovitch looked upon Vronsky as a man taking an important part in a great cause, and Koznishev thought it his duty to encourage him and express his approval. He went up to him.

Vronsky stood still, looked intently at him, recognized him, and going a few steps forward to meet him, shook hands with him very warmly.

"Possibly you didn't wish to see me," said Sergey Ivanovitch, "but couldn't I be of use to you?"

"There's no one I should less dislike seeing than you," said Vronsky. "Excuse me; and there's nothing in life for me to like."

"I quite understand, and I merely meant to offer you my services," said Sergey Ivanovitch, scanning Vronsky's face, full of unmistakable suffering. "Wouldn't it be of use to you to have a letter to Ristitch—to Milan?"

"Oh, no!" Vronsky said, seeming to understand him with difficulty. "If you don't mind, let's walk on. It's so stuffy among the carriages. A letter? No, thank you; to meet death one needs no letters of introduction. Nor for the Turks . . ." he said, with a smile that was merely of the lips. His eyes still kept their look of angry suffering.

"Yes; but you might find it easier to get into relations, which are after all essential, with anyone prepared to see you. But that's as you like. I was very glad to hear of your intention. There have been so many attacks made on the volunteers, and a man like you raises them in public estimation."

"My use as a man," said Vronsky, "is that life's worth nothing to me. And that I've enough bodily energy to cut my way into their ranks, and to trample on them or fall—I know that. I'm glad there's something to give my life for, for it's not simply useless but loathsome to me. Anyone's welcome to it." And his jaw twitched impatiently from the incessant gnawing toothache, that prevented him from even speaking with a natural expression.

"You will become another man, I predict," said Sergey Ivanovitch, feeling touched. "To deliver one's brother-men from bondage is an aim worth death and life. God grant you success outwardly—and inwardly peace," he added, and he held out his hand. Vronsky warmly pressed his outstretched hand.

"Yes, as a weapon I may be of some use. But as a man, I'm a wreck," he jerked out.

He could hardly speak for the throbbing ache in his strong teeth, that were like rows of ivory in his mouth. He was silent, and his eyes rested on the wheels of the tender, slowly and smoothly rolling along the rails.

And all at once a different pain, not an ache, but an inner trouble, that set his whole being in anguish, made him for an instant forget his toothache. As he glanced at the tender and the rails, under the influence of the conversation with a friend he had not met since his misfortune, he suddenly recalled *her*—that is, what was left of her when he had run like one distraught into the cloak room of the railway station—on the table, shamelessly sprawling out among strangers, the bloodstained body so lately full of life; the head unhurt dropping back with its weight of hair, and the curling tresses about the temples, and the exquisite face, with red, half-opened mouth, the strange, fixed expression, piteous on the lips and awful in the still open eyes, that seemed to utter that fearful phrase—that he would be sorry for it—that she had said when they were quarreling.

And he tried to think of her as she was when he met her the first time, at a railway station too, mysterious, exquisite, loving, seeking and giving happiness, and not cruelly revengeful as he remembered her on that last moment. He tried to recall his best moments with her, but those moments were poisoned forever. He could only think of her as triumphant, successful in her menace of a wholly useless remorse never to be effaced. He lost all consciousness of toothache, and his face worked with sobs.

Passing twice up and down beside the baggage in silence and regaining his self-possession, he addressed Sergey Ivanovitch calmly:

"You have had no telegrams since yesterday's? Yes, driven back for a third time, but a decisive engagement expected for tomorrow."

And after talking a little more of King Milan's proclamation, and the immense effect it might have, they parted, going to their carriages on hearing the second bell.

Chapter VI

Sergey Ivanovitch had not telegraphed to his brother to send to meet him, as he did not know when he should be able to leave Moscow. Levin was not at home when Katavasov and Sergey Ivanovitch in a fly hired at the station drove up to the steps of the Pokrovskoe house, as black as Moors from the dust of the road. Kitty, sitting on the balcony with her father and sister, recognized her brother-in-law, and ran down to meet him.

"What a shame not to have let us know," she said, giving her hand to Sergey Ivanovitch, and putting her forehead up for him to kiss.

"We drove here capitally, and have not put you out," answered Sergey Ivanovitch. "I'm so dirty. I'm afraid to touch you. I've been so busy, I didn't know when I should be able to tear myself away. And so you're still as ever enjoying your peaceful, quiet happiness," he said, smiling, "out of the reach of the current in your peaceful backwater. Here's our friend Fyodor Vassilievitch who has succeeded in getting here at last."

"But I'm not a negro, I shall look like a human being when I wash," said Katavasov in his jesting fashion, and he shook hands and smiled, his teeth flashing white in his black face.

"Kostya will be delighted. He has gone to his settlement. It's time he should be home."

"Busy as ever with his farming. It really is a peaceful backwater," said Katavasov; "while we in town think of nothing but the Servian war. Well, how does our friend look at it? He's sure not to think like other people."

"Oh, I don't know, like everybody else," Kitty answered, a little embarrassed, looking round at Sergey Ivanovitch. "I'll send to fetch him. Papa's staying with us. He's only just come home from abroad."

And making arrangements to send for Levin and for the guests to wash, one in his room and the other in what had been Dolly's, and giving orders for their luncheon, Kitty ran out onto the balcony, enjoying the freedom, and rapidity of movement, of which she had been deprived during the months of her pregnancy.

"It's Sergey Ivanovitch and Katavasov, a professor," she said.

"Oh, that's a bore in this heat," said the prince.

"No, papa, he's very nice, and Kostya's very fond of him," Kitty said, with a deprecating smile, noticing the irony on her father's face.

"Oh, I didn't say anything."

"You go to them, darling," said Kitty to her sister, "and entertain them. They saw Stiva at the station; he was quite well. And I must run to Mitya. As ill-luck would have it, I haven't fed him since tea. He's awake now, and sure to be screaming." And feeling a rush of milk, she hurried to the nursery.

This was not a mere guess; her connection with the child was still so close, that she could gauge by the flow of her milk his need of food, and knew for certain he was hungry.

She knew he was crying before she reached the nursery. And he was indeed crying. She heard him and hastened. But the faster she went, the louder he screamed. It was a fine healthy scream, hungry and impatient.

"Has he been screaming long, nurse, very long?" said Kitty hurriedly, seating herself on a chair, and preparing to give the baby the breast. "But give me him quickly. Oh, nurse, how tiresome you are! There, tie the cap afterwards, do!"

The baby's greedy scream was passing into sobs.

"But you can't manage so, ma'am," said Agafea Mihalovna, who was almost always to be found in the nursery. "He must be put straight. A-oo! a-oo!" she chanted over him, paying no attention to the mother.

The nurse brought the baby to his mother. Agafea Mihalovna followed him with a face dissolving with tenderness.

"He knows me, he knows me. In God's faith, Katerina Alexandrovna, ma'am, he knew me!" Agafea Mihalovna cried above the baby's screams.

But Kitty did not hear her words. Her impatience kept growing, like the baby's.

Their impatience hindered things for a while. The baby could not get hold of the breast right, and was furious.

At last, after despairing, breathless screaming, and vain sucking, things went right, and mother and child felt simultaneously soothed, and both subsided into calm.

"But poor darling, he's all in perspiration!" said Kitty in a whisper, touching the baby.

"What makes you think he knows you?" she added, with a sidelong glance at the baby's eyes, that peered roguishly, as she fancied, from under his cap, at his rhythmically puffing cheeks, and the little red-palmed hand he was waving.

"Impossible! If he knew anyone, he would have known me," said Kitty, in response to Agafea Mihalovna's statement, and she smiled.

She smiled because, though she said he could not know her, in her heart she was sure that he knew not merely Agafea Mihalovna, but that he knew and understood everything, and knew and understood a great deal too that no one else knew, and that she, his mother, had learned and come to understand only through him. To Agafea Mihalovna, to the nurse, to his grandfather, to his father even, Mitya was a living being, requiring only material care, but for his mother he had long been a mortal being, with whom there had been a whole series of spiritual relations already.

"When he wakes up, please God, you shall see for yourself. Then when I do like this, he simply beams on me, the darling! Simply beams like a sunny day!" said Agafea Mihalovna.

"Well, well; then we shall see," whispered Kitty. "But now go away, he's going to sleep."

Chapter VII

Agafea Mihalovna went out on tiptoe; the nurse let down the blind, chased a fly out from under the muslin canopy of the crib, and a bumblebee struggling on the window-frame, and sat down waving a faded branch of birch over the mother and the baby.

"How hot it is! if God would send a drop of rain," she said.

"Yes, yes, sh—sh—sh—" was all Kitty answered, rocking a little, and tenderly squeezing the plump little arm, with rolls of fat at the wrist, which Mitya still waved feebly as he opened and shut his eyes. That hand worried Kitty; she longed to kiss the little hand, but was afraid to for fear of waking the baby. At last the little hand ceased waving, and the eyes closed. Only from time to time, as he went on sucking, the baby raised his long, curly eyelashes and peeped at his mother with wet eyes, that looked black in the twilight. The nurse had left off fanning, and was dozing. From above came the peals of the old prince's voice, and the chuckle of Katavasov.

"They have got into talk without me," thought Kitty, "but still it's vexing that Kostya's out. He's sure to have gone to the bee house again. Though it's a pity he's there so often, still I'm glad. It distracts his mind. He's become altogether happier and better now than in the spring. He used to be so gloomy and worried that I felt frightened for him. And how absurd he is!" she whispered, smiling.

She knew what worried her husband. It was his unbelief. Although, if she had been asked whether she supposed that in the future life, if he did not believe, he would be damned, she would have had to admit that he would be damned, his unbelief did not cause her unhappiness. And she, confessing that for an unbeliever there can be no salvation, and loving her husband's soul more than anything in the world, thought with a smile of his unbelief, and told herself that he was absurd.

"What does he keep reading philosophy of some sort for all this year?" she wondered. "If it's all written in those books, he can understand them. If it's all wrong, why does he read them? He says himself that he would like to believe. Then why is it he doesn't believe? Surely from his thinking so much? And he thinks so much from being solitary. He's always alone, alone. He can't talk about it all to us. I fancy he'll be glad of these visitors, especially Katavasov. He likes discussions with them," she thought, and passed instantly to the consideration of where it would be more convenient to put Katavasov, to sleep alone or to share Sergey Ivanovitch's room. And then an idea suddenly struck her, which made her shudder and even disturb Mitya, who glanced severely at her. "I do believe the laundress hasn't sent the washing yet, and all the best sheets are in use. If I don't see to it, Agafea Mihalovna will give Sergey Ivanovitch the wrong sheets," and at the very idea of this the blood rushed to Kitty's face.

"Yes, I will arrange it," she decided, and going back to her former thoughts, she remembered that some spiritual question of importance had been interrupted, and she began to recall what. "Yes, Kostya, an unbeliever," she thought again with a smile.

"Well, an unbeliever then! Better let him always be one than like Madame Stahl, or what I tried to be in those days abroad. No, he won't ever sham anything."

And a recent instance of his goodness rose vividly to her mind. A fortnight ago a penitent letter had come from Stepan Arkadyevitch to Dolly. He besought her to save his honor, to sell her estate to pay his debts. Dolly was in despair, she detested her husband, despised him, pitied him, resolved on a separation, resolved to refuse, but ended by agreeing to sell part of her property. After that, with an irrepressible smile of tenderness, Kitty recalled her husband's shamefaced embarrassment, his repeated awkward efforts to approach the subject, and how at last, having thought of the one means of helping Dolly without wounding her pride, he had suggested to Kitty—what had not occurred to her before—that she should give up her share of the property.

"He an unbeliever indeed! With his heart, his dread of offending anyone, even a child! Everything for others, nothing for himself. Sergey Ivanovitch simply considers it as Kostya's duty to be his steward. And it's the same with his sister. Now Dolly and her children are under his guardianship; all these peasants who come to him everyday, as though he were bound to be at their service."

"Yes, only be like your father, only like him," she said, handing Mitya over to the nurse, and putting her lips to his cheek.

Chapter VIII

EVER SINCE, BY HIS BELOVED BROTHER'S DEATHBED, LEVIN HAD FIRST GLANCED INTO THE QUEStions of life and death in the light of these new convictions, as he called them, which had during the period from his twentieth to his thirty-fourth year imperceptibly replaced his childish and youthful beliefs—he had been stricken with horror, not so much of death, as of life, without any knowledge of whence, and why, and how, and what it was. The physical organization, its decay, the indestructibility of matter, the law of the conservation of energy, evolution, were the words which usurped the place of his old belief. These words and the ideas associated with them were very well for intellectual purposes. But for life they yielded nothing, and Levin felt suddenly like a man who has changed his warm fur cloak for a muslin garment, and going for the first time into the frost is immediately convinced, not by reason, but by his whole nature that he is as good as naked, and that he must infallibly perish miserably.

From that moment, though he did not distinctly face it, and still went on living as before, Levin had never lost this sense of terror at his lack of knowledge.

He vaguely felt, too, that what he called his new convictions were not merely lack of knowledge, but that they were part of a whole order of ideas, in which no knowledge of what he needed was possible.

At first, marriage, with the new joys and duties bound up with it, had completely crowded out these thoughts. But of late, while he was staying in Moscow after his wife's confinement, with nothing to do, the question that clamored for solution had more and more often, more and more insistently, haunted Levin's mind.

The question was summed up for him thus: "If I do not accept the answers Christianity gives to the problems of my life, what answers do I accept?" And in the whole arsenal of his convictions, so far from finding any satisfactory answers, he was utterly unable to find anything at all like an answer.

He was in the position of a man seeking food in toy shops and tool shops.

Instinctively, unconsciously, with every book, with every conversation, with every man he met, he was on the lookout for light on these questions and their solution.

What puzzled and distracted him above everything was that the majority of men of his age and circle had, like him, exchanged their old beliefs for the same new convictions, and yet saw nothing to lament in this, and were perfectly satisfied and serene. So that, apart from the principal question, Levin was tortured by other questions too. Were these people sincere? he asked himself, or were they playing a part? or was it that they understood the answers science gave to these problems in some different, clearer sense than he did? And he assiduously studied both these men's opinions and the books which treated of these scientific explanations.

One fact he had found out since these questions had engrossed his mind, was that he had been quite wrong in supposing from the recollections of the circle of his young days at college, that religion had outlived its day, and that it was now practically non-existent. All the people nearest to him who were good in their lives were believers. The old prince, and Lvov, whom he liked so much, and Sergey Ivanovitch, and all the women believed, and his wife believed as simply as he had believed in his earliest childhood, and ninety-nine hundredths of the Russian people, all the working people for whose life he felt the deepest respect, believed.

Another fact of which he became convinced, after reading many scientific books, was that the men who shared his views had no other construction to put on them, and that they gave no explanation of the questions which he felt he could not live without answering, but simply ignored their existence and attempted to explain other questions of no possible interest to him, such as the evolution of organisms, the materialistic theory of consciousness, and so forth.

Moreover, during his wife's confinement, something had happened that seemed extraordinary to him. He, an unbeliever, had fallen into praying, and at the moment he prayed, he believed. But that moment had passed, and he could not make his state of mind at that moment fit into the rest of his life.

He could not admit that at that moment he knew the truth, and that now he was wrong; for as soon as he began thinking calmly about it, it all fell to pieces. He could not admit that he was mistaken then, for his spiritual condition then was precious to him, and to admit that it was a proof of weakness would have been to desecrate those moments. He was miserably divided against himself, and strained all his spiritual forces to the utmost to escape from this condition.

Chapter IX

THESE DOUBTS FRETTED AND HARASSED HIM, GROWING WEAKER OR STRONGER FROM TIME TO time, but never leaving him. He read and thought, and the more he read and the more he thought, the further he felt from the aim he was pursuing.

Of late in Moscow and in the country, since he had become convinced that he would find no solution in the materialists, he had read and re-read thoroughly Plato, Spinoza, Kant, Schelling, Hegel, and Schopenhauer, the philosophers who gave a non-materialistic explanation of life.

Their ideas seemed to him fruitful when he was reading or was himself seeking arguments to refute other theories, especially those of the materialists; but as soon as he began to read or sought for himself a solution of problems, the same thing always happened. As long as he followed the fixed definition of obscure words such as *spirit, will, freedom, essence,* purposely letting himself go into the snare of words the philosophers set for him, he seemed to comprehend something. But he had only to forget the artificial train of reasoning, and to turn from life itself to what had satisfied him while thinking in accordance with the fixed definitions, and all this artificial edifice fell to pieces at once like a house of cards, and it became clear that the edifice had been built up out of those transposed words, apart from anything in life more important than reason.

At one time, reading Schopenhauer, he put in place of his *will* the word *love,* and for a couple of days this new philosophy charmed him, till he removed a little away from it. But then, when he turned from life itself to glance at it again, it fell away too, and proved to be the same muslin garment with no warmth in it.

His brother Sergey Ivanovitch advised him to read the theological works of Homiakov. Levin read the second volume of Homiakov's works, and in spite of the elegant, epigrammatic, argumentative style which at first repelled him, he was impressed by the doctrine of the church he found in them. He was struck at first by the idea that the apprehension of divine truths had not been vouchsafed to man, but to a corporation of men bound together by love—to the church. What delighted him was the thought how much easier it was to believe in a still existing living church, embracing all the beliefs of men, and having God at its head, and therefore holy and infallible, and from it to accept the faith in God, in the creation, the fall, the redemption, than to begin with God, a mysterious, far-away God, the creation, etc. But afterwards, on reading a Catholic writer's history of the church, and then a Greek orthodox writer's history of the church, and seeing that the two churches, in their very conception infallible, each deny the authority of the other, Homiakov's doctrine of the church lost all its charm for him, and this edifice crumbled into dust like the philosophers' edifices.

All that spring he was not himself, and went through fearful moments of horror.

"Without knowing what I am and why I am here, life's impossible; and that I can't know, and so I can't live," Levin said to himself.

"In infinite time, in infinite matter, in infinite space, is formed a bubble-organism, and that bubble lasts a while and bursts, and that bubble is Me."

It was an agonizing error, but it was the sole logical result of ages of human thought in that direction.

This was the ultimate belief on which all the systems elaborated by human thought in almost all their ramifications rested. It was the prevalent conviction, and of all other explanations Levin had unconsciously, not knowing when or how, chosen it, as anyway the clearest, and made it his own.

But it was not merely a falsehood, it was the cruel jeer of some wicked power, some evil, hateful power, to whom one could not submit.

He must escape from this power. And the means of escape every man had in his own hands. He had but to cut short this dependence on evil. And there was one means—death.

And Levin, a happy father and husband, in perfect health, was several times so near suicide that he hid the cord that he might not be tempted to hang himself, and was afraid to go out with his gun for fear of shooting himself.

But Levin did not shoot himself, and did not hang himself; he went on living.

Chapter X

WHEN LEVIN THOUGHT WHAT HE WAS AND WHAT HE WAS LIVING FOR, HE COULD FIND NO ANswer to the questions and was reduced to despair, but he left off questioning himself about it. It seemed as though he knew both what he was and for what he was living, for he acted and lived resolutely and without hesitation. Indeed, in these latter days he was far more decided and unhesitating in life than he had ever been.

When he went back to the country at the beginning of June, he went back also to his usual pursuits. The management of the estate, his relations with the peasants and the neighbors, the care of his household, the management of his sister's and brother's property, of which he had the direction, his relations with his wife and kindred, the care of his child, and the new bee-keeping hobby he had taken up that spring, filled all his time.

These things occupied him now, not because he justified them to himself by any sort of general principles, as he had done in former days; on the contrary, disappointed by the failure of his former efforts for the general welfare, and too much occupied with his own thought and the mass of business with which he was burdened from all sides, he had completely given up thinking of the general good, and he busied himself with all this work simply because it seemed to him that he must do what he was doing—that he could not do otherwise. In former days—almost from childhood, and increasingly up to full manhood—when he had tried to do anything that would be good for all, for humanity, for Russia, for the whole village, he had noticed that the idea of it had been pleasant, but the work itself had always been incoherent, that then he had never had a full conviction of its absolute necessity, and that the work that had begun by seeming so great, had grown less and less, till it vanished into nothing. But now, since his marriage, when he had begun to confine himself more and more to living for himself, though he experienced no delight at all at the thought of the work he was doing, he felt a complete conviction of its necessity, saw that it succeeded far better than in old days, and that it kept on growing more and more.

Now, involuntarily it seemed, he cut more and more deeply into the soil like a plough, so that he could not be drawn out without turning aside the furrow.

To live the same family life as his father and forefathers—that is, in the same condition of culture—and to bring up his children in the same, was incontestably necessary. It was as necessary as dining when one was hungry. And to do this, just as it was necessary to cook dinner, it was necessary to keep the mechanism of agriculture at Pokrovskoe going so as to yield an income. Just as incontestably as it was necessary to repay a debt was it necessary to keep the property in such a condition that his son, when he received it as a heritage, would say "thank you" to his father as Levin had said "thank you" to his grandfather for all he built and planted. And to do this it was necessary to look after the land himself, not to let it, and to breed cattle, manure the fields, and plant timber.

It was impossible not to look after the affairs of Sergey Ivanovitch, of his sister, of the peasants who came to him for advice and were accustomed to do so—as impossible as to fling down a child one is carrying in one's arms. It was necessary to look after the comfort of his sister-in-law and her children, and of his wife and baby, and it was impossible not to spend with them at least a short time each day.

And all this, together with shooting and his new bee-keeping, filled up the whole of Levin's life, which had no meaning at all for him, when he began to think.

But besides knowing thoroughly what he had to do, Levin knew in just the same way *how* he had to do it all, and what was more important than the rest.

He knew he must hire laborers as cheaply as possible; but to hire men under bond, paying them in advance at less than the current rate of wages, was what he must not do, even though it was very profitable. Selling straw to the peasants in times of scarcity of provender was what he might do, even though he felt sorry for them; but the tavern and the pothouse must be put down, though they were a source of income. Felling timber must be punished as severely as possible, but he could not exact forfeits for cattle being driven onto his fields; and though it annoyed the keeper and made the peasants not afraid to graze their cattle on his land, he could not keep their cattle as a punishment.

To Pyotr, who was paying a money-lender 10 per cent. a month, he must lend a sum of money to set him free. But he could not let off peasants who did not pay their rent, nor let them fall into arrears. It was impossible to overlook the bailiff's not having mown the meadows and letting the hay spoil; and it was equally impossible to mow those acres where a young copse had been planted. It was impossible to excuse a laborer who had gone home in the busy season because his father was dying, however sorry he might feel for him, and he must subtract from his pay those costly months of idleness. But it was impossible not to allow monthly rations to the old servants who were of no use for anything.

Levin knew that when he got home he must first of all go to his wife, who was unwell, and that the peasants who had been waiting for three hours to see him could wait a little longer. He knew too that, regardless of all the pleasure he felt in taking a swarm, he must forego that pleasure, and leave the old man to see to the bees alone, while he talked to the peasants who had come after him to the bee house.

Whether he were acting rightly or wrongly he did not know, and far from trying to prove that he was, nowadays he avoided all thought or talk about it.

Reasoning had brought him to doubt, and prevented him from seeing what he ought to do and what he ought not. When he did not think, but simply lived, he was continually aware of the presence of an infallible judge in his soul, determining which of two possible courses of action was the better and which was the worse, and as soon as he did not act rightly, he was at once aware of it.

So he lived, not knowing and not seeing any chance of knowing what he was and what he was living for, and harassed at this lack of knowledge to such a point that he was afraid of suicide, and yet firmly laying down his own individual definite path in life.

Chapter XI

The day on which Sergey Ivanovitch came to Pokrovskoe was one of Levin's most painful days. It was the very busiest working time, when all the peasantry show an extraordinary intensity of self-sacrifice in labor, such as is never shown in any other conditions of life, and would be highly esteemed if the men who showed these qualities themselves thought highly of them, and if it were not repeated every year, and if the results of this intense labor were not so simple.

To reap and bind the rye and oats and to carry it, to mow the meadows, turn over the fallows, thrash the seed and sow the winter corn—all this seems so simple and ordinary; but to succeed in getting through it all everyone in the village, from the old man to the young child, must toil incessantly for three or four weeks, three times as hard as usual, living on rye-beer, onions, and black bread, thrashing and carrying the sheaves at night, and not giving more than two or three hours in the twenty-four to sleep. And every year this is done all over Russia.

Having lived the greater part of his life in the country and in the closest relations with the peasants, Levin always felt in this busy time that he was infected by this general quickening of energy in the people.

In the early morning he rode over to the first sowing of the rye, and to the oats, which were being carried to the stacks, and returning home at the time his wife and sister-in-law were getting up, he drank coffee with them and walked to the farm, where a new threshing machine was to be set working to get ready the seed-corn.

He was standing in the cool granary, still fragrant with the leaves of the hazel branches interlaced on the freshly peeled aspen beams of the new thatch roof. He gazed through the open door in which the dry bitter dust of the thrashing whirled and played, at the grass of the threshing floor in the sunlight and the fresh straw that had been brought in from the barn, then at the speckly-headed, white-breasted swallows that flew chirping in under the roof and, fluttering their wings, settled in the crevices of the doorway, then at the peasants bustling in the dark, dusty barn, and he thought strange thoughts.

"Why is it all being done?" he thought. "Why am I standing here, making them work? What are they all so busy for, trying to show their zeal before me? What is that old Matrona, my old friend, toiling for? (I doctored her, when the beam fell on her in the fire)" he thought, looking at a thin old woman who was raking up the grain, moving painfully with her bare, sun-blackened feet over the uneven, rough floor. "Then she recovered, but today or tomorrow or in ten years she won't; they'll bury her, and nothing will be left either of her or of that smart girl in the red jacket, who with that skillful, soft action shakes the ears out of their husks. They'll bury her and this piebald horse, and very soon too," he thought, gazing at the heavily moving, panting horse that kept walking up the wheel that turned under him. "And they will bury her and Fyodor the thrasher with his curly beard full of chaff and his shirt torn on his white shoulders—they will bury him. He's untying the sheaves, and giving orders, and shouting to the women, and quickly setting straight the strap on the moving wheel. And what's more, it's not them alone—me they'll bury too, and nothing will be left. What for?"

He thought this, and at the same time looked at his watch to reckon how much they thrashed in an hour. He wanted to know this so as to judge by it the task to set for the day.

"It'll soon be one, and they're only beginning the third sheaf," thought Levin. He went up to the man that was feeding the machine, and shouting over the roar of the machine he told him to put it in more slowly. "You put in too much at a time, Fyodor. Do you see—it gets choked, that's why it isn't getting on. Do it evenly."

Fyodor, black with the dust that clung to his moist face, shouted something in response, but still went on doing it as Levin did not want him to.

Levin, going up to the machine, moved Fyodor aside, and began feeding the corn in himself. Working on till the peasants' dinner hour, which was not long in coming, he went out of the barn with Fyodor and fell into talk with him, stopping beside a neat yellow sheaf of rye laid on the threshing floor for seed.

Fyodor came from a village at some distance from the one in which Levin had once allotted land to his cooperative association. Now it had been let to a former house-porter.

Levin talked to Fyodor about this land and asked whether Platon, a well-to-do peasant of good character belonging to the same village, would not take the land for the coming year.

"It's a high rent; it wouldn't pay Platon, Konstantin Dmitrievitch," answered the peasant, picking the ears off his sweat-drenched shirt.

"But how does Kirillov make it pay?"

"Mituh!" (so the peasant called the house-porter, in a tone of contempt), "you may be sure he'll make it pay, Konstantin Dmitrievitch! He'll get his share, however he has to squeeze to get it! He's no mercy on a Christian. But Uncle Fokanitch" (so he called the old peasant Platon), "do you suppose he'd flay the skin off a man? Where there's debt, he'll let anyone off. And he'll not wring the last penny out. He's a man too."

"But why will he let anyone off?"

"Oh, well, of course, folks are different. One man lives for his own wants and nothing else, like Mituh, he only thinks of filling his belly, but Fokanitch is a righteous man. He lives for his soul. He does not forget God."

"How thinks of God? How does he live for his soul?" Levin almost shouted.

"Why, to be sure, in truth, in God's way. Folks are different. Take you now, you wouldn't wrong a man. . . ."

"Yes, yes, good-bye!" said Levin, breathless with excitement, and turning round he took his stick and walked quickly away towards home. At the peasant's words that Fokanitch lived for his soul, in truth, in God's way, undefined but significant ideas seemed to burst out as though they had been locked up, and all striving towards one goal, they thronged whirling through his head, blinding him with their light.

Chapter XII

LEVIN STRODE ALONG THE HIGHROAD, ABSORBED NOT SO MUCH IN HIS THOUGHTS (HE COULD NOT yet disentangle them) as in his spiritual condition, unlike anything he had experienced before.

The words uttered by the peasant had acted on his soul like an electric shock, suddenly transforming and combining into a single whole the whole swarm of disjointed, impotent, separate thoughts that incessantly occupied his mind. These thoughts had unconsciously been in his mind even when he was talking about the land.

He was aware of something new in his soul, and joyfully tested this new thing, not yet knowing what it was.

"Not living for his own wants, but for God? For what God? And could one say anything more senseless than what he said? He said that one must not live for one's own wants, that is, that one must not live for what we understand, what we are attracted by, what we desire, but must live for something incomprehensible, for God, whom no one can understand nor even define. What of it? Didn't I understand those senseless words of Fyodor's? And understanding them, did I doubt of their truth? Did I think them stupid, obscure, inexact? No, I understood him, and exactly as he understands the words. I understood them more fully and clearly than I understand anything in life, and never in my life have I doubted nor can I doubt about it. And not only I, but everyone, the whole world understands nothing fully but this, and about this only they have no doubt and are always agreed.

"And I looked out for miracles, complained that I did not see a miracle which would convince me. A material miracle would have persuaded me. And here is a miracle, the sole miracle possible, continually existing, surrounding me on all sides, and I never noticed it!

"Fyodor says that Kirillov lives for his belly. That's comprehensible and rational. All of us as rational beings can't do anything else but live for our belly. And all of a sudden the same Fyodor says that one mustn't live for one's belly, but must live for truth, for God, and at a hint I understand him! And I and millions of men, men who lived ages ago and men living now—peasants, the poor in spirit and the learned, who have thought and written about it, in their obscure words saying the same thing—we are all agreed about this one thing: what we must live for and what is good. I and all men have only one firm, incontestable, clear knowledge, and that knowledge cannot be explained by the reason—it is outside it, and has no causes and can have no effects.

"If goodness has causes, it is not goodness; if it has effects, a reward, it is not goodness either. So goodness is outside the chain of cause and effect.

"And yet I know it, and we all know it.

"What could be a greater miracle than that?

"Can I have found the solution of it all? can my sufferings be over?" thought Levin, striding along the dusty road, not noticing the heat nor his weariness, and experiencing a sense of relief from prolonged suffering. This feeling was so delicious that it seemed to him incredible. He was breathless with emotion and incapable of going farther; he turned off the road into the forest and lay down in the shade of an aspen on the uncut grass. He took his hat off his hot head and lay propped on his elbow in the lush, feathery, woodland grass.

"Yes, I must make it clear to myself and understand," he thought, looking intently at the untrampled grass before him, and following the movements of a green beetle, advancing along a blade of couch-grass and lifting up in its progress a leaf of goat-weed. "What have I discovered?" he asked himself, bending aside the leaf of goat-weed out of the beetle's way and twisting another blade of grass above for the beetle to cross over onto it. "What is it makes me glad? What have I discovered?

"I have discovered nothing. I have only found out what I knew. I understand the force that in the past gave me life, and now too gives me life. I have been set free from falsity, I have found the Master.

"Of old I used to say that in my body, that in the body of this grass and of this beetle (there, she didn't care for the grass, she's opened her wings and flown away), there was going on a transformation of matter in accordance with physical, chemical, and physiological laws. And in all of us, as well as in the aspens and the clouds and the misty patches, there was a process of evolution. Evolution from what? into what?—Eternal evolution and struggle. . . . As though there could be any sort of tendency and struggle in the eternal! And I was astonished that in spite of the utmost effort of thought along that road I could not discover the meaning of life, the meaning of my impulses and yearnings. Now I say that I know the meaning of my life: 'To live for God, for my soul.' And this meaning, in spite of its clearness, is mysterious and marvelous. Such, indeed, is the meaning of everything existing. Yes, pride," he said to himself, turning over on his stomach and beginning to tie a noose of blades of grass, trying not to break them.

"And not merely pride of intellect, but dulness of intellect. And most of all, the deceitfulness; yes, the deceitfulness of intellect. The cheating knavishness of intellect, that's it," he said to himself.

And he briefly went through, mentally, the whole course of his ideas during the last two years, the beginning of which was the clear confronting of death at the sight of his dear brother hopelessly ill.

Then, for the first time, grasping that for every man, and himself too, there was nothing in store but suffering, death, and forgetfulness, he had made up his mind that life was impossible like that, and that he must either interpret life so that it would not present itself to him as the evil jest of some devil, or shoot himself.

But he had not done either, but had gone on living, thinking, and feeling, and had even at that very time married, and had had many joys and had been happy, when he was not thinking of the meaning of his life.

What did this mean? It meant that he had been living rightly, but thinking wrongly.

He had lived (without being aware of it) on those spiritual truths that he had sucked in with his mother's milk, but he had thought, not merely without recognition of these truths, but studiously ignoring them.

Now it was clear to him that he could only live by virtue of the beliefs in which he had been brought up.

"What should I have been, and how should I have spent my life, if I had not had these beliefs, if I had not known that I must live for God and not for my own desires? I should have robbed and lied and killed. Nothing of what makes the chief happiness of my life would have existed for me." And with the utmost stretch of imagination he could not conceive the brutal creature he would have been himself, if he had not known what he was living for.

"I looked for an answer to my question. And thought could not give an answer to my question—it is incommensurable with my question. The answer has been given me by life itself, in my knowledge of what is right and what is wrong. And that knowledge I did not arrive at in any way, it was given to me as to all men, *given,* because I could not have got it from anywhere.

"Where could I have got it? By reason could I have arrived at knowing that I must love my neighbor and not oppress him? I was told that in my childhood, and I believed it gladly, for they told me what was already in my soul. But who discovered it? Not reason. Reason discovered the struggle for existence, and the law that requires us to oppress all who hinder the satisfaction of our desires. That is the deduction of reason. But loving one's neighbor reason could never discover, because it's irrational."

Chapter XIII

AND LEVIN REMEMBERED A SCENE HE HAD LATELY WITNESSED BETWEEN DOLLY AND HER CHILdren. The children, left to themselves, had begun cooking raspberries over the candles and squirting milk into each other's mouths with a syringe. Their mother, catching them at these pranks, began reminding them in Levin's presence of the trouble their mischief gave to the grown-up people, and that this trouble was all for their sake, and that if they smashed the cups they would have nothing to drink their tea out of, and that if they wasted the milk, they would have nothing to eat, and die of hunger.

And Levin had been struck by the passive, weary incredulity with which the children heard what their mother said to them. They were simply annoyed that their amusing play had been interrupted, and did not believe a word of what their mother was saying. They could not believe it indeed, for they could not take in the immensity of all they habitually enjoyed, and so could not conceive that what they were destroying was the very thing they lived by.

"That all comes of itself," they thought, "and there's nothing interesting or important about it because it has always been so, and always will be so. And it's all always the same. We've no need to think about that, it's all ready. But we want to invent something of our own, and new. So we thought of putting raspberries in a cup, and cooking them over a candle, and squirting milk straight into each other's mouths. That's fun, and something new, and not a bit worse than drinking out of cups."

"Isn't it just the same that we do, that I did, searching by the aid of reason for the significance of the forces of nature and the meaning of the life of man?" he thought.

"And don't all the theories of philosophy do the same, trying by the path of thought, which is strange and not natural to man, to bring him to a knowledge of what he has known long ago, and knows so certainly that he could not live at all without it? Isn't it distinctly to be seen in the development of each philosopher's theory, that he knows what is the chief significance of life beforehand, just as positively as the peasant Fyodor, and not a bit more clearly than he, and is simply trying by a dubious intellectual path to come back to what everyone knows?

"Now then, leave the children to themselves to get things alone and make their crockery, get the milk from the cows, and so on. Would they be naughty then? Why, they'd die of hunger! Well, then, leave us with our passions and thoughts, without any idea of the one God, of the Creator, or without any idea of what is right, without any idea of moral evil.

"Just try and build up anything without those ideas!

"We only try to destroy them, because we're spiritually provided for. Exactly like the children!

"Whence have I that joyful knowledge, shared with the peasant, that alone gives peace to my soul? Whence did I get it?

"Brought up with an idea of God, a Christian, my whole life filled with the spiritual blessings Christianity has given me, full of them, and living on those blessings, like the children I did not understand them, and destroy, that is try to destroy, what I live by. And as soon as an important moment of life comes, like the children when they are cold and hungry, I turn to Him, and even less than the children when their mother scolds them for their childish mischief, do I feel that my childish efforts at wanton madness are reckoned against me.

"Yes, what I know, I know not by reason, but it has been given to me, revealed to me, and I know it with my heart, by faith in the chief thing taught by the church.

"The church! the church!" Levin repeated to himself. He turned over on the other side, and leaning on his elbow, fell to gazing into the distance at a herd of cattle crossing over to the river.

"But can I believe in all the church teaches?" he thought, trying himself, and thinking of everything that could destroy his present peace of mind. Intentionally he recalled all those doctrines of the church which had always seemed most strange and had always been a stumbling block to him.

"The Creation? But how did I explain existence? By existence? By nothing? The devil and sin. But how do I explain evil? . . . The atonement? . . .

"But I know nothing, nothing, and I can know nothing but what has been told to me and all men."

And it seemed to him that there was not a single article of faith of the church which could destroy the chief thing—faith in God, in goodness, as the one goal of man's destiny.

Under every article of faith of the church could be put the faith in the service of truth instead of one's desires. And each doctrine did not simply leave that faith unshaken, each doctrine seemed essential to complete that great miracle, continually manifest upon earth, that made it possible for each man and millions of different sorts of men, wise men and imbeciles, old men and children—all men, peasants, Lvov, Kitty, beggars and kings to understand perfectly the same one thing, and to build up thereby that life of the soul which alone is worth living, and which alone is precious to us.

Lying on his back, he gazed up now into the high, cloudless sky. "Do I not know that that is infinite space, and that it is not a round arch? But, however I screw up my eyes and strain my sight, I cannot see it not round and not bounded, and in spite of my knowing about infinite space, I am incontestably right when I see a solid blue dome, and more right than when I strain my eyes to see beyond it."

Levin ceased thinking, and only, as it were, listened to mysterious voices that seemed talking joyfully and earnestly within him.

"Can this be faith?" he thought, afraid to believe in his happiness. "My God, I thank Thee!" he said, gulping down his sobs, and with both hands brushing away the tears that filled his eyes.

Chapter XIV

LEVIN LOOKED BEFORE HIM AND SAW A HERD OF CATTLE, THEN HE CAUGHT SIGHT OF HIS TRAP with Raven in the shafts, and the coachman, who, driving up to the herd, said something to the herdsman. Then he heard the rattle of the wheels and the snort of the sleek horse close by him. But he was so buried in his thoughts that he did not even wonder why the coachman had come for him.

He only thought of that when the coachman had driven quite up to him and shouted to him. "The mistress sent me. Your brother has come, and some gentleman with him."

Levin got into the trap and took the reins. As though just roused out of sleep, for a long while Levin could not collect his faculties. He stared at the sleek horse flecked with lather between his haunches and on his neck, where the harness rubbed, stared at Ivan the coachman sitting beside him, and remembered that he was expecting his brother, thought that his wife was most likely uneasy at his long absence, and tried to guess who was the visitor who had come with his brother. And his brother and his wife and the unknown guest seemed to him now quite different from before. He fancied that now his relations with all men would be different.

"With my brother there will be none of that aloofness there always used to be between us, there will be no disputes; with Kitty there shall never be quarrels; with the visitor, whoever he may be, I will be friendly and nice; with the servants, with Ivan, it will all be different."

Pulling the stiff rein and holding in the good horse that snorted with impatience and seemed begging to be let go, Levin looked round at Ivan sitting beside him, not knowing what to do with his unoccupied hand, continually pressing down his shirt as it puffed out, and he tried to find something to start a conversation about with him. He would have said that Ivan had pulled the saddle-girth up too high, but that was like blame, and he longed for friendly, warm talk. Nothing else occurred to him.

"Your honor must keep to the right and mind that stump," said the coachman, pulling the rein Levin held.

"Please don't touch and don't teach me!" said Levin, angered by this interference. Now, as always, interference made him angry, and he felt sorrowfully at once how mistaken had been his supposition that his spiritual condition could immediately change him in contact with reality.

He was not a quarter of a mile from home when he saw Grisha and Tanya running to meet him.

"Uncle Kostya! mamma's coming, and grandfather, and Sergey Ivanovitch, and someone else," they said, clambering up into the trap.

"Who is he?"

"An awfully terrible person! And he does like this with his arms," said Tanya, getting up in the trap and mimicking Katavasov.

"Old or young?" asked Levin, laughing, reminded of someone, he did not know whom, by Tanya's performance.

"Oh, I hope it's not a tiresome person!" thought Levin.

As soon as he turned, at a bend in the road, and saw the party coming, Levin recognized Katavasov in a straw hat, walking along swinging his arms just as Tanya had shown him. Katavasov was very fond of discussing metaphysics, having derived his notions from natural science writers who had never studied metaphysics, and in Moscow Levin had had many arguments with him of late.

And one of these arguments, in which Katavasov had obviously considered that he came off victorious, was the first thing Levin thought of as he recognized him.

"No, whatever I do, I won't argue and give utterance to my ideas lightly," he thought.

Getting out of the trap and greeting his brother and Katavasov, Levin asked about his wife.

"She has taken Mitya to Kolok" (a copse near the house). "She meant to have him out there because it's so hot indoors," said Dolly. Levin had always advised his wife not to take the baby to the wood, thinking it unsafe, and he was not pleased to hear this.

"She rushes about from place to place with him," said the prince, smiling. "I advised her to try putting him in the ice cellar."

"She meant to come to the bee house. She thought you would be there. We are going there," said Dolly.

"Well, and what are you doing?" said Sergey Ivanovitch, falling back from the rest and walking beside him.

"Oh, nothing special. Busy as usual with the land," answered Levin. "Well, and what about you? Come for long? We have been expecting you for such a long time."

"Only for a fortnight. I've a great deal to do in Moscow."

At these words the brothers' eyes met, and Levin, in spite of the desire he always had, stronger than ever just now, to be on affectionate and still more open terms with his brother, felt an awkwardness in looking at him. He dropped his eyes and did not know what to say.

Casting over the subjects of conversation that would be pleasant to Sergey Ivanovitch, and would keep him off the subject of the Servian war and the Slavonic question, at which he had hinted by the allusion to what he had to do in Moscow, Levin began to talk of Sergey Ivanovitch's book.

"Well, have there been reviews of your book?" he asked.

Sergey Ivanovitch smiled at the intentional character of the question.

"No one is interested in that now, and I less than anyone," he said. "Just look, Darya Alexandrovna, we shall have a shower," he added, pointing with a sunshade at the white rain clouds that showed above the aspen tree-tops.

And these words were enough to re-establish again between the brothers that tone—hardly hostile, but chilly—which Levin had been so longing to avoid.

Levin went up to Katavasov.

"It was jolly of you to make up your mind to come," he said to him.

"I've been meaning to a long while. Now we shall have some discussion, we'll see to that. Have you been reading Spencer?"

"No, I've not finished reading him," said Levin. "But I don't need him now."

"How's that? that's interesting. Why so?"

"I mean that I'm fully convinced that the solution of the problems that interest me I shall never find in him and his like. Now . . ."

But Katavasov's serene and good-humored expression suddenly struck him, and he felt such tenderness for his own happy mood, which he was unmistakably disturbing by this conversation, that he remembered his resolution and stopped short.

"But we'll talk later on," he added. "If we're going to the bee house, it's this way, along this little path," he said, addressing them all.

Going along the narrow path to a little uncut meadow covered on one side with thick clumps of brilliant heart's-ease among which stood up here and there tall, dark green tufts of hellebore, Levin settled his guests in the dense, cool shade of the young aspens on a bench and some stumps purposely put there for visitors to the bee house who might be afraid of the bees, and he went off himself to the hut to get bread, cucumbers, and fresh honey, to regale them with.

Trying to make his movements as deliberate as possible, and listening to the bees that buzzed more and more frequently past him, he walked along the little path to the hut. In the very entry one bee hummed angrily, caught in his beard, but he carefully extricated it. Going into the shady outer room, he took down from the wall his veil, that hung on a peg, and putting it on, and thrusting his hands into his pockets, he went into the fenced-in bee-garden, where there stood in the midst of a closely mown space in regular rows, fastened with bast on posts, all the hives he knew so well, the old stocks, each with its own history, and along the fences the younger swarms hived that year. In front of the openings of the hives, it made his eyes giddy to watch the bees and drones whirling round and round about the same spot, while among them the working bees flew in and out with spoils or in search of them, always in the same direction into the wood to the flowering lime trees and back to the hives.

His ears were filled with the incessant hum in various notes, now the busy hum of the working bee flying quickly off, then the blaring of the lazy drone, and the excited buzz of the bees on guard protecting their property from the enemy and preparing to sting. On the farther side of the fence the old beekeeper was shaving a hoop for a tub, and he did not see Levin. Levin stood still in the midst of the beehives and did not call him.

He was glad of a chance to be alone to recover from the influence of ordinary actual life, which had already depressed his happy mood. He thought that he had already had time to lose his temper with Ivan, to show coolness to his brother, and to talk flippantly with Katavasov.

"Can it have been only a momentary mood, and will it pass and leave no trace?" he thought. But the same instant, going back to his mood, he felt with delight that something new and important had happened to him. Real life had only for a time overcast the spiritual peace he had found, but it was still untouched within him.

Just as the bees, whirling round him, now menacing him and distracting his attention, prevented him from enjoying complete physical peace, forced him to restrain his movements to avoid them, so had the petty cares that had swarmed about him from the moment he got into the trap restricted his spiritual freedom; but that lasted only so long as he was among them. Just as his bodily strength was still unaffected, in spite of the bees, so too was the spiritual strength that he had just become aware of.

Chapter XV

"Do you know, Kostya, with whom Sergey Ivanovitch traveled on his way here?" said Dolly, doling out cucumbers and honey to the children; "with Vronsky! He's going to Servia."

"And not alone; he's taking a squadron out with him at his own expense," said Katavasov.

"That's the right thing for him," said Levin. "Are volunteers still going out then?" he added, glancing at Sergey Ivanovitch.

Sergey Ivanovitch did not answer. He was carefully with a blunt knife getting a live bee covered with sticky honey out of a cup full of white honeycomb.

"I should think so! You should have seen what was going on at the station yesterday!" said Katavasov, biting with a juicy sound into a cucumber.

"Well, what is one to make of it? For mercy's sake, do explain to me, Sergey Ivanovitch, where are all those volunteers going, whom are they fighting with?" asked the old prince, unmistakably taking up a conversation that had sprung up in Levin's absence.

"With the Turks," Sergey Ivanovitch answered, smiling serenely, as he extricated the bee, dark with honey and helplessly kicking, and put it with the knife on a stout aspen leaf.

"But who has declared war on the Turks?—Ivan Ivanovitch Ragozov and Countess Lidia Ivanovna, assisted by Madame Stahl?"

"No one has declared war, but people sympathize with their neighbors' sufferings and are eager to help them," said Sergey Ivanovitch.

"But the prince is not speaking of help," said Levin, coming to the assistance of his father-in-law, "but of war. The prince says that private persons cannot take part in war without the permission of the government."

"Kostya, mind, that's a bee! Really, they'll sting us!" said Dolly, waving away a wasp.

"But that's not a bee, it's a wasp," said Levin.

"Well now, well, what's your own theory?" Katavasov said to Levin with a smile, distinctly challenging him to a discussion. "Why have not private persons the right to do so?"

"Oh, my theory's this: war is on one side such a beastly, cruel, and awful thing, that no one man, not to speak of a Christian, can individually take upon himself the responsibility of beginning wars; that can only be done by a government, which is called upon to do this, and is driven inevitably into war. On the other hand, both political science and common sense teach us that in matters of state, and especially in the matter of war, private citizens must forego their personal individual will."

Sergey Ivanovitch and Katavasov had their replies ready, and both began speaking at the same time.

"But the point is, my dear fellow, that there may be cases when the government does not carry out the will of the citizens and then the public asserts its will," said Katavasov.

But evidently Sergey Ivanovitch did not approve of this answer. His brows contracted at Katavasov's words and he said something else.

"You don't put the matter in its true light. There is no question here of a declaration of war, but simply the expression of a human Christian feeling. Our brothers, one with us in religion and in race, are being massacred. Even supposing they were not our brothers nor fellow-Christians, but simply children, women, old people, feeling is aroused and Russians go eagerly to help in stopping these atrocities. Fancy, if you were going along the street and saw drunken men beating a woman or a child—I imagine you would not stop to inquire whether war had been declared on the men, but would throw yourself on them, and protect the victim."

"But I should not kill them," said Levin.

"Yes, you would kill them."

"I don't know. If I saw that, I might give way to my impulse of the moment, but I can't say beforehand. And such a momentary impulse there is not, and there cannot be, in the case of the oppression of the Slavonic peoples."

"Possibly for you there is not; but for others there is," said Sergey Ivanovitch, frowning with displeasure. "There are traditions still extant among the people of Slavs of the true faith suffering under the yoke of the 'unclean sons of Hagar.' The people have heard of the sufferings of their brethren and have spoken."

"Perhaps so," said Levin evasively; "but I don't see it. I'm one of the people myself, and I don't feel it."

"Here am I too," said the old prince. "I've been staying abroad and reading the papers, and I must own, up to the time of the Bulgarian atrocities, I couldn't make out why it was all the Russians were all of a sudden so fond of their Slavonic brethren, while I didn't feel the slightest affection for them. I was very much upset, thought I was a monster, or that it was the influence of Carlsbad on me. But since I have been here, my mind's been set at rest. I see that there are people besides me who're only interested in Russia, and not in their Slavonic brethren. Here's Konstantin too."

"Personal opinions mean nothing in such a case," said Sergey Ivanovitch; "it's not a matter of personal opinions when all Russia—the whole people—has expressed its will."

"But excuse me, I don't see that. The people don't know anything about it, if you come to that," said the old prince.

"Oh, papa! . . . how can you say that? And last Sunday in church?" said Dolly, listening to the conversation. "Please give me a cloth," she said to the old man, who was looking at the children with a smile. "Why, it's not possible that all . . ."

"But what was it in church on Sunday? The priest had been told to read that. He read it. They didn't understand a word of it. Then they were told that there was to be a collection for a pious object in church; well, they pulled out their halfpence and gave them, but what for they couldn't say."

"The people cannot help knowing; the sense of their own destinies is always in the people, and at such moments as the present that sense finds utterance," said Sergey Ivanovitch with conviction, glancing at the old beekeeper.

The handsome old man, with black grizzled beard and thick silvery hair, stood motionless, holding a cup of honey, looking down from the height of his tall figure with friendly serenity at the gentlefolk, obviously understanding nothing of their conversation and not caring to understand it.

"That's so, no doubt," he said, with a significant shake of his head at Sergey Ivanovitch's words.

"Here, then, ask him. He knows nothing about it and thinks nothing," said Levin. "Have you heard about the war, Mihalitch?" he said, turning to him. "What they read in the church? What do you think about it? Ought we to fight for the Christians?"

"What should we think? Alexander Nikolaevitch our Emperor has thought for us; he thinks for us indeed in all things. It's clearer for him to see. Shall I bring a bit more bread? Give the little lad some more?" he said addressing Darya Alexandrovna and pointing to Grisha, who had finished his crust.

"I don't need to ask," said Sergey Ivanovitch, "we have seen and are seeing hundreds and hundreds of people who give up everything to serve a just cause, come from every part of Russia, and directly and clearly express their thought and aim. They bring their halfpence or go themselves and say directly what for. What does it mean?"

"It means, to my thinking," said Levin, who was beginning to get warm, "that among eighty millions of people there can always be found not hundreds, as now, but tens of thousands of people who have lost caste, ne'er-do-weels, who are always ready to go anywhere—to Pogatchev's bands, to Khiva, to Serbia . . ."

"I tell you that it's not a case of hundreds or of ne'er-do-weels, but the best representatives of the people!" said Sergey Ivanovitch, with as much irritation as if he were defending the last penny of his fortune. "And what of the subscriptions? In this case it is a whole people directly expressing their will."

"That word 'people' is so vague," said Levin. "Parish clerks, teachers, and one in a thousand of the peasants, maybe, know what it's all about. The rest of the eighty millions, like Mihalitch, far from expressing their will, haven't the faintest idea what there is for them to express their will about. What right have we to say that this is the people's will?"

Chapter XVI

SERGEY IVANOVITCH, BEING PRACTICED IN ARGUMENT, DID NOT REPLY, BUT AT ONCE TURNED THE conversation to another aspect of the subject.

"Oh, if you want to learn the spirit of the people by arithmetical computation, of course it's very difficult to arrive at it. And voting has not been introduced among us and cannot be introduced, for it does not express the will of the people; but there are other ways of reaching that. It is felt in the air, it is felt by the heart. I won't speak of those deep currents which are astir in the still ocean of the people, and which are evident to every unprejudiced man; let us look at society in the narrow sense. All the most diverse sections of the educated public, hostile before, are merged in one. Every division is at an end, all the public organs say the same thing over and over again, all feel the mighty torrent that has overtaken them and is carrying them in one direction."

"Yes, all the newspapers do say the same thing," said the prince. "That's true. But so it is the same thing that all the frogs croak before a storm. One can hear nothing for them."

"Frogs or no frogs, I'm not the editor of a paper and I don't want to defend them; but I am speaking of the unanimity in the intellectual world," said Sergey Ivanovitch, addressing his brother. Levin would have answered, but the old prince interrupted him.

"Well, about that unanimity, that's another thing, one may say," said the prince. "There's my son-in-law, Stepan Arkadyevitch, you know him. He's got a place now on the committee of a commission and something or other, I don't remember. Only there's nothing to do in it—why, Dolly, it's no secret!—and a salary of eight thousand. You try asking him whether his post is of use, he'll prove to you that it's most necessary. And he's a truthful man too, but there's no refusing to believe in the utility of eight thousand roubles."

"Yes, he asked me to give a message to Darya Alexandrovna about the post," said Sergey Ivanovitch reluctantly, feeling the prince's remark to be ill-timed.

"So it is with the unanimity of the press. That's been explained to me: as soon as there's war their incomes are doubled. How can they help believing in the destinies of the people and the Slavonic races . . . and all that?"

"I don't care for many of the papers, but that's unjust," said Sergey Ivanovitch.

"I would only make one condition," pursued the old prince. "Alphonse Karr said a capital thing before the war with Prussia: 'You consider war to be inevitable? Very good. Let everyone who advocates war be enrolled in a special regiment of advance guards, for the front of every storm, of every attack, to lead them all!' "

"A nice lot the editors would make!" said Katavasov, with a loud roar, as he pictured the editors he knew in this picked legion.

"But they'd run," said Dolly, "they'd only be in the way."

"Oh, if they ran away, then we'd have grape-shot or Cossacks with whips behind them," said the prince.

"But that's a joke, and a poor one too, if you'll excuse my saying so, prince," said Sergey Ivanovitch.

"I don't see that it was a joke, that . . ." Levin was beginning, but Sergey Ivanovitch interrupted him.

"Every member of society is called upon to do his own special work," said he. "And men of thought are doing their work when they express public opinion. And the single-hearted and full expression of public opinion is the service of the press and a phenomenon to rejoice us at the same time. Twenty years ago we should have been silent, but now we have heard the voice of the Russian people, which is ready to rise as one man and ready to sacrifice itself for its oppressed brethren; that is a great step and a proof of strength."

"But it's not only making a sacrifice, but killing Turks," said Levin timidly. "The people make sacrifices and are ready to make sacrifices for their soul, but not for murder," he added, instinctively connecting the conversation with the ideas that had been absorbing his mind.

"For their soul? That's a most puzzling expression for a natural science man, do you understand? What sort of thing is the soul?" said Katavasov, smiling.

"Oh, you know!"

"No, by God, I haven't the faintest idea!" said Katavasov with a loud roar of laughter.

" 'I bring not peace, but a sword,' says Christ," Sergey Ivanovitch rejoined for his part, quoting as simply as though it were the easiest thing to understand the very passage that had always puzzled Levin most.

"That's so, no doubt," the old man repeated again. He was standing near them and responded to a chance glance turned in his direction.

"Ah, my dear fellow, you're defeated, utterly defeated!" cried Katavasov good-humoredly.

Levin reddened with vexation, not at being defeated, but at having failed to control himself and being drawn into argument.

"No, I can't argue with them," he thought; "they wear impenetrable armor, while I'm naked."

He saw that it was impossible to convince his brother and Katavasov, and he saw even less possibility of himself agreeing with them. What they advocated was the very pride of intellect that had almost been his ruin. He could not admit that some dozens of men, among them his brother, had the right, on the ground of what they were told by some hundreds of glib volunteers swarming to the capital, to say that they and the newspapers were expressing the will and feeling of the people, and a feeling which was expressed in vengeance and murder. He could not admit this, because he neither saw the expression of such feelings in the people among whom he was living, nor found them in himself (and he could not but consider himself one of the persons making up the Russian people), and most of all because he, like the people, did not know and could not know what is for the general good, though he knew beyond a doubt that this general good could be attained only by the strict observance of that law of right and wrong which has been revealed to every man, and therefore he could not wish for war or advocate war for any general objects whatever. He said as Mihalitch did and the people, who had expressed their feeling in the traditional invitations of the Varyagi: "Be princes and rule over us. Gladly we promise complete submission. All the labor, all humiliations, all sacrifices we take upon ourselves; but we will not judge and decide." And now, according to Sergey Ivanovitch's account, the people had foregone this privilege they had bought at such a costly price.

He wanted to say too that if public opinion were an infallible guide, then why were not revolutions and the commune as lawful as the movement in favor of the Slavonic peoples? But these were merely thoughts that could settle nothing. One thing could be seen beyond doubt—that was that at the actual moment the discussion was irritating Sergey Ivanovitch, and so it was wrong to continue it. And Levin ceased speaking and then called the attention of his guests to the fact that the storm clouds were gathering, and that they had better be going home before it rained.

Chapter XVII

THE OLD PRINCE AND SERGEY IVANOVITCH GOT INTO THE TRAP AND DROVE OFF; THE REST OF the party hastened homewards on foot.

But the storm clouds, turning white and then black, moved down so quickly that they had to quicken their pace to get home before the rain. The foremost clouds, lowering and black as soot-laden smoke, rushed with extraordinary swiftness over the sky. They were still two hundred paces from home and a gust of wind had already blown up, and every second the downpour might be looked for.

The children ran ahead with frightened and gleeful shrieks. Darya Alexandrovna, struggling painfully with her skirts that clung round her legs, was not walking, but running, her eyes fixed on the children. The men of the party, holding their hats on, strode with long steps beside her. They were just at the steps when a big drop fell splashing on the edge of the iron guttering. The children and their elders after them ran into the shelter of the house, talking merrily.

"Katerina Alexandrovna?" Levin asked of Agafea Mihalovna, who met them with kerchiefs and rugs in the hall.

"We thought she was with you," she said.

"And Mitya?"

"In the copse, he must be, and the nurse with him."

Levin snatched up the rugs and ran towards the copse.

In that brief interval of time the storm clouds had moved on, covering the sun so completely that it was dark as an eclipse. Stubbornly, as though insisting on its rights, the wind stopped Levin, and tearing the leaves and flowers off the lime trees and stripping the white birch branches into strange unseemly nakedness, it twisted everything on one side—acacias, flowers, burdocks, long grass, and tall tree-tops. The peasant girls working in the garden ran shrieking into shelter in the servants' quarters. The streaming rain had already flung its white veil over all the distant forest and half the fields close by, and was rapidly swooping down upon the copse. The wet of the rain spurting up in tiny drops could be smelled in the air.

Holding his head bent down before him, and struggling with the wind that strove to tear the wraps away from him, Levin was moving up to the copse and had just caught sight of something white behind the oak tree, when there was a sudden flash, the whole earth seemed on fire, and the vault of heaven seemed crashing overhead. Opening his blinded eyes, Levin gazed through the thick veil of rain that separated him now from the copse, and to his horror the first thing he saw was the green crest of the familiar oak tree in the middle of the copse uncannily changing its position. "Can it have been struck?" Levin hardly had time to think when, moving more and more rapidly, the oak tree vanished behind the other trees, and he heard the crash of the great tree falling upon the others.

The flash of lightning, the crash of thunder, and the instantaneous chill that ran through him were all merged for Levin in one sense of terror.

"My God! my God! not on them!" he said.

And though he thought at once how senseless was his prayer that they should not have been killed by the oak which had fallen now, he repeated it, knowing that he could do nothing better than utter this senseless prayer.

Running up to the place where they usually went, he did not find them there.

They were at the other end of the copse under an old lime tree; they were calling him. Two figures in dark dresses (they had been light summer dresses when they started out) were standing bending over something. It was Kitty with the nurse. The rain was already ceasing, and it was beginning to get light when Levin reached them. The nurse was not wet on the lower part of her dress, but Kitty was drenched through, and her soaked clothes clung to her. Though the rain was over, they still stood in the same position in which they had been standing when the storm broke. Both stood bending over a perambulator with a green umbrella.

"Alive? Unhurt? Thank God!" he said, splashing with his soaked boots through the standing water and running up to them.

Kitty's rosy wet face was turned towards him, and she smiled timidly under her shapeless sopped hat.

"Aren't you ashamed of yourself? I can't think how you can be so reckless!" he said angrily to his wife.

"It wasn't my fault, really. We were just meaning to go, when he made such a to-do that we had to change him. We were just . . ." Kitty began defending herself.

Mitya was unharmed, dry, and still fast asleep.

"Well, thank God! I don't know what I'm saying!"

They gathered up the baby's wet belongings; the nurse picked up the baby and carried it. Levin walked beside his wife, and, penitent for having been angry, he squeezed her hand when the nurse was not looking.

Chapter XVIII

DURING THE WHOLE OF THAT DAY, IN THE EXTREMELY DIFFERENT CONVERSATIONS IN WHICH HE took part, only as it were with the top layer of his mind, in spite of the disappointment of not finding the change he expected in himself, Levin had been all the while joyfully conscious of the fulness of his heart.

After the rain it was too wet to go for a walk; besides, the storm clouds still hung about the horizon, and gathered here and there, black and thundery, on the rim of the sky. The whole party spent the rest of the day in the house.

No more discussions sprang up; on the contrary, after dinner everyone was in the most amiable frame of mind.

At first Katavasov amused the ladies by his original jokes, which always pleased people on their first acquaintance with him. Then Sergey Ivanovitch induced him to tell them about the very interesting observations he had made on the habits and characteristics of common houseflies, and their life. Sergey Ivanovitch, too, was in good spirits, and at tea his brother drew him on to explain his views of the future of the Eastern question, and he spoke so simply and so well, that everyone listened eagerly.

Kitty was the only one who did not hear it all—she was summoned to give Mitya his bath.

A few minutes after Kitty had left the room she sent for Levin to come to the nursery.

Leaving his tea, and regretfully interrupting the interesting conversation, and at the same time uneasily wondering why he had been sent for, as this only happened on important occasions, Levin went to the nursery.

Although he had been much interested by Sergey Ivanovitch's views of the new epoch in history that would be created by the emancipation of forty millions of men of Slavonic race acting with Russia, a conception quite new to him, and although he was disturbed by uneasy wonder at being sent for by Kitty, as soon as he came out of the drawing room and was alone, his mind reverted at once to the thoughts of the morning. And all the theories of the significance of the Slav element in the history of the world seemed to him so trivial compared with what was passing in his own soul, that he instantly forgot it all and dropped back into the same frame of mind that he had been in that morning.

He did not, as he had done at other times, recall the whole train of thought—that he did not need. He fell back at once into the feeling which had guided him, which was connected with those thoughts, and he found that feeling in his soul even stronger and more definite than before. He did not, as he had had to do with previous attempts to find comforting arguments, need to revive a whole chain of thought to find the feeling. Now, on the contrary, the feeling of joy and peace was keener than ever, and thought could not keep pace with feeling.

He walked across the terrace and looked at two stars that had come out in the darkening sky, and suddenly he remembered. "Yes, looking at the sky, I thought that the dome that I see is not a deception, and then I thought something, I shirked facing something," he mused. "But whatever it was, there can be no disproving it! I have but to think, and all will come clear!"

Just as he was going into the nursery he remembered what it was he had shirked facing. It was that if the chief proof of the Divinity was His revelation of what is right, how is it this revelation is confined to the Christian church alone? What relation to this revelation have the beliefs of the Buddhists, Mohammedans, who preached and did good too?

It seemed to him that he had an answer to this question; but he had not time to formulate it to himself before he went into the nursery.

Kitty was standing with her sleeves tucked up over the baby in the bath. Hearing her husband's footstep, she turned towards him, summoning him to her with her smile. With one hand she was supporting the fat baby that lay floating and sprawling on its back, while with the other she squeezed the sponge over him.

"Come, look, look!" she said, when her husband came up to her. "Agafea Mihalovna's right. He knows us!"

Mitya had on that day given unmistakable, incontestable signs of recognizing all his friends.

As soon as Levin approached the bath, the experiment was tried, and it was completely successful. The cook, sent for with this object, bent over the baby. He frowned and shook his head disapprovingly. Kitty bent down to him, he gave her a beaming smile, propped his little hands on the sponge and chirruped, making such a queer little contented sound with his lips, that Kitty and the nurse were not alone in their admiration. Levin, too, was surprised and delighted.

The baby was taken out of the bath, drenched with water, wrapped in towels, dried, and after a piercing scream, handed to his mother.

"Well, I am glad you are beginning to love him," said Kitty to her husband, when she had settled herself comfortably in her usual place, with the baby at her breast. "I am so glad! It had begun to distress me. You said you had no feeling for him."

"No; did I say that? I only said I was disappointed."

"What! disappointed in him?"

"Not disappointed in him, but in my own feeling; I had expected more. I had expected a rush of new delightful emotion to come as a surprise. And then instead of that—disgust, pity . . ."

She listened attentively, looking at him over the baby, while she put back on her slender fingers the rings she had taken off while giving Mitya his bath.

"And most of all, at there being far more apprehension and pity than pleasure. Today, after that fright during the storm, I understand how I love him."

Kitty's smile was radiant.

"Were you very much frightened?" she said. "So was I too, but I feel it more now that it's over. I'm going to look at the oak. How nice Katavasov is! And what a happy day we've had altogether. And you're so nice with Sergey Ivanovitch, when you care to be. . . . Well, go back to them. It's always so hot and steamy here after the bath."

Chapter XIX

GOING OUT OF THE NURSERY AND BEING AGAIN ALONE, LEVIN WENT BACK AT ONCE TO THE thought, in which there was something not clear.

Instead of going into the drawing room, where he heard voices, he stopped on the terrace, and leaning his elbows on the parapet, he gazed up at the sky.

It was quite dark now, and in the south, where he was looking, there were no clouds. The storm had drifted on to the opposite side of the sky, and there were flashes of lightning and distant thunder from that quarter. Levin listened to the monotonous drip from the lime trees in the garden, and looked at the triangle of stars he knew so well, and the Milky Way with its branches that ran through its midst. At each flash of lightning the Milky Way, and even the bright stars, vanished, but as soon as the lightning died away, they reappeared in their places as though some hand had flung them back with careful aim.

"Well, what is it perplexes me?" Levin said to himself, feeling beforehand that the solution of his difficulties was ready in his soul, though he did not know it yet. "Yes, the one unmistakable, incontestable manifestation of the Divinity is the law of right and wrong, which has come into the world by revelation, and which I feel in myself, and in the recognition of which—I don't make myself, but whether I will or not—I am made one with other men in one body of believers, which is called the church. Well, but the Jews, the Mohammedans, the Confucians, the Buddhists—what of them?" he put to himself the question he had feared to face. "Can these hundreds of millions of men be deprived of that highest blessing without which life has no meaning?" He pondered a moment, but immediately corrected himself. "But what am I questioning?" he said to himself. "I am questioning the relation to Divinity of all the different religions of all mankind. I am questioning the universal manifestation of God to all the world with all those misty blurs. What am I about? To me individually, to my heart has been revealed a knowledge beyond all doubt, and unattainable by reason, and here I am obstinately trying to express that knowledge in reason and words.

"Don't I know that the stars don't move?" he asked himself, gazing at the bright planet which had shifted its position up to the topmost twig of the birch tree. "But looking at the movements of the stars, I can't picture to myself the rotation of the earth, and I'm right in saying that the stars move.

"And could the astronomers have understood and calculated anything, if they had taken into account all the complicated and varied motions of the earth? All the marvelous conclusions they have reached about the distances, weights, movements, and deflections of the heavenly bodies are only founded on the apparent motions of the heavenly bodies about a stationary earth, on that very motion I see before me now, which has been so for millions of men during long ages, and was and will be always alike, and can always be trusted. And just as the conclusions of the astronomers would have been vain and uncertain if not founded on observations of the seen heavens, in relation to a single meridian and a single horizon, so would my conclusions be vain and uncertain if not founded on that conception of right, which has been and will be always alike for all men, which has been revealed to me as a Christian, and which can always be trusted in my soul. The question of other religions and their relations to Divinity I have no right to decide, and no possibility of deciding."

"Oh, you haven't gone in then?" he heard Kitty's voice all at once, as she came by the same way to the drawing room.

"What is it? you're not worried about anything?" she said, looking intently at his face in the starlight.

But she could not have seen his face if a flash of lightning had not hidden the stars and revealed it. In that flash she saw his face distinctly, and seeing him calm and happy, she smiled at him.

"She understands," he thought; "she knows what I'm thinking about. Shall I tell her or not? Yes, I'll tell her." But at the moment he was about to speak, she began speaking.

"Kostya! do something for me," she said; "go into the corner room and see if they've made it all right for Sergey Ivanovitch. I can't very well. See if they've put the new wash stand in it."

"Very well, I'll go directly," said Levin, standing up and kissing her.

"No, I'd better not speak of it," he thought, when she had gone in before him. "It is a secret for me alone, of vital importance for me, and not to be put into words.

"This new feeling has not changed me, has not made me happy and enlightened all of a sudden, as I had dreamed, just like the feeling for my child. There was no surprise in this either. Faith—or not faith—I don't know what it is—but this feeling has come just as imperceptibly through suffering, and has taken firm root in my soul.

"I shall go on in the same way, losing my temper with Ivan the coachman, falling into angry discussions, expressing my opinions tactlessly; there will be still the same wall between the holy of holies of my soul and other people, even my wife; I shall still go on scolding her for my own terror, and being remorseful for it; I shall still be as unable to understand with my reason why I pray, and I shall still go on praying; but my life now, my whole life apart from anything that can happen to me, every minute of it is no more meaningless, as it was before, but it has the positive meaning of goodness, which I have the power to put into it."

About the Author

LEO TOLSTOY (1828–1910) WAS BORN TO A NOBLE RUSSIAN FAMILY AND RAISED AS AN ARISTOCRAT. HE studied law at the University of Kazan but never completed his degree, and took to managing the family's estate at Iasnaia Poliana at age nineteen. Tolstoy began writing in 1850, and some of his earliest fiction was based on his experiences serving as an officer in the Russian army, which he joined in 1851. His first novel, *Childhood,* was published in 1852. Tolstoy was part of a Russian literary scene that included Ivan Turgenev, Ivan Goncharov, and Aleksandr Ostrovsky, when he published his short novel *The Cossacks* in 1863. That same year he began writing *War and Peace*, which was published in six volumes between 1868 and 1869. Tolstoy's chronicle of the Napoleonic War and its impact on Russian life and culture was praised as a modern epic and acclaim for the book earned him renown as one of Russia's leading writers. *Anna Karenina,* which Tolstoy began writing in 1873 and published in 1875, reinforced that reputation. In the course of writing the novel, Tolstoy experienced a spiritual crisis that led him to question the teachings of the Russian Orthodox church. Activities and writings related to his conversion led to his excommunication in 1901, but earned him international regard as a progressive thinker. For most of the two decades he devoted himself to theological studies and publishing criticism of contemporary government, life, and art. In his final years, Tolstoy wrote several dramas and founded a non-profit publishing company. His last full novel, *Resurrection,* was published in 1899.

LIBRARY OF ESSENTIAL WRITERS

2007

LEWIS CARROLL *Complete Works*

◆

JOSEPH CONRAD *Complete Short Stories*

◆

JAMES FENIMORE COOPER *Five Novels*

◆

DANIEL DEFOE *Five Novels*

◆

GUSTAVE FLAUBERT *Five Novels*

◆

E. M. FORSTER *Four Novels*

◆

ERNEST HEMINGWAY *Four Novels*

◆

LEO TOLSTOY *Three Novels*

2006

JANE AUSTEN *Seven Novels*

◆

CHARLOTTE BRONTË *Four Novels*

◆

CHARLES DICKENS *Five Novels*

◆

ALEXANDRE DUMAS *Three Novels*

◆

GEORGE ELIOT *Four Novels*

◆

THOMAS HARDY *Five Novels*

◆

NATHANIEL HAWTHORNE *Five Novels*

◆

O. HENRY *The Fiction*

◆

HENRY JAMES *Five Novels*

◆

JACK LONDON *Six Novels*

◆

W. SOMERSET MAUGHAM *Five Novels*

◆

EDGAR ALLAN POE *Fiction and Poetry*

◆

SAKI *The Fiction*

◆

ROBERT LOUIS STEVENSON *Seven Novels*

◆

BRAM STOKER *Five Novels*

◆

MARK TWAIN *Five Novels*

◆

JULES VERNE *Seven Novels*

◆

H. G. WELLS *Seven Novels*

◆

EDITH WHARTON *Five Novels*

◆

OSCAR WILDE *Collected Works*